BEAUTY AND THE BURGLAR.

CHARLES PEACE;

OR,

THE ADVENTURES

OF A

NOTORIOUS BURGLAR.

FOUNDED ON FACT AND PROFUSELY ILLUSTRATED.

LONDON :

G. PURKESS, 286, STRAND, W.C.

CHARLES PEACE
OR THE
ADVENTURES OF A NOTORIOUS BURGLAR

CHARLES PEACE.

BIOGRAPHICAL SKETCH.

CHARLES PEACE *alias* JOHN WARD, whose life and adventures form the subject-matter of our story, has gained for himself a reputation equal, if not superior, to the lawless ruffians, Jack Sheppard, Dick Turpin, and others of a similar class. He is a union of various elements.

In more senses than one he was a local character.

Born in Sheffield he was, in early days, trained according to the customs of the day, and when about eight or ten years of age was one of the foremost amongst his companions in any game of audacious fun.

He was always considered a "rough," even amongst his earlier associates, and it is said that he was dreaded by the children with whom he played. At ten years of age he had to assist his father who was named

No. 1.

Joseph Peace, in the earning of the daily bread for the family.

Mr. Joseph Peace was a man well respected. He was what is known in Sheffield as a "little master," but in commercial terms would be placed as a "file manufacturer." He had a large family, and amongst his children was this lad, who has achieved such notoriety in the world.

Charles Peace, from his very boyhood, was wild. It is said that there was no adventure to be undertaken in regard to which he had any fear; neither did he require twice telling when he was requested to lead the way in any mischievous plot.

Mr. Joseph Peace was a man of religious inclinations, and was a member of the Wesleyan body. He occupied a house in George-street, Langsett-road, a thoroughfare which is now known as Gilpin-street.

He had a taste for music, and played the "bass" at the Wesleyan Chapel, Owlerton. When ten years of age Charles Peace commenced to take lessons on the violin, his instructor being his father, who rather prided himself on the way he could play the double-bass.

His son Charles was a diligent pupil, and ultimately, having acquired a proficiency in the instrument, be started in life as a sort of successor to Paganini—fiddling most successfully on one string, and only failing to achieve some distinction because he lacked the patience which was necessary to make the stage his "field of fame."

Yet he was always an artist.

If he did not discern for himself a sufficiently splendid career in art, amateur violinists who lived in the neighbourhood of Greenwich, Peckham, or Blackheath had sufficient reason to regret Mr. Charles Peace's devotion to music.

They found that some undiscovered burglar was abroad who had a good taste in the selection of fine instruments.

Mr. Peace indeed had a passion for violins; and if he spared a service of plate sometimes, he was never known to leave a really good fiddle behind.

He was distinguished, too, by his general cultivation and by his devotion to the fair sex. As his good fortune grew, so did the number of inamoratas increase, yet he never seems to have really deserted the wife whom he married.

In housekeeping his taste was luxurious, and he invariably moved into more aristocratic neighbourhoods as he prospered in the art and mystery of burglary. And here comes out the singular phase of his character.

There is no doubt his fame and fortune as a housebreaker culminated in the period between the Bannercross murder and his apprehension at Blackheath; but he appears to have previously enjoyed a reputation as a cracksman.

How does it happen, then, that he could settle down to the life of a picture-frame maker at Sheffield?

The circumstances would not be so mysterious if he had not really made picture-frames; but it appears that he actually worked at the trade. There is some mystery here which requires to be explained. It is difficult to believe Peace turned honest in a fit of repentance; he would, in all probability, have some other object, which has not yet been made clear.

But, indeed, Peace's character in Sheffield is altogether in singular contrast with his character as exhibited elsewhere. His behaviour to the Dysons, as it was described in Mrs. Dyson's evidence, was very much like that of a lunatic.

There appears to have been a singular absence of motive, both for his general conduct and the murder which he is said to have committed. Instead of being the ingenious and cautious Charles Peace of the London burglaries, he is simply an indiscreet and violent criminal.

Equally in contrast was his behaviour on the two occasions when he appeared in the prisoners' dock. In London he was whining and supplicatory; in Sheffield he was reckless and defiant. This change may, perhaps, be accounted for on the grounds that he had a chance in one case, and no chance in the other; but other contradictions in his character are not so easily explained.

Without doubt he was a cunning, bold, and fearless scoundrel of the old heroic type. The history of his many exploits, of his clever disguises, of his extraordinary escapes from punishment, and of the success with which for many years he contrived to live on burglary, even in these days, when we have a large and well-organised police force, cannot fail to excite surprise in the minds of every citizen.

His career is almost unique in the annals of crime. Not only the boldness and skill which he showed in committing his depredations, but his remarkable success in eluding the vigilance of the police, must be regarded as being altogether uncommon. Working entirely alone in his burglarious course, he seemed to command success.

We are told that even dogs felt the influence of his power, and failed to give any alarm on his approach. As for locks, bolts, and other means of security, Peace simply laughed at them. If he made up his mind to get into a house he got into it, and the booty which he appropriated was exceedingly valuable.

Probably many of the stories which are told of his exploits have only an element of truth, but the substratum on which they rest is doubtless constituted of actual facts. Scarcely less remarkable than his success as a burglar was the skill with which he contrived to escape detection by the police.

Although he had been living openly in London, walking even into Scotland-yard itself, he was not recognised as Mr. Dyson's murderer; and his eventual detection was owing to the accident of his capture at Blackheath.

Peace certainly possessed remarkable ability in effecting an almost impenetrable disguise. He has boasted of his contempt for the police, and his confidence seems to have been abundantly justified.

The history of his life presents a combination of passion, craft, cruelty, great spite, and audacity, such as is rarely to be found in any single being.

But Peace has boasted of his ability to deceive the most astute constable or detective. As a proof of this we quote the following personal narrative of one of his old pals. We give it in the words of the narrator:—

"Once on a time, no matter where, no matter when, Charley Peace told me the whole story of his life after that little indiscretion which resulted in the death of Mr. Dyson, at Bannercross.

"It is a narrative of events which have never yet been made known to the public. It presents points of uncommon interest, for everybody has wanted to know how he escaped on that fatal night—how he was disguised, where he went, and how he has lived, down to the days when he reappeared at Peckham, and spent his days and nights after the manner now familiar to the public through the special commissioner of the *Independent*.

"I shall not trench on the latter well-known period.

But I shall fill up the blank in his biography with these autobiographical episodes, for they are almost entirely his own words. I give to you, Mr. Editor, ample credentials to convince you that this is a genuine narrative, for I know, by the way you have stood former tests, that wild horses will not make you break confidence.

"So nobody need take the trouble to come fishing about either you or me for further 'information.'

"Imagine, then, a circle of choice spirits assembled round Charles Peace, under circumstances calculated to make him loquacious.

"'They talk,' said he, 'about identifying me! Why I could dodge any bobby living! I have dodged all the detectives in London many a time. I have walked past them, looked them straight in the face; and they have thought I was a mulatto.'

"Then he asked us if we knew how he did it; and said 'Just turn your faces away a minute, and I'll show you.'

"We turned our heads away, and when we looked again we found he had completely altered the expression of his countenance, and so entirely distorted and disfigured it—save the mark!—that he did not look like the same man.

"He threw out his under jaw, contracted the upper portion of his face, and appeared to be able so to force the blood up into his head as to give himself the appearance of a mulatto.

"Then he laughed heartily at his cleverness; went through pantomimic gestures that would have done credit to 'Quilp,' and again boasted of the many times he had 'put on that face,' and walked past the cute detectives in London and elsewhere.

"We then made allusion to the clever way in which he dodged the police and got away from Sheffield on the night of the murder; and he at once went off into a long story of his escape, telling it with almost fiendish glee, and occasionally laughing joyously at his exploits. He said:—

"'After that affair at Bannercross I went straight over the field opposite, and through Endcliffe Wood to Crookes, and round by Sandygate. Then I doubled and came down to Broomhill, and there I took a cab and was driven down to the bottom of Church-street.

"'I got out and walked into Spring-street, to the house of an old pal. There I doffed my own clothes and disguised myself. I stopped there a short time, and then I went boldly through the streets to the railway station, and took train for Rotherham. I walked from that station down to Masbro', where I took a ticket for Beverley.

"'On reaching Normanton I left the train, retaining my ticket, and took a ticket for York, where I put up that night. The next morning I went to Beverley, and then walked on to Hull.

"'I got in an eating house near the docks, where I stopped a considerable time, and did a 'bit of work' —(meaning, of course, committed a few robberies).

"'Then I went to Leeds, and from Leeds to Bradford; and from Bradford I went to Manchester. I was there a short time and then I went to Nottingham; and in a lodging house there I picked up Mrs. Thompson.

"'Whilst we were together one night, an inspector, who had heard I was there and suspected I was a "fence," came and said to the landlady—"You have got a lodger here—have you not?" She said, "Yes, he is upstairs."

"'He said he wanted to see me, and upstairs he came into our bedroom. When I saw him I said,

"Hullo!" He answered, "Where do you come from?" and I told him from Tunbridge Wells. "What is your name?" he asked. "John Ward," said I. "Well," he said, "what trade are you?"

"'At that I let out and said, "What's that to you what trade I am? What do you want to know for?"

"'He told me he wanted an answer. "Then," said I, "if you do I'll give you one—I am a hawker!" "Oh," said he, "a hawker. Have you got any stock?"

"'I told him my stock and licence were downstairs, and if he would step down my wife and I would come and show him all. He was as soft as barm and went down.

"'I said to Mrs. Thompson, "I must hook it," and, hastily dressing myself, I bolted through the window and dropped into a yard, where I encountered a man, who was surprised to see me. I told him there was a screw loose, and the bobbies were after me with a warrant for neglecting my wife and family. I asked him not to say I had gone that way. He promised he would not.

"'To leave the yard I had to go through the passage of a public-house, and at the door stood the landlady. She was frightened to see me without stockings or boots on; but when I told her the same tale as I had told the man in the yard she said it was all right, and I passed on.

"'I took refuge in a house not forty yards from that I had left, and in a short time I got the woman who kept it to go for my boots, and she brought them.

"'Soon after that I did a "big silk job" in Nottingham, and then, finding the place was getting too hot for me, I left it and went back to Hull. I had made several visits there before, and had given my wife money to maintain her.'

"Peace then told us how he paid no less than three visits to Sheffield after the murder, and more than once encountered one of the most astute and experienced inspectors of the force, but his disguise was so perfect that he passed unnoticed.

"Whilst in Sheffield he committed, he said, several robberies, and he particularly called attention to his adventures in a house at the corner of Havelock-square. 'Do you mean,' we asked, 'at Barnascone's,' and he said, 'Yes, that was the place. The family were out, and there I did very well. I got several rings, and brooches, and £6 in gold.' The policeman said he saw me, but he didn't. I saw him and blocked him, and he never saw me.'

"Peace declared to us that he was in Sheffield when the inquest was held on Mr. Dyson. Afterwards he returned to Nottingham, picked up with Mrs. Thompson, and went on to London with her, where his life and exploits are now matter of history.

"Peace went on to mention the names of several Sheffield people whom he met at different periods in London; and that part of his astonishing story has been confirmed in a remarkable degree by one of the persons himself.

"More than a quarter of a century ago he worked in Sheffield with Mr. William Fisher — in those days known as Bill Fisher—and they remembered each other very well. One day Mr. Fisher was walking across the Holborn-viaduct, when he saw the well-remembered figure approaching him.

"Their eyes met, and Mr. Fisher exclaimed—'That's Peace!' He turned to look again, but Peace had disappeared as if by magic, and was nowhere to be seen. About a week after, Mr. Fisher was going down the steps leading from Holborn to Farringdon-street, and about midway he again encountered Peace.

"Mr. Fisher gave information to the Sheffield police, and the news was sent to Scotland-yard that Peace was in London.

"'But what,' said Peace, 'was the use of that, when I could walk under their very noses and not be recognised?'

"Again a demoniacal grin overspread his face, and again he went through a series of pantomimic gestures, and set us all laughing.

"It has been conceded that he could be exceedingly good company when he liked, and we assure you he had our attention whilst he related these, the most extraordinary chapters in his history."

The personal appearance of Peace is thus described by one who paid a visit to Newgate while the burglar was awaiting his trial. He is a man about 5 ft. 3 in., with white hair on his head, cut very close, and bald in front of the head; but the razor had lately done this.

His eyebrows are heavy and overhanging the eyes, which are deeply sunk in their sockets; a chin standing very prominently—and, as if to make it more so, the head was thrown back with an air of half self-assertion, yet half-caution.

The lower part of his cheek-bones protruded more than was their wont in years gone by; but he had apparently some bruises recently, and had had his whiskers shaven off since he was last seen at Sheffield.

In addition he wore a pair of large brass-rimmed spectacles. Peace was professedly a religious man. The neighbourhood thought him so, and probably he thought so, too; so he associated with the good folk who congregated in the edifice, but never made himself conspicuous.

He trifled with Fate. She had made him rich in worldly goods, although they were not his own. Some idea of the magnitude of his operations may be gathered from the fact that there is evidence in the hands of the police that would convict him of no less than fifty burglaries.

The property he obtained is valued at several thousand pounds, but the burglar as a rule does not realise even one-fourth of the value of the property he appropriates.

The charges of "receivers" in every branch of the profession are of an unusual character, but it has been asserted upon reliable authority that he was a burglar years before the events which have made him so notorious.

It is quite twenty years since he worked at a rolling mill at Millsands, and it was while following this employment that he broke his leg. This accident appears to have thoroughly disgusted him with hard work, and as soon as the injuries were cured he went to Manchester.

Here he appears to have fallen into bad company, and to have been the leading spirit of a gang of burglars. In the small hours of the morning Peace and his confederates were tracked to a lonely house at Rusholme, and the police succeeded in obtaining an entrance.

After a desperate struggle Peace was secured, and a great quantity of the stolen property was recovered, but not before the officers had been severely handled. At Old Trafford he was sent to penal servitude, but he played the "good boy" and was let out on a ticket-of-leave.

After his Old Trafford sentence he returned to Sheffield and took a small shop in Kenyon-alley. Here he used to amuse his acquaintances by showing them the dexterity with which he could pick the most stub-

born lock. He soon resumed his old courses, and made the acquaintance of Millbank.

The career of the notorious culprit whose doings are chronicled in this work furnishes the novelist with a moral. It will be clearly demonstrated to those who peruse these pages that, sooner or later, justice overtakes the guilty, and that it is impossible for the most astute and cunning scoundrel—such as Peace has proved himself to be—to escape punishment.

A life of crime is always a life of care, for the hearts of the guilty tremble for the past, for the present, and for the future. The author of the "Life of Peace" reprobates in the strongest degree that species of literature whose graduates do their best to cast a dignity upon the gallows, and strive to shed the splendour of fascinating romance upon the paths of crime that lead to it—to make genius tributary to murder, and literature to theft, to dignify not the mean but the guilty.

Let crime and its perpetrators be depicted as conscience sees them, as morality brands them; let them stand out in prominent but repulsive relief. There is yet wanted a picture of crime and its consequences true to nature and conscience, and it is hoped that the present serial will, in some measure, supply that want.

The author proposes to present to his readers the felon as he really is—to describe facts as they were found—to present pure pictures of guilt and its accompaniments.

He does not desire to make use of artificial colouring, believing that the interest in the work lies in its reality. The felon appears just as he is, as crime makes him, and as Newgate receives him—successful, it may be, for a season, but arrested, condemned, scourged by conscience, and cut off from society as unfit for its walks.

Of all the members of the family of man few have been so rapidly forgotten as those who have been swept from the face of the world by the fiat of the law and the hands of the public executioner. Yet the guilty and the unfortunate have left biographies behind them that speak to future generations in awful and impressive tones.

If they were inflictions on the past generation, they may be made useful in the present age as beacons to the reckless voyager—voices lifted up from the moral wrecks of the world speaking audibly to listening men "of righteousness, and temperance, and judgment."

CHAPTER I.

OAKFIELD FARMHOUSE — THE BURGLARY — DESPERATE ENCOUNTER—VILLAGERS TO THE RESCUE.

OUR first scene opens at a picturesque-looking farmhouse situated on the outskirts of a pretty little village within a few miles of Hull. Oakfield Farmhouse—so called from a number of patriarchal oaks poising their lofty heads in the rear of the establishment—was in the occupation of two substantial yeomen named respectively John and Richard Ashbrook, their only sister Maude being mistress of the bright and cheerful abode.

In the earlier portion of the day our two Yorkshire farmers had been out on a shooting expedition. They brought back with them two friends—fellow-sportsmen. They were driven home by the rain, which fell in torrents, and rendered further sport impracticable.

"I knowed how it would be," said Richard Ashbrook to his companions. "These beastly river fogs always bring wet, and the clouds have been as 'bengy' (full of rain) for some time—as bengy as could be."

When the party reached Oakfield their garments were saturated with wet, and clung to them like a second skin.

"I have got a fire in the big bedroom—a good blazing fire—for I guessed how it would be," said Maude Ashbrook, as she received her guests at the door. "You'll all of you have to change your things. Mercy on us, you are dripping wet, John!" she exclaimed, placing her hand on her brother's shoulder.

"Our friends will stop and have a morsel of something to eat and drink for the matter o' that," observed Richard.

"Indeed no—I think not," said Mr. Jamblin, one of the farmer's companions.

"Ah, but he will," returned the farmer. "None of yer think nots. Come, friends, get thee in. We don't intend to part with thee so easily."

Mr. Jamblin smiled, shrugged his shoulders, and obeyed. The other friend of the farmer's, a Mr. Cheadle by name, followed Jamblin.

After dinner had been served, "clean glasses and old corks" were festively proposed by the host. Some bottles of genuine spirits and a box of Havannas were placed on the board; an animated discussion on things agricultural and political followed, while ever and anon Jamblin and Cheadle would rise from their seats, repair to the window, and, flattening their noses against the panes thereof, would endeavour to distinguish a star in the sky, or the first beams of the rising moon.

But the sky remained black and gloomy, and continual pattering of the rain was distinctly heard.

"It's no good, my fine fellows," observed Richard Ashbrook. "You are in for it. The rain has set in for good, so you had better make up your minds to stop where you are. 'Any port in a storm,' as my uncle the captain used to say. Nobody will ever expect you home, such a night as this."

"You are very kind, Ashbrook, but——"

"Oh, bother your buts! I tell you I've got a couple of beds for ye. They are small iron bedsteads, both in the same room; but you don't mind roughing it for one night, surely."

The farmer's two friends accepted the offer, and prepared themselves to pass the hours merrily. This they had no difficulty in doing.

Several games of whist were played, after which the host was called upon for a song. He was not quite in tune, but that did not matter. The other singers were equally deficient in that respect; but what was wanting in skill was made up by noise.

Most of the ditties had a good, rattling chorus, which each singer interpreted according to his own fancy. After sundry libations, and much protestation of friendship and good-fellowship, the hour arrived for repose, and the two farmers, their visitors, and Maude betook themselves to their respective sleeping apartments.

As Richard, who was the last, was about to ascend the stairs, he was touched gently on the elbow by a tall long-haired young woman, who was one of the domestics in the establishment.

"Well, Jane, what's up now, lass?" inquired the farmer.

"Hush, master. This way." She drew him back towards the entrance to the kitchen, and said in a low, mysterious tone of voice, "Are the guns loaded?"

"Two of them are. But what of that?"

"Load the others."

"Why, dash it—what ails thee, girl?"

"Nothing, master. I can't tell why, but I feel timmersome like, and fancy something bad is going to happen."

"If loading the other guns will do thee any good the remedy is easy enough," observed the good-natured farmer, who at once proceeded to charge the other weapons.

"Thanks, Mr. Richard, thanks!" exclaimed the girl, in a tone of evident satisfaction.

The farmer repaired to his bedroom, taking the two guns—his own and his brother's—with him. At his suggestion his two friends had carried up their weapons into their bedroom in the earlier portion of the evening. This might appear a little singular, but John Ashbrook had playfully observed to Cheadle and Jamblin that there was sometimes a hare to be seen out of the bedroom window, feeding on the orchard grass of a morning.

"And so," he observed jocosely, "if you see one to-morrow morning you will of course be able to knock him over."

"We will do our best should there be one," said both gentlemen.

In less than half an hour after the party had broken up all the inmates of Oakfield House were soundly sleeping.

All save one.

This was Jane Ryan, the girl who had exchanged a few parting words with her master, or, more properly speaking, with one of her masters, for John and Richard Ashbrook were partners.

A strange sense of coming evil had taken possession of the girl, who sat moodily and dejected in the kitchen long after the other members of the household had retired to rest. Jane did not feel disposed to seek repose; she was restless and disturbed, albeit she was quiet, moving from place to place in a stealthy way, in direct variance with her usual manner.

"I cannot sleep," she murmured; "and so I will e'en keep watch for one hour or more."

She put some fresh coals on the kitchen fire, before which she sat for some time absorbed in thought.

Leaving her there, we will take a survey of the exterior of the house and its surroundings.

It was two o'clock in the morning. The rain had ceased; the moon was shining brightly, and covered the fields with a pale, lustrous light; the stars sparkled in the rain-drops which were hanging from the leaves, and so clothed the trees with a mantle of diamonds.

All was silent in the fields, for the birds and insects of the night were torpid till summer came once more.

All was silent in the yard—the cattle sleeping on their beds of straw, and the fowls upon their wooden perches.

Seen by the pale moonlight the old farm-house was a picture worthy of an artist's pencil.

On the northern side of Oakfield ran a narrow lane, skirted by a dense mass of foliage, which threw the lane into sombre darkness. The lane itself rose abruptly as it neared the farm, which stood on the upland.

In this lane the forms of three men might be seen. The first of these is Charles Peace. Standing facing him is the notorious "cracksman" Ned Gregson, better known by the name of the "Bristol Badger." The last of the three is known as "Cooney;" he is a tinker by trade, but he is a sort of jackal to rogues of a greater degree than himself.

The three men are in close converse. They had

come suddenly to halt, as if doubtful as to their course of action.

"I tell yer it's right as the mail," observed the tinker, in a tone of confidence. "The farmers have sold their wheat, and there's a mighty good 'swag' in the house. Only yer see, Ned, old boy, yer must not be too rash. Be keerful—be very keerful."

"What do yer mean?" inquired the Badger.

"Well, it's just this, old man, the farmers—least-ways so I heerd at the 'Six Bells'—have had two blokes with 'em to-day, a poppin' at the blessed birds, bad luck to them; and from what I could gather from Tim, the two blokes are a stoppin' there to-night."

"What matters about that?" said Peace. "We don't intend to wake the gentlemen."

"All right—so much the better," answered the tinker. "I'm for doing things in a quiet sort of way, I am."

The Badger uttered an oath, and his ill-favoured countenance wore an expression of disgust.

"Do you know where they keep the shiners?" he asked.

"Oh, yes; I think that'll be all right. I haven't been in the house to mend the bell wires without a keeping my eyes open. Ah, ah!"

"Stow that, yer fool!" exclaimed the Badger. "Wait till yer out of the wood afore yer laugh."

"All right, Ned, I'm as silent as the grave."

"When were you at 'The Bells,' then?" inquired Peace.

"I had a game of skittles this afternoon."

"At what time?"

"Between three and four o'clock; or it might be a little later. Can't say to half an hour or so."

"And that's how you came to know about these two sporting chaps?"

"Right you are. Tim gave me the tip."

"You haven't been fool enough to push your inquiries too far?" said Peace. "Tim, as you call him, might suspect."

"He suspect?" returned the tinker, indignantly. "Not he. I was as good as gold."

"It's no use making a long palaver about the matter," ejaculated Gregson. "Let's to business."

The three burglars made direct for Oakfield House. In the space of a few minutes they were busily at work to effect an entrance, but they found this by no means so easy a task as they had imagined. The windows and doors of the habitation were carefully secured, and, although they knew it not at the time, there was one inmate of the establishment keenly alive to every movement.

This was Jane Ryan, who was aroused from her lethargic reverie before the kitchen fire by a sound which was new to her ears.

Jane started and rose from her seat.

"I said something was about to happen," she murmured, pressing her hand against her side. "I could have taken a Bible oath of it."

She paused for a few moments, apparently in doubt as to what course to take; presently she appeared to have decided upon her line of action. She glided from the room with long, stealthy, and noiseless steps, carrying her shoes in her hand.

A sudden surprise awaited her two young masters.

They were awoke from their sleep by a hand placed upon their shoulders. They stared around them sleepily, as yet not realising the real state of affairs. It was dark in their bedroom, for the moon was behind a cloud.

When it gleamed out, they saw Jane Ryan standing before them. Her arms were naked to the shoulder; her eyes glistened with a strange light.

She held a loaded gun in her hands.

The Ashbrooks were perfectly bewildered when they beheld this strange apparition awaking them in the silent hours of the night.

"Jane!" exclaimed Richard Ashbrook, suddenly calling to his mind the warning given him in the earlier part of the night by his faithful and devoted servant. "Jane—what's the matter? Speak, girl."

"Hush!" she murmured, placing her finger on her lips; "make no noise, or it may be fatal. Listen."

Both the farmers listened till their ears tingled, but they could hear nothing.

A thought crossed the minds of both almost simultaneously, that the girl was (to use the expression they made use of afterwards) off her head.

The brothers stared at each other in mute astonishment.

"I can't hear anything," said John Ashbrook.

"Don't speak, master, but watch and wait; you will hear," said Jane, in a low whisper.

She was standing as if in anxious expectation—one hand raised to her ear, the other grasping the fowling-piece.

The two Ashbrooks listened again, and as the moonlight ebbed slowly from the room like a great white wave streaming back towards the sea, they heard a thin scraping sound, which was unlike anything they had heard before. This mysterious sound was followed by deep and heavy blows.

"Are you satisfied now?" said the maid.

"What is it?" they inquired.

She answered in a low, hoarse voice—

"Robbers, burglars, assassins!"

The two farmers stole hastily but silently from their beds.

Jane immediately left the room.

They at once proceeded to arouse Mr. Cheadle and Jamblin. All this was done as noiselessly as possible. When the four men were up and dressed, Maude Ashbrook joined them, declaring that she would not leave the side of her brothers upon any consideration.

They left the door wide open, and all crouched together in a corner.

The sound of the burglars' tools soon ceased—a sign that they were worked by practised hands.

Indeed, no more skilful "cracksmen" existed at this time than Charles Peace, the Badger, and Cooney —the two first-named men have never been surpassed.

The farmers and their friends silently awaited the movements of the robbers, who had without doubt, by this time, effected an entrance into the house.

The party in the bedroom stood prepared for any emergency—they all cocked their guns.

"Let us have no firing, except in self-defence," said Mr. Cheadle. "There are four able-bodied men here, and it must go hard with us if we cannot hold our own."

"I shan't be at all particular about peppering the scoundrels, whoever they may be," returned John Ashbrook. "A set of lawless, midnight marauders— fellows of their stamp do not deserve pity or consideration."

They now heard muffled footsteps in the room beneath them, and immediately afterwards similar sounds were heard on the stairs.

They began to breathe a little quicker, and grasped their guns more tightly.

A gleam of light fell across the threshold.

They could see a slipper lying there—one that Maude had dropped.

The burglars had probably perceived this, and thence argued that people were afoot, for the light disappeared, and they could hear whisperings outside the door.

The big bedroom, as it was called, was a square chamber, barely furnished. The two bedsteads had been placed close to the window on the left-hand side.

Round and about these beds the six besieged persons were crouched or seated.

The moonlight poured in at the window in such a manner that while the whole of the opposite side, except one corner, was as light as day, the little nook by the beds was buried in impenetrable darkness.

The one dark corner on the opposite side was formed by the chimney, which jutted out some little way into the room.

They listened breathlessly for some moments, till they fancied that they heard a board creak inside the room close to the door; and at that moment, as if by magic, a voice issued from the corner of the chimney.

"We are armed with loaded revolvers; if you come a step nearer we fire!"

The lurid flash of a pistol flamed within the room, and they heard a ball strike sharply against the wall.

Maude betrayed their hiding-place with a shriek, and fell fainting in her brother John's arms.

A loud report rang in their ears, and the room was filled with a thick, sulphurous smoke.

By the light of the powder's flame when the first shot was fired, there was one who had seen the robber's face—a face, once seen, not soon to be forgotten. The dark cavernous eyes of the "Badger" had been distinctly visible to Jane Ryan, who gave a scream of triumph and revenge.

It was but momentarily that she had caught sight of the forbidding features of the miscreant; but it was enough for her purpose.

She levelled her master's gun at the supposed spot where the robber was; and as she fired, something fell heavily upon the floor.

A shudder passed over them like a cold wind. They drew their breath and heard the same whisperings outside the door.

John Ashbrook placed his sister behind himself and his brother. There was an interval of silence; they began to hope that the burglars had gone, when presently they perceived something on the opposite wall.

They watched it with fascinated eyes. It was a small, dark shadow, creeping towards them along the wall.

It was the shadow of a man's hand.

Then they heard a harsh, rustling sound, as if something was being dragged along the floor.

The robbers were taking away the dead body of their comrade.

They did not dare to move, for they knew the burglars were armed to a far greater extent than they were, and exposure might prove fatal.

Ten minutes passed thus; ten minutes of frightful suspense to these farmers—who were brave but not phlegmatic—who now fought men for the first time, and fought them in the dark.

They could not possibly tell how many there were of their enemies. To fire the only three remaining charges they had would have been an act of madness; they therefore thought it prudent to keep these in reserve for the grand or final conflict.

But the worst was over, as far as the Oakfield housebreakers were concerned.

Presently the eager tramp of men's feet echoed from the road before the farm, and a dozen rough voices were heard bawling to each other.

The besieged party rushed to the window, and saw in the front of the house one of the village constabulary force, who was accompanied by a posse of strong-bodied youths of the immediate neighbourhood. In addition to these there were shepherds armed with crowbars, stablemen with their pitchforks, bird-keepers with their rusty fowling-pieces, woodmen with their bill-hooks, and a tall relation of Jane Ryan's with a substantial kitchen poker.

The reports of the gun and pistol in the dead hour of the night had aroused the whole neighbourhood.

As may be readily imagined, the strong reinforcement at once dispelled all anxiety or doubt in the minds of the farmer's household.

Three men were instantly mounted, and started off in the dark to the three nearest railway stations. The rest were invited into the kitchen to wait till daybreak.

There had been an unprecedented number of burglaries committed at several houses in the neighbourhood within the space of a few months—hence it was that the rustic population were so keenly alive when any signal of alarm was given.

To capture the robbers was the wish of every one assembled at Oakfield on that eventful night.

With the first streaks of dawn the party congregated in the yard, and took counsel on the best means of pursuit.

"If they have been carrying a body with them they can't be very far off," said Mr. Jamblin.

"They are lurking about somewhere hard by, I dare say," said the police-officer.

"Where's Jarvis?" cried Will, the carter. "He'd be the boy to find 'em for us. He'd ketch 'em if they burrowed underground like a rabbit."

"Would he?" ejaculated the policeman. "He must be a clever chap."

"Aye, that he be," returned another rustic.

"Have you got any more of his sort in this neighbourhood?" asked the officer.

The rustics made no reply.

"Who is this Jarvis you were speaking of?" inquired John Ashbrook.

"Jarvis, sir? Why, him as 'listed some years ago, and fought under Lord Clyde in the Injies. Arter that they sent him to the other Injies, where the red men be, and they've taught him a power of strange tricks. He came here wi' us, but he's got lost since, or summat."

"No, I baint lost, Joe," said a tall young man, whose left cheek was one great red scar, and whose face had been bronzed by no English sun.

"Why, sure enough, it is Jarvis!" exclaimed Mr. Ashbrook. "Give us your hand, lad. Sure enough I shouldn't ha' known ye, they've knocked ye about so."

"Aye, that they have, Master Ashbrook," returned the soldier. "But tell us, neighbour, what you can about this night's business."

"You shall know all I know," answered the farmer; who thereupon put the soldier in possession of all the facts with which the reader is already acquainted.

When he had finished, the soldier said, "I'll be bound for it that the body of the dead or wounded man is not very far from here."

"You think not?"

"Ah! that I do. We came up so soon that they'd have no time to get far away with that load upon their backs; and most likely they've been forced to hide it in a slovenly way."

CHAPTER II.

CAPTURE OF THE BRISTOL BADGER—MURDER WILL OUT—CHASE AFTER CHARLES PEACE—HIS MYSTERIOUS ESCAPE.

THE sudden disappearance of Charles Peace and his two companions upon the arrival of the villagers excited surprise in the minds of all who had assembled at the farm-house. The police officer did not choose to commit himself by any expression of opinion. He was not a man given to loquacity where silence was requisite. He did not, however, attempt to deny the assertion made by soldier Jarvis—namely, that the robbers were not far off.

Enjoining the villagers to stay where they were and to carefully avoid treading over more ground than was absolutely necessary, the young soldier accompanied Mr. Ashbrook to the kitchen window, where the entrance had been forced by removing the glass with a diamond—or "starring the glaze," as it is termed in the burglar's phraseology—and after this had been done panelling the shutter. It was this last process that aroused Jane Ryan to a sense of danger.

Jarvis carefully examined the ground beneath the window, and pointed to some footprints in the wet earth which led towards the straw yard. In one place they were so plain that every nail in the soles could be distinguished.

"They are the impressions of a strange foot—that's certain sure," observed Ashbrook.

"We are on the trail of one of them," returned Jarvis. "I dare say they thought they could do as they liked among yokels, but we've got the trail and I mean to keep it."

The speaker walked slowly across the yard, following the tracks with his eye as a bloodhound would have followed them with his nose.

"They're in this barn, Master Ashbrook," he said, stopping before one of the doors. "No, they baint, though, they're come out agen and gone along the wall. But they've left their dead mate behind 'em. See how different their track is now; they tramples quite close alongside of each other, while afore they carried the body from shoulder to shoulder, and so were forced to walk one behind and a little way apart."

The villagers gave a murmur of astonishment.

"Ah, he knows how many blue beans make five," said the carter, as he took out the peg by which the folding doors were kept closed.

"I don't feel quite so sure about the footsteps," remarked the policeman; "they don't appear to me to tally with the others."

"If I'm mistaken, we shall have to try back," answered Jarvis. "Of course, it is just possible we are on a false scent. Ah! what is this?" The speaker pointed significantly to some drops of blood upon the straw in front of the barn. "What say you to that?"

"Blood, without a doubt," observed the constable.

"That's where they laid him down when they opened the barn door."

"Ah!—dare say—most likely."

The villagers were open-mouthed with wonder. They, one and all, voted the soldier a necromancer.

The doors were flung wide open, and they sprang over the rack into the body of the barn. There had been some threshing done the day before, and there was a vast heap of chaff just outside.

While they were gazing around, a low moan, as of one in pain, fell upon their ears.

"Keep quiet, lads," exclaimed Jarvis; "leave this matter to me and the constable. Keep where you are. We can none of us tell what next will happen."

"Here's footmarks on the chaff, and blood on it also," said the constable, who took a few steps further inside, whereupon his eyes lighted on the prostrate figure of a man lying in the corner on a heap of straw.

He flashed his bull's-eye on the face of the wounded burglar, and uttered an exclamation of surprise.

The Bristol Badger lay helpless, and bathed in blood.

Jane Ryan, who had followed the constable and Jarvis, gave a slight scream.

"Don't take on so, woman," said the constable. "He's only got his deserts."

Heedless of this observation, Jane went close to the wounded burglar and peered into his face.

"Dost know who this here is? I'll tell ye!" she exclaimed, in a voice of concentrated rage; "he's the murderer of my sweetheart. I should ha' known him out o' ten thousand."

There was a murmur of unmixed surprise at this observation.

"What beest thee saying, Jane?" said the farmer, scratching his head. "Hast ever seen 'im afore?"

"Aye, sure enough I have, master. It was not for nothing that I sat up this night. I knew summut was about to happen, but never guessed it would turn out like this."

Gregson endeavoured to rise to his feet, but the attempt was a futile one; he was too weak from loss of blood.

"What has that false, wicked woman been saying?" he inquired of the policeman.

"She accuses you of murder," was the brief rejoinder.

"She's mad. I never saw her before."

"What's to be done wi' this man?" inquired the farmer of the constable.

"He's my prisoner, anyway," answered the latter. "Best see and have his wounds attended to, and then we will take him to the look-up. You charge him, I suppose?"

"Yes, with burglary."

"Attempted burglary," chimed in the cracksman.

"And I charge him with wilful murder!" exclaimed Jane Ryan.

Having said this, she folded her arms upon her breast and relapsed into gloomy silence. There she stood, colossal as an Amazon, in her sublime strength, beautiful as a Judith in her just and fearful vengeance.

A hurdle was brought by some of the villagers, and upon this the ill-fated Badger was placed; he was then carried into the farm-house, not, however, before the constable had taken the precaution to handcuff him, for he was known to that astute officer as a ruffian of no common order. He was, however, run to earth, having been, in a manner of speaking, hunted down by a woman.

A doctor was sent for, who bandaged his wound, which, although severe, was not likely to prove mortal—certainly not unless some unfavourable symptons set in.

While all this clatter had been going on, Charles Peace had contrived to conceal himself in a neighbouring coppice, from which he durst not emerge while the village folk were prowling about.

When Gregson was conveyed into the house the majority of the villagers wheeled off; at the same time Jarvis, however, was still endeavouring to trace out

THE " BRISTOL BADGER " SHOT BY JANE RYAN.

the Badger's companions. He came too near to the coppice where Peace was concealed to be at all pleasant to a gentleman of his retiring habits, so Peace was fain to avail himself of a neighbouring hedge, on the other side of which he crept along on all fours.

Having gone some considerable distance by this means of progressive, he imagined that he was out of sight, and betook himself to the open field, across which he ran at the top of his speed. His movements were however not unobserved by Jarvis.

The latter caught Mr. John Ashbrook by the leg. The farmer was mounted on his bay mare, and said: "There goes one of them; ride down the lane and intercept his flight, while I run across the field. We shall have him yet."

The farmer needed no second bidding. He rode at the hedge which skirted the lane. With one stroke

from the long corded whip, and one cry from the rider's lips, the gallant animal bounded over the hedge like a flying deer.

"Wouldn't 'a brushed a fly off the top twig," exclaimed Ashbrook, triumphantly. "Now, for my gentleman. Dall it, if this won't turn an eventful night, especially if I catch that rascal."

While the farmer was riding down the lane, Jarvis and several others were in hot pursuit of the fugitive.

Peace became aware, much to his discomfiture, that every movement he made was plainly visible to his pursuers, and he deeply regretted having taken to the open field.

He ran his hardest, and had the satisfaction of getting into the lane before any of the pursuing party had even reached the field.

Ashbrook, as he was trotting down the lane, saw the

No. 2.

fugitive jump through a gap in the hedge. The farmer urged on his steed, being now under the full impression that the capture of Peace was reduced to a certainty.

In a brief space of time he came within a hundred yards of the enemy.

"I've got him now!" exclaimed the farmer. "He's mine as sure as my name's Jack Ashbrook."

But there's an old adage "that it is as well not to reckon your chickens before they are hatched."

Peace was in imminent danger, but he was an astute, cunning rascal, who was up to every feint and dodge in all cases of emergency. He, nevertheless, was fully impressed with the fact that matters were growing serious—much too serious to be pleasant. He turned round and boldly faced the horseman.

Drawing a revolver from his pocket, he watched till Ashbrook came within range of the shot, then he fired. At this time he could not have been more than twenty paces from the horse and its rider.

A bullet was lodged in Mr. Ashbrook's right shoulder. The wound was not a very serious one certainly —not enough to place the farmer hors de combat, but the effects of the shot proved more disastrous in another way.

The mare, who was a high-spirited animal, became restive from the pistol's flash. She reared, then stumbled, and threw her rider heavily to the ground. Peace rushed forward and struck Ashbrook two blows on the head, which produced insensibility.

He then made for the mare's head. Turning her sharply round, he led her some paces from the scene of action. He patted her on the neck, and strove as best he could to overcome the effects of the fright caused by the flash of his weapon. The mare became comparatively quiet and tractable.

Peace jumped on her back, and rode off at headlong speed.

While all this had been taking place in the lane the mob of persons in the field had increased considerably in numbers; but the foremost of them were a long way from that part of the lane where the short but decisive struggle had taken place.

Two other horses had been brought out from the stables at Oakfield, but some time necessarily elapsed before they could be saddled; and when Mr. Cheadle and Mr. Jamblin mounted them for the purpose of giving chase, Peace was so far ahead that the chances were remote of finding him.

He knew the bye-roads of the neighbourhood perfectly well, and took very excellent care to choose a circuitous route. As he was riding along he listened every now and then to ascertain if there were any sounds of horses' hoofs to be heard, but none were as yet audible. He felicitated himself upon this fact, arguing therefrom that his pursuers had gone another road.

"I shall give them the double; they are on the wrong scent," he ejaculated, in a tone of satisfaction; "but even when the worst comes to the worst all that will be left for me will be to make a stout fight of it."

He had unlimited faith in his own power, skill, and address in confronting and overcoming difficulties; and his confidence did not desert him on this occasion.

Presently he came to three cross roads, and was hesitating which to take—calculating the while the chances of detection with his accustomed coolness.

While thus engaged he descried a mounted patrol on a formidable-looking horse, coming at a measured pace towards him.

To turn and fly was his first impulse, but upon second consideration he thought it better to put a bold face on the matter.

The mounted policeman came forward, and regarded him with a look of doubt and mistrust.

"Good morning, friend," said Peace, in a cheery tone. "Better weather than it was a few hours ago."

"Yes," returned the other. "Where might you be journeying to this early hour?"

The speaker regarded him with a searching glance. This, however, did not in any way discompose Peace, who, throughout his career, plumed himself upon being able to throw dust in the eyes of the constabulary.

"Ah, I'm sorry to say my errand, or rather the cause of it, is one of a painful nature. A poor gentleman is at death's door, and I have been sent off for the doctor. In cases of this sort minutes are precious. Let me see, yonder's the nearest way to Hull, isn't it?"

"Yes, the right-hand one. But who is in such extreme danger?"

"A farmer—Mr. Ashbrook. Poor fellow, it is a chance if he recovers, so they seem to think."

"I know both the Mr. Ashbrooks perfectly well. Which one is it that's so bad; they were right enough yesterday?"

"Mr. John Ashbrook.'

"Umph! that's strange. What's the matter with Mr. John?"

"He was thrown—horse reared and fell upon him. His injuries are very serious."

"I'm sorry to hear this, but—" and here the speaker regarded Peace with a still more searching look, "it's his horse you are riding."

"Yes, that's right enough; it is.'

'Then who are you going for?"

"Dr. Gardiner."

While this conversation was taking place, Peace had so distorted his features that recognition was almost impossible. He was an adept at this. By constant practice he was enabled to throw out his under jaw, lift up his eyebrows, and so alter the expression of his features that he defied detection. This is now pretty generally acknowledged.

"Well, I must not let anyone detain me very long in a case like this," he observed, carelessly. "So farewell for the present."

The patrol made no reply. He did not, however, feel quite satisfied that all was quite right; at the same time he did not consider it his duty to offer any obstacle to Peace's passage along the road, which led directly to the town of Hull.

Peace trotted along till the patrol was lost to sight, then he pulled the bridal rein of the mare, and turned her into a narrow lane which ran at right angles with the road.

"That fellow suspects something," he murmured; "and for two pins he would have collared me there and then. The sooner I part company with the mare the better it will be for both of us, I'm thinking."

He dismounted, opened a gate which was at the corner of a meadow, and led the mare into the field; then he took off the saddle and bridle, which he threw into a ditch, gave the animal a sharp crack with his whip, shut the gate, and left her to herself. This done, he proceeded merrily along on foot.

Messrs. Cheadle and Jamblin had meanwhile been riding to their hearts' content, but they did not catch the most distant glance of the man of whom they were in search. No wonder, seeing that they had lost all traces of the fugitive, and had been journeying in an opposite, or very nearly in an opposite direction to the one taken by Peace. They had, therefore, the gratification of riding many miles upon a bootless errand.

They returned, vexed and dispirited, to Oakfield House, where they found John Ashbrook in bed, with his sister and the village surgeon in close attendance upon him.

The latter had extracted the bullet, and strapped up the head of the sufferer, who was, he said, doing as well as could be expected. Certainly there was no immediate danger.

The farmer had an unimpaired constitution, and, although sadly bruised and knocked about, would in all probability soon get the better of his wounds.

Peace, when he came to the end of the lane, turned into a road, where stood a small beerhouse, of a primitive character, with a good dry skittle-ground at the back.

He knocked several times at the side door of this establishment, but received no answer to his repeated summonses. It was evident that all were asleep within.

He called the landlord by name, with no better result. While thus engaged, a man came forward from the opposite side of the road, and said—

"Why, what's up now, Charley? Want to get in?"

Peace turned round in some alarm, but was a little reassured upon finding the speaker was a friend of his.

"Hang it! I'm as tired as a dog, and wanted an hour or two's rest," said Peace.

"Tired! where have you been to?"

"Playing the fiddle to a party some miles away from here. They could not accommodate me with a shakedown, so I've had to trudge it."

"Come along wi' me, my lad," said the good-natured groom. "You shall have an hour or two's rest in my little crib over the stable."

Peace gladly availed himself of his friend's offer.

A hue and cry would be raised throughout the neighbourhood of the attempted burglary at Oakfield House and the surrounding districts, and Peace, young as he was at this time—he had only just turned twenty—was fully impressed with the necessity of using caution.

No one would dream of his being in the groom's sleeping apartment. The latter informed him that he had to take the carriage up to London, and that he should not return from the metropolis for several days.

"But that aint of no kind o' consequence," said the groom. "You can sleep away to your heart's content, only when you do leave mind and lock the door. You can give the key to the stable-boy."

"I'm sure I do not know how to sufficiently thank you, Jim," observed Peace in his blandest tone and manner.

"There's no call for thanks, lad. You've done me a good turn afore now, and one good turn deserves another."

Peace was conducted by his companion into the small sleeping chamber.

"There you are," said the latter, pointing to the bed. "In less than half an hour I shall be at the station; make yourself comfortable. We shan't meet again for some days, that's quite certain, and so good-bye for the present."

"Good bye, Jim, and many thanks."

Then, as the man was about to pass out, Peace said, quietly—

"Oh, by the way, there is no occasion for you to say you have seen me, or, indeed, I've been here. It's a little private matter I've been about. You understand."

"A nod's as good as a wink to a blind horse," returned the other, with a chuckle. "No one will know anything from me, Charlie."

After the departure of his friend, Peace was too disturbed in his mind to sleep. He watched from the little window of his dormitory the carriage and pair, driven towards the railway station by his friend, the groom.

When the vehicle was lost to sight, he walked towards the door, took the key out of the lock, and fastened the door on the inside. In a few minutes after this he stretched himself on the bed, and sank into a deep sleep—the village clock had struck eleven before he awoke.

He now began to consider his course of action; he felt perfectly secure from observation in his present quarters. No one would for a moment imagine that he was safely ensconced in one of the apartments of the stables adjoining a gentleman's house.

He thought it best to watch and wait; it would not do to be too precipitate; in the dusk of the evening he might creep out and get clear off.

He found in the groom's bedroom some bread and cold meat, which served him for a meal, and he prepared himself to pass the lonely hours as best he could. The day wore on tediously enough, but the longest day must have an end. And when the grey mists of evening began to encircle the objects seen before so distinctly from the window, Charles Peace prepared to take his departure.

He disguised himself in so complete a manner as to almost defy detection. He made himself up as a hawker. He took the precaution to always carry a hawker's licence, made out in a fictitious name; the licence itself, however, was genuine enough.

He heard, as he descended the creaking stairs, the boy whistling in the stable. Agreeably to the directions he had received, he handed the key to the lad, at the same time dropping a shilling in his hand.

The lad stared with astonishment, which was not unmixed with alarm.

A few words from Peace soon reassured him.

"But ye've been 'nation quiet all the day though," said the lad, with a broad grin.

"People generally are quiet when they are asleep, my lad," was the ready rejoinder.

"Ugh! 'spose so."

Peace did not want to have further parley. His purpose was served, and he therefore proceeded on his journey.

CHAPTER III.

COMMITTAL OF GREGSON—JANE TELLS A TERRIBLE TALE—BROXWELL GAOL.

THE most celebrated cracksman of his day, Ned Gregson, alias the Bristol Badger, was certainly the least fortunate of the three ruffians who contrived to effect an entrance into Oakfield House. He was run to earth. After he had been carried on the hurdle into the farmhouse the village surgeon made a superficial examination of his wound, which was of a fearful nature; the whole of the charge from the gun fired by Jane Ryan had entered the burglar's chest, and the loss of blood was enormous. The only wonder was, that Gregson had not been killed outright; but he was not the sort of man to be so easily disposed of. As far as physical strength was concerned he was a perfect giant; this he had proved on many occasions.

He was more than double the age of Peace, with three times his strength. Nevertheless, as far as the guilty and lawless lives of the two men were concerned, there was not much difference between them; they were both criminals of the worst type, their whole career being one of profligacy and crime.

Gregson was taken away to the lock-up in charge of the constabulary, who procured an ambulance from the hospital. The divisional surgeon was sent for; every care was taken of the prisoner; and all that skill and attention could do to preserve so valuable a life as the burglar's was, as is usual in such cases, not wanting.

When sufficiently recovered Gregson was examined before the stipendiary magistrates. The facts deposed to were plain enough, and the prisoner was committed for trial upon two distinct charges—namely, murder and burglary.

Mr. John Ashbrook had by this time sufficiently regained his strength to leave his room and look after his farming stock, but he was not as yet up to his usual form.

"This extraordinary charge of murder," said the farmer to Jane, one afternoon, as he reclined upon the sofa in the front parlour, "it seems just like a romance. Strange that you should have recognised the ruffian by the pistol's flash on that eventful night."

"I should have known him out of ten thousand. His face was as familiar to me as if I had seen him but yesterday."

"Tell us all about it, Jane."

"Well, master, it's a sad and sorrowful tale, which I have kept locked up in my own breast for ever so long, but it is but right you should know all about it."

"Right lass, right you are; go on. What made you imagine that the house was likely to be attacked? You asked me to load the two other guns."

"I did, because I felt assured that danger was at hand."

"Why so?"

"I had a dream—twice I dreamt the same thing—and then I went over to Mother Crowther and consulted her. She can read the future—being—being a wise woman."

"She is a wise woman indeed if she can do that," remarked the farmer, with a smile; "what did she say?"

"She consulted a book, cast my nativity, and told me that in less than three days I should see here or hereabouts the murderer of James Hopgood."

"And who might he be?"

"He is dead now; he was my sweetheart," answered Jane, hanging down her head.

"Oh, your sweetheart—eh?"

"Yes, before I came here I lived at Squire Gordon's. A kinder master never lived. James Hopgood was a carpenter by trade; he had been doing some work for the squire—building some outhouses, and while the work was going on he slept in the house."

"How long ago was this?"

"Aye, it must be nearly six years."

"You've been here over four."

"That's true. Indeed, it must be more than six years. I cannot say to a certainty; but they've got the date—the pleece have."

"No matter, that's quite near enough—six years or a little more. What happened then?"

"I will describe all to you, just as it occurred. James Hopgood was in the kitchen; he and Mary, my fellow-servant, were having supper together. I was in the back kitchen, when all of a sudden we heard a scuffle in the passage, and my master cried, 'Murder!' James rushed past me, and flew up the kitchen stairs. Then we heard a heavy fall in the passage; this was followed by some low moans. I went up to see what

was the matter, and found my master stretched on the floor of the passage, with blood flowing from a wound in his left temple. I endeavoured to raise him, but was unable to do so. He was a stout, heavy man, and I had not strength enough to lift him."

"Was he killed?"

"No—oh, dear, no; he recovered afterwards. But the worst remains to be told. Oh, master, these be tears that are a flowin' from my eyes. I can see it all now, as if it occurred but yesterday."

"Yes, your master, the squire, you found him senseless. There's no hurry, girl, take your time—don't flurry yourself."

"While I was looking at my poor master, I caught sight of James Hopgood and the burglar—him as I shot down in the big bedroom. James had closed with the ruffian, who, as far as I could judge, was striving to shake James off; but he was not able to do this so easily; they wrestled like two serpents. I felt sick and faint; but, notwithstanding, I had sufficient strength left to hasten to young Hopgood's assistance. I saw the flash of an open knife in the pale moonlight, saw the gleaming of the desperate wretch's eyes, and in another moment the knife was buried up to the hilt in James's breast. He fell with a deep groan, and never stirred hand or foot afterwards.

"I rushed forward, and caught his murderer by the handkerchief which encircled his throat. After this I lost all consciousness. When I came to I found myself on the wet grass of the lawn—the ruffian's handkerchief was firmly grasped in my right hand."

"Why, Jane, my girl, this is indeed a horrible story, and have you kept this all to yourself for these last six years?"

"Indeed I have; but, waking or sleeping, one burning thought has been in my brain. It is this—to avenge the death of my dear and true-hearted James."

The farmer was bewildered—partly dazed by the fearful tale he had been listening to. He turned his eyes towards his sister, who had crept into the room to listen to the appalling narrative.

"Did you know of this?" inquired Ashbrook.

"I knew a shocking affair of some sort took place at Squire Gordon's when Jane was there, but I never knew till now its precise nature. I understood that some young man was murdered—that is all. How and by whom I was never told."

"And was the man never discovered? An attempt was made to find him, I s'pose?" asked the farmer of his servant.

"Government offered a reward of a hundred pounds; a description of the man was printed on handbills, which were sent, so they said, to every police-station."

"With what result?"

"With none, except the arrest of a poor harmless fellow, who never set foot in the squire's house, and who had no more to do with the crime than you or I have."

"And the handkerchief?"

"That I have kept. The knife also with which the murder was committed was picked up on the lawn; that, too, I have preserved. They are both now in the possession of the pleece. Ah! we shall bring it home to the deep-dyed villain. I felt certain that, sooner or later, he would be caught, the murderin' thief."

"What became of the squire?"

He left England for good, and settled in Brittany. He has a daughter who is married there."

"Is he still alive?"

"I believe so. I never heard of his death—oh! I'm pretty sure he's alive."

"Do you think he could identify the man?"

"He told me after his recovery that he saw his features distinctly, and that he would be able to swear to him. It appeared that Gregson was making his escape from the house with the things he had stolen, when he was suddenly and unexpectedly confronted by the squire, who had come over the fields, crossed the lawn, and entered by the back door of his residence."

"We've all of us had a narrow escape," said Maud Ashbrook, "and it will be a warning to us for the future."

"I'm glad Jane shot the fellow down," observed the farmer. "She's a true-hearted, brave girl—not, mind ye, but it would ha' bin better for him to have fallen by the hands of one of us men."

"No, master, no," cried Jane, in a deprecating tone. "I am the most deeply injured, sick and sore of heart—I who have sworn to devote the remainder of my life to discover the slayer of James Hopgood—I was the most fitting person to hunt him down. It has been done, and he will not escape now."

Jane had given her evidence before the stipendiary magistrates in the clearest and most lucid manner. She swore positively to the prisoner Gregson, whose features she declared had not changed since she saw them so distinctly on that fatal night. Her fellow-servant also identified the prisoner, whom she saw, so she averred, through the back-parlour window at the time Jane had hold of him by the handkerchief.

He was also recognised by several of the police as a well-known burglar, who had been convicted several times.

Gregson, who was about as hardened a ruffian as it was possible to conceive, knew and felt that his game was up; nevertheless he clung to the hope, as most criminals do of his class, that he might escape the last dread sentence of the law—perhaps his life might be spared.

He was taken to Broxwell Gaol; his custodians conducted him through the lodge, then he passed through a square with a green plot of grass in the middle, encircled by a gravel walk.

It was like a college quadrangle.

Gregson looked at the grass and the turnkeys who came out to meet him. He was conducted up a flight of stone steps, and one of the turnkeys who had joined him and the constabulary who had him under their charge tapped at a thick oak door, which was covered with iron nails and secured with a gigantic lock.

They were admitted immediately into a little room, which was almost entirely filled by a clerks' desk and stool.

Upon this stool was seated an old man, with a pair of iron-rimmed spectacles on his nose, making entries in an account-book.

The turnkey who had opened the door to them now closed it with an ominous sound.

The key clanked loudly in the lock.

The Bristol Badger was in prison.

The turnkey unlocked another door and disappeared. In a few moments he returned, dismissed the constable, and ordered the prisoner to follow him.

They entered a snow-white corridor, which was lined with iron doors, and above with galleries, also of iron, bright and polished.

Gregson was placed in a cell, for some time in the company of a single turnkey, who stood by him, rigid and voiceless as a statue, watchful as a lynx.

The "cracksman" assumed an air of dejection, and kept his eyes fixed upon the ground.

He had only partially recovered from his wound. From this a vast number of shots had been extracted; but several more, it was thought, still remained in the flesh.

The burning pain in his chest had not entirely left him, although it was not nearly so insupportable as at first.

Presently the door of the cell opened, and a gentleman in plain clothes came in. He had a ruddy complexion, with a brown moustache and beard.

Gregson recognised him immediately. He was the governor.

The recognition was mutual.

"So," he said, "you have come here again?"

"They've brought me here," muttered the cracksman.

"Precisely. Of course you know the usual forms prescribed by the authorities. We must put you through the ordeal of a warm bath.

"Turn on the tap, Wilson," said the governor; and in a few minutes the bath was filled with hot water.

They took off his handcuffs, and then stood by him as he undressed.

"Do you know, governor, that I've been wounded—well-nigh to death? It's too bad to put a cove in hot water in my state."

"Wounded, eh? We'll send for the doctor."

The prison surgeon was brought into the room.

He glanced at the wound, which still presented an angry appearance.

"The bath won't hurt you. There is no necessity for you to immerse your chest or shoulders in the water. In my opinion you will be better for it."

"All right," returned Gregson; "you shall have your way. I'm not one to make things disagreeable."

And forthwith he jumped in.

The governor paced the corridor for the next ten minutes or so under pretence of superintending the arrangements of the prisoners' dinners, which ascended from the kitchen on a great tray by means of mysterious machinery.

On his return he called another turnkey, and ordered him to have the prisoner's clothes brushed and cleaned.

"You have got plenty of money," he said to Gregson. "You are suffering from a severe wound. We don't wish to deal harshly with you."

"I'm much obliged, I'm sure," returned the Badger.

The governor took no notice of this last observation, which, to say the truth, was half conciliatory and half sarcastic.

"We will therefore allow you to wear your own clothes, and to procure your own meals from an eating-house if you prefer it."

"Yes, I do prefer it, if it makes no difference."

"So be it, then. You will see by the printed copy of the rules which is hung up in every cell that you are not allowed more than one pint of wine or one quart of malt liquor daily, and that, if you undertake to board yourself, you must do so altogether. Besides this you will be allowed books to read and paper to write upon, and other little comforts, under my supervision, as I have no desire to treat you with unnecessary severity during the brief period that will elapse while you are awaiting your trial. I hope you will conduct yourself in a proper and becoming manner."

The cracksman nodded, and seemed by his demeanour to appreciate the lenity which the governor displayed.

"You are very good, sir, I'm sure," he muttered. "I wish all gentlemen in your position were equally kind and merciful."

The governor bowed in a dignified manner, and then left the cell. The turnkey returned with Gregson's clothes, and stood by him as he dressed. He was then conducted to Cell No. 15.

There they showed him how to ring the bell, how to pull the slide from the grating when he wanted fresh air, and how to manage the water taps and the bed furniture.

They also informed him that when he wanted anything from the town there was a prison servant attached to the establishment whose office it was to run errands for the prisoners who were waiting for trial.

The turnkeys made these explanations with a courteous accent, for turnkeys have a sort of veneration for great criminals.

And Ned Gregson, in this respect, was a man of mark.

The prison officials went out of the cell backwards, as if they were retiring from a royal presence; they locked the door with an ostentatious noise that they might thereby strike a wholesome awe into the mind of their prisoner.

Gregson sat himself down upon the wooden stool in his cell without moving.

The bitterness of his thoughts it would not be so easy to describe.

He remembered with harrowing distinctness the most remote incident of the night upon which the ill-fated James Hopgood fell beneath the fatal blow.

"And that cursed woman!" ejaculated the Badger. "Who would have dreamt of her being an inmate of the farmhouse? And the oily-tongued Peace, he has got clear off, I'll dare be sworn; and the chances are that he is now playing that old fiddle of his—whilst I —I—"

Here he uttered an impious oath, and then lapsed into silence again.

He sat for two hours a prey to the most agonising thoughts.

At the expiration of that time he uttered curses loud and deep. He ran frantically round his narrow cell.

One of the turnkeys opened the door, and told him that he must make less noise. There was a punishment for making an outcry of that nature, and he pointed to one of the printed rules.

The "cracksman" answered with a howl of rage, and squatted abjectly on his stone floor.

The turnkey, who was pretty well used to scenes of this nature, and who, therefore, made due allowance, repeated his warning and shut the door.

Soon after this the prison servant brought a wooden tray in.

There were two dishes, each surrounded by a pewter cover. One contained three slices of roast mutton, floating in lukewarm gravy; the other contained four good-sized potatoes.

Gregson, who was still on the floor, looked at them supinely.

"Governor! thought you would like a little dinner," said the man kindly; and he propped up a slab which was hanging from the wall, placed the tray on it, reached down a salt dish from a shelf in the corner, where it had grown dusty, in company with a bible and two hymn books.

"Will you take beer or wine?"

"I want wine," said the Badger, sulkily.

"Very good, I will bring you a pint; it's against the rules to have any more."

He drank some of the eating-house sherry, which, bad as it was, encouraged him to eat a few mouthfuls. This awoke him from the stupor into which he had fallen, and which had been almost akin to madness.

CHAPTER IV.

PEACE RETURNS TO BRADFORD—THE SLEEPING BEAUTY— HIS DISGUISE AS A ONE-ARMED MAN—THE ROBBERY AT DUDLEY HILL.

LEAVING the guilty man to his reflections, we will now return to the hero of our story.

Charles Peace, after he left the groom's little bedroom, succeeded in getting clear out of the neighbourhood, without attracting any observation.

As he trudged along he reflected that it would be advisable not to return to Hull. The hue and cry raised in consequence of the events already described would reach Hull, and search would be made by the police in that town.

What had gone of Cooney Peace had not the remotest idea. Whether he had escaped or been captured it was not possible for him to say; neither did he concern himself much about the fate of the tinker. In cases of this sort he felt that self-preservation was the first law of nature.

As he was proceeding along he was overtaken by a covered cart. He persuaded the driver thereof to give him a lift on the road. By this means he managed to get many miles on his journey. Having made up his mind to take up his quarters at Bradford, he, on the first opportunity, took the train to that town. He was acquainted with a girl at Bradford, who was, to a certain extent, attached to him. She was a mill-hand. She was possessed of a considerable share of personal attractions.

It was evening when Peace arrived at Bradford, and in the streets were throngs of persons. The factory hands had knocked off work; some were hastening homewards, others were making for some favourite house of entertainment, and groups of inveterate gossips were to be seen in various parts of the town.

Peace walked jauntily along one of the main streets. Having threaded this, he turned round and retraced his steps. He seemed to be wandering about in a desultory way.

A group of girls emerged from a turning out of the street. Three peals of laughter proved that they were in a merry mood.

One of the girls came suddenly forward, and struck Peace in a familiar manner on the shoulder.

"What! Charlie?" she ejaculated, in a tone of surprise and delight. "Who would have thought of seeing you at Bradford?"

"Bessie dear," said Peace, "don't talk so loud; I've not been in the town half an hour, and——"

"What brought you here?"

"I came to see you, my charmer."

The girl made a grimace—she didn't quite believe what he said, but, nevertheless, felt flattered.

Although one of the working class, she was very beautiful—her features being delicately chiselled, and her form being cast in one of nature's choicest moulds; for the rest she was giddy, thoughtless, and her morals were not of the highest order. Her name was Bessie Dalton.

"And your mother?" inquired the girl.

"I left her at Hull," returned her companion.

The two walked on in close converse for some time. They passed through several streets, and eventually arrived at an unpretending-looking house, where Bessie lived.

They both entered, and Peace was introduced to the landlord, and took one of the furnished rooms, which were let out to work people. He had a tolerably fair share of money, which would suffice for his immediate wants; and in the course of a few days he succeeded in getting some odd jobs in picture framing. In the evening he contrived to pick up a few shillings by playing the violin at some of the houses of public entertainment.

He was a man who could make himself agreeable enough when it answered his purpose to do so. He was in no way deficient in conversational powers; was tolerably well informed upon most subjects, and generally ingratiated himself in the good graces of most persons with whom he came in contact.

To a certain extent the girl, Bessie Dalton, was proud of him. He was far ahead in many ways of the working population of Bradford, who, one and all, voted him a right good fellow.

For a short time he led a tolerably quiet life.

But it was not in his nature to earn a respectable living for long without having recourse to his evil courses.

He became straitened in circumstances, and once more he essayed to replenish his exchequer by his midnight excursions.

Since the disastrous affair at Oakfield House he had made up his mind to carry on business on his own account.

He would have no accomplices. None should know of his depredations save the girl Bessie, in whom he had implicit confidence.

And it is but justice to her to note that whatever may have been her faults she never betrayed Charles Peace.

He was for the first time made up as a one-arm man. He had for a long time contemplated disguising himself in this way, and the better to carry out his purpose had moulded a piece of gutta-percha, to which a hook was attached, his hand, when drawn up, fitting into the socket of the gutta-percha.

When this instrument—if it can be so termed—was on no person in the world would have guessed that he was anything else but a one-armed man.

Disguising himself after this fashion, and staining his face so as to represent a mulatto, he one night started upon one of his lawless expeditions.

He passed quickly out of the town of Bradford, and made direct for a small but handsomely-built house, just on the outskirts of Dudley-hill.

The house, which was built of stone, with bay windows and a handsome portico in front, was in the occupation of a wealthy gentleman, who was a retired mill-owner.

Shrewdly guessing that a pretty considerable amount of moveable property would be found within this habitation, Peace had determined to pay it a visit.

Upon his arrival in front of the house he opened the garden-gate with a skeleton key, closed it again, and began to mature his plan of operations.

There was a garden in the front and rear of the villa, which stood by itself on the brow of the hill. No other habitation was near it—certainly none within a quarter of a mile.

Peace deftly climbed up to the balcony which stood in front of the first floor window. This balcony was half filled with evergreens, and these completely concealed him from any chance passenger—not, indeed,

that there was a single living person to be seen abroad save himself.

The windows were what is termed French ones; they opened in the centre, and swung back on hinges, like folding doors. He had not much difficulty in lifting the bottom bolt of these; the top one had not been pushed into its socket.

He now had to operate upon the shutters; these were fastened by an iron bar, which ran across them.

Stooping down so as to conceal himself behind the evergreens, he began to bore holes in the shutters with a small centre-bit. After working industriously, but at the same time as noiselessly as possible, for some little time, he succeeded in making an aperture in one of the shutters, sufficiently large for his hand to pass through. He then lifted up the bar, and pushed open the shutters.

In another moment he was in the first floor front room. He wore at this time women's cloth boots, over which were goloshes, also women's, so that his footsteps were as noiseless as a cat's.

He carefully closed the shutters after he had effected an entrance. Then he began, by the aid of his dark lantern, to make an inspection of the apartment, which was sumptuously furnished. It contained plate and valuables, which must be worth a considerable amount.

Peace opened cupboards and drawers. In one of the last named he found a bag of gold and a roll of bank notes. An elegantly-wrought silver cup, presented to the mill-owner by his workpeople, shared the same fate as the other articles; and, taken altogether, the valuables abstracted from this one room was a rich booty for the most rapacious mercenary burglar.

Peace was, however, hungering for more. He passed out of the front room and gently opened the door of the back. All was still. He entered; when, to his infinite astonishment, he found it tenanted.

He stood transfixed with wonderment. On a couch, the head of which was near the window, was stretched a young female of such surpassing loveliness that even the callous heart of the burglar was touched.

The pale moonlight streamed through the lace curtains, and revealed a picture upon which the burglar gazed with fascinated eyes.

The young maiden was in a deep slumber, her head was thrown back, resting on one exquisitely-formed arm, a long tress of glossy brown hair fell over her partially-revealed bosom, and the moist, ruddy lips were parted, disclosing the pearly teeth.

The *pose* of the figure was perfect, and if there ever was a living personification of the " Sleeping Beauty " most assuredly the lovely maiden, who moved the senses of the burglar to wonder and delight, was that one.

Peace was spell-bound—he had never beheld in his life anything so matchless, so surpassingly beautiful.

He stood speechless and immovable with admiration. The power of volition seemed to have entirely forsaken him.

" How matchlessly beautiful she is !" murmured the burglar. " What a paragon of perfection; indeed—indeed, I have never seen aught so fair !"

His eyes were rivetted on the couch upon which the young creature reclined.

The room was furnished with all the appliances which wealth could supply, or taste could suggest. Every piece of furniture in that elegant apartment was of the choicest and rarest manufacture. It seemed to the enhanced eyes of the robber to be the personification of a Paphian bower—at once bewitching, poetic, and almost fabulous.

On the mantel-piece was a small clock of rare workmanship. This elegant timepiece was set with jewels, which sparkled and scintillated beneath the rays of his lantern.

Each picture that hung upon the walls was a perfect gem. The chairs were covered with brocaded silk, and the articles of *virtu* observable in almost every part of the bedchamber were too numerous to particularise. It will suffice to note that they served to make up an *ensemble* perfectly unique.

But all these things paled before the lustre and beauty of the sleeper.

Much has been said about the might and majesty of beauty, and no one will deny that a lovely woman is nature's crown of triumph.

She is, beyond all else, the fairest thing in the creation.

Charles Peace was touched. He longed to clasp in his arms the fair maiden who was slumbering so tranquilly.

He had, whilst gazing on her, almost forgotten the purport of his visit to the mill-owner's villa; but was in a measure reminded of the same when he looked at the various articles in the room.

Creeping forward he sought to gain possession of the gold watch on its stand by the toilette-table. He moved forward a step or two, but suddenly became motionless again, as the sleeper heaved a soft sigh and shifted slightly her position. She did not, however, awaken, but the motion revealed something more of her charms.

The heart of the burglar beat audibly.

He hesitated how to act. Grasping with his right hand the revolver he invariably carried with him, he watched the maiden with the eyes of a lynx.

Not that he meant doing her any harm. He hardly knew what he meant. For a time he was subdued, but the greed of gain returned to him, and he placed his hand upon the watch.

"No," he murmured, after a pause, "I will take nothing of her's—nothing."

"I am well repaid by looking at one so lovely."

He withdrew his hand from the watch and retreated some two or three steps backwards towards the door of the room.

Then he became immovable again.

"This will never do," he muttered. "If I go on like this I shall run the chance of being discovered; and how then? No, I must away at once, and yet, hang it, she is so very beautiful!"

He again rivetted his eyes on the form of the sleeper, upon which he once or twice cast the rays of his lantern.

"I'm a weak, silly fool to be overcome thus—an idiot. Bah! there must be an end to it."

He turned round and crept through the half-opened door. Down the stairs, with faltering steps, he then proceeded. He entered the front parlour, and then the back. He stripped them of as many valuables as he could conveniently carry, and then passed out of the house by the back door.

All this had been done without his disturbing any one.

Taking his way along the garden he passed out into the high road. Not a soul was to be seen. The night was clear and bright; and he walked on for a good half mile. Upon arriving at the end of a lane which ran out of the road he halted, looking the while to the right and left.

He saw the back of a policeman going down the lane, and prudence dictated that he should go in the opposite direction.

He walked on with rapid strides, and succeeded in reaching his lodgings at Bradford. Having let himself in with a latch-key, he made direct for his own little room without disturbing any one.

Peace had several orders on hand for picture-framing, and for the next two or three days after the burglary near Dudley-hill he worked industriously at his trade—if we can bring ourselves to consider that to be his legitimate occupation.

He could turn his hand to a number of things—picture-framing being one. This was supplemented by carpentry, wood-carving of every description, and, last not least, he was a violinist of no inconsiderable ability.

Had he chosen to conduct himself in a discreet and proper manner he might have made, if not a shining light, certainly a respectable member of society.

The booty he had obtained from the mill-owner he, of course, carefully concealed. He had already changed one of the notes in a quarter where there was not much fear of detection.

While working at his trade, in a shed at the bottom of the yard of the house in which he had taken up his quarters, he was surprised at seeing a stranger enter the yard in company of Bessie Dalton.

"A friend of mine," said the latter," introducing her companion to Peace. "He is on a charitable expedition. A poor fellow was severely injured at Ludlow's mill, and he has since died. His wife and two children are in the greatest distress. My friend is getting up a subscription for his widow."

"Very creditable of you, I'm sure," remarked Peace, turning towards the stranger. "I am but a working man myself, as you see, but I will willingly give my mite."

"Thank you. It is hardly fair, perhaps, to ask you, as you are a comparative stranger to us. Still, at the same time, it has been well said that many can help one.

Peace put his hand in his pocket, and gave the man five shillings.

"I can't afford much, but what I can spare you are welcome to," remarked the burglar. "Totally unprovided for—are they?"

"Yes; I am sorry to say he was not in any benefit society, although he had put his name down in one, and would no doubt, have been elected at the next meeting."

"All these things are sad, very sad. What does the widow purpose doing?"

"Well, I must tell you that the little sum subscribed, whatever it may be, will be applied to meet her immediate wants. After then we shall endeavour to raise a sum sufficient to set her up in business—some little shop, perhaps. Her husband's employers have promised their assistance, and Mr. Knight, the organist at the church, has promised his services at a benefit concert we thought of giving."

"Not a bad idea."

"The rector will also give us his patronage, besides several other influential gentlemen in the town."

"And I'm sure, Charlie, you will have no objection to give your services," added Bessie.

"In what way?"

"Well, of course, I mean in the way of music. You can play the violin, you know."

"Would you have any objection?" said the stranger.

PEACE, THE BURGLAR, RANSACKING THE DRAWERS.

"Not the slightest. If my services are of any use you may command me; but there must be the arrangement as to programme and the style of music. Also whether you desire me to play a solo or otherwise."

"I am not able to say at present; but this can be arranged by those who understand these matters better than I do. I aint much of a musician myself, although I am very fond of hearing music either vocal or instrumental."

"Have you any vocalists?"

"We shall have some volunteers—some of the choir will, of course, do some part-singing; besides there are

No. 3.

... as well as one or two professionals, have agreed to come forward on this occasion. Oh, I ... say we shall have a tolerably good concert. Mr. Knight presides at the piano, and he has consented to play the accompaniments to the vocalists."

"So easy task," remarked Peace, "especially if he is not acquainted with the performers."

"No—so he says. Would you like to see him?"

"Who?"

"Mr. Knight."

"Is will be necessary for me to do so before the night of the concert. Otherwise we shall be all at sea."

"I will mention the subject. You will find him, I'm sure, in every respect a gentleman, who, I dare say, will be happy to make the acquaintance of a brother artist."

"I'm obliged to you for your good opinion," said Peace with a sort of bow, which was half obsequious and half satirical.

"In the cause of charity we are all of us brothers; and on what evening do you purpose giving this concert?"

"As soon as possible. It would be as well, I think, to strike while it's hot. It must certainly be within a fortnight—or a week, if it can be arranged. Do you play sacred music——"

"I do not care to play anything else. If I consulted my own inclination I should confine myself to sacred music—not, mind you, that I have done so at present."

"Oh, he can play anything and everything," chimed in Bessie Dalton. "Nigger melodies, dance music, comic songs, serious and sentimental."

"There, that will do, Bess," cried Peace.

"Well, you know you can. What's the use of being modest when you've got—ahem, talent?"

"There, gently, girl; leave people to judge for themselves."

"Oh, I've done; sorry I spoke," answered the girl, ...

"I will not detain you, Mr. Peace. Allow me to offer you my most sincere thanks. I shall have the pleasure of seeing you again in a day or two."

The speaker offered his hand to the burglar; there was the usual interchange of courtesies, and the visitor took his departure.

"You ought to make something out of this, Charlie," said Bessie Dalton.

"How so?" returned Peace; "I am to give my services gratuitously."

"True; but it will be the means of introducing you to a lot of swells and rich people, whom you can afterwards call upon and leave your card. You see I've an eye to business, old man."

"Well, yes, certainly, there's some use in that. Some of them may want pictures framed."

"Who are these for?" said the girl, pointing to some frames which had been just finished.

"For a Mr. Vcreon, up the hill. There's not much beauty about them, he's as mean as Lucifer. Indeed, they are all pretty much alike as far as that goes. It's a hard job to get a living by working for the trade."

"You should have a shop of your own."

"May be I shall later on—that is, if I settle in Bradford."

"You are not going to leave me again?" said the girl, ...

"Please heard do," returned Peace, with a smile.

"..."

"Cut it off ... her strap—that's all."

"Men never give girls credit for any feeling," said Bessie, pouting.

"Yes, they are all of them selfish by nature."

"Who?"

"Why, the men, of course."

"You don't mean what you say."

"Don't I?"

"No."

"Only saying so to please you—is that it?"

"I've no doubt it is."

"Well, here's something better than words, lass. Here's a couple of quid for you, to buy a new dress, or anything else you may want."

"Oh you dear, good fellow; and is this for me?"

"Certainly, seeing that I gave it of my own free will."

The girl clapped her hands with delight, gave her companion a kiss, and pocketed the money.

CHAPTER V.

THE CONCERT.—PEACE AS A PUBLIC ENTERTAINER.—THE SURPRISE.

THE ill-fated weaver who had succumbed to the injuries received in the mill in which he worked was a man of steady habits, an excellent husband and father, and altogether a worthy member of society. He was, in consequence, greatly respected in the town. A committee of influential persons was formed for the purpose of carrying out successfully all the necessary arrangements for the forthcoming concert.

Peace, who was to a certain extent popular with a section of the operatives, was introduced to Mr. Knight, the musical director of the proposed entertainment. At the first interview a discussion took place as to the part he was to play on the eventful evening. He tried over several difficult pieces with the pianist, who professed himself well satisfied with the burglar's ability.

"I see you have paid some attention to chamber or classic music, as well as sacred," observed Mr. Knight.

"I commenced with sacred," returned Peace, and always took great delight in both, but at the same time it doesn't go down with the multitude so well as livelier strains, such as ballads, music-hall songs, and nigger melodies."

"We are most of us aware of that," observed the director and pianist, "and hence it is that we purpose dividing the entertainment into two or three parts. The first will be devoted to the better class of music, both sacred and secular; the next will be a mixed entertainment, consisting of varieties of various descriptions. You can, of course, appear in one or both parts. The first we shall have no difficulty in arranging. Your assistance will be required in several pieces which I may say are of exceptional beauty, and will require very careful rendering. We must have a few rehearsals before appearing in public. Can you find time to attend these?"

"I will make it my business to do so."

"Good. And now, as to the second part, Mr. Peace?"

"I leave it to your better judgment."

"Nay, I think you are the best qualified to determine as to that," returned his companion, courteously.

"If I might suggest, then," said Peace, "I will come on as a nigger, give a sort of medley entertainment, finish up by performing on one violin only. I have been tolerably successful in this, and find it generally pleases the people."

"I've no doubt it does. We've got a young gentleman—a volunteer—who is well up in nigger melodies.

would you like him to assist you in this part of the
performance?"

"Yes, most certainly. He will black his face, I suppose?"

"Oh, most willingly; anything would please him
better. I will introduce you to him, and Cooke will be
our little difficulty, I think, about the matter. You
can consult together."

This matter being satisfactorily settled, nothing
remained but the rehearsals.

These were attended with unvarying punctuality,
and the several performers got tolerably perfect before
the night on which they were to appear.

A large building—one of the parish school-rooms,
and which was frequently made use of as a lecture
hall, was placed at the disposal of the managing committee.

Bills containing a programme of the performance
were posted all over the town, and on these the name
of Charles Peace figured as the "Modern Paganini,"
who would, by special desire, perform on one string
only, after the manner of his great predecessor.

Little did those who purchased tickets for the concert imagine that they were about to listen to the performance of one of the greatest and most notorious
burglars of modern times.

Peace at this time was led or rather fell into good
society; and he was too astute and cunning a rascal to
show the cloven foot. He was discreet and very
proper in his conduct, and indeed it may be said that
he was highly popular in the select circle in which he
moved.

Peace throughout his career was fond of notoriety—
this has been evidenced in the latter part of his sinful life—and he looked forward with something like
pleasure to the evening upon which he was to appear
in conjunction with some worthy and honourable gentlemen who were acting in unison in the cause of
charity.

The Bradford people, in common with those of
Birmingham, Liverpool, Norwich, and other manufacturing towns, love music for music's sake; this is
evidenced by the enormous gatherings at the festivals
held at these great centres.

The assertion made by people of other nations that
the English are not a musical people is without a
shadow of foundation—this fact is well known to all
who are conversant with the subject.

When the doors were opened at the school-room in
which the entertainment was to take place crowds of
persons rushed forward to obtain seats. The area
was filled in an incredibly short space of time.

Before the time the performance commenced the whole
place was full from floor to roof.

Bessie Dalton, in company with Mrs. Bristow, the
wife of an artisan residing in the parlours of the house
in which Peace lived, had taken up her station at the
entrance some half an hour or more before the public
were admitted.

Bessie and Mrs. Bristow therefore contrived to get
a tolerably good position in the fourth row of the
area.

A young man, evidently moving in a superior class
to themselves, had been of essential service to the two
friends in protecting them from the pressure of the
crowd during their progress towards the entrance.

He took a seat beside them.

After waiting patiently for some considerable time
the audience began to be restive.

Many began to hammer on the boards with their
feet, while others clapped their hands.

"Play! Play! out it!" exclaimed one or two of them.

"What are they waiting so long for?" inquired
Bessie, of the gentleman by her side.

"Oh! it is time the performance commenced," he
answered, "and the people are getting impatient.
They ought not to do so, seeing that the performers
give their services gratuitously; and then, too, very
many of them are novices, and, perhaps, appear publicly this evening for the first time."

"Certainly," said Mrs. Bristow. "People are so in-
considerate—so unreasonable."

These were stereotyped phrases which the speaker
was accustomed to make use of on every occasion.

The gentleman merely nodded his acquiescence to
the proposition.

A burst of applause announced the appearance of a
young man on the platform, who proceeded in a most
deliberate manner to place the piano in a better position. When this had been done he placed some music
on the instrument, and drew forth a small music-stand,
which he furnished in a similar manner.

Having completed these arrangements he retired.

A titter was heard in the house as he left.

Nobody knew why or wherefore.

Mr. Knight now came forward.

He was well known to most of those present, and,
as a natural consequence, he was loudly cheered.

He bowed, and then sat down to the piano.

He played a difficult piece by Mendelssohn in a masterly manner. It was too long to encore, so they contented themselves with applauding it.

The performer still retained his position at the
instrument.

A group of choristers entered. These were composed of boys and adults.

They sang a selection from the "Messiah" in a way
which appeared to give great satisfaction, some portions of it being encored.

Two other performers now made their appearance,
the first being Charles Peace, the other a tall gentleman, whose name was not announced; he, however,
bore in his hands a base viol.

Two chairs were brought forward in close proximity
with the piano, and on these the musicians sat.

After the usual formula of scraping and twanging
the strings, one of Beethoven's magnificent symphonies
was attacked—to use a newspaper phrase.

It was played with great feeling, being, in fact, a
gem to those who could appreciate first class music.

It was re-demanded.

"That was well played—was it not, sir?" said Bessie,
to the gentleman.

"Oh, dear, yes; highly creditable to all three of the
performers—exceedingly good!"

While this had been going on, Peace appeared to be
a little disconcerted. Despite the encore, he arose from
his seat, and was about to make a precipitate retreat;
but Mr. Knight signified by a movement of his hand
and head that the symphony was to be repeated. Notwithstanding this, Peace still hesitated.

At length he returned to his seat.

Many persons attributed his manner to timidity, and
the tender-hearted gave him a vociferous round of
applause by way of encouragement.

They were, however, quite mistaken in their surmise.

Timidity was not one of Peace's characteristics.

There was another and more potent reason for his
trepidation.

It was this.

In one of the side boxes sat an elderly gentleman and
a young lady.

The features of the last-named were familiar to the violinist.

She was the beautiful and ravishing creature whom he had seen slumbering at the millionaire's house on the night of the burglary.

She was within a few paces of him, being in one of the lower boxes, and she looked the very personification of female loveliness.

Peace was bewildered. He did play his part in the symphony, and he played it well, but it was a desperate struggle to get through it. Any other man placed in a similar position must certainly have broken down.

And as it was Peace was very nearly doing so.

He would have given anything he was possessed of to have been spared this trial, for most assuredly it was the greatest trial he had as yet experienced.

He had in a measure recovered his confidence when the symphony was given for the second time; nevertheless he kept casting furtive glances in the direction of the box in which the young lady was seated.

The performers bowed and retired.

"Three pieces have been successfully got through, and as yet there has been no apology," said a young man behind Bessie and her companion.

"What do you mean?" observed another of the audience.

"Why, only this—that in entertainments of this sort, where amateurs are to appear, there is generally some hitch, some mistake, and as a natural consequence an apology has to be made."

"Oh, no doubt we shall have one before the evening is over."

A young lady was now led on by the director. She had a piece of music in her hand, which shook and trembled like an aspen bough agitated by a passing breeze.

It was painfully evident that she was nervous, and those who have experienced that sensation upon facing an audience for the first time will, I am sure, pity her.

She was set down in the programme for Haydn's canzonet, "My mother bids me bind my hair."

Luckily for her the piece in question has a lovely introductory pianoforte prelude. This gave the singer time to recover her first shock at seeing the sea of heads before her.

There was no help for it—she had to commence. The prelude was over, and in faltering accents she began to warble Haydn's plaintive music. But her throat was dry and husky—a thing by no means uncommon with nervous singers, and even the applause she received did not appear to lubricate it.

It was evident she had a magnificent organ—I say organ advisedly, as it is a term invariably made use of by musical critics, and if they don't know who should? Vulgar, commonplace people would perhaps call it a voice, but that's no matter; organ is the "properer" term, as Artemus Ward would say.

The young lady, however, could not possibly display her full powers in consequence of timidity; yet she did contrive to get through the piece creditably. In the morning she had sung it in Mr. Knight's room magnificently.

But despite her shortcomings the audience encored her.

She, however, bowed and retired.

There was a clamour for her return.

The director had to rise from his seat for the purpose of bringing her back, but she declined.

The clamour continued.

Mr. Knight apologised, and pleaded indisposition, a cold, and hence the young lady's inability to repeat the canzonet.

The tumult was hushed.

Charles appeared—he was accompanied this time by a harpist.

A trio for harp, piano, and violin. This proved to be a very taking piece; it seemed to give general satisfaction.

It was encored.

It was not, however, repeated, the performers substituting another in its stead. This was done to give a greater variety to the entertainment.

After another song and a harp solo, the first part was brought to a conclusion by the choir singing a magnificent chorus from one of the oratorios.

While all this had been going on, the young man or gentleman it might be, who sat beside Bessie, was unremitting in his attentions to her and her companion, Mrs. Bristow, who, albeit a married woman, was not much older than the girl.

In the second part of the performance Peace made a still greater impression on the audience, who applauded him to the very echo.

After two or three popular ballads had been sung, he and another young man came forward with their faces blacked, as a couple of nigger delineators. After some patter, in which some old jokes were given, Peace commenced a mild and meek-like prelude on the violin, his companion the while working vigorously on the concertina.

The sounds he produced from his instrument were so novel, not to say bewildering, that the house was convulsed with laughter. He imitated animals, the shriek of the railway whistle, the noise of a passing train, and a variety of other noises which were familiar to all persons present.

After which he threw aside all the strings of the instrument save one, and upon this he played, *a la Paganini*. Of course no one present had heard his great predecessor, and most persons took it for granted that the performance of the black gentleman before them was most wonderful. It was certainly received with greater favour than many admirably performed pieces in the earlier part of the evening.

When the two niggers left the stage there was a general clamour for their reappearance.

They returned and favoured the company by giving a few more specimens of their musical eccentricities.

The concert was universally acknowledged to be a great success. It was brought to a close by a well-known elocutionist delivering a parting address, which a local poet had written especially, as a conclusion to the evening's entertainment.

The chairman of the committee then came forward, and thanked all present for their attendance.

After partaking of some of the wine and other refreshments provided for the performers by the managing committee, Peace prepared to take his departure; but he did not find it so easy to get away, there were so many persons present who sought to detain him.

In addition to his brother artists, who were by this time loquacious enough, he had to run the fire of many of the town's folk, who were very profuse in their thanks for the diligence and attention he had displayed in furthering the ends of charity. Some who had partaken pretty freely of the champagne went further, and spoke in laudatory terms of his talent.

He was, of course, greatly flattered by these encomiums, as many better men have been under similar circumstances both before and since; but he was uneasy, and was desirous of beating a retreat.

There was good reason for this. The young lady whose acquaintance he made for the first time at Dudley Hill was among the throng of persons in the little room, which had been placed at the disposal of the artists.

There was something so heavenly and bewitching in the expression of the face of this fair young creature that Peace felt abashed and crest-fallen in her presence. He found it impossible to meet the glance of her dark, lustrous eyes without quailing. Conscious of his own weakness in this respect, he was fearful lest it might be observed by others.

He therefore, upon the first opportunity that presented itself, passed out of the room unobserved, and crept along the passage towards the side door, by means of which he gained the street.

Then he breathed again more freely.

He saw Bessie Dalton and Mrs. Bristow some distance ahead, in company with a gentleman, and walked on quickly, that he might overtake them; but his progress was checked by a shabby, dilapidated-looking man addressing him—

"Be your name Peace, sir?" inquired that personage.

"Maybe it is, and maybe it is not. What matters it to you?"

"I've got a letter."

"Indeed. Who from?"

"I don't know the party's name, but he said I was to give it to you."

Peace snatched a dirty piece of paper from the speaker's hand, opened it, and read the following words, which were written in a miserable scrawl—

"Dear Charlie,—'Cheeks' (a flash name for an accomplice) is nabbed—want to see you—am at the 'Bag o' Nails'—hard by—bearer will show you where it is—don't delay. Yours, COONEY."

"Here in this town," muttered Peace to himself. "How can he have possibly guessed? Why, of course, my name in the bills. Curse it, I must have been mad to play in my own name."

"Any answer, sir?" said the man, touching his forehead.

"Answer. Well, yes, I s'pose so. He wants to see me. Where's this house, the 'Bag o' Nails?'"

"Not a quarter of a mile from here."

"Very good, then I'll go at once with you."

Peace and his dilapidated companion walked on in silence for some time; they threaded three of the dingiest and most miserable streets in the town. The locality was in consonance with the character of the tinker.

"Do you know the person who gave you that letter?" said Peace.

"I've seen him once or twice before, I think. Don't know much on him. Guv'nor does, I believe."

"Umph. Has he been long in the town?"

"Came yesterday, I b'lieve."

They now arrived in front of a dirty-looking beershop, which was the house they were bound for. The man, who was potman to the establishment, led the way in. He passed the bar, and pointed to a room in the rear of the premises.

Peace entered. A solitary person was in the apartment. This was Cooney.

"Well," said Peace, offering his hand, "we meet again once more. How goes it with you?"

"Precious bad—jolly bad; haven't got a stiver. Am bust up—that's how I am."

Peace took hold of one of the ricketty wooden chairs, which he drew towards the fire, and sat down beside his quondam pal.

"You managed to give 'em the slip, then?" said Cooney, with a chuckle. "But the old un's grabbed."

"So I've heard. It was a bad night's work altogether."

"Aye, that it was."

"How did you manage to get away?"

"I gave 'em the double," returned the tinker, with a grin. "I'll tell yer all about it another time, if so be ye're interested in a miserable bloke like me, which aint at all likely, seeing as how yer a-keeping company with the hupper classes."

There was a tone of irony in the man's manner which jarred upon the feelings of Peace, who, however, thought it best to take no notice of it.

"We'd better have something to drink first, and then I can hear what you have to say," remarked Peace, as he touched the bell.

Glasses of grog were ordered and promptly served. Peace paid for the liquor, and gave the potman a shilling as a gratuity.

"Here's to our noble selves," said the tinker, raising his glass to his lips. "Ah, that does a cove a world o' good!"

"Well, now, then, we'll proceed to business," observed Peace. "You're hard up."

"I'm done up—bust up, and ha' been pretty nigh starving. That's how I am, and seeing as how I aint got bite nor sup—same what we've jest now had in—I've made so bold as to lay my case afore one who won't send me away empty-handed—leastways not if he 'ave the means to hold a 'elping 'and to a pal vot's in distress."

"I'm in no very good position myself, but whatever I can spare you are welcome to."

"Blessed if I didn't say so. I know'd it—vot yer can do you vill do."

"Yes, here's a quid for your immediate wants. It's all I can spare now, for I must tell you I've cut the old game—don't intend to have any more of it."

"Oh, goin' to do the respectable, eh?" said Cooney, with a very low whistle. "That's yer game, is it?"

"Yes, I am at work now at my old business, and to that I intend to stick. No more night work for me—it's a deal too risky."

"Vell, perhaps you are right. But I say, old boy, can you spare another quid?"

"Yes, provided you leave the town and don't bother me any more."

"Oh, ye've no call to be afeard. I aint a-goin' to stay in this here place—not if I know it."

"Good—then here's the other."

"Thanks—you're a good fellow Charlie, arter all, but I 'spose yer'll be glad to get shut o' me—eh? Here the speaker winked his eye.

"Well, you see we are on a different lay now."

"Right yer are, old man. Vell, there, I aint a-goin' to bother yer; so make yer mind easy on that score, but the old un, Charlie, it's duced hard lines wi' him."

"Ah, he's charged with murder—is he not?"

"Sartin shure he is."

"How came that about?"

"I'll tell yer. Yer see, the Badger, some years ago, cracked a crib in the country, and, as ill luck would ha' it, jest as he vos a-making off with the swag who should cross his path but the blessed old fool hisself. He'd up an' give him one for hisself. A young man as vos a-keeping company vith the servant rushes forward and ketches 'old o' Gregson. Vell, there the two vere struggling like anythink on the grass plat, and Gregson

could not get away just as how, although he tried his
utmost.

"O, he's a deep 'un?"

"He, ah! he said if he could—leastways, that's
what I've heard. Vell, vot does the Badger do but he
whips out his knife, and stabs t'other chap to the heart?
Then the gal comes at him, and clutches hold of his
throat. He managed to shake her off, but you see he
left something behind—the handkerchief he wore
round his neck and the knife."

"But what has that to do with the affair at Oakfield
House?"

"Ah! it's a deal to do wi' it—it has. You shall hear.
The last part on it is like a play—better nor any play,
that's what it is. Yer see, as I said afore, the Badger
gets clean away, a reward is offered by Guv'ment,
likewise a reward by the old bloke—him as was robbed
and knocked down in the passage. The bobbies set to
work, the whole biling on 'em, but they never got the
blind side of the old un. Vell, this is six year ago—
aye, more than six year it is now, and a durin' them
six years the gal has had but one thought—this was to
ketch the murderer of her love, and she's a done it,
Charlie—there aint no mistake about that 'ere—she
done it. The Badger, like a fool, fired a pistol at random when he were in that bedroom. The gal sees his
face by the pistol's flash, and she shoots him down—
that's what she does."

"Of course we know he was shot, but I did not
know who by."

"By the gal, I tell yer. She's been afore the magistrates, and has sworn to him like anythink, and she
means to hang him—leastways, it won't be any fault of
her's if he doesn't swing. Ah! it's all up with the
Badger," said Cooney, with a sigh, at the same time
draining off the liquor left in his glass.

"It's a bad bisness—a precious bad bisness, there
aint no manner o' doubt on't."

"It is, indeed," returned Peace; "but it is a lesson
to both of us—a lesson I hope you will profit by."

"Oh, there aint no call for you to preach, or to try
and make me better nor I am. But I am sorry for the
old un—he was always square enough with me—
always."

"I tell you, Cooney, sadly and seriously, that if you
don't intend to profit by the warning already given to
both of us, I shall; and I advise you to follow my
example."

"Oh, I'll profit by it one way or t'other; I sed as
how it 'ud come to this sooner or later, he was so rash,
so headstrong. Didn't I always say that I liked
to do business in a quiet sort o' way? Answer me
that."

"I admit you did," said Peace in a conciliatory tone
of voice. "But now we must part—I durst not stay
any longer," he added rising from his seat.

"Are yer agoin'?"

"Yes, you don't want anything more of me."

"No, not a morsel. I'm thankful enough for what
you have given me—but I say, Charlie, you're a
knockin' up a tidy business in this town, aint yer?"

"Oh no; but very middling at present. What are
your movements?"

"I leave to-morrow morning—and so good-bye and
good luck to you."

The two companions in crime shook hands and
parted.

Peace, when he reached the street, walked on as fast
as possible. He was greatly relieved when he lost
sight of the beershop in which this interview had taken
place.

Peace greatly regretted having lost any time to do
with the Badger or his jackal, Cooney. Their association with odious characters and desperate lawless had
doubtless a marked influence on his after career. If
he had got into trouble once, through other rough and
lawless companions; he saw it was folly to intrude, and
went alone upon his predatory and nocturnal visits;
and these, as it afterwards transpired, were singularly
successful and lucrative.

CHAPTER VI.

BROXWILL GAOL—GUILTY OF WILFUL MURDER—PEACE SEES THE LAST OF GREGSON.

WHILE Peace was in comparative security, and enjoying immunity for his past crimes, the hours were
rolling away sadly enough with Mr. Edward Gregson,
alias the Bristol Badger, alias the Old Un. He was
caught in a net from which he was not likely to escape.
He was deeply impressed with this fact.

The day appointed for his trial was close at hand,
the nearer it approached the more anxious, nervous,
and fidgety, he became. He was anxious to obtain the
services of some leading barrister to conduct his defence, but he had not funds come out for that purpose.

His sister, who was married to a drunken, worthless
fellow, was the only person who stood by him in the
hour of his extreme need. She went, at his request,
from one to another of the burglar's quondam associates, for the purpose of raising a sum sufficient for
the defence.

At Gregson's direction she waited upon Peace, who
was not a little disconcerted when she presented herself at his lodging in Bradford. He, however, did
more than many of the others did—he gave her a few
pounds.

He also spoke words of kindness to her, and
expressed a hope that the verdict would be more
favourable than anticipated.

And now let us return to Gregson, who had been
confined in one of the model cells of Broxwill.

The little money he had with him at the time of his
capture, he had spent entirely upon sumptuous
dinners.

Gorging himself, like a boa constrictor, he would fling
his enormous frame upon the hammock-like bed, which
oscillated beneath his weight, and slept from dinner
time to dinner time.

Thus did the earlier portion of his imprisonment pass
pleasantly enough.

It is true that he sometimes complained of the regulation respecting the quart of malt liquor, but upon the
whole behaved himself very quietly.

In fact, as he was almost invariably asleep, it could
hardly have been otherwise.

But, alas! one dreadful morning he was informed
that his money was all gone, and that he must, for the
future, content himself with the prison diet.

He knew from experience what that was.

A mug of gruel and a piece of bread was brought
him for his breakfast. He surveyed it with contempt,
and emptied it away into the slop.

He did not care about breakfast or tea. He liked
being fed once a day, like the lions in a menagerie, or
the bull terriers in the room.

His anxiety was great to see what his hot dinner
was. It happened to be a soup day; and his disgust
on finding that he was to dine off a little thin broth and
a piece of bread defies description.

He entreated the warder, in the sweetest tones his
rough voice could command, to bring him something
better than that.

The murder only laughed at him.

From threats he passed to threats, and from threats to a savage blow with his fist, which would have felled the jocund official had he not parried it with the iron door, which rang beneath the shock, and covered the brawny hand with blood.

He howled with pain, and stretched himself on his bed in sulky silence.

After this he became a little more tractable; contenting himself with grumbling at everything that was brought him.

His sister paid him a visit. She informed him that she had obtained some money towards paying counsel for his defence.

Upon hearing this he seemed greatly pleased; despite his recklessness and bravado, he had become sad and serious as the time for the opening of the assizes approached.

He still clung to hope, even as a drowning man might cling to a spar.

At length the day arrived on which the trial had been appointed to take place. The facts connected with the charge of murder were simple enough.

Jane Ryan, who had become by this time a sort of heroine, was the chief witness; but there were others who were to be called as witnesses for the Crown, who to a great extent could corroborate her evidence.

Jane, when placed in the box, was calm and self-possessed.

She swore most positively to the prisoner as being the man who stabbed James Hopgood. She averred that she had a distinct and vivid recollection of every minute circumstance attendant upon the crime committed on that fatal night.

The counsel for the defence by a series of cross questions and innuendoes, strove to throw a doubt upon her testimony.

But Jane never wavered for a moment. Her answers were clear and concise. Every word she uttered bore the impress of truth.

Her cross-examination was continued for so long a time that it became wearisome.

There was, of course, the usual wrangling between the advocates as to what was admissible as evidence.

Objections were taken to some of the questions put to the witnesses, and an appeal was made to the judge, who overruled certain objections, and admitted others.

Jane's former master and her fellow-servant were called next. They both swore positively to the prisoner as the same person who stabbed the young carpenter.

Eight other witnesses were examined, amongst whom were the two Messrs. Ashbrook and the policemen.

The weight of evidence was clearly against the prisoner, and after retiring for a short time the jury returned a "Verdict of Guilty," upon the charge of wilful murder.

The judge passed sentence of death upon the prisoner in the usual form, and Gregson, who did not display the slightest emotion, was taken back to Broxwill gaol.

Jane Ryan, who had borne up with wonderful firmness and fortitude throughout the trial, now gave way. After the sentence was passed she swooned, and was carried out of court in a state of insensibility.

"Poor girl," said Richard Ashbrook; "we none of us know what it cost her to get through this day's business. Perhaps it's the recollection of her sweetheart's death, this. It can't be any sympathy she feels for that miscreant."

"No—tis not saint that as does it," said a female. "The poor dear soul has nerved herself

up to go through a trying part, and she's broken down now it's over. It's a chance if she ever outrights this day's business."

"She's none of your weak sort of bodies," observed the farmer. "Jane' got a brave heart."

"May be she has, sir; but the bravest of us are a little overcome at times," returned the woman.

With care and attention Jane Ryan was soon sufficiently restored to be taken by the good-hearted farmer and his relatives to Oakfield House. She was with good kind friends, who strove in every possible way to restore her to her wonted health and spirits.

But a canker worm was at her heart. And those about her acknowledged to themselves that she was no longer the same Jane whom they had known in an earlier day.

*   *   *   *   *   *

There were but a few grains of sand remaining in Time's hour-glass for the hardened criminal, Gregson. The morning of his execution was at hand.

Let us visit the street before Broxwill gaol before the fatal day.

It was Sunday night, at eleven o'clock; the public-houses had closed and forced the people into the air, which was rain—into the street which was mud.

A vast crowd was already collected before the gaol, and were watching the ominous preparations for to-morrow.

The new act for carrying out the last dread penalty of the law within the precincts of the gaol had not as yet passed, and the public were permitted to see the last throes of the doomed. Now, even the representatives of the press are denied that privilege.

There were lanterns placed at intervals of several yards down the whole length of the street. Dark shadows might be seen flitting round these lights.

The harsh sound of iron striking stone rose in the air.

They were digging holes in the ground with picks and iron crowbars.

At the end of the street, at the farther extremity of the prison, there was a yard surrounded with iron spikes.

The door of this yard was open, lights trembled in its mysterious depths.

A group of men and women stood near it; a policeman was stationed at each side of the door.

Occasionally men carrying large iron bars and wooden posts passed out. These, planted in the ground, were formed into a barrier that the mob might be kept at a certain distance from the scene of execution.

Gradually the group in front of the yard increased into a crowd.

As at every quarter of an hour the church bell gave forth its solemn notes they clung closer together, and peered over each other's shoulders into that black space from which indefinite sounds were raised and which was guarded so vigilantly by its two sentinels.

They heard the noise of wheels and cried joyfully—

"It's coming! it's coming!"

But they became silent as, drawn by three horses, a strange vehicle passed them.

It was a large square cart of enormous size, upon four low, broad wheels. It was painted black.

It passed slowly up the street, and halted before a small door which opened from the prison into the street.

From the interior of the prison sprang three men in their short sleeves. They dragged with them a huge pole, and erected it towards heaven.

A low murmur ran through the crowd. This was a portion of the gallows.

How strange and absorbing is the interest of every class in all that pertains to death !

Many of those assembled round Broxwill Gaol, remained there all night. These were, of course, the "roughs."

But it must not be for a moment supposed that the interest was confined to them.

Numbers of persons belonging to the middle and upper classes had engaged seats at windows of those houses commanding a good view of the scaffold.

As the night wore on the throng of persons diminished in numbers. There were, however, many around the apparatus of death when the first few streaks of dawn were visible in the horizon.

In an hour or so after this people debouched from all quarters of the town, hurrying on towards the fatal spot.

As the minutes flew by the multitude increased.

The salesmen of hot potatoes, coffee, pies, and other delicacies, were threading their way through the crowd.

Some loud-voiced fellows began to cry out the last dying speech and confession of the notorious murderer, Gregson, better known as the Bristol Badger. They recited some doggrel lines as they took their way along, which persons of a powerful imagination might suppose to be the production of the wretch ' - wb was about to die.

The windows of the houses commanding a view of the ghastly scene now began to fill with people.

In them too, many of the fair sex were to be seen.

The crowd before the scaffold became denser—people, as is usual on occasions of this description, push and elbow each other. An English crowd is bound to do this.

" Where ye're shovin' to ?" said a tall youth to a brawny looking man, who to all appearance was a navigator. " Jest keep yer elbows to yerself."

" It aint my fault, yer fool," said the navigator. " It's the people behind who's a pushing."

" Well, then, you're strong enough, and can keep 'em back if you like."

" Don't you be so cheeky, young fellow," returned the other; " you aint everybody."

" Give him a dab in the eye," said a voice behind.

" I shan't be at all particular about that if he gives me any more of his cheek."

" Hush ! Order !" ejaculated another of the crowd. " This aint a time to be a-quarrelin'."

" Right you air, old man," said another.

" Pies, all hot—all hot," shouted out an itinerant vendor of those delicacies. " Here's some of the right sort, all hot."

Several persons became purchasers. The morning air had given them an appetite, and they devoured the pies with evident relish.

A man in a black suit, with a white necktie and a low crowned hat, proceeded to distribute tracts to the gaping throng.

In a few moments he got unmercifully chaffed, but heedless of this he proceeded on his mission.

The hours passed on. It was nearly eight o'clock.

A man in a sable suit, bent form, and a feeble step, made for the door of one of the houses opposite to the gaol. He wore green spectacles, and to all appearance was a cripple, with a false arm. He passed through the doorway, and in a few moments after this had taken up his position at one of the front windows of the second floor of the house he had entered.

He seemed to be a broken, afflicted creature, who was past the meridian of life. His form was bent with premature age or disease—it was not possible to say which.

This person, who was disguised so completely that his own mother would not have known him, was our hero, Charles Peace.

He had come to see the last of Ned Gregson.

His make-up suggested a Dissenting minister. He seated himself by the side of a tall, thin, serious-looking person, of quiet manners and gentlemanly appearance.

The prison bell began to toll.

Then, as if by presentiment, the crowd became more orderly, the men ceased their jests, and the vendors their cries.

" It is nearly time for the carrying out the final act of the law upon the poor condemned wretch " said the tall gentleman to Peace. " What must be his feelings now ?"

" Ah, sir ! the thought is terrible. It is painful to dwell upon. What, indeed, must be his feelings ?"

Here he heaved a profound sigh.

" I have never attended an execution," remarked the other ; " and now my heart begins to fail me. I wish I had kept away. And you——"

" I, like yourself, have never witnessed a scene of this nature, but, having come, I shall endeavour to fortify myself as I best can."

" I am not an advocate for the abolition of the punishment of death," remarked Peace's tall companion. " I frankly own that I do not believe it can with safety be done away with."

" Most assuredly not," returned Peace, in the mildest tone of voice. " In the interests of society it is requisite that the guilty should not escape punishment. The murderer is unworthy of sympathy from his fellow-man."

" I am quite of your opinion—indeed, I may say that you express my sentiments to the very letter."

Peace bowed, and his face wore a complacent expression, which was altogether at variance with its ordinary appearance.

His companion was evidently quite taken up with him.

" The man who is about to suffer has been convicted upon the clearest evidence of a most dastardly and cold-blooded murder. The circumstances which led to his discovery are a little singular ; and, indeed, I might say romantic."

" So a neighbour of mine was saying," observed Peace. " I am not acquainted with all the particulars."

His companion gave a succinct but graphic account of all those facts with which the reader is already acquainted.

" How very singular !—how remarkable !" exclaimed Peace, adjusting his spectacles when his companion had ceased.

A short thick-set man, with dark piercing eyes, a close-cut grey beard, now appeared on the scaffold, at which he took a hasty glance.

This figure presented a weird-like appearance.

" There he is !" said several voices.

" Who is that ?" said Peace.

" Calcraft, the hangman," answered his companion.

" Oh, indeed. What has he come for ?"

" To see that the arrangements are made in a satisfactory manner. He has made one or two mistakes lately, and I think the old man is getting a little nervous."

PEACE ESCAPES FROM THE POLICE, AND SEEKS SHELTER IN A YOUNG GIRL'S BEDROOM.

It was quite true that Calcraft had had one or two mishaps; but these, it is said, were attributable to circumstances for which he was in no way responsible. He certainly fulfilled the duties of public executioner creditably for nearly fifty years, during which period he made use of what is known as the "short drop."

His successor, Marwood, advocates and makes use of the "long drop," and many have affirmed that his mode for putting criminals to death is the most merciful of the two; but when doctors (I mean hangmen) differ, who shall decide?

Calcraft has now retired. He is seventy-nine

No. 4.

years of age, and was, when I last saw him, in tolerably good-health for a man of his years.

The name of the gibbet's victims have been legion; for until a very recent period our penal code was most severe. We have hanged not only the murderer, the ravisher, and the incendiary—not only the burglar, the highwayman, and the forger, but the sheep-stealer, the petty thief who purloined a roll of cloth or a loaf of bread from a shop-counter. If any nation ought to know how to hang, it should assuredly be the English.

Decapitation has been a mode of death reserved for aristocratic culprits, although in the " Halifax gibbet" and the Scottish " Maiden " some faint resemblance to the guillotine may be traced. But we have always obstinately refused to employ the machine, adapted from the mediæval types by the benevolent French physician, and have stuck manfully to the gallows.

Formerly the convict doomed to the " triple tree" used to be flung off a ladder. Then we grew more humane, and made him stand with a noose round his neck in a cart, which was drawn from under him at a given signal.

Ultimately, in the middle of the last century, being under the necessity of hanging a lord—the noble convict was Laurence Earl Ferrers, who had murdered his steward—the scaffold, with a trap-door secured by a bolt, and flapping down from under the criminal's feet, was devised for the express accommodation of the murderous peer.

This was in the reign of George II.; and we have not advanced one step since then in the way of hanging.

The " new drop " is more than a hundred years old, but nothing has been done to render the grim agency more efficacious.

When the bolt is drawn and the drop falls, Marwood asserts, according to his arrangement, that the neck of the criminal is at once broken, and that death is instantaneous. This is his theory; but in practice, we believe that in nine cases out of ten the wretched culprit dies from suffocation.

A murderer, it may be urged, deserves no better fate.

He has shown no mercy to others, and has no right to expect that mercy should be shown to him.

We adhere to the notion that hanging is the shortest and swiftest mode of killing; and Marwood has declared that if he were condemned to death, and had to choose the mode of execution, he would certainly prefer hanging to any other.

Peace remained silent and thoughtful when Calcraft appeared on the scaffold. The latter, after a glance round, returned to the gaol.

Shortly after this the prison door opened slowly. One of the gaolers stood in the portal.

There was now a cry of " hats off," and a thousand heads were bared, a thousand faces upturned.

One would have believed it was a performance at the theatre they were witnessing.

Gregson appeared, bound and pinioned. This was the signal for groans and hisses, which were, however, supressed by the more discreet and better-behaved portion of the throng.

Behind Gregson was the chaplain, with an open Prayer-book in his hand, the sheriffs in their robes, the officers of the gaol, the myrmidons of the gallows.

A regiment of policemen encircled the scaffold with their truncheons drawn.

A trembling ran through the crowd, which resembled the waves of the sea beneath the first blast of the north wind.

This was followed by a murmur like that of the waves when the wind lashes them into wrath.

The crowd became hushed and silent.

The chaplain began to read the service of the dead.

The Badger looked sullenly upon the ground, presently he raised his head and examined the faces beneath him as if there was some one whom he wished to find.

He withdrew his eyes almost reluctantly, and turned them upon the officers behind him.

At this sign the clergyman moved on one side, and Calcraft approached.

All was hushed into silence, deep and terrible as that of the tomb.

Gregson had already made one step towards his death—he now placed himself on the drop.

Calcraft adjusted the noose around the miserable man's neck, then passed a strap round his feet and secured it with horrible deliberation.

He drew a white cap over his eyes and mouth—then he disappeared beneath the gallows.

For an instant Gregson stood motionless upon his open tomb.

The eyes of Charles Peace were rivetted on the form of his quondam companion.

The bolt was withdrawn from below; there was a frightful crash; a black chasm opened beneath the feet of the culprit, whose body swung round and vibrated in the air.

Then commenced those struggles, which, we are informed, are merely muscular and involuntary, but which nevertheless are sickening to behold.

Charles Peace was in no way moved by the appalling spectacle, albeit he affected to be overcome, and buried his face in his hands.

His newly-made acquaintance, however, was visibly affected. The expression of his countenance was indicative of the most profound sorrow.

In a few minutes the crowd before the scaffold recovered from the shock.

A motionless figure dangled from the rope. It was evident enough to all the spectators that life had fled.

Gregson had paid the penalty of his crimes.

The crowd swayed to and fro; several groups of persons took their departure in various directions.

During the whole of the melancholy proceedings the pickpockets were industriously plying their vocation.

More than one of the light-fingered gentry had been given into the custody of the police.

This was a common thing at the time of public executions.

Full two-thirds of the multitude had in the space of a quarter of an hour bent their way homewards.

Many, however, still remained to witness Calcraft's re-appearance on the scaffold for the purpose of cutting the rope from which the body of the murderer was suspended.

Those that remained were, of course, the roughest and least sensitive of the throng.

Their thirst for the horrible appeared to be insatiable.

The unprincipled scoundrel, Gregson, who, as a just penalty for his manifold crimes, suffered death on the public scaffold, was a ruffian of the very worst type. Educated to crime from his earliest youth, his conscience, which had never been tender, became, as years passed over his felon head, " seared as with a hot iron."

If we were to take a retrospective glance at his career from the day that he first enlisted in the " Devil's Regiment of the Line " until the last dread sentence of the law was carried out, we should find abundance of evidence to prove that the way of the transgressor was hard. As we have before signified, "A life of crime is always a life of care."

Gregson found to his cost, despite his callous nature, that this axiom was a true one; nevertheless, he was so steeped in vice and immorality that he found it impossible to reform or mend his ways.

Throughout his whole life there was not manifested one trace of mercy or generosity such as was attributed to the old highwaymen.

On all occasions he displayed a spirit of almost animal ferocity, shown to all who interfered with him.

Gregson, in fact, loved crime—the double life it involved, the excessive danger it created, and the cynical enjoyment it yielded him of doing always the worst thing he could think of.

The man was so radically bad—so naturally prone to wickedness—so utterly dead to the whispers of conscience—that he was a foul blot upon the face of nature.

He was a sort of wild beast, who waged ceaseless war against society.

It is indeed a sad thing to reflect upon that in this civilised country, with the means of education and moral training open to the poorest and humblest in the land, such monstrosities as Gregson and Charles Peace should have existence.

But we will not dwell further upon this painful theme. Gregson, as we have seen, has paid the penalty of his crime.

The career of Peace it is our purpose to chronicle. In doing this it will be necessary, as this work progresses, to diverge occasionally to note the actions and doings of other groups of characters with whom Peace was more or less connected.

Charles Peace, when he had seen the last of Gregson, rose from his seat, and moved slowly towards the centre of the room, which was more than half-filled with sightseers.

The tall gentleman who had sat by his side during the execution also rose, and prepared to take his departure.

"This is a scene when once witnessed is not easily to be forgotten," he observed to Peace. "I assume, sir, you are like myself, but too glad it is over."

"I am, indeed, sir," answered Peace, in oleaginous accents.

"You do not desire to remain longer?"

"Oh, dear me, no."

"Nor I. We will get away as speedily as may be convenient."

"By all means."

The two companions descended the stairs, and gained the street. This done, they walked side by side until they had got clear of the gaol and its ghastly surroundings.

It transpired, in the course of conversation, that Peace's companion was journeying in the same direction as our hero, who expressed himself very well pleased at having his company on the road.

"We have met for the first time this morning, sir," observed Peace; "allow me to express a hope that we may meet again under more auspicious circumstances."

The gentleman bowed, and said, "I hope so, I'm sure. Any way, we shall not meet again under similar circumstances, for I tell you frankly that this is the first, and it will be the last, time of my being present at such a scene."

They walked on for some little distance further, and came within sight of a roadside inn, with seats and alcoves in its front.

"I think a little cold brandy and water will do us both good," said Peace. "What say you?"

"As you please, I have no objection," was the ready rejoinder. "As a rule I do not take any spirits in the morning, but this is an exceptional case."

The two strolled in the grounds in front of the hostelry, and glasses were ordered and paid for by Peace.

"It is a terrible thing to see a fellow-creature put to death—terrible to even the most callous and unimpressionable. But it is a necessity—an absolute and imperative necessity."

"Undoubtedly it is."

"I do not complain of the law as it stands," observed the other; "I think it a just and reasonable law; for the very least a member of a civilised community has a right to expect at the hands of his fellow-citizens, should he fall by the blow of an assassin, is that his murderer, after being convicted by a jury of his countrymen, should be put to death. What say you?"

"I am of the same opinion as yourself."

"I think the mischief arises, or has arisen, on more than one occasion, by the injudicious use made of the prerogative of the Crown. Villains of the deepest dye have been respited, while criminals of a lesser degree have been executed. This, I think, has materially weakened the effects of the punishment of death. It is not only unjust, but is manifestly injurious. It is by the reliability of punishment—by the certainty that punishment follows conviction—that we can hope or expect it to act as a deterrent from the commission of crime. I have given the subject some consideration, and I could cite many instances in which the clemency of the Crown has been made use of in an unjust and most injudicious manner."

"I am not so well up in the subject as you are," remarked Peace, who throughout his life was always ready to moralise; "still, at the same time, I see the force of your argument."

"Well, sir, I will instance a case which came under my own knowledge. In the year 1844 I had a brother residing at Battersea, and, when in the metropolis, I was in the habit of paying him a visit once or, indeed, sometimes twice a week. One evening I was crossing Battersea Bridge, on the left-hand side going from the Bridge-road, when all of a sudden I observed a woman on the opposite side running along with her hands to her throat, from which a stream of blood was flowing. I was, as you can readily imagine, moved to an extremity of fear at the heartrending sight. The poor creature proceeded onwards with tottering steps, and did not stop till she had reached the 'Old Swan' tavern, on the Battersea side of the bridge. This was kept at that time by a man named Goslin, who was a friend of my brother."

"And what followed?" inquired Peace.

"You shall hear, for I remember every incident in this fearful tragedy as clearly as if it had occurred but yesterday. The woman rushed in front of the bar of the 'Swan,' and fell on the floor, deluging the place with her blood. Her throat was cut from ear to ear. I arrived at the tavern just in time to see her fall, and to also see her breathe her last."

"And who was her murderer?"

"A man named Dalmas. It transpired in the course of the subsequent inquiry that he had been paying attention to the murdered woman, whose name was Macfarlane. She was a school teacher, and had half supported the odious wretch who so cruelly and remorselessly took her life."

"And the motive—jealousy, I suppose?" said Peace.

"Nothing of the sort. The ill-fated woman, Macfarlane, was engaged to be married. She wrote to Dalmas, informing him of her engagement, to which he did not presume to offer any objection, neither had he any right to do so; indeed, he clearly understood that she was about to make an alliance with a gentleman, which would place her in a much better position in life. Dalmas wrote a very kind letter to her, in which he requested her to meet him on the Middlesex side of Battersea Bridge that he might bid her a last farewell, declaring that he was about to return to his native country, France, but did not like to leave without bidding her good-bye. She acceded to his request, and met him at the appointed time. The wretch proceeded to carry out his fell purpose unperceived, and while behind his victim he drew a razor across her throat, and inflicted such a fearful wound that she did not survive many minutes—certainly not more than five or six minutes. The wretch, after his barbarous act, coolly walked through the turnstile on the Chelsea side, and succeeded in making his escape."

"And was never caught, I suppose?"

"Oh, yes, he was; the police captured him in the course of a few days, and brought him in a four-wheeled cab to the Millman-row Police-station. Strange to say I saw him taken there. Well, to cut a long story short, he was tried and convicted upon the clearest evidence. There was not the faintest shadow of doubt as to his guilt—indeed he did not attempt to deny it. The murder was cold-blooded, premeditated, and brutal. Most assuredly, if any man ever deserved hanging certainly it was the wretch Dalmas, for there was not one redeeming point in the whole case. Well, sir, what do you think happened?"

"I cannot say."

"To the surprise of everybody the fellow was respited. Why or wherefore no one could possibly tell. No one has ever been able to account for the strange caprice of the executive. I don't believe there was an attempt made to even get up a petition to spare his worthless life. I don't believe there was a single individual—certainly none that I ever heard of—who was not perfectly assured at the time that the law would be suffered to take its course. Indeed, as far as I can remember, everybody was thunderstruck upon seeing it announced in the public papers that Dalmas had been respited."

"How very extraordinary!" remarked Peace. "And what became of him?"

"Oh, he was of course doomed to penal servitude for his natural life. He is at the present time in Portland prison, dispensing the medicines. He was a chemist by profession. He has been kept all these years at the expense of the public, and the probability is that he has found himself much more comfortable during his incarceration than he did when earning, or endeavouring to earn, a precarious existence outside the walls of his prison house."

"It seems hardly possible."

"I have been giving you a plain narrative of facts," returned the other, "and I can vouch for the truth of all you have heard fall from my lips; but this is only one of the cases I could cite to prove to you or anyone else the injudicious use made of her Majesty's prerogative."

"A scoundrel who would be guilty of such an atrocious crime was utterly unworthy of the clemency of the Crown," said Peace. "It seems to me most singular that mercy should be extended in such a case."

"It surprised everybody—none more than myself. I shall never forget the death of that poor creature in front of the bar of the 'Swan.' It has made so lasting an impression, that we have been, and still are at a loss to imagine the sympathy—the misplaced sympathy, I may term it—for those who imbrue their hands in the blood of their fellow-creatures."

"But I do not believe for one moment in the sincerity of anyone who endeavours to screen a murderer," observed Peace.

"Neither do I, sir—neither do I," ejaculated his companion. "If it became a personal question if a murder had been committed in their own immediate circle, they would be the first to demand the assassin's life. We have a practical instance of this in the Marquis of Boccaria, who, while the sheets of his work against capital punishment were passing through the press, did his best to get a servant hanged who had stolen his watch."

It was evident to Peace that the topic was a favourite one with his companion, for he gave one or two more instances of a similar nature to Dalmas's case.*

After some further discussion the two companions took their departure from the roadside inn, and walked on towards their respective destinations. When the time came for them to part company Peace's picked-up friend gave him a card, with his name and address on the face, and said he should be glad to see him at any time he could make it convenient to call. Peace thanked him, and promised to pay an early visit.

And so the two parted.

When left to himself, Peace had more time to think over the sad event of the morning. Gregson's fate made an impression on him, but it is to be regretted that this was but of a transient nature. He was too fond of adventure, too prone to wrong-doing, to allow the miserable end of his brutal and guilty associate to take deep root in his heart, or have any influence over his future actions or way of life. He returned to his lodging, it may be a sadder, but certainly in no way a better man.

CHAPTER IX.

THE OLD FARM HOUSE—THE MASTER PASSION—JANE RYAN.

THE winter has passed away and spring has come again.

All that remains of the much-dreaded Gregson is a few mouldering bones. His body was buried within the walls of the gaol, and the quick lime in the coffin has done its work.

Let us return to the scene of the opening chapters of our tale.

Oakfield House presents a charming picture of rustic beauty in the sweet spring time. In the yard there are milch cows and cart horses, with fowls fluttering, chirping, and pecking.

Stables and barns with tiled and slated roofs, and strong oaken doors through which as they stand ajar, one can see the busy shirt sleeves of the labourer.

* The description given by the speaker, of the murder on Battersea Bridge, is true in substance and in fact. The trial of Augustus Dalmas, for the murder of Sarah Macfarlane, took place, June 14th, 1844. The prisoner was found guilty; there was not one extenuating circumstance in the case, and no possible plea for a respite. Dalmas is at the present time, or was a few months ago, at Portland, in a responsible situation as dispenser of medicine to the sick, and his life is not one of hardship or suffering. He must be now close upon seventy years of age, if not more.

A blue river and a long line of willows, a fine view of the arable country—chalk hills and clay valleys—an orchard with a great stone pigeon-house rising from the midst and towering over all the trees. A rookery which is silent, for all the birds are feeding in the fields, and a little hamlet in the distance seen here and there between the leaves.

These are the leading and most noticeable features of the fine old English homestead known as Oakfield House.

But the picture is unfinished, as every picture is unfinished without a human figure. It is to colours upon canvas what the eye is to the face, what the sun is to the sky.

At the side door of the homestead is a young woman. She is attending to a throstle suspended from the wooden porch in its wicker cage. Her face is pale, its expression is sad and thoughtful. It is evident that she has been early acquainted with sorrow.

It would be difficult for many, who had known her in earlier years, to recognise this young woman as the once gay and sprightly Jane Ryan.

A strange change has come over Jane. She moves about the house, and grounds attached thereto, in a mechanical and listless manner. Her household duties are attended to with even greater care and thoughtfulness than heretofore; but a settled melancholy seems to have fallen upon her, her cheeks are wan and pale, her features are thinner and more delicately chiselled. It is painfully evident to all within the farmer's domicile that Jane is a prey to a deep-seated, and, it is feared by some, an incurable sorrow.

Nevertheless, she does not complain—does not for a moment admit that she is otherwise than in her wonted health.

Those about her, however, are of a different opinion. The Ashbrooks shake their heads. Miss Ashbrook, in answer to her brother's questions, murmurs, "Fading away."

"Poor girl, she cannot forget the past, and, to say the truth, it be no wonder," said the farmer's sister on more than one occasion, when the question was discussed.

"This is an upright straight for'ard good gell!" exclaimed Richard Ashbrook. "That what she be, and I donna' like to see her thus. Ye must do your best, Maude, to cheer her up."

"I ha' done so, many and many a time."

"Ah! that be but right and proper. I cannot see why she should take on so. The past be passed away, it canna' be recalled. But ha' left its traces behind—any one on us can see that," observes John Ashbrook. "Let the lass alone—maybe she'll get over it after a bit."

But the getting over it did not seem so easy as the good-natured farmer might wish.

Jane, as days and weeks flew by, seemed to grow more sad and thoughtful, and more than one of the rustics gravely remarked that she would go off her head if she gave way too much.

Everyone declared that she was a truthful, honest girl; indeed, she was a general favourite. It is little to say perhaps that she had not an enemy.

During the period which elapsed between the burglary and conviction of Gregson, she was looked upon as a sort of heroine, and numbers of well-to-do folks paid a visit to the farmhouse for the avowed purpose of making her acquaintance.

This popularity—or notoriety would, perhaps, be the better term—did not afford Jane any gratification; on the contrary, she was ill at ease when in the company of strangers, especially so when allusion was made to the circumstances connected with the crimes of burglary or murder.

She was a girl possessed of acute feelings—remarkably sensitive—though few persons would, perhaps, have given her the credit of possessing this latter quality, the reason for this being that she was reticent and undemonstrative.

In addition to all these characteristics, she was deeply imbued with superstition—was, in fact, a fatalist, and believed that all things were pre-ordained, and that it was useless for anyone to struggle against the decrees of fate.

The good pastor of the village strove in vain to dismiss from her mind this idea.

Jane heard all he had to say, but remained inflexible, affirming that her own life was a proof of this theory. Twice she dreamt that a burglary would be committed at Oakfield House on the very night that it did take place. A warning voice told her that the murderer of Hopgood would be one of the burglars—this came to pass.

It was in vain for anyone to deny the truth of these assertions, which, as we have already seen, were made manifest to wondering thousands; and it would be equally useless to deny also that similar warnings had been given in similar cases. The dead body of Maria Martin, of Red Barn notoriety, was discovered through the agency of a dream. This was incontestably proved upon the trial of William Corder, her murderer.

We are not for a moment assuming that it would be wise of anyone to put trust in dreams, signs, or omens of any sort—such an act would be the worst of folly.

Superstition is a blight, a mildew, and a curse to all who come under its fatal influence, and to a certain extent it was a blight upon the young life of Jane Ryan.

She had borne up for years hopefully and trustfully, in the full belief that the death of her lover would be avenged.

Now that this had come to pass, Jane felt that her mission was fulfilled. She had little to care for, nothing to hope, and it mattered not to her how her future course was shaped.

She consulted the wise woman who had prognosticated the appearance of Gregson at the farmhouse. The woman told her to forget the past, and look hopefully to the future, which is about the best advice she could give.

But Jane found it difficult to forget. A shadow had fallen upon her like a funeral pall.

One afternoon, while sitting alone in the breakfast-room of Oakfield, she met with a surprise. She had been at needlework. She put this aside, and leaning her head on her hand, with her elbow resting on the table, she fell into one of those deep reveries which had been so frequent with her of late.

A hand was placed on her shoulder, whereupon she gave a slight scream. Upon looking up she found Mr. Richard Ashbrook by her side; his brother John had gone with his sister to pay a visit to a neighbouring agriculturist.

The farmer smiled, and said, good-naturedly—

"Why, Jane, lass, thee beest eas'ly frightened."

"I did not know anyone was here," she answered, "and I was a little startled, and that's the truth."

"You've got very timursome o' late. Tell me, girl, what ails ye? Ye gets paler and thinner every mortal day; and ye see we are getting a bit concerned."

"Oh, I'm all right," she answered, with a faint smile. "There's nothin' amiss wi' me."

"Aye, but there is, gell. I tell 'ee thee is getting in a bad way. Dall it, I do not want to see ye go melancholy mad."

"Oh, I shan't do that."

"Jane," said the farmer, in a more solemn and serious tone than he was wont to assume; "ye been a thinkin' an' a thinkin' till your brain becomes all of a whirl. Tell us, lass, what ails ye, and if anything can be done to put thee right it sha' be done. You know, Jane, we all o' us are as fond o' ye as if—as if ye were our own flesh and blood. Your troubles are our troubles, an'—well, what was I saying? Oh, you must not look like that."

"How am I to look, then?"

"More natural like."

The farmer stood for a few moments after this silent and thoughtful.

Presently he drew a chair beside Jane's and sat down. Upon this the girl was about to rise when he motioned her to keep her seat.

She looked surprised, but said nothing.

There they both sat for a short time without exchanging a word. Presently Richard Ashbrook broke the silence, which was becoming painful and perplexing to both.

"Ye must know," began the farmer, "that I ha' something to say to ye. That be why I came here. I don't want to open old wounds afresh, but there is a reason for yer droopin' and droopin' as ye have been for ever so long a time, and I mean to know what it be."

"I s'pose you can guess?"

"Maybe I can; but I want to have it from yer own lips."

"Oh, sir, ye don't want me to tell 'ee more than ye already know?"

"Ye've mourning for one that be dead and gone. Is that it?"

The girl nodded her head.

"I knew it—I could ha' sworn it. Well, Jane, it is no discredit to ye; still at the same time, gell, thee knows that the wisest and the best of us cannot recall the dead to life, and to cherish a hopeless sorrow is neither wise or discreet. I don't wish to pain ye, but I tell ye plainly that you are altogether wrong. You are young, and although yer have gone through a deal o' trouble that is no reason why you should let the past embitter your life."

"You are quite right, Mr. Richard—it shall not do so."

"But it does, lass, anyone can see that it does. Tell me, do yo think yourself the same gell as came here some five year and a half agone?"

"I hope I am," she murmured; "time has changed me a little, I suppose."

"Jane," said Ashbrook, "we are one an' all of us fond of ye. I had somethin' to say that mustn't go unsaid. Listen—ye'd not disgrace any man, and ye'd be no discredit to any farmer as the mistress o' his house—as his wife—do ye understand what I mean?"

"Yes."

"Well, then, I don't want to see 'ee fade away before my very eyes, under my very nose. I can't and won't stand that, an' ye shall not if I can help it."

Then he took her hand in his own and said, in a voice broken by emotion—

"I love ye, Jane."

Then he placed his other arm across her shoulders and said no more.

The pale cheeks of Jane Ryan were suffused with a deep flush of red, in another moment they became paler than ever.

"Ah! ah!" she ejaculated, after a pause—"ah, Mr. Richard, ye do not know what ye've been sayin'."

"Don't I?" said the farmer, resolutely—"don't I?"

"I do not think so."

"Well, then, if it comes to that, I will say it agin. I love ye. I'll deal honest and fair by ye. If thee likest, if ye'll consent, ye shall be my wife."

He drew her towards him, and imprinted on her lips the first kiss of pure love.

"Ye mek no answer," he murmured. "Speak, gell."

"I bid ye think agen, Mr. Ashbrook," answered Jane. "Think agen."

"I have thought of it over and over agen. What need is there o' further thinkin' when a man has made up his mind?"

"You are too good and kind to me, that's what you are," said his companion. "Much too good, an' that be the truth on't; but, my dear master, you deserve someone better than myself, and it may not be. My heart is bruised and broken, and it be a poor offering to any man. Seek someone more worthy of ye. Ah, Mr. Richard, ye make the hot scalding tears come to mine eyes, which ha' been dry these many a year."

She ceased suddenly, bent forward, buried her face in her hands, and burst into a passionate flood of tears.

The farmer was touched. He was more than this— he was fairly overcome.

He was quite unprepared for this violent demonstration of grief.

"I be sorry I've hurt your feelings, Jane, truly sorry," he murmured.

"Don't say anything to me. Don't say kind things. Oh, how truly wretched I am!" interrupted Jane.

"Wretched!" he exclaimed, in a tone of surprise.

"I had never counted on this."

"And is an honest man's love a thing to be despised?" he said, with something like indignation in his tone.

"No, my dear master, it's a thing to be proud of," returned Jane, throwing her arms round his neck, and embracing him tenderly. "It would and ought to make any girl proud and happy—any but me."

"Ah, that's it—is it?"

"What do you mean?"

"You love another."

"Now, I'm sure you do not mean what you say. I did love another—him as is dead and gone these six years ago an' more."

"Ah! true. No one else?"

"Certainly not. It seems strange to me that you should ask such a question."

"Does it?" said the farmer, musingly, gazing, at the same time, abstractedly through the lozenge panes of the lattice window of the apartment. Then, after a pause, he added—

"I don'no but what you beest right. I dou'no what med me ask such a question."

He again became silent and thoughtful. He was doatingly fond of the young woman by his side—much more attached to her than he had supposed, or, indeed, cared to confess.

A suspicion crossed his mind; it was vague and shadowy at first, and did not assume any tangible shape. It was this—

"What if Jane had formed an attachment in the neighbourhood?"

He had never given that a thought before, not until after he had avowed his love.

The thought was agony. Poor Ashbrook was a man of impulse. He had never throughout his life been accustomed to consider twice before he spoke. He was hasty and at times brusque in his manner; for the rest he was as upright and honest as the day, and was quite incapable of doing a mean, paltry, or ungenerous action. Of all men in the world he was, perhaps, the one least able to bear a disappointment or a repulse from the woman he loved.

The bare supposition of a rival—and it might be a successful one—was gall and wormwood to him.

"Ye've heard what I've bin sayin', Jane," said the farmer, in a tone of voice which, to say the truth, was in strange contrast to its usual tone.

There was a mournful cadence in his voice which his companion never remembered to have heard on any former occasion. He proceeded with his discourse slowly and deliberately.

"As I ha' just sed," he observed, thoughtfully. "You've heard the few words that ha' fallen from my lips, and, hark 'ee, it aint because I'm in a better position than ye are, Jane, that I would seek by word or deed to control ye in a matter which concerns ye more perhaps than aught else. I've no right to control ye. A woman cannot help her likins' and dislikins' any more than a man, and if ye cannot find it in your heart to look upon me wi'—wi' eyes o' favour—"

"Mr. Richard—Mr. Ashbrook," interrupted the girl, with sudden warmth, "you not goin' to tell me that you believe for a moment that I would turn from ye—that I would not lay down my life gladly and cheerfully for you or your'n—at any turn, at any time, or do aught that a poor creature like myself could do to help and benefit you. Ah, ah! if ye doubt this ye do me but scant justice."

"I do not doubt it—I should be worse than a fool to doubt it," said the farmer, bending fondly over her.

"Spoken like yourself—your own good self!" exclaimed Jane.

Ashbrook did not deem it advisable to press the question further. He contented himself with imprinting a kiss on the girl's forehead, and said gently—

"You are troubled. Now, think over what I've bin a-sayin'; we'll talk further on this matter another time."

And with these few parting words he crept softly out of the apartment and went abroad in the fields.

"She must ha' bin mighty fond o' the young carpenter," he murmured, as he took his way over the meadows. "Mighty fond, to keep the memory o' him green for so long a time. Wimmen they're strange creatures—the best on us can't mek 'em out at times, and yet—yet—dall it, I do love that gell, and that's the honest truth."

CHAPTER

PEACE HAS ANOTHER NOCTURNAL ADVENTURE.

For some considerable time after the death of the Badger, Peace worked regularly at his trade. Orders came in pretty freely, and as Bessie Dalton had prognosticated several gentlemen associated with him at the concert given for the benefit of the weaver's widow took great pleasure in recommending him to their friends as a skilful and reasonable carver and gilder.

Had he chosen to do so he might have established a very good business in the town of Bradford, but the greed of gain and the spirit of adventure, as he termed it, was for ever urging him on to commit lawless acts. Hence it was that steady industry became after a while distasteful to him.

His course of life presents us with a melancholy picture—cunning, roguery, wholesale plunder, and reckless bravado. The old adage of "once a thief always a thief" was exemplified in him.

His thin, firmly compressed lips gave one an impression of a man who, if put to it, would stick at nothing to gain his ends. There was a wolfish look about his face, his eyes appeared more like the eyes of a wild beast than of a human being; he had a good square head and altogether looked like one who had both the head to plan and the hand to carry out any villainy on which he had set his heart.

As we have before noted Mrs. Bristow and her husband occupied the parlours of the house in which Peace lodged. Bristow was a smith by trade; in addition to this he was a wretch, who drank horribly, treated his wife—who was a pretty little woman of decent parentage and belongings—with the greatest brutality.

Drink, it has been observed, is the curse of the British workman; the fatal prepensity has led to the commission of numberless crimes.

Our courts of justice furnish us with a black catalogue of atrocities, assaults, and murders, committed by habitual and confirmed drunkards.

If the veil could be lifted, and the desolate and miserable home of the drunkard shown in all their hideous deformity, a picture would be presented which the most phlegmatic and unimpressionable would shudder to look upon.

It is a sad reflection that nothing can be done to purge the land of this terrible scourge.

Bristow had an amiable, forgiving, and patient wife. Her life, since she had been united to her drunken husband was one of sorrow and suffering.

She had for her companion, and to a certain extent this was a solace to her, Bessie Dalton, who on many occasions had sheltered her from the domestic storm which burst over her defenceless head.

The gentleman who had been the companion of these two women on the evening of the concert saw them to the door of their residence after the performance was over.

He took the liberty of calling the next day. He was introduced to Bristow, who, for a wonder, was perfectly sober, and when in this state he was a decent, well-behaved man enough.

He was very respectful in his manner, and thanked his visitor for the kindness and consideration he had displayed in protecting his wife from the rougher portion of the crowd gathered in the entrance hall.

The interview was but of brief duration; after an exchange of civilities the stranger took his departure.

And he called several times after this, and saw both Bessie Dalton and Mr. Bristow.

Ultimately, however, these visits culminated in a scene which we shall have to describe in a future chapter.

Our more immediate business now is to put the reader in possession of all the incidents connected with the escapade of our hero.

Peace, as we have already noted, could not comport himself in a becoming manner for any great length of time.

He had been looking about for a convenient "crib to crack." He had, to use a cant or sporting phrase, "spotted" a large warehouse which stood at the east end of the town, and had come to the conclusion that there would be but little difficulty in his effecting an entrance.

The place was left in charge of a night watchman, whose vigilant eye Peace felt assured he could easily avoid.

It was his custom at this time to wear women's boots. He had on the same pair which he made use of when he entered the millowner's house at Dudley Hill.

Once in the premises, there would not be much difficulty in abstracting all valuables which were in any way portable.

He was over-confident on this occasion. He, however, took the precaution to disguise himself by wearing his false arm and colouring his face, which presented the appearance of a mulatto.

He was under the full impression, to use another sporting phrase, "that he would be able to walk over the course."

The town of Bradford was enveloped in a mist when Peace sallied forth upon his marauding expedition.

He did not start from his lodgings, but had been for an hour or two at a quiet respectable coffee-shop. From this place he started upon his expedition.

There were but a few stragglers in the streets at this time, for the hour was late, and most of the operatives were fast asleep in their beds, save a few of the most irreclaimable, who were in the parlours or skittle-grounds of the public-houses.

In the course of about twenty minutes, or from that time to half an hour, Peace arrived at the warehouse which he had chosen as the scene of his operations.

He glanced furtively around.

Not a solitary passenger was in sight.

The warehouse stood in a part of the town where few chance pedestrians were to be seen even in the busiest part of the day. Now there were none, and the burglar therefore had it all to himself.

He tried the lock of one of the side doors with more than one of his skeleton keys, but was not at first successful in shooting back the bolt.

He was, however, not a man to be easily baffled. On many occasions he has boastfully displayed to his companions his ability in tampering with locks of every description.

After some further efforts he managed to turn back the lock. This done, he gently pushed against the door, which he found was fastened by a top bolt—the bottom one had evidently not been driven home into its socket.

He had now but one thing to contend with, this being the top bolt. He had provided himself with a small piece of flexible steel with a sort of claw at its end, wherewith to operate on this.

A considerable space of time elapsed before he was enabled to successfully surmount this difficulty.

At length, however, by patience and perseverance, combined with skill, he contrived to send back the bolt from the socket by slow degrees.

This done he opened the door, entered, and closed it after him, so that it might not attract the notice of any of the police.

He found himself in an enormously large apartment, which was more than a third filled with goods of various descriptions.

The windows of the warehouse were covered with dust and dirt, and the place was in comparative darkness.

Peace carried no dark lantern with him on this expedition; but he had provided himself with a box of silent lucifers, which were warranted to "ignite only on the box."

He struck one of these, and was about to take his way up the stairs to make an inspection of the upper portions of the building when, much to his surprise and chagrin, he was confronted by the night watchman, who emerged from a wooden hutch in one of the corners of the warehouse.

"You audacious scoundrel!" exclaimed the watchman, springing like a panther upon Peace, in so sudden a manner that he had no time to elude the man's grasp.

"Leave go," cried Peace, in a voice of concentrated passion; "unhand me, or it will be worse for you."

"I'm not going to part with you so easily—you're my prisoner," answered the porter, winding his fingers around the collar. "You're caught, my gaol-bird, this time, and no mistake."

The lighted lucifer had fallen from Peace's hand upon the first assault, and the two men were struggling for the mastery in comparative darkness.

Physically speaking, the watchman was the most powerful of the two, but he had neither the skill, coolness, nor cunning of his more wary opponent. The struggle was a short but desperate one.

The burglar tried every feint and dodge to gain an advantage. By a sudden and adroit movement he tripped up the watchman, who fell on his back, his antagonist falling upon him at the same moment.

Peace lost no time in making the best use of the advantage gained: he placed his knee on the man's chest, and removed his hands from about his throat.

In another moment the burglar was sent backwards by a well-directed blow from his antagonist's clenched fist.

The watchman ran to the door which he opened, then in a stentorian voice he shouted out—

"Help! Murder! Police—police!"

The cries for assistance were taken up and repeated by one or more persons in the street.

Peace made for the wide open staircase which he began to ascend rapidly.

The watchman, perceiving this, gave chase.

The burglar seeing that another struggle was imminent, and being in no way desirous of risking the chances of a second encounter, had recourse to a cunning stratagem.

He waited at the top of the first landing for his pursuer who rushed forward, never for a moment dreaming of the reception that was in store for him.

Peace waited till the man came within reasonable distance; he then kicked out with his right leg and struck his pursuer with his foot full in the face. The latter rolled from the top of the first flight of stairs to the bottom.

Peace heard strange voices below, which he concluded, naturally enough, proceeded either from the police or a chance passenger in the street.

Feeling that he was in a critical position, and that there was now no possibility of his escaping through the door, by which he had effected an entrance into the premises, he made at once for the roof.

The warehouse was a five-storied one, and he did not pause until he had reached the topmost story.

As he had anticipated, he discovered a trap-door, by means of which he could, in all probability, be able to reach the roof of the building.

He drew some bales of goods underneath the trap, and upon these he mounted.

The door was fastened on the inside by two bolts. These he endeavoured to draw back, but they were rusty, and not easily removed.

He heard footsteps ascending the stairs; heard also voices.

Every moment was now precious.

If he could not succeed in drawing back the bolts, his capture was certain.

THE CHASE AFTER PEACE—MIRACULOUS ESCAPE.

He drew a jemmy from his coat-pocket, and getting a leverage from the side of the trap, he drew back one bolt; he was enabled now to raise the trap on one side.

He sprang up from the bales of goods and contrived to pass through the opening. This done he closed it.

He now found himself on the leads of a flat roof.

The building was immensely high, as most structures of this nature usually are.

As far as the eye could reach the chimneys and roofs of the houses of the city lay before him like one vast panorama.

He stood on a dizzy height, from which there did not appear to be any means of escape.

He began to despair, but a shuffling noise at the trap-door moved him to further action.

He ran to the extreme end of the roof, and found, much to his delight, the roofs of houses, some twelve or thirteen feet below.

He looked over the parapet of the warehouse at the roof beneath him.

He cast a furtive glance at the trap, which he discovered was being removed.

The police were on his track.

Urged almost to desperation, he laid hold of one of the coping stones of the parapet; he threw his legs and body over, and then for a moment or so hung in mid air.

To let go and drop on the roof of one of the houses was indeed a desperate alternative.

But, desperate as it was, he felt that the attempt must be made.

He had by this time gone too far to recede.

He let go his hold of the coping stone, and dropped upon the slanting tiles of the house beneath.

He alighted with comparative safety.

Sliding down the roof, he gained the gutter which

No. 5.

ran round the house. Then he stooped down and hid himself behind the low wall in front of the gutter.

By this time the policemen and the night watchman were on the leads of the warehouse. He knew this, for he heard their voices distinctly in the night air.

"He's stepped it," said the watchman. "He's given us the slip after all our trouble, the audacious scoundrel."

Peace heard these observations, and remained as quiet as possible in his place of concealment.

"He's made off over the roofs of those houses," said one of the police officers.

"Impossible!" exclaimed the watchman. "No mortal man could reach them from where we are standing. Oh, no—impossible!"

"You don't know what these fellows can do," returned the constable. "They're like cats—they've got nine lives."

The speaker flashed his bull's-eye in all directions, but no burglar was visible.

Peace was stretched at full length in the gutter, and the low wall in its front effectually concealed him from observation.

But the situation in which he found himself was in no way a pleasant one; but he was as cunning and stealthy in his movements as an old fox.

If he attempted to stir, he knew that discovery was certain.

He, therefore, remained speechless and motionless.

"Have you got such a thing as a ladder?" inquired one of the constables of the watchman.

"Yes, there is one in the yard. Why?"

"He's hiding somewhere on the top of yonder houses. We shall nail him yet, if we can get a ladder."

"Come down to the yard at once, if you think that," said the watchman. "An excellent thought. Come this way."

The speaker and the two policemen retraced their steps, crept through the trap-door, and hastened towards the yard in search of the ladder.

Peace heard every word they had spoken, and was thereby apprised of their movements.

He waited till he felt assured they had left the roof of the warehouse, then he peeped out from his hiding-place.

Not a soul was to be seen.

Abutting out from the roofs of the row of houses on which he had so successfully dropped were a number of dormer windows, with lozenge-shaped panes. Peace crept along the gutter upon his hands and knees, and tried the first window he came to.

It was fastened. He tried another with the same result.

Presently he discerned, at no very great distance off, the faint glimmer of a light from an adjacent window. He made for this at once.

He opened it with the greatest care, and crept softly in.

A young and pretty servant girl was partly undressed, and was about to retire to rest.

She gave utterance to a faint scream as the burglar entered her sleeping chamber, and modestly covered her neck and shoulders, which were bare, with a shawl.

"For the love of mercy, how came you here, sir?" she inquired in evident alarm.

"My dear young lady," said Peace, in his most persuasive tones, "do not be alarmed. Take pity on a poor fellow who seeks your protection."

"Protection, you must be some madman, or else—a —a burglar."

"I am neither. At the present moment I am in the depths of trouble. You can save me—you will, I am sure. You have a kind heart—I can see that by your face, which wears on it a sweet expression. Oh, do take pity on me!"

He threw himself on his knees before her, and again pleaded in such an eloquent manner that the young woman was touched.

She hesitated, not very well knowing what answer to make to such an appeal.

"What trouble are you in, then?" said she.

"I've had a dispute, a quarrel; blows have been exchanged, and, if I cannot escape from the officer who is after me, I'm a ruined man—ruined for life. You will have compassion on me. You cannot find it in your heart to refuse your aid to a distressed and afflicted man."

"What do you want me to do? If you are discovered here my character will be lost. Go—go at once, or I will call for assistance!"

"Nay, you cannot mean anything so cruel—I'm sure you cannot!" he exclaimed, in a beseeching tone.

"Will you go, sir?"

"Yes, if you will only show me the way. This little affair will blow over in a day or two. Matters can be arranged; but if I fall into the hands of the police I'm lost. Now do you understand a miserable fugitive asking you to protect him? You cannot—you will not refuse."

"How can I protect you?"

"Simply by this. The police are on my track; let me out at the back door of the house; I can then make my escape. Now do you understand?"

"What have you been doing for the police to be after you?"

"I've told you. A quarrel—an assault."

"You are a very strange man. I do not understand how you came here."

"I'll tell you all another time. Show me the way to the back door, and I will go at once and trouble you no more. Quick, no time is to be lost. You will do this, and heaven will reward you. But stay—here is something as a recompense for this little favour."

He took a sovereign from his pocket, which he handed to the girl.

She drew back indignantly.

"No, sir!" she ejaculated. "I'll have none of your money."

"Very well," he answered; "so be it. Trust me, I shall find the way of rewarding you some other time. Now let me out."

"I run great risks. Suppose my master or mistress should hear us descending the stairs."

"I will make no noise. They'll not hear us."

The girl took the light, and crept softly downstairs. Peace followed.

The back door was soon unfastened, and the burglar imprinted a kiss on the hand of his benefactress.

"You can jump over the wall at the end of the garden, and reach the court at the back," she whispered. "Now go."

She closed the door and refastened it; then she betook herself to the window of the back parlour, and saw her strange visitor jump over the wall into a neighbour's garden. He then climbed another wall, and gained a side street beyond.

"Oh, gracious goodness! how glad I am he's got off. What an extraordinary man!" she ejaculated.

"Poor fellow, he seemed in the depths of trouble, I shall learn something more about the affair in the morning, I'll dare be sworn."

She crept softly up the stairs and reached her own room without disturbing any of the other inmates of the house.

Meanwhile the police officers had obtained the ladder from the adjoining yard; this they reared against the side of one of the houses which was in close proximity to the warehouse from which Peace had so successfully escaped.

The constables ascended the ladder, clambered over the roofs of the houses, but as the reader may readily imagine, they were in no way successful in obtaining sight of the fugitive, who by this time was far away from the scene of action.

The policemen were much disconcerted, but were, however, not at all disposed to give up the search without further efforts.

They observed the glimmer of the light from the window of the servant girl's room; the latter had by this time returned to her apartment in the roof, and was preparing for bed when she was startled by a loud rap at the window.

"Who's there, and what do you want?" said she, in breathless accents.

"Open the casement—a burglar is in the house. Open at once!"

"Don't be afraid, girl; we belong to the police."

"But I am very much afraid, and that's the truth," returned she, unfastening the window and throwing it wide open. "Good kind gentlemen, for the love of mercy tell me what's the matter?"

The constables made no reply, but sprang into the room. The girl drew back in undisguised alarm.

"It's most disgraceful to force an entrance into my bedroom—that's what it is," she ejaculated petulantly.

"Now, young woman," said one of the constables. "Answer me truthfully. Have you seen a man making his way over the roof?"

"Certainly not, with the exception of you and your companion; you are the only persons I have seen."

"No one has been here."

"Why, goodness me, no. Haven't I told you so already?"

"You're quite sure of that?"

"Quite sure."

The policemen glanced round the apartment, looked under the bed, in the cupboard, and, in short, everywhere they could think of.

"Strange!" ejaculated policeman No. 1.

"Most remarkable," returned No. 2. "Where can he be hiding?"

"Can't possibly tell." Then, turning to the girl, he said, "Hark ye, young woman, a burglary has been committed in the adjoining warehouse; the robber has escaped, and we have reasons for believing that he has sought shelter in this house."

"A burglary!" exclaimed the girl, giving utterance to a loud scream. "What have I done that I should be treated thus?" Having said this she burst into tears.

The door of the bedroom was opened, and a tall gentleman, with a thick grey moustache, appeared with a drawn sword in his hand. He had hastily huddled on his clothes, and was swathed in a long dressing-gown.

For the rest his countenance was indicative of rage and indignation. He was a retired Indian officer.

"What is this noise and altercation about?" cried the half-pay captain, regarding the constables with a malevolent look. "How is this that the sanctity of my private abode is thus violated? Speak! Dost thou hear?"

One of the policemen briefly explained the particulars of the attempted burglary, and the remarkable escape of the robber.

"You have exceeded your duty. How dare you enter the maid's bedroom in this precipitate—this, ahem! unseemly manner? Do you suppose for one moment that anyone belonging to my establishment would harbour burglars? I say you have gone beyond all reasonable limits; and, ahem! I tell you frankly, that the matter shall not rest here. An Englishman's house is his castle, and it is not to be invaded by the officers of the law, without—I say without a reasonable excuse."

"I hope we have a reasonable excuse, sir."

"I say you have not; don't contradict me, man, I will not condescend to bandy words with you. This matter shall be inquired into."

"What is your number?"

"46 T."

"Good, and yours?" he enquired, turning to the other.

"49 T. But will you allow me to explain——"

"No, no. I will not. I don't want any explanation now. At a proper time and in a proper place you will have to account for this scandalous behaviour—forcibly entering a young girl's bedroom upon such a shallow pretext I say it does not admit of explanation. I will answer for the honesty and integrity of this girl —let that suffice. Zounds! gunpowder and smoke, I am perfectly astounded at your audacity!"

46 T said he was exceedingly sorry that there should have been any misunderstanding, but they thought it probable the thief might have been seen passing the window."

"Ridiculous, positively absurd," ejaculated the choleric captain. "You are a pair of blundering idiots. The thief, if there be one, which I do not for a moment admit, would not be fool enough to enter a respectable house and arouse the inmates in his endeavour to escape. The idea is perfectly preposterous."

"It is most unfortunate that you view the matter in this light," said 46 T, "and I deeply regret that we should have offended you, sir, but it has been done in the exercise of our duty."

"Duty be hanged! A pretty story truly, that you are to disturb people in the dead hours of the night, wake them from their peaceful slumbers, frighten the maid almost into hysterics upon the miserable plea that you thought the robber might have sought shelter here. I tell you, sir, that the very thought of such a thing is insulting to me and to all who dwell in this house."

While this altercation had been going on the girl had seated herself on the edge of the bed and gave utterance to a series of sobs and hysterical cries.

"Don't you worry yourself, Mary. You've done nothing wrong, my poor girl," said her master, in a kind tone of voice. "You've nothing to be ashamed of, or indeed to be alarmed at. Dry your eyes, girl, and be of good cheer."

"I'm sure—I—ha—ven't done anyone an—in—jury —and I don't know why I should be treated like this."

"Don't fret yourself; nobody blames you," returned her master. "The righteous have naught to fear."

The captain strode towards the window, which he closed and fastened. He then threw up the shutters. This done, he turned towards the two constables, and said, as he approached the door—

"This way, if you please. It would be idle to prolong this scene. The maid wants to seek repose. She has been kept up later than usual, in consequence of a few visitors we've had this evening. You will, therefore, please follow me."

The two policemen obeyed. The master of the house closed the door of the bedroom, and, with a light in one hand and a sword in the other, he led the way into a room below.

"Now, gentlemen" (he emphasised this last expression), "since you have taken upon yourselves to enter my premises as trespassers—I cannot call you anything else—I do not desire to part with you without first of all seeing that you search every room in the house."

The constables felt that they had made a great mistake; this fact they were forcibly impressed with, and they were seriously concerned at the issue.

"We don't desire to search—" stammered out one.

"I insist!" interrupted the captain. "There is now an imperative necessity for your doing so, and, further than that, I insist as a satisfaction to all parties."

The officers bowed. They were conducted by their guide into one room after the other. It is, perhaps, needless to say that everything was in the same order as when the occupants of the habitation had retired for the night.

Nothing was disturbed. There was not the faintest indication of any stranger or robber having entered the premises.

"You will, I'm sure, pardon us," observed one of the policemen. "We feel now that we have been too precepitate; but I hope you will consider, sir, that the reason for our being so was a desire to further the ends of justice. Mistakes will occur with the best and most cautious constable. I trust you will accept our apology, and say no more about this error—for error it most assuredly is."

The captain was choleric, impetuous, but he was not vindictive. His anger passed away, and he was the chivalrous, generous, high-minded officer whom his worst enemies acknowledged to be a gentleman.

"Enough!" he observed. "You have been greatly mistaken, and I confess that I was greatly incensed, but that is over now. I am not the man to do anyone an injury for being over zealous in the discharge of what they deem their duty. You are satisfied that there is no robber lurking about here—I am satisfied that you did not mean to give offence; so let the matter be forgotten. Certainly it shall not be made public by me."

"We thank you, sir, most sincerely for your kindness and consideration," exclaimed both constables. "We thank you again and again."

The gallant officer unbarred the front door of his habitation, bowed courteously to his companions, who returned the salutation, and passed into the house.

"We have made a pretty muddle of this business," said one of the constables, to his companion; "what I call a regular muddle. It's lucky the old gentleman cooled down. I thought he meant reporting us."

"So he did at first, but he thought better of it."

"Ah! he's haughty, but he's a gentleman. But as to that slippery customer, how he has got clear off will, I fear, remain a mystery."

The policemen went back for the ladder, which they replaced in the yard.

The night watchman remained outside of the captain's house, near by for the constables, who, of course, informed him of all that had passed therein.

The watchman was in no very good humour; he was suffering from the effects of the kick he had received from Peace while ascending the stairs.

Every bone in his body ached. In addition to this

he found that his right ankle was sprained—so, taken altogether, he was in no enviable plight.

CHAPTER IX.
PEACE RETURNS TO HIS LODGINGS.—A VIOLENT SCENE.—
THE ACCUSATION.

THE notorious burglar whose deeds it is our purpose to chronicle during the progress of this work, succeeded, as the reader has doubtless already surmised, in getting clear off. After scaling the two walls in the rear of the captain's house he found himself in a narrow unfrequented street, or, more properly speaking, court or alley.

He proceeded at once to make as much alteration in his appearance as possible. By the aid of his handkerchief and a little water he removed the stain from his face.

It has been asserted that he made use of walnut juice for the purpose of altering the hue of his skin.

This is a mistake. Walnut juice is not so easily removed. The pigment he employed was a finely-ground powder mixed with beer. This, when rubbed on the surface of the skin, gave him the appearance of a mulatto; and he had only to draw on a close-fitting black wig to make the disguise complete.

Peace, when representing a nigger, on the stage had, of course, to make up with burnt cork and beer, and it was this that first gave him the idea of using a brown powder in lieu of the cork to so successfully assume the appearance of a half-caste.

It had, moreover, this advantage; after his nocturnal depredations were over he could wash the colouring off his face in a few seconds, and remove his wig. This done, Charles Peace was himself again.

The disguise was so perfect that detection or identification was almost impossible.

The stain, as we have already observed, was removed, the wig was taken off, the false arm removed, and Peace felt quite secure.

He walked gaily along in an easy self-confident manner, not for a moment caring about a chance encounter with any member of the police force.

The self-possession and assurance of the man surpassed all belief.

He was, however, greatly chagrined at the unsuccessful nature of his raid upon the warehouse, and he could not disguise from himself that he had escaped almost by a miracle.

Nothing daunted, however, by his dangerous adventure, he walked gaily along till he reached one of the main streets of the town.

Here he was met by the two policemen who had made such a vain endeavour to capture him.

One of the constables flashed his bull's-eye full in the face of the burglar, who bore his scrutiny with the utmost complacence.

"You'll know me again the next time we meet!" said Peace, with cool assurance.

"May be I shall," returned the constable. "Where are you coming from, and whither are you going?"

"That's my business; but, if you wan't to know, I'll tell you. I'm going to my own home, and I've been on a visit to a sick friend. You may as well know all. My name's Charles Peace; I'm a carver and gilder—and a musician to boot. Anything else you want to know?"

"Have you seen any one pass as you came along?"

"Well, no one in particular. Oh, yes!—there was a dark-looking man—a mulatto, he appeared to be, with one arm; he was running at the top of his speed."

"Which way did he go?" asked the policeman, eagerly.

"He ran down that street—the second turning to the left."

"How long since?"

"Not a minute ago."

The two constables made off in the direction pointed out by Peace.

"Good!" ejaculated the latter, with a grin. "I hope you will find the gentleman!"

He walked on at a more rapid pace, and did not pause until he had reached his own habitation.

He let himself in as usual with his latch-key, and crept softly upstairs.

For the next few days he worked industriously at his business, and behaved in a proper and discreet manner.

One or two of his friends, or rather patrons, paid him a visit, and gave him fresh commissions, and he deemed it advisable to keep as quiet as possible till the excitement consequent upon the attempt at burglary had somewhat subsided.

Like other affairs of a similar nature it was but a nine days' wonder; the general impression being that it was the work of some tramp, who was in all probability a stranger in the town. Anyway, the aforesaid tramp was never discovered.

John Bristow, the man who occupied the parlours in the house where Peace lodged, had been for some days "on the drink." His poor wife, during this period, had had a sad time of it. Her husband neglected his work, drank to excess, and conducted himself in a manner which was almost intolerable.

Bessie Dalton strove in vain to pacify the brute, who came home in a furious state.

It would indeed be a terrible picture of man's brutality, and woman's forbearance, were we to record all that passed in the drunkard's miserable home.

One night Peace was aroused by piercing screams, which proceeded from Bristow's room.

"For mercy's sake, Charlie," said Bessie Dalton, "go down to that wretch; there'll be murder done. I'm sure there will if they go on like this."

"It's a thankless task to interfere between man and wife," answered Peace. "Best let them settle their own disputes."

"I tell you Bristow's mad, and knows not what he's doing. I cannot and will not remain quiet while this is going on. If you don't care about interfering I will."

She rushed downstairs; Peace followed.

Bessie opened the door of the front parlour, and found the room in the utmost disorder. Chairs were overturned, and the lamp upset and broken.

Bristow had his fingers round his wife's throat, and appeared to be endeavouring to throttle her.

"You inhuman monster!" exclaimed Bessie, catching hold of the back part of the collar of the man's coat, and dragging him back with all her force.

"Now, look here, Bristow," said Peace, "don't be a fool. You've got a good wife, and you don't know how to treat her. A man's a coward who lays his hand upon a woman."

"Ish he?" returned the ruffian, turning savagely upon the speaker—"ish he? Then I'll lay my hands upon a man, that I may teach him to mind his own bushnis."

Having given utterance to these words he sprang upon Peace like a wild beast.

The latter deftly slipped out of his grasp, and gave him a push, which sent him sprawling backwards.

He rose to his feet, and was about to commence another attack, when Bessie Dalton, who was a lion-hearted little girl, threw herself between the two combatants.

"I'm not afraid of you, big as you are," said Bessie. "So if you want to hit anyone, hit me."

With a look of drunken stupidity Bristow poised himself on his legs, which, to say the least, were particularly shaky at this time, and contemplated the girl with something like admiration.

"Thee bee'st a plucky un, thersh no denying that. I don't want to harm 'ee——"

"I wish I was a big strong man," exclaimed Bessie, in a spiteful tone. "That's what I wish."

"And why, my pretty little spitfire?" inquired Bristow.

"I'd give you a good thrashing—that's all.

"Ah! indeed; then I'm glad you're not."

He flung himself into a chair, and looked the very personification of imbecility."

"You ought to be ashamed of yourself, Bristow; upon my word, you are a disgrace to the neighbourhood."

"Am I?" said the man, with a short jerk of his body, and a stupid nod of his head; "a dishgrace, eh?"

"Certainly you are—everybody says so."

"Look here, I aint a-goin' to stand any o' your cheek, blow me if I do—no, nor any of your preaching either. What are you, I should like to know?"

"A thousand times better than you are!" exclaimed Bessie Dalton.

"Ish he?" This was said in a drawling tone and jeering manner.

"Yes, he is."

"I'm not so sure about it. Why, Lord love yer, gal, don't ye know what he ish—a burglar! Do ye hear—a burglar!"

Had a bomb-shell exploded in the room it could not possibly have caused greater consternation than did this declaration.

Peace was pale with rage.

"You infamous liar!" he exclaimed, in a voice of concentrated passion, walking up to the speaker, and shaking his fist in his face.

"Were it not that I respect your poor, ill-used wife—were it not that you are in a beastly state of intoxication, I would fell you to the earth."

Bristow laughed derisively.

"You—you fell me to the earth," he repeated, in a sneering tone.

Peace by this time was wild with fury.

Seeing that a desperate scene of violence was likely to take place, Mrs. Bristow flung herself in front of her husband, and said, in a deprecating tone—

"John—John, for mercy's sake do not make so foul a charge;" then turning to Peace, she murmured, "Take no notice of what he says, Mr. Peace. Do not heed his words. He knows not what he's saying."

"Don't I?" returned Bristow, with another jerk and a nod. "don't I? I aint to be gammoned if you are. I know my way about."

"Silence! Hold your tongue, John. Do be quiet!"

"You think I'm a fool, I 'spose,—eh?" said Bristow, in continuation. "How about that young swell—that lad of a chap 'as comes here? Be he arter you or Bessie? I'm a fool, am I?"

"Abuse me as much as you like—I am used to it; but don't take away other persons' characters," ejaculated the miserable wife.

"Oh, Mr. Peace, he'll be sorry for what he's said to-morrow. Take no notice of him. Pray don't, for my sake."

" For your sake I would do much; but he will have
to answer for this; not now, perhaps, for he is not
sober, but he will have to answer for it, and that he
will soon know to his cost."

" Shall I? Oh, very good. I'll answer for it whenever you like."

" John, be quiet," urged the unhappy wife.

" Well, then, send for something to drink."

" You've had enough."

" Have I? Then I'll have more!" exclaimed Bristow,
rising from his chair and staggering towards the door.
" Who's got any money? Have you got any, Mr.
Burglar ?"

Peace, who was standing near the door, lost all command over his temper. He struck the man a terrible
blow between the eyes which felled him like an ox.

The women both screamed with fright.

A policeman, who was passing, entered the parlour,
and found Peace and Bristow wrestling like two
athletes.

" Now then," said the constable; " let's have no more
of this, or I'll lock you both up."

He parted the two combatants, who stood glaring at
one another like two wild animals.

" He took me unawares, and gave me a prop atween
the eyes," said Bristow, who was by this time a little
sobered.

" He's been beating his wife, the wretch," said Bessie
Dalton. " Been trying to throttle her."

" Do you charge him ?" inquired the policeman of
Mrs. Bristow.

" Oh, dear no. He was not sober at the time. I
don't want anyone to be charged."

" I told you chap that he were a burglar, and he
didn't like to hear the truth," ejaculated Bristow, with
a chuckle.

" The man's mad drunk—he's been creating a disturbance the whole of the evening, and, because we
came into the room to prevent murder being done, he's
been as insulting as possible," said Peace. " He ought
to be locked up, to prevent him from doing further
mischief. Will anyone charge him ?"

" No, there's no charge, policeman," answered Mrs.
Bristow, quickly.

" Well, I'll tell you what it is, if I hear any more
noise or row, I'll lock you up upon my own responsibility ;" this last speech was addressed to Bristow.

" All right; now we understand one another,"
answered the latter, in the same sneering tone which
he had adopted during the whole of the evening. He
was maudlin drunk, mischievously disposed, and
tantalising.

" I'll have no more to say to the worthless vagabond,"
remarked Peace, preparing to leave. " You must use
your own discretion in dealing with him, but before I
go I must tell you that he is a dangerous character,
and a nuisance to the house, and, indeed, to the whole
neighbourhood," and with these words, our hero strode
out of the apartment, being in no way disposed to
prolong a scene which might compromise him.

He felt that the time had arrived for him to beat a
retreat; he adopted this course from strategic reasons.
There was no telling what further might fall from the
lips of Bristow, who was evidently mischievously disposed.

Peace, therefore, made for his own apartments
upstairs.

Bessie Dalton, however, chose to remain in the
parlour to defend her friend, Mrs. Bristow, or Sophy,
as she called her.

The policeman, who was a very efficient and worthy

member of the force, gave the inebriate a long lecture.
He was well acquainted with the character of the
latter, as disturbances and scenes of violence were
unhappily but too frequent.

After the departure of Peace, Bristow toned down.

He said to the constable that he had been a little
hasty—had been, in fact, worried about one or two
matters within the last few days; but that he was
sorry he had lost his temper. He could see it all now
as plainly as a book; still, at the same time, he
declared " that he was not going to stand any more of
that fellow's cheek."

Of course he alluded to Peace, from whose blow he
was still smarting. Indeed, one of his eyes was
blackened, although probably he was not aware of this
at present.

The policeman, after a few more words of warning,
left the two women and Bristow to settle their differences as best they could.

Soon after this Bristow went to bed, and in a few
minutes was sleeping soundly.

The house was quiet for the remainder of the night.

CHAPTER X.

PEACE HASTENS UP TO LONDON—CUNNING ISAAC—THE
JEW " FENCE "—THE VISIT TO SHEFFIELD.

THE words that had fallen from Bristow could not be
forgotten by Peace, who began to be seriously concerned.

He was quite unable in any way to account for the
expressions made use of by the ruffian in the parlour.

From whence could he have obtained his information ?

Had it been noised abroad that Peace was the man
who effected an entrance into the warehouse, or had
Cooney been in the town and split upon him?

Some mysterious agency had been at work.

Bristow could not have dreamt that he was a
burglar. He was too besotted and stupid a man to
divine it from anything he had seen.

Somebody must have given him secret information.
These thoughts passed rapidly through the brain of
our hero.

" This place is becoming too hot for me," murmured
Peace, while working in his shop in the back yard.

" Some enemy is at work, and to remain here much
longer would simply be an act of madness. No, I
must away, and that, too, as speedily as possible, but
I will not let any one know my intentions—no, not even
Bessie. That Bristow is a dangerous fellow—when
the drink is in him he cares not what he says."

Peace had concealed in his rooms a number of valuable articles which were the proceeds of his burglaries.
He did not care about running any risk by disposing
of the same in Bradford; neither did he feel disposed
to leave anything behind when he quitted the town. He
therefore packed them as closely as possible in a hair
trunk which he had procured for the purpose.

All this was done as quickly and secretly as possible
while Bessie Dalton was away at the mill where she
worked. When she came home in the evening she
found Peace busily occupied in the shop with his
picture frames.

He appeared to be as cheerful as usual, but he was
maturing his plan of operations.

On the following morning he paid the landlord his
rent, together with the amount due for the week's
notice, alleging that he had just received a telegram
announcing the fact that his mother was in London
dangerously ill, and that he was therefore compelled to
hasten to her bedside without further delay.

The landlord did not for a moment doubt the truth of this statement.

Peace put his traps in a fly he had hired, and was driven to the station.

He took the first train to London, arriving in the metropolis in the early part of the afternoon.

A four-wheeled cab conveyed him to Whitechapel

In that classic locality dwelt a Jew with whom Peace was well acquainted.

He had on more than one occasion disposed of his ill-gotten wares to the Israelite in question.

The Jew was called "cunning Isaac" by the professional gentlemen who had dealings with him.

Peace was driven to a coffee-shop, near to the Jew's residence.

Here he engaged a bed, his trunks were safely deposited in the back room; he had some coffee in the public room, and in the dusk of the evening he proceeded to the Jew's house, carrying with him, in a large bag, the greater portion of the property he had brought with him.

"Ah, Mishter Peace, your servant. I'm happy and proud to see you. Vat can I do for you? Have you anything in my vay? Bishness is bad—wery bad it ish. Nothing stirring but stagnation, as our friend O'Callaghan used to say."

"You just stop your clatter, Isaac, and don't call me by my name in a public shop. What I have to say to you must be said in your own private room."

"Chertainly, my tear friend, chertainly! This way if you please."

The burglar was conducted into a large back room, which presented the appearance of an old curiosity shop. It was crammed full of articles of almost every conceivable description.

"There now, take a chair, and make yourself at home. I'm happy and proud to see you," ejaculated the Jew, rubbing his hands together.

"There's quite enough of that. You're about as glad to see me as I am to see you," observed Peace.

"Vell, then, ve von't say any more about it. Let's to bishness. You've got something for me, I dare say."

His visitor opened his bag, and placed a number of articles on the table.

These consisted of gold trinkets of various descriptions, silver plate, spoons, forks, and fruit knives, but more noticeable than all the rest was the massive silver cup which the burglar had purloined from the mill-owner's residence at Dudley Hill.

On this was engraved the owner's name, and the inscription signified that it had been presented to the master by the workpeople employed in his establishment.

The Jew examined each article separately, and shook his head in a deprecating manner as some of them came under his inspection. This was a way he had so that he might thereby depreciate them in the eyes of the party who offered them for sale. Some young hands were taken in by his manner, which to say the truth was never very encouraging.

"Oh, I see—plated," he would ejaculate, when handling a genuine silver article, which he would push on one side as worthless. These little pleasantries were habitual with him.

It is a well-known fact to those who are acquainted with the subject that the burglar or thief never realises half, nor, indeed, in many instances a third, of the value of the property he purloins.

The sacrifice he has to make in obtaining ready cash for the same is enormous. The Jew "fence," as he is termed, who purchases the goods obtains by far the largest booty, and this is done with but little risk. The receivers, as a rule, are seldom captured and brought to justice, it being at all times most difficult to prove their guilt.

"Well," said Peace, after the Jew had finished his scrutiny of the various articles, "will they suit you?"

"Umph, there are some good things among them, but ash to the others, vell I don't care much about them."

"Don't have them then," returned his companion.

"I'll have them all at a price."

"Yes, I understand what that means—at your price, about a quarter of their value."

The Jew regarded the speaker with a half angry glance.

"I give the utmost I can afford at all times—to my friends especially. Indeed, Mishter Peace, I often lose by my purchases; bishness ish pad—there are no buyers, money is tight. You don't know how hard it is to get rid of goods, some especially. Now, there's that presentation cup—vat can I do with it? See the risk I run in——"

"Get out!" cried Peace, testily. "Put it in the melting pot—risk be hanged. You can't gammon me, you old sinner."

"Oh, Lord! to hear him talk, it's as good as a play," said the Jew, once more rubbing his hands together. Then, suddenly changing his tone, he said—

"Tell ye vat I'll do—give you fifty pounds for the lot."

"Very kind of you, I'm sure. Fifty pounds for goods that are worth a hundred and fifty in weight of the silver alone."

"Ah! but you forget the solder—you never thought of the solder. Besides I must have some little profit. I can't live on air."

Peace knew perfectly well, when he paid a visit to the establishment, that there would be a long time lost in haggling before he could get a moderately fair offer from Isaac. He had come prepared for this.

"I won't take fifty, or anything like it," said Peace, putting some of the articles back in his bag.

"Yer vont—eh?"

"I know where I can get more, and not far from here either."

"Vere ish it? Tell us vere it ish. Vill he pay of me?"

"I'm not going to let you know where it is."

"Vill you take sixty? There's a good offer. I shall lose by them."

Peace shook his head. No, he would not take sixty.

Ultimately a bargain was struck, and Peace accepted seventy-five pounds for the articles, and he esteemed himself particularly fortunate in realising that sum.

"Ah, that's a pad job about the 'Badger'—a very pad job—poor fellow, he vos bowled out at last."

"He was too headstrong. It was partly his own fault, so I've been told," remarked Peace, as he passed out of the shop.

He slept that night at the coffee-house, and on the following morning took the train to his native town, Sheffield.

He called on his mother and found her in her accustomed health and spirits. It is said that he was her favourite son, but we have no positive proof of this.

Soon after his arrival in Sheffield he wrote a letter to Bessie Dalton, in which he informed her that he had left Bradford for very excellent reasons—the place had become too hot for him, and a change of air was necessary for his health. This, he asserted, was his only reason for leaving—his love for her (Bessie) was as strong as ever. Nevertheless, there was an imperative necessity for them to be separated for a while.

He, however, sent her a small sum of money occasionally, and bade her keep up her spirits until they met again.

He had brought with him a sum which would suffice to keep him for some little time, and before this became exhausted he knew pretty well how to obtain more, but for some weeks after his arrival in his native town he was much more careful than he had been heretofore.

He picked up a very decent living by playing the violin at various houses of public entertainment in the town, and, to all appearance, he was a well-behaved, proper sort of young man enough.

It was shortly after his return to Sheffield that he become enamoured of a young girl. This, the first and indeed only honourable attachment he ever had for one of the opposite sex, was not crowned with success.

The circumstances connected with the life of the object of his new-formed attachment are of a nature singularly romantic, and as our history progresses her career, as shadowed forth in this work, will form a touching episode in the drama of every-day life.

There resided in the town of Sheffield at this time a widow lady, named Maitland. She was possessed of a small income, and led a quiet life. Peace, who had been introduced to her by one of the neighbours, was anxious to improve the acquaintance, his reason for this being a sudden passion for her daughter Aveline.

When once bent on any object he was not a man to be easily thwarted.

Aveline Maitland was possessed of no inconsiderable share of beauty. She was exquisitely formed, graceful, with small delicately-chiselled features, which were singularly sweet in their expression. Taken altogether, there was an air of refinement about her that might well inspire any man with the master passion.

It is somewhat singular that such a radiant, fair young creature should have touched the heart of a man of so coarse a mould as Charles Peace.

But so it was. He saw her by chance at her mother's residence, and he was struck with her grace and beauty.

Her influence over him was so powerful that for a short time he became quite an altered man.

He dressed with scrupulous care, was soft and gentle, and indeed it might be said winning in his manner.

Aveline Maitland, utterly unconsious of the fact that she had made a conquest of her mother's visitor, treated him with courtesy, and conversed freely with him upon the various topics of the day.

Mrs. Maitland gave a party one evening. Peace, who heard of this, volunteered to play the violin to the dancers.

The widow availed herself of his services, and he made himself particularly agreeable to all the guests.

After this he procured a box at the theatre, and escorted the widow and her daughter. During the performance he was most polite and attentive to both the females.

It was a source of great trouble to him, however, that the fair Aveline did not offer him any encouragement. On the contrary, he could not conceal from himself that she was cold and distant.

Nevertheless he did not despair. It is an old adage, "That faint heart never won fair lady." Peace was mindful of this. Most assuredly his was not a faint heart at any period of his career.

He was determined to woo and win Aveline. This time he was desperately in love, but there is another declaration made by a great poet—namely, "The course of true love never did run smooth." It would be hardly worth while to make an effort to ascertain whether Peace's passion for the fair Aveline could be included in the category of "true love;" there was so little truth about the man throughout the whole of his sinful life that the reader will find it difficult to believe of him being inspired with a pure and holy love for one of the opposite sex.

One thing, however, is quite certain, he believed himself to be desperately in love, and comforted himself in much the same way as other mortals do under similar circumstances.

"What is love?"

The fevered head, the palpitating heart, the visions beautiful and young, clothing our every day in a transient paradise, when the voice is heard deliciously exulting, or weeping passionately loud into the pillowed night.

Is this love? Slim girlhood answers yes.

Or is it the interchange of soul and soul, of which all life is typical? A staff in the traveller's hand, music to the soldier's march. Ah, such is love, sweet love!

Peace, as we have already seen, was a man of action. He was not one to beat about the bush, or let the grass grow under his feet, and in a very short time after his introduction to Mrs. Maitland and her charming daughter, he determined upon making a declaration to the latter of his undying and unfading love.

He had before this presented Mrs. Maitland with a handsome timepiece, the frame of which was most elaborately and beautifully carved by his own hands.

He had in his possession a ring set with diamonds, rubies, and other precious stones. This he purposed presenting to the daughter upon the first opportunity that occurred.

The widow's cottage stood on the outskirts of the town of Sheffield. In the rear of the habitation was a small but well-cultivated garden. In this, one fair spring morning, Aveline Maitland was to be seen. She was seated in an alcove, or summer-house, as it was termed, reading.

Charles Peace, who had been watching her from the road, thought this a favourable opportunity.

He unfastened the wicket gate by the side of the garden, and entered.

His manner was soft and gentle. Taking off his hat, he paid his respects to the widow's daughter, who rose from her seat and shook him by the hand.

"Pardon me, Miss Maitland, for this intrusion upon your privacy; but I have that to say which cannot possibly remain any longer unsaid."

The young lady regarded the speaker with a look of surprise, and requested him to be seated.

Peace proceeded. "In the first place, I have a favour to ask, which I hope—nay, I feel convinced—you will not refuse."

"What is its nature?" inquired his companion.

"I wish you to accept this little present," said he, drawing forth the ring; "to accept it as a token in remembrance of me."

"Sir!" exclaimed Aveline. "Mr. Peace, you greatly surprise me."

"You are not offended, I hope?"

"No, certainly not. And I hope you will not be offended when I say I could not think of accepting it."

PEACE'S ENCOUNTER WITH THE DOG "BRUNO."

Peace's brow darkened. To say the least of it, this was a bad beginning. He did not press the question.

"Miss Maitland," he said, in continuation, "you will, I hope, not object to hear what I have to say?'

She signified, by an inclination of the head, that he might proceed.

"Well, said Peace, "I don't know whether you have been able to divine my feelings, or to guess the secret which is locked up in my heart; but I feel that the time has come for me to be outspoken. From the very first moment I saw you but one absorbing thought haunted me. A mighty and overpowering passion took possession of me, and held me in bondage. As time went on, it became more intensified. Take pity on me!"

"Pity, and for what?"

No. 6.

"I am your slave, your devoted slave. It is little to say, perhaps, that I never knew what love was till I saw you."

His companion gave utterance to a cry of surprise, or it might be alarm.

"Ah, my dear young lady, if you only knew how, sleeping or waking, your image is before me, if you only knew——"

"Enough of this," cried Aveline ; "we are not on the stage playing two parts in a fashionable melodrama; you must be less demonstrative."

"I will, as it so pleases you. Listen : I have money at my command sufficient to supply you with every ease or luxury you may desire. Only give me hope—do not drive me to despair. I love you so much that it would be indeed a blessing to devote my whole life to you. Tell me—may I hope ?"

"Hope what ?"

"That you will look with favour on me."

"Mr. Peace I have already signified that you surprised me—now I am fairly astonished. What am I to understand by the words you have been uttering ?"

"I desire you to accept me as a suitor for your hand, and on a future day I hope to become your husband."

Miss Maitland rose from her seat.

"There must be an end of this," she said, with something like anger depicted on her beautiful features.

"You refuse then—you doom me to perpetual misery."

"I don't know what you mean by perpetual misery, but I must tell you frankly that I feel it my duty to at once declare that I cannot for a moment receive you as a suitor, and once and for all I bid you never again to allude to this subject."

Peace was miserably disappointed. He felt humiliated. The reception he had met with was in every way unsatisfactory.

He did, in his way, really love the young woman to whom he had made so sudden and unexpected a declaration.

Her candour and prompt answers cut him to the quick.

He had no right to expect a young lady, who was so immeasurably superior to himself, to treat him in any other way than she had done; but the audacity, assurance, and conceit of the man were beyond all bounds.

He had hoped to carry the fortress by storm, but the attempt turned out an ignominious failure.

"I cannot tell you, Miss Maitland, how supremely wretched you have made me," said Peace.

"I am sorry to give pain to anyone, but at the same time I have felt it my bounden duty to be explicit. You have my answer. Let me beg of you, as a personal favour, Mr. Peace, not to ever again refer to this subject."

"May I inquire the cause of this aversion, if I may so term it ? Is there a rival in the case ?"

"I do not feel myself bound to answer such a question," returned his companion, in a tone of offended dignity. "Neither do I think our relative positions entitle you to interrogate me thus, I might say, rudely. Our interview is at an end."

She moved towards the house.

"I hope we part friends. You're not offended with me ?"

"Well, no ; but I think you have acted without due consideration. There has never been anything in my manner or bearing towards you to warrant this familiarity. But let that pass. I bear you no ill will. On the contrary, I hope and trust you will see the mistake you have made, and so farewell."

She offered her hand to Peace, who took it and raised it to his lips.

She withdrew it somewhat hastily, and walked with rapid strides towards the back door of the cottage.

Peace found himself alone.

He had some difficulty in mastering his feelings.

Rage and despair seemed to have seized him, and had he not respected Aveline Maitland as much or, indeed, more than he admired and loved her, the probability is that he would have burst out in one of those violent fits of passion which he generally displayed when thwarted in any object upon which he had set his heart.

But there was something so polished in the manner of the young girl that he was in a measure disarmed and held in bondage while in her presence.

After the departure of Miss Maitland, Peace remained for a few minutes like one stupified.

He presently recovered himself, and walked slowly along the gravel path in the garden until he had reached the gate.

He opened it, passed through, and crept down the lane which skirted the side entrance of the widow's residence.

He cast one long lingering look at the cottage, heaved a deep sigh, and walked on with accelerated speed.

"I've been too precipitate," he ejaculated, as he proceeded along; "much too precipitate, and by my rashness have lost the only woman I ever loved—the only woman. How could I have been such a fool? Not, perhaps, that she would have been persuaded to listen to my suit, not in any case; but I have thrown away whatever little chance I had. Well, she gave me a plain and positive answer. And it's likely enough that some one else is after her."

As this thought passed through his brain he uttered curses loud and deep.

Crestfallen, and in a state bordering on distraction, he reached Sheffield, where he joined a lot of boon companions, in whose company he vainly strove to drown the sorrow which weighed so heavily upon his heart.

For the next few days he was in a state of nervous excitement.

He could not forget the words that had fallen from the lips of Aveline.

Did she suspect aught? Had some mischievous busybody been speaking against him ? It was likely enough. There must have been some powerful influence at work. The more he reflected upon the subject the more he felt assured that some one had given her a timely caution. Who could it be ?

He ferreted about in all quarters; made inquiries of a number of persons from whom he thought he might obtain the desired information, but was unable to get the faintest clue to anyone. He pushed his inquiries still further, but was in no way successful.

He frequently bent his steps in the direction of the widow's cottage, where dwelt the woman for whom he was ready to make any sacrifice. He hovered about the house and grounds in a state of hopeless and almost incurable despair.

It was even some solace for him to contemplate the habitation, and to conjure up, by the agency of imagination, the fair young creature moving about from room to room.

One day, while traversing the lane, he heard voices in the garden ; they proceeded from the other side of the hedge which skirted the grounds.

Peace came to a halt—listened most attentively. He could hear the low, musical tones of Aveline, and hear also the voice of a man in close converse with her.

His heart beat audibly, his pulse quickened.

"She has some one with her," he murmured.

Moved by a sudden impulse, he crept by the side of the fence until he had gained the extreme end of the garden. A quickset hedge ran along this, through the interstices of which Peace was able, unobserved, to obtain a view of the summer-house, upon which his eyes were now riveted.

He saw Aveline Maitland seated therein. By her side was a tall, handsome young man, whose looks denoted the state of his heart. He was whispering loving words to her—so Peace imagined, and was by no means mistaken.

It was evident that he was saying something that pleased her, for ever and anon she smiled.

Peace's brain seemed to be on fire, his knees knocked together, and his whole frame shook with ill-suppressed passion.

"Tom Gatliffe, as I'm a living man!" he exclaimed. "He then is my rival, the sneaking hound! Ah, if I had only known this before!"

He ground his teeth with rage, and watched the lovers with the eyes of a basilisk.

It would have been too plainly perceptible, even to a casual observer, to say nothing of the penetrating and suspicious glance of Peace, that the young lady in the alcove lent an attentive ear to the soft, low sentences breathed by her male companion.

Peace became furious as he gazed upon the loving pair; nevertheless, he found it impossible to leave the spot. The foliage behind which he hid was sufficiently dense to screen him, but even if this had not been the case, he was wound up to such a state of desperation that he would not have much cared had the faithless Aveline and her companion become aware of his position behind his leafy screen.

Indeed, the thought crossed his mind more than once, of emerging from his place of concealment and confronting them.

But, upon second consideration, he came to the conclusion that no possible good could result from such a course of action, and therefore determined to keep where he was till the interview was over.

He would watch and wait.

The conversation was carried on between the two for some time, after which they both rose and walked slowly towards the house.

Peace was not sufficiently near to hear a word they said, but he judged, rightly enough, that their discourse was a pleasant one—being, in fact, made up of those airy nothings which are the golden dreams of life's morning.

The situation in which he found himself was, to say the least of it, a most trying one—it would have proved to be so to the most apathetic, but to a man of Peace's temperament it was all but insupportable.

"She can be haughty and distant enough when it suits her purpose, the deceitful minx," he ejaculated, with bitterness; "but at other times she can be all honey. Bah! a plague on them both! That mealy-mouthed Tom Gatliffe, with his fine set speeches and goody-goody manner, has turned the gal's head—that is the reason of her flouting me the other day."

The lovers now entered the cottage, and Peace crept along the side of the hedge till he had reached the lane.

He sat down on a neighbouring stile and began to reflect—if a chaotic mass of fugitive thoughts rushing through an overheated brain can be called reflection.

What should he do? How should he be avenged?

Was it possible to break the golden fetters which bound the two together.

These were questions he found some difficulty in answering.

He had known Tom Gatliffe from boyhood; indeed, at one time they were schoolfellows. He was jealous of him even in those early days, for Tom was a diligent pupil, and in every way so superior to Peace that as a natural consequence they were never at any time what might be called pals.

"He was always a proud, conceited upstart," exclaimed Peace. "Always thought a deal of himself, and went in for the virtuous, and looked down upon me with something like contempt. That was bad enough, but worse has followed—he's stolen from me the only girl I ever loved. I hate the fellow, curse him!"

He rose from his seat and walked rapidly down the lane, muttering anathemas against Gatliffe and all his belongings. This did not appear to satisfy him, so he turned round and retraced his steps.

He had no settled or defined purpose in so doing, and, indeed, he hardly knew why he turned back, unless it was occasioned by a reluctance to lose sight of the cottage in the occupation of the widow.

He was so restless, so little himself, that he acted altogether in an erratic way.

In the course of ten minutes or so he caught sight of a solitary figure at the extreme end of the lane.

Peace came to a sudden halt; to all appearance from what he could make out the solitary messenger was none other than the detested Tom Gatliffe.

In a minute or so after this he was assured of this fact; with rapid strides the young man hastened along.

Peace waited; this was just what he desired. His face was distorted with passion, and wore on it a demoniacal expression.

Heedless of the coming storm young Gatliffe walked merrily along until he caught sight of the malevolent countenance of his quarrelsome schoolfellow.

"Ugh, it's you, is it?" said Peace, with inexpressible disgust, both in his tone and manner; "you, eh?"

"What's the matter, my friend?" inquired Tom.

"Friend be hanged," answered Peace, "you're no friend of mine." "What do you do crawling about here? Tell me that. Oh, you may put on one of your sanctimonious looks, but it won't deceive me. I say again, what do you do here?"

"Upon my word, Peace, you conduct yourself in a strange manner. Has anyone offended you?"

"Never you mind whether they have or not; you are lurking about here for no good purpose. Where have you come from?"

"Well, from the house of a friend of mine."

"You are full of friends—everybody's your friend, I s'pose. Is your friend's name Maitland?"

"You are quite correct in your surmise—it is."

"I thought so, and I suppose, if I may make so bold as to inquire, it is not so much the widow who has attracted you to the house as the daughter?" This was said in a tone of bitter irony.

"What if I refuse to answer impertinent questions?"

"You will refuse. You dare not answer them—you're a mischief-making, lying, canting humbug. It is you, and none but you, who have poisoned the mind of Miss Maitland against me—Charles Peace—do you hear?"

Tom Gatliffe was perfectly astounded. As Peace

gave utterance to these last words his countenance seemed to darken with the darkness of a curse.

"Look here," said Gatliffe, in a more serious tone. "For the life of me I do not understand what you mean; but I tell you frankly that I am not disposed to be insulted and abused—the more so since I have not by word or deed done you the slightest harm."

"It's a lie—a miserable lie!" yelled Peace, poking his face forward towards the speaker, and making a hideous grimace.

"Are you mad? What on earth possesses you?" inquired the other.

"Haven't you just left Miss Maitland?" cried Peace.

"Suppose I have—what's that to you?"

"Oh—oh—what is it to me! Why, only this—she looked with eyes of favour on me until you set her against me."

"Looked with favour on *you!*" said Gatliffe, with ineffable disgust. "Me set her against you? Why, Peace, you are beside yourself. Listen. I have known the Maitlands for years; and, long before you set eyes upon either, was the accepted suitor of the daughter. And neither you nor any other man shall come between me and Aveline Maitland—not even a peer of the realm."

"Don't you fancy you're going to carry it off with a high hand, you despicable, crawling reptile!" exclaimed Peace, in a paroxysm of rage. "There's not a word of truth in what you've been saying. I know full well who I have to thank for turning her against me—you, none but you."

With these words he rushed at Gatliffe like a wild beast. He wound his fingers around his throat and endeavoured to throttle him.

In his fury he foamed at the mouth; and, had he been possessed of a weapon, doubtless something serious would have happened.

Gatliffe was a tall, athletic young man, who, in fair fight, would be able to overcome Peace with the greatest ease.

He had stood his taunts and insults with commendable good temper, but there is a limit to the forbearance of the most patient man.

He caught Peace round the waist, lifted him up, and threw him from him with the greatest ease.

Peace picked himself up and rushed forward again at his antagonist, who by this time had become a little angry.

He delivered a well-directed blow on his opponent's chest, which knocked him backwards.

Finding that he was overmatched, Peace picked up a large flint stone, which he hurled at Gatliffe, who was seriously bruised in the thigh from the blow.

He rushed rapidly forward, and, clutching Peace by both arms, he pinioned him, and rendered him powerless to do further harm for the present.

"Let go, coward—let go!" exclaimed Peace.

"It's you who are the coward, you spiteful, vindictive little brute. You ought to be ashamed of yourself —that is if you have any shame in you. Think yourself lucky you've escaped a good thrashing, for it's what you deserve," said Gatliffe.

Peace made frantic efforts to release himself, but he was unsuccessful.

Gatliffe, in addition to having great personal strength, had on more than one occasion carried off the prize as a wrestler.

He was a quiet, well-disposed young man enough, and was at all times the very last to quarrel, but when once aroused he was well able to take his own part.

"Are you going to leave go?" cried Peace, after a series of ineffectual struggles.

"Not unless you promise to behave better."

"I wont promise—I'll die first."

"Very well, then; I shall keep you prisoner till a constable comes—that's all."

"A constable?"

"Yes, a policeman. Will you promise?"

"What?"

"To conduct yourself like a sane person."

"I wont promise anything. I hate and despise you for a sneak as you are."

"You were always an abusive, audacious fellow, even as a boy," returned Gatliffe. "And a man who knows you as well as I do must be a fool to take any notice of your blustering."

Two farm labourers who had witnessed the conflict from a neighbouring meadow, now came forward and proffered their services to Gatliffe.

"You've got a bit of a madman, aint ye, master?" said one of the men. "May be he's escaped from his keeper."

"You impudent wretch!" ejaculated Peace.

"What be going to do wi' him?" said the other rustic. "He deserves ducking in the horse pond—that be the best way to serve him."

"He's flung a big stone at 'ee," said the other; "better take him to the police station."

"Oh, there's no occasion for that," answered Gatliffe. "I think he may go about his business now. If he's got any sense he will do so at once."

And with these words he let go of Peace, who deemed it advisable not to attempt any renewal of hostilities.

"Now go your way," said Gatliffe. "You are smarting under some real or imaginary wrong; hence it is, I suppose, that you have fallen foul of me."

"I haven't done with you—depend upon that," cried Peace. "You've got the better of me now, I admit, but that does not settle the difference between us."

"Get away, you stupid fellow," returned Gatliffe; "you don't suppose I'm afraid of a man like you. Be off, and give me no more of your impudence, for if you do, I tell you candidly you wont escape again with a whole skin."

Peace made another hideous face, after which he jumped over the stile and threaded his way through a narrow pathway which ran by the side of a corn-field.

Gatliffe watched him for some little time—he then turned towards the two farm labourers and laughed.

"He's a spiteful, vindictive rascal," said he; "there's no doubt of that."

"He be vicious, an' I should say from the look on 'un a bad lot," observed the ploughman. "There aint much on 'im, but what there is is all fire and brimstone, an' it dont take much to set it alight."

CHAPTER XI.

THE PROPOSAL—MRS. MAITLAND BECOMES COMMUNICATIVE.

HUMILIATED and crestfallen, Peace returned to his old haunts at Sheffield. He solaced himself by writing a long and affectionate letter to Bessie Dalton, of whom he had taken but little notice for some time past; now he endeavoured to make amends for his neglect.

The excuses he made for this were, as a matter of course, mainly drawn from his own imagination, which, as far as false statements were concerned, was at all times fertile enough.

He mixed freely with his boon companions and played the violin nightly at one or more of the sing-songs held at the public-houses in the town. He had "the gift of the gab," as it is termed, could converse glibely enough upon most topics, in addition to which he had quaint sayings and amusing ways, which went far towards ensuring him a cordial reception from the frequenters of the houses he chose to honour with a visit.

In many ways Peace was a remarkable man. He was a consummate scoundrel from the outset to the close of his career, but he could be, when he chose, a very plausible one.

Had he not been this he could never have imposed upon so many persons as he did.

But, despite his well-affected hilarity, grief lay heavy at his heart when he thought of the beauteous Aveline Maitland.

Her image was for ever presenting itself to his vision. "But she's far beyond my reach," he would murmur. "She never would have listened to me under any circumstances. No, she's too far removed from such as me."

The more he thought over the matter the more he became impressed with the fact. The only wonder is that he had not arrived at this conclusion from the very first.

His successful rival, Tom Gatliffe, had been on terms of the closest intimacy with Mrs. Maitland and Aveline. His love for the latter had grown with his growth and strengthened with his strength. He positively worshipped the fair young creature who had so enslaved him, but for a long time he had remained silent upon the subject which engrossed his whole thoughts.

Young Gatliffe belonged to what is called the industrial class, but he had received an education superior to the generality of men in his station of life. He was by trade an engineer.

Patient, self-reliant, and industrious, he had won for himself a good position in one of the leading firms in Sheffield. His employers had great confidence in him, and he was a young man who gave early promise of pushing his way in the world. He was steady, frugal, and had already saved a considerable sum of money. He had of late become more persistent in his attentions to Aveline.

The end of this may be readily divined.

He avowed his love, and proposed.

Aveline did not refuse. On the contrary, she accepted him upon the condition that he was to broach the subject to Mrs. Maitland.

The young engineer was in an ecstacy of delight at his success so far.

Soon after his encounter with Peace he bent his steps towards the widow's cottage, and sought an interview with its mistress.

Mrs. Maitland shrewdly guessed the object of his visit.

She conducted him into the front parlour, closed the door, and sat herself down in one of the arm-chairs, motioning her visitor to be seated in another.

"My dear Mrs. Maitland," said Gatliffe. "It is indeed a subject of most serious import, as regards my own happiness, which has occasioned me to seek you. For a long time past I have been attached to your daughter—possibly you might have guessed this."

The widow nodded.

"Ah, as I supposed."

"And Aveline?"

"I have told her all—told her that a great golden blaze of light seemed to fall upon me when I first beheld her. I love her and have avowed my love. She bade me seek you—bade me ask your consent. That is why I am here."

"I see and comprehend most fully. You love one

another. Well, Mr. Gatliffe, you are not the first man who has been struck with Aveline—but let that pass. I esteem and respect you, and, as far as I am concerned, there will be no impediment in the way."

"I think you too worthy a fellow to offer any objection to—you have my consent. As far as that is concerned, consider the matter settled. But there are other considerations." she added, in a more serious tone.

"Considerations!" he exclaimed. "Possibly you allude to my position in life."

"Oh, dear me, no—not for a moment."

"Pray explain. Let me know the worst," he ejaculated, in evident trepidation.

"In the first place," answered the widow, "I must inform you that Aveline is not my daughter."

"Not your daughter, Mrs. Maitland! Impossible!"

"No, but I am quite as fond of her as if she were my own child, but she is not, and I think it but right and proper that you should be put in possession of all the facts. She is not my daughter."

"Whose daughter is she then?"

"That I cannot tell you. I have adopted her, and brought her up from infancy."

"I am indeed surprised."

"That is no more than I expected. Listen! You are perhaps not aware that I was at one time matron to the Derby Infirmary. It was while acting in this capacity that I first met with Aveline, who was then between two and three years old.

"There had been a collision on the line. Many persons were seriously injured, while some were picked out of the carriages dead.

"One poor lady was brought into the infirmary in a dying condition. When discovered, strange to say, a little girl, supposed to be her daughter, whom she clasped in her arms, was found to be uninjured; they were both conveyed to the infirmary.

"The mother was in a state of insensibility. After she had been attended to by the surgeon she rallied a little, and murmured once or twice, in a half dreamy state, the word 'Aveline.' The child answered to the name, and went to the bedside of the sufferer.

"We endeavoured to get the poor lady to tell us who she was, but she was too ill to speak, and the doctor forbade us making any more inquiries for the present.

"It was a pitiful sight, for you must understand that there were many other poor creatures besides her who required immediate attention, and of course it was the duty of myself and the nurses under my direction to see to them without a moment's delay.

"While thus engaged one of the nurses came to me, and whispered in my ear that the lady in bed No. 14 had breathed her last.

"I hastened to the spot, and found that her words were but too true. The child was crying, and I directed one of the women to take it into the house I occupied, and tell Rebecca, my servant, to take charge of it till I came."

"And its mother?"

"Had passed away, as I have told you. Many others succumbed to the injuries they had received. Most—nay, indeed, I believe all—were identified by their relatives—all, save the lady and her child.

"For these no claimant could be found. Not the faintest scrap of intelligence reached us from any quarter to give a clue to their identification.

"The lady to all appearance belonged to the upper class. She had a sweet face and features of delicate mould; but who she was it is not possible to say. Neither do I think it likely now that we shall ever ascertain."

"Goodness me—how singular! And had she nothing about her to denote who and what she was?"

"She wore round her neck a double gold locket, containing the portrait of a gentleman on one side, on the other was a likeness of the deceased lady, and, in addition to her wedding ring, she wore one with a motto and crest inside it. A description of her and the child, together with the jewellery she had on, appeared in the list of the dead and missing in the public papers at the time, but no one came forward to claim either the living or the dead."

"Can such things be possible?" exclaimed Gatliffe.

"My dear sir, they are of frequent occurrence. If we could know the number of missing and unclaimed persons which every year furnishes us with, it would surprise most people. But what I am telling you now are simply facts which have come under my own observation."

"And the mother, what became of her remains?"

"After every effort had been made to discover her relations, and we had given it up as hopeless, my husband paid for her funeral, and he said, at the same time, that he would never part with the child. Poor dear soul! he kept his word. She was by his bedside when his gentle spirit passed away. He almost worshipped Aveline, and she was equally attached to him. She has been indeed more than a daughter to us."

"And have you the locket and the two rings?"

"They were kept in the hospital for some years, but upon my retiring, I begged them of the governors, and they at once gave orders for them to be handed over to me. I have them now."

"And do not intend to part with them, I hope?"

"Certainly not. I consider they belong to Aveline."

"Why, Mrs. Maitland, this is indeed an extraordinary story."

"I have thought it a duty incumbent on me to furnish you with all the particulars. If, after hearing them, you are still disposed to have Aveline——"

"If!" ejaculated the young engineer. "You do not for a moment suppose I have any desire to cancel our engagement. No, my dear madam, it is an additional reason for my cherishing and protecting her."

"Well, Tom, I hope—nay, I am sure—you will make her a good husband; and I frankly admit, if it had been left to me to select one for her, I should have chosen you."

Gatliffe sprang to his feet, put his arms round the speaker's neck, and kissed her fondly.

"Tush, tush, you silly boy," said the widow, "what do you want to be kissing an old woman like me for?"

She was, however, not in any way angry with her companion.

"Is Aveline a Christian or surname, do you think?" queried Gatliffe.

"I took it to be a Christian name from the fact that the mother called her child to her bedside by it, and the little thing answered to it with the greatest alacrity. It is her Christian name now. She'll not change it when she marries, I suppose," added the widow, with a smile.

"I shall never call her by any other. You know, Mrs. Maitland, I am but in humble circumstances, but I have enough to give my dear Aveline all she can desire, and I hope in a short time to be more prosperous."

"Ah, as to that, riches are not everything, though many persons think they are—I do not, however. By the way, Tom, do you know that Mr. Peace made Aveline an offer?"

"Yes, I've heard so; but she wouldn't listen to him."

"No, I candidly confess that I had rather a good opinion of him at one time—not as a suitor for Aveline, but I thought him good-natured and kindly disposed."

"Probably he may be so."

"But I have very much altered my opinion with regard to him—very much indeed," returned the widow, with forcible emphasis.

Gatliffe refrained from offering any remark. It was evident, from his manner, that he did not want to dwell further on the subject.

Aveline now entered the room, whereupon her lover rose and embraced her.

"It is all settled, dearest," he exclaimed, in a tone of delight. "You will learn the full particulars from Mrs. Maitland."

"So you have been having a *tete-à-tete*, it seems."

"Yes, we have, my child," said Mrs. Maitland, "and a very satisfactory one it has proved to be."

"I'm glad of that," murmured Aveline. "You both seem well pleased."

Young Gatliffe thought it was time to take his departure. He was elated with the successful nature of his interview with the widow, and thought it best to leave her alone with Aveline.

CHAPTER XII.

THE BURGLARY AT WOOD-HILL—AN UNEXPECTED MEETING.

IT would not be edifying to the reader to chronicle all the marauding expeditions in which our hero was engaged at this period.

The money obtained by the exercise of his musical ability did not content him for long. He visited several houses after nightfall, and if the booty obtained was not large he escaped without detection.

He had "spotted," to use his own phrase, a house standing in its own grounds at Wood-hill, within a few miles of Sheffield.

The place seemed so isolated and looked so tempting, it being in the occupation of some rich person, that Peace determined upon paying it an early visit.

At the back of the house was a conservatory. This could be reached from one of the back rooms. Indeed, it might be said to form part of the room itself.

Peace, who had noted all these things when passing the place in midday, had determined upon his plan of operations.

He scaled the iron railings which ran round the front garden, and made at once for the greenhouse. To obtain an entrance into this was a matter of no great difficulty.

The two folding doors of the parlour led into the conservatory. These were, as a matter of course, fastened, but not very securely.

The burglar, who, as we have already seen, was an expert in dealing with locks and bolts, began by ascertaining, as nearly as possible, the nature of the fastenings.

With a bit of bent wire he picked the lock, and one of the doors yielded to his pressure.

He found the top bolt had not been drawn home into its socket, and an aperture was disclosed sufficiently large for him to withdraw the bottom bolt with one of the instruments he had brought with him. The bolt was pulled back, and the door was flung wide open.

All this had been done in so quick a manner that none of the inmates were disturbed.

Peace entered the back parlour, and found therein a considerable amount of portable and valuable property. By the aid of one of his silent lucifers, he possessed himself of a number of articles, which he placed together on the table, with the intention of removing them upon his return from the other rooms, which it was his purpose to ransack in a similar manner.

He went into the front parlour, and took from it a still richer booty, which he placed by the side of the first heap.

This done, he crept cautiously upstairs, and entered the front drawing-room on the first floor.

This was furnished with most costly articles. The burglar was quite charmed with the appearance of the apartment, still more so with its contents.

He now for the first time made use of one of the long screws which he used so frequently in the after part of of his lawless career.

Closing the door, he bored a small hole in it with a bradawl; into this he inserted a long, pointed screw, which he turned with a screw-driver, and by this means fastened himself securely in the room.

No one would be able to gain an entrance.

With one of his lucifers he lighted a small wax taper, which he placed on one of the hobs of the grate. Then he proceeded to open all the drawers and cupboards, from which he abstracted a number of valuables. These he placed in his bag.

He felicitated himself upon the successful nature of the expedition; the proceeds of his night's work would undoubtedly realise a considerable sum of money, even at the Jew's price.

As may be supposed, he did not leave much behind that there was any possibility of carrying away.

The examination of the room, the turning over the various articles, and abstraction of the same, took a longer time than he had expected; nevertheless, he deemed himself quite safe, as the door was securely fastened.

When he had selected all that he intended to take away with him, he blew out his taper, and began to withdraw his long, thin screw. This done, he cautiously opened the door, and peeped out.

No one was visible.

Turning round to reach his bag, his coat-tail caught the branch of a candelabrum, which fell to the floor with a loud crash.

In another moment he was alarmed by the barking of a dog, and in the next a fierce animal rushed into the room, and sprang at his throat.

Peace was greatly alarmed. The whole household would, in all probability, be aroused.

"Curse the hound!" he muttered; at the same time grasping the dog's throat with both hands, so as to silence him, and at the same time, if possible, to throttle him.

A struggle ensued between the burglar and the dog, which, short and desperate as it was, seemed an age to Peace.

He flung his canine opponent with all his force to the other end of the room; but the dog was not easily cowed; he came on once more.

Peace had expected this. As the animal approached, he struck it a terrific blow on the head with his jemmy. For a moment the poor creature was stunned.

Peace shouldered his bag, and was about to make off, when he received a cut on the forehead from some weapon, which caused a thousand sparks to flicker before his eyes.

He struck out right and left with his jemmy at a dark figure in the doorway.

In another moment he was in the grasp of a powerful man, whose features were not distinguishable, the room being at this time in almost utter darkness.

"Scoundrel—villain!" exclaimed his opponent; "you shall not escape me."

Peace made no answer to these expletives.

He had but one thought—this being to get away. He struggled desperately, and fought like a tiger.

The two combatants fell to the floor, rolling over together. Peace kicked and struck out with his fists, but for all he could do he could not shake off his resolute antagonist.

The dog, who had now in a measure recovered from the blow, set up a loud barking.

He, with a noble instinct, rushed to his master's assistance and caught Peace by one of his legs, who kicked the animal savagely with the other.

"Down Bruno—down, boy," ejaculated Peace's opponent.

At these words the dog ceased further hostilities.

Peace by a supreme effort rose to his feet, but he was still in the grasp of his enemy, who also rose.

The noise and barking of the dog aroused another inmate of the house; this was the servant girl, who hurried on her things and hastened to the scene of action with a lighted candle in her hand.

"For mercy's sake, Mr. Gatliffe, whatever is the matter?" she inquired.

Peace's heart beat audibly. He was in the hands of Tom Gatliffe.

By the light of the candle which the girl carried he beheld the well-known features of his rival.

"Heaven be merciful!" exclaimed the latter, who despite his disguise at once recognised Peace. "Can it be possible?"

He regarded the burglar with a look of bewilderment.

Peace was abashed; panting and puffing like a grampus, he drew back and supported himself against the edge of the cheffonier.

The two—the honest man and the rogue—regarded each other in silence for a brief space of time.

"I had never counted on this—I am appalled," exclaimed Gatliffe. "A robber, a thief, a burglar! It surpasses all belief!"

A stream of blood trickled down the face of our hero from the blow he had received at the commencement of the conflict, but he was heedless of this. The exposure, the terrible discovery made by young Gatliffe, afflicted him more than aught else.

"What have you to say for yourself—can it be possible that you have sunk so low as this? I can hardly realise the fact, which, however, is but too evident. I would that some other person had made this discovery."

"It's no use making fine set speeches," returned Peace; "here we both are. It is not a pleasant meeting for either of us, but we must make the best of it."

"What has been the matter?" inquired the girl. "Shall I go for James, or a policeman, or what?"

"You had better go for a policeman; but stay, where is James?"

"In the room over the coach-house, I suppose."

"Well, we don't want his assistance—go for a policeman. The station is not far hence—go, there's a good girl."

The maid placed the candle on the table, put on her shawl, and sallied forth.

When she had gone Gatliffe closed the door, locked it, and put the key into his pocket.

"Now," he said, turning to Peace, "you are my prisoner."

"So it seems," returned the latter, who had by this time recovered his assurance; "but may I inquire what you do here? You are not master of this house—are you?"

"I am not, but one of my employers is. He's away in the country, and during his absence I have taken charge of the premises. Insolence will avail you but little. You might have got me into trouble, imperilled my position—nay, almost ruined me—had you got clean away with the things you have purloined."

"But I've not got away, and it's no use supposing I have," interrupted Peace. "It is a bad business, but can't be helped. Do you mean to tell me that you are going to hand me over to the police?"

"It is my duty to do so."

"Duty, be blowed! Look here, we've had a word or two. You've robbed me of the only woman I ever cared for. It's driven me to distraction—that's what it's done—else I shouldn't be here. It is all your fault —but, there, I bear you no animosity. Let bygones be bygones. I tell you I've been driven to distraction. Do you hear?"

"Yes, I do."

"Well, then, if you are the same generous Tom Gatliffe as I knew years ago, you wont be hard upon your old chum."

"What would I give to be out of this difficulty?" exclaimed Gatliffe, in a tone of sadness. "Do, for mercy's sake, mend your ways. Never make another attempt of this sort. It is, I hope, your first false step —let it be your last."

"It shall be—I promise you that. It shall be the last," he answered, with well-simulated hypocrisy.

"For the sake of those who are near and dear to you, do not, I charge you, stray from the path of honesty. A burglar—a midnight robber! It appears almost too terrible to believe. What am I to say to my employer?"

"You need not say that we were in any way acquainted. The attempt was made, and you frustrated it. That is all. I'm in your power, and throw myself upon your mercy. Let me go."

"If I do, justice will surely overtake you, sooner or later, unless you mend your ways."

"I will," cried Peace. "Be assured of that. Now, Tom, the minutes are flying rapidly. Even now the police may be on their way here. Let me get clear off while there's yet time."

"But how can I without compromising myself? It is most repugnant to my feelings, most painful for me to give you in charge. But what am I to do? How can I help it?"

"Open the door, and say I slipped out of your grasp, and got away. Nothing is easier. Or open the window, I can drop on the grass plat. Whichever you please, only—time—time presses."

Gatliffe hesitated for a moment, then he took the key out of his pocket, unlocked the door, flung it wide open, and said, in a hoarse whisper—

"Go. Get you gone! I imperil my own position, but we are known to each other from boyhood. Away at once!"

"You're a good fellow, Tom; I always said so," murmured Peace. "Now I am more than ever assured of it. I shall not forget your kindness. But a few days ago I hated you, and could have killed you. Now I esteem and love you."

"Go to —— no more of this," returned his companion. "All I ask of you is that you never again suffer yourself to forfeit my good opinion by any discreditable or dishonest act."

"Trust me, Tom, I will not," said Peace, as he flew with rapid steps down the stairs, and passed through the back parlour, and from thence into the conservatory.

In a few minutes after this he was clear away from the scene of his operations.

After his departure Tom Gatliffe remained in the front drawing-room a prey to a thousand conflicting thoughts.

The unexpected and singular encounter that had taken place was altogether of such an extraordinary nature that he seemed bewildered and perplexed.

He had never for a moment imagined that Peace had been pursuing a lawless career, and the sudden discovery he made that night fell like a thunderbolt upon him.

Gatliffe was a young man of the strictest integrity, of the highest moral rectitude, and he felt supremely miserable when he reflected upon the incriminating facts, which had been made but too painfully manifest, in connection with his schoolfellow Peace.

He would have given half he was possessed of not to have been in the house at the time of the burglary.

Generous, kind-hearted, and forgiving as he was by nature, he found it impossible to blast the prospects of one whom he had known, almost on what might be termed the threshold of existence.

He glanced at the burglar's bag, which contained so many valuable articles, and, as he did so, a shudder passed through his frame.

"I fear this is not his first offence," he murmured, shaking his head sadly. "Young as he is he may possibly be old in crime; but perhaps I do him wrong, yet he was certainly disguised in so cunning and complete a manner that few besides myself would have known him. Certainly his disguise was perhaps the most surprising part of the whole business. Oh! this is all very terrible. I feel wretchedly depressed."

Footsteps were now heard ascending the stairs, and in another moment the servant girl entered the room. She was accompanied by an inspector of the police and a constable.

"Where is the prisoner?" said the inspector.

"He has escaped," answered Gatliffe.

"Escaped!" iterated the inspector. "Surely you have not been foolish enough to let him get away. How did it happen?"

"You shall hear. I had him in this room and kept guard over the entrance. He pleaded for mercy, but I told him I had a duty to perform. All at once, after remaining quiet and submissive for some time, he sprang towards the door. I caught hold of him to arrest his passage; in doing so my foot slipped, and he lost no time in taking advantage of this accident, and succeeded in releasing himself from my grasp. It was all done in less time than it takes me to tell it. He flew downstairs."

"Well, you followed, of course?"

"Yes."

"And could not overtake him?"

"I had very nearly done so, when he rushed into the back parlour, closed the door, and locked it. I ran round the conservatory, searched everywhere I could think of, but was unable to find him. Oh! he has escaped, but it is no fault of mine."

This, as the reader may guess, was not a truthful statement, but it was the only course Gatliffe had left to get himself out of the difficulty.

The inspector looked at the constable—then they both gave a glance at Gatliffe, who, as a natural consequence, felt greatly disconcerted.

BESSIE DREW FORTH FROM THE PAPER A HUNDRED POUND NOTE.

"Well, it is very unfortunate — exceedingly so," observed the inspector. "Should you know the man again?"

"Oh, dear, yes; I've no doubt I should."

"So should I," exclaimed the girl. "I should know him out of a thousand. He had a dark skin, and appeared to be a mulatto."

"Is that so?"

This last query was addressed to Gatliffe.

"Yes, she's quite right—that was what he appeared to be—a half caste, a creole, or mulatto."

"Ah! several burglaries have been committed by a man of that description. I am much mortified at his having made his escape."

"It is indeed very much to be regretted, but it is

no fault of mine. I hope you don't think it is," said Gatliffe.

"I don't say it is any *fault* of yours," returned the inspector, testily. "I only say it's unfortunate, that's all—confoundedly unfortunate, when you've bagged your bird, to let him fly away. I say again, it's unfortunate; but talking wont mend the matter. Let's search the house, Jawkins."

This was addressed to the constable.

"You see this?" remarked Gatliffe, pointing significantly to the bag.

The constable opened it, and drew forth one article after the other in the usual systematic and professional manner invariably adopted by gentlemen of his profession.

"He meant walking away with a tolerably rich booty," observed the inspector. "Ah! he knew his business—not the least doubt of that."

Gatliffe was ready to sink through the floor; he was so abashed and humiliated at the contemptible part he had been playing, which was, to say the truth, altogether foreign to his nature.

After the bag had been emptied of its contents the police-officers proceeded downstairs. They were followed by the young engineer and the servant girl.

The other pile of valuables was discovered on the table in the back parlour. These of course underwent inspection. During the examination of each separate article Gatliffe was perfectly appalled at the magnitude of the projected robbery; but he said nothing, being, in fact, too depressed to venture too many observations.

"Here is where the rascal gained an entrance into the premises," pointing to the folding-doors which led into the conservatory, which gave unmistakeable indications of the marks made by the burglar's instruments.

A rapid and rigid search was now made in the grounds, both in the rear and in the front of the house.

But no burglar was discovered.

The services of Bruno, the faithful dog, were enlisted in this search, which, however, turned out to be fruitless.

The constables returned to the house. They were evidently deeply mortified at the escape of the robber, and could but ill conceal their vexation.

"He's given us the slip," said the inspector. "Got far away by this time, I've no doubt. It's very annoying, but it can't be helped."

"I'm sure I am very sorry to have given you so much unnecessary trouble," murmured Gatliffe. "The more so since I found it impossible to detain him. I wish you had come a little earlier."

"We did not lose a moment after the young woman informed us of the affair. You take my advice," remarked the inspector, addressing himself to Gatliffe, "the next time you collar a 'cracksman,' stick to him. Don't let him slip through your fingers."

"Mr. Gatliffe held him fast enough," said the servant, in a tone of indignation. "He's not the man to give in easily. He had a most desperate struggle with the burglar before I left; and had it not been for him and Bruno the house would have been well-nigh stripped."

The inspector nodded his assent in acquiescence of this last proposition.

"We will take the bag with us," he observed, as he made his way to the drawing-room. "It may afford some clue to the robber."

Upon entering the upstairs room, he discovered on the floor the "jemmy" with which Peace struck the dog. It had fallen out of his hand during his struggle with Gatliffe.

This was also carried away by the police. Upon their return to the station orders were issued to the men on duty to keep on the look-out for the next few days for a man answering to the description of the burglar.

But the bird had flown—he had also changed his plumage—and he was, moreover, too cunning a bird to be seen in the neighbourhood for some time—certainly not till the attempted burglary was a thing of the past.

Gatliffe was in a state of trepidation for some days. The false statement he had made to the police officers caused him the deepest anxiety.

It was altogether so repugnant to his feelings to deviate from the truth that he felt humiliated at having been compelled, by the force of circumstances, to trump up so specious a tale to cover the flight of Peace.

He accused himself of having aided and abetted a burglar in his lawless attempt at robbery.

This was, however, viewing the matter in its worst light. If Gatliffe had erred it was from the best motive; it was to save one whom he had known for many years. He had not the faintest notion, when he connived at his escape, that he was dealing thus mercifully with a callous and hardened criminal.

But Peace, it must be acknowledged, was a remarkable man in many ways, not the least of these being his wondrous power of imposing upon persons with whom he came in contact.

It is at all times difficult to gauge accurately the character of culprits of this class.

In a popular history of British criminals the biographer, introducing a certain infamous rascal, remarks very justly that as a rule the recorders of rogues and vagabonds endow them with qualities they did not possess, and credit them with exploits they never performed.

Hence follows, in the opinion of this judicious commentator, "the difficulty of finding out and appreciating, as they merit, genuine anecdotes of these heroes." Burglars suffer, like bards, from theft of their reputation, and the notorious shoplifter is as liable as the eminent statesman to be saddled with misdeeds he never committed and defrauded of distinction actually earned.

The Newgate chronicle we have quoted tells us in a word how this comes to be.

If any man makes himself distinguished by crime a hundred stories are set in circulation, putting down things to him which he knew nothing about. Peace is no exception to this rule.

A leading London paper reported that he had paid a visit to Chislehurst as a private gentleman, who desired to build a habitation of a similar character—the real object of his visit, however, being to gain a knowledge of its interior for the purpose of carrying out a burglary on a large scale.

There is not a shadow of truth in this report. Peace was never at Chislehurst; neither did he ever contemplate breaking into the place.

It is a long time happily since this sort of scandal engaged the tongues and thoughts of the British public.

The days are gone by for ever when each county in England had its outlaw, whose achievements filled the "lying trump of fame," and agitated society with a pleasing fear unfelt among our modern sensations.

When, however, at rare intervals, some superior villain appears above the lawless crowd, we find the old tendency to make the most or worst of him lingers not dead but sleeping.

Our hero is an instance in point.

We doubt, indeed, if any individual named in the long black bead-roll of the criminal calendar has inspired more invention, or figured in so much fancy, as Charles Peace.

His midnight adventures have not that strong flavour of exciting romance we find in the histories of bygone marauders.

He was practical to austerity, and never made a move that was not calculated and carried out to answer a severe business purpose.

No doubt, as we have before observed, his artfulness, his daring, and other qualities made him a remarkable man.

Unhappily for himself and his endowments, which would have enabled him to win a respectable position in an honest career, appear to have been singularly fitted for the life he chose to follow.

Although he has been charged with many offences he never committed, it may be safely believed that during the thirty years or so he was preying upon the public he has done an enormous amount of mischief.

A poet is said to be one in ten thousand. A man of the special capacity of Peace is far more rare.

He seems like the conquerors, and produces on his fellow-men the same sort of hope that he may be the last of his class.

Probably there is not another man in England who could have run the race of this criminal—by night a thief and a murderer; by day a citizen of credit, who went abroad without fear in the busy haunts of men.

The miserable failure he had made in attempting to rob the house of which Gatliffe was the custodian did not abash him.

He was to be seen in places of public resort at Sheffield on the following day.

Indeed, he mixed more freely with the townspeople than he had done heretofore.

It is our purpose in this work to throw a light on the actions and deeds of its lawless hero; not for the purpose of holding him up as an example, but rather as a warning.

His career furnishes us with a proof that a life of crime is always a life of care.

Disgrace, obloquy, and punishment are the sure attendants on the footsteps of a criminal.

Some few days after his last unsuccessful escapade, Peace was standing outside the principal post-office in Sheffield.

He had been to inquire if there were any letters for him.

He expected to receive one from Bessie Dalton, who, in accordance with his instructions, directed her epistles to the post-office to be kept till called for.

Peace had received several, but for some little time past none had arrived.

He was debating with himself as to the cause, when, much to his surprise, he descried Tom Gatliffe hastening on in the direction of the spot where he was stationed.

It was not possible for him to avoid being recognised, and, to say the truth, he had no desire to do so.

He waited till Gatliffe came up to him.

His countenance denoted that he was a little concerned at the rencontre.

Gatliffe posted some letters, and then turned towards Peace with a look of deep sorrow.

"You remember the promise given to me on that terrible night?" said Gatliffe, in a whisper.

Peace nodded.

"I do," he returned; "shall always bear it in remembrance. Be in no way concerned about me. I've seen my error, and am now a different man."

"I hope and trust you are. Now, Peace," said the young engineer, in a more serious and persuasive tone, "let me conjure you, let me beg of you, never to fall into a similar error. It must have been the arch-fiend who tempted you to commit such a monstrous act."

"Say no more about it. Let it be forgotten. You have been in no way compromised, I hope."

"I must tell you frankly that I found myself in such a terrible scrape, when the police arrived, that I was constrained to do more for you than I have ever done for myself. I had to tell a most deliberate falsehood, but let that pass. You will, I am sure, be mindful of your promise. You are young, possess ability, and may yet win a good position in life. But do not be tempted. If you are in want of money at any time drop me a line, and what I can spare in the way of a loan for a short time you are welcome to. Only do not, I charge you, attempt to rob or plunder. I am sure I wish to be everything that's kind to you; but lately I have heard things which seem to strike me with horror."

"What have you heard?"

"I will not pain you by repeating."

"Oh! don't mind that. The plain truth is at all times the best. What have you heard?"

"Well, then, if you must know, the police informed me that there had been several burglaries committed by a person answering to your description."

"And surely you are not fool enough to believe such a statement. They always say that. They think it so clever. My description, indeed! They wont tell me so."

"I don't mean a description as you now appear, but as you were on that dreadful night."

Peace laughed.

"Ah, I see," he muttered. "Why, I wonder even you knew me, disguised as I was."

"I wonder myself."

"Would they know me now, do you think?"

"Not at all likely, I should say."

"And Aveline Maitland—what of her?" inquired Peace, in an altered tone, for as he inquired a sudden pang seemed to shoot through his frame.

"What of her?" repeated Gatliffe; "why do you inquire?"

"Don't be jealous—she is nothing to me."

"I'm not likely to be jealous."

"You are engaged to her?"

"Yes, I am."

"I thought so. Well, I wish you every happiness—that's all I have to say; but a short time since she drove me to desperation—I did not much care whether I lived or died; now that is past—I'm getting over it."

Gatliffe looked surprised. There was an earnestness in his companion's manner which went far towards giving assurance of the speaker's sincerity."

"You'll not forget all I have said, neither will you forget your promise—and so farewell," said Gatliffe, with a nod, as he took a somewhat abrupt departure.

"Farewell," repeated Peace. "My ways are not your ways," he added, when the engineer was out of earshot."

"Hang it all! what can be the reason of Bessie's silence? Two letters unanswered—something must be up. Has she turned against me?"

This thought seemed to a little depress him; not

that he had any right to expect anything else, seeing that he had neglected her in a most heartless manner. He reflected for some little time, and then said—

"I shall have to go over to Bradford, I expect—that's what I shall have to do. Bessie's a sharp clever girl, and I mustn't lose sight of her. A plague upon that drunken brute, Bristow! Had it not been for him I should not have had occasion to leave Bradford."

His soliloquy was brought to a close by a female addressing him by his Christian name.

It was his mother, who, with all his faults, regarded him with a glance of fond affection.

"Well, Charlie, you rover, now I have found you I don't intend to let you go," said the old lady, playfully. "You must come along with me."

"Where to?"

"Where do you suppose? You must come home. Surely you can spare your poor mother a little of your company?"

"All right, then; homewards we will go," cried Peace, leading the way in the direction of his parent's house.

CHAPTER XIII.
THE DRUNKARD'S HOME—THE ASTOUNDING DISCOVERY.

PEACE's misgivings with regard to Bessie Dalton were not without foundation. To say the truth, she had become duly impressed with the fact that he was intensely selfish.

A number of circumstances conspired to convince her of this, and what liking she had for him at one time was now very considerably diminished.

Bessie was quick-witted, clever in many ways, and was withal kindly disposed. Certainly at this time, at all events, she could not be considered cold or heartless.

But there were other and more cogent reasons for her failing to communicate with Peace. These will be made manifest in the course of this chapter.

Bristow went from bad to worse. His desire for drink became insatiable—indeed, it might with truth be designated a disease. Unhappily for himself and those belonging to him, it appeared to be a disease that was incurable.

For days together this miserably-besotted wretch would be in a state of intoxication.

He had several associates who were nearly as bad as himself. The consequences attendant upon the fatal propensity may easily be guessed. His work was neglected. By degrees his apartments were stripped of everything he could turn into money, and his unhappy wife led a life in comparison to which that of a galley slave was an enviable state of existence.

It is not, it cannot be possible for a writer to depict with anything like adequate force all the misery to be witnessed in the home of a drunkard. Mr. J. B. Gough, the temperance orator, has said that there was no power on earth that tended so much to the degradation and ruin of young men, morally, physically, spiritually, religiously, and he might say financially, as drink. "I have held the hands of dying men in mine," says the orator; "I have laid my hand upon the burning foreheads, and moistened the dry lips of many drunkards, while I have heard such stories as have made my heart ache and my eyes stream with tears. They were wrecks of men of genius—men of education—men of power—men that might have made their mark in the world, going out—oh, so fearfully—into the blackness, and darkness and hopelessness, of the awful future."

The great poetical genius of America—Edgar Allan Poe—gasped out a life the world could ill spare in the agonies of a drunken debauch. Robert Greene, worn out with debauchery and completely shattered with diseases which were a consequence of his ill-guided indulgences, was carried off, it is said, by a surfeit of red herrings. There is no sadder book in literature than his dying homily, "A groat's worth of wit bought with a million of repentance." Poor Lee, the author of the "Rival Queens," died like a dog. He had, it has been said, carousing with a party of friends, none of whom had the grace to see him home.

In the morning he was found dead in the streets, which were covered with snow.

A dray had passed over his body, whether before death or after is not certain.

Hundreds, nay thousands, of other instances could be cited of the fatal effects of intemperance.

But the evil is not confined to a class. It is widespread, and saps and undermines the moral principle of the working classes of this country to an extent which is almost incalculable.

Bristow furnishes us with a sad example of this pernicious and fatal propensity.

He had become an incorrigible and irreclaimable inebriate.

He returned after a debauch of some hours' duration to his miserable lodgings at Bradford.

He had spent what little money he had about him. This it was that caused him to leave the pot-house and bend his steps homewards.

As a rule he seldom came back till past midnight.

His industrious little wife, who worked for the trade, was plying her needle and thread when her husband entered.

"What, John!" she ejaculated, in a tone of surprise; "you're early."

"Am I?" he ejaculated, flinging himself into a chair. "S'pose I am—what of that? I'm not wanted—is that it?"

It was very evident from his tone of voice, as well as his manner, that he was in a quarrelsome mood.

His wife made no reply, but kept on with her work.

"You're a deal too good for me—you are," he muttered. "Pity you threw yourself away upon me."

Still no reply.

"D'yer hear what I am sayin'?" shouted out the ruffian, in a louder tone.

"Of course I do."

"Then why don't you answer?"

"I have answered."

"No, yer haven't, leastways not in a proper manner. D'yer think I'm a stock or a stone? Curse it, you're always at work—always."

"I suppose there's no harm in that."

"I say there is," he returned, with a nod.

He was bent upon fastening a quarrel upon the woman, but did not know very well how to begin.

"I'll put my work on one side, then," said his wife.

"Oh, go on. Don't mind me. I'm nobody. Haven't been anybody for a long time past."

Here he burst out into an idiotic laugh.

Seeing the mood he was in, his wife abstained from making any observation.

This had the effect of aggravating him.

"Has that fellow been here to-day?" he inquired.

"Who do you mean?"

"That mealy-mouthed sneaking chap. You know who I mean well enough."

"No, he has not, or at any rate if he has I have not seen him."

"Ugh! not seen him, indeed. I don't believe it. It's a lie."

"You can say what you like, and believe what you like, for the matter of that."

"Don't you give me any of your cheek, my lady. I aint a going to stand it. Do you hear?"

"Yes."

"Very well, mind what you are about. I'm not a fool. I know all about your little capers. I say he has been here."

"If he has it was without my knowledge."

"Silence. Don't contradict me; I won't stand it!" exclaimed the ruffian, bringing his fist down upon the table with violence. "You're not going to gammon me, mind you that."

He rose to his feet and moved towards the fireplace. After looking on the mantel-piece he went to a chest of drawers which stood at the further end of the room. He opened one drawer after the other, and in one of the small top ones he discovered a paper packet which contained a few shillings in silver.

He drew it forth, and was about to thrust it in his pocket when his wife sprang forward and grasped his hand.

"John—John!" she ejaculated, in a tone of terror; "what would you do? Give it to me."

"I shan't do anything of the sort."

"It is not yours. It is my hard earnings, and it's all I've got to pay the rent. If you meddle with it we shall be turned into the street—you know that as well as I do."

"Let go, I say!" he ejaculated. "I'll soon show you who is master here. Let go, will yer?"

"No I will not. You cannot be so cruel as to rob me of this?"

"Cruel—rob!" he cried, in a fury. "Leave the matter to me. I'll pay the rent when it suits me."

Here he burst out into another mocking laugh.

"John," said his wife, in a beseeching tone, "you are not going to serve me like this. You shall not spend this money in drink, not if I die for it."

"Oh—oh! indeed. You are likely to die, let me tell you that, if you don't mind what you are about."

Mrs. Bristow was in an agony of despair. She knew perfectly well that if she suffered her husband to depart with her little hoard there would not be the most remote chance of her seeing it again.

"There is an old saying, "Tread upon a worm and it will turn," and the unhappy wife was an example of this.

She clung to her husband with a firmness which fairly astonished him.

"You shall not take away the money, John. I tell you you shall not have it. Give it me back at once."

"Get out; don't talk to me, woman!" exclaimed Bristow. "Leave go, or it will be worse for you."

"I will not leave go; I will call for assistance."

He endeavoured to shake her off, but she was wound up to a pitch of desperation, and would not part with him.

He dragged her across the room, and strove to reach the door.

Seeing his intent, she put out all her strength to detain him.

"Let go, I say!" he shouted out, in a stentorian voice.

Once more he strove to shake her off.

Not succeeding in this, he struck her in the face, and tore her garments from her back.

He struck her several blows after this, and finally succeeded in flinging her from him.

Then with the howl of a wild beast he rushed towards the door: in doing so the side of his body came in contact with a small dressing-table, upon which was a looking-glass.

The table was upset, one of its legs was broken, and the plate of the glass was shivered into fragments.

Then Bristow rushed out of the house.

His wife sat on the side of the bed, sobbing convulsively.

Thus ended a scene—the accumulated horrors of which we have purposely avoided giving in all their full detail.

Bruised and bleeding from the effects of the blows inflicted by her husband, the wretched woman cried as if her heart was about to break.

Very soon after Bristow's departure Bessie Dalton, upon her return from the factory, let herself in with the latch-key. As she entered the passage she heard sobs and sighs proceeding from the back parlour.

She was at no loss to divine that something was amiss.

Opening the door of the room she was appalled at beholding Mrs. Bristow seated on the side of the bed in a terrible plight. The clothes were torn off her back, so that the upper portion of her person was nearly in a state of nudity.

Her lip was swollen, her nose was bleeding, and one eye was in an incipient state of blackness.

To add to the horrors of the scene the furniture was upset, and the miserable apartment gave unmistakable evidence of the violent scene which had just taken place.

"For mercy's sake do tell me what's the matter?" exclaimed Bessie Dalton.

"Oh, don't ask me—don't speak to me!" answered the wretched wife. "I wish I was dead—I wish I had never seen that inhuman wretch."

"It is as I guessed. Then Bristow has been here. It is he who has done all this. But do bear up, dear—bear up," said Bessie, going at once for a bason of water, with which she washed the bruised and bleeding face of her companion.

"Ugh, the drunken, good-for-nothing beast," she ejaculated; "and has it come to this?"

"It has. I only wish he had killed me outright—then there would have been an end to my misery. As it is there does not appear to be any end to it."

"But you must leave him. It would be worse than madness to remain longer with such a ruffian. How did it occur?"

"He came back, much to my surprise, much earlier than usual. He had been drinking heavily, that I saw at a glance, and did all he could to aggravate me; but I was determined not to lose my temper if I could help it. He then got up and searched about the room and opened all the drawers, in one of which he found the silver I had put by to pay Parker two weeks' rent. He threatened to turn us into the street unless we paid."

"And what then?"

"He snatched hold of the paper which contained the money, and was about to thrust it in his pocket, and because I tried to get it from him he became furious. He has beaten me most unmercifully, as you see."

"If you live any longer with this infamous man you will have yourself only to blame. Go away this very night. Do not remain another hour under the same roof with such a diabolical wretch."

"Where can I go?"

"Anywhere. Do you suppose that I would remain if I was in your position? Ah, dear, you are too meek and mild. He should have me to deal with."

"You could do nothing with him. Nobody could. He's past cure, Bessie. At one time I had some hopes of reclaiming him—now I have none."

"He'll never be any better," said Bessie Dalton. "That I have seen and known for a long time past. He's a lost man."

"Ah," ejaculated Mrs. Bristow; "it was an ill-fated day when I first set eyes upon him. I was warned and cautioned by those who knew him better than I did; but like a fool I was heedless of their warning. I've paid the penalty of my obstinacy. Many a time I have prayed to be released from this odious thraldom, while at other times I have contemplated flight. Now I am resolved. I will no longer live with him, not under any circumstances."

"Well spoken. I am glad to hear these words fall from your lips, dear," said Bessie, putting her arms round the neck of her companion and kissing her fondly. "Your words give me hope and comfort. Do not change your determination. Go this very night. Go at once."

"But look at me. See how I am disfigured! What will people think of me?"

"Let them think what they like. Tell the truth; you've nothing to be ashamed of."

"I hope not."

"I am sure not. If you remain here you will be murdered. Of that I am as well assured as that he will never reform. I say one day or another you will be murdered. Ah! no, dearest. You must not change your mind upon this. Come, dry your eyes. There, that's better. You are beginning to look a little more like yourself. Oh! how I should like to have the wretch flogged! I haven't patience with the monster."

"What have I done that I should be punished thus?" murmured Mrs. Bristow.

"You've been too easy with him."

"Ah, Bessie! don't say that. It's all very well for a woman to talk about controlling a drunken man. It is quite impossible. Do what you will, treat him with harshness or kindness, the end is the same. But too well I know that."

"Well, I'll not vex you by offering any further observations upon that subject. Doubtless you know best. One thing, however, you can do."

"What is that?"

"Why, leave him. Take a situation, far away from this town. I would rather beg my bread in the public streets than subject myself to the brutality of such a ruffian."

"You are quite right, Bessie. Such a course is the more bearable one of the two."

"Suppose he should come back, how then?" said Bessie, in a tone of alarm.

"Ah, he will not come back till he's spent the whole, or the greater portion, of the money. There's no fear of that."

"To say the truth, I don't think there is. But how he's knocked about the things," said Bessie, glancing at the overturned table and the broken glass.

"He upset them as he went out. The looking-glass is broken. That is a fatal sign. No luck in this house after that."

"Don't be superstitious," cried the girl, lifting up the table, and endeavouring to replace it in its position.

"It won't stand, dear. One of the legs is broken," said Mrs. Bristow.

"Never mind."

Her companion propped it up as best she could.

Then she stooped down and began to pick up the pieces of the glass which had fallen from the frame.

These she placed on the table.

She then lifted up the glass. As she did so, something met her eye. It appeared to be a thin piece of paper, which had been concealed between the plate of the glass and the wooden back.

"Mercy on us! what is this?" exclaimed Bessie.

She drew out the paper, and held it forth. Then, with a sudden scream, exclaimed, in a hissing whisper—

"A HUNDRED POUND NOTE!"

"Heavens above! what do you mean?" cried the miserable wife.

"Well, seeing's believing," answered her companion. "I'm not much of a judge of these matters; but if I am not mistaken, this is a genuine Bank of England note for one hundred pounds."

"How came it there? This looks like sorcery. Ah, Bessie, dear, you are playing me some trick. It cannot be."

"But, my dear, it is. Look here." She drew towards the side of the bed, and placed the note in the hands of Mrs. Bristow.

"Well, this is most wonderful—most incomprehensible. Can you account for it?" said the latter.

"Indeed, I cannot. Where did you get this glass from?"

"Bought it at a broker's shop in the town."

"Give the note to me, I'll take charge of it," cried Bessie, clapping her hands.

"Yes, you had better do so; but I say, dear, suppose it should be a forged one?"

"Oh, lor! I never thought of that; but I've no doubt we shall find it all right enough."

"Let us hope so."

"You have given me your word that you will leave this very night," said the girl. "You are not going to break it?"

"No! Oh dear no."

"You are sure of that?"

"Certainly. What makes you think otherwise?

"Never mind my thoughts. Swear that you will leave this place. If you refuse ——"

"Well, what if I refuse?"

"I will burn this note before your very eyes," exclaimed Bessie Dalton, holding it over the fire.

"What would you do? Are you mad, Bessie?"

"Swear!" ejaculated the girl.

"If it's any satisfaction, I do swear. In the name of the most High and Mighty I pledge myself to leave this house to-night."

"And never to return to it from your own free will."

"And never to return to it from my own free will."

"That is enough. Now I feel assured that you are in earnest. So am I; for I tell you plainly that I shall not rest till I see you out of the house."

"Upon my word you appear in a monstrous hurry to get rid of me."

"No matter about that. You'll have to go, and it's no use making long faces about it. Come, dear, put your things together, and we'll away at once."

"We! are you going, then, as well?"

"I purpose bearing you company for to-night, at all events."

"And whither are we to go?"

"Leave that to me. I have an old friend who lives but a few miles hence. We can stop with her for to-night, and in the morning we shall have a little leisure to arrange our plans for the future."

"You're a brave girl, Bessie; I wish I had your

nerve," said Mrs. Bristow, who proceeded at once to look up several garments which were necessary for her immediate use.

Bessie Dalton went upstairs to her own apartment, and brought therefrom a capacious carpet bag, which she haded to her companion.

Poor Mrs. Bristow was suffering terribly from the blows inflicted upon her by her brutal husband. She was sadly bruised and disfigured, but bore up as best she could.

She had one sincere friend in the hour of her affliction, this being Bessie Dalton.

"Put all you want in the bag," said the latter, "and bid adieu for ever to this miserable place, in which you have suffered so much."

"I intend to do so—rest assured of that."

While the unhappy wife was thus engaged her companion once more proceeded to examine the shattered looking glass.

As yet she had but taken a curious glance at the article in question. Now she made a more searching and minute inspection of it.

She removed the remains of the plate from its front and then uttered an expression of surprise and wonder. The back was literally lined with Bank of England notes.

Bessie's head seemed to swim as she made this unlooked-for discovery.

"Heaven be merciful to us!" she exclaimed. "See here, there are more of them—a whole heap."

"What!" ejaculated Mrs. Bristow, whose heart was by this time beating audibly. "I feel as if about to swoon."

"Bear up, dear," said her friend. "You have nothing to fear, but everything to hope. Here are several notes for a thousand pounds. You are an independent woman, and the possessor of fabulous wealth. Be of good cheer. A bright future is before you. Now we know what to do."

"I feel quite overcome — completely prostrated. Can it be? Is it possible? Or is it all deception?"

"Never you mind, we shall soon be able to ascertain all about this wondrous gift presented to us—or rather to you—by Dame Fortune. I tell you there are notes for thousands, and you are rich—immensely rich."

"I find it hard to believe."

"No matter, you will soon believe it."

"But where, in the name of all that's wonderful, can all these riches have come from?" said Mrs. Bristow, passing her hand across her aching forehead.

"Will you leave the matter in my hands?"

"Of course I will."

"Very well then, so be it. There is a mystery about this affair which neither of us for the present can fathom—that we may take for granted; but the property belongs to you, and for the present I will take charge of it."

"Ah! do so. You are much more quick-witted and clever than I am, and I need hardly say I would trust you with my life."

Bessie Dalton folded up the notes, flew upstairs again to her own room, and returned with a pocket-book.

In this she carefully placed the notes, and then thrust the pocket-book in her bosom.

"So," she ejaculated, "they are safe for the present —safe until we can learn something more about them and their real value. Now, are you ready to leave?"

"Yes; but—ahem—I—"

"Well, what?"

"Hadn't I better write a letter to John, bidding him farewell for ever?"

Bessie shrugged her shoulders and smiled.

"It's more than he deserves," she said, "but as you wish it, do so."

CHAPTER XIV.
THE FLIGHT—A CONFIDENTIAL FRIEND—THE ROLL OF NOTES.

MRS. BRISTOW had screwed her courage up as best she could, but now that the time had arrived for her to leave her home she felt a pang shoot through her heart.

She pictured to herself her husband's return home after his debauch, his awakening in the morning, and his bitter remorse. Dissolute, debased, and worthless fellow as he was, his ill-used and miserable wife had some compassion left for him, some latent love of which she found it difficult to dispossess herself.

This is almost invariably the case with ruffians of this class. We are furnished with numberless instances of this in the reports of assaults upon women heard in our public police-courts.

The injured woman almost always finds some excuse for her brutal husband, and it is likely enough that Mrs. Bristow would never have left her home, however badly she had been treated, had it not been through the instigation and by the advice of her friend Bessie Dalton.

Mrs. Bristow had seated herself in front of a little table—pens, ink and paper were before her, the last-named being already blotted by her tears.

"What shall I say to him, Bessie?" enquired the wife of her friend.

"How should I know? If it were my case I would not trouble myself to write. Wish him good-bye and say you are going abroad, that's the best thing to do."

"Abroad?"

"Certainly. Don't let him imagine you are going to remain in this country; say you are going abroad to seek your fortune in a strange land, that's the way to put it."

"He wont believe it."

"It doesn't matter what he believes—only don't give him an idea that it is any use his endeavouring to find you out."

"I wish you would dictate the letter."

"Very well. Are you ready?"

"Yes."

"Then go on."

"DEAR JOHN,—I write these few lines to tell you that I find it impossible to remain under the same roof with one who has treated me with such unkindness and cruelty. My cup of sorrow is full to the brim. If I remain here I feel convinced that I shall meet with my death at your hands. For both our sakes it is therefore better that we should part. Never expect to see me again in this world. I leave England to-morrow; you will do much better without me. I do hope and trust that you will see the error of your ways and lead a better life.—Your miserable wife,
                                    "MARIA BRISTOW."

"That will do; won't it?" said the girl.

"Oh, dear, yes. My head is in such a whirl that I find it impossible to collect my thoughts. That will do very well, I think," returned Mrs. Bristow.

She folded up the letter, put it in an envelope, addressed it, and placed it on the shelf where her husband could not fail to see it.

This done she felt greatly relieved.

"Now let us away at once," cried the girl. "Give me the bag."

"But where are we going to?"

"To Stanningley. An aunt of mine lives there, a

dear old soul. We can remain with her as long as we like, but there's no occasion for us to stop unless we choose."

"How far is it?"

"Oh, it must be over five miles, but we must have a fly."

"And the money?"

"I've got enough for our immediate wants."

The girl had not spent the last sum. Peace had sent her, in addition to which she had some of her own little savings.

A fly was procured. As they were about to step into this, the gentleman they had met at the concert, at which Charles Peace appeared, now accosted them.

"Well, ladies, whither away in this hurry?" said he, in a tone of surprise.

Bessie put her companion into the fly, then she hurried towards her male friend.

"Ah! Mr. Chipp," she ejaculated, "how glad I am we have met with you! Something has occurred— something terrible," as she nodded towards the passenger in the vehicle.

She proceeded to give a rapid account of the assault upon Mrs. Bristow, and wound up by informing her friend that his wife had left him for good and for all.

"It's not to be wondered at," said Mr. Chipp. "The only surprise to me is, and has always been, that she consented to live with the brute for so long a time."

"I want to see you, sir, about a little matter of business. Want your advice, but have not time to explain matters now."

"Very well, I shall be much pleased to see you to-morrow, if that will suit you; if not, on the following day. You know the hotel I'm stopping at?"

"Yes. If I can manage to see you to-morrow, I will most certainly do so, or the day after."

"Very good—I am at your service."

He now drew close to the vehicle, and shook its inmate warmly by the hand.

Mrs. Bristow had taken the precaution to wear a thick veil, which she wore down, so that the injuries done to her face were not discernible.

"I am pleased to have met you," observed Mr. Chipp; "and, believe me, I hope and trust a more happy future is in store for you."

He raised his hat to both females, and went on his course.

Bessie Dalton jumped into the fly, and the driver pushed forward in the direction of Stanningley.

Bessie chatted merrily during the greater part of the journey, but her companion remained sad and thoughtful.

Upon the travellers arriving at their destination, Bessie conducted her companion to a small, mean looking cottage, in the rear of which was a large and well-cultivated garden.

The place was primitive enough in appearance,

Bessie Dalton unfastened the front door, which was opened with a small latch, and entered the parlour.

An exclamation of surprise, which was not unmixed with pleasure, proceeded from its solitary occupant.

"Why, Bessie, lass, who ever thought of seeing you?" cried a well-known voice.

"My dear aunt," said Bessie in reply. "I have brought with me a very near and dear friend of mine, Mrs. Bristow, of whom you have often heard me speak."

"You are welcome," observed the old lady, addressing herself to her visitor. "I am much pleased to make your acquaintance. My niece has made me

familiar with your name. Sit down." The speaker handed a chair as she made this last observation.

The three women were very soon on the best of terms, and an animated conversation was kept up for the best part of the evening. A frugal supper was served by the hostess, and Bessie Dalton and Mrs. Bristow shared the only spare bed in the establishment.

They had, however, but a short period of rest that night, both being in too great a state of excitement to make sure of unbroken slumber.

They rose early, and having dressed, bethought them of what to do.

"I've thought over and over again the best course for you to adopt," said Bessie, who had already been tacitly acknowledged to be commander-in-chief; "and the more I consider, the more I feel convinced that my first idea is the best."

"And what might that be?" inquired her companion.

"You will become a fine lady—that's what you are destined to be."

Mrs. Bristow laughed at the naive manner of the speaker.

"Ah, you may laugh; but I tell you that's what will happen. I've laid it all down as nicely as possible. Listen. There is no place in England, so I've been told, equal to London for concealment. You must take up your abode there, change your name, and no one will suspect that you are the wife of a poor mechanic."

"Change my name!"

"Most certainly you must do that. Pass yourself off as a widow."

"I should never have the courage to do that."

"You must; don't tell me you haven't courage. What matters—who's to know? You have money, and to the possessor of money everybody pays homage. We all know that."

"You certainly are a most extraordinary girl," observed Mrs. Bristow, in a reflective manner. "What in the name of goodness could have put such thoughts into your head?"

"Common sense; that's all, my dear. I am only using common sense in a matter which, to say the truth, requires a considerable amount of that useful commodity. To remain here, or anywhere else in this county, would be the worst of folly. Change your name, take quiet, respectable apartments at the west end of London, and make your life as happy as possible. You have suffered enough, and deserve to taste a little of the sweets of life. Do you see that?"

"Ah, I acknowledge the truth of your observations."

"Very good. And now, first of all, let us make an examination of the little store. Lock the door, dear. We don't want anybody prying into our secret—not even my aunt. In a case like this, it's best to keep one's own counsel."

Mrs. Bristow rose suddenly from her seat, and crept softly towards the door, which she locked.

"Now for it," said Bessie. "Now for the notes."

She drew them forth, and placed them on the dressing-table.

The first upon which her eye lighted was a note for the sum of one thousand pounds. This was followed by many more for a like sum. In addition to these there were many for one hundred, two hundred, as also others for smaller and larger sums

Reckoning the whole of them up they represented an amount exceeding fourteen thousand pounds.

THE YOUNGER SERVANT STRUCK PEACE WITH THE MOP, AND LAID HIM SENSELESS.

The two women were astounded at the prodigious sum.

"What say you to that?" inquired Bessie.

"I feel like one who is walking on a precipice, and expects every minute to topple over. That's how I feel."

"You'll get used to it in time. Oh, you'll get used to it, believe me."

"But are the notes genuine?"

"I do not doubt it for a moment. You had now better take charge of your own property; sew them up in your stays. That will be the best plan till we see what can be done with them."

"But where can we get notes for so large an amount changed without exciting suspicion?"

"That will require a little thought. It won't do to be

too hasty in a matter of this sort. If one note is good they are all right, depend upon that. I have an idea."

" What is it ?"

" You've got one for fifty pounds ?"

" Yes."

" I will ask Mr. Chipps to change it. " He'll have no objection to oblige either of us."

" But he'll want to know where we got it from."

" I will tell him, my dear—a legacy, a legacy. Don't you see it was bequeathed to you by a relative? I have promised to see him either to-day or to-morrow. I will take this note with me."

" As you please. I leave it to you. Indeed, without you I know not how I should get on at all."

Having agreed upon this course of action Bessie Dalton in the earlier portion of the day started off for the town of Bradford, leaving her friend in charge of her aunt.

The looking-glass in which the notes were found was originally in the possession of an old miser, named Nathan Schreiber.

He was a refiner, and dealt in metals of every description. In addition to this he was a usurer.

Living in an old dilapidated house in one of the back streets of his native town he contrived to drive a prosperous trade; but throughout his whole life declared he was miserably poor.

He was plagued by a number of poor relations, some of whom, it is believed, robbed him.

Anyway, in the last closing years of his life, he was under the impression that his rapacious relatives would send him out of the world before his time.

This thought haunted him by day and by night.

He was eccentric to the last degree. He grew old and feeble, and prior to his last illness he unfastened the back of his looking-glass and laid the notes carefully on the silvering at the back of the plate.

This done, he replaced the backboard in its original position, and felt a grim satisfaction at glancing at the glass on the table by the side of his bed, upon which he shortly breathed his last.

As a matter of course after his decease the house was pretty well filled with his relatives.

A search was made for a will; none could be found. The effects he left behind, however, realised a considerable sum.

The distribution of this was the occasion of a wrangle, and the acrimonious feeling evinced by some of his heirs was in no way creditable to them. The property left by old Schreiber was sold by public auction.

A tradesman in the town bought several articles of household furniture. Among them was the looking-glass containing the notes. The tradesman afterwards became bankrupt, his furniture was sold off, and a broker bought two lots, in one of which the glass was included.

Mrs. Bristow afterwards purchased it of the broker for the sum of fifteen shillings. The end of this we have already seen.*

---

* The concealment of notes to a large amount between the plate and back-board of a looking-glass is true in substance and in fact. A case similar to the one described came under the writer's own knowledge. Many years ago, in Cheshire, a woman in a humble position of life accidentally broke a looking-glass which she had had in her possession for very many years. To her infinite surprise she discovered a number of bank-notes, concealed at its back. The case attracted considerable attention at the time, and she handed the property so found over to the stipendiary magistrates, who ultimately decided that the property so found was hers, and the notes were consequently returned to her. There are many persons now living who can attest to the truth of this statement, which proves the oft-repeated adage that "truth is strange—stranger than fiction."

When Bessie Dalton reached the hotel at Bradford she inquired for Mr. Chipp, and was at once shown into a room where she found her friend seated.

She entered into a full description of the assault on Mrs. Bristow, and wound up by informing him that the latter had left him for good, but did not as yet know where she was to take up her quarters.

It would appear that Mr. Chipp had, for some reason which was best known to himself, been desirous of continuing the acquaintance of the two females he had met for the first time at the concert given for the benefit of the weaver's widow and children.

He had paid frequent visits to the house in which Bessie and her friend resided, and had at all times taken great interest in them; and therefore, Bessie, who was the most self-possessed of the two, had no compunction in seeking his advice on the present occasion.

"She's had a legacy—a little money left her," said Bessie, "and my advice is that she sees no more of that wretch of a husband of hers, but go up to London at once, and see if she can get something to do."

"The best advice you can give her."

"And I've brought with me a fifty pound note, which we don't know where to get changed. Perhaps you can oblige us ?"

She handed him the note—not, however, without some misgivings.

He looked carefully at it, and appeared perfectly satisfied.

"I have not so much money about me, but I can give you a cheque if that will do. You can get it changed before you return."

"Oh, thank you, Sir! That would be indeed a favour."

"Not at all," said her companion, carelessly. "Happy to have it in my power to oblige you."

He drew the cheque for the required sum, and handed it to the girl.

Then, with a smile, he said—

"Then, I suppose I am going to lose sight of you ladies."

"Oh dear, I hope not, Sir !"

"Umph ! Do you go with your friend ?"

"I have not decided as yet. Poor thing ! She is sadly borne down just now, and needs some one to be with her. I suppose I had better see her on her journey."

Mr. Chipp nodded assent to this proposition, and murmured—

"Yes, it would be better for you to do so."

"You see, we are not at all busy at the factory," said Bessie; "and I can be well spared, for a short time at all events."

"It does not appear to me that they are busy anywhere," observed her companion. "I shall not remain much longer in this town, but return to London before next week is over. Have you heard or seen anything of the fiddler ?"

He alluded to Peace, whom he had, since the night of the concert, invariably designated as the fiddler.

"I have not heard from him lately," answered Bessie, carelessly.

The gentleman smiled, but made no further inquiries.

Bessie now took her departure, and bent her steps in the direction of the bank. Upon presenting the cheque, she elected to take the amount in gold.

She then returned to her aunt's residence, and made Mrs. Bristow acquainted with the successful nature of her expedition.

In a few days after this the two women started off for the metropolis.

CHAPTER XV.
PEACE MEETS WITH A TARTAR—THE CAPTURE, AND ITS RESULT.

PEACE paid frequent visits to the post-office to inquire for letters; none, however, arrived. He could not in any way account for Bessie Dalton's silence.

Had she turned against him?

Or had her picked-up friend persuaded her to leave Bradford?

These were questions he was unable to answer.

Something had occurred—of that he felt certain.

Perhaps Bristow had set the girl against him.

"But no," he ejaculated. "She's not such a fool as to listen to the counsels of that drunken brute."

He dispatched another epistle to her lodgings at Bradford.

In a day or two after this it was returned to the post-office at Sheffield.

On the envelope was marked, "Gone away. Not known where."

His worst fears were confirmed. He uttered anathemas loud and deep not only against Bessie Dalton, but the whole sex generally. He was wild with fury, and, like M. Mallet, tore up the letter in a thousand pieces.

"The perfidious, worthless, little hussy," he ejaculated. "The ungrateful, deceitful minx to serve me like this. Gone away, and not known where. Oh, she's made a bolt of it, that's quite certain. There's no dependence to be placed on women—they are all alike. Once out of your sight you stand but a poor chance. Still, hang it all, I never expected she would have served me like this."

He had a burning desire to know the reason for her leaving Bradford, and as the days passed over this feeling became intensified.

He could not rest without making an effort to clear up the "mystery," as he termed it.

He took the train to Bradford, and hastened at once to his old quarters in that town.

Bristow was not at home. This he was glad of. He inquired for the landlord, who at once made his appearance.

"So Bessie Dalton's left, I hear?" said Peace, after the usual civilities had been exchanged.

"Yes, Mr. Peace, she's gone. So also has Mrs. Bristow, and I don't expect her husband will remain long. He'll have to 'bunk' if he goes on as he has been of late."

"Mrs. Bristow left!" ejaculated our hero. "Did she go with Bessie, then?"

"Yes, they were sworn friends, you know, and when one left, why I suppose the other did not care to be left behind."

"And pray can you tell me the reason of their leaving?"

The landlord entered into the particulars of the quarrel between husband and wife and the desperate assault made on the latter, and wound up by saying, "Everybody saw how it would end. She couldn't stand his cruelty any longer, and, therefore, left him. It's the wisest thing she ever did."

"And Bessie?"

"Oh! she went with her."

"Do you know where they've gone to?"

The man shook his head.

"Not I," said he. "It is not likely they would let anybody know that; but I've been told——"

"What?"

"That they are both gone abroad—to America or Australia—so I've been given to understand."

Peace was perfectly astounded.

"Gone abroad?" he iterated.

"Well—yes; and the best thing they could do. They are both young and good-looking, and will do a great deal better in either of those places than they did in this over-taxed country. Working people have not much of a chance here."

The speaker was a Radical of the most pronounced type, and attributed the greater part of the ills which afflict the working class to over-taxation and an oppressive aristocracy.

Peace was in no mood to discuss the question—he was too much overwhelmed by the account given by the landlord of the women's sudden flight.

"I shouldn't bother myself much about them, if I were you, Peace," said the landlord. "It's all for the best, depend upon that. They behaved fair and square to me, and I wish them both well."

"Yes—right you are—I won't bother myself. They are gone, and joy go with them. Thank you for the information."

And wishing the man a hearty farewell, he took his departure.

He visited some of his old haunts in the town, and lodged for the night at a coffee-house.

In the morning he returned to Sheffield.

He was ill at ease—restless and fidgetty—everything appeared to be going wrong with him.

Though apparently pursuing at this time the vocation of a picture-frame maker and picture-dealer, he had, as we have already seen, made "overtime" at intervals with varying success. The illustrations which have been given of his career have in many instances shown that he obtained most valuable booty. But the number of occasions on which he failed in his depredations are not so well known; the reader, however, may rest assured that it was not all smooth sailing with him. He had, as it will be our purpose to show, a number of reverses and many narrow escapes.

The course which he generally pursued was to "prospect a district well" and make himself thoroughly acquainted with the general movements of the police in it.

Next to pick out the places which offered at once the chance of a good haul, with the least possible risk, and having done this, gather in the harvest with as little delay as possible and then disappear from the district.

No wonder the police were baffled.

On the night prior to his leaving Sheffield, Peace had an adventure, which at the time taxed his inventive genius.

He had obtained an entrance to the back premises of a fish shop which was situated at the back of the Cemetery-road. This would be between eleven and twelve o'clock at night.

He was "operating" upon the back window of the place, intending as usual to "borrow" something, when very unexpectedly the proprietor of the establishment returned from the theatre in a cab.

Peace heard the vehicle stop and before he had time to get out of the yard the proprietor came into it.

Seeing Peace, he said—

"What do you want here?"

The visitor, after the manner of many other people, said "oh nothing!"

The fishmonger was far from satisfied, and made a demonstration as though he was about to seize the little fellow.

But Peace had used every bit of the time available

during the brief conversation, for the consideration of the best means of escape, and he had formed a loop-hole.

Jumping upon the boundary wall he dropped over, and fell a considerable depth into the river Porter, which flows past there, but is shallow at that point. In point of fact it is like a large weir. He did not move in the darkness, but kept close to the wall, so that the astonished fishmonger should not know whether he had gone down the stream or up it.

Afterwards he quickly walked up it, past the back of Napier-street, and came out above Andrew-lane, but not without a good soaking.

Had he succeeded in his attempt to break into the shop he would not have got much, as the proprietor had placed his cash in a place of safety.

This is one of the many faithful accounts of his various escapades; but the reader must be apprised that it occurred subsequently to the events we are now chronicling in this and the preceding chapters. It is cited as an instance of one of his many failures. We have, however, to record one which was more igno-minious and disastrous.

Peace remained in Sheffield for some little time after his return from Bradford. He paid several visits to localities which lay at more or less distances from that town, and succeeded in possessing himself of a number of valuables, but he felt unhinged and grew tired of his native town.

Once more he paid a visit to Hull. The Oakfield House burglary, described in the opening chapters of our work was no longer fresh in the recollection of the inhabitants of that town, and Peace felt quite sure that he would not be recognised by any of the constabulary.

The love of change and adventure had most likely prompted him to shift his quarters for awhile, and transfer the scene of his operations to another locality.

Soon after his arrival in Hull he began to look out for the places most available for his purpose, and con-trived to commit some daring robberies without detec-tion.

He had noticed a small villa which stood on the out-skirts of a village, a few miles from Hull. The house was far removed from other habitations.

It was very tempting, not to say inviting, to the burglar.

Peace had played his violin at a beer-shop in the neighbourhood—that is how he came to notice the Gothic cottage, as it was termed.

To obtain an entrance would be matter of no great difficulty. Most of the inhabitants in the neighbour-hood went to bed early, and rose with the lark.

It was between ten and eleven o'clock at night when Peace arrived at the villa in question.

A flight of steps led up to the front door. A bay window, with stone balustrading in front and a por-tico above, jutted out from the first storey of the habi-tation.

When Peace had reached the lawn in front of the house, he hesitated for a short time, before he made up his mind as to which was the easiest mode of access.

He came to the conclusion that it would be best to perform on the door. He had but little difficulty in picking the lock of this. The door yielded to his pres-sure, but he found that it was fastened by an inner chain, the end of which ran into a hollow tube.

It was impossible to effect an entrance without releasing the chain.

Peace drew from his pocket two pieces of wire, both of which were bent at the ends.

With these he believed he could push back the chain, release it, and enter.

While occupied with one arm through the aperture disclosed by the partially open door, the two French windows above were thrown open, and a woman's head and shoulders were visible.

Peace, whose back was towards the window, was quite unaware of the fact that his movements were watched.

Indeed, so intent was he on his work that he did not hear the noise occasioned by the opening of the window.

He was not so successful as he had anticipated in pushing back the chain; and while manipulating with his accustomed skill and perseverance he was suddenly awakened to the position of affairs by receiving a terrible blow between the shoulders, which seemed to take his breath away.

He faced round suddenly, when much to his discom-forture he received another blow on the side of the head, which caused a thousand lights to flash before his eyes.

"Oh, you nasty burglarious wretch," exclaimed the old woman above, who was his assailant. "You murderous villain!"

The speaker was flourishing a long house broom, with the thick end of which she delivered another blow on the burglar's head.

Peace was quite unprepared for this unlooked-for assault; he caught hold of the broom and swore a terrible oath.

A struggle now ensued between the two, Peace held firmly on the end of the broom, and the old woman above clung tenaciously to the handle.

"Murder! thieves! police! help!" screamed the woman, in a shrill penetrating voice, which rang like a clarion note in the night air.

"You nasty, ugly, good-for-nothing, thieving scamp!" she continued. "You hideous, murderous wretch!"

Peace was terribly bruised; a noise as of rushing waters was in his ears, and his temples throbbed and ached most terribly.

By a violent effort he wrested the broom from the hands of his assailant.

He was wound up to a state of fury, and lost his usual prudence.

To be so unmercifully beaten by a woman was positively intolerable.

In all his adventures he had never been so cruelly used.

But he would not be baffled—he would have reprisals.

He jumped on to the top of the stone facing of the balustrade which ran in front of the house, and, broom in hand, struck a defiant attitude.

"Don't you think to master me, you vile, dirty slut," he ejaculated; and, with these words, he aimed a blow at his enemy, who very prudently retired into the interior of the room.

The only effect the blow had was to smash one of the front windows.

"If I can only get in," muttered Peace, "I shall be all right. I'll soon silence that old Jezebel. Without doubt she has been left in charge of the house. I'll give it her, worth her money, when I do get in. Curse it, how my head aches!"

He balanced himself on the top of the stonework, as deftly as an acrobat; then he caught the edge of the balcony with the big end of his broom, and was pre-paring himself for a final spring when another actor came upon the scene.

A buxom servant girl appeared at the open window. She was armed with a mop.

Seeing that Peace was about to scale the balcony, she threw out the mop much the same as a Zulu does his spear, and delivered such a terrific blow on Peace's face that he was hurled back, and fell upon the gravel path in front in a state of insensibility.

The old woman and her maid were masters of the field. Their foe remained prostrate and helpless in front of the citadel.

Again the cries " Help! Police!" rose in the air. They resounded far and near.

The servant girl now brought to the window a pail of dirty water, which she threw over the vanquished burglar.

This had the effect of restoring him to consciousness. He made an effort to rise, but he was so dizzy, so utterly prostrated, that he was almost helpless for a time.

The mistress and her maid had the prudence not to sally forth till assistance had arrived, for they were by no means certain as to the real state of the enemy. He might, after all, only be shamming, and it would not be advisable to risk an engagement in the open field.

They had recourse, therefore, to "sound the alarm," by repeated screams and cries for assistance.

Much to their delight, a constable opened the garden gate, and flashed his bull's-eye in all directions.

By the light of his lantern he discovered Peace stretched on the garden walk.

"Now, then, get up, man," said the constable to Peace.

"I can't," exclaimed the burglar. "I'm all but killed by those she dragons."

"You can't lie here all night. Get up, I say. What have you been doing?"

"Oh, don't ask me," said Peace, in a whining hypocritical voice. "Those infamous women!"

"Don't listen to what he says, policeman," interrupted the old lady. "He was breaking into the house, but we caught him just in time—only just in time."

"Do you charge him?"

"Certainly. Take him in custody. Of course I charge him—the dirty blackguard!"

Another constable now presented himself, and the two carried Peace into the back parlour of the little cottage.

He presented a most pitiable appearance. Two great bumps as big as an egg were visible on his head; in addition to this his nose was bleeding, and a scar was observable on his face; this last being from the effects of the mop which had been handled so dexterously by the servant girl.

He was, moreover, wet to the skin, from the contents of the pail.

He had never been so cruelly dealt with before.

With his head between his hands, he groaned and moaned in a most piteous and abject manner.

"You've got the worst of it this time, old man," said one of the policemen. "Are you sufficiently strong to walk to the station?"

"Me strong! I feel as if about to breathe my last," cried Peace.

The two constables conversed apart for a little time —then one left the house. He returned with a ponycart.

"Now, then," said the other, addressing himself to Peace, "as you are not able to walk, my man, we've got a conveyance for you."

"I'm very bad," said our hero, with a groan.

"Can't help that. Get up, man."

The two policemen, without more ado, lifted up the wounded burglar, and bore him *nolens volens* towards the cart, which stood just outside the garden gate.

Peace was lifted into this by his captors, and the vehicle was driven towards the station. During the journey Peace whined and moaned in a most piteous manner, declaring all the way that he was an ill-used man.

After being examined and attended to by the divisional surgeon, he was locked up for the remainder of the night.

CHAPTER XVI.
THE EXAMINATION AT THE POLICE COURT.

PEACE had been placed in a tolerably comfortable bed; his clothes were dried and brought into his room by early dawn. He was requested to get up; and, when dressed, was conducted to one of the cells adjoining the court, there to await his turn for examination.

He found, upon entering the cell in question, that it contained another occupant besides himself.

His companion in misfortune was a tall, slim young man, apparently twenty or thereabouts. In appearance he was what some persons would call genteel; certainly there did not appear to be anything of the ruffian about him.

Peace regarded him with a searching glance, but did not offer any observation.

To say the truth, he was miserably depressed. Every bone in his body ached, his temples still throbbed, and the bumps on his head were as sore and troublesome as they well could be.

Presently the young man—whose name was Green— addressed Peace.

"What are you up for?" said Mr. Green. This being a slang expression for "What are you charged with?"

"I don't know at present," answered Peace, sulkily. "What are you up for?"

"Slinging my book"—a professional term for picking pockets—"but I'm as innocent as the babe unborn," added Mr. Green.

"Oh, of course," returned Peace; "so am I."

Mr. Green whistled and looked up at the roof of the cell.

"You just mind your own business," said our hero, "and speak only when you're spoken to."

"All right, mate," returned Mr. Green, "there's no occasion to be humpy with a fellow—but there, I've done."

Leaving the culprits in their narrow prison house we will enter the court. The bench of magistrates have taken their places, the night charges are as yet not over. There were the usual amount of drunken cases, assaults upon women, and others of an unimportant nature. The last assault case is being heard; two men were in the dock with bruised faces and torn garments, with unkempt hair and unshaven beards; taken altogether their appearance could not be considered prepossessing.

A tall, well-dressed gentleman was in the box giving his evidence. He had a long, aquiline nose, the skin of which had evidently been damaged some few hours before.

He told his story in a quiet, undemonstrative manner. It appeared, according to his statement, that, as he was turning the corner of a street in the neighbourhood, two men suddenly sprang upon him and tripped him up.

He fell upon his face, and his nose was seriously injured. Being under the impression that the men were bent upon committing a robbery he shouted out lustly for the police. A constable came and he gave his two assailants in charge.

"And do you believe that they intended to rob you?" inquired the stipendiary.

"I certainly was under the impression at the time that they were about to do so, but I should be sorry to say so now after what I've heard. They committed an assault; the effects of their violence I feel now."

"Did they strike you?"

"No, I don't think either of them did, but they sprang upon me."

"Did you see them before the assault?"

"No, sir. They appeared to spring suddenly out of a narrow passage. The attack was so sudden that I am unable to say with anything like exactness where they came from."

"What have you to say to this charge?" inquired the magistrate of the prisoners.

"Please, yer honour, it's all a mistake," said one of the culprits. "Quite a mistake, I assure you. Nobody ever thought of hurting the gentleman in any way. I'm very sorry for what has occurred, and humbly beg his pardon, yer worship."

"That's no answer to the charge. After violently assaulting a passenger in the street in the manner you have done, it is but a poor satisfaction to the injured party to beg his pardon."

"Well, gentlemen, I'll tell yer how it happened if so be as ye'll listen to me."

"I'm all attention. Proceed."

"It happened in this 'ere way. I was a walking down King-street last night when I seed this 'ere man—his fellow prisoner—he says to me, says he, 'Do yer want any o' this?' and with that he up with his fists, and put himself in a boxing attitude. Well, yer honour, saving yer honour's presence, I warn't a goin' to be put upon like that, and so I says to him, 'You aint the man to give it me.' 'Aint I?' says he. 'No, ye're not,' says I. Well, gentlemen, them words were 'ardly out o' my mouth, when he gave me a dab in the eye."

"And you retaliated, I suppose."

"I landed him one on the nose. With that he strikes out, and lets me have it on the jaw. Seeing as how he was a little too long in the reach for me, I closed with him, and we were a strugglin' and a strugglin' like anything. He forced me down a narrow passage, and tried to bump my head agen the wall of the court, not this court, yer honour, but the court or passage as runs out of King-street. Well, arter that I gets one of my feet agen the railing, and I shoves him out of the court with all my might. Just at that time, yer honour, the gentleman was a passin', and we both on us ran full butt agen him, but it warn't no fault o' mine, indeed it warn't."

The man had told his story in such a naive manner that roars of laughter proceeded from the body of the court, in which the bench joined.

"Do you know this man? Your fellow-prisoner, I mean," inquired the stipendiary.

"No, yer worship. I never set eyes upon him afore he sed 'do you want anything of this?'"

"What have you to say to the charge?" said the examining magistrate, addressing the other prisoner.

"I'm very sorry, gentlemen," returned the man. "What he's sed is all true enough. We were having a mill, and the gentleman 'appened to be coming by, and that's how it was. I've never been in trouble afore, gentlemen."

"What are you? What's your occupation?"

"I'm a groom, yer worship."

"You are a pair of silly troublesome fellows, and ought to be heartily ashamed of your conduct. It seems hardly possible that two men, who are perfect strangers to one another, and who, moreover, had no quarrel or dispute to settle, should break the peace in the foolish and ridiculous manner you have done. You really deserve to be imprisoned. However, as the gentleman whom you have assaulted does not wish to press the charge, we shall discharge you upon the payment of a fine of ten shillings each."

Upon this the men were removed.

It appeared afterwards that they were unable to pay the fines, only being able to muster up twelve shillings between them.

The gentleman, however, generously made up the difference.

This case concluded the night charges.

Mr. Green was now brought into court.

His countenance was the very personification of simplicity and injured innocence. He made a most respectful obeisance to the magistrates, and looked benignly at the spectators.

Mr. Green had the misfortune to be charged with picking pockets.

It was said that he was "a snapper-up of unconsidered trifles," but his appearance belied the accusation.

The charge was read over, and the usual formalities gone through. The prosecutor was then put in the witness-box and sworn.

He stated that a crowd was collected in consequence of an accident in the street. A horse had run away; the wheel of the chaise he was dragging came into collision with a lamp-post, the chaise was overturned, its occupants precipitated into the roadway, and picked up in a senseless condition; the shafts were broken short off, and with these the horse galloped off.

The prosecutor was looking at the broken vehicle in the road when he felt a tug at his watch, and saw it fall against his waistcoat.

Turning round he seized Mr. Green by the collar, and promptly charged him with the theft, upon which the young gentleman burst into a flood of tears, and pitifully exclaimed two or three times—

"Oh, my poor dear mamma!"

So ingenuous indeed was Mr. Green's manner that his fervent protestations of innocence would in all probability have had their effect upon the prosecutor had not the watch itself—such was the cruel irony of fate—been seen at the very moment to drop from his hand.

The case was, therefore, very black against Mr. Green.

The prosecutor, however, seemed to give his evidence with reluctance, being under the impression that it was the youth's first offence.

"What have you to say to this charge?" inquired the magistrate.

"I hope you will be merciful to me," said Mr. Green. "I'll tell you the truth, sir. I've been led away by bad company day after day, and that's what's brought me to this—it has indeed, sir. I trust you will have mercy on me as this is my first offence, and I'll take good care it shall be my last, for I would not let my father and mother know, for this would break their hearts, and get me a bad name. I hope you will have the case settled here to-day, as I have been waiting a week, for I did not have nothing to do with the watch; but I leave it to you, sir, to determine. Only I am anxious that my dear father and mother should know nothing of the dreadful charge."

"It is quite impossible for any rational person to believe in your innocence after the evidence that has been offered," said the magistrate. "Still you are young, and may have been led into crime through bad associates, but that is no excuse."

"Oh, do have pity on me!" exclaimed Mr. Green. "I'll tell you the honest truth."

The story which Mr. Green, to use a forensic phrase, invited the bench to believe, did great credit to his ingenuity, but there were other ugly facts brought forward which went far towards prejudicing him in the eyes of all present.

Mr. Green said in continuation:

"I came to Hull a short time since upon a little matter of business. In the train I met a young man who invited me to his house. When the train got to the station all the people got out, so did me and the young man. Soon after our arrival in the town we seed a crowd of persons in the street. The young man sed to me, 'Here, I'll get this gentleman's clock,' and he went up to this gentleman (pointing to the prosecutor) and pulled it out. He wanted to give it to me, but I would not take it, and the gentleman caught hold of me. This is how I got into this. But he (alluding to the prosecutor) did not get the right one, though I was with him. Gentlemen, have mercy on me do, for I am guilty of being with that young man who got away, but who ought to be here instead of me."

The policeman who took the prisoner into custody, and was on the spot at the time of the robbery, was put in the box, and swore distinctly that he saw the watch drop out of Mr. Green's hand.

"Oh, Mr. Policeman!" exclaimed the young gentleman, "how can you say such a thing?" Then, turning to the magistrates, he said, "It was a young man by me, gentlemen, and he ses to me, he ses, 'Hold this ere,' and he shoves the watch into my hand, an' with that the constable he catches 'old of me and ses, ses he——"

"You must ask the witness what he said."

"Thank you, sir, I will," returned Mr. Green. "Now then," said he, turning to the witness, "now then, wasn't there a young man a standin' by me when you came up?"

"No—certainly not; there was no young man by you."

"Ah! Mr. Policeman," ejaculated the prisoner, in a deprecating tone, "how can you say so? Think again."

"There was not," repeated the witness.

"I don't know what my father and mother will say to this, gentlemen," exclaimed Mr. Green, blubbering. "I would not get my father and mother in any disgrace not, for anythink. I will take good care I never get into bad company again. When I get over this I will go home and be happy with my father and mother. Gentlemen, have mercy on me, gentlemen. If I come here again you may do as you like with me."

Mr. Green, with all his cunning and affected innocence, showed a more than usual confidence in human nature, if he imagined that he could impose upon the bench of magistrates with so hackneyed a plea.

His line of defence was as well known between St. Paul's Church-yard and Farringdon-street, as is the *Proprià que Maribus* at Eton.

The magistrates, after consulting together, elected to send the case to the sessions.

The prosecutor was bound over in his own recog-

nisances, and Mr. Green, "like Niobe—all tears," was taken back to his cell.

Peace, who had given the name of Parker when arrested, was now placed in the dock.

He glanced round the court to see if his female assailant was there to press the charge.

To his dismay he beheld the elderly female sitting on a bench by the side of the witness-box.

She was a tall, sharp-featured, angular, bony woman; her cast of features and general contour denoted inflexible determination.

Peace presented a most rueful appearance; two plasters covered the large and painful bumps on his head.

His face gave unmistakable evidence of the blow received from the housemaid's mop.

Mrs. Pocklington, the prosecutrix, had engaged a solicitor to conduct the case.

After the usual formalities had been gone through, the gentleman in question rose and briefly narrated the circumstances which had led to the capture of the prisoner on the preceding night.

Mrs. Pocklington was then put into the box, and gave a succinct account of all that had transpired.

"Upon my word, Mrs. Pocklington," said the chairman, when the lady had concluded, "it would appear that you are well able to protect yourself."

"I hope I am," returned Mrs. Pocklington, sharply. "It is not the first time an attempt has been made to break into my house."

"I never attempted to break into her house, gentlemen," cried Peace. "Don't believe what she says; she's almost killed me."

"What were you doing at the front of her residence, then? And what right had you to be there at all? It is clearly a case of attempted burglary, but you had better reserve your defence; we have other witnesses to examine."

"Thank you, sir," said Peace; "I will not make any further observations at present."

The servant girl was now placed in the box. She corroborated the evidence given by her mistress.

The two constables were next examined. They proved that the large lock of the door had been forced open—proved also that house-breaking instruments were found upon the prisoner, together with a bunch of skeleton keys—"and all these facts pointed to one conclusion," said Mrs. Pocklington's lawyer—"namely, that the prisoner is a professional burglar."

Unfortunately for Peace, this was proved beyond all question. A detective was placed in the box, who said he knew the prisoner well, that he had undergone one month's imprisonment in December, 1852.

Peace denied this in a most positive manner; nevertheless his assertions had but little effect upon the bench, who decided upon sending the case for trial.

"I've been punished quite enough, I should think," ejaculated Peace, "considering I never intended to rob the house—but——"

"If you take my advice," said one of the stipendiary magistrates, "you will reserve your defence. Anything you say now will be given in evidence against you, and it will in no way effect our decision. If you have a legal defence, reserve it till your trial comes on at the sessions. Do not prejudice your case by offering any observations."

"I am obliged to you, sir, for your advice," returned Peace. "I have a defence, but if you have decided upon sending it to the sessions it is no use of my speaking now. Before I go, however, I hereby solemnly declare that that wicked old woman has not spoken the truth; she has committed perjury."

"Don't you dare to insult me, you nasty ugly little villain," exclaimed Mrs. Pocklington, rising from her seat and shaking her umbrella menacingly at the speaker.

"Hush! Silence! Order in court!" cried the usher.

"Sit down, madam, if you please," said one of the magistrates.

The old lady did as she was bid, but she kept rocking herself to and fro, muttering the while to herself inarticulate sentences.

Peace was removed, and found himself once more in his cell, in company with the ill-used Mr. Green.

Another prisoner was brought in—he was charged with horse stealing.

CHAPTER XVII.

THIEVES IN THE LOCK UP—A HORSE-STEALER TELLS THE STORY OF HIS LIFE.

THERE were an unusual number of charges to be heard at the court on the day in which Peace was examined. A gang of poachers were charged with an attempt to murder a gamekeeper in the neighbourhood. The prisoners who had been committed were therefore removed from the cells to make room for the fresh arrivals.

Peace, Mr. Green, and five others were conveyed to a lock-up which was situated at about two miles distant from the court. They were to remain there till the prison van returned to take them to the county gaol.

The lock-up in question has long since undergone demolition, and indeed at the time of which we are writing it was only occasionally used as a temporary and supplementary prison-house for offenders.

It was part of a large building originally erected as a receptacle for fraudulent debtors.

Peace and his companions were safely deposited in the prison van which conveyed them to what was in reality only a wing of the substantial-looking building.

They were conducted into a large lofty stone-room, with windows near to the ceiling, much after the fashion of Millbank prison.

In front of these were strong iron bars.

A long massive table stood in the centre of the cheerless apartment, and around this were arranged a number of chairs.

A cheerful fire was burning in the grate, and in front of this ran some strong iron bars as high as a man's chest. These were supported and braced by iron uprights.

When Peace and his fellow-prisoners entered this place they found several other offenders already assembled therein.

The massive door, studded with iron nails, was slammed to and locked from the outside.

"What do they mean by bringing us to a crib like this when we are committed to the county gaol?" said Mr. Green, in a tone of disgust. "I shall enter an action agen them for unlawful detention."

"You are particular," cried a man seated at the corner of the fireplace. "You'll be taken to the gaol soon enough, but it won't be till after the rising of the court."

"You seem to know all about it," returned Mr. Green. "Thank you for the information."

The batch of prisoners who had but just arrived now possessed themselves of the requisite number of chairs, and arranged themselves in a group apart from the others.

There was a dead silence for some time after this.

Peace was moody and thoughtful, and every now and then regarded his companions with a furtive glance.

He did not recognise any person with whom he had been previously acquainted.

"You all of yer look confoundedly down in the dumps," said the man who had been charged with horse-stealing. "It's no use giving way. Make your miserable lives as happy as you can—that's my motto."

The man who gave utterance to this speech was about thirty-five years of age, and five feet seven in height, with a remarkably firm-knit frame.

His face was bronzed, his hair and eyes were jet black, the former hanging in ringlets over the latter; his mouth was coarse and sensual; his legs were slightly curved, which added to the general strength of his figure.

He wore a sloped-cut, dark-green coat, with metal buttons, a striped vest, which hung half-way down his thighs, over which were broad-striped corduroys, buttoned over the top of the knees, with loose cloth leggings, having gilt buttons to match.

On the whole his appearance denoted a groom possessing great muscular power, and a bully of ferocious determination, who would not hesitate a moment to carry out any undertaking in which he had embarked. For the rest he did not appear to be depressed by the situation in which he found himself placed; he was cheerful and loquacious.

"Listen to me, mates," said this personage, rising from his seat. "If, as our friend has said, we are to remain here till the rising of the court, we shall, I'm afraid, find the time hang heavily on our hearts."

"If we do, there's no help for it," said Peace, looking hard at the speaker.

"Right you are, my lad," returned the other, who then proceeded with his discourse. "I was just a-thinkin'," he observed, "which among us has the honour of being the biggest rogue. We've all been guilty, gentlemen, of doing something which has brought the wrath of our enemies down upon us. I myself am here for taking an airing on a pad one fine moonlight night. Now, I say, I wonder which is the biggest rogue in this batch of injured gentlemen?"

"Oh, shut up; that will do," said a voice from the further end of the room. "What does it matter?"

"Well," returned the other, "as far as that goes, I don't know how it does much matter; but it aint in my nature to sit still like a dummy when in such good company as I now find myself. Let us relate to each other our own lives and doings. It will amuse some on us."

"You begin with yours, then," said Peace. "You've got the jawing tackle on, and won't stand still for want of words, I dare say. I'm quite willing. What say you, gentlemen?"

There was a murmur of many voices, and some of those present expressed their willingness to listen to the story.

"Good, then; here goes to keep the game alive. I can say I am not related to any of the hupper classes; leastways not as I knows on—my impression being that I was born under a hedge: I am a gipsy: this I dare say you have already guessed. Well, let me tell you a gipsy's life is not without its charms. I believe I was cradled on a horse or a donkey, but this is what I've heard other people say.

"DON'T YOU DARE TO INSULT ME, YOU NASTY UGLY LITTLE VILLIAN," EXCLAIMED MRS. POCKLINGTON.

"My earliest recollections bring to my view seven or eight hooped tents on the skirts of a common, eight or ten stunted sorts of horses, and five or six donkeys with here and there a fire on the ground, kettles hanging over them hitched on a cross-stick, supported by others fixed in the ground,

"Myself with four or five other children of my own age might be seen rolling on the grass just washed and refreshed by the morning dew.

No. 9.

"There, aint that a picter? But, Lord love yer, them days are passed, and the honourable race of gipsies are rapidly passing away before modern improvements, as they are termed—and be hanged to them.

"Aint it a picture—a gipsy encampment, I only ask ye that?"

"It is, without a doubt, quite a picture," said Peace.

"I see you are a sensible man, sir," remarked the gipsy; "but let me proceed with my story

"As I grew up I was reckoned the best climber and runner in the camp. My elder brother, Ralph, undertook my edication.

" ' Will,' ses he, one day, ' come along with me.' He took me to a pond at the remote corner of a common when he laid me down on my face across the edge of the bank.

He then covered me with briar, and giving me proper instructions went and drove the geese all that way, quietly to the spot where I lay.

As they waddled to reach the water, I, from under the boughs, grabbed at their legs and secured two on 'em. Didn't I have a tuck-out when I got home off one of the geese ?"

There was a roar of laughter at this part of the narrative.

"After this I got on fast in life ; new scenes every day opened to me, and horse-dealing and horse-stealing became part of my business.

"We attended races and fairs, where the girls of our camp told fortunes, the old women set up togs for the children to throw at three shies a penny. My brother and others followed the thimble and garter rig, while I and father at times skirted the towns and villages to job swap horses.

"Sometimes I was sent off with a horse fifty miles away from his former acquaintances, there to await the arrival of our clan.

"When I was fifteen years of age I could ride and leap a 'oss with any jockey in the kingdom. A 'oss I liked better than anything in the world, and a prad has got me into my present difficulty ; but it can't be helped.

"It happened one day, as my brother and I were taking four chopped 'osses to a fair (we never ventured into a market with a prigged prad), a pack of hounds crossed the road, and presently a lot of swells came leaping over the hedge arter them. One of the last of these, togged in a scarlet coat, came rolling over the 'oss slap at Ralph's feet.

" ' Hallo !' said Ralph, ' a regular spill.'

"Over went the 'oss on the t'other side into the field. ' She'll gallop home,' said the huntsman.

" ' No she won't,' said I, and away I goes with my pony arter her. Well, I had a good chase, but I nabbed her, and getting into the saddle slap, I gallops back and took the hedge and ditch like a good un into the road where Ralph was rubbing down the swell.

" ' Good lad,' said the huntsman. ' Why he can ride a bit.'

" ' Ride,' said Ralph ; ' I believe you, master.'

" ' Try her again,' said the swell.

"So I puts the mare over the hedge and back agen, like a buck in full chase.

" ' Well done, excellent ; you're a brave boy,' exclaimed the swell cove. ' Do you want a place, my lad ?'

" ' I could do very well with one, sir,' I answered.

" ' Very well ; if you do come to my stables,' said he, and with that he handed me his card.

"Well arter he had gone I thought of what he sed, and the next day I run over to the gentleman's stables, when I met a chap cleaning a curb chain.

" ' What do want here ?' said the man.

" ' I want to see your master,' I replied.

" ' Do you ?' he returned, with an impudent mocking laugh.

" ' If you take my advice, youngster, you'll just hook it.'

" ' I shan't do nuffin of the sort,' ses I.

"He laid hold of a long riding whip, and told me to be off.

" ' Don't you think I am afraid of you, big as you are,' I ses.

"With that he aimed a blow at me with the whip.

"I dodged on one side, and caught hold of the lash.

"We had a tussle. I wrested the whip from his hand, and gave him a sharp blow over the legs with the butt end of the weapon.

"Arter this we had a set-to. I floored him twice, when up comes my new master.

" ' Leave the lad alone,' said the swell, addressing himself to my antagonist. ' You're a deal too fast.'

" ' He tried to break my leg,' answered the man.

" ' I've seen the whole affair from the garden. You were the aggressor,' said the gentleman, who then bade me follow him into the house.

"He took me into a fine room in which were seated several gentlemen, I s'pose they called themselves ; and found them to be a fast lot. But I was a little surprised to hear them ' my lord' my master, and he ' Sir Edgar' and ' Sir Thomas' them.

"Well, the upshot of it was that they made bets that I would lick the groom, whom they called Andrew.

"We had a set-to. The fight lasted over five and twenty minutes, and I was declared victor.

"After this I had a chair among the swells, and drank wine out of a tumbler, and the footman brought me some sandwiches, while they talked of a lot of things in slang that puzzled me.

"I understood, however, that horse-racing, steeple-chasing, and dog fighting were the main subjects of their discourse.'

" ' You give a rare account of the aristocracy,' said Peace.

" ' I've had pretty much to do with them,' returned the gipsy. ' Well, the first night I went to bed in my lord's house I couldn't sleep a wink, the bed was so soft and uncomfortable. I got up early, and cleaned out the kennel. About eleven o'clock my lord and his friends came down the yard.

" ' Well,' ses he, ' have you had a look at the stud yet ?'

" ' No, my lord,' says I ; ' your chaps wouldn't like that.'

" ' They'll have to learn better manners,' said my lord. He then had 'em all turned out—eight or nine on 'em there were. ' Harkye,' said he to the men, ' this is my training groom,' pointing to me ; ' so for the future attend to his orders as coming from me. Put up the bar, and bring out Redfern, Curband, and Beeswing. We are going to have some leaping. Now,' he said, addressing himself to me ; ' there will be some crack steeple horses here presently, and you must see what you can do with them. Jump up, and give these a breathing before the others arrive. Have the saddle put on which you like.'

" ' I don't want a saddle, my lord,' ses I ; and up I jumped on a grey horse, named Custard, as I afterwards learnt.

"After I had made a few leaps, I placed shillings between my knees and the 'oss's sides, and the same under my seat, and to their astonishment cleared the bar without displacing them.

"My lord was evidently delighted. He drew me on one side, out of earshot of the rest, and said, in a whisper, ' You shall be my steeple-race jockey, but mind, don't show all you can do at present.'

" ' All right,' says I.

" ' I had no idea Custard could do so much till you rode him.'

"'Why, my lord,' said I, 'I knowed the grey horse when a baby. I could win all the steeplechases in the country with him.'"

"Why, how came you to know the horse?" inquired Peace.

The gipsy looked at the questioner with one eye only.

"Why, Lord bless us," he answered, with a merry twinkle in his eye, "father and I knowed every 'oss as was worth knowing in every country we travelled in, and got money by carrying information about 'em from place to place.

"Well, a great race was to come off soon after this. My lord had taken the field twenty to one over and over ag'in against Custard for the steeplechase which was to be run on the following week, so he stood to win eight thousand if I could bring Custard in a winner, and that I felt I could make sure of.

"But I must tell you, however, that my lord and I, after being so nutty upon one another, all of a sudden on this morning began to wrangle. First he began teaching me how to ride. Well, I couldn't stand that nohow.

"I'm for commanding a 'oss light in the mouth, riding him as with a silken rein as fine as a hair, and which you feel afraid to break. My lord, who was a yokel in the management of 'osses, though he was good at a-getting money on 'em, as you shall hear presently, always gave his lads instructions to hold their 'osses tight in racing.

"Now, if a 'oss bears on his rein in running it makes him open his mouth, and pulls his head up, which frets him, and causes him to jump with his forelegs open, and run stag-necked, locks his wind, and soon tires him. 'Osses that run sprawling, with a part of the rider's weight in their mouth, can never win a race if at all matched. I, however, likes to keep a 'oss together with a good bridle hand, being careful not to pull on the rein, or he can't rise to the fence when he gets up to it.

"Arter a deal of argufying for some time, his lordship gave in, and told me I had better ride as I liked.

"Well, I did have my own way, and the consequence was that I won four races with Custard, and a rare swag of money did my lord make.

"He was entered for the fifth race. Well, you must know that a few days afore this came off a great bull-headed man, who was a bruiser by profession, and a scoundrel by nature, come and ses to me—'Look here, Will, can't Custard and you lose the race that's coming off? It's all right; you are to lose it—so his lordship says.'

"'Oh, indeed; that's to be the little game—is it?' says I. 'I can't give you an answer at present, my noble.'

"So I goes to my lord, and blows the pumping, and all about the losing game.

"'Well,' said my master, 'whatever the gentleman' —he meant, of course, the bruiser—'tells you to do you must consider as my orders. You will be well paid.' I didn't like the task, but there was no help for it, I was bound to obey. But Custard didn't seem to see it, and he would have run the race; so at the last leap but one I tumbled off and left him to do as he liked, and of course he lost it."

"What a dirty piece of business!" said the man by the fireplace.

"Disgraceful!" exclaimed Mr. Green. "You ought to be ashamed of yourself."

"It wasn't nice," said the gipsy, "and went against the grain. When I was limping across the field as if I was hurt, didn't my lord swear at me like a good un

afore everybody? He called me every name he could think of, but I bore it all like a lamb.

"I always thought my lord looked shy at me after this, and never treated me on the same footing as before.

"The truth is, if you once make yourself a rascal to serve a rich man he never likes to see you under his nose any more.

"About a month after this the 'bruiser,' whom I had never seen before the race, sends a gig over for me from the next market town, and when I gets there, 'Well,' says he, 'my lord is going to sell his stud, and bids me say that he shall not want your services any more. He has sent you fifty pounds as a present.' He handed me a note for that amount, which you may be sure I collared.

"'Well, I am sorry he's going to part with his stud,' said I.

"'It's a pity a young fellow like you should lose a good berth,' observed the 'bruiser.' 'I am, however, glad to say that I've got you a situation in one of the first breeders' establishments in the kingdom.'

"Then, pointing to a thick-set man in the room, he said, 'This person will drive you to the place with this letter, and you'll be all right—better off, indeed, than you were in your old place.'

"I assented, and he placed me in charge of the little man whom he called Jim. He was a well-known tool of the 'bruiser's.'

"'What sort of a shop is this you are a takin' me to?' said I to my companion.

"'Oh! it is as right as the mail,' answered he in a cheerful tone. 'Good as gold—that's what it is. If you mind what's said to you, and keep your eye on the main chance, you will be made for life. You'll find it far better than serving a lord.'

"I did not like to inquire any further, but made up my mind to wait patiently till I knew more about matters, but could not help thinking, however, that there was something in the wind. The next day I went with him about fifty or sixty miles off to my new situation, which I was told was a topping establishment— the biggest one there was in the sporting world.

"'What will be my duties?' I inquired of Jim.

"'Well, you see, old man,' he answered, 'you'll only be engaged as helping groom; but what of that? The guv'nor he's a liberal sort, he is, an' he'll make it up to you, so that you'll find it as good as the situation you have just left.'

"Well, I was installed in my new office, and found things comfortable enough. I had not been there more than a fortnight when Master Jim again made his appearance. He was mighty friendly, took me and treated me to a rattling good dinner, which I washed down with a plentiful supply of wine.

"He asked me if I wanted money, and said, at the same time, that I might, whenever I fancied a horse, have part of a bet in his book; in fact, I found him most amiable and considerate. But I wasn't a born fool, and knew perfectly well what the pretended friendship of betting men was worth.

"He kept the game up all the winter, and came to see me frequently till the spring meetings came on at Newmarket.

"I expected something was up, and I was not mistaken.

"My master had a colt and filly both of the best promise of the season.

"He was a big card in his way, and went in heavily for betting.

"When I got to Newmarket with the colt and filly

there was Mister Jim all honey and butter as usual, and now came out the murder."

"You may well call it murder, you vagabond," exclaimed one of the prisoners. "I know all about the villainous transaction, and lost my fortune by that and other swindles of a similar description."

"Well, don't fall foul of me, master," cried the gipsy, who eyed the speaker curiously. "There's no call to use hard words now, seeing that we are here in limbo together."

"Go on," said the other prisoner. "I acknowledge that it was not your fault, but those who bribed you. Go on; I will not again interrupt you."

"Well, as I said, out comes the murder," said the gipsy, in continuation.

"Jim followed me when away from the stables like my shadow, till late one evening he got me into a by-lane.

"I saw something was a coming from the expression of his countenance, and I was not mistaken.

"'I want to say a few words to you upon business matters,' said he.

"'All right,' ses I; 'fire away. I'm all ears.'

"'Well,' he murmured, 'this is a queer world, and there are a lot of queer people in it. Some on 'em are fools, and some are rogues. If you try to live honestly you are doomed to remain a beggar, or next door to one.'

"'I found that out a long time ago.'

"'Did you? Ah, 1 suppose so. I think we shall be able to understand one another.'

"'Ah, I dare say we shall—leastways, I hope so. I aint too particular, you know.'

"'I have brought with me a hundred pounds. You may have it upon one condition.'

"'And what might that be?'' I inquired.

"'Your colt and filly!' he replied, with a meaning look. 'In my pocket are six balls. I want one given to each of them to-night, one to-morrow morning, and one again to-morrow night.'

"'Oh!' I ejaculated, for his proposition had almost taken my breath away. 'That's it, is it? You want me to poison the poor brutes.'

"'No, no,' he quickly answered; 'not poison—only opium; the animals will be all the better for it—their legs will be saved. They will go down in character for this two thousand stake, but come out another day low in the list, to the surprise of the knowing ones.'

"'I don't like the job,' I exclaimed, 'that I tell you plainly—I don't like it at all.'

"'That may be, but you'll do it—you must!'

"'When am I to touch?'' said I.

"'Immediately after the race comes off. Our people are honourable, and just in all their dealings.'"

"Oh, oh!" exclaimed half a dozen of the prisoners, simultaneously.

"In a manner of speaking," returned the gipsy. "That's what Jim wished me to understand. He said he would take their word for thousands.

"Well, I took the balls—the colt and filly ran like cows, and I got the coin.

"Three times afterwards I did the physicking game while in my employer's service. I believe he suspected something, and discharged one man after another, till it came to my turn, and I was sent adrift without a character.

"'And serve you right, too,' said Peace. 'What else could you expect?'

"I had no right to expect anything else, and if I had I should have been disappointed. I was now like a fettered dog, obliged to crouch before the glance of my keeper. Jim had only to say do this or do that, and I was forced to obey.'

Duplicate keys were given me to enter stables by night, and when these did not answer I broke open the doors to hocus 'osses for those who gave out their orders, till at last I and three others had a command to poison the water from which a whole stable of race-'osses were supplied. The game was now up; my employers made a fortune and escaped all danger."

"They were, however, suspected, but as they had touched the blunt and obtained credit of being down to a thing or two they were followed more than before.

"One of their tools was grabbed and had six years of it. I and two others cut our sticks just in time.

"After a twelvemonth's hide we came back, but we could not get anything to do. Jim told us that we had managed the thing badly, and that his employers had cut him off without giving him a 'quid' for his trouble.

"'Foul deeds deserve foul play,' said the moody prisoner in the corner. 'It is the moral law, and grievous ought to be the penalty exacted from all who take part in them. Retributive justice has overtaken you,' Bandy-legged Bill. You perceive I am acquainted with your nickname. But what became of the lord, your former master?

"'Why,' replied the gipsy, 'I knowed he was in it all from first to last, and had picked me up to serve his own ends. I dogged him one morning going down to the stables.

"Please, my lord," says I, coming the crawl to him, 'I am an ill-used man.'

"'Indeed! And who has ill-used you, Will?' he asked, as if he had been my best friend. So I took courage, and up and told him all.

"'And who is Jim Dempster?' said he, when he had heard me out, looking as innocent as a blessed saint.

"'Why, the agent of your friends who belong to the big betting firm where I was after I left you. Jim is the little man you spoke to the other day at Ascot about the running of Butterfly.'

"'My friends, you scoundrel! How dare you call those fellows my friends?' he cried out. 'Perhaps you, too, are a friend of mine, as you have been my groom and rode my horses. Don't you have the audacity to speak of such persons as my friends again.' Then turning as serious as a barn owl, he looked me in the face, and continued, 'You have escaped the law, my man, this time. Take my advice, quit bad company, and turn to an honest course of life. But, mark me, if ever you cross my path again, and are impudent enough to speak to me, I shall give you into custody on your own confession,' and away he strode to the stable.

"'Hang it all, this is cheeky for a youngster, lord or no lord,' says I. 'I don't think I could have done it better myself.'

"I can't tell you how I lived for the next two or three years. It was, perhaps, something after the manner of the dog who has no master—to day, I might be feeding on garbage; to-morrow, snatching a bone from a smaller and weaker dog; and a third time, waiting for the refuse of those who were over-gorged. Like a fly, I dipped into every man's cup that came into my way; but, strange to say, all this time it never came into my head to look back on a gipsy's life."

"Shall I tell you why?" muttered the man in the corner. "There is a charm in a vagabond's wayward life which none but a vagabond can appreciate."

"What is a gipsy's life but that of a vagabond state of existence?" inquired Peace.

"True," returned the other. "Granted, but not precisely in the same degree as the one he had been following. He had known what a wayward life was in the country, but the town loafer's life was new to him, and brought fresh charms—yes, charms, I will call them. There is positively a fascinating spell in a life of monetary casualty which is a mystery to those who are well provided for in life. Even the extreme of misery does not break the spell. Sadness oftentimes twines itself around the strings of the heart, while it releases and softens them.

"I knew a corner in a tap-room of a public-house resorted to by cadgers which was called the dead man's corner, because numbers of decayed beggars had made it their sleeping place, and in that spot one had breathed his last. The seat was frequently at a premium among aged beggars."

"Ah, I say, draw it mild, old man," said several voices.

"It's a fact," returned the man in the corner.

No two specimen of the human species cou'd form a stranger contrast than the gipsy and the man in the corner, or the "Croaker," as the former designated him.

The gipsy was full of robust health, of life, and animation.

The "Croaker" resembled more the skeleton of a murdered man than a living subject.

The attenuation of his figure conveyed to the mind the horrible idea of a man just terminating his life under a sentence of starvation.

His eyes resembled dirty gray glass, and a countenance, when unmoved, adorned with features cut in marble, or moulded in cast iron, impressing those who looked on him with the idea that for once nature had made a man without feelings or affections.

Warmth, ardour, sensibility, and the sentiment of friendship had all, however, reigned successively in the collapsed breast of that frame, of which nothing was left but the bare walls, lighted by the last flickerings of the vital spark of that intellect which had brought reflection and worn him to the bone.

He was a mere wreck. Remorse for an ill-spent and sinful life had eaten like a canker worm into his heart.

Peace was particularly struck with the emaciated man who sat in the corner, and who every now and then offered some observation as the gipsy shadowed forth his career. He would have liked to learn something of his history, and indeed it was understood that he was to be the next speaker.

"Get on with your biography," said the man in the corner.

"I've not much more to tell," returned the gipsy. Let's see, where was I?

"Oh, I was down at low-water mark, and didn't know how to get on. One cold, dark, rainy, boisterous night, the whole of which I had passed in the streets penniless and hungry, drove me almost to desperation. It had often come into my head to knock down and rob the first person I met, but every crime requires a beginning before it can be done with ease and firmness."

"True," ejaculated the man in the corner, "I know it well. If Jem Dempster had put you on to poisoning the trough at starting you would have backed out; but he first put you on to hocussing, and you soon came to the poison like an old un in the trade."

"Cease moralising," called out several of the auditory.

"The morning was dimming the already dimmed lamps when at the corner of Park-lane I saw a chap who had been in the stables with me.

"He recognised me and spoke a few words of comfort after I had told him my story; he did more than this—he lent me a little ready cash. He informed me that he was in a good situation, being groom to a gentleman in North Audley-street. He was a right good sort and stood by me like a brick, helping me in every way he possibly could during the time I was out of collar.

"Well, to cut a long story short, after this I became an 'oss dealer, in which honourable profession I remained, till one night a cunning 'oss coaxed me to put the saddle on his back, and would not be satisfied till I got into it: when he rode away with me—for which they put me in quod instead of the 'oss.

"Now, my old ourang-outang," said the gipsy, addressing himself to the emaciated man, "let us have an account of your times when you were in the land of the living."

"I had thought," responded the prisoner addressed, "that I had some weeks since achieved a victory over memory and buried all recollections of the past. I had shut myself wholly in passive resignation to the future without suffering myself to revert to the bygone events of my life, the frequent reference to which had previously worn me to the object you now behold. But that man," pointing to the gipsy, "has broken down the barrier within which I had taken shelter. He has, in a few words, informed me of the causes of my ruin. His villainies have brought me here.

"The family of which I am an unworthy member was more distinguished for its ancestors than for its possessions."

The speaker had got thus far when the ponderous lock of the door was turned, and a police sergeant and two constables, accompanied by a prison warder, entered.

"Now then, prisoners, this way," said the sergeant.

The culprits rose from their seats. Peace, the gipsy, Mr. Green, with several others, were conducted to the prison van, or "Black Maria," as it is termed by criminals.

The cadaverous-looking man was abruptly cut short in his narrative.

Most persons will doubtless remember having seen the ominous-looking vehicle called "Black Maria" going to and from the various police offices and the metropolitan prisons. It is not unlike a hearse in external appearance, and is suggestive of one of the darker phases of metropolitan and provincial criminal life.

On mounting the steps of the sable vehicle Peace was ushered into a passage running up the centre from end to end of her Majesty's carriage. A number of dark doors were on each side, through one of which he was gently pushed by one of his janitors.

He then found himself shut up in a close box on a seat, not too well ventilated nor too clean.

This was not the first time he had been inside a prison van. He had not been much impressed with its comfort on the former occasion, when he first made its acquaintance; now he was disgusted with it, for it brought to his recollection the many ignominious circumstances connected with his first conviction.

When the outer door was shut and locked the vehicle proceeded on its journey.

His companions in misfortune or crime—whichever of the two it might be—did not appear to be so depressed, so moody, and so thoughtful, as our hero.

He heard the sound of their voices in his narrow compartment.

Some were calling to each other by name, it might be said, in a jocund and familiar manner. Mr. Green's voice was distinctly audible above the hubbub of the rest.

" He's a sharp sort of a chap that gipsy," murmured Peace. "I should have liked t'other cove to have time to tell his tale. Ah, this is a bad business. What a spiteful, vindictive old cat!"

This last observation of course referred to the relentless Mrs. Pocklington, from whom he could not hope to secure clemency. He was perfectly well assured that she would " prosecute to the utmost rigour of the law," to quote the words so often to be seen on warning sign-posts.

On arriving in the court-yard of the county gaol, the prisoners were marshalled in a narrow-vaulted passage, where they were made to stand in a row.

The deputy-governor, in plain uniform, attended by a cordon of officials, was ready to receive them. He was a tall, military-looking personage, with a broad face and a large bushy beard.

He gave a short preliminary cough, and took from the conductor of the prison van a number of papers, one for each prisoner.

He glanced at these, and then proceeded to call out the names, which the prisoners answered to, some in a jaunty, and others in a quiet tone and manner.

Having satisfied himself that the requisite number of culprits were then and there present, he folded up the papers in a mechanical manner.

When this ceremony had been gone through the new arrivals were conducted to their quarters.

The cadaverous-looking man was the first to be removed. He looked so weak, so borne down, that even the officials regarded him with something like compassion. To their credit we must record that they treated him with kindness and consideration—that is, as far as the rigid prison discipline would allow.

Peace was told to follow a warder. The bumps on his head were still very painful, and, taken altogether, he presented a most pitiable and abject appearance. He said to his janitor, as they went along, that he had been most cruelly used, and told him, moreover, that he was perfectly innocent of the charge upon which he had been committed.

The warder was so accustomed to hear statements of a similar character from prisoners that he did not take much heed of Peace's declaration of innocence.

He merely nodded, and ushered his prisoner into a stone cellar-like place, where there were a number of small rooms with baths in them.

Peace was directed to enter one and undress. He obeyed without making any observation, knowing well enough, from his former experience of prison life, that it would be useless to offer any objection.

When he had undressed his clothes were taken from him, and underwent a careful scrutiny—the pockets in the garments were turned out, and all prohibited articles removed.

All this was done in a methodical, systematical way. An inventory of these things was taken, and Peace was told that any of his friends, on calling to see him, might take them away.

" I don't know why I should be stripped of all I possess, but if it's the rule I suppose there's no use murmuring," said Peace.

"It is the rule," quietly observed the warder. " You are treated precisely the same as all the other prisoners. Now you must have a bath."

" I've no objection to that," cried Peace.

The bath room was scrupulously clean; the water looked as clear as crystal, and Peace plunged in.

On re-dressing, he was conducted by the warder up a flight of stairs into a large, lofty hall, on each side of which were galleries.

In each gallery was a warder in uniform. With the exception of the halls and corridors the building was almost entirely divided into an immense number of small apartments. These were homely inside, but exquisitely clean.

Prisons at this time might be said to be in a transition state. In some the old system remained in full force. The two systems vary in their aims. Under the old, prisoners awaiting their trials were allowed to mix together in wards.

In such places as these the criminals of the olden times—common thieves, pickpockets, burglars, and others—had, no doubt, many of them, in their own way, a jolly time of it.

They were supplied with provisions by their pals and relatives, and were not compelled to live on prison fare.

As many as twenty would be found at times in one of these wards under the old system, which were nurseries of crime—so it is said—the old hardened felon contaminating the young and inexperienced.

Then, as now, the prisoners did not do any labour before trial, but after conviction they were sent to correctional prisons.

Under the new system the prison is intended to be a penal hospital for the cure of diseased and contagious souls.

The one in which Peace found himself was of the latter class.

On his reaching the first gallery a number was shouted out in a loud voice by his attendant. One of the warders came forward and conducted Peace to his cell.

He was told what to do in case he wished to speak to a warder. It was pointed out to him by his custodian that everything was clean and in its place, and that he was expected to keep it so.

He was also informed that if he liked to pay another prisoner for cleaning his cell he could, by permission of the governor, have it done for him, but otherwise he would have to do it himself.

All these matters he knew, but he did not care to say so. He also knew by heart the printed list of rules to which his attention was next directed.

He said he was too ill to clean his own cell at present, and would rather pay another prisoner to do the work.

He was very clever at shamming illness, but on this occasion he really was in a weak state.

The door was shut with a horrid discordant sound, and Peace then was fairly caged, and felt miserable to the last degree.

He remained for some time moody and thoughtful. After awhile he rose from his seat, and proceeded to examine his narrow prison house. It was a stone or brick-arched room, some fourteen feet by seven; the furniture was in no way superfluous. A bedstead, consisting of the side walls of the apartment; polished steel staples were fixed in these walls, two on each side, at an elevation of about two feet and a half. The occupant's mattress has two short steel hooks at each end, these are hooked into the staples, so he lies across his abode. A deal table, the size of a pocket-handkerchief, also a deal seat; a bright copper wash basin, fastened to the wall, with a water tap over it so ingeniously contrived, that turned to the right it sends a small stream into the basin, and to the left into a bottomless close stool at some little distance. There were three shelves in one corner.

An iron enamelled plate, a tin mug, wooden spoon, and salt box, and a piece of soap were arranged on the two lower shelves.

"How cursedly clean and staring everything is," exclaimed Peace, in a tone of disgust. "The things seem to glare at you. Ugh! this is about the most contemptible piece of business I ever knew; but, law, they'll never convict upon such a trumpery charge."

He was under the full impression that he would be acquitted.

A great many people are committed by magistrates for trial that are not found guilty. There are many cases where a magistrate will not take upon himself the responsibility of deciding a case, which he prefers being disposed of by the verdict of a jury.

It does happen sometimes that a perfectly innocent man is committed for trial, and it does appear hard, not to say unjust, that he should be subjected to the many indignities and privations which prisoners have to endure.

The law holds that every man is innocent till he is found guilty, and there should certainly be some better arrangement in respect to prisoners who are awaiting their trial.

We question much whether it is advisable for them to be sent to the same prison with others who are convicted.

Many a man at the close of his trial has left the court "without a stain upon his character." Yet he has had to pass through a painful ordeal, which possibly he will not forget for the remainder of his life. This ought not to be.

Men untried should be treated very differently from the way they are so long as they are kept secure from escape; the main object of their detention is effected. But a man who is unjustly accused, sent to prison, and afterwards proved innocent, bears with him the unpleasant reflection that some mischievous and evil-disposed person is sure to be found who will whisper mysteriously to others "So-and-so was charged with larceny, but he was acquitted."

With some persons the very fact of having been accused would be prejudicial, but these are things the reader may perhaps exclaim, "It is not possible for the wisest of us to prevent!"

Granted; but that is no reason why every precaution should not be taken to protect the innocent man.

These observations, however, do not apply to such hardened offenders as Peace, who is included in the category of habitual criminals, or, to make use of a stronger term, professional thieves.

CHAPTER XVIII.

PRISONERS AWAITING TRIAL—THE ASSIZES—PEACE'S DEFENCE.

PEACE, as may readily be imagined, deplored having made an attempt to enter the "Gothic Cottage" in the occupation of Mrs. Pocklington. He came to the conclusion that that was one of the most stupid things he had ever been guilty of.

His first night in the county gaol was by no means an agreeable one.

The first night in any prison is generally one of bitterness and gall to the unhappy prisoners; but our hero felt humiliated at the contemptible part he had been playing to be knocked about by an old woman until he was rendered nearly senseless, and in that state to be captured without even making an attempt to escape, was most aggravating.

The more he reflected upon the matter the more humiliated did he feel.

His sleep was broken and disturbed during the greater portion of the night.

At six o'clock in the morning he was aroused by the resonant sound of a large bell. He arose and hurried on his clothes.

The door of his cell was thrown open by a stalwart warder, who passed on to make room for the deputy governor and another warder. This last-named personage carried in his hand a large book.

"Do you wish to see the doctor?" inquired the governor.

"Thank you, sir," returned Peace. "I do not think there is any necessity for that. I am better than I was; the bruises on my head are less painful."

"And your cell. Do you intend to clean it yourself, or procure a substitute?"

"I'll do my best to clean it."

The name he had given at the police-court was now entered on the list in the warder's book.

Two brushes were then given him, with which he was directed to polish the floor of his cell; and the warder instructed him as to the regulation mode of stowing his hammock and mattress on the shelf, and folding up his blankets and rug.

All these details are easy enough to those who have been accustomed to manual labour, but they are of course very hard to one who has been gently nurtured, or moved in a respectable sphere of life.

This is why prison discipline falls with such unequal force upon different classes of culprits. To a navigator, excavator, or labourer of any description, the tread-wheel is a mere trifle in comparison to the effect upon those who have never been used to manual labour.

Every morning Peace had to go on his hands and knees and polish his cell floor, as well as wash and scrub the table, stool, basin, and every article in the room.

This was not a particularly hard task to him, while to others it would have been one of infinite labour.

When the brief interview with his gaolers was over, his breakfast was served through the little trap in the door. It consisted of a pint of gruel and a slice of bread.

A starving man will eat anything, it is said; but I expect many of my readers would have turned aside in disgust at the breakfast.

Peace devoured it with something like a relish.

There can be no possible reason for denying unconvicted prisoners the luxury of a cup of tea or coffee for their morning's meal.

We never could "abear," as Mrs. Gamp says, gruel under any circumstances.

But, of course, all men are not constituted alike.

After breakfast he was told to prepare for chapel.

On stepping outside his cell he was directed to turn round with his face to the cell door, to take his Bible, prayer, and hymn-book in his hands, and to hold them behind his back.

This, again, is an unnecessary piece of assumption on the part of the prison authorities when dealing with an unconvicted person—one, indeed, for aught they know, may be as innocent of the crime laid to his charge as they are themselves.

He had ample opportunity of contemplating the outside of the door, and seeing how the various mysterious appliances connected with it were worked.

Being of a mechanical and, in many respects, ingenious turn of mind, he was naturally interested.

He regarded with great curiosity the spy-hole over the trap-door, and was at no loss to comprehend how it was constructed.

It was evident enough that the inmate of the cell could not see any person on the outside, but it was equally clear that a watcher outside could command the entire range of the prisoner's apartment.

A number of prisoners were assembled in the passage; Peace was told to join them.

Then the whole of the culprits were marched along the stone passage until they came to a large low-roofed hall.

From this they ascended a dark winding staircase, which led into the chapel.

Peace observed among the motley group the gipsy, Mr. Green, the cadaverous-looking gentleman who was about to give the history of his life in the lock-up, together with many others whose faces he recognised.

The last-named looked even more ghastly than ever.

Nods were exchanged, but not a word was spoken by any of the prisoners.

The chapel was a good-sized lofty room. In it were two large cages—large spaces parted off with iron bars.

Over these was a gallery, with a thick curtain in front, which had been constructed for the exclusive use of the female prisoners.

In one of the cages were about sixteen, who had been tried and sentenced, and were waiting to be drafted off to the several prisons or convict establishments.

All were cropped and shaven close, every vestige of beard being removed, and their hair cut down to about an inch in length.

They were clad in rough grey jackets, trousers, and vests, with coarse blue-striped shirts,

While the male prisoners were assembling the female portion were coming into the chapel by another door, and sat in their own gallery, quite out of the sight of the male prisoners. Two female warders sat behind the female prisoners, and two male warders took their station on each side of the males.

The congregation was of a very motley character: the generality of the boys were poor and ragged; some of them were very keen-eyed and restless in their manner—others were apparently the children of respectable parents.

Presently the chaplain entered in his white gown, followed by an elderly warder, who officiated as clerk.

During the devotional exercises most of the prisoners leaned forward on the seat in front of them.

On one side of the pulpit and reader's desk was the governor's pew, in which was seated that awful functionary. He was a tall, elderly man, with a partially bald head.

When the service was over and the chaplain had retired, the governor was the first to lead the way out. The door was unlocked by his deputy and down stairs the prisoners were marched in military order.

"You look very ill, sir," whispered Peace to the cadaverous-looking man who was now next to him.

"Going home," returned the other. "It matters not whether they convict or acquit me, my race is nearly run."

"Silence," exclaimed a warder.

Not another word was spoken. The prisoners went along with their hands behind them like so many school-boys. The ceremony was humiliating to the last degree.

Peace was directed to cross over to a little office where the governor was standing,

He was then told to take off his boots and stand under a post with numbers on it, with a sliding piece of brass in its centre.

It was a machine for measuring his height.

This was recorded in a book by a clerk.

He was then asked his name, his age, where born, the date of his birth, trade or profession, married or single, together with a variety of other questions, which in most cases were seldom answered truthfully; nevertheless it was a ceremony which had to be gone through.

After it was over he was introduced to the chaplain, whose room was in close proximity to the chapel.

The manner of the rev. gentleman was kind and conciliatory. He asked Peace if he could read and write; the answer was in the affirmative.

"Have you got good legal advice?" inquired the chaplain.

Peace informed him that he had written to his mother to retain the services of an able advocate, and he felt quite sure that he should be acquitted, as he had no felonious intent.

"I hope and trust you may. I feel assured that you will have a fair trial," said the clergyman, who then informed our hero that he could have any books he liked from the library in the prison to beguile the hours during his imprisonment.

"You are very kind, sir, and I have to offer you my heartfelt thanks," said Peace, who was touched by the first words of consolation he had heard since his incarceration.

"In writing to your friends," said the divine, "I must give you a warning. All letters are opened by the governor before they leave the prison."

"Then I think it most unfair," cried Peace.

"We will not discuss that question; it is a rule which is invariably carried out, and therefore I deem it my duty to inform you of it. I advise you also to destroy all letters that come to you as soon as read."

"I will most certainly do so, sir," returned Peace, who again thanked the chaplain most sincerely for his information and advice.

He returned to his cell in a much more composed state; he looked hopefully to the future. After all, things were not so bad as he had at first supposed.

Soon after he had returned to his cell he received a visit from the governor, who, like any other commander-in-chief, was attended by his aide-de-camp.

"They're very attentive to me," all of a sudden muttered our hero, as he caught sight of the governor, who inquired if he wanted anything, looking up and down the cell with a searching glance.

"I'm told I may have a few books to read," said Peace.

"Certainly—by all means you can."

"Then I should like to have one or two."

The prison official nodded, and before Peace had time to make any other requests he had vanished.

Half an hour after this a number of books were brought to the prisoner to choose from.

He selected two, which he was allowed to retain, with the understanding that there were more at his service when he had perused the two volumes.

The records of prison life are necessarily monotonous. The poor prisoners find to their cost their state of existence especially so; but it is impossible that it should be otherwise.

PEACE AS AN ETHIOPIAN MINSTREL.

We have endeavoured to give as faithful a picture as possible of the treatment of prisoners while in gaol awaiting their trial.

Many an innocent man has to put up with all the indignities we have described, and has been forced to suffer in silence, for no one seems to have much sympathy for persons who have the misfortune to be wrongfully accused.

They must get out of the scrape as best they can.

The public, however, every now and then awakens to the fact that a great wrong has been done, and then an outcry is raised, and it goes to sleep again.

We have an instance of this in the case of a clergyman who had the misfortune to be suspected of having committed what is known as the Coram-street murder.

This case is of a remarkable and exceptional character, and incontestably points to what might be termed spasmodic sympathy or charity, evinced on many occasions towards foreigners by a certain section of the people of this country, who deem it expedient to close

their eyes to far more deserving cases of suffering endured by their own countrymen, while they are lavish in their subscriptions to recompense a foreigner.

Many of our readers will doubless remember the particulars connected with the tragedy in Coram-street.

On Wednesday, Dec. 25th, 1873, a dreadful murder was discovered to have been committed at 12, Great Coram-street, Brunswick-square, the victim being a woman named Harriet Buswell.

She had been seen on the previous night at the "Count Cavour" hotel, in Leicester-square, with a foreign gentleman.

The woman and her male companion left the hotel together.

It appeared that two persons, one of whom was the deceased, called at a greengrocer's shop near to Coram-street.

On the Christmas morning she was found by the landlady of the house in which she resided dead on her bed, with her throat cut under the ear, severing the jugular vein, and there was another deep gash lower down.

Life was quite extinct.

The door of the room in which she was found was locked on the outside, and the key taken away ; but, strange to say, there were no marks of blood on the door, nor on the walls or bed, as if the blood had spurted from the wounds.

The face of the victim was perfectly calm, but on the forehead there was the distinct print of a thumb, and a little lower down the mark of the palm of the hand in blood, as if, after the first wound had been inflicted, the poor creature had been held down by the left hand while the second wound was inflicted.

The appearance of the man who went home with the unfortunate woman was described by the inmates of the house, but he left without any one observing him.

Suspicion fell on a German clergyman named Hessel. The waiter at the "Count Cavour" hotel and the greengrocer at whose shop Harriet Buswell called with the gentleman who accompanied her home, swore most positively Hessel was the man who was in company with the murdered woman on the night of the 24th (Christmas Eve), and that he and Harriet Buswell called at his shop and purchased some apples.

Dr. Hessel was examined at Bow-street, and his legal adviser said that he was in a position to prove an *alibi*, the prisoner being at an American hotel in the east end of the town during the whole of the evening in question (Christmas Eve).

He asked for a remand of eight days for the production of witnesses.

This was granted, and on the next examination Dr. Hessel was released, the *alibi* being deemed a sufficient proof of his innocence.

This is a brief epitome of the case. There were, however, one or two other suspicious circumstances of minor importance, which it is now not necessary to dwell upon.

The evidence of the waiter and greengrocer, both of whom had ample time and opportunity of observing the features of the accused, was so direct and positive as to justify his detention.

Many suspected persons have been remanded upon much lighter testimony—have endured all the hardships of imprisonment without any expression of regret on the part of the executive or the public, but a loud outcry was raised at the injury sustained by Dr. Hessel.

There was a general desire on the part of the public to send the ill-used gentleman from these shores—not only compensated in pocket, but compensated in mind and feelings.

In the cruel penitentiary called the "House of Detention," says a daily paper, at the time of his imprisonment, he was treated as a felon ; and every untried man, however innocent, obtains there a sharp foretaste of the punishment that follows conviction.

Dr. Hessel gave a vivid description of a few of his experiences in the Clerkenwell torture-house.

The pens of indignant journalists were actively at work to chronicle the sufferings of the accused gentleman.

The writers for the Press suddenly discovered that the treatment of prisoners and suspected persons generally was a scandal to this country.

Our present system has been in operation a good many years, and it was therefore the more surprising that it was not assailed before, and still more so that it has not been so since.

A general feeling of regret was expressed by all classes—from the Queen to the artisan—that the doctor should have been subjected to so much annoyance, inconvenience, and indignity.

What can be more "gushing" than the following document, which was handsomely engrossed and written both in English and German, and presented to the German doctor :—

" On behalf of the committee of English and German gentlemen acting for the Rev. Godfrey Hessel, pastor designate of a German Lutheran congregation of Moniz, in the Brazils, we beg to state that he was arrested in London upon a false accusation, and after a most searching investigation—overwhelming evidence having been given establishing beyond a doubt his entire innocence of the false and cruel charge—was, on January 30, 1873, acquitted by the presiding magistrate, amidst cheers from the court, as free from suspicion. The acute and unmerited sufferings which Dr. Hessel had to undergo by a grievous and palpable error having called forth a national subscription, the amount, consisting of £1,250, is hereby offered him as the testimony of the universal sympathy felt for him by all classes, and with the assurance that the sincere wishes and prayers of many thousands of German and English friends for his health and happiness, and a long and prosperous career, will follow him to his destination."

Knowing as much as we do of the merits of the case we cannot do otherwise than designate the above effusion as being what our transatlantic cousins would call " bunkum."

Upon the first examination at Bow-street Dr. Hessel's legal adviser declared that there were ten or a dozen persons staying at the same hotel as the accused, and that they were all engaged in distributing the various articles attached to a Christmas tree.

It was not a little remarkable that some of them did not come forward to give evidence on the first hearing.

Eight days were allowed to pass over, and on the second and final hearing of the case only two witnesses were produced to prove the alibi.

One of these was the night porter of the hotel, the other being a young German, who professed to be a personal and intimate friend of the prisoner.

The murderer of Harriet Buswell has never been discovered—indeed, upon the discharge of Dr. Hessel the matter seemed to drop ; no attempt was made to arrest any other person.

As far as the unfortunate woman, Harriet Buswell, was concerned, her fate did not seem to affect people in the slightest degree, the only regret being that the reverend gentleman should have been wrongfully accused.

Taken altogether, the Coram-street tragedy and the circumstances surrounding it must be deemed of an exceptional character.

The sum of money subscribed on this occasion is without precedent in any case of a similar nature.

Some years before this a clergyman of the Church of England was convicted of indecent assault upon the testimony of two little girls.

He was sentenced to a long term of penal servitude for several years, was imprisoned in one of our convict establishments, and was forced to endure all the hardships, labour, and misery to which convicts are subjected.

It transpired afterwards that he was perfectly innocent. This was proved beyond the shadow of a doubt. The girls confessed that they had been tutored by their aunt to give false evidence, and that there was not a shadow of truth in any of their statements.

The clergyman, the Rev. Mr. Hatch, was released, the girls convicted of perjury, and there was an end of the matter.

The injury sustained by Mr. Hatch cannot be estimated with anything like accuracy—it is incalculable; yet we never heard of a single shilling being subscribed for this cruelly used gentleman, who was as guiltless as any one of the readers of this work.

But we should bear in mind that he was an Englishman; had he been a German probably the case would have assumed quite a different aspect.

In referring to the Coram-street case, the *Cologne Gazette* said at the time that the English sympathy with Dr. Hessel had taken too material a shape to be altogether appropriate.

Sympathy in itself was merited, but, beyond that of repayment of costs and free fare to Brazil, no pecuniary recompense was due to the clergyman.

We expect most of our readers will endorse the opinion expressed by the German journalist.

Peace was never much of a reader at any period of his life, but during his incarceration he relieved the tedium of the hours by perusing the volumes he had selected from those brought him from the prison library.

After the Governor's diurnal visit all the prisoners were called out, and marched off into a stone yard enclosed in iron bars on two sides—on the other by stone walls.

In this place Peace had an opportunity of having a look at his fellow-prisoners.

All grades of society were represented by the motley group, from the City merchant to the wretched street Arab.

For nearly an hour did the prisoners go round the yard in regular order, much after the fashion of soldiers. Two warders were there to keep order, and interdict any talking between the prisoners.

On certain days in the week the detectives and warders from other gaols came to take stock, and see if they could recognise any of the new comers.

Sometimes one would be called into the corner of the yard to undergo a closer scrutiny, and it was amusing to see how coy and bashful the hardened offenders looked while this ceremony was taking place; acquaintances were claimed that were by no means cordially reciprocated.

In some cases a photograph was produced by a detective and compared to its living prototype.

The moment the detectives came into the yard those whom they sought would either slink past in hopes of not being recognised, or else assume such a look of injured innocence that they thereby betrayed themselves at once. Many an "old bird" was detected by thus overdoing it.

It is customary for the detectives, before entering the yard, to have a good survey of the prisoners exercising from some unseen corner. They then mark the bearing and look of the prisoners, before they are aware that the detectives are near; on entering they note any change in their demeanour.

The new man—the greenhorn—is not aware that officers are present, for they are invariably dressed in plain clothes, but the old hand knows full well the purport of their visit, and finds it difficult to maintain his composure under such trying circumstances.

Mr. Green unfortunately attracted the attention of a tall, military-looking man, who claimed acquaintance with him, but the young gentleman's memory was at fault; he could not and would not own to a little affair which had taken place some eighteen months back.

"I assure you, upon my honour," said Green, "you are quite mistaken—you are, indeed. I never was at Warwick in my life."

The detective smiled, shook his head, and passed on.

The gipsy did not appear to be recognised by anyone; neither was Peace.

Certain days in the week were visiting days. Peace was looking forward to a visit from his mother, to whom he had written. She presented herself at the prison on the next visiting day, and was conducted by a turnkey to that part of the prison where the inmates are permitted to see their relatives, who have to converse with them through wire gratings, with a space of some three or four feet between them, in which sits a warder.

The visiting goes on for an hour or more. Those prisoners who have friends come to see them stand in a row against these railings, and their friends opposite. As a matter of course, everyone is talking at once with his own friends, and the consequence is there is a constant clatter kept up during the whole of the time.

All are too interested in their own affairs to take any notice of what is going on between his neighbour and friend.

Peace exhorted his mother to procure the services of a counsel whom he named, and in whom he had great confidence.

"Be of good cheer, my dear boy," said his parent, "I have already seen the gentleman you name, and he has promised to do his best for you."

"That old catamaran will swear anything, I feel assured of that," cried Peace. "But he'll be able to bowl her out if you tell him what sort of customer he has to deal with—a she dragon, a very devil, that's what she is."

"Don't lose your temper, Charlie. It's no use doing that now you're behind the bars."

"I should like to—"

"Hush! don't go on so—be patient," interrupted his mother. "There, keep up your spirits; all will be well, I dare say."

"They treat everybody in this place as if they were convicted felons."

"It's a burning shame, that's what it is, but it's no use making any complaint. If a fellow does that he gets worse served. I've done nothing against the laws, but it makes no difference. The biggest rogue gets the best of it in places of this sort."

"Well, it is only for a short time; the sessions will soon be on, and there you'll have justice done you, let us hope."

"Umph! Hope told a flattering tale, mother. But, hark ye! I want to see the lawyer to give him the necessary instructions for preparing my defence. Do you hear? I must see him."

"I've arranged all that. He will be here in a day or two's time. Don't fret or worry yourself; we are doing all we can for you."

"I have no doubt of that; but it's hard to be cooped up here."

While this conversation had been taking place there was a hubbub of voices from the other prisoners and their friends.

Interviews of this nature are in many cases painful in the extreme, especially when the friends or relatives of a prisoner are introduced into the interior of a gaol for the first time.

At the expiration of the time appointed for these visits, Peace and his companions returned to their respective cells.

Soon after this he had an interview with his solicitor,

to whom he explained the whole of the circumstances connected with the alleged attempted burglary at the "Gothic Cottage."

His legal adviser took notes for the preparation of his brief, and told his client that the line of defence he purposed adopting would in all probability be deemed an answer to the charge, and that he looked forward with confidence to an acquittal, unless some further incriminating evidence was presented in the course of the trial.

"You have all the facts, sir," returned Peace, "but of course there is no telling what that infamous old woman will swear."

"Oh! we don't intend letting her have it all her own way," observed the lawyer. "She'll be subject to a searching cross-examination."

Peace was in much better spirits after the interview with his lawyer, who had said, in the course of conversation, that it was as trumpery a case as he had ever had to do with.

The day of trial at length arrived. The prosecutrix and her witnesses were in court when Peace was placed in the dock.

After a few preparatory remarks from the counsel for the prosecution, Mrs. Pocklington was sworn.

She deposed to the facts already known to the reader, her evidence being in substance much the same as that given before the bench of magistrates.

Mr. Serjeant Jawkins rose and proceeded to cross-examine the prosecutrix.

"When did you become aware of the fact that a burglar—as you are pleased to call the prisoner—was endeavouring to effect an entrance into your house?"

"When I opened the drawing-room window."

"And pray, madam, what was your reason for opening your window?"

"I heard a scraping noise at the front door, and suspected there was something amiss."

"And you saw the prisoner at the door of the house?"

"Yes."

"Which he was endeavouring to open?"

"Certainly—so I imagined."

"We don't want to know what you imagined. Will you swear that he was endeavouring to open it? Now be careful in your answers."

"It appeared to me that he was doing so. The door was partly open."

"It was a dark night, was it not?"

"Rather dark."

"And pray how long did you look at the prisoner before you struck him with the broom?"

"Oh! not long."

"I should suppose not; but can you give us an idea how long it was—five minutes or five seconds, or more?"

"It was not five minutes."

"Nearer five seconds—eh?"

"I can't say exactly. It was not long."

"And so, Mrs. Pocklington, you deemed it expedient to act promptly. You commenced a most vigorous assault upon the prisoner without stopping to inquire whether he was a thief or a visitor?"

"I was sure he was not a visitor."

"How could you be sure? Did you see his face when you first struck him?"

"No, his back was towards me."

"Is it your practice to assault persons with a house-broom?"

"I object to that question," said the counsel for the prosecution, rising and interrupting his learned brother.

They are all brothers in a court of law.

"Upon what grounds, brother Matchley?" inquired Serjeant Jawkins.

"As irrelevant."

"I hope his lordship will rule that my questions are relevant."

The judge signified that question might be put.

It was again repeated.

The witness said sharply—

"No, it is not my practice to do so."

"Then it is fair to assume that this is an exceptional case," said Serjeant Jawkins.

"You have not told us, Mrs. Pocklington, if you heard any one calling out or shouting before you opened the window and commenced hostilities?"

"I did not hear any one call out."

"You are quite sure you did not hear a man's voice before you discovered the prisoner at the door of your house?"

"I did not hear any voice."

"Is the prisoner a stranger to you?"

"I never saw him before to my knowledge."

"Is he also a stranger to your maid-servant?"

"I believe so."

"Really, brother Jawkins, I think you are out of order. How is the witness to know whether he is a stranger or not to the servant? Ask the young woman herself when she is in the box."

"I thank you for your suggestion, brother Matchley. It would be the best course. I have no further questions to put to the present witness."

Mrs. Pocklington retired, and the servant-girl was placed in the box. After she had deposed to facts connected with the case, she underwent a severe cross-examination, which took a humorous turn, eliciting laughter in the body of the court, which was, of course, immediately suppressed.

When the examination of the police was concluded, Mr. Serjeant Jawkins rose for the defence. He said—

"My Lord and Gentlemen of the Jury, I must confess that this case appears to me singularly weak, as far as the evidence for the prosecution is concerned—in point of fact, there is no proof whatever that the prisoner contemplated committing a burglary. The pugnacious prosecutrix came to that conclusion at the outset, and she has done her best to substantiate the charge, which, however, I submit, is in no way proved. It is my duty to inform you that the prisoner declares that he had no felonious intention whatever. According to his statement, he had, on the night in question, an appointment with a young woman to whom he is paying some attention. They walked about together for an hour or so, and he was led to believe that she was a domestic in service in one of the houses in the village. After he had parted with her he went to the "Running Horse," a well-known public-house in the neighbourhood, where he had some ale and a game of skittles. He remained at this place about an hour and a half, or it might be nearly two hours. He then left, and bent his steps homewards. As he was proceeding along he, according to his statement, observed the door of the prosecutrix's residence partially open. He entered the garden, went up to the door, and found it fastened with a chain, which he endeavoured to slip back, being under the impression at the time that his "young woman" was inside. He called her by name several times, but received no answer. While thus occupied he all of a sudden received a blow on the back. He turned round, and was struck again on the head. It is not at all surprising to any of us that he should lose his temper. After the infliction of a third blow from his female assailant he naturally enough became furious. He wrested the broom from her hand, and strove to get at her by springing on the balcony. Would he have done this if his intentions had been felonious? Not at all likely, I should say. He was then placed *hors de combat* by another blow from the housemaid's mop. A very little more and the prisoner would have been killed outright, and you would have been spared the trouble of trying him on the present charge. Gentlemen, I submit to your consideration all these circumstances, which require your consideration. I do not believe for one moment, when you have weighed over the matter in your minds, you will ruin the prospects of this young man—blast his reputation, it may be, for life—by returning a verdict of guilty upon such a groundless and trumpery charge. There is no proof of felonious attempt—no proof whatever that he was actuated by any other instinct than curiosity in being at the door of the prosecutrix's house. I admit that he acted in a most imprudent and indiscreet manner—so have many other young men under similar circumstances—but I emphatically deny that he had burglarious intentions."

"Burglars' implements were found upon him, you should remember, Brother Jawkins," observed the judge.

"So the police aver, my lord," returned the advocate. "Indeed, they are so prone to put the worst construction in cases of this sort, that it would not surprise me if they called a toothpick or a pencil case burglars' tools. The prisoner denies this. He asserts that the implements found on him are nothing more or less than tools which he uses in his business."

"What is his trade, then?" inquired a juryman.

"From what I have been informed I am led to the conclusion that he is a sort of handy man at two or three trades—he has worked as a smith, he has turned his attention to mechanical appliances, and is the inventor of a crane of a novel description. This is his rough draught of its form."

Mr. Serjeant Jawkins held forth a large mechanical drawing, which the judge and jury understood as much about as they did of the Sanscrit language.

Nevertheless the diagram had its desired effect.

"It is quite clear," said Serjeant Jawkins in continuation, "that no robbery has been committed. Nothing has been stolen from the house of the prosecutrix, and I maintain that it is equally clear that no robbery was contemplated. The prisoner has been roughly and, I may say, unmercifully used by the pugnacious Mrs. Pocklington and her valiant servant-maid. But, hardly as he has been dealt with by the relentless prosecutrix, he will, I feel assured, be recompensed by an acquittal from the hands of a jury of his countrymen."

Mr. Serjeant Jawkins sat down. He had done his best for Peace, whom he had defended with wonderful skill.

The Judge summed up in a few words. He said, after a review of the evidence, if the jury had a doubt as to the prisoner's intentions, they were bound to give him the benefit of it.

They returned a verdict of not guilty without leaving the box.

"I knew Jawkins would pull you through," whispered Peace's attorney, as his client entered the prisoners' waiting-room. "You may think yourself lucky, young man."

"I do; and am very thankful to you for suggesting the line of defence," returned our hero. "Believe me, I shall be for ever grateful."

Many of the other prisoners who were tried in the same court were not so fortunate.

Mr. Green was not successful in imposing upon the judge and jury. Unfortunately for this young gentleman, he was "well known to the police." More than one constable came into court to claim his acquaintance.

Mr. Green's recollection failed him. He did not remember to have met the constables before. He put on a look of injured innocence, and again burst into tears. But all this display of grief and contrition had but little weight with the court.

Mr. Green was found guilty.

He was sentenced to one month's imprisonment with hard labour.

He cried as if his heart was about to break.

The gipsy was tried on the same day as Peace and Mr. Green.

It was not clearly established that he had stolen the horse, but it was proved that he had taken it away from its owner's stable, and rode off with it.

His defence was that he intended to return the animal, but he utterly failed to establish this satisfactorily.

He was found guilty. But as it was his first offence, or, more properly speaking, the first time he had been convicted, he was sentenced to six months only.

"It's a lottery, quite a lottery," observed the gipsy to Mr. Green.

"I never thought you would get more than me."

"I've been very unfortunate," returned his youthful companion. "It's those bobbies as did it. It warn't of no manner of use my coming the good boy business while they were in court. But I say, old man, do you know your friend is dead?"

"What friend do yer mean?" inquired the gipsy. "I didn't know as I had any."

"Why him as interrupted you in the lock-up."

"Dead—is he? Poor chap."

It was true enough. Two days before the assizes commenced the ill-fated man breathed his last. He was born and bred a gentleman, was of an ancient and honourable family, but in early life was afflicted with a fatal propensity for gambling and betting.

All the years of his life were wasted, his moral principles were undermined. He was, of course, a prey to sharpers.

He became reckless, lost his status in society, and ultimately, in the dire straits in which he found himself, had recourse to forgery.

His family, to save his reputation, paid the forged bills. Nevertheless, the man could not turn aside from his evil course. He had got into a vortex, a sort of maelström, from which he could not release himself. His end we have already chronicled.

It is not easy to estimate the pernicious effects of betting in this country.

It affects all classes, impoverishes the wealthy, makes criminals of the middle and lower classes of the community, fills our gaols, and is, in point of fact, the ruin of scores of thousands of persons, who, but for this fatal propensity, would, in all probability, have continued to be respectable and honourable members of society.

Nothing tends to demoralise the youth of this country compared to the practice of betting.

It is quite time the Legislature should take active measures to suppress, as far as lies in their power, this widespread evil.

CHAPTER XIX.

PEACE'S PROVINCIAL TOUR—THE "OLD CARVED LION."

WE now arrive at another phase in the history of the criminal whose career we are shadowing forth. Peace, after his release, returned to his native town, and resided for many months with his mother.

To all appearance he was a good citizen, and an industrious man enough, who managed to earn sufficient for his own requirements.

It was not known in Sheffield that he had "been in trouble." Those who were interested in his welfare were in great hopes that he would turn from dishonest courses and taste the sweets of honest industry.

Certainly for a long time after the "Gothic Cottage" affair he was more circumspect in his conduct and general behaviour. For the greater portion of his life he seems to have lived on the border line of respectability and decent dulness, and at times appeared to settle down to an honest life.

But he deliberately chose evil for good—the old craving for adventure and excitement would come over him again, and he would plunge headlong into the realms of desperate lawlessness to re-emerge shortly in the daylight as a quiet and steady young member of society.

His single-handed self-reliant way of going to work is perhaps the most notable of his characteristics.

He trusted to himself and no one else.

Whilst this saved him from the danger of weak and treacherous accomplices, it made much larger demands upon his audacity and self-possession.

Thus it came to pass that thousands for whom a vulgar career of crime and violence has no attractions are compelled to feel some interest in a man who is almost unique in the annals of crime.

It is not so much, however, for his commanding superiority in any one department of criminal activity as for the rare combination of his various talents that Charles Peace commands attention.

He was a veritable genius, who reached a high level of excellence in many branches of his profession.

There have been more daring highway robberies and more extensive burglaries than any which he is known to have committed.

But few men have caused more widespread terror, or created more profound attention by the suddenness and the brilliant success of their exploits.

It would be a great misfortune if the boldness and fearlessness of this bad man were to blind even the most thoughtless to the utter worthlessness of his character.

In shadowing forth his lawless career we are under the impression that it will act as a warning to those who peruse these pages.

It will prove beyond all question the truth of the axiom, "That a life of crime is always a life of care."

In nothing does his baseness more transparently appear than in his miserable apologies and self-justifications with which his religious experiences are interlarded.

Assuming, as we are anxious to do, that these pious utterances of his later days are not wilfully insincere, they nevertheless betray an utter moral blindness.

He was very willing to call his past life wicked in general terms, but for his worst transgressions he had some extenuating plea, which destroyed the validity of his assumed penitence.

If he could have been turned loose upon society again, one can hardly venture to hope that his future life would have corresponded with his edifying conduct in gaol.

The curiosity of the public to know all about Peace and his life need not be regarded with too despondent an eye.

If any adventurous and high-spirited youth sees anything to admire in our hero's career he will do well to remember that the grandest successes of a criminal course are at the best but wretched failures.

Peace had probably a far smoother life than most offenders of equal activity.

Yet he spent some considerable part of his time in prison, and in the full noontide of his prosperity hardly reaped as much fruit from his misapplied talents as those talents would have yielded in any honest walk of life.

Peace's strongly marked preference for the revolver was fatal to the picturesque development of his talents.

The truth is, that the particular offender had no special affection for blood-shedding.

Strong as were the fascinations of a criminal life, he chiefly had an eye to business.

In the heat of passion, or with a view to save himself, he was thoroughly unscrupulous about taking life, but he was not anxious to compromise himself by any needless slaughter.

Yet for coolness, promptitude, and self-reliance he has seldom been surpassed.

He never suffered himself to be betrayed into any acts of overwhelming fatuity and oversight such as those which have often led the most skilful to their ruin.

In him there was an assemblage of qualities such as one man rarely possesses.

Peace took great interest in carving, architecture, and works of art of every conceivable description. While at Sheffield, during the few months he remained a decent member of society, he paid frequent visits to the museums and other institutions, and he promised to compete for the prize in wood-carving in the forthcoming exhibition.

But the old feeling for change and adventure came over him, and he determined upon leaving his native town for a while. Business was not very brisk with him at this time—so he thought it advisable to shift his quarters.

He had purchased a number of cheap, showy, attractive-looking prints, together with a large collection of photographs, many of which were copyright, being reproductions from well-known pictures.

In addition to these he had a number of other photographs, which it would not have been advisable for anyone to sell, seeing that they rendered the vendor liable to imprisonment under Lord Campbell's Act.

But this Peace did not much care about.

He felt assured that he was well able to evade the law.

Having renewed his hawker's licence and packed up his goods in as small a compass as possible he bade adieu to his mother and friends at Sheffield and set out on his pilgrimage.

A wandering life was consonant to his general disposition and temperament.

Shouldering his pack with his stout oaken stick and his dog, "Gip," he commenced his journey.

It was only spring time, and he had the best part of the year before him. He paid a visit to Worksop, Huddersfield, Marborough, and Barnsley, calling at several hamlets and villages of lesser note.

He made a long stay in the last-named place; he met there a young man who was a "nigger delineator," as they term themselves in the advertisements in a certain theatrical paper. Peace found in this person a congenial spirit, and they took a commodious room in the town and gave "nigger" entertainments three nights in the week—namely, Saturdays, Mondays, and Wednesdays. The two first were the most profitable, the working class being usually more flush of money.

Peace and his brother artist were tolerably successful, playing on most occasions to a small profit. They would in all probability have continued these performances had they not been brought to a close by Peace's companion signing articles of engagement with a troupe who visited the town on a provincial tour.

Peace, therefore, left and proceeded to the next town with his wares.

In some of the places he visited he was tolerably successful. He sold many prints and photos, and realised a fair profit.

Sometimes he put up at a roadside inn, while at others he took lodgings in a quiet, respectable cottage for a few days.

At this time his life could not be considered in any way disreputable—he was sober and industrious.

It is true that during his peregrinations he was in no way particular about disposing of prints and photos of a contraband nature, but he used a great amount of discretion in his dealing in goods of this description.

It was towards the close of a bright autumnal day that he arrived wearied and footsore in sight of a roadside inn, which stood half-way between two villages in Yorkshire. The sign of this wayside inn was the "Old Carved Lion."

Over the facia of the establishment was a wooden effigy of the king of beasts. Who carved this hideous animal it is not possible to say—it was about on a par with others one sees in houses of public entertainment in the metropolis and elsewhere.

About thirty yards off the "Old Carved Lion" stood a handpost, with its four white arms pointing down the four cross roads.

Some few years before there had been only one handpost within four miles of this spot, and that so defaced and overgrown with moss that it was impossible to decipher a letter.

But fortunately, a nobleman who lived in the neighbourhood happened to lose his way among the dark woods which encircled it, and did not arrive home till his soup was ice, his fish rags, and his sirloin of beef a cinder.

An order was consequently passed by the bench that handposts should be erected in all the parishes under their surveillance at every cross road and turning—the expenses to be defrayed by the funds of the respective parishes.

In rural districts, before any improvements are permitted to be made or nuisances removed, a human being must die or a person of note be inconvenienced.

In the days of the defaced handpost, before railways were in vogue, the "Old Carved Lion" had been a large coaching hotel, furnished with an unbounded amount of accommodation for man and beast.

At the time we make its acquaintance the landlord had turned small farmer, and had aggrandised his stables into barns, and degraded his spare bedrooms into lumber garrets.

However, the good, dry skittle ground still remained, and the hum of voices and incessant rumbling from within proved that this scientific game did not lack supporters.

It was a low cattle-shed kind of place, with benches down the walls and at either end.

On the opposite corners were two small tables, fitted with mugs and pipes.

A portly individual in a white apron filled up the doorway as Peace arrived in front of the old village inn, in the front of which was a horse-trough, a large chestnut tree, and a post bearing at its top the sign of the house.

"Good day, friend," said Peace to the host of the "Carved Lion." "I'm wearied and footsore, and crave a little rest and refreshment."

"Both are at your service, neighbour," returned the landlord, making way for the new comer by withdrawing into the bar.

Peace entered the parlour, and in a few minutes a mug of of ale, together with some cold meat and pickles, were served him, which he devoured with evident relish.

Meanwhile those in the skittle ground were busily occupied.

"Come on, lads, another ge-ame!" cried a lusty, young fellow, with his sleeves rolled up to his shoulder. "Come on, mates, one more. Ye doant mean to say ye ha don yet."

"I doant know 'xactly what to say about it," replied a middle-aged man, who was also in his shirt sleeves. "I tell ye what it be, ye a deal too good for me, a doubt."

"Noa—noa, come on," returned the other, with the mellifluity of a Whitechapel skittle sharper. "Never fear, guv'nor, luck will be sure to change. Doant be so quavery mavery over it. Let's have one more pint for I'm jolly dry."

"You start first, then."

"Get out of my way some of you chaps, and make yourselves look less," said the young man, in a voice prophetic of victory.

Taking from the ground a wooden missile in the shape of a cheese, he poised it between his fingers as if it had been a pebble, and, casting the whole weight of his body, pitched the ball towards the upright pins. It struck the front pin on the left shoulder, and, pirouetting round the ring, knocked all down.

"Brayvo—brayvo!" cried the rustics, knocking their great mugs against the table. "A floorer."

"That was a squiver," said one of them. "Nothing like a flat ball to tiddle 'em over."

"Fust hoss to Bill," cried another, chalking down one on the table.

"You've got your Sunday play on to-day," said the other, as he took the ball in his hands.

His throw was less fortunate.

Only one pin fell, which, after rolling among the others and creating a false interest for awhile, calmly subsided in the dust.

"There, I give 'ee the game and the pot. There's no tackling ye at skittles to-night, that's sartin; and I can't make no how of it either."

"Who's next—next?" cried the victor. "Will e'er a one of ye have a shy for a pot, or wont ye? I'll tak two to one I gets the three fronts, and I'll take it even I floors 'em."

"I'll back Billy agen 'ee for a gallon, if ye like," cried a man.

"Nay, nay," cried a loud but not inharmonious voice; "if old Nick were here——"

"Hoosh! hoosh!" shouted out half a dozen of the throng.

"Who cares about your hooshing? I beant afeared

of no mortal thing; no immortal, for the matter of that; neither man, beast, or sperrit."

The voice came from a young woman, who was finely, though perhaps almost too lustily, formed.

"Ye're all a pack of fools!" said she, giving her head an indignant shake. "A frightenen yourselves about Mother Brickett's ghost. Who is there as has seen it, I should like to know?"

"I ha'," said a man. "I wer a walking across the common here, when I found a somethink white and ghastly walking by my side."

"How big was it?"

"About my height, as nigh as can be. An' it never sed a word. An' just as I was ready to drop, it fanished away."

"And then we all knows," said another, "as only t'other night her voice was heard in the passage by the tap-room where she called Brickett three times by name, and many bein' by. An' it was only yester-night as she came and patted the white cow while Clara wer a milkin' on it."

"This be very sartin," said a tall, pale woman, with a child in her arms: "if she could come back arter she'd gone she 'ould. Her mind was all here when she died. When she was in her last hour her little darter came up to see how she was agoin' on. 'Mind the bisness,' said she, quite sharp; and when Brickett came up, she sent him down pretty quickish. 'Don't mind me, mind the customers'—them were her last words. And she were an audacious woman after money, sure alive."

There is hardly any country place in the United Kingdom but owns some superstitution, which many of the inhabitants have full belief in.

At all ages, and in every place, there have been found many who have entertained the belief that at certain periods the dead are permitted to revisit the earth for a brief period; and it was said in the neighbourhood that the deceased landlady of the "Carved Lion" could not rest in her grave without, in disembodied spirit, occasionally hovering about the old hostelry.

She had been a hard-fisted, money-loving woman in her time, and the frequenters of the inn were wont to talk about her ghost being seen on the common, in one of the dark lanes or elsewhere, in the "witching time of night."

"She must have growed a good bit since she died," said the woman, who had been called Nelly, "for she was a good deal shorter than that gawk there when she wur here. It's all nonsense, I tell 'ee. If people goes to a better world they don't want to come back to a place like this, and if they go to another place——"

"Hoosh—hoosh!" exclaimed several voices.

"Get along with 'ee with yeer hooshing. It's only the truth that I am speaking," exclaimed the young woman.

Doubtless an altercation would have ensued, but the subject was dropped upon the appearance of a stranger.

This was Peace, who had finished his repast in the parlour, and strolled into the skittle-ground.

"Your sarvant, sir," said one of the rustics to Peace.

"Give you good evening, friend," said our hero. "Good evening to one and all."

The villagers made room for him on one of the forms which ran by the side of the building, and Peace sat himself down.

"Ha' the first drink of the new pot," said a broad-shouldered man to a companion by his side, "an' don't 'ee cuss and swear. I hate to hear a man swear for nothing."

"I'm not going to drink your froth for 'ee," returned the other. "I'll ha' some. An' you'll find it as thick as molasses, I'll warrant. Bricket poured a lot of beer into a barrel without clearing out the dregs, and a prutty mess he's made of it. The way business is done here now would make his dead wife walk if anythin' could."

"What, yer grumbling agen as usual?" said another of the company. "Don't be a runnin' down Bricket, for he's a good sort."

"Who says he aint?" cried Nelly; "but some people are never satisfied."

"Right you are, lass!" exclaimed several, for it was evident enough that the young woman was a general favourite.

"Aint nobody seen nothin' of never a hat nowhere?" inquired a thin old man in a querulous voice, twisting in and out of the crowd like a ferret in a rabbit burrow.

"One 'ud think your silly old head were inside on it a wanderin' about like that there," said Nelly.

"Don't 'ee say much to him," whispered the woman with a child in her arms. "Poor Nat Peplow has aged wonderful these last three years. He don't seem like the same man."

"Ho, ho!" guffawed a rustic. "There aint much left of Nat now—

> Poor old hoss! poor old hoss!
> Once I eat the best of hay,
> And lived in a foine stall;
> But now I eats the short grass
> As grows agen the wall.
> Poor old hoss! poor old hoss!
> Thee must die."

"Ah! ye may laugh and sing," said Nat, shaking his head and his voice quavering. "I mind the time when I used to troll that same ditty to grey hairs. It's right it should fall back on me now."

"Poor old hoss!" chanted Nelly.

"But when I wur young I was as lissom as ever a young man here. I taint so strong now as I should be, though when my feyther wur eighty years old he could carry a sack of wheat up a ladder into a granary; and my mother's hair when she wur an old 'ooman was as black and shiny as jet, and growed over her shoulders like a wild colt's mane.

"I don't know rightly what mak's me weaker than they. My arm be a' withered up like a burnt piece of pig's flesh, an' my poor chest do hurt me when I breathes. I think the beer can't be so wholesome and nourishing as it yoosed to be."

And Nat, taking his half-pint mug from the table, peered into it and found it empty.

"Why it's run out!" he cried.

A hoarse giggle from a sun-burnt country lad pointed out the culprit.

"All run out a' the top, I s'pose," he added, resignedly. "Now, Bricket, let's have another half-pint o' twopenny, and draw it thickish, 'cos I aint had my supper."

Nat always liked his beer by instalments of half-pints, because he thought that he got more that way.

Sometimes he drank as many as eight half-pints, on which occasions he would chuckle gravely in his sleeve, and persuade himself that he had cheated the landlord of a noggin.

"GOOD DAY, FRIEND," SAID PEACE, TO THE HOST OF THE "CARVED LION."

Peace had by this time become familiar and on friendly terms with many of those who were assembled in the skittle-ground. The young fellow who had been playing when we first made the acquaintance of this establishment, asked Peace to have a game.

"Don't 'ee p'ay wi' him, master," said Nelly ; "he be's too much for any on 'em here, and ye won't ha'

much chance wi' him unless you are a good hand at the game."

"I'm not much of a player," returned Peace, "but what matters that ? We are only going to play for amusement or for a mug of beer. It don't much matter who wins or loses."

"Please yourself, then—it aint any business of mine."

"Let 'em alone, Nell—there arnt no skittle sharpers here," said a man at one of the tables. "Let 'em be, lass."

Nell shrugged her shoulders, and sat herself down on one of the forms.

The players went to work in good earnest. Peace succeeded in knocking all the pins down at one go.

This exploit was greeted with loud bravos.

His antagonist, however, was equally successful, and the game resulted in a draw. Another game was played; this Peace lost.

"I've done better than I expected," said he, "and I think I had better leave off now. I am evidently no match for you."

"Come," said Nell, "if ye're done skittlin' let us be going in doors, and ye can finish yer ale there."

Many of them now left, those that remained repaired to the parlour.

CHAPTER XX.

THE OCCUPANTS OF THE PARLOUR—A CONVIVIAL PARTY.
PEACE bent his steps in the direction of the bar of the establishment.

As he was proceeding along, a voice shouted out—

"Yer're beant a goin' to leave us, sir, be'est thou!"

"No, no, friend," returned our hero. "I shall join you in a minute or so."

"Aye, that be right," exclaimed the same voice.

Peace went in front of the bar, and said to the landlord—

"I don't want to go any further to-night. Can I have a bed here?"

"Ah! surely," answered the host; "for as many nights as thee likes. The more the merrier."

"Good. Then that's settled."

He returned to the parlour. Over the mantel-piece of this was a smoke-bleached board, on which was inscribed, in dingy yellow letters—

When first I came I some did trust,
And did my money lend;
But when I asked for the same
They soon forsook their friend.
Now my cure is no man's sorrow—
Pay to-day and trust to-morrow.

However a scrawl of chalked hieroglyphics on the bar door proved that the practice of the publican was less resolute than his professions.

"I think I'll ha' another half pint," said the old man, who had been called Nat. A little girl, who served the beer and tobacco brought in the liquor the old man ordered.

"Ye've travelled a greatish distance, may be?" said one of the company to Peace, glancing at his boots, which were begrimed with mud and sand.

"Pretty well, as far as that goes. I can't say exactly how far I've walked, not knowing the ground."

"Ah! I see. A stranger to these parts."

"Yes. I'm on a tour."

"For pleasure?"

"Well, no, not altogether pleasure—business. I'm a picture-frame maker by trade, and deal in prints and photos. Would you like to see some of my wares?"

"Ah! that un should," said several.

"Well, then, so you shall."

He was about to open his pack when a noise of footsteps was heard descending the stairs, and in another moment the broad form of Farmer Wilmot filled the doorway.

"Here, my lads," said he. "It isn't often I give you a treat; but as I've sold my whate and got a good price for it, and as, moreover, this be my son's birthday, I'll give 'ee somthing to drink his health."

He placed several pieces of silver in the girl's hand, and said—

"Give it 'em out in the sixpenny, my little maid, and then what they do drink will do 'em good."

The rustics gave a loud cheer and thanked him again and again for his generosity.

He appeared to be well known to all present, with the exception of Peace, who never remembered to have seen him before.

"Good-by, lads, and don't mek beasts on yourselves. Ale, in moderation, won't hurt anyone; but too much on it is good for no man. Good-night to all."

And with these words the honest farmer mounted his grey mare, which was standing at the door of the hostelry, and trotted off in company with two friends, similarly mounted.

"I be downright glad he's sold his whate," said one of the rustics. "He aint all eyes and ears like some measters, and he knows how to let a poor man off his first fault."

"He was one of us once, ye see, sir," said another, addressing himself to Peace. "He's bin taught to eat poor man's bread and to do poor man's work, and he knows what it is as comforts a poor man's heart. It is only such as he as pities the poor. The rich and idle don't pity, know not what hard work, nor hunger, nor sufferin's loike."

"Aye—that be true enough," said Nat. "He's as good as gold, an' his 'art be in the right place."

"I hope he'll get home safe and sound," said Peace; "but I suppose there aint many robbers about this part?"

"Lord, love ye, no—never a one," cried several voices.

"You've forgotten young Measter Boucher," quavered the aged Nat. "I be an old man, but I mind things better nor you do, seemingly. He was a drivin' home from Bilstoke Fair, and just as he was agoin' up a bit of a hill, with trees on both sides, he felt heavy on his chest, as if he had a fit comin' on, only instead of a fit it was a stout rope, which two men held across the road, and tiddled him over out of his gig. And when he was down they was on him in a minnit, and plundered him of his watch and ten yellow sovereigns."

"That's the story he went home and told his mother," said Nell, scornfully, "but I can pretty well guess how it was. Some of them flaunting hussies got and colly-fogled him into the booths to dance with 'em, and while he wer a thinkin' how pretty he wer a doin' his steps, whip! goes his money and watch out of his pocket into theirs."

This speech was greeted with roars of laughter.

"Ah, Nell, thee boest a knowin' one," cried several.

A portion of the beer the farmer had paid for was now brought in by the little waitress. It was handed round in brown mugs to the company. The farmer's health was drunk, also that of his son.

Peace opened his folio of prints, plain and coloured. Several were spread out upon the table, and regarded with curious and inquiring eyes by the occupants of the parlour.

Peace had pictures to please persons of different tastes. Some were bits of rustic scenery, farm-yards, horses ploughing, hay-making; others consisted of highly-coloured sporting subjects, such as hunting, ratting, and deer stalking; but, as it would never do for an itinerant dealer in these commodities to confine himself to one particular class of art, he had specimens of every conceivable variety, suitable to persons of opposite tastes; pictures addressed to persons of a devotional turn of mind formed a large element in his stock in trade. The Holy Family, the head of our Saviour, together with three young gentlemen in surplices, casting up their eyes, were there in abundance; also a young lady clinging to an impossible-looking cross, her garments dripping with wet, was another. This fine specimen was called "The Rock of Ages," the title of the young gentlemen in surplices being, "We Praise Thee, O Lord." He had also large photos of the "Light of the World," together with a variety of others of a similar character. These subjects went down with some of his customers, while others would not honour them with a cursory glance.

One print, entitled the "Labourers' Best Friends," was greatly admired by the frequenters of the "Old Carved Lion."

The subjects represented were a substantial piece of fat bacon, a quartern loaf, half a cheese, a foaming tankard of ale, and a clay pipe.

"Ah, that be summut loike," exclaimed several, "I call that wonderfully natural, as real as life itself; I should loike to ha' that. How much be it, measter?"

"Cheap enough," answered Peace, "only half-a-crown."

"Umph, I wish it was in a frame."

"I'll undertake to frame any of my prints at cost price."

"Do un, now?"

"Yes, you can have a frame from a shilling to a sovereign—according to the quality."

"I'll come and sit by you," said Nell to Peace, "because you are a clever man, I'm thinking."

"I am very much flattered, I am sure," he answered with a smirk.

"So un ought to be," said another of the company, "it aint many as Nell condescends to flatter."

A young peasant and peasantess, as Mark Twain would say, making eyes at one another after the approved fashion, attracted the young woman's attention.

"Now I call that a wonderfully well done picture," said she.

"Do you like it?" asked Peace.

"Yes, very much."

"Well then I shall beg of you to accept it.

The girl coloured up, not rightly understanding his meaning.

"What be hesitating about, Nell?" said old Nat, "Don't ye understand it's given to you as a present?"

"Oh, I cannot think of having it without paying for it."

"But I desire you to do so—nay, I insist," cried Peace, rolling up the print in a sheet of paper, and handing it to the young woman.

"Oh, I didn't mean to beg it of you," said she.

"I know that—I give it to you of my own free will; so say no more about it."

This act of generosity produced a favourable impression on all present, and Peace became very popular. Several present bespoke prints, and after the whole of them had been inspected they were packed up and put aside for the rest of the evening.

The whole of the company then sat down to enjoy themselves, and, to say the truth, in their homely way they did so, very much more so than many of their betters.

"Ah, I yoosed to be mighty fond of pictures," said old Nat, "but, lord, I don't seem to ha' the taste for anything loike I had formerly. When a man gets old and well nigh worn out he's not so easily pleased as the young uns—be he, measter?"

"Well, I suppose not, friend," returned Peace, "but

we shall all get old and worn out if we live long enough—we ought not to forget that."

"Now none of your croaking Nat," said a lusty young fellow. "You're good for many years yet. Come, jest give us a song, old man. Nat's been a foine singer in his time," observed the speaker in a whisper to Peace.

"Oh, I dare say."

"Fond of music, sir?" enquired another.

"Yes, I'm a bit of a musician myself. If our friend will oblige I'll give you a tune or two upon the fiddle."

This seemed to have a magic effect upon the villagers, who thumped the tables till the pots and glasses danced on the board.

"Will 'ee, though? Oh, that be grand!" exclaimed several. "Now, Nat, just mek a beginning."

"You must excuse me, sir, if I break down," said the old man, apologetically; I aint what I yoosed to be."

"He's never satisfied unless he's telling us that," cried a voice. "Come, old man, fire away."

Old Nat cleared his throat with one or two preliminary ahems, and then, in a high treble, trolled a nautical ballad—the first verse of which described the loves of a youth and village maiden, who plighted their troth under a linden tree; the verse ended with a mournful refrain, which was as follows:—

> Now this ere Jack he was hard-hearted,
> Which no true lovyer ought for to be;
> And this here Sall be soon deserted,
> All for to sail on the salt sea.

The words of the ballad described the anguished feelings of the forlorn and broken-hearted girl, who wanders about her old haunts in the village in a half demented state—for never a word does she hear from her cruel and heartless lover.

There is, it would appear, very good reason for this, for the ship in which the young man sailed foundered at sea, and Jack was cast upon a tropical island, where he remained for three years.

At the expiration of that time he was taken on board a passing vessel, and returned home to find his Sall dead beneath the turf in the village churchyard.

The pathetic ditty concludes thus. The young sailor is supposed to be addressing some villagers assembled in the churchyard:—

> Says this ere Jack, with deep emotion,
> "In this world there's now no rest for me;
> My poor Sall's heart I've surely broken,
> All through my sailing on the salt sea."

It was evident enough that old Nat must have had at one time a sweet and sympathetic voice, and even in his decline there was something of it remaining.

Any one who has travelled through the rural districts of England and paid an occasional visit to old roadside inns cannot fail to have been struck by the quaint and curious ditties that are trolled by the villagers.

Many of them are singularly characteristic.

Where these extraordinary specimens of musical composition all come from—for their name is legion—is perfectly surprising.

In most cases the singers never had a copy of the song they sang; and, indeed, if they had, they would in all probability have been none the wiser, seeing that they were quite unable to read the notes.

They learnt it from some one, and he or she learnt it from somebody else, and so on till the original source of the melody is lost in the deep "backward abyss of time."

When we consider with how easy a transition we may pass from the accents of speaking to diatonic sounds, when we observe how early children adapt the language of their amusements to measure and melody, however rude—when we consider how early and universally these practices take place, there is no avoiding the conclusion that the idea of music is co-natural with man, and implied in the original principles of his constitution.

The principles on which it is founded, and the rules by which it is conducted, constitute a science.

The same maxims when applied to practice form an art; hence its first and most capital diversion is into speculative and practical music.

Go where you will, and you will see how wonderfully music and song are blended with the most laborious occupations of humble life, not only as the natural breathing of cheery thoughts and gladdening hopes, faiths, and feelings, but as giving nerve, measure, and harmony to the physical forces of men bending to the most arduous toil.

We will say nothing here of the influence of martial music on the weary battalions of an army on a forced march.

That illustration would not be apposite to the point we are considering.

Anyone who has travelled by sea and land, and visited different countries, must have been struck with the variety—the use and universality—of the songs of labour.

Who that has crossed the Atlantic, and been awakened at night by the " Merrily, cheerily," of that song with which the sailors hoist the great mainsail to the rising breeze, can ever forget the thrill of those manly voices ?

There they stand in the darkness, with the salt sea spray in their faces, and the tarred rope in their hands, holding the long and ponderous yard against the mast, until their rollicking song reaches the hoisting turn, and all their sinews are strung to the harmony of a unison to the telling pull.

Everywhere and in all ages, the week-day music of the world has been the songs of labour by men and women at their toil, and by the birds of heaven singing to them overhead and around them.

And no ear drinks with richer relish the melodies of these outside songsters—no home more safe and welcome does the swallow find than under the eaves of the poor man's cottage.

Go through the densest courts and lanes of Spitalfields, and see what a companionship of bird life the silk weavers maintain in their garrets, even when the loaf is too small for their children.

The papers recently published a touching and beautiful illustration of the fondness which working men show for singing birds.

When the first English lark was taken to Australia by a poor widow, the stalwart, sunburnt, hard-visaged gold diggers would come down from their pits on the Sabbath to hear it sing the songs they loved to listen to at home in their childhood.

An instance still more interesting has been noted lately in connection with one of the large manufacturing towns in North Wales.

The men, women, and children employed in the factories, not many times a week heard the lark's song, or the music of the free birds of heaven.

These loved the bright air and the green fresh meadows too well to sing many voluntaries in the smoky atmosphere of the furnace and factory.

Thus the cheap concerts of these songsters cost the operatives of the mills long walks beyond the brick and mortar mazes of the town.

But thousands thought them cheap at that price.

" Ah! I mind the time when I sang that very song in this room, more than twenty years agone," said Nat.

" Aye—better than that," said a middle-aged man. " It was on the very night that Lord Ethalwood lost his son—the last on 'em as was left. He aint bin the same man since."

" And who might that be ?" enquired Peace.

" Well, his lordship," returned the other—" the owner of the foine estate on the top of the hill, called Broxbridge Hall."

" Ah! a fine place, is it ?"

" Yes, surely—a should think it was."

" Well, never mind about that, his lordship aint half so happy as we are, I'll bet a crown," said another of the company. " Who's for the next song ? Come, Nelly, can't you give us something soft and sentimental, eh ?"

" Nay; I must be for getting home," answered the girl, " an' leave you men folks to yourselves."

She was about to depart, but as Peace had commenced a preliminary flourish on his violin, she sat down again.

The violinist played a fantasia, introducing a number of popular airs which seemed to delight his audience amazingly.

When he brought this part of his performance to a close he was encored.

He then imitated the noises of animals in the farmyard; this sent the rustics into perfect ecstacies of delight.

" They had never heard anything so perfectly natural in their born days"—so they one and all declared.

" Well, thee just does know how to handle the fiddle," said one.

" And mek it speak like a Christian," said another.

" It be a gift," observed another.

Nell now rose to go, but she was not permitted to do so, until she had favoured the company with a song. In a rich contralto voice she sang the following :—

I love the shepherd's artless rhymes,
  A shepherd's joys revealing ;
I love the songs of ancient times,
  Their notes of simple feeling.
They echoed o'er my native hills
  When last I wandered near them,
And now mine ear with rapture thrills
  In distant climes to hear them.

When hopes that could the heart entrance,
  On airy wings have vanished ;
When all the dreams of wild romance
  From memory's page are banished.
Such strains the heart awhile may soothe,
  'Mid foreign wilds deserted,
Though all the joys that pleased our youth
  Have one by one departed.

Sweet as the dream of former years,
  When sleep the eyelids shrouded ;
Sweet as the star that oft appears,
  When all the rest are clouded.
Sweet as the warbler's latest strain,
  When storms the year have shaded;
Or ling'ring rose that decks the plain
  When all the rest have faded.

" Excellent! Admirably sung !" exclaimed Peace. " I'm quite delighted with your voice and your manner of singing."

" I must not stop any longer," said the girl; " I expect I shall catch it as it is. Good-night to all !"

And with these words she tripped out of the room.

The landlord now entered.

" Ye be making merry to-night, friends," said he.

"Ah, surely it's a poor heart as never rejoices. Sit down, Brickett, we ain't goin' to let ee off."

The host of the "Old Carved Lion" did as he was bid.

"Yo've got a bit o' a musician here, among ye," he observed with a merry twinkle in his eye as he glanced at Peace.

"Yes," said old Nat; "another Paganini—that's what the gentleman be."

"How do you know? You never heard Paganini," returned the landlord.

"Aint I? that's all you know about it. I remember my poor feyther a taken me to the theatre when the great fiddler gave a morning performance, and there was a sight of people there surely—and that be a few years ago."

"And what was it loike?"

"Oh, wonderful—never heard anything equal to it. Not but what our friend here is very good and plays a deal in his style. Any more beer to come in, Mr. Landlord?"

"Yes, the farmer's money aint all run out. Will ye ha' the remainder in now, or stop till you get it?"

This venerable joke seemed to be relished by the customers.

The beer was brought in, which was relished still more.

"Now, Nat," said a young fellow. "Here's a pot o' beer for 'ee if yell sing another song. How will ye have it, hob or nob?"

"Hob" is beer placed on the hob to warm; "nob," beer on the table.

"None of your warm beer for me," cried Nat. "Dont 'ee know what my uncle used to say? When my back wont warm my bed, sed he, and when my belly wont warm my beer, sed he, it's time I were gone, 'cos I aint no yoose to the world, and the world aint no yoose to me."

"That's a good saying, I don't doubt, but pitch us a stave, old man."

"The landlord's got more staves than any on us here. Ask him."

"Ah, let's hear Brickett," cried several.

"I aint a goin' to make any fuss about the matter," said the landlord; "I'll do my best."

"Brayvo, brayvo!"

"So here goes while my head's hot—

Come where the heather bell,
Child of the Highland dell,
Breathes its coy fragrance o'er moorland and lea;
Gaily the fountain sheen
Leaps from the mountain green,
Come to our Highland home, blithesome and free.

The red grouse is scattering
Dews from her golden wing,
Gemmed with the radiance that heralds the day,
Peace in our Highland vales,
Health in our mountain gales,
Who would not hie to the moorland away?

Come, then; the heather bloom
Woos with its wild perfume.
Fragrant and blithesome thy welcome shall be;
Gaily the fountain sheen
Leaps from the mountain stream,
Come to the home of the moorland and lea.

"That's something like, Bricket. You've sung it better than ever, and it's a rattling good ditty," cried a voice. "Here's your health, and long life to 'ee."

A large amount of "brown October" had been consumed by this time, and some of the company were giving indications of being nearly "Three sheets in the wind."

There had not been such a merry-making at the "Carved Lion" for many a day; this was attributable in the first place to the liberal supply of beer furnished by the farmer who had sold his wheat, and in the second by the presence of Peace, who fraternised with the rustics in a free and easy manner, which to them was quite charming.

Bricket knew pretty well when his customers had had enough, and he was, therefore, somewhat anxious for some of them to make a move.

Peace was asked to favour them with a little more music—a request he at once acceded to. When he had concluded the landlord touched him on the shoulder, and Peace followed him into the bar parlour.

"They're a merry set of fellows," said he, "but it's almost time for them to give over for to-night."

"Certainly," returned our hero. I'm quite of your opinion. We've had a very pleasant evening—let it now be brought to a conclusion."

"They'll never go away as long as they hear the fiddle going. I know 'em too well for that."

"Then I wont play any more. Enough is as good as a feast; besides I'm tired, and shall be glad to get rest.

"I'll go in and wish 'em good night, and then retire to my bedroom."

"Don't do so on my account."

"No, but I shall upon my own."

Peace went back into the parlour, and told the company that he needed repose, and was about to retire; he wished them all good night. There was a vast amount of shaking of hands, and reiterated expressions of gratitude and friendship, after which Peace was permitted to take his leave, with the understanding that he was to join them on the following evening.

In less than half an hour after he had retired the parlour of the "Carved Lion" was tenantless.

CHAPTER XXI.
PEACE BECOMES ACQUAINTED WITH THE LANDLORD OF THE "CARVED LION."

OUR itinerant print-seller did not want any rocking that night; he had walked many miles in the course of the day, and was dead beat. He did not wake until morning.

Upon leaving his bedchamber he found his breakfast laid in a large apartment on the first floor, called the club-room.

In this place the members of two or three clubs were accustomed to hold their weekly or monthly meetings. The room was large, with a bay window at one end and a smaller one at the other. The walls were covered with pictures and prints of various descriptions in dingy and faded frames.

Peace was shown into the room by the little maiden who officiated as waitress. She was a rosy-cheeked, bright-eyed girl of about fifteen or sixteen summers.

A substantial breakfast was served; this our hero did full justice to, after which he arose and examined the pictures on the walls. While thus engaged the landlord entered to pay his respects to his guest.

"The top of the morning to thee, friend," said Brickett, "I hope you had a good night's rest."

"Yes, thank you, excellent," returned Peace. "You've got some fairish things here in the way of art," he added, carelessly.

"Some on 'em are not bad—so I've been told. My poor father took great delight in picking up pictures and such like at sales. He was a better judge nor what I am."

"Some of them are very good indeed, and some of them, of course, but indifferent. This one must always expect in a miscellaneous collection, but the frames are little the worse for wear."

"I've bin goin' to have 'em done up ever so many times, but, lord, it ed run into money, I fancy."

"Not much," returned his visitor, musingly; "not a great deal, I fancy. If I stop here for a while I'd give you an estimate."

"And don't you think of stopping?" enquired the landlord, who was much taken with our hero.

"Well, that depends upon what business I am likely to do in the neighbourhood. I shall be able to tell you more about it to-morrow or next day."

"Good, I hope un 'ill be successful; we've got a goodish many well-to-do folks about here."

A thin, short man, in a rusty suit of black, with dark rimmed spectacles, now ascended the stairs and entered the "club-room," as it was termed.

This personage was the parish clerk.

"Your servant, sir," said the landlord to the new comer.

"We shall want the room on Monday next, Brickett," said the clerk.

"It is at your disposal, Mr. Overton."

Brickett now introduced Peace to the gentleman in rusty black, and made him acquainted with his occupation.

"From London, sir, I presume?"

"Yes, from London," answered the print-seller. In expeditions of this sort he invariably gave people the idea that he had come direct from the metropolis. As a rule country folk paid greater attention to one hailing from the great city.

"Show Mr. Overton some of your goods. He be a judge of such like commodities," said the landlord, who at all times displayed a willingness to further the interests of his customers.

Peace's stock, or rather a considerable portion of it, was at once brought forth.

The parish clerk's attention was directed more especially to the sacred subjects. He inquired the price of the large photo of the "Light of the World." It was Peace's practice to lay it on a bit, as he termed it, when he found the fish bite; and he did not neglect to do so on this occasion.

Mr. Overton had made up his mind to have the photo, but he shrugged his shoulders, and said he was a poor man.

"Well," said our hero, "I want to do business. "Is there any other you would like?"

After a deal of consultation the clerk chose another.

"Well, I'll let you have the two for eighteen shillings. That's the lowest I can say for them," cried Peace.

"Then I'll have them," said Mr. Overton.

"And would you like them framed?"

"Oh, of course I must have frames for them."

"Of an ecclesiastical character?"

"It would be all the better."

"I will do you the frames cheaper than anybody—that is, if I can get enough orders to make it worth my while to stop in the neighbourhood for a few days."

Mr. Overton paid for the prints, and the framing of the same was a matter to be considered hereafter. He then took his departure.

"Bagged one bird!" exclaimed the landlord, slapping familiarly on the shoulder. "You mark my words—it'll bring 'ee luck, an' ye won't regret stopping at the 'Old Carved Lion.'

"I should like to stop as long as possible, seeing that its landlord is such a good sort."

"You'll do a decent stroke of business afore you leave."

"I hope so."

Peace now shouldered his pack, whistled to his dog "Gip," and sallied forth. He paid a visit to some of the shops in the neighbourhood, and disposed of some prints and photos.

The prices he obtained for them were so low that he did not get much profit, but it was better than nothing, and kept trade moving.

He called at several private houses, and at some he was very successful. He returned to the "Old Carved Lion" in the afternoon, deposited his pack, and had a late dinner.

Taken altogether he came to the conclusion that matters were by no means unpromising.

Towards evening he went for a stroll to learn a little more of the neighbourhood.

As he was taking his way through a long lane he met the girl whom the occupants of the parlour had called Nelly.

There was of course a mutual recognition.

"Well," said our hero, "how did you get on last night? Did you get scolded when you returned home?"

"No," answered Nelly, tossing her head contemptuously. "It was only my fun. Aunt seldom scolds me; she knows I wont stand it."

"Oh! you live with your aunt—do you? Ah! I wish I was your aunt."

"Why?"

"Then I should have a merry, cheerful companion."

"Get out, talking such foolishness," cried the girl.

"I'm not joking—I am very serious."

"Do you take me for a fool?"

"No, anything but that. But I am glad we've met. You'll be able to tell me all about the people in the neighbourhood, and can be of great service to me if you will."

"If I will. What do you mean?"

"Why, in the way of business, you know."

"Oh, I didn't understand you; but what does that matter? Are you going to stop here—at the 'Lion,' I mean?"

"I'm not going away just yet. I want to see a little more of you."

"You are such a funny man, and tell such droll stories. Where did you come from?"

"London, my dear, from London. Did you like the print?"

"Oh, yes, ever so much."

"You'll like it better when it's framed. Bring it to the 'Lion' and I will frame it for you."

"What will it cost?"

"Do you want to know?"

"Yes."

"Then I'll tell you if you'll pay for it now. It will cost just this."

He put his arms around the damsel's neck, and imprinted on her lips a kiss. They were ripe and ruddy, and he felt that he was amply paid.

"Oh, you wretch," exclaimed the girl; "you've got the impudence of the old gentleman, you audacious fellow. I don't like you at all, not a bit! How dare you?"

"Now don't be angry, my pretty Nell," said Peace, in a wheedling tone. "For the life of me I could not resist the temptation. Forgive me."

"You're a nasty, impudent fellow, that's what you are."

While Peace had been indulging in this little innocent

flirtation a lusty young fellow had been watching the two from an adjacent meadow. He ground his teeth with rage, and clenched his fists in a threatening manner, but both our hero and the girl were ignorant of his being near the spot.

"Now," said Peace, "whither are you going?"

"What's that to you?"

"There's no harm in the question. It deserves a civil answer."

"It's no business of yours where I'm going."

"Perhaps not; but I say, Nell—I call you Nell because I don't know you by any other name—let me accompany you for a little way."

"I don't want your company, and wont have anything to say to you."

"But tell me where you live."

"I shan't."

"Ah, yes, you will."

"I tell you I wont."

"You're very unkind. I thought we were friends, but unhappy is the man who places trust in a woman."

The girl looked surprised. Peace spoke in such a mournful tone that she hardly knew what to make of him.

"Was he in earnest, or only jesting?"

"Well," he added, "if you won't have anything to say to me, so be it—these things are hard to bear."

"Get along, man," exclaimed the girl. "What on earth are you talking about? Are you daft? I'll go my way and you go yours."

"So be it, then, but you'll bring me the picture to frame. I have another and a better one for you, remember that. Good evening—good-bye, Nell."

"You've got my name pat enough. Good night."

She held out her hand, Peace grasped it with ardour, and again bade her good-bye.

She passed through the lane with rapid steps—he watched her as she proceeded along.

When she had gone a couple of hundred yards or so, he followed at a respecful distance.

"She's a charming creature, so impulsive—so ingenuous, but I wont bother her any more just now. She's a little nettled, but she'll come to, I don't doubt that. She's not one to bear malice, or to sulk either, if I read her character rightly."

He let her go her way, and turned out of the lane into a bridle road which ran at right angles with it.

At this time he had not the remotest idea as to who and what she was, but he knew there would not be much difficulty in ascertaining all about her, either from Bricket himself, or one of the frequenters of his house.

Peace walked about the locality for half an hour or more after the girl's departure, and noted all the leading residences in the neighbourhood. Although but a village he had passed through, it was a long straggling one, and was more densely populated than he had first supposed.

He now returned and bent his steps in the direction of the "Carved Lion."

When within a couple of hundred yards or so of that well-known "house of entertainment for man and beast" he was suddenly confronted by a powerful-looking rustic who sprang out of an adjacent copse.

The fellow was an ugly-looking customer, and the expression of his ill-favoured countenance denoted that he meant mischief.

"Well," said our hero, "what might be your pleasure?"

"You be's the man I ha' bin a waitin' and watchin' for, and now I've got 'ee."

"Much obliged, I'm sure; and pray, now that you have got me, as you are pleased to term it, what may be the nature of your business?"

"I'll dall soon let 'un know that," returned the rustic, turning up his cuffs. "I intend to ha' it out wi' 'ee."

Peace was puzzled to understand the man's meaning or his intent. He was at first under the impression that he meant robbery.

"If you are a footpad I must tell you that you are much mistaken in your man. I'm as poor as a church mouse—so let me pass without more ado."

"Noa I wun't let 'ee pass, not afore I give 'ee somethin' for yerself. Ye be a pretty varmint to be a takin' liberties wi' my gell."

"Now, look here, my man," said our hero, in a much more serious tone of voice. "I'll tell you frankly I'm not going to submit to impudence from an ignorant yokel like you, and if you don't get out of the way I'll mark you, big as you are. Your girl, indeed, and who is she I pray?"

"Ye know well enough. Don't 'ee think ye can gammon me? I tell 'ee yer're a dirty blackguard—that's what 'ee be."

"You're an impertinent fellow. Are you drunk, mad, or what?" said Peace.

"I'm neither, but 'ee doen't come betwixt me and her, not if I know it."

"If you give me any more of your impudence I'll chastise you on the spot."

"Oh, oh," exclaimed the other, mockingly, "you chastise—well dang it, that be a good un; we'll soon see who's the best man of the two."

And with these words the speaker up with his fist and delivered a straightforward blow. It was as strong as a horse's kick, and had it taken effect as the countryman intended, it would certainly have gone hard with our hero.

The blow was well meant, but like many other well-meant things it missed its mark. Peace, who had been expecting the attack, warded it off, and sprang back some three or four yards; he then ducked his head and ran with all his force full butt at the chest of his powerful antagonist.

The effect was magical; the man was sent reeling, and fell on his back full length on the hard road.

He was never more astonished in the whole course of his life.

Peace, who was wonderfully agile at this time, had given him no time for reflection, and to say the truth the rustic had never counted on this novel mode of attack.

He was partially stunned by the fall, but recovering himself a little he rose to his feet. Peace did not give him time to pull himself together, but again ducking his head and running forward with all his might he again laid his foe prostrate.

"Now then, my fine fellow, that will teach you to be a little more cautious. You are too great a coward to hit one of your own size."

Once more the man regained his feet, but it was evident enough from his staggering that he had been seriously injured.

Wild with fury at being mastered by so insignificant-looking man as Peace, he rushed forward to annihilate if possible his active and cunning adversary.

He let fly with his right and left, but Peace was far too artful to allow him to get within reach; he again sprang back and, whirling round the stick he carried, he delivered a terrific blow therewith on the countryman's right temple.

Peace's dog "Gip" now sprang at the man and laid hold of one of his legs.

The countryman cried out "Murder!" several times.

"Call yer dog off—call him off! It bean't fair."

"If you've had enough I'll call him off," said Peace.

"Call him off then. Drat it, he's got hold of my leg. Do'ee call him off."

Peace did as he was bid.

Then, panting, bleeding, and fairly cowed, the village athlete stood for awhile humiliated and crestfallen.

"You've brought this on yourself, my fine fellow," said our hero. "You're a big strapping chap, but you see size and strength aint everything. Take my advice, and think twice before you commit an assault upon those who have never done you any harm, and with whom you have no just and reasonable excuse for quarrelling."

"Didn't you meet Nell in the lane? Answer me that."

"I am not bound to answer every fool's question," returned Peace. "What if I did meet a young woman in the lane, or anywhere else for the matter of that, am I to be called to account by a fellow like you? You must be little better than a born idiot to suppose such a thing for a moment."

"I'll ha' it oot wi' 'ee some other time."

"Will you?"

"Yes, I will."

"Look here, my friend," said Peace, "you may think yourself lucky in being let off so easily this time. The next time you attempt to lay hands on me I'll put a bullet in your brain. I'm in earnest, and mean what I say. I will shoot you if you endeavour to again assault me. So now beware."

The man rubbed his eyes and looked hard at the speaker.

"Do you comprehend?" inquired the latter.

"I hear what you say."

Strongly built and muscular as he was, the countryman was by this time as weak as a rat; his knees seemed to give way under his weight, he felt giddy, and was fain to cling to the gate by the side of the road for support.

He was fairly mastered.

"Why, Giles, what be the matter wi' 'ee?" inquired two young fellows, who had seen the affray three fields off, and who now arrived on the scene of action.

"Has the little 'un bin too much for 'ee?"

"He's a devil, that what he be—a devil!" exclaimed Giles, nodding towards Peace.

"You will understand," said the latter, addressing himself to the new comers, "that he attacked me in a violent manner without any reasonable excuse. I never saw the fellow before in my life—have had no quarrel with him until he chose to abuse and assault me, and I desire you to distinctly understand that what I have done has been only in the way of self-defence."

"Why, he's big enough to eat 'ee," observed one of the men, "and ought to be ashamed on himself."

"Go on," exclaimed Giles, "hit a man when he be down, it's the way wi' 'ee all."

"You're simply a blundering fool, and ought to have a month or two on the mill to tame ye," cried Peace. "I'm not at all certain that you didn't intend to rob me."

"Ah, no, he aint one of that sort. Don't 'ee think that, sir," returned the other rustic.

"Well, I hope I'm mistaken. Let it pass. I am mistaken, put it in that way, and so good night."

With these last words, Peace proceeded on his way, and in a few minutes afterwards was safely ensconced in the snug parlour of Bricket's hostelry.

When the time came for the regular frequenters of the establishment to arrive, the topic of conversation was the encounter we have briefly described.

The man Giles was an ill-tempered, overbearing fellow, who was not liked by the village folk, and his discomfiture at the hands of Peace was deemed a good joke by most of them.

The only wonder was with them all, that such a slight-built little fellow could have secured so easy a conquest, and, as a natural consequence, Peace was the hero of the hour.

It was not the first time he had made use of his head as a weapon of defence.

It was a trick he had learnt in early youth—a trick he never forgot. He had, as we have already seen, great coolness and self-possession when in any situation of danger. He was always remarkably active and quick in his movements.

His victory over the village athlete was more attributable to the swiftness and suddenness of his attacks than aught else.

The countryman was as strong as an ox, but he was slow and awkward, and was knocked out of time by his agile and cunning adversary before he had time to recover from his first surprise.

Peace was received by the company in the parlour in a way which was most friendly and flattering—indeed he seemed to be a special favourite with the frequenters of the "Carved Lion," and of course he took good care to make himself as agreeable as possible.

He told a number of amusing stories, played his violin, and was a sort of oracle in the old hostelry. Bricket was greatly pleased with him since he drew customers to his house, being, indeed, a sort of "lion" for a time.

CHAPTER XXII.

PEACE'S BUSINESS ARRANGEMENTS—A VISITOR FROM THE HALL.

FOR some days after the incidents which have been chronicled in the preceding chapter, our hero was actively employed in search of fresh customers. He was by no means unsuccessful, for in a short time he had contrived to obtain a very fair connection.

The orders for frames flowed in apace, but as yet he was not able to execute the commissions for want of a workshop.

He consulted the landlord of the "Carved Lion," who was well acquainted with the neighbourhood and its surroundings.

"I've got a fairish amount of orders," said Peace; "and it's likely that others will follow; but there is a little difficulty in the way."

"And what might that be?" inquired Bricket.

"I can get all my materials easily enough," returned Peace; "but how about a place—a workshop?"

"Ah, I see, of course. You want a snug crib in the neighbourhood?"

"Yes."

"I think I can arrange that. You know Charlie Styant?"

"No indeed, I do not."

"Oh, yes, you do. Not by name perhaps, but you've seen him, an' he knows you well enough."

"Well, what of him?"

PEACE THREW HIS ARMS AROUND NELL'S NECK, AND IMPRINTED A KISS ON HER RUBY LIPS.

"He's a carpenter and cabinet-maker, and has a big workshop just at the end of Dennet's-lane. I dare say he'll be but too glad to let 'ee have part of his shop?"

"Do you think so?"

"Of course I do; nay more I'm pretty nigh sure o' it, and ye'll find him a nice young fellow in the bargain. He'll do anything he can to oblige a fellow-tradesman, I'm sartin sure o' that. Shall I speak to him?"

"I wish you would; but I'm giving you a great deal of trouble about one thing and another."

"Dall it, what's the use of a man being in the world if he can't mek hisself useful to a fellow creature? Besides, we all on us want to make it worth your while to stop as long as possible."

"You are very good, I'm sure. Just speak to this young carpenter and see what he says about it."

No. 12.

"Right you are. It shall be done this very morning."

Peace shouldered his pack and went round to his customers.

Upon his return in the afterpart of the day his landlord informed him that he had spoken to Styant, who expressed his willingness to let part of his shop for a few shillings a week.

"And you can have a bench all to yourself," observed Bricket.

"Nothing can be better. How far is it from here ?"

"Not a quarter of a mile; but we'll go round and have a look at it," said the landlord, putting on his hat. "Nothing like striking while the iron's hot is an old motto of my father's."

The kind-hearted landlord conducted Peace to a long low building built of wood, with a slate roof, at the end of Dennet's-lane, as it was termed.

He introduced his companion to a young man whom Peace recognised as one of the frequenters of the parlour of the "Lion."

"Now ye two are to be better acquainted. Just cast your eyes round, Mr. Peace, and see if this place will suit ye."

"It will suit well enough if I am not incommoding our young friend."

"Ye can have this bench and this end o' the shop all to yerself," said Styant. "I aint got so much business at present as to want the whole shop."

"I don't know how long I may want it," observed Peace; "that all depends upon what orders I get, but it will certainly be for two or three weeks."

"If it's two or three and twenty 'twill be all the better," observed the carpenter, with a smile.

This little matter being satisfactorily arranged, the landlord and his guest bent their steps in the direction of the hostelry.

"Yer had a tidy old scrimmage with Master Giles t'other evening, hadn't 'ee ?" observed the farmer, as they took their way along.

"Yes," answered his companion.

"Short and sweet, wa'nt it, like a donkey's gallop ?"

"It was short, but there was not much sweetness about it."

"About the girl Nelly, eh ?"

"So he said. Is he a lover of hers ?"

"Lord love you, no ! not a bit on it ; but he's spooney on her, so I've been told. But she won't ha' anything to say to 'un. Nell knows too much on him for that."

"He's an impudent, ruffianly fellow."

"But ye tumbled him over like a sack of whate."

"I didn't give him much time for reflection."

"So I heerd," exclaimed the landlord, bursting out in a loud laugh.

"It was as good as a play. The fellow aint liked by any o' his mates; he's a sulky, ill-tempered hound."

"Is Nelly in service ?"

The landlord shook his head.

"In business ?"

"Partly so."

"Does she live near here ?"

"Yes; hard by."

"With her parents ?"

"Noa, she aint got none. She's an orphan."

"Oh ! An orphan ?"

"Yes."

"Does she live by herself, then ?"

"No; with an aunt. The old lady keeps a shop in the next village, and does a little in the market gardening line. She has a large strawberry ground, which is pretty well frequented during the season. Oh, she drives a tolerable trade, what wi' one thing an' another."

"And Nell ?"

"Well, yer see, she's a clever lass, and makes herself generally useful; but she's been a bit spoilt."

"In what way ?"

"Her aunt lets her do pretty much as she likes, but Nell's a good sort and a general favourite, although she is sometimes a little uppish. Is there anything more ye want to know ?"

"No—oh, no," said Peace, colouring slightly.

The two walked on in silence for some minutes after this.

"She was a great favourite with my missus," observed Bricket—"she who is dead and gone now, an' she wasn't a woman to take a fancy to everybody. It was not many as pleased her."

"Ah ! I don't wonder at Nell being a favourite."

"Why ?"

"Because there's something so genuine and ingenious about her manner, and she appears to me to be singularly straightforward for a woman."

"I'm glad you sed for a woman," observed Brickett, coming to a sudden halt and looking hard at the speaker. "I be very glad you sed that."

It was now Peace's turn to laugh.

"You're a bit of a philosopher," he said.

"I mind the time when I wanted all the philosophy I was possessed on; so would you, if you'd been in the same position as I was; but, lor', it bean't no use looking back. We none of us know what we've got to go through in this world, and it's a blessing we don't; leastways that be my opinion, 'cos yer see, Mr. Peace, if so be as we did we should sink down and fall as flat as stale beer afore our journey was half over. We've all our trials an' our troubles, an' arter all I s'pose happiness is pretty well distributed among us. It bean't the richest or the most fortunate as are the happiest. Look at my lord at yonder foine estate, who's a rollin' in wealth; he be a miserable man—much more miserable than either on us."

"I don't know whom you are referring to."

"Why, Lord Ethalwood."

"Ah ! I don't know him."

"But you've heerd on him, I 'spose."

"No, I've not."

"Well, that be strange."

"You seem to forget that I am new to the neighbourhood and its inhabitants."

"Ah, true, I did not think of that. At some other time I'll tell 'ee all about him, but may be ye'll hear from somebody else afore long."

Having made satisfactory arrangements for his workshop, Peace sent orders to a wholesale house in London to forward him several books of gold, together with some lengths of maple wood and German gilding, which would serve his purpose for the manufacture of cheap frames. When the parcel of goods arrived he set to work in earnest; the orders he had received for the inexpensive frames were much more numerous than his commissions for the better class of goods ; he, however, managed to do pretty well with both class of customers.

One morning as he was leaving the "Carved Lion" to betake himself to the workshop, he observed at the bar a powdered lacquey, arrayed in all the paraphernalia of dazzling garments appertaining to persons of his class.

Peace was struck with his appearance, as well he might be; for he was a finely formed man, over six feet in height, with a broad chest, huge limbs, and a proud bearing.

He was decked out in the most gorgeous of liveries, with plush breeches, white stockings, and a large shoulder knot and tags falling over his shoulder.

This radiant individual was conversing with the landlord, who treated him with great deference.

Peace honoured the lackey with a cursory glance as he passed out of the inn.

Upon his return later in the day, Brickett called him into the bar-parlour and said—

"Did you see our swell footman as you passed out this morning?"

"I couldn't help seeing him," returned our hero; "he was so big, and was, moreover, so dazzling, that it was impossible to pass by without noticing him. Who is he?"

"One of Lord Ethalwood's servants—that's all."

"Humph! Well, he's a credit to the establishment, as far as appearance goes, that's quite certain."

"Yes. Well, now just listen to me a moment or so. He came here this morning to order some chartrouse, some bottles of seltzer and soda, together with many other things. It appears that the servants are going to have a party all to themselves. His lordship is in London——"

"And they take the opportunity of enjoying themselves during his absence. Quite right and proper."

"No, not altogether that; his lordship knows of the little affair, which is to come off in a day or two—has given permission, in fact. The butler, who has been in the family for the last thirty years, is a great favourite with his lordship. The butler's fellow servants purpose presenting him with a watch and chain, as a token of their respect and esteem."

"Also very right and proper, I suppose."

"Now, don't be satirical, old man," observed Brickett, with a smile. "Just hear me out. Henry Adolphus——"

"Who is he?"

"The footman."

"Ah! I see; the footman."

"Yes. Well, as I was a saying, Henry Adolphus told me this morning that they were, in addition to other festivities, going to have a bit of a dance. But how about the band?"

"Have Weippert's from London."

"Hang it, don't be so contrary! Two or three musicians will be all they will require. Will you be one?"

"Me! Most certainly, if you desire it."

"You won't lose anything by it."

"Oh, dear, I should suppose not."

"Henry Adolphus has heard of you, and asked me if you were stopping here. I sed yes, in course; and I also sed I was certain sure you would be ready when they required your services."

"You're as good as a father to me," observed Peace, with a smile.

"An yer know, although they are but servants, they are big people in their way at the hall, let me tell 'ee that. And they can do a chap a good turn when un loike."

"I shall be most delighted to make their acquaintance—of that rest quite satisfied. Make what arrangement you like with regard to me—I will do my very best to fulfil it."

"Right you are, old man—leave the matter in my hands."

Two days after this the footman again made his appearance at the inn; he had more orders to give to the landlord—more arrangements to make.

Brickett conducted him into the parlour and introduced him to our hero, who was at the time having his mid-day meal.

"This is the gentleman I wer a speaking to 'ee about Mr. Peace, sir," said Brickett—addressing himself to the flunkey.

"Glad to make your acquaintance, sir," said Henry Adolphus.

Peace bowed.

"I am very glad to meet you, sir," said he.

The footman gave a dignified bend of his body, and handed our hero a card.

It was an invitation to the party to be held at the servants' hall on the following night.

"An you'll have no objection to oblige them with a tune or two?" said the landlord.

"Certainly not, that's understood. Are there any other performers to be there besides myself?"

"A cornet player and a gentleman who plays bass," answered the footman.

"I should like to see them, so that we may know what we are going to do together."

The landlord and his visitor conversed together apart for a minute or so, after which Henry Adolphus said—

"If you see them 'ere to-night or to-morrow morning, will that suit you?"

"Yes, that will do very well."

In the evening of that same day a pale-faced young gentleman, with weak eyes, and a military-looking young man with a heavy moustache, presented themselves at the "Carved Lion," and inquired for Peace.

The first named was the bass-viol player, the other being the gentleman who performed on the cornet.

The three performers repaired to Peace's workshop, where they had one hour's hard practice. This enabled them to keep together—certainly well enough for a beginning. They had another turn at their instruments on the following morning.

The eventful evening arrived. Peace was not permitted to sally forth from the "Carved Lion" without an escort. The landlord and several of his parlour customers insisted upon accompanying him up the hill, on the brow of which was situated the noble mansion known throughout the county as Broxbridge Hall.

Brickett, who had received a card of invitation, was to come later on. He, however, went up to the great gates and lodge at the entrance, and rang the visitors' bell. The porter made his appearance in answer to this summons, whereupon Bricket explained to him in a few words who Peace was, and the reason of his visit.

Our hero was then left in charge of the porter, who conducted him into the servants' hall.

Peace was perfectly astounded at the grandeur and beauty of the place, which had been decorated with flags, garlands, rare and choice exotic plants, and presented all the appearance of a baronial hall of the olden time, such as Nash and Cattermole knew so well how to depict.

The place was crowded with throngs of visitors; the servants, relatives, and friends, together with a vast number of the tradesmen in the neighbourhood, formed on contingent.

In addition to these the parish schoolmaster with some of the elder boys, a few agriculturists, who rented small farms under his lordship, and last, not least, was the girl whom we have known as "Nelly."

Peace had been under the impression that he was

going to a sort of "high life below stairs," about which he had heard so much.

He was, however, of quite a different opinion when he beheld the vast throng of gaily-dressed persons, surrounded with all the appliances which wealth and art could furnish.

He felt perfectly bewildered at the grandeur of the scene, which at this time was lighted up by the rays of the setting sun, which found their way through the many coloured diamond-shaped windows of the apartment.

Henry Adolphus, who was at the further end of the hall, caught sight of our hero as he first entered. With courtly politeness the prize flunkey hastened forward to give him welcome.

"It's vary good of you, I'm shaw," said that personage, after the usual greeting, "vary good to do us the 'onour of being present this hevening. Will you keindly step this way ?"

Peace was conducted by his host towards one of the side tables; here he was introduced to a quiet, sedate, bald-headed, respectable-looking man, whom Henry Adolphus informed him was Mr. Jakyl.

This was Lord Ethalwood's butler.

Had he not been informed otherwise Peace would have concluded that it was his lordship himself.

Mr. Jakyl was reticent by nature; the few words he did utter, however, were courteous and patronising enough.

The butler, however, had so many persons to see, and such a number of little arrangements to make, that he did not remain many minutes in one place.

He was constrained to leave Peace rather abruptly.

"What wine will you take, Mr. Peace ?" said Henry Adolphus.

"None at present, I thank you," returned our hero.

"You must 'ave one glass with me. What say you—champagne ?"

"Thank you, yes."

Two glasses of champagne were filled, and the burglar and the flunkey hobbed and nobbed. Presently the latter's attention was called to another part of the room.

Soon after his departure Peace caught sight of Nelly threading her way through the throng. He hastened towards her.

"You here !" said he in a whisper, when he had reached her side.

"Me—yes. Is there anything surprising in that ?" returned she, with a toss of the head.

"Well, I don't know that it's surprising; it's gratifying to me, at any rate, and makes me feel supremely happy."

"Does it ?"

"Of course, you know it does. How is it you have never shown up since that night ? I've been watching the hours."

"There, that will do. Spare yourself the trouble o' talkin' like a booby. That sort o' thing won't go down here."

"You are a most extraordinary girl," returned Peace. "Hang me if I know what to make of ye. At one time I thought I was a bit of a favourite, but now——"

"Well, what are you a sayin' ?"

"Now you positively flout me at every turn. Of all the persons in this assembly you are the only one I know."

"Ye doesn't know much on me, do 'ee ?"

"Not much, but I want to know more. I wish to become better acquainted with one who has made so great, so favourable an impression on me."

"What brought yer here if yer doesn't know any on 'em ?"

"Because I was invited."

The weak-eyed bass-viol player and the military-looking cornet performer now came forward and offered their hands to Peace, and his conversation with Nelly was therefore brought to a premature close for awhile.

Peace discovered in the course of conversation with his two fellow musicians that an addition had been made to the orchestra—a harpist and a flutist had volunteered their services.

"But positively I tremble," observed the young gentleman with the weak eyes.

"What at ?" cried Peace.

"Well, you see, in case there should be any mistake. We certainly ought to have been introduced to the flutist and harpist, so that we might have had a little practice."

"We shall manage well enough, I dare say," observed the bass-viol player.

A cold collation had been spread out on the huge table in the adjoining room, into which the assembled guests were now conducted.

Mr. Jakyl was to have taken the head of the table, but he had been throughout his life a modest, unobtrusive man, and at his earnest request the village schoolmaster, Mr. Magnet, consented to occupy that place of honour.

He was supported by the bailiff on one side and the head gardener on the other.

All these arrangements had been duly weighed and considered. To many the sitting down at the table was a mere matter of form so far as partaking of the repast was concerned; there were some, however, who did ample justice to the viands placed before them.

After the meal was concluded and several toasts had been drunk, Mr. Magnet rose, and, in a sonorous voice, spoke as follows :—

"Ladies and gentlemen, you will, I am sure, give me your attention for a few minutes. I will not make any large demands upon your patience, but will explain in as few words as possible my reason for my addressing you on this occasion. I am deputed by the members of Lord Ethalwood's domestic establishment to speak on their behalf, and my only regret is that the task was not assigned to a more efficient representative. ("No, no." "Hear, hear." "Can't be in better hands.") That may be your opinion, but it is not mine; however, I will do my best. I think we shall all agree upon one subject, that being the regard and esteem in which our worthy friend, Mr. Jakyl, is held. For nearly thirty years he has had the honour of enjoying the confidence and good opinion of his lordship, and in addition to this his urbanity and kindness cannot fail to have been duly appreciated by all members of this establishment. It is, therefore, with feelings both of pride and pleasure that I present to him, on behalf of the members of this household, a gold watch and chain, as a token of their respect and friendship."

The article in question was now brought forward, enclosed in a handsome case, and laid before the butler by the page.

"Before concluding," said Mr. Magnet, "I shall call upon you to join me in a toast. I need hardly indicate what it is—'Long life and happiness to Mr. Jakyl.' "

This was of course the signal for vociferous applause, which made the servants' hall reverberate to the very echo.

The butler rose in some precipitation, and said he

could not find words to express his feelings, but that he was duly impressed with the honour which had been shown him ; and that, in short, the company were all kindness, and he was all gratitude.

Several other healths were proposed and drunk, and the company now began to assume that of a highly festive character.

There was a vast amount of wine-taking, of mixed conversation, and a noise as of many tongues speaking at once.

One of the young farmers sang a hunting song, with a "tally ho!" chorus, which was rendered vigorously, if not musically.

People had evidently come to enjoy themselves, and they did so to their hearts' content.

Henry Adolphus had been constrained—from the force of circumstances, of course—to partake of wine with so many persons that he was in an effervescent state.

All of a sudden, to the surprise of everybody and the dismay of a few, he rose to his legs for the purpose of addressing the assembly.

"Sit down—don't be so foolish—do pray sit down," cried one of the female servants, frowning at the footman.

"Ish all right, I know what I'm 'bout!" exclaimed Henry Adolphus—"have a dooty to perform."

"Are you mad ?"

"Mary Hann, don't be personal. Be quiet, my girl, be quiet." Then in a louder voice he shouted out, "Mr. Charman !"

"Order, chair !" said Mr. Magnet.

"Mr. Charman and gentlemen," said the footman, "I need not tell you that I'm unaccustomed to public speaking, but I cannot let this hevening pass hover without—without doing what I consider to be a justice to our worthy charman. Gentlemen, Mr. Magnet has put himself out of the way to oblige us. Every one of us can lay our 'ands on our 'arts and say that he has expressed our feelings a deal better than we could have done ourselves. (Hear, hear.) Now, I want to tell you that we ought to be grateful, and I cannot let the hevening pass hover ——"

"Henry Adolphus, do sit down."

"Mary Hann, shut up," said the footman. "I will have my say."

"Oh, it's dreadful. Do get him to sit down."

"We have a little interruption here, Mr. Charman, but that does not matter. I cannot and will not let the hevening pass hover without doing what I consider to be my dooty. Gentlemen, one and hall, my hobject in addressing you is easily expressed, and I intend to keep the hobject in my heye. I'm going to ask you to drink the 'ealth of Mr. Magnet, and at the same time I want you to join me in thanking 'im for all his kindness."

The health of the chairman was drunk with enthusiasm, and, much to the delight of those around him, the pertinacious flunkey sat down.

He had by this time imbibed enough to float a four-oared cutter, and the only wonder was that he did not make a greater fool of himself.

The chairman responded in an amusing speech, and the hilarity was very soon at its height.

It was intimated that everything was ready for the dance, the next room had been cleared, and the musicians were playing some lively strains.

There was a general exodus, most of the company betaking themselves to the ball-room.

Peace and his coadjutors comported themselves very well—the music was bright, crisp, and inspiring.

The musicians were stationed in a gallery at the end of the room, and Peace had no opportunity of mixing with the throng of dancers beneath.

He commanded, however, an excellent view of all that was going on, and was by no means consoled by seeing the girl Nelly dancing with one partner after another, without even condescending to regard him with a passing glance.

This, of course, was irritating to a man of his choleric temperament, but there was no help for it; he was compelled to submit with the best grace he could.

There was a number of young and pretty women among the throng, and, as a matter of course, a vast deal of flirtation took place in the course of the evening.

Mr. Jakyl was evidently anxious that neither his fellow-servants nor his guests should overstep the bounds of prudence.

Some of the young farmers were far too demonstrative and noisy to please the discreet and prudent butler, who, to say the truth, would in all probability feel greatly relieved when the festivities of the evening were brought to a termination.

Those who lived some distance from the hall now began to take their departure, and, in the course of another hour, more than half the visitors had left.

Mr. Jakyl came up into the gallery and personally thanked Peace and his confederates for their services. He at the same time placed wines and other refreshments before them.

He was certainly a well-behaved, considerate man, who never failed to look after the comforts of those who came within his sphere of action.

The guests at the hall now began to leave rapidly and the evening's amusements were brought to a close. The musicians were thanked once more by the butler, Henry Adolphus, and many others of the household, and our hero returned to the old "Carved Lion," in company of its genial landlord, who had been footing it merrily for an hour or more.

CHAPTER XXIV.

LORD ETHALWOOD—A CHRONICLE OF PAST EVENTS—THE SHADOW ON THE HOUSE.

FOR some four or five weeks after this Peace was busily engaged in executing the orders he had received from people of almost every denomination. It was evident enough that he did not intend to shift his quarters for some time, as orders were falling in pretty fast, and he had promised Bricket to regild his frames before he left the village.

Lord Ethalwood returned to Broxbridge Hall. Before introducing him to the reader, we must, for the purpose of our history, give a brief chronicle of past events. He had the reputation of being proud and haughty to a fault. Austere and inflexible as he was in outward appearance, he was not deficient in the softer and more tender promptings of the heart; but he was proud—this fact his best friends could not deny, and therein, perhaps, lay the secret of all his trials and troubles.

He was proud of his name, of his lineage, of his unsullied honour, proud of the repute in which he was held, of his high standing in the county.

As a river gathers force and strength from every tributary stream, so he made every gift heaven had bestowed upon him tributary to his pride.

It was a grand old place he owned, in the county in which he was born. Broxbridge Hall had everything to recommend it. Situated on the summit of a hill, with acres and acres of land spreading out on all sides, fine old woods, fertile land, through which which a silver stream wound its sinuous course, and a house of the old Elizabethan type, together with a princely income. Nevertheless this man was not happy.

Nay more, he was supremely wretched.

No wonder a shadow had crossed over his house—a shadow deep and sinister.

The misfortunes that had befallen him and his were, to a certain extent, attributable to circumstances beyond his control; but he had added to these misfortunes by his own indomitable pride.

People, in speaking of him, said he was just and generous, but very proud.

He was a rigid observer of class distinctions. He paid all persons the honour due to them, and he expected the same in return.

"The Ethalwoods came in with the Conqueror," he would say. "Had fate ordained them to be kings, they would have known how to reign. Old as the line is, there is not a blot on the escutcheon. No Ethalwood ever forfeited his honour."

It is an axiom as old as the hills—much older, it may be, than the honoured line of the Ethalwoods—that pride must have a fall.

Never, surely, was the truth of this more terribly exemplified than in the life of the nobleman now immediately under our notice.

Bertram Lord Ethalwood, married a young creature of surpassing beauty. She was nobly born, but vivacious and volatile. She bore him three children—two sons and one daughter.

The first blow that fell upon our nobleman—a blow which fell upon him "even as a flail falls upon the garnered grain"—was the elopement of his wife with an officer attached to the Indian army.

The injured husband did not show externally any signs of the sorrow which weighed so heavily on his heart. He sued for a divorce, which he obtained without opposition.

His wife, shortly after this, died in Calcutta. It was a relief to him when he was apprised of her death.

He did not marry again, but he loved his daughter and was proud of his sons. His children were the delight of his heart—the very light and brightness of his home was his daughter.

A beautiful, gay, high-spirited girl, who had all the Ethalwood spirit with its attendant pride. Her father literally worshipped her; he watched her beauty as it developed day by day; he pleased himself by fondly imagining what a glorious future was before her.

He could not bear to part with her, and would not upon any consideration be persuaded to send her from home.

He had governesses and masters for her—he did his best to ensure her a good education at home, but it was, perhaps, the most imprudent thing he could possibly do. He made no allowance for girlish gaiety or exuberance of spirits, and the result of this was that the girl began to look upon her home as a sort of prison.

She loved her father, had the greatest respect for his character, but still at the same time she looked upon him as a sort of gaoler, and gloried in evading his rules.

Her brothers she did not see a very great deal of. They spent very little time at Broxbridge Hall; they went to Eton and from thence to Oxford, and were principally under the charge of tutors.

Lord Ethalwood had impressed upon them in a

most marked manner the nobility of their race and the obligation they were under to keep their name unsullied and honour unstained; he left the rest to their teachers.

The name of Lady Ethalwood no one in the household durst mention; his lordship had given orders to that effect. Even his sons and daughter never once alluded to their dead mother.

Whatever they knew or had heard about her they had the prudence to keep to themselves.

The years flew by and the Honourable Miss Ethalwood was approaching her eighteenth summer, and her father was looking forward to the time when she would be presented at Court and take her place among the ladies of the fashionable world.

He almost dreaded this ordeal, for he felt that she would, as a natural consequence, become hurried on into a vortex of pleasure, and be constrained to keep up an incessant round of visits; but a greater evil, a more serious estrangement, was destined to take place before the dreaded time arrived.

When his lordship took up his quarters in his town residence he left his daughter at the old ancestral home, where, during his absence, she reigned supreme. This just suited her, for, like her father, she was immensely fond of having her own way.

With all his intellect and acquirements, how blind was the haughty nobleman to the common affairs of life—how little did he reckon upon the danger which beset his daughter's path at this time!

An Italian professor taught her music and singing. He was, as many Italians are, a remarkably handsome young man, and he had a voice which was simply magnificent.

Bending over the piano, and turning over the leaves of the music, he had ample opportunity afforded him of coming in close contact with his fair pupil.

His visits—or lessons would be the more correct term—were much more frequent during his lordship's absence than they were when he was residing at Broxbridge; even the servants could not help noticing this.

A thought came into the head of the music-master —indeed, it had been there for a very long time; it was this—

"What a grand future I shall make for myself," he murmured, "if I woo and win the Honourable Miss Ethalwood!"

To do the Italian professor justice, he was really not actuated by mercenary motives. He had conceived a passion for his pupil, and, as a natural consequence, she became aware of this without his uttering a word relative to so important a subject.

The professor had all the qualities to captivate one of the opposite sex.

He was light-hearted, animated, had no inconsiderable amount of passionate eloquence, and was, in short, a very dangerous man to hover about a thoughtless and inexperienced girl.

The Honourable Miss Ethalwood inherited much of her father's pride, but that was not much protection when her heart was touched.

In a very short time she became infatuated with the handsome young Italian.

To make use of a common phrase, she was over head and heels in love, or, as Mr. Artemus Ward would say, "I cannot tell you how *muchly* she loved him."

Meanwhile, while all this was going on, Lord Ethalwood had not the faintest notion of the coming storm, and even if a suspicion had crossed his mind he would have dismissed it, for it would have seemed as probable to him that his daughter would fall in love with one of his grooms as with her music-master.

He returned to Broxbridge Hall, and demonstrated all his old fondness for his daughter, and did not observe at this time that her manner was at times constrained.

The professor's visits were now few and far between, but the love between the two grew stronger—the Italian grew bolder—he asked his fair pupil to meet him at an appointed spot in the neighbourhood.

She foolishly consented, and on one occasion when her ardent admirer told her in passionate accents how dearly he loved her she owned that the feeling was reciprocal.

It is not easy to determine whether it was love or ambition that prompted the Italian to make the declaration—it might be both.

It was, however, a base betrayal of trust and a cruel fraud—a most unpardonable deception, a most dishonourable deed.

They plighted their troth. The professor asked the young lady to broach the question to her father.

She drew back a pace or two, and exclaimed—

"Mention it to my father! You must be mad to make such a proposition."

"He would never consent?"

"Consent! He would die first. Oh, you do not know him."

The Italian shrugged his shoulders, and looked on the ground in a desponding manner.

The lovers parted.

A day or two after this the Italian went to Broxbridge Hall for the purpose of giving his usual lesson. He met his lordship in the passage, who bowed stiffly and passed on.

"Can he suspect anything?" murmured the professor, "or is it the natural pride which all the English aristocracy have, more or less? Ah, she's right enough! It will never do to mention the subject to him. Ha, ha, we must elope!"

He told his pupil of the meeting, and informed her also that her parent was stiff and haughty in his manner.

"That is not unusual with him," she answered. "It's his way. Do not take any notice of it."

"Does he suspect aught?"

"No. Oh, dear no!"

While this love-making had been going on there was one in the house who had her own private reasons for suspecting something was amiss—this was the housekeeper in the establishment.

She was under the impression that a little harmless flirtation was taking place, but she had no idea of its nature or extent. Had she been aware of this, in all likelihood she would have mentioned the subject to her young mistress or his lordship.

She, however, deemed it expedient, for divers reasons, to remain silent.

The very last person in the whole establishment to suspect the state of affairs was the master of Broxbridge.

He had unlimited faith in the integrity of his daughter, and, indeed, to say the truth, there was not much excuse to be made for her, save that she was charmed with her lover's handsome person, his musical voice, his fascinating and engaging manners. She was infatuated—so much so, indeed, as to be heedless of the great wrong she was doing, but she had now gone too far to retract.

She consented to elope with her music-master, who had repeatedly suggested a clandestine marriage.

She persuaded herself that he was a gentleman, although a poor one. He was an artist, a man of polished manners, and equal in many ways to her father's friends and companions—in some respects he was their superior.

Poor, giddy, thoughtless girl, she knew but little of the world. Had she mixed more in society she would have hesitated before she took the first false step which led to untold misery both to her and hers.

The end came. She stole one afternoon from the time-honoured walls of Broxbridge, and eloped with Signor Montini.

It would be impossible to describe the despair of Lord Ethalwood when he heard of his daughter's flight. He was frantic for a time, after which he was preternaturally calm; but a storm raged within more terrible than any sudden burst of passion. She had written to him avowing her love for Montini, and informing him at the same time that she took it for granted he would never give his consent. Hence it was she had consented to a clandestine marriage. She implored him to forgive her, to pity and pardon her for her disobedience.

No member of the old Inquisition could have looked more relentless and spectral than did the lord of Broxbridge when he read this epistle.

"She has passed from me, even as did her mother," he ejaculated, in a low deep whisper. "Even as did her mother," he repeated, like the burthen of a song. "Fool that I was, I never counted on this blow."

He took an oath never to look upon her face again. Dear as she had been to him, he was resolved upon thinking only of her as one dead.

This terrible oath he kept unbroken.

He knew but little of Montini, and, strange to say, he was not so embittered against him as might have been supposed. The full measure of his wrath fell upon the head of his undutiful thankless daughter. His love for her had changed to the most deadly hate, which neither time nor circumstances would change.

He was relentless. As far as he was concerned, the noble sentiments conveyed in the words of a celebrated poet, "To err is human; to forgive, divine," never for a moment passed through his mind.

She had brought disgrace upon him. She had sullied the name of Ethalwood by running away with a low-born foreigner, a miserable teacher. The thought was agony. He never would acknowledge her—never more.

It was something fearful to witness the inexorable determination of the injured and unforgiving father, who never for a moment reflected that he was in some measure responsible for the misfortune which had befallen him. Had he been less exacting, given her a wider sphere of action, the chances would have been she would not have been forced into the error which brought with it so much misery.

CHAPTER XXV.
THE CHILDLESS MAN—IN THE HANDS OF FATE.

THE two sons of Lord Ethalwood were perfectly astounded when the news reached them of their sister's elopement with Signor Montini.

They might and, indeed, ought to have taken her part; but they knew pretty well the hopelessness of any appeal to their father, who was not a man to give way when he had once made up his mind.

They had, indeed, seen so little of their sister, had been so estranged from her for so long a time, had left her so entirely to their father's disposal that they did not hold themselves responsible for her actions.

Nevertheless, they found it difficult to comprehend how she could have so forgotten herself.

Lord Ethalwood made no loud complaints.

To all appearance he was as calm and impassible as of yore.

If any one attempted to condole with him he held up his hand in a deprecatory manner, which enforced silence.

His sorrow—his anger lay too deep for words.

He did not interrogate any of the household about his daughter's mode of life, or make any inquiry about Montini.

Servants as a rule are loquacious enough with regard to the movements of their superiors. His game-keepers could, and, indeed, would have told him of rambles in the woods of Broxbridge, of stolen meet-ings in the grounds, but their lord and master at once repressed them.

He forbade them ever to mention the names of either the Italian or their young mistress.

The men of course deemed it expedient to keep silent.

The housekeeper began to open her mind to his lordship.

"I do not desire, madam, to enter into the question, and therefore beg that for now and hereafter you will hold your peace. The past has passed away; let it be forgotten."

The housekeeper made a curtsey and retired.

In a few days after this she received a notice from his lordship, who was then at his town residence, to quit his service.

He did not return till the notice had expired, and she had taken her departure.

She was sagacious enough to understand the cause of her dismissal.

His daughter's lady maid and two other female servants were also discharged.

Upon Lord Ethalwood's return to Broxbridge, he summoned his butler, Mr. Jakyl, to his presence. He was sitting alone in his library at this time, and before him rose, like so many ghosts, all the hopes he had centred in his beautiful daughter. He remembered her as a lovely laughing child—as a merry and artless girl. His brow was dark, and his eyes were red with weeping.

Despite his pride, his sternness, his terrible con-tempt and scorn, there was something pitiful in the proud man's silent, solitary despair.

Never again was he destined to hear the gay young voice—never more to watch the beautiful face. She was worse, ten thousand times worse, than dead. If she had been snatched from him by the icy fingers of death, he could have loved her still—could have visited her grave—he could have spoken of her, but she was dis-honoured and disgraced—she had brought scorn and contempt down upon the very name of Ethalwood.

"Ahem! did you ring, my lord?" said the butler, who had crept so quietly into the room that his master was not aware of his presence. It was a way he had—he was a very soft and gentle in his move-ments.

"Ah, it's you, Jakyl."

The butler bowed.

"Yes, I rang—let me see, what was it for? Ah, I remember. You know the handwriting of your late mistress?"

"Yes, my lord."

"For the future I desire you to look carefully over all the letters addressed to me before I see them, and, should there be any in the handwriting of your late young mistress, destroy them."

"Destroy them?"

"Yes, sirrah; burn them—that's what I mean."

"Yes, my lord," returned the butler with another bow.

He was surprised, but was too discreet a man to let any expression of it be seen on his countenance, which was as inexpressive as that of a wax doll.

He withdrew from the apartment in the same noise-less way in which he had entered.

After this time Lord Ethalwood lived as if he had no daughter.

Mr. Jakyl was the only person who knew how many heart-broken letters came to Broxbridge Hall; he never referred again to the subject to any living creature. He knew very well the uncompromising nature of his master, and knew, moreover, that it was more than his place was worth to be outspoken on so painful a subject.

So time passed on, and the name of the young girl who had been his idol in days gone by was never even mentioned; all trace of her had disappeared, and she was as one dead, and to all appearance even the fact of her having had existence was entirely forgotten.

His two sons he took great pride in. He hoped and expected that they would do honour to his name.

Reginald, the eldest, was proud and haughty like his father. The younger one was soft and womanly; he had not by any means so robust a constitution as his brother, but he was a general favourite, being espe-cially kind and considerate to all who came within his influence.

He was his father's pet, for he never thwarted his parent in any of his whims and fancies; indeed it might be said that he was obedient and yielding to a fault.

Lord Ethalwood could not conceal from himself that this young man had a hectic flush at times, and showed decided symptoms of weakness, or it might be of early decay, and he was seriously concerned when the family physician informed him that his second son required the greatest possible care.

His lordship trembled at the thought of losing one who was so endeared to him, and he could not bear him out of his sight; he was therefore his constant com-panion, either at Broxbridge or his town residence.

Reginald took great delight in athletic sports, was a member of a yachting club, was a daring rider, and attended most meets in the county and elsewhere.

His father did not much concern himself about him, leaving him to do pretty much as he liked; for he used to say, with a smile, that Reginald was strong enough for anything, and was well able to take care of himself.

Judge of his horror, however, when, one afternoon, he received the sad intelligence that his son, Reginald, had been thrown from his horse while following the hounds in a distant part of the country; and that when picked up the young man was found to be dead. His neck was broken, and he never moved after the fall.

This blow fell with a deadening weight upon the miserable and despairing father.

He could not at first realise it, and it was not until he saw the body of his dead son that he could be brought to believe in the irreparable loss he had sus-tained.

There were people who at this time, and indeed afterwards, said that he was justly punished for his indomitable pride; and many averred that he had brought most of the troubles on himself.

Such is the charitable construction some people put upon the misfortunes of others.

But the cup of his sorrow was not yet full.

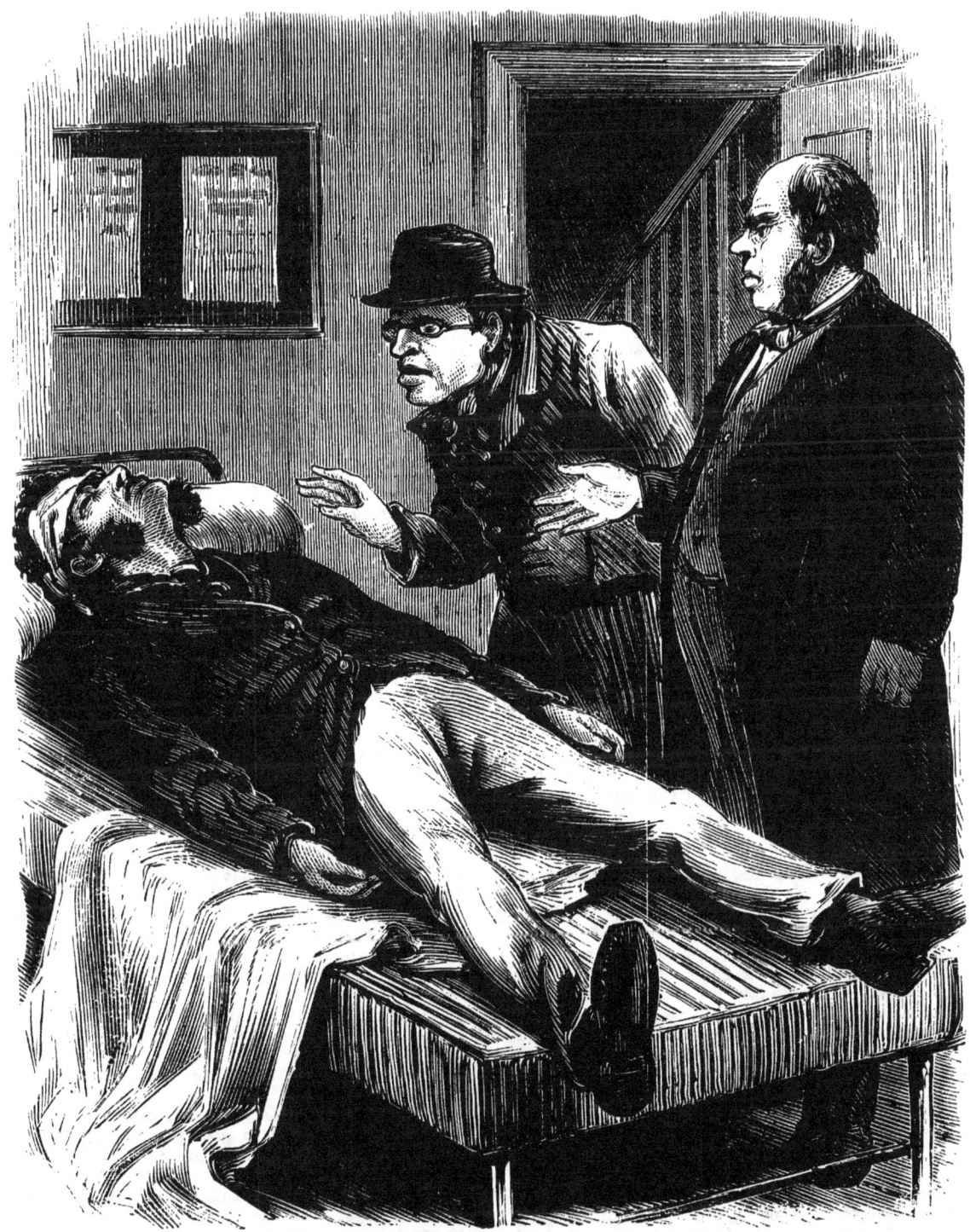

THE LAST LOOK AT JOHN BRISTOW.

A terrible change came over the unhappy and ill-fated nobleman about this time. Long years of toil could not have aged him as his sorrow did. His hair grew white, his face became livid, his eyes lost their wonted fire; and albeit he bore himself bravely under the deep affliction which had fallen upon him, it was easy to see that he was no longer the same man. A shadow had fallen upon him and his, and he was constrained to suffer in silence.

Reginald was interred in the family vault. A noble scion of the house of Ethalwood was gathered to his fathers with all the pomp and ceremony usually accorded to the illustrious dead.

His only remaining son, Herbert, was now his

father's chief, and indeed it might be said only, care.
He had no other prop for his declining years, no other
to look to as the direct inheritor of his title and
estates.

His anxiety about his son, Herbert, was almost pitiful to witness; he was for ever by his side, watching
with a jealous care.

It was pretty generally understood by all that the
young man was acutely sensible of the loss he had
sustained by the death of his brother, Reginald, to say
nothing of the mystery in which the fate of his sister
was enveloped.

He durst not make any inquiries about her, and even
if he had he would have been none the wiser, seeing
that nobody knew aught about her. He therefore
mourned the loss of each in silence.

He was, physically as well as mentally, incapable of
bearing any great affliction, and it is likely enough that
the untoward events which had taken place in a
measure tended to hasten his decline.

Nothing, however, could have saved him, so his
medical attendant declared, for he was suffering from
the worst form of consumption.

This fact, however, was kept from his father for as
long a time as possible.

Lord Ethalwood hoped against hope. He could not,
and would not, up to the very last, believe that his only
remaining son was slowly but surely passing away.

"Remember, Herbert, you are the last of the Ethalwoods, my son, the last of our name. Our race all
depends upon you. It behoves you, therefore, to take
great care of yourself. Live, live, for my sake."

Then he would sit down and watch the thin features
of the young man with the deepest anxiety.

Whether he believed in the possibility of his recovery,
or whether he clung to hope as a last refuge, it is not
possible to say.

It was perfectly evident to all the inmates of Broxbridge Hall that their young master was daily becoming weaker and weaker, and the end most of them
guessed, and even hinted at.

There were many who said the father's excessive
care helped to kill him.

Observations of this nature are cruel enough under
any circumstances. In this case they were most unjustifiable and unpardonable.

Busybodies who came to the house declared that the
young man had too many doctors, too many nurses,
and had taken too many remedies. Those who knew
best, however, were perfectly aware that his death was
inevitable.

The fiat had gone forth, and no medical skill could
arrest the approach of death—Herbert sank to his last
sleep in his father's arms. Lord Ethalwood was left
alone in the world.

CHAPTER XXVI.
THE SOLITARY STUDENT—THE FALL OF AN ANCESTOR—
HIS RESTORATION BY PEACE.

THE melancholy series of events which we have recorded in the two preceding chapters occurred long
before the period in which the action of our story
takes place.

Let us now follow the thread of our narrative.

We have already signified that Lord Ethalwood
returned to Broxbridge Hall very shortly after the
servants' party, at which our hero had played no
insignificant part.

In a small room, called the study, "a thin, tall,
aristocratic man, of three-score years and ten," is
seated; around the walls of the apartment are ranged

glass bottles, crucibles, together with a variety of
other articles, emblematical of a chemical laboratory.
The solitary occupant of the studio might be taken
for a necromancer of the middle ages, so spectral and
weird-like is he in appearance; and at times his deep-
sunken eyes seem to light up and flash with un-
wonted fire, while at others they are cold, inexpressive, and passionless.

His long bony fingers are busily occupied in reaching ever and anon some ponderous volume, the pages
of which he scans with a curious and absorbing
interest.

This old man is Lord Ethalwood, who, despite his
years and the sorrow they have brought, is still firm
and vigorous—still full of active intellectual life.

He is a philosopher—a searcher after truth—a solitary and silent worker in his old ancestral home.

To him the wonders revealed by scientific research
have been a solace and a comfort in the hours of his
affliction.

He has pursued his studies with unwearying industry; has never relaxed, but has worked as hard—
and, indeed, harder, perhaps—than many men whose
means of existence depended upon their own exertions.

There is good reason for this: the recluse at Broxbridge needed some occupation to drive away the
miserable thoughts which at times took possession
of him.

Without some such employment his life would have
been one long sorrow.

He had made chemistry his study, he had also dipped
deeply into the science of astrology, and when wearied
of these he followed up his train of observations in
astronomy.

At the top of his palatial residence he had erected
an observatory.

This was furnished with a large telescope, which was
said to be the finest in the country. He had always
had a taste for scientific pursuits; in the later years of
his life it was a passion with him.

He had little else to occupy his thoughts, for he had
long since withdrawn himself from society, and with
the exception of a few choice friends he did not much
care about mixing with what is called the fashionable
world.

Nevertheless he was not altogether a recluse: with
those who knew him best he was the same genial,
courtly, high-bred gentleman, whose presence was
deemed an ornament in any fashionable or aristocratic
coterie.

But a deep shadow had fallen on the house of Ethalwood—a shadow which no ray of sunlight dispelled.

For an hour or so the master of Broxbridge remained
in his studio, working out some difficult problem in
chemistry. Presently he arose, passed out of his
laboratory, and made his way to the observatory.

To reach this he had to pass through the picture
gallery, on the walls of which were ranged in chronological order portraits of his dead ancestors.

He seldom passed through the picture gallery without taking a glance at the long line of portraits, the
very contemplation of which seemed to take him back
to brighter and more glorious days.

He was proud of his ancestors, many of whom had
been identified with the history of the country.

A miserable sense of depression and loneliness came
over him as he contemplated the time-honoured works
of art. He thought some of his race looked reprovingly
on him out of their dingy frames.

At his death there would be an end to the unbroken
line of the Ethalwoods. He had no son to inherit the

title and estates, which would go to a distant relative, whom he held in utter aborrhence. This thought was perfect agony to him.

He turned abruptly away and made for the observatory, and strove to drown his sorrow in the depths of science.

In a short time, however, he again sought the laboratory. As he arrived at the door of the picture gallery he was startled by a loud noise, a sort of clatter and crash—so it seemed to him—which reverberated through the whole apartment.

He hastened forward, and beheld a cloud of dust.

When this had cleared away he was enabled to ascertain the cause of the strange sounds. The portrait of Gervase Lord Ethalwood, with its massive oak frame, had fallen to the floor.

The master of Broxbridge was greatly affected. His pale face became a thought paler, and his limbs trembled.

A superstitious fear seemed to creep over him.

He looked upon the circumstance as an ill omen.

Had fate in store for him any greater trial?

For awhile he stood motionless and spell-bound, his eyes being all the while riveted on the fallen picture.

His ancestor, Gervase Lord Ethalwood, was deemed the most honoured of his race. He had distinguished himself both in the field and in the senate—had enjoyed the confidence of his Sovereign.

"This is a most remarkable circumstance—the more so since it happened while I was at the entrance of the picture gallery," murmured Lord Ethalwood. "Most remarkable—and—and significant."

As he was hesitating how to act he observed at the other end of the gallery the well-known features of Mr. Jakyl, who was advancing in his usual quiet and unobtrusive manner.

"Oh, it's you, Jakyl!" said his lordship, walking up to the picture. "Do you know of the accident?"

"I heard a noise, my lord," returned the butler, "and hastened to ascertain the cause."

"The picture, the likeness of my great ancestor—it has fallen."

They both looked at the object in question.

"The rings have given way," observed Mr. Jakyl, pointing to the rings through which ran the cords which supported it.

"Strange, most unaccountable!" ejaculated the nobleman. "Most incomprehensible."

"Well, my lord, it is not so surprising after all," returned the butler. "The wood is decayed."

"Umph! You had better lift it up and place it against the wall, then get the steps and hang it up in its place."

The butler gave utterance to an expression of surprise.

"What's the matter?" enquired his master.

"The wood on which the picture is painted is perfectly rotten. I am afraid to touch it in case it should fall to pieces."

This was found to be the case. The picture of Gervase Lord Ethalwood was in such a decayed state that the panel on which that marvellous man had been painted was like touchwood, which had been so wormeaten that it threatened to tumble to pieces.

"I dare not touch it, my lord," said Mr. Jakyl, in evident concern.

"The only wonder is that it should have hung so long in its position. How long has it been painted, my lord?"

"More than three centuries. What do you propose to do? Send up to London. Telegraph at once to a

frame-maker to come immediately. I would not have the painting injured by unskilful treatment, not on any account."

"Send to London?" repeated the butler.

"Of course, that will be the best plan."

A bright idea occurred to the butler, who said in a half apologetic tone, "We have a very clever young man from London working in the neighbourhood, who, I think, would be able to make a good job of it."

"What is he, and who is he?"

"He's in the picture line, my lord and is very clever, so I'm told. His name is Peace."

"Do you think he is a skilful workman?"

"Oh dear me, there's no question about that."

"Very well. Send for him at once; there will be no harm in hearing what he says. Send for him, Jakyl."

And with these words Lord Ethalwood returned to his laboratory.

Peace, who was at work at his shop in Dennet's-lane, was surprised to receive a message from the Hall, commanding his immediate attendance, upon a matter of urgent business.

He put on his best attire and presented himself at Broxbridge.

He was at once taken into the picture-gallery by the prudent and well-behaved Mr. Jakyl.

Mr. Peace made a careful examination of the picture.

"It's all to pieces," he observed to the butler, "and if you attempt to move it it will crumble into dust. I never saw anything so gone. The wood on which it is painted is literally powder. It will require all my skill to make a job of it."

"Do you think you can restore it? Don't undertake it unless you see your way clear, for I must tell you frankly that his lordship sets more store by this than anything else in the whole establishment."

"If I can't do it, nobody can," returned Peace; "but don't let me get you into trouble. If you have no confidence in me send to London."

"I will consult his lordship," observed the butler, proceeding at once to the laboratory.

He returned with his master.

"Well," said the latter, addressing himself to Peace, "how about this picture? Can anything be done with it? I don't mind the price—only I want it made sound."

"And it is no easy task, my lord," answered our hero, "seeing that it is so old and decayed; but I will do my best with it."

"Tell me how you intend to proceed with your work?"

"The surface of the picture is not much injured. The dry rot, as it is termed, has not affected the painting, but it has left the wood like a honeycomb. What I purpose doing is to make a plaster of Paris bed for it. When the face of the picture is once safely deposited in this bed of plaster it will be then my business to make the panel upon which it is painted firm and secure."

"And, pray, how is that to be effected?" inquired his lordship.

Peace smiled, and said—

"By a process I use in cases of this sort. It is an invention of my own, and I think when the work is completed your lordship will acknowledge that it is a very ingenious one."

Lord Ethalwood looked hard at the speaker.

"It may be, but I am still in ignorance as to your mode of operation. I understand chemistry, and should like to hear something more definite about your process."

"The panel on which the portrait is painted is so decayed that you might put your finger through it with the greatest ease. I intend to fill up all the interstices with a solution, which, when set, will make it stronger than ever. When done it will last for centuries, but the difficulty will be in effecting this without injury to the surface, and before I begin I must inform your lordship I cannot be answerable for any injuries to the painting which are at present not discernible, but which may present themselves in the course of the restoration."

"You seem to be intelligent enough. Do your best —only I charge you to use the greatest care. You will bring your materials with you and work here, I presume."

"I cannot do otherwise, my lord; any attempt to remove it would be attended with positive destruction."

"Very well, Mr. Jakyl, you will see that the picture-restorer has all he requires," said Lord Ethalwood as he left the apartment.

Peace returned to Dennet's-lane with the understanding that he was to commence operations at the Hall on the following morning.

He was in some trepidation as to the success of his enterprise, which, to say the truth, required all his skill and care to ensure a satisfactory result; but he was not a man to be daunted by trifles.

On the following morning, therefore, he proceeded to the picture gallery with several bags of plaster of Paris.

His first proceeding was to see if he could with safety remove the panel from the frame, which was almost in as bad a state as the panel itself.

He found that he could not do this with safety; the panel would not bear forcing with the chisel. He therefore prepared a bed of plaster for the frame as well as the picture.

He oiled the surface of both, and, with the assistance of the young carpenter, in whose shed he worked, he succeeded in placing the picture and frame in its bed of plaster.

This was effected happily without any mishap.

His next process was to work into the wood with a fine soft brush a solution formed of oils, resinous gums, and driers. After he had saturated the worm-eaten wood with this, driving it well home to the back of the oiled surface, he left it to dry till the following day, when a similar process was gone through, with the addition of a little cement.

What remained of the honeycombed rotten wood had by this time become fixed and firm—there was no fear of its crumbling into powder.

On the third day he mixed up his patent solution as he termed it. This consisted, like the first coating, of oils, resinous gums, driers, and a larger proportion of cement. Warming the whole in an iron ladle he poured its contents on the back of the picture.

This, like the rest, was left for some hours to set, and on the following day he poured on more of the same composition, until the whole of the injuries to the wood were filled up.

This last process was witnessed by Mr. Jakyl and the footman, both of whom professed to be deeply interested in the proceedings.

Lord Ethalwood himself examined the work after Peace had left, and expressed himself well satisfied with it as far as it had gone.

In a day or two the composition was set as hard as

a rock, and our hero lifted up the frame from the plaster bed, not, it must be confessed, without some anxiety.

As he expected he found a number of small holes, about the size of a pin's head, made by his composition on the painting itself.

Luckily these were chiefly in the background of the picture, only two being observable on the face of the dead Gervase Lord Ethalwood.

Peace removed the panel from its frame—it was as firm and solid as a piece of slate—he placed it on an easel and looked carefully at its surface.

"Well," said Mr. Jakyl, "it's all right, with the exception of those ugly spots."

"It was impossible to avoid showing these; the fact is the decay in another year or so would have gone so far as to destroy entirely the whole of the picture. We may think ourselves lucky it's no worse," observed Peace.

"Yes, I suppose so, but his lordship will think them a great disfigurement," observed the butler.

"You had better ask his lordship to have a look at it."

"I am very well satisfied with the work."

Lord Ethalwood was communicated with. He accompanied his butler into the picture gallery.

He glanced at the portrait of his great ancestor, whose features were as dingy and faded as they well could be; this was more especially observable as the representation of the old nobleman was brought to the light.

"I hope your lordship will be pleased with my work," said Peace. "It has been one of the most difficult tasks that I have ever undertaken; but you wil find, I think, my lord, that you have now a picture more endurable than any in your gallery."

"Yes, it does you great credit," returned the nobleman; "great credit, I admit. But these spots, they are sad blemishes."

"They were holes in the painting itself, which, in another year or two, would, in all probability, have become like a colander."

"Ah, yes; I see. I suppose so."

"But, with your permission, my lord, I will make the work perfect—so perfect, indeed, that no human eye will be able to detect the slightest fault or injury to it. Will your lordship trust me with the picture for a few days?"

"What, take it away? Oh, dear no. I should not like that."

"I cannot very well do it here."

"And why not, I pray?"

"Well, in the first place, I shall require assistance. These spots must be carefully gone over with colour, and—besides, several other things will have to be done to it."

"All of which, I presume, can be done here? If not, it must remain as it is, until such time as I meet with a good restorer."

"Then, as you wish it, I will endeavour to do it here," returned Peace.

It was so arranged. In the course of a few days, our hero sent for a well-known man in the trade, who was an adept in that branch of the profession.

The effigy of the valiant Gervase Lord Ethalwood was subjected to the restoring process. The dirty brown—or black varnish would be the more correct term—was removed by means of powdered cuttle fish. Then the spots were carefully picked out with colour, which had to be matched with that already on.

After this the face of the old earl was glazed, and

when this had been done, the transformation was positively magical.

Lord Ethalwood was delighted. He ordered a costly frame from our hero. In this the restored picture was placed, and then hung up in its original position in the gallery.

He inquired of Peace what he was indebted to him; the answer was twenty pounds. Lord Ethalwood wrote a cheque for fifty, which he handed to our hero.

Nothing could be more satisfactory than this little stroke of business.

Peace returned to the "Carved Lion," and told Brickett of his success, and there was a general rejoicing at the hostelry on the following night. Peace at this time had no reason to complain of fortune's favours; he was doing a good business, had been singularly fortunate—had made a number of friends, and had every reason for pursuing an honest course of life; but he, nevertheless, soon began to be restless and dissatisfied. It must, however, be acknowledged that for a long time after his introduction to Lord Ethalwoods palatial establishment, he continued to lead a respectable life.

He was much taken with the girl, Nelly, but she did not seem to offer him any encouragement. This not a little vexed him, for when they first met she appeared amiable enough. He did not very well know what to make of her.

But what concerned him the most was the mysterious disappearance of Bessie Dalton; this he could not in any way account for. He would have given anything to clear up that mystery.

CHAPTER XXVII.
THE END OF THE INEBRIATE.

VERY soon after the events had taken place which have been described in our last chapter, Peace, much to his astonishment, had a rencontre with a person who was perhaps the very last in the world he would have expected to meet.

Our hero had to take some work home to a customer who resided at about a mile-and-a-half's distance from his workshop. One fine bright sunshiny afternoon he bent his steps in the direction of the habitation in question.

As he was proceeding along a bye road he discovered in the distance a miserably-clad, cadaverous-looking man, whose features he remembered to have seen before, although they were, to say the truth, strangely and sadly altered.

At first he was in some doubt as to the identity of the traveller, but as he approached nearer he was surprised in no small degree to find that the miserable-looking man was none other than John Bristow, whom the reader will remember as Peace's fellow-lodger in the town of Bradford.

Peace was fairly taken back when he recognised Bristow; he would if it had been possible have avoided a meeting, but as this could not very well be compassed, he determined to put the best face on the matter.

What could have brought Bristow to this part of the country was his first thought?

"Was he in search of anybody? Had he any communication to make?"

These were questions he could not answer satisfactorily.

Bristow was in a most miserable plight; his clothes were ragged and torn, and hung upon his attenuated frame like those of a scarecrow; he looked the very personification of squalid misery. Peace never remembered to have seen such a sudden alteration in anyone.

"Is this the right road to Saltwich?" said Bristow, addressing Peace, whom he evidently did not at first recognise.

"You'll have to turn round to the right when you reach the finger-post at the end," returned Peace.

The man started.

"Good luck to you, mate!" he ejaculated. "Why hang it all, if it isn't Charles Peace."

"You are right, and pray, in the name of all that's wonderful, what brings you to this part of the world, John Bristow?" enquired our hero.

"One place is the same as another to me now," returned his companion. "It matters little where I go or what I do. Everything goes wrong with me—has been going wrong ever since I last saw you. It appears likely to go wrong for the remainder of my life."

"Why, mercy on me! you are so strangely altered," said Peace, "that positively I hardly knew you. What has brought you to this? You look twenty years older."

"Do I?" he exclaimed, with one of the jerks or nods which were habitual to him. "Do I? Well, I suppose I do. Anyway, I feel more than twenty years older. I've had a bad time of it—have been in the infirmary—and am next door to starving, that's how I am."

"And have you left the old shop?"

"Left it? Lord, love ye, long—long ago! Haven't had any regular employment for ever so long. They gave me the sack soon after you left Bradford. I get a job when I can, and that's not very often. I'm on the tramp now to see and find something to do, and haven't a blessed mag about me."

"All this is very sad. And your wife?"

"My wife? She took her hook without giving me an hour's warning."

"Where is she?"

"Umph! I should like to know, but I never shall now, I suppose. Oh, she's turned me up. You see, we had a bit of a quarrel, and——"

"You were always having quarrels when I knew you, but whose fault was it—not hers?"

"That's true enough—it was mine. Well, I bear her no ill will. I hope she's happier now. But look here, Charlie, we had some words. I'm sorry for what I said. You don't bear malice, I suppose—there's my hand."

"Let bygones be bygones," said Peace. "You've been your own enemy more than anyone else's. I'm sorry to see you so down, but——"

"I know what you are going to say—it is my own fault. Well, if it is I am the sufferer; but, I say, do you happen to have a trifle you can spare an old chum? Something to help me on my road. I hope to get a job at Saltwich, and if I do I will return you what you may be able to lend—upon my soul I will, and no gammon."

"I am a struggling man myself, but still I'll do something—here's ten shillings. When you have the means to pay it me back do so."

"You're a right down good fellow, Charlie," exclaimed Bristow, in evident delight, "and I am sorry I said what I did, but you know well enough that I didn't mean it."

"That will do—enough upon that head. Pull yourself together, and keep away from that cursed drink; it is that alone which has made you the wreck you are."

"Ah, I am a wreck—you are right enough! I am a wreck, that is true enough. I'm not the Jack Bristow you knew some three or four years ago."

"And what about Bessie ?" said Peace. "What of her ? She left her old quarters about——"

"About the same time as the missus. Ah, they both took their hook at the same time. I don't think the old woman would have had the heart to go by herself. I'll never be brought to believe that. She wouldn't ha' gone had it not a' been for Bessie."

"And have you no idea where they went ?"

"Said they were going abroad, that's all I know. Gone to America, Australia, or some such place. But, lord, I've given over thinking about 'em. What's the use ?"

"I don't know that it is of much use, but I cannot understand the reason for so sudden a flight."

"Oh, there's good reason for the matter of that, leastways as far as my old woman is concerned. I don't believe she ever cared a great deal about me, and that's the honest truth. Well, latterly you see, she got fairly sick of me."

"You have nobody but yourself to blame for that."

"So you always told me. Well, one thing is quite clear, I can't afford to keep a wife now—can't keep myself."

"You ought to be able to do so with common prudence. You are a skilful workman, and, with ordinary care and attention, might earn a respectable livelihood."

"At it again," exclaimed Bristow with a coarse laugh. "The same old game—moralising. What man was ever made sober by preaching I should like to know ?"

"And do you never intend to reform ?"

"Me ? Ha, ha! I'm afraid I'm too far gone for that."

"Then I should be ashamed to acknowledge it, if I were you—that's all I have to say about the matter, Bristow ; you are positively incorrigible."

"You're a good fellow, Charlie, but curse your preaching. I never could stand that ; but there, I don't mean to offend you."

"Oh, you don't offend me. What I say is for your own good. It is no business of mine, you may answer. Perhaps not, but nevertheless it is my duty to offer you some advice, however unpalatable it may be."

"You ought to have been a parson, Charlie, upon my word you ought. You'd ha' made your fortune in the preaching line."

"Well, say no more upon the subject. I have business to attend to, and so we must part."

"Where am I to send to you ? Where do you hang out now ?"

"I am constantly on the move, am travelling, but if you want to communicate with me, address a letter to the post-office, Sheffield, and it will be sure to reach me."

"You're a good fellow. There's no house near where we can have a parting glass? Just one, you know, to show there's no animosity."

"There is no house near, and so think of what I have said, and farewell till we meet again."

"Good bye, Peace, and good luck attend you," said Bristow, shaking his companion by the hand, and so the two parted.

Peace proceeded with his picture frames towards the house of his customer, and John Bristow went in the opposite direction.

"Strange, remarkably strange, my meeting with that man," he murmured, as he walked along. "And so he knows no more about Bessie and his wife than I do myself. It is altogether most mysterious and in-comprehensible, but there's something in the background which has not yet come to light."

After delivering his frames he returned to his workshop, where he was occupied for an hour or two. He then sought the hospitable parlour of the "Carved Lion."

On the following morning, while he was at breakfast in the club-room, Brickett came in and said with much concern—

"This is a sad business at Saltwich."

"What is that ?" inquired Peace, looking up from his smoking and fragrant cup of coffee.

"Ah, of course—I forgot you haven't heard."

"No. What is it ?"

"A poor fellow has been found in the road in a dying condition."

"Who is he ?"

"No one seems to know. He is a stranger to these parts and is supposed to be a tramp."

"Indeed !—is he in any way injured ?"

"Most seriously, they say—skull's fractured. They have taken him to the workhouse."

"Is nothing known about him ?"

"Well, it appears that he had been drinking heavily for some hours, and the last house he called at the landlord refused to serve him. He became so violent that he had to be ejected. After that he offered to fight everybody ; at length he was persuaded to go away. The last time he was seen alive was in Bedhall's-lane ; and at the end of this, near the high road, he was found in a dying condition."

"Dear me, how very terrible ! Has he been subjected to violence ? Has anyone attacked him ?"

"They seem to say not. When last seen he was running like mad. The supposition is that he stumbled and fell, his head striking against a heap of stones near to where he was found."

Peace began to be seriously concerned.

"What sort of a man was he ?" he enquired.

"I don't know, but there's a carter outside who saw him."

Peace rose at once, and proceeded to the front entrance of the house.

A man was giving his horses some hay and water in front of the hostelry.

"Here, Jem," said Brickett, "tell the gentleman what kind of man it was who was found on the Saltwich-road in a dying condition."

The carter scratched his head and remarked—

"What sort o' man ? Well, un seemed a tallish chap, looked like a tramp."

"Pale or dark ?"

"Dunno. Ye see his face were smothured in blood, so un couldn't say."

"Had he dark bushy whiskers ?"

"Yes, sticking out on the side on his cheeks."

"Had he on a ragged fustian coat and moleskin trousers, much the worse for wear ?"

"Yes, un 'ad."

"And short cropped dark hair ?"

"His hair was a bit short."

"Ah, thank you. Will you have a mug of ale ?"

"Aye, thank 'ee, zur, I will."

The ale was drawn and drunk with evident relish by the carter, who was apparently not much discomposed by the sight he had witnessed some hour or two before.

Peace returned to the club-room. He was followed by Brickett.

"Well," said the latter, "how about the description ? Do 'ee know aught about the stranger ?"

"I am afraid I do," returned Peace, who then proceeded to make his companion acquainted with his rencontre with Bristow.

"And it is just possible," he said, in conclusion, "that the miserable besotted wretch spent the money I gave him in drink. I say it is possible—nay, more, it is most probable."

"If I were you I'd just run over to Saltwich and see if it be he—that is, if you can spare the time."

In less than half an hour after this Charles Peace rang the porter's bell at the workhouse.

He was conducted by the master into a small apartment. An iron bedstead was in this, on the mattrass of which was stretched the dead body of a man.

One glance sufficed.

It was the last mortal remains of John Bristow.

The whole affair had been so sudden, the denouement to the tragedy so swift, or it might be said electric, that Peace stood appalled.

"You know him, then?" said the master of the workhouse.

"I did know him years ago, but never dreamed it would end thus."

"There will be an inquest," said the workhouse official.

Peace nodded.

"If my attendance is required you know where to find me—at the 'Carved Lion.'"

And, with these words, he left the chamber of death.

An inquest was held on the body, and the conclusion arrived at was that the unfortunate man had stumbled, and fallen head foremost on a heap of granite. Blood was found on one of the pieces of granite.

He had evidently afterwards crawled to the end of the lane, where it was assumed that he had sunk from exhaustion and loss of blood. He must have remained in a helpless and senseless condition for some hours.

Death resulted from injuries to the head and exposure, joined to a shattered constitution, the effects of drinking to excess.

The jury returned a verdict of "Accidental death."

Unhappily for society, John Bristow's is not a solitary case of the but too frequent indulgence in this fatal propensity.

Within the last week or so the papers have recorded a fatality at the Alexandra Palace which, in most of its features, resembles the wretched end of John Bristow.

The increase of intemperance in this country in the present day is an inexhaustible theme for moralists, economists, and philanthropists.

Drunkenness is the parent of crime, of pauperism, and of misery and degeneracy. It is not possible to calculate the evils that ensue from the pernicious and demoralising effects of a maddening propensity for drink.

The wretched and careworn doubtless fly to it as their only solace. For a time their spirits are raised, but a reaction soon takes place, and at any cost they must procure more stimulants. The end of this may be readily imagined.

How to deal with this gigantic national vice, on which, as yet, no impression has been made, is a question not so easily answered.

If there is one thing more certain than another, it is that, as wealth outstrips culture, sensuality outstrips refinement.

The illiterate millionaire who feasts his guests on turtle and champagne is about the counterpart of the ignorant artisan, who, out of his week's earnings, treats a less fortunate comrade to a bottle of whiskey or gin.

England for many a day has been brought up in the worship of Mammon and Bacchus, and we are afraid, despite the efforts of the Legislature, intemperance is a vice which we must lay to our account for many years to come.

This, it must be admitted, is very sad to reflect upon.

A return, which was moved for by Mr. Henley last session, has recently been issued, showing the population and number of persons taken into custody for drunkenness and disorderly conduct in each city and town in the United Kingdom, for the years 1851, 1861, 1871, and 1876.

The number of arrests in each of the three countries shows a steady increase in the years named.

In England, in the year 1851, 70,097 persons were taken into custody, of whom 44,520 were males and 25,597 females; and each successive period shows a marked increase, until 1876 the total was 104,174—67,294 males and 36,880 females.

The returns for Scotland and Ireland showed an increase in a still greater proportion.

Education, we are told, is to effect a change; it will convert intemperate, improvident, and demoralised millions into sober, frugal, and independent citizens. It has not done so as yet, that is very certain, but we must wait till it does.

CHAPTER XXVIII.
THE WORTHY VICAR—A FRIENDLY COUNSELLOR.

LET us return to the halls of the rich and great. In the library at Broxbridge are seated two venerable-looking gentleman; the first of these is Lord Ethalwood, his companion being the white-haired old vicar. They are both students, only in different ways. The rev. father in God, Canon Lenthal, was a special favourite with the master of Broxbridge.

"But you will pardon me, my lord," he observed, in his soft, mellifluous voice. "The time, I think, has arrived when it is your bounden duty to look to the future. I have no desire to allude to painful subjects, but I really think your wordly affairs should not be forgotten."

"My children are dead, sir," returned the earl—"have been dead for very many years—and every hope of my life has been destroyed. I bow to the decrees of Fate; but the last thing an Ethalwood lays down is what the world is pleased to term his pride."

"My dear and very excellent friend," said the vicar, "that may be true enough—without doubt it is absolutely true in every sense of the word; but, nevertheless, that is no reason for you not turning your eyes towards the future, which is to one and all of us inevitable. Look around you and consider who is to succeed you—who is to carry on the glories and the honours of your grand old race?"

"I have no next of kin save a headstrong, wild, dissipated nephew, who is unworthy for a place of honour—unworthy to represent the ancient and honoured line of the Ethalwoods."

"The more reason, then, is there for you making an effort while there is yet time."

"Make an effort!" exclaimed the Earl. "Can I restore the dead to life?" he added, with supreme bitterness. "Can I call back the loved ones who have passed away?"

"Assuredly not."

"Then what do you mean by an effort?"

"My dear Lord Ethalwood, I have no desire to offend you, but assuredly you can be at no loss to divine my meaning?"

There was a pause. The nobleman made no reply. Like Othello, he gnawed his nether lip, and looked persistently at a large silver salver that blazed on the sideboard beneath the rays of the midday sun, which found their way through the oriel window of the apartment.

The vicar felt that he was treading upon forbidden ground. He, however, determined upon proceeding.

"I think you have not duly considered the matter, Lord Ethalwood," he observed, in the same quiet tender way. "Nay, I am sure you cannot have done so. You have a daughter."

"I have no daughter—she died years ago."

"Died?"

"She has been dead to me—dead—for full five and twenty years."

"True, she may be dead. But, even assuming this were the case—assuming it for argument's sake——"

"Well, what then? We will assume it for argument's sake."

"She may have left children—may have left a son and heir to the title and estates. You have said that her offence was an unpardonable one."

"So it was. No living man will dare to dispute the point with me."

"Do not be so choleric, my very dear old friend. I grant what you say. Her offence is perhaps unpardonable, but that is no reason for the innocent being similarly punished. You really must allow me to be plain-spoken when a subject of this nature——"

"You are plain-spoken," exclaimed Lord Ethalwood, as his pale face became still paler, "very plain-spoken."

He arose from his chair and walked with rapid strides up and down the room.

"You are moved," said Canon Lenthal. "The subject is a painful one, without doubt, but it may appear like egotism on my part when I express a hope that you might possibly be induced to listen to me more complacently than you would to any other. Now sit down, my lord, and view the matter in a better and more becoming spirit."

Lord Ethalwood made no reply, but again took his seat at the table in front of the vicar.

"How could I," he muttered, "bring the child or children of that base, low-born Italian within the walls of Broxbridge?"

"They are his children, no one will for a moment deny, that is, assuming there are any. Should there be issue of his marriage with your daughter they belong to your race—they may even resemble you in features, and in disposition also."

"I hope not."

"Do not say that, my dear friend—let us hope they do. They may even have the grand old Ethalwood spirit, the force, the nobility, and honour of the race from which they descend in a direct line. In a direct line, mark you—you cannot deny that."

"I do not seek to deny it."

"Very well, they have a greater right to succeed to the title and estates than any other living person. You may be proud, but that is no reason why you should not be just and reasonable, and I maintain that it would not be right to pass over your lineal descendants. After all there is something in a rightful claim which the best and worst of mankind generally acknowledge. It would be manifestly unjust to set it aside."

"Really, my esteemed and reverend sir, I must tell you plainly that your argument is based upon no foundation whatever; you are jumping at a conclusion. My undutiful daughter may have no children."

"That I admit. She may not. I am only suggesting that some effort should be made to find her. She may be dead—life is, at best, held but on a frail and uncertain tenure, but that is no reason for your remaining persistently in the dark."

"Ah! so many years have elapsed that the task would not be likely to turn out satisfactory in any way, even if I were disposed to consent."

"But you will give your consent. Let me prevail upon you to do so," observed the good old vicar. "Some effort must be made to find out whether your daughter is alive or dead—that is the first thing to be done."

"We have not the faintest clue. Five and twenty years have passed over. You seem to forget that."

"No, indeed, I do not. I have thought over this matter more often than you can possibly imagine, for I must tell you it is a subject which has troubled me much for years past. I have abstained from breaking it from feelings of delicacy, as I felt that I had no right to interfere between father and child; but it has occupied my mind very much, nevertheless, and it has, moreover, caused me the deepest anxiety."

"Pray say no more. Accept my best thanks for your kindness and consideration. I will think the subject over, and then determine upon my course of action."

"No time like the present."

"You are very persistent," observed the earl, with a smile—it was the first that irradiated his features for many a day.

His companion looked upon it as a good omen.

"I have one or two calls to make at the other end of the village, and, upon my return, will call in again," said the vicar. "Think over what I have said. In less than an hour I will see you again."

"Good. I shall look for you, then, at the expiration of that time."

The rumbling of the wheels of the vicar's chariot were heard on the hard dry road, and Lord Ethalwood was alone once more.

He did think the matter over after the departure of Canon Lenthal, and his heart softened.

"He is right—oh, he is quite right! I am childless—have no kith or kin that I know of. I must and will take active measures, and see if she be still alive."

He sat down at the table, and buried his face in his hands.

The hour sped by, and the vicar returned, agreeable to his promise.

"I have taken your advice, and have thought the matter seriously over," said Lord Ethalwood.

"And what is your ultimatum?" inquired Canon Lenthal.

"To institute inquiries without further delay."

The two friends sat down once more, and began to discuss details in a serious and business-like manner.

To the great surprise of the vicar, he learnt from Lord Ethalwood that he had never heard a word of his daughter after she left Broxbridge.

"Most singular," murmured the good pastor. "But did she never write to you?"

"I believe so, but all the letters have been destroyed."

"Where were they addressed from?"

"I don't know. I never saw them. I gave orders to my butler to destroy them. Oh, we shall never be able to learn anything of that, I am convinced. Nevertheless I will endeavour to do so."

"How will you proceed?"

CHARLES PEACE AND THE DETECTIVE OFFICER.

"Place the matter in the hands of my lawyer—he will know how to act."

"I am most delighted to find that you have listened to my advice, and hope and trust that you may be successful," exclaimed the vicar. "In a few days' time I hope to hear good news. Farewell, my friend, and that your efforts may be crowned with success will be the earnest prayer of your old friend."

No. 14.

The two shook hands, and Canon Lenthal left Broxbridge in much better spirits than when he entered.

Mr. Chicknell, the earl's lawyer, who had been telegraphed for, arrived about noon on the following day.

He was at once shown into the library. Lord Ethalwood had by this time become excited and restless. He explained the whole business to his legal adviser.

"Oh," observed the latter, when his client had concluded. "You now desire to find her out ?"

"If it be possible. It seems to me to be most hopeless."

"Nothing is hopeless in the hands of efficient persons," returned the man of parchment. "Leave the matter in my hands. I know a clever fellow belonging to the detective department at Scotland-yard."

"Detective department!" exclaimed the earl, in evident disgust. "Is my daughter to be traced by a man whose business it is to hunt down common thieves ?"

"My lord, I pray of you not to be so hasty. Detectives are employed by all sorts of people for all sorts of purposes, and for this reason they are especially qualified to deal with cases of this sort. They'll find out in a week probably more than I could in months."

"Well, as you please. You know best."

"I will do my best for you, rest assured of that," said Mr. Chicknell. "The very moment I obtain the least scrap of information I will either write or wire to you without delay."

The active little lawyer returned to London that very afternoon.

Weeks passed over after this. Mr. Chicknell wrote several letters, but they contained but little intelligence.

At last one came which was more cheering. The Italian professor and his wife had been traced first to London, where they had lived some months, and in all probability had spent what little ready money they had. From the metropolis the Italian had gone to Leeds, where he earnt a living by teaching. He and his wife had taken lodgings in that city, and there a child was born.

From what could be gathered it would appear that Montini found it a hard task to maintain a lady brought up in the lap of luxury, and the young couple had to submit to a number of privations.

There were persons residing in Leeds who remembered both the professor and his young English wife.

Indeed, some of the Italian's pupils, now grown up to middle-aged people, attested to the fact that Montini's wife presented her husband with a little girl, and the register of her birth and baptism was obtained in the town.

Matters, therefore, looked a little more promising, and the old earl watched for the post each day with the greatest anxiety.

From Leeds they went to Harrogate. In this place they were supposed to be struggling for some time in adverse circumstances, and while there the professor became seriously ill—so bad indeed that his life was despaired of.

A doctor who attended him, and who still practised in this fashionable watering-place, gave a very sorry account of the Italian's health, which, he said, was much broken while Montini was under his care. His impression, at the time, was that he could not live more than three or four years.

Mr. Chicknell, in his letters to the earl, informed the latter of all these facts ; at the same time he expressed his sincere regret that there did not seem to be much chance of obtaining more information, as the clue seemed to be lost after the professor and his wife left Harrogate.

The supposition was that they returned to London, but this was merely surmise; there was no direct proof of them having done so.

For some time after this the matter remained in abeyance, and the anxiety of the bereaved nobleman increased as the weeks flew by.

He proceeded up to town, and waited upon Mr. Chicknell at his chambers, Paper-buildings, Temple.

"Can nothing more be done in the matter ?" he inquired of the lawyer.

"I fear not, my lord. Certainly not at present," answered his legal adviser.

"Surely, Mr. Chicknell, you do not intend giving over making further inquiries. The case is a most serious one as far as I am individually concerned, and we must not let the matter rest. I do not care what expense is incurred, but you must do your best to clear up the mystery," said Lord Ethalwood.

"We appear to have come to a dead lock, but that is no reason for our abandoning the search as hopeless," returned his companion. "Mr. Wrench, of Scotland-yard, has had the case in hand, and has striven as hard as any man possibly could have done to bring the matter to a satisfactory conclusion. I think the best plan will be for him to wait upon you at Broxbridge, and you can then hear what he has to say. You will find him a most intelligent officer."

"I wish you would communicate with him at once, then."

"He is not in town this week, but the moment he comes back I will convey to him your expressed wish, and he will hasten at once to Broxbridge."

"I shall be anxiously awaiting his appearance," said the earl, who took his leave, and returned to his country seat.

CHAPTER XXIX.

THE NOBLEMAN AND THE DETECTIVE—A CONSULTATION.

IN a few days after this a gentleman presented himself at the outer gate of Broxbridge Hall, and told the porter that he desired to see the earl upon important business.

"Show Mr. Wrench in at once," said Lord Ethalwood to Jakyl; "of course I want to see him."

The detective entered, and introduced himself to the nobleman, who desired him to be seated.

"Well, Mr. Wrench, my solicitor informs me that there is a dead lock in this business ; can nothing more be done ?"

"Oh, we can do a great deal more, my lord," observed Wrench; "but you must acknowledge that I am furnished with such slender material, and then there's the lapse of time, and many other things against us."

"Admitted—still you do not give up all hope."

"Well, no, I'm not accustomed to do that. I am glad we have met, my lord, for many reasons—you will, I am sure, pardon me if I am plain-spoken."

"Certainly, speak as openly and frankly as possible. I desire you to do so. Up to the present time I am free to confess we have been baffled."

"I have done all that man could do, but my efforts have not as yet been crowned with success ; I expect you to give me all the information you can."

"Certainly, that is but a just and reasonable request."

"You will not be offended, therefore, if I inquire about one or two little matters ? Just tell me if you have any of your daughter's letters, which she might probably have sent here after her departure ?"

"I have never seen any of them," said Lord Ethalwood.

"That's most important—did anybody else ?"

"I gave orders to my butler to destroy them."

"Do you think he would remember any of the postmarks ?"

"I never thought of that," exclaimed the earl, with a start.

"Probably not, but it is the very first thing that occurred to me. Did any letters arrive?"

"That I cannot tell you."

"Where is your butler? Is he in your service now?"

"Dear me, yes—he has never left it."

"Will you be kind enough to summon him?"

Lord Ethalwood touched the bell. A servant entered.

"Tell Mr. Jakyl I desire to speak with him," said his master."

In a minute or so the butler entered the library.

"Will you leave it to me to put the necessary questions?" inquired the detective, addressing his lordship, who felt a mere child in comparison to the sagacious officer.

"Certainly," he answered, without hesitation.

Mr. Wrench cleared his throat, and focussed his eyes upon the smooth and placid face of the butler.

"I have one or two questions to put to you," said the detective. "In the first place, did any letters arrive here from the Hon. Miss Ethalwood after her departure from Broxbridge?"

Mr. Jakyl stood aghast—he could hardly believe that he had heard aright.

"Did any letters arrive?" he paused, and glanced nervously at his master.

"Go on. Answer, Jakyl, you have my permission."

"Yes, sir; several arrived after the departure of my young mistress, but——"

"You were told to destroy them," observed the detective. "Did you do so?"

"I would rather not answer the question," said the butler, in evident trepidation; then, turning to Lord Ethalwood, he murmured in an under tone— "If I have done wrong, my lord, I hope you will pardon me. I did not destroy my young mistress's letters."

"A very discreet and sensible man," ejaculated Mr. Wrench. "And pray why did you disobey his lordship?"

"Because I hoped that at some time they might be useful."

"You have displayed great wisdom in your course of action—you cannot be too strongly commended, Mr. ——. I don't know your name."

"Jakyl."

"Well, Mr. Jakyl, you have acted in a very proper manner. I hope his lordship is of my opinion."

"I am," returned the earl, with undisguised pleasure. "I think Jakyl has been most prudent. To say the truth, I have always had the greatest confidence in him."

The butler bowed, and hardly knew how to comport himself under the praise which was so lavished on him.

"I must tell you frankly, Mr. Jakyl," said the detective, "that I am engaged in instituting a rigorous search for your master's daughter; so if it be in your power to give me any information which may aid me in my inquiries, it will be a boon to us all."

"I wish I could, sir."

"Well, not now. I don't mean at present, but if anything occurs to you, out with it at once."

"I will. Now, my friend, let me have the letters without further delay."

The butler looked again at his master.

"Fetch them at once, Jakyl. You have heard what Mr. Wrench has said. The matter is in his hands."

The servant left the library, and in a minute or so returned with a packet of papers tied with silk cord. He handed them to the earl, who pushed them towards the detective, saying, as he did so—

"I have not the courage to open them just now. You can do so."

"I will not open them," answered Mr. Wrench; "but, with your permission, will take a note of the postmarks and dates."

He sorted them, placed them on the table in chronological order, pulled out his note-book, and made entries therein. Then he closed the book, and said—

"This looks a little more promising. I have some material now to work upon. At your leisure, my lord, you can peruse the contents of the epistles, and possibly there may be something which may be of service to us in the pursuit of this inquiry."

"I will go carefully over them when I am a little more composed," observed the earl.

"Good. I shall not return to London just at present, for special reasons. I deem it expedient to remain in this neighbourhood."

"Will you take up your quarters here?"

"No, I thank you, my lord. It would be best, I think, to put up at an inn. There will be more chance of my picking up information in a place of public resort. We have our own way of doing business," observed Wrench, with a smile.

Lord Ethalwood bowed and smiled also.

The very last thing he thought of doing was to dictate to the sagacious officer, who, in affairs of this sort, was so much his superior.

"From the postmarks on the letters I see your daughter and her husband have paid a visit to several other towns besides those in which I have made inquiries."

"Other towns—eh?" exclaimed the earl.

"Yes, one is Sheffield and another Bradford. I shall make it my business to visit both places. Ah! the case is not so hopeless as Mr. Chicknell seems to imagine."

"I am glad to hear you say so. Pray Heaven we may be successful; it will remove a weight off my heart."

The detective looked at the speaker and observed, quietly—

"You ought not to have let the matter go so long without ascertaining something respecting the young people's whereabouts."

"Of that you must allow me to be the best judge," said Lord Ethalwood, with all his old pride and hauteur.

Mr. Wrench saw at once the mistake he had made in hazarding an observation which sounded very much like a reproof.

"But you have a duty to perform, sir," observed the earl, "and I doubt not that you will not shrink from carrying it out to the best of your ability."

The detective bowed and answered in the affirmative.

He then rose and took his departure, promising his patron to wait upon him again in a day or two.

Mr. Wrench inquired of the butler the most convenient house in the neighbourhood for him to put up at.

Mr. Jakyl, as a matter of course, recommended him to go to the "Carved Lion," and he at once bent his steps in the direction of that well-known hostelry.

Lord Ethalwood had not sufficient fortitude to open his daughter's letters in the presence of any one, more especially that one being a detective.

It was a task he had reserved for another occasion.

Soon after the departure of Mr. Wrench his lordship mustered up courage to break the seals of the epistles.

As he did so a tremour seemed to pass through his frame.

A deep sigh escaped from him as he opened the first letter. In this the letter referred to her elopement as a playful piece of diplomacy, never for a moment assuming that it would be deemed an unpardonable offence by her parent.

She asked him to forgive her, and not be angry with his pet, as she had done that which had made her happy for life.

Lord Ethalwood tossed the epistle on one side with something like contempt or disgust.

The second letter was a little more serious in tone. In it she was lavish in her praise of Montini, who she said was the kindest and most considerate of husbands, he was so good, so clever—in short, there was no one like him.

She besought her father to write, if only a few lines. She would not and could not believe that he intended to cast her off.

"The infatuated senseless girl!" ejaculated the earl. "I never would have believed she could have so forgotten her position in life. For the life of me I cannot understand it."

These two communications were followed by imploring letters, in which she told him how hard the world was using them, and what miserable struggles they had passed through.

But in this as in all others she spoke in the highest terms of her husband, who she said did his best to maintain a respectable position in the world; this was done for her sake more than his own, "and if," she said in conclusion, "you only knew him half as well as I do, you would admire and esteem him; nay, more, I believe you would be proud of him."

"She must have taken leave of her senses," ejaculated the earl. "The wretched Italian must have bewitched her, the silly, senseless girl. Oh, but all this is hard to bear!"

He remained for some time after this lost in thought. Presently he opened another epistle.

This announced the birth of a daughter; it was, of course, a fine child, and was, so the writer avowed, "the very image of its mother, and was an Ethalwood, —this everyone would acknowledge upon the first glance, and she will be named after me," wrote the ill-fated wife. "Some day I hope you will see the little dear, and when you do I hope you will forgive me for your grand-daughter's sake. She, at any rate, has not done anything to offend you."

"It all seems to be like a dream," murmured the earl, as he broke the seal of another. This came from Harrogate, and its tone was both melancholy and despairing. Montini was dangerously ill—he was not able to follow his avocation, and his unhappy wife implored her father to hold out a helping hand and send them money without delay, as they were reduced to the greatest possible extremity, and positively wanted the common necessaries of life.

Lord Ethalwood dashed the letter down on the table, smote his forehead with one hand, and uttered an expression indicative of the most poignant agony.

"I never thought it would come to this," he muttered, rising from his seat and pacing the apartment restlessly. "Poor girl, she must indeed have changed to beg for assistance! Oh, what would I give now to have her here by my side, in—in the winter of my life—in my old age!"

He fell into his chair and burst out into a passionate flood of tears.

Retributive justice had overtaken the proud, uncompromising, relentless nobleman, who cried like a child.

* * * * * *

Mr. Wrench wended his way along till he reached the well-known house of entertainment for man and beast, kept by the equally well-known Brickett. The detective was not a man to make himself common by mixing up with any knot of strangers—not unless he could make it answer his purpose to do so—he therefore requested to be shown into a private room, and, after partaking of some refreshment, he proceeded to glance at the memoranda he jotted down in his notebook.

"Humph," he murmured. "The young couple seem to have visited a good many towns; I suppose things were running cross with them. It's a queer business, take it altogether, and the earl is a starchy sort of customer, as unforgiving as the devil, and as proud as a peacock. Well, I wouldn't change places with him for all his wealth and title. He's what I call a stunner. No two ways about him. But 'he's down among the dead men' this time, it would appear—is what our Transatlantic friends would call 'cornered.' I must find out all about his daughter for him, that's certain— that is, if it be possible. The question is, how it is to be accomplished."

Not being able to answer this question with anything like satisfaction to himself, Mr. Wrench lighted a cigar, rang the bell, and ordered some brandy cold.

He had not indulged in many puffs at the "fragrant weed" before Brickett made his appearance.

"Oh, your pardon, sir," said the landlord; "but be your name Wrench?"

"Yes, my friend, it be."

"A servant from the hall wishes to speak with you."

"Let him come up then."

Henry Adolphus made his appearance.

"His lordship told me to call and see if you were comfortable 'ere, as if not a bed will be provided for you at the hall."

"I'm all right, my man. Shall do very well here. Give my respects to his lordship, and say that I am quite comfortable. Anything else?"

"No; I b'leve that is hall."

Henry Adolphus retired.

The sounds of music and merriment in the parlour reached the ears of the detective.

"You appear to have a merry set of people below," said he to Brickett.

"Yes, sir, they enjoy themselves in their own way."

"Somebody's playing the violin."

"Yes; it's a gentleman who's stopping here for a short time, and he generally gives my parlour customers a tune or two after working hours—after the day's work is over."

"He does not handle the instrument badly. Is he a professional?"

"Well, partly so, I believe. He is in the frame and picture line of business—a traveller."

"Ah, indeed! A traveller, a picture dealer, and musician all in one—he's a good sort."

"Yes, he's a very good sort—there aint much doubt of that; has seen a deal of the world, and has visited pretty well every town in the three counties."

"Oh! is that so?"

"Would you like to go downstairs into the public room?" inquired the landlord.

"Not now, I thank you—some other evening perhaps. Did I understand you to say that this violinist and picture-frame maker was stopping here?"

"He is for the present, until his orders are completed.

Why, Lord bless us, he's done wonders at the Hall, and has been highly complimented by Lord Ethalwood himself."

Brickett now put his customer in possession of all the facts relative to the restoration of the decayed portrait of his lordship's great ancestor.

"Ah, he must be a smartish sort of chap. Thank you," observed the detective, who very shortly after the foregoing conversation was conducted to his bedroom.

In the morning he was shown into the clubroom where breakfast was served. Peace was partaking of his morning meal.

The detective bowed and sat down on the opposite side of the table. He looked at our hero with evident curiosity, but did not remember to have seen him before.

During breakfast the two conversed upon several topics, which were however not of a personal nature.

Peace did not know who his companion was; neither did he take the trouble to inquire. He concluded he was some commercial man who had rested there for the night, and the probability was that he should not see any more of him.

In this, however, he was mistaken.

Our hero went to his workshop, and Mr. Wrench remained behind.

He reflected for some little time, and then rose from his chair and went downstairs.

Brickett as usual was behind the bar.

"Is that the violinist and picture dealer—the one I had breakfast with?" he inquired.

"Aye, surely that be he."

"He's a sharp customer, a downy sort of card—isn't he?" said Mr. Wrench.

"He's got his head screwed on the right, way if that's what you mean," returned the landlord, a little sharply.

"Yes, that's precisely what I do mean. Where does he hail from?"

"Hail from? I dunno."

"He's been travelling about the country, you say?"

"That 'im hus—been to every mortal place, so I've heerd."

"Ah, just so. Where is he to be found now?"

"Found! He works in Dennett's-lane."

"And where is that?"

"Not a quarter of a mile from here. Why?"

"I will give him a call. What might be his name?"

"Peace—Charles Peace. Be you going to call on 'im now?"

"Yes."

"Then I'll show 'ee where his place is."

The landlord went to the door of the house, and pointed out the lane in question to his customer.

"There at the further end of that," said he, "you will find a wooden shed, and in that you will see 'im at work."

"Thank you," said Mr. Wrench, who at once proceeded in the direction pointed out by his host.

CHAPTER XXX.

MR. DETECTIVE WRENCH AND CHARLES PEACE.

Mr. Wrench was a man who pursued his inquiries with the greatest pertinacity; he was not accustomed to let the "grass grow under his feet."

It was a maxim of his, and one indeed the truth of which had been made manifest, that "you sometimes obtain the most valuable information from a source which appeared at first glance the most unlikely to be fruitful."

It occurred to him that it would be quite as well to interrogate our hero before he (the detective) proceeded to the other towns visited by the missing pair. Possibly the itinerant frame-maker might have some knowledge of the person or persons of whom he was in search; anyway there would be no harm in putting the question to him.

"Who knows—" murmured Mr. Wrench, as he took his way along the lane—"who knows but this fellow—who, it would appear, is a sort of Admirable Crichton, in his way, if one is to believe the landlord of the 'Lion'—may not have come across someone in his various wanderings who may have been acquainted with the Italian professor, who was a musican? It is certain that, to a certain extent, the picture chap is a musician—so here goes for it."

He was by this time at the door of Peace's workshop, at which he gave a modest knock.

It was opened by our hero.

"Good morning again," said the detective. "I want to have a little conversation with you; but you are busy, perhaps. Some other time will do as well."

"Oh, come in—you won't hinder me," returned Peace. "I can go on with my work, and you can have your say. Be seated."

He handed his visitor a rickety Windsor chair, which, to all appearance, had been put together in the last century.

Mr. Wrench sat down, and Peace, with his book of leaf gold in one hand and the pad in the other, went on with his work.

The detective cleared his throat, and then said, carelessly—

"I understand that you have visited a number of towns—of course you naturally would do so—in the exercise of your vocation. Am I right?"

"Yes; I've been about a goodish bit."

"Oh, yes, so I hear. Well, now, I must be candid with you. I am in search of an Italian professor and his wife. The former was a teacher of music; but it is more than twenty years since anything has been heard of either."

"Twenty years!" exclaimed Peace. "It is, then, not at all likely that I should know anything about them. I was but a child at that time."

"True, but they may be alive now, you know."

"Ah, that's another matter. What might be the gentleman's name?"

"Montini."

Peace shook his head.

"Never heard of such a person," he ejaculated. "Don't know any one of that name."

"Ah, I was afraid it would be before your time," observed Mr. Wrench.

"Therein consists our greatest difficulty—the lapse of time."

"That's a remarkably beautiful frame you are gilding—just my sort."

"Not bad," returned our hero, "but I have had a deal better under my hands; but I'm sorry I can't help you to find the persons you are seeking. What town did they reside in?"

"Ah, several. I will read you over the names."

Mr. Wrench drew out his pocket-book, and ran over the list of places which he had copied from the postmarks on the letters at Broxbridge Hall.

"You know," he said, when he had finished the list, "I don't want any information from you without paying handsomely for it. It is most imperative that I should find these people, if they be still alive."

"Oh, is it?" cried Peace. "Well, look here, I can't tell you anything about them, and if I could——"

"You wouldn't, is that what you mean?" said his visitor, sharply.

"Don't be quite so fast. I know nothing about you, and don't even know your name."

Mr. Wrench drew a case from his pocket, and gave our hero his card. On it was—

Mr. DETECTIVE WRENCH,
Scotland-yard.

"Ah!" ejaculated our hero. "That's it—eh?"

"What?"

"A criminal affair. Some poor crow is wanted."

"Nothing of the sort. I pledge my word as a gentleman, and——"

"A detective," added Peace. "Go on, governor."

"I tell you it is nothing of the sort. The facts are simply these. The lady eloped with her music master. Her relatives cast her off—now they are anxious to find her. Let me disabuse your mind of a false impression."

"I never knew or even heard of such a person as Montini, and am therefore unable to assist you; but have you no clue to them—no letters?"

"Oh, yes, we have letters. That is how we know the different towns they visited. The last one is from the lady. She announces the birth of a daughter, who is named after herself."

"What name might that be?" inquired Peace, carelessly, removing the superfluous gold from the frame.

"Aveline," returned the detective.

"Aveline!" exclaimed Peace, in a tone of surprise, which he found it impossible to suppress.

"Yes. Have you ever met with one bearing that name?" eagerly inquired Mr. Wrench, who was at no oss to comprehend that one chance shot had told.

"Yes, I think so. The name seems familiar to me."

"My dear sir," exclaimed the detective, rising from his Windsor chair, and approaching nearer to his companion, "if you can let me know about this person you shall be rewarded handsomely. It is a most uncommon name, and it may furnish us with a clue to the missing person."

"It is not a very common name, I admit; but then there may be hundreds of persons who bear it."

"You know one, it would seem. Can you tell me where she's to be found?"

"You take me by surprise," observed Peace; "and I cannot quite call to mind just at present where I met with such a person. I know it must be a long time ago. I will think the matter over, and see if I can assist you."

Mr. Wrench saw plainly enough that Peace was not to be caught tripping—he was too wary a customer for that; he therefore deemed it advisable not to press the question further at that time. He therefore said, in an off-hand manner—

"Well, you will see what you can do for me, like a good fellow, as I am told you are, and so farewell for the present."

"Aveline!" ejaculated our hero, when he found himself once more alone. "What can be the meaning of this inquiry? He cannot be in search of the Aveline Maitland I knew—and loved," he added in a tone of dejection; "but no, that is not possible."

Peace was fairly puzzled. He had no predilection for detectives. They were a class of men whose acquaintance he had no desire to cultivate.

When his day's work was finished he returned to the "Carved Lion."

"The vicar has been here inquiring for you," said Brickett. "I told him where you worked, but he said he would call here again later on."

"The vicar—and what might he want? Going to give me an order for some Oxford frames, I suppose—eh?"

"No, I don't think so. It's private business, I believe. You see, old man, people are beginning to take notice of you."

In less than an hour after Peace's return Canon Lenthal called again at the inn.

He was shown into a private room in which our hero was seated.

The vicar was introduced by Brickett.

"You will pardon this intrusion, sir, I hope," said the minister, "but I wait upon you at the request of Lord Ethalwood, whom I believe you have some knowledge of."

"I've worked for his lordship."

"So he informed me. Well, Mr. Peace, I understand that you have some knowledge of a lady whose Christian name is Aveline. Possibly you would not care about furnishing Mr. Wrench with all the particulars concerning her. I can readily comprehend that, and hence it is that I pay this visit. It is to assure you, sir, that you will be conferring an inestimable favour upon Lord Ethalwood by giving him the address of the lady in question. His lordship had a daughter named Aveline, she has been lost to him for years, and——"

"The young lady I knew could not possibly be his daughter," cried Peace. "She is too young for that."

"Admitted, but the circumstance is a most remarkable one—I mean the coincidence as to the names. I am here to make an earnest appeal. Let me entreat and implore of you to give all the information you can."

Peace considered for some little time; presently he said—

"Under the circumstances of the case, I feel that I should not be justified in refusing. I will furnish you with what information I have in my power to give."

"I am overjoyed to hear you make such a declaration. Will you confer with Mr. Wrench, or give me the particulars?"

"I will confer with Mr. Wrench, if you desire it."

"That will be the best course. Accept my most sincere thanks," said the vicar, offering his hand to Peace. "I felt assured my appeal would not be made in vain."

Well pleased with the result of his interview, Canon Lenthal hastened back to Broxbridge Hall.

On the following morning, Charles Peace put Mr. Wrench in possession of all the particulars he was able to furnish in respect to the young lady, whom he had known as Aveline Maitland, but who had become Mrs. Gatliffe three or four years since.

The detective listened to the details with the greatest degree of interest. He was under the full impression that they might ultimately turn out to be of great service to him in tracing Aveline Ethalwood.

"I will at once proceed to Sheffield, Mr. Peace," he said, in a cheerful manner. "It is indeed a most fortunate meeting—I mean, of course, ours. Should I be successful you will be duly rewarded, for I am free to acknowledge that you rendered me all the assistance it is possible for anyone to do similarly circumstanced."

"I wouldn't be too sanguine," observed Peace. "The young woman, whose name and address I have given, you will find, I fear, will be of little service, but it is not for me to dictate or anticipate. Make whatever use you think fit of the information you have obtained in so singular and unexpected a manner."

"I will at once to Sheffield," repeated Wrench. "It may turn out a fiasco, but that is no reason for my remaining inactive."

The detective was driven to the station by Lord Ethalwood's coachman, and in a few hours he was at the door of the cottage which had at one time been in the occupation of Mrs. Maitland.

He was informed by its present occupant that the former tenant had left; she went to live with her daughter and son-in-law at Rotheram, soon after their union.

Mr. Wrench hastened thither. He was informed that they had all left the town, and were residing somewhere in London.

The detective was not to be baffled. He waited on Tom Gatliffe's former employer, and one of the partners informed him that their late foreman was managing a business in the Euston-road.

He put up at one of the leading hotels in Sheffield, having determined upon proceeding to the metropolis on the following day.

CHAPTER XXXI.
THE HOME OF THE WORKING MAN—THE ARRIVAL OF A STRANGER.

SINCE his marriage with Aveline Maitland the reader has heard but little of Tom Gatliffe. The young engineer was the best and most loving of husbands; he worked steadily at his business, and in every respect was persevering in his endeavours to improve his position; but trade at the works where he was employed was not nearly so flourishing as it had been prior to his marriage. He, in common with his fellow-workmen, suffered by the depression.

After remaining two years at Rotheram he accepted an offer to take the management of some works in London.

He had another reason for doing this. His young wife had grown tired of Sheffield, Rotheram, and their surroundings, and yearned to be a denizen of the great city about which she had heard so much, but of which she had seen so little.

Aveline Gatliffe showed symptoms of discontent—she wanted some change of scene.

Her husband took a charming house at Wood-green, which he furnished, not grandly, perhaps, but with every comfort which persons in their station of life could desire.

Here he, his wife, and their child—a beautiful little boy of about three years old—were located.

Let us pay a visit to the home of the British workman.

At the door of the habitation stands a young and beautiful woman. She is barely two and twenty, but does not look even as old as that; her hair of shining brown looks like gold in the sunshine; her eyes are of violet blue; her dress is quite plain, but the homely material only showed the grace and beauty of her figure to greater advantage. Such are the most noticeable features of Aveline Gatliffe.

One might have wondered how she—living in a cottage, the wife of a man who worked hard for his daily bread—came by this dainty beauty, this delicate loveliness which would have been fit dowry for a duchess.

The young wife's gaze was directed down the road which led to the station; the rays of the setting sun cast long shadows across this from the trees which skirted its sides.

Presently her countenance was irradiated with a smile. She heard the sounds of approaching footsteps, she hastened onwards, and in a few minutes she saw her husband in the distance.

"Ah, dearest, you've been waiting and watching for me. Is it not so?" cried Tom Gatliffe.

The young woman smiled and nodded; then they walked slowly home together.

"I hope you have not been dull to-day," said Tom, when the two entered the parlour. "I don't like to see you dull."

"I have been as lively as usual," she answered.

"Umph, that's not saying much, darling," returned the husband in a tone of banter. "Not much, you'll admit. At present the place is new and strange to you. In time you will be more used to it."

"Shall I?" she murmured.

"Why of course you will."

"Make haste and get rich, Tom dear; then we can have a grand house in London."

His countenance fell as he listened to her. For a long time she had appeared discontented with her lot, and this had been a sore trouble to Gatliffe, who found, as others had found before him, that matrimony was not all smooth sailing.

As yet there had been no storm, but distant rumblings of thunder had been heard.

He drew the beautiful face of his young wife towards him, and kissed it with a fondness which spoke more eloquently than words.

"My dear Aveline," he murmured, "our little house is to me more beautiful than a palace. The reason is plain enough—it contains you."

She looked up into his face and smiled faintly.

"And I am sure you are of the same opinion," he added.

"It is well enough, Tom, but——"

"But what, dear?"

"Oh nothing; the time will come, let us hope, when we shall own a grand mansion and have all sorts of beautiful things."

The young engineer looked troubled. This was not the first time by many that he had heard her express a similar wish.

"I don't know what to make of her," he muttered to himself. "Of late a change appears to have come over her."

"Look here, Aveline," he said, more solemnly, "mark what I say; I don't think you will be ever happier than you are now. It is not the place—it is not grandeur that ensures happiness—it is a contented mind; that you have."

"Well, I hope I have."

"You ought. I have; your beauty makes my heart glad, your love makes earth heaven to me."

"Mercy on us, what a speech after four years of matrimony! Oh, you dear old fellow," she ejaculated, clapping her hands together—"dear good old Tom!"

He laughed outright.

"Go on," he exclaimed.

"Well, then, I will. Shall I tell you that I long for this great bright world that you despise?"

"Then I don't, and there's the difference. If we were rich and lived in the great world you speak of so rapturously, you would belong to so many others. Others would delight in your society and follow you with praise, and then I should be jealous. Here, I have you all to myself, which is the very thing I desire."

"Will it be very long before you are rich?" she enquired carelessly.

"My darling, how can I possibly tell, and after all what does it matter? How often have I told you that riches do not bring happiness?"

"It may be so, but I should like to try."

She did not perceive how her words jarred upon his sensitive nature. An expression of pain passed over his fine features, and he said no more for some little time.

He sat down and ate his evening meal in silence.

"I hope I have not offended you," said his wife.

"I do not believe it possible for you to do so," returned he. "You ask me when I shall be rich. I have two or three inventions—one I was about to work out with Charles Peace."

"Oh the horrid man!" Don't have anything to do with him."

"I don't intend, but he has great ingenuity nevertheless; but let that pass. The inventions I am now endeavouring to bring to perfection may turn out successful. If only one of them does so I shall be a rich man; then I suppose you will be satisfied."

"Oh yes, that would be glorious; but it's not certain, I suppose."

"My dear, nothing is certain in this life," he said quickly. "Positively nothing, except hard work for us all."

For some time after this both husband and wife remained silent. She cleared the supper table, and he lighted his pipe.

She sat herself down by his side. Presently she said—

"Tom, I should dearly like to know who I am."

He started, and glanced quickly at her.

"Who you are—you are my wife."

"Yes, I know, but who my mother was, and my father. It is strange that there should be such a mystery hanging over me."

"What puts that into your head all of a sudden?"

"I don't know, I'm sure. My mother was a lady, and I am, moreover, sure that I am one myself, although I have been brought up in a homely manner. No matter for that—I am a lady myself—you may laugh at me, but I feel like one, or rather how I imagine a lady should feel. I love all things bright and beautiful. I detest everything mean, paltry, and contemptible. You think I am discontented, but this is not so. Nevertheless, I am free to confess that I have tastes which, perhaps, will never be gratified—longings which never can be realised. Is it my fault that a dark mystery hangs over me?"

"Life itself is a mystery," he answered. "The world is full of mysteries. You must not give way to these gloomy thoughts—you must not indeed, dearest."

"No, I will not."

"My darling," said Tom, noting the sad tone in which the reply was made, "whatever induced you to think riches must necessarily bring happiness?"

"I don't know, indeed," replied his wife. "There are times when the monotony of this life seems more than I can bear."

"You would find the same monotony in any sphere of existence. What says the poet—

Life is as tedious as a twice-told tale,
Vexing the dull ear of a drowsy man.

But there is surely no reason, dearest, why we should endorse the sentiment."

"None whatever, Tom. You are kindness itself," responded his wife, with a loving kiss.

"By the way, I have not as yet told you that a strange gentleman called at the works to-day. He wanted to see Mrs. Maitland upon very pressing business."

"Ah, is that so? Who is he?"

"I haven't the faintest idea. He said his name was Wrench. Do you remember if your mother ever knew a person of that name?"

"Not that I ever heard of. What did you tell him?"

"I gave him her address."

* * * * * * * *

Mrs. Maitland resided with her niece, whose house was within half a mile of Tom Gatliffe's residence. While the foregoing conversation had been taking place the worthy old lady was having a *tête-à-tête* with the sagacious detective, who had explained to her his reason for waiting upon her.

Mrs. Maitland narrated to him all the circumstances connected with the young girl Aveline, whom she had adopted and brought up as her daughter.

She explained to him how she had fallen into her hands when little more than an infant; explained to him also the accident on the line, how the mother and daughter were brought into the infirmary at Derby, with the death of the former, together with all those particulars which the reader has read in an earlier portion of this work.

Mr. Wrench was charmed—he was perfectly delighted with the successful nature of his visit, and felt perfectly assured that he was on the right scent.

"And the trinkets—the articles of jewellery, madame," said he, "are you still in possession of them?"

"Oh, yes. Nothing would have induced me to part with them, except to those who require them for the purpose of identification."

"Quite right, madam. I presume you will have no objection to intrust them to my care for a few days? They are quite safe in my hands. It will be needful for Lord Ethalwood to examine them."

"Cannot you do so? I will fetch them at once."

The old lady went upstairs, unlocked an iron safe in which the trinkets were deposited, and returned with them into the parlour.

She placed them before the detective, who examined each article carefully.

"Well, what do you make of them?" inquired his companion.

"There can be no doubt about the matter," said he. "One of the rings bears the motto and crest of the Ethalwoods; and, as far as I can judge at present, this portrait bears a close resemblance to Lord Ethalwood's daughter."

"Then my little protégée, my darling child, is——"

"The grand-daughter of a nobleman."

Mrs. Maitland's breath was almost taken away at this announcement.

"Wonderful—more than wonderful!" she ejaculated. "And is it possible that she has been left uncared for and unacknowledged all these years?"

Mr. Wrench shrugged his shoulders. "It would appear so," he said, "but there are reasons for this my dear madam, very strong reasons. I suppose if I give you a receipt for these articles you will permit me to take them to Broxbridge Hall. I pledge you my word of honour, that, come what may, they shall be returned to you in the course of a few days."

"Oh, indeed, I cannot do that."

"I swear they shall be returned in a week."

"I don't like to part with them. If they should be lost."

"They will not be lost. I will answer for that."

PEACE FIRED, AND WOUNDED THE GIPSY JUST AS HE GAINED THE BANK.

"Oh, I dare say you will be careful enough, but still I hardly know how to act in a case of this sort."

"We can do nothing without them. Will you accompany me to Broxbridge Hall, and bring them with you?"

"I am not well enough to bear the fatigue of travelling so far. I have not as yet recovered from a serious illness."

"I leave the matter in your hands. I can get an order in the course of a day or two for you to produce them, but it would be saving a great deal of trouble if you would accede to my request. Yet once for all I must tell you, madam, that Lord Ethalwood counts the hours till I return. He is in the greatest state of anxiety. I have his written authority to act in this matter, the same as himself."

Mr. Wrench pulled from his pocket a document in

the handwriting of Lord Ethalwood, bearing his signature and seal, by which Mr. Wrench was empowered to act according to his own impression in all matters concerning the inquiry he was pursuing.

Mrs. Maitland put on her spectacles, and perused the document in question.

"It is altogether a most wonderful affair," said the old lady. "To think that all these years should have gone by without any inquiry being made after my little pet. Still, I suppose, I have no right to refuse you; only, you see, I'm loth to part with these articles. Perhaps I had first of all better consult those to whom they in reality belong."

"And who are they?"

"My adopted daughter and her husband."

"I would not presume to dictate, madam, but at the same time you will do wisely, I think, by not mentioning the subject to either the lady or her husband till we know whether she is the person, or rather the daughter of the person, I am seeking. That would be the most prudent course. It would be an act of cruelty to raise hopes, which, after all, might have no foundation in fact."

"That is true," returned Mrs. Maitland. "I will not mention the subject at present to either of them."

"If you are mistrustful of me," said the detective, with a smile, "you can send these articles of jewellery to Scotland-yard. It amounts to much the same thing, for they will be handed to the officer who has charge of the case, and that is myself, as you are pretty well assured of by this time, I suppose."

"I hope you do not imagine, Mr. Wrench, that I am casting any slight on you by my hesitation—far from it. I have every confidence in you. I ought to have, seeing the trouble you have been at to find out his lordship's missing daughter or descendants. You had better give me an acknowledgment for the receipt of these articles, and take them with you without further delay. Please let me know, at your earliest convenience, the result of your interview with Lord Ethalwood."

"That you may depend upon, madam."

"It is to me most extraordinary how you found me out," said the widow as she was proceeding to pack up the jewellery in its case.

"I doubt if I should—perhaps never—have succeeded in doing so, had I not by the merest chance in the world met with a townsman of yours—a Mr. Peace," returned the detective.

"Mr. Peace!" exclaimed the widow, in a tone of surprise. "Dear me—how very remarkable!"

"Yes, very. He was acquainted with you some four or five years since."

The widow nodded. "Yes, he was," she said sharply. "Mr. Peace, eh? Well, he is the last man in the world I should have thought of."

The jewellery was placed in a morocco case, and handed to Mr. Wrench, who at once wrote out a receipt for the same. He then placed the case and its contents in the breast pocket of his coat, and took his departure, well satisfied with the result of his visit.

CHAPTER XXXII.

THE RETURN TO BROXBRIDGE.—A MIDNIGHT ALARM AT THE "CARVED LION."—A CHASE, AND AN ESCAPE.

MR. WRENCH was under the full impression that he was a remarkably clever fellow. This fact, however, he had been duly impressed with on very many occasions, but perhaps he was never better pleased with himself than when he left Mrs. Maitland's residence with the proofs of her reputed daughter's identity. He had ascertained from the amiable and worthy

widow herself, that Aveline had a beautiful little boy, who was between two and three years old. This he considered a valuable piece of information, in addition to the facts with which he was already furnished.

Taken altogether, our detective congratulated himself upon being singularly fortunate.

He went by train that same night to Broxbridge Hall, and was rather vexed when the model footman told him that his master was some miles away. Lord Ethalwood was on a visit at the house of a distinguished baronet.

"And his lordship will not return till late to-morrow evening, or it may be the day hafter," said the radiant Henry Adolphus.

Mr. Wrench had no other alternative than to await the return of the earl. It would never do to take the liberty of seeing him at his friend's house.

"He's a bumptious starchy sort of customer," murmured Mr. Wench, "and stands a good deal upon etiquette, and all that sort of thing. I must eke out the time as best I can until he returns. Hang it all, what does he want to go away for at this particular time?"

Mr. Wrench made the best of his way to the hostelry kept by Brickett.

It was market day, and there were a number of strangers in the "Lion," in addition to its regular frequenters.

A noise and clatter as of many voices were heard proceeding from the public room, as the detective arrived at the front entrance of the house.

"You are unusually busy, it would seem," said he addressing the landord, and glancing significantly at the carts and other vehicles in front of the habitation.

"Yes, I have had a regular rush of it all day," returned the landlord, "but I'm glad to see 'ee back, sir, and hope as how ye've brought good news."

"Pretty well for that. Where is Mr. Peace?"

"He be in the parlour, keeping 'em all alive. Shall I call him?"

"No; I'll go in there myself."

Upon entering the public room Mr. Wrench found it three parts filled with people, most of whom were in some way or other connected with agriculture.

Peace rose from his seat and drew near the detective, who had taken his place in a corner near the door.

It was not Mr. Wrench's usual practice to make persons acquainted with his movements or proceedings, but in this case he felt that Peace had a perfect right to know, and he therefore narrated to him the successful nature of his expectations.

This, perhaps, was not altogether a prudent thing to do in a public room, even though the conversation between the two was carried on in a tone which was but a little beyond a whisper.

But our detective was under the full impression that there were none present who even comprehended their discourse, and certainly none who were in any way interested in the same.

But even detectives, with all their caution, are sometimes at fault.

This has been made apparent recently to a very painful extent.

The Kurr and Benson case took people by surprise, and shook the confidence of the public in police detectives. Everybody vaguely felt that an official inquiry must be held. Our detectives are seldom men of much education.

In books of superior fiction they figure as prodigies of acuteness, but the testimony of all who come in contact with them professionally is that they are rather dull and unenterprising, and somewhat thirsty officials, and that the chase of a criminal will be much stimulated by occasional consultations at bars and public-house parlours.

They have sprung from the ranks, and have gained promotion for qualities which are chiefly of use in tracking down and "running in" a receiver of stolen goods, or in apprehending a notorious pickpocket who was "wanted."

The ordinary detective is of service in watching the movements of ticket-of-leave men or persons under the surveillance of the police.

In short, he is a match for the stupid, small-brained criminal, but he is of little use when society bids him capture gentlemanly rogues with plenty of money, ingenuity, and address.

It is, however, unavoidable that, if crime is to be tracked, there should be a set of policemen acting in secret.

It is obvious to what dangers the men who are thus employed must be constantly exposed.

The atmosphere in which they live is not a wholesome one.

They have to mix in an insidious manner with the criminal classes—to resort to all sorts of tricks and stratagems in order to collect particulars which could not be obtained in a straightforward way.

Moreover, men in such a position have a great deal of power in their hands, and may be tempted to use it nefariously, by making terms with those after whom they are sent, and by giving them hints of danger or opportunities of escape.

Detectives have, in the ordinary course of their duty, to place themselves in equivocal positions with those with whom they are watching and studying, in order to get proofs of their guilt, and there are doubtless cases in which appearances may be against them, though they are only loyally fulfilling their duties to their superiors in ferreting out the secrets of suspected people.

What is wanted under such circumstances is a very cheap system of supervision and control.

Officers employed in this way ought to be bound to keep a detailed diary of their proceedings, and to report continually to headquarters what they have in view and what they are doing.

Something ought also to be done to raise the character of the men and perhaps the rate of their pay.

It is quite certain that our system is at fault somewhere.

Mr. Wrench was an officer perhaps a little beyond others of his class As we have already seen, he was persevering and intelligent, and Mr. Chicknell had acted wisely in securing his services for Lord Ethalwood.

Charles Peace was perfectly astounded when he became aware of the facts detailed to him by the detective.

He had never heard of the jewellery taken from the dead body of the lady in the infirmary—had never for a moment imagined that there was any doubt about the paternity of Aveline, whom he implicitly believed to be the daughter of Mrs. Maitland.

He was almost bewildered by the discovery made by the officer, who gave the details in a matter-of-fact sort of way, which left no doubt as to their accuracy.

Mr. Wrench remained in the public room for some time drinking with Peace, to whom he stood divers and sundry potations. After this he whispered to our hero that he was about to retire, wished him good-night, and betook himself to his bedchamber.

Peace did not leave the parlour for an hour or two after the withdrawal of his companion.

He played several pieces on his violin, much to the delight of the assembled guests, and then in his turn retired to his room.

He was, however, too restless and fidgetty to seek repose. He sat himself on the edge of his bed and thought over all the strange incidents which had come to his knowledge in respect to Aveline.

The whole affair seemed to be like the disjointed fragments of a nightmare.

"Was it possible that Aveline, whom he had loved in an earlier day, was a descendant of a great and honoured line?"

"I say it seems like a dream," murmured Peace, "altogether like a dream to think that I should have proposed to one of such high birth; but no, it cannot be. To think, also, that I should be the means of tracing her out—that is still more wonderful."

While thus ruminating he was startled by a noise as of something heavy thrown against the window of his little room.

He arose suddenly and threw open the casement.

Something was flung into the window. It fell upon the floor.

Peace picked it up. It was a small pebble, around which was a piece of note paper.

"What's the meaning of this?" exclaimed our hero, peering curiously out of the window.

No one was to be seen.

He sat down again and unfolded the paper, spread it out on his knee, and saw written thereon these words:—

"Be cautious. Keep watch and ward. Somebody's in the house, a stranger, who is of no good. Take warning!—A FRIEND."

"I can't make this out. 'Somebody's in the house who is no good.' Curse it, I wish the writer had been a little more explicit; this is most incomprehensible."

Again he looked out of his window in every direction, but could not see a living creature.

The handwriting on the paper he failed to recognise.

"This is most remarkable," he ejaculated. "Who is in the house, I wonder, that means no good? Some robber, I suppose—some suspected person. Well, I'll have my revolver handy in case of any attack; but after all it may only be a grim joke of one of my parlour acquaintances?"

He tried to persuade himself that this last hypothesis was the correct one, but signally failed in doing so.

Not a sound disturbed the unbroken stillness of the night.

Peace was not a man to give way to idle or groundless fears.

Nevertheless he could not but acknowledge that the circumstance was singular, and, taken altogether, was of an exceptional character.

"Who could have thrown the stone and paper into the room?" murmured he. "If it came from a friend why did he not show himself?"

During his sojourn at the "Carved Lion" he had made it a practice to have his dog Gip sleep in the same room as himself, and he had not departed from that rule on the present occasion.

He had with him also a six-chambered revolver, which he had not come too honestly by. He had, in fact, stolen it when in Sheffield.

He had always a passion for fire-arms, as also for musical instruments, and had never been very particular how he obtained either.

He glanced at "Gip," who was lying on a rug placed for his accommodation near the door of his room.

The animal looked wistfully at his master.

"Well," murmured our hero; "no one will be able to enter the apartment without my hearing it, for Gip will be sure to give an alarm. At the same time it would be as well perhaps to take this precaution."

He walked towards the door and slid the bolt into its socket.

Then he sat once more on the side of his bed.

"It may be after all but a hoax of some mischievously-disposed fool!" he exclaimed. "In all probability such is the case. Any way, I shall not put myself about, or take further trouble in the matter."

He remained for an hour or so after this, watching and waiting, but could not detect the faintest sound.

All was silent within the house, and all was silent without.

He got fairly worn out, and threw himself on his couch without undressing, drew the rug over him, and sank to sleep.

How long he had remained thus he could not say, but he was awoke by a low moan or whine from Gip, who, upon discovering his master awakening, wagged his tail and came to the side of the bed; then he crept towards the door and sniffed at its base.

"Something's amiss," whispered our hero. "The sagacious brute hears or noses somebody—that's quite certain."

He crept softly to the door, against which he placed his ear.

He heard the sounds of soft footsteps on the outside, but they were so faint as to be hardly audible.

With revolver in hand he awaited the issue.

The dog in the meantime was in an evident state of anxiety.

Peace, before stretching himself on his bed, had taken the precaution to place his lighted chamber-candle in the fireplace, which effectively prevented its feeble rays penetrating into the passage on the outside.

"Somebody or something is stirring," he muttered "I can't stand this state of suspense any longer—so here goes."

He slid the bolt back as noiselessly as possible, and flung open the door.

A flood of moonlight streamed in from the window on the landing.

Beyond this was a wide oak staircase, and ascending this he beheld a strange-looking figure, clad in a long steel-coloured cloak.

To all appearance the figure was that of a woman.

But Peace had never remembered to have seen any such person in the hostelry since he had dwelt there.

"Holloa there—who are you? Speak, woman," shouted out Peace.

No answer was vouchsafed to this.

"If you don't speak and say who you are I'll fire. I've a loaded pistol in my hand. Do you hear? For the last time I say speak, if it only be to save your life."

The figure turned the angle of the stairs, but made no answer.

A buxom servant wench opened the door of her bedroom, and exclaimed—

"Mother Brickett's ghost!"

She then uttered a series of piercing screams, and rushed back into her room in a state of abject terror.

Peace made for the bottom of the stairs, and fired one chamber of his revolver.

He did not aim at the receding figure, his object being only to frighten.

In this he succeeded, as far as the inmates were concerned.

Mr. Wrench came out in his night shirt, pale as a parsnip. Brickett made his appearance in the passage, and exclaimed, in a loud voice—

"For mercy's sake, tell me what's the matter! Are there robbers in the house, or what?"

"It be missus's ghost, that's what it be!" exclaimed the servant girl, from her bedroom. "Ah, woe is me that I should live to see such a dreadful sight!"

"You little fool," cried Peace, "hold your cursed tongue, will you? Ghost, indeed!—more like a robber."

"I've lost the jewels; they've been stolen!" said the detective. "Lost them! Don't let anyone leave the house."

He returned to his bedroom, slipped on his trousers and boots. Meanwhile Peace turned to Brickett, and said—

"Who's in the house besides ourselves? Any stranger?"

"Yes, one."

"Which is his room?"

"No. 9, on the next floor," said the landlord, who had never been so puzzled and alarmed in his life.

Peace rushed back into his bedroom, snatched up the chamber candlestick, and flew up the wide staircase, never pausing till he had reached the upper floor. The door of the No. 9 bedroom was wide open.

Our hero entered the apartment, which was tenantless. He rushed into each of the other rooms on the same floor.

One was occupied by the little maid who acted as supplementary waitress—another was tenanted by an old woman, and another was where the potman slept. All the occupants were scared at beholding our hero with his revolver in one hand, and his chamber candlestick in the other.

In answer to his queries they one and all declared they had neither seen nor heard anybody about since they had retired to rest, with the exception of their interlocutor.

At the further end of the passage was a double window, which opened sideways on hinges, as is often the case in old English houses and inns. One of the casements of this was partially open.

Peace's suspicions were aroused at once. He ran to the window, threw it back, and looked out. At the further extremity of the roof he beheld the figure of a man who flung himself off the roof on to one of the branches of a large chestnut tree, by means of which he reached the ground in safety.

"He's got clean off, and done it very cleverly, I am free to confess," exclaimed Peace; "but we may yet hunt him down."

Mr. Wrench in a state of trepidation now made his appearance.

"Have you discovered anything?" he ejaculated, in a tone of the deepest anxiety.

"He's off," cried Peace.

"Who?"

"How should I know? The robber, whoever he may be. But not a moment is to be lost. Follow me."

Our hero descended the stairs with the speed of an antelope, and was followed by the detective. They both made for the front door, which unfortunately for them was locked and barred most securely.

"How shall we get out of this cursed house?" cried Wrench.

"Here, Brickett—Brickett!" shouted out Peace. "Bring the keys and open the front door."

The landlord hastened to the spot, and undid the fastenings.

Then Peace, without another word, sallied forth.

It is an old saying, "set a thief to catch a thief," and it was never more exemplified than in this instance.

No one, however, at the time suspected that our picture-frame maker was a notorious burglar, who, however, it must be admitted had been conducting himself in a very proper manner.

He ran out into the high road, and saw at about a hundred and fifty yards the figure of the same man he had seen on the roof.

"He's got a good start, it's true," he observed to the detective, "but here goes," and with these words Peace ran after the fugitive at the very top of his speed.

He was followed by Mr. Wrench, who, as a matter of course, ran his hardest.

They had the satisfaction of finding that they gained upon the robber, who had, unfortunately for him, injured one of his ankles in dropping from the tree.

Had this not been the case the chances would have been all in his favour.

Peace and Mr. Wrench found they were gaining rapidly on the robber. This acted as an incentive for them to put forth their energies to the fullest extent.

Beyond the fields which the fugitive was now traversing was a narrow stream—a small river. This, although possibly he did not know at the time, would form a barrier to his progress.

Peace ran better perhaps than he had ever done in his life, and this is saying a great deal. He was far ahead of the detective, who was by this time winded, and was within from twenty to five-and-twenty paces of the robber, who had now come close to the river.

His capture seemed inevitable; but being well-nigh driven to desperation, he made a flying leap, and plunged into the stream just as Peace had made sure of seizing him.

The thief was evidently an expert swimmer. He struck out and made for the opposite shore.

"Curse him! he'll get clear off after all," shrieked out the detective, in an agony of despair. "Can you swim?"

"No, I can't, and I don't intend to try," returned Peace. "Can you?"

"A little, but not well enough to venture with my clothes on in a running stream like this."

"Then wait till he reaches the opposite bank," cried our hero, levelling his pistol.

The robber now got into shallow water, through which he waded as quick as possible.

Peace fired and wounded the fugitive, who staggered, but had sufficient strength left to run behind a large granary in the opposite meadow, which sheltered him from any further discharge from the revolver.

"He's wounded and wet to the skin. He can't run far. I'll after him," exclaimed our hero, who made for a small wooden bridge, situated at about sixty or seventy yards from where he stood. He reached the bridge in the space of a minute or two, passed over it, and gained the field beyond.

He then ran towards the granary.

All this had been done so rapidly that Mr. Wrench did not very well know what his more active companion was endeavouring to compass. The wooden bridge was concealed by a dense mass of foliage, and

Mr. Wrench did not know of its existence. He was therefore greatly surprised at seeing Peace run rapidly across the opposite meadow, and stood watching his movements with the deepest anxiety.

The robber was equally surprised at beholding Peace. Seeing his danger he once more took to his heels.

"If you don't stop I'll shoot you down like a dog," shouted out his pursuer, in a voice of thunder. "You can't escape. Yield, and save your life while you have a chance."

"I know that voice," cried the man. "Don't fire, old fellow. I'm cornered, and give in."

Peace rushed forward and collared the speaker.

"Don't you know me?" said the man.

"Why, hang me if it isn't the gipsy."

"That's right enough; it is the gipsy, who's nearly done over. What with water and fire I've had my dose. But I say, old fellow, you aint agoin' to hand me over to the 'crushers.' You don't want to see a fellow lagged? Look here, this is all I've taken—it is as I'm a sinner. There it is; I give it up. Let me go!"

Peace took the case of jewels from the gipsy. He opened it, and saw that the articles corresponded with the description given by the detective.

"I don't want you to be quodded," said he, "but I shall just have a search before I let you go."

"S'help me goodness," ejaculated the gipsy, "that's every blessed thing I've taken; I swear to you it is, and I'll take my Bible hoath on it. I wouldn't deceive you. Lord! how my leg do pain me."

He turned his pockets inside out, and convinced our hero that for once he had spoken the truth.

"No more burglary bis'ness for me," cried the gipsy. "I aint good at it. One pill's a dose."

"What made you attempt this one?"

"Well, if yer must know, I was put up to it by a swell. Ah! you've sent a bullet into my leg, and maimed me for life, perhaps, and a stopped me a getting a couple o' hundred quid—that's what you've been and done. But you'll let me go?"

"I don't know how you are to get clean off. I expect the officer here every minute."

"I've got a fast trotting prod not fifty yards hence. If I've strength enough left, which I think I have, to mount him, the devil himself wont catch me when once on his back."

"Go your way then—I will return," cried our hero, as he thrust into his coat pocket the much-treasured jewel case, and made again for the wooden bridge.

He passed over this, when he was met by Brickett and the detective.

"Well," said the latter, "he's got clean off, then, after all?"

"What matters that?" whispered Peace to the officer. "This is all you want—isn't it?" and he handed the case and its contents to Wrench, who could not conceal his delight.

"I am greatly indebted to you. Accept my most heartfelt thanks," murmured the detective. "You have indeed afforded me most timely assistance."

"Keep dark for the present," whispered Peace. "We can discuss this subject at our leisure. For the present, let it be known only to ourselves."

The detective nodded, and bent his steps in the direction of the "Carved Lion."

CHAPTER XXXIII.

THE MORNING AFTER—A VISIT TO LORD ETHALWOOD— THIEVES AND "THIEF CATCHING."

Mr. Wrench and his two companions returned to the

inn, all the occupants of which were in a state of alarm. They had no definite notion of the actual cause of the commotion any further than that some stranger had been creeping mysteriously through the apartments of the old hostelry—for what purpose they were at a loss to divine. The servant girl declared most positively that Mrs. Brickett's ghost had paid a visit to the establishment on that eventful night. She was most positive in her declaration as to this fact, for she saw her with her own eyes, and nothing in the world should persuade her to the contrary.

Mr. Wrench and Peace did not contradict this statement; on the contrary, they affected to believe it, albeit they were well aware that it was without a shadow of foundation in fact.

None of the occupants of the inn, however, could conceal from themselves that some secret and mysterious agency had been at work.

Brickett was puzzled—in fact, he was in a state of fog, and could not see his way at all clearly.

He said, in answer to the detective's queries, that a dark-looking man, who was to all appearance a gipsy, had presented himself at the house just before closing time, and inquired if he could have a bed for a night or two.

The landlord answered in the affirmative, and the stranger, after partaking of some refreshment, retired to the room, No. 9, on the upper floor of the house.

This was all the landlord knew of his customer. He seemed, so Brickett declared, to be a quiet respectable sort of man enough.

Mr. Wrench did not offer any observations when this information was given, but he had his suspicions nevertheless.

The whole household had been so disturbed that there was but little rest for them during the remainder of the night.

The detective and our hero met in the morning, in the club-room, where they had their morning meal together.

"This has been a planned thing," said Mr. Wrench to his companion; "that rascal would not have entered my room—opened the drawer of the bureau in which the case was deposited, and stolen the same, had he not been fully aware of both its importance and value. I do much regret that he was not captured."

"I think you will act as wisely in keeping the affair as quiet as possible," returned Peace. "What possible good could accrue from his being brought to justice? answer me that. None at all—it would have only been a needless and unnecessary exposure, at which the earl would have been greatly mortified."

"There is some reason in that."

"Very great reason, I should say—you cannot for a moment suppose that his lordship would like his private affairs dragged before any court of law for the sake of a public prosecution. Rest assured, my friend, that we have acted wisely in letting the rascal go about his business. In any case, even assuming he had been convicted, blame would attach itself to you."

"So it would—I admit that. You take a very sensible view of the matter. Let the matter blow over, and say as little about it as possible," returned Mr. Wrench, with sudden warmth.

"You have shown great wisdom throughout, and I have once more to return you my most sincere thanks."

"Oh, there's no need for that" replied Peace, carelessly. "One thing is, however, quite certain: the gipsy cove was employed by some one to abstract the jewellery from the bureau. There could be but one object in this—to remove the traces of identity."

"I came to that conclusion some hours ago. You are quite right, and we have had a narrow escape—a very narrow escape," said Mr. Wrench, with something like a shudder. "Had they succeeded in carrying it off I don't know what would have been the consequence. To me it would have been most disastrous. I see good reason to be thankful for the issue. But who could have thrown the paper and stone into your window? I haven't the faintest notion, but probably I may discover before very long. Anyway, I shall make inquiries. But for the present I must bid you good-day, for I have business matters to attend to," said Peace, rising from his seat and making towards the door of the club-room.

"Good day for the present," returned the detective, and so the two parted.

In a few minutes after this Henry Adolphus, his lordship's footman, presented himself, and informed the detective that the Earl and Mr. Chicknell were awaiting his appearance at the Hall.

Mr. Wrench lost no time in paying his respects to his two employers. He made them acquainted with the successful nature of his expedition to Wood-green, his interview with Mrs. Maitland, and wound up by producing the trinkets, which had been so miraculously rescued from the clutches of "Bandy-legged Bill," the gipsy.

Lord Ethalwood snatched the case and its contents from the officer. He examined the trinkets, and as he did so a bright flush overspread his features.

"The very image of the long-lost Aveline!" he exclaimed directing the lawyer's attention to the portrait of his daughter. "There can be no doubt as to the identity." Then, turning to the detective, he said, "You have displayed wonderful ability, sir, in the conduct of this case, and deserve my warmest commendation."

Mr. Wrench bowed, but did not offer any observation. Possibly he was mindful of the old adage "That a modest man on his own merits is dumb."

"We" (he spoke in the plural) "have brought the matter to a satisfactory conclusion," observed the lawyer.

"As yet it is not concluded, Mr. Chicknell," returned the Earl.

"No—ahem—of course not. Much remains to be done. Your lordship is quite right—it is not concluded, but it is gratifying to know that we have been successful thus far. The ring bears the Ethalwood crest, I believe."

"It does."

"An additional link—I may say an important one—in the chain of evidence."

"I am told," said the earl, addressing the officer, "that some robber, some unprincipled scoundrel, made an attempt to steal these articles from the inn, either last night or early this morning."

"That is true, my lord, but we were too sharp for him," said Mr. Wrench, with evident vexation—"much too sharp."

"Oh! it would be adding to the other favours already conferred upon me if you could by any means ascertain who the villain was."

"I will do my best, my lord," returned Wrench.

"Thank you."

"Well, I think, that is all we have to say at present, Wrench," said Mr. Chicknell. "I will see you later on."

The detective took the hint, bowed, and retired.

"Confound it!" he murmured, as he descended the stairs. "Who could have told him of the attempted robbery? 'Ill news travels fast' is an old saying, which is borne out in this instance."

For the remainder of the day Peace was actively employed in an endeavour to find out the man who had created such a disturbance at the "Carved Lion" on the preceding evening; but, as he had anticipated, he found this by no means an easy task.

The gipsy had got clear off. There were traces of his passage along the high road by the marks of blood which had poured from his wound, but they gradually became fainter, after which they were no longer distinguishable.

Wrench had proved himself to be a proficient in that department of his profession known as "thief catching," but he was by no means sanguine of success in this case. Neither did he care much about it, for he argued that no possible good could accrue by the arrest of the gipsy; certainly, none as far as he (the detective) was concerned. In point of fact, it would be a needless exposure of his own want of caution.

Thieves as a rule are remarkably cunning, and to capture them is no easy matter.

Captain Fenwick, head constable of Chester, wrote some time back an interesting letter on "Modern Thief-catching." It is estimated, said he, that there are at large in this country about 40,000 individuals who are either known thieves or under the suspicion of the police; nearly 3000 are yearly liberated from the convict prisons alone; and a large proportion of them are lost in the crowd until they find themselves back in prison again.

Considering the influence of these persons on society in the way both of depredation and contamination, it will be readily perceived that thief-catching is a matter of considerable moment.

Captain Fenwick in his epistle reviews the various means which have been adopted from time to time to identify depredators, and to save the public from being victimised by habitual criminals.

When the telegraph system was adopted it was probably thought that its use by the police would cripple the operations of the professional thief.

As a fact it has been and is still used with some success for the purpose, but even at the present day, with the system and its immense ramifications in full working order, the "dangerous classes," as they are termed, manage to exist in strong force.

Photography lends its aid in the same direction.

Twenty years ago the police established what are known as "routes," and many an old gaol bird has been recognised by that means.

When a prisoner has been arrested, and it is suspected from his familiarity with the prison rules and for other reasons that he is known to the police, notwithstanding his air of pastoral simplicity, he is photographed, and his "picture" is circulated.

In a few days it is returned with an accumulation of information signally fatal to the prisoner's assumed innocence, and largely in the public interest.

Instead of a "moon" (a month) in the local gaol he finds himself before a jury as an old offender, and ultimately back again to a convict establishment.

But photography is not always quite reliable, and it is not even imperative upon an untried prisoner to sit for his photograph, and only "chumps" (the inexperienced) consent; and, although after conviction a prisoner is duly "taken" and carefully registered, his personal appearance naturally changes this change, as in the case of Peace, is sometimes assisted by art.

As a rule, prison photographs are not excellent specimens of photographic art.

The *pose* is not perfect, nor the subject carefully focussed, and the result of the defect is not removed by a normal squint or a twist of the features at the critical moment.

Officialdom felt this drawback, and to meet it to some extent a "black book" was devised.

The "Habitual Criminal Register," as this book is termed, is an imposing-looking tome. In six years and a half the names of nearly 180,000 persons were registered in its pages. In every case the criminal had been more than once convicted on indictment for serious crimes against the community.

This formidable catalogue was compiled for the most part by men whose names are to be found in it and printed at "Her Majesty's Prison, Brixton."

There is a curious irony in the fact that some of these gentlemen should be employed to perfect a scheme destined to react upon themselves and their fraternity.

Yet with all these precautions a goodly proportion still evade the clutches of the law.

By the free adoption of aliases, identifications through the *Hue and Cry*, and even by means of photographs, have often failed.

Amusing exceptions, it is true, have occurred, one woman, who had provided herself with sixteen aliases, being convicted for the thirty-ninth time.

Lieut.-Colonel Du Cane says in his preface to the first volume of the "Register":—"It is, I believe, the first time that an attempt has been made to furnish all the police of this or any other country with information in such a complete and readily accessible form respecting the individuals of the class against whom they are carrying on their operations, and the first time that such a work has been carried out in a prison."

The latest attempt, however, is to checkmate and deal with the habitual criminal in the register of their "Distinctive Marks and Peculiarities."

The name only has proved an uncertain means of tracing their antecedents. It is found, however, that many of these people bear about with them some mark or peculiarity, which answers much better.

Thus of 2914 persons who were liberated in 1876 nearly one-half were indelibly stamped in this way, and this information is now carefully arranged in the new register.

A thief may assume any name he pleases—the chances are about even that he is ear-marked, and known more certainly than by name.

This register is a curiously interesting production.

The first issue shows who are "deaf," "very deaf," "men of colour," "blind of one or both eyes," those who squint, or have a "glide," or a "cast" in their organs of vision.

Twenty-five per cent. have "broken, or crooked noses," and a few have "their ears slit."

The mania for tattooing, which it will be remembered even the "Claimant" was not free from, exists largely among thieves.

There is first of all the "D," (deserter from the army), which occurs very frequently, two "D's' almost equally so; some have even three "B C's," (bad characters) appearing on the left sides, of a sufficient number to justify the conclusion that a bad soldier is often something more.

The variety of marks upon the chest is very extensive.

Sometimes they are the initials of the owner's name, or of his sweetheart's.

The presence of the Union Jack is presumed to indicate patriotism of some sort.

Here and there occur a ship in full sail, the masonic emblems of square and compass, and a few adopt such mottoes as *Dieu et mon droit*, "Now or Never," and so on.

The arms are extensively used for this kind of art, every fourth criminal being tattooed with some device.

The variety indeed is almost endless, and the extent in some cases enough to make a Maori jealous.

The sun and moon figure over and over again; anchors, fishes, mermaids, and hearts (pierced with Cupid's arrow and other devices) are also frequent.

Then there are flags, swords, guns, and implements of war in abundance.

Among other devices we come upon such as "Mary." "In Memory of My Parents," &c., &c. The hand is very fruitful in its "particularities," and the legs are laid under contribution in the same way.

The reader will pardon this digression, as this notice of the means by which the police are able to detect the "wanted" when they are "known," has interest for the public, as well as the constabulary.

It is calculated to induce a more general scrutiny of suspected thieves, with a view to discovery of peculiar marks, and in future the "information" received by the police may prove more useful in thief-catching.

CHAPTER XXXIV.
LORD ETHALWOOD AND HIS SOLICITOR.

"We have been singularly successful, my lord," said Mr. Chicknell, after the detective had taken his departure. "We have not succeeded in finding your beloved daughter, but we have found your grandchild, who is beautiful, and who is moreover the image of her mother."

"How do you know? You have not seen her," observed the earl.

"That I admit, but Wrench has, and we can take his word."

"What does Mr. Wrench say about her husband?"

"He says he is a fine handsome fellow. Not of high birth, it is true; but he is a superior man of his class."

"And what might that be?"

"He is an engineer."

"Does his wife seem warmly attached to him?"

The lawyer smiled.

"I am a better judge, my lord, of the merits of a law case than of a lady's affection," he returned; "but from what I am given to understand the union between the two was what is termed a love match."

"Bah! a love match!" exclaimed the earl, with something like disgust. "A love match, indeed!"

A silence of some minutes' duration succeeded this last speech.

The earl glanced at a portrait of one of his ancestors which hung on the wall of his room.

He sighed, and said, sadly—

"It would seem that the Ethalwoods have fallen very low during my lifetime; their name is sullied, their honour tarnished. But I am not unmindful of the respect due to myself and my ancestors. I cannot and will not receive the husband of my grandchild in this house. A man of that kind is not fit companion for me or mine."

"I am sorry for this," murmured the lawyer, "very sorry, but I suppose it cannot be helped. What do you propose then, my lord?"

"At present it is not easy to determine upon my course of action, but I am resolved upon one point. Nothing whatever shall induce me to recognise this miserable mechanic. But I will adopt my granddaughter, I will make her a wealthy heiress—she shall have the large fortune which I purposed dividing between my two sons, and I will also adopt her son. He shall be my heir, but this must be conditional."

"And what is that?"

"She must live apart from her husband. There must be a separation—a legal one if it can be compassed. If not, they must part by mutual consent."

Mr. Chicknell made no reply.

"Do you understand what I have been saying?" asked the earl, testily.

"Oh yes, my lord, I comprehend most fully, but I cannot conceal from myself that there may be some difficulty in carrying out your views."

"None whatever. I can see no difficulty."

The lawyer shrugged his shoulders, but made no answer.

"Really, Chicknell," observed the earl, "you seem to be offering imaginary impediments. You must look at this matter from my point of view, not from your own. I suppose you know enough of me—you ought to do so by this time—to be perfectly aware that I am not a man to be dictated to."

"I would not presume to dictate to you," observed the lawyer.

"I tell you that I will, under no circumstances, receive this young woman's husband here. Let that suffice. It is needless for me to reiterate this."

"Yet you would receive his child?"

"He is of my own race, but his father is an alien. The boy has noble blood in his veins—the father has none. The former has a strong claim on me—the latter has none whatever. You must see this; nay, I am sure you do."

"Yes, I can understand that, but——"

"Well, sir, but what?"

"For the life of me I cannot see what this young man has done that you should seek, my lord, to tempt from him the wife he loves."

Lord Ethalwood uttered an expression of disgust.

"If you are his champion," he said, bitterly—"if you plead his cause so pertinaciously, in opposition to my expressed wishes, say so at once, and I shall know how to obtain the services of another legal adviser."

"I much regret you should for a moment imagine that I have not your interest at heart. Why should I be the champion of a young fellow whom I have never seen? I have always had the privilege of speaking plainly, and it is not because I have done so in this case that I should merit your censure. However, if you have no confidence in me, my lord, it is competent for you to obtain better advice—or rather advice more in accordance with your own views."

"Pardon me, Chicknell, I have been somewhat hasty. What I said was without due consideration, so let it pass; but you must do your best for me. Of course I have no desire to place the affair in any other hands than yours."

"If you have been hasty, I acknowledge frankly that I have been mistaken."

"In what?"

"I thought your delight would have been so great at our success that you would have for the nonce sunk all considerations as to social distinction. I find I am mistaken. I do not wonder at the revolt of the poor against the rich, of the opposition and bitter animosity displayed by one class of the community against another class."

"YOU COWARDLY SCOUNDREL!" SAID THE NEW-COMER TO PEACE: "HOW DARE YOU STRIKE A WOMAN?"

Lord Ethalwood looked at the speaker in some surprise, but his countenance did not, however, wear an angry expression.

"I don't think," he observed with a smile, "that we shall agree upon this great social question, and it is therefore idle and useless to discuss it. I have my views, which it would appear are identical with your own. I do not like you any the less for plain speaking;

nevertheless my opinion remains unchanged. I will receive my grandchild Aveline and her son, but I will not countenance her husband."

"It is my bounden duty to act according to the instructions received from your lordship," said the lawyer. "Tell me what you wish me to do."

"You had better hasten at once to Wood Green, and let my grand-daughter know who she is. I should like you to bring her and her son back with you, if this be possible. I will, in the meantime, consider over the proposition we will make to her."

" I will act in accordance with your instructions."

" But you do not like the commission?" said the earl, quickly. " You need not reply, Chicknell; I see you do not."

" Gentlemen in our profession are constrained to undertake commissions which at times may be neither pleasing nor palatable to them. I will do my best to further your views."

The earl bowed, and then said, in a quieter tone—

" There is another little matter, Mr. Chicknell. We have to attend to this picture-frame maker, Mr. Peace. He has been of essential service to us, and certainly deserves some recompense."

" Certainly; that was understood."

" What do you propose ?"

" He's a poor man. Fifty pounds would be deemed a liberal recompense."

" I will get you to take him a cheque for a hundred."

" Ah, that will be ample—more than sufficient."

" You will see what he says—how he receives it."

The lawyer nodded. The earl drew the cheque, and handed it to Chicknell.

" You wish me to present him with it before I leave ?"

" Certainly ; do so at once."

Mr. Chicknell remained at Broxbridge Hall till the following morning after the foregoing conversation. He sallied forth, and bent his steps in the direction of Peace's workshop.

The frame-maker was hard at work. A few brief words sufficed to explain the reason for his visit.

He handed the earl's cheque to our hero, who accepted it, and at the same time expressed his sense of gratitude, and said it was much more than he had any right to expect.

This little bit of business having turned out perfectly satisfactory, Mr. Chicknell took the train up to London, and from thence proceeded to Wood Green.

Upon his arrival at Gatliffe's residence he discovered the young wife in the garden, which ran at one side and in the rear of the house.

Mr. Chicknell raised his hat in a most courtly manner as Aveline advanced towards the gate at which he was standing.

" Mrs. Gatliffe, I presume ?" said the lawyer.

The lady answered in the affirmative, and unlocked the gate.

" I am a stranger to you, madam," he observed, apologetically; " but the business I am engaged in makes it a matter of necessity that we should confer together."

" Do you wish to see me or my husband ? If the latter he is not within, and will not return home till the evening."

" It's you I desire to communicate with, not your husband."

Mrs. Gatliffe looked surprised, but did not make any reply.

She opened a side door, and conducted her visitor into the front parlour.

The lawyer was struck by her appearance, as well he might be. She was dressed in a neat stuff gown, which fitted tight to her graceful and symmetrical figure, and he thought she was the very personification of female loveliness without the aid of any meretricious adornment.

He entered the parlour and was handed a chair by the mistress of the establishment.

" You will, perhaps, be no wiser," said Mr. Chick-

nell, with a smile, " when I inform you that I am solicitor to Lord Ethalwood, seeing that in all probability even the name of his lordship may be unknown to you."

" It is."

" Well, madam, it must remain so no longer, as it is requisite that you should know who you are."

A bright flush overspread the beautiful features of Aveline Gatliffe.

" Who I am !" she murmured. " Indeed—indeed, sir, I have yearned to know this for very many years past."

" I am not surprised at that, madam. Let me at once inform you that you belong to the aristocracy of this country."

" Oh, sir, are you serious ? Can this be possible ?" inquired Aveline, in a state of the deepest anxiety.

" I am dealing with facts which are incontrovertible," said the lawyer, in a more serious tone. " Listen, madam."

Slowly, deliberately, and with singular clearness, Mr. Chicknell proceeded to make his companion acquainted with all those circumstances connected with his case, as he termed it.

He passed lightly over the elopement of Aveline's mother with the Italian; neither did he dwell upon the painful scene in the infirmary after the accident on the line, but he gave her to understand that the articles of jewellery taken from the dead body of her parent were in the possession of Lord Ethalwood. Mr. Chicknell made the young wife acquainted with every grain of evidence, which taken altogether proved most incontestably her identity.

As Aveline listened her wonder-struck countenance lost much of its wonted colour; her lips grew white as lilies, and her eyes dilated with an expression which was something akin to terror.

He finished his narrative, the last words of which were of serious import.

A mist seemed to float before her eyes.

" Am I really that great lord's grandchild ?" she gasped forth with evident effort.

" You are so beyond all question," returned the lawyer. " You are undoubtedly the daughter of Aveline Beatrice Ethalwood, who ran away from home with her music master. You are the grandchild of Lord Ethalwood, the master of Broxbridge and its rich dependencies. The child playing there (pointing through the window of the apartment to the little boy on the grass plot) may be one day an earl, and you yourself may be a wealthy heiress; but I regret to say that there is one condition attached to all this."

" A condition !" she replied, her face recovering its colour, her eyes flashing light. " I am bound to accept the condition, I suppose? You do not know how I have always longed to be rich and great."

The lawyer smiled.

" It is not for me to dictate. I have only to make the proposition, which it will rest with you to either accept or refuse."

She looked surprised and said—

" There will be no condition too difficult for me to accept."

" I am not so sure of that," said Mr. Chicknell. " Lord Ethalwood is a very proud man—I should say no man living is prouder. He has the greatest reverence for what he calls the honour of his house. Think how he valued it when he treated his daughter as one dead because she married beneath her. I will be explicit and plain-spoken—the exigencies of the case necessitate my being so. Lord Ethalwood will receive you as his grandchild; will give you a large fortune; will make your son his heir; all, upon one condition.

"And what is that?"

"That you will leave your husband, whom he considers low-born, and promise never to see him again."

Aveline uttered an expression as of sudden pain.

"These are indeed hard terms, sir," she exclaimed. "It might be said cruel proposals."

"They are what I have been instructed to make to you," returned the lawyer, with a shrug.

"Leave my husband, who is the best and kindest that ever woman had! I would not do it for any consideration. He loves me, and I will not consent to break an honest man's heart."

"I expected this answer," said Mr. Chicknell, "and it therefore does not surprise me; but if I might suggest, madam, it would be that you take time to consider the matter. This is but just and reasonable."

"You have no right to tempt me thus by making such an offer," she exclaimed, in an angry tone.

"I have simply done my duty," he answered, "by acting in accordance with the instructions received from my client."

"Tell this proud nobleman that I will never give my consent to such a course of action."

She looked so lovely in her pride, her anger, and her tears, that the lawyer wished his client could have seen her at that moment.

He waited patiently till her indignation had in a measure passed over—then he said—

"There will be no harm in your seeing his lordship," he said. "On the contrary, it might have considerable weight with him, and turn him from his obstinate resolution. He requested me to say that he would be overjoyed to see you and your little boy at Broxbridge Hall."

"Did he?"

"Yes. He said I was not to leave until you had consented to accompany me."

"I will see him, then. I accept his invitation, but I cannot leave without first of all consulting my husband."

"Who, in all probability, will not give his consent."

"He will not refuse if I tell him I have promised my word."

Mr. Chicknell inquired of his companion when she would have her husband's answer.

"I will speak to him on the subject when he comes home this evening."

"And if he consents you will accompany me to Broxbridge to-morrow."

Aveline replied in the affirmative.

The lawyer took his departure, with a promise to see her again on the following morning.

Tom Gatliffe, when he returned home that evening, was perfectly bewildered when he had been made acquainted with all the circumstances connected with his young wife. A foreboding of evil took possession of him —he was forcibly and painfully impressed with the fact that the discovery was not unattended with danger. He could, however, refuse his wife nothing, and therefore gave his consent for her to accompany the lawyer to Broxbridge Hall.

On the following morning Mr. Chicknell presented himself. Aveline and her child were arrayed in their best attire, and left their cottage in Wood Green under the protection of the man at law.

A telegram had been sent to Broxbridge, advising its owner of the visit. An open landau awaited them upon their arrival at the station. In this Mr. Chicknell and his two companions were driven to the hall.

As they approached the fine old mansion Peace passed the carriage. His eyes were rivetted on the face of its female occupant, Aveline; he thought she looked more lovely than ever.

It was the first time he had seen her since the rejection of his suit in the garden of Mrs. Maitland's house.

A host of contending emotions rushed through his brain as he witnessed the arrival of the carriage at the great gates of the hall.

"She does not condescend to honour me with a passing notice," he ejaculated, in a voice of concentrated passion; "the stuck-up, proud minx, and but for me she would never have been discovered. Curses on it, I was a fool to give any information—worse than a fool. Much thanks shall I get from either her or her bumptious husband."

He turned out of the high road and made for his workshop, but he was ill at ease. All the worst passions of his nature were in the ascendant, and he did not care about following his usual avocation.

For a long time he remained moody and thoughtful in his workshop. He was laying plans for the future.

The sight of Aveline seemed to have produced a sudden revulsion in his mind. He could not bear to see her under any circumstances; but to find her in such an exalted position was most intolerable. And yet he had been mainly instrumental in bringing this about. Now it was done he bitterly regretted. Such is the strange perversity of the human character.

CHAPTER XXXV.

THE LOVERS—PEACE BECOMES FURIOUS—VIOLENT ALTERCATION—PHILIP JAMBLIN TO THE RESCUE.

WHILE all these events had been taking place Charles Peace had paid frequent visits to the house and gardens in possession of the girl "Nelly," for whom he had conceived a passionate fondness. He had become on tolerably familiar terms with her aunt, and had on more than one occasion flirted with her niece. Nelly did not dislike him, and, although she did not encourage his attentions, she did not positively reject them. To a certain extent she felt flattered by the court and homage paid to her. Her conduct, as far as our hero was concerned, was nothing more nor less than a bit of harmless coquetry.

With Peace it was far different. He hoped to win the girl; otherwise he would not have troubled himself so much about her, and it is likely enough that he would not have remained so long in the neighbourhood had it not been for her.

After the robbery at the "Lion," and the chase of Bandy-legged Bill, Peace endeavoured to ascertain who threw the missile into his window on that eventful night.

He taxed several of the villagers with it, but they one and all denied in a most positive manner having given the timely warning.

It afterwards occurred to him that it might be Nelly, and he mentioned his suspicions to her.

She laughed, and after a little hesitation acknowledged that she was the culprit. She informed Peace that she was mistrustful of the gipsy, whom she had seen in her aunt's strawberry ground with a strange gentleman, with whom he was conversing in almost a whisper. From the few words of the conversation that did reach her ears she was under the impression that a deep-laid plot was hatching; and afterwards, upon finding the gipsy had taken up his quarters at the "Carved Lion," her suspicions were in a measure confirmed, hence it was that she had recourse to the little stratagem which was of such infinite service on the night of the attempted robbery.

"You are a good girl, and are worth your weight in gold," cried Peace, when Nelly had concluded. "Indeed, I don't know what I should do without you."

He placed his arm round her neck, and drew her towards him.

"There, get away, do!" exclaimed the girl, slipping out of his grasp. "I never knew a man so forward and impudent as you are."

"And I never knew a girl so uncertain and capricious as you are," returned he; "so now we are even. But I say, Nell, darling——" he was about to make an amorous speech, when the voice of the owner of the establishment was heard, and Nell said, quickly—

"There's aunt calling me; I must indoors."

"But I want to speak to you—have something to say of the greatest importance."

"Some other time will do as well," she returned, with a laugh.

"Will you meet me to-morrow evening at the corner of Dennett's-lane, and hear what I have to say?"

"Perhaps."

"Nay, don't say perhaps; you must come."

"Very well; I will, if possible," and with these words the girl ran down the gravel walk and entered the house.

It was in the evening of the day on which Aveline Gatliffe had paid a visit to the earl that Nelly had promised to be at the end of Dennett's-lane.

Peace anxiously awaited her appearance.

He remained in his workshop silent and thoughtful.

He was calm, but it was that sort of calmness which presaged a storm.

To say the truth, he was getting tired of the quiet and respectable sort of life he had been of late leading. The old feeling of restlessness and yearning for adventure had come over him, and his mind was in a sort of chaos.

"Will she come?" he murmured, looking furtively down the lane, "or will she make some miserable excuse for stopping away when next I see her? She's a riddle—a mystery, which I find it difficult to make out."

Another half hour passed away, but no Nelly. The sun had already sunk, and the shades of evening were beginning to descend.

He arose from his seat, passed out of his workshop, closed and locked the door, and again looked down the lane.

He beheld in the distance the figure of a woman. It was that of Nelly. His heart leaped with delight.

"You're precious late, my lady," said he, as she approached.

"Be I? Well, I couldn't get away before. It beant no fault of mine if I be late. Now, then, what be ye a-going to tell me?"

"You shall learn all in good time," cried he, putting her arm in his, and strolling along the narrow footway.

"You see, Nell, it's time, I'm thinking, that I should be plain spoken. I find, my lass, that I care a deal more for you than I first imagined. You see, I don't know how much longer I shall remain in this village—not long, I expect. The fact is, I've grown so fond of you that I don't like to leave—nay, more, I don't intend to leave until you give me an answer one way or the other."

"An answer—what about?"

"What do you suppose it's about? Can't you guess?"

"No."

"Well, I'm sorry for you. Don't I tell you that I'm attached to you—that I love you?"

He drew her towards him, and covered her lips and face with burning and passionate kisses.

She was surprised and annoyed, made as much resistance as possible, and pushed him from her.

"What possesses the man," she cried, "to be mawling a gal in this fashion? If I'd ha' known of this, I wouldn't ha' come."

"Now, Nell," cried her companion, "why do you seek to tantalise me? You must know by this time my feelings with regard to yourself. Listen to me for a few moments. You know I've been doing a good stroke of business; I am greatly respected by all who know me. In addition to this I have been patronised and made much of by the Master of Broxbridge ——"

"What has all this to do with me?"

"I am telling you these things to prove that I am worthy of you. I am well-to-do, and have every reason to suppose you care something about me."

She laughed derisively at this last observation.

His countenance grew dark and wore a malignant expression, but by a violent effort he suppressed his passion for a while.

"And be this all you wanted to see me for?" she inquired.

"All!" he reiterated, "and enough too, I'm thinking. Now do be a little reasonable. Do you suppose I should have been dangling after you for so long a time for nothing? I tell you again and again, Nelly, that I doat on you."

Here once more he threw his arms round his companion's neck, and embraced her with passionate fervour.

"There, that will do. You certainly are the most daring man I ever came across. Have you anything more to say?" she enquired, in a coquettish manner.

"Yes, a deal more," he returned. "I want to fix you firm and fast before I leave—I want you to give me a promise."

"What be that you want me to promise?"

"Not to have anything to say to any other chap when I am gone. You must consider yourself engaged to me."

She made no reply, but looked thoughtfully on the ground on which they were walking.

"Do you hear—do you understand?" he inquired.

"Yes, I think I understand."

"And you answer—"

"I aint a goin' to mek any promise."

"What!—you refuse, then—and why? Tell me why? Why don't you answer? Do you want to drive me to madness, you cruel thoughtless girl?"

"I aint a goin' to mek any promise, I dunno what other answer to mek."

"I'll take you up to London and you shall see all the fine sights, and be a fine lady," he said in a wheedling tone. "Come, Nell, say you will be mine."

"I won't say nuffin' o' the sort, not at present."

"Why not?"

"I don't know enough of you," she answered with the greatest simplicity; "that's one reason."

"And the other?"

She made no answer.

"The other!" he shouted in a voice of thunder. "There is someone else in the case—is that it?"

"I won't answer you."

"Then you have been making a fool of me all this time," he cried, in a voice of concentrated passion. "You treacherous infamous girl; but I'll let you know, my lady, that Charles Peace is not to be trampled upon with impunity—understand that."

He caught her by the wrist and held it with the grip of a vice.

"Let me go—ye hurt me—let me go !" she exclaimed in some alarm.

"Not till you give me the name of my rival. Until you do that I will not release you."

He dragged her forcibly along the pathway, and displayed such an excess of fury that the girl was seriously alarmed.

"I must ha' bin a born fool to ha' come here, and I be rightly served. Let me go !"

"Answer my question first—his name—tell me the fellow's name and I'll then release you—not before. You've played me false, and you know it."

He had by this time become more like a maniac than a rational being.

Nell struggled desperately to release herself from his grasp, but although a strong-built muscular young woman she found herself almost powerless in the grip of her persecutor.

"Have I wasted all my thoughts all this time over one who is so base and worthless?" he ejaculated with supreme bitterness. "Am I to become the laughing stock of the whole neighbourhood ?"

"I wish I'd never seen you. I hate you !" cried Nelly, in a spiteful tone. "What have I done to be treated thus ?"

"One word and we are friends for life. Say you will be mine," said he.

"I will say nothing till you let me go."

"I'll have your answer one way or the other," shouted out Peace, drawing a revolver from his pocket. "By the heavens above, I will make you answer me."

At the sight of the weapon the miserable young woman uttered several piercing screams.

A tall young man jumped over a neighbouring stile, and with one blow from the stout ash stick he carried struck the weapon out of Peace's hand ; then he delivered another terrific blow on our hero's head, which sent him back reeling and half stunned.

"You cowardly scoundrel," exclaimed the new comer, "to lay your hands on a woman."

The speaker was about to inflict further chastisement, whereupon Nelly interceded.

"Spare him, Mr. Jamblin," said the girl. "He be mad, and knows not what he has been doing. He be mad, I'm sure o' that."

"What have you to say for yourself, sir ? What is the reason for this outrage ?" inquired the young man, addressing himself to Peace.

"What business is it of yours ?" answered our hero. "There is a reason, and a very strong one. But, hark ye ! Don't you bully me, or it will be worse for you. I'm not afraid of you, big as you are."

"I've seen your face before," observed the newcomer. "It's familiar to me."

"Have you ?" cried Peace, making a hideous grimace. "Then you've the advantage of me, for I never saw your ugly mug before ; and what's more, I don't want to see it again."

"Do you remember a burglary at Oakfield House, some time ago, eh ?"

"No, I don't. Do you ?" inquired Peace, who was by this time a litle less confident in his tone and manner.

"Yes, I do. A man named Gregson was shot by a woman, and afterwards expiated his crimes on the public scaffold. If I mistake not, I met you on the night of the burglary. I've an astonishing power of remembering faces."

"Have you ? You're a mighty clever fellow in your way ; but it so happens that I never heard of any such burglary, and don't know any house bearing that name. You seem to know more about it than I do. Were you one of the burglars ?"

At this last observation the young man rushed forward and was about to strike Peace, when the girl, Nelly, threw herself between the two, and begged her protector to spare him.

"Say no more, Nell," returned the young man. "I won't harm him. Though for the life of me I can't understand why you should seek to protect him."

"Go your ways, you ugly little vagabond," said the stranger, addressing Peace. "If you remain here much longer the chances are you will find yourself handed over to the police constable, who is coming this way."

Peace in this instance considered discretion to be the better part of valour, and, hurling several anathemas at the girl and her protector, he made off.

He hastened at once to the house of the village surgeon, where he had his head dressed, declaring that he had received the wound in conflict with what he chose to term a ruffian.

He was by this time thoroughly sick of Broxbridge, which he determined upon leaving forthwith. He had been jilted and derided by a girl to whom he had become attached, had been chastised by a young man, who evidently knew all about the Oakfield House burglary, which he had believed had been quite forgotten, and so there was every reason for his leaving the neighbourhood. On the following morning he packed up his traps, had them conveyed to the station, and bidding Brickett good-bye, with a promise to return in a few weeks' time, he beat a retreat, and hastened up to the metropolis, to find therein a new scene of action.

CHAPTER XXXVI.
A YOUNG POACHER—THE INDIGNANT AGRICULTURIST.

THE name of the young man who came so opportunely to the rescue of Nelly was Philip Jamblin. The reader will doubtless remember the two visitors to Farmer Ashbrook's house on the night of the burglary at Oakfield. These personages, Messrs. Cheadle and Jamblin, gave chase to Peace after his escape over the fields described in the opening chapters of this work. The Jamblins and Ashbrooks were old friends.

Philip's father was the owner of a large farm situated at about a couple of miles' distance from Broxbridge ; he held this under a lease from Lord Ethalwood. The place was known as Stoke Ferry Farm.

Mr. Jamblin, senior, was a farmer of the old school, who had worked his way up in the world by dint of skill and industry. He it was who paid for the plentiful supply of beer to the occupants of the parlour of the "Carved Lion," on the night when Peace first became acquainted with the establishment.

Mr. Jamblin had in his service a ne'er to-do-well, wayward, good-for-nothing sort of lad, called Alfred Purvis, whose parentage was not clearly established. A gentleman of independent means, residing in the neighbourhood, had paid for his support during the earlier years of his childhood, and when he became old enough he had placed him with Mr. Jamblin to learn the farming business, if it can, with propriety, be so termed.

But the lad Alfred was a sore trouble to the farmer. He was mischievously disposed, and was for ever getting into scrapes.

As he is destined to play a secondary part in this drama, it will be necessay to introduce him to the reader.

Some few days after Peace's departure from Broxbridge, Mr. Jamblin became furious at a discovery he had made.

He was striding up and down the great stone kitchen of Stoke Ferry Farm, with his arms swinging round his head like the sails of a windmill, and his face growing redder and redder every moment.

He was a kindly-disposed man enough, and was greatly esteemed by his workpeople, but he did not like anything under-handed.

His youngest daughter Patty was leaning against the table, and trying to pacify him as best she could.

"Don't lose your temper, father," she murmured, in a soft low voice. "After all it's only one, and surely that's no great matter."

"Only one!" cried the indignant agriculturist. "That be true enough, lass; but how are we to know if he aint killed twenty—the young warmint?"

A dead hare, which was lying on the dresser with a wire round its neck, explained the subject of their conversation.

Mr. Jamblin glanced at it with a look of rage and disgust.

"He'll never come to any good—never, as sure as I'm a born man," he ejaculated; "there beant no manner of doubt about that."

"Haven't you often said that boys wouldn't be boys if they weren't a little mischievous?" said his daughter.

"Don't talk nonsense, gell. Boys' meescheef be boys' meescheef, that be true enough; but it doesn't do to ha' too much of it at one time. I tell 'ee he won't come to any good. He aint a common boy—he's a changeling, that's what he be; there's something remarkable about him. Ever since he's bin here he's bin a sore trouble to all on us, and I wish I'd never set eyes on the young bastard. After he had bin with me a little time and I sent him out in the fields bird-keepin', he begged and prayed of me to take the long gun with him, and I did let un take it. 'You won't know how to use it now you've got it,' sed I. 'Oh yes, I shell,' sed he; and I'm blessed if he warn't right, for directly he got into the fields he let fly at a flock of my house pigeons and brought down four, and took 'em into the veeledge and sold 'em. He'll never come to any good, Patty, you mark my words. Them as commence being bad as early as he did seldom find the right road arterwards."

"Oh, he'll know better as he gets older," said Patty.

"Not a bit on it; not a morsel of improvement will be found in him. I tell ee what makes me most afraid on him," said the farmer, sinking his voice to a whisper, "it's the way he's got of reading a durned lot o' books. It's my belief as they puts him up to no end of things as he'd never ha' thort on without."

"Oh, father, there aint any harm in reading."

"I tell ee there is, I aint no 'pinion of that printed stuff, Patty. When I opens a book it reads all black to me, and whatever's black's bad, so folks say, and it arnt that only, this lad is so clever with'ut. I sent him to a day school to get a little scholarship because the vicar wished me to do so, but he soon beat the lot on un, missus inclooded."

His daughter laughed outright at this speech.

"It be all very well for you to make merry over it, gell; he's allers got a book in his hand now, arter his day's work, or what he calls his day's work, is over."

"He's read all I've got in the best parlour, and there's a frightful sight on 'em there, so he gets about borrowin' books from the neighbours. Blessed if I don't think he would swallow the biggest library that ever was, and think nuffin of it."

"Well, he'd better be reading than be getting into mischief."

"Sam seed him busy about the hedge last evening, and this morning he bein' fust in the ground went to look at the place, where he found this big leveret ketched in a wire as dead as a door nail."

"Here he comes," said Patty, looking through the window.

The farmer gave a sort of a grunt of displeasure, and a tall, light-haired boy ran into the room.

He was full of life and spirits, and as audacious in his manner.

He wore no coat or smock, but a waistcoat with long sleeves and a pair of fustian trousers bound below the knee with leather straps to prevent them from dragging in the mire.

His boots were of the usual clodhopping description, in weight about four pounds, and studded with nails like the door of a prison.

Although his costume was not particularly becoming, there was something in his voice and manner which showed that he was of a different race to the other labourers on the farm.

Nevertheless there was something in his countenance that betokened an absence of moral principle; a restlessness, and an expression of cunning seemed to pervade it.

There was something in his grey eyes which to a physiognomist would have afforded food for speculation and inquiry.

Mr. Jamblin sprang forward and seized the youngster by the collar, at which he did not appear to be surprised.

"You audacious circumventing young wagabond," shouted out the farmer; "I've been a waitin' for you, my pretty manakin. I'll teach you to put metal collars round my hares' necks, you rascal."

"Will you, master?"

"Yes, I will. What have you to say for yourself?"

"What have I say? Well, if you will listen I'll tell you, sir."

"Go on, and look sharp about it, then."

"Aint hares wild animals, the same as rats, foxes, and such like?" said the boy. "When I made a new sort of trap and caught the rats for you, which nobody else could do, didn't you praise me and acknowledge it was a clever contrivance?"

"You young rascal!" cried Jamblin. "Don't 'ee think to shield yourself by your book larning. Wild animals, indeed. I'll flay 'ee alive, you viper."

The farmer seized hold of a stout stick which was lying on the table.

"There was a farmer lagged the other day for killing a boy," said the lad, in an insolent tone. "So don't lay it on too strong, master, for fear of your own precious life."

"You insolent ruffian!" exclaimed Jamblin. "Hang me if I ever met with your like, and hope I never shall for the matter o' that."

He rained a heavy shower of blows upon the boy's back and shoulders, which he bore without flinching or even uttering a cry.

The farmer was surprised.

"He's a hardened callous rascal that no mortal man can mek anything on, and that be the solemn truth."

"He won't do it again—I'm sure he won't, father," pleaded the girl.

"Won't he? I'll wager he will. Good words or bad blows are wasted on such as he."

Then, turning to Alf, Jamblin said—

"I tell 'ee, my lad, I'll serve 'ee in the same way as we serve a dog who runs out and eats his game. To-morrow I will tie this leveret under your nose and your hands behind your back, and let 'ee nose at it for a day or two—that's what I'll do."

And, with these words, the indignant agriculturist stalked out of the kitchen.

The boy watched him across the yard, and when the farmer was lost to sight he unbuttoned his waistcoat, and passing his hand round his back produced a quantity of napkins with which he had padded himself.

He had been expecting some such castigation, and like an old soldier had recourse to stratagem.

The heavy blows fell harmless upon his back and shoulders.

No wonder he bore all with such patience and equanimity.

In cunning he was more than a match for his master, or indeed the whole of the establishment.

Patty could not refrain from laughing when she beheld the artifice resorted to by her companion in the kitchen.

"You are a sharp one, Alf, and no mistake," she cried.

"But you won't peach—won't tell the governor?" said he.

"No—no. Let us hope his anger is all over by this time."

"He won't forget his promise about the hare, I daresay, but what of that? It won't hurt me."

The lad was quite right—Jamblin did not forget the promise he had made.

"Look here, men, just pinion this young scoundrel. We'll teach him a lesson he won't easily forget," cried the farmer to his labourers in the yard on the following morning.

The men obeyed and the boy's arms were fastened firmly, so that there was no possibility of his raising them.

The hare was then slung under his chin.

"Now, my lad, see how that suits you," said Jamblin. "It shall hang there till you promise never to do the same thing again."

He was driven out of the yard by the farm labourers, who one and all detested him for his mischievous ways, and therefore they enjoyed the fun immensely.

"Now then, youngster, go and make a sight o' yourself till noontime," cried the carter, thrusting young Purvis forcibly through the open gate into the high road.

"Who cares for a pack of fools like you?" exclaimed the lad, walking rapidly away from the scene. A chorus of laughter reached his ears as he took his way along the road.

He was certainly under the impression that he cut a most ridiculous figure, adorned as he was with his furry companion, but there was no help for it; he was constrained to hear the sneering remarks passed on him by the passengers, equestrian and pedestrian, he met with on the road.

He had also to endure the jocose and playful cuts with the whip with which the carters saluted him as they went by with their long teams of horses. But he bore all these indignities with the greatest fortitude; nevertheless a burning spirit of revenge smouldered within his breast—a spirit which some day or other would burst into a flame.

He walked on without deigning to offer any reply to the vexatious and sneering observations with which he was greeted.

An hour or more had passed over without his meeting with anyone who would take compassion on him. Presently he espied, at some little distance ahead of him, a little boy coming in the opposite direction.

It suddenly occurred to him that he might make a friend of the urchin, but the latter, believing him to be one of those fabulous animals he had read of in children's good story books, or fables, as they are sometimes termed, screamed, and attempted to fly.

"Come here. I want to speak to you," cried Alfred Purvis. "Don't run away. Come."

But the little fellow was too much alarmed by the extraordinary appearance of the speaker to approach any nearer, and, after hesitating for a few seconds, he made off in the opposite direction.

"Don't run away, you little fool," cried the farmer's boy; "I only want to speak to you for one moment—something of the utmost importance. Don't run away, there's a good fellow; you have no call to be frightened of me."

But the little fellow was frightened, and all the other could do in the way of persuasion failed to restore his confidence.

Alf Purvis said no more in the way of remonstrance, but ran after the fugitive as hard as his legs would carry him.

Encumbered with the hare, and pinioned as he was, he managed to get within a few yards' distance of his younger and less agile companion.

The latter screamed with fright, and, turning out of the high road, flew into an adjoining meadow.

His pursuer followed fast on his heels. In another moment, Alf had overtaken the boy, with whom he came in collision, both falling on the grass together.

"Oh, mercy! What shall I do? Oh, oh!" sobbed the urchin.

Alf held him down by one knee, and then said, in a most conciliatory tone—

"You've no occasion to be a snivelin'. Nobody will hurt you. I want you to do me a favour. Come, there's a good fellow; you won't refuse, I'm sure. Don't you know me?"

"No I don't."

"I work at Stoke Ferry Farm, and they've tied my hands behind me; that's what they've been and done. Now you get up, and I'll tell you what I want you to do."

The speaker rose to his feet.

"Now, then, we're all right. Get up, young un, and come behind this hedge."

His companion after a little hesitation obeyed, with a show of reluctance. His large eyes opened to their fullest extent when he had a full and closer view of Purvis, and he was evidently still in a state of wonderment.

"Now, then," said Alf, "I want you to cut the ropes which fasten my arms. Have you got a knife?"

"No."

"Well, put your hand in my pocket, and there you'll find one."

"In your pocket?"

"Yes; lift up my frock on the right hand side, and drive your hand in my pocket. Why do you hesitate?"

"I'm afraid."

"But you must not be afraid. You're a dear good little fellow; anyone can see that, and I dare say are your mother's pet," cried Alf, stooping down and giving his companion a kiss.

The latter plucked up courage and drew out a knife from the other's pocket.

"Open it," said Alf.

This was not an easy task to one of his tender years, but after one or two efforts he succeeded.

"Excellent. Now go behind me and cut through the rope. Don't be afraid, you won't hurt me. Hack away as hard as ever you can. Ah, ah, we'll show them a trick or two. That's right—hack away."

The celebrated rope trick, as practised by the Davenport brothers, and other impostors, was not known at this time—hence it was that the pinioned lad was powerless without assistance.

"Perseverance overcomes all obstacles," is an old saying, and in the due course of time the rope was severed.

Young Purvis was once more free. He seemed to breathe again with fresh life. He threw the cords scornfully on the ground, unfastened the hare, and shook himself in a satisfactory sort of way.

"You're a jolly good little fellow," he exclaimed, giving his companion a penny by way of reward.

"I'm sorry I haven't in my power to give you more, but I shan't forget you. I'll make it up some other time."

The boy took the penny and looked wonderingly at the speaker, who presented altogether a different appearance.

"Now, youngster," said Alf, "you've done all I have required of you, and so good-bye. You've made a free man of me."

The little urchin scampered off, and Alf Purvis found himself alone.

CHAPTER XXXVII.

ALF'S RESOLVE—HIS MEETING WITH THE WHITECHAPEL BIRDCATCHER.

THE dinner hour came and passed away, but the inmates of Stoke Ferry Farm saw nothing of Alf Purvis. Mr. Jamblin was surprised at this, for the boy as a rule had always been punctual enough at meal times. The farmer grew fidgetty; he half regretted having made an example of the lad for an offence which, after all, could not be considered to be one of a very grave character.

"That young scapegrace is in his sulks, I expect," said Jamblin to his daughter. "An' may be he's got the hump so strong on him that he'll be for stoppin' away for awhile."

"Never fear," answered Mr. Philip Jamblin; "he'll come back again when he's had his fling and hunger begins to set in. He'll come back fast enough then, I'll warrant."

"I'm not so sure of that," returned Patty. "He's got a mighty spirit of his own. He's a lad one might lead, but I don't think he's easy to drive."

"He's an obstinate, audacious young varmint, that's what he be, an' one as no one can do much good with. Let un stop away an' he likes," cried the farmer.

He rose from his seat, and sallied forth into the fields.

"I think, Phil, that father was a little hard upon him, to hold him up to the ridicule of all the farm people, and then to drive him forth to be the laughing-stock of the whole neighbourhood."

"Oh, I don't know; it's no more than he deserves. The lad is always up to mischief, and has been an endless source of trouble and anxiety to us. If I could have had my way I would have got rid of him long ago."

Seven o'clock came, and Mr. Jamblin, the elder, returned to the farmhouse again.

"So that impudent young scamp aint returned yet, it seems," cried the farmer. "He be making a long stop on it."

"I hope he will come back," said his daughter, in a tone of sadness.

"You hope! What do you hope for? If he does come back he shan't stop, I tell 'ee that. I'll see the squire, and get shot of un."

"Have a little more patience with him. He won't be so wilful after a bit."

"Patience, gell! I dunno what thee art thinkin' about. I think we've all had patience enough. Wilful! He'll mend as much as small beer is likely to do in harvest time. Some on us will ha' to break un of his bad habits. I aint much yoose at that, it would seem."

"But when he returns you will wait awhile, and try him a little longer?" said Patty, coaxingly, winding her arms round the old man's neck.

"Umph! ye be a wheedling lass," he returned. "Very well, I will wait and see if he be likely to change. Say no more, gell. You know better than what I do what a fool ye can mek o' yer old father. Say no more; ye shall ha' yer own way in this as in all other things."

"Ah, that's said like my own dear father," murmured Patty.

But the night passed over as the day had done, and no Alf Purvis presented himself at Stoke Ferry Farm; as bed time came the members of the household exchanged blank looks, although they said but little. Each member of the family could not conceal his uneasiness.

Although they said but little each member of the family could not conceal their uneasiness.

Let us return to him whose absence was the cause of this anxiety.

After the departure of the urchin who had rendered such signal service to Alf, the latter walked over the fields and bethought him of what to do.

"I won't return again to that dalled place," murmured he. "I've had enough of the guv'nor and his low-bred crew of workpeople. Oh that I were a man, and able to fight my way in the world without the help of anyone! If I go to the squire he'll give me a long lecture, and take me back to Stoke Ferry Farm. I don't know what to do."

He looked at the sun—it wanted about an hour to noon, his dinner time.

He resolved to stroll about and amuse himself birds' nesting. Anyway he would not return till the evening—he could do without his dinner for once in the way; besides he had a slice of fat bacon between two thick pieces of bread in his pocket; these he had stolen from the larder without any one observing him.

Yes, he'll go birds' nesting.

He walked across field after field, and soon reached a small common which was covered with furze bushes, slanting thorn trees, and yews.

This place seemed to have considerable attractions for him. The aspect of nature is always beautiful, but rugged, savage, uncultivated nature this lad loved the most. Perhaps the reason of this might be traced to his occupation as a tiller of the soil.

As he entered the grass road which ran through the middle of the common he overtook a man who was walking slowly along, looking on all sides of him, and stopping every few steps to listen.

PEACE AT THE ARGYLL ROOMS.

Alf knew pretty well every inhabitant of the locality by sight, but he never remembered to have seen the individual he now came across for the first time.

"Who can he be, and what's his game?" he murmured; "he's a queer-looking sort of customer. I'll just watch and see what he's up to."

The man had a short pipe in his mouth—he was tall, but stooped slightly, which took somewhat off his

height. His clothes were travel-stained and dilapidated, and the beard on his chin seemed to be of some days' growth.

For the rest, his skin was of a deep brown, partly attributable to dirt and partly to his natural complexion, which was what might be termed swarthy. As to his age it would have puzzled any one to tell except those who had been acquainted with him for years—he might be seven and thirty, or he might be sixty.

On his back he carried a huge bundle, which was as large and heavy as a pedlar's pack, but of a very different shape.

Alf's curiosity was aroused—he had never seen any one of a similar character in the neighbourhood. He felt instinctively that the brown-faced man with the bundle was a brother sportsman, but he could not quite comprehend the reason for his stopping every now and then to listen, and then walking on in such a careless desultory manner.

"He's a bit of an original in his way, a sort of curiosity," murmured the boy. "He's up to something and I mean to know what it is before long."

The mysterious sportsman had by this time reached the small "clearing" (to use an American phrase) where the cottagers had been permitted to cut furze for their firing.

The stranger had all this time been quite unaware of the presence of the farmer's boy.

He threw down his bundle and raised himself to his full height; he then stretched forth his arms, which were evidently stiff and cramped from the constrained position they had been in during his journey.

This done he reflected for a brief space of time, after which he stooped down and began to untie his bundle and spread out its contents.

"He's a rum un. Let's see what his next move is," cried Alf, who deemed it expedient to keep as quiet as possible.

He, therefore, stretched himself full length on the grass.

When the boy saw the brown-faced man bring forth a large net his eyes began to shine, and lying on his stomach, with his face between his two hands, he watched the movements of the stranger with the greatest possible interest.

He saw the net, which was about twelve yards square, spread flat upon the ground, and then secured by four small pins (called *stars*), which left, however, a considerable space of net on either side unoccupied.

Then the brown-faced man placed something covered with green baize-cloth in the centre of the net, and, having carefully examined his apparatus, he uncoiled a long line, which was looped and run within the edges of the net.

He then raised the green baize, disclosing a goldfinch in a wire cage.

"My eye, he's an artful old buffer, and knows his way about!" murmured Alf.

The man glanced around.

"Blessed if I didn't hear a voice, or somethin' of the sort," he ejaculated.

He adjusted the lines of his net, and looked up at the sky—then he glanced around once more.

"Holloa, you, sir, what are you a doing there? Want to frighten the birds—eh?" he exclaimed, catching sight of the boy for the first time.

"I hope I aint in the way, or a doing any harm," cried Alf, in a beseeching tone. "I'm only doing the looking-on part. I hope you don't mind, please, sir?"

"Umph," returned the man, with a puzzled expression of countenance, "you've been 'nation quiet, my young bloke. I didn't know there was a soul about; but, look here, my lad, I'd rather you shift your quarters if it don't make any difference to you, 'cos why it's like enough you'll frighten the birds away if you stop there."

"All right, guv'nor, I'll go wherever you like."

The man made a sort of crook with his forefinger, with which he beckoned the lad.

"Just you stir your stumps," he said, "and come here by the side of me."

"All right, that's just what I should like—it will suit me above everything," cried Alf, with evident delight.

He and the brown-faced man hid themselves behind a bush, the latter holding the line and peeping through the interstices of the foliage.

As soon as the goldfinch felt the sun and light it began to sing.

"That's the call bird," whispered the man. "He'll draw a lot presently if we have luck."

It must be owned that there is a most malicious joy in these call birds to bring the wild ones into the same state of captivity, which may likewise be observed with regard to decoy ducks.

Their sight and hearing excel that of the bird-catcher. The call birds do not sing as a bird does when in a chamber; they invite the wild ones by what they, the bird-catchers, call "short jerks," which when the birds are good may be heard at a great distance.

The ascendency of this call or invitation is so great that the wild bird is stopped in its flight, and, if not already acquainted with the nets, alights boldly within on a spot which otherwise it would not have taken the least notice of.

Indeed it frequently happens that if half the flock are only caught the remainder will immediately afterwards alight in the nets and share the same fate, and should only one bird escape, that bird will suffer itself to be pulled at till it's caught, such fascinating power have the call birds.

While we are on the subject of the jerking of the birds we cannot omit mentioning that the bird-catchers frequently lay wagers upon whose call bird can jerk the longest, as that determines their superiority.

They place them opposite to each other by an inch of candle, and the bird who jerks the most before the candle is burnt out wins the wager.

We have been informed that there have been instances of birds giving one hundred and seventy jerks in a quarter of an hour.

It may be here observed that birds when near each other seldom jerk or sing.

It is a singular circumstance that the male chaffinches fly by themselves, and in the flight precede the females; but this is not particular with this class of bird.

When the larks are caught at the beginning of the season it frequently happens that forty are taken, and not one female among them.

An experienced birdcatcher informed us that such birds as breed twice a year generally have in their first brood a majority of males, and in their second of females.

The method of birdcatching must have been long practised, as it is brought to a most systematical perfection, and attended with much trouble and expense. The nets are a most ingenious piece of mechanism.

They are from ten to twelve and a half yards long, and ten yards and a half in width, and no one on bare inspection would imagine that a bird, who is so quick in all its motions, could be caught by the nets flapping over each other till he becomes an eye-witness of the process.

After the birdcatcher and Alf Purvis had taken up their position in the clump of foliage, they waited patiently for more than a quarter of an hour.

The adjacent trees and shrubs resounded with chirpings and carollings.

"I like to hear them twitter," said the boy.

"It looks like business," returned his companion. "Pretty—aint it?"

"Oh, jolly, and no mistake. I wish I knew the business."

The birds gathering courage began to flutter down upon the net, which soon swarmed with linnets, yellow-hammers, and tit-larks.

"Pull the string, guv'nor," said Alf.

"Wait a bit, youngster. I want some bullfinches."

"I can hear 'em piping all around. There's lots on 'em about these thorn trees."

The bullfinch, though it does not properly belong to what are known as singing birds or birds of flight, as it does not often move farther than from hedge to hedge, yet invariably sells well on account of its learning to whistle tunes, and sometimes flies over the fields where the nets are laid, the birdcatchers have often a call-bird to ensnare it, though most of them can imitate its call with their mouths.

It is remarkable with regard to this bird that the female answers the purpose of a call-bird as well as the male, which is not experienced by any other bird taken by the London bird catchers.

The man in the bush imitated the call to such perfection that in a short time he had the satisfaction of seeing six cock bullfinches in the net, which began to present the appearance of an aviary. They were beautiful little creatures, with their blue bullet heads and their scarlet breasts.

They were clothed in red and purple, like the kings of ancient Tyre.

The man gave his rope a sharp tug, and the flaps or wings of the net closed and held them all prisoners.

The poor things beat themselves fiercely against the net, uttering piercing cries, while the call-bird still sung as if in savage triumph from his wire cage.

"Beautiful!" ejaculated the boy. "I call that something like."

The birds were gathered by the large brown hand of their ensnarer, and with Alf's assistance they were placed in a large hamper, which formed part of the fowler's equipage.

"That's a good haul, ain't it?" inquired the lad.

"Middling, not so bad. I've had better, and a good many worse."

"Do you happen to know of any nestesses round here?" he inquired.

"I don't mean the common sorts. D'ye know of a bottletit's anywhere?"

"I know one—in fact I was going to collar it when I met you."

"How far is it from here?"

"Not a hundred yards from where we are now—just ready for eggs."

"I don't want no eggs, but I'll give yer a pint o' beer for the nest—that is unless ye want it yourself."

"I don't particularly want it," said the boy, who was going to show the man the nest for nothing; but he now declared he couldn't afford to part with it under sixpence."

"It's worth that if it be a good 'un. I'll give you sixpence—that is, when I've got the nest."

"All right. Come this way," cried Alf, who showed the man the nest, which was imbedded in a little bunch of gorse.

Instead of tearing it out the fowler cut the branch with his knife, thus preserving it furze and all.

He then handed his companion the sixpence.

The bottle tit, or long-tailed tit, builds the most beautiful of all English nests. It is oval in shape, like a leather bottle, and outside is one mass of that crisp white moss which one finds on apple trees and old gate-posts. There is one tiny hole the circumference of a child's finger, and the interior is choked to its very mouth with soft and downy feathers.

These nests sell at a high price in towns to egg-collectors, closet naturalists, and buyers of curiosities.

"You'll make your money of that, guv'nor. It's a stunner—aint it?"

"Not a bad one of its sort; but, lor' love ye, the job is to find a customer. It's only one here and there who knows what's worth buying and what's best left alone. Still, ye see, it won't hurt by keepin', and it won't die, as many of the birds do. I've been very unlucky wi' my birds of late?"

"Have you, though? They croak, I s'pose?"

"That's it; right you are. They do croak, and no mistake. Howsomdever, it can't be helped. Do you know of any more nests, young shaver—some with bigger eggs, you know?"

"Ah! you mean some of *the other sort?*"

This is a cant term among poachers for those eggs which are preserved by the hand of the law.

The fowler started, and looked at the speaker with his right eye only.

"You're a queer young bloke," he muttered, "down as a hammer, and no mistake. Oh! you're fly, my lad—fly to a thing or two—there aint no manner of doubt about that 'ere!"

Alf laughed. He was much charmed with his companion's quaint and curious ways.

"I know of one nest—eleven eggs, old bird sitting," he said, in a tone of exultation. "Just your book, I should say."

"That's the style, Polly. Bring 'em to me, my lad, and I'll give you a shilling."

"If you'll give me a shilling I'll show you the nest, and let you take it as you did the bottletit's. I want money, I can tell you."

"I s'pose you do. That's by no means an uncommon complaint."

"Well, you can have it if you like—only say the word."

"And fork out the bob—eh?"

"Yes, that's a bargain, you know."

"Well, look here, my little ace of trumps, that may be all very well; but how am I to know if you wont round on me afterwards?"

"I never rounded on anybody in my life," cried Alf, in a tone of indignation.

"Umph, I'm jolly glad of it; but you've got a pair of queer grey peepers. I'm always keerful how I do business with grey peepers."

"I didn't make my peepers, and it's no fault of mine if their colour don't please you. I know one or two shady customers who have black and brown peepers."

"You're a deal too artful for my money, and you see I don't want to be led into a scrape, which is easier for a cove to get into than out of by long chalks."

"Look here, then," cried Alf, pulling out the hare from under his smock; "I snared this, and have had a thrashing for it. I'll sell you this if you like, and then one will be as low in the dirt as 'tother in the mire."

The bird-catcher stared with surprise, and exclaimed quickly—

"Didn't I say as how you was fly? I'm blessed if you are not too good for a God-forgotten place like this."

"I want to leave it, and I will, please the pigs,"

returned the lad. "I don't care what I do so long as I haven't to go back to Stoke Ferry Farm."

"Is that where you come from?"

"Yes."

"Who and what are you?"

"I'm an orphan, and have been brought up by Mr. Jamblin."

"And who is he?"

"A farmer; and one as thinks a lot on himself."

"And you want to leave him?"

"Yes."

"And seek your fortune in the great world, eh?"

"That's it. You've just hit it."

"Well, come, lad, sit down and let us have a bit of dinner together. You're peckish, I 'spose, by this time?"

Alf drew from his pocket the two pieces of bread and the slice of bacon.

"Oh, you carry your prog with you, it seems. Not a bad plan. But just reach that basket—we shall find something better in that."

The two commenced their repast.

"Where are you bound for after you've done for the day?" inquired Alf.

"For London. Whitechapel; it aint a haristocratic part, but it's a busy sort of place in its way."

"I should like to go with you."

"Well, then, you shall, youngster. So that's soon settled."

CHAPTER XXXV.

PEACE IS INTRODUCED TO A GAMBLING CLUB.

CHARLES PEACE, as we have already signified, had become sated of the village in which he had led so reputable a life for a no very inconsiderable period; indeed, if we take into consideration the erratic and adventurous nature of the man, it is a matter of no small surprise that he should have continued to be a respectable member of society for so long a time.

But his new sphere of action had many attractions for him.

In the first place, it had the charm of novelty; in the next, he was petted and made much of by the landlord and the parlour customers of the "Carved Lion;" and last, though not least, he had been greatly taken with the girl, Nelly.

A sudden revulsion, however, took place, and our hero determined upon seeking "fresh fields and pastures new."

He was possessed of a considerable sum of money; for, in addition to the amount he realised by following the business of a frame-maker, and a dealer in works of art, he had the hundred pounds which the earl had sent by his lawyer as a bonus.

He was bent upon seeing something of London life, and therefore hastened at once up to the metropolis.

London has attractions for provincial and country people which perhaps no other city in the United Kingdom possesses, albeit its native population are in a measure heedless of its many attractions.

It is a wonderful city nevertheless, as the following facts uncontestably prove :—

London (with all its suburbs) covers within the fifteen miles radius of Charing-cross nearly seven hundred square miles.

It numbers within its boundaries four million inhabitants.

It contains more country-bred persons than the counties of Devon and Gloucester combined, or 37 per cent. of its entire population

Every four minutes a birth takes place in the metropolis and every six minutes a death.

Within the circle named there are added to the population two hundred and five persons every day and seventy-five thousand annually.

London has seven thousand miles of streets, and on an average twenty-eight miles of new streets are opened and nine thousand new houses built every year. One thousand vessels and nine thousand sailors are in port every day.

Its crime, unfortunately, is also in proportion to its extent.

Seventy-three thousand persons are annually taken into custody by the police, and more than one-third of all the crime in the country is committed within its borders.

Thirty-eight thousand persons are annually committed for drunkenness by its magistrates.

The metropolis comprises considerably over one hundred thousand foreigners from every part of the habitable globe.

It contains more Roman Catholics than Rome itself, more Jews than the whole of Palestine, more Irish than Belfast, more Scotchmen than Aberdeen, and more Welshmen than Cardiff.

Its beershops and gin-palaces are so numerous that their frontages, if placed side by side, would stretch from Charing-cross to Chichester, a distance of sixty-two miles.

If all the dwellings in London could thus have their frontages placed side by side they would extend beyond the city of York.

London has sufficient paupers to occupy every house in Brighton.

The society which advocates the cessation of Sunday labour will be surprised to learn that sixty miles of shops are open every Sunday.

With regard to churches and chapels, the Bishop of London, examined before the House of Lords in the year 1840, said :—

"If you proceed a mile to the eastward of St. Paul's you will find yourself in the midst of a population, the most wretched and destitute of mankind, consisting of artificers, labourers, beggars, and thieves, to the amount of from three to four hundred thousand souls. Throughout this entire quarter there is not more than one church for every ten thousand inhabitants, and in two districts there is but one church for forty-five thousand persons."

Peace, who had but a slender knowledge of the great metropolis, put up at a snug hotel which was frequented by many of his townsmen.

He had at this time no very clear idea as to his movements or future plan of action, and therefore, like Mr. Micawber, thought it best to wait patiently for "something to turn up."

He had abundance of ready cash for his necessities for some time to come, and when that was gone he was perfectly well assured he would find the way to obtain more.

He was never very long in making new acquaintances.

At the hotel where he was stopping he fell into the company of a young man named Kempshead, with whom he at once fraternised.

Kempshead was rather a go-a-head sort of young gentleman, and was therefore well adapted as a companion to Peace.

He was well acquainted with every phase of London life, was well up in all the cant terms and slang sayings which, unfortunately for the moral tone of society are considered requisite by the young men of the present day to indulge in and make use of.

The word "awful" had not come into fashion at the time of which we are writing, but there were others of an equally objectionable character.

The English language is assuredly sufficiently comprehensive for the expression of thoughts or ideas without being supplemented by slang or Americanisms. We shall have to dilate upon this subject in a future chapter of this work.

"Well, governor," said Joe Kempshead to Peace, as they were seated at the table in the public room of the hotel, "what's to be your little game to-day—the exhibition, a morning performance, or what?"

"Haven't made up my mind as yet," returned our hero, putting aside the paper he had been reading. "What are your movements?"

"I am obliged to go into the city—business matters, you know; but in the after part of the day I'm at your service—say about five, or between that hour and six. We can go together somewhere after then, and see what's to be seen. What say you—shall I meet you here?"

"Yes, I will be here at about six."

"Let's have dinner together at that hour, then."

"Agreed."

"Then we shall have the evening before us."

Mr. Kempshead parted with his newly-made acquaintance with this understanding, and proceeded into the city.

Peace bent his steps in the direction of the Kensington Museum.

He had heard a good deal of this place, where he found an almost countless number of objects, which had for him a special interest.

Throughout his life he had always evinced a great fondness for works of art and mechanical appliances, and the exhibition of patent articles in the museum was to him one of its most noticeable and attractive features.

He, therefore, found no difficulty in disposing of his time till the dinner hour. Upon his return to Sanderson's Hotel he found his friend awaiting his re-appearance.

Dinner was served, which was done ample justice to by both gentlemen. It was washed down by divers and sundry glasses of Rhenish wine.

Our hero had thrown aside the habits of the humble artisan, and went in for an aristocratic course of regimen.

He was not adapted for it—neither did it suit him; but there is an old saying, "When at Rome do as Rome does." Peace was mindful of this, and gave himself all the airs and graces of a high-born patrician.

An hour or two passed over, during which period Mr. Kempshead lounged on the sofa, puffed his fragrant weed, and partook of a cup of black coffee.

"Now, then, what shall us boys go in for?" he said, addressing himself to Peace.

"I'm in your hands, and leave the matter to your disposal," returned the latter.

"Very good—so be it. In the first place, old fellow, I want to introduce you to a little drum, which is not far from here. It's a club I belong to—the members are a jolly lot of fellows. By the by, do you play?"

"Do I what?"

"Do you play—gamble?"

"At present that is not one of my accomplishments."

"Surprised at that. Every fellow does that sort of thing nowadays. Couldn't get through the world, you know, without doing something in the betting or gam-

bling line. Still, you've no occasion to play unless you like. There's no harm in looking on."

"Oh, I'll go," cried Peace.

"Right you are; we'll, be off at once then."

The two friends sallied forth from the hotel. The club to which Kempshead alluded was situated in a dingy street at the west end of the town. It was ostensibly a proprietory club—the proprietors thereof drove a tolerably profitable trade.

It had been established as a social club for gentlemen, but its real character was that of a betting crib or gambling house; or "hell" would be the more expressive term.

There are hundreds of such establishments in this great city—betting and gambling is one of the vices of the age. A case which has but recently come before the Lord Chief Justice furnishes us with evidence as to this fact.

A Turkish gentleman instituted proceedings in an action for libel against the proprietor of a well-known newspaper. The paper in question contained an article, in which the plaintiff was denounced as a professional gambler or "black leg."

It was proved in evidence that both parties had lost and won as much as fifteen hundred pounds in one night. The gambling transactions were not confined to this country, but were practised in France and Germany.

The case will doubtless be fresh in the recollection of most of our readers, and comment thereon would be superfluous.

After arriving at the club, Mr. Kempshead spoke a word or two to the man in the hall, ascended the stairs, and entered a large room on the first floor. He was followed by Peace, who was introduced to several of the members of the club by his friend Kempshead.

The object which first attracted his attention was a long table which ran along the centre of the room, the farther end of which was about the distance of three feet from the opposite wall.

At its end was a fine light gas chandelier; each of the lights had over it a large green shade, which was much of the same character as those used in an ordinary billiard-room.

And under the lights was the apparatus with which the game of roulette is played.

This consists of a mahogany frame about eighteen inches square, and three or four inches in height; on it is fixed on a pivot a horizontal wheel about a foot in diameter, the top of which is divided into thirty-seven alternate red and black squares, each of which is marked with a number.

Surrounding the wheel is a little slanting ledge bounded by a raised edge.

The centre of the wheel is held by a thick brass handle, from which extend four ivory branches.

The whole machine is something like the toy "teetotums" fixed in boxes, which are sold freely in the shops.

From the apparatus described, extended along the table, is a green cloth divided by lines worked in white silk into the large portions.

In the margin on one side of the top division is worked the word "under," and on the opposite side the word "over."

The margin of the middle space contains the words, "even" and "odd," and at the opposite sides of the last section of the green cloth are two squares of cloth, one black and the other red.

The cloth is also divided into thirty-seven equal squares.

The uninitiated reader will by the foregoing description be able to form a tolerably accurate notion of the gambling machinery used in playing the game of roulette.

It must, however, be understood that "rouge et noir," and other games were played at the club-house into which Peace now found himself for the first time introduced.

Kempshead endeavoured to explain to him the manner in which the game was played.

A short bald-headed gentleman, who wore a military coat, and had a remarkably thick and dark moustache, and who had been introduced to Peace as Captain Draper, now sidled up to Kempshead and said, nodding at Peace—

"Does your friend play?"

"Well, no, I can't say he does—he's a novice. Ahem, a young man from the country."

"Ah, ah! capital—I see," returned the captain, with a loud military laugh.

Everything he did or said impressed you with being "loud." Doubtless the reader has met with a man of this description.

It is marvellous what a number of captains are to be found in gambling houses, billiard saloons, and other places of public resort.

If you are in doubt about a man it is quite safe to put him down as a captain or a stockbroker.

But the captains are by far the most numerous, and in many instances the most doubtful.

Captain Draper had, of course, a stentorian voice, which doubtless had been acquired by his constantly giving the word of command to the gallant troop of which he was the head.

"Your friend will not refuse to take a glass of wine with me?" said Draper to Kempshead, in an easy off-hand manner.

"He will be most delighted to do so, I've no doubt."

The three gentlemen moved towards the sideboard.

This was an important feature in the appointments of the room. Upon it rested a goodly array of bottles—and such bottles no one out of the gambling world ever saw in their life.

They were redolent not only of wines and spirits at of wickedness.

No other bottle had so insinuating a shape, so graceful a neck, so smiling a mouth, and such an irresistible-looking cork. As far as their external appearance was concerned they were faultless, so also was the brilliant and seductive-looking sideboard.

The thought arose in Peace's mind, "Where do these dangerous bottles come from. Are they manufactured for the exclusive use of the members of this highly respectable and aristocratic club, or does some wealthy member make them a present to the establishment for the use of the delectable members thereof?"

This last hypothesis does not seem to be the correct one.

The brands on them are unknown to fame. None but a sporting man could recognise the name of the maker.

Are they supplied by an adventurous gentleman of the Hebrew persuasion, who finds enough supporters in the villainous world to employ spirit importers, manufacturers, bottle makers, and label printers? The aforesaid gentleman of the Hebrew persuasion is, of course, constrained in his multifarious business transactions to lend money at sixty per cent. occasionally—only occasionally—and then it must be to good men and true.

"What will you take?" said the captain. "Shall we have a bottle of sparkling?"

"My friend does not much care for champagne. If I might suggest, he would like some brandy and seltzer."

"Yes, I should," remarked Peace.

"Then we'll have a pint of sparkling between us," said Draper.

A waiter came forward and attended upon the three gentlemen.

"Ah," remarked the captain, carrying the glass to his eye. "When I was in India this sort of tipple did go down, I can tell you."

"No doubt," said Kempshead.

"'Give Draper his fizz,' Lord Gough used to say, 'and he'll carry any position.' And by Jove, sir, he was right. I remember——"

"Aw, cap'n, 'aw do you do?" said a young man who had just entered the room. "Want to see you, cap'an."

"Oh, do you?"

"Ya'as. Most particular business; that fellow's turning nasty; talks about writing to the guv'nor, and all that sort of thing. He's a cursed bore."

"I'll see to that," returned Draper. "We'll talk the matter over by and by."

"You must see to it, old fellow. 'Pon my soul you must, and no flies."

"All right; I will."

The languid swell strolled towards the table.

"What's up?" inquired Kempshead.

"Oh, the old story—overrunning the constable, that's all. Wine and women, sir," said the captain, turning towards Peace, "would double up any man sooner or later."

The captain, having finished his drink, joined the languid swell and Kempshead, and Peace took stock of the company, which, by this time, was far more numerous than when they first entered the precincts of the unhallowed ground.

Some of the members were seated at the tables, and others stood behind them. The banker took up his position by the roulette.

Before him was a heap of gold, which had been turned out of a cash-box that stood on the table.

In one hand he held a stick, about two feet long, across the top of which was fixed a triangular piece of wood.

This is technically known as the "rake."

He was not altogether an ordinary-looking individual—such as one meets with in places of public resort. It struck Peace that he was playing a part, and this inference was a tolerably correct one.

He was decidedly clever, or he would not have been chosen for the position he occupied.

There was an engaging manner about him; he was loquacious, and affected to be more of the pigeon than the hawk.

But if anyone arrived at any such conclusion they would make a false estimate of his character.

Still, he was eminently qualified for his position. He spoke broken English at the commencement of the evening, but, strange to say, this wore off as the hours flew by.

He was a thin sallow-faced man, with a shrewd expression, and captivating manners.

He said, addressing those present, "We are all friends here; all know one another, and we are here for amusement, that's all."

Several of the members assented by nods to this proposition.

The croupier seemed satisfied.

"He loved play," he said, and here he shook a

pound's worth of "counters" in his white long-fingered hand.

Gambler, indeed! Not he.

He was no gambler, but he loved play to beguile the tedium of what would be otherwise his lonely hours.

He loved society, and was glad to see so many faces around him with which he had been familiar for years.

He certainly did talk like a father—not to say like a saint—to the members of the club.

The hot feverish players smiled grimly at his eloquence.

He was the only talkative man in the room.

There were many there who were not quite so cheery. They were evidently bent on business, not gossip or badinage, and to judge from their apparel their business did not please them much.

"Only for amusement," pleaded the little sallow-faced man, "that's all—only amusement. No stake larger than half-a-crown. We none of us want to be ruined. We play only for amusement. This is a social club. We are all brothers here. We all know that. Only for amusement, gentlemen."

He kept repeating this sentence, even as the raven in "Barnaby Rudge" was wont to repeat "Never say die."

Indeed, to say the truth, the little croupier reminded one very much of a raven.

"Would you like to have one turn, and try your luck?" inquired Kempshead of Peace.

"I don't know anything of the game; but, being here, I must do as others do, I suppose," answered our hero.

"As I said before, gentlemen, we play only for amusement," again remarked the croupier. "It's all fair and aboveboard at this establishment."

Mr. Kempshead drew to the table, and purchased eight round pieces of ivory, each about the size of a shilling, for which he paid the bland and smiling croupier one sovereign.

Peace handed his friend a sovereign, and requested him to purchase eight pieces for him.

Opposite to the two friends was a bald-headed florid-complexioned man, who, Kempshead informed our hero, was a large merchant in the City. He was supposed to be very wealthy, but was a frequent visitor to the club. As a rule, he preferred *rouge et noir* to roulette.

Near to the florid-faced man were two young fellows of gentlemanly appearance, speech, and demeanour; but the gambling contagion had seized hold of them, and their whole souls seemed intent upon the whirling of the roulette.

Peace placed a counter upon the red patch of cloth. His companion had already put one on the black patch, which he had forfeited.

The general banker now gave the roulette a twist with the handle, and at the same time a marble shot round the circling edge.

The little ball flew round and round in one direction,

and the roulette spun in the opposite, until at length the impetus of the marble was insufficient to keep it upon the slanting surface of the frame, and it sank upon the still twisting roulette and settled into a pocket opposite one of the squares.

The square in question was a red one, and the banker handed Peace another counter, value two shillings and sixpence.

Meanwhile the vivacious croupier kept the ball rolling, and continued the game, with many quaint and curious sayings, which seemed to be especially diverting to most of the members and visitors present.

He hospitably invited Peace to drink, enumerating a long list of refreshments for him to choose from; but our hero politely declined. He was bent upon keeping himself as sober as possible—indeed, drinking was not one of his vices; neither was gambling—he had enough bad qualities, in all conscience, without adding either of these to the list.

Peace varied the proceedings by placing another counter upon the margin marked "even."

The ball spun on, and the roulette turned, and ultimately his half-crown was raked up by the banker, as an odd number had been marked by the little marble.

Varying fate attended his efforts, but in the end he left off a loser of about fifteen shillings. Kempshead, on the contrary, was a winner.

"I suppose you've had enough of it for one evening?" said the latter to Peace, who answered in the affirmative.

"Very good; we'll be for making tracks, then."

"What is the name of your club?" inquired Peace, when they had gained the street.

"It is called the 'Tumblers'."

"What a singular name! How came it to be christened that?"

"I don't know. The idea is, I believe, that if the members tumble down they know how to pick themselves up again."

CHAPTER XXXIX.
THE TWO PERILS—LONDON BY NIGHT.

ANYONE at all acquainted with metropolitan life cannot fail to have been struck with the number of objects which seem, by some mysterious agency, to fade away and disappear altogether.

Years ago, when the disappearance of Mr. Speke (not the "great discoverer," but the great discovered) attracted so much attention, the papers were full of stories of similar mysterious absences of some people who had gone out some day, "in their usual health and spirits," and never came back again, nor been heard of, dead or alive, since.

It is impossible they could have been all murdered.

It is astonishing the number of persons who are missing annually, and who are never heard of more.

Take city life in prosperous times—what lots of new undertakings are daily set on foot, which utterly fail and languish in bad years.

What becomes of the "runners" who, in times of commercial infliction, are so well known in every office?

Individuals who are agents for the sale of all manner of speculative securities, who invite you to realise a swift and easy fortune by purchasing a lead mine in the antipodes, or a coal field at the North Pole, or by taking shares in a projected company for journeying in balloons to the moon.

At seasons of commercial depression these individuals disappear as completely as the summer grasshoppers vanish at the approach of winter.

In an equal degree—the old land-

Places disappear in an equal degree—the old landmarks are passing rapidly away from London. Holborn-hill has gone, Temple-bar has vanished—or the last remains of it will in a few days—Vauxhall-gardens, Cremorne, are things of the past, and the once famous Argyll-rooms have received a knock-down blow.

It is to this last-named place that Peace and his friend are about to pay a visit.

After leaving the "Tumblers" Mr. Kempshead, who

was what is called a late bird, proposed that they should drop into the Argyll-rooms. Peace gave his assent to the proposition, and the two companions paid the entrance fee and entered the inner penetralia of that establishment.

They found the place thronged with persons of both sexes—the female, if anything, predominating. A few hired professionals were dancing mechanically and languidly to a very indifferent band.

People did not go to the Argyll to dance; they went to see and be seen. It was a recognised meeting place—for ladies and gentlemen shall we say ? Perhaps males and females would be the more correct term.

If any one went there for the entertainment they were sure to be miserably disappointed.

The same remark will apply with equal force to the Mabille in Paris, which is dull and depressing to the last degree.

Not so, however, with the Argyll in its halcyon days. There was always a certain amount of life about it, and albeit they were many of them "frail," some of the most beautiful women in the world were wont to display themselves at this celebrated establishment.

Peace, who was always an admirer of the fair sex, was perfectly charmed with the array of beauty which met his gaze.

He and Kempshead strolled through the place, observing as they did so its most noticeable features.

"I never would have believed it unless I had seen it with my own eyes," he exclaimed.

"Believed what ?"

"Why that such immense throngs of persons should visit these rooms—then the women! I wouldn't have missed seeing this on any account."

A fair Cyprian now came to the front, and asked them to treat her with something to drink.

She had evidently some little knowledge of Kempshead, whom she addressed in a familiar manner.

There was, however, nothing remarkable in this, since most of the ladies who were in the habit of paying nocturnal visits to the Argyll were generally pretty familiar with most persons, whether strangers or otherwise.

"My friend is of a retiring disposition," said Kempshead.

"Indeed! I'm sorry for him, poor fellow," returned the girl; "but let the gentleman speak for himself."

Peace drew towards one of the refreshment counters, and asked the lady what she would have.

She elected to have a glass of port wine.

This was ordered, with seltzers and brandies for the two gentlemen.

"Your friend is from the country ; is he not ?" said the lady.

"Yes; he's the celebrated 'young man from the country,' about whom you have heard so much."

"I thought so. Going to stop long in London, sir ?"

"Not very long," said Peace, eyeing the questioner.

"Have you got a sweetheart here ?"

"Where ?"

"In London."

"I haven't been here more than two or three days."

"Then perhaps you want one. Shall I be your sweetheart ?"

"You are a deal too pretty, my dear. This is a lovely girl, isn't she," said our hero, chucking her under the chin, and turning towards his friend.

"Oh, dear yes; a most charming creature !"

Then all three laughed as if something clever had been said.

"Here's to our better acquaintance, darling," said the young lady, raising the glass to her lips. "I hope you'll come and see me before you leave London."

"Come and see you ! I don't know where you live."

"I live at Brompton."

"With your parents ?"

"No—with an elder sister. I shall be delighted to make your acquaintance. My place is not half-an-hour's ride from here. Let's have a cab and I'll show you where it is."

"No, not to-night, my dear, I am otherwise engaged ; but on some other occasion I shall be most delighted."

"Yes, on some other occasion," chimed in Kempshead, putting his arm in that of his friend, and sauntering towards the door of the establishment.

"It's too bad to take him off like that," said the girl, pouting. "One would think you were his keeper. Ha, ha !" She laughed what was meant to be a merry laugh, but it was forced, hollow, and unreal.

Peace and Kempshead passed into Windmill-street, and in a few seconds were at the corner of the Haymarket.

The throngs of persons who were assembled here and in the adjacent streets seemed to Peace to be almost incredible. It appeared as if all the women in London had, by common consent, assembled in this quarter of the town.

It is not possible to convey to the minds of those of our readers who never witnessed the night scenes in this locality, some twenty or five-and-twenty years ago, the appearance it presented.

Women dressed in the height of fashion, many of them being possessed of a rare order of beauty ; languid swells, sporting and betting men, together with others of a still less reputable character, congregated together in one heterogeneous throng.

Anyone seeing these assemblies for the first time would naturally come to the conclusion that the metropolis was a city devoted to nothing but pleasure.

Peace was astounded—as well he might be. He had heard of these gatherings, had seen a good deal of provincial life, but the reality far exceeded any description that had been given him.

"My word !" said he to Kempshead, "London is a place. What on earth brings all these people here ?"

His companion shrugged his shoulders.

"It is always like this, every night the same, that's all I know. It's a promenade—a sort of carnival; but let us go down the Haymarket."

The two companions threaded their way through the throng of people. At about half-way down the street a still denser crowd was collected. From this proceeded at intervals cheers and loud peals of laughter.

The young men elbowed their way in the crowd, and then discovered the cause of the merriment.

A gentleman in a tourist's suit was standing on his head in the middle of the cab rank. He was cheered and encouraged by some of his boon companions, as well as the cab-drivers.

"Did you ever see such a consummate donkey—the fool ?" ejaculated Kempshead. "He calls himself a gentleman, I suppose ?"

"Bravo—bravo, well done !" shouted several of the throng.

The crowd grew denser and denser, and in a short time the pathway became blocked up.

A tall policeman came forward and addressed the simpleton who was making himself so ridiculous.

"Now, then, enough of this," cried the constable. "Do you hear ? Give over and move on."

"All right, old man, I'm not hurting you or any one. Mind your own business, and I'll mind mine."

ALF GAVE HIS ASSAILANT A BLOW, WHICH SENT HIM REELING.

"Give over, I tell you," said the policeman. "You are causing an obstruction, and I shall have to take you into custody."

"He's not doing any harm, Mr. Policeman," said one of his pals; "he's only doing it for a wager—let him alone."

'Don't mind what the bobby says," called out a voice from the crowd; "he daren't do anything. A

gentleman has a right to amuse himself after his own fashion."

The constable stooped down, caught the offending party round the shoulders, and lifted him on his legs.

"Now, you make the best of your way home. If you don't it will be all the worse for you."

"I'm a gentleman, and shall do as I like," you

impudent fellow," cried the young man in the tourist suit. "Don't you lay hands on me."

He was not particularly sober, but he knew what he was about—but he was larkish—determined upon having what he called a spree, and appeared to be mischievously disposed.

The policeman was resolute, and told him if he endeavoured to repeat the offence he would lock him up.

His friends had the prudence to draw him forcibly away.

"Did you ever see such a little fool—who on earth is he?" said Peace.

"Oh, he's a gentleman bred and born," answered one of the bystanders.

"There cannot be a moment's question about that."

"Then he ought to know better."

"He's eccentric—a little eccentric, playful."

"Ah."

The crowd began to disperse, at the stern demand of the police-officer.

In ten minutes after this the little gentleman in the tourist's suit was again at his mad pranks.

He was standing again on his head, near to the corner of Panton-street, and as a natural consequence, another crowd assembled to witness his vagaries.

The same policeman again came forward—he had by this, time lost all patience with the offender.

"Now then," he cried in an angry tone, "you know what I told you."

"What! may'n't I amuse myself here then?" argued the young man, perfectly unmoved.

"We've had enough of this," answered the constable. "Since you are determined to get yourself into trouble, don't blame me."

He lifted up the obstinate little fool, collared him, and dragged him along towards the station-house. As he did so a crowd of persons followed and abused him. Another constable came up, and the prisoner was locked up.

In the morning he was taken before the magistrate at Marlborough-street, and fined.

This little incident is one of the many scenes enacted by brainless fellows with more money than wits. It is an actual fact, and was reported in the papers of the period, in addition to which it came under the writer's own observation.

"There are a good many fools in the world, and that fellow is one of them," said Kempshead; "but I've another little place I want you to visit. Come this way."

The speaker turned down Jermyn-street. He was followed by Peace. The two arrived in front of a house on the left side of the street in question, which to all appearance was a coffee-shop. It was a great unobtrusive-looking establishment, with ground-glass windows in its front, on which were inscribed the words "Coffee Room."

"This little drum is worth seeing," said Kempshead. "No one but the initiated would dream that such a place existed."

The two went down a narrow passage, and reached a pair of small folding doors. Peace's companion opened one of them, and said to a man inside, "All right, Sam."

The man touched his hat, and they then passed in. To all appearance it was a coffee-shop. There were compartments, seats, and side tables, such as are seen in ordinary houses of that description; but these were filled with magnificently attired women and aristocratic looking gentlemen, who were quiet, well-behaved, and reserved in their manner.

It was said by Peace's chaperon that more than one titled person was present. At the end of the room was the bar, in which was seated a mahogany-faced gentleman, with an aquiline nose, who was evidently an Israelite.

He came forward from this inner penetralia, and shook Kempshead warmly by the hand. He was introduced by that gentleman to Mr. Charles Peace.

"What shall we have?" said Kempshead. "A cup of green tea?"

"Yes, if you like."

"Two cups of green tea, Isaacson, if you please."

These were brought by a waiter and paid for by Kempshead.

Peace discovered that the so-called "green tea" was cold brandy and water, and he was informed by his friend that black tea, with sugar, was warm brandy and water, but in both cases the grog was brought in an elegantly-shaped cup and saucer.

Other refreshments were served in this delectable establishment, which was kept open, in defiance of the law, during the greater portion of the night.

It was a quiet snug retreat for ladies and gentlemen who did not want to be seen in places of more public resort, such as the Argyll and the Holborn.

The writer of this work was taken there from his club some years ago, between one and two on Sunday morning, by one of the most renowned of London theatrical managers, in company with an actor of celebrity.

The place was not interfered with for years, the reason being that it was patronised by many of the upper ten thousand. The Jew who conducted it carried on the concern, small as it was, sufficiently long to amass a large fortune.

He was unmolested by the police authorities, and, although he had no spirit licence, he contrived to serve brandy and other liquors in the guise of cups of tea and coffee.

It has been with truth often said that "one man may steal a horse, while a less favoured one must not look over the hedge."

While Peace and his companion were seated at one of the tables, taking stock of the company, a private soldier suddenly entered the sacred precincts of this hallowed establishment.

The porter told him to leave—that he could not be served with anything.

The soldier was "half seas over," and, striking a defiant attitude, declared his money was as good as anybody else's, and that he would be served.

The landlord came from behind the bar, and informed this valiant son of Mars that he was in a club-house, and none but members could be served.

This did not satisfy the soldier, who was disposed to be troublesome, for he was too powerful a man to be forcibly ejected, and of course every one present dreaded a row.

A tall gentlemanly-looking man with the greatest composure rose from one of the tables, and, walking up to the side of the soldier, whispered something in his ear.

The effect of this was perfectly magical.

From a lion the soldier became a lamb; he slid through the folding doors, and disappeared like a sprite in a pantomime.

"You possess a potent power," said Kempshead to the gentleman. "How did you contrive to tame the wild animal?"

"I merely mentioned the name of his commanding officer," replied the other.

"Wonderful. It shows what discipline does."

The company assembled in the coffee-room took no notice of Peace or Kempshead, whom they doubtless looked upon as beneath them, and as there was nothing more to be seen they arose and took their departure.

They had not gone very far before they were brought to a sudden halt.

A fashionably dressed woman, who was walking behind them, touched Peace on the shoulder—he turned round and stared her full in the face.

"Well," said he, "what do you want with me?"

"Don't you know me?" cried the female."

"No, I can't say that I do, but your voice is familiar to me."

"Don't you remember Laura Stanbridge, Charlie?"

"Why of course, mercy on us, it is a long time since I set eyes upon you. Laura, dear me, yes, I know you well enough. I haven't seen you for ever so long—not since you left Sheffield."

"No, not since I left Sheffield."

"I'll take my hook," said Kempshead to Peace. "You can follow me on to the hotel. I suppose you have met with an old acquaintance?"

"I shan't be long after you," murmured Peace.

"Right you are," returned Mr. Kempshead, walking rapidly away.

CHAPTER XL.

PEACE PAYS A VISIT TO THE HOUSE OF AN OLD ACQUAINT-ANCE—THE BOY BIRDS-NEST SELLER.

For a minute or two after his friend's departure Charles Peace stood gazing at the features of the young woman before him. She presented altogether such a different appearance to the girl he had known at Sheffield that he stood wonder-struck, thoughtful, and irresolute.

"You've become such a fine London lady that it is not surprising I failed to recognise you when we first met," he said, after a pause.

"No, I'm a good deal changed, I've no doubt, although perhaps I do not see it myself; but you will remember, Charlie, that I was but a slip of a girl when we were in the habit of meeting."

Her companion nodded.

"And I've gone through a good deal since then," she said in continuation.

"Ah, no doubt. What are you doing now, and where do you live?"

"Not many minutes' walk from here. See me home, and we can talk over old times."

"See you home?"

"Yes, I will show you where I live, and you will then be able to give me a call when you have an hour or two to spare."

The girl put her arm in his, and the two walked on together till they reached a street in close proximity to Regent Circus.

She stopped at one of the houses in the street, and gave a gentle rap at the door, which was opened by a neat, modest-looking, maid servant.

Laura Stanbridge conducted her visitor upstairs, when the two entered a large and elegantly furnished apartment on the first floor.

"Now then," she said, "make yourself at home, Charlie. We are no strangers to each other, and I've got a lot to say to you."

Peace sat down, while his companion went into an adjoining room to take off her bonnet and mantle.

"She's a mysterious party," he murmured. "What can she be up to now, I wonder? Seems to be in pretty good feather anyhow."

The girl returned, and sat herself down opposite to her male companion.

"Well, in the first place you are surprised to see me, and in the next you are not able to reckon me up," said she, laughing. "That's it—isn't it?"

"Ah, as to that, Laura, I think most of us reckoned you up when you were at Sheffield; but what you are doing now, of course, I'm unable to say."

"I'm creeping—creeping along."

"We have not met for ever so long a time," said the girl. "and now you have come I'm not going to part with you without first of all having a talk about old times."

"Umph!" muttered Peace; "you seem to be flourishing, my lady—everything very comfortable, and all that sort of thing, eh. I wonder how it's done?"

"What do you mean?"

"Why, you've got a snug place, and seem to be doing it up pretty brown. Are you living here all alone?"

"No. I have a friend, a female companion, who shares the expenses with me."

"Ah, that's all right. I suppose a personal friend?"

"Yes; we work together."

"What at, if it's not an impertinent question?"

The girl burst out in a merry mocking peal of laughter.

"I see—I understand, the same old game, I suppose," remarked Peace.

She nodded.

"I might have guessed as much. 'What's bred in the bone,' &c. You knew the old adage."

"Now, don't you be quite so cheeky, Master Charlie," returned his companion. "What is a lone, unprotected female to do in a great city like this? Tell me that."

"You know more of the great city than I do, and as to what a lone female is to do, my charmer, why that all depends."

"I've not seen you since I left Sheffield. Tell me, does any of our old pals ever mention my name?"

"Not one that I ever heard—not since you slipped away so cleverly. No one seems to have troubled their heads about you."

"Ah, people are soon forgotten in this world. You know my mother is dead?"

"Yes, I knew that long ago. My word, you had a narrow escape, my lady—were as near as possible being nabbed and quodded."

Peace had known Laura Stanbridge from her earliest childhood. She was a native of the same town as himself, and like him she was a lawless character. When but little more than a child she began to steal. Her mother had encouraged her acts of petty larceny.

When a little girl she had worked at one of the factories in Sheffield, and while thus employed she robbed her employer, who himself forbore from prosecuting her on account of her youth.

She was, however, discharged without a character; bad training, bad companionship did the rest, and she became an habitual thief, but somehow or other was fortunate enough to escape the meshes of the law.

Her last robbery in the town was of an extensive nature; it was carried out under the direction of a gang of thieves. Her companions in guilt were tried, convicted, and sentenced to various terms of imprisonment.

Laura Stanbridge managed to escape by leaving the town in a clandestine manner.

She hastened up to London, where all trace of her was lost.

Since then but little was known of her, but without doubt she had been carrying on her lawless practice to a considerable extent in the metropolis and its suburbs.

The contemplation and description of such characters as this woman is not perhaps a pleasant theme to discourse upon, but we should remember that she is only one out of many offenders of a similar description. Their name is legion, even in the days in which we are writing.

We have more than once hinted that a correct history of crime and criminals has long been a desideratum, because much of the history of the times is involved in the prevalence of particular crimes and in the career of criminals.

In every age and country, since the foundation of society, events have been occurring of which, though too minute and fugitive for the rapid page of history, it must be regretted that no record has been preserved.

Few that have written on crime and criminals have kept in view anything but the *crime* or *criminal*, and the holding up of *both* to the execration of mankind.

They have seldom sought for those proximate or remote causes which may have led to the commission of crimes by individuals, and occasioned whole classes of hardened offenders.

Investigation by comparison is the surest road to knowledge; the whole system of daily intercourse throughout the world is carried on by it.

The most exact of the sciences obtains its positive results by no other means.

The passing over all the circumstances connected with the exciting causes to the commission of crime is the result of a motion of very general prevalene.

It is thought that by allowing crimes to be palliated by circumstances we lessen the effects of public examples; but whenever it is proper to publish accounts of persons and events it is always desirable that the truth should be spoken.

And although the task of chronicling the career of such a blot upon the face of society as Laura Stanbridge may be in a measure repulsive, it is nevertheless true to nature.

She had been so early trained in the committal of unlawful acts that she could never go right afterwards.

It is a sad thing to reflect upon that there are in this country thousands of women who are, morally speaking, of much the same type as the woman Stanbridge.

She forms, in point of fact, a companion picture to that of the hero of this work, and it will be our duty, as impartial historians, to shadow forth her life and actions in all their native and hideous depravity.

"Yes, Charlie, I had a narrow escape," observed the girl, in a tone of exultation; "but it is not the only narrow escape I've had—not by a good many; but you know, old fellow, we've all our trials and troubles in this world. You've had yours."

Here she winked at her companion in a manner that was not in any way agreeable to him.

"But tell me, old boy, all about my old pals in Sheffield. What has become of them? As the song says, 'Where are my playmates gone?'"

"Some are dead; some married, and others are serving her Majesty in places where they haven't much chance of deserting, seeing that they are so well guarded and looked after with such care."

"I understand. Poor devils!" cried Laura, with another laugh, which was so loud and discordant that it jarred upon the ears of her companions.

"You make merry over the misfortunes of your friends," he observed, deprecatingly.

"Friends!" she exclaimed, in a sneering tone. "How many have I in this world, I should like to know? Friends, indeed! where can you find them? There are many who may call themselves your friends, but who would nevertheless sell you without pity or remorse if they could profit by the bargain."

"You speak with bitterness, my lady. I have never sold or betrayed you."

"Pardon me, Charlie, I was not alluding to you. Dismiss any such idea from your mind. We were always pals—let us continue to be so."

She drew her chair close to his, and took one of his hands within her own. She had the cunning of the serpent, for in some respects she had much of the fascinating powers which that reptile is supposed to possess; but Peace was not likely to be made a dupe of, as he knew pretty well the character of the woman who was so demonstrative.

"You don't forget your old companion. You don't forget the time when we were boy and girl together?"

"No, I don't forget, Laura."

"Then why this coldness?" she remarked, looking into his face with her soft seductive eyes.

"Look here, old girl, I hope you have not brought me into this crib to make love to me. If you have, it's a bit of a sell, that's all I have to say. We know one another pretty well. We ought to do so by this time. I wish you well, and am glad to find that you are in so comfortable a position. I shan't lose sight of you—shall drop in occasionally to see how you are getting along, for, as I said before, I wish you well."

The woman comprehended his meaning, and at once altered her tactics. She withdrew her hand from his, went to a cheffonier, and placed on the table a decanter of wine and glasses.

"We'll have a glass together before you leave," she said, in a careless manner.

"I have had quite enough already—indeed, more than enough," he returned.

"Ah, that's it—is it?"

"Yes, that's it. You see, old girl, I've been knocking about with a young spark for some hours, and feel that I've had quite enough. However, I won't refuse to take one glass—just to show that there's no animosity."

Two glasses were filled, and the companions drank by way of good fellowship.

Peace remained for some time after this, giving the woman a short but succinct account of their old associates at Sheffield.

It had arrived at the small hours of the morning when he took his departure, and returned to Sanderson's Hotel.

* * * * * * * *

Many days have passed over since our hero's visit to Laura Stanbridge.

Our scene shifts, and other characters appear on the stage.

It was evening in London.

A drizzling rain was coming steadily down; the pavement shone under the glittering gaslights as if it had been smeared with oil.

The streets were slush and mud, which a band of men in tarpaulin hats and coarse blue jackets were scraping to a heap, and piling in a cart with huge wooden instruments, half spade and half rake.

It has been said that London is paved with gold; few of us, however, have been fortunate enough to pick up a nugget, or even a few grains of that precious metal.

Nevertheless it is quite true that, by the refuse of the streets, large sums are realised.

Although the weather was so cheerless the streets were thronged with men and women, whose rapid movements and anxious looks explained that it was business, that patron saint of the great city, which had called them from their comfortable domiciles, their families, and their friends.

There was one, however, in the public thoroughfare who had no comfortable home, no family, and but few friends.

This was a wretched-looking boy.

He was standing opposite the Charing-cross railway station, not very far from the entrance to the Lowther Arcade.

The arcade itself was, as is usually the case in wet weather, crowded with loiterers, who looked at the tempting articles on the stalls, but did not purchase. They had, in fact, only sought shelter till the rain gave over.

Ever and anon an individual would emerge from the precincts of the arcade and hail a passing omnibus, which was of course full inside. The Metropolitan Railway had not at this time extended as far as Charing-cross, and the omnibuses had it pretty much their own way.

The boy, who was so heedless of the falling rain, had long fair hair, which fell down upon his shoulders in clustering curls; his features were well moulded, and denoted a superior organisation to what one expects to see on those of the London street Arabs, who, as a rule, are common and coarse enough—indeed, they might have been esteemed handsome had they been fuller and less dejected.

His eyes were clear and grey, and were now fixed upon the pavement or upon what he was holding in his hands.

His attire was by no means becoming—he had on a dirty smock frock, which fell below his knees, as if to hide the corduroy trousers which hung down in rags, which were splashed and encrusted with mud.

He held in his hands a large basket filled with birds' nests and thin speckled eggs.

The boy was Alf Purvis, who had run away from Stoke Ferry Farm, and had been brought to London by the Whitechapel bird-catcher.

Alf's experience of London life up to the present time had been anything but satisfactory. His patron, the birdcatcher, during the period he remained with him, had been kind enough, but it happened, unfortunately for poor Alf, that the honest and industrious snarer of feathered songsters had a wife—and such a wife !

She was a termagant of the worst description. In addition to her many other accomplishments she drank, and led her husband such a life that penal servitude was luxury in comparison to it.

The birdcatcher caught a severe cold, and fell sick; he sought refuge in the hospital.

After his departure the wrath of his better-half fell upon the ill-fated Alf, who, in self-defence, was constrained to give the shrew as good as she sent. The consequence was that he was turned out of the house, which he was told never to enter again. Before this climax had arrived he had been scratched and beaten most unmercifully by his mistress.

In fact, he had been a source of incessant wrangling before the birdcatcher sought refuge in the hospital.

He had to shift for himself, and strove to earn a living by selling birds' nests and eggs in the street.

But, poor lad, he had a hard time of it. It was not, however, so much the hardships he had to pass through as the associates he was constrained to mix with that formed the foundation of his erratic and criminal life.

Had he remained with Mr. Jamblin he might have turned out a respectable member of society.

He was, as the farmer said, naturally " wiciously " disposed ; but, by good training and careful culture, he might probably have been led into the right path.

He displayed a great amount of patience and endurance in waiting for customers on this particular evening.

Presently a gentleman in a mackintosh, with a brown silk umbrella over his head, stopped before the young ornithologist, and said—

"What have you got there, my lad—are they for sale ?"

Alf started from his reverie, and his countenance became irradiated with a smile.

A gentleman had been attracted by his wares, and perhaps he might be a customer.

The boy made a most respectful obeisance, and said—

"Yes, sir; they are all for sale. Do buy of a poor lad, who's been waiting for hours for a customer."

"Umph. I don't know that any of them will suit me, youngster. What might these be ?" he inquired, pointing to one of the nests.

"I'll tell you, sir. Those you pointed to are dishwasher wagtails; some call 'em so, 'cos their tails are always twiddling like a woman's tongue."

He thought of the birdcatcher's wife when he made this observation.

The gentleman laughed.

"Upon my word, you are quite a cynic," he remarked. "Well, and how about the others ?"

"Do you want to know 'bout 'em all, sir ?"

"Yes, certainly, make me as wise as yourself. You're a sharp lad, it would seem."

"These dishwashers, sir, are three pence each," said the boy.

"These," pointing to another set, " are butcher birds, or hedge murderers ; they're pretty eggs—aint they, sir ?"

"Yes, they are very pretty."

"But the birds themselves, them as lays these eggs, are cruel brutes."

"Indeed, how so ?"

"They'll ketch little birds, and spike 'em on a thorn just as an insect-collector sticks a pin through a butterfly, and then they take to stripping the feathers off on 'em, and eat 'em up morsel by morsel.

"These be house sparrers, and their eggs vary in colour most of all birds. Some are quite white, though not often, and others are almost black. They're two-pence."

"Ah, they are common enough," remarked the gentleman.

"Yes, sir, they are common, but look at these. This is a golden-crested wren's nest, with nine eggs; they are not at all common."

"I suppose not."

"They are very rare indeed, sir, and the eggs are so tiny and brittle it's the hardest work in the world to blow 'em without breaking 'em; it's the smallest bird in Europe, so I've b'en told—the very smallest, and it's sixpence, being choice and rare."

"Humph ! you've got some of all sorts, it seems."

"This is a cuckoo's egg, and it is quite a curiosity,

not often got hold on   I'll let it go cheap, as I want money. I'll take fourpence for it."

"The cuckoo's a shy bird, isn't it?"

"Ah, very shy. Don't often catch sight on it, though you hear it pretty often at certain seasons of the year. It makes no nest of its own, but lays its eggs in the hedge-sparrer's nest, and the sparrow sits on it, and warms it, and hatches it along with its own eggs; so the young cuckoo is brought up with the young sparrers, and when he gets strong and hungry ho gets spiteful, too, and hoists all the t'others out of the nest, and so gets all the food hisself. It ain't fair, but there's a good many things done in this 'ere world that ain't quite the thing."

"By men as well as birds, my lad," remarked the gentleman.

"You're right, sir, by men and women too," returned the lad, who was still mindful of his shrew of a mistress.

"You are really quite an oracle."

"Well, sir, which will you buy?" said Alf, who by this time had come to the conclusion that he had wasted a sufficient number of words without any purport. "Which would you like best? The hedge chaffinch is the prettiest, but the golden-crested wren and the cuckoos are the rarest."

"Oh, yes, they are both very pretty, but I am afraid I cannot be a customer to-day. You are an intelligent lad. Some other time when I'm passing this way. I can't take them home in this rain."

"I'll take 'em wherever you like. I don't mind the wet, I'll take 'em home for you."

"No, not to-day. Some other time; but you're an intelligent lad."

And with these words he walked away.

"There's for you, the humbug!" cried Alf, as a cloud came over his face. "I might have known he was not one of the buying sort; he only stopped to amuse himself. An intelligent lad. I'm glad he said that, it's so consoling when you've got empty pockets and are a shiverin' with cold. Well, it made me forget my troubles for awhile."

He tried to sing to keep his spirits up, but his efforts in that way were not crowned with success.

Presently a tear rolled down his cheek as he thought of the comfortable farm-house which he had left to seek his fortune in a city where the poor may die on a doorstep unheeded and uncared for.

"I don't think much of the London people as far as I have seen of 'em at present; I ain't altogether in love with 'em. A poor devil like myself stands a deal better chance in the country. Nobody as I've met with here will offer a hungry lad bite nor sup not to save his life, and I am as hungry as Jowles' dog—that is certain."

He walked on to the entrance of the Lowther Arcade, in which a dense throng of persons had collected.

Two ladies were waiting for a Hammersmith omnibus. Their attention was directed towards the young birds'-nest seller. "Ah!" exclaimed one, "do look at that miserable-looking boy—he's drenched with rain, Anna Maria dear; how thankful you ought to be that you are not in his position, poor fellow!"

"He does look wretched," said Anna Maria, who was the younger, and by far the best looking of the two, "let's ask him what keeps him out in the rain."

"He's got birds' nests to sell; don't you see?"

"Ah, so he has."

The speaker beckoned to Alf, who made his usual obeisance, for privation had taught him to be patient and polite to all.

He had been taught by experience that ladies seldom bought eggs or nests—not unless they had children with them, which neither of the two in question seemed to have.

Still he was not disposed to throw a chance away— perhaps these might be an exception to the rule—there was no telling.

He drew nearer, and stood close by them.

"How wet and cold you must feel, my poor lad!" said Anna Maria.

"Yes, marm; but I'm used to be out in all sorts of weathers."

"You are from the country, I suppose," said the elder of the two.

"Yes marm, country bred. I was a farmer's boy till a couple of months ago, when a bird-catcher brought me up to London to seek my fortune, though I can't see as how I've bettered myself as yet."

"No, I should assume not. Dear me, and is this your trade?" inquired the elder lady.

"Yes, marm; when I first come up I was pretty comfortable, but the birdcatcher caught a cold, was took ill, and went to the hospital; then my troubles commenced."

"Was he kind to you?"

"Yes, as kind as could be. I should have been all right if he hadn't been took ill—that's what's driven me to this. I have to do business on my own hook, and it aint always as good as it might be."

"Dear me, only to think of that, now," said the old lady, turning to her companion. "A lad like this, too; extraordinary—most extraordinary."

Then, turning towards Alf, she inquired where he got the eggs from.

"They come from all parts. Mostly from Witham and Chelmsford, mum," answered Alf. "Chelmsford is about thirty miles from Westminster-bridge, Witham eight miles further. I go out of town for 'em three times a week. I start generally about dusk, and walk all night. I like that better than walking in the sun; besides, one can't rest in the night time."

"Dear me, how astonishing!"

"When I get there," said Alf, in continuation, "I skipper it under a hedge, and get a couple of hours' sleep. After this I set to work in earnest. It's uncertain about meeting with what I want, but one must take the chance of that. I go on until I do succeed. Sometimes I climb tree after tree, and find no eggs in the nests, or else young birds, which are no use to me. But this aint all. When I've been away two nights and a day, and worked hard, and got a lot of eggs, I have a hard job to sell 'em."

"But, my good boy, don't you know that it's very cruel to take away the eggs of the poor birds?" cried the elderly female. "You ought to consider that."

"I s'pose it is, marm; but other people do the same. There's lots of nesters besides me, and they are a deal more lucky; for some in our trade have what they call a connection, and a goodish many get their orders beforehand, and so they know what they can make sure of, whilst I have to take my chance. I've been about the streets for the whole of this blessed day, and have scarcely sold anything at all."

"How do you account for that?"

"Well, you see, marm, it's been so wet, and there aint been many young gentlemen about, that's the reason. Young gentlemen are my best customers, and if I don't sell anything to-night, I'm sure I don't know what I shall do."

"Are you so badly off, then?"

"I haven't had anything to eat the whole of the day."

"I am very sorry for you—extremely sorry."

"I don't so much mind going without my grub, but unless I get some money I shall have to sleep in one of those dreadful lodging-houses. My regular place is Whitechapel, but I am too tired to walk there. I generally give up trading long afore this, but I've gone on late to-night in the hope of selling a nest or some eggs."

"Ah! all this is very sad; I'm quite troubled to think that you should be so unfortunate," murmured the lady.

The other lady had gone a pace or two from them. She was anxiously looking down the Strand in the direction of the City.

"But how will you get on in the winter time of the year?"

"Winter!" exclaimed Alf; "I never thought of that. I don't know what I shall do then. Beg or starve, I suppose."

The lady bent her head at that moment, her companion gave a scream, and waved her umbrella in the air.

"Please give me a trifle for a night's lodging, ma'am," said the boy, addressing himself to the younger of the two ladies.

"Yes, certainly," she said. "Aunt, you've got my purse in your bag; I want it for a moment."

"Want it—what for? Here's a Hammersmith omnibus waiting."

"Don't go away without giving me something," cried Alf, in piteous accents.

"Anna Maria, what can you be thinking about? We shall lose the omnibus if you don't leave off chattering to that dirty little fellow."

"Let me have the purse."

"I can't get at it without wetting myself through. Give him something another time. It doesn't do to place any reliance upon what boys of his sort say. Do come, or we shall be left behind. Come, Anna Maria."

"Now, ma'am, look sharp, please," bawled the conductor. "Jump in, ladies, if you're going."

The door of the omnibus was held impatiently open. The ladies ascended the steps and took their seats in the vehicle, which was driven rapidly down the Strand.

The poor birds' nest seller was again disappointed this time. He had hoped to extract a small sum from his female questioner.

"Ah!" he ejaculated, "I'm very unfortunate, that's what I am. I have been so the whole of this blessed day."

It was still raining, and he was drenched to the skin. His feet were sore with walking, and every bone in his body ached.

He was sick at heart—felt fairly worn out. It was no use his waiting any longer in the streets—there was no one to buy, and nobody seemed disposed to give him alms.

Hunger was gnawing at his very vitals. He was supremely wretched—more miserable than he ever remembered to have been.

He walked slowly and sadly on towards Trafalgar-square. As he went along he counted the flagstones by way of amusement, if such a term could with propriety be applied to him under the present circumstances.

He arrived at the corner of Parliament-street. He knew that there were several low lodging-houses in the back slums of Westminster. He dreaded, as well he might, having to pass the night surrounded with the very dregs of society.

But there was no help for it. He knew that he must sleep, or try to sleep, or he would faint under his next day's work.

It is true he might go to the casual ward of the workhouse, but of this he had an instinctive horror. He had never been in one, but he had listened to the vivid descriptions of those who had.

He stood at the corner of Parliament-street, irresolute and chapfallen.

A man looked curiously into his face.

The boy raised his head, and saw two gentlemen standing by the side of him.

One of these was Charles Peace; the other, the friend he had picked up at Sanderson's hotel.

"Birds' nests—eh, youngster?" cried Peace.

"Yes, sir. Do, for mercy's sake, buy some, either eggs or nests."

"I'm going to the theatre, my lad, and can't be bothered with things of that sort."

"Won't you buy?"

"No, certainly not. Where do you hail from?"

"Broxbridge."

"I thought so. Well, here's something to keep the devil out of your pocket."

Peace presented the boy with a shilling. At the sight of this he was in perfect ecstasies.

"Oh! thank you, sir—thank you," he ejaculated. "May Heaven reward you!"

"Shut up; that 'ill do," cried Peace, with a deprecating gesture—then he put his arm in that of his friend's, and the two walked away.

"He's a rare good sort—a stunner," cried Alf. "No nonsense or collywabbling about him; he outs with a shiner at once."

He passed down Parliament-street and bent his steps in the direction of Westminster.

CHAPTER XLI.

THE LODGING-HOUSE IN WESTMINSTER.

ALF PURVIS had waited patiently, like Mr. Micawber, till something turned up—the good Samaritan, who had relieved him in the hour of his despair, being, as we have already seen, our hero Charles Peace. There was good reason for this.

Peace had been attracted by the boy, whose features were familiar to him.

Upon a closer inspection he discovered that he was the lad whom he remembered having seen about the neighbourhood of Broxbridge during his sojourn in that locality, and hence it was that he had presented Alf with the shilling.

Peace did not care to make any enquiries as to why the lad was in London, as he had his newly-formed friend with him, and, therefore, contented himself by giving the much-prized coin.

Had he been alone he would have questioned Alf, but, under existing circumstances, prudence directed that he should refrain from doing so.

Peace at this time was passing himself off as a gentleman of independent means: to make use of a common phrase he was "cutting a dash."

How long his means would last, or how long the character would suit him, time would show.

He did the grand at this time to his heart's content, and half persuaded himself that the life of a gentleman was his proper and legitimate sphere of action.

Alf Purvis wended his way down Parliament-street towards Westminster. He was ravenously hungry, and upon his reaching Tothill-street his attention was directed to an eating-house on the opposite side of the way.

In the window of this the savoury steam from the joints proved to be too much for him; he crossed over and gazed wistfully at the dainties displayed so temptingly in the shop.

He entered and ordered a plate of meat and vegetables; these he devoured, as may be imagined, with infinite relish. He was still hungry, so he finished his repast with a slice of pudding, or "plum duff," as it is termed.

After he had paid the reckoning he had but fourpence left out of the shilling Peace had given him.

He confessed to himself that he had been reckless and extravagant, but had enough left to pay for a bed.

He now directed his steps in the direction of a well-known lodging-house situated in one of the streets leading out of the one in which he had regaled himself so sumptuously.

Upon his arriving at the establishment in question he found that externally it did not present a very inviting appearance.

It was a low large building, which he at once boldly entered. At the side of the passage there was a glass window drawn up, and a kind of ledger or counter, on which were two piles of small round tickets. Behind the counter was a small room just large enough to hold a deformed old man, and a brawny forbidding-looking woman—some such woman as Eugene Sue describes in the "Mysteries of Paris" as the "Ogress." The title would apply with equal force to the Westminster landlady.

"Now then, young shaver," cried the man, "what's your pleasure, fourpenny or twopenny, eh? Twopenny, I suppose," he added, glancing at the lad.

"No, guv'nor," returned the latter, "I want a fourpenny."

"Oh, you're one of the haristocratic customers—are you?" said the man, in a jocular tone.

"You'd better make him fork out. I should like to see his money first," cried the woman, folding her arms across her breast like an Amazon.

"Now then, boy, down with the dust," said the man.

Alf fumbled in his pocket; he wanted to keep a penny in his pocket for a loaf in the morning. He drew forth threepence.

"That won't do, you fool," said the landlord; "why here's only three browns."

"He hasn't got another, I'll take my davy of that," observed the woman; "it's just as I expected."

"Well, it's only a matter of a penny," implored Alf, in his most persuasive tones; "don't be hard upon a cove. I've had a bad day of it 'cos of the wet. Trust me for this once. I will pay you to-morrow—indeed I will."

"To-morrow be blowed," exclaimed the man; "that game won't do here. You know our prices, you know our rules; we don't give credit. If we did we should be in the union in quick sticks."

"Well, that's right enough, master, I daresay, but look here," said Alf, showing his basket, "this is how I make my living. Will you take some of these and keep them till I pay you the penny back again?"

"Umph, well I don't know—they are not ugly," said the housekeeper, looking at them curiously and turning them over in his hands; "you're a country lad, eh? Who'd have thought of seeing birds' eggs in a back slum in Westminster? Well, London is a place, surely."

"It's hard lines to be walking about all day in the wet without even so much as one customer," said the boy. "You can take the cuckoos if you like—that's the best one—or you can take any of the others, whichever you please."

"I used to go arter them myself years and years ago, when I was a kinchin. Ah, it puts me in mind of brighter and happier days. They minds me of my old mother, and how she used to scold me, because it was so cruel, she said—bless her dear heart."

"Don't get sentimental, you old fool," cried the woman, in a tone of disgust. "Them days are past wi' both of us."

"Right you are, missus—long since past," returned the man. "Well, hand us over an egg, and here's the ticket for a fourpenny room."

"Nonsense, Joe," said the woman. "What do you want with a trumpery egg? Give the boy a penny back and a twopenny ticket."

"Well, it's hardly worth wrangling about," returned the landlord. "A penny won't hurt us much either way."

As they were talking a man came in, and, drawing a large piece of bacon from his pocket, flung it on the counter.

"How much do you want for it?" said the lodging-house keeper.

"Sixpence."

"Sixpence for a bit of *sawney* ! (stolen bacon). Can't give more than a joey for it."

"Hand it over then, you mean ravenous old land shark."

The money was laid on the counter and collared by the new comer.

Two children came in. One of them paid for his bed and supper with fish *got from the gate* (stolen from Billingsgate), and the other with *flesh found at Leadenhall* (meat stolen from the butchers' stalls in that market).

"That's the way to get your grub and your shakedown," said the woman, addressing herself to Alf.

"So it appears, marm."

"Some bring a *Moses* (second-hand wearing apparel), some prigs tea from the docks, and there's many as brings *hens and chickens*."

These are the cant terms for publicans' larger and smaller pewter measures, which go to the furnace and melting pot instead of to the fire and the dripping pan.

"Give me back a penny and I'll have a twopenny ticket," cried Alf, who did not care to argue the question further.

Before going upstairs he went into the kitchen of the lodging-house.

This was a long quaint room, its walls covered with disgusting figures; the floor was covered with dirt, and a wooden seat projected from the wall all round the room.

In front of this was ranged a series of tables on which lolled men and boys.

A number of inmates were grouped round the fire, some kneeling, washing herrings—of which the place smelt strongly—others without shirts seated on the ground, and others drying the ends of cigars they had picked up in the streets. As for the assembly, it was of the most heterogeneous description.

Some were, like Alf, in dirty smock frocks; others in old red plush waistcoats, with long sleeves. One was dressed in an old shooting jacket, with large wooden buttons; a second in a blue flannel sailor's shirt; and a third, a mere boy, wore a long camlet cloak reaching to his heels, and both the ends of the sleeves hanging over his hands.

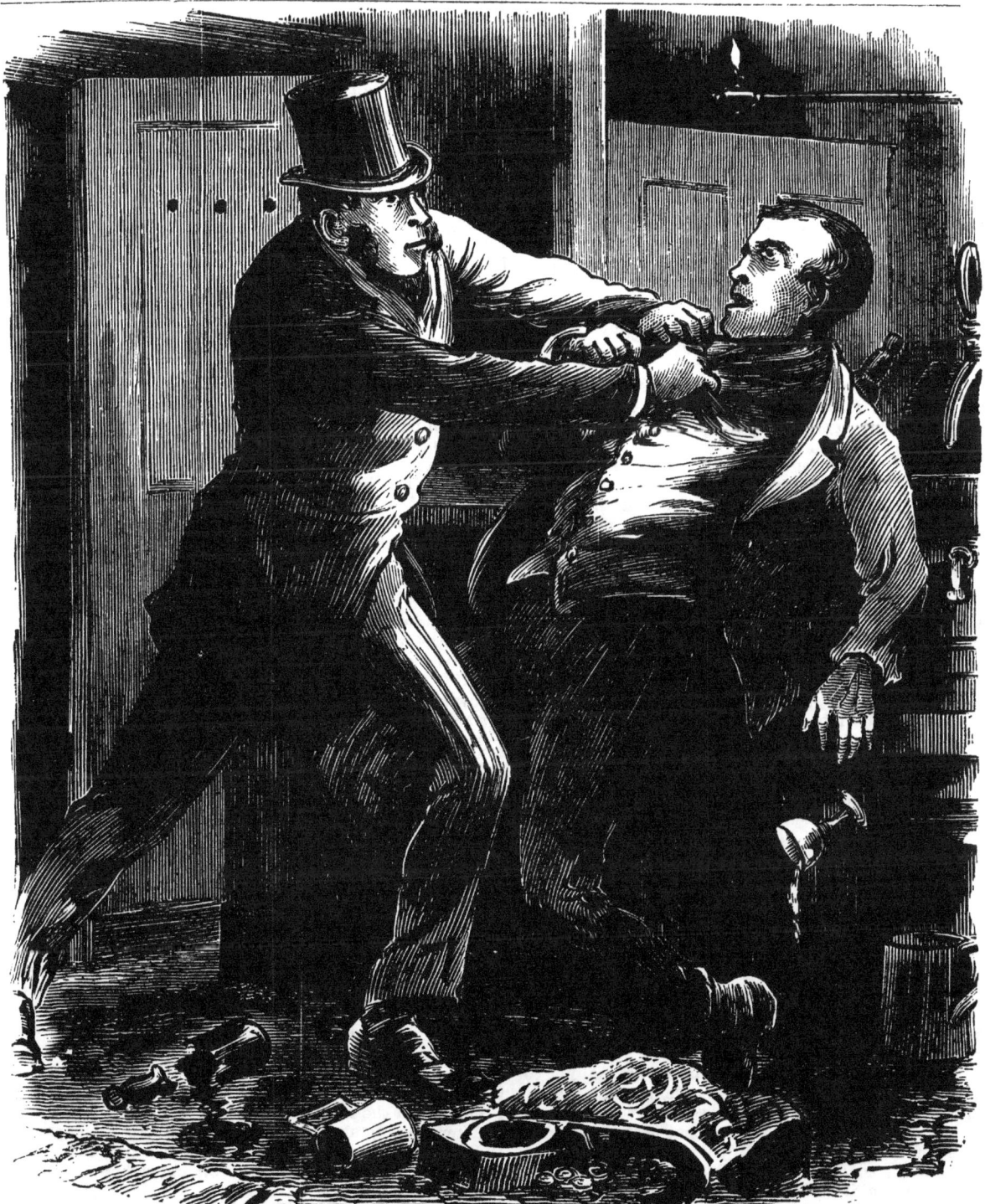

"DON'T MAKE ANY ROW," SAID WRENCH; "YOU ARE MY PRISONER NOW."

The features of the lodgers were of every kind of expression. Alf Purvis was certainly the best-looking of all present, even disguised as he was in his wretched attire.

Here the thieves and cadgers who frequented the place enjoyed their supper before going to bed, and here they might be seen employed in a dozen various occupations.

One was frying bacon, another mending an umbrella, a third washing his shirt in a hand-basin, while the majority were smoking short pipes and conversing in whispers.

Alf Purvis, who had gone to the fire to dry his things, was pushed on one side by a hulking fellow with a red herring on a fork.

Unfortunately for the lad, his smock frock came in

No. 19.

contact with the handle of the frying-pan, which was jerked from the fire, its contents falling in the hearth.

The owner of the bacon was a strapping lad. With a horrible oath he sprang forward, and struck Alf a terrific blow on the jaw, which sent him reeling.

"It wasn't the yokel's fault," cried one of the men at a side table. "At him ag'in, young un."

To be thus assailed for an offence which was committed, in reality, by the herring toaster, was not to be borne.

The bacon frier was half a head taller and a deal bigger than the birds'-nest seller; but the latter had pluck. He rushed at his assailant and gave him a straightforward blow on the mouth, which astonished the young bully.

"Well done. Bravo, little 'un!" cried a dozen voices. "Give it him right from the shoulder."

A ring was formed, and the two lads went to work in real earnest.

Alf Purvis received several ugly knocks; but he was so agile and rapid in his movements that in a few minutes his antagonist's face bore unmistakable marks of the other's blows.

At length the young bird's nest seller rushed in and gave the bacon frier a floorer.

"We've had enough of this," cried a man, in a velveteen jacket. "Stop it—stow it, I say. If you don't, blow me if I don't give the pair of you a thrashing."

The combatants were separated, and peace was proclaimed. Alf was declared victor.

Two women were seated in one corner of the room; their dress and demeanour denoted that they were merely visitors, who had been attracted to the spot by curiosity or some other motive.

One of them was quite young and extremely good-looking, the other was elderly.

They had both been witnesses of the short but decisive battle between the two boys.

They were whispering to each other.

"I could see at a glance that he was no common boy," murmured the younger female. "He's a brave little fellow—that's quite evident."

"Oh! clearly so," returned the other; "but what of that?"

"I tell you he comes from a good stock—I'm sure of it. I'll wager my existence that his father was a gentleman. Look at his hands, how small and delicate they are; look at his beautifully-formed features. Perhaps you can see no further than his smock frock."

"Perhaps I am not able to understand these matters as well as you," answered the elder female, looking abstractedly on the dirt-begrimed floor of the apartment. "We haven't all the same powers of observation."

"I dont think I am mistaken in my estimate of the lad. I don't believe he is a low fellow, like the rest of the lawless young ruffians we see around us. We are all of us liable to mistakes; but that is the impression I have formed of him."

"I don't say you are mistaken. Have your way. Speak to him, if you will."

"I am determined to do so," said the youngest of the two women. "You may think me self-willed—that you have often said—but what of that?"

Alf Purvis had been looking curiously at the speaker during the foregoing conversation. When he had first entered the kitchen he had not been aware of their presence; but now his attention was attracted towards them, and his eyes were rivetted on their faces.

The younger of the two women beckoned to the young birds'-nest seller.

He drew towards them, having already guessed that their discourse related to himself. In this he was not mistaken.

As he approached, an extraordinary thing happened. The old woman and the boy started at the same moment, and each gazed earnestly into each other's eyes, which were lighted up with a mingled expression of curiosity and surprise.

The effect was most remarkable. They both stood for one moment as if rendered motionless by some sudden thought, and petrified into stone.

This feeling, however, was but a transient one, and soon passed away. The woman turned impatiently on one side, as if to crush and smother the weakness which appeared reasonless because it was intuitive.

But she could not conceal from herself that some mysterious and overpowering influence had been plainly manifested for a brief period. What it was she was at a loss to discover.

There is always a reason for these magnetic impulses, which, instead of welcoming and cherishing, men and women but too often drive by main force from their hearts.

Alf Purvis stood motionless before the females.

"You're a brave little fellow," said the younger one. "What is your name, my lad?"

"Alfred Purvis, marm."

"Ah, just so, and your trade?"

"I've been brought up to the farming business, but am now on my own hook. I'm a birds'-nest seller—that is when I can get any customers."

"And do you like the calling?"

"Pretty well."

"Oh, not very well—eh?"

"I should like it better if I could see my way towards something for the winter. It's hard lines sometimes in the summer, but I don't know how I shall get on in the cold weather. The birds don't have no families when the snow is on the ground; they've enough to do to pick up enough for themselves at that time."

"Quite true, boy." Then, turning towards her companion, she said in an under tone, "You see the poor lad is no fool, as I said; and he has pluck at heart for all his poor thin body and pale face."

The elder woman nodded, but said nothing.

"I was right!" exclaimed her companion; then turning towards Alf, she said, "I suppose you have run away from home, or something of that sort—eh?"

"I wasn't used well, and I did leave of my own accord. I half wish I hadn't now; but it goes against the grain to return to Stoke Ferry Farm."

"Ah, that's where you came from?"

"Yes, marm. Do you know the place?" cried Alf, in a tone of evident anxiety.

"Not I, indeed, never heard of it before you mentioned the name. You street boys are a funny lot. After running about you cannot bear to be kept indoors, or be under any sort of control. It is natural it should be so, I suppose. Do you know how to read and write?"

"Ah, yes, marm, I can write pretty well, and as to reading I'm never tired of it; nothing pleases me better than an interesting book."

"Indeed—I should have hardly thought you could have much time for reading."

"I have not since I've been in London, but before I left the farmhouse I had lots of time every evening."

"And what kind of books do you like best?"

"Those that have lots of shipwrecks or battles in

them," said Alf, quickly. "I love battles, and tales of pirates—those are my sort."

The girl gave a murmur of assent or pleasure. It was like the purring of a tigress.

"And travellers who fight with lions, tigers, and all sorts of wild animals," said the boy, in continuation. "And big knights, with polished armour, who kill dragons and rescue ladies. Oh, I can read anything of that sort. I like any book as makes me feel venturesome, but I hate them as keeps on talking and talking over nothing."

The girl burst out in a loud laugh.

"Well, my brave young fellow, I think I may be able to do something for you. Will you call upon me tomorrow if I give you my address?"

"Yes, marm, I will be sure to do so."

She wrote something down on a card, which she handed to Alf.

As she gave him this she slipped a shilling in his hand, and then she and the old woman rose and left the kitchen.

Alf Purvis was in a state of wonderment and delight. He changed his ticket for a fourpenny one, and proceeded upstairs to his luxurious sleeping apartment.

The reader must not suppose that we have presented to him the horrors of low lodgings, however, in the brief sketch given of the one in which Alf Purvis sought shelter. At this period those places were foul blots upon a civilised city. They were the nurseries for young thieves and lawless characters of every conceivable description. Personal narratives are given in "London Labour and the London Poor" by persons who have frequented these dens.

"Nothing can be worse than the health of these places," says one witness.

Without ventilation, cleanliness, or decency, and with forty person's breaths perhaps mingling together, they are the ready resort of thieves and all bad characters, and the keepers will hide them, if they can, from the police, or facilitate any criminal's escape.

I never knew the keepers give any offender up, even when rewards were offered. If they did they might shut up shop.

These houses are but receptacles, with very few exceptions, for beggars, thieves, and prostitutes. The exceptions are those who must lodge at the lowest possible cost.

Fights, and fierce fights too, are frequent in them, and I have often been afraid murder would be done.

I never saw a clergyman of any denomination in any one of these places either in town or country.

In London the keepers know very well that stolen property is brought into their house. In some cases they will buy—in others it is disposed of to some of the other inmates.

The influence of the lodging-house society on boys who have run away from home and have got thither, either separately or in company with lads who have joined them in the streets, is this—boys there, after paying for their lodgings, may exercise the same freedom from every restraint as they see persons of maturer years enjoy.

This is often pleasant to a boy, especially if he has been severely treated by his parents or his master. He apes and often outdoes men's ways, both in swearing and loud talk, and so he gets a relish for that sort of life.

After he has resorted to such places—the sharper boys for three and the duller boys for six months—they are adepts at any thieving or vice.

In the same work the statement of a young girl of sixteen years of age is given.

The narrative is that of a fallen female who was accustomed to sleep in the low lodging-houses where boys and girls were promiscuously huddled together. The account given disclosed a system of depravity, atrocity, and enormity, which certainly could not be paralleled in any nation, however barbarous, nor in any age, however dark.

The facts detailed are gross enough to make us all blush for the land in which such scenes could be daily perpetrated.

Happily for the morality of the lower classes, legislation has done much to abate the evil; the low lodging houses of the present day are under the surpervision of the police, who have done much to abate the evil which was so justly complained of. Nevertheless, the scenes which take place in lodging houses in the courts and alleys of London are, even at the present time, a scandal and disgrace to a Christian land.

The indiscriminate mixing of the sexes, the crowding of large families in one miserable room, does more to demoralise the youth of this country than those unacquainted with the subject can possibly imagine.

The language made use of by children of tender years is something shocking. The writer of this work has heard words fall from the lips of girls who were little more than children that were of too horrible a nature for him to repeat under any circumstances whatever.

CHAPTER XLII.

AT BROXBRIDGE HALL—THE TEMPTER AND THE TEMPTED.

WE left Aveline Gatliffe at the door of Earl Ethalwood's seat, known as Broxbridge Hall. The engineer's wife and child were conducted into the presence of the proud old lord, who was anxiously awaiting their appearance.

Mr. Chicknell introduced the visitors, and at first there was an air of restraint and timidity upon the part of Aveline, and a certain amount of hauteur in the manner of the earl. This, however, soon wore off.

"I think, my lord," observed the lawyer, with something like triumph in his tone, "that there cannot be much mistake in the matter. If any doubts did exist in the mind of your lordship they are now dispelled."

The earl nodded.

"It is Aveline, Aveline risen from the dead—my own Avaline."

"You hear what his lordship says?" cried the lawyer, addressing himself to the lady.

"I do, sir," she answered. "I am so wonderstruck that I hardly know how to comport myself, or to thank you sufficiently for the interest you have taken in the welfare of one who was to you a perfect stranger."

"I have had a duty to perform which I have endeavoured to carry out to the best of my ability," answered Mr. Chicknell. "I may observe that it was a difficult and delicate task, but it is at all times a pleasure to me to meet with the approval of my client and yourself."

While these few remarks were being made the earl had been gazing intently on the young woman, and he nearly lost his self-possession as his eyes fell upon her beautiful face.

Aveline, who did not know very well what to say or do, observed, quietly, to the earl—

"I am sure you will love me for my dear mother's sake."

She had all the Ethalwood grace of manner and movement.

The earl was touched, for she had crept up to him and laid her hand gently on his arm.

He kissed her on the forehead; he looked at the violet eyes, with their golden light; he laid his hand on the shining masses of waving hair.

Then he sighed.

He was thinking of other and earlier days in his troubled life.

His memory conjured up the image of the wife who had proved so false to him, who fled with her paramour, and died in a foreign land unheeded and uncared for.

How about the young creature before him ?

Was she to be trusted ?

Time will show.

"I shall learn," said he, in answer to her question, "to love you best for your own sake, and no other."

"Ah!" ejaculated Aveline, a little disconcerted, "for my own sake ?"

"Yes," he answered. "I think you good and true —nay, I am sure of it. Is this little fellow your son ? You seem to me to look so very young that I can hardly believe you are a mother, or that I am a great grandfather," he added, with a smile.

"You mustn't tell people that, my lord," observed Mr. Chicknell, in a bantering tone.

"They'll find it out without any one telling them," answered the earl, taking the boy in his arms, and, placing him on his knee, looking at him with evident interest.

"He has something of the Ethalwood face," he said, musingly.

"Ah! most undoubtedly. I saw that from the very first," cried the lawyer. "Indeed, to say the truth, he resembles your lordship in a most remarkable degree."

"You think so ?"

"Certainly. It is plain and palpable enough to the most obtuse observer. Quite the Ethalwood cast of feature."

Aveline proved, to her grandfather's delight, that she too had some of the old Ethalwood spirit and pride. Although the magnificence of the interior of Broxbridge Hall was enough to startle and surprise one brought up in a humble sphere of life she did not express surprise, but was perfectly self-possessed.

There was an air of refinement about her which went far towards propitiating the proud old nobleman, who, if he disliked any one thing more in this world than another it was vulgarity, or even anything that bordered on it.

In this respect he had no reason to complain of his grand-daughter, whose natural grace of manner won upon him the more he became acquainted with her.

He was, in short, delighted with her; she seemed to bridge over a wide gulf which separated the present from the past.

The long, long, solitary years he had passed had made him something of a misanthrope, now a new light broke in upon his gloomy path which seemed all of a sudden to be irradiated with sunshine.

If he could only have this young and fair creature all to himself, make her his darling, how happy would he be ! But then there was a husband in the way. This last-named he would not countenance nor receive, not under any circumstances.

These thoughts rushed rapidly through his mind as he sat nursing and fondling the little boy.

"You will be my guest for a short time. You will do me the pleasure of remaining at Broxbridge," said he, suddenly, "so that we become better acquainted."

Aveline turned towards Mr. Chicknell and said, "It was understood, was it not, that I was to remain for a short time ?"

"Oh, yes, certainly," returned the lawyer. "I told Mr. Gatliff so; that's a distinct understanding."

The earl's countenance darkened.

"I have no desire to coerce or control you in any way; indeed I have no right to do so, but still as a favour— "

"There is no favour in the matter, my lord," cried Aveline, "I will remain with you for the present."

"Spoken like a scion of the house of Ethalwood," exclaimed the earl, in evident delight.

The wife of the young engineer was taken by the housekeeper of Broxbridge into a superb suite of rooms, which had already been prepared for her. She was wise enough not to give expression to the surprise she felt at the grandeur of the apartments.

There was a day and night nursery for the boy, and there was a neat smiling maid to attend to him.

A suite of four rooms had been set apart for the sole use of Aveline herself. These were magnificent and luxurious as though they had been for a queen. They consisted of a boudoir with rose silk hangings, rare pictures, fragrant flowers, exquisite statuary, and furniture of the most modern beautiful design ; a sleeping chamber, all white and gold; a dressing-room, filled up with every luxury that the proudest lady in the land could not fail to be satisfied with; and a small library, where she could read, write, or study at will.

As a matter of course, she was treated with the greatest deference by all the servants at Broxbridge.

"I hope you will find all you desire in these apartments," said the housekeeper, "but should you require anything else your orders will be attended to without a moment's delay."

"These are intended for me, then ?" returned Aveline, looking round at the beautifully furnished rooms.

The housekeeper answered in the affirmative.

A pleasant-looking maid now entered, and, after smiling and dropping a curtsey, she said that Lord Ethalwood had deputed her to attend upon his grand-daughter.

Aveline took this for granted, and did not appear at all astonished.

The wardrobe doors were opened by the obsequious maid-servant, and an extensive assortment of costumes were displayed.

Aveline saw wondrous treasures of satin, silk, and lace dresses that had been sent from Paris; Cashmere shawls and mantles of the richest velvet. There was also provided everything necessary in the way of gloves, fans, slippers, &c. Nothing had been forgotten.

Aveline's face grew pale with wonder as she gazed.

"Shall I help you, madame, to dress for dinner ?" inquired the maid, and Aveline, with some little trepidation, consented.

The girl had selected a demi-toilet, a dress of rich blue velvet trimmed with white lace. She arranged the wavy masses of light brown hair so as to show its silky abundance, she placed a white camelia in it, and then she opened a jewel case that lay on the table. It contained a suite of pearls, a beautiful necklace, bracelet, and ear-rings.

When her toilette was complete and the last finishing touch had been given by her attentive hand-maiden, Aveline looked at herself in one of the survey glasses which reflected on its face the whole of the figure, and she was perfectly dazzled at her resplendent appearance.

Could it be possible that the lovely, radiant, magnificently dressed woman was the wife of Tom Gatliffe, a poor working man?

The white graceful neck and exquisitely moulded shoulders were fair as the soft gleaming pearls—the rounded arms were perfect in shape as the small white hands.

She smiled to herself.

It seemed hardly possible that she could have been so transformed.

It has been said that beauty unadorned is adorned the most, but it would be in vain to conceal that the most beautiful woman is not enhanced by the aid of elegant attire and rendered still more radiant by glittering jewels.

"I wish poor Tom could see me now," she murmured, "he would hardly recognise me. Indeed, to say the truth, I hardly know myself."

She went down to the drawing-room where the Earl and Mr. Chicknell awaited her.

They both looked up in wonder as the magnificently-attired girl entered the room.

The old lord was profuse in his compliments. He was evidently proud of his grand-daughter's aristocratic appearance.

"She is an ornament to the old walls of Broxbridge," cried the lawyer, "and I congratulate you, my lord, in possessing such a charming companion, whose presence here imparts so much happiness."

Aveline blushed. She was not accustomed as yet to the compliments which fall so glibly from lips of men of good breeding.

She went through the ordeal of dinner with great calmness and self-control.

But there were many things which, in some measure, made her feel uneasy. She had never partaken of a meal of such an elaborate description. The number of courses seemed to bewilder her.

The banquet was served with the greatest care. The services of gold and silver plate, the rare wines, the exotics, and the luxury which seemed to abound everywhere, half startled her.

She took the initiative from her grandfather—she watched what he did, and imitated him.

"She is clever, and can be easily taught. Three months under the careful tuition of some accomplished high-bred woman," murmured the earl to himself, "and she will be fit for any society."

"I hope and trust you will find yourself so comfortable here," said Mr. Chicknell, addressing himself to the young lady, "that you will not object to remain for a very long time."

"Ahem! I cannot be made more comfortable. My only fear is that I shall be spoilt," answered Aveline; "and besides, I must not forget my husband."

The earl held up his hand deprecatingly.

"I must entreat of you not to mention his name," he said, quickly. "Pray do not."

Her face flushed with anger; she was about to make some sharp retort, but had the prudence to smother her rising anger, and forbore from making any reply.

Mr. Chicknell adroitly turned the conversation with the tact and address of an accomplished courtier. He engaged the earl's attention upon one or two topics which were favourite ones with him.

The cloud passed over, and the earl took his *protegée* to the picture gallery. He talked pleasantly to her, and allowed her to see how greatly she was admired by him.

Without ostentation, without boasting, he gave her some faint idea of the glories of the house of Ethalwood. He was well up in the history of his ancestors.

He showed her ancient armour that had been worn by the heroes and warriors of his race.

He showed her the pictured faces of men whose voice had ruled the land. He showed her the portraits of ladies whose names had been proverbial for beauty and grace.

"I point out these things to you, my child," said the earl, "so that when I am gathered to my fathers you may keep the remembrance of our ancestors green in your memory; for it has pleased heaven to make known to me that there is yet a living descendant of our long and honourable line, who will, let me hope, wear with credit the honours which, in good time, will be his."

"To whom do you allude, my lord?" said Aveline.

"I cannot refer to any other than your son."

The young girl by his side smiled wanly, but her heart was too full to make any reply.

"We shall have to discourse on this subject on some future day," said he, still in the same measured and melancholy tone and manner he was wont to assume when referring to family matters. "Yes, some other day," he repeated.

She bowed her head, and clung closer to him.

Something struck her just then that he was a strange weird kind of man, who seemed to have the power of drawing her closer and closer towards him, until he held her in perfect subjection.

This was but a fugitive thought, but as it passed through her brain she became more reserved in her manner.

"I doubt not but we shall understand each other pretty well," said he; "and I am sure you will do your best to meet my views. I am old, and old age is exacting."

"I will not hear you say so," cried Aveline.

He stooped down, drew her towards him, and kissed her on the cheek.

She passed upstairs to her own suite of rooms, and he returned to the banqueting hall.

Aveline, upon reaching her own rooms, sat down and wrote a long letter to her husband.

In this she described all that had taken place during the day; she informed him also that a grand future was in store for their son, and furthermore that she durst not offend the earl, who had requested her to remain for a short period as his guest, and, under the circumstances it was impossible for her to refuse, and so he must make himself as comfortable as possible during her temporary but unavoidable absence.

Gatliffe, as may be readily imagined, felt lonely during the absence of his wife, for he was not a young man who had at any time sought companionship in the society of those who were frequenters of a public-house.

However, as there did not appear any help for it, he took refuge in the house of Mrs. Maitland, his mother-in-law.

In a few days after her introduction Aveline Gatliffe began to feel more at home at Broxbridge. She became accustomed to its splendours, to its many charms, to the new and beautiful life that opened to her.

She had always yearned for rank and power, and felt assured that sooner or later she would find herself in a higher sphere. In this, as we have seen, she was not mistaken.

Whether the allurements and follies of fashionable life were destined to bring with them unalloyed happiness she had yet to find out. At present she was well satisfied.

She looked back with wonder at the time she had

passed at Sheffield, at Rotherham, and lastly at Wood Green.

How had she borne the quiet seclusion of these places and everything she now valued most? She began to look with contempt upon her past career. Nevertheless she was not disposed to discard her husband, but who, to say the truth, appeared at this time a sort of blot on the landscape.

Lord Ethalwood was most careful and adroit in his treatment of her.

He studiously avoided saying anything that she could openly resent, but at the same time he lost no opportunity at sneering at low-bred persons, and in a pointed manner made frequent allusions to men and women of quality, who were so far removed from the commoners.

Class distinctions he believed in like some old feudal lord. He endeavoured to imbue Aveline with the same notions as himself, and it must be admitted that to a considerable extent he succeeded.

The time soon came when, so far from feeling annoyed with him when he was riding his favourite hobby, she coincided with him in his views.

Mr. Chicknell did not attempt to interfere. He saw pretty clearly his client's course of action, and let him carry it out after his own fashion.

"My grandchild will not leave me, Chicknell," said the earl to his lawyer. "I feel assured of that."

"Not leave you? Not return to her husband, my lord?"

"Well, not at present."

"Ah, that's another matter. Not at present perhaps, but what causes you to arrive at such a conclusion?"

"I will tell you; her master passion is vanity. She is good in every sense of the word as far as I can judge, but she has more vanity than affection."

"My lord, I trust not."

"Do you? then I think you will be disappointed. I have known women—women of our own race too—who would have laughed all wealth to scorn, who would have sacrificed anything, given up their lives, for their love—women of noble nature who would have trampled all the allurements of wealth under foot, but Aveline is of a lighter nature. I have made a study of her character. Her master passion is vanity."

"I shouldn't have supposed so."

"But it is, Chicknell. She will stay with me because I can administer to her vanity, and her husband cannot. Now do you understand?"

"If it be so I am sorry for it, my lord. But assuming it is—I will assume you are better informed on the subject than myself—assuming it is, that is no reason for her being so tempted, no reason for her to be estranged from the husband she loves, or did love, I suppose."

"Yes, I believe she did and, indeed, does."

"Well, then, it seems an act of injustice, not to say cruelty, to separate man and wife by any such means."

"There is one thing you and I can't agree upon, Chicknell."

"What is that, my lord?"

"You are a radical, and are a self-elected champion of the lower orders. I am not. I have no sympathy with people of that order. You have, I suppose."

"I have sympathy with every class, high and low, if they be honest and good members of their class."

"Enough of this!" exclaimed the old nobleman, angrily.

"I have done, my lord," exclaimed the lawyer. "You

sent for me. I presume it was in reference to business matters."

"It was."

"I am at your service."

"It is essential to my happiness—my peace of mind —that this young creature should remain with me—be my adopted. I have not many more years to live; but I cannot part with Aveline. You will say I am selfish, perhaps—that does not much concern me; but you will admit, with all your radical notions, that it is not seemly—not consistent with the ordinary usages of society—that a scion of the house of Ethalwood should be mated to a common, low-bred workman. It is, in point of fact, most intolerable."

"It is unfortunate, I admit," said the man of parchment; "but the contract took place before you were even acquainted with your grand-daughter, and I do not see very well how it can be rescinded."

"It can be rescinded, and must be!" exclaimed the earl, with sudden vehemence.

"Mr. Chicknell, you know what I want."

"Ah—a divorce!"

"That's my meaning. Now you are talking like a sensible man. A divorce—how is it to be effected?"

The lawyer shook his head.

"There is no possible plea for such a course of action. Can't be done."

"It can't?"

"No."

"You must manage it by some means; I will accede to any terms. See this workman; propose a legal separation to him. Offer him what you like; fellows of his nature are always to be had for money. Every man has his price; put the question home to him— say I will agree to settle upon him a large yearly stipend for the remainder of his life, that furthermore his son will be heir to the title and estates of Ethalwood, that his wife will be mistress of Broxbridge Hall, and move in the best society. All this to be done upon one condition—that he consents to a divorce, and does not trouble us any further."

"Ah! this is as you would wish it to be. There is, however, I fear, one insurmountable difficulty in the way. The young engineer loves his wife too much to part with her."

The earl bounced up from his seat in a perfect fury.

"Pshaw!" he ejaculated. "Are you mad, Chicknell? Do you suppose that men of his stamp have any fine feelings? Do you imagine that they would let them— assuming they had such—stand in the way of their own advancement? But that we have to see. All I want you to do is to try. Make the proposition to him. You can do that, I suppose?"

"I can do it of course; but it is early yet. Besides, what about your grand-daughter? If she objects, there is an end of the matter."

"True. Yes, that is true enough. But she won't object after I have made known my wishes."

"Possibly not; but it would not be wise to move in the matter for the present. When the matter is a little more advanced, and you have ascertained that your grand-daughter will offer no obstacle, then I will see what I can do with her husband. If he consents to resign her, he is not the man I take him to be; and I must tell you frankly that I do not like the task, which, however, I will perform to the best of my ability."

"She will have to give up her husband, or give up all claims upon me," said Lord Ethalwood. "Understand that most clearly."

"I understand, my lord," returned Mr. Chicknell.

CHAPTER XLIII.

THE THIEF AND THE THIEF CATCHER.

CHARLES PEACE, who still remained an inmate of Sanderson's Hotel, and enjoyed, if we may so term it, the society of Kempshead, upon returning one evening was a little surprised at beholding, through the glass window of the door which led into the landlady's private room behind the bar, a face which was familiar to him. Mr. Wrench, the astute detective, was in close converse with Mrs. Sanderson. He, however, did not observe our hero, who passed on into one of the public rooms.

Peace thought it a little singular, but said nothing about it to anybody.

However, a similar circumstance took place on the following night. As he and Kempshead were passing through the bar Peace saw the back of Mr. Wrench, who, as on the preceding night, was talking to the landlady.

He and Kempshead exchanged significant glances as they went up stairs.

"Did you see that chap in the bar parlour?" inquired the latter of Peace.

"I can't make out his little game—is he sticking up to the widow?"

"It is not possible to say, but I should think not," returned Peace.

John Sanderson, the proprietor of the hotel bearing his name, had been dead for some three years, and the business was carried on by his widow, who, to say the truth, had been the presiding genius of the place during her husband's lifetime.

Of late Mr. Wrench had paid such frequent visits to the establishment that many others besides Peace and his friend were under the impression that the detective was paying court to the amiable and comely widow.

In this, however, they were mistaken, as will very shortly be demonstrated.

Mr. Wrench only attended professionally, if we may make use of such a term.

For a period of many months' duration—for more than a year—a systematic course of robbery had been carried on at the hotel.

Money was missed from the till, and the cash-box, silver plate, spirits, wines, table linen—in short, almost every description of portable articles disappeared in a most mysterious and unaccountable manner.

The servants were suspected; one after the other had been discharged; a fresh set of assistants were engaged, still every now and then articles, money, and other property was missing, and, taken in the aggregate, the losses by robbery represented a very enormous sum.

Mrs. Sanderson was advised to place the matter in the hands of the police.

Mr. Wrench was deputed to clear up the mystery, and, if possible, to trace out the offending party or parties.

He waited upon Mrs. Sanderson, who made him acquainted with all the facts connected with the case.

Mr. Wrench considered the matter over, examined the premises, listened to the voluble landlady's account of the matter, after which he arrived at one conclusion—it was this, that the robbery was not committed by anyone engaged in the establishment, but by a thief, who, by some means only known to himself and his confederates, effected an entrance into the premises after the household had retired to bed.

Mrs. Sanderson said she could not believe that possible, as all the locks were exactly in the same state in the morning as they were when the household retired for the night.

Mr. Wrench smiled and said—

"Is the outer door bolted when you close?"

"No, it is never bolted," returned the widow; "and for this reason. My regular customers, those who are likely to be late, are supplied with keys with which they can let themselves in. It is only those who have used the house for a number of years, and who are well known to me, that I entrust with keys, and then it is only on special occasions."

"And these are gentlemen you have full confidence in?"

"Oh, dear me, yes. They are of the highest respectability."

"Ahem—yes—I dare say," observed the detective. "Knavery is not confined to a class, Mrs. Sanderson."

"My dear sir, you would not for a moment suspect——"

"I do not suspect or accuse anybody," interrupted the detective. "Some person enters the house at night—of that I feel convinced."

"You think so?"

"I do. The question is, how are we to find out the guilty party?"

"That I must leave to you."

This conversation took place in the little room at the back of the bar.

Mr. Wrench rose from his seat and cast his eyes around, then he walked into the bar itself and glanced at an article of furniture which in shape and size very much resembled a large wardrobe.

"What is that, Mrs. Sanderson?" he inquired, pointing to the article in question.

"Oh, that is a large press, or cabinet, which my husband had made for the purpose of stowing away plate, linen, and other articles."

"Ah! I see; it has folding-doors. Can I open them?"

"Yes, if you like; here is the key."

The detective opened the doors, and found that the cabinet had three large shelves, which ran from side to side.

"We must remove these," he said, turning towards the landlady; "then there will be room enough."

"For what?"

"For me to take up my position for the night. I shall want a small stool to sit upon, and a few holes bored at the top for the admission of air."

"Take up your position there, Mr. Wrench!—what for?"

"To watch and wait patiently till my gentleman arrives," returned the detective, with the utmost composure.

The widow was astonished.

"But you'll be stifled," cried she.

"I hope not," he observed, with a laugh; "as in that case my man will have it all his own way. Now, you must not, upon any consideration, say a word to anyone about my plan of action; secrecy, in matters of this sort, is the very first consideration. The shelves must be removed, and holes bored at the top. This will have to be done by a man in our employ."

The widow nodded.

On the following morning a workman was sent by Mr. Wrench, who removed the shelves and made all the other necessary preparations.

In the evening, the detective crept into the press, and found it sufficiently commodious for his accommodation. He was a little cramped, it is true, or would be so, after a sojourn therein of some hours' duration;

but this inconvenience he felt bound to submit to in the exercise of his vocation.

A small stool was placed inside the cabinet, the doors of which were then closed and locked by Wrench.

So far matters were satisfactorily arranged.

The reader should be apprised that what we are about to describe is a narrative of an actual occurrence, which is, in every way, true, even to the minutest detail.

On the succeeding night the thief-catcher was prepared to take up his station in his narrow prison-house. He remained conversing with the landlady in her little bar parlour till all the household had retired to bed.

As a natural consequence the impression now became pretty general that he was an accepted suitor of the widow, and neither he nor the lady took the trouble to contradict it.

When the house was quiet, and no one any longer visible, Mr. Wrench unlocked the folding doors, and, like the Davenport brothers, entered his cabinet, taking care at the same time to lock himself therein.

The gas was turned off, and Mrs. Sanderson retired to bed.

Mr. Wrench kept watch and ward.

In one of the doors in front of him two narrow slits had been made. These were sufficiently large for him to observe the actions of any one behind the bar, while at the same time they were so constructed as not to admit of anyone seeing him.

In fact he was in Cimmerian darkness which no human eye could pierce.

The hours wore slowly on with our detective. His situation was by no means an enviable one. His position was cramped, and his small prison-house was cheerless and lonely; but detectives have to submit to every kind of inconvenience, and Mr. Wrench did not murmur.

The night wore on—as it waned the hall clock of the establishment struck hour after hour, but no burglar or robber disturbed the unbroken stillness of the hostelry.

Before any of the household was astir Mr. Wrench crept out of his cabinet, opened the front door of the house with the key the landlady had given him, and made the best of his way to his own residence, where he snatched a few hours of welcome and refreshing sleep.

His first night's purgatory had been attended with no good result.

He had been prepared for this. Possibly there would be no attempt at robbery for a week or more. It was impossible to tell.

On the following night he waited again on the widow, and told her of his non-success.

"I do not like you to submit to all this annoyance," cried she. "Perhaps it would be as well to give it up and try some other means."

Mr. Wrench shook his head.

"No my dear lady," he said. "We don't give a case up so easily. If I have to keep sentinel over your establishment for a month or more I shall not be disheartened. I shall make sure of my man sooner or later—that is unless he has been warned by some one."

"I have not mentioned the subject to a living soul," cried Mrs. Sanderson. "It is not likely I should do so after the caution I received from you.

"I am well assured of that, madam; these matters generally require time and patience. We shall succeed eventually, I've no doubt."

Again, as on the previous night, Mr. Wrench betook

himself to his sentry-box, where he again passed many cheerless hours, with no better result.

He left at daybreak, and made his appearance at the hotel a little before closing time.

"He is a most devoted and punctual lover," said one of the chambermaids to the cook. "I call him a model man."

"An' aint he good-looking? He's a little too good for missus. What's his business?"

"Something in the City, I believe." This answer was given at random—something in the City is such an indefinite term.

Mr. Wrench again took up his position.

For eight consecutive nights he went through the same formula.

He was getting a little tired of the painful monotony of his task, which, up to the present time, had been a thankless and fruitless one.

On the ninth night, about half-past two o'clock in the morning, which, to say the truth, sounds a good deal like a bull, for how can it be night if it is morning? But, of course, the reader will understand we are speaking figuratively.

About half-past two, or it might be a little later, Mr. Wrench pricked up his ears. He heard the sound of a key turning the lock of what he supposed to be the outer door. He was assured of this upon hearing the door gently closed.

Then soft footsteps were audible in the passage, and the little flap of the counter was thrown back. A man passed through and came behind the bar, then all was silent for the space of a few seconds.

Mr. Wrench was on the tiptoe of expectation.

The bird was coming into the net.

The striking of a lucifer was the next thing he heard. One gas-burner was ignited; it burnt very feebly as the strange visitor had only partially turned it on, nevertheless there was sufficient light for Mr. Wrench to observe the actions of his man through the slits of his sentry box, for he felt perfectly assured that it was his man.

The detective was too practised a hand to emerge from his place of temporary concealment. He must make sure before he pounced upon his prey.

The man drew from his pocket a bunch of keys. With one of these he opened the till, and, gathering up its contents, he slid the loose coins, gold and silver mingled together, into a canvas bag; this he placed in a small carpet bag which he had already deposited on the counter.

After this he went to the plate basket and abstracted therefrom several spoons and forks. He seemed to have a perfect knowledge of the place, and evidently understood where everything was kept.

He laid hold of a bottle of the best French brandy, and regaled himself with a couple of glasses from the same; this done, he put the bottle with two others in his carpet bag, having previously wrapped the bottles in some napkins he found in a drawer.

He now proceeded to open the cash box. In this were several Bank of England notes; these, like the other articles, were thrust into the carpet bag.

Mr. Wrench, with his hand on the key in the lock of his folding doors, was watching the robber with intense interest.

He was preparing to make a sudden spring, but as the robber was engaged in unlocking drawer after drawer for the purpose of obtaining further booty, the detective thought it would be just as well to let him have his full swing.

PEACE CREPT TO THE TABLE AND STEALTHILY LIFTED THE WATCH.

On one of the shelves was a box of cigars; the thief took a couple of handfuls of these, and which he pocketed.

After this had been done he turned round and took hold of one of the decanters containing wine. He poured out a glass of this, and while he was conveying it to his lips the doors of the cabinet were suddenly thrown open.

Mr. Wrench rushed forth, and, with one pan?..r ?i?e bound, grasped him by the throat with both hand?

The swiftness and suddenness of the attack w.. ? .: fectly electrical.

The robber trembled like an aspen bow s?.?.e?. ?. the blast. His knees gave way, and he wo?ld ? .?t certainly have fallen had he not been held ?? ?? ?r. Wrench.

No. 20.

His countenance was of an ashen hue.

"So, my man," cried the detective, "you're caught at last. I've been watching for you for a long time."

"Let me go!" cried the burglar, endeavouring to release himself.

"Look here," said Wrench, "it's no use your endeavouring to get away, or make any row. You are my prisoner."

"I aint got the strength of a blessed hinfant!" cried the robber. "I'm done as dead as a hammer, but don't put the darbeys on a cove."

"I certainly shall," returned the detective, slipping on the handcuffs with admirable adroitness.

"S'help my tater I am done brown this time, and no mistake."

The detective turned up the gas and rang the bell violently. Mrs. Sanderson was aroused from her slumbers. She hurried on her things, and hastened to the scene of action.

"We've caught him, madam; I knew we should," said Wrench, when the landlady made her appearance. "You had better go to Marlborough-street with me, and charge him."

"Oh! you scoundrel!" exclaimed Mrs. Sanderson, addressing herself to the prisoner. "It's you, eh?"

"Do you know him?" inquired the officer.

"Yes; he was boots here for a short time—about two years ago. Oh! the base, infamous man!"

"Lay it all on me," cried the prisoner. "In course, when a cove's down kick him. Oh! lay it all on me, but I aint so much to blame. Let me off, missus, and I'll tell ye all about it."

"Don't have anything to say to him, madam," said the detective, "but follow us to Marlborough-street as soon as possible."

Peace, who had heard the commotion, emerged from his bedroom half-dressed, and looked over the banister.

He was met by Mrs. Sanderson, who was returning to her room to put on her bonnet and shawl.

"What's the matter?" inquired Peace of the landlady.

"We've caught a burglar, and I have to go and prefer the charge against him," answered his hostess, as she passed into her sleeping apartment.

Our hero's curiosity was aroused. He had another look over the banisters, and beheld Mr. Wrench, whom he knew well enough, in charge of a handcuffed man, who was his prisoner.

Peace drew back. "Cooney!" he ejaculated. "Well, this is most astonishing!"

It was true enough. The robber was indeed "Cooney," whom doubtless the reader will remember as being concerned with Peace and the Bristol Badger in the burglary at Oakfield farmhouse, described in the opening chapters of this work.

Peace deemed it advisable to retire to his own apartment. He did not care to claim acquaintance with the robber. As it was, he had escaped recognition by the merest accident.

"I shall have to fight shy in this case. Cooney is nabbed, and will have to take his chance," he mused, when he had gained his own room.

The burglar was marched off to Marlborough-street. Soon after his arrival there Mrs. Sanderson presented herself.

It was impossible for any case to be clearer. The particulars were entered into the charge-sheet, and the prosecutrix was told by the inspector to be at Marlborough-street in the forenoon.

Mr. Wrench had safely bagged his bird.

When the case came before the magistrate it transpired that Cooney had a confederate.

A man who had held a situation as head waiter at the hotel had planned and contrived the series of artful robberies which had been so successfully carried out, during the period of a little more than a year.

He had provided himself with duplicate keys of all the locks in the house, the interior of which he was very well acquainted with.

Cooney, who had throughout his life always taken a subordinate part in the various depredations in which he had been engaged, had consented to become the tool of the head waiter.

He entered the hotel with the keys provided by his principal, and laid his hands on the most portable and valuable articles within reach, while the waiter waited outside the hotel, and generally contrived to take the lion's share of the plunder.

He guessed what was up when he beheld Cooney handcuffed, pass out of the hostelry in company with Mr. Wrench. He did not stop to inquire, but made off without a moment's hesitation, leaving the unfortunate Cooney to his fate.

The case against the prisoner was as clear as it well could be.

Mr. Wrench's evidence was more than enough to ensure a conviction.

So convinced was the robber of this that he pleaded guilty, and threw himself upon the mercy of the court.

He was told by the detectives that if he chose to give up the names of his accomplices, he would be dealt with more leniently and receive a lighter sentence.

He said that he had but one accomplice, this being the head waiter whom he named.

In the course of a few days the latter was hunted down and taken into custody. He was convicted, and sentenced to five years' penal servitude, for a considerable portion of the property previously stolen from the hotel was found in his possession.

Cooney was let off cheap; he had one year's imprisonment, with hard labour. And so ended the robbery at Sanderson's Hotel.

Many hundreds of similar robberies are committed in the metropolis, every year, and in many cases the culprits manage to escape justice for very long periods.

It is perfectly astounding the amount of thievery going on daily in the metropolis. And it is not confined to a class, but permeates through every section of society.

CHAPTER XLIV.
PEACE PURSUES HIS LAWLESS CAREER—THE BURGLARY AT HIGHGATE.

OUR hero, as we have already seen, had been leading for a long time past a reputable sort of life—indeed, the company into which he had fallen at Broxbridge had caused him to turn his thoughts in another direction. Had he remained there it is just possible that he might have abstained from the pursuit of dishonest courses.

But now the spell was broken.

His funds were at a low ebb, and he did not feel disposed to leave London empty handed. He must levy black mail on the inhabitants of so wealthy a city.

He reasoned with himself in a self-satisfactory way, never for a moment acknowledging that he was in any way a wrong-doer.

Indeed, the sophistry and hypocrisy of Peace was one of his most marked characteristics, and the examination of the character of such a man is a curious study.

It is not only the tissue of audacious crimes of which he is known or suspected to have been guilty, which provoked the eager interest of the community. There is some curiosity to know the mental and moral whereabouts of a man who stands all by himself.

There have been men who have gradually grown up to be practical and dexterous criminals.

Natural qualifications and acquired capabilities have conspired to make them hardened and practical offenders.

Others have leapt up at one bound into daring and accomplished law breakers.

Under the stress of some urgent necessity, or powerful temptation, they have done a deed fit to make men's blood curdle in their veins.

Peace does not, however, come into either of these two classes.

Practical he was to a certain extent, but his habituation to crime was voluntary and wilful.

He chose his walk in life, and determined not to stop short of the most distinguished excellence.

His daring dexterity and self-possession would have made for him a splendid career in any walk of life where his "imperial" customs could have been legitimated by authority.

Then, after robbing and murdering half the world, he might have grasped the highest honours of a peerage, and died in the perfect odour of sanctity.

Peace had just that laxity of moral nature which would have made him a thoroughly unscrupulous instrument in the hands of a lawless power.

But he lacked the golden opportunity, and became instead a desperate criminal.

The arrest, trial, and conviction of Cooney and his confederate had no other effect upon Peace than causing him to give up all idea of remaining longer in "Sanderson's Hotel."

He had narrowly escaped recognition. At present he stood well with Mr. Wrench, and naturally enough he had no desire for the astute detective to be enlightened as to his antecedents or real character.

It was therefore necessary for him to be cautious.

He had a large amount of material connected with his business, consisting chiefly of frames, prints and tools, which had been packed up, and were still at the goods department at the London station, and he had still many commissions to execute.

He took two unfurnished rooms in the neighbourhood of Leather-lane, Holborn, and had his stock-in-trade removed to his new lodgings.

One room he proposed using as a workshop, the other he could make occasional use of as a dormitory.

His newly-found friend, Kempshead, had left London upon a tour to some of the leading towns in the capacity of a commercial traveller; he had, therefore nothing to regret in leaving Sanderson's, so he paid his bill, and moved to his new quarters.

He had thoughts of returning to his native town, Sheffield, but as yet London had many allurements for him, and he was loth to leave it.

He set to work in his new quarters, and sent some frames and prints to some of his customers at Broxbridge, but the spirit of adventure which had lain so long dormant now asserted its sway, and he began to make nocturnal excursions, and returned with the booty to his bare and gaunt-looking apartments, which were, however, in a short space of time pretty well stocked with the proceeds of his various robberies.

Having recommenced this dishonest career of life, he carried on his depredations with the greatest assiduity.

The burglaries he had carried out so successfully were chiefly confined to the north side of London.

He had noticed during his excursions a large red brick mansion at Highgate, standing back from the road with an avenue of gigantic trees in its front.

It was a fine specimen of an old manorial edifice, and had in all probability been originally built by some nobleman or rich commoner.

It was too large and not sufficiently modern to suit the taste of a citizen of the period, but from its commodiousness and the healthiness of its situation it was eminently qualified for a school.

It had been repaired and beautified, and was now known by circulars and advertisements as "Miss Chickleberry's Finishing Academy for Young Ladies."

Peace thought it worthy of a visit—so one moonlight night he bent his steps in the direction of Highgate.

At this time there were not many pedestrians or equestrians passing along the road even in broad daylight. At night there were none, and the burglar therefore felt assured that he should have it pretty well his own way.

Two large wrought-iron gates guarded the entrance to the broad gravel walk which led to the vestibule of the house.

Not a light of any description was discernible at the windows of the habitation.

Peace scaled the wall, and then found himself in the front garden or shrubbery.

He crept silently along until he reached the side of the mansion; passing along this he arrived at the garden in its rear.

It was at the back of Miss Chickleberry's residence that he proposed effecting an entrance, for beyond the garden itself were a number of fields used for grazing purposes.

A death-like silence reigned around, which was only broken occasionally by the mournful sighing of the branches of the trees as they were agitated by a passing breeze.

He concluded that all the inmates were fast asleep—at any rate he hoped they were.

He had provided himself with a capacious bag, as he had been given to understand that there was a considerable amount of silver plate, which he concluded it would be his pleasing duty to remove.

Two men-servants slept in the rooms over some stables which were about a hundred and fifty yards from the house, which, with the exception of a boy who acted as page, was occupied by females only.

But, Peace being a ladies' man, this did not much matter.

The most serious matter for consideration was how to effect an entrance without disturbing the sleeping garrison.

Our hero had turned his attention to this long before the night of the proposed burglary.

The schoolroom appeared to be the weakest point of attack.

It jutted out from the house itself, and was fastened most insecurely—doubtless it had been originally a ball-room in the days when the habitation boasted of liberal occupants. Anyhow it was most alluring to the eyes of our burglar.

At its end was a bay window with lozenge-shaped panes set in lead.

Peace found but little difficulty in removing one of these; but the room was secured by shutters, which were, however, old and rickety; but, nevertheless, they were not so easily opened as he had at first supposed. They resisted all his efforts.

There was no other way left but to bore some holes with his centre-bit, and then to remove a portion of the panel.

This he proceeded to do without further delay, of course performing the operation as noiselessly as possible.

In a short time a portion of the panel was removed. He then put his hand through the aperture and lifted up the bar of the shutter.

He then unfastened the window and gained an entrance into the schoolroom.

All this had been done without anyone being aroused.

The burglar then paused for a brief space of time, and bethought him of his next proceedings.

He had coloured his face, and otherwise disfigured himself, in accordance with his custom when engaged in marauding expeditions of this nature.

He slid over his boots a pair of list slippers, and crept noiselessly into the passage. At the end of this was the reception-room, where the parents of the young ladies were shown into the presence of the mistress of the establishment.

On the table of the reception-room several pieces of plate were ostentatiously displayed, which had been from time to time presented to Miss Chickleberry, either by the parents of her scholars or by the pupils themselves.

They of course had a most imposing appearance, and did not escape the eye of the burglar, who at once transferred them to his bag.

In addition to these he possessed himself of an ormolu clock and several other articles of value.

He could have now returned from the scene of his depredations with a large booty, without running any further risk, but he was not a man so easily satisfied.

He was bent upon going into the other rooms of the house, and it would appear the greater the risk the greater was the charm to him.

Placing his half-filled bag on one of the desks in the schoolroom, he crept softly upstairs.

Not a sound, save from his own movements, broke the stillness of the night.

He entered one of the upstair rooms. This was a prodigiously large apartment. In it were a number of beds, which were occupied by Miss Chickleberry's scholars.

Peace was quite enraptured with the galaxy of sleeping beauties which suddenly met his view.

Young ladies, ranging from the ages of twelve to sixteen, were peacefully slumbering in the grand old bedchamber. Some of them were of a rare order of beauty, but all looked so calm, so gentle, and so innocent, that even the callous heart of the burglar was touched.

Here lay a girl whose glossy, raven tresses fell over a polished shoulder as if in sport—the sleeper was a brunette; in the next bed to her was a blonde, with light brown hair and an alabaster skin; beyond these were fair young creatures of different types, some with thin regular features, which were almost statuesque in their outline, others with full, round faces, in which sat the rosy hue of health.

Our hero was an admirer of beauty, especially when it referred to the opposite sex to his own; but it would not do to fall into a reverie over the display of fascinating creatures before him.

He observed several gold watches on the little tables beside the beds, and to gather these up was the first consideration.

He went to the first table, took the watch from its stand, and slid it into his pocket.

Then he crept on to the next and possessed himself of that, and so on till he had ten or a dozen watches in his pocket.

Having effected this he turned round and made for the door. Just as he was about reaching this he was astounded at beholding the large round eyes of a young girl, of about eleven or twelve, gazing full into his own.

She did not utter a word or even attempt to move.

As he passed her bed she murmured "oh," in almost a whisper.

Peace concluded, naturally enough, that she was paralysed by fear.

That she was awake he knew perfectly well, for her eyes were fixed intently on him.

He went to the side of her bed, and said, in a whisper—

"My girl, if you stir or move, or endeavour to give the slightest alarm, your life will be forfeited. Do you understand?"

He drew forth his revolver, and pointed significantly to the barrel.

"Say nothing, keep quiet, and you are safe."

The girl nodded, but made no other answer.

"Remember!" whispered Peace, as he passed through the door, "as you value your life, keep silent."

He passed into the passage, closing the door of the young ladies' dormitory gently as he did so.

At the further end of the passage or landing was a door. This was suddenly opened, and a tall, angular, severe-looking lady presented herself.

This was Miss Chickleberry herself.

The moment she caught sight of the burglar she gave utterance to a piercing scream. She flew back into her bedroom, still screaming and calling loudly for assistance.

"Silence, woman!" exclaimed our hero, entering her bedchamber without ceremony. "Are you mad, to make all this row and clatter for nothing?"

"For nothing!" cried Miss Chickleberry. "Oh! you monster! Help! Murder! Robbers!"

"Will you hold your cursed tongue?" exclaimed Peace, now seriously alarmed. "If you don't ——"

He produced his revolver.

At this the schoolmistress became perfectly frantic. It was in vain that he pointed the muzzle of the pistol to her temple, and threatened to take her life. She would not be pacified.

He had no desire to shoot her, but she must be silenced. He placed his hand over her mouth to stifle her cries.

She struggled desperately, and was very nearly releasing herself from his grasp.

He lost his temper, and struck her on the head with his clenched fist.

"She'll arouse the whole neighbourhood," he murmured. "There never was such a dragon."

He caught sight of a cake of glycerine soap on the washstand.

He thrust this into her mouth, then tied her hands behind her with a handkerchief.

His impression was that after this she fainted, but he did not stop to ascertain. Taking the key out of the lock of her door, he locked her in from the outside.

A chorus of screams now proceeded from the young ladies' dormitory.

Several by this time had rushed out into the passage in their night dresses, with naked feet, on the cold floor of the landing.

"Back—back into your rooms, girls!" cried Peace,

in an authoritative tone. "You've no occasion to be alarmed. No harm is intended."

"But Miss Chickleberry. What of her?" cried one of the pupils.

"She's all right, quite right," answered Peace, flying down the stairs with headlong speed.

Upon reaching the schoolroom he snatched up his bag and fled from the house.

He jumped over the back garden wall, gained the meadow beyond, and made for a wood which was at no very great distance.

In endeavouring to reach this he ran into the arms of a policeman.

"Unhand me, fellow," he ejaculated. "If you don't it will be the worse for you. Leave go, I say."

"You are my prisoner," said the constable.

"Prisoner be hanged! What for? I haven't done anything. Nobody has charged me. You are exceeding your duty."

"And I will, I'll take my chance of that."

Peace made a desperate effort to slip from the constable's grasp, and a struggle ensued, in which both fell.

But the officer, who was bent upon doing his duty, still retained hold of the robber, who kicked and fought like a madman.

He was unable to draw out his revolver; had he been able to do so the chances were that he would have shot the policeman without pity or remorse. He managed to regain his feet to be again thrown down by the constable, who placed his knee on his chest and endeavoured to slip on the handcuffs.

Peace, however, managed to frustrate this attempt, whereupon his antagonist drew his staff, and said he would make use of it if he offered further opposition.

Our hero now felt that he was at the mercy of his captor, and ground his teeth in rage and despair.

"Take your knee from off me, and I will do as you wish, and go with you quietly," cried Peace, who though it best to temporise, and see if any other chance of escape presented itself.

He was perfectly astounded in another moment at hearing a voice exclaim—

"Let the man alone, you brute!"

A terrible blow was delivered from behind, with some weapon, on the head of the policeman, who was laid prostrate.

His helmet had fallen off in the struggle with Peace, and the blow, therefore, was more effective.

The policeman was evidently partially, if not wholly, stunned.

"Fly—fly! This way!" exclaimed the same voice as he had heard before. "The bobby is knocked out of time—follow me."

The speaker led the way into the wood, and Peace followed, bag in hand.

"Now old man, sharp's the word," cried the same voice. "There'll be a rare hue and cry presently. Keep along this beaten pathway; that's it."

They passed through the wood, and arrived at a narrow lane full of ruts.

In this was a horse and cart.

"Jump in, old man," cried the stranger.

Peace jumped into the cart—his companion did the same and drove off at a sharp trot.

"Well, hang me if I'm not knocked silly," cried our hero, "why if it aint Bandy-legged Bill."

"Right you are, my child," returned the gipsy, "one good turn deserves another. You let me off the 'Carved Lion' business; I've just come up in time to return the compliment."

"How came you on the spot?"

"How came I? Why I heard the scream, and thought murder was being committed, so I dropped out of the trap and made for the old red house. Then I seed you and the bobby a strugglin'; so I ups and gives him one for himself, and the best thing for both on us to do now is to take a circumbendibus route to London—not but what I think we shall be able to dodge 'em. I've got as pretty a little tit in this ere cart as any man need wish to drive."

"Hang it, but you are a jovial fellow, Bill, after all," said Peace, "and I shall never forget this kindness."

"Well, ye see it's a poor tale if we can't help one another on a pinch like that. But where do you hang out? You seem to me to be like a will o' the wisp—here, there, and everywhere."

"I've been stopping in London for a little time, but shall soon return to Sheffield or some other place. Gad, it is fortunate that you came up as you did."

They had by this time emerged from the narrow lane and were proceeding along one of the high roads.

A mounted patrol who was coming in the opposite direction regarded them with an inquiring and suspicious look.

The gipsy, who was driving, slackened his speed and wished the officer "good night."

The greeting was returned, not in a very cordial manner, however.

"I thought he meant mischief," said the gipsy. "It was quite a toss up whether he overhauled us or not."

"What have you got in that bag?"

"Something I shall be very glad to get rid of. Silver plate, with names and dates engraved on it."

"Oh, scissors, that's awkward! We should be done brown if any of the bobbies did overhaul us."

"If you have any fears don't hesitate for a moment. Drop me, and I'll take my chance."

The gipsy laughed.

"No, no, old man!" he cried. "In for a penny in for a pound, is an old saying. We'll take our chance. I aint a going to desert a pal, or turn tail like a cur."

He drove on at a sharp trot, and reached London in safety; dropping Peace at the corner of Leather-lane, he promised to give him a call in a day or two, then wishing him good night he drove off.

Our hero let himself in with his latch key, and after washing the colour off his face, and attending to other business matters, he turned in for the night, and slept soundly till the morning.

CHAPTER XLV.
A VISIT TO THE CRYSTAL PALACE—THE UNEXPECTED MEETING.

As may be imagined, there was a rare hue and cry, both at Highgate and the adjacent neighbourhood, for some days after the burglary at Miss Chickleberry's establishment for young ladies, and as a natural consequence the facts of the case lost nothing in the hands of the gossips who recounted the terrible outrage.

The schoolmistress herself was said to be at death's door, in consequence of the brutal treatment she had received at the hands of the ruffian who had so mercilessly attacked her.

The valiant policeman was also seriously injured, and the amount of property stolen was of course enormous.

Notices were sent to the several metropolitan police stations, and all that could possibly be done to trace the robber was at once set on foot.

Meanwhile Peace was quietly working at his trade in Leather-lane.

He had, on the following day, disposed of the plate

to a Jew fence in Whitechapel; the watches he secreted in the premises he occupied.

He had effected so complete a change in his personal appearance that it was hardly possible for anyone to recognise him as the man who had carried out so daring a robbery; indeed, the policeman into whose arms he ran when making off from the premises had but a transcient glance at him; his impression was that he was a mulatto, and he was so described in the "Hue and Cry."

This in itself would have been sufficient to put the detectives on the wrong scent, and thereby to defeat the ends of justice.

Peace did not stir out from his workshop, save in its own immediate neighbourhood, for some days; and no one for a moment suspected that the quiet, mild-spoken, industrious artisan of Leather-lane was the real culprit.

A week or two passed over, and the burglary at Highgate became a thing of the past; at the expiration of which time, Peace committed some more burglaries in a different neighbourhood. These were on a minor scale, but he contrived to escape detection.

By these, together with the Highgate robbery, he managed to amass a considerable sum.

About this time crowds of persons were flocking to the Crystal Palace to witness the performances of the renowned Blondin, the hero of Niagara, as he was termed in the posters and advertisements.

There never was a greater furore displayed by sightseers of the metropolis and elsewhere than on this occasion.

Blondin was the "lion" of the day, now he is a very lamb—equally as clever, it must be admitted, as when he first came in our midst, but the novelty has worn off, as the novelty wore off some years before with Van Ambrugh.

Peace, who was a lover of daring deeds and adventure, perhaps more than anyone else, could not leave London without seeing the prince of rope performers. He, therefore, determined upon paying a visit to the palace at Sydenham.

He was not a man easily moved to terror, but it has been said, and it would be useless to attempt to gainsay it, that somewhere deep down in the human heart there is a corner devoted to the instinct of horror.

This fact has been evidenced at all times and in all ages, and although the world is said to have grown more civilised since the days of gladiatorial exhibitions in ancient Rome, when gaily dressed ladies placidly witnessed a man being devoured by wild beasts, the love of the horrible still remains.

Blondin, when he first came into this country, revived in the British breast the old feeling of the Romans in the circus.

His daring deeds on the high rope, which, to say the truth, were appalling to witness, drew a greater concourse of people to the Crystal Palace than any other has done either before or since.

He was the rage. Tens of thousands of wondering eyes were rivetted on him as he performed such dexterous feats on the rope. People were fascinated as they watched the acrobat play with the chance of death at such a dizzy height.

We are a Christian people, much given to church and chapel going, and it would be rank heresy therefore to say that our natures would revolt at the sight of a martyr bound to a stake.

Happily the days are over for such an exhibition. The days are past also for bull baiting, badger baiting, cock fighting, and even for fistic contests.

Nevertheless, we expect human nature is much the same as it was hundreds of years ago.

It is true we stick a silk hat upon our heads, and put an eye glass on one of our orbits, and disguise the ladies of our family in pull back gowns and high heels; the love of the horrible is not even scotched, much less killed.

A Christian company sit and stand about the floor and galleries of some great building ostensibly devoted to the arts, to see the wonderful Zazel flirt with the King of Terrors.

They watch the graceful creature shot from a cannon, holding their breath as she flies through the air and alights safely in the net.

Then the poor girl, carrying her life in her hand, in obedience to the bond of service with her worthy master, walks along a wire as high from the earth as a low cloud in a hilly country, in peril of imminent death.

We do not pay to see the clever manner in which Zazel balances herself, because, if the feat were performed at a lower and safer altitude, there would be few, if any, spectators.

And this will apply with equal force to Blondin. His performances on the low rope were much more graceful and difficult, but they were not so popular as his high-rope feats.

It is the element of danger and the probability of an accident which gives piquancy to the exhibition.

It has been said that a gentleman of independent means attended for years Van Ambrugh's exhibition of wild beasts, in the full expectation of seeing him one day devoured by one of the savage animals.

Some years ago, when a travelling blacksmith murdered six persons at a lonely habitation at Denham, the lane leading to the scene of the tragedy was thronged with the carriages of the nobility, the occupants of which offered large sums to the policeman in charge of the house for permission to see the dead bodies as they had fallen when struck down by the hands of their murderer.

The gate post at the entrance was probably cut away by persons who possessed themselves of a piece of the same as a trophy or memento of the tragical event.

In fact, the hitherto unfrequented lane leading to the house presented the appearance of Rotten-row on a summer afternoon, so thronged was it with carriages and equestrians.

Who therefore will deny that the instinct of horror does not still exist?

If this were not so, what would become of our acrobats, our sword swallowers, fire-eaters, and fire kings?

Peace, before setting out from Leather-lane, made as great an alteration in his personal appearance as possible.

He had cultivated a moustache and imperial; he dressed himself in a long black coat of the clerical type, put on a white tie also of the clerical pattern, and stuck on his head a felt hat.

An eye-glass completed his transformation, which was so perfect as to defy recognition.

Taking his ticket at Blackfriars, he was whirled down to the palace with all convenient speed.

He found the place thronged with gaily dressed people; it appeared as if all London had turned out, as by common consent to do homage to the hero of Niagera.

Most of us know what the Crystal Palace was at this time.

If you desired to meet with a few of your friends,

people you had missed sight of for a given space of time, you had only to go there; somebody would be sure to recognise you and claim your acquaintance.

Peace, who now paid a visit to the palace for the first time, was delighted with the attractive nature of its most noticeable and leading features. Apart from the world-renowned Blondin, he found numberless objects of interest to engage his individual attention.

He passed from court to court, examining objects displayed therein with an eye of a connoisseur.

He always found great pleasure in contemplating works of art, whether ancient or modern; and, although but little versed in history, he would linger lovingly over any choice or rare specimen of art workmanship of a bygone age.

This, indeed, was one of the many strange contrarieties of his character, which would lead us to the conclusion that he was destined by nature to cut a more respectable figure in the world than that which is but too plainly evidenced by his lawless career.

While in the Pompeian Court somebody addressed him by name.

He looked up and beheld Brickett, the landlord of the "Old Carved Lion."

"Ye be looking at the wonders of this grand place all by yourself," said Brickett, clapping his friend on the shoulder.

"Well, who would have thought of seeing you?" returned Peace. "I thought you never moved half a league's distance from the old inn."

"Neither do I as a rule, but I've been obliged to come up to London about a little matter, so I thought as how I'd just see this wonderful rope-dancing chap; but I go back agen to-night."

"Ah, well, I'm jolly glad to see you, Brickett."

"The same as regards yourself," returned the landlord; "but I s'pose you haven't cut us entirely. There's lots of people inquiring after you, and good people, too, who want to know when you are coming back. There's plenty of work for you, mind that, when you do return."

"All right; we'll see about it in good time. How does his lordship get on with his newly-found relative?"

"So well, I hear, that he's not disposed to part with her—not upon any consideration. She's tumbled into a good thing, and no mistake; but, lord, she is a sweet creature—a loveable creature."

Peace sighed.

"Yes," he answered, sadly, "she is, so I've been told."

"And let us hope she'll be a comfort to the old man —indeed, I'm sure she will."

"No doubt."

"And she ought to be thankful to you—so I've heard."

Peace made no reply.

"So I've heard," replied the landlord. "It's only what I've heard."

"May be she has," returned Peace, carelessly. "People in this world soon forget those who have rendered them a service; but let that pass. She's the earl's grand-daughter, I suppose, and it is not at all likely she'd care to remember or recognise me."

"Ah!" ejaculated Brickett, looking hard at his companion, "I suppose not."

There was a murmur from many voices and a shuffling of feet.

Blondin was about to go through his performance on the high rope.

Peace and Brickett left the Pompeian-court and

took up the best position they could to witness the hero of Niagara go through his marvellous feats.

The worthy host of the "Carved Lion" stood spellbound with astonishment.

He declared he "had never seen anything like it in his life, and that it quite surpassed his expectation."

Peace was of the same opinion.

When Blondin had finished the two made their way to one of the refreshment-bars, and had some cold meat and ale, which Brickett would insist on paying for, after which he bade our hero a hasty adieu, saying that he had to catch the train which was to take him down to Broxbridge.

Before parting he was very profuse in his protestations of friendship, and then he extorted a promise from Peace that he would very shortly pay another visit to the "Carved Lion."

"He's a rare good sort," murmured our hero, after Brickett had taken his departure; "one of the best and most cheery of landlords I ever met with."

Having given expression to this sentiment, Peace sat down at one of the side tables in front of the refreshment bar, and was for some time apparently lost in thought.

People passed to and fro, but he was so abstracted as to be heedless of all that was passing around.

It was singular, but it was nevertheless true that the very name of the village of Broxbridge or the remembrance of its associates seemed to have a depressing effect upon him.

He liked Brickett, and to a certain extent liked also many of those who frequented the parlour of the "Lion," and he had been fortunate and prosperous while in the village, but despite all this perhaps the very last thing he would think of would be paying it another visit.

Peace was of a jealous disposition. He could not bear to think of his treatment at the hands of the girl Nelly.

In addition to this another, and a higher order of female, had in an earlier day treated him with scorn.

Aveline Maitland, to whom he had made honourable proposals at Sheffield, had cast him on one side to become the wife of his old schoolfellow, Tom Gatliffe.

By an exceeding strange concurrence of circumstances, had been attached to the village in which Nelly dwelt, and indeed where she had been born and brought up.

This was the reason for his hating the very name of Broxbridge, and at the bottom of his heart sat despair and humiliation.

He bitterly regretted ever having given the information which led to the recognition of Aveline as a descendant of the Earl of Ethalwood.

But it was useless to repine, now that the past could not be recalled.

Bad man as Peace was, these circumstances were active agents in hurrying him on in his lawless career. In a great measure they rendered him callous and reckless.

He took a jaundiced view of life, and became the hardened and unscrupulous criminal, whose daring exploits have so astounded his fellow-countrymen.

We do not offer these observations in palliation of his guilt, for to say the truth there was never much good in the man.

But at the same time it is a fact which is incontrovertible, that circumstances in a great measure create criminals, even as they do heroes.

After ruminating for awhile Peace rose from his seat and strolled into the grounds attached to the palace.

He saw many things there which were of sufficient interest to dispel the gloomy thoughts which a few moments before had taken possession of him.

He met at the ornamental gardens one or two persons with whom he was acquainted. The society of these afforded him some relief, as the current of his thoughts were directed in a different direction.

He became all of a sudden gay and festive, and again had recourse to one of the refreshment bars.

It may have been observed by the reader that the Crystal Palace is a thirsty place, or rather a place which creates thirst. Anyway, a very fair amount of liquids of various sorts are consumed therein.

But a surprise which was perfectly overwhelming awaited our hero, who, after parting with his companions, sauntered about in a most desultory manner.

All of a sudden his eyes were attracted to one of the first-class refreshment rooms.

He could hardly credit his senses.

At one of the tables in the room sat a young and beautiful female, dressed in the height of fashion.

Her arms, head, and bust glittered with jewels.

Her costume was perfection.

Peace thought he had never beheld any woman so elegantly dressed, or one possessed of so aristocratic an appearance.

Could he be deceived? Was he dreaming or awake? The features of the female were familiar to him.

"It cannot be!" he ejaculated. "I must be mistaken. And yet the likeness—the similitude—is most remarkable; but, Lord bless me, it never can be her!"

He paced backwards and forwards for some little time, not knowing very well how to act.

To the first-class refreshment room aforesaid his attention seemed to be attracted.

He kept advancing towards the door, peeping in and then retreating again, but he found it impossible to leave the spot.

He was under the impression that the elegantly-dressed female tricked out in such gaudy costume was none other than the long-lost Bessie Dalton.

And yet she was so completely metamorphosed in every way that he had some doubts as to her identity.

Possibly he was mistaken.

But he could not leave the palace without satisfying himself upon the subject which so deeply concerned him.

He passed through the doorway into the refreshment-room and strolled on till he came in front of the elegant young female, who looked like one of the first ladies in the land.

He gazed at her in both surprise and admiration. There could be no doubt about it—she was Bessie Dalton, but oh, how changed!

He had known her only as a chrysalis—now she was a butterfly with gaudy wings.

He walked boldly up to the table by the side of which she was seated, and exclaimed in a hissing whisper—

"Bessie!"

The young woman looked up, and said, carelessly, "On, it's you—eh? Well, you are a stranger."

"And whose fault is that?" cried Peace, as he shook her jewelled hand which she held forth. "Whose fault is that?"

"Ah, that would not be so easy to say, if there is a fault."

"What is the reason for you not acknowledging any of my letters? You've served me nicely; leaving Bradford without letting me know where you had gone.

you and Mrs. Bristow. Now I have met with you I mean to know all about your movements."

"Do you?"

"Yes, I do," said Peace, resolutely, and with something like anger in his tone.

"Well, you see, my dear fellow," said Bessie, in a languid tone, "there were many reasons for our leaving, and as there were also many reasons for our preserving our incognito, I was not able under the circumstances to write a farewell letter to you, and have now to apologise for my seeming neglect, which I assure you was not wilful."

Peace was perfectly astounded.

The easy self-assurance of the woman proved that she was evidently no longer the same in manner and ideas as he had known as a factory hand.

He was perfectly astounded, and to use a nautical phrase, was completely taken aback.

"You've used me badly enough," he exclaimed, "and as far as your apologies are concerned they are not worth a rap. Where did you and Bristow's wife fly to? They told me at the house that you gave out you were going abroad."

"Certainly we did. We wished it to be understood that such was our intention."

"But you never had an idea of leaving this country."

"Certainly not; you are quite right in your surmise. We never had an idea of leaving the shores of England, but you see, Peace, there were special reasons for our wishing it to be understood that we had left the land of our birth. You see we sought concealment—this was not so important, as far as I was concerned, but with Mrs. Bristow the case was different. There was an imperative necessity for her to seek seclusion; this she has found, poor thing, and her life, I am happy to say, is now one of unclouded sunshine."

"Sunshine be ——," cried Peace. He was about to make use of an oath, but the lady held up her fan, and by an effort he restrained himself.

"Look here, my lady," he cried, after a pause. "You're coming it pretty strong. You've got fine feathers and make use of fine words, but don't you think you can deceive Charles Peace. I can see through you, for all your affected airs and graces. You've got an admirer—are under the protection of a gentleman, I suppose. Eh?"

"I must request you to be a little more cautious," said Bessie, perfectly unmoved. "In the first place you must not address me in language which is in every way objectionable. Our paths in life are as dissimilar as well possible for two persons to be. I have been long since shunted—to make use of an expressive simile—on to a different line to yourself, and I must request you to keep your place as I shall keep mine. I wish you well, entertain the most friendly feelings towards you as far as your own happiness and welfare are concerned, but for the rest—for the rest," she observed, conveying a spoonful of strawberry ice cream to her lips, " we are separate and apart."

Peace was indignant beyond expression; he had the greatest difficulty to restrain himself from striking the speaker.

"If you give me any more of your cheek," he cried, in a hissing whisper, "I'll slap your face."

"You had better not, Mr. Charles Peace," said his companion; "upon my word you are sadly forgetting yourself."

"What do you mean, you stuck-up, conceited little hussy, by treating me in this way? Separate and apart indeed! I'll soon teach you a lesson about that, my lady. Where do you live?"

PEACE AND BESSIE DALTON.

"I decline to answer your question; and, indeed, if you do not behave yourself better, I shall decline to have anything further to say to you. I wish you well, and don't bear any animosity towards you; but at the same time must beg you most distinctly to understand that I am not disposed to submit to taunts or insults from anyone—still less from you."

"I am not going to let you off so easily," said Peace. "It's no use you endeavouring to ride the high horse with me. I intend to know where you live, and, in addition to this, I am determined to know all about you."

"Are you?"

"Yes, I am."

"Then you'll have to find out as best you can; for I must tell you frankly that you will have no information from me."

"Do you suppose, you little fool," exclaimed Peace, in a voice of concentrated passion, "that I am going to let you have it all your own way—that I'm going to give you up now I have found you? If you do, you are greatly mistaken."

Bessie Dalton made no answer, but continued to help herself to the strawberry-ice before her.

Her self-possession — her refinement and graceful deportment—fairly astonished her companion.

"Do you hear me?" he cried.

"I cannot fail to do so," she answered, "seeing that you speak vehemently."

"Will you write down your address?"

"Most certainly I will not."

"Then I'll follow you, if it's for twenty miles. You shall not escape me."

"There must be an end to this, Mr. Peace," said Bessie Dalton, in an altered tone. "Your words and manner are most objectionable, and I must decline to have any further converse with you."

"You decline?"

"Most emphatically. Be good enough not to trouble me any further. Our interview is at an end, and I must request you to leave, or, at any rate, not to press your society on me."

"Did any one ever hear of such audacity?" exclaimed Peace, in a perfect fury. "Do you suppose that I am to be taken in by your fine airs and graces? Play them off upon somebody else—they are thrown away upon me. I don't appreciate them—don't believe in them; so the sooner you return to your own natural character the better. I am not to be tricked or hoodwinked. Where do you live, and what are you doing? Don't toss your head; I must and will have an answer."

"Once more I tell you not to interfere with me," cried Bessie. "I do not choose to hold further parley with you. As one whom I knew some long time ago I have been courteous enough to exchange a few words with you. Now I wish I had not done so, for your tone and manner cannot be considered otherwise than offensive in the eyes of any well-bred person, and I therefore request you to leave, as I do not choose to be subject to your insults."

"Insolent minx!" exclaimed Peace, seizing the speaker by the wrist, which he grasped with an iron grip. "You shan't escape me—you have played me false, you have been carrying on a nice game without doubt. But you will find, my lady, that you won't have it all your own way, now. I'm not to be shaken off. I will know what you have been up to, and where you are residing. I swear by the Lord above us that I will not leave till you have told me."

As he gave utterance to this speech he shook her angrily, and grasped her wrist with such force that the bracelet she wore was forced into her flesh and produced acute agony.

She gave utterance to a slight scream and called for assistance.

One of the waiters at the establishment who heard the angry altercation beckoned to a stalwart policeman who was near the entrance, who at once came forward.

Peace's countenance wore at this time a most diabolical expression.

"What is the matter, madam?" inquired the constable, in a respectful tone.

"This man is both threatening and annoying me. In the absence of my friends and relations, who are in the grounds but will return shortly, I am constrained to appeal to you for protection."

"Certainly," returned the policeman. "Now, then," he said, sharply, addressing himself to Peace; "you be off, or else I will take you into custody."

"Leave me alone, officer. I know what I'm about. Don't you interfere between man and wife."

"Wife!" exclaimed Bessie; "I'm no wife of his. Don't listen to what he says; he does not mind what falsehoods he tells. My husband is in the grounds. All I want you to do is to remove this insolent fellow."

"Do you give him in charge?"

"If he won't go quietly I must do so, I suppose."

Peace let go his hold of Bessie, and seemed to be a little staggered at her last observation.

"You go about your business. We don't want any row here!" cried the policeman, taking Peace by the collar and dragging him towards the door. "We don't allow ladies to be insulted with impunity. So you must leave. If you don't, I shall lock you up."

"Lock me up! What for?"

"For a breach of the peace—for creating a disturbance. You take my advice and get clear off while you can, or it will be worse for you."

Peace had no desire to make the acquaintance of the inspector at the station-house, and he had, therefore, no alternative but to submit.

"I want to say a word to her before I leave," he exclaimed, nodding towards Bessie.

"Say it, then, and go."

Our hero was half beside himself with ill-suppressed passion.

"Hark ye!" he ejaculated, bending towards the female, with a hideous grin on his ill-favoured countenance, "you have carried it off bravely this time, but I'll have my revenge. I'll find you out, expose you, and bring ruin upon your head, you deceitful, worthless, despicable huzzy!"

"It is out of your power to do me any mischief. You are beneath contempt," answered Bessie, turning away.

"Now then, no more of this. Be off!" cried the constable, in an angry tone. "Be off, I say."

There was no help for it. To avoid being forcibly ejected Peace had to leave the refreshment room with the best grace he could.

But rage and despair sat at his heart. He never was more astonished than he had been by Bessie Dalton's treatment of him.

He went out into the grounds in a state bordering upon frenzy. He found it difficult to believe that so complete a change had come over the pretty little work girl whom he had been so intimate with at Bradford.

She did not seem to be like the same person. Her costume was magnificent, her manners were polished, her actions graceful, and, taken altogether, her whole appearance denoted that she was moving in the best society.

"Her husband," she said. Was she married? Possibly so.

This thought did not in any way add to his composure. On the contrary, it seemed to fret and chafe him. He generally viewed affairs from his own standpoint; perhaps he was not singular in this respect, for there are multitudes of other persons who make it a practice to do precisely the same thing.

He persuaded himself that he was an ill-used man—that his most intimate associates turned against him for no imaginable reason, and he therefore declared war against the whole human race. How well he carried this out the history of his life but too plainly demonstrates.

He considered that Bessie Dalton had acted towards him in a manner which was altogether incomprehensible.

She had treated him—so he considered—with the basest ingratitude, when in reality she had but cast aside a man who was not worthy a moment's consideration.

At one time she had been in a measure attached to the selfish, unscrupulous burglar, but that time had long since passed away.

"My word!" he ejaculated; "but she knows how to ape the fine lady. I never should have thought it was in her. She certainly plays the part to perfection, the pretentious overbearing little devil! Well, this little affair knocks me completely silly. What on earth can she be doing? She's evidently got into a good position by some means or other. It's altogether a mystery. It appears to me that everybody gets shoved on in this world but myself—Aveline, Bessie, and Lord knows who else besides!"

He paced the grounds of the palace in a restless and troubled manner. His mind was ill at ease. He had been singularly unfortunate in his escapades with the fair sex.

He had wasted his thoughts and time at Broxbridge over the girl Nellie, and now he was treated with scorn by an old flame, whose absence had caused him so much concern.

All this he found hard to bear.

He did not remain long in the ornamental grounds of the Palace. In fact, he was sick of the place, and therefore at once made for one of the entrances, and passed out of the building.

As he turned off to the road leading to the station a surprise awaited him, which well-nigh took his breath away.

An open carriage, drawn by a pair of high-stepping magnificent horses, passed him.

In it sat Bessie Dalton and a gentleman of aristocratic appearance on one of the seats.

On the other reclined Mrs. Bristow, dressed in the height of fashion, with a male companion on the other.

As the vehicle wheeled by Peace became completely overpowered.

"The devil!" he exclaimed. "John Bristow's wife! The John Bristow who died on the public highway, and whose body I identified at the workhouse. His wife and Bessie Dalton riding in a carriage and lolling in the lap of luxury! It seems like a dream. Have they come into a fortune, or what? It is most unaccountable."

This discovery seemed to trouble him more than his treatment in the refreshment-room. He went back to his rooms in Leather-lane in a state of doubt, surprise, and bewilderment.

"It seems I did not go to the Crystal Palace for nothing," he ejaculated. "Well, this beats all I ever heard of."

CHAPTER XLVI.

ALF PURVIS IN HIS NEW HOME—A FRESH LINE OF BUSINESS —PEACE AND LAURA STANBRIDGE.

WE left Alf Purvis at the lodging-house in Westminster. On the following evening, at six o'clock, he presented himself with a faint single rap at the door of a house in one of the streets leading out of Regent-circus.

He was admitted by a buxom maid-servant, who ushered him into the back kitchen.

"Missis expected you would come," said the girl, "and desired me to tell you to take a bath and wash yourself before you put on these clothes, which you are to wear."

She pointed to a suit of second-hand garments, which were hanging on the back of a Windsor chair.

A huge tub half filled with hot water was on the floor of the kitchen.

The girl pointed to this, and said :—

"You will do as I tell you?"

"Yes," answered Alf.

The girl left the room, and the boy had his bath and put on his new things.

Although he had been accustomed to work at Stoke Ferry Farm he did not resemble in any way the rough country lads one is accustomed to see in the agricultural districts.

He had a well-knit figure, a white glossy skin, a fine and almost feminine cast of features, and hair, after it had been cleaned and combed, which shone like virgin gold.

When his ablutions and toilette had been completed, he was called by the maid-servant, who was in the front kitchen.

He entered, and sat himself down on one of the chairs.

"Missus will see you presently," said the girl.

Alf nodded, and quietly awaited the interview which was to follow. He felt a great deal more comfortable than he had done for a long time.

He glanced complacently at his new things, as a scholar surveys his bombazine gown, and a bishop his first pair of lawn sleeves.

In about half an hour he was shown up to the first floor, and there he found the two ladies whom he had seen on the previous night at the lodging-house in Westminster.

The young lady who the maid had told him was Miss Stanbridge appeared to be the real mistress of the house.

She professed to be very pleased to see him, and spoke in a kind manner when addressing him.

Alf was quite charmed with her. He did not remember to have seen anyone who pleased him better.

She asked him several questions about his former life, and soon extracted the history of all his offences and troubles.

At first he touched very tenderly upon the former, but Miss Stanbridge's manner encouraged him to make a clean breast of it. She seemed to view misdemeanours in so charitable a light that he took heart of grace and told her all.

She laughed immoderately when he gave her an account of the hare being tied round his neck, and his selling it after all to the bird ensnarer.

She inveighed against the game laws as bitterly as any sworn abolitionist could have done.

Alf Purvin was duly impressed with the justness of her remarks, as her sentiments coincided with his own.

She concluded by saying that it would be just as fair and reasonable to make laws for birds' eggs as for hares, and that so far from blaming a starving fellow-creature for taking one animal out of a wood which perhaps held hundreds of them, she could scarcely blame him for taking a sheep or a goose or a fowl from those that were over-rich to give to those who were poor.

She was anecdotal also. He was highly entertained at the story she told him of an old nobleman who was a confirmed invalid, and invariably took a constitutional early morning walk before breakfast.

One day, in going through his preserves, he met a

164

CHARLES PEACE;

strange, black-looking, forbidding-featured man, coming in the opposite direction.

The nobleman knew perfectly well that he had no business there, and so walking up to him he said, in an angry tone,

"Now, fellow, what are you doing here? Eh?"

"I'm taking a walk," answered the man sulkily; "And pray, if I may make so bold, what are you doing here?"

"I'm talking a walk, also?" returned the nobleman, "to get an appetite for my breakfast."

"Ah," muttered the man, "I'm taking a walk to get a breakfast for my appetite."

The nobleman did not ask any more questions, but walked on without more ado.

This story pleased Alf immensely.

The speaker now paused as if waiting for him to answer her. He observed that her eyes were searching him through and through, while the elder woman was gazing at him with a peculiar expression of tenderness mingled with pity.

"I think I shall be able to find employment for you," said the younger of the two—"that is if you don't mind work. I will supply you with much better articles to sell in the streets or anywhere else, and if you are a good boy you can make this your home for the present."

"Oh, thank you, marm," cried Alf. "I'm sure I'll do all I can to serve you." He said, in continuation, that it was very hard to have no bread to eat, and no means of getting any, but still he thought that honest people were the happiest, and they were often the richest too, for he'd heard a thief say only a few nights before that an honest shilling went farther than a stolen crown, and certainly the thieves he had seen were very poorly clothed, and dirty, and hungry; it did not seem as if they thrived on their trade.

At this the old lady smiled, and Miss Stanbridge did not vouchsafe a reply.

There was a pause, after which the elder of the two females asked him if he had any father or mother.

And when he said he could not remember either, and that when he asked about them he was told to hold his tongue, since he was an orphan, she started and asked him quickly what part of England he came from.

He said Broxbridge, at which his questioner started, repeating the word after him in a slow, thoughtful manner.

Her emotion did not escape the observation of Alf Purvis.

"You won't find yourself badly treated here," said Miss Stanbridge. "If you do, it will be your own fault. I intend to send you out to sell different articles for me, and I shall give you a commission on all you sell."

"Thank you, marm."

"Then, as you will get your bed, board, and clothes for nothing, you will be able to put by what money you earn, which, in the course of time, let us hope, will amount to a good round sum. That will be an encouragement for you to persevere."

"Certainly, marm. I will try my hardest."

"Good lad. I think we understand one another."

The boy saluted her with his head and hand.

He was delighted with the prospect which opened before him.

That night he enjoyed the luxury of a clean, comfortable bed, such as he had not known for a long time —certainly not since he had left Stoke Ferry Farm.

The next morning he had a good breakfast in the kitchen in company with Susan, the housemaid.

When he had partaken of his morning's meal he was told that his mistress wanted him.

She was at breakfast. On the sideboard was a glass vase with a dozen gold and silver fish in it.

"Now, Alf," said the lady, "look at these. Do you know anything about them?"

"Oh, dear, yes! I know a good deal about them."

"You do?"

"Yes, I know everything about the street trade in live-stock, and about almost every other kind of street trade, for when I could afford it I used to go to a sixpenny lodging-house, or else had fourpennyworth at the Drury Chambers."

"What has that to do with it?"

"Well, you see, marm, there's a good many people, who are in all the street trades, goes to both places, and by asking questions and listening to their patter, I got put up to a pinch of snuff or two. That's how I came to know about these things, for you see I was always looking out for a better trade than birds' nests, which is but a poor one, make the best on it."

"Oh, I see, you've had more experience in those matters than I had at first imagined. Can you tell me what that is worth?"

"A thing is worth what it 'll fetch."

"Yes, I know; but that is no answer to my question. What do you suppose is the value of that?"

Alf. Purvis went up to the sideboard and examined them with the eye of a connoisseur or practical dealer.

"They were brought here this morning," added Miss Stanbridge, glancing at her elderly companion, who had just entered the room, and with whom she spoke in a low voice, pointing at the fish.

"They ought to fetch eighteen pence a pair, but it all depends upon the customers you meet with. Here's one pair of large silvers that are honestly worth four or five shillings of anybody's money. Large silvers are scarcer than large golds."

"Are they?"

"Yes, marm, they are, indeed."

"Well, now you must see if you can sell some of them. You've no objection?"

"None in the world."

"Where will you go? How will you set about it?"

"What I should do with these would be to walk Kensington way. On the outskirts of London they say is the best line for these. I should walk along the street crying them, and when I saw any children at the window I would knock at the door, for children crave rarely after gold fish. If I am asked where they come from I shall say some on 'em were brought from China and some from Portugal, and some from the Injies; then they'll be sure to buy 'em. People are so fond of anything that comes a long way off."

Miss Stanbridge laughed.

"You're a strange lad," she ejaculated—"an old head upon a young pair of shoulders. So you would do that, eh?"

"Certainly; all's fair in trade, and the fun of it is that the Essex fish are the best of all, being bred in cold weather, while t'others have to be bred in warm ponds, and are not anything like so hardy."

"You'll do, I can see," said his patroness.

"But did the man bring a hand net with the fish, marm?" inquired the boy. "It don't do to mess 'em in your hands."

"No, I don't know that he did; but I dare say we have such a thing. My dear," she said, with a dubious smile, "will you go to the lumber-room, and see if you can find one?"

Her elderly companion hesitated for a moment, then

went upstairs. In a few minutes she returned with a bundle of nets of various cordage, with handles of stained wood.

These the boy said he might be able to sell with the fish.

Susan crammed a huge packet in his pocket which contained bread and meat—this was to serve him as a dinner; and he went gaily into the streets.

He returned in the evening in the best of spirits, having been unusually successful.

His good looks, his clean clothes, allied with his cheery manner and lively chatter, won for him plenty of customers.

He was very well satisfied with his day's work; so also was his mistress, who was no niggard in her praise.

He went out again and again, and in the course of three or four days the vase was empty.

He was called up into the drawing-room and regaled with a glass of spirits and water.

"You've done well, Alf, and I'm much pleased with you," said Miss Stanbridge. "Did you tell your customers that your fish came from foreign parts—you young rogue?"

"I was obliged to pitch it a little strong with some of them. I told 'em this fish came from one place and that from another. There, I have done wrong," he added, with a look of humility.

"Dear me! no. All's fair in trade," said his mistress. "People in this world like to be humbugged—I'm quite sure of that; besides, it doesn't do to be too particular. Why, lor bless me, when I was of your age I didn't stick at trifles, I can tell you—not a bit of it."

And she followed up these observations by telling him a series of stories about the pilferings of her childhood, in such a manner that the boy did not understand that these were thefts she was describing so pleasantly. He was entertained, and thought she was very kind and condescending. So, indeed, she was.

But it was the condescension of a ruthless, remorseless woman, with the face of an enchantress and the heart of a demon.

She had the boy in her toils, and as our story progresses, we shall see what she made of him.

Alf Purvis went to bed that night in a state of mind which was at once happy and confused.

Happy because he had six shillings in his pocket, confused because he was not accustomed to whiskey and water, and because the doctrines which his mistress's anecdotes appeared to inculcate were so different to those which Mr. Jamblin had been accustomed to propound.

He considered the matter over before going to sleep, and came to the conclusion that one must be wrong. It was clear, however, so he thought, that the citizens of the metropolis and the rustics of the country, just as they dressed in two different styles, so viewed questions of morality from two points of view.

Which view was right he had not at present determined.

It would be a blessing indeed for him if he had never left the roof of the honest old farmer.

He expected to find another consignment of gold fish on the sideboard on the following morning, but in this he was mistaken.

For the next few days he was sent out with second-hand telescopes and opera glasses.

He did not much care about this occupation; he was not so successful.

He had to stand all day at Tower-hill, or by the docks, and waylay the seafaring men as they passed by.

They were hard customers to deal with—they were not to be talked over; were too wide awake, and were not particular in their expressions.

In addition to this, he was forestalled by a number of Jew dealers, who dealt in articles of that description.

At the end of the week he returned disheartened, and told his mistress he couldn't get on at all to his satisfaction.

The sailor gentleman, he said, would always insist on trying his telescopes before they would make the least bid for them, and when they did bid they showed themselves much more at home in the matter than he was. They beat him, for even when they were drunk they seemed to understand them just as well.

"I suppose," cried his mistress, "that they were accustomed to look through telescopes when they were drunk aboard ship. No wonder so many vessels are lost. I haven't patience to think of such persons; but how about the opera glasses, Alf?"

"Oh, they're no good at all; nobody would even look at them. When I offered them they said, 'Get out. What do we want with opera glasses, you little fool? Better wait till we get opera boxes.'"

"Well, we must start you in another line," said his mistress. "Don't be disheartened. You can't always be successful."

Alf was a little despondent when he retired to rest. He found himself in such comfortable quarters, and was so well cared for, that he dreaded lest his non-success should cause him to be turned adrift.

To be again in the streets, with no friendly hand to help him, he naturally enough dreaded, more especially as he had now tasted the sweets of a comfortable home, for it was a home to him who had been for so long a time a sort of Arab, or outcast.

On the following morning, at his earnest solicitation, his mistress allowed him to try his luck for another day with the telescopes.

Upon his returning in the evening he discovered, much to his surprise, a gentleman at the door—this being none other than the good Samaritan who had presented him with a shilling at the corner of Parliament-street.

He touched his forelock, and made a respectful bow to the stranger, who eyed him in a most inquiring and searching way.

"Umph! I hardly knew you again," cried Peace, for it was he.

"Got a suit of new togs, it appears."

"Yes, sir."

Susan now opened the door, and Mr. Peace inquired if the mistress was in.

He was shown into the first floor.

He had no reason to complain of the reception he met with from his quondam companion—Laura Stanbridge—who professed herself delighted to see him.

"Well, Charlie," she ejaculated, after the few first civilities had been exchanged; "this puts me in mind of old times. I began to think that you had given me the cut; but I suppose you have been pretty well engaged, or I should have seen something of you."

"Middling. You see, before I leave London I thought it just as well to see a few of the sights. Perhaps I shan't have another chance for a goodish while, you know."

"Ah! just so. Then you are only here for a time—you intend returning to Sheffield?"

"Yes, I suppose so."

"I see, a bird of passage—eh?"

Peace smiled. Then, after a pause, he said, quickly—

"But, I say, Laura, old girl, who was that boy I saw at the door as I came in ?"

"A fair-haired lad ?"

"Yes, and good looking. I hardly knew him."

"Have you seen him before, then ?" inquired Miss Stanbridge, in a tone of surprise.

"Aye—surely."

"Dear me ; how remarkable ! You know him, then ?"

"Well, I know about him—have seen him several times in the neighbourhood of Broxbridge."

"Oh ! that's where he came from."

"I suppose so. He was with farmer Jamblin. How is it he is here ?"

"Poor fellow ! he was starving, and—and—well, I made him useful, and gave him board and lodging."

"Ah !" murmured Peace, looking down on the floor of the apartment. "Well, I suppose it's all right ?" here he whistled.

His companion burst out into a loud laugh.

"You're not getting nasty particular, I hope ?" she ejaculated.

"I suppose the boy is nothing to you ?"

"Nothing at all."

"Do you know any of his relatives—his father or mother ?"

"Not I ; but he hasn't got any. He's an orphan—so I've been told. As to his late master, Jamblin, it would not much matter if he were at the bottom of the sea ; but let us pass on to something which more immediately concerns me. I want you to do me a favour."

Laura Stanbridge clapped her hands together, and said joyfully—

"Certainly, old man, with pleasure. What is it ?"

"You are mistress of this house, I suppose ?"

"Yes. All right ; go on."

"And you can let me have the use of one of the top attics for a night ?"

"Of course I can, for as many nights as you like for the matter of that. But, I say, what's your little game ? You have something on—that I can see plain enough."

"You are right, I have. Between us there should be no concealment ; there should be mutual confidence."

The girl smiled and nodded.

Peace went on.

He could be plausible enough when it answered his purpose.

"Well, this is it," he said in continuation. "A crib is to be cracked, and I want to gain the roof of this block of buildings. I can do so easily enough by creeping through one of the windows of your attics. That's plain enough for you, isn't it ?"

"Most unmistakeably plain. You want to get through one of the attic windows. Well, and what then ?"

"The rest is my business. Once on the roof I shall know how to work. What say you ? Will you oblige an old pal ?"

"I dare not refuse you so trifling a favour ; but you must understand, Charlie, that if I am suspected, and a search is made in this house, I am done for. At present I am not suspected, but—"

"You have no call to be alarmed ; I shall emerge from the window. Close it after me, and no one will be any the wiser."

"Let us hope such will be the case."

"You don't care about running any risk to serve a friend—is that what you mean ?"

"I have not said so, Charles. It is you who will have to run the risk. You are welcome to the use of the room, or rather the window. Take care, however, you don't fall down and break your neck."

"Where does the maid servant sleep ?"

"In the back room second floor."

"Does anyone occupy either of the attics ?"

"No. One is used as a lumber room, the other as an occasional bedroom, but not often. You can occupy it if you like."

"That is precisely what I wish to do."

"The matter is easily arranged. You can have a latch-key and let yourself in after we are all in bed. Creep upstairs, and enter the room. Let me at once show you the way to it."

Laura Stanbridge rose and conducted Peace into the attic in question.

He said nothing could be better adapted for his purpose.

It was agreed between the two conspirators that the door should be left unbolted, and Peace was at liberty to enter at what hour he thought best suited for his purpose.

His female companion presented him with a latch-key, and after some further conversation and protestations of friendship on either side, he took his departure, well satisfied with his diplomatic arrangement.

It was not, however, without considerable misgivings that Miss Stanbridge had yielded to his request, and had it not been that she was in his power, and therefore dreaded to make him her enemy, she most likely would have given him a point-blank refusal. As it was she had no other alternative. She knew the man she was dealing with, and therefore deemed it advisable to temporise. Peace had taken her by surprise, and had talked to her in such a plausible way that she was thrown off her guard, and had given in without the faintest show of resistance.

CHAPTER XLVII.

THE ATTEMPTED BURGLARY AT THE JEWELLER'S — PEACE HAS ANOTHER NARROW ESCAPE.

CHARLES PEACE appeared to be like the tiger, who, after tasting human flesh, had an insatiable appetite for fresh victims.

He had contemplated the burglary he was about to put into practice for some weeks, and had well considered the matter before his interview with Laura Stanbridge.

Within a few doors of her residence was a jeweller's shop.

Peace's object was to obtain an easy access to this.

He had ascertained that the owner of the establishment in question did not reside on the premises—he had a house at Fulham for himself and his family.

After the day's business was over he repaired thither, leaving his housekeeper, a maid servant, and one of his assistants in charge of his town residence.

The maid servant was constrained to sleep out of the house, having to attend upon her mother, who was dangerously ill ; consequently the only occupants of the establishment after closing hours were a young man, who was the jeweller's assistant, and an old woman, who acted in the capacity of housekeeper.

Peace, therefore, came to the conclusion that if he gained an entrance into the house there would not be much difficulty in obtaining possession of a large amount of property.

Between the hours of one and two o'clock in the morning he let himself into Laura Stanbridge's house, and closing the street door noiselessly he proceeded upstairs, and reached the attic without disturbing any of the inmates.

Here he remained for some little time before carrying out his plan of operation.

He then ruminated for a brief period, and quietly opened the lattice window.

He peered forth—the noise of distant wheels of some passing vehicle was the only sound which broke the stillness of the night.

He crept through the open casement, and gained the gutter, then he closed the window and passed along till he reached the roof of the adjoining house.

He cast a hasty glance around, and came to the conclusion that his movements were unobserved by any prying or inquisitive eye.

He felicitated himself upon his success thus far, and so silently and stealthily passed on to the roof of the next house, and so on till he had reached the one upon which he had to perform.

His purpose was to effect an entrance by removing the trap door in the roof; having reached this he at once set to work, but some little time elapsed before he succeeded in sliding back the bolts.

But he was, as we have already seen, an adept at this sort of business, and eventually the trap was removed, and he passed through the opening.

The rest was, of course, an easy matter. He placed the trap in its original position, and dropped into the loft.

He now felt assured that he was about to meet with triumphant success.

In this, however, he was greatly mistaken.

A gentleman in one of the adjoining houses, who had been working till a late hour in writing for the Press, had observed his movements from the top window of one of the houses which commanded a view of the jeweller's.

His attention had been attracted to the figure of a man passing over the roof.

He rose from his seat, drew back the curtain of his window, and watched Peace's proceedings.

When he saw him remove the trap-door and creep through the opening he naturally enough suspected that something was amiss.

He was well acquainted with the jeweller, and knew perfectly well that he was at Fulham; he knew, moreover, that there were but two persons sleeping in the establishment.

He at once put on his coat and hat and sallied forth, and bent his steps in the direction of the nearest police-station.

Peace in the meanwhile was busily engaged in collecting together all the valuables he could lay his hands upon. These he placed in a heap on the counter of the shop.

The housekeeper and the shopman were all this time sleeping soundly.

While engaged in his depredations he heard the sounds of voices outside and saw the fitful flashing of lights against the windows of the residence.

He closed the door of the shop, locked it, and put the key into his pocket, then he proceeded upstairs into the front room, first floor, and listened.

People were astir in the street.

He peeped through the window blind and saw three or four policemen in front of the house.

"The devil!" he ejaculated, perfectly astounded at the discovery. "Bobbies! Here's a pretty go; I'm done as brown as a berry."

He drew back from the window blind, and began to seriously consider what was to be done.

It was too plainly evident that the police, from some cause or other, were on the alert.

To return by means of the roof was now an impossibility, as his movements would be seen and capture certain. What was he to do?

It required all his fortitude to meet the urgency of the case.

Escape appeared impossible. Doubtless the back premises were being watched as carefully as the front of the house.

But Peace was equal to the occasion, and hoped to be master of the situation.

Any way he resolved upon a bold stroke of policy.

Several loud raps were given at the front door.

Peace took off his coat, and, opening the window of the front drawing-room, rubbed his eyes as if just aroused from slumber, and, peering forth, said, in a drawling tone—

"What is the matter, policeman? Is the house on fire?"

"No, sir," answered one of the constables. "No; but you've got a burglar inside your premises."

"Goodness me!" exclaimed our hero. "I'll come down and let you in. A burglar, eh."

He went to the front door, which he unfastened, and said, in a tone of well-simulated alarm—

"Don't let him escape. Search the house, and—and place a guard at the door."

Two policemen at once proceeded upstairs, another kept guard over the entrance, while a fourth was on the opposite side of the way, flashing his bull's-eye on the screened windows of the establishment.

"There is a fire somewhere," said Peace, in a confidential tone, to the nearest policeman. "Of that I am quite certain. Don't you smell something burning?"

The man sniffed, and said he could not smell anything.

"It's at the back—that's where it is," cried our hero. "Come this way, policeman."

As he said this, he walked leisurely along the front of the house, which was a corner one, and led the way to the street by its side. The policeman followed.

At the back of the jeweller's was a mews.

"There!" exclaimed Peace. "It's there!"

The policeman, thrown completely off his guard—he was quite a green hand—walked a few steps down the mews, and looked about in the vain effort to discover the fire.

This was Peace's opportunity—it was one he did not fail to avail himself of.

With the speed of an antelope he ran down the side street, turned the corner and was lost to sight before the policeman had retraced his steps and gained the corner of the mews.

He looked round for Peace, but even at that moment he did not suspect anything was amiss, concluding that he had returned to what he deemed was his own house.

The housekeeper and shopman were aroused from their slumbers by the constables who had been searching the premises.

No burglar was to be found, but a coat and hat were discovered on the sofa in the drawing-room; these belonged to Peace, who was by this time far away.

"Where is the governor?" inquired one of the policemen.

"Governor!" exclaimed the jeweller's assistant. "He's at Fulham."

"It's taken him a short time to get there," cried the

man at the door, "seeing that he was here not five minutes ago."

"Here!" ejaculated the housekeeper. "Oh, it's impossible—he left hours ago."

The policeman exchanged blank looks—the truth for the first time dawned upon them.

"What sort of a man is the governor?" inquired one, quickly.

"A tall, stout gentleman, with big bushy whiskers," answered the shopman.

"Well, this is a sell," murmured another constable. "Why I'm blessed if that fellow wasn't the burglar." Then, turning to the man who had kept guard at the door, "You had no right to let him go, Jenkins. It was your duty to detain him."

"Don't blame me—it's no fault of mine. Why I could have sworn he was the master; so would anybody."

"You had no right to let him go."

"But I don't know that he has gone."

There was a loud peal of laughter at this declaration. Everybody is so clever after a mistake has been made and discovered.

And this was clearly a very great mistake.

A search was at once made in every direction for the missing robber; bull's eyes were flashed in all directions, the adjacent streets underwent inspection, as did also several houses which were known to be the resort of thieves, but Peace was by far too artful a rascal to seek refuge in any of these; it was not his practice to do so at any period of his life.

The police were at fault. There was, however, one consolation. Nothing had been stolen. Not an article of any description had been removed from the premises.

On the contrary, something had been left behind—this being our hero's coat and hat, which the police took possession of as trophies.

They, however, could not conceal from themselves that they were greatly in fault. They had no right to allow anybody to leave the house without ascertaining whether he was connected with the establishment; but our hero, who was far more quick-witted and prompt in action than the constables, had thrown them off their guard.

His manner was so ingenuous and inspired such confidence that the police took it for granted that he was either the master of the house or else his confidential man.

Never surely did men make such a palpable blunder.

Peace having got once clear off, ran his hardest until he had reached Seven Dials.

Then he observed, at some little distance off, a policeman taking his lonely round.

As he was without his hat and coat, he deemed it expedient to seek concealment.

He went up a narrow passage and hid himself in a dark gateway till the patrol of the night had passed.

He watched him from his hiding place and saw him walk with measured steps on his beat.

Luckily for him, the policeman walked on without suspecting for a moment that anything was wrong, and Peace did not emerge from his safe retreat till he felt assured that the watchful guardian of the night was far removed from the spot.

He then sallied forth, and crept cautiously along a narrow dark street which led into Long-acre.

A four-wheeled cab, driven by a sleepy driver, drove into sight.

Peace at once hailed it. The cabdriver looked surprised, as well he might be, at seeing a man in such a strange costume.

"What's up?" he cried, looking down at our hero.

"Why, I'm in a devil of a pickle; that's what's up," returned Peace.

"I've been to a masquerade, and some vagabond has stolen my hat and coat. I haven't very far to go, but don't like to walk home in this plight. Drive me to the corner of Fetter-lane."

"I'm taking the horse and cab to the stables, and don't want another fare," said the driver, who was evidently like the animal he drove—fairly done over.

"It isn't far," said our hero, "I'll pay you well. Drop me at the corner of Fetter-lane."

"You're a rum un," answered the man. "Jump in."

Peace did not desire any further altercation—he opened the door of the cab and jumped in.

The vehicle rumbled over the stones, passed through Great Queen-street, then Little Queen-street, and proceeded along Holborn till the corner of Fetter-lane was reached; then it was brought to a halt.

"There you are," cried Peace, handing the driver half-a-crown. "Now I am within a dozen doors of my own home."

The cabman took the proffered coin and drove off.

Peace went up Fetter-lane, and looked to the right and left, but no one was visible.

He waited till the noise of wheels had passed away, and then he went back to the corner of the lane.

If he could reach his lodgings in Leather-lane without attracting attention all would be well. How to complete this he had not at that moment determined.

Should a chance policeman be in Holborn, or in any of the adjacent streets, a man without a coat and at that hour in the morning would be sure to attract his attention and excite suspicion.

Peace had been wonderfully successful thus far, but there was no telling what might follow; whether he had better walk leisurely along or make a bolt of it, he could not for the moment determine.

At length, after a little reflection, he thought it would be best to adopt the former alternative; he therefore crossed Holborn in a quiet, easy, self-confident manner.

A half inebriated pedestrian, who was reeling homewards, called out——

"Hallea, governor, taking a moonlight airing?"

Peace made no reply, but passed on till he had reached the corner of Leather-lane, without attracting the notice of any one else. In a few seconds after this he gained the side door of his own residence.

But he would not enter without first of all ascertaining that no one was watching his movements.

He peered cautiously around. All was silent, not a solitary individual was visible.

He slid the key into the lock, opened the door, and entered. Then he closed it as noiselessly as possible.

He felt that he had escaped by almost a miracle, but did not at the same time feel assured that all danger was over.

He ignited a small hand lamp, which he placed in the grate, so that its rays should not be visible at the window of his room.

He began to reflect on the events of the past hour or two, and had some misgivings when he remembered that his coat and hat had been left behind in the house he had entered.

He was well assured that the former did not contain any papers or other articles which would lead to his identity.

PEACE ENTERS THE JEWELLER'S HOUSE.

The coat itself he had bought ready-made at a shop in Bradford, so that there was no fear of his being recognised by means of that garment, since he was not known to the shopman who served him.

The hat bore no maker's name on the inside.

He was, therefore, well satisfied that he could not be traced by that means.

But there was no telling.

Clues to thieves were sometimes obtained in an extraordinary manner, and he did not feel altogether assured of his safety.

However, he had no alternative but to quietly await the issue.

If Laura Stanbridge rounded on him he was lost: but he did not for a moment imagine she would do so—certainly not unless she was hardly pressed.

No. 22.

He thought all these matters over before he turned in for the night, and bitterly regretted having attempted to rob the jeweller's shop, since it had been attended with such disastrous consequences. The more he thought of the matter the more puzzled he was. He could not understand the reason for the sudden appearance of the policemen in front of the house.

Some one must have given an alarm.

Who could it be ?

Not Laura Stanbridge. That was not probable, as she would thereby incriminate herself.

He was not aware that his actions had been closely watched from the top window of one of the opposite houses.

"Somebody's pulled the string," he murmured ; "that's quite certain. Who can it be ? Ah, it never does for a man to trust to any one ; and this is a lesson to me—a lesson I shall rarely fail to profit by."

He was by no means comfortable when he retired to bed. He was troubled in his mind, and had in consequence but a restless night.

On the following morning, upon reviewing the events of the preceding night, he was forcibly impressed with the egregious blunder he had made, and his own want of foresight.

It is true he had successfully eluded justice up to the present time, but he did not feel in any way assured that the police would not yet find a clue to his whereabouts. He had a considerable amount of stolen property concealed in the premises he occupied. To dispose of this was his first consideration.

After he had partaken of a hearty breakfast, he packed up his spoils in as small compass as possible, and at once set out with the same to the Jew fence in Whitechapel.

Old Isaac was at his post, and upon the goods being handed over to him for inspection, he began as usual to deprecate their value.

This Peace was well used to ; it was a way the Jew had. He had many pleasant little ways, which were at once tantalising and irritating. But it was now imperative for our hero to get rid of the articles, even if he had to make a greater sacrifice than usual.

Isaac was never at a loss to reckon up his customers ; he saw that Peace for some reason or another was constrained to part with the goods.

The Jew offered about one-third their value.

This was indignantly refused, and their owner was about to replace them in his bag, when the Jew, after many shrugs and wry faces, made an advance in the price.

"I won't take it ; I'll smash them all up first, you rapacious old sinner !" cried Peace.

"Vell, vell, smash 'em up ; much good that'll be. I thought you'd more sense than to talk in that way. S'help me goodness, I do my best for all of you. I always dosh my besht. You never that, Peace. You never find me anything but honest and straightforward in my dealings with you."

"Leave honesty out of the question. It don't sound well from your lips. Some of the watches are good enough, but the others—— well, they're such duffers —upon my shoul they are—I wouldn't tell an untruth, not for anything."

"Get out," exclaimed Peace, in an angry tone. "You not tell an untruth ! Bah ! You get worse and worse, and I shan't come again unless you mend your ways. I know where to dispose of them, man. Don't you think you're the only bloke who does things on the cross,"

"Well, then, there—I don't like to turn away a customer, particularly an old friend like yourself. I'll give you thirty pounds for the lot."

"What ! for the clock and plate included ?"

"Vell, yes, of course I mean that. Be reasonable, don't be too extortionate. Ve must all live."

"Honestly if we can," said Peace, with a smile.

"Yes, honestly, my son. As honest as the world will let us be. Lord, how people do try to best one another in this world ! There, I'll give you thirty quid. Vat say you ?"

"I say I want more, and I won't take thirty quid."

"How much more ? Tell me, how much more ? Now don't take them avay, I vant to do bishness if I can, even if it is but at a small profit. Ve must live."

"I'll take forty. I ought to have fifty at the very least, but I can't do with less than forty, for I am just now very hard up."

The Jew shook his head, and said he couldn't give forty.

After a deal of haggling, a bargain was struck, Peace took four and thirty pounds for goods which were worth considerably more than double that sum in the very lowest market, but he had no alternative, and the rapacious Jew suspected this.

As a rule Peace generally managed to get more from the Israelite than any of his compeers.

In many cases old Isaac obtained articles purloined by professional thieves for a third or even a quarter of their value.

Peace pocketed the money and returned to his rooms in Leather-lane.

He, however, deemed it advisable to leave his lodgings for a few days, till the attempted burglary at the jeweller's was not quite so fresh in the recollection of the police authorities.

He wrote a letter to Laura Stanbridge, requesting her to call and see him.

This he sent by a boy.

In less than an hour after its delivery, his old Sheffield companion presented herself.

"Well, Charlie ! What's up now that you have sent for me ?" said Miss Stanbridge. "Anything amiss ? Have they found your crib ?"

"No, not at present," returned our hero. "But you see, old girl, this little affair has been a great mistake. I managed to dodge them, but my coat and hat have been left behind ; and, therefore, I think it as well to bunk—to leave this place for a few days."

"Certainly ; the best thing you can possibly do. Well !"

"And I was thinking, if you could spare that lad, just to take charge of it in the daytime, he could answer all questions, and say that I had gone into the country with some frames that had been executed for a customer. Do you see ?"

"I see plainly enough. But, my dear Charlie, that would never do. The boy is known in my neighbourhood ; and, if he were to be seen here by—by the police, they would suspect that I had something to do with the affair, and it would be my ruin if inquiries were set on foot. No, I don't think we can risk that."

"Oh !" murmured Peace, glumpily. "You won't oblige me, then ; that's what you mean ?"

"I don't mean anything of the sort ; but, for both our sakes, it is well not to put trust in the boy."

"Has he peached ?" inquired our hero, sharply. "If he has, I'll ring his young neck."

"Peached ! No, certainly not. What on earth could have put such a thought in your head ? Peached ! No, of course not !"

"Who gave notice to the bobbies, then ?"

"Who? Why, a gentleman who saw you climbing over the roofs, from one of the top windows of a house opposite."

"Hang it all, I have been a fool! Never thought of that."

"That's how it was. Everybody knows that in the neighbourhood."

"Ah, then, it won't do to leave this place in charge of the boy, I must get some one else."

"You have had a narrow escape, and so have I," said his companion.

"Do they suspect that I reached the roof from your house?"

"No, I am glad to say they do not; if they had I should have been sure to have heard of it. No one, I believe, suspects you were concealed in my house—nevertheless we've had a narrow squeak for it."

"Keep dark—say nothing about the subject to any-one. Hear, but say nothing."

"Trust me for that. You must manage your matters better next time; this has been a most unfortunate business; but never mind, you are out of the fire. I would offer to take charge of your place myself, but have other matters to attend to, and even if this were not the case it would not be prudent for me to risk being seen here."

"Certainly not—I do not desire you to do so. You've said enough, Laura. I'm sorry any act of mine should have placed you in jeopardy, but there is now no reason for your being alarmed. You had better not remain any longer. Should I want to see you I will send a letter, and make an appointment for a meeting at some other place."

"Don't you think I am complaining, Charlie, or am likely to desert you. All that I can do to serve you at any time you may count on. Even now I don't like to leave you to shift for yourself, but I don't think they've got the faintest clue. The coat and hat are at the station, so I've heard, but they've not been able to trace their owner. So be of good cheer, old man, and better luck next time," said Laura Stanbridge, as she took her leave.

In less than two hours after her departure Bandy-legged Bill, the gipsy, dropped in.

Peace was very glad to see him, and recounted all the incidents of the attempted burglary at the jeweller's, which the gipsy listened to with evident interest.

"We'll dodge them even if they do find their way here," exclaimed the gipsy. "Let us consider what is to be done in this matter. Two heads are better than one."

CHAPTER XLVIII.

JANE RYAN—THE CLOSE OF A TROUBLED LIFE.

WE must turn back to earlier scenes in our narrative that we may gather up the tangled threads of this tale.

The reader will remember the burglary at Oakfield farmhouse, described in the opening chapters. He will call to mind the Bristol Badger being shot down by the girl, Jane Ryan, who afterwards gave her evidence at the trial of Gregson, which went far towards ensuring the conviction of the hardened criminal.

Gregson had ruthlessly murdered the girl's sweetheart some years before the period of the Oakfield House burglary.

Jane Ryan had watched and waited, and she had not done so in vain. An inward monitor had whispered to her that sooner or later she would be instrumental in hunting down the man who had robbed her of one whom she valued beyond all else in the world.

She felt that her mission was fulfilled after Gregson had expiated his crimes on the public scaffold.

But the death of this wretch did not remove the canker worm which had found its way into the heart of the young girl. It did not blot out from her recollection the terrible and appalling scene of her lover being stabbed to the heart on the lawn of her master's house.

Jane Ryan became an altered woman; she was, as we have already intimated, deeply embued with superstition, and, moreover, under the impression that her days were numbered. Nothing could dispossess her of this idea.

The last time we took a glance at Jane was in the fourth number of this work, when Richard Ashbrook told her the story of his love, and asked her to become his wife. The interview between the two was of a a touching and tender nature. Jane did not positively refuse, but she bade her master seek somebody who was more worthy of him than she was herself. She told him also that she was mourning for one who was dead and gone.

All this was not particularly complimentary to the substantial and honest yeoman, who began to suspect that there was some other rival in the field. He could not for a moment understand that she could be so true and constant to the dead carpenter.

He was as honest as the day, would not wrong man or woman, or indeed any living creature, but his powers of perception were but limited, and Jane was a puzzle to him.

Poor man, his was by no means a solitary case; hundreds and thousands of women, both before and since, have puzzled and perplexed men of far greater intellect than he could boast of.

Richard Ashbrook considered the matter over. He reasoned with himself, and endeavoured to quench the fire which burnt within his breast.

He was advised to try a change of scene, and left Oakfield for a while upon a visit to Mr. Jamblin, of Stoke Ferry Farm.

He flirted with little Miss Jamblin, who was at this time not out of her teens. He went out shooting with her father and brother, and passed many jovial and enjoyable evenings with his old friends.

But despite all this he could not forget Jane Ryan; her image was for ever presenting itself to his vision.

His friends were discreet and considerate enough not to mention her name; they knew perfectly well his feelings towards her, and hoped that "he would get over it."

But Ashbrook did not find it so easy to get over it as he had imagined.

"When a man is over head and ears in love," said Mr. Jamblin, senior, "it takes a strong rope to pull him out of the pit into which he has fallen."

"She be a rare good un of her sort," said the old farmer to his son one day; "but she be naught but a serving wench after all."

"And Master Richard can do better. He ought to strike at higher game."

"Pipple ought to do a number of things they don't do," answered Young Jamblin. "It ain't easy for a man to right himself when he be capsized by a woman, no matter whether she be a serving wench or a duchess—and for the matter of that in many cases one be as good as 'tother."

"Eh, lad!" cried the farmer, opening his large eyes and staring at the speaker. "Them's your sentiments?"

"Well, yes, and I aint ashamed to confess to them."

"Don't you tumble into the same pitfall as Richard

Ashbrook," said his father in a much more serious tone. " Mind ee don't do that."

Young Jmblin burst out into a loud fit of laughter.

" All right, father ; you've no right to be afeard, as far as I'm concerned.

James Ashbrook now entered the room and cut short the conversation.

" Ah, Master Richard, exclaimed the elder Mr. Jemblin, " Patty tells me you be home-sick and be goin' to leave us. We can do a little longer wi' ee."

" I do not doubt that," returned Ashbrook, " and the change has done me a world of good, but——"

" Oh, aye, but I know what ee's goin' to say—you've got your own affairs to look after and all that sort of thing. Well, please yourself—every man knows his own bis'ness best."

" He's not going as yet," cried Patty, who now entered.

' And why not, lass ?" enquired her father.

" Because I won't let him," returned the young girl, perking up her pretty features in a most comical way. She was the pet of the family and her father doated on her. She was always good-humoured, and had withal a keen sense of humour.

Farmers' daughters, as a rule are not lusty, broad-shouldered wenches with big red arms and necks like bulls, as some of you probably suppose, nor are they the unsophisticated creatures, green as their own meadow grass, soft as their own butter, the stereotyped guile-less victims of stereotyped wicked squires, as drama-tists and writers of rural tales would have you believe.

They can display as much finesse in their best par-lours as any peeress in her gilded drawing-room ; and although they might be at a loss to understand the intricate compliments of a Belgravian roné, they play their plebeian gudgeons with as light a hand as ever tortured a titled trout in a West-end mansion.

In describing Patty Jamblin I present to you a fair specimen of the class.

She was long-haired, and blue-eyed with a clear white skin.

Her hands and forearms were a little red and rough from manual labour, but her neck and forehead were like polished ivory.

Her eyes were mild and candid, and could be roguish when they pleased.

Her hair was chestnut, and instead of being tortured into ringlets, as is the fashion among farmers' daughters, it was worn plain.

She was very partial to both the Ashbrooks, and during the sojourn of Mr. Richard in her father's home had striven to make him as comfortable and happy as possible, by unremitting attention.

Indeed, her cheery manner and pretty ways had done much to dispel the gloom, which he had found it so difficult to shake off.

When left alone with her father's visitor she be-sought him to remain a little longer as an inmate of Stoke Ferry Farm, and he could not find it in his heart to give a denial to the request.

He did remain for another week or so ; nevertheless, despite the pleasant society in which he found himself, he could not forget the thoughtful pensive girl of Oakfield House.

Upon his returning home Richard Ashbrook found his brother and sister anxiously awaiting his return home. The greetings were cordial and affectionate, for the Ashbrooks were a most united family, and it was seldom, indeed, that anything transpired that in any way disturbed the harmony of the establishment.

Jane Ryan, as usual, was busily engaged in her household duties, which she went through in a mechanical unobtrusive manner.

She had never at any time of her life been loquacious, being in fact reserved and thoughtful in her manner ; of late she was so to a degree which, to persons of a lively temperament, was in a measure depressing.

Upon seeing James Ashbrook her face became irradiated with a smile, which, if wan and faint, was ineffably sweet in its expression.

It was wonderous to see the tender solicitude, the care and consideration displayed towards her by the honest horny-handed farmer.

Rough man as he was, when in her presence he was as soft and gentle as a woman.

He watched her moving about the house in an abstracted, half-caressing manner, which it is not easy to describe by words, but which has been, nevertheless, felt by all who came within her influence.

Certainly, if ever a man was devoted to one of the opposite sex, that man was Richard Ashbrook.

His attachment was not so much expressed by words as by manner.

Weeks and months passed over, and his fondness for Jane became deeper and more intensified.

He made her a study—he strove to please her by numberless little acts of kindness and consideration, which were but little or nothing in themselves, but might be likened to straws borne upon the surface of the water, which showed which way the current ran.

Everybody knew perfectly well that matters could not go on thus for any great length of time.

Either the young farmer would have to press the question still closer, or else give up all though s of the girl.

As to sending her away, that was not to be thought of for a moment.

His brother and sister would not consent to such a course, to say nothing of Mr. Richard himself.

And so, after a long, and, it might be said, almost silent, wooing, and watching, Richard Ashbrook once more took heart of grace, and besought Jane Ryan to become his " for better or for worse."

His brother and sister were at this time paying a visit to the Jamblins.

" Jane," said Mr. Richard, one evening, when the day's work was over, " I want to ha' a word or two wi'ee, lass. So when ye've finished cleaning up, just step into the parlour for a while, will'ee ?"

" If you desire me to do so," returned the girl, with a faint flush.

" Yes, I do, if thee beest willing."

She nodded, and said—

" I will be with you presently."

" Aye, do, gell, the sooner the better," cried the farmer, as he left the kitchen, and proceeded into the best room of the establishment.

In a few minutes Jane, having washed and touched herself up, entered.

Her master handed her a seat.

He was in a great fluster, and it was easy to see that he was but ill at ease.

Jane sat down.

" I dunno whether you guess why I ha' desired to speak to 'ee," he said, in hurried manner ; " an it does not much matter whether 'ee do or not, for what's to be sed can't remain any longer unsed, and that's the truth on't. You see, Jane, it beau't o' no yoose for a man to fight agen anything he ain't got any power to grapple wi'. It's against common sense—we none of us can do it—a man aint no yoose agenst a ghost or speerit."

"I don't understand your meaning, Mr. James,' murmured Jane.

Neither did she, and to say the truth the farmer did not quite understand it himself. He had endeavoured to take a high flight—to make a simile—which now that he had uttered it seemed to be quite inapplicable to the subject in hand.

"I mean," he said, endeavouring to come nearer to the mark, "you see, I mean, gal, we ain't any of us got any control over ourselves as far as affairs of the heart are concerned. If a man loves a woman as I do you (this was a home thrust), it's no yoose telling him to find somebody more worthy of him, and all that sort of thing, cause he don't think anybody is more worthy of him—he believes the woman he loves is more worthy and better than any other in the world."

Jane nodded, but made no other reply.

The farmer went on—he was certainly floundering a little, but had made one or two palpable hits nevertheless.

"And so, Jane, my dear gell, I ha' thought over and over agen of what you sed when I asked you to become my wife, and I ha' endeavoured to think no more of you, but find it ain't of no yoose. Love is summat like the wire worm; when it once effects an entrance it aint so easy to extract it."

The simile was not perhaps an elegant one, but it was pretty well for a farmer.

"Have you thought of what I sed to ye, now many months ago?"

"I have thought of it, master," said Jane, with a mournful cadence in her voice, " and I've thought how proud and happy I ought to be, seeing how devoted, how kind you are in every way, but it is not so much on account of myself as it is for you that I have hesitated."

"Hesitated?"

"Oh, Mr. Richard, you want a bright, cheerful companion, not a poor broken-hearted creature like myself. If I could forget the past—if I could be the same as I was a few years ago, the matter would be different. As it is, I know not what to do. Do you persist in pressing the suit?"

"Do I persist? Of course I do," cried the farmer. "Shall always persist while both of us are alive."

"Oh! while we are alive?" repeated Jane Ryan.

The farmer looked surprised—not to say a little alarmed.

"Well we are not going to die, as yet let us hope."

"No; let us hope not."

"And if you marry me," he exclaimed, suddenly assuming a tone of confidence and cheerfulness. "You're so good a girl that you'll live for my sake."

His companion smiled, and wound his arms round her neck.

"Now I've got 'ee," he ejaculated, "and you consent to be mine for better or for worse?"

"I consent!" cried Jane. "It is to be, and I consent. How is it possible for me to do otherwise?" she ejaculated, looking up towards the ceiling. " Yes, Master Richard, I consent."

Richard Ashbrook felt as if a load had been lifted off his heart. He clung to her, and covered her face with passionate kisses.

Thus ended his wooing. When his brother and sister returned from Stokeferry Farm he made them acquainted with all that had occurred, which did not at all surprise them.

Then the village gossips, as well as their more immediate neighbours, had prognosticated how it would end.

James Ashbrook purchased a farm adjoining Oakfield. He and his brother were partners, but Richard furnished the residence attached to the adjoining farm. To this he took his young wife after their union, which took place in less than six months after the proposal and acceptance of the same by Jane Ryan.

If Richard Ashbrook had been a devoted lover he was an equally devoted husband. He treated his young wife with uniform kindness, and indulged her in every thing.

In a twelvemonth she presented her husband with a daughter, which he declared was the image of herself.

After this the shadow which had fallen upon her, and which marriage had failed to dispel, became deeper and deeper still.

For her husband's sake she endeavoured to assume an air of cheerfulness, and strove as best she could to make him believe she was happy. He did his best to make her so, but despite all this there were many in the neighbourhood who shook their heads, and said that Mrs. Richard Ashbrooke was fading away. She believed so herself—had always been under that impression. What she told the farmer before her marriage was true in substance and in fact.

She was a broken-hearted creature, and not all the wealth in the world—not all the attentions of her devoted husband could remove the cankerworm which had crept into her heart.

Some persons are affected by sorrow for the departed in the smallest degree possible—they are enabled to forget the past and look hopefully to the future; while others are struck down with such force that they are never able to rally—people are so differently organised.

It is true Jane Ryan had lived on for some years, but it was a sort of living death. Even her marriage was but a gilt and painted funeral.

She had given her hand, and, indeed, her heart—or what remained of it—to the honest devoted man who led her to the altar, and since the union she had been a loving and exemplary wife, but she could not divest herself of the miserable fact that her days were numbered. The end came.

*   *   *   *   *

In a large darkened room of Richard Ashbrook's house the wan figure of a woman is stretched.

The bedstead on which she lies, with its heavy hangings, presents something of a funereal aspect.

Its occupant is Jane Ashbrook.

She is calm, placid, and resigned. Her features wear a chastened and almost angelic expression. The ruddy hue of health has long since left them; this is succeeded by a delicacy of the skin which is something akin to wax-work.

She does not moan or murmur, but remains more like an immovable statue than aught else.

The dusky shadows of figures are creeping about the room. These are James and Richard Ashbrook, and their sister, Maude.

The sick woman has been dozing for an hour or more. Presently she opens her eyes, and murmurs the name of her husband.

He is by her bedside in a moment, and bends fondly over her.

"You are better, Jane—say you are better," he says, in an anxious tone.

"Better, because nearer home," was the response.

An expression of anguish passed over the features of the farmer.

He sits himself down in a chair by the bedside of the sufferer, and remains silent and thoughtful.

Maude creeps up to the sick couch, kisses her sister-in-law fondly, and in a minute or so after this leaves, in company with her brother James.

Richard is left alone with his sick wife.

He is a strong, powerful man, full of robust health, but feels now so borne down as to be almost prostrate.

For weeks his wife had been thus—a mere shadow of her former self. Her malady appeared to be incurable.

Dr. Bourne, her medical attendant, had been unremitting in his attention; but he confessed himself quite unable to define the nature of the complaint—it appeared to him to be more mental than physical, and for that reason it was beyond the reach of medicaments.

He did his best, however, but failed to arrest the decay which was so silently and secretly taking place.

The door of the room was gently opened, and Doctor Bourne entered in company with the nurse.

He looked at his patient, felt her pulse, watched the expression of her countenance for some little time, and then shook his head.

"Worse!" whispered the parson.

"Weaker, decidedly weaker; you must give her as much nourishment as possible."

He went to a side table and wrote a precription, then he left.

The nurse went down-stairs to show the doctor out. Mr. Ashbrook left the sick chamber and met her upon her return.

"What does he say about his patient?" he enquired anxiously; "anything else?"

"She is weaker, and requires careful watching and the utmost care," returned the nurse.

"What is your opinion, Mrs. Deacon? Tell me candidly—for you have an opinion—and are a good judge in matters of this sort."

"Well, sir, 'while there's life there's hope,'" said the woman.

She did not compromise herself by giving expression to this hackneyed quotation.

"Yes, that we all know," muttered the farmer. "That's but a poor consolation.

"You had better get a little rest now, I will sit up for the next two or three hours with your mistress."

The nurse retired, and Richard Ashbrook returned to the sick chamber.

He sat himself down in an easy chair. In a short time after this his wife sank into a sound slumber, and the farmer himself dozed.

He was awoke by the sick woman softly calling him by name.

"What is the day of the month, Richard?" enquired his wife.

"The day of the month; it's the twenty-first."

"The twenty-first of October, isn't it?"

"Yes. Why do you ask?"

"Ah, nothing particular. You see, my dear good husband, I was not born under a fortunate star. I had my nativity cast a long time ago, and the horoscope proved that I was born under an unfortunate star. It showed also—" she paused suddenly, and closed her eyes.

"What, dear—what did it show?" inquired the farmer.

"That between the twenty-first and twenty-fourth of October, 1874, a change would take place. Now I know what it means."

The farmer felt like one who had received a heavy blow.

He comprehended her meaning, and big beads of perspiration fell from his temples.

"She believes that she is about to die." he murmured; "but this is very terrible.

"Ye mustn't gi' way, Jane—mustn't gi' way to superstition," he cried; "there beant a mossel o' truth in these horoscops—not a mossel o' truth in anything o' the sort. Don't 'ee believe a word o' such nonsense. May be after all it's that what's making 'ee so ill."

His wife smiled.

"My own dear Richard," she murmured, "don't give way—be of good cheer."

He wound his arms around her, and embraced her fondly.

Presently the nurse entered the room, and bade him seek rest.

He retired to a sleeping chamber adjacent to that occupied by his wife; the few broken sentences she had uttered troubled him much, but hope as yet had not deserted him.

The next day Mrs. Ashbrook appeared to be a little better—was more cheerful; but as it waned, and evening crept on, she seemed to be quite listless and heedless of all around.

Those about her thought she needed repose, and did not trouble her with unnecessary questions.

"Where is Maude—let me see her?" she said all of a sudden to her nurse.

Maude was her daughter, who had been so named after her aunt and godmother, Richard Ashbrook's sister.

The child was brought in and placed in her mother's arms.

She hugged the little thing, who gently sank to sleep on her mother's bosom.

An hour passed—mother and child were still locked in a close embrace.

Doctor Browne came. He glanced at the two figures on the bed, and then looked eagerly at the nurse.

"I think they are both asleep sir," said the latter.

"How long have they been so?"

"For nearly an hour."

"Please remove the child? Mrs. Deacon."

The nurse drew the little thing from off her mother

"One is asleep," said the doctor in a solemn voice, which seemed to go through the heart of Richard Ashbrook, who had followed the doctor into the room.

"But it is the sleep of death."

Farmer Ashbrook uttered a terrible cry. He fell into a chair, and burst into an agony of grief, which was dreadful to behold.

His wife, Jane Ashbrook, was dead!

She had passed peacefully and silently away. There was no expression of pain on her countenance, albeit she had died of a broken heart.

The wretch Gregson had suffered death for the murder of young Hopgood, but the fatal blow received by that ill-fated young man was the cause of another death. Jane Ryan had perished therefrom.

It is true she lived for ten years after the loss of her sweetheart, but she never recovered from the effects of the terrible scene she had witnessed, and hers is not a solitary instance of cases of this sort—albeit, the world knows but little of them.

Life is like a fountain fed by a thousand streams that perish if one is dried. It is a silver chord twisted with a thousand strings that part asunder if one is broken.

Thoughtless mortals are surrounded by innumerable dangers that render it much more strange that they escape so long than that they almost all perish so suddenly at last.

We are encompassed with accidents every day to crush the decaying tenements we inhabit.

The seeds of disease are planted in our constitution by nature.

The earth and atmosphere, whence we draw the breath of life, are impregnated with death; health is made to operate its own destruction.

The food that nourishes contains the elements of decay; the soul that animates it by vivifying first, tends to wear it out by its own action; death lurks in ambush along the paths.

Notwithstanding this truth is so palpably confirmed by the daily example before our eyes, how little do we take it to heart!

We see our friends and neighbours die, but how seldom does it occur to our thoughts that our knell may give the next warning to the world.

CHAPTER XLIX.
LAURA STANBRIDGE AND HER PUPIL.

AFTER leaving Charles Peace in Leather-lane, Miss Stanbridge came to the conclusion that for the future it would be advisable for her to be a little more cautious in her dealings with her old playmate and quondam companion.

She was a lady who had her own battle to fight in the world, and as far as want of principle was concerned she was quite adapted to hold her own against any odds.

Upon returning to her own domicile she found Alf Purvis in the kitchen, in company with Susan.

"You may have a holiday for the rest of this day, Alf, and to-morrow we will commence business again."

"Thank you, marm," cried Alf, "May I go out?"

"Yes, where you please; but mind and be home early in the evening. I don't approve of late hours."

The boy sallied forth and wandered about from one place to another, returning soon after nightfall.

"To-morrow you will have to go out lace-selling," said his mistress, upon his entering the house.

"Yes, marm," answered Alf, in a cheerful tone, "I'll do my best."

In the morning of the following day she brought down from the lumber-room a large tray filled with quantities of "edgings," viz., the kinds of lace used for the bordering of caps, &c.; some braid and gimp, some lace articles—such as worked collars and undersleeves—and some lace of a superior quality, which, however, was English.

This latter kind, she told him, was called "driz" by the street sellers, and that he should offer it to ladies as rare and valuable lace smuggled from Mechlin, Brussels, and Valenciennes.

The braid and gimp, she said, was very little in demand, and the whole street-trade was now so indifferent that the only way a man could get a fair profit on what he sold was by "palming"—that is, giving short measure.

"Would you like to learn how to do it, Alf?" she inquired, and without waiting for an answer, she took a yard measure from the table behind, and cried, in a loud street voice:—

"Three yards a penny edging!" Then she measured three yards with her wand, and showed him how she "palmed" the lace by catching it in short with a jerk of the fingers.

"Let me try," cried the boy, quietly, and in less than half an hour he palmed to perfection.

Young Purvis, when he had accomplished this important piece of manipulation, sallied forth.

He patrolled the favourite "pitches" of the lace business—namely, the Borough-market, Walworth-road, Tooley-street, and Dockhead, Bermondsey.

He told his customers that he was a lace-maker from Millyham, and that the edgings were his own and his old father's work.

This tale, which he related with eloquence and sometimes with tears, worked largely on the feelings of his auditory, and whilst compassionate sailor-girls gazed tenderly on his handsome and grief-stricken features, his sobs extracted sympathy from their hearts.

The next day he went to the houses in and about Regent's Park, and towards Maida-hill. There he sold his pseudo Mechlin to the old dowagers, and his worked collars or "edgings" to their housemaids.

He felt a pleasure in cheating these dames, who, while trying to cheat Government, were trying to cheat the whole of their fellow-countrymen; but he felt a pang in clipping the measures of those pretty servant-girls, who gave him such bright smiles and words, and to whom pennies were so precious because they were so hardly earned.

However, he consoled his conscience with the Machiavellian maxim, "All's fair in Trade."

It had become his motto, as it is the motto of those Jesuits of commerce, who say that all is fair which is foul, false, and thievish.

It was his panacea for the heart's qualms, as it is the panacea, for heaven knows how many thousands in London who rise and fast behind their counters till they have stolen the price of their breakfasts.

He told his mistress how he had succeeded by chicanery in realising a good sum for her.

She complimented him.

"There's no harm hoodwinking your customers," she said. "Besides, all's fair in trade."

As he repeated this sentence after her he thought that the elder of the two women sighed.

He had ascertained from the servant girl that this lady's name was Grover.

He lay awake that night, trying to guess who Miss Stanbridge and Mrs. Grover could possibly be.

He did not think they were real ladies.

In the first place he had met them in a house that was frequented by only the scum of the London streets.

Besides that, there was something very different about them to the young ladies who sometimes stopped him to ask questions about his nests in the Bayswater-road or in Grosvenor-place.

Miss Stanbridge, it was true, had the voice and manners of a lady, but in those of Mrs. Grover he had often detected something which reminded him of the rustics among whom he had been brought up.

And yet it was extraordinary that they should always go out in the afternoon, which he knew was the fashionable hour for ladies to go out, and dressed in gorgeous array.

It was singular.

They could not be bad women, argued the young rogue, but always stayed at home in the evening, and though a great many visitors (whom he was never permitted to see) came after dark, he was shrewd enough to understand that these could not be lovers, because his mistress always took off her fine clothes when she came home.

He also observed that these mysterious visitors were never shown upstairs, but always into a room on the ground floor, and that there Miss Stanbridge came down to them. Peace was the only person who was accustomed to go into the drawing-room, and the boy was under the impression that he was a relative of either one or the other of the two females.

Another singular thing was this : the room upstairs looked out upon the back-yard, as did the kitchen.

He was always sent out by this back yard, which led through a mews into the street from which Peace had made his escape on the eventful night of the attempted burglary at the jeweller's. He was told never to come in at the front door.

And the ladies themselves always went out and came in by the back way, which, although he was unacquainted with the manner of gentlefolk, appeared to him to be a very eccentric proceeding.

To show you how slight is the step from fraud to felony I will continue the history of this poor boy who had fallen into the power of one who knew well how to harden a heart for crime.

In Alf's little garret there was an empty book-case. He had often wished there were books in it, and had often thought of asking his mistress whether she could lend him any, for he had no doubt there were some within the mysterious lumber-room, which seemed to possess almost everything that mortal man could think of.

One night he went to bed at eight o'clock, when, much to his surprise, he saw a number of odd volumes in the book-case.

This was a great boon to him, for as we have already seen he had always been passionately fond of reading.

He went to the case, and caught hold of one which first came to hand, and having undressed himself with a rapidity known only to boys, he sprang into bed and at once began to eagerly devour the contents of the volume, which happened to be "The Lives of Celebrated Highwaymen and Pirates."

The work was exactly suited to his taste.

As he read the exploits of these lawless and daring men he was so fascinated that he read without interruption till the candle had died away in its socket.

He lay thinking of what he had read, and watching the thin dusky light as it crept towards him across the room.

He rose at daybreak with his eyes red and watery, and his mouth parched.

Slinging his lace bag over his shoulders, he went downstairs into the streets, where he walked for hours with his eyes now drooped upon the pavement, now raised towards the grey clouds of early dawn.

Two hours afterwards a woman stole into his room with a wolf-like step.

When she saw that the candle had quite burned down, and that there was a book lying on the bed, she gave a terrible laugh, and clapped her hands.

An hour afterwards, another woman entered the room.

But, when she saw the candle and the book, her wrinkled face grew painful, and she sighed deeply.

Then she drew a book from her bosom, and placed it on a table by the window, returning the other to the shelf.

When Alf came home to breakfast, Susan asked him what made him look so pale.

His eight hours' work had never seemed so long and weary as they did that day.

He walked about mechanically, and sold but little, for in great towns customers have to be run after, and almost inveigled.

He was thinking of his book, and longing for the night to return.

He even took the precaution of buying a candle in case they gave him a short one to go to bed by.

At tea-time Susan complained that she could not make him understand a word that she said.

He told her that he was very tired, and went to bed an hour earlier than usual.

As he was undressing his eyes fell upon the book which was lying upon the table.

He determined to begin with that, and, as it was such a small one, he thought that perhaps he might be able to read it through.

The first few lines showed him that it was a moral book, which inculcated good principles.

He glanced impatiently down the page, intending to throw it aside, when a sentence caught his eye.

He turned the page, and read on.

It was a book which had been written by a good and earnest teacher for the assistance of those who might be under some peculiar temptation, or on the threshold of some great crime.

It was written in simple but beautiful language.

It was written with the heart as well as the pen.

Every word in the book was a good spirit, which flew towards the poor soul tottering on the brink of the abyss, and which held it back with tender arms, and whispered to it to turn back and be saved.

When he had read this book the poor lad sank into a calm and refreshing sleep, and awoke in the morning determined to be honest and industrious, and to think of thieving no more.

But he was still too proud to pray.

He relied upon his own heart, which he thought was strong, but which yielded and broke beneath him like a wooden plank which had been rotten and decayed.

He little knew how difficult it is to repent.

Remorse is only regret. Repentance is to regret and amend.

That very day he cheated a customer, and chose to believe that he had not done very wrong.

That very night he returned to his "Lives of the Highwaymen," and felt relieved when he could not see his good book anywhere in the room.

Next morning as he went downstairs he heard female voices apparently in angry altercation.

He stopped at the door, and listened.

He heard his mistress say—

"I ask you again what made you put that book there ?"

"I could not help it," answered the other, which he knew by the voice was Mrs. Grover. "I can't tell you how it is, but my heart kindles towards that boy; I feel as if I could look at him for ever. I tremble when I hear his voice. There's something about him which makes me younger and sadder to think of. I don't—nay I cannot—tell you what I mean."

"You will, perhaps, have the goodness to answer my question," said Miss Stanbridge. "What made you put that book there ?"

"I don't know. I tell you again that my heart warmed towards him, and I wanted to—to—"

"You wanted to baulk me; I know that perfectly well without your telling me so—to baulk me."

"I do not want to do anything of the kind. I have no desire to interfere with you in any way."

"But you do so, nevertheless. After all the time and money I have spent my plans are to be spoilt by a foolish old woman who does not even know why she wishes to spoil them."

"You are quite wrong in your view of the matter."

"Am I ?"

"Most certainly you are."

"Well, then, let me tell you that I'm of a different opinion—you have interfered in a matter which does not concern you."

PEACE TURNED THE KEY, AND THE MASSIVE DOOR OF THE SAFE SWUNG OPEN.

At the close of the day on which Alf Purvis heard the foregoing conversation he was called into the drawing-room, and his mistress congratulated him upon his skill in palming edgings upon the wives of Tooley-street, and Marlow lace as Valenciennes upon the dowagers of Maida-hill.

Alf felt flattered. It was not often his mistress praised him, and when she did so he knew he was in more than usual favour.

"Do as I tell you," said Miss Stanbridge, in continuation, "and you will soon make money. I started in life as you are doing now, and you see that, though I am very young, I am not so badly off. I contrive to live respectably without the assistance of anyone."

Her looks and manner were at this moment most deceptive; anyone who gazed upon her would have said she was a girl who had just been released from the durance of a boarding school.

She was young in face, but in heart she was old as a hag who had lived years in crime.

She spoke of the books he had been reading, and told him several stories about thieves with such eloquence that his interest was aroused, his imagination ran riot, and he was perfectly charmed with her discourse.

While all this had been going on the old woman kept glancing anxiously at Alf, trying to repress her sighs.

"Oh!" he exclaimed, "what a jolly time those highwaymen must lead of it! I should dearly like to lead such a life."

"You would be afraid of the prison and the gallows," cried his mistress, bursting out into a loud laugh.

"Not I, marm. I should have to take my chance like the rest of them. To be in prison is no more than being in the streets—so I've heard 'em say who have been there; and one may as well end one's life in the air as on a mattress."

His mistress again laughed as if he had said something marvellously funny, but Mrs. Grover was evidently greatly concerned and indeed hurt at the turn the conversation had taken.

A shade of displeasure passed over her features, and this was not lost upon Alf Purvis, who refrained from expatiating on lives of lawless robbers. Alf therefore lapsed into silence.

Mrs. Grover meanwhile watched his countenance with intent, so also did Miss Stanbridge, who said after a pause—

"Alf, have you ever been to a London theatre?"

"No, marm, I was never inside a theatre in my life," he returned.

"Would you like to go to the play?"

"Oh, rather," ejaculated the boy.

His mistress smiled, and went out of the room, taking Mrs. Grover with her. She returned and said—

"Well, Alf, you shall see a performance to-night. You have been diligent and deserve a little relaxation."

She was about to put on her bonnet and shawl when Susan entered the room, and said a gentleman wished to speak to her.

Miss Stanbridge inquired the name of her visitor, and the servant girl said it was Mr. Peace.

Our hero was at once shown upstairs. As he entered he glanced furtively at the boy, who was told to go into the kitchen with Susan.

"Anything up?" muttered Miss Stanbridge.

"No, nothing fresh," returned Peace. "But you are about to go out—I shall not detain you. Some other time will do as well."

"I was going to take the lad to the theatre," said his companion.

"All right, old girl, I'll go with you if you've no objection."

"I shall be most delighted to have your company."

Peace, Miss Stanbridge, and the boy sallied forth. To the latter's inconceivable awe, a cab was hailed and procurred.

Alf sat diffidently on the extreme edge of the back seat, and surveyed the gorgeous interior of the vehicle, from the ragged rug to its dingy roof, as a parson's daughter views for the first time the vaulted expanse and the hollow-sounding stones of Westminster Abbey.

After half an hour's ride the cab stopped, and the driver coming round to the door informed them that they had arrived at their destination.

They passed through the entrance and gained the hall. Miss Stanbridge paid for three seats, and they were shown into one of the private boxes.

The house was a very large one, and Alf as he gazed around was lost in wonderment at its gigantic proportions. He had never been in an establishment of this description.

The pit and gallery were crammed with people, those of the lower class predominating. Some of the men were in their shirt sleeves, many of the women carried in their arms babies with bald heads and sturdy lungs; many coster boys were also present, who were overflowing with merriment and wit, while the atmosphere reeked with the mingled fragrance of orange peel, stale ginger beer, and corduroys.

As the boy was gazing round the house the audience were beginning to grow impatient and personal.

Having discovered a gentleman in full dress in one of the boxes, a lubberly lad called out in the voice of a stentor.

"Three cheers for the bloke in white kids!"

This was responded to and assisted with cat calls and hootings as they observed the discomfiture of the used-up Belgravian, who had wandered among these barbarians to receive amusement, not to contribute to it.

This was followed by shrill whistling from the gods above, the stamping of feet, and conversation carried on by some of the occupants of the pit with those in the gallery. The noise was perplexing and almost deafening.

"Now, then, you catgut-scrapers," exclaimed a voice, "tune up. If we aint a goin' to have any acting to-night, play 'God Save the Queen,' and let's go home."

A costermonger in the gallery began to chant a well-known music-hall ditty, which was at this time enjoying an extensive share of popularity; numbers of men and boys joined furiously and tunelessly in the chorus, and this, together with the stamping of the feet of those who were endeavouring to keep time to the melody—if such a term can be justly applied to it—served to amuse the "gods," as they are called, most immensely.

Peace could not refrain from expressing his disgust at these proceedings.

He had an ear for music, and the abominable din and clatter overhead disturbed his equanimity, and ruffled his temper.

To remonstrate with the noisy ruffians would be only making matters worse.

The leader of the band at length made his appearance from beneath the stage, and, just as his face filled the trap-door which led into the orchestra, it was struck by a sucked orange, thrown by some miscreant from the back of the pit.

The house laughed till it nearly cried. An effort was made by the police to find out the delinquent, but it was not attended with success.

Miss Stanbridge bought a bill of the play.

The first piece was one of those romantic dramas which small playwrights pillage from the French—a sin which is not visited upon the thief, but upon those who receive the stolen goods—with their ears.

The plot was of such an intricate and impossible nature that Alf Purvis was totally at a loss to understand the meaning of what was going on.

To say the truth, this was a matter of no very great moment.

If he did not derive much pleasure from the weary polysyllables and the heavy rant of the people on the stage, their spangled robes, the lights and the music, and the novelty of the whole scene, were sufficient to amuse him during its hour of performance.

The tongues of the coster boys had not been idle all this time, and while any good dramatic point was picked out with wonderful acumen, inefficiencies, either in the acting or in the stage management, were treated most unmercifully.

Nor would they permit the play to proceed till they had got a good view of the stage.

"Higher the blue!" was shouted when they found the sky too low; and "Light up the moon!" was the cry when they observed the chaste orbit growing dim.

"Did you ever hear a more uproarious ill-behaved audience?" said Peace, to Laura Stanbridge.

"It's their way," returned his companion. "If they were not permitted to express themselves after their own fashion the gallery would be empty."

The scenes were shifted—not very accurately, it must be admitted. In a castle at the back of the stage a large gap was left.

An indignant chimney sweep called out—"Ve don't expect no grammar here, but you might shove the scenes to!"

At this the people were convulsed with laughter.

Between the first piece and the heavy sanguinary melodrama which was to follow, the bills advertised a comic song by the celebrated Bill Rasper.

This was pretty sure to please the audience, as it was what is termed a topical song, consisting chiefly of hits at popular personages, and sneers at the aristocracy.

By this time the half price had come in, and the gallery presented an extraordinary appearance—a vast black heap slanting to the roof, dotted with faces, and striped with shirt sleeves.

When there was a clapping of hands the whole mass twinkled as if their dingy hands were so many rays of light.

The rails in front were adorned with the bonnets of the ladies, who did for comfort that which, in the dress circles of the West-end, is done for fashion.

These bonnets became marks for the boys at the back, who, seated upon the shoulders of their friends, or upon the spikes which crowned the partitions, played at pitch and toss with nut shells.

Once more greetings were exchanged between the gallery and pit, and sometimes family secrets were revealed.

"Then you aint brought Poll with you after all," cried a voice from the pit.

"No," answered a man in the gallery—"no, I aint. 'Cos why—she's got the hump."

"Oh! Jerusalem; that's the time o' day, is it?"

The comic singer, dressed as only a comic singer can dress, in a chocolate-coloured coat, a waistcoat with a large floral pattern, and pegtop trousers of the most ultra description, and a watch chain, as thick and massive as a ship's cable, now made his appearance.

His nose was deeply tinged with red, and he had an old umbrella of the Mrs. Gamp species under his arm.

He was greeted with loud and prolonged applause.

The orchestra struck up, and the comic gentleman commenced his song.

As he finished his verse he looked up to the gallery to help him out of the chorus, saying, "Now, then, gentlemen, the Hexeter Hall touch, if you please."

The song was called " Keep your weather eye open, my boys," and it was vociferously "angcord" by the noisy multitude, who were flattered at being permitted to lend their services in the chorus.

The gentleman with the large umbrella had his work to do. He was called on again and again, and had to sing fresh verses containing more pointed allusions to persons and events of the time.

When the audience consented to part with their favourite, the curtain rose for the representation of a transpontine melodrama of the most pronounced and formidable description.

It was a little incongruous, but had, nevertheless, all the elements to commend it to the appreciative audience, for whom it had been written by a veteran playwright who dealt in such hotly spiced commodities.

It would be expecting too much of us or any other man to describe the plot after the fashion of the newspaper critics, for to say the truth the incidents in the drama were too chaotic and heartrending to admit of their being placed before the reader in black and white.

The leading personages may, however, be briefly described.

In the first place, there was a wicked baronet, who persecuted the heroine of the piece. She was, as a matter of course, an innocent and artless seraphic creature, entitled the "Lily of Ludgate."

The aforesaid baronet suborns a ruffian of the deepest die, called "Black Hugh."

This personage has committed an endless number of crimes; he is cast into gaol, from which he contrives, after the approved fashion, to make his escape.

He is followed by a detachment of soldiers (supers), who fire at him as he creeps over the castellated roof of his prison house.

To see him gain the rocks beyond this, and plunge from a giddy height into a foaming cataract beneath, was a sight which, happily, is only to be seen on the stage of a transpontine theatre.

He buffets the waves "with lusty sinews," succeeds in reaching an island in an impossible sea; and from this he puts off on a raft, constructed by himself and a nigger, who is, like himself, a castaway.

He describes this in glowing language in the third act.

Eventually he is shot, and staggers on the stage. All of a sudden he becomes repentant, and makes a dying confession.

To see him point his accusing finger at the wretched baronet, and to see also the " Lily of Ludgate " let down her back hair by the footlights, and to hear the gasps and sobs she gives utterance to as she listens to the tale told by Hugh, who sets all things right before he dies, is altogether beyond our powers of description.

It had a visible and marked effect upon the house.

An itinerant vendor of lemons and oranges, who evidently belonged to the Hebrew persuasion, whispered to a companion in the gallery that the piece "wash very deep."

After his confession, Black Hugh raised himself up, gave a gasp, and fell on his back as dead as a stone.

The baronet was loaded with chains, and the "Lily of Ludgate " fell into the arms of the rightful heir, who had been carried away in the earlier part of the drama by Black Hugh, who was evidently a favourite actor with the frequenters of the theatre.

He rolled his eyes, and pronounced his words as only an artist of his accomplishments and powers could pronounce them.

During the progress of the play the whole theatre shook with enthusiasm and applause, and when Black Hugh had safely escaped from his painted prison-house, the shouts of exultation were deafening, and were repeated till the roof rang again.

But then we must remember that crime and the

penalties of crime are so different in the world and on the stage.

On the stage there is not the cankering remorse, the ever-trembling fear, the start at each voice which speaks, the shudder under each hand which is placed upon the shoulder.

On the stage the prison walls are of wood and canvas, and the public will not permit hanging.

On the stage, then, the law has no terrors, the judge with the black cap is a jest, the condemned cell a jovial cider cellar, the gallows an empty puppet for a Christmas pantomime.

Alf Purvis had, during the performance of the melodrama, been most deeply interested with the action of the piece. His mistress placed her hand upon his shoulder, and asked him if "Black Hugh" was not a bold, and fearless man.

"He's a brave chap, but the baronet was the worst of the two, and ought to have been shot instead of Hugh. Don't you think so?"

"Yes, I do, my lad," returned Miss Stanbridge.

"You'll make something of that boy before you've done with him," whispered Peace. "I dare say you find him an apt pupil."

"And what if I do, Charlie?" said the woman, in an offended tone. "It doesn't matter to you, I suppose."

Peace shrugged his shoulders, but made no reply.

A cab was hailed, and the three playgoers were conveyed to their destination. Peace parted with Miss Stanbridge at the door of her house, and returned home on foot to his rooms in Leather-lane.

Miss Stanbridge poured evil words into the ear of the boy, who listened to them greedily. He was ambitious in mind—he was dishonest in heart. He longed to be one who was known and feared while he was alive, and who should be spoken of and written of after he was dead.

Upon his return home, Alf Purvis missed Mrs. Grover.

He asked his mistress what had become of her.

"She has gone away," said Miss Stanbridge. "I had set my mind on something, and she was foolish enough to oppose me."

"Oh," murmured Alf, "I'm sorry for that."

CHAPTER L.

A VISIT TO THE BLACK MUSEUM—PEACE AND BANDY-
LEGGED BILL—THE BURGLARY AT DENMARK-HILL.

AFTER the attempted robbery at the jeweller's Peace had deemed it advisable to leave his quarters for awhile.

Bandy-legged Bill had agreed to take charge of the premises till he returned.

Peace therefore betook himself to a coffee-shop at Putney, where he slept for several nights after his mishap.

He took the precaution, also, of altering his appearance as much as possible, and to carry this into effect he had made a suit of clothes dissimilar in every respect to those he was accustomed to wear; but, to say the truth, all these arrangements were quite needless, for the police had never had the faintest clue to the real culprit, and in a short time gave the matter up as hopeless.

Indeed, to say the truth, they were so ashamed of their own want of foresight, that they were but too glad to let the recollection of blundering die out as speedily as possible.

The constable who had but recently joined the force was made a scapegoat by his companions, who threw all the blame upon him.

He was reprimanded by the superintendent, who enjoined him to be more careful for the future.

The young fellow promised not to make such a mistake again if he could help it, and justice was satisfied, and the majesty of the law vindicated.

Peace's coat and hat, which had been left behind at the jeweller's, were for some time in charge of the police. When all hope of finding its owner had been given up the garments in question were conveyed to what is termed the "Black Museum" in Scotland-yard.

This place is one of the sights of London, but it is rare indeed that any stranger is admitted into its sacred precincts. The uninitiated may possibly feel some interest in a description of this receptacle for criminal curiosities.

We subjoin an account of the place, which the reader may rest assured is genuine.

"Take care how you step," said a courteous official, who preceded the visitor up a staircase in one of the houses in Scotland-yard, and opened a door on an upper story.

"We are obliged to throw a great deal of this about;" the substance in question was a disenfecting powder.

The room into which we were conducted was a large bare-floored apartment, with barred windows, fitted up with wide shelves, which were divided into compartments, and their contents were liberally sprinkled with the all-pervading powder.

The room is that in which the articles of property taken from convicts are stowed away until they are claimed by their owners.

Of course there was not much chance of any one coming forward to claim Peace's hat and coat from the stand in the centre of this receptacle, of the objects of the "unlawful possessor" class, to which a large room up stairs is also devoted.

Overhead is the "Black Museum," in which during the last three years *pieces de conviction*, which until then had been kept indiscriminately with the other property of criminals, have been arranged and labelled, forming a ghastly, squalid, and suggestive show.

On entering the lower room the visitor is struck by its odd resemblance to a seed shop.

Hundreds of hooks stud the rims of the shelves and the sides of the compartments, and from them are suspended hundreds of little packets neatly made up in brown paper, tied with white twine, and severally distinguished by large parchment labels, each bearing a neat inscription.

The packets contain small articles taken from the prisoners, who in due course, after they are discharged from prison will be brought to Scotland-yard, and their portraits taken by force should they object to that process.

The larger things are deposited in the compartments of the shelves, and every item, no matter how insignificant, is entered into the proper register.

A motley collection are the larger articles, with a preponderance among them of grimy pocket-books and greasy purses.

But there are valuable things in some of those parcels, and downstairs in the officials' room is a massive iron safe, fitted with sliding shelves, in which is kept a large collection of watches, rings, choice pins, scent bottles, pencil cases, and other jewellery, which are either the lawful property of prisoners or have been found in their unlawful possession and confiscated, but for whom no owners have been discovered.

Among the watches are some beautiful specimens.

One in particular, taken from a costermonger, of exquisite workmanship and ornamentation, is valued at fifty pounds,

The prisoners' property room is scrupulously clean and tidy, but the look of it is forlorn and squalid, the powder lying thick on everything, and the scent of moth and rot is in the air.

Great bales of cloth and woollen stuff occupy the shelves of the central stand.

They are shaken and beaten and turned, but all to no avail; the moth and rot get at them, and the unwholesome weirdness peculiar to once worn but long unused garments is upon the articles of wearing apparel which are hung or folded up in the room.

This impression comes more strongly upon the visitor when he goes up higher still into the topmost apartment, where heaps of clothing hang upon the walls—some new, some worn.

The heaps of shawls have a draggled and furtive look, and some children's clothing has a touch of its inseparable prettiness, even here.

Old books, a picture or two, some worthless table ornaments, innumerable articles which could not be described or classed except as odds and ends, form a portion of the collection which goes on accumulating, and which has no ultimate destination.

What is to become of all this? asks the visitor, and is answered to his surprise that nobody knows, that the things are nobody's property, and nobody has the power to do anything with them.

A piece of information which makes them more ghastly and nightmare-like to the imagination than before.

An ever-growing dust heap formed of thieves' clothing and unlawful possessions, which nobody can cart away to distribute or bury out of sight for evermore—an accumulating banquet spread for the moth, the rust, and the rat—the contents of these rooms are far from pleasant to think of.

It seems supremely ridiculous, but it is a fact, that nothing but a legislative measure could rid the premises of these rotting garments, out of every fold of which one might shake with the dust an image of squalor, crime, and punishment.

Outside the door of the " Black Museum " is a shelf in the wall of the landing place.

The visitor passing it is aware of a huddled heap of dirty coats, a serge gown, and a coarse kind of rug—the skin of an animal, with red and white hair upon it.

Under the shelf, on the floor, lies some rough packing cloth.

He passes the heap carelessly, and enters the museum.

What are his first impressions of it?

They are various. That it is like a bit out of a gamekeeper's room, with a bigger bit out of a smith's forge, a touch of a carpenter's workshop, a broad suggestion of a harness-room, something of a marine store complexion (and a good deal of its odour), a lump of an open-air stall in front of a pawnbroker's shop, a little of the barrack-room gun-rack, with no bright barrels, enforced a general air of a lumber-room, with just a dash of an anatomical museum; but above all, and increasing with every moment's prolonged observation, a likeness to the cutlery booth in a foreign fair, the articles being so rusty that the said booth might have been shut up for full half-a-century, and the salesman and his customers were all ghosts.

Opposite the door, and on the face of the wall to the right, are displayed on a wooden shelf with iron rings, which convey to the visitor a hint of the open-air stall

in front of a pawn-shop in a very small way of business indeed, a common looking-glass in a wooden frame, four black glass buttons, two wisps of rope, a pair of trumpery ear-rings in card-box, two bullets, a pipe, a cluster of soft light brown hair wound round a pad, a comb, a pocket-knife, and a little wooden stand covered with glass, are the most noticeable articles. On the shelf to the right are a dirty Prayer-book, a pocket dictionary, a pair of boots, a gaudy bag worked in beads, and the crushed remains of a woman's bonnet, made of the commonest black lace, and flattened into shapelessness.

In both these instances the other impressions of the place came in too, for over the shelf fronting the door hung workmen's tools, hammer, and cleaver, and spade, and beside them to the right is just such a bundle as adorns the walls of a marine-store. It consists of a gown, a petticoat of cheap, poor stuff, bearing dreadful dim stains, and a tattered crinoline.

The visitor is in the presence of the objects which perpetuate the memory of two peculiarly horrible crimes.

The soft, brown hair is that of Harriet Lane, murdered by Wainwright; the buttons and the earrings are those which were found in the earth where her body had been buried.

The bullets were taken out of her skull. The object under the glass case is the several pieces of her skin which completed the identification of her body. The wisps of rope dragged her out of the earth under the warehouse; the cleaver, the hammer, and spade are the implements with which the horrible deed, which led to Wainwright's detection, was done.

The knife was Thomas Wainwright's, the pipe was Henry's, and when the visitor is leaving the museum he will be shown in the pack-cloth on the floor under the shelf outside the door the wrapper in which the dismembered body was packed, and one of the dirty coats—a horrid thing, with its hideous rents and smears—Wainwright's vesture on the occasion.

The coat of the captain of the " Lennie," with the gash in the cloth, torn by the knife of his murderer, and eaten through and through with rot and moth, is not nearly so disgusting an object; and as for the serge robe of that poor rogue, " Professor Zandavesta," and the little cloak of the confiscated " anatomical " wax African, who grins awfully in one corner of the museum, a real skeleton hand and arm considerably hidden behind him, they are quite cheerful to look at in comparison.

The Prayer-book and the other pitiful objects upon the shelf to the right were found on the body of Maria Clousen, who was murdered in Kidbrook-lane; the blood and mud-stained clothes were hers, and they contrast with grim-irony as evidences of an unpunished crime, with the all-gory objects which tell of one brother hanged and the other transported.

Along the wall, on the right side of the room, is ranged a choice collection of guns, crowbars, and " jemmies," the latter implements of the housebreaking industry, which admit of great variety, and are susceptible of highly artistic handling; and among them is a pair of tongs unevenly rusted, and with a dirty paper book written all over with incoherent sentences attached to it.

The tongs are those with which a man named Macdonald killed his wife some four or five years ago. He was hanged, as also were many of the proprietors of the horrid labelled assortment of hammers, knives, including the bread-carving and pocket varieties, razors and pistols which suggest a booth in a fair.

There is dried blood on all the knives and razors, and some of the hammers also, and every one of them stands for a murder or suicide.

In a terrible number of cases they record the murder of a wife by her husband.

Several of the pistols, mostly beautiful weapons, are the instruments of suicide, and each is labelled with the name, date, and place.

The simple suicides are almost all among the higher class of society; and when the visitor asks how the pistol, with which a gentleman of wealth and station shot himself, came into the keeping of the museum, he is told—

"The family mostly do not like to have it, and so they ask the police to take it away."

In a corner hang the clothes of the Rev. J. Watson, who murdered his wife at Stockwell, the horse-pistol with which he shot her, and the heavy hammer with which he knocked the nails into the chest, in which he proposed to hide her body.

So carefully had the murderer washed his trousers and his coat-sleeves, that the blood stains could only be observed with difficulty at the time of the investigation.

But since the coat and trousers have been hanging on the Black Museum's walls, the stains have come out close and thick.

"We have often noticed that," the visitor is told.

The frightful weapons used by the "Lennie" mutineers are here neatly ranged under the photograph of the ringleader, "French Peter."

Hard-by is a bundle of letters, forming the correspondence which furnished much of the evidence against Margaret Waters, the baby-farmer.

How much sin, shame, sorrow, and cruelty that small dusty bundle represents it would be hard to say.

A small billycock hat, with a mask fastened inside the broad rim, into which is packed a purse, a comforter, a small lantern, and a life-preserver with a terrific lump of lead on it, is quite a cheerful object to turn to from all these grim relics of worse crimes, though the burglar who formerly owned the life-preserver informed the police—who seized but also rescued him, having come up upon hearing his cries when he was caught between the iron bars of a window, through which he was escaping on a false alarm—that he had thoroughly intended to "do for" anyone who should interrupt him with that convenient weapon.

A large assortment of burglars' tools is not the least suggestive object here.

The weapons of the thieves' war upon society are models of good workmanship, and of the adaptation of means to ends.

When the neatest "centre-bit" of the carpenter's shop is compared with the deft, swift, noiselessly working instrument which goes into an iron shutter as a cheesemonger's scoop goes into a "fresh Dutch;" when one looks at the wedges of finely-tempered steel working between the zinc side-bits; at the two home-made dark lanterns, contrived with extraordinary cleverness out of a mustard tin and metal match-box respectively; at the rope ladder and the "beautiful litte jemmy," in a carefully buttoned red flannel case— this small, powerful tool is made of a piece of a driving wheel belonging to the finest machinery, and the metal was, of course, stolen to make it; at the bright, slender, skeleton keys; at the safe-breaking tools— which make one think that there is nothing like the old stocking in the thatch after all—one is amazed at and sorry for the misused cleverness and perverted inventiveness to which these things testify.

Among the skeleton keys is one delicate little contrivance which, at a first glance, one might take for an ornament to a lady's chatelaine; it is, in fact, a double instrument for picking latch keyholes, one part forming the key and the other lifting the spring.

This pretty trifle was made from the brass clasp of a purse, and used with such success by the inventor that in a short time he found himself in prison.

While one is actually inside the Black Museum one cannot be amused at anything, but by the time we have turned into the Strand the impression of the dreary reliquary of crime has so far passed away that one can smile at the story told of the impudent simplicity of this poor clever thief.

"When he was discharged from prison," said the curator of the Black Museum, as he restored the delicate dangling little bit of villainy to its place, "the man came here and asked us to let him have it back."

*   *   *   *   *   *   *

In a few days Peace returned to his lodgings. He was informed by the gipsy that all was going on well. No stranger had been to Leather-lane to inquire for the industrious and exemplary frame-maker.

"And so, old man, you needn't bother yourself any more," cried the gipsy.

"There will be no more stir in the matter. But you've done me a good turn, Bill, and I shan't forget it. How are you getting on?"

"How? Much the same as usual—anyhow. But I'm not driven so much in a corner as I have been once or twice in my life. I do a little with horses, and have got a swell as 'll fork out a couple of quid or so when I'm regularly hard up. He's a rum sort though. I can't quite reckon him up; he's so 'nation sly and mysterious. He it was who set me to work to prig the jewels at the 'Carved Lion.' My eye, wasn't he riled when he heard of the end o' that night's business; and it was all through you, you beggar," cried the gipsy, with a laugh. "But Lord love ye, I don't think any the worse on ye for it—not a morsel."

"Oh!" murmured Peace; "he set you to work to get the jewels, did he?"

"Yes."

"I wonder what that was for."

"I don't know."

"But I think I do."

"You don't mean that!"

"Yes, I do. They were the chief evidence in proof of Aveline Gatliffe's identity, and this swell, whoever he may be, has reason for not wishing that identity to be established. Who, and what is he?"

"Well, that I am not at liberty to make known," returned the gipsy. "He's a swell in his way, but he aint of much account as far as I can learn—leastways, he's a hot-un in many ways, so I've been told. I met him by chance when I was with my first gov'nor, and he weren't much to boast on."

"Oh, he has a motive, depend upon that, and a strong one too, I should say; but it matters not—it does not concern either of us.

"Not a bit."

Peace and the gipsy had now become what might be termed cronies or pals. To say the truth, the latter had displayed a considerable amount of faithfulness and disinterested friendship for our hero—much more than he really deserved.

In the afternoon of that day "Bandy-legged Bill" brought round his pony trap and took Peace out for a drive.

During this little excursion our hero had an eye to business. He never failed to look out for houses which he thought best adapted to his purpose. He preferred those which stood in their own grounds, detached from any others, and those also that were not near the high road, along which a policeman might be passing.

While out with the gipsy his attention was attracted to a handsome residence situated in the neighbourhood of Denmark-hill.

He noticed the place, and as he did so promised himself the pleasure of paying it a visit at no distant day, or rather night.

The gipsy, who had noticed the attention he had given to the house, pointed with his whip to the habitation in question and said, jocularily—

"The very place for you, old man—eh?"

Peace nodded.

"It's a tempting-looking crib, I must confess," he murmured.

"And is occupied by some wealthy bloke, I'll wager," said the gipsy.

"Oh, I dare say. No doubt."

"I aint good at that sort of business, but I'll drive you here any night you like, and wait for you with the trap till the job's done. Of course for a consideration," observed the gipsy, with great gravity; "business is business all the world over."

"You shan't go unrewarded, Bill."

"I don't expect half, but I must have something."

"Agreed. To-morrow night will do."

"Will it? Then I'm your man."

This little matter being settled the two friends parted at the corner of Leather-lane, the gipsy promising to call for Peace at half-past ten or from that to eleven o'clock on the following night.

In tracing the lawless career of a great criminal like Charles Peace it is not requisite to trouble the reader with a full discription of all his depredations. The leading events in his career it is our business to chronicle.

As a rule he committed most of his daring burglaries without the assistance of confederates or accomplices; but this was not always the case.

In the earlier part of his life he had many lawless companions.

At Sheffield and Manchester he was associated with a band of desperadoes.

The burglary we are about to describe was not undertaken alone, and possibly it was for this reason Peace had made one or two signal failures, and in consequence had escaped in a most marvellous manner on both occasions.

He therefore gladly accepted the service of the gipsy, in whom he felt he could place implicit confidence.

From a psychological point of view the character of Peace presents rather a curious study.

He seems to have been one of those exceptional beings in whom there was an almost innate criminal propensity, and whose infamous practices were in themselves as great a source of pleasure and satisfaction as the booty derived from them.

Mrs. Thompson, his companion in the later period of his life, has declared that he committed lawless acts for the love of adventure.

Not long ago a distinguished German psychologist said that his studies led him to regard the impulses of criminal nature in the light of natural laws.

He said that an "anthropological change," or, in other words, a defective organisation of the brain lies at the foundation of the criminal propensity of habitual thieves, murderers, &c.; that the cerebral changes were of so gross and palpable a nature as to admit of eas

demonstration in the post-mortem room, and that they might even be recognised during life by a careful examination of the criminal's head.

Whether the conformation of Peace's cranium or brain was different from that of most people we will not venture to say, but, judging from his photographs, a man like Professor Benedikt, of Vienna, might certainly find some further data for his doctrines by an examination of Peace's head.

Be this as it may, we have no doubt the cerebral organisation of such a hardened and determined fellow as Peace must have been very different from that of ordinary individuals, although we do not for a moment believe that the difference was of so gross and palpable a nature as to be detectable after death, much less before it.

None the less true, however, is the materialistic view of the criminal propensity—a view which, unfortunately, precludes all hope of our ever permanently ridding society of such characters.

As long as human nature is as it is, we shall have amongst us thieves, murderers, forgers, et hoc genus omne.

No amount of education, no penal codes, no force of example, no religious or moral suasion, will deter such men from their evil courses, or induce them to lead an honest life.

Indeed, the very propensity which seems to be "born and bred" in their flesh is fanned and encouraged by the morbid interest and sympathy of society, which considers itself outraged by their acts.

When well-dressed ladies contend for the opportunity of looking at these villains through their opera glasses, and "special correspondents" are "told off" to watch and record every change in the features of the criminal, and every word or whisper that escapes his lips, can we wonder that such men may even feel as much pleasure and pride in being infamous as their more discreet neighbours do in being honest?

Bandy-legged Bill kept his appointment, and on the following evening he drove up to Peace's door at about twenty minutes to eleven.

Peace in the meanwhile had been reconnoitring in the course of that day, in the immediate vicinity of the residence upon which he was to perform.

From what he could gather in the neighbourhood he was led to the conclusion that there was a considerable amount of property in the house. The mistress and children were said to be away on a visit to a relative. The master, who was a rich city merchant, was at home.

All these facts he had wormed out of the idlers and gossips about the place.

Before the gipsy made his appearance Peace had stained his face, and otherwise disguised himself; his implements were brought forth from their hiding place; these were in a small box, which is thus discribed by Mrs. Thompson:—

"He always had with him a red box. This he generally had left at the nearest station to the house he was about to operate on, wth a notice outside that it was to be called for.

"His tools consisted of a jemmy about fourteen inches long, having a screw at one end and a chisel at the other, which could be used as a plane also. He also carried a block of wood, which he required when using the jemmy, and a knife like a pork butcher's, which he used in cutting through panelling.

"The screw end of the jemmy was for use when the chisel end could not get a purchase in a door.

"He seldom carried lock-picks, having a wonderful

facility in making use of a piece of wire, with which he has been known to open locks of the most intricate nature.

"One great cause of his success," says the woman Thompson, "was the fact that he wore small 'fours' ladies' boots without nails; and the police, when they were put on his track, always thought the crime had been committed by a boy, judging from the footsteps."

"Here I be, old man," cried the gipsy, as Peace presented himself at the door. "Are you ready?"

Peace handed the red box to his companion, then went back into his room again, and returned with a bag and his dog Gip, both of which were placed in the cart.

In another moment the vehicle was rattling over the stones with its two occupants.

"What have you brought the dog for?" inquired Will.

"He may be of service; if we have to leave the trap I'll warrant me that he won't let anybody overhaul its contents."

"All right, guv'nor; you know best," cried the gipsy. "So on we goes, and may we be successful, and have good luck, which is what, I know, we both deserve. Eh, old man?"

"Oh, we both deserve it," answered Peace. "But people never get their deserts in this world; they either get ten times what they ought to have, or none at all. However, it isn't of much use complaining."

The vehicle went rapidly over the stones till the macadamised road was reached, and in due course of time the travellers came within sight of the palatial dwelling which had lured them to the spot.

"Now," said the gipsy, "where had I better wait with the trap?"

"There is a narrow lane runs by yonder house, wait there. If a bobby says anything to you, tell him you've lost your way, and are uncertain which road to take. But lor, it's so far removed from the high road, and is, moreover, so dark, that you will not be seen."

Peace alighted with his implements and bag, and crept through the shrubbery in front of the house.

The gipsy drove slowly on to the dark lane.

No other persons besides their two selves were to be seen.

Peace passed through the grounds unobserved by any one.

He then took a survey of the residence he was about to perform on.

No lights were visible at any of the windows, and to all appearance the inmates of the house had long since retired to rest.

Peace had been informed in the early portion of the day that the owner and his domestics were early people; he therefore concluded that the inmates were asleep.

But as he had met with one or two failures he was more than usually cautious on this occasion, so that he might render the possibility of discomfiture still more remote.

We have on a former occasion made reference to the long screw he occasionally employed in his predatory excursions; these were most ingeniously constructed. At the end of each screw was a sharp point, and the worm was so well made that the screw itself could be forced into the wood of a door without even making a hole first with a gimlet or bradawl.

A small screwdriver was the only implement required to drive home the screws.

They, however, worked much more freely or easily when a small hole was bored.

Peace was furnished with these on the night in question, and to cut off the retreat of the inmates, should any of them be aroused, and to baffle the police, should they endeavour to enter the premises without his permission, he thought it just as well to secure the front door.

He, therefore, at once proceeded to insert two of his patent screws—one near the top, and the other near the base of the door.

This done, he went to the back of the house. Here he saw two doors, one of which opened on to the lawn.

He secured both of these in the same way.

When this had been done, he climbed a spout and got on the balcony, which ran in front of one of the back windows.

He then proceeded to effect an entrance as speedily and noiselessly as possible.

He had but little difficulty in doing this, for the window had been left unfastened, owing to the carelessness of one of the maid servants, who had shot back the clasp presumably in a hurry, for it did not overlap the opposing window sufficiently to prevent its being drawn either up or down.

The shutters, however, were fastened, but very insecurely; Peace had therefore but little difficulty in throwing them back.

All this had not occupied the space of more than three or four minutes, and the movements of the burglar had not been seen by anyone, either from within or without.

Peace dropped gently on the floor of the apartment, which was covered with a thick Turkey carpet.

He had on at this time a pair of women's boots, and his footsteps were almost as soft and noiseless as those of a cat.

The room in which he found himself was furnished in the best possible manner, but there were not many articles therein which were sufficiently portable to be transferred to the burglar's bag, and Peace did not therefore waste much time in examining its contents.

He ignited one of his silent matches, and took a cursory but rapid review of its most noticable features.

Before leaving it, however, he drew back the shutters and opened the bottom window sufficiently wide to admit of his passing through in case of any surprise or alarm.

He crept downstairs and entered the front parlour. In this there were several articles of value, which he at once deposited safely in his bag.

He then proceeded towards the back parlour. This was fitted up as a library. To all appearance the owner of the habitation made use of it for business purposes, for on a library table there were spread out vast heaps of papers, tied up in bundles, with letters, ledger account books, and other objects usually found in a merchant's counting house or a lawyer's office.

In a recess at one corner of the room was a large iron safe; this at once attracted the burglar's attention. Closing the door of the room softly Peace drew from his pocket a curled waxed taper, the end of which he ignited with one of his matches.

He then made a careful examination of the safe, which, he felt assured, contained property—possibly notes and gold were encased therein.

Drawing forth his bent wire, he endeavoured therewith to pick the lock.

He twisted and turned the wire in every possible direction, but was not successful in opening the safe. But he was not a man, as we have already seen, to give up a thing easily,

"OH! MY LORD," SAID AVELINE, "PITY AND PARDON ME."

He had set his heart upon ransacking the safe, and to leave the house without effecting this object was the very last idea that would enter his mind.

He persevered with most laudable ambition, but the lock was too much for him—it was of peculiar construction.

He tried his skeleton keys with no better result. He sat down in one of the library chairs, the very image of despair; he never remembered to have been so baffled.

He had another turn at the door of the safe, which was as immovable as the Rock of Gibraltar—a place, by the way, he was afterwards destined to become acquainted with.

He now made an attempt to force open the door with his jemmy and the piece of wood he carried with him, but it resisted all his efforts, and he at last began to despair.

A sudden thought struck him—the key of the safe was doubtless somewhere in the house. Probably the owner of it had it in his pocket.

Peace crept up stairs again. Not a soul was to be seen. No one was in either the back or front room first floor.

He went up cautiously to the next story. In the front room of this he heard some one snoring.

He concluded that this was the master of the house. He opened the door for about an inch, and peered in —a man, with a dark beard and a moustache, was in bed.

He was evidently sleeping soundly. On a chair, by the side of the bed, were several garments.

There was just sufficient light for the burglar to discern these.

He felt the time had come for him to make an effort. Grasping his revolver in his right hand he crept on all fours to the side of the bed, watching as he did so the face of the sleeping man with the eyes of a lynx.

He placed his hand on a pair of black trousers, and felt something heavy in one of the pockets. Gathering them together in a heap he crept back towards the door, which he passed through in safety.

When on the landing he rifled the pockets, in one of which was a large bunch of keys.

He slid downstairs and gained the back parlour, or library, as it was usually termed by the household.

Once more he ignited his wax taper, and breathed more freely.

To his infinite delight one of the keys fitted the lock, which was turned back; then the massive doors of the safe were thrown open.

Peace looked curiously at its contents. One shelf contained a mass of documents, some books, and other articles which were of no value to the burglar.

But on one of the other shelves there was a cash-box and two canvas bags.

"All right," murmured Peace; "this is worth fighting for. My word, but it is lucky I thought of the keys being in the house."

The bags were at once placed in the one he had brought with him, the cash-box was opened with a small key he had found on the bunch abstracted from the gentleman's pocket.

Between fifty and sixty sovereigns were in the cash-box, together with a roll of notes. It is needless to observe that these found their way into Peace's pocket.

A gold cup, a silver salver, and a box containing jewels were also in the safe. These were placed in the burglar's bag to keep company with the other valuables.

Peace had been fortunate enough to have a good haul, and, having been so far successful, he thought it best to get clear off with his booty while the coast was clear.

He at once made for the back-room first-floor. From the balcony of this he let his bag gently down on to the grass plot beneath with a small piece of cord; then he climbed over the balcony, and hanging for a moment by his hands, he dropped from thence on to the grass.

Unfortunately for him, his coat-tail swept down one of the shrubs in a flower-pot; this fell on to a glass skylight over the back kitchen.

The crash of glass awoke one of the maidservants, who jumped out of bed, and, opening one of the back-windows, peered forth.

She saw a man running across the grass plot towards the shrubbery by the side of the house, and at once suspected that something was amiss.

Panting and almost breathless, Peace arrived at the spot where Bandy-legged Bill was awaiting his re-appearance.

He jumped into the cart, and told his companion to drive off at once.

Bill urged on his pony to its fullest speed, and in a very short time he and his companion were far away from the scene of the burglary.

In a short time they reached Leather-lane in safety, without the faintest degree of suspicion being attached to them.

The burglary at Denmark-hill was pronounced to be a great success both by the principal and his abettor.

Peace presented his companion with fifty pounds as a recompense for his valuable services.

It was a great deal more than the gipsy had ever expected, and he expressed himself more than satisfied—indeed, he was modest enough to intimate that it was more than he deserved.

Meanwhile the inmates of the house at Denmark-hill were aroused from their slumbers by the screaming of the servant girl, who had seen the burglar make a precipitate retreat over the lawn in the rear of her master's house.

Her fellow-servants jumped out of their beds, huddled on their things, and hastened at once to see what was the matter.

The owner of the establishment looked in vain for his trousers, which our hero had so cleverly possessed himself of.

The gentleman sought for another pair, but his wardrobe as well as the drawers in his room were locked, and his bunch of keys was not at hand.

Wrapping himself in his long dressing gown and drawers, and putting his feet into his slippers, he sallied forth.

The open safe, the black trousers on one of the chairs of the library, together with the missing property, clearly demonstrated that a burglar had been in the premises.

A search was at once instituted for the robber, but without any satisfactory result.

The merchant was furious.

He ordered one of his man-servants to hasten at once to the station and give notice to the police.

But here a difficulty presented itself.

The front door could not be opened. Peace had firmly secured it with his screws.

The whole party rushed to the back entrance, which was equally well secured.

Everybody was astonished, as well they might be. It seemed like sorcery.

One of the man-servants unfastened the shutters of the front parlour, and threw open the window, and by this means succeeded in leaving the premises.

In about a quarter of an hour he returned with three police officers.

The usual formula had to be gone through. A list of the missing articles, as far as these could be ascertained, was made by the inspector, who declared the robbery had been committed by a practised hand.

He was perfectly right, but this was but poor consolation to the owner of the property.

He asked the girl if she could identify the burglar. She answered in the negative.

She had only seen his back. His face she never caught sight of, and even assuming she had, identifica-would have been almost impossible.

There was not even a remote chance of discovering the depredator, and Peace was perfectly well assured of this.

The booty he had obtained by this burglary was considerably over two hundred pounds, after deducting the fifty he had given to Bandy-legged Bill, and as he had received a letter from his mother urging him in the strongest terms to return to Sheffield, he determined upon quitting the metropolis and taking up his quarters in his native town.

CHAPTER LI.
MISS STANBRIDGE AND HER PROTEGE—A VISIT TO A THIEVES' HAUNT.

IN a few days after our hero's successful expedition to Denmark-hill he packed up his things, had them conveyed to the station by his friend Bill, and after calling upon Laura Stanbridge and bidding her farewell, he started off to Sheffield.

He gave the gipsy a pressing invitation to pay a visit to him soon after his return.

We have now to describe another phase in the history of the boy Alf Purvis. Since the departure of the old lady, Mrs. Gover, his mistress had been more than usually kind to him, making something like a companion of him during the hours of relaxation.

One evening she said to him " Alf, I want you to go with me to the east end of the town. I purpose taking you to a place which I think will be interesting to you."

"Thank you, marm. When am I to go?"

"At once—therefore get ready without delay."

Alf did as he was bid, wondering all the while what was up, but he said nothing, wisely keeping his thoughts to himself.

When ready his mistress led him to the door. There was a cab waiting outside, but Alf remarked that the horse was a fine animal and well groomed, and that the driver wore no badge upon his coat.

"Now, then, jump in," cried his mistress; he obeyed, and was followed by Miss Stanbridge.

The driver of the vehicle, without waiting for the usual instructions as to where he was to drive to, set off at a brisk pace towards Trafalgar-square.

The cab rattled along down the Strand, which was full of noise and light, and through the ponderous arch of Temple Bar into the City, grave, dark, and silent as it is by night alone.

In a short time the vehicle passed along Leadenhall-street, Aldgate, lighted only by the street lamps, and here and there by a faint gleam from a window of some cigar shop or tavern; then they entered a street so broad, so bustling, that one would have fancied oneself in one of the great thoroughfares of the West-end, were it not for the small size of the houses and the squalid appearance of the inhabitants.

They had passed the boundary between wealth and poverty, between vice and crime.

They were now in a new world, among a race of men who were governed by different customs, by different fashions, by different codes of morality from those of civilised London.

They had crossed the frontier of Aldgate pump, and had reached the land of costermongers and thieves.

They were in Whitechapel.

It is strange what distinctive features different parts of London have.

There is a mixed population in every district, more or less, and there are unfortunately dishonest people in every quarter of this great metropolis; but the unrighteous congregate thickly in many districts which appear to be the homes of the lawless.

At one time Westminster had an unenviable reputation, at another time Whitefriars, which was known by the name of Alsatia. St. Giles's, and the Dials, and many other parts of London have still an unwholesome odour.

An interesting book might be written by detectives, who are for ever engaged in searching for thieves in their well-known resorts.

It was Saturday night when the boy and his mistress arrived at Whitechapel, and the street they were in, which was as broad as Piccadilly, presented an extraordinary appearance.

Butchers' stalls extended down to a considerable distance; the pavements were lined with retailers of fried fish and potatoes, of fruit and vegetables, and a thousand miscellaneous wares, which were displayed to view by means of stout brown paper candles, which, prepared in a peculiar manner, afforded an excellent light.

In some cases the vendors of wares made use of naphtha lamps in lieu of the candles.

Alf Purvis was watching this scene from the window of the cab with great delight, for he was familiar with the neighbourhood, which reminded him of the poor bird-catcher, who had brought him up to London.

"You know this part of London—don't you?" enquired Laura Stanbridge.

"Yes, marm, very well. Whitechapel was the first place I came to after leaving the farmer."

"Ah—so I think you told me."

The cab now suddenly wheeled to the right, and went through a labyrinth of dark and wretched streets, in which nothing could be seen except a few shops full of rags and bones, and placards offering a farthing a pound for the bones, and a penny for the rags.

The cab stopped at the corner, and the driver came round and opened the door.

"Will you get out here," said he, addressing himself to the young lady, "or shall I drive further on?"

"I think this will be near enough for my purpose," she answered. "We are close to Little Mint-street?"

"Yes—quite close."

"Good, then, we'll alight;" and, springing out, the lady walked down the street with the assurance of one who was well acquainted with the locality.

Alf followed his mistress. He did not know what was about to happen, but had some misgivings.

For the locality he had no predilection, for his early experience of it had taught him that it was a place to be avoided; but, situated as he was, he had no other alternative left than to merely submit to the dictates of his patroness.

After a few minutes he heard a whistle and the rumbling of a train. He started, and said—

"There's some railway here, I s'pose?"

"Yes," returned his companion, "the Blackwall. We shall get under it presently."

By the light of a lamp he saw a smile pass over her features.

A strange feeling of doubt and mistrust took possession of him.

"Why was he brought hither? It seemed most singular."

They were soon beneath the arch of the railway, when, instead of passing through it, Miss Stanbridge turned and pointed to the right.

Alf shuddered. They were standing at the mouth of a narrow street, as black and repulsive as a cavern.

It ran under the railway for some distance, the archway being propped up by iron posts.

Thus this street was always dark—it was a tomb; its inhabitants were buried alive, the only sun was the hot blaze of the engines which passed over their heads.

"What a queer street for people to live in!" exclaimed Alf. "I didn't know there was such a street."

"Didn't you? Well, we live and learn. The people are as queer as the habitations," returned his mistress, with a merry laugh.

Alf thought there was not much to laugh at. In fact, he was more disposed to feel dispirited and depressed.

This was not to be wondered at, for the locality was a perfect den of iniquity. The street was inhabited chiefly by women, who were the most abandoned and criminal of their sex; they were foul abusive creatures, and here they lived—a republic of demons.

The boy felt intuitively that he was in the unwholesome atmosphere which was breathed by the very worst of the human species. He shuddered and crept close to his companion, who took him by the hand and led him along the street."

"You seem to be a little disconcerted," said she. "What's the matter, Alf?"

"I shall be glad when we are out of this vile street," he returned.

"Oh, don't be alarmed, my boy—there's no one will harm you."

"I don't like the place," cried Alf.

If he had been disgusted with the place upon first making its acquaintance, he was still more so as he proceeded along.

At the sound of strange steps lights gleamed on all sides, and women emerged from every door. Many of them were only partially clothed, and the appearance they presented was perfectly loathsome. Their faces were swollen with drink, and the expression of their features was simply disgusting.

They surrounded Alf like a set of harpies, and he became positively frightened.

Laura Stanbridge, however, came to his rescue. She spoke to them in an authoritative tone, which could not be misunderstood by them, albeit the language she made use of was not comprehended by the boy.

Her words, however, seemed to have the desired effect, for the wretched besotted creatures parted on one side, and let the two passengers pass without any attempt at further molestation.

Alf Purvis was delighted when they came to a small lane branching out of the street under the railway. This was as dark as Erebus.

There were no lights and no houses, only a dead wall on each side.

"Well, this beats all," cried the boy. "This *is* a place."

"Yes," murmured his mistress. "We must be careful how we proceed along."

She produced a bull's-eye lantern from her pocket, and made the light therefrom precede her as she walked.

"Isn't there danger?" inquired her companion.

"None in the least."

"Oh, I'm glad to hear that."

The lane ended in a yard and in a tall dingy house, which appeared as if it had been uninhabited for years.

Taking a stone from the ground, Laura Stanbridge knocked several times against the door, and then, pausing for a moment, gave a single rap.

"Are we to go in here, then?" inquired the boy.

"Yes, certainly. This is our destination."

The door swung open, and they entered.

But they had not yet gained the unhallowed precincts of the mysterious habitation.

Alf was watching the movements of his mistress with evident anxiety.

Another door was before them with a glass window above it.

Miss Stanbridge wetted her finger and rubbed it across the window in such a way as to elicit a loud screeching noise.

The effect of this was magical.

A face appeared at the window, which was protected by huge iron bars.

"Who's there, and what's your business?" said a voice.

"A lady and a lad on the fly," returned Miss Stanbridge.

"It's the voice of the duchess," said the voice above.

"Yes, it's the duchess," answered Laura. "All right."

The door was opened, and they went down some steps into a large room.

Alf's eyes wandered over this with all the curiosity of a lad who finds himself in a scene which is new and strange to him.

His companion, however, seemed perfectly at her ease, and the most noticeable features of the apartment were quite familiar to her.

There were two long tables from fireplace to fireplace, running parallel with each other.

They were laid with greasy napkins, iron plates, chipped tea cups filled with salt, two small stone jars filled with mustard, and knives and forks chained to the table.

A number of candles in the shades nailed to the wall, lighted the room. These being never snuffed were appropriately invested with *thieves*, which streamed in large flakes upon the floor, the seats, and the backs of the guests.

In this place professional thieves and ruffians of every description were accustomed to congregate, and here numberless robberies were concocted. It was the resort of lawless men, who waged ceaseless war against society.

Here they were accustomed to boast of their exploits as if robbery was a thing to be proud of. The place was a foul den, a very plague-spot—which, however, it seemed out of the power of anybody to remove.

The police knew perfectly well that it was the resort of thieves, but for some reason or another it seemed to be beyond the reach of the law. There are hundreds of similar places in London.

One fireplace was black and empty, but the other blazed with an enormous fire—the temple of a blear-eyed salamander-like old woman, upon whom were fixed, in one long look of hunger and anxiety, the eyes of a vast assemblage of men and women who were seated at two tables, clad in disguises at once loathsome and appalling.

"He's not a bad sort," said a black-bearded man to Miss Stanbridge "him as keeps this 'ere establishment—he'll do a bloke a good turn at times."

"Yes, so I've heard," she answered.

The man went on :—

"He's one of your rough and ready customers, but he's none of your smile-in-the-face-and-cut-your-throat blokes, for all his ugly mug and swivel eye."

"Where is he?" inquired Alf, who began to be interested.

"Aint here at present, young shaver," answered the

man; "leastways I don't see him anywhere in the room."

"And who are those persons?" inquired the boy, nodding towards the group at the table.

"Those? Oh, they are cadgers," answered the man, with something like contempt in his tone, "only cadgers."

The waitress of this delectable establishment, "Limpey Meg," as she was usually termed, now came towards them, flourishing in her hand a brown napkin.

"Well, Meg; still as nimble on your pins as ever?" cried the dark-bearded man. What's the news, lass? All quiet? Any 'crushers' been here?"

"No, never a one," answered Meg; "all quiet, plenty of business, and no inquiries, that's the way to say it," she added with another flourish of the napkin.

In a few minutes after this a yell was raised, the tables were covered with joints and vegetables served up on iron dishes. It was not long before they were all served, and it was a strange sound to hear the noisy clattering of knives and forks upon the iron dishes, and the tinkling of the chains.

Laura and her protégé watched all these proceedings, none of the dinner party taking the slightest notice of them—indeed, they did not appear to be conscious of their presence, albeit, the boy's companion was known to the majority if not to all of them.

Presently Limping Meg came forward again and spoke in a respectful manner, and in an under-tone to Miss Stanbridge.

"Ax yer parding, marm, but perhaps you might be a wanting to see the Smoucher?"

"Where is he, Meg?"

"He's up in his room with the cracksman, and a lot more. They be full o' b'isness."

"He'll find time to see me, I daresay," returned Alf's mistress.

She passed through a large apartment and went upstairs to a room on the first story, which was small and almost filled with ragged men and women.

In this room also was the dark-bearded man whom Alf had conversed with below.

"What are they doing, sir?" inquired the boy.

"Making a cadger," returned the man who then whispered to a short, thick-set fellow next to him, who whispered to somebody else, and Alf heard them saying as they glanced at his mistress—

"That's Laura Stanbridge, the most famous she-fence in London, and she cuts it fat at the West-end of the town."

Then the men nodded mysteriously to one another.

Laura, however, did not seem to hear what they said. If she did she deemed it prudent to keep silent.

The most noticeable person in the room was a thin-featured man with a bushy beard, seated at a small table; low cunning was depicted on his ferret-like features. In front of him, on the table at which he was writing, was a bundle of papers; by the side of the man was a pale boy in rags.

Alf looked inquiringly at his mistress, who informed him in a low whisper that the man with the grey beard was known as the Smoucher. He was a writer of begging-letter petitions, and was employed in fabricating all sorts of documents for the brotherhood who frequented the establishment.

He was, in fact, the accredited secretary to thieves of all denominations. He was thoroughly versed in flash language, and sometimes the epistles he wrote were couched in language which, to the uninitiated, would be quite unintelligible.

We give two specimens, with translations of the same, of the phraseology made use of by thieves, and the reader may rest assured that these are reprints from documents which have been found on the persons of criminals.

FLASH LANGUAGE.

"DEAR DICK,—I have seen the swag chovey bloke who christened the yacks quick. I gave him a double finnip. I am now on the shallow. I have got the yacks, so do not come it fight cocum. I am at the old padding ken, next door to puddling crib. I am gadding the hoof, but quick be a duffer, now on the square. I want a stalsman buttoner to nail prads. I last week worked the nulls. I have lost my joiner mun now."

TRANSLATION.

DEAR DICK,—I have seen the person who bought the watches, and he altered the name in them immediately. I gave him a ten pound note for doing it. I am now going half naked to avoid suspicion. I have got the watches back again—therefore do not turn informer. Be wary and sly. I am stopping at the old lodging-house, next door to the boys' lodging-house. Do not say a word, but be very quiet. I am going about without shoes, but shall soon turn hawker. I am at present honest. I want a partner. Will you come and join me, and then we will commence stealing horses? I last week got through a great many bad five shilling pieces. I have left my fancy girl. Be sure you say nothing.

Another :—

DEAR BILL,—I have seen Cheeks. You must meet us at the old mushroom faker's at eleven; if not there go to the old padding ken—bring all your screws. The case of a bloak is planted, to be cracked, plenty of finnips, also some long tailed ones; be mum with your joiner, fight cocum, and be cocum with boozing kens, only a bloak and a shikster in the case, except a pig. Be cocum crabshells; a goun off was last week booked by a fly through crabs. I have seen a kidsman, who will fence two finnips three finnips. There are no flys about.

TRANSLATION.

DEAR WILLIAM,—I have seen "Cheeks" (a flash name for an accomplice), and you must meet us at the old umbrella mender's at eleven o'clock, and if we are not there go to the old lodging house. Bring with you all your housebreaking instruments. We have arranged to break the house of a gentleman who has plenty of five pound notes, and also some large bank notes. Be sure you do not name this to your fancy girl. Be careful what you do, and keep from drinking shops. There is nothing in the house but a gentleman and a lady and another person. Do not put on your own shoes, a brother thief did last week and was taken by a policeman. I have seen a person who trains boys to thieve, who will take all the five pound notes at ten pounds for fifteen. There are no policemen in the neighbourhood.

The den of mystery to which Laura Stanbridge had paid a visit contained ruffians of every conceivable description.

Lolling in an arm-chair behind the table, with a huge junk of bread and meat in one hand, and a glass of gin and water in the other, and a short black pipe in his mouth, was a burly ruffian, with strength written in his brawny arms and broad shoulders and prominent heaving chest, with villainy in his deep hollow eyes and his cropped black whiskers and eyebrows, which were half an inch apart.

This was the cracksman—a famous burglar, and a

pal of the Smoucher in all the lays which the latter devised and the former accomplished.

This huge miscreant had been at one time a boon companion and accomplice of Gregson, whom he resembled in a remarkable degree.

The untimely end of the Bristol Badger failed to have the slightest effect in turning this callous criminal from his evil ways.

"Now, young man," said the Smoucher, looking up from his papers, "you said you could read, I think?"

"Yes, a little, sir. I've been to school."

"All right, so much the better; nothing like education. Your friends say you are to try your luck at cadging in the country, where people's green and food's cheap. Take this paper and chalk up on the post of every door you go to one of these marks, according to the character of the people you meet with there; that will act as a clue to any brother cadger who may chance to come after you as to what treatment they are likely to expect."

The paper contained a series of marks or signs, which are known only to cadgers.

The boy took the paper and thrust it into his pocket.

The man at the table then gave him several recipes for disfiguring his body so as to present the appearance of burns or scalds, together with other accidents, all of which he laid down to his young pupil in a most systematic business-like manner.

Alf Purvis was astonished at these mysterious proceedings, but he remained silent.

A man now came up to the table and said to the Smoucher—

"What do you charge for a petition?"

"Eighteen pence," was the answer.

"Well, then, let's have one."

The Smoucher placed two ink bottles before him—they were filled with ink of two different shades. He then spread a bit of paper under his hand and began writing.

"He's a stunner at using the pen," said one, looking on. I wish I knew how to do it."

"You'd soon find yourself in the 'steel' if you did, old man," cried one of the party.

The Smoucher, having finished the document upon which he was engaged, folded up the same, creased the paper as if it had been long written, and after examining the signatures attached thereto of ministers and church-wardens, he dipped his fingers under the fireplace, and smeared it with ashes, to the infinite delight of the lookers on, who swore that there wasn't one in twenty who wouldn't take it for a real concern.

The man, having folded this precious document in his green *kingsman* or green silk pocket handkerchief, and placed it in his hat, after the manner of the Persians, departed.

A little more business was transacted in the same manner, and then the cracksman, Laura, and the boy were left alone with the smoucher.

"Well, Laura," said the latter, in a pleased tone, "who would have thought of seeing you here, and you've brought a stranger with you?" he added, glancing at Alf Purvis. "He looks too genteel for this place."

"He's sharp, and willing to learn."

"Ah, I see; you want him taught—wish to have him put in training, eh?"

Laura Stanbridge nodded.

"Well, if you mean business, he must be brought regularly up to the trade—or profession, more properly speaking."

"Certainly, that is right enough."

"And who do you think of binding him to?"

"That's just the question I was going to ask you."

"Me? I don't know what answer to make."

The Smoucher leant his head on his hand and began to ruminate.

"There's a gentleman we both on us know," said the cracksman, "an' both on us respect. His name is Mathew Furness. He began life as a half shallow in the streets; from a shiverer he became a cadger, from a cadger he became duffer (pedlar), from a duffer he became an area sneak, a shop bouncer, and a fogle-tugger. From a fogle-tugger he became a swell mob-bite, and then a rampsman, and then a cracksman. He has ascended from the very foot to the very summit of his honourable and scientific profession. And besides that he is up to all the other little games of life that are worth knowing. He has been a 'shoful man' and a 'smasher,' and a racecourse flat-catcher, and he's as famed a fence as Ikey Solomon or Laura Stanbridge, the Swell-street (West-end) Adam Tiler."

"There's no doubt Matt's a great man—a very great man," said the cracksman, meditatively.

"And who so well adapted to take my young gentleman in hand?" cried Miss Stanbridge.

The Smoucher had not vouchsafed any reply to the adulatory harangue.

"The only question is, will he do so?" said Laura.

"I'll do my best," returned the man of many letters.

"You'll do nothing of the sort. Not if I know it," cried a voice from the further end of the room.

The speaker was the landlord of the establishment. He had short black crisp hair, a swivel eye, and his features were certainly not handsome.

"Well I am blest, this beats cockfighting," cried the burglar. "What business is it of yourn, Sam?"

"I'll make it my business," returned the landlord. "It shan't be done, I tell ye. I wont have anything of the sort take place in my house. We all know what we are, but that's no reason a younker like that, who in all likelihood is gently bred and born, should be ruined for life."

"There's an end of the matter, Sam," said the Smoucher. "I for one wont have any hand in the business."

The tables were suddenly turned. The landlord's word was law; he held the life and liberty of his customers in his hand, and if he chose to round on them it would go hard with all.

Miss Stanbridge was unprepared for this issue. She took the boy by the hand and led him out of the room.

"I hope you'll have a better office when you come here again," cried the landlord as she descended the stairs.

She made no reply, but went into the room below.

While all this had been taking place a woman had been stationed outside the den of iniquity, clinging to the iron railings which ran round the front of the habitation; her eyes were directed towards the windows which shone so brightly.

She watched intently, but could not see the groups of persons in the large room, but she heard the confused sounds as of many voices.

She heard also obscene and blasphemous ribaldry, which were greeted with shouts of horrible laughter.

She clung closer to the railings, and heaved a deep sigh.

A boy's voice clear and melodious rang from that abode of infamy and crime, and soared like a lark's carol towards the sky; but although the voice was musical it was sullied by the words which it pronounced.

The woman heard the voice. In her eyes shone a strange and lurid light. She moaned upon the pavement, and tore her grey hairs while the tears poured down her cheeks.

Had any one seen this strange woman their hearts would have been moved to pity, so supremely wretched did she appear.

" He is there with the pestiferous odious crew of wretches," exclaimed the woman. " He is there—I hear his voice. Ah, why do I love this boy? What secret and unknown power is it that draws me like a loadstone to this accursed spot? I cannot help it. Why do I take an interest in this poor lad? He is naught to me, and I dare not see him again. I am in her power, and she has neither pity or remorse."

The woman arose, pressed her hands to her temples, and shuddered.

Taking one last lingering glance at the thieves' haunt she turned, and hastily left the spot.

Laura Stanbridge and Alf passed through the den, and walked on till they came within sight of the cab, which was waiting for them. They entered the vehicle in question, and were driven rapidly home.

Soon after this the first streaks of dawn and yellow glimmers of light appeared above the housetops.

And the creatures of vice were creeping back to their homes with pale and haggard countenance; and the creatures of labour were rising while it was yet dark, and the great city was waking once more to its toils and its sorrows, its pleasures and its sins.

CHAPTER LII.

THE EARL AND HIS GRAND-DAUGHTER.

WE have now to return to other characters in our story.

Aveline Gatcliffe made a protracted stay at Broxbridge Hall. Like a giddy moth she fluttered around the candles of the rich and great, and in her new sphere of action felt something like pride and satisfaction.

She was made much of not only by the old nobleman, but by his visitors—by the vicar, the lawyer, and a host of other people—so that she was fain to stop very much longer than she had at first contemplated.

Lord Ethalwood talked to her of the great world—of its brilliant pleasures and its honours. He told her how such beauty as hers would command universal homage; that in London, even amidst the noblest of ladies, she would be a queen.

He tempted her with the most costly jewels, with the most magnificent dresses and lavished luxury upon her.

She had the use of a luxurious carriage; she had servants to wait upon her, hand and foot.

He tempted her through her love of the beautiful; he surrounded her with everything that was most graceful and choice; he cultivated her taste, and he spoke highly of her appreciation.

He tempted her through the innate refinement that had always distinguished her—he ministered to her in every possible way. He spoke always with the greatest contempt of poverty, of all approaches to vulgarity, and he spoke with the most condescending pity of those whose position in life was inferior to his own.

Day by day Aveline loved her new life more and more; it was so pleasant to wander in those splendid grounds, under the shade of the ancestral trees; it was so pleasant to live in those delightful rooms, with their thick, soft carpets, their superb furniture, those rare pictures and the profusion of flowers—to have carriages, horses, jewels, dresses, every luxury that imagination could devise.

It was so pleasant always to have a purse full of money, to know that she had never to trouble about ways and means, to have respect, homage, flattery shown to her.

She thought with a shudder of the little cottage at Wood Green; she contrasted her husband, in his working clothes, with the polished gentlemen she saw around her.

She was weak of soul, weak of purpose, weak of heart, weak of will. The past, with its poverty and privations, became hateful to her. She loved the present, she dreaded the thought of returning to her humble home, of giving up her jewels, of growing again accustomed to an obscure life. How she would miss the grandeur, the luxury, the magnificence of Broxbridge Hall !

Yet she loved Tom, loved him as dearly and deeply as her light nature would allow her to love. There were nights when her pillow was wet with tears, when she sobbed as though her heart would break, but with the morning sunshine these thoughts would be scattered and dispelled.

She never forgot her husband. There was hardly an hour in which her heart did not turn to dear Tom, but she was vain, fond of luxury, easily persuaded, and the love of self, the love of wealth and magnificence, was stronger than her love for him.

Then, when Lord Ethalwood thought the love of present surroundings had taken deep root, he again addressed her in reference to the all-important subject.

Aveline and her child had been looking over a book with characters cunningly wrought on vellum. It contained the chronicles of the house of Ethalwood, and had been the work of years.

The earlier chronicles dated back some centuries, and the missal, which was quaint and curious, had been originally commenced by an old monk. Lord Ethalwood explained to his granddaughter the many parts of the volume which were to her unintelligible.

" My child, my own Aveline," said the Earl, closing the volume, " it is fit and proper that you should know something of your illustrious ancestors, especially as this little fellow is destined, by God's blessing, to carry on the line in his person. Have you thought, my darling pet, of what I hinted at during the first few days of your visit ?" said he, in a more serious tone.

" Thought !" cried she. " Alas, my lord, I have thought of many things—indeed, to say the truth, I am always thinking."

" You are now in your proper sphere," he said, quickly, " and I hope and trust you have no desire to leave it."

" No," she answered, hesitatingly. " No, my lord, I should be ungrateful indeed if I did, but then there's my husband."

Lord Ethalwood held up his hand reprovingly.

" I charge you, Aveline, as you love this boy, as you respect me, not to mention that man's name in my presence." He said this in so severe a tone that Aveline grew alarmed.

She fell on her knees before the earl, and placed her hand softly on his.

" Oh, sir !—oh, my lord !" she ejaculated. " Pity and pardon me. I did not mean to offend you—indeed I did not, but——"

" But what, Aveline ?" he inquired, coldly.

" I fear you will be angered."

" No, go on. Be frank with me."

" I am sure, my lord, you are of too generous and just a nature to blame any woman having some consideration for her husband, whom she has sworn to honour, love, and obey."

"This is simply ridiculous. You must have been reading some highly-coloured romance, or perchance a melodrama. Let us return to sense and reason. I will not attempt to influence you—will not make use of either threats or entreaties. I will simply lay before you both paths in life; you shall choose as you will. You must either give up your husband, or—give up me!"

"Ah! my lord, you cannot mean it?"

"I do. I am not accustomed to say what I do not mean."

"I am well assured of that, my lord," she answered; "but you are not unreasonable, and will have some consideration for your granddaughter, who has every desire to please you and to act in accordance with your expressed wishes."

"Pause, my child," said the earl, "and sit ye down. If you have every desire—which I do not doubt—to listen to my counsel, I shall not have any reason to complain or be dissatisfied; but promises are one thing, and performance another."

"I hope you do not think so badly of me as to suppose I should forfeit my word."

"I have the best opinion of you," said Lord Ethalwood, handing his fair companion a seat; "but for divers reasons, Aveline, I must be plain with you," he added. "I shall not seek to influence you. I simply lay both paths in life before you. It is for you to make your election. If you make up your mind to return, and take your boy with you, so be it—I will not reproach you; but for his sake, if for none other, I charge you to duly consider this matter."

"I have considered it."

"With what result?"

"Oh, sir, I am in duty bound to obey you; but this is my first visit. You can have no possible objection to my returning to Wood Green for awhile, and consulting my husband."

"Oh, as to that, I must admit that your request is but reasonable. You are at liberty to return whenever you please; but as to taking the advice of a man who is so immeasurably inferior to me and mine, that is not to be thought of."

"I do not mean to take his advice. All I desire is to explain to him how I am situated."

"Ah, I understand. You can explain to him, but I suppose you propose returning to your proper sphere. I have already told you that your fate is in your own hands. You have to choose between rank and wealth, poverty and obscurity. Do not think I shall ever change, my dear Aveline. If you desire to remain with this young engineer, so be it. If, on the contrary, you decide to remain with me, I will make you heiress of all my fortune, and your son shall be my heir-at-law. You shall have every advantage I can offer you. I will find some lady accustomed to the usages of good society and the ways of the world, to give you two or three months' instruction, so that you may be fitted to mix with the proudest in the land, and then next season you shall go to London. You shall be mistress of Broxbridge Hall and one of the most magnificent mansions in the metropolis.

"You shall be a queen, a leader of fashion, you shall have unlimited wealth, more than you can possibly desire, and your boy, your beautiful child, shall succeed to a large fortune."

The face of Aveline Gatliffe flushed as she listened, and then grew suddenly pale.

"And what is the condition of all this this, my lord?" she inquired.

The earl did not make any immediate reply. He gazed intently in her face as if he would read her innermost thoughts—then, after a pause, said, in a firm tone of voice—

"That you give up your husband, who—but I need not tell you what he is—and be with me, be my adopted daughter."

"The proposal is cruelly hard."

"Not so hard as you think," he rejoined. "Rank always has its penalties. How many queens have married for the good of their kingdom, and have given up the men they really loved? How many noble ladies at the call of duty have married men whom they have positively disliked? You do not understand these things, my dear Aveline. Not at present, but let us hope you will do so in good time."

"I confess I do not," she answered, sadly.

"Well, my darling, you are not required to suffer in a like degree. You have but to leave a man whose tastes, habits, and manners do not and cannot possibly accord with your own."

"I have never had any reason to complain of my husband," she answered quickly.

"Bah!" he ejaculated, "do not offend me by laudatory encomiums on one who is so far beneath you; but enough of this. You must think this matter seriously over, my dear Aveline. You know my wishes, and I do hope and trust you will endeavour to act in accordance with them.

"I shall do my best," she answered, sadly; "but I suppose you will not forbid my returning to Wood Green for a short time—only for a short time?"

"I should not be justified in refusing this request," he murmured, bending over her and kissing her fondly. "I am an old man, Aveline," he observed, thoughtfully, "and the few years that may be yet in store for me would be brightened by your presence. Think of that, my child, and do not deem me harsh or exacting. Your husband I can never receive. Weigh the matter well over before you decide. For both our sakes it would be desirable that you should follow my advice, but I leave it for you to determine; and so, my child, return to your home at Wood Green as soon as you please, but remember all I have said to you."

Aveline Gatliffe rose from her seat, embraced the old nobleman, and crept softly out of the library.

Later in the day Mr. Chicknell made his appearance at Broxbridge—the earl had sent a telegram to him to come down as soon as possible to the Hall.

"I am glad you've come, Chicknell," said Lord Ethalwood, when the lawyer entered the library— "glad for many reasons."

The man of parchment rubbed the palms of his hands together, and smiled grimly.

"Be seated," said his patron.

Chicknell drew a chair towards the table and sat down.

"Well, my lord," he murmured. "Is everything going on as you desire?"

"Pretty well. You have not seen this young man, I suppose?"

"I have not deemed it expedient to do so at present —not till I received further commands from your lordship."

"You have acted with your usual discretion."

"Thank you, my lord."

"But a truce to compliments. Let us to business. My granddaughter is desirous of returning to Wood Green."

"I LEAVE IT FOR MY HUSBAND TO DETERMINE," SAID AVELINE.

"Ah!" ejaculated the attorney.

"Yes, but only for a time. Understand that, only for a short period."

The lawyer nodded.

"I think she is disposed to accede to my wishes—at least, that is my impression."

"I am delighted to hear it."

"Well, this being so, I have thought it best to humour her; let her have her own way; she'll soon be glad to return to Broxbridge."

"You think so?"

"I feel assured of it; but that is not of any imme-diate moment. What I have sent to you for is to beg a favour."

"There is no favour Lord Ethalwood can possibly require from so poor an individual as myself."

"Aye, but there is. What I want you to do is to escort my granddaughter to her husband's house. After then it would be advisable for you to see Mrs. Maitland, who, from what I have heard, is a sensible worthy woman. Wrench spoke in the highest terms of her."

"I will make it my business to see her."

"Yes, and you can explain many things which may be most important for her to know—such as our relative positions, my determination as regards this low-bred fellow, my wish to place Aveline in her proper sphere ; and in addition to all this you may tell her that the only way open to effect this desirable object is for this young man to give up all claim upon the lady who has demeaned herself by becoming his wife. I leave the matter for you to arrange. I don't mind allowing this young fellow a handsome income ; in point of fact I commission you to arrange with him. If he is open to reason I will settle a certain sum on him for the remainder of his life, provided he agrees to sign a deed of separation."

"I'll do my best to carry out your wishes, but the task is by no means an easy one."

"Tut, man, I'll dare be sworn it is much easier than we either of us anticipate. Fellows of his class are not likely to refuse a competency for life. If you play your cards well the matter will be easy enough. A deed of separation, signed by both parties, would be most desirable. Don't you see that, Chicknell ?"

"Doubtless it would, as far as you yourself are concerned."

"You are not wanting in penetration, and are well adapted to bring this affair to a successful issue. Nay, I am sure you will be able to do so if you choose," said Lord Ethalwood, with pointed emphasis.

"If I choose," repeated the lawyer. "I do hope your lordship will do me the justice in believing that I shall not shrink from the performance of what I deem a duty."

"I am sure of that ; pardon my expressing any doubt, but to say the truth, Chicknell, I appear to be full of doubts and fears. Aveline must return—that is quite certain. She must see this low-bred fellow whom she calls her husband, but she will return to Broxbridge. I feel assured of that, for she has pledged her word, which I do not think she is likely to forfeit, and in addition to this there are other cogent and weighty reasons for her to seek the hospitable walls of her ancestors."

Mr. Chicknell bowed, and said he quite coincided with his lordship in the opinion he had expressed.

In two days after this conversation Aveline Gatliffe and her little boy left Broxbridge under the charge of Mr. Chicknell, who accompanied them to Wood Green.

Upon arriving at their destination they found nobody at the little cottage, save a little girl, who had been engaged by Mrs. Maitland to wait upon Gatliffe, who was expected home in about an hour.

Aveline took off her things, and awaited the return of her husband.

The lawyer paid a diplomatic visit to Mrs. Maitland.

Tom Gatliffe's joy knew no bounds when he beheld his wife and child seated in the parlour.

The meeting between husband and wife was of a tender and touching nature.

The former seemed almost beside himself with joy—the latter, however, although as affectionate as could

very well be desired, displayed at times a certain restraint.

"You have come back, my own darling Aveline," exclaimed Gatliffe, "and will, I think, never leave me again."

His wife made no reply to this.

"Eh, dearest ?" he again murmured. "Do you mean never to leave me again."

"Well, Tom, that depends upon circumstances you know. I cannot promise—indeed it would be unjust and wrong to do so. The earl, my grandfather, is an old man, and old people are at times whimsical. I fear I shall have to return."

A dark shade passed over the features of the engineer, who looked hard at the speaker.

"Have to return ?" he murmured.

"I suppose so ; but don't let us trouble ourselves about that."

She placed her arms round the neck of her husband, who for her sake forbore from asking any further questions.

For some days after Aveline's return nothing occurred to disturb the harmony of her small domestic circle ; albeit the engineer could not fail to note the air of refinement which seemed to surround his wife, and pervade all her actions. He grew alarmed.

There came one evening when Tom Gatliffe sat in his garden a prey to most anxious thoughts. The sun was setting, and the birds were singing in the green depths of the trees.

He had returned home that evening, and had found Aveline with a sad pale face standing listlessly at the cottage window.

The smile that usually greeted him was absent from her pale face.

He loved her too fondly to offer any remonstrance—he went up to her and embraced her tenderly.

She appeared listless and abstracted, and took but little notice of his endearments.

He was pained and troubled, and said, after a pause—

"My dear, you don't appear to be well. Are you poorly ?"

"No—oh, dear, no," she exclaimed, flinging her arms round his neck, with a low passionate cry, and hiding her face against his shoulder.

"I am sure you are not well," he repeated. "Something's the matter."

"There is nothing the matter—nothing at all. What puts such a thought into your head ? You seem to have such strange fancies."

"Me, fancies ?"

"Well, yes—more than you used to have."

"My dear girl, what will you say next ?" he exclaimed, with a hollow attempt at a laugh, which, to say the truth, was a dismal failure, for deep down in the bottom of his heart sat fear—a terrible, nameless, ill-defined fear.

"I cannot quite understand you, Aveline," he said sadly. "You are so changed, so variable, so unlike your own sweet self. One moment you are here with your arms clasped round my neck ; the next, you are cold and reserved, and as haughty as though you were a princess and I your slave. At times you seem to love me ; and then, again, you seem to despise me. I cannot make it out. One day I think you are perfectly happy ; the next, you are silent and engrossed with melancholy thoughts. Aveline, there must be a cause for all this. You are tired of your husband, and feel it hard to dwell in this humble abode. Tell me if this is not so ? I can bear it. Do not hesitate to speak the truth; for it is far better for me to know the worst than be kept in a state of suspense."

She clasped her arms round his neck and said he was the dearest, best, and truest of husbands.

He sighed deeply as he soothed her. What had come to this lovely young wife of his?

He little dreamed of the terrible struggle in the heart of her whom he had believed at one time to be all his own.

"I am afraid to say what I think," cried Gatliffe, "and perhaps it had better remain unsaid."

"I wish you to say what you think. Nothing would please me better," she answered. "Tell me what it is."

"Why, that you are more attached to your grandfather than your husband."

"Ah, shame upon you to make such an observation!" cried she.

"I hope I am not mistaken. But tell me, has this proud earl ever invited me to his grand house?"

The young wife's face became suffused with a deep blush. She hardly knew what reply to make.

"Oh, I am convinced he has not," said Gatliffe.

"No, he has not."

"He need not be afraid. I am not good enough for him, and shall never trouble him," he exclaimed, with something like bitterness in his tone.

Aveline was pained. She could not find it in her heart to make her husband acquainted with the insurmountable barrier which separated him from the earl—a barrier which nothing could remove.

It seemed to her that her very soul was rent in twain.

She longed, with an intensity of longing, for the wealth, the position, the grandeur, which she had left behind at Broxbridge.

It seemed so cruel that she should be deprived of all these glorious advantages because she loved her husband, and was constrained from a sense of duty to remain with him.

How happy would she be, installed at Broxbridge as mistress of the grand old mansion!

No wonder, when she thought of this, that she grew sad, silent, and unhappy.

The little cottage became unbearable then, the needful little economies most hateful, the husband for whom she was sacrificing so much a source of aversion.

Then a sudden fit of remorse would seize her—she would prove her love for him by every possible means—she would laugh and sing, all to show him that she was happy—she would utter a thousand little extravagances about their little home and her affection for it.

And then would follow the reaction, and she would be intensely wretched again.

So matters went on for three long weeks, until her health began to give way.

A nobler woman, having once determined to make the sacrifice, would have abided by it; not so with her, however—she wavered even while she believed herself most firm.

She looked ill—her face was always either flushed or white, her hands trembled; she was nervous, hysterical, and unlike herself.

In vain her husband tried everything to please her; he was, if possible, more unhappy than herself.

She could not be contented with her lot at Wood Green. It was not possible for her to forget Broxbridge and its surroundings

It had been such a glimpse of paradise to her. Now the gates were shut and she was debarred from entering.

So the fourth week dawned.

She was in receipt of a letter from the earl. It was couched in the most affectionate terms. In it the writer inquired when she would return to the home of her ancestors.

She did not deem it prudent to show this epistle to her husband, as his name was not mentioned therein, but it contained an intimation that Mr. Chicknell would pay her an early visit.

Meanwhile the astute lawyer had been endeavouring to bring Mrs. Maitland over to the earl's way of thinking.

He had not as yet made known to the lady his client's proposition for a deed of separation.

Matters were not ripe enough for that at present. He must play with fish before he landed it.

Mrs. Maitland, who was honest and straightforward, besought him to speak plainly but kindly to the young engineer. She said that perhaps it would be best for all parties if Tom Gatliffe consented to Aveline taking up her abode at Broxbridge—that is assuming the earl was obdurate, and no other course remained open.

Mr. Chicknell paid many visits to Mrs. Maitland, and felt assured she would do her best in bringing matters to a satisfactory issue.

While all this had been going on, Tom Gatliffe could not conceal from himself that his wife was in a great measure estranged from him.

It was painfully evident that she yearned to be again at Broxbridge.

How all this would end it was not so easy to say.

One morning, before Gatliffe had started to the works, Mr. Chicknell presented himself, and demanded to see the owner of the cottage.

Gatliffe received him stiffly, but courteously.

The lawyer was a wary old soldier, who was not accustomed to jump at a sudden proposition or conclusion.

After some preliminary remarks he told Gatliffe that Earl Ethalwood was ill, and that he most particularly desired to see his granddaughter.

He laid a great stress on this last word.

A feeling as of sudden faintness came over the engineer.

"Wishes to see my wife, sir?" he said quickly.

"Yes, if you can spare her for a few days, it would be deemed a special favour. You see, my young friend, the earl has been accustomed to receive homage and obedience from his inferiors, and, indeed, from his equals in many instances, and he is, from this very circumstance, exacting and uncompromising. I don't say it disrespectfully—for a more honourable gentleman does not live—but he is headstrong and self-willed, and cannot brook contradiction."

"Ah, indeed! That is but natural, I suppose. Well, sir, what do you require—my consent to the absence of my wife?"

"Well, yes, if you have no objection."

"Since our marriage she has been accustomed to have her own way in everything. I have never thwarted her or offered any opposition to her expressed wishes. If she wishes to go, there is an end of the matter."

"Better ask her—hadn't we?" returned Chicknell.

"As you please."

Gatliffe arose from his seat, opened the door, and called his wife by her Christian name.

She hurriedly entered the parlour. At the sight of the lawyer her face became irradiated with a smile, which was not lost upon her husband, who explained to her the reason for Mr. Chicknell honouring them with a visit.

"The earl ill?" cried Aveline, in a tone of alarm. "I'm sorry indeed to hear that. Anything serious?"

"Ahem! No, nothing very serious. His medical attendant says he requires rest, and a change of air when he gets better. There's nothing to be alarmed at—that is, as far as I can learn. And so what say you, my dear lady?" inquired the lawyer, in oleaginous accents.

"As far as I am individually concerned, I should hasten at once to Broxbridge," answered Aveline; "but I leave it for my husband to determine."

"He will not offer any opposition to that, I am well assured," returned Chicknell, with a winning smile, who, throughout the interview, did his best to conciliate the engineer.

"You had better go, dear," said the latter.

Aveline went to his side, and placing one arm round his neck as he was seated in his chair, she then, addressing the lawyer, said—

"I hope you will tell the earl, my grandfather, what a good, indulgent, kind husband I have got, for it is but right and proper he should hear this from other lips beside mine own."

"I will tell him so, rest assured of that. Shall feel a pleasure in making this known to him," said the lawyer.

"I cannot remain longer. My time is up, sir," observed Gatliffe.

"Then I will not detain you," said the lawyer. "I shall, I dare say, have occasion to see you shortly upon a little matter of business, and so farewell till we meet again."

Soon after Gatliffe's departure his wife and little boy started off in company with the solicitor, and reached Broxbridge Hall early in the afternoon.

CHAPTER LIII.
THE ALLUREMENTS OF WEALTH AND RANK—THE DESPAIRING HUSBAND.

WHEN Aveline Gatliffe arrived at the earl's residence she found its owner by no means so poorly as she had anticipated.

Her grandfather had a slight cold, which for obvious reasons had been magnified into an attack of a much more serious nature.

His cold soon disappeared after Aveline had taken up her abode once more at Broxbridge. It was a ruse on the part of the attorney to excite sympathy—a ruse which answered his purpose very well.

Now that Earl Ethalwood had his darling Aveline once more with him he was determined not to part with her, not if he could help it, and seeing that he had wealth, station, and power, the chances were that he would be able to hold his own against any odds.

Her stay at Broxbridge was much more protracted than it had been on the occasion of her first visit, and gradually the truth began to dawn upon the engineer. Mrs. Maitland had pointed out to him the desirability of not offering any opposition to the expressed wishes of so great and influential a personage as Lord Ethalwood.

She told him that if he had proper consideration for his wife, and care for her future prospects, he would let her remain as mistress of the earl's establishment.

At this Tom Gatliffe burst into a fit of passion, and vehemently anathmetised, not only the earl, but the aristocracy generally. He was so violent that the good lady had considerable difficulty in pacifying him.

"If she chooses to stay away of her own free will, so be it. She'll be no wife of mine if she does—that's all I have to say."

"Don't be unreasonable, Tom," cried Mrs. Maitland.

"The earl is now stricken in years, and in the common course of nature he cannot be long here. If only for your boy's sake, you ought to give way. A grand future is before him, if the earl chooses to make him his heir, which he has promised to do."

"What have I done that I should be cast adrift? Why am I not permitted to enter the house of which my wife is supposed to be mistress? Tell me that."

"You have not done anything, but the earl has a prejudice."

"Against whom?"

"Against all who are not nobly born. It is altogether most unfortunate as far as you are concerned, but you must remember, Tom, I never deceived you. I told you all about Aveline when you proposed and asked my consent. You knew perfectly well that there was a dark, impenetrable mystery hanging over her at that time. We cannot see into futurity, and not anyone of us could have guessed that she was nobly born. Think of all these things, and be patient."

"Patient, mother! When a man is robbed of a wife whom he dearly loves, you preach patience? I will write and ask her to come back."

"It would not be wise to do so, but you can of course do as you think best."

"I will write. She has been gone away seven weeks, and in none of her letters does she make the slightest allusion to returning home."

"Well, then, write to her," said Mrs. Maitland hastily; "write."

Tom Gatliffe wrote a somewhat hasty epistle to his wife, in which he expressed a wish for her return. If she had made up her mind to desert him, he besought her to let him know.

In reply to this Aveline informed him that she could not leave Broxbridge without incurring the displeasure of its owner, as she had promised to obey him in all things.

At the same time she informed him that her love was as strong and powerful as ever, and that she would never voluntarily desert him. Still for the present it was expedient that they should remain separate and apart.

It cost her many a pang to indite this epistle, but the urgency of the case required it, and she had no other alternative.

The letter bewildered him. At first he could not realise it, but in a little time slowly and clearly the terrible truth came home to him.

Aveline had forsaken him for mere vanity, wealth, and luxury.

She had given him up and left him for ever.

When his mind had quite grasped that truth, a terrible cry came from his lips, and he fell into a chair in almost a prostrate condition.

When he recovered he sat for long hours in that room which was never again to be brightened by his wife's presence.

Then hot anger, fierce invectives succeeded—anger so wild, so frantic, that he was for the time like a madman.

Who had taken his darling from him? She would not have left him of her own free will—he felt convinced of that.

Who had tempted her? He cursed the proud lord who had robbed him of his treasure.

Then he was reminded by her letter that it was of her own free will that she had done it.

She had left him that she might enjoy wealth, luxury, and splendour.

She had left him and blighted his life—had broken his heart; had slighted his love for—money!

"And what will not either man or woman do for money?" he cried, with supreme bitterness. "Anything—everything!"

He struck his forehead with his clenched fist.

"Had I handed Peace over to justice, which I ought to have done, the chances are that this fatal discovery would never have been made—for fatal it has proved to me; but it is right that I should be punished for my dissimulation and falsehood on the night of the burglary committed by that scoundrel, Peace."

Gatliffe knew perfectly well that there was legal redress for him. He could claim his wife and claim his child, but he would not resort to such a course—he was too proud. If she had voluntarily left him, let her go.

The law of the country might force his heartless wife to return—might compel her to come back to him; but he disdained any such assistance—he held the law in contempt.

"She was light and vain," he murmured. "She was always that ever since I've known her. She had my heart in her hands—that she knew well enough; she has broken it, and thrown it away. For her sake I would have borne starvation, ignominy, and death—she, with a few cool words, gives me up for money!"

Tom Gatliffe's trouble seemed to warp and change his whole nature—it hardened him as nothing else could have done; yet to no living man did he make any complaint.

He said nothing of what had happened; he went about his work for some days as usual, but with a grim determined look on his face.

He had a strange desire. He wanted to see Peace—not that he had any respect or friendship for the man—far from it—but he wanted to know how the discovery relative to Aveline's paternity first came about. Peace would be able to give him this information.

Meanwhile his wife was in the enjoyment of wealth, luxury, and every earthly delight and comfort; if these could give her happiness she ought to be well satisfied, and to a certain extent she was. It is true at times she confessed to herself that the part she was playing was not altogether without its darker aspects.

She had not used her husband well, and she was much surprised that he had not chosen to answer her last letter. She thought he would be sure to write—there would perhaps be a passionate appeal to her to return—a passionate cry for love and pity.

She must answer that as well as she could. The die was cast now. She was as inflexible as the earl her grandfather—for she was an Ethalwood. Poor thing, she was proud when she thought of this—it was the very nature of the Ethalwoods to be uncompromising and unyielding—therefore, come what would, she could not alter her decision.

Still it was somewhat singular that Tom should have not thought it worth while to make an appeal—it was annoying.

She waited in vain for a letter from her husband. She would have been glad to have heard from him, if it were only two or three lines just to say how he was. She was piqued, and not a little vexed; she felt hurt.

She longed to know what he thought of her conduct, what he suffered, if he was unhappy. Unknown to herself in the midst of the splendour with which she was surrounded, she was still longing for his love. What strange inconsistencies there are in the human character! Any way she could not fail to acknowledge to herself that Tom was not selfish, and she did not feel

that she could say the same of those by whom she was surrounded. Her mind and thoughts might be said to be in a state of transition.

It is true that she was made an idol of in her new home—she was surrounded with stately grandeur.

If her head ached every remedy and every luxury was offered to her, but there was no Tom to soothe and comfort her until the pain had ceased.

She missed him more than words can tell, and for some little time after her last letter to him she was undergoing the pangs of remorse.

The earl, who was an adept in reading characters, saw this. He judged that the young wife could not give up her husband without experiencing some sharp pangs, and in this he was not mistaken.

He did all he could to rouse her. He gave a grand dinner party, to which the leading notabilities of the county were invited, who paid homage to the mistress of Broxbridge, to whom they were most profuse in their compliments.

The earl ordered a magnificent costume from Paris for his granddaughter, who was delighted.

In the novelty and excitement she forgot her sorrow, and from that hour the world took possession of her.

Lord Ethalwood kept most faithfully every promise he had made her. In this respect he was the soul of honour.

He busied himself in getting together every legal proof of her identity, and in this he succeeded even beyond his anticipation.

No one could for a moment question the fact of her being veritably his grandchild.

But as the world is censorious, he deemed it advisable to put the question beyond the reach of cavillers.

Then he formally declared his great grandson his heir, and made his will, bequeathing to Aveline, his beloved grandchild, a fortune, which was to have been divided between three of his children, and which would have made each of them rich.

These arrangements seemed to give him more pleasure than they did Aveline, who felt that after all she was but a mere puppet in the hand of her courtly relative.

Nevertheless, she was thankful for the consideration displayed in so profuse and munificent a manner by the earl, who seemed so solicitous for her welfare and happiness.

Indeed, to say the truth, she seemed to be his idol.

He proposed introducing her into fashionable and aristocratic circles, but before doing this he was impressed with the necessity of placing her under the care of some experienced lady, who would induct her into the usages of what is termed good society.

At present she was natural and unsophisticated. These qualities, excellent as they were in themselves, were of no great value to one who was destined to mix with the upper classes.

No one knew this better than Lord Ethalwood, for, as we have already observed, he was a close observer of human nature.

He therefore looked about for an instructor and companion for his well-beloved granddaughter, and he succeeded in finding the very person of all others he most desired.

Lady Marvlynn, relic of Sir Eric Marvlynn, was a lady most admirably adapted for the purpose. She knew everybody "who was worth knowing," to use her own words, had the history and genealogy of every titled family by heart, was good-natured, loquacious, courtly, and a gossip; and the earl felt assured that she would take a pleasure in preparing his grand-daughter for the new sphere of action in which she was destined to move.

Her ladyship consented to educate the beautiful girl so as to fit her for her new position.

"She will never be accomplished," said Lord Ethalwood. "That we cannot help. It would be useless to attempt to teach her French and German; but she knows something of music, can play tolerably well, and sings very sweetly. As for other accomplishments we must dispense with them. Teach her to take her place gracefully as mistress of my house; teach her all the little details of etiquette that every lady ought to know, and she will be no discredit either to me or her tutor—at least, I hope not."

"She's a charming girl—a loveable creature; so unsophisticated—so ingenuous; so much warmth of temperament — so much refinement. I am most delighted to take her under my charge, my lord; most flattered that you should have entrusted me with the pleasing task."

"I am glad you like her, for without all would be of no avail."

"Oh, my dear Lord Ethalwood, I undertake my duties con amore. It will be a labour of love. What am I saying? Labour, indeed; it will be recreation—a pleasant pastime for me. You know since the death of poor dear Sir Eric I have had but little to engage my thoughts—have sought in vain for an object upon whom I could place my affection. Pardon my blunder. Your granddaughter is not an object. Ah—ah!"

And the dowager laughed immoderately at this sally.

The earl joined in chorus.

"She's a wonderfully good-natured creature," he murmured to himself, "and Aveline will doubtless get on very well with her."

He was quite right in this surmise, Aveline did get on exceedingly well with the gossiping, merry, elderly lady, who had always something pleasant to say; sometimes it was about the movements of the upper ten—sometimes it was biographical or anecdotal.

In her society Aveline found the hours pass gaily and merrily away.

The result of her companionship with Lady Marvlynn was a perfect success.

The little deficiencies of manner were soon toned down, the musical voice took a more delicate and silvery tone—the actions and movements, always graceful, became more graceful in their high-bred elegance.

Aveline was so quick in learning to adapt herself to her new sphere that Lord Ethalwood wondered at her marvellous progress.

When she had been with Lady Marvlynn for three months, one might have thought that her whole life had been spent at Broxbridge.

"You have produced a visible change in the manner and demeanour of my pet," said Lord Ethalwood; "I cannot sufficiently thank you for your valuable instruction."

"Don't thank me, my dear Lord Ethalwood," exclaimed Lady Marvlynn. "She has natural grace, is so remarkably impressionable, so easily moved—her appearance is so distingué and her manners so winning, I assure you that she will bear the very highest polish. She is a diamond—a very gem of the first water. Still I do flatter myself she has greatly improved since I first became acquainted with her. I admit that, but at the same time am not vain enough to suppose for one moment that it is attributable altogether to me. I've done my best, and now the dear girl will be an ornament to any society or coterie."

The earl smiled—he liked to hear Aveline praised by others besides himself.

When the London season opened Lord Ethalwood took Aveline to his town residence in Mayfair.

She made her début in the great world, and was received there with every flattering demonstration.

The earl's prophecy was realised—her marvellous grace and beauty created a perfect furore.

More than ever he at this time regretted her unfortunate and ill-assorted marriage; but for that there was no rank she might not have attained.

The only thing that reconciled him in the least to it was the fact of the child's existence.

There opened then to Aveline Gatliffe a most brilliant life. Nothing she had ever dreamed of equalled the magnificent reality.

There was, however, one drawback.

She had one dispute with her grandfather—he was desirous that she should relinquish the name of Gatliffe, and that she would not consent to do.

She looked at him with flashing eyes, and her face flushed up with anger as he made this proposition.

"I have broken my husband's heart," she said, in a tone of sadness; "I have deserted him, my lord—I have embittered his life. All this is bad enough, but I will not give up his name. I was proud enough the day I bore it first, and you have no right to ask me to give it up."

These were the first angry words she had spoken to the proud old earl—the first that had ever fallen from her lips since he had known her.

He was astounded at her boldness, and murmured, "The Ethalwood spirit. I could never have believed it had I not heard her utter such a bold defiance."

He saw it was useless to urge the point—she had evidently more determination and spirit than he had given her credit for.

Nevertheless he was deeply mortified.

Aveline was known as "Mrs. Gatliffe," Lord Ethalwood's beautiful grand-daughter.

People at first used to ask where was her husband—who was he?

And the answer was—

"She married a man much beneath her, and is separated from him."

After a time they ceased to ask, and the beautiful Mrs. Gatliffe became one of the queens of the fashionable world.

She enjoyed life, she gave herself up heart and soul to the spirit of gaiety. No party, no ball or soirée, was complete without her.

She was indefatigable in the pursuit of pleasure.

Lord Ethalwood smiled as he watched her.

"I was not mistaken in my estimate of her character," he thought. "She has forgotten her husband."

He became warmly attached to her, chiefly because her great beauty and popularity flattered his pride.

He loved her, too, because she so closely resembled her mother.

There were times too, when Aveline Gatliffe, looking around her, said to herself—

"I did well. If the time and the choice were to come again, I should do the same. It would have been cruel, such a life as mine in a mechanic's cottage; it would have been cruel and unjust to deprive my darling boy of this grand heritage."

Such is the sophistry people use in cheating themselves into the belief that they have acted right in casting aside their natural ties for the blandishments of the world—for the acquirement of wealth and power.

We shall see in good time if these brought happiness and a contented mind.

CHAPTER LIV.
PEACE'S LIFE AT SHEFFIELD—THE ROBBERY AT CROOKES-MOOR HOUSE—TRIAL AND CONVICTION.

WHILE Tom Gatliffe was bearing up as best he could against the deep affliction that had fallen on him, and while his wife was being fêted, flattered, and spoiled, Charles Peace, the burglar, was pursuing his own erratic course in his native town of Sheffield.

He returned thither with a considerable amount of cash, the produce of his Denmark-hill burglary.

His mother, at this time, was in a state of poverty, and his sister was in indigent circumstances.

Peace at once hastened to relieve their immediate necessities, and in a short time after his return to Sheffield, his funds dwindled down, so that he very shortly became again hard-up.

He eked out his living in all sorts of odd ways. Now mending a clock, and then framing a picture in the intervals, no doubt dealing to some extent with the "fence" of his old comrades in crime.

One night, while playing his violin at a public-house in Sheffield, he met with a girl with whom he had been acquainted when quite a lad.

She had been at one time an intimate friend of Laura Stanbridge's, and her association with that unprincipled female had done much towards leading her into evil courses.

As Peace was leaving the house with his violin under his arm, he was accosted by the girl, whose name was Emma James.

"Don't go away like that, Charlie," cried she, as our hero was about to leave the house. "It isn't often we meet."

"Well, Emma lass, how goes it with you?" returned Peace, shaking her by the hand and chucking her under the chin. "What are you doing now?"

"Nothing at all at present; business is bad and it's a struggle with most of us—leastways, I know it is with me; but we won't talk in front of a public bar."

The two passed out into the street.

"You've been having a fine time of it lately, I hear," said Emma James. "You've been to London, and all sorts of places, besides—I suppose you are well up for money."

"You are greatly mistaken, Emma. I have made a little this time, but it's nearly all gone."

"Well, where do you live—which way are you going?"

"I'm living in the same house as my sister Mary."

"And where might that be?"

"In Bailey-lane."

"You know Mary?"

"Of course I do—or rather I did. I have not seen her for so long a time, not since Laura left the town in such a sudden and mysterious a manner."

"Ah, Laura, of course you knew her. You will be surprised to learn that I met with her in London by the merest chance in the world."

"And how was she looking?"

"So well, so beautiful, so grandly dressed, that at first I did not know her."

"Then she's cutting a dash in London—a big swell, I s'pose?"

"Yes, doing the trick somehow or other. How I can't tell, that's best known to herself."

"Some people have the devil's luck as well as their own. However, she was always a clever girl, and knew her way about as well as most persons. But I

say, Charlie, is it true that Mrs. Maitland's daughter, she whom young Gatliffe married, turned out to be the grand-daughter of a nobleman?"

"Yes, that's quite true, Emma. She may thank me for all she's got; I found her out and was the first to fire the train. Oh, yes, all this is true enough. She's left Tom—so I hear."

"More shame to her. He was the best of husbands, and doated on the ground she walked. Everybody knows that."

"What matters? She's got into good quarters, is now so far removed from him, so much above him, that she's sent him to the right about. It's the way of the world, my darling—has always been so, and always will be, I suppose."

"Well, you've put her into a good thing, and I daresay she is grateful."

"Bah!" exclaimed Peace, "don't be a fool, Emma. Grateful indeed! She didn't condescend to even honour me with a passing notice as she entered Broxbridge Hall."

"Didn't she, though?"

"No, not even a nod."

"The proud, ungrateful upstart."

"Here's my little drum," said Peace, opening the door of the house with his latch-key. "Come in and see Mary."

The girl did as she was bid, and the three were in a short time after this in familiar converse.

A few days after this Emma James became an inmate of the establishment.

She lived with Peace for a short period, during which he made her useful in disposing of property the proceeds of his various robberies.

It was not possible for him to remain long without having recourse to his dishonest practices. To this propensity he joined a great love of playing the fiddle and a fancy for birds and animals.

He committed several burglaries at Sheffield about this time, and in most cases he patronised the west end of the town.

His favourite plan was to pick out good substantial-looking houses with a portico.

Taking advantage of a favourable opportunity he would climb up the columns and enter the house by the window over the doorway.

He was partial to the hour when the family were at dinner downstairs, and he went about his business with such celerity that he usually had a good booty out of the house before the diners had got to the length of the kickshaws and trifles with which they finished their feast.

No doubt while he lifted valuables upstairs he did so to the clinking of glasses and the play of the knife and fork downstairs; the merry jest and animated conversation, no doubt, doing him good service in drowning any little noise he might accidentally make in the course of his operations.

Cunning and clever as our hero was he might have escaped "trouble" for a long time, but for his passion for the society of the softer sex.

Emma James was taken into custody for offering for sale a pair of boots acquired in their way of trade, and Peace coming to her rescue was lodged in durance vile.

The scoundrel, as we already signified, resided in the in same house with James and a married sister; and a search of the latter's house, made by the police, brought to light a large quantity of stolen property.

Then the amiable brother and sister tried their hardest each to shift the onus of the crime on each other.

The reports of the magisterial examination and trial of Peace and his two confederates cannot fail to be interesting to the reader.

In the *Sheffield and Rotherham Independent*, of October 14th, 1854, we find the following :—

STEALING WEARING APPAREL.

TUESDAY.—Present—W. Overend, Esq., R. Bayley, Esq., and H. W. Wilkinson, Esq.

Emma James, Mary Ann Nield, and Charles Peace, all residing in Bailey-lane, were charged with stealing wearing apparel, jewellery, and trinkets from Mrs. Platt, Mr. R. Stuart, and Mr. H. E. Hoole.

A large number of articles of wearing apparel, &c., was placed upon the table, and Inspector Sills said he and Policeman Marsland had found most of them at the house at which the three prisoners lived in Bailey-lane. Some few he had found upon the persons of the prisoners, and one dress he had found in a house in West-court, Westbar.

A female named Skinner said she lodged with her sister, Mrs. Platt, and that Mr. Platt's house was robbed on the evening of the 29th August. Some of the articles produced had been taken away at that time.

Mr. Raynor now asked for a remand, to give time for the case to be got up.

Mr. Wilkinson inquired if prisoners had anything to say why they should not be remanded.

The male prisoner replied that he had got the things from his sister (one of the female prisoners) for money owing to him.

Mr. Raynor said he had no doubt it would turn out that the man was the thief, and that the women were innocent. It was very dastardly in Peace to seek to criminate his sister for the sake of clearing himself.

Remanded until Friday.

The same paper of October 21st, 1854, contains the second examination.

RECOVERY OF A LARGE QUANTITY OF STOLEN PROPERTY.

At the Town Hall, yesterday, Charles Peace, Mary Nield, his sister, and Emma James, were placed at the bar on several charges of felony.

On Monday last James offered a pair of boots in pledge at the shop of Messrs. Wright, of Westbar, which answering the description of a portion of the property stolen from the residence of Mr. H. E. Hoole, she was detained.

The prisoner Peace then came forward and claimed the boots, and was given into custody.

Inspector Sills and Sergeant Marsland then searched his house in Bailey-lane, and there found a large quantity of jewellery and wearing apparel, the proceeds of robberies effected at the residences of Henry Elliott Hoole, Esq., Crookes Moor House; R. Stuart, Esq., Brincliffe Edge; Mr. George Fawcett Platt, of Priory Villa, Sharrow-lane; and Mr. Brown, of Broomhall-street.

The houses of all these parties had been robbed by effecting an entrance through the bedroom windows in the evening before the windows were closed and fastened for the night.

The first charge on which evidence was taken was that of the robbery at Mr. Hoole's.

Lydia Frayman, the cook, proved that on the evening of the 12th of September seven pairs of boots were stolen from Mr. Hoole's dressing-room, and that from finger marks on the portico pillar it was evident the thief had climbed the portico, and thence entered the room by the window, which was left open till nine o'clock that evening. She and the coachman identified

two pairs of boots, traced to the possession of Peace, as part of the stolen property.

The next charge was that of robbing the residence of Mr. Stuart, of Brincliffe Edge.

Mr. Stuart proved that on the night of the 29th September they retired to rest about half-past ten. A gold eyeglass belonging to Mr. Stuart was missing from the top of a chest of drawers. The bedroom window was unfastened and open till they went to bed. The following day she found that there had been stolen from a chest of drawers in the bedroom, which had been unlocked, the following articles, viz. :—Three small boxes, containing £3 5s. in money; a diamond ring set in plain gold, a garnet and pearl ring, a garnet ring, an enamelled mourning ring with "Forget me not" on it, an oval cornelian brooch set in enamelled gold, with a garnet sprig on it; a gold brooch set in hair, a small imitation tortoise brooch, gold drop, and jet earrings, a jet necklace, a black velvet purse with gold clasp, and worked with gilt beads; a gold hoop with rose, thistle, and shamrock worked round it; a gold watch chain, with gold seal and key; a jet chain, some jet beads, a set of seed coral beads loose, two children's coral necklaces, three purple enamelled studs set with diamonds, an enamelled mourning ring with "Betsy Frith" and the date engraved inside, a small pearl box lined with crimson velvet, and a small French paper box, containing old coins. The whole of these articles, with one or two exceptions, had been recovered by the police, and were produced and identified by Mrs. Stuart.

An assistant to Mr. Hammond, of Church-street, proved that the prisoner, Nield, pawned the set of diamond shirt studs for 5s.

Margaret Scotton, of West-court, widow, proved that on Monday last the prisoners brought a silk dress, rug, a pair of Wellington boots, and other things, to her house. After Peace's apprehension, James handed to her several gold rings and other jewellery, and asked her to take care of them till she returned. In the evening, James was brought to her house by Inspector Sills, to whom witness gave up the rings, &c.

Mary Ann Roberts proved that she resided in Bailey-lane, next door but one to the house in which Peace, Nield, and James lived together. Last Monday, James brought a small box and a bundle of clothes into her house, and asked her to take care of them. The box was locked. That afternoon the police came to search Peace's house, and as they were going away she called Sergeant Marsland into her house, and gave him the box and bundle. The box was found to contain part of the jewellery stolen from Mr. Stuart's.

Edward Parker, of Kenyon-street, boot-closer, proved that a month ago Peace sold him a garnet ring for two shillings. The ring was too large for him, but he got it altered. Yesterday Inspector Sills came to him, and he gave the ring up.

The prisoner Nield made a statement, admitting that she had pawned the diamond studs and other things; but declared that she had been brought into the snare by her brother, the prisoner Peace. She had seen Peace wearing some of the rings, and also the diamond studs, several times, and did not know but that he had come honestly by them.

Peace said his sister (the prisoner Nield) had given wearing apparel, jewellery, &c., to James, whom he was about to marry. Nield had given James these things in payment of a debt of thirty shillings, which she owed him.

The girl James made a similar statement.

THE COWARDLY RUFFIAN DEALT A CRUSHING BLOW ON THE HEAD OF THE YOUNG FARMER.

The prisoners were fully committed for trial on these charges, but were ordered to be brought up again on the Tuesday, when evidence would be given, proving that other property found in their possession was part of that stolen from Mr. Platt's, of Priory Villa, and Mr. Brown's, of Broomhall-street.

HOUSE ROBBERY.

TUESDAY, OCTOBER 21ST, 1854. — Present — The

No. 26.

Mayor, J. Jobson Smith, Esq., G. P. Naylor, Esq., V. Corbett, Esq., W. Jeffcock, Esq., and R. Bailey, Esq.

Charles Peace, Emma James, and Mary Ann Nield, who were last week committed for trial on charges of robbing the houses of Mr. Alderman Hoole, of Crookes Moor, and Mr. Stuart, of Brincliffe Edge, were again brought up, charged with robbing the house of Mr. George Platt, of Priory Villa, Sharrow-lane.

The house was entered by the chamber window (which had been left open) some time between eight and ten o'clock on the night of Monday, the 28th of August, and a large quantity of ladies' wearing apparel stolen. A plank taken from an adjoining building in course of erection was found reared against the wall. There had been traced to the possession of the three prisoners, two Canton crape shawls, two silk dresses, a satin jacket, a Thibet shawl, a black satin shawl, twenty yards of black silk, and other articles. Some of these had been pawned at Messrs. Wright's, in West Bar, Mr. Hammond's, Church-street, and others had been left by the prisoners in the care of Mrs. Roberts, residing next door to them in Bailey-lane, and Mrs. Scotton, of West Bank.

On Friday, Peace stated to the magistrates that these articles were brought to his house by his sister Nield, who made a present of them to James, to whom he was about being married. To-day he stated that a man named Bethley gave them to him to take home as a present to his sister. Nield said she knew nothing of the story Peace had told the bench. He brought the things to the house, saying he had bought them, and she pawned some of them for him.

Committed for trial at the Sessions.

TRIAL AND CONVICTION.

At the Michaelmas Quarter Sessions, Charles Peace, joiner, Emma James, spinster, servant, and Mary Ann Nield, married, felt-dresser, were indicted for stealing a quantity of rings, brooches, and other jewellery, from the house of Mr. Richard Stuart, at Brincliffe-crescent. Mr. Overend prosecuted; the prisoners were undefended.

The house was robbed on the night of the 30th August, and the prisoners were proved to have pawned portions of the stolen property, and others were found in their possession.

Peace in his defence said a watchmaker, named Bethley, in Divison-street, had kept his sister (Nield) for some years, and she had had three children by him. Bethley not having given her any money lately sent the jewellery and a bundle of wearing apparel by him to her, instead of money.

The female prisoners declined to say anything in their defence.

The jury found all the prisoners guilty of feloniously receiving the property knowing it to have been stolen.

Evidence was also given that Peace had been previously convicted of felony.

Mr. Maude said there were two other indictments against the prisoners for robberies at the house of Mr. H. E. Hoole, of Crookes Moore, and Mr. George Platt, of Sharrow-lane.

The court thought it unnecessary to proceed with these cases.

Peace was sentenced to four years' penal servitude, and the female prisoners to be imprisoned for six months each to hard labour.

CHAPTER LV.

AFTER CONVICTION—A GLIMPSE AT PRISON LIFE.

CHARLES PEACE had not counted on receiving so heavy a sentence, and at first he was much borne down. He had been for a long time under the notice of the constabulary, who felt assured that he had perpetrated a series of robberies without being brought under the ban of the law. Had the authorities been oblivious to this fact, perhaps eighteen months, or at the most two years, would have been the maximum punishment awarded to him.

"Penal servitude," says an authority on this sub-ject, "is a thing many people hear and read of a great deal, but about which only a certain number know really anything."

Mr. Charles Reade has touched the question in a masterly manner in his powerful romance of "Never Too Late to Mend," but happily for the welfare of society at large, and criminals in particular, modifications have been made in the treatment of prisoners since the publication of Mr. Reade's work.

Peace, as we have already seen, was selfish and unscrupulous.

He would have sacrificed his sister without the slightest compunction of conscience if he could thereby have saved himself.

It transpired, however, at the trial, that he was the principal, his sister and the woman James being but accomplices.

The bench took a righteous view of the question, and our hero simply got his deserts.

He, however, endeavoured to make out that he was an ill-used man.

After the sessions had come to a conclusion, he was taken in the prison van with a batch of convicts to the gaol where they were to undergo the first probationary term of their sentences.

With a heavy heart, Peace once more entered the "Black Maria," which was to convey him to a convict establishment, with which he had never had any previous acquaintance.

When the prison van arrived at its destination the convicts were told to alight.

The first thing on entering the prison, each man was released from his handcuffs, and told to seat himself on a long bench in the passage.

Peace, during the progress of the van through the town, had been greatly annoyed at the shouting, screaming, and laughing of his fellow prisoners, who were, however, now much more quiet and comparatively well-behaved.

They were all subjected to a new and to Peace a most painful operation.

He was well aware that it would be next to useless, if not quite hypocritical, for one in his position to lay claim to any considerable delicacy of feeling, or to be over scrupulous in matters of common decency.

But there were occasionally, however, he found, even amongst convicts, those who will bear a pretty long period of imprisonment, during which they are subjected to a variety of contaminating influences, and yet not have their susceptibilities completely destroyed. Of these he was one, and he felt that the treatment he had to undergo was conceived in a barbarous spirit, and was fitted to destroy utterly any feelings of self-respect which his previous experiences had left in him.

Every part of his body was minutely inspected immediately on his arrival, in order that he might not take any money or tobacco into the prison.

Doubtless it is very desirable and even necessary that every precaution should be taken to prevent such articles finding their way into prisons—at least on the persons of prisoners; but the fact remains that, notwithstanding these inspections, both money and tobacco do find their way into prisons.

The trials of skill and invention which go on between the convict and the inspector, like those between artillery and iron plates, have as yet only proved that, given the power of resistance, the power of overcoming it will be found.

One of his fellow-prisoners verified the truth of this conclusion by taking five sovereigns into prison with him, notwithstanding all the care and experience exercised by the inspector.

Every prisoner on first entering the convict service has to undergo nine months of seperate confinement in a cell by himself, working in that cell, and never leaving it except for exercise or to go to chapel.

During that nine months no remission is given; but for the remainder of his time, if he obtains the full quantum of eight marks a day, which, curiously, he earned by good conduct and the completion of his day's work, whatever that may be, he is allowed a remission of equal to three months in each year, or one-fourth of his sentence, except the nine months.

The full amount of marks for a man to earn in a year is 2920.

If less than this number is earned, so much remission is lost.

It is seldom that a man goes through the whole of his service without losing some marks.

The day after the arrival of our hero and his fellow-prisoners they were all ordered to strip a second time for medical examination, and as a considerable time elapsed before Peace's turn came he had to remain in that state rather longer than was good for him.

It was useless to complain, he had to submit to the humiliating process with the best grace he could.

When the inspection was concluded, he had his hair cut after the approved prison fashion, and was put into his cell to make mats.

His cell was white as the driven snow. His domestic duties were explained to him, and he was informed a heavy penalty would be inflicted if a speck of dirt was discovered on the wall or floor of his cell, or if his cocoa-bark mattress should not be neatly rolled up after use and the strap tight, and steel hook polished like glass, and his little brass gas-pipe glittering like gold.

He listened to all these injunctions with exemplary patience, having made up his mind to be, if possible, a model prisoner. He had in view the remission of his sentence, which was only to be gained by exemplary conduct.

To a sanguine or irritable temperament the monotony of prison life is almost insupportable.

Peace was nearly getting into trouble on the first Sunday he spent in prison for a very unintentional violation of the prison rules.

In accordance with these rules, convicts are not allowed to turn their heads in any direction in the chapel; if they do so it is the duty of the attendant officer to take them before the governor, who, in all probability, will punish them for their disobedience.

It is fair to assume that those who framed these rules had some good end in view in being stringent in the matter of posture in religious service.

The difficulty with Peace was to discover whether the spiritual welfare of the prisoners or the preservation of a more than military discipline amongst them, even in matters of religion, had appeared to them to be of the greatest importance.

It is probable, however, that neither of these considerations decided the question, but that the principal object of these regulations was to preserve in the convict mind, even in the act of worship, the idea of punishment in a perfectly lively and healthy condition.

Be that as it may, on Peace's first Sunday in chapel with his English Prayer-book before him he found himself quite unable to follow the chaplain in the services in which he was engaged.

Turning over the leaves of the Prayer-book in the vain hope of finding the proper place, and happening to cast his eyes over the shoulder of a prisoner in front of him in order to find it, the movement caught the eye of the officer who sat watching every face. Peace saw from the stare and frown which followed, indeed, that he had committed some grave offence.

He immediately resumed his proper attitude, and sat out the service as right as his neighbours, and so escaped the threatened punishment.

"They are jolly particular in this establishment," mused Peace. "Mustn't even look, it appears."

Nothing, however, was said to him by the official, but he felt that he had narrowly escaped being reported.

Every day the prisoners, male and female, old and young, were made to attend chapel, and twice on Sundays.

The appearance of the sacred edifice quite upsets the idea of "freedom" in religious worship.

The chaplain's pulpit is perched high up against the wall at the end, so as to enable him to get a view of his entire congregation; otherwise this would be impossible, for while the larger number of adult male prisoners occupy the body of the chapel, the women and children are partitioned off on either side by a tall partition, which quite precludes the possibility of their seeing beyond.

Before the great space where the men sit is a pair of tall iron gates, and they are ranged on seats rising one above another with warders in attendance, who are constantly on the watch.

The men are expected to look steadfastly before them, regarding through the iron bars the preacher in his pulpit; they must raise or lower their prayer-books with elbows squared, and all at once, like soldiers in a drill.

They must not scrape their feet against the floor without having afterwards to explain the reason of such a movement. They may scarcely wink an eye, cough, or make any noise without danger of rebuke or punishment.

It is a terrible and humiliating state of servitude these miserably guilty creatures have to endure, but with all this it does not seem to deter them from the commission of crime, for many, as soon as they are released, have recourse to their old practices until they are again caught, and sentenced to another and longer term of imprisonment.

Peace began to be weary of his monotonous life. One morning he said to the under turnkey.

"I say, my friend, how long am I to be cooped up in this cheerful little abode—not the whole of the time, I hope?"

"Prisoners are not permitted to talk out of hours," said the turnkey, looking straight before him, but not at his questioner.

"Ah! I beg your pardon, guv'nor; meant no offence."

The turnkey, whose name was Wilson, looked hard at the prisoner, and seemed lost in thought.

Peace felt a little uncomfortable. Perhaps the man would report him to the governor.

"I beg your pardon again; I hope I've not offended you."

The man shook his head and walked away.

"I'm sorry I spoke," muttered our hero to himself.

The turnkey returned.

"Now, then, No. 34."

"Well," cried Peace, "what's up now?"

"Prisoners shut their own doors," returned the man.

Peace closed the door of his cell.

"Lively," he ejaculated, "not to say encouraging.

Well, I am blest, this is a place a cove's got to lock him-self in, it appears."

Peace had gone through the usual formula of prison life; one working day was just the same as another.

He did his share of work, and his custodians had no reason to complain of him as far as industrious habits were concerned; he kept his cell scrupulously clean.

The cell in which Peace was confined was small enough in all conscience. It was not much over seven feet in length, and four feet five inches in breadth; its height being a trifle over eight feet. By the side of the door was a small window of thick rough glass, and beneath this was a little flap table, which had to be let down when the hammock was slung.

As may be readily imagined, there was nothing super-fluous in this narrow prison house, only just enough to admit of a human being existing in the narrowest possible compass.

Over the table was a small shelf. Below the shelf, and at the opposite end of the cell to the window and flap table, was the hammock, which was rolled up in the smallest possible compass, and strapped against the wall.

There was a water spout, so ingeniously contrived that turned to the right it sent a small stream into a copper basin, and to the left into a bottomless close stool at some distance.

There was also a small gas pipe tipped with polished brass.

In one angle of the wall was a small commode or open cupboard, on whose shelves were ranged a bright pewter plate, a knife and fork, and a wooden spoon.

There was a grating at the bottom of the door for the air to come in, and another for foul air to go out if it chose.

An ordinary stable bucket with iron handle and hoops was on the floor alongside of a low wooden stool, a small hand broom, and in a corner under the table a scrubbing brush and flannel. Two tin tallies, with the number of the cell, prison, and hall, hanging behind the door, completed the furniture of this lively and cheerless apartment.

The cellular system has, however, many advantages, and is a far better arrangement than that adopted in the earlier days of prison management.

At one time English gaols were denounced by Howard and others " as schools for instruction in iniquity," and there can be but little doubt that to an extent this was true.

The poor dandy priest, Dr. Dodd, who was executed for forgery, spent six months in Newgate before he suffered death by hanging, and during part of his time he was forced to herd with the common rabble. The change from the caresses and luxuries lavished on him by the silly devotees of his green-room theology to the riot and ribaldry of the gaol sorely tried the unstrung nerves of the pet preacher. When at last he was ac-commodated with a separate apartment he wrote a poem, entitled "Thoughts in Prison," in which he copiously lamented the evils of association and his own personal miseries.

The case of the unfortunate divine-about-town made a great sensation. He really was hardly dealt with, for he had done all he could by confession and resti-tution to atone for his crime.

Dr. Johnson fought for him nobly.

Twenty thousand people signed a petition for his pardon. Consequently, when the ill-fated divine was hung and the poem published, hundreds of fine ladies and gentlemen read, and perhaps deplored, his watery blank verse, and thus most unexpectedly felt a transient interest in the question of prison discipline.

But a change has come over us since the days of Dr. Dodd and Fauntleroy; though it would appear that the sympathy evinced by a certain section of the community for murderers is still extant.

The Rev. John Clay, who was for many years chap-lain of Preston Gaol, in discussing the question of prison discipline, says : " If we regard the prisoner as a moral patient, the paramount object is to render him as amenable as possible to the reformatory process. The tendency of separate confinement is to lower the bodily organs and weaken the faculties.

" The discipline must be modified to correct this ten-dency. The prisoner probably lived a life of gross animal indulgence.

" Accordingly his animal propensities must be first lulled to sleep; this is most effectually done by the repressing power of isolation.

" Plenty of fresh air, therefore, brisk exercise, and suitable diet are necessary.

" If the diet is too low, it will turn depression into despondency; if too high, it will produce excitement and irritability.

" The god of criminals is their belly, and to baulk the belly god to the utmost extent is both wise and just.

" In consequence of lowering the vital energies, the brain becomes more feeble, and therefore more sus-ceptible.

" That is to say, the man becomes more impressible, though this is not the invariable result.

" The cell will sometimes only increase the reserve of the sullen, the stupidity of the dull, the idiotcy of the feeble, and the craft of the cunning.

" Solitude is indeed a terrible solvent, but the main element in a man's character will sometimes withstand its potency when all other characteristics are melted down.

" But, as a general rule, a few months in a separate cell renders a prisoner strangely impressible.

" The chaplain can then make a brawny navvy cry like a child—he can work on his feelings in almost any way he pleases. He can, so to speak, photograph his own thoughts, wishes, and opinions on his patient's mind, and fill his mouth with his own phrases and language."

In common with most philanthropists, the Preston Gaol chaplain considered that almost all crime was traceable to three closely-linked causes, drunkenness, ignorance, and the habit of living in filthy, over-crowded dwellings.

But he maintained that these, in their turn, were due in a great measure to the want of sympathy and intercourse between the upper and lower classes. This cause the late Justice Telford animadverted on while on the bench within a very short period of his death.

Of course the effect produced by the solitary cell depends on many other things, such as temperament, previous habits, &c.

The sluggish, lymphatic man, with small lungs and small brain, adapts himself easily to his solitude. Good food, light work, and a sufficient allowance of visits to break and cheer the monotony of his cell, reconcile him to his position; he becomes almost as passive as a vegetable.

Uniformly submissive, he gives no trouble, and makes an excellent prisoner.

On the other hand, the large-lunged, large-brained man of sanguine temperament is affected very differently. To him the cell is a severe punishment; he chafes and frets under restraint, and most likely grows irritable and sullen.

Probably he breaks the prison rules.

An ignorant, stupid gaoler would try by sharp punishment to coerce a man of this kind to submission, but to goad and madden him still more would be the only result of such an attempt.

Not improbably a duel between prisoner and gaoler would be provoked, and perhaps some tragedy, like that enacted at Birmingham Gaol, be the issue. The details of this tragedy are treated in a masterly manner by Mr. Charles Reade in his "Never Too Late to Mend."

Those who are in the habit of having prisoners under their charge hear some extraordinary stories of crimes.

While Peace was undergoing the probationary term of the sentence passed upon him, more than one member of a light-fingered family of some celebrity were inmates of the same prison.

A brief sketch of this family, every member of which Peace knew perfectly well, is given in the gaol chaplain's report, which, as it is reliable, may furnish the reader with some little insight into criminal life:—

"Trained thieves and pickpockets," says the chaplain, "differ from mere tramps, both as requiring a far greater amount of plunder to support them, and as more constantly and actively seeking it.

"While the tramps are always pedestrian, and are content to herd in the most sordid lodging-houses, the professional thieves resort to ale-houses and taverns, travel by rail, and altogether maintain a style of living unattainable by meaner rogues.

"They differ again from the 'resident bad characters,' inasmuch as they never work if they can help it, but live entirely upon the fruits of their daily villainy.

"Though Preston is not yet of sufficient magnitude and importance to maintain a body of resident pickpockets, it seems to repay the trouble of frequent visits from members of the Manchester, Liverpool, and Sheffield corps. The great majority of cases tried at the sessions, in which it was thought necessary to inflict transportation, have been professional thieves whose head-quarters were at Manchester.

"At certain periods of his life Peace made that town his head-quarters also.

"I have had repeated conversations with many of these professionals, and I shall need no apology for entering into details.

"The first case to which my special notice became attracted was that of three young men, two of them only boys, and a girl apprehended for a shop robbery at Preston—an offence seldom ventured upon by thieves of their class because considered "dangerous"—i. e., involving greater risk of detection than their ordinary practice, and a severe sentence in the event of a conviction.

"The names of the culprits were John O'Neill, Richard Clarke, Thomas O'Gar, and Ellen O'Neill.

"On committal their true characters were at once apparent.

"On their trial numerous previous convictions at Manchester, Liverpool, and Wakefield, &c., were proved, and being once more found guilty, sentences were passed upon them to secure the public for some years from their depredations.

"These unhappy convicts who, previous to their trial, were cautious and reserved, underwent a change afterwards.

"Individual separation, and the consequent working of memory and reflection upon minds too young to be quite hardened, produced the usual result.

"One after another, and each ignorant of what their associates had done or purposed, they gladly availed themselves of the opportunities to unburden their memories, if not their consciences.

"The following is a sketch of the history now under notice, and I am too well assured that hundreds of similar sketches might be made by any one who has the opportunity of studying from the abundance of models supplied by the great towns of this country:—

"An Irish soldier, named Clarke, on his discharge from the army, with a pension of a shilling a day, settled first at Stockport and then at Manchester with his family, consisting of his wife, three boys, and two girls.

"The father occasionally worked at his trade as a shoemaker, and could have earned a comfortable living by it.

"The two elder boys and the elder girl obtained employment at the factories; the girl, however, after a little time exchanged her occupation for domestic service, in which she continued a year or two.

"The parents, as is too frequently the case, bestowed no moral or religious care upon their children, who in consequence soon picked up bad companions, and beginning with petty theft, like Laura Stanbridge, at such places at Knott Fair, gradually entered upon a course of systematic crime.

"The second son, Richard, led the way, and all the rest of the children, with the exception of the youngest girl, followed in quick succession.

"At first the parents remonstrated, scolded, and gave good advice, but never hesitated to accept all that was offered to them of their children's ill-gotten gains.

"In a short time the father became 'a great drunkard,' while the mother, it is evident, encouraged and assisted practices which provided her with the means of enabling her and her husband to live in idleness and luxury.

"The man does not appear to have quitted Manchester, but the woman took a more active part in the proceedings of her children, frequently making long journeys to meet one or other of them on discharge from prison, and occasionally making herself useful in passing stolen bank notes.

"One of the occasional associates of this family, named James O'Neill, attracted by the skill and success with which the girl exercised her vocation, after a short courtship married her.

"'The askings,' said Ellen, 'were put up at Leeds, and I filled up the three weeks by going to Sheffield and York. At the first-named place I fell in with an old friend of mine, named Charles Peace, who advised me to think twice before I threw myself away as he termed it. I got about £10 or £11 at both places together.'

"After O'Neill's marriage with Ellen Clarke he was supported almost entirely by his wife's skill, living, like her father, in a constant state of drunkenness, and only making himself useful now and then by shading off—i.e., screening the operations of his more adroit and acute partner.

"A great extent of country was traversed by this gang on their plundering expeditions, making Manchester the centre of their operations. They organised expeditions to all parts of the kingdom, or, to speak accurately, they started in a spirit of errantry, with no more plan than might be involved in the determination to remain a long time away, and to visit as many places as might hold out a good chance of booty. Now associated, now separated, forming temporary leagues with new comrades, occasionally caught and sentenced to *short imprisonments*, they roamed the country, 'working' the fairs, markets, railway stations, steeple-chases, &c., &c.

"'About this time,' said Richard Clarke, 'I was fifteen, and my gains were between £9 and £10 a week.

"'It went in keeping my mother (to whom remittances were made by Post-office orders) and in public-houses.

"'I was dressed like a gentleman's son, with a cap, a round jacket, and a turn-down collar.'

"Though young Richard was cautious, 'I never ran a chance,' said he, 'of throwing myself away—i.e., taking more than I wanted, and running unnecessary risks.'

"Sometimes, indeed, he did not look for money because he had enough.

"Ellen Clarke and the youngest boy, Edward, were the boldest and most successful of the family, and the girl as well as the mother was not wanting in a certain kind of family affection.

"We find her starting from Manchester to Gloucester in order, if possible, to obtain a councillor for Richard, who had been put back for trial on the charge of picking pockets.

"Unsuccessful in her object, however, and leaving Richard in Gloucester, she occupied some time in travelling about, chiefly in Yorkshire.

"She went to Hull to meet her eldest brother John on his discharge from prison there.

"'I waited till he came out,' said she, 'and then he leathered me for being away from home.'

"Ellen Clarke, indeed, possessed a natural disposition which, had she been blessed with Christian parents, might have contributed to their and her own credit and happiness.

"Her narrative throughout betrays the wish to palliate their conduct, and at her interview with them after her conviction she appeared quite forgetful of herself, and only solicitous to assuage their anxiety about her, and to warn her brother Edward from his dangerous courses.

"This determined and skilful girl-thief of seventeen, who at the latter period of her short run of crime was not satisfied with less than a weekly booty of £10 or £20, trembled very much when she made her first successful essay upon the pocket of a young woman, from which she abstracted eighteenpence.

"'I met,' said she, 'the young woman again in a short time, and she was crying ; I heard her say the money was her mother's. I cried too, and would have given her the money back, but I was afraid of being took up.'

"What an affecting contrast between this girl's character and fate as they were and as they might have been.

"And how sad to think that our backward civilisation possesses as yet no means of saving from moral destruction thousands who, like this poor child, possess natural qualities which by God's blessing would amply repay the labour of cultivation.

"As I have said, after sentence was pronounced upon the gang, the reserve and hardihood which the different members of it had previously exhibited, gave way.

"Richard Clarke was the first to yield ; his sister, who seemed more attached to him than her husband, next softened.

"O'Gar, whose demeanour had always been quiet and humble, after meeting with his mother, entirely threw off his obduracy.

"It has been the long-established practice in this gaol to permit interviews between convicts newly sentenced to transportation and their near relations with more frequency than is usually allowed, partly from a feeling of compassion to all the parties, and partly from a hope that in such cases as the present one, warning may be taken by those who witness the convict's misery should they be in any danger of treading in his steps.

"I was present at two meetings between the Clarkes and their relatives.

"The visitors on the first occasion were the father, the boy, Edward Clarke, and a young man introduced as a cousin.

"They were all expensively dressed for their station ; the father's appearance was rather prepossessing, the boy, though good-looking and well clad, showed to an experienced eye the unmistakable and undisguisable physiognomy and manner of a bold and practical thief.

"Creditable natural feelings were shown by all parties, and many tears were shed by all but the girl, who seemed most anxious to keep up the spirits of the others.

"Old Clarke, habituated to the short imprisonments of his children, seemed unable to conceive that he saw them in a more serious predicament. Almost the first words he spoke were—

"'Don't fret. Sure you'll not be here more than five months. I've sent a letter to General W——, and he'll soon get you off.'

"The convicts themselves were well assured that such expectations were utterly vain, but the father could not be made to comprehend that General W—— neither could or would interfere with the course of justice.

"After the interview Richard Clarke told me that the young man introduced as a cousin was no relative at all, but a former associate, then living with the old Clarke's, and named M'Giverin.

"At the second visit there came both the old Clarkes, O'Neill's mother, Edward Clarke, the younger sister—a fine-looking child of eleven—and a girl who lived with the Clarkes as Richard's mistress.

"Old Clarke, not content with bringing M'Giverin again, also introduced another 'cousin,' a well-dressed man of thirty.

"When Richard Clarke, the convict, was asked who these two men were, his father slipped forward and answered for him, repeating the falsehood he had already told, and persisting in it until his son plainly declared the real name and character of the two 'cousins.'

"When remonstrated with for practising such duplicity at such a time, all that could be obtained from the wretched man was—

"'Well, sir, I ax your pardon. Sure I did not know the rules of the place.'

"At one moment he appeared oppressed with the bitterest feelings, and the next was chatting with an air of eager satisfaction.

"When his relatives had gone Richard Clarke made the following statement—

"'My little brother told me this morning that last Saturday night he got £15 in sovereigns at the Bank Top Station, and that yesterday (Monday) he got £5 in Manchester. The two men that came to see me this morning are Thomas M'Giverin and Henry Kelly. M'Giverin has been a thief about five years, and has two brothers who are thieves. Kelly is about thirty years old ; he has been a thief in all ways about twenty years. He is only just out of Liverpool Gaol, where he got six months for a watch. I think him and M'Giverin came to see me out of curiosity—to see whether I was *hard* or no.'

"I have dwelt longer on the history of this family of pickpockets than may seem necessary, but I have done so from a desire to lay open as far as I can what is too little known, the character and proceedings of this portion of *la classe dangereuse*, to impress upon the public the enormous loss it sustains by their depredations, and to suggest the necessity of resorting to more efficient means for the repression of the evil, which, I believe, to be greatly on the increase.

"There are now many thousands of pickpockets robbing at the rate of £300 to £1000 a year, who boldly follow their trade under the idea—too much justified by past experience—that their particular line of practice involves but small risk of transportation, while its gains are certain and easily obtained.

"Even when apprehended 'legal assistance' is generally forthcoming to aid the chances of escape.

"A short time after the conviction of the Clarkes a boy named O'Brien, alias Johnson, alias *Slaver*, was caught in the attempt to pick a lady's pocket in Preston.

"The boy's accomplice, a man who had trained him, and who lived upon the produce of his robberies, escaped and reached Manchester in time to secure the professional services of a rather celebrated attorney, who came to Preston to appear for 'Slaver,' and extricate him from his dangerous position.

"The boy's skill as an apprentice pickpocket made it worth his master's while to incur the expense of £10 for having the best 'professional aid.'

"'Slaver' was convicted, however, as a rogue and vagabond, and sentenced to three months' imprisonment."

We must conclude this chapter on prisoner and prison life, and recur to this interesting subject in a future number, as we have to chronicle a much more heinous offence than robbery, this being the taking of human life.

Peace had not been many weeks in gaol before another prisoner was lodged therein charged with a capital offence.

CHAPTER LVI.

THE LOVERS—A WARNING VOICE—THE MURDER OF MR.
PHILIP JAMBLIN.

SINCE the castigation Peace received from the hands of Mr. Philip Jamblin and the flight of the boy, Alf Purvis, we have had occasion to take but one cursory glance at the inmates of Stoke Ferry Farm, this being on the occasion of Richard Ashbrook's visit to the hospitable English homestead.

The observation made by Mr. Jamblin, sen., to his son, Philip, respecting his falling into the same pitfall as young Ashbrook, had special significance.

After the departure of Peace from the neighbourhood young Jamblin had paid frequent visits to the grounds and house owned by Nelly's aunt.

It was pretty plainly demonstrated to most persons who took the trouble to interest themselves in such matters that the farmer's son had a sneaking fondness for Nell Fulford.

This was very wrong, seeing that he was supposed to be engaged to a young lady in a very superior position to Nell, but despite this an attachment was formed, and, as far as Nell herself was concerned, there was but little doubt that it was one of a self-sacrificing nature. This fact was afterwards but too clearly demonstrated.

For many months after Peace's departure a course of love-making was carried on between young Jamblin and Nell.

They did not appear to be able to break the spell which bound them—a spell, indeed, which ended in the death of one and long years of sorrow for the other.

But Nell was infatuated with the handsome young farmer, who had been her valiant champion when persecuted so persistently by our hero.

The man Giles, who had been worsted in a conflict with Peace, was also a devoted admirer of Nell's.

He was a moody, morose, vindictive fellow, whom nobody liked, and had left the neighbourhood long before Peace.

Whither he had gone no one appeared to know, and, indeed, to say the truth, nobody seemed to care.

Thus matters stood when, at the close of one market day, Mr. Philip Jamblin arrived at the old "Carved Lion."

He dismounted from his horse and went into the public room of Brickett's hostelry. He had some business to transact with a malster whom he had appointed to meet there.

When this was over the two had divers and sundry glasses together, and soon after nightfall Jamblin's steed was brought round to the front door of the inn.

The young farmer remounted, and trotted leisurely along Dennett's-lane in the direction of his own home.

Upon arriving at that part of the lane where Peace's workshop stood, he, much to his surprise and pleasure, beheld Nell at some little distance off, awaiting his coming.

"Why, sweetheart, who would have thought of seeing you, at this hour, too, when all good lasses should be at home?" said the former.

"Ah! Master Philip, she answered, "I was sartin sure you'd be for coming this way, and that's why I be here."

"Ah! I see. Well, I'm glad to see thee, Nell, but ye bee'st a looking a little pale, I'm thinking."

"Am I?"

"Yes, I fancy so; however, it may be but fancy after all."

"May be it is."

"And may be it aint."

"You've come from the market?" she said, quickly.

"I was there for a goodish while in the early part of the day, but I've just come now from the "Carved Lion.'"

"Ah! I see; that's why yon didn't call at annt's."

"I had a little business to do—had to meet a customer at Brickett's. Now, don't be jealous; it wasn't a leddy or a lass."

"And bee'st thee going home, then?"

"Aye, surely, I hope to get home some time to-night. Why, what ails thee, Nell, dear?"

On either side of the lane in which they were conversing ran a high thick-set edge. Nell glanced at the opposite side to that on which she stood, and placed her finger on her lips.

She then laid hold of the bridle, and drew the horse some little distance forward. Then she glanced again at the hedge.

"What's up?" cried her companion.

"Hush!" she whispered. "Somebody has been watching us from behind the hedge, and has heard every word we have said."

"My darling girl, you are full of strange fancies to-night," said her lover.

"It be as I ha' told ye," she answered. "I seed a

pair of dark flashing eyes a-gleamin' through the branches."

"And what matters if anybody has been 'a listnin'? Much good will it do 'em."

She drew his horse still further on, and again glanced around.

"It be of no use yer shakin' yer head," said Nell. "I see'd him as plainly as I see you now."

"Well, what if you did, lass? Who was it? That pedlar fellow, Peace?"

"No, not him."

"Who then?"

"Giles Chudley. That's who it was. He did not think I saw him, but I did; and he means mischief."

"Who cares for an idle, good-for-nothing like that?"

"Come back, Master Philip; come back, as you love your poor Nell. For her sake come back."

"Come back to where?"

"To the 'Lion.' Don't go home to night. I am a poor, weak fool—weak as water. I've no head or heart of my own when your eyes be a-shinin' on my face, and when your words be a-whisperin' in my ears. Oh, Master Philip, ye know well enough how silly, how miserably foolish I've been."

The young farmer was touched; he reproached himself at that moment, and would have gladly recalled the past, if that had been possible.

"I can ill bear reproaches, Nell, although I well deserve them; but no man is wise at all times, and the most prudent women are not always as careful as they might be, and to say the truth they mostly pay the penalty, which is hard."

He leant forward over the side of his horse, and placed his hands on her forehead. Then he said, in a voice of touching sweetness—

"Thee bee'st trembling, Nelly."

"I feel timmersome loike, and something whispers in my ear that you ought not to go home to-night. If ye do it will go hard wi' both on us."

He tried to laugh away her fears, but she would not be so deceived.

A horrible foreboding had seized her, and she endeavoured to turn his horse's head in an opposite direction to the one he had been taking.

"Well, you are in a strange mood to-night; something's upset you."

She shook her head.

Young Jamblin's face grew cloudy and dark. He did not very well know what to make of her.

Presently he said—

"I've done ye wrong, lass—I'm free to confess that, but ye shan't suffer for it. We'll settle matters all right enough, and if there be no other course left, no one can say anythin' agen ye when thee beest my wife."

The girl uttered a cry which seemed to come from the depths of her heart.

"Be of good cheer, darling," cried her companion, "and don't ye give way to doubts and fears. I'll show ye that I'm not the man to forget one so truthful and trusting as ye have been."

"I do not mind about myself; it be for you that I'm fearful and timmersome."

"And for what reason are you so fearful?"

She put her lips to his ear, as if the words she whispered were too terrible to be spoken aloud in that lonely place.

He laughed, as with one hand he smoothed the soft brown hair over her forehead.

"Don't you have any fear about me. I'm well able to take very excellent care of myself. No—no, Nelly,

it won't do; you're not going to frighten Phil Jamblin by any such groundless fears."

"Oh, don't turn away," she cried; "do come back to the 'Lion.'"

"But, my dear girl, what will the guv'nor and my sister say at my stopping out all night without letting them know?"

"I'll let them know—I'll send a message by Stephen," she exclaimed, gently.

"And they'll put me down as a milksop—as a craven. Ah, no, lass—that would never do!"

"Suppose you were ill?"

"But I am not ill—was never better in my life."

"Ah, Philip, you must let me have my way for this once—only for this once—you know," she murmured, in a soft and beseeching manner.

But it was of no use—the farmer was obstinate, he could not or would not see the force of her argument, or yield to her powers of persuasion.

He told her again that she was a prey to groundless fears.

She looked at him sadly.

"Ye be more obstinate and harder than I took ye for," she cried.

He smiled, and placed his hand on her shoulder caressingly.

He found that she was still trembling, even more than before.

"Philip!" cried the girl, creeping closer to him, "I tell ye again this be no fancy; and even if it be, there would be no harm in your giving way to me for this once. I've tried to forget what happened between us two not long ago, when your head was lost to pleasure, and when my heart was lost to you; but I tell ye that something will soon see the light which will prevent my forgetting that foolish hour."

A shudder seemed to pass over the frame of the young farmer, who was evidently deeply moved at this declaration.

"Oh, Nell," he murmured, "it is I who have been to blame."

"I do not reproach you," she answered. "I meant to have kept it all from you, that I might suffer for it; but I tell ye of it now that I may ask ye by that which is your'n, and your'n alone, not to go further to-night, but to turn back and put up at Brickett's house. I implore ye to do this kindness by that which will soon mek' me love or hate ye more. Oh, Philip Jamblin, for the love of mercy hearken unto me. I ask ye by the memory of the happy hours we have spent together, by the remembrance of the past and hope for the future, not to return to Stoke Ferry Farm this night. I've watched and waited for ye, that I might give thee timely warning."

"But, my dear Nell, you seem to be full of fancies to-night. No harm will come to me. I will see ye to-morrow, lass. I shall have good news for you then."

The girl shook her head and looked mournfully at her companion, who did not fail to note that her eyes were filled with tears.

His limbs trembled with emotion—he was greatly troubled; but, even at this time, he was under the full impression that her forebodings were conjured up by the agency of an over-heated imagination.

He drew her towards him, and covered her face with burning and passionate kisses.

Then he bade her a hasty good-night, and urged on his horse.

Half stupefied and numbed the girl stood as immovable and passionless as a statue.

"THERE'S BIN FOUL PLAY, MATES—MASTER PHILIP'S BIN MURDERED!" EXCLAIMED THE MAN.

In a few moments she aroused herself from her lethargy, and, placing her hands against her temples, uttered a deep-drawn sigh; then she started off at full speed in pursuit of Jamblin.

She heard the clattering of his horse's hoofs, but he was far away and out of sight. She ran after him like one possessed, and never paused till fairly exhausted.

Then she sat on a stile by the side of the road, and, burying her face in her hands, sobbed convulsively.

"All is of no avail," she ejaculated; "a wilful man will have his own way."

The sky gathered over with clouds, and rose towards the moon.

A cold wind swept over the surface of the earth and

muttered among the branches of the trees. The clouds grew darker and heavier ; the moon was darkened by a small black cloud.

Nell still sat silent and dejected on the stile. She gave a low and plaintive wail.

Meanwhile Philip Jamblin, heedless of the warning he had received from his sweetheart, was making the best of his way towards Stoke Ferry Farm.

He passed safely through Dennett's-lane, and reached a bridle road, which was nearly at right angles with it.

This road, or rather the greater part of it, was sheltered on either side by tall trees, hedges, and underwood. At noontide in summer it was a charming retreat, but at night it was lonely and cheerless.

The farmer had not gone a very great distance after turning out of the lane before he had sufficient reason for disquietude, or indeed alarm ; his horse became restive and pricked up his ears. Jamblin, however, held him well in hand, and proceeded along with greater caution.

In a few minutes after this the animal stumbled, but quickly recovered itself.

A terrible blow was delivered from behind by some unseen person full on the head of young Jamblin.

"You scoundrel !" exclaimed the young farmer, who although partially stunned had not lost his presence of mind. Grasping the thin end of his riding-whip, he whirled round the handle, which was loaded with lead, in the hope of striking his mysterious and unseen assailant.

The horse he was bestriding now fell, and Mr. Jamblin, who was a powerful, active young man, sprang to his feet to confront the enemy.

He beheld a big hulking fellow, who was armed with a hedge stick, standing in front of him.

Jamblin struck out with his whip, the blow from which was received on the upraised left arm of his assailant, who again aimed a blow at the head of the other. This Mr. Jamblin turned on one side with his whip.

Perceiving now that it was a question of life or death he advanced a step or two, raised the handle of his riding-whip, with which he struck another tremendous blow. The man, however, drew back his head, and instead of alighting on his head the blow was received on the upper jaw, his lip was laid open, and two of his teeth were knocked out.

The man was driven to desperation, and the struggle after this was but of short duration. The cowardly ruffian stepped back a pace or two and delivered a crushing stroke on the head of the ill-fated young farmer, who fell to the earth helpless and powerless.

Then the murderer rained a series of merciless blows on the prostrate man, thereby reducing him to a state of insensibility.

All this had been but the work of two or three minutes at the most.

But the diabolical wretch had not as yet completed his murderous work. Drawing a clasp knife from his pocket he inflicted with its blade a severe gash in the throat of his victim.

Ruffian as he was he was also a coward. As he was stooping over the dead body of the farmer he became alarmed.

He thought he heard the sound of approaching footsteps, and the knife, which by this time was covered with blood, slipped out of his hand.

He searched for it in vain. The ground was strewed with fallen leaves, and the knife was nowhere to be seen.

Big drops of perspiration fell from the murderer's temples on his horny hands as he was groping about for the missing weapon.

A horrible thought took possession of him. It was this. Possibly the instrument with which the deed was done would rise up in judgment against him, and be the means of his identification.

He shook and trembled with fear—a death-like spasm crept through his heart.

He became almost frantic, and turned over the leaves in the hope of finding the knife, but his endeavours were not crowned with success.

As he was thus engaged his eyes fell upon the pale, ghastly face of his victim, which was turned upwards towards the sky.

Fearful lest he should be discovered by some chance traveller, he arose to his feet, and ran off as fast as his legs would carry him.

He soon reached a place known as Larch Green. At one part of this was a stagnant pool of water.

He knelt down beside this, and washed his ensanguined hands.

While thus occupied, he saw the figure of a man approaching. He was some distance off, but he could see that the stranger's attention was directed towards him.

The murderer flew in the opposite direction over several meadows, never pausing till he felt assured that he was far removed from the scene of death.

Then, panting and groaning, he crept into a dense thicket of trees.

After waiting here a considerable time, with his heart knocking against his ribs, he emerged from his hiding-place, and fled precipitately, he knew not nor cared not whither.

But during his flight he had attracted the attention of another observer.

Henry Adolphus, the earl's footman, had been sent by his master with a message to a landholder and a baronet.

The radiant footman, upon returning from the errand on which he had been sent, thought it a little singular that a man should be running at headlong speed over mead and meadow.

He paused and watched the fugitive, and, as he did so, muttered to himself—

"That chap aint after no good, I'll be sworn. I expect he's been doing a little prigging on his own account. Howsomever, it aint no bis'ness o' mine, and as to catching him, it aint to be thought of. What's every man's bis'ness is no man's bis'ness."

And so, consoling himself with this trite axiom, Mr. Henry Adolphus pursued his dignified course homewards.

He had no occasion to go down the road where the body of the dead man lay, and hence it was that our radiant footman escaped having his feelings shocked, which, to say the truth, would have been a terrible thing to a man of his delicate organisation.

He reached Broxbridge utterly unaware of the fact that a near neighbour and a tenant of his master's had been foully murdered, and that the dead body of the murdered man was lying in a road the end of which he—Henry Adolphus—had passed as he trudged home.

Upon reaching Broxbridge he did not go at once to the Hall.

He just dropped in at the "Carved Lion," to have a "cooler" and a little friendly chat with the landlord. The aforesaid "cooler" not having the desired effect, Henry Adolphus supplemented it by another, insisting at the same time upon Brickett joining him.

"That's a deal better," said the footman, after he had swallowed the contents of his second glass. "I've put on the steam coming home, and felt as hot and dry as a salamander."

"I've had a goodish turn myself," returned Brickett, "and have only just come in. Any fresh news?"

"None as I know on," observed the flunkey, "only that I saw a queer-looking chap a-running like mad over Squire Curtis's meadows."

"You did, eh? What sort of customer was he?"

"Oh! an ugly, evil-looking fellow, as any one would wish to be shut of."

"A tall chap with a black beard, and bushy eyebrows?"

"Yes, something after that fashion, as far as I could see; but I was a long way off. He seemed to me to have a cut or bruise on his ugly mug."

"The very same!" exclaimed Brickett.

"Do you know him?"

"No; but I saw a chap answering that description washing his face and hands in the pool at Larch Green. When he caught sight of me he made off. He's been up to something, I'll dare be sworn—burglary, or summut of that sort."

"I shouldn't wonder, if it be the same as I saw."

"Should you know 'im agen?"

"I might; but I aint quite certain about that?"

Brickett remained for some time silent and thoughtful after this.

"I hope as how he aint been up to mischief," he said, presently. "I do hope that; but I tell 'ee candidly, Master Henry, I didn't at all like the look of the varmint, and had it not been that I aint so lively on my pins as I used to be, I should have med arter him, and no mistake."

"Oh, it's all right enough, I dare say the fellow's been having a set to—a mill with someone, that's how I take it, and may be he's got the worst of it."

"I dunno' so much 'bout that; from what I could see of him he looked a good deal like Giles; him as worked at Stoke Ferry Farm some year or two agone. If it war he, which I somehow think it war, he be's a deal altered."

"Giles, eh? Well, now you mention it I don't know, but it might be he."

"I shouldn't loike to swear to 'im, but that's the idea I formed at the time, but may be we shall larn more 'bout 'im afore long. He aint a much good, anyhow."

"Well, Mr. Brickett, I must be for moving—so, good-night," said Henry Adolphus, who at once bent his steps in the direction of the hall.

CHAPTER LVII.

THE RIDERLESS HORSE—CONSTERNATION AT STOKE FERRY FARMHOUSE—DISCOVERY OF THE BODY OF THE MURDERED MAN.

THERE was not a merrier or more light-hearted girl than Patty Jamblin in the whole county.

Her dulcet voice and ringing laugh brightened the old farmhouse like a ray of sunshine.

No wonder, then, that she was her father's pet; for, albeit she never crossed him by word or deed, she mostly managed to have her own way.

But on this eventful evening Patty was sad and serious.

Whether the deep blow that was about to fall on her and the old farmer had been by some strange mysterious influence foreshadowed, it is now impossible to say.

Patty was dejected, and, indeed, it might be said, sorrowful—a circumstance very unusual with her.

There are moments, however, when our hearts are open of their own accord to melancholy impressions.

This will occur at times to the most vivacious of the human species. At such times a tone of music will bring tears into our eyes, or some simple tale or sight of suffering will fill us with presentiments of a terrible misfortune. Such appeared to be the case with Patty Jamblin.

As the sun sank below the earth, and the curtain of darkness fell softly over Stoke Ferry House, the nightingale pouring forth his first sweet song, Patty dropped into her easy chair and covered her face with her cold and trembling hands.

Her brother had not returned.

She watched and waited—waited anxiously. Something whispered to her what was to happen next.

There are times when a quick succession of "next" is found merely soothing; but there are times of reactionary languor when there is not left force enough to watch when that which we attend to is the rhythm only.

Thus we may find the ticking of a clock nothing—indeed, to mention this is commonplace.

But what a dreadful effect may be produced upon the mind by the sudden cessation of the ticking of the clock when once a certain experience has to be gone through!

Who that has counted the beatings of a pulse or listened to the flutterings of a breath, watching for the next and the next and the next, and coming at last to the one which has no next, can bear without agony to hear a watch or a clock stop ticking, or to hear any rhythmical sound cease suddenly?

One of the most horrible moments in my life was a moment in which the rhythmical noise of a common saw, heard over the parapet of a bridge in London, stopped suddenly when I was listening for it. In the distance the sound was softened; it had a sough with it which reminded me very painfully of the sound of human breath, but when it ceased I thought I could bear no more in this world, and longed to be at that moment taken away.

Of course the emotion of that moment was imparted from my recollection of a moment of which it was the symbol, but I think the cessation of something with a beat in it has always a terror for me.

"Can you draw an inference?" said Coleridge to the clown. "Yes, sir," said the clown, "a cartload of them."

That is the way with most of us. We are too eager to draw a cartload of inferences, and when we find the inference will not be drawn we suffer.

This was the case with Patty Jamblin. She was unable to draw an inference as to what was to follow: she only knew that she was depressed and distrustful.

There is a peculiarity about the next thing, remember —that it is sure to happen, and what a blessing there is in certainty!

We know the difficulty of holding in check our tyrannical habitual mode of passing on.

Every second of time in our experience throws out a pontoon bridge to the next.

We live by a clock that has two sets of hands on the same dial-plate. One is right and the other is always too fast.

Patty was sitting in the parlour. Sometimes she would start upright in her chair and listen eagerly; then she would try to reproach herself for expecting her brother Philip so soon.

He was detained, doubtless, had met with some friends, boon companions, who had prevailed upon him to pass a social hour or so with them.

She endeavoured to persuade herself that he was no

able to return from some cause which was not explained. It would, however, be made manifest upon his return.

She felt that she must do something to break the monotony and suspense which she endured, and which every minute became more painful.

She took from the book-case a volume, with which she strove to beguile the tedium of her lonely hours. She read till her eyes ached, and then she cast aside the book.

"Why am I thus troubled?" she murmured. "Philip has been from home much later than this on many occasions. After all there is no reason for alarm, but— but I do wish he would come home, and father is away too, which makes me still more anxious."

The poor girl sighed to herself as she glanced at the clock, the hour hand of which pointed to eleven.

"I wish one of them would come back," she exclaimed. "I've a good mind to send for father, but he would only call me a little fool for my pains, and yet he knows I am all by myself, and he ought to consider that. I feel wretchedly lonely."

She arose and went to the window.

The sky gathered over with clouds, and a cold wind muttered among the branches of the trees, and strewed the ground with brown and yellow leaves.

The clouds grew darker and heavier and rose towards the moon, which was still shining brightly.

Poor Patty went again to the book-shelf and took another volume from it at hazard.

It was a romance of the last century, written with exaggeration, but with terrible force.

It was not calculated to solace the recluse in Stoke Ferry Farm; but there was a fascination in its glowing pages, and Patty read on, her eyes rivetted on the pages of the volume, which contained accounts of murders and ghosts.

Her form stiffened like a sitting corpse; her eyes protruded; her lips uttered low gasps at every gust of wind which shook the casement. She started as if she had received an electric shock.

At last she could bear it no longer. The very words in the book seemed to have become blood-red, and long black spots ran up and down the page.

The farmer's daughter was fairly overcome, and she let the volume fall to the ground, and in the extremity of her fear ran to the window for fresh air; she leant out, and looked up to the sky, listening.

Listening and watching for the next thing.

"Oh!" she murmured, pressing one hand against her side, "but this suspense is dreadful—too dreadful to bear. Where can Philip be, and father too? He ought not to leave me thus."

She remained with her eyes fixed on the black vault of heaven; her heart beat audibly.

"Heaven protect and preserve me," she ejaculated— "preserve me and mine!"

As the clock struck twelve she heard the faint ring of a horse's hoof. It came nearer.

"It is he. It is Philip," she exclaimed.

She listened more intently. The sound rang harshly on her ears—she felt sick and faint.

A horse passed the window, snorting savagely. It appeared to her to be like some war charger whose rider had been stricken down in the field of battle.

She uttered a scream which rang like a clarion note in the midnight air. Then she called aloud for assistance.

"Joe—Stephen—help—help!" exclaimed the unhappy girl.

She heard the clattering of men's footsteps on the hard road.

They were giving chase to the flying horse, which passed on snorting savagely, foaming at the mouth, and riderless.

"Joe—Joe!" shrieked Patty to one of her father's labourers, "for mercy's sake tell me what's the matter. Speak, I pray you."

The man looked in at the window, and said in a kind tone of voice—

"We none on us know at present, but don't 'e be frightened, missus. Summut's amiss, but maybe it aint o' much consequence. Cheer up, and wait till I coom back. There aint no call for no alarm—leastways not as we knows on at present."

Patty sank into a chair, and felt as if about to swoon.

The man passed on.

In a few minutes after this two of her father's servants passed the window, leading a riderless horse.

They carried lanterns in their hands, and were looking intently and examining the animal. Patty said nothing, but, pale and speechless, awaited the issue.

The horse was taken to the yard, which was at the side of the farm-house. It was the identical yard from which the boy, Alf Purvis, had been ignominiously driven with the hare round his neck some year or two before.

The farmer's men exchanged blank looks.

"It looks precious queer, and may be as how it's an ugly bis'ness," ejaculated the carter. "Mr. Philip's bin thrown, for sartin."

"He's not a man to be throwed easily," said Joe. "I dunno think the cob's bin down."

"Yes, he has," cried Stephen. "This off side be covered in mud and slush. There's bin an accident o' some sort."

"An accident?"

"Aye, surely summut very near it. Look at his knees."

The speaker held down the lantern in front of the horse.

"Why, heaven save us, what be this on the saddle?" exclaimed another.

"Here, man, hand us over the lantern."

By the fitful glare of the light they saw a stream of blood on the saddle, and the horse's flanks.

A low moan proceeded from all present, and they stood petrified with astonishment.

"The saddle be wet!" cried one.

"Ah! surely, that it be—wet wi' blood!" exclaimed another. "There's been foul play with our young master."

While all this had been going on, the elder Mr. Jamblin, who had been playing cards at a neighbour's house, had been suddenly aroused to a sense of danger; he soon hastened homewards, and upon catching sight of his men around the house, he exclaimed, in a tone of indignation—

"What be all on 'ee doin' there? Aint one man enough to attend to a horse? Do it take five to stable a steed? Speak, some on 'ee. You've got tongues in yer heads, I s'pose?"

But none of his men seemed disposed to speak. No one appeared to have the courage to declare the real state of the case.

Puffing and panting Mr. Jamblin hastened up to the riderless steed.

"Where be Mr. Philip?" he cried.

"He aint coom back as yet, zur," said the stableman.

"Then where be he?" was the next question.

"We none on us know; Pepper (that was the name of the horse) has been down."

Mr. Jamblin wiped the perspiration from his forehead.

"Bin down, and Mr. Philip not here," he ejaculated. Then turning to his men he said, in a voice of thunder—

"Look here, men; what be the yoose o' yer standing here like a set o' stockfish? Ye've got eyes and legs I 'spose; why don't some on ye start off and see if ye can find your young master?"

"We'll go at once," cried several, simultaneously.

"I have not a morsel of doubt as to the road he would take," exclaimed the farmer. "He came from Brickett's, and would pass through Dennett's-lane, and then reach Larchgrove-road. Go, some on 'ee, at once in that direction."

Four of the men at once went in search of their young master. They carried lanterns, which, as they advanced steadily and cautiously along the road, swayed like the censers of priests above the altar.

The clouds had by this time melted away; the moon and stars shone brightly.

The rustics passed on till they reached the end of Larchgrove-road. Here they turned down, and as they entered the shadows of this cheerless place a cold chill fell upon them, for they seemed to feel that it was like entering a churchyard at midnight.

"I dun'no what to mek of it," said one. "The cob might have shied at summut, but Mr. Philip aint easily throwed."

"And yet it be certain that some accident ha' taken place. It may be hard to say what it is. It may be worse than any on us think."

They flashed the lanterns in every direction, but failed to find as yet any solution to the mystery.

They walked slowly and sadly along, examining every portion of the way as they did so.

As they neared the end of Dennett's-lane a cry from the foremost party caused a sudden panic.

"What be the matter?" cried the other.

"Matter!" exclaimed the man in front. "Here be our young master lying like one dead. There's bin foul play, mates—Master Philip's been murdered!"

They now gathered round the body of the dead man.

They lowered their lanterns and gazed at his wan features, which too plainly denoted that life had departed.

They looked into each other's faces, and gave a simultaneous cry.

The open gash in the throat, the fractured skull, and the deep pool of blood were evidences of the terrible tragedy which had been enacted.

Philip Jamblin had always been a special favourite with the labourers on Stoke Ferry Farm. It will therefore be readily understood that the sight of his remains had a powerful effect upon those who went in search of him.

At first the farm labourers were too much appalled to give expression to their feelings by words.

They stared at the ghastly face in stupid astonishment, then they moaned, and glanced around, as if they expected to see the assassin lurking in some dark corner.

But all was silent—as silent as the grave.

"Who ha' done this deed?" exclaimed Joe Doughty. "A blighting curse cling to 'im whoever he may be. A blighting curse."

Footsteps were now heard proceeding from the further end of the road.

The men glanced in the direction from whence they proceeded.

"It be measter a comin' this way," they exclaimed.

Joe Doughty walked rapidly on in the direction from whence the footsteps proceeded.

In a moment or so he came up with his master, who, hastening to the spot where his son lay in his last sleep, said—

"How now, Joe," cried the farmer. "What be the matter, man? What's amiss, eh?"

"You mustn't go any further. Bide where ye are, measter. Dunno' attempt to go any further," said Joe.

"And why not? Speak—can't you? Mr. Philip's been throwed?"

"Worse than that," said the man. "Oh, Mr. Jamblin, ye mustn't go no further!"

He laid hold of the farmer by the coat, and drew him towards the trees by the side of the road.

Jamblin looked at him, and as he did so his face became preternaturally pale. There was that in the conduct of Joe which made his master tremble like an aspen bough beneath the blast.

"Summat's happened," said the farmer, in a low hoarse whisper.

Joe nodded, but durst not trust himself to speak.

There was a pause, after which Jamblin said, in a voice of perfect calmness—

"Tell me what it is?"

He was a huge brawny fellow, with a bronzed face, and having hands with thews and sinews like a giant, was this Joe Doughty; but when the farmer's words fell upon his ears—they were spoken in a tone altogether so different to that he had been accustomed to hear—that, athlete and giant as he was, he seated himself on a felled tree which lay by the side of the road, and burst into tears.

The sight of this man, sobbing and crying like an infant, so affected Jamblin, that he was fairly overcome, and had not the power to move.

He looked at Joe, and then at the vault of heaven.

"He be taken from us, measter," said the latter, still sobbing; "and he was the best an' truest friend I ha' ever known; an' I would ha' given my life—ten lives, if I 'ad 'em—only to ha' saved his. But it's no yoose a bellowin' or a crying, it be all over now."

"All over!" said the farmer. "What is over?"

"He be dead and gone, measter."

When he heard these last words, Mr. Jamblin made a movement towards the scene of the tragedy.

Joe rose suddenly, and caught him by the skirts of his coat.

"Ye mustn't go there, measter, indeed you mustn't. 'Twill break your heart to see the sight I ha' seen. Bide where ye be."

"Let me go," cried the farmer. Do 'e think I am afraid to look the worst in the face?"

"Bide here awhile," repeated the man.

"But I must and will know what's the matter."

"Measter Philip be murdered!"

At these words the farmer stepped back several paces.

"Murdered!" he repeated. "And by whom?"

"I dunno. But I will afore long. By the heaven above, I swear never to rest night or day till I hunt down the infamous wretch who ha' done this foul deed," exclaimed Joe Doughty, raising his right hand above his head. "I ha' said it, and I mean it, as God is my judge."

"I must look upon my son," cried Jamblin. "So don't 'e seek to detain me, Joe. Leave go!"

"If it's to be so, I'll go wi' 'e, measter," replied the latter.

And so the two walked on together towards the

fatal spot, for Joe Doughty would not trust his master to go alone.

When they arrived at that part of the road where the dead body of the young farmer lay, the men with the lanterns were more affected by sight of their master than they had been by looking at the stark form of his son.

The agony expressed on the countenance of the elder Mr. Jamblin was painful to behold.

He said nothing, but his looks were more eloquent than words.

After he had contemplated the heartrending sight for some little time, he turned towards Joe, who silently led him from the spot.

"It is as you sed—he's been foully murdered," whispered Jamblin.

"Get thee back, my dear measter. We will bring the body home."

"Home?" iterated Jamblin.

"Yes, sir, unless you wish it otherwise."

"Poor Patty," cried the farmer ; "it will break her heart."

"Better get home and leave the rest to us," suggested Joe. "My young missus had best hear it from your lips."

"You are right, I will return," said the farmer. "I leave the arrangements to you—I dare not stop longer."

He walked away with rapid strides, and Joe hastened back to his companions.

They placed the body on a hurdle, then they covered it over with a couple of sacks, and bore it along until they reached Stoke Ferry Farmhouse.

They had the discretion to place it on a bench in a granary, the door of which they locked, and when all this had been effected in a gentle and thoughtful manner the farmer was made acquainted with the whole proceedings, at which he expressed his satisfaction.

Patty Jamblin went into hysterics, and the village surgeon was sent for, who pronounced her to be in a very dangerous state.

After recovering in a measure from the first shock she remained in a prostrate condition, and appeared to be but partially conscious of all that was going on.

Her father was more concerned about her than aught else, and perhaps this was a merciful dispensation of Providence.

As it was, to a certain extent it diverted his thoughts from the great and irreparable loss he had sustained.

CHAPTER LVIII.

AFTER THE MURDER—THE INQUEST.

THE terrible crime committed in Larchgrove-road, the news of which spread like wildfire on the following morning, caused a thrill of horror for miles around. At Broxbridge, Sulwich, and a host of other places, it formed the sole topic of conversation.

As the cry of fire will frighten the worst sluggards from their beds, so did the tidings of the frightful murder awaken the whole country from its lethargy.

At the present day crimes of a like nature seem to excite but little sympathy—indeed, it is surprising the apathy displayed by the public; regard or pity for the victim or victims of an assassin is never for a moment thought of. Not so, however, was it in the case of the young farmer who met his death in a manner described in our last chapter. Men ran through the streets and stood in knots by the corners, and sat in circles in the alehouses.

There was but one look in their faces—there was but one thought in their minds—this was the earnest desire that the murderer of Philip Jamblin should not escape the fate he so justly merited.

On market day there was a mournful meeting at the ordinary, and most of the farmers wore crape on their hats or sleeves.

The Jamblins were greatly respected, and every one thought of the bereaved father and the suffering sister.

"Poor Phil Jamblin—he was as brave and honest a chap as ever stepped in shoe leather," they said, as they shook their heads; "and never did a morsel o' harm to any one. I'd hang the scoundrel, whoever he may be—hang 'im on the first tree at hand and try 'im afterwards."

"But who could ha' done it?" said a neighbouring farmer. "Phil never harmed nor quarrelled wi' a soul in his life—leastways not as I ever heard of."

"It must ha' bin some stranger as did it—a tramp, perhaps," cried another. "There's no saying for sartin."

Many of the young farmers were not content with lamenting Phil, but they scoured the country upon their hunters, examining every strange face with suspicion, and asking questions of all the publicans in the neighbouring villages and towns.

Throngs of persons of almost every denomination flocked to the "Carved Lion." It had been "noised abroad" that Brickett saw the murderer washing his hands in a pool of water at Larchfield Green. This was enough to bring hosts of inquirers to his house to learn the truth from his own lips.

The worthy host of the "Lion" repeated his statement until he became weary of the narration; but his customers would not let him have any rest—he was forced to comply with their demands.

Every scrap of information connected with the tragedy was eagerly sought after, and retailed afterwards to the wondering village folk.

Exaggerated stories got abroad, and numberless theories were propounded. Somebody who remembered the thrashing Peace received at the hands of the murdered man kindly hinted that he might have committed the crime from motives of revenge.

Brickett was most indignant at this suggestion, which he declared to be both false and scandalous.

It was not possible for Peace to be accused of the murder, seeing that he was in gaol doing his four years at the time it was committed; he was secure enough.

The constabulary took active measures to bring the guilty party within the meshes of the law. Constables were dispatched in every possible direction; notices were sent to the various stations, but as yet no clue had been found to the fugitive.

Miss Jamblin was in a critical state. The surgeon who attended upon her found her weak and dejected as a woman about to die.

Her face was furrowed by the traces of the scalding tears she had shed; her pulse was faintly fluttering like a wounded bird.

As for her father he said but little. It was, however, but too plainly shown that a strange change had come over him, and those about him whispered to each other that the old gentleman would never be the same man again.

The inquest was to take place at the "Carved Lion," and for the convenience of the coroner and jury the body of the murdered man was brought from Stoke Ferry Farmhouse and placed in one of the private rooms of Brickett's hostelry.

There could not be a moment's hesitation in arriving

at the conclusion as to the cause of death, but it was necessary for the usual formulæ to be gone through.

Of late years the examination of the witnesses, and wrangling of the legal gentlemen engaged in the case, have caused the coroner's inquiry to be protracted to a needless length.

It is either one of two things : the inquiry is knocked off with unseemly haste, or else carried on beyond all reasonable limits.

The fourth of Edward the First, the original Coroner's Act, which gave an appointed official the right to inquire into the causes of sudden death within his jurisdiction, was no doubt at that comparatively lawless period an eminently necessary piece of legislation.

In those days deeds of violence, tavern brawls, and mysterious deaths, were of daily occurrence, and doubtless this was the primary reason for the establishment of a legal court of inquiry, and it cannot be concealed that it is needed in our own times.

In remote districts the inevitable coroner's inquiry, which is sure to follow any and every case of sudden and violent death, is a precautionary measure for the safety of her Majesty's subjects. It acts as a deterrent against crime, and assists the criminal courts in arriving at just verdicts.

But it is felt in cities and large towns that the coroner's court is an expensive and withal fussy antechamber to the justice-room of the stipendiary magistrate, and that some alteration is needed in the conduct of these inquiries.

The old fashion mode—and indeed one which was followed in the case of the Larchgrove-road murder—of holding coroners' courts in the parlours of public-houses, within hearing of the noise and ill-timed jollity of the tap-room, and of laying the corpse in some shed at the back yard of a beershop, among the cans and pewter pots, is very objectionable.

The practice degrades the dignity of justice.

There are, however, still more important objections, in the lack of legal training for which too many of our coroners are conspicuous, and in the needless waste of public and private time and money in examining witnesses—in speeches of counsel, who wrangle, ask irrelevant questions, badger witnesses, and retard instead of aid the course of justice.

This of late has grown almost insupportable.

The first inquiry in what is termed the Balham mystery was a mere sham. The second was carried on to a most unwarrantable length—with no good result.

And in the late Richmond murder the public had reason to deplore the license of advocacy, and the shouts of laughter proceeding from persons in the body of the court were a disgrace to a civilised community.

Upon the coroner and jury assembling at the "Carved Lion" no such unseemly merriment took place.

Everybody present conducted themselves in a becoming manner, and many were deeply affected, as the evidence was heard in almost breathless silence.

It was not of a nature to fix the guilt upon anyone person in particular, nevertheless the facts went far towards pointing to one man as the guilty person.

But the links in the chain of evidence were detached. There was, however, good reason for supposing that they would be strengthened and be made more compact after further investigation.

The knife which the murderer had left behind was found, and was produced by the police on the inquest. In addition to this two human teeth were discovered at a short distance from where the body lay ; one of these was broken short off, the other was perfect.

These were considered most important facts, as in the event of the suspected man being captured, the teeth might serve for the purpose of identification.

Brickett was the first witness called. He deposed to the facts already known to the reader. He said he was under the impression that the man washing his hands in the pool at Larch-green was Giles Chudley, but he would not undertake to swear that it was him.

Henry Adolphus gave his evidence in a very creditable manner. He explained the circumstance of his seeing a man running across the meadows. He appeared to be wounded, and from what he could make out the fugitive was bleeding from the nose or mouth, he could not tell which, as he was too far off. He was quite certain, however, that the man was hurt in some way.

Another and more important witness was next examined.

At no very great distance from Larch-green stood a small habitation called " Jawbone Cottage."

This name was given to the place in consequence of the jawbones of a whale being on either side of the gateway at its entrance.

When placed in their position they formed a pointed arch, around which climbed honeysuckle and clematis.

No one, however, would have taken them to have been bones—certainly not at the first glance.

In Jawbone Cottage resided a farm labourer, his wife, and two children ; the eldest of these being an intelligent little girl, of eleven or twelve years of age. She was brought forward as a witness.

It appeared from what she said that her father and mother had gone from home in the after part of the day on which the murder took place, to see her elder brother off, who was going to sea.

They did not return, however, till late ; the witness and her sister, a child of five years old, went to bed at the usual time, but the witness, who had a swollen face which was very painful, and prevented her from sleeping, got up and looked out of the bedroom window, in the hope of seeing her parents coming along the road.

While thus occupied she observed a great man washing his face and hands in the pool of water on the green. She was so frightened that she hardly durst breathe, but she watched him for some time ; she saw that his lip was cut open, and that his hands and face were covered with blood.

After this she withdrew from the window and covered herself over with the bedclothes. Mustering courage to go again to the window, she found the man gone.

She was asked to describe him, and in reply said—

" He had dark bushy eyebrows and a beaky nose."

She was then asked if she would know him again.

After some little hesitation she said she thought she should be able to recognise him, but was not certain.

Her evidence was taken down very carefully by the coroner's clerk, as it was believed to be very important, as far as the after proceedings in the case were concerned.

After the little girl's evidence there was a pause in the proceedings. The coroner looked at his summoning officer, who looked at the inspector of police who had the case in hand ; then there were whisperings and a low murmur from those assembled in the court, out of which the police inspector took his way ; then he returned again, and said something in a whisper to the coroner, who said out loud—

" In the interests of justice it is most desirable that

she should be heard; but if she is too ill, and has a doctor's certificate to that effect, we have no other alternative than to adjourn the inquiry."

"I will do what I can," answered the police-officer, who again left the court.

In a minute or so he returned, and nodded significantly to the coroner.

All was now so hushed that, to make use of a common phrase, "you might hear a pin drop."

It was generally understood that the girl Nelly was about to make her appearance, and everybody was on the tip-toe of expectation.

Wan and pale, and the very personification of sorrow, the unhappy girl was now brought in by two female attendants and the police inspector.

She was placed in the space set apart for the witnesses, and seemed to be so overcome that all present were under the impression that she was about to swoon. She bore up, however, in a manner which surprised everybody.

"Your name is Ellen Fulford, I believe?" said the clerk.

"Yes, sir," she returned, in a voice which was scarcely audible to any one save those who were in close proximity to the speaker.

"Now, don't be alarmed, Miss Fulford," said the coroner, in a kind tone. I do not doubt but this is a painful ordeal for you to go through. We will not ask needless questions or protract it longer than may be absolutely requisite. Take your time in replying to the few interrogations we have to put."

Nell bent her head in acknowledgment of the consideration shown towards her, and the examination proceeded.

She was asked if she saw Mr. Philip Jamblin on the night of the murder, and replied in the affirmative.

She gave a long account of her conversation with him, which took place near the workshop at one time in the occupation of Charles Peace.

Then a juryman inquired if Peace now resided in the neighbourhood.

"I believe not, sir," said Nell.

"Oh, you believe not—you don't know, for certain, then?"

"He has not resided in this neighbourhood for some time. He left a little under two years ago," said the inspector. "As far as he is concerned we are well able to let you know. He was convicted at the last sessions at Sheffield upon a charge of burglary, since which period he has been doing part of his time. He was sentenced to four years' penal servitude."

A murmur ran through the court at this declaration.

"What did he say?" inquired Brickett, of a policeman who stood next to him. "Charles Peace convicted of burglary! It can't be; I dunno believe it."

"Silence; order in the court!" shouted the usher.

"Well, I'm staggered—regularly dumbfounded!" murmured the landlord. "It bean't true."

"Order!" was again called, and Brickett remained silent, but he had half a mind to give an open contradiction to the inspector's statement.

"It's right enough," whispered the policeman. "He's quodded. Hold your row."

"Now, Miss Fulford," said the coroner, addressing himself to the witness, "you have given us, I dare say, a very faithful account of your last interview with the ill-fated young man, Mr. Philip Jamblin. But of the warning you gave him—which, I am sure, everyone must regret that he did not heed. You say a man was

behind the hedge during the earlier part of the conversation?"

"Yes, sir. There was a man."

"Could you see his features?"

"Yes. Most distinctly."

"Were they familiar to you?"

"They were."

"Then you knew him?"

"I did. His name is Giles Chudley."

"This you swear?"

"I do."

"You are quite positive as to his being Chudley?"

"I am quite positive."

"Can you describe his appearance?"

"I dunno that I can. He is a tall, strong fellow, with a brown face and bushy eyebrows."

"With a beaky nose?" inquired the coroner, referring to the girl's evidence.

"Yes, his nose is a little beaky."

"That will do, Miss Fulford, we will not trouble you any further to-day. You have given your evidence in a most satisfactory manner."

Nell was taken out of court. What it cost her to go through the ordeal was only known to herself.

The coroner summed up. He said all the evidence went in one direction, this being to throw a dark shade of suspicion upon the man Chudley. Still at present it was not clearly established that he was the murderer of Mr. Jamblin, and if the jury had any doubts they had better not declare him guilty by their verdict. This was but a preliminary inquiry. It was clearly demonstrated beyond all cavil that Mr. Jamblin was foully murdered; it was therefore their duty to declare this by their verdict.

The jury were some time considering, but ultimately returned a verdict of—

"Wilful murder against some person or persons unknown."

Thus the proceedings ended.

"Well I never!" cried Henry Adolphus, when they had all left. "Mr. Peace convicted of burglary!"

"Oh, there must be some mistake," returned Brickett; "it can't be our Peace—'taint at all likely—'taint reasonable to s'pose such a thing. Why, he was one of the best fellows out."

"So everybody sees; but it's 'ard to know people nowadays. Still, I can't b'lieve that tale."

"The p'leece ought to know," suggested a man, holding in his hand a tankard of ale; "if they doesn't know, who does?"

"You just shut up," cried the landlord. "Nobody asked your 'pinion. I tell 'ee they do not know—so that's enough."

"All right, guvner, I be dun; you know these matters a deal better than what I do, I dare say."

After the departure of the coroner, the jury, witnesses, and constables, the people in the "Lion" threw off all restraint, and conversed freely on the all-absorbing topic. They commented on the evidence with great acumen—I mean rustic acumen.

Everybody agreed upon one point, this being for the murderer of young Jamblin being brought to justice in the shortest possible space of time.

When the funeral of the murdered man took place all the populations of Broxbridge and the surrounding districts turned out to do honour to the obsequies of the young farmer.

It was a touching sight to witness the crowds of men, women, and children who swelled the throng of mourners.

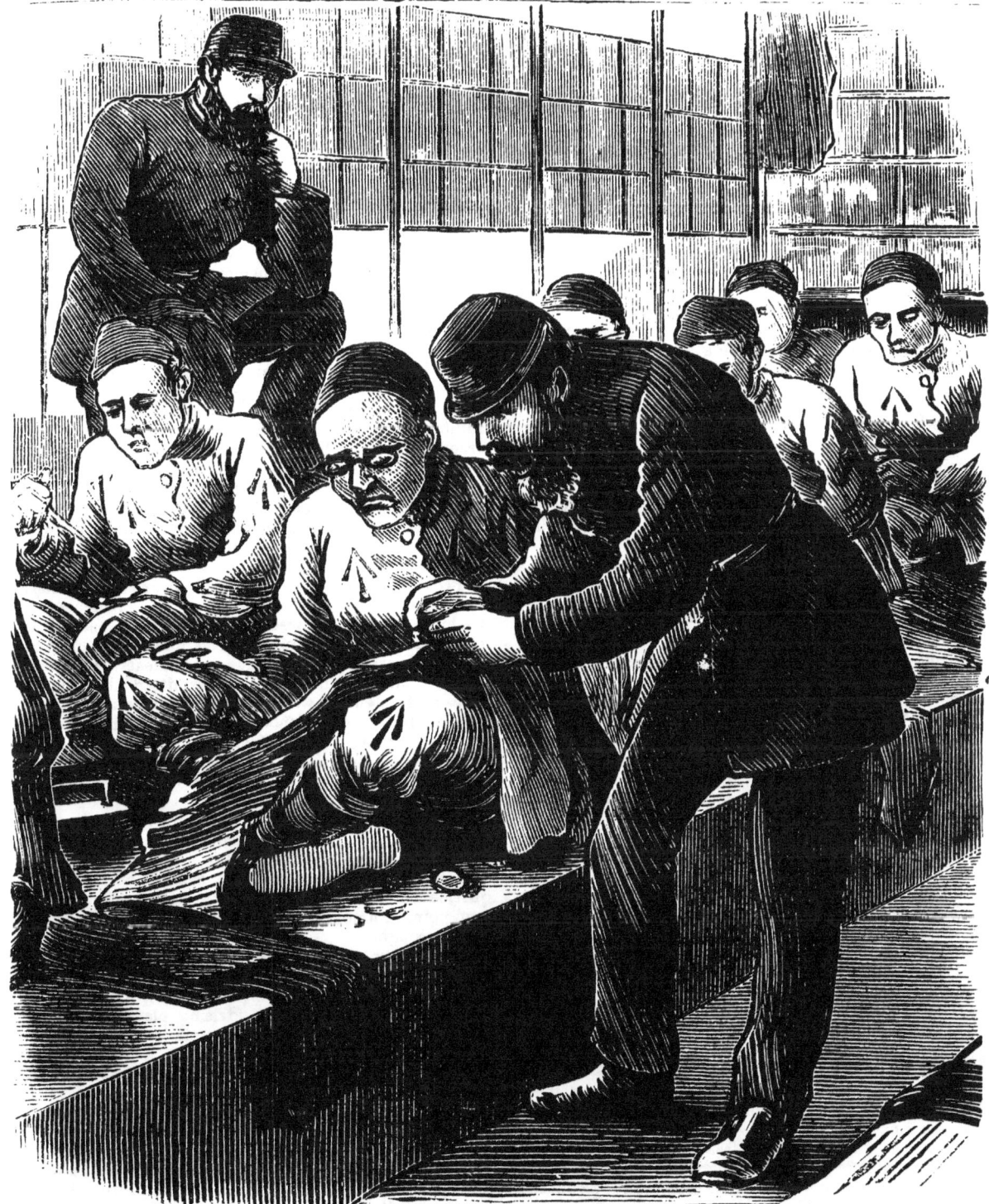

PEACE IN THE TAILOR'S SHOP.

Lord Ethalwood's carriage followed. In this were Mr. Jakyl, Henry Adolphus, his lordship's housekeeper, and head gardener, and when Mr. Jamblin bared his white head beside his son's grave, the tears fell thick and fast down the faces of the women and children, as well as many of the men.

Joe Doughty sobbed convulsively, and it was indeed a day of general mourning, which was heartfelt as it was creditable. There is something of the old heroic chivalrous spirit yet to be found in the rustic population of this country.

There is something of romance and legendary lore left also, but these things are fast fading away. It would be a consolation to most of us if we could persuade ourselves that the better instincts of our nature were not fading away also.

Convulsions have taken place in the moral world. The people of this country have undergone a change—whether for the better or for the worse it is not so easy to determine.

CHAPTER LIX.
MYSTERIOUS MURDERS.

DAYS and weeks passed over, but no clue was found to the murderer of Philip Jamblin. Every effort was made by the police, both London and provincial, but with no satisfactory results.

No one appeared to know where Giles Chudley had gone to after leaving Broxbridge, and nobody seemed to understand how it was that he had returned so suddenly on the night of the murder, and then be spirited away in such an extraordinary manner.

Many of the rustics were under the impression that Nell Fulford might have made a mistake as to the identity of the man behind the hedge in Dennett's-lane.

They did not say much, but shook their heads and muttered—

"No gell could make certain sure of any one behind such a thick hedge."

"Maybe she's mistaken," suggested another.

After short detached observations like these the rustics in Brickett's parlour would lapse again into silence.

Men who are employed from dawn to dusk in such a solitary occupation as ploughing or spreading manure, without perhaps hearing the sound of a human voice all the time, are not likely to be voluble or ready speakers.

They contract silent and ruminating habits, and taciturnity is one of their most marked characteristics. There is no analogy between the "men of the plough" and the British workmen in manufacturing towns.

A group of agricultural labourers will sometimes sit together smoking and drinking for a whole evening, and the nearest approach to a sociable chat will be occasional jerky observations, few and far between, fired off like conversational minute guns.

It is an inevitable consequence of the occupation and mode of life of the men in question.

The farming population of Broxbridge and the surrounding neighbourhood were, however, aroused from their wonted apathy and inactivity by the murder in Larchgrove-road.

Every minute particular was retailed at the village alehouse or elsewhere, and the oft-repeated question was asked—

"Be the man found out yet?"

And when the answer was given in the negative the countenance of the questioner was expressive of regret and disappointment.

Miss Jamblin, for the first few days, was in so serious a condition as to cause the greatest anxiety to those around her.

When the terrible news reached Oakfield House, John and Maude Ashbrook at once started off for Stoke Ferry Farm to administer what comfort they could to the old farmer and his daughter.

They did much, by their presence and kindness, to assuage the grief and melancholy which had found its way into the farmer's homestead.

To say the truth, the Jamblins and Ashbrooks were almost like one family, and Patty was never suffered to be alone: either John Ashbrook or his sister was by her side, and very frequently both were with her.

Lord Ethalwood had been most kind and considerate to the Jamblins.

He sent round Henry Adolphus every day to inquire how Patty was—whether she was progressing favourably or otherwise—he also sent his own family physician to see her.

In addition to all this, he had handbills printed, offering a hundred pounds reward "to any person or persons who would give such information as would lead to the conviction of the murderer of Mr. Philip Jamblin."

Notwithstanding all this, no one was arrested.

It is most extraordinary that so many crimes of this nature should remain undetected; and it is still more extraordinary how soon public interest ceases in cases of this sort. When we consider the number of murders which are known to have been committed, the perpetrators of which are at the present time at large, and who may, for aught we know, be seated by our side in trains, in omnibuses, or places of public resort, the reflection cannot fail to appal the most apathetic and unimpressionable of her Majesty's subjects.

No lesson can be more powerful to teach man the fallibility of his own judgment than the success so frequently attending the efforts on the part of guilt to baffle and mislead. How frequently have we seen a chain of circumstances, pointing apparently with irresistible force to some particular conclusion, suddenly disjoined and scattered by the eliciting of a new fact, by which the pursuit is led away in a totally different direction?

Providence, in its wisdom, has seen fit to limit man's mental vision, and has made many things mysterious to him. It has allowed the hand of the assassin to cut short many a virtuous and valuable life, and permitted the crime to go, in this world at least, undetected and unpunished, and has even permitted the criminal to pass through life without "compunctious visitings" one qualm of conscience. Mocking, as it were, the wisdom of man, it has suffered life to be taken away in the broad glare of noon, in the middle of the crowded city, in the heart of a skilfully-trained police, without the faintest clue to the murderer.

On the other hand, it has given to the criminal the silence of midnight, and the solitude of the forest and plain, and every aid, as it were, for concealment and escape, and suddenly, without even an effort, human justice has laid a denouncing finger on the guilty head, and pointed it out to the world where most unsuspected and unsought.

One slays his victim almost in the face of the ministers of justice, and escapes without haste and rapid flight; another adopts measures of precaution, and exhausts ingenuity in devising places of concealment, and is detected with his victim's warm blood on his hands.

How fruitless are the most elaborate devices for concealment when the hand of heaven is raised to expose the guilt!

Among the many unavenged murders and failures of justice in the great city of London, around the history of which hang so many mysteries in its many phases of life, where frequently the helpless children of hard poverty fall victims to the lust of the wealthy, the death of the young unfortunate girl, Eliza Grimwood, occupies a prominent place.

On the 26th of May, 1838, the whole metropolis of London was startled and horrified by the discovery of the murdered body of Eliza Grimwood, a remarkably handsome young woman, one of the gay belles of London of that period, who by some misfortune or other had been allured from the path of virtue.

She was found terribly mutilated lying on the floor

of a house of doubtful repute, at No. 12, Wellington-terrace, Waterloo-road.

At the inquest held at the "York Tavern," before Mr. Carter, it was elicited that the unfortunate woman, who was about twenty-five years of age, lived with George Hubbard, a bricklayer, but that the deceased went out of an evening to the various theatres, for the purpose of forming the acquaintance of gentlemen to bring home and pass the night with her, and by this means she maintained herself and her paramour.

From the evidence it appeared that some person had gone home with her on the night in question.

The man was, to all appearance, a foreigner, and there was every reason for believing that he had committed the murder, but from that day to this the scoundrel has escaped detection. Not the slightest clue was ever found which might serve to lead to his detection.

The year 1837 was characterised by a large number of atrocious murders, and also by the frequency of brutal garotte robberies.

On the 3rd of November in that year, as Mr. Isaac Butcher, a well-to-do farmer, of Colne Engaine, Essex, was returning from Colchester market he was pounced upon by two men in a lonely part of the road, murdered, and robbed.

One very shocking feature in the case was that his own brother came up shortly afterwards, and was the first who recognised him.

It was believed at the time that the murderers were probably tramping labourers, but no one was ever arrested, and the matter has ever remained a mystery.

A diabolical murder was committed at Chingford Hatch, Woodford, Essex, on Sunday morning, the 21st of June, 1857.

The unfortunate victim was an aged woman, seventy-two years of age, who acted as confidential housekeeper to Mr. and Mrs. Small, farmers of that place.

On the morning in question the house was left in charge of the poor old lady whilst her master and mistress went to attend divine service in the parish church of Chingford. On their return the deceased, whose name was Mary White, was found weltering in her blood. A man named Geydon was suspected. A reward of £200 was offered by Government for his apprehension; but from that day up to the present period no clue to the commission of the murder has ever been discovered.

The celebrated Waterloo-bridge mystery, which caused such a stir in the metropolis, cannot be readily forgotten. On the 9th of October, 1857, a carpet bag was found upon one of the stone ledges of an abutment of Waterloo-bridge. It contained portions of the mutilated remains of a person, evidently murdered and deposited thereon, together with a portion of wearing apparel saturated with gore.

The toll-keeper at the bridge said he remembered seeing a person, dressed as a woman, come up from the Strand side on the previous night, about half-past eleven. She had a carpet bag with her—to the best of his belief the bag in question was the one she had, as he particularly noticed a large flower in the centre of the pattern. The remains were examined, the clothes were hung up in Bow-street station, where thousands of persons inspected them; but, notwithstanding this, like the other crimes, has remained a mystery.

On the morning of the 9th of April, 1863, a very atrocious and mysterious murder was discovered in a house of evil repute, No. 4, George-street, Bloomsbury, St. Giles's, one of the very worst parts of the metropolis.

The unfortunate girl in this instance was a shirt-maker, named Emma Jackson, who resided usually with her father, mother, and brother, at No. 10, Berwick-street.

The unhappy girl used to maintain herself as long as she could solely by her needle; but when this failed her, through shortness of work, she occasionally stayed out at night to eke out a livelihood by prostitution.

The inquest, which was holden at the "Oporto Stores," Broad-street, Bloomsbury, before Dr. Lankester, coroner, showed that the deceased went as early as seven in the morning, on the day in question, to the brothel, at No. 4, George-street, with a man, and on asking for a bedroom, were at once shown to one by the young servant in charge, which they then took possession of.

As she did not come down in the course of the day, the parties belonging to the house went upstairs, and on going to her room were horrified to find her lying across the bed with her throat cut.

Dr. Weekes was the first witness called. He stated that he had made an examination of the body of the deceased, and in addition to finding her throat cut discovered that both her arms and legs were smeared with blood. There were also stains of blood on both thighs. On the left buttock was a mark of the grasp of two fingers. In the neck there were four punctured wounds, two in the front and two behind. There was a considerable effusion of blood on the membrane of the vertebræ, particularly to the right of the spine. There was a very clean cut three-quarters of an inch long. He thought deceased must have been asleep when the first cut was inflicted. The cause of death, he believed, was partly owing to suffocation, and partly owing to loss of blood, as blood had been diffused in considerable quantities both from wounds in the internal jugular, and the veins in part of the trachea. After the second wound he believed that the deceased was dragged into the position in which she was found. In answer to a question by a juror he said he thought the deceased had no power to make any noise after the first wound. In answer to the coroner he said he believed that when he first saw the deceased she had been dead from nine to twelve hours. His belief was that the wounds had been inflicted with a common pocket-knife. In his belief he was decidedly of opinion that the deceased did not receive the wounds in the position in which she was found, but that she was placed in that position by her murderer. She could have had no power of calling out after the wind-pipe had been separated.

The jury, after hearing evidence, returned a verdict of wilful murder against some person or persons unknown.

The matter was then left in the hands of the police.

Among the suspicious circumstances reported was the fact that on the evening of the murder a man went into a draper's shop at Stratford, and bought a new shirt.

The one that he was wearing, together with his clothes, was smothered with blood. When buying the shirt he, in course of conversation with the shopkeeper, said that he had had a quarrel with his wife, and that in the scuffle she had wounded him.

There was a general impression that this was the man and that he was making his way through Epping Forest towards the sea-coast.

Nothing further was heard of the affair, and this also has remained an unexplained crime.

The whole metropolis was thrown into a state of

surprise and excitement on the night of Wednesday, the 11th of April, 1866, by the discovery of a terrible and mysterious murder at Messrs. Bevington and Sons, leather merchants, of Cannon-street, City.

The unfortunate victim was an elderly widow lady named Mrs. Millsum, who, together with a cook named Elizabeth Lewes, were always left by the firm in charge of the premises at night. On the night of the murder, it appears that she was discovered lying just inside the passage leading from the street-door upstairs.

On examining her, she was weltering in her blood. It transpired that while the two servants were upstairs, after the shop had been shut up, and the firm gone to their country residence, the bell of the street-door was rung.

The deceased said to her fellow-servant—

"Ah! that ring is for me. I know who it is," and immediately went downstairs.

She was down a considerable time without any suspicion being occasioned in the mind of her fellow-servant, as the deceased was often in the habit of going down and standing at the door for a considerable time.

When she was first discovered it was surmised that she had perhaps killed herself by falling downstairs, but a further examination proved, beyond doubt, that a terrible murder had been committed.

Mr. May, surgeon, who examined the body, said that when he saw deceased lying on the floor he observed two wounds on the head and face. There was a very deep wound on the side of the head. There was also a wound on the forehead, and one over the eye, and five stabs on the face. He believed that the wounds had been inflicted by a small iron poker or iron crowbar.

A man, who was suspected, was arrested; but there was no material evidence against him, and he was discharged.

The murderer of this ill-fated woman has never been discovered.

A still more extraordinary crime was committed on Wednesday, July 10th, 1872.

Two persons, a mother and daughter, were murdered in a small shop, situated in Hyde-road, Hoxton.

The ill-fated women were ruthlessly assassinated in broad daylight in the very heart of a crowded thoroughfare.

What renders the case more remarkable is that a number of shops, the owners of which drove a thriving trade, were directly opposite to the one in the occupation of the two victims (Mrs. Squires and her daughter).

At twenty minutes past one on the morning of the 10th of July a boy went into a coffee-shop next door to Mrs. Squires' house, and said he had seen blood on the counter of the unfortunate woman's shop.

Upon going in to ascertain the cause, a most horrible spectacle presented itself.

Behind the counter was discovered the body of Mrs. Squires in a pool of blood, with her hand to the right side of her head, which was shockingly injured. The daughter was found with her head in the parlour and her legs in the shop. She was also covered with blood, and her head battered in.

The police at once reached the house, which they found ransacked from top to bottom, and in the parlour was found a clock that had been knocked down, which had stopped at twelve, at which time, no doubt, the deed had been committed, as the doctor who was called in said he should think they had been dead about two hours.

Inquiries were set on foot, and every possible means taken to discover the perpetrators of this dreadful crime, but without avail—like the rest it has been shrouded in impenetrable mystery.

The Ladbroke-lane murder will be remembered by most persons. A girl named Margaret Clemson was found by a policeman in the lane in question frightfully wounded; her skull was laid open in several places (a portion of the brain was protruding from one of the wounds). She was just able to exclaim—"Oh, let me die!"

She was conveyed to the hospital, where after several days of intense agony, she expired. The murderer is at present at large.

Some short time after this the dismembered portions of a female were found in the Thames. A murder of an atrocious nature had been evidently committed, but neither the identity of the woman was established, nor was her assassin discovered.

The body of a boy was found in a lane at Acton some years ago; he had evidently met with a violent death, but the perpetrator of the foul deed escaped discovery or punishment.

In addition to these we could cite numberless instances of crimes of a similar nature.

The Wallaces, husband and wife, have never been arrested for the alleged murder of a lady at Brompton.

The murderer of Harriet Buswell, who was found dead in a bedroom in a house in Great Coram-street, is still at large.

Mrs. Samuels, an old lady whose head was battered in by a hat rail at a house in Burton-crescent, her body being found in the kitchen by a lodger, is another case which demonstrates but too clearly an escape from justice. A woman named Mary Donovan was arrested on suspicion, but after one or two magisterial examinations she was discharged.

Then again, more recently, we have the Euston-square mystery, as it was termed. An old lady, of eccentric habits, named Miss Hacker, took lodgings in Euston-square. She was missing for a year or more, when by the merest accident, her body was found in the cellar of the house in question. Suspicion fell upon a servant girl, named Hannah Dobbs. She was tried at the Central Criminal Court and acquitted.

It would be manifestly unjust to allege that the jury were not quite right in arriving at the conclusion they did. Nevertheless, it was clearly established that the ill-fated woman had met with foul play, and her murderer or murderers have escaped the doom they so justly merited.

When we add to this list the number of murders in which the bodies of the victims are never discovered at all, an appalling list of horrible atrocities is presented to the imagination; indeed, it is hardly possible to calculate the number of crimes of this nature which are annually committed in the metropolis and other parts of the United Kingdom.

It is quite time that some more stringent measures should be taken by the executive.

It may startle many when we declare, according to the Government statistics, that, during 1856 and 1865, one thousand eight hundred and seventy-five murders were unpunished and unaccounted for. But the Home Office publications disclose some serious discrepancies when the number of murders found by coroners' juries are collated with the number of murders brought to punishment.

Speaking broadly, and assuming for the nonce that each murder has been committed by a different individual, it would appear that more than four-fifths of the murders pass unpunished.

This calculation, of course, only relates to crimes of this nature which are discovered. The undiscovered ones would swell the list to an extent altogeter incalculable.

In the interests of society it is requisite that crimes of this nature should not go unpunished.

The very least to be expected, if a member of a community, fall by the hands of an assassin, is that every means should be taken to bring the offender to justice; and when his guilt is established, death should follow as a natural consequence.

It is by the reliability only, and undeviating certainity that punishment follows conviction, that we can hope that it will act as a deterrent from the commission of crime.

But of late years the current seems to have been running in an opposite direction.

There has been a tendency on the part of a certain section of society to make heroes or martyrs of those whose infamous crimes have caused them to be condemned by a jury of their countrymen.

But too frequently every possible excuse is offered for the guilty man, no matter what the enormity of his crime might have been. There are, therefore, a thousand chances of escape.

Sometimes there is an informality in the indictment —as in the case of Charlotte Winslow, the wholesale child murderess; and owing to the ridiculous blunder she escaped.

In other cases there is a doubt about certain evidence being admissible ; attorneys wrangle during the magisterial examinations, which, in most cases, are of an unnecessary length. Witnesses are bullied, all sorts of irrelevant and impertinent questions are asked them by some audacious legal gentleman who thinks it a fine thing to become the champion of a prisoner who is perhaps a disgrace to the name of man.

Everything that is possible for the most ingenious advocate to suggest to turn aside the sword of justice is not wanting, and even after the jury have delivered their verdict and the judge has passed sentence on the prisoner, a knot of busy bodies write letters to the newspapers for the purpose of impugning the judgment of both judge and jury, and the case has to be reconsidered or retried at the Home Office.

These irrational and illogical people are to be found everywhere, and there are some who take a delight in piling stumbling blocks in the way to impede the course of justice from the sheer spirit of opposition, and being different to other persons.

It is really astounding the growing sympathy displayed for murderers within the last few years. We do not remember a solitary instance of pity being displayed on the part of the public for any murdered person.

Strange to say this idea never enters anybody's head. The central point of attraction is the criminal himself, and of late the public have gone further than this—they have subscribed liberally towards a fund for murderers' wives and relatives.

Some alteration in the mode of administering justice will have to be made, as we are going on at present. The evil is beginning to assume gigantic proportions, and nobody's life will be safe.

CHAPTER LX.

THE EARL AND THE FARMER—MR. WRENCH ENGAGED.
OWING in a great measure to the kind ministrations of her father and her two friends, John and Maude Ash-

brook, Miss Jamblin recovered from the terrible shock she had received from her brother's untimely end. She was sad, it is true, and her spirits seemed to be crushed, but she was no longer in a dangerous state, and was able to converse freely with her companions, and view matters with something like a spirit of resignation.

One morning the inmates of Stoke Ferry Farm House were surprised at seeing Lord Ethalwood's carriage being driven up to the front door of the house, his lordship himself being in the vehicle in question.

The footman signified that the Earl desired to speak to Mr. Jamblin, who was of course a little disconcerted, as it was the first time he had been honoured by a visit from so distinguished a personage.

The earl was shown into the best room, and the farmer, in a great state of flustration, entered at once to pay his respects to his landlord.

"Your servant, my lord," said Jamblin; "and many thanks for all your kindness and consideration."

"I am glad to meet you," said the earl, offering his hand, "Pray be seated, Jamblin."

The farmer obeyed. His visitor proceeded—

"I have deemed it a matter on duty to wait upon you for the purpose of offering what poor consolation I can in the hour of your affliction," said the earl, in his usual measured accents. "You have sustained a loss, Mr. Jamblin, which we all of us know to be irreparable, and no one is more sensibly impressed with this painful fact than myself ; but you must strive, my worthy friend, to bear up against this severe trial as best you can."

"Ah, my lord, I ha' striven, and be a-strivin' now," exclaimed Jamblin, in broken accents, "but it ha' bin a sore trial—a terrible trial, and that be the truth. Mek the best on it I'll try."

"We've all our trials and troubles in this world, Jamblin. Up to the present time the police have been unsuccessful in their search for the man who committed this atrocious crime. I have offered a reward, as you doubtless know, but it has not been attended with any satisfactory result at present."

"It's very kind of your lordship to take such an interest in this matter, an' I hardly know how to sufficiently thank 'ee."

"There is no need for thanks, but I've been thinking that it would be as well to have recourse to other means to trace out the scoundrel who has imbrued his hand with the blood of an honourable young man."

"Other means?" repeated the farmer, not knowing very well what his visitor was driving at.

"Yes, if it meet with your approval. I dare say you heard that I had occasion to employ an experienced and intelligent detective in a matter of business which was both difficult and intricate—but he succeeded ; and for this reason I have the greatest confidence in his discretion and ability. I will, if you have no objection, enlist his services in this matter, which concerns both of us, but you in particular. The gentleman's name is Wrench."

"I've heard on him. Yes, a very sharp, clever fellow, I've bin told."

"Yes. Well, you have no objection to my placing the matter in his hands ?"

"None in the least."

"So that matter is settled. I shall send him to you, and you will have to give him all the information you can."

"Certainly, my lord."

"And now there is another matter to which I have to make reference. My man tells me that your daughter is somewhat better."

"She be far better than she bas."

"Is more herself?"

"She's not quite herself at present—that none ov us can expect—but she be better—a deal better."

"Change of scene is requisite for her. She'll never get well without a change; there are too many things in Stoke Ferry to remind her of a dear brother who is gone. I think it would materially hasten her recovery if she paid a visit to the hall."

"To where?" inquired Jamblin, who hardly dared trust his ears.

"To Broxbridge Hall—to my residence. My granddaughter would do everything in her power to make her life as cheerful and happy as possible."

The farmer was astonished. The great Lord Ethalwood to invite his daughter as a guest at his manorial residence!

It was hardly credible. He did not know what reply to make.

Lord Ethalwood was reported to be proud to a fault, and such condescension on his part was, therefore, the more surprising.

"I beg yer pardon, my lord. It be very kind on ye to do my poor gell so much honour, but——"

"Well, Jamblin, but what, my friend?"

"She's as good a gell as ever cheered a father's heart, but she a'nt fit company for thee or thine. It be kind and considerate of you, my lord, an' I shall never forget this offer, which, after all, you would not think it right of me to accept."

"I am not in the habit of making any offer or giving any invitation with the idea that it will be declined," said the Earl, haughtily. "I wish and desire Miss Jamblin to be my guest for a few days—or it may be a few weeks. At Broxbridge new scenes will be opened to her, and these will do much in assuaging her grief. Don't misunderstand me, Mr. Jamblin, I shall be glad to receive her. She will be a companion to my granddaughter Aveline."

The farmer's breath appeared to be taken away; he made no reply, but bowed in a manner, which, under any other circumstances, would have been extremely comic.

"You will make her acquainted with my wishes, and assure her that she is not asked out of mere compliment," said the earl, in continuation. "If she feels herself well enough to leave home my granddaughter will receive her to-morrow, or as soon afterwards as may be agreeable to herself. Make it agreeable to yourselves. And, touching the other matter—I mean with regard to Wrench—that I will see to."

The earl rose, and, bidding the farmer good morning, entered his carriage and was driven off.

Mr. Jamblin was a little dazed, and it took him some minutes to gather his thoughts together.

When this had been done he sought John and Maude Ashbrook, who were in the garden at the rear of his house.

He made them acquainted with all that had transpired in the best parlour.

His young friends were equally as astonished as himself, but they both coincided in the opinion that Miss Jamblin ought at once, without hesitation or delay, to pay a visit to the earl's palatial residence.

Maude went upstairs to communicate the intelligence to her friend Patty.

"He be a real gentleman, every inch on him," said the farmer to young Ashbrook; "that I always knew, but I didn't think he was so tender-hearted."

"His manner is usually austere," said Ashbrook, "but I suppose it's the way wi' most of the big pots—

but he's none the worse for that. His heart's in the right place. And so he's going to employ a detective?"

"Yes he be."

"What is your opinion? Do 'ee think it wer' that Giles, as used to work here, as did the foul deed?"

"I dunno, but I 'xpect it be. He was always an evil-disposed fellow."

"And his motive?"

"Ah, there you beat me. Some people do deeds o' this sort without any motive; but you see," said the farmer, sinking his voice to a whisper, "poor Philip got hampered and cajoled by that gell Nell Fulford, an' it be true enough what's been sed over and over agen, there never was any mischief in this world but what a woman has summut to do wi' it."

"Oh, hang it, don't blame poor Nell. She did her best to save Phil. If he'd harkened to her counsel the chances are that he would be wi' us now. Don't blame Nell."

"I don't blame her, but it were a bad business his ever taking up wi' her. He ought to have know hisself better; but there it was to be, I 'spose, an' it ain't o' no use making matters worse by thinking o' all these things; but I tell 'ee, John, it ha' been a sore trouble to me."

As the old farmer said this his eyes filled with tears, and he turned away and entered the house.

Miss Jamblin was prevailed upon to give a reluctant consent to pay a visit to Broxbridge Hall, and on the day following the earl's interview with Jamblin, the carriage was again at the door of Stoke Ferry House. In it was Aveline herself, who had come to fetch Patty Jamblin, who was taken by storm and whirled on to Broxbridge before she had time for reflection.

It is needless to say that the farmer's daughter was treated with the greatest kindness and consideration by Aveline Gatliffe.

Meanwhile, the earl had telegraphed to Scotland-yard for Mr. Wrench, who hastened down to Broxbridge by the first train.

"Lord Ethalwood wanted to see him on most important business," so the telegram said.

What this was Mr. Wrench was not able to divine, so he thought it just as well to drop into the "Carved Lion" before ringing the big bell at the Hall.

He had a long conversation with Brickett, who told him all the news.

"And depend on it that's what the earl wishes to see you about, leastways that's my opinion. He'd gi' any money to find out the murderer of Phil Jamblin."

After picking up all the information he could Mr. Wrench waited upon the earl.

"Well, my lord, I am here again at your service," said the detective.

"If you will kindly explain to me the nature of the business it shall receive every attention."

"It is this, Mr. Wrench—a brutal murder has been committed in Larchgrove-road. It is now some weeks ago since it took place, and the police have failed to find the guilty person."

"I want you to give the matter your undivided attention, to strive in every possible way to find out the man."

"You are acquainted with a good many people in this neighbourhood—push your inquiries in every quarter. Do your best."

"That you may rely upon my doing."

"Yes, but you see, Mr. Wrench, I don't know why it is, but the police seem to me to be so often in fault."

"In what way, my lord?"

"Perhaps I am wrong in making use of so strong an

expression. I don't know that they are positively in fault, but certainly, scoundrels of the very deepest dye seem to contrive to elude them. I cannot see why this is. I should have thought, with the extensive machinery we have in the shape of a well-organised police force, together with the detective department, that it would have been next to impossible for a man who was well known to be concealed for any length of time."

The detective smiled, and said, "You have no idea, my lord, of the difficulties of detection. They are almost incalculable. I am sure we all of us do our best. If we don't succeed, it is some unknown cause which lies far beyond our reach. Every effort has already been made on the part of the local constabulary as well as the metropolitan. Nevertheless, it will never do to give the case up as hopeless. I am ready to set to work at once."

"Thank you. I am glad of that, as I have great confidence in you. That I need hardly say, seeing that you have given me such unmistakable proof of your ability. I have jotted down all the particulars in reference to the case," said the earl, drawing from his desk a paper, "and at the same time I have made marginal notes and suggestions there. You will use your own discretion about adopting them or rejecting them as you please. The *modus operandi* I leave to you. What money you require Mr. Chicknell will furnish you with, and I do hope and trust you may be successful."

Mr. Wrench bowed, took the paper, and promised to set actively to work, and the Earl felt assured that the murderer of Philip Jamblin would not be long at large.

CHAPTER LXI.

ANOTHER GLANCE AT PRISON LIFE. PEACE'S NEW OCCUPATION.

WHILE all these events were taking place Charles Peace was becoming better acquainted with prison life. He was getting fairly sick of the wearisome monotony of his solitary mode of existence, and although he contrived to get through the quantum of work assigned to him each day, he found it by no means an easy task.

Mat making was the hardest work done in the gaol in which Peace was confined, and when this was supplemented by picking oakum, as it was in his case, it became still more so.

But the work was not so severe a punishment as the solitary nature of his existence. Even if he were not allowed to speak to his fellow-prisoners, there would be some consolation in seeing others at work besides himself in one of the large wards.

He had "taken stock," as it is termed, of all the prison officials who had come under his notice. The chief warder of that portion of the prison where he was confined was a portly, pleasant-spoken man of the military type.

He had been a petty officer in a regiment of dragoons, and had seen a good deal of service. His name was M'Pherson, and a good-natured, good-tempered officer he was, but Peace only caught sight of him occasionally.

The under-warder, who had him more particularly in his charge, was rather of a saturnine disposition, and Peace felt that he was not a sort of man he could take in his confidence.

He, therefore, made up his mind to bide his time.

Peace received the greatest kindness and attention from the Rev. John Clay, chaplain of the gaol.

This gentleman gave him the very best advice it was possible to offer under the circumstances.

Peace took the first opportunity afforded him of asking the chaplain what he had best do to get transferred into one of the working wards of the prison.

"It is out of my province to interfere in such matters," said the chaplain; "but your best plan will be to speak to M'Pherson."

"Oh! not the governor?"

"No; it's left to M'Pherson. He is a privileged warder, and does pretty much as he likes in respect to the working arrangements."

"Good," muttered Peace to himself. "A nod's as good as a wink to a blind horse. I shall profit by your advice."

So when he next caught sight of the head warder going his rounds, he touched his cap respectfully, and said—

"I beg your pardon, sir, but can I have a word with you?"

"What is it, my man?" inquired his janitor.

"When is it likely for me to do my work in one of the wards?"

"When? Well, I don't know as I can tell you just now. Do you know any trade? Can you work with the thread and needle, or what?"

"I am a carver and gilder by trade, but can do smith's work as well, and know something about weaving."

"We'll find you a billet shortly, and put you through your facings. Go back to your cell; I'll see what can be done."

"I thank you, sir, I'm much obliged—very much obliged," cried Peace, again touching his cap.

The reader must not consider Peace fawning or cringing in addressing the prison officer as "sir." It was a rule in the service that whenever a prisoner addressed an official or "officer," as they liked to be called, he was to use the word "sir."

Peace had heard that a great deal of weaving was done in the gaol; these were coarse goods, afterwards used for prison shirts, sheets, towels, pocket handkerchiefs. The fabrics so manufactured are afterwards made up in the tailor's shop or sewing ward.

The bakery and kitchens were all worked by convicts under the superintendence of special warders. Certain numbers of the warders and assistants are sufficiently well skilled in the various crafts to enable them to superintend and instruct those men who are placed under their charge in their respective gangs or wards to learn or work at a trade.

The chief warder made inquiries of his subordinates as to the general demeanour and conduct of Peace; the account they gave was satisfactory, and some two or three days after our hero's interview with him, M'Pherson entered Peace's cell, and said in a conciliatory tone—

"Well, my man, as I have had a good account of you, I don't see that there is any reason for your not making yourself useful. Come this way."

Peace followed the speaker, and was shown into a ward where a number of men were busily occupied on various articles.

A bundle of coarse cloth was thrown down by the chief warder.

"We are going to make a tailor of you," he said, jocosely, to Peace.

"I am much obliged, sir, but I am not much of a hand at tailoring."

"No matter, you are willing to learn, I suppose?"

"Oh yes, quite willing."

"Very well, undo that bundle."

Peace did as he was bid, and found various pieces ready cut out for a similar jacket to the one he had on.

"I suppose you know what these are for?" said M'Pherson.

"For a jacket."

"You are quite right, my man." Then, turning to a man beside him he said, "Give him a needle and thread, and we shall soon see if he takes kindly to the business."

Peace was fitted with a thimble; they gave him a bunch of thread, a piece of beeswax, a needle, and a pair of scissors.

"There you are—now you are set up in business," said M'Pherson, "and can stitch away to your heart's content."

"We don't expect very great things from you at first. See what you can do; if you get into a muddle, you'll have to undo your work and re-sew it."

"I am afraid——"

"Oh, you must not be afraid. Stick to your business, and we'll make a good workman of you before your time is up. I shall give an eye to you and see how you get on."

"I am much obliged, sir, for all your kindnes," cried Peace.

M'Pherson put up his hands deprecatingly, and walked away.

He was a kindly-disposed man, and was generally liked by everyone in the prison. He was never austere or overbearing in his manner; but he would not be trifled with. If a man did not behave properly or gave him unnecessary trouble, and did not conform to his rules, he very soon got rid of him by getting him removed to some other ward.

He took a great pride in the men under his charge, and it was considered quite a favour by most of the convicts to be placed under his charge. He certainly contrived to have the pick of the convicts, and weeded out those who were of obstinate or refractory dispositions. Indeed, M'Pherson was not inaptly termed the "old soldier," and this he certainly was in many ways.

He was an excellent officer, and his superiors were duly impressed with this fact. He had his peculiarities (who has not?), but he was a worthy, kind-hearted man.

Peace had felt assured of this when he first made his acquaintance, and he strove by diligence and good conduct to propitiate him.

The jacket, however, was a little above his comprehension; but he did his best, and while he was at work M'Pherson came and gave him some valuable hints, and he managed to put the garment together much better than he had anticipated.

"It's not at all bad for a first attempt," said the warder. "You'll do after a bit; with a little more practice you'll be a first-rate hand. Persevere, my man; Rome wasn't built in a day. You like this occupation better than mat-making I suppose?"

"Oh, dear me, yes."

"Very well, go on. If you are in any difficulty, ask me, and I'll do what I can to make a soldier—I mean a tailor of you."

The convicts in the gaol where Peace was confined underwent a mild course of treatment. The treadwheel had been entirely removed.

It was first established in 1826, and certainly effected some little improvement on the previous system as a means of deterring from future offence, but when views on prison discipline became more enlightened, and the reformation of a prisoner became an object of greater solicitude than his punishment, it was found that the treadwheel was useless, and worse than useless. When the body was undergoing compulsory and painful exer-

tion the mind was irritated and harassed by the ever-present consciousness of punishment.

The labour least liked by prisoners is the treadwheel. Its use is to raise sufficient water for the use of the establishment to an immense tank fixed in the roof.

Hand-pumping was at first tried with such questionable success that the labourers were suspected of "shirking," and to prove the charge against them a jury of free workers were called in and set to the task, but, having that blessed privilege, after a trial they dropped the pump handles, and flatly declined "to have any more of it."

The treadmill answers better, but it is fearfully hard work for the treaders. The "wheel" itself, as at present used in some of our prisons, extends the whole length of the shed by the wall and revolves on an axle.

Attached to the wheel or rather drum are projecting pieces of board six inches in width and about nine inches apart.

Overhead is a short bar for the operator to grasp with his hands, and when the wheel is started he has no foothold and no rest until his period of treading is at an end.

For full twenty minutes he must constantly first raise his right foot and then his left as though he was walking upstairs, and this at a rate of about sixty times for a minute.

Fancy having to ascend one thousand two hundred stairs in twenty minutes—to ascend to the monument three times over in that short time, and then to be released that you may sit in a box like a church pew in the same shed and pick oakum for a further term of twenty minutes by way of a rest, and then three times to the top of the monument again?

And it is not as though the operator trod on the open wheel. He must not speak to his neighbour—he must not see him.

It must be terrible work for a fat man. It is possible for such a one to lose three stone in as many months.

Happily for Peace he was spared this dreadful infliction, as the gaol in which he was confined did not at that time contain a treadmill; therein he might deem himself fortunate.

His new occupation pleased him well enough, it was far better than being cooped up in a narrow cell.

One day when he was deep in the mysteries of trying to put the different pieces of the jacket together, and comparing them with his own, which he had taken off, he was visited by an assistant schoolmaster, who brought him a Bible, prayer and hymn-books.

He made him write a few verses of a psalm on a slate to see his handwriting, and finding it tolerably satisfactory, told him he need not attend school, but during the hour each week when the other members of the ward were at their lessons, he would be at liberty to read or write, and need not continue his work.

He also asked if he wished to write to any of his friends at the next school day or default.

If Peace did not exercise the privilege within a month he would lose it.

He, therefore, deemed it advisable to book himself to write the very first opportunity.

He was anxious to write to his mother, and when the day arrived that he was to write home he was directed to go to the end of the ward, where he found a number of small tables—one of which with an inkstand, a pen, and a piece of blotting-paper.

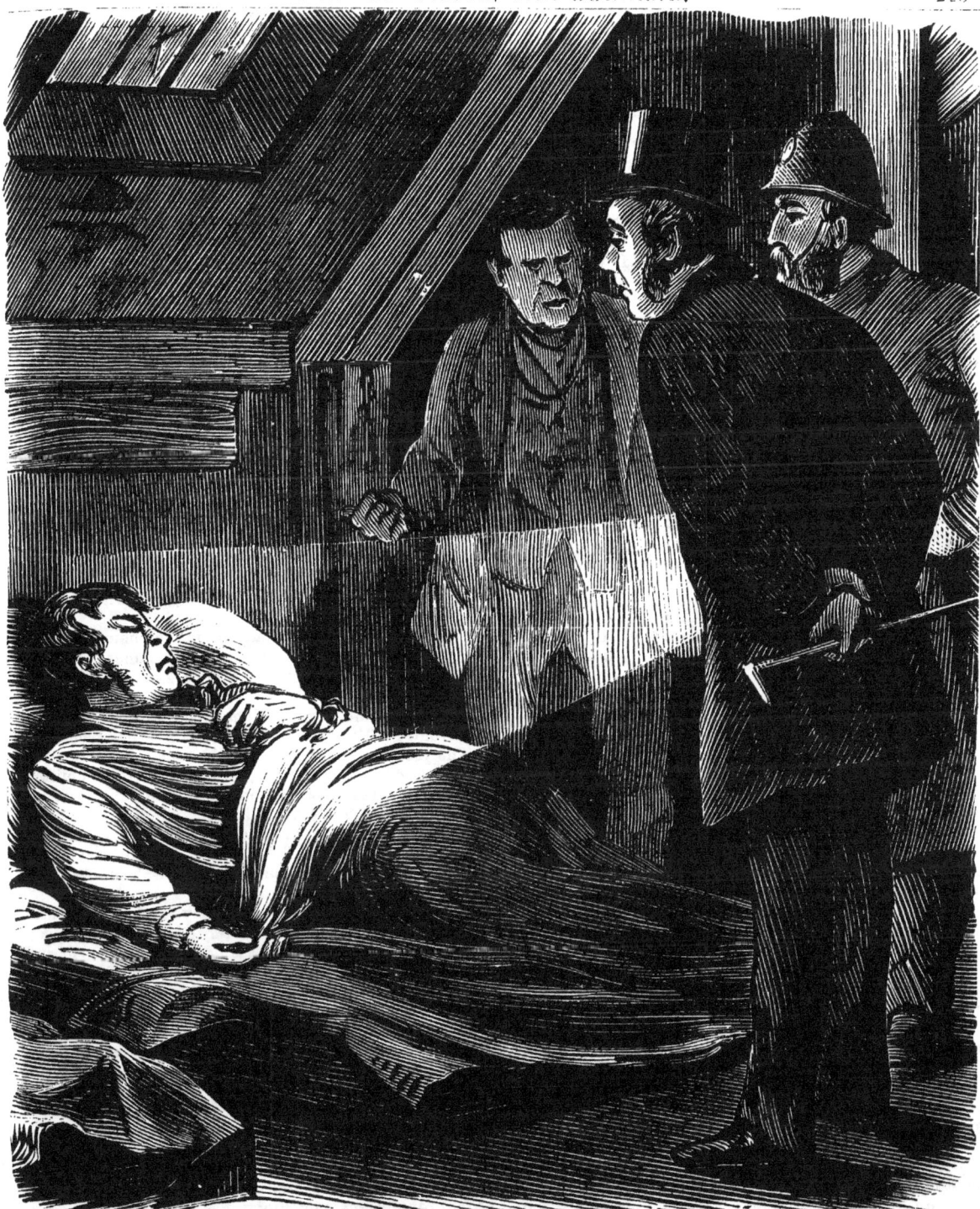

SEARCHING FOR A MURDERER.

He took into his cell a sheet of regulation paper that had been brought to him, on which was already written his name, official number, and the date.

A few lines of printing gave him directions.

He was not to infringe; he was to confine his writing to the ruled lines—not to write between them or to cross his letter; he was not to give any information respecting any other prisoner or any prison news; was not to write to any improper person, or use any improper language.

Every letter to or from a prisoner is examined by the deputy-governor, who initials it and passes it on to the chaplain. He also reads and initials it. Each strikes out anything he considers as infringing the rules, or as improper either for a prisoner to know or communicate.

Knowing his letters to be subject to both an official and clerical examination, Peace was as careful as possible as to what he said.

In the course of a few months he became a tolerably good workman at the tailoring business, and M'Pherson had frequent occasion to compliment him. This worthy fellow took a pride in his ward and the people under his charge, and it was generally acknowledged that every prisoner felt grateful to him, and did his best to keep the old soldier in good humour. He was, in fact, a favourite with the ward. He was always kind to the men under his charge, and it was very rare for his kindness to be abused.

Every day for an hour the prisoners were marched down into the yard for exercise, and some of the able-bodied men were set to work to pump supplies of water into the large cisterns at the top of the yard. Others were set to sweep and roll the gravel of the exercise grounds, and sometimes all the stonework in which the iron railings were fixed were cleaned by the prisoners.

The dinners were served in oblong-shaped tins, divided in the centre into two compartments, with a lid to each.

The division in the centre came up so as to form a convenient handle.

The dinners were kept pretty hot, and the meat and vegetables were well cooked—indeed there was but little to complain of as far as the living was concerned. The food was plain and homely, but wholesome, and the meat was of good quality. Sauces were, of course, not thought of, but there was a plentiful allowance of fresh vegetables.

Cabbages and parsnips were frequently served out, also rice, peas pudding, harricot beans, and preserved potatoes.

One hour was allowed for dinner, and a bell rang at twelve, and frequently in Peace's ward all the dinners were served out before the bell began.

Many of the trades, such, for instance, as tailors and shoemakers, "knocked off" work at six o'clock, and then got their supper, after which they retire to their cells, but they must do some kind of work until the bell sounds eight o'clock, when they may cease, and are privileged to spend the ensuing hour in reading or meditation, or washing themselves, when the bell tolls again, and a clatter of hammock hooks, as long and precise almost as the grounding of arms at a military review, resounds through the corridors, and the prisoners may go to bed.

Reading during this hour is of course a great solace, and cannot be too highly estimated.

With some prisoners it is a necessity, and if the authorities were to deprive the better class of convicts of this boon many of them would doubtless be driven insane.

When the prisoner can read the beneficial workings of the mind are much aided. Although Peace was not what might be termed a great reader—that is, when outside the walls of a prison—he fully appreciated the benefit to be derived from good books during his lonely hours in a prison cell.

At this time all sorts of systems of prison discipline were tried in the gaols throughout the United Kingdom.

Firstly, there was the discipline of Pentonville, now mitigated by horticulture, &c.; secondly, there was the academic discipline, which flourished for so long a time at Reading; thirdly, there was the semi-cellular system, then in partial operation in Birmingham; fourthly,

there was *encellement* with hard labour at crank, and similar contrivances enforced at Winchester, and in a still more primitive fashion at Leicester; and fifthly, there was a "mixed system" still working with great success, and no drawback, at Preston and elsewhere.

All these systems and the effects upon the prisoners were submitted to the consideration of a committee who had been appointed by Government to inquire into the subject.

After examining many witnesses, and long discussions, the committee reported strongly in favour of the discipline of Preston.

At Great Wakefield prison, for instance, the justices had begun with Pentonvillian rigour, and in less than two years adopted all the Preston modifications.

But still the committee hankered after some method of treatment more sharply penal than that at Preston seemed to be.

The influence of able editors crops up in many portions of the report, which was an attempt to make the unpopular system satisfy the cry for cheapness and austerity.

The Reading plan, therefore, of plenty of sleep and study, with no manual employment except by way of "recreation," was thoroughly repudiated, and some obnoxious resolutions passed in favour of more work, coarser food, and less artificial warmth.

Unfortunately, however, the committee went further, and voted that hard labour was incompatible with individual separation, citing Leicester gaol as a model for imitation.

In this gaol prisoners had cranks in their cells, and were forced to turn the handles 14,000 times a day, and if they refused to work they were starved or flogged into submission.

This discipline had produced the notable result of frightening all the tramps from the neighbourhood.

The justices flattered themselves that some of their prisoners were reformed; as, however, the re-committals for serious offences were not diminished, they were in this respect probably sanguine.

In fact the crank variation of the separate system was the very thing which the public had been crying for. It satisfied the requirement of able editors and the justices.

It was in vain that Messrs. Clay, Field, and others protested that the cell without any addition was already penal to the very verge of safety; that Mr. Osborne, of Bath, who spoke from what he had seen in his own gaol, stigmatised crank labour as torture, and foretold the inevitable consequences.

The committee adhered to their opinion, the public approved, and even Sir J. Jebb, who should have known better, appeared as quite a connoisseur in patent cranks, and spoke strongly in their favour.

To such august authority the magistrates in various districts bowed at once, sharpened their discipline, and laid in a stock of cranks.

It was solemnly believed that there was a reformatory as well as a deterrent potency in the appointed 14,000 revolutions per diem, yet to warrant such a belief there was not even the plea that the irksome toil was productive.

It was impossible to find grist for all the penal mills, and the justices were therefore compelled to put their rogues to barren air grinding.

Among the earliest converts to the efficacy of sharp discipline in general, and penal air grinding in particular, were the borough justices of Birmingham.

They were but acting in perfect accordance with the popular philosophy when they ousted Captain

Maconochie, and proceeded to rectify his benevolent eccentricities by appointing a strict disciplinarian, duly instructed to adopt the deterrent method.

At the end of two years the public became anxious that the new governor should give an account of the management of the gaol.

There were ugly rumours afloat which called for immediate investigation.

The sickening tragedy brought to light by the inquiry elicited a unanimous outburst of indignation from the whole country.

The doctrines of the deterrent system had required, it seems, that a certain miserable lad should turn the handle of a stiff crank 10,000 times a day.

Being unwilling, or much more probably unable, to perform the task, it was necessary, in vindication of the deterrent system, to starve him into submission.

As this was found to increase both the unwillingness and the inability of the poor boy, it then became inevitable (as the deterrent system was on the verge of a breakdown) to strap him tight to his cell wall for hours together in the attitude of crucifixion, and when this failed to supply the requisite will or muscle—nay, rather to occasion deadly faintings—then drenching with cold water, as an immediate restorative, and a further inducement to exertion, were superadded.

The devices of the deterrent system were not even then exhausted, but the unhappy boy's powers of endurance were, and, therefore, he rendered further measures unnecessary by hanging himself.

Other stories illustrative of the method of unkindness nearly quite as revolting as this were raked up in the course of the inquiry, and not a few reminiscences of minor atrocities.

The history of this case is most powerfully and graphically given in Mr. Charles Reade's novel of " It's Never Too Late to Mend."

The governor was very properly dismissed.

As a rule felons will submit to these hateful punishments, but the exceptions are numerous.

Some men will rebel, and force the "felon tamer" to some means of further punishment, and the duel between felon and gaoler once begun will be grimly fought—the one, unaided and reckless, will struggle with wild-beast fury; the other, put on his mettle and sorely irritated, will harden into ferocity.

Such a conflict will always terminate either in the prisoner's victory or else his murder or suicide.

When the inquiry at Birmingham gaol was over it was found advisable to submit its prototype at Leicester, the model of crank discipline, to a similar scrutiny. The second investigation was not much more favourable than the former to the deterrent system.

It appeared that there too the felons and the felon breakers had been driven into fierce collision.

And if the inquiry had been extended (as it well might have been) other prisons would have been found in which gaolers and turnkeys had been forced to strange extremities in their endeavours to coerce stubborn convicts into conformity with a radically pernicious system.

Of course the investigations at Birmingham and Leicester produced a reaction against the method of unkindness, and the nation has grown wiser by experience. Cranks, and such like contrivances, have been abolished in most, if not in all of our prisons.

But Peace was not subject to the miserable labour on the treadwheel, or the still more wretched employment of turning the handle of the crank, and all things considered, he had very little to complain of.

The chaplain paid him occasional visits, and gave him the best advice. It would, indeed, have been well for him if he had given greater heed to the counsel of this kind and considerate minister, who, during his long official services, strove earnestly and persistently to improve the moral tone of those who came under his humanising influence.

The chief warder, Mr. M'Pherson, was always busy on Saturdays. Just before dinner was served each man had a bundle of clean clothes handed him—shirt, stockings, towel, and pocket handkerchief; and every alternate Saturday flannel drawers and vest.

These he had to put on during his dinner hour, and after the meal was over the dirty things were collected.

M'Pherson had, on these occasions, always something to say, some pleasant remarks to make to one or more of the men under his care. He had, of course, his favourites. Those who behaved well, and gave the least trouble, he took the greatest notice of; but he was uniformly kind and pleasant to all.

On Saturday, also, the prisoners were supplied with the regulation allowance of bath brick, cleaning rags, and every alternate Saturday a portion of soap which would suffice them for a fortnight.

Sunday was a quiet day; there was no hard work, but the convicts had to go to church twice, and to exercise in the afternoon.

The warders presented themselves in full dress, and those who had served in the army or navy displayed their medals. M'Pherson had several, and generally cut a most respectable figure on the Sabbath—not that there was any pride or ostentation about him. He felt it a duty to show the honours he had won in the service of her Majesty, for whom he had a great reverence.

Indeed, there was not a more loyal man in the prison, or indeed anywhere else, than the "old soldier," as he was termed.

Peace, as we have seen, was a cunning rascal; he could dissemble and "play the good boy" with the best of them, and he managed to ingratiate himself in the good graces of M'Pherson.

Artful old soldier as the latter was, Peace was more than a match for him as far as dissimulation and hypocrisy was concerned.

In our former chapters on prison life we gave the reader a circumstantial account of a "light-fingered family." An unexpected confirmation of the statements of O'Brian, the Clarkes, &c., with respect to girl pickpockets, was supplied by the late Mr. Thomas Wright, of Manchester.

That gentleman informed the chaplain of Preston gaol that while pursuing his benevolent labours amongst the outcast and friendless in the New Bailey, he came in contact with a little girl who had been brought over some time before from Dublin, and was apprehended for a robbery from the person of a lady under circumstances which showed great skill and long practice in the child, and at the same time that she was an instrument—an apprentice pickpocket, working for concealed employers.

A part of Flanagan's account seemed to bear directly on this child's case, and Mr. Wright put down in writing what he remembered of it.

We quote his words to prove that these poor infants are sacrificed body and soul to Mammon in his most hideous form.

Mr. Wright says—

A little girl, whilst an inmate of Salford Gaol, related that she had been brought from Dublin by two women on purpose to pick pockets. They dressed the poor child in the character of a little maid, and, thus attired, she followed a lady into a silversmith's shop, in King-street, and succeeded in extracting from her pocket a purse, which contained twenty sovereigns.

She afterwards followed a lady into the fish market, and again succeeded in extracting this second lady's purse, with which she was making off, when the lady discovered her loss.

The fishmonger said no one had been near her but her little maid. She declared that she had no little maid with her.

The child was overtaken and placed in the charge of a police officer.

When searched she had upon her the two purses. She was tried at the following sessions and sentenced to six months' imprisonment.

I apprised her father a little before her liberation. He came over, and I have not since heard of them.

Some time back much of the crime of this description was committed by children, most of whom came from Ireland.

Flanagan's account is this—

These girls are natives of Dublin. When at home they live in Thomas-street, in the Liberty. When they come to Manchester they are quite plain in their dress, and no person on earth would suspect them. I believe there is nowhere their equal in being expert at ladies' pockets. When they first came to Manchester they stole a large amount of money in shops and omnibuses.

When an omnibus leaves Market-street, for Oxford-road, Cheetham-hill, or elsewhere, they get into it, and being dressed like any gentleman's girls, with one of those French baskets in their hands, nobody suspects them ; they get close beside a lady, and contrive to place their shawl or mantle over the lady's dress pocket, which shades their hand ; the rest is an easy matter.

When these two girls and their mother and myself were having a glass of liquor, they told me they often sent twenty pounds to their parents in Dublin.

To the progress of civilisation in one particular is attributable much of the increased crime as regards pocket picking.

Railways, while they have added to convenience and luxury, to a great extent have also increased the demand for skilled thieves—so much may be done by them in trains, in the stations, and at the attendant omnibuses.

Yet surely these encouragements and facilities to crime, arising out of the railway system, are susceptible of counteraction.

It is well deserving of note that a fashion in dress may lead to a fearful increase of crime and criminals.

Flanagan and the Clarkes, as well as other " authorities " on the subject, declare that ladies' outside pockets cause many boys and girls to begin " wiring."

For this department of the thief's business men and women—unless of low stature—are unfitted, and therefore the master thief, who has become too tall for practice, takes on pupils, by whose gains he is maintained in " style."

" At this time," Flanagan affirmed, " there were at least ten times as many boys ' wiring ' as there were when I was young. Kelty, who has been up to everything for twenty years, trains these boys. He has pointed to a lad and said to me, 'There's one of my bringing out !' "

We have necessarily branched off from the more immediate purpose of our story for the purpose of putting the reader in possession of many noteworthy facts connected with the history of crime and criminals. The commixture of ignorance and knowledge—ignorance of good and knowledge of evil—

brought to light by the examination of prisoners, is astounding even to those who might be supposed accustomed to it—viz., to governors and chaplains of gaols—while it is unfortunately a matter of incredulity or indifference to those who, would they only believe it or look into it, might exercise great influence in bringing about a better state of things.

Many of the great pickpockets, whose names we have recorded, were associates of Peace, who, however, was never known to work with them in their vocation; he never practised this branch of the profession, but confined himself to robberies in dwelling-houses.

Even while working out his sentence in gaol, Peace had an opportunity afforded him of indulging his natural fondness for birds.

For some unascertained reason, two squares of glass had been removed from the window-frame of his cell. Peace placed some crumbs of bread on the ledge, and these soon attracted the notice of the birds.

First of all a few sparrows found out the dainty crumbs, and alighted on the stonework and picked them up.

The prisoner inside was greatly cheered by the companionship of his little feathered friends, who, in a short time, understood that food was placed there for them, and therefore paid regular visits to the grating of the prisoner's cell.

There is a well-known print called " Liberty and Captivity," in which a bird is depicted singing outside the window of a prison, while the captives within are listening to his matin.

This might apply to Peace. His sparrows did not sing, but they chirruped most incessantly. By degrees they got bolder, and sharpened their beaks against the iron bars of the grating. These saucy little creatures afforded him considerable amusement.

Throughout his life he had always evinced a fondness for birds and animals, which, to say the truth, was a remarkable characteristic for a man of his hardened nature.

Any change from the daily routine of prison life was, as a matter of course, a great boon to the convicts, and when M'Pherson informed the men under his charge that many of them would be told off to whitewash the gaol, they were much pleased at the prospect of the new employment.

Peace was to be one of the party, for the season for whitewashing had come, and the prison was to be done throughout.

The work was by no means laborious—indeed it was deemed a sort of pastime by the men who were appointed to perform the task.

The wash was made with lime, and as is usual in such cases, large flat brushes were used.

Peace soon proved himself to be an expert in the use of the whitewash brush.

He had also a good knowledge as to mixing the materials used in the process.

While engaged with the whitewash gang he obtained a good deal of information about the interior arrangements of the prison.

He and his fellow-workmen were at work for more than a week on the walls of the gaol.

Three days were devoted to the passages and in the sick wards, and three days in the women's wards.

But they saw nothing of the female prisoners, as before they went to work the ward to be whitened was cleared out, not a single occupant of it being allowed to remain.

They had, however, left several memorials on the walls of their prison-house.

A good deal of objectionable language and wretched scrawls disfigured the walls of the cells occupied by the male prisoners. Many of the sentences displayed thereon were blasphemous, indecent, and profane.

The practice of scratching their names and writing all manner of things, doggrel lines and coarse couplets, on the walls, wheresoever they may be, seems to be a confirmed habit with the people of this country, both high and low. Every public building furnishes us with instances of this stupid mania. As it is in the outer world so it is in gaols and other public institutions. Take, as a sample, the following—which, with many others of a like nature, were found in the men's cells—

Whillem Meagram came here from the steel
May 10th 1854—5 years for slinging his hook—
Him as prigs vat isent hisen—
When hes cotched vill go to prison—W. M.

Some of these inscriptions proved to be unusually amusing to the whitewashers.

Peace, however, had never evinced any predilection for indulging in this foolish propensity, and he professed to be greatly disgusted at the language made use of by the women on the walls. Many sentences were appended which were grossly indecent, and in some instances these were illustrated artistically. Peace had heard that when a woman is bad she is more debased than many of the opposite sex, but he was under the impression that a certain amount of modesty lay dormant in the most abandoned.

When he saw what the female persons had scratched upon their cell walls the illusion was dispelled.

He was surprised—as well he might be—that such disgraceful inscriptions and drawings were allowed to remain on the walls.

When separate confinements were first introduced as a system in this country, public feeling was opposed to it in no slight degree.

The "solitary" cell was held up for disapprobation, not merely as being too severe, but as driving its miserable inmate to insanity.

In the course of time, however, the cell was regarded more favourably; its special worth as a prime agent in promoting a criminal's moral amendment became pretty generally admitted; and one of the able and powerful exponents of general feeling — tacitly mentioning the cell—distinctly advocates the duty of aiming at the reformation of the culprit.

No one can expect that any system of imprisonment can by human means be successful in every case, but it does not follow that the measures adopted in "separate" prisons are in the greater number of instances wholly inefficacious.

Every precaution is taken that no man shall make his escape, and the first care naturally is that he should not be possessed of any tool or instrument of any kind that is at all likely to be made use of for such a purpose.

Constant care and watchfulness is therefore kept over the prisoners.

Peace would have gladly availed himself of any chance of setting himself free, but it was too plainly demonstrated to him that any such hope would be altogether illusionary.

He found from experience that the watchful eyes of his janitors were constantly on those who were under their charge.

Always while the men were bathing the officers examined their clothing.

One day, on going in after exercise, Peace was surprised, on passing the doors of several cells, to see everything in the greatest confusion.

"Something's up," he murmured to himself; "I wonder what it can be?"

He was mistaken, however; the warders were only using necessary precaution.

On reaching his own cell he found that some one had been placing everything in "admired disorder;" books were thrown in one corner, bedding was unrolled—everything in his cell had been displaced, and a very close inspection had been made of each separate article.

His first impression was that some suspicion attached to him.

Possibly the warders were under the impression that he had concealed some instrument. He did not care for this, as any such supposition was altogether erroneous. He deemed it expedient to take no notice of the overhauling of the articles in his cell.

He learned afterwards that it was by no means an uncommon practice for the warders to institute a rigid search in the cell in the presence of the prisoner, who also had to undergo a personal inspection.

This was generally done after the following fashion. Two officers would enter a prisoner's cell—one stands before and the other behind the culprit, who is made to strip off every article of clothing he may have on.

The one in front examines each article, and throws them one by one on the floor of the cell.

The warder behind watches intently to see that the prisoner does not "palm" anything—in other words, to conceal by sleight of hand any contraband article he might wish to conceal.

Such a thing as a rusty nail being found on a prisoner would excite suspicion, and get him into serious trouble.

It would be taken for granted that he secreted it for the purpose of making his escape upon the first opportunity that presented itself.

We have in an earlier chapter alluded to "tobacco" being conveyed into prisons. This article does find its way into our convict gaols, and this "noxious weed," as non-smokers term it, is a constant source of annoyance and trouble.

Smoking is altogether out of the question, one puff from a pipe or cigar would be detected in a moment; none of the prisoners even have the temerity to smoke, but many of them do continue to get tobacco which they chew.

The question is where does it come from? Who brings it into the prison? No one is able to tell; every precaution is taken to prevent such an article finding its way into gaols, but the fact remains that money and tobacco are smuggled in, notwithstanding the strict surveillance exercised by the authorities.

Prisoners will have tobacco, and tobacco cannot be got without money, so that both must be obtained, and the result has been that the more rigorous the inspection the greater the ingenuity required to evade it, and it would be impossible for the convicts to do this without the assistance of the warders. These men are not proof against bribery, as was evident upon the examination of Kurr and Benson.

These astute rogues argued from experience that every man had his price.

Some of our prison warders are beyond the reach of temptation, while others are open to a bribe.

The "pals" or friends of a prisoner soon find out an official who is assailable, and set about "squaring" him—they come "the artful dodge," as they term it, and arrange with some warder to "sling their friend in quod" some "'bacca."

But few words are spoken after this arrangement is

made. A sign is given to the friend outside that his request has been attended to.

As much as ten shillings, or, in some cases, a sovereign, is known to have been given for the supply of an ounce of "bacca." It only costs the warder a few pence, the profits arising from the supply of the "contraband" articles are of course enormous.

The solitary cell is a sore trial to prisoners under the most favourable circumstances, for, as a rule, men of this sort are gregarious. But its painful monotony and loneliness are doubly hard to the one who is denied the use of the weed, which, from long habit, has become almost essential to his very existence.

No one unacquainted with the use or abuse of the fragrant weed can imagine for a moment the sacrifices its devotees will make to procure it.

Sometimes a warder who deals in the article is "bowled out," then he gets into trouble—the chances being that he will lose his situation and be sent adrift without a character; but, as a rule, the prisoners who get supplies this way seldom or ever "round" on the warder; but there is this danger of discovery: The prisoner who gets tobacco may, perchance, in a generous moment give a piece to a fellow prisoner, or a mate "smells" it and discovers what he has got.

The secret once so divulged, his mate soon finds out who the "blooming screw" is that "slung the smash"—that is, brought in the much-coveted article. Then the unfortunate warder is likely to come to grief. All goes on smoothly enough till the two mates "chip out," or the "blooming bloke," the obliging officer, falls foul of the possessor of the secret, not dreaming that the man knows anything about the contraband trade he has been engaged in.

The prisoner, smarting under some sharp act of discipline on the part of the tobacco-supplier, determines upon having his revenge, and humiliating his janitor, he quietly bides his time till the chief warder or governor comes round, when he asks to speak to him, and "blows the gaff."

A circumstance of this nature took place with a man who was confined in a cell close to the one occupied by Peace. The man was a moody, contemptible ruffian, and had given some trouble to one of the warders in charge of that portion of the building. When M'Pherson came round he accused the officer of having conveyed "bacca" to one or more of the prisoners.

"It is against the rules of the prison to supply tobacco to prisoners," said M'Pherson. "Send Mr. Morgan here!"

Mr. Morgan, the accused officer, presented himself.

"How's this, sir?" said M'Pherson in an indignant tone. "No. 74 accuses you of supplying tobacco to the prisoners. What have you to say to the charge?"

"It is not true, sir," Morgan replied.

"I hope it is not, sir—I hope and trust it is not," returned M'Pherson, who was, however, under the impression all the while that it was, although he appeared to think otherwise.

"It is quite true, sir," returned No. 74, "'Cakey' gave me some."

"Who is Cakey?"

"No. 89, sir," said Morgan.

"Well, we will hear what he has to say."

No. 89 was brought forward. He was asked if Morgan had supplied him with tobacco.

"No, sir, he never has," replied Cakey.

It was a nickname he went by. He was staunch and true, and swore most positively that the charge was without foundation.

No. 74 said that Cakey had given him a portion of the tobacco and that Peace had seen him do so.

Peace was now brought forward and interrogated. He denied having seen any tobacco in the possession of No. 74, or any other prisoner.

"We've only got your bare word for the fact, which is contradicted by two other prisoners," said M'Pherson, addressing himself to No. 74. "In addition to this, your word is not of much value, seeing that you are a notorious liar. Take the men back to their cells."

The men were locked in their respective cells, then M'Pherson turned to Morgan, and said—

"You must be more careful, sir. If anything of this sort is brought under my notice again, I shall report you."

Having delivered himself of this speech, he turned on his heel and walked away. Morgan felt that he had had a narrow escape.

The chief warder, who was perhaps one of the most kindly disposed men in the whole prison, did not forget the circumstance, which, however, he never afterwards alluded to.

He took an early opportunity of getting No. 74 transferred to another part of the gaol, and so the matter ended.

We have devoted rather a lengthy chapter to Peace's prison life, as the outside public know but little of the inner working of our convict prisons, and the various modes of discipline practised therein, but we must now turn to other scenes in this life drama.

CHAPTER LXII.
MR. WRENCH'S WANDERINGS—THE SEARCH AFTER A MURDERER.

IT is astonishing how long a criminal may be at large after he is "wanted," provided he gets away from his well-known haunts. Murderers have contrived to elude the vigilance of the police for a considerable space of time, and some have never been arrested for the crime they were supposed to have committed.

Some few years back two boys committed a murderous assault on an old lady at Norton Folgate. After leaving their victim for dead, the young scoundrels made off. Months elapsed and no trace of them was found; and it was by the merest accident in the world that one of them was discovered. He was convicted upon a charge of larceny, and while undergoing penal servitude for the same, a boy, residing in the neighbourhood of Norton Folgate, recognised him. Luckily for the would-be assassins, the old lady recovered from the terrible injuries she had received, and her two assailants were tried and sentenced to penal servitude for the brutal assault.

We have a similar instance in Good, who was ultimately convicted of murdering a woman, and cutting up the body of his victim, at Roehampton, in Surrey. He made his escape, and many months elapsed before he was discovered. He was a groom at the time of the murder, but had in early life worked as a brickmaker, and it was while following this occupation, in a remote district in the north of England, that he was discovered. But his identity was established by the merest accident; and had he been a little more cautious the probability is that he would have got clean off.

Mr. Wrench felt that he had a difficult task in hand. He searched in vain for Giles Chudley at most of the cheap lodging-houses and thieves' haunts in the metropolis. He sent notices off to the police-stations in the provinces, but he was no nearer to the suspected man.

There was one great difficulty in the matter. Mr.

Wrench did not know Chudley—neither did any of his coadjutors.

He had a description given him of the man, but this was very vague, and could not be relied on. Nevertheless, our detective took every possible means of tracing out the fugitive.

After a rigid and exhaustive search in London and the suburbs, Mr. Wrench began to think seriously of his next best course of action. Certainly the case, as far as it had gone at present, did not look very promising.

Chudley was country born and country bred. The chances were that he would secrete himself in some sparsely-inhabited rural district. The question was, where to look, and this Mr. Wrench could not very well determine.

From information received at Scotland-yard there was reason to suppose that a man answering in many points to the description given of Chudley had been seen tramping along one of the roads leading to Liverpool.

When Mr. Wrench was put in possession of this fact, it at once occurred to him that the murderer of Mr. Philip Jamblin was journeying to that town for the purpose of shipping himself for one of the colonies.

He at once determined on paying a visit to Liverpool without further delay. But here another difficulty stood in the way. How could he possibly make sure of his man, even assuming he was fortunate enough to come across him?

But Mr. Wrench was not easily baffled. He telegraphed to Lord Ethalwood, begging him as a special favour to send the girl, Nell Fulford, off at once to Liverpool, with instructions for her to go to the police-station and inquire for him, Wrench.

The earl was quite as anxious as Mr. Wrench was to bring the matter to a successful issue. He deputed Mr. Jamblin to communicate with Nelly, and make known to her his wishes.

She at once expressed her willingness to go in search of the murderer of her sweetheart.

Joe Doughty, who heard of the intended expedition, begged of his master to be permitted to go also, and so, after a few hours' notice, Nell and Joe set out together.

Upon their arrival at Liverpool they at once made their way to the police station. A constable was directed to conduct them to the house where Mr. Wrench was stopping.

"Ha'ee got any clue to the scoundrel, sir?" said Joe, when he caught sight of the detective. "I do hope un 'as."

"Not at present," returned Mr. Wrench. "Don't you be too forward, my man. Just keep your tongue between your teeth. I don't want anybody in this town to know our business, and an indiscreet word or two may spoil all. So don't you open your mouth about the matter. Don't say anything to a single individual. Do you understand?"

"Ah, I see, beg pardon; I won't say a word."

"Very well, that's all right, my man. When I need your services, which, to say the truth, I hope I shall shortly, I'll let you know. In the meantime keep dark, be as close as an oyster."

Joe nodded and scratched his head. He came to the conclusion that Mr. Wrench was a wonderful man, and he was overawed by his manner, which was incisive and commanding.

"And my dear Miss Fulford," said the detective, turning towards his female visitor; "it is, I am sure, very kind and good of you to come all this long distance to

further the ends of justice, especially as you are at the present time not in your usual health."

"I dunno care 'bout myself, sir," returned Nell. "I would go to the end of the world to hunt down the vile wretch—who—who ha' taken an innocent and honourable man's life."

"Certainly, of course, a very proper feeling—very proper indeed," cried Wrench. "I wish every one was of the same opinion as yourself, Miss Fulford."

"And I am at your service, sir. Have you met with anybody—any suspected person?"

"Not at present. You will have to wait in this town till I have made all the inquiries necessary."

"Ah!" murmured Nell, who was disappointed at not being engaged on active service at once.

Mr. Wrench conducted her to a lodging he had engaged, and told Joe that he was to remain with him.

Mr. Wrench's first night in Liverpool was spent in examining a number of low lodging houses, which were used by tramps, thieves, and the lower class of itinerants.

He took with him Joe Doughty and a sergeant belonging to the constabulary of the town.

He was an experienced hand, and knew most of the habitations of this class.

In many of these places there were assembled scores of the most degraded and vicious members of society, who were lying in ambush, as it were, like tigers in a jungle, ready to spring upon and make a prey of anyone who came within the precincts of their lair.

Prisons, tread-wheels, penal settlements, gallows, were all vain and impotent as a punishment.

The ragged schools and city missions were of no avail as preventives of crime, so long as the wretched dens of infamy, brutality, and vice, termed "padding kens," continued their daily and nightly work of demoralisation.

Mr. Wrench and the Liverpool constable entered one of these wretched receptacles for the homeless and lawless. As the miserable occupants were stretched on their dirty shake-downs, the policeman flashed his bull's-eye in all directions.

Some of the occupants rolled over, and covered their faces with their begrimed bed-clothes, while others were fast asleep heedless of the visit of the "crushers," and many of them for the nonce feigned to be slumbering.

It would be difficult, and indeed almost impossible, to describe to the reader the revolting nature of many of the places visited by the detective and his companions.

As the policeman flashed his light on the men in these unwholesome dens, Joe Doughty examined each countenance, but failed to find the man of whom they were in search.

One of the largest establishments of this class was kept by an Irishman named O'Flanagan, and after an inspection of a variety of these places the searchers bent their steps in the direction of that well-known place.

As they entered they were greeted by the mistress of the establishment, who was standing behind a sort of counter, which separated the front entrance from her own private parlour.

"Och, good luck to ye, Mr. Wrinch," cried the woman, in a strong Irish accent. "An' it's mighty plaz'd I am to set eyes on your own swate fatures. Won't ye be afther coming in and saying a kind word or two to a poor old sinful crathur like myself?"

"How are you, Biddy, and how are you getting on?" said Wrench.

"Oh, by the powers, I'm glad to see ye—an' sure,

thought you had forgotten your ould frind entirely—an' bedad, your broight frind's with ye—well, the more the welcome. Step inside, Mr. Wrinch—an' sure, the masther's not at home, but that's no rason that you should not be spaking to his wife."

The three personages went behind the bar and entered the little room beyond.

"Ah, sure you are as welcome as the flowers in May, Mr. Wrinch, I need not tell you that—and what will you be afther takin—you and your frinds?"

"Nothing just now—we've come on business."

"Oh, sure now, it's business ye've come on," cried the woman in an altered tone. "An' I 'spose, if I may make so bould—I s'pose now, that it's afther some dirty blackguard, that you are—an' bad luck to him."

"Something of that sort, I must confess," returned the detective, with a smile, " and for old acquaintance sake, you'll serve me if you can."

"Faith an' I will, if it lies in me power; and isn't it a good turn ye did me when I was in the depths of throuble—and am I likely to forget it? Divil a bit, an' what might it be that you may be wanting me to do—Mr. Wrinch?"

"You mustn't speak quite so loud, Biddy," said the detective.

"An' its qute I'll be as any church mouse."

Mr. Wrench drew from his pocket the bill relating to the murder in Larchgrove-road; but, unfortunately reading was not one of Mrs. Flanagan's accomplish-, ments.

She seemed unable to comprehend that the document was headed with the word murder.

"Ooh, by the powers," she ejaculated, " it's some murthering spalpeen you'll be afther, Mr. Wrinch?"

"Yes, and a hundred pounds reward will be presented to any person or persons who shall give any such information as may lead to his conviction," said the detective. "I will read you a description of the man of whom we are in search."

"Shure now, it isn't blood money I'd be taking," said Mrs. Flanagan, after the detective had done reading; "no, not even to save my own blessed life; but if I could put you on the track of the murtherin' villain I would."

"Have you seen a man answering to the description I have given?"

"Faix, no—divil a one. I wish I had. Whisht now, do you think he's in Liverpool?"

"I have every reason to suppose so—that is why I have paid you this visit. We must have a look at all the people here."

Oh, by Jasus, ye'll not find the dirty blackguard here, Mr. Wrinch. It's mighty particular we are, both Dennis and myself. We don't let beds to onrespectable piple. It's thrue now, some years ago I was in a little bit o' thrubble, as you know Mr. Wrinch, but ye see, darling, it taught me a lesson, and bedad I've profited by it intirely. Ooh, but it's particular we are, both Dennis and myself, an' anyway, Mr. Wrinch, you don't suppose that we would harbour thieves or murderers."

"I don't suppose you do. I'm not accusing you, woman. All I say is, if you have seen a man answering the description given, tell me so frankly. You had better do so."

"Do ye hear 'im now? Did ye iver hear the loike o' that?" cried Mrs. Flanagan. "As if I wouldn't tell him at onst, if I had it in my power, which it's sorry I am I haven't. More's the pity. But ye'd better have a look at all the boys, and satisfy yerself. Mother o' Marcy, but this is a bad business. An' is it to any o' the lodging houses that ye've bin, Mister Wrinch."

"Yes, we have, but you, being so well acquainted with the town and its people, would be more likely to detect a stranger."

"Oh, sure you are complimintary," exclaimed the woman, who rose from the seat, and conducted her visitors to a large shed-looking place, which was one of the dormitories of her establishment.

The detective and his two companions passed through this place, and examined the features of the inmates. Many of them present were well known to both the police-officers, and some were strangers, but there was not one there answering the description of the man.

They returned to the landlady's private room no wiser than before.

"Shure, didn't I tell ye that ye couldn't find the murtherin' blackguard here. Oh, its careful and particular we are, Misther Wrinch, and small blame to us; haven't I three childer of my own to look afther, an' haven't I known what it is to offind the law? That's our rason for our pickin' and choosin' our lodgers."

"That will do Biddy—you are a model landlady, I dare say."

"Faith that I am, mine's the best managed, 'padding ken,' in all Liverpool; it's kept dacent and sweet, and used by the betherest sort of tramps, and such like, and it's sorry I am that you can't find the big ugly blackgurd you are looking for, but if Biddy Flanagan can do ye a good turn, never fear, but she'll do it. May be you might find the man ye want at the fair."

"What fair?" inquired Wrench, quickly.

"At Nantwich Hoiring Fair. As your man is in the agricultural line may be he'll be afther going to the fair."

"A good suggestion," said the detective. "When is it held?"

"On the 29th of this month."

"Thanks, it's worth consideration, but we won't detain you longer, and so good night."

"But you'll be for calling agin, I suppose, before you lave the town?"

"Oh, certainly. We shall not lose sight of you. Besides, you know you may pick up some information."

The landlady looked mysterious, and nodded.

Her three visitors took their departure.

"She knows more than she cares to tell," said the sergeant to Wrench.

"You think so?"

"Yes I do."

"Then we shall have to pay her another visit."

"There are only two ways to work her. Either to weedle her or put the screw on."

"We've nothing to put the screw on for—have we?"

"I can say we have, but she's to be worked."

"By money?"

"Not by the reward; that she wouldn't accept upon any consideration."

Mr. Wrench returned to his lodgings very much disappointed. He had hoped to gain some information as to the whereabouts of his man, but his search in the various " padding kens " of Liverpool had been of no avail.

He determined upon going to the docks on the following day, with the view of ascertaining, if possible, what vessels were about to set sail, and who were their passengers.

Liverpool is a big place, and it is not possible to do much in the way of hunting for a person therein in one day, or indeed in a week.

"WALK UP, LADIES AND GENTLEMEN; JUST GOING TO BEGIN!" HE SHOUTED.

Mr. Wrench did not despair. Something might turn up in the course of a few hours which would alter the aspect of affairs most materially.

He felt certain that Mrs. O'Flanagan could aid him if she chose, but he would not go to her again till he had exhausted his other resources.

In the morning he proceeded by himself to the docks. He went over several vessels, had intercourse with shipowners, captains, stevedores, and provision merchants—was, in short, industriously occupied till nightfall, but failed to reach the desired end.

It was likely enough that he had been misinformed.

Giles Chudley might not be in the neighbourhood of Liverpool after all.

But it would not do to arrive at that conclusion too hastily.

The police informed him that more than one person had declared a man answering his description—or at any rate, something near it—had been seen within a few miles distant from the town.

But then, men of his class are so much alike, and people are so prone to jump at conclusions.

Mr. Wrench knew but too well the difficulties attending identification—mistakes were so frequently made.

He spent another day visiting all sorts of odd places in the town, and at night he went to the music-halls, taking Joe Doughty with him.

To say the truth, this honest countryman was having a fine time of it; he had seen more of life in the few days he had been under the detective's charge than he had in the whole course of his preceding career.

Doughty was entertained, and considered that he was playing an important part; but he would have been far better pleased at finding the murderer of Master Philip.

He was under the impression that there was not much chance of their meeting with Giles Chudley, but as far as that was concerned he was not a competent judge, not having had any experience in the art of thief-catching.

In the course of the following day, Mr. Wrench paid another visit to Mrs. O'Flanagan.

On this occasion he deemed it prudent to go alone, being under the impression that the loquacious landlady might be more communicative in the absence of strangers.

"An' sure, now, it was my own self as said you wouldn't be afther laving the town without jist giving us a frindly call; an' it's happy and proud I am to see ye, Mister Wrinch. Any news about the murtherin' divil?"

"None at all, Biddy. My search has not been attended with any satisfactory result."

"Oh, maybe the thief o' the world has hooked it intirely, an' won't show up at all."

"It looks like it. But I say, missus," whispered Wrench, in a confidential tone, "you might be a little more candid."

"Oh, bother! What's that you'd be afther saying? Do you think I'd kape onything from the likes o' ye?"

"I hope not."

"Whist! aisy now. Jist come here. Aye that's it. Well, thin, you mustn't go a screamin' and a roarin' all over the town."

"Dear me, of course not. Go on, Biddy."

"Well, then, a few nights ago there was a strange chap whom nobody seemed to know came here for a night's lodging. Well, Wrinch, be the powers, but I must spake my mind to an ou'd frind, the vagabond couldn't slape, so some of the bhoys tould me, and kept tossin' about and a sighin' and a groanin' all night. In the morning he was off, never sayin' nothink to nobody."

"And his appearance was it anything like the description I read to you?"

"Faith, it was—so Pat Murphy said."

"And who is Pat Murphy?"

"He's just one of the boys, one of the regular customers. Begorra he's as good as goold is Pat."

"No doubt. Anything more?"

"Ah, now I dunno that there is. Oh, yes. Pat understood him to say that he was bund for Nantwich."

"Mrs. Flanagan I am deeply indebted to you; accept my best thanks," exclaimed Wrench. "Should anything come of this, you will not be forgotten."

"Oh, kape me out of the bisnis intirely. Do not mintion what I've tould ye to a soul, but make the best use of it. Sure now, don't I owe you a debt of gratitude? And it's myself as nivir forgets a kindness. Aisy now, kape dark, and say nothin' about this or I shall be ruined."

"You may rely upon me," said the detective, again thanking his informant as he passed out of the "padding ken."

Mr. Wrench kept his word. The information he had received from Mrs. Flanagan might be of essential service, or it might turn out a myth. Anyway, he was determined upon following up the slender and uncertain clue he had obtained so unexpectedly.

He at once set off to the town of Nantwich, and took with him Nell Fulford and Joe Doughty.

CHAPTER LXIII

MR. WRENCH AND JOE DOUGHTY—A VAGRANT'S LODGING HOUSE.

THE glories of Bartholomew Fair, of Greenwich, and a host of others in the neighbourhood of the metropolis have long since passed away, and it is not at all likely they will ever be resuscitated. But fairs of various descriptions are still held in many parts of England, but they are considerably shorn of their leading attractions.

Mr. Wrench's motive for hastening to Nantwich was to be present at the hiring fair at a small hamlet within a few miles of that place.

On Pack-rag Day (the 29th of September), the serfs of agriculture pack up their clothes and seek fresh masters.

And on this day the farmers, dressed in their Sunday clothes, ride to the mansions of their landlords, their faces bright with honest pride, their leather bags filled with gold coins and bank notes.

The scene has been faithfully depicted in Wilkie's celebrated picture of the "Rent Day."

The landlords, seated before their blue bundles of quarter's bills, receive their tenants with smiles of welcome and gratitude—that is, if the latter are furnished with the amount of rent due.

In some parts of England it is still customary among the lords of manors and proprietors of large lands to give a dinner to their tenants on the rent days, as shown in Wilkie's well-known picture.

But these quarterly feeds are now rapidly dying out of date, and will soon no longer exist, except in the hall of some youthful squire, who may be gifted with a dramatic passion for revivals.

Like fairs, these convivial gatherings are fast becoming obsolete.

In the year referring more especially to this history, the hiring fair to which Mr. Wrench was about to pay a visit happened to fall on quarter-day; so all the farmers of the neighbourhood paid their rents early, and rode on to the place to engage their carters, shepherds, and farm maids for the ensuing year.

Mr. Wrench was not a man to be a day behind the fair. He came to a halt at a small village within an easy walk of it the day before its fun and frolic was to commence.

He put up at a roadside inn, and secured the best bed in the establishment for Nell Fulford.

This done, he explored the neighbourhood, having for his companion the redoubtable Joe.

Near to the junction of three cross roads, there stood, at the time of which we are writing, a low-looking beershop bearing the sign of the "Travellers' Rest."

This place was a vagrants' lodging-house, and as Mr. Wrench and his rustic companion came within sight of the house the detective regarded it with a considerable amount of interest.

After surveying it for some time he said to Joe Doughty—

"As far as the accommodation is concerned I don't know that I can recommend it, but if you don't mind taking up your quarters in it for one night it would be as well. Tramps, thieves, and vagabonds of all sorts are accustomed to pay nightly visits to the 'Travellers' Rest,' as it is termed, and it is possible you may be able to pick up some information respecting the man of whom we are in search.

"If I thought that, I'd stop there this very night!" cried Joe.

"I wish you would."

"Don't 'ee say another word upon the matter, guv'ner—I'll be one among 'em."

"And you can see me in the morning at the 'Dun Cow.' I would join you, but the chances are that some of the tramps in the 'Travellers' Rest' would know me, and that would be fatal to us. You are a stranger—keep your eyes and ears open, and your mouth shut, and who knows but you may gain the hundred pounds reward?"

"I beant a-goin' to take a shilling on it, coom what may," returned Joe, in an indignant tone.

"Very well, my man, that you can please yourself about."

"Noa, not a penny."

Mr. Wrench and Joe returned to the "Dun Cow," this being the roadside house in which the former had taken up his quarters.

Our detective was a diplomatist in his own peculiar way.

His object was to remain as unobserved as possible till the day of the fair, but his rustic friend was appointed to what might be termed outpost duty.

When night came on Joe was dispatched by the commander-in-chief to the vagrants' lodging-house.

The house in question had at one time been a respectable habitation.

The lower part was built of brick, once red and flourishing, but now dirty and dingy; and about half-way up were boards, once painted white, which took the place of their more solid neighbours below. They were what was called weather-boards, and ran along one over the other, in order that the rain might drop off them to the ground.

The walls below were substantial enough; the yard gate and large fore-court were amply covered with tall grass or graceless weeds.

The gate that once was closed each night by the smart and active ostler now stood back on one hinge, resting, therefore, partly on the ground.

And the stables once filled with prancing or neighing, or, at least, well-fed steeds, were at this time only warmed by the breath of beggars, too poor even to pay a groat for a night's lodging, and who compounded with their host for a twopenny night's straw in the outhouses.

Occasionally, indeed, some benighted and bestormed waggoner, unable to reach the usual place of his sojourn, would unwillingly or unwittingly stop at the "Travellers' Rest," and allow his horses to share the same fate as the beggars who surrounded them. But such visits were few and far between, and even waggon horses would avoid if they could "the vagrants' lodging-house."

The "Travellers' Rest" was one of those houses which was known by all classes of mendicants, whether belonging to the *silver* class, or what are styled by all well-informed travellers *barkers*, to the *lurkers* or begging letter-writers to the *shallow coves* or impostors, who in various garbs obtain clothes from the compassionate and charitable to a great amount, and then sell them to the dealers as left-off garments—too often spending the produce in ardent spirits—to the shallow motts or females, who, like shallow coves, go nearly naked through the world, begging ever for clothes, ever obtaining them, and yet never clothing themselves, but selling them for food, for lodging, for drink, and for the enjoyment of every conceivable vice, as well as to the separate race of beggars and match-sellers, who live by the ordinary tales, true or false, of real or supposed misery, and in which class is to be found much more of suffering than crime, and of destitution and heart-rending woe than we are either accustomed to believe or like to inquire into.

It has been well said that one-half of the world does not know how the other half lives, and the history of mendicants of every degree would furnish the outside public with strange revelations, many of which would appear almost incredible.

The mendicant poor are in every way a different race of beings to the working population of this country.

They have signs of their own, a language of their own, plans and schemes of their own, or rather for their own class, homes of their own, or rather barns and out-buildings, reserved by compassionate farmers and land-owners for them. They split society into fractions, calculate with tolerable accuracy all their chances, and could tell in many cases how much they should receive in a week.

Generally speaking, they are distrustful of each other, living in a constant state of fear of arrest and imprisonment, concealing their own names even from their commonest associates, and changing their announced plans and movements in less than an hour, as they saw with a prophet's eye a lion in their path.

But then how different are their classes!

There's the systematic vagrant, whose life has been one of constant and unchanging mendicity.

There is the occasional vagrant, who begs after pea-picking season is over and after hopping has terminated, in order to raise money to go back to London or to the county to which he belongs.

There is another class of occasional vagrants, who migrate from a district where poverty and misery assail them, to the place of their nativity or of their former brighter fortunes, seeking for halfpence on their way to provide for their daily wants as they press on-wards.

The vagrants in large towns and cities, and principally in the metropolis, are the very worst class.

They are in eight cases out of ten rank impostors.

They go about with statements of losses by fire, shipwrecks, and accidents.

They obtain counterfeit signatures of clergymen and magistrates to declarations of having lost their property by fire.

In a preceding chapter we have given a description of how these precious attestations were manufactured by the "smoucher," and the account given of this clever concoction of false documents is substantially correct.

Those who work with the *slum* and *delicate* (the statement and book of subscriptions) furnished them by the "smoucher," often raise large sums of money, which they expend in vice and profligacy.

The shipwrecked mariner's lurk used to be one of the most frequent and lucrative.

A person of this character, known by the nickname of Captain Johnstone, followed the lurk of a shipwrecked captain for many years.

He was an excellent writer, and had a respectable appearance—so the unwary were deceived, and he was enriched.

It was said that he obtained some thousands of pounds by his mendacious statements.

When any account of a shipwreck appeared in the newspaper which seemed likely to suit his purpose he would write out a new statement (slum), and provide a new book (delicate), and then set to work with the utmost zeal to obtain subscribers.

Polish counts, who had been driven from the land of their birth by Russian tyranny, used at one time to infest London, Liverpool, Manchester, and Bristol, but this form of begging has gone out of fashion.

"The victims of accidents," wholly counterfeit, "the sufferers from sickness," quite unreal, "the deaf and dumb lurkers," who seem to be deprived of speech and hearing, "the servant out of place," who cajoles the domestics at gentlemen's houses, "the colliers who have suffered from water suddenly bursting into a coal pit," and yet who never saw a coal pit, "the starved-out weavers," who go about with printed papers or small hand-bills, representing that they are out of employ, although they have never seen a loom, "the cotton-spinning lurk," with that trick of leaving printed appeals and calling again for them and alms, though they know as much about diamond mounting as cotton-spinning, are a few of the dodges of active, cunning, and shameless mendicants.

There was, some years ago, a celebrated man named "Cheshire Bill," who was at one time a cotton-spinning lurker.

He travelled throughout various parts of England for more than fifteen years as a vagrant. Once he was a "shallow cove," and represented himself as a ship-wrecked sailor. Then he was a "carpet weaver in distress," and sang through the streets to obtain "browns and wedge" (halfpence and silver). Then he was a cotton weaver from Manchester, singing through the streets in company with others, having a clean white apron round him. After this he was on the collier's lurk, and carried a written paper, stating that he had suffered from a dreadful accident at Bilston in a coal pit.

Then he turned watch-seller, afterwards a simple roadside beggar, and finally a cotton-spinner out of employ, selling cotton said to be of his own spinning, and out of which he managed to make a profit of a hundred per cent.

"The calenderer's lurk" is another trick, and the doggerel poetry, in which their appeal is made to the "kind and generous public," contains amongst a variety of other verses the following record of their own virtues and charity when, as they pretend, they knew better days:—

> Whene'er we saw one in distress
> We strove to help him through;
> But now we cannot help ourselves—
> We have no work to do.

The systematic writers of begging letters are also much more common in London than in the country, and rejoice in the name of "highflyers."

Year after year they invent new cases with different hands, and sometimes their wives or mistresses, where they are known themselves, present their "appeal," and thus avoid detection, and collect an abundant revenue for the sins as well as the necessaries of life.

Well would it be for society at large if the vagrants of Great Britain were confined to these impostors. The remedy would be easy. Their extinction by imprisonment and transportation would not be difficult.

But alas! mixed up with these untrue and unreal appeals to the sympathy of our nature are thousands and tens of thousands of cases where sickness, accidents, death, want of work, inadequate wages, and the other ills of life to which sorrowing man is heir, have given to the squalid, starving, wretched, and abused applicants the right to ask for food, or to seek in the "unions" they so much abhor the bread of existence.

Joe Doughty had been accustomed throughout his life to fare but roughly. He had, however, never made the acquaintance of a low lodging-house, and did not, therefore, know the habits and manners of the people who are accustomed to patronise establishments of this description.

When he arrived in front of the inhospitable looking place known as the "Travellers' Rest," he hesitated. All was as still as death. Joe's courage appeared to fail him, and he was half inclined to go back to Mr. Wrench.

The balance was turned in an opposite direction in a few seconds. "A cadger on the fly" (a beggar on the road) with his female companion and three children came up, and made straight for the door.

They entered, and Joe Doughty, seeing that they were well acquainted with the house, followed them.

The landlord of the house looked at his new customers from the door of his small inner room—or bar parlour, as it was termed out of courtesy. He was a man with an eagle eye, but withal a good-humoured cast of features In a familiar tone and manner, he said to the cadger who had entered—

"Well Mike, what luck old man? Which is it, 'browns or wedge,' eh?" Meaning, in plain terms: "Well, Mike, what success have you had? Is it halfpence or silver?"

"Not much 'wedge,'" replied the cadger, in a discontented tone. "Browns is the order of the day—people are getting jolly stingy. It's a selfish world, make the best of it."

As he made the last observation, the cadger walked towards a large back room on the ground floor, which was the vagrants' apartment.

Joe Doughty followed, without either a word of civility or salutation with his host or his customers.

He sat himself down on a bench originally rough and uncomely, but which had been polished by the much sitting of the vagrants thereon year after year.

The sight presented to our honest countryman was neither cheery nor inviting, but Joe had made up his mind to take things as they came, and not to murmur under any circumstances.

As long as he was not interfered with he was perfectly content, and did not find fault with the company in which he found himself.

"Come here," said the man, whom he had followed into the house, addressing himself to his companion and children.

"Out with your scran (broken victuals), and let's have it. I'm as hungry as a half-starved dog."

Joe looked round. The room was filled with vagabonds of every possible description, but they were of a diversified character.

Near the fire, which was composed of dead burning embers and coke, sat an old man, whose hair was white as the driven snow, and who, to all appearance, was between seventy and eighty years of age.

His eyes appeared to be bright and piercing—certainly they were undimmed by age or care, and he fastened them on Joe Doughty for some considerable space of time. It was evident that he recognised a stranger in the countryman, whom he was endeavouring to reckon up.

"These be hard times, my friend," said the old man, addressing himself to Joe.

"Aye, that they be, master. Work be scarce, and money be scarcer still."

"Umph, yes. It's a bad neighbourhood for *high-flyers*," remarked the old man.

Joe, who did not understand the meaning of the term, said, haphazard, "I suppose it is, sir."

"Yes, very bad."

"But times 'll mend, let us hope," observed Joe.

The old man shook his head, and lapsed into silence.

The room was about eighteen feet long by fourteen or sixteen wide. In the daytime it was lighted by two windows which looked out into a sort of half yard and half garden, where there was a pump of good water, and a large stone sink.

The floor consisted of dirty boards, which were, however, sanded every morning.

The room had neither prints, pictures, blinds, or curtains, such articles being deemed altogether unnecessary.

There were, however, strange to say, no broken panes in the windows; but two ventilators whirled round in the upper portion of them, through which the hot air and smoke from the pipes gained egress.

The fireplace was at the farther end of the apartment.

Around the wall, and fixed to it firmly, were a line of benches, before which were tables, on which the vagrant opened his bag, his towel, his basket, or his wallet.

The favourite benches were those which were placed at the top of the room from the fireplace to each side, which were, in fact, cross benches.

Those who arrived last were obliged to content themselves with the forms which were not fixed.

The tables were by no means crowded, but they were tolerably full.

Having discovered a vacant place about the right centre bench, which was fixed to the wall, Joe Doughty made his way to the spot, but as he pushed his way along he met with a reproof from a female, whose supper he disarranged in passing by.

Joe apologised, and the female was gracious enough to accept it, and express herself well satisfied.

This little incident passed unnoticed by the rest of the occupants, all of whom appeared to be intent upon their own business arrangements.

Joe, when he had taken his place, had another glance at his companions, who, to say the truth, would have afforded a painter an excellent study for his canvas.

By the side of the old man sat one of the prettiest girls Joe had seen for many a long day. She was travelling, or, in other terms, begging with her grandfather, who sat next to her.

Whether she was his grandchild no one could tell; she passed as such, and the two were inseparable. Her age was about eighteen.

There was a light in her eye, a rapidity in her step, a fascination in her smile, and a playfulness in her jests and tone, which were quite captivating.

Joe had not come to the "Travellers' Rest" to lose his heart, but the young girl engaged his attention in a remarkable degree.

"She be a purty creature," he murmured to himself, "and be a deal too good for a place like this 'ere."

He did not know, when he apostrophised her, that she had been corrupted by depraved society, and was miserably callous to all moral sentiment.

The old man, her reputed grandfather, "did the *lame lurk*" during the day—that is, shammed lameness, and at night had his leg unbandaged, and could walk nimbly enough across the room.

He was a picturesque old scoundrel, and his grey hairs doubtless helped him more than his lameness, and enabled him to smoke his pipe, drink his pint, and supply half the same quantity to the girl who devoted herself so uncomplainingly to him.

The old man was now and then irritated by the whispering of "an out-and-out swell vagrant," who sat next his grand-daughter and endeavoured to flirt with her.

But the girl did not encourage the amorous swain; she shifted her seat to the other side of the old man, who fell foul of the "swell," whom he soundly rated.

"Shut up! stow it!" exclaimed several, addressing themselves to the young man. "You aint everybody, and the girl don't want to have any of your fine speeches."

The young man, finding himself in the minority, desisted from further importunities.

Joe Doughty's attention was now attracted to another object, this being the landlord, who had entered the room, and, after having spoken to several of its occupants, he came in front of Joe and said—

"Out or in, young man?"

Doughty, who did not know what he meant, affected not to hear him.

"Why don't you answer?" said the landlord. "Out or in?"

All of a sudden it occurred to our obtuse countryman that the question might relate to his sleeping accommodation.

"Oh, in, if you please, sir," said Joe.

"All right, young man. Fourpence to pay, if you please. You'd like a bed to yourself, I s'pose."

"Oh dear me—yes," returned Doughty.

"Very well—down with the browns. Sharp's the word."

Joe took out his fourpence, and placed them on the table all in halfpence.

"Oh, that's it—is it?" said the landlord, as he discovered three harps on the reverse side of the halfpennies.

"*Harp's* the word this time it would seem," said he.

Joe Doughty did not know what he meant by this last observation.

"I thought *harping* had gone out of fashion in these parts," said the landlord as he walked away, "but it appears I am mistaken. Dick Baynton was nabbed yesterday, as was a month at Jeeks, the grocer's, and now's in the lock-up for the "sizes."

Doughty was in a fog—he was under the impression that the words that had fallen from the lips of his host more particularly concerned him, as several present regarded him with a fitful glance.

Presently he mustered up courage, and said to the old man who had previously addressed him—

"What does he mean?"

"Who?"

"The landlord."

"Oh nothing particular; he takes you for a *palmer*."

Joe was as wise as ever, but he concluded that a palmer must be a scounrel of some sort.

"What makes him do that?"

The old man explained matters; he told Doughty that there were a class of thievish vagrants called *palmers*, who visit shops under the pretence of collecting *harp* halfpence, and to induce shopkeepers to search for them they offer thirteen pence for a shilling's worth, when many persons are silly enough to empty a large quantity of coppers on their counters to search for the halfpence wanted.

The *palmer* is sure to have his hand amongst the treasure, and while he affects to search diligently for the *harps* he contrives to conceal some halfpence in the palm of his hand, and when he removes his hand from the copper always holds his fingers out straight, so that the shopkeeper has no suspicion that he is being robbed.

This explanation was to a certain extent satisfactory, but Doughty did not feel complimented by being taken for a vagrant of that class; he however did not trouble himself much about the matter.

The girl who acted as waitress to the establishment now presented herself, and Joe ordered her to bring him "a pint of beer."

"Penny, threehalfpenny, or twopenny?" said she.

"The best you have, my gal," returned Joe, who forthwith pulled out of his pocket some slices of bread and butter and a piece of German sausage, which Mr. Wrench had provided him with; for, as the astute detective observed, "When at Rome do as Rome does—every tramp brings his *prog* with him, which he devours before going to bed; and you must do the same."

The landlord's suspicions were now confirmed. He, as well as the majority of those present, had but little difficulty in reckoning Doughty up. A fourpenny bed, twopenny beer, and bread, butter, and German sausage were fare and accommodation worthy of a *palmer*.

The pint of beer was brought. Joe asked the old man to have a pint as well—which the latter accepted.

The girl who acted as waitress was what might with justice be termed a character. She was short, crooked, one-eyed, lame on the right leg, flat as a pancake, long as a herring, yellow-white, with a sharp nose, and a mouth the shape of an old-fashioned semicircular door scraper.

She wore a low dark cotton gown with a neck handkerchief which might have been white at the time of the Reformation. Her gown sleeves were tucked up above the elbows, and her gown was pinned up behind.

She was certainly more useful than ornamental, and her life was a hard one. As far as work went she was a wonder, her master never supposing the possibility of her being tired or worn out. She was on the trot from morn to night, from week's end to week's end. Whatever good qualities she might have been possessed of had long since disappeared in consequence of the evil association she was constrained to submit to.

She was sullenly stupid, and at times insolent, but she went round and round from January to December, like a horse in a mill, and never complained of the hard life she was leading.

It is true she occupied her present post because nobody else would employ her as a waitress.

As a rule, hotel-keepers and publicans like smart-looking girls to serve in that capacity.

The landlord was a big strapping fellow, who had passed some months of his earlier days in a metropolitan prison for sundry acts of petty knavery, but the discipline of the gaol did not suit him, and he therefore made up his mind to "pull himself short up," as he playfully explained it.

He married, and took the "Travellers' Rest," which he obtained for a "mere song."

He was as strong as a giant, and stood over six feet in height, with strong sinewy limbs.

No one would think of attacking him single-handed, and he was therefore well adapted by nature to be the chief of a vagrants' lodging-house, for he was more than a match for the most desperate or daring mendicant.

His wife was altogether of a different mould. She had once been handsome, but coarse language, coarse associates, combined with a predilection for strong drinks, had converted her into a faded and fallen beauty—a mere shadow of her former self.

When the landlord had seen his customers supplied with the requisite quantity of beer, he turned to a thickset, wild, savage-looking man who had a small bull-dog at his feet, and who travelled with another man much like himself.

The wild, savage-looking man had jet black hair, an old brown leather belt, and a little sack thrown across his shoulder.

He was a "prig," and belonged to that class of vagrants who are adepts in drawing a purse, watch, or pocket-book from persons in crowded places. Races, fairs, and prize fights were the most favourite places with him.

His companion was so much like him that Joe came to the conclusion that he was his brother.

One was talkative, and the other taciturn, and Jim Morgan (for such was the eldest brother's name) gave all the orders and superintended all the arrangements. He was evidently commander-in-chief.

The eldest might have been twenty-five, the youngest some three or four years younger.

"In or out, gentlemen," said the landlord, as he eyed the two with something like doubt and suspicion.

"Why what do you suppose we come here for?" returned Jim Morgan.

"It aint my bis'ness to 'spose anything," said the landlord. "I only ask a question, which perhaps you will answer at your leisure."

At this sally there was a roar of laughter from the company.

"You're mighty clever in your way, no doubt," cried Morgan, "and in course you are duly appreciated. Your question I will answer at once. We want two separate beds, or the largest-sized double bed which you have to spare."

"Right you are," returned the landlord; "we won't make any bones about the matter. No. 9, first floor, two beds in the room, that will suit you all to pieces. If it don't you can accommodate yourselves elsewhere, or out, if you prefer it."

"You're jolly independent, but no matter, it's the nature of the animal," said Morgan.

Joe Doughty had been listening to the foregoing conversation, and hence it was he was oblivious to the fact that a stranger had entered the room.

The new-comer threaded his way through the assembly until he had gained the further end of the room.

It was at this time that Doughty's attention was attracted towards him. There was something in the movements and gait of the man which made Joe pause and consider.

He looked hard at the new-comer, and saw that he was a man with a bushy beard, long elfin locks, and a green shade over his eyes. He did not appear to be acquainted with any of the vagrants, and Joe thought this a little singular.

He seated himself on one of the benches and remained moody and silent for some little time; after which he rose suddenly, and wended his way back to the entrance of the room.

As he passed along there was a peculiarity in his

movement which caused Joe Doughty to regard him with a searching glance.

"I dunno what to mek on him," murmured Joe. "'Taint a bit loike the varmint I am in search of: but he be creeping along in a rum sort of way—a deal arter the fashion o' Giles—but it can't be him—and yet, I don't feel quite sartain—I'll wait and watch. Maybe he'll coom back and let un see a bit more on him."

But Joe was wrong in his surmise. The man with the green shade and bushy whiskers did not return.

Half-an-hour passed over, and the stranger did not again reappear.

The landlord came into the room once more to attend to his customers. As he passed, Joe said—

"What has become of the man with the green shade over his eyes?"

"Oh, he's hooked it," returned the host. "Didn't like the looks of you all—he's a deal too particular for his money."

"Has he gone away?"

"Yes he's stepped it, and arter paying for his shake-down too—he's a rum un."

"Gone, eh!" exclaimed Joe, scratching his head and looking wonder-struck.

"Ah, surely; what's the odds? We can do well enough without a varmint loike him. Let him go, and be hanged to him."

Joe Doughty was perplexed—the man's sudden departure troubled him. He sat silent and thoughtful for some time, and then he took himself to his bed in one of the upstairs rooms.

But the situation in which he found himself was so new and strange to him that it was a long time before gentle sleep closed his eyelids.

By early morn he arose, and sallying forth from the vagrants' lodging-house, he at once hastened to the "Dun Cow," and there awaited, in the breakfast room, the appearance of Mr. Wrench.

CHAPTER LXIV.
THE HIRING FAIR.

WHEN Mr. Wrench made his appearance in the public room of the "Dun Cow," Joe, after a little circumlocution, explained to his chief his adventures of the previous night.

As the latter listened to the account of the stranger in the vagrants' lodging-house, and his sudden departure, his countenance was irradiated with a smile.

"And this fellow went away without saying a word to anybody?" said Wrench.

"He never so much as opened his ugly mouth," returned Doughty.

"Ah, who knows, but he might be the man of whom we are in search?"

"He warn't a morsel loike 'im."

"He wasn't?"

"Noa, not a morsel, 'xcept his walk, and that war a goodish bit arter the style of Giles Chudley's."

"All right, Doughty, I don't think you have spent a night in the lodging-house in vain; but you must be hungry. We'll have breakfast, and then make the best of our way to the fair."

Breakfast was ordered and served. Nell Fulford joined her two companions, and did the honours of the table.

While partaking of their morning's meal the detective and his two companions observed throngs of persons passing the window, rushing even at that early hour to the fair.

"They are taking time by the forelock, Miss Fulford,"

said the detective, looking towards the window of the parlour.

"Oh, yes; it be always loike this at fair time. People coom from all parts, far and near."

"There is one thing I wish to impress on both of you," observed Wrench, "and that is to keep as quiet as possible. We'll see all that's to be seen, but we won't appear to be looking for any one. We are only here to enjoy the fun of the fair—that's all."

"Fun!" cried Nelly, with a sigh.

"I don't expect for one moment, Miss Fulford, that you, or indeed any one of us, will have much enjoyment, but as far as that is concerned it is quite a secondary consideration; but we must appear to be attracted hither for amusement. Let us hope something more important will follow."

His female companion inclined her head in tacit acquiescence, and Joe said he'd have nuffin' to say to anybody.

The fair was held at a small market town, which was built on the banks of a river. As far as architectural beauty was concerned, it was not much to boast of, for the streets rivalled those of Cairo, which are said to be the narrowest and dirtiest in the world, and central is the market-place.

In this market-place the fair was held, though many of the booths and canvas-covered stalls extended down the Egyptian thoroughfares, choking them with impassability.

For one hour or so after breakfast the occupants of the parlour of the "Dun Cow" contented themselves with watching the passengers in the road from the bay window of their snug little apartment.

Mr. Wrench had letters to answer which were sent from Scotland-yard. There was one also from Lord Ethalwood, in which the writer besought him to do his best to discover the murderer of Mr. Philip Jamblin.

A detective's life is both an anxious and an arduous one, make the best of it.

The earl's letter, of course, had to be answered by return of post. Mr. Wrench had little or nothing to communicate at present, but he deemed it expedient to write off and inform his lordship that his injunctions would not be disregarded.

When he had finished his correspondence, which was necessarily very brief, the detective informed his two companions that he was ready to accompany them to the fair.

Many of our readers are doubtless very well acquainted with the most noticeable features of a country fair. When held in a picturesque locality it is a sight worth seeing.

Fairs and wakes are of Saxon origin, and date back for many hundreds of years. The former were instituted in England by Alfred, in the year 886.

Wakes were established by order of Gregory VII. in 1049, and termed Feriœ, at which the monks celebrated the festival of their patron saints.

Fairs were established in France about 800 by Charlemagne, and encouraged in England about 1071 by William the Conqueror.

They may be said to be identified with the history of our country.

It was early in the day when Mr. Wrench arrived at the fair with his two companions, but nevertheless crowds of persons were already assembled.

As they joined the body of the people the noise was almost deafening, but a noise so like that of people enjoying themselves that he must have been a flinty philosopher who could get out of temper with it.

No gathering of this sort was complete without

Richardson's celebrated show, in which a melodrama of a most touching nature was enacted in the brief space of twenty minutes, or from that to half an hour.

Richardson himself at this time was gathered to his fathers.

He was a dumpy, pock-marked man, with a red face and a long brown coat.

Reading and writing were not included in his accomplishments, but he was a kindly-disposed, persevering, honest little man, much given to dirt and the drama, who contrived by praiseworthy industry to amass a large fortune.

It was his boast that some of our most celebrated actors and actresses were, at one time or another, included in his troupe.

The late Edmund Kean in his early career acted at Richardson's show.

The great Mrs. Pritchard, who played with David Garrick, began life as a performer at fairs.

Numbers of similar instances could be cited of other distinguished members of the theatrical profession who were wont to strut their hour upon the stage at shows and booths.

Although Richardson had passed away the booth in the fair still bore his name, albeit it was in other hands.

"Walk up, ladies and gentlemen—just going to begin!" shouted out a leather-lunged individual on the platform of the show.

"The Bleeding Nun; or, the Midnight Hour," was the powerful drama about to be represented.

While the gentleman with the never-failing lungs was addressing the yokels, a clown was going through some antics on another part of the platform.

After this a brass band struck up playing the most discordant music it is very well possible to conceive.

Mr. Wrench and his two companions ascended the steps which led to this temple of the drama, paid their money, and after waiting a considerable time in the interior of the booth had the satisfaction of witnessing the drama in question.

When they came out after the performance they were asked by the gentleman on the platform how they liked it, and of course said they were very much pleased.

Upon this the touter turned triumphantly to the gaping crowd below, and again shouted out, "Now's your time, gentlemen and ladies—just going to begin!"

The formula was gone through over and over again during the whole of the day.

As to dwarfs and giants and giantesses they were innumerable, together with curiosities both natural and unnatural.

An Irishman made up as a red Indian, and called "Yokoomaua, the celebrated fire-eater," undertook to put the end of a red-hot poker into his mouth, across his tongue, and on the soles of his naked feet.

Then there were swings, roundabouts, gold gingerbread, gingerbread nuts, Wombwell's brass band playing their loudest tunes, a horse with two heads and six legs, a mermaid, a wild man caught in the Black Forest, a learned pig, waxwork exhibitions, performing dogs and monkeys, acrobats, Mademoiselle Clotilda Favirini, the celebrated tight-rope dancer who had performed before most of the crowned heads of Europe, a sword-swallower, a Chinaman (hailing from Dublin), who threw sharp-painted swords at another Chinaman hailing from Cork), the Cork Chinaman standing all the while with arms outstretched against a board against which the swords were thrown within the eighth of an inch of his body.

Added to all these was the snapping of guns at the nut stalls, the artificial screams of the young women, and the hoarse guffaws of the young men.

Peace and quietness were out of the question; throughout the livelong day there was a ceaseless row and clatter.

The crowd was composed of three distinct classes—first those who came for amusement only.

Smockfrocked bumpkins and gaily-dressed lasses, who had taken a fresh lease of servitude, and who had been permitted to enjoy a genuine holiday and witness sights which were only to be seen at fairs; clergymen and other professional men of *status* and respectability, who walked awkward through the crowd, trying to look as if they were not enjoying themselves; a score or so of boys from an adjacent boarding school walking in couples like prisoners out for exercise, with the head gaoler in black trousers and blue spectacles, anxiously clearing a way before them; and above all a rosy-cheeked housemaid, who, having stolen half-an hour's liberty under pretext of an errand, was taking a sip at those waters which Solomon affirmed to be so sweet.

Some came only upon business.

Mr. Wrench and his two companions were included in this category.

Austere old maids, who scowled upon the circus, and sneered at the wild beasts; farmers and farmers' wives; of the temperate-in-drink and intemperate-in-religion genus, who, like the Caliph Omar, deemed it necessary to make a hell of this world in order to merit the heaven of the next.

A goodly sprinkling of pickpockets; a host of young persons with painted faces and comical smiles; and, let us add for the benefit of my small readers, all the people engaged in the various places of amusement, from the pretty girl who looked so happy as she danced on the tight rope, down to the red and white-faced clown, who said such funny things that you nearly split your sides with laughing.

And there were a great many people who went to the fair both for business and pleasure.

Farmers and their wives, of the true old Saxon sort, who went to hire their servants, and to spend their money, artful little hussies who intended to enjoy themselves, dancing in the booths, and to pick up fresh acquaintances, or to pull some irresolute swain over that matrimonial precipice, on the brink of which he had long been oscillating, and the great mass of boys and girls who had come, to use their own words, "to see the woild beasteses, and to get bound to the varmers."

It is incident to a fair that persons shall be free from being arrested in it for any other debt or contract than what was contracted in the same, or at least promised to be paid there.

Fairs of this sort were generally held once or twice a year, and by statute they were not to be held longer than they ought.

Also proclamations were to be made how long they were to continue, and no person was allowed to sell any goods after the time of the fair was ended, on forfeiture of double the value, one-fourth of which was to go to the prosecutor, and the rest to the king.

That was a toll usually paid in fairs on the sale of goods, and for stallage, picage, &c.

Fairs abroad are either free or charged with toll or impost.

The privileges of free fairs consisted chiefly—first, in all the traders, &c., whether natives or foreigners, who were allowed to enter the kingdom, and who were, under royal protection, exempt from duties, tolls, &c.

CAPTURE OF GILFS CHUDLEY.

They were established by letters patent from the prince.

Fairs, particularly free fairs, make a very considerable article in the commerce of Europe, especially in the Mediterranean and the inland parts of Germany.

The most celebrated fairs in Europe are those of Old Frankfort, held twice a year, in spring and autumn, the first commencing the Sunday before Palm Sunday, and the other on the Sunday before the 8th of Sept.

They are famous for the sale of all kinds of commodities, but particularly for the immense quantity of curious books, nowhere else to be found, and from whence the booksellers throughout all Europe used to furnish themselves.

No. 31.

Before each fair there is a catalogue of all the books to be sold thereat printed and dispersed, to call together the purchasers, though the learned complain of divers unfair practices therein, as factitious titles, names of books purely imaginary, &c., besides great faults in the names of the authors and the titles of the real books.

The fairs of Leipsic are held thrice a year—one beginning on the first of January, another three weeks after Easter, and a third at Michaelmas.

Besides these, there are a host of others held in various parts of the Continent.

England was at one time famous for its fairs, and even in the present day there are numbers held annually.

Stourbridge Fair, near Cambridge, was by far the greatest in Britain, and, perhaps, in the world. Bristol is next on the list.

The only fishing fair in this country is the one held at Great Yarmouth.

In addition to these there are fairs for butter at Ipswich; in Norfolk, for Scotch runts; at Bettford, for sheep; and a host of others in the leading towns of England.

The place visited by Mr. Wrench and his two companions was, as we have already signified, a hiring fair.

Those who offer themselves as grooms place a piece of sponge in their hat-bands; the shepherds, a tuft of wool; the carters, an inch of whipcord; and the boys of all work, a bunch of blue and green ribbons.

When a farmer wishes to engage a man he finds out a strong-limbed, clear-eyed young fellow. When this has been done they haggle.

Both fight hard for their money and their money's worth, and will often separate after half an hour's argument to look out for softer men.

If a bargain is struck the farmer gives the man a shilling.

This is called the *festin shilling*, or *God's penny*; after receiving which the man is the pursuer's slave, and should he not appear at the time appointed is liable to be sent to gaol.

It is, however, by no means a rare practice for a man or boy to engage himself at a fair on Thursday for 6s. per week, we will say; at a neighbouring fair on the Friday for 8s. a week, and at another on the Saturday for 10s. a week; closing with three offers and only holding to the best.

Farm servants are as hungry after money as the workmen in many of our manufacturing towns, and they are not the innocent creatures which novelists and dramatists would lead you to suppose.

Mr. Wrench had kept his eyes open throughout the livelong day. He had, in company with Joe and Nell Fulford, visited most of the shows, but had not met with the man he was in search of, but he did not feel disposed to give up the search as hopeless.

He partook of a substantial meal with his two friends in a small public-house, which stood just outside the fair.

Night drew on apace, but the devotees to pleasure were not sated. They had come to see all that could be seen, and the village carnival was just as crowded after nightfall as it had been during the bright and sunny hours of the day.

The quietly-disposed village folks retired to their beds. This was a mere matter of form, for the noise in the streets placed sleep out of the question.

Now, indeed, the real fun of the fair commenced.

Now the whole company of the very minor theatre were assembled upon the outer platform, and the man with the leathern-lunged voice was as vociferous as ever. He was a little hoarse with constant shouting, but this did not matter—he contrived to make himself heard.

The company on the platform went through a wild pantomime, in which the clown was ill-treated by everybody.

He was unmercifully whipped by a man in jack-boots, but was heedless of the punishment which, to say the truth, did not appear to affect him in the slightest degree. He contented himself with making grimaces in revenge, at which the people laughed till they cried again.

They had come to enjoy themselves, and it did not take much to move them to laughter.

The external preliminaries having been concluded on the platform of Richardson's celebrated booth, the *dramatis personæ* retired behind the curtain, the man with the leathern lungs shouting out at the top of his voice—

"Now's your time, good people; walk up—walk up! You'd better by half come in at once, if you means coming; we are just going to begin. Grand spectacular romantic melodrama as 'ud move the heart of a stone. This way, gentlemen!"

The harsh clang of unmusical instruments from within, the shaking of the tent, and the delighted shouts of the audience proved the interesting fact that there were still some spots in the world where theatrical announcements were not impostures.

The wild beasts had been fed, Wombwell's brass band had finished their last tune, and the shaven-cheeked, greasy-headed performers were packing up their instruments, chewing their sore lips, and stretching their cramped and weary limbs.

Life and jollity now rolled towards the dancing booths, washing into its stream all those who had been shooting at the nut stalls, or who had been to see the calf with six legs, the wonderful donkey, or the live mermaid, or had been peeping in at the panorama of the "Orful Massacres in the Injees," in which the artist, wisely sacrificing truth to effect, had painted the murderous Sepoys as black as saucepans, with blubber lips, frizzly hair, white waistcloths, and long spears, dripping with gore.

Between two gingerbread stalls there was a brave battle between the crowds.

Crowd No. 1 making for public-house, L.H.; crowd No. 2 pushing for dancing-booth, Op.

Both crowds were composed of free Britons, who will never believe that retreats are sometimes judicious.

Three men in particular might have been seen pushing first one way and then the other, as if they rather enjoyed the scramble than otherwise.

This did not escape the observation of the others, who cried—

"Now then, you sir, keep yer elbows to yerself. You aint everybody."

"You're another!" cried a voice.

"Don't ee give me any o' yer cheek, young man, or you may get a prop in the eye."

"Heigh, my Jack-o'-dandy, you'll spile yer pretty govers if ye shove us common people about like this 'ere," observed a rustic to a young swell.

"Look at the old bloke with the green goggles, how uneasy he is to find himself somew'eres. Keep still, old gentleman—we'll make it all right for you arter a bit."

"Order—silence! Where are you shoving to, yer

fool ?" cried a stout farmer. "Haven't ye ever bin to a fair afore ?"

"Take care of your pockets !" cried a policeman, from the outside, "you as has got anything in 'em," he added, with official sarcasm.

"All right, bobby, we're fly—all on us regularly up to the knocker."

"Don't squeesh—don't squeesh !" cried a Cockney costermonger, with the good humoured raillery of his class. "If there's one thing as I hates more than another, it is to be squeeshed. The doctor says as how my constertootion won't bear it."

"Oh, Bill !" murmured a female voice from the abyss.

"Vell, you knows I can't bear it, Sall," returned the costermonger. "You knows as how I've a delecate constertootion.

"Bear up, old man—don't ee gi' way," observed a rustic.

"Oh, you big hulking beast," screamed an old woman. "You've bin and torn my best dress by a treadin' on it wi' yer great hob-nailed boots."

"Mek him pay for ut, mother," suggested a plough-man. "Give 'im in charge o' the pleece."

"Pleece, pleece !" shouted out the old dame.

"What's the matter, ma'm ?" said a constable.

"Matter, indeed ! this hulking fellow has torn my gownd from my back—that's what be the matter."

"It can't be helped. It was an accident, you ought to keep out of the crowd."

At this there was a roar of laughter.

The old woman became furious.

"You're as bad as he is," she exclaimed, shaking her umbrella at the constable. "What good are you ? What are you paid for, I should like to know ? You ought to be ashamed o' yerself to let an honest woman be used in this way !"

The policeman offered to conduct her out of the crowd, but she would not listen to him. She went on abusing the whole force in general and the luckless constable in particular.

This little incident seemed to be interesting to the multitude, who pushed and shoved to their hearts' content.

It is impossible to say how long this contest might have lasted had not several persons cried out that they had been robbed, and called out to the police. The old woman declared that she had had her pockets picked.

Three policemen now charged the crowd and knocked down an old man and two boys who had done nothing.

After which they clumsily noted down the depositions of the plundered ones in their pocket-books, with looks of solemn authority and words of the obscurest promise.

Half-an-hour passed, and the two crowds ceased their contest.

Mr. Wrench and his two companions, who had become hemmed in, were now enabled to make their escape; they had been borne along by crowd No. 1, and during the rush they had no means of extricating themselves.

When, however, they got clear of the mob of malcontents, they passed out of the fair with all convenient speed.

At some short distance they discovered a small tavern, bearing the sign of the "Lord Cornwallis."

They made for this, to partake of some refreshment.

A large flag, the Union Jack, was suspended over the front of the house, at the door of which stood a few soldiers of that unwashed stamp which

haunt the dens of Orchard-street and the purlieus of Birdcage-walk.

There was an awe-stricken semicircle of rustics at a little distance, before whom stood an enlisting sergeant —his features bloated and reddened from beer and alcohol—beckoning with his naked sword in his hand.

He had the gift of the gab, and the words he was giving utterance to fell glibly enough from his lips.

"Now, my fine fellow," he cried, in a thick husky voice, "don't hesitate. A fine chance offers itself. Take the Queen's money, and join our gallant comrades in the East. Now's your time; but don't all speak at once. Happy is the man who enlists in our crack regiment. We want a little help just now to thrash all them black-faced, black-headed scoundrels who've been butchering the poor women and children. You won't have another such a chance, and so don't hesitate—don't hang back like a pack of curs. I see around me a fine lot of fellows. Come, now, you with the white dudley, we can't go on without you. You know there isn't such a pair of shoulders as yours in the whole army. You're cut out for a sodger, and it's a real sin for a handsome young fellow like you to be wasting your precious life following the plough when you might be making a fortune in Injia. There's heaps of gold there, and you are sure to get promoted. Say the word. Take the Queen's shilling, and you'll come back a general with white stars on your breast, and a mahogany box full of yellow sovereigns. You won't refuse—you're not one of that sort. I've had my eye upon you, and you'll thank me for making a man of you. What say you, comrade ?"

"Don't ee do nothink o' the sort, lad. Don't ee listen to what ee ses," cried a woman, standing by. "I know what he be. He only talks loike that cos he gets so much a head for every fresh fool he takes in. Take the Queen's money, indeed ! Let him keep it. If it was to a man's good to go a sodgering, d'ye think they'd want to tempt him with a shilling ? Go to the wars, and what will ee get for it ? A bit o' ribbon or an iron cross may be. It's a hard world for humble folk: In war they does the fightin', and others get the reward ; in peace they does the hard work, and others collar the money. Don't ee be kiddy kilted into it, my lad. They mek the gentlemen generals, not the private sodgers, and all the plunder goes to the government as stays at home, not to them as risks their lives for it abroad. He can talk and tell lies by the bushel, but don't ee be gammoned by him—and don't ee bleeve a word as he ses."

The rubicund face of the enlisting sergeant became redder than ever as he listened to the words which fell from the lips of the young woman.

He was greatly incensed, and looked upon her with ineffable disgust.

"You are an audacious impudent hussy !" he cried, with the fierce gestures of a Hamlet at the Bower Saloon, "and some wholesome chastisement would do you good, my lady. If you were a man, I'd give you something for yourself, but a British soldier never raises his hand against a woman."

Having delivered himself of this heroic declaration, he turned towards the rustics, and said, in a confidential tone—

"You've got too much sense to take any heed of what a poor half-witted creature like her has to say. Anyone can see that she has not got her right change."

"You've got your change, old man, and no mistake," returned the woman, giving him a playful push in the chest which sent him reeling against the wall. "Why, you're screwed, old man," and added, "You're a nice sort of gineral, ain't ye?"

The clowns, who invariably join with the stronger side, hailed their hero's discomfiture with loud shouts of derisive laughter, and closing fearlessly round him, chanted the cynical refrain—

A sargint stepp'd up to me, and asked me for to 'list,
I bid him stand back, and I showed him then my fist,
Tooral rooral, tooral la.

The sergeant was a big bulky man, but owing to sundry potations he was a little groggy on his pins. He, however, felt very much inclined to give his assailant a sharp box on the ear, but the chances were if he did so that he would raise the ire of the male portion of the assembled throng, and prudence directed him to pass the matter over as lightly and good-humouredly as possible.

"A woman's more than a match for the best of us, mates," he said in a jocular manner. "My principle is to let them have their own way. I never argufy with 'em—am too old a soldier for that."

"That's the way to serve out them 'listin' sargents," cried the woman, taking no heed of the last observations made by the gallant son of Mars. "They bring more sorrow and heartaches upon the poor than all the tax gatherers and squires' stewards can do. Why, Willy, you ha' got gay ribbons on to-day," she ejaculated, catching sight of a young man who was known to her in the crowd. "Hast caught a master with all thy finery?"

"Don't you know the British colours, my girl?" said an old soldier, standing by. "Your Willy has enlisted."

Her countenance now wore a troubled expression.

"Oh, Will," she murmured, in a low, respectful voice, "and ha' ye left your poor mother to starve or go to the House? But there, it's no yoose talking now. Words can't free a bound man, nor yet any money that she or you could find."

"Never fear," said the young man. "I'll come back rich and make her and you happy."

He said this in a faint voice, having but partially recovered from the quartern of gin, under the influence of which he had been imprudent enough to enlist. He now began to feel qualms as to his future welfare.

"I should ha' felt this more at one time," murmured the woman. "For you've bin kind and good to me, Will, and it doant tak' me long to count my frinds. But now I've only one thought in my head and one grief in my heart. I can't think nor feel of anything but this sore trouble, for it be a trouble as will cling to me for many and many a long and weary day."

She ceased, and those around were at no loss to comprehend that the speaker's heart was too full to admit of her saying more.

The young man who had been called Will hung down his head, and but for very shame he would have sobbed; but situated as he was, surrounded by his companions, he bore up as best he could.

The woman turned her back upon the young recruit, and went half-way down the tavern passage; it was blocked up by soldiers who appeared to be discussing the character of their acquaintances.

"He's got an oil bottle in his pocket," were the first words she caught. "An' so has your brave 'listing sergeant," said the woman, "an' bad luck to him an' all such smooth-tongued varmints."

"Don't you speak ill of the sergeant, young woman," said a soldier. "He's a cooty to perform."

"Has he?"

"Yes, he's right enough, but I don't like a man as puts salt into his own beer and sugar in mine, at first sight too. "'Taint natural or seemly that he should."

"'An who be that there," inquired the woman.

"Ah, no one as you knows," returned a rustic.

"But who be it, no matter whether it be my bis'ness or yourn?"

"An old man, my dear, as has been pouring melted butter down our backs, and talking to us as if we were all field-marshals or generals."

"Ye sodgers want to keep all the blarney to your own mouths. But what sort of man be he?"

"Short and dirty, like a winter's day, with a green shade over his eyes."

"A green shade!" exclaimed Mr. Wrench, glancing at Joe Doughty. "An old man—eh, my friends?"

"Well, he aint a young one—leastways, to judge from appearance."

"Appearances are sometimes deceptive," observed the detective.

"Well, that be true, guv'nor. We all on us find that out some time or another, but he aint no good."

"There's some truth in what he said, though," cried another of the soldiers—"that it's us privates as wins all the battles, while the generals take good care to keep out of harm's way."

"Ah, my lad," said an old soldier, joining the group of idlers, "that's all very well as far as it goes, but you might as well put a horse in a gig and tell him to drive himself up to London, as to set an army at an army without a general to hold the reins. And it wants a brave man to be general in a fight when the cannons are roaring, and the wounded are groaning, and the smoke is thickening. It's hard work to keep one's head cool to see what regiments want help and what regiments can do by themselves. I tell you it aint easy work either for the generals, the captains, or the privates. But here we are—sorry soldiers, to block up the passage in this fashion, and none offering to move to make room for a pretty girl to pass."

This last observation applied to Nell Fulford, who had silently and quickly drawn towards the entrance of the passage.

"Now, then, soldiers, make yourselves a little less, and let this young woman pass."

Several of the men withdrew at once, and Mr. Wrench and Joe passed through and gained the public room beyond.

"Keep quiet. Our business is to watch, but don't either of you say anything till I address you," whispered the detective, as they took their way along.

The three entered the room, in a dark corner of which they seated themselves. Wrench ordered some beer and sandwiches, which were brought.

They all three of them glanced round the room, and soon perceived the subject of the soldiers' conversation. He was a bent, long-haired man, with a green shade over his eyes, and dressed in a kind of cloak with loose sleeves.

At the next table, with a huge cheese before him, and glass of cold brandy and water at his side, sat a stalwart, broad-shouldered man, with a hard square cast of face.

Near the window lolled a young gentleman, who was well dressed and be-jewelled, and who had a lighted cigar between his kid-gloved fingers.

He must have wandered in there for a few moments from curiosity, unless he was one of those gentlemen by birth but not by breeding, who drink the dregs of society by preference.

Mr. Wrench recognised these as the last-named two men who had been so energetic during the hustle.

"Bring us a greybeard of Husser and Squencher," said a rustic in a smock frock, who was seated near to the detective. (A greybeard is one of those jugs commonly used in ale-houses with the face of an old man on it. Husser and Squencher is a drain of gin and a quart of beer mixed).

"That was a bad job," observed a rustic, addressing the man in the green shade, "that 'ere job in Larch-grove-lane."

"I've not heerd on it," said the man with the green shade; "what was it?"

When Nell Fulford heard the man with the shade speak she gave a start, and half rose from her seat. Mr. Wrench placed his hand on her shoulder, and by a motion of his head signified that she was to remain quiet.

She obeyed, and shrank back farther into the corner, behind a settle, and listened with gleaming eyes.

Situated as she and her two companions were, they could not be seen by the man with the green shade.

The rustic, who had already alluded to the tragedy, now gave a brief account of the same for the edification of those present.

"These things are most horrible," exclaimed the young swell with the cigar. "Most terrible. What motive had the scoundrel? I suppose plunder."

"Noa, it warn't that," said the countryman. "Leastways, I think not," he added, drinking from his mug and setting it down upon the table with a bang. "It warn't done for money, measter—'cos ye see the young farmer hadn't bin robbed, so I've bin tould."

"No doubt it were done out o' spite or revenge."

"Like enough somethink o' that sort," observed the man with the shade, who, after this last observation, appeared to fall into a reverie.

"And be you a stranger in these parts, measter?" asked the countryman, with provincial curiosity. "If it be a fair question, leastways?"

"Yes, I only came here this morning. I wan't, if I can, to get——"

Nell Fulford could not remain longer passive. She bounded like a panther across the room and sprang upon the man with a horrible shriek, which rang through the apartment with appalling distinctness.

"Wretch! murdering villain! We've found you at last," she cried, clasping him by the neck with superhuman force. "It be he," she shouted, in a voice of triumph, "it be Giles Chudley!"

The room was filled in an instant.

"The woman's mad," exclaimed one of the newcomers, dragging her from the man.

"Mad!" she cried, and with inconceivable strength she broke from the man's grasp, and darted upon the murderer of her sweetheart.

She tore off his wig, which she flung upon the floor.

The company assembled in the parlour of the "Lord Cornwallis" saw before them a man with fluttering, conscience-stricken eyes, and hands clasped imploringly towards them.

"I am innocent!" he exclaimed. "Take her away."

Joe Doughty rushed forward, overset one of the tables as he went along, and sprang at the throat of Chudley.

"I'll ha' yer heart's blood!" he yelled, in a voice of concentrated passion.

He caught the affrighted man by the throat with both hands, and pressed him against the wall.

Chudley's face became purple, and it was evident that he was undergoing the process of strangulation.

"Leave go your hold," cried a soldier at the further end of the room. "Do you want to kill the man."

"I'll ha' his life, if I die for it!"

By this time the utmost disorder prevailed. Mr. Wrench came forward and besought Joe Doughty to release the culprit.

"I'll not let 'im go for you, nor no man!" cried Joe.

"We won't see murder committed," said several rustics. "Forward to the rescue!"

"Doughty, do as I bid you—let go your hold."

His first paroxysm of passion now having in a measure subsided, Joe released his man, upon whom Mr. Wrench had already slipped a pair of handcuffs.

"I did not do it!" exclaimed the prisoner.

"Did not do what?" said Joe Doughty, thrusting his fist within an inch of the pallid, mottled face. "Lying won't sarve you now; you're nabbed, and the hangman's rope is ready for you."

"He says he did not murder Mr. Philip Jamblin," cried Nell Fulford.

"You see he knows what he is charged with, although he's never been in these parts afore this morning."

The landlord of the "Lord Cornwallis" now entered the room. He was in a great state of flustration, and became seriously concerned as he beheld a terror-stricken man upon whom the eyes of all those present were intently fixed.

"What is the matter, gentlemen?" inquired Boniface.

"Murder's the matter; that's all, my friend," answered Mr. Wrench. "And this man is my prisoner."

"Prisoner! Are you in the force?"

"I am a detective from Scotland-yard. I know my duty; let that suffice."

"Well, this is a pretty business," exclaimed the landlord. "Never had such a thing as this occur in my house. I can't make it out rightly."

"It will be made pretty clear very shortly, I expect; but that does not much matter as far as you are concerned."

"It's no business of mine, that be sartin," said the landlord, "but I wish it had taken place anywhere but here. Howsomever, it can't be helped."

"What be goin' to do wi' yer man, measter?" cried a countryman.

"What do you suppose, you silly fellow," answered Wrench; "take him to the lock-up, to be sure. Doughty, just go outside and bring in a policeman or two."

"Ah, ah! that is if ye can find 'em," observed the countryman. "They're seldom in the way when they be wanted."

At this sally many of the rustics who were present burst out in a loud guffaw.

The landlord and one of his barmen proceeded to replace the table which had been overturned, and picked up the shattered glasses which lay upon the floor.

A dead calm succeeded the storm and tumult which had been raging but a few minutes before.

Joe returned with two policemen, who promptly obeyed the orders given by Wrench, who handed his prisoner over to them, and he was forth with marched off to the village lock-up.

"Dall it all," cried the countryman, "but this be but a sorry ending to the fair."

The young gentleman with the flowing locks and kid gloves had quietly withdrawn from the scene immediately after Nell had sprung upon Chudley—he was followed by the man who sat with the huge lump of cheese before him.

Their sudden flight struck Mr. Wrench as being a little singular ; he, however, did not make any remark in reference to the same.

Everybody in the room seemed all at once to become serious, and reflective. The noise of many voices had ceased.

The soldiers were as stiff and formal as on a parade day, and those in the parlour who had partaken a little too freely of strong drinks appeared to be sobered by the sight they had witnessed.

For the remainder of the night there was little else talked about in the parlour of the " Lord Cornwallis " but the capture of the wretched man who was arrested upon the grave charge of murder.

CHAPTER .

THE BENCH OF MAGISTRATES—EXAMINATION OF THE PRISONER.

MR. WRENCH had frequently declared that he sometimes came upon a culprit of whom he was in search when he least expected, and this observation was borne out by the capture of Chudley, which was as unlooked for as it was extraordinary and fortuitous.

He had good reason to congratulate himself upon the issue. After seeing his man safely under lock and key he sent off that night a telegram to Broxbridge, informing Lord Ethalwood of the arrest of the accused.

Early on the following day he took his prisoner per rail to Broxbridge, Nell Fulford and Joe Doughty returning with him.

The prisoner's first examination before the bench of magistrates created a degree of excitement which was almost without a parallel.

It so chanced that his examination took place on market day.

A country town is only awake once a week, and that is only on market day. At other times houses may be open, shops may be open, and eyes may be open, but houses, shops, and people are fast asleep. The houses resemble mausoleums, the shops are cold and still as pictures, and the citizens who walk about do not seem to know where they are going, what they are doing, or why they are out of doors.

But on market days everybody and everything is alive. The tradesman no longer props his front door and yawns down the empty streets—he is behind the counter bowing and skipping like a French dancing master.

His shop is not filled with impatient customers like a shop in London on Saturday night, but with patient customers like a shop in the country on Saturday morning, for the good old housewives only go shopping once a week, and consider it too serious and sacred a business to be lightly hurried over.

Everything is full. The inns fill the farmers as the farmers fill the inns—the yards are full of carts, the stables full of horses, heads are full of business, hands full of wares, hearts full of hope or joy or discontent.

The streets are filled with ragged idlers indigenous to the town and its vicinity, with market women who erect temporary barricades with donkey carts, and hen coops, and fruit baskets, towering towards the sky.

With clumsy cubs of peasant farmers, with felt hats, fustian frocks plush waistcoats, brown leather breeches, sky-blue stockings, and great greasy shoes big as wheelbarrows.

In addition to all these there are to be found homespun specimens of agriculture, who shone years and years ago in Mr. Morton's comedies, with grey hairs, red faces, and top boots, heavy riding whips, and sentimental hearts—for all but their day labourers.

There are also to be seen a set of mysterious bloods who drive dog-carts as high as Haman's Ladder, and steeds strong and fiery as the coursers of Phaeton, who wear smart green frocks, fancy waistcoats, jockey boots, peach-blossom corduroy breeches, and hats lodged jauntily on the left ear—who, once settled in the market-room of their favourite tavern, drink like fishes, smoke like lime-kilns, and sit like hens, and who display three sample bags in the corn market with all the grace of a Rothschild who negotiates a loan upon 'Change.

The news had spread abroad that the murderer of Phil Jamblin had been captured by a clever London detective, who had been on his track for weeks past.

It also became known that he was to be had up before the bench of magistrates, of which no less a person than Lord Ethalwood himself was chairman ; and his lordship was a "sharp 'un," they averred. "He could see his way through a four inch deal board."

It was a busy day for Mr. Wrench when "his man," as he termed him, was brought before the " beaks."

He had seen the earl immediately after his return, for the purpose of arranging all the necessary preliminaries.

Enough evidence would be offered to warrant a remand—there would not be much difficulty about that; but before the committal the case would have to be gone more fully into.

Giles Chudley, in common with most criminals of his class, hoped to escape the punishment he so justly deserved.

A man put upon his trial for a capital offence has so many chances in his favour that nothing but the strongest and most conclusive evidence will suffice; and even when this has been offered by the prosecution, the jury will not return a verdict of "guilty," and when once acquitted, as we all of us know, a prisoner cannot in this country be put upon his trial a second time for the same offence.

This surely ought to be amended.

In Scotland the jury, when there is not sufficient evidence to justify them in returning a verdict of guilty, return one of "not proven," and the prisoner can be tried again if any additional evidence is obtained.

Many years ago a man, named Spollin, was charged with the murder of a railway official in Dublin; the trial was conducted in a hasty and slovenly manner, and he was acquitted.

It transpired afterwards that two witnesses who could have proved the guilt of the prisoner were never examined at all.

If he could have been retried there was abundance of evidence to ensure a conviction.

What was the sequel ?

The wretch Spollin had the audacity to deliver a series of lectures upon murder in general, and the one he had been charged with in particular.

People paid their money to listen to the scoundrel's statement.

Spollin declared that he was giving these lectures to realise a sufficient sum to take him abroad, as he had no chance of obtaining employment in this country.

He was an ignorant illiterate man, and his " lectures " as he called them were contemptible ; they were worse than this—they were an insult to the public, whose indignation became aroused.

The last he gave imperilled his life, for a portion of the audience boldly accused him and would not allow him to proceed till he had confessed to the murder. He admitted himself to be guilty.

A rush was made towards the platform, and Spollin made his escape by a side door.

Giles Chudley was advised by his friends to say nothing himself, but to engage a solicitor to defend him. He agreed to this proposition, and sent for a gentleman who was supposed to be a sharp practitioner.

His learned adviser told Chudley to leave the matter in his hands. He spoke so confidently, and was really so delighted in having the case, that the prisoner plucked up courage, and began to think that he should ride over the difficulties with which he was surrounded.

It was a most singular circumstance—but it was true, nevertheless—that Giles, who was but a poor farm labourer, should have ample funds at his disposal to pay his solicitor handsomely for his defence.

As he alighted from the prison van, which drew up by the side of the court-house, Giles was saluted with a storm of groans and hisses.

Mr. Philip Jamblin was a young man who had been universally respected, and his murderer, as a natural consequence, was as universally execrated, and in all probability, had the populace got hold of him—had he not been protected by a cohort of constables and warders—he would have been subjected to Lynch law.

The magistrates had taken their respective seats, the chief clerk had mended and nibbed a favourite quill pen, Mr. Chickrell was busily engaged in arranging his papers at one of the tables in front of the chief clerk, and Mr. Wrench was rushing about in the greatest state of anxiety. He had his witnesses safely ensconced in an adjoining room.

The court was crowded to excess, and it is perhaps needless to say that it was about as inconvenient and ill-ventilated one as it is well possible to conceive.

Every eye was directed towards the prisoner as he entered the dock. Low murmurs arose from the crowd.

"Silence—order!" shouted out the usher. "Hoosh! less noise if you plase."

Mr. Wrench was called.

He gave a brief but circumstantial account of the arrest of the prisoner, Giles Caudley, together with a number of other immaterial matters relative to the case.

The worthy host of the "Carved Lion" was the next witness.

He deposed to all the facts which had come to his knowledge on the night of the murder.

Mr. Slapperton, the prisoner's legal adviser, rose to cross-examine this witness.

"Pray, Mr.—For the moment I forget your name."

"Brickett."

"Ah! yes, precisely. Well, Mr. Brickett, you say you saw a man stooping down and washing his hands in the pool at Lurch-grove-green?"

"Certainly, I did."

"Yes. Where had you come from—that is, what brought you to the Green?"

"Why, my legs, of course," returned Brickett.

At this there was a titter in the court which was immediately suppressed by the watchful and industrious usher.

"Don't bandy words with me, man," said Slapperton.

"I again ask you where you had been?"

"To a customer of mine."

"Oh! Had you partaken of any refreshment, or, not to put too fine a point on the matter, had you been drinking?"

"I had not."

"You were perfectly sober?"

"About as sober as you are now."

At this last observation there was another titter.

"Your answers are by no means satisfactory, and personal remarks are both unseemly and impertinent," said the lawyer, in a severe tone. "I will not ask you any further questions. The Court will be able to draw their own inference of your conduct and demeanour. You may stand down."

Henry Adolphus, radiant in his new livery, was placed in the box.

His statement was much the same as that sworn to on the inquest.

"And that's all you know about the matter?" said Mr. Slapperton.

"Yes, sir, that is all," answered the footman.

"Look at the prisoner. Does he resemble the man you saw running across the fields?"

"I shouldn't like to say for certain, but he does resemble him."

"Oh! indeed. In what way?"

"In many ways. His eyes are like the man I saw, but since the night of the murder he has grown a beard."

"Be careful, sir," cried Slapperton. "He has grown a beard since the night of the murder? You don't happen to know that he is not the man at all?"

"No, I do not happen to know that," returned Henry Adolphus. "My impression is that he is the man I saw."

"Why, just now you said you could not say whether he was or not. Do you know that you are contradicting yourself—perjuring yourself, in fact?" said the lawyer, turning triumphantly towards the bench.

"I think you are in error, Mr. Slapperton," said Lord Ethalwood. "The witness says he was, and still is, under the impression that the prisoner was the man. He has never said positively that he was. I think you will find that he has not contradicted himself."

"I bow to your decision, my lord," observed the lawyer. "It is quite clear that your servant is unable to identify the prisoner."

"Identification under the circumstances described must necessarily be difficult."

Mr. Slapperton bowed, and the witness left the box. Ellen Fulford was then called.

She gave a detailed account of her interview with the deceased in Dennett's-lane, and in addition to this she described the recognition and capture of the prisoner in the parlour of the "Lord Cornwallis."

She was infinitely more calm and self-possessed than she was when giving her evidence on the inquest.

Mr. Slapperton rose to cross-examine her.

"Pray, Miss Fulford, will you tell us whether you met Mr. Jamblin in Dennett's-lane by appointment, or was it an accidental meeting?"

"I waited for him, as I expected he would pass that way."

"Ah! I see; you desired to speak to him?"

"Yes, I did."

"I believe he was a lover of yours—was he not?"

"We had kept company and walked together."

"He was attached to you?"

"I believe he was."

"And you were also attached to him? The feeling was reciprocal, I suppose, eh?"

The witness did not make any reply. There was a dead silence in the court.

"Why do you not answer my question?" said the lawyer.

"I don't know that you have any right to put such a question."

"Oh! but I have," he returned, with a chuckle; "a perfect right. You must allow me to be the best judge of that."

Mr. Chicknell came to the rescue. He rose, and addressing the bench, said—

"I strongly object to any such question being put to the witness. It is irrelevant."

"I do not see that it bears upon the case," observed Lord Ethalwood, "but if Mr. Slapperton insists——"

"I do insist, my lord," cried Slapperton, "and I greatly object to Mr. Chicknell interfering with me in my line of defence.

"I have a duty to perform—a duty I shall not shrink from, but perform fearlessly. I think I shall be able to prove that the young man who is now under examination is innocent of the charge preferred against him."

As he made these observations he thumped the table, and looked defiantly round the court.

"If it is essential for you to have an answer from the witness it would be wrong for us to interfere. Proceed with your examination," said Lord Ethalwood.

The question was again put.

"He was my accepted suitor," said Miss Fulford, after some hesitation.

"You were engaged to be married to him?"

"He would have married me if he had lived," said the witness, bursting into tears.

Everybody in the court felt for her, everybody but her questioner.

The situation in which she was placed was indeed a most painful one.

But the pertinacious Mr. Slapperton was determined to make himself as conspicuous as possible.

He did not often get the chance of being engaged in such a big case, and he was bent on making the most of it.

"Pray, Miss Fulford, were you not acquainted some time ago with a person named Charles Peace?"

"I did know Mr. Peace when he resided in this neighbourhood."

"Ah, I thought so! And was he also a lover of yours?"

Miss Fulford became red with indignation.

"No, he was not. He paid me some attention, it is true."

"Very marked attention, was it not?"

"Mr. Slapperton, I think you are quite out of order," remarked one of the magistrates. "The man Peace has been in prison for some considerable time, and I for one strongly object to you introducing his name in this case."

"I shall not shrink from doing my duty," said Slapperton, perfectly unmoved. "I affirm most positively and emphatically that I am quite justified in the course I am pursuing. If the bench is of an opposite opinion I have no alternative but to submit to their decision, but I shall do so under protest—I say under protest."

The magistrates conversed together, after which the chairman said—

"My brother magistrates and myself think you are exceeding the limits which ought to circumscribe an advocate in a preliminary examination. It has nothing to do with the charge against the prisoner, and the fact of the witness having one or more admirers or suitors is matter altogether irrelevant. Good taste ought to guide you, and prevent any undue reference to subjects which must necessarily be painful to dwell upon or even to refer to."

"My object is to elicit the truth, my lord. The questions I have to put are perfectly relevant. You must pardon the observation, but I claim to be best judge in respect to my line of defence. The witness has already admitted that she received—I will not say encouraged—the attentions of Charles Peace, who at the present time is a convict undergoing a term of penal servitude."

"That is admitted."

"That being so, I have one or two other questions to put to the witness, which, in the interest of my client, I am constrained to ask."

"Proceed, sir," said Lord Ethalwood, haughtily.

"Pray, Miss Fulford, may I ask you if you are aware that the man Peace and the prisoner had a hostile encounter?"

"I believe they had."

"Oh, you believe so; you are not certain?"

"I was told so."

"By whom?"

"By many persons."

"By Peace himself?"

"No, not by him, but by the neighbours."

"Can you give us their names?"

"Mr. Brickett was one."

"And do you know also that the ill-fated Mr. Jamblin committed an assault upon Charles Peace?"

"I do."

"What was the reason for the assault in question?"

"Mr. Peace was rude to me in Dennett's-lane. He was in a violent passion, and dragged me forcibly along. I strove to get away and screamed, being terrified at the time. Mr. Jamblin rescued me."

"And did he strike Peace?"

"Yes; with a stick he was carrying."

"And did Peace leave the neighbourhood after that?"

"Yes, immediately afterwards."

"Were you attached to him?"

"Really, Mr. Slapperton, you are quite out of order. I object to the question."

"Oh, if you object, sir," returned Slapperton, in a sarcastic tone, "then I presume the court will coincide with you."

Without waiting for the decision Nell Fulford said in a loud voice—

"I was not attached to him."

"Thank you, madam, I am much obliged by your courtesy," cried the persevering advocate in an ironical manner, casting at the same time a withering glance at Chicknell.

Mr. Slapperton had come for the express purpose of asking every possible conflicting and painful question of the witnesses. It was his aim in doing so to distinguish himself as a fearless advocate, and thus create what he termed a "sensation." But the latitude of counsel has increased since his day, and recently it has been a scandal to our courts of law.

Whether, as some people tell us, the quality of the bar, and of police-courts in particular, has deteriorated of late years, whether it is assumed at present the plea of "public interests" covers every excess of zeal and every abuse of privilege which an advocate may permit himself, or whether it is that the inquiries before the magistrate, which have of late years grown to such inordinate dimensions, afford an entirely new field for the display of such excesses, we will not undertake to say. But the fact is indisputable. Nor are the discreditable scenes which distinguished the court-house at Richmond during the examination of Kate Webster, the only ones which have recently drawn attention to the growing coarseness and inquisitorial tyranny with which cross-examinations are conducted.

EXAMINATION OF ELLEN FULFORD.

It was not merely in examining witnesses that the counsel for the prisoner on this occasion indulged in observations which ought not to have been tolerated for a moment by anyone who may be presiding over the proceedings in a court of justice.

It is perfectly true that great latitude must of necessity be allowed to counsel in their efforts to extract the truth from obstinate or interested witnesses.

But in the hands of an accomplished advocate, who is a gentleman at the same time, this need never degenerate into bullying or browbeating.

There are witnesses, of course, on whom tenderness or courtesy would be wasted, and for whom no cross-examination can be too searching or severe.

But where an advocate, through want of skill or self-control, applies to one class of witnesses mode of treatment only applicable to another, it is time for the judge or justice to interfere, and to protect respectable persons from gross outrages and indignities.

Nell Fulford had a series of questions put to her by Mr. Slapperton, which, naturally enough, raised the indignation of the bench.

It would be difficult to fetter an advocate by any hard and fast rules, and both judges and magistrates naturally felt great reluctance in interfering with him in the discharge of his duty.

But the former have a task to perform as well, and any delicacy which they may exhibit in fulfilling it should be met by corresponding delicacy on the part of the counsel in the case.

It is much to be regretted that this is not invariably forthcoming, and that if the particular kind of cross-examination satirised in the person of Mr. Serjeant Buzfuz has, to some extent, gone out of fashion, something nearly, if not quite as bad, survives among our criminal lawyers.

In inquiries conducted before magistrates this license is painfully conspicuous.

It appears very often as if an ordinary bench of magistrates—we are not, of course, speaking of police magistrates—were frightened by the presence of a hectoring, genuine Old Bailey barrister.

It is absolutely monstrous that any of our fellow-citizens should be liable at any moment to be placed in the witness-box, and compelled, on pain of commitment, to answer the most insulting questions about his past career, and about all his relations and connections.

Judges themselves do not always interfere with sufficient promptitude to check these abuses of advocacy.

And magistrates, as we have already said, too often seem afraid to do so.

But there is one person, at all events, who might do something to check the practice, and that is the witness himself.

If it were found that witnesses made a practice of refusing to answer questions raking up their whole past lives, in order if possible to discredit their veracity and respectability, the system must inevitably collapse.

A general public protest against this iniquitous practice, represented by the frequent spectacle of witnesses being committed for contempt of court, would soon bring counsel to their senses.

So far, therefore, the public has the remedy in its own hands.

A few martyrs to this legal tyranny, in the shape of witnesses preferring imprisonment to submission, would work a wonderful change in our law courts.

And it is by no means improbable that an improvement in these might be followed by improvements elsewhere, and that the intangible entity called "public interest" would not so often be allowed to shield the most unwarrantable breaches of confidence and invasions of domestic privacy.

Every man of course knows what he has to expect if he ventures to criticise the procedure of a court of law, or the conduct of a judge or barrister.

He is treated with contempt, as a person who must necessarily be in total ignorance of the subject under consideration.

In all professions there is a tendency to regard the comments of the outside public as not only worthless but impertinent.

The practice of the law is a comparative mystery to all but the practitioners themselves.

The forms of the court, the rules which regulate the examination of witnesses, what evidence is admissible and what is not, the very phraseology in which lawyers communicate with each other—all subjects of which nobody can acquire any knowledge whatever by the light of nature; and this consciousness of ignorance on the part of the public disposes them to look with a kind of awe on the interior of a court of justice, and to be very much at the mercy of any one of the hierophants who shall think proper to rebuke the presumption of an audacious and uninstructed critic.

It is too often forgotten by both sides that the professional man himself labours under disqualifications scarcely less serious than those of the intruder whom he ridicules.

The lawyer's experience, his familiarity with technicalities so formidable to the unprofessional mind, and his personal acquaintance with the working of our judicial system, enable him to speak from a point of advantage in contending with a lay disputant, by which the latter is apt to be abashed.

But the layman, on the other hand, is free from those ideals which upset the judgment of the lawyer; he is not defending a system in which he has been bred, the details of which he has mastered with great difficulty and which long habit has taught him to consider irrepressible.

It is always a moot point whether professional or non-professional men make the better reformers.

For our own part we incline to think the latter are more likely to become so, from the very fact that they are enabled to take an independent and unprejudiced view of the law as it stands.

The first have the knowledge and experience; but they cannot see themselves from without or appreciate the criticism of common sense, when brought to bear upon their long-established maxims.

The second can take broader views of the questions submitted to their judgment, and see the immediate defects of existing rules and regulations, though they are not always able to comprehend the full consequences which might flow from their suggestions.

It must readily be owned, therefore, that such animadversions ought to be uttered with some diffidence, and received with considerable caution.

But he must stand up for the right of the public, to protect itself against the abuse of privilege, when those who ought to protect it are forgetful of their duty.

Witnesses in our courts of law are entitled to be treated with common courtesy.

They ought not to be exposed to the insolence and contumely of pettifogging lawyers and tenth-rate barristers, who have nothing to recommend them out their wigs and their unblushing impudence.

An incalculable amount of mischief accrues from the latitude allowed to counsel. Witnesses have a natural dread of being subject to the painful ordeal of impudent questions being put to them by a bullying coarse-minded legal freelance, and hence it is that there is a natural reluctance on the part of many persons to give their testimony at all, and the consequence is that many scoundrels escape the punishment which they so justly merit.

Mr. Slapperton was a bright sample of an unscrupulous cross-examiner. He was not to be put down.

It is true that the magistrates on the bench were gentlemen, but that did not matter to Slapperton. He had come into court to make a sort of gladiatorial display, to produce as much effect as possible, and, to do him justice, he did his best to carry out his object.

"I have been successful in getting certain admissions from the witness," said the lawyer, addressing himself to the bench; "and I suppose I may proceed with my cross-examination without further interruptions?"

"You are at liberty to ask what questions you deem requisite," said one of the magistrates.

"Do you know, Miss Fulford, if the late Mr. Jamblin ever met Charles Peace after the conflict in Dennett's-lane?"

"I dunno, but I think not. Mr. Peace left Broxbridge on the day after, or it might be two days afterwards. I be pretty sure he never saw Mr. Jamblin agen."

"I think you said that you were engaged to Mr. Jamblin?"

"I have not said so."

"Indeed! Then I must have misunderstood you."

"She said she kept company with him," observed the chief clerk, referring to his notes.

"Ah well, that's pretty much the same thing, I suppose," returned the lawyer, with a short, dry laugh.

"It depends upon what construction you put upon the declaration," suggested Mr. Chicknell.

"Just so. Well, that is how I construe it. The witness said Mr. Jamblin would have married her if he had lived. Did you not?"

This last query was directed to Nell.

"I believe he would ha' done so," she answered, hanging down her head.

"As an honourable man he was bound to do so. Was he not?"

"He was an honourable, good young man."

"Ah, no doubt, but that is no answer to my question."

"I cannot gi' ee any other answer," said the trembling girl.

"Oh, but you must. In plain words, you were already his mistress, and hoped to be his wife. Was that not so?"

"Mr. Slapperton, I must tell you plainly that I think your conduct is most unwarrantable," cried Lord Ethalwood, "and will not allow such a gross act of indecorum to pass over without expressing my disapproval of the same."

There was loud applause in the court as these words fell from the lips of the chairman.

"Order!—Silence!" shouted out the usher, in his usual nasal twang.

"I am sorry to differ with your lordship," observed Slapperton. "It is not my practice to act in an indecorous manner, but——"

"Silence, sir!" exclaimed Lord Ethalwood. "Your conduct is most reprehensible. Have you no consideration for the young person in the box? Have you no regard for her feelings? I will not and cannot sit on this bench and allow any female to be insulted."

"Insulted?"

"Yes, grossly insulted! How dare you presume to make such an observation as you have done in an open court?"

"Because I deemed it requisite—for that simple reason. The prisoner at the bar is a poor man, in a humble position in life. It is my bounden duty to see that he is not the victim of prejudice. It is also my duty to lay before you all these facts which bear directly and indirectly on the case, and in doing so I am constrained to be plain-spoken. I don't create these painful facts. It is no fault of mine that I am, from the force of circumstances, compelled to put questions

which, although painful for me to ask, and are perhaps still more painful for the witness to answer, have nevertheless to be submitted. I must tell you frankly that I will not shrink from doing my duty."

"You cannot proceed, Mr. Slapperton, in opposition to the ruling of the bench. That you know as well as I do," said Mr. Chicknell.

"But as yet the bench have not decided the point."

"We have," said one of the magistrates; "and our decision is unanimous. Your last question to the witness is not admissible, and we cannot reprobate your conduct too strongly in putting such a query, or the bad taste you have displayed by the innuendo accompanying it."

"I have done," said Slapperton. "Let it pass, then. I have no alternative left but to bow to the wise decision of the bench. It appears to me that I am so restricted and subject to so many indecorous interruptions, while vainly endeavouring to pursue a just and proper course of cross-examination, that I am unable to do justice to my client."

"I think your remarks are quite uncalled for, and are, at the same time, in very bad taste," observed one of the sitting magistrates. "You have full liberty to ask any questions of the witness which may bear upon the case; but to enter into private matters, which are altogether irrelevant, cannot be permitted."

"I maintain that the private matters, as you are pleased to term them, do bear upon the case. You, however, appear to be of a different opinion—so I will proceed with other points."

Then, turning towards the witness, Mr. Slapperton said—

"You stated before the coroner that, when you were conversing with Mr. Jamblin in Dennett's-lane on the night of the murder, you saw the face of a man through the hedge. Is that so?"

"Yes, it is."

"And did you see his features distinctly?"

"Most distinctly."

"The night was a dark one—was it not?"

"Rather dark."

"And there are no lamps in the lane?"

"No. None."

"And yet you were able to distinguish the features of the stranger?"

"Ee wasn't a stranger."

"How do you know?"

"'Cause I saw his face, and knew him to be Giles Chudley."

"You must be gifted with wonderful eyesight. Do you mean to say, upon your oath, that the prisoner at the bar was the man?"

"I do. It was none other than he."

"This you swear most positively?"

"Yes, I swear it agen an' agen."

"Once will do, Miss Fulford. It seems almost incredible that you could recognise a man under the circumstances. Pray, did you expect to see the prisoner there?"

"No, I did not."

"Why not?"

"'Cause he had left the neighbourhood, and hadn't been seen for a goodish while."

"I have no doubt that you are speaking conscientiously, Miss Fulford; still at the same time you must not be offended if I suggest that you are mistaken. It would, I dare say, astonish you to learn that the prisoner was not in the neighbourhood on the night of the murder. Perhaps you would not believe this if I proved the fact upon evidence?"

"I should be astonished certainly."

"Are you about to prove an alibi?" said Lord Ethalwood, in a tone of surprise.

"I am instructed to say that evidence will be offered upon that point," returned Mr. Slapperton; "and I am, therefore, most anxious to hear all that Miss Fulford has to say. She is positive, but she may be mistaken. It is a very common thing for a witness to be mistaken as far as the identification of an individual is concerned."

"Ah, that is generally admitted, I think, by most professional gentlemen. You are quite right in your course of cross-examination as far as that is concerned, for it is one of the leading and most important points in the case."

"You will pardon me, my lord," returned Slapperton, "but my hypothesis is that the witness is mistaken. We must bear in mind that there are so many persons in this neighbourhood who might be taken for the prisoner, especially if they were behind a hedge on a dark night.

"In the first place people are much more similar than we always remember, without disputing or accepting the extraordinary idea which exists in so many countries, and is the basis of so many fables, that every man has his 'double' somewhere—an individual absolutely identical in appearance with himself. It is quite certain that most extraordinary likenesses do exist among persons wholly disconnected in blood; that there are faces and forms in the world which are rather types than individualities; people so like one another that only the most intimate friends and connections can detect the difference. I trust, my lord, that you do not deem the observations I am making out of place, seeing the importance of the subject in hand."

"Not at all—I think them both right and proper."

"Very well, my lord, that being so, I will, with your permission, enlarge more fully on this. The likeness of Madame Lamotte and Marie Antoinette is a well-known historic instance, and there are few persons who have not, in their own experience, met with something of the same kind. I have myself twice. In one case I was on board ship in which were two passengers who neither were, nor by any possibility could be, connected by birth or any other circumstance whatever, except in caste. Oddly enough, they were unaware of the likeness which was the talk of the ship, dressed in the same style; but from some inexplicable revulsion—I am stating mere facts, gentlemen—disliked and avoided each other. In a six weeks' voyage, and with a tolerably intimate acquaintance with one of the two, I never succeeded in distinguishing them by sight; and of the remaining passengers, certainly one half, say thirty educated persons, were in the same predicament."

"That appears most extraordinary," exclaimed the bench.

"I pledge you my word and honour that it is a fact," returned the wily advocate, who was riding his hobby to the fullest extent.

"In the second instance the evidence is far less perfect, but sufficient for the argument I am now advocating."

"One day when in Bond-street I stopped short utterly puzzled by the appearance of one of my closest connections but two yards off. Clearly it was he, yet he could from circumstances by no possibility be there. Still it was he, and I advanced to address him, when a momentary smile broke the spell, yet leaving behind the impression. I could have sworn to him in any court of justice.

"The likeness was really astounding, quite sufficient to have deceived any number of policemen unacquainted previously with the other man. And this just brings up the point I want to make—is it not just possible—is it not rather a serious supposition when my client and our criminal procedure is considered—is it not just possible that something like colour blindness affects this matter of identification—that there are a host of persons whose evidence upon any question of identity, though perfectly honest, are worthy of very little trust? That men upon this as upon most other matters are guilty of an uncommon carelessness like that which makes testimony about figured statements so often valueless."

"The witness speaks most positively," said Lord Ethalwood. "Nevertheless, I for one, quite agree with you upon the doubts and difficulties attending identification, but there are other witnesses besides the one at present under examination who bear out her testimony."

"Not in a positive manner, my lord. I have every reason for believing that they are mistaken."

No further questions were put to Ellen Fulford, who was told to stand down.

Matilda Lucas, the little girl who resided with her parents in Jawbone Cottage, was next placed in the box.

She deposed to seeing a man washing his hands in the pool of water at Larchgrove-green on the night of the murder.

She swore most distinctly that the prisoner was the man.

"Now look at the prisoner, if you please," said Mr. Slapperton.

The child regarded Chudley with a curious glance.

"Now, my good girl, take your time, consider well before you answer. Is the prisoner like the man you saw at Larchgrove-green."

"He beant so loike him as he was," returned the girl.

"Ah! no—I thought not," said the lawyer, "but something like him, I suppose."

"Ah! yes, he be the same man as I saw, only he's got a big beard now, which he had not then."

"That would make a difference, of course. You can't swear to him. Now, mind what you say."

The little girl hesitated, and did not make any reply.

"Don't you hear what I say?" cried Slapperton.

"Yes, sir."

"Well, what say you?"

"The man I seed a washin' his hands was Giles Chudley."

"It was?"

"Yes, sir."

"Of that you are quite certain."

"I be quite sartin o' that."

"How can you be certain?"

"Because I know'd him so well, that is why I be so sartin. I know'd him by his brown face, beaky nose, an' bushy whiskers."

Mr. Slapperton was disappointed. The girl's answers were so natural and truthful that every person in the court was impressed with the fact that her evidence could be relied on, and Mr. Slapperton felt that he would be only making matters worse by subjecting her to a severe and searching cross-examination.

"She is a truthful witness, my lord," said the lawyer; "that is, an honest witness who speaks what she believes to be truth, but it does not follow that she may not be mistaken."

"She has given her evidence remarkably well," observed one of the magistrates, "and is a very intelligent little girl."

"Now I have one or two more questions to put," said Slapperton. "When you looked out of the bedroom window of the cottage, was the man's back towards you or his face?"

"His face wur towards me."

"And it was rather a dark night—was it not?"

"Noa, not whar I seed the man. The moon was a shinin' quite bright loike."

"Was his face in shadow?"

"I dunno that it wur; I know'd it wur the face o' Giles Chudley—of that I be sartin sure—and his mouth wur a-bleedin'."

Slapperton felt that it would be worse for him—so ceased all further questioning; and he therefore said in a tone of affected satisfaction—

"That will do; I am quite satisfied—have no further questions to ask."

The little girl left the box.

The divisional surgeon was called. His evidence was to the effect that he had examined the prisoner's mouth—the front teeth (incisors) were missing; and the two teeth picked up by the police in Larchgrove-lane corresponded in size, structure, and colour to the others in the prisoner's jaw.

Mr. Slapperton affected to treat this circumstance as of quite minor importance. He said that there were very few persons who had not shed some of their teeth, and it was quite impossible for the most skilled surgeon or dentist to say positively that those found belonged to the prisoner.

The magistrates, however, appeared to be of a different opinion, and a long discussion ensued between them and the prisoner's advocate.

Both agreed, however, that it would be a question for a jury to decide.

There was a *prima facie* case made out, and further adjournment was, therefore, deemed unnecessary.

The bench then decided upon fully committing the prisoner for trial upon the charge of "Wilful murder."

Mr. Slapperton would not allow the day's proceedings to be brought to a close without making a last appeal on behalf of his client. He was perfectly aware that all he might say would not alter the decision of the stipendiary magistrates; but he had come for the purpose of making himself as conspicuous as possible, and was bent upon having his say.

"I should be sadly neglectful of my duty to my client," said the pertinacious advocate, "if I suffered him to be committed upon this dreadful charge without offering some remarks upon the evidence we have heard. I do not for one moment impugn the veracity of the several witnesses. All I say is, that they are mistaken; they are labouring under a wrong impression, and at the same time I am under the impression that their judgment is warped by a strong amount of prejudice, which, perhaps very naturally, has influenced them in so marked a degree. It has been said by a great thinker and writer 'that it is easier to remove a mountain than a prejudice.' Without doubt most of the witnesses believe what they have deposed to. They are obstinate as far as their evidence is concerned, and to argue with an obstinate man is to confirm him in his opinion."

"I think you are mistaken, Mr. Slapperton," observed Lord Ethalwood. "I do not see that any obstinacy has been displayed by any of the witnesses. On the contrary, the witness Brickett and my footman have been very careful in giving their evidence. They neither of them would swear positively."

"That I admit, my lord. Do not for a moment imagine I had any desire to complain of them. As far as that goes, they are without doubt truthful witnesses. So, indeed, is Miss Fulford, but, nevertheless, I find it hard to believe that she saw the prisoner through the hedge so as to recognise him; but, even assuming she had, this fact does not prove that Chudley was the murderer of Mr. Philip Jamblin. He might be lurking about the neighbourhood, waiting for one of his quondam companions. It does not necessarily follow that he is guilty of this fearful crime, because he happened to be wandering over the fields near to Dennett's-lane. He might be out 'sweetheart-hunting,' watching for some rustic damsel—even as Miss Fulford was watching for her faithful swain."

"I do not say it does," returned Lord Ethalwood. "We none of us say so; but, nevertheless, it is one link in the chain, and it must be admitted on all hands that it is an important link."

"I confess I do not attach that importance to it that you do," said the lawyer, in a careless tone; "but I do say that it is a question of mistaken identity. We are all apt to believe that the difference in faces is very great, and not dependent upon accidental features; yet it is almost certain that no such difference exists—that men are as nearly alike as animals appear to be.

"Take, for instance, in evidence of both these propositions, the carelessness of our usual glance, and the similarity among men—a fact which most persons can test for themselves. Look at the conflicting evidence as to identification in the Tichborne case.

"No man on landing at an Indian or Chinese port for the first time can for a few days tell one native from another, and yet they are quite as unlike as so many Englishmen, because, in addition to every other distinction, their complexions cover a wider range of colour, but, being similarly dressed, they seem for a few days as much alike as so many sheep, who are all alike to a Londoner, but among whom a shepherd or a dog makes no mistake.

"Now, if men were much unlike—more unlike than the sheep are—no such curious haziness would be possible, nor would it be if the observer were unconsciously in the habit of studying the form and character of each face.

"We have, as a rule, no such habit, but unless an artist or a policeman relies unconsciously on accidental circumstances—colour, hair on lip or chin, expression or peculiarity of some one feature—and should that by any accident disappear, he is utterly puzzled.

"One-tenth, at least, of Western mankind, is consciously or unconsciously, short-sighted, and never see in any true sense.

"Then a great number of persons are subject to sudden and sometimes erroneous impressions, and with country people especially, when once an idea enters their head, they are very reluctant to part with it.

"It would be out of place for me to cite cases of mistaken identity; that must be reserved for the trial, for it is quite clear that you intend to send the case for trial."

"Unquestionably, Mr. Slapperton," said the chairman. "We cannot do otherwise. There is abundance of evidence to warrant us in committing the prisoner, and, whatever your line of defence may be, you had better reserve it for a higher tribunal."

"Enough, my lord, I will not pursue the question further. I do hope and trust, however, that whatever little ability I may possess will suffice to make manifest to the jury whose duty it is to try the prisoner that he is guiltless of the heinous crime with which he stands charged."

The examination was at an end. The prisoner was committed on the charge of wilful murder, and the witnesses were bound over to appear at the ensuing sessions.

CHAPTER LXVI.
THE COMPANY AT THE "SHOULDER OF MUTTON" INN.

As we have already intimated it was market day, and as a natural consequence the court, the streets, and the public-houses were crowded to overflowing. The chief topic of conversation was, as a matter of course, the great murder case.

In close proximity to the court-house stood a well-known inn, bearing the sign of the "Shoulder of Mutton," and to this establishment Mr. Slapperton bent his steps. He was a man who courted publicity, and, if it was attainable, popularity also. He was a great talker, an adept at laying down the law, and he felt that he cut what he called a respectable figure in the court, and refreshment after his arduous duties was absolutely requisite ; besides, he had one cr two clients to meet at the "Shoulder of Mutton."

Although his conduct had been very reprehensible and pugnacious while in court, there were many who admired what they were pleased to term his "pluck," and upon entering the public room several of its inmates rose from their seats and shook him warmly by the hand.

"So, Measter Slapperton," cried a broad-shouldered grazier, "you warn't a goin' to let the big wigs ha' it all their own way."

"There are two sides to an argument, my friend," returned the lawyer.

"An yourn be the roight side, I s'pose," cried a voice from the further end of the room.

"Well, I hope so. That remains to be proved," answered Slapperton, making the best of his way towards an ante-room, in which the dinner he had ordered was about to be served. Here two of his clients awaited him.

After he had received their instructions, and devoured his substantial repast, he returned to the public room, which was filled with well-to-do agriculturists.

Mr. Slapperton seated himself, sipped his port wine, and lighted his cigar. He felt that he was the "observed of all observers," and this flattered the legal gentleman's vanity.

There was a sort of running fire of observations on the all-absorbing topic.

One farmer, more pertinacious than the rest, turned towards the attorney, and said—

"An' do ye think as how they'll bring it hoame to the murdering scoundrel, zur."

"I don't give an opinion without the usual fee," observed Slapperton.

This retort was greeted with loud and continuous guffaws.

"You've got ee change, old man," said one.

"It aint no yoose trying it on wi' a lawyer," cried another.

"Oh, there's no secret about the matter, gentlemen," said Slapperton. "It is simply a question of identity. If the witnesses are mistaken, which I affirm they are, it would be wrong indeed to hang a man upon their testimony. So many questions arise in cases of this sort. Fatness and thinness are great aids to recognition, yet they are temporary, dependent sometimes on mere accidents of health. We have all of us met friends whom we have not seen, say, for three years, who have grown wider if not wiser in the interval, and whom we should not, without speech, have recognised."

"That be true enough," said one of the company. "I ha' had the thing occur to me."

"So have I," said the lawyer, who was on his favourite hobby. "I can say so positively."

"You're not agoin' to mek me b'lieve that ee be innocent, identity or no identity," cried Brickett, who was one of the company.

"Oh, it's you, eh ?" said the lawyer, looking curiously at the speaker. "I shall not endeavour to do so. You heard what I said about prejudice ?"

"Yes, I did, and it beant true. There be no prejudice in the matter. I could have sed more if I'd bin amind."

"Ah, I dare say; but now, with respect to identity, I think of the excessive difficulty with which the memory retains a face. Portrait painters of half a century's standing will tell you that they hardly retain the impression of a sitter five minutes, though they have been studying him keenly, that their own first touches from him as he sits are invaluable helps ; that they would all, if it were convenient for art reasons, like to keep a photograph in full view for their work when the original is away. We think we remember, but in five minutes we forget, the half of a friend's face nearly as perfectly as we forget the whole of our own. Clearly if identification were as easy as we are apt to believe, we should not so forget faces. And their expression ? Doubtless, expression being, so to speak, an intellectual rather than a physical fact, stirring and rousing the intellect of the observer, his secret and almost instinctive likes and dislikes, remains longer fixed in the mind than mere feature. The witness who arrested Judge Jeffries might have forgotten his face, did forget it, in fact, for Jeffries when seized had only changed his wig, but he could not forget the ferocious glare of those insufferable eyes. But expression changes quickly, may change permanently. We all say every now and then, 'His face is quite changed,' while nothing is changed except, perhaps, the expression and the colour. Madness, extreme anger, drink, will all change a well-known face till it is almost irrecognisable."

"That may be all true," said one of the company, "but somehow or another I do not think there's much mistake 'bout that chap—he did the murder right enough."

"Aye, an' sure he did," cried Brickett, "as sartain as I'm a speakin' now—the black-hearted villain. It aint a morsel o' good for any one for to be trying to argue us out o' our seven senses. He be the man and none other."

"Yes, that's your opinion," said Slapperton, "but it is not right and proper to hang a man upon mere opinion or hearsay."

"Certainly not," said an elderly gentleman, who was a stranger to them all. "It is requisite to have the clearest and most unanswerable evidence when a man is put upon his trial for a capital offence. I've seen a good deal in my time, have been to most parts of the world, and in early life I was concerned in a trial—was one of the jury in fact—and but for me the man would have been hanged."

"Noo—noe," cried several, with wondering looks.

"All juries do not always agree," said Slapperton; "but perhaps our friend will give us the benefit of his experience."

"Aye, do, sur. Let's hear all about it," cried several.

"Speaking of a jury's disagreeing," said the old gentleman, "I myself was once the cause of such an occurrence, and I can't say that I ever regretted it since it saved not only the life of the prisoner, whom I believed to be an innocent man, but my own life."

"Why, how was that?" inquired several.

"It is really quite a romance in its way," he replied, "and if you care to listen, I'll go through it once more.

"It happened many years ago when I was in the United States. Very shortly after I came of age I was summoned on a jury. As it was my first experience I did not attempt to escape serving, as older men are apt to do.

"The only important case that came before us was the trial of a young man for the murder of his own father,

"I won't go into the particulars any more than is necessary for the story.

"The crime was a most horrible and unnatural one, and to look at the frank, boyish face, and believe him capable of it, seemed impossible.

"The evidence was entirely circumstantial, yet gradually as its terrible weight accumulated, an abundant motive was found in the son's desire to inherit at once the father's immense wealth, as it was shown they had recently quarrelled, that hot words had been given and returned, that the young man had publicly threatened his father's life.

"One by one the jurymen by my side lost faith in the prisoner, and finally when it was clearly proved that he was within five rods of the murdered man, almost after the fatal shot was heard, that he had an empty pistol in his hand, that the ball taken from the wound evidently belonged to the pistol, and that he acted most strangely and unlike an innocent man when found at this time.

"There was only one man on the jury who had not already made up his mind for the terrible verdict— guilty. That man was myself.

"Somehow or other I could not believe the man before me was guilty of the crime charged.

"At the last moment after the judge had charged the jury the prisoner started up and asked if he might say a word for himself.

"Upon permission being given he spoke in a manly voice as follows:—

"'Gentlemen of the jury, his lordship has just charged you to find a verdict entirely upon the evidence. If you do, you will convict me, and add one more to the long list of unfortunate one's who have been victims of circumstantial evidence.

"'But I charge you here, in the presence of God and man, to find a verdict according to your own belief, and may some one among you believe me at this moment when I say, as God hears me, I am an innocent man.

"'You will say I acted wrongly, gentlemen—I grant it myself, if you look at the mere law of the question.'

"It was an unusual speech to make at such a time— one, perhaps, which should not have been permitted. It made quite a sensation in the court, and as the prisoner sat down his fearless eye caught mine for an instant, and I felt, and he felt, that I was the man of whom he spoke, for at that moment with a certainty that amounted to positive conviction I *knew* that he was innocent.

"The other eleven men came to a decision almost instantly after leaving the box. They said the prisoner was undoubtedly guilty, and I, for a while, said nothing. I felt that the man's life was in my hands, that I was in that hour not bound by whatever any man or body of men might say or think, but that I had a solemn question to decide. I said to my fellow jurymen,

'Gentlemen, I cannot and will not stand with you in a verdict of guilty against the prisoner, as I believe him to be innocent.'

"That was my decision, and all the arguments and objections they could bring forward during a long confinement could not change it.

"On the fourth day we were discharged, and the prisoner set free.

"Much was said against me; I was even accused of having been bought up by the young man's family, which was a very wealthy and influential one, and even to this day if I go back there I should be pointed out as the man who sold his verdict. But it had been a matter of conscience with me, and I could not regret it. I have yet to tell you how it was the means of saving my life.

"Shortly after the trial, and more because of the ill-name it had given me than anything else, I removed to New York, started in business there, and found myself some years afterwards a prosperous merchant, yet somewhat broken in health. On the latter account I determined upon a sea voyage.

"I went to Fayal for several seasons, travelled a year or so on the Continent, and finally, having in a great measure recovered my health, I took passage by steamer to New York.

"Somewhere about mid-ocean we experienced a terrible storm. I think the steamer was by no means so seaworthy as she should have been for a voyage at that time of the year (it was in September); at any rate a single night of rough weather strained her severely, and at breakfast next morning it was whispered about that there was a leak forward, and that the water was gaining on us in spite of everything that could be done—all the while, too, the violence of the storm increased rather than diminished.

"Two of the steamer's boats had been disabled in the storm; a rush was made for the remaining three by the cowardly crew; one was stove in launching, and the other two swamped, and their occupants left helpless in the water before they had put half a dozen yards between them and the ship.

"Indeed no boat, however staunch, could have lived in such a sea.

"As soon as it became definitely known that the vessel was making water, I had gone below and reassured the affrighted lady passengers as well as I could, and helped them to secure their life-preservers. Indeed so assiduous had I become in the latter office that I had neglected to save one for myself, and when suddenly an appalling cry came from deck, and we rushed up just as the ship seemed in her last death struggle, I was entirely destitute of any means for keeping afloat. I succeeded, however, in getting possession of a large plank, and while the passengers were jumping overboard all around me I stood calmly by the rail waiting for the last moment.

"Beside me I now noticed for the first time a man of about my own age.

"He had a life-preserver strapped to his shoulders, and, like myself, appeared to be waiting for the final shock.

"'You have no life-preserver?' he said, interrogatively.

"'No,' I answered, 'but this plank will, I think, serve me as well. There seems to have been an insufficient supply of life-preservers—I could get no more.

"'Take mine,' he said, and without a moment's hesitation began to unfasten it. I said I would not think of such a thing, and put out my hand to stop him.'

"What he might have said further was cut short by

a sudden thrill that ran through the vessel from stem to stern.

"With all my might I flung my plank from me, and sprang after it in the water.

"Then I remember feeling a sharp blow on the head, and seeing a thousand flashing lights, and then all was blank until I awoke to consciousness, to find myself fastened firmly to the plank by the strongest of lashings—a pair of human hands and arms. I felt, too, something about my shoulders which almost without thought I knew to be a life-preserver.

"The sea was dashing violently over me, and nearly smothered as I was all the time, it was some moments before I fully comprehended the situation.

"I saw now that the arms which upheld me were those of the man whom I had spoken to just before I left the vessel.

"He was supporting himself and me, too, by means of the plank.

"'What is the meaning of this?' I gasped, as soon as I found my voice.

"'You struck your head against the plank, when you came. You were floating like a dead fish. I jumped over, and brought you back to the plank.'

"'How long have I been this way?'

"'About an hour, though it seems half a day.'

"'Well, I can hold on for myself now,' I said. 'How shall I ever repay you for what you have done? I owe my life to you.'

"'But mine has belonged to you for twenty years,' he said, with strange significance, and I noticed that his voice was feeble with continued exertion.

"Just then the waves swept over us more furiously than ever.

"As soon as there was a lull, I asked again—

"'How came I with this life-preserver?'

"'I put it on for you, and you must keep it.'

"'Why must I?'

"'You don't remember me,' he said. 'You don't know that it was you who once saved me from a dreadful death, but you will recollect me when I tell you that it was I who was tried for murder twenty years ago in M—— Court-house.'

"He paused again, and feebly strove to collect himself.

"The frank boyish face that I remembered was gone, but his eyes were the same that had met mine that day when the prisoner had uttered his strange words to the jury.

"'Yes,' he went on, ' you were man enough to acquit me, because you believed me innocent, and you were right. I repeat it here in this hour of death—for I shall not be alive an hour hence—I was innocent. It was another who committed the crime, and I would have died rather than betray him.'

"Still another long pause, and then again he went on with great effort—

"'Aye, you saved my life, but I sometimes wonder if it was well you did so. I have seen no happy moment since then. I have wandered up and down the earth with the brand of Cain upon my life, and men have everywhere found it out, and turned from me.' He reached out his hand to mine, and as I took it he said—'I am getting weaker and weaker, and there is no good in my hanging on here any longer.' He wrenched his hand away from mine and said—'Heaven preserve and protect you!' and before I could make a motion to detain him he had let go his hold, and a passing wave swept him away out of my sight, and out of my life for ever. Gentlemen, that is the end of my story, which, I assure you, is a true one. I was saved, of course, else I should not be here to tell the tale. I was picked up just at dark, when I had relinquished all hope."

"Dall it, but that be a wonderful story," replied several present.

"And how came it that he was so near being found guilty? He were innocent, I s'pose?" said one of the farmers.

"As innocent as you are yourself," replied the stranger. "It was a case of mistaken identity. The prisoner resembled the actual murderer in a most remarkable degree, but the man who had committed the crime was a great friend of the prisoner, who would have suffered death rather than have betrayed his friend."

"It's a deal more than I would do for any man," observed Brickett.

"Very likely not, but men are very differently constituted. It is perhaps more than any one of us would do."

"The case bears out my argument," said Slapperton; "but it is by no means a solitary instance. I will give you another. At a certain assizes, which it is not necessary for me to name, although many of my professional friends are intimately acquainted with the facts, during the trial of a prisoner for burglary there arose a difficulty—this being a clear proof of the prisoner's identity.

"Baron Alderson, one of the most celebrated judges, in the course of his summing-up, being anxious to impress upon the jury the necessity of caution in the case before them, spoke as follows :—

"'At one of the first assizes at which I was present soon after entering the profession, a prisoner was charged with the murder of a woman who lived in a secluded cottage about two miles distant from his own house.

"'Evidence was given as to what might be regarded as a motive for the offence, and as to language having been let fall by the prisoner indicating hostility to the deceased. On that account, I presume, it was that the moment the crime was known suspicion fell upon the prisoner, and search was at once made for him.

"'He was arrested shortly after the crime had been committed at a place which was not his house, and was at once identified by a host of witnesses, some of whom had seen him shortly before the murder going by a road which led from his house to the scene of the tragedy. Others saw him immediately after it had taken place returning by another and more circuitous route which led to his own house.

"'Some of these witnesses were intimately acquainted with him, as intimate as the witnesses were who gave their evidence to-day with the accused. Others knew him by sight only, and others described him as identical in height, dress, and general appearance with the man in question.

"'One man who met him going to the fatal spot spoke to him and received an answer, and confidently deposed to his identity from his voice, as well as from other circumstances.

"'A woman who knew him well, and who kept a turnpike gate, near which was a pathway leading to the deceased cottage, remembered the prisoner passing through the gate on the night in question.

"'Footprints were observed near the scene of the murder, which, though indistinct, corresponded with those of the prisoner, and were traced along the pathway leading to the place.'"

"Ah! I doan't believe in footprints!" cried a farmer present.

A BATCH OF CONVICTS ON THE WAY TO DARTMOOR.

"Nor I," returned the lawyer, who then continued his narrative in the judge's words: "Well, gentlemen, in addition to all this the man was spoken to on his way home by one who knew him, and none of the witnesses were aware of any reason other than that of guilt, which might have induced him to go to the place at which he was taken into custody.

"'Now the evidence of all these witnesses presented

a striking correspondence in respect to time, each having noticed the man at nearly about the same hour.

"'In short, so great was the testimony showing the prisoner to have approached the scene of the crime shortly before it was committed, and his departure from the spot soon afterwards, that these circumstances seemed conclusively established, and the only

No. 33.

question which appeared to cause any anxiety in the mind of the judge was how far the circumstances were established, coupled with the motive, the malice, and the footprints, to compel belief in the commission of a crime of which more direct evidence was wanting.

"'The case for the prosecution was closed, and the prisoner was called upon for his defence.

"'He called only one witness. It was the gaoler, who deposed that on the day of the murder, and for some time before and for three days afterwards, he had the prisoner in his custody for another offence, of which he was acquitted, the gaoler himself having been present at the trial.

"'The prisoner himself made one observation, which was, that the reason he could not make up his mind to go home was that, having been adjudged innocent, he did not want his neighbours to know that he had ever been in gaol.

"'Gentlemen,' said the learned baron, 'I need not tell you the result.'

"Nor need I tell you the result," observed Mr. Slapperton, addressing himself to the company in the parlour of the "Shoulder of Mutton," "of an accusation turning on a question of disputed identity, where the judge himself thought it necessary to recall so striking an experience for the caution and guidance of the jury. What say you, Mr. Brickett?"

"Ye be too much for me, I doubt," returned the host of the "Carved Lion." "Ye'd mek me bleeve black was white."

"You are obstinate, my friend, and, I'm afraid, a little prejudiced," observed the attorney; "but after all it is but natural."

"If I stop much longer you'll persuade me that my eyes ain't no good to me, and that I've got colour-blindness or something o' that sort. I never seed such a chap in all my born days as what ye are," said Brickett, rising from his seat.

"Don't go, my friend," said Slapperton, good-humouredly. "We'll make a lawyer of you in time. To succeed in the legal profession a man requires either a great deal of talent, or else a great deal of impudence."

"One o' them two you've got a pretty good stock of—I won't say which it be," cried Brickett.

This last observation was greeted with uproarious laughter, and the host of the "Carved Lion" was applauded to the echo.

"Excellent—very good, indeed!" cried Slapperton. "I should not have supposed you'd have had it in you, but you are sharpened up to-day. You see what it is to be in my company."

"Well, I must be for going," said Brickett.

"Don't 'e be in such a might hurry," observed a farmer. "I shall be for starting myself in less than half an hour, and am going your way—so sit down and make your life as happy as you can. We are all on us friends here, and my company be better nor none, I s'pose?"

"All right," cried the landlord of the "Carved Lion." "When you be ready I'm at your service."

"Truly a most complacent man," said Slapperton. "A little obstinate perhaps, but not a bad fellow in the main."

"I s'pose you mean the lion's main?" cried a rustic wit.

"Oh, yes, I see our friend here keeps the 'Carved Lion.' Very good indeed for an off-hander," observed the lawyer; "and as most of you represent the agricultural interest," he added, in continuation, "I'll give

you the particulars of a case which came under my own observation, as doubtless it will amuse you.

It was at Northamptonshire Sessions several years ago that a man was indicted for stealing a duck. The facts are simple enough, and you won't require any stretch of imagination to comprehend the case as it was presented to the judge and jury.

As the prisoner was walking along the highway he was seen by a witness, who was journeying the same road, to enter a field, the gate of which opened on the highway, and seize a duck under his arm.

You must understand that he continued to walk in the same direction in which he had been going before, and that a little higher up on the road before him was the farmhouse belonging to the farm from which the duck was taken.

"Gad, he must ha' had the impudence of a highway-man's horse!" exclaimed one of the party.

Mr. Slapperton continued: This and the fact that he was apprehended with the duck under his arm, and was unknown to the witness or the constable, was the sole evidence adduced by the prosecution.

"And warn't that enough?" said one of the company.

You shall hear. The defendant's counsel said, "I understood you to say that you were walking behind the prisoner?"

"Yes, sir, I was."

"Can you tell me how far behind?"

"Well, as nearly as I can guess, it might be a hundred yards or more."

"Oh, a hundred yards, and did you know there were ducks in the field into which he went?"

"Oh, yes, I'm quite sure of that, for I heard them quacking."

"What! at that distance? They were making a great noise, then?"

"Yes, a very great noise."

"And did you see the dog that was worrying them and causing them to make that noise?"

"I didn't see any dog."

"You didn't, eh? Pray let me understand what you did see. When the prisoner went up to the gate, did you see the ducks?"

"Oh, dear me, no. That was not possible; the ducks were round the corner, loike. You couldn't see 'em till you got close up to the gate."

"Then if a dog was worrying the ducks, you would not see the dog till you got close up to the gate?"

"Certainly not."

Chairman: "Did you hear any dog—and when you got to the gate, did you see one?"

"No, my lord, I did not see any dog at all."

"But," said the counsel, "as you were so far behind the prisoner, and you could not see the ducks, there might have been a dog there, although you did not see it."

"I don't think there was one—still there might have been one, but I am quite positive that I did not see one."

"And he never heard one," said the chairman.

"No, my lord," returned the counsel. "You see the ducks were making a very great noise."

"If the dog barked—which, in such a situation, he most likely would—his bark must have been heard," said the chairman.

"Not necessarily so, my lord."

After a little re-examination as to whether there were any marks of a dog's teeth upon the duck's neck, the case was closed for the prosecution.

"Gentlemen of the jury," said the counsel for the

prisoner, "from the questions which I have put to the principal witness called for the prosecution you will have already anticipated the case I have to submit to you on the part of the defendant. He is a perfect stranger to this part of the country, and has fallen a victim, far away from his friends, to his efforts to rescue a helpless creature from suffering.

"He was passing along the highway thinking only of getting to the end of his journey, and little dreaming of the misfortune which was in store for him. When he came to the gate, hearing a noise, which the witness has described, his attention was attracted to the cause of it, which was a little dog worrying one of the ducks, and of course alarming the rest. The prisoner, I am informed, is a kindly-disposed, humane person, and it frequently happens that these qualities cause their possessor to get into trouble which a less considerate person would perhaps avoid. He was too late to be of much service to the poor duck, but the dog ran away at his approach like a little mischievous cur, as he doubtless was. This is the reason why the witness never saw the dog. The prisoner rang the poor bird's neck to put it out of its pain. I trust any one of you would have done the same under similar circumstances.

"And yet this humane action has brought this worthy man before you under a disgraceful criminal charge, of which, however, I feel confident you will acquit him.

"What can be more absurd than to suppose for one moment that a man who intended to steal a duck would go in the broad daylight, and take it from a field, and wring its neck and put it under his arm within sight of a witness a hundred yards behind him, and then having carefully provided this evidence of his guilt would carry the stolen property in the direction of the owner's house where it would be certain to be identified? My lord very properly put the question whether the witness heard the dog barking, but my learned friend unintentionally cleared up that difficulty by suggesting, in a question to the witness, that the dog might have seized the duck by the neck. Now, if a dog has a duck's neck or any part of a duck in his mouth, I think that it is quite enough to account for the animal not barking; so much for the witness not *hearing* the dog. As for his not *seeing* him, it would be very odd if he had, when my client had gone into the field and frightened the dog away before the witness came up.

"Gentlemen, as the unfortunate man before you is debarred by the law from giving evidence in his own defence, and the only other witness to the transaction has been called for the prosecution, I have necessarily no evidence to lay before you; but as the only witness whom you have heard admits *there might have been a dog although he did not see it*, I confidently ask you to act in accordance with the humane maxim of the law, and give the prisoner the benefit of the doubt."

"Well, gentlemen," said the chairman, "I need not recapitulate the evidence. I have heard the tale of a 'Cock and a Bull,' but I never heard till this day of a tale of a dog and a duck. Consider your verdict."

The jury did so, and without leaving the box returned a verdict of

"Not Guilty."

The learned counsel for the prosecution sang a song very well, and entertained his brethren that evening at mess, and many evenings afterwards on circuit also, with the song of "The Dog and the Duck," to each stanza of which was appended a remarkable chorus, which no type unadapted to music can effectually render. One stanza only I remember.

The witness swore he saw no dog,
The counsel said "So be it,"
But then you know there might have been a dog,
Although you did not see it.
Bow, wow, wow,
Tow, row, row,
Whack fol de riddle diddle,
Bow, wow, wow.

The story was told me by one of the counsel concerned in the case, who, however, took care to add (as I am told he always did) that he would not have me suppose that the plea put forward so successfully for the defence was an invention of the defendant's counsel, but that it was contained in his instructions.

The other counsel in the case, after a long and successful career at the bar, where his wit and good humour made him beloved, and his learning respected by all who knew him, ended his days on the bench, his elevation to which was the proper recognition of an honourable and distinguished career.

The foregoing amusing case is included in legal cases under the title of "Twelve Tales of the Law."

"Didn't I tell 'ee that these lawyer chaps can mek anybody bleeve black's white?" cried Brickett, when Mr. Slapperton concluded. "He meant prigging the duck, depend on that."

"You're a prejudiced man," said Slapperton. "All's fair in love, trade, war, and law."

The company in the parlour of the "Shoulder of Mutton" had a longer sitting than usual, and they now began to break up. There was no end of shaking of hands, as by ones, twos, and threes, they took their departure.

CHAPTER LXVII.

REMOVAL OF A BATCH OF CONVICTS—PEACE TAKEN TO DARTMOOR.

THE events we have been describing—the search after, the capture, and committal, of Giles Chudley—were unknown to Peace; indeed he was in entire ignorance of the murder of Mr. Jamblin.

Through the long weary hours of his imprisonment he was looking forward through the darkness which enshrouded him to the day of his liberation as to a bright and unsetting star.

Its clear white ray pierced the clouds which hung dark and heavy over him, and shed light and hope within him, for it told him that behind those clouds there was a light and a day which would yet dawn upon him, wherein he could work and redeem the past.

As he lay upon his bed and gazed out of the window of his cell, watching the birds dart hither and thither in a clear blue sky, thoughts of the time when he should be free arose in his mind and cheered his desponding heart.

Through the silent hours of the night he watched the myriad stars shining in the midnight sky, glancing glory from far-off worlds, and thought the while which among that radiant, silent throng was his.

He looked forward to the day when he should be cast into the world again.

Can it be wondered at that under the influence of these feelings he bitterly regretted having pursued such a reckless and lawless career? He had seen enough and heard enough from the prison chaplain to be forcibly impressed with the errors of his ways.

He had met with men whose whole life had been spent in constant warfare against society, and who had no other intention, on regaining their liberty, than to continue the struggle to the bitter end—

The murderer, cheerful and complacent over the verdict of manslaughter; the professional garotter, in whose estimation human life is of no value, troubled only at being so foolish as to be caught; the professional thief, the pickpocket, the skilled housebreaker —every one of them sound in wind and limb, intent only on their schemes and "dodges," to extract the sting from their punishment—all longing for the time when they and society would cry "quits," and they be at liberty to pursue their career of villainy.

With these, the vilest of the vile, and also with the hoary criminal who knew no home save the prison, who preferred it to the poor-house.

He had been shut up many months without a glance at the external world and its doings; he had not seen a newspaper or heard a scrap of news of any sort, and it was, therefore, some relief to him when he was informed that he was to be transferred with the next batch of convicts to Dartmoor.

He never reflected at this time that perhaps he might possibly find the discipline much more severe in that place.

Dartmoor, as most of our readers know, is an extensive and remarkable tract of land on the north-west of Exmoor. It comprises an area of three hundred and fifty thousand acres, one-third of which is termed Dartmoor Forest.

During the revolutionary war a French prison was erected on the moor, which has been transformed into an agricultural settlement for the poor. Part of the buildings are now occupied by a company established to extract naphtha from peat.

The prisons were commenced in 1806. They are built of granite found on the moor.

Two of the prisons, a row of houses for subordinate officers, and the chapel walls, were erected by French, whilst the interior of the chapel was fitted by American, prisoners, who received from Government a small gratuity for their labour.

At one period of the year as many as ten thousand prisoners were confined within the walls—the site of the prisons—which comprise a circular measurement of thirty acres, and is about one thousand four hundred feet above the sea. The mortality in the prison at Dartmoor is, therefore, from the healthiness of its situation, much less than any other town average.

Public attention has of late years been directed to this place in consequence of the prisoner Arthur Orton, or the "Claimant," as he has been termed, undergoing penal servitude there.

On the morning upon which the convicts were to be removed from Preston Gaol four omnibuses were drawn up, and into these the batch of prisoners were conducted.

To say the truth, they did not present a particularly respectable appearance, cropped, shaven, and habited in prison clothes as they were; but this, after all, did not trouble them much.

The moment they left the walls of the prison every man in a short time became loquacious—the silent system was no longer in full force, and a certain amount of latitude was allowed; the men were permitted to talk and chatter as they liked, and it is easy to conceive that they did not fail to avail themselves of this privilege.

The omnibuses rumbled along the streets with their distinguished passengers, who looked through the windows in a curious inquiring manner. Their attention was very naturally directed to the contents bills of the morning papers displayed outside the newsvendors' shops, every line of which was eagerly devoured.

The theatrical posters, too, displayed on the adver-

tising stations of the clever and enterprising firm of Willing and Co. interested them in no small degree.

They saw the names of new pieces, of new actors and actresses, with which they were much gratified.

Like boys let out from school, they were in the best of spirits, forgetting for the nonce that they were but exchanging one prison-house for another.

When they reached the railway station a crowd collected to see them alight. They could hear the remarks of the people, which were by no means complimentary, and two or three of the gang of convicts made use of coarse expletives in an undertone.

The warders in charge of the convicts did not give them much time to indulge in idle curiosity; the prisoners were hustled into a large third-class carriage and told to take their seats. They obeyed sulkily, and those next to the windows thrust out their heads and began begging for tobacco from those who were on the platform.

"Now then, guv'nor—you with the barnacles I mean"—cried one, "we are all down in the dumps. Give us a bit o' 'bacco, you won't miss it, ever so little a bit." The speaker held out his hand and a costermonger emptied his tobacco box, the contents of which he placed in the hand of the prisoner.

"Good luck to ye, and many thanks," cried the latter.

"Aint one of you got never such a thing as a cigar about you?" said another convict.

Three cigars were thrown in at the window by a heavy swell.

"Thank you, sir, you're worth your weight in gold. I wish there were more like you in this world."

"Get down, we've had enough o' this," said one of the warders, in a commanding tone.

"All right, guv'nor," cried the convicts. "Don't draw the string too tight," said a prisoner. "If so be as the gentleman is in a generous mood it won't hurt you or anyone else to let us have the benefit on it."

"We'll take what's given you and look sharp about it," returned the warder.

"We aint proud any on us," said the prisoner, addressing himself to those on the platform. "A pennorth o' shag will be acceptable, but cheeroots and cigars we shall be grateful for."

Several of the throng on the platform burst out in a loud laugh, and cigars and tobacco were supplied in a most generous manner.

"We shan't forget this kindness," cried one or two of the convicts; "and you've no call to be afeard that we shall rob any of you. Come what may, we aint such wretches as people suppose us to be, for all that we are in a bit of trouble just now."

"I hope you will mend your ways, and that your hearts may be turned from wickedness," said a tall, thin man, with a white choker, thrusting at the same time a handful of tracts in at the carriage window.

"Oh! I say, guv'nor, give us something better than these; they ain't of no use."

The tract distributor made no reply, but made off without further ado.

"One of the goody-goody sort," murmured a convict. "Aint much to be got out of any of his kidney. He aint my sort."

"Sit down, men," again repeated the warder; "we are just going to start."

The prisoners sat down, and in a few seconds after this the carriage began to move, and they were on their journey.

Peace, during his incarceration in Preston Gaol, had

made the acquaintance of a professional "cracksman," or burglar, who hailed from London.

He had, however, been "landed" at Manchester, where he had committed a number of daring robberies. He was a man of fair education, good appearance, and considerable natural ability, much above the average of his professional brethren.

He had been living luxuriously in London on the fruits of his professional skill. Till now he had escaped all punishment, with the exception of a few months' imprisonment for a "mistake" committed at the outset of his career.

Seeing in Peace a kindred spirit he fraternised with him, and they sat next to each other in the train.

They carried on a conversation in whispers, the words of which were inaudible to the warder who sat at the further end of the carriage.

"Oh, yes," observed the cracksman. "I have no reason to complain—I've had a pretty goodish run of it, all things considered, but they nabbed me in Manchester. Did I tell you how it happened?"

"No," whispered Peace. "How was it?"

"Well, you see, one of my pals showed me an advertisement of a Manchester jeweller, wherein he boasted of his safe having successfully resisted the recent efforts of a gang of burglars. I said to my pal, 'Get Jim, and let us go down to-morrow by the mail train to Manchester, and we will see what this man's safe is like.' We all three went down, inspected the jeweller's premises, and decided upon doing the job through an ironmonger's shop at the back.

"We had got the contents of the ironmonger's till, and were just through the intervening back wall when the 'copper' (policeman) heard us, and signalled to another 'bobby' (policeman) to come and help him."

"Oh that was an ugly situation," remarked Peace.

"Yes," whispered his companion, "it was an unfortunate affair altogether, but there was no help for it. I sprang out at once, for I saw the game was up, and escape was all I thought about."

"But you did not succeed in getting clear off."

"I shouldn't be here if I had," returned the convict, sulkily. "I wish I had never undertaken the job. I made a desperate fight for it, though, and was nearly getting away when the 'bobby' belaboured me most unmercifully with his staff. But I did not give in till I got knocked down insensible. My pal was more fortunate—he bolted and got clean away. Jim and myself got 'copt' (caught), and as we had first-class tools on us, new to the authorities here, they gave it us rather hot."

"Ah, that they would be sure to do. Let them alone for that. But do you think you could have opened the safe?"

"Could I! Certainly. I would have managed it somehow, although I candidly confess it was a jolly good one of its sort. I should not have wasted much time in trying to pick the lock."

"What did you intend to do, then?" inquired Peace.

"Well, you see," said the other, in a reflective manner, "safes do give us chaps some trouble at times, but they're to be mastered. Casey could open any safe, and there are many others in the profession equally clever as him. I flatter myself I'm one, but this you will say is vanity."

"I don't say anything of the sort. What one man can do another ought to accomplish."

"You've heard of Casey?"

"Oh, yes, he's in quod, aint he?"

Peace's companion nodded.

"Yes," he said. "Poor Casey isn't likely to trouble anybody outside the walls of a prison for a jolly long time to come. They've given it him worth his money."

"Yes, but about the safe? How did you purpose opening it?" inquired Peace, for whom the conversation had special interest.

"Well, I'll tell you," answered his companion. "I did not intend to set to work on the lock—that is, not make any attempt to pick it. My plan was to drill a hole, and get into the 'jack.' When this was accomplished I could, with an instrument I had with me, get moving power sufficient to open any safe."

"You could?"

"Oh dear, yes! The great difficulty is to get the time. The work I can easily do; but then Jim, my pal, is one of the best locksmiths in England, and he's as true as steel. I always take him with me for a job of that sort. But, mum, the warder's got his eye upon us," said the "cracksman."

This was true enough, but, situated as he was, he was unable to hear one word of the foregoing conversation. The other prisoners were laughing and talking so that there was too much din and clatter for the warder in charge of them to comprehend the nature of the discussion between Peace and his companion.

The officers in charge of the prisoners allowed them to have it pretty much their own way in respect to social gossip.

As the train proceeded on its journey the prisoners continued to converse together in whispers almost incessantly.

They appeared to be, all of them, in excellent spirits, and to judge from their demeanour, lively conversation, and the occasional fits of laughter, anybody would have come to the conclusion that it was a holiday party of pleasure-seekers, instead of being convicts about to be transferred to a penal gaol.

Peace recognised among his companions many faces that were well known to him.

One young man, who in every respect was superior to the rest, particularly attracted his notice.

He was a stranger to our hero; but there was a sad and thoughtful expression on his features which enlisted Peace's sympathy.

He was very handsome, and did not appear to be more than twenty years of age.

He had been town traveller for a wholesale City house in London, and, unfortunately for him, got mixed up with a fast set of young men about town, and contracted habits of extravagance.

He was introduced to an actress, "fair but frail," and became fascinated with her charms to such an extent that the salary he received was not commensurate to supply her wants.

She persuaded him to try his fortune on the stage. He was under the impression, poor young man, that he had all the requisites to ensure success, but soon found out, however, that it takes years and unwearied industry to climb the ladder which leads to dramatic fame.

The sequel may be readily guessed. He embezzled a considerable sum of money from his employers. He was prosecuted by the firm—they said, "for example sake,"—and he was sentenced to five years' penal servitude.

He was irretrievably ruined. While in prison he listened to the counsel of several hardened offenders, who schooled him for a career of crime and vice.

It is a well-known and acknowledged fact that in this country felony is so lucrative and so far from hazardous that it thrives, and will thrive.

It appears from the judicial statistics that, while

incidental crime is decreasing, habitual crime is growing.

Transportation no longer carries off our thieves, who are discharged at the rate of about two thousand a year into the general population.

It is more than probable that a great proportion of these liberated prisoners re-enter the ranks of the criminal class.

The money spent on the repression of crime, ten millions a year, is amply sufficient to effect the purpose. But, as yet, it has been spent in vain. If things continue in the present course, we may look for another panic ere long. The subsidence of that in 1856 was as irrational as its rise. In deference to the popular outcry a show was made for a time of restraining the issue of the licences, and the country was appeased. But the real evil, the discharge of criminals unreformed by their past treatment, and without a check on their future conduct, continues unabated.

It is to be hoped that when the indignant terror of the public is once more aroused it will not again be squandered on the wrong object—the unlucky ticket of leave. But we must not be too sanguine. It is the nature of the bull to vent his fury on the red rag instead of the matador.

It must, however, be conceded that a man really anxious for self-restoration may pass through Portland or Dartmoor uncontaminated, and even derive some benefit from the discipline, defective as it is; but such instances are rare.

The young man who had attracted Peace's attention became utterly reckless and debased while in the last-named prison.

He became instructed in all the manœuvres of the habitual criminals with whom he associated, and his face became quite changed, as well as his mind.

It assumed that peculiar expression so prevalent among hardened offenders, which to the initiated is unmistakeable. A "leary look," in which fear, defiance, and cunning are blended together.

His was one of the many instances of evil communication sapping and undermining all moral principle.

The train in which the convicts were did not go direct to Dartmoor.

They had to change on to another line.

Upon the arrival at the station they were ordered to get out, and here they were, as at the time of their starting, surrounded by a curious throng of gazers.

"Keep your peckers up," cried a cab-driver, "and mind you are good boys for the future."

"All right, cabby—when I come out I shall want you to drive me to the Hoperoor," returned one of the prisoners.

"There, that will do; you are not brought here to chaff cabmen," said one of the warders. "The less you have to say the better."

"Give him his head for a little bit," observed the cab-driver. "He'll be reined up tight enough before long, I fancy."

"You mind your own business," said the warder.

"All right, guv'nor, sorry I spoke. Lord, you have got a crew under your charge, and no mistake," and with these words the man drove off.

The prisoners begged hard for tobacco of persons on the platform, and that, as well as money, was handed to them.

"Oh, I say, master," cried one, addressing himself to a young man of the Dundreary type, "can you spare us that paper when you have done with it?"

"Certainly, it is at your service," replied the gentleman, handing the newspaper to the other.

"It's against the rules," observed the warder. "Prisoners are not allowed to read newspapers."

"Only for this once."

"No, it's against the rules."

"But we are not in prison now. Mayn't a cove have a squint at the news while he's in the train?"

"Ah, let him have the newspaper; you can make him give it up before the train reaches its destination, you know," said the gentleman to the warder.

"I don't like to be too hard with them, but it's against the rules," replied the warder, walking away.

The prisoner thrust the paper into his pocket, and no further notice was taken of the action.

"I'm blest if I can read it now I have got it," murmured the prisoner, as he stepped into the other carriage which was to convey him to Dartmoor; "but there's some of 'em as can."

The train had not proceeded very far on its journey before the man drew forth his prize.

"I say, mates, I've got a newspaper. Will any on you read it out loud for the benefit of all of us? Please, sir, you won't object to it, please," he said, touching his cap and addressing the officer in charge.

"You know as well as I do that it is against the rules," replied the officer, "but as it has been given to you, and you are not now inside the walls of the prison, I consent."

"Ah, thank you, sir—thank you," cried several.

The young man to whom allusion has already been made was asked to read aloud for the benefit of the other prisoners. He was the best educated man of the whole party, some of whom could not read at all, while others could read but imperfectly.

The paper in question was a Sunday morning edition of one of the weeklies.

It contained reports of the trials at the Middlesex and Surrey Sessions, and the young man began at these, after which he read a portion of the police reports, then his eye lighted on a line in broad-faced type, "THE MURDER IN LARCHGROVE LANE; Examination and Committal of the Prisoner."

"Eh, what's that?" cried Peace. "In what lane?"

"Larchgrove."

"Let's have it," cried one of the convicts. "The whole true and particular account."

The young man began to read. As he repeated the name of Mr. Philip Jamblim Peace started.

"Do you know him?" inquired the "cracksman," who sat next to him.

"Yes, very well."

The reader continued. The murdered man, the detective engaged in the case, the several witnesses, together with the chairman of the bench of magistrates, were as familiar to him as household words.

He was in a feverish state of excitement and drank in every word with the greatest avidity.

Everybody in the carriage was interested, even to the unimpressionable warder, but not in an equal degree to Peace, who was absorbed as he listened to the thrilling narrative.

"Well, I'm blessed," exclaimed a young pickpocket, "but it is a big case."

"Hold your jaw, you young fool," cried a prisoner; "let's hear all about it."

The evidence of Brickett and John Adolphus had been gone carefully through, then followed the examination of Ellen Fulford.

"My eye, he's giving it her pretty hot," said the cracksman, "and doesn't he cheek the beaks?"

"I call him a **right-down** good 'un," observed another.

It would be difficult to describe the sensation produced when the young man read the following passage from the report:—

"Pray, Miss Fulford, were you not acquainted some time ago with a person named Charles Peace?"

The reader paused suddenly. Every eye was directed towards our hero.

"Jemmy Johnson squeeze me, but if that aint a cawker," exclaimed one of the prisoners.

"Order—silence!" said the warder, who began to repent having permitted the reading of the newspaper. He, however, found it impossible to repress the exclamations and inquiries which came from all sides.

"Why, was she a fancy girl of yours?" said one.

"Well, I never," cried another.

"But aint it lucky he's in quod?" observed another.

"If it had not been for that he might have been charged with the murder."

"I wish you'd all hold your tongues, and mind your own business," cried Peace, in a petulant tone. "If you want to hear the case, keep silent; if you don't, shut up."

"Well, don't speak so sharp. It's no fault of ourn," said a man on the opposite seat.

"Don't take on so because the girl's jilted you," cried another.

"You hold your clatter, you fool," said Peace.

"Now then," said the young man, who had been reading, "there isn't much more of it, and so just keep quiet that I may finish the case."

The prisoners obeyed, and the reader continued.

Several more questions were put to the witness regarding Peace, and our hero was greatly relieved when Ellen Fulford's examination came to an end.

Never in his whole life had he been so astonished, and for the rest of the journey he remained moody and silent, hardly exchanging a word with any one, with the exception of his friend the cracksman, who, of his own accord, made Peace acquainted with his offence and the sentence which had been passed upon him.

There is a certain amount of forbearance displayed by prisoners. They make it a rule never to ask a man what he is in for. If a man likes to be communicative that's another thing, but it would be deemed impertinent of a fellow-prisoner to question him on the subject.

The badge on his left arm gives his sentence as well as his number, so there is no reason to inquire "what he has got."

The "outing," as some of the prisoners termed their journey from one prison to another, was now nearly over.

When the train came to the end of its journey, omnibuses were found waiting at the station, to take the convicts to Princetown, on Dartmoor, where the gaol is situated.

To say the truth, the men had behaved very well, all things considered. They had not given their janitors much trouble, and much to their credit, be it said, they had not made use of any objectionable language. Slang words they could not help introducing in their discourse, as they form part of their vocabulary.

They at once entered the omnibuses, which were driven at a moderate pace, for the road and hills necessitated a slow mode of progression.

Peace, who had chummed up with the cracksman, sat next to him as heretofore, for the men were permitted to take their places according to their own fancy, and there were distinct little coteries inside the prison the same as in the outside world.

As soon as they had got a few miles out of the town they were told to alight and walk up the steep hills—to say the truth, the journey was mostly up hill.

Princetown chiefly consists of the barracks and houses of those connected with the prison; in addition to these there are a few shops kept by tradesmen who supply them. It is rude and rugged in character, and possesses but few attractions, if any. It is true some portion of the land is under cultivation—the remaining parts of the place is composed of granite, gorse, heather, and bog.

It was while walking up one of the hills that Peace and his companions beheld for the first time, at a distance, their new prison-house. As they came upon the piquets of the Civil Guard (uncivil would be the better term), armed with their rifles and bayonets, they were impressed with the rigid discipline carried on at the place.

Upon reaching the prison, a gloomy, cheerless, heavy-looking granite building or series of buildings, surrounded by a high wall, Peace's heart seemed to sink within him. He turned to the "cracksman" and said—

"This is a God-forgotten place."

"Not cheerful—not very cheerful-looking, is it?"

Peace made a face and then groaned.

The gate is one of the most gloomy pieces of architecture it is well possible to conceive—indeed, the whole aspect of the place was cheerless and depressing to the last degree.

As soon as the convicts arrived at the gate they were received by several warders, who conducted them into the receiving wards, where all was prepared for their arrival.

Their chains and handcuffs were removed, and they soon found themselves in a long passage about twelve feet wide, lighted by a skylight.

It was made painfully manifest to them all that the discipline at Dartmoor was much more strict than at Preston, and there were not a few who deeply regretted having left that well-regulated gaol.

"I expect we shall have a lively time of it here," whispered the cracksman to Peace.

"Out of the frying-pan into the fire—that's about the size of it," murmured Peace.

The prisoners were taken in ten or a dozen at a time to the bath-room, where they were told to perform the usual ablution. This ceremony occupied some time. At length, however, Peace's turn came. He was taken with the cracksman and eight others down a passage and across a yard. Two warders in charge of this last batch pointed significantly to a number of baths which were all of a row; they were about four feet six inches square and three feet deep.

A wooden seat ran along the whole of the baths, which were about twenty or more in number; behind the seats was a passage.

The convicts sat on the seats with their backs to the passage and facing the water, to undress, while the prison officials marched up and down.

But other ceremonies had to be gone through. When the bathing was over, the men were conducted into a large room leading out of the passage. In this room there were a number of forms. In the centre of the apartment was a table, and at the end of this, facing the door, sat the chief warder.

He was a handsome, pleasant-featured man, somewhat above the middle height, and it was evident that he was an old soldier, for he bore on his breast several medals won on the battle-field. Behind him was a gentlemanly, courteous man, who was the deputy-governor.

At the side of the table sat the doctor with a book before him, and a bundle of papers to which he ever and anon referred. These papers consisted of reports from the other prisons of the men who were sent to Dartmoor. Peace's party consisted of thirty-seven.

After they had been in the examining room a minute or so, they were told to strip. There was no alternative but to obey, repugnant as it was to many, or indeed all of them; but when a man is sent to a goal to undergo penal servitude, he is constrained to leave all sense of decency, modesty, or shame outside, and it is much to be regretted that some better regulations are not made in this respect.

Indignities of this sort are not necessary—they are worse than useless. They have a debasing, and baneful effect upon the prisoners, lower their moral tone, and render them callous.

In a minute or so after the order every man was as bare and naked as a Pict.

The chief then left his seat, and stood up beside the table, and every man paraded himself before him. This scene is at once degrading and disgusting.

After the inspection they were directed to go over to the other side of the apartment, where they found thirty-seven bundles of clean clothes awaiting them.

Each prisoner helped himself to a clean bundle, and donned the garments as quickly as possible.

While the dressing was going on the officials in the room were conversing on the leading topics of the day in an unconcerned manner.

The ceremony which had just been gone through was one of such frequent occurrence that the prison officials looked upon it as a part of their ordinary every day duty, but to a person who has to undergo it for the first time it is something appalling, especially if he happens to have been well brought up or has any self-respect. To the hardened offender it is a matter of no moment.

The doctor was a very kind, considerate gentleman, who paid every attention to those under his care. He called each man before him whose medical report required him to take special notice of, and examined him, comparing any deformity with the written description, and when, if he found it necessary, he questioned the prisoner upon matters relating to his constitution and general health.

He was a sharp observer of human nature, and could almost tell at a glance whether the man he was questioning spoke the truth or otherwise.

" Well, Peace," he observed, as that personage came before him, " there is nothing much the matter with you, I believe—that is, so far as your general health is concerned."

Our hero was surprised at hearing himself addressed by his proper name instead of his number. He was not aware, however, that the doctor had adopted the same method with all the prisoners who had come before him. It was a way he had, albeit it is not the usual custom in convict prisons.

" Yes, sir," returned Peace, who had passed on to make room for another of the batch.

When all were dressed as far as flannels, shirts, drawers, and stockings were concerned, the men were marched out and resumed the outer clothes which they had arrived in, and which had all been carefully examined by one or more of the prison attendants. Every pin a man had stuck in a jacket was removed.

The men were now fitted with boots, some with two pairs of water-tights.

These were for the prisoners who were destined to work out of doors in the swamps and quarries. The strongest and most able-bodied were selected for this employment. All the caps were altered; they had to be turned down according to the regulation pattern and securely stitched in to the required shape.

The selection of those articles took some time, and while it was going on the warders were operating upon the men's heads and beards.

Peace and his companions had their hair cropped as close as scissors could make it. The cropping at Dartmoor is a sort of mania with the officials, who delight in denuding the men of their hair, and making them look as much like convicts as possible.

When all were supplied with clothes they were called in, a few at a time, and each new-comer received a new register number and a small card, a small brush, a comb, and a towel.

Those who required spectacles were desired to give their names to be submitted to the prison surgeon. As each batch was finished off and received their register number and ticket, they were marched away to their respective prisons and wards.

Peace felt very much depressed, and would have given anything to be back in his old quarters. He felt assured that his life at Dartmoor would be a wretched one.

Just as he and some half-dozen others arrived outside in the yard, the warder told them to stand in a line against the wall.

" What is this caper for ?" whispered our hero to a companion.

" Silence !" exclaimed the prison official. " Prisoners are not allowed to talk."

The tramp, tramp of many feet was now heard. The outside gang were returning from work. They came on in long lines, two abreast, each gang with its officers in military style, and keeping excellent step and time, but the men looked desponding and careworn.

Poor wretches, there was good reason for this. The work upon which they had been engaged was arduous enough, and in addition to this the ground under foot was little better than a dismal swamp.

At the inner gate of the prison stood the chief warder. He was saluted by every officer as the gangs came up.

Everything is done at Dartmoor with military precision. The number of men being brought back from the quarries or elsewhere, together with the number of the gang, was called out by the officer in charge.

This was checked against the number that had left the prison in the earlier portion of the day.

Peace, as they marched along, was duly impressed with the fact that it was a melancholy spectacle he was witnessing. The wretched convicts came in gang after gang till some three hundred men or more, according to his calculation, must have passed through. Every officer, as he reached the lodge gate, delivered up his rifle, bayonet, belt, and cartridge-box to the armourer, who with his assistant stood ready to receive them.

When all had arrived, and the working parties were safely within the walls of the prison, the Civil Guard closed up the rear, and there was an end to the melancholy tramp of men doomed to wretched daily servitude.

As the poor wretches passed the knot of new comers they regarded them with a curious and inquiring glance, for they knew perfectly well that they had but just arrived from some other convict prison; but not a word was spoken.

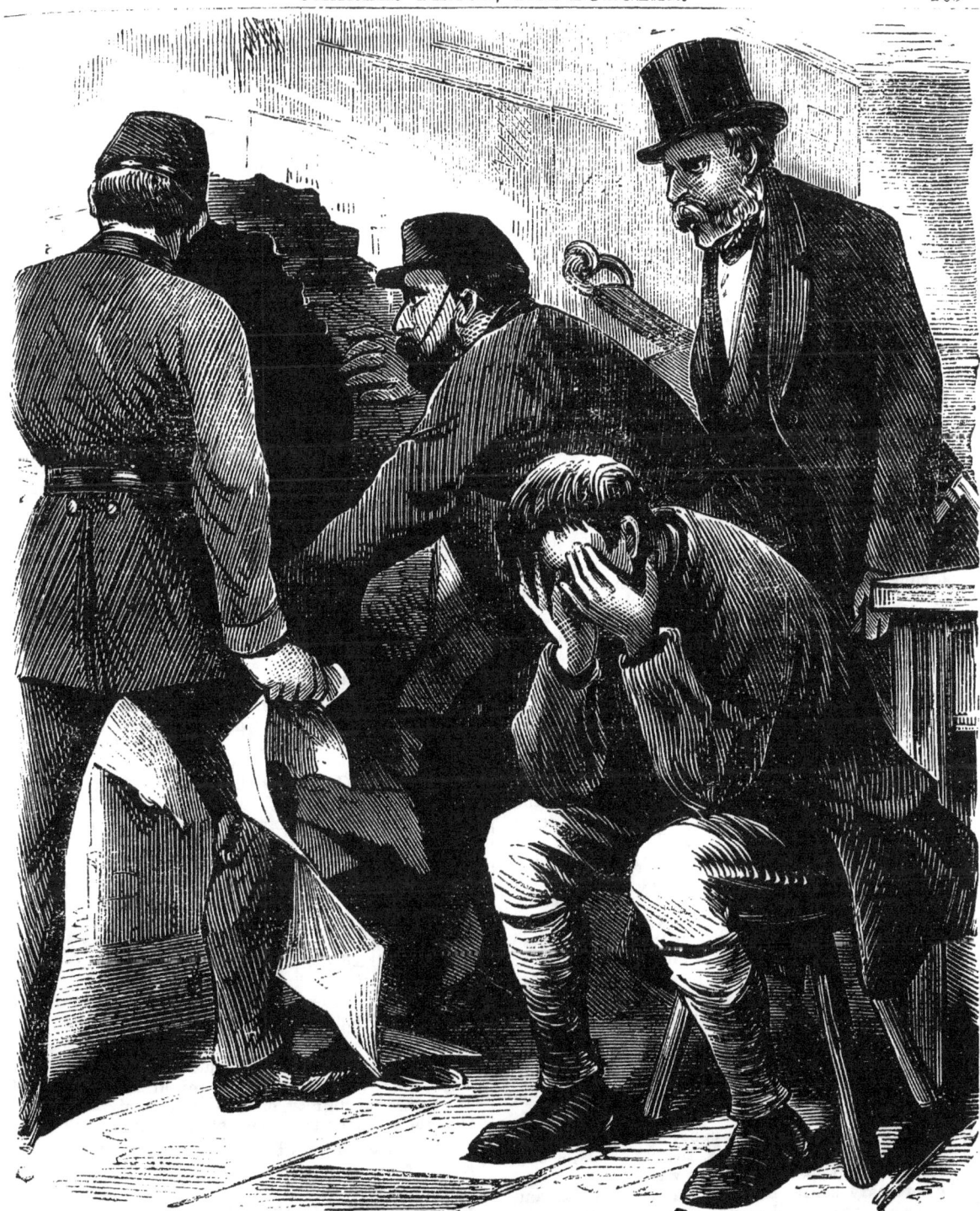

DISCOVERY OF CHUDLEY'S ATTEMPT TO ESCAPE.

Peace and his companions were then conducted into No. 4 prison. This was a large granite building originally constructed for the French prisoners, but now adapted for modern convict appliances.

Since its original construction it had undergone a complete change, as far as its interior arrangements were concerned; it was remodelled upon the plan laid down by those who are so well versed in all the requirements for the reception of convicted felons.

All the floors were taken out, and the galleries of cells were constructed one over the other in four tiers. There are about fifty cells on each landing or gallery, and five landings reached by two flights of stairs, one on each end of the hall.

No. 34.

These halls are called A hall and B hall, and there is only one communication between the two, this being in the middle of the ground floor. The whole of the cells and their supports are constructed of iron, the sides and doors being corrugated iron, and the floor both of cells and landings thick slab slate.

A strong iron rail runs along each landing. No prisoners happened to be there when the new batch of convicts arrived, and the new comers were now mounted up to the top floor of all.

Over the door-cell was a proper receptacle for a small card with the prisoner's numerical register on it.

"What is the number of your gang ?" said the warder to Peace.

"I don't know the number, sir," answered our hero.

"Not know your number ?"

"No, sir. When at Preston I worked in the tailors' shop, but the number of the gang I don't know—indeed, I never did know it."

"Oh, well, that is not of any great importance. If you can't tell me we must do without. Go in there, and the warder of the landing, Mr. Dring, will soon be here."

Peace entered, and the moment the door was closed he saw what a little dark hole he was thrust into—indeed, it was some minutes before he could make out anything distinctly.

He was curious about his future home, and as soon as possible he proceeded to make an examination of the same.

It was like most places of that description—small enough, certainly, not more than seven feet long by four feet six inches in width, and, as far as he could judge, about eight feet in height.

By the side of the door was a narrow window of thick rough plate-glass, beneath which was a small flap table, that had to be let down when the hammock was slung. Only at this table, and immediately close to the window, was there light enough to see any object distinctly. Over the table and under the window was a narrow shelf, on which to place a candle.

Peace glanced curiously around and surveyed each object with a curious and inquisitive eye. The general appearance of the place was much the same in its leading features as the cells in other convict prisons.

A wooden shelf ran over the door from side to side of the cell. On this spare boots and shoes, together with cleaning rags, were kept.

Opposite the door, about five feet from the ground, was another and wider shelf. On this was arranged the bedclothes, done up in a neat, round, compact roll, a tin pint mug, a tin plate, a small brass candlestick, with a curiously contrived pair of snuffers, made ingeniously out of one piece of tin, a tin knife, a wooden spoon, a wooden salt, and an ordinary school slate.

Below the shelf, and at the opposite end of the cell to the window and flap table, was the hammock, neatly rolled up and strapped against the wall.

An ordinary stable bucket, with iron handle and hoops, was on the floor alongside of a low wooden stool ; a small hand broom, and in a corner, under the table, a scrubbing brush, and two tin tallies, with the number of the cell, prison, and hall, hanging behind the door, completed the furniture of the cheerless receptacle for the felon.

Peace surveyed the several objects with a look of resignation. He had by this time been pretty well used to the most noticeable features of apartments of this sort. His attention was now directed to the ventilation of his new abode.

This was of a very primitive principle. There was a gap at the bottom of the door to let air in—the door in fact was made five inches too short—and over the shelf whereon the bedding and utensils were stowed, were some dozen round holes an inch or so in diameter, to let the air out. Each door had a peep-hole with a cover to it.

By the time Peace had completed his inspection the gangs came up, they made a rare clatter and noise, and it seemed to him that they took a delight in making as much disturbance as possible.

In the hall in which he was confined, there were about two hundred convicts, rough, coarse brutes, who, in many respects, resembled caged animals, who only wanted the opportunity to wreak their vengeance upon anyone who came in their way. But they were kept under control, and were so securely guarded that there was not much chance of them getting the upper hand of their janitors.

As each man entered his cell, he slammed the door as hard as he could to vent his spleen and spite upon it for his day's hard and monotonous toil.

"There's a nice lot of boys in here," murmured Peace —"a set of savages, I fancy. Well, it does not much matter, I suppose, but I wish I was back at Preston."

He had hardly given expression to this wish, when he heard a clatter of tins, which at first he could not make out ; this was followed by a shouting between the warders below in the hall and those on the landings.

Presently he heard a warder shout out—

"Can't you put out your tins and your brooms ?"

Peace's door was opened, and a dark-whiskered man peered in.

"Don't you hear me ?" he said.

"I heard your voice, sir," said Peace, in a soft and submissive tone. "What do you wish me to do ?"

"Humph ! You are one of the last batch, I suppose ?"

"Yes, sir. Only came in to-day."

"Ah, I see. Well, then, put out your broom like that," and here he pointed to the broom at the next cell; "and your tin mug and plate."

"Oh, I didn't know," returned our hero.

"Mind you attend to what I say now you do know, my man."

"Yes, sir."

While the warder was explaining this, the principal in the hall below was shouting to him for his "roll," the number of men he had upon his landing.

This the warder ascertained by running along the landing and counting the brooms.

As soon as the roll is called the brooms should be taken in. It is, to say the truth, not a very dignified way—for a man to put in his appearance by means of a broom—but dignity, or even common civility, is never thought of in the treatment of convicts.

Peace had a pretty good sample of this ; not knowing the rules of the place, he left his broom out, a warder came and kicked it so violently that it was a wonder it did not go through the partition.

"This is a lively sort of establishment," murmured Peace, who, after this, kept as quiet as possible. He had made up his mind to conform to the rules and give as little trouble as possible ; but at present he was in ignorance as to what these were.

Soon after the broom incident he heard a further noise of opening and shutting of cell doors till at last his own was flung open, and a little six-ounce loaf of bread was handed him, and he found that his tin mug that he had put outside was filled with gruel.

"My supper, I suppose," he murmured. "Not a sumptuous repast, it is true, but better than nothing."

He sat down on his stool and devoured the dainty meal with something like a relish.

While he was partaking of his frugal repast all appeared to be quiet in the prison, the reason for this being that the other convicts were similarly occupied.

Both cells on each side of the one occupied by Peace had tenants also.

In about half an hour the man in one kept knocking, and wanted our hero to enter into conversation, but as he judged this was against the rules he did not deem it advisable to take any notice of the summons, and so he let the man knock until he was tired, and gave it up as hopeless.

In the other cell he heard every now and then a curious clanking noise which he could not make out. This he took no notice of, for he was determined not to compromise himself in any way, or to incur the displeasure of the officials.

At present he was new to the place, and deemed it advisable to play a "safe game," as he termed it.

Nevertheless he was greatly disturbed and annoyed by his noisy neighbour, who seemed to keep up an incessant clatter throughout the livelong night.

The next morning he discovered what it was that so disturbed him. His neighbour was what is called a black-dress man, who wore fetters and a heavy chain, one end of which was fastened with rivetted rings round each ankle, and the middle of it was held up to his waist by a strap.

Doubtless many of our readers have seen the print of Captain Macheath in the condemned cell at Newgate. The fetters on that fabulous hero of Gay's opera resembled those worn by the black-dress man of Dartmoor.

His dress was parti-coloured, of black and drab—one side one colour, one the other; the front of one sleeve black and the back drab, and the reverse with the other sleeve.

The same with the breeches or knickerbockers, which were fastened with buttons down the sides of the legs, to admit of their being fastened with the fetter on.

The costume was not picturesque, but then the reality of prison life is so vastly different to that shown on the stage! In this man's case it was miserably wretched, albeit he richly deserved the hardships he was compelled to endure.

He was condemned to this punishment for either striking or threatening an officer, and for this offence he had been "bashed," or flogged, besides.

It is not often a flogging is inflicted, only in extreme cases. Night and day the refractory prisoner has to wear his manacles; in bed or out of bed, it was just the same, and every time he moved in bed they clanked and rattled, making so strange a noise that Peace was sorely troubled as he lay in his cell during the lonely hours of the night.

Sometimes, in turning, the manacled prisoner would strike his fetter against the corrugated iron partition of the cell.

Peace pitied the poor wretch, but he had the prudence not to offer any observation.

Mr. Dring, the chief warder, had, as may be imagined, no sinecure.

The duties of his office did not admit of much leisure time for relaxation, and when he returned from his tea he had yet plenty of work before him.

The fifty men on his landing had all their wants to be attended to, and our worthy prison official was not accustomed to shirk his duty.

He was a peculiar man in many respects, but want of attention to those under his charge was not one of his faults.

He was a strict disciplinarian, but in the main was a kindly-disposed man enough.

Sometimes he would "take" to a man, as the convicts termed it.

When this was the case the prisoner was all right; he was treated with civility and consideration, which, all things considered, is saying a great deal; but woe betide the man who was in his black books! He had it pretty "hot," to make use of another phrase of the prisoners.

Mr. Dring had seen something of the world before he made the acquaintance of the interior of one of her Majesty's gaols.

He had served her aforesaid Majesty on land and sea.

He was at one time of his life attached to the Royal Marines, and after fighting his country's battles in that capacity for some years, he rose to the rank of sergeant-major, and those who happen to know what an old sergeant-major of the Marines is will understand that a man must get up very early in the morning, and be a cute fellow to boot, to take the wind out of the sails of Mr. Warder Dring.

He was a quiet, orderly, unobtrusive man, and, from his general demeanour, many were under the impression that he was as mild as a lamb and as green as a middy; but those under his charge soon found out their mistake when they came playing pranks or trying on the hanky-panky business.

Mr. Dring was down upon them at once. There was no man in Dartmoor Prison better adapted to deal with convicts and command their respect than the old marine.

To those who were straightforward and well behaved he was the most considerate and kind master it is well possible to conceive.

But when he once found out a man playing him tricks, deceiving him, and disobeying the rules and regulations of the gaol, he would lead him a fine life. Peace reckoned up the chief warder with something like accuracy, and he did his best to propitiate him.

When he came his rounds he regarded our hero with a searching glance.

"Ah," he observed, "you are new to the place. Well, here's soap, salt, and cleaning rags."

"Thank you, sir," said Peace, touching his cap.

"But stay, you must give me your jacket to be badged," said Mr. Dring.

Peace pulled off his jacket with the utmost alacrity. His janitor gave him another to wear in the meantime; he also gave him a clean pair of sheets, and told him where to place each article, and supplied him with a candle.

Peace thanked him again and again.

"When you hear 'beds down' called out," said Mr. Dring, "you must prepare your hammock for the night. Do you understand?"

"Yes, sir, I will do so."

"But you must not do it till you hear the word given outside."

"No, sir."

"Well, that is all, I think—you will not forget my instructions?"

"Certainly not."

"Good. You've got a queer pair next to you—I mean in the cells adjoining yours. Have nothing to say to them, and if they make a noise, which I expect they are pretty sure to do, take no notice of them."

"One makes a terrible noise."

"Ah, the prisoner with the manacles—yes, I know —well, that can't be helped; it's no fault of ours that he is constrained to wear the fetters."

Peace bowed, but did not offer any observation.

Mr. Dring left him to go to someone else.

Peace had nothing to read, and did not like to ask for a book or two in his present early stage, so he had nothing for it but to sit and listen to the noises that were going on, and there were a few.

As far as the acoustic principle of Dartmoor is concerned it is something very near perfection; indeed, it is aggravatingly resonant.

The entire block of four hundred cells in that part of the prison in which Peace was confined were framed in iron.

The consequence was that there was hardly a door slammed in the whole building that did not vibrate more or less throughout the cell. This fact was made manifest to every prisoner upon first entering Dartmoor; after being there for some little time the men got used to the noises.

The effect when every cell door in the whole hall was slammed at once is not easy to describe; it was like a volley of musketry.

Peace remembered what Mr. Dring had told him, and being anxious to obey that worthy functionary to the very letter, he watched and listened for the signal "beds down."

When he heard the order given he let go his hammock; all the other convicts did the same, and the consequence was that the whole fabric seemed to be shaken.

Peace was pretty well used to prison hammocks, and therefore had no difficulty in arranging his.

Some men on their first acquaintance with these snug resting places make a great muddle of them.

Sometimes a hammock strap would give way, and let the man down on to the hard stones of his cell; but Peace, who was an old soldier in looking after his own comforts, if they could be so termed, took very excellent care to see that his straps were all right.

The warders never object to give a man a new strap or two if any of his old ones are worn out.

At Dartmoor the convicts had very little to complain of as far as sleeping accommodation was concerned.

Each man has a good, warm, comfortable bed, and a plentiful supply of covering, which is invariably clean indeed. This could hardly be otherwise, seeing how frequently it is changed.

It is true there is no bed in a hammock, nor is one needed, but the prisoner has two good blankets (three in the winter), an excellent rug, and two stout linen sheets, with a wool or hair pillow.

The hammock is as comfortable as need be—indeed, many of the prisoners never had such luxurious sleeping accommodation when outside the walls of a prison.

Soon after "beds down" was sounded a warder was heard coming up the stairs to see that every candle was put out.

There are gas lights along each landing-railing, so that there is more or less light in every cell.

After the warder had made the necessary inspection with regard to the candles a bell was sounded, which is the signal for the day-warders to leave the prison, as the night warders come on duty.

When this occurs every man is expected to be in bed, and if the night watch finds him up he is liable to be reported, and reporting means puishment by loss of marks or otherwise.

At regular intervals throughout the night one of the warders comes round and looks into each cell.

By placing the bull's-eye of his lantern against the glass of the window, and peeping through the spy-hole in the door, he can see plainly enough if a man is in bed or not.

Many a time was Peace awoke with the sudden flash of the bull's-eye upon his face.

CHAPTER LXVIII.

GILES CHUDLEY IN PRISON.

GILES CHUDLEY had ample funds at his disposal, and he told the sagacious Mr. Slapperton not to spare any expense in preparing his defence and securing the services of a clever counsel to conduct his case when the trial came on.

Mr. Slapperton had several interviews with the prisoner after his committal, and in common with many others was at a loss to account for the amount of money he had in his possession.

Some averred that Chudley had rich relations, who had come forward handsomely in the hour of need.

He had friends—that is quite certain, but they were not related to him. The reader will remember that at the time of Chudley's capture there were two strangers in the parlour of the "Lord Cornwallis." One was a young swell, the other a broad-shouldered, square-headed man.

The young swell was none other than the boy Alf Purvis, who now assumed all the airs and graces of a fashionable young gentleman, and who, moreover, was one of the most accomplished pickpockets in London. The other, the man with the broad shoulders, was the London "cracksman," who was introduced to the reader when Laura Stanbridge and young Purvis paid a visit to that delectable establishment known as a thieves' haunt in Little Mint-street, Whitechapel.

These two personages had effectually concealed Chudley in various parts of the metropolis after he had committed the murder in Larchgrove-lane.

They had supplied him with funds to go abroad. In point of fact, they were about to see him on board of a vessel at Liverpool, but imprudently chose to pay a visit to the hiring fair.

The result of this act of folly we already know.

Purvis detested the Jamblins, and he, as well as Laura Stanbridge, thought Chudley had done a meritorious act by ridding the world of young Mr. Philip; anyway, they befriended his assassin, and supplied him with funds, both before and after his capture.

Mr. Slapperton, after having received the necessary instructions for the wretched man's defence, spoke most confidently of the result of the trial. He told his client that the chances were clearly in his favour, and that in all probability the jury would return a verdict of "Not Guilty."

Giles, however, was of a different opinion. He was an ignorant low-bred ruffian, but he had a certain amount of low cunning, which, to say the truth, is a qualification that most criminals of his type generally possess. However, he put as good a face on the matter as possible, and affected to believe what his solicitor told him.

But he was reflective, and thinking of certain plans which he had formed. His low cunning now came out with additional force.

One burning thought was for ever in his brain; it was this:

"How could he effect his escape?"

If he could succeed in doing this, there were those

outside who would effectually conceal him from the bloodhounds of the law.

As far as this was concerned the prisoner was not far out in his reckoning.

The reader will remember that in No. 28 of this work we gave a chapter on mysterious murders, and cited many cases in which the perpetrators of crimes of this nature have successfully eluded the vigilance of the police—one of these instances being a murder which was committed at Chingford by a man named Geydon, who in many respects was similar to Giles Chudley.

Since the publication of these cases in a number of this work, issued only five weeks ago, Geydon has given himself up.

For twenty-two years he has, despite the £200 reward offered by Government at the time of the murder, remained under cover.

This, to say the least of it, is a remarkable circumstance, and it is still more remarkable that we should have brought the matter so recently under public notice in this work.

Giles Chudley, as we have already intimated, was bringing all the intellect he had to bear on the one cherished idea which had taken possession of him.

The sessions would come on in about a month. He had that time before him, which he was determined if possible to make use of. In a month there were thirty days, in these thirty days there were seven hundred and twenty hours; a third of the time would be devoted to sleep, to meals, and to times when he could not work, but what of that? There were plenty of hours left for him to accomplish his purpose.

And if all went on well he would accomplish it.

Having come to this resolution he watched and waited for a brief period, never hinting to a living soul that he had any fear respecting the issue of the forthcoming trial.

He assumed an air of cheerfulness, and spoke confidently of the result. He said his innocence would be proved, and that he hoped to leave the court without a stain on his character.

After his trial he judged rightly enough that he would be confined in a stronger cell, and have a warder night and day with him, who would watch him as they watch men who are doomed to die, and whom despair so often inspires with unnatural strength and cunning.

Both these qualities he possessed in a remarkable degree; the last-named prompted him to allay suspicion, and to make everybody around him believe that he had no fear for the future.

He sent a message to the governor, requesting to see him.

The governor was a particularly kindly-disposed man, and was indulgent to a fault. He came at once.

"Do you wish for anything, my man?" he said, addressing himself to the prisoner.

"I'm very dull, and doan't know what to do wi' myself," said Chudley. "You were kind enough to say that I might have books and papers."

"I didn't know you took an interest in books or their contents, or that you cared about reading. However, I am glad to find I've misjudged you. You can have what books you require from the circulating library. You'd better pay a month's subscription, and then you can look over the catalogue, and select those which take your fancy."

"Thank you, sir. How am I to get them?"

"The messenger will fetch whatever you require."

"I shall read a goodish lot o' books," said Chudley, smiling. "Was always fond o' reading."

"Oh, yes; just so—I dare say," remarked the governor, carelessly.

"And I can't sit here all by myself wi'out having summut to do."

"Certainly not; besides, they will keep you out of mischief. Idle people are always mischievous."

"Out of meescheef!" cried Chudley. "Well, I loike that; what meescheef can a poor devil loike me do?"

"You might scrawl on the walls, or tear down the rules, you know," observed the governor, with a smile.

"Oh, I might, sartenly, but I aint loikely to do nuffin o' the sort. I hope I know how to behave myself in prison or out o' prison."

"I dare say you do, my man. Is there anything else you want before I leave?"

"Thank 'ee, sir, that be all."

The governor despatched the messenger to the nearest library, and then left the cell. As he passed along the passage he called the turnkeys before him.

"I can't make out that man," he observed. "What can be his reason for asking for books? Just you keep an eye upon him."

"We are sure to do that, sir; but he don't give much trouble, and seems to make sure of getting off."

"Oh! he does—eh?"

"Yes, sir."

"That may be put on. I wouldn't put too much trust in him. I may be mistaken; but I believe him to be a very artful, cunning fellow. I say again, keep your eyes upon No. 9."

The turnkeys promised to do so, but they could not very well see any reason for mistrust or doubt.

At four o'clock Giles Chudley was summoned to chapel, and was ushered into a long line of fellow-prisoners, clad in the uniforms of convicted crime.

All the officers accompanied the prisoners into the chapel in the manner we have described in a preceding chapter.

The warders stood in the gallery above the seats of the convicts, every movement of whom they commanded with their eyes.

It seemed to Chudley, however, that he was the leading object of attraction, for glancing carelessly round the building, as people usually do when first entering a place of worship, he observed several pairs of eyes accompanying his own in whatsoever direction he turned them, and also that several more were fixed upon him in one long steadfast glance.

He could not help noticing this, at which he felt greatly annoyed. He had not calculated the deep interest men of every denomination take in the actions and demeanour of a murderer.

The glance he had taken at the most noticeable features of the chapel, cursory as it had been, put him in possession of the fact that the windows of the building were only protected by one bar, which fell down the centre, and which left an opening on each side sufficiently small to prevent a sudden escape and sufficiently large to admit of a slim man squeezing through with time and trouble.

He was in a state of feverish anxiety. He clenched his teeth, and endeavoured to prevent his emotion being perceived by the eyes in the gallery.

To deceive whom he did not look round any more, giving his attention not to the chaplain, for that would have been a transparent act of hypocrisy, and sufficient in itself to have excited suspicion, but to the title-page of the prayer-book and to other indifferent little matters, as any one else who had been sent to church by compulsion might have done.

But his mind was actively employed, and his whole thoughts were engaged upon his pet project.

He was trying to guess first what the chapel windows opened out upon; secondly, whether the chapel door was locked at night.

An answer to the first question was soon made by the rattle of carriage wheels, which he could hear distinctly, and sometimes he fancied he could catch the faint hum of voices and footsteps, which gave him hopes of escape and liberty.

There was not the least question about the chapel being close to the street or some public thoroughfare; if he could only get there he could easily escape. But he had seen that there was a lock on the door—a massive lock which might give him a great deal of trouble, and take him hours to pick with such rude instruments as alone he could possibly obtain.

Besides, he was by no means an adept in the manipulation of locks, and this he bitterly regretted; but, nevertheless, he did not despair.

Happening to look on the floor he could scarcely believe his eyes when he saw a good-sized needle there.

It had probably been dropped by one of the female prisoners, who at the regular chapel hour sat together in a large pew, surrounded by a red curtain, but occupied the seats of the male prisoners when attending the school class which was held in the chapel once a day.

He considered for some little time, not knowing very well how to act; the needle would be of service, and he must obtain it by some means.

A few minutes after this he happened to drop his hymn-book. He picked it up again directly, and with it the needle, which he secreted in his shirt sleeve.

As he returned the hymn-book to the ledge of the pew, he took care to display the palms of both his hands, that no one might suppose they contained anything besides his book.

No one who knew Giles Chudley would have given him credit for possessing so much acuteness; but the situation in which he found himself called forth the latent powers of his mind, which had heretofore lain dormant.

As the convicts and other prisoners were being marshalled out of chapel, Giles blundered against the door, apparently by accident, so that it almost shut.

He took hold of the lock to swing it open again, and, in so doing, slipped the needle into the keyhole.

"Can't you see your way out?" cried a warder.

"Oh, I beg your pardon, sir; it was an accident," returned Chudley.

"Forward! this way," said the official, and the line of men marched on.

All was well so far. It was evident that the warders did not suspect that anything was amiss.

He could examine the lock the next day as he went out, and if the needle was still there it would be a proof that the door had not been locked.

The contrivance was an ingenious one, but then we should remember that men whose lives are at stake have their wits sharpened in a remarkable degree.

Chudley returned to his cell. He opened his books, disfigured them with notes on the margin, much to the disgust of the librarian, and littered them together as if he had been diligently employed with them; but he was too excited to read; he could not even sit or remain still for any length of time; he paced to and fro, thinking and muttering to himself.

By day and by night the same thought haunted him.

At dusk a turnkey came in and lighted his gas. As soon as he heard the key in the lock he sprang to his stool, and was poring over his books before the door was opened.

He had the cunning of the serpent, and flattered himself that he could assume anything or conceal anything while the great lock was being turned by the gaoler.

"It is a most fortunate thing the lock makes such a noise when turned," he murmured. "I do hope they won't oil it."

But as yet he did not see his way clear for the accomplishment of his object.

The whole of that night, and on the following day also, he was cudgelling his brains for some solution to the grand and all-important question.

It seemed almost like wasting precious time, but he knew that it would be folly to begin working with his hands till his plans were matured and his calculations had been fully made.

The half-hour of evening prayers seemed to be an age.

He quivered all over with impatience and anxiety.

There was no help for it—he had to wait patiently. The time having expired, he passed out with the others as usual. As he did so he thrust his finger into the key-hole. An icy tremour shot through his frame.

The needle was still there. Never surely did so insignificant an object have such a powerful effect upon a man as did this little needle. It whispered into his ears delusive words of hope and comfort, of escape and freedom.

If he could only work through his cell door into the corridor, from which the chapel was entered, the rest was an easy matter. He felt assured this could be accomplished, and was confident of his ultimate success.

But much remained to be done. His plan of operations was simple enough in theory, but it had to be put into practice.

It would be no very difficult task to turn his bed-clothes into a rope, and when this was done he could let himself down from the chapel window.

Upon his return from chapel he found Mr. Slapperton awaiting him.

The lawyer had a number of questions to put respecting the leading points in the case. He had a long conference with his client, and as heretofore spoke hopefully of the result of the trial.

Giles Chudley assumed an air of confidence, which, to say the truth, he was far from feeling. However, he humoured his legal adviser, but said nothing about the scheme he had in his head.

After Mr. Slapperton had left, Giles knelt down before the door and scrutinised the lock.

After a minute examination of the same he came to the conclusion that it would be easier for him to dig a hole in the wall close to the lock, to wrench the staple away, and then force back the bolt as if it was being unlocked by a key.

He felt assured that this would be the best plan, but as he was rising from his knees he discovered something in the centre of the door which strangely enough had entirely escaped his attention before.

There was a small round grating a little larger than a man's eye: a flap of iron hung before it on the other side.

Giles was astonished, as well he might be, at the discovery, and still more so at it having escaped his notice.

While he was staring at it and fingering it with a considerable amount of curiosity he heard a soft step, so soft that he did not think it was so close to him.

"Some one on the watch," he murmured, as his heart beat audibly.

The flap was gently raised and its place was taken by a large brown eye, which sternly surveyed the interior of the cell.

As if satisfied with the impression it had made, the eye disappeared, and the iron flap descended as noiselessly as it had been raised.

Giles Chudley felt relieved when the scrutiny was over.

"Ah, ah," he muttered, "I did not reckon on this, but I am glad I made the discovery. This is a hound that does not bark; I must act with caution."

He resolved to begin work as soon as it was dark, and watched the shadows one by one as they fell through the little window upon the door of the cell.

Having matured his plans he was burning to put them into practice.

When once outside the walls of his prison-house he would be safe.

So he thought and fondly hoped; but how to get out was the question.

He waited till the turnkeys, who brought the prisoners their suppers of bread and gruel, and lighted their gas, had gone their rounds.

He then wrenched off one of the hooks, upon which his bed was suspended at night, and crept cautiously towards the door.

He was afraid to begin, for the sounds of voices met his ear, and he judged that some of the prison officials were about. He was very soon convinced of this, for the voices became more distinct.

He was constrained, therefore, to await for a more favourable opportunity.

Deeply mortified at this circumstance he heaved a deep sigh, and sat himself down upon his wooden stool.

He felt supremely wretched, and endured an hour of almost insupportable agony. During this time he stared vacantly at the white flame which flickered from the gas-pipe, and calculated what he should do when he had made his escape.

When he heard a clock strike eleven he sprang from his seat, and grasping the hook with which he hoped to obtain his freedom firmly in his right hand, he again knelt before the door.

Not a sound broke the stillness of the night. He set to work vigorously, and struck the hook into the stone. A cloud of white dust flew from it, he raised his weapon again, when the noise of a footstep fell upon his ear.

He paused and listened. It was a slow, regular step, like that of a sentry on guard. He did not move, but waited patiently till the sound had passed, till it had grown faint, till it had become inaudible.

This was a most unfortunate circumstance. It required all his skill and address to baffle his janitors.

One false step and all his schemes were scattered like leaves before the autumn blast.

He felt sick at heart. There was a haze before his eyes, and horrible lights flickering, and strange noises murmuring.

Something seemed to be swinging to and fro inside his head like the pendulum of a clock; big drops of perspiration oozed from his temples.

He was now very well assured that the corridor was watched by both day and night, and it was therefore impossible to force the door without running the risk of discovery—it was impossible to enter the chapel without being seen.

He was baffled, and could have cried in the agony of his despair.

He must resort to some other means.

He felt his way back to his seat, and sat there till the grey light of morning shed its cold wan rays into his cell.

The light, ghastly as it was, appeared to inspire him with strength and hope, for he now rose, drove the hook back into the wall, removed the white dust which was scattered on the floor, and, suspending his bed to the hooks on each side of the cell like a hammock, flung himself upon it, and, wore out with watching throughout the livelong night, fell into a sound sleep.

His first night's experience had not inspired him with much hope; on the contrary, it had almost driven him to despair; but there is an old saying, that a drowning man will catch at a straw, and Chudley, despite the difficulties that were in the way, still clung tenaciously to his fondly-cherished scheme.

The turnkeys in attendance on him observed nothing remarkable in the demeanour of No. 9, except that he was always occupied with his books; so busy was he with them that he hardly honoured the prison officials with even a cursory glance when any one of them entered his cell.

This was most remarkable in a man of his class, and the officials could not help noticing this.

"He's a queer sort of customer," said one—"one of the oddest chaps I ever came across. I sometimes think he hasn't got his right change."

"Ah! don't you run away with that idea," said another turnkey. "He's a jolly sight more artful than people suppose."

"Well, but the fellow takes such strange fancies. Sometimes at his books, sometimes he's writing away like mad, and yesterday he wanted parcels and big sheets of white paper, because he must try his hand at drawing. I suppose he thinks himself a sort of genius."

"That man is a mystery," said the deputy governor, joining the men, "but more knave than fool—mind you that. Keep your eyes well upon him."

It is possible, despite the difficulties and impediments in the way, that Giles Chudley would have succeeded in making his escape had it not been for one circumstance, which proved fatal to him.

It was this.

In the same prison was confined a man who was charged with piracy and murder on the high seas. He was a ruffian of the most pronounced type, and if report spoke truly he had committed no end of atrocities; but report, we must remember, is not always to be relied on.

Nevertheless the nautical miscreant was most unquestionably a bad lot.

Upon being brought to the gaol he gave himself all the airs and graces of a West-end swell, and found fault with everything and everybody.

He said the cell in which he was confined was dripping with wet, and gave him the ague. He was in consequence of this transferred to the cell next to the ill-fated Giles Chudley.

After being immured in this a few days, he said it was worse than the other.

The turnkeys were sick of listening to the man's complaints. At length he said he wanted to see the governor.

"Oh, you want to see the governor, do you?" said the turnkey in attendance, with an air of irony. "What do you want to see him for? Make him apply to her Majesty for better dinners, I suppose?"

"Don't you be so cheeky, young fellow," observed the pirate, "'cos it's no use your trying to bullyrag me. Never mind what I want to see him for, that's my business. I can see him if I like—I read it in the rules; o you shut up. If you don't go and tell him I'll report ou."

"I never said I wouldn't tell him, did I?" and the turnkey as he banged the door in a rage.

"I ain't a-goin' to stand any of their nonsense," muttered the pirate. "I know what discipline is, an' I'll see it enforced, if needs be."

"Well, No. 8, what is the matter now?" said the governor, at he entered. "Anything amiss with this cell?"

"I don't much like it. 'Cos why—I can't get any sleep o' nights."

"Indeed! Not well, I suppose; you had better let the doctor see you."

"I don't want no doctor—I want peace and quietness."

"And I hope you have both."

"No, I aint. There's some of your men at work in the yard below all the blessed night, and I can't sleep for the noise."

"Eh!" ejaculated the governor. "Indeed—men at work all night; that's contrary to my orders."

"Well, all I know is, they are there. All night they are a-scratching and a-scratching, like a lot of big rats."

"I think I know who it is," remarked the governor, in a careless manner. "Just under the window here, isn't it?"

"Yes, that's where it is—the exact spot."

"Ah, the vagabonds, they will work out of hours and disturb people. I'll see and put a stop to them. When do they begin—about dusk?"

"Some little time after nightfall, and they go on till it's light. I never hear it in the day time."

"I am glad you have spoken of this, my man. You won't hear it again. If you do send for me."

"All right, and thank you," returned the pirate.

Seven days had elapsed since the night on which Giles first began putting into practice his plan of escape. On the eighth day the prisoner was still in bed, although it was half-past ten o'clock. He was aroused by the unlocking and opening of his door, but he did not move from his hammock.

He was a little surprised, however, upon beholding the governor, accompanied by two turnkeys, enter the cell.

The governor, who, like most governors of prisons, was a retired military officer, and on this occasion he was arrayed in his best uniform, looked more than usually severe and imposing. He twirled his heavy iron-gray moustache, and glanced suspiciously around the cell.

"You are taking it easy," he observed, addressing the prisoner. "Do you not know, sir—and if you do not it is time that you did—that to be in bed at this hour is against the rules and regulations?"

"I know it, sir," said Giles, springing out of his hammock, and muddling on his clothes, "but I doan't feel at all well, and ha' had very little sleep all night."

"Oh, that I can readily believe," observed the governor, in a tone of sarcasm. "Not well—eh? Perhaps you are over-fatigued."

Chudley was greatly alarmed at this last observation.

"Eh, do you hear, my man?" inquired the governor.

"I don't see how that can be. I aint had nuffin' to tire me," returned Giles.

"Haven't you? Well, there may be other reasons."

At a signal from their chief the two turnkeys proceeded to search the bed-clothes with great care. They also searched the clothes the prisoner had on, and those lying on his stool (for he was but partially dressed).

They found nothing, however, to excite their suspicions.

The governor was evidently disappointed.

"No instrument or weapon of any sort," he murmured.

"No, sir, nothing. Nor do we miss anything from the cell."

The governor, who had been standing with his arms behind him in a Napoleon-like attitude, appeared to be lost in reflection.

While the examination of the garments had been taking place he watched the countenance of the prisoner with the eyes of a lynx. He had succeeded in intercepting one furtive glance.

"Umph! You miss nothing, eh?" said he.

"No, sir."

"How about the hasp to the window?" The turnkeys looked astonished when they found that it was not in its proper place.

"It must be concealed somewhere, and has been taken away for a specific purpose. What that purpose is we can readily guess."

Giles Chudley felt as if about to faint.

"What have you done with the hasp?" said the governor to the prisoner.

"Me, I aint seen nuffin' of it; somebody must ha' taken it away afore I came here."

The governor shook his head.

"No, my man," he said, "that story won't do. It is concealed somewhere, I have no doubt."

The turnkeys turned over all the things and made another search, which was as fruitless as the first.

Their chief contemplated the window with some curiosity.

"Can't one of you climb up to that?" he inquired.

"Yes, sir, certainly; that's easily managed," returned one, who, addressing his companion, said, "give us a back, Jewett."

The latter obeyed, and the other of the turnkeys, who was the lighter of the two, sprang upon his comrade's back and clambered up to the window.

The panes were made of fluted glass, which were very difficult to see through. In addition to this a louvre light, or "copper light," as the prisoners call them, was hung before the window.

It was a great shade made of galvanised iron, which prevented the prisoner from seeing anything else even when the window was opened.

This, however, was never allowed. There was an express rule and punishment for climbing up to the window. The prisoners had to content themselves with the mouthful of fresh air per day which was admitted by the grating.

It must, however, be admitted that there was abundance of air for them as a rule. There is seldom or never any reason for complaint as far as ventilation is concerned.

"Search the louvre light!" said the governor, and he looked Giles Chudley hard in the face as he gave this order. At the same time he twisted his moustache with a sort of malicious hilarity.

Chudley's knees knocked together.

The turnkey drew forth the hasp, which he held forth triumphantly. It had been chipped at the end, and was covered with dirt. It had evidently been used on the prison stones.

AVELINE GATLIFFE AND MISS JAMBLIN ARE HANDED OUT OF THE BOAT.

The governor tapped at the wall with his Malacca cane. After two or three minutes' sounding he came upon a part of the wall which yielded to his stick. Both the turnkeys sprang forward and grabbed at it with their hands.

Giles Chudley fell upon his stool, and, covering his face with his hands, groaned aloud.

An opening in the wall was discovered almost large enough to admit a man.

The hole had been pasted over with sheets of white drawing paper, smeared with prison gruel, which made admirable glue; and these, when powdered over with the white dust of the stone, became not an imitation but a *fac simile*.

No. 35.

An exclamation of surprise proceeded from the turnkeys and their chief.

"Ah!" exclaimed the latter, "we now know the reason for the pirate being so disturbed at night. This is no more than I expected. We have made the discovery in good time."

"It has been cleverly managed, sir," observed one of the turnkeys.

"Certainly, very clever indeed; but all is of no avail."

The three prison officials, however, could not refrain from admiring the masterpiece of industry and art. They remained for some time examining the aperture in the wall.

Presently the governor turned towards Chudley, who sat on his little stool the very personification of despair, and said in a severe tone—

"Since you have been under my charge you have had every indulgence it was possible for me to give, consistent with my duty as governor of this prison. What return have you made for this? The answer is but too apparent. With the basest ingratitude for all the kindness shown to you, without the slightest consideration for me, you have striven secretly to effect your escape. Had you succeeded I should have been disgraced and severely censured. You are a worthless fellow."

"I be sorry for what I ha' done, and ask you to forgive me, but for all that I be doubly sorry that I ha' bin found out. Liberty is sweet, but it aint o' no jouse talking about that now," returned Chudley.

"I will take good care another such an opportunity is not afforded you. Henceforth you will be confined in a stronger and more commodious cell, and I warn you not to make another attempt to escape; indeed, it will be my duty to see you have no chance of doing so. Dogs that bite us when we fondle them must go to dirty kennels and rusty chains. Dixon, you have your orders."

The turnkey touched his cap, and said "Yes, sir."

"And see that my instructions are attended to. The prisoner is a dangerous character; he has the cunning of the serpent. Keep watch and ward over him. Do you understand?"

"He shall be well looked after, sir."

The governor turned upon his heel, and strode majestically out of the cell.

Chudley did not seem to be aware that the prison's chief had taken his departure.

The wretched man sat on his stool almost in a state of stupefaction.

He had drained the cup of bitterness to the very dregs, and did not appear to care what became of him. The misery that had fallen on him was supreme and overpowering.

The turnkeys spoke to him, but he did not answer or take any notice of what they said.

One stepped forward, and shook him roughly by the shoulder.

"Now, then, get up and stir your stumps. Do you hear?" he exclaimed.

"Oh, aye, I hear. You mun ha' it all your own way. What do 'e want me to be after?"

"Get up, man, and follow us," was the answer.

"It doan't much matter where I be; one place is as good as the other," he answered, rising from his seat, and casting a woe-begone look round his narrow prison-house.

He was so broken down that he hardly had strength enough to follow his janitors from the cell.

They took him down a flight of steps through a yard.

In this yard was a covered building fitted up with little cells, each of which contained a crank and a prisoner.

Chudley heaved a deep-drawn sigh, and passed his hands across his eyes, which were filled with tears.

The turnkeys retained him there for a few minutes to see the prisoners at work, and then conducted him to a corner of the yard in which there were two iron doors.

One of these was unlocked, and he was forcibly thrust into a low, damp cell, the walls of which were covered with damp, and which emitted a cold, earthly smell, as if it now tasted the sun and fresh air for the first time.

It was in a cell similar to the one in which he now found himself that the pirate had been confined previous to his being transferred to the one next to the cell Chudley had just left.

He sat down upon the rough stones, with his elbows on his knees and his face in his hands.

He remembered then that he had been within a few hours of liberty—he had been robbed of his life when he had almost grasped it with his hands.

The thought was agony, and he uttered a low, plaintive cry.

Besides this, he had seen his fellow-prisoners at work; he had seen how they obeyed the orders of men who spoke to them, not with words, but with gestures and with bells.

He knew his life in the prison had been one of indulgence and comparative luxury, when contrasted to the poor wretches he had seen in this part of the gaol.

Their infamous dress, their white faces, their servile compliance, had filled him with terror and dismay.

Hope—the last solace of the wretched—seemed to suddenly take wings and fly away.

He looked up at the window, which was little less than one great iron bar; he sounded the walls, so thick and strong; he breathed the air of his new cell, and it chilled him to the bone.

"Am I to remain in this miserable place?" he inquired.

"Yes, until your trial comes on," replied one of the turnkeys. "Don't blame us; it's all your own fault."

"But if I promise to remain quiet and behave better?"

"The governor won't believe you. It aint likely, I should say."

"But I will promise. Tell him to be merciful. I be sorry for what I ha' done."

"No good your saying that. He's lost faith in you. You've nobody but yourself to blame."

Chudley groaned and said no more.

The door was shut with a loud bang, the lock was turned, and the prisoner was alone.

Two hours afterwards, when the turnkeys came in with his dinner of gaol soup and his prison bread, they found him crouched in the farthest corner of the cell, gnawing his hands, and uttering low groans.

He was also trembling all over, and his eyes had a lack-lustre vacant expression like those of a madman.

They exchanged glances and shook their heads, and when the prisoner was shut in again they threw out hints that he might endeavour to commit suicide.

To say the truth, they were not very far out in their reckoning; Chudley had thoughts of suicide at that time, but he had not the means to put it into practice.

CHAPTER LXIX.

AT BROXBRIDGE HALL—THE EARL AND HIS LAWYER.

"I SUPPOSE you have heard the news, my lord," said

Mr. Wrench to Earl Ethalwood, "the prisoner, Chudley, has attempted to escape."

"Indeed!" exclaimed the earl, in a tone of surprise. "No I have not heard anything about it till this moment; but I hope and trust he was not successful."

"No; it was discovered only just in time. A few hours later and he would in all probability have succeeded."

"Miserably-guilty wretch!" ejaculated the earl. "Give me the full particulars.

Mr. Wrench entered into a detailed description of the events which have been described in the previous chapter. When he had concluded he said—

"It is a pretty convincing proof that the prisoner is guilty, and will prejudice self in the eyes of the judge and jury."

"Ah, no doubt; but the evidence is conclusive, and cannot lead but to one conclusion. What say you?"

"Yes, it is pretty clear for the matter of that; but one never knows what may take place—juries sometimes take such singular freaks in their heads. From what I have been able to gather, Mr. Slapperton is going to offer evidence to prove an alibi."

"Which he will fail in doing. Take my word for it, Mr. Wrench, this as well as other rumours we have heard have not truth for their basis. The man is guilty enough. My brother magistrates agree with me in that opinion. As to Slapperton, he is not worth notice. He's a noisy wrangler, who is bent upon making as much display as possible for the purpose of gaining popularity; and in this respect it is just possible that he has succeeded to a certain extent. There are, and I suppose always will be, a certain class of persons who admire a blatant, unscrupulous lawyer."

"Oh, there can be no question about that, my lord —none whatever," returned the detective.

"I am glad you agree with me in this. Well, we acted wisely, I think, in committing the prisoner without any adjournment. I do not hold with protracted examinations. It has been truly remarked that, under the old system, an inquiry into a criminal charge before a magistrate was less an investigation of the entire circumstances of the case than an examination of the prisoner. Certain broad facts were stated, certain leading witnesses were examined, and the prisoner was then requested to explain himself. In serious cases he was closely and sharply questioned; and abundant testimony as to this practice may be found by turning to the newspaper reports of the proceedings before the magistrates in the *cause célèbre* of the murder at Gill's Hill. Thurtell, Hunt, and Probert, being suspected of the murder of Mr. Weare, were examined by the bench as to their complicity, and, their evidence being considered unsatisfactory, they were duly committed for trial."

"I am not able to speak from my own personal knowledge," said Mr. Chicknell, "as it was before my time; but I have carefully read the reports of the case, and I may say that it is much to be regretted that the practice of questioning the prisoner has been discontinued. Now we always treat great criminals with so much consideration and deference that they must not be annoyed, or their feelings hurt by being asked questions. The modern system is virtually to induce the prisoner to hold his tongue very tenaciously indeed, while the lawyers are encouraged to be as discursive and verbose as they please. The value of the evidence one way or the other is heavily discounted. The real facts of the case get mixed up in an inextricable tangle, heavy expense is entailed on the country, and almost ruinous costs are incurred by the prisoner."

"But what sense is there in these forensic wrangles?" said the earl.

"They may be, and doubtless are, very fine sport to the legal gentlemen engaged in the case, but they are essentially futile, and in the end are detrimental to the interests of justice."

"There is hardly an instance of a case being heard without them," said the detective. "Of course it is not my business to comment on the practice in these cases, but I have been compelled to listen with exemplary patience to wordy passages of arms between astute and sometimes irate barristers and witnesses quite as cunning of fence, but better able to keep their temper."

"You are a martyr, Wrench—a suffering martyr," exclaimed Chicknell, bursting out into a laugh, in which the earl joined.

"I don't put it so strong as that, sir. It is the magistrate who is the martyr. He is bound to sit patiently while a multitude of perfectly irrelevant matters are introduced, discussed, and squabbled over. It is as clear as noonday that his decision cannot be influenced one way or the other by these interminable debates; still the lawyers, being paid to talk like Mr. Slapperton, are praiseworthily anxious to earn their fees."

"But touching this man—the prisoner, Chudley," inquired the earl, bringing the discussion to an end— "he will be well looked after now, I suppose; more rigid measures will be adopted by the prison authorities?"

"Oh, there is not the least doubt of that, my lord. There will not be the most remote possibility of his effecting his escape."

"He appears to be a much more acute, daring fellow than we were led to suppose."

"The skill, perseverance, and ingenuity he has displayed have surprised everybody," answered the detective, who, after some further conversation, took his departure.

"And now Mr. Chicknell," said the earl, shortly after Wrench had left, "in dealing with the Larchgrove murder I am actuated by a sense of justice and my duty to the public as a magistrate. There is a private matter which more immediately concerns me—doubtless you will be able to guess what this is."

"You allude to your grand-daughter, I presume," observed the lawyer, in an undertone.

"Precisely—you guess rightly; but the matter rests more specially with the young man she was imprudent and indiscreet enough to marry."

Mr. Chicknell nodded. He thought that was the safest course to adopt, very well knowing to what his client's observations were tending.

"I say again the matter rests more with this young engineer—this—ahem, Gatliffe."

The attorney nodded again.

"You see, Chicknell," said the other in a confidential tone, "I really don't think matters can go on thus. There is an imperative necessity to bring them to an issue. Aveline is now—if I may make use of the term —naturalised; she feels her position—is proud of it, and has, I hope, nothing to regret—she certainly ought not to; but still something remains to be done, not only to secure her fealty to me, but happiness for herself."

"Happiness?" repeated the lawyer.

"Certainly, Mr. Chicknell; most undoubtedly— happiness, contentment, peace of mind, or whatever other term you may choose to make use of to convey my meaning. We will not quarrel about words, which, after all, are but signs or symbols for the expression of ideas, passions, or sentiments."

"I understand your meaning. Pray proceed, my lord."

"Well, then, to begin with. I, as you already know, have placed my grand-daughter under the charge of an accomplished lady, who has so well instructed her that she is now well versed in all the usages of good society. So much so, indeed, that she is pretty generally acknowledged to be, if not a highly-cultivated, certainly a well-bred young woman."

"No one in the world would attempt to dispute that, my lord."

"This being so, it is desirable that she should never have the chance to return to her husband, or any of his associates. Consequently, a legal separation is an imperative necessity."

When the earl had come to this part of his discourse he regarded his companion with a look which seemed to pierce him through.

"Ah," murmured the lawyer to himself, "he's boring at the old subject."

"Do you hear what I say? An imperative necessity!"

"Certainly, my lord. The chief question is, how it is to be accomplished."

"It is easy enough if set about in a proper manner. Have you seen this young Gatliffe?"

"I have, more than once."

"Well, and did you make any proposition to him? Did you carry out my expressed desire?"

"I did, my lord."

"With what result?"

"He seems to me to be perfectly indifferent. He is quite willing to resign all claim to his wife; but, to say the truth, he is so strangely altered, so utterly broken down and apathetic, if I may so term it, that——"

"Well, what? Speak unreservedly, Chicknell."

"That I pitied him."

"Bah!" exclaimed the earl, in a tone of ineffable disgust. "Pity, indeed!"

"You told me to speak unreservedly," observed Chicknell.

"Ah, true, I had forgot. Well, you have done so. But now to business. Will he consent to a separation?"

"Certainly; he has told me that."

"Aveline has many admirers. It would afford me great pleasure to see her united to some scion of the aristocracy—somebody in her own sphere. This is my most earnest desire, and this is sure to come to pass if she can be released from the odious bonds which bear so heavily upon her."

"If she desires to marry again we must obtain a divorce."

"Precisely; that is what I desire."

"Ah, that's another matter," observed the lawyer. "It can only be obtained upon one or more of these pleas—cruelty, adultery, or desertion."

"Well, can't you plead one of these?"

"Yes, but we have to offer sufficient proof, and this we are unable to do, as far as I can see at present."

"Hang it, Chicknell, surely there must be some way of getting over this difficulty?" exclaimed the earl, in a tone of irritation. "It must be done."

"I don't see how. Certainly it would be an unopposed suit. Gatliffe would not offer any objection."

"I will settle a handsome annuity on him for the remainder of his life. Tell him that."

"I have done so."

"And what said he?"

"It is not a money question. Virtually he has given up all claim to his wife, and he is willing to resign her legally, but he will not receive one shilling for so doing. There is a great deal of chivalrous spirit about him, which, I must tell you frankly, I greatly admire; but chivalry is one thing, and the law of England is another. You, as a magistrate, must be perfectly aware of this."

"I have no belief in the chivalry of a person of his class; but we are not here to discuss fanciful and fabulous forms of chivalry. You must obtain a divorce at any cost—mind you that."

Mr. Chicknell laughed.

"You are very positive, my lord," he observed. "I suppose you would not like me to manufacture evidence, as it is termed."

"Certainly not. The end can be obtained by some other means; only I tell you again, Aveline must be released from the tie which is, to say the truth, the very bane of her existence."

"I will consult my partner, and determine how to take action in the suit. I will then communicate with your lordship."

"Enough. So let the matter rest for the present. But pray hurry on the matter at as early a day as possible."

"And now, Chicknell, having arranged this business thus far, let us return to the prisoner Chudley. The assizes will soon be on, and the case will be taken as early as possible. You know, I suppose, that Miss Jamblin has been staying with us—the reason for this being change of scene. Aveline is very partial to her, and I think it best that they should be out of the way when the Larchgrove-lane murder case comes before the court; and I have arranged that they should both go to my house in the metropolis, and stay there till this painful business is over. Chudley will of course be convicted."

"I should suppose so, but I will not answer for it, as Wrench says—and he has had a pretty good insight into matters of this sort. Juries take such strange crotchets in their heads. Still it is fair to assume that he will be convicted."

"In any case the two young ladies had better be out of the way."

While the foregoing conversation was taking place in the reception-room of the grand old hall, Patty Jamblin and Aveline were in the pleasure grounds.

They had for a companion and protector a Mr. Frank Wrexford, son of Sir Mathew Wrexford, the baronet from whose house Henry Adolphus was coming on the night of the murder.

Patty, pale, silent, and thoughtful, was no longer the sprightly, mirthful girl, who had been the light and life of Stoke Ferry Farm, but she had greatly improved in health and strength since she had been at the Hall.

Young Wrexford, who was an Oxford oarsman, persuaded the young ladies to permit him to give them a row on the lake in the pleasure grounds of Broxbridge. While plying his oars he kept up an animated conversation, told them a number of amusing anecdotes, and paid marked attention to the earl's grand-daughter, who, however, did not appear to offer him any encouragement.

Aveline, like a true Ethalwood, was proud, and it was not every one she took to.

The boat sped on over the glassy surface of the lake.

"I should like to see you both in better spirits," said Wrexford; "but past events, I suppose."

"It is hardly worth while, or, indeed, prudent, to

refer to past events," cried Aveline. "Let us look to the future."

"Ah! that is always the wisest course. The past is out of your reach, and cannot be recalled; the future may bring us unclouded sunshine, and a recompense for the past."

"I am sure it's very kind of you to take compassion on us, poor creatures," observed Miss Jamblin, hardly knowing very well what to say.

"It is a pleasure—an indulgence—on your part to trust yourselves with so poor a waterman as myself," returned the young man; "but say when you would like to go on shore."

The ladies said they were in no hurry, and in about half an hour after this the boat was put in shore. The rower held the prow, and offered his arm to each lady as they alighted. He then left them to pay his respects to the master of Broxbridge.

"He's very nice—isn't he?" said Patty to her companion.

"Pretty well—middling," returned Aveline.

"I do not quite understand all he says," observed Miss Jamblin.

"Oh, you'll understand his fine speeches and metaphors in good time—that is if you know him long enough. He's well enough, but not altogether my sort."

"Why, what's the matter with him?" inquired the unsophisticated farmer's daughter.

"I don't know that there's anything particular the matter with him, but he's artificial, that's all."

Henry Adolphus now came into the grounds and informed his young mistress that the earl wished to speak to her and Miss Jamblin.

Both young ladies hastened into the hall.

CHAPTER LXX.

THE TRIAL AND CONVICTION OF THE LARCHGROVE-LANE MURDERER—THE PLEA OF WITCHCRAFT.

THE day at length arrived upon which Giles Chudley was to be tried, and there were many who believed he would get off. The court was crowded to excess, and when the prisoner entered the dock those who had known him in an earlier day were astounded at the miserable appearance he presented.

His features were lined, thin, and haggard, and he was but a shadow of his former self. Nevertheless, he strove to bear up bravely under the terrible ordeal.

To use a common but expressive phrase, "you might have heard a pin drop" when the counsel for the prosecution rose to open the case.

He did so in a fair, impartial, and masterly manner, neither stepping to the right nor the left, to dwell unnecessarily on the leading facts, either for or against the prisoner.

Whatever opinion we may form of wrangling attorneys, third or and fourth-rate barristers, who, in many cases, are so particularly pertinacious and obtrusive in inquiries at our police-courts, there can be but one in respect to a leading counsel, whose business it is to conduct the prosecution, or who is retained for the defence upon the trial of a prisoner for a capital offence. The arguments on both sides are pretty generally fine specimens of calm and subtle reasoning of cultivated intellects.

And we have no reason to complain of the judges of our land. If there is one thing Englishmen have to be proud of, it is the wisdom and honesty of their judges.

We need not go over the case again. It will suffice to declare that as it was presented before the judge and jury at the assizes, it was much stronger and more compact and complete than when heard before the bench of magistrates. There were two additional witnesses whose testimony corroborated those who had already been heard in respect to the prisoner's identity.

Mr. Slapperton instructed counsel, and he was greatly hurt at the latter not entering more fully into his favourite plea of mistaken identity; but the gentleman retained for the defence had too good a knowledge of law to allow himself to be dictated to by a provincial attorney.

Two men were brought from London as witnesses for the defence.

They swore positively that the prisoner was in their company in the metropolis on the night the murder was committed.

They were two unprincipled scoundrels who had been produced by Alf Purvis and Laura Stanbridge to perjure themselves, in the hope that they might save the prisoner from the dreadful fate that awaited him.

Nobody in court believed one word they said, and their testimony was rather prejudicial than otherwise; but Mr. Slapperton would insist upon their being called.

Many of my readers will remember that a similar course was adopted in the Muller case.

Two women swore that he was in their company on the evening upon which Mr. Briggs was murdered.

There was not a shadow of truth in their statement, and, as in Chudley's case, nobody believed them.

The counsel for the defence, seeing that the question of Chudley's identity was fairly established, had no other course left open to him than to strive, by every means in his power, to reduce the crime to manslaughter.

He argued, therefore, that a quarrel had taken place in the lane between the prisoner and the murdered man; that the latter had struck him several blows with his riding whip (the prisoner's cut lip and the loss of two of his teeth established this fact), and that, after this assault, Chudley caught hold of a hedgestake, with which he defended himself.

This, under all the circumstances, was the best defence that could have been made, and it caused the jury to deliberate one hour and a half before they delivered their verdict.

It is possible it would have had the desired effect had it not been for the murdered man's throat being cut.

At the expiration of the time already mentioned the jury returned into the box.

Upon being asked by the clerk, "How say you, gentlemen? Do you find the prisoner guilty or not guilty?"

"We find him guilty," answered the foreman. "Guilty of wilful murder."

"And that is the verdict of you all?"

"It is."

The prisoner was asked if he had anything to say before sentence was passed upon him, when to the surprise of those assembled in court he entered into a long rambling statement, which, to say the truth, was little else than a specimen of ignorance, stupidity, and bigotry.

He said that he was not guilty of wilful murder—that a "cunning woman," whom he declared to be a witch, had cast her spells upon him, and that she, and she alone, was answerable for the crime that had been committed.

The gist of his argument was that he was bewitched, and was therefore in no way a free agent.

He, however, admitted that he had slain his young

master, who was, as well as himself, under the spell of the person whom he was pleased to call a witch.

The judge said that it was difficult to conceive that at the present period such gross ignorance could exist. He besought the wretched man to prepare for the fate that awaited him, and passed sentence in the usual manner, which Chudley listened to with the utmost composure.

No one had anticipated that Chudley would put forth such a miserable plea in the vain endeavour to cover his guilt.

But it is in vain for us to endeavour to conceal the fact that the belief in the supernatural exists still to a large extent in the country towns and villages of England.

Our ancestors, even up to the commencement of the eighteenth century, were strong believers in the existence of witchcraft, and it is not surprising that they were so, for it is a fact our ancient law-books are full of decisions and trials upon the subject.

All histories refer to the exploits of these instruments of darkness, and the testimony of all ages, not merely of the rude and barbarous, but of the most enlightened and polished, give accounts of these strange performances.

We have the attestation of thousands of eye and ear witnesses, and those not of the easily-deceived judges only, but of wise and grave discerners.

Standing accounts had been kept of well-attested relations.

Laws in most nations have been enacted against practices in witchcraft. Those among the Jews and our own cases have been determined by judges, who, as regards other legal matters, are revered, and their names handed down to us as legal oracles and sages, and to all appearance upon the clearest and most decisive evidence, and thousands in our own nation as well as others have suffered death for their vile compacts.

Those who are labouring, either as individuals or in social institutions, to raise the level and improve the tone of life among the mass of the people, are repeatedly confronted by disheartening evidence that gross superstition and ignorant credulity still exist amongst us to a lamentable extent.

Even comfortable farmers with their wives and children, small shopkeepers in the country towns, and working men and women in large towns, are to be found among the dupes of fortune-tellers and witchfinders.

Whether, through the agency of School Boards, education will reach down deeper into society than it does at present the next generation must show; but nothing less than mental improvement, whether by school, by healthy literature, or other agencies, will cure the evil.

It is a few years over the century and a half since the last execution for the "crime of witchcraft" took place in these islands.

Caithness was the scene of this legal murder, and the victim was a miserable old woman, who was done to death by order and warrant of David Ross, sheriff of the shire.

It was the last tragedy of something like four thousand, for this is the computation of those who were sacrificed to Caledonian superstition between the Act of Queen Mary "Anentis Witchcraftes" in 1563, and the final brutality perpetrated in 1722.

We are assured, indeed, that the glamour of the ancient necromancy has not yet died out among our northern neighbours. Just before the rebellion of '45 the Dissenters published an Act of Presbytery, formally denouncing the repeal of the penal statutes against witchcraft as "contrary to the express law of God," and the reason of all the misfortunes that afflicted the nation.

It is curious, by the way, to note how prominent priests and preachers have been in battling the magicians, and with what particular ferocity of spirit they urged the crusade.

While the Popes invoked the tortures of the Inquisition and promulgated the famous *Malleus Maleficarum*, or "Hammer for Witches," the clergy after as well as before the Reformation took their cue from the persecuting Pontiffs.

Even in the United States they led the merciless war against the children of Satan, and pious fanatics, like Cotton Mather and the minister of Salem, were guilty, with the best intent, of barbarities unspeakable.

We find it boldly stated by the author of the "Waverley Anecdotes," that the doctrine urged by the Dissenting Presbytery in the time of the Young Pretender is still taught from the same pulpits, and believed in by the far larger number of their adherents.

This appears very startling. But it is quite explicit, as is the further allegation that a belief in witches prevails even at the present enlightened period among the lower orders in Scotland, "whatever may be their religious persuasion."

This is a strange and scarcely credible character of a canny, shrewd, and hardheaded race. However, the land of Ossian has been an eerie place from remote ages. In this region of mists and mountains the very atmosphere favours *diablerie*, and fosters the supernatural.

Shakespeare's terrible trio will keep Scotland and sorcery linked in deathless association long after the lingering faith of the credulous shall have died out like the credulities that have waxed, waned, and faded ever since mankind had intelligence enough to colour with poetry the harsh and bare realities of life.

Scotchmen claim King David as a compatriot; they have as good a right to the Witch of Endor. Probably, if the truth were known, they are not singular in their superstitious conservatism. It is not yet a hundred years since a witch was burnt at Glarus, in Switzerland.

In the year of the great French Revolution a judicial execution for witchcraft took place in the Grand Duchy of Posen.

Here in England we did better and worse. We stopped hanging witches half-a-dozen years sooner than the Scotchmen.

But it is only sixteen years ago since we drowned a reputed wizard in a pond at Hedingham, in Essex.

It has been our aim throughout this work to give the reader a faithful view of certain sections of society as they exist at the present time.

Superstition is still rife in the land, and Chudley's plea is but an average sample of the ignorance and bigotry which still exist.

As a proof of this, we cite the following case which was heard only a few weeks ago at the East Dereham Petty Sessions :—

A young man named William Bulwer, of Etlinggreen, was charged with assaulting Christiana Martins, a young girl living near the Etling-green toll-bar.

The complainant said that Bulwer came to the tollhouse, abused her with language of the foulest description, and struck her with a stick, without any provocation from her. Defendant, called upon to account for his conduct, told the magistrates that complainant's mother, Mrs. Martins, was a witch, that she had charmed him so that he got no sleep from her for three nights.

He went on, " One night, at half-past eleven o'clock, I got up because I could not sleep, and went out and found a 'walking toad' under a clod that had been dug up with a three-pronged fork. That is why I could not rest; she put this toad there to charm me, and I got no rest night nor day till I found this 'walking toad' under the turf. I got the toad out and put it in a cloth, and took it upstairs and showed it to my mother, who threw it into the pit in the garden."

The witness further informed the bench that the witch " went round this here 'walking toad' after she had buried it, and I could not sleep."

Her daughter he believed to be as bad as the mother, and hence his natural indignation, loss of temper, and act of violence. Their worships appear to have been taken seriously aback by this extraordinary story.

The chairman asked the police superintendent if he knew the witness and could answer for his sanity. Superintendent Symonds answered that he could do so with perfect confidence.

Mr. Bulwer may be a thoroughly rational being in all other matters save witchcraft, and he even here is quite coherent from his own point of view and according to his lights. It was in grim earnestness of conviction that he denounced as " bad enough to do anything" the witch who had the wickedness " to go and put the walking toad in the hole, like that, for a man which never did nothing to her."

We have no doubt, moreover, that the defendant expressed his sincere opinion when he declared that Miss Martins' mother was " not fit to live," because she " looks at lots of people, and she will do some one harm."

Clearly Mr. Bulwer sees in Mrs. Martins a sorceress endowed with the awful gift of the evil eye, a baleful glance from which is potent enough to sour the milk or spoil the butter, to blight an infant from beauty and health into a puny changeling, and even to sow the seeds of slow decay in the robust frame of manhood.

Mr. Bulwer very properly resents the disposition of this enchantress to exercise her diabolical spells upon him, and if he were allowed to take the law into his own hands we should in all likelihood find him adopting an old-fashioned and summary mode of self-protection.

It will hardly cure a rooted belief, such as that by which this yokel is possessed, to fine him twelve and sixpence for assaulting a witch's daughter.

Moreover, the magisterial decision, besides displaying an irritating indifference to the danger in which he stands, must seem doubly harsh to this young man, since it was imposed in face of his offer to bring the " walking toad" into court as evidence for the defence.

The brick which proved the house Jack Cade lived in was not more conclusive testimony.

This case of witchcraft at Etling-green will appear the more remarkable if we just apply a brief comparison.

The last execution for witchcraft in England was that of a Mrs. Hicks and her daughter, aged nine, who were hanged at Huntingdon in 1716 for selling their souls to the devil, and raising a storm by pulling off their stockings and raising a lather of soap.

This was the sort of diabolism those weird sisters used to work, and such was the machinery they used.

Thus, in the two most frightful cases of witch-torturing in Scotland—those of Janet Comphat and Bettie Laing—the overt act was of a kind to raise more than a doubt of the sanity of those who believed it.

The Pittenweem witch, Beatrix Laing, after many a Walpurgis and much riding of broomsticks with impunity, ordered nails from a blacksmith named Patrick Mourton.

Being otherwise occupied, he refused to make them, whereupon she went off muttering. A week afterwards the honest blacksmith, passing the old woman's door with another man, saw a vessel with water outside the threshold.

In this vessel there was a burning coal, and the dreadful portent striking the terrified Mourton with an impression that it was a charm being wrought against him, he concluded, in the vein of William Bulwer, that the witch was not fit to live.

So he gave information, and Beatrix Laing, having been first tortured with the boots, the capsie-claws, the pilniewinks, and other instruments conducive to confession, was ultimately, by the ministers and magistrates, delivered over to the rabble, who had "three hours' sport" before they finally tormented the life out of her.

When we read of a parish, gathered, with the connivance of its clergy, to press a wretched old woman to death under a door, and then drive loaded waggons backward and forward over her body, on the suspicion that she has been, by demoniac arts, causing the crops to fail, the kine to perish, and the fair and happy to pine and die, it seems that the Christian Englishman of the First George was quite another being from his descendant of the Victoria era.

But this case of Martins v. Bulwer shows that there are good folk among us yet who believe in witchcraft, and would, if they had their way, make short work of its professors.

It was noticed that the sixty or seventy persons who lynched the suspected wizard in Essex, in 1863, were all of the small tradesmen class, not a single agricultural labourer being concerned in the tragedy.

Perhaps it is too soon to expect that a superstition which was gravely treated by a British monarch only two centuries earlier, and which fired judges like Sir Matthew Hale and jurists like Sir Thomas Browne to hang scores of women whose only crime was being old, ugly, eccentric, or morose, should have entirely disappeared from the masses of the population.

Nevertheless its existence, especially as William Bulwer betrayed it, is well worth the study of those social reformers who wish, as their cant has it, to exalt the people before correcting their ignorance.

That witchcraft in this country was believed in, and punishable by death, is borne out by our judicial statistics.

Barrington estimates that the judicial murders for witchcraft in England was thirty thousand in two hundred years.

Matthew Hopkins, the " witch finder," caused the judicial murder of about one hundred persons in Essex, Norfolk, and Suffolk, in 1645—7.

Sir Mathew Hale burnt two persons for witchcraft in 1664.

Northamptonshire and Huntingdonshire preserved the superstition about witchcraft later than any other counties. Seventeen or eighteen persons were burnt at St. Osyths, in Essex, about 1676; and two pretended witches were executed at Northampton, 1705, and five others seven years afterwards.

In 1716 Mrs. Hicks and her daughter, aged nine, as already stated, were hanged at Huntingdon for the same offence.

Credulity in witchcraft abounds in the country districts of England.

On the 4th of September, 1863, a poor old paralysed Frenchman died in consequence of being ducked as a wizard at Castle Hedingham, in Essex, and similar cases have occurred since that date.

CHAPTER LXXI.
THE LAST HOURS OF THE CONDEMNED.

THE wretched criminal, Giles Chudley, during the period which elapsed between his condemnation and execution, was deeply impressed with the awfulness of his position. He was, nevertheless, calm and composed.

The prison officials declared that he was remarkably docile, and exhibited a capacity and eagerness for instruction, which was singular in a man of his type. He was visited by his aged mother and sister, and the interview was, as may be readily imagined, of a painful character.

Throughout this terrible trial, however, he preserved his fortitude and resigned demeanour with a singular absence of excitement.

The chaplain of the gaol zealously continued his ministrations, and the unhappy man appeared to profit materially.

He was communicative to his spiritual adviser, and said that he was perfectly satisfied with the verdict of the jury and the sentence which had been passed upon him.

At the same time he declared that he should never have committed the crime for which he was about to suffer had it not been for the spell which had been cast upon him by the "cunning woman," who he declared was nothing more or less than a witch.

He said he was perfectly assured that he was in her power for months before the commission of the murder, that she it was who caused him to be in Dennett's-lane when Ellen Fulford met his young master.

Before that she had set Peace on to him, and it had always been a matter of surprise to him that she had not caused him to take Peace's life, which he believes he should have done had he not left Broxbridge so suddenly.

The superstition and bigotry of the man was one of his most remarkable characteristics.

There were a number of persons who sympathised with the unfortunate misguided man, and a petition was prepared by the industrious Mr. Slapperton, praying for a respite of the culprit.

As is usual in cases of this description a goodly array of signatures was attached to the document in question.

It was not, however, deemed advisable to make Chudley acquainted with the efforts which were being made on his behalf—efforts which, it would perhaps be needless to say, were entirely futile.

The petitions of this nature almost invariably follow a conviction for a capital offence.

It is astonishing how illogically and irrationally some persons reason upon the punishment of death.

We have one broad fact to deal with—namely, that all that a man hath he will give for his life; that no fear can operate on him like the fear of death; that every man calculates upon the chapter of accidents bringing up something in his favour as long as he lives and breathes; and, in fact, the words which Shakespeare put into the mouth of Claudio are not more eloquent than true.

Remove this powerful deterrent, or restrict its operation, and we must be prepared for very mixed results.

At the present time each case is taken on its merits, and the chances are that no man is ever hung now for what is understood to be "murder of a second class."

There is no valid reason for asserting that the substitution of imprisonment and hard labour for death, as a punishment for murder, would more effectually deter men from the commission of that crime. Nothing that has been brought forward by the abolitionists leads us to believe so, and the direct testimony of those best acquainted with the criminal classes negatives such a supposition.

It is generally admitted that the most reckless and violent have a thorough fear of the gallows, which secondary punishments do not inspire. It will perhaps be answered, "why not hang for everything?" If death be the best deterrent, and society has the right to inflict it, "Why not bring the coiner and forger to the gallows as of old?" The answer is that murder is a crime so pre-eminently hurtful to society that it is advisable to distinguish it by a punishment above all others, and by one which may be held up before the eyes even of a man who is undergoing the most extreme sentence for a minor offence. Secondly, the crime of murder is contradistinction to ordinary crimes of larceny, or fraud, and is generally the offspring of that kind of savage disposition, which only the fear of death will effectually control. If the opinions of those conversant with prisoners are to be taken, there does exist a salutary fear of the death penalty among the worst class of the population.

A man will rob a house and waylay a traveller, but in the heat of his act, or in the very height of his fury, he will know how to hold his hand and avoid the actual killing of a human being.

It is said, and, we do not doubt, with perfect truth, that the reason why the proportion of murders to minor offences is so small—why the deed so often stops short of the capital offence, even at the risk of leaving a witness of the scene—is, that there is among the criminal classes the very strongest fear of actually causing death.

They know that the pursuit will be far more keen if a murder be in question, and that, if caught and convicted, a very different doom awaits them.

If this be the effect of the law, it is certainly a most important advantage to society, and one that certainly should not be thrown away in deference to either sentimental humanity or the vague theories of abstract justice.

In his speech at Mr. Spurgeon's Big Bethel Mr. Bright used the following strong language on the subject of capital punishment:— "Notwithstanding such defence as can be made for it the gallows is not only the penalty but the parent of murder." As this remark about the gallows is founded on a delusion, to some extent popular, it may be as well to devote a few lines to its refutation.

The idea that the gallows is the parent of murder is founded upon the statistics which show the decrease of that crime since the abolition of capital punishment for minor offences.

The abolitionists say that since murder has decreased in proportion to the restrictions placed upon the exercise of the last penalty of the law it would decrease still more if that last penalty were altogether abrogated.

This conclusion is, however, a transparent *non sequitur*. It is obvious that when burglary, sheep-stealing, and other offences were punishable with death a housebreaker or other criminal would resist to the last, even to death, in order to escape detection.

CHUDLEY VISITED IN PRISON BY MR. JAMBLIN AND HIS DAUGHTER.

He knew that whether he murdered his captors or not his punishment would be the same, and consequently it was his intent to carry deadly weapons with him and to use them if interrupted.

Punishment was not sufficiently cumulative, and, after a man had arrived at a certain degree of crime, he knew that no offence, however great, could add to the penalty consequent on detection.

Thus it happened that a highwayman or burglar was indifferent whether he took your money or your life, or both, and thus the restriction of capital punishment to the offences of murder alone restricted also the frequency of the crime itself.

Peace often declared that he never took human life if there was any means left open for him to escape without having recourse to such a dreadful alternative.

He was, perhaps, the most reckless scoundrel of modern times, but "fired wide," as he termed it, to frighten his pursuer, whose life he had no desire to take.

It is very questionable indeed whether he intended to kill Mr. Dyson when he fired at him, but in this case he seems to have lost himself, and to have been worked up into a sort of furious kind of madness; but his conduct, as far as the murder of Mr. Dyson is concerned, does not accord in any way with his former acts.

If, however, capital punishment were altogether abolished the completeness of the chain would be destroyed, and offenders whose crimes had already occasioned them to fear penal servitude for life would be encouraged again to resort to violence in order to escape detection.

It has been shown conclusively, on more than one occasion, that the punishment of death, while best for the protection of society, could not be compared in cruelty with the alternatives suggested by the would-be abolitionists. The horrors inflicted upon a man by immuring him in a living tomb without hope are too horrible to contemplate.

The deterrent effect exercised by the punishment of death mainly consists in its appearing more rigorous than it is; its real severity is much less than is supposed.

It is, perhaps, true that the cold-blooded premeditating murderer commits his crime with the full knowledge of the punishment he must suffer. This, however, is no argument for the abolition of capital punishment.

For such men our laws are not made, and it is best that such wretches should be destroyed like beasts of prey.

The evidence of prison governors and warders before the Royal Commission went to show that the lives of turnkeys and warders would not be safe from such men, devoid of hope; and the idea of holding out to them any expectation of being once more let loose upon society is quite out of the question.

Shortly after the condemnation of the wretched man, Joe Doughty presented himself at the prison gate with an order from the sheriff to see the prisoner. He was at once conducted into the cell in which Chudley was confined.

"I could not rest without seeing ye," said Joe Doughty. "I want ye to say you bear me no ill-will. What I have done has been done in the cause of justice, an' it warnt no fault o' mine that ye be in your present position. What say ye, Giles? Speak, man."

"I don't blame you, Joe. I never have done so. It be right that I should be brought to justice, an' ye did nothing more than your duty. I wish, when ye laid hands on me in the parlour of the 'Lord Cornwallis' that yer grip on my throat had been a little harder. I should have been spared a world of anxiety and misery."

As he spoke he gave his hand to Doughty.

"You bear me no ill-will?" cried the latter.

"No—none whatever. I bear no ill-will to any mortal man. Why should I? I forgive as I hope to be forgiven."

"Ah, that be good—I'm glad to hear 'ee say so. I was that angry when I saw 'ee in the 'Cornwallis' that I could ha' killed thee then and there, for I was as savage as a meat hatchet; but that be all over now. We ha' known each other for goodish many years, Giles, ha' worked together for Lord knows how long, an' I be sorry for this bisness. How came 'ee to do such a thing?"

"How?" cried Chudley, "Dunno myself. I was bewitched. People won't bleeve me when I tell 'em, but I was, Joe. I was under a spell. How is Nell Fulford?" he inquired, suddenly.

"She be broken down, but is better nor what she were—a deal better, I think."

"Ah!" exclaimed the prisoner. "When I saw her a talkin' to Mr. Philip in Dennett's-lane my heart seemed to be a fire loike, an' my head was all of a whirl. I could see she were a listnin' and a listnin' to what he were a sayin'. I could see she had eyes and ears only for him. And this drove me wild loike. And then—— But you know the rest."

The miserable man covered his face with his hands and heaved several deep sighs, which seemed to shake his frame to the very centre.

Joe Doughty placed his hand gently and mildly on the shoulder of the prisoner, and said, in a broken tone—

"Ye must bear up—indeed you must. There be one above who sees and knows all our hearts, and he will not desert 'ee, he will not desert a truly repentant sinner, Giles. Mind 'ee that, mate, and think o' that while 'ee have time. Do 'ee understand?"

"Aye, aye, I understand."

"Well, then, be mindful o' what I ha' bin sayin'."

"I ha' bin mindful of it; and Mr. Jamblin, how be he, and Miss Jamblin?"

"Ah, they are neither of them much to boast of. The old gentleman is sadly broken. He looks ten years older."

"Does he?"

"Ah, more—a goodish bit more than ten years. He'll never be the same man again; but I won't pain 'ee by talking about him or his. What be done can't be undone, and it aint o' no use trying to call back the past, because the past don't belong to no man. Think o' that, Giles, ask for forgiveness. Is there any request you have to make—anything you wish me to do for 'ee? I pledge my word to carry out your wishes as far as lies in my power."

"I dunno that I want 'ee to do anything," said the prisoner, hesitatingly. "I have done with the world, but still I should loike 'ee to see Nell Fulford, and tell her that if I had not loved her so much I shouldn't have been so jealous."

"Oh, it will never do to tell her that, Giles. Better say nothing about it now."

"Well, perhaps you be right. Well, then, ask her to forgive me."

"She will do that, poor girl, without the asking."

"An' she was fond o' him?"

"Of who?"

"Mr. Philip."

"Ah, surely, that she were—more's the pity."

"Yes, more's the pity for all of us."

"I will tell her what you say."

"An' you may tell her and maister that I aint so much to blame as people suppose. I never meant any harm to Mr. Philip, and never should ha' dun any harm to him if the witch who had me in her power had not made me go to Dennett's-lane on that fatal night."

He still insisted that he was in the power of an evil counsellor at the time he committed the murder, and this belief he clung to even when he ascended the scaffold.

It was not simulated—not a paltry excuse to cover his guilt but a species of bigotry or superstition, which could not be eradicated.

Joe Doughty made no reply to the last observation. He knew perfectly well that it would be useless to argue the question with his companion, who throughout his life had been most obstinate and self-opinionated on the questions of evil spirits.

"Well," said Joe, after a long pause, "ye be goin', let us hope, where there be no warlocks, witches, gnomes, or evil speerits o' any sort, so let that pass. Ha' ye anything else to say—any other request to mek?"

The prisoner hesitated.

"I dunno as I have."

"Think agen, I be in no hurry," said Joe. "I haint in no hurry."

"Noa, nuffin else," said Chudley, "only do 'ee speak a good word for me to maister and Miss Jamblin. I should loike to see un once more afore I dies."

"I will tell 'em what you say, but can't promise that they will come," said Joe.

The two men shook hands cordially, and, after a few more words of counsel and consolation, Doughty passed out of the cell, and returned to Broxbridge.

He was greatly relieved in his mind at having seen the murderer of his young master. He had done his best to bring him to the bar of justice. Nevertheless, deep down in his heart there nestled a feeling of regret.

Bad man as Chudley unquestionably was, now that he was condemned, Joe Doughty could not rest satisfied without "making it up wi' him," as he termed it, and hence his visit to the gaol.

The governor and prison chaplain took special pains to impress upon the wretched man the fact that there was not the slightest chance of his gaining a reprieve, and Chudley had said nothing to indicate that he had any hope that his life would be spared.

It was thought, however, by those in attendance on him that he scarcely realised the full extent of the crime of which he had been found guilty.

Strange as it may appear, people took an interest in the prisoner, Giles Chudley; and there were many who believed that her Majesty's prerogative ought to be exercised in his case.

The venerable vicar of Broxbridge, Canon Lenthall, paid a visit to the prisoner, and did his best to bring him to a sense of the great change which awaited him. Chudley listened to the admonitions of the reverend gentleman, but still persisted that he had been a mere puppet in the hands of a wicked and designing woman.

The worthy vicar, upon returning to Broxbridge, made the earl, Mr. Jamblin, and his daughter, acquainted with the mental condition of the wretched man.

A long consultation and conversation took place, and a day or two after this the porter of the gaol in which the condemned man was confined, while looking out of his lodge, saw a gentleman and lady crossing the street towards him.

The lady was pale and sad-looking, the gentleman was tall and broad-set, with the ruddy sunburnt face of a man who had spent his life in the country and open air, but his step had lost its elasticity, and lines of sorrow were observable on his features.

He was draped in black, which farmers in the country believe to be the proper and fashionable costume for Sundays, holidays, and visiting days.

It was easy enough for anyone to divine that these two persons were bent on some mission which was new and strange to both of them.

The farmer made a formal bow to the porter, whom he believed to be governor at the very least, and handed him a sealed letter.

The porter said in a careless tone—

"An order from Lord Ethalwood."

The farmer nodded.

"An order to see the gaol?"

"If you please."

"Certainly—pass on."

The farmer and his daughter did as they were directed. They happened to meet the head turnkey in the quadrangle—he received them with a grin of recognition and respect. He knew them both, and guessed the reason for their paying a visit to the prison.

He had so great a respect for both that he would have shown them over the gaol, even without an order from Lord Ethalwood or any one else.

The two strangers were none other than Mr. Jamblin and his daughter. This the reader has doubtless already divined.

They had never been inside the walls of a prison before, and were awe-struck as they were shown all the mechanical wonders of the place.

Mr. Jamblin inquired if he could see the condemned man, Giles Chudley.

The head turnkey, who had been expecting this, like a cunning fellow as he was, affected to be surprised. He raised his eyebrows and gave a short cough.

"See the condemned man?" he murmured. "This is not a visiting day; besides, I must have an order from one of the visiting magistrates."

"Lord Ethalwood told me he had given me the order," returned Jamblin.

"Oh, I see," observed the turnkey, looking at the paper. "Yes, he has included it in the visiting order. It's all right Mr. Jamblin. You can see the prisoner; this way, if you please."

He descended some steps, and the farmer and his daughter followed him.

"In what state of mind does this guilty man appear to be?" inquired Patty.

"He isn't so restless as he was, miss," said the turnkey, "not by a long way, nor is he so unruly. Before trial he was awdacious to be sure, made a desperate attempt to escape, cut through the wall, and nearly got away."

"Did he, though?" exclaimed the farmer.

"Ah, that he did, and no mistake. After his attempt at escape we handcuffed him—it was by order of the justices we did it," he added, cautiously.

"And quite right, too, I should say," returned Jamblin.

"Yes, quite right, sir. Well, he was that stubborn that when we came to look at his handcuffs after three days we found them shaved down as thin as a sixpence just by rubbing 'em together. That was just before his trial, and after his trial he seemed so meek and quiet that the deputy-governor said I might take him out for a walk in the yard with the *darbies* or the *slangs* on. And would you believe it, sir? You see that high wall there. I assure you I only turned my head for a moment, and when I looked round he was right on the top of the wall. How ever he got up is a marvel to me. He must have climbed up at the corners like a cat."

"Dear me, is it possible!" exclaimed the farmer. "I shouldn't ha' b'lieved it on him unless you had told me."

"Fact, sir, I assure you, though none of us said anything about it to the authorities. However, when he was up there," continued the man, with a laugh, "he had only to come down again, which he did without a murmur, and went on with his walk as if nothing had happened."

"What an odd thing!"

"Yes, strange—wasn't it ? But you see he must have thought that this here was the outer wall, instead of which it's the drying-yard between that and the street, and another wall topped with revolving iron spikes. Oh, he was precious artful."

The prison chaplain came out of the cell as they approached it. The turnkey touched his cap.

"Been to see the prisoner, sir ?" said he.

"Yes; he's bigotted and superstitious to the last degree, but he is deeply sensible of the great crime he has committed, and of the change which awaits him."

The chaplain passed on.

"Oh, father, perhaps we had better turn back," cried Patty, in a state of alarm.

"Nay, nay, gell," returned the farmer; "as we have come thus far, we may as well see un; it be our only chance, and as he told Joe that he would loike to ha' a last look at us, why it be our duty to see 'im."

"You need not be afraid, miss," said the turnkey, "he's calm enough now, and is quite resigned."

"Oh, he be—be he ?" said Jamblin.

When the farmer and his daughter entered the cell they inhaled a cold mephitic atmosphere like that of a funeral vault; one pale ray of light filtered thorugh the iron bars ; faint and solitary as a last hope, it could not illumine the whole of the cell.

They found themselves in the most horrible of twilights—the twilight of a dungeon.

When their eyes become accustomed to this sombre light they beheld a man seated on a rough wooden stool; he was ironed hand and foot; he was frightfully thin, wan, and worn ; his eyes wore a hollow dejected look.

Mr. Jamblin failed to recognise in the miserable prisoner the stalwart ploughman who for years had been in his employ; he shuddered, the change was so awful.

When Giles Chudley recognised the two visitors he gave a start which resembled a spasm.

"We've coom, Giles," began the farmer, in a voice broken by emotion.

"I know it; ye ha' coom to upbraid me," interrupted the prisoner. "Go on—I deserve it, maister. You, too, whom I ha' most injured, be coom, too."

"Not to upbraid ye," observed Patty. "It is not likely we should pay ye a visit to do that."

The felon condemned to death gave the speaker a smile of welcome, and, rising, presented his clumsy seat to her.

She hesitated for a moment, and then sat down.

The turnkey, with the instinctive delicacy of nature's gentlemen, stood as far from them as he could. He would have left had it not been against the prison rules.

Duty compelled him to be present—not to obtrude.

There was a silence for several minutes ; neither of them knew what to say. It was Patty who spoke first. She rose from her seat and drew back to the side of her parent, upon whose shoulder she placed one of her hands as if to support herself.

For, to say the truth, the poor girl was deeply moved, and trembled in every limb.

"We have come to you, Giles," said Patty, in a low sweet musical voice, "to tell you how sorry we are that you should have brought yourself to this, and we hope that before you die—you will try and drive out all malice and hatred towards us from your heart, as we have driven all from ours."

The convict made no reply. He looked intently at the speaker, and then seated himself once more on his stool.

"Ye hear what my daughter ha' bin sayin'," observed the farmer. "What answer ha' ye to mek ?"

"You forgive me, then ?" said the prisoner, in a low breathless tone.

"Aye, surely; it aint loikely we shonld do otherwise. It be but natural when 'ee's about to leave the world. We do forgive 'ee."

"Yes," said Patty softly, "we forgive you from our hearts."

"Heaven bless you! Heaven bless you !" cried the prisoner, as he wrung their hands with his, which were chained. "I thought that you would when I asked Joe to tell you I could not leave the world without asking your forgiveness."

"Ah !" he said, in continuation, "you do not know how bitterly I have been punished for my cowardice and treachery, and this be the consequence," he ejaculated, glancing at his chains.

Patty sighed—the sight was a painful and touching one.

The prisoner went on telling them how he had been in the power of an evil woman, and how he had been driven to desperation on that fatal night, and what miseries he had endured since then.

As he gave this recital they closed their eyes that they might not see his face, which was distorted with agony.

The door of the cell was suddenly opened, and the venerable Canon Lenthall entered.

"I am glad you have consented to see the prisoner," he said, addressing himself to the farmer and his daughter; "glad for many reasons."

The farmer nodded and said, "It was not loikely, after what you told us, that we should fail to coom. But he be sadly altered."

"Ah, sartin sure I be," said the prisoner, with a hoarse laugh. "You see the chill of the grave be already upon me; man's hopes and man's heart canna' live for ever, though the hopes be high and the heart be young. I may die before the gallows claims me—think o' that."

"I hope you are in a better frame of mind and are embued with a due sense of the awfulness of your position," observed the canon.

"I be all that, reverend sir. Perhaps you will tell me—you who are so good and so religious—why I have been saved so long, why I was tempted to commit so dreadful a crime, and why I am doomed to die on the scaffold ?"

"We cannot understand how the corn grows in the earth," said the vicar, "how birds fly in the air, how insects crawl across a ceiling, how then can we understand the mysterious ways of the Creator ?"

"You are right," returned Chudley, sharply. "I have probably bin created, like thorns and nettles, for some mysterious purpose."

"That may or may not be," returned the vicar. "Providence is like the sun—when we first look at it we are dazzled and blinded ; we believe that it is faultless. But art and science—those dangerous tutors of man, which teach him little, but which cannot teach him much—show him that there are spots upon the sun, apparently so spotless, and, perhaps, if he could understand the nature of these apparent blemishes he would worship with greater faith the majesty and effulgence of the Deity."

The prisoner looked at the speaker and bowed his head reverently.

The words he had been listening to had a visible effect upon his superstitious, ignorant mind.

"It be a blessing to hear 'ee talk," he murmured.

"Has your mother paid you a visit?" inquired Patty.

"Yes, she war the first to coom. I ha' seen her," said the culprit, in a softened tone.

"I'm glad of it," said Patty. "You will not be angry with me if I ask you something?" she added.

"Angry with you?"

She hesitated, and then said—

"If I ask you whether you do fear the tribunal which awaits you in the other world."

"Fear!" he cried, in a husky voice. "What wretch is there condemned to death who does not quake at the sound of his own voice—who does not shudder at his own thoughts? When pepple are wi' me, though they be my gaolers, when the sun shines upon me, though it be wi' only one pale ray, I feel that I can look the worst in the face, but when I be alone, and in darkness——"

He paused, as an icy tremour ran through his frame. "I could silence[the] turnkeys both by [words and a bold front, but I cannot silence my own conscience—that's not possible. Night arter night I reproach myself for my crime. Night arter night a baud o' pale specters, the witch at their head, flit past me, and point at me wi' their thin bony fingers, and reproach me wi' their red and sunken eyes. Oh, it is horrible, surely."

"And do you never pray to be released from these dreams which come from remorse?" said Patty Jamblin.

"It is too late to pray now. My prayers would not be listened to."

"You are mistaken," said the vicar. "The prayers of a repentant sinner are always heard and answered.

"Ah, I do not know how to pray," he muttered. "No one ever taught me that."

"I will teach you," said Patty Jamblin, and she knelt down upon the pointed stones and raised her hands towards the one ray of light which faint but beautiful fell like the eye of the Omnipotent upon her upturned face.

Slowly and sullenly the criminal fell upon his knees. The farmer also knelt, and the turnkey bared his head and lowered it, that he might listen to the prayer.

Soft and melodious as the murmurings of distant water, the farmer's daughter's voice rose from the depths of that dark cell, and pleaded with Heaven for the sinner's soul.

The fountains of that hard and ignorant man's heart were at length opened, and tears flowed from his eyes for the first time.

Patty ceased, then the venerable vicar, in a solemn and sonorous voice, gave utterance to an extemporaneous but beautiful prayer well adapted to the occasion, and after this Giles Chudley became an altered man.

Jamblin and Patty left, but Canon Lenthall remained with the prisoner for an hour or more after they had taken their departure.

It was thought strange by many who were acquainted with all the *dramatis personæ* connected with the tragedy in Larchgrove-lane, that Giles should never at any time have expressed a wish to see Ellen Fulford.

Without doubt he was devotedly attached to the girl, having been an admirer of her for the best part of his life, and there can be but little question with regard to the motive for the commission of the crime for which he was about to suffer.

Everybody attributed it to jealousy, and this was a righteous conclusion.

Nevertheless, Chudley did not request to see her, or send any message by those who would have delivered it.

After his interview with his master and his daughter, he seemed content, and did not appear to have a wish for further visitors.

Mr. Slapperton, it might be said, almost forced himself into his presence.

The only effect of the lawyer's visit was to disturb and distract the wretched man's thoughts from other and more weighty matters. But the irrepressible Slapperton was heedless of this.

As the time for the final day drew on he was informed by the governor that he could not be permitted to see the prisoner any more.

At this Slapperton was greatly incensed.

Since his interview with Patty and her father, Chudley had eaten well and slept well every night till the night of Saturday, when it was noticed that he did not sleep so soundly.

To the last he maintained that he was under a spell and in the power of a witch.

He occupied the same cell in which he had been confined, and was never for a moment left alone; and at night, in addition to the warder sitting up with him, another officer was patrolling in the corridor outside the cell.

The books he was supplied with were a Bible, a Prayer-book, "Hymns Ancient and Modern," a Scripture picture book, and "Bunyan's Pilgrim's Progress."

When the governor and the sheriff announced the day appointed for the final act of the law being carried out, he evinced no further emotion than a low moan, and then said he was quite prepared to meet the dreadful fate that awaited him, and which he knew was inevitable.

On Sunday night, the condemned man, after being visited by the chaplain, who was unremitting in his attendance on the culprit, was locked up at the usual hour, eight o'clock. He partook of supper, and afterwards had some beer.

He asked if he might be allowed to smoke, and being answered in the affirmative, he lighted his pipe, which he seemed to greatly enjoy.

At a little before nine o'clock, the night warder took charge of him.

After conversing for some little time Chudley retired to rest. He gave no trouble—so his attendant said.

After going to bed he sank into a peaceful slumber, from which he did not awake till past four on the Monday morning.

He opened his eyes and stared round the cell, and, upon his eyes meeting those of the warder, he said—

"What is the time now?"

"Ten minutes past four," was the answer.

"Oh, no later than that?" he returned.

He then went off to sleep again, and did not wake till he was aroused by the entrance of the chief warder. It was now six o'clock.

Giles Chudley got up and dressed himself with more than usual care.

He was asked if he would have any breakfast, and said he could not eat anything, but he, however, had a cup of tea.

Soon after this the governor of the prison entered the cell, and said, "Chudley, the time approaches, and we want you."

"I am ready, sir," returned the prisoner, who was then introduced to Calcraft.

At the sight of the grey-headed man, with dark malicious-looking eyes, the unhappy wretch trembled.

"Get it all over as quickly as possible," he whispered to his executioner.

Calcraft nodded. He never was a man of many words—that is, when engaged in his professional duties.

He was the very antithesis of his lively successor, Marwood, whose manner is brisk, cheery, and self-reliant. Calcraft, on the contrary, was morose, and as close as an oyster.

Chudley offered no resistance to the process of pinioning, which was performed with the hangman's usual skill.

A leathern belt, about an inch wide, was buckled round the culprit's waist, and to this his wrists were fastened down by small but stoutly-made straps.

His arms were fastened just above the elbows, and drawn back as far as it was possible to do so without giving him unnecessary pain, and then connected with the belt round the body.

The procession to the gallows was then formed. It consisted of the chaplain, the governor, the under-sheriff, and another gentleman whose name did not transpire.

When the prisoner appeared on the scaffold there was a low murmur like the moaning of the sea from the immense crowd assembled in front of and around the gallows.

Chudley was deathly pale. A glance at his face showed that he was suffering intense agony, and it was only by the exercise of a powerful control that he was able to bear up and meet his fate with anything like fortitude.

He took a hasty glance at the upturned sea of faces before him.

He then gave a piercing look at the uprights and cross beam, and pendant rope now swinging lightly in the morning breeze.

The sight of the ghastly engine of death seemed to unman him.

He trembled violently, and those who were near him afterwards declared that his hair stood literally on end. Presently he appeared to recover himself somewhat, and he placed himself under the beam, on the spot pointed out by Calcraft, and indicated by that functionary by a chalk mark. The chaplain, who stood about a yard and a half from the culprit, went on with the burial service, while the other members of the sad procession ranged themselves behind the doomed man.

Chudley again scrutinised the faces of the spectators in front of him, but he was unable to recognise any person whom he had known. He was too affected to single out any.

Calcraft lost no time in making the preliminary arrangements, and, stooping down, he fastened a strap round the wretched man's legs.

As soon as he felt the hangman's touch, Chudley seemed as if about to swoon ; he gave utterance to a short prayer, and swayed his hands to and fro in a manner which was piteous to behold.

The executioner next proceeded to adjust the rope round the man's neck, but he displayed none of that professional coolness which he was usually credited with. He was agitated and nervous, and it was some little time before he could adjust the noose to his satisfaction.

At length, however, this task was accomplished, and stepping back a pace he produced from his pocket a white cap which he drew over the prisoner's head.

The miserable convict during the whole of this painful period of suspense was ejaculating appeals to the Almighty for mercy in a muffled voice, the pitiful

tones of which will long ring in the ears of those who heard it.

He was scarcely able to stand upright by reason of the shaking of his limbs, and when Calcraft, after putting on the white cap, left him for the purpose of pulling the fatal bolt he nearly fell backwards, but quickly by a powerful exertion of will he resumed an erect position.

The chaplain repeated " I am the resurrection and the life," the fatal bolt was withdrawn, and the man fell like a plummet.

There was of course the usual " thud." It is impossible for any newspaper reporter to describe an execution without making use of that expressive and favourite word.

His struggles were terrible to witness, and it was quite four minutes before they ceased, and he could be fairly pronounced to be dead.

He was hung with what is called the short drop—which Calcraft invariably made use of. He declares to this day it is by far the most humane and preferable of the two.

Within the last few weeks we have been favoured with long dissertations upon the various modes of putting criminals to death.

A morning paper has given space in its columns for the insertion of several letters under the heading of " Bungling Executions."

The gallows is a dreadful alternative to have resort to, but it is one which cannot be safely dispensed with till some other mode of putting criminals to death is substituted.

No doubt the ghastly apparatus of the scaffold, the halter, and the drop is a shocking topic for public discussion, but the controversy, crude and well-nigh grotesque as it is in form, opens a field for inquiry, the consideration of which calls for curious attention.

It so happens that at the present moment there are only three nations in Europe which retain the undeniably clumsy and barbarous custom of putting human beings to death by suspending them to a beam with a rope round the neck.

Those three nations are Great Britain, Russia, and Turkey. France, Italy, Belgium, and Greece employ a highly-perfected guillotine. Spain and Portugal adhere to the swiftly-killing and painless garotte. Germany, in the rare instances in which capital punishment is inflicted, uses the sword.

We share with our estimable ally, the Turk, and with despotic Russia, the honour of strangling malefactors in the good old conservative fashion.

Impalement seems to have been abandoned, the bowstring appears to have fallen into disuse, and the gallows appears to offer an additional advantage in the circumstance that the patient can be hanged first, and decapitated afterwards.

The apparatus in Turkey is that fine old institution, the gibbet, to which a malefactor can be at once strung up without any nonsense in connection with long and short drops, the efficacy of which have been so frequently discussed by the press of this country.

We have been hanging rogues and others in England for considerably more than a thousand years, but it should be extremely humiliating to us as a civilised, scientific, and mechanically ingenious people that we are as inexpert hangmen as in the days of the Saxon heptarchy.

It would be as well if half a dozen mechanical engineers and practical anatomists were commissioned by the Home Secretary to draw up a succinct report on hanging—distinguishing between the phenomena of strangulation and those of vertebral dislocation, and deliberate on the question of long *versus* short drops.

Marwood has declared on more than one occasion that his method is the most merciful one that has ever been put in practice; but the veteran Calcraft denies this assertion.

The public at large are perhaps indifferent as to whether an assassin dies from a broken neck or from strangulation, but there is a widely-spread feeling that no more physical pain than is absolutely necessary should be inflicted on the miserable wretch.

Marwood's system should be subject to careful tests and exhaustive analysis, and if it is pronounced efficient he should enjoy immunity from further criticism.

If, however, the man's method is faulty he should be directed to execute his victims in a more workmanlike style.

In any case, the recent discussion on "Bungling Executions" may be of service, as it is not improbable that advancing civilisation may some day devise a better mode of carrying out the last dread penalty of the law in a more satisfactory manner than that adopted at the present time.

A few French medical men revived some short time ago the strange paradox of the elder Sue—the famous anatomist, whose son was the author of the "Mysteries of Paris," "The Wandering Jew," and other popular works of fiction—that the action of the guillotine is not so painless as people have been led to imagine, and that the sensation does not cease for some moments after the head has been separated from the body. Dr. Sue's arguments have been long since ably, and it would seem conclusively, refuted, and the fact that decapitation, skilfully performed, is an operation of anything beyond instantaneous pain to the criminal has been once more distinctly affirmed by the most eminent scientific authorities in France.

After this resuscitated dispute died away, Professor Haughton, of the University of Dublin, came forward with a learned and exhaustive disquisition on the economies of hanging, and on the best way of killing a murderer without causing him unnecessary agony. The Professor quoted a statement of the surgeon of Newgate that under Calcraft's *regime* he had frequently seen the criminal struggle for more than twenty minutes before he became inanimate.

The retired executioner may be left to fight his own battles as regards his aptitude of putting people out of the world.

Those who know him best are perfectly well aware that he is not likely to trouble himself about what people say; but the medical officer of Newgate—we are not aware to what particular one Professor Houghton refers—is doubtless aware that convulsive muscular action may be prolonged for some minutes after the suspended culprit has ceased to experience any sensation.

Professor Houghton tells us that the "old system of taking the convict's life by suffocation is inhumanely painful, and necessarily prolonged, and revolting to the spectators whose duty it is to be present;" that the object of an effective execution by suspension should be the immediate rupture of the spinal column through the fall, and that the use of the long drop, which by habit has become known as the Irish method, is not only much preferable from a humanitarian point of view, but is the only method by which the desired object can be effectively attained.

It may be as well to hint to the professor that, to judge from an illuminated Anglo-Saxon manuscript in the "Harleian Miscellany," the severing of the cer-

vical vertebræ occupied the attention of our ancestors centuries ago.

Every executioner, from Derrick to Brandon and from Brandon to Jack Ketch, has done his best to break the criminal's neck, either by sitting astride his shoulders as the culprit was swung, or by pulling his legs from beneath.

As regards the long drop, a few years since the Irish method was but too painfully manifested at Dublin by the fact of a criminal who was given too long a rope and too sharp a fall so that his head was completely severed from his body.

Suffocation was never "systematic" in cases of hanging in this country, and the custom is immemorial of adjusting the knot of the rope under the sufferer's left ear, in order that death might be instantaneous.

Professor Haughton thinks that Marwood has done wonders by placing the knot under the criminal's chin, but a Spanish executioner could very much improve on Marwood's method by exhibiting the capacity of that compact and efficient machine for rupturing the spinal column, called the "garotte."

CHAPTER LXXII.
CHARLES PEACE LEAVES DARTMOOR.

WE must now return to our hero, who, probably many of our readers may think has been left too long unnoticed; but it will be remembered that we left him in good hands. He was well looked after, and month after month wore sadly away, until at length the time approached upon which Peace was to regain his liberty.

He had been very diligent and well behaved, and had earned the requisite number of marks.

Discharges take place in various ways, but Peace was not at all particular about the method or manner of his liberation, provided he left the cheerless walls of Dartmoor.

As we have stated in a preceding chapter, when a man is first of all convicted, his clothing is confiscated, and on his discharge the prison authorities give him other garments in place of those which have been taken from him.

This is part of the prison arrangements that requires reform, and which, doubtless, will be to seen before long.

At the present time two courses are adopted.

If a man joins the Prisoners' Aid Society, he has a small sum allowed to him, which is handed over to the society to purchase clothing; but if he does not, an outfit is given him, but this bears upon it unmistakable evidence that the man has been a convict.

This is neither fair nor just.

It is true the clothes men leave Dartmoor in are cut well, made well, and in most instances are tolerably good fits, but the material is of the very worst quality, being a shoddy imitation of tweed, with a twill or pattern printed on it, and any one would be at no loss to know where it came from, for there is nothing like it made outside the walls of a prison, and such stuff is hardly worth making up into garments, for it is rotten, and will bear no time.

A good serviceable material might be obtained at a trifling more cost, and the discharged prisoner would then have a rough suit of clothes which he would not be ashamed of wearing.

It is ridiculous to measure a man, and spend skilled labour in cutting and making well-fitting garments which will not hang together for a month.

The under clothes there is very little to find fault

with, the stocking and flannels are as good as need be. The materials of the boots in general are of a good quality, and the workmanship excellent.

As far as the hat is concerned nothing can be much worse.

But taken altogether the rig out is most unsatisfactory, indeed; so worthless is it, that if a man were to go straight from prison to Monmouth-street or Petticoat-lane, and is lucky enough not to be caught in the rain, the dealers in new and second-hand clothes will allow him the magnificent sum of six, or at the most, seven shillings for the whole turn-out of coat, vest, trousers, hat, and handkerchiefs.

They are sent abroad, as no one in this country will buy such rubbish.

Due attention has not been given to this subject by the executive.

Men when they leave prison should have every possible inducement for them to return to an honest course of life.

The prisoner who goes to the Prisoners' Aid Society in London is not compelled to accept the clothes which the gaol officials provide.

He is sent up to town for discharge, and the society, out of the funds at their disposal, buy him some decent garments, which he is not ashamed of appearing in.

Peace, however, did not belong to any society of this nature.

When he was discharged from Dartmoor he had, therefore, no alternative than to leave the prison in the clothes furnished him by the authorities.

When he was about to leave he was informed by the governor that a letter had reached the prison, which was addressed to him. It contained an enclosure (a Bank of England note for twenty pounds).

The letter was singularly short and ambiguous. It was as follows :—

" Accept the enclosed from an old friend and companion. Turn from your evil courses, and take heed of the future."

Peace was surprised at the contents of the epistle, and still more so at the enclosure. He could not divine from whom it had come. At first he was under the impression that Earl Ethalwood had sent it, but upon second consideration he dismissed the thought from his mind. The earl would not have been so secret— there was no reason for his being so.

It must have been sent by some friend; possibly Laura Stanbridge had forwarded him the amount, which was, of course, most welcome and acceptable.

In this, however, he was mistaken. The letter and enclosure had been forwarded by his quondam companion, Bessie Dalton, who had, however, at this time changed her name as well as her mode of life. We shall have to refer to her in a future chapter.

Peace was, as a matter of course, greatly delighted at being so suddenly and unexpectedly put in possession of the sum, which would suffice for his more immediate necessaries.

He asked one of the warders if he could get the note changed for him before leaving Dartmoor.

The warder mentioned the matter to the governor, who gave Peace gold for the note.

And shortly after this our hero bid farewell to his prison associates, and was conducted with several others to the station by two warders.

Two of his companions were bound to London. Men who have been convicted in the metropolis are sent there for discharge. If they are Prisoners' Aid Society's men they travel up in convict's dress, and one or more

warders go with them, as the case may be. And, strange to say, a marked difference is made in the treatment of the discharged prisoners.

Those who are convicted in the provinces leave Dartmoor without handcuffs, and with the hands and limbs free, as Peace did on this occasion. Those who have to be taken to London for discharge are manacled and handcuffed, as if fresh caught. Why is this ?

No man going up to London for discharge is likely to run away from a warder; he would be a fool if he did, for until he is completely discharged he has no licence, and if he did abscond he would be liable to arrest as a convict at liberty without leave.

All the convicts know this, and it is not at all likely they would infringe the rules when they were within a few hours of liberty.

The handcuffing of a man under such circumstances is quite unnecessary. It is worse than this, being in short an indignity which is at once cruel and useless. So long as he has any time to serve, and there is any inducement for him to run away, chains and fetters are perhaps needful; as a convict in a convict's dress few would recognise him.

When he goes to London on his discharge journey he has grown his hair, beard, and whiskers.

He travels with other people who are also bound for the metropolis, who, seeing him with the darbies on, know very well that his ornamental bracelets are not the insignia of honour.

The chances are that they may take particular notice of the man, and one may possibly see him at work a week or two afterwards, and view him with repugnance, if not with disgust ; anyway they would look upon him as a person to be studiously avoided.

This is hardly fair to the discharged prisoner, who should certainly, upon regaining his liberty, be permitted to have a fair start in life, and every facility should be offered him to return to an honest course.

Before leaving Dartmoor every prisoner has his photograph taken, and his carte-de-visite is supplied to the various police offices he has to go to for report.

On Wednesday all the prisoners for discharge that week have arrived in London, and in the morning a number of detectives come and take stock of them. The men stand in a row, and the detectives from Scotland-yard and Old Jewry, together with policemen from other stations, come and make themselves fully acquainted with the men who are to be let loose in their districts.

Each man is compared with his photograph and the written description of him. Of some men the police take no notice, or very little ; others they take special care to become thoroughly acquainted with in every particular, and examine them most carefully. They know perfectly well who are likely to be in their hands again.

This ceremony, until very recently, took place in the Queen's Bench Prison in the Borough—that old-fashioned prison for debtors, Chancery victims, and first-class misdemeanants; the prison from which Johnson, the celebrated smuggler, escaped; the place of which Sheridan said no man's education was completed until he had been in the Bench; but the place around the walls of which so many associations cling, is now a thing of the past; its final doom was determined on some time back, and, like Temple Bar, it will live only in the remembrance of the public through the agency of contemporary chroniclers.

For a long time before its final doom it had undergone a remarkable change; it was neglected, forlorn, and its old glories had passed away.

PEACE PAYS A VISIT TO A JEW CLOTHIER.

No longer were its walls marked out with racquet courts—in the olden days the imprisoned debtor could not have lived without the racquet court—but debtors and Chancery victims were no longer confined there.

After the abolishment of the Imprisonment for Debt Act, it was abandoned, and shorn of all its former attractions—for it had attractions without doubt.

It was used as a soldiers' prison, and so it continued for some time, until at length that was discontinued, and the poor old Bench fell farther into decay; it was merely used as a place from whence to discharge convicts.

Men leaving Dartmoor on Monday night arrived at the Bench, or Queen's Bench, on Tuesday morning, where they remain, doing nothing, till the day of their discharge, which takes place one day during the same week.

Prisoners on licence, generally termed ticket-of-leave men, have to report themselves once every month at the police-station of the district where they reside, and to show how they are earning their living.

As a matter of course it is not at all likely any of them will pronounce themselves thieves by trade or profession; and everyone has what is termed a "stall," that is, he professes to be some handicraft or trade by which to designate himself, and which, in most cases, is mere subterfuge—a blind or stall to his real proceedings.

The police are well aware that the pretext is a shallow one, and that in all probability the man has returned to the dishonest course of life which he followed before conviction, but the farce has to be gone through.

If a man moves from one district in London to another he must within four-and-twenty hours of his arrival report himself at the nearest police station, so that watch and ward may be kept over him.

The stoppage of transportation brought the administration of criminal justice to a dead lock. To meet the difficulty the Ministry prepared and passed with all speed a measure, since known as the first Penal Servitude Act.

As a final acknowledgment that it was England's duty to consume her own criminality, and for the sanction which it gave to various important principles, this Act (which became law in the autumn of 1853) has, notwithstanding, many serious flaws, very valuable provisions.

In the course of execution, however, it was stultified into complete failure.

Altogether the first Penal Servitude Act was a complete failure, and in the session of 1856 it was found necessary to reconsider the whole question. The session was too far advanced to allow the report presented to be transformed into an Act that year, but when Parliament met again in February, 1857, the requisite bill was the first ministerial measure introduced, and in spite of the Chinese wrangle and the dissolution it became law before the end of June.

There is little fault to be found with the second Penal Servitude Act.

To lengthen the sentences according to the old scale, to make some portion remittable, to permit the issue of licences, was all required from the measure, and all this the measure accomplished.

The notion that prevails at the English Home Office is, that a discharged prisoner's best chance is to obtain a situation under false pretences.

That he could never obtain employment if his felonious antecedents were known, and that his dismissal from any place he had procured under a false character would be the immediate result of their discovery, is taken for granted; and perhaps, while the English convict prisons remain what they are, and the public distrust of their reformatory power continues in consequence unabated, this belief is well grounded.

It is probably true, therefore, that the acknowledged ticket-of-leave and the avowed police surveillance might possibly impede a man's return to honesty.

As far as Peace was concerned, however, it was a matter of no moment.

He had numberless opportunities afforded him to pursue an honest course of life, but it was not in his nature to be otherwise than a hardened criminal.

There is no question about this; albeit his character

in other ways is of a most indefinite and contradictory nature.

Though Peace has given evidence of having a thorough contempt for human suffering, it is asserted that "he could not kill a mouse" if he had been requested to do so.

He further declared that if he had to kill his meat he should have to go without it all his life. Whether from curiosity or interest he had studied carefully the major portion of the Scriptural writings, and read opinions on them, and manifested much skill in controversy on theological questions. One afternoon, when Peace lived in Brocco, he had a long conversation with the Rev. Dr. Poller on religious topics.

On the departure of the vicar of St. Luke's Peace thus summed up his ideas on the subject—

"I believe in God and I believe in the devil, but I don't fear either."

Peace took his standpoint on this that "man was the creature of circumstances," and supported his argument by quoting authorities on the subject.

From his youth upwards he had been fond of curiosities.

He regularly visited the Museum, and as each addition was made to it he inspected the new object of interest with care. Anything with carving upon it came in for a large share of his attention.

But he revelled among the models most, and if there was one branch more than another in which he excelled it was the making of models of cathedrals and monuments in cardboard, which he embossed and traced with a variety of patterns.

There is one at the present time in Sheffield—a memento of the deaths of four members of his family.

It is about a yard in height, and made of cardboard, the outlines of the embossed work on it being traced with silver.

It represents a monument after an ecclesiastical design, like the main turret in Gloucester Cathedral, and has every pinnacle cut as cleanly as though carved in ivory.

It is mounted on a slab, approached on all four sides by steps—these and the slab being covered with black velvet.

There are four tablets sunk in the lower squares of the monument, one on each side, and on these are placed the names of the relatives deceased.

As a specimen of workmanship, it is without equal in its line in Yorkshire.

Peace expressed his intention of adding to the attractions in the Sheffield museum.

He decided on constructing one of these "monuments," and of presenting it for exhibition in that institution.

Those whose memories it was to perpetuate were the Rev. Canon Sale, the Misses Harrison, and the "Christian poet," Montgomery, whose names he would have engraved on tablets to be placed in the sides of the structure as already described.

He actually commenced the work, and would have completed it, had he not taken to other courses.

After receiving his discharge Peace made the best of his way to London.

One reason for this was that he was not so well known in the metropolis as at Sheffield, and before returning to his native town he was desirous of making a change in his costume; the other reason was that he had for his companions two convicts who were discharged at the same time as himself. One of these was the housebreaker who had been convicted at Manchester for burglary; the other was a regular London thief, whose acquaintance Peace had made in the parade ground of Dartmoor—the last named was a cheery gossiping gentleman, who appeared to be on good terms with himself and everybody else.

"Well, we've all done our dose," said the London thief, whose name was Baxter, "and are glad enough to leave that blooming place. I hope neither on us 'ill see its dark walls again, and bad luck to it. I think it's the worst prison as ever I was in. Why Millbank's a king to it."

"Ah! I never was at Millbank," said Peace.

"Oh, no, s'pose not—you aint a London man, and may be that this is your first lagging. Ye see I've had some 'xperience—been to all sorts of places. Lord, a bloke gets used to it in time. I did a seven year stretch before this, and was at the Gib three out of it."

"At where?" inquired Peace.

"At Gibraltar."

"Ah! indeed. How did you like that?"

"Oh! got on there like a 'ouse a'fire. Bless you, that is somethin' like a stab. Why I was as jolly and 'appy as a sandboy; had it pretty much my own way. Why they serves you out bacca there regularly every week, and precious good stuff it is, and no mistake; but, ye see, I was fortunate, I was," said the speaker, in a more confidential tone—"very fortunate. I was servant to one of the officers, and a right-down good chap he was. I was as right as the mail till the cholera came; then it went 'ard with a good many, me amongst the rest."

"The cholera, eh?" exclaimed Raynton, the burglar.

"Yes, an' a blooming time I 'ad of it. Ugh, it makes my blood run cold to think on it now. Ye see, it aint like no other disease—it's down upon you like a thousand of bricks afore you know where you are. It don't give a fellow no time, and I tell ye I was that frightened at the sights I seed that I didn't know whether I stood on my 'ead or my 'eels—it's a fact. You've no idea what it is like at the Gib. I'm told it was bad enough here, but it couldn't be anything to compare to what it was there. I never seed anything like it. Why I've stood next to a bloke in the morning at early muster, and helped to bury him the same night."

"Oh, gammon and all," cried Raynton.

"No gammon about it, old man. I'll take my Bible oath on it. You don't understand it. Don't yer know that the place is so blooming hot that a chap won't keep, and what's the consekence? He's got to be buried at once."

"And were you an officer's servant all the time?" inquired Peace.

"No, not all the time. You see, the cholera cleared off a lot of the prisoners—they died like rotten sheep. And not only the convicts but the sojers as well; and so as my guv'nor couldn't find any one else he took me. Ah! he was a good sort, surely. I was precious sorry when the time came for me to leave the island. Before I was an officer's servant I worked in the galleries a making casements for the guns, and precious hard work it was; but it was better than the work at the quarries at Dartmoor; besides, there wasn't that strictness and cursed ceremony. At the Gib a fellow could say his soul's his own, and that's more than he can say at Dartmoor. At Gibraltar we also made great tanks to 'old the water. Some of the boys couldn't stand the wet, but I didn't so much mind it.

"It certainly was owdacious at times, but you see we warnt dressed in different sort of togs; we had white canvas jumpers and trousers."

"Ah," said Peace, "and you needed a costume of

that sort, I dare say; but did anyone ever manage to escape?"

"Did anyone? I should just think they did too. You see the Spaniards were very good as far as lay in their power; they'd always help a bloke if he was once over the lines. Say what ye like about the foreigners, they're a jolly sight better than our people in many ways—a precious sight. They aint like the blarney fellows about this place who pounce upon a poor devil, and give 'im up directly for the sake of a paltry five quid that the Government gives 'im. It's every man for hisself and God for us all in this country. Still Dartmoor is better than Chatham."

"I thought you said it was the worst place you were ever in," observed Raynton.

"It's the worst place I've been in for a goodish while, but when I said that I forgot Chatham. It certainly aint so bad as that—leastways, not to my thinking. There's many a bloke there as is druv to suicide—it's such a 'ell upon earth. I hope I shan't have to go there again. One chap, while I was at Chatham, threw hisself down in front of the engine as works the trucks of earth out of the new dock, and was cut in two. Poor fellow, he'd been bashed (flogged) twice, and the warder had been going on at him so that he couldn't stand it any longer, and so he ups with his pick and chucks it straight at him on the shoulder. Just as he'd done this he sees an engine coming, so he saved 'em the trouble of ' bashing' him again. He chucked himself in front of it, and in a second or so all was over. Poor fellow, he was not half so bad as they tried to make him out, but he was nervous and irritable, and couldn't stand being jawed at during the whole of the day. Ye see many of the men at Chatham are drove into being regular devils by being constantly nagged at by the blooming officers. It aint in the nature of man to stand being continually bullied, as some of the poor devils are. Them as 'as got pluck in 'em turns savage, and small blame to 'em; but them as 'aven't knocks under, and does the meek and mild bisness, same as I did. But it's hard lines, either way—precious hard lines—and no mistake; and lots ov 'em die, and it is considered to be a 'appy release; but lor, I don't expect either of you two know the ins and outs of prison life as yet," said the loquacious Mr. Baxter.

"We neither of us profess to have the experience that you appear to possess," returned Raynton. "Have you ever been to Portland?"

"Have I? I should rather think I had! Well, let me tell you. Portland is a precious deal better than Chatham, though Portland aint altogether what you may call an inviting sort of place—far from that."

Peace and the burglar, or the other burglar we ought to say, smiled at this last observation. The speaker's manner was so *naïve*, there was a careless, free-and-easy, confidential tone assumed throughout his discourse, which was rather amusing than otherwise.

The fellow was as callous, and as utterly devoid of all moral principle as it is well possible to conceive. He talked of the crimes he had committed, and of the various terms of punishment he had undergone, as a soldier might tell of his escapes on the battle-field, or the wounds he had received in the service.

He was but one of many of the same type to be found at Dartmoor, Spike Island, Portland, and other convict establishments.

It is true men of this class, while undergoing penal servitude, have the benefit of the ministration of the chaplain, who in most cases does his best to impress upon them the error of their ways, but it is a sad reflection that many, and indeed most, of these wretches are beyond the reach of moral or religious influence.

At Millbank there is a service, or rather was—for the prison is now no longer in use—of the Holy Communion once every three months.

At Dartmoor there is a Communion regularly every Sunday, and the prisoners take it in turns.

Every man was invited to join by the chaplain, who no doubt meant well, but it is very questionable whether his beating up for recruits in the way he did was judicious, as many men attended with the idea of currying favour by so doing.

Peace, who throughout his life professed to be a religious man, was most constant in his attendance; he affected to be remarkably devout. The hypocrisy of the man formed a very large element in his strange and diversified character.

The conduct and language of many of the other convicts gave evidence that they had no real or sincere appreciation of the solemn and sacred service they took part in. Indeed, most of them were in entire ignorance of its nature, and were like a set of puppets going through a performance.

Disgraceful scenes frequently occurred, even in chapel, but it would be in no way edifying to the reader for us to give a detailed account.

Of them it will suffice to note that there are at Dartmoor and other convict prisons in this country wretches, monsters in human form, who seem to be of a different organisation to ordinary men.

The outside world and inexperienced in matters of this nature can have no notion of the barbarous nature of some of the prisoners, who are mere brutes in mind and demons in heart.

To describe them and their crimes when at large and their conversation and acts within the prison walls would so disgust the reader that he would throw aside this work with horror and disgust.

Neither is it necessary or proper to pollute the minds of our readers by entering more fully into a subject which is both painful and depressing to dwell upon.

There are, of course, degrees of morality, or rather immorality, even in the most depraved, but it is pretty generally acknowledged by prison officials that the worst characters generally belong to the class known as *roughs*, and the worst of all are the *London roughs*.

Their language, habits, and mode of life are so radically bad that they may be pronounced irreclaimable, and for this reason: they were debased and utterly lost before they reached man's estate.

They are literally wild beasts, whose animal instincts predominate to the almost total exclusion of any intellectual or moral feeling, and with them kind words or good counsel must necessarily be thrown away.

There is but one mode of effectually dealing with them—brutes they are, and as brutes only can they be punished and coerced, and that is by the lash.

We have strong objections to flogging in the army and navy, but consider it to be the only efficient way in dealing with garrotters and ruffians who commit savage assaults upon either man or woman; in short, it is the only punishment that they dread, or that can exercise any influence as a preventive for crimes of this nature.

The man Baxter had passed through almost every gradation of crime; he had been a thief from his childhood, and so he remained upon reaching man's estate.

He was, however, not an unmitigated ruffian.

To say the truth, there was more of the sneak about him than the ruffian. As to moral principle, he had none.

His favourite " lay " was pocketpicking, and this he had practised to an extent which might be said to be almost unlimited.

He was very communicative to Peace and Raynton, the three companions in crime being the only occupants of the carriage.

" Well, old man," said Raynton, " you'll be a little more careful how you ' sling your hook' after this dose, I expect."

" I shall be as careful as possible, but lor bless ye, a cove may be as careful and artful as blazes, but he's bound to be ' pinched' sooner or later. Can't be helped, it's part of the business."

" That's right enough," remarked Peace; " but what places do you work as a general rule ?"

" I used to do all sorts of places, but my ' lay' lately has been chiefly in the churches or chapels. I used to tog myself up in black with a white ' squeeze' on Sunday, and go to two or three different places of worship. I dare say you'll be a little surprised when I tell ye that I've 'eard all the crack preachers in London, and, except when the May meetings were on at Exeter Hall I never went crooked any other day but Sunday. I used to do a bit in the smashing line; that was when I had a clever partner—but she's dead and gone now."

" She ! Did you have a woman for a partner ?" said Raynton.

" Why, of course; I've had several. I never had nothing to do with any ' Moll' who couldn't cut her own grass " (earn her own living).

" Oh, I see."

" But after she turned me up—which she did long afore she died—I stuck to the light-fingered business. You see, every man has his own particular ' lay.' Some go to public meetings, to races, fairs, and such like, but I always stuck to the churches and chapels, and did a quiet respectable business. A cove does better in the high church, where there's a lot of show and singing. The people there have got plenty of money, but I took precious good care not to go to one place twice within a month; but then you see there's plenty of them, and so there's no call to be too hard upon one establishment. But you must have a crowded congregation, else it's not a morsel of good trying to work it; besides it aint safe."

" Safe or not," said the burglar, " it seems you got ' pinched' in one of your pet places."

" Well, in course I did; but blokes have been ' pinched' everywhere and anywhere. As I told yer before, we can none on us guard against that. A cove makes a great haul sometimes at a race-course or railway-station a deal more than he might do in a church, but he runs greater risks, unless he's very fly indeed; but guess both of you have been working on a different ' lay.' I never succeeded in ' cracking a crib;' it's out of my line. Haven't got the nerve for it I s'pose."

Peace and Raynton exchanged glances. They were neither of them bright specimens of human nature, far from it ; but still it seemed to strike them both at the same moment that they had been listening to a man who spoke of pocket picking and earning a living at it as if it were a recognised and legitimate trade.

They both smiled, after which the conversation appeared to lag.

It was presently brought to an end, or rather turned into a different channel by two passengers who entered the carriage upon the arrival of the train at the next station.

Upon the three discharged prisoners reaching the metropolis they repaired to the nearest and most inviting-looking hostelry about.

They drank each other's health in a most cordial and convivial manner, which was quite touching to behold.

Mr. Baxter was most profuse in his protestations of friendship and good fellowship, and said he hoped as how they were not going to part for good and for all, but that he hoped to meet them, not on the Rialto, but at some of the accustomed haunts where gentlemen of his profession were wont to congregate.

Peace and Raynton both declared that they hoped to have the pleasure of meeting with Mr. Baxter on a future occasion.

That gentleman thereupon said that he might be able to put them up to a dodge or two, and that if he could it would afford him great pleasure to be of any service to both of them.

At length they succeeded in shaking him off.

Peace and Raynton walked on together for some little distance—they were chums or cronies who understood each other pretty well; a sort of friendship, if it could be dignified by such a term, had sprung up between them.

"Which way are you going?" said Raynton—"eastwards or westwards?"

"Westwards," returned Peace.

"Ah, just so, the very opposite direction to the one I am about to take. Well, old man, we've borne our 'prisonment together, and have been on pretty good terms, all things considered. I suppose you are like myself, not quite certain as to your future course of action, but I suppose you don't mean to turn me up—cast me on one side now that you are a free man?"

"Certainly not, Raynton, far from that."

"Well, then, before we part I'll just give you my address, or rather one where a letter will be sure to reach me. If you do write, be careful how you word it, for I've a wife and two kids to look after, and it's as well to keep the missus in the dark as to where we first met."

"All right," returned Peace, "you needn't be afraid of my saying anything—that is, anything you don't want me to say."

Raynton wrote down the address, which he handed to his companion, after which they repaired to another house, where they had a parting glass, and wishing each other better luck for the future they separated.

Peace, as we have already seen, had ample means at his command for his immediate wants.

He now began to reflect a little, that he might determine how to shape his course.

He glanced at the suit of clothes which had been furnished him; then he shook his head. He did not like them, and the first thing therefore was to get a new rig out.

He walked rapidly on in the direction of a new and second-hand clothes shop, kept by a gentleman of the Hebrew persuasion.

He knew the shop perfectly well; it was about a mile from the spot where he had parted with Raynton.

But it was rather late, and possibly it might be closed. There would, however, be no harm in seeing.

He hastened on, and in the due course of time arrived in front of the shop, which was open.

Peace entered. An old Jew poked his head out of a small back room in the rear of the shop, and upon observing Peace came forward.

"Vat can I do thish evening for you, my friend? Coat, vest, troushers, or vat?"

"I want a suit—a regular rig out," said Peace; "and you must give me what you can for the suit I've got on."

The Jew placed his hand on the collar of the coat Peace wore, and then made a face.

"Yes, I know; that will do," said our hero. "See what you've got. I want, in the first place, a black frock coat."

"New, or second-hand?"

"New, if you've got one to fit me."

"Ve alvays manage to fit our customers. Got something to suit everybody."

"Well—look sharp."

Peace tried on one garment after another until he succeeded in finding one that fitted him.

The same process had to be gone through with trousers and vest, for the accomplishment of which he was conducted into the private room.

"There," cried the Jew, in a tone of triumph—"couldn't be better if they'd been made for you. Never saw a better fit; you look quite the gentleman."

"Stow that! I don't want any of your gammon," cried Peace. "I'm not going to give you three pound ten for duffing things like these, so don't you think it."

"S'help me goodness they were never made for the money!" said the Israelite. "I shan't get five shillings out of the bargain. No—I wouldn't deceive you—not five shillings."

"Get out! I shall give you two pound ten and the suit I've taken off."

"Vat, theshe! they're not vorth carrying avay. Shoddy, nothing but shoddy. Never saw such rubbish in the whole course of my life."

"You know where they have come from, I suppose?"

"Oh, yes, I think I can guess. Her Majesty made you a present of them."

"Right you are, and that's why I want you to have them. Now then, don't keep tossing them about. What are you going to allow me for them?"

"Five shillings—not a penny more, and then I shall be loser. Not a farthing more than five bob. Oh, they are not vorth puying at any price; only, as you're a customer—and ——"

"There, that'll do; shut up. Will you take the two pound ten or not."

"I can't—pishness is pishness; but, at the shame time, one mush live."

"I'll take two pound fifteen—there!"

"Peace buttoned up his coat, looked at himself in the glass, and felt that he cut a respectable figure; so, without further haggling, he gave the Jew the required sum, and strode into the shop."

"You look all the gentleman except——"

"Except what?" exclaimed our hero, freely. "None of your nonsense—except what?"

"The hat."

"Ah, that's true. Have you got one?"

"Yes. A pot hat or a pilly cock?"

"A pot hat."

When Peace was fitted with a hat he strode out of the shop with all the airs and graces of a man of fashion.

CHAPTER LXXIII.

LAURA STANBRIDGE AT HOME—A CONFERENCE AND A SCENE.

THE reader will remember the young scapegrace, Alf Purvis, who was driven from Stoke Ferry Farm with the hare round his neck. He had now grown up to a slim, handsome young man, with an almost feminine cast of features.

His education was by this time completed. His instructor and trainer, Laura Stanbridge, in conjunction with her lawless associates, had transformed the country lad into one of the most expert and daring young London thieves of the period.

Alf was lost, irretrievably lost, and no one who knew him at the farm-house could recognise him as the boy who gave such trouble to Mr. Jamblin. He was so completely metamorphosed, personally as well as mentally.

We have had, during the progress of this work, occasion to give the reader some little insight into the lives and careers of juvenile and adult pickpockets.

Alf Purvis was the most accomplished one of the whole fraternity. He had a certain amount of education, was quick-witted, aristocratic in his appearance, and was, therefore, a dangerous person to be let loose on society. He had, moreover, for his accomplice a woman, even more dangerous than himself—a sort of harpy or beautiful demon, if such a term can with propriety be applied to one of the softer sex.

Alf Purvis frequented places of fashionable resort, and had the faculty of obtaining an entrance to select coteries in a manner which was altogether unaccountable.

He was, in short, the George Barrington of his day. His manners were so soft and winning that he was able to deceive and hoodwink his betters.

It is terrible to think of the change which had come over the farmer's boy.

Let us pay a visit to the house at the back of Regent-street. It was one of those hours of the night in which honest folk are asleep, and fools revel, and thieves work.

The vermin of society, like the vermin of the woods and fields, shun the light of Heaven, in which they see the effulgence of an Omnipotent power.

A man, with his face muffled by a cloak, was walking quickly through the courts and alleys which join Regent-street to Piccadilly.

The last of these passages ended in a mews, which we have already described.

Upon his arriving at this place the pedestrian came to a halt, and, glancing furtively around, he affected to be expecting somebody.

Drawing himself under the wall, he looked round till he saw a shadow on the pavement, and heard a step quick, cautious, and as stealthy as his own.

He looked round again, and seeing no policeman in sight, he gave a low whistle, and as soon as it was responded to, advanced into the middle of the road. The other man did the same, and then said in a whisper—

"Any crushers ?"

"No; the man on the beat has passed a few minutes since—the coast is clear."

"Make tracks then."

The two men went down the yard, and thence into a narrow deserted street, in which stood the house in the occupation of Laura Stanbridge.

They knocked in a peculiar manner at the door of the house, which to all appearance was uninhabited, for shutters were up before all the windows.

Any one, however, who supposed the habitation was without an occupant would be greatly mistaken.

The knocks were heard and answered on the instant.

A maid servant opened the door, when, without a word, the two men went in.

The girl locked the door after them, bolted it top and bottom, and finally secured it with a chain, which made it resemble the door of a prison.

All this had been done in the space of a few seconds.

"Is the missis in, my dear ?" said one of the men, in a tone half husky and half oleaginous.

"Yes, sir," returned the girl. "I think she's been expecting you; or, if it's not you, it's somebody else. You will find her in the little parlour."

The men looked at one another, nodded in a mysterious self-satisfied manner, and entered the room.

The little parlour in which they found themselves was furnished in a grotesque and peculiar style. The chairs were all of a different shape, size, and pattern. The carpet would have suited a large dining-room in some palatial mansion, and the paper a summer boudoir; while the dark oak bureau, in one corner of the apartment, frowned with all the sternness of antiquity upon a new and fashionable maple-wood cabinet in the other. As to any furniture en suite, as the modern advertisements have it, that was altogether out of the question.

The pictures, however, which disfigured the walls were all of the same caste and quality, equally indifferent in morality and art.

They consisted of portraits of celebrated criminals, executions, highwaymen stopping carriages and coaches, smugglers attacked by the preventive men, and pirates committing atrocities on the high seas.

"I thought she said her mistress was here," observed one of the men.

The other shrugged his shoulders and said, " She aint far off, I'll wager."

They took off their capes and comforters and sat down.

Both these personages have been already introduced on the night Laura Stanbridge paid a visit to the thieves' haunt in Whitechapel.

One was the "Smoucher," the other was the " Cracksman," and perhaps such another pair of scoundrels could not be found in the metropolis.

The Smoucher threw himself into a chair with the perpendicular back of the Elizabethan age —the Cracksman luxuriated in the soft depths of the latest patent spring.

Presently the sounds of footsteps were heard in the passage, and Miss Stanbridge entered. She was dressed in the height of fashion, and certainly looked what might be termed captivating.

"Glad you've come," said she, with a smile. "You managed to get here without meeting with any impediment ?"

"It was all fair sailing," returned the Smoucher. "No Queen's service men to overhaul us, but we took care to come by different roads, and walked the quiet sides of the streets."

"Where's the Prince ?" inquired the cracksman.

The Prince was a nickname they had given to Alf Purvis—now, however, no longer Alf Purvis, but Algernon Sutherland.

"He's not come, but won't be long, I expect," said Miss Stanbridge.

"Oh, in course he's not here," cried the cracksman. "Aint likely. He's dancing after some pretty face, and forgot all about our chapel, and all about the traps, too, I s'pose. I never saw such an owdacious chap. He'd follow a girl into a police station if he fancied her."

Laura Stanbridge tapped the ground impatiently with her feet. It was evident enough that she was vexed.

"What business is it of yours ?" said the Smoucher. "I make it a rule myself never to interfere with a young man's private affairs."

"I aint a saying anything against him," observed

the other man, "only I 'spose there's no harm in speaking one's mind. Concerning the women the Prince is as weak and wivery-wavery as a cabman that's lived on Haymarket gin."

"Well, and if he is, what of that? It's his only fault. He's a star—a regular out and outer. What wonders he's done for us already. Why, he knows more than any of us, and he's little more than a lad now."

"Ah, he's a right down good un—a regular stunner," cried the cracksman, with the enthusiasm of a true connoisseur. "He did that last job to rights."

"Lord, missus," said Miles Slann, the Whitechapel cracksman, "if yer'd been there yer heart would have melted to see how he walked into them safety locks. Chubbs are puzzlers to him, but at the hanky-panky business, the light-fingered part of the profession, there aint any one to touch him."

"Ah, he's very clever—there isn't the slightest doubt of that," said Miss Stanbridge.

"Clever! I just think he was. He does yer credit, and it's a good thing yer picked up with him when he was so young. He's been well taught, and I say agen he does yer credit. He does all on us credit," repeated Mr. Slann, in a still more forcible manner.

"Don't speak in so loud a tone, you noisy wretch!" exclaimed Laura. "Can't you say what you have to say in a lower tone?"

"Oh, I beg pardon, I forgot. We are not in Whitechapel now, but among the aristocracy. I forgot."

"Well, don't forgot next time," suggested the Smoucher.

"All right, governor. It's a way I've got, 'specially when I am speaking of the Prince; but Lord bless him he never keeps his own long. His blunt is blewed as soon as it is got."

"Hush!" cried Laura Stanbridge. "I hear his step—he has come in by the back way."

"Oh, you know his step—do you?"

"I should think I did. Silence, hark—yes, 'tis he!"

A tall, slim, young man entered the room. His features were almost womanly in their grace and beauty, but there was an expression upon them which it would be impossible to define, and which seemed to emanate from the eyes more than from any other feature, which were of a cold and cruel grey.

"I hope I haven't kept you waiting," said the young thief. "I know I am a little late, but it couldn't be helped, and so now to business, pals," he said, in a clear, sharp voice, every tone of which bespoke promptitude and decision. "You've both of you been too rash. There's no doubt, after that last job which you made such a mess of, that the blue bloodhounds will soon be after you."

"We shall be *chanted in the leer* (advertised in the papers) to-morrow," said the cracksman, in the brutal language of his craft. "We must *speel-to-the drum* (go into the country), captain."

These men, old in crime, already recognised him as their master.

"Yes," he replied, calmly, "you must make up your minds to go into the country, or to cross the herring pond. You are too well known in London to remain here with safety."

"Well, we must hook it, I s'pose," said Miles Slann. "There aint no help for it. Look here," he said, in continuation, addressing himself to his younger companion, "you were born and bred in the country, though nobody would believe it, to look at you now. Are there any "plants" to be made there nowadays?"

Mr. Algernon Sutherland crossed his legs in a sym-

metrical manner, and passed his hands through his flowing locks.

"Umph!" he ejaculated. "I hardly know how to answer your question. In the country dwell a race of men called farmers, who utterly disbelieve in banks, those nefarious institutions which have extinguished highway robbery—the high art of our profession—in order that they may pillage percentage from the million, and, by breaking now and then, utterly ruin the father-less and the widows. But these farmers, who are honest fellows in the main, ride home from market at a particular season of the year with a twelvemonth's income in their pockets, which season is the autumn, now close at hand."

"Oh, aint that fortunate?" cried the Smoucher. "But are there no banks in the country, then?"

"Plenty for gentlemen and tradesmen, and those exceptional farmers who prefer such custody to that of their own clumsy cudgels and rusty blunderbusses. However, they are all compelled to have large sums of money in their houses for the payment of their labourers on Saturday night."

"Just the place for our money," cried the Cracksman. "Let's have a country tour for the benefit of our health. I don't feel up to the knocker myself, and fresh air is needful. Besides, we aint wanted in London—leastways, if we are "wanted," which, in course, is likely enough, why it's as well to give the 'crushers' the trouble to run down to our country seat. Ah, ah! If there be kens to crack and heads to break on the main toby we're all there. What if we do get done for a cramp, and end our days at Tuck-up Fair? There's no need to say die on a dunghill, or talk without meat or drink. So, Lorry, let's have somethink that way, if you please."

"You are a good one for prog and lush," said the Smoucher. "If you were going to be 'topped' to-morrer, you'd ask to die with your mouth full. But take care, old sinner, he who cuts much beef has more belly than brains, and that won't fit in our trade, you know."

"Let him have his way," observed Laura Stanbridge. "He takes pretty good care of himself, and is not likely to starve when food is to be got; but blue ruin's ruina-tion, and a flash of lightning (a glass of gin) has been fatal to many a man before now."

"You must go separate at first, my lads," said the young pickpocket, "and disguise yourselves. This is easy enough; we have plenty of togs here for that pur-pose. We can find whatever you want in that way."

"You're as good as father, brother, and son to us, that's what you are," said the cracksman.

"If either of you should get boxed into the jug, one of us must help the canary bird out of his cage, and cheat the beaks again. I will write down some notions I have on the point, and you shall decide upon them afterwards. Bring me some pens and ink."

Laura Stanbridge rose from her seat, and took from a side table a handsome bronze inkstand, some writing paper, and pens; these she placed before the young man.

"All right, that will do," said the latter, who pro-ceeded to write down instructions for his two associates in crime.

While the Cracksman was eating and the pickpocket was writing, the Smoucher whistled a popular thieves' air in an undertone, and Laura Stanbridge remained apparently in deep thought, glancing furtively at her *vis-à-vis.*

The four personages formed a strange contrast; the woman presented the appearance of a handsome patrician lady, the young man to all appearance belonged to the "upper ten," and the Smoucher and the cracksman were unmistakeable ruffians of the most pronounced order.

The young man presently handed the paper to his two confederates.

The Cracksman frowned over it, not because he disapproved of the ideas, but because he found it difficult to decipher the words in which they were conveyed.

Honest English was as unintelligible to him as the hieroglyphics of thieves would be to us.

Having mastered the preliminary obstacles, however, he testified his delight by knocking down a chair on each side of him with his fist, and handed it to the Smoucher, who, on reading it, appeared no less charmed with its contents.

Laura Stanbridge rose from her seat, and crept out of the room.

Then they drew close together, and conversed for some time in a low and earnest tone.

An hour afterwards the two men passed out. This time each carried a large parcel under his arm, and each with a satisfactory nod went his way.

Algernon Sutherland, alias Alf Purvis, was left alone in the little parlour.

He appeared to be perfectly at his ease and utterly indifferent to the position of his companions in crime or the dangers which beset them both.

"Bah!" he ejaculated, taking a choice Havana from his cigar case. "They are a pair of ruffians without doubt, and must take their chance. I have given them the best advice, which, if they have sufficient prudence to follow, may help them out of their present scrape."

He lighted his cigar, and puffed therefrom thin wreaths of vapoury smoke.

Laura Stanbridge now returned, and entered the room.

She now wore a moire-antique dress, which displayed to advantage her bust, and hands white as Parian marble.

It was evident that she had made a careful toilette, for her attire was of the best and in excellent taste.

The grey-eyed young man was not accustomed to be taken by surprise, or give expression to his emotions, if he had any, in a demonstrative manner; still he did just raise his eyebrows and honour his female companion with an inquiring glance as she re-entered the room.

He acknowledged to himself that she was very beautiful, but round her eyes and mouth there were lines and wrinkles unnaturally deepened by the life of anxiety which she had led.

Nevertheless, all things considered, she looked well, and was by no means a faded beauty, albeit the bloom had in a measure left the peach.

"Alf, dear," she said, walking towards him, "I have something to say to you—a few words concerning my own happiness."

"Indeed! Well, to begin with, I must inform you that I am no longer Alf Purvis, the farmer's boy, from Stoke Ferry farmhouse—nothing of the sort, my dear. I am Algernon Sutherland."

"Of course, I know that. But in speaking to one who has been so long my pet, I addressed him by his real name—dont't you see?"

"Oh, I see," returned the young gentleman, puffing carelessly at his cigar. "But, my dear girl, you ought to know—but, of course, you do—that there is nothing real in the existence of a thief; it is as ephemeral as that of butterflies, ladybirds, and other poetical insects. I have changed my name as I have changed

my habits, my language, my associations, and my honesty."

Mr. Algernon Sutherland took two or three more long and vigorous puffs at his cigar, which had been trying to go out under cover of his eloquence.

"I will call you what you wish," she answered in a gentle manner and tone of voice, "if you will only listen to what I am going to say."

"All right, Lorry. Say what you like. I will listen complacently enough, and of course if it concerns yourself, I will promise to be deeply interested. Can I say fairer than that?" he added, with a chuckle.

"Get away, do, with your nonsense. You do love to be satirical, but that is little to the purpose. You spoke of changing, Alf—for I still cling to the name by which I have known you so long—and that very word has strengthened me in my determination."

"Your determination—eh?"

"Yes."

"And what might that be—to reform?" I hope you are not about to meet me with a long moral dissertation upon the past, the present, and the future?"

"And if I did, there would not be much harm in such a discourse. If I did wish to make reparation for the past by a brighter and less guilty future, there would be nothing to be astonished at."

"Oh, wouldn't there?" he remarked, carelessly.

"No, of course not."

"Well, go on. Fire away."

"Alf, I have been a thief ever since I can remember," said his companion, "and, oh, how I bitterly repent the crimes which others taught me! How sincerely I desire to atone for them by a life of virtue and repentance!"

She buried her face in her hands. Sutherland, as he now termed himself, withdrew the cigar from his mouth, and indulged in a sarcastic smile. To say he was astonished would perhaps be making use of too strong a term. He was a young man who was not easily astonished—but he was amused.

"Would you hear my history, Alf?" she said, as she raised her voluptuous eyes, which were now moistened with tears.

"Your history?" he repeated. "Yes, I should like to hear it. Proceed."

"It will, perhaps, make you take compassion on me. It was my own mother who first taught me to steal, who beat me when I returned without money, who trained me to look upon the gallows without fear or horror, as other children are taught to look upon a happy death-bed and a peaceful grave. I was very quick and nimble, and soon made myself proficient in picking pockets and counter snatching."

"So I should suppose," remarked her companion.

As soon as I could find I could steal for a living I worked on my own account, but let my mother have enough to keep her comfortably.

I was engaged with others in a robbery at my native town, Sheffield; my companions were arrested, but I contrived to give the police the slip, and hastened up to London; my companions were convicted, but I escaped.

In London I went into the service of an old woman, who dressed me in fine clothes and sent me to churches and theatres, where my lady-like looks enabled me to mingle with rich people without their suspecting that I was a thief, and to steal such numbers of watches, bracelets, and other articles of jewellery, that before I was seventeen I was as celebrated as Moll Cutpurse of old.

MISS LAURA STANBRIDGE DOES A FAINT.

By escaping from the clutches of the old Jewess, who thought she had me as her slave for life, and by diligently saving my money, I was enabled after some time to purchase the lease of this house, and enter upon a new and safer line of business—I became a receiver of stolen goods.

"And your friend?" said Algernon, carelessly.

"Oh, the lady you saw here when we first became acquainted."

"Precisely—the old lady."

"She was of service to me."

"So I should imagine, else you wouldn't have had her here."

"No, I met her at a rural lodging-house, playing at

hide and seek with the police about attempting infanticide or something of that sort. I do not know where she is now. We had some words, and she took herself off. After I met with her I used to ply my trade of shoplifting in fashionable quarters, parading her as my duenna."

"Oh, she could ply that part well enough, I dare say," observed the young man, dryly.

His companion proceeded—

"Thus you see, Alf," said she, "that few have had more experience in theft than myself, and few have had such success."

"I should say very few."

"Very few, indeed. I have never been in prison—I am rich, I have had nothing to discourage me, and if it were possible for a thief to be happy I ought to be so. But I am not—I am supremely miserable."

"You surprise me. Not happy?"

"No, far from it."

"I, on the other hand, am a thief pursued by justice, who, fortunately for me, is blind to fact as well as fiction, and yet you see I am perfectly happy and contented with my lot."

"You are happy now because you are tasting triumph for the first time, but be assured it will soon turn bitter in your mouth. You are happy now because you have earned the respect of villains, but the time will come when you will sigh for the goodwill of honest men."

"Umph!" muttered Algernon, "this is an entirely new line of business—preaching morality. Well, I am prepared to entertain the question. What do you propose?"

She placed her white hands upon his shoulders, and her lips upon his cheek.

"Might we not marry, dear Algernon?" she said, in soft beseeching tone. "How happy I should then be! We would travel on the Continent, give up all our old associates, and lead a new life. We would see all the grand sights in the world, and after that," she added, in a voice hushed as a sigh, as melodious as a song, "we would retire to some quiet nook in the country, and there dwell in delicious solitude. Say, dearest, if I may hope for this happiness?"

Her gliding step, her glittering eyes, her fragrant but fiery breath as she approached made her resemble a serpent which uncoils itself to spring.

He shuddered in spite of himself.

Then he rose, and exclaimed, in a voice of thunder—

"Marriage! And you can give utterance to that word as applied to our two selves?"

"Ah!" she cried, as she clenched her hands, and recoiled a few steps, "What is the cause of this outburst?"

"You have told me your history," returned he, recovering his *sang froid*, and lighting a fresh cigar at the dying ashes of his first. "Permit me to relate to you the history of another young lady, for I feel assured that you will find it wondrously interesting. Indeed, it is altogether so romantic that it would appear to many persons quite incredible, but it is correct in every particular—so I have been given to understand. The tale is so instructive that it becomes an actual warning to all who might by chance be acquainted with its heroine. Her name was Margaret Oughton."

The woman uttered a horrible cry. Algernon Sutherland closed his eyes and allowed the smoke to curl voluptuously from between his lips.

"Her name was Margaret Oughton. She was the daughter of a cotton operative. When she left her native town she met with a gentleman in London who was struck with her beauty. He feared to marry her;

the reason for this—or rather one of the reasons—was that he was old, and she was very young. Poor man, he was wondrously smitten with the fair young creature, who told him, with embraces, that she loved him. He was vain, and therefore believed her. He believed those embraces to be pure, which were as meretricious as those of a *fille-de-joie*.

"He married her, and before a month had passed away he found that she had a lover. He ought not to have been astonished at this, and the probability is that he was brought to look upon it as a very natural sequence; anyway he forgave her. In return this angelic young wife robbed him of every farthing she could lay her hands on and eloped with her lover."

"I was his tool—a mere puppet in his hands. I was at his mercy; he made me do it. I had no power to refuse," cried Laura Stanbridge.

"Liar and murderess! That man, your partner in vice, your accomplice in crime, was discovered lying in the high road, his face covered with frightful spots, and all the signs of death by poisoning within his frame. Therefore, my dear Lorry, since I have no ambition to play Duncan to your Lady Macbeth, or to have my tea sugared with arsenic any morning that you happened to sit down to breakfast in a bad temper, I politely decline your kind offer."

She looked at him calmly for a moment, gave a low moan, and fell like a corpse upon the floor.

He surveyed her with the inquisitive look of a prizefighter, who wishes to see what effect his "punishment" has had upon his adversary—a look in which sympathy is the least ingredient.

"Ah," he murmured, thoughtfully, "a knock-down blow—not with the fist, but with hard words. Well, this appears to be genuine, and, I suppose, must be attended to."

He poured out some brandy in a wine-glass, and knelt down by the side of the prostrate woman. He forced some brandy into her mouth, which he made her swallow. It seemed to revive her, for she opened her eyes and sighed.

I write "seemed," for Laura Stanbridge had only pretended to faint, in order that she might gain time to think.

She had been studying a part while she had been lying prostrate on the ground.

She made an effort to rise, and then groaned. Her companion placed his arms round her waist, and raised her to her feet. Then, with one arm round her, he held her in a half-fainting condition.

It so chanced that at this particular crisis Peace, who had been let in by the servant girl, gave a rap at the half-open door of the little parlour, and not receiving any answer thereto, he entered without further ceremony.

He beheld Laura Stanbridge in the arms of a fashionably-dressed genteel-looking young man, and felt that he had intruded at a *mal-apropos* time.

"Beg pardon," cried Peace. "Didn't know you were engaged."

"Oh, come in," said Algernon. "The lady's better now."

"Bless me, fainting fit, I suppose. How very sad!"

He took a tumbler off the sideboard, half filled with water, with which he moistened the forehead and temples of his old playmate.

"That will do—I am all right. Why it's dear old Charlie!" she ejaculated, catching sight of the well-known features of our hero. "Well, I am glad to see you—oh, so very glad! The sight of you has quite restored me. Sit down, Charlie."

"But you," inquired our hero—"how do you find yourself now?"

"Oh, better. I'm all right. Don't concern yourself about me," said Laura Stanbridge, throwing herself into an armchair, and smoothing her brown hair across her brows.

"I will see you later on," remarked Mr. Algernon Sutherland, as he glided out of the apartment. "Farewell for the present."

He gave a graceful waive of his hand, and passed on into the passage.

In another moment the front door of the habitation was gently closed, and Peace was left alone with his lady companion.

"Who is that gentleman?" he inquired, after Sutherland had taken his departure.

"Who? Why, don't you know?"

"How should I? Don't remember to have seen him before."

"Why, you old mufti, it's the boy, Alf Purvis—now a boy no longer, but a heartless young scapegrace, an ungrateful hound!"

"Ungrateful, eh?"

"Ah, that's it. As base as he is ungrateful."

"The boy who used to be with farmer Jamblin?"

"Certainly—didn't you know him again?"

"Dear me, no. Why he's quite a swell, gives himself all the airs and graces of the nobility. My word, but he's strangely altered."

"Ah, Charlie, you may well say that. He is altered. He owes everything to me, and a pretty return he makes for it."

"Would round upon you when he has the opportunity I suppose—eh?"

"It doesn't answer his purpose to do so at present, but he has shown his teeth and, doubtless, will bite in good time."

"Ah, Lorry," cried Peace; "what falsehood and dissimulation there is in this world! One does not know whom to trust. The longer a man lives the more forcibly he becomes impressed with this melancholy fact. I never thought very much of that lad. There's nothing open or candid about him, and he has a cruel, treacherous pair of eyes, but make your mind easy and get rid of the fellow."

"I shall have to do so, I expect, but it cannot be done at present. But I say, old man, how is it I've not seen anything of you for so long a time?"

"For a very excellent reason," returned Peace, with a smile. "Her Majesty required my services."

"Ah, I forgot you were landed at Sheffield for a little affair at Crooksemoor House. That was an unfortunate piece of business—but these things can't be helped."

"I left Dartmoor but a day or two since, and came up to London just for a day or two. A kind friend sent me a letter, in which was enclosed a twenty-pound note. I guessed where it came from, and so have called to thank you."

"I did not send it," exclaimed Laura Stanbridge, suddenly. "If I had thought of it I certainly should have forwarded you something—but, to speak frankly, the idea never occurred to me."

"You did not send it? The handwriting looked like yours, and I made certain——"

"You are mistaken. I have not sent any letter to Dartmoor—indeed, I did not know you were there. I should have thought they would have sent you to Parkhurst."

"Not sent it?" muttered Peace, scratching his head in a puzzled and perplexed manner. "Who the devil did send it, then?"

"That's more than I can tell you. Still, if you are hard-up, and want a little coin, you can have something to be going on with. The least we ought to do is to help each other in a case like this."

"I don't want any money at present. Haven't I already told you that I had twenty quid when I left that cursed place? Well, it's consoling to find that one has a friend, although it is an unknown one. But about this young fellow," cried Peace, suddenly changing the subject. "You've been having a row with him, I suppose."

The woman nodded.

"Is he a ruffian?"

"He's destitute of feeling and of gratitude."

"But Lorry, my girl, I hope he hasn't been base enough or brute enough to raise his hand against you."

"Oh, lor, no, it hasn't come to that. Oh dear no. We had a little bit of a dispute, that's all."

"Ah, and he was insolent, and, ahem, abusive, I suppose?"

"No, not that."

"What then?"

"He was jeering, taunting, and aggravating, and I lost my temper."

"And fainted."

"Something very much like it, but enough upon this head; come, let me help you to a glass of wine, or perhaps you would prefer a little brandy?"

"That would be better, certainly."

"Well help yourself, old man, and make yourself at home."

Peace mixed himself some brandy and water, and also a glass of the same for his companion, who had by this time in a measure recovered from the effects of the scene which had taken place between herself and Mr. Algernon Sutherland.

"I suppose you have had a nice time of it since I saw you last?" observed Miss Stanbridge. "Dartmoor is not an inviting or cheerful place, they tell me."

"I should think not, but I got on and made a good many friends. A great deal depends upon how a chap conducts himself, and I took pretty good care to be on the safe side. I gave them as little trouble as possible, and won the good opinion of the prison authorities; but, lor' bless you, Lorry, you've no idea of the wretches to be found in that heart-breaking place—fellows without fear or shame—monsters, in fact, who are worse than wild beasts."

"Oh, I dare say some of the very worst people it is possible to conceive find their way into prisons of that sort. Well, here's better luck in the future, and, as that gentleman with the gingham umbrella said, 'Always keep your weather eye open, my boy.' But you have not told me how the old lady is?"

"I haven't seen mother, or any of them as yet. Came straight to London, you know."

"Oh, yes, I forgot—so you told me. Well, give my love to all our friends at Sheffield when you do return. By the way, Emma was in the last swim—wasn't she?"

"Yes, she and my sister got six months' each."

"Ah, Master Charlie, you were always sweet on that girl."

"Nonsense—no such thing," returned Peace, indignantly.

"Ah! yes you were; you can't deceive me. I tell you you were sweet on her, and may be now for aught I know. Well, there's many a worse sort than Emma."

"A jolly sight worse," said Peace.

His companion laughed.

"There, didn't I tell you so? Ah! Charlie, you can't deceive me. Well, I should like to see Emma. Tell her to give me a call if she should come to London, which it's likely enough she may do."

"All right, I'll tell her—that is, if we meet again."

The two quondam companions continued their conversation about matters past and present for upwards of an hour, after which he bade Laura Stanbridge farewell and "took his hook," as he termed it.

The grey mists of evening were descending over the mighty city as Charles Peace threaded his way through the streets in the direction of High Holborn. As he approached Middle-row he saw at a few yards' distance a face which had been familiar enough to him in his earlier days.

He started involuntarily, for the face that attracted his attention was so strangely altered that at first he was in doubt as to its being the one which had been so familiar to him.

He came to a sudden halt, being in doubt as to his course of action.

"Charles Peace!" exclaimed a man, coming forward and offering his hand. "Speak, man. You do not fear or mistrust me—me, your old chum, Tom Gatliffe."

"So it is you, then?" ejaculated Peace.

"Why of course it is—didn't you know me?"

"Yes, oh dear yes, of course I did, but we have not met for so long a time and—well, to say the truth, you are greatly altered. You've grown a beard or something, which has quite changed your appearance, but —but—Tom I'm jolly glad to meet you."

"Ah!" murmured the young engineer, "I am indeed altered—not the same Tom Gatliffe you knew years ago; but I have been wanting to see you for a long time, and this meeting is very opportune. Still following your old business?"

"Yes! I am not doing much just now—so thought I would run up to London for a day or two."

"Ah, I have got a lot to tell you, but we can't talk in the street upon private matters. Where can we have a glass together?"

"Here's a quiet little crib just hard by—my time's my own, and I am quite at your service. Come this way, and I'll show you where it is."

"The 'Blue Posts' will do well enough," returned Gatliffe.

"Too noisy and crowded. I'll show you a better place. Come along."

The two companions walked on until they came to a quiet, unostentatious-looking public-house.

They entered and Peace led the way to a small dingy parlour, which was tenantless. Gatliffe rang the bell and ordered some wine.

Glasses were filled, and they drank each other's health.

By the flare of the gas-lights Peace had an opportunity offered him of taking a more steadfast and searching glance at his companion. He noted the alteration which time or sorrow had made in his appearance.

Tom Gatliffe was still handsome, but lines of care were distinctly visible on his well-formed features. The eyes had sunk deeper in their sockets, and there was a dark hue around them which Peace had never observed before.

He was not a very impressionable man, but he was much concerned at the evident change for the worse in the manner and appearance of the young engineer.

"You seem to be taken aback," cried the latter.

"You didn't expect to meet me, and are surprised, I suppose."

"I didn't expect to meet you, I admit, but for all that I'm jolly glad to see you, for barring one thing we have been the best of friends, and I owe you much."

"Ah, the one thing you refer to," remarked his companion, in a slow and melancholy tone, "is what I more than anything else have been wishing to see you about. You know, I suppose, that Aveline and myself are separate and apart. We are strangers. It is no fault of mine that we are so—it is her wish that we should be so. She has left me, Charlie, left me for wealth, position, and rank. I am not good enough for her now—now that she is a lineal descendant of an earl."

"Are you separated, then? Are you divorced?" cried Peace.

"We are separated, but not actually divorced; but I offer no obstacle, and I believe that the earl, her grandfather, is about to obtain a divorce. Well, after all, it is perhaps but a natural consequence. I am not fit to mix in the society in which they move."

"My word, but you take the matter in a most self-sacrificing way. She's your lawful wife. Why don't you exercise a husband's authority, and insist upon her returning to her home?"

"I don't care to do that. If she won't come of her own free will, let her go her ways. I have done with her for good and for all. She was always vain, Charlie —always yearned for wealth and grandeur. Now she has both, and I hope she's satisfied. That question has been settled long ago. What I have been anxious to see you for is to learn from your own lips how it first came about that she was traced and proved to be what she most unquestionably is, the granddaughter of that high and mighty nobleman. You brought it about, or were the main instrument in doing so. Don't imagine for a moment that I am about to upbraid you."

"Well, you see, it was just this. When I was staying at Broxbridge, a detective—a Mr. Wrench—came and made some inquiries about some blooming Italian professor and his wife. I told him all I knew, never thinking for a moment that they had anything to do with your wife. I told him all I knew, and he was a 'cute chap, and a decent sort of fellow enough for a detective—mind I put that in—for a detective—and the earl, too, was a good sort in his way."

"Ah, you know him, do you?"

"Certainly. I did some work for him—restored a picture, and made him some frames. He behaved in a very handsome manner to me, and I have every reason to speak in the highest terms of him. Well, as I was saying, I gave Wrench all the information I could; he followed up the clue, and you know the rest. But lord bless me, Tom, I don't know as you've lost much. As you were saying, she was always vain, and when I saw her in the carriage, being driven to the front entrance of Broxbridge Hall, she never so much as condescended to give me a passing nod—there's for you! And she knew at the time that I had been the chief means of proving her identity, and bringing her to all this grandeur, which she loves better than anything else, it would appear—better than her husband, better than her duty."

"Yes, yes, that is right enough," cried Gatliffe, testily; "but she's not so very much to blame—she has been wrought upon and over-persuaded by those about her."

"Rubbish, gammon!" cried Peace. "It's not much persuading she wanted—not a bit of it; it's her own free will. But, there, I don't want to pain you by these remarks; but it's what everybody says—everybody but you."

"I am satisfied, and am exceedingly glad I've seen you."

"I tell you what I'd do; but, of course, you have done so."

"Done what?"

"Insisted upon the earl allowing you a handsome income for the remainder of your life."

"I will not touch a penny of his money. Would starve first. Do you think I would consent to sell my wife?"

"Ah, well, that's a matter of taste," returned Peace. "I know which way the cat would jump if I were in your place; but, of course, all that is, as I before observed, a matter of taste."

"Ah," murmured the young engineer, with a deep-draw nigh, "it is astonishing what different views men take in matters of this sort."

"You take it too much to heart, I'm thinking," cried Peace.

"What makes you think so?"

"From your appearance, as well as from your manner."

"I am not like the same man, I admit, and yet I have no reason to complain. When Aveline was with me I had a struggle to get on to support her in a manner that she had a right to expect and desired. Since she has left me I have prospered beyond my most sanguine expectations. Two of my inventions have turned out much more perfect appliances than any one ever supposed, and they bring me in a handsome yearly income, in addition to the one I receive at the works; so that I am, as you may imagine, a prosperous man."

"But still you are not happy," suggested Peace.

"Not altogether, I admit."

"Hark ye, Tom. Don't let your happiness be disturbed by a woman. A man's a fool to do that."

"There's a good many fools in the world then," returned Gatliffe.

"Admitted, but that's no reason that you or I should add to their number."

Gatliffe made no reply. He was silent and thoughtful for some little time, after which he said, in an altered tone—

"And now with regard to yourself. You have not told me how you are getting on. Don't be offended, but if you are in need of cash—ready money, you know."

"I am not in need of any," cried Peace. "Not at present at any rate."

"Should you be."

"Well, what then?"

"You know where to apply—to me."

"A letter addressed to Mr. Gatliffe, London, will reach you I suppose?" returned our hero with a laugh.

"I will give you my address. I am still at the same place—Wood Green. Come and dine with me some Sunday."

"I can't. I return to Sheffield to-morrow, but when next in London will do so. Rest assured I shall keep the address."

And with this promise the two friends parted.

"Ah!" mused Peace, as he took his way to the coffee shop where he had taken up his quarters for a night or two, "he hasn't heard of the Crookhsemoor House business, and does'nt know that he has been hobnobbing with a convict just discharged from Dartmoor. So much the better. After all, Tom's a good fellow, and to say the truth he appears to have lost a good

deal of his upstart ways. I s'pose it's trouble as has done that for him."

CHAPTER LXXIV.

PEACE RETURNS TO HIS NATIVE TOWN, SHEFFIELD—HE TAKES UNTO HIMSELF A WIFE.

ON the day after his interview with Tom Gatliffe Peace returned to Sheffield.

The first visit he paid was to his mother, who was overjoyed to see him. It has been alleged that he was her favourite child. Be this as it may she always demonstrated a great amount of affection for him.

The poor old lady was not much to boast of as far as education or social position is concerned, but she was not credited with either refinement or gentility. Nevertheless, it is likely enough that she had occasion to deeply deplore the evil course some of her progeny fell into, more especially the ways of her son Charles.

The matrimonial alliance which Peace had contemplated forming with the discreet and virtuous Miss James was rudely interrupted by the sentence passed by the judge upon Charles Peace for the Crooksemmoor House burglary. Miss James and his sister had to do their six months as accomplices of the greater villain.

When Peace returned after the expiration of the time he had passed in "durance vile" he found that Emma James had not been so constant as he had fondly hoped.

The fact is she was thoroughly disgusted with the course he had taken at the time of the trial. He had vainly striven to throw the onus upon the two women. Miss James therefore allied herself—matrimonially or otherwise, it would perhaps be hard to say—with a young man more congenial to her own disposition, and Peace was fairly jilted.

This did not trouble him much. He was vexed at the time, but that was all. He consoled himself by flirting with several of the opposite sex.

Upon his return to Sheffield he resumed his old practice of playing the violin at public-houses. Although this was not particularly remunerative it brought him in some little ready cash, and in the day time he hawked spectacles and other articles.

It was during his peregrinations that he first met Hannah Ward, whom he is said to have married in July, 1858. This, however, is a little doubtful, for according to the prison statistics he was not discharged from gaol till the October of that year.

This is a matter which we shall find it difficult to determine, and we therefore give Mrs. Thompson's version.

He went long distances sometimes (observes that charming lady). It was on one of these excursions that he first met Hannah Peace—not Hannah Peace, if you please, but Mrs. William Ward.

I will tell you what he told me about their first meeting. It was at the side of a canal on the road to Hanley, in Staffordshire, he met Hannah, who had a baby in her arms, then six months old.

She stated, after they had got into conversation, that she was going along that way to find out her brother-in-law, who was the only friend she had in the world.

She was then a widow of William Ward, a pensioner, and she told Peace so. He asked her what she was going to do if she did not find her brother-in-law, and she answered, "I think of committing suicide."

Peace said, "You are surely not going to do that—a nice-looking woman like you." She was much older than he was, and I have no doubt was a good-looking woman.

Peace said that they stayed all night at an inn. He

promised her that if she would live with him he would prove a good father to Willie.

They went to Worksop for a while, and when there he perpetrated several burglaries in the neighbourhood. I can't tell you how many. But there, if I had taken his advice, I would have put down everything and written his life.

That child is now Willie Ward, who is twenty-one years of age, and Peace is not his father.

He (Willie) never showed strong affection for Peace, but when he came to live at our house in London he would do anything for me.

I think Peace took Mrs. Ward and her child to Sheffield and introduced her to his mother as his wife there.

The testimony of Mrs. Thompson, however, it must be admitted, must be looked upon with distrust, if not with suspicion—and whether this is the true story of the meeting it is not so easy to determine. It is, however, quite certain that after his marriage or connection with the woman whom he always acknowledged as his wife, that he resumed his old courses.

He professed at this time to be earning a living by hawking spectacles and cutlery, but his ingrained fondness for entering the houses of others and for appropriating goods that did not belong to him had not been eradicated by the prison discipline to which he had been subjected. His unhappy wife soon found out the character of the man with whom she had formed an alliance.

Peace at this time had no possible excuse for committing the numerous robberies with which he is credited. He was well able to maintain himself by an honest calling, and in addition to this he had friends who were both able and willing to assist him in an emergency.

It was not many weeks after her marriage that Mrs. Peace's eyes were enlightened as to the extra professional avocation of her husband, by a visit of the police to her house. His alliance with this ill-fated woman did not appear to have any influence over him, in the shape of turning him from his evil courses.

It would be a great misfortune if the boldness and fearlessness of this bad man were to blind even the most thoughtless to the utter worthlessness and depravity of his character.

In nothing does his baseness more transparently appear than in the miserable apologies and self-justifications with which his religious experiences are interlarded.

Assuming, as we are anxious to do, that these pious utterances of his later days are not wilfully insincere, they none the less betray an utter moral blindness.

He was very willing to call his past life base and wicked in general terms, but for his worst transgressions he had some extenuating plea which destroyed the validity of his assumed penitence.

If he could have been turned loose upon society again, one can hardly venture to hope that his future life would have corresponded with his edifying conduct in gaol.

The curiosity of the public to know all about Peace and his life need not be regarded with too despondent an eye, provided it goes no further than curiosity.

But whilst qualities like his command so much reverence and win such high rewards in other fields of activity, it would be vain to hope that our full-blooded and high-spirited youth will not see something to admire in his career.

If there are any such they will do well to remember that the grandest successes of a criminal course are at the best wretched failures.

Peace has probably had a far smoother life than most offenders of equal activity. Yet he has spent no inconsiderable part of his time in prison, and in the full noontide of his prosperity hardly reaped as much fruit from his misapplied talents as those talents would have yielded in any honest walk of life.

Thomas Carlyle, the philosopher of Chelsea, bewailing the degeneracy of the age, complains that we no longer, as in the old days, worship heroes.

To us it seems there is no lack of hero-worshippers in the nineteenth century, but that our heroes are of the wrong sort—imperial tricksters like the Third Napoleon, garotters of liberty such as Bismarck, and super-cunning criminals of whom the man who suffered on the scaffold for the murder of Arthur Dyson, at Bannercross, on the 29th of November, 1876, was a shameful example.

There are thousands of kindly, well-nurtured folk, with a taste for the marvellous, who openly proclaim their sympathy for Peace.

They tell us that every time he went out to rob, and, if necessity should arise, to murder, he carried his life in his hand: that he waged a daring and unequal war against the police and society; and that his courage, his resources, and his presence of mind in moments of the utmost danger, point him out as a man capable of greatness in a legitimate calling.

The argument is as worthless as it is spacious, for those very qualities are shared in greater degree by predatory wild beasts of the jungle. If, however, sympathy for this sort of social outlaw were confined to ladies and ladylike men, very little harm to society would ensue.

The mischief lies on another and a lower level.

It is a notorious fact that the criminal classes are themselves unduly proud of this sort of superlative villain; and if by any chance he were, at the eleventh hour, to elude the hangman, there would be much joy in many thieves' kitchens.

Nor does the public danger arising from such a career as that of Peace end there.

His evil example, in spite of its fatal ending, is calculated to debauch the wild imagination of foolish lads, and every atom of sympathy wasted upon him, every misguided attempt to cast the glamour of romance around his sordid, rapacious, and beastly life, is as a hand held out from the darkness to help the saplings of crime up the steps of the gallows.

Our sympathies are not for such as he.

We are sorry for the respectable man whom he sent suddenly out of the world, the man whom he sought to rob of his honour, and did rob of his life, with as little compunction as he was wont to display in robbing his neighbours of their goods and chattels.

We wonder how sane men can feel, much less express, sympathy for the midnight burglar. A man leads an honest, laborious, and thrifty life, and after many years of self-denial surrounds himself with home luxuries, such as plate, jewellery, clocks, and what not.

Suddenly a thief comes in the dark, and in a moment casts the shadow of irreparable loss over the decent citizen's existence.

Admit that the robber does display a certain sort of brute courage; so does the fox when he steals the poultry; so does the tiger that lies crouching in the jungle and waits for the unsuspecting traveller.

But the farmer traps the fox, and the hunter shoots

the tiger, and perhaps praises their courage—over their carcases.

Peace, as we have already demonstrated during the progress of this work, was a very fair musician, a clever carver and gilder, and a man of good natural ability in many ways.

He was very proud of his proficiency in those arts, which he displayed even in prison, once carving the wood pulpit for the prison chaplain.

His favourite device in prison, indeed, for obtaining lenient treatment was to exhibit a kind of universal "handiness," which conciliated the officials, until, though he had once headed a mutiny, he twice obtained remissions of his sentences.

He was ingenious, too, as well as artistic. He was a mechanician of some skill, having invented and made the false arm on which he greatly relied to conceal his crimes, as no one would suspect a one-armed burglar, and if advertised, he would be described as a one-armed man.

When father told us (continued Willie) where he was stopping, we asked him if he was not afraid of the sergeant's seeing his hand.

He said he could not see it, as he covered it up.

We asked him how he did it, and he took from his pocket the guttapercha arm you have heard about.

He told us he made it himself, and he certainly is very clever at making things.

He had got a piece of fine guttapercha, and he made it into a tube large enough to allow his arm to pass down it. Secured to the bottom of the guttapercha was a thin steel plate, in the middle of which was a hole with screw thread.

Into this hole he screwed a small hook, and at meal times he said that he took out the hook and screwed into the hole a fork which he had made for the purpose, and with it he used to eat his meals.

At the top of the guttapercha was a strap, which he used to fasten over his shoulder, and in that way keep the thing in its place.

No one who saw it could have told that it was not a false arm. He made his own tools, which were at once exceedingly simple and exceedingly effective, and once made a saw out of a piece of tin-plate.

He had, moreover, very considerable histrionic faculty, acting all sorts of characters to the police, whom he specially liked to deceive, and "changing his face" in a way which astonished those who knew him best, and made them declare that even they could not recognise him as he passed in the street.

He certainly could effect remarkable change in a moment, and the one which most disguises dark faces, by bringing the blood into his face till he looked bloated, instead of thin, and this without holding his breath, or any preparation.

There can scarcely be any doubt that he could have lived, and lived well as a carver and gilder; while as an engineer, with his gift for invention, and his very peculiar daring, which was not so much courage as a force of will, enabling him to do exactly what he intended to do, he might, had he possessed any virtues, have risen to competence and credit.

He was just the man for a mining engineer in a dangerous mine, or to superintend torpedo experiments, or in fact to perform any one of the functions in which ingenuity and recklessness have to be displayed at one and the same time.

He had the power, as he showed in his leap from the railway-carriage at Darnall, of compelling himself to accept any risk, however appalling, that stood in the way of his design, and this without losing the full control of all the intellect he possessed.

That form of courage is very rare—the impulse caused by danger seldom increasing both the courage and the brain-power even of brave men. It was noticed by the comrades of General Picton and Lord Gough that this was the case with them, and noticed as a peculiarity very exceptional even in armies.

Peace's daring seems to have been of this kind, and never failed him by night or day, under any circumstances of danger or solitude, any more than it fails a ferret or an otter.

That such a man should have deliberately elected to lead a life of unsuccessful crime and violent crime can be explained only by an inborn propensity to evil, which, if Mrs. Thompson's sketch of her paramour's life is in any part correct, seems to have distinguished Peace.

For, be it remembered, he was no successful criminal, living in luxury through a long life, and only found out by accident at last.

From the time he was nineteen, and robbed Mrs. Ward's house in Sheffield, to his final arrest, a period of twenty-eight years, Peace was always a hunted man, always in danger from the police, and so repeatedly convicted, that he passed sixteen years of his life, more than half the period of his criminal career, in penal servitude; and his last sentence, of which only a year had elapsed, when he was tried for murder, was for life.

His "life of luxury" was only the life of a small tradesman who prospers, and was maintained by constant exertion at a risk which, in spite of his daring and his health, made him an old man before he was fifty—so old that the police thought him too feeble for the usual fetters to be needed.

The bravest dread assassination, and it was that kind of terror, always present and always invisible, which Peace had constantly to face.

It was in spite of constant detection and severe punishment—once including a prison flogging—that Peace persisted in a career of crime, much of which, like his shooting at policemen, and, above all, his murdering Mr. Dyson, was entirely unnecessary, and, as it were, a superfluity of evil.

That he did murder Dyson intentionally seems, on the face of the evidence, certain; and whether his own account of his relations with Mrs. Dyson, or her account, or the third and most probable theory—that she was a foolish woman of a vulgar type, who accepted attentions from vanity, and was concealing something in her evidence, but not much—is the true one, does not signify a jot.

If the evidence was true, Peace resolved to shoot Dyson whenever Dyson's jealousy became inconvenient, and did shoot him, and if that is not murder there is no such crime.

The man, in fact, liked crime for crime's sake, and it was not possible for him to remain long without having recourse to his old practices—he was irreclaimable.

After his marriage he installed his unhappy partner in a house at Sheffield, and professed to be earning a living as a hawker.

It is quite certain that at this period of his career he was looked upon with suspicion by the police, who watched him most zealously; but he was so specious a rascal, that he half persuaded them he was pursuing an honest course of life.

Returning one day from one of his depredatory excursions, he met Sergeant Marsland, one of the officers who gave evidence against him in the inquiry respecting the Crookam-house robbery.

The sergeant regarded him with a look of suspicion.

"Well!" cried Peace, with the utmost effrontery, "what are you stagging me for? Suppose I'm doing something on the cross, eh? You fellows can never let a chap alone. When he is disposed to be honest he's hunted about like a wild beast because he was once in trouble."

"Don't you be so cheeky, my friend," observed the sergeant. "I haven't accused you of doing anything wrong, neither shall I, unless there is strong reason for my doing so. I only hope you are acting on the square; and if you take my advice you'll continue to do so. You don't suppose we—any of us—want to see you go wrong?"

"Well, then, you just leave me alone, and don't be watching me about in the way you and others of your calling have been doing. I'm right enough. Have got a wife to look after, and don't mean to get into trouble again, if I can help it."

"I am glad to hear you say so," returned the police officer. "And understand, Peace, that I shan't interfere with you as long as you keep clear of the law. It does not afford me, or any of us, pleasure to get you into trouble."

"Oh, doesn't it?"

"No, certainly not. I tell you again to keep as straight as you can, stick to your business, and act on the square, and nobody will interfere with you."

"I only ask you to leave me alone. I am all right enough now, but it isn't any reason because I have been once in trouble that I should be for ever suspected, and watched or followed about."

"I will take no notice of you provided you keep clear."

"All right—that's understood then," cried Peace, in a cheery tone.

The police-sergeant made no further reply, but walked on at a steady, measured pace.

"The stealthy beggars have got their eyes upon me," murmured our hero, "and I must act with caution, or I shall be 'copped' as safe as houses."

To "work" at Sheffield, as he termed it, or in other words to commit robberies in that town, was not to be thought of; he, therefore, paid occasional visits to other towns, and on many occasions he went about disguised as a navvy, pretending to be looking for work, but he was really "spotting" the houses he meant to attack.

He broke into a clothes warehouse at Bradford, and was detected in the act, and, to cover his escape, he fired "wide" at a policeman and the watchman.

This adventure put an end to his depredations in that town for some considerable period, for he was, naturally enough, afraid to pursue his favourite calling after the narrow escape he had had.

He therefore changed the scene of action, and betook himself to Leeds, where he remained for three weeks, during which period he forwarded remittances to his wife at Sheffield.

While at Leeds, he met with an adventure, which caused him some anxiety, for it was only by a miracle that he escaped discovery.

He entered a house on the outskirts of the town just as it was getting dusk.

He proceeded at once to the front floor of the establishment, and possessed himself of several articles of value.

As he was engaged in transferring them to his bag, he heard footsteps on the stairs. Quick as lightning he flew out of the room, and managed to reach the next story without attracting the notice of any of the occupants.

The room in which he now found himself was an elegantly furnished sleeping apartment. He stood breathless, listening to the movements of those below.

He heard the sound of a female voice addressing a companion, who was evidently another female, to judge from the tones of the voice.

To his horror he heard the footsteps of two persons who were evidently making for either the room in which he was ensconced, or else one on the same floor.

He was seriously alarmed, but did not lose his presence of mind.

He looked out of the window of the bedchamber, and saw several persons on the lawn in front of the house, they were playing at croquet.

Escape by means of the window was, therefore, impossible, his movements would be sure to attract the attention of the croquet players, and if he passed out of the room through the door, he would, in all probability, be confronted by the two females.

At such a crisis as this every moment was precious. "What could he do?"

A sudden thought struck him. In the bedroom was a large press or wardrobe. A key was in the door of this. Peace withdrew it as noiselessly as possible, crept into the press, and then locked himself in.

Any way it would give him time to determine upon his course of action. Possibly the ladies were about to enter some other apartment.

He listened till his ears tingled again. He was not kept long in suspense.

The footsteps on the floor told him that other inmates were there besides himself. He knew also that they were of the softer sex.

He breathed as softly as possible and durst not move. The words which fell from the lips of the newcomers he heard most distinctly.

A horrible thought crossed his mind. It was this—

Suppose the articles he had purloined were missed, a search would be made, and the doors of the press would be broken open without ceremony.

He felt half inclined to unlock the door and make a rush for it, but then the fact that there were some dozen persons or more on the grass plot warned him of the danger attendant upon such a course.

No, he would patiently await the issue.

The two personages who had entered the bedroom were the mistress of the house and her maid. He very soon became aware of this from the conversation which was being carried on.

The lady sat herself down before the looking-glass, and the maid began to dress her hair.

She was about to make an elaborate toilette before sitting down to dinner. Through the keyhole of the door of his prison-house Peace commanded a view of both females, and was, therefore, able to appreciate to its full extent the elaborate performance that was going on. He inwardly cursed the absurd customs of ladies adorning themselves before presenting themselves in the banquetting room.

He watched the long tresses of the beautiful woman as they fell over her shoulders, and were gathered up by the taper fingers of her handmaiden. The time occupied in dressing and decorating the head seemed to be an age to the imprisoned burglar—who was half stifled in his hiding place.

"I don't like the way you've arranged my hair," said the lady, viewing herself in the glass. "It appears to be drawn too much back, Kate."

PEACE ESCAPES THROUGH THE BEDROOM WINDOW.

"Well, marm," said the girl, "it's as you wished; but if I might be allowed to have my own way I should dress it as I did on Tuesday last. I am sure you looked lovely then."

"Hush, you silly girl. Don't flatter."

"No, madam, I'll leave that for the gentlemen to do; or rather, I mean, I'll let them speak the truth."

"Well, do it as you did it the other night. You shall have your way."

The hair had to be undone, and further manipulations had to be gone through, much to Peace's disgust.

The sound of merry voices, which proceeded from the party on the lawn, reached the apartment, and occasional bursts of laughter were also audible.

"The major's voice," said the lady.

"Yes, marm, what good spirits he is in to-day! He's always merry, but he's more than usually so now. Oh, he is a nice gentleman."

"Yes, kind and considerate to every one, and he's so full of anecdote, too."

"He's been in the Crimea—has he not, marm?"

"Oh, dear yes, all through the Crimean war—at Balaclava, Inkerman, and Sebastopol."

"Oh!" murmured Peace; "there's a major in the case, eh. This is lively. I'm in a pretty pickle, and it will be a wonderful thing to me if I succeed in getting clean off. Hang the woman!—how long does she intend to sit before that blooming glass?"

Our hero soon discovered that only part of the toilette had been performed.

The lady had to change her dress, but luckily for Peace the garment in question was not in the wardrobe. Had this been the case he would have been lost. He had the satisfaction of seeing her maid produce the dress from some part of the room which he was not able to ascertain. He was, therefore, greatly relieved upon beholding the mistress of the establishment disrobe, and put on the costume which was handed to her by the maid.

It took some time to arrange this in a satisfactory manner. Jewels, cuffs, and collar had to be added, and after some further time had been expended in adornment the lady and the maid crept noiselessly out of the room.

Peace felt greatly relieved.

The question was, how could he manage to get clear off. He unlocked the door of the wardrobe and peered out.

No other person was in the bedchamber besides himself. He looked out of the window, the croquet players were no longer visible.

They had in all probability betaken themselves to the dining-room. He felt assured of this as he heard the confused number of voices proceeding from the lower portion of the house.

He waited till he thought they had taken their seats at the dinner-table, then he went to the landing and listened.

A savoury odour found its way up the staircase, and the clatter of dishes was distinctly audible.

"Now is my time," murmured the burglar.

He passed down the front flight of stairs and beheld servants passing to and fro in the hall.

What was to be done? His retreat was cut off. If he attempted to descend into the hall detection was certain, and to remain where he was would be almost as bad.

By this time it was nearly dark on the outside of the house, but the blaze of light came from the rooms below and the gas lamp in the hall. Peace was sadly perplexed. Every moment he expected the articles he had purloined would be missed.

He went once more to the window. In the front of the house was an old vine, one stem of which was near to the side of the window.

When he made this discovery he at once determined upon his mode of escape. Hanging the bag containing the stolen property round his neck he crept out of the window, and supported himself by the stem of the vine by means of which he managed to reach the grass-plot in front of the house.

He had hardly succeeded in doing this when he heard shouts and cries of alarm proceeding from some persons in one of the rooms at the basement of the habitation. He did not wait to ascertain the reason

for the cries, but fled as fast as his legs could carry him, and vaulting over the railings which encircled the garden he reached a narrow bye-lane.

He still heard cries in the distance, and saw several persons emerge from the side gate of the garden.

Two or three shouted to him, and ordered him to stop, but Peace knew a trick worth two of that. He fled, but found, to his dismay, that a party of gentlemen had rushed off in pursuit of him.

He heard the clatter of their footsteps on the hard road.

Shouldering his bag he rushed madly on until he reached a dense thicket of trees; into this he crept and passed on as quickly as the nature of the trees and underwood would admit.

He now arrived at the open country again; running across two meadows he came to a narrow pathway skirted by two hedges.

At the end of this was an old dilapidated-looking mansion, on the front of which was a board with the words "To be Let or Sold" written on its face.

Peace passed through the hedge by the side of the mansion, and made for the back door. He succeeded in turning the lock of this by means of one of his skeleton keys.

He opened the door, slid in, and closed it noiselessly after him. Then he bolted it from the inside.

He was now the solitary occupant of a large red brick building, which had the unenviable reputation of being haunted, and hence it was that it had been so long tenantless.

But, cheerless and dilapidated as the place was, it afforded him a temporary shelter, and as no one suspected that he had effected an entrance he was safe for the present.

He listened and heard the clatter of horses' hoofs—the footsteps of men, who were carrying on an animated conversation.

"I tell you he went this way," cried one; "I saw his shadow on the path. He's not far ahead, and can't escape us, the villain."

"No—no!" cried another, "he turned down the lane to the right, and is, doubtless, making for the high road."

"Well, if you are so positive about it, Vensill, have your own way. You and one or two more go that road, while I and some of the others go my way."

"All right—so be it. We will separate into two parties, and hunt the scoundrel down."

"Very wise of you to do so," murmured Peace. "You may go to the devil for what I care! I wish you success."

The party of pursuers separated into two detachments, and soon the silence of the night was still and unbroken, as far as the ruined mansion or its occupant was concerned.

Peace had with him one of his long, thin screws, and if any attack had been made on his place of refuge he had made up his mind to fasten himself in one of the rooms by means of the screw, but as the pursuing party had left him unmolested in his retreat there was no occasion to have recourse to such an alternative.

He felicitated himself upon the successful nature of his ruse. It was not likely the enemy would return that way, and if they did it was still less likely that they would make any attempt to storm him in his castle.

He was therefore determined to remain concealed till such time as he might reasonably suppose that his enemies had given up the chase as hopeless.

The old habitation in which he found himself was cheerless and depressing to the last degree. He soo found out that it was infested with rats, for he heard them squeaking and scampering about in all directions.

Fond as he was of animals, rats were not included in the list. He held them in the greatest abhorrence, and so when the throng of persons on the outside had taken themselves off he stamped and knocked against the walls to scare away his four-footed associates.

The house was miserably dark and dismal, and he would have been greatly relieved if he had a light.

But this was not to be thought of; if he ignited his wax taper it would most likely betray him, for anybody passing the house would be apprised of his presence by the gleam of light from one of the windows. He had therefore no other alternative than to endure the gloom of the place as he best could.

An hour passed away—an hour of misery and suspense—an hour of bitterness and depression.

Still Peace did not deem it safe as yet to sally forth.

He might pass the night in the old mansion and leave by early dawn, but he was not disposed to do so. Sleep would of course be out of the question.

There was not a solitary article of furniture in any of the rooms.

He was not a superstitious man, but, nevertheless, could not conceal from himself that the place seemed to be admirably adapted for the haunt of witches, warlocks, and gnomes.

Anyway Peace was most anxious to leave it as soon as possible, but it would not do to be too precipitate.

The party of gentlemen who had started in pursuit of him might be looking about, and Peace deemed it advisable not to give them a chance of effecting a capture.

Miserable and lonely as were his quarters, they were preferable to running a chance of being sent to penal servitude.

He therefore waited for nearly another hour, at the expiration of which time he sallied forth, bag in hand.

No one was visible; he argued that the party must have returned to the house, so shouldering his bag he walked boldly on, taking care to keep on the dark side of the road as he watched for the appearance of any chance wayfarer.

Two or three men passed him, and, as they did so, wished him good night, but they evidently belonged to the working class, and he had no misgiving as to them.

In a short time he reached the high road, when, at some distance ahead of him, he beheld a night patrol. He took good care to conceal himself in a bye lane till the officer of the law had passed; then he emerged from his place of concealment, and proceeded along with greater confidence.

CHAPTER LXXV.

PEACE AND THE TRAVELLING SHOWMAN—THE COMPANY AT THE "BLUE DOLPHIN"—THE SHOWMAN'S LEGEND.

PEACE had not gone very far before he came up with a travelling caravan.

The vehicle in question was going at a slow pace, it was heavy and cumbersome, being, in fact, a sort of wooden home on wheels.

Peace could not at first quite make out what it was, but upon closer inspection he came to the conclusion that it was a show, such as one sees at fairs. The driver was seated in front of the vehicle trolling a merry ditty.

"Good night, my friend," said Peace.

"An' good night to you," returned the driver. "Bedad, but this is not the most lively road for a man to thravel."

"No," said Peace, "it is not; but you have the advantage of me. I have many miles to travel on foot, and I am as tired as a dog. You couldn't give a chap a lift, I suppose? I'll pay for the accommodation."

"Faith, and may be I could; but who and what are you?"

"A traveller—a poor hawker."

"Och! Sure now, I aint the man to refuse a favour o' that sort. Which way are you going?"

"Anyway, as long as I can get a lodging for the night."

"You seem a quiet, dacent, sort of man, and, as the saying is, any company is better than none, so jump up—you can ride by the side of me."

"I am sure, you are very kind," cried Peace.

The caravan driver brought his vehicle to a halt, and Peace was but too thankful to avail himself of the offer.

When he had taken his seat the lumbering wooden house was again set in motion.

"An' sure it's not much room there is for the dhriver and his friends on this mighty big machine. But there's good reason for that—the room is wanted for the inside passengers."

"Inside passengers!"

"By the powers of St. Patrick, yes! and not much to spare, either."

"What have you got inside, then?"

"What! why great natheral coorosities—sarpints, kangaroos, a baboon, and a few monkeys. Oh, they are amoosing crathurs, an' as sinsible as Chrishtins."

"Oh, I dare say."

"The guv' has gone on in the other caravans to the fair, which is to take place—bedad, I don't know rightly where it's to take place, but I'm to be there some time to-morrow."

"Oh, you're in the travelling show line, are you?"

"The guv'nor is—I'm only an ondherstrapper, as you may call it—a sort of handy man. But there's a power of work to get through in one way and another."

"Then where are you now bound for?"

"Is it where I am goin' you mane?"

"Yes."

"Och, sure, but it's at a bit of a roadside house I'm afther making for—'The Blue Dolphin.'"

"And where is that situated?"

"Where? Sure, now, an' it'll be about a mile or so this side of Pocklington."

"Ah," said Peace, remembering the name of Pocklington but too well.

It was a Mrs. Pocklington who prosecuted him for attempted burglary, and who had committed such a ferocious assault on him with a house broom.

"But may be you don't know the place. The name is not familiar to you."

"Ah! but it is most familiar," returned Peace; "and if they can accommodate me, I think I will put up at the 'Blue Dolphin.'"

"Ah! bedad, but they must accommodate you. They're dacent people enough, and aint particular at all, at all."

The two chatted familiarly during the whole of the journey, and the conversation did not flag or come to a conclusion till the house in question was reached.

Mr. Dennis Macarty—that was the name of its driver—who was, it is perhaps needless to say, a native of the "Emerald Isle"—took good care to see his animal safely housed for the night, and after this had been done he joined Peace in the snug little parlour of the establishment.

Mr. Macarty seemed to be well known to the landlord, the landlady, as well as the frequenters of the house, all of whom addressed him in a familiar and friendly manner.

"And how's business, Mr. Macarty?" inquired a sedate-looking little man in the public room.

"Ooh, murdher, it's mighty bad, intirely, and has bin so for a goodish while. We've got some of the most intherestin' natheral coorosities, but they don't dhraw as they ought. May be we do a roaring business in wan town or at wan fair, but the next two or three places are, bad lcok to 'em, that bad that we dhrop a power of money. Ooh, by Jabers, things are not what they used to be."

"And you've seen a goodish bit in your time?" said another of the guests.

"Bin all over the world—no, I don't quite mane that, but I've bin everywhere in the United Kingdom. But people seem to have lost heart."

"That's true enough—we all find that out," cried Peace; "at least I find it so in my line."

"An' what might that be, if it's a fair question?" said the sedate little man.

• "An' sure it's in the hawkin' line that our frind is," returned Macarty.

As the steaming glasses of whiskey and water went round, the company became loquacious and assumed a festive character.

Mr. Macarty was full of anecdote. He had stories to tell which elicited roars of laughter, and was voted a most genial companion, which, to say the truth, he most unquestionably was.

After treating them with several amusing anecdotes, he all at once came to a halt, and said sharply—

"Ooh, sure now, did I ever tell ye about the biggest man in all Ireland?"

"No, never!" cried several.

"I never did?"

"No."

"Then, bedad, I'll tell it ye now."

"Ah, do, Macarty ; let's have it."

It's a sort of legend, and may be ye never heard anything of the kind. It's all about Jack Grady and the joiant. First and foremost ye must know Jack was mighty proud ov his size, and ov bein', as he used to say, the greatest man in all Ireland, an' sure enough he was tremendious big. He was more nor seven feet in hoigth, so I've been tould, and had a carcass on him like an eighteen-gallon kag.

"Oh, draw it mild !"

Ah, but I wouldn't desave you, it's thrue for him. Well, one day when Jack comes thrampin' down into Leenane, to get himself measured for a pair of brogues, for he was mighty savin' upon shoe leather, by raison of his weight, he goes into the shop of the brogue maker, wan Farrell by name, a little atom of a man, wid a sharp tongue of his own, who used to take grate divarsion out of big Jack, by gibin' him an' makin' all sorts of dhroll collusions to his bulk and diminsions.

"Top of the mornin' to you, Jack," says Farrell.

"I think you might say Misther Grady to yer bet-thers," returns Jack.

"My bethers! What d'ye say?" cries the little man. "And for why, now? Is it becase yer big and bulky, and ate more bacon for yer breakfast than would kape a family for a week? Arrah! what good are ye at all, at all, except in filling house room? And, for the mathther of that, I saw a biggar man than you are only yesterday, an' he hadn't half your consate."

"That's a big lie, anyhow," says Jack—" a regular whopper. Botheration, but everyone knows that I'm hebiggest man in all Ireland."

"Devil a lie," cried the other. "There's a biggar and finer man than you in Ballinrobe this minnit, and what do you think they are doin' wid him? Why, they are showin' him to the people for twopence in a raree show, just as they do wid the wild bastes. Bedad, if you are wise you'll go and show yourself for twopence. It's all you are good for."

"You dirthy spalpeen. By St. Patrick, but I'll dust yer jacket for your impidence," and with these words Jack makes a wipe at him wid a bit of a stick he used to carry—it was like the mast of a Galway hooker was that same switch.

But ye see, my friends, the little brogue maker was as nimble as a bounding acrobat, an' he skipped away just in time, an' Jack almost knocked out the wall of the cabin wid the whack he gave.

Well, he knew of ould there was no ketchin' Farrell to gi' him a basting, so he made it up wid him, for, to give him his jew, he never bore malice, and was a grate dacent sort of man.

"Ooh, look here, now, I don't want any more of your mighty big lies, so kape your tongue betwane yer teeth, and measure me for the brogues."

Farrell obeyed, and his customer left, but ne was mighty unasy in his mind about the man at Ballin-robe.

"What ails you?" said his wife, upon his return. "Ye don't same yerself at all at all."

"Don't consarn yerself about me," cried Jack. "I'm right enough."

But his wife knew betther. She axed him to sit down to supper, but he refused—and he refused also to take a shaugh at his pipe, he was that heavy in his heart.

"Maybe he's fallen in love wid some forward jade he's met wid," murmured his wife.

Jack was quiet, silent, and a bit thoughtful—an' whin he turned into bed, he says, "Waken me airly for I've got a thransaction at Ballinrobe," and wid that he goes to slape, determined to make a complate dis-covery of the whole matther before he was a day oulder.

In the mornin' he set off for Ballinrobe; but as bad luck would have it, when he got there, the carrywan wid the joiant was gone and all that they could tell him was that it tuk the Castlebar road.

Off goes our frind post haste widout waitin' to take bite or sup, and at last about six miles out of the town he sees the carrywan standin' by the roadside.

It was a big yalla chay made in the shape of a house, wid an illigant hall door and glass windies to it, and "O'Shannasey's Pavilion" wrote in big letthers over them, an' the people belongin' to it was sittin' on the grass by the side of the road aitin' their dinner aff the top of the big dhrum, an' sure now I was one of those, for I first larnt my business wid old O'Shannasey.

The guv'nor was there as well, and a mighty clever fellow he was, too. He used to do thricks wid knives and forks, and crumple a large buck rabbit quite small and put it in his wesket pocket.

"Oh, I say," cried one of the audience.

Oh, divil a bit am I afther spaking ony unthruth.' He done it as asy as anythin', and there was a north countryman wid one leg, who was mighty handy at a Highland fling, which was a bit of a cooriosity for a cripple, you'll all acknowledge.

"Ah, yes, certainly," exclaimed several. "Anybody else ?"

Sartinly. There was a young woman who used to dance in throusers wid frills to them, and take the money in a tambourine when the people went to see the show. An' people did go to see shows in those days.

Besides all thase there was the joiant, but the moment they saw Jack Grady comin' puffin' down the road, they made him lave off actin', and crawl into the carywan, not likin' to let him be seen too chape.

"Health and prosperity to ye all," says Grady.

"And bedad the same to ye, sir, an' the top of the mornin' to ye," cried the showman.

"An' sure now I've bin teuld that ye have a joiant in yer show. If this be so, might one jest ha' a look at 'im ?"

"By the powers, you're a bit of a joiant yerself I'm afther thinkin'," says a young woman, laughing at him quite pleasant.

"Them's my raisons, my darl——, that's to say miss," says Grady, very respectfully, for he was struck intirely wid her, never seeing the like afore. She was a weeshy little crathur, dressed out wid fine ribbons, wid a sallow face, and a spot ov ruddle on each cheek like a poppy in a corn field. But then she had a purty nate foot, and them was faymale accomplishments Jack was mighty partial to.

Well, my frinds, to make a long story short, when they hard he had come all that way to see the joiant they agreed to let him have a look for a bob, tuppence being the regular price on show days, but this was a private view, and cheap at a bob.

So the long man was brought out, an' he an' Jack stud up beside aich other, an' sure enough, Grady wasn't within a head of him, but then he wasn't within three feet as big round the body as Jack, and when they came to talk of sthrength and fell a wrastling, Jack threw him on his back with the greatest aise.

Jack was quite plazed at overcomin' the tall un—so much so, indeed, that he got quite friendly wid the whle ov us, more especially wid the young woman, and when the one-legged man pulled out a pack of cards and proposed a game he went in, as good manners dictated, and av coorse got rooked most awful.

No wondher; he was wake as wather when girls was present, and instead of mindin' his play he was carryin' on wid the young woman, and she encouragin' him, all to spite the long un, who was by way of courtin' her. While this was goin' on the showman was eyein' Jack, and remarkin' "how thunderin' big he was."

"He'd make a mighty good property," says he to the one-legged man.

"That he would, sir, and no mistake," says I.

"The other fellow won't last long," said O'Shannasey. "He's gettin' quite wake on his legs."

"He niver was sthrong on thim," says the cripple; "but he says it comes from lyin' doubled up in the carywan."

"That's all blather," says O'Shannasey; "it's goin' he is. I wish we had this chap in his place, so as not to be left widout a joiant at all."

"I wondher could we coax him to jine us ?" says Wan Leg.

"I much doubt it," returned the showman.

"See," says I "how Biddy is puttin' the comether on him. Suppose we give her a hint. She's the divil for deludhering, anyhow."

"You see what ye can do wid her."

Upon the first oppoitunity I took Biddy aside, and made her sinsible, and explained my maning to her, and then the cards was put away, and a dhrop of the "crathur" brought out, and they all fell to dhrinkin'.

"I don't know if any ov you here have remarked that big men never stand the dhrink."

"I have often remarked it," cried Peace. "They seldom do."

Well, then, he was no exception, but the rason must be that he'd bin fastin', not forgettin' also that the young woman never let his glass stand empty. Jack was very soon obfusticated.

Then they all got into the carrywan, Jack hooraing like anything.

Then they had some more of the "crathur," until Jack tumbles on the floor speechless.

"You gev him too much," says the showman.

"Devil a bit," says Biddy; "you lave him to me."

So they doubled up Jack and crammed him into a part of the carrywan that was made for the great say sarpint, and put a stuffed mermaid under his head for a pillow.

When they got into Castlebar Jack was sleepin' beautiful, so they left him quiet and paceable where he was; and in the morning, when the people began to clusther round the consarn to see the coorosities he was sleeping still.

Well, there was no cause to rouse him, for the say sarpint he was lying with couldn't bo exhibited in regard to being bruk to pieces by the joultin' of the machine over the bad roads.

So the showman began callin' the people to step up and see the great Portugee joiant an' the Injin jugglar (maynin' himself—the ould imposther!), and the grate rowling picther of the goold diggins, and the rest of the wondherful things, every wan of them lies, more or less.

"Plenty of the more, and very little of the less," said Peace.

"Oh, bedad, that's thrue enough," returned Mr. Macarty. Well, the wan-legged man took to futtin' it in the Highland fling, and pounding away like a pavior on his wooden leg, and Biddy all the time turnin' the handle of a machine like a young winnowing machine, and gettin' illigant music out of the same. It wasn't long before the people began to step up in earnest. First one and two, then in bunches, till the interior of the carrywan was nigh thronged. I wish they'd do the same thing now. But the wan-legged man every now and then would quit dancin' and come inside and pack them like pickled herrins, to make room for more; puttin' all the tall ones in the back, an' all the short ones in front. Well, while they wor waitin', an' the showman outside screechin' always that he was just goin' to begin, whether it was the trampin' an' the talkin' that woke him, I dunna, but anyhow Jack began to mutter to himself, an' snore that sthrong that the whole convaniency thrimbled.

"My, oh," says the people, "what's that ?"

An' some said it was the Injin juggler; an' more said it was some other wild baste roarin'.

"I'm fearful," says one.

"I'll not stay," says another.

"Here, misther, let me out," says another.

"What's the matther ?" says the showman.

Whin they tould him, he was fairly amplushed, not knowin' how to get out of it, for he was afeard of ruinin' the characther of the show, eyther by lettin' them go in a fright, or lettin' on that it was only a dhrunken man.

"Lave it to me," says the wan-legged man in a whisper.

"Leedies an' jintlemin," says he, "reshume yer pleeces. There's no call for alarum at all at all," says he.

"What is it ?" says they.

"The Royal Bingal tigyer," says he.

That was enough for some of them.

"Here, give us back our money," says they, "an' let us get shut of the roarin' baste."

"There's no money returned," says he.

"Well, we won't stay to be ate for the lucre of tuppence," says they.

"He won't ate ye," says he.

"For why not?" says they.

"Becase he's a studdy, responsible baste," says he. "I tell you," says he, "he's the royal Bingal tigyer prisinted to the Queen by the Imperor of Chany, an' our propriethur is now taking him home to her Majesty, an' he's confined wid six big goolden chains an' a padlock."

Well, whin they heard that an' about the chains they wor tuck wid a curiosity to see him. But no, sorrow a sight would wan-leg give them.

"It ud be high thrayson," says he, "to make a show of a baste that's the Royal property, and av it kem to the Lord Leftinint's ears he might cut the head off the propriethur:" and in coorse this made them all the more rampagious to get a look at the baste.

How and however, at last he purtinded to come round.

"I durstn't show him to yez," says he, "but there's a chink here convanient to the door, and if any lady or gintleman gives me tuppence more ov coorse I can't purwint them from peeping through it;" the cunning bla-guard knowin' well in his heart that all they could see by raison of the darkness was the tip of Jack's nose and the knees of his small-clothes as he lay doubled up foreninst them.

As ye may guess, the tuppences kem in middlin' lively, and the people was five deep at the chink in a brace of shakes.

"Oh, dear, oh!" says one, "do ye mind his eye. It's as red as a coal o' fiyer."

"Hut, man, that's his nose," says another.

"An' the big legs he has of his own!" says another.

"Are they sthriped?" says one in the back, "I'm told tigyers is sthriped all over."

"Bedad, they are," says the other, "for all the world like cordheroy."

An' so they wint on, the crathurs, though sorrow a much could they see barrin' a big lump of somethin' gruntin' in a corner. But they didn't like lettin' on to one another that they hadn't got the worth of their money.

Maintime the news flew like wildfiyer through the town, an' man, woman, an' child, gentle an' simple, kem crowdin' up to look at the royal Bingal tigyer, and wid them kem one Mullins, a grate ould miser of a chap.

To be sure he began castin' about for some way of seein' the tigyer chape, so what does he do but when no one was lookin' he creeps in undher the wheels of the carrywan, and begins thryin' for a chink of his own, and as good luck would have it he finds a hole where a boult had fallen out of the boords, just convanient to Jack's ear.

As he was looking through this he hears Jack talkin' an' grumblin' to himself in his sleep. So he cocks his ear and listens. "Faix," says he, "you're a dhroll Bengal tigyer. May I never if it isn't Irish he's spaking." And with that he takes a bit of a sthraw and prods Jack in the jaw. "Ow!" says Jack. "That was a grate roar," says the people inside.

"What are ye, at all?" says Mullins in a whisper.

"I'm the greatest man in all Ireland," says Jack, dhrowsy-like.

"Throth, then, ye don't take up much room av ye are," says Mullins.

"Thrue for ye," says Jack, "I'm bint double like a cod in a pot, wid my heels in my mouth a'most."

"An' what brought ye there?" says Mullins.

"Erra, how do I know?" says Jack, goin' aff to sleep again.

"Do you know where ye are, avick?" says Mullins.

"Sorra a know I know," says Jack; "may be it's in Purgathory I am, for my head is shplittin' in two halves, an' I'm a'most desthroyed wid a pain in the small o' my back. Moreover, my tongue's as dhry as the flure of a lime-kiln. Av it's in Abraham's bosom ye are there, give us a dhrink o' wather an' I'll be obleeged to ye."

"Sure, it's a mighty big mishtake you're a making," says Mullins. "You're not in glory. Aren't ye in O'Shannasey's Pavilion, and aint the people a-lookin' at ye for tuppence ahead?"

Well, my frinds, when the mention of that an' the tuppence sthruck Jack's ear, he remimbered all of a suddint all about it, an' how little Farrell was gibin' him wid bein' only fit for a peep-show.

An' wid that he lets wan roar out of him ye'd have hard at the other ind o' the barony, an' sthraitened himself powerful.

The timbers of the carrywan wasn't over sthrong, an' they shplit an' cracked wid a noise like tundher, an' the dacent people begins screechin' "The tigyer—the tigyer!" an' goes rowlin' and tumblin' down the stips for all the world like pitatees spilt out of a creel. Sich murdher never was seen since Castlebar was a town, wid the hurry they were in.

An' maybe the showman wasn't in as big a fright as any of them, for all he knew it was a Christin an' no tigyer; an' faix he tuk to runnin' as well as the rest of them.

And so did Wan-leg, but in his hurry he druv his wooden leg into the dhrum, which delayed him.

Whin Jack got himself loose, the first thing he done was to go and bate the jiant, for, as he said afther-wards, it was all along of him that he got into the shcrape at all. An' he bate him that wicked that it's my belief he'd be batin' him this minnit av it wasn't for the young woman that wint down on her two binded knees to him not to kill him all out.

So he wint at the wan-legged man, but he being a cripple, an' more betoken entangled wid the dhrum, there was no glory in batin' him; so Jack threw him an' dhrum body an' bones into the sthreet, and wint ragin' afther the propriethur to bate him.

Well, the end o' the matther was that Jack had to go before the magisthrates that was sittin' at petty sisshins that same day for assault and batthery, and ruinin' the property of Mr. O'Shannasey; but the magisthrates said sarve him right, an' if he summonsed Jack for tattherin' his consarn Jack might summous him for false imprisonment—so it was even betune them, an' dismissed the case.

But Jack was never the same man afther. It tuck all the pride out of him to be made a tuppenny rareeshow. And many a time afterwards he used to say, in the bittherness of his heart, that was all a big man was good for nowadays, when there was no fightin' or any other divarshin going on.

The occupants of the parlour of the "Blue Dolphin" were greatly amused at the story told by the loquacious and genial Mr. Macarty, who, to say the truth, had no inconsiderable amount of ability in giving effect to a humorous narrative.

"But did it really occur?" inquired one of the company.

"Did it? Why, ov coorse," returned Macarty. "Do you think I'd be afther invintin' a pack of lies? Sure I was there at the time myself, an' remember it as if it tuk place only yistherdy."

"You must draw a line of course," remarked the little man.

"Ooh, but we niver dhraw a line in our business, divil a bit," said the showman. "I don't suppose any ov yez have the slightest idaya of the devices and fakements we have to resort to. Why a legitimate an' genuine article in many cases does not atthract half as well as a 'fake.' Every exhibitor knows that. Faith, you may draw a line as much as you plaze, but a man who undherstands his business will soon jump over it, or else bedad he'll have to starve. It's the same in iverythin'."

"That's right enough," said Peace. "A 'fake' will do more than a legitimate thing. I'll just give you a case in point. My father was a showman, or rather head man to one. He was a tamer of wild beasts."

"Your father! Ochone, I thought you were a boy after my own heart when I first met you," cried Macarty. "Bedad, we must have a friendly glass together at my expinse."

Glasses were ordered.

Peace proceeded.

When my father was travelling with Kensett's menagerie, and the proprietor was doing a good business in most of the provincial towns, business began to drop off in consequence of an opposition show visiting the same places as Kensett's. There was not room enough for both at the same time, and Mr. Kensett as a natural consequence was greatly annoyed. At one town the opposition shop (Barlow's menagerie), as it was termed, carried everything before them, the reason for this being that they had one of the largest ourang-outangs that had ever been brought to this country. The creature was said to bear a remarkable resemblance to the human species, and crowds upon crowds were to be seen daily making their way to Barlow's establishment. Kensett shifted his quarters, and moved on to the next town, under cover of the night. He had not, however, been many hours there before Barlow made his appearance. Poor man, he was perfectly furious when he found that a similar course was adopted by his rival at other towns. Business fell off painfully, and the question was what was to be done under these perplexing circumstances. The ourang-outang was the central point of attraction.

One evening, after a wretched day's business, my father was smoking his pipe with Mr. Kensett, who was at this time down in the dumps—and, as you may imagine, my father was not in the best of spirits. He had been performing with his wild animals to comparatively empty benches.

"He's potted us—knocked us out of time, that's quite certain," said Mr. Kensett.

"He carries all before him," returned my father, "and why? because he's got an ugly brute—the ugliest I ever saw—of the monkey tribe. One never knows how to deal with the public. They are so capricious and uncertain."

"Uncertain be d——d!" shouted Kensett, "there's no mistake about the matter! they are pretty certain to desert me for my rival—that is, as far as we can see at present."

"Luck may change, sir," says my father.

"It may and it may not—more of the latter than the former. Ah, it's a bad look-out for the remainder of this tour."

The two companions lapsed into silence for some little time after this, and puffed away at their pipes.

Presently Kensett said, in a reflective manner—

"How about Old Jemmy?"

"About what, sir?" inquired my father.

"Old Jemmy."

"I don't know anything about him further than what you know."

Mr. Kensett struck his knee in a self-satisfactory manner.

"I have it, old man," he exclaimed. "A bright idea has occurred to me. I have it. We will be down upon this Barlow, and take the wind out of his sails, who please the pigs."

"I only wish we could," says my father.

"But we will. Listen, you must transmogrify old Jemmy. He'll do well enough for a Pongo, or wild man of the woods, just arrived from Africa.

"We'll work the oracle, and double up Barlow."

"How's it to be done?" says my father.

"Shave his haunches, then colour them, encase the upper portion of his body with long hair, shave his face and colour it in the most hideous manner it is possible to conceive. I will get out large bills announcing the arrival of a savage monster in this country, which is exhibited now for the first time. 'The missing link.' Don't you see? Now I've given you the hint, and it only remains for you to carry it out. No one so well adapted to manipulate a case of this sort. You'll be able to make something of him. Do your best, old man, and upset the opposition shop."

My father tumbled to the proposition at once.

"It shall be done, sir," he said emphatically, "and we'll take our chance."

Well, with that, on the following day he set to work.

Poor old Jemmy was a venerable specimen of the ape species, he had been in the show for years, and was as tame and harmless as a kitten, and would let you do anything with him.

The hair was shaved off his posteriors, a long, shaggy coat of dark-brown hair was sewn round the upper portion of his body, the hair on the lower portion of his face was clipped quite close, then his face was coloured, and he was so completely metamorphosed that his own mother would not have known him.

Taken altogether his appearance was at once extraordinary, and like nothing that had ever been seen before or since, I think I may add.

A collar was put round his neck, to which a strong chain was attached, and the end of the chain was attached to an iron bar running across the back of the cage. By this means poor old Jemmy was kept in an upright position and compelled to walk on his hind legs.

It was, no doubt, a sad trial to the poor brute, who, however, bore it complacently enough. When all was in readiness Mr. Kensett shifted his quarters to the next town, having previously beplastered its walls with gigantic posters announcing the arrival of a large Pongo or wild man of the woods, who was so fierce that visitors were cautioned not to approach too near the bars of the cage.

Such a monster was surely never seen before. Jemmy was the very personification of ugliness and ferocity.

Kensett's show was thronged with visitors all day long, and there was a perfect *furore* with the populace, who expressed themselves immensly pleased with the great natural zoological curiosity.

A history of the animal, how it was caught, the nature of its food and general habits was given in a hand-bill presented to each visitor as they entered the menagerie.

It was related how, in a visit of a British man-of-war to the island of Borneo, a party of the sailors were permitted on shore, and entered one of the dense forests which abound in that island.

After some time spent in the search for fruit the party came upon an open glade, and right opposite them, where the forest again commenced, they saw a tree violently shaken.

They rushed forward to ascertain the cause, and saw what they thought was a native woman leap lightly from the tree and disappear in the forest.

But a hairy monster remained in the tree, and seemed in a furious passion, which was redoubled when he saw the sailors.

Breaking a branch from the tree, the wild man (for this was what he was) bounded to the earth, faced the strangers, and then turned to run.

But the tars had been too smart for him, and having surrounded him, he was brought to bay and captured, after a sturdy use of the branch of the tree.

The "history" went down very well with the women folks, for the writer averred that when the wild man was first seen he was busy belabouring his wife, and thus suffered capture.

Barlow came upon the scene of action and advertised his ourang outang, which was really a fine specimen, but the creature paled before the effulgence of his painted rival, and Kensett's counterfoil brute fairly eclipsed the one in the opposition shop. Barlow was furious.

He denounced Kensett as an impostor, and the rival showman had a set-to in the market-place to the infinite diversion of the town's folk; but all was of no use—the "wild man of the woods," "the missing link," as Kensett termed him, carried everything before him, and Barlow's show was comparatively deserted.

"Is it possible that people could be so silly as to be taken in with such a barefaced imposture?" said one of the company.

"My dear sir," returned Peace, "in this world are found people silly enough for anything. But it was a barefaced imposture, I admit, seeing that old Jemmy's face had been shorn of its hair."

"Och, by the powers!" cried Macarty, "people like to be humbugged and imposed upon. Bedad it was a mighty clane thrick, and desarved to sucsade."

The good folks in the parlour of the "Blue Dolphin" had perhaps never in their whole lives learned so much about the doings of showmen, and, as a natural consequence, the evening passed away pleasantly enough.

After some further conversation the party broke up, and Peace and Mr. Macarty repaired to their respective rooms.

Our hero, upon first entering the house, had requested to be shown into the bedroom he was to occupy, saying that he wished to have a wash; his real object, however, was to secrete the bag containing the valuables he had purloined in some quiet corner.

He found in the room a chest of drawers, most of which were empty; into one of these he placed his bag, then he closed the drawer, locked it, and put the key in his pocket.

When this had been done he felt tolerably secure. It was not likely that any person would break open the drawer for the purpose of inspecting the contents of his bag.

He therefore returned to the public room, where he passed the evening in the convivial manner already described.

Upon retiring for the night, he opened the drawer, and found his bag in precisely the same position as he had left it.

He therefore tumbled into bed and slept soundly till the morning.

Upon proceeding downstairs he found, upon inquiry, that his picked-up friend Macarty had risen some hour or so before.

He was at this time in the stable, attending to the inmates of his wooden house.

He greeted our hero in a most cordial manner, and after his animals and reptiles had been fed, returned to the breakfast-room of the establishment with Peace.

"We gave our friends a good dose of jaw last night," said our hero, with a smile.

"Och, sure it's just as well to kape the game alive. I make it a rule to be friendly and familiar wid all people. There's no tellin' what one may want, and a good word from the natives of a town or village may be of sarvice to men of my kidney—but see, breakfast is ready, let's fall to."

A very substantial repast had been provided by the hostess of the "Blue Dolphin," to which the hungry travellers did justice to.

When the meal was over, Mr. Macarty, who was evidently a man of business, made preparations to start on his journey.

"You are in a great hurry to be off, my friend," said Peace. "Have you far to go?"

"Arrah, an' it's not far; but the governor doesn't like to be kept waitin'; besides we've a power of work to do before we let in the British public—that is, if they will come in, an' bad luck to them."

"Good luck to you and yours," cried Peace; "and may you prosper, as I am sure you deserve to do. Any way, I have to return you my most heartfelt thanks for your kindness—to say nothing of your company."

"By jabers, you're puttin' the pot on in the blarney line, anyhow," returned Macarty; "but we undherstand each other intirely, and good luck to you, and many on 'em."

Peace laughed, and said—

"Well, I'm sorry to part with you, but there is, I suppose, no help for it?"

"Faix, an' there is," returned Macarty. "You can make shift wid the same sate ye had last night, and maybe ye'll be a bit more on your journey when you raich Pocklington."

"Pocklington!"

"Ah, shure. I don't know where ye are bhound for, but maybe one place is as good as another to a hawker."

"Oh it don't much matter which road I travel for the matter of that, and since you are so pressing I'll accept your kind offer."

"An' its welcome ye are—as welcome as the flowers in May."

The caravan was by this time in front of the "Blue Dolphin." It looked bright and radiant by the light of the early morning sun, the brass knocker on the door had an extra polish, the horse was well groomed, and taken altogether it was a most respectable turn out.

"There!" said Macarty, pointing to the yellow machine. "It's fit for a prince, bedad; it's as clane as a new pin, and as bright as a newly-polished silver tankard."

"And its driver?"

PEACE VISITED BY A DETECTIVE.

"Aisy, now, aisy. Well, its dhriver is as sharp as a steel thrap. Now then, are you ready?"

"Quite ready; but wait a bit, I must fetch my luggage and pay the reckoning. When this has been done I am at your service."

Peace went into the house, settled with the landlord, and returned with his bag, which he had made into a parcel with brown paper and string. He got up in front of the caravan, which was driven off by the good-natured Mr. McCarty.

Peace felt perfectly well assured that he was safe from the prying eyes of the police while he sat beside his newly-made friend McCarty, who evidently believed him to be a hawker, never for a moment suspecting the depredations he had been committing.

The Irishman drove his yellow house or caravan direct on to Pocklington, and upon his arrival at the last-named place he introduced our hero to his governor.

Peace made himself very agreeable, and entered freely into conversation with the showman, who was greatly taken with him.

He conducted him into all the caravans of which he was proprietor, and expatiated upon the interesting nature of their contents, and wound up by placing before him a cold collation, with some bottled ale and wine, and insisted upon his partaking of his hospitality.

Peace was nothing loth, and expressed himself particularly grateful for the attention shown him.

After remaining for an hour or so with the proprietor of the shows, he took his departure and made his way to the nearest railway station, booked for Sheffield, and in due course of time found himself once more in his native town.

He had but little difficulty in disposing of the property he had possessed himself of in the palatial mansion at Leeds, but as he had had a very narrow chance of being detected he deemed it advisable to leave that town alone for awhile.

Upon his return to Sheffield he worked industriously at his business for some weeks, and those who were in the habit of seeing him during this time were under the full impression that he was a sober, well-conducted man.

So to all outward appearance he was, and it is likely enough that, had he chosen to pursue an honest calling for the future, he would have done well and prospered.

But it was not in the nature of the man to continue long without having recourse to his evil practices.

His house was very respectably furnished. His partner, the mistress of the domicile, did not thwart him, but strove as best she could to make her husband's home as comfortable as possible.

He had a goat (which he had taught to perform many tricks), a monkey, two dogs, some guinea pigs, and a cat or two—he had always displayed throughout his career a great partiality for animals—and he was an adept in taming them, and putting them through various performances for the amusement of himself, family, and friends.

Indeed he might have succeeded very well as a trainer of animals for performing purposes; as we have already signified he was clever in many ways, but his abilities, such as they were, went for nothing. They were overshadowed and submerged by his passion for criminal pursuits.

Nevertheless, those who knew him best, and were in the constant habit of seeing, have declared that it was difficult, nay almost next to impossible, for any one to believe him to be a lawless and unprincipled ruffian, which was afterwards but too plainly proved.

He played at this time in the evenings at various public-houses in Sheffield. He had taught his goat to stand on its hind legs and dance to the sound of his violin.

This little animal is said to have been a most docile and amusing creature, and Peace made a considerable amount of money by its antics.

He was always welcomed at the public-houses he was accustomed to visit, and made a great many friends, but he lost them as soon as made, for there was nothing reliable in the man, and it was, therefore, impossible for any one to place much faith in him.

CHAPTER LXXVI.

THE ROBBERY AT MESSRS. ARNISON AND CO.'s.

FOR some considerable time Peace appeared to be leading a respectable sort of life. His violin-playing in the evening, and the commissions he executed in the way of picture-framing and other odd jobs, brought him in sufficient for his immediate wants, but this did not content him.

He must have a turn at some house, and lay his hands on all he could conveniently carry away.

It so chanced, when he was taking home some frames to a customer on the outskirts of the town, that he met with an old pal whom he had missed sight of for years.

As he was walking along, the sound of a low whistle fell upon his ears. Peace looked round in the direction from whence it proceeded. He beheld at some distance off the dark features of a man which were very familiar to him.

Peace halted at the corner of the next street, and the stranger came up with him.

"What! don't you know me, you old sinner?" cried the man.

"Know you? Why of course I do—it's Bandy-legged Bill."

"Right you are, old man; Bill it is."

"Well, this is a surprise. Why, what on earth brought you to Sheffield?"

"What do you suppose? To see an old chum, to be sure."

"I am glad to have met you, Bill. And how goes it with you?"

"Hardly enough. Have to scratch for a living—like the hens—and don't always get much when I do scratch. And how goes it with you?"

"Nothing much to boast of—got pinched four years ago."

"Ah! so I heard, but you are all right now. Where do you hang out?"

"I'm married, and have settled here in my native town."

"Ah, I see, a reformed character," said the gipsy, making a face. "Given up the old business, I s'pose?"

"Partly."

"Oh! Only partly?"

"Well, I should be telling a story if I said otherwise."

"I wish you could put me up to a job; I am down below water mark."

"Ah, for the matter of that, I dare say we shall be able to work something together. I say again, I am glad we have met. Come along with me as far as I am going. I've got to deliver these frames; when this has been done, we can talk over matters."

"Right you are, Charlie; my time's my own."

The two companions in crime walked on, till the house Peace was making for had been reached. He delivered his frames, and then returned to his own residence in company with the gipsy, whom he introduced to his wife as an old and esteemed friend.

Dinner was served and every attention was paid to Peace's guest, who made himself quite at home; he was a gentleman who had very little pride about him, and did not want much pressing to partake of the dainties placed before him.

He was, however, a little reserved before his friend's better half, and did not touch on subjects which would in anyway compromise his host.

An hour or two was passed after dinner pleasantly enough. Peace played several tunes on his violin, trotted out his animals and made them go through their performances, after which he and the gipsy retired to his workshop where they smoked the pipe of peace and talked upon subjects which more immediately concerned themselves.

"And so you are drifting about in troubled waters in an unsatisfactory way?" said our hero.

"I get a haul now and then," observed the gipsy, "but then there is a long gap between; then ye see I get cursedly hard up sometimes. I get a greenhorn to purchase a 'screw' (an unsound horse) at a topping price, and in course when I pull off a bargain of this sort it sets me up for awhile, but greenhorns are not so easy to lug hold on nowadays; 'blokes' are getting jolly too artful—and it's only by nows and thens I lands one of that kidney. Still I have done pretty fairish at times in the horse-coping line; but there are too many in it, Charlie—and it ain't what it used to be by a long way."

"How about your aristocratic friend and patron?" inquired Peace.

"Oh, hang him, he's been fleeced right and left, and has run through a sight of money. It's the way with those swell blokes—they prey upon one another."

"Well, I've got a bit of a job on hand," said our hero, in a whisper, drawing his chair nearer to that of his companion, "and if you like to stand in, say the word."

"Ah, you've no call to ask that ere question. I'll stand in, whatever it may be, and shall be but too glad to do so. Out with it—let's know the lively little caper."

"I'll tell you all about it, but——"

"But what?"

"I suppose I can rely upon you?"

"Rely!" exclaimed the gipsy. "Did you ever find me round upon you or anybody else? No no, old man, I have my faults, a good many, perhaps, but that is not one of them. I stand by my pals, come what may, have always done so."

"I believe you always have, Bill, but excuse my asking the question. I've always found you right enough. Well, then, listen. I can gain an entrance into a warehouse not very far from here, where a considerable amount of valuable property can be obtained if the matter is skilfully worked."

"All right—fire away—I'm your man."

"I'll show you the premises whenever you like, and I shall not find any difficulty in concealing myself there and waiting patiently till the work people knock off work. When this has been done, I have the place to myself, for, strange to say, there is no porter left in charge of the place."

"Ah, sizzers, but that's grand—nothing could be better."

"What I want you to do is to walk carelessly outside the premises, and watch till the police on beat are changed."

"That I can easily do."

"And when the constable on duty has gone his rounds, to give me notice, either by tapping at one of the windows, or else by a whistle. When I know the coast is clear I shall know what to do."

"I'll take my davy of that, old pal," cried the gipsy, with a loud laugh. "It shall be done to rights, as far as I am concerned."

"But what we shall have to carry away won't go into a particularly small compass, that's the worst part of the business, but we shall be able to manage it all right enough, I dare say."

"Won't go into a small compass?"

"No; but never mind, I'll show you how it is to be worked. Now then, if you've a mind we'll just step round to the warehouse, and take a careful observation."

"With all my heart, I'm ready if you are."

The two companions in crime sallied forth, and in a short time reached the establishment which was to be the scene of their operations.

They did not like to linger too long near the premises lest they should attract attention, but the cursory glance they had sufficed for their purpose, and they crept like two thieves, as they were, into a narrow dark street on the opposite side of the way, which effectually screened them from observation.

It was arranged between the two that the robbery was to be carried out on the following night.

Before the workmen knocked off Peace watched his opportunity, and crept unobserved into the premises, and contrived to conceal himself in one of the cellars. Here he waited patiently till closing time.

The place was locked up, and secured by massive bolts and bars—so carefully secured, indeed, that it was supposed to be burglar-proof. So, indeed, it might have been had not one been already concealed in the premises.

When he felt assured that everybody had left, Peace, like a cunning rascal as he was, crept from his hiding place. He had brought with him a sack, an old one, for a new one would not have answered his purpose.

Sealskins and embroidery were the valuables he was desirous of purloining. He was well acquainted with the interior of the premises, as years before he had done an occasional job therein in the way of mending machinery and carpenter's work.

He had, therefore, but little difficulty in laying his hands upon the goods he so much coveted. He thrust sealskin after sealskin into his bag, together with satin and embroidery; in a short time the sack was very tightly filled.

At a rough calculation the property it contained would represent as much as from two to three hundred pounds—that is, assuming the articles were sold at the manufacturers' prices.

He was now prepared to make clean off with the booty the moment the signal was given by his accomplice from without.

Bandy-legged Bill was a stranger to Sheffield and unknown to any of its inhabitants, and he was therefore not likely to attract much observation.

Peace had watched and waited as he had done on many other occasions. In cases of this sort he displayed an amount of passive endurance which, to say the least of it, was most remarkable in one of his active temperament.

He was greatly relieved upon hearing a gentle tap at one of the back windows of the warehouse.

He looked out and beheld the gipsy, who intimated by a sign that the coast was clear.

Peace lost no time—he passed out of the premises.

He placed the sack on the shoulders of the gipsy, and bade him follow him.

He boldly walked down the Haymarket, passed the side of the Town Hall, and made for some stables in the vicinity, one of which he rented.

He opened the door of this with his key, and then he and Bandy-legged Bill passed in and locked it from the inside.

There was light enough for their purpose. The sack was deposited in one corner of the stable and covered over with loose straw.

At one time Peace had kept a pony trap. This, however, had been sold soon after his conviction. But our hero upon obtaining his release had again become tenant of the stable, in which at the present time was a goat, some rabbits, guinea pigs, and fowls. A horse and trap he intended to purchase, but the stable was useful for a variety of purposes, the concealment of property being one.

"So far we are safe," cried Peace, "but we must be off with the booty by early dawn, certainly before the people arrive at the warehouse."

"What do you call early?" said the gipsy.

"A little after five or from that to six. These things must be far away from the town before any hue and cry is raised."

"And how is it to be worked?"

"You meet me here a little after five, and I'll tell you."

"All right, guv'nor—I'm only a hunderstrapper, you know. You are the commander-in-chief. I does as you tell me."

"You see you are a horsey-looking man—I am not."

"Well, wot of that?"

"It is but natural for a horsey man to be carrying a sack of corn or tares, or what not."

"All right—I tumble. I will be here at a little after five."

With this understanding the two rascals parted company. The gipsy took up his quarters in a beer-shop, and Peace returned to his own domicile.

He was mindful of his appointment with his man Friday, who, to say the truth, was quite as faithful to our hero as Defoe's grateful black.

Upon arriving at the stable at the appointed time, he found his trusty confederate awaiting his appearance.

The gipsy again shouldered the sack, and was conducted by Peace towards the tramway terminus, and they took up their position at the corner of Blonk-street, where they waited for the next moving tramcar.

When it came up Peace and the gipsy took their seats in it, but the conductor would not allow them to take the bag inside, so they deposited it on the platform of the carriage near the driver.

By this means they got it conveyed to Pinfield-lane, when they both got out, went past the brickyard, and continued their course towards Darnell.

"It's a plaguy nuisance that the fellow would not allow us to take it inside. Had he done so we should have got clean away," said Peace, "but there's no help for it. We must do the best we can."

"It'll be all right, I dare say," returned Bill. "We haven't much reason to complain as far as we've gone at present."

"I am not altogether satisfied," said Peace, "and under the circumstances I think it would be better to hide the sack for awhile."

"As yer please. Yer know best."

Peace turned aside into a field, and bade his companion follow up. He then took the sack from the shoulders of the gipsy, and hid it under a hedge.

"It will be all right there for a short time," said he. "In the meantime we can consider what the next move is to be."

The gipsy scratched his head; he did not much like leaving the property there, but he had the prudence to say nothing.

The two repaired to a neighbouring public-house, where they had some breakfast. After this they took a stroll together, being still in doubt as to their course of action.

"If that 'ere blessed old sack is discovered, it's a case of pickles," said the gipsy; "and I aint at all sartin, mind yer, that it won't be."

"Neither am I," returned Peace; "but it's better to lose the goods than be pinched."

"Look here!" cried Bill. "Two heads are better than one. Let's go back, and I'll put you up to a move."

Peace, who was hankering after stolen goods, did as his companion desired; he went back to the hedge.

The gipsy commenced gathering some green stuff a thing he had been accustomed to do when leading a wandering life among the gipsies.

"What is all this for?" said Peace.

"You shall see," returned his companion, who, after gathering an armful of the green stuff, crammed the same into the mouth of the sack, and made it appear as if it was full of the same stuff.

"Now do you understand?" cried Bill.

Peace nodded. "I see," he said.

"If anyone asks what you have got, tell 'em as bold as brass that you've got green meat for your rabbits, guinea pigs, and such like.

"An excellent idea. Cram it well with the green stuff."

The gipsy placed more of the same inside the sack.

"Now we'll take it with us, at all risks," said Bill.

"We'll do so, if you like. I certainly don't fancy leaving it here to be overhauled."

The two companions walked through Darnell in a perfectly easy, self-satisfied sort of way.

The gipsy carried the sack into a field on the side nearest the railway station, and deposited it in a place which he considered more secure.

His judgment proved correct, for no one during the day found out its place of concealment.

"Let it bide there till such time as you make up your mind to put it away, or dispose of its contents," said the gipsy, as he and Peace took their way over the fields.

"I think that will be its last resting place for to-day," observed our hero. "When evening comes on, we shall be able to get clean off with it. In the meantime we must make ourselves as contented as circumstances will permit."

They amused themselves as they best could, and to do this more effectually they paid a visit to an exhibition of works of art and antiquities in the immediate neighbourhood.

Peace took great pleasure in places of this description, and found no difficulty at any time in spending hours therein.

But Bandy-legged Bill had no taste for anything of the kind.

If it had been a horse-fair or a cattle-show he would have been greatly pleased; but he made the best of it, and listened complacently enough to his companion's explanation of the several articles on view.

After emerging from the museum, they wandered through the green lanes, and when the dusk of the evening set in, they took the sack from its place of concealment, and Peace went with it to Sheffield by train.

Upon arriving at the Victoria station, he booked for Manchester, and took the whole of the stolen property with him.

The gipsy remained behind, with the understanding that he was to call at Peace's house on the following day.

At Manchester Peace managed to dispose of the whole of the property, and netted thereby a considerable sum of money, as at that time seal skins were all "the rage," and those he had obtained were of the choicest quality, and cut according to the newest, and therefore most fashionable, patterns.

He did not get nearly their value, but burglars, as a

rule, sell the produce of their robberies at ridiculously low prices, the receiver having in all cases the best of the bargain.

It was singular that Peace, considering the enormous amount of property that fell into his hands during his career, should not have amassed a large sum of money, but it seldom happens that the professional thief or burglar, however successful he might be, is enabled to put much by out of his ill-gotten gains.

There are many reasons for this. Few of them are provident, and nearly all are in the hands of the receivers, and money come by dishonestly goes as fast as it is gained.

It is well said that one shilling honestly earned goes farther than pounds obtained by fraud and robbery.

As far as we can gather Peace was not a gambler or a drunkard; indeed, we have not heard that he indulged in excesses of any description. He certainly had a penchant for the opposite sex, but it would appear that he kept under subjection all the females with whom he was connected.

He was tolerably liberal to them—never let them want for anything if he could help it—but certainly did not maintain them on a very extravagant scale.

When returning to his house in Sheffield, he found himself well up in funds, but he said nothing to his wife respecting the sudden accession of wealth.

She, poor woman, doubtless suspected from whence the money had come, but she had the prudence to keep silent on the subject.

Peace had a great objection to be interrogated by any of his family. Indeed, such a course would be sure to put him out of temper, and when in a passion he was a very terrible and vindictive man.

Those about him knew this well enough from bitter experience, and came to the conclusion, therefore, that the wisest course to adopt would be to let him alone and not pester him with vexatious or troublesome questions.

On the morning after his visit to Manchester the gipsy presented himself at Peace's house. He found him in his workshop with apron on, busily occupied with his frames, as if nothing had happened.

"Well," cried Bill, "you are a card; blest if you don't deserve a medal or statue. Never saw such a chap in all my born days. You're a stunner, and no mistake."

"What the devil are you talking about?" cried Peace. "Hold your row, and sit down."

He handed the gipsy a stool.

"Now, then," said Peace—"what is there to be surprised at?"

"What? Why you look for all the world as if you were the most hardworking, industrious tradesman as ever was, working away for dear life. You'd deceive the devil—that's what you'd do—with ease, and think nothing of it."

"Ah, I dare say—that's all very well; but I should find it difficult to deceive you, old man; but stow your chaff."

"Well, how did you get on at Manchester?" said Bill.

"Oh, as right as the mail. Got rid of them all, and nobody any the wiser."

"My word! but that's clever—turned them into ready cash, eh?"

Peace nodded. He drew from his pocket some notes, which he handed to the gipsy.

"Finnips!" cried the latter.

"Well—what of that? They are right enough; but if you want some gold, here you are."

He placed in the hand of his companion several sovereigns, which made the eyes of the gipsy glisten with pleasure.

"And is this for me? Am I to keep both notes and gold?"

"Yes; it will set you up for awhile."

"You're a downright good fellow, Charlie. Many thanks," said Bill, pocketing the amount.

"And now you had better be off for the present. You can look round in the evening, if you like."

"Yes, I will just drop in for an hour or so; so good-bye for the present."

In about two hours after the gipsy had taken his departure, the well-known form of a detective was visible at the window of Peace's workshop.

He tapped at the door, which Peace opened.

"You are busy. Can I come in?"

"Yes, come in, Mr. Stallard. What's up now?" said Peace, carelessly, as he laid on the leaf gold to one of his frames.

The detective glanced furtively around.

"You seem to be looking two ways for Sunday," cried Peace. "Anything amiss?"

"There's been a big robbery at Messrs. Arnison's," said Stallard.

"Never! When?"

"Either Tuesday night or Wednesday morning, we suppose."

"Ah, much property gone?"

"Oh, dear me, yes—a good deal."

"And have you found out the robbers?"

"Not as yet," observed the detective, regarding Peace with a searching look.

"I'm sorry for that," said the latter.

"Yes, and so am I."

"It's a bad business."

"Very bad."

"And pray now, if it's a fair question," said our hero, leaving off his work for a moment or two, "is that the reason of your visit to me?"

"Well, it's our duty to go anywhere and everywhere for the matter of that—not to leave a stone unturned."

"Oh, I see. Well, Mr. Stallard, all I can say is that I cannot give you any information, for I know nothing about the affair. I'm endeavouring to earn an honest livelihood, and you must admit it doesn't look well to my customers to see a gentleman of your inquiring mind here."

"I have a duty to perform," said Stallard; "I thought perhaps you might possibly be able to give me some information."

"How the devil can I give you information upon a subject upon which I know nothing?" cried Peace in a fury. "Perhaps you think I had some hand in the robbery?"

"Oh, dear no, I never for a moment suggested such a thing."

"Perhaps the best plan will be for you to search the house and satisfy yourself," said our hero, throwing open the doors which led into the lower rooms of the habitation.

Mr. Stallard was taken aback all of a sudden. He came to the conclusion that Peace was innocent, and that he—the detective—was making a fool of himself.

"There is no occasion for you to be out of temper, Peace, not the least occasion. Nobody suspects you."

"I would much prefer your searching the place—I'm not afraid of you or any of your comrades. It isn't because a man's been in trouble that he should be hunted down like a wild beast."

Peace's effrontery was perfectly overwhelming. So

much so that the detective was fairly imposed on. He was duly impressed with the mistake he had made, and with a few more apologetic words left the workshop without further questioning.

"Umph!" ejaculated our hero, "that's the way to stall them off. He's got nothing against me—that's quite certain. It was a mere try on. I wish the idiot had searched the house; much good it would have done him."

Every effort was made by the constabulary to find out the robber or robbers.

It was generally supposed at the time that there was a gang at work who only paid "flying visits" to the town, and all efforts to trace the property were fruitless.

Peace laughed in his sleeve, and then went on with his usual daily vocation as if nothing had happened.

CHAPTER LXXVII.
THE DESIGNING WOMAN AND HER VICTIM.

WE now enter upon a fearful study. It is that of a heart which, though young, is seared, withered, and depraved, and which can no longer throb for aught that is good or noble.

It is that of a mind which is strong to resolve, patient to wait, relentless to execute. It is that of a woman who possesses the face of an angel, and the furious passions of a demon.

Laura Stanbridge had once in her life become human. She had loved. She had loved the boy Alf Purvis with as intense and fiery a passion as an Eastern queen.

She had offered this man her love, which was as lurid as her rage; he had refused it, and in refusing it he had told her the terrible secret of her own life. By some means he had discovered the crimes of her girlhood—adultery, theft, murder. For this she hated him, and with no common hate—for this she determined to be avenged, and with no common vengeance.

Retiring into the depths of her black heart she pondered over various schemes for inflicting a terrible vengeance upon the man who taunted her, insulted her, and refused her love.

Little did Alf Purvis suppose that he had such a bitter, relentless enemy to deal with. He paid her but little attention, was away for days and even weeks at a time. She was too proud to condescend to inquire about his movements, and affected an air of indifference about all and everything concerning him.

They had been partners in crime—now they were working out their own ends separately and apart. Indeed it is surprising that the young pickpocket had not taken himself off altogether; only there was this to be said: with all his assumed bravado he stood in fear of Laura Stanbridge, who was more than a match for him as far as cunning and duplicity were concerned.

But a new actor is about to appear in this part of the drama—one, however, who is already well known to the reader.

One evening, when a grand concert was given at St. James's Hall, Laura Stanbridge sallied forth, paid the price of admission, and entered the Hall. Every seat was occupied. She found out that she was a little too late to obtain a place—so she stood and listened to the music.

A young man who sat close to where she was standing rose from his seat, which he begged her to occupy. She was thickly veiled at this time, but her eyes gleamed through the veil.

Raising it, she disclosed a face which was pale, chaste, and beautiful as that of a Madonna.

"I cannot think of turning you out of your seat, sir," she said, in a voice of ineffable sweetness.

"Nay," returned the other, "I must beg of you to be seated. I can do very well here. Do, pray, take the place."

She smiled sweetly, and sat down.

The performance proceeded.

He noticed that she was expensively dressed, and presented altogether a most aristocratic appearance.

He stood by her side and conversed with her upon the quality of the music and the executants of the same.

He was greatly pleased with her society, and when the concert came to an end offered to escort her out of the hall.

She fixed her eyes on him. As he glanced at those eyes, so full of languor and love, he started and blushed.

She did not blush, but she looked modestly on the ground.

They passed out of the hall together, and descended the staircase, and reached the Piccadilly entrance.

He asked her if he might have the pleasure of putting her into a cab or seeing her home.

She answered him in a confused tone—

"But I do not know you, sir," she said, gently.

"That is true," he answered, with a sigh.

"Still I must admit that I am very pleased to have met you, and at the same time have to thank you for your kindness."

They were in Piccadilly at this time.

"Perhaps you wish me to leave you," he murmured.

"No, I do not say that."

"Have you far to go?"

"Not very far—hardly a quarter of a mile."

He reflected for a few moments, and then said—

"I should like to prevail upon you to take some refreshment if it be only a glass of wine and a biscuit."

"Certainly; I accept your kind offer."

They went into the nearest confectioner's, and had some refreshment.

The young man gazed abstractedly around the place, and then sighed.

"I think you must have heard some bad news," said she, munching a sponge cake.

"What makes you think that?"

"You are sad and preoccupied."

"No no, my dear lady. To say the truth, I am no sadder than I have been for a long time past."

"Ah! something troubles you—I feel certain of that. I am afraid you are in love."

He started.

"Oh! dear me, no such thing," he exclaimed, vehemently.

"Pardon me, I know I must appear very rude. Let us go."

She rose, went out into the street, and he followed.

"You do not need me to tell you that sorrow is robbed of half its bitterness if we have any one to share it with us," said Laura.

"Indeed, that is very true," he murmured.

"But we can't discuss topics of this nature in the public street," she added.

"Ah, I forgot. May I see you home?"

"If you like."

They walked on together till the house in the occupation of Miss Stanbridge was reached. She paused in front of this, and said, "Now, my friend, we must part."

"You reside here?" said he.

"Precisely; your surmise is correct. The hour is

late, and I dare not ask you in, but——" here she bent her eyes on the ground.

"But what?" He was going to say dearest, but luckily he checked himself.

"Well I don't interdict your giving me a morning call when passing this way."

"And your name? You forget, my dear madame, that you have not as yet favoured me with your name."

"Neither have you, sir, favoured me with yours," she returned, handing him her card.

He gave her his in return, bade her good night, raised his hat, and went his way.

"Gatliffe—Gatliffe," she ejaculated, when she had reached her parlour and glanced at the card; "surely I have heard that name on somebody's lips before now. Umph, I think I have played my part pretty well. I shall have the extreme pleasure of seeing the gentleman again. I wonder who and what he is. We shall see."

Miss Stanbridge retired to rest, well satisfied with the evening's adventure.

Between eleven and twelve o'clock on the following morning the maid came into the parlour, and gave her mistress a card.

On it was "Mr. Thomas Gatliffe."

"Show the gentleman in," said Miss Stanbridge. "'Gad, he's not lost much time," she murmured, when the girl had left.

"As I happened to be passing this way," said Gatliffe, as he entered, "I thought I would take the liberty of giving you a call to inquire how you are after last night's fatigue."

"You are very kind, I'm sure," returned Laura, handing her visitor a chair; "and I need not add that I am pleased to see you, as it gives me assurance that I am not forgotten."

Gatliffe's manner was a little constrained—to say the truth, he was not altogether at ease.

In the first place he was surprised to find the lady the only occupant of the room when he entered.

He had expected to see some of her relatives present. He did not know the character or the ways of the alluring creature whom he had imprudently chosen to visit.

He was miserably dull and wretched in his lonely home at Wood-green, and it is therefore not surprising that he should be glad of almost any change to break the painful monotony of his existence.

"Now tell me," observed Laura, in a playful sportive manner, "what do you think of your newly-formed acquaintance by the morning's light?"

Gatliffe looked confused, and did not very well know what answer to make.

"I think you look remarkably well," he muttered, "and only wish I looked half as well."

"Oh! you flatterer. But come, let me beg of you to have a glass of wine."

"Thank you, I had rather not."

"Nay, but you must."

"I'm a business man, and have much to attend to, and therefore seldom take anything in the morning."

"A little brandy and seltzer won't hurt you. Bah! don't make a wry face—you are strong as a young Hercules."

"Am I? I dont feel so," returned Gatliffe, with a smile.

He, however, consented to quaff the contents of the proffered glass.

"I dare say you think me a singular sort of person," remarked his companion; "and, to say the truth, I believe I am."

"I have never said so."

"Possibly not; but you have thought so, doubtless. Our acquaintance has been made in a casual accidental manner; but it sometimes happens, you know, that acquaintances of this sort ripen into a lasting friendship. I hope it may prove so in this case. At present we know but little of each other."

"Yes, at present."

"But there is no reason this should always be so. You are in business?"

"Yes, foreman to a large engineering firm."

"And are single, I presume?"

"For the present, but ——"

He hesitated.

"Enough, I do not seek to pry into your secrets. You are very good and kind—of that I am perfectly well assured; and that is quite enough for the present."

Gatliffe thought her manner was very charming and ingenuous, but he was at a loss to know whether she was mistress of the establishment or not, and he was too diffident to make any inquiry.

"I must take my leave now," he ejaculated.

"What! going so soon? Dear me, yours is a short visit."

"You see, my time is not my own, and when I tell you that, I am sure you'll excuse me."

"Oh, certainly. But I suppose I shall have the pleasure of seeing you again."

"Yes, on the very first opportunity."

"Then I will not attempt to detain you, Mr. Gatliffe," said she, rising and offering her hand to her visitor.

"He's by no means forward or fast," she murmured, when he had gone.

"He wants bringing out. I shall work him all right enough. He's a bit smitten, that is very clear. I wonder whether he has a wife. I rather fancy he has. It is most fortunate that Alf is away in the country with his select companions. I shall have to deal with that fellow in a way he little expects, but for the present I have enough on hand."

She dressed herself in fashionable garments, and sallied forth.

She paid a visit to several places of public resort, and amused herself for that day.

She expected to see Gatliffe on the succeeding one, but he did not make his appearance.

Three days elapsed. On the fourth he paid her another visit.

He was reserved and thoughtful, as on the previous occasion.

She told him that she had two tickets for the opera stalls, and asked him if he would like to make use of one—they were numbered seats, of course, and he might please himself about coming—any time would do, she herself would make use of the other.

He took the ticket, and promised to be there as early as circumstances would permit; then he left the same as before.

"He wants a mighty deal of humouring, and is evidently shy. No matter for that, I shall find means to banish his shyness. Good—doubtless he will be there; anyway I shall."

She made a most elaborate toilette, with bare arms, a low-necked dress, together with all the devices which the ladies of the upper ten have recourse to when paying a visit to the opera in the full height of the season.

It is needless to say that Miss Stanbridge looked

extremely lovely. Art had done something towards improving her personal appearance.

When her toilette was complete she desired her maid to go for a four-wheeler, in which she was conveyed to the opera-house. Upon taking her seat she found the adjacent one unoccupied. Tom Gatliffe had therefore not yet arrived.

Possibly he might think better of it, and not put in an appearance—there was no telling. However, she made up her mind to assume an air of cheerfulness and wait patiently.

He did not arrive till after the overture had been played, and the curtain drawn up. Upon presenting himself he was full of apologies for being so behind hand, saying that he had been unavoidably detained at the works.

Laura Stanbridge pouted a little, but accepted his apologies with grace and good humour.

At the close of the first act an animated and pleasant conversation was carried on between the two—the same formula took place during the succeeding intervals in the performance. The gentleman ordered ices and other refreshments for the lady.

When the opera was over, Laura Stanbridge passed out of the stalls with her friend.

"I must get you to fetch a cab, dear," said she, "for I have come in my opera cloak just as you see me."

"Certainly, by all means," returned Gatliffe. "You wait here. I won't be more than a few seconds."

He returned, conducted her into the cab, and got into the vehicle himself.

He sat by her side, a little reserved perhaps, but in far better spirits than she had ever seen him.

When they arrived home the supper things had been laid, and the table "groaned," to make use of a hackneyed phrase, with the best of everything it was possible to procure.

Gatliffe looked surprised.

"You are going to have some supper with me, of course?" suggested Laura.

"Umph, oh, yes," he replied in a half hesitating manner.

Miss Stanbridge cast aside her opera cloak and stood before the young man in a costume of the most faultless description.

Her arms and the upper portion of her bust were bare, and Gatliffe was taken completely aback at the elegance of her attire and the beauty of her form.

He, however, said nothing, but sat down to supper, the girl waiting on her mistress and her visitor.

When the supper was over, and the things removed, Miss Stanbridge said to the girl—

"You may go to bed, Lucy. I shall not require you any more to-night. I will see my friend out. But stay, before you retire bring in a little hot water in the kettle."

The girl did as she was required, and then took her way upstairs.

At the request of Laura Stanbridge Gatliffe lighted a cigar and mixed himself some grog.

An hour or more passed away.

* * * * * *

The two companions were seated in the parlour, side by side—the hour was late, but Gatliffe still lingered.

"You have told me your sorrows and troubles," said his female companion, "and no one can sympathise with you to a greater extent than myself, for I too have been deserted by a cold, cruel, heartless man, but it is all over now and I strive to forget the past—the bitter past."

After this exordium she told her companion a specious tale, in which she made herself a most self-sacrificing creature.

She wound up by declaring that she was living on her means all alone in the world.

"Alone—eh?" cried Gatliffe. "Well, yes, I had a female companion, it is true, and a young man whom I have brought up, making this place his home; but he is like the rest, ungrateful and selfish."

She sighed, and drew her chair nearer to his.

"Ah! if I could find but one sympathising friend," she murmured; "for, oh! Mr. Gatliffe, we can none of us live only for ourselves. It is not in the nature and order of things—is it?"

"I don't think it is," he murmured, glancing at her dark, dreamy, voluptuous eyes—glancing at her marble bust, which was at this time a little more revealed than it had been upon their first entrance into the parlour.

"You agree with me, then?"

"As far as that is concerned, I do," he returned.

"I expected you would do so, and your wife is so unmindful of this. You love her, I suppose?"

The engineer made no answer to this query.

"It is evident enough you do," observed his companion.

"I did. It was impossible for me to do otherwise. When I first made her acquaintance I thought her the most charming creature I had ever seen."

She placed her hand on his, and looked earnestly into his face.

He grasped her hand and drew her towards him. Her head fell upon his shoulder, and he inhaled the fragrance of her breath. A tremour seemed to creep through his frame; he placed his arm round her neck, and pressed his lips to hers in one long, lingering kiss. She made no resistance.

Presently she wound her arms round him and returned the embrace. She breathed into his ear words of endearment, and Gatliffe was fairly enthralled; his hand accidentally came in contact with her bosom.

"You will not leave me to-night, dearest?" she murmured. "It is too late for you to think of returning home. You will not be cruel enough to leave me all alone after this brief interval of happiness?"

Gatliffe was bewildered; he knew he was acting in a most indiscreet manner, but had not the courage to break the spell that bound him.

The clock on the mantel-piece struck two.

"Goodness me—is it so late?" he ejaculated.

"It is late," said his companion, "but what of that? The hours fly swiftly by when in the society of those we love."

"But I really must be thinking of going."

"Why so? You cannot reach Wood-green to-night, seeing that it is now morning, and what does it matter?"

"Upon my word," said he, "I have been so charmed, so pleased with your society, that it appears I have forgotten all else."

"And so you ought," she cried, with another embrace.

"Ah," he murmured, "I am powerless in your arms, and even unable to exercise any will of my own. This ought not to be."

"Why not? I am pleased to think I have such power over you. Ah, Mr. Gatliffe, we are neither of us accountable to any one, and if—if—you find happiness in my society——" She broke off abruptly, and hid her head on his shoulder.

Gatliffe, who had been quite unprepared for this display of affection, was no longer master of himself. He took her on his knee and kissed her passionately.

GATLIFFE AND LAURA STANBRIDGE.

Laura Stanbridge, who had been playing her part to perfection, smiled.

She had him in her toils. Of that she felt assured. Unimpressible, and in a measure phlegmatic as he had been to the allurements of a designing woman, he was now, to make use of a nautical phrase, fairly capsized.

The beautiful creature in his arms affected to love him, and he, poor weak fool that he was, believed her.

"Now, dearest!" he exclaimed. "Will you excuse me? May I go?"

"As you please," she answered, pouting.

"It is not as I please. It is for you to determine."

No. 41.

"You would not think of leaving at such an hour.
Are you not contented?"

"Certainly, but ——"

"But what?"

I shall compromise you by remaining.

She laughed. "Ah! don't mind me," she cried.

"But the hour—ten minutes to three."

"Well, I know that. When you desire to retire you have only to say the word. There is a bedroom already prepared for your reception This house is my own; I am mistress here, and am a lady of independent means —what more do you desire to hear?"

Gatliffe had a very natural wish to know a great deal more, but he had the prudence not to broach so delicate a question.

"Oh! nothing—nothing more," he stammered out.

"Good—you are weary. I will show you to your sleeping chamber," said his companion, lighting a wax candle, and rising from her seat.

Gatliffe made no observation, but rose also.

The lady led the way upstairs and conducted her visitor to an elegantly-furnished bedroom on the second story of the house.

She placed the light on the toilet-table, and then turned towards the bewildered young man.

"You will be able to rest tranquilly here till morning, dearest," she murmured.

Gatliffe nodded. Then he sprang forward and caught her in his arms. He pressed her form to his, and covered her with burning and passionate kisses.

"Enough!" cried Laura. "Good night. Susan will be up early, and you can have breakfast at what hour you please," and with these words she passed along the passage.

Gatliffe closed the door of his bedroom, sat down in one of the chairs, and endeavoured to collect his thoughts—his head was in a perfect whirl.

"She is a beautiful creature," he murmured. "A lady of independent means! Eh! what a strange adventure! Well, I have no reason to complain."

He threw off his clothes and tumbled into bed, but he was too much disturbed in his mind to sleep. He thought over and over again of his mysterious inamorata. It would have been in vain for him to deny that he was very much taken with her.

He believed that he had made a conquest, and that she had conceived an overpowering affection for him. Who and what she was he found it difficult to determine; neither did it much matter—love levels all distinctions.

When he arose in the morning he went into the parlour, where the breakfast was served by the maid, who informed him that her mistress would be down in a few minutes.

Presently Laura Stanbridge made her appearance. She was attired in an elegant morning costume, and seemed to be none the worse for her carouse on the preceding night. She did the honours of the table with infinite grace, and paid every possible attention to her guest.

Gatliffe was charmed with her manner. He thanked her for all her kindness, and when the morning was over told her that he must leave to attend to his business at the works.

She acquiesced and offered her hand. Gatliffe drew her towards him and embraced her; then he took his departure with a promise that he would pay her another visit.

The more he thought over his adventure the more puzzled he was, but he could not keep long away from the woman who by this time had him enthralled.

He visited her again and again until he became a regular frequenter of the establishment. He slept there two or three nights out of the week. As time went on all restraint was thrown off, and Laura Stanbridge became his mistress.

Those who had known him in his earlier years would have found it difficult to believe that this could have come to pass.

But so it was. He was no match in cunning and duplicity to the heartless woman who had him in her toils.

When he thought of Aveline he felt abased and humiliated. He could not at first realise the depths into which he had fallen. The events of the last few weeks seemed to him more like a dream than an actual reality.

CHAPTER LXXVIII.
HUNTING UP EVIDENCE FOR A DIVORCE—MR. SLINGSBY SET TO WORK.

WHILE the intrigue was being carried on between Laura Stanbridge and her victim, Tom Gatliffe, Aveline's grandfather was in deep consultation with his lawyer as to how a divorce was to be obtained for his darling pet, who was by this time moving in the best society, and surrounded by fashionable admirers. Mr. Chicknell did not know very well what course to advise.

The earl was persistent in his demands. A divorce he was bent upon having, at all hazards.

An opportunity most suddenly and unexpectedly presented itself.

Mr. Wrench was commissioned to wait upon the engineer at his house at Wood Green.

He called several times, but could not succeed in meeting with the owner of the establishment.

He ascertained from the loquacious servant in charge of the place that her master came home only occasionally. She said, in answer to the detective's persistent inquiries, that Mr. Gatliffe had been for some time past in the habit of remaining in London, in consequence, as she alleged, of pressure of business at the works.

Mr. Wrench heard all she had to say, and very soon began to draw his own inference therefrom.

"Stays in town, does he?" murmured our astute officer. Umph! there is some special reason, for this business is all very well in its way, but there may be another cause. Formed some new connection perhaps, illicit love and all that sort of thing. The case looks more promising. If I succeed in finding out anything the earl, my patron, will be in a state of delight, but after all it's too contemptible and paltry a business for me to be engaged in. Well, we will see what can be done. Something's in the wind—that's quite certain. The question is, how is it to be worked?"

Attached to the staff of gentlemen of which he (Wrench) was a distinguished ornament was a man who was a sort of supplementary or occasional detective— his name was Slingsby.

His services had been frequently called into requisition to hunt up evidence for his superiors. Mr. Slingsby had no objection to push his inquiries in channels where his superiors did not choose to venture. He was a sort of sleuth hound, who would stoop to any mean artifices to obtain the desired information.

Mr. Wrench, upon his return home, sent for Slingsby without further ado.

"Well," said the last-named, when he was closeted with his superior, "Naggs said you wanted to see me."

"Naggs was right—sit down," returned Mr. Wrench.

"Anything on hand? Any fresh business?" inquired Slingsby.

"Yes; if you will have a little patience you shall hear."

"I'm all attention, sir."

"Very well. In the first place there is a young man named Gatliffe, who is by trade an engineer. He resides at Wood Green."

"I can go there, and soon ascertain about him."

"Don't you be so fast. I don't want you to go to Wood Green. To do so would be an act of the greatest imprudence. Besides, I have already been there myself. What I want you to do is to watch him as he leaves his work. He is foreman to an engineer in the Euston-road. I will give you the name of the firm and the number of the house. He generally leaves the works at six in the evening, but sometimes he stops till seven or eight, and indeed on special occasions even later than that; but, as a rule, you will be able to make sure of him between six and seven, or from that to eight. You understand me thus far."

"Oh, perfectly. I quite understand, Mr. Wrench."

"Very well. What I want you to do is this—when he leaves, follow him and notice where he goes to. It's probable he may make for the station; in which case push your inquiries no further, as you may rest assured that he is about to return to his own home."

"But if he doesn't do so?"

"If he does not, follow him and see where he goes to. This done, come to me."

"And what's he been up to—forgery or something of that sort, I suppose?"

"Nothing of the kind. He has not done anything wrong—at all events, nothing against the law."

"What is he wanted for, then?"

"He is not wanted. All I require for the present of you is to ascertain where he goes to on the nights he does not return to Wood Green. We have good reason for believing that he has taken up with some woman. Should this be the case we must learn more about it."

"Then that's all you want me to do at present."

"That is all. Here is the name and address of his governor. Now do your best. I have written underneath the address, between the hours of six and eight, and here is his photograph, by which you will be able to recognise him."

"All right, Mr. Wrench. Never fear, I'll find out what you want;" and with these words Mr. Slingsby took his departure.

On the following night he watched the entrance through which the workpeople passed in and out of the works in the Euston-road.

In the course of half-an-hour or so he observed Gatliffe pass through the door, and Mr. Slingsby followed at once. He was, however, much disappointed at finding his man make direct for the railway-station, and had in accordance with his instructions to give up the chase for that night.

On the succeeding evening he was again at his post, and very shortly before seven Gatliffe again passed out of the building—this time to look a different direction. He walked on westwards, and entered a coffee-shop, where he remained for about half-an-hour or more, Mr. Slingsby keeping watch and ward on the outside.

He saw Gatliffe emerge from the coffee-shop, and then walk on at a smart pace, the detective following at a respectful distance. After this the young engineer went into a hosier's shop, and purchased a pair of gloves.

He then made direct for Covent Garden Theatre,

paid the entrance money, and went into the Promenade Concerts.

The detective did the same, and kept a sharp eye upon the movements of his man, who in the course of a few minutes was joined by a female, in whose company he remained for the whole of the evening. When the performance was over the two, upon reaching the street, called a four-wheeled cab, into which they both got. When the vehicle was driven off Mr. Slingsby jumped into a hansom, and told the driver to follow the four-wheeler.

The driver of the hansom obeyed the order given him, and in the due course of time the four-wheeler was brought to a standstill at the house in the occupation of Miss Stanbridge.

Mr. Slingsby saw its two occupants alight and enter the house in question; then he discharged his cab, and watched the house for some considerable time.

He saw a light in the parlour, and saw also the shadows of two or three persons, one of which appeared to be that of a man, the others those of females.

He remained watching the house for an hour and a half, or perhaps two hours; then, when the front parlour was in darkness he went his way, well satisfied with his night's adventure.

Early on the following morning he waited upon Mr. Wrench to make him acquainted with the successful nature of his expedition.

"You have done well, wonderfully well, Slingsby," said the detective. "Nothing could be better. You are quite certain as to his identity."

"Oh, quite certain—he is the image of the photograph."

"Say, rather the photo is the image of him."

"Yes, it is. There cannot be any mistake as to that; and the lady—do you know her?"

"No, never saw her before."

"A fashionable party, I suppose?"

"Oh, dear yes, quite up to the knocker."

"Good-looking?"

"Yes, she's what you would call a fascinating sort of woman, and appeared from what I could see of her to be quite the lady. When I say a lady, I mean of course one of doubtful repute."

"Ah, just so. That is no more than I expected. So much the better."

"The better?"

"Certainly, the matter will be more easily worked."

"Most likely; but what is to be my next proceeding?"

"You have to watch him again, and see if he pays another visit to this establishment. When this has been done we will consider our next course of procedure."

Mr. Slingsby acted in accordance with the instructions given him by his superior.

He was at the works in the Euston-road on the following night, but the result was not quite so satisfactory. Tom Gatliffe went to the railway-station, and made for his home at Wood Green.

He did the same on the following evening, but Mr. Slingsby did not despair. He kept his man steadily in view, and never missed a single night from his post.

All this time Gatliffe was in ignorance of the surveillance which was kept over him.

On the third night he bent his steps in the direction of Laura Stanbridge's residence, the detective following at a respectful distance.

The gentle rap which Gatliffe gave at the door caused it to be opened by the servant girl, when without a word the visitor entered.

Mr. Slingsby remained curling his heels on the pavement on the opposite side of the street.

Presently the owner of the house came out with her admirer.

Mr. Slingsby judged rightly enough that the two were going to some place of entertainment. He did not deem it expedient to follow them, but went his way, and returned to his post a little before eleven o'clock.

In about half an hour after that time the lady and gentleman returned, the former letting herself and her companion in with a latch-key.

A gleam of light shot from the parlour window as on the first occasion, and Mr. Slingsby watched the house until he concluded all the inmates had retired to bed, then he returned to his own lodgings, very well satisfied with his night's work.

"It is pretty clear we have run him to earth," said Mr. Wrench, when his emissary made him acquainted with all the facts which had come to his knowledge. "You have done this job to-rights, Slingsby. Everything is satisfactory, as far as it goes, but, of course, much remains to be done. For the present, however, let the matter rest till I have seen my employer; then I will let you know how to act. Say nothing to anybody; keep quite quiet, and we shall win in a hand canter."

"All right, sir; I am to do nothing till I hear from you."

"Nothing whatever."

When Mr. Slingsby had taken his departure, Mr. Wrench rubbed the palms of his hands together in great glee.

"Ah, I wasn't far out in my surmise!" he ejaculated. "I thought there was a woman in the case. Well, I should never have thought it of him, for, to say the truth, he appeared to be altogether a different sort of man; but, Lord, one never knows whom to place faith in. Still he seemed so discreet, so high-minded, so far removed from temptation. But, then, after all, it is but a natural consequence. Here's a fine handsome young fellow finds himself suddenly deserted by one who, if the truth must be told, ought to have cleaved to him through good and bad fortune. Yes, it is but natural that he should form another connection, and it is withal most fortunate, as far as we are concerned."

He put on his hat and gloves, and sallied forth.

He made the best of his way to Mr. Chicknell's chambers.

The lawyer was perfectly staggered when he heard the news.

"You don't mean it? Can it be possible?" he ejaculated.

"Fact, sir—an indisputable fact."

"Do you think he is living in open adultery with this woman?"

"I fear—or rather I fancy so."

"Umph! sit down. Pray, be seated, Mr. Wrench. The earl must know of this; he will be most delighted."

"There's but little doubt of that, sir."

"None—none in the least, Wrench. Dear me, you have done well. The only obstacle in our way is at once suddenly and unexpectedly removed."

"Not quite."

"Eh, what do you mean?"

"We must have proofs."

"Ah, true. But these are easily obtainable, I suppose, eh?"

"I don't suppose there will be any great difficulty in the matter; but as yet only half our task is accomplished."

"Umph! Certainly that's right enough, and the other half, as you term it, is perhaps the most difficult part."

"It must be managed, sir—that's all I know."

"Yes, most decidedly; that is quite clear. The earl has the highest opinion of your ability and discretion. He speaks in the most flattering terms of your—ahem!—your wonderful powers of penetration."

"Does he? I am sure I am much obliged to his lordship for his good opinion of me," cried the detective, with a short laugh.

"Oh, I am not joking, Wrench. Don't imagine that," observed the lawyer.

"I don't for a moment suppose you are, sir."

"And so he's taken up with a woman of doubtful repute—has he? Dear me, it seems almost incredible."

"Well, it's only as we suppose at present, sir. As I said before, proofs are necessary. It would never do to jump hastily at a conclusion. I have never been accustomed to do that."

"No, no, of course not. That we know perfectly well; and so, upon second consideration, it would be perhaps just as well to hold the matter over for the present, and not mention the subject to the earl till we have clearer evidence."

"I should not do so, not till such time as we are more certain of our bird. He will fall into the web, I dare say, in good time."

"And what do you propose doing then?" inquired the lawyer.

"Well, sir, that is the reason for my waiting upon you. He has been seen in places of public resort with this woman; he has been seen entering the house with her, and there is every reason to suppose that he has remained there all night; but this, as you know, is not positive evidence. We must have more than this."

"Certainly; that is quite clear—much more. Do you know any of the inmates—any servant in the house?"

Mr. Wrench shook his head, and said, "Not a soul—not one person."

"There is a servant, of course, or servants?"

"Only one, I believe."

"Oh! only one—eh?"

"As far as I have been able to ascertain."

"And is she to be got at? Most domestic servants are."

"Well, that remains to be seen. I have not made any attempt to enlist her in our service, and for this reason: should she be faithful to her mistress—which is more than likely—it would be putting them on their guard."

"Just so; that is clear enough, Wrench. Well, I cannot do better than leave it in your hands. You know what is requisite—proofs, clear and unmistakeable proofs, that he has committed adultery."

"When I obtain further information I will see you again," returned the detective, as he left the lawyer's chambers.

Mr. Wrench pondered over the matter.

At present he could not very well see his way. He had, as he termed it, a delicate and difficult bit of steerage.

A rash or imprudent step might ruin all.

He was by no means disposed to tamper with Miss Stanbridge's servant. He had ascertained that she had been a long time with her present mistress, and the people in the neighbourhood said she was "true as steel."

The detective, therefore, concluded possibly enough that the girl might prove a troublesome customer.

He sent for Mr. Slingsby, with whom he had a long consultation.

In the end it was agreed between the two that other attempts should be made before having recourse to the servant for information.

Mr. Wrench now came to the front. He watched the house in the occupation of Laura Stanbridge, and made several inquiries in the neighbourhood in a careless manner.

He ascertained by the merest accident that a charwoman was occasionally engaged by the maid servant to clean the house and do the rough work of the establishment.

This was just the sort of person Mr. Wrench was desirous to meet with.

A few shillings would go a long way with a woman of that description, and the chances were that she had a tongue, which she could make very good use of.

He had ascertained that she was known as Mrs. Mumms, that she was a widow, with a son and a daughter. The son was shopboy to a greengrocer in Jermyn-street, the daughter was in service in one of the western suburbs—Richmond or Twickenham it was said—but there was no positive certainty as to this.

Mr. Wrench elected to try the son, to begin with. He went to the greengrocer's where he worked, and bought some fruit, had the satisfaction of seeing the lad in question, but he did not deem it advisable to make any inquiries of him at that time—he awaited a more fitting opportunity.

On the following morning he paced up and down Jermyn-street till he saw young Mumms come out with his basket on his arm.

Mr. Wrench waited till he came by his side, then he said—

"Hold hard for a moment—I want to ask you a question."

"Yes, sir," said the lad, coming to a halt.

"Do you happen to know the name Crowdace in this neighbourhood?"

"Can't say I do. What street does he live in?"

"I have been told he lives in Ryle-street."

"Don't know the name."

"Sure?"

"Quite sure."

"Do you know the name of Stanbridge?"

"Oh, yes, I know that name. I'll show you where she lives if you want her. I shall have to pass the house."

"I don't want to see her. What I want to know is, has she a lodger with her of the name of Crowdace?"

The name of the gentleman whom the detective was inquiring for was of course a pure invention.

"I never heard that she had, but mother will be able to tell you; she works there occasionally."

"Is there any gentleman lodger there?"

"Well, there you bother me. She don't take no lodgers, I believe, but there is a gentleman or two there occasionally."

"Is she a married lady?"

"I don't know as she's what you might term a married lady, but still she may be for aught I know; but mother will be able to tell you more about it."

"Where does your mother live?"

"Close by here; I'll show you if you like."

"Do—there's a good chap."

Mr. Wrench slipped a shilling into the boy's hand, for which he appeared to be duly grateful.

He took the detective to a narrow court, and halted in front of a dirty-looking house with five bell handles one above the other on the side of the doorway.

He rang the third bell, whereupon a woman, wiping the soap suds from her bare arms with her apron, made her appearance in the passage.

"Mother, a gentleman wants to speak to you," said the greengrocer's assistant, as he left to go his rounds.

"Your sarvint, sir," said Mrs. Mumms, coming forward.

"Oh, your son informs me that you know Miss Stanbridge. Is that so?"

"Yes, sir, I work for her at times."

"Ah, just so. Do you happen to know if she has had a gentleman named Crowdace lodging at her house?"

The woman shook her head.

"I never heard the name before," said she.

"And you don't know, I suppose, whether there is anyone of that name lodging in the same street?"

"Well, sir, not as I've overheard. There may be, but its unbeknown to me, if there is."

"My object is simply this. A gentleman of that name is missing, and his friends are anxious to ascertain something about him."

"Ah, I'm sorry I can't tell you."

"Will you be kind enough to make inquiries in the neighbourhood for me? If you succeed you will be handsomely rewarded."

"I'll do my best."

"Good. Here is a card with the name written thereon. Good morning, Mrs. Mumms."

"Will you call again, sir?"

"Most certainly I will, in a day or two."

This was certainly going a most roundabout way to obtain the desired information, but Mr. Wrench's object was to throw the woman off her guard.

There could be no possible harm in his inquiring for a fictitious individual. His doing so would not arouse suspicion. In the due course of time he hoped to have Mrs. Mumms as an ally.

He called again upon her; of course no such person could be found. He gave her five shillings for her trouble, and engaged her on the day as charwoman to his own establishment.

She came and cleared up his house. He treated her liberally—gave her a plentiful supply of beer and gin, and she was greatly pleased with her new employer.

She went her ways, and in about a fortnight was again hired by our cunning detective.

In the evening she was directed by Mrs. Wrench to dust and clean her husband's library. While she was occupied with this task Mr. Wrench entered. The charwoman was about to withdraw, but the detective requested her to remain.

"Don't go, Mrs. Mumms," said Wrench. "I want to have a little conversation with you. Sit down."

The woman looked a little surprised, or it might be alarmed, but did as she was requested.

Mr. Wrench closed the door of the room, and then took a seat himself. As a preliminary, he insisted upon his companion taking a glass of something short. This done, he proceeded to business.

"I cannot find the person of whom I am in search," said he. "Will you just answer one or two questions. Mind you, I will make it worth your while. I don't expect anybody to work for nothing."

"In course not, sir. You're a different sort of gentleman to that."

"Well, you see, Mrs. Mumms, it has occurred to me that probably the party to whom I allude is passing under a different name."

"Likely enough, sir; but I hope as how he aint bin doing anything wrong."

"Oh, dear me, no such thing. But, now, tell me—there is a gentleman living at the house owned by Miss Stanbridge, or has been, eh?"

"She's always had a relation—a cousin or nephew I believe he is—living with her. She brought him up from a mere lad, so I've been told, but he aint there so much as he used to be, and of late I've not seen much of him."

"Ah! a relation, eh?"

"Yes; so I believe, but he's not the party you are in search of. He's been there for years."

"And is not there somebody else?"

"Yes, lately there has been."

"And do you know his name?"

"Certainly—Mr. Gatliffe."

"You've been given to understand. Now tell me plainly. This Mr. Gatliffe is living with her not as a lodger but as— Well, you know what I mean, you are a woman of the world, Mrs. Mumms. Please answer me truly."

"I shouldn't like to say, sir. It aint no business of mine. There's a good many couple a living together as aint man and wife, but that's nobody's business but their two selves. They both on 'em act on the square as far as I'm concerned, and there's no call for me to round on 'em."

"A very proper observation on your part. I wish everyone had your discretion, Mrs. Mumms; but you need not be afraid of speaking frankly to me. I know they are living together without your telling me so, and you know it."

"S'pose I do, what of that? He's a fine honourable young fellow as ever stepped in shoe leather, and everybody likes him."

"That is true enough, but he is not there always—only occasionally."

"No, he's not always there; but I do hope and trust that you don't intend him any harm."

Mr. Wrench burst out into a loud laugh.

"Oh, dear me, no. Harm indeed! Of course not. What could have put that into your head?"

"Oh, I begs parding, sir. Meant no offence, but I should be sorry to get anybody into trouble."

"You are not likely to do that. Now answer me one question before you go. See, here are five sovereigns, if you answer me truly."

Mrs. Mumms was astounded at the sight of five sovereigns. Her breath seemed to be taken away.

"Do you consent?" cried her companion in a severe tone.

"What do you want me to do?"

"Speak the truth, that's all. Mr. Gatliffe and Miss Stanbridge occupy one bedroom when he visits the house. I know they do, but that is one thing—I want to hear it from your lips."

Mrs. Mumms took up the corner of her apron with which she wiped her lips, then her nose, and lastly her eyes.

"You hear what I say. Give me the desired information and the five pounds are yours. Why need you hesitate? If you won't tell me I shall have no difficulty in finding somebody who will, possibly for a tenth part of this sum."

"Well, then, they do occupy but one bedroom."

"In short, he is to all intents and purposes her husband—in every respect but the marriage ceremony?"

"I should suppose so, but I do hope you are not going to bring them into trouble. I wish I had not said anything about them."

"Don't you be alarmed; nobody will interfere with your pair of turtle doves," observed Mr. Wrench, with a short laugh. "Be of good cheer, Mrs. Mumms, and take up the money."

He handed the gold pieces to his companion, who wrapped them up in a piece of dirty, crumpled paper, and transferred them to her pocket, without saying a word.

"What is the name of the girl who is servant to the establishment?" asked the detective, carelessly.

"Her name? Oh, Susan."

"Susan what?"

"Susan Tarver."

"Thank you." Mr. Wrench wrote it down on a sheet of note paper which lay on the table before him.

"What do you want with her?" cried the charwoman, in a tone of alarm.

"I want nothing of her."

"I hope you won't mention anything about this to Susan—I do hope that."

"I promise you not to do so; neither is it likely, seeing that I don't know her and have no desire to make her acquaintance."

Mrs. Mumms now rose and left in a state of trepidation, for she half-repented of having given the information for which she had been so liberally paid, but when she got home she was in better spirits and was well satisfied with her day's work.

Mr. Wrench had now obtained as much as was necessary for his purpose, the cumbrous and expensive machinery of the law could be put in motion as soon as Mr. Chicknell and his aristocratic client chose. Mr. Wrench hastened to the lawyer's office, and after this the sagacious attorney hastened down to Broxbridge.

CHAPTER LXXIX.

THE EARL AND HIS LEGAL ADVISER—A WIFE'S TREPIDATION.

MR. CHICKNELL knew perfectly well that he would be a welcome visitor to his client's ancestral home, and he was in the best of spirits when he passed into the vestibule of the grand old mansion.

Earl Ethalwood was busily engaged in his laboratory when the lawyer made his appearance.

Aveline and Miss Jamblin had been sent to London for a change, under the charge of the good-tempered and vivacious Lady Marvlynn, so that the master of Broxbridge was without the companionship of the young ladies or the *gouvernante*.

He consented to part with them upon the condition that their visit to the metropolis was not of too protracted a duration.

To say the truth, Aveline did pretty much as she liked, and her grandfather did not oppose her in anything but the one grand wish of his life—this being a divorce from her low-born husband, as he was pleased to term him.

Mr. Chicknell gave his patron a succinct account of those circumstances with which the reader is already acquainted.

The earl was thunderstruck.

He had never for a moment counted on such an issue, but in the goblet of pleasure he drained there were a few drops of bitterness.

His pride was wounded.

Although he affected and, indeed, did treat the very name of Gatliffe with unmitigated disgust and contempt, he did not like the idea of his being so faithless to even the memory of his wife.

To take up with a woman of Laura Stanbridge's class was most reprehensible.

"He's a low-bred hound, and in saying this I have said all," cried the earl. "I always told you so, Chicknell, and we have had many wrangles—if I may so term them—upon this subject. However, the worst is over now, and we have every reason to be thankful that the fellow has acted in such a discreditable way. Nevertheless his conduct rather surprises me."

"It has surprised me, my lord, and it will surprise many others, I expect—more particularly your grand-daughter."

"Poor girl! She clung to his memory with a pertinacity which was most remarkable."

"She is not to be blamed for that, my lord."

"I say she is!" cried the earl, in one of his tantrums —"I say she is! It is the only thing we disagree upon —have always disagreed upon."

The lawyer shrugged his shoulders, but did not offer any observation in reply.

"Mr. Wrench has done exceedingly well in this business, as, indeed, he always has done, and he shall not go unrewarded. Now what are your ulterior proceedings."

"Matters are now simplified, and a divorce can be obtained without any difficulty."

"You have enough evidence?"

"Wrench says so. It will, of course, be an unopposed suit, that is already understood."

"Dear me, Chicknell, this is indeed joyful news. It seems to remove a weight off my heart, and give me renewed life and vigour. I cannot sufficiently express to you my sense of gratitude. Do, my dear friend, set to work at once. Lose no time, but avoid as much exposure as possible. I don't want any public scandal."

"You need not be under any apprehension, my lord; we shall run it through the court as quietly and expeditiously as possible. We have a plea, and that will suffice our purpose."

The earl rose from his seat, rang the bell, and ordered wine and refreshments to be served. He was in a perfect delirium of delight, was loquacious, cheerful, and passed many flattering encomiums on the wisdom and zeal displayed by his legal adviser.

Chicknell had never seen him in such spirits. The dream of his life was about to be realised, and his darling Aveline would be separated for ever from the connection which he deemed a blot upon his escutcheon.

It did not occur to him that Gatliffe was the father of the boy who was destined on some future day to represent the long line of the Ethalwoods; had he thought of this possibly there might have been a few drops more of bitterness in his cup of pleasure.

Mr. Chicknell remained at the hall that night, and on the following morning hastened up to London to institute a suit in the Divorce Court, agreeable to the instructions received from his client.

Meanwhile Aveline was enjoying an uninterrupted round of pleasure in the metropolis. She was surrounded with hosts of fashionable swains, who flattered her to her heart's content.

Lady Marvlynn knew everybody, and everybody knew Lady Marvlyvn.

She was one of those active, quick-witted, good-natured busybodies whom everyone appeared to like. She had the entrée into every coterie of fashionable society, and could say smart things without giving offence to any one.

Miss Jamblin was not taken everywhere with Aveline and her chaperon, but she saw more pleasure than she had seen during her whole life at Stoke Ferry Farm. Her position at the earl's town house was a sort of union of friend, companion, or lady's maid to the greater star in the firmament, Lady Aveline as she was termed.

Of course Aveline and the farmer's daughter were to pay a visit to the opera before they returned to Broxbridge Hall. Lady Marvlynn had made her two young friends understand that they must see Patti.

She was the rage at the time. People felt disposed to fall down and worship her, and declared that there never was such a singer.

The same remark has been made when other celebrities have been alluded to, but that does not much matter. Patti was in the zenith of her popularity, and possibly she was at her best about this time.

So the two young ladies, Lady Marvlynn, and the Honourable Tufnel Oxmoor seated themselves in the earl's carriage, which made direct for the grand entrance to Covent Garden.

It is needless to say that the house was crammed—it being a Patti night.

The opera was "La Somnambula," one of her earliest triumphs—the opera in which Malibran, many years before, had so entranced the town by her matchless vocalisation and marvellous histrionic powers.

Lady Marvlynn, having adjusted her opera-glass to the right focus, began to proceed to take a survey of the leading notabilities in the stalls and boxes. She pointed out to Aveline many distinguished persons, and gave a running commentary on them.

"Ah!" she exclaimed, "as I live, there is my old friend, the Marquis of Fincairn. I've not seen him for an age, indeed; but he's looking remarkably well. I wonder who the lady is he has got with him?"

"Don't you know?" said Oxmoor.

"No. I confess I do not."

"It's Totty Pinkstream, who was the reigning belle in Paris some short time since," observed Oxmoor, in a whisper. "He doats on her—so I'm told."

"Bah! he's an old fool then."

"Oh, Lady Marvlynn!" cried the gentleman.

"Hush, don't speak so loud—and that's the Totty we have heard so much of. Well, she's distinguished in appearance, but not particularly beautiful."

"She's not bad-looking, and has a lovely pair of eyes."

"I allow you gentlemen to be the best judges of female loveliness," said Lady Marvlynn, hiding her face coquettishly behind her capacious fan.

Her companion bowed, but made no reply.

"Who is that lady in the second box from the stage?" inquired Aveline.

"Who, my dear? Well, that's the Countess of Lanfoil—very charming, isn't she, and dressed in such good taste? Her husband chooses her dresses, I have been told, and is very proud of her, but she is cold and unimpressionable, and cares but little for him. She has, however, hosts of admirers."

"What! a married woman have admirers!" said Patty Jamhlin. "How very odd."

"Not at all, my dear; but hush, they are about to begin."

The band struck up and played the overture, the curtain was raised, and the performance commenced. When Patti made her appearance she received a perfect ovation—the applause was prolonged to an inordinate extent.

Aveline and Miss Jamblin were both delighted with her. No wonder, seeing that they had never heard her equal.

When the first act was over, Aveline said—

"She's grand—truly magnificent!"

"Yaas," drawled Oxmoor, "very good, indeed. A most delightful creature—a child of impulse."

"And cultivation," suggested Lady Marvlynn.

"Oh, of course, she has cultivation—that's generally admitted."

"Nature has something to do in forming a singer, and art also. It is the union of the two that helps to form a great artiste."

"Spoken like an oracle," said the gentleman. "Upon my word, you are a practical philosopher, a critic, and a commentator all in one."

"You flatter."

A gentleman opened the door of the box and peered in.

"Ah, Rolf, how are you? Come in," said Oxmoor, addressing the new comer.

"Let me introduce you. Lady Marvlynn, Mr. Rolf, theatrical critic to the *Portsoken Gazette* — Lady Aveline, Miss Jamblin."

They all bowed and smiled, as is usual in such cases.

"She's very fine to-night, better than usual, I think—is she not?"

"Yes, excellent," returned the critic.

"Wonderful singer, is she not, sir?" observed Lady Marvlynn, not knowing very well what to say.

"Yes, has a magnificent organ."

"There you go again," cried Oxmoor. "A magnificent organ! A voice is not an organ."

"It is not a barrel organ, I admit," said Rolf.

"No, nor is it an organ at all. It is produced by the vocal and respiratory organs. By means of these organs a sound, or a series of sounds, either better or worse, as the case may be; but the voice itself is not an organ. I positively and emphatically deny that it is."

"I have heard you say something of the kind before," returned Rolf. "Perhaps you are correct in your theory. After all, it is but a figure of speech. It is necessary to speak by the card, it would appear, when addressing the Honourable Tufnel Oxmoor."

"Oh, I can't cope with you fellows of the press, you know," observed the young aristocrat, twirling his moustache.

His friend laughed.

"I should like to have a voice, or organ as you term it," said Oxmoor. "I would astonish their weak nerves."

"You can't astonish any person's nerves," cried Lady Marvlynn, "that is impossible."

"And why not, pray?"

"Astonishment must proceed from the brain, or sensorium. Nerves are but threads of communication from the brain, and are not sentient. There are, it is true, nerves of voluntary and involuntary action, but they are incapable of being astonished. The phrase is, therefore, quite incorrect."

"Ha, ha!" laughed the critic. "You've got your answer now, Oxmoor. I would not presume to contradict her ladyship. The only answer I can give is that it is like your 'organ,' a mere figure of speech."

"As you are so very particular, it is just as well to be correct, you know," said her ladyship, tapping her friend on the elbow with the end of her fan. "Don't you see, Oxmoor, dear boy?"

"Ah, I see and feel, too," he returned, with a good-humoured smile.

The curtain drew up for the second act, and cut short this playful badinage.

Aveline Gatliffe had been charmed with the magnificent vocalisation of the prima donna, with the admirable orchestral effects, and the grandeur of the scenery; indeed, her attention had been so fixed upon the performance that she had given but little heed to the conversation which had been going on in the box.

Now she had no longer ears and eyes for the performers on the stage.

She turned deadly pale, and something seemed to deaden the pulsations of her heart.

She saw a gentleman in the fourth or fifth row of stalls; by his side sat a lady dressed in the height of fashion.

The gentleman was whispering soft words into her ear—so Aveline judged, for ever and anon she turned her face towards his and smiled.

At first she could not bring herself to believe that the gentleman was her husband, Tom Gatliffe, but she was but too well assured of this fact when she scanned the pair through her opera-glass.

She saw that he was attired in a dress suit, and that his companion was a woman of extreme beauty. She saw also, with the penetrating eye of a jealous woman, that they were on the most friendly and familiar terms.

She felt like one who is about to swoon. Her colour came and went, and the very tremour seemed to pass through her frame, and her evening's amusement was at an end. She would have given worlds to be at home in her own boudoir.

How to sit out the performance she could not divine. Had she been by herself she would have left there and then, but, situated as she was, such a course was quite impracticable.

It was in vain that the voice of the gifted singer gave expression to the most seductive and entrancing strains. It was in vain that the chorus and orchestra poured forth a flood of melody.

Aveline heard them not. Her attention was revitted upon her husband and his fair partner.

"The green-eyed monster" was pressing with a leaden and oppressive weight upon the jealous wife, who forgot at this trying hour that she had deserted her husband for wealth and luxury.

"I hate and despise him," she murmured, with supreme bitterness. "He never was my equal. Now he is a false, deceitful monster. How I despise him!"

"What is the matter with my darling pet?" exclaimed Lady Marvlynn, leaning forward, and whispering in the ear of her young charge.

"Oh nothing—nothing at all."

"Nay, my dear, something seems amiss. You look pale, and do not seem yourself. Tell me what it is? Do you feel faint?"

"I have a headache—the heat is oppressive," cried Aveline, not knowing what excuse to make.

"Ah, you cannot deceive me, my child. I feel assured that you are not well. When this act is over we will retire for a while."

"I shall do very well where I am."

But Lady Marvlynn was of a different opinion; so when the act drop fell she conducted her friend into the lobby, and from thence to the refreshment stall, where Aveline had some cooling drink.

"You are not looking at all well, dear," said her ladyship. "And there must be some reason for this."

"There is a reason," whispered Aveline, "and a powerful one, but do not breathe a syllable to anyone."

"My dear, do you suppose ——"

"No, no! I do not suppose. You have too much discretion."

"What is it, then?"

"In the stalls my husband is seated."

Lady Marvlynn gave a prolonged "Ah!" and looked astonished.

PEACE ENTERTAINS HIS FRIENDS.

"And is he alone?" she inquired.

"No, he is not; he has a lady—I mean a female—with him; but take no more notice of this—I am better now."

They returned to the box, and secretly, unobserved by any one, Aveline directed Lady Marvlynn's attention to Gatliffe and Laura Stanbridge.

Her ladyship nodded, but said nothing.

"Lady Aveline is overcome with the heat, which, to say the truth, is most oppressive," observed Oxmoor.

"Yes, no doubt. She's fresh from the country, and not used to London life, hot theatres, overpowering gaslights, and all that sort of thing, you know," said her ladyship, coming to the rescue.

No. 42.

When the third act was over Oxmoor, to the great relief of Aveline, took his departure, upon the plea that he had to meet someone at his club who was about to depart for Calcutta, and prior to his departure the members of the aforesaid club had invited him to a farewell supper.

Whether this plea was a pure invention mattered but little. The troubled wife was but too glad to be relieved of his company, for she felt that he had his eyes upon her for nearly the whole of the time he remained in the box.

It was a great relief to her when the curtain fell upon the performance, the last two acts of which had been entirely lost upon her.

Before she left the box she observed Gatliffe pass out of the stalls with his female companion. She remained in the cloak-room longer than there was any occasion for, that she might give time sufficient for her husband and Laura to pass out of the theatre.

She felt assured that she should faint if by any chance or accident she met them face to face.

Enveloping her head and shoulders in a shawl she passed through the grand entrance, and tripped into the earl's carriage. When once in this vehicle she felt that she was safe.

Her husband and his fair enslaver would not be likely to cross her path. She was silent and thoughtful during the journey home, and Lady Marvlynn, who was at no loss to divine her thoughts, had the good sense to refrain from making any observation upon a subject which she knew must be a painful one.

She therefore contented herself with giving a running commentary upon the evening's entertainment, and her conversation was chiefly directed to Miss Jamblin, who was at a loss to understand the reason for the altered demeanour of Aveline.

To say the truth, the farmer's daughter's experience of fashionable life did not in any way make her discontented with her own humble sphere. The more she saw of the "upper ten," as they are termed, the more assured she was that real happiness was as little known or experienced by the votaries of fashion as it was by those who could not aspire to so exalted a position.

Patty was a simple-minded unsophisticated girl, who had but little taste for the blandishments of wealth and power; nevertheless she had become greatly attached to Aveline, who, throughout their brief acquaintance, had treated her with uniform kindness. She was, as a matter of course, much pained to find her so sad and thoughtful, and had sufficient penetration to comprehend that there was some powerful cause for this.

What the cause was she was at a loss to divine.

When they returned to the earl's town mansion Aveline excused herself upon the plea of indisposition, and retired to her own room. She kissed Patty and Lady Marvlynn, and then withdrew.

"She's not well," said the farmer's daughter, after she had left the reception-room.

"No, not very well. You see, my dear, she is so excitable, so remarkably impressionable, so delicately organised that it does not take much to upset her. Poor Aveline, she's very sensitive."

"I think she is, but there has been nothing to put her out—that I am aware of—nothing has occurred to-night."

"Ah, dear me, no, nothing—positively nothing—except the heat and over-fatigue, but after a night's rest she'll be herself again."

"I hope so, I'm sure," murmured Patty, who did not, however, see that the excuses offered by the diplomatic

Lady Marvlynn were sufficient to account for the distraught manner of Aveline. However, she did not venture to disagree with her ladyship, and so sat down to the supper-table with the best grace she could.

We have intimated that Lady Aveline returned to her own chamber. When she had reached this she closed the door, bolted it, threw herself in an easy chair, and burst into a passionate flood of tears.

"I never would have believed it," she exclaimed. "The perfidious monster! I abhor and contemn him, and never wish to set eyes on him again."

With all her affected indifference and love of position, she still had, deep down in the bottom of her heart, some latent love for the man who, in an earlier day, she had sworn to love, honour, and obey.

How unmindful she had been of this vow we have already seen; but, notwithstanding that she had cast him on one side and given him up for the new sphere of action which presented itself to her with so much witchery, she could not bear to see him whispering soft words in the ears of a rival—and such a rival!

The thought was a maddening one, and as it passed through her brain the tears fell thick and fast from her swollen eyelids.

She was glad, however, to have her hour or two of poignant sorrow alone, and under the present circumstances could ill brook companionship.

She sat for some time in her bedchamber a prey to tumultuous and agonising thoughts. She would have liked half an hour's interview with the gentle and good Mrs. Maitland, who had been more than a mother to her. Did she know the sort of life Tom Gatliffe was leading?

She upbraided herself for neglecting Mrs. Maitland. If it could be arranged she would like to have her at the hall. She resolved to send her an invitation when she got back to Broxbridge. The earl would give his consent. He would not be cruel enough to make any objection to one who had been so many years the guardian of his grand-daughter.

Aveline retired to bed and sobbed herself to sleep, which throughout the life-long night was fretful, broken, and disturbed.

On the following day, at her own request, she returned with Lady Marvlynn and Patty Jamblin to Broxbridge Hall.

CHAPTER LXXX.

HOME LIFE OF CHARLES PEACE—A MUSICAL EVENING—
THE DETECTIVE'S STORY.

As far as outward appearance was concerned, our hero at this time was leading a quiet, respectable sort of life. He was to be seen at work in his shop for the greater portion of the day, and was on friendly and familiar terms with most of his neighbours.

In the evenings he entertained his visitors in a rational way—playing his violin and singing duets with his step-son—so that most of his friends regarded him as a genial fellow, a little egotistical perhaps, but withal an agreeable companion.

He appears to have had remarkable control over animals and birds, having at his house the billygoat before alluded to, two cats, three dogs, several guinea pigs, a parrot, and a cockatoo, together with a collection of canaries and other song birds.

His family gave him but little trouble: indeed, they ministered to his pleasure during his hours of relaxation—and, with all his faults, it is pretty generally admitted that he was remarkably kind and indulgent to his docile pets.

The sociable evenings in his house at Sheffield were in many ways pleasurable ones.

The police speak of him as being a clever fellow, who, as a cracksman, was A1 in his profession.

The London police speak of him with respect, and it takes a good deal for them to get over their contempt for provincial people in the burglarious and other professions.

Though he gave evidence of having a thorough contempt for the suffering inflicted on persons, it has been asserted "that he would not kill a mouse" if he had been required to do so.

He further declared that if he had to kill his meat he should have to go without it all his life.

Whether from curiosity or interest, he had studied carefully the major portions of the Scriptural writings, had read opinions on them, and manifested much skill in controversy on theological questions.

One afternoon when Peace lived in the Brocco he had a long conversation with the Rev. Dr. Potter on religious topics, and astonished that gentleman by the knowledge of the subject.

Even the most prejudiced against the convict, and who knew anything of his antecedents, admit that he was not a man adicted to drinking intoxicating liquors. He appears to have had a horror of a drunken man, and it is asserted that he never exceeded, save in very rare instances, the bounds of moderation.

This, the more remarkable, seeing that his fiddling at public-houses would lead him into the habit of taking more than was good for him. It is, however, quite clear that he had strength of mind sufficient to resist any such temptation.

One evening, when it so chanced that our hero had one or two friends in his parlour, Bandy-legged Bill happened to drop in.

"Ah, you are engaged. I'll call again some other time," said the gipsy.

"No time like the present—come in you old cripple," returned Peace, "and make your miserable life happy."

Bill did not want a second invitation. He was introduced to the company present, and sat himself down.

"We are just having a little practice," observed Peace. "This young girl is a pupil of mine."

The gipsy glanced at the person alluded to, and beheld a sweet-looking child, who, to all appearances, was about ten or eleven years of age. She held in her hands a flutina.

"A pupil, eh, and a very clever little thing, I'll dare be sworn," said the gipsy.

"Pretty well," returned Peace; "but you shall hear and judge for yourself. Now Esther, dear," this was addressed to the girl, "let the gentleman hear what you can do, or rather what we can both do."

Music was placed before Esther, then Peace led off with his violin, while the child accompanied him on the flutina.

The duet was most creditably performed. The girl was a little nervous at first, but gradually gaining courage as she proceeded, did credit to her master.

The occupants of the room were loud in their praises, and the general impression seemed to be that Peace's pupil was a prodigy. Without going so far as this, it must be admitted that she was possessed of considerable ability, and her master was very proud of her.

She was the daughter of a poor operative; Peace therefore gave her lessons gratuitously. He had an eye to business, however, and very shortly after this he took her with him to public-houses where she sang and played duets with her master.

"And who has taught you to play so beautifully?" said one of our hero's visitors, addressing herself to the child.

"Mr. Peace; I never had any other master," she answered.

"Ah, but you don't know half her accomplishments. She sings like a nightingale. Now, dear, let the gentleman hear you sing. Let's have the 'Life Clock.' Come, don't be bashful."

After some hesitation the child commenced, Peace playing a violin accompaniment. The words were as follows—

There is a little mystic clock,
　No human eye hath seen,
That beateth on and beateth on,
　From morning until e'en.

And when the soul is wrapped in sleep,
　And heareth not a sound,
It ticks and ticks the live-long night,
　And never runneth down.

Ah! wondrous is that work of art
　Which knells the parting hour!
But art ne'er formed nor mind conceived
　The life-clock's magic power.

Nor set in gold nor decked with gems,
　By wealth and pride possessed,
But rich or poor, or high or low,
　Each bears it in his breast.

When life's deep stream 'mid beds of flowers
　All still and softly glides,
Like wavelet's step with a gentle beat
　It warns of passing tides.

When threatening darkness gathers o'er,
　And hope's bright visions flee,
Like the sullen stroke of the muffled oar,
　It beateth heavily.

When passion nerves the warrior's arm
　For deeds of hate and wrong,
Though heeded not the fearful sound,
　The knell is deep and strong.

Such is the clock that measures life,
　Of flesh and spirit blended,
And thus 'twill run within the breast
　Till that strange life is ended.

The voice of the singer was singularly sweet and sympathetic. The ditty was simple, but the words were set to a flowing melody, and the young, fresh voice of the little maiden entranced the ears of her audience.

"My word, Charlie, but she is most charming," cried the owner of a public-house in the immediate neighbourhood. "You must bring her with you when you next come."

"She's too diffident at present to sing before all you ruffians," cried Peace, with a smile. "No, no, guv'ner, I want her to do better things than that."

"Well, but it 'ud be good practice, you know," observed the gipsy.

"Possibly; but she's not my daughter, and I can't do as I like. She's only my pupil, and is at present but a beginner."

"She does jolly well for a beginner, old man," cried the publican, "and there's a lot in her. She's a lump of talent—any one can see that."

"Shut up," said Peace; "you'll make the child vain."

"Well, I'm sorry I spoke, if you take it like that."

"Here, this is your sort of customer," observed Peace, making a motion to his billygoat.

The animal at once stood on its hind legs, and, as its master played a merry tune, danced to the sound of the music in a most comical and grotesque manner.

The occupants of the parlour laughed till they cried again.

Peace put the goat through a number of tricks and antics, which were irresistibly droll.

"He's a regular stunner, that's what he is," said the gipsy. "I'd give the world to have an animal like that; but, lor bless you, I suppose I shouldn't be able to do much with him. Horses are more in my line."

After this performance was over Peace went through one with his two dogs, who were as docile as the goat; they seemed to understand every motion or look of their master.

The little singer, Esther Genge, petted and fondled the animals, who seemed to know her almost as well as they did their master.

"Why don't you do a show, old man of this happy united family?" observed Bandy-legged Bill.

"It aint so easy as you imagine, and costs a lot of money in moving about from town to town," said our hero.

"Ah, I 'spose it does."

"Ah, yes, you want a lot of the rhino to begin that sort of business; besides that, I should soon get tired of it."

"Well, pitch us a stave, Charlie," said the publican; "fire away."

"My voice isn't up to much," observed Peace, "but I'll do my best."

With this he played a long prelude on his violin, and then sang the following:—

> HOLD YOUR HEAD UP LIKE A MAN.
> If the stormy winds should rustle,
>   While you tread the world's highway,
> Still against them bravely tussle,
>   Hope and labour day by day.
> Falter not, no matter whether
>   There is sunshine, storm, or calm,
> And in every kind of weather
>   Hold your head up like a man.
>
> If your brother should deceive you,
>   And should act a traitor's part,
> Never let his treason grieve you,
>   Jog along with lightsome heart.
> Fortune seldom follows fawning,
>   Boldness always is the plan;
> Hoping for a better dawning
>   Hold your head up like a man.
>
> Earth, though e'er so rich and mellow,
>   Yields not for the worthless drone,
> But the bold and honest fellow,
>   He can shift and stand alone.
> Spurn the knave of every nation,
>   Always do the best you can,
> And no matter what your station
>   Hold your head up like a man.

Of course everyone professed to be delighted with the ditty.

Peace at one time had a very fair voice, but it told better in concerted pieces, not being so well adapted for solos, but he sang in time and tune. His knowledge of music could not fail to ensure that.

In the course of the evening he sang a duette with the little girl.

This was executed with remarkable precision, and created quite a furore.

Singular to relate, one of the persons present was a retired detective, who had been introduced to Peace by Mr. Wrench.

He knew perfectly well that our hero had been in trouble, and had done his four years but that was no reason for his discontinuing his acquaintance with Peace, who he hoped and believed was at this time a reformed character.

"Upon my word, Peace," said Mr. Hilton, the detective alluded to, "you ought to do well; for—I don't say it out of flattery—you are clever in many ways."

"It isn't the most clever persons who get on in this world," remarked Peace. "I am afraid, if we examined closely, that the contrary is the case. No one ought to know this better than yourself."

"A man can't do much nowadays without capital," remarked the publican. "He may strive and work his fingers to the bone, but unless he has the fore horse by the head it aint of much use."

"There's a great deal of truth in that," returned Hilton; "but we come into the world without anything, and when we go out of it we can't take anything with us, so I suppose it's pretty much the same in the long run."

"Our friend here has seen something of life, mind you that," said Peace. "He's been a celebrated man in his day. You wouldn't believe it, to look at him, that he has been a detective; but you see," he added, with a smile, "we are all honest people here, and so it does not much matter."

"All honest till you are found out, old man," cried Hilton.

The company burst out in a roar at this last observation.

"We must be a little cautious," remarked one of the company.

"Ah! don't mind me; I've given up the business long since," said Hilton.

"You found it a harassing sort of life, I suppose?"

"Well, I don't know that I did. I have often heard it said that the best part of my life must have been a harassing and painful one, but it was not without its pleasures. The scene of my operations was chiefly in the city of Edinburgh, and as my reputation grew I was obliged to get up at midnight to pursue thieves and recover property, often with little or no clue, and was constrained to trust to chance and wait, like Mr. Micawber, till 'something turned up.'"

"And something generally did turn up," said Peace, with a knowing wink at the company.

"Well, yes, generally, I admit; for I need hardly say if any profession nowadays can be enlivened by adventure it is that of a detective officer."

"With the enthusiasm of a sportsman whose aim is to hunt and shoot innocent animals, he is impelled by the superior motive of benefitting mankind by ridding society of pests, and restoring the broken fortunes of suffering victims."

"Charming occupation," suggested Peace.

"It's all very well for you to make game of our business, my friend, but let me tell you that the ingenuity of the detective is taxed, while it is solicited by the sufferers and repaid by the applause of a generous public. I need hardly say how very much is due to decision in the business of detection. A single minute will often peril the object of your inquiry, and then it does not often happen—at least I have not found it—that the patience that is required in ferreting is joined to the power of dashing at an emergency."

"You can't expect an impetuous man to be patient," observed Peace. "All are not constituted alike, but it requires a man of exceptional qualities to hunt down thieves or robbers, and, as you say, inflexibility of purpose or decision is absolutely requisite."

"My friend, M'Levy," said Hilton, "who was a celebrated man in his day, and who perhaps brought more offenders to justice than any other man of his class, gives an instance, in his work called 'The Curiosities of Crime,' of the value of decision."

"Does he? and what might the case be to which he alludes?" inquired Peace, who was always interested in anything appertaining to crime or criminals; it was an interest which might be said to be engrained within him.

"If you wish to hear it, I can't do better than give it in his own words, for he was a far better hand at telling a story or narrative than I am myself," said Hilton.

"On the 4th of January, 1852," says M'Levy, "as a man whose name has by some mischance been omitted from my book, was going along the head of the Cowgate, he was instantaneously set upon by three young men, thrown down, and robbed of his watch. A man of the name of W. Duncan, who came up at the moment to lift up the stunned victim, met the robbers as they made off. It was dark, and he had a difficulty in catching marks, so as to be able to identify them. All that he could say when he came to the office was only general, so that it would have been impossible to proceed with any certainty on his description. In addition to this disadvantage, it happened that any information that I could get from him was got at the door of the office, where I met him as he hurried in. I was just on the eve of setting out on a hunting expedition, accompanied by my assistant, Reilly, with a draper, who had got taken from his shop a quantity of goods, and whose case was urgent. How can I get so much from Duncan—enough to point my mind towards three young men—David Dunnett, Robert Brodie, and Archibald Miller—the last of whom I knew to be a returned convict."

"Ah, you knew the gentlemen, eh?" cried one of listeners.

"Not me," said Hilton. "I am giving you the narrative as M'Levy tells it in his work."

"M'Levy!—what a rum name!" observed the publican. "A Scotch Jew, I suppose?"

"Nothing of the kind. M'Levy was an Irishman by birth, though he followed the avocation of a detective, like myself, in the city of Edinburgh. Of course it was impossible," says M'Levy, "that the man could give me a description of all three, but he said sufficient for me to draw my own conclusions, for when once a gang is formed, they generally act in concert, so that if you get a clue to one, the other birds are easily trapped. The particular line of the suspected persons, I knew perfectly well, was robbing from the person, and knowing this, I was more easily led to the conclusion that they were the guilty parties—at least such was my impression. It was only that, not a positive or absolute conviction; and, indeed, so much was I taken up with the draper's business, that I sent Duncan to report regularly."

"Duncan?"

"Yes, Duncan is in his grave now, and nothing can touch him further," remarked Mr. Hilton, sententious."

In the circumstances (continues M'Levy narrative), the affair was soon out of my mind, occupied as I was with the poor draper, who sighed for his goods, and no doubt thought that I was the man to repair his loss.

A reputation thus gets a man into toils, but I hope I never regretted this consequence, so long as I could give my poor services to anxious, and often miserable victims.

How often have I walked through Edinburgh in the middle of the night, and far on in the morning—when all were asleep but those who turn night into day—accompanied by some silent man or woman, groaning inwardly over a loss sufficient to break their fortunes and affect them for life—threading dark, noisome wynds, entering dens where nothing was heard but cursing, and nothing seen but deeds without shame, endeavouring in the midst of all this sea to find the sighed-for property, or detect the cruel robber.

Wearied to the uttermost, I have often despaired, at the very moment when I was to pounce upon what I sought, redeem my spirits, and render happy my fellows.

In the present case I had a task of the same kind. We went through a great part of the Old Town, upstairs and downstairs; through long dark lobbies, and into all kinds of habitations, but the draper was not that night, at least, to be made happy.

We had entirely failed, and were all knocked up by disappointment and fatigue.

If the robbery at the Cowgate had scarcely taken hold of me when we set out, all interest had passed away, if not all recollection.

Some hope had taken us over to the far end of the Pleasance, and we were returning by that street. The hour was late—between twelve and one o'clock—and a dark night, every sound hushed.

We were worn out with fatigue, and were fit only for our beds. I think we had got as far as the foot of Adam-street, when up came three young fellows, so rapidly that they were within a yard of us before they saw us or we saw them

I did not hesitate a moment. "Seize them!" I cried.

We sprang upon them on a sudden impulse. I seized Miller and Dunnett each with a hand while Reilly engaged Brodie.

A fierce struggle ensued, as you can readily imagine, during which I cried, "Search Brodie."

And no sooner was the cry raised than Brodie threw something away from him as far as he could throw it. The sound of the article seemed to be music to the ear of the draper.

He ran at once to the spot and picked up a silver watch. The very "ticker" that had been taken from the man in the Cowgate three hours before.

In the meantime the struggle continued, and no man but those who have had to deal with robbers can form an idea of the energy they display when caught suddenly after an exploit.

Then the worst passions are aroused, and the terror of apprehension gives them a power which is perfectly marvellous. Were this not so criminals would never escape as they have been frequently known to do out of the hands of courageous and determined officers.

At length, and receiving some aid from our valiant draper, who lost the sense of his loss in a kind of revenge against the class from which he had suffered, we succeeded in quelling them, whereto we were probably aided, too, by passengers who stopped to witness the row.

We landed them all safely, and they got their reward. Brodie, who had the watch, was sentenced to seven years' transportation; Miller, the returned convict, got two years' imprisonment; against Dunnett, not proven, for there was no proper identification. I have said that Miller was a returned convict. I am not sure but that the old notion that punishment tends to reformation hangs yet about many minds. For God's sake, let us get quit of that.

I have had through my hands so many convicted persons, that the moment I have known they were loose I have watched them almost instinctively for a new offence. The simple truth is, that punishment hardens.

It is forgotten by the hopeful people that it is clay they have to work upon, not gold, and, therefore, while they are passing the material through the fire, they are making bricks, not golden crowns of righteousness.

Enough, too, has been made of the evident enough

fact that they must continue their old courses because there is no asylum for them.

You may build as many asylums as you please, but the law of these strange nurslings of society's own maternity cannot be changed in this way.

I say nothing of God's grace—that is above my comprehension—but, except for that, we need entertain no hope of the repentance and amendment of regular thieves and robbers.

They have perhaps their use—they can be made examples of to others, but seldom or never good examples to themselves.

"There are instances of reformation, I suppose," said one of the company. "Once a thief, always a thief, is not a very humane doctrine."

"There are instances, of course, but they form the exception to the rule," observed Mr. Hilton. "But that the habitual criminal, as he is termed, will always exist, is, I fear, fated; but modern experience tells us that they may be diminished by simply drawing them when very young within the circle of civilisation, in place of the old way of keeping them out of it."

"Some will never reform, do what you will," remarked Peace, "and this is a very sad reflection."

He could moralise with the best of them, and went on for the space of several minutes discoursing upon the question of the treatment of the criminal part of the community. He blamed the government more than the public, or, indeed, the felons, and talked so morally, and in such a proper manner, that his listeners were charmed with his discourse.

Then when the subject began to prove wearisome he played a fantasia on his violin, and made the little girl, his pupil, dance to the sound of the music.

His guests appeared to enjoy themselves—indeed they could hardly fail to do so for Peace, in addition to being an entertainer, played the part of a host in a highly satisfactory manner. Mr. Hilton was the first to leave. After his departure the publican said—

"Ah! a very nice chap, that friend of yours."

"Yes, pretty well, for a detective."

At this observation they all laughed, as a matter of course, and some chaffing went on which Peace bore with admirable good temper until the remainder of the company left, with the exception of Bandy-legged Bill, who remained behind to have a *tête-à-tete* with his boon companion and accomplice in crime.

CHAPTER LXXXI.
THE RETURN TO BROXBRIDGE HALL—THE FARMER AND HIS DAUGHTER.

LORD ETHALWOOD was a little surprised upon finding his grand-daughter returning so suddenly. He had expected her to remain in the metropolis for another fortnight at the very least. He was, however, but too glad to have her back, and, therefore, did not care to inquire the reason for her sudden return. He knew her to be capricious—a little wilful—and concluded that she was satiated of pleasure, and was, therefore, but too glad to have rest and quiet at Broxbridge—any way, he felt he was the gainer. He soon discovered from her manner that she was much more reserved and serious than she had been prior to her visit to the metropolis; the reason for this he could not very well make out.

The crucial question, if we may so term it, had to be put—the intelligence in respect to the law proceedings had to be made known to Aveline.

This difficult and delicate task was reserved for the diplomatic Lady Marvlynn, for the earl did not care to broach the question himself. He was too dignified for that—besides, it would come better from her female adviser and friend; and so, after a playful prelude and a good deal of beating about the bush, Lady Marvlynn came to the point, and informed her young charge of the legal proceedings.

Aveline looked awe-stricken.

"And, pray, who has had the presumption to give these orders without consulting me?" she exclaimed. "I am the fit and proper person to determine, and no other."

"My dear child," said Lady Marvlynn, "you really must not spoil your beautiful features by displaying this excess of anger. Who do you suppose—not me, surely?"

"I have not accused you as yet, Lady Marvlynn," cried Aveline. "It will be time enough for you to answer when I do."

Her ladyship laughed good-humouredly.

"You know, my dear girl, that whatever you choose to say will always be taken in good part as far as I am individually concerned—so leave off pouting. Sit down and lend me your attentive ear, or rather ears."

"Well, what more have you to say?" returned Aveline, dropping into the nearest chair.

"The earl your grandfather, the head of the house and master of Broxbridge," said Lady Marvlynn, emphasising her words with more than her usual care, "has thought fit in his wisdom to take upon himself the responsibility of getting you released from the thraldom which, to say the truth, has been to him for a long time almost insupportable."

"To him?"

"Yes, my dear, to him, and—but this is only hypothetical — he presumes that it is insupportable to his darling pet also, for what constitutes his happiness or misery applies with equal force to his grandchild."

"And have you told him?" exclaimed Aveline, as her brow darkened.

"I have told him nothing," said her ladyship, still more emphatically. "It is not likely I should do so, and you will pardon the observation, but it is by no means complimentary to me to offer such a suggestion."

"Oh, pardon—pardon me! I was wrong, I know it!" cried Aveline, throwing herself forward and clasping her companion round the neck with every expression of fondness.

"Say no more, darling, upon that head. You will find it indeed difficult to offend me. This is but a passing cloud; but my charge must learn to control her feelings—she really must. In the fashionable world these sudden emotions are quite out of place—they are, indeed. Well-bred people never suffer themselves to give way to violent demonstrations. Besides, dear, anger or rage is a sore destroyer of beauty."

"I care not for beauty, and am but as nature made me. I will not give my consent to this suit against my husband."

"You surely do not mean to say that you will oppose the wishes of Earl Ethalwood?"

"Oh, I don't know what to do!" said Aveline, bursting into a flood of tears. "I am the most miserable creature in the whole creation."

"I should have thought——" exclaimed her ladyship, pausing suddenly.

"Should have thought what?"

"Well, I don't know. May I speak plainly?"

"Certainly."

"And you promise not to be offended?"

"I promise."

"I should have thought, after what we both witnessed at the opera, that you would have no hesitation——"

"And assuming it was a mistake—an error, he might have gone thither with some relative—a friend's wife, perhaps. It surely must be so."

Lady Marvlynn shrugged her shoulders and shook her head.

"We are most of us prone to put the worst construction on the matter in cases of this sort."

"All I can say is, I hope we have."

"But you do not think so?"

"I confess I do not."

"Very well. Nothing ought to be done till we have made further inquiries, if it be as you think."

"As I think?"

"Well, say me, if you like. If it be so, then, indeed, I shall not hesitate for one moment."

"So be it, Aveline. We will make further inquiries, and so let the matter rest for the present. You are a dear darling girl," and with these words the speaker embraced her young charge fondly.

"Do not pain the earl by any allusion to this subject for the present," cried her ladyship.

"I promise not to do so."

And so the interview ended.

Patty Jamblin, who had returned with Aveline, did not remain long at Broxbridge Hall. She was anxious about her father, and on the following day hastened at once to Stoke Ferry Farm.

The honest old farmer was almost beside himself with joy when his eyes lighted on the sweet and innocent face of his only child.

She was the only solace he had in his declining years, and for her he seemed to live. Patty was pleased to find that the old man was looking very much better than she expected to see him.

It had been a sore trial, the loss of his son Philip, but he had borne up against the misfortune with great fortitude, and appeared to be more himself.

"I dunno how I shud 'a got on wi'out ee," said the farmer, "hadn't it a bin for John Ashbrook. He took compassion on the old man, ye zee, and has gi'en me as much of his company as he could well spare."

"I'm sure it's very kind of him, said Patty, "and I shall always feel grateful for the timely service he has rendered. Where is he now?"

"Oh, he be here."

"Here?"

"Well, lass, not 'xactly here, I don't mean that; but he be about a lookin' after the men. Ye see he's been my right hand, aye, and the left too I'm thinkin'."

Patty found Stoke Ferry Farm as clean as a pink, both inside and out.

During her absence it had been put in thorough repair. It was never much out of order, but now it was a perfect model in its way.

The house was a substantial affair, as red and ugly as a British uniform, relieved at the corners with white stone facings.

Whether the farmer had sent word to John Ashbrook or not it would be difficult to determine. The fact, however, was clearly demonstrated.

Patty had not been in the house half an hour before Ashbrook made his appearance in the large room which served as a parlour.

He was, as usual, very attentive to the farmer's daughter, and that was all.

But anyone who saw them together would not be far out in their reckoning if they came to the conclusion that he had a sneaking fondness for her.

Old Jamblin was a sociable man, and very few evenings passed in which some neighbour did not drop in to smoke a pipe, have a glass of grog, or a hand at short whist.

During Patty's absence John Ashbrook had paid frequent visits to her father.

After her return he did not seem disposed to leave at all.

"Dall it! but John 'ud mek her a good husband," muttered the farmer. "The Jamblins and Ashbrooks wer med to run in pairs. Patty and John 'ill go together as nat'ral as half-and-half."

As these were his sentiments he gave the young people every opportunity of sweethearting, as he termed it.

And he was perpetually finding excuses for putting on his thick boots to go into the yard.

Jamblin was known to be a rich man. His father had left him a good sum at his death, to which he had been adding for years.

The only wonder was that his daughter had not a host of candidates for her hand.

By-and-bye it came to be rumoured among the old women who gossipped over their brown sugar and tea, and among the farmers and dealers on "'Change" on market day, and among the servants in their Sunday strolls, that John Ashbrook, of Oakfield House, was keeping company with Miss Jamblin, of Stoke Ferry.

As soon as this fact was established Stoke Ferry became the focus of twenty radiating hearts. Then intelligent agriculturists could only discover that Patty Jamblin was a catch both for wealth and beauty by the time that a good-looking and (for a farmer) a passably talkative young man had got a footing ahead of them.

But this, doubtless, most of my readers may have observed is often the case. On Sunday evenings Stoke Ferry was like a fair, and the consumption of spirits and tobacco would have shed honour upon an assemblage of medical students; but even gin and water did not embolden these visitors to make more than sheep's eyes at the fairy who had drawn them there.

These silent tributes flattered her vanity without putting her to the trouble of paining their's. She had, however, one suitor who was really unfortunate.

This was no other than Mr. Nettlethorpe, a new neighbour of Jamblin's, but a man whom he despised; he was one of the most cheeseparing, meanest men in the whole county.

At one time he had been a money-lender, but of later years he had chosen to try his hand at farming, about which he knew next door to nothing.

Although Jamblin had a great antipathy to him, he could not, as a neighbour, be positively rude to him.

"I hate the man," said Jamblin, "but one can't shut the door in his face. Pipple say he's been dangling after you, but of course you think nothing of such a varmint—a fellow with a set of cows not worth opening and shutting a gate after. Why, you might hang yer hat on thur hipbones. He a farmer! A pretty notion he has of farming. He let his plough stand to kill a mouse, and instead of dunging twelve cartloads to the acre, as everybody else does, he doesn't dung twelve barrowfuls. And his horses, too! He thinks it's a saving to starve 'em till they've got as weak as chickens, and can't do any work. Why, you can see 'em reel as they go up the road."

"He has a very nice house," said Patty.

"Nice, indeed. It's Mock Beggar Hall, foine outside, but nat'rally barren within. There aint much more than carp pie for his wife in the larder, I'll be bound, for he beant the sort to keep more cats in his house than'll kill mice."

" He's got a very nice sister."

Farmer Jamblin burst out into a loud laugh.

" Has he ?" he cried ; " well that's a matter of 'pinion, Patty. She be as wretched and ignorant a little nat'ral as ye'd find in a day's tramping. Did I ever tell 'ee ? I was riding by the house one day, and she came out with her back h ir flying loose, and crying ready to split herself. Dear, dear, thought I, brother been took with a fit of remorse and killed hissolf. 'Oh, Mr. Jamblin,' cried she, ' what shall I do ? My poor duck is so ill—she's got fast on the nest and I can't move her off.' Oh, oh, that was a larfable ditty."

" But she hasn't been brought up to farming, father," suggested Patty.

" That beant it, gell. She be mean and close-fisted like her brother. Do you know what she did ?"

" No."

" She watered the men's beer when she sent it out to 'em in the hay harvest. Why, if you put one drop of water into beer it's spoilt directly. It is so different to spirits. She ought to have been made to drink it." The farmer paused suddenly, and then said, in a lower tone, " but here, as I'm alive, comes the very man hisself. I say, Patty, can't 'ee manage to chuck him off somehow ? I can't send him away, and it gives me the sick every time as I sees him."

She answered with a cunning little smile. Her father went out into the fields, and Mr. Nettlethorpe found Patty alone in the parlour, sewing.

He stammered a good morning, and sat down clumsily on a chair.

Nettlethorpe, the miser-farmer, as he was called—for in many respects he resembled the far-famed old Elwes—was a tall meagre-looking man with bright red hair.

He carried pinch and starve in broad letters upon his features, which were angular, and also on his clothes which were patched and threadbare.

" Are you not well, Mr. Nettlethorpe ?" inquired Patty, with an appearance of interest, as she saw her visitor shifting about on his seat as uneasily as if he had been on the top of a kitchen oven.

" Quite well, thank you. The fact is, I—I came over to—to see you."

" Oh, indeed, you flatter me."

" Do I ? I think not. I did not mean to do so, but—"

" Yes, exactly, I understand. Pay your respects to me and all out of pure disinterested friendship."

" That's just it."

" So I thought ; but you have some dust on your coat," said she, patting him on the shoulder under the pretext of dusting it.

This made her lover blush from the nape of the neck to the tip of his long, ungainly nose.

It also emboldened him to seize her hand and to cry—

" Oh, Miss Jamblin, you are so good and kind, so beautiful, and you make me feel so happy."

" Do I ?"

" Oh, yes, indeed you do. Will you consent to make me happier still ?

" How can I do that, Mr. Nettlethorpe ?"

" By giving me your hand. By consenting to become my wife and mistress of my house."

Mr. Nettlethorpe appended a huge sigh to this request. It might have been a gasp of relief—it might have proceeded from some tenderer emotion.

Patty at first turned away her head—it might be supposed to hide her maiden blushes—it might be to

conceal a roguish smile—or, probably, to consider her answer. Then she said—

" But your sister is mistress of your house now, and perhaps she might not like to part with the keys," observed Patty, keeping her countenance in a most wonderful way.

" She shall leave the house directly you come into it. I pledge my word as to that. She can go back to her mother, who resides in London."

He glanced at her with what he intended to be an expression of love, but it struck her as being irresistibly comic.

Nettlethorpe regarded the coy beauty with a somewhat dubious expression.

Patty remained silent.

" What say you ?" he inquired.

" Oh, I am afraid to answer. You know I have such a prodigious appetite. I am afraid I should eat you out of house and home, and folks do say that you don't often light the kitchen fire in your house. I couldn't bear the idea of being starved."

" You shall have anything you wish, my dear Miss Jamblin," cried her red-haired supplicant, with a sudden impulse of prospective generosity. " You shall go shopping yourself, and marketing yourself, just whenever you please."

" I fear, sir, I should not be stewardly enough for your wife, and that you would be too stewardly for my husband. Were it in my power to give you my hand, I must tell you candidly, Mr. Nettlethorpe, that it never would be yours. When I marry, I marry a man not a savings-box; a man who spends his money, and does good with it, and who does not keep it piled up in a heap till it decays; a man who does not think it sinful or extravagant to enjoy a few innocent pleasures, and who will give me a good dinner and eat one himself every day in the year."

" Miss Jamblin, I am astounded. Do you suppose I am so mean that I should begrudge my wife the necessaries of life. A good dinner ! You don't suppose I am likely to starve you, or anyone else, for the matter of that ?"

" I will take good care you don't starve me, Mr. Nettlethorpe."

" You wrong me—indeed you do. These observations are most uncalled for."

" Are they ?"

" Most certainly they are. But I see how it is—some mischievous, evil-disposed person has been prejudicing you against me——"

" No such thing ;" your name has not been mentioned to me by anyone, and I am sure nobody has spoken against you. It is not at all likely."

" Then am I to understand, madam," exclaimed the miserly farmer, " that you decline to listen to my suit ?"

" You may understand that without a doubt."

" And why, pray ?"

" I am already engaged, Mr. Nettlethorpe. This is a very cogent reason."

" Then why couldn't you say so at first, without all this cursed preaching ?"

" Your hat, Mr. Nettlethorpe !"

" When you have spent all your money, come and borrow some of me, and you shall have it at sixty per cent."

" Your stick, Mr. Nettlethorpe !"

" Dash the stick ! Let it stay where it is. It'll do for your husband to lay across your back when you've made a fool of him."

THE NOTTINGHAM SILK ROBBERY.

"Thank you. I will keep it in memory of you."

Nettlethorpe burst out of the room, and went home, snapping like a mad dog at everything he met.

"I've got rid of your pest," cried Patty, when her father entered the parlour, after Nettlethorpe's departure; "and I don't think we are likely to be troubled again with him for some time to come."

"Hast thee given 'im his answer, lass?" said the farmer.

"Well, I fancy so."

"An' what did 'ee want, Patty?"

"He made me an offer."

"Of what?"

"His hand and heart."

The farmer burst out in a roar of laughter.

"He must be mad to mek' such an offer. His hand and heart! Why, the mean hound hasn't got any. Heart indeed! But ye gev' him an answer? Ye'd be sure to do that."

"Oh, yes, he's got his answer, father."

"Good gell. It be loike 'is impudence. I hate 'im as I hate the measles or wire worm. An' he aint o' no good to man nor woman either."

CHAPTER LXXXII.
THE NOTTINGHAM SILK ROBBERY—HOW PEACE DID IT.

FOR some time after his last escapade Charles Peace continued to work industriously at his business. It must not be supposed, however, that during this period he refrained entirely from his evil practices.

He was at work occasionally at night at habitations within a short distance of Sheffield; but he was specially careful, and did not venture upon what he termed a "big job."

No one at this time suspected that he was carrying on his depredations in such a secret and covert way.

He had refilled his purse by disposing of some plate, which was the private property of a merchant at Hull.

When the summer came again he contrived and carried out a robbery on a more extensive scale.

He had for a long time contemplated making an incursion on a large warehouse in Nottingham. He had journeyed thither, and had made a careful inspection of the scene of his proposed operation.

Bandy-legged Bill had to act in concert with our hero, who felt assured that he would be successful in his forthcoming enterprise.

During the latter months of the year, when fishing on the Trent was considered good, a man of fairly gentlemanly appearance, with black hair and a closely shaven face, presented himself at one of the boating stations at Nottingham.

The manager came forward and asked our hero what he could do for him.

"Ah, you see, I have but indifferent health," observed Peace, "and a change of scene is absolutely necessary, so my doctor says. I think of having a week's fishing."

"Yes, sir, and I have no doubt you will benefit by the change," returned the manager. "Do you require a waterman?"

"No, I can manage very well by myself; all I need is a boat. My tackle I have with me at a house in the neighbourhood. I want a good-sized boat, for, let me see, say a week or so."

"Yes, sir, we can accommodate you. Step this way, if you please, and make choice of a boat."

Peace accompanied the speaker to the appointed spot, and after much consideration and haggling a bargain was struck for the fishing-boat.

The required deposit was paid, and Peace on the following morning brought down to the water's side a considerable amount of tackle, rods, lines, baits, and all the requisites for an experienced angler.

His manner was so urbane, and he spoke in such a quiet unostentatious manner, that the boat proprietor was quite taken with him, believing him to be a gentleman of independent means, who was a devotee to the sport.

After some conversation as to the best places on the river and other topics, Peace got into the boat and rowed down the stream. Prior to his starting he said that he had to meet some friends, who, like himself, were about to have a few days' sport on the Trent. He was, as a matter of course, accepted as a profitable customer.

The day was fine and bright, and the water was as clear as crystal, and Peace, as he drifted down the river, was well satisfied with the proceedings thus far. He moored his boat on the river's bank and threw in his line. He remained at what he deemed a likely spot, and pulled out three or four fish.

Peace has been described in the newspapers "as a little insignificant man with grey hair," but at this time his hair was raven black—made so by artificial means—and to all appearances he was a professional man; he might be a doctor or else a clergyman—it would be difficult to say which.

Certainly no one would have taken him for a mechanic; neither did his appearance or manner suggest that he belonged to the working class. He could assume an air of gentility when it answered his purpose to do so. As we have already indicated he was a man of what might be termed a Protean character.

The few chance wayfarers who observed him in his boat were doubtless under the impression that he was a gentleman of independent means. This was precisely what he wished to appear.

After angling for some time he went further down the river, making apparently for a more favourable spot.

After spending some considerable time at his well-beloved sport, he made for a neighbouring house, where he had his midday meal. Here he met with some brother sportsmen, who joined him for the remaining portion of the day, and when night came on he put up at the house by the river side, where he had a bed.

By early morn he again betook himself to his boat, and drifted further down the river, until he arrived in sight of the silk manufactory upon which he proposed operating.

In the after part of the day Bandy-legged Bill made his appearance.

"Well, old man, how goes it?" said the new-comer, in a whisper.

"All right so far. Have you got the trap with you?"

"Yes; I've put it up at a beershop close by here."

Peace at this moment pulled out a good-sized bartel.

"My eye! but you've got a whopper there, Charlie, and no mistake," cried the gipsy.

"Don't call me Charlie. If anybody sees us you are my man—don't you understand?"

"A nod's as good as a wink to a blind horse. Your servant—I tumble," returned Bill.

"I'm supposed to be a gentleman now," said Peace, with a chuckle.

"Ah, I see; and you know how to play the part, which, to say the truth, is altogether beyond me. Howsomedever, I do very well for a slavey; nobody is likely to take me for a gentleman."

"So much the better."

"But how about the bisness? When is it to come off?"

"To-night, if all goes well."

The gipsy gave a low mysterious whistle.

"And about this 'ere child?"

"You had better meet me at yonder point," said Peace, pointing to a turn in the river. "Be there between eleven and twelve to-night, and take care to have the trap in readiness."

"There's a grove of trees just by that spot, which will suit us to rights. The pony and trap shall be there at the time you name."

"Don't disappoint me, you old sinner," said Peace; "if you do, it will spoil all."

"Did you ever find me in the rear when I was wanted at the fore?" inquired the gipsy.

"No, I never have. Only it's as well to have a clear understanding."

"I will be there at yonder point. But how about 'cracking the crib?' Don't yer want my assistance?"

"I think I can manage that very well by myself."

"There's a bloke as sleeps on the premises—so I've heerd," cried Bill.

"The devil, there is! What—a sort of porter, or something of that sort, eh?"

"So I've heerd."

"Well, then, perhaps it would be just as well for you to come round to the warehouse."

"And leave the trap in the grove of trees."

"Just so."

"At what time?"

"Say eleven, or from that to half-past."

"Now go," said Peace. "For I don't want you to be seen by anybody, if we can help it. Remember, from eleven to half-past."

"I'll not forget." And with that promise the gipsy sheered off, leaving Peace alone in the boat.

"A good faithful fellow," he murmured, after his friend's departure. "It's not many I put trust in, but he's fair and square enough."

As the shades of evening descended Peace moored his boat, and threaded his way through the bye-roads and green lanes. He sought seclusion, which he succeeded in obtaining—seclusion till the hour arrived which had been appointed for the robbery.

He found the time hang heavily enough on his hands, and hardly knew how to employ himself; waiting and loitering about is not pleasant under the most favourable circumstances; but in the dead of the night, enshrouded by dark shadows, and with no other sounds but the splashing of water and the mournful sighing of the trees, the watching and waiting was inexpressibly dull.

However, it had to be endured like all other human ills and trials, and Peace endeavoured to put the best face on the matter. He trolled in a low tone a popular ditty, and strove to be as cheerful as possible.

It was some satisfaction to him that he had not met with a solitary individual in his wanderings—this was just as he could have wished.

At length the appointed time drew nearer and nearer. Peace made for the back of the silk manufactory, and waited patiently for the sounds of footsteps.

Bill was true to his appointment. Presently his companion heard the rustling of the decayed leaves which strewed the ground, and he was at no loss to conclude that his confederate was approaching.

He was correct in his surmise.

A low whistle was heard, which Peace answered by a similar sound.

The two robbers were very soon in close conference.

"Any blokes about?" said Bill.

"Not a living soul besides ourselves—at least, none that I have seen. And you?"

"All's still and quiet. The gentlemen who live in these ere parts go early to roost, it would appear. And how about cracking the crib?"

"Leave that to me," said Peace. "It's an easy job enough, I fancy."

The speaker led the way to the side of the premises.

Peace set to work on one of the windows which with his accustomed skill he contrived to open. The window was drawn down, the gipsy gave his companion a "leg up," and in another moment our hero was inside. He had on at this time some yachting boots, the soles of which were made of vulcanised india-rubber, and his footsteps were almost noiseless.

Passing through the room he had entered, he crept downstairs and undid the bolts and other fastenings of the front door.

This done, he beckoned to his companion.

"I wonder where this man sleeps?" he murmured.

"Haven't the slightest idea," returned the gipsy.

"No matter, it's as well to be prepared, however," he muttered, drawing his revolver from his coat pocket. "I never have recourse to this, except in extreme difficulty," said he.

"Ah, don't settle anyone's hash," cried the gipsy, moving forward.

"Don't you come in—leave it to me. You can't slide about so silently as I can. Don't you come in unless you hear me give the alarm. Wait and watch just inside the passage and keep guard over the door."

"All right. On yer goes then."

Peace did go on. In one of the rooms on the basement, he found a man and his wife in bed, fast asleep. He did not, of course, attempt to disturb their slumbers, but assuring himself first of all that they were actually asleep, he withdrew, closing the door gently after him.

He then inserted into it some of his long thin screws, so that the porter and his wife, if they should by any chance be disturbed, would find themselves close prisoners in their bedchamber.

It was not at all likely they could break open the door before our hero and the gipsy had got clean off.

Having performed this little bit of business in a way which was satisfactory to himself, Peace proceeded upstairs into the warerooms.

He found in these an immense amount of property—silks of every hue—but he chose rolls of black silk, this being more saleable.

He brought down as much as he could well carry, and then went upstairs for more, for he was unconscionable in his demands, and stuck at nothing.

Agreeable to his direction Bill took a considerable portion of the booty, which he laid carefully in the boat. Then he returned for more and placed the same with the other rolls.

In a very short time the boat was pretty well filled, and no more black silk could be found. However, Peace laid his unholy hands upon some coloured silks.

They had now as much as they could conveniently take away. Peace emerged from the house and hastened to the banks of the river; he was followed by the gipsy, both the robbers at this time having their arms full.

All this had been done without attracting the notice of any one. The two men jumped into the boat, which sped along over the surface of the stream swiftly and almost silently till the point made by the bend of the river was reached.

Near to this point was the grove of trees where the gipsy had tethered his pony.

The boat was moored again, and the goods taken therefrom as rapidly as circumstances would permit, and transferred to the cart.

But before this was done ten trusses of tares, which Bill had brought with him, were taken out of the vehicle, and when the silks had been packed and been made to occupy as small a compass as possible the tares were thrown on the top, partially covered with a piece of tarpauling, and the gipsy was ready to start on his journey.

He was instructed by Peace to make the best of his way to London.

"I'll go a little way with you, Bill," he said, "and put up at a hotel, and the sooner I am housed the better. There will be a rare outcry in the morning, but that matters but little, I shall be in my boat."

"Ah, ah!" laughed the gipsy; "it's as good as a play. Strike me silly, but this is about the cleanest job that mortal man ever did."

"You must get safely to London, and we are not as yet safely out of the fire."

"I shall reach London right enough—have no fear about that."

"Ah, I don't fear, but still it's just as well not to shout before you are out of the wood; but you know what to do when you get there?"

"Get rid of the goods as soon as possible."

"Yes, and there won't be much difficulty about that if you go to the address I gave you. The name is—"

"Stanbridge," cried Peace's companion.

"Right you are. See her, and say you come from me, and she'll work the oracle. She's up to every mortal dodge."

"I'm afraid she'll be too much for me—I aint much of a hand in dealing with women; they're a jolly sight too artful for me."

"You do as I tell you, and all will be right. There's no call for you to be mistrustful. You may rest assured that I am sending you to the proper party. See her, and if she can't do the job herself she'll find somebody who can."

The gipsy nodded assent to this proposition, and as the vehicle he drove came in sight of a road-side commercial hotel he brought his pony to a standstill.

Peace alighted, wished his companion good night, and entered the hostelry, where he remained till morning.

By early dawn he was up and doing. He swallowed a hasty breakfast, and took his departure, making his way direct for the river's side.

He unmoored his boat, and pulled it between three and four miles down the stream. He then began to angle with all the keen relish of a persevering sportsman.

He was tolerably successful, and drew out a number of fish, some of which were of good size. There were other persons in boats engaged in a similar occupation, and in the due course of time Peace managed to scrape acquaintance with those who were nearest to him.

One was an old gentleman, who was a good companion, being loquacious and full of anecdote. He was, he informed our hero, devoted to the sport, and the extraordinary "takes" of fish that had at various times fallen to his share were perfectly astounding.

Peace had the prudence to hear all he said, and say but little in return. He did not know a great deal about angling, and he was therefore anxious not to betray his ignorance.

He, however, affected to believe all his companion said, for it was his "game," as he termed it, to make as many friends as possible. Certainly, under the existing, circumstances, this was the wisest course to pursue.

He said in reply to the old gentleman that he enjoyed the sport, but could not boast of being a particularly skilful angler, but he was willing to learn.

Upon this his companion gave him a few useful hints, and said that fishing had been one of the chief pleasures or pastimes of his life. He had fished in Scotland, Wales, Norway, and a host of other places.

He did not succeed in pulling out more fish than Peace, but that did not much matter—he would have done so if they had bitten more freely.

"Much sport, gentlemen?" said a young man who had been walking along the bank of the river.

"Middling, only middling, as far as I am concerned," returned the old gentleman; "but then I've not been long here. This gentleman has done pretty well."

"Yes, but then I've had four days of it, this being my fifth," cried Peace. "I mustn't complain, I suppose—still, I might have done better."

"Ah, that's what we all say," observed the man on the bank. "But have you heard the news?"

"What news?" inquired the old gentleman.

"Why, very bad. Spearman's silk-mill was broken into last night, and some hundreds' worth of property stolen."

"Never!" cried several of the fishermen. "Broken into—eh?"

"So it is supposed. Indeed, there cannot be much doubt about that."

"It seems incredible that so many dishonest people should be in the world," said Peace, in a deprecating tone. "It is indeed a most melancholy reflection."

Then, addressing himself to the man on the bank, he said, in a careless way—

"And where is this mill situated, sir?"

"On the bank of the Trent, about five miles from here, or a little less, perhaps."

"Dear me, I'm very sorry to hear it. And have they any clue to the robbers?"

"None at present, I believe."

"But they will have. Oh, they will have, let us hope," remarked Peace, with well-simulated sympathy.

"Hope told a flattering tale, my friend," said the old getleman, who was of a cynical turn of mind. "The chances are that they will never find out the culprit or culprits—they never do. The police are sure to go on the wrong scent."

"Perhaps it was some one on the premises who committed the robbery?" suggested Peace.

"Very likely, sir—nothing more likely," cri d the old gentleman, as he pulled out his line and rebaited his hook.

Another passenger now came along the pathway by the side of the river. He, like the first gentleman, was full of the robbery, and it was perhaps needless to say that he gave another version of the affair.

His theory was, that somebody was concealed in the warehouse for the whole of the day, and when it was closed and the porter and his wife were fast asleep, he crept forth from his hiding-place and let in a band of men, who ransacked the place and made off with a large amount of property.

He also stated that the porter and his wife had been drugged.

People are so remarkably fond of dealing with the wild and wonderful.

"It's a very sad and bad business," remarked Peace, "whichever way it was done; and it is to be hoped that justice will overtake the scoundrels."

His fellow-fisherman coincided with him in the opinion he had expressed, and looked upon him as a man whose highly moral principle made him indignant with the miscreants who had been guilty of so lawless an act.

He was not known, or rather recognised, at Nottingham, and none for a moment suspected that the highly moral and sensitive gentleman was the real culprit.

Peace laughed in his sleeve. The amusement it afforded him was, of course, known only to himself.

He amused himself with his brother anglers for the whole of that day, and when evening set in he repaired to the public-house called the "Seven Stars," and made himself very agreeable to the frequenters of the parlour.

He had, before giving over for the day, agreed to meet some of his brother anglers at the same spot for another day's sport, and he was again to be seen in his boat as heretofore.

He did this to lull suspicion—that is, if any was likely to be attached to him. While occupied in fishing with what to all appearance was a party of his own particular friends, he felt he was perfectly safe.

The police went far and near in search of the burglars; they made desperate efforts to trace the stolen goods. They arrested an unfortunate tramp who was seen lurking about the neighbourhood on the preceding day. There was, however, not a tittle of evidence against the poor tramp, whom the magistrate at once discharged.

It was of no use people saying that they had arrested the wrong man—they shook their heads and looked mysterious.

As he had been arrested they clung to the opinion that he had a hand in the robbery.

The poor wretch wanted the common necessaries of life, and was of course perfectly innocent of the charge made against him; but he was a tramp, and that was enough for the police, and they assumed, as illogically as they usually do, that he knew something about it.

This was all they could do in the matter, and so after a hubbub and outcry for a week or so, the matter was given up as hopeless.

Peace took back his boat, settled with the proprietor, and made the best of his way to Sheffield.

His wife at this time presented him with a daughter.

Meanwhile Bandy-legged Bill arrived safely in London with the booty obtained at the mill.

He waited on Laura Stanbridge, and gave her a note from Peace.

The silk was safely deposited in a loft over a stable, which was in the occupation of a friend of the gipsy's. The same friend had no difficulty in divining that Bill was doing something on the cross, but as he received a handsome sum for the loan of the loft he saw and heard but said nothing.

The most accomplished and daring thief finds it difficult to get on without the assistance of one or more confederates. Laura Stanbridge accompanied the gipsy to the loft in question and inspected the goods. She was of course to have something for her services, and it was ultimately decided to remove the silk to her house.

This was done.

Doubtless most of my readers are aware that there are in London establishments kept by honest tradesmen, who are in a large way of business, and whose buyers are instructed to purchase goods at their own discretion, without being rude enough to ask any questions of those who offer them for sale.

This practice has been carried on for a number of years. It would be invidious to mention names. The fact of purchases being made in the manner described is incontrovertible, and the fact also that the honest tradesman very often, in the way of business, becomes—innocently enough perhaps—a receiver of stolen goods.

Laura Stanbridge, when the silks were in her possession, got a young man who had been in the trade, but who had at one time been unfortunate enough to mistake his master's money for his own, to offer the rolls of silk for sale. At one of the aforesaid houses before referred to they were purchased at about fifteen per cent. below the market value.

The vendor had to be paid handsomely for his trouble—so had Miss Stanbridge; so also had several other persons; but with all these drawbacks Mr. Charles Peace obtained for the goods half as much again as he would have got from a Jew receiver; so that all things considered, he had done a lucrative stroke of business. Bill, of course, stood in, but Peace had the lion's share.

CHAPTER LXXXIII.
STOKE FERRY FARM HOUSE—THE LOVERS—A CONFIDENTIAL TETE-A-TETE.

PATTY JAMBLIN, as we have already seen, contrived to rid herself of her most obnoxious and objectionable admirer. She had, nevertheless, to make use of a common phrase, "many strings to her bow."

Numbers of soft-hearted irrepressible rustic swains hovered round the central figure of Stoke Ferry.

As time went on, John Ashbrook became more deeply enamoured of the pretty Miss Jamblin.

It was generally understood that he was the favoured suitor, for Patty, albeit a little wilful and capricious, had eyes and ears for him more than all the rest.

Old Jamblin was a farmer of the old school. He was, like most of that class, a little prejudiced; it may be said, very prejudiced, as far as his political opinions were concerned. Free trade and the abolition of the corn laws he had opposed to the utmost of his power, and a Radical he hated worse than a tax-collector.

Do not blame him for these opinions. Do not laugh at farmers, for they are men who have worked hard, and who have been ill-treated.

This nation once made it legal to have a free trade in corn, and corn alone. They had the bread cheap at the expense of the farmers.

"And not contented with cheating them," observed Jamblin, "they jeered at them too."

"Ah," say the free traders, "Bobby Peel was going to kill three farmers a week, but there is one or two of them left alive yet."

Yes, for when that law was passed the English yeomen, whom fools call idle grumblers struck their broad breasts with their hands, and resolved to struggle hard against their foreign foes.

It was a hard battle for them, this fight with farmers whose land cost them little, and who had few taxes to pay.

And as they were growing fagged and faint, and were forced to fall back upon their hard-earned savings, the Crimean war began, and the cry was for meat to send out to the land of strife and famine. The nation which had bled the farmers had now to bleed for them, and to buy their sheep or oxen at fabulous prices.

Thus the Emperor of Russia saved half the English farmers from ruin.

As we have already signified, Jamblin was a farmer of the old school, whose favourite maxim was—

He who by the plough would thrive,
Must himself either hold or drive.

He acted throughout his life in accordance with this precept.

He chose for his wife a farmer's daughter—one of the old-fashioned sort—an adept in the economies of the stables and pig-sty, and a perfect genius among the milk-pails.

Having presented him with a son and a daughter,

she expired in the act of lifting a large brewing-tub, which was out of its place in the back kitchen.

Although his wife had perished a victim to her love for *ne plus ultra* housewifery, Jamblin reared up his son and daughter in the same line of education which proved so beneficial to himself.

And sometimes he would recite this old adage in a kind of chant, beating time with his fingers on the kitchen dresser:

The man to plough,
The wife to cow,
The boy to flail,
The girl to pail,
    And your rents will be netted.
But the man tally-ho!
The wife piano,
The boy Greek and Latin,
The miss silk and satin,
    And you'll soon be gazetted.

"When you grow up to be a man, Phil," he would say to his son, "and I have grown old, you shall live in the big house and farm Stoke Ferry all to yourself. You stick to your trade like wax, my boy, and you'll have a red face when you come to be old, and a sound liver, a strong jolly heart, aye, and your pocket full of yellow-boys, tew."

When Philip was talked to like this he would go to work with hoe, spade, or sickle, as if were a young hero cutting himself a path to glory with his sword. His father's words gave him thoughts which cheered him to his work far more than the black muddy beer which was sent out to them in stone or leather bottles. And sometimes, as he plodded across the fallow fields while the last red clouds in the west were fading into white, and while the dew was rising like a fog from the meadow grass, he would stop and fold his arms upon his breast, and, looking up to the sky, dream that he could see a farm-house with a great straw yard and massive barns and countless heads of cattle.

But by daylight he gave himself no time for reverie. Even at nooning, when the labourers were enjoying their dinner and siestas, his mind was full of business, and questions streamed from his lips as water from a bucket overthrown.

"Phil will be a great man," his father used to say; "he does his work like a free horse, an' is allays peerin' about to pick up wrinkles. His heart's in his call, an' that's the head thing to look after."

But poor Phil was not destined to fulfil the farmer's predictions; he was cut off when on the very threshold of life—stricken down by the hand of an assassin.

His connection with Nell Fulford had been a source of anxiety to the farmer long before his son's death. It was a subject he never afterwards made reference to; but although he was silent on the subject he had not forgotten it.

One evening when Patty was away (she had gone to the hall to spend a day or two with Lady Aveline, at her ladyship's special request), Jamblin had for his companion John Ashbrook.

Strange to say, on the evening in question there were no chance droppers in—the reason for this being, perhaps, the absence of Patty.

The two farmers were seated in the parlour before a bright, cheerful fire.

"Kitty," said Jamblin, addressing himself to a red-faced, red-armed servant girl, who was kept more for use than ornament, "go down to the cellar and bring up a big jug of the October old ale out of that little cask in the corner."

The October ale, which was several years old, and of unrivalled strength and flavour, never moistened throats except upon holiday occasions.

The girl knew her master disliked to be questioned, so taking a bunch of keys from the shelf, she glided out of the room and returned with the ale.

"Now, gell," said her master, "go upstairs into my room, and on the top of the shelf of the left hand cupboard, you will find a jar of 'bacca in it, under a lead weight. Bring two or three screws of that, will you?"

It was real Latakia, which had been smuggled over from Turkey by a parson's son, a midshipman in the navy, and presented to the farmer in return for hospitalities.

Kitty gave one stare of astonishment before she complied. She had never known the old man treat himself to the October ale and the Latakia tobacco on the same evening, but she said nothing, and hastened on her errand.

When she returned, Jamblin said—

"Reach down from the shelf in the parlour two of those cut glasses."

This was too much for Kitty, who could hardly believe her ears. The cut glasses in question had never been used—so she had been told since the death of her master's wife—they were called Mrs. Jamblin's glasses.

"Do you mean the best cut glasses, sir?" inquired the girl, almost breathless with astonishment.

"Yes, you little fool!" roared the farmer. "What for d'ye want doddlin' and starin' like a stuck pig? I thought I spoke plain English tew." The beer and tobacco were all placed on the oak table at the farmer's elbow.

"Well, measter John," said he, "it be's a poor heart as never rejoices, and now we be free from them chaps who drop in at times when mebbe they're not wanted, we'll enjoy ourselves in our own humble way."

The glasses were filled and Jamblin held his own up in the air and looked at the bright liquor it contained.

"I will gi' 'ee a toast," said he. "Here's everybody in the world's good health, 'cept farmer Nettlethorpe."

They both drank the toast, after which John Ashbrook burst out into a loud laugh.

"Poor Nettlethorpe!" he exclaimed.

"Poor, indeed," returned Jamblin. "I'll tell 'ee why I don't drink his good health. It is because I want farmer Nettlethorpe to die. He's a puddin' mean man, and tries to make his land as thin and poor as his cattle, and his cattle as poor and thin as himself."

"He's what I call an apron-stringed farmer," said Ashbrook. "He was a grocer, and now he's taken to farming. He'll find it a poor catch."

"You don't say much, John, but what you do say aint a great ways off the mark. He will find it a poor catch for all he tries to strip two skins off a cow, and would stoop any day to take a farthing off a dunghill wi' his teeth. I dare say ye've heard in yer Sunday travels 'em tell that he who changes his trade often makes soup in a basket."

"If a man was bred and born a farmer," said his companion, "and could tackle hold of the right end of the stick, and mek the quarters meet as should be, I don't think he'd want to change his trade—that is, if he has got a farm worth working, but land 'ill beat any man."

The old farmer gave a laugh of pleasure, disguised as a cough; then he asked for his pipe, and having filled the bowl with the Turkish herb, dipped the stem into the beer to sweeten the clayey morsel to his mouth.

He then leant back in his chair in an attitude of

placid enjoyment. His friend filled his pipe and began smoking also.

For some little time neither of them spoke. Jamblin's eyes, though half closed, were directed towards Ashbrook. The two human funnels were absorbed in a fragrant weed.

"I feel somehow, John, that I be gettin' an old man, and may be I shan't be able to look after Stoke Ferry for many more years. It's of no use denying the fact or attempting to conceal it. I ain't what I was, an' ever since my poor boy's death I aint had the heart as I used to ha'."

"You must not talk like that, Mr. Jamblin; you are not so young as you were, it is true, but you are hale and hearty as yet."

"As yet — that be a good term; but I ain't got the pluck as I ought to ha', an' I've been thinking, lad —well I've been thinkin' of a lot of things. Now there's Patty, you know——"

"Yes, and as good a girl as ever stepped."

"That be right enough—I am glad to hear thee say so. Well, although I be old I ha' got eyes in my head and know how many blue beans mek five—an' I can see pretty plainly, John Ashbrook, that you are sweet on the gell, and it may be that she's a bit partial to you. This is only as I guess," he added, pointing over his shoulder with the end of his pipe.

"Be I right or be I wrong?" he said, sharply.

"Why of course you are quite right. I am glad you have broached the subject, which, to say the truth, I was about to enter upon myself. Mr. Jamblin, I need hardly tell you how dearly I love your daughter, I have done so for years past, but——"

"But what? Don't 'ee begin loike that, John. The only butt there is in the question is one filled with the best stingo, which is to be broached when the health of the bride has to be drunk."

"It does one good when you talk like that," cried Ashbrook, bursting out into a laugh.

The old man indulged in a merry chuckle also.

"But I must beg you to listen to me for a short time," said Ashbrook. "You see, Mr. Jamblin, things are not so rosy with us at Oakfield as they used to be. There are many reasons for this. The farm has not been so profitable of late, and we've had some heavy losses. Poor Richard has not been the same man since the loss of his wife—you know, of course, she died of a broken heart."

"Ah, poor gell, so I heard. That scoundrel Gregson, the burglary, his execution, enough to make one shudder to think on."

"You know also that the man Peace who was here some time since—he as your son gave a thrashing to, he was concerned in the burglary at Oakfield."

"Was he though?" cried Jamblin, taking the pipe out of his mouth and staring at the speaker.

"Yes he was, but let that pass. As I was saying, Richard, poor chap, took it in his head to have a turn at brickmaking. He fancied he had found a vein of earth well adapted for the purpose, and he's sunk a deal of money on the speculation, which we shall none on us see back agen, I'm thinking."

"Foolish lad, what does he understand about bricks?"

"Well, Mr. Jamblin, I am not a rich man but a poor one, and that has been my only reason for not asking your consent, you understand?"

"Umph, well yes, I think I do. Well, John, I'm sorry you've bin goin' to the bad of late, but it can't be helped; it aint no fault o' yours, that I be quite sartin

on. And as far as Patty is concerned, it won't mek much difference."

"She may have more wealthy suitors."

"She may certainly, or she may not; but in any case it won't make much difference. If you loike her, which I blieve ye do, and she loike you, we'll strike a bargain."

John Ashbrook shook the old farmer warmly by the hand.

"I cannot tell you how supremely happy you have made me," he murmured, "and only wish I had a fortune to lay at your daughter's feet."

"But you've got time afore ye, lad. Ye're young, and ha' got common sense."

"No one can be too clever for a farmer. I haven't been in the world without knowing that."

"You're right, John. The more a man larns our trade the better he finds out how little he really knows, an' I've often thought that if God gave a man the grace to live a thousand years, like Methusalem of old, he wouldn't be able to tackle the ins and outs of the weathers, and manners, and stock, and markets, and all the rest of it. Well, John, most people who have saved a little money and bought a little land like to keep their children waiting for it till they die, and then folks wonder there aint more tears shed over burials. Now, I aint one of that sort. My daughter is now my only care, and if so be as she and you make up your minds to be one—which I dare say ye have for a long time past—ye shall have a fair start in life. You've got your head screwed on the right way, lad, and what I put by for poor Phil shall be yours."

"Oh! Mr. Jamblin, I have no right to it."

"I tell 'ee ye have, and that's sartain. You shall have a good start, and as Oakfield Farm aint what it was, let Richard and your sister have it. You can work this for awhile under my direction, and in time, when I be gathered to my faythers—well, then it'll be yours and Patty's. There, I can't say much fairer than that."

The farmer sent forth vigorous puffs of smoke from his pipe after he had delivered himself of this speech, and his companion, who was perfectly overwhelmed by his generosity, could not for the moment find words to express his gratitude.

"I am sure I can never be sufficiently thankful to you, Mr. Jamblin," he ejaculated.

"Nonsense, lad. Haven't we known each other for years and years? The Jamblins and Ashbrooks ha' been staunch friends for more than half a century. Your poor fayther and myself went to school together when mere yonkers—and that be a few weeks ago," cried Jamblin, bursting out into a loud guffaw; "only a few weeks ago, John."

"Ah, sir, time runs on pretty fast with most of us; and what appears but a few months or years perhaps bridges over a long gap in a man's lifetime."

"That be true, lad. Well, as I was a sayin', the Jamblins and Ashbrooks ha' bin firm friends for more than a lifetime, and setting aside Patty, I've neither chick nor child, and therefore she be my only consideration. Mek her a good husband, John, and I be sartin sure she'll mek you a good wife; and so, lad, we ha' a clear understanding. There, boy, my hand on it!"

The two friends shook hands once more, and they drank each other's health in some whiskey toddy, and did not retire to rest till an unusually late hour.

Patty Jamblin returned on the following day, and after a cordial greeting the old farmer went abroad in the fields, leaving the lovers to themselves.

"I expect you and father have been enjoying yourselves to your hearts' content during my absence," said Patty to John Ashbrook.

"We've made ourselves as contented as we could under the circumstances," returned Ashbrook.

"Ah—so I should suppose. You can do very well without me, you two cronies."

"Indeed, we cannot, neither of us. But we have touched on a question during your absence which concerns both of us. Oh, Patty! I am thankful and grateful to Providence that we have spoken so freely to one another."

"What on earth do you mean?"

"Just this. Your father has given his consent. There is now no impediment in the way of ——"

"Impediment! Pray tell me what I am to understand by this."

"You cannot guess, then, my darling?"

Miss Jamblin coloured, and stammered out the monosyllable, "No."

"I say he has given his consent freely and unconditionally. What say you to that?"

"I wish you would speak a little more plainly."

"Oh, Patty! surely you who are so quick-witted will find it easy to divine my meaning. You do not need to be reminded of my devotion to you. You do not need me to plead my own cause, for, to say the truth, I am a very dunce in affairs of this sort. You do not require me to tell you how dearly and fondly I love you."

"Upon my word, you are growing eloquent all of a sudden."

"It is the first time I ever was, then; but, Patty, say something. Tell me, do you——"

"Do I what?"

"Give your consent? There, dall it, I am a plain-spoken man, and am but a poor hand at pleading my own cause. You know what I mean."

"Do I?" inquired the little coquette.

"Why, of course you do. Will you be mine?"

"Yours?"

"Yes."

He drew her towards him with his arm round her waist, and his heart going, as he afterwards said, "nineteen to the dozen," he embraced her passionately.

"Your answer, darling. Give me an answer."

"You are in such a mighty hurry, John. You don't give one time for reflection."

"But you have reflected long ago."

"Ah well, there may be some truth in that."

"There is—there is a great deal of truth in it. If you don't know your own mind now you never will; but it's of no use you making any attempt to oppose your father's expressed wishes," he added, with a smile and a kiss. "No dutiful daughter would do that, you know."

"Oh, then, according to your showing I am to have no voice in the matter?"

"Your word is law—I obey it most implicitly; but you will not be so cruel as to—well, cast me off."

"No, I don't say that."

"Well, then, what do you say?"

"That if I am not your wife, I'll be no man's wife, John. That's what I say."

Ashbrook uttered an expression of delight.

"Oh, Patty, my own, my dear, dear Patty!" he ejaculated.

"And so you and father have settled the business between you—eh?"

"No, do not misunderstand me. It was left for you to determine."

"But I suppose now you had the vanity to believe that I shall do so in your favour."

"I confess I had."

"So I thought. Well, John, you are not mistaken, you see, and what did father say then?"

"Oh, he said a good deal more than I expected, and his kindness quite overpowered me. He spoke of poor Philip."

"Ah, I thought he would do that," said Miss Jamblin, her countenance changing in its expression. "I cannot forget Phil—he never will, rest assured of that. And what else did he say?"

"I told him of our altered circumstances."

"That did not make any difference, I'll be sworn."

"None in the least. He said the money he had put by for his deceased son should be mine, and that I was not to trouble myself about being not so well off as I have been; but lor, Patty, it would take me a long time to tell you the whole of our conversation. It is enough to declare that he does not make money a consideration, or the need of it an impediment to our union."

"Ah, John Ashbrook, my dear father may be a little wilful and opinionated, but his heart is right enough. No one knows that better than myself; but there, you know there is Richard and your sister Maude. What will they say?"

"That is all arranged. Richard is not the same man he was a few years ago, and, without Maude, I know not how he would get on at all."

"He's never got over the loss of Jane."

"Never, and I fear never will. You see Jane was a fatalist, a believer in destiny, was strangely superstitious, believed in omens and signs and all that sort of things, and somehow or other at times I am afraid she has imbued my brother with the same notions."

"You think so?"

"Sometimes I do, while at others I hope I am mistaken, but taken altogether it has been a bad business."

"What! his marriage with Jane Ryan?"

"I don't say that. He loved her if ever man did love a woman, and she was worthy of him, for a better, more true, and honest gell never broke the bread of life. This is one thing, but her heart was bruised and half-broken when she gave her hand to my poor brother."

"Ah, John, a deep shadow has fallen over you and yours, even as it has done over me and mine, but these are things over which we have no control, and yet they both spring from the same cause or nearly so."

"You are right, Patty. A shadow has fallen on Oakfield."

"But we are no worse off than our betters—perhaps not so badly off, in many ways. A shadow has fallen over the inmates of Broxbridge Hall, and Lady Aveline is not without her troubles; neither is the earl, her grandfather."

"I suppose not."

"By no means. Did my father say anything about the lad that used to be with us—the boy Alf Purvis?"

"No, he did not mention his name."

"What can have become of that young scapegrace? We have had no tidings of him since he left here with the dead hare tied round his neck."

"How very remarkable!"

"It is singular, I must confess. I know father would be glad to learn something about him; but he never will, I suppose, now."

"I fancy not, but he's better lost than found, if all be true I've heard."

THE ATTEMPTED ESCAPE FROM WAKEFIELD GAOL.

"Yes, that's right enough—at least, I suppose so," cried Miss Jamblin, who after this was lost for some time in reflection.

"I am the happiest man alive," exclaimed John Ashbrook. "You are to have your own way in everything—that has been agreed upon."

"Has it? I am glad to hear you say so, because, you see, we all like to have our way."

"Ah, but you are not to be crossed in anything, and, to say the truth, darling, it is not at all likely you will be. I love you too much for that."

"Promises are one thing——"

No. 44.

"And the performances of them are another—that's what you were about to say."

"You are very clever to be able to anticipate one's thoughts," said the farmer's daughter, with a merry laugh, "but I think I may trust you."

"Be assured you may. You will have no reason to repent of your choice, although I say it as should not say it, to make use of a common phrase."

"I do not for a moment doubt it, John. I accept you with a right good will, and with all my heart."

The young farmer embraced her fondly, and nothing now remained but for the happy day to be named.

In a few days after this it became generally known to all who took interest in such matters that John Ashbrook and old Jamblin's daughter were shortly to become man and wife.

There were of course a number of disappointed swains, who had to repine at the loss they had sustained, but we are happy to be able to state, upon reliable authority, that no serious results attended their discomfiture. They solaced themselves by seeking "fresh fields and pastures new," and bore their fate with becoming fortitude.

The wedding ceremony was performed on a grand scale, and on the day on which it took place Stoke Ferry Farm was filled with guests of every denomination. Lord Ethalwood honoured the nuptials with his presence, and his grand-daughter, Aveline, was one of the bridesmaids; Maude Ashbrook, and her brother Richard, were of course there, and the good people in the neighbourhood had not seen such a gathering or such a scene of festivity for many a long day.

The bride looked lovely, as all brides do under similar circumstances, or said to do, which is much the same thing.

Farmer Jamblin was a little thoughtful, or it might be said downcast, this being attributable to painful reminiscences in respect to his son; but when the ceremony had been performed, he rallied and was as cheerful as the best of them.

After the bride and bridegroom had started on their wedding tour, he became silent and thoughtful again. He had, however, for his companions Maude and Richard Ashbrook, who had arranged to stay at Stoke Ferry for a few days to keep him company.

CHAPTER LXXXIV.

PEACE'S LAWLESS CAREER—CAPTURE, TRIAL, AND CONVICTION—HIS ATTEMPTED ESCAPE FROM WAKEFIELD.

WE must return again to the hero of our story. To say the truth the life of this man is little more than a record of his escapades, troubles, and trials, and a detail of the various robberies in which he was engaged. The scoundrel's hypocrisy forms a large element in his character.

He was professedly a religious man; the neighbours thought him so, and possibly he thought so too; so he associated with the good folk who congregated in the sacred edifice, but never made himself conspicuous.

Peace trifled with Fate. She had blessed him with worldly goods, though it must be confessed that they were not his own, and his consummate impudence led to his apprehension.

One of the inspectors who had been concerned in his capture, expressed his opinion of Peace's character in these words:—

"There is not another demon in Europe like him, unless it's the Czar. What sort of scoundrels they have in Asia I don't know."

The words were graphic, but they were spoken with such vehemence as to show that even the London police were surprised at the revelations which were made.

Another said, "He mistook his hunting-ground; there is not sufficient room for brigandage in England; he ought to have gone to Sicily." The general opinion of the police was one rather of wonder mixed with surprise, but with a certain admiration for the fellow's cleverness in his profession.

The more inquiries that are made into the past history of Peace, the more does it appear that he was a head and shoulders above the ordinary criminal. He appears to have had ingrained in his nature a cruelty of mind and firmness of purpose which nothing could baffle. He always objected to poverty, and as he did not seem to be over fond of hard work—though at times he certainly did follow his business of a picture-frame maker with something like assiduity—he chose a career of crime as the most fitted to maintain him in luxury.

When eighteen years of age he lived with his mother at Walker-street, Sheffield, and was employed in Millsand's rolling mill.

At this time he developed a passionate love for music, the instrument on which he most excelled being the violin. He was welcomed at the various public-houses in the vicinity on account of the readiness with which he was always willing to exhibit his accomplishment without direction, and there are many people residing now in Sheffield who can remember with pleasure evenings spent in Peace's company.

He was at this time known by a little goat-carriage in which he was accustomed to drive the child who was his pupil, and who was introduced to the reader in a previous chapter.

This singular equipage usually attracted great attention, and many no doubt remember him by his goat excursions.

His course from this time became a downward one, and from one excess he fell into another. He was living with his wife and stepson on good terms, and ostensibly his business was that of a picture-frame maker.

He became acquainted with a neighbour who was notoriously dishonest, and the pair spent a good deal of time together.

They planned a daring robbery of wine, which they managed to successfully carry out. The booty was concealed in a field until the hue and cry should have ceased.

For some considerable time he and his accomplice managed to carry on their depredations with impunity; but justice, however, at length overtook them, and again Peace was brought to the bar of justice.

Indeed he passed, as we have already signified, a very considerable portion of his time in prison; but penal servitude in his case, as in so many other instances, did not appear to have a deterrent effect.

No sooner was he released than after a short period of honest industry he again had recourse to his thieving propensity. We subjoin a report of his trial and sentence.

BURGLARY AT RUSHOLME.

George Parker, alias Charles Peace (aged 30), and Alfred Newton (aged 25), were charged with having burglariously entered the house of Elizabeth Brooks, at Rusholme, near Manchester, and stolen therefrom a quantity of silver plate and other property. Mr. Higginson prosecuted; Mr. Fearnley defended the prisoner Parker, and Newton was defended by Mr. Camhbell Foster.

Mr. John Aitken, a gentleman residing with Miss Brooks, stated that about six o'clock on the morning of the 3rd of June he discovered that an entrance had been effected into the dining room by forcing open the window, and upon examination it was discovered that a coat, some papers, and a cigar case belonging to himself, and a picture, a cash-box, fourteen silver spoons, and two sugar tongs, the property of Miss Brooks, had been stolen. Information was given to the police, and a search being made in the fields near the house, nearly the whole of the property was found in an old sewer. Officers were set to watch the place, and on the prisoners approaching the spot with a hamper for the purpose of removing the property, they were apprehended, and after a violent resistance safely lodged in Bridewell. The missing cigar-case was found in the possesion of Parker, who stated in the first instance that he found it, and afterwards that it had been given to him.

On behalf of the prisoner Parker witnesses were called to prove that he came from Sheffield to Manchester only a few hours before he and Newton were captured, and several witnesses were called to prove that Newton was in Sheffield at the very time that the burglary was committed, and did not leave that town for Manchester until the next morning.

It was contended on behalf of the latter prisoner that he would have no motive for committing the crime with which he was charged, as he was a well-to-do tradesman, having money in the bank. The explanation given of their attempting to remove the stolen property from the sewer was that they had accidentally found it whilst taking a walk together.

Both prisoners were found guilty of receiving the property knowing it to have been stolen.

A former conviction was proved against Parker, and he was sentenced to six years' penal servitude. Newton was sentenced to fifteen months' imprisonment with hard labour.

Peace was sent to the Old Trafford Gaol. We must pass over the period of his imprisonment for this offence, as other and more important events in his life have to be chronicled.

Peace, though a desperate character, could appear as meek and mild a man as ever handled a six-shooter.

The result of his playing the good boy was that he was let out on ticket-of-leave, and society once more suffered for the relaxation of the law's severity.

After his Old Trafford sentence he returned to Sheffield, and took a small shop in Kenyon-alley. There he used to amuse his acquaintances by showing the dexterity with which he could pick the most stubborn lock. He soon afterwards resumed his old practices, proving the truth of the old adage, "Once a thief always a thief."

He carried on his business for some time in Kenyon-alley, and it was while here that he displayed some considerable amount of ability as an actor. Mr. John Tait, schoolmaster at Consett, gave an account in the *Consett Guardian* of a visit Peace paid to his school. He says, "Many of my old scholars well remember Peace performing the gravedigger scene in "Hamlet." His acting was admirable, but the contortions of his countenance and the amazing transformations he effected in his visage baffle all description." Mr. Tait further states he visited Mr. Dawson's school at Spennymuir about the same time, and performed the same part as he did at his school, with the addition of decamping with two musical instruments he had borrowed, and attempting to persuade a girl to elope with him.

His life in the several convict prisons in which he was confined would fill a volume, but as we have given an account of his sojourn at Preston and Dartmoor, this will suffice for the present.

In serving his time at different periods, Peace made the acquaintance of the prisons of Millbank, Chatham (where he was flogged), and Gibraltar.

His handiness caused him then as at other times to be employed as a sort of general utility man about the prisons, doing odd jobs in which tact and dexterity were needed.

It was after his earlier convictions that Peace was sent to Gibraltar, where, with other convicts he was employed on Government work, and was there known to be anything but a quiet sort of man to have in charge.

This, however, must be considered an exception to the rule, as in most cases he was tolerably well conducted when undergoing the various terms of imprisonment.

At Gibraltar he especially incurred the hatred of a servant there, named Baynes, who, he found, was stealing firewood.

It appeared that Government allowed firewood in certain proportions for the use of the men stationed there, and Peace, after watching him, caught him in the act of taking firewood and disposing of the same.

He informed the authorities of this, and the result was that Baynes was discharged. However, by some means or other the latter became employed as a warder at one of the great convict establishments, and subsequently our hero found himself under his care.

It may be imagined that, though a convict's life is far from a pleasant one, that of Peace was, if anything, more unpleasant than usual. The warder paid off one or two old scores, and never let an opportunity pass of showing his aversion, and making Peace's life as uncomfortale as possible.

However, in the due course of time, the convict was discharged, and returned to Sheffield.

In the summer of the year before his arrest at Blackheath, Peace was in the City on business, and had occasion to pass over London Bridge. His hands were not covered, for at this time he wore no gloves; he was simply clean shaven, and well dressed. Midway on the bridge, who should meet him but the warder who so much detested him?

Of all the men he would rather not have faced, this, with the exception of a Sheffield detective, was the one.

However, he walked straight on, and though the warder looked at him, and actually turned, he never stopped, and thus once more Peace escaped detection and apprehension. Had he been "tackled" there and then, doubtless he would have made a desperate resistance, and what the result would have been can only be a matter of conjecture—for at this time he never went out unarmed.

When in confinement Peace, during his leisure moments, used to employ himself in studying mechanics. He was, as we have already signified, exceedingly fond of watching machinery in motion, and had a good idea with regard to its essentials—he having, in the earlier part of his life, worked at a rolling mill.

At Dartmoor he suggested some very important improvements in the machinery used there.

His notions were tried, and then adopted, and up to the present time they have not been superseded, there having been no improvement upon them.

Indeed, many of his inventions were adopted in other of the convict establishments.

Whatever Peace undertook, whether it was a burglary or a piece of other handiwork, he always did it well, and in that sense he may be said to have been a successful man, but in that sense alone.

During his imprisonment for the Rusholme robbery his poor wife had a hard time of it. In addition to the boy, Willie Ward, she had a child by Peace to look after.

The lonely wife had to sell up her home to provide the means of defence at his trial, and afterwards she began to keep a shop—the little bow-windowed shop so well known in Kenyon-alley. Hither came, one night in the summer of 1864, the returned convict, released on ticket-of-leave.

It was now that Peace again commenced the picture-frame making, which was the ostensible business of the remainder of his life, and for a time he seems to have been industrious and to have done well.

The wretched criminal had many good chances of placing himself in a respectable position, but was so steeped in crime that he would not avail himself of the chances thrown into his way.

For some time he led a more creditable life; he worked for Closer's, in Gibraltar-street, and afterwards he was manager for Peters, in Westbar-green. Then he engaged a workshop at the end of Kenyon-alley, and found so much to do that from having only a boy he employed two journeymen to help him.

In this way he got a good business together, and the place being too small, he made the unfortunate venture of taking a shop in West-street, two doors from Rockingham-street.

The moment he got there his luck seemed to turn, and the takings were not so great in a week as they had been in Kenyon-alley in a day.

This exasperated him, for he was not a man who could ever do upon a small income. What he did with all the money he obtained by his extensive robberies must for ever remain a mystery.

Not satisfied with the business in West-street he gave the shop up, and migrated, with his family, to Manchester. He took with him a stock of frames, but he had not been there a fortnight when he was once more in the hands of the officers of the law for doing a job at a house in Lower Broughton. He was caught in the act, and his excuse for such clumsiness was that he, who was usually strictly temperate, had partaken of several glasses of whiskey and water, and did not know what he was doing.

We subjoin an extract from a Manchester paper, containing a brief report of the trial and conviction of Peace :—

George Parker, alias Charles Peace, was indicted for breaking into the dwelling-house of Mr. W. R. Gemmell, Addison-terrace, Victoria Park, on the night of the 20th of August. Mr. Gorst prosecuted ; and Mr. Torr defended.

The servants and Mr. Gemmell were disturbed about 4 o'clock in the morning by a noise outside the house. On going downstairs they found that some person had got in through the scullery window, and that £3 7s. 4d. in money, an opera glass, a pipe, and other things, had been stolen from the dining-room. The prisoner was arrested near the house, about five o'clock, by Police-constable Norris, who found upon him the whole of the stolen property, and several burglarious tools.

Mr. Torr raised a point as to whether the case was one of burglary or of simple robbery from a dwelling-house. It appeared that the scullery window was a horizontal sliding one ; and his lordship ruled that the mere sliding back of the window, whether fastened or not, was sufficient to constitute a burglary. It was

not necessary that anything should be broken—the mere act of removing anything that prevented an entrance was enough. The jury found the prisoner guilty of burglary.

The prisoner, a grey-headed man, begged in piteous accents for mercy for himself and his children.

His lordship said he found that the prisoner was convicted at Liverpool in 1859, and sentenced to six years' imprisonment ; in 1854 he was sentenced to four years' imprisonment; and before that he had been convicted of housebreaking. If he had really been penitent, it was not likely that he would have committed the present offence, and that, too, in a manner which showed that he was prepared to go all lengths in housebreaking. Not only, however, did he commit this burglary, but on the very same night he broke into another house, from which he stole some plate ; but that charge would not be gone into. Under the circumstances, his lordship thought he could do no less than sentence him to be kept in penal servitude for the term of seven years. The prisoner then implored permission to be allowed to see his family, and his lordship said the proper authorities would decide that point.

The court then rose.

Peace, when he parted with his wife after his conviction, was sadly borne down. He bitterly regretted having indulged in strong drink. He had indeed put an enemy in his mouth to steal away his brains.

"It's no use blubbering," he said to his weeping wife; "it's done and can't be helped. I was a fool to muddle myself, and make such a miserable mess of the business; but drink will knock over any man. Look here, now, aint it aggravating to be lagged for years because a chap was stupid enough to be boozing in the morning? It's hard lines——"

"It's hard for me, as well as yourself," returned his companion. "What is to become of us?"

"You must do the best you can, old girl; and when I return I'll make it up to you. I'll lead a new life, and cut this sort of business."

"It's time you did, Charles. If I thought——"

"Thought be hanged!" interrupted the convict, petulantly; "I tell you I will, and so there's an end of the matter."

"Seven years is a long time."

"I know that, you stupid; I know it from sad experience, and don't want you to remind me of it. All this is sad enough, but my trouble is about you. It is not so much for myself that I care, but for you. Not, mind you, that a seven years' stretch is a thing to be proud of or pleased with. It's a hard sentence, that's what it is. Ain't it, guv'nor?"

This last observation was made to a warder who had charge of him.

"I don't know that it is, considering all things," returned the warder.

"Oh, no; you chaps never do think a cove gets more than he deserves."

"Well, you see, there were previous convictions against you—that's why you've got it so hot."

"I was driven to it. Business was bad, and I was without a mag."

"That's no reason for laying your hands upon other people's property," suggested the warder; "but I don't want to pain you by my reproaches. I am sorry for your misfortune—sorry for your wife and child's sake."

"Thank you, sir; you are very good, I'm sure," observed Mrs. Peace, wiping the fast-falling tears from her swollen eyelids.

"It is not the man only who suffers—it is his family," said the warder. "They are to be pitied the most."

"What's the use of pity?" cried Peace. "Did you ever know it do any good? It aint worth a rap—pity indeed. No one will help her or me—not that I know of."

"I hope there is some one. Have you any friends?" This last observation was addressed to the woman.

"No, none. None that can give me any assistance. Those I know are as poor as myself."

"Now, then, prisoners, this way!" shouted out a man in the lobby in a stentorian voice. "This way for prisoners."

Peace bade a hasty farewell to his wife, kissed his infant daughter, and was conducted to the "Black Maria," which was standing at one of the side doors of the Court-house.

Mrs. Peace returned home in a very wretched frame of mind, as may be readily imagined. She did not know how to eke out a living for a short time after the conviction of her husband.

She kept a little shop in Long Millgate, Manchester, but before long she went back to Sheffield, and got employment in charing, and in the bottling department of a wine merchant. There were some few who took compassion on her, and strove to put something in her way.

She was an industrious frugal woman, who did her best under most trying and disheartening circumstances.

At first she lived in Prippet-lane, but afterwards in Orchard-street, where Peace's mother lived.

In 1865, shortly before leaving Kenyon-alley, there had been a son—John Charles—born, but he did not live to see the return of his father.

Peace was taken to Wakefield gaol. The usual formalities were gone through, which were much the same as those described in some of the earlier chapters of this work.

Peace, as we have observed, was a handy man enough, and this was soon found out by the authorities of Wakefield prison.

For the first few weeks after his introduction he was set to work at oakum-picking; but as time went on, and the warders and deputy-governor became better acquainted with his habits, he was set to work at whitewashing, painting, and doing other odd jobs in the prison. He contrived to make himself generally useful, and in addition to this he succeeded in impressing the chaplain with the fact that he was a very devout person, who had seen the error of his ways, and who was moreover duly impressed with the necessity there was for him to reform.

He had been convicted thrice; this fact he could not conceal; but when once he had another chance given him he said he would avail himself of it, and that nothing in the world should ever induce him to stray again from the path of rectitude.

He talked so plausibly, entering into elaborate disquisitions upon certain portions of the Scriptures, that the chaplain was fairly imposed upon by the hypocritical prisoner.

Some repairs were being done in the prison, and Peace was one of the gang employed for this purpose. He worked industriously with his mates for some days.

Although he was a cunning, clever rascal, and was unscrupulous and daring to boot, he does not appear to have rivalled the celebrated Jack Sheppard, as far as attempts at escaping from prison are concerned.

As he was at work the thought crossed his mind that he might succeed in effecting his escape, and when once this idea entered his head he did not rest till he laid out his plan of operation.

The repairs he was executing gave him an opportunity of smuggling a short ladder into his cell. No one for a moment suspected what he was meditating, and, indeed, it would appear that much more latitude was allowed him than usually falls to the share of a convict.

He managed to secure a piece of zinc, and took an opportunity of nicking it so that it would answer the purpose of a saw. When shut up for the night he set industriously to work.

The cell in which he was confined was not of a modern structure, with stone walls and an arched stone roof, such as are now invariably used in all our convict prisons.

The roof was plaster; in the centre of it ran a beam. Peace had ascertained this before he began his operations. It did not take him long to make a hole in the ceiling. When this had been done he set to work with his zinc saw to cut through the beam.

The cell was one of the top ones; it was in close proximity to the roof. This he had also ascertained—if he could once get on the roof, he felt the rest would be an easy matter.

The chances are that he would not have succeeded in any case, but he was bent on his project, and was in a state of nervous excitement until it was carried out.

"I'll do them yet," he murmured. "If I gain the roof I shall be able to give them the slip, and there will be one prisoner less in Wakefield gaol—that's all. Ha, ha!" he laughed, at the prospect of doing his janitors.

For the greater part of the night he was at work, but the progress he made was so slow, in consequence of the clumsy instrument with which he worked, that daylight came before he had made a hole sufficiently large for him to pass through.

"The warders will be round presently," he ejaculated; "and if I am not clean off before they make their appearance I am lost."

He set to work with renewed vigour; the perspiration fell in thick beads from his forehead and temples. An exclamation of delight escaped him: the aperture was sufficiently large for his purpose.

He crept through the hole, and then seemed to breathe more freely. He laid hold of the top rail of the ladder, which he was in the act of drawing up after him, when the cell door was opened, and an official exclaimed in a voice of alarm—

"Halloa there—what's this? Come down!"

Peace made no reply. The moments were now precious to him. The officer advanced and endeavoured to seize the ladder. Peace gave him a blow with it in the chest, and knocked him down.

The man uttered an exclamation of rage and pain. But Peace did not wait for further parley: he drew up the ladder and ran along the roof in the greatest state of excitement.

After running over the roof he got on to the prison wall, and he was making his way along there when a terrible misfortune befel him: the bricks were loose, and it was impossible for him to keep his balance or maintain his foothold. He fell. It was supposed that he had fallen outside.

There was by this time a hue and cry after him. Consternation sat on the visages of the warders, and the whole place was soon in an uproar.

The deputy-governor asked what was the matter. The warders said that a prisoner had escaped.

"How and by what means?" cried the deputy-governor.

Nobody appeared to know. Davis, the warder who had been pushed down by Peace, not chosing to stop and explain matters, hastened at once into the governor's presence, and made him acquainted with the facts which had come under his knowledge. After this he ran round the outside of the prison in search of Peace, whom he did not succeed in finding.

Peace had really fallen inside the prison wall, not far from where some servants were looking out from the door of the governor's house; but, notwithstanding their close proximity to him, they had not seen him either before or after his fall, the reason for this being that their attention was directed away from him.

The general impression was at this time that our hero had succeeded in making his escape, and the governor and deputy-governor were greatly incensed at what they termed the carelessness of the men in charge of the convicts.

The prison officials were in no enviable frame of mind; they expected to be called over the coals, and were ransacking their brains for excuses to offer.

Peace, finding that the governor's servants had not observed him, determined upon a bold stroke. With the cunning of a hunted fox he slipped past the room in which they were at this time, entered the governors' house, and ran upstairs.

No one for a moment supposed that he was loitering about the premises. Indeed, every one was fairly puzzled, and could not in any way account for his sudden and mysterious disappearance.

People were started off at once in quest of the fugitive.

Upon Peace reaching one of the upstair rooms of the house, he stripped off his prison clothes and dressed himself in a suit of the governor's.

This done, he watched patiently for an opportunity of escape, but none came.

A throng of persons were in the lower rooms of the habitation, and, for the present at least, escape was impossible.

Even if he had the temerity to drop from the window, he would be sure to be recaptured, for there were numbers of persons—policemen and warders—gathered round the walls of the gaol.

Peace was wild with fury. He was within eight of liberty, which was, however, denied him.

He thought it best to remain concealed in his hiding-place till the aspect of affairs changed.

But no change appeared likely to take place.

An hour passed.

Then another half hour, at the expiration of which the room door was suddenly opened, and several piercing screams proceeded from a maid-servant, in whose room Peace was secreted.

He strove in vain to silence the girl by placing his hand over her mouth for the purpose of stifling her cries.

But the attempt proved futile. She was too much alarmed, and her voice was so shrill that it would have awakened one of the seven sleepers.

"Hold your deuced tongue, you little fool!" exclaimed Peace. "Nobody will hurt you."

But the mischief was already done. It is just possible that the maid might have connived at his escape if she had considered twice about the matter; as it was, he was lost.

He knew and felt this, as the noise of ascending footsteps fell upon his ears.

The governor, with a cohort of prison officials, now entered the apartment.

Peace cut such a rueful figure, and presented altogether such a comical appearance in the governor's clothes, which were a world too wide for him, in addition to being too long, in this respect resembling two towns on the Continent, namely Toulouse and Toulon, that more than one of the party could not refrain from laughing, the governor first setting the example himself.

"So, sir," said he, "this is how you repay the kindness shown to you—is it?"

"Oh, I am very sorry for what I've done," said Peace, in a whining tone of voice, "but liberty is sweet, and penal servitude is a sore trial. I hope you will take a merciful view of the matter, for I don't suppose it would have made much difference to anybody if I had got clean away—as it is I am to be pitied."

"You are a hypocritical, worthless fellow," observed the governor; "and the sooner we are rid of you the better. You are not worthy of consideration, and as to kindness, it's thrown away upon you. But whose clothes is the rascal wearing?" he observed, as it suddenly occurred to him that the garments looked very much like his own.

"He's got on your clothes, sir," said one of the warders.

"Upon my word, his impudence exceeds all bounds," cried the governor in a fury.

"I couldn't find any others to put on," whined Peace. "I'll take them off at once."

He began to undress, slipped out of the garments in question, and put on his prison attire.

"Has he any accomplices?" inquired the governor.

"I think not, sir," answered Davis.

"I have a great mind to recommend a sound flogging."

"Oh, pray don't, sir; I ask your pardon. Pray have pity on me, if you please. I declare most positively that I intended to lead a new life, to reform, if I had got back into the world, and I intend to do so, under any circumstances. I pledge my word as to this."

"Your word!" exclaimed the governor, in ineffable disgust. "Your word, indeed! There, take him away; place him in one of the refractory cells."

Upon hearing these words Peace made a most piteous appeal to the governor, who, in reply, told him that he might think himself fortunate at being spared a flogging.

The refractory or punishment cells, as they are termed, have double doors, which are kept locked to effectually prevent any communication from without. The prisoner, on entering one of these dark cells, which do not admit a single beam of light when the doors are closed upon him, finds everything as silent as the grave.

The furniture of these wretched places consists of an iron bedstead, securely fixed in the floor, and a water closet.

There is also a bell to communicate with the officers of the prison, and a trap in the door to convey food, as in the other cells.

When under confinement in these places the prisoners are kept upon bread and water.

The bedding at night consists of a straw mattrass and a rug, handed in at nine o'clock in the evening and taken away in the morning, when a tub of water is given to the prisoners for the purpose of performing their ablutions.

Peace was conducted back to the gaol by the warders, one of whom unlocked the door of one of the refractory cells, and the wretched prisoner was thrust into the dark and cheerless receptacle.

Without doubt even a temporary or short imprisonment in a dark cell is a terrible punishment to most men.

When Peace heard the door slammed to his heart sank within him. A cold shudder passed through his frame as he breathed the mephitic black air, which seemed to be more like a fluid than an atmosphere.

His allowance of bread and water had been given him as he made the acquaintance for the first time of his dark prison-house.

"Oh!" he exclaimed; "and to think it should come to this! Had it not been for those loose bricks I should be breathing the fresh air now—be at liberty—but this is, indeed, most horrible. Ugh! this wretched darkness—this appalling gloom!"

He sat down on the side of his bed and pressed his hands to his temples, which were throbbing painfully. He remained for some time lost in thought.

"I am but a poor, silly fool after all," he presently ejaculated. "Why should a man like me shudder at the darkness. What does it matter when one's asleep whether there be light or not? How long am I to remain here, I wonder, and what will be their next move?"

He endeavoured in vain to penetrate the gloom—endeavoured to make out the objects in his cell, but all to no purpose.

It was the first time in his life that he had been immured in a refractory cell—he had heard the horrors of the place described by those who had suffered confinement in such places—now he had to learn them by his own bitter experience.

After all it is better than being bashed (flogged)," said he, "but it is bad enough, and a little of it goes a long way."

"If I keep still I shall be benumbed with cold. I must endeavour to get some exercise."

He groped to the wall, and keeping his hand on it, went round and round like a caged wolf. This exercise seemed to afford him some temporary relief, which, however, was but of a transient nature. He groaned and gnashed his teeth—the silence and gloom seemed almost insupportable. He sat himself once more on the side of his bed.

"What have I done that I should be punished thus?" he ejaculated. "Endeavour to gain my liberty. Every person would do that if he saw a chance; he'd be a born idiot if he did not."

He sat rocking himself to and fro—trying not to think of anything, for now the miserable nature of his position seemed to fall upon him with additional force.

"If they would only let me have one ray of light, however feeble, I would not complain. Nay, I would be satisfied, but this impenetrable gloom is more than mortal man can bear. I shall go mad. In a short time they will let me out of this place a howling maniac."

He stretched himself on his bed, and endeavoured to sleep, but every now and then he started as if an adder had stung him; he started and groaned, then he turned round, covered his face with his handkerchief and remained quiet for awhile.

If he could only sleep he would be satisfied, but he found this impossible. The place was cold, damp, and cheerless.

He arose and crept towards the door of the cell.

What would he give to see it opened and have free passage accorded him?

He listened at the door for some time; he could not detect the faintest sound, save the beatings of his own heart.

He shouted out as loudly as he could, and his voice reverberated through the cell, making strange and uncouth echoes.

He beat his fist violently against the door, the only effect of which was to bruise his hands; no one answered—there was nothing for him but darkness, silence, and solitude.

"They have no compassion, no feeling, and have left me here to die!" he ejaculated. "Oh, the merciless wretches!"

A thousand fugitive thoughts flitted through his brain; the incidents of his life were pictured before him with inconceivable rapidity.

He had some feelings of remorse, and made good resolutions for his future conduct, which were afterwards broken, like others he had made when in trial and suffering, and now remorse and memory contracted themselves on one dark spot in Charles Peace's history.

Fear came upon him, an icy tremour crept through his frame, and a feeling of faintness came over him.

Once more the past rushed by with tenfold force. All this was bad enough, but worse followed.

He fancied something supernatural passed him like a cold blast.

His limbs shook as with palsy, and his teeth chattered. Thick beads of perspiration oozed from his forehead and temples, and coursed down his cheeks.

He cried most piteously for help. He said the cell was full of evil spirits—uncouth forms were flitting about him—horrible faces were grinning hideously at him. He screamed and cursed, and prayed, and dashed himself frantically against the door, and ran round his cell like a mad person. But no one came to his assistance. He flung himself once more on his bed, and uttered a plaintive moan.

How long a time he had passed in his miserable prison house he could not possibly tell—to him it appeared an age. He was, however, aroused from his state of lethargy by the cell door being suddenly flung open, and when this had been done he beheld Davis—the man he had knocked down with the ladder—peering in. The warder tossed in the rug which was to cover him for the night.

Peace sprang from his rude couch, and rushed towards the door.

"You'll kill me, that's what you'll do," he said, in a whining voice.

"How long am I to be shut up in this cursed place? Tell me that. How long?"

"I don't know—the governor has not determined."

"It's cruel—monstrous, inhuman."

"It's your own fault, you've nobody to blame but yourself."

"Don't go. Pray, don't go."

"What do you want?"

"I'm not well—want to see the doctor."

"You are all right. Don't think to gammon us again."

"It isn't gammon. I pledge you my word that it's the solemn truth. May I see the governor?"

"He's not in the way just now, and I don't suppose he would see you if he were. I am sorry for you, and thought better things of you. You've had every indulgence."

"I know it, and am grateful for it."

The warder laughed.

"Don't jeer at my misfortunes. May I have a light?"

"Certainly not; I can answer that question. No lights are allowed in the refractory cells. You have your answer, and so ——"

The warder suddenly slammed the door to, and Peace was left in darkness again.

"Wretches—barbarians—inhuman monsters!" he ejaculated, and in the bitterness of the moment he felt disposed to cry.

The prison authorities were, however, more considerate and merciful to him than perhaps he had any reason to expect.

After two days' confinement in the refractory cell he was taken out and placed in an ordinary prison cell, and in a few days after this he left the gaol with a batch of convicts, who were bound for Millbank. The officials at Wakefield were but too glad to be rid of him.

CHAPTER LXXXV.

PEACE BECOMES ACQUAINTED WITH THE INTERIOR OF MILLBANK PENITENTIARY—A BRIEF DESCRIPTION OF THE PRISON.

MILLBANK PENITENTIARY, as it was termed, is now a thing of the past. The new prison at Wormwood Scrubs will supersede a place of some historic history. Probably not many Londoners of the present generation know the history of the huge ugly building which occupied the left bank of the Thames between the Horseferry-road and Vauxhall-bridge.

It figures on the maps as a series of six pentagonal structures arranged round a central sexagon.

The forbidding structure was, until very recently, an ordinary prison, whither convicts were sent for separate confinement for the first nine months of their sentences of penal servitude, before they were drafted off to the convict prisons at Portland, Chatham, Portsmouth, or Dartmoor.

Its history as a "Penitentiary" closed more than thirty years ago, when Sir James Graham told the House of Commons it was a failure.

The place itself was one of the early results of Howard's efforts to improve the condition of prisoners, and all the methods of prison discipline which have since been practised have been associated with it.

Howard withdrew from the scheme before even the site had been fixed on, and it was taken up by Jeremy Bentham, who wished to realise his idea of the Panopticon or Inspection House, "in which any number of persons may be kept within reach of being inspected during every moment of their lives."

Bentham agreed with the Government to build a prison, and bought the land at Millbank of Lord Salisbury for £12,000, but the scheme fell through, though eventually the Penitentiary was built, and received its first batch of convicts in June, 1816.

In its management the new institution was meant as an experiment in the humanitarian treatment of crime.

The place was not to be a prison, but a penitentiary, and the convicts were not so much to be prisoners as penitents. Men who knew trades were to work at them and teach others.

Captain Griffiths, the present Deputy-Governor, in his "Memorials of Millbank," just published, describes it as at this time "a huge plaything; a toy for a parcel of philanthropic gentlemen, to keep them busy during their spare hours."

Visitors were taken to it as a show-place, where the prisoners read and went through religious exercises to the great edification of the company.

At Christmas they were regaled with roast beef and plum pudding, after which they passed a vote of thanks to Archdeacon Potts, the visitor, and sang "God save the King."

Punishments were rarely inflicted, and then only after report to the visitor. The first prisoner who was released from the penitentiary was a woman who, being dressed in her new clothes, was taken round to see her fellow-penitents, who were duly addressed by Sir Archibald Macdonald, the visitor, on the improving spectacle.

Next day as she left the place of her temporary detention the other women were at their cell windows, and vociferously cheered the first subject of the new discipline as she went forth into the world. Convicts thus treated soon began to give themselves airs.

One charged with stealing the matron's tea was so hurt as to be thrown into fits. Some of the women refused to have their hair cut short, and were allowed to retain their locks.

One Sunday the Chancellor of the Exchequer and some friends were at the prison service when a riot arose from the objection of some women to brown bread. The Chancellor addressed the men after the women had been removed, and promised to represent their complaint to the Home Secretary. The rebellious spirit, however, continued, and eventually had to be suppressed by punishments. The failure was charged on the officials, not on the system, and the Penitentiary continued to be conducted, as Captain Griffiths says, like a big school.

The populace called it "Mr. Holford's fattening-house," and it was suggested that the guards and warders were not needful to keep the rogues from getting out, but to prevent honest people from rushing in.

One of the services which Millbank has rendered in return for the half million of money squandered on it may be said to be the complete explosion of the idea on which penitentiaries were based.

Millbank was the first penitentiary, and the last, in the full sense of the word.

From the very first the place was a perpetual source of anxiety and dispute.

Before it was finished Sir Robert Smirke had to be called in to rebuild it, and it had only been opened a few years when one of the most terrible epidemics in prison history broke out among its occupants, necessitating their removal to the hulks.

When it was again occupied the same weak system seems to have prevailed.

The power of persuasion to reform criminals was thoroughly believed in, and nobody seemed to doubt that a year or two in Millbank would change any rogue into an honest man, if he were at all capable of reformation.

Only such as were considered hopeful were sent to the Penitentiary, and it required the failures of years to convince the public mind that the system of petting and patronising was the wrong one.

Parliament had not even given the governor the power to inflict corporal punishment; and a Parliamentary committee reported that the situation of convicts in Millbank "cannot be considered penal; it is a state of restriction, but hardly of punishment." In 1826 the prisoners began to revolt even against restriction.

For some years the place was the scene of continual rebellions and disturbances, and Parliament at length authorised whipping.

THE LAWYER AND AVELINE GATLIFFE.

This was inflicted in the first instance on a man named Sheppard, who had beaten an officer in presence of other prisoners, but it was done with great gentleness, and when it was over the scoundrel made an edifying address to his fellow-prisoners.

One of the most celebrated cases of incorrigible perversity was that of Julia St. Clair Newman, which was often discussed in Parliament, and investigated by a select committee of the House of Lords.

She was apparently a Creole who had been educated in France, and came to England as a swindler. She looked like a gentlewoman, but had been imprisoned several times before she was sent to the penitentiary to be reformed.

Here her conduct alternated between fits of uncontrollable fury and passionate appeals for sympathy.

She feigned illness, pretended to be insane ; sometimes embraced the female warders vehemently, at others flung her gruel in the face of the chaplain; would one day make her clothes into a doll, and another compose a long and critical examination of the character of the Queen, who had just then come to the throne.

Her influence all through the prison was most mischievous, and at length she had to be removed to Bethlehem.

There it seemed impossible to restrain her, and the effort was given up. She was at length sent out to Van Dieman's Land in the "Nautilus," and was no more heard of. She was only one of the Millbank failures.

After the confession in 1843 of the breakdown of the penitentiary system, the great prison became a kind of second Newgate.

In Newgate, however, as Captain Griffiths points out, the worst criminals soon pass beyond human ken ; at the great depot prison they at least continue alive.

The calendar is full of names which have become historic in the annals of crime. Not to come down to the times of Orton, the names of Robson, Redpath, Poole, and Pullinger recall frauds which were conducted with a cleverness, and for a long time with a success, which only a genius for swindling could have attained.

"Jem the Penman," the master mind of a gang of forgers, who made great hauls before they were caught, looked like a drunken sot in prison, but conducted himself fairly well.

One remarkable criminal was a practising surgeon, who had married wives in various parts of the country, and having got possession of their money, trinkets, and clothing, had deserted them.

He spoke several languages, and one of his favourite feats in prison was to write the Lord's Prayer in five different languages within a circle the size of a sixpence.

His conduct at Millbank was most exemplary, and he, like other prisoners, eventually went to the Antipodes and married.

An "honourable and reverend" gentleman, who was convicted of forgery, and sentenced to transportation for life, became almost imbecile and useless in confinement; he, too, went to the colonies, where he "was last heard of performing divine service at an outstation at the rate of a shilling a service."

A military man, of good family, who had become a gambler, and was convicted of enormous swindling transactions, proved in detention an idle, good-fornothing rascal, who would do no work, and expected to be waited on.

Another ex-military officer was sentenced to seven years for striking the Queen. No motive could be found for the act, but in prison he declared that his sole object was to bring disgrace on his family, as his father had offended him. He was leniently treated, was popular with the officers, and eventually went to Australia.

These glimpses which the records of such a prison as Millbank give of men who have disappeared from the world are like scenes from Dante.

All hope, however, is not abandoned even when the gates of Millbank close behind a criminal. He still belongs to the world he has left.

A way back is kept open for him; and, though his old friends may know him no more, he has usually a chance of redeeming his position, perhaps under another name, in another land.

Upon Peace and his companions in crime arriving at Millbank, the first thing that was done on entering was to take the handcuffs off each convict ; they were then told to seat themselves on a long bench in the passage.

Presently two chief warders arrived, accompanied by a medical officer and a clerk.

On their appearance the prisoners were told to rise and stand to attention. One of the chief warders walked along one line, and claimed more than one of the party.

By the time that certain preliminary preparations had been gone through, and the name, case, and crime of each prisoner had been entered into a book in the office, it was twelve o'clock, and dinner time.

The new comers were informed that presently they would be asked what religion they were. Each man might please himself what he chose to be, but what he elected he must stick to.

The bill of fare for each day of the week was read out to them. The allowance given to each person was quite sufficient to support life, and keep him in good health.

Luxuries were, of course, never thought of. Coarse plain food was all they had any right to expect, and certainly it was all they got, but the cost of prisons forms a very large item in the expenses of the country.

Up to the time the prisons were taken over by the Government, it appears that the cost of maintaining the prisoners, exclusive of convicts, had been slowly but gradually diminishing, and it is not improbable this movement will now continue even more rapidly.

It appears from the volume of judicial statistics lately issued, that the average for the year 1876-7, of £28 16s. 7d., calculated on the total cost, is less than the corresponding average for 1875-6 by £1 9s. 5d.

The average, omitting the extraordinary charge for buildings, &c., is less than the corresponding amount for 1875-6 by £1 4s. The average yearly charge per prisoner, depending in a great degree on the number of prison officials maintained, and the daily average of prisoners, varies greatly in different prisons.

It is, of course, affected also by extraordinary charges of buildings, loans, &c. The lowest average cost per prisoner for 1876-7, as for 1875-6, is at Salford County Prison, where, with a total staff of 65 officers, and a total daily average of 900 prisoners in the latter year, and of 66 officers, and a total daily average of 966 prisoners in 1876-7, the average cost per prisoner was £14 6s. 1d. in 1876-7, and £15 12s. 5d. in 1875-6.

In Durham County Prison, with a total staff of 42, and a daily average of 641 prisoners, the average cost per prisoner was in 1876-7, £17 0s. 2d.

In this prison for the previous year, with a like staff of 42, and with a daily average of 625 prisoners, the average cost per prisoner was £17 17s. 6d.

In Preston County Prison, with a staff of 36 officers, and a daily average of 435 prisoners, in 1876-7 the average cost per prisoner was £16 14s. 10d.

In this prison for the previous year, with a like staff of 36 officers, and with a daily average of 405 prisoners, the average cost per prisoner was £19 12s. 10d.

The highest average cost for 1876-7 was, as in the previous year, at the Lincoln County Prison, where, with a total staff of 9, and a daily average of 12 prisoners, the average cost per prisoner was £107 10s. 11d. the average cost for the previous year, with a staff of

9 officers and a daily average of 9 prisoners, £133 19s. 10d. per prisoner.

The average cost per prisoner, in the following 13 prisons, in the year 1876-7, exceeded in each case the sum of £50—namely, Wisbeach; Hertford, County; St. Alban's, County; Great Stukely, County; Newgate, City and County; Peterborough, Liberty; Oakham, County; Bury St. Edmund's, County; Ripon, Liberty; Beaumaris, County; Cardigan, County; Dolgelly, County; and Presteign, County Prison.

The average cost per prisoner in the following four prisons, in addition to the three previously mentioned, in the year 1876-7 was in each case under £20—namely, Devonport, Borough, £19 16s. 3d.; Kirkdale, County, £18 1s. 3d.; Liverpool, Borough, £18 2s. 2d.; and Manchester City Prison, £17 16s. 7d The different sources from which the prison expenses for the year were defrayed, and the amount received from each were as follows :—

From prison receipts, inclusive of profits of prisoners' labour, £64,855, or 11·0 per cent. of the total amount from local rates and funds was 69·1 per cent. total, and from public funds £116,769 or 19·9 per cent. of total.

The principal and proportions for the year 1875-6, under various heads, were, from prison receipts, £65,387, from local rates, &c., £400,712, and from revenues £110,300.

It will be seen by the foregoing statistics that the criminal population of the United Kingdom absorbs a vast amount of money annually from the pockets of the ratepayers for the maintainence of convicts.

This is a lamentable state of things, but under existing circumstances there is no help for it.

After the rules had been read, Peace and his fellow-prisoners were ordered in batches of four or five into some cells, each man having given to him previously a loaf of bread and a piece of cheese of excellent quality.

Here Peace was kept for a long time, but he could hear that the officials had returned and were engaged with the fresh arrivals he had for his companions—three ruffians of the very worst type—these being indeed, London thieves, and he had as little to say to them as possible.

Not being pleased with his associates, he got up on a table under the window, and looked out on the Pentagon yard.

"What are you up to?" cried one of his fellow-prisoners. "Want to see as much as you can of the blooming place. An' much good it ell do yer."

Peace made no reply, but looked out. Walking round the yard, or rather the division nearest to the cell window, he observed a number of prisoners marching round the yard, about five or six yards apart.

In the centre stood an imposing-looking warder in uniform, with a staff like a policeman's in his hand.

Each man was dressed in a short, loose, ill-fitting jacket and vest, and baggy knickerbockers of drab tweed, with black stripes one and a half inches in width. The lower part of the legs were encased in blue worsted stockings with bright red rings round them, low shoes, and a bright grey and red worsted cap. It struck Peace that they were very much like supernumeraries at a theatre, but all over the garments there were hideous black impressions of the broad arrow, the "crow's foot" denoting that the articles belonged to her Majesty.

After inspecting the prisoners at exercise, Peace descended from the table, and stood silent and dejected in the cell.

Presently the door was opened, and he and his companions were ordered out.

Peace was directed to go to the end of the passage, where the principal of the receiving ward was standing. He had to undergo the usual formula of the bath. A bundle was handed him, which contained a complete suit of clothes of the same picturesque pattern as those worn by the prisoners he had seen exercising.

He was then called into a room where the doctor was, and here he saw the chief warder—an enormous man with the voice of a Stentor, who looked dreadfully stern and resolute, but who was, nevertheless, a kindly-disposed man enough—this he afterwards found out; there, to his surprise, he was shown a bundle which he at once recognised as the clothes, even to the hat and boots, he had worn before his conviction—his last habiliments of freedom.

"You know what these are, and whom they belong to, I suppose?" said the prison official.

"Yes, they belong to me," Peace returned.

"All right," said the other, throwing them into a corner, where a pile of similar bundles were lying.

After he had undergone the usual examination by the doctor, a card was given him with a number on it, which he was told was his number, to which he was to always answer, as prisoners left their names behind them.

All this he knew perfectly well from sad experience, but he was too artful to let it appear that he was well acquainted with prison life.

They would find that out in all probability quite soon enough.

When fully equipped, and feeling very uncomfortable, he was marched down a passage and through a door at the foot of a winding spiral stone staircase into the Pentagon yard, across this and through a gate or two in the dividing railings into a similar door, up a spiral stone staircase like the first one he had passed—one flight, two flights, three flights, to the very top where he was transferred by the warder who had conducted him so far, to the care of another warder, and he at once pointed out the way along the passage to a cell, the door of which he opened, and introduced him to the quarters he was to take up during his sojourn at Millbank.

The little ticket with his number was taken from him, and placed by the warder in a rack over the doorway. This done, he locked Peace in.

Each convict establishment has a governor, deputy governor, and one or more chief warders. At the time of Peace's incarceration in Millbank it had no less than three, who had under them three grades of officials—principals, warders, and assistant warders.

The slang name for all the prison officials is "screws," all are armed in some way, the leading officials wear swords, the warders and assistant warders are armed with truncheons, which are carried in cases at the side, much the same as those worn by the police.

When with a gang of men at outdoor work these truncheons are replaced by a short rifle and bayonet. In addition, there is at Dartmoor and other prisons away from London, the civil guard, armed with rifles and bayonets, who do military duty in guarding the place.

Millbank was so near to the barracks at Westminster that there was little need for a special guard. Every block of buildings and every ward in Millbank prison was in communication with each other, and all radiated from the centre of the whole establishment. Though to an outside observer it looked like a number of detached buildings, it was possible to visit every cell and every ward without once going into the open air.

The numberless windows which were seen on the outside of this prison were not, as many erroneously supposed, the windows of prisoners' cells. These windows served to light the passages running between them and the cell gates and doors. Every cell had a strong iron gate, opening outwards into the wide strong corridor or passage, and a wooden door opening inwards to the cell. Opposite the door was a large window, about three feet square, looking into the inner yard of the Pentagon.

The round towers at the corner of each angle of every block of buildings, surmounted with pointed roofs, contained the spiral stone staircases leading from the ground-floor to the top landing.

There were four stories of these cells, all of which were alike and of good size, being about ten feet square.

On each floor were sinks and water supply, and other conveniences for the wants of that corridor. Captain Arthur Griffiths has written an admirable work upon this prison, which he entitled "Chronicles of Millbank," and the reader who desires to know more about a place which possesses an historical interest, cannot do better than consult that work.

The history of punishments is parallel to the history of civilisation, for every advance made in the direction of a humane and intelligent treatment of criminals has marked a progressive step in contemporary manners and modes of thought.

Among barbarous peoples the penal measures were barbarous; as the world has grown older and wiser punishments have become less cruel, and been based on wider principles.

At first the object of punishment, whether by death or torture, was vengeance; only after long years was it directed to suppress crime; and it is in these more enlightened days that the system has developed into one which, while it is assigned to correct the wrong-doer, endeavours also to reform him, and prevent others from following his ways.

It seems at first sight surprising that confusing ideas with regard to the means and methods of punishment are the growth entirely of the present century; but so it is, and the work under notice most usefully reminds us of the various mutations those ideas have undergone, and of the immense change which has been made within a hundred years in the views of statesmen and philanthropists with regard to penal reclamation.

"The Memorials of Millbank" are, in that, a description, full of instruction and charged with interest, of the process of evolution through which our prison system has reached its present excellence.

Captain Arthur Griffiths begins his work with a picture of the condition of affairs in the time of Howard, long before Millbank was built or thought of, and a terrible picture it is he draws.

Prisons were overcrowded, ill-ventilated, damp, pestiferous. The gaol fever, a disease now happily unknown, carried off, according to Howard, "more people than were put to death by all the public executions in the kingdom."

And those were times in which capital punishment was inflicted for the most trivial offences. Prisoners brought into court communicated the infection to judges, barristers, jurors, and spectators; and at Taunton in 1730 bench and bar and hundreds of people in court died from the disease.

The prisons were not only pesthouses: they were places of torture, and gambling, and vice. The gaolers were inhuman wretches, as mercenary as they were cruel, and their chief aim was to make their positions profitable to themselves.

Howard's revelations stirred first of all the Duke of Richmond, who built a new and improvised prison at Horsham for Sussex; and soon after that, when transportation to the American colonies was abandoned, the Legislature resolved to build a gaol to which should be sent criminals heretofore ordered for transportation.

Here it was hoped, to use the words of the Act, "that solitary confinement, accompanied by well-regulated hard labour and religious instruction, might be the means under Providence, not only of deterring others, but also of reforming the individuals and turning them to habits of industry."

This extract contains the seed from which, after long controversy and the failure of a scheme which honest but unpractical Jeremy Bentham attempted to carry out, the Millbank Penitentiary grew; and it contains, too, it appears to us, the secret of the repeated failures which governor after governor and successive Legislatures met with when the great experiment was under trial.

The cost exceeded £350,000, which was a much larger sum at that date than it would be to-day to expend in a philanthropic enterprise, and is a proof of the earnestness with which the Government embarked in the task; but the money was almost thrown away.

It was for a long time the old, old story of zeal without knowledge.

Ministers and their advisers made the mistake of overrating the capabilities and moral qualities of the class they had to deal with.

The committee of supervisors, who were virtually the rulers of the prison—which was another mistake—fell into a similar error.

The governor and officers seem to have done the same; and nothing but trouble was in store for Millbank for many years to come.

The story of the first volume is a sad one.

It is one long series of struggles between well-meaning but weak authorities and turbulent incorrigible prisoners in a chronic state of insubordination. Even this was not all.

The place was built on a faulty site; structural defects were constantly appearing, and the prisoners more than once were laid prostrate with a then mysterious disease, which turned out afterwards to be due to unsound sanitary and dietetic conditions.

Leniency was the key-note of the prison system. Men and women the most depraved, the most irreclaimable, were to be reformed by moral suasion. There was practically no punishment, no discipline, no order.

The governor was fettered by the supervisors, the officers were lax because there was no organisation, and the consequence was there was constant mutiny, escapes, or attempts to escape, which, despite altered arrangements and new regulations, continued for years.

It was not until long after—not until transportation to the new Australian colonies commenced—that this evil was cured, and it is instructive at the present juncture to read that it was cured by the use of the lash.

No other form of punishment was so efficacious; no other mode of correction so feared. The prisoners who witnessed the sufferings of their fellows appear to have been cowed.

The women, who were always worse than the men—and here Captain Griffiths receives ample confirmation in a work published by a prison matron in 1862—

seem only to have been controlled when it became known that they too might be treated—though it does not transpire that they ever were—with the same severity.

Corporal punishment, however, was only needed to correct offences which it is evident a stricter discipline from the first would have prevented.

In the course of years the Government discovered how little was to be hoped from moral suasion. Time and experience brought wisdom in their train, and ultimately the old order changed, giving place to new.

The original scheme of a penitentiary was abandoned, the whole system was re-modelled, changes were made which we have not room to describe, and the prison was devoted to a different purpose and a different class of criminals—*i.e.*, those on their road to the transport ships; and later on, when transportation was finally given up, as the first gaol of the convict under sentence of penal servitude, on his road to Portland or other establishments of the kind.

Captain Griffiths in his second volume interweaves with his narrative of Millbank some interesting chapters descriptive of the system adopted in transportation to the colonies and the mode of life of the convicts there.

A singular similarity exists between the errors of the one system and the other. In the earlier days of both the Government was too hopeful. They expected too much from the unpromising material they had to work upon.

A reaction from the horrible condition revealed by the labours of Howard carried them too far in the other direction, and it was the reaction from this which led ultimately to a complete reversal of the old scheme of secondary punishment, the abandonment of transportation, and the establishment of the systems we have at present.

Peace got on pretty well at Millbank; the warders were kind to him, and he behaved himself in the best possible manner, and his attempt to escape from Wakefield appeared to have been forgotten: anyway, it was never alluded to. It was some relief to the monotony of his prison life, when he was set to work with other prisoners to clean the windows of the establishment.

It fell to his share to work at the infirmary, and while engaged on the windows in that part of the prison, he felt very much depressed, for the sight presented to him was indeed a most piteous one.

To see fellow-creatures stretched on a bed of sickness is a sorry sight at the best of times, but when the bed is in a prison cell, with an iron gate at its entrance, securely locked, and the thought comes over you that the chances are that you may be in a similar position, it is enough to depress a man.

Peace was greatly affected as he, as noiselessly as possible, polished the infirmary windows.

He remembered at that time the accident that occurred to him in the rolling mills where he worked; and he remembered also his own long illness and tardy recovery after his leg had been set; but then he had a mother and sister to attend upon him, and he was a free man—in humble circumstances, it is true—but, nevertheless, free.

As he thought of being seized with illness in a convict prison, he shuddered.

The miserable patient, under these circumstances, has not one kind or sympathising face to smile upon him.

The chances are that he is rudely tended by some fellow-prisoner, and he has to take his chance—and

a very poor one it is—as to the sort of man whom the authorities have thought fit to appoint as hospital nurse.

In most cases men who volunteer their services in cases of this sort do so for the purpose of shirking hard work, and but too frequently they feast themselves on the few little dainties ordered by the doctor, of which they rob the sick man when a warder's back is turned. It is in their nature to do these sort of things; they have no compunction, no pity, no mercy. There are of course exceptions; sometimes indeed a convict makes an excellent nurse, but as we before observed the sick man has to take his chance; he has no voice in the matter. To complain would be of little avail; prison officials are so used to complaints that they take but little heed of grumblers, as they call them.

To be ill whilst a convict is sad—to die a convict is terrible, and yet there are hundreds, and indeed, thousands, who are doomed to such a miserable fate. When a convict is sentenced to be imprisoned for his natural life, it of course means that he is to die in prison.

To die at sea, and to be cast into the waves, rolled up in a hammock with a shot to carry the poor soulless body deep down where no mortal eye may see it, seems a sad and piteous fate. Anyway it is not pleasant to reflect on.

To be shot down, or mangled by the bursting of a shell while fighting one's country's battles, yields, at least, some satisfaction to those who risk their lives in honour's cause; but to die a convict, to be buried in an unknown, uncared-for grave, thrust into a prison coffin, filled up with dirty sawdust, as Peace had seen them done at Dartmoor, so that the ragged old shirt given out to do duty as a shroud may be served for other purposes, is but a sorry end for a man who had once lived respected and beloved.

Peace was very glad when his window-cleaning job was over, he did not feel at all well, and the idea crossed his mind that probably he might be very shortly down upon the sick list, and be sent to the infirmary.

This reflection was by no means a pleasant one; however, in the course of a few days he was in better health and spirits.

Nothing after this disturbed the dull dry monotony of his prison life, but as the year was drawing to a close, he daily got more and more anxious to know what penal establishment he was to be drafted to after he had gone through his probationary term at Millbank.

He had gathered scraps of information from several prisoners who professed to know a great deal of the subject, but he did not place much faith in anything they said, for, as a rule, prisoners' "yarns" are not particularly truthful; nevertheless, he listened to what they had to say.

One man, "an old lag," said the next batch were going to Chatham, and it very soon transpired that he was correct in this surmise.

In about a fortnight after this Peace became acquainted with the station to which he was to be drafted.

While dinners were being served the chief warder said to him—

"8642, collect all your letters together. Tie up your work, and put all your flannels on."

"Going away, sir?" said Peace.

"Yes," returned the warder.

"Where to, sir?"

"Prisoners must not ask questions—it's against the rules."

"I shall know soon enough, I dare say," growled Peace.

"Well, Chatham, if you must know," exclaimed the warder.

"Thank ye, sir, I'm much obliged; I'm sorry to leave, though."

"Daresay you are. There, no more words. Pass on."

Peace now knew that the end of his quiet, though solitary, time was about to be brought to a close.

He dreaded very much being brought into daily and hourly contact with some of the ruffians and black-guards he had been able to keep at a respectful distance while at Milibank, but there was no help for it.

The batch had to finish the remainder of their respected sentences at Chatham.

Thirty of them soon found themselves in the same corridor in which they had been received upon first entering Millbank, and after the usual formalities had been gone through they started on their journey, and were soon whirled down by train to their destination.

CHAPTER LXXXVI
LORD ETHALWOOD AND HIS ADVISERS—MR. CHICKNELL MAKES A PAINFUL REVELATION.

THE commotion created by the marriage of John Ash-brook and Patty Jamblin had long since subsided and the bride and bridegroom returned to the old farm-house.

The usual amount of visits were paid, and the "happy pair" were suffered to settle down into their own natural unobtrusive mode of life.

Meanwhile Mr. Chicknell had been very busy in the Divorce Court for the purpose of obtaining a decree nisi in the case of Gatliffe v. Gatliffe. The reader will remember that we left Aveline and Lady Marvlynn together discussing the all-important question in a previous chapter.

It appeared that the earl's grand-daughter, however, had a will of her own. She would not consent to be made a mere puppet in the hands of others, and after her interview with Lady Marvlynn she reconsidered the matter, and boldly declared that the suit should not proceed.

The earl lost his temper—this was a very wrong thing for him to do, considering his years and high social position—but he displayed his anger to Lady Marvlynn, who was good enough to act as a convenient buffer to break the shock which otherwise might have been attended with much more serious consequences.

"She must have taken leave of her senses, the silly, wayward girl," he cried, in a fury. "My dear Lady Marvlynn, you must give her a good talking to. Tell her I am greatly incensed."

"I have told her so—I have talked to her, my lord," returned her ladyship.

"Well, and what said she?"

"Ah, she has said enough in all conscience. I think her pride is wounded—her feelings are so easily worked upon, she is so very impressionable, so sensitive."

"All this I know perfectly well," interrupted the earl, "have known it for a long time past, but what of it? You surely don't mean to tell me, Lady Marvlynn, that my grand-daughter is so unjust, so unreasonable, so undutiful, as to persist in offering an impediment to what she knows and believes to be essential to my peace of mind?"

Lady Marvlynn shrugged her shoulders, but made no reply. It was a way she had when in any great difficulty.

"I must request you to return me an answer, madam," said the earl, with hauteur.

"I have striven—I have done my best, the very best I could, I am sure, my lord; you will acknowledge this?"

"Yes, I do."

"But the poor child still clings to her husband."

"Clings to her husband!" exclaimed the earl, in a perfect fury. "I say she must be mad—positively bereft of her senses; but, enough of this, if she persists in her obstinacy—well then, the tie between us is broken. I cannot, and will not, submit to this indignity. With her my word should be law."

"And so it is, I hope."

"We've a pretty sample of it now. Chicknell is in despair; he can't move a step further in the business —nay, he declares he won't. Am I to be bearded in my own house? Am I to be set at defiance? You must see yourself, Lady Marvlynn, I have strong reason for complaining."

"I don't deny it, my lord. Don't be so excited, and listen calmly to me. Will you promise to do so?"

"Well, yes, of course I will," said the earl, seating himself by the side of the library table. "Proceed, madam, I am all attention."

"If my dear pet were convinced that her worthless husband was living in open adultery with a woman of doubtful repute—if she had indisputable proofs of this, then I think she would give up all thoughts of him for now and hereafter."

"But haven't you told her?"

"I have made her acquainted with as much as I thought it prudent to do."

"But she has witnessed quite enough with her own eyes. Did you not tell me that this man was at the opera with the shameless hussy with whom he has taken up?"

"Really, my lord, you must pardon me for a moment. The fact of a gentleman and lady being seated side by side in the stalls of the opera-house does not in itself incriminate them. The lady might be a relative, a friend's wife, a country cousin, or what not."

"Ah, true—there is something in that."

"Very well. As you admit my argument thus far, it is not in any way surprising that Aveline should refuse to believe her husband to be as guilty as we know him to be."

"But hang it, madam, you can tell her, I suppose?"

"I can, of course; but I have not done so."

"And why not, pray?"

"Ah, for many reasons. I love her as much as if she were my own child. You may believe me or not, Lord Ethalwood, but I do."

"I do believe it—but what of that?"

"This: No woman ever quite forgives another for running down her husband or exposing his foibles, or his vices—if you like that term better. That is why I have not chosen to be the accuser in this case. You will acknowledge—albeit unwillingly, perhaps—that I am right."

The earl made no reply.

He was silent for some time, and seemed to be much troubled.

Presently he offered his hand to his companion, who shook it warmly.

"I am answered, Lady Marvlynn," said he. "You have taught me a lesson. What you have said is but a proof of your discretion—your perspicuity—your intelligence. You would have been overstepping the line which prudence and good sense draws for all of us. Questions like these are at all times difficult to deal with, and in my haste and zeal I had overlooked this fact, and I have to apologise to you for pressing you upon the point. I see now, my grand-daughter, who, to say the truth, has much of the Ethalwood in her, will not yield without good and sufficient cause."

"And I admire her for it," cried Lady Marvlynn, with some warmth.

"You *are* her friend," said the earl, musingly. "A wiser and more truthful one no woman ever had."

"I understand her better than you do."

"Without a doubt. The Ethalwoods never understood one another. This has been the bane of their happiness."

He sighed and leant his head on one hand. Then he repeated, in a solemn, melancholy tone—

"The bane of their happiness."

Lady Marvlynn did not venture upon any remarks. Before her sat an honourable gentleman, across whose features a fleeting expression passed.

It would be difficult to define this; it appeared to be a combination of emotions, in which sorrow, regret, and disappointment were combined.

"I will bethink me," he presently said, "as to what is best to be done in this business. As for my reasoning with her that it is not to be thought of; but doubtless I shall find some other way."

"Let either Mr. Chicknell or Mr. Wrench have an interview with her, and convey to her the unwelcome intelligence. It will come better from them than either of us two," said Lady Marvlynn. "It matters not what they say as business men."

"You are indeed a wise counsellor," cried the earl, tapping her on the shoulder. "Nothing could be better; the suggestion is an excellent one, which I will act upon immediately. Chicknell will be here in an hour or so, and I can arrange with him without further delay."

Lady Marvlynn, feeling that the subject of their conference was at an end, rose, made a curtsey, and left the apartment.

When the lawyer arrived, which he did in the course of two or three hours after the foregoing conversation, he was made acquainted with the nature of the commission imposed upon him, to which he at once acceded.

The earl went out to pay a visit to a neighbour. Mr. Chicknell sought the Lady Aveline, who consented to receive him in her own apartment.

After much bowing and scraping, the astute attorney consented to bring himself to an anchorage on the soft velvet seat of a carved oak chair.

After a preliminary cough, he began as follows—"This little business which the earl, your grandfather, is so anxious to get settled, is at present in *status quo*, the reason being the disinclination on the part of your ladyship to act in concert with his legal advisers, and I have, therefore, my dear madam, taken upon myself the not very pleasant task of seeing you on the subject."

"I am very glad to see you at all times, Mr. Chicknell," said Aveline. "As a friend of our house, you are welcome."

"Ah, thank you!" returned the lawyer, not very well liking her manner. "I felt assured that I should be. We cannot get on without your co-operation—indeed we cannot. Ahem! it's no use attempting to disguise that."

He laughed as if he had said something remarkably pleasant and witty. Aveline only nodded.

"It's like driving a bent nail in an oak plank," murmured Chicknell; "but no matter;" he then went on, addressing himself to the lady. "You see—ahem!—

I have felt it a duty incumbent on me to learn your wishes with regard to the pending suit from your own lips. Am I right when I say that it was first instituted with your full consent?"

"Certainly not. I never did give my consent."

"Dear me, that's most unfortunate; but as we have proceeded thus far, I presume you won't offer any opposition. You certainly ought not to do so."

"Indeed! I claim to be the best judge in this matter, and do not care to be made a mere puppet in the hands of others. Pray, why ought I to give my consent?"

"Well, as your ladyship has put the question so plainly, I am bound to answer it. In the first place, I do not think you would be justified in opposing Earl Ethalwood's expressed wishes, and in the next"—he paused——

"And in the next," cried Aveline.

"You are quite justified in getting rid of a man who has brought such discredit on you and yours."

Aveline rose from her seat, her eyes flashing with indignation, and her whole manner was indicative of the most violent emotion.

"And pray, Mr. Chicknell," said she, "who has deputed you to make such a statement? In what way has my husband brought discredit on me and mine? I have yet to learn that he has done aught to disgrace either himself or me."

"You must pardon me, madam," said the lawyer, in no way moved by the anger of his companion. "It is, to say the truth, no pleasant task I have undertaken; and allow me to say that if it is repugnant to you to hear the truth I will remain silent, and never again allude to a subject which is evidently most painful to you. We professional gentlemen have, at times, very unpleasant revelations to make, but I would not—nay, nothing could induce me to press a question which, possibly, you have no desire to hear."

"I do not quite understand you, sir. But you have my full permission to proceed. Pray go on."

"My dear young lady," said Chicknell, in oleaginous accents, "you must learn the truth. Your husband is living in open adultery with a woman of more than doubtful repute. That fact is established. We have indubitable proof of it."

Aveline turned pale, trembled slightly, and sank into a chair.

She made, however, no reply.

"You have heard what I have said?" said the lawyer, in continuation. "Indubitable proofs! If you doubt this I will bring an officer who will convince you of the fact."

Still no reply.

"Mr. Gatliffe is, at the present time, living with a lady of the name of Laura Stanbridge."

"He must be strangely altered," said Aveline—"so altered that I find it difficult to believe that he should have so far forgotten himself."

"We are dealing with facts," returned the lawyer; "facts which have come to our knowledge by chance or accident. Nevertheless, such facts are quite incontrovertible. We have the clearest and most unanswerable evidence of your husband's guilty intercourse with the woman Stanbridge, and I presume my word will suffice for the purpose, without entering into all the painful details."

Aveline leaned forward, placed her elbow on the table, and, burying her face in her hands, she burst into a passionate flood of tears. Her hysterical sobs touched the heart of the lawyer, who placed his hand kindly on one of her shoulders, and standing over her, said in a sympathetic tone of voice:

"My dear Lady Aveline, I cannot express to you the sorrow I feel at seeing you thus borne down. Believe me, nothing but the imperative necessity of making the revelation has induced me to be thus outspoken. I had no other alternative left, and have been constrained to enter thus fully into this business. Do, pray, try and bear up, and meet the case with becoming fortitude."

"You have said enough, Mr. Chicknell. You have convinced me. I feel hurt. My pride is wounded, but I shall not offer any opposition to the proceedings you have taken at the instigation of the earl, my grandfather. Release me as speedily as possible from this odious bondage. I desire to be disunited from a man who is so utterly unworthy of my consideration."

"Do not think that I have sought you for the purpose of maligning the man who is at the present moment your lawful husband. He is not worthy of such a distinction. I say this most emphatically—he is not worthy of even a passing thought."

"Enough, sir," interrupted the unhappy wife. "It is hardly worth while pouring out your vials of wrath upon him. It will suffice for our purpose that you bring the suit to as speedy a termination as possible."

"It shall be done, madam, as speedily as possible. Do not let this unfortunate business cause you any anxiety. Be of good cheer, and look hopefully to the future. Remember you are surrounded by friends who are deeply concerned in your happiness and future welfare. You will, I am sure, do me the justice to believe that I have your interest at heart, and that at all times you may rely upon, not only my advice, but upon my warmest and most disinterested friendship."

"I do not doubt it, Mr. Chicknell," said Aveline, drying her eyes. "And so you know now your course of action. Accept my best thanks."

They shook hands, and the lawyer took his departure, very well satisfied with the result of the interview.

In the course of a few weeks the divorce was obtained without opposition on the part of Gatliffe, and Lord Ethalwood felicitated himself upon the fulfilment of the crowning wish of his life.

CHAPTER LXXXVII.

PEACE'S DISCHARGE FROM PRISON—THE RETURN HOME.

WE must pass over the period of Peace's incarceration as a convict, and take up his history from the time of his discharge.

As the long-looked-for day began to approach the prisoner, as is usual in such cases, was permitted to grow his hair.

Three months' permission is given for this purpose; the regular once-a-week "clip" is no longer insisted on, and the prisoner has become what in common parlance is termed "a permission man."

As the weeks pass by the hair grows. Peace had never at any time an abundant crop, and at this period he was nearly bald. Nevertheless, the few straggling hairs he had left were suffered to grow their full length.

One fine morning No. 8642 (George Parker, seven years') was called out on parade. Peace fell out when he heard these welcome words. He was marched before a principal warder and the governor, and interviewed as to his intentions on discharge.

He was asked kindly enough by the governor where he was going to take his discharge to? What occupation he thought of following? If he had a wife, or family, or friends?

Peace said he was desirous of returning to his native town, Sheffield, in which place he had a wife.

A kindly admonition as to his future good conduct was given by the governor, who informed him that a gratuity would be given him upon the day of his release.

But a certain ceremony had to be gone through. Peace was drafted off with a batch of other permissive men to the photographers' room, where the whole party had their cartes de visite taken.

On the Saturday morning preceding the day of liberation, another ceremony had to be gone through. The prisoner is taken to the store-room, called the tailors' cutting-room; here he has to change his clothes, his prison garb is taken off, and, in its stead, a suit of clothes is furnished him, in which he is to enter the world again.

Peace was glad enough to have a new rig out, after which he was marched off by a prison official to an open space of ground adjoining the gaol; at this place some fifteen or twenty persons were assembled. This assembly of persons consisted chiefly of the detective police, who inspect minutely the man who is about to be discharged.

Peace bowed to the throng of detectives, who made some jocular remarks, the nature of which our hero understood but too well. "Ah, I see, No. 8642, name George Parker, sentence seven years."

"Yes, sir," returned Peace; "that's quite correct."

"Convicted of burglary, sent here from Millbank?"

"Yes."

"Where are you going when you obtain your discharge?"

"To Sheffield."

"Well, you will have to report yourself every month; don't forget that, Parker; if you do, you'll get into trouble."

"I won't forget, sir"

"Good."

"Have you a business?"

"Certainly."

"What is it?"

"I am a picture-frame maker by trade."

"And a burglar by profession, eh?" and at this sally the speaker and his companions burst out into a hearty laugh.

"I've been in trouble, as you all know," cried Peace, in an angry tone; "but that is no reason for my being jeered at. When a man's down kick him is an old saying."

"Well, then, we'll say no more about it," said the officer. "I didn't know you were so thin-skinned. Take my advice, stick to your business, and don't get into trouble again."

"Thank you, I will remember your warning. I will not get into trouble again."

After this Peace was fitted with a pair of boots, and his outfit, if it could be so termed, was now complete. He was informed that he would be presented with a gratuity of three pounds before he went out of the prison.

Any sum would be, of course, acceptable to begin the world again with. Three pounds is not a large capital, it must be admitted, but it is better than nothing.

In the due course of time Peace received a visit from the stewards' clerk, his object being to obtain our hero's signature on a stamped receipt for the whole of the munificent gratuity, and his signature also to several forms which he has to sign without revealing the contents of the aforesaid forms. This is a matter of no very great moment, for if he did peruse them the probability is that he would not be much the wiser.

PEACE RUSHES FORWARD AND MAKES A FULL BUTT AT MR. DYSON.

After this ceremony had been gone through the clerk handed Peace a copy of "Her Majesty's license to go at large during the remaining portion of his term of penal servitude," in which her Majesty hereby orders George Parker, within thirty days from the date of this order to report himself, which is signed by the Home Secretary or his deputy.

This licence is given subject to the conditions endorsed on the document, upon the breach of any of which it shall be liable to be revoked, whether such conduct is followed by conviction or not. The conditions are of course very stringent; nevertheless, they are but too frequently evaded or broken despite the surveillance of the police. The reader will understand this when

No. 46.

he is informed that the conditions are as follows:—
"The holder shall preserve his licence and produce it when called upon to do so by a magistrate or police officer." This for his own safety he generally does. "He shall abstain from any violation of the law." This he does not always do, for ticket-of-leave men are constantly getting into trouble through lawless acts. "He shall not habitually associate with notoriously bad characters, such as reputed thieves or prostitutes."

It frequently happens—more frequently than otherwise—that licence men do associate with disreputable characters.

"He shall not lead an idle, dissolute life without visible means of obtaining a livelihood."

Most discharged convicts profess to have some honest calling, or a "stall" they term it, and it is putting too fine a point on the matter to dispute this fact for the police, in most instances, are well aware that the business or calling which these men profess to follow, is nothing more than a mere sham, but it is out of their power to prove this.

If his licence is forfeited or revoked in consequence of a conviction for any offence, he shall be made to undergo a term of penal servitude equal to the portion of his term which remains unexpired when his licence was granted.

We have discussed the question of licences, or men let out on ticket-of-leave, in a former chapter of this work.

"The ticket-of-leave men," as they are termed, have been an endless source of trouble to the honest citizen and the police, and, as we pointed out, the whole system wants remodelling.

Another printed paper was handed to Peace which had superscribed on it his name and number. After this the following admonition was given:—

"Take notice, you are required by Act of Parliament to report yourself to the chief police-station of the locality to which you may go, within forty-eight hours of your arrival therein, and if you change your residence from one police district to another, you must report it to the police-station to which you last reported yourself, before you go. If you omit any of the above particulars, you will be guilty of a misdemeanour, and upon conviction will forfeit your licence."

Peace was duly impressed with the importance of the document handed to him, which, however, he did not attempt to read.

After he had partaken of the dinner ration served to him, the cell door was unlocked for the Scripture-reader. This gentleman turned to the convict with a benign smile, and said in a soft tone, "And so, Parker, I have to congratulate you that your day of release has arrived. It cannot fail to be most gladly welcomed by you."

"It is," returned our hero.

Peace's visitor handed him a Bible and prayer-book and said, "I hope you will profit by a careful study of these. I have as the rule dictates written your name, number, and date of your discharge inside the cover. These books are supplied to all convicts on discharge."

"I am very much obliged to you," said Peace, who, however, was by no means pleased with having books in his possession with a record of his discharge written therein; but he did not deem it advisable to make any comment on this.

"I hope you will lead a new life, and I am sure I am only echoing the sentiments of the gaol officials when I say we all wish you may prosper, so long as you keep in the right path."

"You are very good," said Peace, with a hypocritical whine which he knew so well how to put on.

The Scripture-reader after a few more remarks took his departure, and in the due course of time an orderly officer unlocked the door again and inquired if he was ready.

"I should just think I was," returned Peace, hurriedly finishing his liberty toilette.

"All right—come this way then," cried the officer.

Peace did not want a second bidding—he was soon outside the cell. The warder placed the hard round felt wide-a-wake on his head, and the truly wretched scarecrow, "her Majesty's licence-holder," was hurried to the entrance gates, where more signing was done, and the official copy of the "licence," signed by one of the directors of convict prisons, placed in his hand.

This was the last ceremony he had to go through. He found an officer in prison uniform waiting to conduct him to the railway station, and the wicket being at length unlocked, the ticket-of-leave man and his conductor passed through.

Peace was once more a free man!

As the two proceeded towards the railway station, jeers and remarks were made by several passengers, which were in no way complimentary to our hero, but convicts on release have to bear these indignities, which, to say the truth, they are subject to, both inside and outside the prison walls.

The officer in charge of Peace presented the governor's order, and obtained a ticket at the same rate as charged for soldiers.

The released convict had by this time regained his confidence. At the request of his conductor he entered the carriage.

The official did not leave him until the train was in motion.

While the train was at a standstill, he gave some excellent advice to his man—this is a way they have—good advice costs nothing—and it may be of service or not—in most cases it has but little effect upon the man to whom it is offered so unsparingly. The officer's last words to Peace were, "Keep in the right path for the future, and mind you report yourself in accordance to the instructions."

"All right! Thank you, sir. Farewell!" cried Peace, who was whirled along at the rate of thirty miles an hour.

After the train had started the passengers began to speak.

They conversed on the weather, the news of the morning's papers.

One passenger, more curious than the rest and who was struck by the uniform of the officer, asked Peace if he belonged to one of the volunteer regiments.

Our hero endeavoured to evade the question by professing ignorance, but his questioner was pertinacious, and so the released convict was constrained to be more communicative.

He told his companion in the train the real state of the case—that he was a convict on release.

This piece of information caused some consternation. The eyes of every person in the carriage were scrutinising the speaker, upon whom they cast glances of suspicion.

Thoughts of robberies and murders flitted through their brains, and they, most of them, shifted their positions and placed their hands on their pockets.

"Dear me, how very remarkable!" exclaimed an old gentleman in the corner. "How singular! I did not know—ahem!—that persons of your class were permitted to travel in carriages occupied by respectable people."

"I'll get out at the next station and go into another carriage if you wish it," remarked Peace.

"Certainly not! We don't wish anything of the sort," observed a broad-shouldered man, who, to all appearance, was, what is termed metaphorically, a "son of Neptune." "At least I don't."

"Nor I!" cried another. "Sit where you are, my man."

"I'm glad you are at liberty again, and hope the trouble you have been through will be a lesson to you, and teach you that honesty is the best policy."

"I don't intend to get into trouble again," echoed Peace.

"Well said!"

The train rattles on, but despite these assurances some of the passengers are ill at ease.

The females bestow compassionate glances at Peace, whose costume causes him to be a marked man; it is in every respect so different to that worn by the other occupants of the carriage.

When the train stopped the old gentleman and two or three others in the carriage discovered that a change would be desirable.

They leave their seats and hurry forward and ensconce themselves in another compartment.

It is pretty plainly demonstrated to him that his room is liked better than his company; or, in other words, he is a man to be avoided.

"All right," murmured Peace. "This is the usual course of things; and what a man has to submit to with the best grace he can. But it does not much matter. I'll soon cast off this precious outfit and make up for a gentleman, and then nobody will be any the wiser."

Before reaching Sheffield, Peace found his wife, his mother and son-in-law awaiting his approach.

The meeting was, of course, an affectionate one, and our hero, with three pounds in his pocket, returned once more to his humble home, where he had "a bit of a jollification," as he termed it, and an indent was made in the three pounds he had brought with him.

CHAPTER LXXXVIII.

PEACE'S LATER CAREER—THE WHALLEY RANGE MURDER.

AFTER his return from penal servitude he followed his trade of picture-frame maker with renewed assiduity. He was very careful to duly report himself at the police station in the district, in which he resided, and it appears from all we can gather that the police treated him generally with the greatest consideration, and never hunted him down as it is termed. Indeed, they had a great reluctance to expose him or interfere in any way with him while following his ordinary avocation.

We have but little to chronicle in respect to Charles Peace from the time of his release up to the year 1876.

Presumably he was following an honest course of life, but we fear this was supplemented by occasional acts of dishonesty and depredation.

He, however, managed to steer clear of the law; and no conviction or even suspicion fell upon him till the year referred to.

It is said that for a short period he opened a provision shop in Hull, and that he left that town suddenly, for what reason does not transpire. After this he was again a picture-frame maker in Darnall.

We now propose following up the record of his career in something like consecutive order that the reader may fully comprehend the events which ultimately led to his conviction upon the charge of murder.

We have it from reliable authorities that at the time of the Banner-Cross murder, his mother—Mrs. Jane Peace—lived in Orchard-street, Sheffield, and she had not seen her son Charles—who by the way was her favourite son—for two years, on account of a difference arising out of his taking Mrs. Dyson to her house one night in 1874.

The precise date at which his intimacy with Mrs. Dyson commenced does not transpire.

Mrs. Dyson, herself, at the Leeds Assizes, spoke to Peace having lived next door but one to her and her husband when they resided in Britannia-road, Darnall, in the earlier part of 1876.

She knew him as a picture-frame maker, and he used to visit the Dysons, and had been, if he was not actually then, on terms of undisputed intimacy with the woman whose husband he afterwards murdered.

Before following the clue to this murder, we must give a brief record of another crime of a similar nature, which happened in the same year.

Without doubt Peace continued his lawless depredations to a great extent while residing at Darnall.

The Whalley Range murder caused great popular excitement.

An innocent man was convicted and was cast for death. He escaped suffering the extreme sentence of the law by almost a miracle.

At the time of the occurrence Peace was there to "work" some houses. He went to a place called Whalley Range.

He had "spotted" a house which he thought he could get into without much trouble.

He was always respectably dressed, so he declared, for he made a point of dressing respectably, and for this reason he knew the police never think of suspecting one who appears in good clothes.

In this way he threw the police off their guard on many occasions.

On the night of the fatal occurrence Charles Peace, in an easy, careless, jaunty manner, walked leisurely through the streets of Manchester.

He had not at this time his friend Bandy-legged Bill with him, or indeed any other accomplice; but he was a self-reliant man, whose object was to pick up what he could without the aid of a confederate.

While walking through the streets in Manchester he occasionally went between policemen, who were exercising their brains as to the burglar who had "done" some houses there.

Peace laughed in his sleeve. He knew the real culprit, but said nothing.

He took his way towards the house he designed to work, and as he went along he passed two policemen on the road.

"I may tell you," says he, in his confession, "I did not go to any house by accident; I always went some days, sometimes weeks before, carefully examining all the surroundings, and then, having 'spotted' a likely house, I studied the neighbourhood both as to the means of getting in and as to getting away."

He walked boldly on until he arrived at the house which was to be the scene of his operation.

The house stood in its own grounds, which were inclosed by a wall, and in some parts a shrubbery.

When the sun shone, and nature was in her best mood, it was most picturesque and lightsome, but in the dead hours of the night it was singularly dreary. This, however, did not matter to Peace, who was bent upon "cracking the crib," as he termed it.

Upon arriving at the place of his destination, he considered for a few moments, and then determined upon his plan of action.

His object was to get into the grounds which surrounded the habitation in the dusk of the evening, and then wait a convenient time to effect an entrance into the house.

There were policemen about whom Peace managed to dodge for a time.

They had, however, observed him, and were, in consequence, on the watch.

This fact he was not aware of; had he been so, the chances are that he would not have made any attempt on the house that night.

He, however, walked into the grounds through the gate, and before he was able to begin his operations, he heard a step and a rustling behind him. He became suddenly alarmed, and turned sharply round, when, to his dismay, he beheld a policeman, whose figure was the same as one of the two he had passed on the road. The constable in question was making the best of his way into the grounds.

He had evidently seen Peace, turned back, and followed.

Peace came to the conclusion that he could not work that night. He therefore doubled, to elude the constable.

For a moment he succeeded, and taking a favourable opportunity, he endeavoured to make his escape.

With surprising agility he sprang up on the top of the wall which inclosed the grounds, but a fresh misfortune now befel him.

As he was dropping down and had cleared the premises, he almost fell into the arms of a second policeman, who must have been planted in the expectation that he would escape that way.

The policeman made a grab at our hero, who was by this time driven to a state of desperation, for he was under the impression that he would be captured, and then his previous convictions would be brought against him, and he would be sent to penal servitude again.

Peace was nettled that he had been disturbed, and his blood was up and all his worst passions in the ascendant, for he had "spotted" the house for a long time, and it had been a favourite project of his to rifle it of its most valuable and portable contents.

"You stand back, or I'll shoot you!" cried Peace, in a voice of concentrated rage.

But the ill-fated young man was brave, and bent upon doing his duty—such officers are a credit to the force, and cannot be too highly commended—but alas! the poor fellow paid a fearful penalty for his gallant conduct.

He would not stand back and let the burglar pass, so Peace stepped back a few yards and fired wide at him, for the purpose of frightening him; but the brave young fellow was not to be intimidated.

Peace, in his whining hypocritical confession, declared—

"That he had a great repugnance to taking human life. I never wanted to murder anybody. I only wanted to do what I came to do and to get away."

Amiable man!

"But it does seem odd after all that I should have to be hanged for having taken life, the very thing I always endeavoured to avoid. I have never willingly or knowingly hurt a living creature. I would not even hurt an animal, much less a man. That is why I fired wide at him. But the policeman, like most Manchester policemen, was a determined man. They are a very obstinate lot, those Manchester policemen. He was no

doubt as determined as I was myself, and you know when I am put to it I can do what very few men can do."

This is Peace's own account of the encounter.

After he had fired wide at the ill-fated young man, Cock, the latter seized hold of his staff, and was evidently bent on capturing the ruffian. He rushed at Peace, whom he was about to strike.

The burglar now saw that he had no time to lose. He was determined not to be captured, and was bent on effecting his escape at all hazards, even if it was at the sacrifice of human life.

He discharged another barrel of his revolver, in the hopes of disabling the arm of the officer, who held the staff.

The ball entered the unfortunate man's breast, and the poor fellow, with a deep groan, fell to the earth.

Peace managed to make his escape.

Policeman Cock had received his death wound, the bleeding from which was chiefly internal.

His comrades came to his assistance and raised him up, but he was in such acute agony that he begged of them to leave him alone.

He was, however, removed, and very shortly afterwards breathed his last.

Peace got clear off, and no one for a moment suspected that he had any hand in the murder.

Suspicion fell upon some young men in the neighbourhood—the brothers Habron. The police, when once they have fixed their minds upon any theory as to the guilt of a person or persons, cling to it with the utmost pertinacity.

The Habrons were aroused from their beds on the fatal night, soon after the commission of the crime of murder.

They slept in a cottage or shed which stood on the grounds, where they worked as gardeners or agricultural labourers, the brothers being in the service of a Mr. Deakin.

William Habron, it was suggested, had threatened to shoot Policeman Cock if he did anything to either him or his brothers; and it was moreover alleged that he had on many occasions displayed great animosity towards the deceased. So the police were under the impression that he was the guilty person.

The trial took place in August, 1876.

The principal, perhaps the only, points condemnatory of William Habron when tried were—firstly, his threats uttered against the unfortunate officer; secondly, his going to the shop of Mr. Moore in order to ask the price of a revolver, and of some ball cartridges; thirdly, that a man wearing a certain shaped coat and hat, similar to those worn by Habron, was seen by two persons near the scene of the murder; and, lastly, the footprint which corresponded with Habron's left boot.

These facts, though circumstantially bearing upon the case in the eyes and minds of the police authorities—eyes that were absolutely prepared, before a single examination took place, to look upon the brothers Habron as the guilty parties—were still too flimsy to any unprejudiced mind to form any solid foundation for placing a man's life in jeopardy, unless well supported by far more grave and weighty evidence.

Indeed, Mr. Justice Lopes, in his charge to the grand jury, pointed out that no firearms had been found in possession of the prisoners, that there was no evidence against John Habron at all, and the only evidence that could be adduced against William was that of wearing a dress similar to that seen, on a dark night, by some persons near the spot, his having used threats, the footprints, and his inquiry for cartridges which he did not purchase.

Mr. Justice Lopes would evidently have not been astonished had the grand jury ignored the bill.

Before commenting on the evidence brought forward under the supervision of Superintendent Bent, it would be just as well to mention one important speech of that officer's, which forms a key at once to his whole working of the case.

He says, " On hearing of the murder I immediately suspected the Habrons."

That Cock was foully murdered none, of course, could doubt; but who fired the fatal shot could not fail to be a matter of serious doubt to any person who read the particulars of the affair in the daily papers whilst the sad event was under investigation.

F. Wilson, a witness on the trial, deposed that John Habron told him that if ever the " Little Bobby " (their nick-name for Cook) did anything to either him or his brother he would *shoot* him.

Mrs. Carter, wife of the landlord of the " Royal Oak," said that if the said " Little Bobby " did not stop persecuting him and his brother, they would *shunt* him through their " gaffer," Mr. Deakin, as he would not be the first policeman they had shunted.

Mrs. Fox gave evidence that John Habron (who was under the necessity of appearing at the police-court on the Monday, to answer the charge of drunk and disorderly conduct, preferred by the deceased) said to her, " If he does me to-day I'll do him on Wednesday."

James Brownhill deposed to John's threats to shoot the officer.

The savage threats made by the acquitted John, and the expression used by William, must have been, to say the least of it, frightfully overrated to bear a construction of murder, and yet that construction was put upon it the result of the trial of this ill-used young man shows.

The next point which was supposed to bear upon the guilt of William Habron is that of his having gone to the shop of Mr. Moore, the ironmonger, to ask the price of and to examine some ball-cartridges (the revolvers were brought out and shown him by the shopman, M'Clelland, unasked for).

Here the witness cannot swear whether it was on Monday or Tuesday the transaction occurred.

But he swore to the man, although he had probably never seen him before in his life, nor, in the ordinary way of business, would he take any more notice of him than he would of any other casual customer.

And, moreover, the other servants in the shop, although having had the same facilities of recognition, did not think it the same man, and declined to confirm M'Clelland's statement.

In addition to this, he neither purchased cartridges nor pistol; so that the visit to Mr. Moore's shop, as a piece of evidence, even if made by Habron, is of no value whatever.

The little item of finding two percussion caps, introduced by Superintendent Bent, was evidently a superfluity, as Mr. Deakin, the employer of Habron, says the caps might easily have been in the waistcoat pocket when he gave it to Habron, as he had been using his gun just before, and had probably put some caps in the pocket.

The actual bullet extracted from the body of the unfortunate policeman was pronounced by an experienced gunsmith to have been fired from a No. 442 pinfire cartridge, which was the largest size but one then made.

The third standpoint in the case made out against William Habron is that of dress and general appearance, which bore a similarity to the dress and general appearance of the man seen near the scene of the murder by two witnesses.

J. M. Simpson, who had been walking and conversing with the deceased, had only just left him when he met this man; he described him as an elderly man, and declared that he walked with a stooping gait.

Police-constable Beanland, whose evidence was perhaps the most important, under present circumstances, in the whole case, said that the man was about twenty-two years of age, and walked quite erect; and from general appearance he thought it must have been William Habron.

The man under notice, says Beanland, went along Seymour-grove to Mr. Greatorex's gate, and he there lost sight of him; and on going to the gate he found it open. He went in at the gate, and examined Mr. Greatorex's premises, but found all right, and then heard two shots, and found the deceased on the ground at West Point.

We next come to that conclusive evidence of Habron's guilt as established by Superintendent Bent —the footprints.

He deposed to the examination of the footprints with great exactitude.

He was totally unable to count the nails in the outside row as they were so closely together, but on the inside row they were thicker nails in one line, and the same number of indentations were visible in the footprints; and there were two middle rows of nails and two nails in the toe; the heel iron was worn, and there were three nails in it.

That Mr. Justice Lindley did not think the evidence conclusive against William Habron, the following conclusion to his summing up will testify. He said:— " With regard to William Habron, was there any evidence that he was on the spot where the murder was committed on the night in question? There was the evidence, such as it was, of the witness Simpson and Police-constable Beanland, and they had the evidence of the footprints, and he asked them to satisfy themselves that the impression was the impression of William's left boot. If they were of opinion such impression was not that of William they would have but little difficulty in dealing with the case. If they were, on the contrary, satisfied the impression was made by William's boot, then came the next question.—What other evidence is there to show when it was made? For that was a serious conclusion for them to make, because, according to the evidence for the defence, he could not have been there the day previously; and the question was, the print would not have been there if not made recently. He then reviewed the evidence in their favour : Firstly, they were of good character. Secondly, when arrested they were where they ought to have been—in bed. Third, no trace of firearms had been found."

After the verdict the learned judge did not, as is usual, express his concurrence in the jury's opinion, but simply said— " You have been found guilty of murdering Nicholas Cock, and it is my duty to pass sentence upon you," and again, a few moments after, " I shall simply discharge my duty by passing sentence upon you."

Notwithstanding the doubt existing after the trial and sentence as to Habron's guilt he had a narrow chance of being hanged, and he would certainly have been doomed to penal servitude for life had not Peace, in a fit of remorse, told the truth about the whole business while under sentence of death in Armley gaol.

Peace had the audacity and hardihood to be present at the trial of William Habron, and looked complacently on while an innocent man was being condemned to death for a crime he (Peace) had committed.

"Some time afterwards," observed Peace, "I saw it announced in the papers that certain men had been taken into custody for the murder of the policeman Cock. That greatly interested me. I always had a liking to be present at trials, as the public no doubt know by this time, and I determined to be present at this trial. I left Hull for Manchester for two days, not telling my family where I had gone, and attended the assizes at Manchester for two days, and heard the youngest of the brothers, as I was told he was, sentenced to death. The sentence was afterwards commuted to penal servitude for life. Now some people say that I was a hardened wretch for allowing an innocent man to suffer for the crime of which I was guilty; but what man could have gone and given himself up under such circumstances, knowing as I did that I should certainly be hanged for the crime?"

CHAPTER LXXXIX.
CHARLES PEACE AND THE DYSONS.

EVERYBODY will agree with us when we declare that Peace's acquaintance with the Dysons is altogether incomprehensible.

How he managed to force himself upon these two persons, how he contrived to have so strong a hold on Mrs. Dyson, appears to be the strangest and most inexplicable part of his career.

He persecuted her with a pertinacity which was almost unparalleled.

Whether he was really attached to her it is not possible to say, but it must be admitted that his conduct at this time was more like that of a madman than of a rational being.

Mr. Dyson, the ill-fated gentleman who was murdered in 1876 by the miscreant Peace, was married in 1866 at Cleveland, Ohio, and took a house at Finsbury. From thence he removed to Highfield, afterwards to Heeley, and again to Darnall, and from Darnall they moved to Banner-cross-terrace.

There is just a short period of the history and phase in the existence of Mr. Arthur Dyson after his arrival in this country from America, says a fellow countryman of his, which may not be uninteresting. Soon after his arrival he made application to the resident engineer of the North-Eastern Railway Company at York for employment as a civil engineer and surveyor, and his credentials were of such a character that an engagement was entered into with him. The character of his occupation in America led to the anticipation that he would be able to find "his way about here," and that in fact his services might prove to be of a most useful character.

On presenting himself for the purpose of commencing his duties, his personal appearance was the source of considerable curiosity and surprise amongst the remainder of the officials in the engineer's office.

He was extremely thin and singularly tall, measuring over six feet; and he wore a low felt hat, as he afterwards explained to one of the staff, for the purpose of abstracting from his great height and from the observation which it had led to amongst those with whom he had to associate.

He cut a singular figure when engaged in his occasional duties as a draughtsman at the table which was general to the rest of the staff, and to mitigate the inconvenience which must have attended his tallness in the performance of this part of his duties, some special arrangements were made by which he might be able to keep a more upright position. Despite his great height, he is described as being as "straight as a poplar."

The general bearing of Mr. Dyson was that of a gentleman, and whether in conversation or written communication with those around him, he never bent from this position, and, as a consequence, commanded general respect.

When he took his engagement in York, he dated from the Firs, near Rotherham, where he said that his wife was residing; and whilst he remained in the ancient city he lodged with a Mr. Waddington, of Holgate-lane.

He was engaged there for only about two months, much of the time being occupied in surveying various stations on the York and Whitby line.

He had at last been sent for this purpose to Grosmont Station, and as after his departure, as it was expected, for that place, nothing was heard of him for a fortnight, inquiry was made at Grosmont, and it was found that he had not been there.

This led to an intimation being sent to him at the address near Rotherham that his return to duty was not required, and to the termination of his engagement with the North-Eastern Railway Company.

Peculiarity was noticed about the unfortunate gentleman, which gave rise at the time to the impression that something preyed upon his mind, and he on more than one occasion, in intimating to one of his superiors a desire that he should be allowed weekly to visit his wife, hinted that he suffered from some domestic trouble.

What the nature of this domestic trouble was it is not easy to say.

Possibly it might be in some way connected with the mischievous, tormenting little rascal, Peace.

While the Dysons were at Darnall Peace was a frequent visitor at their house.

Mr. Dyson, for some considerable time after his first becoming acquainted with our hero, conceived a certain amount of partiality for him, and, in consequence of this, Peace soon became on intimate terms with both husband and wife; his connection with the latter has never been clearly established.

It is, however, quite certain that his attentions to Mrs. Dyson were most marked and persistent.

She went about with him to various places of amusement, and was with him also at the Sheffield summer fair, 1876, and also to several public-houses—this was proved at the magisterial examination.

This familiarity with Peace greatly annoyed Mr. Dyson, who was a discreet, equably-disposed, well-conducted man.

He was greatly incensed at his wife's intimacy with our hero, and as time went on he spoke his mind pretty plainly, but Peace was not a man to be snubbed easily—he openly defied Mr. Dyson, and continued his persecutions of his erratic wife.

It is certain that for a considerable period he had a powerful hold of her—not of her affections perhaps, but her vanity was such that she continued on friendly terms with him long after her husband had expressed his dislike to the man.

One afternoon she had been with him to his brother's public-house, where, it appears, there were singing and dancing.

She bent her steps in the direction of Darnall. Peace insisted on accompanying her, and as the pair were proceeding along they came in sight of a well-known roadside inn, with a garden in its front; here they stopped and had some refreshment.

"It's no use your thinking of giving me the cut, old woman," said Peace. "I'll stick to you while I've life, and I'm not going to be shunted."

"I wish you'd hold your tongue, or, at any rate, not speak so loud," cried his companion. "I never met with such a man in all my life."

"I am devotedly attached to you, and you know it," whispered Peace; "and nothing in the world shall make me give you up."

"You are talking like a fool."

"No matter about that—I'm saying what I mean. I tell you again, I won't be cast off. I love you too well for that. Do you hear?"

"I hear, of course; but I have a kind good husband, and must not listen to your nonsense."

"It is not nonsense—it is the solemn truth. You don't know what sort of man you have to deal with. I would give up everything for your sake. Can a man say fairer than that?"

"I don't want you to give up anything for my sake. All I want is for you to keep at a respectful distance."

"Then I won't do anything of the sort," cried Peace, in a fury, and making such a hideous grimace that his companion was frightened.

"I won't—not for you or any one else," he repeated in a louder tone.

"Do, for goodness' sake, mind what you are saying," murmured his companion.

"I do mind, and I hope you do also. I tell you again, I won't give you up. We've been companions and friends for a long time, and it is not because your stately, mighty big fellow of a husband has taken a dislike to me that our friendship is to cease. Listen; I've got a good lump of money, and it will be yours if you'll only consent to fly with me."

The woman burst out into a loud laugh.

"Fly with you!" she exclaimed. "You must be mad to make such a proposition. No, no, my friend; I know what is right and proper."

"I'll make you do so," he exclaimed, making another grimace, and regarding her with a malicious grin, which was more like that of a satyr than a human being.

He caught her by the arm, which he pinched with savage grip.

"Leave go!" she ejaculated. "What have I done that you should treat me thus?"

"I'll never leave you, never give you up as long as I have life," he returned.

"Oh! you tormenting man! I will not remain with you any longer."

"You shall!" he returned quickly. "You shan't leave; I won't let you. Don't think to get the better of me, my lady. You shan't go."

Mrs. Dyson gave utterance to a faint scream, when, to the surprise of her and her pertinacious companion, Mr. Dyson came in front of the arbour in which they were seated.

"What is the matter?" he inquired. Then, for the first time, catching sight of Peace, he said, in a tone of anger—

"How is it I find you, sir, annoying my wife again? I must request you to abstain from this unseemly conduct. If you do not, I shall take means to prevent you."

"Shut up!" cried Peace, "and mind your own business. This is a public place, and as such, I have as much right to be here as you have. So shut up, I say."

"You are an impertinent fellow," said Mr. Dyson, seizing him by the collar, and dragging him forcibly from the alcove, "and deserve a thrashing."

Peace slipped deftly from the grasp of his assailant,

and retiring back for some little distance, he bent down his head, and rushed forward, making a full butt at him.

The attack was so sudden and unexpected, that Mr. Dyson fell to the ground with considerable force, and was for the space of a few minutes utterly powerless and prostrated.

One of the waiters of the establishment came to his assistance, helped him up, and there was a general expression of surprise and disgust at the cowardly action. A search was made for Peace, who had however, deemed it prudent to beat a retreat.

He was nowhere to be found.

"The contemptible, despicable little wretch!" exclaimed Mr Dyson. "The spiteful, malicious scoundrel!"

"He is the torment of our lives, dear," returned Mrs. Dyson. "Oh, I do wish we could find means of being rid of the ruffian."

"I'll get a summons against him, and punish him, as he deserves to be punished."

"That's the best plan, sir," observed the landlord. "There are plenty of witnesses who can speak to the assault."

"The man is our evil genius, I do believe," said Mr. Dyson. "I have thought so for some time. He has been the bane of our existence, and has caused us more anxiety and trouble than I can at the present moment describe. He's a most venomous creature."

"He's a reptile, that's what he is!" cried Mrs. Dyson. "But, never mind, dear, we can take measures to bring him to justice."

Mr. and Mrs. Dyson returned home; the former was greatly disgusted with Peace's conduct, and upbraided his wife for having consented to be his companion. The latter offered every possible excuse, and said that it was no fault of hers, that she was afraid of him, that he was a dangerous designing man, who persecuted her in a manner which was altogether unaccountable.

In his reply to this Mr. Dyson said she must have given him some encouragement, or he never would be so pertinacious.

After a wrangle Mr. Dyson left the house and proceeded in the direction of the line where his services were required, and his wife strove to calm herself as best she could.

Evening came on, and as she sat at her toilette in one of the upstairs rooms of her domicile, she was suddenly aroused by some sand or gravel being thrown violently against the window panes of her bedroom.

She looked out and beheld Peace at the side of the house.

"What do you want now?" cried she, opening the window.

"You," he returned, whereupon he threw a pebble stone, round which a piece of paper was wrapped, into the open casement.

"Go about your business; I will have nothing to say to you," said Mrs. Dyson.

"Won't you? I know better than that. Read!"

She unfolded the paper, and read its contents, which were as follows:—

"Don't flatter yourself that you can elude me. I am here, as you see, again. Come down, or it will be worse for you."

"Go away!" said Mrs. Dyson, looking out. "I don't want to have any conversation with you, and I positively refuse to come down."

"You do?" screamed Peace, making a face at her. "You refuse?"

"Most positively."

"I'll break into the house, and force you to hear me!" he cried, with a malicious grin. "You know enough of me that I am not likely to take such an answer. I will make you do what I wish."

"Oh, you horrible man!"

"Horrible—am I?" He drew a revolver from his pocket. "You will make me do something horrible if you don't mind," he ejaculated.

"I'll call my husband, and let him answer you," returned Mrs. Dyson.

"Your husband, the poor fool!" said Peace, in a jeering tone. "Do you think I am to be deceived? Your husband is far away. But if he were at home it would be much the same. Come down and let me in."

The wretched woman was so alarmed, that she went down from the upper room and opened the front door.

"For mercy's sake, Peace, do go away—there's a good fellow. I must not and will not have anything to say to you, after your cowardly conduct."

He tormentingly laughed at this last observation.

He placed one arm round her shoulders, drew her towards him, and endeavoured to embrace her.

She was a powerful woman, and struggled desperately to release herself from his grasp.

A violent struggle ensued, in which Mrs. Dyson struck Peace repeatedly with her clenched fist; but his perseverance was beyond all bounds.

He fought like a demon, and his conduct, taken altogether, was like that of a perfect madman.

How long the conflict would have continued, and what would have been its issue, it is not possible to say, had it not been for the unlooked-for assistance arriving.

A policeman, who happened to be passing, attracted Mrs. Dyson's attention. She called to him, and he at once came to the rescue.

"Take this man away," she said.

"Do you charge him?" inquired the constable.

"No. All I want of you is to take him away. Remove him from these premises."

"Now then, you sir," said the officer, "move on, or I'll lock you up."

He gave Peace a push, which sent him reeling.

"You keep your hands to yourself, and don't assault me," said he, "or I'll lodge a complaint against you; mind you that."

"Will you go? If you don't—well I shall know what to do."

"You're a big man in your own estimation, but a very little one in everybody else's," returned Peace, who, however, thought it best to get clear off; and so, making mocking gestures as he went along, he went his way without further ado.

It was a great relief to Mrs. Dyson when he was out of sight; but she was not at all certain about his returning shortly.

However, he did not trouble her again that night.

This attack, together with a variety of others of a similar nature, was the reason the Dysons had for leaving Darnall.

They took a house at Bannercross, to be farther removed from their tormentor.

The trouble and misery brought upon the Dysons by Peace is almost incalculable. We cannot do better than place before the reader Mrs. Dyson's own account of her connection with the murderer of her husband:—

"When we went to Darnall," said Mrs. Dyson, "our troubles began.

"But for our going there, Mr. Dyson would probably have been still alive, and I should have been spared all that has happened since.

"You will naturally ask how I became acquainted with Peace. It was impossible to avoid becoming acquainted with him.

"Besides, at that time I did not know the sort of man he really was. He lived the next door but one to us at Darnall, and he used generally to speak to Mr. Dyson on going in and out.

"Mr. Dyson was a gentleman, and, of course, when Peace spoke to him he used to reply.

"But Peace wasn't content with a merely speaking acquaintance. He wanted to force himself upon us. He did all he could until he succeeded in accomplishing this.

"One of his favourite means was to place his parrots and his other birds upon a wall. He would then call our attention to them, and to what they could do, and thus get us into conversation with him.

"Introduction! you say. No, there was no introduction. He introduced himself, and would have you to talk with him whether you would or no.

"At first Mr. Dyson did not object, and Peace became a constant visitor to the house.

"He was plausibility itself. To hear him talk you would have thought him the most harmless of men. I am certain that much which he has succeeded in doing, both before and after the murder, is the result of the power which he has been able to exercise by his tongue and manner.

"Of course, when we went to Darnall we did not know what he was. To us he appeared to be simply a picture-framer in anything but good circumstances, for he had but little business to do, and his wife used to go out every morning washing bottles.

"We considered they were poor. I am, of course, now speaking of the time when we first went to live at Darnall. Mr. Dyson soon began to tire of him. My husband had travelled much, and could converse well on many subjects.

"Peace was plausible enough, but his language was not good; in fact, he very soon began to show that he was anything but a gentleman. Mr. Dyson could not stand that; and, besides, he had seen something which disgusted him."

"Do you mind telling me what that was?"

"Well, it was some obscene pictures, and my husband said he didn't like a man of that kind, and wouldn't have anything more to do with him. Besides, another thing greatly repelled Mr. Dyson. It was this. Peace wanted to take him to Sheffield to show him what he called the 'sights of the town.'

"Mr. Dyson knew what that meant, and being, as I have said, a gentleman, he became much disgusted at Peace and annoyed that he should force his company upon us.

"My husband had been accustomed to different society. But we couldn't get rid of him. We were bound to show him common politeness. Though he must have seen that we didn't want his company, he forced himself upon us.

"He would, for instance, drop in just when we were sitting down to tea, and we were compelled almost to ask him to have a cup.

"His constant visits to the house at last became intolerable to us, and then it was that my husband placed his card in the garden, desiring Peace not to annoy him or his family.

"When he found that he could no longer gain access to the house, Peace became awfully impudent.

THE BANNERCROSS MURDER—PEACE THREATENING MRS. DYSON.

"He would, for instance, stand on the doorstep and listen through the keyhole to what we were talking about, or look through the window at us.

"His persecutions at this time became almost unbearable. He did everything he could to annoy us. I was not afraid of him, and should have taken the law into my own hands, but my husband would not

hear of such a thing. He always advised me to keep quiet.

"I could not stand his impudence and the way in which he went on. I had not been used to such society as his proved to be, and I rebelled against it. I can hardly describe all that he did to annoy us after he was informed that he was not wanted at our house.

"He would come and stand outside the window at night and look in, leering all the while; and he would come across you at all turns and leer in your face in a manner that was truly frightful.

"His object was to obtain power over me, and having done that, to make me an accomplice of his. I have told you that when I knew him first I thought him to be a picture-framer, and nothing more. Since then, however, I have learnt a good deal, and much that was difficult to understand has been made plain. He wanted me to leave my husband! Positively to leave my husband.

"'What should I do that for?' I said.

"'If you will only go to Manchester,' he answered, 'I will take a store (American for shop) for you, and will spend £50 in fitting it up. You shall have a cigar store, or a picture store. You are a fine-looking woman. You look well in fine things, and I will send you fine clothes and jewellery, and if you wanted to pawn them it would be easy. The pawnbroker would think everything all right. Suppose, for instance, you had a grand pair of bracelets on, all you would have to do would be to go into the pawnbroker's, take them off your wrist, and say, 'I want to pawn these things.' He also said, 'If you will only do what I want you, there shall not be such another lady in England as you may be.'

"At the time I couldn't understand what was his object. Of course, I see it plain enough now. I did not suspect he was a burglar.

"He was living at Darnall, making picture frames whenever he could get any to make, and his wife was apparently assisting to keep the house together by washing bottles at a wine and spirit merchant's. How could I know that he was anything other than he represented himself to be?

"I was suspicious. I remember on one occasion he offered me a sealskin jacket and several yards of silk. Of course, he couldn't have come by them honestly. I now know they must have been part of the proceeds of a burglary. And well I should have looked if I had accepted them! I should then have been quite in his power.

"But I knew better than that. I declined his present, and told him that if he had a sealskin jacket and some silk to spare, he had better make a present of them to his wife and daughter.

"I also told him that they wanted them much more than I did, and that if I desired to have a sealskin jacket, I would wait for it until my husband bought it, and that if he couldn't I was content to go without. Some time afterwards he offered me a gold watch; but I wouldn't have it. That, of course, was stolen.

"I consider that he offered me these presents as one means of getting me into his power. I would have nothing to do with him, and so he tempted me with sealskin jackets, and silks, and watches. I remember when he was speaking to me about Manchester, he said—

"'If you will only go, I'll fix you up there nice. You will have a splendid business, and will live like a lady.'

"'Thank you,' I said, 'I always have lived like one, and shall continue to do so quite independently of you.'

"I was getting downright mad with him, because of his constantly bothering me. What he wanted me to go to Manchester for was to pass off his stolen goods—at least that is my opinion. He never said so in so many words, but he could have had no other object.

"To do this, he wanted first to get me in his power, and not only did he try, but other members of his family did their best. When he found that he could not succeed by fair means, then he tried what threats and persecutions would do.

"He once came into my house, and said as I would not do what he wanted, he would annoy and torment me to the end of the world.

"'Don't you ever come into my house again,' I said, 'or ever darken its doors.'

"But it was no use my saying that. He still came whenever he could get in, and when he couldn't, he watched for me and followed me wherever I went. I have known him to go to the railway station and say to the booking clerk after I had taken my ticket, 'Give me a ticket for where she's going.' That's how it was he followed me to Mansfield, and then came into the same house there where I and my companion were staying. That was, too, how it was that he was seen with me in the streets.

"So it was as regards his being with me in the fair ground, about which so much has been made. I went to the fair with a neighbour and her children, and when we got into the photographic saloon my intention was to have the children photographed. I had no intention whatever of having myself taken with Peace, but he stood behind my chair at the time my likeness was taken.

"That was quite unknown to me, though, at the time. You can have no idea, unless you know the man, how he persecuted me and attempted to get me within his power. I remember doing something in the kitchen, and my back was turned to the door. Hearing a slight noise, I turned round, and then I saw Peace standing just inside the door.

"The expression on his face was something dreadful. It was almost fiendish—devilish. He had a revolver in his right hand, and he held it up towards me and said, in an excited and threatening manner—

"'Now, will you go to Manchester? Now, will you go to Manchester?'

"I did not shriek, but I cried out 'No, never! what do you take me for?'

"Finding that I was firm, he dropped his hand, and went out; but I can assure you I was frightened at the time.

"He had a way of creeping and crawling about, and of coming upon you suddenly unawares; and I cannot describe to you how he seemed to wriggle himself inside the door, or the terrible expression on his face.

"He seemed more like an evil spirit than a man. I have told you that when we knew him first we thought him a rather nice old man; but I soon found out, after he had taken against me, that we were sadly mistaken in our impression of him.

"He turned against me solely because he could not make me do as he wanted. I would not have done as he wished for anything in this world. He wanted me to be an accomplice in his doings.

"That has been his endeavour all through, and because he could not succeed he turned round on me and was determined to have his revenge. He thought he could handle me as he liked, that I was a weak sort of a woman, and could be got over like others who have been associated with him; but he found he was mistaken.

"I was terribly tried by him, though, and at last I was frightened—I don't deny it. There have been times when I haven't feared him, and when I should have thrashed him if Mr. Dyson would have allowed me.

"I once did give him a good hiding, because he had

insulted and annoyed me, but perhaps I had better not say much about that now. I used to be especially afraid of him at nights, because he had a habit of continually prowling about the house, and of turning up suddenly. He would, too, assume all sorts of disguises.

"He used to boast how effectually he could disguise himself; and I was afraid of his coming in some guise or other at night, and carrying out his threats.

"He was very determined. I never saw anything like it in my life. I have been about a good deal, but I never saw such determination and persistency as he has. It seems to me there was scarcely anything which he couldn't accomplish if only he was determined to succeed.

"He once said, 'I never am beaten when I have made up my mind. If I make up my mind to a thing, I'm bound to have it, even if it cost me my life.' You could not shake him off, do what you might. The only way to get rid of him was to knock him down as I once did.

"Determined as he was one way, I was equally determined the other, and that was why he never succeeded with me. He once made use of this expression to me: 'I don't care how independent you are, I'll get hold of you some way or other.' But I said as firmly as I could, 'Never!' and so I have always said.

"We went to Bannercross because we were afraid of Peace. Before going there, my husband took out a warrant against him. That was in July, 1876, and as soon as Peace knew of the warrant he left the town. It was soon after this that Mr. Dyson decided to go to Bannercross.

"What became of Peace I never knew, except that I heard he had gone to Manchester. He suddenly disappeared, and I did not see him again until on the very day that our furniture was being removed to Bannercross. I and my husband saw him coming out of our new house there.

"So annoyed and irritated was I at this that I really should have caught hold of him, and held him until a policeman could have been fetched. But my husband would not hear of such a thing.

"Just fancy Peace coming out of the house we were going into! I really felt quite mad at it. This was on the 25th October, and I did not see him again till the night of the murder.

"I didn't really know that Peace was a burglar until after the murder. If I had he would never have entered our doors. But what I know now explains a good deal. For instance, when we were out walking together, if I happened to look into a shop window, he would say to me, 'Is there anything there you would like? If there is I will get it for you before morning.'

"He would say that if I looked into a jeweller's or a draper's shop. I did not know what he meant then, but I do now. My suspicions were aroused, for I used to see him leave his house at Darnall in the evenings with a little satchel under his arm, and he would come back early in the morning carrying a large bundle. The satchel, I suppose, contained his housebreaking implements. He often used to go to Manchester with this satchel. He came to my door one morning just as he was going to Manchester. He then had his satchel with him. Looking into the room where I was, he said—

"'I'll have you alive or dead. I'll have you, or else I'll torment you to the end of your life.'

"On another occasion, when I had defied him, he said—

"'I'll make you so that neither man nor woman shall look at you, and then I'll have you to myself.'

"I answered, 'Never. What can you do? What are you capable of?'

"'No matter,' he replied, 'I'll do it.'

"My opinion of Peace is that he was a perfect demon, not a man."

CHAPTER XC.

THE BANNERCROSS MURDER—PEACE'S ADVENTURES AFTER THE DEATH OF MR. DYSON.

THE Dysons found it impossible to shake off Peace, who continued his annoyances to them with a pertinacity which occasioned them the greatest possible trouble and anxiety.

Peace was irrepressible; he was most ingenious in the way of persecution.

He followed Mrs. Dyson about, threatened her, and watched outside the house to catch sight of her.

It was in vain that Mr. Dyson sent him a communication, requesting a cessation of his visits. This, coupled probably with a discountenance of Mrs. Dyson's friendship, seemed to almost madden Peace, who swore to be revenged on them both.

But too well did he carry out his wicked purpose.

In July, 1876, he threatened to blow out their brains, accompanying the threat with pointing a pistol at the head of Mrs. Dyson.

A warrant was taken out against him for this, but he evaded apprehension, while continuing to annoy the family, and on October 29 the Dysons removed to Bannercross, with the hope of being free from his disagreeable visits; but on the very night they removed Peace appeared at Bannercross and confronted Mrs. Dyson, saying in a malicious tone of voice, "You see I am here to annoy you, wherever you may go."

Mrs. Dyson remonstrated with him, and told him "he was a wretch."

Peace only laughed derisively at this, and said, "he was not to be shaken off, that he would follow her if it was to the end of the world."

Just one month after this he went to Bannercross at eight o'clock in the evening, and perpetrated the murder for which he afterwards suffered death.

Peace proceeded to Sheffield the night after the trial of the unfortunate young man, William Habron, and he went to Bannercross in the evening.

At the back of the house where the Dysons lived, which was in one of the houses in the terrace called Bannercross-terrace, there was a low wall.

Peace wanted to see Mrs. Dyson—so he afterwards declared—he knew the house very well. He stood on the low wall at the back of the house. He was well acquainted with the back premises as also the front, and he knew that the bedroom was at the back.

For some time Peace's eyes were directed towards the apartment in question; presently he noticed a light at the window.

The blind was up, and he could, with tolerable distinctness, see her carrying a candle and moving about the room.

The guilty man watched her for some time, and saw that she was putting her boy to bed.

He then "flipped his fingers," as he termed it, and gave a sort of subdued whistle, to attract the attention of Mrs. Dyson, as he had frequently done before at different places.

He had not long to wait, the assumption being that she was aware of the presence of her tormentor.

Anyway, Mrs. Dyson left the bedroom, went down stairs, and entered the closet.

Peace got down off the wall and gained the yard. He then went towards the passage of the house.

According to his own statement, the only object he had in paying a visit to the house was to induce Mrs. Dyson to withdraw the warrant which had been taken out against him. Whether this was the real purport of his visit has never been clearly established—we have only his bare word for it, but that is not very reliable testimony. He said "he was tired of being hunted about, and not being able to go and come as he liked."

Mrs. Dyson, according to his account, became very noisy and defiant, and made use of fearful language against him.

Peace became angry, and taking his revolver from his pocket, he held it up in her face, and said:

"Now you be careful what you are saying to me. You know me of old, and know what I can do.

"You know I am not a man to be talked to in that way.

"If there is one man who will not be trifled with by you or anybody else, it is Charles Peace."

She was highly incensed, and would not take warning, and continued to threaten Peace, who soon became wild with fury.

All the bad passions of the man were now dominant.

While loud and angry words were being exchanged, Mr. Dyson made his appearance.

It was most unfortunate for him that he came forward.

Peace threatened to shoot Mrs. Dyson, who took refuge in the closet.

Peace turned round and fired twice, the first shot striking the wall, and the second striking Mr. Dyson in the temple.

Peace saw the unfortunate gentleman fall, but was not aware at the time that he had received his death-wound.

His murderer rushed into the middle of the road, and stood there for a brief period, apparently hesitating as to his course of action.

He was, as may be readily imagined, under the greatest agitation, and as he observed a number of people gathering about, he at last decided to fly.

He jumped over the wall on the other side of the road, and as he did so a packet of letters fell from his pocket, just as he was jumping over the fence.

Mr. Dyson died in about an hour after he had been shot.

Peace managed to effect his escape.

How he contrived to get clean off has been a matter of surprise to everybody; and how he afterwards managed to elude the vigilance of the police and continue his lawless career in London and the suburbs, is still more surprising.

The following is his own version of his movements after the murder.

"I want it to be properly understood," says Peace, "that, from the moment I left Bannercross on the 29th of September, 1876, I felt sure of making my escape.

"I felt I had no cause to do so, for I knew that I had done nothing wrong; for in the first place when it happened, I came down the passage and stood in the middle of the road not knowing what had happened.

"I did not know whether to run away or walk away, till I heard Kate (Mrs. Dyson) scream; and then not knowing what had happened, I took across the road and fields to Hentcleff (Endcliffe) crescent. I then walked to Broomhill Tavern, and took a cab into Church-street.

"I then went to see my mother, and remained with her for more than half an hour. I then went down to the Attercliffe railway station, and took the train for Rotheram.

"I then booked from Masborough for Hull, but having got into the York part of the train (not knowing) in place of the Hull part, when the Hull part of the train was liberated from the York part at Normanton I was taken forward to York.

"I remained at York in the Railway Hotel in the station yard all night. I took the first train next morning for Beverley. I took the next train for Cottingham. I went from Cottingham to Hull.

"I went to see my wife and family at 27, Collier-street; this would be about ten o'clock in the morning. I had been away from my family a fortnight, and was talking to them in the kitchen when I heard two dectives (detectives) talking to my wife in the shop, asking if a young man of the name of Peace lived there.

"My wife said 'Yes; but he has gone to Sheffield to see his grandmother,' thinking that they meant my son.

"But I in the kitchen, hearing this, felt that it must be me they meant, went upstairs into my son's bed-room, put the window up, and went between the two roof's of the building, and remained there till the detectives had searched the house, and when they had gone out I came back again into the kitchen of my own house, and took my things and began to wash myself; but before I could finish washing myself I heard them in the shop again, so I went upstairs through the windows between the roof till they had searched the house and gone out again. So I then went down again into the kitchen.

"My wife and daughter were sobbing fit to break their heart, for they did not know what was the matter and I could not tell them.

"So I washed me, and put on my clothes, and bid them all good-bye, and went out through the window again between the roofs. I remained there again for some hours, till just before dusk.

"I then went down the spout at the further end of the building, which brought me into the next yard but one, and went to a woman's house that dealt at our shop, and told the woman I had to get away out of the shop over a warrant, or something of that, and asked her if she would go into our house and ask my wife to send me something to eat out, but mind the detectives did not hear and see her, and I had my tea in this woman's house.

"I then asked the woman to let me go through her kitchen window in her back yard and also go ask the woman in the next yard if she would let me go through her kitchen window, and pass through the house into another yard.

"She went and asked and got consent, so that I went through the window and house into the other yard. This was three clear yards away from my house. It was then just dark.

"I walked out of the passage end, and turned to the left down Collier-street, towards the fair ground, and went away—but not out of the town—and got lodgings; and I remained in Hull for nearly three weeks, and done some places for money.

"I then left Hull and booked for Doncaster. I then booked from Doncaster to London. I then took the underground railway to Paddington, and booked from Paddington for Bristol. Bristol was the first place I saw a reward out for my apprehension."

" I remained in Bristol till January. I booked from Bristol to Bath. I stopped at Bath all night. I booked from Bath to Oxford, and in the carriage with me there was a police sergeant on his way to Stafford Assizes. We rode and talked together to Dickcot Junction (Didcott Junction), and arrived there in the middle of the night.

"We slept together in the waiting-room for four hours, and then went forward to Oxford by first train. We then shook hands and parted; he went forward to Stafford and I remained at Oxford all day.

"I then booked for Birmingham. I remained at Birmingham four or five days. I then went on to Derby.

"I stopped at Derby at an eating-house oppersite the railway, and there was a young man there just joining the police force, and the police-station was not more than 150 yards from there. I remained at Derby for something more than a week.

"I then went to Nottingham, and took lodging at a little shop three or four doors from the police-station on the Burton-road right oppersite a timber-yard where I was stopping, and the police-station is at the corner of Leanside.

"I remained with them till they left there and went to live with them in a yard a bit lower down, that led out of Leanside into Narrow Marsh, but not more than fifty yards from the police-station.

"I remained with them some time, working Nottingham and the towns round about. I then went to live with Mrs. Adamson, a buyer, next door to the 'Woodman Inn,' in Narrow Marsh. It was there I became acquainted with Mrs. Thompson.

"Upon one occasion I booked from Nottingham to Sheffield, but got out of the train at Ely (Heeley) station, and walking past the police-station at Highfield. Inspector Bradbury was stood at the police-station door, at about seven o'clock at night, and I passed close by him, and he did not know me.

"Then I went right away up to Sharrow, and crossed over quite close to Bannercross, down into Hescle-hall (Ecclesall) road, turned down towards Sheffield, and crossed through Broomhall Park, into Havelock-square.

"I that night did a house over at the corner of Havelock-square. They was away from home. I got about £6 in money and a lot of jewerley.

"The watchman on the beat fancied he heard something in the house, but I saw him stop the sergeant when he came his round, and I got away backwards. By certain papers I brought out of the house they called them Barney Swincourse (Barnascone). I went to Ely (Heeley) Railway Station, and from Ely to Nottingham.

"At Nottingham I done a big tailor and draper establishment and took a lot of overcoats."

It was at the last-named place, as he declares in the above statement, that he met with the woman who played so conspicuous a part in Peckham.

Mrs. Thompson's name was Susan Gray, and she was lodging at a house where Peace had apartments.

It is said that she was married to a commercial traveller named Bailey, but discarded him for Peace; and it was while at Nottingham that a detective surprised them in the night.

There had been a robbery in the town, and the officer was in pursuit of the thief. Peace induced the constable to go down stairs, stating that he was a pedlar, and would bring down his pack for examination. He escaped, half dressed, through the window; and the

officer, after waiting for some time, returned to find the bird flown.

Peace afterwards talked of this with great glee.

He afterwards returned to Hull with Mrs. Thompson, and six months subsequently to the murder at Bannercross had the audacity to take apartments with a police-sergeant in Albany-road, near to Hengler's Circus. Peace and his female companion were the front parlour lodgers, and as the sergeant kept other lodgers, mainly "professional," Peace was quite at home, and the life and soul of the company.

While residing with the sergeant he committed one of his daring burglaries, and frequently had conversations with his landlord about the supposed burglar. The pair stayed here for nearly two months under the names of Mr. and Mrs. Thompson.

From Hull they went to Lambeth, changing their quarters to Greenwich, and finally to Peckham. It was here that Mrs. Thompson found out who and what her companion really was.

He told her he had never been married; and rummaging among his boxes one day, Mrs. Thompson discovered a funeral card in memory of his son, aged four. The name Peace at once disclosed the real character of the man to whose fortunes she had allied herself.

She charged him with being the Bannercross murderer; which he did not deny. Then his whole manner changed. He had been kind to her up to that period; but he now took an opposite course, and tyrannised over her.

Mrs. Thompson, it must be admitted, was much addicted to drink and snuff-taking to an inordinate extent.

She used to frequent public-houses. She was prohibited from going out, but could have as much as she liked to drink at home.

It then occurred to Peace that if Mrs. Thompson had thus found him out his wife and his step-son, whom he had left in Hull, might divulge the secret. He therefore devised a plan, and Mrs. Thompson was compelled to fall in with it.

Both went down to Hull, and Mrs. Thompson one fine day presented herself at Mrs. Peace's home with a letter, in which Peace expressed his penitence for all the misery he had caused her, and said he was most anxious to make her some reparation.

He told her he was now in a good position, and could not bear to see her drudging at Hull. Finally he prevailed upon her to go to London with her son Willie, stating that he had bought a business in Tottenham-court-road, and that he would pay a year's rent in advance, and never come to molest her if she desired him not to do so.

She believed him, and journeyed up to London—agreeable to his request—poor confiding woman as she was.

On the morning after the murder, according to his account, he walked into his mother's house, to her great surprise just as she was sitting down to breakfast. Willie Ward and two other relatives were there at the time, and perhaps their presence disconcerted him, for he left again directly for the purpose, as he said, of seeing his brother Dan.

He promised to return shortly, but did not go back till ten o'clock the same night, when he had a wild expression in his eye, his face was discoloured, and his clothes daubed with mud.

He told his mother that he had "been and shot Mr. Dyson," assigning as the reason that he had taken out a warrant against him for using threatening language and that if it were brought before a magistrate his prison life would go against him.

He hastened at once to clean himself, and after saying "Good-bye" to his mother he left the house never to see her again in this world.

Peace, as we have before observed, took great delight in boasting how he could deceive the police, and often declared—

"That he could dodge any detective in existence."

The fact of his having baffled his pursuers is doubtless to be ascribed to his facial peculiarities, especially the length and mobility of the lower jaw, and the flexibility of his muscles. This was one of his most remarkable characteristics. He said to some friends one day—

"Do you want to know how I dodged the bobbies?" and on receiving a reply in the affirmative he said, "Well, I will tell you," then he asked them to turn their backs to him a bit.

They did so, and were astounded to find that Peace had completely altered the expression of his face, and so protruded his chin and curled his lip that under ordinary circumstances it would have been impossible to recognise him, especially as he had by the peculiar contortion of his features forced the blood into his face until he looked like a mulatto. One of the inspectors said—

"No wonder you could get clear from Sheffield when you can change your face like that."

Whereupon Peace laughed and said—

"I can do more dodges. I can dodge any detective."

The circumstances surrounding his connection with the Dysons form the most remarkable and inexplicable portion of his career.

It would appear that he completely lost himself in his infatuation for Mrs. Dyson; his usual caution forsook him, and he run greater risks in the pursuit of Mrs. Dyson than he did by any of his daring burglaries.

The end we know. He paid the last dread penalty of the law for the murder of the unfortunate gentleman who fell a victim to his bloodthirsty spirit of revenge.

When the Dyson's first went to live at Eccleshall, some five weeks before the murder, Peace made it his business to wait upon the vicar, the Rev. E. Newman, to warn him against the new arrivals in his parish.

He then told Mr. Newman some most incredible stories, making grave charges which it would be indelicate and unjust to even hint at.

Mr. Newman was incredulous that things could be as Peace represented them, and asked him how it was that he had chosen to make such statements to an utter stranger.

"My object," promptly replied Peace, "is to put you on your guard."

It struck Mr. Newman at the time that there was something behind, but Peace persistently stuck to his story. As it was not believed he left the vicarage, stating that he would return with proofs such as would leave no doubt of his speaking the truth.

The following particulars of a subsequent interview will be read with interest at this time :—

"At twenty minutes past six on Wednesday evening (November 29th), 'a thin, grey-haired, insignificant-looking man' presented himself at the front door of Eccleshall Vicarage. He rang the bell and announced himself as Peace, stating to the servant that he desired to see Mr. Newman.

"When Mr. Newman saw him Peace at once produced what he called his 'proofs' of the statements he had made about the Dysons on his first visit. He represented himself as a very respectable man—indeed,

taken at his own estimate he was about as near perfection as he could get, and he attributed all the troubles and wickednesses into which he had fallen to the people he has now so fearfully revenged himself upon.

"He said he had come to Mr. Newman 'to make a confession—a clean breast of all his wickedness.' Mr. Newman tried to turn his thoughts to the only source of forgiveness, but Peace would have none of his counsel. He was determined to confess to Mr. Newman, and then began a narrative, which, in the abundance of the abominable, is beyond belief.

"His allegations were not only wicked, but most extravagantly wicked. Peace put himself forward as having been all that was right and proper until Mr. Dyson became jealous of him.

"He told Mr. Newman that he said to Mrs. Dyson, 'That they had better give him (meaning her husband) something to talk about,' and that from that day commenced all his trouble.

"Peace produced to Mr. Newman a vast number of letters, photographs, cards, and other things, and was eager in pressing them upon the vicar, adding that he could bring any number of the same sort. His great grievance against the Dysons appeared to be the issuing of the warrant against him.

"Owing to that he had to break up his house and become a fugitive in the land. He consulted a solicitor, who advised him that he was liable to four actions if he did not make himself scarce. So he was obliged to 'dodge' the authorities.

"This trouble seems to have made him almost mad, and the mere recollection of it roused his wrath as nothing else could. He spoke in words of forgiveness —forgive the word!—of Mrs. Dyson; but nothing could exceed his hatred of her husband, the person whom, if his own story was to be believed, he had most deeply wronged. He said he was determined that wherever the Dysons went he would follow them. He had quarrelled with his own wife, and would never go back to her again.

"Peace added that he had come to Sheffield that morning with his daughter to see a relative, and having a little time on his hands he thought he would go up to Mr. Newman's with the proofs he had promised. On his way up he said he had ascertained—as he had ways and means of doing—that Mr. and Mrs. Dyson were at home, and he knew how they were (making another charge against him).

"Going out and while on the door-step, he turned to Mr. Newman and said, 'I won't call at the Dyson's to-night, but I will call at the Gregory's.' He then left, bidding Mr. Newman a cheerful 'good-night.'

"He left the vicarage at twenty minutes to seven, Mr. Newman being indeed anxious to get rid of him, as he had a meeting to attend that evening. It afterwards transpired that Peace had gone to Gregory's shop.

"He would get there about seven or shortly afterwards. Mr. Gregory was not in, and Peace left, going down the road as if returning to Sheffield. He was watched as far as a lamp, 150 yards from the house. Very shortly after he must have returned and secreted himself in Mr. Dyson's garden, with the dreadful purpose of murdering that gentleman."

The following remarks were made by a journalist on the interview at the time :—

"There can be no doubt that when Peace sought that remarkable interview with the vicar he had meditated murder and decided upon his diabolical plan.

"All the time he was talking in Mr. Newman's study he must have had murder in his heart, and the revolver with which he meant to do it would be in his pocket, probably loaded.

"Had Mr. Newman known the desperate character to whom he had granted the interview he would not have sat so easy in his study chair. Peace could only have one purpose in his visit. He knew that after he had done the deed he would have either to shoot himself or fly the country, and his communication to the vicar therefore was in the nature of a last will and testament.

"He evidently desired the public to know his side of the transaction, and the clergyman of the parish would naturally occur to him as the most likely party to entrust it with.

"His communication, however, is of such an atrocious character that its publication is simply impossible, apart altogether from matters of truth and justice. There can be little doubt that Peace is a great liar.

"He gave Mr. Newman the idea that he was a superior kind of workman and rather a respectable person. He was guarded in his language, composed in his manner, and during the whole of the interview never betrayed the slightest indication of the horrid business he had in hand.

"The fine character he gave himself, however, was all a fable. He has been frequently in prison, and small and insignificant as he is he has served a term of penal servitude for a daring burglary at Salford."

It is pretty clearly established that Peace wanted Mrs. Dyson to leave her husband and take up with him, and doubtless he would have had very little compunction in deserting his own wife, and leaving her to shift for herself as best she could.

He was a man who would not let anything stand in his way when he was bent on any particular project, and would sacrifice friend or foe without pity or remorse.

A more unscrupulous man never lived, and there can be but little doubt as to the fact of his being impelled by a blind fatuous spirit of revenge to commit the Bannercross murder as it has been termed.

Every effort was made by the constabulary to find out the perpetrator of this outrage, and the probability is that the real culprit would never have been discovered had it not been for the attempt on the life of the policeman, Robinson.

An arrest was made some time after the commission of the crime.

On December 9th, 1876, Police-constable Barker apprehended a man at Barrow-in-Furness who was strongly suspected of being Peace, but Inspector Twibell, who was sent up to identify him, found that a mistake had been made. Early last year the same man was apprehended at Hexham, and until Police-constable Boreham had been able to prove his non-identity it was firmly believed that the murderer had been run to earth.

Upon inquiry, however, it was found that the man was not, as had been supposed, the celebrated Charles Peace, and he was therefore liberated.

The murderer of Mr. Dyson and police-constable Cock now deemed it advisable to bid adieu to the scenes of depredation and heinous crimes. He had succeeded in persuading his wife to hasten at once to the metropolis. The poor broken-down woman had not the heart to refuse the miscreant. As we have already signified she left Hull for London.

We now arrive at another phase in the history of this great criminal.

CHAPTER XCI.

PEACE'S DOINGS IN LONDON AND THE SUBURBS—HIS HOME LIFE AT EVELINA-ROAD, PECKHAM.

AFTER changing his place of residence two or three times, Peace ultimately settled himself permanently at Peckham with his two housekeepers—Mrs. Peace and Mrs. Thompson—together with Willie Ward, his step-son, and it was at this time that he committed a series of burglaries in the suburbs of London, which are altogether unparalleled in the history of any criminal.

The house he had chosen for his residence was No. 5, East-terrace, Evelina-road, Peckham. It was very conveniently situated for the masterly operations of the crafty burglar's nefarious art; he selected it manifestly with an eye to business.

It was the end one of a row, and was bordered with a hedge on one side, that abutted on the Palace railway embankment, near the Nunhead Station. A gateway leading to the rear of the house gave entrance to an ordinary vehicle, and the exits from the dwelling were so numerous that a rascal of Peace's type would rarely be so ambuscaded as to block his flight in case of surprise, however cleverly contrived.

He came into the neighbourhood as a retired gentleman, possessed of a modest competence, which would enable him to live quietly without business cares, and also enable him to indulge little whims in a scientific direction, in which indulgence he gave out that he had lost thousands.

Mr. Cleaves, the greengrocer at the corner, was commissioned to "move him," as Mr. Cleaves says, from Greenwich, where he had been living a retired and peaceful life, allowing his days and nights to ebb in the cause of science.

Mr. Cleaves charged a sovereign for the job of transporting, and the convict was so beneficent as to add 2s. and a fried steak and beer, in appreciation of the services rendered.

The furniture was costly, and somewhat extravagant for a man of the convict's simplicity, there being two suites of drawing-room furniture, and loads of knick-knacks that only a luxurious taste would covet, and a heavy purse undertake to own.

But unquestionably a large amount of plate and a considerable collection of pictures that the convict owned were not transported openly in Mr. Cleaves' vans, but forwarded secretly from Greenwich to Peckham.

The neighbours in the course of a few weeks made acquaintance with the new comer, but none of them divined the being he was, although most of them seemed to have thought him singular.

He was a man of independent means, yet he had no servant. He was able to maintain a pony, and ride behind it in a gig.

Yet in the small house of two parlours and a kitchen and three bedrooms he had two women living, one of whom is conjectured to have been his wife, and who certainly had borne him a son, and the other had passed as Mrs. Thompson, Peace himself proclaiming that his name was Thompson.

How the real wife and the mistress, or how both the mistresses came to live in one house, is only to be explained by the knowledge that both of the women had of the convict, and their fear of being held accountable as accessories after the fact in his crimes. The mixed family did not live in harmony.

Mrs. Thompson had frequently a black eye, and indeed was rarely without one, and shrieking and cursing were not uncommonly heard proceeding from the house in the midnight hours and in the afternoon.

Peace was very rarely seen in the morning, or until late in the day. People in the vicinity who gave the matter any attention supposed he was busy with his scientific invention, of which he was fond of talking in an effusive manner.

He conveyed the impression that he was a man of moral tone.

"I would not do anything to injure the poor," he said one day to the greengrocer, as he pulled out a handful of sovereigns, the number of which the greengrocer magnifies into seventy; and when in conversation with the landlord of some new houses near the "Rail oad Tavern," he informed Mr. Gosling that he did not approve of public-house fellows who went to the bar so early in the morning.

This was a reflection upon the milkman and the greengrocer, who had presumptuously saluted him.

Nevertheless, he occasionally invited his neighbours into his mansion to take something, and by all accounts he was a jovial host.

He was possessed of seven or eight guitars and almost as many violins, and in his leisure moments he took pleasure in musical performances that brought out to the full the qualities of the instruments.

The greengrocer owns a musical bell of glass, which belonged to the convict. When he came outside the gate in the afternoon, and took a cast around the sky with his furtive eye, Peace was communicative and critical to whoever was passing that knew him, and he especially delighted in a chat about crime and criminals with the watchful policemen of his district.

In conversation, he had an odd habit of digging his hands deep into his pockets, and twisting himself round in the pantomimic contortions of a clown. Social visits were never paid, and, except informally, he did not encourage them to his house.

The large menagerie of pets that he formed at Peckham was certainly extraordinary for so unpretentious an establishment, but he was a gentleman devoted to science, and might be allowed to indulge a hobby for zoology.

Whether he was really attached to animals is doubtful, for there are many traits of his nature that indicate he was cruel and remorselessly selfish.

The collection embraced thirty-two guinea pigs, some goats, cats, dogs, canaries, fowls, pigeons, and he had a pony which apparently was much beloved, and which he wept over with tears of regret when 'Tommy" died.

Some of these pets he had trained to execute tricks wonderful enough to earn a showman his living. His pony especially had a marvellous obedience to command. At a word he would rear up and remain standing, and at another word he would lie down and remain as if dead.

In short, "Tommy" had been trained to be a silent partner in burglary. The custom of Peace was to go out during the day, with Mrs. Peace and Mrs. Thompson and the son in his trap, himself driving, and take a survey of the mansions he intended to rob during the night, and the precise spots to which he would carry the booty for subsequent recovery and resetting. He made two attacks, as the neighbours express it.

He went out early in the evening when the family were downstairs, and robbed the house upstairs, and later in the evening, or far on in the morning, when the family were upstairs, he roamed through the lower regions and abstracted the heavy articles of plate and gems, of pictures, and all valuables that were portable and transmutable into money. He went out alone on these expeditions.

The son, Willie Ward, was seen by the greengrocer at Forest Hill one morning at six, driving rapidly, as if he had business; and the greengrocer's man saw the son on two occasions out early in the morning. It is surmised that the son took these early rides in the vehicle, by arrangement with the father, for the purpose of collecting the plunder of the night, and conveying it in an unsuspicious way to the town.

Peace encountered a man at Lewisham one night, who had passed Nunhead, and was obliged to walk back. The two had a most interesting conversation upon botany, in which science Peace seems to have laid magnificent foundations for studying, having selected for culture, in a plot of thirty square feet, several hundreds of choice plants.

The pony went out from Peace's stables at most unearthly hours, and sometimes the neighbours woke up when it returned. One night the driving in at the gate was furious, and the pony knocked over the gate, and made such a racket that the attention of No. 120 policeman was drawn to the circumstance.

The policeman was on the threshold of discovery but suspected nothing. Peace unquestionably had just returned from an expedition with spoils, but when he saw the officer he blandly invited him in, although it was one o'clock in the morning, and lifting up the lid of a long box, he explained that he had been engaged in perfecting an invention for raising sunken vessels, which he and a Mr. Brion were about to patent.

"And you know it would not do to let people know about this in the day-time," added the convict, upon which the policeman drank his health, and hoped he didn't intrude, and assisted Mr. Knight, the milkman adjacent, to re-adjust the gate on its hinges. On another occasion the convict was surprised while occupied at two o'clock in the morning in his back-yard.

The milkman had returned home with his waggon, and was astonished to discover old Peace at work in the garden digging.

"It's only me, Mr. Knight," said Mr. Peace, as he heard a door grate, and discovered the milkman scanning his midnight toil. The milkman went nearer, and perceived that Peace had dug a hole long enough and deep enough for a grave, and Peace explained that the exhumed earth was intended for potting, and that the hole would do for manure from the stable.

But Peace played it on the milkman some time later than this to a prodigious extent.

"Poor Tommy" died, and was lamented with bitter lamentations by his bereaved master, and a few days afterwards the bland Peace, with a truly sympathetic manner, went to the milkman, and said, "Mr. Knight, I see your stable is very damp, and I don't like to see any animal treated to damp quarters. Since 'Tommy' died I have had no use for my stable, and you might as well put your pony in there, where it is dry, and you know I am a man of means, and will take every care of him. In fact I am very fond of animals." The milkman had commiseration for his beast, and stabled him in Peace's stable.

The convict considerately said he would not charge anything, and he showed an interest in his charge by providing a new bucket for the pony, and supplying good litter. But in the mornings the milkman noticed that his pony was often bespattered thickly with mud, and was eating hungrily from the manger.

PEACE STRIKING MRS. THOMPSON.

He threatened to kick his stable-boy for not having scrubbed the beast down, but was astonished, on reckoning with himself, to remember that on the previous evening he had both washed and curried the pony with his own hands. In addition to these strange manifestations, the pony from having been a brisk trotting animal suddenly developed a turn for laziness,

and was, in fact, as jaded and listless a trotter as could be seen on the road.

The milkman never found the reason why his pony was dispirited. It was Box and Cox in the stable, with the pony in the *role* of both, and the play lasted three months.

The pony obtained repose when the brutal midnight

No. 48.

driver was arrested after his murderous attack on the police-constable at Blackheath. Peace's pets were not chosen without some regard to his profession.

He had studied dogs; and it is said that, stranger as he must have been in his burglarious prowls about mansions, he never had any difficulty in silencing the most ferocious mastiff or impudent terrier.

It was a sight to see him on a Sunday walking through Peckham, followed by the six dogs that owned him as master.

The impression of the neighbours about his appearance was exceedingly various. When abroad on his raids he was accustomed to stain his face, and some considered him a retired Jew from Ratcliff-highway.

The lower part of his face was mobile to a surprising extent, and he could at will assume a disguise very bewildering.

He allowed it to be understood that his left arm was maimed; he wore across the palm of the hand a dark bandage, and when he sat down to meals he fastened on the arm an apparatus of indiarubber, into which as a socket a fork was secured. It was all a blind to produce the belief that he was weak and helpless.

His house at Peckham was most beautifully furnished. In the drawing-room was a suite of walnut-wood, worth fifty or sixty guineas; a Turkey carpet, mirrors, and all the et ceteras which were considered necessary in the house of a gentleman of good position.

Upon the bijou piano was an inlaid Spanish guitar worth thirty guineas, the result of some depredation, and said to be the property of a countess.

His "sitting room" was a model of comfort: there was not a side table missing where it appeared requisite. In every essential it was fit for an independent gentleman, and even the slippers which were provided for his convenience were beaded so as to show their value.

The residents of Peckham wondered, for the favours in the way of burglaries which for a year past had seemed the exclusives of Lambeth and Greenwich, recommenced in that neighbourhood.

The police were again on the alert, but of no avail. The public press called attention to this abominable state of things; householders lost their goods, and Charles Peace prospered. He added to his earthly store of wealth and furniture.

Peace had always loved a "bit of music." Even in his less prosperous days he had bought a wooden canary which could sing a song, and as the residents of Peckham wondered why, in addition to the robberies of plate and jewels from their abodes, there was always sure to be a good fiddle missing if it had been near the plate, yet the store of musical instruments in Peace's dwelling gradually and more surely increased.

At length he had so many musical instruments that his new sanctum would not hold them, and he was obliged to ask a neighbour to place a few in his house.

He was considered, as before observed, to be a "gentleman of independent means," and as he "never played anything but sacred music" people believed him to be a discreet and proper sort of man.

His home life at Peckham appears to be quite different to that of his previous career—to say the least, the occupants of the house in the Evelina-road were not altogether a happy or united family.

Peace, with the heavy burthen of the murders on his conscience, was in many respects an altered man. He had his hour of conviviality and relaxation, it is true, but he was soured in temper, and at times was brutal to his two female associates or housekeepers.

Despite his bravado and cruelty he was afraid of them turning round upon him, and accusing him of the Bannercross murder.

Clever as he was he found it no easy task to get along with the two ladies of his house.

He could manage his two cats, his three dogs, his billygoat, his Russian rabbits, his seven Guinea pigs, his young thrushes, his collection of canaries, his parrots, and his cockatoo—to say nothing of his pony —for which he had an inordinate affection. This varied family gave him little trouble till the the pony died.

His pets, indeed, afforded him much amusement in the quiet hours of the afternoon, before he went on his evening expeditions. But two "wives" were too much for him. All the stories which have been told about his domestic surroundings are either grossly exaggerated or altogether untrue.

When Peace arranged to live at Peckham he sought out Mr. S. Smith, of Ryde-villas, St. Mary's-road, who had several houses to let. Peace had a large number to choose from, and he at last hit on No. 5, East-terrace, Evelina-road—"the first house through the viaduct." I was directed to it.

Mr. Smith, however, is a careful man. He does not let his houses to everybody who asks to become his tenant. He knew not "Mr. Thompson," and demanded references.

Mr. Thompson was evidently prepared for the request, and at once offered to give him any number, which he did, driving Mr. Smith over to Greenwich for the purpose.

Mr. Smith was perfectly satisfied, and let him have the house, which was admirably adapted for Peace's purpose.

It was the last house in the terrace. The railway is close to it, and when he went out on his midnight business he was not obliged to use the front door, as he could slip out at the back, steal up the embankment, cross the railway, and find his way to the quarry he had "spotted" during the afternoon excursions when he drove his ladies out for an "airing"—always in the direction of the better-class houses towards Blackheath and Greenwich—"cribs which were worth cracking," as a policeman put it.

No. 5, East-terrace, was rented at £30 a year, and Mr. Thompson paid his first quarter all right—the landlord lacks the last quarter, though he knows where the furniture is, and can follow it if he pleases.

One curiosity of the establishment Mr. Smith found after his tenant left—the crucible which Peace must have used to melt down the jewellery he got in his burglaries, and which he wanted to put off the possibility of detection.

Since Thompson's real character came out, Mr. Smith tells me he might by selling bits of his goods as relics have recouped himself for his rent and more, the morbid curiosity of visitors having been equal to anything of the kind experienced in the case of previous remarkable criminals.

The new tenant appears at first to have favourably impressed Mr. Smith, for he found himself frequently at No. 5 taking tea with Mr. and Mrs. Thompson and the other lady. Everything, he tells me, was very clean and comfortable.

Mr. Thompson was a kind and pressing host; the best of everything was put on the table, and the appointments in china and silver, to use the landlord's own words, "were always up to the knocker."

Thompson conversed freely on the various subjects of the day, took an interest in politics, and impressed his guest with the intelligence and knowledge he possessed.

Whilst Mrs. Thompson deftly served the tea, her husband enunciated his views on the different topics he had found to interest him in the newspapers, of which he was a diligent reader. It may interest Russophiles to know that this distinguished character took a great interest in the war, and favoured their views of the question.

Mr. Smith tells me that though he frequently talked about the war, he never indicated his views in his presence.

Another gentleman, who was the recipient of Mr. Thompson's opinions on more than one occasion, says that he expressed very general regret that nations could not find a more humane way of settling their differences than by the sword.

He wanted to know what our Christianity and civilisation meant by countenancing such murderous ways of deciding disputes.

He thought that the Turks had shown themselves a cruel race—he admitted they had good qualities, particularly in the matter of abstaining from intoxicants, which was a hobby of Mr. Thompson's—and he was glad that they had been punished for their cruelty. The Emperor of Russia, he held, had undertaken a high Christian mission, and our Government were greatly to blame in interfering with him.

He was confident that the Ministers would be punished (that was a favourite word of his) for their interference with the only Power which had shown any practical sympathy for the "suffering races," and so on.

With tea, toast, and talk, and anything in season from the neighbouring greengrocer's at the corner, the evening passed pleasantly away, the later hours being filled up with music by Mrs. Thompson, Mr. Thompson and the boy "Ward," who had been taught to play on many strange instruments until he was almost equal to Peace himself in his proficiency.

Shortly after tea, Mr. Thompson would quietly rise from his chair, and the guests—usually only one, or at the most two—would take the hint and leave, Mr. Thompson apologising by saying that he was not quite so strong as he once was, and late hours being detrimental to his health and opposed to his habits, he was obliged to go to bed at what other people would consider very early hours.

This idea he seemed anxious to impress upon the neighbourhood, and succeeded in doing it.

Mrs. Long, who lived near him for the most of those six months, tells me that they were very early people— "the light," she says, "was out at No. 5 before any other house in the neighbourhood."

The explanation, of course, is easy. Peace might ostentatiously lock his front door at half-past ten, and half an hour after, when the people supposed he and his family were sleeping the sleep of the just, he would be stealing out at the back, climbing the railway embankment, and off on his midnight raids, which always meant robbery and plundering, and, if necessary a murder.

Mrs. Thompson played a most conspicuous part throughout the latter part of Peace's career. How she and Mrs. Peace could have consented to live under the same roof with the burglar Peace is altogether unaccountable.

The ladies of the house in the Evelina-road are thus described by one who had an opportunity of learning something of the doings in that abode of bliss.

I am afraid (says the narrator) I must knock on the head a good many of the stories that have been printed about Peace's establishment, as well as about his ways of life.

In the first place he had no servants at all. There were in the house, in addition to himself, the younger person who passed as Mrs. Thompson, the other elderly woman, who gave herself the name of Mrs. Ward, and a lad of seventeen, who was named Willie Ward.

Tempted by the stories about Mr. Thompson being a gentleman of independent means, a girl once offered herself as domestic servant.

"She saw a man," she says, "who told her he did not believe in servants, as they were always gossiping."

Probably Peace had too much experience of the information to be got from servants' loose tongues to have one about his own premises.

That girl did not get the place. Mrs. Ward, I find, acted as a kind of working housekeeper.

She is described to me as having usually the appearance of a cross between a washerwoman and a monthly nurse, wearing an apron, her arms akimbo, and altogether a slattenly, unlovable, unclean-looking personage

Mrs. Thompson, on the other hand, was a likely lady for a companion. She was much taller than Peace, walked in a firm manner, carrying her head with a somewhat jaunty air, until latterly, when Peace's cruelties "took it out of her," as a neighbour put it to me.

She was a good figure, inclined to full habit, had pleasing brown hair, which she sometimes wore in curls; a good, fresh complexion, dark eyes, Grecian nose (but no snub), and altogether, as I have said, a person of a rather attractive appearance.

She dressed well, and never appeared to want for anything, Mrs. Long and other neighbours telling me that her wardrobe must have been very rich, and extensive, as she never wanted for changes of dresses— appearing sometimes in tightly-fitting costumes, and at others in richly trimmed and fashionably-cut jackets, donning for the afternoon drives a superb sealskin paletot.

The neighbours say that Mrs. Thompson's weakness was drink.

The boy who piloted me about Peckham told me that the first week they came he fetched 4s. worth of whiskey for Mrs. Thompson, "who," he added, "was a very nice person when she was herself," meaning when she was sober.

Mrs. Long, to whom Mrs. Thompson seems to have confided her troubles, believes that she would not have "gone to the drink" if it had not been for the cruelty to which she was latterly subjected.

But that she *did* drink is beyond dispute.

Indeed, the old woman, Mrs. Ward, gave it out to Mrs. Cleaves, a most intelligent neighbour, from whom I had many most interesting details, that her principal business at No. 5 was to watch Mrs. Thompson, whose drunkenness grieved Mr. Thompson very much.

He was a very temperate man himself, and could not do with drunken people about him.

Mrs. Ward was eloquent about Peace's liberality to the younger woman.

"He did not care," she said to Mrs. Cleaves, "what she costs him in dress; he never refused her anything she asked, and what was very kind of him, he always bought it and brought it himself."

Of course he did, the clever scoundrel!

He knew the places to get his goods on easy terms.

"She could swim in gold if she liked," said Mrs. Ward, on another occasion. "He does not mind what he gives her, he is so fond of her, if she would only keep off the drink." That was good Mr. Peace's greatest trouble, "and that," added the old lady, carefully removing a tear from the corner of her eye, "frequently puts him out, and makes him angry, till I'm afraid the neighbours hear him."

And the neighbours did hear him. Frequently, there were sounds of quarrelling at No. 5. In the shrill tones of a boy's voice would be heard the cry, "Don't, father, don't," succeeded shortly after by the shriek of a woman.

When the storm had reached this height it speedily subsided. It was no part of Peace's plan to be a noisy neighbour. These disturbances, however, were repeated, and the neighbours knew that things were not going well at No. 5.

They wondered why it was that the afternoon, or the early hours of the evening, should be selected for these scenes, which in ordinary households usually come on later in the evening; but they were not sufficiently curious to follow the matter up.

On one occasion when the boy's voice was heard, as imploring "father" to stop, the shriek of the woman who was evidently suffering some outrage, was so agonising that a person passing ran up the steps and knocked for admittance.

In an instant everything was still. The man who could strike the woman was equal, no doubt, to gagging her mouth when her cries attracted attention. Mrs. Ward, the next day, always made a point of explaining the sounds in her own way.

Mrs. Thompson had been drinking again, and Mr. Thompson was angry with her. She did wish Mrs. Thompson would leave off the evil habit, as she was sure it would break the heart of her husband.

Her husband all this time seemed more bent on breaking Mrs. Thompson's head than his own heart, but Mrs. Ward played her part well—so well that some of the neighbours appear indisposed even yet to believe any good whatever of the poor creature who, in an evil hour, linked her fate to the burglar and murderer.

One time Peace's cruelty reached a crisis.

Mrs. Thompson ran from the house, and sought shelter from Mrs. Long, who lives in Kimberley-road, a short way off. Thompson, she said, had struck her insensible, and amongst other marks of ill-usage she pointed to her eyes, which were frightfully discoloured.

Her face was cut—the effects of a blow he had given her with his fist. He always wore a large diamond ring—sometimes two of them—and that afternoon, Mrs. Thompson having offended him at tea, he coolly rose up from his seat and "landed her" a couple of frightful blows on the face.

This was the outrage which had roused Mrs. Thompson to leave the house whenever Peace's back was turned. She began to tell Mrs. Long her miserable story.

She had met Thompson—she did not say where—and believing he was an honest man, as he represented himself to be, able to keep her in a comfortable position, as he also represented, she began to receive his advances favourably.

He told her the old story about his being a gentleman of independent means, with a liking to travel about. She listened, and was deceived. Not so her mother and father. Both of them took an instinctive dislike to the plausible villain who came after their daughter.

She did as many other daughters do, and will do to the end of the chapter—she believed the stranger, and left her home with him.

She insisted that she was properly married to him

at church—which, if true, would add bigamy to Peace's other offences against the law—but never gave any indication where the ceremony took place.

"I never quite liked the man," she said, "even though I disobeyed my parents to follow him; and on my way to church to get married, a strong feeling took hold of me to turn back. How I wish now I had done it."

Then she would burst afresh into tears, and exclaim—

"But it serves me right. It is but a just punishment upon me for disobeying my parents. They did not want me to have anything to do with the man, and I ought never to have spoken to him. It was a sorry day for me I ever saw him."

She went on to say that she had relatives in a good position in the North. "I wonder," she cried, "if my brother would take me in."

Her brother, she told Mrs. Long, was a medical man, and her sisters, of whom she had several, were well married.

She asked Mrs. Long if she would advise her to write to them. Mrs. Long thought that would be the best thing she could do, and here came a strange bit of feminine jealousy, which showed of what a contradictory compound some womenkind are made.

"Mrs. Ward" passed in the pony trap along with Peace, evidently going out for a drive. Mrs. Thompson, in a moment, was herself again.

"No," she said, with decision, "I'll not leave him. That woman's in my place, and he would no doubt like me to leave; but I won't, I'll go back to my husband, and assert my rights."

And back she went to be brutally abused as before, to bear upon her face and body the marks of his blows, and to endure all the mental agony which was now hers as the truth gradually oozed out about her husband's real character.

Mrs. Thompson found too late what sort of a man she had so imprudently taken up with. About this time the real character of Peace was presented to her in all its hideous deformity. But she found it difficult and next to impossible to detach herself from the cunning and cruel rascal who held her bondage. It was not possible for her to be an inmate of the house in the Evelina-road, without having some inkling of the goings on in that delectable establishment. Numberless boxes were coming and going. Thompson or Peace was absent at strange times. On the evenings he was absent he returned at all hours, nobody knew when or how, but with his return was associated an accession of worldly goods.

How these were obtained those around him could make a shrewd guess, but neither of his housekeepers had the temerity to ask any questions.

Mrs. Long, who was in a great measure Mrs. Thompson's confidant, declared that up to two months before No. 5 became famous, her friend Mrs. Thompson had no guilty knowledge of Peace's nefarious doings. We are, however, of a different opinion.

We find it impossible to believe in her innocence, particularly in the face of her flight and continued concealment out of the way of the police; but she managed to make many people in Peckham believe it, and we are only repeating their version of the story as it relates to her.

They believed that Peace got to know that Mrs. Thompson was uneasy, and redoubled his vigilance over her.

This is likely enough. He certainly, according to

credible authority, treated her at times in a most brutal manner.

Mrs. Peace or Mrs. Ward, as she was called at this time simultaneously, became more than ever watchful over her charge.

So, taken altogether, it was a pretty family party at Peckham.

The stories of drunkenness accounting for the quarrels became more frequent, and if Mrs. Thompson visited any of the houses she had been accustomed to drop into at Peckham, Mrs. Ward was quickly at her heels.

One day when she went to Mrs. Long's, the old woman haunted the house till she came out. That very day Mrs. Thompson seemed terribly distressed. She appeared to have some dreadful load on her mind, which she was anxious to communicate to some one. At last she burst out with a cry—

"Oh, Mrs. Long, if I could only tell you everything —if I could but find the courage to make you acquainted with all I know!"

Mrs. Long, who was getting rather uneasy about Peace, for whom she had a strong but unaccountable aversion, did not encourage her to say any more.

She was afraid it would get her into trouble, as she had been given to understand that Thompson—it is immaterial whether we call him Peace or Thompson— disapproved of his wife's visits to the house.

This he knew through Mrs. Ward, the constant spy upon the other's movements.

Every effort was now made to keep Mrs. Thompson a close prisoner in the house.

The Longs at that time kept a dairy, and used to supply the Thompsons with their milk, where the little girl delivered the milk in the morning.

Mrs. Thompson would come for it, but at her back was the old woman to see and hear what passed.

Ultimately the Longs were told not to send any more milk—Peace and the old lady evidently hoping in this way to cut off the communication between the two houses.

On the evening to which we more particularly refer, Mrs. Thompson said "he," meaning Peace, had gone to the theatre, and she did not know when he would be back.

She had seized the chance of running out unknown to Mrs. Ward. She deceived herself. At that very moment Mrs. Ward was at the door, waiting and watching for her return. And that evening she repeated the visit to Peace, who, in Sheffield phrase, "paid" the poor wretch severely for her call on Mrs. Long.

On that night Mrs. Thompson was in great fear. She trembled all over her body, as she disclosed to Mrs. Long that she felt in danger of her life, adding, now and again, "Oh that I could tell you what I know— oh, that I knew what to do!"

It would be interesting to know if Peace really did play in the orchestra of any London theatre. Mrs. Thompson sometimes accounted for his frequent disappearances at night in this way, until she began to know better, or rather worse, and even she seems to have been undecided between fear of telling the truth and shame of keeping up the old lie in the face of Peckham.

Peace told her that he occasionally played in the orchestra—not that he needed to do so, but simply through love of music, and because, as he boasted, he was pressed to do so by the conductor, who said he was the best "bow" he had.

Peace's skill on the violin, of course, is well known,

having long earned him the distinctive title, of which he was particularly fond, of "the modern Paganini."

It is not unlikely that one night he operated with his violin in the orchestra to Blackheath ladies and gentlemen, in one of whose houses he the following night operated with equal skill with the burglar's tools, supplemented by a knife and a revolver slung to his wrist by a leathern thong.

One day Mr. Long was walking down Evelina-road, when he met Mrs. Thompson, to whom he spoke as usual. She seemed in a hurry and disconcerted, passing on at a quick pace, and not stopping to speak, as was her wont.

Further on he met Thompson, moving along with rapid strides and carrying an ugly-looking whip in his hand, which he was handling in a nervous yet vicious style.

"Good morning, Mr. Thompson," said Mr. Long, adding, "Mrs. Thompson is just a little before you."

Long held out his hand, which Thompson shook as usual, then nodding quickly, said "Good morning—I'm in a hurry," and he expedited his walk till he overtook her he was after, and then they slowly returned to the house together.

What happened there did not transpire till some time after when Mrs. Thompson took to pouring into Mrs. Long's sympathetic ears the story of her "married" life at No. 5.

Thompson, when he got her inside, used his whip about the wretch's shoulders, and beat her with the butt end of the stock, to frighten her into doing what he wanted.

The fact was, he began to be suspicious, and as a consequence his usual caution foresook him.

That scene in the street, which took place some two months before his capture by Robinson, was the most impudent thing he did at Peckham, and there is reason to believe that he was then contemplating another change of residence, where Mrs. Thompson's tales would be in less danger of getting through the neighbours to the police.

Had he not "tried" that house at Blackheath, or had he succeeded in doing it and getting off, Peckham would speedily have lost the society of the independent gentleman with the interesting household.

Peace's life at this time must have been something terrible to think of—that is, assuming he had any feeling or conscience, which, to say the truth, is very questionable.

With all his cunning he must have been in constant fear of detection.

His wife was faithful enough to him, but he had good reasons for mistrusting the woman Thompson; who was prone to gossiping, and given to drink, and who was, moreover, kept under subjection by cruel usage and a system of espionage; but, with all this, there was no telling how soon a man might be compromised by means of an incautious word, and it required a wonderful amount of pains and trouble to keep watch and ward over Mrs. Thompson, who, to say the least of her, was anything but a prudent woman.

In addition to all this, Peace had to elude the vigilance of the police. This he continued to do successfully enough for a considerable period, but it was not done without a vast amount of dodging, and even while at Peckham he was disturbed by them.

One morning the local policeman noticed a light in Thompson's house at an unusual hour—about two o'clock. He was afraid things were not quite right, and was unwilling to let so estimable a citizen be robbed.

He knocked loudly at the door. All was silent. He knocked again, and then there shuffled along the passage some one who cautiously opened the door.

When Peace saw it was the policeman, and heard his business, he was instantly himself—the cool, impudent rogue that he was.

Flinging open the door, he insisted upon his coming in, saying—

"We are working here at all hours of the night at present. The fact is, I am busy on an invention by which I expect to make my fortune over again—it is for raising sunken ships, and I hope to start with the 'Eurydice.'"

And the interested constable went in and had the invention explained to him. It is more probable that at that time Peace was busy at his crucible melting down some stolen goldware, and that he first cleared away all signs of the work and substituted the model of his patent to produce before the policeman. On one occasion Peace had a "scare."

A "Long Firm" had been established at Peckham, and two detectives—one rather famous in his profession—came over from Greenwich.

At that time, an assistant to Mr. Cleaves—a man named Thomas, who looks after the removal of furniture—was helping Peace to erect his stable. Peace's quick eye noticed the detectives stop opposite his house.

He said, "Thomas, are these not two policemen in plain clothes?" Thomas said they were. He knew one of them—naming him as the famous M——.

Peace was frightened for the moment, but was reassured when Thomas told him they had come to inquire about a "Long Firm" case, mentioning one man he knew they were after.

"Oh! ——," said Peace, "the damned old scamp! Why can't he get his living in an honest way?"

Had the famous M—— known he was in sight of the Bannercross murderer, I fancy he would have let the other "old scamp" slide for the moment.

Thomas tells me that Peace did not go out much after his pony died.

That event seemed to take the heart out of him. He was accustomed to trot his pony very fast, and he always went out in the afternoon "prospecting."

When his pony became ill he showed the greatest solicitude for its recovery, walking it up and down at a most gingerly pace, and stroking it tenderly, while nothing was too good for it to wear, or too expensive for it to take.

Mrs. Thompson used to tell Mrs. Long that, however great a villain he was, he was very kind to dumb creatures, and would not let anyone hurt a hair of their heads.

Mrs. Long has got his favourite black cat, and is very anxious to get possession of "Rosie," a dog which had a great liking for Mrs. Thompson.

Once, when Peace struck her, Rosie sprang at him and bit him severely.

Rosie has disappeared. Every morning Mrs. Thompson cut down a big loaf for Peace's pets, which he always saw fed himself. He was very careful, too, about their being cleaned, making it his rule to get down on his knees and scrub the stable flagstones himself.

Thomas once said to him jestingly while the stable was being built that "it was a good amusement for him—it kept him out of the public-house." "The public-house," said Peace, "is the ruin of all. I never go there. Keep out of it, my friend, if you would be a respectable man and do well."

As a matter of fact he did go to the public-house. He would take one glass, never any more, though he would pay for any quantity for other people. He usually went to the Hollydale Tavern, Hollydale-road, and he never sat down. "He always stood up, near the door," it was said, "as if he was ready to make a run for it."

Meanwhile robberies went on night after night, and the magnitude of the depredations, together with the immunity of the burglar, was a matter of surprise to everybody. Letters appeared in the papers complaining of the inefficiency of the police, but all was in vain. Peace for a long time escaped discovery or capture. The wonderful way in which he disguised himself is most remarkable, and we doubt if it has ever been equalled by any other criminal, either great or small. We have already said that Peace was very careful in hiding his mutilated hand. That hand might have been to Peace what his heel was to Achilles. The tenant of No. 5 was more careful about keeping the missing finger from the not very prying eyes of the Peckhamites. He did not look like a man who was much given to the wearing of gloves, and anything new that way seemed to sit clumsily upon him, but upon the left hand he usually wore a glove, and to outward appearance he had the usual complement of fingers. He got over the difficulty by having one glove finger padded. When he had forgotten his glove, which was on very rare occasions, he pushed his left hand into his breast, and loitered about, but did not care to talk to anybody.

But, more important than the glove expedient, were his other measures to conceal his identity. He treated his hair in a variety of ways. After the Bannercross murder he eschewed beard and whiskers altogether, and in addition to getting rid of them he shaved his forehead, thus giving himself the appearance of a person with a bald head. In talking, the neighbours can now recollect how strangely he used to "lift up," as it were, the whole front of his forehead, and let it quickly settle down again. When he elevated his eyebrows—he had not much in that direction to elevate, and these were usually "doctored" in various ways—it seemed to him as if the whole of the front part of his head went with them.

Indeed, this interesting old gentleman had begun to amuse his nearest neighbours by what they considered his little oddities and innocent eccentricities.

He was fond of wearing a wig, and he seemed unable to decide upon any given kind or colour of wig. At one time he would show the carefully-arranged locks of hair—not one awry—which always indicate the work of the peruke-maker—in the glossiest of black; then a few grey hairs would give him a venerable aspect, and anon he would fall in love with a pleasing brown, which the neighbours thought was a close imitation of the tresses of Mrs. Thompson. So much was he given to change that some people thought that the tenant of No. 5 was a trifle "cracked"—or, what Yorkshire people call, "silly"—in this respect.

Another method he had of disguising himself was the way in which he coloured his complexion. Peace had, no doubt, picked some walnuts in his day, and the singularly effective dye which exudes from the outer shell had not escaped his attention. It was walnut-juice he used to impart to his face that peculiar tinge which would enable him to pass himself off as a half-caste. Mrs. Cleaves, the lady to whom I have already repeatedly referred, includes walnuts among the articles she sells at her premises four doors off. "Mrs. Thompson" or "Mrs. Ward"—I forget which at this moment—used to ask Mrs. Cleaves to be good enough to save the walnut shells for her, and Mrs. Cleaves gave one or other of these "ladies" a basketful at a time, frequently wondering what the people at No. 5 could want with so many walnut shells. One day feminine curiosity got the better of her, and she asked Mrs. Thompson, who said Mr. Thompson had a secret of making "ketchup" from walnut shells, and that was what they used them for. Another day, the man Thomas, while he lived next door, observed his neighbour, "Mr. Thompson," emptying some dark shell out of a black bottle, and he was curious enough to ask the mistress—by "the mistress" he meant Mrs. Thompson—what that stuff was. She replied that "he" had been trying his hand at pickling walnuts, and had spoilt them.

An intelligent young Peckhamite said that he and other lads had begun to notice something very peculiar about Mr. Thompson's back hair. He sometimes wore a low hat which fitted loosely to his head, and the wind would occasionally "ruffle up" the hair at the back. They could then see that there were distinct colours, which were no doubt caused by the dyeing with walnut juice. He must have used it very freely about his face, chest, neck, hands, and arms, and well down his body, and on his legs, for when the police stripped him he looked even darker than the half-caste he professed to be. I am told that almost every morning he could be seen picking the shells of walnuts and throwing the nuts away.

Peace, as we have already seen, was as cunning as a fox, and in fact as far as scruples were concerned, he did not profess any. He would resort to any artifice for the purpose of carrying out his notorious practices. How "he obliged a friend," is very well remembered by the inhabitants of Peckham to this day.

CHAPTER XCII.

AN OUTCAST IN LONDON—THE GIPSY'S TRIALS AND TROUBLES.

THE London career of Charles Peace was the most remarkable and daring one it is well possible to conceive. Indeed, we have nothing on record equal to it in the life of any criminal of ancient or modern times. We shall have occasion to shadow this forth in the succeeding chapters of our work.

We have followed the footsteps of our hero up to the time of his becoming a resident in Evelina-road, Peckham. For the present we shall have to leave him, that we may turn back to an earlier period and chronicle the doings of some of the other personages who have figured on the stage of our drama.

Mr. William Rawton, the gipsy, better known to the reader as "Bandy-legged Bill," left Sheffield after Peace's last conviction. To use his own phrase, he saw "the game was up," and that his quondam companion had a "pretty good dose." The gipsy, therefore, turned his thoughts in another direction, and sought out his patron, as he was pleased to term him.

The gentleman in question was distantly related to the Ethalwoods, but he was the black sheep of the flock — a restless, careless, ne'er-do-well, who ran through his patrimony by betting largely. In addition to this, he had other vices, which are too numerous to mention. To do him justice, however, he had been kind to the gipsy on several occasions. He advanced him money when very hard pushed, and put many jobs in his way.

It was, therefore, a sad blow to Rawton when he was informed of his patron's demise. He felt that he had lost a good friend, and deeply deplored the loss.

In addition to this misfortune, another befel him.

The groom in Park-lane, who had been so staunch and true to him in times of great necessity, mistook his master's property for his own, and had to decamp to save himself from a worse fate. So the ill-fated gipsy was left without a friend in the metropolis.

He went from bad to worse, and finally became so reduced that he was on the verge of starvation.

"He deserved no better fate!" the reader may exclaim. Possibly so, but it is hard for a fellow-creature to be in the most opulent city in the world without being able to obtain the common necessaries of life. Nevertheless, this is of almost daily occurrence.

The reports of similar cases in our public newspapers furnish us with proofs of this.

We have no desire to enlist anybody's sympathy for wretches like Charles Peace, or Bill Rawton, or others who figure in this work; but starvation in a land of plenty is a melancholy fact which every right-minded person must of necessity deplore.

Starving, homeless, friendless, despised, and desperate, Bandy-legged Bill wandered through the streets of the metropolis.

It was a cold winter's night, and the gipsy's teeth chattered, and his limbs trembled.

"Nothing remains for me but death," he ejaculated, "for most assuredly my life must soon come to an end if things go on in this way. The crimes and injustice of others have brought me to this, not my own."

This is the specious way scoundrels of this type invariably delude themselves by false reasoning.

"It aint been my fault," he repeated. "I always acted on the square with all my pals. Curse it!—but it's hard lines to be in this sorry plight. I'll cast all conscience scruples in one scale hereafter, and will be an outlaw as well as an outcast. A man gets no thanks for being honest in this world. I am at war with the world, even as mankind are at war with me."

Bill crawled towards a street lamp as if he could derive warmth from its flickering flame.

"I aint a bit like myself," he exclaimed. "Am as weak as a rat, and as down-hearted as a man just sentenced to a 'lagging.' Peace is better off than I am; he has food and shelter, such as it is, at the expense of Government. I should like to be in his place just now, and the chances are I shall be before long."

The hour was late—approaching towards midnight, and the street in which he was stationed was pretty nigh deserted. Presently he heard the measured tread of a policeman, and the gipsy not being desirous of an official interview with the arm of the law, skulked away and hid himself in a dark alley until the constable had passed on.

"I must find some place to crawl to, but where?" exclaimed Bill. "That's easier asked than answered. Mercy on me! how my teeth do chatter! I wish the night was over; but, lor', what's the use of wishing that? Morning will bring me no relief."

Presently he heard footsteps. He guessed shrewdly enough that they were not those of a policeman. He grasped a thick cudgel he had in his hand and said, "Now for it!"

A well-dressed gentlemanly-looking person was advancing towards him with stately tread. He was a handsome man, in the prime of life, and was evidently a favourite of fortune; yet the expression of his face was evil.

The gipsy sprang forward, and grasped him by the collar of his coat.

"Quick! haul over your cash!" he exclaimed, "or I

will knock you senseless. Do you hear? I'm driven to desperation, and money I must have."

"Well," exclaimed the gentleman, "you are either a madman or else one of the most audacious fellows I ever met with."

"I am no madman. If you refuse or attempt to utter a single cry for assistance I'll brain you."

"You are a most extraordinary man."

"Your money!—I am starving. Do not drive me to desperation. I am not to be trifled with. Do not drive me to commit murder."

"Upon my word you really amuse me," said the gentleman. "I thought the time was past for footpads or highway robbers, but we live and learn, it would appear. Unhand me."

"Not until you have given me what I demand."

"If I summon a policeman and hand you over to justice, which, to say the truth is my duty, you will be severely punished. But as you are starving, according to your own account—"

"I am dying with hunger, and don't care about being sent to prison. It's preferable to dying like a dog in the streets."

"I will take compassion on you. This is something like an adventure. Again I say, take your hand from my coat. I will assist you. There, will that satisfy you."

"It will," observed the gipsy, in a softened tone; "for once I have met with one who has compassion on a fellow-creature."

"You would not be very scrupulous, I suppose, in rendering services for kindness received—eh?" inquired the gentleman.

"Scrupulous!—well no, not very."

"I should imagine not."

"A starving man is not likely to be over particular," said the gipsy, laughing bitterly, and looking attentively at the face of his questioner.

"Well, then, you must understand that this is not the place for a conference. I rather think you will suit my purpose. So, if you will accompany me, I will take you where you can enjoy both warmth and food. Then we can talk over this business. Follow me."

Bandy-legged Bill strode onward.

He and his companion threaded their way through a number of streets, through which the winter's blast howled dismally.

Nothing can be more desolate than the deserted streets of a great city at midnight.

The busy thoroughfares are as silent as the grave, and every house seems a tomb enclosing some tremendous secret.

What if, in the silent hours of the night, the walls of the dwellings should suddenly become transparent, revealing all that might be passing inside?

What astounding disclosures would be made!

Imagination shrinks from the picture, appalled.

"Here we are," said the gipsy's companion, pausing before a house of handsome exterior, and leading the way down into the basement.

Over one of the windows of this basement was a gilded sign, bearing the name "Doctor Bourne."

The doctor unlocked a door, entered a room, and turned up the gas.

The gipsy now found himself in a very comfortable apartment fitted up like a surgery. There was a book-case, surmounted by the usual skull—there was the inevitable skeleton grinning in a corner—there were anatomical pictures, a case of surgical instruments, shelves of bottles and phials, nice sofas, a crimson carpet, and a highly-polished stove, in which a cheerful fire blazed.

"Sit down, my man," said the doctor, with an air of superiority and condescension.

The gipsy thanked his host, and seated himself.

"Now in the first place I must get you something to eat and drink," said the doctor. "By my faith, but you look like a starved cat, and yet now I glance at your face it seems familiar to me."

"Does it? We have never met before, not to my knowledge."

"No, no, of course not—I know that. Our spheres of life are widely different, I hope; but what the devil ever brought you so low as to set you prowling about the streets at night, dressed in rags, and threatening to brain people with a bludgeon?"

"The story of my life is hardly worth the telling," returned Bill.

"Well, I should suppose not, but I suppose your downfall is partly owing to drink."

"Partly," observed the gipsy.

"Ah, so I thought."

The doctor unlocked a cupboard and took from it about two-thirds of a cold boiled ham, a loaf of bread and sundry other articles, which he placed before Bill, inviting him to fall to and help himself.

The starving man needed no second invitation; he ate most ravenously. Meanwhile the doctor, rummaging in the cupboard, brought forth more eatables, which he placed before his guest.

After the gipsy had satisfied his hunger a glass of warm grog was mixed by his benefactor, which the gipsy was nothing loth to partake of.

He was, however, greatly puzzled at the reception he met with—it was altogether so much out of the common order of things, and he was curious to ascertain in what way his services were required, for he was acute enough to divine that all these attentions were not shown him without some ulterior object.

"Ahem—you spoke of some service, something you required me to do. May I ask its nature?" observed the gipsy, carelessly.

"Oh, we won't enter on the business just now," said Bourne. "It is not of any immediate importance, but I suppose you will pass your word to do me a good turn when I require you to do so?"

"It is only my duty, sir. Anything I can do shall be done, provided it be such as a man can consistently perform."

"Yes, precisely. Well, we will discuss this question when we are better acquainted with one another."

"He's jolly artful," murmured the gipsy to himself, "and don't let every fool see his cards. Well he's not to blame for that."

"By the way," said Bourne, "you have not told me your name?"

"My name?"

"Yes; don't be afraid. I am not likely to hand you over to justice," and at this the doctor laughed.

"I don't expect you are. Well, I am not ashamed of my name. It is William Rawton—Bandy-legged Bill my pals call me, because, you see, my legs were a little warped in the drying process."

The doctor gave an involuntary start. "Rawton, eh!"

"Yes, Bill Rawton. Have you heard the name before?"

"Well, I rather think some of my patients have mentioned that name. To all appearance you are a gipsy?"

"Yes, I was born a gipsy, but our camp broke up years and years ago."

DR. BOURNE QUESTIONING BILL RAWTON, THE GIPSY.

"Have you been a jockey at any time of your life?"

"I should rather think I had. I might say that I was, in a manner of speaking, brought up on the back of a horse."

"Oh, that accounts for it. I have heard your name mentioned by some of my sporting and aristocratic patients."

"And who might they be?" inquired Bill.

"I cannot at the present moment call to mind. You are a single man, eh?"

"I am single now, but I have been married."

"Ah, I see. Wife dead, I suppose?"

"I haven't seen her for years, but she may be alive for what I know."

Then suddenly looking hard at his questioner, he said, in an altered tone—

"What makes you ask that question ?"

"Faith, I don't know why I made the inquiry. I was thinking if you had any one to share your troubles."

"No, I have not, and what's more, I dont want anyone to share my misery. It's hard lines for one ; it would be doubly hard if there were two doomed to the misery I have had to endure."

"You are quite right, my friend, it would."

The gipsy regarded the speaker with another furtive glance.

"By the way, you are not getting on. Let me mix you another glass—the night is cold, and drinking in moderation is beneficial. I am not an advocate for total abstinence."

"Nor am I," observed Rawton, with a laugh, "but of late I have been compelled to be a total abstainer."

"Another glass and a cigar ?"

"You are very kind, sir, I'm sure. I won't refuse, since you are so pressing."

The grog was mixed, and the gipsy lighted a cigar of the first quality.

"Take it altogether this is a strange night's adventure," observed Bourne. "Most remarkable. It pleases me, and for this reason : I am fond of searching into the character of man, and I feel convinced your history must be strange one."

"I've seen something of life. Have had my ups and downs, more of the latter than the former, and as I feel just now—or rather as I did when we first met—I don't think there is much worth living for in this world—not as far as I am concerned at any rate."

"You mustn't give way to despondency and look at the dark side of the picture. Brighter days may be in store for you—who knows ?"

The gipsy shook his head.

"I doubt it," he observed, sententiously.

There was a pause, after which the doctor said, carelessly—

"And so you have been married, have lost your wife, and don't know where she is ?"

"Haven't the slightest notion, and don't care to inquire. Ah, she left me of her own accord. It must be—well, let's see—ah, it must be getting on for twenty years ago."

"Dear me, how very remarkable ! Did she"—then pausing suddenly, as if to check himself, the doctor added, "But then I don't know that I have any right to inquire into your private affairs, which, after all, cannot be of any great interest to me."

"Oh ! I don't mind telling you the whole history if you think it worth listening to. You see, in my early youth I was a very different sort of chap to what I am now—I was what you might call a smart young fellow, who got on pretty well with the girls."

"Oh ! I dare say. No doubt."

"But since those days I've had a rough time of it, and had fallen into evil ways. At one time I associated with the upper classes - not quite as a companion, I don't mean that, but I was in the secrets of a few of the big guns—but, zounds ! that is all past now. I've come down right on my haunches, and the chances are I shall never get up again. This is a beautiful flavoured cigar."

"Yes, I've got a very choice brand; the best I've had for many a day." The doctor lighted one for himself. "Very good flavour indeed. Well, as you were saying—go on with your history."

"Oh, I was merely observing that I was at one time thought a goodish bit of by some heavy swells."

"Yes. Proceed. And your wife—was she with you at this time ?"

"We didn't live many months together."

"Not many months ! Your nuptial bliss was, indeed, of but a short duration."

"No, not many months. You see she was too good for me. The fact is, she was but a chit of a girl when I married her, who didn't know her own mind. It was a runaway match. I was passionately fond of her at the time, but I found out afterwards that I had made a mistake. She was a delicate sensitive thing, had been well brought up, and I was not the sort of man she ought to have chosen for a husband. She soon found that out. She got sick and weary of me, and——"

"And what ?"

"Well, we parted. She said she wished to leave me, and I knew she would do so in any case, whether I liked it or not ; so I thought it best to consent to a separation. 'Cause, you see, she had an admirer."

"An admirer, eh ?"

"Yes."

"A gentleman—a man of property, I suppose."

"Oh, yes, a baronight. She went to live with him. He took her over to India, and I have never seen her from that day to this. If she's alive, which I don't feel at all certain about, I hope she's happy, for she was a right down good sort."

"And pray, my complacent friend, is it a fair question to inquire the name of the baronet ?"

"I don't mind telling you. Sir Digby M'Bride was his name."

"And he went to India, you say ?"

"So I was told."

"Sir William has been dead for the last fifteen years," said the doctor. "He fell on the field of battle, like a brave soldier as he was."

"Did he though ? I never heard that bit of news before."

"It is a fact, I assure you."

"Did you know him then ?"

"No, not personally, but I was acquainted with those who did know him. What was your wife's maiden name ?"

"Hester Teige. Upon my word you seem greatly interested about her," cried Rawton, with sudden warmth.

His companion coloured slightly. "No, oh dear no—not at all. You are mistaken," he ejaculated, endeavouring to assume an air of indifference. "I know not why I asked the question, but I suppose she passed as Lady M'Bride."

"I dare say she did. She might have done for aught I know. She may have had a good many names in her time. She went on the stage, so I was told, and played under another name."

"Oh, indeed, then possibly she's had some strange alternations of fortune."

Rawton shook his head.

"I know nothing about her. She's passed away, and is nothing to me now—has not been anything to me for years."

"You are evidently a character in your way. You've endeavoured to play the part of a highwayman—not very successfully, it is true—but you've made the attempt, and doubtless you have played many other parts in the drama of life. I must learn something more of you. Take my advice for the future—abstain from the committal of any lawless act. I have a wish to befriend you; for the present I will give you some temporary assistance—something to help you over your immediate difficulties—and for the rest you have my permission to visit me again, when I will see what can be done for you."

The doctor gave Rawton a sovereign, which the latter took, and at the same time overwhelmed his benefactor with thanks.

"That will suffice," said Bourne. "I am glad to be of service to you, and will see what more can be done. Possibly I may be instrumental in procuring you a situation, but you must first of all be furnished with better garments than those you have on at present. Well, we will see what can be done."

"You are very kind, I'm sure, and I ought to be grateful. Indeed I am, much more than I can express."

The gipsy rose to take his departure, being under the impression that his company was not wanted any longer.

"You can give me a look in to-morrow, or next day, if you like. The most convenient hour to see me is after seven o'clock in the evening. As a rule my professional duties are over by that time, except in urgent cases, which happily don't occur every day."

"I'll make bold to call again if you will permit it."

"Certainly I desire you to do so," returned Bourne, as he accompanied his visitor to the door.

Rawton was about to pass out of the house when the doctor beckoned him back.

"What might you want?" he inquired.

"Oh, just this," returned Bourne. "It is a matter of no very great moment, and which I cannot exactly explain at present, but could you procure your marriage certificate and bring it with you when you call again?"

The gipsy was dumfounded, and hardly knew what reply to make.

"Can you do so?" again repeated his companion.

"Why what on earth do you want a worthless bit of paper like that for?" ejaculated the gipsy. "It aint of no use to mortal man."

"Well, that's a matter it is hardly worth while discussing, but I take it for granted that you wish to oblige me."

"Most certainly I do."

"Then you will greatly oblige me by doing this little favour."

"But what for?"

"As a matter of good faith—as a proof that you have not been deceiving me."

"Deceive you in what way?"

"It will give me assurance that you have spoken the truth."

"Oh, that's it. You don't believe a word I have been saying, then?"

"I believe all you have said, but I tell you again, I should be much more satisfied if you would bring with you the marriage certificate when you next call. Now do you understand?"

"Of course I understand, as far as it goes. Well, I'm blest if this aint a new start."

"Well, never mind. Let it be for the present. I will explain more fully when we next meet. Now go, for I am perishing with cold."

The gipsy bade his companion good night, and left the house without further ado.

CHAPTER XCIII.
THE UNEXPECTED DISCOVERY—HUSBAND AND WIFE.

Mr. WILLIAM RAWTON, after he left the doctor's establishment, betook himself to a common lodging-house, where he slept for the remainder of the night.

He had found a friend, it is true, and the assistance afforded him was most welcome, as it saved him from perishing from actual want and privation; but the more he considered the matter over, the more puzzled he was to account for Dr. Bourne's manner and demeanour. That there was something beneath the surface Bill had guessed long before he took his departure from his patron's house. What that something was he could not possibly divine or even guess.

The thought crossed the gipsy's mind that the certificate of his marriage was wanted to prove his (the gipsy's) identity, and possibly criminal proceedings would follow.

He did not like the doctor's manner; he did not like his looks, or indeed the man himself.

Anyway he deemed it expedient not to be in too great a hurry to oblige his patron, about whom he was desirous of learning a little more.

Rawton's elopement and marriage with Hester Teige was a sort of boy-and-girl attachment, which was in reality but little more than a nine days' wonder. Both the contracting parties found out their mistake, and it is likely enough that the gipsy was as glad to be rid of his bargain as she was to leave him.

Hester Teige was a beauty. In addition to her personal charms, which were of no mean order, she had grace, and an air of refinement which went far to commend her to persons in the higher walks of life.

The history of this fair but frail woman would fill a volume.

She had passed through various phases of life—had been the pet and idol of some of England's proudest aristocracy.

Then when the sunny days of her youth had passed away she was left to the tender mercies of one who ruled her with a rod of iron.

As far as Bandy-legged Bill was concerned he had altogether forgotten the young and attractive girl whom he imprudently chose to marry. The only wonder was how such an ill-assorted match could ever have taken place, or how any well-educated young woman could have ever consented to be led to the altar by such a commonplace personage as our friend the gipsy. But so it was.

Bill had certainly one quality to recommend him—he was brim full of good nature, and was at this time one of the best tempered fellows out. He was goodnatured enough to resign his wife to better hands, and after this had taken place he never afterwards interfered with her.

The gipsy husbanded his resources as carefully as possible. He could make a small sum go a long way when it suited his purpose, and the sovereign he had received from Bourne would last him some little time; besides, the chances were that a further advance would be made when that was gone.

He did not deem it advisable to call the following day; but at about half-past seven in the evening he presented himself on the succeeding one. The doctor was in, and the boy who answered the bell showed him into the surgery.

"Ah—it's you. Sit down, my man, and I'll attend to you presently."

The gipsy seated himself.

"Well," said the doctor, after the boy had left, "so you are here again. I hope you have been conducting yourself in a proper and discreet manner."

"I've done my best, sir; but it's hard lines with those who cannot get anything to do. I don't mind what it is, so long as I can earn an honest living."

"I'm glad to hear you say that. But, you see, my man, I am afraid you have lost your character—is that not so?"

"I won't deny it, sir—I have."

"Yes; by dishonest practices. Eh?"

"I don't deny that. I have been in trouble."

"Ah, I thought so. Have you brought that certificate?"

"No; I am sorry to say I have not; but of course I can get it if you wish me to do so."

"Confound the man! What's the use of saying if I wish? Haven't I already told you what I wished?"

"Very good, sir. The next time I come will do, I suppose?"

"It must do."

It was very evident that Bourne, for some cause or another, was in a bad temper.

At this juncture the boy entered the room, and said that Mrs. Moncroft wished to see his master.

"Oh! Mrs. Moncroft. Eh?" exclaimed the doctor. "Dear me. I will see the lady."

"Shall I leave, sir?" inquired the gipsy.

"No; don't go. I wish to have a little conversation with you, but—ah, you had better go into the consulting room and wait till I am disengaged. Walter, show this gentleman upstairs into the back room; he will wait."

"Yes, sir," said the lad, who conducted Rawton into a dingy apartment above what was called the surgery. In a minute or two after this a fashionably dressed comely-looking woman was shown into the apartment in which Dr. Bourne was seated.

"He aint altogether what you might call a nice-tempered, amiable sort of gentleman," murmured Rawton, as he seated himself on the well-worn sofa in the room to which he had been conducted. "He's far from that, I'm thinking; but then we all of us have our faults and weaknesses. Shortness of temper seems to be one of his. I confess I can't quite tumble to him. However, we shall see how he turns out as time goes on. It's jolly hard lines for a cove to be dependent on a stranger, but he aint the sort of man to do the generous all for nothing; leastways that's my private opinion. I hope I don't do the gentleman an injustice."

Mr. Rawton whistled and beat a tattoo on the head of the sofa just to beguile the tedium of the hour. As he was thus engaged he heard the sound of voices, which appeared to come from the front parlour of the establishment. He paused and listened attentively; then he turned pale, and his heart seemed to sink within him. He listened again—two persons were conversing. One voice was strangely familiar to him.

He rose from the sofa, and walked hurriedly across the room. He partially opened the door, and stood spell-bound with astonishment.

"It's many a long year since I heard that voice, or rather a voice like it; for I must be mistaken—it aint likely, and it's well-nigh impossible; and yet the sound is so unmistakeable that it seems to knock me over."

He heard the light step of a female in the passage. He opened the door and peeped out. A maid-servant was passing along the passage.

"I say, my dear, just a word with you, if you please," said Mr. Rawton.

"I am not your dear, sir," returned the girl, with a pout.

"Beg pardon, meant no offence, but you see I don't happen to know your name."

"Well, what do you want?" cried the girl.

"May I ask who it was I heard talking in yonder room?"

"Who? Why me and missus."

"Ah, and who might your missus be?"

"Mrs. Bourne, of course, who do you suppose?"

"I don't suppose anything. She's the doctor's wife then?"

"Yes, certainly. What makes you ask such a stupid question? Just mind your own business."

"Now don't be angry. You are a charming girl, as beautiful as the flowers—I mean, as a butterfly."

"Get along with your nonsense—do."

She was about to pass on, but he detained her.

"What on earth do you want?" she ejaculated.

"Only a word—only a word or two." He drew her into the back parlour.

"Now, then, what do you want?"

"Where is your mistress?"

"In the front parlour."

"Oh, will you do me a favour?"

"That depends upon what it is."

"I want you to go back to your mistress and ask her if she knew a man named William Rawton."

"And what if she does?"

"Well, then she will remember the name if she is the person I suppose her to be. Now do as I tell you, like a good girl, as I am sure you are."

"You are a queer sort of fellow; ask her yourself."

"No, I would not think of doing such a thing. I ask you again to oblige me by doing this."

"There's not much difficulty in the matter. I will do as you desire."

The girl flitted past her questioner, hurried along the passage, and entered the front room.

When she had reached this Rawton heard a faint scream, and in a few moments after this the maid servant, pale and flurried, returned to the gipsy.

"Well!" exclaimed the latter.

"Well—it's not well. When I mentioned the name of Rawton, my poor mistress was ready to faint; and when I left she had not recovered."

"Ah!" said Bandy-legged Bill, "I am not surprised. I am almost inclined to do a faint on my own account; but did she make any inquiries—did she say anything else?"

"Yes; she told me to ask who and what you were, and wished to know if you wanted to see her."

"I do want to see her," returned Bill, "if only for a few minutes. I should like to see her. Tell her so. I don't know your name."

"My name is Amy."

"Well, then, Amy, say I want to see her, if you please."

The girl went to her mistress and delivered the gipsy's message.

In a minute or so after this an elegantly dressed aristocratic-looking female entered the doctor's consulting room.

"You wished to see me, sir," she observed, with hauteur, addressing herself to the gipsy.

For a moment Bill was so taken aback that he could not find words to express himself. He stood gazing abstractedly on the wan features of the fair creature before him, and found it difficult at that moment to feel assured as to her identity.

"I beg your pardon, madam," he stammered, "but you see I thought, as I listened to the conversation which was going on in the opposite room, I recognised a voice I had heard afore, though it be ever so many years back since I heard it."

"I do not quite understand your meaning, sir," observed his companion.

"Pray may I inquire whom I am addressing?"

"You do not know me, then?"

"I confess I do not."

"I am Bill Rawton, the gipsy."

Had a bombshell exploded in the room Mrs. Bourne could not possibly have been more astonished. She staggered back several paces and sank into a chair; she became deathly pale, and her whole appearance was indicative of terror intermingled with despair.

"You, William Rawton?" she presently ejaculated. "It is not—it cannot be possible. Rawton has been dead for more than fifteen years."

The gipsy slowly shook his head.

"You are mistaken, madam," he said in a tone of abject humiliation, "I am that man."

"But he was drowned in Harcott's Mill, I heard, years and years ago."

"A man, supposed to be Rawton, was drowned there, and there was an inquest on the body, but it was not me."

"I am ruined, undone, and the most miserable of mortals," exclaimed Mrs. Bourne, wringing her hands. "What has brought you here, and what is the object of this visit?"

"Do not be alarmed. It has not been my own seeking. I am here by the merest accident, and the very last person in the world I expected to meet here is yourself."

"I am appalled! Gracious heaven, what am I to do? And you—are in the depths of poverty, I presume?"

"That is so; but do not suppose I mean you any harm. We have been strangers for twenty years—let us continue to be so."

"And my husband—do you know him? But of course you do, else you would not be here."

"I know something of him."

The miserable woman shuddered, and pressed her hands to her throbbing temples.

"My cup of sorrow is full to overflowing," said she with extreme bitterness. "Exposure, disgrace, ignominy are before me. Oh! why have you come hither? and in such a garb too! Oh! but this is indeed terrible! Does the doctor know who and what you are?"

The gipsy hung down his head.

"I am answered," she cried. "For mercy's sake tell me what you want. If it be money, I will give you what you need, provided you do not come here again."

"I shall not trouble you," he exclaimed; "and I will not accept any money from you, seeing that I have forfeited all claim upon you; but I should like to have half an hour or so's conversation with you, not on account of myself, but on your account. Is this man kind to you?'

"What man?"

"Doctor Bourne."

She approached the speaker, and whispered into his ear the monosyllable, "No."

The gipsy nodded significantly.

"Tell me when I can see you without fear of interruption. I've something to tell you; but it's likely enough you've a bit to tell me."

"May I trust you?"

"You may, as heaven is my judge."

"On Thursday next the doctor will be away. He has to attend a patient in the country. You can see me on that day any time after five. But, hush! that's his footstep."

And with these words Mrs. Bourne hurried back into the front room. She had done so but just in time, for the doctor ascended the stairs immediately after she had disappeared, and, putting his head into the room where the gipsy was, he said, in a loud, pompous tone—

"I shall not have time to attend to you to-day, my man; so you had better call again. Do you hear?"

"Oh, yes; I hear, sir," returned Bill. "I will call to-morrow or next day, whichever will suit you best."

"Either will suit me; but I am busy just now."

Bill Rawton passed out of the house. When he gained the street he saw that there was an open carriage at the front door of Bourne's house. In this was seated a fashionably-dressed lady.

Presently the doctor emerged from the portico of his residence, jumped into the carriage by the side of the lady, and the vehicle rumbled over the stones.

CHAPTER XCIV.
BILL AND THE DOCTOR'S WIFE—A TALE OF SORROW AND MISERY.

MR. WILLIAM RAWTON, when he left the doctor's residence, returned to the wretched lodging-house where he had taken up his quarters for a brief period during his sojourn in the metropolis. The events of the last two or three days had made a deep impression on him.

He was not a man given to sentimental or moral reflections upon either the past, present, or future, but he was, nevertheless, forcibly impressed with the remarkable series of coincidences which had recently taken place, and the appearance and manner of the woman whom he had wooed and won in the outset of his career gave unmistakable indication of the dark mystery which was hanging over her and enshrouding her even as a funeral pall.

Bandy-legged Bill was puzzled—there was evidently something lying beneath the surface, but what that something was he was at a loss to divine.

He felt abashed and humiliated when in the presence of Mrs. Bourne, and had it not been for his strong desire to learn something more about her, the chances were that he would never have sought her again; but he was "down upon his luck," as he termed it, and did not know which way to turn. He had never in the whole course of his life been at so low an ebb as at this particular period; nevertheless, to do him justice, it was not for himself that he was so much concerned, as for the woman whom he had known in an earlier day as Hester Teige.

Bill Rawton, beyond a certain amount of good nature, had but little to recommend him. He had been a dodger and a cheat from boyhood, and his moral principles had in no way improved as he grew older. Nevertheless, deep down in the bottom of the heart of this coarse, common man there was one touch of honour and good feeling. Under any circumstances he would not of his "own free will" round upon the girl whom he had once loved; nay, more, he would not harm her by word or deed; and if he had thought she was happy in her present position he had sufficient respect for her never to trouble her again with his presence. For he had sunk so low in the social scale that he felt he was a disgrace to her. When he thought of this his dark, swarthy face wore a troubled expression, and something like a tear stood in his eyes. Many of my readers will find it difficult to believe that anything good and pure could be found left in the callous and hardened nature of the gipsy. My answer to this is, that it is nevertheless a fact. Bandy-legged Bill is sketched from nature, and many of the incidents I have described in his course are founded on actual facts, and are in short real occurrences.

Bill pondered over the words which had fallen from the lips of Doctor Bourne, and as he did so he felt they had a significant meaning. What this was he could not at present determine.

"He thinks me a bad lot, of course," muttered the gipsy. "And I suppose he's not far out in his reckoning. I look about as great a wretch as it is well possible to conceive—so people tell me. They seldom flatter a bloke who is so low down as I am at present. The fact is, I'm ashamed to pr sent myself at a respectable house. That's not to be wondered at."

He glanced at his ragged dirty garments, and as he did so, his countenance wore an expression of disgust.

"I don't know as I shall go there any more," he exclaimed with sudden warmth. "It isn't the cheese for me to do so. I shall only disgust her. Let things take their chance. I can but call when I am better off, if that ever comes to pass."

He drank the lodging-house coffee—or a decoction of horse-beans would, perhaps, be the better term—and sallied forth. He had no particular place to go to, no business to transact, and was certainly not a pleasure-seeker, but, like the rest of the idlers in the great human hive, he paced the streets and stared about him. In the course of an hour or so, he discerned a face which was not unfamiliar to him. A fashionably dressed lady turned her head as she passed by, and came to a sudden halt. The gipsy was bold enough to walk up to her, as her manner seemed to be encouraging.

"Goodness me, it is you, then, but how strangely altered!" said the lady.

"I hardly know myself, and it's a wonder you recognised me, Miss Stanbridge," cried Bill.

"Why what in the name of all that's wonderful have you been doing with yourself? You look the greatest ragamuffin out," observed Laura Stanbridge. "Why, my friend, you are down upon your luck."

"I should just think I was, and no mistake."

"And Peace—Charles Peace—what became of him?"

"Don't know. He had seven years, and I haven't set eyes on him since he came out. He's left Sheffield."

"Left Sheffield, eh! And is he in London? I should suppose not, or I must have seen something of him?"

"No; I don't think he can be in London."

"And you—what are you supposed to be doing?"

"Nothing at all at present."

The lady laughed. "Then how do you live?"

"I don't live; I exist; how I cannot tell you."

"Why, Rawton, this is a bad business."

"Precious bad; but there are others as badly off as myself. I am too honest for this world."

And here the speaker laughed, but it was a forced hollow sort of laugh.

"Well, I am vexed to see you in such a sorry plight; but you'll never do any good while you present such a wretched appearance as this. Call on me this evening."

"Where? At the old place?"

The woman nodded.

"At what time?"

"You will be sure to find me in after eight o'clock."

"I'll call, if you give me permission to do so."

"Good! Call by all means. Adieu for the present. You won't forget?"

And with these parting words she tripped lightly over the pavement.

"Ah! I'll call; she may depend upon that," muttered Bill, after she had left; "there won't be any harm in my giving her a look in. Probably she may put me up to a thing or two. A clever woman—a mighty clever woman—and isn't she up to the knocker? As fresh as a four-year-old, and jolly well groomed to!"

When the specified time arrived, Mr. Rawton gave a modest knock at the door, and was thrown into the presence of the mistress of the house, who treated him hospitably enough. A substantial repast was placed before him, together with some old ale. The gipsy elected to partake of the last-named beverage. He was not much of a hand at wine, but as to malt liquor, he could take any quantity of it.

"Here's to you, marm," said he, raising a foaming tankard to his lips. "My respects and thanks at the same time. You aint one of those who deserts a cove when he's down, and I aint one as is likely to forget your kindness."

"Never mind that. I don't want any protestations. Eat and drink, and make yourself as happy as you can under existing circumstances. And so Peace had to do his seven years—had he?"

"Well, I 'spose they let him off after a five years' stretch; they usually do that if a man behaves himself anything near the mark, and he'd be sure to get the blind side of them, if any man could."

Miss Stanbridge was silent for some minutes.

"Oh!" she at length ejaculated, "poor Charles! he was very unfortunate to be nabbed; but the wisest men are caught napping at times."

"You've known him for a long time, marm?" inquired Bill.

"Dear me, yes—since I was a child."

"He was always square enough with me. I've no reason to complain of him. I only wish I knew where to find him."

"Why?"

"Because I don't think he'd let me go away empty-handed."

"Neither do I intend you to go away empty-handed," cried Bill's companion.

The gipsy looked hard at the speaker.

"Do you mean it?" he said.

"Of course I do. You must not go about in your present plight. Everybody suspects a man who is in rags—and the police in particular. You must make a better appearance."

"I wish I could."

"Aye, but you must, my friend. Now, look here—I will advance you five pounds. You can pay me back when you are better off, you know."

"Ah, my dear good creature, I'll pay you back the first money I get hold of—never fear that. Five pounds! It's a little fortune to me just now."

"Will you promise to make good use of it?"

"Yes, I do promise."

"And not give way to drink?"

"It aint likely."

"I don't know so much about that. I am afraid it is more than likely."

"I have suffered too much for that. You may trust me—believe me you may."

"Well, I will trust you. See, here are the five sovereigns. This sum will suffice for your present necessities. Possibly, in a week or two's time, you will be able to turn yourself round and get something to do. You are not a fool, and I hope you are not an idler."

"I am not afraid of work, marm."

"No, no; Peace told me. I know but little about you from my own personal knowledge, but I am proud to say that Charley always spoke well of you, and it is for his sake that I am rendering you this timely assistance."

"I don't know how to thank you sufficiently. You are a downright good sort, and no mistake; and I shall never forget your kindness," observed Bill, who was really grateful for the service rendered him.

He pocketed the money, and, after again expressing his thanks, took his departure.

He proceeded at once to the nearest clothier's, and had what he termed "a complete rig out." He then returned to the lodging-house, where he washed, shaved, and put on his new garments.

When this had been done, he did not appear to be the same man. His appearance was not aristocratic, it is true, but he looked a respectable member of society. In addition to this, he felt in better spirits and looked hopefully towards the future.

"If I am not up to the knocker," he observed, "I am at any rate neat and tidy, and don't look the forlorn and dilapidated wretch I did yesterday. Oh, I shall do, and I don't mind paying a visit to the doctor's establishment. To say the truth, I did feel downhearted when I last called there."

The gipsy made himself pretty comfortable till the evening, which had been appointed for him to pay a visit to Mr. Bourne.

He counted the hours till the time arrived.

As the hour approached he made himself look as presentable as possible, and then bent his steps in the direction of the doctor's residence. He gave a timid knock at the door, which was presently opened by the servant girl, Amy.

To his inquiry, "whether her missus was in?" the maid gave a nod, and the gipsy entered. He was conducted into a room on the front floor, in which was seated the doctor's wife.

"Ah, 'tis you," she said; "I am glad you have come."

"Are you alone?" inquired Bill.

The answer was in the affirmative.

"You are in much better trim than when I first saw you," she said, glancing at his attire.

"Yes, a little better."

"How came that about?"

"I have had assistance from a friend, marm."

It is astonishing how respectful he was towards her. He treated her as a superior being to himself, and was humble and submissive to the last degree. He could not fail to observe that she looked pale and delicate, and that a settled melancholy seemed to be indelibly fixed on her thin but beautiful features.

"You have something to tell me," she observed, languidly.

"Ahem—yes," he stammered, not knowing very well what to say.

"In the first place, be good enough to inform me how you became first acquainted with Dr. Bourne?"

This was an awkward question—not a very agreeable one to answer—but the gipsy thought it best to tell the truth; so he made his companion acquainted with the attempted highway robbery, and all that followed after this.

"You have sunk so low as that," she murmured, as a dark shade of sadness passed over her countenance. "Oh, but this is very dreadful!"

"I was driven to it, and bitterly regretted the act," he returned, turning away his head. "Had I known—"

"It is of no use repining—it is done," she interrupted; "so let that pass. Now for the rest."

"I don't so much regret the lawless act I was guilty of, not half so much as letting him know that I was married. He wants my marriage certificate, as

I have already told you—what for I am at a loss to imagine."

"He has a motive, and a strong one, or he would not be so importunate. I know him, and can read him like a book. Don't give him any further information upon that or any other subject."

"I will not. I am sorry I said so much."

"Dear me, this is the most wonderful thing that ever occurred. It seems to me to be altogether impossible. I deemed you dead—I felt assured of it; and now in the hour of trouble and travail you rise up in judgment against me—you whom I have not seen for nearly twenty years."

"Don't imagine I am likely to trouble you," cried Bill; "I'd sooner cut off this hand than harm a hair of your head. When I leave this house it will be for good and for all, and you may rest assured that, as far as you are concerned, Bill Rawton, the gipsy, will never cross your path. He'll change his name, and no one will ever know that he is crawling about on the face of the earth. No, no, Mrs. Bourne; you have nothing to fear from me. This meeting is an accidental one, but our ways—our paths of life—are too far asunder for you to be in any fear of being troubled with my presence. I'll go this very moment if you wish it."

There was a tone of sincerity in Bill's manner which went far toward's reassuring the doctor's wife.

"You speak fairly enough, and I have no reason to doubt you; indeed, in earlier days I was taught by experience that you were mindful of me, and never that I can remember thwarted me in one solitary instance."

"You told me the last time we met that you were not happy. Is that so?" inquired the gipsy.

"Alas! yes. Happy! I am supremely miserable, more wretched than I can possibly tell you."

"And the reason for this?" he inquired. "You are the mistress of this establishment, are the wife of a physician of good repute."

"Good repute!" she exclaimed, with bitterness.

"Well, I should imagine so; and I hope I am not mistaken?"

"It is hardly worth while discussing that question. It was an unlucky hour that you ever met with my husband. Most of all fatal for me. You have made him acquainted with too much already, and he will never rest till he gets all from you."

"He'll get no more from me," exclaimed Rawton; "I wish my tongue had been cut out before I told him what I have; but, Lord bless us, I had no idea I was doing anything wrong—had no notion that it would injure anyone, still less you."

"Ah, you don't know all, or you would not talk like that. Listen. This man—this Doctor Bourne, my husband—hates me—he wants to be rid of me at any cost. The lady who was with him when you were last here is a rich widow, to whom he is paying attention. I am the one person too many in this house, and at any cost or sacrifice I must be removed. He has tried poison, but as yet has not succeeded."

"Poison!" exclaimed Rawton, turning suddenly pale. "Do not tell me that."

"It is a fact; I know it but too well. Every day, every hour I am in fear of my life. Oh, the miserable life I have led!"

She paused suddenly, and her eyes were suffused with tears.

Bill Rawton was touched. He could hardly believe his senses.

"The wretch!" he ejaculated — "the abominable, merciless wretch. If I thought that I'd——"

"Hush, silence! Don't be rash. It was wrong of me to say thus much, but it was done without due consideration. It is enough to know that he wants to get rid of me either by fair means or foul. I have good reason to know this. He has been placed in his present position through me, or, rather, through one who was my protector."

The gipsy gave a prolonged "oh!" The real state of affairs began to dawn upon him.

"That's it—eh?" said he.

"Yes, it is," answered Mrs. Bourne. "He married for the handsome dowry he had with me. Nothing else induced him to make me his wife."

"And who gave the dowry—if I may make so bold as to inquire?" said Rawton.

"Oh, it's no secret; I'll tell you—Lord Fullerton. It answered Bourne's purpose, for at that time he was a poor man. With the money he had with me he was enabled to make a good appearance, without which a doctor has but little chance of getting on. He is mercenary, cold, cruel, and crafty, and is desirous of espousing the rich widow you saw in the carriage with him the other day. I am the only stumbling-block in the way. Now do you understand why he wanted the marriage certificate?"

"Well, not exactly. How is it possible that he could connect my marriage with you?"

"Doubtless he has heard of something of the sort. Perhaps he is better acquainted with my past history than either you or I imagine. There is no telling. If the idea once entered his head he would cling to it as a drowning man is said to cling to a straw."

"Well, this quite gets over me—I never heard of such a thing. I wish I had died of starvation before I saw the varmint. That's all I wish, and bad luck to him! I'm knocked clean out of time, and no mistake."

"I have told you all, because I believe I can trust you. If he could prove a former marriage, he would have no scruples in casting me adrift without a shilling in the world."

"He'd never do that, surely."

"Aye, but he would. Too well I know it. It was a most fatal night for me when you met the doctor, for it will bring ruin and disgrace upon me."

"Ruin and disgrace!" exclaimed Bill, in a tone of deep dejection and concern. "Your words drive me mad. I wish—I—I can't express myself. Hang it all, I have been a fool; but, never fear, I'll make it all right, if it costs me my life."

"How can you possibly do that?" said Mrs. Bourne. "The mischief's done. You have been most rash and imprudent. Oh, that I could see my way out of this difficulty!"

"I confess I have been imprudent, but what of that? It was not done wilfully. Who could or would have supposed for one moment the doctor's object in questioning me so closely about my private affairs?"

"He seldom takes the trouble to question people closely upon any subject without a special reason. He has the wiles of the serpent, the cunning of the fox. Oh, he had an object in so kindly becoming your patron; he has some well-devised scheme in his head —some plot to be rid of me."

"I would not stay with such a wretch if I were you," exclaimed Bill.

"I would leave him to-morrow—be too glad to leave him—upon certain conditions. I cannot consent to go out of this house penniless; but enough of this.

As I before observed, the mischief's done, the train is formed, and it cannot be undone. I do not blame you, William Rawton. You had no desire to injure me, nevertheless I cannot conceal from myself that your presence here is likely to prove fatal to me."

"Fatal to you—how so?"

"Oh, do not torment me with questions," cried Mrs. Bourne. "The mischief's done. This man—this Dr. Bourne, my husband—if he could by any means in his power find out that I had been married years and years ago, would not scruple to put the machinery of the law to work to ruin and crush me. He would be but too glad of the chance of prosecuting me for bigamy."

"Bigamy—he can't do anything of the sort. In the first place, you were what the law calls an infant at the time; and, in the second place, there was an inquest on the body of a man who was found drowned in a millstream, and whose body was identified as that of William Rawton, or supposed to be him."

"Ah! supposed won't do."

"Well, hang it all, if my existence is so baneful to you—if there is no other way of repairing the mischief I had so unwittingly done—then I can throw myself into a millstream, or any other way to make an end of myself. I am only an encumbrance on the face of the earth. It is quite time for me to trot off into another world."

"Peace! don't be so rash. Your death would not make any difference now; and if it did, it is perfectly purposeless to make such a suggestion. I will consider the matter over, look at it from every point of view, and determine what had best be done."

"Ah, I think I shall have to determine," remarked the gipsy.

"You! What do you mean? How can you determine?"

"Well, you see it's simply this. It unfortunately happens that I have been imprudent enough to blow the gaff; but I beg pardon—you don't understand this sort of language?"

"I confess I do not."

"Well then I've let my tongue run too fast—that you understand?"

"Most certainly I do."

"If it costs me my life I'll put matters straight. He may be jolly artful this same doctor, and no doubt he is; but I'll take good care, if so be as it lays in my power, which I believe it does, to circumvent him."

"Your language is altogether so foreign to what I have been accustomed to listen to that I hardly know what reply to make."

"Don't you trouble yourself to reply. I know my way about. It is true I have been most imprudent, but I will repair the evil. Oh! Mrs. Bourne—Hester I used to call you—be of good cheer; do not give way to despair. I can see my way out of this business."

"But how? Tell me how."

"Never you mind. Leave it to me."

"I cannot possibly do otherwise now."

"Very good, then rest satisfied. I think I can see through his little caper. I never liked him—now I hate and despise him, 'specially after what you have said. I'll do him yet as dead as a nail. But——"

"But what? Do you want my assistance?"

"In what way? You can't render me any."

"I mean as far as money is concerned."

"I don't care to take money from you. Still a trifle would be of service. I can return it you at some future time."

Shortly will be published, "The Life and Recollections of Calcraft the Hangman," in Penny Weekly Numbers.

BILL RAWTON SEARCHING THE CHURCH REGISTER.

"I will give you what you require, for I believe you are sincere, and mean what you say."

Opening her desk Mrs. Bourne drew therefrom several gold pieces, which she placed on the table in front of the gipsy.

"Take what you require," she said. "The money is at your service."

"I will not rob you of a shilling!" exclaimed Bill, resolutely. "Not a penny."

"You are much more self-sacrificing and scrupulous than I gave you credit for. I say again take what you require for your immediate necessities. Surely you are not so proud as to refuse what is offered freely, and with the best intentions."

The gipsy hesitated.

"Well," he observed, after a long pause, "perhaps you are right, marm. I may need a little ready rhino to carry out a little bit of business on my own account.

"I hope it is not a dishonest one," cried Mrs. Bourne, with some concern.

"You've no call to be alarmed. What I am agoing to do is right enough—leastways what I hope to do."

Mrs. Bourne had no very exalted notion of her companion's honesty, or way of life, about which, however, she knew nothing, but she guessed rightly enough that he had fallen into evil courses, and was therefore a discredit to her, and all who might happen to be acquainted with him; nevertheless she felt assured that he would not willingly harm her by word or deed. It was a terrible thing that he had become acquainted with her husband, as from this very fact ruin and disgrace might fall upon her in a way that she had never for a moment contemplated.

"I will not make any further inquiries," said she. "All I might say would not alter your course of action, and therefore the least said the better, but I am free to confess that I tremble for the future. Your presence here has been most fatal to my happiness and peace of mind. If this man, my husband, could find any means of getting rid of me he would be but too glad to avail himself of the same, for I feel assured that I am a stumbling block in his way, which doubtless he will find some means of removing. Oh, no one knows but myself what I have suffered—what daily, what hourly dread I am in of this man. What if he should find out the church in which we were married? What if he should produce the certificate of the same? Oh, why has all this come to pass? I deemed you dead; could have sworn it."

"You have not seen or heard anything of me for over twenty years, and you had a right to conclude I was dead. He can do nothing, rest assured of that. Hang him, I'll take very good care that he won't have it in his power. Be of good cheer, marm; when next we meet I hope to bring you good news, and so farewell for the present."

Rawton rose from his seat, and, taking four sovereigns from the heap of gold before him, he descended the stairs and passed out of the house.

"Oh, heaven save me," ejaculated Mrs. Bourne, "I am now in his power, but still I think I may trust him. I hope so, lost and fallen man as he is. Oh, Amy, it's you?"

"Yes, marm," answered the girl, who had crept into the room immediately after she heard the gipsy take his departure. "But how troubled you look!" cried the maid, as she glanced at her mistress. "What does that dreadful man want?"

"Oh, he's better than you suppose him. He wanted a little assistance—that's all."

"Why, he's quite a swell to what he was the other day. I hardly knew him when I opened the door, he looked so respectable. But he has such odd ways, and is so familiar—too familiar by half, to my thinking."

Mrs. Bourne laughed. It was the first time she had done so for several days.

"Who then is he, Amy?"

"Well, marm, I think so; not rude, you know, but he makes use of such odd words, and has such an easy, confident manner with him. Oh, he's a card in his way—there's no doubt about that."

"Yes, he is a character; but there is no occasion for you to mention to the doctor that he's been here."

"Me, marm? Lord bless me, no—I wouldn't think of doing such a thing."

"Because, you see, he's a man I knew when little more than a child. He appears to be so strangely altered since those days that I can hardly believe him to be the same person. He's evidently quite a lost man; but this is only as I guess, for I know nothing of his mode of life, which, however, I fear, is not altogether a respectable one."

"I wonder what the doctor wanted him here for. He wouldn't have encouraged him unless he had some motive."

"That's not your business—neither is it mine," observed Mrs. Bourne, reprovingly.

"No, of course not, marm; anyway it aint any business of mine."

CHAPTER XCV.

MR. WILLIAM RAWTON'S CUNNING DEVICE—THE MISSING PAGE.

WITH all the gipsy's faults—and it must be confessed he had a few—want of consideration for Mrs. Bourne was not one of them.

He saw pretty clearly that a concurrence of circumstances, as unlooked for as unpropitious, threatened to environ the doctor's wife in a labyrinth of difficulties. It is true that, morally speaking, no blame could be attached to her for consenting to become the wife of a needy and heartless physician.

She had not the faintest notion that Rawton was in the land of the living. Indeed, she had quite forgotten in the vortex of fashionable life that such a person ever did exist; but facts are stubborn things, and there was no getting over the horrible one which so immediately concerned herself.

Nothing would please Dr. Bourne better than having it in his power to cast her adrift on the world, to be released from the tie that bound him, and to espouse the rich and fascinating widow whom he had been dangling after for so long a time.

He knew perfectly well that his present wife regarded him with the greatest possible aversion, and the chances were that she would offer no impediment to a divorce, provided he gave her only a portion of the dowry he had received from the nobleman who was her former protector, but Bourne's cupidity was so great that he could not bear to part with money. His device was to obtain a release by other means.

He had learned from a gossiping mischief-making Frenchwoman, who, at one time had been lady's maid to his wife when she was in India with Sir Digby McBride, that in her early youth her ladyship, as she was termed, had been espoused by a gipsy named Rawton. Indeed the lady's maid in question aided further than this, she gave the doctor a small miniature, which she said was a correct likeness of the gipsy in question. This the doctor treasured, and it was from this same miniature that he traced some similarity in the features of Bill Rawton, when he met him on the eventful night of the attempted robbery.

Well might his wife say that he had the cunning of the fox. He had a motive, and a strong one too, in patronising the gipsy. His motive was to worm out of him all respecting his—the doctor's—wife. He had already become possessed of facts which he deemed might be of infinite service to him in carrying out his nefarious and contemptible plans.

He had, as may be readily imagined, married the nobleman's cast-off mistress for the purpose of his own personal aggrandisement.

It was not a very creditable course of procedure; nevertheless it is one which has been frequently adopted. Bourne had no very nice sense of honour, and not much self-respect, or he never would have acted as he had done throughout the greatest portion of his selfish life.

He now thought he saw his way out of the difficulty. He believed if he could obtain the certificate of the marriage of the two persons named, William Rawton and Hester Teige, his own marriage contract would be rendered thereby null and void.

The chances were that he would have found out that he was, after all, only deluding himself with false hopes ; but he was very much charmed with the idea, and believed in its efficacy.

Bill Rawton was under the impression that the plea would not hold good—nevertheless, he was sorely troubled in his mind. There was no telling ; he did not understand much about the law—certainly not that part of it which related to matrimonial and divorce suits, but he was determined not to throw a chance away. He felt that he had already done an incalculable amount of mischief, and was determined to repair the evil at all hazards.

How he proposed to do this we shall presently see.

While at the common lodging-house, he met with Cooney, whom the reader will remember as being connected with Gregson and Charles Peace in the Oakfield House burglary described in the opening chapters of this work.

We have had no occasion to take notice of Cooney since he was captured by Mr. Wrench in the bar of Sanderson's hotel. Since that time Cooney had gone through a series of gradations in crime.

How he obtained his living when Bill Rawton lighted on him it would be difficult to say. He did not, however, appear to be in very prosperous circumstances, being, as of yore, very glad to turn his hand to anything.

The gipsy came to the conclusion he was just the man for his purpose ; so he at once made a pal of him, and told him what he required him to do.

Bill Rawton was married at a primitive village in Hampshire, called Wratton, and to this place he forthwith proceeded in company with Cooney.

"It's a delicate little bit of business we are going on," said Rawton; "and will require a good deal of artfulness to work properly, but it must be done, that's certain. It is not a profitable job I admit, but we must take the fat with the lean."

"All right, old man," said Cooney. "I don't much care what it is, as long as it's worked to rights. Let me know what I've got to do, and I'll be on to it like a shot."

Upon arriving at the village in question Mr. Rawton was more communicative to his companion.

"Now, old sinner, I am going to the church."

Cooney opened his eyes to the fullest extent.

"To the church, eh ! Oh, I tumble ; the plate I spose ?"

"No such thing. I want to search for a register."

Cooney nodded.

"And when I give you a signal, all I want is for you to throw a stone at one of the windows of the church, and then take to your heels."

"Well I'm blessed, if you aint a rum un. What ! break a window. What's the good of that ere ?"

"Never you mind, do as I tell you, and all will be as right as the nail. I know every inch of the ground in this neighbourhood, and every stone in Wratton church."

"Does yer ?"

"Certainly."

"And what's the good on it if yer do ?"

"Nothing in particular as I can see ; but that ain't the question. You play your part, and I'll play mine. Yours is an easy one enough."

"It aint wery difficult, if that's all you want me to do."

"That's all ; but here we are at the church."

The two confederates passed through the gate, and reached the churchyard.

"Ah, it's the same old place—not altered in the least," cried the gipsy. "Just the same, but how changed to me !"

"Ah, out that ; don't go for to be sentimental. You aint come down here to moralise," cried Cooney. "I say, leave that to some other bloke ; it's out of our line."

"Perhaps you're right ; but, you know, this place I remember when but a bit of a boy, and I haven't set eyes on it for many and many a year."

"At it again," cried Cooney, with a sort of double shuffle. "Well, I'm blest. It's the green trees and the dicky b'rds as does it for you. Makes you feel alloverish like, just the same as ye'd be if yer were once more on your mountain heather—like the man who ses his 'art's in the islands."

Mr. Cooney, after this speech, indulged in a prolonged whistle.

"There's no occasion for that," observed the gipsy, reprovingly. "We've come on very serious business, and must look very grave."

"Mustn't indulge in unseemly mirth, as our parson used to say. Werry good, I'm all there—not, mind you, but this is quite a new line of business to me."

"But you are equal to anything."

"In course I am."

"So now keep quiet. Listen. Do you see that little window in that part of the church which abuts out ?"

"Yes, I does see it, with these 'ere blessed eyes."

"Good. There's nobody about just now, which is all the better, as we must not be seen together. I have shown you the window ?"

"Yes, yer have."

"At that end of the church there is a clump of yew trees—you can easily conceal yourself in those."

"I'll go at once then."

"No, not now ; all is not ready at present. Wait patiently. I am merely explaining what you are to do, because if we don't pull this off this time we shan't have another chance ; so we must be careful not to make a muddle of it. I shall have to go round to the clerk's house I expect, for he doesn't seem to be here. What I want you to do is this : go out yonder into that lane, watch, and wait there till you see me and the clerk enter the church."

"Yes."

"But don't be seen yourself if you can help it."

"All right—drive on."

"When you see us enter the church together, creep down from the lane where you have been stationed, and conceal yourself in the clump of yew trees ; then keep your eye fixed on that little window."

"Yes, and what then ?"

"You will see me looking over a big book. When I draw my hand across my forehead, thus, throw a stone at one of the end windows, and make off as fast as your legs will carry you ; but mind, Cooney, don't attempt to throw the stone till I have given the sign."

"Oh, no, in course not. I aint likely to do that. And what else ?"

"You are pretty sure to get clean off. Make for the station, and remain in the waiting-room till I come. Now, you understand ?"

"I hopes as how I do."

"Now make off, and I will go and find the clerk."

Cooney at once betook himself to the lane, and Rawton returned to the village.

Upon arriving at the clerk's house, he found that worthy at dinner—so he took a stroll till the meal was over, and then called again.

He explained his business, saying he wished to get a copy of the register of two persons who were married at the church some twenty or two-and-twenty years back.

The clerk was a very old man, with tottering limbs and defective sight; he had held his present office for over fifty years. He carried with him a huge bunch of keys, and walked by the side of the gipsy conversing in a friendly manner till they reached the church.

"You are not quite certain as to the year, you say," he observed, as he opened the door of the sacred edifice.

"No, not quite certain, but I can't be very far out."

"The names you have with you?"

"Yes, they are Jane Jenkins and Robert Bessant."

"I dare say we shall find them. This way, if you please."

Rawton was led by the old man into a small apartment, in which were a number of ponderous volumes ranged on shelves.

"We had better search the volume for 1858 first."

"As you please."

"Have you the paper with the names?"

"Yes—here it is."

The old clerk began to look over the book. Page after page was gone over, but no such names could be found.

"Can I be looking over the volume for the preceding year?" said Rawton, carelessly.

"Oh, certainly, sir, if you please. My eyesight is not so good as it was, but my memory is good, and I think I can recollect two persons bearing the names here written down."

The gipsy meanwhile turned over the pages of the other volume. He soon came to the page on which his own name and that of Hester Teige was inscribed. He slid a piece of paper between the leaf and turned over the others. Then he drew his hand across his forehead.

Immediately after this a loud crash was heard. The sound reverberated through the aisles with terrible force.

"Mercy on us, what's the matter?—some accident to the church!" cried the gipsy, in a tone of alarm. "Pray see what it is."

The clerk was seriously alarmed, and, upon the impulse of the moment, rushed out into the body of the church.

This was Bill Rawton's opportunity. With almost incredible rapidity he drew forth his penknife, which he had kept open in his coat pocket, passed the blade along at that side of the page which was fastened to the book, and drew it forth; then, folding it up, he thrust it into the breast pocket of his coat. When this had been done he went out of the little room and anxiously inquired what was the matter.

The clerk informed him that some evil-disposed person had thrown a stone at the church windows, one of the panes of which was broken. The stone was picked up inside the edifice.

"The mischievous, audacious scoundrel!" exclaimed Rawton. "Shall I try and catch him? He can't be far off."

"I wish you could."

"I'll try," said Rawton, who at once rushed out. He brought in a lubberly boy, who was staring, openmouthed, at the broken glass.

"It aint me as did it, sir—indeed it aint. I never heaved a stone at the window," cried the lad, bursting into tears.

"Oh, it's you, Jim Starling—eh?" said the clerk. "And if it wasn't you, perhaps you can tell who did it."

"I dunno. I heard a smash, and saw the window shivered, but I did not see him as heaved the stone."

"Was there anyone else about besides him?" said the clerk, addressing himself to Rawton.

"I did not see anyone else."

"This must be inquired into. It's a most scandalous, wicked act, and you must do your best, Starling, to find out who it was."

"Yes, I will, sir—I will do my best."

"Am I to let him go?" said Rawton.

"Yes, I suppose so. Ah, yes, he is well known here. I don't think he would be wicked enough to do such a thing, for we consider him to be a well-conducted lad; but as I said before, it must be inquired into. A reward must be offered, and the police must be made acquainted with the circumstance. Dear me, sir, young people of the present day are not a bit like those I remember when I was young; they are audacious, mischievous, and uncontrollable; but, as I said before, this matter must not be allowed to drop without a searching inquiry."

"No, certainly not. I'm a stranger to these parts," observed Rawton, "and certainly never expected to find such a lawless act committed like this in open daylight. It so alarmed me that I have not as yet recovered from the shock."

"I dare say not, sir; I can well understand that, and indeed I am very sorry," replied the clerk, apologetically, "extremely sorry. Such a thing never occurred before. I can't make it out; but your pardon, sir; you have not found what you want."

"No, the interruption was so sudden and unlooked for that for the moment I had almost forgotten my errand."

The blubbering boy scampered off the moment he was released, and the clerk and Rawton returned to the room.

"May I take the next volume to this?" said the gipsy.

"Yes, sir, if you please."

Rawton turned over the leaves of the other volume and in the space of a few minutes found the two names of which he professed to be in search, but which, as the reader can readily imagine, he cared nothing about. It so chanced that he remembered the persons bearing these names being married in the year 1852, and they did very well as a blind to his proceedings.

When he found them he professed to be very anxious to have a copy of the entry in the book, which the clerk at once proceeded to make. The clergyman had to sign it as a matter of form, and when this had been done, it was handed to the gipsy, who paid the usual fee, wished the clerk good day, and walked rapidly on towards the station.

"I've done my worthy friend, the doctor, now, and no mistake. Hester can defy him. After all there was not much to fear, but I should have been on the grizzle, and as savage as a meat hatchet if he'd got the better of her. It was about as neat a job as I can remember doing, and Cooney did his part to rights, just in the nick of time. Nobody will be any the wiser, and the chances are the leaf will never be missed; but if it is I can't help it."

Upon arriving at the station, he found Cooney seated in front of the refreshment bar, devouring the remains of half a pork-pie, which he washed down with a pint of bitter.

"Thought you'd never come," he cried, upon catching sight of the gipsy; "been waiting here till I was so hungry that I couldn't hold out any longer, so thought it best to stick up a score to you."

"Gammon and all," said Rawton. "They don't give credit at these places."

"I aint paid for nuffin as yet."

"Then I will," said Rawton, who forthwith put a shilling on the counter and called for a pint of the best Burton, paying for that and what his friend had had at the same time.

When the two entered one of the carriages of the next London train their tongues were unloosed, for there were no other persons besides themselves in the compartment, and they had purposely forborne talking about the business that had brought them down before the barmaids and loiterers in the refreshment bar. All restraint was, however, now thrown off.

"Well," said Cooney, "how did you work it—all right?"

"Right as the mail. Never did anything so neatly in my life. Went out and collared a boy for throwing the stone."

"Oh scissors! What a spree!"

"Yes, and did the indignant to rights, I can tell you. The old clerk took it all in like a gudgeon, and was mighty civil and obliging."

"Oh! he's a very decent old boy."

"Well," said Cooney, "this one is about the rummest start I ever knew. Coming all these miles for the purpose of throwing a stone at the window of a church. Why, when you come to look at it in a serious light it seems ridiculous, don't it?"

"Oh! as for that, in a manner of speaking, it is ridiculous; but what of that? It has answered our purpose. You don't want more. I suppose we've done what we came to do. It's a matter of duty—leastways as far as I'm concerned, and as to you a trip in the country, and a sniff of the fresh air won't do you any harm."

"It's the dicky birds and the trees and the green grass as does it. Makes you preach like a parson, and talk like a book—blowed if they don't; but I'm glad you've brought it in all right. Why, Lord bless us, I wonder what has become of Charles Peace—haven't set eyes on him for years."

"He got into a little bit of a mess at Sheffield," observed the gipsy, "and had to do seven years' 'stretch.' Since his conviction I haven't seen anything of him."

"Nor don't know what he's up to, I s'pose?"

"No, haven't the slightest notion. Poor Charlie! He was always straight and square with me. Many people run him down, but I speak of a man as I find him."

"Same here. He was always right enough; but Lord bless you, things aren't a bit like what they used to be—you can't trust anybody nowadays."

"That's true enough, Cooney—you're right there, old man."

"But, I say," observed the gipsy's companion after a pause; "what might be yer little game at this blessed old church? You haven't come all the way for nuffin, that's quite certain."

"For nothing—why of course not, 'taint likely."

"Well then, what's yer lay?"

"Merely to serve a friend, that's all."

"Hang your artful old eyes, it's something more

than that. I 'xpect you'll make a jolly lot of couters out on it."

"Nothing of the sort—I shan't make a single quid out of it. I pledge my word that it is a mere matter of friendship."

"S'help my taters, I'm jolly glad to find there's so much friendship left in the world, but it's hard to believe for all that."

"You can please yourself about believing it. I have only to say again what I've said is the solemn truth."

"All right—I don't want to pry into any man's secrets. You've done the trick cleverly, and that's what you may call a jolly artful dodge and no mistake, but I'm as dry as a piece of old chunk. Stand a drop of something to drink at the next station'"

"Right you are—you shall have as much as you like."

When the train arrived at the station the two companions repaired to the refreshment bar, and regaled themselves with some "heavy wet."

Upon their arrival in London, they betook themselves to their lodging-house, and Bill Rawton presented Cooney with two sovereigns for his services, which the latter considered a handsome recompense. The gipsy, with all his faults, had never been a mean or selfish man, and, certainly, in this case, he did not take the lion's share, but he was well pleased with the result of his visit to the village church, and was, consequently, in the best of spirits.

He considered he had put into practice a master stroke of diplomacy, and began to ruminate upon the best course to adopt in seeking an interview with Mrs. Bourne.

He had no desire to see the doctor—he wished to have a tête-à-tête with his wife.

CHAPTER XCVI.
THE GIPSY AND MRS. BOURNE—THE SURPRISE.

RAWTON deemed it best not to venture paying a visit to Mrs. Bourne without first of all making sure that the doctor was from home.

How this was to be ascertained, he could not at first determine, but after some consideration had been spent in reflection, he elected to send Cooney with a note addressed to Mrs. Bourne, with strict injunctions that it was to be delivered into her hands, and if this could not be conveniently done, Cooney was to return with the letter and wait a more favourable opportunity.

It took him some time to indite the brief epistle, which was couched in very guarded, albeit not in very elegant, language but it sufficed for the purpose.

Cooney was as hang-dog a looking rascal as it was well possible to conceive, but the gipsy had no other person to send upon whom he could rely—his messenger was by no means a fool—although of a common coarse type and as ignorant as a "hack horse;" but he was artful and was not easily "cornered," to make use of an American phrase, so away he went upon his mission. The maid servant opened the door and Cooney asked if her mistress was disengaged.

"Suppose she is. What do you want with her?" inquired the girl, looking at the speaker with evident mistrust and suspicion.

"I don't want anything with her, my dear," returned Cooney, in oleaginous accents.

"Don't dear me, man," cried the girl. "What's your business?"

"Is the doctor in?"

"I don't know."

"Is your mistress alone?"

"If she is I'm sure she won't see you."

"Well, you're a nice-looking girl, but a little sharp, but that don't matter. Now listen."

"I am listening. Go on, and be as quick as possible."

"I've got a letter for your mistress," said Cooney, in a strange whisper, "which must be delivered into her own hands."

"A begging letter I suppose."

"No, it aint no begging letter, nuffin of the sort. You were never more mistaken in your life, but it's a letter from a friend, and is of the greatest importance."

The girl laughed derisively.

"You're on the wrong tack, my lady," observed Cooney, reprovingly. "Don't be so cheeky, because it aint becoming in young females to be cheeky."

"Get out with your impudence. Give me the letter at once, and I will take it up to Mrs. Bourne."

"All right, my lass, there it is; but don't you be agivin' it to anybody else. Do yer hear?"

"Yes, I hear," cried the maid, tripping lightly upstairs with the missive in question.

"She is a pretty creature," murmured Cooney, as he was waiting in the passage. "A jolly nice gal, but a little pert; but I like her all the better for that. Don't care a bit about your smooth-tongued wenches."

In a minute or so the maid returned and handed an envelope with no name or address upon it to Rawton's messenger.

"You are to give that to him," said the maid, in a more subdued tone of voice.

"Thank you kindly," returned Cooney. "Oh, but you are a darling, and no mistake."

"Get along with your impudence. I never met with such a rude man in all my life."

"Oh—don't say that."

"Go away at once. You've got your answer—so now be off."

Cooney sallied forth, and the door was slammed to the moment he had passed out of the house.

He took the answer he had received to his pal, Bill Rawton, who tore open the envelope, and drew forth a slip of paper, on which was written these words—

"If you desire to see me, call to-morrow evening at about half-past seven."

"That's all right," cried the gipsy. "I'll be there."

"She aint altogether the most amiable girl I've met with," observed Cooney

"Who aint?"

"Why the maid-servant. But she's jolly good-looking, and I 'xpect she knows it."

"You haven't been fool enough to chaff the doctor's servant? Why, she's a most respectable, well-behaved young woman."

"Aint no manner of doubt about that ere," returned Cooney.

"I am sorry I sent you."

"Why, it's all right enough—aint it?"

"Yes; but it strikes me you've been too forward with the girl."

"Nuffin of the sort. Is it likely?"

"Well, if I must say what I think, I feel certain that there's nothing more likely. You ought to know better."

"Well, I'm blest! Do you expect a bloke to stand like a mute at the door of a gentleman's house?"

"There, shut up! Enough of this," observed Rawton, who made a shrewd guess of what had taken place. "He never could keep his tongue still," murmured Rawton, "and I suppose never will. However, it doesn't much matter I suppose."

On the following evening, at a little before the appointed time, Bill Rawton left the lodging-house, and made direct for the doctor's house.

As he came within sight of this he observed the boy in the street with a basket of medicine bottles on his arm.

"Hallo, young gallipot!—just one moment, my lad," cried Rawton.

"Yes, sir."

"Is your master in?"

"No."

"Oh, then, I'll just call and leave my card. When do you expect him to return?"

"He didn't say when he would be back."

"All right. I may as well call. Good night."

"Good night, sir."

"Oh, he's not in; so much the better for my purpose," said the gipsy, as he gave a gentle knock at the door, which was opened by the girl Amy.

"Do you want to see missus?" said she.

"Yes, if she's disengaged and alone."

"She's quite disengaged, and told me to show you upstairs."

Bill was conducted into the front room, first floor, where he found Mrs. Bourne, pale and anxious, awaiting his appearance.

"So," said she, "you are here again. I concluded you had something to communicate, and am glad you have come at the specified time. My husband is not in the way, and we can converse without fear of interruption. Be seated, and proceed to business at once."

The gipsy dropped into the nearest chair.

"It would be a sore trouble to me if I thought my presence here and my interview with the doctor, and the words I have spoken, might cause you trouble or anxiety."

"They have caused me great trouble and anxiety, but let that pass. I do not blame you. What you have done—the information you have given—places me in the utmost peril: but, as I before observed, it is no fault of yours. Pray tell me what you purpose doing? It appears to me, if you have any consideration for me, that you had better avoid this house, and not present yourself here again. You will thereby avoid being cross-questioned by my husband, who, from what I can gather, wishes to extract all he can get from you."

"He will get nothing more from me—remember, not a smell. Of that I will be as silent as the grave. If I do open my mouth at all it will be to deny all I have said. You say I have placed you in a situation of extreme peril?"

"I believe you have. And you would agree with me if you knew all. Doctor Bourne will not rest, night or day, till he has found out the church where we were married. This done, he will have proof which will be fatal to me."

"He will find no proof, madam," said Bill Rawton. "I have taken good care of that."

"How can you talk in such an inconsistent and unreasonable way? How is it possible for you to remove a record so indisputable? The books in the church contain a register of this unfortunate and fatal marriage."

"I told you, when last here, that I would repair the evil I had done. I have kept my word. There is no record of our union—none whatever. And no living man can procure it—except myself," cried Rawton, in a solemn tone of voice.

"You are speaking more like a madman than a sane person.

"Am I?"

"I should imagine so."

"You are mistaken. Listen to me for one moment. I say there is no record. The leaf in the book containing the certificate of the marriage between William Rawton and Hester Teige is no longer in the books of the church. I have it here."

As he said this Bill Rawton drew forth the page he had abstracted from the breast pocket of his coat. He handed it to his companion, who was bewildered and awe-struck.

"In Heaven's mercy what have you done?" she ejaculated.

"Read and judge for yourself," he returned.

She did read, and her face became as pale as death.

She was so overwhelmed with astonishment and fear that she could not find words to express herself.

"I have kept my word," he said slowly, and with something like melancholy and remorse in his tone. "I have at all risks contrived to make you a free woman—free, as far as I am concerned, and free also from the danger which threatened you. Bear witness, Mrs. Bourne, for you alone can do so, that I have been mindful of your interest, that I have shown a desire to shelter and shield you. The tie which bound us was cancelled years and years ago. Now it no longer has existence. It has passed away, and will never rise up in judgment against either of us—never."

He took the paper in his hand, thrust it into the fire, where in a few moments it was consumed.

Mrs. Bourne looked at him in a state of stupefaction, but he was calm and quite unmoved.

"William Rawton," she presently exclaimed, "I never would have believed this of you, certainly not, unless I had been witness of it and seen it with my own eyes. I have found a champion and friend where I least expected to meet with one. I know not how to express myself. I never dreamed you had so much magnanimity in your nature. How can I possibly recompense you?"

"I don't want any recompense," observed the gipsy. "What I have done has been done for your sake. Perhaps you will find it hard to believe this, but it is a fact nevertheless. I aint of much good in this world, and nobody has a good word for Bill Rawton the gipsy. Nobody cares about him, who is at best an outcast and a blot upon the face of the earth; but it may be in the years that are to come that one person will think well of him, and remember he was not altogether the selfish and abandoned wretch people suppose him to be. If that one thinks well of him—remembers him with something like gratitude—he will be amply rewarded for the favour he has conferred upon her."

Mrs. Bourne was touched, her eyes were moist with tears, and she stretched forth her hand which the gipsy clasped fervently, and respectfully raised to his lips.

"I am glad to have been of service to you," he cried. "This is the brightest hour I have known for many a day, and the remembrance of it will last my life."

"Oh! Rawton, how much I have reason to be thankful for what you have done. I tremble when I reflect upon the act you have committed. Suppose it should be discovered, what then? What a risk you have run!"

"It will not be discovered—rest assured of that. I am in no fear of the consequences."

"But it's a dreadful alternative, and a most discreditable proceeding. It's direct robbery."

"Nothing of the sort."

"Oh, yes, it is—there's no denying it."

"Well, suppose it is, what does it matter. You are not bound to know anything about it—nobody is bound to do so. Don't you be concerned about the matter; it's right enough."

"Right! I think it's very wrong, sinful, and wicked."

"Ah, that all depends upon the way you look at these things. I see no harm in it—not a morsel of harm. However, it's done, and done to save you."

"I know that, and am, of course, duly grateful; but it is a terrible alternative."

"There was no other left, as I could see, and it was the wisest course. Any way, it makes you safe, and that's all I care about."

The conversation was cut short by the sudden and unexpected entrance of Dr. Bourne into the room in which his wife and the gipsy were seated.

They were both astonished, and not a little alarmed at his appearance.

"You here, eh!" he exclaimed, in a tone of anger, addressing himself to Rawton.

"Right you be, doctor," returned the gipsy. "I'm here, as you see."

"And pray, sir, if it is not an impudent question," observed the doctor, with bitter irony, "may I inquire how it is that I find you holding a secret conference with my wife? But I need not ask. I can make a pretty shrewd guess."

"If you can guess, I wouldn't trouble myself to inquire, if I were you," said Rawton, nothing moved.

"You are an impudent, low-bred fellow," cried Bourne, in a towering passion. "How dare you have the impertinence to address this lady, and what can you be thinking of to encourage the visits of such a low ruffian, madam?"

This last observation was made to his wife, who was too distressed and overcome to make any reply.

"You were out," said Bill, "and I asked to see your lady. 'Spose there's no great harm in that?"

"Harm!" cried Bourne. "Don't imagine you can deceive me. I ask you again, what brought you hither?"

"Why my legs, of course; I ain't got a carriage, and so had to walk."

"Hark ye, my man, let me have no more of your impudence, or I shall find means to punish you. I say, again, what business have you here holding a conference with Mrs. Bourne, who ought to be ashamed of herself to be seen conversing with such a ruffian. Answer my question without any more ado."

"You're so sharp upon a cove that you don't give a chap time to answer. Well, if you must know, I wanted to leave a message with the lady."

"It's a lie—an impudent lie; you wanted to do nothing of the sort. You think I cannot see through you, I suppose, you shameless woman."

"Hold hard, guv'nor—one at a time, if you please," cried Bill.

"You will be pleased to address me in a more respectful manner, my man. Do you hear?"

"Yes, I hear."

"Now, madam," said Bourne, turning to his wife, "will you kindly enlighten me on this subject? What is the reason for this man being here?"

"He is your acquaintance, not mine," said Mrs. Bourne.

"Thank you for the compliment. He's a robber, a

thief, and a disgrace to a civilised community; and this is the man you choose to encourage here, is it?"

"I do not encourage him—I have told him to go away."

"Yes, that's quite true; she has told me to go away and not come here any more, and I have promised to do so."

"You are not going away just yet, my man," cried the doctor. "I have a goodish bit to say to you."

"Ah, that being the case, it's lucky I am here."

"You are very well acquainted with this lady it would appear—eh?"

"I don't know what you mean," returned Bill.

"Don't you?"

"No."

"I know what I mean—look at her."

"Well, I am looking at the lady."

"You've seen her before years ago—haven't you?"

"Me, no; not as I know of."

"You can't deceive me, you scoundrel—she is your wife."

At this, Bill Rawton burst out into a loud laugh, which a little disconcerted the doctor.

"My wife," cried Bill. "Why, doctor, you're a little touched in the upper story, I'm thinking."

"I say she is your wife."

"Do you?"

"Yes."

"And I say she's not."

"And never was?"

"And never was."

"Well, my man, you have any amount of audacity—that I frankly admit; but it won't be of much service to you in this case. You have already acknowledged your name to be William Rawton."

"I have passed as William Rawton."

The doctor started.

"You haven't got the right sow by the ear as yet, doctor," observed the gipsy, with the most admirable self-possession. "Him as you call Will Rawton was drowned years agone in Harcott's millstream."

"Audacious liar!" exclaimed Bourne, in a fury; "think not to disprove your identity."

"I don't intend to do so; but, as I observed before, you've got the wrong pig by the ear."

"Then you are not William Rawton?"

"I have passed as him—that's all."

The doctor made no answer to this. He quietly walked into an adjoining room, without even so much as uttering a word. Presently he returned with something in his hand.

It was a miniature.

"Look at this," he said, holding it before the gipsy.

"Yes, I see it; it's a picture, and a very pretty one, too—a likeness of somebody, I 'spose?"

"A likeness of yourself, my man," said Bourne, in high glee.

"Of me?"

"Most certainly, and an admirable one it is, or was, for it was taken about twenty years ago. It must have been wonderfully like at that time—I should say most remarkably like the original."

"Not having seen the original I can't say," said Bill, perfectly unmoved.

"The original is yourself, my man."

Bill shook his head.

"That won't do; look at the nose, it's a mile too long, and the picture is not in any way like me—leastways as far as I can see—but if you say it is, of course I give in to your superior judgment."

"I say it is a portrait of William Rawton, and that you are he."

"Very good—have it your own way. It does not make much difference to me. I don't quite see what you are driving at, but that is of no great consequence, I suppose?"

"It is of very great consequence to me though."

"Is it?"

"Yes, and so, my very excellent friend, you may as well confess all. You will have to do so, you know, sooner or later. You are the lawful husband of this lady."

"Get out—me her husband!—it's false," exclaimed Bill. "You must think me a fool to believe what you say."

"I shall find means to prove the truth of what I'm saying," said Bourne, in a confident tone.

"I am sure you won't. What's your little game? Do you want to get rid of your wife—eh?"

"Your wife."

"No; yours, if you please. Of all the capers I ever heard of this is about the rummest. Why, you must have been swallowing some of your own medicine, doctor, and it has flown to your head, and driven you silly."

"Don't you give me any more of your impudence, fellow," cried Bourne, in a fury. "I am in no mood to stand it. Your audacity is exceeding all bounds; but I know very well how to deal with a man of your type. You will find it difficult, or, indeed, I may say impossible, to deceive me. This miniature which I hold in my hand is in itself quite sufficient to prove your identity. You are William Rawton, the gipsy—the same William Rawton who was wedded some twenty years ago to Hester Teige—the beauteous and fascinating Hester Teige, as she was afterwards called," continued the doctor, in a sarcastic tone.

"Am I?"

"Yes, you are; and I think you will find it difficult to disprove my statement."

"All right, governor; have it your own way," cried Bill, with an aggravating laugh. "All right. Have it your own way. It does so happen, however, that Rawton was drowned in a mill-stream, and that, for special reasons, best known to myself, I chose to call myself by his name."

"Then you told me a false and wicked lie on the evening when we first met, but I know which story to believe.

"Pray, sir, how is it I find you here in company with this lady? Answer me that. Shall I tell you?"

"If you like."

"It is just this: you are here plotting together for the purpose of determining how you can best deceive me. But do not think you will succeed in your nefarious plans. Still at the same time I have to apologize for disturbing a tête-à-tête between husband and wife," observed the doctor, with aggravating sarcasm.

Mrs. Bourne, who had purposely abstained from saying anything more than the occasion absolutely required, now observed in a deprecatory tone—

"I do hope and trust, Mr. Bourne, that this conversation will be brought to a close as speedily as possible, if it be only for my sake."

"For your sake, madam!" exclaimed her husband with a sneer. "Upon my word that is really a good joke. It is really amusing. I think, madam, I shall have no very great difficulty in dissolving the galling and odious tie which binds me to so amiable a partner. A prior marriage with a gentleman who is still alive

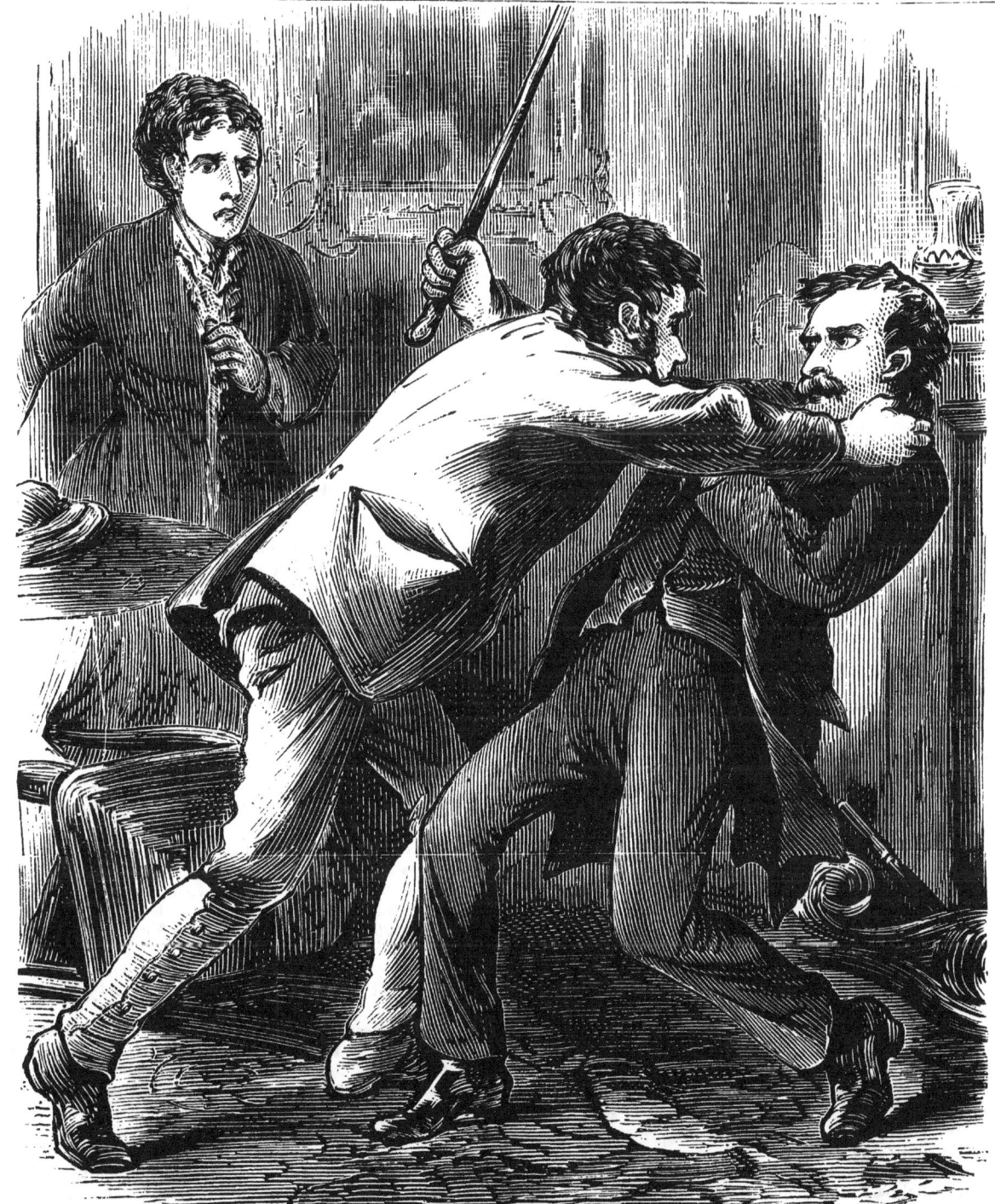

"YOU AUDACIOUS MISCREANT," CRIED BOURNE, STRIKING THE GIPSY WITH HIS WALKING STICK.

will suffice for the purpose. Mr. William Rawton, who is here present——"

"I am not William Rawton," interrupted the gipsy.

"Then who are you?"

"What do you want to know for?"

"No matter; I do want to know—let that suffice."

"Then I don't choose to tell you; let that suffice; but even if you could prove me to be Rawton, which you never can, what would it matter?"

"Then this lady would be the wife of two husbands," cried the doctor, bowing with mock gravity; "don't you see that?"

"No, I don't."

"Ah! but I do."

"Oh, so you think; but you are mistaken," observed the gipsy, perfectly unmoved; "never were more mistaken in your life."

"Am I?"

No. 51.

"Yes; you are most miserably mistaken. Shall I tell you why?"

"I am always glad to receive information, especially in this case, as it is a subject which concerns myself."

"Right you are, doctor; I s'pose it does concern yourself. Well, then, the young girl named Hester Teige was married to a gipsy; there's no denying that; but what sort of marriage was it?"

"What sort?"

"Aye, what sort, indeed! She was married in the gipsy's camp—after the manner of gipsies—married by the father of the tribe, with the sun for a witness, and the green sward for her couch. As far as the legal part of the business is concerned, it wasn't any marriage at all. So you may take your change out of that."

As he brought this brief speech to a conclusion, he burst out into a mocking laugh.

"You lying scoundrel!" exclaimed Bourne, in a paroxysm of rage. "You contemptible, deceptive hound—it is false—and I will prove you to be a liar as well as a thief—you unmitigated ruffian!"

"Go on, governor, lay it on thick. Your hard words won't hurt me; cause why? I'm too much used to them."

"You shameless abandoned woman," cried Bourne, turning towards his wife. "I have disgraced myself by my connection with you. What have you to say to this fellow's declaration?"

"I don't choose to say anything. You have heard all he has said, and can judge for yourself. You have brought this scandal upon yourself; but it was not done without a cause. I decline to argue the question with you."

"Insolent strumpet!" exclaimed the doctor, striking his wife on the side of the head. "Hence—get out of this house at once."

"Hold hard!" cried Bill, stepping between the enraged husband and his ill-used wife. "Hit a woman! You are a coward and a bully. If you want to hit anyone pitch into me."

"Stand out of my way—you dirty lying thief," cried Bourne.

"Look here, if you give me any more of your cheek," said the gipsy, "or attempt to lay hands on this lady I'll smash you—that's what I'll do with you, and no flies."

"You audacious miscreant!" cried Bourne, almost beside himself with rage, and striking the gipsy over the head with his walking stick.

Bill at once let out with his right and left in rapid succession, hitting the doctor some terrible blows in the face, which were delivered direct from the shoulder. Bourne was so taken aback by the suddenness and vigour of the attack that he had not time to recover himself.

"I'll make you smart for this," he said, presently. "You can't escape me, you scoundrel. I've two officers below." And as he uttered these words he rushed towards the door, calling out for assistance at the same time.

The gipsy intercepted his passage, and levelled him to the floor with one powerful blow from his clenched fist.

In falling the doctor's head came in contact with the fender, and he lay on the hearthrug, speechless and senseless.

At this crisis the sound of a low whistle fell upon the ears of Bandy-legged Bill, who judged rightly enough that danger was at hand. He went at once to the door of the apartment, closed and locked by them he bethought him of what to do.

"Oh merciful heaven, save and succour me," ejaculated Mrs. Bourne, wringing her hands. "What have you done?" She glanced at the prostrate form of her husband. "Perhaps murder."

The noise of ascending footsteps on the stairs was now heard, and another whistle was given by somebody outside the house.

"This is indeed terrible. You will be captured; ruin and disgrace will fall upon me. Oh, unhappy and fatal was the hour you set foot in this house."

"I'll leave it for good and for all," returned Bill, "and never of my own free will enter it again."

"Leave—but how?" inquired Mrs. Bourne. "Hark, they are knocking at the door and endeavouring to break it open."

Bill Rawton felt that not a moment was to be lost; he flew to the back window of the apartment and threw it open.

Then he thrust his head forth and took a rapid survey of the surrounding yards. Abutting out from the window was the roof of a washhouse. To drop on this was no very difficult task, but even when this had been done, the gipsy did not see any way of getting clear of the yards in the rear, and the sides of the doctor's residence were surrounded by walls and houses, and he did not see any place for concealment. Nevertheless, he felt that to remain where he was would most assuredly end in his capture. There were one or two little matters against him which rendered an interview with police officers in no way desirable. Rawton had risked much for the sake of Mrs. Bourne. He had acted towards her with a spirit of magnanimity, which was the one bright spot in his shadowy character, and it is but fair that he should have full credit for the better impulse of his nature, which prompted him to save the woman whom he had once loved.

The officers were beating violently against the door of the apartment, and demanding immediate admittance.

"Fly!" cried Mrs. Bourne. "Get clear off while there is yet time."

"It is evident you have done something wrong, and the police are on your track. Doubtless my husband has brought them hither. Fly! for mercy's sake hesitate no longer!"

"Hammer away, my sweet pets," cried Bill, as he heard the thumps at the door. "My name's Walker."

He crept through the window, hung by his hands for a moment from the sill, and dropped safely on the roof of the outhouse. From here he slid down into the yard. Then he looked about him for a moment or two, not knowing very well what next to be at. He felt pretty certain that some of the neighbours would soon observe his movements from the backs of the surrounding houses, and therefore prompt action was required in his present emergency, for he did not intend to be taken if he could help it.

He jumped over the wall and reached another yard, which was paved. He soon discovered he was in close proximity to a stable.

A man was cleaning some harness in the yard, where he now found himself, and while thus occupied he looked at the gipsy in an inquiring and, it might be, a suspicious manner.

"All right, mate," said Bill. "You've no call to be afeard. I've just given a bloke a prop in the eye, and another on the sneezer. We've had a bit of a scrimmage, and the bobbies are after me."

"Who have you been mugging, then?" said the ostler, with a laugh.

"Why, a doctor."

"What name?"

"Bourne."

"Oh, scissors! What, that varmint!"

"Ah, you're right, he is a varmint. But, I say, just let me come inside—there's a good fellow."

"Inside where?"

"The stable. Anywhere to get out of sight."

"I'd step it, if I were you."

"That's just what I want to do."

"Come in, mate, I won't turn my back upon a man whose in a bit of a mess, which I 'xpect you are."

"In a jolly mess, and no flies."

The gipsy crept into the stable, and his newly-formed friend went on cleaning the harness as if nothing had happened.

Both remained for some time inside the stable without saying a word. Presently his friend, the ostler, said, in a low whisper—

"I say, old fellow, there's some blokes a looking out of the window of the doctor's house."

"The devil," murmured Bill, "I wish I was out of this. They'll be in the yard presently I expect. Tell me when they draw in their ugly heads."

"Hush, stow magging," cried the man in a whisper. "Hold your row, you fool."

The gipsy did not venture to speak after this timely admonition, but awaited the issue in breathless suspense.

In a few moments after this the harness cleaner entered the stable.

"You'd better step it," he observed.

"Yes, that's all very well, but how? Show me the way, and I'll be off in the twinkling of a bedpost."

"I don't know who you are," said the ostler. "You may have committed murder, for aught I know; but I don't like to give a cove up, unless he's a downright bad un."

"Oh, get out—murder, indeed! I tell you, all I've done is to floor the doctor; but he's got his knife into me for other reasons. I can't explain all to you now, but show me the way to escape. Could you take me through the house?"

"I can, of course, but you may be seen, and then there will be the devil to pay!"

"Well, I'm sure you're a good sort. Take pity on a poor chap. Come, now, just think it over. A man is never the worse for doing another a good turn."

"Who and what are you?"

"Well, if you must know, I was a jockey. Now, I'm in the horse-training line."

"I guessed as much by your looks. Wait a bit; I'll just have a squint, and see if the blokes are there or not."

The speaker went out into the yard again, and glanced at the back window of the doctor's residence, then he returned to the stable.

"They've hooked it," he ejaculated. "Now's your time. Follow me."

Bill Rawton did not need a second bidding. He passed quickly out, went up a narrow passage by the side of the stable, and then entered the back door of the house to which it was attached. Passing quickly along this until he reached the end of the hall, he came to the front door of the establishment.

The ostler opened this, placed his finger on his lips to enjoin silence, and Bill emerged into the street.

It is needless to say perhaps that he walked as fast as his legs would carry him.

He had succeeded, thanks to the ostler, in getting clear off.

Leaving him for awhile, we will return to the room from which he had escaped.

The hammering at the door continued for some time after Bill had dropped on to the outhouse. Mrs. Bourne did not know what to do.

On the floor lay her husband in an insensible condition. Who the men were outside the room she could not very well determine, but she judged rightly enough that they were officers of the law.

She was, however, in no way disposed to admit them till Rawton had sufficient time afforded him to effect his escape.

The poor woman was in a terrible state of fright and trepidation, and she stood, pale and irresolute, wringing her hands, in the centre of the apartment.

"If you don't unlock the door, we will break it open," cried a voice from the outside.

"For mercy's sake, what's the matter? Do say what you want!" cried Mrs. Bourne.

"We want to see the doctor. Open the door without further ado."

"But I am afraid. Doctor Bourne has had a desperate struggle with some man, and is lying senseless on the floor. Are you friends or enemies?"

"Friends. We are detective officers."

Mrs. Bourne unlocked the door, and our old friend, Mr. Wrench, entered, in hot haste. He was accompanied by another person, who was a detective from New York.

"What is the meaning of all this, madam?" said Wrench. "Your husband lying senseless, and you alone with him! Please to account for this as best you can."

Mrs. Bourne briefly explained the conflict that had taken place, and said that the man who had struck her husband threatened to take her life if she opened the door. She wound up by declaring that he had made his escape through the window.

"Foiled!" ejaculated Wrench. "Our man has given us the slip. But no matter, I shall be able to find him."

"What has he been doing, gentlemen?" inquired Mrs. Bourne.

"We have to arrest him upon the charge of horse-stealing—that's all," observed Wrench.

"But my poor husband? Pray see to him at once."

The two officers lifted up the doctor and placed him on the sofa.

The movement seemed to revive him, for he slowly opened his eyes and exclaimed, in an anxious tone—

"Where is he?"

"Who, sir?" inquired Wrench.

"That infamous wretch, the gipsy."

"He has escaped, but don't trouble yourself about that, we shall catch him. How do you feel now?"

"Very bad—my head swims—I——"

He ceased speaking, having swooned.

A doctor in the immediate neighbourhood was sent for, who at once proceeded to make an examination of the injuries received.

He said there was nothing to be alarmed at; there was a contused wound at the base of the skull. This had, in all probability, been caused by the head coming in contact with the fender, but in addition to this there were two or three abrasures and contusions on the face.

The patient was weak from shock to the system and loss of blood, but there was no danger to be apprehended.

The injuries were strapped up, and the doctor ordered

him to keep his bed till his medical adviser's next visit.

"I care not for myself," said he to Wrench; "all I am anxious about is that miscreant. Lose no time in hunting him down. Don't let him escape if you can possibly help."

"I dare say we shall be able to find him, sir. Leave that matter to me and my friend Shearman."

"Ah, just so, you have not introduced me to the gentleman."

"I beg pardon, I have not. Mr. Shearman, of the New York detectives; Shearman, Doctor Bourne."

"I should have liked to make the doctor's acquaintance under more favourable circumstances," observed Shearman, dryly. "But, let us hope he will be himself again in a day or two."

"There is not the least doubt of that," said Bourne; but, meanwhile, do your best to capture that ruffian."

"Wrench and Shearman drew aside and had a long conversation, which was carried on in whispers.

"Not at present; there will be time enough for that," cried Wrench, in a louder tone — "plenty of time."

"Good; so be it, then," ejaculated the Yankee.

"I tell you no time is to be lost," exclaimed the doctor, who was under the impression that they were discussing the mode of proceeding to be adopted in reference to Rawton.

"We will do our best, rest assured of that, sir," observed Wrench, quietly. "In the meantime, keep as quiet as possible. Good evening. We both wish you a speedy recovery."

"Thank you. Good evening, gentlemen."

The two detectives then left the patient to himself.

Doctor Bourne's head and temples were throbbing, and he was in great pain, but consciousness had returned, and he was already much better than anyone would have supposed.

"I wonder who that fellow is Wrench brought with him? A detective from New York, he said. Strange! What made him bring him here, I wonder. Our constabulary is sufficiently effective without enlisting the services of officers belonging to America. It seems a strange thing to me that Wrench should be in such close companionship with a mysterious man like that. From New York, eh?"

He tossed about in an uneasy manner, and kept harping upon the subject for some time; presently the medicine he had swallowed took effect, and he sank into a sound slumber.

CHAPTER XCVII.

WATCHING AND WAITING—A TETE-A-TETE BETWEEN TWO
DETECTIVES.

WHEN Mr. Wrench and his companion descended to the basement of the house they were invited into the parlour by the mistress of the establishment, who placed before them wine and brandy—they both elected to have a glass of the latter.

"How do you think the doctor is? He seems very prostrate," said Mrs. Bourne.

"I think he's going on all right, madam," returned Wrench. "He's weak, of course, but is far better than we had a right to expect, considering the damage to which he has been subjected."

"You think so?"

"Oh, dear me, I feel assured of it. You need not be under any apprehension. He'll soon be himself again, but we must now look after our man—that is the next duty we have to perform."

"You allude to his assailant, I presume?"

"Precisely—to the man Rawton. It will be joyful news to you, I expect, when you hear of his arrest."

"It's an unfortunate business, Mr. Wrench—very unfortunate. Rawton was not so very much to blame.

"Indeed!" exclaimed Shearman. "The attack was not made for the purpose of robbery, then?"

"Dear me, no. There was a dispute—a wrangle—and words were used, and the doctor struck him first."

"Oh, oh!" cried Shearman, glancing at Wrench.

"It does not matter," returned the latter. "He is wanted—is charged with horse-stealing; this assault is only a secondary sort of affair, but of course it will have to be inquired into when we get our man. Did you see which way he went, madam, after he got out of the window?"

This last query was addressed to Mrs. Bourne.

"No, I did not," she answered.

"If it is not an impertinent question," observed Shearman, "may I inquire how long you have been married to Doctor Bourne?"

"Sir!" ejaculated the lady.

"Pray excuse the observation. Do not imagine, madam, that I am inquiring out of mere idle curiosity. Gentlemen in our profession seldom do that."

"I confess I am at a loss to understand the reason for such a question, but there is no secret in the matter—indeed, there is no reason for secrecy. I have been married to the doctor between five and six years."

"More than five years of wedded bliss," ejaculated the American.

"I have not said so."

"Ahem! No. But I infer it. I hope the inference is a correct one, for your sake."

"I do not as yet see what you are driving at, sir," returned Mrs Bourne, a little nettled, "and for the life of me cannot understand what my wedded bliss, as you term it, has to do with you."

"Pardon my friend," cried Wrench, coming to the rescue, "he's at times too plain-spoken, and, I think I may add, a little too inquisitive, but it is a way he and his countrymen have, and which, I am sure, or at any rate I hope, you will overlook."

"I am not offended with the gentleman, but he is to me a perfect stranger. That you must admit. And —well, to speak plainly, he is a little peculiar for a stranger."

"I beg ten thousand pardons, my dear madam," said Shearman. "I will not offend in a like manner again."

"I have already told you, sir, that I am not offended. Let that suffice."

"Let it suffice also for the present," observed Shearman, "that as time goes on you will be able to discover the reason for my query, which, as I before observed, was not made out of idle curiosity."

"Good evening, Mrs. Bourne."

"Good evening, gentlemen," said the doctor's wife, as she saw her two visitors to the door.

"Now, Shearman," ejaculated Wrench, when they had got some little distance from the house, "you have your duty to perform and I have mine. In the first place, I must see and find my man."

"Certainly, by all means; the sooner the better, say I. Am I in your way?"

"By no means. I shall be glad of your company, if you've nothing better to do."

"I've nothing to do at all just at present."

Mr. Wrench made direct for a public-house called

"The Bag o' Nails." This place was nearly opposite the common lodging-house to which Rawton was known to repair. The detective's object was to keep watch and ward over the entrance to the lodging-house from the front-floor window of the public opposite. He argued shrewdly enough that as the night wore on, the gipsy would pass in to the lodging-house in question, and when this had taken place, Mr. Wench proposed paying a visit to the establishment and capturing the runaway horse-stealer.

The front room first floor of the "Bag 'o Nails" was used by the Foresters, who held their weekly meetings there. On the evening in question it was vacant, and this Mr. Wrench knew perfectly well.

The detective was known to the landlord of the house, and a few explanatory words in the bar parlour with that worthy sufficed to make him comprehend that our two detectives wanted the use of the room for a few hours, and this was at once acceded them.

They took up their station close by the window, but like bashful gentlemen as they were, they did not court the public gaze. Far from it—they concealed themselves, as well as they could conveniently do so, behind the thick wire blind which obscured the lower part of the window. There was a flaming gaslight immediately in front of the lodging-house, so that there was but little difficulty in observing those who entered the place after dark.

Some brandy cold was ordered by the two detectives, who, after it had been brought in, closed the door, and took up their stations.

"You know best, I suppose," said Shearman, "but I should say the fellow would never be fool enough to betake himself to his old quarters since he must know he's wanted."

"Well, he's hard up, and has no other place to go to, I believe. Anyway, there is a chance, and I don't care to miss it."

It is weary work watching and waiting in cases of this sort, and the outside world has probably no idea of the patience and unremitting attention which detectives have at times to exercise.

In this case, however, Wrench had a companion, and that in a measure beguiled the tediousness of the hours.

"The doctor's wife must have been a beautiful woman in her early days," said Shearman. "Indeed, she is so now, to my thinking."

"Oh, yes, very beautiful at one time, and was thought a good deal of in the fashionable world."

"Has been kept by one or more, I suppose?"

Mr. Wrench nodded.

"Bourne married her for money, I should imagine."

"For nothing else, money and patronage."

"Ah, just so. That I should imagine. Don't hit it very well together, eh?"

"Do people ever hit it who contract marriages of that description?"

"Perhaps not. Still there are exceptions."

"Very few."

"He's a bad lot."

"Dear me, yes, a very bad lot."

The conversation began to flag, and the first hour passed slowly away. Two more glasses were ordered, and two cigars, and the watchers shifted their seats and prepared themselves for a long sitting.

"You've seen a goodish bit in your time, Wrench?"

"Yes; and so have you, I expect?"

"Certainly; but the life of chaps like us is very different, I should imagine, in the States to what it is in this country. You see, there is such an extent of territory, and it would puzzle a Philadelphia lawyer to tell which way your man has taken. But, mind you, your London thief is a match for all the world in cunning—he hasn't any equal, I should say."

"None whatever," returned Wrench, puffing blue wreaths of smoke from his cigar.

"Your man don't make his appearance as yet."

"No; and it's precious tedious, this waiting. But don't you stop unless you like."

"Ah, but I do like. I don't find it tedious. We are all right here, in a snug room quite to ourselves. Did I ever tell you of a midnight adventure I had in the new country?"

"No, I don't know that you ever did. Let's have it. Anyway, it will break the monotony of the evening."

"No one knows better than yourself, Wrench, that a detective's life is full of incident and adventure. One hears this remark often enough, but few out of the force reflect upon what a multitude of remarkable circumstances and events such an experience does cover. You must know that at one time I was night policeman in the New York force."

"Oh, were you? I didn't know that," said Wrench.

"Yes, was only a night policeman at the commencement, and I must say, that notwithstanding the many disagreeable things connected with the calling, on the whole I liked it."

"Ah, you would not like it in this country."

"Possibly not; but I did there, and took an interest in my business. Perhaps this is why I was in several instances more successful in certain matters of importance connected with our profession than were others of my companions, and eventually attracted the head of our department. At all events, I received a note from our chief, and was agreeably surprised upon calling, to find that I was to be removed from the position I then occupied, and was to be put upon special duty as a detective officer."

"Oh, that's how it came about, eh?" said Wrench.

"Yes, and you—?"

"I commenced as a detective, but proceed."

"We have had an eye upon you, Shearman," said our leader, "and in addition to you being a brave and efficient officer, certain matters show you to be ingenious and incorruptible—the characteristics which should be vital tests in the selection of our detective force; so you know the reason of your promotion."

"He was quite right," observed Wrench. "I am sorry to say that corruption creeps in to no small extent here—I don't know how it is in America."

"Oh, bad enough. I thanked him for my good fortune, and so much that was flattering confused me not a little."

"Now, Shearman," said he, after I had concluded, "we are about to put you on a trail that will test your powers to the utmost, and one which, if successfully followed up to a favourable termination, will establish your reputation as a detective."

I eagerly listened to the details which were placed before me, and made careful and copious notes of the same; and when I left the office it was with the determination never to return unless as a successful man—that is, as far as this case was concerned.

With an excess of caution I said nothing to my old companions about the change in my circumstances, for I had determined to be as faithful as I possibly could. The facts of the case were as follows :—

A bank robbery, so bold and startling as to create a good deal of excitement, even in those days of sensation, had been perpetrated a few weeks previously on one of our State institutions, and the whole matter had been accomplished in such an exquisitely adroit and skilful manner as to baffle hitherto the most persistent attempts to discover the clever operators.

A large reward had been offered for the offenders, but all seemed useless, and the losers had about made up their minds that the affair must go to their profit and loss account.

I had little hope that I, so inexperienced, could succeed, where men thoroughly educated and disciplined by years of practice had signally failed, and almost grumbled that the department had put me upon such a case for my maiden attempt; still I determined to do my best.

Of course, my first move was to carefully examine the premises where the robbery had taken place, and discover, if possible, some clue to the villains.

From the style of the work they were undoubtedly experienced hands, but I was too new to the brotherhood to determine with any degree of probability as to the identity of the men from the character of the job, like others who had preceded me.

I found nothing which would apparently throw the faintest gleam of light upon the matter, and in fact said as much to the president, as I was about to leave the place.

The stone bank building joined the wooden building of the cashier, and was accessible from his rooms by a glass half door. It was plain enough that the thieves had effected an easy entrance into his house, and passing softly through his sleeping chamber, had gained the interior of the bank and the vaults by removing a pane of glass from the upper part of the door, and had escaped by opening a window from the back of the bank from the inside.

The vault locks, themselves, had been destroyed in a common way, by the agency of gunpowder. While I was talking with the president, I stood idly drumming on the sash where the glass had been removed, and as I turned away, felt a sharp pain like the prick of a needle upon my right forefinger, and upon looking at my hand found that it was bleeding slightly.

Naturally my first thought was that I had been cut with a piece of glass broken off in the sash when the pane was first removed, but not liking to overlook anything, however trivial apparently, I privately turned back, and upon examination, to my joy extracted from the wood-work the ragged end of a penknife blade, which had perhaps been used to remove the glass.

I examined it intently, and found that the fracture was peculiar—rather a longitudinal one than the ordinary breakage straight across the blade. I said nothing of my discovery, but put the piece carefully away, perhaps for further use.

Now all this seems a very small matter, but I well knew that a very slight clue would sometimes lead up to an important disclosure; still there was nothing at present to do, but to take the cars and return to New York.

I had been riding for over an hour, quite amused by an animated political discussion between two gentlemen who sat directly in front of me, and, indeed, had come to the conclusion that they were both more than usually intelligent and interesting talkers, when a little incident put me once more on the extremest official alert.

It chanced that a boy passed through the car with a basket of fruit and confectionery for sale, and my companions each bought an orange, a thing common enough, and which almost escaped my notice.

I happened to be looking at the one who sat on the inside, as he took out a knife and began to peel his orange. An exclamation of annoyance which escaped him caused me to glance at the knife, when, to my astonishment, I noticed that part of the blade was gone, and, singularly enough, the fracture startlingly suggested the fragment that I had rescued from the bank window.

I fancied I saw a look exchanged by the two men, but kept quiet and cool. My next move was to call back the boy, although I had refused to buy as he passed, and purchased an apple.

This done, it was a delicate venture to request the loan of the aforesaid knife, pleading the loss of my own. As we had had some little conversation previously, he could hardly refuse, and, indeed, passed it with no apparent hesitation. I had, of course, taken care to have the fragment handy, and, when unobserved, tried the two. They were two parts of one whole.

I was satisfied that I held the knife that cut out the bank window, but whether the man in possession of the same was the robber or not, was uncertain, but of course now I had nothing to do but follow up the trail opening before me.

I returned the knife with thanks, and gave myself up to a severe study and scrutiny of the two, so that I could never forget or mistake them at any other time; but to my surprise, I discovered that to a great extent I was baffled in this by what seemed a design on their part.

Instead of proceeding direct to New York, as I had supposed they would, at the next station they got out and took seats in a car running on a branch road towards the interior of the State.

Of course I had nothing to do but to follow. I saw that they glanced suspiciously at me as I entered, and fancied that I detected a look of anxiety on their faces, but said nothing.

"It's best to say nothing in cases of that sort," observed Wrench. "Many of our chaps spoil all by opening their mouths when they ought to be closed."

"Oh, and so do ours, but we can none of us be wise at all times."

"Well, how did you get on after that?"

"You shall hear."

It was near nightfall when we all three dismounted at a lonely station, where a large old-fashioned house seemed to be the only indication of life about the place.

I must needs make some explanation of my course, so I casually told them that I had come down into that part of the country to look up a desirable farm, with the idea of purchasing if suited.

They accepted my explanation without comment, and as they informed me that the adjacent house was used as a sort of tavern, I accompanied them there, and engaged lodgings and supper, taking occasion to ask our host, a withered old fellow, in an audible voice, if he knew of any good farms for sale in that region.

Of course I had to listen to a string of tedious enumerations in reply, but it answered my purpose very well, and I saw that my companions seemed easier than before.

There were four other fellows in the great kitchen, and rough-looking chaps they were, too, and had I met them in the purlieus of Five Points, or Cow Bay, I should have instantaneously set them down as a quartette of arrant cut-throats and burglars; however, out here in the country that was hardly likely, and they were doubtless honest enough drovers or horse jockeys.

I was, however, considerably worried when I saw a silent but unmistakeable look of intelligence pass between my gentleman friends and these fellows, and I speedily made up my mind that I was in the midst of a gang of desperate characters, and that my only safe way would be to leave the place, if possible, by the very first morning train, as I had ascertained that this being a branch road no night trains passed. I was well armed, but what could one man do against six such fellows as these?

About nine o'clock I was shown to a large unfurnished room overhead, and, to my consternation, found that I must share my bed with one of these worthies; but fearful of exciting suspicion, I made no objection, but only partially undressed, and lay down not to sleep, but still pretended to do so, and was soon breathing deep and heavily.

Everything was quiet until about midnight, when my companion stirred, got up in bed, and I was sure bent over me to see if I slept.

I lay very still, and he, evidently believing that my feigned breathing was real, crawled softly over me, and stepped out upon the floor, where, hastily dressing, and taking a parting glance at the bed, he silently left the room. I heard him descend the stairs, and the next minute I was at the window.

It was quite light without, and shortly I saw my friends steal out of the house, and move in the direction of the station. An impulse seized me, and I was quickly upon their track. I had no idea of their purpose, but I was sure that it was no good one.

I soon reached the station, and almost stumbled upon them, but had presence of mind enough to conceal myself in a dark shadow, in time to escape detection, but where I could overhear their conversation distinctly, from which I soon learned that not only had I discovered the missing bank thieves, but come into possession of a number of other facts of great importance.

It seems that they had become suspicious of me, and had determined to leave the place in the night, with which idea they had determined to break open the door of one of the railroad buildings, and stealing a hand-car, make their way with that to a junction some seven miles down the road, and there take an early train for the West.

I heard the door burst open, and the muttered oaths as the party discovered that the car usually there was that night, unluckily for them, gone. It was then that I was seized with an irresistible desire to cough; in vain I struggled against it; it would come, and it did.

I had hardly time to dart away when they were in full pursuit, and despite my utmost efforts, I was caught, knocked down, and borne back to the station; and now my heart failed me entirely, for I was completely disarmed, and I knew by the scowling glances, that I was in the deadliest peril. Still, I had only done my duty, and I determined if I must die, to do so like a man.

There was little said to me, but I saw that they were deliberating as to the best way of disposing of me, and when two of them approached me, I thought that my time was come, indeed; but it was not to be so yet, for they pushed me into the empty car-house, and shut the door, leaving me to my reflections.

I soon found out the motives of this; the house was to be fired, and I was to be burned alive! to destroy every evidence of guilt! I attempted to cry out, but the roll of thick cloth in my mouth stopped that effectually.

The thought of my poor wife and child drove me to despair; could I have had a chance to die in conflict, selling my life as dearly as possible, it would be easy to such a death as this; but to be confined in a dark room, unable to move or speak, or to make a single effort for my own relief, to helplessly lie and listen to the crackling of the fire, and feel the gentle warmth at first, grow to a savage, terrible, horrid torture fiend eventually lapping the moisture from my bones and blood, and swelling my black and blistering tongue till, consumed by its own rage, it fell a foul and withered cinder in the common ruin.

What a decree of deadly, deadly fate it seemed that only a week before, the night train that would at least have saved me from this kind of death, had been taken off, and no relief could come until eight o'clock the next morning, before which time nothing distinguishable would be left of me.

I already choked with the smoke that came rushing in through the loose sides of the building, when something tore past the station with what seemed to me a scream of frantic exulting joy and hope. My heart leaped at the sound, and with a tremendous effort I snapped the cords that bound my arms.

It was the whistle of an approaching engine, and I knew that, as this was one of the few watering places on the road, they would certainly stop there.

My captors heard it, too, and in a minute I heard them at the door. I prepared myself for a rush, and, as it hastily swung open, I darted out, and struck wildly right and left at the desperate fellows who surrounded me.

They fell upon me with knives, and I felt myself, although a very powerful man, and fighting as only a strong man can fight in the last extremity, half-blinded, badly cut, and gradually sinking under the terrible assaults of one huge fellow in particular. I slipped over an old dry-goods box that stood near. The fiend had me by the throat in an instant, and, poising his monstrous bowie-knife over my head, cried out—

"D—n you! what can save you now? You miserable spy! This and this!"

I heard a terrible voice cry, and then came the crash of a revolver, and the hand at my throat relaxed, and with a loud cry, my assailant fell heavily backward. I gained my feet, and to my utter amazement, saw the two gentlemen that I had first met on the train, struggling desperately with the other three.

I was weak and wounded, but I did what I could to help. I heard a roar and a rumble, and a great blazing eye came out of the night, and an engine and car loaded with labourers stopped at our feet.

I fell to the ground, and only knew that we were helped upon the train. When I came to in earnest, three days afterwards, I found two smiling and somewhat familiar faces at my bedside, who unravelled the tangled skein of my night adventure.

I found my two companions to be detectives from Chicago, who, in the guise of swell mobsmen, had made the acquaintance of the real criminal in our party of that terrible night, and had gone down there with the *supposed* intention of participating in a burglary already planned, but with the real purpose of preventing the robbery and arresting the party, with the assistance of others lying in wait at the selected house.

But I had interfered with all their plans, and they had not dared to reveal themselves to a stranger, when with such a large party. Still at the same time I came so near being burned, they had made up their minds, despite the risk, to attempt a rescue, but the fortunate arrival of the train solved the difficulty partially. While with the robbers, a few days previously, they had come into possession of the peculiarly broken knife that had attracted my attention, and had retained it, thinking something might come of it, as there did, for the crime was traced beyond a doubt, to two of the prisoners, and they received a sentence that will probably furnish them with lodgings for a life time.

You can imagine what this lucky exposure did for me. Had I not have been a new man in the force, the Chicago men would probably have known me.

"Ah, yes; there is a great advantage in not being known; we all find that out," said Wrench. "It's a great drawback, and causes us no end of trouble."

"Does your man know you?"

"What Rawton, Lord bless you, yes—know me? Why I gave evidence against him in a former case."

"Oh," cried Shearman, "I shall have to tell you one or two more of my adventures, then."

While this conversation had been taking place, and the two detectives had been keeping watch over the entrance to the common lodging-house, a man with a shambling gait had made his way to the "Bag o' Nails." This personage was Cooney, and, as the reader will doubtless readily imagine, he had not paid a visit to the place without a purpose.

His object was to have a word or two with the potman of the establishment, to whom he was very well known.

Cooney's circle of acquaintances, if not very select, might be considered extensive. Potmen he looked upon as his natural associates; anyway, he generally managed to ingratiate himself in their good graces.

Cooney entered the taproom of the house, and drew the potman on one side in a mysterious manner.

"I say, Dick, old man—a word with you," whispered Cooney. The two went into the passage.

"Well, what's the row?" cried the potman.

"Just give us the straight tip. You've got two blokes—upstairs in the front room, first floor, aint you?"

"There are two gentlemen there, I believe."

"Guessed as much. Gentlemen with eyes like gimlets, as can pierce through a four-inch deal board. Eh?"

"I don't know about that."

"They hail from Scotland Yard."

"That's about the size of it, I fancy."

"Thank you, Dick. That's all I wanted to know. Been here long?"

"An hour and more."

"I see rocks ahead. Good night."

Cooney did not want to make any further inquiries. He saw which way the land lay, and acted accordingly. There wasn't much chance of the gipsy making his appearance at the lodging-house for that night, or a good many more after. Cooney "blew the gaff," gave the alarm, and of course Bill Rawton was very shortly far away from the scene of action.

The night wore on.

Mr. Wrench and his anecdotal lively companion began to consider the case as hopeless. The latter had done so on the outset, and Wrench was fast inclining to his friend's opinion.

But Wrench was a most persevering officer, and was not one to give up easily when he had made up his mind to any course of action.

"I guess we shall have to go away as wise as we came," said Shearman, with a short, dry laugh. "The fellow's fly, and it's no use watching the dark shadows cast on yonder door."

"I fancy not. I shall give it up for to-night; but I shall have him before many hours are over our heads."

"I hope you may; but what are you going to do now?"

"Cut it. Are you ready?"

"I have been a long time ago."

The two friends passed out of the club-room, and descended the stairs. The obsequious landlord came out of his bar-parlour.

"Are you off, sir?" said he.

"Yes," returned Wrench. "It's been a bit of a sell, but it don't matter. The bird has flown."

The landlord gave a mysterious nod, and the detectives took their departure.

CHAPTER XCVIII.

THE WOUNDED MAN AND HIS BETTER HALF.

IN the course of a day or two Doctor Bourne was sufficiently recovered to sally forth and attend to his professional duties. He was in no very amiable frame of mind, and his temper was not improved when he learnt from Mr. Wrench that Rawton had not been arrested. He offered a handsome reward for his apprehension, albeit he was in no way concerned in the charge of horse-stealing, but he was furious when he thought of his assailant, whom he hated with no common hate. Rawton had deceived him. He had done more than this, he had insulted him, and committed a violent assault. All this was bad enough, but a number of other circumstances conspired to irritate the doctor, which filled his bitter cup to overflowing.

Mrs. Bourne had, of course, a fine time of it. She saw as little as possible of her selfish and overbearing partner.

He was morose and snarlish; answering her in short sentences, and treating her with the utmost contempt. At length, however, after a few days had passed over, he became more outspoken.

"And so, madam," he said one afternoon, "you and your worthless infamous champion and protector have done your worst. You have chosen a thief and a ruffian of the very worst type for your companion. It is a pity you did not take yourself off with him. I should then be rid of a pest and a nuisance."

"I am perfectly well aware, sir," said Mrs. Bourne, indignantly, "that my presence here is obnoxious to you. I would gladly go, and would be thankful to be released from this odious thraldom."

"Then why the devil don't you go? Nobody wants you to stop. I am sure I don't," he added, sarcastically.

"You wish to be rid of me, and have done so for a long time past. Do not for a moment imagine, sir, that I do not know the reason. If you were an honourable man, which you are not, you would at once agree to a separation."

"Agree! 'gad it would be the most desirable thing that could happen. Agree, indeed!"

"You had five thousand pounds settled on you on the day I became your wife. Resign that, or a portion of it, and the tie which binds us can be dissolved. You are then a free man, and will be at liberty to marry the rich lady upon whom you have an eye. Upon that condition I will resign all claim to you."

"I am much obliged, very much obliged, I am sure;

"MR. BOURNE—DOCTOR!" EJACULATED WRENCH, WHO SUDDENLY ENTERED THE ROOM.

but does it not occur to you that I can obtain a release without acceding to any such condition?"

"I know your mercenary, grasping nature; you would not willingly part with a shilling of the money."

"No, I don't intend to do so. Certainly not to such a shameless, abandoned woman as you are. I was a fool—worse than a fool—to be cozened into marrying a common harlot."

"Mr. Bourne, your language is intolerable. What were you at the time? What are you now? I will proclaim you to all the world as a brute and a ruffian, for such you are. If you had one spark of manhood in your coarse, callous nature you would blush at such observations."

"Thank you, madam, for your good opinion. We know each other pretty well, I believe, and there's no very great love lost between us. I shall find the means of proving your marriage with William Rawton, not-

...standing the assertion made by that wretch as to its being an illegal one. When I am in a position to prove it—which I soon shall be—out of this house you go."

"I am in danger of my life while I remain here," exclaimed his wife.

"What do mean, madam?" he returned sharply.

"Oh, you know what I mean."

"Liar and adultress!" he exclaimed, in a violent fury. "I demand to know what you mean. You know well enough that I am not a man to be trifled with. Explain yourself."

"I say, I believe my life to be in danger—that is my answer."

"Who cares what you believe? Your life—it doesn't much matter how soon it comes to an end—certainly, not as far as I am concerned. You are an adept at dealing in innuendoes—I deal with facts. I wish to be rid of you."

"I am well aware of that. My life has been for a long time almost insupportable, and it would indeed be a joyful hour when I could feel assured that I was about to part from you, so that I might never see you more."

"The feeling is quite reciprocal, madam," said Bourne. "I hope the hour is at hand, for both our sakes. You have passed through many grades in the social scale; you can now return to the arms of your admirer and protector—your ruffianly husband—who is a thief, and for aught I know may be a murderer as well."

"You base, infamous man," cried Mrs. Bourne, in a perfect frenzy, "you have not one spark of honour in your whole composition."

Upon the impulse of the moment she caught hold of a scent bottle, which stood on the table, and hurled it at her husband. It struck him a sharp blow on the left cheek.

He sprang forward and struck his wife with his clenched fist. Then he wound his fingers around her throat, and pinned her to the wall.

"You common harlot," he exclaimed, "I'll make an end of you at once, and take all consequences."

He pressed the unfortunate woman's throat with such force that she was half strangled. She made a desperate struggle to release herself, and called out for assistance, being under the impression at the time that he would carry his threat into execution; but her cries were soon stifled by her brutal husband.

Fortunately for her the street-door had been opened by the maid in answer to a gentle rap, and Mr. Wrench, hearing a noise in the front parlour, entered without any ceremony.

The detective was awe-struck at beholding Mrs. Bourne purple in the face, and her husband grasping her remorselessly by the throat.

"Mr. Bourne—doctor!" ejaculated Wrench, dragging at the same time the man he was addressing from his wife, and thrusting him forcibly into one corner of the room.

When this had been done, he said, "How is this, sir? You are sadly forgetting yourself, it would seem."

"Leave me alone. Don't you interfere between man and wife," exclaimed Bourne. "I know what I am about."

"Do you? Well, and so do I."

"I have a good reason for all this. You don't know the provocation I have had."

"I have nothing to do with that. I will not allow an assault of this nature to take place in my presence without interfering. I know my duty, Mr. Bourne, and am surprised at you."

"You would not be if you knew all."

"I know a great deal more than you imagine," said Wrench, with admirable coolness.

"A parcel of lies she has been telling you, I presume."

"No such thing. This lady has never spoken to me about your disagreements. You are mistaken."

"She would not scruple to malign me to you, or anyone else."

"I say I am very much shocked at your conduct during the scene I have just witnessed. I sympathise with you, madam," said the detective in continuation, and turning towards Mrs. Bourne.

"God knows I need sympathy; I am weary of life," cried the lady.

"Silence! hold your tongue, woman!" exclaimed her husband.

"Mr. Bourne, do let me endeavour to prevail upon you to be a little more temperate, and conduct yourself in a more becoming manner."

"I'm not to be lectured or dictated to by you, sir," was the reply.

"I have no desire to dictate to anyone, but in a case of this description I am of necessity constrained to be outspoken."

"Oh, go on, sir, pray go on. I am not master in my own house, it would appear."

"I hope you are. I should say, judging from appearances, that you are very much the master."

"I'll get a warrant," said Mrs. Bourne, "and swear that I am in danger of my life. I can do that, I suppose?"

"You can do it, of course," returned Wrench. "But it would be a very great exposure for a gentleman in your husband's position."

"I don't care if it is."

"She does not care for anything, and has no regard for my interests. She is a worthless woman, Wrench. I am very sorry to be obliged to say so, but it is a fact."

"You don't believe him, I hope," observed Mrs. Bourne, quietly.

"He does not mean what he says, madam—I am sure of that."

"I do," ejaculated the doctor. "I say she is a worthless, infamous woman."

"I am sure you don't expect me to believe you."

"Indeed, but I do."

"Well, we will not discuss that question, Mr. Bourne. You are out of temper, and say a great deal more than you mean; but let that pass. I hope and trust there will be no recurrence of this scene of violence."

"I want to have nothing to say to her. I hope and trust to be in a position before many days are over my head to get rid of this abusive woman."

Mrs. Bourne made no further observation, but quietly left the apartment.

"Well," said her husband, after she had retired, "have you any good news for me? Is that scoundrel still at large?"

"We have not as yet been able to meet with him, but hope to do so before long."

"Hang it! but that's most unfortunate. I concluded, when I saw you, that business had brought you hither."

"Well, so it has. It is partly business matters that I have come upon."

"Ah, indeed, just so. And what is the nature of the matters you speak of?"

"Upon my word, doctor, I don't know that I am in position to tell you precisely. I have come hither for the purpose of inquiring what time it will be convenient for you to see Mr. Shearman?"

"Mr. Shearman? What!—that detective from America?"

"Yes."

"What can he possibly want with me?"

"That you had better hear from his own lips."

Doctor Bourne looked puzzled, or, it might be said, a little disconcerted.

"From his own lips?" he iterated.

"If you please. That, I think, would be the best course."

"Upon my word, Wrench, you are monstrously mysterious. What has the man to tell me?"

"I am not able to say."

"Ah, very well, I will see the gentleman. I hope he will bring me good news. Perhaps a rich relative has died abroad, and left me some thousands—eh?"

"I don't think so," observed Wrench, quietly.

"Or it may be that I am the owner of some unclaimed property. Such things have taken place before now."

"They have, I admit; but I would not buoy myself up with any such fallacious expectations."

"Oh, you don't appear to be at all hopeful or sanguine, but at any rate I trust this active and intelligent Yankee will bring me good news of some kind."

"You will learn all when you see him," observed Wrench. "The case is in his hands—not mine."

"Case! What do you mean? What case has he in hand that can possibly concern me? I never saw the man before in my life that I am aware of. Not till you brought him here."

"That is likely enough."

"And has he ever seen me before?"

"I believe not."

"Hang it, Wrench, you are most confoundedly mysterious. I wish you would be a little more communicative."

"When will it be convenient for you to see Mr. Shearman?" said the detective, not appearing to take any notice of the doctor's query.

"When? Oh, any time that may be most convenient to the gentleman."

"Any time is no time, Dr. Bourne. You had better state the day and the hour."

"Certainly. Will to-morrow evening suit?"

"Very well, I should imagine. And at what hour?"

"Let me see. I am rather busy, it is true; but will eight o'clock do, or between that and nine?"

"It will suit Shearman, if it does you."

"So be it, then; I will be in then, and shall be glad to receive your friend between eight and nine o'clock."

"Agreed, doctor; I will make a point of being here. I am quite sure of that."

"Shall I have the pleasure of seeing you as well?"

"I cannot promise; besides, it would be perhaps advisable for him to confer with you without the presence of a third party. The case has been entrusted to him to conduct."

"Oh, indeed," cried Bourne, in a tone of mistrust. "But here—you must not go, my dear friend, without a glass of wine or some refreshment. What will you take?"

"I would rather not have anything just now, if you'll excuse me."

"Umph! I see how it is; you are a little out of sorts just now. Probably this may be attributable to the scene you have just witnessed; but permit me, in justice to myself, to assure you that there was a strong reason for my being so moved to anger. It is not possible to make you acquainted with the nature of the provocation I have received from the woman."

"I do not desire to inquire into your domestic troubles—for such I suppose them to be," said Wrench, rising; "I hope there will be no further violence displayed on either side."

"There shall not be as far as I am concerned. I pledge my word as to that, Wrench. I lost my temper, I admit; but it is all over now. I shall be more guarded for the future. Thank you for your good advice."

"I wish you a good evening, sir," said the detective, with something like dignity in his tone and manner. "My friend, Mr. Shearman, will be here at the time specified. Good evening."

"Good evening. But I say—one word before you go."

"Yes, what is it?"

"There is no occasion for you to mention the outbreak—the fracas—you have been witness of. Do you see?"

"Yes. I will not mention it to any one."

"You pass your word as to that?"

"I do. Once more, good-night."

CHAPTER XCIX.

MR. DETECTIVE SHEARMAN IS OUTSPOKEN — A STORY OF WOMAN'S WRONGS AND MAN'S BASENESS.

DR. BOURNE, after Wrench had taken his departure, was calm and thoughtful; he was by no means so self-confident and overbearing in his manner as heretofore. Indeed, he might be said to be considerably cowed, why or wherefore it would, perhaps, not be so easy to determine, but the storm of passion had passed over, and was succeeded by a dead calm.

The doctor busied himself in his surgery. He had to make up several prescriptions, with which he purposed drenching his patients. Nevertheless, the compounding of deleterious drugs occupied some time.

It served one good purpose. While thus engaged Bourne's mind was in a measure released from the weight that seemed to oppress him; but despite his employment a foreboding of coming evil seemed to fall upon him. This he found it impossible to dispossess himself of.

Late in the evening he sallied forth, paying a visit to one or more of his familiar acquaintances. With this he whiled away the time till long past midnight. All the occupants of the house had retired to rest. This is precisely what the owner of the establishment desired.

He did not trouble himself to inquire after his wife, for at this time they occupied separate apartments, and saw as little of each other as possible. To say that there was no love lost between them would be but making use of a very mild figure of speech. As far as Bourne himself was concerned he cordially hated the woman whom he had sworn at the altar to cherish and protect. If any one had come to his bedside with the news of her death they would have been greeted as a messenger bearing glad tidings, but no one had come with such welcome intelligence, and Bourne slept peacefully, albeit his slumbers were now and then disturbed by strange, uncouth, and fantastic visions.

What greater misery can by possibility fall upon any one than to be compelled to live with a person whose presence is repugnant and abhorrent, yet the man and woman—the doctor and his wife—had submitted to this torment for years.

He never loved the woman he had espoused, but in the earlier portion of the period of his intimacy with her—and, indeed, for the first year or two of his married life—he had liked her. Had this not been the case, he would never have made her his wife, but the liking no longer existed. It was succeeded by a deadly and rancorous hate, which of late had become intensified.

When he saw her on the following morning, he maintained a dignified silence, and the miserable pair did not exchange a word. Whatever it was necessary to say was conveyed through the medium of Amy, the servant girl, a faithful little maid, who was very well used to these scenes. She liked her mistress, but had no very great predilection for the doctor.

Bourne was from home the greater part of the following day. He came in shortly before seven o'clock in the evening, and betook himself to his surgery.

At twenty minutes after eight he heard a loud rap at the front door. He started, and listened. He heard the well-known voice of Shearman, who was speaking to the servant.

There was no mistaking it for the voice of the detective, who had an American twang, and was altogether dissimilar to any of the other visitors to the doctor's residence.

"Show the gentleman in here," said Bourne to Amy, when he was informed by the girl that the American was in the passage.

Mr. Shearman entered the surgery in an easy, self-satisfied sort of manner; he was smoking a cigar, which he at once took out of his mouth and placed on the mantelpiece.

"Pardon me, doctor, I forgot for the moment that the Virginian weed might be objectionable to gentlemen of your profession."

"By no means; I am a smoker myself, and have no kind of objection to the fumes of tobacco. Pray continue your smoking. I shall in all probability join you shortly."

"Oh, well, if you've no objection."

"None in the least. Pray do not stand upon ceremony, my friend."

Mr. Shearman took up his cigar, the end of which he replaced between his lips.

"So you are pretty punctual, it would appear," observed his companion.

"Ya's; always make it a rule to be up to time, if it s possible."

The doctor placed a chair for his visitor.

"Oh, thank you—much obliged, I'm sure."

He seated himself, and stretched out his long thin legs with the utmost complacency.

The doctor looked at him inquiringly, but his countenance gave no indication of either pleasure or anger; it was a perfect blank.

"Wrench said you had something to communicate to me. I assume that his statement is correct."

"Perfectly correct; but you are not in any hurry—that is, I 'spose you've got an hour or two to spare?"

"Certainly; I am quite at your service."

"Ah, that's well, because it's a matter which will require some little time. I don't like to jump at conclusions, doctor; I like to take matters in regular order. You understand?"

"At present I do not understand the nature of your business, but I dare say I shall do so in the due course of time."

"There is not the least doubt of that," remarked Shearman, sending out several blue wreaths of smoke from his Havanna.

"That is well," observed Bourne.

"You know, or at least you can imagine, that every man has his own way of going about business. I have mine, and if you please I will begin at the beginning. The tale I have to tell you is a little singular, and I think there is an air of romance about it, considering all the circumstances of the case; but I deem it but fair and just that you should be put in full possession of all the particulars. It may be better for you."

"For me?"

"Well, for me, for you, for everybody. That's my view of the matter. I may be mistaken, but I think I am not."

"It is not for me to dictate, Mr. Shearman, or even to suggest; I am here to listen."

"Hadn't you better light up?" said the detective, offering his cigar-case to the other.

"Yes, perhaps it would be as well."

The doctor drew forth a cigar, which he lighted.

"Now we are on equal terms," observed Shearman, with a laugh.

"Confound the man!" muttered the doctor. "When is he going to begin?"

He had not long to wait.

"You see, doctor, I must take you over to the United States, for that's where great part, and, I may say, the most important part, of the events I have to describe took place."

"Oh, indeed. In the United States, eh?"

"Ye-es," drawled the American. "Wall, some years ago there resided at Baltimore a gentleman of the name of Leaven."

The doctor started, and gasped out—"Yes. Well, what of him?"

"He was a planter, tolerably well to do. He had a daughter, whose baptismal name was Clara. She was a wild, hair-brained, giddy little flirt, I've been told, but that's not much to the purpose. Mr. Leaven had the misfortune to lose his wife before his daughter Clara was fifteen years of age, and, as a matter of course, the loss was a severe one, as far as the gal herself was concerned, for she was deprived of a mother's care just at the time when she most needed it. However, misfortunes of this kind are inevitable, and cannot be averted. In addition to his daughter, the planter had two sons, who were, however, younger than the gal. They were a little wayward and self-willed. But the planter loved his children so much that he was blind to their faults or foibles—for to speak the truth, if I am to judge from what I've been told, neither the boys nor the gal had anything much the matter with them—certainly nothing very serious; but you follow me, I hope," suddenly ejaculated Shearman.

"I beg your pardon, but I don't quite understand your question," observed Bourne.

"Oh, don't you? You follow me—that is, you understand the narrative as far as I've gone."

"I should indeed be a dunce if I could not do that."

"Ah, 'xactly, that's all right then. Where was I? Oh, the sons and the daughter. Wall, matters went on right enough for some considerable time after the old lady's death. She was not very old by the way, but I call her so to distinguish her from the younger members of the family. I say matters went on all right enough for some time. Clara Leaven had her admirers, with whom she flirted to her heart's content. One of these was a Britisher, who was very persistent in his attentions to the young gal. Wall, ye see, the planter, for some reason or another, didn't like this gentleman —perhaps the reason for this was his being a Britisher, for prejudice does run high with some. Anyway he did not approve of him as a suitor to his daughter's hand."

"The old story, I suppose," observed the doctor, with a sickly smile. "A hard-hearted parent and a self-willed, disobedient child."

"I s'pose we may call it the old story," returned the detective. "She was a little fool—that's what she was; but it is not much use dwelling upon that now. She gave the Britisher encouragement, and I suppose she fell madly in love with him. That's what I've been told. Her father, when he discoverd the state of her mind towards him, became furious. He threatened to lock her up, to take her life, if she acted in disobedience to his expressed commands. If his daughter was a little fool he was a big one, for that was not the way to quench the flame which had been kindled. Women, and gals in particular, are so perverse that by opposing them in affairs of this sort you clench the nail more securely—on the other side."

"Really, Mr. Shearman, I do hope you have not come hither for the purpose of reciting a love story to a hackneyed man of the world like myself. If it concerned me ——"

"If!" cried the detective. "There's the point, which I hope to arrive at in good time."

"Oh, well, that being the case, I have no other alternative than to complacently listen."

"I think you'd better hear me out, doctor—indeed I do. Wall, as I was saying, Leaven led the gal a devil of a life. He wasn't altogether a tyrant or anything of that sort, but he was impetuous, and liked to have his own way. He did his level best to corner the Britisher, who, however, in the end proved too much for him. A parent hasn't much chance against a favourite lover of his daughter, and so Leaven found out. As to giving his consent, that was altogether out of the question—not to be thought of for a moment. What was to be done under the circumstances? The old expedient—an elopement. Clara Leaven was under the delusion that her parent would forgive her, and matters would be made up after the marriage, so she consented to fly with the Britisher."

"And pray, Mr. Shearman, what was the name of the 'Britisher,' as you are pleased to call him?"

"His name?" cried the detective, "oh, Wagstaff. Doctor Wagstaff he called himself."

Bourne's countenance became of an ashen hue.

Mr. Shearman relighted his cigar, which had gone out during the recital, and puffed away vigorously.

"I am burning him all on one side, doctor, Gone out, and a relighted weed is always a bit obstinate."

"Take another. You won't do much good with that."

"I will take another."

Mr. Shearman threw the half-smoked cigar behind the fire, and then re-commenced his narrative.

"Yes," he said, "the Britisher's name was Wagstaff. He was an artful cuss as ever stepped in shoe leather, so I've been told. He planned and carried out the elopement, the gal of course assisted him, the two were married and settled in Texas. After the lapse of a short time Clara Leaven wrote to her father to beg his forgiveness. He forwarded her some money, but informed her that he would not consent to receive her husband upon any conditions whatever. He was firm and staunch in that resolution, and his sons could not turn him. So there was no help for it. The young and loving pair had to shift for themselves, but in justice to the planter it must be said that he sent his daughter several sums of money, stating at the same time that nothing would please him better than to have her back, but it must be without her husband. Wall, you see, doctor, the gal clung to her partner even as the ivy clings to the ruined wall. She would not return home, although it was said that she had by no means a bed of roses in Texas. To make use of a common phrase, she found out in the due course of time that she had outlived his liking, but she never told anybody this but one person."

"And who might that be?" inquired Bourne.

"That was a young black gal, who had left the plantation to follow her mistress, whom she accompanied in her flight. She made a confidante of her sable companion, who was a liberated slave, and 'Tilda,' as she was called, was in possession of all her secrets."

"Your story is doubtless very entertaining, sir," observed the doctor; "but, for the life of me, I cannot see how it can in any way concern me."

"I hope to arrive at that point presently," returned Mr. Shearman. "Do, pray, permit me to deal with the case in my own way."

"Oh, certainly—I will not interfere with you."

"So the happy pair lived in Texas for some months —over a year, or it might be a year and a half. Before the expiration of that time Mr. Leaven died somewhat suddenly from disease of the heart. The land and stock were sold under the hammer, in accordance to the will he had left. The bulk of the proceeds was left to the sons; some few hundreds—I don't know precisely how many—being Clara Wagstaff's share. Shortly after the demise of her father Clara grew suddenly sick. The circumstance was a little singular, but it is not more strange than many others one hears of of a similar character. Well, to cut a long story short, the young wife died. The cause of death was not clearly established, but the doctor who attended her in her last hours gave the requisite certificate, and she was buried."

Mr. Shearman at this point of the narrative paused.

"Very sad—a very sad story," ejaculated Bourne, casting his eyes up to the ceiling.

"Ya'as, most melancholy, aint it?" said his companion.

"Very much so, indeed. And the husband——"

"Oh, wall, he had, of course, the money left to his wife. It wasn't a great deal, I believe, but it sufficed him to run the rig in Texas for many months. He led a life of pleasure, and "blewed" the greater part of the money. Then he sloped, and returned to the old country—so people say; anyway, he was not heard any more of in the 'States.'"

"Not heard of, eh?"

"No. To make use of a nautical phrase, he slipped his moorings, and was not seen any more."

"Perhaps he's dead?"

"And perhaps he aint," said Mr. Shearman. "That all depends. You see, I have paid a visit to this country for the purpose of finding him out."

"Oh, indeed! I hope you may be successful."

"Tha—ank you." Mr. Shearman rolled the end of his cigar in his mouth. "I think I shall go away wiser than I came, but that don't matter."

"And what do you want to 'find out'—this man, Wagster, did you say?"

"Wagstaff."

"Ah, just so. What do you want to find this Wagstaff out for, then?"

"We must not jump at conclusions," returned Mr

Shearman; "that would never do. You have as yet only heard part of my story."

"True, I am most anxious to hear the conclusion."

"Aire you? Wall, then, you shall. You must know that after the planter's death the war between the Federals and the Confederates took place. The North and South went at it like hammer and tongs. Both the young Leavens were engaged throughout the terrible and sanguinary war. The Southerns had a hard time of it, but they fought for their homes like lions, and the odds were against them, and, despite their valour and heroism, they were whipped in the end. I guessed they would, but they were brave fellows, and deserved a better fate."

"Oh, I know all about the war to which you refer."

"No doubt. Well, I'm only mentioning it to account for the occupation of the two Leavens. One, the youngest, fell on the field of battle, the other is now a farmer in South Carolina. Ye must understand that he never knew the whole particulars concerning his sister's sudden and, I may add, mysterious death."

"Mysterious!" exclaimed Bourne, suddenly.

"Ya-as, it was a bit mysterious."

"Was it?"

"Ya-as."

"How so?"

"I'll tell you. As I before observed, Silas Leavn settled in South Carolina. Shortly after his arrival there he began to reflect seriously upon the sudden death of his sister. It may appear strange that he should let so many years pass over without troubling himself to make any inquiries, but the fact is he didn't suspect anything was amiss, and took it for granted that she had died of a broken heart. In South Carolina he met with some persons who hailed from Texas, who resided there when Mr. and Mrs. Wagstaff were there. Wall, they told Silas a lot of things about the young people, which greatly surprised him. They hinted at foul play, and said that the ill-fated Clara had been poisoned."

"Poisoned!" exclaimed Bourne, in an evident state of trepidation. "Gracious Heaven! I hope there was no ground for any such statement."

"I am pretty sure there was. Wall, you see, when Silas Leavn heard all these things it occurred to him that he had better try and find the girl Tilda in the first place, and after that he might make further inquiries."

"And did he find her?"

"Oh, ya-as, he found her. She was at work on a plantation a good many miles from his own, it is true, but he found her nevertheless, and engaged her as a help on his own farm, for she was a faithful, hard-working darkie. She told him a lot more."

"What did she tell him then?"

"Ah, she up and told him as plain as the letter O that she believed her dear young mistress was done away with."

"Oh! it's not at all likely upon the very face of it. Calumnies—all calumnies."

"Wait a bit, doctor. The case was placed in my hands, and I need not tell you that I did not let it go to sleep. It had been slumbering for a good many years, but when I had hold of it I was not disposed to let it rest."

"Quite right. What did you do then?"

"I got an order to exhume the body, so that a post-mortem might be made, and an inquest held."

"Excellent device. Nothing could be better."

"A good move—wasn't it?"

"Oh, dear me, yes, most admirable."

"I thought you would say so."

"And so a post-mortem was made?"

"It was."

"With what result?"

"It was clearly established, beyond all cavil, that the ill-fated young woman had died from the effects of a mineral poison."

When Mr. Shearman uttered these last words, he regarded his companion with a searching glance.

The doctor quailed before the piercing eyes of the detective. In appearance his face resembled that of a corpse rather than that of a living being.

He endeavoured to muster up an air of intrepidity to his brow, but it was plainly perceptible that he was a prey to a deadly and sickening fear.

Shearman affected not to see this, but it did not escape his notice.

"The poor creature died by poison—did she?" said Bourne, after a pause.

"Yes, doctor, that has been clearly demonstrated."

"Was it a case of suicide, then?"

"No, murder!" exclaimed the detective, sententiously.

"And whom do you suspect?"

"Her husband."

"Mr. Wagstaff?"

"He went by the name of Wagstaff when in the States, but we concluded that he would not be fool enough to pass under the same name here, and I believe the presumption is a correct one."

"Ah!" ejaculated the doctor, gasping for breath, "you astonish me."

"I thought I should. Now do you want to know in what way this story concerns you?"

"Sir — Mr. Shearman — what can you possibly mean?"

"I always like to do things in a straightforward, upright sort of way. Before coming to that part of the evidence which so seriously affects you, I have deemed it advisable to put you in possession of those facts which lead up to the main issue. This is but fair to a suspected person, and one I invariably adopt when circumstances will admit of my so doing."

"You are still speaking in enigmas. I again ask in what way does the case concern me?"

"I don't want to ask you any questions, Doctor Bourne," said the American. "I should not be justified in doing so, and I may observe that I don't want you to make any statement. It would not be advisable for you to do so, since you might criminate yourself."

"Criminate myself, sir!" cried the doctor, rising suddenly, and regarding the speaker with an eye of flame. "Are you mad?"

"I hope not. Let me come at once to the point. We have reason to believe that Dr. Wagstaff, of Texas, and Doctor Bourne, of London, are one and the same person."

"Gracious Heaven! what do I hear?" ejaculated the miserable man. "Me accused of a heinous crime of this nature! It is monstrous, scandalous, and most improbable."

"Well, doctor, I hope you may be able to prove your innocence, but I have a duty to perform, and, unpleasant one as it may be, I have no other alternative than to execute it."

"Mr. Shearman," said Bourne, in a whining tone, "surely you are not serious?"

"Ah, but I am. I've my own way of doing business. It's different, perhaps, to the ways of detectives of this country, and I must inform you that I hold in my possession a warrant for your apprehension upon the charge of wilfully murdering Clara Wagstaff."

"But I am not Wagstaff, Shearman; you are mistaken. I swear you are mistaken."

"Don't swear, doctor; you will not be benefitted by so doing. There is no help for it; you will have to meet the charge."

Bourne looked down upon the floor in all but hopeless despair.

He remained silent for a brief period; then, as if suddenly something had occurred to him, he raised his head, and glancing at his companion, said in a conciliatory tone—

"Let us arrange this matter, Mr. Shearman. Give me a little time, and I shall then be in a position to prove my innocence. As far as recompense is concerned, you had better name your own terms."

"I never accepted a bribe from any man," said Shearman, indignantly, "and it is not likely I should do so now. You are my prisoner!"

"My God, this is indeed horrible!" exclaimed the conscious-stricken man, falling into a chair in a perfect state of prostration.

"I cannot help you, doctor, but you had better meet the charge like a man. It is of no use attempting to shirk it; the matter has gone too far for that, and the weight of evidence too strong."

"Too strong—eh!" said the doctor, looking up.

"I fancy so; but, of course, I may be mistaken."

"But I tell you again I am not the man. I never passed under the name of Wagstaff—never in my life. What proof have you of it?"

"That you will hear when the first examination takes place."

"And when will that be?"

"To-morrow, I believe."

"This is a false and malicious charge got up to ruin me."

CHAPTER C.

THE INQUIRY—THE END OF A MURDERER.

ALTHOUGH Doctor Bourne was what might be termed a black sheep, he was in a good position; he mixed with a respectable class of persons, and was in tolerably fair repute as a medical man.

The darker side of his character was, of course, not known to those whom he counted as his friends.

Some people, gossiping and mischievously disposed persons, hinted that he was not the best of husbands; that he was a mercenary grasping man, but nobody was prepared to hear that he was a murderer.

His social position caused him to be treated with some degree of consideration, and bail was accepted pending the serious and weighty charge made against him. He had not much difficulty in obtaining the necessary sureties, after which he returned home. The offence with which he stood charged was committed in America, and the prosecution sought, by means of the extradition treaty, to take him over to that country for trial.

The doctor hoped, as other culprits have hoped both before and since, that the identification would fail to be established, and at the outset of the proceedings he buoyed himself up with this delusion. But Mr. Shearman had managed the case with a considerable amount of skill and tact, and he was not at all the sort of man to let the accused escape through any neglect or want of forethought.

When the first examination took place before the sitting magistrate, the counsel for the prosecution gave a brief but succinct recital of the leading events. He dwelt with much force upon the sudden and mysterious death of Clara Wagstaff, who appeared, so he averred, to be in sound and robust health but a few days before her decease.

Suddenly, and without any perceptible cause, she was stricken down with insupportable and violent pains in the viscera.

A doctor was called in, who declared her to be suffering from inflammation of the bowels. He prescribed and attended her with the greatest assiduity, but despite his remedies she gradually sank and expired in her husband's arms, who was said to be overwhelmed with grief at the loss of his partner.

The body of the ill-fated woman was interred, and her husband, after a short period of mourning, plunged, so it was alleged, into a vortex of dissipation.

The theory that the young woman came by her death from natural causes, which were beyond the control of man, was very generally accepted. Some few, however, at the time of her decease, were a little mistrustful. One in particular, the black girl, Tilda, shook her head, and said she was not at all satisfied with the manner of her mistress's death, which she declared to be strange and mysterious, and in every way suspicious. She spoke her mind pretty freely at the time, with no better result than being reviled for what people chose to call her scandalous and wicked aspersions. So the matter dropped, and, as years passed on, the death of Mrs. Wagstaff was forgotten by the inhabitants of the neighbourhood. And it was not until Mr. Silas Leaven instituted inquiries, that the real facts of the case were brought to light. The body was exhumed, and the presence of arsenic was detected in the stomach, intestines, and other organs of the body. A sufficient amount was recovered to prove beyond all question that the poor creature had been poisoned by that deleterious drug. Two doctors from America, who made the post mortem examination, gave their evidence at the police-court, and their testimony was unanswerable.

Up to this point the case was as clear as the sun at noonday. The next question was, how far Dr. Bourne was connected with the case. Was he the man who passed as Wagstaff, and who married the planter's daughter?

In proof of this a photograph was produced of the person known as Wagstaff; it bore a most remarkable similarity to the accused—that is, if allowance was made for the difference in his age now and at the period when the photo was taken.

The magistrate, however, was of opinion that the photo, although valuable as collateral evidence, was not in itself sufficient to establish identity.

When the doctor heard this he smiled—hope dawned upon him, and he emphatically declared that he was not the man.

But the case did not rest on the photo alone.

Two persons, who had resided at Texas at the time of the lady's death, were present at the inquiry, and were placed in the box.

One swore to the prisoner most positively, and the other would not go further than that he was the gentleman whom he had known as Mr. Wagstaff to the best of his belief; further than this he would not undertake to say.

"I confess," observed the magistrate, "that the case assumes a grave aspect, and certainly cannot be permitted to drop without a searching inquiry, but at present I fail to see that the identity is clearly established. It is true, one witness swears to the person being the man, but it is possible—nay, indeed, probable—that he may be mistaken."

"He is not mistaken, sir," said the counsel. "And that I hope to be in a position to prove to your satisfaction in the course of two or three days at the latest."

"How do you propose to do that?" inquired the worthy magistrate.

"By producing the black servant who lived in the house with Mr. and Mrs. Wagstaff at the time of the unfortunate lady's decease. She is well acquainted with the countenance and general personal appearance of her late master, and if she recognises the prisoner as the husband of the now dead lady, I assume the case is established as far as the identity is concerned."

"If she does recognise him, and can swear positively to his being the person, then it is established, and all difficulties will be removed. When do you expect her?"

"She ought to be here now. She may arrive to-morrow or the next day. In fact, she is hourly expected."

"That being so, it would be best to adjourn the case for a week, perhaps."

"Will that be long enough?"

"Oh, I should imagine so. She is sure to arrive before the expiration of that time—at least, we hope so."

"She will be the only other witness, I presume, you are likely to call?"

"No; there will be another—a lady who was on intimate terms with the Wagstaffs when they resided in Texas. She is also well acquainted with the personal characteristics of the murdered woman's husband."

"Where was this photograph taken?" said the magistrate, glancing first at it and then at the prisoner.

"At Baltimore, I believe."

"No, New York," said Shearman. "I purchased it myself in that city."

"And are you sure it is a representation of Mr. Wagstaff? We have at present no proof of that, you know."

"It has been recognised by a number of persons in Texas who were acquainted with the person it is supposed to represent. Indeed, many of the inhabitants have copies of it, presented to them by Mr. Wagstaff himself."

"It is to be regretted that one or more of them are not here."

"But two are here, sir."

"And who may they be? and why have you not called them?"

"The two gentlemen who have already been examined can speak to the photo being a representation of Mr. Wagstaff," said the counsel.

"Then let them be recalled."

The two witnesses from Texas were again placed in the box. They both swore that the photo in question was a representation of Mr. Wagstaff as he then appeared.

"I adjourn the case till this day week," said the magistrate.

"I hope, sir, you will accept good and substantial bail for the reappearance of my client," said Bourne's solicitor. "We have not had any time allowed us to meet this charge. My client is a gentleman moving in a good position in society; he is greatly respected by, I may say, all who have the honour of his acquaintance, and a charge of this nature presses with a heavy overwhelming weight upon one who, we hope and trust

it will be proved beyond all controversy, is perfectly innocent."

"I am not likely to prejudge the case, and should, indeed, be sorry by any observation of mine to prejudice Doctor Bourne in the eyes of the world or his associates," observed the magistrate. "Still you must admit—indeed, every one must admit, I think, who has heard the evidence—that the case cannot be dismissed without a searching inquiry. I hope and trust that the prisoner may be in a position, on the next inquiry, to rebut the grave testimony that has been given against him here to-day. I, however, deem it advisable, for many reasons, not to enter into any discussion upon the merits of the case in this early stage of the proceedings. I will accept good and substantial bail for Doctor Bourne's reappearance at the next examination."

"Thank you, sir. With the usual notice?"

"Yes, with the usual notice. There will be no difficulty in the matter, I suppose?"

"None whatever. Doctor Bourne can produce bail to any amount."

In the course of the day bail was offered and accepted, and the doctor was liberated. He returned home, miserably depressed—dejected and sick of heart.

He had not counted on the array of evidence which had been presented on the first examination. His legal advisers endeavoured to comfort him with the assurance that as yet there was not enough to send the case for trial. Much depended upon the girl Tilda.

She might break down. Anyway she would be subjected to an exhaustive and searching cross-examination. Then came the question of an alibi; when everything else failed an alibi was the invariable recourse of an accused person. Was it possible to get up one? Such things had been done, and in some cases they had been successful. The doctor clung to this as the drowning wretch clings to a straw, but he could not, at present, see his way clear as to working it successfully.

He returned home, and at once made for his surgery, where he remained for hours still and thoughtful. The clouds which had been gathering over his head seemed to be darkening and thickening.

What was he to do? Could he fly and escape the avenging arm of the law? It had been made painfully manifest to him at the examination before the magistrate that his enemies or accusers were on the alert; they did not intend to let him escape.

Certainly not if they could help it. Mr. Shearman had acted in a business-like way throughout the inquiry; he had hunted up evidence in the States with the greatest assiduity, and had succeeded in obtaining information connected with a number of smaller and less important circumstances connected with the death of the ill-fated woman.

At present, Bourne had only been made acquainted with a portion of the evidence to be preferred against him. Much of it was kept in the background, but what had been given before the magistrate was of a most damnatory character.

Bourne appeared to be almost paralysed at the array of evidence. He trembled for the future; an oppressive and all but insupportable weight seemed to press upon him.

Just as he was about to accuse his wife of bigamy, so that he might be rid of her, and be free to marry a third wife, in the shape of a rich widow, a fearful accusation was brought against him, which in any case would hurl him from his present position, if nothing worse happened; but the chances were that he would have to suffer a dreadful and ignominious death.

"DEAD!"

They would take him over to America to try him—so his solicitor informed him—and he knew perfectly well that prejudice ran high against him when he resided in Texas, and the probability was that this feeling had been strengthened and intensified, so that if there was a chance of bringing the charge home to him, a Yankee jury would be sure to return an adverse verdict.

Dr. Bourne, therefore, could not conceal from himself that he was in imminent danger.

He knew himself to be guilty of the charge preferred against him, and was in consequence scourged by conscience, and in a state of fear and trepidation.

Nevertheless, he was in hopes that the evidence in respect to the identity would break down.

The crime had been committed many years ago, and

No. 53.

if he could throw discredit on the witnesses there might be some chance of upsetting the whole case. Much depended upon the girl, Tilda. Bourne was in hopes that he was so much altered in appearance that the black slavey would be a little puzzled, and would fail to recognise him.

It is thus that criminals of every degree have been from time immemorial accustomed to delude themselves with hopes that in most cases have turned out fallacious.

The doctor affected to put as bold a front on the matter as possible, but he studiously avoided his wife, and she had no desire to force herself into his company. It had been at best but a miserable state of affairs as far as their domestic happiness, if it could be so termed, was concerned, and it was a relief to both when they were apart. Consequently they saw as little of each other as possible.

Mrs. Bourne, however, was not altogether in the dark in respect to the state of affairs as regards her husband. Her faithful attendant, Amy, who like, most servants, was something of a gossip, made her mistress acquainted with the full particulars of the grave charge made against her master. Mrs. Bourne was perfectly astounded at the revelation. She had never for a moment supposed that her husband had contracted any marriage previous to his nuptials with her. He had throughout their acquaintance signified that he was a bachelor.

"Ah!" murmured the unhappy wife—"my suspicions were not groundless. I have indeed escaped almost by a miracle; but, after all, I cannot find it in my heart to believe him guilty of such an atrocious crime."

Facts, however, are stubborn things, and there was no getting away from those made manifest on the first magisterial inquiry.

Mrs. Bourne was now very careful in examining minutely what she partook of in the house of her suspected husband—who, however, had very little opportunity at this time of tampering with either food or drink; he was too much occupied with his own guilty thoughts, and in devising some scheme to turn aside the course of justice. He went about, as usual, paid visits to his patients, and endeavoured to make out that the whole affair was a wicked conspiracy on the part of some evil-disposed persons who owed him a grudge. There were many who believed this view of the matter; for it is at all times most difficult to believe a man you have been intimately acquainted with capable of committing a crime of such enormity.

The few friends the doctor possessed rallied round him on this occasion, and sought to console him with words of comfort. Prone as the world is to look upon the dark side of the picture, the most hardened offender has at times a few faithful followers, and the doctor was not an exception to the rule; nevertheless it was pretty generally buzzed about that he was in a precarious position, and that those engaged for the prosecution were using every endeavour to bring the murderer of the dead woman to the bar of justice. The matter was canvassed at several fashionable clubs, in select coteries, and by the public generally; indeed, it was the universal topic of conversation at the West-end of the town, and many bets were offered and taken upon the issue of the next examination.

Two days of suspense had passed over. On the third, as Doctor Bourne was getting into his brougham, he saw at the corner of the street two persons looking eagerly at him. His heart seemed to sink when he discovered that one of these was the black girl, Tilda, the other being Mr. Shearman.

"Oh, golly!" exclaimed the black girl. "that's 'im, massa; I could swear to him out of ten tousand. It's Massa Wagstaff, as did away wi' missus."

"Hush! mind what you are saying, girl," cried Shearman. "Remember you are in England, and people are not permitted to speak their minds as freely as in the States."

"Dunno 'bout dat," returned Tilda. "I knows 'im, an' I mean to tell all 'bout de cuss, come what may."

"Silence! Come along, and cease your clattering, you foolish wench," said Shearman, dragging her forcibly from the spot.

Doctor Bourne broke down; his last hope was gone. It was evident enough that Tilda would swear to him —we won't say till she was black in the face, for that she was already—but she would swear to him while she had the power of speech.

Bourne felt convinced of this. He knew pretty well the temperament and disposition of the young woman who had come across the seas to give evidence against him. He knew that she would not budge an inch when she had once made up her mind.

She had years before been forcibly impressed with the fact that her mistress had met with her death through foul play, and at the time of her decease she had not scrupled to say so.

She had been throughout her life devotedly attached to the planter's daughter. This is not at all surprising, seeing that "Tilda," as she was termed, had been a "help" in the family since she was little more than a child.

"Curse her!" exclaimed Bourne through his clenched teeth. "I wish the ship that brought her over had sunk to the bottom of the sea before she set foot on these shores. The game is up—they'll prove their case, and I am lost—lost!"

He was so miserable, so completely overcome, that he would fain have burst out into tears, but his eyes were dry and bloodshot, and his tongue was hot and parched; there was a singing in his ear like the murmur of rushing waters; his temples throbbed painfully, and he fell back in the cushions of his brougham in a state of prostration.

Something seemed to whisper to him, "Can't she be bribed?" At this suggestion hope dawned again upon him for a moment, but it was only for a fleeting moment or so, and he came to the conclusion that bribery in her case would be an impossibility.

"What was he to do? what would be the end of this terrible business? Death on the public scaffold."

This thought was a maddening one. He struck his forehead with his clenched fist, let down the window of the vehicle, and gasped for air, for he felt as one about to faint.

Mr. Shearman would be too much for him—that was but too painfully manifested. On the next examination he could complete his case, and then in all probability he would be given into the custody of the American representatives. Bail would, of course, be refused, and it was not very difficult to see how it would all end.

Doctor Bourne, upon arriving at his own residence, endeavoured to muster up an air of intrepidity to his brow. Upon alighting he told his coachman that he should not go out for the remainder of the day. Then, having signified this much, he opened the street door with his key and made at once for his surgery.

He remained there for two or three hours making up some prescriptions. The medicine boy came in and sallied forth with his basket of drugs, after which the doctor went into the front parlour.

When dinner was laid he was informed by the maid servant that her mistress was indisposed and begged to be excused at the dinner hour, adding that she, Amy, was to take her up a basin of soup and a small portion of fish into her bedroom. This was done, and Bourne sat down to his solitary meal.

He was glad, however, to be by himself. He did not believe in the indisposition of his wife, and deemed it only an excuse. Perhaps he was not very far out in his suppositiom. He did not care to meet her, nor she him; and, so as far as that went, they were both satisfied.

He had no appetite, but swallowed several glasses of wine, which he supplemented by a small modicum of cognac. Then he endeavoured to swallow a few mouthfuls of food. This he found no easy task. His throat was inflamed, and his tongue seemed to cleave to the roof of his mouth. Nevertheless, he felt constrained to make a pretence of dining, and to say the truth a most miserable pretence it was. However, it had to be gone through.

He was very quiet and reserved, and only hazarded a few chance observations to Amy, who was struck with the paleness of his countenance and his distraught manner. However, she did not appear to notice it, and spoke to her master in her usual respectful cheery manner.

Bourne looked at her for a moment, and then heaved a deep-drawn sigh.

What would he have given at that time to be possessed of a conscience as pure and untroubled as his servant girl !

The dinner things were cleared away, and Bourne took a medical book, which for some time he appeared to peruse with interest.

The grey dusk of the evening was succeeded by the gloom of night, and the girl lit all the branches of the chandelier.

Her master was busily occupied with his book and did not appear to be aware of her presence, or if he was, he did not care to take any notice of her. The night wore on. Bourne left the front parlour and entered his surgery.

His countenance was pale and haggard. It was indicative of some settled and defined purpose. There was a fixed and rigid expression about the mouth, and an almost savage look darted from the flaming eyes.

He sat himself down in his chair, and then bent his body forward, resting his head on his hands, while the elbows were supported on the table before him. His breathing was heavy and troubled, and his whole attitude was one of abject despair. Presently he rose from his seat, went towards the bottles, which were ranged on some shelves at the side of the room. He took one after another in his hand, and examined their contents with the eye of a connoisseur.

He selected one and placed it on the table near to a medicine glass, then he sat down again.

The terrible and appalling nature of his thoughts at this time it would be impossible to describe.

He took the glass stopper out of the bottle, emptied the contents of the bottle into the medicine glass, and swallowed the liquid with one gulp.

And then? Well, there was silence in the room— silence deep, dark, and impenetrable.

A few fleeting hours passed over, the night waned and passed away, the second hour of the morning arrived. All the inhabitants of the house had retired to rest—all save the master of the establishment.

There was a violent ring at the night bell, which was unanswered; a second summons was given, whereupon the servant, Amy—who had hastily slipped on her things—descended the stairs and opened the door. A man servant stood on the steps outside.

He informed the doctor's maid that his mistress was seriously ill, and desired Doctor Bourne's attendance immediately. The doctor had been retained as accoucheur to the lady in question, and the man said that not a moment was to be lost.

"I will tell Doctor Bourne," said the girl, "and am quite sure he will be with your mistress in less than a quarter of an hour, or perhaps before that."

The messenger upon this assurance took his departure. Amy closed the street door gently, and made direct for her master's bedroom. She knocked at the door, but received no answer. She called him by his name, and then knocked louder, but still no answer. In cases of this sort ceremony could be dispensed with. She opened the door, and entered the room, which she found tenantless.

"Perhaps he's gone there," she murmured. "He knows Mrs. Curtis is near her time. It is possible he may have gone there."

She paused for a moment, and pressed one hand to her side as a troubled expression passed over her countenance.

She looked at the bed. It was just the same as she had made it in the morning. It was evident enough that no one had occupied it since then.

"I did not hear him go out," she murmured, "and I believe he was in the surgery when I went to bed."

She crept downstairs without awaking her mistress, and made direct for the surgery.

She could see through the crevices of the door that a light was still burning.

She knocked, but received no answer.

Then a vague shadowy fear seemed to take possession of her, and she was half afraid to enter, but being a girl of high spirit, and one who was not easily cowed, she opened the door and entered.

She saw the figure of her master in his high-backed chair.

To all appearance he was slumbering.

"Mr. Bourne—doctor!" cried Amy. "You are wanted immediately, if you please. Mrs. Curtis is very ill!"

The figure in the chair did not stir or give any indications of life. The girl cried out in something like a terrified voice, but she did not succeed in arousing her master, who had fallen back in his chair with his legs stretched out like one who had suddenly sunk into a deep slumber.

"I can't wake him! What on earth shall I do?" cried the girl. "How very strange and how fearfully pale he looks."

There was a small hand-lamp on the table. Amy seized hold of this and by the aid of the flame examined the features of her master.

"Heaven save us!" she ejaculated, "he must be in a fit or else——"

She did not complete the sentence, but examined the features of the doctor more minutely. She placed her hand on his shoulder, shook him, and called him again by his name.

Then she shuddered and crept out of the room like one bewitched. She hastened upstairs and aroused her mistress, who was sleeping soundly.

"For Heaven's sake do tell me what's the matter, Amy? You look like a person who has just seen a ghost."

"Oh, ma'am, if you please I don't know what to make of master, he looks so strange. I am afraid something's happened to him—he appears to be in a fit."

"Where is he—in his bedroom?"

"No, in the surgery."

"In the surgery at this hour! It is just upon two o'clock," said Mrs. Bourne, as she glanced at the time-piece on the shelf.

"He hasn't been to bed, that's quite certain, and I told Thomas, Mr. Curtis's footman, that he would be with her in less than a quarter of an hour. Whatever are we to do?"

"I'll get up at once," cried Mrs. Bourne, springing out of bed and arraying herself in her capacious dressing gown.

"In the surgery—eh?"

"Yes, ma'm, sitting in his chair."

"Ah, he's all right enough, I dare say. Don't give way to groundless fears—let us hope you are mistaken."

Mrs. Bourne put her feet into her slippers, and, accompanied by her faithful handmaiden, she went downstairs.

She entered the surgery, and glanced at her husband. Then a bolt of ice seemed to shoot through her heart.

"Where is Peter?" she inquired.

"In bed, I suppose."

"Go and rouse him at once. Tell him to put on his things and go off at once for Doctor Garnet. Quick! not a moment is to be lost."

"What is the matter with the doctor?" inquired Amy, in evident trepidation.

"Matter, girl, something very serious. It appears to me that he is dead."

At these words, the girl uttered a sort of shriek, and flew upstairs for the boy Peter.

The young urchin was not long in bundling on his things.

Upon descending below he found his mistress in the front parlour.

"Go as quickly as possible to Doctor Garnet's house, ring the night bell, and say I want to see him. We fear something has happened to Mr. Bourne. Do you hear?"

"Yes, ma'am, I'll run all the way."

"Good lad, and mind you don't return without Dr. Garnet," cried Mrs. Bourne, seeing her messenger to the door.

Dr. Garnet lived but two streets off. He had been accustomed to attend to Bourne's practice when that gentleman was away from home.

He was a little alarmed, however, upon being informed of the urgent nature of the case. He had seen Bourne a day or two before, and considered him to be in excellent health.

He was a little depressed, it is true, but nothing to speak of—certainly not to give rise to fears as to his health.

Garnet was a little fussy bald-headed gentleman, with a soft musical voice, and a conciliatory agreeable manner. He was very popular with the ladies, to whom he was at all times remarkably attentive.

"Dear me, this is a very sad business," he ejaculated, as he proceeded to make a careful toilette, for Garnet made it a rule never to be caught en deshabille. "Very sad. Poor Mrs. Bourne, it must have greatly alarmed her. Did you say your master was insensible, my lad?"

"I aint seen him, sir," returned the boy; "but missus said he was, and Amy could not get him to speak."

"Ah, we will see what ails him. Over work, worry, anxiety of mind, that's the remote cause, the proximate may be—be—well, apoplexy perhaps."

"Tell your mistress I will be with her in a few minutes."

"If you please, sir——"

"Well, what?"

"She said I was not to return without you."

"Oh, very well, my man, go down stairs and wait, I will be with you shortly."

The lad went down as requested. Presently he was joined by Dr. Garnet, who hurried off at once to his patient. As a matter of course he found Mrs. Bourne anxiously awaiting his appearance.

"My dear Mrs. Bourne, let me beg of you to bear up against this trial, for such it must prove to be in any case, but we none of us know how soon we may be stricken down; but this is of so sudden a nature that——"

"It is sudden, Dr. Garnet, both sudden and unaccountable."

"We shall be able to account for it, my dear madam, there is not the slightest doubt about that. But where is the patient?"

"In the surgery."

"I will see what can be done for him," said Garnet, with the same soft voice—the same mellifluous and measured accents—for he never at any time permitted himself to be betrayed into an expression of surprise. To use a common phrase, he invariably took things in a quiet sort of way.

He entered the surgery, and glanced at the face of Bourne; then he felt his pulse, and then placed his hand on the region of the heart; then he lifted up one of the eyelids and looked at the pupil of the eye.

This done, he drew a chair up to the table and sat down, placing at the same time another chair for the mistress of the establishment.

"Well, doctor, what is it?"

"It is very plain what it is, Mrs. Bourne; but let me beg of you to bear up against this terrible trial."

"What is it?" cried the lady.

"It is death!" returned Garnet. "But the cause which led to it we have yet to determine."

"My husband is dead then?" exclaimed Mrs. Bourne. "Then there is no hope?"

"None whatever. He has passed away peacefully and tranquilly, and to all appearance without pain. Be thankful for that."

The bereaved wife burst into tears. He had never been at any time an affectionate partner, or even a passable sort of husband, but the suddenness of the blow quite unnerved his widow, who demonstrated an amount of feeling which few would, perhaps, have given her credit for.

"Dead!" she iterated in sorrowful accents, "and the last time we met we parted in anger."

"There is no occasion for you to make that declaration, my dear lady; people will talk quite soon enough without you giving them a handle for their discourse. Say as little as possible upon that subject, which is nobody's business but your own. Poor Bourne, I confess I was not prepared for this, but after all, everything is for the best."

"I do not understand your meaning," said Mrs. Bourne.

"Umph, no, perhaps not. When was the doctor last seen alive?"

"When he went into the surgery—in the early part of last evening."

"And by whom?"

"By me, sir," returned Amy.

"And did he appear in his usual health at that time?"

"He looked very pale, and his manner was strange."

"How strange?"

"He seemed to be in trouble about something—so I thought."

"Oh, likely enough, girl; the probability is that he was very much troubled in his mind. He gave indications of that when I last saw him, but not to so great an extent as to suggest this act."

Mrs. Bourne looked hard at the speaker, but said nothing.

"What a strange odour there is in the room, doctor," observed Amy.

"Odour, girl—of what description?"

"Like peaches."

"Umph! Ah—yes, there is, I admit."

He took up the medicine-glass, which had fallen upon the floor after its contents had been swallowed by the dead man, and smelt it.

"It proceeds from this," observed Garnet, in the same soft voice as heretofore. "Yes, that is from whence this odour proceeds. Let us return into the next room, my dear madam."

Mrs. Bourne rose from her seat and went into the front parlour with Doctor Garnet. Amy and the boy made their way into the kitchen, after carefully closing the door of the surgery.

"I shall purposely abstain from making any observations upon the state of mind of my friend, Bourne, prior to his decease. In fact, it will be as well, I think, to say as little as possible upon the subject, certainly not till the inquest is held."

"Inquest!"

"Yes, my dear madam. There must be an inquest. That is a *sine quâ non*. It is pretty clearly demonstrated that Bourne has died from the effects of poison, and there can be but little doubt, I think, that he took it of his own free will."

"What poison has he taken, then?"

"Prussic acid! That is as far as I can judge at present. I must beg of you, my dear friend, not to disturb anything in that room—in fact it had better be locked up, and either you or I will take charge of the key."

"Oh, you had better do so. I would much prefer it."

"Well, I will if you wish it. Let us lock the door at once."

Garnet and Mrs. Bourne went out of the front parlour. The former locked the door of the surgery and placed the key in his pocket; then they returned to the parlour once more.

"These things will occur," said Garnet, casting his eyes up to the ceiling. "In fact they do so, I may say, almost daily. Death is terrible at all times and under any circumstances—that is a truism everyone must admit; but all things considered I really do not think there is any great reason to repine in this case. I have lost an old friend and companion, and you have lost a husband, and we have, of course, both of us reason to mourn. Still, matters might have been worse."

"They might have been, I admit," said Mrs. Bourne.

"This is a shock to you, a sad blow," cried Garnet, placing his hand on her shoulder with well-simulated kindness of manner. "Let me again beg of you to bear it with becoming fortitude. I will be with you in the morning after I have given notice to the coroner. Till then, adieu, my dear madam. I need hardly say that it will afford me great pleasure in being of service to you in this matter."

"You are very kind, I am sure, Mr. Garnet. Accept

my thanks. At the present moment I find it difficult, and indeed, I may say impossible, to realise the terrible reality which has been presented to us so suddenly."

"Of course not. I can well understand that," observed the oily-tongued doctor; "but do not worry yourself, the worst is over. I was not prepared for such an ending, but all things considered, it is after all but a natural sequence, and not so much to be regretted as we at first supposed."

"Not to be regretted, Doctor Garnet?"

"Umph. Well, no, not so much, my dear madam."

"What do you mean? Are you of opinion that my husband was guilty of the charge preferred against him?"

"Really, Mrs. Bourne, you must excuse me. You cannot expect me to answer such a query. I should not be justified in hazarding an opinion at this early stage of the inquiry. Still you know people will draw their own conclusions after what has occurred. Be thankful that you are here."

"I now perfectly understand your meaning."

"The lady died from the effects of poison; that has been established beyond dispute," said Garnet. "Who administered it is another question. The prosecution says my late friend, Doctor Bourne; but assertions are one thing and proof is another. This is a question, however, which I think we had better not attempt to discuss just now. Good-night, or rather morning, my dear friend. I will see you as early as possible to-morrow."

And with these words the fashionable physician took his departure.

CHAPTER CI.

AFTER THE DEED—THE SALE BY AUCTION—MRS. BOURNE PAYS A VISIT TO MR. THOMPSON.

THE news of Doctor Bourne's sudden departure from the world, together with the manner of his death, spread like wildfire. It was in every person's mouth. Would-be wiseacres shook their heads and said "it was no more than they expected." Rich dowagers and antiquated maiden ladies said it was very shocking, and that the poor dear man had been persecuted by a lot of good-for-nothing Americans who were envious of his position and fair fame.

Everybody had something to say upon the subject—the diversity of opinion was most remarkable.

Meanwhile the dead body of the doctor remained in the chair, in precisely the same position in which it had been found, till the day appointed for the coroner's inquest.

The inmates of the house and Doctor Garnet were of course the chief witnesses. A feeble attempt was made to prove that death resulted from disease of the heart. There was, as usual, a great deal of hair-splitting, and the medical evidence was contradictory. But the facts were so clearly manifested that after a short deliberation the jury returned a verdict "that the deceased died from the effects of prussic acid, taken while labouring under a fit of temporary insanity."

Everybody appeared to be satisfied with the verdict, and the last remains of the doctor were interred with great pomp and ceremony. Upon the cavalcade reaching the grave many hundreds of persons were to be seen awaiting the arrival of the hearse.

To say that there was not a dry eye in the assembly would be but to make use of a newspaper reporter's stereotyped phrase.

As far as grief was concerned there was but little,

if any at all, but there was a vast amount of curiosity, and it was this that had drawn the people to the spot.

Strange to say Doctor Bourne, to the surprise of everybody, and to his wife in particular, died intestate; Mrs. Bourne, therefore, took out letters of administration.

As may readily be imagined she was not permitted to have it all her own way—the doctor's relatives stepped forward to have a wrangle over the effects.

He died worth a great deal more than was supposed, and the widow's share of the property was quite sufficient to maintain her handsomely; so that after all the American plotters, as they were termed by some, had really done her a very great service.

She was released from a thraldom which had daily become more and more painful, and she was rendered independent for the remainder of her life—proving the old adage, "that no evil occurs but some good comes from it."

It was necessary for the better distribution of the property that the furniture and personal property of the doctor should be disposed of, and consequently a public sale took place. Everything was brought under the hammer.

The number of curiosity hunters and sightseers who flocked to the house during the three days appointed for the sale was prodigious.

Every class of the community seemed to be represented on this occasion, Jews and brokers being, as usual, the most prominent.

Some of the articles fetched fancy prices, while others went at sums considerably below their value.

The aristocratic and more wealthy class of bidders went in for the pictures and articles of virtu.

The reader will perhaps be in no way surprised to learn that Charles Peace attended the sale. He purchased a violin.

Bourne had at one time taken lessons of an eminent professor of that instrument, and in early life had amused himself during his leisure hours in practising, but he never made much of a hand at fiddling.

However, his violin was sufficiently good in tone and quality to tempt our hero to bid for it, and he became the purchaser at a ridiculously low sum.

Peace had always a penchant for visiting places of public resort, and the probability is that he was attracted to the sale by the circumstances connected with the dead man.

He knew that Bourne had been accused of murder—this fact in itself was quite sufficient to excite the curiosity of Charles Peace.

There was, it must be admitted, something like a grim jest in a murderer purchasing a murderer's musical instrument at a public sale.

Rawton, or Bandy-legged Bill, as he was more frequently termed, kept his word; he never again paid a visit to Mrs. Bourne. He had not been seen or heard of by any of the detectives since he had effected his escape.

Mrs. Bourne very much regretted not having had any tidings of him.

She did not wish him to be captured—far from that, but he had behaved so well to her that she was desirous of forwarding him some money as a recompense for his exertions on behalf of herself.

Bill, however, contrived to remain perdu, and the doctor's widow had lost all trace of him.

She was the more concerned about this since she was about to leave the house she at present occupied, and then there would be but little chance of her ever again communicating with the gipsy.

This reflection seemed to have a depressing effect upon her, for it occurred to her that perhaps Bill had been captured and cast into prison without her knowledge, and when the thought crossed her mind she was more than ever deeply concerned about him.

The servant girl Amy, who happened to be looking out of the window watching the throngs of persons going in and out of the house, cried out in a surprised tone—

"Well, I declare, if there isn't the man who brought the letter to you just gone in!"

"What man, and what letter do you allude to?"

"Why, that impudent forward man who brought a letter from Mr. Dorton or Rawton. I don't know his right name."

"Gone inside, did you say?"

"Yes, ma'm."

Mrs. Bourne reflected for a few moments, and then said—

"I wish you would go downstairs and see if you can find him. Do go at once, there's a good girl—it is rather important."

"And if I do find him?"

"Oh true, if you do, I never thought of that. Well, you can ask him for the address of Mr. Rawton."

Amy was under the impression at the time that the man would not give the required address, but she said nothing.

Her mistress again urged her to go downstairs, and she obeyed.

The sale-room was thronged with visitors, who chaffed and bantered each other, to say nothing of the auctioneer, to their heart's content. At a public sale all restraint is thrown off, and people say and do what they please.

Amy, who was a remarkably pretty girl, had to run the fire of a series of observations, which doubtless were meant to be flattering and complimentary, but which were, however, very distasteful to her.

Presently she caught sight of the person whom she was seeking.

This was Cooney, who had just dropped in to see if he could get a job to do in the way of porterage, and if, at the same time, he could pick anything up, it would suit him better.

The girl beckoned to him, and he came forward out of the crowd.

"What, my charmer!" he ejaculated. "I said as how you'd think better of me as time went on. Well, I'm jolly glad to see you—and how's the missus?"

"Come this way," said Amy, drawing him towards the passage.

"Vell, what is it?" inquired Cooney, who now began to be a little alarmed. "Out wi' it. Let us know the whole and true particulars."

"I wish you'd hold your tongue, you fool," said Amy. "You've a great deal too much to say. Listen to me for a moment, if you please."

"Vell, aint I a-listenin' to your sweet voice?—In course I am. I like to hear you speak."

"Can you give me the address of Mr. Rawton?"

Cooney gave a prolonged "Ah!" and looked puzzled.

"Don't you hear? I want Mr. Rawton's address."

"Do you?"

"Yes—at least missus does. She sent me down for it."

"Vell, you see, my pretty pet, I can't give it."

"And why not?"

"For a good reason—he aint got no address."

"But you know where to find him, I dare say?"

"Yes, I might find him, but he won't come here any more."

"Wait till I have asked missus."

"Wait where?"

"Here, or in the sale-room, anywhere you choose, but don't go away till I come downstairs."

"I won't."

Amy tripped upstairs and told her all that had passed between herself and Cooney.

"Ah, no, he won't give the address—of course not. We can't hardly expect him to do so; Rawton is at hide and seek. There is but one way to get over the difficulty. I will write a letter and this he will deliver to Mr. Rawton."

She sat down and penned a hasty epistle to Bandy-legged Bill.

"There," she said, handing it to Amy, "give him that and tell him to deliver it to the party to whom it is addressed. But stay, better give him something for the favour. Here is half-a-sovereign, slip that into his hand when you give him the letter."

"I think he's a sort of a man who is quite open to receive a bribe," cried Amy, bursting out into a laugh, as she descended the stairs once more.

"Oh, gi' him this—eh?" said Cooney. "Right you are, Mary. It shall be done, and no flies. What! half a quid. S'help me bob, I wish I could find a few more of your sort. Your missus is a stunner, and no mistake."

"Do hold your tongue, you donkey."

"Vell, I'm blest. Don't like to hear a cove speak —don't yer?"

"I don't care about listening to your conversation."

"Why, what's the matter with it?"

"It doesn't please me—that's all. You have a deal too much to say."

"All right, darling, then. I'll remain mum. So I'm to give this to Bill?"

"You are to deliver it into the hands of Mr. Rawton."

"And bring an answer?"

"Yes, if you can, that will be all the better, but we leave here the day after to-morrow—remember that."

"I'll be here afore you leave, please the pigs!" cried Cooney, as he left.

"What a common brute!" exclaimed Amy, after he had left. "He is a coarse common sort of man, but I suppose he will keep his word—at least, I hope so, for missus seems to be very anxious about Rawton for some reason or another, which I can't quite make out."

Cooney was sufficiently faithful to his pal the gipsy not to let anybody know his hiding-place; but he had very little difficulty in delivering the letter to its rightful owner on the evening of the day upon which it had been placed in his hands by the girl, Amy, whom he still declared to be the most aggravating, charming creature he had ever set eyes upon.

On the following day he returned with an answer to the epistle which had been entrusted to his care.

"I'm here again," said he to Amy, when she opened the door; "I can't keep away from you. You're in my thoughts by day and by night; I can't sleep for thinking of you."

"I don't intend to listen to any more of your nonsense, you impudent vulgar fellow," returned the girl, in an angry tone, "and so you'd better conduct yourself in a more becoming manner. If you don't, I shall have to tell my mistress, who, I am sure, will forbid you coming again to this house."

"What for? I aint said or done nothing that any

one can complain of. Here's a jolly sell. Well, I'm blowed."

"Silence, let me have no more of this. Have you got an answer?"

"Well, in course I have, but you won't give a cove time. I never seed such a pretty little tartar in all my born days."

"Give me the answer if you've got one."

"Didn't I tell you I had? Here it is. Am I to wait outside or come in?"

"Oh come in," cried Amy, in a pet, slamming the door violently. "I shall be glad when we are rid of you."

She went into the parlour.

"Ah, I aint fortunate wi' women or gals, never was," murmured Cooney, looking meditatively at the hall clock. "Charles Peace is the man for that sort of business. He'd make any on 'em b'lieve black was white if he'd a mind to. Howsomever, it don't much matter, I s'pose. They've been a deal of trouble to Charlie—that's sartin sure."

Amy returned, gave Cooney two half-crowns for his trouble, and told him to be off.

"You're in a jolly hurry to get rid of me," said he. "I'll give ye the two half bulls if you'll——"

"Well, what?"

"Let me have one kiss."

"Get out, you wretch. If you don't— Well, there's a detective in the back parlour."

"Oh, crikey!" exclaimed Cooney. "I'll step it if you please, my dear, but you might——"

"Hush!" cried the girl, "he'll hear," and she pointed significantly to the door of the back parlour.

She found this ruse a most admirable and efficacious one, for Cooney hesitated no longer. He as noiselessly as possible passed out of the house, and was lost to sight in an incredibly short space of time.

Amy laughed.

There was no detective in the house, but she had got rid of a troublesome customer by the mere mention of such a personage.

The contents of the letter which Mrs. Bourne received from Rawton proved to be sufficiently satisfactory to that lady. The epistle was a brief one.

The gipsy congratulated her upon being rid of what he chose to term a tyrannical and worthless husband, and at the same time he said he did not require a recompense or even thanks for whatever he had done for her.

It was enough for him to know that she was relieved from an oppressive thraldom, that she was now her own mistress, and that he had been of some little service to her, or at any rate what he had done was with the view of rendering her a service.

That, however, was all over now, and he bade her a final farewell, but as the chances were that she would not be contented without knowing where to address him, he informed her that any letter forwarded to Mr. Thompson, Evelina-road, Peckham, would be sure to reach him; the said Mr. Thompson being an old friend of his would be sure to know where to find him.

So far the letter from Rawton was explicit enough, and Mrs. Bourne felt that all communication was not cut off from herself and the man to whom she owed a deep debt of gratitude.

"Poor fellow," she ejaculated, "he's self-sacrificing and magnanimous enough. His conduct to me is, I presume, the one bright spot on his character—perhaps the only one, for it is evident enough that for years he has been leading a lawless and depraved life. Dear me! but this is all very terrible. I do not desire, however, to see him again, and shall, therefore, as far as that is concerned, take him at his word; but, this Mr. Thompson, I wonder who he can be—some worthless character I suppose. Well, I can leave him a cheque or bank-note enclosed in a letter addressed to Rawton. Yes, that will be my best course."

When the sale was over and the goods removed, Mrs. Bourne took furnished lodgings in Somerset-street, Portman-square.

As yet she had not determined her course of action.

She thought of taking up her residence in Paris for awhile.

She spoke French fluently, and understood something of German.

Indeed, she was what is called an accomplished woman, who shone in society as a sort of star.

She was a good musician, an excellent singer, and, as we have already signified, had at one time been an actress of no inconsiderable merit.

But with Dr. Bourne she had been buried as far as the external world was concerned. She was so depressed, so miserable, that she had not the heart to go into society to the extent she had done before her fatal marriage.

After her husband's death she was sought after and patronised by the upper classes in a way that not only astonished her but numbers of others besides.

In fact, she was more popular than ever. Although the bloom on the peach had long since disappeared, and the springtime of her life had passed away, she was still a beautiful woman, and was capable of making herself very agreeable in society.

In addition to all this there was a halo of romance cast upon her—her career had been a most remarkable one—that was pretty generally admitted, but the culminating point was reached when her husband was accused of a murder committed years before his marriage with Hester Teige.

Mr. Shearman and his confederates were miserably disappointed when they heard of Doctor Bourne's suicide.

No end of trouble and money had been expended in getting up the case against the guilty doctor; and it certainly was very mortifying to the American detective to find himself "cornered," as he termed it, by that "artful cuss."

Mr. Shearman was baulked just as his prey was about to fall into his hands.

It would have been quite a triumph for him to have escorted Bourne to the States, proved his guilt, and had him executed.

However, as he could not pot his man, he contented himself while in this country in seeing all the sights he possibly could in the great metropolis, and these, as the reader can imagine, were not a few.

Mrs. Bourne looked very well in her widow's weeds, which, however, she purposed throwing off as early as custom and the usages of society would admit.

She had not been very long in her new quarters before she determined upon paying a visit to Rawton's friend, her object being to leave a sum of money for the gipsy with Mr. Thompson.

The doctor's two vehicles, together with the horses, had been sold, but his widow had purchased a neat unostentatious-looking brougham for her own use. She had been so long accustomed to a carriage that from force of habit she felt constrained to have one.

She had taken with her into her lodgings in Somerset-street her maid Amy, who was a faithful girl and devotedly attached to her mistress. The brougham was ordered, and as the doctor's widow did not care to

wait upon a stranger without a companion, she took Amy with her.

Peace's house in the Evelina-road was a decent, respectable-looking habitation enough, but in its external appearance it certainly could not be described as aristocratic-looking. Its general appearance is doubtless familiar to many of my readers from the representations of it which have appeared in several of the illustrated papers at the time of Peace's arrest for the attempted murder of police-constable Robinson.

Anyway, it was a far better sort of habitation than Mrs. Bourne had expected to see, for she was under the impression that Rawton's friends must be of the very lowest class.

Mrs. Thompson opened the door, and to Mrs. Bourne's inquiry as to whether Mr. Thompson was within, she was answered in the affirmative.

She was shown into an elegantly furnished parlour, and saw there an old gentleman looking over a draft which he had before him, stretched out on the table.

Upon the widow's entrance he looked up from the chart or draft, and made a sort of bow, which the widow returned.

"Pardon my intruding upon you, sir," said Mrs. Bourne. "You are Mr. Thompson, I presume."

"Yes, madam," said Peace, "Pray be seated."

"You are a friend of Mr. Rawton's, I believe."

"Eh—of who did you say?"

"Mr. William Rawton, or Bill Rawton, as he is more familiarly termed."

"Oh, certainly, yes, I know Bill Rawton perfectly well, but he is certainly not in London just now—is far away, I believe. What might you want with him?" inquired Peace or rather Thompson, with a suspicious look.

"I have no desire to see him, Mr. Thompson, but he has rendered me a service, and I am desirous of offering him some recompense for the same."

"Oh, I see; that's a different matter altogether. It will be very acceptable to him, I have no doubt."

"You've got a grand work here, sir," said Mrs. Bourne, glancing at the paper on the table. "You are in the engineering line, I suppose?"

"Well, I do a little in that way; this is a draft of an invention a neighbour of mine and myself are about to patent."

"I hope it may prove successful and lucrative," said the widow.

"I hope so, I'm sure, for his sake. Luckily for me, I don't depend upon those sort of things. I am possessed of independent means."

He spoke so confidently, and was withal so plausible and urbane in his manner, that Mrs. Bourne was rather taken with him than otherwise.

"Well, as I was observing, Mr. Thompson," said the widow, "I have no desire to see Rawton, but he has informed me by letter that anything I might leave for him with you would be sure to fall into his hands. Is that correct?"

"Perfectly correct. I will undertake to give him anything you may entrust to my care."

"I am greatly obliged, I'm sure."

Mrs. Bourne took from her pocket a large-sized envelope, containing two ten pound notes and a slip of paper with a line or two written thereon, saying who had sent them. The envelope was addressed to—

"Mr. William Rawton, care of Mr. Thompson."

"Will you be good enough to give your friend Rawton this?" said the widow.

"Certainly, with the greatest of pleasure. And to say who it comes from?"

PEACE JUMPS INTO HIS PONY TRAP.

"I have signified that inside—from Mrs. Bourne."

"Dear me!" exclaimed Peace. "Not the widow of Dr. Bourne, at whose house a sale has recently taken place?"

"The very same; I am the lady."

"How very remarkable."

"Indeed—in what way?"

"I attended the sale merely as a matter of curiosity —that is all. I purchased a violin, which I presume was the property of the deceased gentleman."

Peace went to a side table and produced the violin.

"Yes," said Mrs. Bourne, "that belonged to my husband. You play, I presume?"

"Yes, a little."

"Dear me, what a singular circumstance! Are you pleased with your bargain?"

"Not a bad instrument," said Peace, carelessly; "it has a mellow, rich tone."

He drew the bow across the strings and ran through a scale or so.

"You know how to handle the instrument, I can see that," said Mrs. Bourne; "dear me, I should have supposed you to be a professional."

"I have played in public," observed our hero.

"So I should imagine; I am a devotee to music, Mr. Thompson."

Peace, or rather Thompson, pointed to the piano in his room, and said "Do you do anything in that line?"

"I used to play very often, but am now out of practice. Indeed, I have not taken much interest in music of late years."

"That is no reason for you not doing so now. See, I have here a charming piece set for the violin and piano. Will you accompany me?"

"I'll do my best," said Mrs. Bourne, who believed at the time that she had met with a kindred spirit."

She sat down at the instrument, and very soon convinced Mr. Thompson that she was an accomplished musician.

They played a duet together. Mr. Thompson did his best, and the piece, it is needless to say, was most charmingly rendered.

"It is not often," observed Mr. Thompson, "that I meet with such an admirable executant. Really, madam, your style is most admirable, and merits the warmest commendation."

"Ah, sir, you flatter; I am out of practice."

"I should hardly have supposed so. However, we will, if you please, try another."

"I am a little nervous," suggested the lady.

"Oh, but you must get over that. Remember we are not playing before an audience, only to amuse ourselves."

Mrs. Bourne thought he was a very nice old gentleman, quiet, unobtrusive, and well-behaved.

As we have before intimated, Charles Peace was a most plausible man, and could deceive the most wary person in the world.

Another duet was gone through with even greater success than the first, and the girl, Amy, who was waiting for Mrs. Bourne in the brougham, wondered what was detaining her mistress. She heard the sounds of music, and was under the impression that the doctor's widow was taking a lesson of some well-known professor.

After the second duet was over, Mrs. Bourne rose from the music-stool on which she had been seated, and said—

"You must now excuse me, Mr. Thompson. My brougham is waiting, and I have several calls to make, and therefore I must, however reluctantly it may be, wish you good morning."

"I am sure I have been most delighted with this short visit, and only wish it could be protracted; but I will not seek to detain you."

"You will remember the letter I have given you for Mr. Rawton?"

"Most certainly I will; it shall be delivered into his hands upon the very first opportunity."

"Thank you very much."

Peace saw his aristocratic visitor to the door; she entered her brougham, waved her hand to the gentleman of independent means and musical proclivities, and the vehicle was driven off.

"I thought you were having a lesson, ma'am," said Amy, after they had got out of the Evelina-road. "I'm sure it sounded beautiful."

"Oh, dear me, no, you silly girl. A lesson, indeed! Only just trying a new piece of music over, that's all. Mr. Thompson is such a nice, genial old gentleman; quite a fatherly man, and I should say he is a most respectable person."

"Is he a professor of music?"

"Oh dear, no—nothing of the sort. He has played in public, though. So he told me."

"I hope you have not lost your heart," cried Amy, bursting out into a merry laugh.

"Hush, don't be so ridiculous! What can you be thinking about? Lost my heart, indeed. I should hope not. He may be very nice in his way, but he's not a sort of man I am likely to fall in love with."

"No, he's not particularly handsome—is he?"

"You mind your own business, girl, and don't be so demonstrative or talkative."

Amy said no more—she felt that she had already said more than enough.

The vehicle was driven rapidly along, and in the due course of time the doctor's widow reached her house.

She threw off her travelling costume, and arranged herself in an exquisitely and faultlessly-made dress. She was about to receive visitors. Throngs of persons now flocked to her house; indeed, she was quite the rage for a brief period, and people who before had taken but little notice of her, all of a sudden demonstrated a feeling of friendship, or it might be attachment, which, to say the least of it, was most remarkable.

She was a woman, however, who had a pretty good knowledge of the world, and the people who lived in it, and could gauge with a tolerable degree of accuracy the amount of sincerity of those who all of a sudden professed to be her friends.

She had had at all times an extensive circle of acquaintances. From the very nature of her position, this could not be otherwise, for although she had not been recognised or patronised by the extremely discreet and virtuous of the upper classes, she had been received as a guest by some of the most wealthy and aristocratic persons in the land; the union with the doctor silenced in a great measure the rumours as to her antecedents. She cared but little for the opinion of the world. Indeed, she had been lectured by her former protectors to contemn it, but deep down in the bottom of her heart lurked sad and bitter recollections, which she could not smother; but despite all this she looked hopefully to the future.

She had always been a well-conducted, lady-like woman, and never indulged in coarse innuendoes or vulgar display. Error had been in a great measure forced upon her; and considering how she had been petted and sought after, it is a matter of surprise that she contrived to remain so quiet and unobtrusive in her ways and habits.

CHAPTER CII.
DOMESTIC SQUABBLES—BILL RAWTON PAYS A VISIT TO THE EVELINA-ROAD.

PEACE'S house in the Evelina-road, to which Mrs. Bourne had paid a visit, has attained a considerable share of notoriety. It is most remarkable how he contrived to live there so long and carry on his lawless practices in the surrounding districts without being discovered. A glance at his house would, at first sight, have suggested the impossibility of his going on for so long a time without being brought to justice.

In the front of him was a row of houses, to the rear were the backs of a whole roadful of dwellings, in which the windows seemed so many eyes looking down into the Peace establishment.

On the railway side he was safe enough, as the embankment was high, and the trains passed within a few yards of his dwelling, but high above his roof. Yet it does seem, looking from the street, as if he must have been observed sometimes by the people in the bedrooms to the rear of that road.

If we take a glance at the back we shall soon find out why Peace managed to escape observation.

The tenant of No. 5 neglected nothing. He had a microscopic eye for what people foolishly call "little things." A master of detail, he made the stable serve two purposes—to house his pony and to conceal his doings.

It was constructed so as to shut off all prospect from the rear. The stable was placed and covered in so cleverly that nothing short of the power to pierce through wooden boards could have enabled anyone to see anything.

To make assurance doubly sure, he had, all round the back, a wooden partition put up—even on the side next the railway, where there was only the hedge to guard against. Timber of fine quality was used for this purpose, and the workmanship was creditable to the carpenter—Peace himself.

A neighbour remonstrated with him once for using such good wood for what seemed to be so common and trivial a purpose.

"Ah," replied Peace, "I know my own business best; money's no object to me, for I like things well done, whatever it costs."

He had a peculiar light which enabled him to show varying colours in rapid succession, and the effect was to dazzle and bewilder the person in whose face it was flashed. He guarded the lamp very carefully.

Mr. Knight, the neighbour who served him with milk, said they were a remarkable lot for playing early in the morning. Frequently when he went out with the milk in the morning he would find Peace playing on the fiddle, and the lad of seventeen, Willie Ward, strumming on the guitar. "And capital music it was too," he added; "sometimes sacred, but they played all sorts as well—operatic and dance music."

Occasionally the boy had the violin and Peace the guitar, and they would go at it for hours, getting a name for the eccentricity which they took pains to encourage on all sides.

Very rarely when Peace was at home was the sound of music unheard, and Mrs. Thompson could do her part on the harmonium. "The old gentleman" was fond of the harmonium; he preferred it to the piano for sacred music.

"There was a fulness and depth about the notes," he said, "which gave the peculiar solemnity he liked in the rendering of sacred music."

There is a tradition that Peace was once induced to go to some Methodist chapel, but we think that this story must be relegated to the region of fiction. Nobody at Peckham believed it, and the gentleman who was said to have taken him denied that he ever did anything of the kind. Peace on the Sunday had always a little chapel of his own, in which the service was exclusively musical.

He read the daily papers with great diligence, yet music had greater charms to soothe his savage breast, so that when he was wrapt up in his harmonies, the papers lay unregarded on the doorstep; and sometimes when the pair of Peaces fiddled and guitared, the milkman, who was not so enamoured of the melodious art, perused the papers to see if they were worth a penny.

Mr. Knight usually delivered the milk at Mr. Thompson's house himself. He gave rather a different account of the appearance of the habitation in the morning from that given by the other neighbours, who were privileged to drop in to tea in the evening. He said that things were very higgledypiggledy. All the kitchen utensils seemed to be in a mess. One morning he particularly remembered seeing all the tea and supper things in the fire-place within the fender, and on the rug in front of the fire was Mrs. Thompson lying full length, with a cushion for a pillow. She had evidently lain there all night; Thompson himself was then "up." Perhaps he had been at an unusual distance that morning. "The family," he said, seemed to live well. They wanted for nothing, but they appeared to have it in a rough and ready fashion. That was his idea of how they lived when they had no visitors, but Mr. S. Smith, of Ryde-villas, who let them the house, declared that at Peace's little tea parties "everything was up to the knocker." Peace's life in the Evelina-road is perhaps the most remarkable period in his whole career; and as far as his lawless depredations are concerned, appears to be almost incredible. But we must not let this little sketch break the continuity of our story.

A few days after Mrs. Bourne's visit to our hero, Bandy-legged Bill put in an appearance. After his escape from the doctor's house he had, as already mentioned, been playing at hide and seek. It was Bourne himself who had aroused the detectives and sought thereby to bring the unfortunate gipsy under the ban of the law, but despite the vigilance of Mr. Wrench, Bill had succeeded in keeping out of harm's way. To explain how this was done would be only a waste of space, which we hope to occupy with more important and interesting details.

Bill Rawton did contrive to "dodge" the detectives —that is sufficient for our purpose. By the merest accident in the world he happened to meet with Peace in the neighbourhood of Whitechapel.

A mutual recognition took place, and an interchange of expressions of friendship, for Peace liked the gipsy in consequence of his always acting fair and square to him. Indeed, it must be conceded to that worthy that he had done a number of acts of disinterested kindness for our hero, and as we have before said, with all Bill Rawton's faults, selfishness was not one of them.

Peace invited him to his house in the Evelina-road, which Bill accepted. They very soon became as good pals as ever, but our hero, albeit he gave his friend an account of his adventures since they had last parted, did not make any allusion to the Banner-cross murder, This was a subject upon which he was remarkably reticent. Soon after this Rawton received the letter from Mrs. Bourne, which Cooney had undertaken to deliver. He then asked our hero if he had any objection to receive any communication for him which a friend of his might at some time or another entrust to his care.

Peace at once expressed his willingness to do so, but told Bill that he was no longer Charles Peace, but Mr. Thompson, and that on no account whatever was the name of Peace to be mentioned to a living soul. He had sufficient confidence in the gipsy to trust him with his secret thus far, and his confidence was not misplaced.

The gipsy was, as heretofore, true to the core.

One afternoon, when he did not know very well what to be up to, as he termed it, he determined upon calling again in the Evelina-road, not that he had the most remote idea any communication from Mrs. Bourne had been left for him in charge of our hero. Upon Bill's arriving at Peace's house he heard a violent altercation in the front parlour; this was succeeded by a scream from a woman. Bill entered, and beheld his friend Peace in the passage giving some straightforward blows to a female, whom he afterwards took by the shoulders and thrust into an adjacent apartment, closing the door and locking her in without further ceremony.

Rawton made no observation, but concluded naturally enough that it was a domestic squabble, the cause of which he was unable to fathom.

"Oh! it's you Bill, eh!" cried Peace, catching sight of his friend. "Come in, old boy."

Peace went into the front parlour, from whence a moment or so before he had emerged in such a towering passion.

"What's the row, guv'nor," said Bill.

"Oh! row—don't ask me," returned his companion. "These women drive me distracted at times. That fool can't keep her tongue from wagging, and I feel like a man who is walking with a lighted pipe over a powder magazine. Sit down."

Rawton sat down, but did not make any further remarks for the present. He was at no loss to see that his friend was in one of his tantrums, and that he had "let her ladyship have it."

"I tell you, those two women are the torment of my life," cried Peace, still irate.

"Two—eh?"

"Well, yes, two, worse luck. It's bad enough to be troubled with one, but two is more than mortal man can bear."

"It's no business of mine," said Bill, "but I should have thought—"

"Well, what should you have thought?"

"One jibber would have been enough for you to do with at a time."

"You are right—they are both jibbers; but then it's no use talking about the matter—every man has his troubles in this world."

"And yours appear to be women—eh, old man?" cried the gipsy, with a laugh, for he was well acquainted with his friend's predilection for the fair sex.

"Now don't chaff me, I tell you—I'm in no mood to stand it."

Rawton said no more. He looked hard at the speaker, and saw that he was still in a great state of flustration.

The gipsy remained silent and thoughtful for some time.

Presently Mrs. Peace entered the room; she started at perceiving Rawton. "Dear me! how are you?" she said, offering the gipsy her hand.

"I'm pretty well for an old un," replied Bill. "We 'aven't met for a good while. How's yourself?"

"Middling—only middling; but I am glad to see you."

"Thank you, marm, an' the same to you."

"Where is Susan?" said Mrs. Peace, addressing herself to her husband.

"Where I put her—in the next room. Hang her! she can't, or rather won't, keep her tongue still. I tell you what it is—she shan't go out of the house at all. I'll stop this little game! I'll tame her, as sure as my name is——"

He was about to say Charles Peace, but he substituted "what it is," instead.

"Nobody wants her to go out," said his wife.

"Well, then, why does she? Merely out of aggravation. But I won't have it. If she does, I shall have to wring her neck, that's all."

"I'll look after her; do not put yourself in these tantrums."

"But you don't look after her."

"Yes; I do."

"I say you don't. If you had there wouldn't have been this row. I am sick and tired of speaking about this."

"She's in the next room; I'll give her a good talking to," observed Mrs. Peace, who was on the point of leaving the parlour.

"Here," shouted her husband, "take the key of the next room. I've locked the self-willed obstinate fool in."

Mrs. Peace took the key, unlocked the door of the back parlour, and went into the kitchen with Mrs. Thompson.

"She wants a deal of watching, that woman does," observed our hero. "And if she is not watched, mind you, she'll most likely get me into a devil of a mess."

"Oh, Jerusalem—will she, though?"

Peace nodded significantly.

"I give in to you, Charlie," said Bill, "you've had more experience with women and such like than I have by a long way. I confess they've generally proved too much for me."

"I'll take good care they don't get the better of me —not if I can help it," remarked our hero; "but let's drop this—I'm sick of it. We will talk about other matters. How fares it with you? Have you managed to keep dark?"

"As dark as the old gentleman himself. Not a blessed crusher has been at my heels. I've dodged them to rights; but I say, Charlie, old man, you've got a jolly comfortable little crib here, snug, quiet, and everything you can desire."

"It would be comfortable enough if it wasn't for anxiety of mind. That 'nd knock over any man."

"Anxiety of mind?"

"Yes. Well, you see, Bill, these women are almost more than I can manage. To a certain extent they have me in their power, and they know it."

"I see—might round upon you at any moment?"

"If they felt disposed to do so of course they could."

"Ah, but they won't do that; leastways, I think not. I can answer for one—the other I know nothing about."

"Umph!" ejaculated Peace—"all the better for you. I wish I had known nothing about her."

"Women will be your downfall, old man," observed Rawton. "There aint any mistake about that."

"Get out; mind your own business. I know my way about, and don't intend them to get the best of me, if I can help it."

"All right, Charlie; I dare say you know best."

"But I'm blowed if I ain't forgot something."

"What's up, then?"

"Why, I've got a letter for you."

"For me? Never!"

"I say I have. A lady—a proper sort of one, too, I can tell you—called here a few days ago, and asked if I knew you. She was as nicely behaved a woman as I ever clapped eyes upon, and her manner was so sweet and gentle, so ladylike, that—well, hang me, if I didn't get quite spoony on her."

"What! another?"

"Oh! as for that it's only in a manner of speaking. Well, after some conversation and a little music we got quite friendly-like."

"Yes, I understand; she knew me, did she?"

"Yes, and left a packet for you. A letter with an enclosure. So she told me. I'll give it you."

Peace went to a side table, unlocked his desk, and drew therefrom the letter which had been given to him by Mrs. Bourne.

Rawton glanced at the writing on the envelope, and turned suddenly pale.

"Why what on earth ails you?" cried Peace.

"Oh nothing, I'm all right."

He twisted the letter in his hands for some little time as if afraid to break the envelope which enclosed it.

"Fire away, old man—open it," said his companion.

"Oh! yes, certainly."

Bill did as he wished, and drew forth a slip of paper and two £10 notes.

"Finnips, eh, Bill?" cried Peace in a voice of surprise.

"Yes; two tenners as I'm a living man."

"Well I'm blessed. What did you mean the other day by saying you had not a friend in the world?"

"I've one or two friends left for all my grumbling," observed Rawton, "and she who sent these is one."

It was easy to see that he was much moved, for as he held the notes his hands trembled, and his countenance was indicative of deep emotion.

"You are a star in your way," said Peace.

"Why?"

"Why, indeed, to all appearance you seem to be knocked silly instead of being pleased as anyone else would be under the circumstances. Who's your friend?"

"Oh, I hardly know what to say to that question."

"If it's a secret, keep it to yourself. I don't expect you are the sort of man to make up to the widow."

"Widow?"

"Yes, she had on widow's weeds when she called."

"I suppose so."

"I know it, and that's better than supposing. She's a downright good sort, I should say."

"You are right; she is a good sort."

"Her name is Mrs. Bourne."

"How do you know that?"

"Because she said so. Why, her husband that was, Doctor Bourne, committed suicide. His furniture and other effects were brought under the hammer, and, strange to say, I attended the sale and bought his violin—that one that you see lying on the top of the piano. We played a duet or two together when she called."

"Did you?"

"Yes. What is there to be surprised at in that we did?"

"Ah! you'd be surprised if you knew all."

"But I don't know all; in point of fact, I know nothing as yet. Certainly not from you."

"No, that is true enough."

"Why, Bill, what's the matter with you? You don't appear to me to be a bit like yourself. Keep your pecker up, old man. There's nothing so very dreadful in receiving two tenners from a pretty woman—is there?"

"Oh, dear me, no, nothing at all; but I am surprised, never expected she would come here or give a thought about me—never expected it—and don't deserve it. I think I'll send them back."

"Don't be a fool. Send them back! Why you must be off your head to think of such a thing. Send back the flimsies—well that's beyond a joke."

Bill Rawton made no reply—he seemed to be at a loss to determine his course of action, and remained for some time silent and thoughtful.

"I say again, you're a star; I can't make you out," observed his companion.

"Well, you see, Charles," said the gipsy, "we've all got our weak places. The most callous cove as ever lived finds that out some time or another, though maybe he don't care to confess it, and somehow or another I aint come off scot-free. The lady as called on you was, when I first knew her, one of the purtiest creatures as ever broke the bread of life. I met her when she warn't but a wee bit of a thing, a chit of a girl, as one might say—and—to meet her was to love her."

"Oh, scissors! it came to that—did it? What you, Bill the gipsy, fall in love with a ladylike person such as she appears to be?"

"It doesn't seem natural, does it?" returned Rawton; "and now nobody would b'lieve it; perhaps can't quite b'lieve it myself. But mind yer, she aint nuffin to me, nor has been for more than—well, getting on for twenty year. I hadn't set eyes on her for all that time, nor she me—supposed her to be dead—I had been dead to her for ever so long a time. Well, you see, Charlie, lately, by the merest accident in the world, I met with her. She was at this time the wife of that doctor chap named Bourne, and I was well-nigh upsetting the apple cart when I got acquainted with old Gallipot. I wished myself at Jericho—in quod—anywhere, rather than where I was."

"What harm did you do, then?"

"A goodish bit of harm—that is, I might have done, but as matters turned out, there wasn't much call for grumbling, though it was a narrow squeak."

"I'm blessed if I know what you're driving at, Bill, and that's the truth. You're getting into a fog, and no mistake."

"No I aint, I sees my way clear enough."

"Glad you do. It's more than I can. How was it that you were so near upsetting the apple-cart?"

"'Cause Gallipot was a varmint, a bad un, and wanted an excuse to get rid of his wife—that's why—don't you see?"

"Not just at present."

"Well, I'll go back a bit."

"Yes, do try back."

"I will. As I was a saying, Charlie, I fell in love with her."

"Oh, gammon and all—shut up."

"But I won't shut up; I did more than this. When she was a chit of a girl as didn't know her own mind, and was anxious to get away from her stepmother, who treated her with the greatest unkindness, she gave her consent and became my wife."

"Your wife!" cried Peace, wheeling back his chair, and regarding the gipsy with an incredulous look. "Why you must have taken leave of your senses."

"No, I aint; what I've said is the solemn truth. She became my wife; but, Lord, it wasn't to be supposed that a purty delicate creature like her would stay with me—it wasn't possible—not likely. She was a deal too good for me, and so in less than six months after our wedding we parted. I gave her up. She went her way, and I went mine. She left the country. Remained in India for some years, so I was told; indeed, I thought she was there still; never dreamed of her being in this country. However, she was, and we met."

"And did you claim her then as your wife."

"Claim her! I should think not. Hav'n't I told you we were separated twenty years ago—divorced?"

"Oh, you were divorced."

" Well, in a manner of speaking we were."

" I'll tell you what it is, old man, you're having a bit of game with me to-day."

" No, I aint—it's all fair and square what I've been a telling yer. It's as right as the mail—aint a bit of falsehood about it—not a morsel. I tell ye I wouldn't harm a hair of her head, and if needs be, if needs be, I'd lay down my life for her. There, I've said it out— I mean it!"

" It is a most extraordinary thing that you should never have told me anything about your having a wife before," cried Peace—" a most extraordinary circumstance."

" I never told anyone, 'cos why, it's so many years ago that I had really forgotten all about Hester Teige, as she was called."

" That was her maiden name, then ?"

" Yes, Hester Teige. She had changed it three or four times, I believe, before she became Mrs. Bourne."

" But how about the bit of a mess you were likely to get into ?"

" You shall hear."

Bill Rawton at this point proceeded to give Peace a succinct detail of all the particulars connected with his visit to Bourne's house, with which the reader is already acquainted.

"Now I understand," observed our hero. " Old Gallipot wanted to come the artful dodge and be rid of his partner without the trouble or risk of putting her out of the way. Very natural, and, all things considered, a wise course, perhaps; but he was floored, it seems, just in the nick of time."

" Oh, I haven't the slightest doubt about the end. If he couldn't be shut of her by fair means he would have done it by foul. She would have been poisoned like his first wife. He was a cold-blooded, cruel scoundrel."

" Upon my word, the story you've been telling sounds more like a romance than an actual reality."

" Perhaps it does; it seems almost like a romance. When I think of the time when I first met with Hester, and what I have passed through since then—what I am and what I might have been, and how gentle and beautiful she was, I feel a heavy weight fall upon me— I feel that I want a heart not made out of human flesh, but out of the nether millstone."

There was a mournful cadence in the gipsy's voice as he gave utterance to these words, which made them additionally expressive, as the sounds fell upon the ears of Charles Peace the burglar.

Then on the bronzed and wrinkled cheeks of Bill Rawton two tears chased their way. They were the first he had shed for many a year. The hard man's heart was softened. The remembrance of his early days—the dawn and noontide of love—seemed to him then like the oasis in the sterile and arid desert, and he leant forward and buried his face in his hands.

To say that Charles Peace was moved by the display of feeling in one from whom he would have least expected to find any genuine sentiment, would be, perhaps, saying too much. But he was surprised; more so, perhaps, than he had been in the whole course of his life.

He might well be so, for many reasons. He never for a moment gave his companion credit for so much chivalrous and disinterested feeling as he had displayed in his endeavours to shelter and shield Mrs. Bourne, and perhaps the reader will find it difficult to believe that a man of such essentially coarse a type as

Rawton was capable of being moved by the higher instincts of our nature.

In answer to this we have but to declare that the gipsy's character is sketched from life; the leading incidents in his career are but records of actual occurrences; his devotion to Mrs. Bourne was the one bright spot on his character, which nothing could dim or diminish. Throughout his life he invariably spoke of her with respect and admiration, not unmixed by a latent but enduring love.

Instances of this kind are by no means so rare as people are led to believe, although, perhaps, they are not outwardly manifested, as in the case of Rawton. The human character is diverseful, and it would not be a pleasing thought, nor indeed would it be correct, to suppose the most callous do not possess " one touch of nature which makes the whole world kin."

" What can be said about Peace, then ?" some of our readers may exclaim. It is true he was a bold bad man, who had but little to recommend him; he was about as bad a sample of the human species as it is possible for us to find. Nevertheless, he had some lighter shades in his character. He was fond of animals, of music; he was not an unkind father. Perhaps there may be what we may term negative qualities, for taken altogether he cannot be deemed anything else than a ruffian or freebooter of the very worst type.

Rawton remained for some time silent, with his head resting on his hands, and Peace was so taken back by the narrative and the deep dejection of the gipsy, that he had not the heart to question him further, and so the two sat in the front parlour of the house in the Evelina-road for some minutes without exchanging a word.

" I've known this bloke for a good while," murmured Peace to himself, " but I'm blessed if he haven't queered me now and no mistake. Hang the fellow ! I'm afraid some parson has got hold of him."

He took his violin and began to play a prelude to a new piece of music.

" Ah, that's right," cried Rawton. " Give us something soft and touching; you know I always like to hear you play."

" You want something lively, old fellow, to cheer you up," returned our hero. " You're down among the dead men just now, and seem inclined to do the snivelling business, which, to say the truth, I should have thought quite out of your line."

" Don't be hard on a cove, Charlie—I'm a bit down, I confess; but, fire away, let's have a tune."

Peace played a surprising bravura air upon his violin. As the strains of music reached the ears of the gipsy his countenance became radiated with pleasurable emotion.

" That's grand, an' no mistake," he ejaculated. " I wish I could handle the instrument as you do; but that I never shall, it ain't in me—not, mind you, but I've a great liking for it—always had."

" Well do you feel better, old man ?" inquired Peace, with a lurking smile upon his countenance.

" Yes, a deal better."

" That's well. Have a dram of brandy—that'll set you to rights."

He passed the bottle towards his companion.

Bill poured himself out a glassful, which he drank off at one gulp.

" You are all right now," said Peace, " or you ought to be by this time. Pull yourself together, and drop the sentimental."

" Ah," murmured the gipsy, " I dare say you think

me a weak silly fool, and, indeed, to say the truth, I think so myself. But you must know, Charlie, that I never think of Hester Teige and of the days when I first knew her, without many bitter regrets for the past."

"Ah, I dare say. It won't do to give way to this sort of thing. Are you spoony on her now?"

"Spoony be hanged!—she's nothing to me, and I am nothing to her. Lord bless yer, what can you be thinking about? Why, she's far above me in every way. What am I, old man? A cadger—a dodger—a miserable wretch who's not worth her notice."

"She has noticed you, though," returned Peace. "Aint she left you two tenners?"

"Ah, true. Well, I rather fancy it would be best for me to return them. Did she leave her address?"

"Not a bit of it. She left no address with me, so you must pocket the affront—that's the best thing you can do."

"I don't like to take her money. I would sooner rob than accept anything from her."

"And why, pray?"

"Because I don't deserve it, and would rather not have a sixpence of her money."

"You don't like to be beholden to her. Is that what you mean?"

"No, it aint that; but I don't like her to think that what I've done was with any idea of getting paid for it. It goes agin the grain for me to receive a single quid from one whom I would serve for the mere pleasure of serving her."

"Well, you are a stunner, and no mistake!" cried Peace. "I never could have believed you had so much honour in you—not unless I had been witness of it."

"I'm a queer chap, Charles, and I dare say I've queer ways, but I am too old to alter now; but there, let us say no more about the matter. We'll talk about something else."

"I think we had better. Perhaps you'll be a little more reasonable upon other subjects. Are you in the mind to take a bit of a drive with me this evening?"

"In course I am; where to?"

"That we will determine by and bye. I am going to have a spin in the pony trap, and shall be glad of your company."

"All right, I'm your man. Never say no to a good thing. Is it business matters you are going on?"

Peace smiled.

"Well, yes, it's all in the way of business."

"What time do you start?"

"Oh, about seven o'clock, I suppose."

"Very good, I'll come round at that time."

"No, don't do that. I would rather you would not. Meet me in the road, and I can pick you up. Do you see?"

"Just as you like, where shall I meet you then?"

"Ah, I don't know, let's see; Spurgeon's Tabernacle will be as good a place as any."

"I'll be there, old boy, only let me know the time."

"From seven to about a quarter or twenty minutes after. I'm sure not to be later than that."

"I'm on. Will be there at seven without fail. Now I'll be off; but, I say, keep yourself quiet, and don't have any more shindies with the women."

"Oh no; that'll be all right," replied Peace, with a laugh. "Don't you bother yourself about my domestic affairs. Good-bye for the present. You won't forget the appointment?"

"Not I—t'aint likely."

Bill Rawton took his departure.

Peace returned to his little parlour, and began scraping away at his violin.

Presently Willie Ward came in and took up the guitar, and they played several duets.

Mrs. Peace, who had been in the kitchen below endeavouring to console Mrs. Thompson, shortly after this presented herself.

"Ah! it's you, eh?" cried our hero. "Well, what about that beauty? Wants to go out again, I suppose, to make as much mischief as possible."

"She does not want to go out, and has promised to remain indoors, but of course she does not like to be kept a prisoner."

"I tell you she must not go out. She can have whatever she likes, and enjoy herself as much as she likes here, but I will not have her trapesing about and letting everybody know our business, and what is going on here."

"I'll take good care she doesn't do that any more."

"That's all right then. I hope you'll keep your word this time."

"Mother's sure to do that," cried Willie. "She does her best, I'm sure."

"I wish I could be as sure of it; but no matter. Now then go on with your music."

The two began to play once more. Mrs. Peace, who had quite enough of their musical entertainments, left the room, and made the best of her way towards the kitchen.

As seven o'clock approached the pony and trap were got ready, and Peace drove off to meet Bill Rawton.

CHAPTER CIII.

BURGLARS AT BLACKHEATH—THE SURPRISE—THE STRANGE MEETING.

IT has been said that Charles Peace carried out the burglaries on the other side of London entirely by himself, and without the assistance of even one confederate, and to a considerable extent the statement is borne out by facts.

Nevertheless, it is quite certain that occasionally he had a helpmate or accomplice, this being none other than Bandy-legged Bill.

Rawton, however, was fortunate enough to escape notice.

He was never implicated in the extensive series of depredations carried on by our hero during what may be termed his London career.

We have it upon good authority that there was another person besides Bill who occasionally accompanied Peace on his predatory excursions—this personage also escaped detection.

It is true that both he and the gipsy only acted in concert with our hero some half-dozen times or so.

As a rule Peace certainly did commit an almost incredible number of burglaries entirely by himself, and this perhaps furnishes us with the series of daring exploits which for audacity and fearlessness are without a parallel in the history of criminals.

But Peace was altogether a character far above the level of the ordinary housebreaker.

His cunning, finesse, his hypocrisy and assumption of the character of a well-to-do respectable member of the community when in his house in the Evelina-road, seems to be altogether outside the barriers which hedge in the lawless class to which he most unquestionably belonged.

The neighbours, as they saw him drive his pony trap along the Evelina-road, said, "The old gentleman has gone out for his evening drive." They saw him go out, but none of them saw him come back. Whither he went nobody seemed to take the trouble to inquire. The supposition was that he was going to pay a visit to some friend who did not live within walking distance, and as Peace made it appear that he was an invalid and was not able to bear much fatigue, they naturally concluded that the respectable independent gentleman had a large circle of acquaintances who lived on the outskirts of London, and to these persons he was accustomed to pay periodical visits.

That he did make it his business to call at the houses of the wealthy in Blackheath, Greenwich, and elsewhere was very certain—the number of houses he entered it would be very difficult to enumerate, and in most cases he brought away with him substantial proofs of his having made a careful selection of the valuables therein.

Upon arriving at Spurgeon's Tabernacle he found Bandy-legged Bill awaiting his appearance. Bill was good at an appointment, and seldom failed to keep any he made with our hero.

"Well, old stick-in-the-mud, are you in better fettle now? Got rid of the miserables—eh?" cried Peace.

"I'm all right now, old man," returned the gipsy. "It was but a passing cloud."

"Ah, so you've still got a touch of the romantic, it would seem. Well, jump up."

The gipsy got into the trap, which was driven off by Peace.

"Where are you making for—any place in particular?"

"I saw a tempting-looking crib at Upper Charlton, and we'll just see if it can be worked to rights."

Rawton laughed.

"I wish I had got your ability, Charlie, and your nerve," said he. "I've tried, but have never been able to manage this sort of business by myself. I expect I'm clumsy. Anyway, I'm a fool compared to you."

"I don't know so much about that. We've done pretty well together at one time—why not now?"

"Oh! I'm well enough to play second fiddle, but aint of no manner of use when left to myself. So you've given up Sheffield and the other towns—have you? Got too hot, I suppose."

"It's not altogether that. I could do well enough in my old quarters, but a change was absolutely necessary."

"I see—a change of air for the benefit of your health."

"Look here, nobody knows me as Charles Peace in Peckham, and so you'd better not mention Sheffield, Manchester, or Bradford, 'cause, you see, if you do, it might get wind, and, if it did, I should be 'copped' as sure as eggs is eggs."

"Oh, you've nothing to fear from me."

"I know that, old boy—I'd trust you with my life, and that's saying something, seeing how few there are a bloke can trust now-a-days. Men are getting more like wild beasts than human beings. As to the people in this world getting wiser or better it's all my eye and Betty Martin."

"That's right enough, they are not near so good I think as they were when I first came into this world," remarked the gipsy. "Look at old Gallipot. He poisoned his first wife, and no doubt intended to polish off his second by the same means."

"He left behind him an excellent fiddle, that's one thing in his favour, seeing that I bought it for a mere song."

"Was that his fiddle you were playing on to-day?"

"Why, of course it was. I told you so."

"Oh, true, I forgot."

"Why your wits are wool-gathering."

"That's better than oakum picking," returned Bill, bursting out into a loud laugh. "I had you there, old man, and no mistake."

"Look here, Bill, it aint worth while for you to remind me, nor for me to remind you of the miseries of prison life. I don't like to think of it—blessed if I do. It seems to send a cold shudder through my frame. I've had enough of it, and don't intend to be 'copped' again, come what may."

"Why, what would you do then?"

"Shoot my man down, rather than be taken."

"Oh, Jerusalem! But——"

"Well, what?"

"That sounds like murder," cried the gipsy; "and we've neither of us come to that as yet, and I hope as how we never shall—never."

Peace was a little discomposed at this speech, which was delivered with an earnestness and power which seemed to go right through him.

"No, Bill, we aint come to that as yet. Let's hope there'll never be any occasion for us to be brought to such an extremity."

"Brought be blowed!" said Rawton. "Prigging's one thing and murder another. If you lift a few things from a crib as you enter, while the owner and his wirtuous family are asleep, why, well and good; the loss of them won't ruin him—indeed, in a manner of speaking, it won't perhaps do him a morsel of harm; but taking human life, old pal, is a horse of a different colour, an' I'd rather give myself up, let alone being 'copped,' than rob a cove of his life. 'Cause, you see, Charlie, life is a precious gift, and when once taken, it be a gift it aint in the power of mortal man to restore; and you know it's dear to everyone ov us, however hard-up and miserable we may be."

"I tell you what it is, Bill, I'm blowed if some sanctimonious parson aint been getting at you—there's no mistake about that."

"You make a jolly big mistake if you suppose that. I aint sed a word to any parson, nor has one sed even so much as a word to me; but that don't much matter. Prigging's one thing, murder's another."

"Well—who says it aint?" cried Peace, petulantly. "We've not come out on a preaching tour—have we?"

"No, I dunno as we have; but you mustn't talk about shooting your man down, 'cause, in the first place you'll be a jolly fool to do so; and in the next the chances are you'll never have a happy hour arter."

"You're a jolly old hypocrite, Bill!" exclaimed Peace, laughing in his turn—"a thundering old hypocrite!"

"Am I? Well, I s'pose I am, if you say so. But them's my sentiments and always were, come what may. I don't intend to go in for murder or manslaughter. As to giving a cove a crack on the head when he becomes troublesome that's another matter, but shooting or stabbing aint in my line, and, as I said afore, I hope it never will be."

"You never know what you may be brought to, so don't you make cock sure of being free from temptation."

"Oh, I aint free from temptation—I admit that, Charlie. Don't you imagine I'm going for to do the sanctimonious, as you term it, because, yer see, it wouldn't fit either on us—not a bit on it. I am game to lift anything as comes in my way, and no gammon."

"If you said otherwise I shouldn't believe you."

"In course yer wouldn't. You might as well expect Cooney to preach morality as me."

"Cooney!" exclaimed Peace. "Have you seen anything of him lately?"

A STRANGE AND UNEXPECTED MEETING.

Our hero now became seriously alarmed.

"Eh. Well, yes, I have."

"For mercy's sake don't say you've seen anything of me. Don't tell Cooney I'm in London; but perhaps you have already done so."

"No I aint, nor do I intend. Do you take me for a fool?"

"Far from that, old stick-in-the-mud. But don't you say a word to Cooney about me."

"I won't—'taint likely."

"He's all well enough in his way, but he's got a precious long tongue, and is too fond of chattering."

"Oh, there aint any harm in the chap; leastways, I never found any. He's fair and square enough."

"That may be, but I again charge you, Bill, to say nothing about my being in London, what I am, and what I am doing. This is most important. Do you understand?"

"I do. Cooney knows nothing, nor shall he."

"That's right. You've passed your word, and I am satisfied."

They had by this time passed Charlton. The curtain of night had fallen over the landscape. Not a star to be seen.

Peace drew the rein, and the pony and trap turned into a dark narrow lane.

"We are within sight of the crib," said Peace. "I shall leave you here in charge of 'Tommy.'"

"Who's 'Tommy?'"

"The pony."

"Oh, I see. Well, and what then?"

"You wait here till I come back. The house is some little distance off from where we are now. So much the better. I don't want the trap to be seen by any chance passenger. Here you are pretty safe from observation, but if a bobby does hail within sight you can drive slowly on—and after he has gone return to this spot or near it. I shall be sure to find you. If I do not I shall give a whistle, and you'll know I am at hand."

"Oh, you are going to crack the crib all by yourself then?"

"I shall manage it better without a companion; besides, some one must be left in charge of 'Tommy' and the trap—don't you see that? Tommy's worth his weight in gold, and I wouldn't lose him for the best man or woman that ever breathed."

"You were always fond of animals, Charlie, and you ain't altered in that respect, I see."

Peace left the gipsy, and proceeded to the habitation he proposed operating on, and Rawton had to content himself as best he could in the dark lane till the return of his companion.

A quarter of an hour passed over, then half an hour; the gipsy felt cold and uncomfortable. He got out of the trap, and walked backwards and forwards in the lane to break the monotony of the hour.

"I wonder how far this place is Charlie was speaking of? I do hope he'll work it to rights. I'm getting jolly sick of waiting, but anyhow I'll stick to my post. He is a stunner, and no mistake."

Presently the moon, which had hitherto been obscured, shone forth, and lighted up the surrounding neighbourhood with remarkable distinctness.

Rawton re-entered the trap; before doing so, however, he reined up Tommy, whom he had loosened, that he might nibble at the grass which grew by the hedge-side.

The gipsy glanced in every direction. In a few minutes, after he had seated himself again in the trap, he beheld at some distance down the road, which ran at right angles with the lane, a man running at the top of his speed. He was at no loss to comprehend that the fugitive was Charles Peace.

He was panting, and almost breathless.

It was evident enough that he had run his hardest. He threw his bag into the trap, put on an overcoat, encased his neck in a red muffler, and exchanged hats with the gipsy.

In the space of a few seconds he made such an alteration in his appearance that none would have known him.

"Drive your hardest!" exclaimed Peace, "and keep as quiet as possible."

The gipsy put Tommy out to the greatest possible speed, and in a few minutes after this they were far removed from the scene of action.

"What's been the matter, then?" cried Bill, after they had got clean away.

"Matter," returned our hero. "I was as near as possible being potted. Just as I was leaving the grounds of the house, who should come up with me but a bobby. 'What have you got in that bag?' says he.

"'That's no business of yours,' says I.

"'Aint it though,' cries my gentleman.

"'No it aint. You mind your own business, and leave respectable people alone.'

"'You'll just let me see what you've got there, my man,' says he, and with that he endeavours to seize hold of the bag.

"'Now then, guv'nor,' says I, 'you're a jolly sight too fast, you are, by a long way. If you give me any more of your cheek I'll report ye.'

"'You are not going away without satisfying me as to what you've got in the bag,' says he; 'just hand it over without further ado.'

"'No; not if I know it.' says I. Well, with that he seizes me by the collar of the coat, when, before he was aware of it, I slipped out of his grasp, and tripped him up. I didn't wait for any further conversation with my gentleman, but ran my hardest; he followed, but you see I had the start of him, and cut across a field, and reached the high road again. By this means I doubled on him, but he was still giving chase when I jumped into the trap. However, he's left behind now; but it might have been worse."

"I am glad you were not driven to extremities," observed Bill, in a tone of satisfaction.

"I am glad of it myself; but I was very near being copped though—precious near."

"Which road am I to take now?" inquired the gipsy, as they came to the end of the one through which they had been travelling.

"Make for Blackheath."

"What! not for Peckham?"

"No, shan't go home just yet; my business is not over."

"Why, surely you don't intend—"

"Aye, but I do. One crib don't satisfy me; have got to work another."

"Well, you have got a nerve, Charlie. After what has taken place, I should have supposed it would have given you the sick of it for to-night, at all events."

"Drive on to Blackheath, I tell you, and leave me to myself."

"To yourself?"

"Yes, I'll tell you what to do presently."

"Right you are, old sinner. I've no right to interfere; so, here goes."

Upon reaching Blackheath Charles Peace got out of the trap, took his burglar's instruments with him, and declared that he was about to effect an entrance into a palatial-looking mansion in the immediate neighbourhood.

"Now, if you like, you can drive Tommy home, and leave me to myself. See, here's the key of the stable."

"I don't care about leaving you to yourself, as you term it."

"It is best for you to do so. There's a goodish many things in the trap, and if we are suspected—which is more than likely, seeing that the cart and pony may be recognised if we are not—and the contents of the bag are overhauled, where shall we be then? No, no, Bill—it won't do to risk it. You make the best of your way to the Evelina-road, put up the nag, hide the booty in the place I pointed out to you, and then step it. If you see either of the women say I am detained playing at a concert in Blackheath. Then you can see me in the morning."

"Oh, very well, if it is to be so, there's no help for it, I suppose. But where are you going to now ?"

"Oh, I've had my eye on one or two little places. Never you mind where they are—I tell you I've not done for the night—not as yet."

" You lick me—knock me silly; I'm not in it," cried the gipsy, with a laugh. "I'm to go back—am I ?"

" Yes—haven't I told you so ?"

" Anything else you want ?"

"No—nothing. Drive on."

Bill turned the horse's head, wished his companion good night, and trotted on towards London.

Charles Peace remained for some little time silent and abstracted until the gipsy was lost to sight, after which he walked on in the most unconcerned manner it is very well possible to conceive. He had before leaving his companion taken off the overcoat and muffler, put on his own hat, and made himself up in a manner which was altogether different to the one he had assumed when starting out on his lawless expedition.

After a walk of some ten minutes or a quarter of an hour's duration, he came in sight of an elegant mansion, situated in its own grounds, which was to all appearance tenanted by some wealthy well-to-do citizen.

The house in question stood not very far from Kidbrook-lane, which has attained an unenviable celebrity for the barbarous murder of the ill-fated girl named Margaret Clewson. This crime, like many others of a kindred nature, remains a mystery to this day.

The murderer of Margaret Clewson is, in all probability, still in our midst. The murder in Kidbrooklane was one of the greatest possible atrocity. The victim lay for hours in a semi-unconscious state by the hedge where she had been stricken down, with fourteen wounds of a most fearful character on the head and face. After lingering in perfect agony and torture for some days, death put an end to her sufferings, but the perpetrator of this horrible crime has never been overtaken by justice—the avenging arm of the law has been nerveless and powerless in this instance.

Margaret Clewson was not able to articulate or express herself in the smallest degree after being taken to the hospital.

When found in the lane by a policeman all she was able to say, "Oh, let me die." Those were the last words she uttered. Many of the inhabitants of Blackheath, Greenwich, and Sydenham believe to this day that her death will be avenged, but we fear the chances are very remote of her murderer being discovered.

Peace walked round the fence which enclosed the garden and grounds of the house upon which he had an eye. As he was making a survey a policeman, who was going his rounds, passed close to the spot where the burglar stood, but the latter was in no way abashed, he walked leisurly on, and watched the bobby going his round till he was lost to sight, then he returned to the habitation.

With one spring he cleared the low wall which ran round the back garden, he then found himself in a dense plantation of trees and underwood, which effectually concealed him from observation.

He then bethought him of what to do. He glanced at the back of the house.

One of the windows of the first-floor room seemed to be available. He might succeed in climbing up to this without attracting anyone's notice.

He paced up and down the garden, being still in doubt as to the weakest point of attack.

While doing so he observed a short ladder stretched lengthways by the side of the wall.

It had been used in the early part of the day by a man who had come to prune the vines.

This would suit his purpose admirably. He rubbed his hands with glee.

"Sent on purpose; nothing could be better," he murmured. "Nothing."

He looked over the wall ; no chance passenger was visible. He reached the ladder, and in an incredibly short space of time he succeeded in opening the back window.

He crept softly into the apartment. He found himself in an elegantly-furnished room full of articles of virtu, with a large wardrobe, in which were articles of female attire, a lady's riding habit, sealskin mantles, and other costly garments.

Peace looked about, and observed by the aid of his dark lantern a number of valuable trinkets and portable property, which quite charmed him to look upon.

He set to work without further hesitation.

In the next room to the one in which he was occupied sat a lady, who was evidently waiting for some one. She heard a noise in the adjoining apartment.

" Dear me, how late it is !" she murmured. "I ought to have been in bed hours ago. Ethel, is that you ?"

Ethel, the ladies' maid, did not answer, and the faint rustle in the back-room, which had called forth the lady's question, ceased the instant she spoke aloud.

The lady was not wanting in courage—she was not nervous—far from it, yet her watch seemed to tick with extraordinary vigour, and her heart to beat harder than common while she listened.

The door of communication between the two rooms was closed. Another door in the smaller apartment opened to the passage ; but this, she remembered, was invariably locked on the inside.

It couldn't be Ethel, therefore, who disturbed her mistress's reflections, unless that faithful handmaiden had come down the chimney or in at the window.

It could not be her husband, for he was far away in the country on a visit to some of his relatives. Still, it was just possible he might have come back ; but even assuming he had, it was not at all likely that he would be groping about in the adjoining room.

The house was very silent—so silent that in the distant corridors were distinctly audible those faint and ghostly footfalls which traverse all large houses after midnight.

A small hand-lamp was burning on the lady's toilette table, but it served rather to show how dismal were the shadowy corners of the large lofty bedroom than to afford light and confidence to its inmate.

She listened intently. Yes, she was sure she heard somebody in the next room.

A step that moved stealthily about. A noise as of woodwork skilfully and cautiously broken open.

She became seriously alarmed. Who could it be ? She endeavoured as best she could to account in some rational and reasonable way for the sounds which fell upon her ear.

One moment she felt frightened, then her courage came back higher for its interruption.

She was a woman who was not daunted by a trifle—still it must be confessed the situation in which she found herself was a trying one.

She could have escaped from her own room into the passage easily enough, and so alarmed the house, but when she reflected that its fighting garrison consisted only of an infirm old butler, and a page boy whom no one could possibly wake, there seemed little to be gained by such a proceeding if violence or robbery were really intended.

Besides, she rather scorned the idea of summoning assistance till she had ascertained the amount of danger.

She remembered at this time the accounts she had heard of the numberless daring robberies which had taken place in that and the surrounding neighbourhoods.

She had laughed at these reports, which she concluded had been greatly exaggerated, but she looked upon the matter in a more serious light now.

It was likely enough that some daring burglar had paid her establishment a visit during her husband's and the footman's absence, for both were away.

She determined upon her course of action. She would know the worst.

She blew out the lamp on her toilette table, and crept to the door of the smaller room, in which our hero was now so busily occupied.

She put her ear to the keyhole, and heard the burglar's movements more distinctly. She laid her hand noiselessly on its lock.

Softly as she turned it, gently as she pushed the door back on its hinges inch by inch, she did not succeed in entering unobserved.

The light of a shaded lantern flashed over her the instant she crossed the threshold, dazzling her eyes indeed, yet not so completely but that she made out the figure of a man standing over her shattered jewel-box, of which he seemed to have been rifling the contents.

Quick as thought, she said to herself—

"Come, there is only one. If I can frighten him more than he frightens me the game is mine."

The man uttered a series of impious oaths in a whisper, and the lady was aware of the muzzle of a pistol covering her above the dark lantern.

She wondered why she was not frightened. It was most remarkable, for her position was one of imminent peril; but she did not lose her presence of mind.

She could distinguish a dark figure behind the spot of intense light radiating round her own person, and perceived besides, almost without looking, that an entrance had been made by the window, which stood wide open, so as to disclose the topmost rounds of a garden ladder propped against the sill.

What Charles Peace saw in the flood of light was an aristocratic-looking woman, decked in the most costly raiment, with her neck and arms sparkling with jewels.

There was such an air of composure and refinement about her that he was fairly bewildered.

"Bessie Dalton, as I'm a living man!" he ejaculated.

CHAPTER CIV.
CHARLES PEACE IS CHECKMATED.

THE pale dauntless woman, with her haughty delicate face, and her loops of brown hair falling over robes of white, stood erect and motionless, confronting the levelled weapon of the burglar without the slightest fear.

To his exclamation she made no reply.

He had never before set eyes on such a sight as this in circus nor music-hall, nor gallery of a metropolitan theatre.

For a moment he lost his heart—for a moment he hesitated.

In that moment his companion was equal to the occasion.

Quick as thought she made one step to the window, pushed the ladder outwards with all her force, and shut down the sash.

As it closed, the ladder, poising for an instant, fell with a crash on the ground below.

"Now," she said, quietly, "you are trapped and taken. Better make no resistance, for the man servant can be summoned if I choose, and I have no wish to see you ill-treated."

Peace was aghast. What could it all mean? Was he awake or dreaming?

"She must be well backed," he said to himself, "to assume such a position as this, and she looked so firm and resolute."

Nevertheless, instinctively, rather than of intention, he muttered hoarsely—

"Drop it, let's have no more of this. One word out loud and I'll shoot you as you stand there."

"Fire away," she answered, with perfect composure. "You will save me the trouble of giving an alarm. They expect it, and are waiting for it every moment below stairs. Light those candles and let me see what damage you have done before you return the plunder."

A pair of wax candles stood on the chimneypiece, and he obeyed, mechanically wondering to himself the while.

His cunning, however, had not quite deserted him, and he left his pistol lying on the table ready to snatch it away if she tried to take possession.

It was thus he gauged her confidence, and seeing she scarcely noticed the weapon, argued that powerful assistance must be near at hand to render this brave woman so arbitrary and so unconcerned.

His admiration burst out in spite of his discomfiture and critical position—

"Well, you're a cool one!" he exclaimed, in accents of mingled vexation and approval. "A cool one and a stunner—I'm blest if you aint!"

"I am not afraid of you, Charles Peace," she returned—"why should I be? You are now in my power."

"Are you, then, mistress of this establishment?" inquired our hero.

"I am, and have been so for some years. What more do you desire to know?"

Peace seemed all of a sudden to be under a spell, and while he acknowledged its strength had no power —nay, had no wish to resist its influence. What had come over him?

He felt almost pleased to know he was at her mercy, and yet she treated him like the dirt under her feet.

"The mistress of this princely establishment—why, Bessie?"

"Don't call me Bessie, if you please, sir. It is my husband and my intimates who have the privilege of addressing me by my Christian name."

"Well, I'm knocked silly," exclaimed our hero. 'I'm sure I beg your pardon."

"That is the very least you ought to do. You must understand most clearly that I cannot permit you to rob this establishment. Return my jewellery at once, if you please."

"I did not know it was your's, or I should not have taken it."

"Much obliged to you for your consideration," said the lady.

"But I say," observed Peace, in a wheedling tone, "don't be so grand and distant. We've not met for years, and at one time you knew well enough that I doated on you."

"Don't talk like that," she cried, holding up her

hand in a deprecating manner. "We have not met for years. I only wish we had not done so to-night, because it only causes me pain and sorrow."

"Oh, I dare say it does, but I'm knocked over. Hang it all, do tell me something about your past life—I mean that portion of it since you left Bradford, when you were——"

"Cease, sir. If you do not behave yourself in an orderly and respectful manner I solemnly declare that I will show you no mercy, but will hand you over to the officers of the law without pity or remorse."

"I do not desire to say anything that may offend you—indeed I do not."

"My husband would never forgive me if he knew I held parley with a burglar and a convicted criminal."

Peace hung down his head.

"Your husband!" he ejaculated. "Then you are married?"

"Of course I am, to as good and kind a husband as ever woman could wish to have. He's very rich, of a good family, and has not a blemish on his escutcheon."

"I'm knocked silly. There's no mistake about it—you might double me up with the blow of a mere straw. This beats all. I've heard of sorcery, and I'm blowed if there must not be something of the sort here."

"Before you proceed with your agreeable discourse," said the lady, "you had better put every one of my trinkets in its place."

Peace at once proceeded to replace the jewels in the case. The other articles he had possessed himself of were also rendered up to their owner without hesitation.

"There, will that satisfy you? It is not at all likely that I should attempt to rob you. I have returned everything."

"That is well, and now——" she hesitated.

"Well you have thrown down the ladder, but I can get clear off."

"Do so then at once."

"Ah, but you must tell me how all this has been brought about. I promise never to molest you again—never to trouble you, but how, in the name of all that's wonderful, have you managed to become a lady of fashion, for such I presume you are?"

"Your surmise is a correct one."

"How has it been done? That's what I want to know."

"By moving in good society in the first place, and in the next becoming the wife of an honourable and wealthy gentleman."

"Good society—how was that managed?"

"Easily enough. We had a good introduction."

"We. Who do you allude to besides yourself?"

"Mrs. Bristow, to be sure."

"What! John Bristow's wife?"

"Certainly—none other. She came into a fortune."

"Oh, came into a fortune, did she? I see, that accounts for it in some measure. And what has become of her?"

"She is all right."

"And has she got a worthy and honourable gentleman for a husband?"

"She has."

"And now before I go—we shan't see each other again, I expect, not this side of the grave—do answer one or two other questions. How did John's wife become possessed of a fortune? Did she inherit it?"

"I suppose so."

"But all her relatives were poor—so I always understood."

"Most of them were, but that's not to the purpose. Mrs. Bristow, as I have already intimated, had enough to support an establishment at the west end of the town. She did not like living by herself, and I became her companion. Is your curiosity now satisfied?"

"Yes. Where is she now?"

"Who?"

"Mrs. Bristow."

"I do not deem it expedient to answer that query, for I am perfectly satisfied that she has no desire to see you. Oh, Charles Peace, let me beg and entreat of you to alter your course of life. What will be your end if you don't—think of that? Have you no thought of the future?"

"Have you ever had any thought about me?" cried Peace.

"Certainly I have. I sent a remittance to you to be handed to you at the expiration of your term of imprisonment."

"Did you send that?"

"Yes, and would most gladly, most cheerfully, assist you if you would become a respectable member of the community."

"Oh, gammon and all, I've tried the respectable dodge, but didn't find it pay."

"I'll say no more. Go your way. You will never be wise or discreet, I suppose. Are you in want of money at the present time?" she said, drawing out her purse, and opening it. "Because if you are——"

"If I am I should not accept anything from you," he cried, with some asperity. "Put back your money and keep it to serve a better purpose. I can be as proud as you when I choose."

"Enough, sir, we will say no more upon the subject, then."

"This appears to me to be more like a dream than an actual reality. You mistress of this grand establishment, assuming all the airs and graces of a lady of fashion. Confound it all, I am knocked completely silly—there's no mistake about it, I'm dead beat. You Bessie Dalton!"

"I am not Bessie Dalton, Mr. Peace, and I must request you to be more guarded in your observations. A wide gulph now separates us—a gulph which nothing can bridge over. Go your ways, and leave me for evermore unmolested."

"I am done, there's no denying that—a gone coon, but after all I see no reason for regret, none whatever. I am pleased to think that you have been so fortunate, madam—that the sun of prosperity shines upon you," said Peace, with something like sarcasm in his tone. "We are separated, and a wide gulph, as you very properly observe, lies between us, but for old acquaintance sake——"

"For old acquaintance sake I would do anything that lies in my power to serve you," said she—"anything to turn you from your evil courses," she added, after a pause.

"Rubbish! Don't preach morality to me," cried the burglar, "because I aint in a mood to listen to it—certainly not from you—or from anyone else, for the matter of that."

"As you please. I do not desire to hold further parley with you; and now——"

"Well, what?"

"I must devise some means of getting you away without attracting the notice of any of the servants."

"You devise? I'll act for myself," cried Peace. "There will not be much difficulty in the matter."

He made towards the window, threw it open, and passed through. He hung for a moment by his hands from the window sill, and then dropped on the gravel walk below.

Bessie Dalton, or, more properly speaking, Mrs. Metcalf, looked out in some alarm, for she feared the burglar's daring escape would be attended with serious consequences.

In this, however, she was mistaken. She observed Charles Peace safe and sound in the grounds at the rear of the house.

He did not speak, but waved an adieu with his hand, and in another minute was lost to sight.

All this had taken place in a much shorter time than we have taken in describing it. Mrs. Metcalf closed the window, fastened it, and then stood irresolute for some little time.

She was aroused from her reverie by the entrance of her maid, Ethel.

"Goodness me, ma'am, how pale and troubled you look," cried the girl. "Whatever is the matter?"

"What has kept you all this time?" said her mistress, in a tone of anger. "I've been waiting anxiously for your return, you giddy, thoughtless girl."

"If you please, ma'am, it aint my fault. As I was coming home, Mrs. Fowler's servant stopped me, and said her mistress was so ill that she was going for the doctor."

"Well, what has that to do with the matter?"

"I just looked in, and saw Mrs. Fowler, who would not let me go till Ann came back."

"You had no right to look in there. You could be of no use in such a case, besides you know perfectly well that you were keeping me waiting. I want to retire to rest. A pretty time of night truly for you to be gallivanting about—you ought to be ashamed of yourself."

The girl had not confined herself strictly to the truth. Female domestics who hold midnight audiences with life guardsmen seldom do; but part of her story was correct enough.

She had called at Mrs. Fowler's house and seen that lady, but she did not remain with her for more than five minutes at the outside.

Ethel, who was a cunning little puss, sought to change the subject, and an admirable opportunity occurred for her doing so.

She caught sight of the shattered jewel-box, and immediately uttered a faint scream.

"Oh, missis, something's amiss. What has happened?"

"A burglar has entered the house," returned her mistress, "and I might have been robbed and murdered."

"A burglar!" cried the girl. "Oh, mercy upon us, and what has become of him?"

"He has made his escape. I caught him in the act of abstracting the jewels from the case, and at the sight of me he sprang through the window and made off. I have reason to be thankful that no worse has happened."

"Well, I never heard of such audacity!" exclaimed Ethel. "The daring scoundrel!"

"That will do. I don't require any further remarks. I am weary, and shall be glad to seek repose. When you are ready I am."

"Oh, dear me, ma'am, of course I am at your service now. Dear me, my heart's in my mouth, and I come all over with a cold shiver. A burglar! I never heard of such audacity. I am so sorry, ma'am."

"Hold your tongue, do," said Mrs. Metcalf. "I will go to bed at once, if you please."

CHAPTER CV.

THE TWO DETECTIVES—CAPTURE OF A SMASHER—PASSAGES IN THE LIFE OF A DETECTIVE.

CHARLES PEACE, as he wended his way homewards after his escapade at Mr. Metcalf's house, was almost bewildered with the singular adventure that had taken place.

He could not in any way account for the altered position of the girl whom he had been so intimately acquainted with years before at Bradford.

He could not fail to understand that she was altered in every way. Her manners did not appear to resemble those of the mill-hand who was at one time his constant companion.

How the metamorphosis had taken place, and how she was able to assume the grace and demeanour of a well-bred woman to such perfection, was a matter he could not account for.

He felt ashamed of himself, if he ever had any shame in him. The better term would perhaps be that he was deeply mortified.

He had been foiled by a woman. He had let her have it all her own way, had given up the stolen property without a murmur or even so much as a feeble attempt to retain possession of it.

This he did not so much regret, for after all it was but the loss of a few trinkets.

He was too great an adept at his art to repine at being baffled in this instance, but he was very much chagrined at being looked down upon by one whom he had considered at an earlier day as an equal if not an inferior.

"She's done the trick, the saucy jade—done it to rights," he ejaculated. "How she has managed it is another question. Well, I'm regularly queered, but I suppose I shall never know the rights of it—never."

He was of course in a terrible bad humour when he returned to his habitation in the Evelina-road, and half regretted not having returned with Bandy-legged Bill, for he would have given almost anything rather than have encountered Mrs. Metcalf.

It was gall and wormwood to him to see her under the circumstances, but it was too late now—he could not recall the past; he had seen her, and the worst was over. He determined upon avoiding such another rencontre.

Peace, as we have intimated more than once, had very little feeling in his whole composition, but he was at times a prey to jealousy, and he was most certainly both jealous and envious in this case—he was envious of Mrs. Metcalf's superior position.

As far as the woman herself was concerned, he cared perhaps but little about her; but he did not like to be lorded over—he did not like the tone of superiority she assumed, and it is likely enough, under any other circumstances, he would have hurled at her a perfect shower of epithets and virulent abuse. He was, however, unable to do so; upon meeting her in her own house, to use his own expression, he was regularly "floored."

Upon arriving at his own domicile he at once made for the stables. He found "Tommy" properly stalled, and the valuables he had purloined carefully secreted by the gipsy in the place he had named.

So far all was satisfactory, and after seeing to this he retired to rest.

The history of the two women—Mrs. Bristow and Bessie Dalton—is in many respects a romantic one. We have not taken note of them for a long time, but doubtless those who have perused these pages will remember that a number of Bank of England notes were found secreted in a looking-glass—behind the plate and back-board of that useful piece of furniture.

The notes represented in the aggregate many thousands of pounds.

When Mrs. Bristow and her faithful companion and friend, Bessie Dalton, arrived in London they changed their names, as they had changed their condition in life.

Mrs. Bristow, although the wife of a working engineer, was tolerably well connected, certainly better than most women in the same walk of life.

She took an elegant suite of apartments in Brook-street, Grosvenor-square, and having ample means at her disposal, she lived in good style, and in the due course of time contrived to get introduced into society, as it is termed—that is, she became acquainted with people who moved in the upper circles.

Bessie passed as her younger sister, and as time went on they both improved, became more polished in their manners, dropped provincialisms as much as possible, and really turned out very creditable specimens of unostentatious gentility, and were pretty generally liked, for their kindliness of heart and unobtrusive manners and demeanour.

They were introduced to Mr. Metcalf, a rich city merchant, and frequently paid visits at his house at Greenwich.

He was seized with a sudden fit of illness—a virulent fever.

Bessie Dalton volunteered her services as nurse, and her attention was so unremitting, her gentleness was made so manifest on many occasions, that it laid the foundation of a deep and endless love which found its way into the heart of Mr. Metcalf.

The result of all this was an offer of marriage, and Bessie Dalton became the wife of, as she told Charles Peace, an honourable gentleman.

Soon after this Mrs. Bristow found a husband in the person of an obese widower, with two daughters.

This is a brief account of the factory hands who rode to rank and fortune upon a bundle of bank notes found in the looking-glass of a deceased miser.

The history is a romantic one, but not more so than we find in the affairs of every day life. Life is full of romance to those who have the wit to see it, and the one we have been describing is based on fact. This the writer could prove beyond all cavil.

But our scene shifts to other characters in this veritable history.

Mr. Shearman, who had so industriously and cleverly ferreted out the murderer of the American planter's daughter, was, as a matter of course, much chagrined when he heard of Doctor Bourne's suicide.

Justice had been baffled and baulked. It is true the end would have been much the same—with this difference, however, instead of coming by his death from the effects of prussic acid, the doctor would have had to meet his fate on the public scaffold.

Mr. Shearman, in common with the majority of his countrymen, had a certain amount of respect, or, it might be said, admiration for the mother country; he therefore embraced the opportunity afforded him of seeing something of London life before he returned to the United States. He was, as we have already seen, on the best of terms with our old friend Wrench, and at the latter's instigation he had put up at Sanderson's Hotel, where, it will be remembered, Peace sojourned for a short period after his leaving Broxbridge. The buxom widow, Mrs. Sanderson, made the American and the persons he had under his charge—these being the witnesses in the Bourne case—as comfortable as possible, and Mr. Wrench generally dropped in on those evenings upon which he was disengaged to have a friendly chat with Shearman.

To all appearance the American detective liked the old country so well that he was loth to leave it. Anyway he remained as long as circumstances would warrant.

The day, however, was drawing nigh upon which Mr. Shearman was destined to take his departure.

"The best of friends must part," said he, as Mr. Wrench dropped in on the evening before the appointed time. "I've enjoyed myself and seen more of the old country than I ever expected to do this journey, and I have to return you many thanks, Wrench, for all the trouble you have been at on my behalf. If you should ever have to come to the States the first person you will inquire for, I hope and trust, will be me."

"That you may rest assured of."

"It's turned out a bit of a frost this business, but it it can't be helped. Confound old Bourne for making away with himself, say I."

"He's gone to that bourne from whence no traveller returns," observed Wrench, with a smile. "Excuse the pun."

"I'd excuse anything in you; but now you have come we'll make a night of it, as possibly it may be the last we shall be able to pass together for one while."

"Can't be done just now," returned Wrench. "Have a little matter on hand."

"The devil! What—something particularly urgent?"

"Rather so."

"What might it be, if it's a fair question?"

"I'm after an old scoundrel whom I hope to take to-night—he's a well-known thief. We've got one or two cases against him."

"What's he been up to, then?"

"Oh, his old caper—smashing."

"Are you going to pull the string this evening, then?"

"Yes, in less than half an hour."

"And after then?"

"Oh, well, then I shall be at your service."

"Very good then, I'll wait here for you—shall I?"

"Just as you like; or you may go with me, if you prefer it."

"I should much prefer it—very much."

The two detectives in a few minutes after this sallied forth from Sanderson's hotel in quest of the "smasher."

"He's an old hand, I suppose," said Mr. Shearman.

"Old hand, bless you, yes; he's been a thief all his life, but he's a stranger to me, or rather was, but a few days ago. I saw a chap yesterday, who had six years' penal servitude; met him by chance in the street. He is leading an honest course of life now, and has been doing so for some years. He's one of the few that have reformed. Well, this old scoundrel, whose arrest for smashing I am bent on I did not know much about. Well, as I was saying, I met the other one, whose name is Kedge. I asked him if he knew anything about my "smasher."

"Know? Of course," said he. "Why you know who he is—don't you?"

"Well, no, I can't say that I do."

"He had ten years for breaking into a public-house in Oxford-street sixteen years ago. Well, after his return from transportation, he goes to the public, calls for something to drink, and as he stood in front of the bar he asked the landlord if he kept the house sixteen years before. 'No,' says the landlord, 'I did not.' 'Sure on it,' says Hardy—that's his name, though he calls himself Mr. Dawes—'sure on it?' says he."

"Quite sure," says the landlord, "who, I fancy, suspected something was wrong."

"Well, then, I b'lieve you're telling a thundering lie. Do you remember charging a man with burglary sixteen years ago?"

"No, I do not," says the landlord. "I never charged anyone with burglary in all my born days."

"I'm glad on it," said Hardy, "for if you'd been the man as got me convicted of burglary, I'd have had yer life—that's all."

"You see, Mr. Wrench," said Kedge, "Hardy wasn't sartin about his being the same man, and it's likely enough the landlord saved his life by declaring he was not the person who kept the house sixteen years before. Of course he was greatly altered in his appearance—so much so that the returned convict did not know him."

"It was lucky for the bung," observed Shearman.

"Very lucky, for he's a desperate old scoundrel is this Dawes, as he now calls himself, but I shall be able to prove several previous convictions against him, I've no doubt, but let me make sure of my man first."

Mr. Wrench made the best of his way to Drury-lane. In one of the narrow turnings, which led from that place to Great Wild-street, the smasher resided, and it was to this turning that our two detectives were bending their steps.

It was the resort of thieves and all sorts of disreputable characters, many of whom were well known to the police. They had got about twenty yards or so down the court or alley, when Mr. Wrench was accosted by a woman who was a native of the Emerald Isle.

"Ah, good luck to ye, Mr. Wrench," said the woman, making a curtsey. "An' it's right ye are this time if any jintleman iver was. Oh, sure, now aint he fast asleep in the front room, and a snorin' like a dozen fat hogs?"

"He's in his room, Winny, is he?" cried Wrench.

"Didn't I see him myself wid my own precious eyes not a moment ago? Oh, bedad, he's a waitin' for ye, and no mistake at all at all."

"That's all right, then, Winny; we'll pay the gentleman a visit."

"Oh, the thief of the world; but he's a dirty circumvinting blackguard, mek the best av him. But arrah don't ye be afther saying a word about me, or maybe he'd be a little rampageous like."

"I won't mention your name—depend upon that," said Wrench. "We never do that in cases of this sort; besides, you know, there is no occasion."

"Thin, I'll be afther going, or maybe he might suspect something. Oh, but ye've jest come in the nick of time. My duty to ye, Mr. Wrinch, and good luck to ye."

The old Irishwoman at once disappeared from the scene. Whither she went Mr. Shearman had not the faintest notion; neither did he take the trouble to inquire.

The detectives now arrived in front of a miserably dirty and dilapidated habitation; indeed, it was so covered with filth, and such an offensive odour came from the place, that Mr. Shearman half regretted having set out on the expedition.

Mr. Wrench went into the passage, opened the door of the front room and entered. He was followed by the American. On a dirty mattress which was on a ricketty bedstead, an old man was stretched—that he was sleeping soundly was evident enough.

Mr. Wrench nodded significantly to Shearman.

"Your man?" whispered the latter.

"Yes, that's my gentleman."

The room was dimly illumined by a gas lamp in the court, the feeble rays of which found their way through the dingy window panes. There was, therefore, light enough to distinguish the features of the sleeping man with tolerable distinctness.

"Now then, wake up, man! you are wanted," cried Mr. Wrench, in a loud voice.

The sleeper uttered a kind of sigh or groan, and then, opening his eyes, he beheld those of an officer looking into his own.

"Curses on you, what brings you here?" cried the "smasher." "Get out—will you? Leave me alone."

"Come, come, Dawes, you're wanted, and you are my prisoner."

"What for? I aint done anything. It's a lie, I aint your prisoner, and don't intend to be."

He sprang out of bed and glared round the room like a wild beast.

"Get away, will you?" cried he. "If you don't—" he paused suddenly, and made a hideous grimace, which he intended for a look of defiance.

"Wall, stranger," said Shearman, "it's no good hollering. You're cornered—aint got a ghost of a chance. The game's up, you'd better go quietly."

"Who are you, I should like to know; and what business have either of you here?" cried the "smasher," making a hideous grimace, which he intended to be a look of defiance.

"If you are going to ride rusty," observed Mr. Wrench, "say so, and we shall know what to do."

"Perhaps you will first of all tell me what you have come here for? I aint done nuthin' as I know of."

"Well, that is a matter of opinion. You are charged with passing bad money—with 'smashing,' and you are my prisoner."

"It's a lie. I aint passed any bad money for ever so long, and so you may take your change out of that, Mr. Wrench."

"I am not here to take any change, as you term it, but I shall have to take you, and you had better put on your coat and hat and come along with me to Bow-street."

Mr. Wrench had observed upon his first entrance a sort of trap-door in the centre of the room. The boards had been cut away so as to afford a place of retreat for the "smasher." Had he succeeded in passing through this into the cellar below, he would doubtless have succeeded in making his escape, but our detective had the forethought to stand on the trap while he was interrogating the man, Dawes.

"You see," he said, with admirable coolness, addressing himself to the smasher, "there is no chance for you to effect an escape, so come on at once. The game is up."

"Curses on you!" exclaimed Dawes. "You're a meddling dirty crew, the whole lot of you, and if I had my way you would have been sent to kickereboo long ago."

"Oh, I dare say—but you see fellows of your class are not permitted to have it all your own way. Now then, man, look sharp. Put on your coat and hat at once, or otherwise I shall have to take you as you are."

The man was only partially dressed, having on only his shirt and trousers.

In appearance he was a ruffian of the very worst type, and had there been a chance he would have offered an obstinate resistance, but he was taken by surprise and did not see very clearly any way of getting out of his present difficulty.

"Vell," he said, in a sulky tone, "if yer vants me, which I 'spose yer do, I'd better put on my togs and be off with you."

A MAGNIFICENT BLACK WAS BROUGHT BY THE OSTLER, AND THE STRANGER MOUNTED.

He went to a corner of the room, drew forth a coat and waistcoat, which he put on in a leisurely manner; then he drew on a pair of highlows and, lastly, his hat. When this had been done he made a sudden rush towards the door in the hope of making his escape, but Mr. Wrench, who had been watching him, was prepared for this; he tripped his man up—and as he lay on the floor clapped a pair of handcuffs on his wrists, and then told him to get up.

Dawes was by this time completely cowed; he rose to his feet, cast a malevolent look upon the American and Mr. Wrench, and then walked towards the door, held firmly the while by the English detective, who conducted him safely enough to Bow-street, where,

No. 56.

after the charge had been entered, he was locked up till the morning, when he would be taken before the magistrate.

"He was disposed to be nasty," said Mr. Shearman to his companion, after they had left the police station, "and is a sort of gentleman I fancy who wouldn't stick at a trifle."

"Oh, dear me, no—a regular bad un. Wouldn't mind what he did if he only had the chance."

"Is the evidence fully clear?"

"It is. We've got him as straight as an arrow. There's half a dozen cases against him. Oh, he's safe to be convicted; he knows that well enough. He is a most daring and determined 'smasher.' Just to give you an idea how these fellows carry on their business I'll tell you of one case. A shop was opened a few days ago in the neighbourhood of Oxford-street. It was a publication and cigar business, which was left in charge of a young girl, the niece of the proprietor. On the day it was first opened one of the smashing fraternity went into the shop and bought half a quire of note paper. He tendered a florin, which the girl changed. Half an hour afterwards another of the same respectable body of men purchased some tobacco. He also tendered a florin, which was changed. Six florins were taken in the course of the day and five shillings. Upon the proprietor of the establishment coming home in the evening he was delighted to find that there had been so many customers; but, alas! upon his looking over his money he found that the six florins and five shillings were all bad ones."

"And where do the rascals get all these bad coins from?" inquired Mr. Shearman.

"They are sent up in boxes or cases from one or more of our provincial towns, and bought by the 'smashers' for next door to nothing. The man I have just 'quodded' has been following the calling for years."

CHAPTER CV.

AT "SANDERSON'S HOTEL"—RECOLLECTIONS OF AN AMERI-
CAN DETECTIVE.

AFTER a little further conversation the two friends reached "Sanderson's Hotel," where Mr. Wrench spent the remainder of the evening with the American.

"I like the old country after all," said Shearman, "though a good many of my countrymen run it down, and, as far as expert thieves are concerned, you beat us into an almighty smash."

"That's a very doubtful sort of compliment," observed Wrench, with a smile, "but I will not attempt to deny the statement. I believe we do. A London rough is a match for any one in brutality."

"By the way," said Shearman, "what became of that horse-stealer, the gipsy, you were in search of? Did you ever find him?"

"No. Well, the fact is, I have given up the search. The gentleman from whom the horse was stolen don't care about prosecuting now."

"Why not?"

"He don't—that's all I know. The fact is, he was persuaded to do so by Bourne, and now the doctor's dead he's disposed to let the matter drop. He says Rawton is not so bad as he has been painted."

"What's your opinion?"

"If I am to speak the truth I am of the same opinion. It was nothing but spite, revenge, or whatever you may please to term it, that made Bourne so bitter with the gipsy."

"'Twas a nice article to give himself airs and graces, and do the virtuous."

"Yes, particularly so—wasn't he?"

"I had one scrimmage with a horse thief which I shan't easily forget," said Shearman. "He was a resolute rascal, surely. I'll tell you all about it. Light up another cigar before I begin."

Mr. Wrench did as he was bid.

"You must know," observed Shearman, who was never so happy as when recounting one or more of his adventures, "that I had been furnished by an Omaha express firm with the means to ferret out a horse thief, by whose operations they had lost some ten animals. Being persuaded by information, too tedious to detail, that the purloiner had gone to Silver Creek, on the Pacific Railroad, I proceeded to that unknown settlement, and immediately commenced operations.

"The man and his habits were so familiar to me from repeated description that I felt certain of identifying him in some of the many faro establishments of the place; or, failing in them, in one of the multitudinous fire-water dispensaries.

"One night I visited all the gambling banks unsuccessfully. The next I proceeded to inspect the drinking places. The first one was a large frame house, which I entered, and, while drinking, quickly scrutinised every face and incident.

"In the middle of the room, upon a huge barrel, stood a red-faced, broad-shouldered Irishman, in his one hand a bottle, in the other a glass; on the floor, close to the barrel's base, crouched an ill-looking mastiff who eyed around savagely.

"At the bar was a tall man waiting the replenishing of his flask. His hat concealed half his face, and a scarlet handkerchief wound round his neck buried in its greasy folds a mass of matted, gipsy-like hair.

"I caught him glancing furtively at me when entering, then saw him turn his back; so I kept my eye brisk for any suspicious incident.

"Suddenly the Irishman, who all along had been afternately singing in his native dialect and absorbing spirits, fell headlong upon the dog, whizzing the glass and bottle across the floor with a crash.

"Simultaneously with his fall out went the light. The reeling man had clutched and wrenched the fixture from the ceiling. Now it was confusion with a vengeance.

"The different card-playing groups, deprived of light, rose from the tables, and each gainer or loser struggled for the little heaps and balls of money.

"Noises from shouts and loud curses from the hard breathing through the clenched teeth of combatants filled the room; and in this pandemonium I nearly gave up all hope of nabbing my man.

"In the midst of the confusion the door opened, the clear moonlight streaming in. Stepping across the sill I saw the man with the red kerchief.

"Ere this I had decided that this one was no other than the thief I was after; so I made a spring towards the door, but came to the ground stunned and bruised. Rising, with bleeding face, I saw that I had fallen over the prostrate Hibernian. I rushed out and ran to my horse—he was gone!

"Clattering hoofs, gradually lessening in sound, told me that the thief had outwitted me—gone on my own horse. I chafed considerably at the discomfiture, but only for a moment, detectives having little time for sentiments of any kind.

"Without any exact purpose, I started off in the direction of the decreasing sound, and suddenly came upon a team of mules.

"In predicaments necessitating immediate action, we sometimes hit upon expedients which at other times might seem ridiculous.

"So now with me; I cut the breeching and traces of the saddle mule, vaulted on his back, and scampered after the appropriator of my horseflesh.

"I knew well that my horse was too fagged for much riding; and as the animal I bestrode was fresh from the stable, I was pretty sure of making my captive, if it was to be determined by speed alone.

"Moreover, my mule being miraculously void of the attributes of his race—obstinacy and slow gait—warmed to work, and gradually the thud of the hoofs ahead became more distinct."

"Ah, you are a good rider, I suppose?" observed Wrench.

"Pretty well—aint you?"

"Nothing much to boast of."

"Ah, but a fellow must know how to ride in America well."

"In twenty minutes, on the moon-lit road, one-fourth of a mile ahead, I saw the man mounting a hillock at a far less rapid pace than mine. At last I come so near that I discerned two pistols stuck in his belt.

"I disengaged my own weapons, but did not fire, the rascal's irregular motion—darting in and out of the skirting woods—excluded the possibility of hitting him.

"I called him to halt, at forty yards, levelled, and then let fly at him; a strange, agonising cry arose at the report; galloping through the smoke, I came upon a prostrate horse, no man.

"A crunching of crisp leaves among the trees betrayed the quick footsteps of the fugitive. Dashing into the woods, at three paces came a shot from the forest gloom, laying my mule stark dead, I leaping off just in time to escape a crushed limb.

"I whipped behind a tree, straining to see my assailant, but I heard and saw nothing; so creeping cautiously back, I found my horse dying and the mule dead. Being a good distance from town, I had no choice but to camp out or foot a weary journey home.

"Mounting a low tree, I espied, far in the woods, a bright fire, which I knew was a camp of railroad labourers.

"After a two-mile walk I entered a circle of gambling, smoking, low-talking men of different nationalities, receiving a rough welcome.

"To my inquiries I found they had heard the shots, but such things were too common to notice; and about ten the most of the camp fell asleep.

"I entered a small log tenement belonging to the boss, the hospitality of which was tendered me by that worthy himself; and the company not being very assuring of safety, prepared to take a watchful sleep.

"The boss, however, was, as he told me, above the generality of his class as to family and education, having come out of the States for the sake of adventure.

"He sat up late, playing with a large, glossy Newfoundland; talking over the topics of the day, and relating many anecdotes of the stirring life in the Western land. Inspired by some excellent punch, I told him my whole adventure, describing minutely the man who had so miraculously eluded me.

"He listened thoughtfully, then said he doubted of my ever capturing him, because of the many desperadoes swarming along the line of the roadsmen—who held law officers as foes to the death, and who would espouse the cause of any rascal against them.

"Finally we both fell asleep, after I had bargained with him for a horse. Aurora had just arisen from her gray couch, as a shout and bustling without made us both leap from our slumber.

"A violent beating at the door, nearly shaking it from its fastening, accompanied by vociferations for the boss, impelled my host to begin rapidly drawing the door bolts, but I clutched his arm and told him to stop, for I had distinctly heard my name pronounced without. We listened; a savage voice yelled:

"'Sind the blackguard out; it's Shearman, the detective, an' shure he's afther Scrubby, the spalpeen! Sind him out, or be jabers we'll have both av ye out, ye bloodsuckers!'

"A pick came hurling, and thrust its four inches through the door; a huge missile fell violently upon the roof, almost coming through. Terribly serious was it becoming. The boss commanded them to desist, but was greeted by a tornado of rocks, spades, &c., thudding over every inch of the edifice.

"Two bullets now buried themselves in the doorpost, three inches more and they would have entered the superintendent's heart. Seeing nothing but our death would allay their drunken rage, the boss declared his intention of fighting to the last.

"We grasped hands and then piled all the available moveables against the door; and then charged the three rifles and four revolvers we had.

"We both ascended into a low loft over the room, the eaves of the roof forming a narrow opening near the floor. We knelt down and peered out. About thirty men, most intoxicated, armed with excavating tools and firearms, were grouped a little way off, gesticulating and reeling at a terrible rate.

"Though divested of his scarlet kerchief, I recognised my horse-thief. Communicating my discovery to my companion, he said that when I first described the rascal he thought he knew him, for his name was entered on the work-list yesterday when he came from Omaha.

"'And depend upon it,' added the boss, 'he has escaped some criminal penalty in other settlements than Omaha.'

"The lull in the human tempest was now accounted for. Part of the crowd were now engaged in belabouring four Chinamen who had refused to join in the assault; the rest were hilarious witnesses of the performance.

"At last, the luckless Celestials being punched into speechlessness, attention was turned on us. Not to betray our refuge, the boss slipped down the ladder and ordered our assailants once more to desist, as we were prepared to kill, if necessary, and determined to rather die than surrender. A renewed bombardment of projectiles inconceivable was their response.

"'Now Shearman,' said the boss, "use your weapon well, for the way things look, I dont think we could procure life assurance policies on any terms. However, we can stand a siege if fire is not enlisted on the enemy's side. We have provisions and water below for a week, and half a cwt. of bullets and powder. But, by Jove, this roof will never stand such missiles as the one that Irishman is picking up; and it is not proof against the balls of that crack rifle your friend o' the scarlet kerchief is loading; so we'll put these planks along this side, and keep them from bringing fire to the door—that would be death. See him! look!

"The Irishman was drawing back to hurl that death and ruin-dealing rock when the boss fired; the man dropped in his tracks, the heavy stone falling on his face.

"The wild drunken crowd rushed at the door with yells of drunken madness. Four small puffs and fla[...]

issued from under the eaves; the rabble drew back pell-mell, leaving three stretched upon the ground.

"Our precise locality being thus discovered, the bullets came thick and fast, and the efficacy of the planks was proven—a dozen balls perforated the roof, but lodged in the stout boards.

"Suddenly I saw the horse thief partially slip from shelter and poise his deadly-looking rifle. I was aware that its contents would pierce our barricades, and not being able to pick the fellow off in his position, I sprang aside, dragging the boss with me.

"Hardly done ere whizz went the ball through a spot of the plank where my brain was the preceding instant, and buried itself in the noble Newfoundland's heart.

"With a mournful cry of agony the brute sprang up, and fell across his master's knees. The boss stroked his glossy coat, then a strange gleam flashed in his eyes.

"We both fired at the slayer—he dropped, then sprang up, and savagely laughing whipped behind a tree.

"By this time, from continual battering, the door hung loosely on its broken hinges; nevertheless, our fire kept the mob from attempting the breach, and finally they retreated far back in the forest, giving us a respite to refresh and contemplate our begrimed and bruised faces, our arms discoloured, and trembling from violent exertion, for we had begun the struggle at dawn; it now wanted one hour of noon.

"Suddenly a wreath of smoke curled up from the tree; firing and shouting again were rampant; and we got a glimpse of the horse-thief darting from tree to tree, at last bringing up behind a huge oak, exactly in front of which and opposite our citadel grew a tall, flexible sapling.

"The man clutched a roaring brand, and I saw his hand cautiously creep around the tree trunk toward the sapling. Then I fired at his huge palm; but he drew it back too quickly. When the smoke cleared away, we saw the sapling bent behind the tree—the man, unseen, busily attaching something to the branches.

"We wondered at these proceedings, but the mystery soon cleared up; the sapling bent back, touching the ground, then sprang forward with elastic violence, and from its branches, like a meteor, darted a glancing, hissing brand, lodging on our frail roof with an ominous thud. In unison came a joyful shout from the villains, who made a rush for the door."

"My word, you were hardly pressed," exclaimed Wrench.

"Ah, it's nothing to what followed. It was a smartish piece of business—take it altogether.

"Pell-mell, firing, &c., on rushed that mass of brutal, drunken strength, thirsting for the lives of us two men. A well-timed volley drove them back, less by four; but on the forest-edge stood the horse-thief, exultingly pointing to the blazing roof.

"The solar rays of noon, the roof in a whirlwind of flame, and the dense smoke made the house a suffocating oven; hot cinders fell upon us, and the floor below in perilous proximity to the powder; glowing coals fell upon our bare breasts, and put us in momentary agony.

"Death stood at our shoulders, and Hope did not accompany him. Seconds now were priceless.

"We dashed down the ladder as a heavy beam fell from the roof, and left the loft open to the shots of the enemy. Quickly the boss pulled up a trap from the floor, pushed me down, sprang in himself, and shut and bolted it.

"The rapid tramp of feet overhead told our escape was none too soon; we heard the reckless fiends tearing away the barricades, shouting in expectant revenge.

"I followed the boss along a narrow, low, excavated passage, till coming into a sort of cellar, which he said was the storage place for the spirits, he exclaimed, hoarsely—

"'Take this pick, and dig for your life, through the wall, upward; after bursting the spirit-barrel, I will do the same.'"

"What a position to be in!" observed Wrench.

"Well, I can't say I have ever had anything so hot as that.

"Neither should I care for such another dose. Of course you understand that I was in uniform, and serving my country as a volunteer at this time."

"No, I did not quite understand that."

"Ah, but I was; although a mere detective, I could handle a rifle with the best of them.

"Well, I need not tell you that I worked as I never worked before—the axe tore down the earth in masses —the darkness, the perilous mystery in that I was doing, the faint-heard shouts of the wretches above, storming about the burning house, the flames roaring, the wood crashing, wrought me up to a herculean frenzy.

"The spirit-cask was now staved; ankle deep in the fiery contents we both worked, like Gog and Magog of yore; suddenly a huge lump of mould rolled down, light and air pouring in upon us. Tear! wrench! a fissure sufficient for human egress presented itself; quickly dragging ourselves through, we stood in a thick clump of low rose bushes, where we lay peering out towards the roaring mass of flame, and through the smoke endeavoured to get a sight of the murderous rascals who ran riot amidst the flames.

"Hark! The riot lulls; a thud of hoofs, a regular monotonous clanking—ah, we knew those sounds. Rushing out of the bushes, we came upon a cavalry squad, holding at bay the drunken crowd.

"We shouted to the officer in charge to order a surround, which was quickly done; then followed explanation. In the excitement of the scene I had almost forgotten the man with the scarlet kerchief; now I thought of him.

"Looking sharply around I espied him creeping off towards the place where the boss's horses were tethered.

"There is the ringleader, Dan Whipple, the horse-thief; in the law's name, lieutenant, I order you to help capture that man!'

"Saying this, I threw myself on the nearest horse, followed by four soldiers; but he had reached the tetherage, and we saw him galloping through the woods, far ahead, saddleless, and managing his nag with a mere halter.

"Our horses and his were about the same mettle, and we gained nothing on him. The soldiers told me they had left Silver Creek in search of this Dan Whipple, who, in the open street, had stolen a mule from a team about to set out with a colonel's camp furniture; that on the road they had come upon a dead horse and the stolen mule with a bullet-hole in his head, being at a loss to account for it; however, they had pressed on in hopes of capturing the outlaw.

"They had not gone far before they heard shots and saw smoke, and after a sharp ride came upon the camp.

"I did not enlighten them in regard to the mule, but kept a look-out for the fugitive. Although during the civil war the popular estimation of Government horse flesh was not very great, nevertheless these Western war steeds were not at all despicable, for they brought us near enough to get a sight of our prey; but just then the mare whisked into the woods and was invisible.

"An ejaculation of a soldier caused me to turn my head, and, fifty feet right behind us, came on the horse the rascal had two minutes before bestrode.

"We looked at each other astonished. One man secured the horse, and I ordered the troops to proceed with me to the place where the thief had darted into the forest. We scrutinised every bush and hollow closely; for the moves of the man were so sudden and unexpected that I looked for a fatal shot from every corner.

"In apparent despair, I ordered the men to face homeward as our prey had certainly escaped us. We had not gone far, however, before I signed them to keep on slowly, while I lightly dismounted and made a large circuit, until I stood hidden in the bush, ten paces from a certain large tree I had noticed.

"Yes, the branches swayed in a manner not at all natural. First a limb rather high up moved queerly; then a lower one; now one farther down; and so the strange motion was communicated till the legs of a man appeared beneath the lowermost branch. I cocked my pistol.

"Gradually the body of the veritable Dan Whipple came down till he hung by the hands. Now was the time. Wishing merely to disable him, I aimed for his legs.

"'Ping, ping,' went those barrels. He tried hard to draw himself up into the tree. Then hung by one hand, with the other endeavouring to detach a weapon.

"But it was too much for him. He dropped to the ground with a heavy thud. I pounced upon him, held him by the throat, my knee on his chest, shouting for the soldiers.

"A cavalryman detached from his saddle a pair of iron cuffs, originally intended for the appropriator of the luckless mule, and the unenviable ornaments speedily enveloped the captive's wrists. The wound not seeming serious, we placed him astride his last booty and started for camp.

"To conclude, suffice it to note, that the rioters were liberated with the exception of a few of the most prominent, who were sentenced to some months' labour at the garrison in Silver Creek.

"There was no convenient penitentiary in the locality; besides men were in demand by the P. R. R.— therefore they were set at large. As for Dan Whipple, it was found necessary, after surgical examination, to amputate his wounded limb; but his thiefship obstinately refused to undergo the beneficial operation, and three days after his capture he died miserably from the effects of gangrene; thus preventing me from taking him to Omaha, to be subjected to lawful justice by the injured express firm—my employers.

"In justice to the departed purloiner of other people's horses so as to obliterate from his record at least one crime, I explained to the military authorities the abstraction of the mule from the team, and was cleared of all intention of joining the profession, of which Mr. Whipple was such a prominent member.

"The labour superintendent, since these adventures were shared, has often met me, and we have undergone the same perils over and over — in words."

CHAPTER CVI.

A GLANCE AT BROXBRIDGE—THE ROBBERY AT NETTLE-THORP—A VISIT TO MOTHER BAGLEY—A STRANGER AT THE FARM HOUSE.

WE must beg of the reader to accompany us once more to Broxbridge, which has been the scene of so many important events in connection with our history. Since our last visit to this place time has made many sad alterations.

Old Mr. Jamblin has passed away from the living things of the earth, and his daughter and son-in-law are in full possession of Stoke Ferry Farm. The old rascal with the scythe, forelock, and hour-glass, has dealt mercifully with the noble earl at the Hall; nevertheless Lord Ethalwood gives unmistakable indications of advancing years.

He does not shoot or hunt so much as he used to do of yore, his fine frame is a little bent, and his step has lost a something of its elasticity; but despite all these drawbacks he is a fine specimen of England's boasted aristocracy, and it is pretty generally admitted that there is not such another aristocracy in the world.

Think of the American honourables, and spit from nausea as they do from fashion; think of the Continental counts, who are as numerous and as dirty as the paving-stones of a London street.

An English nobleman has the breeding of a French marquis before the Revolution, the majesty of a Spanish hidalgo, the phlegm and equanimity of a German baron. He can show you a pedigree which has no beginning, for its roots are buried in the obscurity of tradition, and which will end only with the world itself. He can show you his name crowned with fresh laurels in each fresh generation, and then he can show you himself—brave and loyal as his ancestors, should his services be needed for his country or his sovereign.

It has been said that we live in degenerate times, that the age of chivalry has passed, and that the English aristocracy are not the proud and noble race they were. And it cannot be denied that some members of noble families are frivolous, enervated, and deficient in mental power, but they are the exceptions, not the rule.

Lord Ethalwood, as we have already intimated, was a fine sample of his order. His leading fault was his indomitable pride and his undisguised contempt for the lower classes.

When his daughter was divorced from her husband he seemed for some time to have taken a fresh lease of his life. As a matter of course the Lady Aveline was surrounded with admirers, and the greater portion of her time was spent in London.

Mr. Jakyl, like his master, was falling into the "sear and yellow leaf," but he had the same soft, unobtrusive, respectful manner as of yore. As to the radiant footman, Henry Adolphus, he got sick of service, and yearned to be his own master.

He jilted the young female he was engaged to, and paid marked and persistent attention to Nell Fulford, whom Peace had been smitten with in an earlier day, and who afterwards became the mistress of Philip Jamblin.

These circumstances, however, did not appear to have any great weight with Henry Adolphus, who, in the course of time, made up his mind to pop the question. At first he was refused, but as he was a man not to be easily cast on one side, and chose to press his suit again and again, he was ultimately accepted, and he led Nell to the hymeneal altar.

After his wedding he started in the green-grocery line, had a big plate-glass front put into the old shop, originally owned by Nell's aunt, and drove a very prosperous trade; he served the hall, Brickett, and a host of the surrounding gentry and tradespeople; and it is but justice to him for us to signify that he made Nell an excellent husband.

Brickett still kept the "Carved Lion," and would often, when in a contemplative mood, wonder what had become of Charles Peace, but it was only to his particular cronies that he would broach the subject, for Peace by this time was looked upon as a daring and hardened offender, and the more discreet portion of the villagers forbore from mentioning his name or making any allusion to him.

Let us now take a glance at Stoke Ferry Farm. The external appearance of this English homestead we described in a preceding chapter.

Now there is seated on the roughly-hewn bench before the front door, a bright-eyed, dimpled-cheeked young woman twittering to a baby which she holds in her arms, the female in question being none other than she whom we have known as Patty Jamblin. She is now Mrs. Richard Ashbrook.

She caresses the child—she talks sweet gibberish to it with her lips; doubtless the words she gave utterance to were but a mere sound to the child, but, to all appearance, it is a pleasing sound, for the little thing "rears its creasy arms" and smiles, and sometimes the young mother, sustaining her offspring with one arm, would stroke its face with her fingers, which were soft and delicate.

And ever and anon she would look down the long white road, which was only lost to view among the dark and distant woods.

She was evidently expecting something or someone, for her glance was earnest and frequent.

Presently her eyes brightened, and she tossed the baby gaily in the air, the infant uttering loud and rapid screams, which no one but a mother or one who had been accustomed to children could have understood to be demonstrations of delight.

The black dot in the distance had now become a man on horseback, who galloped towards the farmhouse enthroned in a cloud of dust.

"It is Richard," cried Patty. "I knew it by the manner he rode—it is he."

She was right enough, it was her husband, who upon arriving at the front gate called lustily out for Joe, the same Joe who had been so intimately connected with the discovery of the murderer of Philip Jamblin. He was still retained on the establishment.

His master gave him injunctions to rub the mare down well.

"I'd no business to put her out to such a pace, especially as there's a bit of a hill. However, she'll be none the worse for it if she's well looked after. A horse should always go cool into the stable—rub her down. I'm desperately behind to-day, there's no doubt about that, but she went along bravely though, and is as good as gold to any man."

"She'll be all right," said Joe. "I'll see to that; don't you concern yourself about her."

"Dear me, you have been a time," cried Patty. "I thought you would never come back; but here you are—and that's enough."

She placed her hand upon his broad shoulder, and rising on tiptoe kissed him tenderly.

He took her in his arms and they kissed each other repeatedly. Oh, it is a pretty sight these meetings of husband and wife after the day's work is done.

When they have been separated for a few hours they greet each other with the warmth which follows an absence of years.

They have carried each other's photographs in their mind; having cherished the emblems all day long, they spring to each other's arms with transports which the forethought has prepared.

What a contrast these two persons afford to the matrimonial life of Mr. and Mrs. Bourne—the one is unalloyed happiness, the other supreme misery.

"And now, sir," said Patty, endeavouring to call up a frown, "what have you to say for yourself? How is it you have kept your wife waiting in this way?"

"Couldn't help it, dear."

"And why not?"

"Well, in the first place, I had got to start 'em right with their sowing for the spring wheat, and after that I made over to Oakfield."

"To Oakfield, eh?"

"Yes, one of my chaps told me John was not at all the thing, and I was a bit anxious, you see."

"And how did you find him then?"

"Oh, only middling—very middling one might say. He don't seem to ha' a bit a life about him."

"Nothing serious, I hope?"

"Oh, no; but Maude, poor gell, troubles herself a goodish bit. Well, it aint to be wondered at. He gets such strange notions in his head. I must go over there for a day or two, and give him a good talking to, else—hang me, if he won't go melancholy mad or summat."

"However, let's hope he'll mend. I suppose dinner's pretty well cooled by this time, eh?"

"It won't be too hot, I dare say, but the girl has set it down before the fire."

The husband and wife went into the front parlour, where dinner was served. Richard Ashbrook was as hungry as a hunter, and did ample justice to the repast set before him.

"I'm sorry to hear so poor an account of John, though," observed Patty. "Very sorry, but he mustn't give way."

"No, of course not; half his ailment proceeds from the mind. The doctor says he's a—hip—adriach, or summat of that sort. I aint quite got hold of the right word, but I dessay we shouldn't be much the wiser if I had."

"It's a longish word, aint it?"

"Oh, yes; an' you've got to jolt it out if you want to make anything of it; but I say, old gell, I've got some news to tell 'ee—summat as 'ill surprise 'ee."

"Lor! Out wi' it, then; tell us what it is."

"Why, I dessay you remember carroty-head Nettlethorpe, him as you used to be spooney on before you were silly enough to marry me."

"Spooney on Nettlethorpe! Get out with you."

"Well, we won't dispute about that."

"Don't be so foolish, Richard!" cried Patty, pouting.

"There, don't be crabby. I was only joking, you know that well enough."

"Go on with what you were about to say."

"Old Nettlethorpe's been robbed."

"Never! Why it will kill him."

"Oh, you may well say that. He's been robbed, house broken into, strong-box opened, and all the money he and his amiable sister had stinted themselves of, for I don't know how many years, gone in one night. Think of that."

"Well you do surprise me," returned Patty. "Poor fellow, it is cruel though, most cruel of anyone to take a man's all."

"It is, you are quite right; but do you know people —a goodish many—say that it serves the beggarly screws right? They starved themselves, and worse than that starved their servants and watered the men's beer at harvest time."

"So father used to say."

"Yes, and he was right; they gave the men shorter wages than any other farmer, and when there was a holiday given all over the land made 'em do work the night before, and that they did, too, and ploughed by moonlight."

"But suppose there was no moon," said Patty, with a laugh, "did they find the men rushlights?"

"Ah, you may make light of the matter, missus, but it's a fact nevertheless. Still I don't wish Nettlethorpe any harm; he's a pinch-and-starve farmer, it is true, but that's no reason for his being robbed, for after all it can't be less trouble to them to lose what they came by hardly and honestly than it is for folks as be more open-handed, and we ought'n be glad that mischief is done to a neighbour, whatever that neighbour may be. 'Never rejoice at nobody's downfall,' my old father used to say, and a good saying it be."

"You are quite right—it must be a hard blow for them, and it must be harder to find that people are glad because of it. But how did it occur? Whoever could have been wicked enough to commit such an act?"

"Oh, there are plenty who are wicked enough if they only had the chance—you may depend upon that; but I haven't heard the particulars. I tell you what we'll do."

"Well—what?"

"Presently we'll go up to old mother Bagley's, and she'll be sure to know the whole history of the affair by heart—trust her for that."

"Excellent thought; we'll pay a visit to the old dame then."

Soon after this Mrs. Ashbrook went upstairs to put on her things, for the purpose of paying the visit agreed upon.

Upon coming down again she found her husband waiting at the front door, when he scolded her goodhumouredly for having been so long with her bonnet and shawl.

This is by no means an uncommon complaint with husbands.

She gave him back his jokes transformed into repartees, and thrust her wrist through the loop of his arm.

They walked along the bare white road for about a mile and a half. As they proceeded along Ashbrook said—

"I tell'ee what it is, Patty—it's my belief that Charles Peace 'as had a hand in this business. People say he's the most desperate and determined burglar out."

"Oh, Richard, dear, be just," returned his wife. "It don't seem fair to accuse a man without the faintest scrap of evidence against him."

"Well, I dunno as it is, but it's just like one of his tricks."

"But he has not been seen in the neighbourhod for years."

They presently turned aside through a gate which opened on a footpath which led to Mother Bagley's cottage.

This humble habitation stood in a field, with no safeguards from solitude but a walnut tree, hollowed by lightning, a pair of apple trees, a microscopic garden of cabbages and potatoes, and a high untrimmed hedge, in which bloomed, side by side, the last convolvuluses of summer and the first berries of approaching winter.

The cottage was small and compact. It did not ramble over a fraction of an acre as most cottages do, and its appearance made one believe that it was not the home of a common peasant.

In point of fact, Mrs. Bagley was the relict of an old servant of the earl's.

When her husband died Lord Ethalwood made her a present of the habitation in which she now resided, and in addition to this he settled on her a small annuity, which sufficed for all her wants.

The earl never let any of his dependents come to want, and this was only one instance out of numberless others of his kindness in this respect.

Mrs. Bagley lived a secluded, almost solitary life, and yet contrived to acquaint herself with every tittle of parish gossip. She knew everything, and anybody wanting information need only to consult her.

Whenever there was a mystery it was to old Mother Bagley that the cronies of the village resorted, as if she had been a sibyl or a priestess of the oracle of Delphos.

The interior of her house was remarkably clean and neat, the articles of furniture were so many varied mirrors, her tiny poker, tongs, and shovel were as bright as a set of surgical instruments, and the very smoke seemed to go carefully up the chimney, curling and twisting and rolling itself into the smallest possible compass, as if doing its best not to leave any soot behind.

Mrs. Bagley was a character in her way—one of those oddities one seldom meets with nowadays. She possessed a Bible, prayer-book, a pair of spectacles, and a snuff-box.

With these she amused herself all day long, or, to speak more correctly, during that portion of it upon which she was not otherwise engaged, for, being a lady of gregarious habits for all her solitary life, she had innumerable droppers in, who were, of course, village gossips.

Like most old peasant women, she was an inveterate tea drinker, and her favourite beverage was always brewing by the fireside.

The teapot was a round, red, little thing about the size and shape of an apple dumpling, with a spout like a baby's finger, and the lid made fast to the handle with a silver chain.

This cleanly old woman took snuff, it is true—of the light yellow pungent species—for she was a victim to headaches, the natural result of incessant twankay or souchong, but she took it without permitting a grain to fall upon her Bible or her dress.

When Mr. and Mrs. Ashbrook entered her unpretending dwelling, she was sitting like "Simon, the Cellarer," in her high-backed chair, enjoying the faint warmth and rosy light of the fire, and bestowing a glance every now and then upon a baby which reposed in a cradle by her side.

Patty saw this cradle as soon as she opened the door, for it was a sight which was pretty sure to attract the attention of any young mother.

She gazed upon the tiny creature with evident interest.

It was a sweet little infant about six months old. Its hair was already dark, and promised to be black as the raven's wing; silky eyelids fringed the pearl-white lids, and its skin was as delicate and soft as satin.

"I say, missus," cried Ashbrook, "what's the meaning of this? What have you been up to? Going to turn baby farmer, eh?"

The old woman laughed good-humouredly.

"No, Master Ashbrook; thanks to his lordship I don't need anything of that sort. The little thing belongs to one of my neighbours. They often bring their children here for me to take care of when they go to work or to market, or anywhere for a day. But won't you take a seat, sir, and you as well, madam?"

"You are very good, I am sure, to take charge of your neighbour's children. What a sweet little thing it is!" observed Mrs. Ashbrook.

"A very nice child, and so good-tempered, too—don't give any trouble," said Mrs. Bagley, rising and wiping with her apron two chairs, which she placed at the disposal of the visitors.

"Thank ye," said Ashbrook. "You are looking just the same as ever, Mrs. Bagley—not a bit altered since I last saw you—not a day older."

"Ah, Master Ashbrook, I be older, and, what be more, I find it out. My back is so weak at times that I hardly know how to hold myself up; but I haven't any great reason to complain, all things considered."

"You are happy and contented—that's the chief thing."

"Well I do hope as I never was one of the complaining sort, poor dear Bagley used to say."

"Oh," thought the farmer, "if I once let her loose on that string, we shall have to listen to her for heaven knows how long."

He therefore interrupted her with a sharp query.

"We have called here, being in the hopes of learning something about the robbery at Nettlethorpe's. Do you know anything about it?" cried Ashbrook, all in a breath.

"Aye, Master Ashbrook; I know something about it."

"Well, then, tell us—there's a good soul."

"It went this way, Master Ashbrook. You must know that, four or five days it might be—I couldn't swear which it was—two men came a drivin' round the country in a gig; I saw 'em myself—one a rare big black-mouthed-looking fellow as ever you'd wish to see."

"Or, rather, wouldn't care about seeing on a dark night in a lonely road—eh?"

"That's more like it, master. Well, the other was a poor weazened bit of a chap as ever you'd set eyes on in a day's travel. The pair on 'em were goin' about like bagmen with japanned tea-trays; but instead of going to the towns and doing business only with the shops, they went round the country and called at the houses themselves, and among others they went to farmer Nettlethorpe's, not to sell trays (for everybody, yourself among the rest know that Master Nettlethorpe aint the man to spill money over such like things), but to take the measure of his kitchen window with a piece of tape."

"Goodness me, is it possible?" exclaimed Patty, in a tone of alarm.

"It be the solemn truth, mum, as sure as I be a speaking to you this very minnit. They not only measures the window wi' tape, but they take the shape of his lock wi' a bit of bread paste."

"Never!"

"Oh, we knows this, because the sarvint caught one man at the window afore he'd quite done, and found a bit of bread crumb in the lock that same evening, but she being a poor silly morsel of a field wench, didn't think no harm 'ud come of it."

"She must have been a born idiot. That's what she must be," cried Ashbrook. "Well, what followed?"

"Harm did come, as we all on us know, for last night the house was broken into by the kitchen window and the passage door; the master and missus were gagged and bound wi' cords by two men wi' crape on their faces, and wi' pistols in their hands, and every farden in the house was robbed right away."

"Oh! but I be very sorry for poor Mr. Nettlethorpe and his sister. They say as how she was senseless for hours, and the doctor had a hard job to bring her to at all."

"I am sorry for both of them, but I tell 'ee that there's summat more to be said in the business. It was only yesterday as farmer Cheadle met me out riding, and he told me about a couple of impudent fellows as had driven up to his house, and one on 'em had got out and come into the kitchen, and asked his housekeeper, Dorcas, if she wanted any tea-trays, and she said 'No.'"

"Is it possible?"

"Yes, and then they told her to go in and ask her master if he wanted any trays, and she said she knew he didn't, because she had bought one for him not long before that, and she had the control of these things herself; and she declared that she wasn't going to trouble her master for nothing. When they saw she wasn't to be got out of the room, they did abuse her frightfully, and she did not stir for all their bullying. Oh, she's a tartar, and no mistake."

Mrs. Bagley heard the farmer out so far, on the chance of picking up some additional gossip, under which circumstances alone she consented to listen to anyone's tongue but her own.

Ashbrook having told his story, she fired away again, and related to him, at full length, all the burglaries which had been committed in the neighbourhood and the surrounding districts for years past.

"Well, I'm much obliged to you for the information you have given us, Mrs. Bagley, and that be all I can gi' ye in return," said Ashbrook, rising, and preparing to take his departure.

"I don't want anything else—nay, not even that—for you are quite welcome, and I be glad to see 'ee and miss—I beg pardon—Mrs. Ashbrook as is, and Miss Jamblin as was."

"But I say," cried the farmer, "your hedge wants trimming; it's the only untidy thing about the place. I'll send a man up to do it for 'ee."

"I am sure you are very kind, sir," said the old woman, dropping a curtsey. "It do mek me wild like, when I sees it, but I aint strong enough to do a job like that, and the earl, if he were to pass by, I know he'd be more annoyed than what I be myself. 'Course, he's a very particular gentleman, and so kind I'm sure I ought to pray for him, for he's been that kind."

"Oh, no doubt, he is to all his tenants, dependents, and, in short, everybody," said Ashbrook sidling towards the door, and nudging Patty to follow him.

"I'll send round one of my people, either to-morrow or next day, depend upon that," cried Ashbrook, as he passed out of the house. "Good-bye."

The farmer and his wife returned home.

"I tell you what it is, Richard," said Patty, "we had best be on our guard, for probably these tea-tray men may pay us a visit—who knows?"

"Oh, we none of us know. The burglary committed at Oakfield House years agone has proved to be almost a curse—certainly it has been attended with fatal effects to one member of our family."

"Fatal! To whom?"

SEIZING A STOUT ASH STICK FARMER ASHBROOK PROCEEDED TO GIVE THE VILLAIN A THRASHING.

"To poor Jane," said Richard Ashbrook. "And it has not ended with her death. John is no longer the same man. I think, of all men in the world, the Ashbrooks have reason to dread any attack of that nature So, as you say, we'll be prepared—to be forewarned is to be forearmed. I'll tell you what I'll do, Patty."

"Well—what?"

"I'll just step round to Brickett's for half an hour or so. I shall learn more about this business at the 'Lion.'"

"Very well—only don't stop late, Richard."

"I'll take good care of that."

"It being market-day there'll be a goodish many people there, I expect."

"Likely enough I may pick up some information."

Richard Ashbrook sallied forth, and in a few minutes' time he was in the snug little parlour of the "Carved Lion."

The room was full of people, many of whom were very well known to the farmer, who was a special favourite with the frequenters of the room.

A young swell, who was a stranger to all present, was holding forth to the yokels. To all appearance he was a gentleman. There was an air of refinement and condescension about him which seemed to indicate that he was of gentle birth.

He affected to commiserate with the person who had been the victim of the burglars, and assumed such a high tone of morality that all present were under the impression that he was a person of great rectitude.

But Ashbrook was not furnished with much more information than he had already gathered from Mother Bagley.

Nevertheless, he remained for some time listening to what the people had to say. As he was about leaving the stranger rose also, and made his way towards the bar. By this time it had commenced to rain in torrents.

"A most wretched night, it must be confessed, sir," said the stranger, addressing himself to Ashbrook.

"Yes, sir. I thought we should have it before morning, but didn't expect it to come on so suddenly."

"This is very awkward," remarked the stranger to Brickett. "Are you sure you cannot accommodate me?"

"I'm sorry to say I'm quite full. This is market day, and I have got more than my average number of visitors. Every bed in the house is engaged."

A magnificent black horse was brought by the ostler in front of the "Carved Lion," and the stranger mounted. It was at this time pouring in torrents. Brickett, who was holding a horn lantern, seemed much annoyed that he could not find the rider a bed.

"Do you know of any other house where I am likely to meet with the accommodation I require?" said the stranger.

"Well, there's the 'Frighted Horse' about two miles and a half down the road, but it's not a place I should like to recommend," returned Brickett.

"What does the gentleman want?" cried Ashbrook. "A bed?"

"Yes."

"Well, you surely are not going to turn him out such a night as this?"

"It goes against the grain for me to do so," said the host of the "Carved Lion," "but there's no help for it as I can see."

"Have you far to go, sir?" inquired the farmer of the stranger.

"Well, that depends upon what luck I have," answered he, with a winning smile. "I've a good horse, and don't much care about a soaking, and must take my chance, I suppose."

"Dall it all, but it seems cruel, Brickett," cried Ashbrook, rubbing his head in a puzzled manner. "Look at the night."

"It seems like cruelty, I admit."

"I tell 'ee what 'ee can do—I can give you accommodation for one night, at all events."

"I am sure you are extremely kind, sir, and I hardly know how to sufficiently thank you for the offer, but I should not like to intrude upon a stranger."

"Oh, ye be quite welcome, for the matter of that," said the good-natured Ashbrook. "I expect you are a stranger to these parts."

"Yes, quite a stranger. I am from London."

"Aye, well you mustn't go back with a bad account of the hospitality of the pipple of Broxbridge—must he, Brickett?"

"I hope he won't do that, Master Ashbrook," said the landlord.

After some further discussion it was eventually arranged that the gentlemanly young man from the metropolis was to become the guest of farmer Ashbrook.

He was conducted by his host to Stoke Ferry Farm, and upon arriving there Ashbrook told his wife to see the things were well aired, and everything got ready in the spare bedroom.

Patty did not quite like the presence of a stranger under the circumstances, but in the course of a quarter of an hour or so she found him so courteous and pleasant-spoken a gentleman that she became more reconciled.

Richard Ashbrook, who was hospitable to a fault, conducted his guest to the spare bedroom, wished him good night, and the inmates of Stoke Ferry farmhouse then retired to their respective chambers.

CHAPTER CVII.

THE STRANGER IS COMMUNICATIVE—BREAKERS AHEAD.

To the farmer's surprise the stranger was up and stirring by early morn; he professed to be a lover of the country, who liked to see the sun rise.

When Ashbrook and his wife had seated themselves at the breakfast table they were informed by their newly-formed acquaintance that his name was Mr. Eric Fortescue, and that he was spending his four weeks' leave of absence from the red tape and parchment of a fashionable Government office to which he belonged.

All this appeared to be natural enough; he had the appearance of a gentleman attached to some such establishment, and the farmer and his wife were duly impressed with the respectability of their guest.

Mr. Fortescue was loquacious and confidential—he said he was fond of riding. Besides his two hours' ride in Rotten-row, between five and seven in the morning, it was his custom to take a long journey on Sunday through the Middlesex meadows, sometimes as far as the hop-fields in Kent, and to spend his annual holiday upon the saddle, with no luggage but the carpet bag, which he strapped upon the pommel, and with no companions but the feathered choristers in the fields and the sweet odour of the wild flowers and the music of his horse's hoofs.

Ashbrook thought him a jolly sort of fellow enough, genial and companionable—indeed, he was charmed with his discourse.

He abounded in anecdote, and revealed to their astonished mind much of the arcana and interior machineries of polite society, which are hidden from the uninitiated by a spangled but impenetrable veil.

He knew, or affected to know, a number of notabilities whose names had reached Patty through the medium of her friends, Lady Aveline and Lady Marolyn, and she was therefore under the full impression that Mr. Fortescue was intimately acquainted with many of the leading personages who figured in the fashionable world.

His manner was engaging, and he was scrupulously polite and respectful.

He hastened to assure his host and hostess that he was ignorant upon many subjects in which they were well versed, by asking them about farming and house-wifery, and listened attentively to their explanations.

In an incredibly short time he became on excellent terms with the master and mistress of Stoke Ferry, and they would not hear of his leaving on that day or the next.

Joe Doughty was sent round to the "Carved Lion" for the gentleman's horse, and it was stalled at the farm-house, carefully groomed, and got ready whenever its master needed it.

Thus matters went on for some days until at length a tacit agreement became established between them that Mr. Erric Fortescue should spend his holidays at Stoke Ferry Farm.

He appeared to be quite charmed with the establishment into which he had been by chance thrown. He went to bed with the linnet, rose with the lark, and breakfasted on fat bacon and home-made bread and butter at half-past seven. His life was one round of pleasure and happiness—so he averred.

After breakfast the horses would be saddled and brought round to the door by Joe, and Mr. Fortescue and Ashbrook would ride over the farm together.

Now ambling along the fallows and watching the progress of the plough—now cantering along the greensward by the road side—now taking a flight of hurdles or a five-barred gate—little matters which the Londoner achieved, to Ashbrook's astonishment, with a seat as firm and a hand as light as his own.

Fortescue was not much of a hand at a gun; he said he did not shoot, but that it always gave him pleasure to see the sport, and often he would take a big stick in his hand and do as tidy a day's beating, so said Joe Doughty, "as e'er a man on the farm."

It certainly was most remarkable how he accommodated himself to the ways of Richard Ashbrook. On market days the latter was quite proud of him.

He would take his seat about half way down the table, and before the first quarter of an hour had passed he would contrive to be on good terms with every farmer at the ordinary.

In short, he was a general favourite.

When dinner was over and glasses round was the war-cry of the knights of the plough, he told them stories till they clapped their hands to their aching sides, and spluttered in their glasses as they vainly strove to drink.

"He was a right-down proper sort of gentleman," the yeomen declared. "There warn't no mistake about that."

He was popular with all classes.

"He comes from another breed nor most Cockneys," said one man. "He aint one of those starchy sort of customers. Dall their rich and stuck-up ways; they's too proud to look at we poor folks, and when we touches our hats to 'em their heads seems as if they were made of ice. But there aint no pride in this gentleman, ne'er a crumb or morsel."

So Mr. Fortescue was looked upon as a right down good fellow on the farm and premises—with all but one.

This was the maid-servant, or household manager, Kitty, whom the reader may probably remember as the same serving wench who waited upon old Mr. Jamblin when he spoke his mind so freely to Richard Ashbrook in respect to his daughter Patty.

Kitty had remained in the same establishment after the death of her old master, and she was now chief domestic to his daughter and her husband.

She had watched the stranger from the very first time he entered the house. He read in her eyes that she hated him by instinct.

These antipathies are common enough with women, and are very difficult to conquer.

It touched his pique, and he resolved to wage war against her, for he knew that she was prejudiced against him, and that to remove any such prejudice in a woman of her class was next to an impossibility.

He addressed her at first with those silly compliments which are omnipotent with most girls of the lower class, because they are mysterious. These she spurned with a contempt which appeared to be genuine; so he changed his tactics and treated her with diffidence and reserve.

Soon, however, his aims were turned to another quarter.

He had liked Patty Ashbrook during the first few days as a pretty and agreeable woman, but of the two his senses had been captivated by the tall, athletic servant girl, whose arms, full of strength and symmetry, resembled those of the Amazons of old, and whose eyes seemed to flash real fire when they encountered his.

But one day he caught Patty looking at him, and in the languishing expression of those beautiful blue eyes, in that language which the eye alone speaks and is never false, he read that she admired him. This was enough, for he was vain, and, we might add, unscrupulous.

It was this look which showed him that she was lovely, that she was a prize which kings might have knelt to obtain.

He wondered how it was that he had not admired her before, as one wonders how one has passed the tuft of grass without detecting the nestling place of the sweet and hidden violet.

This look was also a reminiscence. He now remembered the dear little child who had so often tried to conceal his faults, and who had given him innocent kisses when he was a boy.

All these things seemed to strengthen him in his admiration for the sweet and gentle farmer's wife.

Once this feeling took possession of him it grew with such strength and rapidity as to be almost overwhelming. His mind very shortly afterwards became filled with this woman.

He would sit in long reveries, dreaming to himself that he held her hand in his, and that she was whispering to him and caressing him tenderly, and at night, when the house was hushed to rest, when all was silent within and without, when the cries of the night birds were heard no more, when the moon was shining brightly and covered him with her pale light, visions more voluptuous still would seize him in their grasp—visions so powerful and intense that they made him rise trembling, almost shrinking from his sleep. And when he awoke he would find that it was yet dark night, and that he was alone, and he would press his hands to his burning brow and sigh, as men sigh when evil spirits are wrestling at their hearts.

Beneath the dark mantle of the night he conceived and plotted a most diabolical design. It was to destroy the happiness of two fond hearts, whom the roses of youth and love had twined lovingly together.

But roses soon wither when touched by a poisoned hand. In this world thorns alone are those which do not die.

And to gratify a whim this wretch would lead a poor woman, in the one weak moment of her life, from peace, from innocence, from happiness for ever! Oh why are men so wicked and women so weak? Why is it that the good are the victims of the bad, and that the foolish bear all the sufferings of the world upon their breasts?

But Mr. Fortescue was under the surveillance of

one who had from the very first looked upon him with eyes of suspicion and mistrust—this was the girl Kitty.

From his fits of abstraction, from the clouds which constantly gathered on his forehead, and from her own indefinable misgivings, she learnt that there was something on his mind, and began to watch him with the eyes of a lynx.

"He's quite the gentleman, and has most charming manners, that everyone acknowledges," said Mrs. Ashbrook, to her serving maid, "and is so greatly interested in farming matters."

"He knows a great deal more of farming and things of that sort than people suppose," returned Kitty. "Don't 'ee mek any mistake, missus—he aint the greenhorn you imagine."

"I never said he was a greenhorn, you foolish girl," said Patty, a little petulantly.

"Well, mum, it aint no business of mine; but I think——"

She paused suddenly.

"Well, what do you think?"

"I shouldn't like to say."

"And why not?"

"Ye might be a bit offended. But I don't think as how he's the man you and master tek 'im to be—'scuse my plain speaking."

"Ah, you are prejudiced, and don't understand people of his class. It is not at all likely you should be able to do so."

"I've got eyes, and plain common sense, I 'spose?"

"You don't like Mr. Fortescue—why or wherefore, I cannot imagine; he's always behaved well enough to you."

"Perhaps he has; but I tell 'ee plainly, I don't like him. I should be telling a lie if I said I did. We can't help our likes and dislikes, none on us; and he isn't one of my sort."

Mrs. Ashbrook broke out into a laugh.

"You foolish girl!" exclaimed Mrs. Ashbrook. "You are both unjust and unfair."

"I don't like his ways, mum, and I think sooner or later you'll be of my opinion, but, as I said afore, it beant any business of mine, so I'll say no more about your newly-made friend."

Patty Ashbrook was greatly annoyed and troubled by these observations, but she deemed it advisable not to press the question further, and so the matter dropped for some little time, but she afterwards remembered all that her maid had said.

CHAPTER CVIII.

KITTY'S SUSPICIONS—HER RENCONTRE WITH FORTESCUE.

MATTERS went on smoothly enough for some days after this, and no reference was made to the visitor at Stoke Ferry. Ashbrook made him his companion as heretofore, and his popularity had not in any way diminished.

One morning the farmer said in a tone of banter, "Come Patty, dear, what have you been about? The tea isn't made, and the cloth isn't laid, and I'm half famished. Has Mr. Fortescue got into your head, or what?"

"Mr. Fortescue!" exclaimed Patty, colouring. "What could induce you to make such an observation as that? Mr. Fortescue, indeed!—'taint likely."

The farmer laughed.

"There, don't 'ee lose yer temper—I didn't mean to offend 'ee," said he.

"Oh, you don't offend me, Richard, but I should say that he's more in your head than in mine."

"That's true enough, old gell, quite true. But hark'ee, Kitty don't think much on him—does she?"

"I believe not."

"Ah, so I thought. Lord bless us, what a funny world it is, to be sure. She says that she's quite sure from his face that he's no good, and that he must ha' given us a false name, because the initials on his linen aint E. F., or anything like it."

"Indeed!"

"Yes, that's what the gell sez, and she aint often mistaken. When Kitty meks up her mind to do a thing I'll back she'll stick to it, but I don't think it at all likely that he would give us a false name."

"Neither do I. I'm glad to hear 'ee say so, wife," returned the farmer. "Very glad. The gell must ha' gone stark crazy, I do believe. Why, a better fellow than Fortescue never breathed—there's no man can hold a candle to him for jokes and stories."

"I believe him to be a very good fellow, and should be sorry to find myself mistaken."

Mr. Fortescue entered at that moment—he was looking pale, and his eyes were gentle and almost pathetic.

Richard Ashbrook was a handsome man enough, but there was something so unmistakably physical about him. His face was red, and streamed with that which is praiseworthy and even scriptural upon the brow of a man who works for his bread, but which is certainly not poetical.

Then his hair was ruffled, and his garments, the offspring of the village sheers, were clumsily put on.

Patty looked at their visitor, who, with features so distingué, with clothes that fitted him like a glove, with perfumes encircling him, appeared to her like the genii of a romance.

The contrast between him and her husband was most marked, which no one could fail to notice.

Mrs. Ashbrook loved her partner quite as much, if not more, than women are accustomed to do, but it must be confessed, however, that she was not insensible to flattery and attention.

The visitor at Stoke Ferry was scrupulously polite and respectful in his manner towards the farmer's wife.

It was his purpose to lure her from her fealty to her liege lord by slow degrees.

Patty had at all times displayed a disposition before her marriage to flirt with those of the opposite sex. She never for a moment thought there was any harm in this, for in the main she was a true-hearted, honourably-disposed woman. Nevertheless, she did give ear to the fulsome flattery bestowed upon her by Mr. Fortescue.

The farmer had full confidence in his wife, and would have trusted her with anybody, but he did not calculate with anything like exactness the viper he was cherishing in his household.

"You're looking a little pale and jaded, Mr. Fortescue," said he. "Leastways, it strikes me so—I hope I'm mistaken, sir."

"I'm tolerably well, thank you," returned the visitor. "But I could not sleep well last night;" here he glanced at Patty.

"That be a bad job," cried Ashbrook. "When a man can't sleep there must be summat the matter wi' him."

"Oh, I shall be all right in an hour or two, I dare say," returned Fortescue, with a laugh. "It's no use giving way to idle fancies."

"Not a bit on it, none in the least. Tek a mug of beer wi' your breakfast and come over to Cheadle's farm wi' me. They've got an ingin there."

"Oh, indeed."

"Yes, ha' another there, and a crust of bread and cheese; then if you're done up you can come back here while I walk over the farm."

"All right, my friend, I will do so."

Long before they had come in sight of Cheadle's farm they heard a low humming sound like the music of a jew's harp, and as they drew nearer the rattle and clanking which formed a deafening accompaniment.

Then they saw a stream of smoke curling over the trees, and on reaching the yard found themselves close upon the thrashing machine itself.

A huge machine with revolving wheels and high narrow funnel and a great iron belly, out of which rolled sheaves of straw.

These the men and women standing by caught on their pitchforks and piled into a rick.

"What do ee' think of it?" cried Ashbrook. "You don't see that sort of thing every day—do'ee?"

"No, I can't say that I ever did see one before—it's a wonderful sight. Do you use it on your farm?"

"Not I," replied the farmer, contemptuously. "I'm one of the old-fashioned sort, and stick to flail and barn door. My men hold to me in the summer when men are gold—so I keep work for them in the winter when work is scarce, and the best on 'em are glad of a job just to keep the pot boiling."

"Ah, and it's a very proper course to adopt. These machines must be bad things for the labourers?"

"Yes, I 'spose they are, but it don't so much matter as far as the thrashing goes. Ye see farmers were drove to hire or buy these ingins—why? Because they couldn't get the thrashing done without. The men round here would sooner be thrashed than thrash any day. Barring my own men, you won't find three flails for miles around. Thrashing indeed! Why if every one hereabouts had to thrash his own corn, there's many as 'ud have to eat their'n in the straw."

"And how about reaping machines?" said Mr. Fortescue.

"Well, they do take the bread out of the poor men's mouths; for you see at harvest time a poor man counts on getting the money to put something on his back and feet. It's all a man with a family can do to buy bread and pay his rent with what he gets a week; but farmers don't like to use machines, and don't do it when they can get men. There's very little difference in the expense, and I always will believe that a man with a head on his shoulders can do his work cleaner and better than a great iron thing with a lot of teeth and wheels."

"Machinery is now made use of for almost every purpose," said Fortescue; "but I had no idea the population was so thin in the country."

"Ah, but it is miserably thin. If we go on as we have been within the few last years our 'bold peasantry,' as they've been termed, will disappear altogether, and I'll tell 'ee why. There's fresh commons enclosed and bits of waste lands constantly taken into cultivation, arable lands increases every year, but the population don't; it drops behind. The young men go to London to be mechanics, or to market towns to learn trades, or to Australiay or Californee to mek fortins—heaven help 'em—and the girls go to service. You can't get girls to field work now, or if you do by chance she comes with a big hoop on, as if she was agoin' to a party. Ugh! I like to see a field wench as she ought to be—in a smock and leather gaiters, not dressed like a milliner, and moppin' and poppin' about as gay as the first lady in the land."

"Oh, certainly, that's right enough," said Fortescue,

"but the question is whether it is to the advantage of women to go to field work?"

"I dunno as it is," said Ashbrook, drily. "It meks 'em dirty, and their homes dirty, and their children are left all day to themselves, and their clothes be soon spoilt. The little they do get is fetched out of the foire like."

Fortescue affected to be deeply interested in the subject. He asked question after question, and Ashbrook replied with oration after oration, for he was never tired of discussing upon farming matters, and was an oracle in his own particular way.

He little thought, however, where his companion's thoughts were wandering all the while.

"A man must have his head screwed on in the right way to be a successful farmer," observed Fortescue, thinking thereby to please his companion.

"You're right, it does—there beant any mistake about that. Many pipple think any fool is fit for a farmer, but they are deucedly mistaken though, and so many of them find out arter they ha' tried their hands at the business."

"But after all it's a healthy pleasant sort of life."

"Aye, it be that—all that."

The two companions walked for some distance together over the ploughed fields.

Presently Ashbrook glanced at his companion in a furtive manner, and said in a tone of something like commiseration—

"Ye beant looking at all the thing this morning, and seem to ha' overdone it in the way of exercise. I think 'ee had better go home and see what the missus can do for 'ee. She'll tackle your complaints better than I can. I know more about physicking horses and dogs than human critters, but she finds all the neighbours in medicine—she do."

"Oh, I have no desire to return."

"But 'ee must. Enough's as good as a feast, and you had more than enough, I guess. Go back, Mr. Fortescue, and keep yourself as quiet as possible."

They walked together as far as the front gate, then Ashbrook pressed his hand warmly, and gave his visitor kind words.

The villain's conscience, seared as it was, felt a momentary pang, but it was only momentary. He walked slowly till a high hedge hid him from the farmer's sight; then he ran at full speed towards the house.

He entered through the kitchen. There he found Mrs. Ashbrook standing over a deal table with a rolling-pin in her hand, a heap of paste on one side, and a dish of apples pared and sliced on the other. Her plump white arms were bare above the elbows, and her fair hair was parted across her forehead and gathered up in a thick cluster at the back of her head. She looked more charming and captivating than ever—so her visitor thought.

She started as Fortescue entered.

"So you're come back, eh? said she.

"Yes, Mr. Ashbrook did not think I could bear any further fatigue, and he advised me to return."

"Oh, well, I hope you are better for your walk, sir, but I fear that our early hours and rough fare do not agree with you."

"It is not that which prevents me from sleeping," he murmured, in a low plaintive voice—"not that," he replied.

"Oh, indeed!" She glanced at him curiously, and saw something in his look which made her avert her eyes.

There was a pause. Presently the farmer's wife said—

" Oh, I dare say you'll be glad when you get back to London."

"Indeed, I shall not," he returned quickly. "I don't care about the metropolis now, and shouldn't be sorry if I never saw it again."

" Why, Mr. Fortescue, what can you be thinking about to say such a thing? You would never be able to submit to the humdrum of a country life."

" I should if I were near you," he answered.

Her face wore a puzzled expression.

He placed his hand on hers, which she suddenly withdrew.

" Mr. Fortescue," she cried, " You don't seem yourself to-day; I don't know what to mek of you."

At this moment Kitty who had been at work in the back kitchen came in. She took up a pail of water which was standing near the door and went out again as if she had not noticed them.

Mrs. Ashbrook had looked uneasy, and had shrunk back a little when she entered.

The scoundrel saw this, and his eyes shone triumphantly.

" I should like to make pastry as well as you do," said he, following her to the table, and standing close beside her.

He pretended to assist her, and sometimes their fingers met, and sometimes his hand encountered as if by accident, her soft bare arm. A faint colour, the harbinger of a blush, tinged her cheeks, and her eyes were lowered upon the table.

She was in a state of trepidation, but did not know very well how to get rid of her tormentor.

" I hope I am not in your way, Mrs. Ashbrook," he said, in a respectful tone.

" Oh, dear no," she returned, " not at all; you will be away the whole of Saturday."

" I'm getting tired of the market people," he answered; " but how can I avoid going unless I fall ill, or something of that sort?"

Her face became crimson, but she made no reply.

" You will not be angry with me if I was to fall ill," he asked, in a whisper, and placing his hand caressingly on her shiny soft hair.

" Mr. Fortescue," she cried, in evident surprise. " I do not understand your meaning—angry! In what way can your movements concern me?"

Kitty came in again.

She darted a panther-like look at Fortescue, who received it with a face of marble.

" I have been showing Mr. Fortescue how to make pastry," said Mrs. Ashbrook to her servant.

" Is the gentleman going to take a situation as man cook, then?" said Kitty, sarcastically.

Mrs. Ashbrook was greatly chagrined at this last observation.

" You are a funny girl," cried she.

" I think it very funny that a Lannon gentleman should be pushing his nose in a farmer's kitchen," observed the maid. " I dunno what to mek on it," and with these words she darted out of the apartment.

" That girl is a great deal too forward—takes too many liberties to my thinking," said Fortescue.

" She will speak her mind," returned the farmer's wife. " But you know she is privileged—she has been here for so many years that she looks upon herself as one of the family."

Mr. Fortescue smiled and shrugged his shoulders, and deemed it best under the circumstances to beat a hasty retreat. Nodding to Mrs. Ashbrook he left the kitchen.

" I wish you'd not be so ready with your tongue before strangers," said the farmer's wife to her servant. " You see what you've done."

" No, I don't."

" Why, you've offended Mr. Fortescue."

" Oh, is that all?" cried the girl with an impudent toss of her head. " It's a good job if he is offended."

" Of that I am the best judge."

" Well, I doan't care for 'un, and never shall. I could take my Bible oath that he be a false man."

" Go along wi' ye—do."

" Well, I've sed it, and mean to stick to it. He's no good—I be sartin sure of that. His ways are not like those of an honest man."

" Kitty, for shame!"

" Ye mayn't loike to hear it, 'cause you and master be taken so much up wi' him; but it don't alter my opinion."

" Nobody asked you for your opinion. Go away and attend to your business."

Kitty left, but she was heard muttering to herself in the wash-house for some time after this.

Contrary to his usual custom, Mr. Fortescue sat up till late that night reading.

His candle died out in the socket, he had no matches in his pocket, and was, therefore, obliged to feel his way up in the dark.

As he passed Kitty's door he saw a light shining through the keyhole.

This he thought was a strange circumstance, and urged by curiosity more natural than refined he bent his head and peeped in.

She was seated on the bed half undressed busy with some work in her lap.

" Oh, female vanity! female vanity!" he soliloquised. " The new ribbon for the Sunday bonnet, or the worked hem for your Sunday petticoat, is sufficient to impel you to almost fabulous exertions; to work your fingers to the bone; to rob you of your needful sleep; to make you burn your master's candles. As men labour to increase their wealth, so women will to decorate their persons."

Filled with these sage reflections, he was about to withdraw his eye from its post of observation, when, to his surprise, the girl placed her work on one side, and rose from her seat.

She proceeded to disrobe herself, and was evidently preparing to go to bed.

" She's a fine woman—that is evident enough," cried Fortescue, who was, however, afraid to risk staying any longer—so he crept up to his own room again. " She hates me and mistrusts me, and will baulk me if she can. She is no contemptible enemy, it must be confessed—is self-reticent and watchful. But I hold a trump card in my hand which she little suspects. Well, we shall see. When you draw your sword, Miss Kitty, you will find that you have only a feather in your sheath."

CHAPTER CIX.

A YOUNG WIFE'S DANGER—THE DENOUEMENT

MR. FORTESCUE managed to sleep pretty soundly, despite his plans and machinations. He was such a consummate scoundrel and hypocrite that he was enabled to carry out his infamous project with the utmost coolness and address.

He had neither pity nor remorse for the friend who had cherished him in such good faith and in such unshaken confidence.

He rose early, in the hope of enjoying half an hour with Patty before her husband returned to breakfast.

He had met her thus the day before, and had told her that he intended to rise earlier the next morning.

To this she replied with one of those looks which women use when they wish to accord favours, but fear to betray themselves by words.

In a few minutes he heard footsteps outside the door; he ran to it before it was opened and said—

"Good morning, Mrs. Ashbrook."

"It is not Mrs. Ashbrook," replied a stern voice. Kitty confronted him.

"It is not Mrs. Ashbrook," she repeated.

He shrugged his shoulders, but beneath this apparent non-challenge he prepared himself for a duel. He saw that the crisis was come, and that his opponent was not to be despised.

"I'm glad we've met," said the girl. "Very glad."

"Indeed, and why, pray?"

"Because I've a serious word to say to you, sir, and the time's come to say it."

"A serious word, my girl. Well, I'm all attention. Say it, then, without further ado. Something strictly confidential, I suppose?"

"I dunno about that; but harkee, Mr. Fortescue, or whatever may be your name——"

"That is my name. You are particular. One would suppose you were a lawyer about to open an indictment. Go on, Kitty."

"Ye mean to act basely towards my young mistress —that's what 'ee mean to do. Oh, none of your lying looks and lifting of hands at me. I be only a common country gell, but I can tell what it is as shines in your eye when you see her, and trimbles in your voice when you speak to her. I can tell what it is as meks you sit thinkin' by day and wander about your room by night. I can tell what it is that's plottin' in your hard black heart as well and better than a lord's lady or a squire's wife."

"Can you?"

"Yes, I can."

"Upon my word you are an astonishingly clever girl. I should not have given you credit for so much penetration. You can read my thoughts, can you, and see into my—my—'black heart,' as you are pleased to term it? I don't know which to admire most—your perspicuity or your politeness."

"It won't do, Mr. Fortescue. I won't be put aside by foine words."

"You take my advice, my excellent and sagacious friend. Look after your pigs and poultry, and don't attempt to meddle in matters which don't concern you."

"Not consarn me! not consarn me! Don't it, indeed? Do you suppose I am likely to stand tamely by and see a white dove carried off by a ravenous kite? Don't it consarn me to see the dear lady I've known from a child on the edge of being ruined for this life, and for the next, too, maybe?"

"Your similes do you great credit," said Mr. Fortescue coolly, paring his nails with his penknife— "very great credit, especially the white dove and kite. I am the kite, I presume, and your mistress is the white dove. Anything more?"

Kitty became furious. She could not stand the fellow's cool impudence and sarcasm.

"Harkee, Mr. Fortescue; if you aint out of this house by to-night's dusk or afore then, I'll tell Mr. Ashbrook, and he'll pitch 'ee out; aye, and I'll help 'im, too. D'ye see this arm? it's bigger than your'n, and it's stronger than your'n, and it's thrashed a better man than you, for all your fine beard and cloth clothes and women's scents."

Mr. Fortescue was perfectly unmoved. He looked languidly at the speaker, and said, carelessly—

"You are a brave champion, I admit; but you are a silly girl, nevertheless—a very silly girl. I have no intention of acting badly towards your mistress; dismiss such a thought from your mind."

"I won't believe it. Be out of the house by the shank of the evening, or Mr. Ashbrook shall towel 'ee till your white skin's black and blue, my London gentleman."

He clenched his teeth, and approached her. Revelling in her vast strength, Kitty waited for him with her bare brown arms folded on her chest.

He poured a fierce whisper in her ear.

She became pale. "Oh, no, no," she cried. "He is dead, and there has never been a breath agen him yet."

He saw her weak point, and attacked her like a fiend.

"Don't tell me," he cried. "I know the whole history. Mr. Philip Jamblin, who was murdered in Larchgrove Lane, had another sweetheart besides the one who gave evidence on the trial. I know who that was."

"It is false," she cried; "but even if he had, what has it to do with you? Do what you like wi' me. Pelt me, put me in the pillory, but not a word agen him."

He went up to her, and said in a soft voice—

"Do not be afraid, Kitty—I will not betray you. I have a secret of yours—you have a secret of mine; let us be friends."

She did not answer him; he left the kitchen, contented with his morning's work.

Matters after this went on much the same as usual at Stoke Ferry Farm for some few days after the altercation between Kitty and Fortescue.

One morning, however, there was a change in the aspect of affairs. Richard Ashbrook was moody and discontented. It was easy to perceive that he was ill at ease, and that something troubled him. What this was his wife was at a loss to divine.

"You seem to be out of sorts," said Patty; "you have scarcely touched your breakfast. Richard, dear, what ails you?"

He did not answer at first. When he spoke it seemed as if there was something in his throat choking him.

"Matter, indeed!" he ejaculated. "To my thinking there's a deal the matter. I've heard bad tidings, and it's upset me."

"Goodness me, what is it, then? Tell me all about it. Is anyone ill?"

"No it beant that. Everybody as we know seems to be well enough. It's not a matter of sickness or disease, nor yet of bones breaking, nor crops failing, nor cattle dying of the rinderpest. It be worse than that I've heard to-day, Patty. I've heard to-day that the man I trusted most in the world—the man I loved loike a brother as one may say—the man I treated as one of my own kin and my own blood—— "

He ceased suddenly, and drew his hand across his eyes.

"That man is trying to ruin me—to rob me of all I hold best in the world—that while my bread has been in his mouth, and my words of welcome in his ear, he has been jeering at me in his heart, and setting snares to betray me and mine."

"Ah, Richard, how very dreadful; but are you sure of this?"

"Quite sure," he returned—"Quite sure."

"Ah! I do hope you are mistaken."

He strode across the room, and gripped her by the shoulder till she winced with pain.

"I tell 'ee there aint any mistake about it," he ejaculated. "If ye had nursed a worm in your bosom till he had turned a viper what would ye do? Would you let the reptile crawl away, alive and strong as ever, to sting other hearts, or would ye crush his head beneath your heel, as ye'd crush a weazel or a stoat? Wouldn't ye crush the varmint? Answer me, Patty—speak, wife."

"You are so excited, so moved, that I hardly know what answer to make; but, Richard, be careful—keep within the law."

"I'll keep within the law, never fear," he answered, with a terrible smile. "But the law, my gell, is hard upon such men as he; and I intend to be hard upon him, or my name's not Richard Ashbrook. The soft-spoken, circumventing vagabond!"

Kitty now made her appearance. She was very pale, but her voice was firm.

"Your horse is at the door, master. Ye'll be late for market unless you are off at once." And she added some words in a hoarse whisper.

The farmer mounted his horse and rode off.

His wife was seriously concerned about him. She sat by herself, thinking and trembling. She had never seen him in such a fluster before, and he had not told her who it was that had behaved so ungratefully, nor what it was that he had tried to do. She was greatly puzzled. Who could it be? She could not determine. Possibly he would give her the whole particulars when he returned from market. Any way, she must rest contented for a while—that is, as contented as she could be under the circumstances.

In a few minutes after Ashbrook's departure, Mr. Fortescue came down stairs. There was an expression of anticipated triumph in his face, cloaked by precaution.

At first Patty's manners were absent and restrained. She was thinking more of her husband's violence than of the fascinating young gentleman who was endeavouring to make himself so agreeable. Mr. Fortescue was a little disconcerted at her indifference, the reason for which he could not very well comprehend; but he strove to hold her engaged, and he succeeded so well that in the course of half an hour of his mellifluous conversation all thoughts of her husband were banished from Patty's mind.

Still she had no idea of doing anything actually wrong. She reasoned to herself that she was fond of being alone with Mr. Fortescue because she liked his conversation, and when her husband was present they talked so much about farming and so little about the world. The association with the Lady Aveline had given her a taste for the gaiety of London life; this, however, had in a measure passed away. She was well satisfied with her present sphere of action; nevertheless, she liked to hear the scandal and gossip which floated about respecting those who move in fashionable society. Mr. Fortescue abounded in anecdote, and seemed to be deeply versed in the movements of great personages. As may be readily supposed, he drew largely upon his imagination, and did not confine himself to the truth. She listened to his discourse, and was charmed. In other words, she wished to gaze into the depths of a horrible abyss, and had invited a murderer of women's souls to lead her to the brink.

Fortescue soon guided the conversation to topics of fashionable life, and with consummate art drew a sketch of matrimonial intrigue—a sketch in which he took care to introduce none of those dark and terrible tints which form the background of such pictures in real life.

She remembered having heard similar narratives fall from the lips of persons she met with in London, when she sojourned there with Lady Marolyn and Aveline, but these were pure and innocent—no comparison to Mr. Fortescue's.

And, as an experienced huntsman does not frighten his quarry by riding straight towards it, but rides round and round, gradually lessening the circle, till the deer having become familiarised with the dangerous object, no longer heeds it—so by imperceptible gradations he approached this foolish deer, who sat listening to all his wicked nonsense with open ears and wondering eyes.

I do not wish to analyse the infernal art with which he excited the senses of an innocent and guileless woman; many who read these pages might take that as a guide—others would refuse to accept it as a warning.

Mr. Fortescue presently poured into her ear a passionate declaration of attachment, which she ought not to have listened to. He hung over her, he placed his arm round her waist, and before she was aware of it, his lips met hers. She struggled to release herself from his grasp, and said—

"Mr. Fortescue, release me. This conduct is unpardonable. Pray—"

She ceased suddenly, for a dark shadow fell across the room, and they both looked up. It was Richard Ashbrook standing on the threshold.

"I am glad you have come," cried his wife.

He made no reply, but with one hand gestured for her to leave the room.

She crept past him with her head bowed upon her breast.

For a few brief moments the farmer stood still as if to reflect. His face was white, but very calm. Presently he made towards the door, locked it, and thrust the key into his pocket; after this he drew down the blinds.

Fortescue, who was perfectly astounded at the sudden appearance of the farmer, was at no loss to comprehend that he was made a prisoner. Trusting to bravado to save him he hummed an air from the last new opera.

"You infamous, deceptive scoundrel," cried Ashbrook; "I've half a mind to shoot 'ee as I would shoot down a fox or a wolf. It would be no more than you deserve."

"Indeed, and why so?"

"You came here a stranger," said Ashbrook, endeavouring as best he could to command his temper for a while; "I gave you a night's rest unasked; for several weeks I have made you live with me, and have treated you to the best of my poor power; I have made you my home your home—I have made my friends your friends."

"I do not deny all this," said Fortescue. "In point of fact, I admit it. But then, my honest yeoman, consider the honour of having a gentleman in your house. I have to return you many thanks for your kindness and hospitality."

"A gentleman!" cried Ashbrook; "God keep me from such gentlemen! A blackguard, you mean—a gambler—and a thief!"

"Have a care, Mr. Ashbrook, as to what you say. There is such a thing as indicting a man for defamation of character."

"Character! you've none to lose, you sneak. You've deceived my wife," said the farmer, raising his voice; "ye've deceived me, poor fool that I have bin; ye've tried to disgrace us both for life."

ASHBROOK RECEIVING THE CHALLENGE FROM "CAPTAIN BRADLEY."

"That I deny. Assertions are one thing and proof is another—remember that, Mr. Ashbrook."

"I call ye a coward and a dirty, contemptible hound, but I don't intend to let 'ee off with hard words—I mean to give 'ee a few hard blows. You won't forget Stoke Ferry, I'll dare be sworn, for many a long day."

"Ah, you are pugnaciously disposed, are you? Well,

we can easily arrange matters. I have a pair of new trigger pistols upstairs, and am ready to give you satisfaction wherever and whenever you please."

"Satisfaction, ye call it, you audacious varmint. Ah, ah! That's a queer sort of satisfaction. Because you've done me wrong I'm to be shot at with a pistol. No, no, my man—I know a trick worth two of that.

This is what I call satisfaction, you impudent monkey."

He sprang to the fireplace and snatched down a stout ash stick which hung over the mantel-shelf, and which he made whistle a sinister melody.

"One minute, sir, if you please," said the wretch, who soon began to tremble for the first time. "You accuse me of being a coward and a scoundrel because I have flirted with your wife. Pray may I inquire if you knew Mr. Philip Jamblin—he was murdered in Larchgrove-lane?"

"What if I did?   Don't 'ee say anything agen him."

"You knew him?"

"Yes.   What of that?"

"Did he flirt with anybody?   Answer me that."

"Dall you, if you speak a word agen Philip, I'll have your life, you cowardly dirty scoundrel. He aint here to take his own part, but I am here, and that's just as well. Dare you speak of a murdered man to me his bosom friend, by all I hold most sacred, before you leave this room, you shall pay in part for the pain ye've made me bear."

Mr. Fortescue was at no loss to divine that the farmer was in earnest. He whirled round the stout ash stick in a most menacing manner. The London gentleman sprang towards the window, which he endeavoured to open, but the farmer was too sharp for him. He caught Fortescue by the collar of his coat, and with herculean strength dragged him from the window, then he belaboured him most unmercifully with his stick, with which he rained a series of terrible blows on his back and shoulders.

Fortescue flew to the fireplace and snatched up the poker. On the instant he received a terrific blow on the wrist, the poker dropped from his hand, which by this time had been rendered powerless, and then another series of blows followed in quick succession.

If any man ever had a sound thrashing, Mr. Fortescue was the man.

"Get out of my house and never darken my doors again," cried Ashbrook, opening the parlour door, and thrusting his visitor forcibly out. The latter did not want a second bidding. He made his exit without further ado. As he was passing the back kitchen which abutted out from the farmhouse, the girl Kitty, who had been watching for his appearance, flung a pail of dirty water over him.

"Take that, you dirty conceited puppy," said she.

Dripping with wet and aching in every limb, Mr. Fortescue flew over the fields as if pursued by some wild animal, and was soon lost to sight.

"Joy go with him!" cried Kitty, "the dirty lying blackguard. I dont think it likely we shall be troubled with him agen, master."

"I hope not," said Ashbrook. "I fancy he's had a pretty good dose."

"And one as ell last him a long time," observed the servant, retreating into the washhouse.

Patty Ashbrook remained sad and silent upon a seat in her own chamber, her face distorted with terror as she listened to the sound of heavy blows and the cries of the man who but a few moments before had been whispering loving words into her ear. She despised him now, but not more than she despised herself. For now she remembered every little act, every word of kindness her husband had ever bestowed upon her. Now she felt that she was an ungrateful wretch, that she deserved to be driven from her home, even as Mr. Fortescue had been.

This last thought flashed upon her like a flash of fire,

and dried up the last glad warm drops of blood in her unhappy heart.

Oh, what a horrible fate it seemed to be—compelled to leave the house in which she had been happy from her earliest infancy—in which she had lived with those whom she loved and honoured most in the world !

She glanced tearfully round the room, as if to engrave everything it contained more firmly on her memory. Perhaps she might never enter that room again.

All was silent below.   Then she heard the door open and shut; then the voice of Kitty; then another interval of silence.

There were then minutes of terrible silence. She heard a slow and solemn footstep upon the stairs. She held her breath; her tears ceased to flow.

She flung herself into a chair, and raised her eyes full of repentance to the pale calm face of her injured husband.

"I've got rid of un for good and for all; heaven be praised for that," said Ashbrook.

"Oh, Richard!" exclaimed Patty; "beat me; beat me heavily, for I deserve it, but do not drive me from you. I could not live away from you."

"I hope not," returned he, placing his broad brown hand upon her shoulders. "Nobody would wish it—leastways not me." His voice was gentle with love, tremulous with pity.

"I say I have got rid of that viper whom I ha' bin foolish enough to cherish. I ought to be set down as a born idiot for my foolishness. But we are none on us wise at all times."

"Oh, Richard!" exclaimed his wife. "You ought to blame me—which no doubt you do. I have been more to blame than you have; but can you forgive me, my dear, honest husband?"

"Can I forgive you?" cried Ashbrook. "You ha' bin a good wife for me for five long years, Patty. You have worked hard for me by day and by night. When I've come home weary, and oftentimes, it may be, a bit ruffled in temper, you ha' always had a sweet word and a kind kiss for me; and do you think, my lass, that I ha' any right to forget all that, and let a silly, foolish hour or so blot out the thoughts and memories of five good years? No, no, my gell. We've been both to blame; I ha' bin more foolish and blind than what you ha' bin."

He took her in his arms and cradled her on his manly breast.

"Oh, Richard," she ejaculated—"my own dear, good Richard !"

"It was more my fault than yourn," cried Ashbrook —"a deal more my fault. I know that now. I put faith in this—this deceivin' varmint. I left him with 'ee. I gave him good chances to pison your mind, and to draw your love from me to him for a little while. More fool me. But your love's all come back agen now—aint it, lass?—and stronger and warmer and truer than afore, if that be possible, which somehow I doant think it can?"

She did not answer him. Her head was upon his shoulder, and her face was covered with her beautiful brown hair. She was still weeping, "but now her tears were tears of joy."

"My dear Patty," cried the farmer. "Heaven be praised! you've bin saved from the teeth of the wolf.'

CHAPTER CX.

MR. ERIC FORTESCUE AND HIS RESPECTABLE ASSOCIATES—
THE CHALLENGE, AND THE RESULT.

MR. ERIC FORTESCUE, alias Alf Purvis, alias Mr.

Algernon Sutherland, smarting with pain, and foaming with rage, made the best of his way to London after he had been ignobly expelled from Stoke Ferry farm-house. He was in a terrible plight—was saturated with the dirty water which had been thrown over him by the girl Kitty, and his back and shoulders were black and blue from the blows that had been so mercilessly showered upon him by Ashbrook, but he contrived to reach the metropolis. For three days he preserved a moody silence, and shut himself up in one room from morning to night.

On the evening of the third day he sent for Laura Stanbridge. He made her acquainted with all that had passed at Broxbridge. She laughed at him, and this made him perfectly furious.

"You make a jest of my misfortunes," cried he. "It's just like women—they are always pleased when they hear of a friend's mishap. I am sick of the world—sick of you and of everybody."

"I dare say you are, but who have you to blame but yourself? You imagine every woman must of necessity be smitten with you. You shouldn't be so vain, my young spark."

"Don't preach to me, you fool. I'm not disposed to listen to your lectures. I have had enough of them."

"Very well, that being so, "I'll make no further observations," replied Miss Stanbridge, with perfect composure.

"What am I to do?" he inquired, after a pause. "Tell me what I am to do. How can I be revenged?"

"I am not able to tell you," said she.

"Confound it, Lorry, you appear to be most indifferent about the cruel treatment your old friend has met with."

"I know not what advice to give you. The whole affair I look upon as a piece of folly. This is the second time you have been thrust forth with cuffs and hard words from Stoke Ferry house. The first time you were not so much to blame, but the last time you were much to blame. I don't know that you deserve much pity," she added, scornfully.

"Hang your pity!—I want none of it. But you've got a good head-piece of your own. Can't you advise a fellow in this business?"

"You must be badly off, indeed, to come to a woman for advice," she rejoined. "When you want to rob a house, do you ask me how to pick the locks? And now that a lusty farmer has insulted you and given you a good drubbing, you ask me what to do. Throw off your fine clothes and your finnicking airs. Alf Purvis, I am only a weak woman, but I need no instruction when I wish to be avenged. Ah! you do not know how sweet it is to be revenged."

She became frightfully pale as she made this last observation, and cast upon him a look as venomous as a viper. He remained silent for some minutes. She watched him eagerly.

"Your friends have been more successful than you have been," said Laura Stanbridge; "they managed to get into Nettlethorpe's house, and carried off all the valuables in a regular business-like way. They were clever, but you are not."

"I am much obliged for the compliment," returned her companion; "much obliged. This is a fitting time to indulge in taunts and sneers. You compare me to the Smoucher and the Cracksman—a low-bred pair of rascals as ever darkened the doors of an honest man's house. I tell you what it is, my lady, you are not the same woman to me that you were, not by a long way."

"That is most surprising—isn't it?"

"It's a fact that I know full well."

"Are you the same? As long as you were an out-cast, a poor wretch, wandering about the streets without a home or a friend, you were civil and tractable enough; but now——"

"Well, go on, Lorry, go on, finish the sentence."

"Now you are vain, haughty, and unmindful of those who have befriended you."

"It is false. I never was unmindful of past favours, but I intend to alter my course of life—to reform, and, if possible, to live honestly."

His companion laughed.

"I mean it," he added—"mean what I say, but I must commit one crime more. I will not rob this man, I will not steal his money, I will rob him of a treasure he holds dearer than his gold—I will take his wife. Thus my heart shall be consoled and my hate revenged."

Miss Stanbridge looked at the speaker in a state of bewilderment.

"You love her then?" said she, as her eyes scintillated sparks of fire.

The young man nodded significantly. "I love her," he repeated, "and will go abroad and take her with me."

"Excellent device!"

"She shall never leave me."

"She will always hate you."

"And I shall always love her. All that the mind of man can conceive, all that the powers of man can execute, I will employ to gain her love. But she shall be mine, I swear it."

Laura Stanbridge writhed as she listened to these words, after which she became very calm.

"You must have taken leave of your senses, my very excellent young friend," she murmured. "You always love her!"

"Yes, always."

"Bah! you are mad."

"Am I? Well, that's a matter of opinion," said he, running his hand through his auburn locks.

"You are vain—that you will admit, I suppose?"

"Nothing of the sort—never was so in my life."

"And ape the manners of your betters."

"Anything else?"

"Which, to say the truth, do not in any way become you."

"Ah, you are jealous," cried he, with asperity.

The face of his companion flushed up.

"Jealous of you, my beauty!" she ejaculated, in a tone of contempt. "Don't flatter yourself, Alf, by such a supposition. We know each other by this time. If we don't, we never shall. Jealous of you, indeed!"

"Well, there's no occasion to be petulant or spiteful, Lorry. Don't lose your temper. Every gentleman must have his private amours, and I like you none the less because I have been carrying on a little innocent flirtation with the farmer's wife."

"Love me! I wonder you can make use of such a term," cried Laura Stanbridge, with something like indignation in her tone.

"We don't want to quarrel. It wouldn't answer either of our purposes to do that."

At this moment there was a knock at the door, and to Fortescue's "Come in," the "Smoucher" and the "Cracksman" entered.

"Oh, you've got back from Broxbridge, then?" said the latter, in a familiar and half-sneering tone.

"Yes, I have," answered Fortescue, alias Alf Purvis.

"You've bin having a fine time of it, captain. Enjoying yourself like anythink, I s'pose?"

"That's my business and not yours, my tea-tray friend."

At this he and the Smoucher burst out into a loud laugh.

"We worked it to rights—did the trick as clean as a brand-new whistle. Got off wi' the swag, and nobody any the wiser. I suppose you've heard the whole history from your old friends at the farmhouse?"

"I've heard all about it. Mr. Nettlethorpe is half crazy, and they say he'll never recover the loss he has sustained."

"Oh, what a pity, poor chap! Everybody is so fond of him, you know; that must be a great comfort to him. It was a good joke, though, your taking up your quarters at the next farm; jolly good that was. I hope as how you've enjoyed yerself?"

"Yes, I have, very much; but don't you trouble yourself about me or my pleasures and enjoyments. You've got to look after yourself."

"Why, captain, you're rather short and sharp with an old pal. Something's upset you."

"Yes; I'm vexed and annoyed."

"What about?"

"Oh, many things."

"Can either of us help you?"

"I don't think you can."

"He's lost his heart," observed Miss Stanbridge, with a merry twinkle in her eye.

The two scoundrels burst out into another and still louder laugh.

"Why, that's nothing new, missus," said the Smoucher. "The captain is easily knocked over by a pretty face. He's so werry susceptible."

"Don't talk nonsense, you fool," cried Alf Purvis, in an angry tone.

"Oh, I've done. Sorry I spoke, for the matter of that."

"But there's an old saying," observed the Cracksman, "and may be it's a wise one—'the course of true love never did run smooth.'"

All present laughed again, all but Alf, who turned away with disgust.

"I'm not disposed to stand any more of your chaff," said he, "and so if you've nothing better to talk about, the sooner you take your hook the better."

"Well, I'm blest," cried the Cracksman, "you are riled about summut, that's quite sartain. I never knew you to be so short in temper as you are to-day."

"I don't want any more of your sneering observations, and I've business to attend to."

"Oh, that's it, eh?" said the Smoucher—"we'll be for making tracks then—come along, mate."

And upon this the two men wished their superior good-day, and beat a retreat.

"You were very sharp with them, Alf," observed Miss Stanbridge when the two had gone; "they meant no harm."

"They are a pair of vulgar common brutes, and I don't choose to give them too much latitude. I am glad to be rid of them."

"And I suppose you will be glad to be rid of me?"

"I don't say that, Lorry; you I can bear with, but I can't bear those fellows when I am perplexed and troubled, which I happen to be just now."

"Is there anything I can do for you?" said the deceitful woman, placing one arm round his neck in a loving manner.

"Yes, I tell you what you can do."

"Out with it, then."

"I wish, as you go home, you'd call upon young Bradley, and tell him to come here as soon as he possibly can."

"I will do so with pleasure. Say you wish to see him?"

"Yes; upon particular business."

"All right; it shall be done, Alf, dear. Done with the greatest pleasure."

The woman took her departure, and in an hour or two after this Mr. Bradley, the young man in question, made his appearance.

He was a genteel, good-looking fellow, of about eight-and-twenty, and was one of Alf Purvis's most particular friends—if friendship can with propriety be applied to such a connection—for, like Purvis, he was a loose fish, a lawless character. He, however, affected to be very partial to Mr. Algernon Sutherland, and was just the sort of man he needed to perform the office which he was about to assign to him.

The greeting between the two was a cordial one, for Mr. Bradley had not seen his young friend since he rusticated at Broxbridge.

Alf at once proceeded to put his friend in possession of all those circumstances which have been described in the preceding chapter.

He, however, passed lightly over the thrashing and his ignominious expulsion from the farmer's house.

"A nasty, spiteful, objectionable, old agriculturist," cried Mr. Bradley, after the narrative had been brought to a conclusion. "He rode rusty—did he?"

"That he most certainly did."

"He's a hog—a swine—a low-bred, vulgar fellow."

"Very low-bred."

"Oh, so I should imagine. But we'll find some means of serving him out. Wife's a pretty little woman, I suppose?"

"Oh, dear me, yes."

"And a great deal too good for such a pig?"

"Much too good. But we will not discuss that question now. I am in need of a confidential friend like yourself."

"Certainly, old boy. I am at your service."

"I have left my portmanteau and things at the farmer's, also my horse. I want you to run down to Broxbridge and demand them."

"Good. That I'll do without a moment's hesitation. You must give me a note, of course?"

"Yes—a note requesting him to give them up to you, and at the same time I purpose sending him a challenge."

"Oh, Jerusalem! a challenge, eh? Capital! That I am to deliver, I suppose?"

"Yes."

"Oh, what a lark! Nothing could suit me better. It's quite in my line. By-the-way, you'd better say the bearer of your challenge is your friend, Captain Bradley."

"I will do so. Captain Bradley, of the Horse Marines."

"Or the Fall Backs. There's magic in the word 'captain,'" said Bradley, rubbing his hands together with great glee. "By-the-way, I ought to put on spurs, and wear a military coat."

"It would be all the better."

"I will do so, and at the same time assume a military bearing. I'll astonish old Mangold Wurtzel; give it him hot and strong, without sugar. Egad! I'll astonish his weak nerves."

Mr. Eric Fortescue, as he called himself, wrote a dignified epistle, in which he demanded all that he had left at Stoke Ferry. This he supplemented with another, challenging the farmer to mortal combat.

Both these precious documents were given to Mr. Bradley, who was quite delighted with his mission.

"You must remember that on this occasion I am Mr. Eric Fortescue; that is the name I gave when I first made the acquaintance of this rustic. Don't forget that."

"I'll bear it in mind; of course I do not know you by any other. I shall say that my friend Fortescue has directed me to wait on you, &c. You can imagine the rest; leave it all to me. He won't accept the challenge, I suppose?"

"I should say not, but press the question. Put the matter home to him."

"I will."

The next day Mr. Bradley put himself in the train, and made the best of his way to Broxbridge. He had been told by his friend to call at the "Carved Lion" before proceeding to Stoke Ferry farmhouse, as possibly he might pick up some information at that respectable hostelry, but John Brickett was as silent as the grave, and studiously avoided referring to the circumstances attending Fortescue's visit to Mr. Ashbrook.

It was a scandal he was in no way desirous of making more public than necessary, and hence his reticence.

Mr. Bradley had therefore no other course than to fight his battle single-handed. He presented himself at the farmhouse, and inquired for Mr. Richard Ashbrook. Kitty, who opened the door, said her master was in the fields, but if the gentleman would call in about an hour and a half's time Mr. Ashbrook would be sure to be in by that time.

Mr. Bradley, upon this, contrived to kill time by a stroll round the neighbourhood. When he returned the farmer was at home, awaiting the stranger's appearance, in the very same room in which he had chastised his ungrateful guest.

The girl announced Captain Bradley, who was at once shown into the parlour.

"Ah! your servant, sir," cried the captain; "Mr. Ashbrook, I presume?"

"Aye, that be my name. What may your business be?"

"It is a delicate and in some respects a painful one," returned Bradley.

"Oh, indeed, I'm sorry to hear that."

"Yes, I am deputed by my friend, Mr. Eric Fortescue, to wait upon you. In the first place I am directed by him to demand the things he left here, together with his horse, which I am to take back to his town residence."

Upon this he handed the farmer the first letter.

"You can take 'em wi' you at once, the sooner the better," said Ashbrook, after he had perused the letter; then thrusting his head out of the front door, he called out, "Joe, Joe."

Joe Doughty made his appearance.

"Go upstairs and bring down Mr. Fortescue's portmanteau," said Ashbrook.

Joe did as he was bid, and in a few seconds returned with the article in question.

"There it be," said the farmer, addressing himself to the false captain. "Now, Joe, let this gentleman have the black horse—him as is owned by Mr. Fortescue."

"Anything else, sir?" said Ashbrook.

"I am sorry to say that there is. I have another and more important letter to deliver. Its nature I am very well acquainted with. Sir, I must inform you that Mr. Fortescue has been grossly insulted, and I

have further to declare that he is a gentleman who never tamely submits to an insult."

"Doesn't ee, though?"

"No, sir. In short, he cannot pass over the indignities to which he has been subjected. No gentleman in his position would be warranted in doing so—not if he had any desire to maintain his status in fashionable and good society. I must, therefore, beg of you to read this second missive. It is a challenge, Mr. Ashbrook. You cannot consistently refuse to give my friend that satisfaction which one gentleman has a right to expect from another."

Richard Ashbrook perused the document curiously; then he burst into a loud laugh.

"Do not treat the matter with unbecoming levity, sir. If you do I shall have reason to feel offended. It is not a time for jesting, Mr. Ashbrook. I therefore demand an answer. Please to name some gentleman who will officiate as your second, so that I may confer with him. That is the usual course we adopt in cases of this sort."

"Do 'ee tek me for a fool, my brave young spark?" cried Ashbrook; "or what?"

"I decline to inform you what I take you to be. All I require is an answer. Name your conditions."

"Conditions! I aint a goin' to mek any conditions wi' the loikes of 'ee, or your friend, as you term him—a circumwenting, deceitful varmint!"

"Have a care, sir. Have a care as to what you say. I will not stand tamely by and hear my friend, Fortescue, reviled."

"Get out! don't 'ee think to bullyrag me. If ye gi' me any more of yer nonsense, I'll chuck 'ee forth, and send 'ee about yer business. Take the fellow's things, and be off while ye've got a whole skin."

"What! threats?" cried Bradley, putting himself into a military and defiant attitude. "Mr. Ashbrook, I am surprised. I will not depart without an answer."

"An answer to what?"

"Respecting the proposed hostile meeting. But I pardon you—you do not understand the usages of polite society. Permit me to explain."

"I want none of yer explanations. Don't care to listen to such rubbish. So ye'd better be off."

"Then am I to say you decline to meet my friend Fortescue?"

"Fortescue!" cried the farmer, with a sneer. "He's no more Fortescue than I am. Don't 'ee come here wi' any more cock-and-bull stories. Why, he's a thief, and the p'leece are arter him. If I were to appoint a place of meeting, he'd be collered and clapped into gaol. Do you see that, my brave captain?"

Mr. Bradley was rather taken aback at this speech. He also had the honour of being well acquainted with the police, and he thought that it was therefore quite time to lower his tone. He assumed for the nonce an air of injured innocence.

"Mr. Ashbrook," said he, "I put it to yourself as an honourable man whether you think it the right thing to cast aspersions upon a gentleman when he is not here to answer you. I do hope and trust that you have not so bad an opinion of me as to suppose for a moment I would lend myself to so dishonourable a proceeding as to espouse the cause of a disreputable character. In common justice you ought to offer an apology, and express your sorrow for making such indiscreet observations."

"Look 'ee here—you can go back to London, and tell this friend of yours that he is found out. His real character is known here. The p'leece will gi'ee more information respecting him than I can. He's a bad egg if there ever was one, and as to this, well, there—"

He tore up the letter which contained the challenge into a hundred pieces, and threw them in the grate.

"Now Mr.—or captain—you had better be off, or, may be, you and I shall quarrel."

"I hope not, I'm sure," returned Bradley. "I have not done anything to offend you that I am aware of."

"There be an old adage, 'Ye may know a man by his friends,—and if Mr. Fortescue, as he choses to call himself, is a friend of yourn— well, I wouldn't gi' much for 'ee; that be all I ha' to say."

"You are complimentary, Mr. Ashbrook," said Bradley, with a sneer.

"Horse be ready, master," cried Joe Doughty from the yard.

There, your—or rather his—horse be ready. Ye'd better mount and be off, or may be we shall find out something about you. What regiment are you captain of?"

"What regiment? oh, the 3rd West Middlesex."

"Oh, you're in the volunteer service?"

"Ahem! yes."

"Well, captain, I wish you may arrive safely back in London. Your horse is ready."

"And you decline to return any answer?"

"Look 'ee here. If that young scoundrel comes in this neighbourhood he will very soon find himself in one of her Majesty's prisons—so 'ee may tell him that from me. And now, if ye'll take good advice, which I think it just as well to |offer 'ee, you'll just mek yerself as scarce as possible, or maybe 'ee may find yerself as deep in the mud as he be in the mire."

"I shall not condescend to have any further discourse with you," said Bradley, assuming as high a tone as possible at parting. He went out into the yard, mounted his friend's black horse, and directed Joe Doughty to take the portmanteau round to the "Carved Lion," handing him half-a-crown for his trouble. He then trotted off, very much dissatisfied with his visit to Stoke Ferry Farm, which he considered to be a most miserable failure.

CHAPTER CXI
THE SURPRISE AND ESCAPE—A DRIVE FOR LIFE.

PEACE, after his encounter with Bessie Dalton, abstained for a short period from his predatory excursions.

The scene in the rich merchant's house at Blackheath had made a deep impression on him, and it is just possible that he had some slight compunctious visitings; but these were of course of short duration.

His house in the Evalina-road was, as we have already intimated, exceedingly well furnished. On his removal from Greenwich a large amount of plate and a considerable collection of pictures were not transported openly in the van he hired to remove the rest of his goods; they were forwarded secretly from Greenwich to Peckham.

It was generally understood in the neighbourhood that he was a retired gentleman possessed of a modest competence, which enabled him to live quietly without business cares, and to indulge his little whims in scientific inventions, in which indulgence he had lost thousands.

The mixed family, as we have already seen, did not live in harmony.

Mrs. Thompson, it has been said, was rarely without a black eye, and shrieking and swearing were not uncommonly heard proceeding from the house. Yet Peace gave himself the reputation of a humane and moral man with a character to maintain, who must

not be familiarly accosted by milkmen, greengrocers, and other people who resorted to public-house bars in the morning.

Peace was very rarely seen till late in the day. People in the vicinity who gave the matter any consideration supposed he was busy with his scientific pursuits, of which he was fond of talking in an effusive manner.

He occasionally invited his neighbours into his house to take something, and by all accounts he was a jovial host.

He was possessed of seven or eight guitars, and almost as many violins. When he came outside the gate in the afternoon and took a look at the weather he was communicative and critical to whoever was passing that knew him, and he especially delighted in a chat about crime and criminals with the unsuspicious policeman of his district.

In conversation he had an odd habit of digging his hands deep into his pockets and twisting himself round in the pantomimic contortions of a clown. Social visits he never paid, and he did not encourage unexpected visits to his house.

At Peckham he formed a menagerie of pets, which was certainly extraordinary for so unpretentious an establishment; but being "a gentleman devoted to science" his neighbours thought he might be allowed to indulge a hobby for zoology.

That he should be fond of animals is strange, seeing the traits of his character have been disclosed, which indicate that he was cruel and selfish to the last degree.

Some of his pets he had learned to execute tricks wonderful enough to earn a showman his living. His pony especially showed marvellous obedience to his command.

At a word this faithful animal would rear up and remain standing on his hind legs, and at another word he would lie down as if dead.

"Tommy" seemed to have been trained as a silent but faithful partner in burglary.

The custom of Peace was to go out during the day with Mrs. Peace, his son, and Mrs. Thompson in his trap, himself driving, and taking a survey of mansions he intended to rob during the night, and arrange about the destination to which he should convey the plunder.

He had two methods of attack. He went out early in the evening, when the family of the house to be plundered were all down stairs, then he robbed the rooms above, or late in the evening, or far on in the morning, when the family were all upstairs in bed, then he roamed through the lower regions, and abstracted the heavy articles of plate and pictures, with all valuables that were portable and transmutable into money. In most cases he proceeded alone in these expeditions.

The pony went out from Peace's stables at most unseemly hours, and sometimes the neighbours woke up when it returned.

One night the driving up to the gate was so furious that the gig knocked over the gate. The noise attracted the attention of a policeman who was on the threshold of a discovery, but he suspected nothing.

Peace had unquestionably just returned from an expedition with spoil, but when he saw the officer he blandly invited him in, although it was one o'clock in the morning, and lifting up the lid of a long box he explained to him that he had been engaged in perfecting an invention for the purpose of raising sunken ships, which he and Mr. Brian were about to patent.

"And you know it would not do to let people know

about this in the daytime," added Peace, upon which the policeman drank his health, hoped he did not intrude, and helped to readjust the gate on its hinges.

Peace, as we have already signified had described himself to the new sphere of respectable neighbours among whom he at this time moved as a "gentleman of independent means," and he was looked upon as one who had done well in the world, but there were more burglaries in the neighbourhood, and Greenwich became almost as noted for these classes of depredations as Lambeth had been. But there was this difference—that whilst the "middle class" people of Lambeth dare not report their troubles to the police and were not allowed the privilege of complaining to the columns of the dailies, the Greenwich "whitebaits" would not sit down so calm with this disgraceful state of things.

Night after night the houses of leading residents in the locality were broken open and quantities of plate, jewellery, and valuables of that description were stolen.

The "gang" who did it were evidently good judges, and selected very carefully before removing anything. Then the police became indignant—the public blamed the police—letters to editors were freely penned, but still the depredations continued.

Then came a lull—Peace, the single-handed perpetrator of all these daring robberies, had taken time to consider, and had decided to again change his residence.

But he had grown in riches, the result of his six months' robberies, and he decided upon taking a better house—one with a more substantial look of respectability about it, and hence it was that he deemed it advisable to remove to the residence which we have already described — namely, the habitation in the Evalina-road.

It is not easy to calculate with anything like exactness the mischief which a scoundrel like Peace has done by his daring exploits.

Man is a creature of imitation, and after the capture and condemnation of our hero, other rogues endeavoured to imitate him.

The evil which Peace did seemed to live after him.

No sooner had the public experienced a sense of relief at having got rid of him than a successor turned up to carry on the business on the same system which he had introduced.

The new candidate for the honours of murder and burglary combined, however, shifted the base of his operations from Blackheath to Hampstead-heath. He was discovered prowling about the grounds of Roselyn House by a constable of the S division.

The policeman on demanding of the man what he wanted there, was answered with a threat, to the effect that if he approached he would blow his brains out.

He, however, did approach, and while attempting to close with the miscreant, received a pistol shot, which would probably have killed him, had it not fortunately struck the bull's-eye of his lantern.

He was slightly wounded, and in the struggle which followed was struck on the head by his assailant with some blunt instrument.

Notwithstanding this he gave the would-be assassin chase, and coming up with him again, closed with the robber, but was too much exhausted to succeed in his commendable efforts to effect a capture.

The man accordingly escaped, and no doubt congratulated himself upon the success which so far attended him in his attempts to follow in the footsteps of the prince of scoundrels whose nefarious career he had endeavoured to shadow forth.

Doubtless many of our readers will remember the case to which we refer, since it was reported in all the London and provincial newspapers.

We sincerely trust that the loathsome memory of Charles Peace will not breed a contagion of burglary.

That crime, however, is infectious was shown by the garotte epidemic from which London suffered some few years ago.

The best preventive against the prevalence of a possible plague of housebreakers is undoubtedly to be sought for in efficient police surveillance.

A stronger force of mounted patrols is wanted in the suburban districts.

That a policeman should be left to encounter an armed burglar single-handed on Hampstead-heath in the dead of the night shows that this particular part of the metropolis at any rate is not properly protected.

In such a place the police should go in pairs, or, if one man is deemed sufficient to guard it, he should be provided with some better protection than a *bâton* against the chances of losing his life through being assaulted by wretches of Peace's calibre.

It appears to us that the police on night duty are distributed very unfairly. In many streets, for instance, where persons are constantly passing all through the night more police than are necessary are to be found, but in some suburban retreats the midnight quietude is seldom disturbed by the constable's measured tread.

You may walk through the leading thoroughfares of the West-end or the tenantless streets of the City at any hour of the night, and meet with a score of policemen, but on a tour of the same distance in the suburbs where all or most of the burglaries are perpetrated, it frequently happens that not a single guardian of the peace is to be met with. There is evidently need for alteration here

But none of Peace's imitators, or rather those who strove to carry on their nefarious practices after his fashion, ever succeeded in reaching the same acme of perfection, if it can with propriety be so termed, in any degree comparable to our hero.

Peace had been leading a sort of cat and dog life for some time past with his two female companions in the Evalina-road. He knew perfectly well that he was like a man who is at the top of a dangerous precipice; the slightest mishap, one false step, would precipitate him into the dark chasm in which sooner or later he was to be plunged.

He, therefore, strove as best he could to keep a tight hand over the woman he most dreaded. He did not care what amount of money he expended in ministering to her wants, with this proviso, that she was to remain in doors. So Mrs. Thompson had her "drops" at home.

She had a weakness for strong drinks, and was an inordinate snuff taker, and, according to Peace's own account, she cost him a pretty penny.

His weakness in respect to women is perhaps the most remarkable feature in his character.

After ruthlessly slaying the ill-fated Mr. Dyson, which crime he perpetrated not for gain, for it was clearly established that the unfortunate gentleman met with his death from the hands of his murderer simply because the latter had a sort of mad infatuation for his (Mr. Dyson's) wife.

And, stranger still, immediately after the commission of the foul deed, he took up with another woman, whom he afterwards had good reason to be in dread of.

Nevertheless, despite all these circumstances, he perseveringly and persistently followed his nefarious calling, even while the sword of justice was almost hanging over his head.

He had at this time perpetrated two murders. He had sent Police-constable Cock, of Whalley Range notoriety, and Mr. Dyson, to their account; and yet he professed to be a moral man in his new home in the Evalina-road.

It would be impossible to follow Peace's footsteps throughout his extraordinary career while engaged in his various depredations in the suburbs of London, but it will be necessary for the purposes of his history to glance at some of the well-recognised events which are, so to speak, almost public property.

It was not likely he would remain long quiet in his suburban retreat—excitement was a necessity with him. He could not sit himself down with his two female companions like other "gentlemen of independent means"—he must be up and doing.

So, early one afternoon, the gate was thrown open and Charles Peace passed through in his pony trap. He had to call on a friend, so he averred, but on this occasion he had with him the lad "Willie Ward."

He was going to give him a ride for a short distance, and purposed dropping him at the "Bricklayers' Arms." Willie was then to return home either by omnibus or the marrowbone stage—whichever he choose—but he was not to go further than the appointed place with his patron and stepfather.

As far as Willie himself was concerned, Peace had no reason to complain, for he was in a measure attached to his relative, and was at all times faithful and obedient to him.

An animated conversation was carried on between the two for the greater part of the journey. The lad would have liked to remain in the trap just to see what the driver thereof would be after, but he durst not express any wish to that effect; so, when the "Bricklayers' Arms" was reached, and Peace brought the pony to a halt, Willie jumped out and retraced his steps without a murmur.

Peace drove on.

He was, as the reader has doubtless already guessed, on one of his marauding expeditions. It was as yet early in the evening—so early, indeed, that few persons would expect burglars were abroad.

Peace, in the due course of time, arrived at Sydenham. He pulled up in front of a roadside inn, gave the pony-trap in charge of the ostler, and said he had to wait upon a gentleman in the neighbourhood, and would return in about an hour.

He was not a man, as we have before observed, who was addicted to drinking, but he thought it just as well to go to the bar and have a small modicum of brandy and water; then he left, bag in hand; the inference being that he was about to deliver some goods at one of the neighbours' houses.

He walked leisurely along till he arrived at a villa residence, built in the Gothic style of architecture. With the greatest possible effrontery he opened the gate and passed into the garden by the side of the house. Nobody appeared to be about, and seeing a bay window half open he crept through, and found himself in one of the back rooms. He peered forth, and seeing the coast clear he ascended the stairs. Somebody at this time was playing on the piano in the parlour, and the noise of the instrument, which was most unmercifully pounded at, effectually drowned the noise of his soft and cautious footfalls.

He found in the upstairs room a number of valu-

able and profitable articles, such as watches, jewellery, and the like; these he at once possessed himself of. The whole proceeds occupied but a small space, and were carefully disposed of in the capacious pockets of his coat. As he descended the pianist was still rattling away at the instrument.

When he reached the passage he found on a dumb waiter several silver spoons and forks; he snatched up these, passed through the bay window by which he had effected an entrance, and got off without being observed by a solitary individual.

The family were out for a drive, and there was nobody in the establishment besides the eldest daughter, who was taking a lesson of her music mistress, and the servants, who were in the kitchen busily occupied in preparing the dinner.

The astonishment of all, when they discovered the robbery, can be readily imagined. Notice was given to the police, inquiries were made, but Mr. Charles Peace laughed in his sleeve, and got clean off; but his evenings work was as yet not over.

He bent his steps in another direction, and after walking about three-quarters of a mile, or a little more perhaps, he came in sight of another house he had "spotted."

In front of this was a conservatory. As on the previous occasion he opened the gate, and entered the grounds.

Then he passed along till he came to the conservatory. He looked through the window, and saw that it was filled with the choicest flowers.

But he suddenly withdrew his head as he heard the sounds of voices, which evidently proceeded from the parlour or dining-room.

He was at no loss to divine that the family were at dinner, and to judge from the number of voices he was under the impression that there were several guests present.

He hesitated for a moment, being in some doubt as to his mode of action. His object was to gain the upstairs rooms, lay his hands on all within his reach, and then make off.

But this did not appear to be so easy a task as he had at first supposed. Probably the servants were passing to and fro, and in such a case discovery would be fatal.

But the greater the danger the greater appeared to be the fascination to a man of Peace's temperament.

He passed along the side of the house and found the back door wide open. He looked in and saw no one. With unparalleled audacity and assurance he crept into the passage, flew upstairs, and inspected the apartments above.

He filled his bag with the most valuable and portable articles he could lay his hand on, and up to this time had been undisturbed, but the question was how he was to get clear off.

If he dropped from one of the upper rooms the chances were that the noise of his descent would attract the notice of some one, besides which the windows were so high up that to descend from them was no easy matter.

"I shall have to risk it, I expect," said he; "go down the stairs and take my chance. It is quite clear they are all of them pretty well occupied in cramming and guzzling. So here goes."

He descended the stairs as quickly as he could, and was making for the back door when he was suddenly confronted by a buxom, red-faced, red-armed servant girl, who gave a start and a faint scream as she caught sight of a strange man.

THE DEATH OF TOMMY.

Peace was perfectly calm and self-possessed.

"Don't be alarmed, my girl," said he, in his softest accents. "Is the governor in?"

"Yes," she said, in the greatest possible state of surprise.

"Ah, that's all right," cried Peace. "Can I see him?"

"He's at dinner just now," returned the maid, completely thrown off her guard, "but I'll tell him you are here if it's anything particular."

"Only a message from Mr. Woodward."

"From who?"

"Mr. Woodward."

The girl had never heard of such a person. It would

be strange if she had, seeing Peace had given the first name that had occurred to him.

"I'll go in and ask if he will see you," replied the girl.

"Do, please," cried Peace.

The maid went into the dining-room to make the inquiry.

This was Peace's opportunity, of which he was not slow to avail himself. He flew out of the house, jumped over the garden fence, and then ran off as fast as his legs would carry him.

"Tell him to wait—I'll see him presently," said the master of the establishment, when the girl announced that a stranger wished to speak to him.

The girl was astonished when she discovered that the stranger was no longer visible. She went out into the garden, looked about in every direction, but could not, of course, see anyone.

She went into the kitchen and made her fellow-servants acquainted with the circumstance. The footman said no doubt the "fellar" was going to call again, and that she, Jane, was a little fool.

She retorted, and for a few minutes there was an intestine war in the kitchen. However, after this was over, and the strange man did not put in an appearance again, matters did not look so rosy. The servant girl was seriously concerned. What could it mean? The affair had to be explained to her master, who was, of course, very angry, and till up to this time no one had suspected that a robbery had been committed, and it was quite an hour before the discovery took place and then there was, of course, a fine hue-and-cry. But Peace long before this had reached the roadside house where he had left his pony trap. But his evening's adventures were not nearly over as yet.

After he had cleared the fence and got far away from the scene of his depredation, he decreased his speed, for he had become winded, and therefore contented himself with walking at a moderate pace. This he continued to do till the public-house was reached. When this had been done, he thrust the bag containing the valuables underneath the seat of his gig and gave the ostler a handsome gratuity.

But now a new danger threatened him. Just as he was getting into his gig he heard a voice exclaim in a tone of surprise,

"Look at that fellow. I do believe it's that scoundrel, Charles Peace."

The voice proceeded from one of the alcoves which were situated in the gardens of the public-house he was about to depart from, and Peace knew the tones of the speaker, who was a Sheffield detective, with whom he had been formerly acquainted. The celebrated exclamation of the Duke of Wellington of "Up, guards, and at them!" did not carry greater dismay to the enemy than did to Peace the words spoken by the Sheffield police-officer.

Peace endeavoured, successfully enough, it must be admitted, to alter the expression of his countenance as he stepped into the gig, but he was panic-stricken nevertheless, and for the moment all his fortitude appeared to desert him. He heard a movement, a shuffling of feet, a ringing of glasses proceed from the alcove in the garden. He did not wait to hear or see any more. He urged on Tommy, who answered by going at a rattling rate; the wheels flew round so fast that you could not see the spokes. Presently the driver came in sight of a steep hill, he turned round and observed in the distance two horsemen urging on their steeds to the utmost; they were enshrouded in a cloud of dust.

Peace grew sick and faint.

"Curses light on them!" cried he; "they are giving chase. One is Stackhouse as I'm a living man."

There was no help for it; the pony had to be put out to the top of his speed.

Peace urged him on with a few sharp cuts of his whip and then by his voice, which had a much more powerful effect. The faithful creature seemed to comprehend that the hour of danger and trial had arrived, for it tore up the hill like a mad thing. The pursuers were perfectly astounded at the speed at which Peace was going.

"But we shall have him yet, Clayton—have him as sure as a gun."

"My brute is panting and roaring like a blast furnace," observed the party addressed. "I don't think he'll hold on if we come to another such a hill as this. Confound it, there doesn't appear to be a level piece of ground in this locality."

"Can't be helped. We must have him."

"Ah! if it be Charles Peace, which I am very doubtful about."

"It's him safe enough. Do you suppose he would go at such a pelting, killing pace unless he knew he was pursued. I am pretty sure about it's being Peace, though he is a bit altered. But there, he's got a regular indiarubber face. He can do pretty much as he likes with it—twist it up in all sorts of ways—I know him of old."

"I am glad you do, and hope you are not mistaken. Lord, how this beast of mine does bump one! He's like a great elephant."

"Put him along—never mind his bumping," cried Stackhouse, in the greatest state of excitement. "We shall soon be up with my gentleman."

Peace knew every inch of the ground, while his pursuers did not. Had this not been the case, the probability is that he would have been captured, for Stackhouse was bent upon having him if he could compass it by any possibility. Neither of the detectives was well mounted; they were on hired hacks, which rebelled against being put to an inconvenient pace. They had not been accustomed to gallop up hill, and resolutely refused to accede to such an unreasonable proposition. Stackhouse's horse became restive, and had he not been a good rider the chances were that he would have come to grief; but the urgency of the case demanded desperate efforts on the part of the detectives.

Peace, when he reached the brow of the hill, turned sharply round into a narrow bridle road. He traversed this, and then took another turning, at the end of which were three cross roads.

Upon reaching this point, which he had done without attracting the observation of those who were giving chase, he took the road which led direct to Forest-hill.

Now he put Tommy out again to the fullest extent of his speed, and, looking back, he could nowhere perceive the two detectives.

He had succeeded in doubling upon them; they did not arrive at the cross roads till long after he was out of sight.

"He's done us," cried Clayton—"given us the slip in a most knowing, clever way. There's no telling which road he has taken, and, to mend matters, my horse is as lame as a cub and as obstinate as a mule."

"He's the very devil himself, I do believe," said Stackhouse. "Why, what a pony he must have to be sure! But it's no use hesitating—which road had we better take?"

"I leave that to you, my friend. I should say, the one which leads direct to London; he would be sure to go that way."

"All right—then on we go."

They did go on, as fast as their two hacks would take them. But mile after mile was covered, yet not the faintest trace could they find of Charles Peace.

Clayton was rather nettled.

"And suppose after all he is not the man. A pretty pair of fools we've been making of ourselves," said he.

"We've had a pleasant evening's ride."

"Pleasant you call it—I can't see it in that light myself."

"It won't do either of us any harm."

"Well, we shan't find him now wherever he may be."

"I'm afraid not. So here is a roadside house, we'll give it up then and dismount."

The two officers went into the house and partook of some refreshment. Meanwhile Charles Peace had been urging on Tommy, who never relaxed his speed till Forest-hill was reached.

It then became painfully evident that the faithful little creature was greatly distressed. He stumbled two or three times, and Peace observed, with the deepest concern, that the pony was all of a tremble.

"My poor Tommy!" he ejaculated. "I fear I've asked too much of you. Hang it," he said, in continuation, "but the pony is bad—can't hold itself still."

The animal in question was in a complete lather, and was snorting and panting in a manner that was painful to behold. Every now and then it gave a cry of pain which went to the heart of its master.

"Ah, my faithful friend," mused Peace; "you have saved my life; but at what cost? and I dare not risk remaining here, though I have every reason to believe that these bloodhounds are no longer on my track."

He had at this time come to a halt, and listened intently to ascertain if there were sounds of coming horsemen. All was, however, quiet, and he had every reason to believe that the danger was over. He therefore let the pony trot along at an easy pace, but even while doing this he found that he every now and then staggered and appeared to be in danger of falling from sheer weakness, so that it was a hard job for him to reach the Evalina-road.

CHAPTER CXII.

A PAINFUL SCENE—THE DEATH OF TOMMY—PEACE'S GRIEF.

WHEN Charles Peace arrived at his own residence he was almost as bad as his steed. It was only by a miracle that he had escaped being captured. Stackhouse was of course very well acquainted with all the particulars concerning the Bannercross murder, and should he, Peace, come across him, an ignominious death would be sure to follow as a natural consequence, for the "gentleman of independent means" felt that he could not impose upon the Sheffield detective. All things considered, it was most necessary that the latter should not trace the murder of Mr. Dyson to his residence in Peckham. Stackhouse, although he affected to be quite certain as to our hero's identity, was by no means so well assured as he professed to be to his brother officer. And in addition to this there were other circumstances which conspired to break the thread of the clue.

Stackhouse was only in London for a few days, and after the chase described in our last chapter, he returned to Sheffield upon other but less important business.

He told the officials there that he believed he saw Charles Peace in front of a roadside inn at Sydenham; but the general impression seemed to be that he was mistaken, and so the matter was suffered to drop.

When the pony had been taken out of the trap, its master saw that it was in a very sad condition; there was no use attempting to disguise this fact, which was self-evident.

Tommy had not been quite right for some days before this. It had a cold, and was out of order in other ways, but nothing very serious was supposed to be the matter. A mash was given, and the usual remedies applied, but the enormous stress that had been put upon it on this ill-fated evening seemed too much for the beautiful little creature.

Peace removed the valuables from his trap, and concealed them in his usual hiding-place. When this had been done he rubbed down the pony, and tended it as carefully and affectionately as a mother does her pet child. He was greatly concerned about the animal, perhaps quite as much so as he had been about himself during the fearful half hour or so he had driven so recklessly to save his worthless life. He was greatly dispirited and depressed, and in this instance he had to keep all his troubles to himself. It would never do to let the women of his establishment know the danger he had passed through, or the real cause of the change that had come so suddenly over his Tommy.

His thoughts, as may be readily imagined, were by no means pleasant ones, and for upwards of two hours did he sit in the stable watching his steed and musing upon the present and the past, and it might be trembling for the future, like a guilty remorseless miscreant as he was, for however callous and selfish a man of his type may be, he cannot be altogether dead to the silent monitor within.

He had obtained a considerable amount of booty by his night's depredation, and it is surprising, seeing the amount of property that fell into his hands, that he was not a rich man. It is a wonder where all the money went to, and the probability is that he did not know himself. It came and it went, how it would be difficult to say.

Upon his entering his domicile, he found both his ladies in the parlour with Willie Ward. As a rule they did not ask him any questions, or rather no more than was absolutely necessary, but they were at no loss to divine that something had "put him out." His brow grew dark when spoken to, and his answers were sharp and by no means agreeable in either tone or manner, and so but little was said by any member of the select family. When he did not desire conversation, he had recourse to an ingenious device—he took up his violin and directed Willie Ward to accompany him with the guitar. He knew perfectly well that his female companions would much prefer "magging," as he termed it, and sometimes he was disposed to indulge them, but he was not on this particular evening; he was not in a mood to listen to their discourse; he therefore laid hold of the fiddle he had bought at the sale of Doctor Bourne's effects, and began to play a prelude. Willie was always but too glad to join in, and he began twanging at one of the guitars.

The two females listened to the music complacently enough, but they, of course, had had quite enough of it, and, first of all, Mrs. Peace went into the kitchen on some excuse or another; in a short time she was followed by Mrs. Thompson. Then a discussion ensued as to the cause of Peace's moody manner, and both agreed that something or someone had put him out.

However, after putting his goat through some tricks

and amusing himself with one or two more of his pets, his ruffled temper became a little more smooth, and Charles Peace was himself again.

The women returned to the parlour. A game or two of whist was played, and then Peace arose, and said he must go into the stable.

"Into the stable?" said Mrs. Thompson, in surprise.

"Yes," cried our hero. "I don't like the look of Tommy—he's very queer."

"I'm sorry to hear that," observed Mrs. Peace; "but he'll be better in a day or two, I suppose?"

"I'm not so sure about that. He's very bad, poor little fellow—refuses his food."

"May I go with you?" said Willie.

"Aye, if you like. Come along."

"Oh, that's what's put him out," said Mrs. Thompson. "I knew there was something the matter. It's the pony. Well, that's a bad job."

"He cares a deal more for Tommy than he does for either of us—you may rest assured of that. But then, you see, the faithful little animal don't cross him; so there is, after all, good reason for his attachment."

"He likes to have it all his own way. It's the case with most men."

"He's got a temper—that all who know anything of him will readily admit. But so have we all, I suppose."

"I hope I've got a better temper than he has."

"I dare say you have; but you mustn't run Charles down. He's not such a bad sort after all—there's many worse than him."

The two women went on bandying words for some time. There was nothing new in this; it was their custom, and had been so ever since they had become acquainted with each other. It was, as we have before indicated, not altogether perfect harmony in the house in the Evalina-road, and wrangles were of frequent occurrence. It was perhaps in the nature and order of things that this should be so.

Meanwhile Peace and Willie were busily engaged in the stables. The pony seemed to be in great pain—he would not take his food for all Peace's coaxing—he was restless and fidgetty; nevertheless he pricked up his ears, and strove to put a better face on matters when spoken to and caressed by his master, but with all this it was easy to perceive that he was not in his usual health. As a rule our hero was not accustomed to give way to despair—his naturally sanguine temperament led him to look difficulties or troubles in the face. Had this not been so, he never could possibly have gone through what he had throughout his guilty and chequered career. Without doubt he was a most remarkable individual. The sanguine man can bridge over difficulties, which one of the opposite nature would perhaps sink under. His future, he will admit, presents the possibility of failure or mischance, as well as the possibility of good fortune and success, but with him the preponderance is immensely in favour of the realisation of his wishes.

Let him make up his mind that the attainment of a certain object is desirable and he has a wonderful knack of persuading himself that it is easily attainable.

He will muse over it until he has clearly realised not merely the bare object that would be all that would present itself to an ordinary imagination, but the thing itself, decked out in all the tinsel and trappings which a fervid fancy can create.

With him it is the goal which shines out large and luminous, and it is the obstacles to be overcome in reaching it that are too hazy and insignificant to be worth serious consideration.

The future always presents probabilities of both, but to the naturally despondent and apprehensive the balance is always in favour of mischance.

Both these peculiarities of character are open to serious objections, and if a man might choose his mental constitution for himself no doubt he would be wise to keep clear of both extremes. For all the ordinary purposes of life the capability of regarding the future under the clear and cold light of reason, untinged by the delusive colouring of hopes and fears, is very valuable.

He who can do this will not be daunted by imaginary difficulties, or waste his powers by needless preparation to meet them, and, on the other hand, he will not court failure by undertaking the tasks that lie before him, and neglecting to make due allowance for contingencies.

But if the choice lay between the over-anxious and the over-sanguine temperament, then for all the purposes of an active and happy life the hopeful is infinitely preferable.

It is just possible that excessive care and caution would in the long run more often prove right in judgment than injudicious hope; but even that is perhaps doubtful.

Not merely the unforeseen, but that which cannot be foreseen by the most anxious vigilance, is so potent a factor in human affairs that the fortuitous and accidental may perhaps be said to shape as many of our ends as all our cares can do.

Moreover, anxiety and fear and morbid apprehension are quite as distorting as high-flown hope and confidence.

But even though it be granted that the more cautious temperament is the safer of the two, any advantage in this way is more than counterbalanced by the pluck and energy which a boundless hopefulness is able to inspire.

There is, it must be confessed, very little "go" to be got out of those who are habitually given to a despondent and over-anxious view of things, however useful they may be as skids upon wheels that are apt to go too fast; while, all the world over, it is an always has been those who are dazzled by the brilliancy and colour in which they themselves deck out the future who have done the greatest deeds and excited the greatest influence.

All history almost has been made, wars have been waged, freedoms have been won, dynasties have been overthrown, reforms have been brought about, inventions have been perfected, not by men who have been pre-eminent for their skill in forecasting difficulties, but by those who have insanely "laughed at impossibilities."

No doubt great caution as well as great hope has been characteristic of many of the foremost men of history, but as a rule the greatest of human works have been accomplished by those whose cautious fears and prudent foresight have continually been borne down by their sanguine temperament or some equivalent to it.

The utterances of oracles, the reading of the stars, omens and prophecies, witchcraft and palmistry, and every other species of infatuation have at all times been called in to inspire just that confident hope with which capricious Nature has so largely endowed some of her children, while to others of them she seems to have denied it altogether.

That an over-sanguine person is incapable of taking

an altogether safe view of things, and that he is always in more or less peril, is true; but it is also true that his very delusions are the source of an energy and daring which must always be wanting to the timorous and despondent.

His infatuation may, no doubt, be regarded as merely a mild phase of insanity, since he will often see that which to the soberest sense is undiscernible, while he often appears blind and deaf to the most obvious facts before him. But if the delusions are akin to those of a madman, the strength and the daring are the madman's too.

Undoubtedly he who has this temperament should be regarded as one of fortune's favourites. The light that leads him on may often prove delusive, but it does not always do so, and even when it does it sheds a cheery glow upon his path that enables him to enjoy his life as he goes along, and at times permits him to revel in the anticipation of successes that are never to be his.

Cowards die many times before their death;
The valiant never taste of death but once,

says Cæsar. In the same sense the hopeful individual enjoys good fortune many times, the anxious and despondent only once; and sometimes not at all.

A more important consideration is the fact that whereas the cares, and worries, and disappointments of life have a natural tendency to intensify the over anxiety and apprehensiveness of those who yield to a proneness in that direction, they tend in an ordinary way to correct the opposite fault.

There are, it is true, some to whom experience seems to bring little wisdom, and there are still more to whom experience brings wisdom, only when it is too late to be very effective; but as a rule the individual who starts in life with a superabundant dash of the buoyant and hopeful in his composition, starts with, no doubt, a somewhat perilous fault, but yet with a fault which time and experience will greatly modify and reduce; while he who is wanting in this faculty of hope has a no less serious flaw in his composition, and one which, unless he strive against it, time and experience will but increase.

The sanguine temperament and self-reliant nature of Peace caused him to surmount difficulties which other men would have sunk under. And had he turned his thoughts and mind more in a proper direction, he had sufficient qualities to have caused him to have cut a respectable figure in the world; but it was not in his nature to abstain from wrong-doing.

He was guided by no moral principle, but had been radically wrong from his earliest childhood.

But we must return to the stable to which Peace and Willie Ward had betaken themselves. The former was much concerned at beholding the pony rear on its hind legs as if in pain; then the faithful animal dropped on all fours again and looked inquiringly at his master.

In a minute or so after this a sudden shivering seemed to seize the pony, who trembled in every limb, at the same time snorting like a war charger.

"Poor little fellow! he is bad," cried Willie, in a tone of alarm. "I never saw him like this before. What can be the matter with him?"

"That's not easy to say. He's dreadfully bad at present, but he'll get better after a bit."

"I hope so."

"Oh! he'll get better."

Peace, despite the symptoms, which were of a serious character, was still sanguine.

He strove to put the best face on the matter, and proceeded at once to prepare a bran mash.

In this he was assisted by his step-son. "Tommy" was the most docile, tractable little animal it was well possible to conceive, and took his mash without hesitation.

"Will that do him good?" said the lad.

"I hope so," returned Peace. "It is a simple remedy, and can't do him any harm."

Peace endeavoured to get the pony to take his food; he led him to the manger, and strove by every means in his power to persuade him to eat.

Tommy swallowed a few mouthfuls of oats, but this was evidently an effort.

Presently he turned away from the manger and lay down upon the clean straw which his master had previously prepared for him.

"We will leave him now," said Peace. "Quiet and rest will do more than we can do for him. Come along."

The two passed out of the stable and returned to the parlour of No. 4.

"How is the poor little fellow?" inquired Mrs. Peace.

"I don't like his looks. Very bad. I wish to goodness Bill would drop in."

"He was here when you were away," said Mrs. Thompson.

"What! this afternoon?"

"Yes, between five and six o'clock."

"Did he leave any message?"

"Said he would call to-morrow, in the early part of the day."

"That's well. Bill will be able to set him right if any man can. I wish he was here now."

"Whatever is the matter with the animal?" cried Mrs. Peace.

"He's been driven at too sharp a pace for one thing, and in the next he has been ailing for some days past. Bill will pull him together."

"I'm sure I hope he may, but ——"

"But what?" said our hero, sharply.

"Why drive him beyond his pace?"

"Mind your own business. What do you know about the matter? Nobody asked you for your opinion, which aint worth much at any time."

His partner was silent. She knew perfectly well that he was irritable, and would, to use a common phrase, "quarrel with a straw," so she said no more.

Peace bore up bravely against adverse circumstances, but his rencontre with the Sheffield policeman troubled him much. There was no telling what might follow. If he discovered the burglar's snug retreat at Peckham the game would be up.

As he reflected on this Peace's brow grew dark, and his face wore a troubled expression.

He had, however, a great desire to conceal from his two female associates the trouble that for a time so seriously depressed him; he therefore assumed an air of bravado, and discoursed upon matters in a reckless and over-confident tone. Luckily at this juncture a neighbour dropped in; this was a great relief, a little music followed, and finally a game of cards, so by this means he was enabled to get through the remainder of the evening. Before he went to bed, however, he went into the stable and had another look at "Tommy," who was evidently in great pain; the poor animal could not rest for long in one position. After attending to him Peace retired to rest.

Between twelve and one on the following morning Bandy-legged Bill presented himself at the house in the Evalina-road. Peace was overjoyed to see him.

"Well, Bill, old man, I'm glad you've called—have been anxiously watching for you," cried Peace.

"Oh, indeed; anything up?"

"Tommy's very bad, cursedly bad. I don't know what to make of him. I want you to see if you can put him right."

"Bad—eh? Attacked suddenly?"

"Well, yes, it is a bit sudden. But come into the stable and have a look at him."

"Right you are; I'll see to him."

The two went into the stable, and Mr. Rawton at once proceeded in the most professional manner possible to make a careful examination of his equine patient.

"Well, what do you make of him?" inquired Peace, in an anxious tone.

"Umph!" murmured the gipsy. "He's as bad as a 'oss well can be, that's what I make of him. He's got a fever."

"A fever!"

"There aint the least doubt of that, and the chances are——"

"Are what?" cried our hero.

"That it ull finish him."

"Don't say that, Bill."

"Aye, but I must say it. I think I ought to know something about 'osses by this time. Can't you see that he keeps grinding his teeth, that his eyes are distended, and that every now and then he is convulsed. His sight and hearing, too, are both evidently affected, and he is unable to swallow."

Peace groaned and said—

"As bad as that, eh?"

"Has he been overdriven?" observed the gipsy.

"Yes, he has."

"I thought so, and by whom?"

"By me."

Peace hereupon proceeded to put the gipsy in possession of all those facts with which the reader is already acquainted.

"Ah, Charlie," said Rawton, after the narrative had been brought to a conclusion; "you've knocked him silly. A 'oss is pretty much like a man in many respects. If you make him do more than he ought to do it's pretty sure to find him out, even as it finds us out. He's a purty creature, was a free goer—he was none of you sleepy-headed brutes. Worse luck, perhaps, seeing as how he's done so much for his master. Why, lor' bless yer, he'd ha' gone till he dropped—that's what he'd ha' done. Don't I know it—haven't I put him into a pelting pace myself afore now?"

"You have, and he was none the worse for it."

"That's just where it is—he was none the worse for it, but I expect as how it was nothing to what you made him do."

"I dare say not, but in my case there was no help for it."

"I don't deny that. I aint a blamin' you. Should have done the same thing myself under similar circumstances, but that doesn't alter matters as far as he is concerned. I'm afraid he's done for."

"Done for! You surely don't mean that?"

"Ye see," said Mr. Rawton, in an oracular manner, "I've had to do with 'osses ever since I was a youngster—a mere kid in a manner of speaking—and can therefore judge pretty well about this 'ere animal. He's got a fever, he's dull and heavy, his head hangs down, there's a chilliness about him, a staring coat, coldness on the surface and at the extremities, and every now and then a shivering fit. These are the first symptoms of what we call symptomatic fever."

"Well, but can't you do something for him?" cried Peace.

"I'll do all I can—that you may rest assured of, but I can't promise you to effect a cure. I may, it is true, but I'm doubtful. He's been overdriven, that is one thing against him, but no doubt the disease would have come on whether he had been overdriven or not."

Bill Rawton went out at once and purchased at the nearest chemist's some drugs, which he made up into laxative balls, two of which he gave to the pony. After this he took a small quantity of blood from his patient, which seemed to afford great relief.

"Oh, you'll pull him through," cried Peace.

The gipsy shook his head.

"I'm afraid of it, Charlie," said he. "It's no manner of use attempting to buoy oneself up by false hopes. I am afraid you must make up your mind to lose the faithful little creature who's done his best for you, and has paid the penalty."

Peace was sadly depressed as he listened to the words the gipsy had let fall. Still he clung to hope, even as a drowning man clings to a straw.

"It's a bad business," he murmured in a sorrowful tone—"a dreadful business. It was a fatal evening, upon which I had to fly for my very life."

"It's ugly altogether," returned Rawton, "for one doesn't know what may follow."

"There, that will do. Don't make matters worse for us by anticipating fresh misfortunes. Look after Tommy, and do your best for him. I'll leave him in your hands."

"Are you going anywhere, then?"

"Yes, to Whitechapel."

"Very well, I'll do my best."

"And so I leave my favourite in your hands for the present."

Peace took his departure, and Rawton remained.

He did not leave the Evalina-road for the remainder of that day.

Peace returned at about dusk.

To his inquiry in the house, he was informed by Mrs. Thompson that the gipsy was in the stable, and that he, the gipsy, had informed her some hour or more ago that the pony was not expected to live.

Peace went into the stable, and found his equine pet stretched on the floor. Rawton was kneeling by its side, and had its head on one of his knees.

"Well," cried Peace—"what news?"

"He's a dead un," returned the gipsy. "All his troubles are over. I've done all it was possible for a man to do, but couldn't save him, poor little fellow!"

Peace sat himself down on an inverted pail, covered his face with his hands, and burst into tears.

"It aint of no manner of use giving way so," said Rawton. "It was to be. I said so the moment I set eyes upon him this 'ere morning. There wasn't a ghost of a chance."

"I've lost my best friend—my faithful companion," murmured Peace. "Ah, Bill, but this is terrible."

"It may be so, but there are worse misfortunes than this. Keep your pecker up, and don't take on so. You laughed at me a few days ago when I gave you an account of Hester Teige. Now you are worse than what I was."

"I would have given anything to have saved him."

"So would I, but it wasn't to be done—so it's no manner of use talking about it; 'cause why, talking or mourning won't bring him to life again."

"Of course, I know that very well, but I can't help

grieving. He was my pet, was to me as faithful and docile as a dog. There never was such a faithful creature, and I have killed him. That's what makes me so miserable—I have killed him."

"You've done nothing of the sort. He was bad at the time, and it is likely enough that he would have died just the same if he had not been put out to such a killing pace. Cheer up, Charlie, it can't be helped, there are other ponies in the world."

"Ah, but not like him, none like him."

"Maybe there are, who knows ?"

"Ah, who, indeed ? Not I."

Despite the exhortations of Rawton, Peace could not readily get over the poignant sorrow he felt at the loss of his pony.

This may appear strange with one of his callous temperament. But the fact remains the same, and many persons could testify to the great grief he demonstrated on this occasion.

It passed over, however, in the course of a few days, and Charles Peace was then himself again.

CHAPTER CXIII.

MISS LAURA STANBRIDGE MAKES A MISTAKE—CAUGHT IN THE ACT.

LAURA STANBRIDGE throughout her lawless career had been singularly fortunate in escaping detection. She was known or suspected rather of being a receiver of stolen goods, and while following this occupation she had as yet not been entangled in the meshes of that net which the law throws out to catch the unwary or less fortunate criminal.

But no one is wise at all times, and such was proved to be the case with Miss Stanbridge.

Actuated by a mad impulse, or, it might be, from the desire of excitement, this unprincipled woman chose to do a little robbery on her own account.

There was no occasion for it, for she was rich, and therefore had not the excuse of extreme need; but nevertheless she could not resist the impulse.

She was stopping for a day or two in a small country town in the north of England.

Clickborne, the place in question, was one of those clean dull towns where the streets are always white, the pavement equally so, likewise the houses.

Some persons called it a pretty place, and, as far as cleanliness and salubrity were concerned, there was perhaps no reason for complaint.

But it resembled a huge white sepulchre—the names over the doors forming the epitaphs, the cries of the commercial vagrants forming the funeral hymn.

This is, perhaps, not a very flattering description of the place, but it is one which a journalist gave in one of the London newspapers. We do not, of course, vouch for its accuracy, for journalists are prone at times to sacrifice truth to effect. That it was clean and apparently dull is beyond all question.

Suddenly, however, the principal street was thrown into a state of the greatest excitement. Windows were flung open, and a crowd of faces protruded. Beggars basking in the sunshine returned to their feet, and to an unpleasant consciousness of their starvation, which, while in a dormant state they had perhaps forgotten; dogs awoke from their slumbers, and aroused the neighbourhood with their sharp barks; pigeons descended and fluttered round the cause of all this startle and disturbance.

There was nothing of any great importance to cause all this flutter and outcry, but the Clickbornites were very impressible, it would appear.

The cause was simply this.

A lady elegantly dressed was walking quietly along the right-hand side of the street, toying with a green silk parasol between her lavender gloved fingers. The Clickbornites watched with a curiosity as unfeigned as it was undisguised.

She was a lady, or supposed to be such—anyway she had the appearance of one, and therefore it was taken for granted that she was such, and she was dressed in the height of fashion—she was therefore not only a stranger but a prodigy.

Now in most country towns there is one shop which is as large as three, and which employs a fabulous number of young men. In some towns it is a grocer's, in others it is a fine art repository, in Clickborne it was a draper's.

Before the door of this well-known establishment one might see at a certain hour handsome carriages, which were driven into Clickborne every afternoon when the weather was fine.

It was also patronised by young gentlemen incipient in dandyism, who attempted with Clickbornian scarfs and collars to rival the exquisites of Bond-street or Belgravia, for it must be noted that in addition to the drapery department there was one devoted to hosiery of every conceivable description.

Every town, remote as it may be, and rude as its inhabitants may appear, has yet its fashionable hours. In Clickborne no one shopped till the afternoon; therefore when they saw the strange lady enter the great shop at noon, the sensation rose to a climax, and the crowd increased. It does not take much to arouse the curiosity of persons who locate themselves in the country; there is generally such a dearth of objects to create excitement that the good folks avail themselves of any excuse for a surprise.

In half an hour's time the lady reappeared. Her veil was raised. Before she wore it down. However, they had time to see that she was beautiful. Her handsome face inspired the male passengers with awe, the females with envy, and the beggars with hope, although hard experience teaches us that the ugliest people are the most charitable. Beauty is a shrine at which we involuntarily worship, and which we ever invest with the attributes of compassion. This is evidenced but too frequently; and it is not possible for the most determined caviller to contravene. In trials we invariably find that there is but little interest manifested by the outside public in a female prisoner who is unmistakeably plain or ugly.

The lady to whom we are now referring was almost lost sight of round the distant corner, when the shop door was suddenly opened and three young men rushed out into the middle of the street with bare heads and a wonder-struck expression on their countenances. On perceiving the lady they gave a shout, and rushed after her like harriers.

The excitement was by this time at its height. What could it mean ? was the question repeatedly asked, but which no one seemed able to answer.

The spectators poured down from their windows to their doors, and from their doors into the street. Something extraordinary had taken place, and everyone was desirous of knowing what that something was.

They saw the shopmen leading back the fashionably-dressed female, who expostulated with them loudly. She was most indignant, and told them that they should be severely punished for the indignity they had offered her.

One of them carried a bundle of lace in his hand, which, with a triumphant wave of his hand, he presented to the owner of the Titanic establishment, who, panting and almost breathless, had come up with his subordinates.

They were immediately surrounded by a horde of men, women, and children, who had come to see what was the matter. These persons cried out in loud voices, and, addressing themselves to the master draper, asked what the poor thing had done.

There was a general feeling of sympathy for the lady manifested by the crowd, some of whom were disposed to take her part at all hazards.

The proprietor of the drapery establishment saw this, and he appealed to them impetuously. He was not very logical, but that did not much matter.

"Was it right," he said to the gaping bystanders, "that he should have, he'd be afraid to say how many pounds worth of lace, lifted out of his shop without trying to protect himself?"

"Oh, gammon and all!" cried a rough navigator, who had been working on the line for the last few weeks.

"No gammon, my man," said the draper, with sudden warmth, "it's a fact. Isn't it a duty I owe to myself and to all my brethren in the trade to resent such an act—to punish the perpetrator? Isn't it incumbent on me as a Christian and a church-goer to expose such dishonest practices? I ask you that."

"I always thought it was the duty of a Christian to forgive his enemies," said the navigator. "Leastways, that's what I've bin taught, guv'nor."

"You mind your own business, my friend," cried the draper, "and I'll mind mine."

"Don't you attempt to cheek me," said the navigator, who stuck to his post manfully—"'cause I tell yer plainly I aint one as ell stand it. You may keep a fine shop, but that's no reason for your being better than other people. Let the woman alone, and if so be as she's done anything wrong, she'll have to answer for it; but I don't b'lieve she has."

"No more do I," cried another.

One of the town's people, touched by the beauty and sadness of the prisoner, put in a word for her. He besought the draper to take his goods back, and pass the matter over as a mistake, which he hoped it really was.

"No, no, my friend," said the tradesman, "I'm for making an example of persons of this description. I'm as straight as an arrow myself, and there is but one course to pursue. I've sent one of my lads for a policeman. I pay him by the day, and I can't afford to let him waste his time."

"But, my dear fellow, consider——" interposed the townsman, who had before spoken.

"I have considered. If it was a poor man who tried to steal something because he was sick or starving, it would be a different thing altogether—I might take compassion on him; but look at the clothes the woman has on, they are of the most costly description. I can't afford to dress my wife like that, although I work hard and have done so early and late for the last thirty years."

"You work hard!" exclaimed the navigator, in evident disgust.

"You don't know what work is. Come along wi' me, and I'll show yer."

"I don't want to have any conversation with you," cried the draper.

"Shut up, then," said the navigator. "Go back to your flarey shop, and let the woman go about her business."

"I have no answer to make to this man," said the other, addressing himself to the crowd.

By this time one of the rural police had succeeded in squeezing his way through the crowd of persons.

The circumstances were explained to him, and the stolen articles displayed. He endeavoured to look as wise as he could, reflected for a few moments, and then said, interrogatively—

"Do you charge her?"

"Of course I do—charge her with robbery, with shoplifting."

"She couldn't lift your shop, old man, if she tried ever so," said the navigator, "so don't tell no lies."

At this there was a roar of laughter from the crowd.

"You have him there and no mistake," cried one.

"So you charge her then?" again repeated the policeman.

"Yes; do your duty," returned the draper majestically, "sawing the air" with his right arm.

"You must come with me to the station-house," said the constable, addressing himself to Miss Stanbridge.

She bowed her head without speaking, and walked quietly by his side.

"I should like to land him one on his nose," said the navigator to a companion in the crowd. "That's what I should like to do."

"What's that you are saying? Have a care," cried a ci-devant detective. "If you don't you will get yourself into trouble, my man."

"Ugh! he aint worth getting into trouble for," answered the navigator; "so I shall step it. Make your mind easy, old penny-three-farthings a yard. I hope she'll be discharged by the beak." And with these words the knight of the pick and spade took himself off.

"I should say she's an old hand," observed the detective. This is a conclusion they generally arrive at in cases of this sort.

"Why is she an old hand?" inquired a butcher of the town. "Tell us that. Do you know her?"

"Can't say that I do," returned the detective, "but, you see, a raw thief would have turned as white as a turnip when the man said 'station-house,' and cried a pailful of tears, pretty nigh. But this moll's too clever to waste words and tears when it's no use. She can see that the old man means pulling her, and she knows well enough, I dare say, that one might as well talk to a post as a 'bobby,' specially a country 'bobby.' Only wait till to-morrow, and you'll see how white her cheeks and how red her eyes will get."

"Well, she didn't look like a thief to me," said the butcher, "and as to her being an old hand, I don't b'lieve it. It's all moonshine."

Laura Stanbridge was lodged very roughly that night, and brought up the next morning before two of the borough magistrates.

As the detective had predicted, her cheeks were very pale, and her eyes inflamed with weeping, but in her case they were real tears.

She bitterly regretted having been so imprudent as to commit so foolish and unnecessary a robbery; indeed, she could not very well understand what induced her to run such a risk, and for the greater portion of the night she was plunged into the very depths of sorrow.

Her tears and protestations of innocence, combined with her beauty, might, perhaps have saved her if her judges had been gentlemen of the country, who, as a rule, take a merciful view of cases of this description. But they were tradesmen.

The injured draper was a magistrate himself, and, though not allowed to act in his own case, sat close to the Bench, which he watched with his eyes.

THE YOUNG CHAPLAIN STARTED AS HE BEHELD THE GRACEFUL FORM OF THE PRISONER.

The consequence was that they committed Miss Stanbridge—or Clara Johnson, as she called herself, upon this occasion—for trial.

After this had been effected the three magistrates returned to their counters—one to sell reels of cotton marked with mendacious numbers; the second to regulate his false weights and measures; the third to superintend the adulteration of articles of food of various descriptions.

The fair culprit was then placed between two policemen and escorted to the gaol, followed by a ragged and sympathising crowd. Indeed, it was impossible not to be affected by her face—so dignified, so pale, and so resigned.

Clickborne Gaol is one of the prettiest specimens of the model prisons in this country. We may contrast it with those of the old style, as we contrast the fairy-like colleges of Cambridge with the grand picturesque but sombre piles of the senior university.

Built of no dark grey stone, but of variegated bricks, which were adorned with fantastic designs and with an assemblage of graceful and picturesque little turrets, it presented nothing of the appearance of a receptacle for thieves and lawless characters, with the exception of thick bars before the windows, and in the ponderous locks attached to the doors.

Laura Stanbridge was conducted by the deputy-governor and the head turnkey of the prison to a building separated from the establishment by the ground in which the prisoners were exercised. The deputy-governor preceded them up a flight of stone steps, and knocked at a small iron door. It was instantly thrown open, and two women of repulsive appearance stood before them. They were both dressed in black, and both had ponderous bunches of keys suspended at their girdles.

Laura was forcibly impressed with the depressing nature of all these formalities, but she bore up as best she could, and endeavoured to put a good face on the matter.

Having handed over the prisoner to the care of these ogresses, the deputy-governor and turnkey returned to their own sphere of action. No man was permitted to enter the female ward but the governor, the chaplain, the visiting justices, and the surgeon; and so, having handed Miss Stanbridge over to the female warders, her two male conductors retired.

The shoplifter would have much preferred their remaining, for, to say the truth, she had more faith in those of the opposite sex than she had in her own.

But the rules of the prison could not be infringed, and she therefore submitted to them with the best grace possible.

She was taken to a reception cell and subjected to the usual course of bathing and searching, with those thousand indignities which felons and suspected persons have to suffer. When this was over she was conducted to her cell, which was on the same model as those of the male prisons, and which has been described in a previous chapter of this work.

Miss Stanbridge was disgusted with her narrow prison-house, and she did not fail to express her dissatisfaction.

"Pray tell me," said she, in angry tone, "is it customary to put prisoners before their trial in such a miserable hole as this?"

"Most certainly it is," was the answer of her janiters. "We have no other cells."

"Then I must tell you plainly that I think it an act of great injustice," said Laura—"of gross injustice! Am I to understand that a prisoner before conviction is treated in the same manner as a prisoner sentenced to imprisonment, without hard labour, after conviction?"

"Well, yes, she is. Unless she happens to have money."

"Oh, indeed. Money, eh?"

"Yes."

"And what if she has?"

"Oh, that makes all the difference."

"Does it? Then it's still more discreditable. Well, assuming she has money—what then?"

"She will be allowed to buy books, clothes, and food."

"Will she?"

"Certainly."

"And bedding and furniture?" she asked, glancing at the bed which was rolled up and bound by a strap, and at a wooden stool with no back to it by the wall."

"You cannot buy furniture; the governor would object to any prisoners making themselves so comfortable in prison. He might perhaps let you have a chair or an extra blanket to your bed; but, of course, we are only subordinates. It rests with the governor."

"Whom I cannot see, I suppose?"

"Oh, you can see him whenever you like. He is a very genial gentleman, and does all he can to make prisoners comfortable who behave themselves—but they must behave properly."

"I am not likely to misbehave myself," said Miss Stanbridge, "but I must tell you frankly that it appears to me that suspected felons are not allowed so many comforts as convicted first-class misdemeanants, who are swindlers, and therefore only felons on a grander scale."

She pointed to the rule which applied to the treatment of first-class misdemeanants, and which she had discovered with her first glance at the printed board.

"We don't make the rules," said one of the female warders.

"I don't say you do. All I object to is being treated like a guilty person before conviction. I am innocent, and this I shall be able to prove when my trial comes on."

The women smiled.

"You don't believe me?" cried Miss Stanbridge.

"Everybody is innocent until found guilty," was the quick response.

"I don't expect much sympathy from anyone here; but that does not so much matter. While I am here awaiting my trial it is but fair that I should be treated with some little consideration."

"Certainly you will be—without doubt."

"I can send for my luggage, I suppose?"

"If you choose to do so you can. Where is it?"

"At the hotel where I was stopping when this shameful charge was made."

"We have a prison messenger, who will fetch your luggage if you pay him for doing so."

"I will pay him," cried Miss Stanbridge.

"You forget, perhaps," observed one of the women, "that you had only seven-and-sixpence in your purse."

"I do not forget. I have good friends who will assist me in the hour of my trial and trouble. I am not without means."

Upon this both the women were much more conciliatory in their manner.

"We will do our best to make you as comfortable as possible," they both ejaculated. "We always do that to those who have the misfortune to be charged with any offence."

"You are very kind, I'm sure," cried Miss Stanbridge, with something like irony in her tone.

"You had better let me keep the seven and sixpence," said one of the female warders, "and pay it to the prison servant to clean your cell, otherwise you will have to do it yourself every morning."

"Clean it myself! Is that in the rules?"

"Yes, it is a rule always exacted."

"Very well, I'll leave the amount in your hands. That will be the best course to adopt—won't it?"

"I think so. There is a bye-law in most gaols against prisoners keeping their own money. Besides, you know you would soon spoil your fine clothes if you elected to clean your own cell, which I suppose you won't think of doing?"

"Well, I don't know about that."

"Then in that case you had better wear the prison dress if you mean to do prison work. It is grey cloth, very comfortable and becoming."

"May I wear it in addition to this dress?"

"Oh, dear me, no; you must wear our dress or your own."

Laura Stanbridge hesitated. "I don't want to be arrayed in the garb of a felon," she ejaculated. "Not unless there is an absolute necessity for my doing so. I will, therefore, wear my own."

She reasoned that in the gloomy dress which these poor criminals wore she would lose many of her fascinations. Besides, it was like putting on a badge of guilt —a thing that was most repugnant to her.

Having invited her to study the prison rules, the warders left her to herself. When alone, she gave full vent to her rage, and paced her narrow den with masculine strides, tearing her lip with her white wolfish teeth.

She bitterly regretted having made the false step which brought her into her present awkward predicament. It was a sort of mad infatuation which had led her to attempt the robbery at the draper's. She could not any way account for the impulse which had so suddenly prompted her to commit such a foolish act.

Crestfallen and humiliated she felt the danger of her position. She felt also its degradation, for this was the first time she had been in prison; but, worse than all, she was fearful of being baulked of that revenge for which she had so long and so patiently waited, and of which she believed herself secure.

Alf Purvis was at large, and she was in "durance vile."

"Oh," she ejaculated, "it is indeed bitter to be locked up here when all was working so well without. I must have been mad to run any risk—worse than mad—seeing that there was no earthly need for it."

She screamed with rage, and climbing up to the window like a cat, she shook the bars with her white hands till the dust flew from the stones.

Uttering frightful imprecations she sank back exhausted.

"This is the worst of folly," she ejaculated; "I cannot escape with my hands and arms. I must use a woman's real weapons—her voice, her beauty, her falsehoods, with a man's mind and nerve to guide them."

She sat down, and, leaning her head against the wall, with her arms folded and her face slightly upturned, she began to reflect — as a mathematician commences the solution of some abstruse problem—as an actress studies the looks and gestures of a new and difficult part.

Man forgets and forgives, but the woman whose pride has been injured can never forget and will never forgive. Alf Purvis had cruelly wounded her vanity, and this vanity, which when flattered will decoy women into vice, when angered will drive them into crime.

Laura Stanbridge had taken a tigress-like fancy for this man, who was so much younger than herself, and whom she had taught to steal. She had spent pains and money upon him, believing that thus she would secure a powerful weapon; but it had proved a weapon with a sharp edge which stabbed the hand that endeavoured to direct it.

Spurned in her passions, thwarted in her schemes, she had conceived an incredible hatred against him.

It is true she had solaced herself by making a conquest, and for a long time nothing disturbed her friendly and familiar terms of intimacy with Tom Gatliffe. This had continued even up to the time of her arrest; but for all this she had not forgotten her hatred of Purvis, whom, sooner or later, she had determined to bring to ruin. Now she was powerless; she trembled when she thought of the exposure and ignominy that might follow.

She was surrounded by stone walls and iron bars— by persons who would be stone to her entreaties and iron against her bribes.

The stern faces of the warders gave her no hope. Besides, they were women.

She had seen the governor for a moment in the corridor. He had scarcely deigned to honour her with a cursory glance as she passed; and as they were taking her through the yards, her eyes, busy as her thoughts, had observed a number of children playing in the garden, which was separated from the yards by an iron railing surmounted with huge spikes, yet enclosed within the walls. The governor was probably old and possibly phlegmatic. It was at least certain that he was married and the father of a large family. He would not be assailable. Her beauty, her falsehood, and dissimulation would be of no avail, as far as he was concerned. It would but be a waste of time for her to endeavour to propitiate him; besides, from what she could gather, he was a man, who, although reputed timid and considerate, was withal a strict disciplinarian and not easily turned from the path of rigid duty which he had followed for so many years.

She ran her eyes down the rules, and from thence discovered that one of the visiting justices was by law compelled to visit each prisoner once a week alone, in order that the presence of the governor or turnkeys should not intimidate the prisoners from making complaints.

This gave her hope, but it was but a transient one.

"Once a week," she ejaculated. "Ah, that is not of any great import. I would it were once a day—then there would be some chance for me. In two or three visits it would be difficult, or indeed impossible, to do much, if anything, but in fifteen or twenty—well, I might yet triumph, but I will watch and wait; it is not possible to say at present what my chances may be."

As she spoke the door of her cell was opened, and a young man of prepossessing appearance presented himself. He was dressed in a suit of black, with a plain white cravat round his throat. His countenance was indicative of deep and anxious thought, and his brow was furrowed with long thin lines. When she saw his face her heart seemed to beat more audibly, her eyes flashed for a moment, then she bent forward her head, and gazed abstractedly on the floor of her cell.

"He is young, and I think impressionable," she murmured, "and has, I hope, a good heart."

Then she took a pose.

CHAPTER CXIV.
THE PRISON CHAPLAIN.

THE gentleman who had so suddenly and unexpectedly entered the cell in which Laura Stanbridge was confined was the ordinary. He was an enthusiast, and during his brief term of office had striven hard to bring the persons he visited to a sense of their miserable position, and the evil effects of criminal careers. In some cases—in very few it is to be feared—he had succeeded in bringing the culprits to a right way of thinking.

His father, William Leverall, returned to England at the age of sixty-five. He had spent his youth and strength in the East Indies, where he had shed so much of his blood. Covered with honourable, but fatal, wounds, he came home to breathe the fresh air of his native land and to die.

He had not succeeded in amassing a fortune, which many less worthy persons than himself had done, for he had never at any time of his life been a devotee at the shrine of mammon. He, however, bequeathed the sum of two hundred pounds a year to his wife and two children. It was all he had to leave them. His will directed that he was to be buried with his hands crossed on his breast, and that his sabre should be by his side.

To pay for her children's education, which in England costs so much, Mrs. Leverall went to service as companion to a rich relative.

Thus, she seldom saw her children; but they were always with her in her thoughts and dreams, and the letters which she received from them gave her the brightest hopes, for they were both affectionate and obedient to a fault.

It was her wish that her son might take honours at the university and enter holy orders. His father had always been religiously disposed, and therefore the pulpit seemed to his widow to be the pinnacle of human greatness. It was far better, she thought, than following the calling of a soldier.

When her son William (he was named after his father) was twenty years of age, it was time he entered for matriculation; but her daughter Bertha was only seventeen, and though accomplished, was too young to commence life as a governess or teacher of music.

So they had recourse to speculation. Mrs. Leverall gave her son sufficient out of her ten years' hard savings to pay his expenses to Cambridge, where he intended to compete for that truest of all lotteries— an open scholarship.

She would have preferred Oxford as the arena of his struggles and trials, because her father and brother had both belonged to one of the colleges there. But then it was more expensive, add every sovereign had to be looked at.

Young Leverall was persevering and studious; he was therefore successful. He returned in triumph, while his mother stifled him with embraces.

Bertha, who was sternly classical, crowned him with a wreath of laurels. Then she gazed at his black and silvery hair, from which the green leaves peeped forth here and there like Dryads sporting in a dark cave.

She gazed at his soft hazel eyes, and at his cheeks, which care and thought had made so pale. Unable to restrain her inexpressible love, she flung her arms round his neck, and kissed him and toyed with his hair till the leaves fell one by one crumpled to the ground.

Mrs. Leverall shook her head, and then burst into tears; she saw it was a bad omen. Her son and daughter laughed at her, for these superstitions are only cherished by children and the aged, as shadows are longest and darkest in the morn and in the eve.

With the little which he had earned from *alma mater*, and with the little which his own mother could afford to give him, he was able to pay his college fees, his room rent, his kitchen bills, and to buy himself clothes. But he was obliged to be very economical, and it was this very economy which drove him within himself and to habits of solitude.

At first fresh from school, where his mother's straitened means had not prevented him from joining in the amusements of his fellows, he would sometimes pause in his work and look and listen with something of envy to the windows which were blazing with light and to the gay laughter, and the loud chorus of the bacchanalian song.

Soon, however, he learned to despise these boisterous pleasures, for he discovered from the faces and words of their votaries that they, despite their forced uproarious merriment, were not so happy as himself.

He would have become a misanthrope had not his heart been touched by a gentler and more refined influence.

A new spirit seemed to seize him. It did not descend in the shape of a vulture or a raven, as it descends upon fanatics and bigots—if it ever descends upon them at all—but rather in the form of a white and gentle dove.

One morning he awoke a different man. He no longer confined himself to his solitary room or pored over his ponderous books.

Stamping out the last spark of foolish pride with the iron heel of an indomitable will, and disregarding the professed scorn of his college companions, he joined them, and talked with them, hoping that some day he might be able to do them good.

When they found that he was unlike the other needy scholars who, to a man, condemned those innocent luxuries which they were too poor to afford, they began to like him, in spite of his shabby clothes and the tallow candles which he burnt over his Whately and Æschylus.

By the time he had taken his degree with high honours there was not a man in the college who did not respect him, and there were many who were deeply attached to him.

Mr. Leverall was a general favourite, and it would have been strange indeed if it had been otherwise, seeing that he was so unassuming, so gentle and kind to all who came within his influence. The old adage of "winning golden opinions from all sorts of people" might be applied to him.

He had studied hard, was an enthusiast, and looked hopefully to the future. But man's hopes are not at all times destined to be fulfilled—indeed, but too frequently the reverse is the case.

His mother spoke to him of those distant and almost unknown lands, where savages, with wandering feet and restless hearts, existed in a state of barbarism.

His imagination was fired by the idea of treading where no white foot had ever trod before, of encountering dangers, of civilising a whole nation to the science and commerce of man, and of leading it to the right faith.

A new society had been formed, who were preparing a crusade against the wooden idols of some obscure Indian tribe in South America.

He applied for the post of missionary. His fame and learning and the great eulogiums which his tutors had passed upon his character obtained him the appointment.

The vessel was to sail in about three weeks, and this time he was invited to spend with one of the members of the society.

He had never been in the metropolis before; his eyes and brain were bewildered by the vast chaos of men and houses through which he hurried in an open vehicle.

The next day he walked out alone to study the great city which he might perhaps never see again.

He was looking with wonder at one of those shops, which are as large and massive as a castle, and pondering upon the wealth and enterprise of his countrymen, when a horrible sight met his eyes.

It was a woman so thin, so miserably thin, that she was almost a skeleton; her bones seemed to protrude through her skin, her eyes were hollow, her features pinched and shrivelled.

She wore no dress but a tattered shawl, which could scarcely conceal her shoulders, and a skirt which hung round her wasted limbs in tatters.

Two infants naked and blue with cold were clinging to her for warmth, which she tried to give them with her attenuated arms.

When he saw this he was nearly overcome. Several persons passed her; some were tradesmen, other professional gentlemen, and some were well-dressed ladies with kind benignant countenances.

With words so faint that they resembled moans, and with hands outstretched, this wretched woman appealed to them for alms, but they passed by without deigning to take any notice of her or her supplication.

This continued for some little time, during which Mr. Leverall looked at each passenger as he or she went by.

Presently a policeman came upon the scene, he ordered her, in a sharp angry tone, to move on. She looked tearfully at his face, saw no mercy there, and was about to leave the spot.

Leverall could bear it no longer—he gave her all the money he had with him, and walked quietly away without listening to her shrill and almost delirious exclamations of delight.

In ten minutes he regretted that he had not gone home for more money, but in ten minutes more he began to learn that it required unlimited means, boundless wealth, to relieve the distress one witnesses in certain parts of the metropolis.

Anxious to learn the worst he turned down the narrowest and darkest street he could find, where the shops were of the lowest and filthiest description, where the atmosphere was tainted as with a pestilence, where the streets were knee-deep in mud and putrid vegetables, where squalid children were paddling about, heedless of the unwholesome atmosphere and its surroundings.

Where all starved, and sinned, and drank—the men to nerve themselves for deeds of crime, the women to gain the high spirits and false smiles wherewith to deceive their victims, the children because their mothers taught them to, and because they were hungry.

It must be conceded that this picture is a repulsive one, but is nevertheless such as one sees in the noisome dens of the great city.

It is in vain to legislate for people of this class so long as their homes and the internal arrangements of their habitations remain as they are at the present period.

It is in vain to attempt to disguise the fact.

Mr. Leverall was in the midst of a populous district, where infants were born and old men and women died with no hand stretched out to feed their bodies, to ameliorate their condition of squalid misery, or to save their souls.

He saw enough in one day to convince him that there were thousands at home who were quite as demoralised as the savages abroad.

That night he sent in his resignation, stating his reasons. Half the mission disbelieved him and called him an impostor—the other half believed him and called him a madman.

His friend remonstrated with him, showed him what a brilliant opening he was about to throw away, and assured him that several missions had been started to ameliorate the condition of the London poor, that every effort had been made to bring about a better state of things, but that in almost every instance the success had not been at all commensurate with the time and money expended.

Leverall had his own opinion upon the subject. He could not bring himself to believe that the mission or those appointed as its agents had set the right way about the work of reformation.

The arguments, therefore, made use of by his friend only strengthened him in his resolution.

The missionaries he had worshipped then were only cowards who abandoned a difficult task at home in order to obtain an easy victory abroad. To him difficulties in his narrow path were but mountains by which he could climb to the goal upon which he had set his heart.

He visited the husband of the lady whom his mother had served as a companion. This gentleman was rich and had influence in several quarters. He had an antipathy to foreign charity and home heartlessness; he was a practical man, who was not easily bamboozled by cant or hypocrisy, and he could not restrain his admiration as he listened to the glowing description of the young man who, on the short but incontestable experiences of a few hours, had given up a liberal income from motives which, to say the least, were both honest and reasonable.

"I think I understand you, Leverall," said his patron. "You think that there is plenty of work at home for a zealous minister—more than enough work in the dens of London."

"I feel assured of it, sir."

"But the task is not an easy one, and hence it is that so many who have undertaken it have given it up as hopeless."

"I do not intend to follow their example," said Leverall, in a tone of confidence.

His companion smiled.

"You will have to cope," said he, "not with untutored savages, who, as a rule listen readily, I am told, to the words of those whom they acknowledge to be superior to themselves, but with men who are seared by crime, brutalised by drink, and embittered by misfortune. At present you are young; you have energy, patience, and hope, but you have no experience."

"That I admit; but experience I shall get as I proceed with my task."

"My very excellent young friend, be assured that no great design has yet succeeded which has not been matured with profound thought and deliberation."

"Without doubt that is so."

"Therefore, all things considered, I bid you think twice before you start on a crusade which might after all turn out, not only immensely laborious, but perhaps in the end unsatisfactory."

"I do not view it in that light."

"Perhaps not, but I do."

"You are without doubt the best judge."

"Well, Mr. Leverall, I have been thinking the matter over for some little time, and I am glad you have come here to seek my advice in the matter. I tell you what I can do—at least I hope I shall succeed, if it meets with your approval. The chaplaincy of one of our county prisons is at present vacant, apply for the appointment, and I will exert my interest in your favour."

"Oh, sir, I am indeed obliged by this kind offer."

"Then you consent?"

"Most willingly."

"In prison you will meet with criminals of the worst type—you will also meet with many whom a timely word of warning will turn to the path of rectitude. It will be a fine arena for you to study the human character, and in a very short time you will have a practical knowlede of erring man. Your salary will not be very large, but will suffice for your immediate necessities, and I will give you a certain sum of money to expend upon books and whatever else you may deem necessary for the good of those placed under your charge. Keep an account of this money, with a diary of your doings, and send them to me every three months."

"Accept my most sincere and heartfelt thanks," cried the young minister.

"When I see that you have grown wise enough to be the leader of a mission," said his patron with a winning smile, "I will liberate you from your apprenticeship."

Leverall applied for the appointment, which he readily obtained, through the influence of his friend and counsellor.

Had Laura Stanbridge been able to see into this young man's heart, which was so gentle and so pure—could she have guessed this divine scheme which was germinating in his brain, and which raised him above all vulgar passions, she would perhaps have despaired of destroying in a few days that which had been implanted at his birth, and which gave promise of such fair fruit.

He was not satisfied with the one hour of communion with the prisoners appointed by the law—it was his practice to visit them all in their cells privately every day.

He had heard that No. 43 was a noted female thief, and he approached her cell with some little mistrust. This statement, however, was altogether erroneous, as many other statements sometimes are, either out of prison or within its walls.

Laura had never been before in trouble—that is, in other words, she had never been in prison, albeit she had been living by dishonest means for a number of years.

The chaplain had expected to find one of those hardened women who are worse than the vilest of men, and who so often replied to his kind words with coarse invectives or obscene jests.

When he entered the cell he started, for he saw a young woman, pale and beautiful, who was seated on a wooden stool, with one hand, limp and motionless, in her lap—with the other supporting her head, half concealed in her beautiful brown hair.

The chaplain gazed for a moment, wonder-stricken, at the graceful form of the prisoner, who was the very personification of grief and resignation. Her manner was subdued, and it might be said refined.

Mr. Leverall thought there must be some mistake. Surely the fair creature before him could not be a hardened offender. He came at once to the conclusion that the authorities were in error, and nothing could dispossess him of this impression.

Laura Stanbridge had observed his start, and the expression of surprise which sat on his countenance. She was about to play a part, and all her hopes depended upon the skill with which she performed it.

"You are one of the fresh arrivals in this gaol, I believe?" said Mr. Leverall.

She answered by an inclination of her head.

"Charged with shoplifting—is that so?"

"Yes, sir," she answered; "I am charged, that is all."

"You hope to prove your innocence?"

"Indeed I do."

"I also hope so."

"Thank you, sir."

He took a volume from his pocket, and said kindly—

"Will you allow me to read to you a little from this book?"

She did not reply by words, but again nodded her head, and then heaved a profound sigh.

"Poor thing! She is in great trouble, evidently," murmured the chaplain.

He then commenced reading. She listened intently, not to the words but to the voice, through the tones of which she hoped to read his heart. She was an adept in divining the disposition of a person by the tone of his voice. She found his was firm and melodious, but also firm and regular in its accent. She looked earnestly at his face through her long eyelashes—an art which is much studied by women, and which she had practised to perfection. In cunning she was almost a match for Charles Peace, and this our hero was very well aware of, for he had at all times been duly impressed with the powers of discernment. He knew her to be a remarkably clever woman, as false and unprincipled as she was clever. These were qualities which were duly estimated by the notorious burglar.

She continued her scrutiny of the prison chaplain, but could discover no symptoms of an amorous or voluptuous temperament in him. His complexion was clear, his forehead high, his eyes mild and open, while his chin was strongly marked and his mouth finely but firmly modelled.

From his voice and face she learnt that he was not only virtuous but firm. Her first glimpse had caused her to hope; her scrutiny almost made her despair. But this shadow of despair strengthened her determination, as those fight most fiercely who stand on the brink of a precipice with their backs to the abyss.

"It is my only chance," she reflected. "If I fail with him—if he will not listen to my entreaties—I am lost, irretrievably lost. I can do nothing with my gaolers—who will be women against a woman and fierce men against the prisoner. I can do nothing with the governor, who is a regulated machine. This man is young and pious—he is in all probability inexperienced and innocent. So much the better for my purpose. He is human—is to be wrought upon—not by gold, but by words, and—well, we shall see."

Absorbed in these thoughts she did not hear what he said to her; she only heard an indistinct sound, like the murmuring of distant waters.

When it ceased she glanced through her eyelashes, and saw that he was preparing to go. As he opened the door he looked at her compassionately.

She listened to his retreating footsteps till they became inaudible. Then she clenched her hands together.

"He started. I have made an impression on him—perhaps he admires me. Ah, I will teach him to adore me."

She gave a laugh, and walked to and fro like a leopardess in an iron cage.

"He looked at me sadly as he went out. Good—that is well. I think he is impressionable, and has, moreover, one spark of pity for me in his breast. Out of that one spark I will raise a fire which may light me out of these accursed walls."

CHAPTER CXV.

LAURA STANBRIDGE HAS CONFEDERATES—A VISIT TO THE PRISON.

THE few shillings Laura Stanbridge had on her when cast into gaol were of course soon expended. She found out that a supply of money was absolutely requisite, and she began to consider how this could be obtained. She had a large balance at her banker's, and a considerable sum in her house at the West-end of London. She had a great objection to doing anything that might advertise her present position to her friends and associates, and she did not care about making a confident of Alf Purvis. She hoped to get through her present difficulty without letting either Alf or Tom Gatliffe know that she had been charged with shoplifting. Unprincipled woman as she was, she had nevertheless a vast amount of pride, and of course this was greatly wounded.

After considering the matter over for some time she determined upon her course of action. Charles Peace was the very man for her purpose. She had befriended him on more than one occasion, and he was in duty bound to do the same towards her. Anyway, she felt that she could trust him, as there was no reason for him to round upon her.

Peace was therefore much disconcerted upon receiving a letter addressed to him in the Evalina-road from his quondam companion, Laura Stanbridge. In it she begged of him to pay her a visit—he was to pass as her brother on this occasion.

"Look here," said our hero, addressing himself to "Bandy-legged Bill," "Lorry Stanbridge has written fool to the end of her name at last."

"What do you mean?" inquired Bill.

"Mean! Why, just this—she's been charged with shoplifting—been caught in a lace net, and they've run her in."

"The devil! you don't mean that? Where did it occur?"

"Down in the country where she went for change of air. Gad, she's got a change now, and no mistake."

"Well, I'm blessed, that's the last thing I should ha' thought of. Why, I thought she was all over money."

"So she is—leastways I've always understood so. She wants to see me to arrange about her affairs—don't care about anybody knowing that she's in quod, and all that sort of thing. That's not to be so much wondered at. It is hard, but you see, Bill, it won't do for me to trust myself inside a gaol—'taint likely."

"But you won't desert her?"

"I'll do what I can—bound to do that—but as to paying her a visit, that's all my eye—won't do at any price. So you see, old man, I've been thinking the matter over, and have come to the conclusion that you might serve poor Lorry."

"Me?"

"Yes, there would be no harm in you running down to Clickborne, and having a squint at her. She wants to arrange a few matters, and keep the whole affair dark, for the present at all events, till she sees how matters go. Perhaps she may be able to pull through, do you see? and in that case her friends here in London will be none the wiser."

"She's not given her own name, I suppose?"

"Oh, Lord, no! She's too fly for that. Well, what say you? Are you willing?"

"In course I am. She's done a good turn when I hadn't a shoe to my foot, or a rag to my back. Will I go?—like a shot! Tell me where it is, and I am all there."

"You are a good fellow, Bill; I always said so, and are the first to help anyone who is in distress."

"Oh, gammon and all! Don't lay it on too thick, Charlie."

"I mean what I say."

"I dare say yer does; but now let's know the rights of it. Fire away!"

Peace explained to the gipsy that Lorry was in want of some ready cash. This he, Peace, was willing to furnish her with. In the next place she wanted somebody to call at her house and inform her maid that she was unavoidably detained in the country.

"As far as the cash is concerned, that there will be no difficulty about; the other matters will require some little consideration. The first thing to be done is for you to see her."

"I'll run down this 'ere blessed day," cried Bill.

"No; to-morrow will do. Start early in the morning, and do your best. You must, of course, not give your own name."

"I should think not—I'll call myself Mr. Bourne."

"Yes, and say you are her uncle. Better to pass as a relative. Her uncle—do you understand?"

"All right, I'm fly. But Lord bless us! this is a pretty business. Why, what could she be thinking about?"

"I expect she did it without thinking; it's the way with women, but she's got her head screwed on right enough, has cut her eye-teeth long ago. I certainly shouldn't have thought she would have let herself be caught tripping in that fashion, but there is none of us know what may happen. It was to be, I suppose; that's the best way of looking at the matter."

"She's proved herself to be a downright good sort to me, and I'd do any mortal thing to serve her," cried Bill, in an earnest tone. "Whatever she wishes I'll do, if it be possible—that's all I can say. Hang it all, but this is a bad business."

"Don't you say anything about it to a soul—mind you that."

"I will not."

"Not to the women of this house, or Willie."

"Oh, dear me, no; I shouldn't think of such a thing. She may still be able to pull through."

"I hope so, I'm sure. Well I never—blowed if this hasn't queered me and no mistake."

"Let's have some grog, old man. It's put my pipe out—to-morrow morning, you say?"

"Yes—by the early train. You will be able to learn more then, for of course she's obliged to be a little pinched in her letter to me, which commences with " My dear brother."

The gipsy burst out into a loud laugh.

"That's a caulker," said he. "She looks a deal more like your daughter, old man."

"There isn't the least doubt of that. She looks wonderfully young, all things considered."

"She's what I call a fascinating woman, and, when togged-up, is right up to the knocker. Well, I am sorry for her, poor soul—very sorry."

Mr. Rawton drained off the remainder of his whiskey-and-water, and did not refuse a fresh supply when Peace pushed the bottle towards him.

Bill could take a pretty good amount of spirits and beer, and did not appear to be much the worse for it. Peace, on the contrary, seldom exceeded the bounds of moderation.

"Keep your head cool for to-morrow's business," said he to the gipsy, "for you'll want all your wits about you to dodge the gaolers and to throw dust in their eyes."

"You don't want to be very clever to do that if t's gold dust."

"Yes, that's right enough. You'd better take a little with you. It will be serviceable, I dare say—that is, if you know how to work it."

"I'll work it right enough; you've no call to be afeard of that."

After some further conversation Bandy-legged Bill took his departure, for by this time Mrs. Peace and Mrs. Thompson had come into the room and put an end to the discussion.

On the following morning Mr. William Rawton took a return ticket to the nearest station to the gaol in which Miss Stanbridge was confined; before doing so he had deemed it advisable to make as elaborate a toilette as circumstances would admit, and looked on this occasion really respectable, and, in addition to this, he had determined upon being guarded in his expressions, avoiding as much as possible any cant sayings or slang expression. His grammar was a little faulty, it must be admitted, but it was wonderful how he could pull himself together, and assume an air of gentility when the occasion required it.

He presented himself at the prison gates, and said he had come from London to see his niece. He was admitted at once, although it was not visiting day, but the chaplain had obtained permission from the governor for No. 43 to see her relatives in the cell in which she was confined, and Bill, or rather Mr. Bourne, as he called himself, was at once conducted up some steps, then through corridor after corridor, till cell 43 was reached.

As he came in sight of it he observed a clerical-looking gentleman emerge from its entrance.

This personage was Mr. Leverall, who glanced at the gipsy.

"Uncle to the prisoner No. 43," observed the warder, in answer to the glance of inquiry given by the chaplain.

"Ah!" said the latter, "you are the young person's uncle—are you?" said the chaplain.

"Yes, sir," returned the gipsy. "It's been a sad shock to her relatives, and has fallen upon me with terrible and overwhelming force. I have come to know the rights of it, for we all of us find it hard to believe."

"I hope and trust—and, indeed, I may say I feel assured—that I have awakened in the mind of your niece a sense of her position, which is, indeed, a most distressing one. She has no friends or relatives in this neighbourhood, I believe?"

"No, sir, not any. All her relatives reside in London."

"You may think yourself greatly favoured in being permitted to visit her in her cell. It is against the prison rules, but the governor has kindly accorded you the privilege."

"I am sure I don't know how to sufficiently express my thanks," said the gipsy, with a look which would have imposed upon the most sceptical.

Mr. Leverall passed on, and Rawton was conducted into the presence of No. 43. As he was passing through the door he slipped half a sovereign into the hand of the warder, who had been instructed to remain with the door half open, in sight of the prisoner and her visitor—so that while in this position he could not fail to hear the whole of the conversation that passed between the two, but the piece of gold had a magical effect; he withdrew out of earshot, and Bill and Miss Stanbridge were enabled to converse without reserve.

"Oh, it's you, Bill," cried the latter; "why hasn't Charlie come?"

"Couldn't—daren't—that's the reason. Well, I never expected to see a niece of mine in this position!" he added, emphasising the word "niece" emphatically.

"My dear uncle," cried Laura, taking up the cue; "I hope you have not come here to upbraid me."

"Far from it; I am here to see what can be done for you, my darling," returned he, putting his arms round her neck and giving a loud smack or two with his lips to make believe that he was kissing her. This little ceremony over, he glanced through the chink in the door, and saw that the warder had withdrawn to the further end of the corridor.

"All right," he said to Laura—"he's out of earshot. Now let's to business. Charlie can't come, but I'm here instead—so fire away while we've got the opportunity."

"You must not say a word to anyone about this unfortunate business."

The gipsy nodded.

"And, above all, nothing to Gatliffe or Purvis."

Another nod.

"Go to my house and tell the girl that I am detained in the country, and shall not return for a fortnight at the very least. I wish you could manage to take charge of the house during my absence. That would be a great relief to me."

"Stop there?"

"Yes."

"But I haven't your authority, and they'd turn me out."

"Ah, dear me, how powerless I am—how very powerless!" cried Laura, in a tone of sadness; "I'm at his mercy—and he would not scruple to do anything."

"I'll help you as far as lies in my power," said Rawton; "that you may depend upon."

"Do, there's a good creature; for I need help just now—and I know I can rely upon you."

The gipsy put five sovereigns into her hand, which she slid into the pocket of her dress.

"That will be enough to go on with, I suppose?" observed he.

"Oh, yes, more than enough; where did you get them from?"

"Charlie."

"Call at the house as often as you can, and see how matters are going on there. I suppose Alf will see that all's right. I hope so, but you keep an eye upon the place and let me know if anything's amiss."

"I will—anything else?"

"I don't know that there is."

The gipsy leant forward and whispered into her ear, "I am your uncle, and my name is Mr. Bourne. Remember that."

Miss Stanbridge nodded.

"And Charles is Thompson—that's understood."

"If you once address him by the other name, he will be ruined. He bid me charge you to remember that."

"But I'm not likely to forget it."

"But you'd better not write to him at all."

"Has he said so?"

"Yes."

"He has his reasons then—I will not do so."

The conversation was continued for some time. Laura Stanbridge felt very well assured that Charles Peace had some very strong motive for concealment. Whether she suspected at this time the magnitude of his crimes, or that he was liable at any moment to be arrested on the charge of murder, it is not so easy to determine, but it was quite clear that he had manifested no disposition to desert her since he had sent down Rawton with remarkable promptness.

She had unbounded confidence in the discretion and faithfulness of the gipsy, and this confidence it is needless to say was not misplaced.

AS HE ENTERED SHE SEEMED CONFUSED AND ATTEMPTED TO RISE.

During their interview she fully explained her position, and laid down the line of action he was to follow. In short, she made him her confidential friend and factotum, and after a long conference, much longer than is usually accorded to prisoners, Bandy-legged Bill kissed her hand affectionately, and passed out of the cell, the door of which was immediately locked by the prison warder.

Bill put a handkerchief to his eyes and pretended to be deeply affected, and apparently overwhelmed with grief he suffered himself to be conducted in silence through the corridor of the prison.

He hastened back to Peace and made him acquainted with all that had passed between himself and Laura Stanbridge.

"Umph!" ejaculated our hero; "it isn't of any use

mincing matters in cases of this sort. I'm sorry for her and will do what I can to help her, but it isn't any reason because one person has tumbled into the water that another should do the same thing in his endeavours to save a friend. I can't go and see her, and won't."

"She knows that, old man. She's a sensible woman, and sees things in a proper light. I will see her as often as she requires me, so that's enough—aint it? You can't do her a morsel of good."

"Of course I will serve her to the utmost of my power," said Peace, "but it must be done without my running any risk. I have got quite enough to contend with here, and if the police are down upon me, or have the slightest idea who I am, the game will be up, and I'm done for. Do your best, Bill, and for mercy's sake keep dark."

"You've no call to be afeard as far as I am concerned," replied the gipsy. "I shall see her again, and see how she gets on; but, Lord, I dare say she'll be able to pull through. She wants me to keep an eye upon her house—which of course I'm in duty bound to do. She aint got altogether what you might call the best sort of people about her! Hang it all, but she has been a fool!"

"A downright fool in this case, and no mistake; but it's too late to talk about that. She's got herself into a scrape, and must get out of it in the best way she can."

"I intend to stand by her, come what may," cried Bill, "and so don't you trouble yourself in the matter."

"You are as good as gold—that's what you are," replied Peace.

Rawton remained for some time at Peace's house, and took his departure therefrom with many protestations of friendship towards Peace and the unfortunate Laura Stanbridge.

CHAPTER CXVI.

THE YOUNG ENTHUSIAST—A WOMAN'S WILES.

MISS STANBRIDGE had set herself a task which required all the tact and finesse she was mistress of to bring about a successful issue. She had the cunning of the serpent, the patience of Job, and hoped to prevail before the drama was played out; anyway, she made up her mind to have a stout fight for it. She was duly impressed with the fact that it would not do to be too precipitate; she must study the character of the man whom she hoped to make her victim.

Two days passed without her being able to obtain any fresh insight into the character of the gaol chaplain. He came in always at the same time, and remained with her the same length of time. He was punctual in his attendance, and equally so in his time of departure.

This was very systematic, but not by any means so satisfactory. He appeared to be fulfilling a duty in a methodical manner; nothing more. Laura watched his looks, his tones, his gestures; weighed them, compared them, and analysed them, and could gain nothing from them that could lead her to hope.

He was earnest in his discourse, was gentle and conciliating in his manner; but then, she judged rightly enough that this was habitual to him. He was so, she imagined, just the same to the other prisoners. She could not flatter herself that he evinced any greater consideration for her than the other inmates in the gaol.

This vexed her. She must have recourse to stratagem, for the time was passing, and she was no nearer the goal upon which she had set her heart.

On the last day she listened to his words as well as his tones. They were words of pity which she could not turn as a weapon against him.

She now began to fear that the look upon which she had built her schemes had not been one of compassion for her beauty, but regret for her sins, and that this was a soul too high above her for her arts to pollute.

If this proved to be the case, she would be defeated in her purpose. Up to this time she had studiously avoided speaking to him. She had not looked at him openly, for thus she counted on exciting his curiosity, but now she determined to use her voice, her eyes, and her blandishments, and to cast forth the first of those silver cords with which she hoped to enmesh his heart.

When he came to visit her at the accustomed hour, he found her upon her knees cleaning the floor of her cell. Her snowy arms were white and naked, her brown hair fell with dishevelled art upon her shoulders, and over that voluptuous bosom which her dress did not entirely conceal.

As he entered, she seemed confused and attempted to rise, looking at him with eyes which appeared to languish, but which were really piercing into the depths of his soul.

He glanced at her for a moment or so, and then turned away with aversion, but without precipitation. He said that he would return when he had visited another prisoner, and these words, so calm and cold, crept like ice through her heart.

He had not evinced the slightest passion or hesitation, but was perfectly calm and self-possessed.

She was vexed—she shuddered. This was not a man! He was either supremely dense and unimpressionable, or else sublime as an angel.

In either case he was impregnable.

She heard him enter the cell adjoining her own, and hastily finishing her task she adjusted her hair, and waited patiently until he had concluded his ministrations to the other prisoner.

He remained with No. 42 exactly the same length of time that he had accorded to her on the previous occasions. It was therefore clear that he made no distinction between the other prisoners and herself.

Upon discovering this she was deeply mortified.

Consumed by bitter thoughts and anxieties, for the first time she omitted to look at him or to even listen to his discourse. For the first time she was deaf to his voice, or as blind to his face as she had wished him to believe.

"Oh, you impenetrable creature!" she exclaimed, when she was again alone. "Oh, you man without a passion! I will not rest till I have found out a flaw in your armour—till I have learnt where I can wound you. You must be human—you must be weak. I bide my time. I must and will triumph."

She dug her nails deep into her flesh, and gnawed her lips, to prevent herself from shrieking aloud.

At the end of two hours, exhausted with rage, she sank back upon the wooden seat, and wiped away the tears which fury had brought to her eyes.

There was a clatter at the door; a trap flew open in the centre, and presented a slide, on which was a bowl of gruel and a hunch of bread—her supper.

At the same moment a stream of white flame burst up into the air and flared and bubbled, making her cell light and cheerful.

She took her supper from the slide, ate it slowly, and replaced the bowl upon the board. Half an hour afterwards the door again clattered and the mug disappeared.

A great bell rang, and filled the whole building with its harsh and monotonous tones.

At this signal she went to the corner of her cell, unrolled her bed, and suspended it from wall to wall after the fashion which has been described in one of our previous chapters. She undressed herself slowly—being engaged in deep thought all the while. She lay down upon the bed; her brow was still dark and disturbed. Suddenly it became irradiated, and the prisoner sprang up in bed, and clapped her hands together.

"Ah, how foolish I have been!" she ejaculated; "but now I understand. How blind I have been! Ah! passionless man, I will conquer you yet. It is my only chance—I will get him into my power!"

The gaslight died out of the leaden pipe; Laura Stanbridge sank back in her bed and fell asleep with a smile upon her lips.

Anyone to have seen her thus would have said she was a young virgin who was dreaming of her honeymoon.

On the following day the chaplain, at his customary hour, paid the shoplifter another visit. He exhorted her to prayer and repentance, and was more than usually earnest in his manner. She listened to him this time, and affected to be deeply moved at the words he gave utterance to. Having fulfilled his duties thus far, he rose to leave the cell. He paused, and laid his hand on the lock. She took advantage of this pause to speak. It was the first time he had heard this voice, which was sweet, plaintive, and dangerous as the voices of the sirens of old.

"Ah, sir," said Laura Stanbridge, with a sigh, "you tell me to pray for mercy and to repent of my sins."

"I do," he murmured.

"And yet you do not even ask me whether I am innocent or guilty?"

He paused for a moment, and looked intently in her face.

"Young woman," he presently ejaculated, "I am not allowed to make myself your confessor. I beseech you to address yourself to a higher power, to Him who knows all our hearts, if you are innocent."

"If, reverend sir," exclaimed Laura, with an injured look, "I am so."

"That is a question I must decline to discuss or offer an opinion on.

"If what you say is true, I hope and trust you will be able to prove your innocence. Will you read a little of this while I am gone?" he added, and he placed a pocket Bible between her passive hands.

She did not answer.

"I will leave it with you," he murmured.

She nodded her head mechanically.

He went silently and almost sadly from the cell. Then she rose and walked slowly to and fro, with her beautiful but treacherous head upon her breast.

She repeated these words several times—

"I am not allowed to make myself your confessor."

In spite of the mild tone in which they had been pronounced, her eyes, which lost nothing, had detected a momentary contraction of the eye-brows.

At length she solved the enigma. Her chaplain had thought of the Roman Catholics as he spoke. Of this she felt convinced. He had therefore a prejudice against them.

"Good!" she murmured, "I have discovered that you have a prejudice, and each prejudice in a man's mind is a crevice in his armour. It will suit me very well to attack him on his weakest side, and it will go hard with me if I do not in the end succeed in my purpose."

When we signified that William Leverall was neither a fanatic nor a bigot, an exception should have been made in respect to one point—he did hold the profession of the Catholic faith in utter abhorrence. It is not possible to find any one man faultless. High-minded and virtuous as was Mr. Leverall in almost every way, he was nevertheless intolerant in this respect, and yet it appears strange that this young man, who had so often emptied his needy purse, who had passed so many sleepless nights, after witnessing a spectacle of human misery or human sin—that this man, who was really devout, should dislike men who were perhaps as devout as himself, and who tried to win souls as even he himself strove to do.

A bitter and poisonous hatred to Popery had been instilled into his heart by ignorant and prejudiced tutors, and by the controversial books and newspapers which they had placed in his hands. It was the one blemish on his white robe.

When he came the next day he found No. 48 with the sacred volume in her hands, and her eyes filled with an ardent gaze.

"Oh, sir!" she exclaimed, as she rose, her bosom heaving and her face stirring with emotion. "Oh, sir, you have saved me. I began to read this book, not because you asked me, but because I was dull; but soon the words began to steal into my heart. I read on and on, unable to withdraw my eyes away. When the light was put out I screamed. In the horrible darkness and silence of the night I heard whispers all around me, and sounds like the rustling of wings in the air, and the words which I had read I read again in strokes of fire on the wall.

"I awoke in the morning with a burning head, and a cold shivering in all my limbs. Again I opened the book, almost fearing to read, and yet unable to resist the strange fascination which it exercised over me. Accept my most heartfelt thanks—you have saved me!"

She burst into tears as she spoke, and uttered words which were stifled with sobs; but all the while she was watching him like a lynx. She saw his hands clasp and his lips flutter for an instant; she understood that he believed in her sincerity, and gave a smile behind her hands—so cold, so sardonic, that it would have served as an offering to the demon who inspired her.

He stayed with her for a longer period than his usual wont. In that time he discovered that she possessed the power of diving through the dead and inanimate letter, and revealing the pearls of the spirit which were beyond the reach of common understandings.

In fact, she was a wonderful woman, for in two hours she taught him not only a lesson in theology, but she had completely studied his character and was learning it by heart.

"Ah," murmured Laura Stanbridge to herself after he had departed, "he is the most virtuous man I ever met with. But so much the better; virtue is simplicity, simplicity leads to concession, concession to vice. That is why many good women fall and are scouted as ruiners, and why artful women, shielding themselves with prudence—the only useful virtue—are respected as moral members of society."

As she lay in her bed that night, she murmured to herself in a state of satisfaction and full confidence in her diabolical machinations—

"He has two flaws in his armour—the one is ambition—laudable in its way—but in all ambitions there is a stamp of the cloven foot. The other is a blind and senseless bigotry upon a certain point. Through one of these I will stab him in the head, and through the other in the heart."

For five days she allowed him to visit her without taking any fresh steps.

Precipitation would be her ruin, and she was too wary to risk taking any false step.

During the succeeding five days she coiled herself slowly and silently round the poor sleeping victim; soon he would be quite encircled in those horrible folds which embraced before they killed.

During those five days she matured her observations of the intricacies of his character, and obtained a certain mastery over him by her prodigious penetration into the meaning of the sacred writings, and by her eloquent and exalted language.

These he ascribed to divine inspiration instead of the human intelligence.

There are men so superstitious upon the problem of faith and inspiration, that they are unable to see things in a practical light.

Without knowing it he already venerated her, for in acuteness and powers of perception she was more than a match for him; and he never for a moment suspected that she was playing a part with one special object.

This gained, she would relapse again into the unscrupulous and sinful woman she had been all through her life.

The warders congratulated him upon the good effects of his ministrations.

"No. 43 was quite a different person now from what she used to be," said one of them to Laura Stanbridge's pastor.

"I believe and hope she is," observed Mr. Leverall.

"Oh, dear me yes, sir," cried the woman, "quite different. When she first came here she'd howl to herself when she thought no one was by, and answer us so surly when any one of us spoke to her, it made a body loathe to go anear her. But now it is quite different. When we go in she's meek and mild, and is always a reading a good book, and she speaks so beautiful, makes use of such soft and loving expressions that it does one's heart good to listen to her, poor soul! I do hope she'll get through the bit of trouble she's got into."

The chaplain's countenance was indicative of the pleasure he felt at listening to the foregoing observations.

"She is in an excellent frame of mind, and feels her position most acutely, I am sure of that," said he.

"She does, poor dear, and every one is sorry for her," cried the canting old crone, who, as the reader may suppose, had been well bribed by the prisoner in cell No. 43.

Miss Stanbridge had been playing her cards pretty well, all things considered. Bribes would not do with the prison chaplain, but she held him in bondage by other means.

Of this she was perfectly convinced, and the sequel proved that she was not far out in her reckoning.

She began to reflect upon her projects, which were still vague and unsettled.

At present they were like dark shadows, which passed backwards and forwards, but which she could not grasp or connect.

She possessed, or supposed she did so, a key to liberty, but she was wandering in the dark, for she had not yet found the door.

She resolved to make him tell her his history. Thus she might obtain a clue to the labyrinth in which she was lost. Thus she might find a fulcrum, without which the most powerful lever is useless.

William Leverall was by this time fairly in the toils of the huntress, albeit she did not realise this herself; but he was so, without perhaps knowing it.

She had so wrought upon him that when he left the cell he could not dismiss her from his thoughts. To say he was in love would be making use of too strong a term; he was fascinated, even as people are said to be fascinated by the piercing eye of the serpent.

His eyes were dull and reddened through want of sleep when he again approached the cell in which Laura Stanbridge was confined.

He had of late visited her several times in the day, and whenever he came he found her always reading.

On this occasion he opened the door softly. She pretended not to hear him.

He gazed upon her with a feeling that almost amounted to veneration. Her pale face and her eyes glowing ardently made her resemble a virgin saint at her devotions.

He was touched, and his countenance was expressive of pity, which, to say the truth, was the index of his thoughts.

He grew more sad when he remembered that, perhaps, in a few weeks she might have to wear a felon's dress and endure a felon's doom.

This thought made him shudder. He fancied that he saw her striving to soar above the shame and ignominy—saw her dragged back into the abyss by the base drudgeries and foul companionship of infamous and base women.

"Oh!" he murmured, "how is it possible to avoid the law? How can she be rescued from her impending doom?"

He remained silent and motionless, still gazing at her sorrowfully.

She divined his thoughts, and her black heart leapt with joy. When he spoke to her she gave a faint scream, and said, apologetically—

"Oh! sir, pardon me; I did not know you were here."

She showed him what she had been reading, and described her feelings with that perfidious eloquence which was one of her chief weapons.

Then she asked him to relate to her his life.

He sat down by her side with his eyes bent on the ground. She was delighted, but did not attempt to give expression to the joy she felt.

Then calmly and in soft low voice he entered upon his history.

He told her all about his college life, his three years at the university, his missionary prospects, his interview with his relative, and his appointment as chaplain to the prison.

He spoke to her of his mother and sister, whom he loved so warmly.

And he laid bare his warm and enthusiastic heart, into which she probed with cold and ingenious calculations.

When he had ended he found her silent and thoughtful, looking vacantly on the ground; he believed that she was buried in a reverie.

But this was not so. She was attempting in these few moments to mould her scheme into a form which could not fail. She threw out a sentence in order that she might feel her way. She watched him keenly as she spoke.

"How long have you been here, then?" she inquired, carelessly.

"Two years," he answered, with a sigh.

"Two years of prison life—of earnest ministrations! Oh! sir, how many hearts have you moved by your eloquence? Had I not met you, I might have been lost. You so good, so noble—"

"Hush, do not indulge in laudation," he said, interrupting her.

"But I must when I speak of you," said she, leaning her head forward till her cheek almost touched his. "Without you my life here would have been insupportable, and the' future," she added, with bitterness, and bursting into tears—"I dread to think of the future."

"Ah!" he ejaculated; "that is a sad reflection."

"Oh, sir," she said, in a tone which seemed to find its way to his heart, "what a terrible position I am in! I behold exposure, ignominy, and disgrace before me. My poor mother will break her heart when she learns what I am charged with."

"Does she not know it already?" he inquired, in some surprise.

"No—oh, dear, no! My uncle thought it best to keep it from her. It may be that the charge against me will not be substantiated, and in that case she will be spared the infliction of knowing her daughter has been an inmate of a prison. I cannot tell you—words are altogether inadequate to express the miserable state of hopeless despair I am in. Think of a respectable family being disgraced—think of the odium and obloquy that must necessarily fall upon me even under the most favourable circumstances. I have not before spoken of my own deep, deep sorrow—my abject despair. I have not pained you by a recital of all my agonising thoughts, because I thought it selfish to do so; but oh, sir, you behold in me one of the most wretched and miserable creatures you have ever met with. At night I think of these things—by day I strive by prayer and penitence to cast aside the heavy shadow which has fallen over me. I ask for mercy—I pray to be relieved from this miserable thraldom."

She ceased suddenly and burst into a passionate flood of tears.

He bent over her and with soft words tried to assuage her grief, which was painful to behold.

"You must not give way to despair. Bear up against the deep affliction which has fallen upon you," he murmured. "Cheer up—brighter days are in store for you, let us hope."

"For me there is no hope."

"You must not say that. Hope never deserts us, however sorely we may be tried. It never deserts the truly repentant sinner—you do not need to be told that."

"Oh, I am supremely miserable," she ejaculated. "If it were possible for me to return to society without disgrace and exposure I would for the rest of my life devote myself to the service of my fellow-creatures. But——"

"But what?" he inquired.

"I fear it is not possible. Can you see any way?"

This was a home thrust, and the chaplain hardly knew what reply to make.

"I am sure you would lead an exemplary life—I hope so—if you obtained your release."

"I would—I swear it!" she exclaimed, with sudden warmth and energy. "I will swear it on this sacred book."

She laid her hands on a volume which was on the table before her.

"All this is very sad and painful," he murmured. "You are respectably connected, without doubt."

"Dear me, yes. Some day I hope to introduce you to my relations."

"There will be time enough to think of that hereafter."

"Ah, hereafter—you are right. It is the present, the miserable, hopeless present, I have to consider; and when I think of that I grow sick at heart. "Tell me what I am to do—you are so good, so pure, and high-minded."

She looked up into his face, and saw that he was deeply moved.

"Forgive me troubling you about my wordly affairs. I feel that I am inflicting pain upon you. Pardon, pardon me."

She drew her hand across her eyes, and again regarded him with a glance which was at once supplicating, caressing, and voluptuous.

He quailed before the glance.

"Tell me—tell me what I am to do," said she, placing her hand upon his shoulder.

A beautiful woman in distress might well move the most obdurate heart, the most unimpressionable of the opposite sex to her own.

Mr. Leverall felt a strange thrill pass through his frame. It was the first time the prisoner had been so demonstrative. His pulse quickened as he felt her soft, pliant hand upon his shoulder.

She was not slow to perceive the effect of her wiles. As a cat with slew, noiseless and stealthy steps approaches her prey, so did Laura Stanbridge approach her victim.

She poured forth another piteous and eloquent appeal, and as she did so drew closer to him.

"My guide—my counsellor—my kind and gentle monitor! tell me what I am to do," said she. "You, who are so wise, have such wondrous powers of perception and penetration, are so well adapted to save and succour one who is at the present moment surrounded with difficulties which appear to be insurmountable."

"I have already given you the best advice I could offer," said he, not daring to turn his head and look at the upturned beseeching face of the siren by his side.

"You have caused me solace which can never be forgotten," she exclaimed, with something like rapture in her tone and manner.

She rested her head on his shoulder, pressing him fondly with her hand on the other.

He did not attempt to withdraw from her embrace. He placed his arm round her waist and drew her towards him.

Their lips met, and being now no longer master of himself, he had one long lingering embrace, which, if the truth must be told, was neither parental nor fraternal.

"He is mine," murmured the charmer, to herself. "He is in my toils, and soon, very soon, I shall be able to mould him at my will."

It was true enough the chaplain was fascinated with the seductive being by his side. He forgot to administer his habitual moral discourse—he forgot all but one thing, this being that he had an alluring and fascinating woman by his side—and he drank deep of his first draught of illicit love.

She had worked unceasingly to bring about the present issue, and she had succeeded far beyond her expectations. The fortress she had been endeavouring to reach for so long a time fell into her hands as suddenly as unexpected.

A smile of triumph sat upon her features, for she felt that the battle was nearly won. She felt assured also that very shortly she should be able to gain her liberty; nevertheless she could not conceal from herself that much remained to be done.

Mr. Bourne, her uncle, had paid her another visit. He had brought her a second supply of money, which had been sent by Charles Peace.

Laura Stanbridge had bribed the female warders in

charge of her so liberally that they were quite astounded at her munificence.

In prisons, workhouses, and other public institutions, money works wonders. It is useful enough, we all of us will readily admit, everywhere and, under all circumstances, but without it the prisoner can do little or nothing—with it he or she can do a great deal.

The female warders were in the pay of Laura Stanbridge.

She persuaded them that she was highly connected, that some of her relations belonged to the upper ten, and they believed her. Small wonder at that, seeing that in appearance she was far above those females they were accustomed to have under their charge, and in addition to this she appeared to have ample means furnished her from those of her relations and outside the walls of the prison.

The chaplain's visit on this occasion was one unusually long—indeed, there is no telling how long it would have been had it not been rudely interrupted.

While seated by the side of his enchantress the alarm bell of the prison was suddenly rung.

This was followed by the shuffling of feet along the corridor, the sounds of many voices, as of people who were conversing hurriedly.

Mr. Leverall judged rightly enough that something unusual had occurred in the gaol.

"My dear Laura," he exclaimed (he had already learned to call her by her Christian name), "there must be some strong reason for all this commotion ; I must, therefore, leave you now."

"You are going," cried the prisoner, pouting. "Well, I will not seek to detain you."

The door was suddenly opened, and a male warder thrust his head in.

He was evidently in a state of alarm, and said—

"Oh, your pardon, sir, but the governor wishes you to attend a patient in the infirmary."

"What is the matter, Martin ?" inquired the chaplain.

"A prisoner has attempted to escape, and is dreadfully injured. The governor thought you had better see him."

"Oh, certainly, by all means I will do so," observed the chaplain, who at once left the cell with the prison official.

CHAPTER CXVII.

THE ATTEMPTED ESCAPE—MURDOCK, THE SMUGGLER.

WHEN Mr. Leverall reached the infirmary he approached the bedside of one of the patients to whom his attention had been directed by the surgeon.

The man appeared to be almost in a state of collapse.

"Is he in immediate danger ?" said the chaplain to the doctor.

"I think not, but his injuries are very serious. He has sustained a compound fracture of the leg, two broken ribs, besides other casualties consequent upon his falling from a high wall on to the stone flags of the yard."

"How very terrible! It's that man Murdock, I see."

"Yes, the smuggler, as he is termed. A most determined, incorrigible ruffian."

Mr. Leverell made no reply to this last speech, but approached the bedside of the sufferer.

"I am sorry to see you in this position, No. 59," observed the chaplain, "very sorry."

"Ugh," groaned the man, "I wish I'd escaped or else have been killed outright. Oh—oh," here he writhed with pain.

"You must bear up against this new misfortune, and have the grace of patience," said the chaplain.

"I aint got any patience left. It's all gone long ago, and I don't want any of your palaver."

"You must not talk like that. Let me read a little to you."

"No, I won't be read to—I don't like it. Leave me to myself."

"But I must beg of you to listen to my discourse. It is useless your being obstinate or refractory."

"Get away, and leave me alone," cried the man in a voice which was something like the roar of a wild beast.

The chaplain began to read after a few further observations, and the man hallooed and shouted like a maniac.

Nevertheless the chaplain persevered, although not a word he was uttering reached the ears of the wretched man.

At this moment the governor came in. He was a tall handsome man, of about fifty-five, with a military stride, and a military voice. He was, in fact, a retired officer in her Majesty's service.

He glanced at the sufferer, who was writhing and making hideous grimaces.

"I am afraid you'll not be able to do much with him—not at present, at any rate," observed the governor, addressing himself to the chaplain ; "still I thought it my duty to communicate with you."

Mr. Leverall bowed to the governor, who glanced at the doctor ; then the three gentlemen withdrew into a corner of the room, and conversed in whispers.

"He's of a most excitable temperament, and as to making any impression on him I frankly own that I believe that to be quite hopeless. Under all the circumstances of the case, he had, I think, better be left to himself. His wounds are dressed, the broken bones are set, as well as we could do them, and in the course of an hour or so I shall prescribe an opiate."

The governor nodded ; the surgeon was a special favourite of his.

"In that case I shall not attempt to address any further conversation to him," observed Mr. Leverall, pocketing his book, and accompanying the governor out of the ward.

"I am glad he's taken his hook—jolly glad," said the smuggler, following with his eyes the receding figures of the governor and the chaplain.

Desperately injured as the man was, and dangerous as were his wounds, these were as nothing in comparison to the madness of his despair at being thwarted in his attempt at escape.

Mat Murdock was a villain of the most pronounced and desperate type. He had for many years of his life been a seafaring man, first as a smuggler, then as a pirate, while at other times he had been in the merchant service.

He had been convicted upon various charges, and had been sentenced to short terms of imprisonment both at home and abroad, and at one time he was the chief of as lawless a set of desperadoes as ever trod on land or sailed in salt water.

At length, however, the law proved too strong for him. He was tried upon the charge of murder and piracy on the high seas. The first charge, however, was reduced to manslaughter, and Mat Murdock was sentenced to penal servitude for life.

He was sent to Dartmoor, and while there he made two attempts to escape. He was such a trouble to the authorities there that they were glad to get rid of him, and an order was therefore sent for his removal.

It was understood that his ultimate destination would be either Portland or Spike Island, but for the time being he was lodged in the same gaol in which Laura Stanbridge was incarcerated.

While here he meditated and matured another plan of escape. He succeeded in removing the bars of his cell, crept through the aperture, and dropped on to the wall which enclosed one of the yards, then began to creep along this in the hopes of arriving at the outer wall, from whence he hoped to drop into the street, but, much to his chagrin, he found himself baffled.

He could not keep his equilibrium, the reason for this being that in one of his attempts to escape from Dartmoor he had been fired upon by the sentry on duty, and had received a bullet in his right hip.

The bullet was extracted and the wound healed up, but it left Murdock partially a cripple. He could not rely upon or make good use of his right leg for ever afterwards; the consequence was, when he was on the wall, its weakness became painfully manifest.

The miserable man was almost powerless; he tottered, swayed to and fro for a moment, then closed his eyes and fell.

When discovered by the prison officials he was senseless.

He was carried into the operating room, where a consultation took place, and the doctors in attendance did the best they could for him under the circumstance, and after this Murdock was placed in the infirmary.

Under the influence of morphia the smuggler was passive and peaceable enough, but the moment the effects of that drug passed away he began howling and screaming like a wild beast.

The bitter mortification he felt at the unsuccessful nature of his last attempt to escape was too much for him.

It drove him frantic, and during the night the manifestation of his rage was so terrible that the patients in the same ward with him could get very little sleep.

On the following day, when the doctor paid his accustomed visit, they one and all complained of the noise made by Murdock.

The wardsman and night nurses corroborated their statement, and the consequence of all this was that the wounded smuggler was transferred to a small room at another part of the prison.

Ill or well, Mat Murdock was a difficult customer to deal with, and not one of the few professional nurses who were in attendance on the prisoners seemed disposed to volunteer their services to wait on the smuggler.

But as we have indicated in a previous chapter, it is a common thing for the prisoners themselves to be appointed as nurses to the sick, and so, after some little discussion, a young man named Walter Knoulton volunteered his services as attendant on Murdock.

There was some reason for this. Knoulton and the smuggler had been on friendly terms ever since they made each other's acquaintance in the gaol where they were both confined.

They had worked side by side in the same shop at mat making, and Murdock had spun many a yarn to the younger prisoner.

Seeing and knowing all this, the officials one and all agreed that no person was better adapted to the task than Knoulton, who was generally acknowledged to be an excellent nurse.

In addition to this he was a young man of rather a superior class. He was well educated, had moved in respectable society, and was generally liked by all who knew him.

Prior to his conviction he held a good appointment in a mercantile house in one of our provincial towns, and was greatly esteemed by his employers, who, it was said, allowed him too much latitude.

His downfall was brought about by a concurrence of circumstances. He began by betting, then he indulged in a plurality of mistresses, besides other little foibles, which it is perhaps needless to mention. The end of it was that to bridge over a difficulty, he made use of his employers' money.

The first time he escaped discovery, as he made up the deficiency just in the nick of time, but he had recourse to the same desperate alternative several times afterwards, and the result was that his defalcations were discovered, and he was given into custody.

He was convicted upon the charge of embezzling, but his prosecutors strongly recommended him to mercy. It was thought that he would have a mere nominal sentence—a few days' imprisonment perhaps—but he had the misfortune of being tried before a severe judge, who never, under any circumstances, gave less than six months' imprisonment; so six months' young Knoulton had, and hence his becoming a fellow-prisoner with Murdock, the smuggler.

It would be difficult for me to attempt to convey to the reader the bold and fearless nature of this man, who, like a caged tiger, was for ever clawing at the bars of his cage. Nothing appeared to intimidate him. After his attempt to escape at Dartmoor he had for several months been forced to work at the quarries in chains weighing some thirty pounds, or more. Every vigilance had been exercised by his guards to prevent the possibility of his flight, and yet the idea of escape haunted his imagination, and became a never-dying, never-yielding monomania.

The thought of regaining his liberty seemed to be the one acting principle of his life. He used to observe to his companions in crime that he would much prefer being executed than having to endure a life-long imprisonment.

Whether this was merely said out of bravado or not we cannot determine, but one fact is quite clear—of all the prisoners in this gaol and others he had been drafted to, he was the most restless and discontented —he of all men else pined most for liberty.

When young Knoulton entered the apartment occupied by the sick man, Murdock gave a grunt of satisfaction, but he said nothing at first beyond that momentary expression.

"Poor chap, he does look bad, though," murmured the commercial, if we may so term him—"very bad."

There was a silence for some time.

Knoulton sat himself down at a side table and began to read. He and the other convicts, who were elected to similar offices to himself, were permitted to have what books they chose from the prison library. This was, of course, a great boon to them.

He read on for half an hour or so, being under the impression that the patient had sunk into a peaceful slumber; but this was not so.

Murdock even at that hour was meditating how he might at some future time effect the object, the thought of which had occupied his undivided attention for so many long and wearisome years.

He knew that young Knoulton was in the room, and he judged, or rather hoped, he had been appointed nurse. This hope he fancied would be delusive if he made any inquiry.

He, therefore, chose for the nonce to maintain a moody silence. He wouldn't be first to speak—not he; he didn't care for any man. He had been befooled and baffled; the world was against him, and he was against the world. These were his first fugtive thoughts upon Knoulton's first half hour or so in the apartment.

The door opened, and the governor entered.

He walked to the bedside of the patient and looked at him for a moment or so, then apparently satisfied with his inspection he said in a kind tone—

"I hope you like your new quarters, No. 95 ? They are much more comfortable, I think, than the infirmary."

The convict nodded.

"Ah, that's well," observed the governor in a cheery tone. "Is there anything you want ? If so, tell me what it is."

"Want ?" repeated Murdock.

"Yes. Can we do anything for you ?"

"Can you ? Yes !"

"What is it ?"

"Give me my liberty !" shrieked the smuggler.

The governor started back.

"You ask impossibilities," said he; "be reasonable. At the present moment your life is in peril. Be patient, No. 95; you are not out of danger for the present, and excitement may prove fatal. Be patient and resigned, and hope for the best."

"Hope! Ugh, that has long since deserted me. I want my liberty."

The governor said no more, but turned away and slowly left the apartment.

"He is incorrigible, and almost unmanageable," he whispered to the doctor. "I never met with such an obstinate man in all my experience."

The doctor nodded significantly, but made no reply to this last speech.

In a few minutes after this, Mat Murdock was left in the charge of Knoulton.

The latter did not seem inclined to force the conversation. He knew the irritable nature of the patient, and therefore deemed it advisable to leave him to his own reflections, which were, to say the truth, bitter enough.

The smuggler tossed about in his bed, groaned, and ground his teeth, but his nurse took no notice of all this; he was well used to scenes of this nature, and was, moreover, well versed in the treatment of such persons.

Presently Murdock glanced towards him, and said in a more subdued tone —

"Have they placed you here to attend upon me ?"

"Yes," answered Knoulton; "I am your nurse. Does that satisfy you ?"

"I'd rather have you than anyone else. Give me your hand."

Knoulton put down his book, and went to the bedside of the injured man, who grasped and shook his hand gratefully.

"Ah! Walter, old chap, I'm pretty well done for. Haven't much life left in me. But I'm thankful that they've allowed ye to be by my side, 'cause, ye see, we've always been friends since we first met—always !"

"I hope so, I'm sure," returned Knoulton.

"Ay, but we have, there's no gainsaying that—good friends and true. Oh, but it was a narrow squeak after all. If it had not been for my game leg, as deserted me when I most needed its service, I should by this time—long ere this—have been outside these accursed walls. Bad luck to the sodger who fired upon me at Dartmoor, may he be —— !" He uttered an impious oath.

"Silence! you must not talk like that. It's no use bearing malice against one who only did an act of duty."

"I wish he had been throttled afore he fired on me. Had it not been for that all would have gone well."

"You really must endeavour to be as calm as possible. Do not excite yourself."

"Not excite myself!"

"No, certainly not; that is if you wish to recover."

"Just Providence, think what I have suffered," cried the pirate. "Nine long long years of misery, and now two months of cherished hopes are crushed in a moment. Shattered, maimed and almost done to death, here I am at the mercy of my gaolers, and the hope of liberty still further from me. Merciful heaven, but its terrible—horrible."

He writhed and moaned in bitter anguish.

"Be patient, Murdock; be contented with your lot."

"Contented!" he ejaculated, bursting out into a mocking harsh horrible laugh.

"Why are you so desirous of gaining your liberty ?"

"Why ? Oh, you know not what it is to endure the horrible drudgery of nine years' penal servitude. If you had, you would not ask such a question."

"Well, perhaps not. Yours is a hard lot, and has been for so——"

"For nine long, miserable years."

"But of what use is liberty to you now ? You are old, Murdock. The best and brightest of your days have passed."

"True, I am old; there's no denying that. You are right—I am old."

"Past fifty, I suppose ?"

"Nearly sixty."

"Well, then, supposing you gained your liberty, what would you do to obtain a living ? You are getting past work."

"I'm not past work as yet," returned the pirate, savagely, "though I am not the man I was; but I can turn my hand to a thing or two still."

"That may be; still you would have a precarious sort of existence. As I said before, the best of your days are over, and you might starve."

The captive smiled.

"Should I ?" he ejaculated. "I know better than that."

"I hope you would not. Still, after your long imprisonment, you would find the outside world strangely altered. Many of your friends are doubtless dead. Others may be in distant parts, and you would, therefore, be thrown upon your own resources. I am afraid, Murdock, you have not duly considered all these things."

"I tell you I have considered all you mention, and more too—a good deal more. Starve—eh ?"

An almost disdainful sneer of triumph curled his lip as he said—

"I am richer than you or any one supposes."

It was now Knoulton's turn to start.

"Richer !" he ejaculated.

The pirate nodded.

"Aye, lad," he murmured. "Riches if I could only get outside these walls—if I could only regain my liberty. Ugh !"

"I don't know what to make of you, and that is the truth," said the young man. "You are a puzzle to everybody. You rich ?"

"Certainly, if I could escape I should be so."

"You are indeed most fortunate."

This was said with a degree of bitter irony, which, while it conveyed a doubt of the truth of the assertion, told how highly Knoulton esteemed the gifts of fortune.

MURDOCK, THE PIRATE, DRAWING A CHART OF THE WHEREABOUTS OF THE HIDDEN TREASURE.

"Would you like to be rich, Walter?" inquired the pirate.

"I should be telling a falsehood if I said the contrary. Do you take me for a fool that you endeavour to deceive me?"

"Belay there," cried Murdock—"hold on a bit, lad. I aint romancing, talking wildly, when I say I can make your fortune. What think you of that?"

"I don't know what to think. It appears to be incredible, but still I am bound to believe what you say, seeing that you can have no motive in declaring that which is untrue. So let it pass. Wait till you are better—till you have recovered. It will be some time before that comes to pass."

"I say I can make your fortune, and you take no heed of my words or warning."

No. 62.

"I do take heed. You would carry out some robbery in which you would have me join. I think I understand."

The pirate shook his head.

"No yer don't," cried he. "If you will assist me to make my escape, we'll succeed the next time. If you will do that you shall be rich, for I will give you half I have."

Walter Knoulton was under the impression at this time that the pirate was light-headed, and he therefore did not take much notice of the declaration he had made.

He deemed it advisable, however, to humour him, for experience had taught him that it was never at any time advisable to contradict patients in the condition Murdock was in at that time.

"You are in earnest—I know that," said he; "and I am quite sure you would keep your word as far as your promise to me is concerned."

"But you don't believe me, for all that," observed the sick man.

"Yes, I do—indeed, I do."

"You merely say that to humour me. Your manner belies your words."

"I tell you I do."

"Good, then—that being so we shall be able to understand each other, and I will take you into my confidence, for I believe I can trust you."

The conversation was suddenly brought to a close by the entrance of the prison chaplain.

CHAPTER CXVIII.
THE INJURED MAN AND HIS ATTENDANT—A PIRATE'S YARN.

GENTLE in his manner and soft in speech, the chaplain approached the bedside of the wounded smuggler.

"I hope and trust, Murdock, that you are more disposed now to hearken to my counsel. Remember you are at the present time in imminent danger, and there is no telling what may be the result of the terrible injuries you have received. There is no telling how soon you may be called away by a power which is omnipotent. Let me conjure of you to make some amends for the past by a sincere repentance. Remember——"

"I don't want to be preached to," interrupted the hardened criminal; "all I want is to be left alone."

"But it is my duty to endeavour by every means in my power to bring you to a right way of thinking, and I should be sadly unmindful of my sacred mission if I neglected you at this time. I must therefore beg of you to hear me."

"I don't want to hear you. I am nearly mad with pain and driven half crazy when I think of being cheated of my liberty. I am done this time, and if I am to slip my moorings, the sooner I do so the better. There, that will do—I don't want any palaver. You can't make matters any better."

"But I hope and trust I can," returned Mr. Leverall. "Nay, I will venture to assert that I am sure I can if you will be a little reasonable. Come, Murdock, you must not, you will not turn a deaf ear to one who is prompted by the purest and best of motives in striving, as best he can, to soften your heart and make you comprehend your awful position."

"I know my position well enough. It is a hopeless one. They've been killing me by inches for nine long and miserable years. They'll never be satisfied until they see the breath out of my body, and then—well, then they may cut me up piecemeal in the dissecting-room as soon as they please."

"Nobody wishes to see you dead, and you are quite wrong in such a supposition. It is not at all likely that anyone in this gaol regards you with personal animosity. It is unjust and unreasonable to suppose such a thing. You are taking a morbid view of things. Now permit me to read to you."

"No, I won't be read to. I don't want any long-worded sermons. I won't listen. Leave me alone."

"But I cannot and must not leave you in your present distress. Remember you have a soul to be saved, and you must listen to the words of One who came into the world to save us all."

"You have me at an advantage," cried the smuggler. "I am powerless, and cannot get away."

"I hope you do not want to get away?"

"Yes, I do."

"He's very self-willed, and won't bear being spoken to," said Knoulton, addressing himself to the chaplain.

"I am perfectly assured that he is self-willed and obstinate, but that is the greater reason for my endeavouring to move him, and bring the unhappy man to a better condition. I am not in the habit of giving up persons of his nature as altogether hopeless."

The chaplain then, in a slow, measured voice, read from the volume he had brought with him. Murdock this time made no objection. He closed his eyes, and appeared to be half asleep, nevertheless he listened to much the chaplain uttered.

The reading lasted some quarter of an hour or twenty minutes. Mr. Leverall was under the impression that the old evil-minded man had profited by his ministrations; he closed the book, and laying hold of the smuggler's horny hand, shook it, and then took his departure—thinking he had done enough for the present, and to continue further would be only to weary the sick man.

"A good, kind gentleman," said Knoulton, when the door had closed on the chaplain, "and he is one who takes a deep interest in all who have the misfortune to be incarcerated within these walls."

"Ugh! He means well, I dare say," cried Murdock.

"I am sure he does—no man ever meant better. I am sure I ought to speak well of him, for he has been both father and brother to me."

"Ah, it may be so; but I am too far gone, do you see? I aint to be piloted into port by any of his kidney, and so it's no use mincing matters. I didn't interfere with him when he let go the jawing tackle; because why—it aint no manner of use. Just heaven, what would I give to be clean out of these waters!"

"And then, if you succeeded in doing so, you would not be much better off, perhaps."

"Shouldn't I? You allow me to be the best judge of that. No better off, indeed! I tell you what it is, Walter—you don't know why I yearn for liberty so much."

"I confess I do not."

The pirate shook his head.

"Ah, that's where it is," said he.

"Why, you must have led a strange life, I should say," observed the young man, "and been witness of scenes that were no doubt of a harrowing nature."

"I've passed through a deal more than I could ever tell you—have sailed to almost every port in the world, and have had a hard time of it occasionally, but it's all over now—Walter, all!"

"Come, take some of this beef-tea," said his attendant, drawing to the bedside of the sufferer.

Murdock, with great difficulty, sat half up, his back and shoulders supported by pillows, and partook of some refreshment, which he seemed to enjoy.

"There, that'll do for the present," said he, handing his attendant the basin. "I feel a little better now."

The hours flew by, night came on, but the sick man was unable to obtain sleep, and young Knoulton sat up and watched him with exemplary patience. As the night waned, its tedium was beguiled by conversation, for when alone with his nurse the pirate was loquacious enough, for nothing pleased him better than spinning yarns, as he termed it, and giving his companion a brief recital of some of the incidents in his earlier career.

Knoulton encouraged him in this, for he argued that it was far better than his brooding over his present misfortunes.

"Well, for the matter of that, I have seen all sorts of sights, both ashore and afloat," said Murdock, "but about as terrible a bit of business it is well possible to conceive was what is termed a "cacciata."

"A what?" said Knoulton.

"A cacciata. It's an Italian word, I believe, but it means a fight with knives or poignards. As I can't sleep I'll just give you an account of it. When I was a young man I did a little business on the cross with an Italian count. He wasn't of much account, but that doesn't much matter, but to talk to him you'd suppose butter wouldn't melt in his mouth. I had left my ship for a time, and visited Rome to see the sights there, and met by chance my old friend the count.

"'Ah, Murdock!' said he, 'what brought you here?'

"'A little matter of business in the first place,' I answered, 'and pleasure in the next.'

"'All right, my friend,' he returned. 'I'm glad to see you. You have seen most of the sights, I suppose?'

"'I have seen a good many.'

"'Have you any further visits to pay?'

"'I don't know that I have. I think I must have seen everything—unless you have something further to show me.'

"'Well, yes,' said the Count, 'you may congratulate yourself, for I think I can show you something this evening that will be both novel and distracting.'

"Just suit me, then," said I, "for you must know, Walter, I was at this time a young hair-brained chap as didn't care a straw what places I visited, or what risks I ran."

"I should imagine you to be all that," returned Knoulton.

"'Well, we shall see,' said the Count; 'I must leave you, for we must not be seen together, and you must leave Rome in the morning, without fail. Not a word of our conversation to anyone. Meet me to-night in front of the Alberti Theatre. Silence, mystery, and may good fortune favour us.'

"Well," observed the pirate, "I couldn't quite get the right soundings, so was just going to heave the lead again, when my gentleman walked swiftly away. I walked on, musing on the mysterious sensation which had been promised me by my friend. Reaching my lodgings, I put on my travelling suit, settled my account, and made arrangements for leaving in the morning, according to the count's instructions. I was at this time a smart young fellow," added Murdock, "and in every way different to what you see me now. Lord bless us, it appears impossible I can be the same person—but what have I not gone through since then?"

"Ah, time changes the best of us," observed his companion. "It will effect a wonderful alteration in me, no doubt, as years go on."

The pirate made no reply, but remained silent for some little time, and Knoulton was under the impression that he was too weak to continue his narrative. Such, however, was not the case, for after a somewhat lengthy pause, he renewed his story.

"As soon as it was dark," said Murdock, "I directed my steps to the Alberta Theatre. It was about eight o'clock.

"I found the count promenading the walk. He was not alone, but was accompanied by a young man with a full Italian face, and who walked and chatted with him while waiting for me.

"For some inexplicable reason my heart began to beat violently when my eye fell upon the count and his companion. With a gesture imposing silence upon me the count whispered—

"'Come, let us lose no time, but get into the carriage.'

"It was with some astonishment that I noticed that I was not presented to the stranger. Nevertheless, so soon as we were in motion we all began to chat as if we were intimate acquaintances.

"The unknown was a person of charming manners and excellent conversational power. Although somewhat effeminate, he had an air of distinction. He had that dull tinge characteristic of the *meridionaux* who drink only water.

"He was about twenty-four years of age; he wore a moustache of fine texture and ebon blackness; and his raven hair contrasted singularly with the whiteness of a neck whose shape would have excited the envy of a woman. He was, in short, one of the handsomest of Italians.

"The carriage rolled on for some ten minutes, and was already travelling obscure streets, which to me were wholly unknown.

"While it is true that I had no fear, I ought to say that the singular circumstances of this nocturnal journey awakened an emotion which bordered on inquietude, and which induced me to break out suddenly—

"'My dear friend, I accepted your proposition with my eyes closed. Now, after all this mystery, will you tell me where you are conducting me?'

"'Your pardon,' said the count in a serious tone. 'I have promised to enable you to assist at a spectacle such as you have never seen, and never will again in all your life; but where this spectacle will take place, I am not permitted to say. I count upon your discretion and rely upon your abstaining from all questions. I have promised you a sensation, and you shall see it; and I guarantee to you that it will be satisfactory as a sensation, for it will be most terrible and most bloody."

"'Bloody,' repeated I, surprised at this confidence.

"'Yes, bloody and terrifying beyond description. There is yet time. Do you wish to renounce this excursion? If you do not have the courage, I will accompany you to——'

"'My friend, I have faith in your loyalty; and I know you will do nothing unworthy the character of a brave gentleman.'

"'Fear nothing,' said the young Italian, in excellent English, 'only wait till in your own country before you speak.'

"A moment after, our carriage halted. We found ourselves in a small square, dimly lighted, a species of *carrefour*, which gave access to four streets.

"We descended and waited till the carriage had driven away and the noise of its wheels was lost in the deserted streets. It was nine o'clock.

" 'Follow us,' whispered the count, 'and do not utter a single word.'

"We proceeded a dozen steps along one of the streets which led into the place, and then the count stopped before a door, and said, in a low voice—

" 'It is here.'

"He pushed gently against the door, which yielded easily; and then we entered a long dark corridor, at the extremity of which there shone a faint light through the curtains of a second door, which seemed to open into some lighted apartment.

"We had walked about half the length of the hall, when the second door opened and there came out a man, who closed it behind him with great care. During the instant that the door was open we heard a murmur of voices, which convinced us that the room beyond was occupied by a numerous company.

"At a sign from the count we all three halted. The man came softly forward until he reached the count, who stood in advance, and whispered some words in his ear, which we could not hear. The next moment he turned to the right and led us to a stairway which seemed cut in the wall, and which, by the faint light, we saw to be filthy beyond description. We followed our guide on tiptoe and in absolute silence.

"We ascended several steps, and found ourselves in front of a door. Our guide took us by the hand, and we groped our way silently into the darkness of what I imagined to be a hall of some kind. The darkness was impenetrable. We were led a short distance, and then all three of us were quietly forced into a species of bruel, or *canapé*—and then we waited.

"What was going to happen, and what astounding thing was I about to witness? Despite my confidence in the count, I could not, in view of our marches and countermarches in the darkness, and all so silently, restrain somewhat of an apprehension.

"Gradually there began to reach us, from in front and below us, the murmur of voices, and which we could not distinguish when we first entered the apartment.

"From such indications as I could possess myself of, I concluded that we occupied a position with reference to those below us, like that of spectators in a gallery to the actors on the stage. These were mere suppositions, however, for the darkness was so intense that I had no means of verifying their justness.

"None of us spoke.

"Suddenly a great noise broke out in the place in front of us. There were cries of joy and enthusiasm; there was a general stamping of feet, and, at the same instant, directly in front of us, a curtain was drawn aside as if by magic.

"I was correct in my surmise that we were in a sort of gallery. We were so placed that, without being seen, or our existence suspected, we could command a complete view of the large room below us, and in which some twenty people were conversing with each other, and throwing themselves about with a demoniacal violence.

"The count whispered in my ear: 'Now we can speak, but we must not permit ourselves to be overheard.'

" 'And now,' said I, 'will you explain the mystery of seeing a score of Italians in a state of intoxication?'

The count laughed slightly, and for an answer he said—

" 'Look attentively.'

As for the young Italian, he revealed his presence only by long-drawn sighs.

"I could now examine at my leisure what passed below us in the room, which was lighted by four miserable lamps, and which gave out more odour than light. Some twenty persons were present.

"They were ordinary men with healthy colour, and whose glances were full of pride and energy. Some of them were advanced in years and were gray; others were mere boys, but all appeared equally audacious and daring.

"At the moment I had taken in these particulars, one of them had mounted a bench and commenced to speak; the rest listened with great attention, and from their attitude, I could infer that the proposition of the orator was received with favour.

"All at once, it occurred to me that these men were not intoxicated. There may have been one or two whose brains were somewhat affected by drink; but none had that brutal and contemptible drunkenness which one sometimes sees among our workmen in the large cities. One would imagine them to be conspirators or bandits, but never drunkards."

"I always understood that the Italians were not addicted to habits of intemperance," observed young Knoulton.

"Neither are they—at any rate as far as my experience of them is concerned," returned Murdock. "If the truth must be spoken I have every reason for believing that the majority, if not all of those present, were as sober as you and I are now."

"Well, we haven't had anything to intoxicate us—that is quite certain," said the young man, with a smile.

The pirate continued—

" 'What is going to happen?' I asked the count in a low voice.

" 'You see all those men,' said the count, in a voice which vibrated with emotion; 'they are mostly young men; in every case, they are robust. Well, my good friend, all these young men whom you see are about to poignard each other—to attempt to kill each other with an unimaginable ferocity.'

"I repressed an exclamation.

" 'What is it you tell me? Why, these men have the appearance of being intimate friends.'

" 'They are; and it is necessary that they should be, and that they should possess a great reciprocity of esteem in order to carry out the terrible combat whose conditions they are even now arranging.'

"I heard this with stupefaction. I tried to believe myself the victim of a joke on the part of my friend; but the tone of his voice left me no room to doubt.

"Besides, the precautions we had taken to assist at the combat of the gladiators; the semi-revelations and mysterious occurrences of the evening did not permit me to suppose that my friend told me anything but the exact truth.

" 'And will this act of savagery take place under my eyes?'

" 'Let me, at first,' said my friend, 'explain to you this singular duel, for it is a duel sustained without enmity, without heat, without anger, for the simple purpose of proving to each other their surpassing courage, and their contempt for existence. This savage recreation, which owes its origin to barbarous ages, is called a *cacciata* from the word *caccia* (hunting). From time to time, when security from the police is certain, a group of persons such as these meet in some secluded locality for the purpose of holding a *caccio*, whose end is solely to test their courage. But hold,' he added, 'that tall man whom you see at the extremity of the hall is about to announce the proposal to fight.'

"At the same moment I heard, in the obscurity, our

young companion rubbing his hands with great satisfaction.

"Although a good deal disturbed at what I had heard, I did not lose a motion of the men.

"Suddenly there arose a great tumult in the hall.

"The man whom the count had indicated by his great stature, pronounced a sort of speech; but he spoke with so much heat and volubility that it was impossible for me to understand a single thing except the word *cacciata*.

"When he finished speaking, each man put his hand in his pocket and drew out an enormous knife, whose blade shone and sparkled with a sinister brilliancy.

"'My God,' said I, 'are they going to cut each other's throats under our very eyes?'

"'Calm yourself,' said the count, seizing my hands with force. 'Reassure yourself, you will see nothing —what is now passing is the worst. Come, be courageous, and do not lose sight of a single movement.'

"The recommendation to calm myself was wholly useless.

"Despite myself I was seized by an undefinable nausea. The belief that I was about to see the room below running with human gore gave me a tremour of horror, and held me spellbound in a condition of horrible anticipation.

"But such is the deformity of the human heart that, notwithstanding I experienced a most frightful repulsion, my curiosity was powerfully interested; and my fear of suffering was more than overpowered by my desire not to lose a feature of the frightful scene.

"At once, and as if obedient to a signal, these twenty individuals commenced to disrobe themselves. But before commencing, and seemingly as a precaution, each placed his knife by his side and within reach. It was a formidable weapon whose variety of form indicated the character of the individuals.

"With supreme calmness, and an assurance that was terrifying, they divested themselves of everything save their pantaloons, which was held up by waist belts. In almost the flash of an eye, they were stripped to the waist and ready for the combat.

"It was, I assure you, a moving and cruel spectacle to see all these robust torsos, with their white or bronze colouring, thus becoming revealed in the feeble, tremulous light of the hall.

"Despite the impending horror of a savage butchery I could not but admire the energetic heads, the fierce glances, and the rude muscularity of the arms now ready to deal out death.

"When they cleared away the tables so as to leave the arena free, all these athletic forms assumed attitudes whose delineation would have made the fortune of a painter of the human form.

"'Now,' said the count, 'the fight is going to commence. The tall man whom you see in the centre of the group is recalling to them the conditions of the sanguinary combat. These conditions are—

"'The lights must be extinguished, so that he who is struck may not know who has given the blow— which is the only means of avoiding repentance on the one hand and hatred on the other.

"'It is not permitted to give a blow below the belt..

"'Whatever may be the severity of the wound which one receives he can neither utter a complaint nor a groan, as the sound of his voice would establish his identity.

"'One who is down cannot be struck. When one is wounded, or wishes to discontinue his participation in the combat, he extends himself at length and is secure from molestation.

"'But so long as there remain two of them erect, who meet each other in the darkness, they strike pitilessly at each other's breasts, and this, despite the fact that they may be friends, relatives, or even brothers.'

"And now, the last table and stool being removed, each individual placed himself, knife in hand, with his face to the wall.

"There remained only the extinguishing of the light before the carnage should commence.

"I followed with a horrible curiosity each phase of the savage tragedy which was about to conclude in the darkness, not more than a dozen feet from where I sat. During those latter preliminaries, I felt such a lively emotion of horror that I could scarcely refrain from uttering a cry in order to reveal our presence, and put an end to the infamous proceedings.

"Had only my personal safety been involved, I should not have hesitated, but my companions were present, and they had not ceased to repeat that the smallest suspicion of our presence would compromise all of us. I was obliged, therefore, to await the termination in silence.

"Soon the tall *sacrophant* extinguished one of the four lamps. Then the second was deliberately put out, and then the third. As I saw him approach the fourth and last one, my heart ceased to beat, and I involuntarily closed my eyes.

"When I opened them it was night, silence, the profound peace of the tomb, and I seemed to be under the influence of a dream.

"At a movement which I made on my seat, and which was more noisy than prudence would permit, the count seized me vigorously by the arms, and his significant pressure seemed to say, silence! At the same moment we heard a certain agitation at our feet; the combatants putting themselves into position for the attack.

"From the depth of the obscurity we could at first hear only what seemed like repressed breathing, and which was scarcely perceptible.

"Doubtless, each was upon the defensive, holding his breath, and acting with great circumspection which would not permit more active movements. But of all this we could see nothing—absolutely nothing; we could only guess at what was passing.

"However, each moment the agitation augmented in the darkness in which swarmed these terrible gladiators.

"The restrained chests began to dilate, and the vague and scarcely perceptible tumult of the first moments began to take a more pronounced form. It seemed to us that we could distinguish, at the least indication, the movements of the combatants.

"We imagined we could see them bounding from one end of the hall to the other, seeking to strike an adversary during the furious *élan* of their passage.

"Little by little, as the blood of the combatants became frenzied, the primitive incoherence of the battle was accentuated by a horrible murmuring. The impact of rushing bodies began to be distinguishable. The clear sound of the knife striking the flesh could be heard; and then falls and hoarse rattles.

"A little later, when the infernal tumult had swollen to its height, there were heard savage vociferations, sounds of suffocation, dull cries, and strange ejaculations uttered in no language and in no recognisable accent, but none the less horrible and lacerating.

"This fearful occurrence, rendered still more frightful by the profound darkness, lasted some twenty minutes.

"At the end of this time, somebody cried, in Italian—

" 'To the floor, everybody!' and in a moment silence reigned, as if by enchantment.

"The same stalwart devil who had extinguished the lamps, now relighted them, one by one. The scene which came slowly into view from the darkness was horrible in the extreme.

"Those who had not been struck during the mêlée immediately began to raise those who were extended in a sea of blood, their chests gashed and their arms slashed by deep blows from the knife.

"A sickening odour filled the already vitiated atmosphere. The combatants pattered across the bloody floor; some crowded about the wounded, others calmly wiped their bloody knives upon their handkerchiefs. Two or three who were wounded, but who had not fallen, with bent necks, examined with cold disdain the wounds they had received.

"The spectacle was at once sinister and yet full of courage, hideous and attractive, abject and full of grandeur. I wished to fly, and yet, when the moment of departure came, it was necessary to tear me away.

"And this is what is known as Cacciata."

"What a horrible scene!" exclaimed Knoulton. "One would hardly suppose it possible that such atrocities could be committed in a civilised country."

"I was, as I have already told you, young at the time, but it made so deep an impression on me that I shall never forget it for the remainder of my life."

"And your friend the count?"

"Oh, he died a violent death. He was stabbed in the street by a hired bravo some years after the tragic affair he had taken me to. He was a bad lot, had sold his best friends, and got himself into some scrape, the rights of which I never know, but it ended in his death. I have seen a good many horrible sights since then, have been cast adrift on the ocean, and only saved by what one might term almost a miracle, and have been driven into this cursed port at last. Oh, how I sigh to be again on the blue water! You cannot understand the misery of my situation—'cause why? You see you have been brought up differently to what I was, and don't and can't feel the punishment of being cooped up under hatches for life. Death is happiness in comparison with it—perfect happiness."

"You must hold up, and not give way to desponding thoughts. If you do—"

"Well, I know what you would say—I shall go to Davy Jones's locker. Yes, that's what you'd say. You are right enough, my lad. Feeling as I do now, I shan't much care if I do."

Young Knoulton looked at the clock, and saw that it was time his patient had his medicine. Murdock swallowed the contents of the glass which the other presented to him, and shortly after this he sank into a fitful slumber.

CHAPTER CXIX.

LAURA STANBRIDGE AND THE CHAPLAIN—AN IRRESISTIBLE APPEAL—THE ESCAPE.

THE attempted escape of Mat Murdock had, by this time, become known to most of the inmates of the gaol, and there were many who deeply regretted that the pirate had been so unsuccessful, for there is always a certain amount of sympathy evinced by prisoners for one who has had tact and address enough to plan and carry out any scheme for breaking through the walls, bolts, or bars of the gaol.

Although most of Murdock's fellow-prisoners sympathised with him, they were discreet enough to refrain from expressing their opinions openly to any of the officials of the gaol.

Laura Stanbridge had learnt the whole history from one of the female warders who had her in their charge. She was by this time on familiar and friendly terms with both of these women, who professed to be greatly interested in her.

The reason for this was obvious enough. Laura had liberally showered her gifts upon them, and hence their altered demeanour towards her.

She had a scheme in her head which she hoped to carry out before the day of trial arrived. She was perfectly well aware that if found guilty she would not have a very lengthened term of imprisonment, but she had special reasons for not running the risk of a conviction. She hoped to get clean away by some means or another.

This designing woman already exercised a powerful influence over Mr. Leverall, who, to say the truth, became each day more and more fascinated with her.

She was always in his thoughts, and he was ashamed to confess to himself the precise nature of these, which, to say the truth, he could not analyse.

He strove, however, to dismiss her image from his mind, but the more he tried the less successful he seemed to be.

It was strange—indeed marvellous—but his was not a solitary case, either with churchmen, heroes, or sages, who are one and all open to the wiles and blandishments of an artful and designing beauty.

While the miserable and ill-fated pirate was tossing uneasily on his pallet, his mind filled with visions of the liberty he was never destined to realise, Mr. Leverall was giving more of his time to the prisoner in cell No. 43 than the exigencies of the case would seem to warrant, but nobody took heed of this.

It is true the two women attendants remarked to each other that the chaplain appeared to be a bit sweet on No. 43, but there was after all nothing surprising in this.

Ministers, like other men, had their favourites in the prison, and it was quite certain, so they averred, that Mr. Leverall had effected a great change in Miss Stanbridge, and it was equally certain, although they did not say so, that she had effected a still greater change in him.

On the morning after Murdock's attempted escape Laura Stanbridge received another visit from the man who passed as her uncle.

Bandy-legged Bill brought her a fresh supply of money, and, in answer to her inquiries, informed her that he had called repeatedly at her house and informed the maid-servant that her mistress would return to London shortly.

He also said that Mr. Gatliffe had made repeated inquiries after her, and that Alf Purvis had been most insulting to him (Bill), declaring that he did not believe he had any authority to visit the house from its mistress.

As may be readily imagined, Bill retorted. In consequence of this a wordy war ensued, and Purvis ordered the gipsy not to show his face there again; but the latter, as he termed it, "was not to be sat upon" by a conceited puppy like that, and he, therefore, told him that if he gave him any "more of his cheek, he'd give him a prop in the eye" as soon as look at him.

They were very nearly coming to blows there and then, but Mr. Purvis was under the impression that he might get the worst of it; so he was fain to be a little more moderate in his language.

"And I'd ha' done it, and no flies," said Rawton.

"There aint any mistake about that; 'taint likely I'd submit to be bullyragged by the young hound, and be hanged to him."

"He's a conceited fellow, Bill," observed Laura. "Everybody knows that, but don't take any notice of what he says. It is isn't worth while."

"I don't know so much about that," returned the gipsy, with a nod. "A sound thrashing u'd do my gentleman a world of good, and he'll have it some of these days, mark you that."

"And how about Charlie Peace—I mean Mr. Thompson?" inquired the fair prisoner.

"Oh, he's as right as the mail. Sent his love to you and all good wishes, but he dursn't come himself, because you see he might be recognised, and then the game would be up, and Charlie would be quodded. Oh, don't think anything the worse of him for it; but he can't come."

"I understand that. I don't wish him to come—it would be the worst of folly for him to do so."

After a short interview the gipsy took his departure, and returned to the Evalina-road to report progress.

As the evening drew on Mr. Leverall entered cell No. 43, and found its occupant reading and in tears.

He was deeply moved, and drew towards her.

"How is this?" he said, placing his hand on her shoulder. "In tears?"

She looked up at him, and made room on the seat.

He sat down beside her.

"You are weeping," he said.

"Oh, sir, you little know the miserable hours I pass when you are away, and I have no friend or counsellor—no one to sympathise with me. What am I to do? How am I to avoid exposure, disgrace, ignominy?"

She sobbed convulsively.

He endeavoured to pacify her, and to change the subject of her thoughts, gave her a succint account of Murdock's attempt at escape, the injuries he had received therefrom, and his present condition.

"Poor fellow!" she exclaimed, when the narrative had been brought to a conclusion; "I can indeed sympathise with him, for I am in much the same position myself. Escape! Do you hear, my kind and benevolent friend—my saviour? If I could escape!"

As she uttered these last words in a low, hissing whisper she crept closer to him, placed her rich ruddy lips close to his ear and repeated them again and again.

He started and almost trembled.

"Do you understand?" said she, her cheek touching his as she made this last inquiry.

"Impossible—quite impossible," he murmured.

"Nothing is impossible to those who have a will, who are earnest and firm of purpose. Nothing!"

He shook his head, but made no reply in words.

"Ah, sir," she ejaculated in a persuasive tone. "Take pity on me, and you will be rewarded, be solaced when you reflect that you have been instrumental in rescuing a contrite woman from the dark abyss which lies before her. You, so good, so gentle, whom I love with all the ardour of an affectionate nature—you will aid me, I am sure you will."

She took his hand within her own soft silky palm, and pressed it with every demonstration of affection.

He knew not what reply to make—his mind seemed to be in a perfect chaos—his temples throbbed, and he felt like one who is on the brink of a precipice.

She poured into his ear a plaintive and urgent appeal.

"My dear young creature, what can I do in this business?"

"Much," said she. "Answer me one question."

"What is it?"

"Do you wish me free?"

"Indeed I do," he answered.

"That is spoken from the heart," said she; "it is genuine. You do wish me well, I feel assured of that."

She bent forward and her beautiful bust became half-revealed by this action, for her dress was unfastened in front (accidentally of course).

But Mr. Leverall was an exemplary virtuous and pious young man, yet he was human, and being so was subject to the passions and frailties which the best and most rigid-minded persons find at times to be all-powerful.

For the first time, perhaps, he discovered that he was enamoured of the seductive creature by his side, and she had sufficient penetration to perceive this also.

She was now convinced that she had won the prize which she had sought with so much patience and industry.

"You will aid me," she murmured, as she placed her cheek against his. "I am sure you will."

He made no reply.

He was what the corner-man of a nigger troupe would call "a gone coon."

The huntress had him in her toils.

"You will," she repeated. "If you could see into this heart!"

She placed his hand beneath the folds of her bodice on her bare bosom.

The young chaplain was astounded—he was in a delirium of delight.

With his disengaged arm he pressed her form, and covered her cheeks and lips with burning and passionate kisses.

*   *   *   *   *   *   *

It was night in the prison.

For a few hours all punishments were past—all cares were forgotten.

It was night in the prison, and all save Murdock and his attendant slept—the guilty with the innocent—the prisoners with the gaolers—the chained with the free.

Pale moonbeams threw a faint light upon the long dusky corridor, and filled it with wild, uncouth, fantastic shadows.

But soon a stranger shadow still—it moved—it glided silently by the wall.

A key turned softly in the lock—a door opened by inches—two shadows floated across the floor.

Another door opened—this time with more noise—it was the door of the corridor.

The moonbeams disappeared. All was dark in the prison—dark and impenetrable as a demon's mind: dark and gloomy as a lost soul's despair.

That night the tolling of the deep-toned bell awoke the frightened inhabitants of Clickbourne from their sleep. It was the alarm bell of the gaol—one of the prisoners had escaped.

The dulcet voice of a woman proved to be a more potent agent than the brawny arms of Murdock the pirate.

CHAPTER CXX.

DEATH OF MAT MURDOCK—THE LAST BEQUEST.

THE extraordinary and unaccountable manner in which the prisoner in cell No. 43 had contrived to get clear of the prison walls was, of course, a matter of surprise to every one, and a considerable amount of blame and censure fell upon persons who were not in any way concerned in it.

The two female warders underwent a rigid cross-examination, but they both declared that they were as much in the dark as the governor himself.

The turnkeys were next questioned; they could throw no light on the subject. There was a great hubbub for the next few days, but not the faintest scrap of information could be obtained whereby the real culprit might be traced.

The governor was very irate; the warders were sulky, and everybody seemed to be discontented. Nevertheless, Laura Stanbridge had succeeded in her purpose.

She had cleverly given her janitors the go-by, and once more she experienced the inestimable blessing of liberty, and she was far too clever a woman to run the risk of being recaptured by any act of imprudence on her own part.

Meanwhile Mat Murdock remained in a precarious position. He was closely tended by Walter Knoulton, whose kindness and attention were duly appreciated by the pirate, who soon began to lend an attentive ear to the exhortations of the prison chaplain.

A change for the worse took place in the condition of the injured mariner some three cr four days after the departure of Laura Stanbridge. Murdock was stricken with fever, and at times he was light-headed.

The night nurse who had been deputed to relieve Knoulton, worn out with fatigue and weary watching, was overcome with sleep, and, while in this condition, the pirate in one of his paroxysms leaped out of bed, wounded and wearied as he was, and caught hold of the iron bars which ran in front of the small window of his apartment and vainly strove to remove them.

He fell to the floor, exhausted and senseless, and it was not possible to say how long he had remained in that condition.

An alarm was given by his attendant when the discovery was made, and Murdock was placed again in bed, but his ultimate death may be attributable to this accident.

But he appeared to have but one dominant idea, this being the desire of escape.

Walter Knoulton returned to his duty, and after this he never left the pirate till the end came.

He found Murdock by this time quite an altered man. He was no longer the dissatisfied, impetuous, unreasonable being, as heretofore; on the contrary, he was passive, resigned, and at times even gentle in his manner—and now and then he would make use of his old nautical phraseology.

"I'm nearly done for," said he to Knoulton, when they were closed in for the night. "It was a bad business your leaving me in the hands of that lubber. He went fast asleep, and it appears I jumped out of bed."

"I've heard all about it. Don't blame the chap; he was worn out and sleep overtook him—it's no fault of his."

"Well, perhaps not, when one comes to consider the matter; but I tell you what it is, Walter; my line is nearly worn out, my lad. There isn't half a fathom to run reef. It's hard for the likes of me to slip my wind in this narrow hammock—deuced hard. I should like to have been going free when I sprang my last for the long voyage."

"Oh, you must not talk like that; with good nursing and proper attention you will recover," cried Knoulton.

The pirate shook his head.

"No," said he; "don't deceive yourself, Walter. My log is made up, and I must founder; I know that

by what the doctor said. He won't be able to keep me afloat for many days longer. Now there's a strange feeling about my heart and head which makes me sure that he gave the right heave of the lead. There, I feel stronger now than at any time since I first fell from that cursed wall; but," added he, in a tone of sadness, "I've seen too many shipmates slip their cables not to know that's my signal for sailing to the other world. Now don't turn away your head, Walter, because my looks upon your face can't be for long, and I don't want them to be shortened. You've been good and true to me. We've only known each other since we've been in limbo, but for all that our friendship has been firm, ever since we first clapped eyes upon each other."

"It has, and I hope better days are in store for both of us."

"You are young and have only to sail in the right direction, and all will go well enough with you, my lad. I hope and trust it may, but as to this ere old hulk that's quite a different matter; but I shouldn't mind if I could be free. You see, Walter, I was very young when I first looked on the sea. I had seen no land then, and as I grew older it seemed to me to be the natural element for men to live on. I had the same thoughts of land as the long-shore people have of the sea, and I have often thought it strange when I have known messmates of mine who have done that, and brought them aboard again. Now when I overhauled it in my mind I have thought there must be something in the land which I had never fetched. I have many times lain and looked at the green fields, but never fancied they were the sea. No, Walter, never; but it would not become me to call them foolish as thought so much more about the land than the sea, for there may be something in home and friends and birthplaces which drains a man's heart. There, ahead of all other things, I have never known any of them; for I was on the sea from the earliest days of my life, and should indeed be blessed if I could slip my cable on it now. But I dare say it's pleasant, as I have heard many of my shipmates say, to be stowed away in an old churchyard which you played about when a boy, and where your kin and friends may always have an eye on your last berth, and the youngsters come and stick flowers on it. I dare say this is all very pleasant, but it is not a thing for me to look or hope for. I have neither family or kin of any sort, no old churchyard as I skylarked about, or youngsters to show their pretty remembrance that it ain't a skulk that is under hatches. I must never leave these walls, even after death, and there'll be no one to point out the spot where I lie."

"No one?" cried Knoulton.

"Well, may be I was wrong there," returned the pirate. "And I'm sure if you thought my sleep would be lighter or more pleasant by pointing it out, or do anything, you would do it—that I am quite certain of. It's something for a man to say he has picked up a friend—a true and staunch one—a thousand miles from his home, in a prison."

"Did you never know your parents?" said Knoulton.

"No, never," answered the pirate. "I wish somehow or another that I had. But what's the use of overhauling that now that my grog is stopped? For, with or without family, I must founder, and, perhaps, it's better that I should. There is nobody to let tears run out of their lee scuppers for my sake. It is better as it is—much better."

Mat Murdock paused from exhaustion, and his face, which had been flushed, now grew deathly pale.

PEACE ENTERTAINS TWO DETECTIVES TO DINNER.

Walter Knoulton saw that it was time he took some nourishment, and he at once proceeded to give him some light nutritious food.

The pirate panted for breath, and a cold clammy perspiration broke out all over him.

He, however, rallied, and, with a faint smile, said in a weak voice—

No. 6 ½.

"That was the first cast of the line—there's very little water—the next heave I shall shoal."

"You are better now, Murdock," said Knoulton. "Cheer up, old man."

"When I first met you," observed the pirate, "I knew pretty well that you would stick to me till the last, and I am not mistaken—no, not mistaken. Well, you see, my friend, I haven't known many as I cared about, few of us have. There is something I would say to you before I sink to my last sleep. I said some few days ago that you should have half I possessed. It seemed ridiculous, I dare say, and you did not take much heed of it, but it's true, nevertheless. You shall be rich, Walter, independent for the remainder of your life. All I have I bequeath to you."

"All you have?"

"Yes, every stiver. Don't think I am wandering, I am in my sober senses. My head was never clearer than it is at the present moment. Listen !"

"I am all attention. Proceed !"

"Will, then, mark what I say. On the beach of St. Michael's, just beyond the rock of Irglas, in a pit six feet deep, ten years ago I hid an iron case containing gold and jewels to a large amount, enough to make us both rich for the remainder of our lives. I shall never live to gain the treasure, but you may and can, if you've a mind to do so."

Knoulton paused, and then added, in a tone of doubt—

"The tale seems scarcely credible, Murdock. You have been a prisoner for more than nine years."

"That's true enough. It's fully that time since Arkenstall and I, being closely pursued, buried the treasure in the spot I have mentioned. A few days after this we were seized at Preston and tried for mutiny and murder on the high seas. I never committed murder, and this I solemnly declare, but we were both convicted of manslaughter. The rest you know."

"What has become of your companion, then ?"

"What—Arkenstall ?"

"Yes."

"Dead, years ago."

"Then you are the only person living who knows of this ?"

"The only one. You need not, therefore, wonder at my desire to obtain my freedom."

"Certainly not."

Notwithstanding all his endeavours to appear indifferent, young Knoulton had listened with deep attention to the pirate's recital.

When he had ceased to speak the young man remained perfectly silent for some time, seeming to balance in his own mind the probability of the story he had just heard.

Casting his eye up for a moment he found those of his companion fixed on him.

He started from his reverie, and said in a dubious tone—

"The story you tell is, to say the least of it, a strange and improbable one. These hidden treasures are a hackneyed subject."

His fellow-convict regarded him with a look of indignation.

"You do not believe me, then, Walter ?" he murmured.

"Nay, I don't say that," was the quick response ; "but how came the iron case to fall into your hands, and who did it belong to ?"

"It would be too long a story to tell you how we became possessed of it—neither does it much matter. It belonged to an English merchant, who is long since dead."

"Oh! then there is no claimant ?"

"Not that I know of."

"Will you promise me one thing ?"

"What is that ?"

"Promise me to search for the treasure after I am dead."

Young Knoulton hesitated.

"Will you promise ?" said the pirate, still more earnestly.

"Yes, I will."

"Good. Well, then, the doctor has left some sheets of paper and a pen and ink on that table. I will make you a rough drawing of the spot where it is buried. I am not much of a hand at drawing, but I've done a chart or two in my time—so let's go ahead."

Knoulton gave him the requisite materials, and Murdock sat up in bed and made a tolerably accurate drawing of the spot and its surroundings. When this was completed, he fell back upon his pillow in a state of exhaustion.

A death-like pallor overspread his features, and he drew his breath with difficulty.

"Give me your hand, Walter," said he. "Ah, that's well, pray for me, my friend. I have heard that when the chaplain prays for a sinner he makes an easier passage aloft, but if you now could say a word or two for me, I am sure it would do more than parson's lingo !"

"I will, indeed—I will, messmate," cried the young man.

"Walter, you couldn't have done me a kinder act than calling me your messmate," exclaimed the pirate, with sudden animation.

"That has done me more good than our doctor's care and attention—that's cleared the turn for my run more than all. Ah, ah, it's pleased me to hear you call me your messmate. I don't like parting with you. You have been very kind to me, very—from the first hour we met. As a dying man, Walter, I have been true to you, and afore I have made a spare hammock, tell me whether you think so ?"

"I do, Murdock. I wish you may be spared."

"Avast there, Walter—avast !" exclaimed the pirate, his voice growing more and more feeble. "You have never forgotten me at any time.

"Come, never turn your head from me. Look on me. Why should you show a wet eye ? Damme, you make my scuppers run over. I—we must part some day, and why not now ? Walter, take your hand from your face if you love me. Let me see your face. Why, that's it. Walter, I've looked my last upon the sea ; there is a haze over it. You had better send a hand aloft, a smart seaman, to keep a bright look-out—it's very hazy. Walter, are you sure the fire was got under—the deck's full of smoke ? Open one of the ports ; and yet I am very cold, Walter. I am shaking. Have I got your hand ? Topman, away ! There—clap on the yard tackles. Stretch out along your tackle full top out. Walter, my friend, God bless you ! Remember the beach of St. Michael's. The pumps are choked."

He paused for a moment, and at first young Knoulton thought he was dead, for his eyes closed, and his face exhibited the ghastly pallid hue of death, but a moment afterwards he opened his eyes and tried to gaze around him. They were dull and glazed, but he turned them anxiously from side to side.

He knit his brows and worked his lips about with an evident desire to speak; he passed his hand through his hair, and at length exclaimed—

"The reef has now struck a hole in her which no carpenter can stop; and the seas that wash over her will wash everything out of her as clean as a captain's steward does a stew-pan. Ah, you may cut away at the masts, but she will not move. You may spare yourself the trouble—here comes a sea that will carry them by the board. Hold on—hold on, mates, for your lives! That sea has fixed her. Cut the lashings of the boat on the boom. The next sea will carry it from the chucks to the quarter. Bear a hand—bear a hand! Here comes the sea, Walter—hold on by me. Where are you? Avast, I am alone! The sea blinds me. I am faint! I cannot swim a stroke! The water gurgles in my throat! Down, down—down—

The last word died on his lips; his features were convulsed, his jaw fell, and all was over with Mat Murdock, the pirate.

It would be a task of considerable difficulty to attempt any description of the sense of loneliness that fell upon Walter Knoulton at this time. Despair seemed to enter his heart. It is true that he had attended upon the sick on very many occasions, but this was the first time he had witnessed the death of a fellow-creature, and he was so supremely miserable that he was well-nigh bursting into tears.

It is equally true, also, that the dead man had doubt-less, for the greater portion of his career, led an evil life. He had been a lawless freebooter, who, from a moral point of view, had very little to recommend him, and was, therefore, deserving of very little sympathy; but Knoulton knew only the best and most favourable side of his character, and he had always evinced a great liking for the old pirate or smuggler. Possibly this might be in some reason attributable to Murdock's being shunned and despised by the other prisoners, who were, however, greatly in dread of him. To Knoulton, however, he had been uniformly kind, and this was proved by the last request he had made. To trace the secret springs of the human heart is beyond the skill or power of man, and, strange as it may appear, Walter Knoulton felt as acutely the loss of his fellow-prisoner as many men feel the loss of a dearly-loved relative.

"He is gone," murmured the young man. "Who can say whether he has passed away, and will not trouble any of us further?"

He glanced at the features of the dead man, which were so calm and peaceful, without any expression of pain on them, and heaved a deep sigh.

Then he bethought him of the paper with the rough draft thereon, and at once proceeded to secrete it beneath his flannel shirt.

It would not be intelligible to any one but himself, and even if the prison authorities discovered it, the chances were that it would not be taken from him if he told them that it was given him as a keepsake from his deceased friend, so he had but little fear as far as the chart was concerned.

But presently a sort of superstitious fear seemed to creep over him, and so powerful was this influence that he thought the eyes of the dead pirate moved. This was but imagination, but it exercised a powerful influ-ence over him.

Young Knoulton had attended on sick persons for the greater portion of the time he had been a prisoner, but he had never before had a patient die under his hands.

It was the first time he had been in the presence of death, and as he glanced at the rigid features of the dead pirate, his heart beat audibly, and a horrible fear seemed to creep over him.

Everything was so still; no sound struck upon his ears; not a faint murmur of any sort; he would have been thankful if he could have heard the faintest indica-tion of a human voice, or any articulate sentence uttered by a living creature. He was for some time so overcome that he found it impossible to rise from his

seat, but remained sad and thoughtful till the unbroken silence became oppressively painful.

Presently he thought he detected some movement from without, as of a warder passing almost noiselessly along the corridor.

He sprang to his feet, and made towards the door; this done, he shouted for assistance.

A measured tread told him that one of the prison officials was going his rounds. Knoulton hammered at the door with both his fists. It was instantly opened, and a tall man with a large bushy beard thrust his head in.

"Well, what do you want?" inquired he, perfectly unmoved.

"Help! come in!—he is dead."

"Who? the pirate?"

"Yes; for mercy's sake come in."

The warder entered and made straight for the bed on which the remains of Murdock were stretched.

One glance sufficed to tell that it was all over with the wretched Murdock.

"Gone, eh?" he ejaculated. "It's rather sudden, but the doctor said there was no chance for him. Well, poor fellow, all his troubles are now over in this world. When did he breathe his last?"

"Not half an hour ago. Oh, less than that."

"Humph! we'll tell the governor," returned the warder, passing again through the entrance to the apartment, and closing the door gently after him, which he, however, locked with his usual caution—re-membering at the time the clatter there had been about prisoner No. 43.

In a few minutes after this the deputy-governor and prison surgeon entered with the turnkey. The surgeon pronounced the prisoner dead.

The last offices were performed, and young Knoul-ton's duties were over as far as the pirate was concerned. They thanked him for his attention, and he was conducted to a cell in another part of the prison.

This was about the most comfortable berth in the whole ship, to make use of the language of the dead pirate, and Knoulton had every possible indulgence it was possible to accord, consistent with the rules of the establishment.

It wanted only six weeks more to complete his term of imprisonment, and during that period he was chiefly engaged in the infirmary, but he could not forget the last words of Murdock, and he had a burning desire to test the truth of his statement as to the treasure which had lain hid for so many years.

CHAPTER CXXI.

MISS STANBRIDGE'S PEREGRINATIONS—HER VISIT TO CHARLES PEACE.

LAURA STANBRIDGE succeeded in reaching London with-out attracting any attention or arousing the suspicions of any one. She walked on for miles until she was fairly worn out with excitement and fatigue; neverthe-less she persevered, being at the time under the full impression that messengers would be despatched from the goal in all directions for the purpose of recapturing her.

This was done, but as frequently occurs in cases of this sort, the messengers went in every possible direc-tion but the right one.

Laura did not deem it advisable to continue for very long in any of the high roads. She went through bye-lanes and unfrequented footpaths, and thereby dodged her pursuers. When fairly worn out with fatigue, so that she could barely drag one leg after the other—to make use of a common saying—she bethought her of what she could do. To betake herself to a house of public entertainment would be running a great risk, as the chances were that these establishments would be the first places the police would visit.

She espied at no very great distance a large-sized barn, and at once made for this as a haven of rest.

She had not much difficulty in unfastening the door, which was only secured by a wooden peg. This done, she crept in and stretched herself at full length upon some trusses of straw. She was so overpowered and prostrated, that she soon sank off to sleep, and did not awaken till the voices of men fell upon her ear. She then suddenly sprang to her feet and looked through the crevice of the barn-door.

It was by this time early dawn, and the hilltops were tinted with the rays of the rising sun.

In an adjacent field she beheld two farm labourers at work, and a milkmaid with her pail.

When their backs were turned she crept out of the barn, and passed into the lane which she had traversed on the night previous.

She had sufficient money on her person for her immediate wants; this had been given her by her friend, Mr. Leverall.

As the milkmaid came along with her pail she wished her a good morning.

She was a good-looking buxom wench, with red cheeks and mottled arms—the very personification of rude health and good-nature.

"An' good morning to you, ma'am," said the girl, staring with wonder, "but ye be up wi' the lark, missus."

"Yes," said Miss Stanbridge; "I lost my way last night and took shelter in the barn till the morning. I could not find any place open."

"Maybe you're a stranger to these parts?" observed the girl.

"Quite a stranger. Don't even know where I am or the name of this place."

"Ye be London-bred and London-born if I aint mistaken?"

"You are quite correct in your surmise. I am a Cockney. That's what you country people term us Londoners."

The girl gave a broad grin and a chuckle at this last observation.

"I dunno how you could manage to rest in such a place as that," said she, nodding with her head towards the barn.

"There was no help for it, my good girl; beggars must not be choosers, you know. But I say—listen to me a moment," added Laura, slipping a shilling into the maid's hand—"can you tell me, like a kind, good girl, as I am sure you are, where I can get a conveyance about here—a post-chaise, or something of that sort? It matters not what it is."

"Where ee goin' too, then?"

"I want to get to the nearest station. How far might that be off?"

"Well, better nor five miles—not a morsel less."

"And, can you tell me where they let out flys?"

"Lord, no—not I. You won't find any here about, I'm thinking."

"Dear me, that's unfortunate. No conveyance—eh?"

"Will ee coom inside the house and see missus?" cried the girl, as if a sudden thought had struck her.

"Ah, that I will; shall be but too glad to do so. Where is the master?"

"There aint no master. He be dead and gone."

"Oh, only a missus?"

"Ah, that be all, but she be a good sort."

"I shall be most delighted to make her acquaintance."

Laura Stanbridge was conducted into a primitive-looking parlour, and introduced to a comely, cheerful-looking old lady, the mistress of the establishment.

"Your sarvint, ma'am," said the old dame. "Glad to see you."

The milkmaid informed her mistress that the London lady had lost her way on the previous night, and had sought shelter in the granary, and, furthermore, that she wanted to reach the railway-station as soon as possible.

"I be sorry you had no better accommodation," observed the old lady, "but ee must be faint for want of summut to eat and drink. Sit ee down, and ha' some breakfast, ma'am. Ye sha'n't go away wi' an empty belly."

"I am sure you're very kind. I have the wherewithal to pay for what I have."

"Tush, tush, child; don't ee be talking after that fashion. You are freely welcome to all I have. It be a poor tale indeed if we can't help a fellow-creature in distress. Don't you see—eh?"

"Yes."

"An' what brought ee to these parts, if it be a fair question?"

Miss Stanbridge hesitated, and turned away her head with mock modesty.

"Oh, well, if it be a secret, don't say a word."

"It isn't much of a secret, as I know of," observed the escaped prisoner. "I came unbeknown to my relatives. Had to meet a young man to whom I have been engaged."

"Oh, I see, lass—I understand; and maybe your parents object to him as a suitor for your hand."

"Yes they do, but—" here she hesitated again.

"You love the chap—is that it?"

"I do." She tried to blush, and partially succeeded. Her companion tapped her playfully on the elbow.

"Well, well," she ejaculated "I don't blame ee. Ha' done the same thing myself years agone. I don't know as ye are to be blamed—we none of us can help our likes and dislikes, and we all like to choose for ourselves in cases of this sort—it is but natural. And did he keep his appointment—did ee see him?"

"Yes; Alf—he is obliged to go abroad, and wrote to me to beg me that I would meet him and wish him farewell before he took his departure."

"Umph, thee beest a brave girl to coom all this distance by yerself. And I be glad ee saw him."

It is, perhaps, needless to observe that the whole of this story was invented on the spot by the acute and mendacious Laura Stanbridge. It was the first that occurred to her, and, as the old adage has it, "any excuse is better than none."

The old lady snapped at the bait, and believed every word the other had spoken.

After Laura had partaken of a substantial breakfast, which, to say the truth, she did ample justice to, she began to consider how she could get to the station.

It was so remarkably early—not six o'clock—that the chances were that she might be able to make a clean run of it and get clear off before the myrmidons of the law were abroad hunting for their prey.

"I wish I could meet with a conveyance, madam," said Laura, addressing herself to her elder companion. "It is essential that I should be in town as early as possible, but I cannot at present see how it is to be compassed."

"Not unless you'll consent to ride in a milk cart," returned the other.

"In a milk cart! Goodness me, I shall be but too delighted. What matters it what sort of vehicle?"

"Well then, I tell ee what ee can do, if ye're amind, and don't care about it. In less than a quarter of an hour Nat will start w' the milk to the station, and he can take you with un."

"Oh, my dear lady, I am so much obliged by this offer! In a quarter of an hour, say you?"

"Aye, surely. It be better nor nine miles. And if so he as ye are in a hurry——"

"I am in a great hurry."

"Well, then, it 'ud take a goodish while to walk—at least it would me. My health ain't so good as what it yused to be, nor my legs either, for the matter of that, but ye be strong and lithe of limb, but still it be too far for ee to walk, so ee'd better go wi' Nat."

As she spoke these last words a raw-boned lad of about eighteen thrust his shook head in at the doorway.

"Oh, here be Nat," cried the old lady; "so that be all right. Now, lad, you're going to ha' coompany to the station."

"Coompany!" repeated the lad. "Who be it, missus?"

"This lady. I know you're fond of the ladies."

The lad blushed up to the roots of his hair, and went his way without further ado.

"Don't care about taking me, I fancy," said Laura.

"Not care! he's but too delighted. Don't ee mind him lass, that's his way—he's rather sheepish and queer wi' strangers. Oh he'll tek ee right enough. Here, Nat—Nat, I say, aint ee got yer ears this morning, or ha' ee left em behind ee? Coom here, lad."

The lad came into the room.

"Now, look here, you've got to tek this leddy to the station—so mind ee drive careful and don't get the wheels into the ruts any more than you can help. Do ee understand?"

"Yes, missus," said the yokel ,scratching his head; "I'll be very careful."

"Good lad. The leddy wants to get to the station as soon as possible. Is the horse put to?"

"Yes, and the milk is in the cart, but yer see, missus, it beant much of a trap—I mean there aint much room to spare. I wish I'd a better turn out, 'taint good enough for the loikes of un." This was said in a whisper, but Miss Stanbridge heard every word.

"I am quite content," said she, addressing herself to the lad. "Nobody knows me hereabouts. If we had to travel through the streets of London, it would be a different matter, you know."

In a minute or so after this the milk cart was at the door of the farmhouse, and Laura, who had gone upstairs to arrange her hair, and to make something like a rude toilette, quickly descended, and after thanking her hostess and wishing her farewell, stepped into the cart and sat herself beside the lad.

"Be careful, be very careful, and mind the ruts," was the last injunction his mistress gave him as he drove off.

"Now for it," murmured Miss Stanbridge. "If we should chance to run across any of the warders I am lost. But the probability is that they won't any of them be about thus early. They never are in places where they are wanted. Not that I want to see any of their ugly visages. Anyway there's no help for it now. I must take my chance as many have done before me under similar circumstances."

The road to the station was evidently not much frequented; for some considerable time after the horse and cart had left the farm house not a solitary passenger or vehicle met the eyes of either Nat or Miss Stanbridge.

So far all went on well.

"Not many vehicles about it would seem," observed the latter.

"No, not many. Seldom is at this time. Ye see it's a cross road, and people doesn't care about driving over it, except them as is obliged, and there beant many of those. It be very lonely by night though."

"So I should imagine, but it's a bright beautiful morning, and the birds are singing so gaily, I wish I could live in the country instead of London."

"Ah, I dessay ye do, marm, but may be ye'd get tired of it after a bit."

"I think not. Don't you like it?"

"Ah, ah," said the lad, with a loud guffaw, "I loike Lunnon. There beant any place loike Lunnon to my thinking."

"Ah, well, it is of course all a matter of taste, and I suppose we most of us like any place better than the one we are in."

Miss Stanbridge did not force the conversation beyond reasonable bounds, but she thought it quite as well to be on familiar and friendly terms with the farmer's boy, who was as good-natured as he was unsophisticated; so they continued to chat familiarly until the station was reached.

Then alighting from the vehicle, she put half-a-crown in the lad's hand, which seemed to have a marvellous effect on him.

At first he obstinately refused to accept the gratuity, but Laura was equally obstinate in forcing it upon him.

He was profuse in his thanks, and when he returned to the farm-house he declared his fellow-passenger to be a perfect "leddy."

Miss Stanbridge took a first-class ticket for London, and then went into the ladies' waiting-room, where she remained till the train was upon the point of starting.

She succeeded in reaching the metropolis in safety.

After paying a short visit to her house in the neighbourhood of Regent-street, and assuring her maid that she was a good deal better for her trip into the country, she set off for the Evalina-road.

She found Charles Peace at home; the time had not arrived for him to sally forth upon his depredating excursions, and he was busily occupied with his mechanical inventions.

"What, Lorrie!" he ejaculated, upon catching sight of his visitor. "Well, I am staggered! What's up? No true bill found, or what?"

"I didn't wait for the grand jury, old man," returned Laura, indulging in a loud laugh.

"Didn't wait—eh?" returned Peace, looking at the speaker from over his spectacles.

"No, Charlie. Gave 'em the slip, my boy. Ah, it's been a lesson to me. I'll take good care never to be caught on the same hook. It's been a hard fight, but I've won, and now ——"

"Well, and now, old girl—what now?"

"It won't do for me to remain in London."

"Oh, that's it—eh?"

"Well, you know, they'll be on the look-out, and to remain at my old quarters would be too risky."

"I don't know so much about that. Lord bless ye, Lorrie, those fellows' heads are as thick as a skittle-ball. If you've got clean off—which it's pretty certain you have, seeing that you are here safe and sound and looking better than ever for your—ahem—country trip—you've no cause to fear. Aint the blokes after me, and haven't I dodged them to rights?"

"Ah, but I'm not a Charles Peace."

"Hush, silence!" cried our hero in a tone of alarm, placing his hand before the mouth of the speaker. Then in a tone more serious he added, "Drop that name for ever more. Drop it—as you love me do this. I am Mr. Thompson. Didn't Bill tell you this?"

"I beg ten thousand pardons! Of course he did. What a donkey I am, to be sure! I am not as a rule so incautious, Thompson," said she, emphasising the last word.

"Enough. Say no more about it, then. But don't forget."

"I will not."

Laura Stanbridge now put him in possession of all the circumstances which took place respecting her escape, and wound up by thanking him most heartily for his kindness.

"Oh, bother that," said our hero; "Bill's behaved like a trump card, which to say the truth he is. Why, Laura, I'd trust him with my life; and if you have gratitude towards anyone it should be shown to him."

"I shall never forget his kindness—never!" ejaculated Laura. "He's worth his weight in gold. Indeed, I could never have believed it possible he had so much goodness in him if I had not had such unmistakeable proof of it. But I shan't remain in London, though; so before I go I will return you the money you were kind enough to send me."

"Any time will do for that; I am not in want of it."

"No time like the present; so here you are, Thompson."

She drew from her purse notes for the amount, and handed them to her companion.

"Oh, if you are so beastly particular, so be it, then," observed Peace, taking them from her and pocketing them.

"There's an end of that, then," said he. "Well, I'm as pleased as Punch to see you once more free. Why it's the first time you've been in gaol—aint it?"

"Yes, the very first, and I hope, Thompson, it will be the last."

"I hope so, I'm sure," returned Peace, in a sanctimonious tone and manner, which would have done credit to a Dissenting minister.

Miss Stanbridge stopped for some little time. After this she was introduced to the two ladies of the establishment, but, of course, not a word was said either by herself or our hero upon past circumstances or the nature of her connection with Peace. The women had to be kept in the dark as much as possible, and certainly their lord and master contrived somehow or other to throw dust in their eyes, which, all things considered, must be deemed almost marvellous to all reasonable persons. But Peace was a wonder in many ways, this being by no means the least remarkable trait in his diversified character.

Laura Stanbridge, as we have already seen, knew very well how to make herself agreeable, and her two female companions declared, after she had left the house in the Evalina-road, that she was a most delightful woman—a declaration which we don't expect any of our readers will endorse.

CHAPTER XXCII.

THE TRIAL OF THE DETECTIVES—PEACE'S VISIT TO BOW-STREET.

ALTHOUGH Charles Peace was what is termed playing a game of hide-and-seek, and to play this game effectually it is usually deemed advisable to court publicity

as little as possible, Mr. Thompson—as he called himself—did not choose to pursue this course of action. He went abroad, and paid frequent visits to places of public resort, and was as self-possessed and confident as if he had no oppressive weight on his conscience, no heinous crimes to answer for. In point of fact, he assumed all the airs and graces of a man who had done nothing but meritorious acts throughout his life.

It was at this time that the town was startled by the extraordinary detective case in which the convicts Kurr and Benson played so conspicuous a part. The confidence of the public was suddenly shaken in the whole system of the detective department of this country, and it was only after an overwhelming weight of evidence had been brought forward, that they could give credence to the startling revelations of bribery and corruption practised by Kurr and his accomplices upon paid officers of the Crown. Far be it from us to stigmatise the whole force as corrupt and unreliable. There are doubtless many good men, many intelligent, active, and praiseworthy officers to be found, but the machinery appears to be too cumbersome to be put in motion with sufficient rapidity to be of much service in cases of murder or manslaughter. We have alluded to this in a previous chapter, and since that was written, events have occurred which strenghten us in our opinion.

The Scotland-yard detective department is, and has been for years past, miserably inefficient in tracing out the perpetrators of the heinous crime of murder, and we are convinced that, sooner or later, it will be requisite, for justice sake, as well as for the safety of the public at large, that some better organised body of men will have to be formed to meet this crying evil.

Murders are rife in the land, and it is perfectly appalling the number of murderers who escape the strong arm of the law, which of late seems to be almost paralysed in dealing with crimes of this nature.

Charles Peace had read in the papers the report of the first inquiry into the charge made against the four detectives. He was greatly interested in the case, for, said he, with a sort of chuckle—

"I think I ought to know something about chaps of that kidney. I've dodged 'em a good many times, and when it answered my purpose I've bribed them; but this I only did when my dodgery failed. I'll go and have a squint at these beauties when they come up for their next examination."

"I'm sure I'd do nothing of the sort, if I were you," observed his wife. "What good can it do you? Talk about women's curiosity, why it's nothing in comparison to yours."

"Mind your own business, you fool," answered Peace sharply. "Leave me to be the best judge of my own actions."

"Oh, well, I've done. You know best, I suppose. I only made the remark for your own good. I shouldn't have thought you had any desire to be seen in Bow-street Police-court."

"I have a desire, and that's sufficient. I'm as safe there as I am here. More so, perhaps."

It may, and doubtless it does, appear singular that Peace should have had any desire to disport himself in the court referred to, but it is, nevertheless, a fact, he was present at one of the examinations of the detectives, and this has since been proved beyond all question.

The court was crowded almost to suffocation when the detective case came on, and Peace had the greatest difficulty in elbowing his way in. The Bow-street court, as most of our readers know, is miserably small, and inconvenient. As far as the public is concerned it could not very well be worse in the way of accommodation. It has for years been acknowledged to be ill adapted for the purpose for which it was constructed.

Peace found this out. He was a little man, and behind him was a man of elephantine dimensions, who kept bearing the greater portion of his weight on his shoulders.

"I wish you'd not press on me in this manner," said our hero to his tormentor.

"I can't help it, the people are shoving behind. Don't blame me."

"Order! Silence in the court!" cried the usher.

"But I'm half stifled," observed Peace. "Can't you make room for me somewhere?"

"No, every place is occupied."

"If you don't like it go out," said the big man.

Peace, who was dressed in a suit of black, with his silver spectacles on his nose, and looked a mild meek old gentleman of the Pickwickian order, again remonstrated in a soft gentle voice.

"What's the matter?" inquired a stout-built good-natured looking man, as he elbowed his way through the throng.

"Old gentleman's hardly pressed, and can scarcely breathe," answered one of the persons in the rear, and who evidently commiserated our hero's situation.

The stout person, who seemed to be dressed in a little brief authority, touched Peace on the shoulder, and said in a whisper—

"Follow me—this way."

Peace, nothing loth, did as he was bid.

He was taken by his conductor from the body of the court and passed in to that portion of it where the lawyers, barristers, and other persons of a nondescript order thread their way. Here he was comparatively comfortable—that is, as comfortable as it is possible to be in this precious sample of a court of justice, which is, perhaps, not saying much.

His conductor stood by his side on the same platform.

"I don't know how to thank you sufficiently for this act of kindness," observed our hero.

"Don't mention it, sir, I beg," returned the gentleman, who, if the truth must be told, had mistaken Peace for another and more exalted person.

Presently the four detectives—Meiklejohn, Druscovich, Palmer, and Clarke—were brought in. They took up their stations, and were joined by Mr. Froggatt the solicitor. Mr. Poland proceeded to state the case. After he had concluded, Mr. Superintendent Williamson was called.

It will be needless for us to give a detailed account of the proceedings, as the result has long since been patent to everybody. It will suffice for our purpose to note that Peace became on friendly and familiar terms with the gentleman who had been of such service to him. They conversed freely during the day's examination, and when the court rose Peace asked his companion to have a glass of wine.

"Well," observed the latter, "I don't mind if I do; but I've not as yet dined."

"Nor have I," said Peace; "are you going to have your dinner in the neighbourhood?"

"Yes," was the ready response.

"Well, so am I. Suppose we dine together somewhere."

"Yes, I'll do so with the greatest pleasure."

They adjourned to a neighbouring tavern, where they met a friend of Peace's companion, whom the latter introduced as a Mr. Shearman, who, it is perhaps needless to mention, was the American detective who had the charge against Doctor Bourne in hand.

Shearman had come over again to this country to "pot," as he expressed it, a runaway Yankee, who was charged with frauds on an extensive scale.

"Mr. Shearman," said the gentleman, addressing himself to Peace; "pardon me, but I don't know your name. I took you for Mr. Belmore, whom I have the honour of knowing."

"My name is Thompson," said Peace; "and I am most proud to have made your acquaintance. I will, with your permission, show you a rough draft of an invention of mine."

He drew from his pocket a drawing of his apparatus for raising sunken ships.

His two companions inspected it, and said it appeared to them to be a most admirable contrivance. This declaration was succeeded by a long discussion upon its merits, and soon after this dinner was served, upon which the three gentlemen sat down.

Peace had not the faintest notion at this time that he was hob-nobbing with two detectives, and it was fortunate for him that Mr. Wrench did not put in an appearance at this juncture.

"Wal," said Shearman, "how goes the case? Ugly against the prisoners?"

"Most remarkably strong against them," returned Mr. Cartridge, Peace's friend.

"I guessed as much. Wal, it's a scandal to your country—a great scandal," observed Shearman.

"Oh, everybody must admit that, sir," returned Peace. "For my own part, I can't see any excuse for these men. They were well paid, would, on retiring, be entitled to pensions, and yet they must aid and abet dishonest persons like Kurr and Benson."

"That is if they have done so," said Mr. Cartridge.

"Do you doubt it after what we have heard to-day?" inquired Peace.

"I should be sorry to prejudge the case; still, as I before observed, it looks ugly—that I readily admit. It is possible, however, that they may be able to produce some rebutting evidence on the trial, which will materially alter the complexion of the case. One never knows what may take place, for it has been often said that truth lies at the bottom of a well."

When the dinner had been dispatched Peace called for the bill, which he insisted on paying, alleging, as an excuse, that he had invited the other two to dine with him.

They both protested against this, but Peace, who was in a liberal mood, would have his own way, and a compromise was therefore effected by the other two being allowed to pay for wine and cigars.

In the course of conversation Peace discovered that he was passing a pleasant hour or so with detectives.

He was a little disconcerted when he ascertained this, but there was now no help for it—so he put a bold face upon the matter, but was at the same time more guarded in his conversation.

Mr. Shearman, as heretofore, told one of his stories about his own exploits in America, and Mr. Cartridge, not to be outdone, narrated the following case of mistaken identity, which for the reader's behoof, seeing that it is possessed of considerable interest, we print *in extenso*.

CHAPTER CXXIII.

MISTAKEN IDENTITY.

"I FELT convinced," said Mr. Cartridge, "that I had got the right man, for all the facts that had come to my knowledge were dead against him, but I am free to confess that there were others who were of a different opinion. I will just give you a circumstantial account view of the case.

"'Send for his friends?' I repeated, in reply to a question put to me by the inspector of a police-station at which I happened to be; 'oh, yes. I see no reason to refuse his request, but I think you are fully justified in not admitting him to bail.'

"The prisoner in question was a tall, fair man, of gentlemanly appearance, who seemed to feel his position acutely. He had lately been brought in on a singular charge of skittle-sharping.

"The prosecutor, a simple-looking countryman, deposed that he had met the prisoner three days before in Westminster, with two other men, and was by them solicited to have something to drink.

"After his compliance, a game of skittles was proposed. Bets were made, and he was ingeniously robbed of eighty pounds in gold and notes.

"The whole of the gang on that occasion made their escape; but the prosecutor met the prisoner while walking in the Strand, and recognising him at once, gave him into the custody of the first police officer he saw.

"The prisoner vehemently protested his innocence, and in no measured terms declared that he was the victim of a mistake.

"He gave the name of Joseph Halliday, and gave a respectable address, which we afterwards found was a correct one; described himself as a civil engineer, and said that he was the scapegoat of the prosecutor's stupidity.

"It was the early part of the afternoon, but the business of the court that day not being very heavy, the magistrate had finished his work and gone home; so that Mr. Halliday would have to remain a prisoner until the next day, even if he were able to prove his innocence in an incontestable manner.

"We were accustomed to see respectable men—that is, externally respectable—brought into the station on charges of skittle-sharping; and so Mr. Halliday's decent exterior did not impress me in his favour in the least.

"He appeared greatly distressed, and said repeatedly, as the charge was being taken, that he was innocent. His manner had the appearance of being genuine; but I never allowed appearances to have any weight with me.

"Some of the rascals who infest the streets and plunder the simple are such clever actors that if they were not incorrigibly idle, they would make a decent living upon the stage.

"I suggested to the inspector that it might be a case of mistaken identity; and, in order to set the question at rest, it would be better to send for the landlord and barman of the 'Duke's Head,' which was the name of the public-house in which the swindle had been perpetrated.

"The prisoner evinced the utmost signs of joy and exultation when he heard this proposal; and the prosecutor made no objection, saying that he was sure their testimony would bear out the charges he had just made against Joseph Halliday.

"Accordingly messengers were dispatched to the 'Duke's Head,' requesting the immediate attendance of the landlord and his barman. In the meantime the prisoner was conveyed into the yard of the station-house and placed in a row with nine other men.

"It was intended that the witnesses we had sent for should identify the prisoner from amongst a number of others.

"When they arrived, the landlord of the 'Duke's Head' requested to be told why he had been summoned.

"'A case of skittle-sharping,' replied the inspector, 'took place in your house three days ago. Would you remember the three men who hired your skittle-ground for the best part of the afternoon?'

"'Perfectly,' replied the landlord; 'there were four altogether, and this gentleman' (turning to the prosecutor) 'was one of them.'

"'You are quite right; but he is the victim of the three rogues. We imagine that we have one of them in custody. He is amongst some others in the back-yard. If your memory serves you, you will have no difficulty in selecting him from his companions.'

"'I don't think I shall have the least trouble. I have a distinct recollection of the whole party,' replied the landlord, following myself and the inspector to the yard.

"The barman we left behind; his turn was to come next.

"It must have been a moment of intense anxiety to Mr. Halliday.

"I was a little curious as to the result, and looked on with expectation.

"The court-yard was a narrow piece of ground, in which men were drilled occasionally. It was covered with gravel and surrounded by a high wall, which, however, in no way obstructed the light, which fell in a bright stream upon the men, who were marshalled in single file, to await the scrutiny of the landlord, who took a critical survey of them, and, without a moment's hesitation, went up to Mr. Joseph Halliday, and touching him on the shoulder, exclaimed, 'this is the man.'

"A shudder of repulsion ran through the prisoner's frame, and he turned ghastly pale. I thought he would have fallen. The inspector smiled, and said, 'An old hand, evidently.'"

"Oh, they generally come to that conclusion in most cases—do they not?" observed Peace.

"Well, I don't know that they do, sir," returned Mr. Cartridge; "but you know we have such a number of shocking characters under our hands, that it is, after all, but a natural conclusion. But I will proceed with my narrative:"

"'Oh! I knew him again in an instant,' exclaimed the landlord, who went back again with the inspector to allow the barman to commence his investigation.

"A tin cup stood under a tap, and seeing the prisoner looked faint and ill, I filled it with water, and presented it to him.

"He drank off the contents at a draught, and regarded me gratefully.

"'You are very kind,' he murmured, in a low tone.

"There was something in his voice that interested me—something quiet and gentle; but the evidence against him was so strong and damning, that I could not bring myself to regard him favourably, or look upon him as the victim of a mistake.

"Presently the barman made his appearance; he seemed an intelligent fellow, possessed of powers of discrimination.

"He walked along the yard and looked steadily at the men who were grouped together for his inspection, and stopped abruptly when he came to Mr. Halliday.

"'This is the one,' he said, triumphantly. 'I could tell him amongst a thousand.'

PEACE DESCRIBING TO THE TWO DETECTIVES HIS PLAN FOR RAISING SUNKEN VESSELS.

"The slender hope which had hitherto animated the prisoner now deserted him, and he fell on the ground in a heap, insensible. It was a terrible ordeal for him to have gone through, if innocent. Stepping up to the inspector, I said, 'This is a remarkable case; but although the evidence seems against him, it is odd—isn't it?—that he should take on so.'

"'I don't know. These fellows are up to as many dodges as there are days in the year. He must take his chance. He'll have a fair trial to-morrow. Perhaps he can prove an alibi. If you take an interest in him you can talk to him. I won't lock him up again till you've done your little bit of palaver.'

"Thanking the inspector, I returned to Mr. Halliday, and was glad to see that he showed signs of returning animation. Some good Samaritan had sprinkled his face with water, and he had opened his eyes.

"By my orders, he was accommodated with a chair, and when he was sufficiently recovered I began a conversation with him.

"'Do you still persist in saying that you are the victim of a mistake, Mr. Halliday?' I exclaimed.

"'Most certainly I do,' he replied, earnestly. 'Some one must have a strong and fatal resemblance to me.'

"'Will you tell me how you spent your time on the day of the alleged robbery?'

"'With pleasure,' he answered; 'but, I presume—excuse my asking the question—that I am talking to some one connected with the police.'

"'I am a detective, and in my professional capacity may be of service to you.'

"'You are very good, and I esteem myself fortunate in having met with you. In the first place, I must tell you that I am a civil engineer by profession, and tolerably well known to people who move in scientific circles. On the day in question, when the man who gave me in charge was robbed and plundered, I was attending a meeting at Muswell-hill and giving evidence as to the advisability of extended sewerage in the vicinity before the Muswell-hill Board of Works. The solicitors to the Board will prove it. The members of the Board will prove it.'

"'Very good,' so far,' I replied. 'Leave your case in my hands and make yourself easy as to the result. I shall, with your permission, instruct Mr. Sea, one of the cleverest practising barristers we have in cases of this kind, to defend you when brought before the court to-morrow morning, and to ask for a remand. You must put up with the worry and annoyance of imprisonment for a few days. Bring all your philosophy to your aid, and I will see if I cannot unravel this tangled skein. By the way, I should like to ask you one thing.'

"'As many as you like,' he replied readily.

"'Does any of your family resemble you in any way? Have you ever been taken for any one else on a previous occasion?'

"'Some years ago,' he replied, thoughtfully, 'my twin-brother was alive, and you would not have known us from one another—we were veritable Dromios.'

"'Is he dead now?'

"'I am sorry to say he is. We were much attached to each other, but he was of a roving disposition and would never stick to anything. I started him in several professions, but he always repaid my kindness by ingratitude, which is hard to bear from a relation. At length, on my refusing to assist him any longer, he ran away to sea, and the ship in which he sailed was subsequently wrecked on a voyage to Malaga.'

"'Oh!' I said, with a prolonged exclamation; I began to see my way a little clearer.

"Wishing Mr. Halliday good-bye, I left the station-house to commence operations. If what the prisoner said about his being in attendance upon the Muswell-hill Board of Works at the very time at which he was accused of being at an obscure pot-house in Westminster, in company with two other men not in custody, to defraud a simple-minded countryman of his money, the case was at an end. I at once left a retainer for Mr. Sea and engaged his services for Mr. Joseph Halliday on the morrow.

"I had a shrewd suspicion that I was about to embark in the investigation of one of the strangest cases of mistaken identity that had ever been heard of; nor was I mistaken, as after events tended to prove.

"I was acquainted with a man of the name of Pegon—a Frenchman—who had, it was popularly believed, been a thief in his own country, although he might have left France through political motives.

"On arriving in England he had taken service in the police force, and evinced such wonderful dexterity in tracking criminals that he speedily became one of our most valued detectives.

"The old saying—set a thief to catch a thief—was, admitting the reports about Pegon to be true, never better exemplified than in the person of the dapper little Gaul. He was not a proficient in the English language; he talked it in a half-broken sort of way, rather amusing than otherwise. It was to Pegon that I betook myself after leaving Mr. Sea's office.

"I found him at his favourite public-house—the 'Three Spies.' He was seldom at home, and when not on business he could always be discovered at the before-mentioned tavern or else at the Welsh ambassador's—the 'Goat in Boots.'

"Pegon had probably a greater acquaintance with the skittle-sharping fraternity than any other man in London.

"He knew them all, and when they occasionally took a trip into the country Pegon would miss the familiar face, find out where he was gone, and telegraph to the police of Birmingham, Manchester, or Liverpool, and they would exercise such a strict look-out that their vigilance would soon drive the sharper back to his old haunts and associates.

"When Pegon met him on his return, he would smile sardonically and say—

"'Back again—eh? Change of air is goot for your 'elth;' and his mouth would distend itself into a broad grin.

"It was rumoured that Pegon was occasionally heavily bribed by the thieves to allow them to remain unmolested; but his superiors took no notice of this scandal, as they always found him an active and intelligent officer; and if a man was wanted particularly, and Pegon was applied to for his apprehension, he was almost always forthcoming at a specified time. Pegon was sitting in the parlour of the 'Three Spies,' smoking contentedly, and drinking out of a pewter pot, which contained nothing stronger than the best old and mild ale. He rose when he saw me, and exclaimed, in a genial tone—

"'Ah, sir, it ees you! How you carry yourself? Sit down—'ere is a chair.'

"Taking out his handkerchief, with true politeness, he dusted the bottom of it, and handed it to me.

"'Good morning, Pegon,' I said; 'I have come to consult you on a matter of some importance.'

"'Yaes—yaes.'

"'Three days ago a countryman was robbed by a skittle sharper at the 'Duke's Head,' in Westminster.'

"'Yaes,' said Pegon, concentrating his attention on what I was saying.

"'To-day a gentleman was arrested on suspicion of being concerned in the robbery. The barman and the landlord swore that he was one of the men.'

"'Ah,' said Pegon, 'that is strange—ver strange.'

"'Have you heard of the robbery?'

"'No, but I have my suspicions; my good friend Toko, and my dear friend Donnymore have been ver flush of their money, and I suspect——'

"'Who is Donnymore?' I ventured to ask.

" 'Donnymore! oh, he ver goot fellow, Donnymore, but he go leetle too far.'

" 'In what way?'

" 'I shall tell you,' replied Pegon.

" 'Donnymore he come to my 'ouse, and he drinking my wine, but that is noting—oh, no, noting. You must know I used to pay Donnymore when I first com to England to show me thing or two I not know much, and Donnymore he shows me the places where thieves go, and give me hint now and then; but Donnymore he ver goot fellow, only he go little too far—just little bit too far. One day he com to my 'ouse and he drinking my wine and smoking my tabac, but that is noting —oh, noting—but he go to drawer, and he steal my stocking—oh, Donnymore, he ver goot fellow, but he go leetle, leetle too far.'

" 'Your stocking,' I said; 'that was not very valuable, I should think.'

" 'Oh, be Gar! it was. I keep all my money in my stocking. Thirty, forty, fifty, hundred pound! Oh, Donnymore, he ver goot fellow; but by Gar, he got leetle too far.'

" 'So you think Donnymore had a hand in this robbery?' I said, laughing at the Frenchman's story.

" 'I be dam well sure,' replied Pegon, slapping his fist on the table. 'I say to myself, aha, Donnymore, my boy, you have been at your old games again. More stocking, eh? Donnymore, take care, sare, you do not go leetle too far.'

" 'Who is Toko?' I asked.

" 'Toko! he Donnymore's pal. They stand in always.'

" 'And the third, do you know him? I believe these fellows always work in gangs.'

" 'Oh, certainement! It most be! Let me see. It most be Fon Beest, the German. I know him. Oh! he is crafty, like one English fox—yaes, I say so!'

" Von Beest I had heard of as a clever German thief, who had once been imprisoned for two years for a daring burglary in Oxford-street.

" 'What do you know about Toko?'

" 'Toko! he is what you say new mans almost; he has not been here 'bove year and half. He is sailor or something; he look like gentleman, and knows how to talk, and Donnymore he make him decoy. Oh, leave Donnymore alone. I have met him before today. Yaes, I know Donnymore; he ver goot fellow, but he go leetle too far—just leetle bit too far.'

" And as the little Frenchman recalled his grievances, he pulled away somewhat vigorously at his pipe, and looked at the sanded floor as if the reminiscence of the gold-laden stocking was painful to talk about.

" After a pause of a minute, he said, 'Oh, yaes! I know Donnymore!' and then he chuckled as if he contemplated revenge.

" 'Where could you find Donnymore and his associates?' I asked.

" 'I say,' asked the astute little Frenchman, 'is there reward offered?'

" 'No,' I replied; 'but Mr. Halliday, the gentleman I was speaking of, who is in custody, is well off, and will, I have no doubt, make a couple of days' work worth our while.'

" 'Bien! that is goot. I like to be on ze square, you know. You vash humbug, I vash humbug, we all vash humbug.. Tiens! you shall hear. Donnymore, Toko, Fon Beest all stay now at the "Crown," King-street, Seven Dials. I have my eye on all of them toujours. I am father—they are my children.'

" 'Let us go, then, and reconnoitre; I want to see if this man Toko resembles Mr. Halliday in any way; if so, the mystery is cleared up at once.'

" 'Of course it is. Well, we will go. I can spot them. I shall not touch Donnymore, I think, for Donnymore he ver goot fellow; but he go leetle too far —just leetle bit too far. Donnymore and me were pals once, confrères. You shall have Toko and Fon Beest, but Donnymore he shall shake loose leg a little longer. Vat you say to that, sare?'

" 'I have no objection,' I replied. 'I only want Toko.'

" 'Bon! You shall have Toko, and I will be liberal —I will throw Fon Beest into the bargain.'

" We shook hands in order to cement the bargain; and leaving the 'Three Spies,' we wended our way to the Seven Dials, and entered the 'Crown.' It was filled with thieves and loose women, their companions. Pegon perceived no trace of the trio we were in search of. Coming near, he said : 'Attendez! they are en haut.'

" On ascending the stairs, we found ourselves in a spacious room, in which singing was going on. It was long and narrow, with a stage at one end, and a succession of tables on each side, with a passage up the middle for ingress and egress, very much after the manner of the cafes chantants in the Palais Royal. The room was tolerably well filled.

" A man who threw himself into the most awful contortions and impossible attitudes, attired in a suit of clothes of a check pattern—something like Mr. Leech's caricature of Mr. Briggs when his mind is on hunting intent—was lilting a ditty respecting 'Sairy's young man,' which seemed to take the audience by storm. The success of this song was only equalled by another, beginning—

A cove he would a macing go,
Whether the blueskins would or no.

An evident allusion to accomplished thieves and baffled policemen. We took up a position from which we commanded an excellent view of the room. I began to look about me, and perceived a couple of bottles of champagne standing on a particular table in one corner.

" At this table three men were seated. I started. Pegon asked me what was the matter. I smiled at my stupidity; I thought I saw Mr. Halliday. My explanation of the singular coincidence was, that the brother whom Mr. Halliday had thought dead had escaped the shipwreck which had induced the belief of his decease, and that on returning to England his innate vagabondism had broken out afresh and he had allied himself with Donnymore and Von Beest.

" 'Who is that?' I asked Pegon, pointing out the man who bore such a marvellous resemblance to Mr. Halliday.

" 'That is Toko, and that is my dear friend Donnymore, while the other is that sacre German Fon Beest. Oh, I will make it hot for Toko and Fon Beest.'

" 'Cannot you go up to them and get into conversation?' I asked.

" Pegon looked at me steadily for a moment, and replied—

" 'You of course my friend. Donnymore, he will jump to see me; but I shall give him the office, and say, it is no business; he is not wanted; and we shall be ver merry. When he is in luck he will spend money like a king; so vill Toko; but Fon Beest he is a screw —no good, no, not to anyone. Come along, mon cher. Baisez moi? Non. It is droll, is it not? Come 'long; let us go to these ruffyans.'

"The Frenchman offered his hand to Donnymore and exclaimed—

"'Ah, how is Donnymore, my ole friend Donnymore? I always say he ver goot fellow, but he once go leetle to far—just leetle bit too far. But we will not talk 'bout that now. I have come out for what you say spree, one lark, and I am rejoice to see you here; and my friend Fon Beest too, and that dear Toko. Toko, how you do? You not shake hands with your own Pegon? That is right. Fon Beest, your hand. That is right also. Now, Donnymore, you make room for us.'

"Donnymore, slightly reassured, made room for us, and we sat down.

"'Ah,' continued the indefatigable Pegon, 'you have been in luck lately. Champagne, vin de ciel. Give me some, Donnymore; I feel very dry.'"

"Donnymore called for some more glasses, and poured out some wine for both of us.

"The more I looked at Toko the more surprised was I at the wonderful likeness between him and Mr. Halliday. No wonder, I thought, that the innkeeper and his barman as well as the prosecutor were deceived.

"The resemblance was something marvellous. I remarked the same mild-looking blue eyes, the same rather broad mouth and thick lips, the same straight nose a little dilated at the nostrils; but there was one thing about Toko which was not observable in Mr. Halliday.

"His face wore a restless expression, as if he had been haunted by the apprehension of arrest. You would have put him down at first sight as a man who had something upon his mind which was eternally weighing upon his spirits and depressing them. He drank heavily.

"His somewhat bloodshot eyes, together with their swollen lids, and the dry, parched, burnt-up, cracking skin upon his lips sufficiently proclaimed the fact of his having addicted himself to spirituous compounds in a wholesale manner.

"Pegon was in his element. He carried on the part he had undertaken with admirable cleverness.

"'Ha—ha!' laughed the sharpers.

"'Pegon's a good judge,' said Toko.

"'Yes, leave him alone,' replied Donnymore.

"'More wine, Donnymore,' exclaimed Pegon. 'Once you drinking my wine; to-day I drinking yours.'"

"Donnymore complaisantly filled his friend's glass, paying mine the same compliment. After Pegon had, to his satisfaction, quaffed the foaming vintage, he exclaimed—

"'Donnymore, you telling me one thing.'

"'Fire away, old fellow.'

"'You will tell me true this one thing?'

"'Yes, half-a-dozen, if you like.'

"'What you going to do now?'

"'Do?' repeated Donnymore, with the light of consternation in his eyes, for Pegon's words seemed to have a strange significance for him.

"'Yaes, what you going to do?'

"'Oh, I don't know.'

"The man looked nervously around him, and eyed the door suspiciously, as if he fully expected to see a body of police standing in its immediate vicinity.

"'Why not try change of air?'

"'I'm well enough.'

"This was said rather surlily.

"'Birmingham is nice place.'

"'D—— Brummagem,' muttered Donnymore.

"'Ah; you not like to leave your friends!'

"'No, I don't.'

"'That is good, shows you have good heart. It is but natural, you are so well known, and have so many friends.'

"He laid a stress upon the last word, and Donnymore looking steadily at Pegon, said angrily—

"'Look here, Pegon—what the deuce are you driving at?'

"'Me! noting, my friend—it is only anxiety for the state of your health.'

"'My health be blowed! What's your little game?'

"'How you talk! as if I ever had little games; but he is so funny, that Donnymore.'

"There was an awkward pause, during which the sharpers looked at one another uneasily.

"'There is that dear Fon Beest,' resumed Pegon. 'His friends could not part with him; he is too precious to them.'

"'Drink your wine and hold your row!' growled the German.

"'Ha, ha!' laughed Pegon.

"'That dear Fon Beest is like one bear with a sore head. He is complimentary too. But I shall have the pleasure of returning his compliment some day. I never forget my debts.'

"'Devil doubt you,' said Donnymore.

"'I wish I was like you, Donnymore,' exclaimed Pegon.

"'What for?'

"'Shall I tell you?'

"'Go ahead.'

"'I would take a Schwostle.'

"'Where's the pull in that?'

"'Oh, you'd soon learn the squeak.'

"It was clear now that Donnymore began to see some hidden meaning in Pegon's apparently objectless remarks. He became more and more uneasy, and it was evident that he came to the conclusion that Pegon was giving him the office in a friendly way. He did not care much for Toko or Von Beest.

"Self-preservation was the first law with him, and he apprehended they were both wanted, whilst he was, through the Frenchman's kindness, allowed to escape. Rising from his chair, in a careless way, he put on his hat.

"'You are not going yet?' asked Pegon, pretending to be surprised.

"'Going! no, not till midnight. I'm game for a spree.'

"'Where you off to, then?'

"'Back in a minute.'

"When his associates heard this they disposed themselves quietly to await his return.

"Pegon muttered to himself, 'Oh, he's fly bird, ver fly bird.'

"After the lapse of five minutes the sharpers began to grow fidgety, and Toko rose to take his leave. Pegon got up at the same time and exclaimed—

"'Have you a minute to spare?'

"'What for?'

"'Just one word—private conversation. You stop here.'

"This was to me.

"Toko and Pegon walked up the room together. Suddenly there was a cry of rage and alarm. I looked up. Two men in the body of the hall were fiercely struggling together. The fight was of short duration. In less than a minute Toko was lying on his back on the floor handcuffed.

"When Von Beest perceived this he turned deadly pale.

"I heard him utter an imprecation upon Donnymore

and his treachery, and then he made a rush towards the door, but Pegon had by this time drawn his policeman's staff, which he carried concealed under his cloak, and as the German attempted to pass him, he struck him on the forehead, and he rolled heavily over upon the floor.

"Toko and Von Beest were both manacled and helpless.

"A smile of triumph flitted over Pegon's face; he beckoned to me. I came up and stood by the side of Toko, who was sitting disconsolately upon a bench.

"The musical performance was arrested, and the people who were in the hall manifested the most lively interest in the proceedings of Pegon and myself.

"I was especially an object of remark and scrutiny.

"'Mr. Halliday,' I said, in a low voice to Toko.

"He started; my words roused him from his listless apathetic mood, and he asked in a hurried voice if I spoke to him.

"'Certainly,' I replied, 'that is your name.'

"'How do you know?'

"'That does not matter; you cannot deny it.'

"'I can—I do,' he vociferated.

"'Your violent asseverations—' I began, when he interrupted me, saying—

"'Whoever says so is guilty of an infamous falsehood.'

"'Possibly,' I replied. 'By the way, have you seen your brother lately?'

"'My—my brother?' he stammered.

"'Yes, the engineer.'

"'Who are you,' he cried, 'and why do you ask me these questions?'

"'I am a detective, and I ask you these questions in order that Justice may vindicate her character and reputation for impartiality.'

"'A detective,' he repeated slowly.

"'I think I said so.'

"'Why, I should as soon have thought of seeing a flying fish or a sea-serpent with a ring through its nose.'

"'You have not answered my question respecting your brother yet?'

"'I have not seen him, nor do I wish to.'

"'What harm has he done you?'

"'Only driven me to ——; but never mind.'

"'He thinks you're drowned at sea.'

"'A good job too—let him think so.'

"'Do you know where he is now?'

"'No,' he replied laconically.

"'He is where you will soon be.'

"'In gaol?'

"'Yes, in a prison.'

"'What!' he cried with a bitter laugh; 'does it run in the family?'

"'Not that either.'

"'Explain yourself?'

"'You are the cause of his arrest.'

"'I!' he ejaculated in astonishment.

"'Yes; he is accused.'

"'Of what?'

"'Of committing an offence, the responsibility of which rests entirely with you. He has been taken up as a skittle sharper."

"'No; you are joking?'

"'I assure you I am speaking the truth."

"There seemed something so exquisitely ludicrous in the idea of his sober, steady-going respectable brother being brought before a magistrate for a disgraceful misdemeanour, that the dissipated scamp laughed immoderately.

"The painful position in which he was did not affect his hilarity or his flow of animal spirits.

"''That is capital,' he said at last. 'I am only sorry he was not committed for trial.'

"''There is no chance of that now.'

"''I suppose not, as I have fallen into your clutches through the infernal treachery of that fellow Donnymore. But I'll be even with him some day.'

"''He had nothing to do with it; you must lay your misfortune to the astuteness of Mr. Pegon.'

"''I wish you and Pegon and the whole kit of you were at the bottom of the sea!' he growled.

"Presently Von Beest returned to consciousness and glanced fiercely around him.

"''Ah,' said Pegon, with cruel levity, 'that dear Fon Beest is himself once more. Do I not pay my debts well? Have I not returned your compliment, my amiable Fon Beest? Come along; you shall go to the 'Government Hotel' to-night, and if the beds should turn out hard come and complain to me and I will get you a new chambermaid. Come here, my dear Fon Beest. Come along, my good Toko.'

*   *   *   *   *   *

"When the magistrate saw Toko he was no less astonished than the prosecutor, who at once admitted that he had fallen into an error which, he trusted, was excusable, owing to the wonderful likeness existing between the brothers.

"Mr. Halliday, the engineer, and Mr. Halliday, the skittle-sharper, must have been cast in the same mould. The prisoner was at once discharged, and his brother placed in the dock.

"Mr. Halliday's joy at seeing his brother once more was considerably damped by the reflection that he had provoked the doom of a felon; and taking me on one side he asked me to add to the favour I had already done him, and try to make terms with the prosecutor.

"I found this worthy rather obdurate at first, but when I told him that Mr. Halliday would refund all the money he had lost, and make him a handsome present besides, his anger gave way, and he consented to withdraw from the prosecution.

"Toko was so much affected by this proof of his brother's good nature that he gave up his evil ways of living, and addicted himself to honest pursuits. He thought it unadvisable to stay in England, so he went to Australia (not at the expense of the Government as he was once ambitious of doing—but by his brother's assistance), and set up in New South Wales as a sheep-farmer; and the last time his friends heard from him he was doing remarkably well, and turning out better than the most sanguine of his acquaintance had ever anticipated; and so ended this marvellous case of mistaken identity."

"Ah," observed Peace, in a quiet, contemplative manner, "we cannot any one of us be too careful in the matter of identity. I myself have on more than one occasion been sadly at fault in this respect, and I should hesitate before I swore to a person, unless there were corroborating circumstances."

"We have most of us been at fault in this respect," returned Mr. Cartridge. "No stronger proof can be given of this than an event which occurred on this very day. When I saw you in the body of the Bow-street Police-court I mistook you for another person. I was under the full impression that you were the individual in question, and hence it was that I was induced to take you to a more convenient part of the court. So you see you have not so much reason, after all, to thank me for my courtesy," he added, with a smile.

"You were of essential service to me, anyway," said Peace; "and, as a matter of course, I am duly thankful."

At this all three gentlemen laughed once more.

"Wal, Cartridge," said Shearman, "I have always said that sooner or later some very great alterations will have to be made in the detective department of this country. We manage matters a great deal better in the United States. Look at the number of murderers who escape in and about London! Why, it's perfectly scandalous. With such a large and expensive establishment such things ought not to be."

"I quite agree with you—it is scandalous," returned Shearman; "but how is it to be remedied?"

"Ah—that's another question, and one I shall perhaps not find it easy to answer; but that some remedy must be applied is, in my opinion, beyond all question. Why, within the last few years you have suffered a host of assassins of the very worst type to slip through your fingers. What am I saying?—that's not precisely my meaning, for you have never laid hold of them at all. Now, there was that case at Brompton—Edith-grove or Maude-grove—I forget which. The two Wallaces, after the death of the ill-fated woman, betook themselves to a cab, were driven off, and not the faintest clue has been found to either of them. Is that not so?"

Mr. Cartridge shrugged his shoulders, and said, "I am afraid it is."

"I'm sure of it. Wal, such things ought not to be. What is the inference? I say again, what is the inference?"

"Can't tell."

"I can—bribery and corruption. You won't make me believe that they would have been all this time at large unless, like Kurr and Benson, they had closed the eyes of the police with gold-dust. What say you, sir?"

This last observation was addressed to Peace, who by this time had begun to be in a little bit of a quandary, for he felt that it was an act of great imprudence to continue in the company of his two associates much longer, but he did not very well know how to bring the interview to an end without exciting suspicion.

"I quite agree with you, sir," he returned.

Then, thinking to change the subject, which was to him by no means an agreeable one, he drew from his pocket again the drawing of his invention for raising sunken ships.

"It would be indeed a favour if either of you gentlemen could put me in the way of laying this draft of my invention before the proper authorities."

With a couple of drawing-pins he fastened the drawing against the wall of the room, and proceeded to point out its merits once more to the two detectives. They knew but little about it, but strove to comprehend its mode of operation, rising from their seats and carefully inspecting the chart in question.

"Ah," murmured Peace to himself, "I wish I was fairly out of this. The Yankee bloke seems ever and anon to look one through. He's awfully cute—I do wish he'd go."

After some further discussion the chart was rolled up again, and Peace placed it in his pocket, whereupon the three gentlemen sat down again.

"Wal, stranger," said Shearman, addressing himself again to Peace, "as we are all here to ourselves, I'll just give you an account of a bit of business I was engaged on in New York. It's a true story, and there ain't no tall talk in it."

"I'm really very sorry," observed Peace, "but I am afraid I shan't have time."

"Oh, bosh, I'll trot it off as sharp and brisk as a donkey's gallop. Here's to our better acquaintance. I am glad to have met you, sir," added the American, raising the glass to his lips.

"And I am equally glad to have met you, sir," returned our hero, who wished the Yankee to the Antipodes. "But you must excuse me."

"Sit down for another quarter of an hour," said Shearman. "We shall be all three of us going at the expiration of that time. Come, light up—have another cigar."

"Devil take these fellows!" murmured Peace to himself. "There is no getting out of their clutches."

He, however, lighted up, and reluctantly consented to remain a little longer.

"My friend, Shearman, can tell you tales of detective life for a week at a stretch," observed Cartridge, with a smile; "and mind you a good many of his stories are both interesting and instructing. One thing I will say for him, he is never backward in obliging."

"Wal, I hope we learn something from each other," observed the American. "It is by the interchange of thought, and knowing something of other men's experiences, in addition to our own, that we may eventually become smart officers. That's my opinion, I make it a rule to listen to all people have to say, whether they be wise or otherwise."

"That's right enough," returned Cartridge.

"So here goes," exclaimed the Yankee.

CHAPTER CXXIV.

STOLEN LETTERS—AN AMERICAN DETECTIVE'S STORY.

"THE Post-office," said Mr. Shearman, "is one of those institutions where scrupulous honesty is required, where very inadequate pay is given—a man is expected to slave like a mule or a camel for something under a pound a week, and to resist temptation.

"Some do it, others do not—they fall. Possibly these latter have wives and children, and cannot help thinking of them as a letter passes through their hands with a little coin inside. It is not a large sum, but it is more than half a week's wages to them, and would enable them to do something for the 'young ones.'

"The post-office, or more correctly the public, is robbed to a large extent annually, and it is impossible to put a stop to these depredations, for although the offenders are detected in some instances, and brought to justice, others escape and become hardened in crime.

"During the year of the last Great Exhibition these robberies became so frequent that it was found necessary to adopt some extraordinary means to check them. The utmost vigilance was exercised by the officials, but they found their efforts unavailing.

"The thefts continued, and the authorities were deluged with letters, stating that money, notes, cheques, and valuables of all descriptions had never come to hand. In the dilemma in which they found themselves placed they had recourse to the police, and Colonel Warner recommended the case to my notice. I undertook it; for it was a task of some difficulty which I found would occupy a week or so most agreeably.

"I was always happier in the harness than out of it. I do not mean to say that I despise reasonable relaxation, but I deprecated any great waste of time. I petitioned to be allowed to learn the business of a letter-sorter, which request was granted at once.

"A few days initiated me into this branch of the business, and I was then drafted into the room in which the latest operations were carried on. Large bags of letters were continually being shunted down shafts.

"When they reached the floor they were eagerly pounced upon and sorted for transmission to all parts of the kingdom. I carefully watched every man, which would seem a useless proceeding on my part, because a spy appointed for the express purpose is continually looking on. He is concealed from view, and gazes through a pane of glass at those who are at work in the room, and of course he detects frauds when they are very frequent.

"This man maintained, for his own credit sake, that the robberies were perpetrated at some other place and not in the General Post-office, but I did not agree with him. It required something more searching than the sleepy vision of a hired spy to detect the skilful thieves who were making a large income out of his carelessness and inefficient efforts.

"The quickness with which experienced men perform their duties is inconceivable to those who have not witnessed their exertions. I found it very difficult to keep my attention sufficiently fixed upon one in particular to be able to remark the peculiarity of his manner. The hands of all of them were here, there, and everywhere at once.

"I pretended to be absorbed in my occupation, although I was in reality remarking everything—one man especially attracted me. There was something so restless in his manner, that from the first time I set my eyes upon him I singled him out as the most likely fellow in the room to be a thief.

"I remarked that he every now and then raised his hand to his mouth. But so rapid were his motions that they resembled sleight-of-hand, and I could not discover what he was doing. This man looked as if he had known trouble, and was thoroughly acquainted with that painful process which is known as being in hot water.

"Perhaps he had been born with ideas above his station. There are people who move in a very humble sphere of life think they ought to have been born peers of the realm, and nothing but monarchical greatness will content others, though the majority of aspirants draw the line at nobility.

"Luxurious notions may have entered this man's head. He may have had a fancy for asparagus, or new potatoes, or lamb and duck and green peas, and his own beggarly salary not 'running to it,' as the phrase goes, he may have thought it no great sin to help himself when the occasion presented itself in a favourable manner. He was not of full habit of body.

"There was something hollow and unsubstantial about him, although he was not much more than thirty years old, if you could judge from his outward appearance, which was not prepossessing.

"I determined, when work was over, to follow this man to his lair and see what he was like at home. The domestic hearth is something like wine. It shows men in their true character. The public-house is not a bad interpreter, but the hearth is the best of all. Work was over at six. At that time the night men came on.

"I afterwards ascertained that the man's name was John Brown. He walked with a quick step along the street, looking behind him occasionally without seeing anything to arouse his suspicion, and entered a public-house, which was situated about half-way up a small court, whose obscurity must have prevented it from being generally known.

"Standing at the bar was a young man of gentle-manly but dissipated appearance, well dressed, and wearing some jewellery which, if real, must have been expensive. When he perceived Brown, he exclaimed—

"'Johannes, my man, otherwise John, I am glad to see you.'

"Brown responded by a nod and a grunt.

"I followed, unnoticed by either party, and placed myself in a convenient position for eavesdropping.

"Brown sat down by the side of his acquaintance, said—

"'Rather later than usual to-day, Mr. Wareham. The bags were rather heavy.'

"'Never mind that. Have you worked the oracle properly?' replied Wareham.

"'About the same as usual, I think; my pockets are pretty well lined.'

"'Turn them out; there is no one here to notice us.'

"'I shouldn't mind something to drink first,' growled John Brown.

"'You shall have it, my pippin. What tap's most to your liking?' replied Mr. Wareham.

"Brown expressed an opinion strongly in favour of beer such as is brewed by Bass on the banks of Trent, which was promptly brought him by an obsequious waiter. After quenching his thirst, he said—

"'Now, sir, I feel better.'

"Putting his hand in his coat pocket, he produced several pieces of money, together with little scraps of paper. He had, I imagined, first of all felt the letters that passed through his hands, and if he detected the presence of gold, he raised the envelope to his mouth and bit off the corner in which the coin had fallen, afterwards placing it in his pocket. He appeared to have about twelve pounds to show as the result of his day's work.

"Mr. Wareham examined the spoil, counted it, and having divided it equally, gave Brown one-half as his share of the plunder. Brown uttered an exclamation of discontent.

"'What are you growling at?' exclaimed Wareham.

"'I ought to have the whole of it. I run the risk.'

"'So you do. But you are obliged to bring all you get to me, because I know your secret. I need not give you anything if I did not like. You ought to be grateful for the generosity with which I treat you; upon my word, Brown, you are a fortunate fellow.'

"'More of a fool than that,' grumbled Brown, who seemed inclined to retaliate, and kick over the traces.

"'I can't agree with you, then.'

"'It don't much matter whether you do or not. I am pretty well sick and tired of this little game. I have a good mind to leave this land and go to Texas or Mexico.'

"'At the expense of the Government,' sneered Wareham.

"'If I went, you'd go with me,' said John Brown, fiercely.

"'Think so? Well, you have a right to form your own opinion.'

"'I, however, don't suppose that such a thing is even remotely possible. I am very well satisfied with my native country; I have found you, and you are a source of profit and of income to me. You are what I may call a pearl of great price. I am unwilling to relinquish you. If I did so, I should be like the man who killed the goose that laid the golden eggs. My dear Johannes, you are necessary to my existence.'

"'You always think of yourself.'

"'Of course; egotism is the primary duty if not the whole duty of man.'

"'I don't know anything about that, but I'm tired of the way we're going on. I would rather be in a prison than lead this sort of life.'

"'Have you ever been in a prison?' exclaimed Wareham, with a searching glance.

"'No, but the time may come for all that. I'm going the right road to be shut up in gaol,' returned Brown, savagely.

"'As we are friends,' said Wareham, 'I don't mind telling you that I have.'

"'You!' said Brown.

"'For a year and a half I enjoyed that pleasure.'

"'I wish you were there now.'

"'Very possibly, my friend, but I really cannot join you in your amiable desire. I am unable to say in the spirit of the hymn, "I have been there and still would go," for it is anything but a little heaven below.'

"'So you had your hand in before you met me?' said Brown, with a malicious grin.

"'Certainly I had; a man must live, and I can declare that I was never any burden to my respectable parents. From my earliest infancy I had a talent for appropriating the property of other people, and I have lived upon my wits ever since I first knew I had any.'

"'What got you into trouble?'

"'An inordinate passion for riding. I always envied people I saw on horseback, and one day as I was loitering about the best part of the town, a gentleman asked me to hold his horse for him, while he entered the house of a friend. I looked upon the request as an insult, and while I held the bridle I ruminated as to the best method of revenge upon the aristocrat who had laid himself open to my resentment. It occurred to me that the best way to punish him would be to rob him of his horse. So seizing an advantageous opportunity, I sprang lightly upon the animal's back.

"'I did not know how to ride. The horse found at once that he had a light weight upon him, and he soon discovered, with equine instinct, that I had never been on a horse before. Setting back his ears, the beast bent his legs under him and set off at a quick pace. John Gilpin going to Edmonton must have felt very much as I did.

"'The horse galloped recklessly and furiously from street to street, and at last landed me in the paternal arms of a blue-coated policeman, who looked after me with the care of a father.

"I was committed for trial, and engaged Mr. Earwig, the celebrated criminal counsel, who did his best for me, and moved the court to tears as he recounted the sad position of this well-connected young man (my father was at the time in Sing Sing gaol for debt, and my mother in the penitentiary owing to a little matter of manslaughter), whose parents were highly respectable.

"'The misguided youth had given way to a sudden impulse of temptation which led him into the commission of a sin, the enormity of which was regretted by none so much as himself.

"'At this juncture of the learned barrister's speech the prosecutor got up, and said he hoped the court would deal leniently with the prisoner.

"'He was willing to make all the reparation which lay in his power.

"'The horse had subsequently run up against an omnibus, broken his neck, and damaged sundry pedestrians in his dying struggles, so it may be imagined that I was not able to make much reparation.

"'The unhappy boy (sobs audible in various parts of the court) narrowly escaped with his life. When he, in an unguarded moment, leaped into the saddle he had no idea that the horse would go on.

"'He had never been in a similar position before, and was so ignorant of the first principles of horsemanship that a donkey might lead him to destruction.

"'No felonious design lurked in my client's head. Steal the horse! Why, gentlemen of the jury (this with a persuasive simper), you might just as well, and with equal propriety, accuse me—me, Mr. Earwig—of wishing to run away with the box in which you are at this moment sitting. (A murmur of incredulity arose from the body of the court, which was instantly suppressed by the energetic efforts of the usher.)

"'No, no, gentlemen, the poor young man whose prospects in life are already partially ruined, owing to his having been placed in the ignominious position in which he is by the precipitancy of the sitting magistrate who committed him for trial; whose character has been aspersed, and whose prospects have been blighted through a strange perversion of the truth, and a misconception of actual facts, never—I say it emphatically, never—contemplated an offence against the common law of the land.' (Applause, and "hear, hear," from a juryman.)

"'Acquit him, gentlemen. You are not the slaves of prejudice. Do your duty as is meet and proper for men of standing and position. Why should you wreak an imaginary vengeance upon an innocent man, for innocent he is, in spite of the allegations that have been made to the contrary? Let him go his ways, gentlemen of the jury, and none of you will sleep the worse for it.'

"'Mr. Earwig sat down in a state of moisture, arising from perspiration and exertion, but his arguments were not so availing with the jury as I would have wished them to be; they found me guilty, and I made the acquaintance with the interior of the State Prison. Profit by my experience, my dear Johannes. If you are of an ascetic turn of mind, and wish to mortify the flesh, by all means step within the pale of the criminal law, and get brought up before the district judge. You will not forget your interview with that terrible functionary in a hurry. I have seen him once, and I do not want to renew my acquaintance with him. Since that delightful period of my existence I have played the part of the monkey who made use of a cat's-paw to pull the chesnuts out of the fire for him. You, my accommodating Johannes, are my cat's-paw. The coins which you bring me from the G.P.O are the chesnuts. My heart overflows with gratitude to you. I regard you as my benefactor, and I wish I could promote you in some way. The days in which Jack Sheppards and Dick Turpins flourished have gone by, but you might be a Redpath or a Dean Paul; I think you have talent enough for a Redpath, and I don't think you would make a bad Roupell.'

"'When you have ended your nonsense I shall be glad if you will tell me,' exclaimed Brown, who had been fretting and fuming during this lengthy speech.

"'My good, my excellent Johannes,' replied Mr. Wareham, suavely, 'I have scarcely commenced.'

"'What I want to know is, how much longer this game is to last?'

"'I can tell you,' said Wareham. 'If you can manage to nail a certainty—by that I mean something worth having—we will divide the swag, and you can go to Mexico when you like. I shall not endeavour to stop you. Can't you rob the California mail? Get yourself put on night duty; do something. If you go on like this, you will get bowled out at last, and we shall have to throw the sponge up.'

PEACE PARTING WITH THE DETECTIVES.

"'I'll try,' replied John Brown, moodily.

"'Think it over, Johannes, and do your best.'

"'I wish I had never given way to your temptation,' muttered Brown, in a low voice, but Wareham did not overhear the remark.

"'I must tear myself away from your fascinating society, Johannes,' continued Wareham; 'I have an appointment with a fly flat (i.e. a clever fool), and he has some superfluous cash which I covet. See if you cannot do something worth talking about. I shall meet you to-morrow at the usual time.'

"Wareham lighted a cigar, and nodding to his accomplice, strutted leisurely out of the place.

"Brown allowed his face to sink upon his hands, and

I heard him say, ' Curse him! may God in Heaven curse him!'

"He remained sunk in a lethargic despair for more than an hour, then he raised himself and left the tavern. I returned home to ponder. It was necessary to put a stop to the nefarious practices that Brown carried on with such skilfulness, and I considered how I should best take action in the matter."

"Which of course you did," observed Mr. Cartridge.

"Wal, I guess so, I never was one to let the grass grow under my feet."

"Ah," thought Peace, "when will he have done. I am on tenter-hooks. Then aloud he said, "I am greatly interested in your narrative—pray proceed, sir."

"All right," returned the American, "I'll jest git this darned weed to draw and be hanged to it. The Britishers always roll their cigars up too tight. It's a way they've got, I suppose."

"Take another," said Peace.

"No, he's all right now, thank you." Mr. Shearman then proceeded.

"I had not the remotest conception how Mr. Wareham became acquainted with John Brown's secret, but one thing I was sure of, and that was that the aforesaid gentleman was a consummate scoundrel.

"In order to understand his character better, and to see with whom I was contesting, I applied to an intelligent officer who was acquainted with almost all the thieves, vagabonds, and rogues in the city.

"The reply I received confirmed my suspicions. Wareham was well known to the police under a dozen of aliases. He had been convicted, and I resolved that he should be so again if there was any virtue in an indictment for conspiracy to defraud.

"I watched the two men carefully for some days, and at last I gained some information upon which I determined to act. They had planned an elaborate robbery between them, and Mr. Wareham's habitual prudence was so far overruled that he consented to take an active part in it.

"Those letters which were registered on account of their containing valuables were also placed in a bag by themselves. Of course there were different bags for different places, but the Cincinnati bag was always a bulky one; they determined to appropriate the contents of that one.

"It was Brown's duty to take certain bags to the lower regions of the Post-office for transmission through the tubes of the Pneumatic Company, which had just been laid down.

"Having overheard all their plans, and made my arrangements accordingly, I concealed myself with one of the watchmen connected with the establishment, in an angle of the wall, where I was free from observation, but able to spring out on a moment's notice.

"Wareham accompanied Brown from above, and assisted him to carry the bags. No one asked him any questions—it was supposed that he had been told off on the same duty. The room in which the opening to the tube was situated was unoccupied by any one except the workmen connected with the machinery requisite to put the valves in motion.

"Browne and Wareham, thinking themselves alone, commenced the execution of their nefarious project. They hastily untied the neck of the small sacks, and plunging their hands in drew out as many letters as they could conceal about their persons.

"They had taken the precaution to have pockets ingeniously sewn on inside their coats and waistcoats, so that the plunder might be more easily distributed about their bodies.

"If they had crammed and stuffed the two ordinary pockets that every coat possessed, they would have bulged out, and most likely have betrayed them.

"I allowed them to satisfy their rapacity, and waited patiently to see what they would do next.

"The mouth of the pneumatic tube was very like the opening of the boiler of a furnace. The bottom part resembled a miniature railroad, and the idea was strengthened by the car or small waggon, which was driven along at an immense pace by atmospheric pressure.

"The waggon was in readiness for the bags, and when the two thieves had robbed the appointed bag of as much of its precious contents as they thought they could safely carry away with them, Brown raised it up and placed it in the waggon.

"I considered this a good opportunity to make my presence known and make a captive of Brown and his dangerous accomplice.

"Stepping from my place of concealment I appeared unexpectedly before them. Brown uttered a terrified cry, and seemed petrified with fear and apprehension.

"To be detected when success seemed most certain was very mortifying. He had made his arrangements to leave the country that very night. I could see by the aid of the gaslight that he was ghastly pale.

"Wareham did not exhibit the symptoms of terror and consternation that characterised the bearing of his less hardened confederate, but he was a little thrown off his guard, nevertheless.

"' Well, governor, what do you want?' he exclaimed in a voice he vainly endeavoured to render calm.

"' What are you going to do with all those letters?' I asked.

"' Letters—what letters?' he replied, with well-affected astonishment.

"' Those you have in your pockets.'

"' I don't know what you mean.'

"' Don't you, really? That's a pity,' I said, in a bantering tone. 'Unfortunately I saw you put them away.'

"' And suppose you did; what then?' he cried, boldly; 'I suppose you want something to keep your mouth shut?'

"The watchman had remained in his hiding-place up to the present time, but now turning half round I beckoned him to show himself.

"He did so.

"' Take that man into custody,' I cried, ' for robbing the post-office.'

"Brown was too much alarmed to make any resistance, and in half a minute the handcuffs were glittering on his wrists.

"Wareham looked on at this with blank amazement; then when it was finished and his friend secure, he burst into a loud laugh and exclaimed—' Sold, by Heavens!'

"The watchman now came to my assistance, and we advanced to Wareham, who retired until he came to the mouth of the pneumatic tube.

"I made sure of catching him, and was already congratulating myself upon having apprehended the prisoners without any bloodshed, when I was unpleasantly forced to remember that there was such a thing as a slip between the cup and the lip.

"Just as our hands were upon him Wareham courageously gave a spring and entered the tube, taking a recumbent position upon the waggon by the side of the plundered mail-bag.

"Seizing the handle he pulled the door to after him. This, I afterwards found, was the signal for the workmen to put the machinery in motion. The bird escaped from my hand just as I was about to seize it.

"I do not think that Wareham imagined the waggon would be at once propelled through the tube; it is more probable that he wished to gain a temporary asylum; but a loud rumbling soon informed us that something was taking place inside.

"Leaving John Brown in charge of the watchman I ran hastily upstairs and asked where the tube discharged its contents. I was told the correct spot. I went hastily into the street and got into the first cab I could see and drove to the place at the utmost speed of which the cab horse was capable.

"On arriving there I proceeded to the post-office department, and found to my inexpressible chagrin that the waggon had duly arrived with its human freight ten minutes before.

"The workmen were surprised to see a man travelling in charge of the bag; but Wareham, elated at his narrow escape, told them that he had done it out of curiosity, and they asked no further questions.

"As may be imagined, he took the earliest opportunity of leaving the office, and I was too late to apprehend him. That, however, did not annoy me very much; I had a satisfactory clue to Mr. Wareham, and by twelve o'clock the next day he was in custody.

"Neither money nor letters were found upon him, so he must have been associated with some gang to whom he had handed over, for the better concealment thereof, the quantity of letters he had stolen.

"He was afterwards induced to relate his sensations when in the tube.

"'The air,' he said, 'felt cold and refreshing, but the darkness was appalling. The waggon was about four feet long by two wide. He disposed his legs as well as he was able, so as to avoid contact with the sides of the tube or any foreign body he might encounter.'

"'He was surprised beyond measure when he found the waggon in motion, but being somewhat of a philosopher, he resigned himself to his fate. The speed at which he was driven along took his breath away, and he was not at all sorry when he arrived at his journey's end.'

"Brown and Wareham were arraigned at the State Sessions. I was the principal witness against them. Brown, at the last moment, finding that he had no chance of escape, having been taken in flagrante delicto, turned State evidence, so that his punishment was comparatively trivial to that of Wareham, who was for a term of years removed from that busy sphere in which he had so greatly distinguished himself, and of which he was so promising a member.

"He was much missed by the school to which he belonged, and many of the thieving fraternity went into deep mourning for what was almost equivalent to the death of their versatile friend."

"I am sure, I hardly know how to express myself," cried Peace, when the American detective had brought his narrative to a conclusion. "I don't know when I have passed such an agreeable hour or two as I have with you two gentlemen, who have given me an insight into matters quite new to me."

"Oh, Shearman can tell you a heap of good stories, and can keep anyone amused for hours," remarked Cartridge. "I'm not in the race with him."

"Oh, you are well matched," returned Peace, forcing a smile, for by this time he had had more than enough of his two companions. "But I must now be off, as I have to meet the gentleman who goes partner with me in some of my inventions. He is a practical man, and is, therefore, able to carry out my ideas."

"I'll tell you what I'd do," said Shearman.

"What?"

"Wal, I would lay the matter before the Admiralty. If you can raise ships by the means you propose—and I don't see why you should not—why, it will be worth thousands to them."

"An excellent thought, sir. I'll take your advice," cried Peace, rising from his seat and putting on his hat.

His two companions followed his example, and they all descended the stairs and passed out of the front door of the house.

Peace hailed a cab; then, wishing the detectives a hearty farewell, jumped into the vehicle, which was driven off, at Peace's request, in the direction of the Ludgate-circus.

"Got rid of 'em at last!" cried our hero, as the cab rattled along. "Gad, but this has been a dose. No more police-courts for me. Why, they'd jaw a horse's hind leg off—and think themselves so jolly clever, too. I've had enough of them—quite enough for the present, at all events."

When the cab reached Ludgate-circus Peace paid the fare, and walked over Blackfriars-bridge.

He thought it just possible that his movements might be watched. Not that he imagined that either Mr. Cartridge or the Yankee suspected him—far from it; but he considered it to be just as well to be on the safe side, and break the continuity of his journey.

He therefore just dropped into a coffee-shop in the London-road and had his tea. He remained there for some little time, and then proceeded once more on his journey. He said nothing to the ladies of his establishment about his rencontre with the detectives, but put Bandy-legged Bill in the full possession of all the facts when that worthy called on the following day. His predatory excursions were continued for night after night, and up to the present time he had escaped detection. But we must leave him for awhile to take a glance at other characters in our story.

CHAPTER CXXV.
THE YOUNG EARL OF ETHALWOOD.

THE reader will understand that a lapse of years has taken place since we last took a glance at the inmates of Broxbridge Hall, and it will be needless to signify that time is an active agent, and many changes have taken place since our last visit to the hall. The Lady Aveline plunged into the vortex of fashionable life, and as a natural consequence had a number of admirers. It was her grandfather's wish that she should form an alliance with a member of the aristocracy. She would then be still further removed from the low-born engineer. There were many suitors for her hand, but Aveline herself did not display any willingness to change her condition; and the probability is that she would not have done so had it not been for the importunities of the earl and the vivacious Lady Marvlynn.

After a good deal of flirtation, hesitation, and irresolution, she consented to become the wife of a baronet of some eight and thirty summers, Sir Gerald Batashall by name.

On the day of her marriage the earl settled on her a princely dowry, and all went on as merry as a marriage bell. The Batashalls were an old family in the West of England; they were proud, like the earl, and the match was considered by everyone to be a suitable and proper one.

The Lady Aveline bore her husband two children, a boy and a girl.

In the meantime, the young heir of Ethalwood was growing up to man's estate; he had been indulged by his mother and spoiled by his grandfather, who made him his pet, and indeed it might be said, almost his idol.

He was sent to college, and when at home had tutors in the house. No expense was spared to make him worthy of the proud position he was to occupy.

He was a generous-hearted impetuous youth, but could not brook control, and the servants averred that he had much of the Ethalwood spirit.

Before he reached his nineteenth year his grandfather breathed his last in the presence of his granddaughter and great-grandson.

The latter came into the title and estates at too early an age, perhaps, but there was no help for it; the earl was full of years at the time of his decease—between eighty and ninety, which is a respectable old age.

After the few months of mourning for his noble ancestor Lord Reginald Ethalwood soon began to have his own views of youth and freedom in the new life which was so suddenly opened to him.

The temple of pleasure was before him, and he soon found his way into its innermost penetralia. For a long time the intoxicating and enervating draught of luxurious indulgence was never absent from his lips until at last he had drunk down to the very lees of the cup, and, as a natural consequence, tasted of satiety and disgust.

His mother could not give so much heed to him as she wished, as she had her husband and her young children to occupy her thoughts, so that the young earl was left to steer his course as best he could. He became *blasé*, discontented, and yearned for a change.

Change of scene, change of pursuit, both were open to him as the natural resources of his condition, and without hesitation he turned to them for relief from the ennui and discontent that had overtaken him.

Among the possessions that had come to him with the patrimonial estates he had inherited from his great grandfather, was a small chateau or hunting lodge on the borders of Switzerland. In the earlier days of his life, the deceased earl had been accustomed to spend a good deal of his time at this place. The Ethalwoods had always a great predilection for sports, and shooting and hunting had special charms for them when in the pride and full vigour of manhood, and hence it was that the chateau in question had at one time been a favourite resort with the father and his sons.

It was built on the side of one of the high spurs of the Jura, in the midst of some of the wildest and most picturesque scenery of that portion of the country which links France with Switzerland.

Except to a few visitors in the summer months the profound solitudes of the mountains were almost unknown to strangers—the valleys and mountain sides being inhabited by populations ignorant of everything that passes in the world beyond the bounds of their native forests.

Erected some three hundred years before, the chateau was a sombre and imposing building. Above it rose a pine forest, dark and stately; below it lay a deep valley.

The whole aspect of the place was one of savage grandeur. Lord Reginald Ethalwood, tired of London fashionable life, made up his mind to seek change in this charming retreat.

He was a keen sportsman: could handle a rifle with the best of his fellows, and, much to the surprise and

discomfiture of his gay and thoughtless companions, he left England for the far-famed retreat on the borders of France. Once arrived there, he gave himself up, with a constantly-increasing ardour, to the hunting of the fox and the wild boar.

He had in a short time grown to like this sort of life; and it might have lasted for many years but for an adventure which cast a shadow over his path—a deep and sinister shadow, which brought with it regret, sorrow, and remorse.

In the ardour of the chase he was led over the highest pinnacles of the mountains; a toppling crag gave way, and he was precipitated into the chasm below. The fall was a fearful one, and he lay stunned and motionless, and to all appearance dead. Some peasants discovered him, and placing him on a litter they conveyed him to the nearest habitation, where every attention was paid him by the kindly disposed mistress of the establishment. But for some days he hovered between life and death. Luckily for him, he had fallen into good hands. Madame Trieste, the owner of the chalet into which he had been conveyed, tended on him with maternal solicitude, and by careful nursing, joined to medical skill, he recovered from the terrible injuries he had received.

Madame had two valuable assistants in nursing the wounded earl, these being her daughter and a servant, so that the English nobleman had every possible attention.

When he recovered he was loth to leave the hospitable establishment. One reason for this was a lurking fondness for Mademoiselle Theresa Trieste — his hostess's charming daughter, in whose society he found great solace and comfort.

Days and weeks had passed over, but the young nobleman still continued an inmate of the house in the occupation of Madame Trieste—he did not feel disposed to leave. He had by this time recovered from his accident, but did not feel inclined to return to his own domicile. Indeed, to say the truth, he had been persuaded to remain by mademoiselle, who had no desire to part with him. Thus matters went on for some time, until a change took place in the aspect of affairs.

On the day in question there was a sort of lull; the dinner passed over in a humdrum way. Madame Trieste was the only one of the party whose good spirits were not forced; Theresa scarcely spoke at all; she appeared to be preoccupied—the reason for this was not made manifest.

Agatha, the servant girl, was even in a still worse condition; it was evident that she had been weeping, for her eyes were red and swollen.

Lord Ethalwood himself felt dispirited, and it was in vain that he strove to assume an air of cheerfulness, and it was impossible for the vivacious Frenchwoman, his hostess, not to observe that there was something the matter with her guest. The woman prudently forebore to make any allusion to his altered demeanour.

"I am but a dull and cheerless companion, madame," observed Lord Ethalwood, when he rose from the table. "The fact is I am not so strong as I supposed, and my long morning's walk has been a little too much for me."

"It is not to be wondered at, my lord," returned the lady. "It will be some time, I expect, before you have recovered your strength."

"No doubt some time, but to-morrow I hope and trust I shall be a little better."

"I hope so, I am sure."

He excused himself upon the plea of weakness, and

retired to his room. Here he sat ruminating for some time, and upon retiring to bed that night, he could not rest, a vision of two girls sleeping under the same roof with him rose up and floated before him, so that repose was impossible.

The next morning he rose earlier than usual, hoping to find health and strength in the fresh mountain breeze.

He was away some considerable time, wandering about in a desultory manner he knew not whither.

When he returned to Madame Trieste's house, he was silent and thoughtful, but was, nevertheless, extremely courteous in his manner. This was habitual to him. He found the ladies waiting breakfast for him.

Theresa looked pale, and appeared to be in a state of trepidation. Her maid Agatha, however, seemed to be keenly alive to all that was passing, for her eyes wandered about from one to another in an inquiring manner.

Madame Trieste was lively and loquacious, and the meal passed over pleasantly enough. When it was concluded, and the party were about to leave the dining-room, a loud barking of dogs in the garden fell upon their ears.

"Oh, a visitor," remarked Madame Trieste.

"Do you expect anyone?" inquired Lord Ethalwood.

"Well, yes, I do, if the truth must be told," returned his hostess.

Theresa started, and a troubled look sat on her beauteous and expressive features.

There was a gentle rap at the door, after which a young man entered the room. He appeared to be about four or five and twenty. He had a well-knit frame, indicating great strength and activity. His features were characteristic of determination and were possessed of a certain amount of manly beauty—albeit, they lacked refinement. His hair was black, and his complexion swarthy.

Madame Trieste held out her hand to him, which he raised to his lips with a kind of rough gallantry. He then shook hands with Theresa, who appeared to be greatly disconcerted.

Lord Ethalwood returned the young man's salutation with the greatest possible hauteur.

"My dear Gerome," said Madame Trieste, in an affectionate tone, "this gentleman is Lord Ethalwood, of whom you have heard us so often speak."

The young man nodded.

Then, turning towards his lordship, she added—"My dear Lord Ethalwood, allow me to introduce you to one of my neighbours, Gerome Chanet. You are both young, both sportsmen, both good-hearted and intelligent, and I hope and trust you will become excellent friends."

Lord Ethalwood bowed stiffly, and turned on his heel.

"My dear Ethelwood," exclaimed the hostess, "do pray shake hands with my young protégé. You English are so singularly cold and unimpressionable."

"Are we?" returned his lordship. "Well, it is constitutional with us, I suppose," he added, with a sickly smile.

Gerome Chanet held out his hand and Lord Ethalwood took it; but there was an evident reluctance on both their parts. Each of the young men divined that in the other he had a rival, or it might be an enemy.

"You intend to spend the whole day with us—do you not, Gerome?" said Madame, assuming an air of cheerfulness.

"Ahem! I hardly know," he returned. "You have a visitor."

"What of that? You ought to be proud to make the acquaintance of so distinguished a gentleman."

"Ahem! Yes, of course."

"Then, why do you hesitate?"

Gerome made no reply to this last observation.

The little party went out into the garden, and seated themselves in a small bower overgrown with honeysuckle and eglantine. Madame Trieste and her daughter took with them their needlework, and all more or less entered into conversation.

It would have been impossible for Lord Ethalwood, without ridiculous affectation and unpardonable bad taste, to refrain from addressing Gerome Chanet.

The young man greatly displeased him, it is true; but he had done nothing offensive, and it would have been in very bad taste on the part of the English nobleman to ignore his presence.

The conversation, therefore, became general. Gerome recounted several wild and exciting stories of mountaineering life, but sedulously avoided making himself the hero of the adventures. He was as modest as he was brave.

During these recitals Lord Ethalwood watched Theresa. She evidently took but little interest in any of the narratives, and her undisguised indifference filled his heart with joy. Now and then, Madame Trieste slightly bent her eyebrows and looked vexed as her eyes rested upon her daughter.

Afternoon arrived. Theresa and her mother returned to the house to see to the preparations for the dinner. Lord Ethalwood and Gerome Chanet were thus left together.

The masks they had been wearing instantly fell from their faces—it was useless to keep them on any longer, and, from the moment of the ladies' departure, not another word was spoken. Lord Ethalwood strolled in the garden, leaving his companion to enjoy his pipe alone in the arbour.

Dinner passed over, and at length the day—which had seemed interminable to Lord Ethalwood—was drawing to a close. Night was slowly approaching, and Gerome Chanet took his leave of the ladies.

In obedience to the request of madame, the two men once more shook hands in the same cold formal manner as before.

Gerome departed along a road leading to the mountains, and every step which increased the distance from the house seemed to lift a portion of a heavy burden that weighed upon the English nobleman's heart.

He seemed to breathe more freely when he felt assured that Gerome was far removed from the house in which he and his rival—for he felt assured he was so—had first met.

As soon as the young mountaineer was out of sight, Madame Trieste motioned Theresa to return to the house, and then taking Lord Ethalwood's arm led him back to the arbour in which a great part of the day had been spent.

"My dear friend," said madame, as soon as they were seated, "here we can converse freely, and I have something to tell you."

"Oh, indeed, madame! I am all attention."

"I look upon you as one of our nearest and dearest friends. I am right in that supposition?"

"Of course you are—perfectly right."

"And, as a proof, I am going to show you how much confidence I have in you. I have introduced you to Monsieur Gerome Chanet—you have had ample opportunities afforded you to converse together—now tell me, without reserve, what you think of him?"

"My dear lady, what reason have you for putting such a question?"

"Never mind; answer it."

"Frankly?"

"Yes. Do you like him?"

"Well, you put a plain question, which, to say the truth, I would rather not answer, but if you insist——"

"I do insist, you perverse creature."

"Well, then, my answer is that I do not like him at all."

"I thought as much."

"Then you are not mistaken."

"And your reasons?"

"He displeases me. It is wrong to be prejudiced against any person, but, nevertheless, I frankly confess that the moment I set eyes upon him I felt towards him the greatest possible aversion."

"How very singular! He is brave and generous."

"That may be; but he is evidently not my sort. I do not like him. I should perhaps find it difficult to tell you the reason for that dislike. All I know is, that it does exist, and I may add it is likely to exist."

"I am very sorry for it."

"Why, my dear Madame? It cannot be a matter of any moment whether I like or dislike Monsieur Chanet. I have met him to-day for the first time, and possibly we may never meet again."

"You are mistaken."

"In what way?"

"This young man," answered Madame Trieste, "will shortly be my son."

"Your son, madame? Impossible!"

"It is a fact, monsieur."

Lord Ethalwood appeared thunderstruck, and he changed colour.

Luckily, however, it was nearly dark, and his altered demeanour was not observed by his companion to its fullest extent. She, however, saw that he was moved and greatly disconcerted.

"I cannot believe it possible," he repeated.

"He is betrothed to Theresa," said Madame Trieste. "The marriage will take place three months hence; all has been arranged and definitely settled."

"And, Mademoiselle Theresa," stammered out his lordship, "does—does she love him?"

Through the increasing darkness the young nobleman could see that the French mother shook her head sadly.

"Does she love this man, madame?" cried Ethalwood, in a more imperative tone.

"No, I do not believe she does," was the answer to this query. "But she esteems him, and feels for him a strong friendship," added madame.

"Oh, indeed."

"Yes, I hope and trust she does."

"But why do you give her to him?"

"Because, though she does not love him now, love may come with marriage. It is often the more solid for coming a little late."

Lord Ethalwood shook his head.

"You do not think so?"

"No, indeed, I should be blind to facts if I did," returned he.

"I do not think so."

It could not possibly occur to the mind of Madame Trieste that in speaking thus she was wounding the heart of her guest and friend. The idea that her daughter, the fortuneless daughter of a poor lieutenant of gendarmerie, might cast her eyes upon a proud wealthy English nobleman never for a moment occurred to her.

"You will understand that what I have told you is strictly confidential," said Madame Trieste, "and you will not, of course, ever mention the subject to my dear Theresa under any circumstances."

"Certainly not—I should not think of doing so. You may rely upon my discretion in this matter."

"Thanks, my lord, a thousand thanks. It is now getting late, and the night air is cool. Will you come indoors?"

"I will rejoin you in a few minutes."

"We shall be waiting for you in the house," she said, as she turned and left him.

It is hardly necessary to describe the nature of the reflections to which he gave himself up on being left alone.

The natural repugnance he had for the young mountaineer was now greatly intensified.

He hated the very name of the man, and half regretted not having openly insulted him—indeed, had he been acquainted with all the circumstances which had since come to his knowledge, the probability would have been that a violent scene might have taken place.

He was at this time greatly concerned and deeply dejected, and his reflections were by no means agreeable ones.

He was suddenly aroused by feeling a burning hand pressed upon one of his own, while a breathless voice whispered in his ear—

"Leave your door open. I must speak with you to-night."

The speaker was Agatha, and she had disappeared before the sound of her voice had died in Lord Ethalwood's ear.

He strove in vain to fathom the intention of the young girl in thus addressing him.

What could she probably have to say of such moment as to impel her to take such a questionable course as that of secretly visiting his room in the dead hour of the night?

It was altogether strange and unaccountable, and he was at a loss to account for the girl's conduct.

Upon rejoining Madame Trieste and Theresa in the house, he seemed so abstracted and preoccupied that his hostess regarded him with a look of commiseration, being under the impression at the time that he was indisposed.

She asked him if he felt unwell.

He answered in the affirmative, being but too glad to avail himself of any excuse to be by himself. He therefore retired to his room.

It was by this time a little after ten o'clock, and he might have to wait a long time for the arrival of the maid.

He opened the window of his apartment, and gazed out. A panorama of beauty lay before him, which was lighted up by the silver rays of the moon and myriads of stars.

Lord Ethalwood surveyed the scene with something like satisfaction, for the temperature was soft and mild, and a light breeze, laden with the perfume of flowers, fanned his cheeks.

But as yet Agatha had not made her appearance.

Possibly it might be, after all, a mere girlish whim—a caprice forgotten almost as soon as expressed.

"What could she have to tell? No matter," murmured the English nobleman, "I will wait patiently. It may be something of moment, or it may be a mere trifle—any way I will wait. I am far removed from friends and home, and my mother in her last letter begs of me to return to London with all convenient speed. Perhaps she suspects that there are attractions in this district, and to say the truth she is not far out——"

His soliloquy was suddenly brought to a termination by a gentle rap at the door, which was afterwards slowly swung back on its hinges, and Agatha, the pretty French waiting maid, presented herself.

"So you have kept your word, my pretty little tormentor," cried his lordship. "It is almost more than I expected."

"You have never known me to break my word," returned the girl, "but we will not dispute on that point. I am here, as you see."

"As I see."

"And I am here for a purpose."

"I do not doubt it, Agatha."

The girl seemed to be in a sort of a tremour; possibly she half repented of her rash and imprudent act, for Lord Ethalwood, upon her entering the room, had carefully and almost noiselessly closed the door. This done, he led her to a seat.

"Ah," sighed Agatha, "it is perhaps wrong of me to visit you thus, but I do not see any other way, and, so, pardon me, monsieur."

"I have nothing to pardon," returned his lordship. "On the contrary, I have reason to be grateful for your disinterested kindness, for I am sure you are prompted by nothing but the best and most unselfish motives in thus presenting yourself."

The girl's face became suffused with blushes as she listened to this complimentary speech.

"Monsieur—my lord!" she ejaculated, "what I have to tell you is serious—nay, it may be terrible."

"Indeed!"

"Yes. You are in danger—imminent danger."

"Pray don't frighten me, Agatha," he said, with a smile.

"Oh, my lord," she returned, "you cannot deceive me. You love Mademoiselle Theresa. Don't shake your head. I say you are enamoured of my young mistress."

"Hush! Do not make such rash assertions. I swear to you," he cried.

"Do not swear, monsieur," she answered, interrupting him. "It is useless your attempting to deny it. You might as well attempt to prove to me that I am the Queen of France, as to that you do not love my mistress."

"Well, for argument's sake—mind, only for the sake of argument—assume, if you like, that I do love Mademoiselle Theresa. What then?"

"Well, then—a young man came here to-day."

"Certainly. What of that?"

"You do not like him. That is in no way surprising; and he hates you!"

"There is not much love lost between us, I dare say. But how do you know he hates me?"

"I have seen the evil looks he cast upon you. I tell you his hate is of a most deadly and venomous character. Ah! monsieur—my lord, have a care, be warned in time. This young man—this Gerome Chanet—loves my mistress to distraction—he doats upon her. Full well I know this. He would gladly and cheerfully lay down his life for her."

"Upon my word, Agatha, he is a most chivalrous, self-sacrificing knight errant—that is, assuming your theory to be a correct one."

"I am not mistaken," said the girl, with renewed emphasis and force.

"Monsieur Gerome Chanet idolises Mademoiselle Theresa, and madame has promised that she shall become his wife."

"This may be the case."

"It is so."

"Well it is, then, if you will have it so."

"It is not I would have it, because I do not like him; neither does Theresa."

"Then she is a fool if she has a man she does not like."

"But then he will be revenged, take a deadly vengeance on the man whom he deems his rival."

"And who may that be?"

"None other than yourself. Oh, my lord, how can you ask such a question?"

"Upon my word, Agatha, you are a most extraordinary girl."

"You do not know the man you are dealing with, but I do," exclaimed Agatha. "He is brave and impetuous, his passions are like a mountain torrent; his father is rich, but his grandfather was a smuggler, who thought as little of killing a fellow-creature as you think of plucking a flower. Gerome takes after his grandfather. Oh, monsieur, be warned in time. If he supposes you supplant him in the affections of my mistress, which you do, he will strike you down in one of the mountain passes without pity or remorse."

"You are drawing a most terrible picture, my dear Agatha."

"Not more terrible than true, my lord."

"What would you advise me to do then?" he inquired.

"You must leave this house at once—you must quit this country, return to your native land, and await the issue of events. I don't believe that Mademoiselle Theresa will give her hand to the young mountaineer after all that has passed."

"You don't think she will. And why not, I pray?"

"Because she has another attachment."

Lord Ethalwood gave a prolonged "oh," but forbore from pressing the question further.

"You can guess who the object of that attachment is," murmured his companion.

"I think you are a wise counsellor, Agatha, and I will think over all you have said and act in accordance with the dictates of my judgment, but to leave this country, to part with you, my charmer, would be, indeed, a terrible punishment."

He caught the French maiden round the waist, pressed her form, and covered her face with kisses.

"Oh, monsou—Oh, pray don't!" she cried, as a deep blush suffused her face and neck. "Pray release me."

"You are my protectress, my adviser, my sweet pet," cried he.

She struggled to release herself from his grasp, and when she had succeeded she opened the door and fled precipitately.

"Ah!" ejaculated Lord Ethalwood, "what a charming creature! So piquant!—so unsophisticated—so loveable!"

CHAPTER CXXVI.
FURTHER ENTANGLEMENTS.

LORD ETHALWOOD, at this particular period of his career, stood a fair chance of getting himself into a scrape. His conduct, albeit that of a gentleman, could not, taking the most favourable view of it, be deemed prudent. He was enamoured of his hostess's charming daughter, but at the same time carried on a flirtation with the maid, which, as discreet persons would say, was in every way reprehensible.

It would have been well for him if he had taken the advice of Agatha, whose acute perceptive faculties enabled her to see the coming storm, which might probably overwhelm more than one of the inmates of Madame Trieste's establishment.

After the girl's departure his reflections were by no means of an agreeable character, for at this time the idea of marriage was the very last thing that occurred to him.

He was embued with much of the aristocratic prejudice which formed so strong an element in the character of his ancestor, the late earl, who before his death had made his great grandson promise—nay, indeed, swear—that he would never contract a marriage with any lady who was not nobly born, and it was therefore impossible for him to give his name to a girl of humble and obscure origin.

He had not duly considered this when he first suffered himself to be allured and fascinated by the beautious and susceptible French maiden.

He was not singular in this respect, for hundreds, and indeed thousands, have been equally reckless both before and since.

His mother all this time was in entire ignorance of the course which was being pursued by her erratic son. She suspected something was amiss, perhaps, but then she argued that all members of the aristocracy must have their private amours—it was but in the natural order of things that such should be the case.

Lord Ethalwood came to the conclusion that he had been both unwise and indiscreet, and the only course open to him was flight; he therefore on the following day intimated to Madame Trieste that he intended to return to his own chateau, and much to his surprise the widow did not make any objection to this, but upon the face of her daughter sat an expression of sadness and almost despair. She, however, did not make any observation.

No doubt she had discovered that a fatal attachment had been growing from hour to hour in the young girl's heart, and like a prudent mother she was solicitous of seeing her daughter married, feeling perfectly well that no good could come of her encouragement of the English nobleman's attentions, seeing that it was not at all probable a gentleman in his position would form what every one must consider a *mesalliance*.

Towards the middle of the day Lord Ethalwood set out for his own residence.

He was not in his usual spirits upon returning to his chateau, and forbore from indulging in the pleasures of the chase.

In consequence of this he felt the time hang heavy on his hands and had serious thoughts of returning to Broxbridge Hall, and plunging again into the vortex of fashionable life. But there was a loadstone which kept him from carrying out this good resolution.

He had passed about a month of dull purposeless existence since his return, when one morning his valet delivered to him a letter in an unknown handwriting.

The unexpected missive came from an old French gentleman who had been at one time an intimate associate of the late earl, who was most anxious to pay his respects to his successor.

Any society was better than none, so in reply to the Frenchman's letter Lord Ethalwood wrote an invitation to the writer, intimating that he would be glad if he would spend a day or two with him at his chateau.

The name of his father's friend was the Chevalier Gustave de Monpres, and punctual to the time appointed the chevalier arrived in a post-chaise at the chateau.

He was a thin man, with a bald head and a heavy military moustache, and although verging on three score years and ten, was as active as a harlequin and as loquacious as a barber.

He very soon made himself known to the English nobleman, whom, he said, was the image of his friend, the deceased earl.

He was most profuse in his protestations of friendship, and passed his arm through that of his host as if he had known him for years, and led him into the park, where he insisted on giving his companion an account of the wonderful adventures he and the late earl had had together, and speaking to the present one as if he were a man of his own age.

He certainly was a most vivacious, amusing old gentleman.

Poor Reginald could not get a word in edgeway. It is true he did not make any great effort to out-talk the Frenchman, being convinced from the very first that he was in this respect "nowhere," to make use of a sporting phase.

The chevalier had sufficient penetration to see that his young friend was rather dispirited, from what cause he could not divine. However, he made up his mind to get at the pith and marrow of the subject before he left the chateau, and he was just the sort of man who was beyond all others the most likely to succeed in such a case.

He told the young earl a series of anecdotes and stories about all sorts of people, and the general tenour of his conversation was what some persons would term free—it partook more of the libertine than the moralist. However, it served to beguile the tedium of the earl's monotonous life, and he was in a measure amused with his vivacious guest.

When the walk in the grounds was over, the dinner was served, and the two gentlemen sat down to what in truth might be termed a costly banquet.

The chevalier, who was a connoisseur in gastronomic matters, tasted all the dishes, did honour to all the wines, and complimented infinitely the talents of Lord Ethalwood's *chef*, whom he declared to be a man of supreme ability and taste.

As the meal progressed the old roué's spirits frothed and sparkled like the champagne he swallowed, but his host remained dull and thoughtful, despite the exhilarating effects of the wine.

His companion could not fail to observe this; he was too much a man of the world, and too great a courtier to rally the earl on the subject. He took a different course: he tacked about, changed the character of his discourse, for he had the protean power of adapting himself to all occasions. He therefore became affectionately insinuating, and even almost parental. This was more consonant with the earl's state of mind at that time.

The chevalier did not seem to be the same man he was an hour or so ago. He was so engaging, so soft and winning, and it might be said earnest and almost pathetic.

"Oh, my dear young friend," said he, "it is well to be young—but, at the same time, the young as well as the old have their cares, troubles, and anxieties, though these in most cases result from different causes. You are preoccupied to-day—there is doubtless good reason for this."

"Nothing in particular," said Ethalwood—"but you must understand that at times I feel the effects of the severe fall I had some time ago."

"Ah, true, no doubt; but if there is nothing more serious than that—well, I think you'll get over it in good time."

THE MEETING OF THE RIVALS.

The conversation was continued much in this strain, when by artfully calculated means the chevalier soon succeeded in drawing from Lord Ethalwood the cause of his preoccupation, and, indeed, of all that had happened in the house of Madame Trieste.

Monsieur de Monpres' eyes sparkled and his whole face was lit with an expression of joyousness when

Lord Ethalwood had finished his confession. He was wholly in his element; he had before him a young man trembling on the brink of a moral abyss, and his was not the hand to be stretched forth to save him.

"Ha, ha!" laughed the old chevalier. "Carrying on a flirtation with the mistress and her maid both at the same time—excellent! Why you are a perfect Don

Giovanni, my young friend. By the way I knew Lieutenant Trieste, the husband of the lady whose house afforded you such timely shelter; but, of course, a man in your exalted station would never for a moment contemplate uniting yourself to a person in Mademoiselle's humble position—that's altogether out of the question."

"It is quite out of the question."

"Good; I am glad to hear you say so, because it proves to me that you are a sensible young man. I should not trouble myself much about the young mountaineer; fellows of his character are not worth wasting one's thoughts over. Bah! she'll never marry him—never—take my word for it."

"Unless I return to England."

"Ah, that's quite a different matter, but you do not intend to return?"

"Not just at present, at any rate," added the chevalier, with a sarcastic smile. "I think I know you too well for that, although our acquaintance is of such short duration. Be of good cheer, and don't give up the girl to a boor like that."

The chevalier took the young man's soul, as it were, and softened it in the fire of passions which he excited with his contaminating breath; then he kneaded it like molten wax, and gave it back more or less after the pattern of his own.

His language had the glitter of the serpent, that seems to caress its victim the better to destroy it. Without once wounding the sensibility of his listener, the chevalier scoffed down all his beliefs, demolished all his illusions.

Lord Ethalwood had heard much of the lax morals of our continental neighbours, and in Monsieur de Monpres he had a bright example.

"Come, come," said the latter, "you must bear a more cheerful aspect. I tell you freely I don't intend to take my departure from your hospitable house until I see you looking bright and cheerful."

The old Frenchman kept his word, for he remained several days with the young earl. During his stay he was explanatory as regards Madame Trieste, whom he described as a very clever and cunning mother, speculating on the inexperience of a young man of name and fortune, with the view of entrapping him into a marriage with her daughter. This, he said, was all fair enough. She had a perfect right to do the best she could for her child, but on the other hand the earl had an equal right to take excellent care not to snap at the bait so artfully presented to him.

Finally he demonstrated that Gerome Chanet, the girl's betrothed husband, was simply a supernumerary called in to play a part, to serve the ends of the chief actors in the drama, by exhibiting himself in the character of a betrothed, to force his lordship into a declaration of love.

Ethalwood listened to all his unprincipled counsellor had to say, and pointed out to him that Chanet was desperately and madly in love with Theresa.

At this the old Frenchman shrugged his shoulders and shook his head in a most significant manner.

When the chevalier had taken his departure Ethalwood felt in some measure relieved. While he was with him he lent an attentive ear to all he had to say, and he was inclined to believe that he was tolerably right so far as the main facts were concerned, but despite this he could not bring himself to believe that the young mountaineer was playing a double game, or acting as a subordinate to others. It appeared to be altogether foreign to his nature; besides, Agatha herself had told him that Chanet was very much in earnest,

and this declaration was proved but too plainly by subsequent events.

"I cannot believe all he says," murmured Ethalwood, "but nevertheless there is much truth in many of his observations. Doubtless he is enabled to see things much more clearly than I can myself. He's a sharp-sighted old gentleman, without a doubt, and he hasn't been too particular at any period of his life. I wonder what the proud old earl could have seen in him to make him his companion. I suppose he did do so? I never heard him mention his name, though. But, Lord bless me! how many years ago must it have been?"

Lord Ethalwood was restless and fidgetty—so much so, that he could not remain any longer at his own chateau; so he determined upon paying Madame Trieste another visit. He longed to learn something about the fair Theresa, and was a little piqued that no messenger had been sent by Madame Trieste to inquire how he was, or bring him an invitation.

As he was proceeding in the direction of madame's house he was met by the chevalier, who was being driven along in his old lumbering post-chaise.

"Going to the widow's—are you?" said the chevalier—"good, excellent! I am going close to where she lives. Jump in, and we'll drive there. That is close to her house; you can then alight, and walk the remainder of the distance alone."

Ethalwood availed himself of the offer, and drove within half a mile or so of his destination. He alighted and walked rapidly on. When he presented himself he found Madame Trieste in her garden. She was alone, and as he passed through the gate she raised her eyes with such a look of astonishment as to almost imply that she did not recognise him.

This a little disconcerted him, and he felt half disposed to turn back and go away in dudgeon. The probability is that he would have done so had not the widow advanced a few steps and exclaimed in a tone of surprise—

"What! my lord? Well, you do astonish me."

"And pray, madame, what reason is there for astonishment? I have not heard from you. Not a scrap of intelligence has reached me from either yourself or your daughter, and hence it is I have deemed it my duty to call."

"Ah, yes, of course," observed Madame Trieste; "yes, quite natural you should do so, and—ahem—have you quite recovered from the effects of your accident?"

"Yes, I hope so."

Her manner was constrained, not to say cold, and the earl was at a loss to account for her altered demeanour.

"I am glad you are yourself again."

"And so you see, madame," he observed, assuming a cheerful, confidential tone, "I could not keep away from you any longer—so I've just run over to see how you all are."

"Certainly; it's very kind of you, I'm sure."

Lord Ethalwood was under the impression from the lady's manner that his presence in her chateau was not altogether desired, but he did not choose to take any notice of this. There might be something amiss, and he was determined, if possible, to find out what that something was.

Without invitation he unslung his game-bag and ascended the stairs leading to the apartment he had before occupied.

Madame Trieste looked a little surprised, but said nothing.

On the landing he met Agatha.

"Gracious me!" she ejaculated—"you here, my friend."

"Certainly. Is there anything astonishing in that? I am here, as you see."

The maid drew back and seemed to be a little disconcerted.

"Like mistress, like maid," murmured his lordship to himself. "It does not much matter—I don't intend to be baffled if I can help it. Hang their blank looks and frigid manner."

Agatha still stood contemplating her mistress's visitor.

"Why, what ails you, my little pet? You look scared."

"Do I?"

"I fancy so. Are you not well?"

"I am well enough, as far as health is concerned."

"Are you in trouble then?"

"Oh, my lord!" returned the girl. "You went away from here leaving sorrow behind you. This you ought to know without my telling you, and you have returned to bring misery and despair."

"Upon my word, Agatha, for the life of me I cannot understand what you mean. Explain yourself."

"Let me pass," exclaimed Agatha.

He endeavoured to detain her, but she refused to answer his questions, and fled along the passage with the speed of an antelope.

"Perverse, obstinate girl!" exclaimed the English nobleman. "What can possess the little jade? The whole household appears to be under some malign influence, which is both extraordinary and unaccountable."

As he passed on towards the apartment he had previously occupied, he observed in one of the sitting-rooms Theresa Trieste, who was reclining in a large arm-chair in a pensive attitude.

"Mademoiselle Theresa," ejaculated Lord Ethalwood, "whence this altered demeanour?"

"My lord!" cried the French maiden — "you here!"

"Yes—may I enter?"

"If it pleases you to do so—you can of course."

Lord Ethalwood entered, and crept up to the chair on which the young woman was seated.

"Tell me," said he in a voice of deep emotion, "the reason for my being received so coldly by the inhabitants of a house where I was wont to receive nought but kindness. Have I done ought to offend you, Theresa?"

"Nothing whatever," was the quick response, "but the aspect of affairs has greatly altered since you were last here, and I am no longer my own mistress—am not free to do as I might wish."

"Not your own mistress? Surely you are not united to that——"

"No, I am not," she answered, interrupting him quickly; "but I was under an engagement which is now broken off. Ah, why did you leave so precipitately?" she added, regarding him with a reproving look.

"Why?" he replied. "For a very cogent reason, Theresa. I learned from your mother that you were affianced to the young man I was introduced to just before I took my departure. I was duly impressed with the awkwardness of the situation in which I so suddenly and unexpectedly found myself, and felt it my duty to retire from a scene in which I appeared to be an interloper. From prudential motives I deemed it expedient to leave."

"Just at a time when your presence was most needed," returned Theresa.

"Just at a time when my presence was least needed —so I concluded."

"You might have consulted me on the subject, my lord, before you took your departure. I am free to confess that I think you have not acted altogether so prudently as you might have done under the circumstances."

"So you upbraid me. This is most wicked. I durst not trust myself here any longer. But oh, Theresa, you have been for ever uppermost in my thoughts, and I could no longer remain away—hence it is I am here now. You will not—you cannot—find it in your heart to censure me—me who would lay down my life for you."

"Ah, sir, these are but words—idle words—the past cannot be recalled, but the actual present is absolute, and the future is terrible."

"Why terrible, Theresa?"

"Do not ask me such a question, my lord. It comes with ill grace from you."

Lord Ethalwood was puzzled, as well he might be. He did not very well know how to construe the meaning of the young girl's words. He remained silent and thoughtful for some little time, and then said in a low tone—

"Possibly I may be mistaken. This young man who has caused us all so much anxiety may not be after all the one you would have chosen for a husband of your own free will, but your mother——"

"He is her choice—not mine," cried Theresa, with sudden energy.

"Tell me frankly, dearest," said Lord Ethalwood, bending fondly over her—"do you love him?"

"No—a thousand times no!" she answered. "I should have thought that was self-evident."

"Theresa," said he, taking her hand within his own, "I thank you for this candid avowal. I have no desire to see you sacrificed on the altar of filial duty or affection. Be bold and resolute—discard him, dearest, send him adrift."

"You wish me to do so?"

"I do most earnestly desire it; since I feel perfectly well assured that your future happiness will be sacrificed by so ill-assorted a match."

He bent over her and kissed her on either cheek as a brother might kiss a sister.

Her face flushed up, and she burst into tears.

"Leave me now, my lord," she exclaimed suddenly. "Madame my mother will wonder what has become of you. Possibly she may suspect something. Rejoin her, I pray."

"But you? I cannot consent to part so suddenly from one I hold so dear."

"Go, my lord; it is not well for you to remain any longer here."

"But when shall we be able to converse further on this subject? When can I see you again?"

"Offer to take me out for a walk towards evening. This you can easily do."

"Enough—so be it. I will do so."

Lord Ethalwood returned to his own chamber, where he reflected over all the incidents of the day. It was evident enough that Theresa Trieste was greatly piqued at his abandoning the field, and leaving her to the control of her mother, and he assumed that she was desirous of evading or cancelling the contract made with Geromé Chanet. This was evident enough, but the earl found himself on the horns of a dilemma. He could not make honourable proposals to the widow's charming daughter, and how to act in the matter he could not very well determine. He came to the conclusion that it would be best to trust to chance. After remaining for some time in his own apartment he deemed it advisable to pay his respects to the mistress of the establishment. So he descended below, and found Madame Trieste at work in the summer-house. She was alone, and Lord Ethalwood without further ceremony entered the rural retreat and sat himself down beside the widow.

"You see, madame, I don't stand on ceremony," said he, in a tone of familiarity, "I take the privilege accorded to an old friend of the family. I come without invitation, and I remain without much pressing."

"You are welcome, Lord Ethalwood," said madame, with a furtive glance at her visitor.

"Ah, that's well. I feel assured of that."

He then inquired about the health of Theresa.

"She has not been at all herself for some days past," observed madame. "Indeed she has been constrained to keep her room."

"Goodness me! I hope she is not in danger," cried his lordship, with well-simulated anxiety.

"I hope not. It would be a source of great anxiety and trouble to me if I thought there was anything serious in the malady of my poor dear child."

"And it would be an equal source of trouble to me."

The widow looked up, but made no reply to this last observation.

"Is your daughter's indisposition likely to delay the ceremony appointed to take place at no very distant date?" observed the earl.

"You ask me a question I shall find it difficult to answer, monsieur," returned the lady.

"And why so, I pray?"

"I am not certain that the marriage will ever take place at all. We can none of us tell what may happen. It is an old saying that 'there's many a slip between the cup and the lip.'"

"But I understood," stammered out his lordship, "at least such was my impression, that all the preliminaries were arranged, and that a special time had been appointed."

"So it had, but what of that?"

"I presume the contracting parties have no desire to withdraw from the covenant?"

"I don't know about that. There is a new aspect in affairs, and one of the contracting parties has imprudently chosen to withdraw."

"Indeed, you surprise me. Which may it be? Excuse my plain questioning. I am deeply interested in all that concerns your dear amiable daughter."

"You are very kind, I am sure," observed madame, with something like sarcasm in her tone.

Lord Ethalwood bowed courteously.

"You surprise me, madame," said he. "One of the parties has a wish to withdraw—eh?"

"It is more than a wish—it is a positive refusal. Theresa will not consent under any circumstances to give her hand to Monsieur Chanet."

"How very remarkable!"

"Not at all so, monsieur. There is nothing at all remarkable or surprising in the matter. Theresa is inflexible."

"But what is her reason?"

Madame shrugged her shoulders.

"Ah, sir," she remarked, "you would be a clever man if you could account for the caprices and fancies of a young maiden. Theresa will not give me any reason. All she says is, that she will not become the wife of Gerome, and he, poor fellow! probably doats upon her."

"Then he is very much to be pitied."

"He is. You are just right—he is greatly to be pitied, but of what avail is pity or commiseration to a despairing lover?"

"Not much avail."

"None whatever."

"I do hope and trust he will get over the disappointment."

"I don't think he ever will."

"That is very sad, indeed. But cannot you divine the reason for her objecting to the union?"

"I have my ideas upon the subject; but these are only surmises, which are vague and unsupported by facts. Still, I am under the impression that there is a reason—what this is I do not care to say."

"Oh, no—I suppose so. Far be it from me to intrude upon family secrets. These are matters which no man has a right to inquire into."

"It is altogether a most unfortunate affair, and one I have great reason to regret. I wish now we had never seen Gerome Chanet. I fancy we should all of us have been spared a great deal of anxiety had we not known him."

"That is likely enough, madame," returned Ethalwood, "but it is impossible for the wisest of us to foresee these things. It would have been well, perhaps, if I had not been so close an intimate of the family."

"I have not said so, my lord."

"No, madame, you are a great deal too considerate to make such an uncourteous observation, but we cannot alter the events which are now past. We have to consider the future, and your daughter's happiness in the years that are to come."

"I am afraid she is tossed about in a stormy sea of trouble at the present moment. How it will end none of us can determine."

"She has a sincere and attached friend in me, and anything I can possibly do to serve her will be most cheerfully done."

"She looks upon you as her friend, Lord Ethalwood. I hope she is not mistaken."

"Mistaken, madame! Do you doubt my sincerity?"

"I have the greatest possible esteem for you," returned Madame Trieste.

The conversation was abruptly brought to a close by the girl, Agatha, making her appearance. She announced the arrival of a visitor.

At first Ethalwood thought it was his rival, but he was presently informed that the new arrival was an old lady who was a near neighbour of his hostess. The latter left the summer-house, and Lord Ethalwood soon found himself alone in the little alcove.

He was ill at ease, troubled in his mind, and did not know very well how to act. The matter could be easily enough brought to a satisfactory conclusion by his openly avowing his attachment for the French maiden, but for prudential reasons he refrained from adopting such a course.

His oath to his deceased relative was an insurmountable barrier, and, in addition to this, there were others of a lesser note.

Nevertheless, he was not disposed to give up the beauteous young female who held him in bondage.

"I am a silly, weak, love-sick fool," he murmured, "to be hesitating and vacillating after this fashion. I haven't a grain of resolution left in my whole composition. What must—what can be the end of all this? Nothing but trouble and difficulty! And yet I appear to be powerless. I cannot—nay, I will not—abandon Theresa."

These words were hardly out of his mouth when the party in question made her appearance in the garden. Lord Ethalwood at once rose to meet her.

She was dressed as if about to go abroad, and he at once remembered her suggestion respecting an afternoon walk.

"This is most kind and considerate on your part," he exclaimed. "I perceive you are ready, and, I hope, willing, to do me the honour of becoming my companion for a short ramble."

The young girl nodded, and said, "You must mention the subject to madame, my mother."

"By all means, Mademoiselle Trieste," said he, leading her to the alcove, and conducting her to a seat. This done, he flew into the house and informed Madame that he and her daughter were about to take a ramble over the mountains for an hour or so. The widow made no objection, and the young man and the maiden were soon far away from the house, taking their way over a narrow footpath, which was the beaten track of travellers who took delight in wandering over the mountains.

The conversation between the two was, as may readily be imagined, of a tender nature. Lord Ethalwood was profuse in his protestations. He told his companion that he found life insupportable when he was away from her, and a thousand other declarations of a similar character, one or two of which would have sufficed to turn the young girl's head.

She listened to him, and, like an infatuated fool that she was, believed all he said. She was flattered by the encomiums he passed upon her, charmed with his protestations of love. He, in his turn, was at no loss to perceive the effect his words had on her, and he felt proud that he had so much power over a young and confiding maiden.

They sat on the promontory of a rock, and looked out at the distant mountains, whose peaks were now gilded with the rays of the setting sun. Here he again poured into her ear the soft and delusive whispers of love, and Theresa Trieste was enraptured by his eloquence, which sounded as sweet and seductive as the Arcadian lutes did to the village maidens of old.

While thus seated together, their arms encircling each other's waist, their hands locked together and touching, a dark form was visible on an adjacent rock. It was that of a hunter, who paused, and whose eyes of flame were instantly fixed on the lovers. This was Gerome Chanet, who stood like a statue—still, silent, and immovable. Fire was at his heart, and the demon of jealousy had him in his clutches.

"Theresa!" he hissed between his clenched teeth, "and with *him*—with the Englishman. Heaven be merciful to me, for I feel as one about to sink into some dark and fathomless abyss."

Neither Lord Ethalwood nor his companion was aware that their actions were being watched by the terrible and vengeful young mountaineer.

When by chance either of them turned their heads Gerome crept behind a mountain peak and stood motionless.

He was the very personification of mute despair.

No wonder. Theresa Trieste had cast him off. The reason was now but too palpable. Gerome felt that he had lost the dearly-coveted prize he had sought with such pertinacity for so many years.

The looks, the attitude, the low whispers which the loving pair were exchanging told the mountaineer of the utter hopelessness of his case.

Theresa would not condescend to even look at him after this.

He felt so supremely miserable at this time that the thought crossed his mind of committing suicide there and then by precipitating himself from the promontory upon which he stood.

But upon second thoughts he made up his mind to make one last desperate effort. He would send a messenger to the earl and ask him to give him an interview. As a gentleman, he could not refuse this request.

Having made up his mind to this course of action, Gerome Chanet crept like a guilty thing over the rocks, and had his dark and miserable hours all alone.

Meanwhile the lovers had lingered, as lovers usually do, much longer than they had intended, and warned by the shadows of the evening, they both rose and made the best of their way back to Madame Trieste's residence.

The widow cast an inquiring look at the lovers. She judged rightly enough that ample time had been afforded them for explanations as to the past and promises and good resolutions for the future. As may be readily imagined nothing would have pleased her better than seeing Lord Ethalwood in the character of an acknowledged suitor of her daughter, but she was far too prudent to suggest or even hint at such a thing. Like a prudent mother she thought it best to leave the young people alone, as in any case matters would not be forwarded by her interference.

The evening passed over pleasantly enough; the inmates of the chateau were more sociable and in better spirits than they had been in the earlier portion of the day. From Theresa's manner Madame Trieste augured that she had had a satisfactory *tête-à-tête* with the earl, and he on his part was more than usually pleasant and animated.

CHAPTER CXXVII.

THE RIVAL LOVERS.

ON the following day Lord Ethalwood sallied forth alone. In the course of his migrations he met the chevalier in his lumbering old postchaise. He affected to be overjoyed to meet his young friend, and rallied him on his intrigue, as he termed it. He informed Ethalwood that he was stopping in the neighbourhood with a friend, to whose house he invited him to spend an evening when quite disengaged. The earl promised to do so, albeit he was not at all disposed to do so, since he was otherwise engaged. However, he felt constrained to treat the chevalier with becoming courtesy; so he took leave of him with a promise to see him again as early as possible.

After his ramble he returned to the widow's house and dined with her and her daughter. In the after part of the day he noticed outside the garden gate a ragged sheep boy making signs and motions to attract his attention. He was under the impression that the lad in question was a beggar, who was about to ask alms, but at the same time he was rather surprised at his pertinacity.

"Confound the fellow's impudence!" he exclaimed thrusting his hand in his pocket, with the intention of throwing him a piece of money; but the lad, who had noticed his action, shook his head, and signified by motions that he wished to speak to him. Upon this, the earl went direct up to the gate.

"What are you nodding like a Chinese mandarin, for, you young rascal?" said he. "Be off, without further ado."

"Are you the English milor who is stopping with Madame Trieste?" inquired the boy.

"And if I am, what business is it of yours, you impudent young jackanapes?"

"Pardon, monsieur, I've got something for you," returned the lad, in a submissive and respectful tone.

"What is it?"

"This letter."

As he spoke he drew from his pocket a large-sized letter, which he handed to the earl. It was carefully folded and sealed, and addressed in a firm, bold hand writing.

"And who may this be from?" inquired Ethalwood.

"Please read it, sir; then you will see who sends it."

The earl broke the seal, and read the contents of the missive, which ran as follows :—

"Milor,—Although far beneath you in station, I claim as a right some explanation for the great wrong you have done me. I have always been given to understand that an English gentleman is never wanting in courtesy towards a stranger, however humble may be his birth, and I hope I am not mistaken. I request an interview. This surely you will not deny me, for I have a terrible reckoning to demand of you. If I were a reckless bravo, a lawless freebooter, I should waylay you and have my revenge, but I am neither of these. You know best how deeply you have injured me, and as a man of honour you cannot refuse to hear what I have to say. I shall await you at the foot of the large lime-tree, which stands at the corner of Alacia Pass. Tell my messenger whether you will be there."

The letter was signed "Gerome Chanet."

"Umph!" exclaimed the earl, "a nice, amiable sort of person to meet; but, however, I suppose there is no other way than seeing the young ruffian."

"What answer am I to take back?" inquired the boy.

"What answer, my lad? Oh, I haven't time to write any reply, but you can tell him I will be there at the appointed time."

"You will be there?"

"Most certainly I will. Here is something for yourself."

He handed the boy a silver coin, which he at first refused. After a little pressing, however, he consented to accept the proffered gratuity.

He then scampered off like a mountain goat, and was soon lost to sight.

"I don't like the business," muttered the earl, "and it strikes me that I shall get myself into trouble. An injured parent or a despairing lover is a dangerous person at the best of times, and from all accounts this young fellow is a sort of fire-eater. Well, I will hear what he has to say."

Shortly before the specified time Lord Ethalwood started off in the direction of the lime-tree named in Chanet's note.

On reaching the spot indicated he found the young mountaineer seated on a large moss-covered stone.

He appeared to be in a depressed state; his head was bent forward, and rested on the palms of his hands, which were pressed firmly against his temples.

The miserable young man was heedless of the earl's presence, so absorbed and abstracted did he appear to be.

"So," exclaimed Lord Ethalwood, in a loud voice, "I am here, agreeable to the request made in your uncourteous and intemperate letter. What would you with me?"

Chanet regarded the speaker with a malevolent look.

"What would I?" he repeated.

"Aye, surely you sent for me. Pray—inform me what for?"

Rising from his seat Chanet made a courteous obeisance, and then said—

"I am not mistaken, then—you have condescended to grant me a meeting?"

"That is evident. Now, your business. Proceed, if you please. In this letter," said the earl, drawing the missive from his pocket, "you speak of a terrible reckoning you have to demand from me. I must frankly confess I do not at present understand the meaning of this expression. Perhaps you will enlighten me, for at the present moment I am in the dark. I hope you are not labouring under some hallucination."

A bitter smile passed over the swarthy features of the mountaineer, who shook his head ominously.

"I will explain, milor, and hope to make you comprehend plainly enough the nature of the injury you have done, and for which I now seek reparation."

"Do so, then, and let it be done as briefly as possible, for I have not much time to spare, and if I had I should not be disposed to a prolix account of real or imaginary injuries."

Chanet leaped over a narrow ditch which formed the boundaries of a wood, and bade the earl follow him.

"What would you have me do? Whither would you lead me?" inquired the latter.

"A hundred paces in the forest," replied Chanet.

"I don't see any necessity to go farther. I can hear what you have to say here. What is your reason for penetrating the forest? Come back."

"We cannot talk here, because we shall be liable to interruption, and what I have to say is for your ear alone."

"You are a strange person, and I don't know that I shall accede to your request."

For a moment or so the idea that Gerome Chanet sought to draw him into the forest for the purpose of murdering him crossed Lord Ethalwood's mind, and he did not, therefore, comply with the demand made by his companion; but reflection quickly banished this apprehension, which, if it was ill-founded, would be an insult to his rival, and might in any case call down upon himself a suspicion of prejudice.

Lord Ethalwood deemed the suspicion an unworthy one, and without further hesitation he followed Chanet. He took care, however, to be upon his guard, and keep a sharp look-out for any sudden surprise.

The two men moved forward for a hundred paces or so, and Chanet stopped in a kind of opening among the trees.

"Well, sir," said the earl, "is this the spot you have selected for our conference?"

"Yes," was the answer. "We can now converse freely."

"Proceed. I am all attention."

"I will."

"Be good enough to abridge as much as possible whatever you may have to say, as otherwise you might exhaust what little patience I happen to possess."

Chanet darted upon the speaker a look as bitter and vengeful as that with which he had first regarded him when they met at the lime-tree, but by a violent effort he controlled his feelings and assumed an air of tranquillity.

"You wish me to be brief, and not trouble you with too many words," said he.

"I do," returned his companion.

"Enough. I will endeavour to explain as quickly as the circumstances of the case will admit."

"Thank you," returned the earl, with an air of condescending hauteur.

"Milor, I will try and be calm and unimpassioned, although my heart seems to be almost ready to burst," exclaimed Chanet. "You will not perhaps be surprised at this when I tell you I love Mademoiselle Trieste. Oh, how fondly, how sincerely, no one knows save myself."

"Surely you have not drawn me hither for no other purpose than to make this declaration. I have been given to understand that you love her. What of that?"

"What of it!—are you mad?"

"Certainly not. You were engaged to her—were you not?"

"Yes, I was to have married her in four weeks from this time."

"That I also understood."

"You did—from whom?"

"From madame, her mother."

Chanet was perfectly astounded at the coolness displayed by his companion.

"Oh, from madame, eh?" he stammered.

"Yes, from her; and are you not going to be married to mademoiselle at the time you have just named —in five weeks from this date?"

"No!" thundered forth the mountaineer. "No, I am not."

"Indeed you surprise me."

"Do I?"

"Well, yes, I confess you do. May I ask why you are not able, or possibly it may be willing, to keep your engagement?"

"Willing!" yelled Chanet in a voice of concentrated passion. "Do not aggravate me—do not taunt me."

"I have no desire to do so—you are quite excited enough already."

"You ask me why I am not going to marry Theresa Trieste. You do not know, I suppose?"

"I cannot say I do."

"I will tell you, then," said Chanet, with forced calmness.

"You will be conferring a great favour on me if you do, my dear M. Chanet," remarked the earl.

"You are the cause of the engagement being broken off—you, Lord Ethalwood, and no other person. Sacre! don't attempt to deny it. You have been the blight in the bud, which sooner or later will destroy so fair a rose. I am ashamed of myself to be pleading and beseeching one who has done me such a deadly injury."

"You have not done so as yet; that is, if you mean me, which I presume you do."

"You endeavour to carry the matter off with a high hand, milor. It is the way with you English; but you can't deceive me. You cannot deny that you have no right to gain the love of my darling Theresa, and by so doing you have robbed me of my betrothed —my future wife and my happiness. Do you think it possible for me to be calm and unmoved under such an affliction?"

"I make every allowance for your excitement, which is, perhaps, but natural under existing circumstances," replied the earl, in the same measured tone of dignity and hauteur he had assumed from the commencement; "but at the same time, Monsieur Chanet, I must observe that you have fallen into a grievous error, which, in justice to myself, I feel bound to correct."

"What error do you allude to?"

"You make a great mistake in asserting that I have robbed you of the love of Theresa. The Ethalwoods never rob or steal."

"You have supplanted me in her affections, then, which is much the same thing, call it by what term you please," cried Chanet. "Like a wolf, you have stolen into the house, and stolen from me the fairest and most beautiful young creature that ever human eyes lighted on. You have driven me to desperation, made my life one long and hopeless sorrow, and now at the present moment I should feel thankful if death would come and release me from my sufferings. Oh, milor, I don't know—you cannot possibly know—the deep, deep affliction that has fallen upon me."

There was an amount of pathos in the manner as well as the words the young mountaineer had given utterance to that for a moment touched the heart of his rival.

"Poor fellow," thought Ethalwood, "he is most terribly in love."

There was a pause, after which the nobleman said in a less cold tone—

"I very much regret that you should take this matter so much to heart; but, upon my word, Monsieur Chanet, I cannot see how you can blame me."

"Not blame you! You have won from me the love of the only woman I had ever loved."

"No such thing. It is a mere supposition on your part. A chimera—a dream."

"It is no dream, milor. It is a certainty."

"But what proofs have you to offer? Assertions without proofs are valueless—everybody knows that."

"Proofs!" iterated Chanet. "Oh, milor, don't deny it. Last night I saw you and Theresa seated on the platform of a rock; your hands locked together, your cheeks touching, and you breathing soft words into her ear. Do you take me for a fool to doubt after what I have seen?"

The earl's face became at once of a heightened colour, and he stammered out—

"We are attached friends, it is true. I won't deny that."

"Friends!" ejaculated Chanet, with ineffable disgust. "Bah, I'm not to be cozened in that way. You are her lover, and she is attached to you."

"You are in error, my friend."

Chanet shook his head sorrowfully and said—

"I wish I could think so."

"I wish you could, because you would then be a more contented man."

"From the day on which I first set eyes upon Mademoiselle Trieste," said Chanet, sorrowfully, "I loved her—loved her with all my heart and soul, loved her with a love which nothing can extinguish—a love which will go down with me to the grave. It is little to say, perhaps, that I would lay down my life for her, and if she asked me to give her up for a more wealthy suitor, a man of title, such as you are, if I thought, if I could believe that it was her own special desire for me to do so I would resign her; and this, it is true, would be a terrible alternative—a miserable sacrifice as far as I am individually concerned, but it should be done nevertheless. My father asked of Madame Trieste the hand of her daughter for me, and my suit was accepted by both mother and daughter. All went on well enough till you came upon the scene, and then——"

"But surely you do not mean to say that I am answerable for the caprices of a young maiden. Was she attached to you? Answer me that question—I mean before I came upon the scene, as you are pleased to term it."

"Well, monsieur, I am free to confess that I don't think she cared for me nearly so much as I did for her."

"I am sure she did not; that's better t\an thinking."

"She did not?" exclaimed Chanet, in a tone of surprise.

"No."

"Not since you have been here—that I admit, for since you made your appearance she became so completely changed that I hardly knew her as the same person. You have poisoned her mind against me."

"I have done no such thing. Look here, my good friend, I charge you to be a little more careful in your observations, or if you are not it is just possible we may quarrel."

"Quarrel!" cried the mountaineer, with a horrible laugh.

"Yes, that was my word. Have you invited me here for the purpose of picking a quarrel with me? It looks like it, and if that be the case I shall take my departure forthwith."

"You must not go yet."

"Must not!—and why, pray?"

"Because I have much more to say."

"You had better be quiet about it then, for I am getting tired of the subject, which, to say the truth, is becoming wearisome."

"Well, then, I will come to the point," said Chanet. "Theresa has refused me, after giving her solemn word to become my wife. What reason is there for this? Now I ask you, monsieur, on what other ground than that of her love for you is it possible to explain her sudden and absolute change of mind and refusal to redeem her promise to me. From her birth Theresa has known but two young men—yourself and me. She loves one of these two. It is not me; therefore it must be you."

"You sum up the case like a judge," said the earl, with a smile. "Assuming your hypothesis to be correct—what then?"

"That is just what I am coming to. Theresa loves you and you love her. Let me ask you one question. Will you marry her? Tell me you will, and I will leave this country to-morrow, and never trouble either you or her again. That is the point I have been trying to reach all the time."

"I am not likely to ask your permission in such a case. What business is it of yours whether I marry her or not? You are begging the question, and I do not choose to be dictated to by my inferiors."

"I do not like you. I disliked you when we first met; now I hate you with a deep deadly hate!" cried Chanet, his countenance becoming lurid with ill-suppressed passion.

"It is as I suspected," he added, with supreme bitterness.

"Is it?"

"Yes; you take it so," he cried, in a half-suffocating voice. "You will not marry Theresa Trieste?"

"I do not choose to answer such a question. I am not called upon to marry all the young girls who may happen to decline the honour of marrying you, Monsieur Chanet."

"Is that all the reason you choose to give?"

"Most certainly it is."

"Then hear me, monsieur. From this moment I claim all the rights over Mademoiselle Trieste, given me as an accepted suitor."

"You are justly entitled to them, I suppose, and welcome as far as I am concerned."

"I will watch over my betrothed and guard her from stain—not her honour, which is unassailable, but her maiden reputation."

"Well, sir, you are at liberty to do so. What has all this to do with me?"

"A very great deal. I forbid you to pass another hour under the roof of Madame Trieste."

"Your insolence is intolerable," exclaimed the earl, in a fury. "Do you suppose I am likely to submit to the dictation of a low-born peasant? You forbid! Be thankful I do not chastise you on the spot."

"I am not to be intimidated—I have a duty to perform," cried Chanet. "I say again I forbid you."

Lord Ethalwood now became furious. He had listened complacently enough to a long and to him a tedious harangue, but his patience was by this time quite exhausted. He closed his fist and shook it in the face of his companion, who folded his arms and looked calmly but resolutely at the earl.

"I ought not to have lowered myself by consenting to this meeting, and now much regret having done so, since it has resulted in my being subject to insults from one who evidently does not know his own or my position. Get thee hence. I will have nothing more to say to you."

And with these words, Lord Ethalwood struck Chanet a violent blow on the chest. The act was, to say the least of it, a most imprudent one, for had the mountaineer chosen to take reprisals—which, all things considered, it was surprising he did not—he could have slain his adversary there and then. Indeed, for the moment, the earl thought Chanet meditated drawing a knife upon him.

He was, however, too honest a fellow for that, and would scorn to take any mean advantage—albeit he was almost trembling with passion. For a brief period both men stood motionless and silent.

CHAPTER CXXVIII.
THE HOSTILE MEETING—A DUEL TO THE DEATH.

IT was pretty plainly demonstrated in our last chapter that the interview between the rivals was working up to a climax, and, to say the truth, it could not possibly be otherwise, unless Lord Ethalwood had agreed to a compromise, by declaring his intention of espousing Theresa Trieste.

This declaration would have at once disarmed Chanet, who had only the interest of his affianced at heart, but it was not to be.

The earl, when he fell in love with the French maiden, forgot the promise made to his ancestor—a promise he held sacred beyond all else.

"So," exclaimed Chanet, "you have chosen to dishonour me by a vile and cowardly blow; but it is, perhaps, just as well, for it must end in the death of one of us."

"Indeed, sir! pray explain yourself."

"I demand satisfaction," cried the mountaineer.

"The Ethalwoods have been accustomed to fight with their equals."

"Do you refuse then? Are you so base?"

"I do not refuse—I am at your disposal. I have brought this upon myself—that I freely admit."

The young earl bitterly regretted his rash act. Not that he was indisposed to any hostile meeting, but he felt both shame and remorse at the action which rage had driven him to commit.

An action which he recognised as being one of odious and unjustifiable brutality. But pride, which was at the bottom of the nature of every member of the race to which he belonged, forbade him from temporising with his adversary.

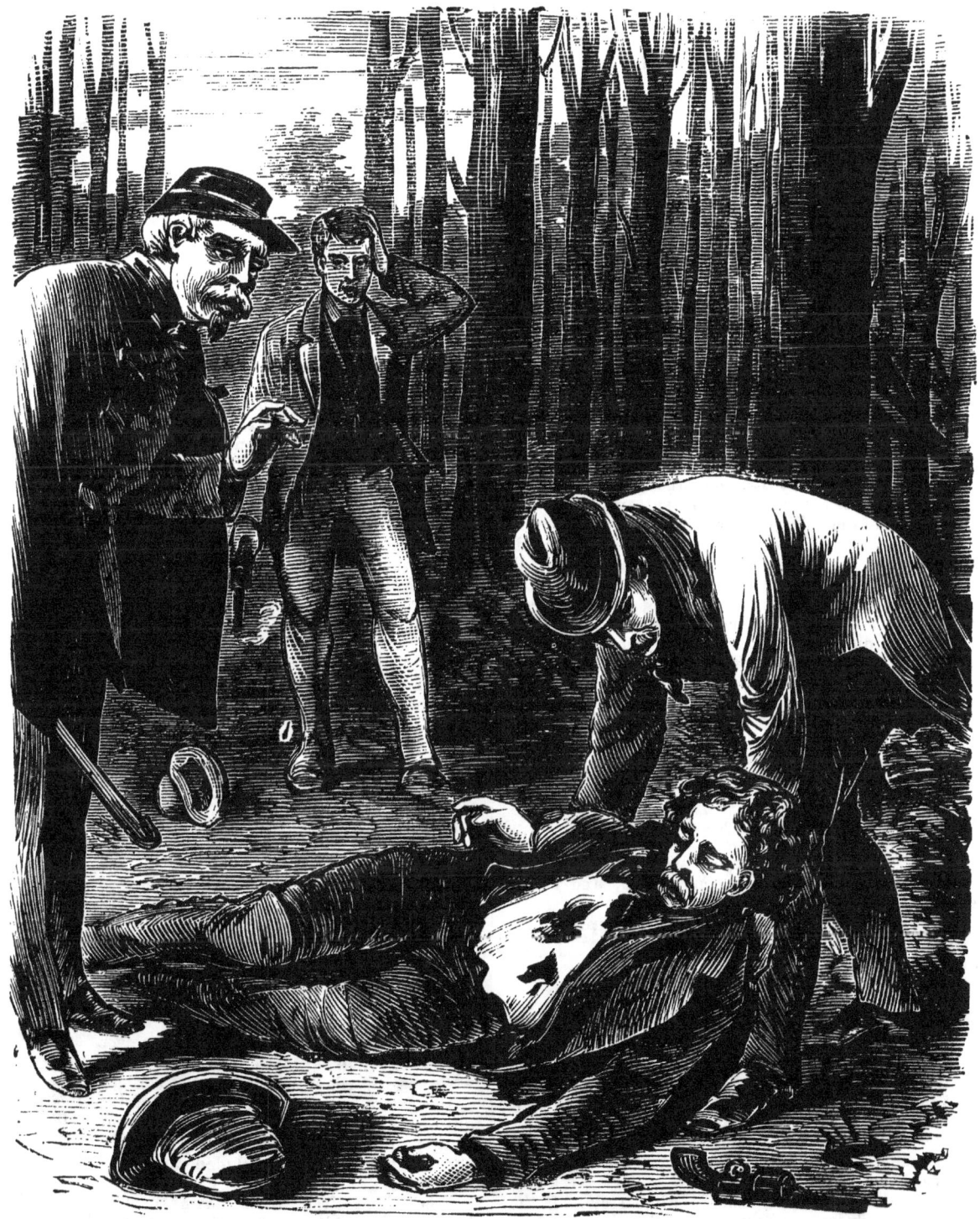

THE DUEL—DEATH OF GEROME CHANET.

"You demand satisfaction, Monsieur Chanet—so be it. Name your conditions. I will agree to anything you propose."

"I suppose by that you mean to confer a favour."

"Nothing of the sort. It is but justice. You are the offended party."

"I am, in more ways than one."

"Admitted; we will not discuss that question. You feel yourself aggrieved or injured, which you will."

"Deeply injured."

"That is understood. What do you desire, then?"

"The conditions I propose will be very simple, and will be as fair to you as they are to me."

"It is simply a question of appointing seconds."

No. 67.

"We do not want any."

"Absurd! A duel without seconds! It is not to be thought of for a moment."

"I hope I am dealing with an honourable gentleman."

"I am sure you are—that's better."

"Well, then, we can trust each other."

"We can do so, of course, but it is not the usual course of procedure; and I strongly object to a hostile meeting under such circumstances."

"But I understood you to say that you were willing to accede to any terms I chose to propose."

"Any reasonable terms. I do not want you to be charged with murder, or myself either, which most assuredly we, one of us, should be, unless we had seconds. Custom dictates that this should be done."

"What do I care for custom, or what I may be charged with?"

"That may be so; but the case is very different as far as I am concerned. I must have some regard for my own reputation, and, therefore, decline to meet you upon the conditions you propose."

"Would you have me brand you as a coward?"

"I must again inform you, Monsieur Chanet, that you would do well by being more guarded in your expressions. As a matter of courtesy I waive all distinctions, and am willing to give you the satisfaction you require, provided the arrangements are in accordance with the recognised rules which are invariably adopted in such cases. Do not for a moment imagine I have any desire to shrink from the performance of what, after all, must be deemed only an act of justice."

"When a duel takes place between two Corsicans," said Chanet, "each of the adversaries places himself at the opposite end of a newly-dug pit, and whenever one of them falls rolls into this grave dug by himself. Doubtless, you know, that in obedience to a physical law—which I will not attempt to explain—a man struck by a bullet in the front of the head or chest falls face forward."

"Very likely. I will not dispute your theory, but I am not a Corsican; neither are you, I presume."

"No, I am not."

"Well, then, this being so, we are governed by the rules adopted by our own countrymen, and therefore is it that I insist upon having seconds."

"I do not wish my dear Theresa to be compromised, and I would, therefore, prefer dispensing with witnesses; but if you insist——"

"I do insist. So there ends the matter."

"You shall have your own way then. You bring a second, and I will do the same. Will that satisfy you?"

"Certainly; and now please to name the time and the place."

"The place must be where you struck me; on that spot must the battle be fought, and one of us must not leave the ground alive."

"Agreed, let that be understood. Now the weapons."

"Six-chambered revolvers—have you one?"

"Yes."

"So have I. We will charge all barrels. If the first shot produces no effect we will fire till one of us falls dead."

"This may be all very well, but it does not accord with the practice of civilised communities," said the earl, carelessly. "It seems to me more like deliberate murder than anything else."

"It is not murder. It is a duel to the death—that is all."

"Oh, I see, a mere trifle, of course, in your estimation, perhaps. Have a care, young man—be not so relentless."

"The injury I have received from your hands admits of no atonement. I am resolved," replied Chanet.

"Well, if that be the case, I will not offer any opposition. Now about the hour?"

"At six o'clock to-morrow evening—will that suit you?"

"I am master of my own time—say six then."

"You will keep your word?"

"There is no fear of that. I will be on the spot at that time with my second, if I can procure one."

"If? Do you doubt being able to do so?"

"No! I believe there will not be much difficulty as far as that is concerned, and so our conference is at an end, monsieur."

The earl bowed, turned on his heel, and took his departure.

"Agatha was quite right," he ejaculated, when far removed from the spot where the strange interview had taken place. "He's a desperate, determined fellow, and means to send me to the next world if he possibly can; but there is no help for it now. I cannot retract: even if I were disposed to do so the chances are that I should be waylaid and murdered. I must meet this young ruffian and trust in Providence. I wish now I had not consented to have an interview with him, but one can never foresee these things until it is too late. Hang the fellow, what is the value of his life in comparison to mine?"

Hurrying on with rapid steps he soon came within sight of Madame Trieste's chateau.

He paused, and endeavoured to assume as calm a demeanour as possible; but, despite his fortitude, he was greatly troubled at the issue of affairs.

He began to consider seriously whether the fascinating and beauteous Theresa was worth the sanguinary encounter which had been appointed to take place on the morrow.

Taking a common-sense view of the question, the conclusion would be that she was not, but hot-headed lovers have generally but a small modicum of common sense left in their whole composition, and such appeared to be the case with Lord Ethalwood, who had, in a great measure, brought himself into his present difficulty.

As to Chanet, he was so wild and furious that it was not possible for him to be brought under the influence of reason.

Upon entering the house of his hostess, Lord Ethalwood put a bold face on the matter, and succeeded in being as cheerful and pleasant as heretofore, but, despite this, an air of melancholy seemed to hover over the little household.

Theresa said but little. She, however, ever and anon cast inquiring looks at the earl, who at such times whispered words of comfort in her ear.

It was not possible for him to determine whether any of them suspected that he had seen Gerome Chanet. If they did they were remarkably silent on the subject, and never in any way alluded to the young mountaineer.

When he retired to his chamber Madame Trieste bade him farewell as if he had been a traveller setting forth upon a journey from which he would in all probability never return. She kissed him affectionately on the forehead, and was more than usually demonstrative in her expressions of friendship.

Theresa had at this time betaken herself to her own apartment.

The earl was a little puzzled at the widow's altered demeanour, but he said nothing beyond responding to the good wishes she expressed.

He was, as may be readily imagined, in no very enviable frame of mind, and on reaching his chamber he looked at his watch, and found that the night had not passed away.

He opened the window of his sleeping chamber, and looked out at the sky. The thought crossed his mind that possibly it might be the last night he had to pass in this world, and this was not a very agreeable reflection.

How different was the aspect of the sky on which his eyes now rested!

And oh, how different the circumstances! Instead of being lit by myriads of stars, the heavens were as sombre as his own thoughts. Nature seemed, as it were, shrouding itself in a mantle of darkness.

In spite of himself he fell into a reverie, and his reflections were tinged with a melancholy which he could not shake off.

What course could he adopt?

He deemed it expedient to sally forth in the morning and consult the chevalier whom he proposed to appoint his second.

He was a brave, gallant old gentleman, and as courteous as he was brave.

No one was better qualified to act in such a capacity, and he felt perfectly well assured that he could count upon his services on such an occasion.

The more he pondered the more convinced he was that there was now no possibility of retreating from the position in which he had been placed by the force of circumstances, conjointly, it must be admitted, with his own rashness and imprudence.

He felt that the position was a false one, and the fatal words, "it is too late," fell from his lips again and again, and he could only resolve to drain the bitter cup which he had madly filled for himself.

He sat for an hour or two ruminating on the aspect of affairs, but the more he reflected the more distressed did he feel, until at length, worn out with bitter thoughts, he threw himself on his couch and sank into a fitful slumber.

On the following morning, immediately after his morning meal, he sallied forth and hastened at once to the house of the gentleman where the chevalier had taken up his quarters.

The man servant who admitted him said that the chevalier had not risen, but he would inform him of the earl's presence, and in the course of a few minutes after this he was shown into an elegantly furnished bijou apartment, in which his friend was seated, sipping a cup of fragrant mocha. He professed to be overjoyed at seeing the earl, to whom he apologised for having kept waiting.

The old Frenchman looked jaded and worn, but he soon pulled himself together, and was as cheerful and vivacious as heretofore.

Lord Ethalwood was of course more than usually grave and thoughtful.

"It is a matter of business I have come upon, monsieur," said he. "Indeed, I may say it is rather a serious business."

"Ah, my worthy friend!" exclaimed the old Frenchman. "A little escapade, I suppose. Well, you may command both my advice and services. I need hardly intimate that."

"I am perfectly well assured you will do your best to serve me," returned the earl. "First and foremost let me put you in possession of all the facts connected with the case."

The Frenchman bowed, and his companion proceeded.

He gave him an unvarnished narrative of the events which led up to the proposed hostile meeting.

"Mon Dieu!" exclaimed the chevalier. "Risk your life in a duel with a low-born peasant, that's not discreet. Bah! It's madness. Positive madness."

"It can't be helped—I must give him satisfaction, I have pledged my word, and my honour is at stake," observed Ethalwood.

"You ought to have seen me before undertaking such a foolhardy enterprise. What, fight with a ruffian of that type! Bah, it's monstrous."

"It is very indiscreet, I admit, but as I before observed, I cannot refuse now, and therefore have come hither to ask you to be my second."

"Oh, oui, certainly; if you are determined to carry out your promise given to this low-bred hound, well, I am at your service."

"I am determined. So don't upbraid me for my rashness and folly. Promise to be ready at the appointed time."

"The fellow is half a savage, and would not scruple to murder you if he had a chance of doing so."

"I do not think that. No, monsieur, he is not without honour."

"Bah! Don't you mislead yourself supposing anything of the sort. You don't know what sort of a man you have to deal with. A duel with such a person—well, I won't say any more, but the whole affair appears to me altogether incomprehensible."

"Why so?"

"How? Why that you should have suffered yourself to fall into such a trap. But you must bring your man down. Now you are in the scrape you must get out of it in the best way possible."

"Then you agree to accompany me, and see fair play?"

"I should not be worthy the name I bear if I refused," cried the chevalier, with a flourish of his right hand, and a significant nod. "Oh, yes, you may rely upon my services in this business—in this unfortunate business. But, my dear young friend, I will not attempt to conceal from you that I am greatly concerned at the course of events—greatly concerned."

"I am not very well pleased myself, to speak the truth, but this is between ourselves."

"We must make the best of a bad job. You are a good shot, that's one thing in your favour—an excellent shot."

"So is he, I should imagine."

"With a rifle," observed the chevalier, carelessly.

"And with a pistol as well, I presume."

"These fellows as a rule are not so good at handling a pistol as a gun. Oh, you'll wing your man, I dare say. Sacre! You must do so; and by gar, you shall."

Ethalwood laughed, and said: "You speak in a confident tone."

"And mean it," cried the old Frenchman. "And now about the place of meeting and the hour?"

"The hour is six o'clock this evening; the place is on the skirts of the forest. I will show you where it is, for we had better go together."

"By all means. We can drive over in my post-chaise."

"That might attract attention. Better walk."

"No, we will drive there. Never mind about attracting attention. I don't care about walking. Let us drive there."

"But we must not have an attendant."

"Well, so be it. I will drive myself. We don't require a coachman. We will go by ourselves. Will you call here for me, or shall I call for you?"

"I had better call here."

"As you please. Let that be understood then. Six o'clock in the evening, eh? It ought to be in the morning, that is the usual course."

"It ought, but the time is named and agreed upon. It is to be this evening at the hour I have named."

"Bah, it does not much matter whether a man is sent out of the world in the evening or the morning for the matter of that."

"I have passed my word."

"Certainly. Now you will find some fine old cognac by your side there. Just help yourself to a glass. It will steady your nerves."

"No, I thank you, I will not take anything just now."

"But you must—I insist, just one glass. You are now in my hands, and must do as I tell you. This is not the first affair of honour I have been engaged in by a good many, and I may say that I have been singularly fortunate bringing my men through. Before we start this evening you will have to take another glass of brandy with a few drops of laudanum in it. It will wind you up like a clock, and you will be able to see through a brick wall. That is my specific for duellists. It's the finest thing to take under the circumstances."

"But I don't require any stimulant."

"No matter whether you require it or not, I intend to have my own way, and you have but to passively submit to my dictation. Leave all to me, I am an old soldier, and know pretty well what is requisite in such cases. My dear young friend, valour is one quality, and a very important element it is, but experience is another. Be of good cheer, for although I say it myself you are in good hands."

"I am perfectly well assured of that," returned the earl, "and esteem myself fortunate in having the assistance and services of so valuable an ally as yourself."

"I am not likely to allow this headstrong young man to ride roughshod over you. Act according to my instructions, and it will go hard with us if you don't polish off your man. I intend you to do so, and that is sufficient for our purpose."

The chevalier Gustave de Monpres was on this occasion, as he had been in many similar cases, determined to have his own way. To say the truth the earl could not possibly have enlisted the services of any one better adapted to befriend him than the chevalier.

He was duly impressed with this fact, and felicitated himself upon having applied to him on this trying occasion.

After some further conversation he took leave of his friend, with the understanding that he was to call for him on his way to the fatal spot.

Lord Reginald Ethalwood returned to the widow's house, where he dined, and strove as best he could to assume an air of cheerfulness, which, to say the truth, he was far from feeling. The day wore on, not very brightly, it is true, but it passed over, nevertheless. On consulting his watch, the earl found that the appointed hour was fast approaching.

Unobserved by any of the inmates of Madame Trieste's chateau he passed through the garden gate and sallied forth, and at once bent his steps in the direction of the house in which his friend the chevalier was anxiously awaiting him.

He was much pleased at being able to leave the widow's residence without attracting the notice of any one, as he thought, but he had reckoned without his host. His movements had been watched; and he had not got more than a hundred and fifty yards or so from the chateau when he became aware that some one was behind him. His attention was attracted by footsteps. He stopped to listen, and then the sound ceased.

"I am full of idle fancies. No wonder," he ejaculated, and once more he continued on his way.

But again the sound fell upon his ear. It was at this time nearer and more distinct.

"Umph, I was not mistaken after all," he murmured. Upon turning round and looking behind him he observed a female which, much to his surprise, he found to be Theresa Trieste.

"You here, darling?" he ejaculated. "Whither are you bound for?"

"It is not a question of whither I am bound for," returned the French maiden. "That is of no import. Where are you going, my lord?"

"Where am I going, Theresa?"

"Yes, where?"

"Well, if you must know, I am about to pay a visit to my friend, Monsieur de Monpres."

"Don't think to deceive me by such a shallow pretext," cried Theresa.

"Deceive you, my sweet pet, it is not at all likely I should attempt to do so."

"I wish I could bring myself to believe what you say is true."

"But it is true. There, see I pledge my most solemn word it is. What more can you desire? Why, my dear girl, you are trembling like an aspen leaf shaken by the winter's blast."

"Oh, my lord, there is something afoot which you are keeping from me—I feel assured there is. A boy brought you a letter yesterday—who was it from?"

"Who? What matters? It was a private matter. I will tell you all about it when I return."

"Tell me who sent that letter, and tell me also what business takes you from our home this evening."

"I have already told you I am about to pay a visit to the chevalier."

"Nothing else?"

"Well, I cannot tell what our movements may be. I am going direct to him now; that's all I am able to say at present."

"Come back with me, and go to the chevalier to-morrow evening instead."

"It may not be. I have passed my word."

"Passed your word?"

"Yes!"

"To meet Gerome Chanet. Is it not so?"

Lord Ethalwood started back in surprise.

"What could possibly have put that in your head?" he ejaculated.

"It matters not how it came into my head. I feel too well assured that such is the case. Oh, my lord, avoid that man; have naught to say to him, and, above all, do not give him a meeting."

"I will bear in mind what you have said. I like him not; but at the same time, my dear Theresa, you must permit me to be master of my own actions."

"I saw a boy deliver a letter to you yesterday at the garden gate. I judged who it was from—Gerome Chanet—and judged also its purport. He would speak to you. Is that not so?"

"Assuming it is, what of that? I am not afraid of Gerome Chanet."

"I am sure you are not, but tell me where he is waiting for you?"

"Waiting! What idle fancy is this? Have I not

already told you that I am going to see the chevalier ? What more do you require ?"

" You shall not go to meet Chanet ! I say you shall not !" she cried, vehemently.

" Who will prevent me if I am so disposed ?"

" I will."

" You will ! Why, my dear Theresa, surely you do not mean me to understand that I am to act under the control of you. By what right do you assume this position ?"

" By what ? By the right of my love—my love for you, wild, hopeless as it is—my love that hangs upon your life, though it may be as the drowning wretch who clings to a spar that will but lengthen his torment and desert him at last."

" I am not complimented by the simile. It is not at all likely that I should desert you. Be reasonable, dearest. I have an appointment, and as a gentleman and a man of honour I must keep it."

While this conversation had been taking place both the earl and Theresa had walked side by side, not very rapidly, it is true, but nevertheless, every step they took brought them nearer to the house in which the chevalier was located.

Theresa Trieste saw plainly enough that the earl was not to be turned from his purpose; entreaties and arguments were alike in vain—so she continued to walk by his side, in the hope of discovering if her suspicions were correct.

He on his part did not appear at all disinclined to have her as a companion, and this threw her a little off her guard.

When she accosted him at first she was under the impression that he was going direct to some appointed spot to meet Chanet.

She had no idea, however, that it was for the purpose of fighting a duel with the young mountaineer, but she dreaded a meeting under any circumstances, and had striven hard to prevail upon her aristocratic lover to return to her mother's residence.

" You seem very suspicious, Theresa," said the earl, in a tone of banter. " I don't know what I have done to give rise to this feeling. However, we are now more than half-way towards the residence where the chevalier is at present sojourning. You will be satisfied, I suppose, if you see me there—see me enter the house."

" Oh, I am satisfied that you are going there, if that is what you mean," she returned. " Monsieur de Monpres is a stranger to me, and it would not be seemly for me to be introduced to him under the present circumstances. Perhaps I had better turn back, and make the best of my way home."

" As you please. Be of good cheer, my darling," exclaimed the earl. " I will return as soon as possible. Let me have a little license to night, and then we will pass a happy hour or so before bedtime. Come, Theresa, do not be so downcast." He placed his arms round her shoulders and gave her a long embrace.

"Oh, my lord, this love of mine will be fatal to one or both of us," she ejaculated. " But of what avail is it to repine? I do love you so."

" I feel assured of that, Theresa; and so I must leave you to a lonely walk home."

" Return as soon as possible."

" I will—I promise that."

And so the two parted.

Lord Ethalwood walked on with accelerated speed. He looked once more at his watch, and found there was ample time for him to be at the place of appointment.

Nevertheless, he was anxious and troubled. Most men are under similar circumstances.

He found upon his arrival the Chevalier de Monpres, dressed in his uniform, looking like an officer in the Old Guard.

" I am glad you have come thus early. Nothing like taking time by the forelock," cried De Monpres, in high glee, for he made it a rule to be in the best of spirits and assume an air of confidence in all cases of this sort. " Why, mon Dieu, are you mad ?" exclaimed the old Frenchman, glaring at his visitor.

" Mad, no ! What's amiss, then ?"

" Amiss ! Goodness me, you are never going to face your man in that costume ?"

" Why not ?"

" What—in a white waistcoat ! It's not to be thought of for a moment. The act of a lunatic, mon ami—a wild lunatic !"

" I do not understand you."

" What, a white waistcoat. Why, it's offering a mark for your adversary. I won't have it. Certain death if the fellow is anything of a shot."

" I never thought of that. I'll button up my coat."

" I won't permit you to wear a white waistcoat, not under any circumstances. Sacre, it's ridiculous. Take it off and wear one of mine. It won't fit you very well I dare say, but that's a matter of secondary importance. Off with your waistcoat without further ado; and an open white shirt front ! Here is a waistcoat which will button up to the throat—that's the garment to fight a duel in."

Lord Ethalwood smiled, took off his waistcoat, and put on the one handed to him by the old officer.

" There," said the latter, " that's better. Offer no mark to the enemy; and now, mark you, we must bring down our man at the first shot, if that be possible. We'll manage it, I have made up my mind as to that, but let me see. Oh, yes, the brandy."

" I don't want any."

" You will have to take it nevertheless."

De Monpres poured out a glass of cognac, into which he carefully let fall a few drops of laudanum.

" That will steady your nerves—make you as bold and fearless as a lion. Top it off."

" Must I ?"

" Yes you must, and what is more, you shall."

Although the earl objected to such a course, he knew it was no use refusing; so he made a virtue of necessity, and swallowed the draught.

" That will put new life into you," cried the Frenchman; " and now the weapon. Have your brought it with you ?"

" Yes, here it is."

De Monpres made a minute inspection of the revolver, which was a six-shot one.

" Yes, a good weapon," said he; " very good. We shall have to load on the ground, that is the usual course adopted in affairs of this sort. The seconds load and the principals fire."

" How about time ?" said Ethalwood.

" We've loads of time. My postchaise is in the back yard, and can be driven off at a moment's notice. Everything is prepared, and may you bring down your man at the first shot—it will save us a deal of trouble. By-the-way, don't aim at the head—at the chest; that's better. Mind, cover him well with your barrel before the word to fire is given, and stand as firm as a rock. Oh, we'll polish the scoundrel off."

" You seem very confident, monsieur—I wish I was the same."

"You must be—you must be confident—it's half the battle. Go in and win."

The loquacious Frenchman rattled on, cheering up his companion by an animated conversation during the whole of the journey. He never suffered Lord Ethalwood's spirits to droop, and certainly he was in all things considered a most invaluable adviser and ally in a case of this sort. Without him the earl would have been quite lost.

Upon arriving at the appointed place of meeting the earl and Monsieur de Monpres found Chanet and a young man awaiting them at the outskirts of the forest.

"You are punctual," said Gerome. "I expected you would be so."

"The Chevalier de Monpres," returned the earl, introducing his friend. Chanet bowed and introduced the young man he had brought for a second as Monsieur Vasseralt. Then there was another exchange of courtesies and the chevalier and Vasseralt drew on one side and conversed in whispers; meanwhile the two principals stood silent and motionless.

"We had better proceed to the glade in the forest without further hesitation," observed the chevalier; "by standing here we may probably attract attention. Forward, gentlemen," added he, as he led the way. The three other gentlemen followed.

"Now, gentlemen, you had better take your positions."

"Perhaps we had better charge the weapons first," suggested Vasseralt.

"As you please, sir," returned the chevalier, "it is not a matter of very great moment. We will charge them."

"The six barrels are to be loaded," said Gerome, "and we are to keep on firing till one of us falls. That is the understanding."

"It is against all rules laid down in such cases," observed the chevalier, "and it is a most murderous and un-Christianlike mode of procedure, but if it is an agreement, of course we must, I suppose, abide by it."

"It is an agreement. Ask your friend," cried Gerome.

"Let it be as Monsieur Chanet wishes; I offer no objection," said the earl.

"I enter my protest against such a course, but will do as you desire me. So be it—the six chambers have to be charged."

The seconds proceeded to carry out these instructions, after which the two principals were placed in position.

De Monpres walked up to the side of the earl and handed him his pistol.

"Be sure you stand firm and aim at his body—not at the head. You'll bring down your man. That fellow has no idea of loading a pistol; in addition to which his powder is of the very worst description. You have every chance in your favour, and must come off victor."

Having delivered himself of this speech the chevalier withdrew.

"Now, gentlemen," said he, "it has been agreed upon that I am to give the signal for firing. It is this: one, two, three—fire! When the last of these words is uttered you discharge your weapons. How say you? Do you understand?"

Both the belligerents answered in the affirmative.

The chevalier glanced anxiously for a moment at his man; then he said in slow, deliberate voice—

"One, two, three—fire!"

Both weapons were discharged simultaneously. The earl was conscious of the fact that a bullet passed within an inch or two of his head.

Gerome Chanet staggered for a moment, threw up his arms, and then fell forward on his face.

"See to your man, Monsieur Vasseralt," exclaimed the chevalier.

Advancing quickly, and in an evident state of trepidation, the young Swiss bent over the prostrate form of his friend, whom he called by name but received no answer. He then turned him over and observed a dark stream of blood oozing from his chest. The ill-fated Chanet breathed one last sigh and expired.

"He is dead! Gracious heaven, he is dead!" exclaimed the Swiss. "Come this way—for mercy's sake come."

The chevalier walked deliberately forward and looked in the face of the dead man.

"It is all over with him," he ejaculated. "He has fallen at the first shot. Well, he brought it on himself, and he has paid the penalty."

"I wish I had not had any hand in this business," said Vasseralt. "I do most bitterly regret ever giving my consent to act as second. It is the first time I have been engaged in such a capacity, and I will take good care it shall be the last. Can nothing be done for him?"

"My good fellow, we cannot restore the dead to life," return De Monpres. "If young men will be rash and hot-headed, and rush into affairs of this sort, they must abide the issue. Your friend is slain, but has died honourably—what more need be said?"

"Oh, but it's very terrible."

"Can I do anything to serve you?" said the courteous old Frenchman. "If so, command me."

"Inform his family of this dreadful tragedy."

"No, I cannot do that. It would not be in conformity with the usual course of events. It is your duty to apprise his friends of the manner of his death—not mine. Permit me as an old soldier to express my most unqualified satisfaction of your conduct throughout the whole of this painful affair, and so good night."

He offered his hand to Vasseralt, which the latter accepted, and then withdrew from the ground in company with Earl Ethalwood, who, now that it was all over, fairly broke down.

"It is of no use your pulling a long face," said de Monpres. "You have reason to be thankful, and I congratulate you. Didn't I tell you how it would end? I knew you would put him to bed with the first shot, and my words were prophetic. Ah, mon ami, he meant mischief. A blood-thirsty scoundrel the world is well rid of! Come, here is the postchaise; let us drive off at once, before the affair gets wind. Jump in."

The earl obeyed mechanically, for he appeared to be in a perfect state of bewilderment. It was the first time he had slain a fellow-creature, and he upbraided himself for the part he had played in the dark and sanguinary crime. He could not conceal from himself that his adversary had been deeply wronged, that he had during their interview in the forest displayed a nobleness of purpose in regard to Theresa, which could not fail to command the respect of all right-minded persons. He was willing to make any sacrifice for the woman he loved, even to giving her up to his rival, if he could thereby have ensured her happiness. The earl pondered over all these circumstances, and acknowledged to himself that he had committed a great wrong.

"It seems to me, my friend," said the chevalier, "that you are letting this little affair disturb your equanimity. Why, Lord bless us, it is after all but an everyday occurrence. The fellow is better out of the world than in it. Cheer up—don't look so cursedly miserable."

"I don't feel very well satisfied with myself, I candidly confess," murmured Ethalwood. "It has been a most unfortunate business."

"No such thing—not as far as you are concerned. On the contrary, it has, to my thinking, been most fortunate. You've got out of a scrape in a most satisfactory and I may say gallant manner. We'll just have a bottle of sparkling hock and a choice cigar, and that will put you all right again."

"Ah, my dear de Monpres, I am afraid it will take a great deal more than that to efface from my mind the fearful incidents of to-night. I feel myself to be a guilty wretch, an assassin, and murderer."

"Mon Dieu, monsieur, you are talking in a wild, incoherent manner. Assassin and murderer—bah! Be reasonable if you please. Don't talk in such a false and ridiculous strain. Come, here we are at our domicile. Jump out, and come in—ha, ha! and make your life happy. I won't have you accuse yourself thus wrongfully. Murder—bah! it is ridiculous."

The chevalier rattled on in his accustomed vivacious and loquacious manner, endeavouring as best he could to reassure the earl, who was, however, despite his friend's playful pleasantries, greatly troubled at the tragic event of the evening. He, however, strove to play up to the exuberant Frenchman, and upon entering the house he drained off in rapid succession several glasses of champagne. Under the influence of the sparkling wine he became greatly exhilarated, and was enabled to listen with something like satisfaction to the lively discourse of his companion, the chevalier.

An hour or so passed away, and then the earl remembered the promise he had given to Theresa.

Making the best excuse he could, he rose to take his departure, but De Monpres did not feel disposed to part with him, and pressed him to remain at the chateau for the remainder of the night.

"You can return to the widow's residence as early as you choose in the morning," said the chevalier.

"I am under a pledge to be back early to-night," answered Ethalwood, "and I am quite sure you will excuse me."

"When a lady's in the case all things must give place," observed his companion, "and therefore I will let you have your own way—but I don't care about your going alone, so with your permission I will drive you there, and see you safely housed. What say you?"

Ethalwood hesitated for a brief period, and then said—

"Perhaps you are right. All things considered it would, perhaps, be just as well for me to have a companion, and I cannot have a better one than yourself."

The postchaise was once more brought into requisition, and the chevalier drove his friend home—or rather to the widow's abode, where he had taken up his quarters. When the vehicle arrived in front of the garden-gate, the earl alighted and begged the chevalier to enter the house that he might be introduced to the inmates.

The chevalier, however, politely declined.

"No," said he, "not now. I will be introduced to Madame Trieste on some other occasion—this certainly cannot be considered a favourable one. No, my lord, I will leave you now, and hope to see you some time to-morrow. Be of good cheer, and do not let this little

affair dash your spirits, and so farewell for the present."

The two gentlemen shook hands, and De Monpres drove off.

CHAPTER CXXIX.
AFTER THE TRAGEDY.

LORD ETHALWOOD had some misgivings respecting the inmates of the chateau he was about to enter. He did not know very well what to say to the widow or her daughter. Being perfectly well assured the fatal deed would be the subject of conversation with everybody in the neighbourhood, and that the whole circumstances would on the following day become known to Theresa and her mother, it was not possible for him to remain silent on the subject. He therefore stood irresolute at the garden gate, not knowing very well what course to take.

To all appearance the inmates of the establishment had retired to rest, for he could not see any light gleam from the window of the sitting-room, and all was as silent as the grave.

The earl at this time felt like some guilty wretch who had returned red-handed from the perpetration of an act of violence.

He strove as best he could to muster an air of intrepidity to his brow, but his heart beat audibly as he passed into the little garden surrounding the house. He observed the faint glimmer of light over the doorway; this proceeded from the small window above the entrance.

He paused for a few moments, and then gently tapped at the door, which was opened by Agatha, who, pale as ashes, started back at beholding him.

"Agatha, dear, what ails you?" inquired the earl, not knowing at the time what to say. "You seem scared, my lass."

"Oh, my lord," exclaimed the maid, "you have returned. Heaven be praised for that!"

"Where is madame?" was the next question.

"She is out—gone to attend upon a neighbour who is dangerously ill. She will not return till the morning."

The earl was thankful for this piece of information.

"Well, it is very good of her," said he, entering the parlour.

"And you——" cried the maid, glancing at him with a look of wonderment.

"I am right enough. Where is Mademoiselle Theresa?"

"She has retired to rest—has been watching and waiting for you till she is fairly worn out."

"It is not so very late, Agatha."

"I don't say it is, but—"

"Well, what, girl?"

"My young mistress has passed a miserable time since you left."

"And why, pray?"

"I cannot tell you any more than she has had a foreboding of evil—a presentiment that something dreadful would happen to-night."

"And you?"

"I have been much the same. But you are safe?"

"Yes, and your fears are groundless, you see."

The girl flung herself into the arms of Lord Ethalwood and burst into tears.

He strove as best he could to comfort her, and presently she dried her eyes and gave a faint smile.

"You should not give way to idle fancies, my darling," said the earl. "What is the matter?"

"You seem so strange—your manner is so different—you do not appear to be like your former self."

"Bah! mere fancies. I am just the same as I always have been since you first knew me."

"Are you?" said Agatha, seating herself in a chair and endeavouring to collect her thoughts, which, to say the truth, at that particular period were in rather a deranged state.

The sound as of a low moan, sigh, or wail, fell upon the ears of the earl; it seemed to proceed from one of the upper rooms.

Upon the impulse of the moment he rushed upstairs. On reaching the first landing he stumbled over something. Upon recovering himself he discovered that it was a prostrate figure of a human being, and upon closer inspection he found it to be the senseless form of Theresa Trieste, who had from some cause or other swooned.

Lord Ethalwood stooped down and raised the senseless Theresa, whom he carried into an adjoining room. He was so overcome with terror and anxiety that he did not know very well how to act, but after a moment's reflection he laid her on a sofa and then sought for some vessel containing water. When this was found he bathed her forehead and temples. She heaved two or three deep-drawn sighs, and then opened her eyes.

"It is you, my lord. The saints be praised you are alive and well," she ejaculated.

"Yes, dearest—I have returned, as you see. And you?"

Ah, my lord—my dear Reginald, I have passed a miserable time, and thought some terrible misfortune had befallen you. For mercy's sake tell me where you have been, and what has happened."

"I have been to De Monpres, as I told you."

"Ah! nowhere else?"

"Why do you ask? I am here by your side. Be satisfied."

"I am more than satisfied."

He knelt by her side, and gazed upon her wan features. He did not remember her ever looking so beautiful as she did at that time. He was absorbed in contemplating her expressive and charming face. The terrible incidents of the night were for a moment or so effaced from his memory—he thought only of Theresa. He leant over her and embraced her tenderly.

Theresa's large eyes were bent upon Lord Ethalwood, upon whom she gazed with an expression of dreamy astonishment, and at first he was half disposed to think that she intended to repulse him, but in this he was mistaken. Tears came to her relief, and in piteous accents she exclaimed—

"I have reason to be thankful, to rejoice—for you are safe. Gracious heaven! it is almost more than I have expected."

Her companion made no reply, but wound his arms lovingly around her.

She entwined her arms about his neck with an *abandon* that proved her heedlessness of the peril in which she was placing herself, but her love for the English nobleman was so strong that she was thereby held in bondage, and prudence was forgotten.

It would indeed have been better for her had she been more circumspect and less demonstrative, but she was impulsive by nature and had not as yet learnt to put a restraint upon her actions.

She had been plunged into almost hopeless despair while he was away—now her spirit seemed to rebound, and she forgot all else save the happy present. The man she loved was by her side, and demonstrating the strongest affection for her.

Alas! a thousand times better had it been for her had her innocence been less perfect. How many tears of unavailing anguish might have remained unshed by her? How many years of bitter remorse might have been spared Lord Ethalwood?

But neither the young maiden nor her lover viewed the subject by the cold light of reason. It is true, however, that the earl had at this time some qualms of conscience he could not fail to acknowledge to himself estranging the affection of a young maiden whom he could not under any circumstances consent to view in the character of a lawful wife.

The earl was not at this time a heartless seducer, but he was so enamoured of the fair Theresa that passion got the better of his judgment and reason. The end may be readily imagined.

"You have not been candid," said Theresa. "I feel assured that something dreadful has happened. Do not conceal anything from me; I charge you as you love me to tell me all. You have met Gerome Chanet, I feel assured of that."

"Well, what if I have?" returned Lord Ethalwood, turning from her. "Suppose I admit it—what then?"

"You cannot do otherwise than admit it, my lord. What has happened?"

"We had a hostile meeting."

"I knew it. I felt assured of that. And how did it end?"

Upon this the earl made a clean breast of it, and made Theresa acquainted with every minute particular connected with the tragedy in which he had played so conspicuous a part.

His companion listened to the harrowing details with forced calmness.

She did not betray outwardly any great emotion, but a heavy weight seemed to fall upon her, and she was supremely miserable.

"What a dreadful ending—what a terrible calamity! Poor Gerome! He was true to the last, then?"

"He was determined to have my life if possible; failing that, he was prepared to render up his own. The end was inevitable. Do not blame me, Theresa."

"I do not blame you, but what a risk you have run! Alas, you did not know the sort of man you had to deal with. Gracious Heaven! how very terrible is all this! But you must not stay in this neighbourhood. His death will be avenged. There are those who will watch and wait for you—those who will not scruple to slay you without pity or remorse. Oh, my dear Reginald, beware in time. Take heed of what I say ere it is too late. Your life may be sacrificed without a moment's notice. You do not know the sanguinary nature of those who watch and waylay unwary travellers in the mountain fastnesses. You are utterly heedless of the risk you run. They would not scruple to take your life to make reprisals for the loss of their comrade. You must not remain here. It would be madness to do so. But oh, how terribly hard it is for me to part with you. But it must be done, indeed it must, dearest. Consider——"

"I have considered," exclaimed the earl; "and I am well capable of taking care of myself."

"You are powerless in such a case as this. No man can guard against treachery—not the most valiant. You must not—nay, you shall not—remain here."

"Whither would you have me fly, then?"

"It matters not—your own country, or to France, anywhere you please, but don't stay here. Oh, Reginald, for my sake promise me to go away."

PEACE BARGAINING WITH THE JEW RECEIVER.

"You take a dark view of the aspect of affairs."

"It is not more dark and dismal than actual reality. Oh, this fatal love! How will it end? In death!"

As she gave utterance to this last speech she burst into tears, and her limbs trembled with excitement.

"Do you hear what I have been saying?" she ejaculated with bitterness.

"Of course I have, my own sweet darling, and with me your wishes are law. I will leave the neighbourhood at my earliest convenience."

"At your earliest convenience! At once! You must do so at once."

"Well, at once, then. So be it; but not to-night."

"No, not to-night. It is already morning."

"To-morrow, then, if you desire me to do so."

"I do desire it. Oh, mercy on me, I am over-whelmed with sorrow and sadness. I repent the past, and tremble for the future."

"I will act in accordance with your expressed wishes. Do not give way to needless fear. Come, sweetest, cheer up—be not so downcast. It is a melancholy ending, but, as I before observed, it was inevitable."

He strove as best he could to pacify the wretched Theresa, whose only thoughts were for his safety. He promised to fly on the following day.

They remained, exchanging words of love and vows of constancy, till the first few hours of the morning had passed away.

When Lord Ethalwood sought his own couch it was with an aching head and a heavy heart that he sought repose. His slumbers were disturbed by hideous dreams, and he arose hot, feverish, and excited.

Madame Trieste had returned, and was in the break-fast parlour when he presented himself. She tossed up her hands and heaved a deep sigh as her eyes lighted on him.

She told him she knew all—knew of the duel and the death of Gerome Chanet, but she did not upbraid him, or express any dissatisfaction at the line of conduct he had chosen to pursue. On the contrary, she said that she knew it had been forced upon him, and that he had no other alternative than to accept the challenge.

The Chevalier de Monpres had taken the precaution of sending to the earl's residence, with the request that his groom should bring round one of his master's saddle horses, and the man arrived at the widow's chateau with a magnificent animal before the inmates of the establishment had finished breakfast.

"It is very kind and considerate of the chevalier," cried Madame Trieste, "and redounds very much to his credit. He, like ourselves, my lord, knows the class of people we have to deal with."

"Yes, I have good reason to be thankful for the active part the chevalier has taken. He has befriended me in a way I had no reason to expect from one whose acquaintance I had so recently made. I owe him a deep debt of gratitude."

"To crown all," cried the widow, "he must be a most worthy man in addition to being a remarkably clever and courteous one."

"I should very much have liked to introduce him to you," observed the earl; "and indeed it would be as well, perhaps, to do so now."

"No, no—some other time. A more favourable opportunity will occur," said Theresa. "Do not linger here for any such purpose."

"Upon my word, mademoiselle, it seems to me that you are in a monstrous hurry to get rid of me," said the earl, with a sickly smile.

"It is only out of consideration for you, my lord," returned Madame Trieste. "My dear Theresa would not willingly part with you unless the urgency of the case demanded it."

"I am well convinced of that, madame—at least, I flatter myself that such is the case," returned Lord Ethalwood.

The groom informed his master that the Chevalier de Monpres had sent a message, requesting the earl to call at the chateau where he was staying as he pro-ceeded on his road home.

"I will do so, Curtis," said Lord Ethalwood. "Ride on and inform the chevalier that I will be with him in less than an hour from this time."

The groom upon this started off, leaving Lord Ethal-wood's horse ready caparisoned at the garden-gate of the widow's house.

"So you are going to ride over to your residence?" said Madame Trieste, "and without an attendant, it would seem."

"Nay, not so," observed the earl. "Curtis will attend me."

"But he has gone on to Monsieur de Monpres."

"True, I shall be by myself part of the way."

"And do you not think that very bad policy?"

"Why so, madame?"

"Suppose two or three ruffians were to attack you—what then?"

"I should have to defend myself to the best of my ability—that is all," returned the earl, with a smile.

"You make light of the matter, my lord. I look upon it from a different point of view. I consider your path beset with danger, and that you cannot be too cautious. You ought not to travel without an escort."

"It would be as well, perhaps, to have company on the road, but it is, after all, of no very great moment. I dare say I shall be able to reach home in safety."

"I hope so, I am sure," said Madame Trieste, "but you don't know the natives of these parts so well as we do."

"Certainly not. I don't pretend to do so."

"They are by nature treacherous, and are not to be trusted."

"I don't intend to put any trust in them, and for this reason I have no confidence in any of the rascals. But, my very dear friend," said Ethalwood, in an altered tone, "there is now an imperative necessity for me to take my departure. I am constrained by the force of circumstances to leave. Before doing so I have to express to you my deep sense of gratitude for all your kindness—which will be remembered for the remainder of my life. Let me, my dear Madame Trieste, assure you that, although from the force of circumstances I am constrained to take an abrupt leave of you, that I shall bear with me the most lively sense of your motherly kindness, and at the same time that I shall always look upon you as one of my most attached friends, for beneath your roof I have passed the happiest years of my life."

"Oh, my lord," exclaimed the widow, "I am indeed proud of the encomiums you are pleased to pass upon me; but although we part now from stern necessity we shall, I hope, meet again under happier circum-stances."

"I hope so, I am sure," said the earl, bending over her and imprinting a kiss on her forehead. "And now, my dear Theresa," he added, "do not think I shall forget you. I shall bear you in my remembrance, and long for the time when we may be reunited."

"Oh, my lord, my heart is too full for me to express myself in words. Be cautious—be mindful of the great peril you are now in, and for the rest let me hear from you. You will not forget your poor unhappy Theresa?"

"Never—never! I swear it," cried the earl, embrac-ing the young maiden with fervour.

He was not disposed to prolong the scene, which, to say the truth, was a trying one. He therefore made at once for the garden-gate and mounted his steed; then with another embrace and a blessing on the in-mates of the chateau, he trotted off.

Theresa Trieste watched the horse and its rider till both were out of sight—then she gave a faint scream and fell back into the arms of her mother.

Lord Ethalwood trotted on until he came to a steep

hill, with the precipitous rocks on either side. He drew the rein and walked his horse up the acclivity. He was ruminating on past events, and for a short time was lost in a reverie, when all of a sudden he heard the sharp crack of a rifle, which reverberated with a thousand echoes through the rocks overhead. A bullet was flattened against a stone wall which stood within a few paces from him.

Aroused to a sense of the danger, which was so immediate, he clapped spurs to the flanks of his steed, and galloped up the hill.

"Ah," he murmured, "a narrow escape. Theresa was right; there are murderous villains prowling about, and the chances are that this may not be the only shot that will be fired."

He did not give much time for his assailant or assailants to take deliberate aim, but put out his high-mettled steed to the utmost, and was thankful when the house in which the chevalier was located came within view. He found his groom awaiting his appearance at the entrance gates, which were thrown open, whereupon the earl rode at once into the yard. The gates were then closed.

De Monpres presented himself, and was overjoyed to see his friend, whom he at once conducted into the interior of the chateau.

"Well," said the old Frenchman, "what news? How goes it?"

"The scoundrels are afoot. I was fired at, and a bullet was flattened against the wall beside the road."

"I guessed it would be so," returned the chevalier. "I was a fool to let you come alone. My dear friend, you don't know what those fellows are. The greatest caution is now needed, for I believe one or more of them have sworn to have your life, but we will baffle them. The worst is now over, and for the rest——"

"Well, how about the rest?" inquired the earl.

"It's just this—you must cut and run. Don't imagine for a moment that such a course of action is discreditable to you; on the contrary, it is most wise and discreet. Of what avail is it seeking to hunt down or bring to justice a parcel of lawless miscreants who lie in ambush? My good fellow, I know what a guerilla war is—have gone through it: they pick you off before you know where you are; and, mind you, they would take a pride in making dogs' meat of you. No, no, my lord, we won't risk that, and to remain here to be a mark for sharp-shooting—why, it would be madness. They have sworn to have your life."

"Have they?"

"Do you doubt it?"

"I don't know what to say—am in perfect ignorance of their movements."

"I think you have already had proof sufficient. I tell you that they lie concealed in all parts. The first question that occurs to me is, how you are to reach your chateau in safety."

"I will ride there."

"You will do no such thing."

"Why not?"

"Because I won't let you—that's why."

"But what would you have me do then?"

"That depends upon circumstances. We will, if you please, hold a council of war."

As the chevalier made this last observation, a stout, good-humoured-looking gentleman entered the room.

"Ah," cried De Monpres, "I am glad you have come back, Monsieur. This is my friend, Earl Ethalwood, of whom you have heard me speak. My lord," said he in continuation, addressing himself to the earl, "Monsieur Jantie, my friend and host."

"I am proud to make your acquaintance," said Jantie, "and have to express my regret that it is not under more favourable circumstances, as I shall not have the pleasure of your society for long."

"No, no, not for long," said the chevalier with a laugh, "you may rest assured of that. The wolves are prowling about, seeking whom they may devour, and my friend, Ethalwood, is a marked man."

"Ah, surely you are taking an unfavourable view of the case," remarked the earl.

"Bah! don't be so dubious," cried De Monpres. "I had it upon the best authority that a group of mountaineers—unscrupulous desperadoes—swore over the dead body of their comrade, Gerome Chanet, to have your life. What more do you need in confirmation of my statement?"

"Is it possible?"

"Possible—it is a fact beyond all controversy."

"And how came this to your knowledge?"

"Well, I don't know that I am bound to secrecy. Monsieur Vasseralt, who after all turns out to be a good fellow enough, gave me the information. Now are you satisfied?"

"Perfectly. Monsieur Vasseralt—eh?"

"Yes, he was my informant; but, mark you, this unholy and sanguinary proceeding was not countenanced or approved of by him. He has, however, given me a caution, a timely warning, which we shall do well to remember."

"The infamous wretches!"

"Ah, but they think it a praiseworthy action. It all depends upon how men view these matters."

"I am beset with difficulties, it would seem," said the earl.

"We'll pull you through—leave the matter in my hands. An old soldier like myself will prove too much for these fellows, I expect," said De Monpres.

"You must place yourself in De Monpres' hands," observed Monsieur Jantie, addressing himself to the earl.

"I have the utmost confidence in the chevalier," observed the latter—"I wish I had his experience and wisdom."

The chevalier bowed courteously, and the conversation was continued in a lively strain. Monsieur Jantie treated the earl with marked politeness and attention, and begged of him as a personal favour to spend the remainder of the day with him. This honour, however, Lord Ethalwood declined, upon the plea that there was an imperative necessity for him to be at his own chateau.

It was ultimately arranged that Ethalwood and the chevalier were to be driven home in one of the close carriages of M. Jantie. The reason for this may be readily imagined.

The sharpshooters from the surrounding hills would be baffled. It was just possible, however, that an attempt might be made by a lawless band to stop the carriage. There was no telling how far the audacity of the men might carry them. It was, therefore, upon the advice of Vasseralt, Chanet's second, that the carriage was drawn under the escort of some half-a-dozen lusty yeomen retainers of Monsieur Jantie. These persons carried loaded weapons, and were otherwise armed to the teeth, and so, with these precautionary measures, Earl Ethalwood and his friend the Chevalier de Monpres contrived to arrive home in safety.

On the following day the earl set out on his journey, and made the best of his way to his native country.

CHAPTER CXXX.

CHARLES PEACE AND HIS UNLAWFUL GAINS—A VISIT TO
MR. SIMMONDS—A SURPRISE AND ESCAPE.

ONCE more we are constrained to return to the Evalina-road, for the purpose of seeing how it fares with the hero of this work.

Charles Peace had up to the present time not only escaped detection, but had managed his affairs with such success that not the faintest breath of suspicion fell upon him.

He was looked upon by his neighbours as the same easy-going, agreeable old gentleman of independent means as he had been deemed ever since the first few months of his life at Peckham.

His musical evenings were as frequent as of yore. He was seen occasionally in the garden and at the front entrance of his habitation, and appeared to be a quiet, discreet person, who to all appearance was what he professed to be—a man of thoughtful, studious habits, and the general impression was that there was no harm in him.

It is true that at times there were evidences of a storm within the house at No. 4, but this was attributable more to the irritable nature of the female residents than to the quiet and unobtrusive master of the establishment.

But Peace, during this interval of time, was industriously pursuing his lawless practices. The number of burglaries that had been committed in the surrounding districts seemed perfectly incredible, but no one suspected that Mr. Thompson had any hand in them.

Peace's house was crammed with articles of almost every conceivable description, which were, as may be easily conjectured, the produce of lawless depredations.

His two female companions must have been perfectly well aware that he was a wholesale and unscrupulous robber, although they both of them afterwards declared that they knew nothing about his numerous burglaries.

This upon the face of it appears to be altogether incredible, but it is perhaps just as well to give them the benefit of the doubt. They might have suspected, but possibly they were discreet enough to close their eyes to actual facts.

The house in the Evalina-road was at this time so crammed full of stolen goods that its occupant deemed it expedient to get rid of the greater portion of the articles.

If by any chance the place underwent an inspection by the police, there would be no possibility of Peace accounting for the possession of such a heterogeneous collection of property.

When in any difficulty he generally called into requisition his faithful comrade and ally, Bandy-legged Bill.

So one evening, when the sagacious Mr. William Rawton was engaged with a fragrant weed and a bit of music at the house in the Evalina-road, Charles Peace broached the subject.

The two women were at this time at the house of a neighbour, and Willie Ward had been sent on an errand.

"I say, Bill, old man," observed Peace, "I am a bit lumbered up here with a lot of things which would be best out of the way. Do you see?"

"Well, I should just say I did see, and no flies," cried Bill. "Why, Charlie, you've got what one might call a regular museum, a sort of old curiosity shop, stowed away in nooks and corners. It would not be particularly healthy for yer if the pleece were to take a review of all the blessed lot—not at all healthy."

"I quite agree with you, Bill. So I've been thinking we had better have a clearance—get shut of the whole blooming lot, eh?"

"Right you are, guv'nor. Turn the whole blessed collection into ready money. Get as many quids as you can for them, and then snap your fingers at the blooming bobbies."

"That's just what I intend to do. So you see, Bill, we will, now the place is all to ourselves, set about the business at once."

"What do you mean?"

"Just this. I've got two or three old hampers in the stable, and I want your assistance."

"All right; I'm on."

"Very well. We will at once proceed to fill the hampers, and to-morrow, please the pigs, will get them off to the East-end, to old Simmonds—he'll give as much as anybody."

"Don't care a great deal about Simmonds—he's not a square sort of chap, to my thinking."

"It does not matter what 'fence' we take them to. All I want to do to-night is to get the goods ready for starting."

Peace lighted a hand-lamp and bade his companion follow him. Then the two conveyed a number of articles to the stables, and when there they packed them up in as small a compass as possible in the hampers to which Peace had made allusion.

The greater portion of the property was safely stowed away in the hampers, which were afterwards tied down with long cord.

All this had been done in an incredibly short space of time. Then the burglar and his horsey companion sat down on the corded baskets and discussed the intended proceedings of the morrow.

"Poor Tommy, my beautiful little pet, is gone!" said Peace, with something like sorrow in his tone. "I shan't get another like him in a hurry, Bill. But it's of no use grieving—it was to be, I suppose, and so there's an end of that matter."

"Ah, poor old Tommy! but lord bless you, nothing in the world would have saved him. But it ain't of no use dwelling on that now. These precious hampers have to be got, somehow or other, to Whitechapel—that's quite certain. There won't be much difficulty about that ere. I'll bring a trap round we can shove 'em in, and the rest is an easy matter. I shall be glad when we've got shut of them."

"So shall I. Are you going to borrow a trap, then?"

"Ah, yes, Joe Starker will lend me one in a minute. There ain't no manner of trouble about that. Say the word, Charlie. Tell me what time I am to be here, and it shall be done like a shot, and no flies."

"Eight o'clock to-morrow evening will do very well, I think."

"All right, guv'nor, eight o'clock let it be, then."

"And drive round to the back yard, without saying a word to anyone."

"I'm on; so be it, Charlie."

This little matter having been thus satisfactorily arranged, Peace and the gipsy returned to the parlour.

Willie Ward had by this time returned, and he and our hero, as usual, began to play duets.

Presently the ladies of the establishment presented themselves, and a social and convivial evening was passed.

Rawton left at a little before twelve, with a promise to be there on the following evening.

Peace, of course, did not go out on a depredating excursion for that night.

Punctual to his appointment, Bandy-legged Bill drove into the back yard of No. 4 at about a quarter before eight on the succeeding night.

Peace was ready to receive him, and the hampers were quickly lifted into the cart, whereupon the two friends proceeded at once in the direction of White-chapel.

"We'll try Simmonds first," said our hero. "Cunning Isaac, as we call him, is a rapacious old scoundrel, who wants things for next door to nothing. Simmonds is worth two of him."

"I don't like either of them, if the truth is to be told," cried the gipsy; "but, lord, they aint any of them worth much, as far as that is concerned. The whole biling of them are a set of bloodsuckers, but there, I dare say you will ask what's a cove to do."

"Yes, that's just where it is. We can't do without them, Bill—there aint any mistake about that. I look upon it that men and women prey upon one another like wild beasts. The 'fence' preys upon the 'cracks-man,' the cracksman—well, he preys upon the public —that is, the rich public—and they in most cases have made their money out of the poor. From the lowest to the highest it is one system of cheating and robbing —that's my view of the matter."

"Oh, you are not far off the mark, it's right enough," returned Bill. "You are never so happy as when you are moralising," he added, with a laugh.

"Ah, you may laugh," cried Peace, "but pray tell me how many persons you know in this world as you can trust—just you answer that question."

"Jolly few, if that's what you mean. You may count 'em on your fingers, and not want all on 'em to do so."

"No. I should think not."

"But, I say, what blooming crib are yer bound for?" said the gipsy; "for we are coming to close quarters, now."

"Oh, we will see what Simmonds says. I shall leave you to strike the bargain. Take one hamper into him, and see what he offers."

"I tell yer what it is, Charlie, I don't care about the job, cos why—he don't like me, and I've no affection for him. You'll do a deal better with him than what I can—so just pop down upon the old rascal, and I think I shall be able to work Isaac."

"Oh, you prefer Isaac, do you?"

"Well, yes I do. Every man has his fancy. Some can get along with one, which perhaps another cove wouldn't be able to work not nohow whatsoever."

Mr. Simmonds's establishment stood in one of the streets which ran at right angles out of the White-chapel-road.

It was not an aristocratic-looking shop, and the immediate neighbourhood surrounding it could not be considered either cleanly or odoriferous.

Mr. Simmonds himself was not altogether a pattern of cleanliness—neither could he be considered particularly handsome. His nose was long, and his mouth was wide. In short, his features, taken altogether, would lead a superficial observer to the conclusion that he was a gentleman of the Hebrew persuasion.

Still Mr. Simmonds had contrived to drive a very profitable trade. He was very well known, and always ready to purchase goods of every conceivable description, and it was not his practice to ask impertinent questions.

He therefore drove a profitable trade.

Charles Peace was very well acquainted with him, and had had with him many business transactions.

A well-known journalist, at the time Peace carried on his lawless practices in the Evalina-road, was desirous of knowing how he disposed of his plunder. "There is more in this question," said he, "than the police were able to discover."

In cases of common burglary the usual course is for the thief to make his way direct to some safe "fence" and drive the best bargain he can of the receiver. But Peace was no common burglar.

The more I enquire into the life and habits of those in his establishment at Peckham, the less disposed I am to believe that Mrs. Thompson acted as a "go-between." Certainly the boy, "Willie Ward," was not entrusted with such delicate missions, and I am pretty certain the services of Mrs. Ward would only be resorted to when things were growing desperate.

The impression at Peckham was, that Peace had a male accomplice, a clever unscrupulous fellow like himself, and not at all dissimilar physically, but even superior to Peace himself.

This surmise on the part of the journalist in question was correct, the accomplice in question being none other than "Bandy-legged Bill."

Upon coming in front of Mr. Simmonds's respectable blishment Peace alighted, and without further ado took one of the hampers into the Jew's shop.

"I am happy and proud to see you," cried Simmonds. "Anything in my way?"

"Yes," returned Peace. "You can look over the articles in this hamper, and see what you can afford to give for them."

"Yesh, yesh, my tear friend, I vill do so, but business is bad and money is tight—still I'll do my best for you."

"I am not going to be chiselled if I can help it," returned Peace; "so don't think to come any of your hanky-panky tricks over me."

"Lord bless us, how suspicious you are! S'help me goodness, I do my best for all of you, my very best. But I say just bring the things into the back parlour, there's a good fellow. Oh, you don't know what risks we run."

Peace dragged the hamper into the small room at the back of the shop. The Jew then began to make a careful inspection of the articles as he drew them forth. He approved them as he did so, putting them down on the tablet of his memory at fifty per cent. less than their intrinsic value.

While thus engaged he dodged and ducked his head, every now and then peering into the front shop through the dingy and dirt-begrimed glass of the door which separated the parlour from the outer shop.

There was, of course, the usual haggling—the price the Hebrew offered was too ridiculous for Peace to accept. Then followed the expletives and oaths, without which no bargain of this description could be concluded. At length, however, Peace consented to take seventy pounds for the goods, whereupon the Jew handed down a fifty-pound note and twenty sovereigns to our hero, who pocketed the same.

The bargain had hardly been concluded when two persons entered the Jew's shop. Mr. Simmonds looked through the curtain which hung over the window of the door of the parlour, and uttered an exclamation of surprise.

"What's up?" cried Piece, in some alarm.

"Two detectives," was the quick rejoinder.

"The devil!" exclaimed our hero, looking into the shop. "And one of them——"

"Well, what?" ejaculated Simmonds.

"One of the blokes I know; and what is worse he knows me."

"And wants you?"

Peace nodded significantly.

"Gracious! However, I would not have a customer of mine 'copped' in my place; no, not for the world."

"What's to be done," said Peace. "Is there any means of escape? I must not be seen by the tall ones or I am a lost man."

"Father, two gentlemen want to speak to you," said a youth in the shop, who was Simmonds's son.

"Fly up-stairs," cried the Jew, "and hook it. I will keep them in conversation. Step it at once."

Peace required no second bidding; he left the back parlour just as the Jew entered his shop.

"Your servant, gentlemen," said he in oleaginous accents. "Vat can I do for you?"

"Have you purchased a watch to day or yesterday, bearing on its face the name of Velluming," said one of the detectives.

"No! Haven't purchased any watch for a week or more."

"You are quite sure of that?"

"Oh, yes—certainly I am."

"Wasn't there a person in your back parlour when we entered?" said the taller of the two.

"Nobody but myself," returned Simmonds, in a confident tone.

The detectives exchanged glances, and conversed in whispers.

"We have very good reasons for doubting your statement, Mr. Simmonds," said one of them.

"Vell, gentlemen, I do hope you believe I wouldn't tell you a deliberate lie. Please tell me your business."

"If you are speaking the truth there cannot be any possible objection to your letting us search the premises."

"But vat for? I haven't done anything against the law?"

"No matter about that. Will you or will you not permit us to run over the premises?"

"I think it is very unbecoming of you to make such a request," said Simmonds; "but I suppose you know your own business best. Search the house if you like."

The two detectives entered the back parlour. Of course Charles Peace was not there. Then they passed out into the passage and began to ascend the stairs leading to the upper rooms.

"I don't think yer acting in at all a proper manner, gentlemen," exclaimed Simmonds, speaking as loud as he could, "and I must protest against such proceedings. Do you think I harbour thieves?"

"We don't *think*," observed the detectives.

"Well, I won't say any more, as I shall be only subjecting myself to insults," cried the Jew. "Rachel!" he said, in continuation, calling to his wife, who was in one of the upstair rooms. "Don't be alarmed, tear. Two strange shentlemen are coming upstairs. They won't hurt you. Don't be alarmed—it's all right, they know their business, and I know mine."

"He must have got clear off by this time, I should suppose," muttered the Jew to himself. "If he hasn't, vell, the Lord help him, for I can't."

Charles Peace, after leaving the back parlour, at once made for the topmost story of the house. In one of the back rooms he found a double dormer window. He passed through this, closed it carefully after him, and then gained the roof.

He must have considered himself hardly pressed, for after going along the slates he got into another house through the window, which he also closed after him.

The room in which he now found himself was unoccupied, but upon descending below he came across a woman, who was the landlady of the habitation. She was greatly surprised at beholding Mr. Peace, who, however, put the best face on the matter.

"My dear madam," said he, "I am sure from your appearance that you are not one to refuse succour to a persecuted man. The police are after me, and I have contrived to elude them for the present. Will you befriend me?"

"How can I do that?"

"By letting me remain here for awhile."

"But you may have committed some dreadful crime, and if such be the case I shall get into trouble for harbouring you."

"Do not be in any way alarmed—I have not committed any dreadful crime. Do I look a man likely to do such a thing?"

"I can't say you do, but appearances are often deceptive. What are you charged with?"

"Oh, a mere trifle. Deserting my wife and children. The fact is, I have been out of work, but now I am doing very well, and intend to rejoin my family. But if I am caught it will be my ruin, for my employer will, in all probability, discharge me. I will pay you handsomely for the accommodation if you will only let me remain here."

The woman, who was naturally kind-hearted, hesitated.

"It is a most extraordinary thing you entering the house in the way you have done. I don't know what to say about it."

"Take pity on me. You will not refuse. I am known to some of your neighbours, who will answer for my respectability."

"Who do you know, then?"

"Mr. Simmonds; he will tell you all about me."

"Ah, Mr. Simmonds—eh?" returned the woman, in dubious accents.

"Yes. Do you know him?"

"I know him as a near neighbour, that is all. Well, you had better come downstairs and sit in the front parlour for a time."

"Oh, thank you kindly. You are a dear good creature. I was sure of that when I first saw you."

"I would much prefer you going away at once."

"So should I, if it were possible, but it is not, and you will let me remain till the coast is clear."

"Come down into the front parlour. What will my lodgers think of me, talking to a perfect stranger in this way? Come down."

"Ah, certainly, with the greatest pleasure."

Peace descended, and was shown into the lady's sitting-room.

"Now, sir," said she, "you must make yourself as contented as possible. I cannot find it in my heart to give you up to the police. I hope and trust you have spoken the truth."

"I swear——"

"There is no necessity to do that. I will take your word, that is sufficient."

"Quite so. I am sure you will never regret doing this act of kindness to a poor fellow in trouble."

"I hope I never may have cause to regret it, but you certainly are a most extraordinary sort of man, and that's the truth."

"It will be all right if I succeed in concealing myself so that I may avoid needless exposure. I intend to return to my family to-morrow, and then there will be an end of the business."

While Charles Peace was concealed in the parlour of the house into which he had so unceremoniously entered, the two detectives ran through the rooms of the Jew's habitation. but they could not discover any stranger in any of the apartments which Mr. Simmonds opened obsequiously one after the other.

The detectives saw they were at fault, and they assumed an apologetic tone, and expressed their regret at having been so troublesome, stating, at the same time, that they had a duty to perform, and that they were in search of a gentleman who was "wanted."

The Jew's son, who had been left in charge of the shop, was a sharp-witted, precocious young gentleman, who, like his father, had an eye to business. He thought it just as well to take the articles, one by one, which his father had purchased of our hero, and place them under lock and key.

In their hurry to secure their man the detectives had forgotten to examine these contraband goods, some of which had the initials of their owner's engraved on their face.

When Simmonds descended into the back parlour with the detectives, he noticed the absence of the goods from the place where he had left them, but he was by far too prudent a man to make any observation or allude in any way to the subject.

"Good lad," he murmured to himself. "Ah, he'll make a bright man—he has cleared all away. So much the better. He's as good as gold—that's what he is."

The detectives remained for some time in the shop, conversing with the Israelite, who thought it just as well to be urbane and conciliatory in his manner.

He was, however, at this time not at all aware of the magnitude of Peace's depredations or the grave charge which hung over his head; neither did he know that one of the detectives hailed from Sheffield.

Peace, in dealing with the Jew, had taken the precaution never to give his right name. The receiver of stolen goods, throughout his acquaintance with him, had been under the impression that he was a well-known London thief.

Bandy-legged Bill, who was waiting at the corner of the street for Peace, did not know very well how to act. He saw the detectives enter the Jew's shop. He was seriously alarmed and trembled for his friend, but he had at the same time unlimited faith in the resources of "Charlie," as he termed him.

Still he did not like to abandon him, and for a brief space of time he debated with himself as to what had best be done under the circumstances.

He was half inclined to alight, enter the shop, and see how matters stood; but upon second thoughts he came to the conclusion that it would be the worst possible policy for him to leave the trap, which contained so much stolen property.

After cogitating for some time he deemed it advisable to drive off without running risk of detection.

And so, while the coast was clear, off he drove.

Bill was very reluctant to abandon the field, but prudence dictated this course of action, and he argued that he could be of no service to Peace under any circumstances—so he drove off far away from the scene of action.

And for his own as well as for his friend's safety it was as well, perhaps, that he did so.

But the detectives, after they left the Jew's house, did not seem disposed to leave the neighbourhood.

The Sheffield man was under the impression that he had seen some one in the back parlour of Simmonds's establishment the features of whom were like those of Charles Peace.

But he was by no means sure of this: he had only caught a fugitive and transient glance of the face through the dingy windows of the door; but whoever it might have been, the man in question—if there was a second person in the little parlour, which he was by no means certain of—had been spirited away in a most extraordinary manner.

The two detectives walked up and down the street more than once, glancing as they passed along at the windows of the several houses, with no very satisfactory result.

It was not at all likely that Mr. Peace would at this time be looking out of the window of the one in which he was ensconced.

He was by far too clever a rascal for that, but the landlady of the establishment saw the officers pass and repass and described their appearance to our hero.

"Ah, it's them safe enough," cried Peace, "they are ooking for me without a doubt, and be blowed to them. My dear madam, I don't know how to sufficiently thank you for this timely shelter. You are my good angel, my protector."

"I hope I am not doing wrong," returned the woman, "but if I am it can't be helped. I'm sure there is no telling who people are nowadays. My dear husband used to say so, and he was quite right—one never can tell."

"Your husband," said Peace, in some alarm—"where is he now?"

"Where is he?" cried the woman, with a shake of the head, "where, indeed? Who knows? In a happier world, let us hope."

"Ah," said Peace—"he is dead then?"

"Why, of course he is. Has been dead three years come next September."

Peace was greatly relieved when he heard that the good gentleman had been removed to a happier sphere, since it would have been rather awkward if he had presented himself and not taken the same humane view of the case that his better half had done.

"Ah!" ejaculated our hero, "life is uncertain, and there is no telling how soon we may go." Here he cast his eyes up towards the ceiling, and endeavoured to look sentimental. "The loss of a dear relative, and especially a husband, is a sad trial."

"It is," returned the widow; "especially when one has to mourn the loss of so good a husband as mine was."

"I am pleased to hear you speak so well of him—it does you great credit," observed Peace, in a sanctimonious manner. "By the way," he added, "do you see those wretched men lurking about?"

"No, I don't see anything of them now," she answered as she peered through the window curtain. "They appear to have gone."

"So much the better," said Peace.

The two detectives, not being able to see anything of the man whom they had been so industriously seeking, went into several known houses which they knew to be the haunts of thieves, but were equally unsuccessful in their search. They lingered about the neighbourhood after this for some considerable time and then took their departure, being about as wise as they were when they first entered the house in the occupatio of the astute Mr. Simmonds.

But Charles Peace, who was a tolerably good judge of the proceedings of detectives of every conceivable description, did not deem it advisable to sally forth just at present; he, therefore, continued in friendly discourse with the woman who had been of such essential service to him.

He placed a sovereign on the table, of which he begged her acceptance; but, although she was not by any means in affluent circumstances, she declined to accept of the gratuity.

Peace, however, would not take any denial, and said he should be greatly hurt and mortified if she did not permit him to prevail upon her to accept of some small recompense for services rendered.

The woman was by no means mercenary. What she had done was simply a matter of kindness and humanity on her part, and she had never for a moment contemplated the matter in any other light than a natural desire on her part to assist a fallen creature who was plunged into the depths of trouble. However, after much persuasion on the part of our hero, she reluctantly pocketted the sovereign.

"I should indeed be sorry if by any chance these men should find you when you leave this house," said the widow, "and therefore I think you had better remain till after dark."

"I am afraid I am in your way," returned the burglar.

"Not at all, sir. You can have a bed and remain all night if you think it advisable to do so."

"There will be no necessity for that," said he—"not the slightest necessity. But I tell you what you can do to serve me."

"What?"

"Have you got anybody who can be trusted to go round to Mr. Simmonds?"

"Dear me, yes. My little girl will go at once, if you wish it."

"Let her go, then."

"By the back way?"

"Yes—that would be better."

The widow went into the passage, and called out in a loud voice the name of "Netty" once or twice.

A little girl of about eleven years of age made her appearance.

"Now, then, tell me what she is to do," observed the widow.

Peace slipped sixpence into the hands of the child, and told her to go to Mr. Simmonds and say he wished to speak to him.

The child did as she was directed, and in a minute or so returned with the Jew.

"Ah, you are safe—eh?" cried Simmonds. "Vell, you've done the trick cleanly, old man. Given them the slip, s'help my goodness; but you're down us a hammer, and no mistake. I'd have been ready to have gone clean mad if anything had happened to you in my place. All the years I've been in business I never had a customer 'copped' at my establishment."

"Have they gone away do you think?" cried Peace.

"Ah, I hope so—and bad luck to 'em—but I won't say for certain. There's no telling what gentlemen of their kidney may be up to, but I think as how you are safe. Come with me, and I'll show you how to get clean off."

Thanking the widow for her kindness, Charles Peace went out of the back door of her residence in company with the Jew.

He found himself in a narrow blind alley.

The Jew led him through a labyrinth of narrow courts, and they then emerged into a wide street. Peace had not at this time the faintest notion of where he was, but Simmonds led him into a house. In

one of the rooms on the basement a group of persons were assembled.

It was evidently the resort of thieves of every description, and was an establishment much after the fashion of the one to which Laura Stanbridge took Alf Purvis when he was a mere lad.

The Jew appeared to be pretty well known to most of the persons who frequented this establishment, for many present spoke to him in a familiar and jocular manner.

Simmonds sent a leary-looking man for a four-wheeled cab, and when the vehicle drove up to the door of the house he bade Peace jump in without further ado.

This our hero did without hesitation, and then the cab was driven rapidly over the stones.

CHAPTER CXXXI.

THIEVES AND RECEIVERS.

THE receiver of stolen goods, from whose establishment Charles Peace had so cunningly contrived to make his escape, was an average sample of his class.

There are hundreds, and, indeed it may be said, thousands of persons of this description in the metropolis and the suburbs.

It has been remarked by many who have a pretty good knowledge of characters of this description that without receivers there would be no thieves, but we do not quite agree with this hypothesis. Thieves it is not possible to eradicate, but certainly the receivers offer every inducement for men to pursue dishonest courses, and it is most remarkable how few are ever brought to justice.

One of the most celebrated men of his time was a Jew, named "Ikey Solomons."

He flourished some forty or fifty years ago, and his transactions with thieves of every description were of a magnitude which appeared at the time to be almost incredible and are said to have rivalled those of the famous Jonathan Wild.

When quite an old man "Ikey" came to grief. He had up to the time of his capture followed his nefarious calling for over half a century, and had managed somehow or other to escape detection.

He was tried at the Old Bailey, but was, to the best of our belief, acquitted.

It has been said that Dickens drew his character of Fagin, in "Oliver Twist," from the celebrated Ikey Solomons, but we are not disposed to give credence to this statement, as Ikey was, beyond the fact of his being a Jew "fence, in every way dissimilar to Dickens's hero.

When the name of Charles Peace was in every human mouth public interest was awakened by the spoils of a receiver of stolen property falling into the hands of the police.

The following paragraph, from a newspaper of the period, will, perhaps, interest the curious and inquisitive reader. It runs as follows:—

"There is at present, at the Bethnal-green Police-station, under the charge of Inspector Wildey, of the Criminal Investigation Department, attached to the K division, and Detective-sergeants Rolfe and Wallis, about one of the most extraordinary collections of stolen property ever seen in this metropolis.

"The goods are laid out in the library and reserve-room of the station, and consist of articles of almost every conceivable kind—at least as far as things of a portable nature are concerned.

PEACE AND THE CABMAN HAVE A LIQUOR AT THE ELEPHANT AND CASTLE.

" First come some dozen or so of gold watches, from the ordinary Geneva to the highly-finished and expensive article from the shop of some first-class London maker ; then come silver watches, gold bracelets, lockets, chains, and guards, rings set with precious stones, silver spoons, forks, and fruit-knives.

" On another table is a quantity of really good elec-tro-plate—one set of forks, spoons, ladles, &c., being marked with the letter B, and are supposed to have been the proceeds of some burglary committed a year or two back.

" On a table in the middle of the room are strewn cigar-cases, meerschaum pipes, small fancy thermometers, mantel ornaments of a superior kind, opera

No. 69.

glasses, books, photograph cases and albums, some with portraits and some without, a large family Bible, a silver snuff-box ('presented to Sergeant Tierney by Mr. and Mrs. Maitland'), Crimean medal, with the Balaclava and Sebastopol clasps, the property of Private Wilson, of the Royal Marines; and three boxes, each containing a dozen silver thimbles.

"On the mantelpiece are some half-a-dozen clocks, some of them of a very expensive kind, and evidently taken from the house of well-to-do people.

"Around the room are scattered coats, jackets, capes, shawls, rolls of flannel, cloth, and linen, about fifty or sixty pairs of new boots, and any number of umbrellas.

"Piled up against the wall are some sixty or seventy workboxes of various sizes and kinds, from the humble article costing only a few shillings to the more expensive article, which probably cost five or ten guineas.

"Cases of claret, champagne, and brandy, railway and carriage rugs, and a host of other things much too numerous to mention, but which do not form a tithe of the bulk of property originally seized—the whole lot, indeed, filling three large vans.

"These things were seized about eight weeks ago by Inspector Wildey, in company with Sergeants Rolfe and Wallis, at a house in Thomas-street, Commercial-road, the proprietor of which has been, for the last twelve years, suspected by the police to be a receiver of stolen property, but so cleverly has he managed his business that until the last week there had been no chance of bringing anything home to him.

"The way in which he was caught at last was as follows:—Two men were apprehended on a charge of burglary, and one of them referred the police to this individual for a character. Inspector Wildey thereupon went to the house, and saw him, and he gave the man in question a most excellent character. From what he saw at the place, however, Mr. Wildey was induced to ask the magistrate for a search warrant, the result of which was that the whole of the property referred to was discovered there.

"Already articles relating to no less than thirty-two cases of burglary or housebreaking have been identified among the things, and fresh identifications are occurring daily.

"It is stated that seventeen years ago this modern Fagin was a poor labouring man, but he now owns some thirty houses in and about the district where he has been residing."

It is not often, as we before observed, that persons of this class are compelled to disgorge their ill-gotten gains, or come within the meshes of the net the law has woven for them.

As a rule, they were by far too cautious and cunning to be caught napping.

But occasionally, and only occasionally, is it that one of the fraternity gets into trouble, and even then he generally manages to slip out of the hands of justice.

During the period between the trial and the execution of that eminent homicide and burglar the late Mr. Charles Peace, the public manifested a not unnatural curiosity to ascertain how he had managed to dispose of the great number of various articles which from time to time had come into his possession in the practice of a profitable but venturesome calling.

This anxious pursuit of knowledge—not altogether for its own sake—on the part of the payers of police-rates ultimately reached the ears of Mr. Peace himself, who, apart from his homicidal and acquisitive tendencies, was, like most other musical amateurs, an amiable and obliging person.

Finding there was not even a remote chance of breaking prison and escaping the attentions of Mr. Marwood, Mr. Peace supplied the police with a full and accurate list of purchasers of stolen property with whom he had had business transactions up and down the country.

If we recollect rightly, a subsequent conditional promise was made on behalf of the guardians of order that the convict's allegations should be thoroughly investigated, and that, if these were found accurate, the persons pointed at should be prosecuted with the utmost rigour of the law.

Whether the promised inquiry was ever commenced we cannot say.

It is, however, an indisputable fact that but for the existence of the class of individuals to whom Peace disposed of his booty, that adroit criminal might have earned an honest livelihood as violinist in an operatic or theatrical orchestra. The receivers are always ready to the hands of the thief.

Even without the assistance of persons of Mr. Peace's profession, the police know of their existence, their whereabouts, and their manner of prosecuting a most lucrative and not sufficiently dangerous trade; but, from a mistaken leniency in the spirit of our law, these worst of criminals are left undisturbed.

The police—often conveniently blind—are nothing if not arithmetical. Armed with a note-book and a pencil, they penetrate into the most secret recesses of a guilty commerce, and, having tabulated the number of "fences" in England and Wales, complacently suffer wrong-doing to take its course.

Either the crime of receiving stolen goods is on the increase, or the receivers are growing less fortunate; since the number of commitments for this specific offence was, according to the latest returns, four hundred and eighty in 1878, against four hundred and fifteen in 1877.

On the other hand, the known houses for the receipt of stolen goods slightly vary numerically from year to year, the average being about one thousand one hundred, and the known thieves and receivers of stolen goods and suspected persons may be roughly estimated at close upon forty-one thousand.

If the net of the law were spread, and these houses shut up and their occupants taken care of, crimes against property would at once fall to a minimum, the criminal courts would soon become idle, and respectable citizens might lie down to rest without fear of the "villainous centre-bit."

Within the last few weeks another case has come under the notice of the police.

It would appear that a great number of robberies having lately been committed in the Western suburbs of London, the attention of the police was called to the flourishing establishment of a marine-store dealer, of Pimlico.

We have no desire to prejudice the case of the person at present under remand. Marine-store dealers are not supposed to traffic in jewels and gold, in the settings of personal ornaments made of the precious metals, from which the gems seem to have been ruthlessly severed, or in household plate from which the crests appear to have been recently erased.

All the same, the marine-store man may have come by such objects of art and luxury in a perfectly lawful manner; and inasmuch as he stands remanded, without bail, on a charge of receiving a stolen silver medal, it is only fair to assume him innocent.

Unfortunately for him his recollection of certain late commercial transactions did not tally with the information of Inspector White and Sergeant Day, of the B Division of police.

It happened that these agents of the law, having occasion to call at the shop to inquire whether its owner purchased any plate that day, the marine-store keeper was so ill-advised, or of such uncertain memory, as to deny the soft impeachment.

Mr. White, however, proved too pressing for him, and, accompanied by his fellow-officer, followed him and his wife upstairs, where they came upon a store of treasure of more than Oriental splendour and variety.

There, upon tables and under beds, and strewn about in confusion, the police found gold coins, travelling bags, bank notes, blue serge, watches, chains, tablecloths, brooches, lockets, studs, silver plate, pieces of alpaca, cutlery, artificial teeth, slippers, shawls, lead, and brass, and articles of almost every description—among other things, certain stolen property traced directly from the prosecuting owner.

It is, of course, within the bounds of possibility that the marine-store dealer may have purchased the articles catalogued in the regular way of business; and he may rest assured that every opportunity will be afforded him to make his title clear, not only to the silver medal, but to every item so opportunely discovered on his premises.

The broken jewellery found at Pimlico may have been accidentally damaged by the manufacturers themselves.

It is possible that the late proprietor of the silver drinking-cup, in the shape of a thimble, with "Just a thimbleful" in blue round the rim, shocked at the temptation to dram-drinking which its possession hourly put in his way, may have adopted a peculiar form of local option and chosen to dispose of the bauble to the shopkeeper for value received.

The pair of gold solitaires engraved with "a cock in the act of crowing" may have offended the æsthetic tastes of their former holder; the gilt whistle may have been found too noisy by its late custodian, and the lockets fitted with hair and the portraits of children need not necessarily have been stolen to have passed into the hands of respectable tradesmen.

We sincerely trust that the accused may be able to prove his innocence to the satisfaction of a British jury.

At the same time, it may not be thought out of place to call attention to the crying evil involved in the existence of a class of persons—quite independently of individuals—who, although shrewdly suspected by the police to be buyers of stolen goods, are left undisturbed to their mischievous avocations.

Stolen goods are habitually disposed of through the medium of the pawnbroker, the leaving-shop, the marine-store dealer, the assayer or dealer in gold or silver, and the professional "fence," the last of whom has reduced his calling to a regulated system, and has his agents in different parts of the country and on the Continent, to whom he consigns parcels of stolen property with all the forms of regular commerce.

If the police could be induced to speak they might recount the histories of individuals who, after long careers of moral infamy in this line of business, have blossomed into respectable retirement in surburban mansions.

They are among the most difficult sort of criminals to convict. The transactions of the firm are generally managed by a strong-minded, subtle rogue, who keeps the majority of those to whom he disposes of his ill-gotten gains in ignorance of his and their true character.

The pawnbroker is generally more sinned against than sinning; for, if stolen property can be traced to his possession, he is forced by law to restore it to the right owner without compensation.

While, however, the pawnbroker is licensed and subject to many disabilities in the prosecution of his calling, the keeper of the leaving shop is a mere unlicensed usurer in a small way, generally ready to advance petty sums on all sorts of portable property without asking questions as to its rightful possession.

Even when this sort of person is not a regular "fence" for the lowest class of thieves, he robs the very poor by taking exorbitant interest. He should be suppressed and eradicated root and branch.

When lead is stolen from the roofs of buildings, or metal fittings purloined from uninhabited houses, such plunder almost invariably finds its way to the den of the marine-store dealer, who also encourages servants to acts of wilful extravagance in the choice and rending down of fat meat by purchasing the residue, without comment or inquiry, as "kitchen stuff."

The pretended assayer and dealer in gold and silver usually has his shop in some respectable part of the town, and in the neighbourhood of *bonâ-fide* establishments for the purchase and sale of the precious metals.

He makes little, if any, display of goods in his window, and the thief once inside his carefully-enclosed shop is safely screened from the gaze of the passers by.

This worthy tradesman has a spout at the back of his counter communicating with a floor above, in which is situated the "soup," or melting, pot.

The thief may hand in for disposal, at well-understood prices, ornaments in the most precious of metals, possibly treasure trove in the shape of some great wrought Saxon collar of gold, or Queen Anne silver plate.

It is all "stock" that comes to the "soup" kettle of this sort of gentry. A few minutes after the chain or ladle, bracelet or salver, is handed across the counter the materials are reduced to their original state.

Form vanishes, and with it most of the chances of detection. These facts are not unknown to the police, and it may well be asked whether the suppression of an avoidable evil of great magnitude and importance would not fairly come within the duties of a public prosecutor.

In the stolen goods department of commerce, as in many other things, prevention is better than cure.

Subject to some few exceptions, a shop within the metropolitan district is a "market overt," the keeper of which is free, without fear of the law, to buy or sell anything he pleases, from a malachite snuff-box to a Prayer-book bound in ivory, or from a cedar-wood work-box to a set of gold solitaires.

Browne has a right, no doubt, to claim that he must be held innocent until the offence with which he stands charged is actually proved.

But the commonest consideration must show the case to be one of very grave suspicion, and the sitting magistrate sufficiently showed his opinion of the facts as put before him when he refused to listen to any application for bail.

Without, however, impugning the innocence of the prisoner in the present instance, there can be no doubt that receiving stolen property, or "fencing," as it is technically known at Scotland-yard, is largely practised in London by the class of tradesmen to which he belongs.

The difficulty the police always have with the "fence" is to bring the guilty knowledge home to him.

The skilled "fence" will purchase nothing the identity of which cannot be at once destroyed without very materially depreciating its value.

Some few years ago the Messrs. Hancock, of Bruton-street, discovered, at their stock-taking, that jewellery—principally consisting of brilliant diamond rings and bracelets—was missing to the value of several thousand pounds.

They said nothing, but put the police on the alert. A few days later a little boy offered a marine-store dealer a small mass of mis-shapen metal tied together with a string.

The boy was detained, and the metal proved to be the settings of the missing jewellery. The boy declared he had picked them up in the mud of the Thames off Battersea, and there was every reason to believe his story.

Evidently the whole of the plunder had come into the hands of a single receiver; the stones had been wrenched out of their setting, and the gold itself had been actually thrown away.

As for the stones, they no doubt found their way to Amsterdam, or the Hague, or Antwerp.

But the "fence" escaped detection, although it is possible that the thief himself was discovered in the person of one of the shopmen, who pleaded guilty to several small robberies, but obstinately denied all knowledge of the larger offence.

When Lady Ellesmere's jewels, valued at fifteen thousand pounds, were stolen from the top of a cab in 1857, they came into the possession of a small shop-keeper and tallyman, who paid rather less than ten pounds for them.

The thieves were ignorant of the true value of their booty, and the "fence" represented that the articles were mere "Brummagem ornaments," worth a few shillings at the most.

The purchase of stolen goods is a trade so lucrative, and offers so direct an incentive to crime in others, that, when it is fully brought home, the offender cannot, in the public interest, be too severely dealt with.

If there were no receivers there would be hardly any professional thieves. Their detection, as we have said, is difficult, for the simple reason that a detected and convicted thief knows, as a rule, that he has very little, if anything, to gain by putting such information as he can give at the disposal of the police.

Were pardons or remissions of sentences more frequently granted as the reward of Queen's evidence, it ought to be perfectly possible to hunt down every professional receiver in the metropolis.

The law finds it at all times difficult to deal with receivers of stolen goods, who, as a rule, contrive somehow or other to baffle and elude its most vigilant and acute officers.

Thieves, however, are less fortunate than receivers: they are frequently brought to the bar of justice, and have to undergo various terms of imprisonment, but it is a most remarkable fact, that in most cases, after the habitual thief has served his time, he invariably returns to his dishonest practices.

It seems almost impossible to effect a reformation in such cases, and punishment is of no avail.

Some men pass two-thirds of their lives in prison, and yet are as hardened and callous as ever.

We do not believe it would have been possible to have effected a reformation in Charles Peace, no matter what mode of treatment had been adopted. He was so radically bad that he was past all cure, and there are at the present time, hundreds and thousands of ruffians preying upon the public, who are equally unreliable.

But Peace was a man of exceptional qualifications. He was steeped up to the very lips in crime, and we shall find it difficult to find a parallel to him either in this or any other country.

Some time since America furnished us with an example of a hardened offender, who in some respects resembled the hero of this work.

The man to whom we allude was twenty-one years a convict, and he is thus described by an American journalist:—

"The attention of many passers-by upon Main-street, in this city, on Tuesday afternoon, says the Jackson (Mich.) *Citizen*, of Dec. 8, was attracted by the somewhat striking appearance of an old man, of slight, wiry frame, but bent by age and toil; dressed neatly, but in plain, coarse garments, that had evidently been selected at random from a miscellaneous collection, and whose actions were rendered noticeable by that vague uncertainty and indecision so characteristic of those who have for many long years been isolated from the world within the walls of a penitentiary.

"As the old man wandered along, keenly observant of every passing object, scanning the features of hurrying pedestrians with a scrutinising gaze, as if in search of one familiar face—anon lifting his head to look upon the bright blue sky above him, and then turning with an interest almost childish in its eagerness, to the contemplation of some trivial scene or object upon which the busy, bustling throng would scarce bestow a passing glance, as he moved slowly along with his withered hand drawing the scanty coat more closely about his shoulders, and yet with an expression of happiness lighting up his countenance, which told that he was oblivious to age and poverty and cold—there were many who turned to look after him as he passed, and wonder who he was and what his history.

"Few they were, however, who knew that the old man was none less than Silas Doty—'Old Sile Doty,' as he is best known to the public—whose startling exploits as a daring, adroit, and skilful horse-thief, burglar, and gaol-breaker were once celebrated throughout the entire country.

"Twenty years, nine months, and twenty-six days of this singular man's life have been passed in hard labour within the massive walls of the State prison in this city, and Tuesday his third term of imprisonment expired, and he came forth into the world once more, a free man.

"Silas Doty was born at St. Albans, Vt., on the 30th of May, 1800, and is therefore over seventy years of age, although his appearance would not indicate him to be a person of over fifty-five. He is a small, wiry-built man, about five feet seven inches in height, and probably weighing about 130 pounds, but still evidently possessed of unusual muscular power—quick and active as a cat, and with a mind evidently vigorous and unimpaired by his long retirement from the world.

"'Old Sile's' personal appearance is rather pre-possessing than otherwise, and when we look upon his pleasant, good-natured face, and observe the merry twinkle in his eye, we find it rather difficult to reconcile him with the reckless, dare-devil horse-thief of our imagination, conjured up by the thrilling tales related to us in our juvenile days.

"'Old Sile' has a very keen appreciation of humour; he dearly loves a joke, and never better than when the laugh is at his own expense.

"He is quite free to relate the experiences and vicissitudes which he has passed through, and the history of them would fill a volume, surpassing in thrilling interest, romantic situations, and striking events, many a work of fiction.

"The earlier years of Doty's life were passed in the State of New York, and were not marked by anything of unusual interest or more than ordinary occurrence. He was brought up upon a farm, and followed agricultural pursuits for a long time after his removal to Lenawee county, in this State.

"He was known among his neighbours as a quiet, inoffensive, good-natured man, possessed of great activity and strength, which rendered him quite a local celebrity as a chopper, mower, &c.

"It was said at one time that he was the 'champion cradler' of the State—certainly of that section in which he resided. He was a man who was not (nor ever had been) addicted to the use of intoxicating liquor and tobacco; but while he was possessed of very many excellent traits, it was pretty generally understood that he didn't have a fine appreciation of the rightful title of personal property, and was prone to convert to his own use any article which he might stand in need of, even though the ownership vested in some other party.

"Yet it must be acknowledged that there were some good points about 'Old Sile's' stealing. He was a philanthropic thief; he would steal from his richer neighbours to aid those in destitute circumstances.

"In fact, there was something about his thefts akin to Claud Duval, Dick Turpin, and those other English knights of the road, whose exploits are handed down to posterity, through the medium of yellow-covered historical works of doubtful moral tendency.

"If one of Mr. Doty's poor neighbours came over to his house and wanted to borrow a log chain, Sile would inform him that he would have one for him the next day, and he would; while some other one of his neighbours would be one log chain short.

"The first charge upon which he was arrested was that of horse-stealing in Lenawee county, in the latter part of 1841. He broke gaol soon after his arrest, but was recaptured and sentenced to the State prison for a term of two years, entering that institution for the first time April 9, 1842. Here he served his full term, and soon after his discharge went to New Orleans, where he engaged as body servant to Gen. Scott, at a salary of 45 dol. per month in gold. He went with that officer to Mexico, and stole Santa Anna's army into a state of destitution wherever he went.

"A great variety of adventures, some of them of decided interest, were sustained by Doty while in Mexico, where he continued filling various positions as cook, waggon-driver, body-servant, &c., until the end of the war, when he returned to this State.

"For a little over seven years it is a statistical fact that he kept out of prison, but he good-humouredly excuses this off by the plea of absence from the State during the most of that time.

"Several times Doty was arrested, broke gaol, and escaped conviction in various ways. One of these cases was one of particular interest.

"Being arrested in the winter of 1850 on a charge of horse-stealing, he was confined in several gaols, but persisted in breaking right out again with such unceasing regularity that he was finally locked up in the Angola, Ind., gaol for safe keeping.

"These quarters, however, did not suit him, and although he was heavily ironed and carefully watched, he soon succeeded in effecting his escape by cutting the bar of his cell window with a small saw which he had manufactured out of the blade of an old case knife.

"At the time of his escape his ankles were fettered with irons weighing thirty-five pounds, but he succeeded in hobbling to the barn of the prosecuting attorney of the county, who lived near the gaol, and appropriated that functionary's horse.

"A short distance from Angola he broke open a blacksmith's shop, and procured therefrom a cold chisel and hammer, which he took with him to the woods and tried ineffectually to free himself from his fetters.

"Failing in this, he remounted and rode a distance of over thirty miles, when he left the horse and stole a fresh one, riding that for a considerable distance, and then abandoned it for another. In this way, and by dint of riding nights, and keeping in unfrequented roads and in the woods, he succeeded in reaching his former residence in Hillsdale county.

"Here, during the night, he went to the house of friends, and by them was accompanied into the woods, and while one held a tallow candle, another succeeded in striking the irons from Doty's ankles.

"Being thus freed from his annoying incumbrance, he proceeded to pick out another horse (although Sile strenuously insists to this day that this animal was his own property), and started for Detroit, intending to cross into Canada, and there dispose of the steed, but upon arriving at Detroit, to his disappointment, he found that the river was but partially frozen, and that a crossing was impracticable.

"He therefore turned his horse's head in the direction of Port Huron, intending to make his way into Canada from that point. Upon arriving at Port Huron, the attention of the officers there was attracted by the jaded, travel-worn appearance of both horse and rider, and Doty was arrested upon suspicion of having stolen the animal.

"This arrest, after all his struggles and escapes, and when his destination was so close at hand, was extremely discouraging, but Sile Doty was a man of iron will and indomitable purpose, and proved himself equal to the emergency.

"He was taken for safe keeping to one of the upper rooms of a hotel, and his hands secured with handcuffs, separated from each other by a heavy iron bar about twelve inches in length, which consequently kept his hands that distance apart. Of course Doty's first move, when left alone, was to seek for some means of escape.

"He found with a proper tool he could unscrew the lock upon the door. He had nothing in his possession but an old spear, but he broke all the points from that in unavailing efforts to unfasten the lock.

"Soon after this the sheriff came to his room, and consented to take Doty down to the stable to look at 'his' horse.

"While in the stable Doty espied a mason's trowel lying upon a box near him, and succeeded in slipping it unobserved into his side coat-pocket, and upon his returning to his room secreted it in the straw mattress of his bed.

"Feigning illness, Doty disrobed with the exception of his shirt, drawers, and socks, which he retained, and prepared for bed, after being handcuffed as before.

"The officers again left the room, but to Doty's dismay they took his clothing with them, and gave him the comforting assurance that at nine o'clock—it was then just dark—an officer would return and remain during the night with him.

"No sooner had the officer reached the door below than Doty was at work at the lock with his trowel.

"Screw after screw fell upon the floor, and the door stood open. Stealthily making his way through the halls, and past the open doors of rooms where persons were sitting, he finally reached a lower floor, and following a rear passage-way, threw open an outer door, and started back almost in utter despair at the prospect before him—the prospect was certainly not an encouraging one.

"About three inches of snow had fallen, and the flakes were still rapidly descending. The situation was not a pleasant one for a man in pursuit of liberty—clad only in a thin shirt and drawers, with light socks —no coat, hat, pants, or boots—heavy irons upon his wrists, and a blank space of unbeaten snow before him to receive his tracks, and to enable the officers to follow him with unerring accuracy; but, as 'Old Sile' expressed it to our reporter, 'a man can never tell what he can do until he makes a trial,' and so he bravely accepted the chances, although they were so fearfully against him.

"Plunging out into the snow and darkness, he ran as rapidly as possible in the direction of a small black-smith's shop, which he remembered to have seen that morning a short distance from the village.

"Here he effected an entrance without much trouble, and fumbling around among the tools, he found a large file, which he screwed into a vice by the aid of his knees, and, alone in the dark, after repeated failures, he succeeded in disengaging his bruised and bleeding wrists from the irons, and once more started out into the stormy night.

"He thought that if he could conceal himself until after the stage passed by, he could then follow the tracks of that vehicle with less fear of detection. Near the roadside was a small marshy spot covered with high reeds, and here the fugitive secreted himself until the stage passed by, when he again took to the road.

"At the first opportunity he broke into a barn and secured a horse, with which he proceeded to Mount Clemens, in Macomb county.

"Here he effected an entrance to a hotel, with the premises of which he was familiar, and helped himself to a complete and comfortable suit of clothing, which he carefully selected from the wardrobes of the various guests with the utmost impartiality, and also procured some slight refreshment from the pantry.

"He then remounted and pursued his journey without interruption to within four miles of Detroit, when he stopped at the house of a friend and left the horse which he had 'borrowed' near Port Huron, with instructions to return it to the owner, which instructions were afterwards fully carried out.

"The indefatigable Doty then proceeded to Detroit, and while there he slipped into the United States Hotel—long since destroyed by fire—and made some necessary additions to his somewhat limited wardrobe.

"From thence it was an easy matter to get into Canada, where for some time he worked at shoe-making, which trade he had learned at the prison; but he soon became involved in a quarrel with his employer, and after thoroughly 'licking' that individual, he came back to this State.

"Several times after his return he narrowly escaped arrest, and became the recognised leader of a gang of thieves who infested the southern parts of the State.

"Soon afterwards he and several of his party were arrested for robbing the waggon of a Jew pedlar from Detroit, who was travelling through Hillsdale county.

Doty was convicted upon this charge, and brought up before the venerable Judge Pratt, then of Marshall, for sentence.

"Nearly everyone has read or heard the story of how Judge Pratt, who was a man of very brusque manner, commanded the prisoner to stand up.

"'Sile Doty,' said the judge, 'how old are you?'

"'Fifty-three,' responded Doty.

"'The allotted age of man,' said the judge, 'is three score years and ten; beyond that this court has no jurisdiction, and therefore sentence you to confinement at hard labour, in the State prison at Jackson, for a term of seventeen years.'

"So, on the 18th day of April, 1851, 'Old Sile' donned the striped suit of a convict for a second time, and served for fifteen years five months and twenty-six days, when, having gained several months 'good time,' he was discharged.

"'Old Sile' then went to Coldwater, in Branch county, but in a few months he was again arrested on a charge of horse-stealing, and upon the 27th of July, 1867, commenced a third term at the prison, having been sentenced for four years.

"Having, by meritorious conduct, gained about eight months 'good time,' he was discharged on Tuesday morning for the third, and, it is to be hoped, for the last time.

"There are scores of incidents in relation to 'Old Sile' that might be related, and would be of public interest, but space forbids their enumeration.

"Mr. Doty left for Coldwater, Branch county, yesterday morning, and intended to reside with his children in that place, and to follow his trade of shoe-making. May success attend him, and may the world deal gently with one who has suffered this severe punishment for his misdeeds.

"Almost twenty-one years of this man's life were spent within those prison walls, and now, an old grey-headed man whose days are almost numbered, he goes forth to start anew in the world, and to endeavour to lead an honest life. This case is a most peculiar one.

"'Old Sile' does not appear to be a bad man at heart; indeed, there are many men occupying important positions and moving in the higher walks of society who are more deserving of the convict's stripes than 'Old Sile Doty.'

"It seems to be impossible for him to refrain from the wrongful conversion of property, and it is a grave question with many as to whether he is morally responsible for his acts."

Charles Peace, when he had engaged the cab, told the driver thereof to set him down at the "Elephant and Castle"—he, from prudential motives, not deeming it expedient to be conveyed to his residence in the Evalina-road. It was his practice at all times to make a sort of break in the journey, that he might thereby baffle any attempt on the part of the police and detectives to trace him to his own residence.

Upon arriving at the "Elephant and Castle" he alighted, and took the cabman in front of the bar, where he stood a friendly glass. Drivers of cabs, as a rule, have a weakness for hot rum and water, and the one in question was not an exception—he elected to have a small modicum of that inspiring beverage; and after it had been consumed Peace paid the fare and discharged the knight of the whip. He remained in the house of public accommodation for some time after the departure of the cabman, and regarded the persons there assembled with a searching glance.

He could not see anyone whom he suspected to be an officer of the law, and concluded that no one was on his trail; but he was duly impressed with the fact of having had a narrow escape—indeed, the number of chances he had of being detected at this period of his career would, if they were all chronicled, appear to be more like a romance than an actual reality. But it is our purpose to sketch the most noticeable and leading events in his lawless and chequered career, and these will, of necessity, occupy sufficient space without entering into every minute detail.

Fortune had favoured him this time, as she had done on many other occasions.

He had succeeded in getting away from the Jew's house, but he was greatly troubled when he thought of Bandy-legged Bill, whom he had missed sight of soon after his entrance into Mr. Simmonds' respectable establishment.

"What had become of him?" was the question he asked himself when in front of the bar of the "Elephant and Castle."

"Had he been captured; and if so, what followed?"

He had unlimited faith in Bill's integrity. As far as he was concerned he was quite certain that the gipsy would never "peach" or turn approver. Still it was an ugly fact to reflect upon, that he had under his charge a mass of stolen goods, which, if discovered, might lead to his (Peace's) detection.

This thought was by no means a pleasant one, and the more he reflected, the more seriously concerned did Peace become.

He was uncertain as to his mode of action, and felt a little reluctant to return home. He, therefore, went into the parlour of the establishment and read the paper, without taking any notice of the few persons who happened to be there at the time.

After this he hailed an omnibus, and made the best of his way to Peckham.

His two female companions saw that he was a little out of sorts, and when this was the case they did not pester him with any extraneous questions.

He was not a nice sort of man to deal with when put out, and he would not have hesitated to inflict personal chastisement on either of them, if they aggravated him.

They knew this perfectly well, and had the discretion to abstain from making any unnecessary observations.

But Peace was ill at ease, and as the evening drew on he put on his hat, and sallied forth for a walk in the neighbourhood.

He never had been what is termed a "public-house man," and only had recourse to houses of that description either when plying his vocation as a violin player, or from necessity.

It is, however, a fact established beyond all controversy that he was not addicted to habits of intemperance. It was while strolling in the neighbourhood that he discovered, much to his delight, the well-known form of "Bandy-legged Bill."

Nothing could be more propitious, for he wished to see the gipsy, beyond all other persons in the world, at that particular time.

As he caught sight of him his features were irradiated with a smile.

"Lord send I may live!" cried that worthy; "but this 'ere is a blessed sight."

"What do you mean?" inquired Peace.

"What? Why to see you safe and sound. So you've managed to dodge them, Charlie, eh?"

"Yes; and you?"

"Well, you see, I thought it wasn't of no manner of use my stopping outside that cursed crib. I wasn't

either of use or ornament, and so, thought I to myself, I shall only be making matters worse by hanging about, 'cause you see I had the stuff in the cart."

"Quite right; it would have been madness to have remained there. So you hooked it, I suppose?"

"I did so. Don't think I deserted you in the time of need; it wasn't no fault of mine."

"You did the best you could under the circumstances. Don't imagine for a moment that I blame you."

"S'help my taters, but I have been in muck and no mistake. Didn't know how it fared with you, and I was in consequence knocked clean silly. Couldn't tell what to be up to."

"What did you do, then?"

"Drove off as fast as I could, and got clean out of the neighbourhood. What would you have had me do?"

"Just what you have, old stick-in-the-mud. And how about the baskets?"

"Ah, that's where it is. That was what cornered me. I thought it best anyhow to take a circumbendebus route, so I had a pretty little drive in the country, all through the buttercups and daisies; but, Lord bless you, Charlie, I didn't enjoy the bootiful scenery, for I was thinking all the while of the mess you had got into, and thinking at the same time what chance you had of getting out of it. So, you see, it wasn't at all a pleasant ride I had—far from it. Howsomever, I needn't ask now how you got on, for you are here, and I'm jolly glad to see you."

"I had a narrow squeak for it, but I pulled through."

"I sed as how you would—blessed if I didn't. You're a stunner, and I had that confidence in you that I felt sartin sure you wouldn't let em cop you, but I warnt sure 'bout old Simmonds. How did he behave?"

"Right as the mail. He turned out a trump card."

"I'm glad to hear it, precious glad."

"Well, and after you drove in the country? What then?"

"Why, I says, says I, this is a bit of a fix. 'Cause, you see, in a manner of speaking, I didn't know very well how to get shut of the stuff."

"Why didn't you take the whole lot to Isaac?"

"What, at that time, when the detectives were on the scent? No, no, Charles, Bill knew a trick worth two of that body; lord bless you, the chances were that they'd visit the houses of every Jew 'fence' in the neighbourhood. Don't you see that, old man?"

"That is true enough. So you did not venture to try an' get rid of the things—so much the better. What did you do after all then?"

"I didn't know what to be up to—didn't know a blessed cove as I could trust at the east end of the town, so after a thinkin' an' thinkin', till my head ached, all of a sudden it occurred to me to make for what you may call the fashionable quarters in London."

"What do you call the fashionable quarters?"

"Why, the west end, in course."

"Oh, I see."

"It occurred to me that the best place for me to make for would be Laura Stanbridge's. She's fair and square enough."

"Oh, Lorrie's all right; no fear of her peaching."

"So I, after I had considered the matter over for some little time, I just brought the mare gently round, turning her head in an opposite direction to the one in which she had been going before, and after going down the green lanes, the high roads and by roads, and finally the streets of London, I found myself at Laura Stanbridge's establishment. So I up and told her what had happened, and she seemed greatly concerned about you."

"You found her alone, then?"

"No, she was not alone when I first entered."

"Had that conceited puppy with her, 'the dandy,' as we call him, I suppose?"

"Oh, no, not him. She had a tall, handsome-looking chap with her, whom she called 'Tom.' "

"Oh, I know, Tom Gatliffe. He has taken up with her. Well, go on—fire away."

"I haven't much more to tell. Lorrie agreed to take charge of the two hampers and so I left them with her."

"You couldn't have done better, so that's all right. So far all is well. Come, let us return home, for, to say the truth, I only came out in the hope of meeting with you."

The two friends returned to No. 4 in a much more happy frame of mind.

CHAPTER CXXXII.

PEACE HAS A FEW FRIENDS—A MUSICAL AND ANECDOTAL EVENING.

IT was arranged between the two confederates, or companions, in crime, that Charles Peace was not to run any further risk by endeavouring to dispose of the property he had acquired by his various burglaries.

There was nothing he dreaded, at this time, so much as falling in with a Sheffield or Manchester policeman or detective.

To the members of the London constabulary force he was not known, and certainly not one of them had at this time the faintest notion that he was Peace. Had this not been the case he never could have escaped detection for so long a period.

So Bill Rawton, who appeared to be a handy man to many, agreed to undertake the disposal of the goods, which he carried out after his own fashion.

Some of the articles Miss Stanbridge agreed to take at a given price, which was perhaps a trifle more than the Whitechapel or Petticoat-lane receivers were likely to offer.

Bill struck a bargain with Laura, who selected the goods which she said would suit her; the rest of the stock she did not care about, so these the gipsy took to Isaac, who, as usual, offered a ridiculously low price, but Bill, like his friend Peace, was very well used to the ways of the Israelite.

Bill haggled with him for some time, and even went so far as gathering the things together, avowing his intention at the same time of going to another shop. Upon this the Jew made an advance in his price, and after a little more conversation a bargain was struck, and the goods were purchased.

Bandy-legged Bill was perfectly well satisfied with his day's work, and upon returning to the Evalina-road he found Peace in close converse with a strange gentleman whom he had never remembered to have seen before.

He came to the conclusion that the party in question was on friendly terms with our hero, for there was a degree of cordiality between the two which caused him to be assured of this.

Peace withdrew to an adjoining room, where the gipsy handed him over the proceeds.

"You have done well, Bill. Indeed, I don't know what I should do without you," cried Peace. "Nothing could be better. We've made a regular clearance, and I am greatly relieved."

"Who is your friend?" said the gipsy, nodding significantly towards the door of the front parlour.

"He is in the engineering line, and has taken in hand one or two of my inventions. Oh, he is a clever fellow—a most genial, agreeable companion, who thoroughly believes in me. He is coming to-morrow evening to spend a few hours with me, and I shall, therefore, be glad of your company, you old sinner; but don't you launch out or say any more than may be needful; let my guests do the talking. Do you understand?"

"I won't say more than is necessary—trust me for that."

Bill and Peace returned to the front parlour. The gentleman who was its only occupant was introduced by our hero to the gipsy as a Mr. Whittock.

He bowed courteously to Rawton, and then resumed his conversation with Peace.

The conversation was confined chiefly to engineering matters, and a long discussion took place upon Peace's various inventions.

It was evident that Mr. Whittock had a great opinion of Mr. Thompson, whom he frequently complimented Bill listened, but said nothing.

Presently the gentleman rose to take his departure.

"I shall expect to see you to-morrow evening, Whittock," said Peace. "We will have a little music, supper, and a friendly game."

"I shall be most delighted, I'm sure," returned Whittock. "I have a friend stopping with me at present whose acquaintance I am sure you will be pleased to make. He has a son who is a beautiful singer. May I bring them with me?"

"Certainly; nothing would please me better. What is your friend's name?"

"Mr. Harker. He is a capital fellow—knows almost everything, has been in all parts of the world, and is excellent company."

"Bring him, by all means, then," said Peace.

On the following day preparations were made at No. 4 for the reception of guests.

The owner of the establishment was overjoyed at the sale of the articles which he had been for a long time most anxious to get rid of, that he was disposed to make merry over the bargain.

He had ample funds at his disposal, and his friend Whittock was a special favourite with him, albeit the friendship between the two was not of very long standing.

It was arranged that Mrs. Thompson should be the hostess on this occasion—the elder female was to attend to the culinary department, and prepare the supper for the guests.

Peace arrayed himself in his best attire; William Ward was got up in a perfectly satisfactory manner, and Mrs. Thompson was carefully watched, so that she might be in a fit state to receive the company.

Some of Peace's immediate neighbours had been invited; these were the first to arrive, after which Mr. Whittock presented himself. He brought with him Mr. and Master Harker, who were introduced in due form.

"I am greatly pleased to see you, and am glad to have an opportunity of making your acquaintance, sir," said Peace, addressing himself to Mr. Harker. "As a friend of Mr. Whittock, you are specially welcome. Mr. Whittock and I understand each other."

"You will shortly astonish the world with some excellent inventions, I expect," returned Harker. "Well, this is not altogether a country for the inventor; America is the place."

AN EVENING PARTY AT EVALINA-ROAD.

"The people are not so prejudiced in America," continued Harker, "and a man has greater chances. The English, as a rule, are slow to perceive the value of any new power of machinery."

"That is true enough," remarked Peace. "They are rather dense, it must be admitted, and are, as you observe, prejudiced. All we can do is to persevere and hope for the best."

Here he called the attention of his guests to several drafts of machinery he proposed to patent.

Those present were duly impressed with the ability of their host—none of them at this time being at all aware of the character of the man who was so modest, so urbane, and so hospitable.

"I look upon my friend, Thompson, as a remarkably ingenious and clever man," remarked Whittock; "and the more you know of him the more impressed you will be with this fact."

"Ah, no doubt; we all agree upon that," exclaimed several.

The social glass was filled, and the company began to settle themselves down for a pleasant evening, which, to say the truth, was an agreeable one to all.

Peace was in the best of spirits.

He had shaken off the dismal forebodings he had felt some three or four days before, and at the request of a neighbour played a duet with Willie Ward.

This was the commencement of the musical portion of the entertainment.

A violin solo followed, after which Mr. Harker said his son gave promise of musical ability, since he had been complimented by the master of the choir to which he belonged. The lad was asked to give a specimen of his vocal powers, when after a little hesitation he sang the following :—

HOPE'S LIFE IS SHINING YET.

'Tis true that time may swiftly pass
    And years as quickly fly,
And every hope that springs to birth
    May wither, fade, and die.

And oh! 'tis true that all our dreams
    May in life's darkness set,
But in the chambers of my soul,
    Hope's life is shining yet.

Thine was not love that could be cooled
    By words or looks of scorn,
Ah, no, it was as pure and deep
    As if of angels born.

Thine was that love which sorrows, storms,
    Nor cruel fate could sever :
It burns on brightly—and it will
    Keep burning on for ever.

To think thee faithless would, indeed,
    Be casting doubts on high—
Would throw a dark suspicious shade
    O'er angels in the sky.

But, oh, within my trusting heart,
    No doubts there are as yet—
The lights of faith and hope are still
    Within its portals set.

The music to which these words were set was simple and plaintive, and well adapted for the voice of a young female or a boy.

The singer had evidently been well trained, for he sang in good time and tune, Peace playing the accompaniment.

Mr. Harker, the lad's father, was greatly pleased at the performance, and passed flattering encomiums on Peace's skill as an accompanist: indeed, it was in every way creditable, and there was a general murmur of applause as the song was brought to a conclusion.

"Your son has got a beautiful voice," said our hero, addressing himself to Mr. Harker. "If he perseveres he'll be a very accomplished vocalist."

"I am glad to hear you say so, Thompson," observed Whittock, "for I know you are a competent judge of these matters."

The conversation was carried on in an animated manner for some little time, after which Peace and Willie Ward played another piece together. Several of the company expressed a wish to hear Mr. Thomp-

son sing. He was in no very good voice, but chanted the following quaint ditty :—

I've been thinking—I've been thinking
    What a world we might possess
Did folks mind their business more,
    And mind their neighbours' less.
For instance, you and I, my friend,
    Are sadly prone to talk
Of matters that concern us not
    And others' follies mock.

I've been thinking if we were
    To mind our own affairs,
That possibly our neighbours might
    Contrive to manage theirs.
We've faults enough at home to mend—
    It may be so of others ;
It would seem strange if it were not
    Since all mankind are brothers.

Oh, would that we had charity
    For every man and woman:
Forgiveness is the mark of those—
    We know " to err is human."
Then let us banish jealousy,
    Let's lift our fallen brother,
And as we journey down life's road
    Do good to one another.

"Excellent—admirable!" cried several voices.

"I call that a fine sentiment," said Mr. Whittock. "I wish men and women would act up to it. There's a great deal too much meddling in this world."

"Yes," said a Mr. Newnham, who was one of Peace's neighbours. "We've quite enough of that sort of thing here in our locality. It's a capital song. I never remember to have heard it before, but I admire it immensely."

Peace glanced at Mrs. Thompson, and made a wry face, at which the company laughed.

Soon after this supper was served, after which a game of whist was proposed, and two sets of partners sat down to cards.

Mr. Harker, who was not included in either of the parties of players, sat down by the chimney-corner, and entered into a lively discourse with some of those who were disengaged.

He was a man who had at his disposal a whole fund of anecdote, and was therefore a great acquisition to the visitors.

He gave a running commentary on the great detective case, which was the general topic of conversation at this time, and cited instances of the mistakes made by the Scotland-yard officials.

"As far as mistakes are concerned," said Harker, "their name is legion, and I, for one, should be very careful in delivering a verdict without the clearest and most unmistakable evidence, for, from my own personal experience, I am able to testify as to the unreliability of suspicious circumstances, which may, by the merest accident, be brought to bear upon a man."

"There is no doubt about that, sir," said Peace; "mistakes are frequent enough."

"Well," observed Harker, "as I am only a looker-on now, and am not engaged to play, I'll, with your permission, first narrate to you what I may term a 'Romance of a Counting-house.' The whole of the incidents came under my immediate knowledge. In short, I was the leading actor in as pretty a little drama as ever man had the misfortune to play in."

"I shall be most delighted to hear it," said Peace, "and so will all our friends, I'm sure.

"It came about in this way. I had married and was going to make my fortune, and therefore (having that laudable end in view) left a good situation in Yorkshire to settle down in Liverpool as a merchant 'on my own account,' and commence to make it without delay. I had not much capital, and so I resolved to economise at first.

"In course of time I imagined the tidy brougham and the country house across the Mersey would certainly come; and one serene September evening, many years ago, I was walking up and down St. George's landing-stage, building castles in the air, wondering whether rents were high at New Brighton, and whether Kate would prefer a pony phaeton to a brougham.

"I am not sorry to add that I still reside in a modest house up Edge-hill way, and that I come to business as Cæsar went to Rome, according to Joe Miller, *summa diligentia*, on the top of an omnibus.

"I was waiting for Mr. Moses Moss to return at eight p.m. to his office in a street hard by—call it Mersey-street—and for the reason that Moses Moss had a furnished place to let which his advertisement called 'two spacious counting-rooms' — goodness knows, I never counted much in the shape of coin; and I did not like the situation; nor the narrow, dark staircase; nor the look of the boy of Hebrew extraction who howled 'Cub id,' when I knocked, and told me 'Mr. Boses would be in at eight o'clock;' but twenty pounds a year was very cheap, so I told my young friend I would call at that time, and look at the 'counting-room.'

"How well I remember that night! The ferry-boats from the Cheshire shore gliding along with their lights twinkling like glow-worms, the vast hull of the 'Great Eastern' just visible in the Sloyne, the squared yards and all-a-taut look of a seventy-four of the old school, showing black and distinct against the daffodil sky, and the lap of the swell against the under timber of the stage—I was inclined to be sentimental; but Mr. Moses Moss claimed my attention, and once more I entered his office and found him awaiting me. He was a little, fat, good-tempered Jew, who spoke decent English, and who, I afterwards found out, was constantly affirming, in season and out of season, that he was no descendant of Abraham.

"'Hillo, Brunton!' he cried, jumping from the chair. 'My lad told me you'd been here. Where have you been these two months and more? Look here, old fellow, I've advertised your place; but you can have it on the old terms.'

"'Some mistake, sir, I believe,' and I handed him a card bearing the inscription, 'Charles Harker.'

"He took it and held it to the gaslight, looked at the back, considered it endways, and pondered over it upside down. Then taking the candle his clerk had brought, he held it close to my face.

"'If you are not disposed to proceed to business, I will bid you good-night,' said I, greatly annoyed at his manner.'

"'It's him, and it ain't him,'' he said aloud. 'Carl could never look a man in the face as this one does. And yet I don't see my way through the features.'

"'There's no necessity for you to trouble yourself about my features!' I exclaimed, opening the door— 'good night.'

"'Stop, stop, my dear sir! and don't be offended. It was all a mistake. All Isaac's mistake, upon my honour.'

"'All a mistake,' echoed young Isaac.

"My curiosity was excited, and, besides, I really wanted the offices; and I therefore allowed myself to be persuaded into mounting the narrow staircase, until we faced a door bearing the name of Brunton on it in white letters, and having the two upper panels glazed,

more, I should imagine, to supply light to the staircase than for admission of light to the office.

"Mr. Moss produced a key, and turning to me with a good-natured smile, said: 'I'd have sworn you were Brunton five minutes ago, but I'm sure now that I was wrong. Carl always swore when he came upstairs, and you haven't. It's Brunton's face all but the eyes, and I'd swear to the eyes anywhere. That is, to the twinkle of 'em, you know.'

"And he unlocked the door and invited me within.

"Walking to the table on which he had placed the light, I took a chair and produced my pocket-book.

"'Before we go further, Mr. Moss, let us quite understand each other, I have no wish to derive any benefits from any virtues Mr. Brunton may possess; and I am going to convince you that I am what I represent myself to be. Be good enough to read that letter.'

"It was from a merchant in the North, only received that morning, and mentioned circumstances which were sufficient to settle any doubts as to my identity.

"Mr. Moss read it, folded it up briskly, and presented it to me with a bow.

"'Sir, I apologise. I confess that up to this moment I fancied it was Carl; but what puzzled me was, that such a surly fellow should take to larking and playing the fool. You are very much like my last tenant, sir, that is all.'

"'Very well; now that matter is settled, let us look at the rooms.'

"The lighted gas showed me a large one, and very barely furnished. There was a large leather-covered table with a desk on it, four chairs, an inkstand, and a partially filled waste-paper basket, and that was all.

"'Rather meagre, Mr Moss.'

"'Now, my dear sir, what more could you want? Would you like a safe? I've got one to spare downstairs, and you shall have it, and a new mat for your feet—I hate haggling.'

"'Let me see the other room, please.'

"It was one which a person sitting at the table would have right opposite to him, and it had no door.

"'It was a clerk's office,' Mr. Moss said, 'and you wanted your eye on such chaps.' I suggested that the principal might sometimes want privacy, whereupon he said 'he had the door downstairs, and it should be hung at once if I wished it.' But having no intention of engaging a clerk at present, I told him it was of no consequence.

"The room was about half the size of the outer one, and contained a desk and stool. There was a large closet for coals and such like matters, and a good allowance of dust and cobwebs all over.

"'I'll have it cleaned up to-morrow,' said Mr. Moss. 'It looks beautiful when clean, and you will find the desk to be real Spanish mahogany.'

"They would suit me well enough, and I told Mr. Moss so; paid him a quarter's rent in advance, and rose to depart.

"'Oh, by the way, Mr. Moss,' I exclaimed, a sudden thought striking me; 'I will send a man to paint my name on the wall downstairs.'

"'Very good, sir. I would do it at once if I were you. Carl was a loose fish, and if you delayed it until you got here, you might be annoyed.'

"'How so? What was he?'

"'Take a cigar first, Mr. Harker, you'll find no better in Liverpool. Lord! how like him you do look when I don't see your eyes!'

"'And yet I have not been thought to resemble a loose fish before, Mr. Moss.'

" ' I didn't mean that. Have you never seen an ugly person resemble a very handsome one ? I have many a time. Well, about Carl. He was here about two years, and call me a Jew if I could reckon him up. He used to come here about noon and work up to eight or nine o'clock at night ; but what business he worked at I could never find out. I know he had a big ledger, and two or three such books ; but a big ledger won't make a business any more than a big carpet bag will, and he always carried one. He would come and smoke a cigar with me now and then; but I never came up here all that time, and he kept his door locked. He always seemed to be expecting a blow, did poor Carl ; more like a rat in a corner than anything else, poor beggar. Well, sir, one morning I found the key on my mat, and found the place just as you see it, and have never seen Carl since. One or two queer-looking men have inquired for him, and asked if he was coming back, and I said most likely he would, and likely enough he will.' "

" ' Not at all an interesting story,' I thought, and felt inclined to yawn in Mr. Moss's face ; but I thanked him for his information, and promised to take possession in three days, which I spent in presenting my letters of introduction, and making other arrangements for the prosecution of my plans.

" At length the eventful day arrived, and I stood in my own office, with my name emblazoned on the door and passage wall. I was waiting for a friend to call on me (who, by the way, had promised to put me in the way of doing some business that very day), and felt impatient for his arrival in consequence.

" The office was clean and tidy, and the floors had been well scrubbed.

" Why hadn't they emptied the waste-paper basket of all that lumber ?

" The office-keeper had lighted a fire, and I took up the basket to perform the operation myself ; but from some cause or other I placed it on the table and began idly to burn the scraps one by one.

" I had nearly disposed of them all when a scrap attracted my attention, and I read it. It was torn so as to leave a few words intact, and it ran thus—

" ' Louise has given your description, and you may rely on our finding you. Forward the plates at once, or——'

" Then another piece was mysterious, apparently a plan of some place or other.

" What did this mean ?

" But I had no time to consider, for my friend entered, and, putting the two pieces of paper in my drawer, I emptied the basket in the fire, and went out with him to do a good day's work.

" Returning late in the evening, I relit the fire, and addressed myself to the writing of two important letters to be posted by half-past eleven that night, in order to be in time for the Cunard steamer, which sailed early in the morning ; and then it was that the black darkness of the doorless room opposite me began to trouble me most.

" It had troubled me before, but on this night it troubled me tenfold. From childhood I have been imaginative, and knowing this, I stirred the fire, called myself a fool, and went on with my letter ; but not for long. My eyes wandered to the black darkness of the doorway, and I began to ransack my memory for statistics of men who could tell by some occult power if any one were hidden in the room they entered ; and I laughed aloud when I remembered that I had read of one sensitive gentleman who by this same occult

power had found that a surgeon's skeleton was in the closet behind him.

" I own I dislike being in the dark, but I will do myself the justice to say that I have resolution enough to overcome the dislike.

" Therefore I proposed to myself to very quietly walk into the dark room which troubled me, and (without a light) look out of the windows, and slowly return."

" I shouldn't have liked the office myself," ejaculated Peace. " You may well call it a romance."

" As for the matter of that, I confess it sounds like one," returned Mr. Harker, " and I assure you every word I am saying is strictly correct. Romance and reality are much more intimately interwoven together than people generally suppose."

" You are quite right there, sir," cried one of the cardplayers, who had been listening so attentively to the narrative that he revoked.

Mr. Harker continued—

" I went. The very first step beyond the threshold dispelled my fears. I could see the glimmer of the stars through the glass, hear the rattle of the cabs outside. Why, it was quite a cheerful place, after all.

" Ha ! there was a shuffling noise there by the closet ! and then my fears returned and overpowered me. I strove to walk out like a tragedy hero ; but my pace quickened as I neared the door and heard the shuffling noise close to me. The next moment a powerful hand was at my throat, and I lay helpless on the floor with the cold muzzle of a pistol to my head.

" I was bound, and dragged into the outer office, thrust into my chair, and confronted by two quiet-looking men, one of whom laid his revolver on the table, saying at the same time, with an ugly sneer—

" ' So, Brunton, we have caught you at last.'

" The speaker was a mild, intelligent looking man of about thirty-five. In a proper dress he would have looked like a High Church clergyman.

" His companion was evidently a foreigner, and I imagine a German.

" He was about fifty years of age, and wore spectacles, and a profusion of beard and whiskers covered more than half his face ; but he had a winning smile and good teeth, which he often took an opportunity to show.

" ' We have found you at last.'

" I am thankful to say that I am not nervous when I see danger, and I boldly replied—

" ' My name is Harker, and not Brunton ; Mr. Moss, the landlord of these premises, has noticed my resemblance to his late tenant, and is satisfied that I am not the same. Depend upon it that I shall make you repent this outrage.'

" I tried to rise to call for help from the street, but the pistol was cocked and pointed at me, and there was that in the man's face which cautioned me against rashness in my helpless position.

" ' Well, I never,' cried Whittock. ' Tha twas a nice pickle to be in.'

" ' It was,' observed Harker.

" ' I will sit down,' I replied, ' and hear what you have to say ; but if I choose to do it, I shall do my best to raise an alarm in spite of your revolver.'

" ' Vel spoke, Carl,' said the foreigner ; ' Louise always says he's a plucky one.'

" ' Now, then, Brunton,' whispered the other, ' let us have no nonsense. We have not met before, it is true, but Louie has so well described you, that putting another name on your door was simply idiotic. Besides, one of our friends has watched for your return, and we communicated with him as soon as we landed. Go free if you like, but we will have the plates.'

"'Dat's de matter vid us,' echoed the German; 've vill have de plates.'

"'I know nothing of any plates,' I cried, 'nor of Louise, nor of you. All I know is that you will see the inside of a prison very shortly.'

"'And you think you can throw us, throw me over in this way? Dou you think you deal with children?'

"'I think I deal with a burglar. Most certainly with a rascal of some sort or other.'

"Here my two friends held a whispered conference. Then he of the revolver turned sharply towards me.

"'Will you marry Louise? Will you give up the plates and marry my sister?'

"'She lofe you like old boots,' added the German; and from which I opine that he prided himself on a knowledge of English idiom.

"In spite of my serious position I was getting thoroughly amused.

"The dark doorway held unknown terrors to my excited imagination; but two commonplace fellows who had made a mistake caused a feeling of merriment, even in spite of the revolver.

"'I am sorry I cannot oblige you,' I replied. 'I am flattered by the lady's preference, but having one wife already, I fear I must decline taking a second; and as for the plates, please explain what you mean.'

"The answer to this flippant speech was a blow on the face, which immediately sent the blood streaming on the floor.

"'You'll remember insulting the sister of Louis Orloff! Here, baron, let us gag him, and search; he will be raising an alarm presently.'

"They thrust a piece of rope between my teeth, compressing my windpipe to make me open my mouth; and there I sat helpless, whilst they turned out the contents of my desk and drawers, not forgetting my cash box, which was opened by a key taken from my vest pocket, and the contents appropriated.

"Knowing that the two scraps of paper I had found in the waste-paper basket and placed in my drawer must have reference to their visit, I watched very anxiously when they opened it.

"But they escaped notice, and I felt that I had got some clue to the mystery, even if these men escaped; and I had quite determined that they should not escape, for I was insecurely bound, and had been working hard to get my right hand free, and, thanks to having a very narrow one, I now found myself able to slip it through the loop which encircled the wrist; but I 'bided my time,' for I saw that a false move might bring a bullet through my head.

"'De plates is in ze oder room, Carl Brunton, mon ami,' said the baron, smiling, and patting my shoulder. 'Vy not say? Vy shoot we you? You do dem so well, ve no get any like dem. And you use dem yourself, and den, Ach Gott, you upset de cart of de apple.'

"'Yes,' I thought, 'and it's odd to me if I don't upset your cart of de apple before long.'

"'Iu dere; in back room?' asked the Baron, with another amiable smile.

"I said 'yes,' with my eyes.

"'See now, my Louis, you were too rough. You into him pitch like dam. So see him amiable.' Then to me:—

"'And you will marry Louise, who lofe you like old boots?'"

"My other hand was free now. I tried to speak, and implored with my eyes for the gag to be removed.

"The baron removed it, and while doing so I resolved on a plan of operation.

"'You will marry Louise, and give us the plates?'

"'I will give you every satisfaction.'

"'That is business,' said Louis Orloff, coming forward. 'First the plates; then you return with us to New York, and keep your promise to Louise. Why give us the trouble? I tell you frankly that the expense will be deducted from your share, and that you will be strictly watched in future. I should have cut your throat but for my promise to Louise. Now, where are the plates?'

"'Look in the closet in the next room, rake out the coals and take what you find.'

"'Good! Come, baron.'

"And they left me to operate on the coals. Springing up, I seized the revolver, darted to the door, and in a moment had locked them in.

"But my triumph was of short duration, for Orloff was on the other side like lightning, the rotten woodwork torn out under his vigorous wrench, and his hand was on my throat before I could grope my way to the stairs.

"Then I knew that life depended on the struggle, and I fought like one possessed, for the revolver. The baron came to his friend's help; but I found time and opportunity to send him reeling to the ground.

"Orloff was the weaker man, but he outdid me in skill, and a dextrous feint threw me off my guard, leaving the revolver in his hand.

"Purple with passion, he fired instantly, and I felt a sharp sting in the left shoulder; and then all earthly things seemed to be fading away, and a world beyond opening to view.

"When I recovered I found myself laid on a mattress on the office table, and my wife tearfully bending over me. There was a calm-faced surgeon too, who showed me the ball he had extracted, and told me to cheer up, for I should be better in a few days, for no harm was done.

"Mr. Moss was there too, and came to my bedside —I mean my table-side—and whispered how he had been called up by the police, who, hearing a pistol-shot, had come upstairs and arrested Orloff and the baron, and finding me on the ground bleeding, had sent for a surgeon and my wife, having found my private address from a letter in my pocket.

"I was only faint from loss of blood; the bullet did little damage, and I preferred getting up, and then gave an account of the evening's adventure, not noticing at the time that a tall inspector of police was in the room.

"'Will you kindly show me those pieces of paper?' he said, advancing. 'I have the men in Mr. Moss's office; but beyond the assault on you, I have no evidence against them; but I know them well.'

"I produced them, and the inspector fastened on the one which seemed to be a plan; then looking around, he said:

"'This is a plan of your office.'

"'Call me a Jew if it aint!' exclaimed Mr. Moss, taking it.

"'Yes, it is certainly a plan of your office. See, here is the doorway, and there comes the other room. Then there is a cross against the fireplace in this room, on what I judge from the lines to mean the fourth board from the hearthstone, and another cross against the sixth from the hearthstone in the other room. Get a crowbar, Mr. Moss.'

"'There's one downstairs.'

"I do believe that if you'd asked for a crocodile, he'd have got one 'downstairs.'

"Crowbar and a policeman to wield it were soon procured, and then the mystery was unravelled.

"Close to where I sat, were unearthed several copper-plates for the forging of Russian rouble notes of various amounts; and in the back room, under the flooring, were found several hundreds of well-executed forgeries carefully soldered up in a tin case, together with correspondence implicating Orloff and the baron.

"It appeared that Brunton was engaged by a New York gang to engrave the plates, and that he had never seen his employers, the agent between them being the Louise before mentioned, whose fair hand I had been compelled to decline.

"Brunton had evidently become frightened, and had fled.

"He was no traitor, or he would have decamped with the plates.

"Perhaps the dread of having to espouse Louise may have had something to do with his flight.

"She was a very handsome woman, if I may judge from a photograph of her found in the tin case, but looked like one accustomed to rule, and who would not hesitate to administer wholesome correction to her spouse.

"Assisted into a carriage which was waiting, I had the satisfaction of seeing the baron and Orloff brought down in handcuffs, the baron regarding me with a sweet smile, and Orloff scowling on me like a fiend. I did not prosecute, for they were so well known to the police as forgers that there was evidence enough for the Russian Embassy to procure a conviction and a sentence of ten years' penal servitude; and in due time I recovered, and dismissed the matter from my mind.

"But I had not heard the last of it. About twelve months after the trial and condemnation of the baron and his friend, there came one night a timid knock at my office door, and my clerk (for I had such a luxury then) ushered in what, at first sight, seemed to be a moving bundle of rags.

"Strictly speaking, the bundle of rags insisted on seeing me, and ushered itself in, in spite of all remonstrances.

"It came and stood before me, and resolved itself into the semblance of a man—a man lean, haggard, sunken-eyed, ragged, and dirty, but with a face something like my own; and without putting a question I knew that I stood face to face with Carl Brunton, and I addressed the rags by that name.

"'I took that name,' the poor shivering thing replied, 'but my name is—but no matter. May I speak to you?'"

"'Yes, go on.'

"'Will you give me some drink first? I have had none to-day, and feel delirium tremens coming on. Oh, how cold it is, and how I shiver!'

"I sent the clerk for some brandy, which he took raw, and with shaking hand held out the glass for more.

"I imagine it is Mr. Moss you want to see, is it not? If so, you will find him to-morrow, at ten o'clock.'

"'No, no, you, I want—I—I am very poor, very poor. Will you give me sixpence?'

"I gave him half a crown.

"'Now, what can I do for you?'

"'I—left some property here when I went away. You won't refuse to give it up? I seem poor, but am rich—ah! so rich!—and I will pay you well.'

"'You mean the forged rouble notes and the plate you engraved them from?'

"'Ah! Who told you that? Then you have found them and used them? I ran away from them, and wished to lead a better life, but they drew me back; and now you have robbed me, and I shall starve.'

"I explained to the poor wretch what had become of his possessions, and how they were found, and inquired if he had not heard of the fate of his accomplices.

"'No; I have been wandering about the country, living in hospitals, because they hunt me down from place to place. They will kill me as they did the Posen Jew and the engraver at Stockholm, all because they demanded a fair share. They are dogging me to-night; one of them is outside now. Let me see, what did I come here for? Oh, sixpence. Lend me sixpence; I'll give you a hundred pounds for it to-morrow.'

"I made a further donation, and, as the man was evidently in a state of delirium, I told my clerk to fetch a medical man. But before he could execute the order the bundle of rags crept down the narrow stairs, sitting on each step, and wriggling by aid of his hands to the next below, whilst we, unable to pass him, looked on, wondering how it would all end.

"The street gained, he stood upright, and, casting a terrified glance around, fled away into the darkness, and we, following the direction he had taken, learned shortly afterwards that a beggar had thrown himself into the Mersey from St. George's landing-stage, and had sunk to rise no more.

"His body was never found, and I, having had enough of Mersey-street, moved my quarters, much to the regret of Mr. Moss, for, quoth he, 'Two of 'em are at Portland, and another at the bottom of the river—so you may call me a Jew if any one troubles you again.'

"But I went; and the office is still without a tenant, and I shudder when I pass through the street at night, and, looking up, see the two black shining windows, like two great eyes watching me, and fancy I can see a shadowy form in rags pressing his face to the glass, and gibbering and bowing at the busy stream of human life which surges to and fro for ever."

When the narrator had brought his story to a conclusion, there was a dead silence for a brief period. The cardplayers had been so interested that their game had been carried on in a loose, desultory manner, and the whole of Peace's guests were more or less wonderstruck.

"You know how to enchain your hearers' attention, sir," observed our hero.

"What I have been telling you is simply a narrative of facts, and, as I before observed, it proves the truth of the old adage that 'truth is strange—stranger than fiction;' but I have to apologise for so rudely interrupting the game."

"There is no occasion for apologies, sir," said a Peckham tradesman, who formed one of the party, "for the account you have given is one which, I think, all of us would have been sorry to have missed."

"I think we shall all of us agree in that," observed Peace.

"But this is a social evening, and all I desire is to see everyone enjoy themselves."

"You might vary the entertainment with a little music, Mr. Thompson," said Bandy-legged Bill. "After this perhaps some other gentleman will tell us another story."

"I am at your disposal, gentlemen," returned our hero. "If you desire to hear a little music, so be it;

but with your permission I will just put some of my pets through their paces."

Having made this observation, he opened the door of the room, and whistled to his dogs.

Two docile animals came bounding into the apartment; they skipped about, wagged their tails, and demonstrated the greatest possible affection for their master.

Peace played a tune on his violin, and made them dance on their hind legs, and go through a variety of difficult and diverting feats, to the infinite delight of the assembly.

"You have a wonderful power over the brute creation," said Mr. Whittock. "Why, you might pull in a lot of money as a public entertainer."

"It has always been a hobby of mine, sir. I take great delight in teaching those faithful creatures—I say faithful advisedly, for the most fortunate of us will acknowledge that they are more faithful, and I may add less selfish than man."

"It is not very complimentary of you to say so," observed Mrs. Thompson, who was at this time on her best behaviour.

"You are right, my dear," returned Peace. "It is not complimentary, but our friends will excuse it. Present company is, of course, excepted."

At this there was a roar of laughter, after which Peace and Willie Ward played another duet.

To see our hero at this time it would have been impossible for any one to guess that he was anything else than a genial, good-natured, kind-hearted, old gentleman, who took a delight in making everybody happy and comfortable around him.

The old adage, "that appearances are oftentimes deceptive," was specially applicable in his case, for he would have deceived the Prince of Darkness himself, his power of dissimulation being perfectly marvellous. In the course of conversation he expressed himself in such a gentle unobtrusive way—assumed for the nonce such a moral tone, and reprobated wrong doing so earnestly, and at the same time so naturally, that it would have been impossible for any one who did not know his manner and mode of life, to imagine him to be the hardened, callous, unscrupulous criminal whose nefarious career we have endeavoured to shadow forth.

"Now, gentlemen," cried Peace, after a pause, "make yourselves at home—do just as you like. Whittock, see to your friends, and help them to all they require. Possibly you know more of their habits than I do."

"They are very well able to take care of themselves," said Mr. Whittock. "If they don't have all they want it's their own fault."

One of the personages introduced by Whittock has been already introduced to the reader; the other was a Mr. Corbet, who had been a captain to one of the American steamers.

He was a weather-beaten, self-reliant man, who, albeit mixing with the company, had not as yet spoken a great deal.

His friend, Whittock, however, was anxious to draw him out, for when once Mr. Corbet did let loose the jawing tackle, he went in for a "pelter."

"This old pirate could spin a few yarns if he chose," said Whittock, nodding towards the party to whom he was alluding.

"Anyone can see that," observed one of the company. "Hang it, Jenkins, you've trumped my trick," he added, in a petulant tone, addressing himself to his partner.

"I beg your pardon, I'm sure," returned Jenkins, apologetically. "How very foolish of me to be sure, I don't know what I could have been thinking about."

"Spin us a yarn, Corbet, and stop this wrangling," cried Whittock.

"I aint up to it," said the captain. "Besides, my experience is chiefly confined to foreign parts, as people are apt to observe."

"All the better, sir," said Peace, "all the more interesting. We lead in this country such a monotonous, hum-drum sort of life that there are positively no incidents worth recording."

"I don't know that," observed Corbet. "None of us can pass through life, I expect, without meeting with some strange adventure, without gaining some experience."

"Oh, we gain experience without doubt, Corbet," said Whittock. "It is hardly possible for it to be otherwise."

"Well," said Corbet, "as our friend has given you a little of his own experience, I don't mind following suit. I don't mean with cards, for that's not much in my line, but I'll just give you another narrative of facts."

"Hear, hear. Fire away, cap'en," cried Whittock and one or two others. "Anything to keep the game alive."

"During the milder months of the twelve constituting a year I occupied myself in running a small steamer from Puntsville to B——, carrying the mails, such as they were, freight, and any chance passengers, which, I assure you, were exceedingly scarce.

"These trips were generally of a monotonous character to the crew of the 'Silver Arrow,' consisting of the engineer, myself, and an Ethiopian deck-hand.

"Once, however, something extraordinary out of the general routine of rounding points, making fast to the long, straggling, desolate wooden piers of the intermediate landings, or the thousand and one little nothings, peculiar to the voyage, occurred, which came near resulting in my death, besides putting me to serious inconvenience, and in a not very reputable predicament.

"One bright June afternoon the 'Silver Arrow' backed from her wharfage at B——, sped gallantly down the sunny channel, lined on either side by rows of carved, lettered, gilt dingy sterns of all nations, and soon, with her bright new paint reflecting in her wake, and her streamers flying, was going down the wide river.

"In high good humour was I, for besides an unusual quantity of freight, three passengers had booked themselves for Puntsville, full fare paid, intending, as they remarked, to participate in a hunting expedition in the game-abounding district of the lower river.

"We had proceeded some twenty miles, darkness was beginning to succeed twilight, when giving the wheel in charge of Dick, the deck-hand, I descended to ascertain if all was in readiness for the passengers in their allotted cabins.

"The 'Silver Arrow' was run on stringent bachelor principles, and no charming *femme de chambre* enlivened us by her silvery vocalisation, or by her clever manipulation administered to our comfort.

"After seeing all correct, I went into my own little cabin, and perceiving the mail-bags in the centre of the floor, where I had carelessly thrown them when the post-office messenger had brought them down, I proceeded to place them in a more secure location, when, as I raised the leathern sacks up, the bottom of one gave away, and out in a thick-spreading torrent rolled a mass of letters and packages.

"Dropping on my knees I raked them in, and then examining the bag found that the mischief was occasioned by the receptacle being charged beyond its capacity, the bottom bursting out from the severe pressure of more letters and packages than to my knowledge had ever at any one previous time constituted the Puntsville mail.

"There I was on my knees with an immense pile of mail matters heaped before me; and I was mentally deliberating what to do with the matter, when softly behind me creaked the door, and in a second a strong set of fingers grasped my throat, bending me back to the floor, and the cold, icy muzzle of a pistol pressed fearfully against my temple.

"He who held me thus I recognised as one of the three passengers—a slightly built, extremely muscular, quick-eyed sort of a man. Physically he was a far better man than I, and the position in which he seized me, rendered me perfectly helpless.

"'Ho, ho! my old bird; robbing the mail, eh? Twenty years in the penitentiary!' said he, in a low, clear whisper, with a peculiarly triumphant sparkle in his sharp eyes.

"I tried to speak, but his grasp on my throat prevented me; he pressed harder, and continued in the same cautious undertone:

"'Lie still, my beauty, or out go your thievish cerebrals; however, I'll let go your throat; but if for a fraction of a second you open your lips, I'll let daylight into your aged anatomy, my venerable, but ungodly purloiner,' and he indulged in a moderate laugh at his own quaint style of expression, as keeping his weapon in a straight line with my forehead, he crept toward the door and gently closed it; coming quickly back, he placed the muzzle against my forehead, saying, mockingly—

"'You are a pretty one to be robbing the President's mail at your time of life, you virtuous old sinner!'

"'You infernal villain,' I broke out, however, not very loudly, because at the first movement of my lips he clapped his hand on my throat, and the revolver pressed harder, and now at half cock, a hair breadth's space between me and eternity.

"By some great effort, however, I managed to blurt out in spasmodic whispers, that the mail had burst; had not been robbed, as could be proved by inspection, and that I wanted to ascertain by what authority he came the detective over me in so forcible a manner.

"Laughingly he took from his pocket a scrap of written paper, held it out of reach, but near enough to be legible, whereon was stated that so-and-so was commissioned by so-and-so to investigate the cause of the numerous losses that had recently occurred on the Puntsville mail route, &c.

"'No use palaverin', my renowned skinflint; you've been caught squarely and fairly in the deed, and you're booked certain for Sing Sing, or some other institution conducted on the same charitable system, and you won't get out for a period—no, not at least till you get the Presidential pardon.'

"The affair was growing more strangely serious than I had anticipated, and still I lay on the cabin floor with the contents of the mail-bag strewn over and around me, the detective keeping rigid surveillance over my every movement, however slight.

"Leaning forward, with his foot he pushed the door partially ajar, pursed up his moustached lips, whistled a bar of some current popular music, and directly footsteps sounded without, and soon another one of the passengers entered the cabin.

"Exchanging a significant look with my captor, he looked around the room with a quick glance, and coming close to my head, dropped down suddenly on his knees, and almost before I was aware of it, had inserted a gag in my mouth, and there I lay, speechless.

"Without losing any time, they seized me by neck and heels and plunged me, without the least effort, into the bunk. Then a heavy cloth, deeply saturated with chloroform, was thrown over my face, and after that, if you except for an instant a confused sound of rumbling machinery and a rushing of waters, I remember nothing.

"When I regained my senses all the cabin was dark, my brain was confused and obfusticated. I managed to get out of the bunk, looked out the narrow window, and saw that surging black water and heavy, threatening, driving thunder-clouds were the only things visible.

"The waves were rising fearfully, the huge white-capped, black-bodied monsters rushed against the boat's side with thuds that made every timber rattle; the paddle wheels were idly beating to and fro; the wind shrieked through the chains that held the smokeless stack, and the 'Silver Arrow' rocked enough to throw nine out of ten fresh-water sailors off their feet. A hundred thoughts sprang up.

"Why had the boat stopped? Where were the passengers? Passengers! Oh, now the whole series of events occurred to my remembrance. Perhaps the engineer and the negro had suspected foul play and resisted the rascals, and had been disabled if not murdered.

"With fearful misgivings I groped along the passage, reached the engine-room, and, stepping across the sill, fell over a human body. I knew where the lamps usually were kept, and after great difficulty succeeded in getting one alight.

"On the floor, lying on his face, was the engineer, but on examination I could discover no traces of violent treatment. However, the odour of chloroform pervaded the room, and I was persuaded that that forcible agent had been brought to operate upon other systems besides my own.

"The engineer was stupefied by the combined influences of chloroform and whiskey, for the odour of the latter was nauseously prevalent; but whether the liquor had been imbibed from voluntary self-indulgence, or from forcible application, the individual upon whom the potent influence was now in operation was in no condition to inform me, and I had no means of ascertaining the fact.

"Then I went upon deck, examining every nook for signs of my quondam passengers.

"I entered the pilot-house, and there on the bench, with his huge hands on the spokes of the wheel, sat the negro deck-hand, and a cloth swathed about his head of a faint chloroformic odour told how he had been rendered non-combatant.

"The storm was fearfully violent now; the boat seemed to be drifting rapidly, and rocked so that I experienced great difficulty in going below.

"The engineer seemed to be reviving, and a bucket of cold water dashed over him brought him quickly to his senses.

"With his assistance I pumped the boiler full, and started the fire, while he told me how one of the three passengers came in the engine room and threw a cloth over his face, and he remembered no more.

LORD ETHALWOOD CONDUCTS CHEVALIER MONPRES THROUGH THE PICTURE GALLERY OF BROXBRIDGE HALL.

"These facts were somewhat mysterious, but danger was all around us, and no time could be spared for discussion, and necessarily we were compelled to direct all our energies towards saving the boat from wreck and ourselves from destruction.

"Despite our danger, however, I could not help thinking of what had occurred, and suddenly it struck me—the mails.

"Leaving the engineer in charge, I rushed with my lamp to the cabin, and there, strewn about, as before, lay the postal contents.

"I examined them eagerly, and in the heap saw a

thick packet directed to the officer of the Puntsville and Rocktown R. R. Co., marked on the outside ' No. 5,' and in small caligraphy in the left-hand corner, ' 6000 dollars.'

" ' No. 5!' And where were the remaining four? I now remembered I had heard that 25,000 dollars worth of endorsed and signed railroad bonds were to be put up for sale in Puntsville.

" There was one package—one-fifth of the total amount—and the other four were stolen! This was what had brought my three gentlemen passengers on a hunting expedition. Yes, for game worth 20,000 dollars, and never a shot fired.

" As I stood in amazement at the daring and cleverness exhibited, and in alarm from the reflection of the responsibility I might incur from the robbery, a huge wave struck the boat, and she almost capsized.

" Hastily collecting the mail contents in the old bag, I shouted to the engineer to turn on all steam, while I ran to the pilot-house and grasped the wheel.

" Slowly the paddles went round, then faster, then the ' Silver Arrow' tore through the black waves under a dangerous pressure of steam.

" Hardly had we attained speed ere a great mountain wave struck her amidships, carrying away the larboard paddle-box and the greater portion of the aft bulwarks.

" The boat rocked and plunged, almost stopped, then the wheels crashed through the splintered timbers that had become inserted in the paddles, and again we bore on, until a loud snap echoed through the boat, the wheels stopped, the ' Silver Arrow,' caught up by the rushing waters, drifted helplessly.

" The engineer, breathless, came up and said the piston-lever had broken, and still we drifted on—to death.

" Another giant wave struck—three feet of water below, and fast filling—still raged the storm and warred the water.

" Two miles from shore, and the black, ghastly, whitened waves roared over the rocky bar, two hundred yards distant.

" In an instant we were close on it.

" I rushed below, seized the mail bags, and unscrewing the cylinder-head, thrust them in, and closed it up. Then they were in a water-tight compartment, safe and recoverable, even if the luckless ' Silver Arrow' went to the bottom.

" As I secured the mails the water was waist high. When I reached deck the waves were beginning to roll over it, and the engineer and negro, whom, it seemed, the terror of the situation had suddenly roused, were launching the remaining boat.

" The starboard boat, I forgot to mention, had been discovered gone when I examined the deck, on recovering from the chloroform's somnolent effects.

" I shouted to them to save themselves by some other means, as no boat could live in such a storm; and then, grasping the chain stays, hauled myself, hand over hand, to the top of the stack, which had not yet cooled, though the fires had been extinguished twenty minutes, and the spray was continually dashing over and around, causing jets of steam to emanate from every spot it touched on the black cylinder.

" I hung there for life, though it scorched my hands dreadfully; and at last I managed to lash myself fast by a bit of rope, which, providentially, I had found in my pocket. The boat sank no deeper. It had grounded on the bar, and I was temporarily safe.

" Then I looked amid the turmoil of waters for the engineer and his companion. Of them I could see

nothing. Half a furlong to leeward tossed the boat, bottom upward. The unfortunate men had gone to the bottom.

" The ' Silver Arrow' rocked fearfully, and jarred and shocked me through every limb, as I hung lashed to the smoke-stack.

" I was fast being spent, when, the storm abating, a boat put out from shore, and without detailing the difficulty of getting aboard, suffice it to say that, half dead, I was rescued, and after a couple of day's recuperation on shore, I got aboard a schooner bound up, and arriving at Puntsville, related what had happened.

" In a few days calm weather returned, the ' Silver Arrow' was raised, the mails were secured, intact, and I mentally resolved to give up steam-boating for a lengthy interval, at least, and measures were taken to recover the stolen railroad bonds through the city detectives.

" Finally it was rumoured that the bonds had been recovered from a city firm, who had purchased them two days after they were stolen; that the party who had sold them could not be found, but his arrest was very probable from the descriptive clues which the authorities had received from a member of the victimised firm.

" And now I became involved in a predicament equalling in unpleasantness that of the clinging to the smoke-stack of the sinking ' Silver Arrow.'

" One day, about a week after the robbery, a gentleman called at the Puntsville Hotel and expressed a wish for a private interview, and when we were alone, produced a warrant for my arrest for mail robbery. Remonstrance was useless.

" He said it was a very unpleasant duty, but the law must be enforced, &c., and as the document was in proper form and legally made out, I could do nothing but accompany him.

" To be brief, I was tried and convicted on the sworn and positive evidence of the senior partner of the firm who had purchased the stolen bonds. He identified me as the man who brought the stolen paper into their office, and to whom he had paid the money for the same.

" In detail his evidence went to the effect that the man had grey mutton-chop whiskers and moustache, brown eyes, red face, and a mole on the left cheek, all of which answered my description exactly.

" In vain my lawyer argued and argued—the evidence was point blank against me, and an alibi could not be proved; for unfortunately the very day on which the bonds had been offered for sale I had gone, starting at sunrise, on a solitary fishing excursion to a little frequented part of the river, and had not met a single person until I came home late at night.

" The trial lasted but one day, and the next I was on my way to the Albany Penitentiary for a term of three years.

" The prison became unusually crowded, and I was compelled to occupy a cell in companionship of another convict.

" We lived together very pleasantly for some weeks, became as intimate as our diverse social station would permit, and in a communicative mood one night my companion related how once on a steamboat he with two other companions had robbed the mail, and after drugging the crew had escaped in a small boat, and he wondered if the old captain was drowned, as he had heard afterwards that the boat had sunk.

" You may know what were my reflections when I heard this, and, to be sure of a witness, I informed the turnkey, and next night he stationed himself immediately outside the door, and in the course of our nightly conversation my fellow-convict repeated his confession, with an addition that he and his two pals had heard that the bonds were to be sent to Puntsville, and had laid their plans as they carried them out; and what was of more immediate consequence to me, how one of them had imitated my appearance, even to the mole upon my cheek, and thus turned the attention of the authorities towards me, and gave them time to get out of the country; and, moreover, that when he succeeded in selling the purloined bonds he had decamped with the proceeds, and had never been heard from.

"He (the prisoner) was incarcerated at the present time for another offence entirely different.

"With the turnkey as my witness I speedily obtained a hearing, and after a series of legal formalities was released from durance vile; and, of course, if I had not then been in comfortable circumstances, very likely I would have instituted an action for false imprisonment, and thereby put sums of money in the pockets of the lawyers and a pittance into my own.

"However, I waived all right to compensation for my injured liberty, having had quite enough of legal experience, and this is what happened to me thirty years ago, when I was a young man."

"I said Corbet could tell you a tough yarn or two," remarked Whittock. "Why, Lord bless you, he'd keep you amused the whole evening. He has tales about all sorts of things, and, what is better, they are everyone of them true."

"This one is, that I'll vow for," returned the captain, "but I don't say all I tell are."

"We don't ask whether they are true or not," observed Peace, with a smile. "It is enough for us to know that we are entertained. So long as the hours pass pleasantly away, and we all enjoy ourselves, what more is needed?

Everybody appeared to coincide in this opinion, and so, after some more music, both vocal and instrumental, one of the guests, who it appeared, had been at one time a station-master in the United States, told the following tale, which we reserve for another chapter.

CHAPTER CXXXIII.

TIED TO THE TRACK—A STATION MASTER'S STORY.

"OUR friend here," said the station-master, "has given you a notion of what a life on the ocean wave is, now I'm just going on a different track altogether. Perhaps the most monotonous unromantic life it is possible to conceive is that of a railway servant, whether guard, engine-driver, porter, or stationmaster, and I dare say you are all astonished at my volunteering a tale about railway life."

"Not at all! No such thing! Go on," cried several.

"Well then, here goes," cried the narrator.

"Along about the years sixty-seven and eight it got to be altogether too common a thing on our line putting sleepers across the track and tearing up rails, to throw the train off, so as to rob the express car; and some of the villains who were caught got pretty severe sentences.

"It so happened that in an especially noteworthy case it was my own evidence chiefly that convicted two of the most precious rascals you ever set eyes on, Tom Jackson and Clint Parker by name.

"They were sent to Joliet for fifteen years, and I was mighty glad to serve as 'humble instrument' in the case, I tell you; though sometimes I did feel kind

of squeamish-like when I repeat to myself the last words Parker said as they took him out of court:—

"'As for you, Joe Townsend' (and he shook his fist significantly in my direction) 'all this comes of the cowardly lies you've sworn to; and I want you to understand that Tom Jackson and me, we aint the men to stay down at Joliet for fifteen years breaking stone. We're goin' to git out, we are, and you may depend upon it we'll be keerful to pay our first respec's to you. We've invented a new kind of sleeper to throw trains off with—eh, Tom?' and he leered horribly to his crony as they passed through the door.

"Those last words of Parker's I turned over in my mind a good many times during the next two years —somehow or other they stuck by me:—'We've invented a new kind of sleeper to throw a train off the track.'

"I kind of felt as though he meant something unusual by that, although I could not make out what. It seemed that I was to find out, though, before many months.

"The house, where my wife and the babies lived was just about three-quarters of a mile below the station, and quite near the track. I generally got through at the depot at half-past eight, as soon as the accommodation went down.

"The night express, which goes through at 9.55, doesn't pull up at R—— at all, and the through freight, which meets it down the road a piece, at W——, of course I have nothing to do with. I might mention here that the road is double-track the entire length; but there is a long bridge at W——, so that the freight always waits there for the express.

"At half-past eight, then, as I say, I was at liberty for the night, and it didn't take me long to shut up the depot and start off down the road for home; and a lonely enough tramp it is, I tell you, even on a bright night, for the track runs all the way through woods and swamps, and it's mighty dark and uncomfortable at best.

"Well, the night I'm going to tell you about was black as the inside of a two-mile tunnel. When I started down the track I almost wished I'd gone around by the highway, for I had to feel my way half the time.

"However, I knew the path tolerably well, and could tell where all the culverts and dangerous places were, pretty nearly.

"So I held up my lantern like the head-light of a locomotive and stumbled along, making pretty good time on the whole.

"I must have been just about half-way home, I guess, when all at once, without the slightest idea on my part that any human being was within half a mile of me, I felt a pair of arms clasped around my waist with a strength it was impossible to overcome; then, suddenly, I was thrown down, the light from a more powerful lantern than mine (which had fallen from my hand and become extinguished) flashed about me, and by its glare I saw three powerful fellows, who, in spite of my struggles, and I am no baby, proceeded to tie my hands firmly behind me.

"I did not recognise them at all till, at length, as I lay there on my back, entirely helpless, one of them snatched the lantern from his companion and held it close down to me, while he brought his own face close to mine.

"'Wall, Joe Townsend,' he said, 'do you know me?'

"'Yes, I know you, Clint Parker,' I answered, as coolly as I could.

"'I thought as how mebbe ye would. I didn't

mean to stay down there to Joliet so long thet my dearest friend would forgit me. I've been thinkin' 'bout you, Joe, most all the time while I was down there gittin' up my muscle-breakin' stone. And here's another feller you may remember—leastways, he aint forgot you, eh, Tom ?'—and I now recognised Tom Jackson, the other prisoner of two years before. The third man I had never seen.

"'This place'll do as well as any, I 'spose,' Parker went on, presently. 'What's the time, Jem ?'

"Jem consulted his watch, and pronounced it to be about nine.

"'All right; he'll have jest about fifty minutes to think things over in and repent having lied about two such exemplary gentlemen as Tom Jackson and myself —eh, Tom ?' and Tom chuckled, approvingly.

"'Now git out all them ropes,' still Parker went on. He seemed to be the leading spirit and spokesman of the enterprise. 'Do ye know what we're goin' to do with yer, Joe ? We aint goin' to throw no trains off the track. Oh, no! Tom and me, we wouldn't do nothin' of that kind—eh, Tom ? But we're goin' to let you throw one off. I told ye, ye know, that Tom and me we'd diskivered a new kind of sleeper for throwin' trains with. We're jest goin' to tie you down here across the track awhile, that's all. We wouldn't do nothin' cruel—eh, Tom ?'

"So their hellish purpose was revealed at last. They were going to tie me to the track and let the train pass over me ! I confess at that moment my limbs actually shook with fear. It was not only death within less than an hour that I was to suffer, but death in a most violent and horrible form.

"Certainly a revenge worthy of two such monsters as stood there gloating over my misery. For a moment I thought only of myself. Then I groaned aloud as I remembered Jennie and the little ones.

"I don't know why I should be ashamed to tell it— I doubt if there are many men who would not have done the same in my place—but I just sank down on my knees then and there, and begged those heartless villains to forego their desperate purpose.

"I might as well have gone on my knees to the great iron monster that would be along in so short a time to crush me.

"They only laughed merrily over my despair, and began their work.

"You'll acknowledge yourselves, gentlemen, that it's rather a dismal lock for a poor fellow to be gagged and bound, hand and foot, and then be tied fast across a railroad track with his neck across one rail and his feet over the other, and to know that in something like half an hour's time a fast express train is coming down that very track without paying any attention to him whatever—and this in a dark, drizzly night, and in a lonely spot where no human being is at all likely to find him.

"And that's the way those double-dyed scoundrels left me—they tied me there fast and firm—they mockingly bade me good-night and pleasant dreams—the leader, Parker, even stooped over me and kissed me with pretended tenderness, and I felt his hot, liquor-freighted breath on my cheek.

"And yet I could not cry out in my agony nor curse them in my desperation as they moved off.

"No words of mine, gentlemen, can describe the horror and agony I felt during the time I lay there.

"You can not half imagine it—I doubt if I can recall it now as it really was myself. I go over it again and again in my sleep to this day—fancy myself once more bound down to that fearful rack, powerless to stir hand or foot, yet striving with almost superhuman force to burst the ropes that bind me— till I finally seem to succeed and awake shrieking from the horrid nightmare, with the sweat standing out in great drops upon my brow.

"But I did not burst my bonds that night. The villains had taken good care of that. There I was in a most painful position, bound by the neck to one rail, and by the ankles to the other, my hands tied beneath me, and my body fastened to a sleeper.

"Oh, God ! how I did struggle to free myself ; how I sought to wrench away my legs ; how I tugged at the cord which bound my wrists ; and then, since I could not get them free, as I thought of the fearful death so soon to come upon me, how I strove to throttle myself with the rope that held my head to the rail !

"How I prayed that I might suffocate there as I lay! I have heard that men have died of terror, but I don't believe it. If such a thing were possible I think I should have perished in those dreadful moments. But I did not. Oh, no ! The murderers were to have their fullest revenge.

"And now, suddenly I grew strangely calm. I philosophised with myself. I said resignedly, that a man could die but once ; and after all, what would it matter an hour hence ?

"Besides, in reality, this was an instantaneous and almost painless end. But my wife and children ! Oh, I would like to live for them. And could I not ? I was not dead yet. If I could only move myself a few feet. Oh, so very few feet ! Yet I could not stir.

"Now, a thought struck me. Could I not signal the train in some way, stop it one little yard, or foot, or inch before it passed over me ? Alas, how ? They would never hear my cries.

"They would never see me in the darkness of the night. No one would know until the morrow, and then I should be, alas! crushed, and mangled, and dead.

"But my lantern—where was that ? I turned my head, and could see it a few feet away where I had dropped it. If I only had it on my breast I could draw up my pocket with my teeth, I thought, and somehow get a match from it, and so light the lantern.

"And in my insane terror I called out to it, and begged it to come nearer, and save my wretched life. You may smile at that, gentlemen, but human nature is weaker than you think, and I believe I am as good a man ordinarily as the most.

"But all this time the minutes were flying by like lightning. Horrible as that hour was to me, I could have wished it was all eternity.

"Every instant I dreaded to hear the train coming. I knew it must be well-nigh time for it now, and I knew that it was on time, for we had telegraphed it an hour before.

"I will not dwell longer on my sufferings. I did not free myself. I could not if the salvation of the race had depended upon it. Nor did anybody come to free me. No one would ever pass that spot on a night like that, and at such an hour.

"Nor was the train behind time. No, I heard it at last ; it was no creation of my excited fancy this time. I heard it at last, first a faint, rumbling sound, that seemed to come from deep down in the earth, beneath me ; then the ground seemed to thrill and tremble ; then the rails rattled a little, then more and more; then I heard the whistle and bell, and then, oh, God ! another instant and it would be upon me. I could even see the reflected glare of the headlight.

"I tried once more to cry out; I struggled again for an instant, with all the power of my being, then I knew that my time was come, and I shut my eyes and lay quite still.

"And the great train came rushing on and on—it was close upon me—I saw it not, yet I felt it to be directly above me. Great heavens! what was this? Was it passing over me and I still living, and feeling it not?

"I opened my eyes; I saw the cars flashing by above and within a few feet of my head. Then the truth flashed upon me. *The train was upon the other track!* The reaction was too much for me, and I fainted dead away.

"When I came to consciousness again, I found myself in my own room at home.

"I had only a confused recollection of the events which had so lately befallen me, but they told me gently all that I did not know of the story.

"I had been very ill, they said, of brain fever. They had found me on the morning of that terrible night, bound fast—not to the railroad-track, but to a tree, just a few rods away from it.

"I was very delirious, and was taken home raving continually.

"I had been sick for a fortnight. Then they asked how it was that I came to be tied to the tree.

"But, alas, I knew as little of that part of the story as they did.

"I told them how I had been seized by Parker and his companions, and tied to the track.

"My lantern, found near the spot, and distinct marks of a struggle, confirmed the story.

"The question was, how did I escape the train, and how did I become tied to the tree?

"My own theory is this: Parker and Jackson were not, after all, so bad as I took them to be. Their revenge had been, not to murder me, but to frighten me terribly; and they certainly had succeeded perfectly. I could see nothing, tied as I was, could hardly turn my head, and they had easily persuaded me into the idea that I was on the down track—that of the passenger-express.

"After the train had passed, they had come to release me before the up freight should be along. They had fastened me to the tree so as to get fully away before I could give any alarm.

"That is the only way I can account for the facts. And though I certainly don't owe the rascals anything for what they did to me, I never think of the affair to this day without feeling a kind of gratitude towards them, and thanking God they were not as black-hearted as I thought they were, after all."

"Well, that's a jolly good yarn," said the captain; "it beats mine into an almighty smash, and no mistake."

"Oh, I don't say that," observed Whittock, "you are both good story-tellers. Talk about the 'Arabian Nights' Entertainment,' I rather fancy we could knock up one ourselves if we had a mind."

"I'm sure we could," returned Peace.

"But the time is getting late, gentlemen," said the captain. "The best of friends must part. Time is on the wing, and all that sort of thing."

"Time was made for slaves," cried one of the party. "Don't go yet."

"No—no; sit down, and make yourself as happy as possible," said Peace, who on this occasion, as on many others of a similar nature, proved himself to be an excellent host and a most genial companion, so that

the small hours of the morning had arrived before the party broke up.

There was the usual amount of leave-taking, shaking of hands, and protestations of friendship.

Peace saw his guests to the outer gate, and then, when all had taken their departure, he returned into the house with Bandy-legged Bill, who took up his quarters at No. 4 for the remainder of the night.

CHAPTER CXXXIV.
LORD ETHALWOOD'S RETURN HOME—REGRETS FOR THE PAST—NEWS FROM ABROAD.

LORD REGINALD ETHALWOOD returned to England a sadder and in some respects a wiser man. He was no longer the gay and light-hearted nobleman whose merry pranks and jovial manner caused his associates to court his company.

A strange alteration in the mode of life and manner of the young earl had taken place. He was grave and thoughtful, and at times melancholy.

A shadow seemed to have fallen upon him, and the recollection of the events that had taken place during his sojourn on the Continent seemed to cling to him with terrible tenacity.

There were a number of circumstances connected with his *liaison* with Theresa Trieste which could not fail to cause him great uneasiness, but beyond and above all there was the fact that he had sent to his account a young man, who, whatever his faults might have been, was true, faithful, and self-sacrificing to the object of his love.

Indeed, Chanet had displayed an amount of chivalry and devotion which could not fail to command the respect of Lord Ethalwood.

Upon returning to his ancestral home Reginald had ample time to consider over past events. He could not but acknowledge to himself that his share in the business did not in any way redound to his credit, and now that he had time and leisure to reflect on the part he had played in the sanguinary drama caused him to upbraid himself for his rash and impetuous course of action.

Lord Reginald, upon his arrival in England, hastened at once to the town residence of his mother, to whom he paid his respects.

Nothing was said about the tragedy of the Jura mountains.

"My dear Reginald," exclaimed Aveline, embracing her son with maternal fondness, "it is indeed a source of happiness for me to see you again in your native land, and I hope and trust you will not again leave the country—certainly not for some time to come—for, oh, my darling boy, you do not know how anxious I have been about you. Consider, Reginald, the position you hold as the representative of an honoured line—the only representative—and consider also how needful it is for you to uphold the dignity of the house of which you are, I am sure, a worthy representative."

"I have duly considered that, mother," returned Reginald.

"And, therefore, it behoves you to be mindful of yourself. Alas! my son, there are many reasons for you to be especially guarded in your conduct. Remember the untimely end of your predecessors—the earl's sons—and the end also of my poor mother. I tremble when I think of the untoward events which have taken place; and it is, therefore, with something like a melancholy foreboding that I charge you to take special care of yourself."

"You need not be any way concerned about me," said Reginald, not very well knowing what his mother was driving at. "I am in good health and spirits. Why, therefore, should you be thus anxious?"

"Are you in good health and spirits? It has struck me that you do not look so happy and contented as when you left for this—this hunting expedition."

Lord Ethalwood burst out into a loud laugh.

"Why, my dear mother," said he, "to hear you speak thus one would almost imagine you to be a fatalist."

"Well, assuming you came to that conclusion, what then?"

"What! You would not have me come to any such rash conclusion, I should imagine?"

"Have you reflected upon past events?" said Aveline. "Have you duly considered the strange vicissitudes of the house of Ethalwood, of which you are now the representative? Have you thought of the untimely deaths of the younger members of that honourable line—of the sad end of your grandmother, and all the events which have led to your being the rightful and acknowledged heir? It behoves you, my son, to be duly impressed with your position, to strive in every possible way to support, to the best of your ability, the dignity of our house."

"I am duly impressed with all this," said the young earl, "and do not need to be reminded of it."

"Ah, Reginald," exclaimed Aveline, "pardon me for being thus plain-spoken. In you I behold the sole surviving link, from the present to the past, of a great race."

"I know that, mother. But why this concern and anxiety? I am well, and am heedful of the trust which is imposed upon me."

"Spoken like my own dear son," said Aveline. "I am sure you will never do aught to compromise or sully the honour of the Ethalwoods."

"I hope not," he added, with something like melancholy foreboding in his tone, for he remembered at the time the sad events which had so recently taken place.

It was evident enough from his mother's manner that she had some inkling of the part he had been playing in the dark drama on the continent—albeit she wisely forbore from alluding directly to it.

She was concerned and troubled about something—what this was Lord Ethalwood could only surmise.

After paying his respects to his father-in-law he returned to Broxbridge Hall, which has been the stage upon which so many scenes of our drama have been enacted.

At Broxbridge he was, in a great measure, secluded from a host of acquaintances who, at that particular time, he was not anxious to meet.

Mr. Jakyl, full of years and servitude, was still the major domo of the establishment; he appeared to be as devoted to his young master as he was to the late earl.

Jakyl was at this time a very old man; he had the same soft, respectful, unobtrusive manner as of yore; indeed, these qualities were even more apparent in his declining years—if this were possible.

The slightest hint given by Lord Ethalwood was considered law by his faithful and venerable servitor, and it afforded the old domestic a considerable amount of pleasure and satisfaction at beholding the earl return to his ancestral home.

Mr. Jakyl was not at all demonstrative—was never gushing, but those who knew him best were at no loss to comprehend when he was pleased or otherwise.

Lord Reginald, after his return to Broxbridge, remained for a considerable time secluded.

He did not court the company of his quondam companions, and his retainers could not fail to observe that he had come back a sadder and more thoughtful man.

It is true he received a few visitors, with his accustomed good fellowship and courtesy, but there was no longer that sportive mad-cap merriment which had marked his course of life before leaving for the Continent.

No one was quite able to account for the altered demeanour of the gay and merry young earl.

Very shortly after his return he received a letter from abroad which seemed to deepen the shadow which had so suddenly fallen upon him.

The epistle in question came from Theresa Trieste. It was couched in the most affectionate language. In almost every passage the writer gave expression to deep and unfailing love, but at the same time the tone of it was melancholy and sorrowful to the last degree. In fact it appeared that Theresa was plunged into the depths of despair.

Her mother had been suddenly and unexpectedly struck down with a fit of apoplexy, and after lingering for a few hours, she expired. This was a sad blow to the earl. Theresa was left with little or no provision, and in addition to this she expected very shortly to become a mother.

Lord Ethalwood was greatly concerned upon learning this. He naturally enough upbraided himself for the part he had been playing, but it was now not possible to retract. The death of Madame Trieste was an event he had not counted on, and it, of course, added to the complication of circumstances with which he had become surrounded by his own imprudence.

But he was in an exalted position, was wealthy, and under all the circumstances felt bound to make some provision for the woman whom he had so deeply wronged.

This was an easy matter enough, but Theresa did not view the matter in a mercenary light. She would have been content to share poverty with her seducer so long as she was near him and was assured of his love.

Lord Reginald did not know what to do under the circumstances. He was still greatly attached to Theresa, and he, therefore, wrote a most affectionate letter to her in reply to the one he had received.

He enclosed a draft for a considerable sum with the letter, and bade her consider him in the light of both a friend and a lover.

The position was both a difficult and a delicate one, and he was therefore specially cautious in wording his letter, not that he had the faintest notion that the unhappy Theresa would take any advantage of any incautious expression, but still he deemed it just as well to be on the safe side.

He also dispatched a missive to the Chevalier de Monpres, bidding him wait upon Theresa and comfort her as he best could.

He also entrusted the arrangements of the funeral of Madame Trieste to his friend, De Monpres.

He begged, as a special favour of the old Frenchman, his attention to these matters, and wound up by an earnest request that he, De Monpres, would pay a visit to Broxbridge.

In a week or two after this the earl was both surprised and delighted when one of his servants announced that a gentleman—a stranger to Broxbridge—was waiting in one of the reception rooms.

Upon looking at the card handed to him by the domestic, the earl saw it was none other than his late second, who desired to speak with him.

The chevalier was at once conducted into the presence of the earl.

"My dear good friend!" exclaimed the latter, "this is, indeed, kind and considerate of you. I know not how to thank you sufficiently for your kindness and attention."

"Well, the fact is, Ethalwood," said De Monpres, "I could not remain away any longer. I felt, naturally enough, that you needed advice and consolation; besides, it was essential for me to communicate with you personally."

"I am overjoyed to see you. Sit down and make this place your home, for some time to come, at all events."

"Ah, but I intend to do that," cried the chevalier, with a shrug and a grimace. "Eh, but you've got a fine old palatial mansion, a grand old place, which I should imagine has stood for centuries—that is, if one is to judge from appearances."

"It is very old—almost as old as our genealogical tree."

"I should suppose so. Well, my young friend, I intend to enjoy myself while I am here, so you mustn't think of assuming a serious or dejected aspect, for I tell you frankly I will not permit it. You are under my care now—do you understand?—and are to be as merry and jocund as possible."

"I will endeavour to be so," returned Reginald. "That is as far as circumstances will admit."

"Bah! circumstances! What have you to complain of? Nothing—positively nothing!"

"Very well, it shall be as you say. I will not repine."

"I hope not, indeed. I am not an envious man, my dear Ethalwood. If I were I should long to be in your position. You have youth, health, wealth, and bear an honoured name second to none within these realms. What more do you need?"

"A clear conscience," returned the earl.

"*Mon dieu*, don't be so weak and silly. You had better have some champagne, and we can talk this matter over at our leisure."

"I won't say no. Let us have some sparkling then, if you have no objection."

"None in the least."

"Ah, I see you are not so bad as I thought," cried De Monpres, raising the glass and pledging his friend with the same.

"Is that better?" said he.

"You received my note, of course," observed Ethalwood, when the first civilities were over.

The Frenchman nodded,

"And—ahem—the funeral, how did that pass over?"

"I carried out your instructions to the very letter."

"I was sure you would do that. A thousand thanks. And poor Theresa?"

"Ah, *mon ami*, she was sadly borne down, poor girl. I thought she would have gone into hysterics, but she is better now—much better. Ah, she will be all right again in the due course of time. These things are always sad, and in her case there was every reason for deep and poignant sorrow. I am thankful for having been of service to her."

"You did your best to cheer her up, I have no doubt."

"My very best."

"Umph, it is altogether a most unfortunate affair, De Monpres, and I need not tell you that it has been a source of trouble to me, which, despite all the philosophy I can bring to bear upon it, still hangs heavily on my conscience."

"Conscience—bah! You have nothing to charge yourself with—have acted in every way as becomes an honourable gentleman."

"Oh, no—no!" interrupted the earl, with sudden warmth.

"That is my view of the matter," observed the Frenchman, "and I am a much older man than you are, and ought to be a competent judge of what is wrong and what is right. Why, my dear young friend, in my young days these things were as common occurrences as possible. Nobody even thought anything of them. You became enamoured of a young and fascinating female, and she was attached to you; well, the end we both know. What do you propose doing?"

"That is precisely why I have been so anxious to see you."

"To seek my advice—eh?"

"Yes."

"You cannot do otherwise than make a provision for her."

"Of course not; but that will not satisfy her."

"No, it will not," said the old Frenchman, as he swallowed another glass of wine. "She seems to me to be what one might call madly infatuated; but, dear me, women are such strange creatures, that one hardly knows what to say to them. She wants to come to this country."

"Yes—so she gave me to understand."

"To be near you—that is her only reason, I believe. Ah, she is infatuated! But you mustn't compromise yourself merely for the sake of a love-sick woman."

"What would you advise me to do, then?"

"Ah, that is a question one finds it difficult to answer upon the spur of the moment."

"But you have thought the matter over, I suppose."

"I have certainly given it due consideration, but then I am not Lord Ethalwood—I am only an old military officer. My view of the case and yours may be diametrically opposite; don't you see that?"

"Yes, I quite understand what you mean, but take another glass."

"Thank you. It is unfortunate for us—and especially so for her—that her mother died at this juncture, but it could not be helped, and it is not, therefore, any use dwelling upon it."

"It is very unfortunate."

"And you know, Ethalwood, I am really sorry for the girl. Perhaps you won't believe me when I say so, but I am, indeed."

"I have no reason to disbelieve you, monsieur—far from it."

"Because, you see, she is placed in a false position."

"Yes, that is quite true."

"But you mustn't compromise yourself. You mustn't do that, come what may."

"I should be base, indeed, if I deserted her, after all that has passed."

"Oh, dear me, no one could think of advising you to do that. Certainly no one who had any respect for you."

"By the way, this is a splendid glass of wine. A little sweet, perhaps, but it's none the worse for that. It is of the finest vintage."

"I am glad it meets with your approval, as I know you are an excellent judge."

"Well, as I was about to observe," said the chevalier, carelessly. "Theresa thinks only of you. You are the father of the child, which is soon to see the light, and I am in some doubt as to what course I ought to advise you to take. I should not like to be instrumental in bringing an encumbrance on you—still, at the same time, I cannot conceal from myself that to leave her to take her chance in those cursed mountains all alone, and without any other companion than her maid, who, to say the truth, is a giddy, flirting little puss, is not altogether desirable."

"I am delighted to hear you say so," cried the earl, "and for this reason, that it coincides with my own view of the question. I am now determined I will have her over here—take a villa for her in one of the London suburbs."

"Or apartments for her in the metropolis."

"Yes, or apartments. Perhaps that would be better."

"Much better. Villas are all very well in their way, but she would be much more cheerful and contented with apartments."

"I think you are right; but that is a question which we can determine upon her arrival. I will write at once and tell her to come over to this country without any delay. What say you?"

The chevalier answered with a shrug.

"I think I am in duty bound to do this—eh?"

"Well, perhaps you are. One thing has been made manifest to me plainly enough."

"What is that?"

"She won't be contented where she is—that's quite certain; and—bah!—after all you can well afford to keep a mistress, or half a dozen or so for the matter of that; and you are quite justified in doing so. They are at times troublesome to a man, but one can't have any pleasure in this world without its alloy. Send for her. Let her come over at once, Ethalwood, before I leave. Possibly I may be of service to you."

"My dear De Monpres, you are as good as a father to me. I don't know what I should have done without you."

"Oh, you would have done well enough, I dare say," observed the chevalier.

"I don't think so."

"Well, we won't dispute upon that subject. I am here enjoying your society and hospitality, and I don't intend to leave you for the present. Certainly not, till I see you out of this little difficulty."

"And how about the mountaineers? Did you see or hear anything of them after I took my departure?"

"I heard a good deal,' cried De Monpres, in a serious tone; "heard enough to fully comprehend that they intended to polish you off if a chance had been afforded them. *Sacre*, I shudder when I think of the bloodthirsty miscreants."

"Ah, they meant mischief then?"

"*Mon dieu* yes."

"But how did you know this?"

"From the young fellow who was Chanet's second. He has behaved in a way which meets with my unqualified approval."

"Has he?"

"Yes, he is an honourable and upright young man and evinced the greatest possible solicitude for your safety. He knew the danger of the situation—knew that a band of mountaineers were in league together to —well—bah—murder you at their earliest convenience, and made me acquainted with the whole of their proceedings. I had three or four of the rascals arrested, but as there was no direct evidence against them they were discharged with a caution. This is all I could possibly do, and I believe that to a certain extent it had a salutary effect. They were intimidated. They knew the eyes of the officers of justice were on them, and they returned to their fastnesses like a set of curs as they are. Still, my friend, despite all these precautions, we cannot conceal from ourselves that your life was not worth a few hours' purchase while you were in the neighbourhood of those treacherous mountains. Neither would it be now if you were imprudent enough to return."

"I am not likely to do that," said Lord Reginald; "not at all likely, for very many reasons."

"I should suppose not."

"Oh, dear me, no; but the day is still young, what say you to a stroll in the grounds?"

"Nothing would please me better, but before proceeding thither will you just let me have a look at your picture gallery?"

"By all means—with the greatest pleasure."

Lord Reginald Ethalwood conducted the chevalier to the gallery in which the late earl so loved to linger, and here it was that Charles Peace, in an earlier day, succeeded in making such a wonderful restoration of one of the portraits which now looked as fresh and bright as when it was first painted.

As the old Frenchman passed through he came to a sudden halt, and stood for some time gazing upon the portrait of the late earl.

"How lifelike!" he ejaculated. "What an admirable representation of my late friend! I should have known it anywhere, and under any circumstances. I never saw a better portrait."

"It is wonderfully well done, monsieur. The artist has caught the habitual expression of his features, which, to say the truth, were generally tinged with a shade of melancholy."

"Say, rather, thoughtfulness," quietly remarked the chevalier. "The late earl was thoughtful and meditative by nature. There were many reasons for this, which it would be needless to dwell upon now."

"You are quite right—such was the case," returned Lord Reginald.

After passing through the gallery, the two friends rambled over the grounds and in the woods on the Broxbridge estate, returning to the hall to dinner.

De Monpres', visit proved to be a great source of comfort to the young earl.

The chevalier had been so mixed up in recent events that he was specially welcome, and was made much of by the master of the hall.

The days passed pleasantly enough. The chevalier had a whole fund of anecdotes at his command, and although advanced in years, he was brimful of jocularity, sparkling repartee, and lively discourse upon present and past events.

The visitors to the hall were quite charmed with him, and Reginald looked forward to his departure with something like sorrow and regret.

But De Monpres was too well satisfied with his present quarters to dream of leaving them at present. He had passed his word to remain in England till the arrival of Theresa Trieste, who had written a reply to the earl's letter, intimating that she would be with him as soon as she possibly could. Theresa lost no time in carrying out her promise.

She had become an object of mark in her mountain home, and the mountaineers regarded her with malevolent looks, in which aversion, not to say hatred, formed the chief ingredient.

They did not attempt to molest her, or offer any positive insult, but she was duly impressed with the fact that there was a general feeling of discontent and animosity towards her in consequence of the part she had played in the sanguinary drama.

"HILLOA THERE, I'VE COTCHED HIM," CRIED MR. ASHBROOK TO THE DETECTIVE.

Theresa Trieste had lost her parent, and she was left alone in the world, with no other protector than Lord Ethalwood.

To remain any longer in the chateau at the foot of the Jura mountains was therefore quite out of the question.

She therefore gladly acceded to the request of Lord Reginald, and made preparations to take a speedy departure from the home which had now no longer any charms for her.

She believed, as many other women have done under similar circumstances, in the honour and integrity of her seducer. Any way she had no other alternative than to trust to his good faith and consideration.

She hastened at once to England, and upon her arrival at Dover she dispatched a letter to Broxbridge, making him acquainted with the fact.

The Chevalier de Monpres had been commissioned to engage apartments for the lady.

Strange to say, he took a suite of rooms in the house occupied by Mrs. Bourne.

The last-named had long before this furnished her house in Somerset-street in the best possible style, and, as it was a much larger one than she required, she had deputed an agent to procure her a lodger.

The courteous old Frenchman applied to the aforesaid agent who recommended Mrs Bourne.

De Monpres waited upon the doctor's widow, with whom he was greatly pleased, and at once engaged the suite of rooms on the first floor.

He was at no loss to divine that Mrs. Bourne was precisely the sort of person Theresa Trieste would, in all probability, get on with; consequently he struck a bargain and engaged the rooms for the young French lady, who was about to arrive from the Continent.

The earl and chevalier met Theresa at the London station, and accompanied her to the widow's house in Somerset-street.

She was greatly pleased with her new quarters, and her countenance became irradiated with a smile as she gazed on the handsome features of her lover.

She hoped for the best, and had not at this time any misgivings for the future, for the earl demonstrated the strongest affection for her, and was profuse in promises. Nevertheless, deep down in his heart was the canker-worm of remorse.

However, he strove as best he could to assume an air of cheerfulness, and after remaining for the best part of the evening with his mistress he took his departure in company with the Chevalier de Monpres.

CHAPTER CXXXV.

SOME PASSAGES IN THE LIFE OF A LONDON THIEF.

ALF PURVIS, alias Mr. Algernon Sutherland, had, with the exception of our hero, become one of the most daring of metropolitan thieves. His genteel appearance and engaging manners were of essential service to him in carrying on his nefarious practices.

In this respect he had the advantage of Peace; but with all these qualities he was not nearly so cunning or artful as our hero.

Nevertheless, Mr. Sutherland was, in his own particular sphere, a young gentleman of note and mark, who was greatly admired and envied by villains of coarser type with whom he was wont to associate.

He was known by the cognomen of the "Dandy," in consequence of his fashionable attire and finicking ways.

A more audacious, unscrupulous young scoundrel it would not be easy to find. As far as pocket-picking was concerned he was a sort of prodigy; but he did not confine his attention to this branch of the profession, as he termed it; he had at times recourse to other means to replenish his exchequer, and of late he had hit upon what he deemed a most ingenious scheme to furnish him with the means of indulging in his extravagant mode of living.

The reader will doubtless remember the "Smoucher," whose acquaintance he made at the thieves' haunt in Whitechapel.

The "Smoucher," as he was termed by his familiars, was an adept in penmanship, and had the faculty of imitating the handwriting of any person in a manner which was at once remarkable and surprising.

It occurred to Mr. Sutherland that he might make very good use of the Smoucher's ability, and he at once put into practice a scheme he had pondered over for a considerable period.

Mr. Sutherland had an extensive circle of acquaintances, and, strange as it may appear, he did, by some means or another, contrive to push himself into certain coteries of respectable society, one reason for this being attributable to the fact that he belonged to one or more gambling clubs in the metropolis.

At these he picked up all sorts of acquaintances, good, bad, and indifferent. He picked up also a vast amount of information at these establishments which he made serve his purpose in many ways.

He occasionally lost large sums of money at the gaming table, which had a certain amount of fascination for him, so that he was a frequent visitor to these "hells." The term is an old one, but it is remarkably expressive.

In the course of play he became possessed of cheques for both large and small amounts, and was, as a natural consequence, in a short space of time very well acquainted with the signatures of persons of wealth and position.

When aground for money, Mr. Sutherland sought the assistance of the Smoucher.

That worthy performed the secret of removing the handwriting on the body of the cheque by some chemicals.

He also removed one or more of the figures, and then wrote in figures to perhaps ten times the amount for which the cheque had been originally drawn.

Mr. Sutherland paid his confederate handsomely for this little favour, and then changed the cheque.

He had done this on very many occasions, and, strange to say, had escaped detection. But the game was a risky one, and it was only under pressing circumstances that he had recourse to this species of fraud; but he was so extravagant, so reckless in respect to money matters, that despite the large sums he gained by his robberies, he was, like most of his compeers, continually in need of a fresh supply of coin.

It was on one of those occasions that Sutherland or Purvis endeavoured to put into practice a robbery on a much more extensive scale than he had as yet attempted. He was not aware at this time that suspicion had been aroused, and that the detectives were at work to run him to earth.

He held a cheque payable at the Saltwich bank. It was for forty pounds odd. This he took to the Smoucher, who, with his accustomed skill, took out the handwriting, and substituted in its stead four hundred pounds instead of the forty.

It was so admirably done that no one could detect the alteration, and Mr. Sutherland, who knew perfectly well that the drawer of the cheque had a large balance at the bank in question, hastened down to Saltwich with the altered cheque. He had for his companion the unscrupulous scoundrel, "The Cracksman," as he was termed. This personage has already been introduced to the reader.

Sutherland and his accomplice put themselves into the train and booked to the nearest station for Saltwich.

Sutherland was to present the cheque while the Cracksman kept watch and ward outside.

When they arrived at their destination Mr. Sutherland made at once for the bank. He was fashionably attired was of aristocratic appearance, and had all the ease and self-possession of a person who was accustomed to move in good society. And he had the audacity of the old gentleman himself.

He walked into the bank with the greatest possible assurance and presented his cheque, which was paid without a moment's hesitation.

He pocketed the money and met the Cracksman at an appointed spot some distance down the road.

"It's all right—got the browns," said Mr. Sutherland. "We had better not be seen walking together. You make for the station as soon as you see me turn down Hagget's-lane. I'll wait for you at the station. Do you understand?"

"All right, Dandy. Best not be seen together till we are out of the wood. All right, I'm fly."

Sutherland walked rapidly on till he reached the lane in question.

He had not gone very far down this when he was accosted by a stranger.

"You have paid a visit to the bank at Saltwich, I believe?" said the latter.

"What business is it of yours whether I have or not?" returned Mr. Sutherland.

"I ask you a simple question, and I must insist upon an answer. Have you been to the bank?"

"If I have, what is it to you?"

"You presented a cheque drawn by Mr. Leathside, and the cheque was paid?"

"Upon my word, your insolence is most remarkable. What have you to do with my business transactions? Stand aside, and let me pass."

"You will have to accompany me. I arrest you upon the charge of obtaining money under false pretences," returned the stranger. "It is of no use you attempting to carry the matter off with a high hand, Mr. Sutherland; you are my prisoner," observed the detective, for such he was. "You are my prisoner, and will have to answer the charge preferred against you."

As he uttered these last words he placed his hand on the Dandy's shoulder.

"Confound your impudence!" exclaimed the latter. "If you attempt to detain me, I'll lay you flat in a brace of shakes."

"You had better go quietly. If you resist it will be all the worse for you. I am a detective."

"What do I care for that? You don't suppose that I am in fear of a detective."

"You had better go quietly. If you are innocent, you have your remedy; but once more I have to inform you that you will have to go with me."

"Upon my word, sir, I am astounded at your impudence. Arrested, and for what, I pray?"

"I have already told you. For obtaining money under false pretences—for forgery. Come, Mr. Sutherland, don't attempt to deceive me, for that you will find to be hopeless. I have a warrant for your apprehension. You are my prisoner."

"Prisoner be hanged. If you attempt to molest me I'll give you the soundest thrashing you ever had in your life."

The detective made no reply, he only smiled.

Sutherland rushed past him and took to his heels, but the officer gave chase and proved that he was as fleet of foot as the young fugitive, whom he overtook, tripped up, and then seized with a firm grip.

The Dandy by this time was duly impressed with the danger of his position. He struggled most desperately to escape from the clutch of the officer, but found all his efforts unavailing.

"You are a foolish young man," cried the detective,

"and are only making matters worse by this violence, which will not serve your purpose."

"Unhand me—let me go," said the Dandy.

"Not if I know it," returned the other.

Sutherland shouted out for assistance, and in a few seconds the Cracksman came upon the scene.

"Have at him," cried Sutherland. "Polish him off if you have any care for me."

With a yell of indignation the Cracksman precipitated himself upon the officer, who was probably astounded at the strength and savage ferocity displayed by his athletic assailant.

The struggle was a short but desperate one. The Cracksman threw the detective, and when he was down pinned him to the earth with his knee upon his chest.

The Dandy laughed. Escape seemed certain. The officer of the law was at the mercy of the two thieves.

It is not possible to say how the conflict would have ended, but assuredly it would have not been in favour of the detective had not another actor arrived on the stage.

The noise of a horse's hoofs were heard on the hard road, and in a moment or so a farmer drew the reins of his champing steed.

"What be this?" he ejaculated. "Two upon one—that beant the right thing. Look here, you ugly varmint, leave go of your man. Do you hear?"

This last observation was addressed to the Cracksman, who, in reply to the same, uttered an imprecation, at the same time pressing his knee more firmly on the officer's chest.

"If ee beant disposed to take heed of words, maybe blows will suit ee better," cried Ashbrook, for such the new comer proved to be.

The speaker whirled round his riding whip, and with the butt end of this he dealt a terrific blow on the side of the head of the Cracksman, who howled with pain.

"Just you let 'im go, or maybe I shall give ee a crack on the crown as'll knock ee silly."

The Cracksman sprang to his feet, and at once made at the farmer, whom he endeavoured to pull from his horse.

But Ashbrook rained such a shower of blows on the head and shoulders of his brutal assailant, that the latter, blinded with the blood that flowed from the wounds, and staggering from the effects of the punishment he had received, like a coward and bully as he was, turned tail, and took to his heels.

Mr. Sutherland, seeing that the odds were against him, followed the Cracksman.

"He'll get clear off," cried the detective. "He can run like an antelope."

"Who do ee want, then?" inquired the farmer.

"The young un, the swell cove."

"I'll ketch him," cried Ashbrook, "please the pigs," and he forthwith put spurs to his horse and galloped after the fugitives.

Of course the Dandy ran his hardest, but he was soon overtaken by the horseman.

"Ye beant a goin' to gi' us the slip, ye circumwenting young vagabond. Not if I know it," cried the farmer, as he came up with the runaway. "Hold hard, you scoundrel. The game is up, and so surrender."

"I'll have my revenge upon you some time or another," said Sutherland. "What business had you to show your ugly mug here?"

"Don't ee gi' me any more of your cheek. If ee do, I'll spoil your beauty for the next three months at the very least."

And with these words the farmer rode full at the

fugitive, whom he collared and dragged along for some distance.

"You will have to answer for this. I shall bring an action against you for assault and battery," cried the Dandy.

"Ah! oh! it be you, Mister Fortescue—be it? Glad we ha' met. So, my beauty, you are run to earth—eh? Don't ee think to get away 'cause you see the 'pleece want ee, and what is more I want the 'pleece to ha' ee, so it be no manner of yoose yer strivin' to get clear off. Hilloa there, I've cotched 'im," cried Ashbrook, shouting out at the top of his voice to the detective."

Mr. Sutherland strove in vain to slip out of the hands of the farmer, who was altogether too strong for him.

Panting and perspiring from every pore, the detective came up with the runaway, and while the farmer held him the officer clapped on his wrists a pair of handcuffs, and made him his prisoner once more. He had now no chance of making his escape, and was therefore fain to submit quietly.

"What be going to do wi' him?" inquired Ashbrook.

"Take him before a magistrate," was the prompt answer.

"Ah, that be best. What be he charged wi'?"

"With forgery."

"Oh, that be all, eh?"

"Yes, and quite enough too. I am greatly beholden to you, Mr. Ashbrook, for the service you have rendered me, for without your assistance I should have hardly known what to have done."

"You're quite welcome, Todd, quite welcome. I be glad I coom up in the nick of time, seeing as how it might ha' gone hard wi' ee. But ye're a brave fellow and stuck to your man like a Briton, and I shall just let un know how gallantly ye behaved,"

"I am sure I dont deserve this praise. I merely strove to do my duty."

"An ye've done it right well. As to this young varmint the sooner he's lagged the better, for he be a rank bad un."

"Do you know him, sir?"

"Know him—I should think I did. He passed himself off as a gentleman, and I like a fool believed him, but we won't enter upon that now, Todd; ye've got yer man—that be enough for both on us. Where be ee goin' to tek un to?"

"To Squire Kensett's."

"Aye, lad, that be the best thing to do."

Mr. Todd marched off with his prisoner, and Ashbrook promised to follow on to the house of the magistrate.

CHAPTER CXXXVI.

THE JUSTICE OF THE PEACE AND THE PRISONER.

MR. SUTHERLAND was run to earth.

It was the first time during his lawless career that he had been brought under the ban of the law; nevertheless, he was by no means so downcast as persons would suppose.

He had unlimited faith in his tact and address, which he hoped would stand him in good stead on the present occasion.

He told Mr. Todd that he was perfectly innocent of the charge, and assumed an air of quiet resignation which was quite charming.

He objected, however, to the ornaments on his wrists, and begged as a special favour to have them removed.

Mr. Todd declined to oblige him, and said that he would have to bear them till they reached the magistrate's house.

Mr. Sutherland made a wry face, and declared that he was an injured person, and that the indignity was quite uncalled for, since he was a gentleman who was well able to meet the charge, and leave the court without a stain on his character.

Mr. Todd only smiled at the last observation, and so the two—the prisoner and the detective—walked on conversing in what might be considered to a casual observer in a friendly and jocund manner.

They had not very far to go, for the magistrate's house was within three-quarters of a mile from the spot where the affray and capture had taken place.

The magistrate and his wife were at this time seated together in the old oak dining-room of their habitation. He was reading the pages of a book on heraldry, watching from the window the broods of rooks who were cawing as they flew from bough to bough.

These two persons lived in that which their tenants believed to be a palace, but which was in reality little better than a prison. They were forced to live in this great house, which they could hardly afford to repair, surrounded by these lands which were taxed in proportion to their extent, but which only yielded income in proportion to their real worth.

The squire was always anxious. He was buried in hopeless poverty, engaged in an endless struggle to keep up appearances.

His wife was always sad. Providence had given her but one real blessing—it was a son—and for this son, who had died in his youth, she had never ceased to grieve.

That is why her face was always pale and her eyes so hollow—that is why she lived but in a reverie, and so seldom spoke. Her thoughts were always in the past; she had nothing to care for in the present—nothing to hope for in the future.

They lived together, and yet so isolated; they seldom spoke to each other—they never quarrelled. Misfortune, which had at first made them cling closer to each other, had finished by making them gloomy, taciturn, almost misanthropical.

They had now learned to nurse their own sorrows in their own hearts, and never to give vent to their troubles by words.

Such misfortunes, however, as they had become inured to were now about to yield to another—poignant, appalling, dangerous.

There was a sound of bustling and voices in the kitchen which reached into the dining-room. The servant presented himself and informed his master that Mr. Todd, of the local police force, wished to speak to him.

The magistrate requested his domestic to show the officer in.

Mr Kensett rose. His face, which had been before melancholy and abstracted, now became dignified and severe.

It was necessary to put on the mask of self-composure which he was obliged to wear before the world.

Mr. Todd entered and made a respectful obeisance.

"Beg your pardon, sir, and yours too, madam," said he, in a conciliatory tone; "but if you please, sir, I've managed to capture the fellow who has been defrauding the bank by a false cheque."

"Indeed, Mr. Todd; I am pleased to hear it," exclaimed the magistrate. "Caught the rascal—have you?"

"Yes, sir. Mr. Wrench sent a telegram from Scotland-yard, and directed us to watch for our man."

"Quite right; very good of Mr. Wrench. He has done well. Where is the culprit?"

"I have him here, your worship."

"Oh here—eh?"

"Yes, sir."

"That's better still. Bring him in; and you, my dear——" observed the magistrate, glancing at his wife.

Mrs. Kensett obeyed his gesture, took the hint, and left the room.

The magistrate was astonished at the aristocratic and gentlemanly appearance of the young man who was conducted into his presence by the police officer.

"Is this the accused?" said he.

"Yes, your worship."

"Under what circumstances was he arrested?" was the next query.

The officer explained all those particulars with which the reader is already acquainted.

"Have you searched him?"

"Yes, sir."

"With what result?"

"The four hundred pounds paid by the bank have been found upon him."

"The cheque is a forged one—is it?"

"The signature is genuine, but the amount has been altered."

"We shall want the drawer and the bank clerks to depose to this fact."

"They will be forthcoming, your worship. I don't think there is much mistake about the forgery."

Mr. Kensett took a volume from his bookcase, which he consulted as to the law in such cases.

"What have you to say to the grave charge preferred against you, young man?" said the magistrate, addressing himself to the prisoner.

"I deny it *in toto*," said Sutherland, in an indignant tone. "It is utterly false. I have changed a cheque, it is true. That I do not for a moment dispute; but as to tampering with it I do not admit."

"Well, if you are innocent, I hope and trust you will be able to prove such to be the case; but you will have to be detained."

"Detain an innocent man! It's most unjust!" ejaculated the prisoner.

"Of that I am the best judge," quietly observed the magistrate. "If you had been innocent it is not at all likely you would have made such a desperate attempt to escape. However, I should be sorry to prejudge the case, and shall, therefore, forbear from making any further observations. Mr. Todd, you will have to bring this young man to the court by ten o'clock to-morrow morning, and be prepared with what evidence you can by that time. Enough must be procured to justify a remand, do you understand?"

"I quite understand your worship."

"Am I to be locked up till that time, sir?" said Sutherland.

"Certainly, you must remain in custody till the morning."

Sutherland approached the table, and taking a pen between the tips of his fingers, wrote two words upon a slip of paper.

When the magistrate read these two words he became frightfully pale.

"You see, sir," said Sutherland, "this is information which would be of material value to the cause of justice. I must, however, decline to enter into the matter before witnesses, and——"

"Clearly so," interrupted the magistrate. "It would not be desirable for you to do so. I don't desire it for a moment."

"Then, sir, all I ask of you is to give me a private interview."

"I am in duty bound to accede to your request. Mr. Todd, the prisoner has secrets of importance to communicate, and will you, therefore, be good enough to wait in one of the upstair rooms?"

"Certainly, your worship."

The magistrate rang the bell. A servant appeared to answer to the summons, and Mr. Todd was conducted into another apartment in the magistrate's house.

When alone with the prisoner Mr. Kensett turned the key of the dining-room, and looked inquiringly at Sutherland.

"Now, sir," said he, "you have the opportunity of explaining yourself. You have written upon this paper *your grandson*. I do not know what you mean. I have no grandson, and if this is but a *ruse*, a trick on your part, I shall take very good care that you shall be severely punished."

"It is no trick or *ruse*," quietly observed Mr. Sutherland. "It is nothing of the sort."

"Well, sir, I fancy you will find it difficult to impose upon me."

"I have no desire to do so, Mr. Kensett. On the contrary, I wish to give you valuable information."

"These are but idle words," cried the magistrate, "a mere sound."

"Permit me to relate to you a little story. I am sure it will not only surprise, but will interest you much. With your kind permission I will take a seat. Am I constrained to wear these handcuffs? They are by no means agreeable."

"Let me hear what you have to say. As to the handcuffs that is a question which rests with the officer who has you in charge," returned the magistrate.

"They are needless appendages, but we will not discuss the advisability of submitting me to this indignity —so let it pass. So if you are agreeable I will at once proceed with my narrative."

"The incident which I am about to relate to you occurred seven-and-twenty years ago, come next September. On the night of the eleventh of that month a woman, with a baby in her arms, proceeded through the bye-road leading to Saltwich. She was in the depths of trouble, so I have been given to understand, and bore in her arms a newly-born infant."

Mr. Sutherland paused, and placed his hand on his forehead as if to collect his thoughts.

The magistrate seemed to be almost stupefied with astonishment, but forbore from making any observation.

The prisoner proceeded—

"The woman's name was Isabel Purvis; she is the heroine of my story."

The magistrate uttered an exclamation of surprise and horror.

"Doubtless the name may be familiar to you, sir," said his companion. "Well, as I have already observed, she went by the name of Isabel Purvis, but her real name was Kensett."

"It is false," cried the magistrate, "utterly false. She had no legal right to the name of Kensett."

"I don't wish to contradict a gentleman in your position," returned Sutherland, "but I think you will find what I have just said is true in substance, and, in fact, her real name was Kensett."

"I am lost!" cried the magistrate.

"Lost in wonder, doubtless, but not yet lost, I trust, in the extensive sense usually applied to that word. But this is digression. To continue : It was a cheerless night, the wind was beginning to rise, and moaned among the trees of the forest by which your house is so gracefully encircled, the rain dashed in torrents against the windows as if the very elements—but you can imagine the rest."

"I can do nothing of the sort, sir. I don't know to what you would allude."

"Well, Mr. Kensett, I assure you that I have every reason for believing that what I am about to tell you is correct in every particular. The woman placed her child on the doorstep of a house, and then fled precipitately; but she did not escape—she was arrested by the village constable upon the charge of attempting to murder her offspring. You were, on that night, seated in this room, as you are now—on one hand a book of the law to assist your memory—on the other hand a Bible—before you a felon. You were alone with this criminal, as you are alone with me now, and you were in the power of this criminal, as you are now in mine."

"In your power ?"

"Most completely. But to my story. This woman, who was charged with abandoning her offspring, was not so bad as people were led to suppose. The father of her child was your own son—was Mr. Robert Everhard Kensett—he went to sea, and the ship he set sail in foundered, and all hands on board were lost."

The magistrate uttered a groan.

"He was not only the father of the child but the husband of its mother."

"I never can—I never will believe it," cried Mr. Kensett, in an agonised tone of voice. "It is not possible."

"It is not only possible but an actual fact. You might have read the Roman history, sir. It is possible that you might have heard of Brutus, the first consul. However, it is very certain you did not attempt to imitate him. You aided your daughter-in-law to escape from this house, gave her some money and exacted a solemn oath from her that she would never trouble you again. That is true—is it not ?"

"I will not deny it. It is true."

"Then it appears to me that you are in my power."

The magistrate tried to collect his bewildered thoughts.

"On that night," said he, "there was a legal paper in the possession of the prisoner. I was, therefore, in her power, but were you to state these circumstances in court you would not be believed."

Sutherland smiled.

"I will not give you the second chapter of my story. You evince but little curiosity, and are perhaps not anxious to have it completed, but remember the words which I have written down, and to which I have not yet given you the clue."

"I will hear you to the end," said Kensett; "but wait awhile, Mr. Todd will wonder what has so detained me."

He went to the door and called the officer by name. Mr. Todd came down from the upstairs room.

"Ah, Todd," cried the magistrate, "it appears that this young man will detain me much longer than I had at first expected You had better have something to eat and drink. The servants will bring you what we have in the house."

"Thank you, sir. It will be very acceptable."

"Good. Then make yourself at home. When this young fellow has finished his—ahem—confession, I will call you."

"All right, your worship, I am in no hurry."

Mr. Kensett shut the door and again turned the key.

CHAPTER CXXXVII.
MR. SUTHERLAND IS TRIUMPHANT—THE AMICABLE ARRANGEMENT.

"Now, sir, you can proceed, if you please," said the magistrate, sternly. "I have consented to hear what you have to say in this matter, but it does not necessarily follow that I place any reliance upon this specious tale of yours."

"Oh, dear me, no. Certainly not. You will, of course, take it for what it is worth. I am not the first man by a good many who has had the misfortune to be looked upon with doubt and mistrust."

"You will be pleased to confine yourself to the facts, and not indulge in extraneous or impertinent observations," cried the magistrate.

His companion bowed and said quietly—

"The facts are in themselves significant enough."

"Are they ?"

"Yes, I hope so. Let me see, where did I leave off ? Oh, I know, at that part of the narrative where you parted with this unfortunate woman. Well, Mr. Kensett, she went her ways. She kept her promise; for from that day to the present moment you have not seen or heard anything of her. Is that so ?"

"Yes, that is so."

The magistrate began to feel a vague fear, and shuddered in spite of himself.

Mr. Sutherland continued—

"The child was taken to the union, where it remained for some three or four years; then it was taken charge of by Mr. Searle, your wife's brother. I believe he elected to be its natural protector, and placed it in charge of an old woman, whose name I do not at the present moment remember, but she was, so I have been told, a most worthy person, and did her duty, was mindful of her young charge. Any way the youngster thrived, and when old enough Mr. Searle apprenticed him to the late Mr. Jamblin, owner and occupier of Stoke Ferry Farm. The farmer had instructions to bring the lad up as an agriculturist. He obeyed the instructions given him by Mr. Searle. By injudicious punishments and injudicious pardons he taught this boy, whose father was dead, whose mother was a fugitive, and whose grandparents dared not acknowledge him, to be mischievous, discontented, and deceitful. Finally, he ran away from his foster father, and a reward was offered for his apprehension, but all efforts to regain this treasure proved ineffectual, and his relatives resigned themselves with Christian resignation to his loss."

Mr. Kensett was perfectly bewildered. He stretched his hand out mechanically towards the bell.

Sutherland only smiled sardonically.

"On reaching London," said he, "after leaving Stoke Ferry Farm, the boy sold birds' nests in the street, till he was adopted by a fence or receiver of stolen goods, who instructed him in the way of cheating, in which he soon became a proficient. He then passed into the hands of one of the most notorious thieves in the metropolis."

"Gracious Heaven !" exclaimed the magistrate, with a deep-drawn sigh. "Can this be possible ?"

Sutherland took no notice of this last observation, but went on.

"In a twelvemonth," he observed, "like Raphael and other great artists the boy had surpassed not only the expectations, but also the *chefs d'œuvre* of his master. At nineteen he became notorious—at twenty-one he became celebrated. Now he is a Claude Duval in politeness, a Lovelace in intrigue, a Richard Turpin on the highway, and will perhaps prove a Jack Sheppard among the prison locks."

Mr. Kensett began to have a dim perception of the terrible secret in store for him.

"This man," continued Sutherland, "this glorious hero to whom the London detectives, if they knew heathen mythology, would attribute the ring of Gyges, which rendered its possessor invisible, is myself, I, Alfred Purvis, *alias* Sutherland, *alias* Fortescue, who have the honour of standing before you now."

There was a pause. The magistrate was deeply moved.

Presently he said, in a tone of anguish—

"Do you mean to say, young man, that you are Alfred Purvis, who ran away from Stoke Ferry Farm?"

"Most certainly I am," answered the prisoner.

"It appears to me to be altogether incredible."

"That is likely enough, sir, but it is a fact. You see, sir," he said, calmly, "how intricate and mysterious are the ways of Providence. By a miracle I was saved from death in my infancy, and why? Most probably you have committed some crime, which has never been discovered. It is I who have been selected as an instrument of retribution. I own I would have preferred that I had been some one else, but——"

"Silence, sir, this insolence is altogether intolerable! Me commit a crime! Are you mad to make such an assertion?"

"Pardon me," said Sutherland. "I did not make the assertion. I only threw it out as a suggestion, as a possibility, but no doubt the hypothesis is incorrect. It does not, however, in any way alter the leading facts connected with the history of your humble servant. You will find it difficult to set aside the relationship which exists between us."

Mr. Kensett rose from his seat, and paced the room with rapid strides.

"It is enough," he presently said. "There is no further need for threats or taunts if what you have been saying is true."

"It is true—every word of it."

"Well, if such be the case, you are the son of my son—you have my blood in your veins—you are a felon."

"That has yet to be proved."

"I hope it never will be, for both our sakes."

"I hope not."

"Ah, but this is indeed terrible; I know not how to act."

"Let me go!"

"I cannot do that. Do you think you will be able to prove your innocence when the magisterial inquiry takes place?"

"You ask me a plain question?"

"Yes, I do."

"And require a plain answer?"

"Certainly."

"Well, then, Mr. Kensett, I don't think I shall be able to prove my innocence, and therefore it is advisable that you aid me to escape."

"I will save you if possible," said the magistate, in a low voice. "But how is it to be effected? That's the question."

"How!" cried Sutherland. "It is easy enough, I fancy."

"Not without compromising myself; I am quite powerless in this case, and yet ——"

"You have no wish to see your grandson cast into a cell?"

The magistrate shuddered.

"Suppose you let me overpower you—tie you to a chair, and then get clear off."

"Impossible!"

"Ah, it's possible enough if you will only oblige me by taking off these handcuffs."

"I dare not do it. No, we will devise some better scheme."

"I am at your mercy—it is not for me to dictate. I leave the affair in your hands."

Mr. Kensett considered for some little time and then said—

"I do not approve of your scheme—it is not practicable; but I shall save you, Alfred Purvis—save you for my poor dear boy's sake. Listen—you will have to submit to a short term of imprisonment—you must be locked up for the night. In the morning you will be brought before the police-court, and evidence will be offered to justify me in remanding the case—this I shall do."

"And what then?"

"Apply for bail, which I will grant. If the case does not assume a very serious aspect, possibly I may feel justified in letting you out on your own recogniances. The rest is an easy matter. Go abroad; get out of the way till the offence is blown over. You can do this, I suppose."

"I shall not trouble myself to come up for a second hearing—you may depend upon that," said Sutherland, with a mocking laugh.

"And if I do this you will promise to lead a new life, and strive as best you can to make atonement for your past errors. Will you promise?"

"Oh! certainly. I pass my word—that is sufficient," replied the prisoner carelessly.

"You are not sincere, and do not mean what you say."

"I declare most positively I do, sir," was the prompt reply.

"I wish I could believe you. Oh! but this is a terrible trial to me. Even now I find it difficult to believe you are the boy who, years ago, worked at Stoke Ferry Farm."

I will give you proofs, sir—incontrovertible proofs, if you need them, before many days are over our heads."

"Peace! silence! Let it pass on. I believe your story, and so that's enough. I see the likeness to my dead son when I gaze on your features. Yes, I believe all you have said. I took no notice of you when a child; now I would risk anything to save you from ignominy and disgrace. Leave it to me."

The magistrate went to the door, and called out in a loud tone for Mr. Todd, who at once made his appearance in answer to the summons.

"The prisoner is persistent in his declaration of innocence, Mr. Todd," said the magistrate, in his habitual official tone of voice.

"Is he, sir?" said the officer. "We know what that is worth."

"Yes—oh, dear, yes—of course, Todd. Still, I do hope the young man, who is evidently well educated, may not be so bad as we think. However, you must take charge of him, and bring what witnesses you have to the court to-morrow morning. By the way, there is, I think, hardly any necessity now for the handcuffs. They can be removed."

"Ah, certainly, your worship, if you wish it."

Mr. Todd, with marvellous dexterity, removed the objectionable ruffles from the wrists of Mr. Sutherland, who was deeply sensible of this little favour. He was then marched off to gaol.

When he and his captor had gone, the magistrate fell into a chair, covered his face with his hands and sobbed like a child.

He had hardly recovered himself from his first paroxysm of grief when the voice of Ashbrook was heard in the outer hall, inquiring of the servant for Mr. Kensett.

The magistrate pulled himself together as best he could, and assumed an air of official sternness.

"Oh, your sarvint, sir," cried Ashbrook, entering the parlour. "I be a little late—leastways later than I had intended. Beg pardon, squire, but I hope I aint intruding."

"Not at all, my friend, so pray be seated," exclaimed Kensett. "I am glad to see you."

"Thanks. I ought to ha' been a little earlier, but it can't be helped, I've been detained. I wanted to say summut about Mr. Todd. He's done his duty, and I am glad I coom up just in time to render him timely service. However, what I wanted to make known to your worship is this, Mr. Todd did his duty and fought like a brick."

"Ah, I have no doubt. Todd is a most efficient officer."

"He brought in the prisoner, I s'pose," said Ashbrook.

"Yes, the young rascal is locked up, and will be brought before me to-morrow morning for examination."

"Ah, just so. Well, Mr. Kensett, I know summat of the varmint; he be a bad lot."

"You know him, Ashbrook—do you?"

"Yes, sir; he passed himself off as a gentleman, and was my guest at Stoke Ferry Farm for some time."

"Indeed, and does your wife know him?"

"My wife!" exclaimed the farmer, wiping his forehead with his bandanna. "Well, sir, she does know him—knows him to be a deceptive, circumwenting, young scoundrel."

"I am glad you have called upon me," observed the magistrate, "because I desire to know as much as possible about the prisoner. As far as I can see at present the charge is not substantiated, but it is not possible to say what evidence is forthcoming."

"He is a bad lot anyway," returned the farmer.

"Appearances are against him, I admit."

"Appearances be hanged! I tell ee that he's a wretched impostor."

"May be so, Ashbrook. Possibly he is so."

"There is no possibility in the matter—he is. I tell ee, Mr. Kensett, that he is a false, deceitful fellow. I shouldn't say this unless I had good reason for it. He's a varmint."

The magistrate smiled.

The farmer was so energetic and impressive that it would have been difficult for any one to have refrained from smiling.

"You are right enough, I dare say," observed the magistrate, "but assertions are one thing and evidence is another. If this young man is guilty we shall know how to deal with him."

"Oh, mek no doubt o' that, not a morsel o' doubt. It aint loikely that he will be able to throw dust in the eyes of an experienced and far-seeing gentleman loike yourself. I will be at the court to-morrow morning, and just tell what I know about him."

"I don't know that there will be any occasion for that, Ashbrook," observed the magistrate.

"Oh, but it 'ud be just as well, your worship. I know summat about the young vagabond, and I be willing enough to do my best to send him to quod."

"Just so; you are actuated by the best motives without doubt, but at the same time we have to consider many things before rashly entering into matters which are after all but pendents on the main issue."

"I do not quite understand you," said the farmer.

"Possibly not; but we will consider this over. Take a glass of wine, Mr. Ashbrook; we do not often meet," said the magistrate, passing the decanter to his agricultural companion.

"Certainly, sir. Here's your very good health, and I may say I am happy and proud to see you," cried Ashbrook, raising the glass to his lips.

"The feeling is reciprocal, I am sure," returned the magistrate. "Your very good health, Mr. Ashbrook. By the way, you observed just now that you knew the prisoner. Will you be kind enough to tell me under what circumstances you made his acquaintance?"

"Sartinly," said the farmer, "I med his acquaintance by the merest chance."

He then proceeded to give his companion a succinct account of all those events which the reader is already acquainted with—the meeting of the young man at the "Old Carved Lion," his taking him to his own house, and the base ingratitude of his guest.

The magistrate was surprised at the narrative, as he well might be. It was a history he was quite unprepared for.

"So you will see, sir," observed the farmer, when he brought his narrative to a conclusion, "that it aint at all likely I bear him any good will; on the contrary I should loike te see him behind the bars of one of her Majesty's prisons."

"Of course, that is but natural, since he served you so badly."

"An audacious, impudent, lying, circumwenting, young jackanapes," exclaimed the farmer. "A wretched impostor, who passed himself off as a gentleman, and sent a challenge to me by a sham captain, who was no better than himself."

"It was a piece of impertinence, I admit."

"That beant the proper term; it was oudacious, beyond all bounds."

"It was so."

"I lose all patience when I think on it."

"No doubt. That is in no way surprising."

"I tell ee, Mr. Kensett, that he's a viper—a serpent as would ha' destroyed my happiness and peace of mind for ever had I ha' given un the chance."

"His conduct was bad in every way."

"It was infamous. But I'll be at the court in the morning, never fear."

"I do not think there will be any occasion for you to attend."

"You think not?"

"Hardly so."

"But I caught the fellow and handed him over to Todd."

"Certainly so. He informed me had it not been for you, Ashbrook, the officer would have been very badly used indeed."

"I'm sure on it, sir; this young feller's accomplice was a desperate ruffian—there aint no mistake about that. My belief is he would not care about committing murder."

"I dare say not. Todd said he was a desperate ruffian."

HE GAVE THE ORDER TO THE PLATOON TO FIRE, AND FELL INSTANTLY.

"He was all that, sir."

"The case is a most remarkable one—remarkable and singular in many ways; but I think we shall not need your evidence upon the first examination."

"Not need it!" cried Ashbrook, in a tone of surprise.

"Well, no, I fancy not. It will be my duty to re-mand the prisoner, and you can give your evidence at the second examination."

"Why not to-morrow? I took an active part in the scrimmage," observed Ashbrook.

"No doubt about that, but we shall have enough to do to hear the evidence connected with the charge."

No. 73.

"As you please, sir—you ought to know best ; but I should have thought my evidence would have been needed."

"Most certainly it will.   The timely assistance you have rendered redounds greatly to your credit, Ashbrook.   Everybody will acknowledge that, but there are other considerations.   The prisoner has made me acquainted with other facts which have greatly astonished me.   Indeed, I may say, have caused me much anxiety.   It would surprise you, I dare say, to learn who he is."

"I know who he is, Mr. Kensett, a circumventing, worthless young scoundrel—I know perfectly well who and what he is, sir.   Don't ee make any mistake about that."

"You know something of his history, but not all."

"Not all—eh ?   Well I 'spose not, but I know enough."

"I say not all advisedly, Ashbrook.   You must not repeat what I am about to tell you."

"Anything told in confidence I am not likely to repeat."

"Very well.   Perhaps you have heard of a lad who was many years ago placed in the care of the late Mr. Jamblin, your father-in-law?"

"Well, what o' that ?   Old Jamblin was as good a fellow as ever stepped into shoe leather, or crossed a furrowed field."

"Nobody will attempt to gainsay that.   He was a most worthy man—but to my story.   This young man who is charged with fraud—this fellow who calls himself Sutherland now, and also passed as a Mr. Fortescue when he was a guest at your house, is the farmer's boy who, years and years ago, ran away from Stoke Ferry."

"Run away !" cried Ashbrook, in a state of bewilderment.   "Look 'ee here, Muster Kensett, I dunno as I rightly understood ee."

"You will do so after a while.   You know, I suppose, that the late Mr. Jamblin had placed under his care a lad who was said to be an orphan ?   The youngster's name was Alfred Purvis, and from what I can gather he was a sore trouble to your father-in-law."

"Well, I have heard so," ejaculated Ashbrook.   "I do remember a lad of that name being at the farm, but he ran away years ago, and has never been heard of since."

"That's right enough, Ashbrook; all traces of the scapegrace were lost.   But, nevertheless, I have good reason for saying that the young man who was arrested to-day is none other than he."

"What !   Alf Purvis ?   Oh, that be impossible.   I wunno b'lieve it."

"I wish I could not believe, but that I find impossible."

"Never, Mr. Kensett—it beant loikely."

"It is so, Ashbrook.   I am afraid it is true."

"Well, I am knocked silly if that be the case.   Why, he aint a mo'sel loike the boy."

"He is altered in every way—that I admit; but he is Purvis, I tell you, nevertheless."

The farmer's breath seemed to be taken away at this announcement.

"You be mistaken, I'm thinkin'," said he.

"No, I am not—I am correct in my surmise."

"Well, ye ought to know a deal better than what I do, seeing as how you have had so much experience; but I'm floored, and that's the honest truth, and completely by the heels !   Can it be possible that this young man, who was a guest at my house and was so friendly and intimate with Patty, can be the boy who

years and years ago was driven from Stoke Ferry by old Mr. Jamblin, with a hare tied round his neck ?   It appears to be perfectly incredible."

"It is a fact, Ashbrook ; at least, such is my impression."

"Well, I be wonder-struck—that's all I ha' to say 'bout it, and as to Patty, she'd be regularly done over when she hears this piece of news."

"There won't be any occasion for you to make her acquainted with it," quietly observed the magistrate.

"I dunno so much about that—ye see, Mr. Kensett, I ha' no secrets from my wife, and I don't b'lieve she has any secrets as she keeps from me.   I'd better tell her all about this business, for she's sartin to hear on it sooner or later."

"You are the best judge as to that, Ashbrook.   Tell her if you think it advisable to do so."

"Oh, aye, I'll tell her," returned the farmer; "but you see, Mr. Kensett, after what you've bin a sayin', I dunno as how I shall go to the court to-morrow.   The lad was a bit hardly dealt by when at Stoke Ferry—so I've bin given to understand, and maybe it 'ud be just as well for me to keep away, and not mix myself up in the business any more than I can help.   I'll consult Patty.   She's got a lot more common sense than falls to the share o' most wimmen.   I'll ask her what she thinks about it."

"Certainly, it would be your best course, and act in accordance with her wishes."

"Aye, may be it would.   Well, I never !   It's altogether a most extraordinary affair—most extraordinary."

"Not more extraordinary than true, Ashbrook."

"No, sir, I aint a sayin' as it be ; but it gets over me, and no mistake."

After some further conversation, the worthy agriculturist bade the magistrate good-bye, and took his departure.

Alf Purvis, whose rather chequered career we have already sketched up to the period of his arrest, was about as unprincipled a young scoundrel as it is well possible to conceive.   The earlier years of his life were in a measure enshrouded in mystery.   He was supposed to be the illegitimate offspring of some gentleman, but this was only surmise.   When an infant he had been left on the doorstep of a house in the immediate neighbourhood of Saltwich.   He was picked up by a farmer's man and taken to the workhouse.   His mother, who had abandoned him, was tracked by a village constable, arrested, and brought before Mr. Kensett.

She told her tale to him, said that the father of the child was his (Mr. Kensett's) son, who had gone to sea.   The magistrate, who had every reason for believing that the story the woman told was a true one, connived at her escape, extracting from her before she left his presence a promise that she would never trouble him again.   He gave her a sum of money and heard no more of her, had never seen her from that time up to the present hour.   Such are the leading particulars connected with the life and parentage of the accomplished London thief.

When the hour arrived for the prisoner's examination Mr. Sutherland was brought into court by Todd, the detective.   His genteel appearance, good looks, and winning manners made him more an object of pity than execration.   The women who were present in the court were unanimous in their opinion that he was an innocent person, or, if not quite innocent that he had been the dupe of more designing persons, for it was not possible to believe that so genteel and well-conducted a young fellow could be a callous offender against the laws of his country.

Mr. Todd and the other members of the police force were, however, of a different opinion. The London detective gave him a bad character, not that he had ever been in trouble before, but he was said to have been a suspected person for a considerable period while residing in the metropolis. It is needless to observe that they were not very far out in their reckoning.

Mr. Todd when put in the box gave a full detail of the prisoner's capture, and the attempted rescue of him by the Cracksman, who was a well-known thief. These circumstances were made manifest enough, and could not by any possibility be contravened. The fact of his having in his possession the full amount he had received for the cheque cashed at the Saltwich bank was also deposed to, and the bank clerk was also in attendance who declared that the cheque had been altered.

This, however, could not be proved positively without the attendance of the drawer of the cheque, and he, it appeared, was at this time in Paris, and the gentleman engaged for the prosecution thereupon asked for a remand.

At the advice of Mr. Kensett the prisoner was represented by a badgering lawyer, who availed himself of every quibble to set aside the evidence offered for the prosecution.

He had not much difficulty in turning the tide in favour of his client, for, to speak the truth, the case for the prosecution was a regular bungle, and Mr. Sharpthorne, Sutherland's legal adviser, damaged it materially.

"I respectfully submit, sir," said Sharpthorne, looking triumphantly round the court and addressing himself to the magistrate, "that there is in reality no kind of proof offered on behalf of the prosecution that this young man has committed any fraud whatever. A cheque has been presented by him and paid by one of the cashiers of the Saltwich Bank. I am instructed by my client to inform the court that he received the cheque in the ordinary course of business—that he was, in point of fact, a perfectly honest holder of the cheque in question, and he presented it in the full faith of its genuineness. I must say I think the bankers have acted in a most indiscreet and, I may observe, a very harsh way, towards a respectable and honestly-disposed young man."

"Respectable and honest—eh?" sneeringly observed the attorney for the prosecution.

"Certainly," replied Sharpthorne, thumping the table before him. "I say advisedly and emphatically, both respectable and honest. The inference is a rational and reasonable one. Every man is honest until he is found guilty."

"The prisoner made a determined attempt to escape. You seem to forget that," observed Mr. Kensett, addressing himself to the blatant lawyer.

"Well, sir," observed the latter, "I should be very sorry—indeed, it would be imprudent for me to contradict you; but permit me to observe that even this has not been clearly established. It is true a ruffian attacked Mr. Todd and endeavoured to overpower him —indeed, he partially succeeded in doing so; but it does not necessarily follow that this was done at the instigation of the prisoner. It is just possible the man in question was a perfect stranger to my client. I believe he was."

"Ah, Sharpthorne, that is going too far," observed the opposing solicitor.

"You may think so, if you please; but I do not think I am exceeding my duty in making such a suggestion. But it is hardly worth while discussing that question; even assuming such were the case, it does not prove anything after all. It does not incriminate this young man, against whom there is positively no proof of fraud or dishonesty."

"The circumstances surrounding the case are suspicious," quietly observed the magistrate. "If proofs are wanting now, possibly they may be brought forward in the due course of time."

"But is this young man to be degraded in the eyes of the world by lying under the stigma of dishonesty merely because a country banker chooses to assume a position which is not supported by evidence? It is a most trumpery charge."

"I object to the word trumpery!" exclaimed the lawyer on the other side.

"You may object as much as you please. Substitute contemptible in place of it if that pleases you better," returned Sharpthorne.

This last observation evoked a peal of laughter from those in the body of the court.

"Order! silence!" cried the usher.

"If there is any more of this unseemly merriment," said the magistrate, "I will commit those persons who indulge in it."

This had the desired effect—the audience abstained from any further laughter.

"I have to express my regret that an unguarded expression made by myself should have given rise to this breach of etiquette," said Sharpthorne.

"Let the subject drop, I pray," observed Mr. Kensett.

"By all means, sir. I am, I hope, the last man to court a legal wrangle. We have to deal with the evidence, and I submit that this is of a nature that, regarding it from a legal point of view, does not in any way bear against the prisoner, who, I maintain, is entitled to be discharged."

"I should not be justified in dismissing the case after the evidence offered," said Mr. Kensett.

"Evidence, sir," cried Sharpthorne, "there is positively none."

"I am not accustomed to allow gentlemen to direct me in the course I am to pursue," observed the magistrate. "I admit the evidence is very weak at present, but there is no telling what may be forthcoming, provided the legal advisers for the prosecution have time afforded them for that purpose; and at the same time, Mr. Sharpthorne, I should be sorry indeed to prejudice the case, or to press badly on the prisoner who to all appearances is a quiet gentlemanly young man. Still at the same time I have a duty to perform. If the prisoner is innocent I hope and trust it will be proved on the next examination. Certainly, as far as I can see at present, there is not a great deal against him. Certainly not enough to send the case for a jury to decide. I think, therefore, under all the circumstances, I should be justified in remanding the case to this day week, and in the meantime I will let the prisoner out upon his own recognisances."

"I hope you will require him to find good and substantial bail, sir," said the solicitor for the prosecution.

The magistrate hesitated, whereupon Mr. Sharpthorne came to the rescue.

"The young man knows nobody in this neighbourhood, and it would be unjust to accede to Hashby's suggestion. I therefore beg of you to bind him over in his own recognisances."

"Yes, that, I think, will be all that the exigency of the case requires, said Kensett." The case is adjourned to this day week, and in the meantime our friend Hashby will have ample time afforded him to obtain whatever evidence he can to complete his case."

"His own recognisances!" murmured the bank clerk. "What does that mean?"

"Why, it means that his worship don't think much of the evidence offered to-day," whispered Sharpthorne. "And to say the truth, it would be strange if he did."

"We are going to fight it, Sharpthorne; and we are, I hope, going to pot our man," said Hashby.

"Are you?"

"Well, yes, I think so."

"We shall see, my friend. Better luck next time, as the butcher said when the rope broke with which he had attempted to hang himself. You haven't scored much to-day."

"That I admit, but it isn't my fault. Was only instructed half an hour before entering the court."

"Oh, by the way, Mr. Hashby," observed the magistrate, "you had better leave the cheque in my hands, and I shall then have time to make a careful examination of the same."

The cheque was handed to the magistrate, who looked at it for some little time.

"I must confess, as far as I can see at present, it seems to be genuine enough. Do you happen to know whether this is the drawer's signature or not?"

"The bank clerks do not appear to have any doubt about that," said Hashby. "But the writing in the body of the cheque and the figures have been altered."

"How could that have been done?"

"Well, sir, it has been done on more than one occasion, for the purposes of fraud, and it is managed in this way: The original writing is taken out by chemicals, then the manipulator imitates the hand-writing of the drawer, and places a much larger amount in than the cheque was originally drawn for."

"It is a very extraordinary proceeding. I do not remember, in the whole course of my experience, meeting with a similar case."

"I deny most positively that the cheque has been tampered with. If it has, it has not been done with my knowledge," exclaimed the prisoner. "The charge is a false and malicious one."

"That is my opinion," cried Sharpthorne, "and if this be the case the matter will not rest here. The bank directors have laid themselves open to an action for damages and false imprisonment. I say, again, it is not at all likely the matter will be allowed to be hushed up."

"Hushed up, Mr. Sharpthorne! What can you be thinking of to make so unjust an observation?" cried the bank clerk. "Do you suppose that we have any vindictive feeling towards this young man?"

"I purposely avoid replying to your query," returned the lawyer. "I have my own opinion of the matter, which, for cogent reasons, I choose to keep to myself."

"But you have cast a slur upon the bank directors, and I say it is not just or proper for you to do so. We have good reasons for acting in the way we have."

"Oh, I dare say," sneeringly observed Sharpthorne. "No doubt you think yourself on the safe side."

"Let there be no squabbling," said the magistrate, interposing. "The bank think themselves justified in the course they have adopted, and it is but fair to assume that they have good reasons for their line of action. It is not at all likely that a respectable and old-established firm would be rash or indiscreet enough to institute these proceedings without due consideration."

"I should hope not," returned Sharpthorne; "but at the same time, sir, we must all admit that people are sometimes mistaken, and I think it will be found that such is the case in this injudicious and uncalled-for prosecution."

"I really do not see that you are mending matters by casting aspersions upon a respectable body of gentlemen, who, from the position they hold in the commercial world, are incapable of acting in an improper or harsh manner."

"I have done, sir. We'll say no more about the matter at present," observed Sharpthorne, with a shrug, as he gathered up his papers and transferred the same into his official blue bag.

The prisoner was bound over in his own recognisances to appear that day week, and there was an end of the case as far as the first hearing was concerned.

Mr. Sutherland had had a narrow escape. He was by far too cunning and dexterous a thief to present himself on the following week.

He contrived to become possessed of sufficient funds to take a trip, and repaired to the Continent, where he proposed remaining till the little affair of the Saltwich bank forgery had blown over.

The bankers were very indignant when they found the bird had flown, and Mr. Todd was, of course, greatly mortified at the issue, but there was no help for it. The police had instructions to make every effort to trace the fugitive, but as too frequently happens in such cases their efforts proved ineffectual, and in the course of time the affair was forgotten, and "the storm in a teapot," as Mr. Sharpthorne designated it, subsided.

CHAPTER CXXXVIII.

THE FASHIONABLE GATHERING AT LADY MARVLYNN'S.

AVELINE GATLIFFE, now Lady Batershall, wife of Sir Eric Batershall, Bart., had long since forgotten that such a person as Tom Gatliffe had existence.

In her new sphere of action, and the two ties in the shape of a boy and a girl by her husband, the baronet, she had little time to think of her earlier career, which appeared to have been blotted out of her recollection.

She loved to be a reigning beauty in the fashionable world, and although time had in some measure robbed her of the freshness of youth, she was still a beautiful and loveable woman, whose society was courted.

She had at times misgivings in respect to her son Reginald, who did not give her much of his society.

There were reasons for this. In the first place, the young earl did not care a great deal about his father-in-law, who, albeit, a good, honest, bluff, English gentleman, was a little brusque in his manner towards his son-in-law.

This was not intentional, but resulted from a habit of plain speaking which he had acquired down in his ancestral home in the west of England.

To Aveline he was uniformly kind and considerate. Indeed, with him her word was law. He knew she had been indulged by her grandfather.

"Spoilt," he would sometimes say, "if it were possible to spoil such a gentle, tender-hearted creature. But there," the baronet would say, "he did his best to spoil her, but she was too much for him, and he couldn't succeed. Hang me, if I think any man alive could spoil my Aveline. No man breathing, sir," and when he gave utterance to this speech the baronet would glare around at the persons he was addressing, and looked as if they had done him some sort of an injury; and so it was pretty generally acknowledged that Lady Batershall was a star in the fashionable firmament.

She did not lose sight of her old friend and instructress, Lady Marvlynn, whom she regarded in the light of her nearest and dearest associate.

The latter had always on hand one or two protégées whom she was preparing to " bring out," as she termed it. It was not possible for her ladyship to remain long idle, some sort of employment was a necessity to her.

She had at this time a young lady under her charge, a Miss Arabella Lovejoyce.

She had become greatly attached to this young girl, who was possessed of a more than ordinary amount of beauty, and could also boast of many accomplishments. She was a " blonde," whom some wicked persons who take a delight in detracting called insipid.

She was, however, by no means deficient in sense.

Miss Lovejoyce had been for some months on the Continent, in charge of a severe vinegar-visaged old maiden aunt, and upon her return to this country Lady Marvlynn gave a grand party in honour of her arrival.

Of course a number of notabilities were invited.

The army and navy were both represented on this occasion, likewise the Church. People of almost every denomination were included in the list of invitations, and amongst them were the Lady Aveline and her husband.

The preparations were on a grand scale.

Lady Marvlynn resided at Upper Charlton. The locality was not altogether so fashionable a quarter as she could have wished, but her house, which stood in its own grounds, was most elegantly furnished. It was a model bijou residence, and contained a suite of reception rooms sufficiently commodious to admit of a tolerably extensive gathering. Besides all this, her ladyship was the very best of hostesses, and strove on these occasions, as indeed she did at all times, to make those around her as much at home and as happy as possible.

Lady Marvlynn was not only appreciated by hosts of persons, but was generally esteemed by all who came within her influence.

It is true she was not what one might say positively rich, and hence it was perhaps that these gatherings were few and far between, but when she did give a party it was done in a proper manner, and it was the fault of those present if they did not enjoy themselves.

When Aveline and her husband presented themselves they found the house full of people.

Many of those present were known to the baronet and his wife, but there were some who were strangers to them.

Introductions as usual took place—the requisite bowing and courtesies followed.

On the lawn were one or two croquet parties, and seated around were groups of persons, who did not play themselves, but elected to be passive spectators.

These had before them iced drinks of every possible description. Aveline took a stroll in the grounds with her friend Lady Marvlynn, who was as lively and loquacious as usual. An opportunity was thus afforded of taking stock of the guests.

" There are many here to day," said Aveline, " who are to me strangers."

" Oh, yes, of course, my dear. That is but natural, you know, but I am sure you'll like them; at least, I hope so. You see that elderly gentleman sitting next to the lady in pink ?"

" Yes. I don't know him—do I ?"

" I think not. He is a most wonderful man, has been in every part of the world."

" He's in the army I should imagine."

" Yes."

" And his name ?"

" Is Major Smithers Smythe. Got no end of medals. Was wounded at Agra in the Sepoy rebellion. Oh, he has a whole fund of anecdote, and tells such amusing stories. I'll trot him out, dear, before the day is over. You'll be quite charmed with him."

" Oh, I dare say, and the other gentleman further on—"

" In a black coat and a white tie ?"

" Yes."

" That's the Rev. Mr. Downbent. He's taken three degrees at Oxford, and is a most eloquent preacher. Oh, you'll like him, I am sure. The slender gentleman on the other side of the grass plot is Sir William Leathbridge, he is conversing with Lord Chetwynd—a very old family the Chetwynds—came in with the Conqueror. His lordship is a quiet, thoughtful man, who, as a rule, does not say much, but he thinks a good deal more, and, entrez nous, he is reputed to be a little gay. Keeps an opera dancer so I've been told, a beautiful Spanish woman, I believe ; but one never knows what to believe nowadays—it may be all scandal. All I know is, that he is very charming, and as to a 'gentleman's private amours, that's no business of yours, my dear,' as poor dear Sir Eric used to say when such topics were broached."

" Who is the one playing now ?" inquired Aveline, glancing towards the party in question.

" That's Captain Crasher. Oh, he's another of the right sort ; will sit and tell you stories till the small hours of the morning—that is, if you are disposed to listen to him."

" And the gentleman with the long hair and dark moustache ?"

" What—the one talking to Arabella ?"

" Yes."

" Oh, dear me—don't you know him ? That's Signor Marowski, the celebrated basso profondo. You'll have an opportunity of judging of his ability, for he is set down in the programme for two of his favourite scenas."

" Ah—you are going to have some music, then ?"

" Dear me—yes. A little bit of a concert, you know. And about an hour, or perhaps more, I think you'll find we've got several crack singers and instrumentalists. We are all lovers of music."

At this point of the conversation a lady met the two speakers in the side walk.

She was dressed in the height of fashion, and evidently strove to assume a juvenile appearance ; but she was not young—neither was she stout ; scraggy would, perhaps, be the better term.

" Oh, glad to have met you," said Lady Marvlynn, " as it affords me an opportunity of introducing you to my friend, Miss Fagg—Lady Aveline Batershall."

" I've not had the pleasure of meeting you before," said the faded spinster, for such she was, " but have often heard your name mentioned by my friend, Lady Marvlynn."

" Oh, I dare say," returned Aveline ; " her ladyship is one of my oldest friends."

" Yes, so I have been given to understand. Most delighted to make your acquaintance."

Lady Aveline bowed somewhat stiffly.

" I am much pleased," said she.

The conversation was continued, but there was no further discourse as to the persons present, and Aveline would have been greatly relieved by Miss Fagg taking herself off.

This, however, she did not seem disposed to do, for she continued to walk by the side of Lady Aveline, apparently oblivious to the fact that she was not wanted.

"I wish, dear," said Lady Marvlynn to Miss Fagg, "you would give a glance at the dining-room, and see if my people are making any preparations for the banquet."

"Oh, if you wish it, certainly," returned the spinster, stepping off like a lapwing.

"Ah, we've got rid of her," cried Lady Marvlynn, with a merry laugh. "I thought you were beginning to get a little fidgetty. You know, dear, I was constrained to invite her. She is one of your dear Sir Eric's distant relatives, and it is not often she gets the chance of a treat like this, for, although I say it myself, I know it is a great treat to her, and the chances are that she'll talk about it for the next three months when she returns to her friends in the village which has the honour of counting her among its inhabitants."

"She's a good sort of person, I should say," observed Aveline, apologetically.

"Ah, dear me, yes, very good, unsophisticated, and all that sort of thing, but she is perhaps a little out of place here."

"Ah, yonder is Lord Fitzbogleton," cried Lady Marvlynn.

"Where? I don't see him."

"Look, through the shrubbery. He is talking to Arabella. How he does follow that girl about to be sure! He is spoony on her—poor man."

"And does she like him?"

"Bah! who can tell? Perhaps she doesn't know herself. She endures him, that is quite certain. But let us return into the house; they don't want our company, I fancy. In cases of this sort it is my maxim 'to let the young people alone;'" and here the widow indulged in another merry laugh.

They went into the house, where they were joined by a throng of persons. In less than half an hour after this dinner was served.

The Rev. Mr. Downbent said grace in an impressive manner, and all present proceeded to partake of the various dishes placed before them.

The conversation soon after this became lively and animated. A few stale jokes were uttered, which elicited as much laughter—perhaps more—than new ones. Healths were drunk, but, as it was a private affair, no speechmaking was attempted.

It was, in fact, a social party, and not a public banquet, and oratorical flourishes would therefore be out of place.

The meal occupied a considerable time—much more than was necessary; but this may be said of all such entertainments. A dessert of a most costly and elaborate description was laid in an adjoining apartment, and to this the greater portion of the guests repaired.

"Now, gentlemen," said Lady Marvlynn, "I must beg of you to do just as you like. Those who wish to smoke are requested to do so, because I believe most of the ladies present will not offer any objection to the aroma of the fragrant weed. I like to see gentlemen smoke—it looks sociable; but I am not everybody, you will perhaps say. Well, that is true enough—so we will effect a compromise, if you please. A room is prepared for the reception of those ladies who object to smoke."

"My dear Lady Marvlynn," cried one of the gentlemen, "this is really too bad. In the first place, we do not care to dispense with the company of the ladies; and in the next, we are, I hope, not such slaves to habit as to persist in smoking in the company of ladies."

"I shall not be satisfied if you do not enjoy yourselves in your own way."

"This is not a barrack-room," said Smythe, deprecatingly.

"Now, major, although I have every respect for your opinion," said Lady Marvlynn, banteringly, "you are not in command here."

"And if I were, I should give way to your ladyship," returned the major.

"The best thing you can do is to keep the party alive by telling us one or two of your adventures," said Lady Marvlynn. "Now don't be disagreeable, major. Let me have my way this once."

"Don't I always let you have your way? Ah, dear me, I only wish I was a younger man."

"I should like to be a little younger myself," returned her ladyship.

Cigars were lighted, the wine was passed round, and the whole party were soon in social and animated conversation.

"Let me see, major," observed Colonel Snappe, who was one of the guests; "were you not present at the execution of the ill-fated Maximilian?"

"I am glad to say I was not," returned Smythe. "But I was in Mexico a short time before that untoward event. You know, I suppose, that the scoundrel Juarez, after Maximilian's death, had the body of his victim embalmed. In the holes made by the executioners' bullets pieces of red velvet were placed, a pair of glass eyes were inserted in the orbits of the dead man, whose body was decked out with most costly garments, and then it was sent on to his relatives."

"How very horrible!" exclaimed Aveline. "I never heard of anything more sickening."

"Very horrible, I admit," said the Colonel; "but such was the fact."

"While I was in Mexico," said Major Smithers Smythe, "facts came to my knowledge which, with your permission, I will relate."

"Oh, by all means, we shall all of us be delighted. Pray proceed, major," cried several.

"The little story I have to tell," said Smythe, "I call a game for life or death. It is as follows":—

"It was night in the camp of Maxmilian's army, and sounds of merriment were heard upon all sides, for soldiers are ever wont to indulge in pleasure, regardless of what morrow would bring forth.

"In a tent in the inner circle of the camp sat two officers at a rude table, upon which was marked with lead pencil a chess, or checquer board, while black and white buttons served for the 'men.'

"Around the tent were stationed guards, and both of the officers were unarmed, while not a weapon of any description was visible in their canvas room.

"They were prisoners: soldiers in the service of Juarez, captured the day before; but their appearance indicated that they were not Mexicans.

"Both men were of tall commanding forms, and of easy, graceful address; but, whereas one had dark blue eyes, and light hair and moustache, the other had eyes that were large and black, with brown hair and moustache.

"Both men were exceedingly handsome, and upon their faces bore the impress of noble souls and hearts that knew no fear.

"A love of adventure had caused them to leave their homes in the north, after the close of the civil war, in which both had fought bravely, and cast their swords with Juarez, to aid in driving from Mexican soil a German emperor.

"Capoul Monteith, the blonde officer, was a young man of wealth and good family, a New Yorker, and a pet in society.

"Garnet Weston, the brunette, was a poor man, a young lawyer in New York, of good, though poor parentage. He was possessed of superior intelligence, and was fast winning a name, when he crossed the path of Mabel Monteith, the sister of Capoul, and a beauty and an heiress.

"So deeply did Garnet love Mabel that he was miserable when not in her presence, and he believed she cared for him; but his pride was great, and he would not offer a pauper hand to a belle and an heiress, and so struggled hard to win fortune and fame in his profession.

"One day, an evil day for Garnet, a pretended friend told him that Mabel was his promised wife, but that their engagement had not yet been made public.

"Like one in a dream Garnet Weston listened, and then in despair determined to seek some more stirring field, where the image of his lost love would not be ever before him.

"A month later found him a cavalry captain in the army of Benito Juarez, where, a few weeks later, he was surprised to be joined by Capoul Monteith, who had also offered his services to the Mexican President.

"In an engagement, two days before they are presented to the reader in their tent, they had been captured and carried into the lines of Maximilian.

"That night in camp they were playing a game of checquers, *pour passer le temps*, and Capoul who was an expert player, was surprised to see how readily he was beaten by Garnet.

"Suddenly a heavy tread resounded without, the sentinel challenged, there was a response, and the next instant three of Maximilian's officers entered the tent, one of whom was an American, a Republican fighting for Imperial Mexico, against the Republic; another was a flashy-looking Frenchman; the third was a Mexican colonel.

"'Gentlemen, I am sorry to disturb you; but news has come to-night that Benito Juarez has executed a captain of our army, and I have orders to select one of you, and march you forth to die in retaliation,' and the American Imperialist looked sad over the duty he had to perform.

"'You cannot mean that one of us must die for an offence against Maximilian by Juarez?' said Capoul Monteith, rising.

"'Even so are my orders, sir; but I know not which to select, for my duty is most painful.'

"'Let the gentlemen play a game for the choice— the loser to die,' suggested the young Frenchman.

"'A good idea, monsieur. Gentlemen, I observe you were playing a game of checquers when we entered —so set to work and play three games—the one who wins two of them to escape, the other to die.'

"'When is this execution to be?' asked Garnet Weston.

"'Within the hour, sir.'

"'Very well, Capoul, I am ready for the game of life and death.'

"Capoul Monteith paced to and fro the tent with quick, nervous strides; he was young, handsome, possessed of vast wealth, and fond of life, and he cared not to be thus shot down like dog; but he was a brave man, and thought of Garnet Weston, whom he had always admired, and half wished to be the loser rather than see his friend die.

"'I am ready,' he at length said, and the two friends, strangers in a strange land, sat down to play the game of life or death.

"Capoul Monteith played with the utmost caution, for, 'if one must die, I have as good a right to struggle for life as has Garnet,' he thought.

"Garnet Weston played with indifference, a quiet, sad smile upon his face, and around them stood the three officers, and the platoon that were to be the executioners of the losing one.

"Ten minutes passed, twenty, and the game was won by Capoul Monteith, whose face flushed crimson, and then paled again.

"Garnet Weston's face never changed an expression, for the same smile rested there.

"The second game passed quickly, Garnet making his moves the instant Capoul had raised his hand, and surprising all by his reckless indifference, but cool manner.

"Five minutes passed, and the second game was won by Capoul Monteith.

"'My God! Garnet, old fellow, I feel for you from my heart,' cried the winner, the tears starting to his eyes.

"Garnet pressed his friend's hand, the same smile upon his face as he said, quietly—

"'I was ever a poor unlucky dog, Capoul; but, my friend, when I am dead look in my saddle-roll, hanging there, and the papers you find please deliver to the proper address, and—and—Capoul, say to—to Miss Mabel I left a farewell for her.'

"'Gentlemen, I am ready.'

"'Curses on your Imperial humanity! Will you slay a man as though he were a hound?' cried Capoul, angrily turning towards the officer, for it cut him to the heart to thus part with his friend.

"'I yield to the fortunes of war, Capoul, and these gentlemen but do their duty.'

"'Come, let it be over,' replied Garnet, and shaking the hand of his friend warmly he was marched away.

"Half distracted with grief, Capoul Monteith paced his tent, his thoughts whirling, and his brain on fire, as he gazed at the stool where a short while before poor Garnet had sat.

"An hour passed, and the American officer of the Imperial army stood before him.

"'Well?' said Capoul, hardly daring to ask the question.

"'He is dead.'

"'God have mercy upon him,' groaned the sorrowing friend.

"'Yes, Captain Monteith, he is dead, and though I have seen many men die I never saw one face death with such perfectly calm indifference as did your friend.'

"'He gave the order to the platoon to fire, and fell instantly; but, ere he died, he wrote this note to you,' and the American Imperialist handed a slip of paper to Capoul, and, turning, left the tent.

"In Garnet's bold hand was written—

"'Capoul,—I gave my life away to save you, for I loved Mabel too dearly ever to let her brother die where I could be sacrificed instead. I dare tell you this now, for I stand on the brink of my open grave. Farewell!—GARNET.'

"A bitter night of sorrow passed Capoul Monteith in that lonely tent, for well he knew his friend had spoken the truth, and when months after the star of Maximilian's crown had set in gloom, and he resigned from the army of the successful Juarez, he wended his way homeward with a heavy heart, for he could not forget that Mexican soil covered the noble man who had fallen a sacrifice to save his life.

"Three years passed away after the game for life or death, and one pleasant evening, toward the sunset-hour, a horseman was riding slowly along a highway, traversing a fertile valley of a South-western State.

"Three years had added more dignity to the face, and perhaps saddened it; but otherwise no change had ever come over Capoul Monteith's fine features.

"Upon his right hand, setting back from the road, was a pretty little farm-house, surrounded by fertile fields, and the sight promising well for a night's 'lodging for man and beast,' Capoul turned in at the white gateway, and rode up to the front door, and dismounted.

"The owner of the mansion descended the steps to greet him, and Capoul Montieth stood face to face with Garnet Weston!

"'My God! has the grave given up its dead?' cried Capoul, in dismay.

"'No, old fellow; you find me flesh and blood, ready and willing to give you a hearty welcome to this my home, left me by an old bachelor uncle a few months since. But, come in; I will tell you all.'

"The surprised and delighted Capoul willingly accepted, and around a well-spread tea-table that evening he heard how Garnet had been carried forth to be most bunglingly executed; but a squadron of Juarez cavalry had appeared and frightened off his executioners, ere the first platoon had retired, and that a watchful ranchero had seized him and borne him to his ranche, where through months of suffering, he recovered, and was able to depart from the house of his good friend.

"But it was long ere he could gain strength enough to reach Galveston, Texas, and there he met an old uncle, who had carried him to his comfortable home with him.

"The kind old bachelor was one day thrown from his horse, and night and day Garnet had watched by his bedside, until death relieved him of his sufferings, and the young man found that his uncle had left him all his wealth.

"'But, old fellow, why did you not write to let me know, for you know not how I have mourned for you?' asked Capoul.

"'I did write to my old law partner in New York, and he said you had moved away, none knew whither.'

"'True; poor Mabel failed in health, and I carried her to Europe, but we soon returned; and to effect a change in scene and air I purchased a fine farm, about two days' journey from here, and there we now live. Mabel is contented, if not happy.'

"'She married——'

"'She married? Fiddlesticks! No, she never had any idea of marrying any man excepting yourself, and you went off to Mexico and nearly broke her heart.'

"'God, I thank Thee,' cried Garnet, and he buried his face in his hands and wept like a very child.

"Three months passed, and the bachelor home of Garnet Weston had a mistress to preside over it—a queenly-looking woman of twenty-two, perhaps, with dreamy, sad eyes, and a face of wondrous beauty.

"That woman was once the heiress and belle of New York—Mabel Monteith—who had, after long years, married her first and only love, through that game of life and death, in the gulf-washed land of Mexico."

"Well," said Colonel Snappe, "it's a moving narrative, and I expect our friends here, as well as myself, are under the impression that Garnet Weston was done

to death. How he managed to escape is the most surprising part of the business."

"Ah, but I am so glad he did escape, poor, dear fellow," cried Arabella; "but it is a most touching story. I wouldn't have missed hearing it on any account."

"By Jove, but it's a splendid narrative—never heard a better," said Lord Fitzbogleton. "I know a fellow, who knows another fellow, you know, who is a capital hand at telling stories, but he isn't up to the major—not by an immeasurable distance."

"Ah, that was a most unfortunate piece of business. It was the first serious mistake the late Emperor made," said the colonel.

"It was not so great as going to war with united Prussia," observed Sir William Leathbridge. "That was his downfall."

"Without doubt, Sir William. Nobody will dispute that for a moment; but he was forced into it; and, after all, much as Napoleon III. has been maligned, he was not so ambitious or remorseless a man as many people have been led to suppose. On the contrary, he was a much more kindly monarch than I at one time gave him credit for. We in this country look at foreign potentates and foreign politics from our own point of view."

"That is but natural, sir," observed Mr. Downbent. "It is in the nature and order of things that it should be so."

"And, in addition to all this," observed Sir William, "I have always maintained that as a nation we are greatly prejudiced, and think we are nearer perfection than any other country."

"Oh, that, I think, there can be no doubt about, Crasher. One thing, however, is quite certain. We appear to be miserably behind hand as far as our detective department goes. Murder is rife in the land, crimes of the greatest possible amount of ferocity are committed, and the perpetrators, for some reason or other, are permitted to escape."

"You have broached a subject, sir," said Sir William Leathbridge, "which is an all-important one—I mean the protection of human life—and I don't believe that under the existing state of things the Government is competent to deal with this question. Why, it is a scandal to this nation."

"You mean the number of murderers who escape detection."

"I do."

"Well, we shall do no good till a different class of men are employed and the whole system is reformed."

"I've got a little bit of a story to tell about a New York detective," said Sir William. "It happened when I paid a visit to the United States."

Everybody, of course, hoped that Sir William would give the narrative, which he did after the following fashion—the details of which we reserve for the succeeding chapter.

CHAPTER CXXXIX.

SIR WILLIAM'S TALE—A MUSICAL MELANGE.

"THERE was at the time I paid a visit to our American cousins," said Sir William, "a sharp, clever fellow named Dixon. He had gained a considerable amount of reputation as a detective, and I believe he well deserved the encomiums passed upon him. Any way, as far as I could judge, he was a remarkably acute man, and he was in addition to this a civil and obliging officer.

MISS ARABELLA LOVEJOYCE AND THE PROFESSOR DELIGHT THE COMPANY.

"The case which I am about to present to you does not, perhaps, possess what I may term the romantic interest of my friend Smythe's story; but it has, nevertheless, something to recommend it, since it serves to show how quickly retribution followed the commission of a horrible crime.

"My story is that of a dead traveller found in a train.
"The train stopped at Dexham's bleak depot long enough to permit a man to spring from the drizzling gloom upon the platform of the through coach, whose doors were locked. The conductor, ensconced from the rain in the express car, did not see the new acqui-

sition to his list of passengers, and the man standing on the platform seemed to be congratulating himself on the success of what he wished to call secrecy.

"When the train moved from the station, whose night-clerk slept in his dimly-lighted office, the unknown passenger quietly drew a brass key from his pocket, and unlocked the door of the coach. When he closed it again, himself inside, it was locked as before.

"He found the car lighted by three lamps, and seemingly deserted. Not a head protruded above the seats, and the air of desolation filled the place. He heard the rain now falling in earnest, beating against the windows, beyond whose panes the blackness of darkness reigned.

"Not far from the fireless stove the new passenger seated himself, and began to brush his hat with a handkerchief. He was in the midst of his work when something like a groan startled him, and he stopped. Leaning forward, he listened keenly, and at length rose and walked down the aisle.

"He seemed satisfied that he had heard a human groan, for he looked into and between the seats, and it was near the forward door that he suddenly came to a halt.

"He stood over a man whose head rested on the crimson cushions of the seat, but whose body lay on the floor.

"From the white lips beneath the silent spectator had proceeded the startling groan, and the eyes moved once when they caught sight of him.

"The unknown passenger regarded the scene for a moment before he stirred a limb. Then he bent over the recumbent man, and with no little difficulty assisted him to the seat.

"'I say it's no use after your murderous blows,' said the stricken one, seeming to regard the new passenger as his mortal enemy. 'You need not strike me again.'

"'I never struck you,' replied the passenger, with a faint smile. 'My kind sir, you have mistaken the person. Will you not tell me how all this came about?'

"It was quite evident that the wounded traveller was near unto death. One quiver after another passed over his frame, and once or twice after speaking he gasped for breath. The single spectator saw this and put his hand on his shoulder.

"'I will avenge you!' he said, stooping over the dying traveller. 'Tell me who did it; I am a detective.'

"The deathly eyes fixed their stare upon him, and when he saw the white lips move he put his ear down to them.

"'Tell Natalie—Natalie—tell her that—God pity me!'

"With the last word the traveller's head fell back upon the detective's hand, and the gurgle of death ran up his throat. Then he turned his face from the light, and the rain-drops that came through a hole in the pane fell upon a dead man's brow.

"'Curse the stupid luck!' said the detective, standing erect. 'He would have told me, I am sure, and my case would not have been difficult. But let me see what I can find upon him by which to work, for I swear I will hunt to the death the man who killed the traveller.'

"An examination of the dead man's pockets revealed nothing concerning his identity, and the detective looked puzzled.

"He found an empty pocket-book and a watch; but they did him no good.

"The man had probably reached his thirtieth year; his hair and well-dressed beard were light, and his lifeless eyes a beautiful blue.

"He was well dressed, but there was no show of ostentation about his garments.

"After the search the detective unlocked the front door of the coach, and with another key which he drew from his pocket unlocked the express car.

"Stepping boldly into it, he startled the messenger, whose hands flew to an inner pocket when he beheld the unsummoned intruder, but no pistol was drawn.

"'No shooting, Tobey,' said the detective, and the messenger, recognising the voice, came forward with extended hands.

"'You take a fellow by surprise, Dixon. I might have shot you.'

"'Oh! I guess not,' laughed the detective. 'Where's Golden?'

"'Asleep in yon corner.'

"Dixon stepped forward, and waked a good looking man, who had fallen asleep on several bales of gunny-cloth.

"'You've got a dead man on the train,' Dixon said to the conductor, when he opened his eyes.

"'A dead man!' cried the express messenger, before the conductor, recovering from his sleep, could utter a single ejaculation.

"'A man as dead as Chelsea! Come and see him.'

"The messenger picked up a lantern, and the two left the car.

"'I recollect him,' said the conductor Golden, looking at the dead traveller. 'He boarded the train at Monterey, and was my only through passenger. There's two stabs in his left breast! You've noticed them, I suppose?'

"'Oh, yes—nothing ever escapes me,' replied the detective, with a smile. 'Do not either of you gentlemen know aught about him?'

"The messenger shook his head without replying, and the conductor said—

"'I've met him once or twice before. I think his name is Hardesty. Concerning his home or his people, I know nothing.'

"A few minutes later, on some sacks stretched on the floor of the express-car, lay the dead traveller. The lamplight fell over his pale face and rendered it ghastly, like the faces of corpses.

"Conductor Golden said that the mystery of the passenger's death puzzled him. He was sure that no other person tenanted the fatal coach when he locked it, after taking up the only through ticket, and giving the proper check.

"The theory of suicide was discussed, but abandoned, as no weapons were found on the passenger's person. The messenger recollected a certain robbery of the company's car works several years prior to the fatal night, and stated that a number of coach keys were then taken.

"In all probability some person in possession of one of those keys had entered the coach at some station, murdered the unknown passenger while the train was in motion, and made good his escape.

"This theory satisfied messenger and conductor, but not the detective.

"'Gentlemen,' he said, calmly, 'this man was killed by an old enemy. His watch, worth at least two hundred dollars, remains on his person, but everything else has been removed. The murderer has carefully removed all traces of his identity, but his shrewdness shall avail him naught. For I tell you,' the speaker's cold but piercing eyes were fixed on Golden, 'I tell you,' he repeated, 'that I will hunt him down and make him pay dearly for his terrible work.'

"'Your hand on that,' said the conductor, putting forth his hand, and the men clasped.

"'Why, there's blood on your hand!' suddenly said Dixon, noting a crimson spot on Golden's member. 'I've a mind to arrest you,' he added, with a smile.

"'Do so, and hunt no further for your man,' returned the conductor. 'I had my hand in the dead man's bosom, hence the gore on my skin. But do you think you'll ever catch the perpetrator of the deed?'

"'Catch him!' cried Dixon. 'In my detective life I have never followed a man in vain. John Golden, you have heard of me in the capacity of a man-hunter, and I promise that you shall be present at the death of your passenger's assassin.'

"'Good! I accept the invitation implied in your words; and Tobey—is he included?'

"'Certainly,' answered Dixon, with a faint smile; and then the conversation was interrupted by the whistle of the engine.

"'We're running into Dayton,' said the messenger, taking up his book. 'I put off a parcel here that is not entered on the books,' and he glanced from the detective to the corpse.

"The coroner's inquest elicited no new facts concerning the dead passenger. The usual verdict that 'the deceased had come to his death at the hands of some person or persons unknown to the jury' appeared in the morning papers. During the day many people viewed the corpse in the coroner's office, but it was not recognised.

"Dixon, the detective, kept about the office the entire day. He scrutinised the face of each viewer of the corpse, and assisted to put the dead into the coffin after office hours. Many people wondered who that strange and commonplace man in the office was, never dreaming that he one was one of the keenest detectives in the United States.

"He left the office at eleven o'clock and passed under the gaslight towards the Merchants' Hotel. This resort was in a distant part of the city, and to gain it the detective would be obliged to traverse a portion of the metropolis infested with thieves, gamblers, debauchees, and wicked people generally. He had traversed it before, unarmed, and did not fear its denizens.

"He set forth alone, and had gained the nearest and best portion of the infested district, when a hand was laid on his arm. He stopped and beheld a young girl looking up into his face.

"'Well, miss?' he said, in a tone that reassured the person, for she came nearer.

"'I saw you in the coroner's office; but I was afraid to come in,' she said. 'I looked in from the curb, and ran off when I thought you were looking at me. Sir, I would like to see him before they give him an unknown grave. He was my brother.'

"Dixon started and turned full upon the pale, sorrowful girl.

"'Your brother?' he cried. 'What is your name?'

"'Natalie Green.'

"'Natalie!'

"It was the last name pronounced by the murdered traveller; and the detective was startled at finding its possessor so soon.

"'Where do you live?' he asked.

"'In a house two blocks down this street. Oh! sir, do not think me one of the sinning. I am not. He drew me from home, and I had not the hardihood to return. I could not face father, though I have not

fallen, and brother George, the dead, has been hunting me ever since.'

"'Natalie, this is no place for conversation,' said the detective. 'In your home you must tell me the whole story. You know what I am, girl?'

"'Yes, a detective,' she replied. 'They don't like such as you in these parts.'

"'I reckon not,' he said, with a smile, and together they walked down the street.

"What followed I need not detail here; the denouement of my story will tell you.

"One autumn night, three months later, a man boarded a train as it was leaving a country station.

"The night was the counterpart of the one that witnessed the finding of the dying passenger in the coach, and the person who had nimbly leaped upon the platform unlocked the car with the sang froid of a privileged person.

"He passed through the well-filled coach, and presently faced the messenger, who was at cards with the conductor. Both men started when they beheld the new-comer; but they soon recognised him and gave him a friendly hand.

"'No man yet,' said Conductor Golden, with a light laugh, as he looked up into their visitor's face. 'The trail is long, and will in time, no doubt, grow tiresome.'

"'But I have reached the end of it!' said the detective, seriously, and the conductor rose to his feet.

"'Good!' he exclaimed. 'Tobey, we will drink to Dixon's success.'

"'You must drink soon, then,' was the reply, and a revolver quietly slipped from the detective's pocket.

"'John Golden,' he continued, 'I arrest you for the murder of George Green. You allured his sister, Natalie, from her home, and swore to kill him because he followed you. That vow you have kept: you met him in your through coach, the night was dark, and he your sole passenger. Then and there you imbrued your hands with blood, and removed from his person traces of his identity. Deny not the charges, for I am prepared to prove each and every one! Tobey, there are a brace of handcuffs in my pocket.'

"The astonished messenger moved towards the detective, when with a cry of horror the conductor leaped to the half-open express door.

"Dixon sprang forward to arrest him, but was too late.

"The train struck a bridge as the form of the conductor disappeared, and messenger and detective gazed blankly into each other's faces.

"'Dead?' asked Dixon.

"'Dead!' responded Tobey. 'If he missed the beams he fell into the river eighty feet below us.'

"'Well, let him go!' said the detective. 'He is the assassin of the man from whose home he allured a sister.'

"The body of John Golden was never found. Among his papers at his boarding-house in the city was found a memorandum book belonging to George Green, and other articles that Natalie identified.

"Thus was the mystery that hung over the dead traveller cleared, and I have but to add that Natalie returned home, and after the lapse of two years, became the wife of no less a person than Jerome Dixon."

"It is very much to be regretted," said the Rev. Mr. Downbent, "that the detectives of this country are not able to unravel the many mysteries which of late have been presented to us in the metropolis. Indeed, to say the truth, they appear to be grossly at fault in this respect."

"We shall never do any good, sir," observed Sir

William, "till a better class of men are employed, and, I may add, prompter and more stringent measures are taken to check crimes of this nature. I have come to that conclusion years ago, and recent events have strengthened me in the opinion I have formed."

"It is a most melancholy state of affairs," said Lady Marvlynn. "I don't pretend to be a competent judge of such matters, but every one must admit that it reflects no credit on a country which is perhaps the most opulent and civilised community in the whole world."

"You are right, my dear lady Marvlynn," returned Sir William. "The number of murders committed of late in this country that we know of is bad enough, seeing that the perpetrators of these crimes are never discovered, even to say nothing about their being convicted; and then how many are there perpetrated which are never brought to light in any shape whatever?"

"This reflection is a most painful one. Looking at the matter with an unprejudiced eye, we must confess that this country has not so much to boast of after all. It is true we put down the traffic in human flesh. We abolished slavery—that is something to our credit."

"Yes, but at what cost, Sir William?" cried Captain Crasher.

"Never mind the cost. It was done—and effectually done."

"After much cost both in money and men," said Crasher. "As we are all of us in what I may call an anecdotal or story-telling vein to-day, I will, if you please, tell you a story of the African slave trade."

"Oh, do; there's a good, dear soul!" cried Lady Marvlynn.

"By all means, madam, if our friends are agreeable."

Everybody declared that they would esteem it a favour if the captain would go ahead; so he at once rushed into the following narrative:—

"Now I am going to tell you a story about 'The Right of Search,'" said Crasher.

"The events I am about to describe," said he, "date back to a period twenty years ago, at which time I was but a newly-appointed midshipman—the youngster of the larboard steerage-mess of the ship of war 'Excellent,' Captain David Hodge.

"As they relate to the right of search as applied to slavers, those of you who are familiar with the subject will pardon a word of explanation for the benefit of those who are not.

"Slaving not being reckoned as piracy by the law of nations at the time to which I allude, no ship was permitted to search another, even though the latter were positively known to be loaded with negroes, unless the two vessels carried the same flag.

"Consequently, any slaver when pursued, if aware of her pursuer's nationality, might run up a foreign flag, and sail coolly away under its protection, her enemy being entirely powerless in the matter.

"This was the state of affairs from the treaty for the mutual suppression of the African slave trade between Great Britain and the United States, in 1842, down to the treaty of 1862, which to some slight extent mended the matter.

"The 'Excellent' had been cruising off the Guinean coast, particularly about the region between Cape Three Points and the Bight of Benin, for upwards of four months now, and nothing to speak of had come of it.

"To be sure, we had all been ashore once or twice to call on the King of Dahomey, the best misrepresenta-

tive of royalty to be found on the western coast at that time, and he had dined us deliciously on shelled peanuts, and pledged our professional health in deep draughts of his villainous *sego*.

"But of our legitimate business in that part of the world we had done little or nothing.

"Nor was this exactly for lack of opportunity. We knew very well that the rascally old potentate was trading off his subjects at the rate of a thousand or so every two or three weeks.

"We would even lie there sometimes and see a slaver go to sea, knowing that her decks below were crowded with miserable negroes. But if we made a movement to pursue, up would go a Spanish or French flag, and all we could do was to let her severely alone.

"Once, indeed, we did circumvent one of them most beautifully.

"We had followed her up when she put out of the river until she showed the stars and stripes, and then, as the breeze was light and the night a promising one, the old man ordered out the barge and sent an officer up to Elmina, ten miles above us, to inform a Yankee sloop of war which we knew to be there. We hung to the slaver all night with the ship, and just at day break, sure enough, there was the American making for her with all sail spread.

When the fellow saw her, he thought to get out of it by running up a French flag, but at this—since change of flag is presumably evidence of fraud—we both pounced upon him, and in half an hour had his crew in irons.

"But that wasn't the story I started to tell. As I say, we were not always as fortunate as that, and after weeks and weeks of hot weather and no prizes, the whole ship's company began to grow desperate.

"One evening, just before twilight came on—or what would be twilight if they had such a thing in those latitudes—we were standing idly along up towards Coast Castle, when a sail was reported as seen over the land, the vessel being just about to emerge from a small bay that makes in just there. Captain Hodge was on deck at the time, and himself addressed the masthead.

"'Do you know her?' was his first inquiry.

"'Can't make her out just yet, sir, on account of the hill,' answered the look-out. 'I should judge, from the size of them tops'ils and the rake of her masts, that it is the big schooner we overhauled last week.'

"A moment after, and the captain hailed again.

"'How is she now, my man?'

"''Tis the schooner, sir.'

"'All right. Keep an eye on her,' and the captain went below a moment.

"Fifteen minutes after we were in full sight of the slaver—for slaver we knew her to be. That low black hull and rakish build could belong to no respectable craft, even if the presence of such could be accounted for just there and then.

"'Now,' cries the old man, again making his appearance on deck, and as much interested in the affair as was I, the most inexperienced youngster in the ship, 'we'll make her show her colours. If she don't recognise us she may show a different flag from what she did before. If so, she is ours.'

"But the stranger was not to be caught in any such way as that.

"She did remember us perfectly well, probably had known precisely where we were every day for the last week, and when a gun was fired she ran up the French flag as innocently as could be.

"Shortly after the sudden darkness of the tropics

came on, the faltering sea-breeze died out entirely, and night set in with the two vessels within half a mile of each other, and hardly likely to change their relative positions before morning.

"At daylight, quite contrary to his custom, the old man was on deck again and inquiring for the slaver. She was still in sight; but a slight land breeze had sprung up shortly before day broke, and she was cautiously edging off to the westward.

"Although she might be perfectly safe according to the law's letter, she did not feel easy in our vicinity any more than a thief does in the company of a policeman. And so the captain remarked to the officer of the watch.

"'Mr. Bright,' said he, 'the nigger doesn't mean to stay by us long, even if we can't touch him.'

"The captain always called all slavers 'niggers' without discrimination or difference.

"Mr. Bright was the second lieutenant, young for his rank, and a man who had won rapid promotion by his decision and intrepidity. His answer was characteristic.

"'And why can't we touch him?' he asked, in a meaning sort of way.

"The captain seemed to understand him perfectly well; but he shook his head gravely.

"'It wouldn't do, Mr. Bright—it wouldn't do.'

"'But nothing would ever come of it, sir. Suppose we should take the fellow with the French colours flying, do you really think any complaint would ever reach the French government?'

"The captain still shook his head.

"'I don't know about that, Mr. Bright,' he said; 'but I don't like to do it. The thing would be unprecedented. It's too bad, too, with the nigger right here in our hands, and we are not at liberty to take hold of him,' and he strode off towards his cabin.

"Yet the lieutenant's idea seemed still to be working in his mind, for just as he was about to disappear he called out again, 'Mr. Bright, you may as well shake out an extra rag or two and keep the scoundrel in sight.' Then he vanished down the stairs muttering something about his extreme curiosity to behold a cursed 'nigger' who could get away from the 'Excellent' when her blood was up.

"So we loitered along after the schooner with what little wind there was, and after breakfast we were surprised by an order coming into the steerage, summoning all the commissioned officers, even of lowest rank, to the captain's cabin.

"We went aft in a hurry and found all assembled around the cabin table, except Mr. Bright, who was still in charge of the deck. Captain Hodge stood at the head of the table. We waited for him to speak.

"'Gentlemen,' he began, 'please fill your glasses. And now here's to the honour and success of the old "Excellent."'

"We drank the toast with great enthusiasm. Then he went on: 'Gentlemen, it is too bad, it is outrageous, the way things are at present. Here have we been cruising up and down here all summer long and hardly a prize to show for it.

"'And now, here is another blamed nigger right before our face and eyes—we know his hold is full of slaves—we can almost see 'em, and if the wind would haul to west'rd a bit hang me if I don't believe we could smell 'em—and yet, because the fellow has run up a French flag, we've got to lose him. Gentlemen, I repeat, it is outrageous!'

"We all asserted clamorously that it was monstrous.

"'And something ought to be done about it,' continued the old man, waxing warmer and more indignant. 'Ordinarily, I can somehow manage to stand it, but this fellow has been dodging here for a week with a rascally lie at his peak, and this time I'm not going to stand it.'

"The captain paused and wiped his brow with his silk handkerchief.

"'Now, gentlemen,' he again went on, 'you all know it was rather duskish last night when we made the fellow show his colours. Are you all perfectly certain what flag it was he hoisted?'

"We all kept silent with a puzzled air.

"'That is to say,' he continued, 'are you all perfectly certain it was the French flag? There was blue in it and red in it. Now, may there not have been white in it, too? In short, may it not have been the British Jack?'

"The captain said this with a queer kind of smile that suddenly betrayed to us his meaning.

"Probably he himself was the most scrupulous officer present—indeed, upon him must the whole responsibility rest.

"If he chose to run the risk it was hardly probable that any of us would hesitate, especially at what we considered a perfectly justifiable piece of deception.

"We had suffered enough already in consequence of this punctiliousness of the home Government about the right of search.

"Up spoke little Bradford, of Southampton—

"'I was in the maintop at the time, sir, and my eyesight is very good indeed. I could almost swear it was British colours she showed.'

"Several others of us made similar remarks in a jocular kind of way; but the captain interrupted us.

"'This is no joking matter, gentlemen. If we seize that schooner while she is under a foreign flag, we deliberately violate the law of nations, and without doubt run the risk of a national dispute. Yet I intend to seize her—on one condition.'

"Here he paused, and looked around the circle of eager faces.

"'Please name it, sir,' said the first lieutenant, seriously.

"'That each of you pledge me his honour that he will everywhere and under all circumstances, unless under oath, insist upon it that she showed the British flag last night.'

"Every man of us immediately declared his willingness to promise this.

"'Mr. Hazleton,' said the captain to me, 'will you ask Mr. Bright to step to the companion-way?'

"I went on deck and communicated to the second luff the captain's request. As soon as he appeared, Captain Hodge called out to him—

"'Mr. Bright, are you sure the schooner showed the British flag last night?'

"'The British flag? Why, she—oh! yes, I am quite sure.'

"'Could you swear to it?'

"'I could do anything almost but swear to it.'

"'Very well, sir. Can you come down a moment? Gentlemen, let us once more drink to the honour of the old ship—and remember that that honour should be as dear to us as our own. And now, Mr. Bright, let us overhaul the nigger as soon as possible, for, by the Great Horn Spoon, we'll have her now if she flies the flag of every nation in Christendom!'

"All sail was immediately made on board the 'Excellent,' and the slaver, seeing that something was up, and that we evidently meant to overtake her, did her very best to prevent it. But, as the captain had said, there were few slavers that could get away from the 'Excellent' when she was doing her best, and a light breeze abeam was her best point.

"Slowly but surely we overhauled her, and at noon were almost within hailing distance.

"The old man was on deck in person, and chose to assume the trumpet and negotiate the whole business himself. He had a powerful voice, and he used it as soon as there was the slightest possibility of its being heard.

"'Come into the wind,' he cried, 'or I'll blow you out of the water.'

"The stranger held straight on. He either did not or would not understand. But a round shot across his bow brought him to. As we drew nearer he called out in the best of English:

"'By what right do you stop a French vessel?'

"'Go to the pit with your French vessel. You were a British vessel last night. Stand by till we send a boat on board.'

"'Two cutters were manned, and under charge of Lieutenant Bright, dispatched to the schooner. Her papers were examined and her character as a British vessel by an American firm was positively established.

"The slaver's crew were put in irons, but left on board their own vessel. An unusually large prize crew was told off, and, to our surprise, Lieutenant Bright was put in charge of it. He was a favourite with the captain, and we had expected the third or fourth luff would go.

"But the truth was, the captain was a trifle nervous about the affair after it was over with, and he was particular about the prize. The schooner's captain had made a good deal of talk about the matter, swearing that the vessel was not English, and that his government would right the matter for him.

"Before Mr. Bright left us for the last time to go on board his new command the captain took him below and had a long talk with him. Then the two came up together, shook hands affectionately, and Mr. Bright went over the side with a farewell nod to us all. Before night the schooner was out of sight to windward.

"A year after, the 'Excellent' having by that time been ordered home, I learned that Bright took the slaver in all right, but reported that her officers and entire crew had, by some ingenious plan, escaped in the long boat before he got away from the African coast.

"Very little had been said about the matter, however, at the navy department, and shortly afterwards Bright had received his promotion. I thought that altogether the thing looked rather strange and I straightway elaborated a theory of my own about the matter.

"By Captain Hodge's orders Bright had probably put the schooner's company on shore before going to sea. The captain thought, I suppose, that they would be less likely to give any trouble about our 'violation of the British flag,' if left in Africa.

"And, as I believe, Bright took home with him from the captain letters to the Secretary of the Admiralty (a personal friend of his) explaining the whole matter and recommending Bright for promotion. At any rate, he was promoted, and we never heard anything more from the captain of the slaver."

"Ah, those were times, sir," said Sir William Leathbridge. "Happily for the world they have long since passed away."

"There are a few white slaves in this country, I believe" said the captain, carelessly.

"That may be; but they are not slaves in the sense we allude to. Many men are slaves to habit; indeed, most of us are, but that is very different to being bought and sold like beasts of burthen."

"Perhaps I have not duly considered the question," returned the captain.

"I do not say that for a moment; on the contrary, no man has had better opportunities than yourself to thoroughly understand the subject, and I take it we are not likely to disagree on its general bearings."

"I hope not, I am sure," said Captain Crasher. "But the evil has passed away, and none of us here, I expect, would wish a return of the old times. Our American cousins have endorsed the opinion expressed by the people of this country, and it redounds to their credit that they have followed the excellent example set by the 'Britishers,' as they term them."

A desultory conversation followed, in which many of the company took part, and soon after this it was announced by the hostess that the concert was about to commence.

Many of the guests had by this time betaken themselves to the apartment where the musical performances were to be given, and the remaining portion of the company rose from their seats and sauntered into the concert-room. They dispersed themselves in groups on the chairs and couches placed around for their reception.

A young lady was conducted to the piano by Signor Marouski, who was, in addition to being one of the chief performers, also master of the ceremonies, or musical director.

The young lady commenced with what might be termed a bombardment of the instrument. Then she ran over the keys with a rapidity which was perfectly electrifying.

It was a show piece she was playing—its name, however, did not transpire. It had the effect of creating astonishment, and that was all she looked for.

She was, of course, complimented, and then retired to give place to a young man with weak eyes and a pale face, who stepped forward to sing a tenor song.

His voice appeared to be weak as well as his eyes, but its tone was sympathetic, and he sang correctly, and with a certain amount of feeling which went to the hearts of his hearers.

A trio for the harp, violin, and piano followed. It was a little too long perhaps, but was very well executed—by artists who were, evidently, well up to their work.

Lady Marvlynn's protégée, Miss Arabella Lovejoyce, was now brought forward by Lord Fitzbogleton. She took her place by the piano, and her master, Signor Marouski, sat down to the instrument for the purpose of playing the accompaniment.

He began by executing a prelude of a most difficult and elaborate nature, after which the vocalist commenced a bravura from one of the well-known operas.

This she attacked with force and vigour, and it was difficult for anyone to determine exactly which to admire most, the signor or his pupil, for they were both so terribly in earnest.

Lady Marvlynn was charmed. The fair Arabella, she afterwards declared, surpassed herself; anyway she did not let the grass grow under her feet, but poured forth roulade after roulade in a most energetic and earnest manner. Her voice was a little thin and sharp—censorious people might say even piercing—but that did not so much matter—she got through her piece creditably, and was, of course, highly complimented at its close.

"By Jove," said Lord Fitzbogleton, "you are weally quite as accomplished a singer as the vewy best professional. My dear Miss Lovejoyce, I am quite enchanted."

"Oh, pray don't," said the pretty pet; "how foolish you make me look, my lord!"

"Foolish! What a remarkable observation! Foolish, indeed! You ought to be pwoud. I know I should be if I had a tithe of your ability."

"Oh, my lord, you are a flatterer, I do believe," cried Lady Marvlynn, coming to the rescue; "but of course I know that anything my dear Arabella attempts to do is sure to please you."

"Indeed you are mistaken, Lady Marvlynn," said the young nobleman; "I am a most wigid cwitic, I assure you."

The speaker conducted the fair Arabella to her seat, and Signor Marouski seated himself once more at the piano; he was about to favour the company with a long scena from a popular opera.

He began by playing a long monotonous prelude of a weird-like character; to judge from the sounds produced the inference would very naturally be that some one was in a state of deep dejection, or it might be despair or agony.

Presently he sang, in a sonorous voice, three prolonged notes. These were repeated several times, and were succeeded by a jerky, quick movement; this appeared to be a sort of recitative or prelude, for the notation was soon of a changed character—still, however, wailing and melancholy, or it might be said depressing.

That clever entertainer, Frederick Maccabe, says, when performing the rôle of a street minstrel—

"Why, lor bless you, there aint much occasion to hunderstand much about music wen you plays to a west-end audience; as long as you play somethink melancholy it's sure to go down with the hupper classes."

Perhaps Signor Marouski was of the same opinion. Anyway, he acted in accordance with Maccabe's instructions.

It was a Wagnerian piece he was executing, and many present declared it to be grand and magnificent. Whether they were able to comprehend its precise meaning it would not be so easy to determine.

However, the Italian professor sang on.

He evidently threw his whole heart into his work. He was a sound musician and an admirable vocalist, but he was imbued with the notion that the "music of the future" was the right sort of thing.

When he came to a conclusion many gave a suppressed sigh of relief, and many expressed their satisfaction by exclaiming, "Grand! splendid! remarkably fine!"

"What think you, Sir Eric?" cried one, addressing himself to Aveline's husband.

"Oh, if you ask me my opinion," cried the baronet, "I must tell you plainly that I consider all this fuss about Wagner is quite out of place."

"Oh, my dear Sir Eric," said Lady Marvlynn, "you don't know what you say, I'm sure."

"Don't I, though?" returned he. "I most certainly do. I consider it humbug. I don't profess to be an accomplished musician and am perhaps not a competent judge. Why, Lord bless us, I'm old enough to remember the time when this man's music was laughed at and scouted in this country."

"That's right enough," observed Captain Smither Smythe. "What a thing is popularity—or becoming the fashion would perhaps be the better term! The English public are afflicted every now and then with a sort of mad infatuation for eccentricity, and are apt to applaud to the very echo things they do not understand. As a proof of this I have only to refer to the *furore* for the Italian actor, Salvini. They made a god of him for a season, and then left him to flicker out and return to his native country a sadder and a wiser man. Doubtless he was duly impressed with the fleeting nature of popularity. Now it is the fashion to have a craze for a composer whose works are incomprehensible to me, and whose beauties are effectually hidden, as far as I am individually concerned."

"Really, gentlemen," said Lady Marvlynn, "you are paying Signor Marouski but a poor compliment."

"Pardon me," said Sir William Leathbridge, "we owe and pay tribute to the talents of the professor. What we are discussing is the merits of Wagner."

Marouski now endeavoured to explain to the company what Wagner had endeavoured to express in the piece he had just executed, and wound up by declaring that the German composer was a great genius.

"I admit my inability to appreciate his beauties," said Sir Eric Batershall, "still I am not singular in the opinion I have formed. In an admirably-written article in a periodical a month or two ago the writer sets forth that, 'Whereas Mozart's opera music has been the delight of every concert goer since the day when it was first written—and this, irrespective of the scenes to which it belongs—Herr Wagner's vocal phrases, detached from the pictures they illustrate, can only strike the ear as so much cacophonous jargon, in which every principle of nature and grace has been outraged, partly owing to poverty of invention and absence of all feeling for the beautiful—partly owing to the arrogant tyranny of a false and forced theory."

"These are strong expressions, I admit," said the baronet; "but not a bit too strong, excepting for the fanatics who have set up the Wagnerian idol, and would coerce the rest of the world into the worship of the fantastic creed they have adopted, just the same as the craze for the pre-Raphaelite school of painting, as it was termed, was endeavoured to be forced on the art-loving world many years ago."

"That is true enough," said Mr. Downbent; "it was a craze."

"A sort of epidemic," returned the baronet; "but hear me for a moment or so. Speaking of Herr Wagner's profuse musical dialogue, and particularly in relation to 'Das Rheingold,' the writer says, 'The recitative in which the scenes are conducted is throughout dry, unvocal, and uncouth, but Glück might never have written to show how truth in declamation may be combined with beauty of form, variety of instrumental support, and advantageous presentiment of the actors who have to tell a story.'"

"Ah, but you English cannot bear to listen to long descriptive recitative passages," cried Marouski.

"I admit that as a rule they don't care about them. Still a great many persons who listen to Wagner's operas will feel the force of the observations I have just quoted. His interminable dialogues, his annihilation of pleasant comprehensible form of music, and his systematic crushing out of melody from his compositions, must eventually cure the musical public, or the small section of it who are with him, of their unhealthy craze. In the meantime, his operas, 'dry' as they usually are, will be revived in the course of the operatic season, and among them 'Tannhäuser' is of course excepted. In this work there are long dreary pass   o wade through, with little else by way of compensation than the gorgeousness of the *mise en scène*. The professional march is truly an inspiration, and in the 'Chant of the Pilgrims,' Tannhäuser's 'Hymn to Venus,' and the shepherds' song, concessions are made to those who demand continuous understandable melody. For these indulgences we cannot be sufficiently grateful, and must congratulate ourselves that 'Tannhäuser' belongs to Wagner's middle period, and not to his later style, from which tune is rigorously excluded."

Signor Marouski smiled, and shrugged his shoulders.

"Ah," said he, "it is always difficult for a grand original genius to make himself understood or to be fully appreciated by the public."

"There are a number of musical geniuses whose works have been popular in this country," observed Smythe, "but I don't expect we shall agree upon this subject; and we have to apologise to our kind hostess for thus interrupting the concert."

"I like to listen to discussions of this sort," returned Marouski, "because I believe that the English people have a much greater love for good music than foreign nations give them credit for. However, as you don't care about Wagner," he added with a smile, "I will give you something from an opera by one of my own countrymen."

Marouski sat down to the piano once more, and sang a recitative air from one of Rossini's operas. He executed it in a manner which was beyond all praise, and the contrast it afforded to his first performance was so powerful that his audience found it difficult to believe that it was the same singer they were listening to. The Italian professor was applauded most vociferously and was evidently well pleased with his success.

"Now you must not tell me, signor, that the last piece is not a hundred per cent better than the first," cried Sir Eric Batershall."

"It all depends upon taste. Each is good in its own particular way."

"Lady Batershall or Aveline, as we have been accustomed to call her, was now conducted to the piano.

She sang a simple ballad with such pathos and with so much feeling that the assembled guests were deeply moved.

After a few more pieces had been performed and songs sung, the musical entertainment was brought to a close.

The conversation became general, the topics discussed were various, and a vast amount of knowledge was displayed by the speakers in what might with truth be termed a most delightful convivial discussion.

Among the company was a learned professor—a great naturalist who had been in many parts of the world—he had been somewhat taciturn during the earlier portion of the day, but Captain Smithers Smythe, who had resided in India for some years, drew him out, and an animated conversation followed upon the great Indian Empire. Professor Mainwaring had a number of interesting anecdotes to tell, and finally concluded with the following narrative:—

"You see," said he, "it is a good many years ago now since I was lost in the forest, but every minute incident, captain, is green in my recollection, aye, as if it occurred but yesterday."

"I can readily understand that."

"Well, it was an oppressively hot day, in the very height of summer, when Carter and myself pitched our tent in a secluded forest tract of land, near the head waters of the Chenaub. I dare say you know the river?"

"Oh, perfectly well," returned Smythe. "You had some fellows with you, I suppose."

"Dear me, yes. Our party consisted of three native servants, besides coolies, who had been engaged at the last village to carry the baggage."

"And who would run away at the first approach of danger," said Smythe.

"They were men you could not place implicit trust in, I must confess. Well, our route lay along a rugged pathway by the side of the river, through dense forests of pine and cedar which clothed its banks to the water's edge, and spread their great branches across its bosom until they nearly met in mid stream.

"A more perfect solitude could scarcely be imagined; indeed, excepting a few birds and a solitary black bear I had slain, when busily engaged performing his toilette in a brook, not another large animal had been seen for several days since leaving the verdant mountain glades of Cashmere.

"Whilst my companion and servants were employed in pegging and stretching out the bear's skin—an operation requiring to be performed when the hide is fresh, as otherwise it will shrivel up and become rotten—I took advantage of the delay, and seizing my gun, strolled through the forest in quest of novelties in the beast or bird line, being then engaged in making collections of the natural objects of the country.

"I had not proceeded far before the fresh run of musk deer indicated the proximity of that animal, which, like the hare, is partial to localities, and may be often discovered by following its footprints.

"I accordingly pushed further and further into the forest, in expectation of meeting a musk at any turn, and until it became evident that my hopes were not to be realised, when finally, getting tired of tracking, I gave up the pursuit, and set off in quest of rare birds.

"Here and there the harsh screams of the speckled nutcracker and yellow grosbeak drew me away in opposite directions, until, after devious swervings to the right and left, it suddenly dawned on me that my pocket compass had been forgotten. What was to be done? In what direction lay the river? It was useless attempting to retrace my footsteps, for, what between the hard nature of the ground, and my soft grass shoes, anything like an impression was impossible.

"I pulled out my watch to find it was four o'clock, thus leaving three hours of daylight. So now in which direction should I proceed? These and many anxious thoughts flashed across my mind, when, shouldering the gun, I stared about for a way more likely than another in the dismal gloom; but not one opening or indication seemed preferable to the rest.

"How often I had changed front since starting could not be surmised; however, a conviction arose in my mind that the way back to camp did not lie in front of the position in which I stood at that moment, accordingly I wheeled about, and set off at full speed in an exactly opposite direction.

"At first a straight ahead course seemed the proper one, but after a time it was apparent that I had been unconsciously bearing off too much to the left, and, as there was a gentle slope in that direction, a feeling kept constantly increasing that this was the watershed of the Chenaub, for the sound of whose troubled waters I stopped constantly to listen, but in vain.

"Uneasiness now grew apace, with the cravings of hunger, whilst the sun declined, and finally the glare on the tree tops vanished, leaving an obscurity which was soon doomed to blacken into night."

LINKED IN FIERCE STRUGGLE, PEACE AND THE FOOTMAN FALL FROM THE WINDOW.

"What a position to be in !" cried Smythe. " Indian forests, as a rule, are not the safest places in the world for a man to put up at, or bivouac in for the night. Beasts of prey, to say nothing of snakes or serpents, are to be found there in abundance."

"Yes, that is true enough, but, luckily, I did not consider all these things. Still, I frankly confess, that

the idea of being lost in a forest made my blood run cold. I could not discern any river, and the idea occurred to me that I might be walking away from it."

" How dreadful!" exclaimed an old lady in a turban, who was listening to the narrative. " Most dreadful, indeed."

" Yes, madam, it was not by any means agreeable, to

No. 75.

say the least of it," returned the professor. "Of course, I need not tell you that I did not know very well what to be at, or how to shape my course, since I was quite out of my reckoning. At length, being perplexed, and not knowing anything about the track I was following, I halted in front of a large cedar. This I determined to climb; my object in doing this was to see if I could, from the upper branches of the tree, discern any object in the distance which might serve as a guide to deliver me out of the labyrinth into which I had got entangled."

" And did you ascend the tree?" inquired the captain.

" Most certainly I did; but I was no wiser; from its very highest branches I could only discern one unbroken forest, and so I descended with despair at my heart, and a foreboding of evil for the future, for by this time I must tell you, that I felt my physical strength giving way. What with fatigue, want of food, and the exertion of climbing the tree, I was pretty well done over."

" A gone coon."

" Precisely. Very much gone, and very despairing also."

" My situation was melancholy and desperate to the last degree. If I had had any companion, anybody to share my troubles, matters would not have been so bad, but I had not a living creature, not even a dog, for my companion, and the solitude was well-nigh insupportable."

" Oh, yes, the beauties of nature are all very well in their way," said Smythe, "and I, for one, am a great admirer of them, but not alone. One wants company in cases of this sort. Enoch Arden felt that in his tropical island."

" As darkness drew near," said the professor, "while seated on a rugged piece of stone, I counted every percussion cap, bullet, and charge of powder. An idea flashed across my brain that by firing off a few shots at intervals and following each report by loud shoutings it might just happen that my companion and the native 'shikari' would discover my whereabouts. Indeed, a presentiment clung to me all along that the camp could not be at any very great distance. How anxiously I listened for a response after every report, whilst my throat ached again with shouting, and how I kept hoping against hope, until all hope seemed to have vanished with the daylight, and now not even the noise of an insect or the murmur of the tree-tops broke the dismal stillness. I had been on my feet for upwards of twelve hours, without intermission, and seeing it was nearly midnight I determined to give up the fruitless struggle, so stretching out my wearied limbs on the hard ground, and placing the gun by my side, I settled down, tired, hungry, and anxious, but still anticipating that the morrow would bring my deliverance."

" My word, but it is a wonder you escaped with your life," said Sir William.

" It does seem a wonder, I confess; but it does not necessarily follow that beasts of prey were lurking about, as our friend remarked; and, indeed, such could not have been the case, or I should not have been here to tell the story.

" Utterly exhausted, I fell into a sound sleep, which lasted several hours; when awaking I found day breaking, with the wind howling through the branches overhead.

" To repair the grass sandals and load with buckshot was the work of a few minutes, when I was once more on my feet and off on the anxious journey.

" Now pushing through underwood; now carefully treading over prostrate rotten stems; here getting foul of dependent branches; then brought to a standstill by a huge patriarch of the forest.

" At length, after wandering for some time, the spoor of a musk deer was visible, and in a few minutes the little creature jumped up before me and fell dead with the contents of my gun in its side.

" Soon a fire was made in the usual native way by see-sawing a slow match in a handful of dried grass or leaves, when, cutting steaks from the haunch and stringing them together on a twig, I roasted and devoured my kabobs with avidity, for, considering that no food had crossed my lips since the previous morning, it would be doing small justice to my appetite to say that I felt other than ravenous.

" However, the savoury repast made me feel wonderfully refreshed, and with a haunch of venison on my shoulder, I proceeded once more through the wilderness of pine trunks, looking intently in every direction for the slightest indication of a stream or a water parting.

" The absence of animal life in the depths of the forest has been frequently observed, and may no doubt be owing to the want of subsistence for the majority of herbivorous quadrupeds.

" However, as I trudged along from the denser to the more sparsely wooded parts, in expectation that a clearing would suddenly open out the country, and show the way towards the river, a musk deer would now and then spring out of some bush, and, in the intervals between its fantastic mode of jumping, would stop and turn round and stare at me in bewilderment, as if it had never seen a human being before."

" Well, I must confess," observed Smythe, "that does appear to be most remarkable. I should have thought that ' tree tigers,' as we term them, would have been there in abundance."

" I saw none, and if there were any they did not trouble me."

" You were a most fortunate man."

" Possibly so. No doubt I was.

" The time must now have been about mid-day, when I came to a gap in the forest, occasioned by the fall of several spruces. Here, whilst examining the spot, a horrible feeling came over me that I had passed the identical opening shortly before dark on the previous day, so that as I pushed along I could not help muttering to myself, 'I am walking in a circle. This comes of always trending towards the left.'

" I consequently started in an opposite direction, and soon found myself on an incline, and before another hour had gained a small torrent, the bed of which was choked up by tall bracken and wild balsams, from whence numbers of the gorgeously attired Monal pheasants rose and fled down the glen, with the metallic sheen of their gorgeous plumage glistening in the sunshine.

" Here, virtually, my troubles seemed to have come to an end for ever. Since the stream was discovered, hopes grew stronger and stronger that if I could follow it up there would be an end to my anxieties.

" At length the narrow gorge gave way to an open valley, and, listening now and then, I fancied I could catch the murmur of distant waters, until the sound finally ended in a continuous roar, and I found myself on a footpath, with the Chenaub rolling rapidly along its rocky bed.

" One problem, however, remained unsolved, ' Was my tent up or down stream?' Now considering the sameness of the scenery, and very irregular, not to say eccentric, windings of mountain footpaths in general, and Himalayan foot-tracks in particular, it would have taken a greater experience of wilderness ways than I could then command to have recognised one object more than another, along the route I had trodden on the way from Cashmere.

"Nevertheless, expecting that footprints might turn up on softer parts of the path, I searched for such indications of man, but without success, and the forest on either side gave no token of commanding positions from whence a survey could be made; consequently, only one of two alternatives remained, either to push up or down the river bank.

"I selected the latter, and after devouring a portion of the venison and pitching the remainder into the river, I pushed down the pathway, in the belief that I must have struck the river above my camp, which might turn up at any minute.

"In this expectation I was sadly deceived, inasmuch as hour succeeded hour, and no trace of my little canvas home became apparent.

"The footpath, moreover, was not always safe; sometimes it ran across a beetling precipice, at others I had to wade streams; finally it led away from the river into the gloomy forest, where at dusk, after clambering up a ledge of rock, I found myself on the brink of a crag, with the river rushing furiously below.

"To have proceeded further that night seemed only to risk one's life, as every minute increased the inability to pick my way in the darkness; so once more all the pangs of hunger and disappointment came back in terrible reality, alloyed, however, with a consolation that I was at all events on the right track.

"The venison I had thrown into the river now rose before my mind, as supperless and disappointed I lighted a fire and discharged my gun, following each report by prolonged outcries, such as the natives of these parts are wont to hail each other with from opposite sides of ravines.

"But it happened that a sudden bend of the river a short distance above the eminence on which I stood broke the sounds, and sent them back in clear echoes one after another."

"And did no one come to your assistance, Mr. Mainwaring?" inquired Avaline, anxiously.

"Not at that time, my dear lady; but of course my gun was the only means that I had of giving an indication of my whereabouts. I concluded, naturally enough, that my friends would be on the alert and institute a search for me. Carter, I knew, would never rest till he had ascertained what had become of me, and I need not tell you that the report of a discharged weapon carries much further than the most powerful human voice, but I made use of both, and soon got quite hoarse from continually shouting.

"The shades of night had now gathered in, when, piling faggot upon faggot, I sat myself down by the blazing fire, and ruminated on what a new day might bring forth. At length, with blighted hopes, and fairly worn out, I once more hugged the gun, and, coiling myself up by the fireside, fell into a deep sleep.

"I was suddenly awoke by some one exclaiming, 'Sahib, Sahib!' and, starting up, found my native hunter, Eli Shah, standing by my side. He had been wandering through the forest all day, and was returning to the tent when my fire attracted him.

"'O master,' he exclaimed, 'we all thought you were dead;' and, untying his girdle, he handed me a parcel of sandwiches. 'This all comes of your not taking your "magic watch" with you;' the name by which he and my other hill servants designated the compass. When I came to reckon the distance

between our encampment and the point where I had struck the river, it was found I had wandered upwards of five miles northwards of the former.

"Thus ended a foolish adventure, which none but a tyro in wilderness wandering would have committed; nevertheless, it was not the last of similar mishaps that subsequently occurred to me in other and far-distant regions, when carried away by the excitement of the chase, and that wild enthusiasm in which the student of nature is prone to indulge."

CHAPTER CXL.
THE SURPRISE—CHARLES PEACE'S NEW PANTOMIME TRICK. HIS UNEXPECTED APPEARANCE ON THE SCENE.

WHILE Professor Mainwaring had been relating the foregoing adventure, Lord Fitzbogleton and Arabella Lovejoyce had strolled through the suite of rooms, engaged in close converse.

The young nobleman, who was greatly taken with the lovely Arabella, evidently desired a tete-à-tete with the fascinating creature.

It is true she cared but little about his attentions—indeed she did not in any way offer him encouragement, and felt more disposed to view the matter in a humorous light than otherwise; but she was like most women—pleased at being made much of by one who seemed to be an admirer.

His lordship could not at present be looked upon in the light of a lover, though it must be confessed that he appeared to be fast approaching that delightful and beautiful state of existence.

He was evidently spooney on Miss Lovejoyce—that is the correct term—albeit it may be a little too expressive.

They sauntered from room to room, roved like butterflies from flower to flower—discoursed on the several articles of virtu which came upon view as they passed along, and being a great admirer of the products of nature, Lord Fitzbogleton, naturally enough, was attracted by a choice collection of exotic plants which were displayed in such admirable order within the conservatory abutting out from the furthermost apartment.

It was equally natural also that he should wish his fair companion to admire the choice flowers as well as himself.

Lord Fitzbogleton had not a very strong voice; indeed, it might be said to be weak. He had, moreover, a slight lisp. This is rather pleasing than otherwise in a female, provided she be young and pretty, but it cannot be deemed a recommendation to one of the sterner sex.

But, despite all these little drawbacks, his lordship was a thoroughly good-natured man, and good-hearted as well, and this is saying a great deal just now, seeing how few possess either of these qualifications.

When the young people had gained the conservatory Lord Fitzbogleton, after passing his remarks on the plants before him and discoursing on their various properties, and which country they were indigenous to, he looked into the face of his companion.

He intended to convey by the look unutterable things, but its eloquence was lost upon his companion.

"Now, I don't know what you think, Miss Lovejoyce, but I call this the most pleasant part of the day. I have never felt so happy as at the present moment."

"I am glad to hear you say so," observed Arabella, looking intently, with the eye of a connoisseur, at the magnificent bloom of a cactus.

"You are? By Jove, that's wery wemarkable! I

hope and trust the feeling is wecipwocal. Indeed, I feel assured it is."

"Oh, certainly, I hope so," returned his fair companion, who, however, had great difficulty in suppressing a smile.

"Well, you know, I am not much of a fellow for argument and all that sort of thing, you know, and I can't for a moment pwetend to tell stories and anecdotes like our fwends in the other room; still, I I can appweciate a good tale if it's well told, and like to hear fellows hold forth, but I much pwefer being alone with a cweature like—well, like yourself, Miss Lovejoyce. You understand my meaning, eh!"

"Oh! certainly, my lord—indeed, I quite understand you."

"I hope we shall soon understand one another better," he returned, looking into her face admiringly.

Miss Lovejoyce made no reply; she appeared to be still engaged in admiring the cactus.

"Confound it! What is there in that flower to attract so much attention?" observed her companion.

"It is very beautiful," she returned, carelessly.

"I do not deny that. I know a fellow who grows these sort of things—takes a delight with 'em, you know. He would tell you the name and properties of any plant in the whole creation—thinks of nothing else, I do believe."

"He is an admirer of nature's products, doubtless, and is a man of taste, I suppose."

"Oh, dear me, yes, but you see some how or other I pwefer animated nature."

"Both animated and inanimate nature have their respective charms," returned the lady.

"I dare say, but why will you be so pewerse?"

"Perverse! I do not understand you."

"Well, now, just look here. I want you to give more attention to me. Don't you see?" cried his lordship, glaring at her through his eyeglass.

She smiled, and replaced the pot containing the cactus in its original position.

"There," she ejaculated, "will that satisfy you? I am all attention."

"Oh, Miss Lovejoyce, you are a charming cweature," said he, taking her jewelled hand within his own.

"I am afraid you are a flatterer."

"Oh, so Lady Marvlynn said half an hour or so ago, but you are both mistaken, I am no such thing. If there is one thing, I plume myself upon more than another, it is my sincerity."

"That is a quality which, to say the truth is rare, my lord, and therefore cannot be too highly prized."

"You think so?"

"Most certainly, I do."

"I am glad to hear you say so."

"Why?"

"Because it gives me hope."

"Hope?"

"Pwecisely; hope and confidence, for, to say the truth, as a rule I do not posses much of the latter."

"Are you wanting in confidence then?" cried the lovely Arabella, with a wicked smile. "That is most unfortunate."

"Yes, I admit it is a misfortune. I know a lot of fellows who have the audacity of a highwayman's horse. Sometimes I wish I had my share of the same."

"I don't like men who are of too demonstrative or of too pronounced a character."

"No more do I," returned her admirer, "but still, you know, a fellow can't get on in the world who is too retiring."

"No, certainly not. It is the happy medium which is most to be desired. But what is so engaging your attention just now, my lord."

"I was looking at this charming wing. It is very chaste in design."

"Do you think so?"

"Yes I do, indeed," he observed looking intently at the ornament on one of her fingers." "I admire it immensely, even as I do its wearer."

Miss Lovejoyce looked down at the tesselated pavement of the conservatory, but she made no reply.

"I'm going to beg a favour of you," said he, after a pause.

"A favour?"

"Yes. Will you grant it?"

"I must first know what it it is."

"But you would not wefuse me?"

"That depends."

"Depends on what?"

"The nature of the request you have to make."

"Well, I was about to say, and, ahem, it may as well be said at once. Don't you think so?"

"Most certainly I do. Proceed, my lord."

"Ah, yes, I will. Well, you know, it's just this—I've got a wing which has been worn by the Queen of Spain. It is a rare jewel—a trinket of the choicest quality."

"Indeed! I should like to see it."

"I not only desire you to see it, but the favour I was about to ask is that you will accept it from my hand, and——"

"And what—the other conditions?"

"That you will wear it in remembrance of me. Do you now understand?"

"Oh, I comprehend; but at the same time, you must pardon the observation, my lord, but I do not see how I can consistently accept it as a gift."

And why not, Miss Lovejoyce—I mean Awabella? You must let me call you Awabella—you weally must. Miss Lovejoyce seems so stiff and formal."

"Well, call me Arabella if that pleases you better."

"It does please me, and so it's a bargain."

"What's a bargain?"

"That I am to call you by your Christian name."

"Agreed then. It is a bargain."

And now about the wring? You must—you will accept it."

"I have not said so.

"Not as yet, but you intend to do so."

"You are arriving at a hasty conclusion, my lord."

"Not at all. So, now don't turn away. I hope I have not offended you."

"Oh, dear me, no; but still, at the same time, I think it would be very indiscreet on my part to receive a present from you."

"By no means. I shall be very much hurt if you refuse. Nay, more, I won't take a refusal."

"For a gentleman who is so wanting in confidence your tone is somewhat dictatorial," said she, with a merry laugh.

"It is for you to dictate, and for me to obey," returned he.

"Very good—very good, indeed. I quite agree with you."

"If you agree with me, I shall consider the question settled."

"What question?"

"The wing."

"Oh, is that all?"

"Yes."

"Ah, my dear friend, you must allow me some brief space of time to consider the matter over. You know, my lord, we must be governed by the rules of etiquette, and, it is, therefore, for me to arrive at some satisfactory conclusion as to what is seemly and proper in a case of this sort."

"Upon my word, Awabella, you talk more like some old sage than as a cheery and fascinating young girl. I don't care to argue questions of this nature. Arguments are altogether out of place in—ahem—in affairs of the heart, you know."

"In affairs of the heart, my lord?"

"Certainly. Now don't you be so pwovoking. I do declare that I have a mind to stop your mouth with——"

He drew her towards him and kissed her passionataly.

"My lord, pray don't. What can you be thinking about?" she ejaculated.

"I think only of you, my darling Awabella—only of you," he replied.

"I am really very sorry you should be wanting in confidence," she returned, pouting.

"Well, I don't care. You'll dwive me to despewation—that's what you'll do."

"It appears to me that you are half way there at the present moment. Do not be so demonstrative. Pray release me."

He had his arm round her waist at this time, and did not seem disposed to comply with her request.

The sparkling champagne he had imbibed seemed to have endowed him with a courage which surprised both himself and his fair companion.

"I think we had better return to the concert-room," observed Arabella.

"Ah, by no means," said he, "we are far better here."

"But I'm positively afraid of you, my lord. Let us return, I pray."

"I can't for a moment consent to such a course. No—no, my dear Awabella; you have said I might call you by that name—this is elysium. The concert-room is but earth."

"Pray, don't be metaphorical or poetic, for it would be more than I could bear just now."

"You are the most tantalising, charming, bewitching creature I ever met with in the course of my life. Oh, Awabella, tell me, dearest, if you have any wegard for me?"

"How can you ask such a ridiculous question?"

"Widiculous, my charmer!" ejaculated Lord Fitzbogleton. "You surely do not for a moment imagine I am jesting?"

"I don't know what to think; you have taken me so by surprise."

"Ah, ah, endeavoured to carry the fortress by storm, as our friend Smithers Smythe would say, but you must allow me the privilege," and here he snatched another kiss.

"It's very wrong and altogether improper," cried Arabella. "If you don't desist I shall be offended—indeed I shall; and when I am once offended I must tell you frankly I am not likely to forget—I won't say forgive, but certainly I shall not forget."

"Now you are angwy."

"I am not very well pleased with you, I candidly confess."

"You do not like me, then?"

"I have not said that. You will please me better by being a little more reasonable. I do not care about so much ardour and impetuosity, and for this reason I doubt its sincerity. Now don't be angry—I do not mean to offend you."

"You cannot do that. I love you too much."

"Love me?"

"Yes, that is what I said."

"Well, my lord, I am bound to believe you."

"And what say you?"

"At present I do not choose to say anything. So let that pass."

"Not say anything?"

"No, certainly not. I am a free agent and reserve to myself the right of placing my affections on the man I deem worthy of them."

"And am I not worthy of them?"

"I do not say you are not."

"But you will not say I am. Is that what you mean?"

"As time goes on I shall be better able to judge. A fortress may be carried by storm, I suppose, but it would be indeed a vain attempt to gain the heart of a woman by any such means—certainly not my heart. I only speak of myself."

"I have no desire to attempt such a course of action," observed the young nobleman, in an altered and more subdued tone. "Pardon me. I ask your pardon," he ejaculated, falling on one knee before his companion.

"Rise, my lord, pray rise; you would not like to be caught by any of the company in this supplicating position."

"I will not wise until you tell me you forgive me," cried he.

"I do forgive you. Be satisfied with that declaration."

Lord Fitzbogleton found out that he was no match for his fair enslaver, whose force of character was far beyond his own. He arose and looked a little foolish. Most men do when they meet with a reproof or a rebuff under similar circumstances.

"You are weally most exacting and hard-hearted," said he, "but, possibly, I have been to blame; but I am sure you will take a merciful view of the case. Now tell me, dearest Arabella, if you feel disposed to take compassion on me. Hang it, but I am a poor hand at pleading my own cause—don't you think so?"

"I hardly know what reply to give to such a question," she observed with a witching smile.

"I am sure you think so, only you don't like to acknowledge it. Come, dearest, let us be friends."

"We are friends, and true ones I hope."

"That's kind of you to say that. I mustn't, of course, I mustn't. I mean I must keep at a respectful distance—eh?"

She laughed again. "I cannot be angry with you, my lord. Indeed, there is no reason for my being so, seeing that you are so candid—and at the same time so very affectionate."

"Hang it all!—don't chaff a fellow. Nobody likes to be made a fool of, you know."

"Certainly not, my lord; and I am not likely to attempt such a thing. And, indeed, I feel perfectly well convinced that I should not succeed if I made the attempt. I both esteem and admire you."

"You admire me—eh?"

"Yes, I see many things to admire in you."

"What are they?"

"Well, in the first place you're remarkably good-natured, and you have, I believe, a good temper; in addition to which I believe you are sincere—at least I hope so."

"Say you are sure of it," he cried quickly.

"As far as I am able to judge at present, I feel assured of it. Will that satisfy you?"

He raised her hand to his lips and kissed it.

The conversation was continued for some time after

this, but we must for the present leave the young people to themselves to pay a visit to one of the upper apartments of the widow's house.

While Lady Marvlynn's guests were engaged in conversation in the concert-room, and Lord Fitzbogleton was engaged in whispering soft nothings into the ear of the fascinating Arabella Lovejoyce, a far different scene was taking place in a chamber above.

James Jabez Jones, her ladyship's footman, was sent up by one of his fellow-servants for his mistress's fan, for her ladyship by this time began to feel the heat oppressive. She had had a day of considerable toil and anxiety, and was consequently in what might be termed a state of flustration.

Now, when Mr. Jones ascended the stairs, in search of the fan in question, he was a little surprised at hearing a sort of subdued noise in one of the upstair rooms.

James Jones was a cautious, careful man—so when the sounds, which were altogether new and strange to him, fell upon his ears, he came to a sudden halt and listened more intently.

Some one was evidently moving about in an adjoining apartment : of that he felt perfectly well assured.

Who could it be ? was the very natural question he asked himself. Not any one of the visitors, for they were all below—probably it might be one of the maid servants. The door of the room was partially open, and through the crevice of this he peeped in. He then saw the figure of a man moving about in what he deemed a stealthy manner.

Mr. Jones was surprised—indeed, it might be said astounded.

From what he could make out, the person in the room was a short elderly man, with a long coat and a sort of wide-awake hat.

"Haint up to no good, I fancy," murmured James Jones ; "leastways that's my 'pinion. Who the devil can he be, and what brings him here ?"

He peered through the crevice of the door, and saw the suspicious-looking party lay his hands on some trinkets, and place them in one of the capacious pockets of his coat.

"Well, I'm blowed," murmured the astonished footman, "if this ere don't take the wind out of me entirely. Why, hang it, the fellow's a thief or a burglar, as sure as my name's Jones ! I'm blest if he aint and no mistake—the audacious circumventing scoundrel !"

It was as plain as a pikestaff—the man was possessing himself of what property he could lay his hands on ; that was too evident.

Mr. Jones was a man of Patagonian proportions—he was tall, and proportionately stout, with a broad pair of shoulders, and unexceptionable calves.

In point of fact, he considered himself to be one of the chief ornaments of the household ; but despite his stalwart frame and athletic limbs, he was what one might term "knocked silly" for a brief space of time.

The situation in which he found himself was altogether an exceptional one.

He was calmly contemplating a burglar or professional thief at work, and James Jones was, as a matter of course, for the moment dumfounded.

The audacity of the man was beyond all bounds.

How he had contrived to effect an entrance into the apartment in question was a matter the puzzled footman could not determine, but it was plainly demonstrated that he was there.

"Well I never !" exclaimed Jones. "It seems altogether impossible, and surpasses all belief, the contemptible, despicable little thief."

The reader will doubtless be in no way surprised when we signify that the robber to whom the footman alluded was none other than our old acquaintance, Charles Peace, who, taking advantage of the family gathering at Lady Marvlynn's, had crept into the house to do a little business on his own account while the festivities were at their height, and had it not been for the little incident of the fan would in all probability have escaped notice, and got clear off without anybody being the wiser. As it was, however, the chances were against him.

Mr. Jones opened the door and entered the apartment.

"Now, then, sir, what are you doing here ?" he suddenly exclaimed.

Peace, whose back was towards the speaker, turned round and looked at the footman.

"You audacious thieving scoundrel !" exclaimed the latter.

"Stand back !" cried Peace. "If you don't, it'll be the worse for you !"

As he uttered these words he drew from his pocket a life-preserver, which he held menacingly forward.

James Jabez Jones was a brave man. To be threatened and insulted by a contemptible little wretch like Peace was more than he could stand.

He rushed at once forward and laid hold of the burglar, who deftly slipped from his grasp, and then with a cat-like spring made for the half opened window of the bedroom.

Jones, who had not been prepared for this show of activity uttered a growl of dissatisfaction, and in his turn flew towards the window.

Once more he laid his hands upon the culprit. Peace, who was at this time kneeling on the sill of the window, preparatory to springing out, now found his situation a desperate one.

He struck out with his life-preserver, but from the position he occupied was unable to use it with anything like effect. With one hand James Jones fairly grasped the collar of Peace's coat, and with the other he held the wrist of the burglar to prevent him from inflicting any more blows with his weapon.

A determined struggle now took place, and our hero, much to his chagrin, found that he was in the grasp of a formidable and powerful antagonist.

"You just let go, you d——d fool," cried he, foaming with passion.

"Not if I know it," returned James Jones. "No, my little beauty, don't think to get off, because it's time your game was put a stop to. So you are the chap as has been committing all these robberies. Glad to make your acquaintance. There's a good many as will be glad to see you."

"Are there ?" cried Peace. "Are there, you ugly dirty flunkey."

He hardly knew what to say bitter enough, but he was determined to run any risk rather than be taken prisoner, and had he happened at this time to be possessed of his revolver, the chances would have been that James Jabez Jones would have received the contents of one or more barrels : but he was without that useful weapon, and bitterly deplored this fact.

Jones stuck to him like a leech, and the burglar found it impossible to free himself from his grasp.

Below him was the roof of the conservatory, in which Lord Fitzbogleton and Arabella Lovejoyce were conversing, altogether heedless of the scene that was taking place above them.

Peace threw his legs off the window-sill, electing to trust to chance. He then hung suspended therefrom, held only by the powerful arms of the footman, who strove to lift him up and drag him on to the sill.

This, however, he found to be an impossibility. Still, he was not disposed to give up the struggle as hopeless.

Peace kept twisting and turning about, in the hope of wearing out his tormentor, and, to say the truth, Mr. Jones soon gave symptoms of distress, as they say in the sporting world; but, to his infinite credit, however, he stuck manfully to his colours, or rather his "man."

Peace placed one of his knees against the wall of the house, and then threw the upper portion of his body backwards.

This had the effect of forcing Mr. Jones partly through the window. Indeed, he was nearly coming through bodily, so sudden and artful had been his opponent's movement.

"It aint no good, you spiteful little reptile," cried the footman. "You aint a going to get off—so don't think it."

"Aint I," sneeringly returned our hero, making such a hideous grimace that the flunkey felt perfectly disgusted, "aint I, Mr. Yellowplush? We'll see presently. Oh, Lord, I wish I had——" he paused suddenly.

"Yes, I dare say you do wish you were on the top of a Brixton bus—eh?"

"Don't you be so cheeky, Mr. Yellowplush, 'cause you see I aint accustomed to give in to the likes of you."

"Aint you?"

"No, I aint, old ugly mug," returned Peace, making a still more hideous grimace.

"You'd do very well to grin through a horse collar, you would," remarked Jones. "Why don't you try it? It's a much more respectable line of business than prigging, I should say.

Mr. Jones found his strength giving way. He did not like to leave go—nevertheless he called out for assistance.

At this particular time a grand piece was being performed by Signor Marouski and two of his pupils, and it was of so furious a character that the dulcet voice of James Jabez Jones was drowned thereby.

Nevertheless, when our hero heard the footman shout out he was perfectly furious and driven almost to desperation.

He placed both knees against the brickwork and gave his body a sudden and violent jerk. The effect was magical.

James Jabez Jones lost his equilibrium, and he and the burglar fell together in a deadly grasp.

A crash followed immediately; the glass of the greenhouse was shivered into a thousand fragments, and two men fell upon the tesselated pavement. In their passage pots and flowers were upset, and worse than all the hat worn by Lord Fitzbogleton was forced over his eyes, where it remained like an extinguisher, his lordship at the same time being knocked over by the concussion, and a scene took place which I shall find it difficult to describe.

In the first place Arabella Lovejoyce, who was under the impression that a thunderbolt had fallen, uttered a series of piercing screams, The company in the further room rose from their seats and rushed pell-mell towards the spot from whence the sounds proceeded, and in a moment the green-house and the adjoining

room were filled with people with anxious and inquiring faces.

The charming Arabella fainted in the arms of Major Smithers Smythe; on the hard pavement of the conservatory lay Charles Peace, stunned and motionless, and at a short distance from him was the prostrate form of James Jabez Jones, with pieces of glass sticking in his unmentionables, and his white stockings stained with blood from the same cause.

Poor fellow, his appearance was rueful in the extreme, but he was not reduced to a comatose state, albeit he was terribly bruised, and was aching in every limb.

Lord Fitzbogleton was making desperate efforts to get his head out of his hat, but at present had not been successful. The broken flower-pots were strewn around in confusion, and the wreck was altogether perfectly appalling.

"For mercy's sake, gentlemen, do tell me what is the matter," cried Lady Marvlynn. "What dreadful accident has occurred? And my poor dear Arabella," she murmured, as she caught sight of her protégée; "pray bring her into the house, major, and let the dear girl be attended to. Oh! merciful heaven, but this is indeed dreadful."

Arabella Lovejoyce was carried into the house, and placed upon one of the couches, where restoratives were applied.

Lady Marvlynn returned to the conservatory.

"What is the matter?" she again cried, in a beseeching tone. "For mercy's sake do speak, some one of you, and explain this dreadful business!"

"My dear Lady Marvlynn," said Lord Chetwynd, "we none of us are able to explain the meaning of this disaster—for such I take it to be."

"Will somebody help me off with this hat?" cried Lord Fitzbogleton, his voice sounding like some pantomimist behind a mask, only a little more muffled.

Two or three gentlemen hastened to the unfortunate nobleman's assistance, and after several efforts the hat was removed.

"Now, then, we shall be able to learn something about the accident," said Captain Crasher.

"I know nothing about it, no more than you do," returned Fitzbogleton.

"James," said Lady Marvlynn, "what is the meaning of this? You are wounded and bleeding."

"Yes, my lady; I am cut about terribly."

"So he is, poor man. Oh, how very dreadful!" chorused half-a-dozen fair beauties.

"Dweadful indeed," said Fitzbogleton. "It's a mercy I've escaped with my life. As it is, I am not at all sure my head is still on my shoulders. But where —oh, where is Awabella?"

"In the next room. Go and see how she is—there's a good man," said the hostess.

His lordship went at once.

"Now, James, tell me how this occurred—but you are bleeding, and perhaps seriously hurt."

"It's the glass, my lady, but I've picked out all the pieces I could find. And who is this strange person?" said his mistress, glancing at Peace.

"He's been the cause of it all, my lady. He's a robber, a thief, a burglar, and I caught him taking a lot of jewellery from one of the upstair rooms. I rushed forward and collared him, then he threw himself out of the window, and I had a hard job to hold him."

"And did you let him go after that?" inquired Crasher.

"No, sir, I wasn't likely to do that. I stuck to him

and he pitched himself backwards. I lost my balance, and we both fell through the conservatory."

"Well, I never heard of such a thing—a burglar in the house, a ruffian of this nature in our midst," ejaculated Sir Eric Batershall. "But you've done your duty and deserve the highest possible praise."

Peace, who had by this time partially recovered, heard the latter part of the conversation; he deemed it prudent, however, to remain as if insensible.

He had a large bump on the back of his head, and was in great pain, but he bore this without even a groan or sigh.

"You had better have your wounds dressed, James," said Lady Marvlynn, "after which you will be able to give us a more lucid and detailed description of all that has taken place."

A medical gentleman who happened to be one of the party made an examination of Mr. Jones's injuries, which he said were fortunately but of a superficial nature. When this had been done he turned his attention to the other patient.

Charles Peace was lifted up and placed on his legs, whereupon he uttered a deep groan.

"Perhaps he is mortally wounded, poor fellow," cried Miss Fagg.

"Poor fellow, indeed!" exclaimed several. "A scoundrel like him is not worthy of sympathy."

But Charles Peace, beyond the bump on his head and divers and sundry other bruises, was not so very bad after all, but he pretended to be at death's door.

This was done in the first place to excite sympathy, and in the next to gain time.

"We shall have to attend to this man," said the doctor. "After which you will hand him over to the officers of justice, I presume."

This last query was addressed to Lady Marvlynn.

"Oh, yes, of course. I suppose so."

"You have no other alternative, my lady," said Sir William Leathbridge. The case is clear enough against him. Some of the articles he has purloined have been taken from his pocket."

"Ah, just so. Dear me, what an extraordinary thing that a burglary should have been carried out while so many persons were in the house."

Peace had a plaister put upon his head by his medical attendant, and pretended to be so seriously injured otherwise that he could scarcely walk.

He was left for a few moments in the conservatory, in which were two or three young ladies of the company, who remained, possibly, to have a good look at so celebrated a character, for they felt certain he was celebrated, although none present had the faintest notion who he was.

He crept towards the door of the conservatory, unfastened it, and then flew across the grounds, in the rear of lady Marvlynn's house.

"He's gone!" cried the ladies, "gone! We thought he could not move."

"Gone!" exclaimed James Jones. "The scoundrel!" And away the wounded footman went to give chase to the fugitive.

Peace soon convinced his pursuer that he was fleet of foot. He ran round the grounds and made for the side gate.

Jones, who soon guessed his intention, sought to intercept him—which he succeeded in doing before he gained the gate.

<hr>

CHAPTER CXLI.
THE VALIANT FOOTMAN AND THE DESPERATE BURGLAR—
THE PRISONER IN THE STABLE—UNEXPECTED RELEASE.

LADY MARVLYNN's guests were doomed to experience another alarm.

It was soon made apparent that the wounded burglar had attempted to make his escape, and some of them were under the impression that it did not much matter if he succeeded in doing so, while others were most anxious for him to be brought to the bar of justice upon public grounds.

Some of the gentlemen volunteered to give chase, and sallied forth, and of course took the wrong direction.

One energetic young man, partly owing to his haste and partly to the darkness, was brought suddenly to a standstill by his neck coming in contact with a clothes-line which ran from wall to wall in the back garden.

His neck came with considerable force against this, and he hit out right and left with his clenched fists at some antagonist who, he believed, was endeavouring to garotte him. His appearance was so comic, as well as the circumstances, that his friends could not refrain from a hearty laugh at his expense, and he afterwards declared that he fully believed that some one was garrotting him, and that he was fighting for his life.

Meanwhile, while this and a number of other incidents were taking place, Mr. Jones had come up with Charles Peace, who was once more in the valiant footman's grasp.

Peace now fought like a tiger; he threw himself down and kicked his assailant unmercifully, and the chances were that he would have got the better of Jones had not the stableman come to the rescue.

"He's the most determined little brute that mortal man ever set eyes on," remarked James Jones. "He is the very devil himself, I do believe."

"We'll devil him," returned the stableman. "The best way to serve a chap of this sort is to prevent him from doing further mischief. He's a kicker, you see, and wants the kicking-strap put on."

And with these words the man fastened Peace's legs together with a strap, after which he pinioned his arms with a rope.

When this had been done, he said—

"Now, Jem, we'll carry him into the stable, and lock him in till we get a bobby or two to look after him."

"You cowardly scoundrels!" exclaimed Peace, in a paroxysm of rage, "you shall suffer for this."

"Go on, guv'nor, take your fill of abuse," returned the stableman. "Did your mother have any more of your sort?"

Peace was carried into the stable and bound to a post. Then the stable door was locked on him, and he was left to his reflections which were anything but of an agreeable nature.

Now, all this had been done in an incredibly brief space of time, and Mr. Jones considered it very cleverly done—all things considered, for, smarting as he was from the cuts and bruises he had received in the recent conflict, he very naturally enough bore our hero no goodwill, and it would have caused our footman great mortification of the little scoundrel, or devil as he termed him, had succeeded in getting clear off after the trouble he (Mr. Jones) had been at.

He returned to the house and made his mistress acquainted with all that had happened.

"Dear me!" said Lady Marvlynn; "but upon my word, James, I hardly think you were justified in binding the man"

"You should have seen him kick and fight, and even try to bite. What could we do with such a—devil?" he was going to say, but he substituted ruffian instead.

AVELINE AND LADY MARVLYNN LETTING PEACE OUT OF THE STABLE.

"Well, I confess I do not understand these things," returned her ladyship. "I hope and trust it is all right. It has so completely upset me that I hardly know what I say or do."

"I am going to send Peter for a policeman, if you please, ma'am."

"Oh, indeed, eh—for a policeman."

"Yes, my lady."

"Oh, very well, perhaps that is the best course. We can consult the constable when he comes, and take his advice in the matter."

"It rests with you, my lady."

"Of course, certainly. Well do as you say—send for a policeman. How are you now? Do you feel better?"

No. 76.

"Oh, yes, I am a little shaken of course, but am thankful that I escaped as well as I did."

"Yes, certainly, we are all thankful. I have reason to be grateful for the energy and courage you have displayed. It will not be forgotten, believe me. Neither is it likely to go unrewarded; but more of this hereafter."

James Jabez Jones bowed and took himself off. As Lady Marvlynn was about returning to her guests she was met by Aveline.

"This ruffian is locked up in the stable, dear, and is not likely to trouble us any more, I hope," said Lady Marvlynn. "I know you will be glad to hear that."

"Oh yes, certainly," stammered Aveline. "I suppose all will be glad."

"Why what's the matter, dear? You seem troubled."

"I have a word or two to say to you in private."

"Of course, my darling pet. Come into this room."

She led her companion into a small apartment which had not been placed at the disposal of the general company.

"This man whom you are about to give into charge for—burglary—for housebreaking——" she paused.

"Well, what of him?"

"Do you intend to charge him?"

"Do I? Well, I suppose so. You heard what the gentlemen said but just now. I was bound to do so on public grounds."

"There are private reasons for your not doing so."

"For my not doing so? You surprise me, Aveline. Name them."

"He is known to me."

"I am astounded. Known to you?"

"Yes," said Aveline, with something like sadness in her tones. "Years ago he did me a service."

"Impossible."

"It is a fact. He was mainly instrumental in throwing a light on the dark and, at that time, impenetrable mystery which hung over the house of Ethalwood. He it was who gave Mr. Wrench the information which led to his discovery of me."

"His name is then——"

"Charles Peace. Oh, Lady Marvlynn, I have every reason for believing him to be a bad man, but I frankly confess I was quite unprepared for this. I did not think he had sunk so low—that he was so callous—so debased—but that is but little to the purpose just now. I have one favour to ask."

"What is it?"

"That you let him go about his business. Do this for my sake. I cannot explain all the circumstances which lead up to this, but I say again let him go."

"You must be mistaken, my dear. It cannot possibly be the man to whom you allude."

"I am not mistaken," said Aveline. "I saw his face distinctly as he stood in the greenhouse. Time has not improved its expression; but it was too familiar to me years and years ago for me to make a mistake, but if you doubt it I will convince you."

"How?"

"Simply by our both going to the stable together."

"We will do so, by all means, if you wish it."

"I do wish it. I desire to do so most earnestly."

"Your word is law with me," cried Lady Marvlynn, who at once left the room and summoned Mr. Jones.

"I wish to see the prisoner, James," said she; "give me the key of the stable."

"You would not go alone, my lady?" said the footman.

"I am not afraid of this man; give me the key."

The sagacious flunkey was surprised, but he handed his mistress the key without any further observation.

Lady Marvlynn returned to Aveline.

"Now, dear, we will proceed thither at once; that is if you are not afraid to face this tiger," for such Jones calls him.

"Oh, dear, no, I am not afraid."

The two ladies hurried along till they had reached the temporary prison-house of Charles Peace. The lock was turned, the door opened, then they entered, closing the door after them.

Lady Marvlynn, who had taken the precautions to provide herself with a flat-glass lantern, now turned its rays full upon the features of the imprisoned man, who was, as already stated, tied to a post, having been previously bound hand and foot.

Peace at this time looked the most miserable dejected wretch it was possible to conceive, and those who were not very well acquainted with his features would have found it impossible to recognise him, but Aveline, or rather Lady Batershall, at once saw that the wretched criminal was the same person she had known in the earlier period of her life.

She started back, and exclaimed in a subdued tone—

"It is he; but oh, how strangely altered!"

At the sound of her voice Charles Peace became deeply moved, albeit he strove to maintain an air of bravado.

"And has it come to this, you unscrupulous abandoned man?" said Aveline. "A common robber—a disgrace to society."

"I'm ill—have been cruelly treated—and don't care what becomes of me," whined Peace, in a cringing tone. "Taunt me and upbraid me as you please. I am powerless, and am at your mercy."

"Yes, at our mercy," said Lady Marvlynn, turning towards her female companion and regarding her with an enquiring look. "Poor wretch, he is at our mercy, and is, moreover, in a sorry plight."

"I don't know you, madam," observed Peace, "but I think if I am to judge from appearances, that you are kind and tender-hearted. The other lady I know perfectly well, and she owes me a deep debt of gratitude, and ought not to upbraid me."

"She does not do so," returned Lady Marvlynn.

"She does not? Well perhaps I am mistaken. But you will admit that it is hard to be treated in this merciless cruel way. Let Aveline Gatliffe speak for herself."

"She is no longer Mrs. Gatliffe but a lady of title."

"I know that, and who caused her to be recognised as a lady of title? People in this world soon forget past favours."

"I do not, sir," cried Lady Batershall, with something approaching to hauteur in her manner, "be less personal in your observations. I find you here a criminal, a thief, an outcast, but at the same time I am ready and willing to render you whatever service lies in my power. Gracious heaven, how terrible is all this! Tell me what you desire me to do."

"I want to be free. If I am given into custody, I am a ruined man, but if you let me free——"

"Well, what then? Will you promise me to abandon your present course? Oh! for mercy's sake tell me that you will reform and lead a new life."

"I will—I promise," cried Peace, in a hypocritical whining tone, "I hereby solemnly swear——"

"Do not swear—there is no need for that," interrupted the gentle Aveline. " Give me your word and keep it—that is all I need."

"I do give you my word. Oh, my lady, have pity on me! My only hope is in you. Remember that mercy is one of the most divine attributes which a woman or a man possesses. Think of my poor wife— of my family, and all who belong to me. You cannot find it in your heart to bring ruin and disgrace upon me and mine."

"I am very sad, and cannot express to you my feeling of sorrow and the miserable state of dejection all this occasions me, dear," said Lady Batershall, not taking any heed of Peace's words, but addressing herself to her companion. "This man I knew years and years ago. At one time he was a respectable member of society—at least so I deemed him. Judge my horror at this night's proceedings—a common robber, a ruffian! It is almost incredible."

"It's no use going on like that," whined Peace. "You don't know how I have been tempted—what troubles I am surrounded with. What's the use of talking of the past, or saying what I was and what I am? Do you think I want to hear about my former life? It is over. I am as you see me just now, in the depths of trouble. If you can serve me, which I very well know you can—do it for old acquaintance sake. There, that's plain enough, aint it?"

"Oh, you bad, wicked man!" exclaimed Lady Marvlynn; but there, I won't say any more upon that head."

"Are you the mistress of this house?" inquired Peace.

"Yes, I am."

"Very good; and do you intend to give me in charge? Say yes or no, that I may know what I am to expect."

"For the sake of this dear lady, I will not give you in charge unless I am forced to do so."

"Forced! Who is likely to force you?"

"No one, I hope."

"And I hope the same. You need not be afraid. I intend to reform if you will only let me have a chance of doing so."

"Are you sincere?"

"Of course I am. I'll lead a new life after this. I've seen the error of my ways, and promise to be as straight as an arrow for the future; only take compassion on me and release me from this miserable bondage. I ache in every limb, and my head goes throbbing like anything. Do cut the cords that confine me; you'll never regret it. My dear good creatures, have compassion on a miserable wretch who appeals to you, and will for the future be as honest and upright as the day. No time is to be lost if you wish to save me, which I feel assured you do. Hesitate no longer, or it may be too late."

"Indeed there is some reason in what he says, dear," observed the kind-hearted Lady Marvlynn.

"I will hesitate no longer," cried Aveline. "Come what may, this man must be free."

Without further ado Aveline at once proceeded to unbind the rope which confined Charles Peace, who in a minute or so was freed from the post, the strap was then removed from his feet, the cord which confined his arms was undone, and once more he had free use of his limbs.

"I shall remember this act of kindness to the last and latest hour of my life," said he. "Oh, my good angels, for such indeed you are, accept my most sincere and heartfelt thanks."

"Now go, say no more in the way of grateful expression. Time presses; hence away at once without further hesitation," exclaimed Lady Batershall, "and remember your promise."

"Be assured of that. I shall never forget it."

Aveline opened the stable door, and Charles Peace passed through. The garden gate was flung open, and the burglar ran at the top of his speed down the lane which skirted Lady Marvlynn's palatial residence. Both ladies listened intently to the sounds of his retreating footsteps, and when these were no longer heard, Lady Batershall pressed her hand to her side and exclaimed, in a low breathless tone—

"Heaven be praised, he is free!"

"Ah! my dear," said her companion, "I know this has been a sore trial for you."

"It has—I freely confess it," was the quiet rejoinder. "I am quite unnerved, and scarcely know what I am doing."

"The horribly debased, lost man!"

"But he will reform—I do not think there is any doubt about that."

"I hope so. I wish I could feel assured of it."

"I feel it difficult to believe that he could have sunk so low as this."

"Do not take on so, dear. Let us hope for the best. I should never have forgiven myself if I had been constrained to hand him over to the officers of justice, but I expect we shall be censured by our friends."

"I expect so too," returned Aveline," but that we must submit to with the best grace we can. Ah! we shall be censured—there is but little doubt upon that subject."

A loud ring at the bell was now given by somebody outside, and upon the mistress of the house opening the gate a policeman presented himself.

"Ah!" exclaimed Lady Marvlynn, "you have come."

"Yes, my lady. There has been an attempted robbery—a burglary in your house, I understand?"

"Ahem, yes. A very unfortunate affair indeed."

"Where is the prisoner?" was the next question.

"He was confined in the stable, but has escaped."

"Escaped!" cried the constable. "How long since?"

"Oh, some little time back, but come in."

The policeman entered, and glanced in every direction as he did so.

"How did he contrive to make his escape, and which road has he taken I wonder; but we'll soon hunt him down."

"One moment, if you please," said Lady Marvlynn. "This man, the burglar, I have let go free, as under no circumstances whatever should I have charged him. I am sorry to have given you needless trouble—regret this very much, but as I did not intend to prosecute, well, you see, I let him go."

"Umph! Well, you know best, my lady, but I think you will have reason to regret it."

"I hope not, but we will talk this matter over presently. Come in and have some refreshment. James Jones will be able to give you all the particulars."

"Who is James Jones?"

"My footman."

"Oh, I see; but had I not better see if I can recapture the scoundrel?"

"No. Do as I bid you. Come into the house."

Lady Marvlynn led the way, the officer of the law following. He was presently conducted into the servants' hall, where he found a well-spread table.

He thought the circumstance a little singular, and could not very well account in anything like a satisfactory manner for the release of the culprit, but he was wise enough to keep his thoughts to himself—to hear, see, and say nothing.

CHAPTER CXLII.

CHARLES PEACE RETURNS HOME—THE BARRISTER'S STORY.

CHARLES PEACE, after his release from the stable, succeeded in getting out of the neighbourhood without attracting the attention of any officious or inquiring policeman.

Used as he had been throughout his lawless career to dangerous escapes and alternations of fortune, this last adventure appeared to make so deep an impression on him that he was quite unnerved.

This is saying a great deal, seeing that he was a man of so essentially a callous nature that the better instincts of his nature were submerged beneath an amount of guilt and atrocity, which, to a casual observer, would appear to be almost incredible.

He could not fail to acknowledge to himself that he had a desperate struggle and a narrow escape. Had Lady Marvlynn elected to give him into custody he knew perfectly well that the hangman's halter awaited him, for Lady Batershall knew perfectly well who he was, and she was too truthful by nature to screen him by any false statements.

He did not for a moment doubt that she would have every wish to do so, but it would become an impossibility if he had been sent for trial.

The world would then know that the respectable elderly gentleman in the Evalina-road, who passed as Mr. Thompson, was the murderer of Mr. Dyson, of Banner-cross.

As Peace thought of this he turned pale and trembled for the future.

He looked at this time a most pitiable object—his head throbbed with pain, and in addition to this his legs and shoulders bore upon them many severe bruises, the result of his fall through the conservatory.

He was, however, not much injured by the broken glass, as his antagonist, the stalwart footman, was the first to fall through the roof of the conservatory, nevertheless he was in a most dilapidated condition, and felt dispirited and sick of heart.

When he had got out of the neighbourhood he betook himself to a small coffee-shop. Here he had some refreshment, and begged permission to go into one of the bedrooms to wash himself, alleging as an excuse that he had been engaged in a fight with some one who had insulted him.

Whether the coffee-house keeper believed his story it would not be so easy to say; however, he affected to do so. The house he kept was not of very good repute, being, in fact, one to which thieves resorted.

Peace, after a wash up, together with a plentiful application of cold water to his head, felt a little better, and after swallowing his coffee and muffin, once more proceeded on his journey.

He was now passable in his external appearance, so much so as not to attract attention; so in the course of half an hour after he had left the coffee-shop he went to the bar of a roadside public and swallowed two stiff glasses of brandy and water.

As we have already indicated he was never at any time a drinking man, but, as he afterwards declared, he was so "limp" on this occasion that he was fain to have recourse to stimulants to wind himself up.

We need not follow his footsteps further—it will be enough to note that he reached his residence in safety. Lady Marvlynn and Aveline returned to the grand room, in which the guests were assembled.

An inquiry was made by several with regard to the prisoner, and a general expression of astonishment very naturally followed, when they were informed by the hostess that he had been set free.

"What!—let the scoundrel go?" exclaimed Colonel Snappe. "I never heard of such a thing. Why, my dear Lady Marvlynn, what could you have been thinking about?"

"He was contrite, and pleaded for mercy," said her ladyship, with a shrug. "I suppose I have done wrong, but I could not find it in my heart to detain him."

"Well, I am indeed astonished," said Lord Chetwynd. "It is positively most reprehensible."

"I expected you would all censure me," observed Lady Marvlynn; "but it is done, and can't be helped now."

"But the scoundrel knocked my hat over my eyes, and would have killed me if I'd given him the chance," exclaimed Lord Fitzbogleton. "He's a wetch whom hanging is too good for. I am sowwy you have let him go."

"So am I; so are we all, I expect," remarked Major Smithers Smyth. "What say you, Mr. Quirp?"

Mr. Quirp was a solicitor of Furnival's-inn, Holborn.

"I always regret hearing of the escape of a robber," said he. "It but too frequently happens that men belonging to the criminal class escape through their victims declining to prosecute. There are many reasons for this. In the first place the duty which falls to the share of a prosecutor is at once an onerous and unpleasant one. It is attended with great inconvenience, loss of time, and in some cases considerable expense, and hence it is that so many object to the task."

"Clearly so," observed Mr. Tangle, another of the company, a barrister in the Temple. "It has always been so. People do not like to be hanging about police-courts, but it is essential in the interests of society that persons should sacrifice their own personal comfort for the public good."

"I dare say Lady Marvlynn has made use of her good sense and judgment in this case," cried Sir William Leathbridge, coming to the rescue. "It may be against the dictatorial opinions or views of our legal friends, but I am quite sure no one ought to blame her or any other woman for leaning to the side of mercy."

"Hear, hear," cried several of the company.

"I would not for a moment presume to dictate," observed Quirp. "It would not be right and proper for me to do so; still, at the same time, I frankly confess I see much to regret in adopting such a course. If you knew how many hardened ruffians, how many habitual thieves escape from this cause, you would, I think, endorse the opinion expressed by myself and Mr. Tangle."

"I am sure they would, and, what's more," chimed in the other lawyer, "there are hundreds and thousands of men in the metropolis and elsewhere who calculate with the greatest possible coolness the chances of detection and conviction, and it is only the reliability and certainty that punishment follows detection that we can hope for any beneficial effect therefrom as a deterrent from the commission of crime."

"Ah, there is not the slightest doubt of that," returned Sir William; "but, of course, there are exceptional cases."

"Very few, I fancy."

"But the wretch knocked my hat over my eyes," cried Lord Fitzbogleton.

"Do be quiet, and leave the other gentlemen to discuss the question," observed Arabella Lovejoyce.

"Oh, if you wish it, I will remain silent."

"I do wish it."

"Weally, Awabella, you are vewy pwovoking."

"And very unjust as well, my lord," remarked Quirp. "The fact of his knocking your hat over your eyes is an additional reason for his not having mercy shown to him."

"Well, gentlemen," said Lady Batershall, "it is not much use discussing the question now. Make yourselves as happy and comfortable as possible, and forget that a burglar has disturbed the harmony of the evening for a brief period."

"Well said," cried Sir William Leathbridge. "I move that we adjourn the discussion *sine die*. How say you?"

"Agreed," cried several.

"And so to change the subject," said Mr. Tangle, "I will just recount for your delectation a case that came under my notice."

"That's right," cried Major Smithers Smythe. "Every man has something interesting to tell of his experience in life, and none are more prolific in that way than you gentlemen of the legal profession."

"I am not about to discuss some knotty point of law," observed Tangle. "I leave that to its proper arena—a court of justice."

"I know as much about law as a Hottentot," returned Smythe. "Still, although ignorant, I'm willing to learn."

"It was in the earlier days of my career," said Tangle, "and briefs were like angels' visits, but few and far between—in fact I had begun seriously to contemplate emigrating to British Columbia, or to some equally distant and desolate locality.

"Fortunately for me and society generally, which sooner or later must recognise my distinguished merits by placing me on the bench, I abandoned the idea of British Columbia, and went to Reading; a beneficent fate rewarded me for my courage in the shape of a big brief with a small fee, to defend two men for conspiring to cheat a young gentleman with more money than brains, by gambling with him and using loaded dice.

"It was a case that had excited a good deal of interest in the neighbourhood, partly from the very remarkable way in which the cheat had been discovered by a stranger who happened to be in the room where the play was going on, and who, suspecting that all was not right, had with a large carving fork pinned the hand of one of the conspirators to the table.

"Underneath it, sure enough, were found the loaded dice, which he had manipulated up and down his sleeve so skilfully that the verdant youth found himself some five hundred pounds to the bad.

"As counsel for the defendants, the aspect of the case was far from inviting, and as the very beery solicitor who instructed me observed, 'It looked uncommon fishy.'

"In that remark I entirely concurred, and folded up the papers with a hopeless sigh, cursing the ill-luck that always brought me the deadest cases.

"In the present instance there was little for me to do but to sit by and hold my tongue—a process, by-the-way, anything but satisfactory to one fond of hearing the sound of his own voice.

"Apart from professional regrets, I could not help feeling that this precious pair of rascals thoroughly deserved all they were likely to get, and the longer they were shut up, the better for the community at large.

"The trial came on in due course, and the two prisoners were placed at the bar. As I looked at them, I was much struck with their gentlemanly appearance and dress, but then I remembered that all that was part of the stock-in-trade of persons of their class, and turning to my brief, prepared to do battle.

"As this is but a subsidiary portion of my story, it is unnecessary for me to linger over the details of the trial. They say that lucky fate often follows on the footsteps of rogues, and in this instance, by some unpardonable carelessness on the part of the constable, the loaded dice which had been found under the hand of one of the prisoners were not forthcoming, and after a great deal of wrangling with the counsel on the other side, the learned judge said that the prosecution in not producing it had, in his opinion, failed to make out a sufficient case to go to the jury, and that he must therefore direct a verdict for the acquittal of the prisoners.

"They were as much astonished and overpowered as myself by the unexpected turn things had taken, and with admirable celerity disappeared from the dock.

"Some four years afterwards I received a very pressing invitation from my old Eton friend, Charlie Forrester, asking me to run down to his place in Devonshire, and spend a few days with him.

"Master Charlie, whose lines had fallen in exceeding pleasant places, and who at twenty-one had come into a very nice estate and some five thousand pounds annually, after tantalising all the marriageable girls in the county by refusing to go to balls and croquet parties, with invitations for which he was pertinaciously pestered from morning till night, had finally taken himself abroad, no one knew whither, and there remained between four and five years.

"When he returned home again he brought a wife with him, a proceeding on his part which excited general discontent and disapprobation.

"But Charlie cared very little what the country folks thought about him.

"He was passionately fond of his wife, and consequently devoted to home, while he occupied his time in regulating the affairs of his estate and improving the breed of pigs. In short, he found within the limits of his park fence all the amusements and society he required.

"His attachment for his wife was not surprising, for she was indeed a most lovely and charming woman, full of intelligence and good sense, and in every way fitted to preside over a household.

"When she and Charlie first met at Pau she was the governess in an English family that was staying there; their courtship lasted but a few days, and one fine morning they met by appointment, and walking together to the church, were married before breakfast.

"Violet Danvers had no idea of the position, pecuniary or otherwise, that attached to Charlie, but her life had been full of troubles, and all she knew was that he had been very kind and good to her.

"Friends and relations she had none," she said; and then, as she rested her head against his breast, and looked up into his eyes, Charles felt that Heaven had sent her for him to love and cherish.

"He told her of his past life, and his wanderings in distant countries, and sought to engage her confidence in return; but she always seemed to avoid all reference to her own past, and would hurriedly turn the conversation into quite another channel.

"Charlie was not of a suspicious nature, and had far too much love and confidence in his wife to fancy that she was concealing anything from him.

"And so Violet came to her new home—to the old

home in which generations of Forresters had lived and died.

"It was not so very long after they had taken up their abode at 'The Lions,' that I received the invitation before alluded to; and as the long vacation had already commenced, and my pecuniary resources were not in a condition to stand a trip even to the seaside, I thought the best thing I could do was to accept the hospitality that my old friend offered me.

"A few days more found me comfortably installed at 'The Lions,' thoroughly enjoying the fresh air and strong exercise that followed, in pleasing contrast to the heated atmosphere of close courts and continuous sitting in dingy chambers.

"I found Mrs. Forrester a most charming and amusing companion, though I could not help being struck by an air of constraint and reserve that at times settled upon her. A very brief acquaintance satisfied me that there was some mystery attaching to her which she dared not reveal.

"One morning at breakfast, Charlie, after reading a letter he had just received by the post, informed us that it was from an old Paris friend of his whom he had met in his traveller days, and who, in pursuance of a long-standing invitation, had written to say that he proposed coming on a visit to 'The Lions,' and would, without waiting for a reply, put in an appearance that very evening.

"Charlie was delighted at the prospect of seeing his old acquaintance, and in the course of a walk over the farm he informed me the name of the coming guest was Murray, and that he was blessed with a great deal of more ready wit than ready cash.

"'Though he is a bit of an adventurer in his way,' said Charlie, 'he is a capital fellow, and the best company in the world.'

"It was very late when the expected guest arrived. Mrs. Forrester had retired to bed some time before As for Charlie and myself, we kept the new comer company while he supped, and when he had done ample justice to the good things before him, it being already in the small hours, bed was voted and carried unanimously.

I was very sleepy, and beyond uttering a mere commonplace or two had taken little or no notice of the stranger; but when he came across the room and held out his hand, which, oddly enough, was encased in a light-coloured glove of some sort, to bid me good night, as I looked him full in the face, he seemed to start for a moment.

"Although his features were hidden by a heavy moustache and huge beard, there was something about them that appeared familiar to me. Where on earth could I have seen him before?

"When I got upstairs into my bedroom, I puzzled my brain with inquiries, but all in vain; I could connect the face with nothing, and nothing with the face, and with that I got angry with myself, and went to sleep.

"The next morning I awoke early, and feeling a strong inclination for a walk before breakfast, tumbled headlong into my cold tub, and in a very short time after had completed my 'toilette,' and was out in the glorious fresh air.

"An hour's stroll brought me back to the window of the breakfast-room, which opened into the garden, and with the appetite of a tiger I was on the point of entering when my step was arrested by the sound of Mrs. Forrester's voice, trembling with emotion, exclaiming, 'Say it is not true!—for pity's sake, say it is not true!'

"What could this mean? Being of a curious turn —my conduct may have been disgraceful, but hereafter I hope to stand excused for it; I moved into a position where I could see into the breakfast room without being seen, and hear all that was said.

"In an arm-chair by the table, her face buried in her hands, and her elbows resting on her knees, Mrs. Forrester was rocking herself to and fro in a way that showed her to be labouring under deep emotion.

"Close to her, in a strangely cool and insolent attitude stood the new comer of last night, stroking his moustache with his gloved fingers.

"'Upon my word, my dear Violet,' he replied to her entreaty, with a measured slowness of speech that made me long to kick him, 'I regret to say that it is true; Arthur Bernard is no more dead than I am. Like Norval's father, he at the present moment feeds his flocks, not, however, upon the Grampian Hills, but in the neighbourhood of the great city of Otago.'

"'But they told me he was dead,' almost shrieked Mrs. Forrester; 'the people who were with him when he died wrote to me."

"'Wrote to you!' interrupted Murray with suspicious eagerness. 'Have you got the letter?'

"'No, I dared not keep it,' she replied, 'lest it should fall into my husband's hands. Listen,' she continued, hurriedly; 'he knows nothing of the past— not even of my first marriage; I have kept it all, everything from him; for pity's sake leave this place, where, save for the thought of that, I have been so happy, and let him remain in ignorance still.'

"'Gently, Violet, gently!' responded the man, unmoved in the least degree by her appeal. 'Firstly, let me observe that, having promised myself a short stay in the country, I can hardly terminate it so abruptly as you desire me; in the next, as in addition to the agreeable change of air, I have met, quite unexpectedly, with an old companion for whom I have been searching ever so many years, and to whom I have a good deal to say, it would be quite impossible to do as you wish.'

"She made no response, only kept her face still buried in her hands as he went on. 'At last, Violet Bernard, the game is in my hands. You laughed at my love, jeered at my protestations of devotion for you, curled up your proud lip at me, and dismissed me from your presence with contempt when I asked you to be my wife. I have not forgotten that, and never shall—never, never! But sooner or later you must hear me; mark, you must! Else——' He paused an instant, and continued, 'I won't threaten, but remember Arthur Bernard lives!'

"At this juncture Charles entered the room, but not before Mrs. Forrester had had time to collect herself; while Murray, without appearing in the least disconcerted, went on making some commonplace remarks about the weather.

"As for myself, this interview, of which I had been an unseen spectator, had naturally aroused varied emotions, and before putting in an appearance at the breakfast table I thought it best to take a walk round the garden to indulge in a few moments' reflection.

"The confession is somewhat humiliating, but I have always been rather fond of interfering in other people's affairs, and in the present instance, having seen and heard all I had, I felt exceedingly reluctant to let the matter drop. The mystery attaching to Mrs. Forrester was not very difficult to unravel—at least in its main feature.

"As for this Murray and the influence he seemed to possess over her, I had long since made up my mind that he was a villain who would stoop to any device, however contemptible, to ensure the success of any evil enterprise in which he might be engaged.

"I determined to use every endeavour to defeat him in his present scheme, though let it not be for a moment supposed that any heroics were mixed up in this resolve.

"I looked upon the whole matter rather as a game of chess, in which by hook or by crook I must check-mate my adversary.

"When I reached the breakfast room, the trio seemed on the best possible terms one with another—Charlie cheerful and unsuspicious as ever, Mrs. Forrester playing nervously with a tiny piece of toast, which she made pretence to eat, but never touched, and Murray eating and talking with equal earnestness.

"'Oh, yes,' he said, as I came in, 'your wife and I, Charlie, have discovered that we are old acquaintances. Curious, isn't it?' Wheels within wheels! What fools we are to fancy our world to be such a huge place!'

"I looked at his face as I sat down at the table more closely than I ever had before, and again the old thought of last night came back to me.

Then my eyes involuntarily settled on his hands; they were still encased in light gloves.

"I do not know what it was that prompted me, but, joining in the conversation, I said—

"'You are right; I often tumbled across people I never expected to see again—mere passing acquaintances. Do you know,' I continued, 'last night when you arrived I fancied we had met before, though then you had no beard and moustache?'

"I could have sworn, and did to myself at the moment, that his hand trembled as he raised his cup to his lips; but a moment after, as he set it down again, he was perfectly calm and cool, while in a nonchalant tone he replied—

"'I must say you have the advantage of me, as I am not aware that we ever met before; indeed, I am quite sure that we never did. Besides, I have worn a beard and moustache ever since one or the other would grow.'

"'Why, when you were in Paris you were as clean shaven as a priest on a feast-day,' burst in Charlie, quite innocently; but Murray, without taking any notice of the observation, turned to Mrs. Forrester, and commenced talking to her about something quite different.

"Slowly, but surely, a conviction was growing upon me that made me pay considerable respect to my impressions of the night before, and determined me to be more watchful than ever.

"My only fear was that Mrs. Forrester, in the weakness of her terror, would take some desperate step, when after all, as I firmly believed, there was not the slightest ground for alarm.

"In the course of the next twenty-four hours, by dint of pertinacious listening and watching, I found that Murray's protestations of affection cooled in proportion as he ingenuously hinted that his silence may be purchased for a reasonable sum—a suggestion that his victim caught eagerly at, only to be the more crushed by the revulsion of feeling that followed when she reflected how utterly impossible it was for her to obtain the two hundred pounds he modestly asked.

"He was treading on dangerous ground, this same Murray; even as he stood there I might have handed him into the custody of the nearest constable on a charge of endeavouring to extort money by threats and menaces.

"Looking at it from a legal point of view, this would have been an excellent course to adopt; but it was the exposure that was to be avoided, and, therefore, it was necessary to adopt different tactics.

"For three days I watched—with what a trial to the patience can readily be imagined—this human spider torturing the poor fly he had got into his web: he cool, courteous, and insinuating as he worked out his scheme; she growing weaker and weaker, and losing all strength and courage, only to find it again to take one last desperate step, and thus for ever put an end to the torture she was suffering.

"Yet all this while her husband seemed to notice nothing amiss with her, though her eyes were often red with weeping, and her face wore a settled look of melancholy and despair.

"Not that he failed in affection or tenderness, only he was one of those men who, in the goodness of their own digestions and the smoothness of their life-stream, look upon dyspepsia as a popular delusion, and cannot understand why any one should be unhappy.

"It was the evening of the fourth day since Murray's arrival, and after dinner I had left him and Charlie discussing a bottle of '54 Chateau Margaux and their old Paris days, and was wandering down a side-path that led into the plantation, when I suddenly trod on something.

"Looking downward, I saw that it was a pocket-book, of somewhat bulky dimensions. There was only one thing to be done—namely, to pick it up, unclasp it, and examine the contents—which, I need scarcely add, I faithfully did.

"This investigation having been satisfactorily accomplished, I placed the pocket-book in my pocket, and strolled on into the plantation, again to reflect what my next move with Mr. Murray should be. I knew the game was in my hands "now;" my only puzzle was, how to play it without making a disturbance.

"Still, what was to be done must be done quickly. As I came to this determination I found myself standing by a small lake that lay in the midst of the plantation; almost at the same moment I heard a groan, as of some one in distress.

Turning eagerly to the direction whence it seemed to come, through the dusk which was now growing into darkness, I saw the flutter of a white dress near the head of the lake. I know not what possessed me, but a thought seized me that sent me tearing through the bushes and brambles with frantic speed.

A few seconds more, and I had caught Mrs. Forrester by the wrist.

"'What would you do, woman?' I exclaimed, breathless.

"She made no answer—only fell fainting at my feet.

"When I got back to the house I found Murray alone in the dining-room, paying the closest attention to a second bottle of the '54 Chateau Margaux, to better appreciate which the lamp had been brought in, so that he might examine the marvellous beauty of its colour.

"Charlie was closeted in the smoking-room with his farm bailiff; in short, the opportunity of an interview alone with Murray, that I so much wanted, presented itself. I was not slow to take advantage of it; and, flinging myself into an arm-chair close to him, poured out a glass of wine, and settled comfortably to my task.

"It was pretty plain that he was anything but pleased at the prospect of a *tete-a-tete*, and seemed not altogether easy in his chair.

" 'I was thinking of taking a stroll in the garden,' he said, half rising from his chair.

" ' A pity to leave such excellent tipple,' I replied; 'besides, it's rather chilly. 'Do you know,' I continued, 'I have been thinking of that observation you made the other night, when I said we had met before, and, upon my word, I believe I was right after all. I have such a capital memory for faces that I cannot imagine myself mistaken."

" 'Indeed,' he laughed, roughly, ' you seem to have great confidence in yourself; unfortunately, as I told you, in this instance you are mistaken."

" 'Well, perhaps I am,' was my answer, as I drew my chair a little nearer to his. "The strangest part of my error was that I fancied you were one of two men I defended at Reading some four years ago, for conspiring to cheat a young undergraduate out of his money by playing with loaded dice.'

"He was far too much on his guard to make any sign; he only said, with a smile, 'You certainly paid me a great compliment.' But I saw that he was drawing away his right hand, which had hitherto been resting on the table. 'It was a remarkable case,' I continued, ' chiefly from the way in which the roguery was detected. The hand of the man who was manipulating the loaded dice was, as yours might be, on the table, to all appearances, in the most innocent manner possible'—with that, as if to give him ocular demonstration of the way in which the cheat had been effected, I took hold of his hand and held it on the table—' when a stranger, who had been sitting at the further end of the room, came quickly to the side of the rogue, and in an instant more had pinned his hand with a carving-fork to the mahogany.' I felt that I had carried the play on long enough, and quickly inserting my finger at the top of his glove, I tore it down the back. He jumped to his feet, and so did I. "You are the man,' I said, ' whose hand was so pinned to the table, and that scar is the evidence I should call, if it were necessary to prove it, Therefore, sit down and hear what else I have to say.'

"He glared viciously at me, lifted his fist as if he would have struck me, and then sank into his chair again.

" 'A man who could try to rob a poor silly boy by such disgraceful means,' I continued, ' could hardly be expected to have any pity on a helpless woman; but, fortunately, I have been a witness of your endeavours on more than one occasion, by threats and menaces, to extort a large sum of money from your host's wife, and that by representing to her that her first husband was alive, and at Otago, New Zealand, when you knew as well as I do that he was dead, and has been so these two years.'

" 'He is not dead,' growled Murray.

" 'He is dead,' I replied, 'and your own pocket-book proves it.'

"As I said this, I held up to him the wallet that I had tumbled upon in the plantation walk, in one of the pockets of which, among a number of other exceedingly suspicious-looking documents, I had found a certificate of the death of Arthur Bernard.

"But as I have been a very long time in telling my story—barristers are proverbially long-winded, you know—I must hurry to a conclusion.

"The morning following our interview, Murray, with many excuses and regrets, found himself unavoidably compelled to return to town.

"As he got into the phaeton that was to take him to the station he kindly whispered in my ear, 'I'll live to pay you out for this yet!' a promise that I

somehow or other fancy he will fulfil some day. Till then I am content to forget all about him.

"As for Mrs. Forrester, the clouds upon her horizon have lifted; she has buried a sad and painful past, and lives in a present, loved as dearly and tenderly as ever by Charlie, who knows nothing, and who never shall, unless she, as I have advised her, has the courage to tell him all, even to the extent that her first husband, Arthur Bernard, was the co-conspirator who stood at Murray's side in the felon's dock.

"I have every hope that she will do this, for the confidence between husband and wife should be as clear as the day at noon."

"Well, Mr. Tangle," said Lord Chetwynd, when the barrister had brought his narrative to an end, "it is a most interesting story of real life, and I expect you gentlemen of the long robe are the possessors of secrets of a similar character, which, in many cases, you are, for various reasons, not permitted to divulge."

"Yes, we are at times the recipients of many a domestic drama or tragedy."

"And did Mrs. Forrester ever make known to her husband the history of her first unfortunate marriage?"

"I believe not. Certainly not that I am aware of. It was a matter I did not choose to interfere in beyond giving her a word or so of advice. No man has a right to interfere between husband and wife, you know."

"He was a base scoundrel," observed Quirp, "and for such men we should have no pity; one hardly knows what punishment such a fellow deserves."

"Solitary confinement, cried Major Smythe. "That's the way to bring a fellow to his senses. If that doesn't succeed nothing will."

"Well, you see," remarked Quirp, "solitary confinement is so terrible that it cannot be resorted to with safety; after a time it has been found to drive prisoners mad."

"Drive them mad—eh?"

"Dear me, yes. Didn't you know that? It is the most fearful of all punishments, and has been tried in the penal prisons of this country and elsewhere. I will give you an account of a prison I visited while this punishment was in operation.

"The prison I am about to speak of was in Philadelphia, to which city an important will case once necessitated my paying a visit. Let me premise here that the solitary system was, at that time at least, practised in American prisons with far more rigour than in English gaols, and sometimes lasted a lifetime, or ended in the madness of the prisoner."

CHAPTER CXLIII.

A VISIT TO A PRISON—SOLITARY CONFINEMENT.

"WHY, Mr. Quirp, have you been in a prison?" inquired Lady Marvlynn.

"I am sorry to say I have been in a good many, my dear madam," returned the lawyer. Not as an inmate—don't imagine that."

Upon this the company burst out into a loud laugh.

"No, only as a visitor," added Quirp. "That is all, and from what I have seen of the internal accommodation of those places I have no desire to dwell therein even for the space of, say, four and twenty hours."

"You are afraid the air would not agree with you?"

"Exactly so. I am quite sure that neither the air, the food, nor the sleeping accommodation would suit me. But I will give you an account of what I saw.

THE "HARVEST HOME" GAMES AT FARMER ASHBROOK'S.

"I had visited a large number of prisoners, when the warder of the Penitentiary said to me, just as we reached the door of a cell whose outward appearance was even more gloomy than those we had visited:—

"'This is the cell of the prisoner I was speaking about—Dick Malden. I have no time to wait at present, but, if you would like to converse with him, I

No. 77.

will lock you in the cell, and call for you, say in half an hour.'

"The warden, in his practical way, was accustomed to allude to his prisoners in much the same manner as the keeper of a menagerie would refer to his living specimens of natural history.

"After all, I thought, there was more reason in this

than appeared at the first glance; for no doubt many of the human hearts which were caged in those impenetrable walls of iron and stone, throbbed with fiercer passions and more savage instincts than ever inspired the breast of any wild beast of the field.

"I had become so used to the warder's manner that, before I assented to his proposition, I was on the point of making inquiries regarding the tameness of the animal within; but I checked myself, and merely signified my assent.

The door was partially opened, and, by a strange sort of turnstile arrangement, I was inducted alone into the cell.

"'Scientific visitor for No. 46!' cried the warder in a loud voice from the outside; then the iron door crashed between us; thud went the shooting bolts, and I heard his echoing steps retreating down the vaulted corridor.

"The cell in which I stood was about ten by fifteen, larger than the ordinary dungeon, and was well lighted by a small grating high in the wall opposite the entrance.

"It contained a small iron bedstead, a small iron table, a small iron chair, and a young man seated on a stool, engaged in pegging shoes with such rapidity that it seemed his life must depend upon completing a gigantic task in an impossibly short space of time.

"But upon my entrance, he threw down his work, and rushed up to me with an eagerly extended hand, and a wild joyous blaze in his eyes (they were very fine eyes —large, gray, lustrous, and expressive), as if I were a brother or a near friend from whom he had long been separated.

"I noticed that the young man was very handsome, even in his degrading prison dress. His frame was lithe and sinewy, his hands and feet small and delicately shaped.

"His face was smooth and beardless as a woman's, his features regular, and singularly handsome, and the contour of his closely cropped head was noble and dignified; yet, with all these redeeming characteristics, there was the inevitable stamp of the born criminal over all.

"His physiognomy was one of those strange, rarely encountered specimens, where, through the mask of good nature, shines forth the glimmering of a depravity so natural to the possessor as to render even him totally unconscious of its existence. But I liked the intensity of feeling with which he grasped my hand.

"'Take a chair,' said he, pushing up the single chair, and seating himself on the side of the iron bedstead. 'I hope you will pardon my vehemence, sir, when I say that yours is the only human face I have seen for, I judge, eight months.'

"'Are you in earnest?' I exclaimed in amazement— for, much as I condemned the system of solitary confinement, I was not aware that it was carried to this extent in America.

"'Certainly, sir,' replied the prisoner, Dick Malden. 'You will perceive, by the peculiar construction of that door, that I cannot even see the face of my gaoler when he brings me food. Even in the chapel, on the Sabbath, our seats are so arranged that we can neither see each other nor the face of the chaplain who preaches to us. We used to have some relief by being able to speak to each other through the water-pipes of the necessary here,' said he, pointing to the apparatus, just below the small grating; 'but they found it out, and now even that avenue of communication is obstructed. They have got us solitary enough now!'

As the young man said this, a wan smile crossed his lips.

"'What is the term of your sentence?'

"'A lifetime.'

"'And your crime?'

"'Murder!'

"There was something terrible in his calm, even tones, and I instinctively shrank back at the dreadful word. Perceiving that the gesture pained him, however, I continued the colloquy by asking—

"'Pray how many times have you been in prison, Mr. Malden?'

"'Call me Dick, sir,' said the prisoner, laughing, but evidently gratified at my civility. 'I have been in prison—in this same prison—five times, when they "copped" me on this last go; I had a pretty sure thing of it, however.'

"'I suppose if you were released to-morrow,' said I, 'it would not be long before you would be back again?'

"'Very likely,' he replied, nodding his head meditatively.

"Then, perceiving the mingled curiosity and incredulity in my countenance, he continued—

"'If you care to hear it, sir, I don't mind giving you some particulars of a thief's story. The last man I saw, about eight months ago, was a sort of a tract distributor, who asked me a great many silly questions about religious matters, of which he himself was as ignorant as that spider on the wall there. He was one of your d——d canting hypocrites, without enough brains to call a congregation into a God-shop, and without pride enough to work for a living, so I turned my back on him at the start. I see nothing but pleasant sympathy in your face, however, and would like the most of my half-hour with you.'

"I gladly assented, and the prisoner-for-life began his story as follows:—

"'I never knew my mother, and my father was a professional thief—at least, he was when I first recognised him as my father. He brought me up as a thief, and I soon proved a wonderful adept, but, in his drunken moments (he was seldom sober) he beat me so cruelly that, when fourteen years of age, I ran away from him, and came from the western city, in which we lived, to this city.'

"'I was an accomplished thief for one so young. There was nothing in that queer Latin of the thief's lexicon that I was not thoroughly conversant with, and, being acquainted with all the secret signals, I was enabled, at almost every point of my journey, to form any variety of acquaintance in my now peculiar life.

"'I could "fake" a "wipe," or "crib" a "spoon," with the best of them, and was not long in teaching the swell-mob of the eastern coast more than they knew, and, moreover, what was not imported from foreign countries either.

"'But, somehow or another, I was not naturally inclined to the profession, and, accident befriending me, I became a lawyer's clerk in Philadelphia.

"'My employer had a very extensive library, and so much did I enjoy reading, that I remained with him for a number of years, improving my mind, and robbing my employer so moderately it was imperceptible.

"'I dressed well, and moved in decent circles, but, when eighteen years of age, I overstepped my modesty, robbed my master of two hundred dollars, and fled, for I knew he would not forgive me.

"'He pursued, arrested, and imprisoned me. This sealed my fate. Allow me to say to you sir, that I know it to be both wrong and impolite, to steal; but in some cases I can convince you that it can't be helped. My imprisonment was of brief duration, but it was sufficient to confirm me as a villain and a wretch.

"'This system of solitary confinement can never reform a criminal. I have tried it for many years, and I ought to know.'

"The prisoner-for-life paused contemplatively, and I could not help wondering at these unusual comments from such lips.

"'No,' he continued, 'they will never succeed in reforming the world that way; I am certain of it. Look at it yourself from my point of view, and you will see it in the same light. Here am I, say, arrested for theft. Grant the crime—what's the use of denying it after you're judged?

"'And I will credit the law by saying this much, that I was never imprisoned unjustly in my life. I am suddenly picked up from the street, and, after a brief trial (I would willingly dispense with that, because my word goes for nothing, and I have no friends), placed in solitary confinement for six months, a year, or two years.

"'No person, sir, who has never undergone the punishment, can even imagine the slow agony of solitary confinement. You could not stand it a year. I, who by this time, should be pretty well used to it, will be able to stand it ten or twelve years longer, when my life-imprisonment will be at an end. Save in the case of such visits as yours, no human face is seen by the prisoner.

"'You probably wondered, when you entered this cell, why I worked so hard. When we first come here, we are given the choice of doing nothing or working. We always prefer the former at first; but not many days of thought—wild, mad, wearing, eternal, lonely thought—are required to drive us to the latter alternative, and we work so hard, so incessantly, in order to forget ourselves, that the authorities make much more out of us than they could out of honest workmen.

"'You see, sir, we must forget ourselves, and that is what we try to do when we work so hard.

"'Well, suppose my term expires, my cell door opened, I am conducted downstairs, change these striped clothes for those relinquished upon entering the prison, and am shown into the street—free to do as I will.

"'Imagine my sensations. I have not seen a human face for years, perhaps, and now, suddenly, I see thousands.

"'I am just as if I were translated into another planet—or like Rip Van Winkle after his thirty years' nap. My clothes are out of fashion, houses have been built where I remember nothing but empty lots. The faces of men and women in the streets seem unreally vivid and distinct.

"'The roar and rumble of the street confuse my brain. I am bewildered, lost. The few dollars I have earned through overwork in the prison are speedily expended for necessities. I am penniless in the world. It is difficult to obtain honest employment.

"'Credentials are almost always required; and who would employ a convict? The only acquaintances whom I meet in the populated streets are those whom I knew of old—fellow-thieves. From these alone I receive the cordial smile of welcome, the warm hand-clasp of friendship. However deeply I may have resolved upon reformation, my old unprincipled feelings repossess me.

"'I borrow money of thieves, visit the old cribs mostly frequented by thieves, meet and become intimate with women—often very pretty girls—who are thieves, and whom I have known before. This is my only sympathy in the world.

"'There is nothing intentionally false or down-dragging in their smiles and their welcomes, because I belong to their tribe, and know that they are really glad of my release from the Penitentiary.

"'Well, thieving is the only legitimate occupation I have. A few weeks' dissipation serves to render me forgetful of my prison experience, hard and bitter as it may have been.

"'My trade is a precarious one—from day to day, from hand to mouth. If the hardships, the danger, the necessary and never-ceasing anxiety of a life of pillage could be presented to the infant mind, I think there would be no thieves.

"'It is terrible, and yet, to one who has been initiated into the wicked mysteries, there is a fascination which cannot be resisted.

"'It is all luck—I may run a day, a week, a month, a year; but, sooner or later, I am sure to feel the cop's accusing grip upon my shoulders—and the eternal dread of this is what gives the wandering glitter which you may have noticed in the thief's eye, and which renders his life a torment of restlessness and fear.

"'Well, after a while, I find myself here again, and immediately pitch in to drown my wretchedness in hard work.

"'The magistrates know me, and treat me as an old customer; and here, in the prison, they regard me as an erratic boarder (permanent enough now!) who will be sure to return again.

"'This is the routine of my own life, and may answer for that of many of my class.

"'I will relate to you the circumstances of my last arrest—and my final one, for I firmly believe that I shall never again quit these prison walls alive.

"'I had just finished a term of four years, and, after praying to God very sincerely, and reasoning with myself very strongly, and come to the determination to lead an honest life, if within the scope of possibility. Fortune favoured me, and I obtained a subordinate position in the office of a prominent lawyer.

"'He knew my history. I told it all to him, and threw myself upon his generosity. He extended his hand nobly to me. For a long time I did not repay his kindness with ingratitude. I suffered more than he thought in my endeavours to be honest.

"'Every day I would encounter the sneers of my comrades in the street, and frequently their curses, but still remained firm in my good resolutions.

"'My employer was an old bachelor. His office was in the front part of his dwelling, which was presided over by his housekeeper, Mrs. Stanton, an eccentric, but kind-hearted old lady. I noticed, casually, that my employer never banked any of his money, and, at the same time, very seldom had much of it upon his person, so out of mere curiosity (I assure you, sir, it was nothing but curiosity), I set myself to find out what he did with it, until one day I discovered, while accidentally traversing an upper hall in his house, that he secreted it somewhere in an old bureau, in his own bedroom.

For several days after this I could not help thinking what a shrewd old fellow my employer was, to deposit his money in such an out-of-the-way place, instead of letting all the world know its whereabouts by the presence of the usual massive and cumbrous iron safe.

"'Well, sir, one bright morning, Mr. B——, my employer, sent me to collect a bad debt for an inconsiderable amount, and, as I left the office, I noticed that the door of the dwelling-house was wide open.

"'I was pretty sweet on Polly, the cook, or she was on me, which was better yet, and I thought it wouldn't do any harm just to run into the kitchen and give her a good-morning kiss. As Satan would have it, Polly wasn't in the kitchen, and there were signs of her having just gone to market.

"'I glanced into the little sitting-room, which Mrs. Stanton nearly always occupied when she was in the house, and, to my surprise, there were signs of her having also just gone to market.

"'Greatly marvelling that such a nice house should be thus left all alone, I thought I would just take a look around the premises, out of mere curiosity. To make a long story short, I found myself presently in Mr. B——'s bedchamber, gazing very curiously at that old bureau, somewhere in which I knew he kept his money. At first my curiosity was genuine, but I gradually began to think how many nice things I could buy if that money was mine.

"'I was sadly in need of a suit of clothes, and was also very fond of dress. I hadn't been on the spree for a long, long time, and, just at this unfortunate moment, my mouth began to water for the wine-cup.

"'Well, sir, it is hardly worth while for me to describe the various phases of temptation which led, step by step, to the evil deed. I was almost as much surprised at myself as any stranger would have been, had he seen me, when a few minutes later, I found myself rummaging through the drawers of that old bureau, in the most nervous and excited manner.

"'I was engaged in this manner when I was startled by a loud scream, and wheeled on my heel to perceive the housekeeper, Mrs. Stanton, looking at me. The thought of my position flashed upon me so strongly and vividly that, for a moment, I was incapable of action.

"'I was too old a bird, however, to be paralysed by fear for more than an instant of time. Her screams continued.

"'In my wild alarm, I sprang upon her and clutched her throat.

"'As I did so, a thousand thoughts flashed through my brain. The consequences which would fall upon me should my employer discover any attempt upon his property—the judge's face, stern and relentless—the words of the prosecuting attorney—the stolid jurymen, with prejudice and hatred imprinted upon their foredooming faces—and then the walls of this accursed prison rose before me, with their stony hopelessness augmented fifty-fold. I continued to choke down her accursed cries more vigorously as these terrible thoughts fleeted through my head.

"'At length she ceased struggling, and, slowly relinquishing my grip, I laid her upon the floor. I then bent over her, with a cold, icy horror at my heart, never experienced before; for I perceived that the housekeeper was dead.

"'I had no control over myself after that, sir. In my wild excitement I rushed to the nearest police-station, hurriedly confessed my crime, and was arrested. At the subsequent trial I was found guilty of murder in the first degree, and sentenced to be hanged. In view of the extenuating circumstances, as they called them, my sentence was commuted to penal servitude for life, and here I am.'

"'Good-bye, sir, and may God bless you! I hear the warden at the door.'

"Tears stood in his eyes as he extended his hand to me, and grasping it warmly I quitted the cell. After the door was closed I heard a great hammering going on within, and I knew that the prisoner-for-life was forgetting his loneliness in the monotonous hum-drum of shoe-pegging."

"Poor fellow," said Lord Fitzbogleton. "What a dweadful punishment it must be to be impwisoned for life!"

"Yes, it is a most melancholy state of existence without doubt," said Smythe: "and, to say the truth, it appears almost miraculous how prisoners are able to bear so severe a punishment, but in most cases they deserve what they get. The wonder is that there are not more escapes, seeing that so many are driven to what one might call a desperate condition."

"When I was in the United States," said Captain Crasher, "escapes and attempted escapes from prison were frequent occurrences, but here in the old country, as our Transatlantic cousins term it, the chances for prisoners freeing themselves from bondage are but few and far between. Nevertheless, even here successful attempts at escape do take place, despite the surveillance kept over the unfortunate denizens of a penal prison. When I was in America many of the convicts of Clinton prison strove to be again on their travels. No less than thirteen tried to escape within the space of two months. Whether this was caused by the neglect of the officers, or the insecurity of the prison, I will not intend to say, but as we are discoursing on prison life, I will just give you an account of the rascals at Clinton, and how they managed to escape, or, at least, tried to do so.

"First, two of their number made their exit from the forge during the night, which is closely guarded inside and out by several of the most efficient guards of the prison.

"Strange to say, these same two escaped from the same place last summer.

"Their names were Samuel Tweed and Henry Austin.

"After leaving the prison they proceeded to a barn in the vicinity, where they procured a horse and waggon, with which they managed to reach the village of Saranac, some six or eight miles distant; but there finding their great enemy, the snow, had not left the premises, and as they were unable to use the waggon any further, the snow being so deep, they concluded to tramp it on foot, and to their sorrow, for they were quickly followed by officers Christian and Hagerty, who succeeded in first capturing Tweed; but, Austin being somewhat of a more daring character, attempted to fight it out, paying no attention to the word 'halt' given by Mr. Hagerty.

"Seeing that Austin meant to try his speed, Mr. Hagerty discharged his revolver over the convict's head, which, as intended, brought him to bay. Finally they were once more secured in their old quarters, and now wear a heavy log chain as a reward of their escapade.

"Not the least daunted by the failure of his brother convicts, William Wallace (no relation of the Scotch chieftain), who was employed as engineer at the rolling-mill, took it into his head to vamose; so, by playing possum with the keeper, he succeeded in leaving the prison.

"He could not have scaled the stockade before the alarm was given, but, alas! the bird had flown, and was not caught for some days afterwards, and then by chance, he being hidden in the woods, heard a gun discharged close by, and, thinking he had been discovered, took to his heels and ran.

"Those who fired the gun were not in search of escaped convicts, but for pleasure, and pleased they were when they saw fifty dollars within their reach, and which they received for the capture of the said William Wallace, who now works in his old shop, but is not engineer, unless he may be called an engineer in a small way, for I suppose it is a matter of engineering to walk with the large shackle and chain which he wears without injuring his ankles.

"So far I have only recorded escapes and recaptures. Now I come to a trial escape (which is a very rare occurrence).

"It was on Sunday, a day of rest (but not for the prison-keepers), that as usual two convicts were sent from their cells to feed the hogs, but instead of laying out the usual quantity of food for the hogs, they laid out an unusual quantity of food for themselves, contemplating beforehand that they would need it on their travels.

"Travels, I say, for travel they did over the pickets, and God knows where, for they were not seen again for ten or twelve days after. One of them, by name Tanner, happened to come across an old acquaintance of his in the shape of the sheriff of the town he was convicted in.

"The sheriff, knowing his term had not expired, at once arrested him and placed him in gaol, there to await an answer from the prison-officers, concerning the escape of Tanner.

"One of the ex-officers of the prison, Mr. John Thompson, who had been sent in that direction in expectation that Tanner would seek his former acquaintances, was soon at the gaol and immediately recognised him.

"From certain information received from Tanner, in regard to the whereabouts of Yates, his confederate, Thompson and the sheriff proceeded some miles further on in hopes of effecting Yates's capture.

"In the meantime, Tanner thought he would try his luck once more; so with very little trouble he succeeded in breaking out of the gaol, since which neither he nor Yates has been heard of.

"Probably Mr. Thompson and the sheriff will learn to profit by that somewhat stale proverb, that 'A bird in the hand is worth two in the bush.'

"Next comes another escape from that stronghold, the forge. Strange to say, among so many guards, a convict could not be seen to leave his fire and ascend to the roof, from there through a sky-light, as Patrick Curly did, not many nights before, but the fortunate was doomed to misfortune, as it proved, for he succeeded in getting no further than Cadyville, where he was captured and brought back, and by two boys, both younger than himself.

"He now wears the reward of his failure in the shape of a heavy chain fastened to the leg, and it is to be hoped he will learn that the way of the transgressor is hard.

"It was on the evening of the 28th of May, some half-dozen of convicts were employed in the foundry (a rather unusual thing, i.e., after six o'clock, p.m.), in charge of three guards, each having charge of two men; but it seems that one of the guards, a Mr. Burdick, was cross-eyed, which enabled him to see both ways; but unfortunately for his reputation, and I have no doubt for his position, he did not see the way that William Shea and Patrick Foley made their exit, and it was not for some time after they had gone before our friend, Mr. B., became aware of the fact.

"When he was told of it he remarked: 'Yes, they are gone, and so is my 75 dols. a month gone.' He being a keeper, was of course at once discharged for neglect of duty.

"Shea, after three days' hard travelling, became so exhausted, that he concluded to give himself up, which he did to two men, for which they received the usual reward of 50 dols.

"Foley, it seems, was somewhat the toughest, for he managed to stay away two days longer, and after travelling, as he says, about a hundred miles and more, he met two men of whom he inquired how far it was from Canada, which they undertook to show him by bringing him back to the prison, which was somewhat about twelve miles distant.

"Foley participated in the joy of the two men who effected his capture, for on entering the prison-gate, being tied down to a waggon, he looked up and exclaimed 'How are you, Canada?'

"The usual reward was received by all parties—viz., 50 dols. for the capture of each—and the captured received their reward by having their head shaved in the shape of a cock's comb, dark cell, and ball and chain; that man-killing machine known as the shower-box being abolished by an act passed by our State Legislature.

"Nothing must do but the Sabbath must be broken, also, the prison windows (which by-the-bye are made of cast iron), by two desperadoes known as James McManus and Washington Roxford.

"The circumstances are as follow:—It seems that when the convict Curly escaped, Charles Richardson, principal keeper, received the information that the said McManus in some way or other assisted him, which justified Richardson in keeping McManus locked up.

"Some time previous Roxford had committed a breach of prison discipline, for which he also was locked up and wore a chain.

"It seems they contemplated to repeat the Sing Sing tragedy, in bucking and gagging the guards, for the material for so doing was found in their rooms; but luckily for Charley Gray, who it seems they intended to select for their victim, they pursued another course, which was to cut their doors, and with a heavy sledge hammer break the cast-iron windows, which they succeeded in doing about nine o'clock a.m.

"While the Sunday school was being held they succeeded in going through the window, but to their surprise they were confronted by several of the guards, who it seems had been on the alert, expecting this for some time. No doubt Charley Richardson rewarded them as they deserved, both being 'hard cases.'

"It is a strange thing that in this enlightened age one of the State prisons should be as far behind the times as to have doors and windows made of cast iron, which is well known to be utterly useless as a safeguard against convicts' escapes, and the convicts know it, too.

"It is to be hoped that some means will be found to make the new prison now in contemplation more secure than the one at Dancmora.

"His Excellency Gov. Hoffman paid a visit to the prison some time since, which was not intended as an official one (he being on a pleasant trip to the trout lakes in the vicinity), but the convicts made it one for him, for out of 500 and odd men there nearly one-half wanted to see him, but of course could not, his stay there being but short; but those that did see him were received very kindly, and those who deserved it, I have no doubt, heard from him in a short time, for he had already pardoned two.

"He had no sooner left the prison than three of the convicts took the notion that they would leave too; but thanks to some of the guards they did not go any further than the main sewer, where they had hidden themselves.

"Their names were Obastio (coloured), Whitehead and Howard; all belonging to that unruly school of boys known as the 'Nail Factory.'

"The guards were aroused in the night, or in the morning, for it was about three, and that, too, on a Sunday morning, by the report of a pistol which was discharged at the convict Hughes, who attempted to break the window with a hammer; but the night-guard, Mr. Kimball, being on watch for such things, quickly made him drop the sledge and cry for quarter. He was not shot, though it was no fault of the guards, for they were determined to make an example of some of those gaol-breakers.

"The convict, Thomas Kelly, was indicted for murder in the first degree, subsequently, for the murder of his fellow-convict, Lorenzo. He was tried at Plattsburgh, the witnesses being mostly convicts.

"A convict there, named Mulligan, a noted river pirate, under sentence of fifteen years, attempted suicide by opening an artery in his arm, and was only saved by the prompt arrival of the prison physician, Arthur S. Wolff.

"Several attempts have been made, of late, in the prisons, upon the lives of officers. In a great many of them they are provoked assaults by the officers, I have no doubt. At least, one came to my notice during my stay.

"It was between a convict named Morrow and Officer Moore. This Moore was a very brutal man, and uses at all times the most abominable language towards his men; and it was a wonder to me that such a man should be allowed in the prison as a keeper.

"Charley Richardson knew this man's character; why did he not take such steps as would cause his removal? On the same day convict Flaherty attempted to cut Officer Cartwright without any cause whatever.

"What is the use of officers carrying firearms, if they have them in such a position that it takes them so long before they can get at them? I have known about six or seven keepers in one prison who could have prevented the beatings they have received by the timely appearance of their pistols, which they keep slung on a belt around behind them, and in a case, which is kept buttoned.

"Convicts know this; so, when they attack an officer they know they do it without chance of being shot. Never do I remember of one case where a convict was shot in attempting to strike an officer, which was getting to be an every-day occurrence."

"Gentlemen," said Lady Marvlynn, "I do hope and trust you have enjoyed yourselves. We have had, I am sure, a most charming and sociable evening. I can speak for myself. The amount of information and interesting matter which many of my guests have kindly furnished us with has been specially acceptable both to myself and many others of the company. There has of course been one circumstance which has broken up the harmony and flow of conversation for a brief period. I allude to the presence of that lawless man whom many of you censure me—and, I admit, with justice, perhaps—for suffering to escape; but at the same time——"

"Say no more upon that subject, my lady," inter-

rupted Sir William Leathbridge. "The fellow has had a respite—is far away by this time. The best thing we can do is to forget that he was present here to-night."

"But he knocked my hat over my eyes, and be hanged to him," cried Fitzbogleton, "and sent Miss Awabella Lovejoyce into hysterics."

"Miss Lovejoyce will forgive him, I dare say," observed the baronet.

"Oh, dear me, yes," returned the fair Arabella, "most willingly."

"I felt assured of that," said the baronet. "Now, ladies and gentlemen, we are, I take it, all agreed upon one point, this being that our kind friend and hostess has acted with her usual discretion, and, all things considered, it is just as well, and it may be a great deal better, that we are rid of the scoundrel."

"Certainly, quite right, Sir William," cried several. "We endorse your opinion most willingly."

"And so this matter being settled," observed the baronet, "and seeing also that we have had a long sitting, and however pleasurable the evening may have been, which it has been to all of us—(hear, hear)—nevertheless, as it is now drawing to a close, before we break up I have one toast to propose, and I am sure, speaking from my own personal experience, and the experience also of most—and indeed I may say, all persons present—that you will join me in doing justice to that toast. I will not tell you how many years I have had the honour of knowing Lady Marvlynn, because you see by so doing I should have to go back to the sunny days of my youth, and this would lead up to the unpleasant fact that I might probably be no longer young—in fact, it might be said that I am getting old. ("No, no," and cheers). Well, we will not dwell upon such an objectionable subject. Her ladyship is the same bright, kind-hearted creature whom I knew, say for the nonce a dozen or so years ago. Time has not changed her, and, as far as I am individually concerned, as years have flown by, my friendship for her ladyship has been strengthened rather than diminished, and I may add that it is a deep and lasting friendship, which I am perfectly well convinced will only end with my life; and, so you see, this being so, I have felt it a duty incumbent on me to propose the health and happiness of Lady Marvlynn. May her future life be one of unclouded sunshine, each day fulfilling the promises of yesterday, still promising to-morrow. My friends, Lady Marvlynn!" cried the baronet, raising his glass.

The company stood up and drank the toast with enthusiasm.

Signor Marouski sang a sort of benediction in choice Italian, which was doubtless very fine, but nobody understood it.

This did not much matter, it was very effective, nevertheless.

Other speeches and toasts followed, and shortly after midnight the guests began to take their departure.

Lord Fitzbogleton was the last to leave. He still lingered by the side of Miss Lovejoyce.

"Your carriage is at the door, my lord," observed the lady.

"I know it," he answered petulantly. "I am perfectly well assured of that important fact. What does it matter? I am master of my own time—have no wife or babies waiting for my return. Hang it, don't be in such a hurry to get rid of a fellow."

"I am in no hurry, my lord."

"I am glad to hear you say so, and now about the

wing. I swear most positively I will not go till I've got your pwomise."

" What promise ?"

" What pwomise! Why, that you will consent to accept the wing as a token of my esteem." He was going to say love, but substituted the other word in lieu of it.

" Your esteem ?"

" Certainly. Confound it, Awabella. I intend to always call you Awabella, you know."

" Well, yes, that, I believe, is an agreement."

" It is, and you won't depart from the letter of the law in this respect."

" There is no reason for my doing so."

" Well, what was I saying ? Where was I ? Oh, I know—about your pwomise."

" We will talk about that when we next meet."

" Indeed, we will do no such thing. We will talk about it now. I will not leave this house till you have given me your word that you will accept the wing as a token of fwendship and esteem."

" That is your determination ?"

" It is."

" Then, of course, as you are so persistent I have no alternative. Be satisfied with the assurance that I will accept the gift."

" I am the happiest of men," exclaimed the young nobleman. Farewell for the pwesent, dearest Awabella. You are an angel—that's what you are."

" Am I ?" she exclaimed, bursting out into a laugh.

" There you go again," ejaculated her companion. " You are so fond of looking at things in a widiculous light. A fellow don't like to be held up to widicule. No fellow likes that."

" No, of course not."

" Then why do you do it ?"

" I have not attempted to hold you up to ridicule," said she, poa.ing.

" No, no, I didn't mean to say that. Pardon me, my charmer, I could not find it in my heart to blame you. You are faultless."

The champagne and other sparkling wines, together with the excitement of the day, had produced a visible effect upon Fitzbogleton, whose utterance was a little thick.

" We part good friends," said he. " Say that you are not offended."

" Goodness me, no !" cried Arabella. " How can I possibly be offended ?"

He would not leave go of her hand, but strove as best he could to explain himself. He was a little foggy, and Miss Lovejoyce thought he would never go.

" If he is often like this," she murmured, " he must be rather a troublesome man."

At length he made a movement towards the door, and after bidding a final farewell, betook himself to his chocolate-coloured chariot, and was driven off.

And so the festivities at Lady Marvlynn's were brought to a close.

CHAPTER CXLIV.

A GLANCE AT STOKE FERRY FARM HARVEST HOME.

FOR some days after Peace's return to the Evalina-road he was in a furious savage state. He did not tell anyone of his escapade at the residence of Lady Marvlynn, but those about him were at no loss to divine that something had occurred which not only roused his temper, but made him as sharp and snappish as a rabid dog.

Mrs. Thompson, who had been putting an enemy into her mouth, incurred his displeasure. With brutal ferocity he struck her mercilessly about the face and head. So violent was his attack that one of the unhappy woman's eyes was closed, in addition to several other bruises, which she received at the hands of her brutal companion; the only wonder is that she consented to remain with him so long.

It was in vain for Mrs. Peace to interfere, for she knew that the chances would have been that she would have been subjected to a similar course of treatment, for Peace ruled his two female companions with a rod of iron.

Bill Rawton strove to pacify the tyrant. He was a man who never at any time of his life treated one of the opposite sex with unkindness, and Peace's conduct towards the " ladies " of his establishment met with Bill's unqualified disapproval.

As time went on, however, the owner of the home in the Evalina-road toned down, and it is said that he expressed his regret for his barbarity—anyway, he became more considerate towards those who might at at any given moment have handed him over to the officers of the law.

But we must leave the brutal burglar for a while, to take a glance at some of the other characters, who figure in this history.

In the succeeding chapters it will be our purpose to chronicle the career of our hero, with something like an unbroken course of action.

It is, perhaps, needless to say that Mr. Algernon Sutherland dodged the police; he did not present himself at the police-court, where the second examination should have taken place, and the magistrate, Mr. Kensett, felicitated himself upon the fact that the young man had contrived to give his enemies the slip.

Many months had passed over since the capture, and fresh examination of Sutherland took place, and the affair had by this time been nearly if not quite forgotten.

It was autumn, and the harvest time was over, the fields were no longer forests of waving corn, but bare and yellow stubble; the yards of the farmers were filled with portly and imposing sacks of corn, warm and sweet beneath thin roofs of pale clean thatch.

Harvest time is the holiday of country labourers—one of hard work and high wages, which is the best holiday of all.

At harvest time men and women, who in some parts of England are still preferred to machines, earn the chance of buying for themselves and families new corduroy trousers, cotton gowns, and nailed boots for the ensuing year.

But there are few (however temperately they may have lived during the other months of the year) who do not spend a great deal of their money on filthy debauches over poisoned beer. This is called the " harvest drunken touch." With some it lasts no longer than one night; with others a week, a fortnight, or even longer. It is one of the sacred impurities of our forefathers, which descend from generation to generation, fathers and grandfathers industriously setting the bad example.

I have to describe a jovial and a far happier scene, and to take you to a *Plat* or orchard, belonging to Stoke Ferry Farm. John Ashbrook was, as we have already seen, a most prosperous man.

It was a bright day for him when he left Oakfield House to take to Stoke Ferry Farm, and to espouse its then owner's charming daughter.

Very different was it with the other brother.

Richard Ashbrook, who had married the girl Jane Ryan, seemed to go from bad to worse after his brother had left him, and his wife died.

He seemed to lose all heart, and the consequence was that his farm was neglected, for the simple reason that he did not appear to care about anything. The result may be easily imagined. Richard was as unprosperous as his brother was flourishing.

Nevertheless, when the harvest festivities were about to take place at Stoke Ferry, John insisted upon his brother and sister doing honour to them by their presence.

It was a goodly gathering. Brickett was present, as were also old Nat, whom the reader will doubtless remember as one of the parlour customers of the "Carved Lion ;" Mother Bagley, the personification of spotlessness in dress, and sedateness in demeanour; and Master John Ashbrook, puffing out his cheeks like the sides of a red balloon, and rubbing his broad brown hands, and Patty as loveable and charming as she had ever been.

There were sports to be played at, and prizes to be contended for; pole-climbing, jumping in sacks, wheelbarrow races blindfold, hurdle jumping, ball throwing, and quoit throwing were the order of the day.

These games occupied the whole of the forenoon, and when six brawny fellows took their places, the whole of their bodies being encased in sacks, with nothing but their heads visible, there was a roar of laughter, and peal after peal followed in quick succession as one or more stumbled, and frantically strove to rise upon his legs again.

When these sports were over, they adjourned to the barn, and commenced an onslaught upon brown loaves, Cheshire cheese, and a barrel of home-brewed beer.

After lunch it was announced that the lamb race was to come off.

Heralds in corduroys spouted it forth with their voices, loud and brazen as trumpets; ballmen cleared the course with their wands of stout ground-ash.

"Come, Kitty," said John Ashbrook, "Why be dull a day like this? Brighten up, lass, brighten up, there's plenty of sun behind the clouds yet, though, for my part I cant see any clouds at all."

"There be clouds, nevertheless, master, said the young woman. "I be thinkin' as how he be dead and gone. The clouds are in my heart, where it's not for the eyes of man to see."

"It may be so, that be true enough, I dessay, lass, but ye see it beant o' no manner o' yoose for a lad or lass a settin' their minds to be for ever a mournin'. Look at my brother—he can't forget, poor chap, the one as be dead and gone. Don't ee follow his example. Look at Joe—he's the honestest and truest lad in the hull county, and he's bin after ee ever so long, but you won't speak to un, though all the maids be a dyin' for un. Don't ee like him, Kitty?"

"I like him well enough—I could not help doing that there, if it were only for his fondness and attachment to Mr. Phillip, but I couldna marry him."

"And why not?"

"I couldna without a tellin' him, and I wouldna do that to save my life."

"Ye be a strange gell, self-willed and wayward, I'm thinkin'. I dessay, if the truth may be spoken, Joe knows all about what you ha' to tell him."

"Does he? Well may be as how he does."

"And so ye see, lass, there beant no yoose your being so obstinate. You must say a kind word or two to Joe or else——"

"Or else, what, master?"

"Well, maybe you and I shall fall out."

"We ha' never done that as yet, anyhow."

"Noa, an' I hopes as how we never shall."

"Tell him what you like then, it won't alter his love, you foolish hussey; and now go and have your thumbs tied."

"What, run for the lamb!" she cried, shrinking back a little.

"Aye, run for the lamb. Ye're the straightest-limbed girl in these parts, and the strongest. Joe Doughty is the Lord of the Harvest, and so, gell, you must be the Lady of the Lamb."

The lamb race, as it is termed, is thus regulated. A young lamb is run for by the young maidens, who have their thumbs tied behind their backs. Whoever succeeds in first seizing the lamb with her mouth, retains it as her prize, and receives the title of the Lady of the Lamb.

The custom is an ancient one—the relic, perhaps, of a less refined age than the present—and it cannot be considered a very elegant performance. Nevertheless, it generally affords amusement to most persons who witness it.

Ten young women had already stood forward as candidates.

It fell to the sweetheart of each to tie her thumbs for her. If by chance any one of them did not happen to have a sweetheart, one of the young men volunteered to perform the amorous duty; and this was perhaps the prettiest part of the sport.

Sometimes there was a little confusion when a belle happened to possess more than one recognised lover.

They would stand watching her with their sheepish eyes, and she would be compelled to choose once for all which of the two she would keep company with for the future.

When Kitty appeared the girls looked at each other anxiously, for they recognised in her a formidable antagonist.

All the young men made way for Joe Doughty, who went up to her and asked her if he might tie her hands for her.

"As well you as any other," was the answer.

She exceeded Ashbrook's expectations, and the forebodings of the other candidates were verified.

Kitty, open-jawed, and as agile as a young leopardess, had soon pounced upon the lamb, and won the prize with her teeth.

Whether she would have been a match for the female acrobat who recently astounded the frequenters of a London music-hall, with the tenacious power and strength of her teeth, is another question, but she took the shine out of all her rustic competitors, and her master, Mr. John Ashbrook, felt proud of the victory she had obtained.

Now the old wives were marshalled into a line to run a race for a pound of tea.

Mother Bagley, who indignantly refused " to beneath herself by joining in such a rabbling concern," condescended, however, to drink hot tea against other dames who worshipped the refreshing beverage.

The scalding twankey brought the tears into her eyes, but comfort to her heart.

Snuff had now become her staff of life, the prop of her old age. To be out of snuff was to be snuffed out —a dead charred wick instead of a bright and constant flame.

A tub of water was brought out and placed in the centre of the plat. Apples were called for, the largest that could be had.

The boys immediately formed themselves into a procession, and proceeded to wassail the orchard, or to go apple-howling, as it was otherwise termed.

DEADLY STRUGGLE BETWEEN PEACE AND CONSTABLE ROBINSON.

One of them had a cow's horn, from which he extracted horribly discordant notes. Then they marched to one of the apple trees and encircled it, chanting a prayer for the next year's crop.

> Stand fast, root—bear well, top—
> Pray the Lord send us a good heavy crop.

> Every twig apples big—
> Every bough apples enow :
> Hats full, caps full,
> Full quarters, sacks full.

They shouted in chorus with the cow-horn accompaniment, rapped the trees with sticks, which each bore in his hand, and concluded the ceremony by

No. 78.

knocking down three monster red-cheeked pippins, which were soon floating in the t b, ready to be mouthed for by the youngsters, who endeavoured to earn them under the same conditions as the lamb race.

Indeed, the sports and pastimes on this occasion were singularly varied and amusing.

Old Mr. Jamblin had, throughout his life, taken great delight in keeping up the old English customs of his forefathers, and John Ashbrook proved a worthy successor, in this respect, to his father-in-law.

At six o'clock they sat down to the harvest dinner, which was spread and served on a table of fabulous length in a corner of the plat, where the grass had been mowed for the purpose.

It was still warm enough for *al fresco* repasts—at least, on such an evening as this, when the air was fragrant, when the nightingale was singing, and when the last rays of sunlight fell goldenly and gloriously upon the scene.

As soon as the sirloins of beef and huge plum puddings had disappeared from the table, and pipes with tobacco had taken their place, a low whisper ran backwards and forwards, and more than one voice cried audibly for Joe Doughty.

Joe had earned the rank of the Lord of the Harvest by reaping more corn than any other labourer on the farm. It was one of the duties of this nobleman to propose the health of the reapers.

He was, like a good many more, "unaccustomed to public speaking. So he rose and said—

"Pr'aps as Master Cheadle was the vice, sitting opposite to Master Ashbrook and all——"

"Strike me into brandy pop, you're a coming it strong, young man," said Cheadle, with affected sternness, "Don't go puttin' your pack upon other pipple's shoulders."

"There, that's just like my Joe," cried Doughty's mother. "He knows I want him to speechify, and he's a tryin' to get out of it on purpose to worrit me."

"All right, mother," cried Doughty, "you shan't be worrited. I aint much of a hand at speechifying, but I dunno as I ought to shirk my duty; so you see I shall ha' to cut the matter as short as the stubble in the whate-fields. I'm a goin' to ax you to drink the health of the most considerate and kindest of masters as ever mortal man had. From the first drop of the dew-cup to what we are drinking now, when ha' we had to ask for beer and couldn't get it?

Chorus of voices: "Never!"

[The dew-cup is the first draught of beer given to reapers before they begin harvest work.]

"We've had kindness always, and beer always, and money always when we have earned it, sometimes afore that wi' some on ye, and to-day we've had sports and prizes as we don't get every day in England; so I ax ye to drink the health of Master Ashbrook."

The health was drunk with wild enthusiasm.

"And, now," said Doughty, "let's hear you join in wi' me in the harvest song, and we'll sing it in the good old style."

When the harvest song (which has appeared too often in print to need further recording) was concluded, John Ashbrook rose and thanked them, and then, without sitting down, sang a song in praise of the "Lord of the Harvest." All rose while Doughty remained seated. At the end of the song Joe commenced a song in praise of the head carter. The company rose again and joined him in the characteristic chorus, "With a halt, with a ree, with a wo, with a gee;"—then the carter sang to the shepherd, the shepherd to the thatcher, and so on.

All these little musical arrangements had been decided on weeks before the appointed day, and it had taken some of the vocalists months to learn their parts.

By the time their complimentary songs were ended it was quite dark. A large camphine lamp, which occupied the centre of the table, supplied the place of the moon, and half a dozen candles played their parts of fixed stars.

"Who's to be knocked down for the next song?" roared the wood-cutter, in his stentorian voice. "It's my call—and I calls on—calls on——"

"Come, say it, and ha' done wi' it," said Nat, peevishly. "It rouses my corruption to hear a growed-up man hogglin' and bogglin' like that 'ere."

"Then I calls on you, Nat."

The rustics laughed, and sang, "Poor old hoss—poor old hoss!"

"Don't ee be fools," cried Joe. "I aint a-going to let ee sing that to-night."

"Spiff a song, ould un, and don't be ranty tanty—coom."

"I bean't ranty tanty," said Nat, "but it meks me rankled to think as we ha' no fitchet pie for supper. We allers yoosed to ha' it, and I can't sing wi'out it, nother."

"We used to ha' fitchet pie, sartinly," said the old wood-cutter, "but we didn't yoose to ha' such good meat nor such fine plum puddings as we's had to-day, and there's no lack o' beer. Pour him out a noggin and then he'll sing."

"There's something better than that coming. My eyes alive, look ee here."

"Buckle-my-buff, and a gallon on it," shouted an enthusiastic clown.

"There's another coming," said the girls, as they set it down upon the table.

The beer mugs were speedily emptied, and sent in half-dozens to the bowl, before which a servant lass, ladle in hand, laboured without ceasing.

"My blessing to all on you," cried Nat, with a devotional expression of countenance.

"Yes, that's all very well, Nat, but we want your song first, and your toast afterwards."

"I doesn't care a dump for yer wants; I'll sing when I has a mind to, and not afore."

"Well, there's plenty as can if you can't."

"Can't. Who says I cant sing? I'll sing e'er a man here for a pint."

And he broke out into the following pastoral:—

THE GAY PLOUGHBOY.

Come, all you merry ploughboys, and listen to my song;
A tale I have to tell you, which doth to love belong.
He that doth rise up early to lead his team with joy,
And so bravely does his duty like a gay ploughboy.
            Like a gay ploughboy.

Says the mother to the daughter, "You seem to love him well—
It seems as if your tender breast all on his head could dwell;
Young lads they are so rakish, young maids they do decoy,
And some day we'll see you on the knee of a gay ploughboy."
            Of a gay ploughboy.

"Oh, no, oh no," said Jenny, "he's just the lad for me;
With him I could live happy, his heart's so gay and free,
And he does rise so early to lead his team with joy,
And he bravely does his duty, like a gay ploughboy."
            Like a gay ploughboy.

Young William in the evening, returning home from plough,
He showed to me a gay gold ring, how could my tongue say No?
"Oh, take this ring, dear Jenny, and the parson we'll employ,
And they may see you on the knee of a gay ploughboy."
            Of a gay ploughboy.

'Twas so they were united, and William goes to plough,
And Jenny rises with delight to milk her spotted cow.
Down in a lonely cottage, where none can them annoy,
Ah, who so happy as Jenny and her gay ploughboy?
            And her gay ploughboy.

"Where's measter?" said a cowboy, addressing himself to the multitude. "Here's the fiddlers coom, and wants to know whether they may stop or no."

"Yes, they may stop," said Nat, in a confident tone. "I'm head man here."

"You've got bit by a barn-mouse already—aint you?" inquired the wood-cutter.

"Or bin to Hatcham Fair and broke both his legs," said Joe.

"That'll be first-class if we ha' a dance, won't it?" said a young lady, with an elegant motion, which was probably intended for a pirouette.

"Dancin'!" cried Nat, scornfully. "Drat it, what d'ye want to be got at dancin' for? We be very well as we are, and I means to call upon the thatcher for a song, cos he and I allers bin such very partikiller friends."

"I aint heard your toast as yet," said the thatcher, "and I've been listening for it hard, tew."

"If you'd listened harder wi them stupid ears, you'd ha' herd me gi' it afore ever I sung. Here's another for ee, you darned deaf adder, 'Two In and One Out'—d'ye know what that be? It's in health, in wealth, and out of debt."

"And a downright good toast too," said John Ashbrook, who had left the company for a while and had now returned, "and an excellent toast, Nat."

"Aye, that it be, measter."

"But what say ee to a dance?" said Ashbrook.

"There, I knew all your pretty girls would like to dance. Tell 'em to come in, some of ee."

Half a dozen scampered off with the glad tidings, and in a few minutes returned with three men, each of whom carried something wrapped up in green baize beneath his arm.

"I want my call answered first, though," said old Nat, "and the thatcher he aint no true friend o' mine, so I calls on——"

"Be quiet, you flabbergullion, talking like that 'ere, afore measter."

"He knows as much about civility as a fly does of a gaiter strap," said the indignant Mrs. Doughty.

"There, when he gets into that drunken guret it aint no yoose talkin' to him. If the angel Gibbriel commed down he'd try and push him out of the way. I never seed such an obstinate fellow in all my born days."

"I intend to ha' my call," cried Nat, "and so I calls on Kitty Morgan."

"I don't know any songs," said Kitty."

"Get out! you know a wheelbarrow full," returned Nat.

"And she can sing even as sweetly as a barley bird (a nightingale)," said the farmer.

There was no getting out of it—so Kitty tried to do her best.

"Very prettily sung, my gell," said Ashbrook when she concluded. "Now for the dance—it will be bull's noon (midnight) else before we begin. The Harvest Lord and the Lady of the Lamb lead off. What's it to be, Joe?"

"'Speed the Plough's' my sort, sir," said Joe, touching his cap; "it's one of the best country dances we have."

"I quite agree with you, Joe — it is," said the farmer. "Now, fiddlers, strike up for 'Speed the Plough.'"

The musicians tuned their instruments, ran over the first few bars, and were satisfied that they were up to the mark, and then dashed off.

"Speed the Plough" was danced through and played

through as country people dance and as country fiddlers play.

As far as vigour was concerned there was no reason to complain. The farmer stopped the dance out, and then left them entirely to their own devices.

This was turned to profit by the fiddlers, who had been secretly paid by him. Disguising this fact, they sent one round with a tambourine, as they were wont to do in public-houses.

On Saturday night and village revels one penny was the accustomed fee for man and partner.

"Now then," cried the musician, going his rounds and jingling the coppers in his tambourine, "now then, for the next dance. Six down; who makes eight? Now then, mates and partners, for double lead through the next country dance. Ten down; who makes twelve? Oh, there isn't a twelve (cheerfully); then we'll go on as we are."

All the other popular dances were done in due notation. "Step-and-Fetch-it," "The Tramp," "Lee Po," "Hands Across," "Six Bond," &c."

"Want more corn vith your galop?" inquired a man, bringing the almost but never quite exhausted musicians some mugs of "Mickle my buff."

"Ah, we shau't hurt to-night," they said. "It's real fiddlers' fare here—meat, drink, and money."

Several single dances were next performed, such as hornpipes, "The Dunhill Parson," "The Broom Dance," "The Pipe Dance," and others of the same calibre, after which a kind of cushion dance, called "Bob-in-the-Bowster," which was provocative of much kissing and enjoyment.

In the meantime the old women were steadily drinking all the while, amusing themselves at same time with a game of cards, called "Laugh and Lay Down," and with another game, which none but rustics can understand, and which is played by inscribing chalk lines both ways upon a table, and making spots between the squares.

Kate Morgan, the Lady of the Lamb, as she was termed on the eventful day, had withdrawn from the throng of merry-makers, and Joe Doughty, who had not ceased watching her the whole evening, followed her.

She turned and saw him. Then his heart, which had been so stout in the furrowed field, began to tremble like a timid bird.

"Well," said his companion.

"I hope as how it is well," he answered. "Kitty, I've got a serious word or two to say to ee."

"Ha' ee?"

"Yes, my gell."

"And what be it then?"

"In foreign seas, so I've bin told, lass, there's fishes as ha' teeth upon their tongues, and there be many a woman as can set teeth upon him which will bite a man's life and happiness in two."

"An' what if they be? Has that anything to do wi' me?"

She looked at him keenly. Poor girl, she had had bitter experiences.

"I want you to understand," said Joe Doughty, in a serious tone of voice, "that the will of a woman has a deal to do wi' me, for ye must know how much my future happiness depends upon one single word uttered by you."

"By me?"

"Aye, lass, that be true enough—by you. Often and often, when alone in the field of waving corn, or it may be yellow stubble, I ha' thought of one who had it in her power to mek or mar me. Now doant ye be shakin' yer head, 'cause what I be sayin' is the solemn truth, and there's no gettin' away from it. Indeed, it it aint o' no yoose tryin'. Where was I? Oh, I know, in the field, either a ploughin', sowin', or reapin', it matters not which; but, anyway, I ha' thought this matter over and over again, and though I ha' not sed anything, not as yet, I ha' felt all the deeper perhaps. Kitty, you must not look so coldly on me; indeed you mustn't. Shall I tell you why?"

"If you like."

"Because I love you, and none other but you. I aint rich, that you know, but I've saved a bit of money, for I haven't bin like a good many others on the farm, a spending what I earn afore I earned it."

"I know you have been careful and frugal," she answered.

"Well, I aint afraid of work—that you know also."

"I do."

"An' if so be as you consent to be my wife, which I hope and believe you will, I shall work wi' greater energy, for I shall ha' something to work for. A man ain't a mite o' yoose in this world if he be all alone, as I ha' bin all these lonely years, and I want ee for a partner, and if I canna ha' ee, then there be no other woman as I care about having. Answer me! Dang it all, say yes or no Kitty, without further ado."

"Hark ee, Joe Doughty," said the woman, with a boldness and energy that fairly astonished him.

"I be not fit for an honest man. I tell ee plainly that, years agone, when you were away from Stoke Ferry, summut happened as will for ever prevent me from becoming your wife."

"It won't do, Kitty; you must find some better excuse than that," said he, placing his hands upon her shoulder. "It wunno do, lass."

"Wunno do!" she ejaculated, in unfeigned surprise. "May be ee don't understand me rightly. I tell ee agen and agen—I ain't fit to be the wife of an honest man."

"And why not?"

"Ye maun to force me into a confession. Well, so be it. I am already a mother."

"What if ee be? Don't ee think I ha' considered all that. He who be dead and gone did ee a wrong, and it appears to me that ye are not the only woman as he wronged, for there's——"

"I know what you are going to say," she said, interrupting him, but, if you care about me, don't ee say a word agen Master Philip, 'cause I can't bear that. Whatever his faults may have bin, it ain't right and proper to be a-talkin' about em now. He was wayward and wilful, and did not take heed of timely warning, but he be dead and gone; he met with a cruel death, and so say no more about 'im."

"You are right—I will not refer to the subject again, seeing as how it be a trouble to ee; but it doesn't follow that, because in a foolish hour you forgot all but your love for him, that ye're no fit to be my wife, and I say agen you must find some better excuse."

"I should not like to ha' a husband taunt me wi' the shame that has fallen on me. I should no like that."

"And do you think, you foolish lass, that I am likely to do so? You ought to know me better—a deal better nor that there."

"Are you in earnest, Joe?"

"Earnest! Dall it, I never was so much in earnest—no not in the whole course of my life."

"And you mean what you say?"

"Of course I do; every word I ha' sed."

"And you'll ha' me for all that ha' past?"

"Aye, lass, I will."

"What be left of my heart be yours," she cried, "and what be left of my life will be devoted to you, and so, if ye'll tek me ye may ha' me."

Her lusty companion wound his arms around her, and embraced her with fervour. And so Joe Doughty and Kate Morgan were betrothed in this simple and homely fashion.

When farmer Ashbrook was informed of the circumstance, he was greatly pleased, and promised to give the bride a handsome dowry; not that Joe had for a moment been actuated by mercenary feelings when he declared his passion and besought the girl to bestow her hand and heart upon him, for he was strongly attached to her, and had never at any time flirted with any other village maiden.

Mr. Philip Jamblin, the ill-fated young man who was murdered by Giles Chudleigh, had not been altogether so circumspect as his relations and friends could have desired.

It was pretty plainly demonstrated that he had seduced two young women before he was sent to his account by the brutal Giles, and there were some evil-disposed persons still living who hinted that the young farmer had been brought to his end from this cause.

He was a free-hearted fine young fellow, who at times let his passions run riot.

Many of his betters are apt to do the same thing. This is evidenced by the conduct of Lord Ethalwood, but two blacks do not make a white, and the late Philip Jamblin was, as we have already seen, not without fault.

We have taken but little notice of Richard and Maude Ashbrook, who had been present throughout the festivities at Stoke Ferry.

They had not taken a very active part in any of the proceedings, remaining for the nonce but passive spectators.

Richard Ashbrook seemed to be a completely broken-down man. He did not appear to have any relish for the sports—occasionally, it is true, a wan smile passed over his melancholy features, but that was all.

He appeared to be thankful when the sports were brought to a conclusion, and pleading indisposition he retired to bed.

For the next few days he grew worse, and it soon became manifest to those about him that his life was drawing to a close. He said he had no desire to live, and that he knew his final time was approaching. He was continually mentioning the name of his deceased wife, Jane Ryan, whose spirit, so he averred, had appeared to him on three separate occasions.

Those about him strove to disposses his mind of this idea, but, for all they could say or do, Richard Ashbrook persisted in his declaration, and so he prepared to settle his worldly affairs.

His brother John, who was almost heart-broken, agreed to take charge of his child and his sister Maude. It was arranged that Oakfield Farm was to be sold, the proceeds of the same were to be handed over to Maude; and in less than a fortnight after the harvest-home at Stoke Ferry Richard Ashbrook breathed his last.

It will be remembered by the reader that the first scene of this history was laid at Oakfield, when Jane Ryan played so conspicuous a part on the night of the burglary by Charles Peace, Gregson, and Cooney.

CHAPTER CXLV.

PEACE'S LAST BURGLARY—A BRAVE POLICEMAN—PEACE'S CAPTURE BY ROBINSON—A VISIT TO NEWGATE.

THE most remarkable and at the same time unaccountable part of Peace's career is certainly that portion of time while he was in the occupation of the house in the Evalina-road, Peckham. It appears almost incredible that he could have remained there for so long a period without being discovered.

After the murder of Mr. Dyson the police were supposed to be on the alert.

Every effort was made, so it was stated, to hunt down the perpetrator of the murder at Banner-cross, but in spite of all this Peace was free from suspicion, and night after night committed the most daring burglaries ever attempted by one solitary individual.

Indeed, had it not been for the determination and courage displayed by Police-constable Robinson, the chances are that the scoundrel, whose deeds have so surprised the world, would be even at the present time at large and undiscovered.

It really does appear most remarkable that so many murderers should be able to elude justice. We have several instances of this since Peace expiated his crimes on the public scaffold.

The Wallaces, who went off in a cab after the death of their victim, have never been arrested.

The Burton-crescent murder—the murder of Miss Hacker, of a servant girl at Harpurhey, near Manchester, of a youth at Rotherhithe, who died from bayonet wounds, and lastly, the woman whose body was found in a tub at Harley-street, one and all remain deep impenetrable mysteries.

But Peace, who although for a time managed to escape detection, was in the end run to earth.

The last burglary committed by this lawless man, whose remarkable career we have endeavoured to shadow forth, proved fatal to him.

At Blackheath, on the night of 10th of October, 1878, a burglary was committed of a most daring character.

On that evening Peace had repaired to the house of Mr. James Alexander Burness, in St. James's-park, Blackheath, and whilst endeavouring to add to his own riches was observed by a constable on duty, named Robinson, but Peace was not a man to be taken easily. Upon finding that he was discovered he rushed into the garden and fired four shots at Robinson, then, with a fearful oath, he, after taking deliberate aim, fired a fifth.

The shots were fired from an American revolver of the newest make.

The fifth struck the constable in the left arm above the shoulder, carried some cloth with it right through the flesh, grazed the bone, and then passing out, went through a gentleman's drawing-room window, and after rebounding on the wall fell on the floor.

But Robinson, though injured, seized the man, and after a desperate struggle threw the fellow to the ground.

A fight took place, and the burglar attempted to draw a sheath knife which was in his pocket; but the officer, though severely wounded, did not lose his presence of mind, and gave his prisoner a few taps on the head by way of a sedative.

When examined it was found that the fellow carried a six-barrelled revolver, and that the weapon was strapped to his wrist.

Young and Brown came up as soon as possible, and the thief was secured, but not until he had been pretty smartly struck with a truncheon.

On being charged with the offence the prisoner refused to give any name or address, and as his face was stained with walnut juice he was mistaken at the time for a mulatto.

The garden was searched, but no confederates were found. Mr. Burness was away from home at the time, but his wife, who was awakened by one of the servants, witnessed the desperate struggle in the garden.

Subsequent examination of the premises by Inspector Bonney, X Division, showed that the dining-room window fastenings had been forced by a crowbar, which was found on the prisoner with other house-breaking tools; and that a hole, 5 in. square, near the lock of the door, which was locked on the outside, was cut, enabling the prisoner to put his hand through and unlock the door—the key having been left in the lock.

Plated and silver articles were removed ready to be carried away, and the prisoner had taken a bank cheque book from a drawer of a table in the drawing-room, and a letter case from a davenport in the library, which had been forced open.

Mrs. Burness said the house was securely locked at half-past eleven o'clock the previous night, and that there were two fastenings to the dining-room window, which had been broken in forcing the window open.

At this time, it must be remembered, there was no suspicion that the man was anything but a burglar, and to prove his guilt as such was the effort of the officer.

To find out his name was very difficult, but after a fortnight's search Bonney discovered that the prisoner was a "respectable gentleman," who at Lambeth, Greenwich, and Peckham, had passed as "Mr. Thompson."

The last residence of this Mr. Thompson, otherwise Peace, was at Evalina-road, Peckham, a most respectable neighbourhood, the house a really comfortable one, and a good garden in front.

The inspector prosecuted his inquiries, and found thirty pawn tickets in the dwelling. These tickets mostly related to property stolen from houses in Greenwich and Blackheath—namely, silver and gold plate, together with jewellery.

The goods had been pawned by one of Peace's "lady assistants," under the obliging name of "Thompson," and were recognised by those who had lost them.

Robinson, although severely wounded, very shortly recovered sufficiently to give his evidence at the magisterial inquiry.

He was shot through the fleshy part of the left arm above the elbow, but fortunately no bone was touched.

The bullets, fired from a six-chambered revolver, were afterwards found, and were produced in court. The firing of five shots before one took effect was attributed to the constable dodging behind some shrubs while he was being fired at.

The following is the description given of Peace in the daily papers at the time of the occurrence:—

"The prisoner is a repulsive-looking man, with protruding jaws and thick lips, of the negro cast, with receding forehead; in height he is about 5 ft. 6 in., but he is not a powerfully-built man. He still doggedly refuses to give his name and address, or any account of himself, but from a knife, which bears a name, being found in his possession when captured, it is thought the police will be able to connect him with a burglary committed in December last. Burglaries have been frequent in the neighbourhood of Blackheath during the past three months, the houses selected being generally those with a garden in the rear, and, although detectives have been specially employed to discover the burglars, they have hitherto failed; but it is thought the man who shot the constable is the principal actor in these burglaries, and from his mode of procedure, and the housebreaking tools found upon him, it is evident he was no novice at his work."

EXAMINATION OF THE PRISONER.

At the Greenwich Police-court, John Ward, aged sixty—(we quote the newspaper reports; Peace, however was not fifty, although he certainly looked ten years older at the time of his capture)—who had previously refused to give his name, was brought up on remand, before Mr. Flowers, charged with burglariously entering the house of Mr. Burness, 2, St. John's-park, Blackheath, and stealing several plated articles; and on a second charge of shooting and wounding Police-constable Robinson, 202 R.

The prisoner, who had his head and face bandaged on the first examination, was now divested of such bandages; and Edward Robinson, the constable, who had his right arm in a sling, was examined.

He stated that at two o'clock on the morning of Thursday last he was on duty in the avenue at the side of No. 2, St. John's-park, leading to Blackheath, when he saw a flickering light in the dining-room at the rear of the house.

Thinking this was suspicious, he went to the next beat and obtained the assistance of Constable Girling, and returned to the avenue, Girling assisting him over the garden wall 6 ft. high, and they kept watch till the arrival of Sergeant Brown, 32 R, who lifted Girling over the wall, and told them to remain there while he went to the front of the house to rouse the occupiers.

On the door-bell ringing, the light used inside the house was immediately extinguished, and he jumped from the wall into the garden, breaking some glass, and Girling got off the wall and went down the avenue to the rear of the garden wall.

The prisoner came out from the dining-room window on to the lawn, and ran along the garden to the back.

He followed the prisoner, who turned round and faced him, and presented a revolver at him.

It was moonlight at the time, and the revolver being presented at his head, the prisoner said—

"Keep back—keep back! or, by God, I'll shoot you!"

He told the prisoner he had better not do so, and he rushed at him; the prisoner discharging three shots in succession, the first two shots passing close to the left side of his head, and the third shot passing over his head.

He then made another rush at the prisoner, who took a more straight aim at him, and fired a fourth shot, when he closed with him, and struck the prisoner on the face with his left hand, guarding his head by raising his right arm.

The prisoner said, "I will settle you this time," and then fired the fifth shot, which perforated the great coat and tunic he was wearing, and went through his arm above the elbow.

They struggled together, and he threw the prisoner on the ground, seizing him with his left hand and knees, and caught hold of the revolver, which was strapped round the prisoner's wrist, and struck him over the head with the revolver.

Whilst on the ground the prisoner put his left hand in a pocket, and said, "I will give you something else."

At this time Sergeant Brown appeared, and assisted Constable Girling up, and took the prisoner from him. The wound in his arm bled very much, and he was taken to the divisional surgeon, and his wound was dressed. He was still under treatment.

Sarah Selina Cooper, under-housemaid, at the prosecutor's house, said that on the morning of the burglary, in cleaning the room, she found a shot on the hearth-rug, and a hole in the window, the shot having struck the wall.

Inspector Browney said he could produce evidence as to the prisoner having been concerned in another burglary.

The prisoner said he had been informed, a quarter of an hour before being brought into court, that he would be again remanded, which was not fair, as he had never before been in custody. Mr. Flowers remanded the prisoner.

When Peace was brought to the Greenwich Station after he had been caught in the act, he presented a most miserable and pitiable spectacle. "Talk of him being taken for a half-caste," said my informant, "he looked more like a black man than a mulatto.

"What with the rough usage he had got in the struggle and the tumbling about on the grass, he was in a desperate plight—clay all over him, his face clogged up with dirt, and the mud oozing up about his neck and stiffening the little hair he had. He was a mealy-mouthed, whining old scamp, and he was as dirty as the devil."

This was not a very official way of putting it; but it was explicit enough for the purpose.

"Did he say anything particular?" I asked.

"Oh, he kept whining away; but the fact was he had been badly 'punished.' Robinson had certainly given him a stiff un on the head."

"And who wouldn't?" asked an approving constable who just looked in. "Wouldn't you, if a fellow fired a revolver at you, and then searched for his knife?"

Of course we concurred, Peace having no sympathisers in the company. "Well," continued my informant, "he had got it and no mistake. Robinson had given him sufficient to settle him for a day. Peace looked dazed and bewildered, and kept wandering in his talk, now and again moaning and crying. When we stripped him we found he was one mass of filth. His shirt was all rags; the marvel is how it hung together; everything about him was similar— he was one of the most miserable-looking scoundrels I ever set eyes upon. In fact he was in so bad a way that I felt sorry for the poor wretch. I had some hard eggs boiled for myself. I gave him one and some bread, which he ate with some difficulty."

When he was locked up he went on in the same way.

"When I looked at him through the grating, he whined out," said the officer, imitating his way of talking, as if his tongue was too big for his mouth, "Oh, would to God, sergeant, you would come in here and knock my brains out—I feel so bad." He was always going on in this way—"Would to God," and "I wish to God," being the phrases which most frequently fell from his lips.

"A canting, whining old hypocrite," said the sergeant to me; "and as for his face, why he was so ugly I cannot understand why any woman would look at him, much less live in the same house with him.

"He was the ugliest, vilest-looking little wretch you would meet in a long day's walk."

When Peace refused to give his name he was over-cunning. The police suspected that a man who would give no name must have unusual reasons for his silence.

So they set their wits to work to find out who and what he was.

When he did give the name of "John Ward" they were not disposed to accept it. The warders of the principal prisons were sent for to see if they they could identify him.

When the warder of Millbank appeared Peace was asked if he knew him.

"Oh, no!" replied the prisoner, with an affectation of great innocence and ignorance. "I never saw his face before. Who is he?" He was informed.

"Ah!" continued Peace, "he never saw me before; I never was in such a prison before. This is the first time I was in such a place," and he looked wearily round his cell with the air of an injured innocent. It was the same with all the other warders who came to look at him.

Peace's old audacity returned to his assistance. He stood up when called, and relying upon his changed appearance—the shaving of his head, the dyeing with walnut juice, and the like—he confronted them with as much confidence as could be put on by an old convict in the presence of those who had been his gaolers.

He succeeded in deceiving all those experienced officers, but just in proportion to the success of his deception was the desire of the authorities to get behind the mask, and they did so at last—not by any sudden revelation, or undetected discovery, but simply by the capacity for taking pains in putting together the many "trifles" which at length connected the burglar Ward with the murderer Peace.

There was something superb about the audacity of this remarkable villain.

After he had somewhat recovered from the "taps" which friend Robinson had given him that memorable morning in the garden at Blackheath, he once more tried on the old canting ways which had in former days served him so well.

In prisons oft he had known the value of playing the part of the penitent, and by his good conduct had been able to get out much earlier to resume his old bad courses.

On the way from Greenwich to Newgate he was himself again.

In the prison van the inmates are divided by wire partitions, through which they can see and talk to each other if they are in the talking mood, as they usually are.

One of the prisoners had got three months for drunkenness. Peace, who was waiting his turn when this person was committed, recognised his face, and at once embraced the opportunity to put a few words of good advice.

He positively commenced to lecture the prisoner on the wickedness of which he had been guilty. "But," remarked the officer, "you should have heard how the other prisoners let out at him."

"They were not going to be preached at by that old canting humbug."

The fellow who had got the three months turned upon Peace and said, "Well, you're a nice one, you are. Here am I got three months for getting drunk; but what have you been doing? Don't ye think I know? Why you've been trying to shoot a policeman, you have. They ought to hang the likes of you."

The sentiment met with the approving plaudits of the other prisoners, and Peace did not continue his discourse, and, what with the sense of mortification at being repulsed, and the candid if cruel remarks of the other occupants of the prison van, had rather an unhappy time of it during the rest of the journey to Newgate.

Peace's journey in the "Black Maria," or prison-van, was by no means an agreeable one—journeys of this description can never be accounted agreeable under the most favourable circumstances, but in Peace's case it was most disheartening.

He trembled lest his identity should become known, and, to say the truth, he feared the worst.

It seemed hardly possible, under existing circumstances for him to maintain his *incognito*, and discovery meant certain death.

Nevertheless he bore up as best he could, and hoped for the best.

The exterior of Newgate Gaol is not by any means prepossessing—the interior is most depressing.

On arriving within the court-yard of the gloomy and repulsive-looking old city prison, from whose debtors' door so many have stepped to pass on to the scaffold, Peace and his companions were let out of the "Black Maria," and conducted into a dark stone passage, and our hero was told to stand in a row with his fellow-passengers.

The deputy-governor, with two warders, received the batch of prisoners, and the constable, who had acted as conductor to the hearse-like carriage, handed over to the deputy-governor a number of papers, one for each prisoner, whereupon the names were called out, to which suitable replies were given. Most of them were "remands" or "committals."

Peace answered to his name in a low submissive tone, and looked as if he felt deeply sensible of his humiliating position.

There was, however, no getting over the fact that he had attempted to murder a police-constable; and, indeed, at this time it was by no means certain that Robinson would get the better of his injuries. He was progressing favourably, it is true, but an unfavourable change might take place at any time.

The prison officials scanned Peace for a few moments, then upon a signal from their superior he was conducted to his quarters by a young man, who treated him with civility and consideration.

It was the first time Peace had been in Newgate, and he did not even at that supreme moment of misery realise the fact that he was driven to his last ditch, and that never again was he destined to become a free man.

Out of the many thousands who pass by this great city prison, how few there are who have any definite idea of its inner penetralia!

A brief account of a visit to the establishment in question will convey to the mind of the reader its most noticeable features.

First of all comes the lodge, as it is termed. We enter this by a door elevated a few steps above the level of the street, in a line with the Old Bailey—this, flanked by dark masses of stone forming part of the wall, which is about four feet in thickness.

This outer door has doubtless attracted the attention of many street passengers. It is about four feet and a half high, and is covered at the top with short bristling iron spikes, the open space above being farther fenced with two strong iron bars with transverse iron rods. There is another massive oaken inner door alongside, faced with iron, of enormous strength, which is only shut at night.

It reminds us of the terrible prisons in the old barbaric times, when criminals were more desperate than in our day, before Howard commenced his angelic mission over the dungeons of England and the Continent.

This door has a very strong Bramah lock with a big brazen bolt, which gives a peculiarly loud rumbling sound when the key is turned; and at night it is secured with strong iron bolts and padlocks, and by an iron chain. The great bolts penetrate a considerable way into the massive stone wall.

The lodge is a small sombre-looking, high-roofed apartment, with a semi-circular iron-grated window over the doorway, and a grated window on each side, and is floored with wood.

On our left hand is a small room, occupied by a female warder who searches the female visitors to the prison, lighted by an iron-grated window; and on our right is an ante-room leading to the governor's office.

Another heavy oaken door, faced with iron, leads into the interior of the prison; and alongside is an iron-grated window communicating with the interior.

On the walls are suspended different notices by the Court of Aldermen in accordance with Act of Parliament.

One of them forbids liquors to be introduced into the prison, another refers to visiting the prisoners, and a third to the attorneys and clerks who should visit them respecting their defences.

The deputy-governor opened the ponderous iron-bolted door leading into a gloomy recess passage with arched roof, conducting along the back of the porter's lodge towards the male corridor and kitchen. On our right hand is a strong door of the same description, leading to the female prison, secured by ponderous lock and bolts.

We meantime turned to the left, and came to another strong oaken door faced with iron. In this sombre passage the gas is kept burning, even at mid-day. As we passed along we saw the sunbeams falling on a stone flooring through an iron grating, opening into the interior of the old prison yard.

On passing through this heavy door, which is kept locked, the passage widens. Here we saw a long wooden seat for the accommodation of the prisoners who are to appear before the governor to have their descriptions taken.

This passage leads, on the right-hand side, into a room called the bread-room, where we observed a warder in the blue prison uniform, who is detained here on duty.

We went with the chief warder into the bread-room, which is also used to take descriptions of the prisoners, being well lighted and very suitable for this purpose.

It has a wooden flooring, and is whitewashed.

In this apartment is an old leaden water-cistern, very massive, and painted of a stone colour, curiously carved, with the City coat of arms inscribed on it, and dated 1781.

There is here also a cupboard containing a curious assortment of irons used in the olden time, as well as a number of those used in the present day, of less formidable appearance.

There are here deposited the leg-irons worn by the celebrated burglar and prison-breaker, Jack Sheppard, consisting of an iron bar about an inch and a half thick and fifteen inches long.

At each end are connected heavy irons for the legs, about an inch in diameter, which were clasped with strong iron rivets.

In the middle of the cross-bar is an iron chain, consisting of three large links to fasten round the body. We found these irons to weigh about twenty pounds.

There is also in this cupboard a "fac simile" of the heavy leg-irons of Dick Turpin, the celebrated highwayman, who plays a conspicuous part in Mr. Ainsworth's celebrated romance, "Rookwood," in which work "Turpin's Ride to York" is not the least attractive feature.

The irons worn by Turpin consist of two iron hoops about an inch thick to clasp the ankle, and about five inches in diameter.

A ring goes through and connects with the iron clasp, which secures the ankle with a long link on each side, about ten inches in length, and about an inch in thickness.

These long links are connected with another circular link, by a chain passing through to fasten round the body. They are about thirty-seven pounds in weight.

It was a saying in the olden time when any body wanted to be extremely bitter, "I shall live to see you double-ironed in Newgate."

But criminals are not so frequently manacled in the present day beyond wearing handcuffs, when it is deemed necessary for security, and in extreme cases in penal prisons by way of punishment for refractory conduct. Those, however, who work in gangs at Portland, Dartmoor, or elsewhere, are chained together, so that there should be no chance of escape. But men condemned to death are not now placed in irons as was the custom in such cases in former times.

There are, however, to be seen now at Newgate some of the old irons which were formally put on prisoners capitally convicted, which they were constrained to wear day and night till the morning of execution, when they were knocked off before they ascended the scaffold.

It was the practice at that time to hang the bodies of prisoners in chains as a warning to other depredators, but this also has been abolished.

There is, in Newgate, also an axe which was made to behead Thistlewood and the other Cato-street conspirators, but it was not used; the bodies of the culprits, after hanging the usual time, were taken down and decapitation was effected by the use of a sword, which was said to be dexterously used by a young surgeon engaged for the purpose.

The axe, which forms one of the curiosities of Newgate, is large and heavy, and weighs about eleven pounds.

There is also a murderer's belt, about two and a half inches wide, for pinioning condemned persons when about to pay the last penalty of the law.

It goes round the body, and fastens behind with straps to secure the wrist, and clasp the arms close to the body.

There is likewise another used by the executioner on the drop for securing the legs. A number of these straps had been used in pinioning notorious murderers executed at Newgate, who tragic histories are recorded in the "Newgate Calendar," and many of these leg-irons had fettered the limbs of daring highwaymen in the olden times, who used to frequent Blackheath and Hounslow-heath, Wormwood Scrubs, and a host of other places on the outskirts of the metropolis.

What thoughts do these memorials of the past conjure up!

The massive and cheerless City prison which contain these ghastly relics give us a glimpse of the rigid discipline of our forefathers.

In the meantime we returned to an ante-room leading into the governor's office on the left-hand side of the lodge, lighted by an iron-grated window looking into the Old Bailey.

There is a cupboard here containing arms for the officers in the event of any outbreak in the prison, consisting of pistols, guns, bayonets, and cutlasses.

We do not expect there is any chance of any outbreak in this City stronghold, but it is of course just as well to be prepared for any emergency.

In convict prisons the governors and warders cannot be too careful, for there some of the most desperate characters on the face of the earth are congregated.

THE PRISONERS AT EXERCISE—PEACE EYEING THE DETECTIVES.

In the ante-room there are two very fine old paintings of Botany Bay, which are hung on one of the walls. There is also a painting of Davies, who was executed years ago for the murder of his wife at Islington. It is roughly executed, and was done by himself before he was apprehended. It is said to be a tolerably good likeness.

His brow is lofty and full, the lower part of the face is perhaps a little sensual, but taken altogether, it is a countenance which does not in any way accord with one's preconceived notions of the type of a murderer. But it is not possible to arrive at an accurate conclusion as to the character of individuals by their facial expression.

No. 79.

Along two shelves over the door of this apartment and on the top of an adjoining cupboard are arranged three rows of the busts of murderers who have been executed at Newgate.

Some of these had a most repulsive appearance and were of the most brutal and lowest type of humanity.

The deputy-governor directed attention to the bust of the miscreant Greenacre who had a very sinister appearance.

It is, we believe, not more than a year and a half ago since his mistress and accomplice, Sarah Gale, died in Van Diemen's Land at a very advanced age.

She was transported for life as an accessory to the murder. She was nearly, if not quite, eighty at the time of her decease.

Another bust pointed out to us was that of Daniel Good, who was executed for murdering a female and mutilating the body, a portion of which he buried in a stable.

The mouth had a disagreeable expression, but his countenance was better moulded than that of Greenacre, and did not give indications of the enormity of the crime he committed.

Good, when the mutilated remains of his victim were discovered, sought safety in flight. At the time of the commission of the crime he was groom to a gentleman residing at Roehampton, but it transpired that in early life he earnt his living as a bricklayer.

He went to some remote country place a hundred miles and more from the metropolis, and obtained work. As may readily be imagined he passed under another name, and it was some months before he was discovered —indeed, it was quite by accident that he was found out.

The woman in whose house he lodged was deeply concerned at his dejected appearance and his restlessness at night.

She heard him sighing and groaning for hours, and suspected that he had something on his mind.

She mentioned the circumstance to one or two of her associates, the police were communicated with, and this led to Good's identification.

" There," said the deputy-governor, looking at a full-length bust, " that is Courvoisier, who was executed for the murder of his master, Lord William Russell. The counsel who defended him—the late Mr. Charles Phillips—declared, as he went into court, that he would get him off, and it was likely enough he would have succeeded had it not been for one circumstance."

" And what was that, pray ?"

As Phillips was addressing the jury in a most powerful speech, a cab drove up in the court-yard, and a woman, who was the landlady of a hotel in the neighbourhood of Leicester-square, brought into court some of Lord William Russell's family plate, which Courvoisier had tied up in a bundle, and left at her house to be called for.

This was fatal to the prisoner. Charles Phillips saw all chance of an acquittal was over. He dashed down his brief, and said no more.

The judge summed up, and the jury returned a verdict of guilty, upon which Mr. Phillips impudently declared they were right, as Courvoisier confessed to him that he committed the murder, just before he entered the court.

Phillips never got over this, and retired from the bar, accepting an appointment offered him by Government.

Upon examining Courvoisier's bust we found the man had a low brow, and the lower part of the face was coarse, or, it might be said, brutal, the neck was full and protruding under the ears.

The upper lip of most of the group of busts was thick, which might possibly be caused by the process of hanging. Some of them had their eyes open, and others shut.

We saw the bust of Lani, who was executed for the murder of a woman of the town in the vicinity of the Haymarket; the wretch strangled her in bed, with his bony, powerful hands, which were preternaturally large, his countenance was brutal in the extreme, and he was a most diabolical, merciless wretch.

Another bust was that of Mullins, executed for the murder of an old lady at Stepney.

This scoundrel was base enough to charge an innocent man with the crime.

He had a heartless, hypocritical expression of face, and we could believe him capable of committing the most atrocious crimes.

On leaving the ante-room, we pass along a gloomy passage, and make our way towards the kitchen.

After reaching the side of a room enclosed with glass panelling, in the centre of a large apartment, with a groined roof, we proceeded along another narrow gloomy passage, lighted with gas, and went into the kitchen, which was very similar in size and general appearance to the lodge, entering it by a small door of massive structure, furnished with locks and bolts.

Opposite to it, fronting the Old Bailey, are two ponderous doors, through which the culprit used to pass on to the drop on the morning of the execution; but the Private Execution Act has done away with this, and the extreme penalty of the law is carried out within the precincts of the gaol.

We are not at all sure that a change has been made for the better.

It is quite true that pickpockets ply their vocation even at the foot of the gallows; but it is equally true that they do so in churches and chapels at the present time, but that is no reason that all places of public worship should be closed, neither is it any reason that murderers should be strangled in secret.

In the kitchen are two coppers sufficient to cook food for three hundred prisoners.

The steam is conveyed away from the coppers by means of pipes that lead though a grated window into the open air.

On shelves were ranged bright tins for the use of the prisoners, and wooden trays to carry the food from the kitchen to the various prison cells.

Leaving the kitchen, and bending our steps to the left, we go along a sombre passage of the same character as the one described.

Passing through a door at the extremity, we enter a covered bridge leading across a court into the corridor of the male prison.

It has four galleries, surmounted with a glass roof, which presents a very cheerful appearance, very unlike the remaining portion of the old prison.

We observed a stair on the outside communicating with each gallery, which is girdled with an iron balustrade.

There is also a hoisting machine, by which provisions can be conveyed to each gallery in the short space of a minute and a half.

There is a machine for weighing the provisions in the centre of the corridor, and a dial over the second gallery.

In answer to our interrogatories, the deputy-governor gave us the following statement :—" The prisoners are brought here in prison vans from the various police courts over the metropolis, being committed for trial by the magistrates.

"The City magistrates commit to Newgate, and send prisoners for remand as well as for trial. The metropolitan police courts only send those who have been committed for trial.

"Those sentenced by the justices of the metropolitan police courts are sent to the House of Correction at Coldbath Fields, whereas those in the City are sent to Holloway Prison.

"Prisoners convicted of a capital offence remain in Newgate until they are executed or reprieved. Some are incarcerated in Newgate for short terms by the judges of the Old Bailey, such as for contempt of court, and others are sent by the House of Commons for a similar offence."

"Newgate," continued the chief-governor, "is a house of detention for prisoners before trial, as well as for those sentenced to penal servitude, kept here for a short time awaiting an order from the Secretary of State to remove them to the Government depots for the reception of convicts. In all cases of murder tried at the Old Bailey, the prisoners are sent here. When convicted they are given over to the sheriff of the county where the offences have been committed. If done in Essex, the murderer is removed to Chelmsford; if in Kent he is removed to the county gaol at Maidstone, and if in Surrey he is taken to Horsemonger-lane Gaol."

On the basement of this wing are the reception cells, and bath rooms, and the punishment cells.

The deputy-governor showed us into one of the cells in the corridor, which we found to be 7 feet wide, 13 feet long, and 8 feet 10 inches high, at the top of the arch. It has a window with an iron frame protected by three strong iron bars outside.

The furniture consists of a small table which folds against the wall, under which is a small wooden shelf containing brushes, &c., for cleaning the cell, a small three legged stool, and a copper basin well supplied with water from a water-tap.

On turning the handle of the tap in one direction the water is discharged into the water-closet, and on turning it the reverse way it is turned into the copper basin for washing. Each cell is lighted with gas, with a bright tin shade over it. On the wall is suspended the prisoner's card.

There are three triangular shelves in a corner of the cell, supplied with bedding, &c., as in other prisons we visited. The floor is laid with asphalte; over the door is a grating admitting heated air, with an opening under the window opposite to admit fresh air at the pleasure of the prisoner.

Under the latter, and near the basement of the cell, is a grating similar to the one over the door, leading to the extraction shaft, carrying off the foul air, and causing a clear ventilation.

Each cell is furnished with a handle communicating with the gong in the corridor, by which the prisoner can intimate his wants to the warder in charge, and the door is provided with trap and inspection plate.

All the cells in the corridor are of the same dimensions and similarly furnished.

On proceeding to the basement we visited the reception cells, which are eleven in number, of the same dimensions as those in the corridor above, and fitted up in the same manner.

There are three slate baths, about six feet long, two feet broad, and two feet and a half deep, provided with footboards. They are heated by means of pipes communicating with the boiler in the engine-room. Two of them are fitted up in one cell, with a dressing-room adjoining.

The other bath is in a long room, where there is a fireplace and a large metal vessel heated by steam, to cleanse the prisoner's clothes from vermin and infection. This resembles a large copper, and is about two and a half feet in diameter and three feet deep, with an ample lid screwed down so firmly that no steam can escape.

The clothes are put into it and subjected to the action of the steam for about a quarter of an hour, when the vermin are destroyed. The clothes are not in the slightest degree injured.

This vessel is heated by means of a steam-pipe connected with the boiler in the engine room. The bath is similar to the others already noticed.

The dark cells are situated at the extremity of the new wing on the basement. They are six in number, and are of the same dimensions as the other cells. No light is admitted into them, but they are well ventilated.

The furniture of each consists of a wooden bench, to serve as a bed—though it is a hard one—and a night utensil; and the flooring is of stone.

There are two doors on each cell. When shut, they not only exclude a single beam of light, but do not admit the slightest sound.

The deputy-governor remarked—

"There are very few punishments inflicted in this prison. Sometimes the prisoners infringe the prison rules by insolence to their officers or making away with their oakum instead of picking it. We have had only two persons in the dark cells for the past two years."

Opposite the bath-room is an engine-room, fitted up with two immense boilers for heating the whole of the prison and keeping the baths supplied with hot water. The engineer informed us that, during the winter, nearly a ton of coals is consumed per day.

The pipes are conveyed into the different cells for the purpose of heating them. Along the walls are arranged a copious supply of iron tools for the purpose of repairing the different locks, &c.

Leaving the corridor of the male prison we returned to the passage across the court, covered with thick glass, where relatives and friends are permitted occasionally to visit the prisoners. On each side of it is a double grating, fenced with close wirework, of about four feet wide, occupied by the prisoners.

The relatives take their station on each side of the passage during the interviews, and a warder is stationed by their side to overlook them. On one occasion we were present when several of the prisoners were visited by their friends.

One of them was a man of about fifty years of age—a Jew—charged with having been concerned in the forgery of Russian bank notes. He was an intellectual-looking fair-complexioned man, with a long flowing beard and a very wrinkled brow, and his head bald in front.

He was very decently dressed, and appeared deeply interested while he conversed in broken English through the wire-screen with an elderly woman, who appeared to be warmly attached to him, and who was profoundly affected with his situation.

He appeared to be a shrewd man of the world. Alongside was a genteel-looking man, with sallow complexion and fine dark eye, who was visited by a tall young woman, decently dressed, who stood with a bundle in her hand. It appeared this prisoner was under remand for stealing clothes from his employers. He looked sullen, and though apparently attached to the young woman, was very taciturn, and looked around with a very suspicious air.

A modest-looking elderly man, with silver hair, genteelly attired in dark coat and vest and grey trousers, stood with a bundle in his hand, and was busily engaged conversing with a little smart woman of advanced years, dressed in a grey dress and dark shawl.

We learned he was charged with embezzlement.

But there is one feature of Newgate's interior a recollection of which will probably abide in the memory of the man who sets eyes on it, long after all else connected with the grim prison is forgotten—the murderers' burying-ground.

When one reads that " the body of the malefactor was the same afternoon buried within the precincts of the gaol," the natural inference is that there is a grave-yard, that there is a spot at the rear of the chapel, very likely, set apart for the interment of those who are sacrificed to the law's just vengeance, and that, though the unhallowed hillocks are devoid of head or footstone, there is a registry kept, by which the authorities can tell whose disgraced remains they cover. This, however, is by no means the system adopted.

The guide, unlocking a door, discovers a narrow paved alley, between two very tall, rough-hewn walls, which are adorned with whitewash. The alley is, perhaps, five-and-twenty yards long, and not so wide but that two men joining hands could easily touch the sides of it, and at the end there is a grated gate.

"This," remarks the civil warder, "is where we bury 'em," and you naturally conclude that he alludes to a space beyond the gate, and that he is about to traverse the alley, and open it.

Instead of this, barely has he stepped over the threshold than he points to the letter " S," dimly visible on the wall's surface, and, says he—

"Slitwizen, who was hanged for murdering his wife and burning her body," and before your breath, sus-pended by the startling announcement, is restored to you, he lays his forefinger on another letter a few inches off.

"Ketchcalf, who cut the throat of his fellow-servant ; Brambleby, who split his father's skull with a garden spade ; Greenacre, who murdered Hannah Brown and afterwards cut up her body," and so as he keeps shifting barely a foot at a time along the face of the whitened wall, he goes on adding to the horrible list, while the ghastly fact dawns on you that every letter denotes a body cut down from the gallows, and that the pavement you are walking on is bedded in the remains of who shall say how many male and female murderers ?

We are comparatively moderate in modern times in the use of the hempen cord as a remedy against man-slaying, but this was nearly a generation since, when business was exceedingly brisk in that line, and a hanging was looked for in the Old Bailey on a Monday almost as much as a matter of course as the cattle-market in Smithfield on a Friday.

Then, as now, the dreadful little lane between the high walls was the only place of sepulchre for those who passed out to death through the debtors' door.

The very paving-stones bear witness to the many times they have been roughly forced up by unskilled hands that a hole may be dug for the reception of the poor coffined wretches who wear quicklime for a shroud.

There is not a whole paving-stone the length of the alley, and they are patched and cobbled and mended with dabs of mortar in the most unhandsome way.

"A very large number must have been buried here at one time and another," I remarked.

" Bless you, yes sir," replied the Newgate warder of long service, "you can't see half the letters. They used to be all over the other wall as well, but, being whitened every year, the letters at last got filled up."

It was not a pleasant idea, and I believe that the cracked and unstable condition of the paving-stones suggested it, but it came into my mind as I scanned the walls and made out scores and scores of ancient letters, showing ghostlike through the obliterating whitewash, what a hideous crowd it would make if those to whom the initials applied could all in a moment be recalled to life.

The narrow alley would not hold them all. There would ensue such a ferocious crushing and striving for escape that there would be murder done over again, and such work for Mr. Marwood that he would be striking for extra pay.

A hundred years ago the public executioners of the metropolis were kept uncommonly busy.

According to the *Newcastle Chronicle*, of July 29th, 1780, there were thirteen criminals hanged in the four days from July 18th to 21st, 1780, and of these ten had been convicted of complicity in the Gordon Riots, the remainder being for highway robbery.

One of the condemned rioters was a Jew, named Solomons. The report of the executions says :—

"Yesterday morning (July 21st), at a quarter-past six o'clock, Thomas Price, James Burn, Benj. Walters, Jona. Stacey, and George Staples, convicts, for riot-ing, &c., in Golden-lane and Moorfields, were called up to prayers, and about eight o'clock the three former had their irons knocked off, put in a cart, and con-veyed in the same order as before to the end of Golden-lane, Old-street-road.

"At their coming out of Newgate, James Burn de-sired the carman not to drive so fast, which was com-plied with.

"On their arrival at the place of execution, the Ordi-nary got up into the cart, prayed with them for some considerable time, when he left them, and they were tied up—shortly after they shook hands with each other, and said, as they had lived together on earth, and died, so they hoped they should live together in Heaven—their caps were pulled over their faces, and they were launched into eternity, while the clock was striking nine.

"The cavalcade then went back to Newgate, and about eleven o'clock, Jonathan Stacey, for demolishing Mr. Malo's house, and George Staples, for demolishing the Romish Chapel, &c., adjoining, were put into the cart, and conveyed to Moorfields, the gallows being fixed directly opposite the ruins thereof.

"They arrived there about a quarter after eleven, when the Ordinary went up to them, and performed his duty, which, being finished, the executioner pulled their caps over their eyes, and they were launched into eternity.

"These poor men prayed in a most exemplary man-ner all the way from Newgate to the place of execution, and never once took their eyes from their books but when they lifted them to Heaven for mercy."

Out of one hundred and thirty-five rioters who were tried, fifty-nine were capitally convicted.

The prison arrangements in the olden time were far different to the present regulations.

The author of a work entitled, "The Penns and Penningtons of the Seventeenth Century," tells the following story of Newgate, which, as we are discoursing on the City gaol, may be interesting to our readers as a contrast to our present prison regulations.

When we came to Newgate (says the narrator) we found that side of the prison very full of Friends, who were prisoners there before us; as indeed were all the other parts of that prison, and most of the other prisons about the town; and our addition caused a still greater throng on that side of Newgate.

We had the liberty of the hall, which is on the first story over the gate, and which in the daytime is common to all the prisoners on that side, felons as well as others.

But in the night we all lodged in one room, which was large and round, having in the middle of it a great pillar of oaken timber, which bore up the chapel that is over it.

To this pillar we fastened our hammocks at one end, and to the opposite wall on the other end, quite round the room, in three stories, one over the other; so that they who lay in the upper and middle row of hammocks were obliged to go to bed first, because they were to climb up to the higher by getting into the lower ones.

And under the lower range of hammocks, by the wall sides, were laid beds upon the floor, in which the sick and weak prisoners lay.

There were many sick, and some very weak, and though we were not long there, one of our fellow prisoners died. The rest of the story is too good to be omitted.

The body of the deceased, being laid out and put in a coffin, was set in a room called "The Lodge," that the coroner might inquire into the cause of his death.

The manner of their doing it is this. As soon as the coroner is come, the turnkeys run into the street under the gate, and seize upon every man that passes till they have got enough to make up the coroner's inquest. It so happened at this time, that they lighted on an ancient man, a grave citizen, who was trudging through the gate in great haste, and him they laid hold on, telling him he must come in and serve upon the inquest.

He pleaded hard, begged and besought them to let him go, assuring them that he was going on very urgent business. But they were deaf to all entreaties.

When they had got their complement, and were shut in together, the others said to this ancient man—

"Come, father, you are the oldest among us; you shall be our foreman."

When the coroner had sworn the jury, the coffin was uncovered that they might look upon his body, but the old man said to them—

"To what purpose do you show us a dead body here? You would not have us think that this man died in this room! How shall we be able to judge how this man came by his death, unless we see the place where he died, and where he hath been kept prisoner before he died? How know we but that the incommodiousness of the place wherein he was kept may have occasioned his death? Therefore show us the place wherein this man died."

This much displeased the keepers, and they began to banter the old man, thinking to beat him off it. But he stood up tightly to them.

"Come, come," said he, "though you made a fool of me in bringing me hither, ye shall not find me a child now I am here. Mistake not; for I understand my place and your duty; and I require you to conduct me and my brethren to the place where this man died. Refuse it at your peril."

They now wished they had let the old man go about his business, rather than by troubling him have brought this trouble on themselves. But when he persisted in his resolution the coroner told them they must show him the place.

It was evening when they began, and by this time it was bed-time with us, so that we had taken down our hammocks, which in the day hung by the walls, and had made them ready to go into and were undressing, when on a sudden we heard a great noise of tongues and trampling of feet coming towards us.

By-and-bye one of the turnkeys, opening our door said—"Hold! hold! do not undress; here is the coroner's inquest coming to see you."

As soon as they were come to the door (for within it there was scarcely room for them to come) the foreman who led them, lifting up his hands, said—"Lord bless me, what a sight is here! I did not think there had been so much cruelty in the hearts of Englishmen to use Englishmen in this manner! We need not now question," said he to the rest of the jury, "how this man came by his death; we may wonder that they are not all dead, for this place is enough to breed an infection among them. Well," added he, "if it please God to lengthen my life till to-morrow, I will find means to let the king know how his subjects are dealt with here."

The Sessions House adjoins Newgate prison.

The older wing is uniform with it in appearance, and was the original Sessions House.

There are seven doors entering into the old court-room; two of them on the side next to Newgate, one of them in the area being for witnesses, and another more elevated being a private entrance for the judges.

On the opposite side there are two doors, one for the jury and counsel, and the other a private entrance for the judges and magistrates who take their seats on the bench.

There is another door behind the bench, by which any of the judges are able to retire when disposed; and on each side of the dock there is a door for the entrance of the witnesses, solicitors, and jury.

The court-room is lighted by three large windows towards Newgate, and by three smaller sombre windows on the opposite side.

The deputy-governor of Newgate informed us, that all classes of heavy offences are tried at the Old Bailey Criminal Court, which is the highest in England. The prisoners are brought from the prison of Newgate and placed in cells under the courts, until they are called to the bar to be tried.

They are then brought into the dock to answer to the criminal charges brought against them. The indictments are read over to each of them, and they are asked by the clerk of the arraigns if they are guilty or not guilty. If they plead guilty, they are ordered in the meantime to stand back.

If they plead not guilty, they remain at the bar until all the pleas are taken of the other prisoners at the dock.

After this is done the jury are called into the jury-box, to proceed to investigate the different cases. The prisoners can object to the jurymen before being sworn.

If the prisoner at the bar is found guilty, he is sentenced by the judge, and removed to the prison. If he is declared not guilty, a discharge is written out by the governor, and he retires from the bar.

In the case of a murderer, he is taken to the court in custody of an officer. He is arraigned at the bar in the same way as the other classes of prisoners. If found guilty he is taken back to the condemned cell, where he is watched day and night until he is executed, which generally takes place within three weeks thereafter.

The deputy-governor stated :—I find the murderers to be of very different characters. Some are callous and ruffian-like in demeanour, but others are of more gentle and peaceable disposition, whom you heartily pity, as you are convinced from all you see about them, that they had been incited to the commission of their crime through intemperance or other incidental causes, foreign to their general character.

We find those to be worst who premeditated their crimes for gain. There have been few murderers here who assassinated from revenge.

I have seen twenty-nine criminals executed in front of Newgate, and was present in the court at the trial of most of them. Palmer was one of the most diabolical characters among penal offenders I ever saw in Newgate, and Mrs. Manning the most callous of females. Palmer was a gentlemanlike man, educated for a surgeon.

By giving himself up too much to gambling and field sports he was led to the murder of J. P. Cooke to repay his losses. He was executed at Stafford, and was only temporarily under our custody here. In person he was strong built, about the ordinary height, and had very strong nerves.

Mrs. Manning was a very resolute woman, but her husband was a very imbecile character, and had been dragged into crime through the strong mind of his wife, who had formerly been lady's maid to the Duchess of Sutherland.

The deputy-governor informed us he had taken notes of the executions in Newgate since 1816, when criminals were hanged for cutting and wounding, burglary, forgery, uttering base coin, &c.

The law was changed in the year 1836 in reference to capital punishments, and the sentence of death is now restricted to murder and high treason. In 1785 nineteen persons, and in 1787 no less than eighteen were executed at one time.

When females are convicted of murder they are asked by the Clerk of Arraigns if they have anything to urge why sentence of death should be passed on them. The matron who sits in the dock beside a female culprit, asks if she is in the family way. A curious case took place in 1847.

Mary Ann Hunt, being convicted of murder, was asked by the Clerk of Arraigns if she had anything to urge why sentence of death should not be passed upon her. She replied through the matron in the dock that she was with child. An unusual step was here taken. A jury of twelve married women were summoned to court, who on being sworn, examined her.

After they were absent for some time, they returned into the Court, and stated that she was not with child. She was afterwards examined by the medical officer in Newgate, and found to be pregnant. She gave birth to a son on the 28th of December following. When before the Court she must have been eight months gone with child.

CHAPTER CXLVI.
PEACE'S EXPERIENCE OF THE INTERIOR OF NEWGATE.

WE left Charles in charge of a prison warder who ushered him into a vaulted apartment of a gloomy cheerless description, like most others in the prison.

Abutting out from this were several small rooms with baths in them, and Peace was told to perform the customary ablution.

This he knew from former experience to be the usual course of procedure; so he undressed without a moment's hesitation, whereupon his clothes were taken by his attendant and carefully examined, and all prohibited articles were removed from the pockets.

An inventory of these things was taken, and our hero was informed that it was against the prison rules for him to retain possession of them; but that his wife or any of his friends, when they paid him a visit, might take them away, and "should you be fortunate enough to be acquitted," observed the warder, "you can have them when you are discharged."

Peace nodded significantly.

"Should I be fortunate enough," he murmured to himself; "I fear there is not much chance of that. Well, you see, young man," he said, aloud, "I don't think there is much chance of my pulling through, 'cause, you see, the case is ugly against me."

"I have nothing to do with that; you are sent here to await your trial, and are, of course, innocent till you are proved guilty," observed the warder, who was evidently a kindly-disposed person.

Peace was informed that he could have the prison allowance of food, or order in what he required, under certain restrictions, from an eating-house on the opposite side of the Old Bailey, and that the money found upon him could be given to his relatives, who would be thereby enabled to pay for the choicest viands from the aforesaid cook-shop.

All this information was conveyed to him in the set phraseology invariably adopted by wardens when addressing prisoners in similar cases.

Peace was never at any time in his life a gourmand, and paid but little attention to the pleasures of the table. Nevertheless, he directed to have his meals furnished by the proprietor of the elegant restaurant outside the walls of the prison.

But this only lasted a few days. From what he could see of the prison fare it was sufficiently good for his purpose, being wholesome and passably good in flavour, so he dropped the Old Bailey restaurant, and contented with the food supplied by the City authorities.

After he had taken his bath, and had re-dressed himself he felt a little refreshed, and he was told to walk in front of his conductor.

He ascended a flight of iron stairs into a lofty hall with a glass roof like a railway station, and on either side of this were galleries one above the other, forming tiers with cells along each, the doors of which were all numbered; a number was shouted in a loud voice by his attendant, when a warder on the first flight told Peace to come up stairs; he obeyed, and was at once ushered into his cell, which he was told must be kept as clean as he then saw it—that it would be requisite to scrub it every day. His attention was then directed to a printed list of rules, with which he was to make himself acquainted.

All these formalities he had gone through on other occasions, but he did not choose to appear as if he knew anything about them; he was desirous of passing off as a green-hand, he had never been in Newgate before and none of the officials knew him—it was quite time enough for him to acknowledge that he had been convicted before upon the charge of burglary when he was recognised by other prison officials.

When the door of his cell was closed, and he found himself alone in his narrow prison-house his heart seemed to sink within him; there was no telling what might be the issue of this capture.

In any case, taking the most favourable view of it, he was certain to be sentenced to a long term of imprisonment.

This was but a natural consequence, and this he was

prepared to undergo, but if by any chance he should be identified as the celebrated Charles Peace, of Sheffield and Banner-cross notoriety, his life would be forfeited.

"Oh," he murmured, "there is that cursed woman who I have never trusted out of my sight since I first became acquainted with her. What will she do? Send me to the gallows, I expect. Oh, I wish I could see Bill Rawton; he's the only man I can rely upon."

After these observations he fell into a reverie; then he proceeded to examine his cell and its furniture. It was much the same as the others he had been shut up in.

It was a brick-arched apartment, about 12 ft. by 7 ft. There was the same description of wash-basin, the same flap table and wooden stool, the enamelled plate, tin mug, wooden spoon, and salt-box, he had been accustomed to in the earlier days of his prison life. At the sight of these old familiar objects his heart grew sick.

"Hang it all! I have been a fool," he murmured. "I can see that plainly enough, now that it is too late."

Oh, how he sighed for liberty at that supremely bitter moment!

The window of his cell was strongly barred and escape was impossible. He climbed up to this, and from it, through a small door, some 10 in. by 4 in., was just able to distinguish the roofs of the houses and the majestic dome of St. Paul's.

The noise of the street traffic fell faintly on his ears, telling of the world outside—that dark receptacle of crime.

Then he heaved a profound sigh.

Should he ever again be mixing with the throng of passengers in the highways and byways of the great city?

It was a query that he could not very well answer; but even at this time hope did not entirely desert him. There might be some flaw in the indictment—some legal technicality which might be used in his favour. There was no telling—such things had occurred and might again.

Anyway he would hope for the best; as Mr. Micawber was wont to say, something might turn up.

He remained for a long time after this a prey to agonising thoughts—the leading subject of these being Mrs. Thompson whom he now more than ever mistrusted.

There was nobody now but his wife to keep watch and ward over her. It is true his friend Bill Rawton might use some little influence over the erratic woman, but then Bill knew nothing about the Bannercross murder, and he debated with himself if it was advisable even now to make the gipsy acquainted with all the circumstances attending upon that horrible crime.

If this were done, Rawton might desert him at a time when he most stood in need of his service.

He was anxious to drive the thoughts of his position from his mind, and so began to make an inspection of the door of his cell, the intricacies of which afforded a welcome relief by diverting his ideas from the misery of his situation.

He had, throughout his life, taken great interest in mechanical appliances, and, to say the truth, it was, after all, but a poor consolation to employ his thoughts upon the solid fastenings of his door, but it was better than suffering the canker worm to gnaw at his heart. In the wall itself adjoining the door, about two feet from the top, was a something he could not make out.

At first he was inclined to think it was a ventilator, but upon further examination he came to the conclusion that he was mistaken.

It was no ventilator. He touched it, and immediately heard a sharp click outside. This made him start for a moment.

A gong bell was sounded, the trap in the door flew open inwards, forming a little shelf, and a voice exclaimed—

"Now then, what do you want?"

Through the aperture Peace saw the face of a warder, not the one, however, who had shown him into the cell.

He did not know very well what answer to make, and the man outside, in a still more emphatic manner said—

"Can't you say what you want? Speak, man."

"Oh," cried Peace, "I beg your pardon for disturbing you, but I should like to have some writing paper, pens, and ink, if it not against the rules."

No reply was given to this request, but immediately the little trap closed with a click as suddenly as it had opened.

"I expect Mr. Warder is a bit riled," murmured our hero. "Well, if he is I can't help it."

Presently he heard a key inserted in the lock, and the door was opened. Then the warder pointed to an inkstand, pen, and a sheet of writing paper, lying on the ground just outside the cell door.

"I am sure you are very kind, and I beg to thank you for this favour," said our hero, in the softest voice possible.

"That will do," cried the gaoler, closing the door after Peace had possessed himself of the writing materials.

"Ah, a man of few words," murmured the prisoner. "They are most of 'em like that. The least said the soonest mended is their motto. However, he's given me what I asked for. I'll write a few lines to the old woman, but I must mind how I word the letter, for I suppose it will be carefully examined before it is permitted to leave the prison."

He occupied himself in writing for some considerable time, and when the hour for bedtime arrived, he unfastened his hammock and retired to rest, sleeping soundly for the greater portion of the night.

At six o'clock in the morning he was roused by the clanging of a large bell, and he knew it was time to get up.

But before he had dressed, the door of his cell was thrown open by a warder, who passed on to make room for the deputy governor and another warder, who carried a book for taking notes of anything worthy of notice.

Peace knew all these formalities very well, and was, therefore, quite prepared for them.

He assumed a respectful manner for the nonce, and, to all appearance, he felt deeply the painful situation in which he found himself placed.

He bowed submissively to the deputy-governor, who took but little notice of the obeisance.

"Do you want to see the doctor?" inquired the prison official.

"No, sir; I am in pretty good health. There is nothing the matter with me, beyond the fact that I am, of course, in great anxiety of mind."

"Just so. Then you don't require medical advice?"

"No, sir."

"Explain to him what he is required to do," said the deputy-governor, turning on his heel.

Two brushes were handed to Peace, and he was informed they were to be used in polishing the floor of his cell. He was also shown all the other arrangements with which, however, it is needless to say, he was already very well acquainted, but he listened to the warder's instructions complacently enough.

Every morning he had to go on his hands and knees and polish the cell floor as well as wash and scrub the table, stool, and bason, and every article in the room.

After breakfast—which was served through the little trap in the door, and which consisted of a pint of gruel and a piece of bread—he was told to prepare for chapel.

As we have, in a previous chapter, given a full detail of the proceedings in the chapel of a prison, it will not be necessary to repeat the same in this place.

It is certain, however, that in chapel and at other places in the gaol opportunities are afforded of prisoners conversing, and it is equally certain that "old lags," on coming into contact with first offenders, delight in polluting their minds.

In due course the chaplain paid a visit to Peace. He was urbane and kind in his manner, asked the prisoner a variety of questions, and it is needless to say that Peace pretended to be contrite, and expressed his regret for having been led into error. He did not say he had been a criminal for the greater part of his life, but he assumed a sanctimonious air. But the chaplain of Newgate, although uniformly kind to those under his spiritual care, had too much penetration to be deceived by Peace's hypocrisy.

No man could by possibility be more fitted for the office than this gentleman. Few men have the gift of dropping in a few words of seasonable advice, judiciously mingled with reproof, than this gentleman.

When Peace regained his cell, after the service was over, he received a visit from the governor duly attended, like any other commander-in-chief, by his aide-de-camp.

He regarded Peace with a scrutinising glance, and inquired if he wanted anything.

"I want to see my friends as soon as possible, and my solicitor to arrange for my defence," said our hero.

"Very well, that is but natural. Write to them and you can have an interview on the next visiting day."

"I have written," cried Peace. "I hope the letter was sent off."

"It was," observed the governor, sententiously. "Anything else?"

"No, sir, I don't think there is anything else, thank you."

The governor retired.

His visits after this were singularly regular. He came, looked round, made one or two observations, and then departed.

Peace did not dare to ask if Robinson, whom he had shot, was progressing favourably or not, but this was a question he was most anxious about.

If the wounded policeman succumbed to the injuries he had received his assassin would expiate the crime he had committed on the scaffold.

One day he asked one of the warders if Robinson was still alive. The question was answered with a nod only, which signified that he was. This seemed to lift a load off Peace's heart, and hope dawned again.

After the governor's diurnal visit all the remanded prisoners were called out and marched off into a stone-paved yard surrounded by high brick walls.

Peace had the strongest possible objection to this arrangement.

He dreaded marching round, as, by so doing, he would run the risk of being detected, and his real identity would become known.

However, he was constrained to follow the instructions given him.

It was deemed necessary that prisoners should have exercise, and so there was no other course open to him than to comply with the usual regulations.

He had a good opportunity of looking at his fellow-prisoners.

They were of all grades of society, from the fraudulent merchant to the small boy who had been taught to pick pockets.

There were forgers, embezzling clerks, housebreakers, and villains of every conceivable type.

Peace glanced at them, protruding his lower jaw the while, and distorting his features in such a way as to render recognition difficult and almost impossible.

"What are you in for?" whispered a youth of the Artful Dodger species.

Peace made no answer.

"I say, old man," observed the precocious youth aforesaid, "you let fly at a bobby—didn't yer? S'help me taters, I wouldn't be in your shoes.

All this was said in a whisper, but it was loud enough for Peace to hear.

"Hold your tongue, yer fool," cried another of the group, addressing himself to the pickpocket. "Can't yer see as how the gentleman don't like it?"

Round and round the yard in Indian file, some three yards apart, did the prisoners march for nearly an hour.

Two warders were there to keep order, and check any talking between the prisoners, but a few chance observations such as we have recorded did at times take place, despite the warders' surveillance.

"Oh, strike me lucky, but the old un has a pretty mug of his own," said the pickpocket, as he caught sight of Peace's profile.

"Now then, no talking," said one of the warders.

"I vasn't a speakin'," cried the pickpocket.

"It was you who spoke, and if you do it again I'll report you," said the prison official.

"Vell, all I sed vas, vat a beautiful old genelman I've got in front of me. There aint any harm in that, I s'pose."

"You hold your tongue. Do you hear?"

"Yes, I hear. "Vell I'm blest. A cove musn't even open his mouth to get a breath of fresh air."

"Silence."

The pickpocket said no more, much to Peace's relief, for the few chance observations he had already made naturally enough attracted the attention of most persons to our hero.

Presently a batch of persons emerged from a side door of the prison, and entered the yard.

They were detectives and warders from other prisons, and had come to take stock, and see if they could spot any "old friends."

Peace walked round and round without appearing to be aware of the presence of the new comers, but he was most anxious, nevertheless.

As he passed along and came within full view of them, he did not recognise any face that was known to him in the group, and hoped, therefore, that it was all right as far as that day was concerned. Nevertheless, several recognitions did take place, for one man was called to the corner of the yard to undergo a closer scrutiny, while one of the prison officials compared a photograph he drew from his pocket with the features of the man in question, and there was no denying the "soft impeachment."

VISITING DAY AT NEWGATE—PEACE'S INTERVIEW WITH HIS WIFE.

The gentleman was known as an "old lag." The acquaintances thus claimed are seldom cordially reciprocated, and in more than one instance Piper at the present moment was found to be identical with Jenkins, of Coldbath-fields, or White, of Holloway. Peace expected his turn to come.

It would, indeed, have been a sore trial if the visitors to the gaol discovered that Mr. Ward, of Blackheath, or Mr. Thompson, of Peckham, was identical with Mr. Charles Peace, of Sheffield; this is what he most dreaded, but it so chanced that on this day none of his friends, either in the "force" or in gaol were present at Newgate. So much the better for him—he had a respite for a while.

Those who were recognised stoutly protested that the warders or detectives were mistaken; they said they had never been in trouble before, and assumed such a virtuous tone of indignation as to somehow shake the faith of their accusers.

An old and astute detective told us that it was not so much the recognising the face and figure of the individual that they depended on in the first instance, as the fact that in nine cases out of ten an "old lag" would betray himself.

Artful as these men are they appear to lose presence of mind the moment the detectives come into the yard.

Those whom they are seeking seem to be but too well aware of the danger that awaits them, and they invariably try to look so perfectly innocent, and slink past in such a shuffling manner, that the chances are they are bound to be "spotted."

But it must be understood that those who are in search of old acquaintances of this sort generally have a good survey of the prisoners, as they are marching round, from some dark window of the prison before they enter the yard. Thus the bearing and looks of the prisoners are undergoing a careful and rigid scrutiny when they are not aware of it.

On entering, the detectives note any change in their demeanour.

The new man, the green hand, is perfectly indifferent as to who sees him—indeed, in most cases, he does not even suspect what has brought the crowd of persons into the yard, his natural surmise being, if he reflects at all upon the subject, that they are mere loungers, who have been brought thither from mere idle curiosity.

But with the old hand the case is altogether different. He looks upon the detectives and all prison officials as his natural enemies, and he cannot preserve his usual equanimity when they make their appearance in the exercise-yard, and hence it is that in most cases the old hand, by some sudden or indiscreet movement, is pretty sure to betray himself.

Many culprits of this class would gladly avoid the customary exercise which is deemed requisite by the authorities to take, and Peace was one of this number; but to refuse would only cause them to be looked upon with suspicion, and would be attended with other evil consequences.

When the customary walk-round in the yard is concluded, the general practice at Newgate is for the prisoners to partake of the mid-day meal. This generally consists of a few potatoes or other sort of vegetables, a few ounces of meat, and a tolerably good supply of bread—the last-named is generally pretty good. Although it is made of coarse flour, still as a rule it is passable enough. When their meat is not included in the list of delicacies soup is given, which is made from the liquor of the meat on the preceding day.

As far as the meat is concerned, it may be good enough, though it consists of the coarsest and most inferior part of the animal, but if any care or attention was paid to the cookery of the beef or mutton it would be eatable.

But this is never done. Huge junks of beef are placed in a copper, unsalted, and boiled as rapidly as possible, and when turned out it presents the appearance of horse flesh. As a rule there is very little fat to it, and it presents a most objectionable appearance.

The English are not versed in the science of cookery, and have yet a great deal to learn from their Continental neighbours, but the beef at Newgate requires a very strong stomach to take to it kindly. This is the more surprising, seeing that the City gaol is under the superintendence of the Court of Aldermen and the Court of Common Council, and every member of these august bodies is supposed to have a great relish for the good things of this life.

It is true that they have a great abhorrence of evil-disposed persons who are indiscreet enough to commit acts which bring them under the ban of the law—such persons must be punished, and ought not to be pampered or fed upon the fat of the land during their temporary sojourn in the City prison. And, to say the truth, they certainly are not.

If the object is to make the meat as hard, unpalatable, and indigestible as possible, and at the same time to impart as little flavour and nourishment to the "soup," the end is attained. But there is really no reason for this—with the same materials properly cooked excellent dinners could be furnished; as it is, the cooking is simply abominable—as bad as can possibly be.

It is to be hoped that a change will very shortly take place in the culinary department of Newgate, for it should be remembered that many persons are sent there who in the due course of time are proved to be innocent of the crimes with which they are charged.

Peace, however, never complained of the food which he partook of without a murmur, but there were others who made wry faces as the unsavoury mess was placed before them.

During the afternoon he was constrained to take another turn round the yard with his companions in misfortune, or, more properly speaking, crime.

On this occasion no detectives or warders paid a visit to the yard, and Peace, therefore, had no misgivings as far as that day was concerned. But he was, however, greatly relieved when he was conducted back to his cell. Anyway he would not be troubled to move out of it again till the following morning.

He was most anxious to see Bill Rawton or his wife. He had more confidence in the former and would much prefer having an interview with the gipsy, but he had already sent letters to both, and expected to see them on the next visiting day.

Certain days in the week are appointed for prisoners to have interviews with their friends or relatives. The friends of prisoners not convicted are allowed to come and see them and converse through wire gratings.

The rules in this respect are stringent enough, and many have declared that they are unnecessarily so. It certainly does appear hard upon an unconvicted person, that he or she should not be permitted to have any private conversation with friends or relatives. But such is the present regulation.

There are two gratings with a space of some three or four feet between them, in which space stands or sits a warder.

Any parcels of clothes or other not prohibited articles are passed first to the warder so that he may be satisfied that there are no contraband things among them, and then, after examination they are handed by him to the prisoner.

The visiting goes on for an hour. The prisoners, or such of them who have friends to see them, stand in a row against the railings with their friends opposite.

Everyone is talking at once to his own friend, and the consequence is that a noise and hubbub is kept up for the whole of the time, and all present are too interested in their own individual matters to heed what is going on between his neighbour and friend, and as far as the warders are concerned they look upon the scene with perfect apathy, and in most cases do not hear anything very distinctly; or, if they do, do not bother themselves with affairs which after all do not as a general rule in any way interest them.

Peace during his first few days' incarceration in the gaol of Newgate had conducted himself in a discreet and proper manner. He was observant of the prison rules, assumed an air of passive resignation, and strove as best he could to impress everybody with the fact that he was a repentant sinner.

The hypocrisy of this man was one of his leading characteristics. One morning, when the governor had paid him his accustomed diurnal visit, he expressed himself dissatisfied with the manner in which his cell was cleaned.

Peace assumed a tone of humility and said he was much pained at incurring his censure, but that he would be specially mindful of the timely warning, and take every care not to incur his censure again.

At the same time he expressed his thanks for the considerate manner he had been treated by the prison officials, whose kindness he should ever be grateful for.

It is said that a soft word turneth away wrath, and Peace after this was treated with the greatest possible kindness, conformable with the rules of the gaol; indeed he played his part so admirably that those about him were disposed to believe that he had fallen into error by some sudden or spasmodic influence which they were at a loss to account for.

CHAPTER CXLVII.
VISITING DAY AT NEWGATE.

PEACE had written a number of epistles to his friends. These, of course, had undergone the usual inspection, but there was nothing in the documents to compromise the writer.

On the contrary, although the language was neither grammatical nor refined, the letters themselves appeared to be those of a penitent and contrite man who bitterly regretted the error into which he had fallen.

The day at length arrived upon which Peace had the satisfaction of seeing his poor ill-used wife and Bill Rawton, the gipsy.

For the behoof of those who have never witnessed scenes of this description we will endeavour to give a graphic account of the interior of the gaol on one of these occasions.

On certain mornings, and at regular hours, small groops of woe-begone tearful girls may be seen in the Old Bailey, exchanging whispers with each other or treading their way silently through the throng of meat salesmen, City policemen, ticket porters, warehousemen, clerks, and shopboys, with which the busy place is full.

The girls look prematurely old and worn, and many of them have the unmistakable expression all noted criminals obtain, while the elder women may be divided into two classes—the callous and the crushed, and in the latter category may be included the wife of Charles Peace.

There is a world of misery behind the defiant as well as the tortured faces one sees here.

All pause at the steps leading up to the half door, behind which the head and shoulders of a stalwart man in uniform are seen, and after a moment's parley they are admitted within.

The object of their journey is nearly accomplished now, for they are about to be allowed to see and converse with husbands, or lovers, with their brothers, or their sons.

These last are taking their prescribed amount of exercise in the prison yards, and it is from behind one of the gratings looking on these that they are permitted to gaze from a given distance upon and exchange words with their visitors.

Between the prisoners and their friends runs a passage of about a yard wide, with another set of iron bars fencing it off from the place where the women stand; so that between the visitors and the visited are two stout barriers and sufficient space to preclude the possibility of articles being handed from one to the other. There are no seats.

The prisoners are told to break out of the line of march, and permitted to advance to the grating of the yard in batches of three or four.

The women who have come to see them stand exactly opposite, within the prison, and all have to press their faces close to the bars to make hearing possible.

If a double set of wild-beast cages were planted in parallel lines, with the ironwork of each facing the others, but a yard or so apart—if the lions and tigers were pushing their noses eagerly at the barriers, as if trying to escape, and if a keeper or two were planted in the intervening space to watch, a fair imitation of Newgate gaol during visiting hours would be obtained.

The gloomy place has been vastly altered and improved during the last few years. Those who only remember its old dark wards, with their long line of oakum-pickers at work in the day time, who saw the condemned cell, say about the time Palmer had occupied it, or Bousfield endeavoured to commit suicide by throwing himself in its fire, would be amazed at the transformation effected in its interior.

Light iron staircases lead to airy galleries, out of which the various cells open, and from the lower floor of which the exercise grounds are gained. The condemned cell differs little now from that appropriated to ordinary prisoners, save that there is accommodation for the warders, whose duty it is to watch the wretch sentenced to die, and who never leave him until he falls from the gallows' drop.

But our present business is with the exercise yards, and the interviews held between their bars. There is a ghastly resemblance between them and the playground of some strict school.

Pacing regularly round, a fixed space being maintained between each man or boy, and the rate of walking in each case the same, proceed the prisoners. It is their wicked, callous faces which make the school simile seem ghastly.

Dangerous beasts moving restlessly to and fro in a vast cage seems much nearer the mark, now that we are among them. Sordid common villainy, theft, forgery, assault, burglary, cutting and wounding, and passing bad money, make up the bulk of the offences with which the men before us stand charged.

A stout florid-faced man, who looks like a country farmer, and who is gesticulating violently through the bars to the cowed and crying little woman beyond them, is in on a charge of horse-stealing. He has been in prison before, and indeed was only out of it ten days when he was again apprehended. A muscular powerful man, he looks as if he could carry off a horse bodily, if necessary; and one wonders what the messages are he is impressing so earnestly on his poor little wife.

A warder is standing near enough to the twain to overhear their talk, but we are assured no effort is made to eavesdrop, the presence of a prison official being insisted on simply as a precautionary measure.

Next to the horse-dealer is a well-dressed young

clerk, whose alleged offence is embezzlement. The elderly woman whose sobs reach us across the yard is his mother.

She seems to be pleading earnestly, and he to be half sullen, half ashamed, but finally to yield to her entreaties, whatever their purport may have been.

The third prisoner being visited is an older man, and the girl talking to him looks like his daughter.

Their interview is far calmer than that of the other two, and seems indeed of a business character; for some clean linen has been brought, and the man is actually talking of the weather as we pass by—a proceeding which we thought a feint, but which, as we were reminded, was natural enough.

The three-quarters of an hour allotted to each interview is doubtless a very precious time.

It can only be had on particular days, and the strongest wish of those concerned must be to compress as many questions and answers into it as possible.

Fancy the painful excitement with which a man about to be tried for some serious crime must look forward to his promised talk with those whom he can trust to act for him outside.

The anxious thoughts, the doubts, the fears, the hopes which agitate him in the solitude of his cell are to all bear fruit in the momentous conversation he is permitted to hold.

The chances of the impending trial, his fate if convicted, the means to be raised for his defence, and the effect upon those dependent on him of his present state, have to be eagerly canvassed; and it is all important that not a moment should be lost.

But this very eagerness defeats itself. Just as it often happens, that when people meet after a long absence, and for a limited time, they fail to recall half the topics in which they are vitally interested, and on which they are anxious to compare notes—so with the imprisoned men before us and their friends.

In the other yards we visited men and women were absolutely staring at each other through the bars, in silence; though the latter had come on purpose to talk, and the former would be shut up again in a quarter of an hour.

In some cases it may have been the dumbness of despair which made them tongue-tied; but many seemed so nervously anxious to express all they had to say that they were unable to arrange their ideas sufficiently to give them articulate shape.

Some of the women treated the whole affair lightly, smirked at the warders, and looked boldly round; but these were the exceptions. The rule both in those waiting and those in communication with their male friends was absolute dejection.

Two other kinds of accommodation are provided for special visitors, both similar in character. The first is an enclosed closet in the centre of the principal corridor, and is for the attorneys; the second is for the prisoners who are Roman Catholics, and who are visited by their priest.

Both have glass sides and roof, and realise "the light closets," upon which Clarissa laid much stress when describing the lodgings she had been entrapped into by Lovelace.

The advice to little children, "to be seen but not heard," is rigidly enforced upon all people inside these two places.

They live, for the time being literally, in a glass-house, and every movement can be seen from almost any portion of the chamber or corridor in which they stand.

Both places were empty during our stay, the only visitors being the women pressing against the iron bars.

It is easy to fill up their vacancy, however; and all but impossible not to realise the scences which take place in the attorneys' box, as well as the priests'.

There are seats here, and a resting-place for papers. It is, indeed, a small office under a glass case, and swept and garnished for the next tenants.

The futile attempts at deceit, the half confessions, the miserable equivocations as to the extent and circumstances of guilt on the one hand; the calm business tone, the remonstrances on the suicidal folly of concealment, the penetrating questions, the practised art with which the truth is wormed out, and the astute assurances of help from the professional advisers on the other, this place has heard.

If glass walls have ears like the neighbours of stone and brick, what strange stories could this little cramped cage reveal!

There are more women in the porter's lodge, as we leave, tearful and miserable as the rest, and waiting their turn for interviews.

They, too, will be conducted to the iron barriers, and utter their broken conversation across the dismal yard of intervening space. The prison of Newgate is so obviously well managed, and the comforts—we had almost written the luxuries—of its inmates are so carefully secured, that its authorities have doubtless sufficient reasons for the rules under which the visits of prisoners' friends may be paid and received.

Still, a vast majority of the inmates are "remand cases;" and as they are all sent elsewhere as soon as possible after conviction, it is difficult to repress a wish that some less restricted mode of communication could be allowed.

Although many of the evil faces we saw marching round were old prison hands, we presume that the law holds them innocent of the particular offences they are charged with, until it finds them guilty.

Again, it must occasionally happen that guiltless persons who have been committed for trial are detained here, and there is something repulsive in the absolutely penal character of the reception they have in each case to give their friends.

The reader will be able to understand from the foregoing description the most noticeable features of the visiting day at Newgate.

Upon the morning to which our history more immediately refers there were two persons among the throng of visitors outside the gate of the city prison—these being Mrs. Peace and Bandy-legged Bill, both of whom had presented themselves at the prison for the purpose of having an interview with the most celebrated burglar of modern times.

Bill had dressed himself in his best attire, and looked quite respectable.

His female companion was tearful, depressed, and appeared to be quite borne down.

When the prison door was thrown open, the motley throng of visitors passed into the entrance.

They were conducted to the place appointed for the visitors, and behind the bars they beheld the man of whom they were in search.

Peace appeared to be perfectly composed. His wife uttered a deep sigh as she reached the barrier which separated her from her husband.

A woman who stood next to her, and who was evidently a native of the "Emerald Isle," set up a most dismal howl as she caught sight of a shock-headed urchin, who was, it afterwards transpired, her youngest son.

"Ooh, bad luck to the spalpeen as brought you to this!—bad luck to him the murtherin' baste," cried the woman. "It's sorry that I am to see ye brought to this anyhow, but it aint no fault of yours. Oh, murder, but my heart is a breakin', it's all through that dirty blackguard, 'Cakey.'"

Cakey was a London pickpocket of the most pronounced type, and he it was who had suborned the ill-fated young Irish lad and taught him to become a thief. (So his mother affirmed.)

She set up such a howl that the other prisoners could not hear what their relatives had to say.

"Now then, less noise there," exclaimed one of the turnkeys. "Don't be howling like that, woman."

"Oh, bedad, it is meself as is the most miserable 'oman as ever broke the bread of life," exclaimed Mrs. O'Grady, "and it is well for the likes of you to be bullyragging a poor broken-hearted mother. I've six childhre, and never a one av 'em iver done aught as they need be ashamed of—never a one, save my poor Dinnis, and may be he's got into a bit o' throuble through that lying, dirty scamp, "Cakey."

Cakey, as he was termed, was the young gentleman who had made himself so obnoxious to Peace in the exercise yard.

"Hold your row, mother," said one of the prisoners, "You aint everybody."

"There now," exclaimed Mrs. O'Grady. "It's well for the likes of him to be thryin' to stop the mouth of a fond and affectionate parent; but hold up your head, Dennis darlin', and don't be afther takin' heed of the dirty spalpeen. Ooh, but it brings tears into my motherly eyes to see ye behind the bars."

"Now, then, there's quite enough of this," exclaimed one of the warders. "You mustn't make such a noise. If you are not more quiet, we shall have to turn you out."

"An' it's turnin' me out ye'd be afther—would it?" cried the woman.

"Yes, unless you behave yourself."

"Oh, murdher, it's the first time I was within the walls of a prison, and I hope it 'ill be the last. Maybe I don't know how to behave mysel', and am wrong entirely. Ooh, sure, now, I've been as well brought up, and that aint saying much, as ony av ye."

After this outbreak the Irishwoman was a little more subdued, and conversed with her son in a lower tone.

"I'm sorry to see you in this pickle," said Bill Rawton to Peace. "It's a precious bad business."

"It is," returned our hero, "but I swear most solemnly that I never intended to do the bobby any harm. I was driven to it—in fact it appears to me to be almost like a dream. How is Sue?"

"She is pretty well," returned his wife.

"Hark you," said Peace, in a whisper; "both you and Bill must keep a sharp look-out—watch over her Do you understand?"

Both his visitors nodded.

"Good! so much the better, there is good raason for this."

"She's all right" observed Bill. "Don't trouble yourself about that; she's right enough."

His wife at this time had decamped from the Evelina-road, but neither she or Bill made him acquainted with this circumstance.

Peace hesitated a moment or two, and then said—

"She can come on the next visiting day. Poor soul, she means well, I believe, but there, when she's had a drop of drink, she will let her tongue run nineteen to the dozen, she'll want a deal of looking after—and you know as well as I do, that we've got a set of gossip-ing neighbours. What do you they say about me now?"

"Oh, they are all of them very kind and say they are sorry you've got into trouble and hope you'll get through better than you expect."

"I never intended to hurt the 'bobby,'—I swear that. Nothing was further from my thoughts, but you see I was half mad at the time, and driven to it."

"All I intended to do was to frighten him; but it's of no use talking about that now; when a man's in trouble people generally look at the worst side of the case."

"Cheer up, old man, and don't give way," cried the gipsy, in a consolatory tone, "Let us hope the judge will look upon the matter in the right light, and deal mercifully with you. How about your defence?"

"I have seen my lawyer and shall be well defended."

"Who will you have then?"

"Oh, one of the very best in the whole profession—Mr. Montague Williams."

"Couldn't have a better, I should say."

"No; but, Lord bless me! what defence is there?" Rawton looked down upon the ground, and shook his head.

"Not much," said he.

"I make up my mind for a long lagging—that's bound to follow as a natural consequence—and if the 'bobby' had died I should have had something worse."

"Ah, but he has recovered—there is no doubt about that," returned Bill, quietly.

Peace nodded significantly, and said, "So I hear."

"Be thankful for that."

"I am thankful."

"And I say, Charlie," whispered Rawton, as he put his face closer to the iron bars, "I saw Lorrie the day before yesterday."

"Yes. What did she say?"

"Sends her love and all that sort of thing, and told me to let you know that if you needed it she would let you have what you want to pay the costs incurred for your defence."

"Umph, it's jolly good of her." Tell her I don't want anything at present. I've got enough to last me till after the trial, but possibly I may avail myself of her offer after then. Ah, Bill, but they've got me pretty tight now. There aint much chance of slipping out of this—none whatever."

A long conversation now took place between the prisoner and his wife. This chiefly related to the disposal of certain sums of money and domestic matters generally.

Mrs. Peace was tearful and broken down, but she strove to bear up against this new misfortune as best she could.

Peace had but little consideration for her. His thoughts were engaged upon his own terrible position.

While he was conversing with his wife, the woman O'Grady set up one of her wild howls again, and interrupted the conversation.

"Can't you be quiet, woman?" said Peace. "A fellow is notable to hear himself speak."

"Ooh, but it's nearly mad that I am—I've seven childhre, and none on 'em iver did anything as they need be ashamed ov, barrin' this poor lad, who has been brought into throuble through that dirty black-guard, Cakey, and bad luck to him."

"I think you told us that before, missus," suggested one of the other prisoners. "The story is a little old."

"It's ould—is it?"

"Well, I think so, but that don't matter. Hold your row."

The Irishwoman began uttering a series of anathemas

against the speaker and lawless persons in general, when a turnkey took her by the elbow, and conducted her away from the scene, telling her, as he did so, that they had had quite enough of her for that day.

Everybody was greatly relieved when she had gone, and the conversation was carried on between the prisoners and their friends without any further interruption.

When the time had expired, accorded to visits of this character, Bill Rawton and Mrs. Peace took leave of our hero, and went sadly on their way home.

For the next few days Peace occupied himself in writing letters, and having interviews with his lawyer, for the purpose of preparing his defence.

Some of his letters were literary curiosities, and as a sample of them we give the reader a faithful verbatim copy of some he addressed to his friend, Mr. Brion.

We have, in the course of this work, made allusions to the inventions of the hero, and it has been pretty generally admitted by those who are competent judges that these were by no means of a contemptible character.

His partner in these inventions was a Mr. Brion, who was a near neighbour of Peace's.

This person was under the full impression at the time that our hero was a respectable gentleman, who was possessed of independent means, and he was never more surprised in his life than when he learnt the real character of the man with whom he had been dealing.

After Peace's conviction for the attempted burglary and attack on Police-constable Robinson, Mr. Brion, of Peckham, made the following statement:—

"The invention spoken of was for the raising of sunken ships; and for the purpose of having it patented, specifications were deposited in the names of Henry Brion, geographer, and Henry Thompson, gentleman.

"Becoming bold over their invention, they offered to the Admiralty to raise the 'Eurydice' and 'Vanguard,' and a similar proposal was made to the German Government in regard to the "Grosser Kurfurst." Peace was told by the Admiralty that outside assistance was unnecessary, and that the naval authorities could do their own work.

"Brion's connection with Peace ended in an estrangement.

"One day Brion had fetched from Peace's house one of the fittings which they had decided to use in their plan of operations, as he required it in order to satisfy a gentleman who was ready to advance £500 to carry out the experiment.

"While doing this Peace came into the house, and was very angry at what Brion had done, and on his going away said that he would settle the matter in a way that Brion did not dream of.

"Mrs. Thompson told Brion afterwards that, as he had put him out so, the wonder was that Peace had not shot him, and added that if Brion had come round to Peace's house, as he asked him to do, Peace told her that he would have shot him.

"The convict had also told her that he could get into Brion's house and despatch the whole of them.

"Brion saw nothing more of Peace until he received a letter from Newgate, which was couched in the following terms:—

"'From John Ward, 1 D for trial, H.M. Prison. Newgate, Nov. 2, 1878.

"My dear Sir.—Mr. Brion,—I do not know how to write to you or what to say to you, for my heart is near broken, for I am nearly mad to think that I have got into this fearful mess, all with giving myself up to drinking; but O, Mr. Brion, do you have pity on me, do not you despise me, as my hone famery has don, for I do not know ware they are, for they have broken up there home and gon I do not know where. So O, my dear Sir, I must beg of you to have mercy upon me and come to see me.

"O do not say nay, for I now that whe you do see me, and know what I am here for, you will weep for me; but I cannot tell you till I can see you, for I have something that I want you to do for me, that is for you to try and find out for me, for I do not know whare they are gon to.

"Give my love to Mrss. brion and to little fredey, but not disspse me now that I am in Prison, and for meary sakke write a letter back to me direct at once, to give hease to my trobel hart. I finish with my love to you all. I am yours recherd JOHN WARD. But do have mercy upon me and come to see me. You can see me heney week day from one till two o'clock, and inquire for John Ward for trial.'

"On November 2nd Brion went to Newgate and asked to see the writer of the letter. To his surprise he was shown his old acquaintance, Thompson.

"Peace said he was a wicked, dreadful man; that he had shot a policeman, but that he only did it as he was driven for money, and asked him (Brion) to come to the court and give him a character. The prisoner also asked him to call on a publican in Middlesex-street, Whitechapel, with whom he had had some dealings, and ask him to give him a character.

"This person, in reply to his request, said that a character would do Peace more harm than good.

"Other letters were received by Brion before the trial at the old Bailey.

"From John Ward, 1 D for trial, H.M. Prison, "Newgate, Nov. 4, 1878.

"'O my dear Friends, Mr. and Mrs. Brion,—I know that you are full of trouble for me been such a nod fool to give way to drink and bring myself into this most fearful alarer; but do forgive me for writing to you and have Pity upon me; and do all you can for me, a moust wretched and miserbel man, that is not fiet to live nor dei, for I am not fiet to meet my God, and I am not fiet to live now that I have disgraced myself, but O do have Pity upon me, and do all you can for me, and I will Pray to God to re Pay you for it agane.

"'Sir, if you have seen my Solictor, or seen Mr. Levy, or heard from or seen my wife, do be kind as to come and see me at once, for O, Sir, I have vely much thet I do want to see . . bring me the stamps and envelops. . . you for, and it will do me much beter than you writing to me, so do be so kind and see to-morrow, the 5th, if you can do and if you have seen my wife or friends tell them to come and see me at once, for I must see them.

"I do also want to see Mr. Levy very much, if you will write and tel him. Sir do not let Doctor Sargent nor heney oughter frinds know of my drisgrase, I conclude with my best love to you all, but come and see me.

"'Yours, "'JOHN WARD.

"'Dear Sir,—I think that the shesions will be on the 18th of Novem.

"'Henry Brion, 22, Philip-road, Peckham-rye, S.E., London.'

"The third letter was as follows:—

"'From John Ward, "for trial, H. M. Prison, Newgate.

"'My dear Sir,—Mr. Brion, will you be so kind as to send me the directions of Mr. Nash, direct at once for

I do want to suppine him to come on my trial to prove that I bougth my guitors of him, for the police have got them for to say that I stole them, but I bought them of him when I bought my ship of him. So do be so kind as to send me his directions this very day, and my dear sir you be so kind as to come and see me yourself on Monday, for I do want to see you Mr. Brion. —I am your an unhappy man, JOHN WARD.'"

It will be seen by these documents, that Peace was a very illiterate man, but it must be admitted, however, that, in conversing with him, he did not appear, from his conversation to be nearly so ignorant as he really was.

He had a very small amount of education, but he had natural gifts, and was, moreover, a hypocrite and deceiver of the most pronounced type.

Peace's arrest caused much consternation in the house in the Evalina-road.

On the morning that Mr. Thompson was missing, there was trouble at No. 4. Mrs. Thompson went to Mrs. Long in great distress. The infatuated woman seemed to be fond of the wretch she had taken up with, despite all his ill-usage.

She said, however, at this time that she did not care anything about him, "if she only knew where he was."

She took to advertising in the newspapers. These brought no response.

She found, on her return, that the old woman had gone away with the boy, and taken with her two boxes filled with valuables.

She instantly took precautions to secure the rest, which she stored away in her own name in a house at Peckham—all except the articles we have already described as having been left elsewhere.

She stayed with Mrs. Long, to whom she first told the story that her husband had gone off to America with another woman, and that she would never see him more.

Her stay extended over ten days, and then, chancing to get a hint somehow as to her husband's whereabouts, she left, telling Mrs. Long that she should write and send her address.

Mrs. Long never heard from her afterwards, but believed in her still, and trusted in the information she had given us she might not do "the poor woman any evil turn."

Two days after Peace disappeared, Mrs. Thompson went to Mrs. Cleaves, a greengrocer a few doors off, whose husband had identified some of the property, and asked her as a great favour to come into the house with her.

She said Mrs. Ward had gone as well as her husband, and there were several boxes, saying, "I am afraid to open them myself. I don't know what he may have been up to. I can't open them unless somebody will help me, because the old devil may have killed somebody, and have packed their bodies in these boxes."

Mrs. Cleaves did not relish the ghastly suggestion, and declined to have anything to do with Mrs. Thompson's boxes, which were ultimately obtained by the police, who had no scruples about searching the contents.

Mention was made at this time of a suspicious-looking crucible in the house in the Evalina-road. It was found, however, that Peace never made use of this. One of his "fences" had brought it to the house in the hope that arrangements might be made for reducing on the spot a large haul of goods to a concentrated shape.

But Mr. Peace preferred to dispose of his plunder in the rough, and did not care to set up a furnace, whose discovery would have been fatal.

He did once try melting silver in this crucible over an ordinary fire, but the attempt was a failure, and it was not renewed.

Peace was quite right when he observed that Mrs. Thompson required watching. But who was to undertake the task now that her lord and master was in durance vile?

Mrs. Peace became duly impressed with the fact "that the game was up" and she was not disposed to remain any longer in her old quarters at Peckham.

The consequence was, that Mrs. Thompson was left to fight her own battles in the best way she could. A description of this woman is given by a journalist, and it is a tolerably accurate one.

"I was privileged yesterday," says he, "to see Mrs. Thompson, the lady who has been so intimately identified with the convict Charles Peace. Mrs. Thompson is a woman of gaunt stature, wizened features, and altogether the very antithesis of the saucy Mrs. Dyson, for whom Peace seemed to have formed such a consuming passion.

"This preference for two women of such opposite appearance may be taken, I presume, as an instance of the happy impartiality of Mr. Peace in his loves. Possibly Mrs. Thompson may owe some of her present uncomeliness to her experience while under the protection of the burglar. That she has undergone much suffering I think certain, from the hard and leather-looking hue of her shrunken face.

"There is an abiding distrust lurking in her cold, restless eyes, which is confirmed by the twitching of her fingers as she speaks to you.

"There are moments when Mrs. Thompson thaws, as it were, when the curiously Mephistophelian mouth, the corners of which curl upwards instead of downwards, with a sharp precision of ominous intent, loses somewhat of its rigidity.

"That is when Mrs. Thompson is face to face with the whiskey bottle. It is then the lady becomes communicative.

"She croons over her connection with 'Charley,' referring to the criminal in terms of admiration and horror combined. It is quite erroneous to say, as some papers have done, that Mrs. Thompson was educated at a boarding school, and is a woman of culture.

"To use her own words 'No, sir, as I was I am. I have brothers and sisters—that is true. But myself, all I can say of myself is, that I disgraced them.' The woman seems to have money, but she appears to be oppressed by a dread that 'Charley' Peace will escape and cut her throat."

Mr. Brion was certainly hardly dealt by. In the first place he had been greatly deceived by the hero of this work, and in the end he had lost a considerable amount of time in rendering assistance to the Government in the prosecution of the Bannercross murderer, and had no adequate compensation for the same.

A writer for the press gives the following faithful account of his visit to Mr. Peace's "friend" at Peckham:—

"How Peace came to live at Peckham is a story which has not yet been told, and, I suspect, will not be known unless it is told by Peace himself or by another party whom I called upon yesterday, and who, I suspect, could say a great deal if he could be induced to say it.

"This gentleman, who occupies a good house in a

leading road, was a great friend of Peace's. The people say that he and Peace were 'always together.'

"Considering Peace's manner of life, that is more than I can receive as gospel; but it is certainly a fact that this gentleman was more in Peace's company than any other person in Peckham. My interview with him was not very encouraging.

"A sharp-witted Peckham boy, who acted as my guide in showing me the residences of the people whose names I had on a card to visit, pointed to the street in which the house was situated, and said, 'You will easily find it; it is the only house on that side where the lower windows are *frosted*, to prevent people looking in.'

"The boy added that the windows were frosted after this gentleman began to be seen a good deal in Peace's company. Sometimes he went and visited Peace at 5, East-terrace, and sometimes Peace came and visited him.

"With the exception of Mrs. S. Smith, who let the house to Peace, the latter kept himself very 'reserved' so far as his neighbours were concerned, and as the neighbours thought that the Thompsons—as they called themselves—were well-to-do people, considerably above their station—they did not like to intrude themselves upon the new comers' notice.

"The house of this gentleman is a better one than that occupied by Peace, and is in a more pretentious road. There is an apartment underneath the level of the roadway, with a large open window, and it was this window which was 'frosted.'

"I saw no other window on the road treated in that fashion. Of course it may have been done simply to prevent prying people from looking in, though none of the neighbours seem to have thought it necessary to take similar precautions.

"Three knocks with the knocker failed to elicit any answer, and I was leaving to try my luck elsewhere, when a comely-looking lady put her head out. Happening to look back at the time, I noticed her, and returned.

"She kept me standing at the door for some time, but eventually, on my telling her as much of my business as I thought it prudent to mention, she asked me in, adding, as she showed me into a parlour, 'I don't think he will tell you anything about that.'

"She closed the door, and left me to myself. The parlour, I had been told, was mainly furnished with articles from Peace's house.

"I sat down in one of the chairs belonging to the walnut suite which had adorned Peace's parlour, and here I may say that if the walnut suite is a fair sample of the 'luxurious furnishings" at 5, East-terrace, you must not suppose that there was anything very palatial about the place.

"In fact, the longer I inquire into this man's establishment the glory of it seemeth to fade away. The suite is a fairly good one, covered with rep, in green and gold stripes, considerably faded by wear—such a suite as the esteemed auctioneer over the way from your office would knock down any day for fifteen or sixteen guineas, and think he had done fairly well for the seller, and not badly for the buyer.

"In the room was also a harmonium, on which 'Mr. Thompson,' 'Mrs. Thompson,' and the boy 'Ward'—of whom more anon—used to play sacred and other music.

"It is a fair-looking instrument, worth perhaps a ten-pound note. There are other nick-nacks which had also been obtained from Peace's establishment.

"While I had been using my eyes in this way a conversation had been conducted in undertones in another room.

"The wife was evidently telling the husband who I was. Then the door opened and there came close up to me a little man, wearing spectacles, through which he peered at me, with his small keen eyes, rather curiously, and 'took me in' from head to foot.

"After he had finished his examination he retired to a chair in the corner. The wife stood by his side, and he pointed me to a seat near the window.

"'What's your name?' he asked me abruptly.

"'Had I not better tell you my business first?' I replied.

"'Your name, sir, your address, and your occupation?—*if* you please.'

"I told him my name.

"'Have you your card?'

"I handed him my card, which he carefully examined, then looked at me carefully as if to see if he could detect any discrepancy between the name on the card and the person who presented it.

"'Now, sir, what do you want?'

"I soon told him what I wanted.

"'You knew Peace very well, did you not?'

"'I knew Mr. Thompson; but before I say any more let me tell you that I have been before the authorities, and expressly cautioned not to say anything to anybody. They have heard my story, and if I am wanted they know where to find me.'

"'Oh, I didn't know you were going to be a witness?'

"'I did not say I was going to be a witness. The Greenwich police have asked me what I know, and I may tell you have warned me against saying any more. I must decline to give any information which may be used ——"

"Here the wife interrupted, 'You have said quite enough; don't say any more." '

"The husband drew up abruptly. I told him he had quite mistaken my mission.

"I had been informed that he was more in Mr. Thompson's house than anybody else, that he had frequently had Mr. Thompson at his house; that Mrs. Thompson and Mrs. Ward had also been there, and that I simply wanted to know what kind of people they were, and how they lived, and was not anxious to know anything about the Blackheath business.'

"'Before I say any more,' he answered, 'I must ask you to promise me as a particular favour that you will not mention my name in any way.'

"'Well,' I said, 'your name has been hinted at already. You have been spoken of as Mr. B——, and I expect the Peckham people know very well now who Mr. B—— is.'

"He did not seem pleased at this information, and was about to tell me something more, when his wife again put the drag on, and kept it on all the time I was in the room.

"'You were working with Mr. Thompson on a patent for raising sunken ships—were you not?'

"'I must decline to answer any questions about that.'

"'Well, but that is a matter about which there is nothing to be gained by reticence. In fact, I know you have got that model in your house now, and that it is enclosed in a box like a plate-chest. I should really, as a mere matter of curiosity, like to have a look at it.'

"It was no use. He entrenched himself behind his spectacles, the wife assisted him to hold the fort of his lips, and nothing further could I obtain from him.

PEACE AT HIS PRISON TOILET AFTER HIS LIFE SENTENCE.

"If it had not been for that excellent lady, I think 'Mr. B——' would have been induced to tell something which has not yet been made public, though he was evidently very anxious not to say anything which could in anyway connect him any further with the 'Thompsons.'

"As I was leaving I tried a parting shot.

"Mrs. Thompson when she left promised to write to you, stating where she could be found. You have had a letter, I am told. There is now no doubt that Mrs. Thompson is merely wanted as a witness. There can be no harm in saying if you have had that letter."

Mr. B—— was about to speak, but his good wife was before him, and with her 'don't say any more—you have said too much already '—a point which I politely disputed with her—'Mr. B——' shook his head, and I left the interesting couple.

"Someone has said that a woman can't keep a secret, and an old cynic offered a reward for the first female who could be found capable of holding her tongue.

"I want the address of the gentleman, for I can conscientiously claim the reward.

"I have found in the person of my friend, Mrs. B——, a lady who can not only hold her own tongue, but that of her husband also.

"I left that house with mingled respect for the excellent good wife, and disappointment that she did not happen, at the time I called, to be out taking a five o'clock tea with some estimable neighbours in the region of Evalina-road, or anywhere else except in her own house and by her husband's side.

"I am convinced that this gentleman and his wife could have told me a great deal as to Peace's life at home, and perhaps something about his life abroad, which he may have guessed at or picked up in his frequent interviews with his friends the Thompsons, of No. 5, East-terrace."

CHAPTER CXLVIII.

THE TRIAL OF CHARLES PEACE FOR BURGLARY.

THE days and nights passed slowly and sadly enough with Charles Peace during the brief interval between his committal and trial.

Take whatever view he would of the case he could not see any gleam of sunshine and hope for the future. It was not possible for any intelligent jury, after hearing the overwhelming evidence which would be brought forward for the prosecution, to return any other verdict than that of guilty upon the charge or charges preferred against the ill-fated man.

Peace, despite his sanguine temperament, was forcibly impressed with this fact. He whined and moaned and declared himself to be an ill-used man.

His relatives and friends had deserted him in the hour of extreme need—so he averred. It was the way of the world, he added, and there was therefore no reason to be surprised at a circumstance, which, to say the truth, was one of almost daily occurrence.

He confessed that he had been greatly to blame, that under the influence of drink and excitement he had committed a most unwarrantable act of violence, but was at the same time truly thankful that the life of the gallant police officer had not been sacrificed. This was one of the greatest consolations he had in the hour of trouble and suffering.

He affected to be so contrite, and assumed such a virtuous tone, that those about him were half disposed to believe he had been led into crime by a sudden impulse : nevertheless the facts were dead against him, and a heavy sentence would be sure to follow conviction.

As the sessions drew nigh Peace became additionally nervous and anxious. He wrote off to several of his friends.

So long as a man is in prison before trial and condemnation he has no work of any sort to do beyond the cleaning of his own cell and utensils.

Books are allowed him, and writing materials, as before observed. Whatever a man writes is inspected and read by the governor, and every sheet of paper is counted, and has to be accounted for.

This course is adopted so that prisoners may be prevented from writing letters to their friends outside without undergoing the inspection of the governor.

The rule is an arbitrary one, and it does not seem to be altogether just. They have no right to be placed under such rigid surveillance before they are proved guilty.

About 420,000 persons in the course of a year pass through the hands of the police in England and Wales. Of these, about 275,000 are convicted, some summarily, others after trial by jury, the former being seventeen times as numerous as the latter.

The great majority of these mean nothing but the slightest punishments, generally fines; but about 70,000 are sentenced to imprisonment. Of these, 6000 in round numbers are children under sixteen years of age, nearly 1000 of whom are committed to reformatories for most of the remainder the cellular prisons probably furnish sufficient correction.

Of the adults rather more than 2000 are sentenced to penal servitude.

Of the 420,000 persons apprehended by the police more than 80,000 are either known or suspected to be criminals by trade, and from 50,000 to 60,000 are known to be living in total idleness and vice.

This is, of course, a terrible state of things, but as yet no remedy has been found to repress crime in the metropolis or elsewhere.

Peace was a criminal of the most irreclaimable, daring, and desperate order, but this was not known to the authorities at—for a certainty—the time of his arrest, but it afterwards became sufficiently manifest.

At length the day arrived on which Peace was to be tried.

He was in close converse with his lawyer on the preceding day, and was informed that Mr. Montague Williams would conduct the defence.

The legal gentleman did not tell his client that the case was in every way a hopeless one, but bade him keep up his spirits and hope for the best.

Before the court was duly opened, barristers and solicitors were to be seen ascending the staircase, ducking mysteriously into ante-rooms, and it was evident enough that there was to be a sort of legal field day.

In the several robing-rooms counsel were dressing like other actors for their parts.

The judge was arraying himself in his robes of office, and everybody appeared to be engaged on some important business.

A court of justice is built everywhere much in the same fashion—a throne for the judge, benches right and left for the sheriff and municipal authorities, boxes on each side for the juries, separate pews for the warder and clerk of the court, convenient seats for the barristers. Then there is the witness-box, the dock, and benches piled tier over tier for the convenience of the spectators, and, as a matter of course, the ventilation is radically bad.

There is also a stone hall outside in which clients congregate till their turn comes on, and witness-rooms.

In addition to this, British witnesses seem to possess an inexhaustible supply of sandwiches in brown paper, and ardent spirits in old medicine bottles : upon these they feed incessantly, partly to kill time, and partly to fortify their moral courage, which they know will soon be tried in public as severely as the integrity of the prisoners.

Up and down a passage which leads to the jury-room and to the private entrances into the court, one may see the attorneys in their Sunday shabby-genteel, and in great bustle and importance, running backwards and forwards, now halting to confab with gentlemen who are relations of the prisoners, or are subpœnaed witnesses—now with the barristers who wear stereo-typed smiles upon their faces, as if law life was a pleasant dream.

The judge entered the court and the usual formulæ had to be gone through. The benches appointed for the use of barristers were tolerably well filled.

The first case to be tried was a charge of embezzle-ment. It did not occupy a great space of time, as it was as clear as the sun at noon-day—that is on days that luminary does condescend to shine.

Peace was anxiously waiting his turn with two other fellow-prisoners. To his ineffable disgust one of these was the lad "Cakey," as he was termed, who had so annoyed him in the exercise-yard. He was charged with picking pockets, in the practice of which he was an adept.

"Strike me lucky," said the audacious young ruffian. "I hopes as how they won't keep us waiting long—don't you?"

"Mind your own business," returned Peace.

"Vell, there aint no call to be humpy about the matter. I spoke civilly enough—didn't I?"

"You are too fast for my book," said Peace. "You're like a sheep's head—all jaw."

"Oh, carry me out and bury me dacent, but you're as good as a play, you are, and no flies," said the pick-pocket. "Blest if you couldn't make a fortin' as a mummer; but I say, old man, I 'xpect you'll get it rather 'ot. What made yer fire yer pop-gun at a 'bobby,' eh?"

"Mind your own business, and don't interfere with me."

"Vell, I'm sorry for yer, and I hopes as how——"

"Hold your tongue, you fool," interrupted our hero. "You'll have euough to do to prove your innocence, I'm thinking."

"Vell, now, we agree this once. I'm of the same 'pinion. They'll be down upon me as dead as a hammer. I'll lay yer half a bull that they give me two 'stretch.' I mek up my mind to that there, but you—vell, I don't know how it 'ill go vith you, old un; but yer had a pretty smart tussle with yer bobby—didn't you?"

"Let the gentleman be," said the other prisoner, who, like "Cakey," was hardly out of his teens. "Yer sees as how he don't like it. I'm ashamed on yer. This isn't a time for chaff—is it?"

"I don't know that it is, but it's better than sitting like a set of mutes—aint it? It's enough to give a fellow the hump to be sitting still a waitin' to be placed in the dock."

The conversation, if it could be so termed, was brought to a close by a man coming in and saying to the young pickpocket—

"Now then, this way."

Cakey was placed in the dock. The trial did not last half an hour. He was found guilty, and sentenced to eighteen months' imprisonment.

He considered the sentence a most lenient one, and left the court in better spirits than he had entered it. He found Peace in the passage when he was returning to the gaol.

"Vat do yer think, guv'nor? Only eighteen months. There's for you—I've lost my half bull."

Peace was too much wrapped up in his own thoughts to take any heed of the playful youth who was address-ing him.

His case was the next, and as he was placed in the dock he glanced furtively round the court.

The first face he recognised was that of Robinson, the policeman, then his glance fell upon several others that were familiar to him, but he did not see any of his Sheffield friends. "So much the better," mur-mured he.

Mr. Poland was engaged in earnest conversation with a police-inspector, while Mr. Douglas Straight was scanning some papers before him.

Peace was conscious that he was an object of interest, for he saw that the eyes of many persons were upon him.

He endeavoured to put on a look of humility and dejection, hoping thereby to excite sympathy.

He glanced at the jury to see if they looked merci-fully disposed or otherwise. One or two jurors struck him as being hard-featured men, who were bent upon doing their duty fearlessly.

It was on the morning of Tuesday the 19th of November, 1878, on which this trial took place. It was of course an eventful day in the history of our hero.

The case was tried at the Central Criminal Court, before Mr. Justice Hawkins, John Ward alias Charles Peace aged sixty (he was so put down, although he had not reached that age by three years) who was de-scribed as a sailor, was indicted for a burglary in the dwelling-house of James Alexander Burness, and steal-ing therefrom a quantity of plate, the property of the aforesaid James Alexander Burness.

He was charged also with feloniously shooting at Edward Robinson, a police constable, with intent to murder him.

Mr. Poland and Mr. Douglas Straight conducted the prosecution for the Treasury.

The prisoner was defended by Mr. Montagu Williams and Mr. Austin Metcalfe.

There was a dead silence when the case came on, and a number of persons from Greenwich, Blackheath, and elsewhere, who had been suffering from the depre-dations of burglars, were present at the trial; and, in addition to these, in an obscure corner sat, unobserved by Peace, Aveline's husband and Lady Marvlynn.

The indictment proceeded with was the charge of shooting at the constable.

Edward Robinson was then examined. He said: On the morning of the 10th of October I was on duty at Blackheath in the avenue leading from St. John's-park, the back of the residence of Mr. Burness. I noticed the flickering of a light in Mr. Burness's drawing-room, and this excited my suspicion, and I procured the assistance of another constable named Girling. The light continued to move about the house, and I was assisted by Girling on to the wall. At this time a sergeant named Brown came up, and he went to the front of the house and I heard the bell ring, when the light was extinguished immediately, and the prisoner jumped out of the drawing-room window to the lawn. When I saw him in the act of running away I followed him, and he turned round and pointed a revolver at my head, and said, "Keep back; keep off, or by —— I will shoot you." I said to him, "you had better not," and he immediately fired three chambers of a revolver at my head. Two shots passed over my head and the third by the side of my head. I made a rush at him and he fired a fourth shot, when I closed with him and struck him on the face with my left hand. The prisoner then said, "You ——, I will settle you this time!" and then fired a fifth shot, which wounded me in the right arm. I seized the prisoner then, and threw him down, when the prisoner exclaimed, "You ——, I will give you something else!" and tried to put his hand in his pocket. I struggled with him and got the revolver from him, and struck him several blows with it. I held him down till Sergeant Brown came up and he was then secured. The revolver was strapped round his wrist. I began to feel faint from loss of blood at this time, and handed the prisoner over to Sergeant Brown and Girling.

Charles Brown, a sergeant of police, proved that he heard the shots fired and the cries for assistance, and said that when he went to the spot he found Robinson lying above the prisoner with a six-chambered revolver in his hand, but it was strapped round the prisoner's arm. On the prisoner he found a silver flask, a banker's cheque-book, and a letter-case, which were afterwards identified by Mr. Burness, and a small crowbar.

William Girling, the other policeman, confirmed the testimony of the previous witnesses as to the five shots being fired, and he also said that he heard the prisoner say that he only did it to frighten him. On the prisoner he found an auger, a jemmy, a gimlet, and other house-breaking implements. The prisoner attempted to get away after he had apprehended him, but he hit him with his staff.

Mr. Bonny, an inspector of the R Division, proved that he examined Mr. Burness's house and found that several places had been broken open with a jemmy.

The prisoner refused to give his name and address, and when he was asked for them, he replied, "Find out."

Sarah Selina Cooper, servant to Mr. Burness, proved that she found a bullet in the drawing-room on the morning after the occurrence.

Mr. Montagu Williams, on behalf of the prisoner, entreated the jury, in the first place, not to allow any prejudice that might have been created in their minds by what they had read about the number of burglaries that had been committed in this neighbourhood to operate against the prisoner, but to be guided solely by the evidence relating to the particular charge. He said that his case was that the prisoner did not intend to murder the constable, but that all he desired was to get away; and he argued that the facts were of a character that tended to support this view of the case.

The jury, after a very short deliberation, found the prisoner guilty upon the first count of the indictment, which charged him with discharging the revolver at the constable with intent to murder him. The jury, at the same time, desired to express their admiration of the courageous conduct of the constable, and expressed a hope that he would receive some reward for the way n which he had acted. The foreman of the jury handed in a written paper to that effect.

Mr. Justice Hawkins: I am not surprised, gentlemen, that you should have made this representation, for the constable has certainly behaved in a very gallant manner.

Mr. Poland said that probably his lordship would like to hear something of the previous history of the prisoner.

Mr. Justice Hawkins said he should be glad to receive any information that could be given to him respecting the prisoner.

Inspector Bonny then stated that at the prisoner's house at Sheffield there was found a large quantity of property, and in twenty-six cases property had been identified by the owners as the produce of different burglaries. The necessary legal proofs were not present in court, but they could be produced on the following morning.

Mr. Justice Hawkins said he did not think it was necessary to postpone passing judgment, as he thought the court was already in possession of sufficient information to leave no doubt as to what course should be taken.

Mr. Read, the deputy clerk of arraigns, then put the usual formal question to the prisoner whether he had anything to say why judgment should not be pronounced upon him.

The prisoner, in reply, said: Yes; I have this to say, my lord, I have not been fairly dealt with: and I declare before God that I never had the intention to kill the prosecutor, and all I meant to do was to frighten him, in order that I might get away. If I had had the intention to kill him I could easily have done it, but I never had that intention. I declare I did not fire five shots—I only fired four, and I think I can show you, my lord, now. I can prove that only four shots were fired. If your lordship will look at the pistol, you will see that it goes off very easily, and the sixth barrel went off of its own accord after I was taken into custody. At the time the fifth shot was fired the constable had hold of my arm, and the pistol went off quite by accident. The prisoner then exclaimed with great earnestness, " I really did not know that the pistol was loaded, and I hope, my lord, that you will have mercy on me. I feel that I have disgraced myself. I am not fit either to live or die. I am not prepared to meet my God, but still I feel that my career has been made to appear much worse than it really is. Oh, my lord, do have mercy on me; do give me one chance of repenting and of preparing myself to meet my God. Do, my lord, have mercy on me ; and I assure you that you shall never repent it. As you hope for mercy yourself at the hands of the great God, do have mercy on me, and give me a chance of redeeming my character and preparing myself to meet my God. I pray and beseech you to have mercy on me."

The prisoner delivered this speech in a calm and earnest tone of voice, and at the conclusion he appeared to be quite overcome by his feelings.

Mr. Justice Hawkins then, addressing the prisoner, said: John Ward, the jury have found you "Guilty," upon the most irresistible evidence, of having fired this pistol five times at the constable with intent to murder him, and I must say that I entirely concur in that verdict, and I do not believe that any other would, upon consideration, have been satisfactory to themselves. You were detected in the act of committing a burglary in the house of a gentleman, and, putting altogether aside what may have been your conduct on other occasions, the circumstances of this particular case are quite sufficient to prove to my mind that you are an accomplished burglar, and that you went to this house determined to rob by fair means if you could, but armed in such a manner that you were also determined to resort to foul means if necessary to escape detection. You have asserted that you only fired the pistol at the constable in order to frighten him, that thus you might be enabled to make your escape. I do not believe you. The shot was fired at his head, and but that he was guarding his head at the time with his arm he would have received the shot upon it, and if that had been the case death would probably have been the result, and you would at this moment probably be receiving a sentence of death. I do not consider it at all necessary to make any inquiry into your antecedents; the facts before me are quite sufficient to show that you are an accomplished burglar, and a man who would not hesitate to commit murder in carrying out that object. Notwithstanding your age, therefore, I feel that I should fail in my duty to the public if I did not pass upon you the extreme sentence of the law for the offence of which you have been convicted, which is that you be kept in penal servitude for the rest of your natural life.

The prisoner appeared to be panic-stricken at the sentence. He uttered a series of moans, and fell into the arms of the warders in attendance, in a state of perfect prostration.

Whether his emotion was real or not it is not easy to say, but certainly on this occasion Peace completely broke down.

He had not for a moment contemplated having so severe a sentence passed on him, and he afterwards said it was a shame, and a most cruel merciless punishment.

At this moment all his bravado forsook him, and his despair and anguish were pitiful to behold.

Radically bad as the man was there were a few persons among the spectators who pitied him and thought him hardly dealt by.

This is invariably the case. No matter how great the criminal, or how many heinous offences he may have been guilty of, misplaced sympathy is sure to follow his sentence.

Lady Marvlynn and Sir J. Battershall were greatly moved when the sentence was passed upon the prisoner.

Her ladyship, from her own personal experience, knew the brutal nature of the man. Nevertheless, she was much affected at the issue of the proceedings.

"Miserable wretch!" she ejaculated. "I should have thought six, or ten years at the most, would have sufficed in a case of this sort, but of course Mr. Justice Hawkins is, I suppose, the best judge."

"I don't think it would be possible to find a better," returned her companion. "I confess I cannot myself see any palliation, any reasonable excuse, for the crime of which he has been found guilty upon the clearest evidence."

"No, I suppose there is none," returned Lady Marvlynn; "but still penal servitude for life! Why it is almost worse than death."

"If Robinson had succumbed to his injuries there would have been but one course left—his murderer would have to suffer the extreme penalty of the law. You do not duly consider the matter, my lady."

"I hope I do. But the Lady Aveline, this will be sad news for her."

"Sad!" exclaimed the baronet. "I do not see how that can be."

"Ah, I know she will be sorry to hear of his untimely fate."

"Really, Lady Marvlynn, you surprise me. I have yet to learn that my wife has any sympathy for ruffians of this type."

"I don't say she has sympathy, but she possesses the inestimable quality of mercy—which blesses him that gives, and him that takes—and she has a feeling heart. That you know."

"Oh, most certainly, No man knows it better. Still I cannot for the life of me understand why you and Aveline are so wrapped up in this man."

"You will not be surprised when you know all."

The baronet made no further remark, but seemed lost in a reverie.

Peace, who was completely overcome, had to be carried out of court.

Mr. Justice Hawkins then directed the prosecutor, Robinson, to stand forward, and, addressing him, said: The jury have expressed their admiration at the bravery you have displayed in this matter, and have also expressed a wish that you shohld receive some reward. In the first place, I hand to you the paper on which

the jury have expressed their opinion of your conduct, in order that you may keep it and refer to it in after life, and that it may be an incentive to future good conduct. I quite concur in the opinion of the jury with regard to the manner in which you have acted on this occasion, and I think the country ought to be proud of you and of the force to which you belong, and I have great pleasure in ordering you a reward of £25 for your gallant conduct.

The prosecutor thanked his lordship, and the proceedings then terminated.

When Peace returned to Newgate after his sentence he immediately came under another class, and his real imprisonment began.

He moaned and groaned as if in deep pain, and there is but little doubt as to his sufferings at this time.

He was conducted downstairs to the same floor as the baths; he made no observation, but was evidently in a state of prostration, but he did manage with assistance to reach that part of the City prison where another painful ceremony had to be gone through.

The garments he had on he was no longer permitted to wear,

They had to be exchanged for those of a convict. Never again was he destined to wear the clothes of a free man.

He had been previously told that whatever clothes he wore would be forfeited.

They were not of much value, it is true, for, at the time of his capture, he was encased in his shabby long-tailed coat, as represented in the illustration on the front page of the preceding number.

This valuable garment, together with his low-crowned hat and other articles that completed his suit, were forfeited to the Crown—doubtlessly have been preserved as relics of the most daring burglar of modern times.

He heaved a profound sigh, which seemed to come from the bottom of his heart, when he was arrayed in the convict garb, with which, however, he was but too familiar.

After he had shuffled into his new attire, he was told to select from a bundle of dirty, greasy-looking things what was supposed to be a woollen cap of the Scotch-bound type; he chose one which appeared to fit him the best, and then the painful ceremony was over.

"I've been cruelly used," he ejaculated. "The sentence was a most unjust one. I never intended to hurt the bobby. I'll take my solemn oath that nothing was further from my thoughts. But my friends will not see me thus wronged without making an effort on my behalf. They will send a petition to the Home Office."

"Well that can be done, of course," observed one of the warders, who felt some commiseration for the wretched man.

"It must be done."

"Time enough for that."

"Penal servitude for life. It's scandalous."

The warders were not disposed to continue the conversation; so they marched their prisoner off to his cell.

Peace found he had to mount higher in the world, to the top landing, and he was located on the north side of the wall, he hitherto having been on the south.

The first thing that struck him on entering his new abode was the smell of tar—good, wholesome, honest tar. He had been described in the indictment as a sailor. Why or wherefore was not clearly made manifest.

It is true that he had been on board ship once or

twice during his chequered career, but he could not lay claim to being much of a sailor, but he soon found out that his long days of comparative idleness had come to an end.

The smell of the tar gave him a gentle hint of the agreeable process of oakum-picking, this being one of the occupations prison authorities had invented for the amusement of the prisoners under their charge.

The cell was an exact counterpart of the one he had left, except that the dust from the oakum had taken off a good deal of the brilliant cleanliness of the floor and walls.

He was most miserable, and found it impossible to regard his new sphere of occupation with complacency. He had passed through a terrible ordeal, had hoped against hope, but now the terrible reality came upon him with redoubled force.

His worst fears became an actual reality: he was a convict, and would remain so to the end of his life. He slept but little during the night—when he thought of his sentence he shuddered. He tossed restlessly in his hammock, groaned and gnashed his teeth.

"A life!" he ejaculated. "It's too bad—a burning shame."

Then he thought of getting his friends to send in a memorial to the Home Office, praying for a commutation of the severe sentence passed upon him.

He clung to this hope even as a drowning man is said to cling to a straw.

The next morning, while he was cleaning his cell, three pieces of junk or old rope that had been part of the standing rigging of some old ship were flung into his cell, with an intimation that he would have a "fiddle" presently.

"Umph!" he ejaculated, "here's some of their cursed stuff. I know what that means—aching fingers and endless toil."

He was perfectly correct in this conjecture.

After some little time a warder he had never seen before, except at a distance, entered his narrow prison-house, and told him that he would have to pick four pounds of oakum every day while he was in Newgate, or else his allowance of food would run short.

"Oh, I dare say," replied Peace. "Then I shall have to go on short commons, 'cause you see I shan't be able to do the quantity you require."

"That's no business of mine," returned the warder; "I don't make the rules. All I have to do is to see that they are carried out."

"Much obliged to you for your information," exclaimed the prisoner; "I've been cruelly used."

"I've nothing to do with that," said the warder, slamming the door of the cell.

"A set of merciless wretches," ejaculated Peace. "I know the ways of them but too well."

He sat down on his stool, and buried his face in his hands.

After he had devoured his breakfast the taskmaster-warder paid him a visit, bringing with him the "fiddle," on which he was to play a tune called "Four pounds of oakum a day."

It consisted of nothing but a rope and a long crooked nail. He showed Peace how to break up the block of junk, and to divide the strands of the rope.

There was, however, but little necessity for the warder to enter into a description of the work, since the prisoner he was instructing knew the odious business pretty well from his previous experience in the ways of prison life.

However, he affected to be a novice, and listened to all the warder had to say, apparently paying the greatest attention to his instructions.

The four pounds did not look so much after all, but when pulled to pieces and divided into strands, it seemed to grow wonderfully in size, and Peace knew the amount of labour required to pick it.

He made a wry face and groaned, but did not complain.

When the strands were all divided his instructor showed him how to pull them to pieces.

Peace set to work, being perfectly well assured that the task must be got through. He soon found out—as others had done before him—that oakum-picking made his fingers and thumbs sore and painful; nevertheless he persevered—the task seemed to be an interminable one.

When he saw how little progress he had made in the first hour his heart seemed to sink, and he remembered the many miserable and lonely hours he had passed in convict prisons.

He was on the side of the gaol nearest to Newgate-street. His cell was on the top floor and the window was open, so that he now heard much plainer the noise of the street traffic, which spoke to him of the outside world.

There was something consolatory in even hearing the sounds of the passing vehicles as they rumbled along in one of the great thoroughfares of the busy city.

At chapel next morning he with others, who had been tried at the same sessions, were marched into a cage under the women's gallery, and locked in. Once a day only were they exercised out of doors, and this took place in a much smaller yard than he had walked in before his conviction.

This was a matter of no very great importance; one yard was as good as another to him.

He bore up as best he could, hoping that sooner or later he might succeed in getting a commutation of his sentence. This hope, however, was never destined to be realised.

Every morning the quantum of "junk" was served out, and in the evening the taskmaster came round with weights and scales to take each man's oakum.

There was no cheating in respect to the requisite quantity of oakum on these occasions.

The prisoner who had picked his full allowance was permitted to have the remainder of his time to himself for the rest of the day; but it was sharp work for the best of them to get through the four pounds of oakum.

Many now found it impossible to get through that quantity. Some could not do as much as two pounds, although they worked from morning till nine o'clock at night.

The old "lags," who were well used to the work, were, in most cases, able to do their quantum.

About three or four days after his sentence, a warder entered Peace's cell with another prisoner, to crop and shave him.

Peace knew this ceremony had to be gone through, and was, therefore, in no way surprised at the appearance of his new visitors.

He begged to be allowed to shave himself, but this request was refused; so he sat himself down, and submitted himself to the operator, who was a regular bungler.

He, however, managed to effect a clean scrape, after which Peace's hair was clipped to about half an inch long. He had not much hair on his head at this time, but what there was had to be reduced to the regular length.

The person who performed the operation was very loquacious; most members of the hair-dressing fraternity usually are so, and Peace's barber was confidential and communicative. He affected to commiserate with our hero, and deprecated in the strongest terms the severity of the sentence passed upon him.

He also told Peace that he (the barber) had done a "lagging" before, and that he was doing a six years' "stretch" at the present time.

This playful conversation was not interrupted by the warder in attendance, who looked on as the operation was performed, and occasionally indulged in a smile as some pertinent remark fell from the lips of the perruquier.

After the shaving and cropping the barber wished Peace good-bye, bade him keep his spirits up, and hope for the best.

What that best was he did not say, but he tripped merrily out of the cell, with a nod to its occupant, and once more our hero found himself alone.

CHAPTER CXLIX.
THE TROUBLES OF MRS. PEACE.

AFTER Peace's arrest, trial, and conviction, the house in the Evalina-road was no longer a home for his miserable partner.

Mrs. Peace and the woman Thompson could not agree, and this, in addition to other circumstances, caused Mrs. Peace to make a precipitate retreat from the neighbourhood of Peckham, and Mrs. Thompson was left to pursue her own erratic course.

There was no help for this. It was not at all likely that the two women would agree in the absence of their master.

Mrs. Peace left Peckham, and at once proceeded to Hull, and from thence to Sheffield. But the police were actively engaged in ferreting out every scrap of information which might lead to the detection of other crimes committed by our hero.

As a natural consequence his miserable partner was suspected, and after some searching inquiries she was arrested and taken before the sitting magistrates at Sheffield, as will be seen from the following report :—

At the Sheffield Town Hall, yesterday, before the Mayor (Ald. Mappin) and W. E. Laycock, Esq., Hannah Peace, a respectably-dressed woman, 58 years of age, of No. 4, Hazel-road, Darnall, the wife of Charles Peace, picture-frame dealer, who murdered Mr. Arthur Dyson, engineer, at Banner Cross-terrace, on the 29th November, 1876, was brought up under circumstances which are at present exciting unusual interest.

The charge against her was that of being an accomplice in the recent Blackheath burglaries, on the ground that certain articles of property found at the house where she is living had been identified as part of the booty obtained at Blackheath.

Prisoner seems a fairly respectable, well-dressed woman, and appeared to feel her position acutely, looking very nervous and uneasy, and occasionally sobbing. She was accommodated with a seat in the dock.

The property includes several parcels of jewellery, a silk dress, two watches, and a patent clock. Mrs. Peace was charged with stealing the property, or of having received it knowing it to have been stolen. A number of persons crowded into the court during the few minutes the case was being heard.

The Chief Constable said: The prisoner has been apprehended on suspicion of having stolen property or with having received it knowing it to have been stolen. I shall put a witness in the box, and after his examination I shall have to ask for a remand for a week.

Henry Phillips said : I am Inspector of the Metropolitan police, attached to the Criminal Investigation Department, and stationed at Greenwich. There have recently been a considerable number of burglaries committed in the neighbourhood of Greenwich and Blackheath. At one of the houses that was burglariously broken into information was given as to a silk dress though I cannot swear to the colour. A little mantelpiece clock was stolen bearing the inscription "Waterbury Clock Company. Patented Sept. 11, 1877," and the stolen clock in every respect corresponds, I believe, with this clock. Some other houses were broken into, and property, corresponding with some of that now produced, was stolen. I believe if a remand is granted I shall be able to get further evidence.

Mr. Robinson (to prisoner) : Do you wish to ask any questions now?

Prisoner (sobbing) : I have not received them knowing them to have been stolen; no, I have not.

Inspector Twibell said : I went with the last witness to the house of the prisoner, who is living at Attercliffe, yesterday. I found in her house and in her possession the property now produced.

The Bench : All of it?

The Chief Constable : Yes, and a great deal more.

Mr. Robinson again asked the prisoner if she had any questions to ask.

Prisoner : I do say that I did not know they had been stolen.

The Chief Constable (to the Bench) : I have now to ask that the prisoner may be remanded for a week.

The prisoner was accordingly remanded for a week.

Early in the afternoon Inspector Phillips, taking with him the stolen property, returned to London.

From inquiries made by our reporter it has been ascertained that Hannah Peace has resided for a considerable period at Hull.

About a month ago, however, she came to Darnall, to be present at the confinement of her daughter, who resides with her husband at 4, Hazel-road, Britannia-road.

Although the house is stated to be in the road, it is really in a court some distance from the thoroughfare —the middle one of a row of seven.

Mrs. Peace brought with her to Sheffield a large box, which she stated contained her wearing apparel and a few "odds and ends."

She gave it out that she had been obliged to break her Hull home up on account of the persistent attentions of the police, who "dogged" her in every direction, and made her life a burden.

The "odds and ends" she brought with her are likely to get her into serious trouble unless she can explain how they included goods which originally belonged to persons in the neighbourhood of Blackheath.

During the time Mrs. Peace has been resident at her daughter's house she has not, as many persons supposed, kept within doors so as to avoid being noticed. On the contrary, she has moved about and freely conversed with her neighbours, who were greatly surprised when the police apprehended her.

The opinion of the neighbours is generally favourable to Mrs. Peace. People are loth to believe that she was the person to connive at the crime with which she is at present charged. They all bear testimony to her good character so far as they could tell.

The daughter and her husband appear respectable people, and have resided at their present address for several years.

After further examination at Sheffield, Mrs. Peace was ultimately sent to London, and on Saturday, Dec. 7th, 1878, she appeared at Bow-street, before Mr. Flowers.

The following is a report of her first examination in London :—

Hannah Peace, wife of Charles Peace, the Black-heath burglar, now undergoing penal servitude for the attempt on the life of a police-constable while in the execution of his duty, was brought up on remand granted by the justices of Sheffield, charged with stealing or otherwise receiving a clock the property of Mrs. Dadson, of 5, Kidbrook-terrace, Blackheath, part of the proceeds of a burglary committed on the 2nd of August. The clock produced in court, was found by the inspector at Darnall, near Sheffield.

Henry Phillips, inspector of the R Division of the Greenwich police, having been duly sworn, said the prisoner, Hannah Peace, had been remanded by the justices at Sheffield several times for her supposed connection with the burglaries committed in Blackheath by her husband, and was, on Friday, finally remanded to London. A small mantel-piece clock had been stolen on the 2nd of August last, from the house of Mrs. Dadson, of 5, Kidbrook-terrace, Blackheath, and corresponded in all respects with one found at prisoner's house, on the 7th November at Darnall, near Sheffield, when he searched it in company with Inspector Twibell. The depositions produced were taken at Sheffield.

Miss Elizabeth Marian Collison Dadson, daughter of Mrs. Mary Campbell Dadson, widow, of No. 5, Kidbrook-terrace, Blackheath, deposed that the clock produced was her mother's property, and was first missed on the morning of the 3rd of August. The house had been forcibly entered on the night previous—August 2nd.

Mr. Flowers : I shall remand the case till this day week. Prisoner, have you anything to say ?

Mrs. Peace, who had been accommodated with a seat during the two or three minutes she was in court, then rose, and in a trembling voice, said : I did not steal the clock, nor did I know that it was stolen. I have no question to ask.

She was then removed from the dock.

There can be but little doubt as to her being a woman "more sinned against than sinning," but the fact of her being the wife of Charles Peace brought her under the ban of the law, and for a long time she was in the depths of trouble, not very well knowing the nature of the charges that were to be brought against her.

It is hardly possible to estimate the anxiety and sufferings the guilty acts of a man like Peace entail upon innocent persons.

When we say innocent persons, we include his unhappy wife, for, despite the array of evidence brought against her, the police failed to prove her complicity in the crimes committed by her husband.

It will be seen by the following report of her second examination that the learned gentleman engaged for the prosecution strove to prove that the ill-fated Mrs. Peace had been guilty of acts which were in themselves most suspicious, if not absolutely criminating.

BLACKHEATH BURGLARIES.—THE EXAMINATION OF
MRS. PEACE.

At the Bow-street Police-court, London, on Saturday, before Mr. Vaughan, Hannah Peace, aged fifty-eight, believed to be the wife of the celebrated Charles Peace, burglar and alleged murderer, was brought up in custody on remand, charged with stealing and receiving a clock and a quantity of other articles, which it is alleged are the proceeds of numerous burglaries committed by her supposed husband.

Mr. Poland, barrister, instructed by Mr. Pollard, the solicitor to the Treasury, appeared for the prosecution. Mr. Walter Beard (Messrs. Beard and Son, solicitors, Basinghall-street, E.C.) was instructed for the defence.

Mr. Poland, in proceeding to open the case on behalf of the prosecution, said in this case the prisoner is charged before you in the name of Hannah Peace with stealing and receiving a quantity of property, the proceeds of a number of burglaries which have been committed in various parts of London. It appears that a man, who was tried at the last sessions at the Central Criminal Court by the name of John Ward, alias Charles Peace, was sentenced to penal servitude for life for shooting at a constable, with intent to murder him, on the 10th of October last ; and he was then in the act of committing a burglary at Blackheath. Now, sir, there is no question whatever that we are in a condition to show that that man undoubtedly was a professional burglar; that he was in the habit of going about to different parts of London, particularly Blackheath, committing burglaries, and taking from houses where these offences were committed valuable property, and disposing of it for his own advantage. The police, of course, endeavoured to find out what had become of the property, and where this man had been living, and they somehow discovered that he had been living at No. 5, East-terrace, Evalina-road, Nunhead, which is in the parish of Peckham, since May, 1878, in the name of John Thompson, and with a woman—a woman, I think, of about thirty years of age—who lived with him as Mrs. Thompson. In the same house the prisoner also lived, and she was then passing, I believe, by the name of Mrs. Ward ; and there was also a young man living there who was called Willie Ward, and he was stated to be the son of the prisoner, or, as she was called, Mrs. Ward. This man (Peace) having been arrested on the 10th October, of course he did not go home that night or the following morning. The persons living in that house must have known that he had been arrested, and the prisoner appears on that day to have removed three boxes, with the assistance of a railway porter, to the Nunhead station, and then to the King's-cross station, and these boxes were taken down to Nottingham. At Nottingham she went, I believe, to a house occupied by some relations of the woman who was passing as the wife of this man, but they, I think, declined to allow these boxes to be brought there, and we find that on the following day, the 12th October, the prisoner went with some portion of the property to No. 4, Hazel-road, Darnall, which is three miles from Sheffield. At that place her son-in-law and daughter lived, a man of the name of John Bolsover, who is a working collier. On Nov. 6th the police went to Bolsover's house at Darnall, and searched the place, and there found a quantity of property, which I shall be able to show you was the proceeds of some of these burglaries. On the 14th of November they made a further search, and found other property. The prisoner, when she was taken into custody, stated that she had received various things, but she did not know that they were stolen. She admitted that she had removed the things, and she stated also that she was the wife of the man who had been living at No. 5, East-terrace, Evalina-

THE WARDER SHOWING PEACE HOW TO PICK OAKUM.

road. When she stated that she was his wife, she was at once asked where she was married, but up to the present time she had not stated where the ceremony was performed.

The prisoner: Yes, sir, I have.

Mr. Poland: According to my instructions she has not stated to the police where she was married. She has given no date; she has produced no certificate. I think she stated that the certificate has been burned. So far as I am at present in a condition to deal with the case from the inquiries made by the police, they cannot ascertain that she is married. What I propose to do, with your sanction, is to prove the arrest and search of the premises, the taking of the house at

Peckham, the removal of the boxes, and the identity of some of the property. Then I shall be able to show you on a future occasion by calling other witnesses that there were found at the cottage to which these boxes were removed near Sheffield, the proceeds of some ten or twelve burglaries.

Inspector Phillips then said, in answer to questions proposed by Mr. Poland : I am one of the inspectors of the Metropolitan police force. On the 10th October, a man was captured at Blackheath, in the act of committing a burglary. Ultimately he gave the name of John Ward, and he was committed for trial as John Ward for shooting at a policeman and for burglary at a house in St. John's Park, Blackheath. On Nov. 5th I went down to Sheffield, and on the 6th I went to Darnall, to the house No. 4, Hazel-road. That is about three miles from Sheffield. John Bolsover, a labourer and working collier, lives there. His wife was there on the occasion when I called, and also the prisoner.

Mr. Poland : Was it stated that Mrs. Bolsover was the daughter of the prisoner?

The witness : Yes.

What name was the prisoner living there in ?

Mrs. Ward, I think. She was generally known there, I believe, as Mrs. Peace ; but I am not quite clear upon the matter.

Was there anybody else in the house ?

There was a boy, who was called Willie. He is about twenty years of age.

Did you understand that he was the son of the prisoner ?

Yes. He addressed her as " mother."

You saw the prisoner, and what did you say to her ?

I had some conversation with her first without telling her who I was. I looked round the room and saw a clock standing upon the chest of drawers, which I knew from the description. I told her I knew the clock to have been stolen from Blackheath. The prisoner replied, " I did not know it was stolen. A tall woman gave it to me five weeks ago." I then proceeded upstairs, and said I would make further search.

Before that time had you said anything to her as to who she was ?

I said, " Do you know where your husband is. Has he been here ?" She replied, " No." Then I said, " I will tell you where he is. He is in Newgate Prison, on a charge of burglary and shooting at a constable." She said, " Oh dear ! What trouble that man has brought me into, to be sure ! He seems to be my ruin everywhere I go." I then searched the top room in company with another officer, and found a large quantity of property.

What did you do in reference to this property ?

I took it into my possession. After I had got the prisoner to leave the house I told her she would be charged with stealing this property, and receiving it knowing it to have been feloniously procured.

Mr. Poland : Did she say anything in your presence as to whether she was Peace's wife ?

Witness : I have a slight recollection of asking her for her marriage certificate, and of her saying that she was married at St. George's Church, Sheffield. I said, " Have you got a marriage certificate to show me ?" She said, " No I have not ; the old man burned it."

Mr. Samuel Smith, builder, said : I live at 68, Rhyde Villas, St. Mary's-road, Peckham. About the latter end of May I was at East-terrace, Evelina-road, Peckham. About the latter end of May I was at East-terrace, Evelina-road, Peckham. I remember a party of four persons calling there. The prisoner was one of them. I knew her as Mrs. Ward. She gave that name. Two of the other persons were known as Mr. and Mrs. Thompson, and the other one of the party was a young man they called Willie. The man known as Mr. Thompson spoke to me, and asked to look over the house, but it was too late in the evening for that. He asked me the rent, which I told him was £30 a year ; and subsequently I let the premises to him. The woman I knew as Mrs. Thompson was a younger woman than the prisoner ; a little over thirty I should think.

I believe you asked Mr. Thompson on that occasion for some reference ?

I did, and he then asked me to go and see where he was living in Greenwich, which I did.

Where was he living at Greenwich ? Do you recollect ?

I do not recollect the name of the street. The house at Greenwich was a respectable house, and I saw prisoner there. The place was respectably furnished, and that satisfied me. I went to the house many times afterwards, and I know from having visited at the place that the man and woman known as Mr. and Mrs. Thompson, and the woman known as Mrs. Ward, and the boy Willie, were living there. Rent was paid me up to Michaelmas. I have got possession of the house now. I heard some time after Thompson had disappeared that a man, who was believed to be him, had been taken into custody.

Thomas Pickering, a porter employed at the Nunhead station on the London, Chatham, and Dover Railway, said : On the 11th October, in consequence of a message I received from another porter, I went to No. 5, East-terrace, Evelina-road, which is about three minutes' walk from the Nunhead station. When I got to the house I saw an old lady. I could not swear that the prisoner was the lady. It would be a person of about the same age. She asked me to take three boxes to the Nunhead station and label them for King's Cross. I went into the house, got the boxes and put them on my barrow. The old lady told me to send the boxes by the five minutes to six train and she would be there. I took them to the station and labelled them for the Great Northern Railway terminus at King's Cross. I did not notice any name or address upon the boxes. After I had taken them to the station the old lady came. She went away by the five minutes to six train that evening.

Examination continued : I have seen a box at the Bow-street Police-station. It resembles the box I brought from the house in the Evelina-road, to the Nunhead station. The other two boxes were similar. I did not know the old lady before, and have not seen her since until to-day.

Selina Karcher said : I am housekeeper and lady's maid to Mrs. Wood, Sunnyside, Leigham Court-road, Streatham. I was so engaged on the 20th August. When I went to bed on that date the house was all safe, but next morning, when I came down, I found that the house had been broken into. From the house I missed a number of things, including a plate basket, a silk dress trimmed with velvet, belonging to my mistress, Mrs. Kathleen, the wife of Mr. Mark Wood. The value of the silver missed was about £30, and the silk and velvet dress, which was a very valuable one, was also worth £30.

Elizabeth Mary Ann Collinson Dadson was next called, and reiterated her statement in reference to the clock taken from Kidbrook-terrace, Blackheath.

Louisa Newman said : I live at Richmond Lodge, Honor Oak-road, Forest Hill, and I am cook in the service of Mr. Charles Perry. On the 5th of August the place was secured for the night, with the exception of the back drawing-room window, which was accidentally left unfastened. Next morning I went into the back drawing-room at about half-past eleven, and found that there were missing several ornaments, amongst other things a tortoise-shell casket and a red cornelian casket. These articles were produced by Inspector Phillips, and are the property of my master. A silver inkstand, a silver goblet, and a flask were also taken, and I believe that the total value of the things abstracted was between £30 and £40.

The prisoner was remanded.

Hannah Peace was brought before Mr. Vaughan, at Bow-street, London, on Wednesday, for the purpose of being formally remanded.

It is definitely understood that Charles Peace will remain in Newgate until the authorities are prepared to proceed with the charge against him of the murder of Mr. Dyson at Banner Cross.

The investigation of the police have revealed the fact of his participation in no fewer than forty-five burglaries, for the most part committed in London, but extending over an area which includes Hull, Manchester, Sheffield, Market Harborough, and Southsea.

It would appear, however, that on the next examination the magistrate thought there was sufficient evidence to send the case for trial.

COMMITTAL OF MRS. PEACE.

At the Bow-street Police-court, on Wednesday, December 18th, 1878, before Mr. Vaughan, the woman who alleges that she is Hannah Peace, the wife of Charles Peace, the burglar, was brought up on remand charged with feloniously stealing and receiving a number of articles purloined by her alleged husband in the commission of burglaries in the neighbourhood of London, and in various parts of the country.

Mr. Poland said that since the adjournment every effort had been made to ascertain whether the prisoner was or was not married. All the evidence went to show that the prisoner was not the wife of Peace. She was living with him as Mrs. Ward, the boy Willie was living there as his nephew; and Mrs. Thompson lived there as his wife, though she was not his wife, and there was evidence that Mr. Thompson used to speak of Mrs. Thompson as his wife.

Emma, wife of William Gardner Shapley, said I live at Seymour Lodge, Peckham Rye. On Monday, the 23rd September, at eleven o'clock in the evening, I discovered that my house had been entered and a quantity of property taken away. A side door had been left open. I missed wearing apparel of the value of £25. I identify some pocket handkerchiefs, a night dress, a pair of slippers, two scarfs, and a pair of silk stockings, which are produced.

Eliza Macdonald said : I live at 16, Kidbrooke Villas, Blackheath, and am housekeeper to Mrs. Sarah Bowcher. On the 10th August, at about ten o'clock at night, the house was fastened up in the usual way and I went to bed, leaving it safe. Next morning I found that the breakfast room window had been broken open and the house entered, and I missed a number of articles from the house. I identify the tablecloth and the silver pickle fork, now produced, as the property of my mistress. I also missed silver spoons and a butter knife.

Mr. Frederick Hanley said : In September I was living at Arbutus Lodge, Denmark-hill. At that time I was at Brighton, when I heard that my house had been broken into and a number of things stolen. I returned in the ordinary course at the expiration of my holiday, and I found that two dessert knives and forks, and a pair of cornelian bracelets had been stolen. From one of the drawers £30 in gold and silver had been taken, and I also missed a set of diamond studs, a diamond ring, and a variety of other rings, of the value, I should think, altogether of £50.

Lousia Tweed, parlour-maid to Mr. Walter Robert Tidd, Upper Denmark-hill, Camberwell, said : On the 18th September, at a quarter to twelve at night, I discovered that Mr. Tidd's bedroom window was open. It had been forced from the outside and the catch broken. I missed a plate-basket, with the plate, both silver and electro, five silver bangles, and a brooch, engraved with a crest and motto.

A quantity of electro-plate was produced to the witness, which she identified as the property of her master. The silver articles stolen were all missing from the property recovered. Witness then identified six table spoons, twelve dessert spoons, twelve forks, eleven teaspoons, one cheese scoop, and a jam spoon.

Inspector Henry Phillips said : The property belonging to Celia Korcher, which was identified on the last occasion, I found at Bolsover's house, at Darnall, on the 9th November; also the clock belonging to Miss Dadson; and the caskets, identified by the witness Newman on the last occasion. The velvet table cover, also identified by Miss Newman, was found by Inspector Bonney. The property identified by Mr. Shapley was found at Bolsover's house on the occasion of the second visit, on the 14th November, with the exception of a chemise, which was found at Nottingham. The table cloth shown to Macdonald was found at Darnall, on the 14th November; the pickle fork came from Nottingham. The property identified by Mr. Hawley was found at Darnall, on the 6th November. The plate identified by Louisa Tweed was found at Nottingham.

Inspector John Bonney, R Division, said : On 5th November I went to Nottingham, No. 11, North-street. I found there a small red box, which had the appearance of having been nailed down, but was open when I saw it. The house was tenanted by a Mrs. Gresham. I took all the things out of the box and brought them to London. The property which had been found at Nottingham was identified by the various witnesses. The red box he found at the house of a Mr. Brion, 22, Philip-road, Peckham Rye.

Inspector John Pinder Twibell, of the Sheffield police, said : On Wednesday, November 6th, I assisted Phillips in searching Bolsover's house, and saw the things found. After the search and removal of the property we went away for a short time, but afterwards returned. Bolsover was present the second time. I said to him, "We have found a large quantity of property in your house, which we have good reason to believe is stolen. There is a clock which Inspector Phillips identifies as part of the proceeds of a burglary at Blackheath. How do you account for this property being in your house?" He replied, "I know nothing about it." I said, "It is here, and you will have to account for it." The prisoner then said, "I brought the clock with me from Hull about five weeks ago." I said, "How do you account for it? It is stolen." She said, "A tall woman brought it to me. I do not know the woman. She said another woman had sent it for me. The other property was in my house nearly two years ago."

Mr. Poland : Has she given any information to you about her marriage ?

Witness : Yes ; she said she was married at St. George's Church, Sheffield, the year before her daughter was born. Her daughter is nineteen years of age.

She could not fix the date other than in that way. I have not searched the register of St. George's Church.

William Bolsover, No. 4, Hazel-road, Darnall, said: I am a miner by trade. I have known prisoner for about five years as Mrs. Peace. She was living with Charles Peace, who told me his real name was Charles Frederick Peace. They lived together as man and wife, and they had a young woman living with them, who was known as Jane Ann Peace, their daughter. There was also a lad named Willie Ward, who, I understood, was a son of Mrs. Peace by a former marriage. On the 8th January I married Jane Ann Peace, at Hull. Peace was not there at the time of the marriage. Mrs. Peace, previously to that, had kept a chandler's shop at Hull. I did not know where Peace then was. He was not at Hull. On Whit Monday I came with my wife to London, and went to No. 4, Evelina-road, Nunhead. My wife was married in the name of Jane Ann Peace, not in the name of Ward. The man whom I had known in Sheffield as Peace I found was living as Mr. Thompson. He came to meet us at the King's Cross Station with a woman (now in court), who passed for Mrs. Thompson. Mrs. Peace was living there in the name of Mrs. Ward, and Willie Ward was also there. On one Friday he gave me some money and I returned home. Willie Ward and the prisoner usually took their meals together, and I had mine with Mrs. Thompson. On 11th October Willie Ward came to my house at Darnall, bringing with him a concertina box and fiddle case. On the 12th the prisoner came to my house. I did not expect her. She had not written to say that she was coming. She told me that she had left a large box at the Sheffield station, and that a man whom she supposed was her husband had been apprehended. She stayed with me. On the Monday I and the lad Willie went to the Sheffield station, and fetched away the box, which was very heavy, on a truck. Willie and I brought it to the house. It was afterwards taken away by the police. Willie afterwards brought another trunk from the Darnall station to my house. After the opening of the boxes I saw things in the house which I had not seen until after the boxes were brought there. Amongst other things, a silk dress which has been shown to one of the witnesses was brought to my house. I had previously seen it at Hull in October.

Eliza Bellfitt, wife of Robert Bellfitt, Great Freeman-street, Nottingham, said: On the 5th November I was living at 11, North-street, Nottingham. Inspector Bonny called upon me there. The woman known as Mrs. Thompson is a sister of mine. About the second week in October, Mrs. Thompson and the prisoner called at my house. Mrs. Thompson introduced the prisoner as Mrs. Ward. They had no boxes with them. They wanted to stay all night, but I had no accommodation for them. Mrs. Ward and Mrs. Thompson both said they were in trouble. When they left I accompanied them to the station. Mrs. Ward went to the station to get a large oval box, which was very heavy, and which they took away with them. The prisoner afterwards gave me a ticket relating to two other boxes belonging to Mrs. Thompson. Mrs. Thompson asked me to take these boxes to my house. In regard to the red box Mrs. Ward particularly requested that I should take care of it for her, as it was a family relic, and, moreover, contained her property. She promised to call for it the week afterwards. The other box—the black box—she said belonged to Mrs. Thompson. Mrs. Ward then went to Sheffield, taking the large oval box with her. After she had gone I took the two boxes from the cloak-room to my house. About a

fortnight afterwards Mrs. Ward called again, and said she wanted some of the things out of the red box. She opened the box and took them out. She went away, again, leaving the box in my care. She took a paper parcel out of the red box and left it with me. It was sealed up. Mrs. Thompson left a table cover; and afterwards came and took her box away, and I kept the small red box and the parcel until the visit of Inspector Bonney on the 6th Nov. Mr. Bonney took out some small pieces of silver—I do not know what they were—and some other things. About a week after that I received some letters from Mr. Brion. Mrs. Brion afterwards called, and I gave her the sealed paper parcel. In December, in consequence of a letter I received from Mrs. Thompson, I sent the small red box by rail to Mr. Brion's.

Cross-examined: I have only known my sister in the name of Mrs. Thompson—never as Mrs. Ward. Her maiden name was Grey.

Is your sister, Mrs. Thompson, in custody?

She is not in custody.

Where is she?

She is in this court.

Henry Forsey Brion said: I am a geographical engineer, and live at No. 22, Philip-road, Peckham Rye. On Sunday, the 19th of May, I called at No. 5, Evelina-road, Nunhead. I went into the breakfast-room. I there saw Mr. Thompson, Mrs. Thompson, Mrs. Ward, and Willie, whom afterwards I found to be William Ward. Mr. Thompson said to Mrs. Thompson, "Suey, will you fetch the child down for this gentleman to see," alluding to a child which had been injured. As she was on the point of leaving the room, while Mrs. Ward and Willie were present, Mr. Thompson said, pointing to Mrs. Thompson, or as he called her Suey, "That is my wife."

The prisoner was then charged in the usual form by the learned magistrate, and in answer to it she said—

"I am his wife, and whatever I did I did through complete compulsion."

The prisoner was then committed for trial.

Mrs. Peace was at this time plunged into a vortex of troubles, and doubtless she bitterly regretted having allied herself with so heartless and unscrupulous a miscreant.

Fain would we pass over in silence the troubles and perplexities with which she found herself surrounded, but it is requisite for the continuity of the story of "the Life of Charles Peace" that we are constrained to record all those events and circumstance which throw a light upon his dark doings and sinful career. His unhappy wife, as we have already intimated was committed to Newgate, and on Tuesday, January the 14th, 1879, Hannah Peace, aged fifty-eight, alleged to be the wife of Charles Peace, the notorious burglar, was indicted at the Old Bailey, London, before Mr. Commissioner Kerr, with feloniously receiving, in the county of Surrey, seven pocket-handkerchief, one night-dress, one pair of slippers, two scarves, and one pair of silk stockings, the property of the wife of Mr. William Gardner Shapley, Seymour Lodge, Peckham Rye, on the night of the 23rd September.

Several other indictments charged her with stealing divers other articles of property; and she was further indicted for harbouring the man Peace.

Mr. Douglas Straight and Mr. Tickell, instructed by Mr. Polland, solicitor to the Treasury, appeared for the prosecution; Mr. Forrest Fulton, instructed by Mr. Walter Beard, for the defence.

Mr. Straight said the case was one of some peculiarity. If a woman were married to a man, the law assumed that any offence like the present with which the prisoner was indicted was committed under his coercion. There was, however, another element in this case which had to be considered—viz., whether there was such independent action on the part of the prisoner, in respect to the disposal of the stolen property, as would lead to the conclusion that the prisoner was to be held criminally responsible. The prisoner was indicted in the name of Hannah Peace, and answered to the indictment in that name. The responsibility, he contended, was thrown upon her to make out the marriage. Mr. Straight proceeded to detail the circumstances of the robbery at Mr. Shapley's, and the course adopted by the prisoner in removing all the property from the house in the Evalina-road, after her husband had been taken into custody, and he remarked that there could be very little doubt that the property so removed by the prisoner was that which was afterwards found. They had made every possible inquiry, and could find no trace of a marriage having taken place.

Inspector Henry Phillips was then examined by Mr. Tickell, and said : In November last a man, named Charles Peace, was convicted of burglary and shooting at a constable with intent to murder. On the 5th November I went to a house, No. 4, Hazel-road, Darnall, when I saw Mrs. Peace, a young man, named Bolsover, who is her son-in-law, and his wife. On entering the house I saw a quantity of property which I knew, from the description, to have been stolen. I was accompanied by Inspector Twibell, of Sheffield. I said that the property on the floor had been stolen, and proceeded to take charge of it. The prisoner said, in reference to a clock belonging to Mrs. Dadson, " I did not know that it was stolen. A tall woman gave it to me about five weeks ago." I told her that Peace had been convicted, to which she replied, " He has been a great trouble to me. He seems to harass my life out wherever I go." I afterwards searched the house, and in the top room I found a silk dress, a set of studs, identified by Mr. Wood, two bracelets, some knives and forks, and other property, belonging to Mr. Hanley, Mr. Perry, Mr. Allen, Mr. Andred, and others. Inspector Twibell was about to open a box, when the prisoner said, " I know what you want ; I will give it you." She thereupon handed to the officer a parcel containing about forty pieces of plate, the majority of which has been identified. The prisoner was taken before the magistrates, and afterwards brought to London. On the 14th of November I again visited the house, when I found two sealskin jackets and the property identified by Mrs. Shapley. On the first occasion she gave the name of Hannah Peace, and said that she was married at St. George's Church, Sheffield, or rather her son said so in her presence. I brought one of the boxes up to London, and showed it to a witness named Pickering, and to Mrs. Bellfitt, of Nottingham. When she said she had been married, I asked her for her certificate, which she said the " old man " had turned some time before.

Evidence was then given as to the robberies that had taken place and in recognition of stolen property.

Mr. Samuel Smith, builder, Peckham, said that in May, a Mr. and Mrs. Thompson, a Mrs. Ward, and a boy, who was called Willie Ward, called upon him in reference to the letting of the house, No. 5, Evalina-road, Peckham. Having satisfied himself of the respectability of these people by going to their residence at Greenwich, he let the house to them. In October, he found that the house had been deserted, and entering by the back way he took possession.

Mr. Henry Forsey Brion, geographical engineer and constructor of relievo maps, living at 22, Philip-road, Peckham, said that, on the 19th of May last he went to Peace's house in the Evalina-road. In the breakfast room he saw Mr. and Mrs. Thompson, and the former, pointing to the latter, said " That is my wife." The prisoner, who was present, made no remark. Between the months of May and August he constantly visited at the house. Mr. and Mrs Thompson appeared to be living as man and wife. In consequence of a communication he received from Peace, in the name of John Ward, witness on the 1st of November called at Newgate to see the writer of the letter, in whom he at once recognised Mr. Thompson. He was previously asked if he knew anything of the prisoner, and declared that he knew neither the handwriting nor the name in the letter. Between May and August they came to witness's house on one occasion. The woman known as Mrs. Thompson was introduced as the wife of Mr. Thompson, and Mrs. Ward was known by that name. In consequence of a communication, witness wrote to a Mrs. Bellfitt at Nottingham, and received from her a small red box.

Robert Mapleson, warder in Newgate, deposed to the interview in Newgate between Mr. Brion and Peace.

Thomas Pickering, porter, in the service of the London, Chatham, and Dover Railway Company, at the Nunhead Station, deposed to taking three boxes to the station on the night of the 11th October, by the direction of the prisoner.

Eliza Bellfitt, wife of Robert Bellfitt, Great Freeman-street, Nottingham, said that in November last she was living at No. 11, North-street, in that town. She recollected the visit of Inspector Bonney on the 6th November. Previously to that Mrs. Thompson, who was her sister, had come to her premises accompanied by the prisoner.

The witness was here admonished by the prisoner (who stood up for a moment for the purpose of being identified) to speak the truth.

Examination continued : They arrived between one and two o'clock in the morning, Mrs. Thompson introduced the prisoner as Mrs. Ward, and asked if they could stay all night, but they could not be accommodated. They said they were in trouble, but did not mention the nature of it. They stayed until four or five o'clock in the morning, and took their departure by an early train. Witness accompanied them to the station, where Mrs. Ward, having obtained a large box, gave her a ticket relating to two others. The box was put into the van. Witness had since seen the box at Bow-street ; it was like the one which the prisoner had with her on the night in question. Prisoner asked that the boxes might be taken to the house of witness, who complied. One of them was a small red box, which the prisoner said was a family relic, and she would call for it. Mrs. Ward went to Sheffield, and witness removed the two boxes from the cloak room. About a fortnight afterwards Mrs. Ward returned, and said she wanted some of the things out of the red box, which, when she went away, she again left in the care of witness. There was also a paper parcel, of which she was requested to take charge. She afterwards gave up the red box and the parcel to Inspector Bonney, who took out some plate and a tablecloth. She subsequently received a letter from Mr. Brion. and on the 25th November handed the parcel to Mrs. Brion. On the 3rd December, in consequence of another letter she received, she took the small red box to the house of Mrs. Brion, 22, Philip-road.

Mr. Fulton: What has become of Mrs. Thompson?
Is she within the precincts of the court?

She is not, I think.

How often have you seen her since this woman
was first given in charge for receiving those goods?

Once.

By Mr. Straight: I knew her when she was living
with Peace under the name of Thompson.

Mrs. Alice Brion, the wife of a former witness, said:
On the 25th November I went to the house of Mrs.
Bellfitt. I received the parcel produced and handed it
to the police.

Mr. Fulton: Is Mrs. Thompson living with you?

Witness: Mrs. Thompson has been living with me.

Since Peace was taken into custody?

She has been.

But did you know, previously to that, that Mrs.
Thompson had been living with Peace as his wife?

I understood she was Mrs. Thompson.

Have you ever seen this unfortunate woman on any
occasion?

Whom do you mean?

I mean the prisoner. Let her stand up.

Yes, on many occasions.

What position did she occupy in the house?

The position of a lodger upstairs. She had two rooms
besides a back kitchen.

And Mr. and Mrs. Thompson occupied the rest of
the house as man and wife?

That is so.

Wm. Bolsover, 4, Hazel-road, Darnall, near Sheffield, said: I knew the prisoner when she was living at
Darnall with Peace and her daughter. I was married
to the latter at Hull on 8th January, 1878. Peace was
not present. On Whit Monday I came to London, and
stayed with Peace at the house in Evalina-road for
eight or nine days. Peace was living with a woman
who was known as Mrs. Thompson, in the name of
Thompson. Mrs. Ward and the boy Willie had their
meals alone, and Mr. and Mrs. Thompson in another
part of the house. On the 12th October the prisoner
came to my house and stated that she saw by the
papers that a man whom she imagined to be her husband had been taken into custody. I took her in, and
afterwards fetched her luggage from Sheffield.

Cross-examined: I have known Mr. and Mrs. Peace
for some time, and believed them to be man and wife.
Their daughter had, I understood, lived with them
from infancy.

John P. Twibell, police inspector, Sheffield, said he
assisted Philips in searching Bolsover's house. Between the 6th of November and the 14th witness was
told by the prisoner that she was married at St.
George's Church, Sheffield, in the name of Hannah
Ward to Charles Peace, the year before her daughter
was born. She was unable to fix the date in any other
way. The witnesses of the marriage were, she said,
John and Sarah Clarke, who are both dead.

This was the case for the prosecution.

Mr. Fulton submitted that there was no case to go
to the jury. Peace and the prisoner had, it was
evident, for many years lived together as man and
wife, and their daughter was married in the name of
Peace. He further pointed out that the prisoner had
given minute facts in reference to her marriage, and
also gave the names of the witnesses. These being
dead, the onus was, he contended, upon the prosecution to make some inquiries.

Mr. Commissioner Kerr then retired to consult with
Sir Henry Hawkins, whose opinion, he announced on
returning into court, very closely agreed with his own,

viz., that a marriage in this case might be assumed.
That was to say, there was very much stronger pre-
sumptive evidence of a marriage between this woman
and the man Peace than there was to the contrary.

After some discussion the jury resolved to give the
prisoner the benefit of the doubt, and accordingly
found that she is the wife of Peace.

No further contention being made on behalf of the
prosecution, the jury, by the direction of the learned
Commissioner, returned a verdict of acquittal against
the prisoner on all counts.

Mrs. Peace had passed through a terrible ordeal.
There were many who averred that she had had a
narrow escape, but in justice to this unhappy woman
it is but fair to state that there was in reality no legal
evidence to warrant the jury in finding a verdict of
guilty.

It is quite true that she had been connected with
the most determined and cunning burglar of the day,
but it does not necessarily follow that she was his
accomplice.

On the contrary, the whole tenour of his lawless
course would indicate that both the women were mere
cyphers in his establishment in the Evalina-road.

No doubt they were cognisant of the fact that he
was a burglar, but they were powerless. Any attempt
to turn him from his sinful course would have brought
down upon them the unmeasured wrath of their
tyrannical lord and master.

After Mrs. Peace's acquittal she lost no time in
taking her departure from the metropolis.

She arrived in Sheffield on the Tuesday night by
the 8.44 Great Northern express, and proceeded to
Darnall at 9.5.

CHAPTER CL.

A VISIT TO NEWGATE—IDENTIFICATION OF PEACE—MRS.
THOMPSON'S PERSONAL HISTORY—RECEIVERS OF STOLEN
GOODS.

FROM what we have been able to gather from persons
whose testimony is in every way reliable, Mrs. Peace
made a precipitate retreat from Peckham after the
arrest of her husband.

The day after Police-constable Robinson bravely
fought the burglar down, in spite of his wounded arm,
and had Peace taken to gaol, the wife of the convict
made preparations for flight. She packed up three
boxes, and had them conveyed to Cleaves, the greengrocer, to Nunhead Station.

She and her son followed them to the station, and
took the train for Darnall, near Sheffield, the place
where Peace lived before coming to London, and at
which he was living when Dyson was shot.

A month after the arrest some of the effects were
sold, and the remainder were carted to No. 22, Philip's-
road, the residence of Mr. Brion, heretofore mentioned
as the joint patentee of the invention for raising
sunken ships.

There is no question that the police were afterwards
made aware of the departure of Mrs. Peace and of Mrs.
Thompson's change of abode.

Mrs. Thompson, although she lived with Peace at
Nottingham after the murder, and lived in company
with Mrs. Peace at Peckham, was not called as a witness for obvious reasons.

Peace was convicted of assault with a deadly
weapon, and it was unnecessary to try him for the
burglary, as the sentence was penal servitude for life.

The representative of the Press Association had an
interview with Mr. Brion. His relationship with Peace
was, he said, a purely business one.

"But for me," he said, "Peace's connection with the murder would never have been discovered. It was I who gave the police the information that put them on the track. Those police would never have discovered anything themselves had not everything been told them and every step they took indicated. How did I become connected with Peace?

"You will know all about that in my testimony at Bow-street, when Mrs. Peace was under examination. I am an inventor, a geographical engineer. I make maps. You know Donald McKenzie, who has gone to Africa to make surveys for letting the ocean flow into the Sahara?

"That is my project. This is the map I exhibited at the Mansion House. (Mr. Brion unrolled a map 20 feet by 12 feet, whereon was delineated very broadly the Continent of Africa and on which was shown, in red dotted lines below the Canary Islands, a kind of gutter through which the ocean is to flow inland and flood the Sahara.)

"Mrs. Thompson went away from here on Monday. I know where she is, but I cannot tell you of her whereabouts. That has all been arranged with the police. She came here with the full knowledge of the police, and all the goods in Peace's house were brought here by their direction and consent.

"The police are aware of everything I can tell them about Peace. I have spent three months in the interest of the public to bring this man to justice, and I was promised by the police that I should have my expenses paid, but here have I been during all that time running around the country and living at hotels, and spending money for the sake of getting at evidence, and now they refuse to pay me anything.

"I have done with the police, although they know all that I have done, and now I have a memorial to the Treasury on the subject.

"I am disgusted with the whole business, and annoyed that for any length of time I should have been associated in whatever degree with such a scoundrel as Peace.

"He was a very interesting man, full of general information, and had acquired a great amount of ability in mechanics. He had an inventive faculty, and could readily understand anything in mechanism.

"He was working away at this idea of his for lifting ships from the sea bottom, and it is now plain that he could not have obtained a patent himself.

"As with all these men of smirched reputation, he had to look around for some one to assist him, and he fastened upon me.

"I used to see him in the mornings, afternoons, and at nights, and he was always pleasant enough, and I never suspected he was what he is.

"His left hand was always bare when I saw it, but when he went to Whitechapel he was accustomed to cover it and pretend that it was injured.

"Whitechapel was where he went with his booty. I expended a considerable sum in my experiments with Peace on his invention.

"I found that he had the idea of raising ships by air force, but that the appliance was faulty, and that no patent would be given for an idea.

"I have a plan of my own for raising ships, and I have offered it to the Admiralty. They have not accepted it, and I intend to raise the 'Vanguard,' and sell it on my own account. The police are aware of everything that Mrs. Thompson has to say.

"They have been cognisant of her movements from first to last, and they knew of her departure from this house, and where she has gone."

The reader will be at no loss to understand that the police were tolerably well informed as to the movements and whereabouts of Mrs. Peace. This is plainly evidenced by her arrest, the examination at the police-courts that followed, and her trial and acquittal at the Central Criminal Court.

After this they confined their attentions to the convicted man who was at this time incarcerated in Newgate, and their chief aim was to prove him to be the murderer of Mr. Dyson.

The capture and conviction of Peace was the universal topic of town talk. Never surely did a criminal create a greater amount of excitement both in the metropolis and the provinces.

Officers were despatched both to Nottingham and Sheffield. The constabulary received information from the Park-road station of the K Division. It was put forth that the prisoner in Newgate was a man apparently about fifty years of age, dark, clean shaved, hair grey, large mouth, large scar on the side of the left leg, and the back of the thigh, three fingers on the left hand deficient, dress overcoat, with velvet collar, and black under coat.

He wore a brown leather belt, low boots, and a brown felt hat.

A Sheffield paper thus chronicles further proceedings:—

Police-constable David Morris was dispatched to London, by Mr. Jackson, with a view to the identification of the criminal in custody at Newgate.

Morris, who was at one time stationed at Darnall, lived for more than a year in the house directly opposite to that occupied by Charles Peace, and was therefore in the habit of seeing him every day, and frequently several times a day.

Morris had with him a letter from his chief to the director of the Criminal Investigation Department, by means of which he obtained admission to the cell.

At half-past one o'clock a telegram from our reporter was received at this office as follows:—

"ST. MARTIN'S-LE-GRAND, 1.30. p.m.

"Peace has been further identified by a Sheffield constable, and there is no doubt he is the murderer."

The telegram, when posted in the window of our publishing department, excited much interest. Shortly after two o'clock the Chief Constable received a telegram from Police-constable Morris as follows:—

"Man in custody is Peace. I am quite positive about his identity."

All doubt, if any existed, has now been removed. The man, John Ward, the notorious burglar of Blackheath—the man who did all his villainies "single-handed," and thus no doubt escaped detection for a longer time than he would otherwise have done—is none other than Charles Peace, the murderer of Mr. Arthur Dyson, at Bannercross-terrace, that dark November night two years ago.

Charles Peace, alias George Parker, alias Alexander Mann, alias Paganini, alias John Ward—the man of many aliases—is trapped at last, and the general hope is that now he is caught there may be evidence enough to make him suffer the penalty of his greatest crime—that which startled this town and district so terribly in the winter of 1876.

A journalist furnishes us with the following descriptive visit to Newgate and the scene at the identification:—

That Charles Peace, the murderer of Mr. Arthur Dyson, of Bannercross, is at last caught there cannot now be the shadow of a doubt. He has been clearly identified by a Sheffield constable, who knew him most intimately.

The result of my researches into the history of this man's career reveals a depth of depravity, hypocrisy, daring, and low cunning, such as have scarcely ever been penned in the annals of crime.

On entering Scotland-yard, and making known my errand—that I desired to prosecute inquiries into the history of the man then in their custody, who was committed for trial from the Greenwich Police-court, on charges of attempted murder and burglary, a man who had given the name of John Ward, the replies given were certainly very courteous, but in no way satisfactory to a reporter in quest of information.

The result was that after about an hour and a half's waiting, and after being interviewed successively by some dozen or two very polite gentlemen, who were evidently "authorities," I was ultimately told, with a smile, by one that they did not give information to members of the Press.

"Why?" I asked.

"Because it's against regulations, and we are not allowed to answer questions."

"Well," I said, "where is this man Ward or Peace confined, because I want to see him?"

He had a short look at me, and after telling an un-truth in the words "He's not in town," took his departure.

However, I knew there had come up to London by the morning train a Sheffield constable whose errand was to see the man "Ward," and that officer was one who had been on the most intimate terms with Charles Peace.

He had seen the murderer daily for months before the commission of the crime, had had him in his house, and had further confided to him some of the "family troubles" of Peace.

The officer was Police-constable (222) David Morris, of the Attercliffe division, and it is due to him that Peace has at length been identified beyond dispute.

The police authorities of the metropolis are true to their word and traditions in this, that if they gain their information with difficulty they hold it with tenacity when they have obtained it. They appear to mistake reporters for Ishmaelites.

After further trouble I succeeded in finding out that at about one o'clock a detective from Scotland-yard would be at the Old Bailey, otherwise well known as Newgate Gaol, and that he would there ask Morris if he could pick out the so-called Peace from a number of men.

How to get it was the question, but I also thought it might be possible *for me* to identify him if I could see him, and so, with a little help from a friend, I got permission from the authorities to go inside and witness.

The approaches to the Old Bailey are of a forbidding character, dark and repulsive. Even the inquiry door has massive iron spikes projecting from the top of it, and as you have to make your applications either through the spikes or over them, you stand a chance of having your chin perforated.

On getting inside there are apparently nothing but bars and big doors, but over one of the doors on the shelf there are conspicuously displayed plaster casts of heads.

These casts are the official representations of all the murderers who have interviewed the hangman within the walls of the prison, and a hideous-looking crew they are.

Seeing that another candidate for the "long drop" has next to be interviewed the effect is not pleasing.

However, there is another delay, and this is accounted for by the fact that the suspected culprit is being "mixed" with some more prisoners, the more to test anyone in the task of identification.

At last the signal is given that all is ready, and after passing through a short corridor a yard is seen, rather capacious and surrounded with cell-doors.

But between the yard and the corridor were double gates of iron, and anyone exercising in the yard had not a shadow of a chance of communication with the outer world.

The iron gates were opened by the governor of the gaol; in front stood the constable and another who had come to see if Peace was in the hands of the police, and in front were twelve prisoners doing "the circular drill."

This is a performance best known to prison officials, and to those who have been "wanted." It consists in this :—

If there is a prisoner in the establishment whose identity needs to be established, and there is anyone attending for the purpose of viewing them, the pri-soner is placed amongst others, and they follow each other in circle.

The suspected prisoner must then be identified. Those who performed the "circular drill" on this occa-sion in the Old Bailey were a curious lot.

First came a young man, of some three or four-and-twenty years, with his neck half hidden in a muffler.

His gait was upright, but there was that cowed look about him which showed him to be "an old prison bird."

Before the march commenced the prisoners took a look at us; they did not know who was "wanted," and our visages were strange to all but one.

Then the march began, and all the prisoners appeared to want to march the double, but they had only a short time of duty.

The second man who passed was an old one, some forty years of age, who wore a swallow-tail coat, and looked most like a defaulting half-starved attorney's clerk.

He gave a searching look, knit up his brows, as if to see "who in creation there could be that he knew," and then apparently satisfied that he was not "wanted," passed on with a livelier tread.

The third but a young man, with a bull neck, who held his head down and stared at the ground, as though afraid of seeing anyone strange, for fear they should recognise him.

He had apparently gone through this class of in-spection before.

Two other young fellows passed, of lively mein, and then there came

ONE WHO WAS WANTED.

A man of about five feet three or four inches in height, with white hair on his head, cut very short, and bald in the front of his head, but the razor had lately done this.

His eyebrows heavy and overhanging the eyes, which were deeply socketed.

A chin standing very prominently, and, as if to make it more so, the head was thrown back with an air of half self-assertion, yet half caution, as though there was a degree of hesitancy in the action.

The lower part of his cheek bones protruded more than was their wont in years gone by, but he had appa-rently had some bruises recently, and had had his whiskers shaven off since he was last seen in Sheffield.

THE IDENTIFICATION OF PEACE BY THE SHEFFIELD OFFICER.

In addition to that he wore a pair of large brass-rimmed spectacles, as if the more completely to make certain of his non-identification.

Slightly bending himself this man approached those who were inspecting the prisoners, and then there was a sudden stop.

"That's Peace," said Morris. "I'd know him any-

where," and the man "Ward" stepped from the ranks and approaching the officer with a look which betokened the most earnest inquiry, asked, "What do you want me for?"

The governor here very severely said, "Go on, sir, with your walk," and Peace returned to his place in the ranks, which were no longer marching.

The other prisoners were now staring at the identified man, and evidently wanted to ask, "What has he done?" but they dared not.

Even Peace had had no intimation given to him that he was recognised as the Sheffield murderer, and until he saw the officer who had come to identify him he had no notion of why he was required to go on this special parade.

The marks which were described as on the missing Peace are all distinctly on him. Before he can appear in the police court at Sheffield on the charge of murder, the Chief-constable for Sheffield will have to apply to a superior court for a writ of *habeas corpus.*

Upon this he will be taken to answer the capital charge now made against him.

After committing the murder on the night of the 26th November, 1876, Peace was completely lost sight of; his career in this life, it was said, was closed, for he had made away with himself.

But Peace was not such a fool as that, for he had no sooner finished the murder than he took to his old game of burglary—an avocation which appears to have had a curious attraction for him.

Subsequent events have proved that Peace went to Hull, and there replaced his waning funds by breaking into a gentleman's house, from which he extracted a large quantity of plate and valuable jewellery.

From thence, after realising on his spoil, he repaired to Nottingham, where a near relative resided, and with her he took up his quarters.

Although it was well known that there was a heavy reward offered for his apprehension, it does not seem that any of his relatives considered it advisable to state who was in the midst of them.

After effecting a very clever warehouse robbery, in which silk goods were the principal booty, Peace appears to have then considered that his proximity to Sheffield was dangerous, and he again changed his abode.

Thus it will be seen that the Sheffield authorities were correct when they stated that they had traced the man to Hull, but there had lost sight of him.

It was believed that he had escaped to the Continent. But not so; the fox had "doubled," and in the Midland Counties, with Nottingham for his centre, was continuing his depredations.

On reaching London some four or five months after the murder, he was not very well off for money, and he took up his residence in Lambeth.

The police in charge of this district then became aware that night after night the most audacious depredations were committed in the district.

There was scarcely a night passed but a burglary was announced, and in as even a succession the statement followed that the thieves had not been caught.

The value of the booty thus secured was exceedingly great, and the thieves—for they were then believed to be a gang—were said to be well rewarded for their audacity.

But the place appears to have become too hot for him, and he then removed to Greenwich, where he occupied a beautiful house, and commenced to furnish it in a most expensive manner.

Whatever Peace failed in, it was not in the want of self-assurance and the belief that he could pass through society as a gentleman.

Though he had repulsive features he appears to have had winning ways in the eyes of some, for he now appears to have decided on engaging a lady to share his improving fortunes.

This "lady" may perhaps figure elsewhere shortly,

and her name will then be found in the police record. But the establishment could not be kept up without "means," and again came the last resort.

Peace had described himself to the new sphere of respectable neighbours—among whom he now moved —as a "gentleman of independent means," and he was looked up to as one who had done well in the world.

We have endeavoured, throughout this strange eventful history, to place before the reader the leading and most noticeable circumstances connected with the career of this sinful man. After his arrest for the burglary and attempted murder of Police-constable Robinson, there was but little chance of his escaping conviction for the Bannercross murder, but there are many who have attributed his identification and subsequent conviction upon the grave charge to the jealousy of a woman, as will be seen by the following extract from a journal of the time.

It has been remarked by ancient as well as by modern writers that wherever there is a piece of outrageous mischief there is sure to be a woman at the bottom of it.

The experience of the present civilised age does not present any instances to the contrary, but rather strengthens the opinions previously held. Charles Peace was clever in one thing, that he knew his "profession" and succeeded in it so long as he did it "singlehanded;" but when he obtained a partner, like many others who have preceded him, his fortunes, though apparently improving, were really on the decrease.

Whilst in Nottingham—and this only happened within a month after the murder of Mr. Dyson—he succeeded in securing to himself the affections of a young female relative.

This young "lady" followed him through his many hazardous adventures until at length the two were in Lambeth, where they occupied a decent house, and to all intents and purposes were a well-conducted pair—the lady being slightly younger than her husband, but as "Mr. Johnson" was well-to-do it was supposed that there had been a marriage of love.

Business in Lambeth proved of a paying character, although those who did the paying were not always aware of the fact until before banking hours in the morning—when the news was brought to their bedroom doors by the earliest risers in the house.

On removing to Greenwich, Peace was accompanied by the young lady who had followed his fortunes, although she might not know the whole of his crimes and there were again commenced the robberies which have made his name so notorious in the criminal annals of the country.

Peace resumed his business; as he had not to press sales on the market he did not care what came to his hand, and being well versed in the legerdemain of the light-fingered fraternity he obtained access to the mansions of the rich around him, and their loss was his gain.

As the aristocrats in his neighbourhood became more indignant, he became more pious, and his immediate neighbours, whilst looking out for the midnight thieves, relied somewhat on his perception and assurances that nothing would be wrong.

But all this time there was in Peace's well-furnished household a young woman who had been misled and wronged.

She had been led to believe that Peace, with whom she had associated in Nottingham, was a steady, hardworking man. Peace had given to her a number of costly goods, he was to her a man of sterling honesty, and then it transpired that he was a burglar.

Then came her time of trial.

The man with whom she was associated was a thief, a burglar, and more than that—and she knew it.

He was a murderer.

But what could she do? It was this man upon whom she was dependent for a subsistence—it was this man who had committed murder once, and whom she knew would not hesitate to commit it again.

So she helped to get rid of the goods which were brought by his nightly marauds, and like other sensible people who are in a mess, she held her peace.

But when Peace and this housekeeper had got to the new home at Peckham, " a cloud came o'er the scene," and the cloud was a woman.

This "cloud" took up her residence in the house of Mr. Peace—otherwise "Johnson," by which latter cognomen he was well known—and then commenced the beginning of the end.

The first victim of Peace's duplicity dared not speak, and the second admirer of him dared not—so between the rivals the burglar had a fair chance of bidding for favouritism.

But when the last " throw" came from the dice-box of criminal ingenuity and the thrower lost, there were left in the house in Peckham a couple of rivals.

One, the latest comer, " realised," and the older and much-injured one gave information which resulted in the disclosures which had now been made public.

By the aid of " the first love" valuable goods were traced to Nottingham and others to Sheffield.

She told the detectives where to work and where to find, and she disclosed the name of her rival, Mrs. Thompson, who was asked to give her address.

Charles Peace, as we have had occasion to observe before, was by no means a man of retiring character, but in respect to audacity and assurance he was certainly able to hold his own with any of those great criminals in whose footsteps he so long and persistently followed. It must, however, be admitted that there was one bright spot in his character.

It was this : after his arrest and conviction he strove by every means in his power to prove the innocence of his wife.

It is certain that he only sought to become acquainted with those who were, in his estimation, likely to be useful to him in an emergency, and this statement has been fully borne out by the latest phase of the case.

A gentleman in Sheffield some years ago bestowed some favours on a member of the miscreant's family, and his name and address had been treasured up, with a view to still further calls upon the benevolence that was once exercised in his behalf.

The gentleman in question was infinitely surprised one morning to receive a letter, which was directed in an unknown hand.

Tearing open the cover he saw a mass of cramped and crooked lines, which ran higgledy-piggledy over the paper, and showed that the hand which had written them might have been more familiar with the "jemmy" and the skeleton key than with the pen.

A further consideration of the document revealed that the author was either a most illiterate man, or that, to suit his own purpose, he would fain appear to be such.

The simple rules of grammar were set at defiance, and the attempts to decipher the letter were so painful that it would have been tossed impatiently aside had not the eye been caught by the signature, " Charles Peace or Ward."

The gentleman at once made all efforts to decipher the letter, which was from no other person than the notorious Bannercross murderer, who was at that time in Newgate.

The purport of the letter was to supplicate the receiver to become bail for Mrs. Peace, who for some time had been in custody in consequence of the vast quantity of stolen property found in her possession by Inspectors Phillips and Twibell.

He coolly went on to ask that counsel should be obtained for her defence, and declared that his wife had no guilty knowledge when she received the goods, but that he forwarded them to her in order that she might convert them into money to supply her needs.

He again and again with some vehemence asserted that Mrs. Peace was an innocent woman, and that the misfortunes into which she had fallen were not attributable to any fault of her own.

It was much to Peace's credit that he thus endeavoured to exculpate his wife, and it is pleasant to record this one good trait in his otherwise debased and odious character ; but he made a fatal mistake in forming a connection with the other lady of his establishment.

Mrs. Thompson (who may be known by some by the name of Susan Gray), the woman with whom Peace was living at the time of his arrest for the Blackheath burglaries, made a long statement as to her own career, and her connection with our hero.

As this forms part of the history of the notorious criminal the reader would be in no way pleased by our suppressing it.

The following is a tolerably accurate description of her personal appearance.

In person she is tall, and considerably above the middle height. Her figure is not robust. Her complexion is fair, and was no doubt at one time good. Her hair is dark and plentiful, and her eyes of a deep blue, what is known as a violet hue.

Mrs. Thompson, at the time I saw her, was dressed in a brown robe, trimmed with velvet to match ; and wore a cloth jacket and round hat, becoming and neat. Both of these articles she removed in the course of conversation.

Her manner was at first frank and agreeable, but as our interview lasted it changed to a fitful moroseness, which was difficult to deal with. Both in person and in manner Mrs. Thompson may be said to be decidedly prepossessing—what may be called a taking woman.

She is manifestly a fairly well-educated woman, and writes a pretty, ladylike Italian hand. The statement she made to me in answer to questions and in course of conversation was as follows :—

MRS. THOMPSON'S PERSONAL HISTORY.

My maiden name is Susan Gray, and I was born in the year 1842, at Nottingham. My parents are very respectable people, and carry on a small business in that town. I am heartily sorry to have brought this disgrace upon them.

In my childhood I went to various schools in Nottingham—to the Trinity School when I was a youngster, when I was also picked out as a singer in the choir.

I continued to attend the Trinity Schools until I was eight or nine years of age, when my parents removed me to the College School.

There I remained until I was fourteen, when I went out to work.

I should not like to state where I was employed, as

it might give pain to persons living, but there are those alive who know that this statement is true.

After I left my first situation I stayed at home and assisted my father in his business as his bookkeeper.

When I was about twenty-eight or twenty-nine years old, a Mr. Bailey one day came for purposes of business to my father's house.

He had occasion to see my handwriting, and asked me if I would make out some bills for him. I obliged him, and from that day I kept his books, and did all the writing he required.

One day he asked me if I would marry him, and, in a spirit of vexation, I having had some little disturbance with a brother of mine, I said "Yes."

We were married on the 10th of October, 1872, but three months after that I left him, on finding out what was his true character, and that it would be impossible for me to live happily with him.

I went next to live with my married sister at Nottingham.

I then worked for my living, employing my time in the manufacture of caps such as ladies and servants wear.

One Sunday evening, perhaps six months afterwards, as I was going to chapel, I met Bailey again. He stopped and spoke to me, and finally induced me to return to live with him.

I stayed with him for nearly a year, when I again left him, and since that time I have not spoken to him, except to obtain from him a weekly allowance, which I continued to enjoy until I met the man Peace, but on my becoming connected with him that allowance was forfeited.

HER FIRST MEETING PEACE.

I met Peace in January, 1877, I think it was. He came to the house where I was living at Nottingham about that time.

One evening, just as I was returning from work, when I entered the house, I saw him there. I shall never forget the impression he made upon me.

I thought him of very singular appearance, and, from what I saw at first sight, I had reason to believe that he was a one-armed man; but that appearance was only the result of one of his tricks and deceptions.

When I went in he said to the landlady, "Is this your daughter?"

I was not living with my sister then. I had left home, and had not spoken to any of my family for a long time.

In answer to Peace's question, my landlady, after some hesitation, gave an affirmative reply.

Some conversation in subdued tones then took place between Peace and my landlady. I ought to have said that this occurred in a house in a district known as "The Marsh," at Nottingham—a very low neighbourhood indeed. Peace had brought my landlady some boxes of cigars for sale.

She said to him, in reference to myself, "You can speak before her; she won't say anything."

Peace then asked her if she would go and see if she could sell the cigars.

This woman, who is since dead, was an accomplice of his, and used to assist him in the disposal of stolen property. Her name was Adamson.

She thereupon went out and sold them, and when she returned gave him 18s., of which sum he returned her 6s. by way of commission.

After that he became a constant visitor, and we always spoke of him as the one-armed old man. He not unfrequently had there his breakfast, dinner, tea, and supper, and at last it became known to me what his real character was.

At first he gave out that he was a hawker, and dealt in various little articles such as pedlars invariably travel with—spectacles, cheap finery, and jewellery, and miscellaneous goods of that description.

At last he openly showed himself in his true character—I mean as a most daring burglar. He brought things into the house which it must be evident to anybody were stolen property.

There were articles of silver plate, timepieces, watches, and even quantities of tea, sugar, and other perishable articles.

I do not know at all where he got these from; but I am perfectly satisfied that they were the proceeds of robberies or burglaries.

This knowledge was kept from me at first. I was led to suppose he was what he seemed to be—viz., a hawker, and a quiet, respectable man.

On one occasion he went out of town, saying he had to go and see his mother at Hull. By his mother he meant Hannah Peace.

Peace on that occasion took £5 to Mrs. Ward at Hull, and stayed there three weeks.

During that time he committed several robberies either at Hull or in the neighbourhood.

I know that to be the case, because when I have been in Hull he has shown me the houses at which the burglaries were committed, and he also told me that on one occasion he had to run for it, when he "fired wide" at a policeman by whom he was in imminent danger of being captured.

The property was disposed of in Hull. He returned after a while to Nottingham. I was out at the time of his return, having business in the evening, for I was still at work and getting my own living in an honest way. I was not earning very much, for work was short, but still it was honest.

On this particular night, on my return home, Mrs. Adamson said to me, "Oh, Mrs. Bailey, who do you think has come back?"

I replied I did not know, to which she made answer, "Why, the one-armed old man, and he has asked for you. He swears he will shoot you unless you go to him."

He was in the house of our next-door neighbour, and previously to that the lady of the house came in, and said, "Oh, Mrs. Bailey, do come in, the old man's gone mad; he wants to see you so bad. He won't be satisfied with anyone until you go."

When I went in I found him "drunk on Irish whiskey."

He said, "Is that you, pet (for by that name he used to call me), I am so glad you have come, where have you been?"

I told him I had just come in from business.

He said, "Oh, I am so glad you have come. I thought you were never coming back. Are you not pleased to see me?"

I said, "Oh, particularly, very; I like you so much."

People must not think by that that I loved him, or because he said in his last letter to me that I did. I got him home, and made him a cup of tea, after which he seemed better.

He went back to the place where he was then residing, for he did not, as I have already said, live in the house with me.

The following day he came to me very early. That day I was rather short of work.

He said he was sorry he had been in such a bad way

and had behaved so rudely. He next asked me to stay at home for the day.

I said "No, that would not do. I should lose my work."

"Never mind that," said he. He reckoned up how much I was earning, and said, "Look here, darling! If you will promise me not to go to work again, I will pay for your board and lodging. And if Mrs. Adamson likes, I will give her 14s. a week for my board, and come and stay, but not sleep here."

There was no accommodation for him in the house. Eventually my better feelings were overruled, and I submitted myself to him. He was invariably very kind to me, and I did not live with him unhappily.

I knew that he made a living on the proceeds of burglaries which he committed, but I never had any of the goods so stolen; and my dresses were bought for me by him.

He said one day he would have given me a splendid ostrich feather, but he had not got them, because the woman of the house at which he used to lodge would not give them up.

I said "It is very strange if you have things where you used to lodge and cannot get them if you don't owe them anything."

He replied "Never mind; I will buy you one."

One Monday night he brought home a black silk dress, polonaise, and a long jacket, which he said he thought would fit me.

I told him I did not wear such things. He offered to buy me some like them, but this offer I also declined.

If I remember rightly, these things were the proceeds of a burglary at Hull, and I believe they have been given up to the police. I have since worn dresses that were stolen, but they have all been given up now to the police.

Mrs. Adamson went with him one day to look at a pawnbroker's shop, into which she wanted him one night to force an entry, but the project never came to a head.

I believe he thought the premises whereon was so much valuable property were pretty sure to be watched.

Mrs. Adamson would have found means of getting rid of the spoil, but he never did enter the place.

I would rather not mention the name of the street in which the shop was situated.

After that he committed a great cloth robbery at one of the factories, and in the course of a week he went again and stole a great number of coats.

He brought several rolls of cloth and the coats to Mrs. Adamson, who disposed of a great portion of the property to persons whom one would have thought to be of unblemished respectability.

In June, 1877, Mrs. Adamson wanted some blankets, and Peace said he could get her any amount.

He went to get some, or, at any rate, to try, but was detected in the act of entering the house.

He made his escape through a stable and through a woodyard.

Resistance was offered by a man on the premises, but Peace pulled out his revolver and threatened to shoot him; and the man, intimidated, let him get clear away.

PEACE'S FLIGHT FROM NOTTINGHAM.

After that he was constantly concerned in robberies until the occasion of the great silk robbery, for the perpetrator of which £50 reward was offered. That was just before we came to London.

The silk was disposed of by Mrs. Adamson, and the detectives came to her house two or three days after.

Ward, as I then called him, and I were sitting together. We were living together you know, sir, then——the fact is we were in bed together. I was asleep, but the noise the officers made on entering awoke me.

I said, "Oh, Mr. G.," that is the name of the officer who first entered the room. He stood astonished when he saw me. "Oh, Mr. G.," I said, "let me get out of this."

He said, "I am surprised to see you, Mrs. Bailey."

The men turned to the convict Peace and said to him, "What is your name?"

"John Ward," was the rather sullen reply.

"What do you do for a living?" the officer next asked.

"I hawk spectacles."

"Where is your licence?"

"I will show it to you when I come down."

"Get up and dress," said one of the officers.

"I shan't before you," was the reply, in the same sullen tone and manner, "but I will be down directly."

They went downstairs, leaving Ward in the room.

I said to Peace, "Let me go out," whereupon he permitted me to leave the room, and went to my next-door neighbour's, where I was very much hurt indeed at the thought of what had happened.

They asked me what was the matter, and I said, "I do not know."

No sooner had I left the room, than Peace slipped on his clothes, and made his escape through the window, squeezing himself between two iron bars which I am sure were not more than six or eight inches apart.

He ran across the road into the house of a neighbour, whom he got to fetch his boots for him, the detectives being at the time in the house waiting for him to come downstairs.

At last one of them shouted out, "Come, young man, you are a long time coming."

No answer being returned, a move was made upstairs; the door was thrust open, and the discovery made that the bird had flown.

Away from the neighbour's house he went to the Trent side, where he walked for a considerable distance.

When he considered himself safe from recognition, he entered a public-house, where he gave a man 1s. and a note for me.

The note was one asking me to go to him at the place where he was staying, but I declined, and the daughter of the house where I was living went to see him in my stead.

I sent him some money by her, and the answer he made me was that he did not care for all the detectives in England; that he would not lose sight of me; that he would not go away from the place without me.

I belonged, he said, to him, and he would not leave the neighbourhood without me.

He sent yet again, and then I met him by appointment in the evening time, and from that time we have always been together.

We came to London together, and took apartments in the Lambeth district, where he began again that career of crime which has made him so notorious.

But here again his character to the outside world was the same as it had ever been.

Though he was always regarded as a passionate man, he was at the same time looked upon as quiet, peaceable, and inoffensive, and in the highest degree respectable.

As a performer upon the violin he was anything but a mean proficient. He mixed very little with his neighbours, to my knowledge, in this locality, and but little was known of that wonderful fund of ingenuity which he undoubtedly possessed.

Often and often have I said to him what a pity it was that he had not turned his abilities to a better account than for the purpose of committing depredations upon the property of his fellow-creatures; but though his manner to me was kind, he would always jeer and scoff at my rebukes.

It would be utterly impossible for me to enumerate all the robberies he has committed. He has told me at times of his having been into as many as four and even six houses in a single night, sometimes with success, and sometimes, of course, without.

During the day it was his custom to remain in bed, preparing himself for his work in the following evening, when he would regularly go out upon his house-breaking exploits.

Sometimes he came in with a great deal of valuable plunder, consisting chiefly of silver and gold watches, rings, and various other articles. After a while I became tired of living at apartments. Some of his friends from Darnall used to stay there.

We only had one room, though it was comfortable and nicely furnished; and as I did not think it decent for them to come and live with us, I insisted upon Peace providing me with a home that I could call my own; and as he was uniformly good to me at that time, and gave me nearly everything that I asked, he promised that I should have one.

He had just previously committed a great robbery, and he asked me if I would take some money for him to some friends of his at a distance, as he dared not write letters. I consented to this, and several times I took money for him to Hull.

Hannah was living in that town at the time, and kept a shop there. I particularly wish that fact to be stated. Several times I took money to Hull, and never less than £5 at a time. Often I took a great deal more.

MRS. PEACE GOES TO LONDON.

One Sunday evening a knock came at the door at the house where we lived at Lambeth. I answered the door; and saw before me a little elderly woman.

"Does Mrs. Thompson live here?" she asked.

I replied, "Yes."

She then said that she was Hannah.

I called to Peace and said, "Jack, you're wanted."

"Who is it?" he asked.

"Come and see," I replied.

He did, and he found to his surprise, I believe, that it was Hannah.

"What brought you here?" he asked.

I interrupted jocosely with the remark, "I suppose the train."

Hannah, however, said, "Didn't you yet my letter? I have been waiting two hours on the look out 'for you."

"I said, "We received no letter. There is no delivery here on a Sunday morning."

"Jack said, "Come in," and she came in. Having looked round our apartment, she said, "You have a nice place here."

Jack asked her if she would have some supper.

She replied in the affirmative, and this I had to get ready. She then began to talk about his friends and of the people whom they both knew, and I learned in the course of conversation that the shop at Hull had been given up, and that she had realised the proceeds.

Peace asked my permission to have Mrs. Ward and the boy Willie in London.

I could not do otherwise than consent, and eventually they came.

Shortly after their arrival we moved to a house at Greenwich, but as we did not live comfortable in the same house, we moved into separate habitations adjoining each other, Mrs. Ward and her son living in one, and I and Peace in the other.

Whilst we were living in this manner Peace made a journey into the provinces—a thing which he now very seldom did. Whilst upon this excursion he committed a great burglary at Southampton.

The police say that the affair took place at Portsea, but I know better; it was at Southampton. By this robbery Peace cleared something like £200—£60 of the money being in gold and silver, and the remainder in Bank of England notes.

These he found no difficulty in getting rid of. There is a place, I am told, where all Bank of England notes can be disposed of without inquiries being made, but I do not feel justified in stating where it is. That is reserved for the Bank of England authorities.

It was upon the proceeds of that excursion that he started his pony and trap, the expenses of maintaining which he found to be great.

In the first place we had no stable accommodation connected with the house we occupied. This had to be paid for, and the cost of the food for the pony was again a very considerable item.

One day I said to him:

"I don't like this neighbourhood; let us remove from here and get where there is a stable connected with the house."

He told me he had seen a place in the Evalina-road, Peckham, and if I would put my things on we would go and see it, which we did.

We inquired next door as to who was the agent or the landlord of the house, and the lady whom we saw kindly referred us to Mr. Smith. We looked over the house, which we both liked very much. Smith and Peace came to an agreement as to the building of a stable.

When Smith asked for references, Peace said to him:

"Oh, come down and see my house."

Smith did so, dined with us, and went away perfectly satisfied, for a few days afterwards we received a note to say that the house was at our disposal.

Shortly afterwards we removed to the house No. 5, East Terrace, Evalina-road, Peckham, where my troubles commenced.

Mrs. Ward and the boy Willie came to live in the same house with myself and Peace, and her presence occasioned much trouble between us. When we were settled, Peace began his system of robberies again.

Oh! many a time have I, by my tears and by my entreaties, kept that man at home.

I was not allowed to move from the house without either one or the other being with me; but though they were so afraid of me, I should never have breathed a syllable against them.

I have been threatened, and he latterly at times ill-used me.

I have had a pistol pointed at my head and more than once he has threatened to kill me. Peace used occasionally to ill-use Hannah cruelly, and in a way I shudder to think about.

On one occasion he threatened me because I had pawned a silk dress, and he was afraid that it might be traced.

Racked by jealousy, a prey to remorse, and the object of constant suspicion, is it to be wondered that I at last took to drinking?

In this respect Peace was again indulgent, for though he jealously guarded me when I went out, at home I could have what I liked, and with drink I deadened my senses, and fled from my shame and despair.

Peace, as a rule, went out nightly, unless he got a good haul, when he would stop at home for a night or two.

What I call a "good haul" was when he was able to show me plenty of jewellery and silver-plate. I have know him bring home sixty-six ounces at a time. His method of procedure being this: he used to be driven of an evening to within a certain distance of the house where he intended to "work."

If the nights were light, Peace used to be concealed all night and return home, say, between six and seven o'clock in the morning, when some one would go out and meet him.

He was very good to his horse, for I should like people to give him his due; and it was only occasionally that he worked it hard.

He often went to his destination by train or by tram, and some one would go with the trap to meet him at the hour and place appointed. When he has come home haggard and black, as I have often seen him, he has said to me, "Well, pet, have you not got a smile for me?"

According as he had been successful, or the reverse, he would say, "Well, I have not done much, my girl;" or, "I have done pretty well;" and then he would proceed to sort out the property, preparatory to its disposal.

I have seen him shake his head sometimes over the proceeds of the night's takings, and say, "I don't think they will fetch much." Then he would tell me of his struggles and his escapes, and the number of houses he had been into.

Once he told me that, in order to get a gold watch and chain from under a lady's pillow, he had to shift her position slightly.

The lady, he told me, muttered something fond, and turned over to her husband, whom she believed to have been the cause of the very slight disturbance occasioned.

Peace abstracted the watch and chain, and came away. I verily believe that, when such adventures occurred to him, he used to come back sick at heart, for, notwithstanding the profession which he followed, and the fact that he had always firearms which he would not have hesitated to use had he been disturbed, he was generally very kind to me, and I am sure he felt such things.

Now, as to the disposal of the property. If it was valuable, he used to send for those persons who bought of him, and obtain for them such a sum of money as he required.

I am not at liberty to say who those persons were, but Peace used to swear that if ever he was taken he would do for them, and confess as to his accomplices, but I hope I shall not be mixed up in that affair.

I always told him he would go to Blackheath once too often. I cannot say more than the persons to whom he disposed of the property were Jews.

Two I know of, certainly, and they will "Jew" me, I expect, if they get hold of me. One day I went with him while he disposed of some property.

He used to take the property wrapped up like drapers' parcels—innocent and unsuspicious-looking enough. He used to treat me with great kindness when Mrs. Ward was nowhere about.

He seemed to be never so happy as when he could get me alone. We occupied the drawing-room floor, using the front room as a sitting-room and the back as a bedroom, the breakfast-room below being my private sitting-room or boudoir, and the rest of the house being devoted to our lodgers.

The care of Peace's animals, of which, by the way, he was extremely fond, devolved upon myself.

It would be as well, I think, to say what they |were, as the collection was heterogenous.

There were ten guinea pigs, every one of which I gave away when he was taken; a goat, two cats, two Maltese terriers, and a cockatoo; and in addition to these, Mrs. Ward kept a Maltese dog, a parrot, a dog, and four pigeons.

When Peace went out at night to work he always took with him a revolver, a "jemmy," a sharp knife, and various-sized screws wherewith to fasten the doors of rooms in which he was "working," so as to ensure his being able to thoroughly ransack them without being disturbed; but he never took skeleton keys, for he was so skilful that he would take out the panel of a door almost noiselessly and with great rapidity.

When the police caught him they caught the cleverest thief and the cleverest beast that I should think there ever was in human form.

Here, Mrs. Thompson, as I shall continue to call her (that being the name by which she is best known), produced to me an old pair of Peace's trousers.

In addition to the usual side pockets, they were fitted with pockets behind on a level with the hip, and in these receptacles he used, she told me, to stow away his revolver, and whatever instruments he had to take with him.

The inside of the trousers on the left-hand side was filled with a piece of oilskin or glazed cloth, to prevent the iron from chafing the burglar's skin.

Mrs. Thompson also showed me how, by turning in his left foot and by bending up his make-believe arm towards his shoulder, the little man used to assume deformity.

I also obtained from her a description of a burglar's stick, as she called it, which Peace found useful in climbing, and an instrument still more remarkable which, she said he possessed, as a kind of portable step ladder of seventeen steps, which he was able to fold into so small a compass that he could go out with it underneath his coat without attracting attention.

It was provided with hooks, for the purpose of fastening to walls and window ledges, but she said he never used it, owing, I suppose, to the fact that it was a clumsy apparatus to affix noiselessly.

After that she continued her narrative as follows:—

Peace never went out without leaving me with a revolver which, I dare say, I should have the courage to use had occasion presented. He had four revolvers altogether, and the three he left at home I destroyed, when I found he had been taken. Yes, as you suggest, I sank them. When he came to London he ceased to appear as a one-armed man, except in the presence of a man whose name I will not mention.

PEACE'S CAPTURE—DISPOSAL OF PROPERTY.

When we saw in the papers that he had been taken Mrs. Ward cried out, "Oh, my poor Charlie—my poor Charlie! I must go—I dare not stay here; Willie, you must go too."

I then asked her, "And what is to become of me then?"

"Oh," she said, "You are young; you can fight your own battle."

She was for selling everything, but I objected to my

furniture being sold, as I thought I might be able to get a living by letting apartments.

My rooms were well furnished, though I had no carpets, and Jack bought every stick that was in them. We divided all the money that was in the house, about £5, and sold the trap, harness, cushions, and rug for £8, though he had given £14 for the trap alone.

It does not matter to whom they were sold, because the man who bought them did not know at that time that we were other than very respectable people, and I should not like to expose him as having had dealings with us.

Hannah took all the moveables. We divided the ready money, and parted.

I was very firm about the furniture, which Jack said he had bought to be my own. If I liked, he said, he would buy me more.

I was to have had a piano on the 14th December last, as a birthday present.

Heigho! I cannot help feeling that I have made a great mistake. It has blotted my life; but there, I am not going to be sentimental any more. I am not a sentimental sort.

Mrs. Thompson then went on to state that when she found herself quite alone she had applied to a gentleman who had befriended her, and through whom she received the following letter from the wretched man in prison:—

"From John Ward,
    "A prisoner in H.M. Prison, Newgate, November 5, 1878.

"My dearly beloved Wife,

"Oh! do forgive me for what I have brought on myself, and the disgrace upon you. Oh! have mercy on me all of you, and do forgive me for my drunken madness and do all you can for me on my trial, which I think will be about the 18th November, so, my dear wife, do have pity upon me and do your very best for me, for I think that you may do me a great deal of good, that is by doing just as I tell you to do. You must go and tell Mr. —— that I do very much want to see him at once about him coming to speak as to my character. I want to see Mr. —— to see if he will come to speak for me, and I want you to go with Mr. —— to Mr. —— to see if he will come forward to speak to my dealing with him in musical instruments, and tell him that I only want him to come forward and speak the truth of me. My dear wife, you must also find everyone of my letters about my income, and also every invoice about my dealing in musical instruments, and give them to Mr. —— for him to take along with his letters to my solicitor, now, at once, and also let them have some of my cards. My darling dear wife, this must really be attended to at once.

"My dear wife, I feel that there is one great favour, that this has been my first offence, and never having been in prison before, so that by your doing your best for me, and with the help of God, hope it may be better for me than may be expected, and as soon as ever this comes to your hands you must come direct to see me, and never mind the disgrace of your having come to see me in a prison, for I must really see you, so do come to see me, and I want to see my solicitor for something very particular, so that you must tell him to come and see me, and give my dear love to Mr. and Mrs. —— and also to my dear friends.

"I am, your ever loving husband,
    "(Signed)   JOHN WARD."

This gentleman, as Mrs. Thompson further went on to state, had been engaged with Peace in the getting out of a patent for raising sunken vessels. To him she applied when Peace was taken, she stating that he had left her and gone off with another woman.

He took her into his house, and under his persuasion she disclosed what she knew of him—not, she said, for her own protection, for she would willingly have been taken herself, but because it was represented to her that she must forward the ends of justice.

I then tried to obtain from her some particulars of the past life of Peace, but as to these she was extremely reticent.

"How did he really escape on the night of the murder?" I asked.

Mrs. Thompson replied—

"I have never breathed this to any one. I have had people try and try, and try over again.

"According to what he has told me, he climbed over a wall opposite Mr. Dyson's house, and walked deliberately over a field.

"He has told me the name, but I do not remember. I got a lot out of him through his dreams, but he never told me he had committed murder. He said it was something else he had to run away for.

"He went direct to his aunt's house. Having first cut off his beard, he dressed himself in a fustian suit, and went across country, committing little depredations to help him on his journey, for he had no money until he arrived at Bradford.

"He did not personate a one-armed man then; that device he did not carry into effect until he was at Hull. He took a room at Bradford and kept two women there, who used to assist him in burglaries.

He has often boasted to me of his achievements in that town and others, and he seemed to find a particular sort of pride in the fact that in one case it took him and one of his accomplices three days to remove some things from a furnished house which the tenants had temporarily left, and which, so far as articles of value were concerned, he literally cleared out.

"He has told me a good deal about his earlier career, but I can't recall it to mind just now. First of all, he told me he was a sort of worker in the iron trade; that ever since he was fourteen he was a thief. Some time between 1852 and 1854 he resided with Mrs. Peace at Manchester. He was brought up for trial on a charge of burglary about that time, and Mrs. Peace had to sell the things in the house they lived in—most of them being stolen—to procure him professional advice upon his trial. He was committed for seven years, and while he was in prison he communicated with her, and always knew of her whereabouts.

"He managed to write more than the police officials knew of, for he had a way of pasting up his letters which he has shown me. When he had regained his liberty, which he told me was in 1858, he rejoined Hannah and resumed his old courses. When he went out on his exploits he wore stockings over his boots to conceal his footmarks."

Mrs. Thompson made various other statements respecting the notorious man who was the subject of our conversation, but they were not calculated to add much to the existing stock of information concerning him.

Either she did not know much of Peace before she went to live with him, or she did not care to make any disclosures; but, as our interview lasted for something over five hours, she must have been tired and her memory confused.

A MOTHER SEEKING HER SON IN THE THIEVES' KITCHEN.

I was not such a barbarian as not to have offered her some refreshment during that period. She took it in the form of steak and onions, rinsed down with brandy and water.

When we parted we were the best friends in the world; she shook me warmly by the hand, and her last remark was, "I have my own character to redeem, and if I have my health and strength I hope to do it."

The foregoing is a faithful chronicle of the account given by the woman Thompson.

We have on more than one occasion given the reader an insight of the mode in which Peace disposed of his stolen property. He did not, however, confine his business transactions in this respect to one receiver, or "fence."

This has been already demonstrated. He had several confederates to whom he disposed of the goods he had so dexterously purloined, but in most cases he had to part with them at what drapers are accustomed to term "a ruinous sacrifice."

This is invariably the case with burglars and robbers of every description. The receiver has always the best of the bargain.

The property must be got rid of, and this the "fence" knows perfectly well.

Peace, in addition to the two other Israelites already introduced to the reader had a Petticoat-lane confederate, who during his London career bought largely of him. This personage was interviewed by one of the special correspondents of the press. We subjoin a graphic account of his visit.

"That's my name, and you're quite right about my keeping a tobacco shop in this lane, and about my buying and selling 'most all kinds of old stores."

This was the reply given to a comprehensive interrogatory addressed by a Sheffield reporter to a middle-aged keeper of a public-house in Petticoat-lane, whose name indicated that he was "of the order of Melchisedeck," and who, rumour said, knew something of the manner in which the convict Peace had invested some of the money it is supposed he must have been possessed of shortly before his arrest.

If the police with their finished machinery and well-trained inquisitors have been able to discover nothing, it was hardly to be expected that the astute Hebrew dealer would allow himself to be trapped into any prejudicial admissions by a newspaper emissary, even though he was simply charged with the high and philanthropic duty of affording that dealer opportunity for clearing from his character aspersions which had been unjustly cast upon it.

Having informed the "old stores" man of the charitable nature of his mission, said the "special":—

"Now, I suppose you never knew or had any dealings with Peace?"

"Me, dealings with Peace! Why, I never heard or seen 'im, except when I was bound over to keep it for six months, 'cause I give a cove a knock in the eye."

At this sally the rowdy-looking congregation in the bar, who had evinced a lively interest in the interview, delivered themselves of a unanimous guffaw. The special smiled blandly, and went on:

"I suppose you have seen what the papers have been saying about your supposed connection with Peace?"

"Oh, yes; I've seen it all. It's all wrong. I'm quite innocent o' this thing. Besides, it aint nothing to do with me. It aint me they mean. It's the other man with the same name that keeps the 'knell' down the lane. If they wrote about me I should 'a took it up; but as they didn't, I shall not trouble about it."

"Glad to find you're so clear of this nasty business; but have you heard much about the rumours here in the lane?"

"No; nothing except what there's bin in the newspapers."

"Ah! then I think I'll call on the man at the 'knell,' and hear what he's got to say."

"Yes, that'll be 'sgood a thing as you can do," said the store dealer; and as the special passed the threshold sounds of merry cachinnation reached him from the idlers at the bar.

Trudging through the snow-slush, with pipe in mouth as an antidote to the many-flavoured, fever-charged atmosphere, the interviewer in a few minutes found himself outside the "knell."

The proprietor having been inquired for, he was summoned from upstairs, and in about five minutes presented himself. He was a very young man. He was in his shirt sleeves.

He was short, but had good shoulders and breadth of chest, and his face, which had a puffiness betokening free application to the pewter pot, was adorned with a nose off one side of which the skin had been almost entirely scraped. A smile was as foreign to him apparently as vegetation to an iceberg.

The interviewer made no attempt to smile upon this young and promising vendor of Old Tom. He did not make another.

There was not the remotest smirk of sympathy or approbation in the countenance of his vis-à-vis.

He listened stoically to a few introductory original observations by the special, such as, "Very unexpected fall of snow this."

"Quite an old-fashioned winter."

"Spring will soon be here now, though."

But on learning the nature of the caller's business he was no longer passive.

His eyes brightened and jumped a bit, and he became loquacious, but continued cynical.

"I haven't got nothing to say about the matter. All I know is that I don't know nothing about Peace or about his money, or his loan society, or anything else. Besides, the newspapers know all about the case already. If they knows s'much, what do they want to send to me about it for?"

"Well, the fact is," answered the special, "the function of a newspaper is to put the public in possession of reliable information. Reports which compromise your honour have been given currency, and although minute inquiry has been made no particle of foundation has been found for them. What I want is to get hold of the facts necessary to put the public au courant with things as they really are, and at the same time afford a much-injured party a means of retrieving his good name."

The short man with the broad shoulders, stuck his hands in his breeches pockets, spread his legs, swung his head to and fro, lifted his eyelashes, and remarked, "Ah! you do—do you?"

Then he turned round to his wife and inquired of her in surly tones why she had called him down, and muttered something to her not at all complimentary to newspaperdom or its labourers.

"Well, look here, Mister. I don't care for what the newspapers say. Let 'em find out what they can. I aint got nothin' to say. All I knows is that if the papers says anything about me they'll be sorry for it, that's all."

"Ah! but they have done so already. They have mentioned both your name and that of your house."

"Well, what if they have? What good have they done?" rejoined the innkeeper, and then he continued, "I've been bothered enough over this matter already, and I don't want to be bothered any more." So saying he left the special in dudgeon.

The rumours which have been afloat anent Peace's confederates in Petticoat-lane have been sufficiently weighty to justify a descent by the police on the houses of the suspected parties.

Nothing criminating was, however, forthcoming, and the probability is that, wanting divulgence by Peace, the public will remain ignorant what has become of whatever money he has stored.

Inspired by the extraordinary statements circulated at this time as to the enormous amount of property alleged to have been disposed of by Peace, and by the reported "finds" of hidden spoil in London, the *Daily Telegraph* writes :—

"For a precedent to the curious museum of plunder now in police custody at Bethnal-green we must go back to the days of that very eminent 'fence,' Jonathan Wild.

"The real character of this remarkable scoundrel has been unfortunately obscured, first in Fielding's masterly 'Jonathan Wild the Great,' which is fundamentally a satire upon the statesmen of his time ; and next in Mr. Ainsworth's foolish and mischievous romance of 'Jack Sheppard.'

"We must peruse the straightforward and dispassionate Old Bailey sessions papers to study Jonathan in his true aspect as a cunning, adroit, and not ill-educated rascal, who first reduced robbing to a system, and organised a detailed scheme for receiving and disposing of stolen goods.

"He started in business on a very small scale as the landlord of a little alehouse in Cock-alley, Cripplegate, where he surreptitiously purchased the 'takings' of the juvenile pickpockets from Moorfields.

"At night he would perambulate the brandy shops of Fleet-street, and traffic with the women who had contrived to rob drunken people of their watches or pocket-books.

"Growing bolder with success, it is on positive criminal record that he convened a meeting at his house of the most notorious thieves in London, and represented to them that if they took their booty to such of the pawnbrokers as were known not to be troubled with scruples of conscience, they—the thieves—would scarcely receive a fifth of the value of the goods which they had stolen ; whereas if they could agree to bring their prizes to him he would make much more liberal terms for them.

"The penalty for failing to constitute Jonathan Wild their receiver-general was simply death. Bad faith was immediately resented by the denunciation of the thief to justice ; and unless he could come to an arrangement with Wild the chances were overwhelming in favour of the robber going to Tyburn.

"Thus Jonathan Wild was not only a preceptor of thieves and a 'putter-up' of robberies, but also a receiver of stolen goods, and a thieftaker to boot.

"Removing from Cock-alley to a house in the Old Bailey, he found at length that he had accumulated an embarrassingly heavy stock of stolen property, and he absolutely purchased a sloop in order to transport his plunder to Holland and Flanders.

"The command of this vessel was entrusted to one Roger Johnson, a noted river pirate ; and Wild's factor at Ostend, and general Continental agent, was a superannuated thief called Randall.

"The sloop—her name, unfortunately, is not mentioned in the records of rascality—having discharged her cargo at Ostend, brought back to England such commodities as lace, wine, and brandy, which were landed at night, and, it is almost needless to say, without the custom-house authorities being troubled in the matter.

"Smuggling and dealing in stolen goods are operations possibly, no longer carried on in conjunction ; still, who shall say that our modern Jonathan Wilds have not their favourite lines of steamers—it is not now necessary that they should buy ships of their own—and that they have not their factors and agents at Continental ports and in Continental cities ?

"Many thousands of pounds' worth of jewellery and bank-note—to name only two sorts of plunder—are stolen every year.

"There must be a mart for this precious merchandise, a mart the whereabouts of which must be perfectly familiar to professional burglars and thieves.

"Bank robbers and pickpockets have been known coolly to admit that the market price for a stolen five-pound note is three pounds ten shillings. Who buys stolen bank notes at this rate ? Who melts down the stolen plate ? Who wrenches the stolen gems out of their settings ? Who sends the unset jewels to Amsterdam and elsewhere ?

"If the police are unable to find out the wholesale dealers in stolen property, and trust to chance to make such a haul as they made the other day in the Commercial-road, might it not be expedient to allow the next professional burglar we catch to turn Queen's evidence against the receivers ?

"No terms can be made with a murderer, and Peace must be left to the gallows ; but most useful revelations might be obtained from a professional housebreaker permitted to turn approver.

"Such a witness, if his evidence proved trustworthy, should receive—strictly or once in a-way—a full pardon.

"Convicts sentenced to penal servitude are not apt to be very grateful for a partial remission of their term of durance ; and, indeed, in the case of Mr. Harry Benson, the Government, it appears, does not conceive that it is under any obligation at all to the convict for having made an exhibition of the old detective force in its full iniquity.'"

In tracing the criminal career of a desperate character like Peace, it is curious to note how prone to wrong-doing he was from his earliest youth. His first theft is thus described :—

"An apple of beautiful hue tempted Eve to her first sin, and it is said that fruit of a similar name first induced Peace to commit a serious theft. In the year 1830 he lived close to the orchard of the Rev. Joseph Smith, whose residence was known as the Plantation.

"The rev. gentleman was the pastor of the flock who worshipped at the Nether Chapel in Norfolk-street. But the 'Plantation' on Langsett-road had a different prospect to what is now the case.

"Then it was in the country really ; on the banks behind the houses were farms and orchards ; beneath the house were meadows sloping to the River Don, which was then alive with fish, trout being plentiful in the waters, and at times a salmon or sea-trout strayed into these higher regions from the Ouse.

"The railway connecting Sheffield with Manchester had not made its black streak across the opposite Old Park-hill, and a pleasant place was the residence of the Independent minister of those days.

"Behind the good man's house was a goodly orchard, and within the enclosure fruit trees which carried crops of heavy, golden fruit.

"The lads of the neighbourhood viewed those crops with envy, and one of the leading spirits among them was Charles Peace, a well-instructed lad, fearless, venturesome, and domineering in spirit.

"He planned the robbery of the pastor's orchard, but being inexperienced, was captured—whilst in an apple tree.

"He had not learnt in those days the wiles and deceits which have since come so naturally to him.

"But he had not to cope with detectives, inspectors, constables, and other professional men, who render life obnoxious to a thief. His captor was actually the parish beadle.

"Had that man lived until these days how proudly he might have said—

"'I caught Peace!'

"But the youthful aspirant to future honours did not obtain the reward he should have had for his speculation.

"He bargained for apples, and instead was taken before the wrathful owner of the fruit, Mr. Smith. The beadle shortly afterwards had a task to undertake which left no mark in local history, but did on the young man who stole the apples.

"Such was the commencement in 'active' life of him who now occupies a cell in Newgate, from thence to be taken to answer a record of crime the which has not been paralleled by Claude Duval, Thomas King, Richard Turpin, or others of that ilk.

"Those men had not the telegraph to compete with, yet failed; Peace had the widespread information of modern days to watch, and yet for a time succeeded.

"The marauders of the old school, above mentioned, defeated justice for a time because on their thorough-bred horses they could outride the messengers of justice.

"Peace had to fight against the magnificent apparatus of science by which information is flashed across a thousand miles in a second of time, and yet he succeeded in baffling all who sought to track him."

The blow that had fallen on Peace and his domestic circle was a terrible one, and in a short space of time, after his conviction, the house in the Evalina-road was tenantless.

A visit to the locality is thus described by an eye-witness:—

"Peckham approached from Greenwich, with a suggestion of sunshine in the sky, looked much prettier to-day. There are some goodly houses along Queen's-road, but as one climbs the hill to Peace's part, the houses taper away till long lines of modest brick buildings meet the eye. Where Peace lived may be called the tail-end of Peckham.

"His house is still to let, and though nobody that I can hear of has been to visit it—except members of the Press—the gentleman who has the letting of it thinks he will get a couple of pounds extra now that it has sprung into notoriety.

"Well, he may. I don't know so much about the peculiarities of the Peckham people; but on this point I am inclined to agree with the lady who lives next door. She wants to let her front room, and has 'Apartments' in the window.

"That card appeals in vain to the eligible young gentlemen who usually want comfortable chambers, and she is afraid that respectable people will not care to come into such a 'dreadful' neighbourhood.

"She considers it a bad day for her when she came there, which she did a week before Peace was found out. Indeed, it was from Peace she had the keys to look over the house. An ominous introduction truly.

"Her idea is that before that house lets again £2 will have to be taken off, instead of being put on, the rent. I agree with her, for I can hear of nobody who has a good word for the house, except perhaps the postman, who told me, as we trudged together through the mud, that 'it wasn't a bad place in his view of it. The Thompsons did not trouble him much—they had very few letters.'

"A neighbour says that when the Thompsons came their house was a treat to look at, Mr. Thompson filling all the front windows with choice and costly flowers, which he carefully tended and watered with his own hands.

"People at Peckham are beginning to be a trifle impatient with inquisitive strangers who want to know about their most famous character. On my first visit to Peckham I looked in on the gentleman who combines the duties connected with her Majesty's mails with dispensing flour and other household necessities to her Majesty's females.

"I asked him if he knew and could tell me where 'Mr. Smith' lived—the party who had let the house to Mr. Thompson? This gentleman shut me up very sharp.

"'I know where Mr. Smith lives, but I don't think I would be justified in telling you, as you would only be bothering him like the rest.'

"I left that establishment with a feeling that my introduction to the natives of Peckham was not encouraging. A few yards further on I saw Mr. Smith's address in the windows of half-a-dozen empty houses, the notices inviting people to apply to 'Mr. Smith, Ryde Villas, St. Mary's-road.'

"I accepted the invitation, and found Mr. Smith a most obliging and very communicative gentleman.

HOW PEACE WAS FOUND OUT.

"I find the police scout the idea that the man 'Ward' was discovered through the jealousy of Mrs. Thompson, the younger of the 'housekeepers' at Peckham, and the professed wife of Peace.

"Those who had to do with the case told me that they had no information whatever from Mrs. Thompson, who never communicated with them, but disappeared as she sniffed danger.

"'How then,' I asked, 'did it occur to you to connect the Blackheath burglar with the Bannercross murderer?'

"'Well,' was the reply, 'we can scarcely tell you. We could not get our evidence so complete as we could wish, and we were obliged to wait for a time. That waiting served us well. Trifles, mere trifles, such as we can scarcely repeat to you, made us believe that this man was 'somebody.' We watched those who came about our place at Greenwich; then we watched those who came about Newgate. We got, after great trouble, a hint or two; we acted upon what we received, and were ultimately able to connect the man 'Ward' with Peckham; then from Peckham we worked Nottingham and Sheffield, and then the case gradually worked itself into shape.'

"For the police it was a lucky thing Mrs. 'Ward' took those two boxes to Sheffield.

"That, I believe, was really the first indication that Blackheath and Bannercross were connected.

"It suddenly flashed across one of the Greenwich division that this mysterious man, who called himself a 'half-caste,' resembled in every respect except one the man so urgently 'wanted' at Sheffield.

"That exception was his hair, particularly the absence of beard and whiskers. Height, breadth, eyes, manner of talking, singularity of fingers, and wide, straddling walk — to quote the police description, 'walking with his legs apart'—all tallied. Put beard and whiskers upon that face, and it was—Peace.

"Inspector Bonny went to Nottingham; Inspector Phillips to Sheffield.

"Phillips was shown a portrait of Peace. He was confirmed in his suspicions. The photograph resembled the man in Newgate so closely that he had no doubt as to the identity.

"The rest of the story you know. How Phillips and Twibell found the property at Darnall in the possession of Mrs. Peace, how the property was identified as part of the proceeds of the Blackheath burglaries, how Police-constable Morris came to London and identified Peace in Newgate, and (as I telegraphed to you) how the Treasury, appreciating the importance of the case in the light of the identification, undertook the prosecution on its own account.

"To Police-officer Robinson undoubtedly belongs in the first instance the credit of capturing Peace. He unquestionably risked his life in his courageous encounter with the desperate convict, and well deserves such recognition as has been suggested by your correspondent.

"Let it not be forgotten, however, that Robinson's share in the transaction terminated there. Without him nothing would have been done; yet after Peace's bullet pierced his arm and the two constables came to his help, Robinson dropped the thread, which was picked up by Inspector Phillips and Inspector Bonny.

"These officers have been indefatigable in their exertions to bring home the graver charge against Peace. Day by day, and night after night they have laboured, and many a night since the memorable evening when Peace was caught in the act, they have slept not, neither have they rested, so anxious have they been to close once for all the career of the dreadful villain whose escape made everybody so uneasy.

"But it should not be forgotten (observed a writer at the time) if testimonials are spoken of, to remember these two officers.

"Robinson was a brave fellow, and acted like a hero; yet if Bonny and Phillips had not used their brains, and set their highly-trained wits to work, 'John Ward' might have been convicted of the Blackheath burglary and the shooting of the intrepid Robinson, and he might have been sentenced to penal servitude for life; but in Sheffield the Bannercross murder would have been regarded as an undiscovered crime.

"To Bonny and Phillips belong the credit of proving that Ward was Peace, that Blackheath meant Bannercross, that burglary was overshadowed by the bigger crime of murder. A wave of relief swept over Sheffield when it was known that Peace had really been captured at last. To Phillips and Bonny was due the fact that he was thought of at all as the man who shot Dyson two years before.

THE TROUBLES OF THE PEACES.

"There is really no peace for the Peaces. Now that Charles Peace, the man of Bannercross, has been caught there are dozens of persons who are anxious to tell all they know about him and his family.

"Several of them have got it into their heads that there is only one family of Peace, the head and front of which now awaits in Newgate the reward of his desperate misdeeds.

"Thus it comes about that several most excellent people are getting uneasy about the name they bear, particularly when they find it connected with some of the early doings of "the insignificant-looking" gentleman who has recently sprung into so much significance.

"The latest instance is that of a family of Peace who lived some time ago in Philadelphia—not the Philadelphia which figures in Sacred Writ, but the exceedingly secular locality of that name which figures in Sheffield.

"Mr. Charles Peace, of George-street, Philadelphia,

has no connection whatever with the Charles Peace of the many aliases, burglar and murderer; neither is it right that his son, who also bears the (in these days) somewhat burdensome name of Charles Peace, should be associated with the person who has proved himself so eligible a candidate for the last attentions of the law.

"It is certainly a trifle too bad, even when people are thirsting for every particle of information about that extraordinary character, that the respectable member of a respectable firm of file manufacturers in Pea-croft, or his son who earns his livelihood in an honourable way in the file trade at Rotherham, should have themselves brought up in public as connected in even the remotest degree with the ruffian who had the misfortune to call himself by their name.

"So that, once for all, readers will understand the Philadelphia Peace and the Bannercross Peace are wide as the poles asunder.

"This incident reminds one of the trouble and suspicion to which many people were put shortly after the murder.

"Peace, it will be remembered, was described as a 'little, insignificant-looking man, with grey hair.'

"There was at once an eager look-out kept for people who answered that somewhat general description. It was a bad time for 'little insignificant-looking men,' and as our local world has a good many people who come fairly within that description, several estimable and other citizens were frequently the object of glances which were not at all flattering in their meaning.

"Two elderly gentlemen were pointed out as greatly resembling the notorious Peace, and enjoyed a reputation on that account only a shade less comfortable than other gentlemen in this district, of most substantial proportions, who up to a short time ago were repeatedly referred to as remarkably like the Claimant.

"Even when a more specific description of Peace appeared mistakes were freely made, though not with the provoking results of a double apprehension, as in the case of that poor tramp at Barrow-in-Furness, who was subsequently apprehended at Hexham, and who complained bitterly—and not unnaturally—to our reporter who interviewed him in prison, that he should have been arrested a second time 'when the police had already let him go once.'

"This poor fellow, to put matters right once for all, made a pilgrimage to Sheffield and called upon the Chief Constable, who, of course, had no more to do with his arrest at Barrow-in-Furness and Hexham than the poor tramp had to do with the arrest of the real Peace by Police-constable Robinson in that garden at Blackheath."

CHAPTER CLI.

A VISIT TO WHITECHAPEL—THE STREET OF WOMEN—A MOTHER SEEKING HER SON.

WE must leave Charles Peace for awhile to gather up the tangled threads of our story, and follow the fortunes of other characters who have figured in this "strange eventful history."

The capture and conviction of our hero, together with the remarkable concurrence of circumstances connected with the history of the most accomplished and desperate burglar of modern times, created an amount of public interest which was altogether of an exceptional character.

This interest was not confined to one class of the populace. It permeated throughout every conceivable class from the highest to the lowest, and as a natural consequence the criminal portion of the community were deeply interested in the fate of one who had proved himself to be so much ahead of any of his compeers in crime.

Peace was looked upon as a sort of hero, Many admired him, and not a few pitied him. His adventurous life, his daring exploits, found favour in the eyes of rogues and thieves of a lesser degree, and his exploits formed the theme of conversation among numberless sections of the lawless portion of the thieving fraternity of London.

We must take a glance at one of the haunts of the dissolute and depraved. It is Saturday night, and the hour is ten o'clock. All London is alive. for Saturday night is the market-time of the poor.

The streets of Whitechapel presented remarkable scenes. Huge crowds passed down them, and bought their Sunday dinners from the butchers' stalls upon the pavement, where joints of raw meat were suspended upon hooks, and which were lighted by pipes of blazing gas. Others crowded into the fried-fish shops and supped ravenously on rank plaice swimming in oil. Others resorted to the taverns, which were adorned with portraits of pugilists, and regaled themselves with Old Tom for which Whitechapel is so famous.

Close to one of these streets, where rioting and business seemed to go hand in hand, there was a narrow lane, silent as death. Gigantic warehouses rising on each side seemed to shut out heaven.

A man was walking down the lane—his appearance was dejected and his eyes were bent on the ground.

When he had come to the end of the lane he dived into a dark alley, which brought him out close to a railway arch.

Hollowed in the side of this arch was a hole like the mouth of a cavern, and running under the railway supported by black pillars was a street.

This was "the street of women," described in the early portion of this work; it was the place where Laura Stanbridge led the boy, Alf Purvis, on a dark night.

Our pedestrian walked along the street, and the women who stood at their doors brawny, repulsive, and naked as the ogresses of old, did not molest him even with their tongues.

They looked upon him with kindness, for they had heard that he was the friend and companion of the celebrated Charles Peace, the burglar, and hence it was that they gazed at him in silence, with something like a feeling of reverence.

He turned down a yard and stood opposite to a house dilapidated and apparently untenanted, but from the cellar windows of which came shouts of laughter and streams of light.

He entered by the same means as those previously described, and having gained the kitchen, which was filled with thieves and beggars, sat down in a corner by himself.

There were several men seated round a table; at a little distance from the rest a tall pale man, who was clad in the dirtiest rags, but who, nevertheless, could afford to drink gin—and doses in large quantities—was speaking.

"It's the greatest pity in the world as that gang got broke up by the beaks; they were an honour to our English gemmen—they were an honour to our land."

"Ye—es," said a man with a white comforter tied over his mouth, "ye—es; so I thought till they got nabbed like that there in the country. That was a pitiful job—old hands like that goin' time arter time on the same beat, and almost on the same lay, with the whole vorld, as one might say, before 'em. It's jolly hard—that's what it is."

"I tell you how it happened," observed another of the company, who was smoking a short pipe, "the whole country laid awake at night a watching for 'em."

"There was somethink under the rose, depend on't," said a red-faced man in a green cutaway, and his whiskers cropped in that peculiar fashion which stamps the habitué of the race-course. "Smoucher and Jim were both high-flyers and knew how to make their books as well as any going; but there's days on which even the knowin' ones gets taken in, though not so often as the knowing ones would have you believe. Well, it's a pity as how they were copped. They'd never have gone into the neighbourhood if it had not ha' bin for the Dandy."

"Vell, there now, I hope as how he aint a goin' to blame Alf for it," said the man with the comforter.

"In conrse not. Who says I do?"

"Nobody as I knows on."

"I remember," said the pale man, "the first night as the Dandy came to this 'ere blessed crib, and sat at this 'ere table and drank Max with Lorrie Stanbridge. She brought him here. I remember it well enough. Why, he was only a boy then, but his eyes were as sharp as needles, and his long white fingers seemed a 'itching for the game even then."

"Ah," soliloquised the gentleman with the white comforter, "Vat a pictur that hand vos to be sure!"

"I was made a cadger on that night in the little room upstairs. The 'Smoucher' used to have it then, just as Lorrie has it now; but as I was a coming out who should I see but these two—Lorrie and the little bloke? I guessed as how he was to be 'chanted the play' too, but I didn't guess as how that smock-faced kid was a goin' to turn out as he has."

"I never liked the 'Smoucher,'" said the sporting man, "though I've often been on the 'flimsy-kiddy' and the 'ring dodge' down at Ascot with him. Still, I'm sorry he was made a target on, which, for sartain I am he has bin."

"But, Jim," said the man with the muffled mouth, "he vas a good sort. S'posin there vas any nasty or ticklish vork to be done on the fly, sitch as breaking a bobby's head, he vas alvays ready and foremost to do it himself, instead of trying to put it on his pals."

"Breaking a bobby's head!" exclaimed another of the party; "'taint so easily done. It's all very well for you chaps to talk, but I say it aint so easy. But, Lord love yer, there aint anybody here as is fit to hold a candle to Charley Peace—he was the man to knock over the bobbies."

"There aint no manner of doubt of that there," said the pale man; "not a shadow of doubt. Charley was a wonder."

"That he was, and no flies," said Cooney, for he it was who had introduced the name of our hero. "He was allers straight and square with me; I aint got a word to say against him. You chaps here talk about the 'Smoucher' and the 'Dandy'—why they were fools compared to Peace."

"I dare say they were, or indeed are," observed the man with the pipe; "but yer see, I never happened to fall across Peace. He was a bloke who, from what I've been told, kept hisself to hisself. Vell, I don't care about blokes of that kidney. 'Live and let live,' that's my motter, and do as ye'd be done by."

"Well, and who says Charlie wasn't one of that sort? He allers acted fair and square with his pals."

"Ah, he was a wonder," exclaimed the man with

the muffler. "He stands alone—there aint a bloke as can come up to 'im. Pity he's been nabbed, 'cause ye see he was a stunner in every way—leastways, I'm only a speakin' from what I've heard."

"Oh, you are right enough," returned Cooney. "You may take your davy about Charlie. You won't find such another throughout England."

"I'm precious sorry for him, poor chap. I don't know as I was ever so broken down in the whole course of my life as when I heer'd of his conviction, 'cause you see he proved himself to be a downright good sort, as far as I am concerned."

"But yer aint seen much of him of late, have yer?" inquired the pale-faced man.

"No, not much; yer know he was like hide-and-seek, and he kept as much to himself as possible; but, law, he wasn't to blame for that, seeing what were agen him, he worked on the quiet, all to himself as yer might say."

"And didn't care about trusting anybody—eh?"

"Right you are, old man," said Cooney, with a nod. "But for all that, I wouldn't mind doing a seven years' stretch if I could see him out of limbo, but Lord bless us, there aint much chance of that now. They've got poor old Charlie pretty tight, and he's done for."

"Will be tried for the Bannercross murder, I 'spose?"

"That's their game—so I've been told."

"Ah!" said the pale-faced man, "this is how we lose our friends; the best on 'em get nabbed, them as we care most about go the first. It's the way of the world."

"Who's that old woman over there, talking to Bandy-legged Bill?" suddenly exclaimed the sporting man.

"Can't say," said the man in the white muffler. "She comes here to see Bill, and seldom speaks to any one else."

"But who is she? Don't you know her name?"

"Oh, yes—she's known as Mother Grover."

"Thank you for the information. I am about as wise as ever. Who is she, and what brings her here?"

"She wants to know about the Dandy, wishes to find him out, so I've been given to understand."

"Does she want to pinch him, the old cat?"

"Ah, no. Hark ye," said the man with the muffler. "She's greatly interested about the Dandy, and I've been told she's his mother."

"Oh, scissors!" exclaimed the sporting man. "His mother—eh?"

"That's about the size of it," ejaculated the other, with a mysterious nod. "She was a bosom friend of Lorrie's years and years ago; but they chipped out, and my lady, I mean Lorrie of course, is a bit too much for her. Oh, there's a mystery about the Dandy and his belongings, but I do honestly believe that yonder woman is his mother."

"It's a rum story, take it altogether," cried Cooney. "That woman is for ever following upon the heels of Bill Rawton. Why I cannot tell you."

There was a dead silence for some time after this, but the eyes of most present were directed to the corner of the apartment where the gipsy and his companion sat.

The last-named were conversing in a low tone, which was but a little above a whisper.

"You are not so callous and hardened," said the woman, "as to be dead to all feeling for another. I ask you to find my boy. You can do so—of that I feel assured. You know Laura Stanbridge, who is his friend, or professes to be so."

"Hold hard," interrupted Rawton. "Don't be quite so fast, mother. I am not her friend. I know her. She has done me a good turn more than once, and I have had it in my power to return the compliment. What of that?"

"What of it? A great deal. She will listen to you, and I wish you to do me a turn. I wish you to help me to find my son."

"I don't believe Lorrie knows where he is, and I am quite certain that I do not, and, what is more, I don't want to know. He's a chap I never cared a bit about—he was a deal too uppish for my money, and thought too much of himself; so you see it ain't at all likely that I can assist you."

"In other words, you won't."

"I would if I could."

"You can—of that I feel perfectly well assured. It was into this house, years ago," she murmured, in a low and concentrated voice—"it was into this very house that she decoyed my poor innocent boy, and I, loving him, I knew not why—crouching on the cold stones outside—shivering under the bitter winds. But ah, woman without heart! your day shall come, and it is nigh at hand."

"Be silent," whispered Rawton. "They will hear you."

"I do not care who hears me."

"But I do. You do not know the people here so well as I do. Your life might be sacrificed if they suspected your purpose."

"Is it wrong or wicked for a mother to strive to rescue her son from the depths of sin?"

The gipsy laughed.

"You make a jest of it—do so," returned his companion.

"Rescue the Dandy—rescue Alf Purvis! Bah"

A shade of sorrow passed over the features of the woman.

"Is he lost, utterly and irretrievably, then?" she inquired. "Answer me, Rawton."

"You and I are not likely to agree upon this subject," returned he. "I must tell you frankly that he is as unprincipled as he is worthless."

"Do you wish to drive me mad?" said Mrs. Grover.

"Certainly not. But you must not place all the faults of this young gentleman upon the shoulders of Lorrie Stanbridge."

"Who taught him? Who brought him up as a thief? She did!"

"We will not argue that question. He proved to be a pretty good pupil, and was not good for much when she took him in hand."

"What has she made of him? Oh, Rawton, you know but too well, although you do not choose to say. Listen to me. I am growing old, have no tie but one, it is my boy; restore him to me, and heaven will bless you. Think of the many dreary and desolate years I have passed—think of all I have suffered, and take pity on me."

"I do pity you," cried the gipsy. "I am sorry for you, but what's the use of that? You cannot be benefitted by my pity or commiseration. I do not know anything about Purvis; if I did I would tell you all I knew."

"But you can find him—I am sure you can if you set about the task with a free goodwill."

"Ask Lorrie Stanbridge. She is the person to apply to. Alf, to the best of my belief, is abroad. He has left his country for his country's good, that is all I know about the matter."

"He did leave England, but he has returned—he

must have returned by this time. You can aid me. Oh, Mr. Rawton, you are kindly disposed, are not sunk so low, but have, I am certain, some good left in your disposition. I am a friend of Mrs. Bourne's, and she speaks of you as a man who is——"

"Who is what?" cried Bill, with sudden vehemence, and interrupting the speaker. "As what? Mrs. Bourne!—do you know her?"

"Yes. Have known her for many years."

"I never heard that—Mrs. Bourne, eh?"

"Yes, the widow of Dr. Bourne. He who committed suicide."

"I know. There is no occasion for you to tell me about that. I know the whole history of his crime, and his end."

"You acted fair enough towards her."

"Well, what of that? Who says I didn't?" cried the gipsy, evidently moved.

"Nobody. If they did I should suppose they spoke an untruth."

"Look here," said Bill Rawton, after a pause. "You want me to help you, and I aint the man to say no to such a request, but that is one thing. I may have the will, which, to say the truth, I have, but I have not the power. I know nothing about this young gentleman—no, nothing about Alf Purvis, or Mr. Algernon Sutherland, as he now calls himself. Let me give you a word of advice. Don't trouble yourself about the young scapegrace. You wouldn't be much benefitted by finding him."

"But he is my son. Oh, sir, think of that."

"I do think of it."

"Well, what then?"

"He is better lost than found."

"Have you so bad an opinion of him, then?"

"I have a very bad opinion of him."

"I dare say he has become hardened, and, as a natural consequence, is despised by many of his associates."

"I am not one of his associates. Please to understand that," said Bill Rawton, "I never cared anything about him—a stuck-up conceited jackanapes. I tell you frankly, I would never have anything to say to him—'cause why?—he wasn't my sort."

"You hate him then?"

"I never liked him, if that's what you want to know."

"Oh, I do not want to know anything about his doings, or about his enemies. All I want is my son. Will you help me to find him?"

"I'll do what I can to serve you, but you musn't bother me as you've been doing lately. If I learn anything about him I'll let you know."

"You promise that?"

"I do. There's a mystery about this young shaver, but it aint no business of mine. You want to see him?"

"I do."

"Well, if I can put you on the scent I will—that's all I have to say. So now you had better step it, for my friends yonder are wondering what business I have with you, so make tracks as soon as possible, or may be we shall get into the mire."

The woman drew from her pocket a piece of dirty crumpled paper, which she handed to Bandy-legged Bill.

"There is my name and address," said she, "and, oh, Mr. Rawton, I pray you to do your best. Restore my son to me, and I shall owe you a lasting debt of gratitude."

"All right, mother," said Bill, pocketing the paper. I'll do my best for yer."

The woman rose and took her departure.

"Vell I'm blest," cried the man with the cutaway coat. "Blow me tight if Bill hasn't got a woman on the hooks. We shall see a big wedding presently, I s'pose."

"I hope she's got plenty of blunt, and that we may be invited, the whole piling on us, to the wedding breakfast," remarked the man with the cutaway coat.

"She's no blunt, you fool, said the pale-faced man. No such luck."

"Ah, I see, Bill's going to marry her for her beauty—a love match, eh? observed another of the party.

"You're a set of noodles to be talkin' like that 'ere," said Cooney. "Don't ye know who she is?"

"No, I don't," returned the sporting man.

"Vell, then, I do. 'Tis Mother Grover, as vas a friend of Lorrie Stanbridge's some years ago."

There was a prolonged "ah!" at this last observation.

"That's about the size of it," observed Rawton. "There's a bit of mystery about the Dandy. He came from a good stock, so I've been given to understand, and the woman who has just left is his mother."

"Tell us all about it, Bill," exclaimed several. "You aint the man to keep anything from your pals."

"I don't know as I've anything to tell you," said Bill Rawton.

"Ah, gammon an' all," exclaimed the sporting man, "but if you are making up to the young and fascinating widow, and the matter is of a private nature, vell, in course ve won't ax any further questions."

"Shut up," cried Rawton. "Making up to her! You must be going off your nut to be a-talking in that way."

"Ah vell, I'm sorry I spoke."

At this last observation there was a loud peal of laughter.

"You've got yer chaffing togs on to-day, it would seem," observed the gipsy. "But there aint no secret in the case. The woman, as I said afore, is the mother of the Dandy—leastways that's what I believe, and I don't see any reason to doubt what she says. She's been on to me for ever so long to find him for her. You know, all on yer, that he aint now on good terms with Laura Stanbridge; why or wherefore this is I don't rightly know, and, as yer all know, he hasn't shown up of late."

"He's got a precious sight too proud to mix with any of us. He was allers a la-de-da stuck up young shaver," remarked the man with the white comforter, "and wasn't at any time quite my book. But that's neither here nor there. He's mizzled, turned tail, and keeps aristocratic company—so I've been told—and much good may it do him—but go on. The old woman wants to find him. I hope as how he's come into a fortune."

"And if he has he'll spend it jolly quick," said Cooney.

"Not the least doubt of that, old stick-in-the-mud," observed another of this choice assembly. "But stow magging—Bill's got something to tell us."

"No, I've not," returned Rawton. "You know just about as much as I do myself, and if any on yer can find the Dandy, why it 'ill be doing the old 'oman a service, and you won't go unrewarded when you give her the tip."

"That's business," ejaculated the pale-faced man. "I likes a chap to come to business without any long palaver. If any on us tumble over my gentleman we shall know what to do. Do you see that, mates?"

WITH A SUDDEN PUSH, SHE HURLED HIM OVER THE CLIFF.

"Aye, aye, governor, we all on us see that," exclaimed several.

"But is it a plant?" suggested the man with the cutaway coat.

"Plant, Lord love yer, no," returned Rawton. "The old 'oman's right enough, right as the mail—I'll take

my davy on that; but she does take on, and no mistake. She'd give her life to find the Dandy."

"But, hang it all, she never took much notice on him when she was with Laura," said Cooney. "It's a rum start, take it all together."

"She didn't take much notice on him at that time, I admit," answered Bill. "But why didn't she?"

"Can't say."

"Then I'll tell yer. She didn't know then that he was her son. Do you understand now, old thickhead?"

"Vell, I didn't understand it rightly," returned Cooney; but I s'pose it's square and straight."

"As straight as an arrow, take my word for it."

"I don't care which way it is," said Cooney. "Blow the Dandy, say I. I only wish I could get Charley Peace out of quod."

"Ah," replied the gipsy, "and so do I. He's worth fifty Dandys."

"Have you seen anything on him?"

"Yes. I saw him on the day of his trial."

"And how was he?"

"Oh, miserably cast down. Couldn't hold up at all."

"Poor chap. It's hard lines. Why, the sentence was a cruel one."

"It was—it was!" exclaimed several. "Everybody says so!"

"And what everybody says must be right—leastways, it can't be very far wrong," said Bill. "But it aint of no manner of use a-talking about that— Charley's potted. There aint much chance now of his ever being a free man, not unless he can get the Home Office to commute his sentence, but I 'xpect there ain't much chance of that."

"Lord bless yer," said Cooney, "yer might jist as well 'xpect to lift up St. Paul's in the palm of yer hand. Commute—blow me tight, there aint no manner of chance of that there—and mind ye, Charley's as right as the mail—never turned round on a cove in all his mortal days. Well, here's to his good health."

The speaker raised a full goblet to his lips and toasted our hero.

The woman known as Mrs. Grover, and who had been pleading so pertinaciously to Bill Rawton, was no other than Isabel Purvis, the mother of Alf Purvis.

The reader will doubtless remember that Laura Stanbridge had with her as a companion a Mrs. Grover when she first took Purvis under her protecting wing.

At this time her companion had no idea that the young bird-seller was her own son, but she had taken to him by one of those unaccountable influences which are past the comprehension of ordinary individuals.

As years passed over her head she comprehended that Miss Stanbridge's protegé was her own offspring.

When the fact became clearly established she was solicitous of finding the young scapegrace, and for this purpose she applied to the gipsy.

Mrs. Grover, or more properly speaking, Isabel Purvis, had in early life been associated with a tribe of gipsies, and here it was that she had made the acquaintance of Bill Rawton.

She knew his wife, and had been mixed up with the wandering tribe, to which he at one time belonged, and hence it was that she sought his assistance in tracing out her son, the worthless young scoundrel, Alf Purvis, or Algernon Sutherland, as he chose to term himself.

CHAPTER CLII.

A POPULAR WATERING PLACE—THE RENCONTRE, AND FEARFUL DENOUEMENT.

LEAVING the unwholesome purlieus of Whitechapel, we must journey to the resort of City clerks, Jews, tradesmen, professional men, and, in short, people of almost every denomination.

Margate, in the season, simply means London out of town. People flock to this place in shoals. It is, of course, requisite for the Cockneys to rejoice in buff slippers, nautical hats, and sea-side costume, and it is equally necessary for them to throng the pier and jetty, and ogle each other with a pertinacity which, it is presumed, is highly satisfactory to themselves, and agreeable to everybody; but our business is not with the select visitors to the jetty or the pier; for the purposes of our story we have to take a glance at another part of the well-known watering-place.

On the cliffs, just where the Infirmary stands, two figures might be seen walking side by side—they are in close conversation—the time is evening—the sun is set, and the vault of heaven is speckled with myriads of stars.

The two persons engaged in conversation are well known to the reader.

One is Tom Gatliffe, of whom we have heard but little of late, and the other is Laura Stanbridge, who, albeit somewhat faded, as far as her general appearance is concerned, carried with her yet the traces of that beauty which, in the years that are passed, stood her in such good stead.

She has lost but little of that fascination of manner which may be likened to that of the wily serpent— but she is more staid and thoughtful—and we may add even more dangerous in many ways than she has been heretofore.

Gatliffe had at one time been perfectly fascinated with her blandishments, and for many years she held him in bondage. Now, however, he could be esteemed only a sort of friend, if such a term could, with propriety, be used; anyway the connection between the two was now severed.

Gatliffe, who had betaken himself to Margate for a change, met Laura accidentally there: people do meet at Margate in a most unaccountable manner, and this was the case with those two. They became for the nonce inseparable companions during their sojourn at at the sea-side.

"It has been well said," observed Laura Stanbridge, "that one has only to go to the sea-side to renew old acquaintanceships. Such appears to be the case with us. My dear Tom, of late you have not thought it worth while to call upon me as of yore. Have had other matters to engage your attention, I suppose."

"Well, to say the truth, I have," returned her companion.

"I judged so. Do not for a moment imagine I am saying this as a reproach. On the contrary I believe, and always have believed, you to be genuine. Still, it would pain me much if it came to pass that we should be no longer good friends and true. You understand my meanings, at our age one does not so easily form new friendship; and this, I suppose, is the reason why I cling so tenaciously to those whom I have known in earlier and, I think I may add, in happier years."

"Happier!" repeated Gatliffe, with something like sorrow in his tone."

"Certainly, happier."

"Oh," answered her companion, "the brightest days of my life have long since passed away, and I have not much to live for now."

"Not much to live for? You are a prosperous man, and have reason to be thankful, all things considered. It is true you have been deserted by one who ought to have clung to you, but I expect you have cast from your mind a woman who has proved herself to be unworthy consideration."

"Silence!" exclaimed Gatliffe. "I do not care to listen to observations of this nature. Do not speak disparagingly of one who, whatever her faults may be, is far removed from either of us. I am surprised at the observations you have made, and I must beg of you not to allude to this subject. Indeed, I am at a loss to imagine why you have chosen to broach it."

"Oh, I have done. She was once your wife, and now——"

"She is nothing to me only an honourable lady, whom I cannot do aught else but esteem and admire; but pray how did you come to know about my connections?"

Laura Stanbridge laughed.

"How?" said she. "Why, my dear Tom, I suppose you will admit that your divorce is a matter of public notoriety?"

"It was so many years ago I wish it to be forgotten. I wish to forget it myself if that be possible."

"Then I will never again allude to the circumstance. My dear Tom, you need not be told that I am not likely to say anything to offend or annoy you. The past has passed away, and we have only to look to the future."

"That is true," said he, "and do you know, Lorrie, I have serious thoughts of beginning life again if that be possible?"

"And how do you propose to do this?"

"Well, I'll tell you. I propose going to one of the Colonies—to America, or Australia, it doesn't much matter which; but I am certain I shall be able to do well in either place, and, to say the truth, I am thoroughly sick of this country."

"Why, so am I," quickly rejoined his companion. "Let us go together, a woman has a better chance there than in England. Take me with you."

Gatliffe made no reply, but appeared to be lost in thought.

"You do not answer," said she. "I'll work and slave for you, and be your faithful friend and companion. Oh, what happiness it would give me, for I love you—and none other but you!"

She placed her arm round his shoulders, drew him towards her, and embraced him fondly. She was like the syrens of old—false and seductive.

"We will talk about this on some future occasion," observed he, for he had not altogether the faith in the woman by his side as he had during the first few years of their acquaintance.

Nevertheless he was in some measure attached to her, and found it difficult to shake her off. She was his evil genius.

At one time he had, like many others, been infatuated with her, but this infatuation had in a great measure passed away. Still, even at this time, she exercised considerable power over him, and most unquestionably she had to a great extent lowered his moral tone.

It has been said, and there is no denying the fact, that we are all creatures of circumstances. Poor Gatliffe had been the victim of untoward events which were far beyond his own control.

There were times when he thought of the woman whom he in the earlier years of his life indulged and almost worshipped, but she had left him for rank and power.

He did not blame—on the contrary, he made every possible excuse for her desertion of him.

He was not, however, aware that his own illicit intercourse with Laura Stanbridge had become known to her very shortly after his intimacy with that heartless, designing, and worthless woman, who lured but to betray.

It is just possible that he might have been prevailed upon to suffer her to accompany him to Australia or America, but a circumstance occurred which put that altogether out of the question.

This it will be our purpose to describe.

Gatliffe and Miss Stanbridge were walking close to the edge of the cliffs, as the moonlight cast its beams on that part of the rocky eminence running from where the Infirmary stands to a place known at this time as Marsh Bay.

It will be perhaps needless to say that his female companion demonstrated the strongest affection for him, and made use of all her blandishments to draw him towards her.

A spectator at a casual glance would have conjectured that they were lovers—albeit they were neither of them particularly young at this time.

They had not gone very far when the figure of a man was observed making towards them. He was coming in the opposite direction to the one they were taking.

Laura Stanbridge was at no loss to understand who the stranger was, and perhaps, of all men in the world, he was the very last she had any desire to see.

As he approached he indulged in a low satirical mocking laugh, which jarred upon the ears of Gatliffe's companion.

"Ah, oh!" he ejaculated. "It is you, eh? and with your fancy man, too! I am most charmed at this unexpected meeting, because it gives me assurance that you are alive and well, which is vastly consolatory. Taking a moonlight stroll, my charmer—eh?"

Gatliffe did not condescend to take any notice of these sneering observations, but he was a little ruffled, nevertheless.

"You will be pleased, or, rather, I shall be, by your abstaining from sneering observations, and if you have nothing better to say, pass on."

"Not till I have a word or two with you, madam," said Alf Purvis, for the new comer was none other than he.

"Not until I have told you a piece of my mind. You think, perhaps, that I am in ignorance of your doings. Who was it that betrayed me, and set on detectives to find out the forged cheque business? A curse light on you!"

"This lady is under my protection," said Gatliffe, "and I must request you to go your way."

"You request?"

"Yes, most certainly; this is not the time or place for you to indulge in personal and impertinent remarks."

"Do not heed what he says," ejaculated Miss Stanbridge. "He is unworthy of notice."

"It is of no use your endeavouring to carry it off with a high hand, you worthless, base woman," cried Purvis. "I know you, my lady. No one knows you better, and it will go hard with me if I don't have my revenge. You have betrayed us. Do you hear, you infamous strumpet?" he added, shaking his fist in her face.

"You audacious young scoundrel!" exclaimed Gatliffe, who was by this time incensed beyond all reasonable endurance. "Begone, while you have a whole skin."

"You threaten, do you? Do you happen to know the character of the woman you seek to shield and protect? Shall I tell you a little of her history? It will greatly interest you, I dare say. Listen ——"

"Get you away, and give me no more of your impudence," exclaimed Gatliffe.

Alf Purvis indulged in a low mocking laugh, which so exasperated his adversary that he raised his fist and gave him a heavy blow on the chest, sending him reeling back several paces.

When he had recovered from this first assault, Purvis rushed at Gatliffe and struck him in the face. The latter closed with his younger opponent, and a struggle ensued, which was, however, but of short duration, for Purvis was no match for the powerful and athletic engineer, who threw him violently to the earth, and when he rose again stood on the defensive.

But by this time Alf had had enough. He stood scowling and swearing at a respectful distance.

"Come dear," said Laura Stanbridge, "Let there be an end to this. I am sorry to have been the occasion of this scene of violence."

"You sorry!" exclaimed Purvis, "Have you any feeling? You care as little about him as I do about you. I am sure a worthless creature like you is hardly worth quarrelling about."

Tom Gatliffe and his female companion walked on, followed by their tormentor, who was bent upon mischief.

He gave expression to a series of taunts and degrading observations, but now that the first outburst of passion was over Gatliffe had no desire to recommence hostilities. Nevertheless he was greatly annoyed at the pertinacity of Purvis, who continued to aggravate Laura Stanbridge in a manner which soon became insupportable.

"You had better discontinue those impertinent remarks. Go your ways. We neither of us have any desire to listen to your impertinence," said Gatliffe.

"I don't want to pick a quarrel with you, sir," returned Purvis. "You have done me no wrong, but as to your companion, she has been the very bane of my existence. She it was, who, when I was a helpless lad, taught me to become a thief. I am not romancing. She has made me what I am. Perhaps you don't know that she is a trainer of thieves."

"Silence! No more of this, you audacious miscreant," cried Gatliffe, in a violent rage.

"And you are her champion! Well I wish you a better office."

"If you persist in annoying us, I will inflict summary chastisement on you, let the consequence be what it will."

"I say again I have no desire to fasten a quarrel on you, Mr. Gatliffe. I believe you to be upright and honourable, but that's no reason for your espousing the cause of one who is so utterly worthless. In the due course of time you will be convinced of the truth of all I have been saying. Take my advice—have nothing to do with that woman. Shall I tell you her early history?"

"I again request you to keep your remarks to yourself," observed Gatliffe, who was at this time overwhelmed with astonishment at the turn the conversation had been taking.

"Well, sir," said Purvis, "on consideration, it is doubtless neither pleasing nor palatable to you to hear the truth spoken, but I warn you to be careful in dealing with the odious woman by your side. In the earlier years of her life she was under the protection of an old gentleman, whom she robbed and afterwards poisoned. I have the whole history of this part of her career by heart—she is an adultress and a murderess. Listen to the story I have to tell."

Alf Purvis was on the edge of the cliffs when he made these last remarks. Laura Stanbridge, who was at this time pale with ill-suppressed passion, sprang forward, and stretching out her arms, she with a tiger-like spring, rushed full at her traducer. Throwing the whole weight of her body in the sudden assault, she pushed Alf Purvis with such terrible force that he reeled and tottered for a moment, then a loud splash in the water told that the ill-fated young man had fallen over the precipice.

"Gracious heavens, what have you done?" exclaimed her companion pale as ashes and trembling in every limb. "He has fallen over."

"And a good job too; I know how to protect myself."

Poor Gatliffe was stupefied with astonishment and fear.

"But this is murder," cried he.

"Not so," returned his companion with perfect composure—"he has *fallen over the cliff*. Do you understand?"

"I will be no party to such an act of atrocity," said he. "Oh, miserably guilty woman, have you no pity, no remorse?"

"Not any for him—none whatever."

Gatliffe, who was at this time almost beside himself, looked over the cliff.

The tide had been at the flood about half-an-hour before the murderous act. It was now flowing out. Gatliffe saw a dark speck on the water, which he judged to be the head of Purvis.

He rushed madly from the spot, and made for a narrow cutting which led to the sea-shore.

But one dominant thought possessed him. He had a burning desire to save the victim of the atrocious outrage.

But how this was to be accomplished he could not very well determine. When he came to the end of the cutting, his eyes rested on a boat, which had been moored against a stake driven into the sands.

He released the boat, jumped in, and rowed his hardest.

Far out in the distance he beheld a black speck, which he believed to be Purvis, who, despite the giddy height from which he had fallen, might yet be swimming for his life.

"Pray heaven it may be so," he ejaculated. "If he is lost I shall never forgive myself."

He pulled lustily at the oars. The sea was rather rough, and although he was a tolerably good rower on the Thames, or any other river, he had but little experience in the management of a craft on the sea; but he did not care much about the danger and risk he was running—he was actuated by a higher feeling.

His object was to save and succour a fellow-creature, and so he bore bravely on. As he did so he heard Laura Stanbridge's voice. Heard her cry out—

"Come back, Tom. The attempt is useless."

He took no heed of the warning, and never stopped till he had come within sight of the black speck. Then, to his dismay and horror, he discovered his mistake. It was but a floating buoy.

He was so moved by this discovery that he was near bursting into tears.

His eyes swept the waste of waters, but he could discern nothing like a human form; yet, nothing daunted, he rowed in almost every direction in the hope of seeing some trace of Purvis.

Darkness now fell upon the scene—some heavy clouds obscured the moon, and sadly and reluctantly the unhappy rower made for the shore.

When he had gained the cutting he moored the boat to the stake, and slowly and sadly crept up towards the cliffs.

"Oh, that I should have lived to see this dreadful sight—this infamous, cruel, and cold-blooded assassination!" he ejaculated. "It is most horrible—most infamous! What is to be done? I feel as if I had been party to a murder, and shall never know what peace of mind means."

His knees seemed to sink under him, and he was so utterly prostrated that he felt as weak as a child.

When he reached the cliffs he was confronted by Laura Stanbridge.

"Well," said she," "the attempt you have made has not proved successful, I suppose?"

"Go, woman!" he exclaimed, bitterly. "I will have naught to say to you. Go your ways, and never—never let me set eyes upon you again. I cannot express to you my disgust and horror. A curse will cling to you."

"He deserved his fate, and it is useless now to indulge in recriminations. He drove me to madness, and upon the impulse of the moment I did an act which in cooler moments I should have shuddered at. Do not upbraid me. It was but a sudden impulse. I was smarting under his taunts, his infamous, slanders, but it is done. The worst is over."

"The worst, woman! The worst is to come—a life of bitter remorse!"

"Well, Tom, I regret——"

"Don't talk to me. Don't call me Tom. The tie between us is broken now and for ever!"

"Do you intend to betray me, then?"

"I know not what to do. I am so supremely wretched that I wish I sank beneath the waves."

"What folly is this? It was an accident—a mere accident. Of course I never intended to hurl him from the cliff. Do you think it's likely? Listen—for my sake you must keep silent. It is known only to our two selves. He fell over by accident—walked too near the edge, and then you did your best to save him. Nothing can be plainer."

"I'll be no party to so infamous a crime. I will not tell an untruth. No, not to save your worthless life. You are a monster, a murderess, and I have done with you."

"I am in your power to a certain extent, I admit. Still, at the same time, permit me to observe that you will do well by holding your tongue, for your own sake as well as mine," she added, with something like a sneer. "Do you understand?"

"Just Heaven! do you dare to threaten?"

"I don't threaten, my friend—I merely suggest, and my suggestion is a very natural and reasonable one, and when you have only considered the matter I doubt not that you will be of my opinion."

Tom Gatliffe was perfectly appalled, not only at the observations which had fallen from her, but at his own position.

If she chose to accuse him of the crime, what witness could he call to prove his innocence?

He could not deny that he had struck the murdered man—that they had a short but fierce struggle.

He felt that he was in a very dangerous position.

All these thoughts rushed rapidly through his brain, and he was almost inclined to look upon himself as an accessory.

"Ah!" he ejaculated. "Cursed be the hour when I first set eyes upon you."

"It's no use you talking in that way. We have known each other for many years. There are numbers of persons who will vouch for that, and so it's no use your endeavouring to shirk the question. This miserable business may, in a great measure, be attributed to my love for you."

"Are you mad, woman?" cried Gatliffe, drawing back with ineffable disgust. "Your love for me! I have brought myself to a pretty pass, it seems."

"No doubt you have, dearest," she returned with perfect composure.

He now saw the nature of the woman with whom he had to deal, and the last words uttered by Purvis seemed to be almost prophetic.

He stood for a moment or two gazing upon the woman who was so callous and hardened that she did not demonstrate the faintest symptom of remorse for the atrocious act she had perpetrated.

"So," said she, "it would appear that you, like the rest, are disposed to round on me. I confess I was not prepared for this, but after all it does not matter."

"I do not understand you, woman," he ejaculated. "I am appalled, and am utterly at a loss. A murder has been committed before my very eyes—a crime so infamous that I stand aghast—and am almost petrified with astonishment. Had I guessed your horrible purpose——"

"Don't make matters worse by abusing me—it will not serve any purpose. It is necessary, for both of our sakes, that we should be friends," she observed, in a low tone.

"Friends!" he exclaimed. "Never again will I consent to even hold discourse with you—never again will I hold out the hand of friendship to a cold, cruel, heartless assassin. Get thee hence! I will not have anything further to say to you."

He turned and was about to take his departure.

"Oh," said she, "it is thus you treat me. Stay a moment, if you please. Possibly you are about to denounce me."

"And if I am it is no more than you deserve."

"We will not argue that question. Do so if you please; but, hark ye, Mr. Thomas Gatliffe, a word in your ear. If you accuse me of committing this atrocious crime, as you term it, I must tell you frankly, I shall be constrained, in self-defence, to declare that you are the murderer of Alf Purvis. So it is, perhaps, just as well for you to understand what you have to expect."

"Infamous, abandoned, and guilty woman!" cried Gatliffe, who was at this time driven to a state bordering on distraction. "I have no fear for myself. Think not to escape by such a miserable device. I both abhor and contemn you. Away, wretch! Away, murderess and adultress; I am far beyond the reach of your malice—go!"

"I shall go when I feel disposed to do so. I am proof against your taunts and abuse, and I should advise you to be a little more temperate in your language. You don't know at present whom you have to deal with."

"I say, go. I will have nothing more to say to one who is so vile."

"Very well, sir, as you please. We are to part in anger, it would seem. The fault is not mine."

"Yours!" exclaimed Gatliffe, casting upon her a look of unutterable disgust. "Part in anger! Away, woman—away! I loathe the very sight of you."

She came forward with the intention of making an urgent appeal to him, but he thrust her fiercely from him, turned on his heel, and without uttering another word fled from the spot.

When he reached Margate he made for the station, booked for London, and hastened on to the metropolis.

Laura Stanbridge, after he had left her so abruptly, remained for some time lost in thought.

"Ah," she murmured, "he'll keep silent upon this subject—I think I know enough of him to be assured of that. He is not likely to turn against me for all his vapouring. I don't think I have much to fear as far as he is concerned; but if he does play me false, well, I have my remedy, which I shall not hesitate to make use of. Anyway, he will find it difficult to come out of the business with clean hands—certainly not without a strong shade of suspicion. Let him do his worst, then, if he means to turn traitor. Yes, let him do his worst. That base, ungrateful boy has met with his deserts. For years I have been thirsting for revenge, but never deemed it would be brought about in this fashion."

She walked slowly on in the direction of a small cottage, which she rented furnished, for a few weeks during the season.

Upon her entering the habitation in question, her maid observed that she looked troubled and careworn. the reason for this alteration in her appearance the girl could not quite understand, but she said nothing, laid the table for supper and then looked inquiringly at her mistress.

" Oh! any visitors? Is that what you mean?" said Miss Stanbridge.

" Yes, ma'am."

" Not any visitors to-night, Jane. Mr. Gatliffe is called suddenly away. I shall be all alone this evening."

The table having been laid, and the supper served, Miss Stanbridge partook of her evening meal as if nothing had happened. Her heart was as hard and petrified as the nether millstone.

CHAPTER CLIII.
THE STOKE FERRYMAN.

Tom Gatliffe, as we have already intimated, went direct up to London, after the terrible scene on the cliffs.

He made up his mind to cast off the woman who had, in days gone by, held him in bondage.

Come what would, he was determined never to have anything further to say to her. But his mind was distraught, and every turn he expected to learn that a body had been picked up off Margate.

However, days passed on, and no news received of the ill-fated Alf Purvis; but Tom could not dismiss from his mind the harrowing circumstances connected with the tragedy, and deemed it advisable to keep silent and await patiently the issue. It would be time enough for him to be outspoken when he felt assured that silence would be criminal.

The infamous woman—the perpetrator of the act of atrocity which we have recorded—remained for a few days in Margate after the event, then she, like her companion, returned to the metropolis.

She was quite calm and self-possessed, and did not appear to have any remorse for the past, or fears for the future.

*   *   *   *   *   *   *

On the side of a dark-rolling river, half buried among willows and rushes, stood a small cottage. Suspended before the door was a large bell, the rope of which swung backwards and forwards in the breeze.

The road which passed the cottage consisted of two huge ruts, with grass growing in the space between; it ended at the river bank.

To this bank were chained two boats—the one a kind of barge adapted for the carrying of vehicles and large burdens; the other one of those small flat-bottomed boats which may be propelled either by oar or pole and which are called punts.

It was Stoke Ferry, the most desolate of all spots on the river as it passes on its course to the sea. The cottage was the residence of the ferryman—the bell was rung by those who wished to be ferried over to the other side.

Some years previously the house and ferry had been put into the auction-room. An old man whom nobody knew had bought them, and had lived there since that day.

He was never seen outside his door, except to ply his calling as a ferryman, and once a month to go to London, where he would always remain a night and return the next day with a face, they said, more pale and stern than before.

He had no servant in the house to help him; he did all his washing and cleaning himself; he took his meat from the butcher, his bread from the baker, and his milk from the farmer's man at the door. He was only known by the name of the Stoke Ferryman.

His habitation was well suited to a misanthrope; it was surrounded by barren fields, exposed to cold winds, and in the winter the river would flood his garden, and would beat against his primitive residence, the walls of which were mossy and green from damp.

The neighbours looked with astonishment upon this man as a sort of natural curiosity. He remained buried in solitude within sight of men; he dwelt amongst waters, and seemed to live in eternal cold and darkness, for no lights ever shone from his windows—no smoke ever rose from his chimney.

When there was a dearth of scandal—it was not often this was the case—but when there was a lull in this respect, the gossips would always fall back upon the Stoke Ferryman.

Some said he was a sorcerer, that he had dealings with the Evil One; some that he was a criminal hiding from the eyes of the law; others that he was only an eccentric individual, who was a little crazed in consequence of a great trouble he had met with in early life.

When the children in the neighbourhood were troublesome and could not be brought to order by ordinary means, they were told that they would be handed over to the Stoke Ferryman, and this threat invariably had the desired effect.

At a little less than a half mile from the ferry stood the habitation and fertile land known as Stoke Ferry Farm, and at about two miles distance or a little more perhaps, was the residence of Mr. Kensett, the magistrate.

It was the hour of twilight. Frogs croaked hoarsely from the damp ditches by the river-side, sometimes an owl flew past with its white ghastly wings and hollow cry.

A woman stood before the ferryman's house. Her face was pale and haggard, her limbs were weary, and her garments were soiled.

She stood there for some minutes in a state of trepidation. Presently she seemed to muster up courage, for she seized the rope and rang the bell violently.

The cottage door was opened, and an old man with a lantern advanced down the garden path slowly towards the gate.

Through the bars of the gate which was secured by a padlock, he examined her face.

" Umph," he murmured, " I suppose you wish to cross over, madam."

" No, I do not. I wish to speak with you," she answered.

" Speak to me! And what might it be upon? Well, I am all attention, proceed."

" I wish to speak to you alone."

The old man extended his thin, horny hand towards the barren, dusty plain, then towards the silent river.

"You may speak here safely," said he, with a grim smile. "We are quite alone, and I do not expect we shall be interrupted by visitors."

"Ah, sir," she cried, in a tone of anguish, "they say you know more than other men, and if this be so, which I do not for a moment doubt, you may be able to render me a service."

"I do not at present see in what way. What is it you desire?"

"To find my son, whom I have been searching in vain for."

The ferryman regarded her for a moment, and then shook his head.

"Do not refuse me the assistance I require. If I do not find my poor boy, I shall die. My feet are blistered with walking, my eyes are sore with weeping, and my heart is pining for him I cannot find. Oh, sir, if you have the power to assist me, you will not—you cannot refuse."

She fell upon the damp ground, and prayed with clasped hands to him who looked at her through her gate.

"Such are women," muttered the misanthrope. "When their own resources have failed them, they make one shallow hope an assurance, and appeal to a poor old man as if he were a god."

"It is my last hope," she moaned.

"What is your name?" he asked, absently.

"I am called Mrs. Grover," she returned, "but that is not my real name."

"And what might be your real name, then?"

"Purvis."

"Ah, indeed. I have heard it before, I think," he ejaculated, as he gave a convulsive start, while his eyes glared at her through the iron bars like those of a caged wolf who sniffs blood in the air.

There was a pause of several minutes—then he slowly unlocked the gate.

"You had better come in," said he.

She entered.

He opened the door of his house and bade her follow him.

She entered a room which was heated by a clear coal stove, and that was why no smoke ever rose from his chimney. It was lighted by an oil lamp suspended from the ceiling,|while huge oaken shutters, and a baize edging to the foot of the door, prevented a gleam of light from penetrating abroad.

The walls and floor were hidden by books; a table in the centre was covered with papers, and with instruments of a kind which she had never seen before.

He trimmed the lamp, and sat down, leaning his face on his hand. He seemed to be lost in thought, but all this while his eyes were bent upon her—his eyes full of sorrow and compassion.

Under other circumstances, the woman would have been frightened, and, as it was, she was not without certain misgivings; she was in the lone habitation of a forlorn and mysterious man.

She was surprised at his pensive attitude, and his singular silence, which appeared to her to be almost preternatural.

"Ah, sir, you already know my errand," said she in a beseeching tone. Do not keep me in suspense. If you can do anything in respect to my poor boy, I feel assured you will not deny me the favour I ask."

"If I can. Ah," murmured the recluse, "does it not strike you as being a little remarkable that you should seek the assistance of a poor old hermit like myself? I have no home, woman—am poor—and, I may say, despised. How can I serve you?"

"I want to find my boy—he who, years ago, was at Stoke Ferry farmhouse.

"From which place he ran away?"

"He was turned away. The cruel farmer tied a hare round his neck, and beat him unmercifully. Small wonder is it then that the poor lad left Stoke Ferry farm for good and for all."

"He did not leave it for good—not for any good, as far as he was concerned."

"He was the son of a gentleman, and could ill brook the cruel usage to which he was subjected."

"We will not quarrel about that, Mrs. Grover," said the ferryman; "it is hardly worth while. Mr. Jamblin was a worthy man—a little headstrong, perhaps, but he was a good man for all that. Do not speak ill of the dead."

"Oh, I don't speak ill of Mr. Jamblin. Still, had he been a little more tolerant, the boy would not have been driven to seek his living in the streets; neither would he have associated with lawless characters."

"Isabel Purvis, the thoughtlessness of man, and the bleeding of your own heart, drove you to a crime—you abandoned the child which you, as its mother, ought to have cherished. Is not this so?"

"It is—I do not deny it. But I have had a life-long punishment."

"True, you have repented. You are punished now, but you will be pardoned hereafter, let us hope," he added, in a lower tone.

She shuddered, and felt half afraid of the mysterious man who spoke so calmly, and appeared to be so self-possessed.

"You have heard my last observations—have you not?"

"Yes," said she, "and they have sunk deep in my heart. It is quite true. My son has led an evil life—so I have been told."

"Who told you?"

"I have heard it from several."

"Name one."

"William Rawton."

"Rawton—Rawton! He's a gipsy—is he not?"

"Yes. Do you know him?"

"I have seen him once or twice—that is all. Cannot he give you any information about your son, whom, it would appear, you are now, all of a sudden, so anxious to see?"

"It is not so sudden. I have been anxious to see him for a long time past. You forget, sir, that it is only lately I have had reasons for thinking he was my son."

"Ah, true, there is something in that. It's a pity you had not known it earlier."

"I divine your meaning," she cried, seizing his hands. "You know he is dead, and do not like to tell me. And yet——"

"Yet what?"

"He cannot be dead, he is so young."

The ferryman rose, and opened a small cabinet.

From this he took a book bound in black, and placed it on the table before him.

Now his face became stern, jets of fire seemed to dart from his deep-sunken piercing eyes.

Mrs. Grover began to tremble.

"In this book," he muttered, in a hollow voice, "are recorded the vile deeds of a woman who is as nefarious as she is alluring."

Mrs. Grover started to her feet.

"What is her name?" said she.

"It would not benefit you if I were to tell you," he answered.

"But I can guess. I think I know whom you mean."

"Do you? Please to say then."

"Her name is Stanbridge."

The old man nodded and pored over his book.

"Am I right?" she inquired.

"Be silent!" he cried, "Have you no wounds in your heart which words will open? Be silent, my friend, and listen to your woes which are kindred to my own.'

He opened the book. She shuddered. There were pages of writing, and the letters were all red.

"You need not be under any apprehension," said her companion. "I am not likely to do you or anybody else any harm, although my ways are not altogether like the ways of other men."

He turned to a particular page in the book.

"Listen," said he. Then he read.

"Isabel Purvis.—Hiding from the police for the abandonment and attempted murder of her child. Repentant, and desirous of gaining an honest livelihood. The daughter of Satan discovers her—she pretends friendship, worms from her the relation of her crime, threatens to hand her over to justice if she refuses to obey her, and to destroy her."

Mrs. Grover groaned.

"Yes, yes!" she ejaculated; "all this is but too true—every word of it. How could it have become known to you?"

"That is my business," said he, turning to another page.

"Alfred Purvis runs away from Stoke Ferry Farm, and sells birds' nests in London. The fiend finds him in a low lodging-house in Westminster, takes him to her den, depraves his mind by slow degrees, teaches him to cheat, places him under a notorious thief, sends Mrs. Grover upon the streets because she, warned by the instincts of a mother's love——"

"I did not know at that time that he was my son," cried the miserable woman.

"Possibly not. Indeed it is certain you did not; but listen. Alfred Purvis was placed under the care of Mr. Jamblin—he ran away to London. In different hands he might have been a credit to his relatives—I say he might—it is not certain—but he might; but under an obstinate agriculturist he became mischievous, and under a fiend——"

"Why do you not continue?" exclaimed the woman. "There is more writing on the page. Go on. Pray go on. I can bear it—indeed I can. I am quite calm, as you see."

He closed the book, she sprang towards him with a yell, but his eyes repelled her; it was not because they were stern—it was because they were so sorrowful. She crept back from him.

"Tell me, sir, for mercy's sake—tell me if he is alive or dead. His grandfather, Lyme Kensett, yearns to see him. Already he has saved this unhappy and ill-fated young man from being convicted—now he wishes to make him his heir. Is he alive?"

"He is," said the old ferryman—"he is alive."

"Bless you for telling me this. It has given me new life. I may yet see him. Tell me where he is. Oh, give him to me!"

The old man shook his head.

"I cannot do that," he slowly answered. "*She* must do that, I cannot."

"She—Laura Stanbridge?"

He bent his head.

"Is she in London?"

He made the same sign.

"Now leave me," he said.

She arose and went to the door and gained the garden beyond. He followed her to the gate. As she opened it he laid his hand upon her shoulder, where it felt like hot steel.

And he hissed into her ear—

"When the cup is full come to me."

CHAPTER CLIV.

THE UNEXPECTED MEETING—LAURA AND MRS. GROVER.

WE are again in London—it is night—the day's work is over with many of the inhabitants of this mighty human hive. But there are thousands, however, whose work commences after dark. Journalists, reporters, printers, and those who minister to the pleasure of the public as entertainers, have each and all to ply their vocation after what are the recognised working hours of the great body of the people.

The doors of the theatres had opened for the second price; from the cafés, saloons, and taverns, of the Haymarket and its purlieus red lights began to gleam—hoarse voices to swear—and this fearful quarter, where, but a few years back, vice and debauchery reigned undisturbed, now began to fill with the votaries of vice and the victims of vanity—men who covered their natures of beasts with the garb of gentlemen—women, who, with sad gaiety and lurid smiles, walked, walked, and walked, in order that they might not starve.

In a dark street near Leicester-square two women met beneath a gas-light. Both started. One of them tried to pass. The other seized her.

"No, I must speak to you, Laura Stanbridge," said the elder of the two.

The woman whom she addressed affected surprise.

"Why, is it really you, Mrs. Grover?" said she.

"Yes, it is me," she answered, gloomily. "It is years since we met, but I knew you in a moment."

"Indeed! In that you had the advantage of me, for at first, I confess, I was at a loss to understand who you were."

"That is likely enough. Time has altered both of us, but me more especially."

"I don't see that it has. But do you want anything of me?"

"Yes, I do, or I should not have troubled to make myself known to you. I desire to have a little conversation with you."

Laura Stanbridge hesitated.

"Humph! Something to say, eh?"

"Yes."

"Perhaps I may learn something from her," she muttered to herself, "better keep in with her."

Then aloud she said—

"You are the last person in the world I should have expected to meet. Still, of course, I am glad to see you."

"Oh yes, I dare say you are."

"Let us enter this café," said Laura.

They entered the establishment in question, which was provided with some marble tables and luxurious ottomans.

It was divided into two compartments.

They passed into the further one, where they could converse with privacy.

First, however, it was requisite to order some refreshment.

"Garcon!" cried Laura.

LAURA STANBRIDGE AND PURVIS'S MOTHER IN THE RESTAURANT.

A waiter, with shaved cheeks, and a small black moustache of the true Frenchman style, answered the call.

"*Une verre de parfait amour*," said Miss Stanbridge.

He bowed, vanished, and returned with a tiny glass filled with a liquor red as a girl's lips, luscious, and perfumed as the nectar of the gods.

No. 86.

"Now, my dear Mrs. Grover," said Laura, as she sipped the beverage and reclined in a voluptuous attitude, "I am all attention. Pray tell me what you have to discourse about. The wickedness and vanity of the world—or what?"

"There is no occasion for you to make a jest of a subject which to me is, alas! a most serious one," returned her companion. "I have come to ask what you have done with my child."

"Your child?" cried Laura, raising her eyebrows. "The person to whom you allude is no longer a child."

"Well, then, my son, if that term pleases you better."

"We will not dispute about terms—I presume you allude to a young man who was at one my time protégé."

"The boy whom you adopted from the streets and taught to be a thief was my son. I always loved him," said the unhappy woman. "I always loved him without knowing why. But he was the babe I nursed at this breast, and carried in these arms, and kissed with these lips—the babe I abandoned when I was mad and foolish, and whom they tore from me, and made me fly for my very life. I never knew this until lately, and I have been searching for you for months past. I asked Bill Rawton to put me on the right track, and I have asked everybody I could think of."

"Oh, indeed."

"Yes, I have."

"This is very curious and romantic ; and you really mean to say that you have not seen or heard of your young friend for all these long and weary years?"

"No never—never once have I set eyes upon him. But what could I do? You threatened me with the police if I tried to baulk you and I was altogether at your mercy. I did not know that he was my darling son, and if I had," she said fiercely, "the rope itself should not have held me back, but I did not know that then. I only knew that I loved him, but I did not know why."

Laura Stanbridge sipped her *parfait amour.*

"This is really very dramatic, Mrs. Grover—very dramatic indeed," said she with perfect composure, "And I suppose there will be no harm in grattfying your curiosity, especially as it may serve you as a lesson not to play at pitch and toss with babies in the future."

"I do not care a pin for your taunts. Jest at me as you will—it will not harm me ; only tell me where he is."

"I should be clever indeed to tell you that, seeing that I do not know myself."

"Have you quarrelled then, and do you never see him then?"

"I never see him and never wish to do so ; he was my friend—he is now my bitterest enemy. I suppose you have heard of Dandy Sutherland, as he is termed."

Mrs. Grover turned pale. "Eh," she murmured, "Then my boy has fallen into his hands? All is lost, all is lost."

"Dandy Sutherland is the Bully Grand of the Forty Thieves, and the standing toast of every boozing ken between Westminster and Whitechapel. While other men have been content to shine in one branch of the profession, the Dandy has made himself master of them all, and is equally notorious as a drummer, as a mobsman, a shofuller, a smasher, and a cracksman. In this last capacity he is only surpassed by the celebrated and famous Charles Peace, who surpasses all others as a daring and accomplished burglar."

The Dandy, therefore, is not to be named in the same day with Charles Peace, but he has other accomplishments—practises other forms of villainy which Peace never attempted.

"Gracious heaven ! Can this be possible ?"

"It is not only possible, but true."

"Admit that it is so, but this does not help me to find my son. Where is my boy ?"

"His genius for calculation would have made his fortune at cards before the hells were abolished," observed Miss Stanbridge, not taking any heed of her companion's queries. "And could he obtain an *entrée* into the 'Ottoman' or 'Cocoa-nut Tree,' where hundreds of pounds are frequently staked upon a game, his skill at billiards would speedily enrich him."

"And is he not rich now ?" inquired the other, stifling her rage that she might obtain the information she desired.

"He was not rich when I last saw him ; on the contrary, he was poor, but this is some time ago. I have not seen anything of him for a long time past. He is unsettled and extravagant. Besides, he is an unprincipled corrupter of our own sex, and so spends more thought upon vice than upon crime. Vice is a safe game because it is played at by all the aristocracy, but it is the reverse of lucrative."

"And this man, this Dandy Sutherland, as you call him, am I to understand that he is an associate of my son's, or is he my boy himself ?"

"Well, to tell you the truth, forlorn and afflicted parent," said Laura Stanbridge, "Dandy Sutherland, with his fifty aliases and his thousand crimes, is no other than the youth whom I had the honour of initiating into his profession."

The mother did not speak. She stared at Laura stupidly as if she had not understood her, but she turned pale, and breathed very hard.

"I repeat," said Laura, "that your son is now called, by the thieving fraternity, Dandy Sutherland, and that he has been compelled to fly from the officers of justice in consequence of a burglary and murderous outrage he has been engaged in, and, I think, seeing that he is wanted by the police, that it is very doubtful about your finding him—for some time to come at all events. If he is caught they'll give it him pretty hot, I fancy," remarked Laura, carelessly, as she sipped her *parfait amour.*

"And you will be glad to see him in trouble. If you say that again I will throttle you," cried Mrs. Grover, with a sudden burst of passion.

"Now don't be noisy, my dear old friend," returned her companion, with a smile. "It is, of course, very dramatic, but we don't want to bring down the house just now—we don't, indeed."

The unhappy mother fell into a chair, and the tears streamed in hot torrents from her eyes. Suddenly she sprung to her feet.

She snatched a handkerchief from her bosom, and showed Laura Stanbridge a golden ring and a slip of paper, on which the ink was brown and faded, as if it had been written years before.

"I will save him yet !—I will save him yet !" cried the woman. "Do you know what I will do ?"

"Can't possibly imagine."

"I will go to him, and will show him this ring and paper, and I will tell him that he is not base born, but born in lawful wedlock, and heir to a squire's land. That will tempt him to turn from his evil ways, and he will go to his grandfather, and, of course, he will not know what my son has been, and what he will never be again, but will make up some clever story, and it will be all right."

"Oh, it must be a wonderfully clever story to put your son straight with Squire Kensett—wonderfully clever, indeed. Why, don't you know that the worthy magistrate in question has already had Dandy Sutherland before him upon the charge of attempting to defraud the Saltwich Bank ?"

"Before Squire Kensett," cried Mrs. Grover, perfectly aghast at this piece of information.

"Most certainly."

"Alf is the squire's grandson."

"Is he?"

"Most certainly, he is the son of Mr. Robert Everhard Kensett—read that," said Mrs. Grover, handing her companion the paper.

"Ah I see a marriage certificate, and your husband—this Mr. Robert Everhard Kensett—is dead."

"Yes, he is. The ship he sailed in foundered at sea and all hands on board were lost."

"How very unfortunate—very sad indeed! But this instrument appears to be genuine."

"When I show it my son he will do as I wish; will he not?"

"No one could refuse to exchange constant anxiety and danger for perpetual substance and respectability."

"You think he will come with me then?" asked Mrs. Grover, for the sake of hearing such words again.

"I am sure of it, if you find him."

"If I find him!"

"Yes, at present that little difficultly stands in the way."

"Oh, how happy I am, and the thought only came into my poor weak head lately. My boy will be a squire, and perhaps they will make him a magistrate. Only fancy his being a magistrate."

"I confess I cannot fancy it. At present he is hunted like a wild beast, and has been compelled to leave the country—so I have been told. He had better keep out of the way, and no doubt he will, for he is cunning as a fox."

Mrs. Grover looked at the speaker anxiously.

"What are you doing with my certificate?" said she.

"I am folding it up to put in my pocket. It is a very important paper, and perhaps you might lose it."

"Oh, no, I am not likely to do that," said the other, earnestly. "I have kept that paper and the ring my husband gave me ever since I was a young and wicked girl. Don't put it in your pocket. I shall want it, you know, to show it to my son."

"But I don't mean to let you show it to your son."

And she sipped her *parfait amour.*

"Not let me! Why not?"

"Because I don't wish your son to become a squire and a magistrate. He would be too proud to remember his old friends."

"Oh, Laura!" cried the miserable mother, "you cannot find it in your heart to hold him back from a life of honesty and drive him to sin and death. Ah, woman, you have made him everything that's bad. Have you not done enough?"

"No!" shrieked Laura, rising to her feet—"no, I have not done enough, for, do you know, woman, how this precious son of yours turned round upon me?"

"No, I never heard."

"Hark ye, woman! I knelt to that man—I, Laura Stanbridge—and he spurned me as if I had been a leper. I became a woman for once, and I was trodden on. Do you think I am likely to serve him—the recreant, heartless scoundrel? No, no, madam. You know little of me if you imagine I can forget the bitter wrong done me. I fostered a serpent, and now I both hate and despise this precious sample of manhood. Go your ways. Do as you will—you cannot count on any assistance from me. Find him if you can—but I tell you once and for all that I have done with him."

Mrs. Grover listened to this sudden burst of fury at first with a shudder, afterwards with an icy calmness. She had taken a resolution. Without replying she moved towards the door.

"Stop!" cried Laura Stanbridge. "Understand me distinctly. I have nothing to say against you personally. I do not dislike you, but as for him——"

"No more. Say no more. You have done your worst."

"Do not be sure of that. Possibly worse is to follow."

Mrs. Grover moaned and sank back in her chair. There was no life in her eyes but one tear which struggled freely down her cheeks—no life in her frame but a slight quivering in her hands.

Laura Stanbridge looked at her with a smile. Then she drew the marriage certificate from her pocket and read it over carefully, and she took the last sip of her *parfait amour.*

After awhile her companion recovered herself. She arose, and, holding up one hand in a deprecating manner, she passed out of the café.

"Unhappy woman!" exclaimed Miss Stanbridge, after she had gone, "She little thinks that she is not likely to see her son this side of the grave. Strange that the body has never been found—drifted out, I suppose, and never will be recovered. All things considered we must deem ourselves fortunate."

CHAPTER CLV.

IDENTIFICATION OF PEACE—CHARGED WITH THE MURDER OF MR. DYSON.

THE incidents described in the preceding chapters came to a denouement; this we shall have to chronicle a few chapters further on. Meanwhile we will put the reader in possession of other facts in connection with our hero.

Charles Peace, at this time occupied the attention of the detectives in a most remarkable degree, and every effort was made to bring the crime of murdering Mr. Dyson home to him.

Every effort was used to give as much publicity to the leading circumstances attendant on this crime. The public were furnished with the following account:—On the night of the 29th November, 1876, a civil engineer named Mr. Arthur Dyson, who resided at Bannercross-terrace, near Sheffield, was shot by a man whom he found lurking on his premises. That man was subsequently sworn to as being Charles Peace, a notorious character, who had been convicted of felony, and who was known to be a desperado.

Immediately after committing the murder Peace decamped across the adjacent fields, and from that time all trace of him was lost. A coroner's inquest, sitting on view of the body of Mr. Dyson, returned a verdict of wilful murder against Peace, and on this a warrant was issued for his apprehension, and it is believed that he at last has been captured.

Peace was an "old bird," and eluded those who were on his track. He was so successful in that, that many believed he had made away with himself by jumping down some old coal pit, and thus hiding his body whilst ridding the world of himself.

But the police officers who had had to deal with him did not believe this story. "Peace," they said, "is not a man to do that; he'll fight before he's caught; he's not dead."

On the night of the murder there was a "handicap" in Sheffield, in which men were the competitors, and the railway stations were crowded with those who were returning home after viewing the pedestrian exhibition.

It was thought that Peace mixed up with this motley crowd and so effected his escape for the time being.

As to where he had gone was a question, but the police were almost as rapid in their movements as was Peace, though for the time being he appeared the most successful in the accomplishing of his purpose—the effecting of his escape.

Within five hours after Mr. Dyson's death the whole of the large towns within a radius of two hundred miles of here had been warned of the crime which had been committed, and the railway stations of Hull, Huddersfield, Leeds, Manchester, Bradford, Liverpool, and Halifax, were most vigilantly watched, and it was known that Peace, being an old hand, knew the thieves' runs and hiding places in those localities.

Notwithstanding every effort there was no indication of the whereabout of the man.

The houses of some of his relatives in Sheffield were searched almost nightly; nocturnal visits were made to the domiciles of other friends, but yet there were no tidings of "Peace," and the closest scrutiny failed to show that he was having the slightest communication with any of those who in Sheffield had been regarded as attached to him, and with whom he had been in the habit of associating.

One Sheffield detective watched the Manchester Railway station for almost a month, but, of course, unsuccessfully.

The almost universally accepted version of the murderer's escape was this—that Peace took train to Hull within a couple of hours after shooting Mr. Dyson.

Indeed, an officer who went to that town afterwards and who knew the "crimping places," as he himself, graphically describes them, said he had no doubt that Peace had been there, and had remained a week or two, but after that there was no trace of him.

There was but one other theory left, and that was that the fellow had taken ship and gone to Hamburg —he being well versed as to the thieves' haunts there.

It should here be stated, however, that before committing the murder Peace went to "a friend" and said he was short of cash. He borrowed £15—and forgot to return it.

Thus it will be seen that he was not short of funds when he set out with the intention of committing the murder—for that he intended to commit one there can be no doubt, although his particular reasons for doing so are, for the present, a complete mystery.

The authorities took care to circulate throughout the police districts of the United Kingdom a complete description of the man who was "wanted," together with photographs of him, showing his visage when shaven, when wearing a beard, and, indeed, under all the appearances he had worn whilst in the hands of the police.

The authorities on the Continent and in the United States received similar advices, but still there was no trace of the man, and this only led the incredulous to be more firmly of opinion that Peace had committed suicide, and would no longer be heard of amongst the living.

It will be seen, from the official notice which we append, that if Peace fell into the hands of the police, there were marks on him which would make him somewhat easy of identification. For his apprehension a reward of £100 was offered by Government. The police notice was as follows :—

"MURDER.—£100 Reward. Whereas on the 29th ult. Mr. Arthur Dyson, C.E., was murdered at Bannercross, Sheffield, having been shot in the head, in the presence of his wife, by Charles Peace, who escaped in the darkness of the night, and is still at large; and whereas at the coroner's inquest, held on the 8th inst., upon the body of the said Arthur Dyson, a verdict of 'wilful murder' was found against the said Charles Peace.

"Notice is hereby given that a reward of £100 will be paid by her Majesty's Government to any person other than a person employed in a police force in the United Kingdom who shall give such information and evidence as shall lead to the discovery and conviction of the said Charles Peace.

"Peace is a thin and slightly-built man, about forty-six years of age, but looks ten years older, five feet four or five inches high, grey (nearly white) hair, beard and whiskers (the whiskers were long when he committed the murder, but may now be cut or shaved off), has lost one or more fingers off left hand, cut mark on back of each hand, and one on forehead, walks with his legs rather wide apart, speaks somewhat peculiarly, as though his tongue was too large for his mouth, and is a great boaster.

"He is a joiner or picture-frame maker, but occasionally cleans and repairs clocks and watches, and sometimes deals in oleographs, engravings, pictures, &c., associates with loose women, and has been twice in penal servitude for burglaries near Manchester."

Besides that Peace was known to be a "good shot," and a quick one.

He had been a daring poacher when a young man, and always carried a revolver on him.

As a "cracksman" he stood in the foremost ranks of the thieving fraternity; he was a capital hand at opening a "safe," and was utterly reckless as to consequences, and notoriously cruel.

Such was the man whom the police desired to apprehend, and it was well known that if he had a chance he would resist his capture, and not hesitate to resort again to the use of firearms. There is now almost every reason to believe that Peace has at length fallen into the hands of the police.

THE IDENTIFICATION.

A prisoner of the notorious character indicated above, was, of course, the object of special care and precaution. As a consequence it was found that there were marks on him of a singular description, and a word or two which he had dropped to a fellow-prisoner gave rise to a suspicion in the minds of the authorities that "John Ward" was not altogether what he professed to be—a half-caste American, and a juvenile in the art of thieving.

Inspector Phillips took the matter in hand, and as a result of his searches, came to the conclusion that the prisoner was no other than Charles Peace, of Sheffield, the murderer of Mr. Dyson.

He examined the prisoner more closely, and found the numerous discolourations and disfigurements on his body to coincide with the police description.

The photograph of the missing Peace was evidently that of this prisoner, and a number of other circumstances tended to prove the identity of the guilty man; so the police came to the conclusion that the man in Newgate was none other than the Bannercross murderer; indeed, it was generally understood that the prisoner did not attempt to deny that he was Charles Peace.

In addition to all this Mr. Jackson was in possession of some valuable information which he was not at liberty to divulge till the inquiry assumed a more definite shape.

Certain legal forms had to be gone through before Peace could be removed from Newgate to answer the charge made against him in the county in which the crime had been perpetrated.

One difficulty, however, stood in the way. The question at this time was, how to find out Mrs. Dyson; without her evidence the case would break down.

Mrs. Dyson was now "wanted" as badly as Peace had been. Some time after the murder she left this country to return to Ohio, United States, and was indeed seen on board the vessel at Queenstown by Sub-inspector Walsh.

There were persons who thought she would not remain long in in America, and that she had returned to this country.

The question was, where was Mrs. Dyson? This was a query which naturally suggested itself.

Her appearance in Sheffield was a matter of great importance, for without her Peace might be kept outside the law which he had so long defied.

The public had at this time, perhaps, as much interest centred upon Mrs. Dyson as upon Peace himself.

There was a general belief, however, that Mrs. Dyson knew a great deal more than she divulged at the inquest—not, indeed, about the actual facts of the murder, but with reference to her previous knowledge of our hero, and her communications and transactions with him.

Certain letters produced at the inquest tended to show that between Mrs. Dyson and Peace much correspondence passed.

This was flatly denied by Mrs. Dyson, who declared that she had never seen the letters before, and in this unsatisfactory condition things remained for some time. When the Bannercross tragedy was occupying public attention, information respecting the appearance, conduct, and antecedents of Mrs. Dyson were read with interest.

Mrs. Catherine Dyson was married at Cleveland, Ohio, about the year 1866, to Mr. Arthur Dyson, civil engineer. In 1873 they returned to England, and lived at Tinsley, with the mother of Mr. Dyson. Afterwards they removed to Highfield, and then to Alexander-road, Heeley.

Darnall was their next abode, and at Darnall Peace first came upon the scene. He took a house near the Dysons, and endeavoured to become intimate. Mr. Dyson treated his advances with coolness. and then Peace altered his tactics, and endeavoured to make disturbances between husband and wife. Failing in this he spread mischievous reports about them, and finally threatened to shoot Mrs. Dyson.

For this a summons was issued against him, and neglecting to answer it, the summons was followed by a warrant. Upon this Peace left the neighbourhood, or at any rate endeavoured to give that impression to those who knew him. Mrs. Dyson, however, never believed that he had gone far.

Though letters, purporting to come from Germany, and signed apparently by Peace, frequently came to the house, she had the impression that he was still about the town, and at his tricks. At this time the Dysons went to Bannercross, where the murder subsequently took place.

Mrs Dyson was then about twenty-five years of age, or half the age of her husband. She was a person of considerable muscular development, and not without personal attractions of face and figure. Her countenance was round and ruddy, her hair raven black, and neatly and fashionably tied up in coils.

After the murder of her husband she appears to have been animated by a profound hatred of Peace, and

naturally so. The various statements she made tend, nevertheless, to show that she had an intimate knowledge of him, and knew his real character.

She scouted the then prevalent idea that he had drowned himself or otherwise put an end to his existence, She was certain, she stated, that he was not so far away, but that he would return and "finish" her.

It was not her husband he intended to shoot, but herself. She regretted she had not a revolver when she met Peace; in that case she should herself have shot him dead. She was convinced that he would escape capture till he had put a bullet through her head as well as her husband's.

Her only protection was to have a revolver herself, and if he came she declared she should use it. These and other statements show the views Mrs. Dyson had at that time.

Her examination at the inquest was looked forward to with great interest. Then it was believed revelations would be made by her as to her knowledge of Peace, but in fact nothing transpired.

She positively repudiated the notion that there was anything kept back, or that Peace was anything more to her than he had been to her husband.

The following are some of her replies in answer to the Coroner, who pressed her very closely upon this point:—

Had there ever been a quarrel between you and your husband with regard to Peace?—No. No quarrel.

You are quite sure that he never quarrelled with you on account of your familiarity with Peace?—No; I am sure he has not.

Has he ever complained of your speaking to Peace? —He did not wish me to speak to him.

Has he ever found fault with you for speaking to him?—No, he has never found fault, because he told me never to speak to him, and I did not.

The letters found near the scene of the murder created a good deal of bewilderment as to what they related to, and who were the authors of them.

These letters were found the morning after the murder by police-constable Ward, in Mrs. Else's grass field, opposite Mr. Dyson's house, and handed over to Inspector Bradbury.

Amongst them was a pink envelope enclosing a cent. American coin, the envelope bearing the words "C. Peace, Esq."

The directions and other writing on the covers were evidently in a woman's hand, and written by one who apparently was carrying on an intrigue with Peace.

These letters and papers were by the police evidently believed to have been written by Mrs. Dyson to Peace, for during the examination of Mrs. Dyson by the Coroner, the letters were handed to the latter, who thereupon closely cross-examined the witness as to her knowledge of them.

The Coroner, in alluding to the letters in question, said—

Have you ever seen this writing before (handing witness a quantity of letters)?—No.

Have you looked at them?—Yes.

Did you ever lend Peace a book?—No.

The Coroner (to the jury): These are letters and memoranda, gentlemen. They are not addressed to anyone—so it is difficult to say what bearing they have on the case. Addressing witness: Did Peace never write to you?—No.

You are quite sure of that?—Yes.

Did he never write asking you to meet him?—No.

The Coroner (to the police) : I suppose some one will give evidence as to where these came from ?

Mr. Inspector Bradbury : Yes.

The Coroner : It is difficult, gentlemen, to know what to do with regard to those letters ; they are not addressed. There is one here. I do not like to read it, because it does not say for whom it is intended. It runs :—" I write you these few lines to thank you for all your kindness ; and so on. It is not addressed to anyone, and might have been written to Mrs. Dyson or not. To witness :

Did you ever write a letter to Peace in your life ?—No, I never did.

Not a scrap of paper of anything ?—No,

You never wrote a word to him on paper ?—No.

Just be careful, please. Do you mean to swear you never have written a word to him on paper ?—No.

Never at all ?—No.

Mr. Bradbury explained that the letters were picked up by a constable about fifteen yards from where Peace was seen to get over a wall. They were found the morning after the murder. Peace had been in the neighbourhood to several places, and showed the papers, which he said were in Mrs. Dyson's handwriting, and written by her at the time she lived in Darnall.

The Jury : Are they all in one handwriting ?—Some are in ink and some in pencil. There is one scrap in Mr. Dyson's handwriting, telling Peace that he would have nothing to do with him.

To witness : Whose handwriting is that ?—I don't know.

Is it in your handwriting ?—No.

Can you write ?—No, I never do write.

The Coroner said they were not addressed, but one scrap was identified by witness as her husband's handwriting. It was, " Charles Peace is requested not to interfere with my family." (To witness.) Do you know Peace's handwriting when you see it.—Yes.

Witness then went over the letters, and thought that some of them were in Peace's handwriting. The writing was similar to that contained in the threatening letters which were at Mr. Chambers's office.

Inspector Bradbury explained that the letters had been given up to the chief constable, who had intended to be present at the inquest, but his brother's death had prevented him.

The Coroner (to witness) : I understand you to say that, with the exception of the threatening letter, Peace never wrote to you, or to him ?—No, I never did.

Was this threatening letter addressed to you or to your husband ?—To my husband.

Then he never wrote to you a threatening letter or any thing else ?—No. The letters threatened both. Peace never wrote to me.

Then again with regard to the pink envelope and the cent coin the following took place :—

Mrs. Dyson (recalled) was examined by the coroner, who said : Are you an American by birth ?—No.

You have been living in America ?—Yes.

Where did you see this coin last (meaning the cent)? —I cannot say where I have seen this. I have seen several.

Do you know where Peace got it ?—No.

Did you give it to him ?—No.

Did you never give a coin at all ?—No, I did not.

The papers, after Peace's identification, published an account of the interview of Peace, before the murder, with the Rev. E. Newman, in which he made charges of a very gross kind against Mrs. Dyson, and produced letters, &c., in support of his allegations. There can be little doubt that these letters are identical with those afterwards found by the police-officer.

It is said that one great object Peace had in view in trying to get Mrs. Dyson to follow his fortunes was that she would be useful to him in disposing of the proceeds of his burglaries. At one time he offered her £50 to take a trip through the country with him.

Peace had a great liking for arms, and succeeded in stealing four revolvers in his burglarious expeditions.

With one of these, a six-chambered weapon, he shot Mr. Dyson at Bannercross, and he used the same revolver when he encountered Police-constable Robinson at Blackheath, and shot him in the arm, just before his capture.

This was his favourite revolver, but he had another, a smaller one, with five chambers, which he practised with at home.

It carried only a very little bullet, not much larger than a pea, and when fired its report was scarcely louder than the crack of a whip. A capital revolver for practice, he frequently used it in his garden, firing at a bottle for a mark, and gaining great proficiency of aim.

The third revolver had seven chambers ; and the fourth ten chambers. The six-chambered one was his constant companion, however. He always carried it loaded, slept with it under his pillow, and kept the other three weapons, likewise loaded, in a drawer within easy reach of his bed, so that if his house had been surrounded by police, and they had endeavoured to arrest him, there is no doubt whatever that Peace would have fought to the last, and that he would have been captured at a terrible sacrifice.

He devoted a good deal of attention to his weapons ; frequently drew the charges and cleaned them, and always had them ready for use.

The six-chambered revolver was wrested from his grasp at Blackheath by the police ; but the other three, together with the ammunition, were sent down to Nottingham, and by a relative of Mrs. Thompson's were dropped into the canal near the town.

The arrangements for conveying the prisoner to Sheffield, to be then and there examined upon the charge of murdering Mr. Dyson, had been made in what was supposed to be a satisfactory manner, and it was at this time that our hero committed one of the most daring acts in his whole career.

On Wednesday morning, of June 22, 1878, Charles Peace was taken in charge of two stalwart warders to the King's-cross Station, for the purpose of being conveyed by express train to Sheffield.

But the proceedings came to a standstill in a most extraordinary manner.

On Wednesday morning by a determined and nearly successful attempt at escape, by leaping from an express train, Charles Peace, alias Ward—notorious as the hero of the Blackheath burglaries, and accused, on the evidence of Mrs. Dyson, of having murdered Mr. Dyson at Bannercross, near Sheffield—added another startling chapter to the strange, eventful history with which the public are already familiar.

The facts of this daring attempt are briefly as follows : —The prisoner Peace left King's-cross, London, by the 5.15 Great Northern train, accompanied by two warders from Pentonville Prison, where he had been confined, and he ought to have arrived at Victoria Station, Sheffield, at 8 54 a.m. The warders, who have been very much censured in Sheffield, have stated that when they brought Peace from London he was exceedingly troublesome throughout the whole journey, and wanted to leave the train whenever it stopped, and indeed when it was travelling.

At Peterborough he was allowed to get out, and the warders had considerable difficulty in getting him back when they urged him to return, as he was keeping the train waiting. He answered them sneeringly, "What have I to do with caring for trains?"

By way of precaution against this annoyance the chief warder states that he provided himself with a number of little bags, and that whenever Peace required it one of them was handed to him, and was afterwards thrown out of the window.

It is clear that the desperado had been on the lookout for a favourable opportunity of making his escape, and at last it came. He pretended great weakness, and used several of the bags on the way.

This may partly account for the fact that he had no irons on his lower limbs. His handcuffs were fastened with a chain about six inches long between them, and another chain for the warders to hold him by.

The point selected was peculiarly favourable to the attempt.

Between Worksop and Shireoaks—so called from certain oaks under which the three shires of Nottingham, York, and Derby meet—the ground is comparatively level; the country is also well adapted by the neighbourhood of the forests, as well as by old lime-pits and coal-workings, to offer temporary shelter to a criminal.

Peace, it is known, is well acquainted with the district, having tramped it repeatedly when some of his many enterprises were unsuccessful.

The warders, through Chief Constable Jackson, of Sheffield, have stated that when the train had passed Worksop, and was going at full speed, the prisoner asked for another bag.

The chief warder gave him one, and he stood up with his face to the window to use it, the under-warder being close behind him.

The window was dropped for him to throw it out, and, quick almost as lightning, Peace took a flying leap through the window. The under-warder sprang forward and caught him by the left foot. There he held him suspended head downwards, Peace kicking the warder with his right foot, and struggling with all his might to get free.

The chief warder, unable to render his colleague any assistance in holding Peace, inasmuch as he occupied the whole space of the window, hastened to the other side of the carriage and pulled at the communication cord to alarm the driver and secure the stoppage of the train.

The cord would not act, and some gentlemen who were in the next compartment, seeing the position of affairs, assisted in the efforts of the warder to stop the train.

All this time the struggle was going on between Peace and his warder, and eventually the prisoner succeeded in kicking off his shoe, and he fell, his head striking the footboard of the carriage, and he dropped on the line.

Supposing that the burglar had been able, as he came very near being, to jump clean through the window and alight on the soft embankment, fortune would also have favoured him in the matter [of a fair start for Sherwood Forest.

The struggle lasted during about two miles, and even after Peace got out the train ran on for about a mile before the speed slackened sufficiently to allow the warders to follow him.

A three-mile start would have given the desperado such a chance of availing himself of the features of a very peculiar country as he of all men would have delighted in. When it had slackened speed sufficiently to allow the warders to alight the express train went on, and the warders hurried back along the line.

Mr. William Barlow, fruiterer, of Retford, who was a passenger by the train in which Peace was travelling, accompanied the warders, and in a plain, unvarnished manner he states that between Shireoaks and Kineton Park he heard a noise, and looking out of the window saw one of the warders with a shoe in his hand.

The train was brought up near the malt kiln at Kineton Park.

The two warders and Mr. Barlow at once got out, and ran back along the line, and when they neared the spot where Peace made his plunge, they found him lying insensible on the line.

He had been dragged for about twelve yards, and appeared much hurt, but when he was moved to the side of the road consciousness returned, and he begged them to cover him up as he was very cold.

A slow train, which is timed to reach Sheffield at 9.20, soon came up.

The warders shouted to the guard that Peace had jumped from the train and was lying there. The train was pulled up, and the criminal, who was now in no condition to offer resistance, was placed in the guard's van.

He was then bleeding profusely, and apparently in great pain, but the guard made him as comfortable as possible under the circumstances.

Meantime, in Sheffield, the scene was highly exciting. As early as six in the morning a crowd began to gather round the Town Hall and at all the approaches, and long before the time the convict was expected to arrive, the assemblage had become very dense. Several persons fainted, and were taken away; but still the crowd waited most patiently until the rumour spread that the convict had escaped.

Then the excitement was redoubled; the people surged backwards and forwards; they almost attempted to force the doors, and the police had hard work to keep their places at the railway station.

When the train which should have brought Peace arrived without him and ten minutes late, the great crowd outside commenced shouting and yelling in a most excited manner, and the utmost confusion prevailed.

The prisoners' van, which was awaiting to convey Peace and the warders, was drawn up opposite the large hall-door.

The train being brought to a standstill, a surprising announcement was made by the guard.

"Peace has jumped out," cried that official. The statement was for the moment treated by the crowd as a hoax, and meant as a "blind" in order to get the platform cleared; but when, instead of Peace, a sword, a bag, and a rug belonging to one of his warders were handed over by the guard to Inspector Bird, it was generally believed that Peace had really escaped, and that the warders were on his track.

It was rumoured at the station that Peace had escaped through the railway carriage window, and had succeeded in making off; but several of the more incredulous, however, would have it that he had been taken out of the train at Darnall, and would be from there quietly conveyed in a cart to Sheffield. Many persons lingered on the platform in order to satisfy themselves of his non-arrival.

At the Sheffield Police-court the few persons who had taken their seats in court by a quarter-past nine o'clock were astonished when, a few minutes subsequently, the chief constable entered, in a state of considerable excitement.

Addressing his audience from the bench, Mr. Jackson said he was sorry to tell them that they had put themselves to inconvenience in attending thus early in the day, all to no account.

"In short," he exclaimed, "Peace has escaped from the warders; at least, that is what I hear."

Meanwhile, the court very slowly filled, and a minute or two before ten o'clock the witnesses for the prosecution were admitted from the magisterial entrance.

Mrs. Dyson, it was noted, looked wonderfully well, and even more collected in her demeanour on Friday last, notwithstanding the fact that she was to undergo the ordeal of a special examination.

She again wore a black hat and feather, but eschewed the veil which before she persisted in keeping drawn close down over her features, and the thick waterproof, with which she formerly enveloped her figure, had given place to a mantle of a lighter description.

Punctually at ten, the stipendiary, Mr. Welby, took his seat. Mr. Pollard and Mr. W. E. Clegg, the prosecuting and defending solicitors, were also in their places, but the dock remained untenanted.

A quarter-past ten, and no Peace. The rumour was whispered around that it was doubtful whether he would be able to appear at all that day, and this view of the situation was strengthened when, after an interview with Mr. Jackson, the stipendiary hurriedly left the court.

Presently Mr. Welby came back and said—

As to this case, in consequence of the injuries the man Peace has received this morning it is necessary to remand him for eight days. Therefore, the case is adjourned for eight days.

There will be nothing further done this morning. Do not disperse in a hurry, for there is a large crowd outside.

Another correspondent telegraphed:—The news was again and again repeated that Peace was dead, but the fact is that this report was founded upon his fall from the carriage. No fears are entertained as to his ultimate convalescence.

On reaching the police-offices at Sheffield, the convict was carried to a cell where he was seen by Dr. Spowart, the police-surgeon, and Mr. Hallam, a surgeon of large experience. They found he was suffering from a severe scalp wound in the head and concussion of the brain, and he appeared in a very exhausted state. He vomited freely, and it was with some difficulty that stimulants could be administered to him.

His wound was carefully dressed, and he was laid on the cell bed, and covered with rugs. After a little time Peace was able to speak to his warders. The Sheffield police cells have the advantage of ample space, light, and warmth.

The furniture in each cell consists of a long wooden bench : but the apartment occupied by Peace has had added to it a mattress and pillows, together with an ample supply of rugs.

There lies the little old man lies, his grey head curled down under the rugs, and near the door stand his two keepers.

During the first hour he was frequently aroused, and brandy administered to him. At first force had almost to be used to get him to take it, but afterwards he drank it without any objection; though at one time, with that thoughtfulness for himself for which he has been distinguished, he expressed a preference for whiskey, "if he must take any stimulants."

The vomiting with which he was at first troubled, soon ceased under the influence of the restoratives, and the medical men have been unremitting in their attention. There are some officers in the Sheffield force who were very doubtful as to the injuries he had sustained, and believe that he has been up to his old cunning and shamming a bit.

These constables stated that when he was lifted up, and the bottle placed to his lips, he ground his teeth and clenched his fists, and appeared to be struggling in a fit.

He was laid on the bench, and force was about to to be used to make him take the stimulant, when one who knew him well said very sternly, "Now, Charley, it's no use. Let's have none of your hankey pankey tricks here. You'll have to take it."

Charley recognised the voice, opened his eyes, and replied, "All right ; give me a minute." A knowing wink passed among the officers, and presently he sat up and took the brandy. Indeed, he seemed rather to like it, for he drank two gills in a comparatively short time.

He is now resting quietly, the only request he makes being that he may be well covered, as he feels the cold, which is in Sheffield exceptionally severe. When the Great Northern express train reached Retford the carriages for Sheffield and Manchester were detached and "made up" for the Manchester, Sheffield, and Lincolnshire Railway.

The compartment occupied by Peace and his warders was a third-class one in a composite carriage, immediately in front of the guard's van.

In the next—a first-class compartment—were Mr. Benjamin F. Cocker, who resides at Retford, and another gentleman.

Mr. Cocker says : " We had got about half a mile past Shireoaks Station when I heard a loud shout from the compartment where I knew Peace was. The gentleman with me said, ' Peace has got out,' and tried to open the window on the near side, but it was frozen fast. I tried the other window, and, opening it, leaned half my body out and tried to pull the communication cord. I saw the warder, who was doing the same thing. The warder said, ' I have got hold of this cord, but cannot make it ring.' After trying this all we could, at Branchcliffe siding we signalled to the signalman ; again and again we tried the cord, and the train slackened speed. As it did so, I exclaimed to the warder, ' You are a nice sort of fellow to let the man get out of your grip.' The warder answered, ' He jumped right through the window in a second. I held on him by the leg, but his boot came off, and of course he dropped then.' The warder's hands were covered with blood, for Peace had kicked him very severely while struggling at the window."

For the present, at least, Peace will remain in Sheffield.

At half-past ten p.m., Chief-constable Cosgrove and his colleagues reported that Peace was slumbering in apparent comfort; but as the warder—who looked very wearied, and who evidently regards his charge as something entirely out of the ordinary run—remarked, "With one eye open."

A little earlier in the evening the medical attendant had found it necessary to order the prisoner a little medicine.

PEACE'S LEAP FROM THE TRAIN.

This he refused to take; "but," said the warder, "it was the doctor's orders, and we were bound to carry them out."

Peace screamed violently, and the warder stated that he found a good deal of force necessary to compel the prisoner to take the potion, which, it is believed, was a slight opiate.

"Even now, after all he has gone through," said the warder, "he seems to have more than the strength of an ordinary man."

The warder added that, having been himself afoot since two o'clock in the morning, he felt much exhausted. After taking the medicine the prisoner was less excited, but did not seem to sleep at all easily.

The police understood that the prisoner was to be retained in Sheffield till all is over. Not only in Sheffield, but at Darnall and Bannercross, where Mr. Dyson was well known, at Shireoaks, Kineton Park, and Worksop, near where the prisoner lived, and all round the district; an unparalleled interest was shown in the prisoner's latest escapade.

The following further particulars are given by a correspondent :

The window was let down, and Peace, stooping in front of it, was using the bag, which the warders thought he was going to throw out as usual. Suddenly, with all the agility of a cat, Peace took a " header," and threw himself out of the window. The under warder sprang forward, and was just in time to catch him by the left foot.

There he held Peace, head downwards, dangling out of the window—an extraordinary sight to those who happened to be passing at the time. Peace with his other foot kicked the warder's hands, and struggled most determinedly to get free from the warder's grasp.

The chief warder, finding the space too narrow to help his associate in the struggle, seized the rope communicating with the guard's van, and endeavoured to stop the train.

Peace, knowing that the window was too narrow to let the other get forward, became more savage and ferocious still, and kicked and wriggled about with great violence.

Still the warder clung to him, and, for a distance of two miles, Peace was hanging head downwards by the carriage side. At last, by supreme effort, he managed to wriggle off his boot, which was left in the warder's hand, and the convict fell on the stepboard of the carriage, from which he bounded upon the ends of the sleepers.

The train was still travelling very rapidly. The communication cord having failed to work until a gentleman in the next compartment, hearing a noise, and suspecting something was wrong, managed to pull the rope, and the warders had the satisfaction of hearing the deep "boom" of the gong.

The train slackened speed and the warders got out and ran back up the line for nearly a mile, where they found Peace lying as he had fallen, having evidently received injuries sufficient to prevent his getting away.

He was conscious, however, and gave the warders a smile of satisfaction as they came up to him. They found him in the act of trying to wriggle the handcuffs off his wrists.

Blood was flowing from a wound in his head. They picked him up, and, as the slow train which arrives at Sheffield at 9.20 a.m. was coming up, they signalled it to stop. The convict was put into the guard's van, where for the rest of the journey the warders kept a sharp look-out.

He asked to be wrapped up in a rug, as it was a very cold morning, exclaiming, "Oh, my head!—oh, my poor head !" precisely the same observation he made when he was brought to Greenwich Police-station, after his encounter with Police-constable Robinson, the morning he was caught.

On his arrival at Sheffield, an immense crowd awaited the train, but Peace was promptly seized by four officers, conveyed to the van, and was soon at the Police-office, where he looked a piteous spectacle.

As he was lifted out of the vehicle and removed inside the police-station he appeared in a very exhausted condition, but after a little time he spoke a few words to the warders and took a pretty stiff dose of brandy, which was administered to him by medical orders.

PEACE'S EFFORT TO ESCAPE.

Various versions were very readily afloat after the express had reached Sheffield as to how this daring convict had succeeded in eluding his custodians, but they were all more or less wide of the mark.

Through the courtesy of the chief constable, we are able to give the following authentic particulars of this last and most astounding feat of this remarkable man.

It appears that when the warders brought Peace from Pentonville on the previous week he was exceedingly troublesome throughout the whole journey, and wanted to leave the train whenever it stopped; and indeed when it was travelling.

At Peterborough he was allowed to get out, and the warders had considerable difficulty in getting him back into the train.

The chief warder adopted a plan of his own on the present occasion, and he provided himself with a number of little bags, and whenever Peace required it one of them was handed to him, and was afterwards thrown out of the window.

From the moment of their leaving Pentonville he appeared to set himself deliberately to work to annoy and irritate and vex the officers to the utmost of his power.

And no one unacquainted with him can form any conception of his matchless powers in that direction.

Having been in prison so many times, he is as well acquainted with the rules which guide the warders as they are themselves; and any infringement of those rules on their part he would quickly detect and make a noise about.

His set purpose seemed to be to provoke them to a breach of the rules, and to serve him as he too richly deserved to be served.

He behaved more like a beast than a human being, until the carriage became almost unbearable.

The train had passed Worksop, and a part of the country was reached which Peace knew too well. All the way down on this, as in his previous journey, he had been adopting the most ingenious and cunning devices to put the warders off their guard, but without success.

Now was his last chance of eluding them, and if he could but escape from the carriage, he could follow, perhaps, well remembered "cuts," steal into Darnall or some other place of refuge, and, profiting by past experience, be no more discovered.

The train was whirling along at express speed; but what of that ? To such a man to regain freedom was worth a supreme effort—though he died in the attempt. He had used several of the bags referred to on the journey, and he asked for another.

The chief warder gave him one, and he stood up with his face to the window to use it, the under warder being close behind him. The window was dropped for him to throw it out, and quick almost as lightning Peace took a flying leap through the window.

The under warder sprang forward and caught him by the left foot. There he held him suspended head downwards; Peace kicking the warder with his right foot, and struggling with all his might to get free.

The chief warder—unable to render his colleague any assistance in holding Peace, inasmuch as he occupied the whole space of the window—hastened to the other side of the carriage and pulled at the communication cord, to alarm the driver and secure the stoppage of the train.

The cord would not act, and some gentlemen who

were in the next compartment, seeing the position of affairs, assisted in the efforts of the warder to stop the train.

All this time a most desperate struggle was going on between Peace and the warder. Peace, whose vitality seemed to be unbounded, was struggling with all his might, quite reckless of the consequences of falling headlong on the rails, or of being caught in the train and dashed to pieces. The warder held on to him like grim death; determined not to let go of him, but unable to secure a firmer grip of his prisoner.

The passengers all down the train had had their attention arrested by what was going on, and were craning their necks out of the windows, astonished at the spectacle which met their gaze.

The train, it is stated, ran a distance of nearly two miles whilst this exciting scene was being enacted; and then Peace succeeded in kicking off his left shoe, which remained in the warder's hand; and he fell with all the force of his own weight and the impelling motion of the train.

In his fall his head struck the footboard of the carriage, and he rolled over into the six-foot between the up and down lines.

The train ran on about a mile further before it could be stopped, and then the warders and others jumped out and ran back along the line in pursuit of their prisoner.

They found him in the six-foot, near to where he had fallen, insensible, and blood flowing from a wound in his head.

They assisted him up, and the down slow train, which was due shortly after, was stopped, and he was lifted into the guard's van.

In a few minutes he recovered so much consciousness as to say, "I am cold; cover me up." Rugs were placed upon him, and in a little while he arrived in Sheffield.

NARRATIVES BY EYE-WITNESSES.

Mr. W. Barlow, fruiterer, of Retford, who attends Sheffield market, was a passenger on Wednesday morning by the fast train by which Peace was travelling.

Between Shireoaks and Kineton Park he heard a noise, and looking out of the window saw one of warders with a shoe in his hand. The train was stopped as soon as possible, but it had run nearly two miles before it came to a stand, and was brought up near the malt-kiln at Kineton Park.

The two warders and Mr. Barlow at once got out and ran back along the line, and when they neared the spot where Peace made his plunge they found him lying insensible on the line.

He appeared much hurt, but when he was moved to to the side of the road consciousness returned, and he begged them to cover him up as he was very cold.

Shortly afterwards a slow train came up, and this was stopped. Peace was put into the van and brought on to Sheffield.

It seems that the escape was managed in this way. As the train was flying on at full speed Peace induced the warder to allow him to open the window.

No sooner was this done than the convict flung himself head first through the opening. The warder seized him by the leg, and held on for some time, but the prisoner struggled so violently that his shoe came off in the warder's hand, and the wretched man fell upon the line.

One of the first persons who reached Peace after his desperate leap was a blacksmith, named William Stephenson, who is at present working at Kineton Park.

He says:—About a quarter to nine o'clock I was standing close to Kineton-park station, when the fast train from London came slowly into the station. Almost everybody was at the carriage windows, and some were craning their necks out, and looking back up the line. We asked what was the matter, and they shouted excitedly " Peace has escaped; he has jumped out of the train."

We knew all about Peace at Kineton Park, and there was a general rush from the platform up the line after the warders, whom we could see just ahead of us.

The guard said they had just stopped for the warders to get out, and we rushed on.

We came up to the warders as they got to Peace, who was lying by the side of the up line about a mile from Kineton-park station in the direction of Shireoaks.

At that point the line runs almost on a level with the surrounding country.

Peace appears to have jumped out of the window on the right hand side of the train, and when the slipping off of his boot released him from the grasp of the officer he fell in the six foot between the up and down metals.

The velocity he received from the motion of the train then rolled him over, and he must have fallen where we found him, or have crawled off the metals of the up line.

He was lying on his back, and was to all appearance unconscious.

Blood flowed freely from a large gash over his right ear, and he did not speak.

Just then a slow train came up from Shireoaks for Sheffield, and that was stopped. We lifted Peace into the guard's van, and laid him on the floor.

He did not say anything about his attempt to escape, but merely said that he was cold, and asked for a rug to be put over him. He was brought to Sheffield.

The people in the train were wonderfully excited, and had seen the struggle from their carriage windows.

After Peace's arrest frequent references were made to the large black rimmed spectacles which he had worn with so much ostentation for the purpose of concealing his identity.

Indeed, they had played almost as conspicuous a part in his case as a certain pair of elegant gold-framed spectacles did when their owner was under the searching cross-examination of a gentleman who on Wednesday occupied a seat on the bench.

Precious as the spectacles of Mr. Peace are to him, they have narrowly escaped destruction. After he had been picked up on the line on Wednesday morning, and taken on to Sheffield, two men named George Hewitt and Wm. Turner walked down the metals to see what could be seen.

Peace had fallen at a place called Harrycroft, between Brancliffe siding and the canal siding, near to Kineton Park; and when the men reached the place and were looking round they saw lying on the line Peace's spectacles. They handed them over to the station-master at Kineton Park.

The warders had evidently been too much occupied with their re-capture of Peace to notice that he had lost his spectacles, or to think about them.

Probably there never was more excitement caused by the expected arrival of an individual who had gained notoriety, through whatever source it might be, than was manifested at the Victoria Station on Wednesday.

Notwithstanding the bitter cold, a concourse of perhaps some thousand persons of all ages and both sexes assembled in the square opposite the court, intent on seeing Peace if possible, and though a large body of police, under the charge of Inspector Bird, did their utmost to keep the crowd from gaining ingress to the platform, the station was crowded.

It was generally believed that Peace would be removed from his cell to Pentonville, and brought down by what is known as the newspaper train, leaving King's Cross at 5.15, and due in Sheffield at 8.58.

When the train steamed into the station some twelve minutes late the crowd had increased very considerably.

Those outside commenced shouting and yelling in a most excited manner, and the utmost confusion prevailed.

The prisoners' van, which was awaiting to convey Peace and the warders, was drawn up opposite the large hall door. The train being brought to a standstill, a surprising announcement was made by the guard.

"Peace has jumped out!" cried that official; and to see the amazement that came over the countenances of Inspector Bird and his men were at once painful and amusing in the extreme.

The affair was for the moment treated by the crowd as a hoax, and meant as a "blind" in order to get the platform cleared; but when, instead of Peace, a sword, a bag, and a rug belonging to one of his warders were handed over by the guard to Inspector Bird, it was generally believed that Peace had really escaped, and that the warders were on his track.

It was rumoured at the station that Peace had escaped through the railway carriage window, just after passing through Welwyn, and that he was once more at large.

Passing from mouth to mouth, this version of the story soon spread far and wide. Several of the more knowing, however, would have it that Peace had been taken out of the train at Darnall, and would be from there quietly conveyed in a cab to Sheffield.

Many lingered on the platform, however, in order to satisfy themselves of his non-arrival, for they seemed to entertain the idea that it was probable he had been secreted in one of the carriages till the course was clear for his conveyance from the train into the van.

But when the latter was driven away without its expected charge, and the police returned to the Town Hall, the crowd commenced to disperse, and by and by the station assumed its normal appearance.

Peace was carried to the first cell to the right of the stairs on the second landing. Under ordinary circumstances a police cell is not the most luxuriously furnished room in the world; but the Sheffield police cells have the advantages of ample space, light, and warmth.

The "furniture" in each cell consists of a wooden bench, and that answers all the purposes of a bed, a chair, a sofa, and so forth. On this bed the convict was laid, rugs were rolled up for his pillow and a heap of rugs was thrown over him.

Mr. Harrison, who was a witness in the case, was at the court, and he was asked to see Peace, but he manifested a decided reluctance to do so; and, indeed, said he would as soon attend upon—well, somebody else, as he would see Peace.

Dr. Spowart, Police-Surgeon of the Walkley Division,

and Mr. Hallam of the Central Division, were promptly in attendance, and they found that he was suffering from a severe scalp wound in the head and concussion of the brain; and he appeared in a very exhausted state.

He vomited freely, and it was with some difficulty that stimulants could be administered to him. His wound was carefully dressed; he was laid on the cell bed and covered with rugs. There were some officers present who were dubious as to the extent of the injuries he had sustained, and believed that he was up to his old cunning and shamming a bit.

When at intervals a little brandy was given to him, he was lifted up and the bottle placed to his lips. He ground his teeth, clenched his fists, and appeared to be struggling in a fit.

He was laid on the bench, and force was about to be used to make him take the stimulant, when one who knew him well said, very sternly, "Now, Charley, it's no use. Let's have none of your hankey pankey tricks here. You'll have to take it."

Charley recognised the voice; opened his eyes, and replied, "All right: give me a minute."

A knowing wink passed amongst the officers, and presently he sat up and took the brandy. Afterwards he took stimulants when offered to him; and he even went so far as to express a preference for whiskey over brandy.

After being thus attended to, he would immediately lie down and curl himself up under his rugs, scarcely leaving even his little grey head visible.

Mr. Hallam visited him at frequent intervals during the afternoon and evening, and on each occasion he found him steadily improving.

The vomiting had long ceased; he took stimulants and food readily, and was indeed going on "as well as could be expected."

When Mr. Hallam saw him late at night, he said he should not come down again unless he was sent for.

I was infected for once by the common curiosity, and instead of waiting patiently to read your report of the final hearing before the magistrates, of the charge of murder against Peace, I betook myself to the Town Hall in good time, in the hope that, if I should escape being squeezed as flat as a red herring in the process of effecting an entrance, I might see the noted prisoner, and admire the tact with which my friend, Mr. W. E. Clegg, would cross-examine Mrs. Dyson.

It soon appeared that I was out in my calculations. I gather from your second edition that this morning "the early birds did not catch the worm," though they did receive the next best thing, the shock of a surprise.

"Peace has escaped" was the cry. I had made up my mind to the disappointment of my expectations, and supposed I should hear in an hour or two that the mangled body of Peace had been picked up on the line, or that the prisoner, maimed and battered, had been found and sent to hospital.

However, I betook myself to the Court to try what was to be heard and seen. We sometimes hear how hard it is to get together magistrates enough to do the business. There was no such difficulty this morning. I should think some of these excellent gentlemen were there to perform a work of supererogation and score an attendance that might count in the scale of merit.

And they were in capital time too. For a quarter of an hour several of them, with sundry non-magisterial friends, were on the bench.

A few moments before the stroke of ten entered Mr.

Welby, the able, mild, and unpretending stipendiary. On his left was Mr. Overend, Q.C., whose genial and ruddy countenance seems to defy the power of years; and on the right was Mr. T. W. Rodgers, with a patriarchal aspect. The audience was curious and excited.

The Mayor did not put in an appearance, but a fair majority of aldermen and councillors were present, and had established themselves in the best places they could get before the doors were opened to the common public.

Mr. H. E. Watson talked last week of "the governing families of the town," but these were, I suppose, the governing men, and as they serve the public assiduously it was meet that they should have a sort of priority. A few minutes after ten enters Mr. Pollard, Treasury solicitor, bland and cheerful, and bowing to the Bench, takes his seat.

A little later appears the prisoner's solicitor, Mr. W. E. Clegg, with no marks of fussiness or anxiety, such as would make a client nervous, but with the self-contained look, assuring those who were interested that all the resources of an active, acute, and trained legal mind were at their service.

Everybody looked and listened. There was the prisoner's dock empty. It contained several chairs, with a pitcher of water and a glass.

The whisper went round that the prison surgeon was in attendance on Peace, and the speculation was —Is he in condition to be brought up? Or, if not, will Mr. Pollard offer the prisoner's advocate the opportunity to cross-examine Mrs. Dyson in his client's absence?

Everybody expected to see Mr. Pollard rise, state to the Bench what had happened, and make a suggestion as to the course to be pursued.

Presently there was a move, and the chief constable made a private communication to the stipendiary.

Mr. Welby left his seat and went out, followed by Mr. Overend and Mr. Rogers.

Then Mr. Clegg, and next Mr. Pollard, were called out. For five or ten minutes there was nothing to do but look round and speculate.

There is but one female in court. How is this? Is female curiosity defunct? Don't the ladies want to see Peace and the woman whose name has been so unhappily mixed up with his, and who may be regarded as one of his victims?

No doubt they do. Never was female curiosity more lively, and this morning there were many early breakfasts, and there was a decided resolution to be in time.

Soon after nine o'clock, quite a bevy of ladies had made their way into the police offices, never doubting that their potent claims would carry them into the court, and secure them the gratification they longed for.

It was a painful duty for the chief constable to make the ladies aware that the examination of the day was likely to take a very delicate turn indeed—so delicate that the presiding magistrate would have to point out to any ladies who might be present the propriety of retiring.

I will not undertake to say that there were not applicants who could have run the risks of all this, but the case was to put to the group so plainly as to induce them all to retire.

But, as I have said, there was one woman in court and the whisper went round "That is Mrs. Dyson."

"Is that lady a widow? I should not have guessed it," was the remark. Certainly she was out of mourning.

I have the pleasure to remark that the lady appears quite to have recovered the shock of her bereavement of two years ago, and that her two voyages across the Atlantic with her sojourn there, seem, judging from her rosy visage, quite to have restored her spirits and established her health.

With every desire to be as complimentary as possible, and to paint female charms with the liveliest colours, I cannot borrow the imaginative language of a pretended interviewer of New York, who has soared into the realms of fiction to find Mrs. Dyson's version of her husband's murder, and to discover the grounds surrounding his mansion, and the servants who were brought to the spot by the screams of their horrified mistress.

The Bannercross cottage is capable of development when seen through a New York telescope. The American interviewer enlists the sympathies and stirs up the credulity of his readers at the outset, by saying Mrs. Dyson is "a young and extremely handsome lady."

One does not want gratuitously to take the edge off so very pleasant a compliment. But if the said interviewer had seen, instead of imagining, Mrs. Dyson, I fancy he would have given us a guess at her weight in pounds—for that is a common ingredient in an American description—and if he had been a good judge, he would have put the figure pretty high.

However, I may satisfy your readers by saying Mrs. Dyson is buxom and blooming; and when Mr. Dyson's heart was pierced by her youthful charms he no doubt showed himself a good judge of female beauty.

It was remarked last week that when she was examined for the prosecution, she wore a veil, and Peace remarking that she kissed the book without raising her veil, insisted that she should take the oath "without a veil between" her lips and the calfskin binding.

To-day she had provided against such an objection, and had discarded the veil, her headgear being a hat with a feather, jauntily set on.

As I am not a milliner, and only saw her sitting, I cannot tell you anything about the rest of her dress, but that her general appearance was stylish and cheerful, and it did not appear that the prospect of being put through the small sieve by Mr. W. E. Clegg had alarmed her—certainly it had not blanched her cheeks.

Well, but while I have been noting Mrs. Dyson and the less notable persons, the magistrates and advocates have concluded their consultation out of court. They resume their places, and then Mr. Welby makes the brief announcement that ends all questions for the day.

A very large proportion of the public were glad to hear that Charles Peace had recovered very satisfactorily from the injuries he had received.

As previously stated, he first refused to take any stimulants, and only seemed to desire to be left alone curled up under a heap of rugs.

Later in the day he revived a good deal; took stimulants freely, and when Mr. Hallam, surgeon, saw him late at night, he found him so much improved that he expressed his intention not to come down again unless sent for.

The necessity did not arise for Mr. Hallam to be again called in. Peace continued to improve during the night, and on Thursday morning, when the surgeon saw him again, he was much better. Peace spent a very restless night.

He tossed about a good deal, and his conduct was altogether so marked as not to escape attention.

The two warders who brought him from London had never both left him since they picked him up on the railway on Wednesday.

One of them sat close by Peace's side throughout the whole night watching his every movement, and not for an instant having his gaze averted from his now more than ever remarkable and distinguished prisoner.

At intervals Peace, as already stated, tossed about a good deal, and then he became quiet, and apparently dropped into a sound slumber.

Presently the watchful eye of the warder has seen him peep stealthily up from under his rugs, evidently to ascertain whether he might risk any move without being watched.

Of course there was not the slightest chance of his escaping from the cells; but if opportunity offered he might make an attempt upon his life. He frequently took stimulants—brandy and milk; and when Mr. Hallam saw him on Thursday morning he found him very much better, and ordered him tea and bread and butter.

When asked " What sort of a night he had had ?" by one of the officers, he replied in that hypocritically whining tone which he knew so well how to simulate, " Not very good. I can't sleep."

He remained lying down under a good supply of rugs, and although hitherto extremely talkative and effusive in his efforts to recognise all who approached him, he now said but little, even when roused to take stimulants.

On Thursday night two members of the borough force were told off to assist the warders in their care of the convict. Two lamps were placed in his cell in such positions as to throw their light full on his face; and near him sat one of the warders and the two policemen.

The second warder rested on a " shake-down" in the corridor while the first kept his watch, and at intervals they changed.

On Thursday night, Peace was reported to be much better, and he asked for soup and other stimulants, which were supplied to him.

Peace's career continued to be one series of surprises, not the least astonishing of which came to light on the morning after his attempted escape. His object in jumping from the train appears to have been not so much to escape as to destroy himself.

He was often heard to express a strong desire to be buried at Darnall. It was there, it will be remembered, that he occupied a little villa residence standing in its wn grounds, and the garden attached to which he cultivated with so much care; it was there he unhappily made the acquaintance of the Dysons, and became so offensive in his friendship that they had to leave the village to escape from him; it is there his married daughter lives; it was there his wife was arrested on a charge of being in possession of goods the proceeds of his burglaries; and to Darnall she returned immediately after her acquittal on the charge at Newgate.

These and perhaps many other associations appear to have endeared the place to him. It is also a remarkable fact that the spot selected by Peace at which to make his daring leap from the carriage was, measured by the rate at which an express train travels, within a very short distance of Darnall Church.

At first it was supposed that the only and real purpose in his mind in endeavouring to give his custodians the slip there was that—hoping to escape unhurt—he knew the country well, and could take short cuts across the fields and find safe and friendly shelter at Darnall. His object, however, appears not to have been to regain his freedom, but to destroy himself.

On Thursday morning, Mr. W. E. Clegg, visited the convict in his cell, for the purpose of receiving instructions from him as to his defence, and before he left Peace drew from his pocket a scrap of crumpled paper, and handed it to him.

As it was contrary to the rules of the Pentonville establishment that a prisoner should have any letter or anything of the kind upon him, the warders asked that the paper might be handed over to them. The note was written in pencil, and read as follows:—

" BURY ME AT DARNALL. GOOD-BYE. GOD BLESS YOU ALL. C. PEACE."

It appears that when a Pentonville convict has a letter sent to him, it is opened and read by one of the officials, and if there is nothing in it objectionable it is initialled and passed on to him.

The scrap of paper upon which Peace had written, and which he had kept treasured up in his pocket, was part of a letter which had been so handed over to him. Where he got the pencil from to write the note, and when he wrote it, is unknown.

From its contents it would certainly appear that his deliberate object in springing through the window when the train was going at express speed was to destroy himself; and, bad beyond description as he is, he seems to have possessed sufficient human feeling to desire that his remains might lie amongst those whom he had known in life.

At intervals during Thursday morning he seemed to suffer much mental distress, and exclaimed with great intensity of feeling, " I do wish I was dead!"

In the face of all these facts the warders, it may be readily imagined, redoubled their already vigilant watch over him, and his slightest movement did not pass unobserved.

Peace's escape from instant death when he leaped out of the railway carriage window was a matter of surprise to everybody. His custodians never expected to see him alive after his fall.

CHAPTER CLVI.

OUTSIDE THE POLICE-COURT—EXTRAORDINARY SCENES.

As was generally expected, there was a most exciting and most unusual scene outside the police-court on the morning appointed for the examination.

On Friday comparatively few people knew that Peace was to be brought before the magistrates, but almost as soon as it was opened the court was crowded to its utmost capacity, the approaches were lined with excited people eager to gain but a glance at the prisoner or Mrs. Dyson, and in the hall on the ground floor were several hundred people who were unable to get upstairs.

Outside a mob surged to and fro, obstructing the traffic in Castle-street, and several free fights occurred between people whose only object seemed to be to get nearer the Town Hall door without the faintest hope of getting in.

This was the state of things when it was not generally known that the proceedings of the Police-court presented a feature of unusual attraction.

But when it had been announced by the stipendiary, and announced in the papers, and was known by everybody, that the prisoner had been " remanded until Wednesday morning at ten o'clock," and that Mrs. Dyson was to be cross-examined, it was generally anticipated that a crowd such as had never before been attracted to the Police-court would besiege the building. Some fears were entertained even that serious results might follow from the immense crush when the doors were opened and everybody in the large crowd made an almost superhuman individual effort to occupy one of the small number of places set apart for the gratification of the public.

The Chief Constable accordingly took every precaution to guard against the rash and ill-judged violence of an excited crowd.

A large staff of police-officers were marshalled in front of the Town Hall, their instructions being to keep the crowd moving as long as possible.

They found on arriving that they had been forestalled by the public, who had already assembled to the number of about 200, and were being rapidly reinforced.

Some of the people who were there had, it is said, taken up their positions as early as five o'clock, and verily they looked it. The cold, raw air had exercised to the full its nipping influence upon them.

Their faces were pallid, with just a dash of blue in the lips, and a dab of carnation on the tip of the nose. Their shoulders were raised almost to their ears, and their coats drawn carefully round their throats.

They shivered occasionally in a most complete and uncompromising manner, but there was even in that shiver an expressed determination to stand their ground to see Peace, even though an insidious fox, in the form of a biting wind, were gnawing to their very vitals.

The unmistakeable meaning conveyed in the shiver was echoed in the ceaseless stamp of feet upon the pavement, as the people endeavoured by that means to keep up something like circulation in their benumbed extremities. There could be no doubt of their intentions.

They had come to see Peace, and they would see him however much they suffered.

But waiting was very monotonous work, and despite the excitement of the occasion, the time passed slowly and wearily along.

The individuals who composed the crowd must have been those "with whom time ambles withal," for the minutes dragged themselves along in the style supposed to be appropriated to "linked sweetness," and each succeeding minute seemed to be longer drawn out than its predecessor.

The crowd was not large enough to get up any enthusiasm, and it was not until towards eight o'clock that anything like life and fun were observable.

Then the new arrivals were frequent and numerous, and what had been the fringe of the crowd became a compact mass.

Castle-street, near the Town Hall, was crammed full of people, and now that it was evident that the whole of them could not get in, an excited and determined struggle for places began and was carried on with vigour up to the time when it was known that their labours had been in vain.

It was an intensely and essentially selfish crowd, and its composition was a medley of a motley character.

Nearly all classes of society were represented in that mass of people, and one extraordinary feature was the immense number of women amongst them.

Men, women, and children were huddled together as closely as it was possible for human beings to be packed.

They were crushed and crushed and crushed again until almost all the compressibility contained in their individual bodies had been utilised, and they were contorted into angular portions of humanity, all of whose sides geometrically corresponded with the sides of other portions of humanity presented to them.

Thus it may be imagined that space was economised at the expense of comfort, but that was a trifling consideration.

The people had come to see Peace.

Comfort was a secondary matter—away with it! So they grinned—those of them who had room to do so—and bore the discomfort good humouredly so long as they did not lose a point in the struggle towards the door.

Those immediately round the door were, of course, the early risers.

They were, without exception, people in the lower classes of society. Boys, who might fairly be classed as *gamins*, with a neglected look and a suspicious air of having been out all night, had taken up front positions, and, having become jammed in by the crowd, were unable to get out, though there was not the slightest probability that the police would let them into the court.

Many of the men were dressed in their working clothes, whilst some of the women had only shawls thrown over their heads.

Further back in the crowd other classes were represented.

Not a few silk hats were observable, dotted about here and there, amid the sober shoal of less demonstrative round felts, and one of the former dodged about in a most amusing manner, as its owner made the most heroic but unsuccessful attempts to defend a fair companion who wore a beautiful sealskin jacket.

There was also a good sprinkling of young men, who would perhaps be looked upon as "swells" by the lower classes, but these young gentlemen did not show any of their distinguishing characteristics, and kept quiet.

As nine o'clock approached the people began to be excited, and their ebullitions of feeling found vent in a series of rushes which produced a swaying, surging movement on the part of the crowd.

This placed in jeopardy the situation of some of the people who had secured what they thought to be good chances of getting in, and they fought manfully to retain any advantage they might have gained.

Their struggles, however, against the surging of the crowd were puerile and utterly inoperative, and their vehement protestations against the injustice of the dispensation was laughed to scorn.

As a natural sequence curses and blasphemy took the place of protestations, but these were alike ineffective, and everybody seemed to devote his attention to swindling everyone in front of him of his position. The slightest rent in the crowd caused by a rush called forth numerous claimants, and angry passions were allowed to rise, without stint in the breasts of those who allowed their chances to pass.

Women as well as men struggled to the front, and as they asserted their rights courtesy retired. *Place aux dames* was an obsolete idea. The women placed themselves on the same level as the men, and demanding the rights extended to men, received courtesy in the same ratio.

Judging by the looks of some of them they did not enjoy the working of the principle, and they would have been only too glad to sink their rights for a little comfort and convenience.

It was a case of every man for himself, and the hindermost, who were supposed to be left in the care of the prince of darkness, were of course the women.

Nine o'clock struck, and the excitement of the crowd

reached fever heat. It was pretty generally known that Peace was to arrive about nine, and it was thought the doors now would soon be opened.

The people on the outside of the crowd saw that it would be hopeless for them to attempt to get into the court, and in the hope of seeing something to recompense them for their trouble they gravitated towards the Castle-green and Water-lane entrances to the Police-offices.

Those who went to Water-lane had the satisfaction of seeing a number of gentlemen pass in the portals of the offices, receive a military salute from the numerous constables posted about the place, and disappear in the long passage at the top of the steps.

Several other people came up the same way, and some having the necessary credentials were passed in, and the others rejected and turned back. One of the funniest scenes of the morning occurred here, when a fat and self-sufficient landlord, accompanied by his gaudily-dressed wife, sailed down Water-lane, and with an important air strutted up the steps, throwing dignified nods at the police-officers.

His wife waddled after him, and they successfully passed the gauntlet of police until they came to the steps.

Here they were tackled in an apologetic but firm manner, and after having been reminded, as they were loth to go, that they were obstructing the passage, they were unceremoniously ordered out.

The spectators who assembled in front of the Castle-green entrance certainly had the best of the day. They were in the very thick of the excitement. The prison van had gone down Castle-green to the station, and Peace was momentarily expected.

He would be concealed in the inmost recesses of the van, but what of that? He would be there. Time sped. It was ten minutes past nine. The train must be late.

No, there was the jingle of the bells on the harness, and the heavy rumble of the wheels was heard as the ponderous conveyance turned out of Bridge-street into the Green. But what—what is this? Why does the van come so slowly? Why does everyone seem so dejected?

Why does not the driver turn his pair cleverly round into the Parade Ground with a triumphant and defiant crack of the whip? What does it all mean?—he can't have escaped.

The suspense for the moment is fearful, almost agonising, and then the word is passed, "He has escaped—jumped out of the train, going at full speed."

A few incoherent sentences convey a world of information, and form the groundwork of numerous rumours. The news spread like wildfire. The crowd in front of the Town Hall is dazed. The strain is gone. No longer do they struggle to get the best places. A feeling of insecurity has come over them.

They think of Peace in the dock as an insignificant old man, but Peace at liberty is a very different individual.

He is surrounded by an air of villainy with a dark background of vengeful intrepidity, and his constant companion is a "six-shooter."

Society feels unsafe, and though an additional lustre has been imparted to the halo of glorious romance which surrounds his life by his latest achievement, a universal hope is expressed that he will be recaptured.

The wildest rumours are floating about as to his mode of escape, and circumstantial details are not wanting as to his having overpowered the warders,

alighted uninjured, and, plunging into a wood, eluded pursuit.

But these surmises are premature. Again the van was brought out, and driven off to the station. These were anxious moments. More than half the people declined to believe the rumour that Peace had escaped.

It was such a likely thing for Peace to attempt, that some one would be sure to suggest it, and thus start a rumour. On the other hand, it was so unlikely that a couple of London warders would allow a little man like Peace to escape, that the majority of the people assembled would not accept the statement.

However, the bringing out of the van a second time gave a foundation to the first rumour, especially when it was now expected that he had been retaken. The van was not long away.

Again the jingle of the bells. The horses came up Castle-green at a smart pace. Triumph was written on the faces of the local police.

The van turned into the yard of the police-station; with a good swing, the doors were banged to and locked, and once more Peace was safe.

Now came another struggle for places, and this was continued fiercely. Traffic had been resumed, however, and every now and then the consistency of the crowd was broken in upon by a vulgar cart, an impertinent hansom, or a blundering 'bus.

The breaches were most trying to the people in the roadway. They must either sacrifice their positions or be run over. As long as they could they stuck to their places, but preferring not to be run over, they relented and ran for it.

Women as well as men were in the way of the conveyances, and it was most funny to see the terrified faces of the women as, after being elbowed out of the crowd by men who coolly took their positions, they suddenly found a horse's nose within a few inches of their faces. Flight was the first thing with them. Then when they were safely out of the way they were frightened, and exhibited a tendency to screaming and hysteria; and subsequently, when all was over, they became vaguely, but virtuously, indignant.

Such scenes as these beguiled the minutes which crept slowly by, until about a quarter-past ten, when it was known that a remand had been granted. More vague rumours flew about for a few minutes, and then the chief constable appeared at one of the upper windows.

Immediately there was a breathless silence, and Mr. Jackson announced that Peace had been remanded for eight days in consequence of injuries he had received. He had made an attempt to escape, but had been recaptured.

A great shout greeted this latter statement, and society once more breathed.

In spite of the obvious wish of the chief constable that it should move on as well as breathe, society did not move on, and for hours hung about the street in the hope of picking up gossip, reliable or unreliable.

Now and then a wild rumour sent a thrill through the crowd. Several times Peace had just expired. Others stated that he was so "smashed that he had to be carried about in a sack."

Then it was given out that he was very little hurt, and was "drinking brandy like mad." And lastly, as might have been expected, that "he was not hurt at all, but was only shamming."

Mrs. Dyson, though only a lesser light by the side of Peace, was somebody, and her appearance was anxiously looked for. But here again disappointment waited on the unhappy people.

PEACE IS VISITED BY HIS SOLICITOR.

She got safely away, and the only thing in the way of a sensation that turned up to gratify the crowd for long waiting was the appearance of the Pentonville warders.

They had occasion to appear in the Haymarket, and, being identified by their uniforms, were made the butt of much unpleasant chaff.

They were followed about by the people, laughed at, jeered, ironically cheered, and asked the most pertinent, yet impertinent, questions.

Eventually they were protected by a strong body of police, and, amid a discharge of chaff, succeeded in gaining the Police-offices.

After this nothing more happened, and as nothing

seemed likely to happen, first one and then another of the members of the crowd dropped off, until finally the last man, sighing over the barren results of all his struggling, scuffling, suffering, &c., cast a furtive eye at the Police-station, and a perfunctory glance at the now lighted Town Hall clock, and departed.

CHAPTER CLVII.

THE EXAMINATION OF CHARLES PEACE UPON THE CHARGE OF MURDERING MR. DYSON—SCENES IN COURT.

PEACE remained in a very prostrate condition, and, according to his own account, he was not fit to make his appearance in a court of justice. It was deemed, however, expedient to proceed with the charge.

Mr. Pollard, on Friday morning, put it to the Sheffield stipendiary whether the "leap for life" which Peace, the burglar, made from the express train was not inconsistent with his innocence of the crime of murder.

Mr. Welby suggested that a convict under a life sentence might have other reasons for the leap than the fear of hanging. No doubt it was with the convict a case of mixed motives.

Had he been able to escape, even for a few days, a lease of life for at least six months would have been secured, as his case would have been kept over till the Leeds Assizes following those which open next week.

Having been remanded for eight days, the desperado, like many less deeply interested, believed that his respite had been secured. Perhaps but for this knowledge the criminal would have played a deeper game by not getting better so soon.

The brandy with milk and arrowroot, which from the first few hours of his capture he took pretty freely, produced such an effect on his sound and wiry constitution that by Thursday evening Mr. Hallam, the surgeon specially in attendance, was able to say that if no change for the worse occurred, he might be brought before the stipendiary on the following morning.

The prisoner has proved such a troublesome and expensive "guest" that the authorities seemed to entertain a strong desire to see him again in Pentonville or such other place of security as it may seem fit to assign him to.

The secret of the examination being held to-day was last night divulged to the press, but only on condition that they should keep it private till the prisoner had been actually brought up.

Of course it was kept yet more secret from the prisoner.

This helped him to sleep last night, and, though he showed himself much more querulous than has been his wont, he took in the morning a plentifully early breakfast.

The surgeon, having seen him, decided that he was fit to be brought up. Soon after ten o'clock the prisoner was accordingly helped out of his cell, but apparently had no idea of where he was being taken.

The warders presently placed him in a large arm-chair in the corridor, and into this he sank with a lengthened sigh, leaning his head on his hands, as if much exhausted.

Then suddenly, with an ugly expression in his eyes, he protruded the lower part of his face across the long table which had been set in the corridor, and exclaimed with clenched teeth, but in a low tone, "What are we here for? What is this?"

The scene might well arouse the criminal's curiosity. Unwilling to cause excitement either to the prisoner or to the public, the authorities had improvised a court in the corridor of the prison, where the light was supplied by candles.

The stipendiary, with his clerks, sat ready to examine the prisoner.

The chief constable was present, also Inspector Bradbury and Police-constable Walsh, who was in charge of Mrs. Dyson. Mr. Pollard again appeared to prosecute, and Mr. W. E. Clegg conducted the defence.

The scene was dreary and depressing. especially as there was no audience for the principal actor to play up to, even had he been so disposed, the public having been excluded.

After several half-whining protests from the convict the stipendiary decided to go on, when, with a sudden change of voice, Peace exclaimed in his old sharp tones, "I wish to God there was something across my shoulders."

He was then plentifully supplied with coverings through which his newly-bandaged head at times could hardly be seen. His high but narrow forehead slopes rapidly upwards, and, though much of his apparent weakness was evidently mere affectation, his wan and haggard aspect was pitiable as well as repugnant.

Towards Mrs. Dyson, who was placed at some distance along the table, he alternately glared, and scowled and leered, and more than once became very excited in his demands for justice when the stipendiary firmly refused liberty to press certain questions which he deemed irrelevant.

Mrs. Dyson was tastefully dressed entirely in black, and without her veil. She seemed in good health, and, though apparently suffering somewhat from suppressed excitement, gave her evidence clearly, calmly, and without a particle of flinching.

The whitewashed walls of the cold corridor did not look more stonily at Peace than did the face of the woman whom he tried to claim as his former paramour.

The absence of spectators was a relief to her, and she stood quietly and without apparent weariness during her long and trying cross-examination.

Mr. Clegg did the best he could for his client, but refused to take any notice of the low mutterings or loud protests of the prisoner.

The stipendiary refused to let the letters be read aloud, but the most exciting passages were given. These documents are a series of comparatively dull communications written on old envelopes and dirty scraps of paper.

Here is a specimen : "How well you never told that man I looked at you out of the window you left me to find out for myself and would not put me on my guard, as I do you. Hope you won't do it again. Don't talk to little Willie much, or give him any halfpennies. Don't be a fool; it looks as if you want people to know the way and—"

A blank occurs here, and the remaining portion of the letter now legible says: "If you are not more careful we will have to say quits. I have told you not to say anything until—"

On the theory of the defence the Willie referred to is Mrs. Dyson's son, aged seven, and William Henry by name. (Mrs. Dyson's reply to every question was a decided repudiation of the suggestion that the letters had been written by her.)

At these repudiations the convict affected to be savagely indignant. Also when Mrs. Dyson said the portrait had been stolen from her room he muttered between his clenched teeth—

"Stolen—stolen—stolen!"

He glared towards the witness with a tragic air, and

then buried his head in his arms, which were stretched on the table.

At another time, when Mrs. Dyson was being questioned as to whether any struggle took place between her husband and the murderer, and replied in the negative, Peace, who had seemed comparatively quiet, shot his head up and made his lower jaw protrude in a loathsome manner, as he glared at the witness.

While Mrs. Dyson's depositions before the coroner were being read the prisoner caused another scene. On being removed to his cell, at the end of the proceedings, his energy seemed quite to leave him; but when his counsel visited him in his cell shortly afterwards the prisoner seemed comparatively cheerful and careless, and gave his instructions and suggestions in quite a business-like fashion.

Only passages from the letters alleged to have been written by Mrs. Dyson were read aloud in court.

In spite of the policy of secrecy followed by the stipendiary and Chief Constable Jackson, a large crowd gathered at the Town Hall, and long before the usual time of opening the doors so great became the pressure against them as to burst them open, and the courts were rapidly filled.

The police were able, however, to clear them without any serious trouble.

People knew that the ordinary business of the Court would commence at eleven o'clock, and they settled down to wait as comfortably as possible for that time, knowing that they would then be able to gain admission.

When the doors were opened to the public, the two courts were soon filled again, and the people rested in expectation till authentic word came that the convict's examination was well-nigh over.

Throughout the time there was greater excitement than at any period since the great Sheffield flood, but the police were able to preserve order.

Robinson, who captured Peace at Blackheath, after such a desperate struggle was in Sheffield, on a visit to some friends, and his frank and yet jovial bearing has impressed very favourably those who happened to meet him.

A suggestion was made that a public testimonial should be presented to him for his bravery, and, in spite of dulness of trade, was likely to be received with favour. Robinson had not seen Peace in Sheffield.

Up to half-past ten at night the prisoner was behaving with comparative composure, and had taken refreshments when he required them.

The following is a fuller account of the particulars of this examination :—

A few minutes after ten o'clock Peace was assisted out of his cell and placed in an armchair in the corridor where the inquiry was held. He seemed to be exhausted, and sinking into the chair he exclaimed, "Oh, oh !" and leaned his head on his hand. He then looked about with an air of surprise, and exclaimed, groaning deeply, "What are we here for ? What is this ?"

The Stipendiary (Mr. Welby) : This is the preliminary inquiry which is being proceeded with after being adjourned the other day.

Prisoner (groaning again) : I am not able to bear it. I ought not to be brought here.

The Stipendiary : Then you must do the best you can. This is only the preliminary inquiry. You are not absolutely obliged to be here—so you must attend as well as you can. You are represented here, and the preliminary inquiry is to be finished to-day ?

Prisoner : I wish to God there was something across my shoulders. I am very cold. Oh dear ! oh dear ! Then am I to be committed to-day ?

The Stipendiary : The preliminary inquiry will be finished, and if the evidence is sufficient you will be committed.

Prisoner : I want to have my solicitor here. Oh dear ! and I want to call my witnesses.

Mr. Clegg : You will have sufficient time for that ; you will have plenty of time to call your witnesses.

Prisoner (groaning) : I am not able to go on. Oh, I am so cold ! (A thick rug was here thrown over him by one of the warders.) I am not able to go on ; I am not. (Groaning again.) This is not justice ; it is not justice.

The Stipendiary : You must take it for what it is.

The prisoner here uttered some words, which were taken to be " Oh, never mind that ;" and afterwards asked that his counsel should come nearer. He seemed to suffer from the cold and the draught of air in the corridor.

Prisoner (apparently recovering himself, and looking more alert, and speaking with more energy) : Then, I say, it is not justice ; it is not justice. Why does not my solicitor prevent this, and ask for a remand. What is my solicitor doing not to prevent this ? Tell my solicitor I want him.

Mr. Clegg : Well, what do you want ?

Prisoner (sharply) : Why don't you ask for a remand ?

The Stipendiary : It is no use asking for a remand at all, I tell you ; the inquiry is going to be proceeded with.

Prisoner (piteously) : It is not justice. I am not able to go on ; you know how I am. Oh, dear, it is no matter if I'd killed myself. It would be no matter. You know how I am, and ought to have a remand. I feel I want it, and must have a remand.

The Stipendiary : Remand will not be granted ; and you had better attend to what is said.

Mr. Clegg : If you want to say anything wait until I am cross-examining Mrs. Dyson, and it can be done then. You had better save your energies until then. The inquiry will be proceeded with to-day.

Mrs. Dyson was then called and sworn. She looked well, but spoke slowly, as if labouring under suppressed emotion.

Mr. Pollard : Catherine Dyson, there were some papers produced the other day in court. Bradbury, will you produce those papers ?

Inspector Bradbury handed in the papers.

The Stipendiary : Those, I suppose, are the papers and the card.

Mr. Pollard : They are the papers produced by Bradbury. (To witness) : Have you seen those papers before ?—Yes ; at the coroner's inquest in December, 1876.

You have seen the first card—the card numbered one. That, I think you say, is the handwriting of your husband on the back of it ?—Yes.

With reference to all the other papers, do you know the handwriting ?—No, I do not.

The Stipendiary : You had better look over them, every one of them, before you speak to them all.

Witness then looked over them, prisoner meanwhile languidly saying : They are not all there. I want to look at them.

Mr. Clegg : Be quiet.

Witness : I do not know whose handwriting it is.

The Stipendiary : You do not know whose handwriting it is on any of them ?—No.

The Stipendiary : You have looked at them ?—I know none of them except the post-card.

Prisoner (interrupting) : I want the milkman called.

The Stipendiary : You had better be quiet. Your time for calling witnesses will come.

Mr. Pollard (to witness) : Were any of those written by your authority ? Do you know any of them ?—Not by my authority. I know nothing of them.

What distance should you say it is from the house that you lived in at Darnall to the house you removed to at Bannercross ?—About five or six miles, to the best of my knowledge.

Mr Clegg : Before proceeding with the cross-examination I should like to recall Mr. Inspector Bradbury.

The Stipendiary : Why so ?

Mr. Pollard : I have a question to put to the inspector that I omitted to ask the other day.

Mr. Bradbury was recalled, and was examined by Mr. Pollard.

Do you produce a bullet ?—Yes (producing it).

From whom did you receive it ?—From Dr. Harrison, on Dec. 8, 1876, the day of the inquest.

Cross-examined by Mr. Clegg : You remember on the last time, Mr. Bradbury, that I asked you if you had seen a photograph ?—Yes.

Have you got that photo now ?—Yes. (Produced a photo) I got it from Mr. Jackson, the chief constable.

The photo was then handed to the stipendiary, and Peace, eyeing it, said in an aggrieved voice : " They have taken it out of the case."

Mr. Clegg, addressing him, said : Will you be quiet ?

Mr. Pollard : I want to ask one or two questions of Mrs. Dyson with reference to these photographs.

The Stipendiary : Certainly.

Mr. Clegg : Perhaps it will be better if you let me finish my cross-examination first.

Mr. Pollard : I prefer to do it now.

Mr. Pollard : Mrs. Dyson, have you any remembrance of being photographed ? First of all, whose photograph is this ? (Handing a photograph to the witness.)—It is the prisoner's and mine.

Where was that taken ?—It was taken in 1876.

The Stipendiary : What part of 1876 ?—I cannot remember the date. It was summer.

When was it taken ?—At Sheffield Fair.

Was it at the summer or winter fair ?

Peace : It was the winter fair.

Mrs. Dyson : I won't say, because I am not sure.

How near was it to Nov. 29, 1876 ?—It was some months before that date ; at the Sheffield Fair.

The Stipendiary : There is a name at the back of the photo.

Mr. Pollard : Will you look at that (handing a small photo to Mrs. Dyson) ?—That is mine.

Had you in the years 1876 or 1875 a photo like that, in that position ?—Yes ; I had one in a locket.

Was it in 1875 or 1876 ?—I had it in 1875.

Can you say at all whether it was in 1875 or 1876 ?—Yes ; I had it in the early part of 1876.

You say you had it in a locket ?—Yes.

Have you that photograph in the locket now ?—No it was taken from me.

How do you mean ?—It was taken out of the house without my knowing how.

It was in the winter ?—Yes, 1875, as well as I can remember.

The Stipendiary ? Before the larger one was taken ?—Yes it was.

Can you say it was the winter of 1875 or 1876 ?—Well, it was about Christmas.

Do you say that the locket was stolen ?—No, the photograph was then out of the locket.

You were living at Darnall then, were you ?—Yes.

Where was the locket when you missed the photograph from it ?—It was in my bedroom.

Did you speak about the loss ?—Yes, I mentioned it to my husband.

Did you make any search for the photo ?—Yes ; I also told an officer before I went to America.

You made a search for the photo ?—Yes.

Did you ever find the photo ?—No.

Mr. Pollard : Is that the locket, or a copy of the photograph that you so lost ?—That is not the original, because the one that I had was taken in Cleveland, Ohio.

Mr. Pollard : And this is a copy of it—is it ?—Yes.

Mr. Pollard : I see that this has the name of F. Barber, photographer, Church-gates, Sheffield.—Witness : This is not the original. The original was taken by Mr. Wragg, Cleveland, Ohio.

Mr. Pollard : Did you ever go to Mr. Barber's to be photographed ?—No, no ; I never had a photograph taken in this country except that one.

Mr. Pollard : Except the one that was taken at the fair.

Mr. Pollard (to the Stipendiary) : That, you see, is done on glass. That was done at the back of the other.

The Stipendiary : Oh, I see.

The Clerk : There was only one photograph taken then ?—Witness : Only one.

The prisoner here put his legs on the table, and the Stipendiary, addressing him, said severely : You must not put your feet on the table.—Prisoner (sharply) : All right.

Mr. Pollard (to witness) : Did you tell any other person at the time besides your husband of the loss of the photograph from your locket ?—I told one of the officers.

That you told us ; but anybody else ?—No.

Mr. Clegg : Besides, if you did it would not be evidence.

Mr. Pollard : Unless the neighbour was—I do not want to put it in her mouth.

Mr. Pollard (to witness) : Was your husband with you that day in Sheffield Fair ?—Yes.

On the day you were photographed ?—Yes.

The Prisoner : Call Daird (meaning the policeman of Darnall)—will you, please ?

At Sheffield Fair the prisoner was a neighbour of yours ?—Yes. I believed him at that time to be a respectable man.

And a picture-frame maker, as you said ?—Yes.

You said you had this (referring to the photograph) with you then. Where was it kept ?—On the mantelpiece in the kitchen.

When did you miss it ?—In a week or so after it was taken.

When did you next see this one (lifting another photograph) ?—I cannot exactly say the day. One day last week, in Mr. Jackson's hands.

In the hands of the police ?—Yes.

Did you give it to any one ?—No ; I did not give it to any one. It was taken away without my knowledge.

Then with reference to the photograph which was taken from your locket—what about it ?—It was taken away without my knowledge.

When was that ?

Mr. Robinson : I have got all that down as in the winter of 1875.

Mr. Clegg : I might as well take this photograph at

once (showing the double one to the witness). Was not that photograph taken in the fair of 1876 ?—In 1876—I think so, as well as I can remember.

The photograph I am now holding ?—Yes, I see.

Was this photograph taken in the fair of 1876 ?—I said I could not remember the date.

Was it during the time that you were residing at Darnall ?—Yes.

When did you leave Darnall, was it on Oct. 29 ?—On Oct. 25, 1876.

Was it at the fair preceding the time that you left Darnall ?—It was at the fair before I left Darnall.

I want now to know, for certain. Are you certain this was taken in the preceding fair before you left Darnall ?—I did not say the preceding fair.

Well, I ask you now ?—I cannot say. I am not quite certain, but I should be able to find out, if necessary.

But I want to know now ?—I cannot say.

You have already said you thought it was the Summer Fair of 1876 ?—I think so, but I am not quite certain ; but it was taken at Sheffield Fair.

I will try and assist your memory. Did you not say before the coroner that you had known the prisoner for about ten months ?—I don't recollect exactly.

At the time you gave evidence before the coroner in December, 1876, how long had you known the prisoner ? —Perhaps near a year.

Had you been with him to more than one fair ?—No.

Had you been with him to what is called a Winter Fair ?—No.

Then the fair at which you had been with him was the Summer Fair ?—Yes.

You say you had only known him a year, and you had not been with him to a winter fair. Now, then, cannot you now say that it was the summer fair of 1876 ?—Oh, no ; I cannot say, because I am not quite sure.

I will try and assist you a little further. How many months was it before you took out the summons against him for threatening your life that you had been with him to the fair ? I cannot tell you how many months. I cannot tell you exactly. It might be two or three months, perhaps. I cannot be quite sure.

When were you married to Mr. Dyson ?—I do not remember the date.

Don't remember the date ? What year was it ?—I can't tell you that.

Do you mean to swear that you can't tell the year when you were married ?—No, I can't say what year.

Not what year ?—No ; but I can find out.

Don you mean to say you don't know what year you were married in ?—I don't.

Where were you married ?—In Cleveland, Ohio ; Trinity Church.

Mr. Clegg : Were there any witnesses present at your marriage ?—Certainly ; my sister, Mrs. Thomas Mooney.

Mr. Pollard : I object to this. I can't see the relevancy of it.

The Stipendiary : She says she can't remember when she was married.

Mr. Clegg : I don't wish to waste time ; but I believe all the questions I ask will have a relevancy to the case.

The Stipendiary : I must trust you to a great extent. I do not myself see the relevancy.

Mr. Pollard : It will do no good to go into the whole history of a person's life from their first years.

Mr. Clegg : I am only starting the question of whether she was married, and I have every reason for asking for full particulars of the facts.

The Stipendiary : If she could remember the year of her marriage I should say the rest was not necessary.

Mr. Pollard (to Mr. Clegg) : Ask when it was about.

Mr. Clegg : If she had told me the year I should have been satisfied. (To witness) : Your sister was one of the witnesses. Who was another ?—Dr. Sargent.

Did you get a certificate of your marriage ? Certainly ; it is with my agent in America.

What is your agent's name ?—Booth, Barratt, and Co., St. Louis, Missouri, United States.

Had you any object in leaving your certificate there ?—I have left other papers there. They are more safe then carrying them about.

The Stipendiary here interposed with reference to the manner in which Mr. Clegg was cross-examining.

Mr. Clegg : In this case it is a question of credibility as to what actually happened, and as this witness is the only person who actually saw what happened I think I have a right to test her credibility in every possible way. I have an object in asking these questions as to her marriage, in consequence of what I am instructed she has told somebody about it. I wish to inquire into it, whether it is true or not.

Mr. Clegg : Was your husband friendly with the prisoner ?—Yes.

Did he frame any pictures for you ?—Yes.

(Prisoner muttered something which was not distinctly heard.)

Did he tell you what they were ?—Yes. One was a portrait of my sister, one of Mr. Dyson, and my brother, and my little boy.

Was your husband's mother not amongst them ?—I think not.

Will you swear he did not frame that ?—No, he did not.

Had your husband a portrait or picture of his mother ?—I had one.

The Stipendiary : What about your objection, Mr. Pollard ?

Mr. Pollard : Of course I make my objection. I was leaving it in your hands.

Mr. Clegg : Will you swear he did not frame a portrait of your husband's mother ?—No, he did not. There was one in a pot frame.

The Stipendiary said something to Mr. Clegg, who replied, " I will show the portrait to you, sir. I do not want to prove anything that is not material."

Mr. Clegg : This is a material object ; a most material object.

The Stipendiary : It is not, in my idea, of sufficient importance to be gone on with.

Mr. Clegg : I think you will see, when I bring out what I want to know about this portrait, that it is a very material object.

The Stipendiary : Very well, I will say no more ; but if it is merely a question of general credibility, it is unnecessary.

Mr. Clegg : Did you ever ask him to frame this portrait—this picture of your mother ?—Yes. I was to get a large one of my mother. I mentioned it to him about framing them, but I never got the photographs.

Did you ask him to frame your mother's portrait ? —Yes ; but he never did it.

Mr. Clegg : Did you write him any letter ?

Mr. Pollard : She gives a reason why she did not ask him.

Mr. Clegg : It is not an answer to my question. I do not care about her reasons.—(To witness) : Did you send him a letter about it ?—No.

Mr. Clegg (holding a bundle of letters in his hand,

and calling the attention of the witness to one marked No. 6) : Look at this letter. Is it in your handwriting ?—No.

Is it in your husband's writing ?—No.

Do you know whose writing it is ?—No, I don't.

Did any person know of your wish that he should frame the picture of your husband's mother but your husband and yourself ?—Not that I am aware of.

Except your husband and yourself ?—Not that I am aware of.

Have you ever seen the prisoner write ?—No.

You will swear that you never saw him write ?—No, I never saw him write. My husband used to write for him. I have seen him sitting at a table with writing materials in front of him.

Can you tell his writing if you see it again ?—I have not see him write.

(Peace here leaned against the table, and looked with great interest at the witness.)

Have you never seen letters purporting to come from him ?—No, I never have, for I did not know he could write, because he used to get my husband to write for him.

As far as you are concerned in reference to this wish, that you wanted the prisoner to frame your photo——

Mrs. Dyson : I did not ask him to frame mine.

I did not ask you that. I said your husband's mother's photo. You did not tell anyone of that ?—I do not remember that I did.

Now, just listen to this letter ; will you take it into your hands and follow it while I read a copy ? Now listen : "Saturday afternoon—I write you these few lines to thank you for all your kindness, which I shall never forget, from you and your wife. She is a good one. Does she know that you are to give me the things or not ? How can you keep them concealed ? One thing I wish you to do is to frame his mother's photograph and send it in with my music-book ; if you please do it when he is in. Many thanks for your kind advice. I hope I shall benefit by it. I shall try to do right to everybody as far as I can, for I can always look upon you as a friend. Good-bye. I have not much time. Burn this when you have read it."

Madame, will you still venture to swear that that paper is not in your writing ?—No, it is not.

Peace : I will prove it, though.

You remember you are upon your oath ?—Yes, I do.

Peace : I want these witnesses of mine called.

You were very intimate with Peace, were you not ?—Yes, I used to go into his house with his wife and daughter.

Have you been together with him, and have you not been to places of amusement together ?—I have been with him, his wife, and daughter.

I did not ask you that. Have you not been alone to places of amusement with him ?—Not to places of amusement. I have been to one place in Sheffield alone with him.

Where ?—I don't know where. Peace said there was a man there who was his brother.

What sort of place was it ?—A public-house.

Mr. Robinson : Did you see that man there ?—Yes, we saw him.

Do you know the name of the street ?

Prisoner (raising himself up, and addressing his solicitor, extending his arm towards Mrs. Dyson) : Ask her about going to the theatre with me.

Mr. Clegg : Have you been to the theatre with him ?—I was with him and his daughter and wife.

Was your husband there ?—No ; but I had other friends along with me.

Have you been with him alone to the Albert Hall ?—To the Albert Hall ?

Yes, to the Albert Hall ?—No, I never was with him alone ; his daughter was with me.

The prisoner again raised himself up, and exclaimed, "Send for Mr. Cowen ;" and then, as no attention was paid to his request, he leaned back again on his rugs.

Have you been to any public-houses together ?—I have already told you I have been to one.

More than one ?—No, not along with him ; but he has followed me into public-houses when I was with my husband. He followed me into one or two at Darnall. I cannot tell you the names of them.

Was one the Duke of York ?—I believe so.

Didn't you use to go there alone ?—I used to go there.

Stop a bit. Did you not sometimes go to that house to get something to drink, and tell the landlord to put it down to Peace, the prisoner ?—No. (Peace muttered something about it being false.) There was no landlord, only a landlady, in the house then.

Oh, you do remember that ? The name is Mrs. Liversidge—is it not ? I ask you now, have you been to the Halfway House ?—Yes.

Have you told the persons belonging to that house to put down the drink you had to Peace ?—Not to my knowledge.

Not to your knowledge ?—No.

Will you swear you have not ?—I cannot swear it ; but I say I never have to my knowledge.

Did you frequent that house ?—I called there two or three times, I believe.

Did you know a person of the name of Goodlad ?—Goodlad ?

Yes. Did you know the pianist at the Star Music Hall, in Spring-street ?—No.

Mr. Goodlad was here called up.

Mr. Clegg : See, that is the man.

The Stipendiary : Do you know that man by sight or name ?—Which one ?

The Stipendiary : Come forward. See, that is him. (Mr. Goodlad advanced.) Look at him, Mrs. Dyson.

Witness : I never remember seeing him before.

Prisoner (groaning) : Call his master ; call his master.

Mr. Clegg : Have you and the prisoner been to the Star Music Hall together ?—I don't know it by that name.

Then I will ask you this question—have you been to a music hall together, and to a public-house ?—He called it a picture gallery. I didn't hear any music there. There was no music there.

The Stipendiary : You had been to a place he called a picture gallery ?—Yes.

Mr. Clegg : Where was it ?—It was in Sheffield.

Can you tell me whereabouts it was ?—I could not tell you the street. I could not find it now.

Have you been to a public-house with him, where there was music and singing ?—We were at his brother's public-house ; and he said his brother was in some music society. I believe so, I am not quite sure.

Have you been to music-hall held at a public-house where there was some music and singing ?—Not to my knowledge.

What ?—It looked as if there was some music because there was a small stage, but there was no music in our time. It was early in the afternoon.

Have you not been at night, when there has been music and singing, and that man who was called has been playing there?—No, I do not remember to have seen his face.

The Clerk: You say you have not been there at night?—Witness: No, it was in the afternoon.

Mr. Clegg: Do you know a public-house in Russell-street, Sheffield, called the "Marquis of Waterford?" —No.

Mr. Clegg (to witness): The public-house that I am talking about now is in the street where the prisoner's brother lived?—I do not know it by name.

But do you know it now I have given you the place? Do you know where the prisoner's brother lived?—I do not know where he lived. He was in that public-house.

Mr. Clegg: Will you call a man of the name of Cragg? (Cragg was brought before the Court.)

Mr. Clegg: Do you know that man?—No, I never remember seeing him before.

That man is the landlord of the public-house that I have been talking about?—I never remember seeing him, but he may have been there and me not see him.

Have you been to several public-houses with him (the prisoner), and had something to drink with him at those public-houses?—No, I had soda water.

Mr. Clegg: Well, that is something to drink.

The Stipendiary: You do not deny that you have been at these public-houses?—I have been there.

But you have not seen these men that have been produced, to your knowledge?—Not to my knowledge.

Mr. Clegg: You have had some drink there?—I have had a bottle of soda water or pop.

Have you had something stronger than either of those two?—No.

How many times have you been with him to these various houses?—Only once.

Where?—The house where you speak of.

But I think you do not know it?—I have been to the house where his brother was.

But I am not talking about the place you call the picture-gallery. I am talking about another public-house altogether.—Oh, I did not understand.

Have you been to more than one public-house with him?—I have been to the picture-gallery and another place with him.

Those are two, and have you been with him to the "Halfway House?"—Not with him.

Or to the "Duke of York?"—Not with him.

Have you and he been out of the town together?— Yes; he followed me one day to Mansfield.

Was any one with you?—Mrs. Padmore and her three children.

When was that?—The summer before we returned.

Was that about the time you had your photograph taken with him?—No; not about the time.

Was it before the fair or after the fair?—I cannot tell you exactly.

Don't take refuge behind "Cannot tell exactly."— I cannot remember the date, and you don't want me to tell a lie.

I don't want you to tell me a lie.—It was in the summer some time.

Before or after the photograph was taken?—I cannot tell you exactly.

Was it immediately preceding or subsequently?—I can't tell you exactly.

Can you tell me whether it was before the fair or after the fair?—Don't remember.

Oh, please do try and remember?—Well, I can't; but I will find out for you.

Was it before or after you had taken out the warrant? —Why, long before.

The Stipendiary: Was it a warrant or summons?

Mr. Clegg: Well, both.

Mr. Pollard: The summons was taken first, and then the warrant.

Mr. Clegg (to witness): It was long before that, you say?—Yes.

Then at the time you went to Mansfield with Mrs. Padmore had you bad any quarrel with the prisoner? —Yes; I didn't want him to annoy me.

Had you had any quarrel?—Yes, because he was a nuisance to me.

That was before you had your portrait taken with him when you went to Mansfield?—I don't remember.

At this point the prisoner groaned loudly several times, and finally caused his head to fall forward on the table, placing his hands underneath. In this position he remained.

Examination continued: Do you say it was two or three months before?—I didn't say two or three months. I said a while before.

What do you call a while?—A month or so—two or three weeks. It might be longer. I am not quite sure.

Before you took out this summons against him, had you any quarrel at all?—Had I any quarrel?

Mr. Robinson: You summoned him for a certain thing. Had you any quarrel before that certain thing? —Not a quarrel, only that he was such a nuisance about the house, calling me a brute, and listening on the door-step to our conversation.

The prisoner here again groaned, and asked for the surgeon.

Mr. Hallam, the police surgeon, felt his pulse. He then suggested that his feet should be raised by being placed on a chair. This was done, and then the prisoner lay back in his arm-chair with his feet curled before him.

Had you any unpleasantness before you went to Mansfield?—He was a constant source of annoyance by his disagreeableness. He used to listen at the door, and jump over the wall, and be very disagreeable indeed. He was a constant annoyance.

What train did you go by when you went to Mansfield?—The afternoon train.

Where did you go after you got there? Was he with you?—He followed us, and came into the house just as we were sitting down to tea.

Do you know a person of the name of Kirkham?— Kirkham?

Mr. Clegg: Call Kirkham. (Kirkham a person about twenty years of age, was brought into the corridor.)

The Stipendiary: Do you know him?—Yes; I remember his face.

Mr. Clegg: You know him now; there can't be any doubt about it?—I remember his face.

Mr. Pollard: Do you know him by name, or only know his face?—I only know his face.

Mr. Clegg: He delivered the milk?—He and his father.

Have you never give him notes, with instructions to deliver them to Peace?—I gave him two receipts.

Two receipts? What were they for? For pictures, framing.

What were they written on?—On paper. I don't know whether there was an envelope. I think only a piece of paper.

Have you not given him notes or receipts?—I have given him two receipts.

I ask you have you not given him notes? No, no notes.

Little scraps of paper?—No, I have given him two receipts.

Where did your husband keep his address cards?—In his writing-desk.

Locked up?—No.

Where was the writing-desk?—In the sitting-room.

Had you no address cards?—I, myself? No.

Did you ever see your husband's?—No.

The prisoner had a daughter named Jane—had he not?—Jane Ann they called her.

Now, then, look at that (showing her a card).—It is in the same writing as the other.

Mr. Pollard: It is an address card. What is its number?

Mr. Clegg: It is "No. 2." (To witness): Read out what it says (handing witness the card).—Witness: I cannot read it, and it is not written very plain.

Then I will try and assist you. You can read?—Yes.

And you can write?—Yes.

This is what it says then: "After he is going out I won't go if I can help it—so see me. Love to Janey."—I did not write it.

Has that card been altered from "Mr." to "Mrs." Look?

Mr. Vickers: Is there some alteration there?—Yes; there is an "s" there.

Will you venture to say you did not use that address card and alter that from "Mr." to "Mrs.?"—I did not alter it.

It is on your husband's address card?—I am aware of that.

Now, do you know a little girl named Hutton?—I don't remember the name.

Do you know a Mrs. Hutton living in Britannia-road?—No, I don't remember the name; but I might know her if I saw her. I can't tell her by name.

Did you not go and meet him there?—No, I never did.

Were you never together in Mrs. Hutton's?—We called together one day, when I was looking after a little girl to go errands for me.

Was it Mrs. Hutton's little girl?—Yes, I believe that was the name.

Will you swear that you never gave notes to her little girl to give to the prisoner?—I will.

Will you give her a pen? I should like to see her write what I shall dictate to her. What do you write with generally—a steel pen or a quill pen?—It does not make much difference, though I usually write with a quill.

Well, write with a steel pen, "I will write a note when I can, perhaps to-morrow." Yes, that will do. Go on and write, "You can give me something as a keepsake if you like, but I don't like to be covetous, and to take them from your wife and daughter. Love to all." You have not written this half as well as the first part.—It is the best I can do.

Now, look at this first line, "I will write to you a note," and look at this card. Now, madame, will you swear that this is not your writing?—That is not my writing.

Now, I will go over these letters. Did the prisoner ever give you a ring?—Yes.

Peace: Did I give her what?

Mr. Clegg: Do you be quiet.

Did you write to acknowledge the receipt of that ring?—Not to my knowledge.

Had you any envelopes in your possession like this?—I cannot say.

Look it well over. It is important.—I cannot say.

Was the prisoner living next door to you when he gave you the ring?—Yes.

The attendant surgeon, Mr. Hallam, here went to feel Peace's pulse, whereupon the prisoner groaned a good deal, and seemed to be very ill. He, however, found his invalid all right, and left him for a time.

Now, then, just look at that letter—that envelope with the writing upon it. Is that your handwriting?—No; it is not my writing.

Did anybody besides you and the prisoner know he had given you a ring?—I don't know. I guess his daughter knew; at least he said so.

Did you know whether the daughter could write or not?—I don't know. I guess she could.

Do you know about when that writing was given to you?—No; I can't remember.

Very well. Now then, listen to me. I am going to read a letter, and you follow me. "I don't know what train we shall go by. I have a good deal to do this morning. Will see you as soon as I possibly can. I think it would be easier after you move; he won't watch so. The r—g (meaning the ring) fits the little finger. Many thanks, and love to Jennie. I will tell you what I thought of when I see you about arranging matters. Excuse this scribbling."

Mr. Clegg: What is the next word—is it "hello?"—I don't know, I cannot tell.

Now, you admit you have received a ring from him?—Yes; he gave me a ring.

Will you swear that is not a letter from you to him?—It is not from me.

Not about putting the ring on, and trying it on and telling him the ring fits?—The letter is not from me.

You will not swear the letter is not from you?—It is not from me.

Did the ring fit?—No.

Did you tell him not?—I did not keep it very long. It did not fit my little finger.

Mr. Clegg: Did you try it on?—Yes, I tried it; but I could not put it on.

What sort of a ring was it?—I could not tell you exactly. It was not worth much.

Do you remember the prisoner's foot being damaged?—No; I do not remember anything about it.

(The prisoner groaned, and his solicitor had a consultation with him.)

Will you swear that you did not write this note to him (producing a letter marked No. 5)? Is that in your handwriting?—No.

Mr. Clegg: I will read it to you.

Mr. Pollard: The witness keeps on saying she did not write the letter to him, or the note. I object that, unless it is proved the thing is connected with the case it cannot be used. She denies that she wrote it.

Mr. Clegg: I submit, then, sir, that you have a most curious coincidence. She admits that the ring is given to her by the prisoner, and yet she denies writing the letter in which the ring is mentioned to her.

The Stipendiary: What does it all lead to?

Mr. Clegg: It leads to this. This woman has sworn now, as she did previously, that she did not write any of the letters, and I am in a position to prove that she did.

The Stipendiary: She distinctly denies it. You have evidence quite enough to damage her credit.

Prisoner (moaning): I demand that justice be done.

The Stipendiary (to prisoner): Don't you interrupt.

Mr. Pollard: I will take your opinion on the subject.

EXAMINATION OF MRS. DYSON.

The Stipendiary : I think enough has been gone into for the purposes of the preliminary examination You can reserve the rest for the trial. I consider that enough has been gone into for the purpose of the preliminary examination.

Mr. Clegg : Supposing that at the trial this man is not defended—a state of things which is not at all unlikely.

The Stipendiary : You know very well that in that case the judge would order some learned counsel to defend the prisoner. I am not going to deal with a state of circumstances that may arise at the trial. It would be presumption in me to provide for want of justice before the judges.

Mr. Clegg : This is a preliminary inquiry, and I can put in whatever I think is for the the benefit of the prisoner. Though it is only a preliminary inquiry I am bound to do it.

The Stipendiary : I rule that sufficient has been asked about those letters.

Mr. Clegg : I shall persist in asking these questions until I am stopped.

The Stipendiary : Then I stop them now. You have quite enough for your purpose.

Mr. Clegg : I don't think I have.

The Stipendiary : You have quite enough. You can prosecute her for perjury if she has spoken falsely as to what has been asked of her. There are two very particular points, on which she has decisively spoken in reference to these letters.

Prisoner : She has done more than that.

The Stipendiary : You may if you have cause, indict her for perjury ; it can lead to nothing else.

Mr. Clegg : Then at present I don't think I have got sufficient, in my opinion, to test this witness's credibility.

The Stipendiary : In my opinion, you have. If what you have asserted is shown to be true, you have more than sufficient to damage her credibility, and more than sufficient to have a cause for indicting her for perjury. Beyond that it is not necessary for you to go, and I rule you shall not go.

Mr. Clegg : How can I indict the woman for perjury unless I put the letters in her hands ?

The Stipendiary : She has looked at them, because I told her to look at them myself. I said to her, "Look at each one, and see if it is not in your handwriting." That is in itself sufficient.

Mr. Clegg : Those letters have been already produced by the prosecution. I have the right to call for those to be read, and if you will not now let me cross-examine her in reference to them in detail, then I ask that the letters be read ; then I can cross-examine upon them, and that comes to the same thing.

The Stipendiary : You should have done that before. It is too late now. I cannot have them read now.

Mr. Clegg : Put that decision on the depositions. I ask that those letters put in by the prosecution be read by the clerk of the court.

The Stipendiary : You have seen them.

Mr. Clegg : I have not seen them. I have not had the opportunity of reading these original letters. By mere favour I have had copies of them sent to me.

Prisoner : It is nothing but injustice.

The Stipendiary : You will take the ruling of the Court, Mr. Clegg, if you please, and have done with it.

Mr. Clegg : I put it to you as a matter of law.

The Stipendiary : I have given my decision.

Mr. Clegg : I object to proceed until these letters are read.

Prisoner : Hear, hear.

The Stipendiary : You can proceed with your cross-examination.

Mr. Clegg : I have a right to have the letters read if I please.

The Stipendiary : You can read them over yourself if you like.

Mr. Clegg : If they are put into my hands I shall read them to witness.

The Stipendiary : Then you may read them.

Mr. Clegg : Very well, then ; that is all I want. The witness has denied that she has had anything to do with them. (To witness) : Have you read them ? —Some of them.

Have you read them all ?—Not all of them.

Then I will read them to you.

Mr. Pollard : There will be no necessity for their being read aloud. Let the witness read them for herself.

Mr. Clegg : I will read this one to you now, if you please. (Reading) : "If you have a note for me send now whilst he is out, but you must not venture, for he is watching, and you cannot be too careful. Hope your foot is better. I went to Sheffield yesterday, but I could not see you anywhere. Were you out ? Love to Jane." Did you write that letter ?— No.

Mr. Clegg : Now I put that letter in. Have you had an envelope in your possession like that (handing an envelope to the witness) ?—I don't know ; perhaps I might have. As regards the envelope, the prisoner used to come for paper and writing materials to my house.

Prisoner : No, I did not ; oh, no.

Mr. Clegg (holding a yellow envelope in his hand) : Have you read the contents of this ?—Yes, excepting something I could not make out.

Will you swear that is not your handwriting ?—I swear there are none of them in my writing.

Mr. Pollard : I think you need hardly put it to her now, because she has sworn over and over again that there are none of them in her writing.

Mr. Clegg (to witness) : Did you ever give the prisoner an American cent ?—No.

Did you ever borrow any money from him ?—No.

Not at all ?—I never did

Mr. Clegg, reading : "Things are looking very bad, for people told him everything. (Then there is something missing.) Pick out F. D." Do you know what that means ?—No.

Mr. Clegg (again reading) : "Do keep quiet, and don't let any one see you." You did not write that ? No ; I did not write that.

The Stipendiary : She says she didn't write these letters.

Mr. Clegg : Well, I wish to question her on the point.

The Stipendiary : I will not have it, and I will have my ruling attended to. It shall not go down on the depositions.

Cross-examination continued : You had a son named Willie ?—William Henry.

How old is he ?—Seven years old last December.

Did the prisoner ever give your son any halfpennies or coppers that you know of ?—No, not that I am aware of.

You have seen that letter as well (handing a letter to witness) ?—Yes, I have seen them all.

Do you know a woman named Norton ?—Norton ! I seem to remember the name. I think I remember the name.

Did you ever write this to the prisoner, "Mrs. Norton is raising h——about what I——(then follows a blank)——. Can you settle it, and send me the prints ?"

Mr. Pollard : Witness denied that she ever wrote the letter, and the magistrate has given a ruling.

Mr. Clegg (to witness) : When you were before the magistrates last week you said that you left Darnall in consequence of the prisoner annoying you ?—Yes, on account of his annoyance.

Had you seen him from July, 1876 up to the time when you left in October ?—No.

Did you know where he was ?—No, I did not. He made himself scarce on account of the warrant I had taken out against him.

Did his family leave the neighbourhood before you left ?—I don't know.

What do you now say was the reason for your leaving Darnall ? Because we were afraid of him. That was the reason. We thought he might come in in the night. We thought we had better go where he would not know where to find us.

It was because you were afraid of him ?—Yes ; he had threatened both my life and that of my husband.

Was the sole reason you left because you were afraid of him ?—Yes ; and we were told that he visited Darnall in female attire.

Did you say that the prisoner had threatened to blow your brains out, and those of your husband ?—Yes ; I said that.

Will you say that he threatened to blow your husband's brains out ?—Yes ; I will swear that threatened to blow out both my brains and my husband's.

Did you state that before the coroner ?—The case was not brought before the coroner.

Were you not examined before the coroner ?—Yes ; on the case of murder, nothing more,

Were you examined as to the death of your husband ? —Yes.

Did you say then that the prisoner had threatened your life at all ?—Not that I remember.

The depositions of the witness were then put in by Mr. Pollard, from which it appeared that before the coroner witness had said that Peace had threatened to blow out both her brains and her husband's.

Had there been any quarrel between prisoner and your husband ?—I say he had been very annoying.

Was there any quarrel ?—I can't say there was any quarrel, because my husband would not speak to him.

Have you ever received a letter from the prisoner at all ?—No sir. Oh ! yes. I have received threatening letters.

Have you got them ?—Mr. Chambers has them, I think.

I am now talking about the night of the murder. Previous to your going into the closet had your son been taken to bed, do you know ?—Yes.

Did you see the prisoner when you were in the bedroom ?—No.

When you were coming out of the closet did you see the prisoner ?—Yes, I did.

Did you say to him, " You old devil, what are you doing here now ?"—I don't remember saying anything to him, but he said, " Speak or I'll fire."

Will you swear that you did not say, " You old devil, what are you doing here to-night ? I should have thought that you had brought enough disgrace upon me ?—I don' remember speaking at all. I was too astonished.

Did he say to you, " I will let you have the notes back again if you will get him to stay proceedings ?" --No.

Did you say, " You know very well he won't do it, as he has placed it in the hands of the lawyers ?"— No ; I did not speak to him.

Your husband then came up ?—Yes.

How far was he from you and the prisoner before you first saw him ?—About two or three feet.

How far is the passage from where you were to the closet ? Close by.

Well, how many yards ?—I can't say.

How far were you from the closet door when you saw your husband ?—Only three or four feet ; I was just at the end.

Whereabouts was the prisoner when he came up ?— The prisoner was going down the passage.

Was he walking or running away ?—He was going at a rather quick pace.

Was he walking pretty quickly away from your husband ?—He was going down the passage.

Away from your husband ?—Away from him.

When your husband was going towards the prisoner did you hear him say, " If you don't stop I'll fire ?"— No.

Did you see the prisoner on the ground ?—How do you mean ?

With your husband. Was there any struggling between your husband and the prisoner ?—No, no.

How far were you away from them when your husband was shot, did you say ?—A few feet off.

Did you hear the prisoner speak to your husband before he fired ?—No, I did not. There was no speaking at all.

Not from the time that he came out right up to the time he was shot ?—No.

Will you swear that your husband and the prisoner were not struggling together on the ground ?—No, they were not struggling. They were not close enough together.

Mr. Clegg : What became of the lantern that you had ?—What became of my lantern ?

Yes, had you it in your hand ?—I threw it down.

Before you saw your husband come out had you the lantern still in your hand ?—Yes.

This concluded the cross - examination of Mrs. Dyson.

Mr. Pollard (re-examining) : Are there some steps coming from the passage into the roadway ?—There are one or two steps.

When your husband fell in what direction did his head fall ?—From the side of the passage.

Did he take any step forward after the bullet struck him ?—No, he dropped instantly.

At the time the bullet was fired did you see whether Peace was down on the pathway of the causeway ?— Yes.

Therefore he would be some few feet below your husband ?—Yes. He was down off the steps on the causeway when he fired the second shot.

And you say he would therefore be some two or three feet below your husband's head at the time he fired ?—Yes.

You were saying something about threatening letters. Between July and October, 1876, did you see any threatening letters ?—Yes.

How many ?—I know of two, and there were perhaps more.

Have you those letters ?—Mr. Chambers, solicitor, has them. Mr. Dyson gave them to Mr. Chambers.

You gave them to Mr. Dyson, your husband, and he gave them to Mr. Chambers ?—Yes.

You don't know whose writing they were ?—They were signed as if from prisoner, and seemed to come from Germany.

(Prisoner : I wish to call witnesses.)

The Stipendiary : It's not time to call witnesses.

Prisoner : Am I going to be committed to-day ? I want my witnesses called before.

The Stipendiary : It's not the time.

This concluded Mrs. Dyson's evidence, who then retired.

Police-constable 235, John Pearson, was next called and examined by Mr. Pollard. Do you know the prisoner ?—I do, three or four years.

Prisoner : Let that person come up here, will you ? I don't know him.

Mr. Pollard (to witness) : Three or four years from now ?—Yes, I knew him about two years before the murder.

You remember the date of the murder of Mr. Dyson in November, 1876 ?—Yes.

Did you receive some instructions from your superior officer to go in search of the prisoner ?—I did. I received instructions the same morning at half past two o'clock.

That was Nov. 30 ?—Yes.

Did you go to any place in Hull which you had any reason to know ?—Yes, I went to 37, Collier-street.

Who was living there ?—Peace's wife, I believe. The same person who had been locked up here in the name of Hannah Peace. She was keeping a shop.

You failed to find him there ?—Yes.

Mr. Pollard : I propose now to take the escape and recapture of the prisoner on the last occasion.

Stipendiary : You have gone after the time.

Mr. Pollard : I put it on the ground of what it is worth, as an element for a jury to consider, whether an innocent person after having been examined, and hearing evidence such as was given on the last occasion, would have attempted to escape as he did.

The Stipendiary : He was a convict, you know, suffering under sentence of penal servitude for life.

Mr. Pollard : Well, I will not press it.

Mr. Pollard then said that was his case.

Prisoner here exclaimed : " I want my witnesses called. Why don't you call my witnesses ?" and then fell down.

The depositions were now read over, Mrs. Dyson's being taken first.

Whilst her depositions were being read the prisoner conducted himself in an excited and somewhat insolent manner. Making a faint of jumping from his chair, he fell back suddenly, calling to be taken to his cell. The warders stepped forward, and he then refused to be removed, and called for his counsel, to whom he began to give instructions in an excited fashion. Mr. Clegg took little notice, and soon after Peace put his arms on the table, laid his head between them, and moaned loudly. He next drew the rug over his head, and made such interruptions that the rug was drawn back, and he was asked to be still. He paid little attention to this request, but kept moaning and muttering till the deposition were read over.

Stipendiary (to Peace) : Do you hear what is said ?

Prisoner (whining) : Oh yes, I hear.

The depositions were afterwards read over of Sarah Ann Colgrave, Mary Ann Gregory, George Brassington, Thomas Wilson, Police-constable Ward, Inspector Bradbury, and Police-constable Pearson.

Prisoner : Cannot you call my witnesses ? What is the use of my having witnesses if they are not called ?

The Stipendiary : Listen to me.

Prisoner : I cannot have them called.

The Stipendiary : Oh, yes, you can, Listen to me. You first of all have to make a statement, and then if there are any witnesses to be called they can be called. Now listen to me. The charge against you is that you wilfully and of malice aforethought did kill and murder one Arthur Dyson, on Oct. 29, 1876. Having heard the evidence, do you wish to say anything in answer to the charge ?

Prisoner : Yes ; I wish to say that——

Stipendiary : You are not obliged to say anything in answer to the charge. What you do say will be taken down, and may be given in evidence against you.

Mr. Clegg : If you take my advice you will simply say not guilty.

The Prisoner : I say I am not guilty, and that justice has not been done to me so that I can prove I am not guilty. That is what I want. I want that. I want justice done me. Why don't they let me call my witnesses, because you are asking me shall my witnesses be called ? Why should they not be called here ? Why ? because I have not the money to pay the expenses.

The Stipendiary : What is it you complain of ?

The Prisoner : I want my witnesses called to prove that I have really not done this.

The Stipendiary : Are there any witnesses to be called ?

Prisoner : Yes, sir.

The Stipendiary : Are they here ?

Prisoner : Yes, sir.

The Stipendiary : Then you must ask your solicitor.

Mr. Robinson (reading) : You say, " I say I am not guilty, and I want my witnesses called to prove I am not guilty."

Prisoner : That is what I said. I have lots of witnesses who can prove that that base, bad, woman has threatened my life, and has threatened her husband's life ; but I can't talk to you, I am so bad. I feel very bad. But she has threatened to take my life often.

The Stipendiary : Is this what you say ?

Prisoner : I say I am not guilty, and I say I have not justice done me to prove I am not guilty, and that I want my witnesses called. (Loudly.) I say I can prove that I have not threatened her life. She has threatened her husband's, and she has pointed pistols and things at me.

The Stipendiary : Have you any witnesses to-day ? You are not taking your trial to-day. This is only a preliminary examination.

Prisoner : I cannot have those witnesses without I pay for them.

Mr. Clegg : I say I don't intend calling any witnesses to-day.

The Stipendiary : Do you care to sign your statement ? Would you like to put your name to the statement ?

Prisoner : I will try.

Prisoner (to his warder, in a very rough tone of voice) : Let me be. Then, taking up the pen, he said, I cannot see.

Mr. Clegg : Just sign it there.

Prisoner then rested his head on one arm and signed his name very deliberately, the capital " C " and " P " being particularly well flourished.

The Stipendiary : You are committed to take your trial on this charge at the assizes at Leeds.

The Prisoner (with eagerness) : hen are they ?

The Stipendiary : They are next week.

Inspector Bradbury was then bound over to prosecute, and the witnesses to appear at the trial.

The Prisoner : Will you let me sit before the fire a bit before I go ? I am really very bad.

Mr. Clegg : He complains of being cold.

Prisoner : You can put me in irons if you like, but put me near a fire.

The Chief Constable : The cells are warm enough. It is only in this corridor that there is so much air.

Mr. Clegg : You will be warm enough in the cell.

Prisoner : I want to see you.

Mr. Clegg : Yes, I will see you.

Prisoner was then removed to the cell, groaning and whining, apparently overcome by the result of the day's proceedings.

Mrs. Dyson laboured under suppressed emotion, but bore the ordeal well. The utmost precautions were taken to keep down excitement in the town, but popular feeling ran very high.

We have during the progress of this work had occasion to refer in more than instance to the latitude allowed to counsel on police examinations. A striking instance of this was made manifest on the several examinations of the prisoner Webster for the Richmond murder, and before then, in a lesser degree, perhaps, a similar instance occurred in the examination of the witnesses brought forward to give their testimony upon the Bannercross murder.

Peace was a daring and reckless burglar. An adept at disguising himself in a style that eluded the scrutiny of the police, he set small value on the vigilance of professional detectives.

The comparative immunity with which he had escaped the consequences of his iniquity induced him to wax bold in transgression.

Even to the last there seemed an idea that he might still be able to baffle justice. Everything a wicked ingenuity could do was done to discredit the testimony on which he was convicted; but the utmost license of counsel was unavailing.

We are not disposed to say anything severe about a barrister struggling with the difficulties Mr. Lockwood was called to combat. In such circumstances the old adage of "No case—abuse the plaintiff's attorney," is a sufficient explanation of what might otherwise appear unseemly.

On the present occasion, however, it was not the attorney, but the press that got abused. In the recent trial of the directors of the City of Glasgow Bank, a similar policy was pursued by a prominent and really able advocate.

But the barrister to whom the defence of Charles Peace was committed passed beyond the duty of counsel in the denunciation of newspapers.

It was thus that Mr. Lockwood delivered himself:

"Never in the course of my experience has there been such a cry raised on the part of those who ought to be most careful of all others in preserving the liberties of their fellow-men and the independence of the tribunals of justice. I say that in this respect these parties have proved false to the great duties entrusted to them, and have not hesitated to raise a merciless cry for blood for the sake of the paltry pennies which they have been able to extract from the public, whom they have tried to gull."

This charge against the press is false. There had really been no attempt to stimulate public antipathy against the Bannercross culprit. In point of fact, a judicious critic might with some show of reason insinuate that the details of the life of Peace had been placed before the public in aspects more attractive than just.

The convict was not at all averse to the notoriety which he had recently achieved. But when his life is carefully scanned from the day that he first enlisted in the "Devil's Regiment of the Line" until sentence of death was passed upon him, it is abundantly evident that the way of the transgressor was hard.

Charles Peace commenced his criminal career before he was fourteen. He was not yet fifty, but already there was unambiguous evidence that premature old age was stealing over him.

Though devoted to crime, Peace never consorted with criminals. This peculiarity in his career constituted his safety. It is mainly because the haunts and habits of criminals are known that they are detected.

The impunity with which, for a very considerable period, Peace was enabled to commit the Blackheath burglaries arose from the air of mystery with which he was surrounded.

It must not, however, be assumed that there was anything heroic in the kind of housebreaking with which he was identified.

Houses in the district that formed the scene of his depredations afford every facility to the "cracksman." But the good fortune which had so often favoured Peace in this region at length deserted him.

A constable whom a revolver could not scare mastered the burglar.

When he was condemned to penal servitude, it was discovered that the culprit had been guilty of a more serious crime. "Information received" enabled the authorities to connect the Blackheath burglar with the Bannercross murder.

That crime was fast fading from the memory of even those amongst whom it had been committed, and every hope of arresting the murderer had been abandoned.

Mr. Dyson's widow was in America, and Peace, who knew this, thought himself safe.

"But, if "justice steals along with woollen feet, it strikes with iron hands."

Mrs. Dyson was brought back from the United States to avenge in the witness-box the brutality of her tormentor.

Her evidence as to all that transpired on the eventful night that her husband fell was too minute and circumstantial to be shaken by even the severest cross-examination.

The line of evidence which counsel was instructed to take only deepened the infamy of the accused.

Even had it been possible to prove an improper intimacy between Peace and Mrs. Dyson, that would have done nothing to mitigate the atrocity of Mr. Dyson's murder.

A most persistent effort was made by Mr. Lockwood to show that, previous to the firing of the shot from which Mr. Dyson fell, there had been a struggle between the murderer and his victim.

On this point, however, the widow's evidence was decisive. There was indeed no necessity that Mr. Dyson should close with the culprit.

Moreover, inoffensive people are not usually anxious to fight ruffians who are armed with "six-shooters."

When Peace was in a difficulty or in a passion, recourse to firearms seemed perfectly natural. Society was his legitimate prey, and in presence of unarmed antagonists the burglar waxed valorous. Rarely has a more wanton murder been perpetrated than that of Mr. Dyson.

The only offence of which that unfortunate man appeared guilty was his abhorrence of the attentions of Peace. To escape them, he removed from the neighbourhood in which the convict dwelt.

The scamp, however, followed the Dysons with a fiendish malignity. When threatening to blow out Mrs. Dyson's brains, Peace had the effrontery to ask a bystander to "bear him witness that she had struck him with a life-preserver." This idea was a pure myth.

The preserver existed only in the foul imagination of the criminal, and the struggle with Mr. Dyson on the 29th November, 1876, was a still bolder fiction. It is possible that the crime was unpremeditated, and that annoyance rather than murder was intended. But a man who makes a revolver the instrument of annoyance cannot guard against the most dreaded contingencies.

Mr. Campbell Foster was justly enough precluded from making any reference to Peace's attempted escape from the railway train. But it is not difficult to understand the motives under which the desperate leap was taken.

If Peace had possessed any confidence in his ability to support the plea set up in his behalf, there would have been no attempt to escape. But he was aware of what awaited him.

He knew enough of Mrs. Dyson to fear that her testimony was not likely to be shaken. Every incidence in her career, so far as it was known to counsel, was reproduced for the purpose of disconcerting and discrediting her. Nevertheless, she left the witness-box with her evidence unshaken.

Thus has Charles Peace been condemned. Hunted down while not yet fifty, there is in every feature of his forbidding face evidence that such a career is as unprofitable as it is criminal.

It is difficult to conceive what this malefactor might have been under other and brighter auspices. But, dedicated to crime from his youth upward, as years passed away, conscience, which in his case was never tender, became "seared as with a hot iron."

When the final stage in his trial was reached, and Peace was asked if he had anything to say, he whimpered out, "Is there any use of saying anything now?"

But in his cell the convict collapses, and his courage proves melodramatic.

CHAPTER CLVIII.

PRISONERS AND THEIR CUSTODIANS.

ONE of the most remarkable and daring exploits of our time, and one which more than any other of his adventures awakened the public mind to the desperate and reckless nature of the man was his attempt to escape while in the charge of his warders in the railway carriage. This might be considered the culminating point of his lawless life, and had he been without handcuffs, and possessed of his favourite weapon—a six-chambered revolver—we would not have given much for the lives of his two custodians. It was indeed fortunate for them that the wild beast under their care was safely manacled, and, indeed, the great body of the people had no idea of the risks run by the servants of the law in dealing with ruffians of Peace's type. We subjoin an interesting account given by an officer, and printed in *Chambers's Journal* of

A PERILOUS RIDE WITH A CONVICT.

One of my journeys called me away to a town in Suffolk, where I was ordered to take charge of a prisoner to be discharged the next day from one of the local goals, in which he had been undergoing a year's imprisonment for a criminal assault.

The man had been let out on a ticket-of-leave from the "Defence" hulk at Woolwich, and had speedily, as it appeared, got into trouble down in the country.

As he was merely "wanted" to complete his original sentence—having broken his ticket-of-leave—there could be no bother about apprehending him inside the prison, and using such precautions for his safe keeping as seemed best to my judgment.

Just as I was about to leave the office in Bow-street, one of my comrades with whom I was rather intimate came in, having finished a journey such as I was myself about to set off on.

"Going out, Tom?" he asked; and on my telling him

where I was bound for, he continued— "Better have this 'barker,' Tom—you may find it useful."

At the same time he produced a small pocket pistol, which he held out for my acceptance.

"I have not got any powder," he added; but here are some caps and bullets."

It seemed needless to remark that this was before the days of revolvers and patent cartridges; we had then to load in the old fashion, and had merely got as far as the introduction of the percussion cap.

I had never before carried anything more deadly by way of protection than a life-preserver, but as my friend seemed to mean a kindness, I made no ado about accepting his offer; and having "capped" it there and then, I consigned it to the side pocket of a pilot coat, which I wore buttoned over my uniform.

My journey down to Suffolk calls for no particular notice. In due time the railway deposited me at my destination, and left me with plenty of leisure to call upon the governor of the prison over night, with a view to my carrying off my charge the next morning. I asked what sort of a customer I would have to deal with, and must confess that I did not feel much encouraged with the reply,

"He is what I would call a nasty customer," was the answer. "He has given us a deal of trouble while we have had charge of him; continually breaking prison rules, and more than once he has tried to commit suicide in the most determined manner by tearing open the veins in his arms with his finger-nails."

This account of matters was not, as may well be supposed, at all enlivening; and when the governor added that the man was a perfect giant, and had been a "navvy" before he fell into evil courses, I began to fear that my work was cut out for me. However, there was no help for it.

The inn where I had taken up my quarters stood right opposite the gaol entrance, and as the street was somewhat of the narrowest, the most complete view of all comers and goers could be commanded from the front of my temporary residence.

Next morning found me seated at a very comfortable breakfast, and the weather being fine, the window of the private parlour was open, affording a perfect view of all that might take place at the prison door opposite.

While I was absorbed in the good cheer before me, I was startled by an exclamation from both the landlady and her daughter, which caused me to look up and instinctively to glance across the street.

"Did you ever see such a big, coarse, and clumsy-looking woman?" exclaimed the younger of my entertainers.

"Or is it a woman at all?" added her mother.

My attention was at once riveted upon the new comer, whom I somehow could not avoid connecting with the criminal it would so soon become my duty to apprehend.

Without saying a word to the two ladies, I carefully and closely watched every movement of the party opposite during the remainder of my morning meal. More than once I caught myself mentally repeating my landlady's query: "Is it a woman, after all?"

The "it" must be excused, as the point was so entirely doubtful. For a woman, the individual was very considerably above the average height, and her whole physique indicated far more than the average strength of womankind.

There was a swagger in her walk, too, most unlike the carriage of a female. I was fairly puzzled, and none the less so that I had twice noticed her ringing the prison bell, and that I knew there was but o. o individual to be discharged that morning, and that it was close upon my time to go and look after him.

I had barely finished my last cup of coffee, when one of the prison warders came across to say that the wife of my prisoner was waiting outside, and had twice made a demand to see him; but that the governor did not care to accede to the request without first consulting me.

After casting the matter over in my own mind for a minute, I told the warder that I did not mind the woman being admitted, but that the two ought to be very closely watched during the interview.

The man re-entered the prison, and within a few minutes I observed that the woman was called in.

Punctual to my time, I crossed over to the prison, and found my charge waiting for me, his wife being still with him, and no one in the room but the governor.

Contrary to my expectations, the prisoner held up his wrists and submitted to be handcuffed with the most lamb-like docility.

When we got out into the street, I suggested, as there was time to spare, that the stalwart pair should have a bit of breakfast at my expense before starting on the journey for town.

I thought the woman seemed a little taken aback at my invitation; however, it was acceded to; and we entered the inn parlour, where I requested the landlady to produce a plentiful supply of ham and eggs; and as the pair preferred ale to tea or coffee, I ordered them a pint apiece.

I had of course to unlock one hand in the order to allow my prisoner the free use of his knife and fork; and, after what I had heard the night before, I thought it was rather risky thing for me to do, as though he might not attempt to do me any mischief, it was just possible he might try to inflict some serious mischief on himself.

All, however, passed off safely, and when breakfast was finished, I told him he must bid his wife good-bye, as I did not want to attract any attention at the railway station. A kiss was accordingly exchanged, the bracelets were again attached to the wrists, and we set off at a brisk pace.

When we got to the station, I learned that the next "up" train was an express, and that I would have to look sharp, as it might be expected immediately, and made but a brief stoppage.

The train, in fact, came in almost to a minute after the information was communicated to me; and I hurried across the platform, got my man into a second-class carriage—the compartment I had only just time to notice was empty.

The whistle sounded, and the train was beginning to move, when the door was flung violently open, and in jumped the prisoner's wife, taking her seat right opposite me.

There was but time for the porter to slam the door, when we were off. It need not be said that I was very far from being satisfied with the look of things, and that I had made up my mind to be carefully on my guard.

I said nothing, being fully determined not to show any uneasiness, though it must be owned I felt much. Before we had gone any great way my prisoner turned sideways to me and said: "Master, my missus and me have some small matters of our own we would like to talk over; and as they don't concern you in the least, p'raps you wouldn't mind looking out of winder for a minute or two while we have our talk."

"That I could not possibly do," was my immediate answer. "My duty is to keep you always under my eye and control; and besides, as you have just said, your domestic arrangements can be a matter of no concern to me, so you can discuss them as freely as you please without minding my presence."

This answer seemed to disconcert both of them; but as if by way of compromise, I at the same moment leant towards the window of the carriage for a moment, and glanced outside.

My hearing is sharp enough now, but at the time I speak as was even more acute. Just as I turned my head, I heard, or thought I heard the man whisper the words: "Both together." Instantly the suspicion flashed across my mind that these words related to myself, and I turned round and faced the couple in a moment.

What I saw in the expression of each of them seemed to warrant my acting with immediate decision. I seized the man between his manacled wrists so that he could not raise his hands.

With an instinctive thought I plunged my right hand into the pocket of my pilot coat, pulled out the pistol my mate had handed to me, cocked it with my thumb, and holding it within a few inches of the face of the woman opposite, I looked steadily into her eyes, and said with emphasis, "If you attempt to stir before we reach the next station you will certainly be a dead woman!"

It was something fearful to notice the immediate change on that woman's countenance. She became of a pallid whiteness, and her lips had the purple-bluish tinge that indicate so unmistakably an access of deadly fear. In the highly-dramatic positions I have just described we sped on until the next stopping station was reached, and that occupied fully more than twenty minutes.

The moment the train came to a stop I thus addressed the woman, keeping her "covered" with the muzzle of my pistol: "Leave the carriage; and, if you value your liberty, make what speed you can to get into hiding."

She disappeared instanter; and I felt a heavy load of anxiety lifted off my mind as she left us, for of all the encounters I most hate, an encounter with a woman is to be classed foremost.

Not a word passed between my prisoner and me during the remainder of the journey to London, which we were no great while in reaching, and where I duly delivered him into safe keeping at Bow-street police-office.

Next morning I had to conduct my prisoner to Woolwich, there to deliver him to the authorities of the hulks, from whom he had obtained his ticket-of-leave. He seemed to have recovered from his scare of the day before, and on our journey spoke freely enough, and with an earnestness that left no doubt of the truth of his communication.

"Master," said he, "I am main glad you kept your head yesterday, and did not lean out of the winder. Had you done so, missus and I meant to have pitched you out, and taken our chance afterwards of getting off.

"I was not very likely to be so easily put off my guard," was the laconic answer.

"Aye, but master, your danger was not over then; for missus and I had made it up that she was to pin your arms—and she could a done it easy—while I was to smash your head with the 'd-rbies.' We should then a took a key, got off the bracelets, and heaved you out of a winder, afore you could come to yourself.

That pistol fairly put us out, for it cowed missus, and she isn't easily cowed, I tell ye."

"But the pistol was not loaded," said I—"nothing but a cap and an empty barrel."

"All the same, master, I'm main glad we failed. Now I've thought it over, I know I could not have escaped. It was known I left in your charge, and that missus joined us. When your body was found, we'd a been spotted at once, and most likely both on us would a swung for it. I'm main glad, I tell you, that you got out of the mess, and I don't bear you no ill-will for having done your dooty as a man and a hofficer."

Never before, to my knowledge, had I been in such deadly peril, and truly thankful did I inwardly feel for the providential escape I learned I had just made. I was glad to hand my murderous-minded charge over to the care of the officers of the "Defence;" and I am thankful to add that I never heard more of him, or wished to do so.

Among the many persons who had been present at the examination of Charles Peace was an old acquaintance—Shearman, the American detective, of loquacious and anecdotal proclivities. After the prisoner's committal he adjourned to an adjoining house where good entertainment was provided for man and beast. In the company of the English detectives engaged in the case, police-sergeants, and inspectors, Mr. Shearman was quite at home. A long, rambling discussion took place, the leading subject being the merits, or rather demerits, of our hero. Incidents in detective life became the order of the day, and, as far as this was concerned, Mr. Shearman, as usual, "went ahead." He told a capital story, which, as this is the last time we shall have to take notice of him, we give in his own words:—

TRACKING A FUGITIVE OVER THE OCEAN.

I am not Pollaky or Paddington Green, neither am I Inspector Webb, nor Detective Bull of the City force, said Mr. Shearman. My status in society is that of a banker's clerk. I hold an appointment in a Midland Counties firm, which I entered upon five-and-twenty years ago.

I had reached what is termed the "ripe middle age," when some months since the even current of my life was interrupted by the following event:—

The establishment with which I have been so long associated is well known, and has gained a reputation by the quiet, respectable character of its business transactions.

It does not indulge in speculative ventures, and hence has escaped many of the misfortunes and missed no little of the agitation which some banking firms have had to encounter.

Occasionally we have been startled by the presentation of a bad note, a forged cheque, and other cunningly-devised schemes of well-practiced swindlers to impose on our simplicity and credulity, which circumstances have forced us into the excitement of judicial investigations.

Thus, from time to time, I was brought into contact with some of the most celebrated detectives of the day. I still remember the feelings of admiration with which I witnessed the skill and sagacity of such men as John Forrister, Leadbeater, the Bow-street officer, Inspector Wicher, and other police officers, in tracking and detecting a swindler.

At that period I little dreamt that my quiet life would be disturbed by an eventful episode, such as I am about to relate.

On the morning of the 28th of September, 186—, I was at my post as usual, when a message from the bank manager summoned me to his presence. I saw at a glance, on entering the room, that something had happened.

My chief informed me that a customer of the bank, whom, for obvious reasons, I will call Mr. Hooker, had absconded.

I was aware, not only that he was under an engagement to liquidate a considerable claim we had against him, but that he had recently fixed a day for the fulfilment of his promise, assuring us that he should be in the immediate receipt of a large sum of money, which would enable him to pay his debt, and leave a balance to his credit in our hands.

The statement of his expected funds was no fiction—he duly received them—but instead of appropriating his newly-acquired wealth to the honest discharge of our claim, he clandestinely left his home, and before the intelligence of his departure had reached us, he was half-way to Canada.

The manager's indignation at the fraudulent conduct of an individual whom he had believed to be an honourable man, and had trusted as such, did not surprise me. Neither was I astonished when he told me he would do all in his power to punish the absconding debtor, if means could be adopted to discover and arrest him in his flight.

It was a matter for serious deliberation. Ultimately, acting on an impulse I could not control, I proffered my services to go in pursuit of the defaulter. They were accepted.

The same evening, in company with one of our directors, I left by the mail train for Liverpool, reaching that place some little time after midnight. The object of this journey was to endeavour to ascertain, through the Liverpool detectives, when and by what ship Mr. Hooker had sailed, as well as his destination, in order that we might arrive at a conclusion as to the propriety of my crossing the Atlantic in pursuit.

Early the following morning we were at the headquarters of the detective police. We related the nature of our mission, and the services of one of their most efficient officers were placed at our disposal.

He was evidently well known at all the shipping offices. In less than an hour he furnished us with every information we could obtain in Liverpool. He ascertained that Hooker had sailed for Quebec seven days previously in the Canada mail packet ship "Belgian," and had booked through to Montreal; and he added the still more important facts that the delinquent had with him his wife, sister-in-law, and two children, and further, that he was in possession of a roll of bank notes at the time he secured the berths.

Had he gone alone I doubt whether I should have had the courage to proceed farther; but the fact of his being encumbered with the ladies, the children, and a large quantity of baggage was a set-off against his seven days' start, and considerably altered my views.

With such a drag on his movements, I felt there was a hope of success, and at once accepted the responsibility of following him.

A berth was secured on board the "China," of the Cunard line, and on Saturday, the 30th of September, 4.30 p.m., I found myself afloat, and the docks of Liverpool becoming fainter and fainter.

Fortunately the weather was extremely fine; and as we steamed down the Mersey the scene and the event was one of unusual interest to me.

The interior of a first-class mail packet just starting on her voyage, and its animated appearance, have often been described. I need only say there were over two hundred passengers on board, and that my im-

A ROPE IS FLUNG OVER LAURA'S HEAD, AND HER ARMS ARE CLOSELY PINIONED.

mediate companions were a French gentleman, a Spaniard and his wife, a Scotch physician (who was in a state of complete prostration three-fourths of the voyage), a ship-builder from St. John's, N.B., and his two daughters, the chaplain of the ship and his wife, and Mr. Tucker, an intelligent man from Philadelphia, who, during the voyage, gave me such valuable infor-

mation, and introduced me to some Canadian merchants on board. These gentlemen subsequently rendered me great assistance in the prosecution of the object I had in view.

One of the most agreeable interludes of our voyage occurred during our detention at Queenstown for the mail bags.

No. 90.

A delay of the mail train enabled us to pay a visit to the lovely Cove of Cork. We landed at the pleasant quay, ascended Lookout Hill, and partook of the hospitality of the Queen's Hotel.

The jaunting cars, negro minstrels, mendicants, men-of-war's men, yachtsmen, and hawkers occupied the foreground, while the cove itself was studded with vessels, among which some of our ironclads and gunboats were conspicuous.

The view was bounded by the islands of Spike and Haulbowline, and the famous lighthouse that marks the entrance to the harbour.

It was about half-past four on the following day week when I was aroused from sleep by the report of a cannon close to our saloon. The first idea that I had on awakening was, that we had struck upon a rock, but my neighbour informed me it was a salute we were firing on entering Halifax harbour.

We had made one of the quickest passages on record; for before five o'clock a.m. on Monday, the 9th of October, we arrived at Halifax, being only seven days and twelve hours from the time of our departure from Queenstown.

I proceeded to Boston, where I remained one day. I left that city for Montreal. I reached the St. Lawrence Hall Hotel in that place at ten a.m. on Thursday, the 12th of October.

I confess that the three hundred miles of night travelling, following so closely on the voyage out, caused me great bodily fatigue, and I suffered much from mental depression.

As I sat alone that morning, some three thousand miles away from home, and as far distant from any friend, I began to reflect whether I had not undertaken a task of too great magnitude.

I was weak enough to regret having left the shores of England upon what now appeared so Quixotic an undertaking. It was too late for regret, and I immediately dispelled my doubts by action.

My first step was to collect my credentials and call upon the solicitors whose advice was to guide my future proceedings. Messrs Roberts & Roe are one of the most eminent firms of *avocats* in Montreal.

On making the acquaintance of the senior partner I felt that I stood in the presence of a gentleman of no ordinary ability—one whose verdict would go far to decide whether my mission would be stamped with "success" or endorsed with "failure."

I related to him as briefly as possible the circumstances which brought me to him; I handed him the power of attorney, and, being desirous of securing his unlimited confidence, I also exhibited to him my letter of credit and introduction to the eminent Canadian house, Messrs. Gillespie, Moffat, & Co.

When I had finished my recital, Mr. Roberts took a few moments for reflection. I watched him narrowly, and I fancied I read distinctly in his countenance that his honest conviction was adverse to my cause.

I found that such was the fact; for, addressing me very deliberately, he said, "I fear your case is hopeless, and that your journey will be a fruitless one."

He explained to me the law of Canada in reference to such cases, and pointed out, that even if I found Hooker, which was in his opinion, doubtful, I could only treat him as a debtor; I could not touch either his person or his goods; that I might bring an action against him for a common debt, with the consolatory thought that after I had spent some weeks in litigation and obtained judgment, Mr. Hooker would run across to the United States and snap his fingers at me and my judgment.

Mr. Roberts was kind enough to say he could not but admire the spirit which had been evinced by our bank, in taking such prompt and energetic action in the matter, and expressed a desire that other large mercantile firms in England would adopt a similar line of conduct, which would prevent Canada, and more particularly Montreal (from its proximity to the United States), becoming the resort of so many swindlers to the mother country.

Naturally I felt for the moment cast down by the revelation of the "hopelessness of my case," and for an instant I contemplated relinquishing all further proceedings; but happily, in a few minutes, this feeling vanished, and I became, as it were, fortified with unusual strength and energy.

I was enabled calmly to reflect upon the formidable difficulty I had to encounter, and instead of abandoning my mission, I resolved to prosecute it to the utmost.

I told the legal adviser that my first step must be to discover the fugitive, and next to give him into "pretty safe" custody, until I could come to a satisfactory settlement with him—disregarding for the time all the terrors of the Canadian law on the question of false imprisonment.

At this period I was introduced to the junior partner of the firm, who subsequently undertook the management of the affair, and by his advice I shut myself up in my hotel, in case Hooker should see me and abscond whilst the *avocat* undertook to send during the day to all the hotels to examine the books of arrivals.

After a wretched time of inactivity I again sought my solicitors to ascertain the result of the search.

It was altogether unsuccessful. I subsequently found that had the official to whom the duty had been intrusted exercised an ordinary amount of vigilance, he would have been able to have furnished me with most welcome intelligence.

His search, however, had been a very superficial one, and I was consequently compelled to return to my hotel sadly disappointed, and wearied both in body and mind.

The following morning I was introduced to the Chief of the Montreal detective police, Mr. O'Leary, a remarkably acute and intelligent Irishman.

He regretted that for a day or two he could not give me much personal assistance, as he was engaged in several important criminal cases at the assizes, which were then being held in Montreal.

I briefly put him in possession of the facts of my mission, and he consoled me with the assurance that, if Hooker were there or in the neighbourhood, he should have no difficulty in finding him.

As I was deprived of the detective's active assistance, I resolved to take a line of action of my own.

I suggested to Mr. Roe that we should make inquiries at the offices of the Canadian Mail Steam Packet Company, in one of whose ships (the Belgian) Hooker and his family had sailed from England.

Mr. Roe acceded to my suggestion, and accompanied me at once to the office, where I was introduced by him to Mr. Allan, the principal partner in the firm.

My object was to ascertain whether, from the official list of the passengers of the Belgian, they could furnish me with any information as to the arrival of the fugitive either in Quebec or Montreal. Mr. Allan at once communicated with the officials at Quebec, where the passengers had landed.

I was employed during Friday in visiting my solicitors and the detective's officers, as well as in making inquiries at banks, post-office, and smaller hotels, but without acquiring the least information likely to prove serviceable.

At an early hour the next morning I started out with a conviction that if Hooker were in Canada I should obtain some clue of his whereabouts before night.

This presentiment did not mislead me, for before three o'clock I effected his " capture," and had him closeted in my solicitor's office in Little St. James-street, with O'Leary and a brother-detective in close attendance.

I will record the events as they occurred that day, which was one of much anxiety and excitement.

When I reached Mr. Allan's office I was informed by the head clerk that a letter had been received from their establishment at Quebec, in reply to their inquiries, containing some important and satisfactory information.

It is true they had lost all traces of the fugitive on his landing at Quebec, and consequently could not have rendered any assistance but for a singular coincidence which occurred a few days previously at Toronto.

The purser of the Belgian had occasion to visit the City of the Lakes, and whilst there he saw and had recognized Hooker as one of the passengers.

The latter believed himself to be perfectly safe, and, not having the slightest idea that any one was in pursuit of him, he invited the purser to take some refreshment, and then voluntarily entered into conversation about himself and family, mentioning, among other things, that his wife, sister-in-law, and children were at the Montreal Hotel, in Montreal, where he intended shortly to join them.

The purser returned to Quebec, and, fortunately for me, was at the office when the letter of inquiry from Montreal was opened. He immediately communicated the above facts to Mr. Allan.

I hastened with the welcome intelligence to my solicitors. It was difficult to decide upon the best course to adopt.

If any direct inquiry were made, Mrs. Hooker would probably communicate with her husband and prevent his return ; after a short consultation we decided to leave the matter in the hands of O'Leary, the detective.

I went for him at once, and fortunately found him at the chief office of police. As I have previously stated, he was a sharp-witted Irishman, of gentlemanly bearing.

After deliberately reading the letter which had been intrusted to me by Mr. Allan's clerk, he took my hand in his own, and, grasping it warmly, he said in his native accent, "My dear sirr-h—it's all right—lave it to me."

On our way to Montreal House he informed me that he knew, and had the greatest confidence in, the landlord, from whom he could obtain every information without exciting suspicion.

We entered the house by the public bar, and of course were at once the object of that curiosity which is invariably manifested when a detective officer appears in company with a stranger in a public place of that description.

The character of O'Leary was too well known for any one to venture upon a remark beyond an inquiry as to the state of his health, and "what would he drink ?"

One cadaverous-looking Yankee put the latter ques-

tion to me, but, as I was a stranger to him, I politely declined to take anything.

I soon discovered that I had committed rather a grave sin, for the Yankee appeared much irritated at my refusal, and advised me if I were going to New York, never to decline such an offer if it were made to me in that city, or, said he, "I guess it will be worse for you."

On returning to O'Leary, I found him carelessly glancing at the names in the arrival book of the hotel.

Suddenly he closed the book, took it in his hand, and gave me a sign to follow him into an inner office.

When the door was closed he opened the book, and putting his finger on Hooker's signature, inquired if that was the man. I replied in the affirmative.

The landlord was then admitted into our council, and a cautiously whispered conference took place.

The landlord informed us that Hooker's wife and children were up stairs in the apartment above us, and that he had stowed large quantities of baggage in an adjoining room.

At that moment Mrs. Hooker was expecting her husband by the first train from Toronto, after which they intended leaving, but where they intended to go he had no idea.

O'Leary advised me to change my quarters from St. Lawrence Hall Hotel to the Montreal House, and keep a watchful eye on the movements of the family, so as to be ready to confront the husband on his arrival.

I hastened to the hotel, removed all traces of my address and railway tickets from my luggage, and entered my name on the arrival book of the Montreal Hotel as Mr. V. Robinson, from Boston.

I lounged about the place with a view to picking up any stray piece of information I could. I heard, among other things, that Hooker had lodged his money in the Merchants' Bank.

I thought this of sufficient importance to communicate to my solicitor at once.

On my return I was somewhat startled by the announcement that Hooker, who had just arrived, was then sitting down to dinner in the public room.

There was evidently no time to be lost, as he had ordered his bill, and would leave in half an hour.

I knew my only chance consisted in playing a bold game.

With the "hopelessness of my case" ringing in my ears, I had not the courage to confront him myself, and yet in half an hour he would be gone.

It was just a question of finding O'Leary and bringing him on the scene of action in those thirty minutes. There was no vehicle at hand.

I ran hastily to the head office of the police, and found to my dismay that O'Leary was not there, nor was there anyone who knew where he could be found.

I retained the services of the chief officer present, secured a cab, and went at full gallop to O'Leary's private residence, where we were fortunate enough to find him.

He immediately entered the cab and we returned to Montreal House, whilst I related to him all that had occurred since I last saw him.

As I told him we should probably find our man quietly taking dinner, his face lighted up with pleasure, and he exclaimed, "It's one of the most beautiful little affairs I have been engaged in for some time past !"

I feared that his zeal might get the better of his discretion.

I again explained to him the full nature of the case, that I could not legally give him into custody, and my only chance of recovering any portion of the money with which he had absconded from England, was to frighten him into some concession before he could procure legal advice.

O'Leary appeared delighted with the prospect of his game, and requesting me to "lave it entoirely in his hards," assured me that in case he were obstinate he would terrify him out of his life.

Ere we reached the hotel I was wrought up to a high pitch of excitement; the time for decisive action had arrived.

Preceded by the landlord, and in company with the two detectives, I ascended the principal staircase, at the top of which was the entrance to the dining-saloon.

The door was open, thus affording us a view of some twenty of the guests, and, among them, of the man in search of whom I had crossed the Atlantic.

He was sitting with his back to us, his wife and sister-in-law being on each side of him.

He appeared in high spirits, and was chatting with the various guests at the table, little dreaming who was standing at the open door, prepared to denounce him, if necessary, as a fugitive swindler from England.

I pointed him out to O'Leary, who calmly remarked, "That's enough," and then, as a second thought struck him, he added, with a spice of Irish humour, "but we'll let him finish his dinner first, for he seems to be enjoying it so much."

In accordance with so odd a request we allowed him a minute's grace. He was then touched on the shoulder by the head waiter and informed that a gentleman was waiting to see him.

Still unsuspecting he arose from his seat and came towards us with a smiling countenance.

O'Leary met him, and with a slight inclination of the head, said, "Mr. Hooker, from England, I believe."

"Yes," was the apparent firm reply.

I thought I could discover an anxious nervous twitching in his face, betraying an under current of guilty consciousness, and a fear that he had not escaped pursuit, as perhaps only a few minutes previously he was flattering himself he had.

I was standing a little in the rear of O'Leary, and thus was partially hidden from observation.

Stepping on one side, and extending his hand towards me, O'Leary said, "Allow me, Mr. Hooker, to introduce you to a gentleman from England, with whom I believe you are well acquainted."

Making an effort to appear calm and unconscious of danger, the swindler deliberately disowned all knowledge of me.

Looking at me, and then turning to O'Leary, he replied, "I do not know the gentleman. He is a perfect stranger to me."

I was unprepared for such a barefaced disavowal from a man with whom I had so often and so lately transacted business.

For a moment I felt staggered by this fresh evidence of guilt.

At length I stepped forward and said, "Mr. Hooker, you know the —— Bank, and you know me as the cashier of that establishment, and you know, too, perfectly well the nature of the business which has brought me to Canada in search of you."

These words, uttered with all the menace and determination I could throw into them, had a marked and striking effect on the conscience-stricken man to whom they were addressed.

His courage instantly forsook him. He trembled as stricken with ague.

Uttering all sorts of miserable excuses for his conduct, he requested that we should retire to a private room, with a view to an explanation and settlement.

I readily acceded to this, and now felt somewhat hopeful of bringing the business to a satisfactory conclusion.

I soon discovered that in this I was fated to be disappointed; for, shortly after we were closeted, he again assumed a bold appearance, and seemed disposed to justify his conduct rather than make any reparation for what he had done.

His principal anxiety appeared to be to avoid exposure before the inmates of the hotel.

This afforded me an opportunity for suggesting a movement I was anxious to effect—viz., an adjournment to the office of my legal advisers.

Taking his arm in mine, and requesting the detectives to follow closely, we left the hotel.

After we reached Mr. Roe's office, nearly two hours were expended in vain attempts to induce the delinquent to accede to some equitable terms of settlement.

He at first appeared very penitent, and, in the midst of his tears, declared that it was his intention, as far as lay in his power, to act honourably to everyone; he begged again and again to be allowed to return to his wife, who, being ignorant of the state of affairs, would be suffering great anxiety from his prolonged absence.

He seemed so sincere in his protestations, that Mr. Roe suggested that I should accede to his request.

This was a moment of great difficulty to me. I did not wish to be unnecessarily severe; neither did I wish to act in opposition to the advice given me by Mr. Roe.

Still I felt sure that I should be losing some of the vantage ground I had gained through the day, if I released him whilst matters were in their present position.

At last I said, "I have a duty to perform, and I cannot shrink one step therefrom.

"You absconded from England, and having incurred expense in finding you, I cannot and will not release you until you have given me some material guarantee that the funds which you have deposited in the Merchants' Bank in this city, shall not be touched until you have made a satisfactory settlement with me."

My determination had the effect of again making him change his tactics. He upbraided me for bringing two detectives to his hotel, threatened vengeance against me for having been given into their custody, and asked me indignantly what I required.

An idea flashed across my mind. I confess it was a piece of strategy, and, conceived as it was in a minute, I could hardly hope that my prisoner would fall into the trap I wished to lay for him.

I replied—

"You are anxious to get back to your family, and I am equally anxious to terminate this painful interview. I will release you on the following conditions:—You shall draw a cheque for the funds (with the exception of a few pounds for your immediate use), which you have placed in the Merchants' Bank, payable to your order and my order jointly, and deposit the same with my solicitor. As a man of business," I continued, carelessly, "you are aware that I shall not be able to touch this money without your endorsement to the check."

I confess I did not draw his particular attention to the fact that he would be equally helpless without my signature.

Neither could he have given one moment's consideration to this feature in the transaction, or he certainly would not have so readily acceded to my terms. He appeared lost to every idea but that of his present escape; he immediately drew up the cheque, which he signed and handed to Mr. Roe.

I was now as anxious to get rid of him as I had been a few hours previously to effect his capture.

It was necessary to have the cheque "initialed" at the bank, which would place such an embargo on his funds as would prevent the possibility of his tampering with them by other means.

It was Saturday afternoon, and a half-holiday. Hurrying away as quickly as we could, we proceeded to the Merchants' Bank. It was closed.

After some little delay we gained admission by the private door. The clerks were leaving, but informed us that no further business could be transacted until Monday.

Monday would be too late; the full nature of my compromise with Hooker would be laid before him by a legal authority, and, perhaps, was at that moment being divulged to him.

Steps might be taken to remove his funds from my grasp. He, too, would be told of the "hopelessness of my case," and would, doubtless, set me at defiance.

I felt that if we failed now I should never recover one shilling of the money; that I should have to return to England beaten and disappointed, with a heavy bill of costs to add to the amount of which my firm had already been swindled.

With desperation I urged my solicitor forward, and we soon found ourselves in the interior of an inner office, where one of the chief tellers and junior still remained.

Fortunately for me and those whom I represented, the principal was a friend of my solicitor.

The cashier had his hat on, the junior was in the act of placing the last huge ledger in the iron safe, when he was stopped by Mr. Roe.

"One minute," he exclaimed to his friend the cashier; "I will not detain you long, but in that ledger you will find an account opened, within the last few days, by a Mr. Hooker from England. He has just given me a cheque for nearly the whole amount, payable to the joint order of himself and this gentleman," pointing to me. "We do not require the cash, but simply to have the cheque accepted by the bank."

The cashier, anxious to oblige his friend, opened the ledger, turned to the account, attached his initials to the cheque, and returned it to us.

The thanks we tendered him were neither few nor cold; and, as we hastily left the bank, Mr. Roe warmly congratulated me on the success of my plot.

I was too overpowered to say much myself.

Begging him to take especial care of the cheque, and under no circumstances to part with it without my authority, I left him, promising to see him on Monday morning.

I wandered down Notre Dame-street, in a state of complete abstraction and bewilderment.

I was overjoyed at the result of the day's proceedings, the exciting events of which had passed so rapidly in succession that I could scarcely realise the agreeable change which during the last few hours had taken place in the aspect of my Canadian affairs.

Of one circumstance I have a vivid recollection. I sat down to dinner that evening with a heart full of thankfulness; and, for the first time since I landed in America, I really and truly enjoyed the viands which were placed before me.

Although I had virtually brought Mr. Hooker to a strait which would compel him to accede to my own terms of settlement, still he evinced at times, more obstinacy than ever; and it was not until after a week that I finally closed with him.

It was early on the morning of Saturday, the 21st of October, that I sought an interview with Mr. South, the solicitor who had been consulted by Hooker.

Fortunately for me he was a highly respectable man. He had, on one or two occasions, intimated his contempt for his client, and that he was heartily sick of the transaction.

I told him that I had fully made up my mind to leave Montreal that night by the mail-train for Quebec, and to take passage in the North American, which would sail from the latter place on the following morning for England.

"If," I said to him, "your client does not accept my terms, I will take his cheque back with me, and make a bankrupt of him—his a-signees shall endorse the cheque *per procuration*, and the whole of the funds will then be sent to England for the benefit of his estate."

The reply was satisfactory.

"I admit," he said, "that the terms you propose are such as my client ought to accede to. He will be here shortly. I will inform him of your ultimatum; and if he still remains obstinate, I shall decline to have anything further to do with him. Will you call on me again at twelve o'clock?"

I kept the appointment punctually. The guilty man was there too, and quite crestfallen. Under the heavy pressure that had been brought to bear upon him he had at length given way. He accepted my terms, indorsed the cheque; and in a few hours, with a draft for the "salvage" money drawn by the City Bank of Montreal on Messrs. Glyn and Co., of London, safe in my possession, I was steaming rapidly towards Quebec.

I landed in England on Thursday, the 3rd of November.

Notwithstanding the hopelessness of my case, I had effected my "capture in Canada," and was enabled to report the same personally at headquarters in less than five weeks from the date of my departure.

CHAPTER CLIX.

SCENE AT STOKE FERRY—LAURA STANBRIDGE LED INTO AN AMBUSCADE—A LOVE STORY TO UNWILLING EARS.

IT was the nineteenth of November, and it had been a cold, gloomy day, and the night descended black and noiseless as a funeral pall upon a corpse.

The railway station was built of red bricks, which the storms of winter had almost turned brown. One gas-light flickered feebly within its case of glass. Two travellers were waiting for the train—one of them reading the advertisements on the walls, the other walking quickly, to keep himself warm.

A bell was rung—two red stars appeared in the distance—there was a low hum, which became a roar, and the train stopped by the trembling platform.

There had been only one passenger. It was a lady neatly dressed, without luggage or attendants.

She was not young, but her features were very handsome, albeit her grey eyes, which had a cold and cunning look, and her low, receding forehead, together with the thinness of her lips, robbed her of half her beauty.

A red-haired man, with a whip in his hand and a copper badge upon his breast, came up and spoke to her, touching his hat. As he spoke he pointed to a large close carriage in the road outside the station, to which were harnessed a pair of strong brown horses.

"I wish to go to Broxbridge Hall," said she. "Do you know the place?"

"Yes, ma'am—the seat of Earl Ethelwood. I know it well enough. I knew it when the old Earl was alive. Ah! me—things are changed since then, surely."

As she stepped into the carriage, she glanced anxiously towards the western sky, where a few rays of light showed that the sun had lately set.

These rays resembled streaks of blood, and cast a lurid glow upon the purple and copper-hued clouds around them.

She drew down the blinds, and, throwing herself back at full length in the vehicle, gave herself up to the meditation of her schemes.

She was roused by the stopping of the carriage. She drew up the blinds and opened the windows. It was now nearly dark, and distant flashes of lightning betokened a storm. The wind also had risen, and moaned among the distant trees.

They were upon the banks of a broad river, which was covered with small but white-crested waves.

The driver gave a peculiar kind of shout, which was answered from the other side by another shout and the ringing of a bell.

The lady began to understand.

They were about to cross a ferry.

She looked back on the road they had come, and which merely consisted of two huge ruts.

She could faintly distinguish the road on the other side, and it appeared to improve but little.

"Is this the only road to Broxbridge?" said she, in a tone of anxiety.

"Well, ma'am, it be," returned the red-haired man, "unless we'ed gone by the pike, which is five miles round. Cattle and men are both used to these roads hereabouts."

"But I thought the station was close to Broxbridge."

"There is a station close by it, but not the one I've brought you from."

"Then they have deceived me, and I booked for the wrong station."

"It can't be altered now, ma'am. We must make the best of a bad job, but you'll be all right enough."

She walked to the brink of the river, and eyed the dark sullen torrent as it ran swiftly past.

She heard the rattling of chains, and, looking up, saw a man crossing the river in a large punt.

In the dusk of the evening the mass glided towards her like some monster ghost, and the noise of the chains added strongly to this impression.

The boat was moored to a post in the bank, the horses were led carefully in, the driver assisted the lady with rough courtesy into the boat, then the ferryman, having unloosed the chain, drove his long iron-pointed pole into the gravelly bottom of the river.

The boat moved slowly and silently through the water, which it cleaved into ripples with its broad bow. The sky was covered with clouds, some long, some narrow and streaky, floated irregularly over the general mass.

They are called mare's tails, and generally forebode rain. The lightning flashes still continued, and once they heard a peal of thunder, faint and dull as an echo.

"The storm is coming up," said the driver, and he patted his horses, which were sniffing the air nervously, and soothed them with those signs and words which form a language between men and the lower animals.

The ferryman appeared to be old and feeble. He bent his face over his pole as he drove it into the ground at the bow of the boat, and followed it into the stern.

"Aye," said he, "the storm is coming up quickly and from what I can see of it at present we shall have it pretty sharp and no mistake."

When the boat grounded upon the sandy shelving bank on the other side, the ferryman stepped out and fastened the chain, averting his face from the boat.

The driver led the horses out of the craft and up the bank, the carriage jolting and rumbling as he did so. As the lady passed out her dress touched the hand of the ferryman.

At this touch he started suddenly and trembled all over, and his eyes followed her savagely.

As soon as she was reseated in the carriage, and had pulled the blinds down, the driver looked back at him significantly.

He nodded and climbed into the rumble, where he sat with his arms crossed, and his head upon his breast.

Laura Stanbridge—crouched within the vehicle, which she had made dark as if her thoughts were too evil to bear the light—did not hear the wind which now howled fiercely above her head, nor the thunder peals, which every moment grew more long and loud.

"Ah!" said she, "I will see this proud earl, and let him know who and what his father is. He little thinks what an amusing tale I have to tell about Mr. and Mrs. Thomas Gatliffe. I will bring him to my feet, and he will be but too glad to purchase my silence at a princely sum. So, Mr. Gatliffe, you spurn me now like the rest —do you? Are meditating mischief, I'll dare be sworn. Well, we shall see. Fool that you were to entrust me with your secrets!"

She uttered a cry of impatience as she saw, from the slow pace of the horses, and the manner in which the carriage hung back, that they were ascending a steep hill.

At the same moment a vivid flash of lightning darted past her eyes, and a peal of thunder, which made the windows rattle, followed it immediately—a sign that the storm was near.

The horses had stopped, and on peering through the front window she saw that the driver was no longer on the box.

She opened the door, and, alighting, found that a tree had fallen across the road. Upon this tree were seated two figures.

"Goodness me, how unfortunate!" exclaimed Laura. What must be done?"

The driver scratched his head, and seemed sorely puzzled.

"I don't know how we are to get to the hall now, ma'am," said he.

"But we must get there by some means or another," cried Laura, in a petulant tone. "How very unfortunate we've been to be sure! Everything seems to go wrong. What do you propose, driver? Just think—there's a good fellow."

"I am thinking, but can't tell what to do for all that."

One of the figures rose and approached them. It was a woman, in the uncouth dress of a female peasant.

"If the leddy wants to see the Earl, a maun see 'im to-night—he's off to Lunnon early the morrow."

"I do want to see him most particularly," said Miss Stanbridge. "My business is immediate. Can you tell me, my good woman, how I can get to Broxbridge Hall? You know the neighbourhood, I dare say."

"I do, indeed," was the ready response.

"And can tell me what to do?"

" Well, marm, my zon and oi be goin' that way, and we can show 'ee if a doan't moind goin' by a rough road through the woods."

" How far is it ?"

"Oh, only a little bit of a step."

" Very well ; then I will go, and trust to you to guide me," said Miss Stanbridge. "I do not see any other course left open."

Having paid the man for the distance he had brought her, she prepared to accompany them.

The woman climbed the bank at the side of the road and passed through an open gate into the footpath which led across a field.

The person whom the woman had mentioned as her son followed behind. Laura Stanbridge turned round in the field to look at him, but the night was so dark that she could only make out a shadowy form, which appeared to be enveloped in a large cloak with a high collar, which completely hid his features. Neither his dress, nor his gait were those of a labouring man, and she began to think that she had acted imprudently in trusting herself so implicitly to two strangers.

"However," she thought, " if they belong to any London gangs, I have only to speak to them in the thieves' patter, and they will not dare to touch me. If, on the contrary, they are yokels, they will be content with robbing me, and I have not much to lose."

They passed from the field into a small gorse common, across another high road, past a couple of lights which, shining in the windows of the cottages, showed that their inmates were already retiring to bed, and over a stile into a shaw or small copse, which skirted the side of the road.

Laura Stanbridge had addressed several questions to her conductress without receiving a reply. She had spoken once to the young man who followed like a phantom on her steps, and he had not chosen to make any answer.

Laura, who possessed the courage of a man or rather of a demon, began to be afraid. The night was miserably dark and cheerless, the way was lonely, the rain descended with much violence and the thunder seemed to shake the earth as it rolled from horizon to horizon.

Sometimes the lightning flashed through the trees and showed her three outstretched branches and their ghastly trunks.

But they could not show her the features of that grey-haired woman, who strode so swiftly before her, nor the face of that young man, who followed with equal speed, and who watched all her movements with glistening eyes.

She was trying to shake off her fears, which appeared to her idle and reasonless, when the woman stopped and pointed to the trunk of a tree, which had been stripped of its bark, and which lay like a naked giant across her path.

" Sit down there, madam," said she, in a voice which she seemed to remember, " sit down, you must be tired."

Laura hesitated. "Tut," said she, " after all, what can be more natural ? One meets every day with people who will not answer questions, and who will yet show every consideration for your comfort."

So she did as she was requested. As soon as she was seated a rope was flung over her head, and her arms were closely pinioned to her side. She struggled violently to free herself, but in vain. She therefore became calm, and said some words in the secret language of thieves.

"You are mistaken," answered the woman, in the same tongue, as she seated herself on the trunk. " I

do not wish to rob you. I wish to tell you a story—that is all."

Laura Stanbridge trembled. She began to suspect that she had fallen into the hands of a mad woman. But by a miraculous effort she recovered her self-possession and said quietly, " Very well, I shall be glad to hear what you have to say, but you need not have tied me. Unloose me first."

" No, madam, I must not unloose you, for when you have heard my story you will try to run away."

" I swear I will not attempt to do anything of the sort. I pledge my word as to this."

" I do not choose to take your word."

" Why not ?"

" For many reasons. I do not intend to let you escape."

Laura was bewildered.

The tones of this woman's voice were firm and menacing, and she fancied they were not unfamiliar to her.

She remembered also the rustic accent with which she had at first cloaked her words, and which must have been used for the purpose of deceiving her.

All this began to resemble a preconcerted scheme.

She waited anxiously, with dilating eyes, and ears bent forward, like the stag which hears the first bay of the distant hound.

" Besides," observed the woman, quietly, " if you tried to run away you might meet with an accident." She produced a dark lantern from underneath her shawl, and flashed the light in front of them.

By the yellow stream of light she distinguished a black opening in the ground, at the distance of scarcely three feet from where they were seated.

She shrank back, shuddering. The woman smiled grimly.

" I do not understand your meaning, or what your purpose is," cried the miserable Laura.

" You will understand all presently, I dare say.

" Gracious heaven ! you are——"

" Mrs. Grover, your old friend," replied the woman. " A light suddenly dawns upon you."

" You do not mean to harm me ?" cried Laura.

No answer.

The question was repeated.

" I have a story to tell," said Mrs. Grover.

" Bah, silly woman ! I have no desire to listen to your tales. I believe you are half crazed."

" No I am not; listen. Once I was a young girl, as innocent and happy as a spring bird, but a gentleman saw my pretty face. He fell in love with me—he wrote me letters. I could show you them if I wished, for I have borne them on my heart ever since. We used to meet on this very spot—it was here that I first felt his warm lips and the pressure of his hand, so soft and small—it was here that I first learned what it was to love—to have a beating heart when he came near me— to tremble with delight when I heard him speak.

" He did not treat me at first as gentlemen treat poor girls. One day he told me to meet him at Broxbridge. I made an excuse for leaving home that day and night, and met him at the corner of a dark street as he had appointed.

" I asked him no questions, I felt no fears. I loved him too well for that.

" He took my hand in his, and asked me if I would go with him. I kissed that hand, and said I would go with him to the end of the world."

" Goodness me, what have I to do with your early days ? What care I for your romantic love story ?"

ejaculated Laura Stanbridge. "Have you brought me hither for no better purpose than this?"

"You will know all in good time. When it was quite dark he took me to a little church which stands about half a mile from the town. In this church there was only one person—it was a young gentleman, in a white robe, who stood at the communion table between two wax tapers, with a book in his hand."

"The woman's as mad as a March hare," murmured Laura.

"My sweetheart drew me towards him, and again took my hand and made me kneel with him. Then I knew that he was going to marry me, and I almost swooned with astonishment and joy.

"The young clergyman read the service in a low and solemn voice. I could hardly speak the answers, my lips were trembling so. A ring was placed upon my finger—a hand pressed mine, and something like a soft flower fell upon my forehead—it was my husband's fond kiss."

"Undoubtedly mad, but I must humour her," thought Miss Stanbridge.

"Ah, how happy were we the first few months! We seldom saw each other, but that only made us love each other more.

"We used to meet on this very spot, and often on that soft bank he would crown me with a garland of fair wood flowers, and kiss me, and enfold me in his arms, and tell me again and again that he loved me as his life.

"And then," she said, plaintively, "he deserted me, and died at sea."

"Ah, it's a sorrowful tale—very sorrowful," said Miss Stanbridge, still, however, thinking that the narrator was most decidedly off her head.

"I had a child," said the woman, continuing her singular narrative. "The neighbours scoffed at me, and called me a wanton and my child base-born. I did not tell them; so I kept my secret as my husband had ordered me."

"Oh! he wished you to do so, then?"

"Yes; made me promise not to divulge it upon any condition whatsoever. After this I was ill awhile, and too weak to work out in the fields. No one would take me into their house because I had a base-born child. This made me mad. I cursed the poor infant for bringing its mother into shame. I tried to destroy it, but my heart failed me, and one night I abandoned it to its fate. Ah! there's nothing like misfortune to harden the heart; it will make a mother murder her own child, and there is no worse crime in the world than that."

CHAPTER CLX.

THE ACCUSATIONS MADE AGAINST LAURA STANBRIDGE.

MRS. GROVER, or, more properly speaking, Mrs. Kensett, relict of Evershal Kensett, Esq., deceased, had spoken the words, which form the conclusion of the last chapter, in a voice which was tremulous and at times inaudible from emotion. After this she fell into a reverie.

The rain still pattered upon the leaves, the lightning still dashed its gleams through the wood, the thunder still rolled menacingly.

By these flashes of lightning Laura Stanbridge might have been seen pale, paralysed, and crouched rather than seated upon the log.

Now she knew by whom she had been captured, and she knew also that she was in imminent danger.

"Help—help!" she cried, in a loud voice. "Help—help!"

Her companion was awakened by these cries.

"You may shout as loud as you like—nobody will hear you. At the same time, if you do so again, I will kill you."

This was enough; Laura became silent. It was evident that this woman was remorseless, and that her best hope to protect her life lay upon the chance of some one passing by.

It was a public footpath. Then she remembered that there was a young man present. He might be corrupted with a look—with a whisper.

She stole a glance towards him; he remained motionless as a statue of black marble, his face hidden by his cloak.

"Who can this man be?" she reflected, "whom she calls her son, and whom I cannot recognise? It must be some one whom she has hired to help her. If so, I may be saved."

She darted another look piercing as a flame upon the mysterious individual. At this look he hid his head.

"Ah, he knows me, and fears to be recognised. It is perhaps, one of my old comrades. So much the better. He will understand that his employer is less powerful than I am."

She half turned her head and whispered—

"A hundred pounds for my liberty."

Mrs. Grover burst into a hoarse laugh.

"She is trying to bribe you. That is because she does not know you."

The figure nodded.

"Woman," exclaimed Mrs. Grover, with sudden vehemence, which made the other start, "what have you done with my son?"

"With your son?"

"Aye, don't echo my words, but answer. Shall I tell you? Infamous wretch, hateful fiend, you have murdered him, and for this as well as for other crimes you have been brought here to die."

"Oh, take pity on me! You do not mean to do anything so horrible. I will give you money, all you may desire, but, oh, I am not fit to die."

"You are not fit to live, and I intend to have your life. Who was it you pushed over the cliffs at Margate? Answer me that."

Laura Stanbridge gave utterance to a piercing scream as these words fell upon her ears. She trembled in every limb, and the first thought uppermost with her was that she had been betrayed by Tom Gatliffe.

"Listen to me—be reasonable," she cried, in piteous accents. "I see now who has brought this about, and know who has charged me with this odious crime."

"Who?"

"Tom Gatliffe!"

The woman smiled sardonically, and shook her head.

"Who, then?"

"Ah, ah, my lady, you want to know too much. You can't deny the charge."

"I do deny it."

"You do!"

"Yes," returned Laura, resolutely.

The man in the cloak passed slowly round the fallen trunk and stood in front of her.

The yellow light of the lantern streamed upon him. He tore open his cloak. Laura Stanbridge screamed with horror. She beheld the pale features of Alf Purvis, who uttered but one word. It was—

"Murdreess!"

LAURA STANBRIDGE HANGED IN ENDEAVOURING TO ESCAPE.

The lantern was hooked upon a branch and flung its ghastly rays upon the surrounding trees, and upon the young man who stood with his arms folded, a cold stern light in his eyes ; upon the convicted wretch who, now cowering to the ground, uttered low moans of terror.

At the same time another figure also cloaked, and with features concealed, issued from behind the trees and stood in the dark shadows of the background, unheard and unseen save by Mrs. Grover, who however seemed to be heedless of his presence.

"Laura Stanbridge," said she, "prepare to meet your fate. In a few minutes you must die."

"Why must I die?" exclaimed the wretched woman.

No. 91.

" What have I done that my life should be thus sacrificed ?"

" Do not fear," answered Mrs. Grover, " you shall be fairly judged, and I will accuse you first."

" You have me in your power, and can of course do as you please with me. It is cruel and merciless to treat me thus."

Heedless of this last observation Mrs. Grover proceeded. " I accuse you," said she, " of decoying my child into your house, of depraving his mind and teaching him to steal, of driving me forth when I attempted to save him. How say you, Laura Stanbridge ? Is that true or false ?"

" It is true, but you must remember that I found him starving, and that I gave him bread to eat, that I taught him to earn money as I earned it, and as you earned it, and, at the time I parted with you, you did not yourself know that he was your son, and could allege no good reason for trying to thwart my schemes."

" That I admit," returned Mrs. Grover after a few minutes' reflection. " We are not likely to disagree as far as that point of your history is concerned."

Laura had a glimmer of hope.

" I accuse you," said her relentless companion, " of urging my son to all sorts of crimes. I accuse you of betraying him to the law. What say you to this, Laura Stanbridge ? Is it true or false ?"

" It is false ! it is false !" she cried " you cannot prove what you say."

" Have you forgotten our conversation in the French café ?"

" I have not forgotten it. I remember every word. I was jesting then ; you know that as well as I do myself. Would you condemn me for a few empty words ?"

The woman made no reply—but her son Alf Purvis, stepped forward and scowled at the prisoner.

" Subterfuge and prevarication will avail you not murderess," said he. " Thrice guilty as you are any plea for mercy will be unavailing. Miserably guilty woman, your hour has come."

" Mercy, mercy !" exclaimed Laura Stanbridge " I never meant to harm you. You drove me to desperation, and I know not what I did. You cannot, you will not turn against me."

Alf Purvis held up his hand deprecatingly. " Silence," said he. " For you I have no pity—you have made me what I am—a thief, and an associate of thieves. This done, you betrayed me and my companions. Not content with this, you hurled me from the cliff ; but Providence, more kind than my companions or friends, watched over me. Fate willed that I was not to perish.

" Exhausted, and all but dead, I was picked up by a fishing-smack, and saved to become your accuser, and the avenger of those whom you have so deeply injured. Laura Stanbridge, are you prepared to die ?"

" Gracious heaven, no ! I am unfit to die," said she, and she made the tears rise to her eyes, and turned upon Alf Purvis, one of those mournful and languishing looks by which the hearts of men are destroyed.

But this look was lost upon him. He knew her but too well.

" Is this all ?" she said, scornfully. " Am I to be murdered ?"

" My son evaded your wiles," said Mrs. Grover. " It is well for him that he did so."

" He offered me his hand and made me love him," returned Laura. " Then, not content with affronting me by a rejection, he became my most bitter enemy. Is it in any way surprising that I should have striven to have revenge for the injuries sustained ?"

" I will not answer you, infamous and merciless woman !" exclaimed Mrs. Grover. " But we have here another victim."

The third accuser now advanced and bared his aged and weather-beaten face. This was the old ferryman.

" And who is this ? Who is this ?" cried Laura Standbridge, her hair undulating and rising over her head as if alive.

Mrs. Grover laughed.

" It is the faithful servant of the man you murdered —the man who patronised and protected you—it is Henry Wincott."

" Oh ! no—no, it cannot be," she cried.

" Yes," said the old ferryman, " I am Henry Wincott—the faithful servant of the gentleman whom years and years ago you robbed and murdered."

She uttered two or three wild cries, which produced a strange and melancholy effect as they died away on the night wind ; then she swooned.

There was a consultation. The three accusers debated for some time.

They had intended taking summary vengeance on the woman who had so deeply wronged them, but a better feeling at length prevailed, and Laura Stanbridge, when she had in a measure recovered from the deep trance into which she had fallen, was taken, bound as she was, to the home of Mr. Kensett, the magistrate, where she was charged with the murder of her paramour, and attempted murder of Alf Purvis.

A long examination took place, and Laura was taken to the lock-up in the neighbourhood.

She was placed in one of the upper rooms of this station, and left alone for the remainder of the night.

Her remorse and miserable thoughts would be difficult to describe. She became duly impressed with the hopelessness of her condition, and during the dark hours of the lonely night but one burning thought possessed her.

This was to effect her escape.

She tore up the sheets of her bed, contrived to unfasten one of the windows of her bedchamber, from which she flung herself, in the vain hope of reaching the ground.

The circumstances connected with the attempted escape were never rightly understood, but she was found in the morning hanging from the open casement quite dead, with the shreds of the sheets around her neck.

Whether she had purposely put an end to her existence, or her death was the result of accident, never transpired, but the close of her sinful life had this miserable ending.

CHAPTER CLXI.

PEACE'S LAST NIGHT IN SHEFFIELD—HIS REMOVAL TO WAKEFIELD—INCIDENTS BEFORE THE TRIAL—A TRUE BILL FOUND.

WE must now return to Charles Peace, who, the reader will remember, was fully committed for trial upon the charge of murder, a report of the examination of which appeared in a previous chapter. Peace entered his cell, and there he soon recovered his spirits, and was more cheerful than he had been since his recapture.

He spent a much better night, and on Saturday morning he appeared refreshed and altogether a stronger man. It may not be, perhaps, out of place to refer here to an extraordinary statement made by Peace at this time.

His relative, who lives in Spring-street, made no secret of the fact that Peace did call on him on the night of the murder. Peace came to his door and found it locked.

He went into the public-house close by and asked for a glass of beer, and seeing his brother there, called him out. They were together a few minutes, and then Peace wished him "Good-bye," and went on to the Attercliffe-road station, and took train at Rotherham.

When he arrived at the Masbro' station, he found there was no train to Beverley for two hours; and he wandered about in the neighbourhood during that time, and when the train came up, he procured his ticket and went on, as stated, to Normanton.

At that time Peace was altogether unaware of the result of his encounter with Mr. Dyson. He saw his victim fall, and he heard Mrs. Dyson scream, and he had no doubt that the second shot had inflicted injury, but it was not until the next morning, when he was at York, and saw the papers, that he became aware that he had committed murder.

He further disguised himself, and took greater precautions than before to avoid detection. In confirmation of Peace's story about having been seen in London, it may be mentioned that Mr. W. Fisher told Detective Carswell—amongst other officers—that he had seen Peace in Holborn.

Peace further stated that in the course of his career he has stolen thousands of pounds' worth of property—diamond rings, gold watches, and, indeed, valuable articles of every description.

On the Saturday succeeding his committal Peace was removed to the county prison at Wakefield.

He was seen in the morning by Mr. Hallam, the police sergeant, for the purpose of ascertaining whether he was in a condition to be removed, and on his certifying that he could safely undergo the short journey from Sheffield to Wakefield, it was decided that he should be taken there in the afternoon.

This intention was observed with the utmost secrecy. But, somehow or other, a rumour got abroad that Peace was likely to be removed, and small crowds hung about the station, and especially in close proximity to the entrance in Castle-green.

The appearance of the prison-van horses on their way through through the town of course led to the supposition that the van was to be used, and the crowds quickly increased. But there was a strong force of policemen on duty in the neighbourhood of the station, and as their orders were to keep the people "moving on," they carried their instructions out very literally.

The spectators indeed might as well have moved off altogether, for nothing whatever could be seen; and when the prison van did come out, it was driven off so rapidly that but a glimpse of it could be caught as it quickly disappeared down Castle-green.

There was also but little to be seen inside the parade ground at the police station, where the prison van was drawn up in readiness to receive its very notorious occupant.

The first intimation that Peace was about to leave his cell was furnished by some of the prison officials bringing down the mattress upon which he had lain since his arrival here, and the rugs or blankets which constituted his bed clothes.

These were placed upon the floor of the van, and an impromptu bed was thus readily at hand. Soon afterwards Peace himself came down. But he did not

walk—whether he could not or because he was still "shamming," is entirely a matter of opinion.

One of his warders, a man of sturdy frame and powerful build, held him underneath his arms, whilst the other warder and Inspector Bradbury, carried him by his legs. In this way he was taken from his cell, down the two flights of stairs, and then out into the parade ground.

If Peace were shamming, he did it admirably. He looked a miserable, wretched object of humanity—a little limp bundle of brown-coloured clothes, out of which peeped a face intensely wan and haggard.

It was noticed that he wistfully and almost pleadingly glanced into the faces of those who were in the parade ground, probably in the hope of seeing some one whom he knew; but there was no time for recognition, for he was carried quickly across the space between the bottom of the steps and the prison van, and placed upon the mattress on the floor.

The warders followed him in. Inspector Bradbury and others joined them; the door was then locked, and the van speedily driven out of the station.

In some mysterious manner the news became known that Peace would go from the Midland station, and a considerable number of people assembled there.

They stood about near to the entrance, of course expecting that the prison van would draw up there, and that a good view would be obtained of the convict as he was brought in. They were disappointed.

Presently several policemen suddenly appeared at the Heeley end of the platform, and immediately there was a rush in that direction.

Almost before the foremost of the crowd could get to the open beyond the platform, the prison van was driven rapidly into the yard and drawn up close to a passenger guard's van, which was in waiting on the siding.

That had been placed there in readiness to receive the convict and those in charge of him. The movements of all concerned were marvellously quick in what they had to do.

The doors of the guard's van were thrown open, and at the same time the doors of the prison van. Out of the latter stepped members of the Sheffield force, and then came the warders carrying their burden.

He was promptly lifted into the guard's van, moaning piteously, and placed on the floor. Then his mattress and rugs were carried in, and a bed prepared for him, and on it he was laid and covered up.

He appeared glad to curl himself up under the rugs and to hide himself from the gaze of the bystanders; for notwithstanding the utmost exertions of the police and the officials at the station, a great number of people got near, and many hundreds more crowded the bridge across the line and other points from which they could see what was passing.

The warders, Inspector Bradbury, and Police-constable Capel, entered the van with the prisoner, and the doors were then shut and bolted.

The people surged round the window, anxious to catch a glimpse of the prisoner, but all that the most favoured could see was what was very much like a heap of rugs on a mattress.

Amongst the crowd was Police-constable Robinson, who was shot by Peace at Blackheath. He came forward and shook hands with the warders through the window, and had a look at the man with whom he had had such a deadly encounter.

After waiting a short time the train from London arrived in the station, the guard's van was pushed up from the siding to it, and the train went on its journey.

The van was detached from the train at Sandal and Walton, and hooked on to the train for Wakefield, where it arrived soon after three o'clock. One of the warders left the van and called a cab, and into it Peace was lifted.

Accompanied by his two warders and Inspector Bradbury, he was driven to Wakefield prison, where he was safely lodged.

The warders were supplied with the necessary documentary evidence that Peace had been handed over to the officials at Wakefield, and later in the evening they set out on their return journey to Pentonville.

They were heartily glad to be released from any further charge of the convict, who since his escape had been a source of great anxiety and trouble to them.

Nothing of importance occurred during the journey. Soon after the train had left Sheffield, Peace threw back his rugs, looked at his custodians, and then asked, " Where are you taking me to ?"

They told him he was going to Wakefield. He gave a groan, rolled himself up in his rugs, and nothing more was heard from him throughout the journey.

Peace, after his arrival to Wakefield, was watched with the utmost jealousy by the officials, and as the convict recovered from the effects of his leap from the railway carriage, he displayed a good deal of irritation at this strict supervision.

He declared that never before was he so closely watched as he was then. His system was recovering its tone, and the effects of the injuries sustained by his leap from the train were becoming less apparent.

REMOVAL OF PEACE TO LEEDS.

On the arrival of Peace at the Wakefield prison, on Saturday, a notice was posted at the principal entrance lodge in Love-lane, warning the officials not to divulge any information to the outside public, and this order was most strictly complied with.

It may be mentioned that Peace was no stranger at the Wakefield House of Correction, for he had been incarcerated there on three or four different occasions, and one of his visits was rendered famous by a most daring act.

A man named Roberts, who lived in Garden-street, Wakefield, and was for many years an officer at the Wakefield Prison, informed a correspondent on the occasion that in 1854 Peace was ordered to be imprisoned for four years, and he was sent to Wakefield.

For some time he worked in the gardens which surround the gaol, and in the evenings after work hours he was in the habit of whiling away the time and amusing himself by cutting out figures and making designs in tin, cardboard, &c., or in cutting tissue paper in various ways for the decoration of rooms.

Subsequently he was employed in what is known as the beaming room in connection with the manufacture of mats and matting, and one afternoon, whilst in charge of Roberts, he succeeded in making his escape out of the room, the door of which had been accidentally left unfastened.

He succeeded in getting upon a wall, and then climbed upon the roof of a house in the prison yard, which was occupied by the late Dr. Milner, who was convict surgeon at the prison at the time of which we speak—1854.

Peace removed some of the slates on the roof of the doctor's house, and made an aperture through which he descended into one of the bedrooms.

Immediately he was missed from the work-room an alarm was raised, and a most diligent search commenced.

In a very short time the daring fellow was found secreted on the top of a wardrobe, out of which he no doubt intended to take a suit of the doctor's clothing and attire himself in them in place of the prison dress he was wearing.

He was at once seized and placed in solitary confinement, when he became violent and made a most determined attempt to destroy himself. He inflicted a very severe gash in his throat, the mark produced by which was still visible.

On the Tuesday night, Councillor Atkinson, cab proprietor, received instructions from Captain Godfrey Armytage, the governor, to have two coaches in readiness at half-past one o'clock the following afternoon, for the purpose of conveying Peace to Armley, and the strict secresy which was enjoined on him was observed to the very letter.

It may be safely affirmed that not a single other person in Wakefield had the slightest idea of the time of Peace's departure, and the fact that all the trains departing for Leeds up to two o'clock on Wednesday were closely watched, showed that the mystery remained as deep as ever.

Even at half-past one on Wednesday morning, when the fast train leaves for Leeds, people were found who, despising the cold, kept a steady look-out for Peace, and frequented the approaches to Westgate Station with the object of satisfying their insatiable curiosity.

Precisely at the preconcerted hour, one of the coaches arranged for was driven into the prison yard, and pulled up in front of the main entrance.

At that moment Peace was being conducted across the vestibule, heavily manacled, and guarded by three warders ; so that as soon as the coach came to a standstill he was at the door.

The proceeding seemed to go altogether "against the grain" with him; at one moment he twisted his face as if in pain, then changing to a scowl, he at last flashed his eyes with evident anger as he was ordered to step into the coach.

This he seemed to do with pain, making it appear that the lifting of his legs was indeed a laborious task. When he had sat down within, three warders, armed with cutlasses and revolvers, got in after him, and then the windows being darkened by blinds drawn down, the coach was driven out.

The whole proceedings, which were under the personal direction of Captain Armytage, and were carried out in the presence of a considerable body of the prison officials, did not occupy much over a minute.

In the lane outside the prison scarcely a single person was stirring, so that the coach got clear away up Back-lane and through St. John's, without any of the general public being any the wiser.

While matters were proceeding at the prison as we have just described, another two horse coach was being quietly walked up Back-lane, and destined to convey an extra body of armed warders to Armley along with those in the first coach.

It was arranged that this second coach should wait at the West Riding Police Depot until the other came up ; but as it was thought that its standing in the open street for some time might attract attention it was driven on for some distance further.

When opposite St. John's Church four warders, who had been sauntering along, got into it, and were driven along in the wake of the convict and his more immediate attendants.

Here another move was made to throw the public off the scent, for instead of keeping the Leeds road, the drivers turned into the Bradford road as soon as they had got out of the town.

Continuing on the route for four or five miles, when they got to the " White Bear Inn," at Ardsley, they turned into the Leeds and Dewsbury road, by which they arrived at Armley Gaol.

CHAPTER CLXII.

THE TRIAL AND CONVICTION OF CHARLES PEACE.

THE eventful day at length arrived upon which the most daring and desperate criminal of modern times was to be tried upon the grave charge of "wilful murder."

" Let Charles Peace stand forward."

There is a scuffling of feet, and a small, elderly-looking, feeble man, in brown convict dress, is helped into the dock, and placed in a chair by stalwart warders.

The Clerk of Assizes states the charge.

" How say you, Charles Peace, are you guilty or not guilty ?"

In a feeble voice, hardly audible, the words " Not guilty " are uttered.

The prisoner's face is impassive, but he takes in all the surroundings with short, quick glances.

The jury is empanelled, the arraignment is opened, and Mr. Campbell Foster rises to address the jury.

The scene is one of much interest. As early as nine o'clock the small portion of the court allotted to the public had begun to fill with eager spectators.

The press enters in force, considerable portions of the court, and also of the gallery above the jury, being reserved for its representatives.

Barristers drop in, eager as the people who are unfamiliar with the courts, and quickly filling their seats, there accumulates a standing group, which remains about the door all day.

The occupants of the court, with scarcely an exception, deport themselves as men and women come to witness a comedy, not a grim tragedy—talking, laughing, joking, and congratulating themselves on their luck in gaining admission on so famous an occasion.

The judge takes his seat precisely at ten o'clock, and the case at once begins.

Mr. Campbell Foster bespeaks the unprejudiced and impartial attention of the jury, and enters upon a lengthened recital of the facts of the case.

The tale is a plain and unvarnished one, but, to be quite candid, that is all the praise that can be bestowed upon it.

A very frank critic might even say that it is somewhat dreary and decidedly commonplace. However, it is listened to with silent attention—by none is it followed with closer care than by the prisoner, who occasionally indulges in a nod of assent, or a remonstrating shake of the head, or now and then leans forward, his head on his hand, and eyes fixed upon the speaker.

The learned council spoke for half an hour.

Then the evidence began, the first witness being Mr. Johnson, who proved the plans put in of the Dysons' house in Bannercross-terrace, and was asked a question or two as to Mr. Dyson's physical appearance.

There was "sensation" in court when Catherine Dyson was called. She stepped into the witness-box, dressed in black, neatly, her jacket trimmed with crape, the somewhat jaunty hat which she had worn at the preliminary examination replaced by a modest bonnet.

She had a veil or "fall" over the upper part of her face, but it was not enough to obscure it. She had a heightened colour, suggestive of rouge, with a slightly sulky expression, and the look of a person who, tensely strung, yet knows what she is about and is resolved to act on the defensive.

She was examined by Mr. Shield, and spoke in a very low tone of voice.

The examination was uneventful; it only repeated the old familiar account of the transactions which led to this trial; and when Mr. Lockwood rose to cross-examine the witness, there was a feeling that now, the preliminary details settled, the real engagement of the day was about to be fought.

The first point on which the opposing forces came into conflict was as to whether or not Mr. Dyson, on the night he was shot, got hold or attempted to get hold of the prisoner.

Before the Coroner and before the magistrate, the witness had professed her inability to say that her husband did not grapple with the prisoner. She now declared positively that he did not, and there was a long struggle on this point.

Mrs. Dyson maintained her composure, during the searching catechising that ensued. Whatever she might have said before, she now said positively that her husband did not get hold of Peace.

Pressed hard for admissions that there was some sort of a struggle between the prisoner and Dyson, the witness adhered to her denial that anything of the kind did or could take place ; and the cross-examination then went on to deal with the photograph taken in the fair.

A good deal of fencing took place as to the precise fair at which this photograph was taken, based partly upon the mistaken assumption that the Peaces went to live at Darnall at the end of 1875, whereas they went there at the beginning of the year.

The witness could not see her way through the puzzle, except that there was some mistake in the dates—which was a very just conclusion at which to arrive.

Nothing was made of this—except to render it evident that no reliable dates could be got from the witness; and, with the positiveness displayed on previous occasions, she repudiated any knowledge of the letters found near Bannercross after the murder.

The journey to Mansfield, on the occasion when Peace followed her there, next came under notice, and the gift of a ring by the prisoner. Then the visits to Sheffield public-houses with Peace—she had been once with him to the "Marquis of Waterford," Russell-street, she said, and might have been twice, but she could not say positively.

The keepers of several of these houses were called and confronted with Mrs. Dyson, but she knew them not, nor did she know (though she avoided positively swearing it) that she had ever had drink at the "Halfway House," Darnall, charged to the prisoner.

Mr. Lockwood was equally unsuccessful in his attempts to extract confessions as to the transmission of notes between herself and Peace. As before the Stipendiary, so now Mrs. Dyson was subjected to a trial in caligraphy, and it may be assumed that the results were not very encouraging to Mr. Lockwood, since he did not pursue the subject further. But the incident elicited a curious example of Mrs. Dyson's composure.

She was passing to Mr. Lockwood the paper on which she had written, with the ink wet. It had actually left her hands, when she took it back and calmly rubbed a piece of blotting paper over it.

Coming down to the day before the murder new

points of much interest were opened up. The witness admitted that she was on that day at the "Stag" Hotel, Sharrow. A little boy was with her—not her own child.

A man followed her in and sat beside her—she would almost swear that the prisoner was not the man—upon which a sort of laugh ran through the court.

She was cross-examined as to her other movements that night, and as to going to a friend's named Muddiman on leaving the "Stag." She swore that she did not tell Peace that she was going there—for she did not see him.

A laugh was caused when Mrs. Dyson pleaded guilty to the soft impeachment of having been "slightly inebriated" at the "Halfway House," but she denied that she had ever been turned out of that house either for being drunk or for being "slightly inebriated."

This concluded Mrs. Dyson's cross-examination, which had lasted exactly two hours, her examination in chief having previously lasted half an hour.

The re-examination by Mr. Campbell Foster lasted only a few minutes, and after a question or two from the Judge, the Court adjourned for luncheon, the general opinion being that Mrs. Dyson had passed through the trying ordeal with great firmness and self-possession, and that the defence had not made a material mark upon the case.

After half an hour's interval the trial was resumed by the production of the Bannercross witnesses.

There were few new features in this, but Mr. Lockwood made a vigorous attempt to damage the credibility of the young man, Brassington, whose testimony went to establish malice and intent on the part of the prisoner.

Peace himself, during this, departed from his customary air of stoical calm, talking rapidly, in a low tone, and evidently challenging the witness's statements in no amicable mood or feeble terms.

The evidence of Mr. Harrison, the surgeon, went to show that the direction of the shot was such as would be likely to be taken by a bullet fired from the low level of the road at a person above, and the questions of Mr. Lockwood, in cross-examination, pointed to the suggestion that certain bruises on the deceased's nose and chin were caused by blows, in a struggle with the prisoner.

But Mr. Harrison did not take to this theory, though as the deceased had fallen on his back when shot, he did not seem quite able to account for these grazes.

Soon after this there took place between the learned counsel engaged in the case a contention of which there had been one or two previous indications. It was a struggle on the part of the defence to force the prosecution to put in the letters found in the field at Bannercross.

Mr. Lockwood wanted the letters to be put as evidence, that he might use them; but he did not wish to put them in himself, because that would deprive him of the last word to the jury, and give it to Mr. Campbell Foster. The point gave rise to much argument, but in the end Mr. Lockwood had to abandon his contention.

After this the prosecution called witnesses who had not been before the coroner or the magistrates. Then followed evidence as to the capture of Peace at Blackheath, and this closed the case for the prosecution.

Mr. Campbell Foster summed up the evidence he had produced in proof of the charge of murder, Peace listening to everything he said with unflinching attention.

Mr. Lockwood's vigorous speech for the defence followed. It contained powerful appeals to the jury, and animated attacks upon the prosecution and the press; but it was an up-hill fight that the learned counsel was so gallantly waging.

He claimed to have utterly discredited Mrs. Dyson's testimony, and urged that the jury could not send to execution any human being on such evidence as she had given.

The theory set up by him as to the actual occurrences at Bannercross on the night of the murder was, that Peace, finding himself pursued by Mr. Dyson, fired his revolver to frighten him from pursuit; but this not effecting its purpose, a struggle took place, and in that struggle the revolver went off accidentally, with fatal effects.

But unfortunately Mr. Lockwood had no testimony behind him to back up this ingenious attempt to reduce the crime to one of manslaughter; and the glamour of feeling in which he had sought to invest the case was quickly dispelled even in the breasts of the most sentimental in court when the learned judge, in a summing-up of a marked fairness and impartiality, placed the plain issues, and the unanswerable facts, about which there could be no question, before the twelve men on whose word the life of a human being hung.

His lordship, who began to speak at a quarter-past six, occupied fifty-five minutes.

The jury, who retired at ten minutes past seven, were absent fifteen minutes, and on their return the prisoner, who had been allowed to leave the dock, was brought back and replaced in his chair, looking limp and wretched.

The warders, who had hitherto sat beside him, now stood, one holding either arm. The Judge resumed his seat, and the jury immediately delivered their verdict of guilty.

Asked if he had anything to say why sentence should not be passed, he replied very faintly, "It's no use my saying anything."

The learned Judge forthwith passed sentence in a few calm, matter-of-fact sentences. There was an utter absence of feeling in court.

The unhappy man heard the sentence with an apparent indifference, bred either of stoicism or despair, and the warders at once raised him to convey him from the dock.

As he stood up he clutched at the rail in front and appeared to wish to speak, but his keepers paid no attention to the desire.

He bowed to his solicitor, and expressed in a word or two thanks for his efforts; then disappeared to his doom.

THE TRIAL.

In the Crown Court at the Leeds Assizes, Charles Peace, described as a picture-frame dealer, forty-seven years of age, was placed upon his trial, before Mr. Justice Lopes, for the murder of Mr. Arthur Dyson, civil engineer, at Bannercross, Sheffield, on the 29th November, 1876.

It is almost unnecessary to say that the case has created the greatest possible interest—an interest not felt simply in Sheffield, but throughout the country.

This had arisen not so much because of the murder itself—for the facts were exceedingly simple—but because of the extraordinary career of the prisoner, his sudden disappearance after the murder, and his subsequent identity as the notorious burglar who kept Blackheath in a state of considerable excitement for some months.

Peace was already under a sentence of penal servitude

for life for shooting at Police-constable Robinson, who apprehended him whilst he was endeavouring to escape from a house which he had burglariously entered at Blackheath.

At that time Peace was known as John Ward, a half-caste, who had, according to his own statement, recently arrived in this country. For considerably more than a week this was all that was known of him.

Then information came to the police, through a woman with whom he had been living, that the prisoner under remand at Greenwich was not Ward, but Peace, who was wanted for murder, and for whose apprehension a reward of £100 had been in vain offered for more than a couple of years.

Subsequent investigations resulted in some extraordinary disclosures. It was found that Peace had been living in a semi-detached villa at Peckham, in company with a woman named Thompson, who was supposed to be his wife; that he kept a pony and trap, and that he lived in a style of considerable comfort.

It was found, too, that he was the perpetrator of most of the burglaries which had for some months past been of almost nightly occurrence at Greenwich and Blackheath.

After his sentence of penal servitude for life the Treasury authorities decided to prosecute him for the murder of Mr. Dyson.

The chief witness, Mrs. Dyson, was then in America, having gone there, to reside with some relatives, a few months after her husband was shot.

A special messenger was dispatched in search of her, and on her arrival in this country, Peace was taken to Sheffield to undergo an examination before the stipendiary magistrate.

His attempt to commit suicide on the way down from Pentonville, by jumping from the train, is too well-known an occurrence to need more than a passing mention.

In consequence of the excitement prevailing, and the great desire to obtain admittance to the court on the occasion of the trial at Leeds, it was decided that only a limited number of seats should be thrown open to the public, all other parts being reserved for those in possession of tickets.

The public seats were taken possession of immediately on the opening of the court at nine o'clock. The other parts of the building were filled within the next hour, and when the Judge took his seat at ten o'clock every seat was occupied.

In one of the galleries were Lord Houghton and a number of guests from Fryston Hall. A large crowd remained outside the hall, but a strong force of police prevented them reaching the doors.

Peace was removed from Armley Gaol on Monday evening, and was placed in one of the cells at the Town Hall, under the care of four warders. He passed a very restless night, and on Tuesday morning was in a state of much weakness and depression. His appearance in the court, of course, attracted considerable attention. He partially walked and was partially carried up the step leading into the dock, and then was placed in a chair in front of the dock.

A warder occupied a seat on either side of him. Unless he was "shamming," his condition was almost pitiable to behold. He seemed so weak that he could scarcely sit up in his chair, but, notwithstanding that, he appeared to take the keenest interest in the case as it proceeded.

On the charge being read to him he pleaded "Not Guilty," but he spoke in so low a tone that he could scarcely be heard.

Mr. Campbell Foster, Q.C., and Mr. Hugh Shield prosecuted on behalf of the Treasury; and Mr. Lockwood and the Hon. Stuart Wartley (instructed by Messrs. Clegg and Sons, Sheffield), defended the prisoner.

Mr. Campbell Foster, Q.C., in opening the case for the prosecution, said he could not disguise from himself, nor from the jury, that the case, from the great public comment which had been made upon it in the various newspapers, must come before them under circumstances calculated somewhat perchance to bias their minds, but before entering upon it he would beg and implore them to put from their minds anything they might have read about the case, and be guided entirely by the sworn testimony which would be given by the witnesses as to the guilt or innocence of the prisoner.

It would be shown, he said, that, previous to July, 1876, the man, into whose death they had to inquire, lived at Darnall, a village about three miles to the east of Sheffield, and now one of the outskirts of the town.

He and his wife lived in a row of cottage houses, and next door, or next door but one, lived the prisoner and a person who, so far as they knew, was his wife.

From being so near neighbours the Dysons got to know the prisoner. He was in the habit of framing pictures, and was employed by them to frame two or three small prints and pictures which they had in the house.

This led to an acquaintance between the prisoner and the Dysons, but at last Mr. Dyson seemed not to like the persistent familiarity with which the prisoner was in the habit of treating them, walking into the house whenever he thought proper, at meal times, and generally obtruding himself upon them.

This annoyed both Mr. Dyson and his wife, and, as a consequence, shortly before the 1st July, 1876, Mr. Dyson wrote on the back of one of his address cards—

"Charles Peace is requested not to interfere with my family."

The card was thrown over the wall into Peace's garden, and the sending of it seemed to have created a bad feeling in the mind of Peace against Dyson, for it would be shown that on the 1st of July, meeting Mr. Dyson, he suddenly commenced an assault upon him, attempting to trip him up and throw him down.

Late in the evening Peace found Mrs. Dyson talking to some neighbours about his extraordinary conduct, and asked if she were talking about him.

She replied that she was, and apparently in a sudden burst of passion he produced a revolver and presenting it at her head said he would blow her brains out—of course using an expletive—and subsequently he threatened to blow her husband's brains out as well.

In consequence of that a summons was taken out against him, but he did not appear, and a warrant was granted against him. He seemed to have known that a warrant had been obtained, and from that time until October he was not seen in the neighbourhood.

To be quite out of the way of his annoyance the Dysons decided to remove, and took a house at Bannercross, a village about three miles to the west of Sheffield, and consequently about six miles from Darnall.

They removed on the 29th, following the furniture by train, and when they arrived at Bannercross the first person they saw was the prisoner. Some conversation took place between him and Mrs. Dyson, and the prisoner said, " I am here to annoy you, and I will annoy you wherever you go."

Mrs. Dyson told him there was a warrant out against him, and he replied that he did not care for the warrant and he did not care for the police. That sort of conversation would tend to show that there was the same bad blood, the same ill-feeling, in the breast of the prisoner against both Mrs. Dyson and her husband which had existed in the previous July.

Mr. Campbell Foster put in a plan of Bannercross-terrace, and described its surroundings to the jury. Prisoner, he added, went to the shop of a man named Gregory at the end of October, and engaged him in conversation, and at that time he was particularly noticed by Mrs. Gregory.

In about a month afterwards he again called, asked if her husband was in, and upon being answered in the negative, he went out and was seen to be loitering about.

During that time he was seen by a Mrs. Colgrave, who was going to Gregory's shop. The meeting took place in the road..

The prisoner engaged her in conversation, and asked if she would take him a message to Dyson's house, asking Mrs. Dyson to come out.

Mrs. Colgrave objected, upon which he made use of a coarse expression regarding Mrs. Dyson. At ten minutes to eight he was seen by a man named Brassington, who met Peace walking in front of the Bannercross Hotel.

They met under a gas-lamp, and prisoner inquired if he knew some strangers who had come to live there.

Witness did not, he said, and Peace showed him a bundle of notes and some photographs, but Brassington put them back, as he could not read.

They separated about ten minutes past eight. The jury would learn from Mrs. Dyson that about that time she had occasion to go to the closet in the yard. To do so she put on her clogs, and had to pass Gregory's back door.

After being in the closet a short time, she opened the door, and saw standing before her the man Peace, who had a revolver in his hand.

He presented it in her face, and said, "Speak, or I will fire."

The woman gave a loud and sudden shriek, and stepping back into the closet, slammed the door and fastened it.

She next heard her husband's footsteps, and Mrs. Gregory also came up, but when she saw Mr. Dyson she went into her own house and fastened the door. Hearing her husband's footsteps, Mrs. Dyson became emboldened, opened the closet door, and advanced towards the end of the passage.

Mr. Dyson passed her, and she saw Peace going out of the passage by the front. When he was a few steps from the gateway Mr. Dyson stepped after him.

According to Mrs. Dyson's statement, he was never near enough to touch Peace. Having got into the road, Peace fired his revolver, apparently at Mr. Dyson. The shot struck the stone lintel of the doorway at the entrance to the passage.

Mr. Dyson continued to advance, and before he had got out of the passage, Peace, who was on the road, again faced round and fired his revolver, and Mrs. Dyson saw her husband instantly fall.

She shrieked out, and was heard by a young man named Whitting to say, "Murder! You villain; you have shot my husband."

The learned counsel then proceeded further to describe how Peace escaped from Bannercross after the murder, and showed that Mr. Dyson died two hours after the bullet entered his temple.

He laid much stress on the fact that in a field which

the prisoner had crossed over on his way from Mr. Dyson's house, a packet of letters was found.

In this packet was the very card which Mr. Dyson had sent to the prisoner requesting him not to annoy his family.

There could, therefore, he said, be no doubt that the man who dropped the papers was Peace—the man in whose mind the card had produced so much ill-will and ill-feeling, and who had dogged the footsteps of the Dysons in the way he had described.

Mr. Foster next proceeded to show that after the murder Peace made his escape, and was not discovered until he was apprehended in the commission of a burglary at Blackheath.

He next showed what took place after his apprehension, and was proceeding to refer to the attempts made by Peace to escape on his way to Sheffield, when

Mr. Lockwood objected to the matter being gone into. He said it would of course be affectation on his part to object to its being mentioned, because it was notorious to everybody, but he certainly strongly protested against the course his learned friend was pursuing.

His Lordship said he considered the reference that Mr. Foster was making was quite unnecessary.

Mr. Foster said he was quite content to leave the matter as it was.

He proceeded to say that if the jury believed the circumstantial evidence which showed the prisoner to have been at Bannercross from seven o'clock up to ten minutes past eight—which traced him across that field, and found on his path a packet of letters, they could not but believe that the prisoner was the man who fired the shot which killed Mr. Dyson.

With what intent did he do it? Did he do it maliciously and with the intent to do the full charge mentioned in the indictment? With what object did he go from Darnall to Ecclesall, hanging about the house, threaten Mrs. Dyson, and tell Brassington the scandalous story of which they would hear?

Did all that point to malice, to malignity, to hate? He thought it did. If the jury came to the conclusion that it was the hand of prisoner who shot poor Mr. Dyson, and if they found that the motive which prompted him to do it was a malicious and a premeditated motive, then he thought they could come to no other conclusion than that the prisoner committed the crime charged, and that he did it with malice aforethought.

Mr. Johnson, of the firm of Holmes and Johnson, architects and surveyors, of Sheffield, produced a plan of Bannercross, showing the house in which Mr. Dyson lived, and the gardens and fields adjoining.

MRS. DYSON'S EVIDENCE.

Mrs. Dyson, whose appearance in the witness-box aroused great interest in court, said she was the widow of Arthur Dyson, who was shot at Bannercross in 1876.

She lived with her husband in Britannia-road, Darnall, and at that time the prisoner resided in the next house.

She knew him then as Charles Peace, a picture-framer, and he frequently visited their house until her husband, annoyed at his visits, sent him a card requesting him not to annoy his family.

In July of the same year the prisoner threatened to blow out their brains, and put a pistol within six inches of her face.

PEACE CONDUCTED BY THE OFFICERS TO THE PRISON VAN.

A warrant was taken out against him for this, but he still continued to annoy them; so they removed on the 25th of October to Bannercross, where they hoped to be freed from his disagreeable visits.

But the very night they removed the prisoner appeared at Bannercross, and said to her " You see I am here to annoy you wherever you go."

On the 29th of November, about ten minutes past eight in the evening, she went to the closet behind the house, and when she opened the door to come out she was confronted by the prisoner, who stood near the closet doorway with a revolver in his hand. He said, " Speak, or I'll fire."

She screamed, and stepped back into the closet and

shut herself in; but, hearing her husband's footsteps in the yard she came out. Prisoner was then in the passage leading to the road; but, being followed by her husband, he turned round and fired.

That, bullet struck the wall, and on getting to the bottom of the passage the prisoner fired again. The second shot struck her husband in the temple, and he fell.

She screamed and the neighbours came, but in the meantime the prisoner had scaled the wall on the opposite side of the road and fled.

Her husband did not speak after he was shot, and died the same night about eleven o'clock.

Cross-examined by Mr. Lockwood : Before going to the closet I put my little boy to bed. The bed-room is in the front. There was a light in the room.

My husband at this time was downstairs reading, and when I went to the closet I left him still reading. I said nothing to him before going to the closet. I had to pass through the room where he was. When I heard him coming I came out of the closet.

[A plan of the premises was then put into witness's hands, and she said she did not understand it very well.]

Cross-examination resumed : I was only four or five feet from the passage leading to the closet when my husband passed me to go down to the prisoner. I could see him plainly, and all that he did. He was going rather slowly.

I am prepared to swear that my husband never touched the prisoner before the shots were fired. He could not get near enough to him. Of course I cannot say what he intended doing.

I remember being before the coroner, but I cannot remember that I said to him that I could not say "whether my husband attempted to get hold of Peace or not ;" but if I did say so it is correct.

The account which I gave to the coroner is the correct one. I cannot swear that my husband did not attempt to get hold of the prisoner, but I can swear that he did not succeed in doing so. I distinctly swear that he never touched the prisoner.

When were you first so certain of this ?—I have been certain all the time.

Were you certain about it on the 24th of January last ?—Yes ; as certain as I am now.

When before the magistrates did you say this : " I cannot say. My husband did not get hold of the prisoner ?" I cannot say that he did not try.

Mr. Lockwood contended that this was not an answer, and a conversation took place between Mr. Campbell Foster and the judge on the matter.

On the question being repeated, Mrs. Dyson said : I cannot swear I did not use the words just quoted. I will not swear I did not. Having heard the words, I still pledge my oath that my husband did not get hold of the prisoner. I don't remember swearing before the magistrates that my husband didn't get hold of the prisoner.

What I said before the magistrate is correct. I noticed how my husband fell. He fell on his back. Nothing touched him before he fell. I will swear that after the first shot was fired my husband did not get hold of the prisoner.

He did not catch hold of the prisoner's arm which held the revolver, and the prisoner did not strike my husband on the chin and nose.

I will positively swear that my husband was never touched on the face except by the bullet which the prisoner fired.

How long have you known Peace ?—Between three and four years. I never saw him before I saw him at Darnall. I cannot say whether I or my husband first made his acquaintance. He lived next door but one to us. My husband began to dislike him in the spring of 1876.

Was he jealous ?—No.

Do you remember showing your husband a photo of yourself and the prisoner ?—Yes. It was taken at the Sheffield fair.

How came you to be photographed together ?—We went to the fair together with some children. The children were photographed, but we were in a sepa-rate picture. I cannot say whether it was the summer or winter fair. It was summer fair, but I cannot say whether it was the summer of 1876. It certainly was not in 1875.

If it was in the summer of 1876, how was it you were photographed with a man of whom your husband disapproved in the spring of that year ?—I think there must be a mistake in the dates. I cannot say. I had known the prisoner for more than a year in November, 1876. I may have known him since the spring of the previous year, but I won't be certain. I cannot say when we went to Darnall. I mean the jury to understand that I cannot tell within three or four months. When before the coroner I stated that we had been in England three years, and that we lived for a year with my husband's mother. I also stated that afterwards we lived at Highfield. We did not remain there more than four or five months. We next went to Heeley, and remained three or four months. From there we went to Darnall. I still say I do not remember when we went to Darnall. We were there a few months before the prisoner. He framed four pictures for us. I remember a conversa-tion about his framing the portrait of my husband's mother. I asked the prisoner to frame it. I mentioned the matter to the prisoner or his daughter, but I can-not say when it was. I did not write to ask him to send the frame. He never sent the frame. I never wrote asking him not to send it. I know nothing about the matter.

Mr. Lockwood : Look at that letter.—Witness, after looking at it, said : It's not mine, and I don't know whose it is.

Another letter was then handed to her, and she gave a similar answer.

Mr. Lockwood next handed to the witness a scrap of paper on which she wrote some words when before the magistrates, and asked her to look at it. This having been done, Mr. Lockwood asked : Did anybody know except yourself, your husband, and the pri-soner, that you wanted the portrait of your hus-band's mother framed ?—His wife and daughter knew.

Did you talk to them about it ?—I mentioned it to the daughter. I remember going on one occasion to Mansfield. That was in the summer of 1876. I don't recollect the month. Mrs. Padley went with me. I had not told Peace that I was going. I went by an afternoon train to Mansfield.

Did you ever write to the prisoner, telling him you were going by the nine o'clock train ?—No.

Did you tell him he must not go by train, " because he (Dyson) will go down with me," and also say, " Don't let him see anything if you meet me in the Wicker. Hope nothing will turn up to prevent it. Love to Janie ?" Did you write that ?—No.

Just look at that (handing up the note just read) —That is not my handwriting. I was not in the habit of dealing with Francis Walker, wholesale and retail grocer and Italian warehouseman, at High-street, Attercliffe.

At any rate, when you got to Mansfield he was there ?—Yes.

And you told him you were going ?—No.

Can you account for his being there ?—No, I can't. He was a constant source of annoyance to me, and was always following me.

Do you remember the prisoner giving you a ring ?—Yes. He gave it to me in the winter ; at least I cannot tell when it was, or the year.

Was it before or after you were photographed together ?—That I cannot say. I cannot say, too, if I showed it to my husband. I know I threw it away. The ring did not fit me.

Did you ever write this : " I do not know what train we shall go by, for I have a great deal to do this morning? Will see as soon as I possibly can. I think it will be easier after you leave ; he won't watch so. The ring fits the little finger. Many thanks. Love to Janey. I will tell you what I think of, when I see you about arranging matters, if it will. Excuse the scribble." Now, did you write that ?—No.

Did you ever tell him that the ring would not fit ?—No.

Are you now prepared to swear that you did not write to acknowledge the ring ?—I did not.

Mr. Lockwood then asked the witness whether she preferred a steel or a quill pen to write with, and Mrs. Dyson said it made no difference.

A steel pen was given to her, and she wrote as follows from the dictation of the learned counsel : " I write to you these few lines to thank you for all your kindness, which I will never forget. I will write you a note when I can."

Mr. Lockwood : That is your best writing ?—Yes.

Witness continued : On one occasion I went to a public-house with the prisoner, but I cannot remember the date. I cannot say where the public-house is. The prisoner told me that there was a picture gallery there. My husband became dissatisfied after that.

Was it in consequence of your going to the public-house with the prisoner that he became dissatisfied ?—No.

Are you sure of that ?—Yes.

Did you tell him you had been to a public-house with the prisoner ?—Yes.

Was it after that he became dissatisfied ?—I can't say exactly. I know a public-house in the same street as that in which the prisoner lived. I don't know it by name, nor do I know a man named Craig as the landlord. I have been to a public-house where there was a picture gallery, and there I had a bottle of "pop."

Did you go to another public-house with the prisoner ?—Yes.

Did you see Craig ?—I don't know him.

Craig was then called into court, and Mrs. Dyson was asked, " Have you not been to the ' Marquis of Waterford ' public-house, in Russell-street, Sheffield, on several occasions, with the prisoner ?"—I may have been once or twice, but not more often.

When you have been with Peace has he not paid for drink for you ?—I have only had " pop " with him.

How many times have you been with him ?—I am sure of once, but I don't know that I have been any more times.

Do you remember when this was ?—No.

Did you tell your husband ?—I told him that Peace had introduced me to his brother.

Did you tell your husband that Peace had taken you to a public-house and paid for drink for you ?—Yes.

And after that he became dissatisfied ?—Yes.

Do you know the Norfolk Dining Rooms in Exchange-street ?—No.

Have you ever been to some dining rooms, near the Market-place, with the prisoner ?—Yes.

Alone, I mean ?—Never alone.

Never alone, you say. Call in John Wilson. (Witness called in.) Now look at that man. Did you ever see him in those dining rooms ?—Not to my knowledge.

Do you remember being introduced to that man by Peace ?—I never remember seeing him before.

Look at him again.—I have looked at him. I will swear I have not been to some dining rooms with Peace on several occasions. I have been to some near the market once. Then we were not alone. There were two children with us. They were my own little boy, and a child of Mrs. Padmore's. I had refreshment there. That was at the time of the Sheffield fair—the same fair at which I was photographed—the same day that I had been photographed with Peace. And these children went to the dining-room.

What had become of your husband ?—He was away from home.

Was he not at the fair ?—Yes. I saw him there and met him in the evening after the photograph was taken. My husband did not come into the fair until evening.

Do you know a music-hall in Spring-street, Sheffield ?

Witness : What is the name of it.

Mr. Lockwood : The " Star."

Witness ; Is it a picture-gallery ?

Mr. Lockwood : I don't know.

A man named Goodlad was called into court, and Mr. Lockwood asked the witness : Have you ever been to the " Star " music-hall with Peace ?—I don't know it by that name.

Have you been to any music-hall with Peace ?—I have been to a place where there is a picture-gallery, and where it looked as if singing went on. There was a small stage and tables and chairs.

Do you remember being introduced to that man by Peace at a music-hall ?—I never remember seeing his face before, except at the Town Hall.

Have you not been three or four times to the music-hall in Spring-street ?—No ; I have only been once. I know a public-house at Darnall, called the " Halfway House." To my knowledge, I have never had drink there which was put down to Peace.

That won't do. Are you prepared to swear that you have not had drink there on Peace's credit ?—Never to my knowledge.

Though the witness was pressed severely on the point, this was the only answer that could be obtained.

I have shown you some letters—have you written a letter to the prisoner ?—No.

Do you know a little girl named Elizabeth Hutton ? Call Elizabeth Hutton.

On the child coming forward, the learned counsel asked : Can you swear you never sent that child with a note to Peace ?—Not with a note.

What did you send her with ?—I sent her with receipts for some pictures which the prisoner had framed. He was in the habit of asking my husband to write out his receipts and letters.

Now look at the child again. Will you swear that child has not brought back notes from Peace to you ? —She brought me one, and I returned it. I can't say when this was, but it was after Peace removed to the opposite side of the street at Darnall. I never gave the child anything for taking notes to Peace. I don't know a man named Kirkham. (Kirkham was here called.) I never gave him any notes for Peace, but I gave him a couple of receipts. Those receipts were for picture-framing. Kirkham has not brought notes from Peace.

Can you swear that?—Not to my knowledge, he has not.

Can you swear one way or the other?—I can swear he has not—not to my knowledge.

Did you ever send that litttle girl for drink to the "Halfway House?"—Not to my knowledge.

By that I understand that you won't swear either one way or the other?—I have sent her for beer, but not to the "Halfway House" in particular.

Now I want to bring you to the night before the murder. Were you, on the 28th of November, 1876, at the "Stag Hotel," Sharrow?—Yes. I was there with Mrs. Padmore's little boy. He is about five or six years of age.

Was anybody else with you?—No.

Mrs. Redfern, the landlady of "The Stag," was called into the court, and Mr. Lockwood asked: Was there not a man with you?—No; I was by myself.

Now (looking at Mrs. Redfern), will you swear that?—A man followed me in and sat down beside me.

Was that man the prisoner?—No.

Will you swear that?—I would almost swear that the prisoner was not the man.

That will not do. On your oath, did not this man go into the "Stag" on that night with you?—No, he did not.

Did he not follow you in?—I don't know that he did, unless he made himself different from what he is now.

On your oath was it not this man?—To the best of my belief it was not. He seemed a man about thirty-five years of age.

What did you mean by saying just now that you would almost swear he was not the man?—Because he was so much in the habit of disguising himself.

So it might have been him? Did you speak to the man?—I don't remember.

Did he speak to you?—He asked me where I had been, or where I was going, or something of that kind.

Did you answer him? Yes, I passed some remark.

Did the man go out when you went out?—Yes, he followed me out.

Do you mean, on your oath, to say that you did not see the prisoner, and that he did not tell you he would come to see you the next night?—No, he did not.

Did he say anything to you?—Nothing particular, because I did not take any notice of him.

Not after you left the public-house?—I did not speak to him after leaving the public-house.

Did you think at the time that it might have been the prisoner?—I had not the slightest thought. I had not been in the fair that night. I passed by. I might have said to Mrs. Redfern that I had been. I had not been in any public-house before going into the "Stag." I had previously been to the house of some friends of mine named Muddiman.

Did you tell Peace that you were going there?—Witness: What had he to do with it?

Answer the question.—Mr. Muddiman does not live at Sharrow.

Will you swear you did not tell him that?—I did not. I did not see the prisoner at all.

How long were you at Mr. Muddiman's?—Perhaps an hour or so.

And from there you went to the "Stag"?—Yes.

Witness continued: I have seen the landlady of the "Halfway House" at Darnall here.

Have you ever been turned out of that house on account of being drunk?—No.

What! never?—No. I have never been drunk in my life.

Will you swear this?—Yes.

Bring in the landlady. Now, will you swear you have never been drunk in this woman's house?—Well I might have been slightly inebriated. (Laughter.)

Will you swear you have never been turned out of the house for being "slightly inebriated?"—No, not to my knowledge.

Mr. Lockwood: Quite true. You might not have been aware of it. That is all I ask you.

Mrs. Dyson was then re-examined by Mr. Foster, who asked: You have been questioned as to whether your husband got hold of Peace. Are you quite sure that he never tried to get hold of Peace?

The question was objected to by Mr Lockwood.

Continuing, Mr. Foster asked: Can you tell me how your husband fell?—The witness: On his back rather slanting.

Was that in the passage or in the little court?—It was in the little court.

What is the width of the court?—It is about twice as wide as the passage.

Did you observe when he fell whether the side of his face went against the wall or not?—He fell close to the wall, slanting, and then on his back.

You have been asked about going to a dining-room, near the market, with two children. I think you answered that you went for refreshments?—Yes. The children were hungry, and I went to give them some refreshment.

My friend has asked you about a man bringing a note to you from Peace. Is that correct?—Yes, but I sent it back again.

Have any others been sent to you by Peace at all?—Not to my knowledge.

My friend got out the last answer from you about Mrs. Norton, that you might have left the house "slightly inebriated." How did it occur?—I cannot tell. I might be slightly inebriated, but I cannot tell.

The Judge: You said the prisoner came to the closet door?—Yes.

How long was it after that the first shot was fired?—About a minute or two? It may be a little more.

What time elapsed between the first shot and the second?—About a second; it was almost immediately.

So far as you could see, did he stand in the same place when he fired both shots?—No; he stood on the lower step when he fired the second shot, and in the yard when he fired the first.

How far was your husband away from the prisoner at the time?—They were about four feet apart. There were only two steps between them. The prisoner was on the bottom step.

This concluded the examination of the witness, and the court adjourned for half an hour.

On the re-assembling of the court, Mr. Lockwood said if the case for the prosecution lasted till five o'clock he should ask his lordship to adjourn the defence till the following day.

His Lordship said that if it would be a convenience to Mr. Lockwood, he would certainly do so.

Mr. Lockwood added that if the case for the prosecution was over before five, he should not then ask his lordship to adjourn, but would proceed with the defence and finish the case that evening.

Mary Ann Gregory, wife of John Gregory, grocer, Bannercross, said she lived next door to the house occupied by the Dysons, and on the night of the murder the prisoner who had previously visited the shop, came again and asked to see her husband, who was away. The prisoner left the house, going down the road. An hour afterwards she saw Mrs. Dyson walking towards the closet, and two minutes afterwards heard her scream loudly. She told Mr. Dyson to go to his wife immediately, and he went directly along the passage. She then heard a banging noise, or rather two noises, and heard footsteps coming up the passage. The next thing she saw was Mr. Dyson bleeding from the head as he was propped up in a chair in his own house.

In answer to Mr. Lockwood, the witness said she heard Mrs. Dyson scream within a couple of minutes of her going into the closet. When Mr. Dyson left to go down in the direction of the closet he walked quickly.

Sarah Colgraves, wife of Thomas Colgraves, of Dobbin-hill, said she remembered going to the shop kept by Gregory on the night of the 29th of November, about half-past seven o'clock. She met the prisoner about thirty yards from the shop, and he asked her if she knew who lived in the second house down the road. She said she did not. He asked if she knew whether they were strangers, and she replied in the affirmative. The prisoner then said, " Do you mind going to the house to say that an elderly gentleman wants to speak to her ?" Before that he had said, " You don't know them ?" and she replied, "No." He then said, " I will tell you. She is my b———." She told the prisoner he had better mind what he said, particularly to strangers, and told him to take the message himself. About ten minutes afterwards she saw the prisoner come out of the passage by the side of the house.

This witness was not cross-examined.

Charles Brassington, living in the Lane End, Ecclesall, said he was on the road near Bannercross, on the 29th of November, standing opposite the Bannercross Hotel, about twenty yards from Mr. Gregory's shop. It was about eight o'clock. The night was moonlight, and he noticed the prisoner walking to and fro on the causeway. Standing beneath a lamp at the time, he could see the prisoner quite distinctly. Peace approached him and said, " Have you any strange people come to live about here ?" He replied, " I don't know." Peace then showed him some photos and letters, and desired him to read the latter. He said he could not. The prisoner then told him that he would make it warm for those strangers, for he would shoot them, and after saying this Peace walked down the road towards Gregory's. He next saw the prisoner in Newgate, walking round the yard along with several others, and he was certain he was the man who uttered the threat at Bannercross.

In cross-examination the witness was severely questioned as to the date when he saw the prisoner and had the conversation with him. He admitted that he could not himself tell the date, but had been told by other witnesses.

Charles Wyville, living at Ecclesall, said on the night of the murder he was in the Bannercross Hotel,

when his attention was attracted by hearing two reports of a gun or pistol. On his going to the door to see what was the matter he heard Mrs. Dyson screaming " murder." He went in the direction of the screams and saw Mr. Dyson lying on the ground, with Mrs. Dyson holding his head.

Thomas Wilson, scythe-maker, of Brincliffe-hill, said he was outside the Banner-cross Hotel about twenty minutes past eight on the night of the 29th of November, when he heard two reports from a revolver. The sound came from Gregory's house, and on looking that way he saw a man run across the road from the end of Bannercross-terrace and get over the wall on the opposite side. It was a moonlight night, but as the man was crossing the road the moon was under a cloud and he did not see the man distinctly. But he heard Mrs. Dyson scream, and on going into the passage from which he had seen the man emerge, he found Mr. Dyson lying on the ground and Mrs. Dyson was holding up his head.

Mr. J. W. Harrison, of Sheffield, surgeon, said on the 29th of November, he was called by Thos. Wilson to see Mr. Dyson, who had been placed on a chair in his own house. He was unconscious, bleeding from the temple, and there was a quantity of blood on the floor. He laid the injured man on the floor and attended to him, but he did not recover consciousness, and died about half-past ten o'clock the same night. Subsequently he made a *post-mortem* examination. On the left temple there was a valvular wound in the skin, flesh, and muscles. On removing the scalp he found in the substance of the brain, running upwards and backwards, a groove, and on the right side of the brain he discovered the bullet produced. It had entered the temple and passed in an oblique line to the right side of the head. The cause of death was the entrance of the bullet to the brain.

By Mr. Lockwood : He found some light abrasions on the nose and chin. He did not think they were caused by a fist, because in the case of abrasions the skin was grazed. A fist he did not think would produce the effect, not even if there was a ring on the finger. The abrasions seemed to have been caused by sand. At the coroner's inquest he might have said he noticed a bruise on the nose and chin as if Mr. Dyson had fallen on his face. That really was correct, and he would adhere to that statement.

Police-constable Ward stated that on the 30th of November he searched in a field opposite Mr. Dyson's house at Bannercross. The field was divided from the house by a road, a garden, and a wall. About fifteen yards from the wall dividing Mr. Dyson's garden from the field he found a bundle of papers, and amongst them Mr. Dyson's card.

At this stage a discussion took place between the counsel on either side and the learned judge in regard to putting in the letters found by this witness.

Mr. Campbell Foster objected to their being put in, on the ground that they were irrelevant ; but Mr. Lockwood contended that his learned friend had gone too far, and that, inasmuch as he had opened the letters to the jury, he was bound to put them in now. His lordship entertained a contrary opinion, and consequently none of the documents were brought before the court.

Inspector Bradbury produced the bullet found by the surgeon in Mr. Dyson's brain.

At the request of Mr. Lockwood, witness produced the photograph of Mrs. Dyson and Peace taken in the fair ground.

He said it was handed over to him by Mr. Jackson, the chief constable at Sheffield.

Mrs. Dyson was here recalled, and in answer to Mr. Lockwood she said the photograph was that to which she referred in her evidence.

This was the whole of the evidence regarding the murder, and Mr. Foster proposed to call evidence of threats used by the prisoner against the Dysons in July, 1876.

Mr. Lockwood objected to this course, but his lordship ruled that the evidence was admissible.

Rose Annie Sykes, wife of James Sykes, Darnall, proved that on the 1st July, 1876, she saw Mr. Dyson coming down the street. The prisoner was following him, and endeavouring to trip him up. On the night of the same day she saw the prisoner take a revolver out of his pocket, point it at Mrs. Dyson's head, and say he would blow her brains out, and those of her husband, too.

Cross-examined by Mr. Lockwood: Witness said she heard nothing about a poker or a threat from Mrs. Dyson that she would would use one. She did not hear about this time of any disturbance with the police, or of Mrs. Dyson being inebriated. She was quite certain about the date, because her little boy was born on the Tuesday following.

James Sykes, Darnall, said on a day in July, 1876, he was with his wife and Mrs. Dyson at Darnall. Peace came up at the time, and Mrs. Dyson said "That's the man that's always annoying my husband." Peace replied, " I will annoy your husband and you and all." At the same time he pulled a revolver out of his pocket, and presenting it at Mrs. Dyson, said, " I'll blow your brains out and your husband's too." Peace then went up a passage, as if he was going into Mr. Dyson's back door. He returned in a minute, and said, " Now, Jem, you be a witness that she struck me with a life-preserver." Witness replied, "No, I will be a witness that you threatened to take her life." He did not notice that Mrs. Dyson had a life-preserver, or that she struck at the prisoner.

During the examination of this witness Peace seemed somewhat excited, and kept muttering to himself.

Jane Wadmore said, in 1876 she was living in Britannia-road, Darnall. She knew both Mrs. Dyson and Mr. and Mrs. Sykes.

On the 1st of July in that year she was talking with them, when the prisoner came up. Mrs. Dyson said to him, "Why do you annoy my husband in the way you do?" Peace replied, "I will annoy you. I will blow your brains out and your husband's too before I have done with you." Peace then went in the direction of Mrs. Dyson's back door, and subsequently went into his own house.

In answer to Mr. Lockwood, witness said she remembered going to Mansfield with Mrs. Dyson. Peace did not accompany them, but he followed them. On their arriving at Mansfield, she and Mrs. Dyson went to a house for some refreshments. Peace followed them right into the room, and called for a bottle of something to drink. She did not leave Mrs. Dyson alone with Peace on the occasion. Mrs. Dyson returned home with her. Peace did not ride in the same compartment, nor did he treat them to anything to drink. She did not accompany Mrs. Dyson to a fair, but she remembered that there was a fair in Whitweek of 1876.

Police-constable Robinson, of the Metropolitan Police Force, related the well-known circumstances under which he captured the prisoner when committing a burglary at Blackheath on the 10th of October, 1878,

and described how he was fired at by Peace three times, and was wounded by the third shot.

Charles Brown, sergeant in the Metropolitan Police, who went to the assistance of the last witness, produced the revolver taken from the prisoner on the occasion.

James Woodward, a gunmaker, of Manchester, examined the revolver produced, and said it contained seven barrels. He believed it was of Belgian manufacture. The bullet produced found in Mr. Dyson's head would fit the barrels.

In reply to Mr. Lockwood, witness said the revolver was of a common description.

This was the evidence for the prosecution.

Mr. Campbell Foster then summed up the evidence. He said, if it was true that Mrs. Dyson was on terms of intimacy with the prisoner, was that any justification for his shooting her husband? He characterised strongly the attempts made to discredit the evidence of Mrs. Dyson, and to prejudice the jury against her; and he showed what a conclusive case this was against the prisoner, even excluding the testimony of the murdered man's widow. But taking Mrs. Dyson's evidence, as reasonable men must take it, the case against the prisoner was irresistible.

Mr. Lockwood then rose (at five o'clock) to address the jury on behalf of the prisoner. In the course of a powerful appeal he declared that there had been a wild and merciless cry for blood, which was a disgrace to the country, and he spoke fiercely against the action of the press in this matter.

This remark elicited a low " Hear, hear," from the prisoner, who listened with the utmost eagerness to the words advanced on his behalf.

The learned counsel maintained that he had placed Mrs. Dyson's evidence in a light which necessitated a most suspicious examination on the part of the jury. It had been all-important to show at the time when Mr. Dyson became dissatisfied with his wife, she was still keeping up communication with the prisoner; and he claimed to have done this. Pointing especially to her prevarication as to the date of the fair at which she was photographed, the learned counsel claimed to have irretrievably shaken the testimony of Mrs. Dyson by means of the persons with whom he had confronted her. He dwelt emphatically upon her answers as to what transpired at the " Stag " Inn on the night before the murder, and her credibility, he insisted, was an essential element, because other than that woman and the prisoner no one could say what took place at Bannercross. The theory he adduced was that Peace fired a first shot to frighten Dyson; that a struggle ensued, and that during the struggle the pistol went off and killed the man. That was not murder, he pointed out. Mr. Lockwood maintained that there was strong corroborative evidence of a struggle. Turning to the letters, he commented strongly on the refusal of the prosecution to put them in evidence. They dared not place in the hands of the jury documents which might throw light upon the case, and might benefit the prisoner. Was not that an additional reason for looking with suspicion upon the woman who was accused of writing them? The whole case depended on Mrs. Dyson's testimony, and it was not upon such evidence that human life should be taken. A detailed examination of the statements of the other witnesses followed, Mr. Lockwood maintaining that all these were consonant with his defence, or were fatal to Mrs. Dyson's statement. He did not deny that his client had been a wild and reckless man, and it would be quite possible for one with such a temperament to use threats which he did not intend to carry out. He appealed to the jury to spare the man's life. However bad he might have been, he was all the less fitted to die. But he had stronger grounds, and he asked whether on the uncorroborated testimony of that woman they were going to condemn this man to die? He concluded with a powerful appeal to the jury.

In summing up, the learned judge briefly defined murder as distinguished from manslaughter. The theory of the defence was that there had been a struggle between the two men; that the first shot had been fired merely to frighten, and that the second was the result of accident in the struggle. If that was the opinion of the jury, then they could not find the prisoner guilty of murder, but it was important to tell them that this was only a theory, and was not supported by a particle of evidence. The jury would be shown a revolver taken from the prisoner, which it was suggested was like the one, if not the same, which had been in his possession on the evening of the sad occurrence, and it would be for the jury to say for themselves whether they thought such a weapon could have gone off accidentally. To press home their theory the prisoner's counsel discredited the testimony of Mrs. Dyson, and it would be for the jury to carefully weigh her evidence. At the same time he would remind them that the case did not rest alone on her evidence.

His lordship having remarked that no one could regret more than he did that the case had been talked about and written of so much, then proceeded to read over the evidence.

THE VERDICT AND THE SENTENCE.

The jury retired to consider their verdict at a quarter past seven, and returned into court ten minutes subsequently.

Having answered to their names,

The Clerk of Arraigns asked: Are you agreed upon your verdict? Do you find the prisoner at the bar guilty or not guilty?

The Foreman: Guilty.

The Clerk of Arraigns (addressing the prisoner): You have been indicted and convicted of wilful murder. Have you anything to say why sentence should not be passed upon you according to law?

The prisoner (very faintly): It's no use my saying anything.

One of the ushers having called for silence,

His Lordship said: Charles Peace, after a most careful trial, and after every argument has been urged by your learned counsel on your behalf which ingenuity can suggest, you have been found guilty of the murder of Arthur Dyson by a jury of your country. It is not my duty, still less is it my desire, to aggravate your feelings at this moment, by a recapitulation of any portion of the details of what, I fear, I can only recall your criminal career. Imploring you, during the short time that may remain to you to live, to prepare for eternity, I pass upon you that sentence, and the only sentence, which the law permits in cases of this kind. (Here his lordship assumed the black cap.) The sentence is that you be taken from this place to the place from whence you came, and thence to a place of execution, and that you be there hanged by the neck until you are dead; and that your body be buried within the precincts of the prison in which you shall have been last confined after your conviction. And may the Lord have mercy on your soul!

The prisoner was then removed from the dock, but before leaving he expressed his thanks to Mr. W. E.

Clegg for the efforts he had made in his behalf, and his appreciation of all that had been done for him.

Immediately after he was handcuffed, and leg chains were put upon him. The prisoners' van was then backed to the inner gate of the Town Hall.

Peace walked along the corridors to the gate, muttering as he went. He was lifted into the van, and he was driven to Armley gaol shortly before eight.

Mr. Keene, the governor of the gaol, accompanied the van. There was one warder outside, and four warders were inside with Peace.

The only meals which he had on Tuesday, at the Town Hall, were breakfast and dinner, both of which he ate heartily.

Mrs. Dyson, attended by Inspector Bradbury, and several of the witnesses for the prosecution, left Leeds for Sheffield the same night by the 10.5 train.

CHAPTER CLXIII.

AFTER CONVICTION—PEACE AT ARMLEY GAOL—INTERVIEW WITH HIS RELATIVES—PEACIANA.

THE accounts which appeared in the several papers of the condition of Charles Peace were at this time most conflicting. Some declared him to be in a sinking, desponding state, and hinted at his committing suicide if he was not carefully watched, while other journalists said he was perfectly resigned to his position, and was preparing, as best he could, to meet his doom with becoming fortitude.

Very much was made of the supposed letters which Peace dropped whilst running away from Bannercross on the night of the murder, and their supposed authorship by Mrs. Dyson.

They formed the subject of much of her cross-examination at the trial, and have been often referred to to show the terms of intimacy upon which she must have been with Peace. We are, therefore, glad to be able to say upon authority that the letters are not hers. That authority is none other than the statement of Mr. Dyson himself.

During the summer of 1876, when Mr. Dyson took out a peace warrant against Peace for threatening and annoying himself and family, he consulted Mr. Chambers, solicitor.

At that time the letters alleged to have been written by Mrs. Dyson to Peace were in existence, and had been seen by Mr. Dyson and other persons.

Mr. Dyson expressed to Mr. Chambers his full assurance that the letters were not his wife's, but were forgeries concocted by Peace for purposes of annoyance. He was anxious that Peace should not be able to bring the letters into court, for he felt sure he would do so, if possible, for the sake of further annoyance and persecutions.

Peace's step-son, accompanied by a friend, visited him in Armley Gaol. The cell was in a sort of cage within the cell, two sides made by the walls, and two composed of iron bars from floor to ceiling. Beyond this was the cell itself, into which no friends were allowed to pass.

The prisoner was dressed and sitting in a rail-backed arm chair, such as is common in old-fashioned public-houses. As the visitors entered his face was turned towards the door, and over his head, behind him, was a gas light.

Seated a little to the left, and looking him steadfastly in the face, was one warder; and behind him, a little to his right, was a second official—not lolling back in their chairs with folded arms, and endeavouring to make their irksome task as pleasant as possible.

Nothing of the kind. They were all attention, ready to spring forward to the convict in an instant.

Willie asked his father how he was, and he replied, "I am a little better, but very weak."

Dropping his head and breathing apparently with difficulty, he repeated, "I am really very weak." He then looked at the friend as much as to say, "Who are you?"

Willie told his father that his friend was the gentleman to whom he referred on the previous day; and the convict nodded, as though gratified to see him. Peace asked respecting the witnesses who could be collected at Darnall.

"There are plenty of people there," he said, " who can tell what sort of a woman Mrs. Dyson is, if you can only get them to come."

Then becoming more animated and apparently wishful to get closer to the bars which separated him from his friends, he made a move as though he would stand up and draw his chair towards them.

Instantly the warders were at his side, and one of them said, "Don't disturb yourself! We'll move you!" Instead, however, of drawing him nearer to his son, they lifted the chair perhaps a foot further from the visitors, nearer to the wall, and more immediately under the gas.

A savage scowl came over his face, and he gave them a look that plainly said, "That was not what I wanted."

An almost painful silence prevailed for a few moments, and then the convict looked at his son and said, "Do you know a house in Westbar, opposite to the top of Bower Spring? There is such a shop and such a shop (mentioning the business carried on in each), and then there is the house I mean."

Willie asked him if he meant the "Little Tankard" or the "Old Tankard?"

The convict said he did not mean the singing-room. It was a little low house, with a shop front. Asked if it was opposite the "Shakespeare," he answered, "Yes, it is opposite the 'Shakespeare.' It is a little beershop, with a passage up the side of it. The window of the snug looked into the passage. One day I was in the snug alone with Mrs. Dyson, and the landlord went out at the front door, down the passage, and peeped in at the window. I want you to get him to come to tell the jury what he saw. He will remember us; try and get him to come."

Peace was then asked if anything occurred during the fortnight between his leaving Hull after the quarrel with his family, and the 29th of November, when Mr. Dyson was shot.

The convict replied, "I went from Hull to Manchester, and after stopping there three or four days, I went to Sheffield. Oh, yes; I went backwards and forwards to Sheffield several times." I saw Mrs. Dyson more than once, and he repeated what he had said several times before, that on the evening of the 28th he was at the "Stag," at Sharrow with her.

The convict was then asked where he went when he left Hull after the affair at Bannercross?

" I went from Hull to Cottingham, then to Beverley, and then to York. I there took train to London; but got out at a little station before I got to London, and went by the Underground to Paddington. From Paddington I went down to Didcot, from Didcot to Oxford, then to Bath, and on to Bristol. They will know that I was down there by this fact, that when going, I think it was from Didcot to Oxford, I travelled in the same compartment as a police-sergeant. He had been somewhere, and had apprehended a young woman for stealing £40, and he was bringing her to lock her up. I sat next to him, and talked to him nearly all the way, and he told me all about the case. He seemed a very smart chap; but not smart enough to know me. If you can find out the day an officer took a girl to Oxford that is the day I travelled there. I stopped in Bristol a few days and did a little 'work,' and then I left for Nottingham, and reached there, I remember, on the 9th January, or about six weeks after I had left Bannercross."

Peace, apparently proud of the manner in which he had gone shoulder to shoulder with the police, went on to tell them how he once lodged at the house of a police-sergeant in Hull. He also entertained his friends with the story of his escape through the bars of the bedroom at Nottingham. It exactly corresponded with the version given more than a week before, and subsequently confirmed by Mrs. Thompson.

The convict seemed pleased to have someone to speak to, and he would laugh when he told them that he once threatened to report an officer for insulting him.

Willie asked him when that occurred.

The convict replied: In the summer after that affair at Bannercross I went down to York to see the races. The militia were up, and one day I found myself standing by the side of Mr. Cooke, who lived next door to us when we were on the Brocco. I think he was doing duty as a military policeman. I knew him, but he did not know me. A row broke out whilst I was there amongst a lot of the militiamen, who were drunk, and presently a mounted policeman rode up to help to quell it. He rode close past me, and his horse nearly knocked me down. I went after him, got hold of his horse's bridle, and insisted on knowing his number. A superior officer came up and said, "Don't stop him now, while the row is on. Come in the morning, if you have a complaint against him." I replied "All right; I'll be there; I'll see if he is to knock people down like that." Of course, said the convict, I did not go to pick him out. If you mention it to Cooke he will remember it.

On Monday Mrs. Bolsover, the daughter of the convict, with her little baby in her arms, and her husband, visited him. Peace, although dressed, was lying down in his little bed, and by his side were his two warders. The convict heard the visitors enter, and roused himself. Seeing his son-in-law, he said "How art thou, Billy?" The young man appeared overpowered, and he was unable to reply. Seeing his daughter, Peace then said, "Come forward, Jennie, and sit down." She stepped forward, and sat on the little seat to the left of the door, but still within the barred enclosure.

" Have you" said he, "brought the baby with you?" The daughter replied that she had. "Then," said he, " Let me look at it." The mother held the child up to the bars, and Peace exclaimed with much earnestness, " God in heaven bless its little soul." Peace asked how his wife was, and whether she fretted much. He was told that she was very poorly and in low spirits. "I should like to see her," he said; "I should like to see her." He then asked what efforts were being made for his defence, and if they remembered a row that took place one day at Darnall when Mrs. Dyson came out of her house with a " potato masher" and challenged any of the neighbours to fight. They did remember such an occurrence, and he asked that some who witnessed it might be called to speak to it.

Mr. Bolsover told him that Mr. Hutton's little girl, who carried notes from Mrs. Dyson to Peace, was coming forward.

PEACE GIVING HIS SPECTACLES TO HIS WIFE AS A KEEPSAKE.

The Convict : I am very glad to hear that. Heaven bless her ! I hope she will come.

Mr. Bolsover reminded him that two persons were in the 'bus with him and Mrs. Dyson when they rode up to the "Stag" at Sharrow on the night before the Bannercross affair, and told him that one of them would come forward and speak to that fact if he was asked.

The convict was pleased, and said, I hope you will tell Mr. Clegg all about that, and look after that witness.

The convict then alluded to the current version of the circumstances under which he jumped from the express train when on his way to Sheffield, and he said the warders stated that one of them caught him by the foot and held him head downwards for a distance of nearly two miles. Nothing of the sort, he said. Before he left London he made up his mind to jump from the train, and to kill himself if he could. When the train had passed Worksop, he stood up on the foot-warmer, put his hands together, and sprang clean through the window. His heels struck the top of the window, and he fell head first on the footboard, and bounded away from the train. He did not remember anything that occurred after that until late in the afternoon. He declared the warder never had hold of his foot—otherwise he could have held him. He had not the slightest intention of escaping; he wanted to kill himself.

Mr. Bolsover told him he understood that the prosecution were going to bring down a gunsmith from London to prove that the bullets found at Blackheath and the bullet found in Mr. Dyson's head were of the same size.

The convict replied that he had four revolvers—a little one that had five chambers, one that had six, one that had seven, and one that had ten chambers. The six-chambered one taken from him at Blackheath carried the same size bullet as the seven chamber. He did not attach much importance to evidence of that sort.

The convict then expressed the hope that Mr. Bolsover would take warning by what had befallen him; told them that he did not care who came forward against him if they only spoke the truth, and then asked to be allowed to shake hands with them. He was told that that could not be allowed; his friends withdrew, and the interview terminated.

Peace is said to have made an extraordinary statement respecting the murder. He stated that on the night Mr. Dyson was shot he was at Bannercross at the request of Mrs. Dyson, with whom he had an appointment. On reaching the house, he saw her go upstairs, and he alleged that she made signs to him signifying that Mr. Dyson was within, and that he (Peace) was not to enter the house. In consequence of these signs he remained outside, and, presently, Mrs Dyson came into the yard with a lighted candle. She went into the closet and he followed her and remained talking to her for some time. At the time there was a warrant out against Peace, at the instance of the Dysons, and he asked Mrs. Dyson to get her husband to withdraw it. She replied, "I can't do it; you know what an old devil he is for cash; he wants £40 to square the matter." At this moment Mr. Dyson came out in the yard, and, according to Peace, a struggle took place between the deceased and his wife, in the course of which a pistol which Mrs. Dyson had in her hand went off. Peace then ran away.

PEACE'S EARLY CRIMES.

We now give some authentic particulars of Peace's childhood and youth. It is said that when, having recovered from two years' illness caused by an accident at Kelham Rolling Mills, he had been in the service of Mr. Edward Smith, and had after that become, under the tuition of one Bethley, a player on the violin at public-houses. There is a tradition that soon after this, having had a quarrel with his sister, he slept out, in an empty house, was caught, and got a month's imprisonment therefor. Whether this be so or not, the next glimpse we get of him is making a highly promising commencement in his future profession. He was charged at the Sheffield Sessions on Saturday, Dec. 13, 1851, along with George Campbell, with breaking into the house of Mrs. Catherine Ward, Mount View, and stealing two pistols, a mahogany box, a bullet mould, and other articles. An entrance apparently had been effected by climbing upon the balcony and

opening the bedroom window. The only property missed was a case containing Mrs. Ward's jewels, a case containing a brace of rifle pistols, and a silk dress. The jewel case was found unopened on the balcony. The prisoners were afterwards found dealing with the pistols; Campbell was discharged, while Peace, who received a good character for honesty from his employer, got one month's imprisonment. This robbery shows how closely Peace adhered through life to the *modus operandi* adopted thus early, and it fixes his then age (19).

A CROP OF BURGLARIES IN 1854.

During the subsequent years 1852-3-4, he continued his musical services at public-houses, and became familiar with company no better than it should be. In the autumn of 1854 he carried on a daring game of house robbery, and it appeared, that on the 13th of October, 1854, Charles Peace, Mary Ann Niel, his sister, and Emma James were placed in the dock of the Town Hall to answer several charges of felony. James had offered a pair of boots in pledge at the shop of Messrs. Wright, Westbar, and on her being detained on suspicion, Peace came forward and claimed the boots, and was given into custody. In Peace's mother's house in Bailey-field, there were found a large quantity of jewellery and wearing apparel (including crape shawls, silk dresses, &c.), the proceeds of robberies effected at the residences of H. E. Hoole, Esq., Crookes Moor House; R. Stuart, Esq., Brincliffe Edge; Mr. G. F. Platt, Priory Villa, Sharrow-lane; and Mr. Brown, Broomhall-street. The houses of all these parties had been robbed by effecting an entrance through the bedroom windows in the evening before the windows were closed and fastened for the night. At Mr. Hoole's the thief had climbed the portico, and from Mr Stuart's a good deal of jewellery had been stolen. The prisoners were clearly proved to have been in possession of this property. The defence raised did not place in a very amiable light the affection subsisting between the sister and that brother who used to avenge the wrongs she sustained at her husband's hands. Each accused the other of being the culprit. At the sessions at Doncaster (October, 20, 1854), Peace (who was undefended) said that a watchmaker named Bethley, in Division-street, had kept his sister (Neil) for some years, and she had had three children by him. Bethley, not having given her any money lately, sent the jewellery and a bundle of wearing apparel by him to her, instead of money. Peace was sentenced to four years' penal servitude, and the female prisoners each to six months' imprisonment.

Peace was described in the calendar at that time as being 22 years of age. The mention of Bethley's name will remind our readers that he was the person who instructed Peace in the art of violin-playing, and Mrs. Neil's connection with the case does not shed much lustre on the family annals. She died we may add by way of completing her history, on the 2nd April, 1859, aged 33.

MARRIAGE AND SIX YEARS' PENAL SERVITUDE.

The matrimonial alliance with Miss James was, of course, rudely interrupted by the sentence pronounced at Doncaster. The tender passion does not seem to have survived his four years of penal servitude. It is believed that Peace served his whole term of four years. This brings us to the October of 1858, and the term of imprisonment conflicts with Mrs. Peace's statement, that she was married to him in July, 1858. On his liberation he resumed his strolling vocation of fiddling at public-houses and feasts. It was at one of these that he met Hannah Ward, a widow, with one son

Willie, and she became his wife. He was then earning a fair livelihood, partly in the way mentioned and partly by hawking cutlery, but his ingrained fondness for entering the houses of others, and for appropriating goods that did not belong to him, had not been eradicated by his prison discipline, and it was not many months after her marriage that Mrs. Peace's eyes were enlightened as to the extra-professional avocation of her husband by a police visit to her house. The police at Manchester, having discovered a quantity of stolen property in a place of concealment, set a watch, and caught, but not without a violent resistance, two men who came to remove the goods. One of the prisoners gave the name of George Parker, and they both hailed from Sheffield. Parker was really Charles Peace, the other being the keeper of a beershop in Spring-street. They were tried at Liverpool Assizes, August, 1859, when Parker (Peace) was sentenced to six years' penal servitude, and his companion to fifteen months' hard labour.

DARING ADVENTURE AT WAKEFIELD.

In serving his time Peace made the acquaintance of the prisons of Millbank, Chatham (where he was mixed up in a mutiny, for his share in which he was punished —flogged), and Gibraltar. His handiness caused him then, as at other times, to be employed as a sort of general utility man about the prisons, doing any odd jobs in which dexterity and tact were needed. It was this sort of work which enabled him to make that daring attempt to escape from Wakefield during one of his sojourns there. Perhaps it is worth while to tell the story in some detail. The repairs he was executing gave him an excuse for smuggling a short ladder into his cell, and an opportunity also of nicking for himself a sort of saw out of a piece of zinc or tin. Thus armed he cut through a beam in the ceiling, made a hole through the plaster, and got through on to the roof. He was just drawing the ladder after him when an official opened the cell door. As he attempted to seize the ladder Peace gave him a blow with it in the chest and knocked him down. Then running along the roof he got on to the prison wall and was making his way along it when, the bricks being loose, he fell. It was supposed that he had fallen outside, and there was a hue and cry after him, but he had really fallen inside, not far from where some servants were looking out from the door of the governor's house. Their attention was, however, directed away from Peace, and with the cunning of a hunted fox he slipped quietly past them into the house, and ran upstairs. Stripping off his prison clothes, he appropriated a suit of the governor's, and watched for an opportunity to escape. But none came; and after being in the bedroom for an hour and a half, he was found and recaptured.

THE PICTURE-FRAME BUSINESS.

At the end of November, 1859, not long after Peace's enforced departure for penal quarters, his wife gave birth to a daughter—now Mrs. Bolsover. The lonely wife had sold up her home to provide the means of defence at his trial, and had afterwards begun to keep a shop—that little bow-windowed shop so well known in Kenyon-alley. Hither he came, one night in the summer of 1864, the returned convict, released on ticket-of-leave, after serving nearly five of his six years.

It was now that he commenced that picture-frame making, which was the ostensible business of the remainder of his life. And for a time he seems to have been industrious, and to have done well. It was in Kenyon-alley that he began this trade, and he worked for Close's in Gibraltar-street. Afterwards he was manager at Peters' in Westbar-green. Then he engaged a workshop at the end of Kenyon-alley, and found so much to do, that from having only a boy he employed two journeymen to help him. In this way he got a good business together, and the place being too small, he made the unfortunate venture of taking a shop in West-street, two doors from Rockingham-street. The moment he got there his luck seemed to turn, and the takings were not as great in a month as they had been in Kenyon-alley in a day.

EIGHT YEARS' PENAL SERVITUDE.

In this state of things the West-street shop was given up, and Peace migrated with his family to Manchester. He took with him a stock of frames; but he had not been there a fortnight when he was once more in the hands of the officers of the law. "Doing a job" at a house in Lower Broughton, he was caught in the act, and his excuse for such clumsiness was that he, who was usually strictly temperate, had had nine glasses of whiskey, and did not know what he was doing. He was tried at the Manchester Assizes on the 3rd of December, 1866, under the name of George Barker, alias Alexander Mann, and he was sentenced to eight years' penal servitude.

HIS LAST RETURN.

Upon that Mrs. Peace for a short time kept a little shop in Long Millgate, Manchester, but before long she came bak to Sheffield, and got employment in charing, and in the bottling department of a wine merchant. At first she lived in Trippet-lane, but afterwards in Orchard-street, where Peace's mother also lived. In 1865, shortly before leaving Kenyon-alley, there had been a son—John Charles—born, but he did not live to see the return of his father, who, on the night of the 9th of August, 1872, re-appeared at home. His eight years' sentence had been commuted to less than six.

Having provided himself with picture-frame making tools, Peace then took a house in Brocco, and lived a few doors from Inspector Twibell, and his family helped him in the business. Here Brahma fowls were kept, and Peace there, besides resuming his performances on the violin, attempted, but without much success, to instruct Willie in the art. The frame-making prospering, there was a removal to Scotland-street. The testimony is that Peace was really industrious at this time, and being particular in the execution of his work he got much custom. His children attended the day and Sunday-schools of the parish church in Queen-street, and he was very strict with them as to the companions and the hours they kept. For himself he had never been known to go to church. He was accustomed to profess his belief in the existence of a God and a Devil, but he declared that he feared neither one nor the other. But he wished his children, he said, to believe in God and to fear Him.

Peace left Scotland-street through a disagreement with his landlord, and removed to Darnall, in the beginning of 1875. The house he chose was a semi-detached one in Milton Villas, Britannia-road. Next door but one, with an unoccupied house intervening (a circumstance which explains one of the letters found in the field at Bannercross), lived Mr. Arthur Dyson and his wife. And these were the materials out of which has to be developed the tragic termination of Charles Peace's career.

The Bannercross murder led to the performance of extraordinary feats in telegraphing. On the day that Mrs. Dyson was under examination in the corridor at the Sheffield Police-offices press messages numbering 180,000 words were telegraphed away. The number of words actually sent away from Leeds in one day, in connection with Peace's trial, was 200,000. The number of words delivered to all papers exceeded 300,000. With respect to Sheffield two special wires were used solely for the local papers. Ten men were specially employed at that end in writing up the news, and at no time throughout the day were they above twenty words behind hand. The news was delivered almost sheet by sheet by special messengers.

SALE OF PEACE'S MUSICAL INSTRUMENTS.

The excitement which prevailed at Mr. Harvey's auction mart, in Bank-street, during the sale of Peace's violins, was only excelled by that manifested at the Sheffield Town-hall when the convict was first brought up for the murder of Mr. Dyson. For several days it had been publicly announced that those celebrated violins which had accompanied Peace in his wanderings would be sold by auction by Mr. Harvey; and on the afternoon, long before the hour fixed, the room was filled by persons who were either intent upon purchasing if possible, or having at least a sight of the instruments.

Scores who were unable to obtain admittance collected outside the premises, and it required the efforts of two policemen to prevent a disturbance amongst the crowd, as there were a great number of roughs, who frequently indulged in shouts and yells.

The proceedings were characterised by no little amusement, and when, in the first place, Mr. Harvey inquired whether there was anyone present "concerned" about the property to be disposed of, he was met by the felicitous rejoinder, "Do you mean concerned with Peace?" and much laughter was created. Mr. Harvey then proceeded to open the sale, and first offered a copy of the "Duke" fiddle.

He said a gentleman had come a distance of 225 miles to look at the fiddles, that he might be able to say he had had Peace's fiddles in his hand. He had also received letters from gentlemen residing at Tunbridge Wells, Manchester, London, and other places, offering to purchase them by private treaty. They were capital instruments, and if Peace had stuck to his music, he would not have been in the position he was now. There was no doubt the man had good as well as bad qualities.

The instrument having been handed round, several tunes were played upon it, and the bidding commenced at £1, followed by offers of £5 and £10. An offer of eleven guineas was increased by steady bids of one guinea each, until a bid of 20½ guineas was made, and at that price the violin was knocked down to Mr. G. C. Millward, provision merchant, York. Mr. Harvey said that £50 had been offered for the fiddle before it was put up for auction, and he firmly believed it was worth quite that to any person. He declared that there was not a bit of pluck in Sheffield, or the fiddle would have sold for double the amount.

The "Kit" violin was next put up, Mr. Harvey assuring his audience that there was no want of genuineness about the original ownership of both instruments. They were first pledged, he said, to pay for the defence of Mrs. Peace, and they had recently been redeemed by Messrs. Clegg and Sons to be sold for the convict's defence. The offer made was 5s., which was quickly followed by offers of £2 10s., £5, £5 10s., £6, £6 10s., £7 10s., £8, and £8 10s., and an offer of £8 15s. being refused, it was sold to Mr. Lofthouse, of the "George Hotel," Bridlington, for £9 10s.

A "Short Grand" piano, formerly the property of Peace, was then offered. An offer of ten guineas was first made, and the bids rising by one guinea each to nineteen, 19½ was offered, the figure slowly rising, by three other bids, to 23 guineas. Half-guinea bids were made in rapid succession, till 24½ guineas were realised, the purchaser being a gentleman from Hull, who desired that his name should not be published.

A violin, made by Peace himself, twenty years ago, was next offered for sale. Bidders were now, however, very scarce, and, though the instrument was of infinitely better tone than the one first disposed of, it only realised about one-third the sum. Mr. Harvey said the violin was now the property of a person named Hewitt, better known by the name of "Little Teddy," who told him that he and "Charley" had played upon the instrument many a time. Mr. John Stansfield, of the Music Hall of Varieties, Leeds, was the buyer, for £6 10s.

No small amount of surprise was expressed that the instruments should have been permitted to leave the town.

PEACE AND MRS. THOMPSON.

It was suggested that there was some secret behind Mrs. Thompson's alleged potent influence over the convict Peace. He sometimes treated her with more partiality and kindness than he did his wife; but when Sue got drunk and pawned the proceeds of his robberies, which he had given to her, he would treat her with as much savage brutality as he ever did his wife, and for days after she would carry the marks of his violence.

Mrs. Thompson, it was stated, was never asked to help Peace to make away with the goods he had stolen; but Hannah was frequently called upon to share in the risk of removing them. In this selection of his tool, Peace knew perfectly well what he was about; and it furnished no proof of his partiality for Sue over his wife.

She was his paramour, and had she been detected in possession of his stolen property, she could have been indicted with him. His wife, as the trial at the Old Bailey proved, could not be punished for making away with such goods, as she was supposed to act under his influence and control.

On the day when Peace's daughter, Mrs. Bolsover, her husband, and his other relatives visited him at Armley Gaol, they implored the condemned man not to see Mrs. Thompson, stating that if he did Mrs. Peace would not come over. When put to him in that way Peace promised not to see her.

Mrs. Thompson called at the gaol immediately after they were gone, in response to a letter she had received from Peace, dated Feb. 9th, saying she would be allowed to see him; but after waiting two hours she had to leave without seeing him. A second letter addressed to her by Peace was, however, read to her by the Governor. For some reason the Visiting Committee were also opposed to letting Mrs. Thompson see Peace.

On Wednesday Mrs. Hannah Peace, her son, Willie, and the nephew, anew importuned Peace not to see Mrs. Thompson, threatening they would not come again if he did so, and they obtained a promise from him that he would not see her. In addition to his promise, they relied on the position assumed towards the woman by the Leeds Visiting Committee, who were indisposed to allow a mistress to visit her paramour in gaol.

It is also inconceivable that, knowing the unenviable position in which she stood to Peace, and knowing that he does not wish to see her; that his friends were strongly opposed to the interview; and that the local authorities had repeatedly refused her admission; that she should still hang about the gaol and persist in her attempts to obtain admission to the cell of the condemned man.

The following is the letter above alluded to, that Mrs. Thompson received from Peace, the envelope being addressed, " On her Majesty's service, Thompson—letter box General Post-office, Leeds, to be called for."

" From Charles Peace, H.M.'s Prison, Leeds, Feb. 9, 1879.

" My poor Sue,—I receive your letter to-day and I have my kind governer's permission for you to come and see me at once so come up to the prison and bring this letter with you and you will get to see me I do wish particular to see you it is my wish that you will obey me in this one thing for you have obeyed me in many thing but do obey me in this one Do not let this letter fall into the hands of the press Hoping to see you at once I Remane your ever well wisher

" CHARLES PEACE."

The letter was written on the usual official paper. Mrs. Thompson took the original with her to Armley Gaol, and at Governor Keene's request, give it to him. One of her friends, who went to the post-office for her, had, however, taken a copy of it. Had Mrs. Thompson gone with this letter at once, she would probably have seen Peace; but she delayed, and the permission to see him was delayed.

LETTERS TO PEACE'S FAMILY.

After the sentence of death had been passed upon Peace his wife and family were astonished at the interest taken in their welfare by people about whom they knew nothing. They received several letters expressing sympathy with them, and other people showed their regard for them by asking that some small article which the convict had used might be sent to them to keep in remembrance of him. It need hardly be stated that none of these modest requests were complied with. The following was one of the latest letters received :—

" Market Place, Middlesbro on Tees,
" Feb. 11, 1879.

" Mrs. Peace,—I Have Taken the Liberty of writing to you under Your Painful Circumstances to ask if any think is beeing done on behalf of Your Husband Charles Peace i mean in the Ways of appealing to the Home Secretary for a Respite for your Husband i have made an Appeal in his Behalf to Mr. Cross the Secretary of State and the Reply is that it Shall have their Carefull attention i hope Some one or at Least a Large number will follow up in the Same line and urge for a Respite of Course i know nothing of your Husband only from the accounts of the Papers which i think as been most erroneous and Must have damaged his case in the Mind of the Public and i fear the Judge and Jury also it is upon this head that i make my appeal for his life to be Spared and i Should like to know if any other Effort is being Putt forth Please write a few lines if You Can or Get Some one else to do it for you and let me Know if you hear of any one that is making any Effort for what is done Should be done quickly and without delay and i hope God in his mercy will uphold You and Yours under Your Most trying Circumstances and i trust by the Mercy of God that Your Husband May not Come to die by the hands of the Exicuitor but i hope his life may be spared that he May depart at Last as is the way of all flesh. i am only a Poor man and a stranger

to you all but never the Less i am doing all that i Can in this matter hopeing you Pardon me for intrudeing upon you in the manner i have done by writeing to you but i fell as tho i Should like to know if any think is beeing done in the way of Partitioning about where You live.—" Yours Respeffully

" E—— W——

" Please write by Return and let me know if any thing is beeing done "

To the above letter the following reply was at once sent :—

" Darnall, Feb. 13, 1879.

" Mr. W——

" Dear Sir,—I received your letter this morning, and on behalf of my mother and family I heartily thank you for your kind and sympathetic letter. In reference to the petition, your letter is the first intimation we have had, and we are not aware that anything is being done in that direction.

" I quite agree with your remarks about the public being prejudiced against my father through the action of the press; for many of the papers have published things that are utterly untrue; but not too untrue or too romantic for the public to believe. The blacker a paper has painted him, and the more romance has been mixed with it, the more it has suited the public appetite.

" With reference to the jury being prejudiced I can only say they took a very short space of time in which to make up their minds to return a verdict of guilty in such a serious case. I thank you for your kind wishes towards us, and am pleased to tell you that Mr. Peace is resigned to his fate, and his state of mind is all that could be desired.

" Hoping you will not think it any intrusion if you wish to write again, I remain,

" Yours respectfully,

" WILLIAM WARD."

The following may be taken as a specimen of another class of letters that were received :—

" Dear Mrs. Peace,—I Hope you Will go and See your Husband Mr. Pease In Reading The Papers I think Hee Is not aware That It was Mrs Tompson Thot Betraid Him ask Him If He Ever Come To Nottinghamshir with Mrs Tompson If Mrs Pease Is Not able To Goo I Hope Some of The Famely Will and Bee Shur and ask Him I Hope God Will Pardon Is Sins Befor The Execusion Takes Plais I Feel Sorry For You all But not For Those Two Wimen I think They Have Led Him To Mor Then He might Hev Don —Yours truly —— I will Right agoin to you."

Charles Peace, while under sentence of death in Armley Gaol for the murder of Mr. Arthur Dyson, addressed the following letters to his son-in-law and son. They were written on one sheet of paper, the one letter following the other. Both the writing and the spelling were much better than in some previous letters received from the convict. The letters will speak for themselves; and will afford additional proof —if proof were needed—of the sort of man he was.

L. P.—C. 4.   H. M. C. P. M. 12—73.

From Charles Peace.

" H.M. Prison, Leeds, 7th February, 1879

" My dear Son-in-law,—I hope this lettr will find you as well as it can do i am Still very week and ill but a little better then i have been. You will know well that i have been perged (purjured) against by three persons in Darnall what I wish to say to you is this do not attempt to avenge the wrong that was done to me by Jim and his wife and Mrs. Padmore, for under my Present feelings i feel no imbetterness against no Person in this world, for if i must be forgiven I must forgive. So, My Dear Son, do you Not Commit yourself in either thought, word, or deed against any of these Persons, but in Place of being in their Company do all you Can to avoid them, and this will keep you from doing anything at each other that will be offencive. I do Send you a form of Prayer that I Compiled Myself before i left Pen ton vile Prison.

O Lord, turn not Thy face from me, but have mercy. Good Lord, have mercy on me. I need not to Confess my life to thee, for thow knows what i have been and what i am. So O My Blessed Lord and Saviour Jesus Christ, have mercy upon me, and wash and cleanse me from all my Sins and Make Me Clean, and save me from the danger of sin and from the Power of Hell. O God do not despise me nor Cast me from thee, but have mercy Good Lord have mercy upon me, and make me what thou would have me to be, to enter into the Kingdom of heaven, and then receive my Poor Soul at the last for Jesus Christs his Sake. Amen. "The Lord have mercy upon me, Christ have mercy upon me. Amen."

"My Dear Son,—I have sent you this Prayer to Show you the State of Mind that i do now feel myself to be in i do not feel no trouble so great as i do my Sinful life against my God i begin to feel that my God will have mercy upon me and forgive me all my Sins and receive my Poor Soul into the Kingdom of heaven i send my best love, thanks and Good wishes to all friends that came up on my trial to Speak for me i do want to see all my family as often as i can do before i die you Can See me any week day but you will have to bring this lettr with you and go the Leeds Town Hall and enquire for Mr. John Thornton magistrates clerk and he will give you every information yo require to see me you cannot see me without an order from him So to Save time and trouble go and see him before you Come to the Prison. I send my Dearest love to my Dear, dear wife and all of you my loving children. —I am Your Wrecthed Husband and Father,
"CHARLES PEACE."

WILLIE'S LETTER.

The above letters are in answer to the following :—
"Darnall, Feb. 6, 1879.

"Dear Father,—We had hoped to have had a letter from you this morning to tell us how you are. Will was in court on Tuesday and heard your trial, and when he came home and told us what the sentence was, it upset us all.

"We did all we could for you, and if there is anything more that we can do, write and let us know. We cannot come to see you as often as we could wish, but we hope you will write to us, and let us know how you are getting on.—Your affectionate son, WILLIE."

INTERVIEW WITH HIS RELATIVES.

On Monday, no fewer than thirteen of Peace's relatives and friends went from Sheffield to Leeds to have an interview with the convict Peace in his condemned cell. There were eleven in the first group, but in their appeals to Mr. Thornton, the magistrates' clerk, for tickets of admission, they were not all successful.

Only five of them—Mr. Daniel Peace (the convict's brother), and his wife, and three of their children—were granted permission to see the condemned man. The others were refused. The second group consisted of Mrs. and Mr. Bolsover (Peace's daughter and son-in-law), and they readily obtained the necessary authority to see him.

On their arriving at Armley, the governor (Mr. Keene) gave them very strict injunctions as to how they were to behave themselves when in the presence of the convict. They were to restrain their feelings, and on no account whatever was there to be any "scene." They were also to be extremely careful what they said to him. Having been thus suitably admonished as to their conduct, they were taken in two parties by the governor to the condemned cell. It was the same that the convict has occupied from his arrival at Armley, and they were simply admitted within the barred-off portion of the cell. He was sitting in a chair, and on either side of him stood a warder, watching his every movement. He seemed very weak —much weaker than when he appeared in the Crown Court to take his trial. Indeed, those who had not seen him for some time were quite startled at his pale, shrunken, weak appearance.

Peace was asked by one of the party how he was, and he replied, in very feeble tones, "I am no better; my head is very bad." From further remarks he made it appear that he was suffering very much from the effects of his jump from the train. He said the wound on his head had broken out afresh, and he was in much pain from concussion of the brain. Proceeding, he said, "I am sorry now that I made such a rash attempt upon my life; I would never do it again."

The governor, seeing the condemned man was becoming somewhat excited, interposed, and urged him to keep himself calm, and not to talk too much. Peace thereupon became quiet, and said little more, except to express a wish to see his wife. The interview allowed to either party was of short duration. The impression they formed was that the convict was perfectly resigned to his sentence, and that we had given up all hope of having his life prolonged. He was wearing the spectacles which the Home Secretary had given instructions that he should be furnished with, and near him were three books, which he had been reading. When the time allowed for the interview had expired, the relatives were exceedingly desirous to shake hands with him, but that was not allowed. The culprit, as one after the other bade him "good-bye," quite broke down, and his grief expressed itself in tears.

INTERVIEW WITH HIS WIFE.

On Wednesday, Mrs. Peace, Willie Ward, her son, and Thomas Neil, a nephew, went from Sheffield to Leeds to visit the condemned man in his cell at Armley.

They left Sheffield by the Midland 9.5 train, and arrived at Leeds at 10.20. After an interview at the Town Hall with the chairman of the visiting justices the necessary order was then given to them, and they went a circuitous route to Armley.

The governor then conducted them to the cell, and the interview with the condemned man lasted more than an hour-and-a-half. He was sitting up, and since Monday the bandages had again been placed on his head. He was exceedingly pleased to see them; and, though weak, he appeared in excellent spirits, and during the whole time the interview lasted he carried on a most animated conversation with them. He gave his wife minute instructions with respect to private matters, about which nothing further need now be said; and as a memento of her visit he took off and handed to her, with the case, the pair of gold-framed spectacles about which so much has been said and written.

Peace had had those spectacles for many years, and he had them on the night he was captured by Robinson. They were then taken from him under the impression that a burglar would not come by a pair of gold spectacles honestly, and that they were part of the proceeds of some robbery. While he was in Pentonville, he asked to be supplied with spectacles, as he could not without them see to read and write, and the pair of brass-framed spectacles which gave him such a grotesque appearance—and which it was assumed he had adopted with a view to better disguise himself—were supplied to him. In his leap from the express train when on his way to Sheffield he lost those spectacles, but others were supplied to him while he was in Armley. A few days previously he wrote to the Home Secretary, asking that his own spectacles might be forwarded to him, and they were sent carefully packed in a small box. He was much gratified to receive them, and as they were almost the only articles with which he could part, he took them off, put them in their steel-bound leather case, and handed them to his wife, asking her to keep them for his sake.

With Willie and the nephew Peace talked with equal freedom, and gave them much good advice. Mrs. Peace had not seen her husband for four months, and she could not but observe the change that had taken place in him. But although he appeared feeble in body—so feeble that he could not walk alone,· yet his mind was as clear as ever it was in his life, and never did he talk more sensibly. He had in his cell a Bible and a Prayer-book, and a number of tracts and letters which had either been supplied to him by the chaplain, or sent to him by sympathising friends. In reading, writing, listening to the exhortations of the chaplain, praying, and in talking, the convict passed his time. He appeared to be not only perfectly resigned to his sentence, but to have no fear of death whatever. Indeed, he expressed a hope that he would have sufficient strength to walk firmly to the scaffold, not in a spirit of bravado, but to show that he was not afraid to die. He asked his wife to forgive him every wrong he had done her, admitting, that had he followed her advice he would not have been in his present terrible position. She freely forgave him. He then said he entertained feelings of ill-will towards no one; and he hoped to receive the forgiveness of everybody towards whom he had done wrong. He spoke in terms of gratitude of the kind treatment he received at the hands of the governor and all who had to do with him, and said he had nothing to wish for at their hands. Towards the end of the interview his remarks were of so kind and tender a character as to affect his relatives to tears, and when they were leaving he entreated them to visit him again, and they promised to do so.

The Central News special reporter, referring to the interview with his family, wrote:—"There was an affecting scene between Peace and his daughter, who carried her baby in her arms. The woman sobbed bitterly, and even Peace himself cried. He inquired in affectionate terms after her mother, and seemed disappointed at her not being among the party. Mrs. Bolsover told him that she would tell her mother of his desire to see her, and that she would visit him. Peace took a great deal of notice of the child, and hoped that God would bless it as well as all his relations and friends. Although he seemed depressed, still he chatted freely and showed no reluctance to talk on any subject. He complained that he had not received justice, and that several of the witnesses against him had perjured themselves. Both Mr. and Mrs. Bolsover reproved him for thinking any more about Mrs. Thompson, and when they learned that he had written to her again, they became quite angry. They begged him

to have nothing further to do with her, as she had been the means of giving him much trouble. Peace reluctantly vowed he would have no more to say to her. After an interview of over an hour the party took an affectionate good-bye of him, some of them promising to come back again if they could get admission."

MRS. THOMPSON AGAIN.

It seems that before leaving Leeds Mrs. Thompson wrote the following letter, and entrusted it to one of her friends to deliver:—

"7th February, 1879.
"To the Postmaster, Leeds.

"Please give the bearer any letters addressed 'Mrs. S. Thompson, Post-office, Leeds, to be called for,' and oblige.   "S THOMPSON, OR BAILEY."

On Monday morning an elderly woman, dressed very plainly, called at the Post-office, and got two letters for Mrs. Thompson, one of which, was, it was known, from the convict Peace. The party receiving the letters must have telegraphed for Mrs. Thompson, for she was seen to enter the gaol shortly after four o'clock. She said she came from London, having left that place early in the forenoon.

She remained within the gaol about two hours, and had a long conversation with Governor Keene, but was not allowed to see Peace, the latter, it is said, declining to see her.

Mrs. Thompson cried a good deal, and said she had had her second journey for nothing. It was stated that this sudden change of the convict's mind was brought about by the visit of his relatives earlier in the day.

A Leeds correspondent telegraphed:—"To the surprise of the officials of Armley Gaol, Mrs. Thompson made her appearance there again on Monday, accompanied by a young man. She drove up to the gates in a cab at dusk, and at once sought another interview with Mr. Keene, the governor. When she applied to the visiting justices, at Leeds Town Hall, on Friday week, she was told emphatically that she could not be allowed to see her former associate. On Monday, she received no more satisfaction. She was not admitted, and she seemed little disappointed."

PEACE'S WILL.

Peace's will was drawn up by Deputy-sheriff Ford, who is a member of a local firm of solicitors. It extended to but four or five lines and devised his property to Hannah Ward or Peace, his wife, the mention of her first name obviating the necessity of legal proof of marriage. The text was not to be published until the day of his execution.

In regard to the former will be made, bequeathing everything to Mrs. Thompson, the latter's sister burnt the document, so that neither Peace nor his family need have any fears on that score. Mrs. Thompson has again made her appearance in Leeds. She was evidently bent on seeing the convict.

On Thursday morning she called at the office of Messrs. Ford and Warren, solicitors, 25, Albion-street. Shortly afterwards, or about noon, Mr. Warren drove to the gaol in a cab with Mrs. Thompson, and, presenting the following letter to Governor Keene, asked him to allow her to see Peace:—

"Prison Department,
"Home Office, Whitehall, S.W.,
"8th Feburary, 1879.

"Madam,—I am directed by the Chairman of the Commissioners of Prisons to acknowledge the receipt of your letter of the 7th inst., requesting to be allowed to see John Ward, alias Charles Peace, a prisoner under sentence of death in Leeds Prison. In reply, I am to acquaint you that by desire of the Secretary of State the Governor of the Prison has been authorised to permit you to have an interview with the prisoner under the usual restrictions, and subject to his wishing to see you, on your presenting this letter at the prison.—I am, madam, your obedient servant,

"C. N. JOSEPH.

"Mrs. Thompson, Post-office, Leeds."

The letter, to which the foregoing was a reply, was as follows:—

"February 7th, 1879.

"Gentlemen,—I beg to be allowed to see the condemned man, Charles Peace, Thompson, or Ward, now in Armley Gaol, Leeds. He has been my reputed husband for years, and he has no other legal wife. He has 'earnestly' desired to see me, and for reasons that can easily be understood. I deeply hope and pray, gentlemen, that you will furnish me with the authority to see him before the end. I will not disturb his mind, but try to sooth him. Imploring you will speedily grant my prayer,

"I am your obedient servant,

S. THOMPSON.

"P.S.—Please address to me, 'Post Office, Leeds, to be left till called for.'"

Governor Keene said to Mr. Warren that since the letter sent by the prison authorities had been received, his (the governor's) authority to allow the interview had been countermanded by the Home Office, but that if Mrs. Thompson had applied at the gaol immediately the letter reached Leeds he should have allowed her to have seen Peace.

Mr. Warren explained that there were difficulties that prevented her doing so, and withdrew, saying he would make a formal application, for leave for her to see Peace, to the Visiting Committee. After proceeding to the Town Hall, and being unable to find any of the members of the Visiting Committee, Mr. Warren went to the office of the chairman of the committee, John Ellershaw, Esq., who declined to accede to Mr. Warren's petition, saying he should not do so unless Mr. Warren could show him a letter from the convict dated since Peace's interview with his daughter, Mrs. Bolsover, stating the convict's wish to see Mrs. Thompson.

MRS. BRION IN LEEDS.

As Mr. and Mrs. Bolsover were returning from Armley to Leeds, they were greatly astonished to see Mrs. Brion, the wife of Peace's friend at Peckham, wending her way to the gaol. She told them that she had come down from London, and was going on to Armley, and hoped she would be allowed to have an interview with Peace.

She expressed great concern for his state of mind, and said she believed if she could see him she should be able "to say something to him that would do him a little good." At that time she had not seen the magistrates' clerk, and had obtained no authority to see Peace.

OFFERS TO HANG PEACE.

After Peace had been tried and condemned, the authorities had several applications to fill the grim office of executioner. These were from amateurs, one of whom, from the neighbourhood of Sheffield, wrote to say that he would undertake the duty gratuitously; whilst another asked the modest sum of only £3 10s. for his services, should they be accepted. It is scarcely necessary to say that no notice was taken of them, and Marwood was engaged to carry out the sentence.

SUGGESTED POSTPONEMENT OF THE EXECUTION.

A letter was forwarded to the Home Secretary on

behalf of the convict, which said: "I hope you will kindly bear with me whilst I venture to address you upon a matter the immediate attention to which must prove of the utmost importance to one who stands condemned to suffer capital punishment, according to the organs of the newspaper press, in the course of the coming fortnight. There can be no disguising the fact that a large number of persons in the metropolis and throughout the country entertain the idea that the prisoner Peace's late trial before the judge and jury was too hurried to be just. Such persons believe that the very circumstances which had been alluded to by the learned counsel for the defence—namely, that the cry for the prisoner's blood and the sensational intelligence of the prisoner's career which had appeared in the columns of the leading organs of the press—had combined to induce the jury to come to their most serious decision in the reported space of a quarter of an hour. A very unpleasant sensation has likewise been created, that the whole matter, namely, the condemnation of Peace, had been previously arranged—had, indeed, been cut and dried. . . . As I am confident that the spirit of justice of English law would rather permit ninety-nine guilty to escape than that one innocent should suffer, and as I feel it would lie upon my conscience did I abstain from laying the 'evil' alluded to before you, I have herewith endeavoured to discharge my duty—a duty which I feel I owe to the prisoner, his sympathisers, and to the best interests of English justice. Certainly, if the sentence cannot be reversed, the impression of unfairness would be removed by postponing the date for Peace's execution."

To this communication the following reply was received from the Home Secretary on Tuesday:—

"Whitehall, Feb. 8.

"SIR,—I am directed by the Secretary of State for the Home Department to acknowledge the receipt of your application on behalf of Charles Peace, and I am to acquaint you that the same will be fully considered. —I am, Sir, your obedient servant,

"A. F. O. LIDDELL."

MR. BRION ALSO CLAIMS A REWARD.

The Central News said at this time Mr. Brion, of 22, Philip-road, Peckham, had prepared for the Treasury a statement of his work in connection with this case, in order that payment might be made him for his services.

It was with Mr. Brion that Peace was engaged in perfecting his invention for raising sunken ships; in fact, witness and the prisoner, in their quieter days, were in the habit of taking a large model ship, which had been built by them for experimenting in regard to the invention, to the pond at Peckham Rye, where they attracted the general attention of the neighbourhood.

Brion claims to have been the first to identify Peace after his apprehension for the Blackheath burglary. The notorious convict, when in Newgate, wrote to Mr. Brion in the name of Ward, on Nov. 3rd, beseeching him to come and see him, and attributing the whole of his misfortunes to drink.

Mr. Brion went to Newgate to see who the man was, and was very much surprised to find it was Mr. Thompson, his friend and neighbour. This fact he at once communicated to the governor of the gaol, and the police, being put on the alert, searched Thompson's house at Nunhead.

The woman Thompson, it will be recollected, had got herself into the meshes of the law by being a party after the crime and acting as a receiver of his stolen goods.

MRS. THOMPSON REFUSED ADMISSION TO SEE PEACE UNDER SENTENCE.

The detectives worked upon her fears, and in this they were aided by Mr. Brion, who heard her drop words of a crimirating character while she was under the influence of drink, so that partly by threats and promises of immunity if she would confess all and assist the officers of the law, the woman informed on Peace.

Mr. Brion received two other letters from Peace, but

they merely referred to making subsequent visits, and arranging for the defence, and getting money for that object, and nearly all the facts narrated by this witness as regards Peace himself were published when he gave evidence before the magistrates.

He appears to have been most anxious to aid the police in their endeavours to recover the stolen property, and the long list of journeys which he undertook at that time with them testifies to the value of his services in this respect.

He was particularly successful in revealing the establishment in Petticoat-lane, where Peace had much of the proceeds of his robberies placed, and by representing himself to the receiver as an accomplice of Peace, and then revealing the results of his interview to the police, the latter were able to act with promptness and decision.

Among the many attributes of Peace, according to Mr. Brion, none were more remarkable than his wonderful ability to hide in the smallest limits.

He could place himself in a box with almost the same promptitude as Mr. Cook, of Egyptian Hall celebrity; in the bottom drawer of a chest, and in a cheffonier he was frequently hidden, while from long practice he was able to hide under an ordinary round table, clinging to the spiral stem in such a manner that even if the table had no cover he would escape the glance of a casual observer.

PEACE'S CYPHER CODE.

A Central News telegram states :—The convict evidently kept fully abreast of the age in all he did, for instead of making use of the ordinary thieves slang, when he had anything of a secret nature to communicate to his friends, he made known his message by means of numerals, each of which represented a word.

This cypher code of his, though somewhat crude and cumbersome, bore a general resemblance to those used by business firms and Government officers. Messages containing the secret cyphers of Peace were usually sent to certain receivers of stolen goods to whom he disposed of the proceeds of his burglaries, and to Mrs. Thompson.

As to Mrs. Peace, or Hannah, none of these messages were sent to her, for, as she says herself, " I am nae schullar." Peace had 144 words at least in his secret vocabulary, as the number ran from 1 to 144. The numbers 27, 13, 21, 39, 40, 98, 100, 101, 102, were respectively the words, " he, me, of, we, call, pet, coming, house, pounds, night, and right." In fact, the code was well calculated to enable him to communicate secretly in respect to almost any matter.

Peace had also another peculiarity. He kept a careful and accurate account of the money he received and expended in his city house. In little pass-books, each alternate leaf of which was provided with blotting paper, he entered an account of his payments and expenditure.

Mrs. Thompson had an interview with Governor Keene at Armley Gaol after Peace's conviction, and he read a long letter to her which he had just received from Peace's hands. The letter was full of most endearing terms, even fulsomely so, the convict calling Mrs. Thompson his "pet" and "darling," and professing undying love for her. Mrs. Thompson wept passionately on hearing it read, and appeared much crushed.

The Central News special reporter, wrote :—As doubt has been expressed respecting the existence of Peace's cypher code, the following is furnished as an accurate copy of it, the original having been for some time in the hands of the police authorities :—

1 one	2 I	3 is
4 oh	5 he	6 to
7 me	8 my	9 in
10 as	11 it	12 at
13 of	14 up	15 on
16 or	18 a	18 aye
19 am	20 so	21 we

22 us	23 but	24 you
25 nap	26 hope	27 they
28 thy	29 was	20 will
31 she	32 well	33 went
34 who	35 has	36 let
37 and	38 can	39 call
40 time	41 still	42 her
43 out	44 four	45 give
46 kiss	47 dear	48 pet
49 there	50 some	51 that
52 had	53 life	54 are
55 poor	56 course	57 come
58 coming	59 where	60 but
61 from	62 much	63 many
64 what	65 this	66 mean
67 when	68 must	69 may
70 road	71 uneasy	72 money
73 love	74 loving	75 every
76 then	77 old	78 how
79 never	80 name	81 Ben
82 sent	83 say	84 —
85 almost	86 friends	87 sum
88 pull	89 post	90 happy
91 wish	92 pain	93 until
94 bear	95 word	96 shall
97 used	98 house	99 back
100 pounds	101 night	102 right
103 write	104 mind	105 oblige
106 cannot	107 sold	108 things
109 said	110 know	111 just
112 railway	113 yes	114 believe
115 about	116 owes	117 told
118 fact	119 belong	120 word
121 since	122 away	123 early
124 such	125 finish	126 best
127 first	128 whose	129 early
130 Monday	131 Tuesday	132 Wednesday
135 Thursday	134 Friday	135 Saturday
136 Sunday	127 home	138 have
139 fancy	140 face	141 washed
142 ready	143 for	144 Johnny

Johnny being of course himself.

PEACE IN THE COMPANY OF MEMBERS OF PARLIAMENT.

We cannot refrain from telling a story of Peace's extraordinary coolness and impudence. He was, as the reader perhaps has heard, the inventor of a plan for raising sunken vessels, and he actually exhibited his patent at Bristol, where, too, he offered £50 for the salvage of a wrecked schooner, though as the money was not forthcoming, the bargain was never concluded.

This invention, however, brought him into the acquaintance of several M.P.'s interested in the subject of his patent, and a friend of ours remembers going with him to the lobby of the House of Commons to see these gentlemen.

Peace conducted himself throughout these negotiations as a quiet, respectable, steady, and apparently well-to-do man. He seemed to be acquainted with most of the prominent M.P.'s, and quizzed them upon their peculiarities; at one time, indeed, it was thought he was the author of some of the political quizzing in *Truth.*

It would, doubtless, surprise Mr. Plimsoll and the First Lord of the Admiralty to learn that they had been in the company of Peace in connection with his patent. But we are told there is no doubt of it. And it was after the Dyson murder.

PEACEIANA.

Peace, it will be remembered, on more than one occasion assumed the *role* of a hawker of spectacles, and he provided himself with the necessary proof had his representation been challenged.

On one occasion, when visiting his friends at Hull, he was asked what he was doing, and he replied, " I am selling spectacles." At the same time he produced a travelling sample case, made of leather and elaborately gilded, and on opening it exposed to view some thirty pairs of spectacles of different kinds.

He never did much in the way of pushing the spectacle trade ; but no doubt the taking of it up assisted to conceal his identity. He had for many years worn the gold-framed spectacles about which so much has since been said. Previous to his murdering Mr. Dyson he only used them when reading or doing fine work ; but afterwards he wore them out in the streets, and was seldom seen without them.

Peace was once terribly annoyed at a disappointment he met with at Croydon. He went down there one afternoon, and selected a house to rob. The same night he visited it again, expecting to obtain a good booty.

He reached one of the bedroom windows and forced back the hasp, but to his chagrin he found that the sash was secured from opening wider than a handbreadth by patent fasteners—those little metal knobs, the shape of an acorn, that screw into a brass socket. He could not, therefore, open either that or any other window within reach.

He returned home in a most ill-conditioned humour, and made no secret how he had been " duffed," but he said he would not be beaten. Provided with the necessary tools, he went to the same house the next night ; took off the strips of wood which held the sashes of the bedroom window in its place, drew the lower sash forward and got into the bedroom.

He then not only gathered up jewellery and other articles of considerable value, but revenged himself for the disappointment he had experienced on the previous night by taking the patent fasteners off the window. When he got home he threw them on the table, and with an air of triumph exclaimed—" There's your patent fasteners !"

A good many versions have been given as to the circumstances under which Peace met with the injury to his hand. The account he gave to his family was that one night in October, while he was living in the Brocco, he was going up Hollis-croft, when a young man struck him. He was about to return the blow, when either his assailant or some companion shot at him with a pistol, blowing off the first finger and otherwise injuring his left hand.

Peace walked to the Public Hospital, where he was treated as an in-patient for a month. He then took his discharge and " doctored his hand himself." The police never discovered his assailant ; and the opinion some of them arrived at was, that the injuries were self-inflicted—accidentally of course. They believed that Peace was carrying the pistol in his pocket, and that it exploded and shattered his hand.

Reference has previously been made to the long screws which formed part of Peace's burglarious implements. It will be remembered that he used these to secure himself from intrusion while ransacking a room, and he also employed them to prevent pursuers from cutting off his retreat.

On one occasion he showed his confidence in them in a remarkable manner. It was night time, and he selected one of a row of houses in a main street at Brixton. He went to the front door and fastened it with a screw.

On going to the back he saw two doors, one of which opened to the lawn. He secured both of them in the same way. He then climbed a spout and entered the house by a bedroom window.

The door of the room he so fastened with a screw that it could not be opened from the outside, and then proceeded leisurely to ransack the drawers. He was just upon the point of forcing open the desk when a servant came to the door, and when she could not open it she began to scream.

There was a rush to both back and front doors, but it was impossible to open them. Peace remained in the room until he had broken open the desk and abstracted it contents, and then he left the house as he had entered it and escaped.

The " specials " of many newspapers drew the long bow very considerably when they began to pile on the agony in describing Peace's appearance when sentenced to death. There was talk among them about fierce scowls, and convulsive twitchings of the mouth, and a pallor that extended to his very lips.

Others descended still lower, and described the tremblings of his limbs, and spoke of him as if carried out in something like a swoon. There was a great deal in all this as imaginary as Dr. Potter's "trembling like an aspen leaf." As the judge pronounced sentence Peace sat with one leg crossed over the other knee, without the symptoms of even a passing tremour.

And as for his face, it was almost expressionless. He had seemed the whole day to be in a sort of lethargy; if there was any change at the end it amounted only to an increase of stupor.

We wonder where Dr. Potter picked up his story about the convict having broken his aged mother's heart ? Possibly from the unreliable source whence many of the other fictions promulgated from St. Luke's pulpit came.

We mean no disrespect to the ancient lady who was wont to hawk tapes and ribbons about the outskirts of the town, but her heart took an uncommon lot of breaking.

As to Peace having dishonoured his mother, if we mistake not she was largely responsible (far more responsible than the father, who received such short shrift at Dr. Potter's hands) for his evil start in life. She is credited with having possessed a pretty accurate acquaintance with the details of her illustrious son's career.

She had a domestic establishment, around which hovered anything but an atmosphere of sanctity ; and our readers know how the poor creature was dragged over to Manchester Assizes to swear to an alibi for her son.

She managed to survive the tragedy, which according to Dr. Potter, broke her heart, by something like a twelvemonth.

Did Dr. Potter receive his intelligence "by electric telegraph ?" That is the latest form of journalistic enterprise—to have news specially wired from Bank-street to High-street, that it may be reproduced from other columns in a surreptitious second edition, and that it may be claimed as confirming statements which it emphatically contradicts.

The account of Peace's doings after the murder may be taken as one among the innumerable episodes which the Sheffield papers were the first to publish. They gave the route he took on that fatal night, and the manner in which he made his escape. That account was contradicted by the journal which was so sure Mrs. Dyson could not be found.

Two days afterwards one print ventured to give a route of its own. It told how Peace went down

Ecclesall-road, on Sharrow vale, through Frog-walk, and into Cemetary-road. The statement by Peace, which was published afterwards showed that this story was the purest fiction.

AN OFFER TO MRS. THOMPSON.

Notoriety has with some people more merit than business qualifications, as the following indicates :—
" J. Myers, Queen's Music Hall, 20, Bridge-street, Manchester, February 10, 1879.
"Mrs. Thompson. Madam,—You will excuse me taking the liberty of writing to you, as I thought I should like you at my house as waitress. If you would like to come to Manchester I could give you 25s. per week, if you think you would like to come. Hoping there is no offence in my proposition.—I remain yours most respectfully.   " JOHN MYERS."

CHAPTER CLXIV.

MRS. DYSONS DEPARTURE—AUTOBIOGRAPHIC SKETCH AND SELF-VINDICATION.

AFTER the trial and condemnation of Charles Peace, Mrs. Dyson left for the United States, and subsequently she conducted herself while in New York in anything but a creditable manner. She left Sheffield for Liverpool on Thursday morning, Feb. 26th. 1879, and later in the day she embarked on board the White Star steamer Britannic (the vessel in which she returned to this country) en route for Cleveland, Ohio. She was accompanied by Police-constable Walsh as far as Queenstown.

Mrs. Dyson was desirous, before leaving this country of contradicting in the most emphatic terms the imputations which had been freely cast upon her character and her morality. She accordingly left the following narrative behind her with an earnest request that, by its publication, she would be set right in the estimation of her husband's townsmen :—

I was born in Ireland, at Maynooth. There I remained until I was fifteen years old. Then, having just left school, I started off by myself to see my sister, who had previously gone off to America. She was living at Cleveland, Ohio, and is the wife of Mr. Mooney, captain on one of the Lake Erie steamers.

Though I only went originally to see my sister, I stayed at Cleveland, for I liked the place, the people, and the life. It was there that I first met my husband. He was then a civil engineer, in the service of Sir Morton Peto, and was at that time one of the engineers on the Atlantic and Great Western Railway.

We married, and spent our honeymoon on a visit to the Falls at Niagara. Coming back from our honeymoon, we went into housekeeping at Cleveland, but we did not remain there long. We stayed only until the section of the line of which Mr. Dyson had charge was finished.

Then he received another appointment—that of engineer to the St. Louis Railway, known as the Iron Mountain Road, and went to reside there. He subsequently became the engineer of other lines then in course of construction, and his last engagement in America was as superintendent engineer of the magnificent bridge which spans the Mississippi, and here his health broke down.

He had been often compelled to lead a very rough kind of life, and it began to tell. His duties made that necessary, for the railways on which he was engaged opened up quite new country. The life, however, had many charms for me. I am a good hand at driving, and am fond of horses. I always used to drive Mr. Dyson. He used often to say that I could drive better than he, and he would sit back in his buggy—

they call them buggies there—whilst I held the reins and sent the horses along.

I liked the excitement of driving him to and from his work, and especially when we were in new country, and he was out surveying. I have driven him through forests where there were bears, and over creeks—they call rivers creeks in America—that were swollen by the floods. The horses have often had to swim.

I remember on one occasion sending the horses and the buggy across a river, and then coming over myself on a piece of timber. Of course such a life has some drawbacks, but I was young and strong, and it possessed for me considerable fascination.

My husband loved me and I loved him, and in his company and in driving him about in this wild kind of fashion, I derived much pleasure.

Afraid? Not I. I did not then know what fear was. Besides, I have a good deal of courage—I think I have gone through sufficient (here Mrs. Dyson's tone was tinged with some sadness) of late to show that—and I always felt safe. To be in positions attendant with danger caused me not fear, but a kind of excitement which, if not always pleasurable, certainly possessed some kind of fascination.

But, as I have said, Mr. Dyson's health broke down, and he was compelled to return to England. This was about four years ago. We first lived at Tinsley, with Mr. Dyson's mother; then at Highfield, nearly opposite the police station; and afterwards we took a house in the Alexandra-road, Heeley. Then we went to Darnall, and it was there that my troubles began. But for our going there, Mr. Dyson would probably have been still alive, and I should have been spared all that has happened since.

You will naturally ask how I became acquainted with Peace. It was impossible to avoid becoming acquainted with him. Besides, at that time I did not know the sort of man he really was. He lived the next door but one to us at Darnall, and he used generally to speak to Mr. Dyson in going in and out.

Mr. Dyson was a gentleman, and, of course, when Peace spoke to him he used to reply. He introduced himself, and would have you to talk with him whether you would or no. At first Mr. Dyson did not object, and Peace became a constant visitor to the house. Our impression of him at that time was that he was really a nice old man. I suppose you have heard how plausible he was? He was plausibility itself. To hear him talk, you would have thought him the most harmless of men.

To us he appeared to be simply a picture-framer in anything but good circumstances, for he had but little business to do, and his wife used to go out every morning washing bottles. We considered they were poor. Mr. Dyson soon began to tire of him. He very soon began to show that he was anything but a gentleman. Mr. Dyson could not stand that; and, besides, he had seen something which disgusted him—some obscene pictures which Peace had shown him. He said he didn't like a man of that kind, and wouldn't have anything more to do with him.

Besides, another thing greatly repelled Mr. Dyson. It was this. Peace wanted to take him to Sheffield to show him what he called the " sights of the town." Mr. Dyson knew what that meant, and being, as I have said, a gentleman, he became much disgusted at Peace and annoyed that he should force his company upon us. My husband had been used to other society. But we couldn't get rid of him. We were bound to show him common politeness. Though he must have seen that we didn't want his company, he forced himself upon us.

He would, for instance, drop in just when we were sitting down to tea, and we were compelled almost to ask him to have a cup. His constant visits to the house at last became intolerable to us, and then it was that my husband placed his card in the garden, desiring Peace not to annoy him or his family.

When he found that he could no longer gain access to the house, Peace became awfully impudent. He would, for instance, stand on the doorstep and listen through the keyhole to what we were talking about, or look through the window at us. His persecutions at this time became almost unbearable. He did everything he could to annoy us. I was not afraid of him, and should have taken the law into my own hands, but my husband would not hear of such a thing. He always advised me to keep quiet.

Amanuensis: It is impossible for you, Mrs. Dyson, to be unaware of the rumours afloat as to the terms on which you and Peace were at Darnall. Would you like to say anything about that matter?

Mrs. Dyson: That is just what I want to speak about. (Here Mrs. Dyson spoke under some emotion and her face became quite flushed with excitement.) That's what I want to speak about, and I want you to do me the justice of writing down just what I state.

The public of Sheffield—the vulgar public I mean—have been prejudiced against me. I have been tried in every shape and form since I came over here to give evidence, and my character and credibility have been made light of. But I want the people of Sheffield to see that I am a different kind of person from that which they have taken me for. They have classed me with Peace and Mrs. Thompson, and others of his gang, but I wish to show them that I am far superior to any of them.

Mr. Dyson did not take a stronger disgust to Peace than I did. In fact, I think I was the first to express my disgust. I could not stand his impudence and the way in which he went on. I had not been used to such society as his proved to be, and I rebelled against it. I can hardly describe all that he did to annoy us after he was informed that he was not wanted at our house. He would come and stand outside the window at night and look in, leering all the while; and he would come across you at all turns and leer in your face in a manner that was truly frightful. How is it that having been so friendly with me and Mr. Dyson, Peace should conceive so intense a dislike to us? Well, I admit that's a matter which has never been clearly stated, and I want it clearly stating now. His object was to obtain power over me, and, having done that, to make me an accomplice of his.

I have told you that when I knew him first I thought him to be a picture-framer, and nothing more. Since then, however, I have learnt a good deal, and much that was difficult to understand has been made plain.

He wanted me to leave my husband. "What should I do that for?" I said. "If you will only go to Manchester," he answered, "I will take a store (American for shop) for you, and will spend £50 in fitting it up. You shall have a cigar store, or a picture store. You are a fine-looking woman. You look well in fine things, and I will send you fine clothes and jewellery, and if you wanted to pawn them it would be easy. The pawnbroker would think everything all right. Suppose for instance, you had a grand pair of bracelets on, all you would have to do would be to go into the pawnbroker's, take them off your wrist, and say, 'I want

to pawn these things.'" He also said, "If you will only do what I want you, there shall not be such another lady in England as you may be."

At the time I couldn't understand what was his object. Of course, I see it plain enough now. At that time I didn't know he was a burglar. But I was suspicious.

I remember on one occasion he offered me a sealskin jacket and several yards of silk. If I had accepted them I should have been quite in his power. I declined his present, and told him that if he had a sealskin jacket and some silk to spare, he had better make a present of them to his wife and daughter.

I also told him that they wanted them much more than I did, and that if I desired to have a sealskin jacket, I would wait for it until my husband bought it, and that if he couldn't I was content to go without.

Some time afterwards he offered me a gold watch; but I wouldn't have it. That, of course, was stolen. I consider that he offered me these presents as one means of getting me into his power.

I remember, when he was speaking to me about Manchester, he said, "If you will only go, I'll fix you up there nice. You will have a splendid business, and will live like a lady."

"Thank you," I said, "I always have lived like one, and shall continue to do so quite independently of you." I was getting downright mad with him, because of his constantly bothering me.

What he wanted me to go to Manchester for was to pass off his stolen goods—at least that is my opinion. When he found he could not succeed by fair means, then he tried what threats and persecution would do. He once came into my house, and said as I would not do what he wanted, he would annoy and torment me to the end of the world.

"Don't you ever come into my house again," I said, "or ever darken its doors."

But it was no use. He still came whenever he could get in, and when he couldn't he watched for me and followed me wherever I went. I have known him go to the railway station and say to the booking clerk after I had taken my ticket, "Give me a ticket for where she's going." That's how it was he followed me to Mansfield, and then came into the same house there where I and my companion were staying.

That was, too, how it was that he was seen with me in the streets. So it was as regards his being with me in the fair ground, about which so much has been made.

I went to the fair with a neighbour and her children, and when we got into the photographic saloon my intention was to have the children photographed. I had no intention whatever of having myself taken with Peace, but he stood behind my chair at the time my likeness was taken. That was quite unknown to me, though, at the time.

You can have no idea, unless you know the man, how he persecuted one, and attempted to get me within his power.

Once I was terribly frightened at him. I was busy, I remember, doing something in the kitchen, and my back was turned to the door. Hearing a slight noise, I turned round, and then I saw Peace standing just inside the door. The expression on his face was something dreadful. It was almost fiendish—devilish. He had a revolver in his right hand, and he held it up towards me and said, in an excited and threatening manner, "Now, will you go to Manchester? Now will you go to Manchester?" I did not shriek, but I cried out "No, never! What do you take me for?"

Finding that I was firm, he dropped his hand and went out; but I can assure you that I was frightened at the time. He had a way of creeping and crawling about, and of coming upon you unawares; and I cannot describe to you how he seemed to wriggle himself inside the door, or the terrible expression on his face. He seemed more like an evil spirit than a man.

He turned against me solely because he could not make me do as he wanted. He thought he could handle me as he liked, that I was a weak sort of a woman, and could be got over like others who have been associated with him; but he found he was mistaken. I was terribly tried by him, though, and at last I was frightened—I don't deny it.

There have been times when I haven't feared him, and when I should have thrashed him if Mr. Dyson would have allowed me. I once did give him a good hiding, because he had insulted and annoyed me, but perhaps I had better not say much about that now. I used to be especially afraid of him at nights, because he had a habit of continually prowling about the house, and of turning up suddenly. He would, too, assume all sorts of disguises. He used to boast how effectively he could disguise himself; and I was afraid of his coming in some guise or other at night, and carrying out his threats.

I never saw such determination and persistency as his. It seems to me there was scarcely anything which he couldn't accomplish if only he was determined. The only way to get rid of him was to knock him down, as I once did.

Determined as he was one way, I was equally determined the other, and that was why he never succeeded with me. He once made use of this expression to me, "I don't care how independent you are, I'll get hold of you some way or other." But I said as firmly as I could, "Never!" and so I have always said.

The statement is not true that your husband was jealous of you and Peace, and so decided to go to Bannercross? Why should he be jealous? There was no cause; for all this time that we were at Darnall I was doing my best to withstand Peace. I know what has been thought and what has been said. (Here Mrs. Dyson spoke excitedly and in a tone of much bitterness.) I think no woman has ever been tried as I have.

Why, ever since I came from America to give evidence, they have been trying me, not Peace. I want the public to understand that I have been tested to the utmost, and yet what has been proved against me? Why absolutely nothing.

All that has been said about myself and Peace is a lie, and I wish it to be put down as a LIE. If you could draw three strokes under the word, so as to make it plainer I should like it done. I wanted this opportunity of saying what I have on this matter. I had no one to speak up for me, I had to speak for myself. I deny what has been said and imputed with regard to Peace and myself, and I dare and defy any one to say with truth that my conduct with regard to him was anything but what was right. We went to Bannercross simply because we were afraid of Peace. What became of Peace after the warrant was taken out I never knew, except that I heard he had gone over to Manchester.

He suddenly disappeared, and I did not see him again until on the very day that our furniture was being removed to Bannercross. I and my husband saw him coming out of our new house there. So annoyed and irritated was I at this that I really should have caught hold of him, and held him until a police-man could have been fetched. But my husband would not hear of such a thing. I really felt quite mad.

This was on the 25th October, and I did not see him again till the night of the murder. There is no truth whatever in the imputation that I was with Peace on the day and night previous to the murder. I say I never saw him from the time of his coming out of our house on the 25th of October till I saw him, pistol in hand, standing outside the closet door on the night of the murder. To say that I did is an abominable and wicked lie. But no one can really say that I did.

It is true certain persons were brought at the trial, but could they say that they had seen me? No, not one of them: and I defy them to say it.

I am aware, as you say, that when I was asked if Peace did not follow me into the "Stag" Inn on the night before the murder, I replied that I could almost swear it wasn't Peace. I know also that it seemed as if my evidence at that point was weak. But I didn't want to swear a lie.

Peace had been in the habit of so disguising himself and of following me about that I should not have been surprised if it had been him. That was why I answered Mr. Lockwood in the way I did. It certainly was not Peace. Of that I am confident.

It is not true, as it was imputed, that I was in the fair with Peace on the day before my husband was shot. I simply passed along the road from the Victoria Station and looked over the wall. Neither is it true that I went with him to any dining-rooms, or to a public-house. That is a lie altogether.

The only place I called at was at Mr. Muddiman's shop, at the top of Pinstone-street, and I went from there to the "Stag" at Sharrow.

If I were to die this minute, I am altogether innocent of seeing Peace or of having anything to do with him from the time of our going to Bannercross till the night of the murder. I cannot put the matter plainer than that, and I want it putting plainly.

As to the letters which Peace dropped on the night of the murder, I say as I have always said—that I never wrote them. They were base forgeries, and were written with an object. I cannot say whether Peace wrote them himself or whether they were written by members of his family, because they, as well as he, tried to get me into their power. But I know what the object was. It was to endeavour to compromise me.

Yet how much has been said about those letters, and how I have been maligned in regard to them! I don't think any woman has been tried as I have, or has been compelled to go through so much. But I have been able to stand up through it all, because I have spoken nothing but the truth. If the letters were mine, the handwriting could have been easily proved. Wasn't I tried in court about it? Didn't they ask me not once, but twice, to give specimens of my handwriting? If the letters were mine, they could then easily have proved it.

The letters must have been manufactured for a purpose. I don't see how else they could have come into existence. So far from writing to Peace after the murder, I never wrote to him in my life. I never heard anything about Peace from the night of the murder until Walsh came over to Cleveland to fetch me.

I was staying at my sister's house there, and Walsh went direct to the house. When told that he had come, I knew at once what he wanted me for, and to his question whether I was willing to go back with him to give evidence against Peace, I said "I would go back if I had to walk on my head all the way."

That's just what I said, and it will show how willing I was to give evidence.

Of course, at the time I didn't know what I should have to pass through, but if it were to come all over again I would do the same. My friends didn't want me to come, and did all they could to dissuade me. I also received a threatening letter from Sheffield. But I was determined to come. My desire was that Peace should receive the justice he so richly deserved.

I didn't really know that Peace was a burglar until after the murder. If I had he would never have entered our doors. But what I know now explains a good deal.

For instance, when we were out walking together, if I happened to look into a shop window, he would say to me, " Is there anything there you would like ? If there is I will get it for you before morning." He would say that if I looked into a jeweller's or a draper's shop. I did not know what he meant then, but I do now.

My suspicions were aroused, for I used to see him leave his house at Darnall in the evenings with a little satchel under his arm, and he would come back early in the morning carrying a large bundle. The satchel, I suppose, contained his housebreaking implements. He often used to go to Manchester with this satchel.

He came to my door one morning just as he was going to Manchester. He then had his satchel with him. Looking into the room where I was, he said, "I'll have you alive or dead. I'll have you, or else I'll torment you till the end of your life."

On another occasion, when I had defied him, he said, "I'll make you so that neither man nor woman shall look at you, and then I'll have you to myself."

I answered, " Never. What can you do ? What are you capable of ?" " No matter," he replied " I'll do it."

He was always wanting to get my photograph, and as I wouldn't give him it, he or some member of his family stole one out of a locket which I had. It was afterwards copied by a photographer in Sheffield, and I have fancied since that he wanted to get my features transferred in some way or other to one of his obscene pictures and so disgrace me.

I cannot understand in any other way what he meant by saying that he would make me so that neither man nor woman should look at me.

My opinion is that Peace is a perfect demon—not a man. I am told that since he has been sentenced to death he has become a changed character. That I don't believe. The place to which the wicked go is not bad enough for him. I think its occupants, bad as they might be, are too good to be where he is. No matter where he goes, I am satisfied there will be hell. Not even a Shakespeare could adequately paint such a man as he has been. My life-long regret will be that I ever knew him.

CHAPTER CLXV.

PEACE CONFESSES HIMSELF TO BE THE MURDERER OF A POLICEMAN NEAR MANCHESTER—THE CONVICT AND MRS. THOMPSON.

IT was understood on the Wednesday night that the convict Charles Peace was expected to confess to having murdered Constable Cock, at Whalley Range, near Manchester—a crime for which a youth of eighteen years of age, named William Habron, had been sentenced to death, and only escaped with a commutation of his sentence to penal servitude for life. Peace, in justice to this young man, made a full and explicit confession. He admitted, with many professions of penitence, that he murdered the officer, and declared Habron to be perfectly innocent of the crime, for which he was at that time so cruelly and injustly suffering.

When, in July, 1876, Peace heard that Mrs. Dyson had taken out a warrant against him, he packed up his " tools " and some other things and prepared to leave Darnall. His family asked him where he was going, and he replied, " To Manchester." He had often been there before. Indeed, it was a favourite resort of his. When he lived on the Brocco, and in Scotland-street, as well as after he went to Darnall, he frequently ran over to Manchester, sometimes remaining there for a week or more.

It is no secret that he went there to commit robberies. There was a man there to whom he sold his plunder, and he would come back to Sheffield with nothing but the proceeds in hard cash. Of course there was nothing remarkable in his going to Manchester, and he confessed that he went there on this particular occasion—as he had often gone before—" to work."

On the afternoon of the 1st August he went round by Whalley Range to select a likely house as the object of his burglarious intentions, and he " put up " that occupied by Mr. Gatrix, at West Point, where three public roads, and an occupation road, converge. Towards midnight he went to the place, and as he was creeping along under the overhanging trees on the opposite side of the road he saw Mr. Simpson and the two policemen, Cock and Beanland, talking together on the footpath.

Presently he left his hiding-place and crossed from Upper Chorlton-road to Seymour-grove, looking distinctly at the officers as he passed. He entered Mr. Gatrix's grounds, but before he could get up to the house he heard a policeman on his track ; and it is a fact that Beanland followed him.

Peace doubled, and attempted to leave the grounds by another way, when he was confronted by Police-constable Cock, who attempted to apprehend him. Said Peace, I told him to " Stand back !" and, to frighten him, I fired one barrel of my revolver. He, however, came towards me, and was about to collar me, when I hit him. By " hitting him " Peace meant that he fired at him ; the officer fell and he escaped.

Peace remained in Manchester for several days, and heard of the arrest of the Habrons, and the committal of John and William on the charge of " Wilful murder." He then left the city and went to Hull.

During the next few weeks he gravitated between Hull, Sheffield, and Manchester several times, and he was in the latter place at the end of November. Incredible as it may seem, he distinctly stated that he went to the Assize Courts and heard the two Habrons tried for the crime which he had himself committed. He was present when John was acquitted, and he heard William sentenced to death.

He appeared to have had no compunctions of conscience whatever at the terrible position in which he had placed the youth. Had the sentence been carried out there is no reason whatever to suppose that Peace would have come forward and confessed to the crime. It would almost seem that his escape from the remotest suspicion at Manchester only made him more reckless, as the night after the trial he went to Bannercross and shot Mr. Dyson.

Since he was himself sentenced to death at Leeds, and he had occupied the condemned cell, he had thought not only of the crime for which he was suffering, but also of that other almost more diabolical act of his at

Whalley Range, for which an innocent man was undergoing punishment. Having given up all hope of life himself, and having nothing to fear from any confession he might make, he decided to do tardy justice to young Habron.

Some days before his execution he asked the Governor to supply him with the necessary paper, pencils, rule, compassses, and so forth, that he might draw some plans. Having satisfied the Governor as to the object for which he wanted them, the articles asked for were supplied. He then began working diligently upon the plans; and the progress of his work was a matter of no small interest, not only to the governor and the chaplain, but to all the officials who had to do with him. The plan which he drew of Bannercross two years after the murder proved that Peace could remember localities, and that he could transfer to paper his recollections. The plans he drew of West Point—for they were in three or four parts—represent very accurately the locality, and on them the precise spot as indicated where Peace encountered Cock and shot him, and the route he took to escape. He completed the plans, and handed them over to the governor, together with a full confession of his guilt.

Peace affected to the extremely sorry for the young man Habron, but he excused himself for not having done him the scant justice he deserved at his hands in a very plausible way. He said that if he had come forward and accepted the responsibility of his act he would have been sentenced to death without any doubt whatever; whereas the one who had to bear it had escaped with penal servitude.

We give the circumstances under which the murder was committed, and it will be seen at once that the crime looks very much more like the work of a man of Peace's experience than of a lad of eighteen, who probably never fired a revolver in his life.

Nicholas Cock, the officer who was murdered, was twenty-three years of age, and had been in the county constabulary about eight months. He was a Cornish man, but had gone from Durham to Manchester to join the force. His beat on the night of the 1st of August was from Chorlton village, along Chorlton-road, to its junction with Seymour-grove and Upper Chorlton-road. The junction is known as West Point, and is near Manley Hall. The officer's beat terminated there, and from that place he would retrace his steps to Chorlton village. The junction is a triangular piece of ground, from which three roads diverge—Chorlton-road, Upper Chorlton-road, and Seymour-grove—and there is also a small occupation road leading from that triangle to Firs Farm.

Cock arrived at West Point at midnight, and there he was met by Mr. Simpson, who was at that time a law student, and whose father resided in Upper Chorlton-road. They walked together a short distance along that road, and meeting Police-constable Beanland they stopped and conversed for a few minutes.

Whilst they were standing they observed a man walk out of the shadow of the overhanging trees in Upper Chorlton-road, and cross over the triangle to Seymour Grove. Here he stopped under a lamp, and, after gazing steadfastly at the officers, passed on. Beanland said to Cock, "Who's that man?" and he replied that he did not know.

They watched the man go up Seymour-grove, but finding that he did not pass the gates leading to the house of a Mr. Gatrix, Beanland said he would go and see who the man was.

The officer accordingly went up to the gate, and finding it open passed in and went up to the house. H

tried both doors and windows, and found them safe, and was turning to leave the grounds when he heard two shots, and saw two flashes of fire.

At the same time he heard some one shout, " Oh, murder, murder! I'm shot, I'm shot!" Scarcely half a minute had elapsed since he had left Cock, and, running back to the spot, he found the officer lying on the kerbstone. He was bleeding from a wound in the breast.

Police-sergeant Thompson, who was on duty in Whalley Range, and had heard the shots, came running up, and joined Beanland, at the same time that Mr. Simpson returned.

That gentleman also heard the firing when he was about two hundred yards from the end of Upper Chorlton-road. At that moment a night-soil cart came past, and the injured man was lifted into it and taken to Dr. Dill's surgery in Lower Chorlton-road.

Cock was unconscious when he arrived there, but after stimulants had been administered he revived a little, and was repeatedly asked who had shot him.

Once he said "I don't know," but afterwards relapsing into semi-unconsciousness, he said "Leave me a-be. Oh, Frank, you are killing me." There was no one named Frank in the room.

He died shortly afterwards, and at the post-mortem examination made by Dr. Dill, a gun-shot wound was found in the breast near the right nipple.

The ball had struck the fourth rib, shattered the bone, and had then gone through the right lung to the spine, where it had lodged. Death had resulted from hæmorrhage, which was very great, both internal and external.

Suspicion fell upon three brothers named John, William, and Frank Habron, the first of whom had been employed for nine years, the second for seven years, and the third for eight years, by Mr. Francis Deakin, nurseryman, of Chorlton-lane. Cock being a young officer, was disposed to take notice of things that older and more experienced men would have tolerated with impunity.

He had not been long in the neighbourhood before he incurred the ill-will of the Habrons, and both John and William were heard to use threats of violence towards him. In July, Cock saw John and William the worse for drink, and he obtained summonses against them.

The case against William was heard on the 27th July, and he was fined 5s. and costs. The case against his brother was adjourned until the 1st August, and between those dates John, on several occasions, and William, at least once, was heard to threaten what they would do to Cock if he was not careful. At the adjourned hearing, John was fined 10s. 6d., and that very night Cock was murdered.

Cock had told his superior officers what these young men had been heard to say, and immediately after his death, Superintendent Bent went with Inspector Whittam and a large staff of officers to apprehend the two brothers.

They occupied one room—a sort of outhouse—upon the premises of Mr. Deakin, their employer; and as the officers went up Chorlton-lane the room was full in view, and they saw a light in the window. Superintendent Bent called up Mr. Deakin, and then went to the outhouse, and found that in the meantime the light had been put out, and the police having rapped at the door, which was opened by one of the brothers, the three were arrested.

Next day the prisoners were brought before the magistrates.

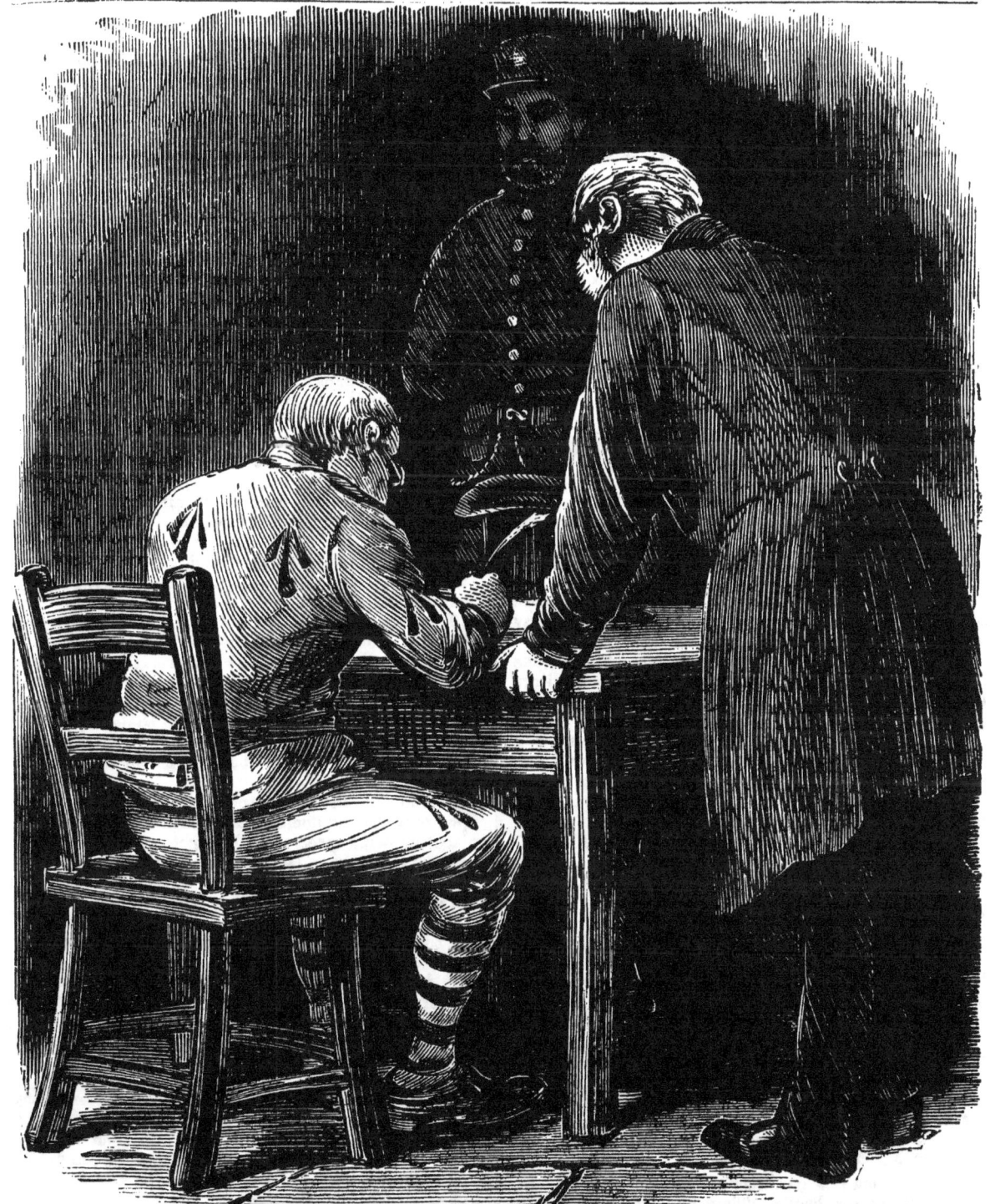

PEACE DRAWING THE PLAN OF THE WHALLEY RANGE MURDER.

CHAPTER CLXVI.

THE CONDEMNED MAN VISITED AGAIN BY HIS RELATIVES—PEACE CONFIRMS HIS CONFESSION.

ON Friday, Nov. 21st, Peace was again visited in Armley by his wife, Mrs. Hannah Peace, Willie Ward, his son, and Mr. and Mrs. Bolsover, his daughter and son-in-law.

Though this visit was intended to be kept a secret

from any but the prison and other officials, this object, very much to their annoyance, was defeated.

At the Normanton station they were discovered by a couple of reporters, and on their arrival at the Leeds station they were met by several others.

Taking shelter in a cab from their persistent attentions, they drove to Mr. Watson's, the solicitor engaged to draw up Peace's deed of gift, and then proceeded to the Town Hall, to get the necessary order of admission to the gaol.

There they had to wait for a couple of hours in consequence of the absence of the clerk to the visiting justices, who had ultimately to be sent for.

Two visits were made by them to the gaol during the day, for there was much business to transact, and this was the last occasion upon which it could be done.

When the relatives arrived at Armley on the first occasion, and reached the cell of the condemned man, they found him in a somewhat perturbed state.

He had got hold of the notion that the authorities were endeavouring to prevent his relations from seeing him, and he was determined that they should not be excluded from visiting him.

He was assured that he was labouring under a misapprehension, and that the relatives who had any claim to see him should be admitted. He thereupon became calm and expressed regret that he had been so hasty.

Peace then conversed for some time about his "deed of gift," and the disposition of his property. He told them that on the previous day Mr. Brion came to see him and spent nearly three hours with him.

He obtained from Mr. Brion a list of the articles retained by him, and which belonged to Peace, and a promise that they should be given up to the proper owner of them.

He also assigned to Mr. Brion the right to make use of three inventions that he had discovered, if they should be worth following up.

Having made the necessary arrangements for the completion of certain legal documents, the visitors left and returned to Leeds to again consult a legal gentleman.

In the afternoon they returned to Armley, and had another long interview with Peace. They found him —as they had found him during previous visits—calm and collected, and prepared to reply to any questions put to him. A number of subjects were referred to.

The chief of them was as to his remarkable confession that he murdered Police-constable Cock at Whalley Range, on the night of the 1st August, 1876.

He was told that a portion of the public had received the statement with considerable incredulity, that some persons would not believe that he had made any such confession, and others that if he had made it he had done it to throw discredit on the police, and that it was still untrue.

He repeated that he had made such a confession, and that he had prepared plans of the locality where the murder occurred.

The plans and the confession he had, he said, placed in the hands of the governor, by whom they had been forwarded to the proper authorities. In due course, he said, it would be seen whether or not he had not made such a confession.

Of course his relatives needed no confirmation of the statement at his hands. They knew perfectly well that he had made such a confession, and, what was more, it was no news to them.

It is true Peace never had a confederate in his work, but he could not do without a confidant. There is perhaps not a crime of any consequence that he had committed that he did not make known to some one.

He, however, exercised great discretion in the choice of his friends, and while he had his liberty he did not suffer anything at their hands.

He had not been back from Manchester among his friends long before he dropped hints that during his absence he had "done the biggest thing in his life."

Months went on, and one day when in a more than usually confiding state of mind, he told a relative the whole story; and it differed in no particular from the story he told in the condemned cell.

He said then that when he heard that the Dysons had taken out a warrant against him he went to Manchester.

He had not been there many days when he put up the house of Mr. Gatrix, at Whalley Range, intending to work it at night.

He went there before twelve o'clock, and it was he whom Mr. Simpson saw cross the road. He did not think the police were watching him when he went in at the gate, but before he got up to the house of Mr. Gatrix, he heard Police-constable Beanland following him.

He turned back towards the road, and jumped over the wall close to where Police-constable Cock was standing.

That officer tried to capture him, and as he would not keep back with the first shot he fired again, and hit him in the chest.

Attracted by the reports of his revolver he heard people coming in both directions, and to escape he jumped over the wall again into the grounds of Mr. Gatrix, and went through them past the place where the Habrons lived, and escaped without anyone having seen him.

The next day he heard of the arrest of the three Habrons, and he followed the course of the proceedings taken against them with the deepest interest.

On one occasion, when speaking of the murder to a relative at Hull, he said he was truly sorry for the young Habron who was sentenced to death, and subsequently let off with penal servitude for life, and said if he could get him his liberty, without sacrificing his own, he would do so.

At one time the crime appeared to weigh so heavily upon him that he declared he would draw plans of the place, showing precisely the spot where the murder was committed, and tracing the course of his flight from it, and forward them to the authorities, with a full statement of the facts, but withholding his name.

He thought, perhaps, that would lead to inquiry, and to the liberation of Habron. He did not carry out his intention at the time, and subsequently he said he should abandon it; but if he ever did get into trouble, one of his first acts would be to try to prove the innocence of Habron.

Peace did get into trouble, and a few days after he had himself been sentenced to death he bethought him of his determination.

He knew there was no prospect of a reprieve being obtained in his case; he knew that, say what he would, no further harm could come upon him; and he therefore set to work upon his plans and his confession, that he might do tardy justice to the young man he had so grievously wronged.

On Monday the Mrs. Peace visited him in his cell he was engaged upon the plans, and a hint was quite sufficient to let her know what he was doing.

When Mrs. Bolsover was with him on Wednesday he had completed his work—done, he said, all that lay in his power to secure the liberation of Habron; a load seemed taken off his mind, and he conversed with her freely on the subject.

He begged of her not to let this additional proof of his baseness trouble either her or the rest of his family, and said if there was anything more that he could do to prove his own guilt and Habron's innocence, he would gladly do it.

To the Rev. J. H. Littlewood, Vicar of Darnall, he told the same story, and when the subject was referred to, Peace adhered to all he had previously said upon it, and declared that he had spoken nothing with respect to it but the most naked truth.

There is no foundation whatever for the story that Peace had spoken about a crime committed by him seven or eight years before, or that he persisted in saying it was as long since he shot the policeman at Manchester.

The fact is that at that time Peace was in penal servitude doing the penitent business and winning a "ticket of leave."

Peace, during his last days, frequently expressed the hope that he would be able to walk to the scaffold.

On this matter he seemed exceedingly anxious; for, courageous as he undoubtedly was, he imagined that if he had to be carried it would look as if he was a coward.

The impression of one who saw him at the time was that he was suffering from partial paralysis of the lower extremities—a result, it might be, of his terrible leap from the train on his way to Sheffield.

His general health had somewhat improved.

He had, from the very moment of his conviction, regarded his speedy death as inevitable, and now that the time was rapidly approaching he showed no fear, nor gave any indication that he was not to meet the last act of justice with composure.

The stealing of the portrait, by Gainsborough, of the Duchess of Devonshire will be fresh in the minds of many of our readers.

It will be remembered that the picture, which was valued at ten thousand guineas, was very cleverly cut from its frame one night, and that since then no tidings whatever have been obtained as to its whereabouts.

The robbery looked like such a one as Peace would commit—it was so cleverly managed, and the thief left no trace behind.

It is not unnatural, therefore, that he should have been regarded as the thief, and we believe he had been seen on the subject by two or three gentlemen interested in the matter.

Peace stated that he did not steal the picture, nor did he know where it then was.

He had also been seen or written to regarding some valuable lace which was stolen some time before, and very urgent requests have been made to him to say where it now is.

But notorious as Peace is for his many burglaries and his successful way of "working" them, there are other burglars besides himself, and it is not surprising therefore that he knows nothing of the lace.

Peace had no actual accomplices; but he found a ready means of disposing of the booty which fell into his hands. The receivers, however, whoever they are, were not likely to suffer by any confession from Peace as to their whereabouts.

We understand that pressure had been put upon him—we suppose by the authorities—to induce him to say where he disposed of his plunder. But he had steadfastly refused to say.

When pressed on this point, his answer had generally been, that if any man were in prison on his account he would now do his best to get him out, but that he was the last man to be the means of getting anybody else into trouble.

The receivers, therefore, are safe so far as Peace was concerned; but we should have thought that Mrs. Thompson could have told all that the police wanted to know.

It may be, though, that Peace didn't tell her all, and that there were some things which he considered it wise to keep to himself.

During the course of an interview, Peace gave his relatives some excellent advice as to their future conduct, and expressed an earnest hope that they would all meet in heaven.

One of his relatives thereupon remarked that the Rev. Dr. Potter, of Sheffield, had preached a sermon about him, in which he said that "all hope for his (Peace's) salvation was gone for ever."

Peace replied, "Well, Dr. Potter might think so, but it's not my opinion." He moreover said that he was confident of his forgiveness and acceptance. Bad and base as he had been, he was yet able to look to his end with confidence and hope.

Peace had always had an objection to having his portrait taken, and it will be remembered how indignant he became at the Sheffield Police-court when he fancied that he was being sketched.

At Newgate, though, he had been compelled to submit to the unwelcome attentions of the prison photographer. This was before he was identified, and the portrait represents him with his lower jaw very much protruded.

A copy of the portrait falling into the hands of the London Stereoscopic Company, it had been multiplied in immense quantities and circulated all over the country.

This had, somehow or other, come to Peace's knowledge, and he wrote a letter to the Governor of Newgate Prison, complaining that he should have allowed his portrait to have been so made use of.

The power which he possessed of protruding his lower jaw seemed to have been a comparatively recent accomplishment. About ten months previously he broke off a couple of teeth.

The jagged stumps bothered him a good deal, and it was whilst working his jaws about to reduce the stumps to something like a level surface that he discovered he could so protrude his under jaw as to almost completely alter the expression of his face.

Upon making this discovery he told his relatives that it would stand him in good stead if he ever got into trouble, as he should be able to deceive the police as to his identity.

That he was firmly convinced of this was evident from the fact from the time of his apprehension at Blackheath until he was identified in Newgate he protruded his jaw in the manner shown in the photograph.

As soon as he was identified and found that the game was up, he abandoned this mode of disguise, and his face assumed its normal expression.

There was no use Mrs. Thompson endeavouring to see Peace, and she might as well have retired from the hopeless task. The fact was, Peace did not want to see her.

It might be that he had discovered by this time that she it was who had first informed the police authorities who it was that Robinson had apprehended at Blackheath.

During the interview with his relatives he was told that Mrs. Thompson had caused a letter to be written to the Home Secretary, asking for an order of admission to see him.

Peace at once replied that he did not wish to see

her, and that the Home Secretary's permission would be useless, inasmuch as he would have to be consulted, and that his permission would most certainly not be given.

The Leeds Central News reporter said :—

"About two o'clock on Friday, Hannah Peace, Wm. Ward, and Mr. and Mrs. Bolsover obtained permits from the Visiting Committee to see the condemned man for the last time.

"The nephew, Thomas Neil, also applied for a permit, but he was refused. On obtaining the orders or permits the party proceeded in a cab from the Town Hall to Armley Gaol.

"They were accompanied by a clerk of Mr. Alfred Watson, solicitor, who was to see that certain papers were signed by Peace. Among the papers in question was a new will and another deed of gift. The object of the visit was to induce Peace to make a new settlement of his affairs, and to take farewell of him. The interview was of nearly three hours' duration.

"During it Peace gave directions for the disposal of his affairs, and the conversation was for the most part entirely connected with private matters.

"A wish was expressed that Peace should not see Mrs. Thompson, but nothing further was said on that score. The parties then said good-bye, but the leave-taking could not be called a sorrowful one. Mrs. Bolsover was the only one that really appeared deeply affected at saying farewell.

"The relations of Peace subsequently drove to the office of Mr. Watson, solicitor, in order that he might draw up certain legal documents defining their respective interests in the property."

A Manchester correspondent wrote :—

"Although the police at Manchester are still without any official information on the subject of Peace's alleged confession of the Whalley Range murder, there is no abatement of the public anxiety in the matter.

"If Peace has really declared himself the murderer, the fact will be a great relief to a great portion of the public in the neighbourhood, for there has always been a strong feeling of doubt about the guilt of young Habron, who is now undergoing his commuted sentence.

"This feeling was expressed soon after the conviction in two petitions for a reprieve, one of which was signed by eight thousand persons, as many signing it probably because of the doubt there was in the case as on account of the convict's youth.

"The report that Peace gave an entertainment in a Wesleyan School, Hulme Hall-lane, Manchester, in August, 1876, is officially denied, but there seems to be no doubt that he was in the city in that month and a series of burglaries committed in the neighbourhood about that time are now attributed to him."

STILL ANOTHER LETTER TO THE CONVICT FROM MRS. THOMPSON.

The Central News reporter at Leeds telegraphed the following correspondence as having taken place :—

"Leeds Railway Station, G. N.
"9.15 p.m., 20th Feb., 1879.

"To Mrs. Thompson.

"I have been to-day and seen Charles Peace, and he has expressed a great wish to have your address, so that he can communicate with you. Will you, therefore, please write to him at once. I send this to you by ——, whom I have just met, and who has promised me to hand it to you.—Yours &c.,

"HY. T. BRION."

Mrs. Thompson at once forwarded the following letter to Peace :—

"21st February, 1879.

"My Own Dear Jack.—I have received information from Mr Brion that you have not altogether forgotten me, and that you don't utterly despise and hate your poor Sue. Oh, Jack, for the love of mercy, as you hope for that mercy which is given to all those who truly repent, do, my Jack, let me come to see you, if only once more. You know in your heart that you ought to see me, your own Sue.

"John, I have not betrayed you. Little do you know how I have suffered, and how I was threatened and tormented. I was only obeying that which you have over and over again told me, to save myself, as I could not do you good. Had I not have opened my mouth, I should now have been in prison like you—two of us instead of one—and that could have done you no good. Darling Jack, do write me asking me to come and see you. Never mind what the people in this world say.

"I can say many things. Darling, don't judge me wrongly, as you know your trouble has made me an altered and different woman. Oh, do take that to heart. I am living here in private lodgings so as to be near you. Now darling, I must and shall be near you. Oh! for all the love you bear me, do let me see you once more upon this earth. Do write me to my solicitor, for if I give my address it will get through the papers, and I am talked about enough. I will tell you where I stay when I see you. God in heaven bless you, and give you strength, is the every thought now of your unhappy Sue. John, write me quickly. Good bless you from my heart.—Yours, SUE."

"Friday.

"Darling,—Since writing you the enclosed, a letter from Mr. Brion has been sent to me, telling me that you want to see me. Oh, John, I am so happy to think this is true. This will be taken to the goal by the person who met Mr. Brion at the station and was kind enough to give me the message. Do, pet, write at once. The bearer will wait for your letter asking me to come, and when I receive it shall come at once. I will tell you where I am staying when I see you.

"Your Own SUE."

CHAPTER CLXVII.
THE CONVICT'S CONFESSION.

THE *Sheffield Daily Telegraph* gave the following as the full text of Peace's confessions to the Rev. Dr. Littlewood, vicar of Darnall :—

When Mr. Littlewood entered the cell he saluted the convict according to the custom he followed when he was chaplain at Wakefield Prison—"Well, my old friend Peace, how are you to-day ?"

Peace looked up at him with a wistful glance, and replied, "I am only very poorly, sir," and then, after averting his face, as if to hide the emotion upon it, he turned round and added, "but I am exceedingly pleased to see you." Mr. Littlewood said, "I should have been much more gratified, Peace, to have visited you under different circumstances. This is a very sad errand for me to have to attend upon you in such an awful position."

The convict shook his head and slightly moaned. "But I assure you," added Mr. Littlewood "that there is at least one person in the world who has deep sympathy with you."

Peace seemed a little surprised at this, and after some hesitation he asked, as Mr. Littlewood paused,

"Who is that?" Mr. Littlewood looked at him intently, and as their eyes met for a moment he added, "It is myself."

Peace seemed overpowered, muttered the words "I deeply thank you," and burst into tears. He remained sobbing for a considerable time, his body quivering, his lips moving as if he was muttering something, and altogether he appeared remarkably moved.

That remark, Mr. Littlewood says, made the criminal as humble as a child.

"I wanted to see you," said Peace after a few moments, to unburden my mind to you. I know I am about to die, and I want to take from my conscience some things which weigh heavy upon it, but before I begin I want to ask you—do you believe I am anxious to speak the truth, and nothing but the truth?" He paused for a minute, and Mr. Littlewood also waited.

Peace then resumed: "I know, sir, I am about to meet my God. I know that He will hear all that I now say in my cell, and that He will require me to give an account not only of what I have done, but of what I am now telling you. Do you believe me?"

Mr. Littlewood intimated that he would, but Peace did not seem satisfied with this, and pressing his face as close to the grating as he could, he said earnestly, "I do assure you, sir, I want to utter nothing but the truth and the whole truth in everything I say."

The convict paused again, and repeated the question in a firmer tone, as if he was determined not to proceed until he was assured that Mr. Littlewood had thorough confidence that he desired to speak the truth.

Mr. Littlewood looked at him carefully, observed his manner very closely, and states that from his experience as a prison chaplain in Wakefield, having had to do with criminals of the deepest dye for many years, his own conviction was that the convict really was in earnest, and as sincere as any man could be.

Peace waited during all this trying time until Mr. Littlewood at last said, "Yes, Peace, I believe you are sincere, and desire to speak the truth. No matter how bad you are or have been, I cannot conceive it possible that any human being in your terrible position could deliberately lie and confirm those lies, knowing that your Creator and Judge is conscious of all you say, and that you will have to give an account of all you utter."

Peace seemed relieved at what Mr. Littlewood said, and after waiting a little he said, "You know, sir, I have nothing to gain and nothing to lose in my present position. I know I shall be hanged next Tuesday. I desire to be hanged. I do not want to linger out my life in penal servitude. I would rather end my days on Tuesday than have that dreadful looking forward to all those years, but I do want as far as I can to atone in some measure for the past by telling all I know to some one in whom I have confidence," and he added, looking up earnestly into Mr. Littlewood's eyes, "I have perfect confidence in you."

Proceeding, Peace said, "I am exceeding grieved and repentant for all my past life, and if I could only undo anything I have done, or make amends for it in any possible way I would"—and he spoke very firmly, "I would suffer my body as I now stand to be cut in pieces inch by inch." He then turned again to Mr. Littlewood, evidently to see what effect his words had upon him, and as the rev. gentleman made no response he asked him again, sharply and firmly, but yet somewhat pleadingly, "Do you really think, sir, I am speaking the truth?"

Mr. Littlewood again assured him that he believed him, and then Peace continued, in lower and mournful tones: "I feel, sir," and he raised his hands wearily, "I feel, sir, that I am too bad either to live or to die, and having this feeling I cannot think that either you or anyone else will believe me, and that is the reason why I ask you so much to try and be assured that you do not think I am telling lies. I call my God to witness that all I am saying and wish to say shall be the truth, the whole truth, and nothing but the truth."

Mr. Littlewood says that at this moment Peace talked with all the earnestness of a judge, and repeated these words with a deliberate solemnity which greatly impressed him. As he spoke he turned not only to Mr. Littlewood, but motioned also towards the warders, as if he were invoking God in the presence of them as witnesses. He was not at all excited, but spoke most rationally and coherently.

"Well, now, sir," said Peace, evidently reassured by Mr. Littlewood's belief in him, "in the first place I understand that you have still the impression that I stole the clock from your day-schools." He waited for an answer.

"Well," said Mr. Littlewood, "I have that impression."

"I thought you had," replied Peace, "and this has caused me much grief and pain, for I can assure you I have so much respect for you personally that I would rather have given you a clock, and much more besides, than have taken it." Then he added, "At the time your clock was stolen I had reason for suspecting that it was taken by some colliers whom I knew."

Peace stopped again. Mr. Littlewood thought he was going to mention the names of the colliers, but he did not, and as the rev. gentleman was not disposed to follow that subject up, thinking it was too trifling compared with the others that were to follow, it was about to be dropped, when the convict turned to him again sharply, and earnestly asked, "Do you now believe that I have spoken the truth in denying that I took your clock, and will you leave me to-day, fully believing that I am innocent of doing that?"

Mr. Littlewood looked at him again, to confirm his own conclusion, and paused for some few moments, as if deliberating what he should reply.

The convict watched him keenly all the time, and seemed rather uneasy at the answer about to be made, but in the end Mr. Littlewood said, "Peace, I am convinced that you did not take the clock. I cannot believe that you dare deny it now in your position, if you really did."

The convict looked immensely relieved, and burst into tears afresh, and it was some time before he was able to proceed. He next abruptly said—

"Now, Mr. Littlewood, about the Bannercross murder. I want first to say solemnly before you in the sight of these men, and in the hearing of God, that several witnesses grossly perjured themselves. Brassington and Mrs. Padmore were two. They have grossly perjured themselves, but I freely and fully forgive them, and hope to meet them in Heaven. You may ask me what their perjury was. Well, they swore that they heard me threaten Mrs. Dyson. That was a lie. I call God to witness that I never did threaten Mrs. Dyson. I tell you, sir, that Mrs. Dyson and I were on such intimate terms that I could not have done so. It would not have suited my purpose to have quarrelled with or threatened Mrs. Dyson."

Here the convict made use of language expressive of his familiarities with Mrs. Dyson which we cannot reproduce in print, but, if true, confirms all that has been alleged on that delicate subject. Without another word he then burst out:

"And now about Whalley Range."

Mr. Littlewood was a little anxious to keep him on the Bannercross murder for a little time, but Peace would have his own way, and he went on.

"I was in Manchester in 1876, and I was there to 'work' some house. I went to a place called Whalley Range. I had 'spotted' a house there which I thought I could get into without much trouble. I was always respectably dressed. I made a point of dressing respectably because I knew the police never think of suspecting one who appears in good clothes.

"In this way I have thrown the police off their guard many a time. I walked through the streets of Manchester, and occasionally went between policemen who were all the time exercising their brains as to the burglar who had 'done' some houses there. On my way to the house that night I passed two policemen on the road. I may tell you I did not go to any house by accident.

"I always went some days, sometimes weeks, before, carefully examining all the surroundings, and then, having 'spotted' a likely house, I studied the neighbourhood, both as to the means of getting in and as to getting away. There were some grounds about that house, and my object was to get into these grounds in the dark, and wait a convenient time for getting into the house.

"I missed the policemen, and for a moment I thought they had not suspected me, and had not come my way. I must have been mistaken. I walked into the grounds through the gate, and before I was able to begin to 'work' I heard a rustling and a step behind me. Looking back I saw a policeman, whose figure was the same as one of the two I passed on the road, coming into the grounds. He had evidently seen me, urned back and followed.

"I saw I could do no work that night, and then doubled to elude him. For a moment I succeeded, and taking a favourable chance, I endeavoured to make my escape. As quickly as I could I jumped on the wall, and as I was dropping down, and had cleared the premises, I almost fell into the arms of a second policeman, who must have been planted in the expectation that I would escape that way.

"This policeman—I did not know his name—made a grab at me. My blood was up, because I was nettled that I had been disturbed, having 'spotted' that house for a long time and determined to do it—so I told him, 'You stand back, or I'll shoot you.' He didn't stand back, but came on, and I stepped back a few yards and fired wide at him purposely to frighten him that I might get away.

"And now, sir, I want to tell you, and I want you to believe me, that I always made it a rule during the whole of my career never to take life if I could avoid it."

The convict said this very earnestly, and looked at Mr. Littlewood as if he expected a further reassurance of his faith in him on that score.

"Yes, sir," he repeated, "whether you believe me or not, I never wanted to take human life. I never wanted to murder anybody. I only wanted to do what I came to do and get away, but it does seem odd, after all, that in the end I should have to be hanged for having taken life—the very thing I always endeavoured to avoid. I have never willingly or knowingly hurt a living creature. I would not even hurt an animal, much less a man.

"That is why I tell you, sir, that I fired wide on him, but the policeman, like most Manchester policemen, was a determined man. They are a very obstinate lot, these Manchester policemen. He was no doubt as determined as I was myself, and you know that when I am put to it I can do that which very few men can do.

"After I fired wide at him—and it was all the work of a few moments, sir—I noticed that he had seized his staff, which was in his pocket, and was rushing at me and about to strike me. I saw I had no time to lose if I wanted to get away at all that night. I then fired the second time, and I assure you again that then I had no intention of killing him.

"All I wanted to do was to disable the arm which carried the staff, and in order that I might get away. But instead of that he came on to seize me, and we had a scuffle together. I could not take as careful an aim as I would have done, and the bullet missed the arm, struck him in the breast, and he fell. I know no more. I got away, which was all I wanted."

Peace then rested for a little, and afterwards proceeded.

"I left Manchester and went to Hull. Some time afterwards I saw it announced in the papers that certain men had been taken into custody for the murder of this policeman. This greatly interested me. I always had a liking to be present at trials, as the public no doubt know by this time, and I determined to be present at this trial.

"I left Hull for Manchester, not telling my family where I had gone, and attended the assizes at Manchester for two days, and heard the youngest of the brothers, as I was told they were, sentenced to death. The sentence was afterwards commuted to penal servitude for life.

"Now, sir, some people will say that I was a hardened wretch for allowing an innocent man to suffer for my guilt, for the crime of which I was guilty, but what man would have given himself up under such circumstances, knowing as I did that I should certainly be hanged for the crime?

"But now that I am going to forfeit my own life, and feel that I have nothing to gain by further secrecy, I think it is right in the sight of God and man to clear this young man, who is entirely innocent of the crime.

"That man was sentenced to death the day before I shot Mr. Dyson. I did not intend—I really did not intend—to kill this policeman, but only to disable him, and then to get away myself, and I call God to witness that his life was taken by me unintentionally.

"I came to Sheffield the night after the trial, and went to Bannercross in the evening. There is a low wall at the back of the house where the Dysons lived, which is one of the houses in the terrace called Bannercross-terrace.

"I wanted to see Mrs. Dyson. I stood on the low wall at the back of the house. I knew the house very well, both front and back, and I knew that the bedroom was to the back.

"While I was standing I noticed a light in the bedroom. The blind was up, and I could see plainly Mrs. Dyson carrying a candle and moving about the room.

"I watched her for some time, and I then saw that she was putting her boy to bed. I then 'flipped my fingers'—and the convict imitated the action to Mr. Littlewood—and gave a sort of subdued whistle to attract the attention of Mrs. Dyson, as I had often done before at other places.

"I had not long to wait. Mrs. Dyson came downstairs—she had evidently heard the signal, and knew I was there—and in response to my call she came out and passed out to the closet. I then got down off the wall into the yard, and went towards the closet.

"I was with her there some time. You may ask what I wanted to do with her there. Well, I did not want to do what people think. I went simply for the purpose of begging her to induce her husband to withdraw the warrant which had been issued against me.

"I was tired of being hunted about, not being able to go and come as I liked. I only wanted the warrant withdrawn. That was my only object, and if I had got that done I should have gone away again.

"Mrs. Dyson became very noisy and defiant, used fearful language and threats against me, and I got angry. Taking my revolver out of my pocket, I held it up in her face, and said, 'Now, you be careful what you are saying to me. You know me of old, and know what I can do. You know that I am not a man to be talked to in that way. If there is one man who will not be trifled with by you or anybody else, it is Charles Peace.'

"She did not take warning, but continued to use threats against me, and angered me. I tried to keep as cool as I could. While these loud and angry words were going on Mr. Dyson hastily made his appearance. As soon as I saw Mr. Dyson I immediately started down the passage which leads to the main road. I was not sharp enough.

"Mr. Dyson seized me before I could get past him. I told him to stand back and let me go, but he did not, and I then fired one barrel of my revolver wide at him to frighten him, expecting that he would then loose me and that I should get off. I assure you I purposely fired wide.

"I was so near to him I could have shot him dead at the first shot, but I purposely fired wide and the bullet hit the gable end of the house. Mr. Dyson kept his hold of me, struggled with me, and at last was about to get the better of me. He got hold of the arm to which I had strapped my revolver, which I always did, and I then knew I had not a moment to spare.

"I made a desperate effort, wrenched the arm from him, and fired again.

"It was a life and death struggle, Mr. Littlewood, but even then I did not intend to shoot Mr. Dyson. This you must remember—my blood was up. I had been angry at what that woman had said to me.

"I had only come to ask that which I thought I should get, and I would have gone away and not troubled them again; but, then, with Mr. Dyson struggling with me, and having fired off one shot, I knew if I was captured it would mean transportation for life.

"That made me determined to get off somehow. I fired again, as I told you, but with no intention of killing him. I saw Dyson fall. I did not know where he was hit, nor had any idea that it was such a wound as would prove fatal.

"All that was in my head at the time was to get away, and if he had not so obstinately prevented me I should have got away.

"I assure you, sir, that I never did intend, either there or anywhere else, to take a man's life; but I was determined that I should not be caught at that time, as the result, knowing what I had done before, would have been worse even than had I stayed under the warrant.

"After firing the first shot I knew then how serious it was; and, whatever was sworn to at the trial, I tell you that we had a scuffle, that it was a life and death struggle, and for a time Dyson had the best of it.

"With my revolver I could have shot him dead at the first, but I did not do so, and when I next fired I could not calculate my aim owing to the excitement. If I had been able to do so I should simply have disabled him and got away.

"After Dyson fell I rushed into the middle of the road, and stood there for some moments. I hesitated as to what I should do. I felt disposed at first to go back and assist Dyson up, not thinking that he was wounded fatally; but I was labouring under great agitation, a number of people were gathering about. I heard them moving and rushing, and at last I decided to fly.

"I jumped over the wall on the other side of the road, and as I did so a packet of letters fell from my pocket just as I was jumping down over the fence.

"It is not true that I deliberately left these letters as a plot against Mrs. Dyson.

"They fell from my pocket. It is not likely that I should leave any letters about to show where I had gone.

"I call God to witness, sir, that I did not kill Mr. Dyson intentionally, and I most solemnly swear that in shooting at him I did not intend to murder him.

"Mrs. Dyson committed the grossest perjury in saying that no struggle between Dyson and myself took place. There was a fearful struggle, and she saw it.

"I want to be assured, Mr. Littlewood, that you really believe what I say. I tell you that if anyone thinks he will see that I never intended murder when I went to Bannercross.

"If I had meant to murder Mr. and Mrs. Dyson, or either of them, I knew the place well enough. All I had got to do was to go to the door, walk in, and shoot them both as they were sitting.

"And do you think, sir, if I had gone there to murder Dyson, that I should have allowed myself to be seen by so many persons? No, I would have gone about it in another way altogether.

"Of course I took Mr. Dyson's life as it turned out, but I did not go there with the intention of doing it.

"It was as unintentional a thing as ever was done, and it would not have been done if it had not been that I was interrupted in trying to get Mrs. Dyson to speak to her husband to withdraw that warrant, and if Mr. Dyson had not been so determined to get me into trouble and to prevent me getting away.

"Now, sir, will you tell me your candid opinion of Mrs. Dyson? I know what they say, but I would like to know what you think of her."

The Rev. Mr. Littlewood was not much disposed to state to the convict, as probably he would be to anyone, his candid opinion of Mrs. Dyson, but Peace insisted, and after a good deal of wavering and hesitation Mr. Littlewood answered him. His answer, of course, has nothing to do with this story.

Peace seemed slightly assured after hearing what Mr. Littlewood had said, and a little later, after resting himself, he added:

"During my life I have never once attempted to take life wilfully. I did not mean to take the life either of the Manchester policeman or of Mr. Dyson. Instead of taking life my object has been to save life.

"I have fired many a hundred barrels at people to frighten them, and I did succeed in frightening them, and in getting away after I had done what I came to do.

"Where they have lost their lives has been when they have roused me, struggled with me, and prevented me getting away, and even then it has been in a scuffle and never intentionally. Of course I have used threats that I would shoot them, but that was only meant to frighten them also.

"My great mistake, sir, and I can see it now as my end approaches, has been this—in all my career I have used ball cartridge. I can now see that in using ball cartridge I did wrong. I ought to have used blank cartridge; then I would not have taken life.

"If I had been captured after firing with blank cartridge in the face of anyone, I should have been able to say when I was taken that it was blank cartridge, and the worst thing that could have been done to me would only have been penal servitude. If I had to do it again I should not use ball cartridge.

"Now, sir, I am very anxious that this man who was committed at Manchester should be set at liberty, for God knows that he is innocent; and in order to prove that I took that man's life I want to tell you something.

"If they will take the bullet which they extracted from his body and examine it and weigh it they will find it was such a one as I was in the habit of using, and would fit my revolver.

"I shot him with the same revolver that I shot Mr. Dyson. In both Dyson's and the Manchester case one reason why fatal wounds were inflicted was, I tell you, because of the struggle, not knowing exactly what I did or the way the bullet would go. My revolver is a peculiar one."

Peace proceeded to describe technically as to its being a self-acting needle revolver, but Mr. Littlewood did not follow him so closely as to be able to reproduce his description. He gave Mr. Littlewood to understand that the revolver being self-acting he had no control over it after the first shot.

"I have drawn plans," continued Peace, "showing the place where the murder was done. I have furnished all the full particulars I have remembered. All this I have done in order that I may clear this innocent man, and unburden my own conscience of the crime before I go to the scaffold, when it will be too late. These plans and particulars I have handed to the governor, and he has told me that he has forwarded it to the Home Secretary."

"What was your object, said Mr. Littlewood, " in telling me all about this murder?"

"Well, sir," said Peace, "I want you to be an additional witness to my confession that I am now making to you that I did commit it."

"Do you want me to take any steps in the matter to bring this man's innocence out?"

"No," replied Peace, "not necessarily. But the fact of my having given this statement to you may be of some service to the young man when I am done with. And now, sir, after my poor body is done with I want to be entirely forgotten by everybody; and after my execution I hope my name will never again be mentioned."

"I also beg that you will use your influence in Darnall in preventing the people from persecuting the dear members of my family. They could not help anything I have done. They could not prevent it. They had not the slightest control over me in any possible way. They have no more to do with all my crimes than the greatest stranger in the land.

"Give my kind remembrances to the different people in Darnall whom I knew. Say to them, sir, that I hope they will be warned by my fate. Wish them good-bye, and tell them that Charles Peace, bad as he is, has still the hope that all of us may meet again in heaven.

"I hope God will give me strength to go like a hero to the scaffold. I do not say this, sir, in any sort of bravado. I do not mean a hero such as some persons will understand when they read this. I mean such a hero as my God might wish me to be. I feel sensible of my position. I feel penitent for all my crimes. I feel in speaking to you that one foot is on the scaffold, and I tell you, sir, before God and before men, that I am deeply grieved for all I have done. I would atone for it to the utmost of my power, and I shall endeavour to die bravely."

A long pause took place. Peace seemed somewhat exhausted, and looked wearied, worn, and anxious.

Mr. Littlewood then touched him upon a very delicate subject which he had determined to broach before he left Darnall. This was on the point of disclosing the names of the receivers who had taken his goods.

"I want you," he said to the convict, " to do me one favour. Will you grant it?"

"I will grant it if I can," replied Peace.

"Well," said Mr. Littlewood, "in the first place, I want you to be submissive and prepared for your great change. You say that you will do anything you can to atone to those you have wronged, and to make reparation for your wasted life."

"I do say so," said Peace; "I am most anxious to do so."

"Well," said Mr. Littlewood, " I can't point you out a way in which you can atone in a great measure to society for what you have done. Your disclosure about the Manchester murder is an act of justice, but there is a wider act due to society upon whom you have preyed. It is due to society still further that you reveal the names of those who have received your stolen goods.

"I have no hesitation in saying that such a disclosure would be greatly to your benefit in the sight of God. You could either make it to me or to anyone you think proper, but it is only your due to society to do it, and you have the best reason in the world for doing it, for you may attribute your present position in a great measure to those persons who have been in the habit of receiving your plunder."

Mr. Littlewood proceeded, "You know you would not have stolen sealskin jackets, silver plate, gold watches, diamond rings, and all those other things if you had not been able to dispose of them. They would have been really of no value to you unless you could have turned them into money. You committed a great injustice to society, and now I ask you to do an act of justice to society, and I ask you to do it as well for your own sake."

"Well, but you see, sir," replied Peace, with great emphasis, "I have always been a man, and I mean to be a man to the end. You know, sir, the public generally look on this kind of thing in the same light as you do. It is quite a mistake. I suppose you mean to say, sir, that if there were no receivers there would be no stealers?"

"Yes," said Mr. Littlewood; "that is what I say and what I think."

"Well, then," replied Peace, "I assure you, sir, that the impression is wrong. Supposing I have taken rings, containing diamonds or other brilliants, directly I have got them in my possession I have taken the gems from the gold, and then no one can swear to them in any court of justice.

"I always did that quickly. I sometimes did it on the night I got possession of the plunder, and before I went to bed. Then I had a crucible in which I melted down the gold and silver into small ingots, and disposed of them by simple weight."

MEMORIALS OF THE WHALLEY RANGE MURDER, DRAWN BY PEACE IN PRISON.

"Well, but, Peace," said Mr. Littlewood, "it seems to me your reply is not a sufficient reason for refusing to give up the names of the receivers of stolen property. If you would do so it would raise you considerably in the estimation of all respectable citizens, and confer an incalculable boon upon this country."

Peace made no response, and Mr. Littlewood continued: "You know, what you say about diamonds

and gold and silver may be all true. I don't dispute with you on that point, but you could not melt down sealskin jackets and things of that kind."

Peace still refused to make any response, and the subject eventually had to be dropped, as he seemed determined on the point.

[The reason Peace did not give the names may be stated here. His property was believed to be in the hands of receivers, and the law of felon's property is now altered. At one time when a felon was hanged all his property was forfeited to the Crown. The law has since taken a more merciful view of the convict's family, and permits the felon to will his property as he pleases. Of course there will no doubt be certain restrictions in the event of the property being identified as the proceeds of burglaries, but a person of Peace's habits would take care that his most valuable property was promptly realised and placed where it could be obtained. It is therefore more than probable that the reason we have stated is the correct explanation—that in the event of his disclosing the names of the receivers they would have cleared out and carried away all the booty, so that the family whom Peace seems disposed to benefit at the last would have received nothing.]

Passing from this subject Peace said to Mr. Littlewood, " Now, sir, may I ask you a favour ?"

" Yes," said Mr. Littlewood, " you may."

" I want you, sir, to preach a special sermon over my case, but I do not want it to be preached till after my execution. I want you to hold me up to the people of Darnall and to the world—to hold me and my career up as a beacon, that all who see may avoid my example. I want all who have known me to have me stated exactly as I am, that in the end my death may not be altogether without service to society.

"You know, sir, that the public of Darnall have nothing to say against me. They will certify to this fact—that I was respected by them. And they had no reason to think otherwise. I never did any of them any harm all the time I was there."

Mr. Littlewood told him that he could not quite see his way to preach a special sermon about his case, particularly as he had already expressed the wish that after he was executed his name should never be mentioned, but Peace held to this point. Eventually, however, Mr. Littlewood was enabled to pass on to some other subject.

" Now, sir," continued Peace, " I think I have told you all I have to say, and I want before you go that you should do me another thing. I should like you to hear me pray."

Mr. Littlewood assented, and Peace, turning to the warders, desired them to help him out of his chair that he might kneel down by his bedside. He also commanded them to kneel down. Mr. Littlewood also knelt close to the grating.

The convict then commenced a long and earnest prayer of nearly twenty minutes' duration. He prayed with great fervency and fluency. First of all he prayed for himself, and asked God for Christ's sake to blot out all his transgressions, and implored that his sins might be washed away in the blood of Jesus, and invoked the Holy Spirit to cleanse and purify his heart.

He referred to each member of his family, and prayed for them with equal earnestness.

From thence he went on to pray for those whom he had wronged, and interjected there a special prayer for Mr. Littlewood and his family, whom he hoped God would greatly bless and prosper.

He then prayed for society generally, all classes of the community, and one special part of his prayer powerfully impressed his hearers.

In a lower tone of voice and with subdued earnestness he prayed most devoutly for those two poor souls he had launched into eternity without any warning or any time to be prepared for their great change.

He prayed that he might meet them before God, and that God would forgive him for such a wicked act,

that they might meet in His presence, and he obtain full forgiveness for his crimes, and that thus meeting and recognising each other they might forgive and forget all that had happened on earth, and enjoy the fulness of God's presence for evermore.

Before Mr. Littlewood left Peace said, " I could like to ask you one thing, sir. Do you think it would be necessary for my own welfare that I should see Mrs. Dyson personally, and ask her forgiveness for shooting her husband ?"

Mr. Littlewood had understood that Mrs. Dyson had gone away, although she really did not leave till the next day, and he told the convict that Mrs. Dyson had left, adding—

" What you want, Peace, above all things, is the forgiveness not of any human being, but the forgiveness of your Maker ; and to that, with my last words to you, I want to direct your attention."

The convict looked perfectly satisfied, and asked Mr. Littlewood to engage in prayer, which he did. Mr. Littlewood's prayer was frequently interrupted by fervent responses on the part of Peace.

"Oh, God," he cried, " answer this prayer ! Have mercy upon me." And he cried and sobbed incessantly.

Though his face was buried in the bed-clothes, the sound of his sobbing was painful to hear, while his whole body quivered with emotion.

The scene was most affecting, and can never be forgotten by Mr. Littlewood or the warders who were present.

On rising from his knees Mr. Littlewood asked for a Bible and Prayer Book, which were handed to him by the warders.

Mr. Littlewood reminded Peace that the day of his execution would be Shrove Tuesday, and the day following that Ash Wednesday, the first day in Lent. He pointed out the peculiar appropriateness of various passages in the Prayer Book, particularly the well-known words of the Communion Service commencing " Let us therefore return unto Him who is the merciful receiver of all true penitent sinners, assuring ourselves that He is ready to receive us, and most willing to pardon us, if we come unto Him with faithful repentance, if we submit ourselves unto Him," &c.

He also directed his attention to the introductory sentences of morning and evening prayer, the Confession and the Absolution, as well as the seven Penitential Psalms, the beautiful words of which might almost have been written to meet the case of a great sinner like the condemned criminal crouching behind his prison bars.

The convict seemed pleased at Mr. Littlewood's attention, and glad to have anything to occupy his mind. He asked the reverend gentleman to turn the leaves down at these passages that he might ponder over them in his cell.

As Mr. Littlewood was preparing to leave, Peace, with tears in his eyes, said, " I suppose, sir, we shall never meet again in this world. I pray God to bless you, and all your family, and I pray we may meet again in heaven."

Then taking the left hand of the warder, who, at the same time, took Mr. Littlewood's right hand, the two parted, the visitor leaving the cell deeply affected by the interview, while the miserable being he had left was lifted wearily back into his bed, where he turned his face to the wall and wept.

CHAPTER CLXVIII.

AFFECTING FAREWELL LETTERS &c., FROM PEACE TO HIS
WIFE AND FAMILY.

PEACE, for a criminal, was a voluminous letter-writer, and after he had been sentenced to death no restriction whatever was placed upon his writing proclivities, and he indulged them to the full. When weary of writing himself, he enlisted the assistance of one of his warders, who penned at his dictation.

More than a week previous to his execution, Peace conceived the notion of writing a farewell letter to his wife, to each of his children and relatives, and to some of his friends, and of handing them to the chaplain when he was on the scaffold that he might post them for him.

He employed his time in writing or dictating these letters, and in a few days he had sixteen completed. He then handed them to the chaplain, who posted them as requested.

The following letters were addressed by Peace to his relatives :—

"From C. Peace. H. M. Prison, Leeds, Feb. 25, 1879.

"My Dear Dear Wife I have been A bace bad man to thee for many years O Dear if I had taken thy advice may years ago this would not have befallen me I need not ask for thy forgiveness for I know that thow hast already forgiven me for all I have done to them and my Dear I do not only forgive thee but I forgive all Persons for I have not any ill feeling against any Living Person. O my Dear wife I do pray to Almighty God for thee and I do hope that he will prosper thee in all thy doings and bring them to the kingdom of Heaven at the last where I hope that thou wilt meet me at the last So O My Dear Lass do not forget that our next meeting Place I hope will be in heaven. So do not forget to Prepare thy self to come.

"My Dear wife I do send you the coppy of some verses that I made when our Dear little John Died and I was at Woking Prison (Nov. 26, 1871, John died)

"They told me gently he was dead
My Dar and lovely child
They led me to the lonely grave
Whear lay my Darling boy

When they laid thee in this silent grave
I was A convict bound
But now I am free to meet and pray
On this thy sacred ground

Great God in Pity look on me
And take my life away
And turn my body cold as clay
And lay me with My boy

But hark me thinks I hear a voice
It is my lovely child
Hark me thinks I hear him say
I am not fit to die

Thou chides me well
My once loved one
And tells me what I am
I am not to live or die
I am such a wretched man

So lay and Sleep My once Loved one
And I will live and Pray
So fare thee well My Darling boy
I'll meet thee in the sky

"O My Dear Wife how can I say good bye to thee for ever but I must say it so.

"Good bye Good bye and may my God bless and bring thee to heaven at the last. Good bye for I am gone there."

Later on Peace wrote a second letter to his wife, as follows :—

"From Charles Peace
"H. M. Prison Leeds Tuesday Febe 25, 1879
to My Dear Wife

"I think that this is a true view of how I stand in this world in the first Place my sentence was Life and with me having ben three in Penerservitue I could not having got my freedom aney more so that I should have to die a misserbel death in Prison at the end. I mite have lived 20 year or more and have died in Prison at the last So my Dear wife I do think that me and you and my children hought to think that it will be for the best of my blessed Lord and Saviour Jesus Christ will hear my Prayers and for give me my sins and receive my Poor Soul into the Kingdom of Heaven. So think of this and tray to meet me thear oll you my Dear frinds I am husband and farther
"CHARLES PEACE.
"God bless you all."

On Tuesday morning after the convict had breakfasted he had a few minutes to spare before being introduced to Marwood, and he employed them in writing the following letters—the last he wrote :—

"From Leeds.
"H. M. Prison thuesday feb. 25, 1879.

"O my Dear wife and famerly I tel you this Grat Joy that I could not tel you yesterday for I could not I have not no fear now for it is all ded up as to ware I am going to I am going to Heaven or to the place ware the good go to that die in the Lord to wate in the Place appointed by God for the good to waite until the resurrection of the dead so do not forget our meeting Place is in Heaven so do come at the last and you will find me thear this letter is wrote 25 minits be fore I do die so I must know say good bye to all so good bye and God bless you all for I am gon to heaven. "CHARLES PEACE."

To his wife he also sent a very beautifully illuminated card. In the centre of a floral wreath was the following :—"The Lord bless thee, and help thee: The Lord make His face to shine for ever upon thee, and be gracious unto thee: The Lord lift up His countenance upon thee, and give thee peace."

On the back of the card the condemned man wrote :—

"My Dear Wife this was sent to me bye a Lady from Hull and as she wishes to me I do wish to thee My Dear wife so good bye for I am gone to Heaven. "CHARLES PEACE."

He also sent her a quarto copy of "The Old, Old Story." It was in two parts—(1) The Story Wanted; (2) The Story Told; with the author's music. On the last page he had written :—

"My Dear Wife, This was sent from London from a Lady at a prayer meeting, where prayers were offered up for me at Eaton-square, London, for to bring before thy poor husband's face his Saviour, finding him a poor lost sinner, and to bring him to his fold, where I also hope thou wilt be brought. "CHARLES PEACE."

LETTER, &c., TO HIS DAUGHTER.

The following is a copy of the convict's letter to his daughter.

"From Charles Peace H M Prison Leeds
"tuesday feb 25 1879

"O My Dear Jane Ann, My Dear child I send thee this letter from the scaffold, so O my Dear child do act up to it all through thy Life so that thou may bring thy Soul to the Kingdom of Heaven at the last ware I hope that thou will meet Me never to Part from Me no more, So My Dear child do above all things in this world Pray earnestly and continually to that only Great and Powerful God who will bless and Protect thee through Life and bring thee to Heaven at the last so my Dear Dear child Let me beg of thee not to fret for me no more then thou can help for it will do no one any good to fret so.

"My Dear child the Darling of my heart I am now compeled to say to thee for ever and ever Farewell for in a few moments time I shall be dead.

"So may the Lord Bless thee and thy baby and prosper you both and bring you to the Kingdom of Heaven at the last good bye good bye and God bless you—Your Farther,   "CHARLES PEACE.

"Good bye good bye I am gone to Heaven."

To Mrs. Bolsover he also sent a photograph, representing the crucifixion, and underneath, in the same handwriting as on the other photograph, is the following : "This man has done nothing amiss. He was wounded for our transgressions." On the back of the card, Peace wrote :—

"For Jane Ann.—My dear child, this was sent from London from a Lady at the prayer meeting in Eaton-square for to bring before thy poor father's face his dying Saviour that died to save him from his sins. And My Dear Child I hope it will bring thee from thine.—To My Dear Child.

"Good bye, for I am gone."

LETTER, &C., TO WILLIE WARD.

To his stepson, Willie Ward, Peace sent the following letter. Those sent to his wife and daughter were in his own handwriting ; the first part of the following letter was written at his dictation :—

"From Charles Peace.

"H.M. Prison, Leeds, Tuesday, Feb. 25, 1879.

"My dear Son,

"I now write to you my last dying wishes and request, that you will take a warning by poor me, and live happy and comfortable with your dear mother. I have handed this to my chaplain when upon the scaffold, and a moment before I die. Oh, let me beg of you in my last moments to give yourself to God, to try and walk in the narrow path that leadeth to eternal life. And may the Great God in His mercy pardon all your sins. And may we all meet in the end at the Right Hand in Glory. I have sincerely prayed to the Great and all powerful God to forgive me all my sins as I freely forgive all who may have sinned against me that those few lines may have their desired effect upon you and that we may all meet in Heaven is the Dying Prayer of your dying father.

"My Dear boy do do all that is wright in the sight of God and man and do not forgate that we have fixed upon our meeting place to be Heaven so I must say good bye good bye and may God bless thee My boy.

"Good bye good bye I am gone."

To his son he also sent a photograph of a painting representing our Saviour as the Good Shepherd. He has a crown of thorns on his head ; no shoes on his feet ; in His right hand He has the shepherd's crook, and on His left shoulder He carries a lamb, with which He is returning from the wilderness to the fold. Underneath, written in capitals, is the following :—"The Son of Man is come to seek and to save that which was lost." On the back of the card Peace wrote :—

"My Dear Child this was sent from London from a Lady at a Prayer meeting where Prayers was offered up for me at Eaton-square, London, for to bring before thy poor father's face his Saviour finding him a lost sinner and to bring him to his fold and I also hope my son that he will bring thee to his fold.

"For William Peace good bye my Dear son for I am gone there."

LETTERS TO HIS SON-IN-LAW.

The latter part of the following letter only is in the handwriting of the convict :—

"From Charles Peace.

"H.M. Prison, Leeds, Tuesday, 25th Feb., 1875.

"My dear son Bolsover.—This is my last letter here upon earth. Let me beg of you to take my dreadful end as a warning. May it be the cause of your leading a godly, righteous, and sober life, so that in the end you may obtain life everlasting. It is the last advice I can ever give to you, for when you receive this I shall be dead. This is handed to the chaplain upon the scaffold for you. May it have its desired effect upon you. I wish you prosperity. May you escape all the accidents to which your profession endangers you. May you live a long and happy life, and at the last, when you are put in the balance, God grant that you may not be found wanting, but that we may all meet at His right hand in glory, there to part no more, is the dying prayer of your poor father, Charles Peace.

"So I must say Good bye good bye and may God bless thee for I am gone to Heaven. Good bye.

"CHARLES PEACE."

LETTER FROM MRS. THOMPSON.

"Tuesday, Feb. 10, 1879.

"Dear Charley,—Why is it, after all my anxiety and trouble to come to see you after your especial desire to see me, and your letter yesterday, asking me to come at once, and now you don't see me? What have I done to not merit to see you? You have turned to me in all your troubles since I have known you. Is it because your relations have been? They had the first chance. Or were your feelings too much overcome I pity you much. I sincerely thank you for your second letter you sent by the governor to read to me. I do forgive you all as you ask me, as I hope to be forgiven. I shall for ever cherish the small scrap of paper torn from your long letter which the governor so kindly gave me in Armley Gaol. As you blame me for all that is being done, in regard to letters and in the papers, let me tell you I am not to blame. How could I have information that you had written to Hannah and Bolsover? You know, dearest, they are no friends of mine, and it is best known to themselves if they were unkindly treated when they came to my house. Had I have been in their position, I would not have come; but that is past. You cannot leave this world without seeing me again. You know I have been faithful and true to you if I have other faults. Now one word—clear your conscience of everything before it is too late."

Across this letter was written the following lines, said to have been Peace's own composition :—

"And while his heart
O can the heart grow cold?
False ones, the tales that in this world are told
Swell in his voice.
He knows not where to end,
Like one discouraging an absent friend."

On an enclosure addressed to Governor Keene was written "Please give the enclosed to my poor John."

The convict, absurd as it seems, was of a poetical turn, and he was very fond of reading and reciting poetry. Indeed, he had a weakness for versification, and had in his time written many a jingling rhyme. One of his favourite compositions that he was wont to declaim began with the lines :—

"Lion-hearted I've lived,
And when my time comes
Lion-hearted I'll die."

When news of Peace's arrest reached the inmates of the house at 5, Evelina-road, Peckham, the Dyson letters, so called, were given by Mrs. Thompson to Willie Ward to burn. Both Hannah Peace and the woman Thompson were in a terrible flutter, as the house contained things that would get them into trouble should the police search the premises. The letters entrusted to Willie Ward were with two or three exceptions all burned, the women foolishly thinking their existence might tend to the incrimination of Peace. This fact was well known to the detectives, it is said. The letters in question destroyed, in whosoever's handwriting they were, are stated to have contained requests for money, and their contents were not such as could have been written by a pure-minded person.

The Central News special correspondent at Leeds wrote that Mrs. Thompson had again made her appearance in Leeds. She was seen at the Post-office. She asserted her faith that she would see Peace before he died. She again wrote to him, as follows :—

"15th Feb., 1879.

"To the Governor of Armley Gaol.

"Sir,—Will you kindly oblige me by giving the enclosed to Charles Peace ?—Yours, &c., S. THOMPSON."

The following was the enclosure :—

"To Charles Peace, Armley Gaol, Leeds.

"Saturday, Feb 15, 1879.

"My own dear Jack,—What do you mean by turning against me—I who have cared for you ? What must I believe ? Hannah is admitted to see you as your wife, and you have most solemnly swore to me that she was not. When you and I went to Hull you told her you would and should marry me, as I alone should be your wife, as you could not part with me. Oh, why am I to suffer like this ? It is killing me. I am prevented from seeing you, and am pointed at in the streets, 'Here comes Mrs. Thompson.' Have I deserved this ? You would not have gone out had you have taken my advice upon the 9th of October [the date of his arrest.] It is most terrible that I am not allowed to see you. All your people are doing all they can to prevent me doing so. The magistrates' committee say I cannot unless you ask for me. John, darling, I must see you once again upon this earth. Darling, remember the last time I saw you. You turned back a second time to kiss me. Oh, I do upon my knees implore of you to see me. I am watched and hunted to death. Is this not fearful ? I do not imagine this, this time eight months ago, that I should have gained such notoriety in the world's history. John, do write me under cover to my solicitor. This is killing me. I have not a friend to whom I can turn upon earth. I cannot write more, for my heart is well-nigh broken. What must I, what shall I do ? God bless you. "Yours SUE.

"Oh, you have spoken harshly to me many times, but, then, when your temper has cooled down, you have come to me. John, Charley, let me see you. I freely forgive you what you ask me in your last letter. I cannot write more. Do ask to see me, John.

"Your own, SUE."

A letter was sent by Mrs. Thompson's solicitor, to the Home Secretary, on 13th Feb., which after stating the result of Mrs. Thompson's application to the Leeds Justices, states certain particulars as a reason why Mrs. Thompson should be allowed an interview with the convict. It is understood that the request had been refused by Mr. Cross.

PEACE AND HIS INVENTION.

The "Central News" special reporter at Leeds said the convict pointedly denied, that Mr. Brion ever knew or learned anything in respect of the invention for raising sunken vessels, except what he (Peace) imparted to him. He charged Mr. Brion with ingratitude in the matter, and said that when that individual first received a hint of the plan, he did not rest content until he had got possession of all the details of the invention. Peace's method for raising sunken ships was to close their hatchways, ports, and any large leaks, and to force air into the hold, a simple trap or valve allowing the water to escape as the air was forced in. He purchased a small model steamer, and having taken out the engines and boilers, altered her to suit his purpose, and attached one of his valves and India-rubber tubing connnected wiih an air pump to the deck. A wooden tank about 7 feet long, 3 or 4 feet wide, and the same in depth was made, and this was filled with water in order to enable Peace to carry on his experiments. The model boat was also on several occasions sunk to the bottom of the Thames, and raised again by Peace's apparatus, a select party of his own and Mr. Brion's friends being present to witness these experiments.

VISIT OF MR. BRION TO THE CONVICT.

The "Central News" special reporter at Leeds telegraphed on Thursday : Mr. Brion, of 22, Philip-road, Peckham Rye, arrived in Leeds to-day about two o'clock. He went to the Town Hall, where he was at once provided with a pass admitting him to see Peace. He immediately took a cab and drove to the gaol, which he reached about half past two o'clock. On entering, he saw Mr. Keene, the governor, who took him to Peace's cell. The greeting between the two men was not over-cordial. Mr. Brion told him the object of his visit was to get a renewal of the statement that he (Brion) knew nothing about Peace, the convict's past career, or that he was other than what he represented himself to be, namely, a retired gentleman. Peace said that such was the case, and he called those present to witness that Mr. Brion knew nothing about his doings ; and the sole cause of the frequent visits to his house was in connection with the invention of raising sunken ships. Peace then asked a number of questions in respect to the Evelina-road house, and what disposition had been made of the effects therein. Mr. Brion told him that so far as he knew everything had been carried off and disposed of, Mrs. Thompson and Hannah having divided the proceeds. He also expressed himself as willing to turn over to anyone whom Peace should name all the plans and papers belonging to him in his possession. This appeared to please Peace, and he became more communicative. He said he was prepared to meet his fate, and that he should send letters from the scaffold to many of his relatives and friends. He professed the greatest esteem for Mr. Brion, and bade him good bye with a considerable show of feeling, saying that the latter should hear from him again. Mr. Brion returned to London by the ten o'clock train.

LETTER TO MR. GOODLAD.

Peace was a staunch friend as well as an implacable enemy. Two of his oldest friends were Mr. George Goodlad and Mr. Cragg, and he was much disappointed when he was informed that they could not be permitted to see him at Armley. He promised to write to them both, and he kept his word,   Amongst the batch of letters handed to the chaplain on Tuesday morning was the following :—

"From Charles Peace H.M. prison. Leeds, Tuesday, 25th February, 1879.

"My dear friend George Goodlad, I send you this letter from the scaffold. It is handed to my chaplain when upon the scaffold to send to you So I hope you will take A. warning from my most fearful fate. You and me have known each other A great number of years, you choose An honest industrious way through life, but I choose the one of dishonesty, villainy, and sin. So my dear friend do take a warning by me for the remainder of your life. I die with the hope that God as heard my prayers and forgiven my many sins, and that in a few moments I may be at his right hand in glory, where I hope we shall all meet at the last Great day. That God may bless and prosper you and your dear Wife and Son and the workmen in your shop and all enquiring friends is the dying prayer of

"Yours CHARLES PEACE.

"Good-bye and bless you all Good bye.

"Mr. George Goodlad, pianist at Milners Concert rooms, and picture gallery off West-bar, Sheffield."

PEACE PREPARES HIS OWN FUNERAL CARD.

At the interview that Peace had with his wife he told her he would prepare a funeral card commemorative of his own death. He said he would endeavour to have it ready to give her when she paid the final visit to his cell. He reminded her of the monument at home, made by himself, and said if she liked she might put it on that.

When he came to do the card he found that his eyesight had failed him; that his hand had somewhat forgot its cunning; and he was unable to complete it. It is the half-finished design of a tombstone, with a floral wreath across the top. In the centre is the following :—

IN
MEMORY
OF
CHARLES PEACE,
WHO WAS EXECUTED IN
ARMLEY PRISON,
TUESDAY, FEB. 25,
1879. AGE 47.
FOR THAT I DON BUT NEVER
INTENDED—

The lettering is in capitals, and occupies about half the card. On the other half the convict intended to have written some lines, but he was unable to do so. He gave it to his wife on Monday, with expressions of regret that he had not been able to complete it.

LETTER TO PEACE FROM AN OLD CONVICT.

The following letter was sent to Peace, and by him handed over to his family on Monday. The original had the signature of the writer in full :—

"Saturday morning, ½ past 1 o'clock.

"My Dear Friend,—You will I trust Pardon Me for Breaking in and Intruding upon you Now at this Most Awfull and Most Solemn time—Most awfull Because you and Me are about to Leave) I may if it be the Will of God Leave this Earthly Tabernacle off before you (this Perishing world for Ever—Luke 21-33, But we Must Both Stand before the Judgement Seat of Christ Dear Friend Your position is fearful Here—But what will it be then. How Shall we appear Before the Judgement Seat of Christ—For I too Dear Friend have a fellow Creatures Life then to answere for and it may be More than One—my Life and yours here as indeed

been a Life of Sin and crime O that it had been Otherwise—But We Can Do Nothing—or Recall the Past— But Blessed be God He Has Shewed both you and Me a Way of Escaping all Bitter torments for the future— Yes only one Way John 14 ch 6 v 3 ch 14 to 18 verses Isaiah 1-18 57 ch 15 v 66 ch 2 verse Matthew 11-23 Psalm 146-3 verse Matthew 10-23—Ah My Dear Friend Many there are that Shew a Cold Shoulder to us Now May God have Compassion and Shew them Mercy for Jesus Christ's Sake—Yes our friends or Most of them in the time of trouble Desert us—But there is a friend that Sticketh Closer than a Brother Proverbs 18-24 and He that Best of all Friends has told me and you to call upon Him in the time of trouble and He will Deliver us—I beg of you Dear Friend to Listen to the Chaplin May God Reward and Bless his Endeavours to bring you to understand your Position —these few Remaining Days I beseach you to Spend in Prayer—and in the Reading of Gods Most Holy Ward—I have indeed found very Great Comfort by Reading that Sacred Volume after asking our Heavenly Fathers forgiveness of the Past—and to open My Eyes to the Blessed truths Contained therein—and I have found in times Past in a Prison Cell that Peace which the World Cannot Give—twenty five years of My Past Life have I spent in Prison—But to be with you Now Dear Friend I would very Gladly Spend five years more—Shall I tell you why Dear Friend Because you and Me are by ourselves Lost—But Jesus Christ Says I came to Seek and to Save that which was Lost—only trust Him He will Save you—Have faith in God. May the Almighty and Merciful God forgive all |Our Sins and Grant You and Me a Place in his Kingdom at the Right Hand of Jesus Christ our only Mediator and Advocate is the Ernest Prayer of Your Friend

"W. O.

"Mile End Road London.

"Farewell Dear Friend I do so much want to Me you in Heaven. Do Come Mercys Door is open for us and Gods hand is Stretched out Still."

FROM A LITTLE GIRL.

The following is a copy of another letter sent to Peace, and on it he wrote, "this was sent to me bye a little girl" :—

"Jesus Christ says He came 'to seek and to save that which was lost.' 'I came not to call the righteous but sinners to repentance., When he was dying he prayed for those who killed Him. 'Father forgive them, for they know not what they do,' and now Jesus, Our Lord is in Heaven praying to God for you. He died on the cross for you, because he loves you and 'wills not the death of a sinner but rather that all should come unto him and have Everlasting Life.

"Oh, don't think you are too great a sinner for Jesus to save. He is ready and willing 'to save to the uttermost all who come to him.' He is longing for you now to believe in Him, and be safe for ever. He has promised 'Him that cometh unto me I will in no wise cast out,' and all you have to do is to repent and ask God to forgive your sins for Christ's sake. We have no need of doing that; we have all sinned and grieved our loving Saviour many times.

"Then think of what follows after this life. Everlasting bliss and happiness with Jesus. But if you refuse to come and be washed in the Blood of the Lamb it is awful to think of what follows—an everlasting pain in hell with devils and damned spirits where 'the worm dieth not and the fire is not quenched.'

"Oh, don't let such an awful fate be yours—you can

prevent it if you will. When Jesus is ready *now, this minute,* to save you, why do you delay?

"What keeps you back?

"A man in the Bible wanted to be saved, but he did not know how to say a long prayer, so he just said, 'Lord, have mercy upon me;' and God heard him and answered his prayer. Oh, may God help *you,* and may you be able to really believe that Jesus loves you, and is waiting to save you.

"We will all pray for you that for our Saviour's sake you may be saved, and we shall then meet you in heaven with Jesus.

"February 10th, 1879."

TELEGRAM FROM IRELAND.

On the 22nd inst. the convict received the following telegram from "M. J., Londonderry, to Charles Peace, Armley Prison, Leeds. Believe on the Lord Jesus Christ, and thou shalt be saved. He is able also to save them to the uttermost that come unto God by Him."

When the telegram was handed to Peace he read it, and said—"This is from Kate Dyson's sister. Her initials are 'M. J.,' and I'll be bound she has sent it." The message seemed to give him a good deal of pleasure; but the impression is that he was wrong as to where it came from.

CHAPTER CLXIX.

SKETCH OF THE CONVICT'S CAREER.

THE life of the hero of this work was, as already indicated, full of strange incidents, which have been duly chronicled during the progress of this history. We subjoin a brief epitome of his career:—

"His father, who started in business as a shoemaker, after a wandering life spent at fairs and wakes, was residing in Nursery-street, Sheffield, on the 14th of May, 1832, the day when Charles Peace was born.

"The lad was sent to school in the town, but did not make much progress, and revealed a strong taste for constructing various articles rather than for learning.

"On leaving school he went to work at a rolling mill, and was there crippled in the leg by a piece of heated steel. In 1853, when a young man, he had gained great proficiency as a performer on the violin, and in company with a number of amateur theatricals, appeared at Worksop as 'The Modern Paganini.'

"At this time, notwithstanding his lameness, he excelled in physical exercises, and was so courageous that he once seized an enraged bull-dog, and beat it until the animal was stunned.

"His first robbery was committed at Mount View, in Sheffield, and for that offence he was sent to gaol for a month. On his liberation he began to associate with thieves, and soon became notorious as a portico robber.

"In 1854 he broke into three gentlemen's residences at Sheffield, gaining admittance by climbing the portico, and carried off large quantities of jewellery.

"Caught again, he was tried and sentenced to four years' penal servitude. Having served that term, he resumed his old life of fiddling and thieving, and in the course of his strolling met Hannah Ward, whom he is alleged to have married.

"Soon after his marriage he went to Manchester, and whilst committing a burglary at Rusholme, on the 11th of August, 1859, was captured, after a desperate resistance, and again sentenced to penal servitude, this time to six years.

"In the summer of 1864, however, he was again free, and commenced business in Sheffield; but it did not flourish, and he returned to Manchester, where he got into trouble about another burglary, and was sent into penal servitude for a further term of ten years.

"In prison he was mixed up in a mutiny, flogged, and then sent to Gibraltar. But his sentence was commuted to six years, and on the 9th of August, 1872, he returned once more to Sheffield, where fo some time he worked industriously as a picture-framer, and lived apparently a most exemplary life, sending his children to the Sunday school.

"About this time his hand was injured by a pistol shot, one of his fingers being blown off; but the injury did not materially interfere with his business, which he continued on his removal to Darnall.

"Whilst living in Britannia-road there, he met the Dyson's; forced himself upon their society; pryed into their affairs, and made himself so objectionable that Mr. Dyson wrote on one of his visiting cards, 'Charles Peace is requested not to interfere with my family,' and threw it into Peace's garden.

"Peace was furious; he sought out Mr. Dyson, tried to trip him up by the heels, and the same night, confronting Mrs. Dyson, revolver in hand, threatened to blow out her brains and her husband's too. A warrant was taken out against him; he escaped to Hull, but returned to Sheffield again on the 25th of October, 1876, when he threatened to annoy Mrs. Dyson 'wherever she went.'

"On that day the Dysons had removed from Darnall to Bannercross, specially to escape his disagreeable visits; but Peace followed them there, and meeting Mr. Dyson near his new abode took out his revolver with the intention of shooting him at that time if Mr. Dyson had offered to molest him.

"Peace returned to Hull, and turned his wife and family out of doors because his daughter ventured to bring up the name of Mrs. Dyson in conversation. He then wandered to Manchester, and back again to Sheffield, where, on the night of the 28th of November, 1876, he alleges that he had another interview with Mrs. Dyson.

"The next morning, the 29th, he visited his mother, and later in the day had an interview with the Rev. E. Newman, at Ecclesall Vicarage, to whom he told a most extraordinary story of his wrongs, and accused the Dysons of destroying his home happiness.

"The same night, shortly after eight o'clock, Peace shot Mr. Dyson. He concealed himself in the yard behind the house at Bannercross, and watched Mrs. Dyson go into a closet. When she opened the door he stood before her with a revolver in his hand, and said, 'Speak, or I'll fire.'

"The woman, greatly terrified, gave a loud shriek, and, stepping back into the closet, slammed the door, which she closed. Mr. Dyson immediately came out of the house, and Mrs. Dyson hearing his footsteps left the closet, and saw her husband follow Peace across the passage. Suddenly she saw the man turn and fire at her husband.

"Mr. Dyson, a powerful man, 6 feet 6 inches in height, was undeterred by the shot, and still pursued Peace, who, on reaching the steps at the end of the passage, again faced round, fired his revolver, and Mr. Dyson fell, shot in the left temple, the bullet penetrating to the brain.

"'Murder! you villain—you have shot my husband!' shouted Mrs. Dyson, who was found by the neighbours supporting her husband's head. Peace escaped across the fields, and Mr. Dyson died two hours afterwards.

Although not certain as to the result of his firing, Peace felt it necessary to get out of the way as soon as possible, and, cutting across the country, he arrived at another suburb of the town.

"In the meantime he slipped an indiarubber band over his head, confining his long white beard closely under his chin, and, putting on a muffler, gave himself the appearance of a man with a short beard.

"Taking a cab, he rode into the centre of the town, and, after bidding good-bye to his mother and a brother, he walked to Attercliffe-road station and went to Rotherham. From another station he went on to York the same evening, and a day or two afterwards turned up at Hull, where his wife was keeping an eating-house.

"No sooner had he entered than the detectives came up to inquire for him. He hastily ran upstairs, and, getting out of a bedroom window, climbed up a spout and got upon the roof.

"When the coast was clear he returned and had dinner, but was again forced to fly to the roof by another visit from the detectives. He escaped at dark, and then assumed that disguise which first deceived his relatives and subsequently enabled him to elude the vigilance of some of the cleverest detectives in the country.

"Finding the police were on his track he left Hull in a roundabout way, and wandered about the country for nearly six weeks. Once he travelled with a police-sergeant, and fraternised with him in the train.

"On another occasion he ostentatiously read to a police officer the bill offering a reward of £100 for his capture. Early in January he turned up at Nottingham, and, taking lodgings in a low quarter of the town, he commenced burglarious operations.

"It was here that he formed the acquaintance of Mrs. Thompson, and after living with her for a short time in Nottingham they went to Hull, and lodged in the house of a police sergeant. Whilst in Hull Peace made considerable stir, and on two occasions was very nearly caught.

"His first 'work' was on a Saturday night. He had broken into a villa residence, and collected a number of articles of value, when the front door opened, and two ladies and two gentlemen entered. He hastened to the first landing, and found to his surprise that the people were coming upstairs. He took energetic measures.

"Drawing his revolver, he fired over the balustrade into the ceiling, and the people, frightened out of their wits, fell downstairs, and Peace escaped through the garden. One of the gentlemen pursued him, but was fired at by Peace, who got safely away.

"On another occasion Peace was stopped by a policeman as he was leaving a house with some booty. The constable asked Peace what he was doing there, and Peace immediately fired at him. The officer fled precipitately, and Peace again got away. Shortly afterwards, finding a constable drunk on his beat, Peace entered six houses in one row, and finished a successful season by a large robbery of plate at the house of Mr. Ansell, a member of the Town Council.

"Returning to Nottingham, he committed several daring robberies, the last of which was a most successful silk robbery, and for the detection of the thief in which case a reward of £50 was offered.

"The police got a clue, and going to the place where he was staying, found Peace and Mrs. Thompson in bed.

"Peace told the officer that he was a hawker, and offered to show him his licence if he would go down stairs. No sooner, however, had the officer left the room than Peace escaped through the window, and subsequently went back with Mrs. Thompson to Hull.

"Peace next moved to London, and took a miserable room in Stangate-street, Lambeth. Here he was ostensibly carrying on the business of a dealer in musical instruments, but it was at this period that his most successful burglaries were committed.

"Breaking into a villa at Denmark-hill, he found a large safe in one of the lower rooms, but not being an expert at opening safes, he went upstairs into the master's bedroom and took his keys out of his trousers pockets as they lay on the bed.

"He took from the safe all the family plate, and obtained for it in Petticoat-lane no less than £250. Soon afterwards he realised £200 by a burglary at Southampton. The greater part of this was in money and the remainder in Bank of England notes. Subsequently he removed to Greenwich, and brought Hannah Peace, his reputed wife, and her son Willie Ward, to live with him.

"Hannah Peace and Mrs. Thompson soon quarrelled, and the family removed to Peckham, where they lived in good style at No. 5, Evalina-road. This was a pretty little villa standing in its own grounds. There were two entrances to the premises—a small gateway leading to the front steps and a carriage entrance.

"The front door opened into a moderate-sized hall, and a large drawing-room communicated by means of folding doors, with a spacious sitting-room behind. The house was well furnished throughout, and, indeed, at the time that Peace took it he must have been possessed of a considerable amount of ready money.

"In the drawing-room were a number of nicknacks, and in the different rooms there were several good pianos and violins. Peace made a number of improvements to the outside of the house, and the 'Thompsons' came to be regarded by the residents as their 'carriage neighbours.'

"Here Peace set up a pony and trap, and in the afternoon he used to ride out and mark the houses which he thought likely for 'business.' At night he would go out and enter the houses, and the pony and trap, which was waiting for him somewhere in the neighbourhood, was driven home at a most furious pace, the proceeds of the burglaries being concealed in the cart.

"It is believed that here he did some good business, but in spite of the fact that he had two women and a young man living with him very little is known of his actual operations. He had some trouble with the women. Mrs. Thompson drank, and Mrs. Peace was jealous, but Peace had no fear of treachery, and he continued most successfully his burglarious career.

"He received regular visits from the receiver of stolen goods, who used to take back good bargains from Evalina-road. At one time Peace endeavoured to melt down the plate he obtained to render its disposal more easy, but this attempt he soon gave up as likely to attract the attention of the neighbours.

"Thus he lived until the 10th October last year, when he was so pluckily captured by Police-constable Robinson. The officer detected him in a burglary in the house of Mr. Burness, at St. John's Park, Blackheath, and, calling the assistance of two other officers, a most determined and prompt effort was made to capture the man who had terrified South East London by his nocturnal robberies, and brought down a storm of reprobation upon the police.

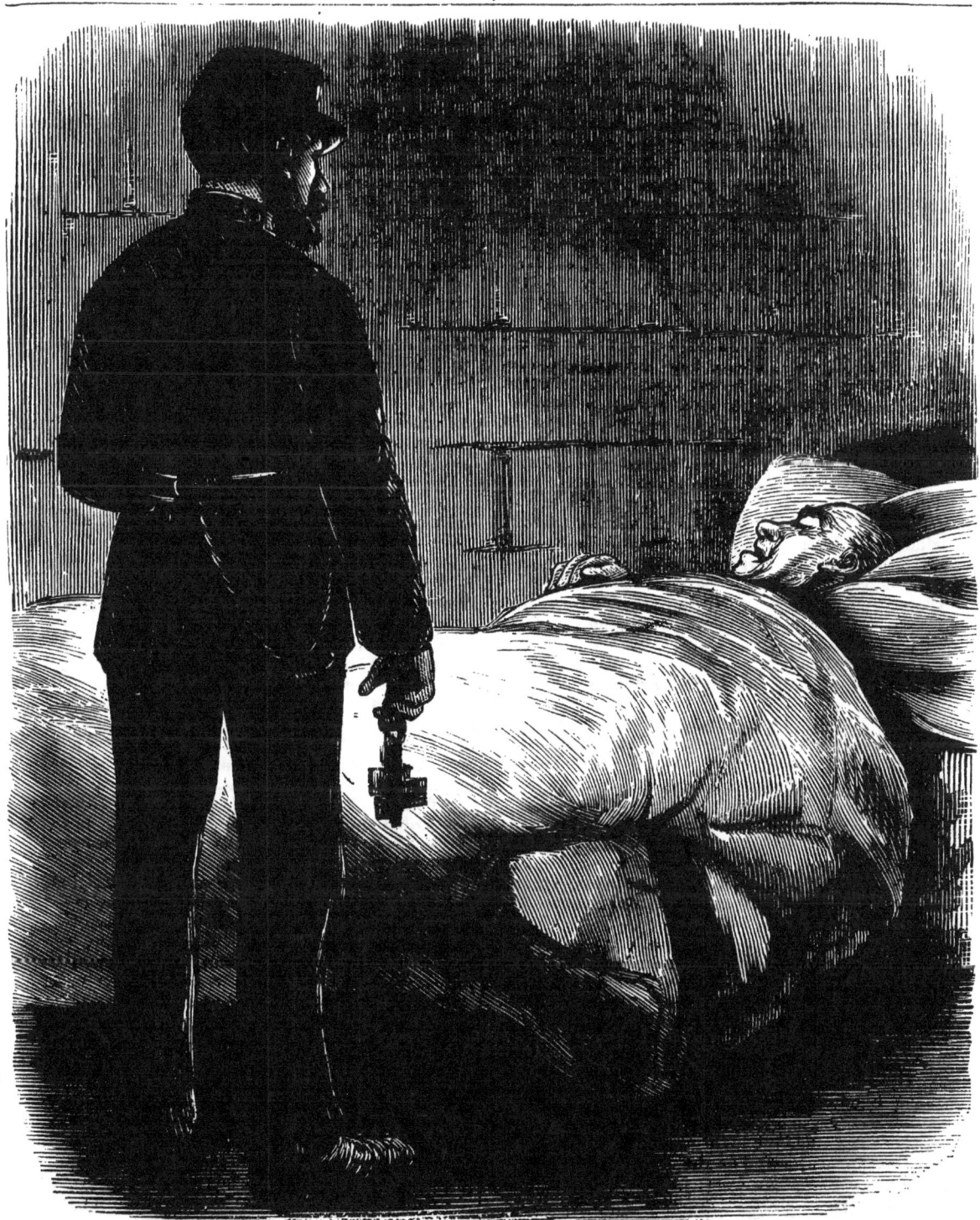

PEACE AFTER HIS INTERVIEW WITH THE REV. MR. LITTLEWOOD.

"Robinson saw him leaving the house and chased him across the garden. Peace drew a revolver and fired five times, the last shot wounding the officer severely in the elbow, but Robinson stuck to his man, and the other officers coming he was secured.

"The news of his arrest soon reached his people in Evelina-road, and the house was stripped of almost everything in a few days. Furniture was sold, and the proceeds of burglaries were removed to Nottingham and Sheffield.

"Then Mrs. Thompson, under pressure, informed the police who their prisoner really was, and whilst the London officers were congratulating themselves on having caught a most successful burglar, the Sheffield police were equally satisfied that the Bannercross murderer was in custody.

No. 97.

"An officer was despatched to America to find Mrs. Dyson, the widow of the murdered man, and before he returned, Peace, under the alias of John Ward, had been sentenced to penal servitude for life for the attack on Robinson. No time was lost in bringing Peace to trial for the graver offence, and on the 17th January he was taken to Sheffield for his preliminary examination.

"He was remanded on this occasion, and he was being taken from Pentonville to Sheffield on the following Wednesday when he made that daring attempt to escape or to commit suicide. He was being conveyed to Sheffield under the charge of two warders, and whilst the train was running at the rate of fifty miles an hour between Retford and Sheffield, Peace suddenly jumped out of the window.

"One of the warders dashed forward and seized him by one foot as he almost flew through the window. He thus had but insecure hold of the convict, who appeared to be almost mad with rage that his attempt had been foiled, and struggled wildly to escape from the officer's grasp.

"With his left leg he savagely kicked the officer's hands, and with his manacled hands grasped the footboard and endeavoured to free his right foot. The other warder, in the meantime, was unable to get to the window, and Peace's boot coming off, he fell on the footboard of the carriage with his head, and bounded off that into the up line.

"The train was stopped after running about a mile, and Peace was found lying insensible where he fell. He had received a severe wound at the back of the head, and was so much shaken that he could not be brought before the magistrates that day, and was remanded.

"On the following day a note was found upon him containing the words :—'Bury me at Darnall. God bless you all. C. Peace.' This, he said, he wrote in Pentonville, because finding that he could not escape he had determined to commit suicide.

"He was sent for trial at the Leeds Assizes, and was then sentenced to death after trial before Mr. Justice Lopes. After his removal to the condemned cell he had paid great attention to the administrations of the chaplain, and was described as having been really penitent and resigned to his fate.

"He also carried on a voluminous correspondence, letters frequently passing between him and his family and Mrs. Thompson. The latter, after having handed him over to justice, most persistently sought an interview with him, but was not allowed by the authorities to see him.

"One of the most extraordinary events in connection with Peace's career was his confesssion of the Whalley Range murder. A young man, named Habron, was then undergoing penal servitude for the crime, which Peace stated he himself committed.

"The murder occurred on the 1st of August, 1876. It was at the time when Peace had the Sheffield warrant hanging over him. He had packed up his housebreaking implements, and left Sheffield for Hull and Manchester in July.

"Arriving in Manchester he committed several burglaries, and on the night of the 1st of August, he went to the house of Mr. Gatrix, at West Point, Whalley Range, to break into it.

"As he was going towards the house he was seen by Mr. Simpson, a law student, and police-constables Cock and Beanland.

"Peace, followed by Beanland, crossed the grounds, and, jumping over a wall into the street, alighted close against Police-constable Cock, who was watching there.

"The officer tried to arrest him, and Peace fired to frighten him; but Cock endeavoured to apprehend him. Peace then shot the constable in the chest, and escaped before the arrival of Beanland, who remained in the grounds seeking the burglar. Three brothers named Habron, who were employed at a market gardener's near, were suspected of the murder, and two of them, John and William, were committed for trial.

"At the Assizes, which took place on the 27th and 28th of Nov., William Habron was found guilty, and sentenced to death, but John was acquitted. A petition was got up on behalf of William Habron, and his sentence was commuted to penal servitude for life. Not long afterwards Peace, under a pledge of secrecy, told his relatives what he had done, and expressed a wish that he could get the young man liberated without implicating himself.

"A few days after he had been sentenced to death at Leeds for the murder of Mr. Dyson, he drew plans showing the locality at West Point, Whalley Range, indicated the spot where the murder was committed, and also wrote a confession of the crime. His plans and confession were forwarded to the Home Office. Peace had a final interview with his brother Daniel and various other relatives on Saturday.

"Though physically prostrate, and suffering much from emotion, the convict expressed himself as prepared to meet his fate, and earnestly enjoined his friends to lead religious and virtuous lives."

As a supplement to the above we add the following details of Peace's early crimes.

"Having recovered from the two years' illness caused by his accident at Kelham Rolling Mills, he had been in the service of Mr. Edward Smith, and had after that become, under the tuition of one Bethley, a player on the violin at public-houses.

"There is a tradition that soon after this, having had a quarrel with his sister, he slept out, in an empty house, was caught, and got a month's imprisonment therefor.

"Whether this be so or not, the next glimpse we get of him is making a highly promising commencement in his future profession. He was charged at the Sheffield Sessions on Saturday, Dec. 13, 1851, along with George Campbell, with breaking into the house of Mrs. Catherine Ward, Mount View, [the mother of the then Mayor of Sheffield] and stealing two pistols, a mahogany box, a bullet mould, and other articles. An entrance had apparently been effected by climbing upon the balcony and opening the bedroom window.

"The only property missing was a case containing Mrs. Ward's jewels, a case containing a brace of rifle pistols, and a silk dress. The prisoners were afterwards found dealing with the pistols; Campbell was discharged, while Peace, who received a good character for honesty from his late employer, got one month's imprisonment.

"This robbery shows how closely Peace adhered to the *modus operandi* adopted thus early, and it fixes his then age (19).

"A CROP OF BURGLARIES IN 1854—FOUR YEARS' PENAL
"SERVITUDE.

"During the subsequent years 1852-3-4, he was continuing his musical services at public-houses, and becoming familiar with company no better than it should be.

"In the autumn of 1854 he was carrying on a daring game of house robbery, and from a report in the papers it appeared that on the 13th of October, 1854, Charles Peace, Mary Ann Niel, his sister, and Emma James were placed in the dock of the Town Hall to answer several charges of felony.

"James had offered a pair of boots in pledge at the shop of Messrs. Wright, Westbar, and on her being detained on suspicion, Peace came forward and claimed the boots, and was given into custody.

"In Peace's mother's house in Bailey-field, there was found a large quantity of jewellery and wearing apparel (including crape shawls, silk dresses, &c.), the proceeds of robberies effected at the residences of H. E. Hoole, Esq., Crookes Moor House; R. Stuart, Esq., Brincliffe Edge; Mr. G. F Platt, Priory Villa, Sharrow-lane; and Mr. Brown, Broomhall-street.

"The houses of all these parties had been robbed by effecting an entrance through the bedroom windows in the evening before the windows were closed and fastened for the night. At Mr. Hoole's the thief had climbed the portico, and from Mr. Stuart's a good deal of jewellery had been stolen.

"The prisoners were clearly proved to have been in possession of this property. The defence raised does not place in a very amiable light the affection subsisting between the sister and that brother, who used to avenge the wrongs she sustained at her husband's hands. Each accused the other of being the culprit.

"At the sessions at Doncaster (October, 20, 1854), Peace (who was undefended) said that a watchmaker named Bethley in Division-street, had kept his sister (Niel) for some years, and she had had three children by him. Bethley, not having given her any money lately, sent the jewellery and a bundle of wearing apparel by him to her, instead of money. Peace was sentenced to four years' penal servitude, and the female prisoners each to six months' imprisonment.

"Peace was described in the calendar at that time as being twenty-two years of age. The mention of Bethley's name will remind our readers that he was the person who instructed Peace in the art of violin playing, and Mrs. Niel's connection with the case does not shed much lustre on the family annals. She died we may add by way of completing her history, on the 2nd April, 1859, age 33.

CHAPTER CLXX
PEACE'S EXTRAORDINARY CAREER.

"THERE is an old Yorkshire saying, 'When it is dangerous to speak the truth, it is wisdom to say nothing,' and that would appear to have been the motto which Charles Peace adopted during the last four or five years of his life.

"We are enabled to continue the narrative, not for the guidance of any who may read it, but as a warning The fact that Peace has now to answer the capital charge is of itself sufficient evidence of the gradations downwards which the pursuit of crime involves.

"The singular episodes in the career of the criminal are stranger even than many a highly imaginative novelist could have portrayed.

"The police have been acquainted with many of them for months, and have been puzzled by them.

"The narratives are obtained from a private source of a perfectly reliable character, and are given accordingly.

"In the course of recent inquiries allusion has been made to certain letters which were addressed to Mrs. Dyson by the prisoner. These letters had upon them the Hamburg postmark, showing they had been posted there.

"From that it was argued that Peace had been living in that town, but the man never left the country excepting once—when sent to Gibraltar. He gave the letters to a captain to post in Hamburg, and his instructions were faithfully carried out.

"That Peace had committed a great number of burglaries and impudent feats of housebreaking there can be no doubt, but his most daring ones have certainly been completed in the metropolis, and during recent years.

"Three-fourths of the thefts which he has committed in this way have been between six and eight o'clock in the evening, and but very few of them after midnight.

"Now that he has been found out to have been the sole perpetrator of some of the robberies, reference to the police books proves the statement as to the hours when these were done to be correct.

"One night Peace repaired to a house in Greenwich, his object being to 'borrow' some jewellery which he knew to be in one of the bedrooms. It was the dwelling of a rich man, and when he reached the second story window at the back he for the first time in his life became acquainted with the use of a patent window fastener. When he had raised the sash about two inches he found it was prevented from going any further upwards by two brass nobs which protruded from the woodwork.

"In addition to that there was another apparatus which prevented him from moving the sash back again —it was locked. He was very much annoyed with this contrivance, but being of a resolute turn of mind he repaired to the same house in a night or two afterwards and took another course, certainly an extraordinarily bold one.

"He took the window frames out bodily, in the same manner as is often done for the removal of furniture in and out of the houses, and entered the house that way. The booty he secured on that occasion was exceedingly valuable.

"There is no doubt that Peace was well prepared for anyone should they endeavour to effect his capture, and there can be no more ample proof of this than the reception he gave Police-constable Robinson. It is believed, however, that had he known there were other members of the police force about besides Robinson, the latter would have had a sorry time of it.

"Whatever is stated to the contrary, Peace was undoubtedly a 'dead shot' when he meant it. He has fired over the heads of many people who have disturbed him in his operations.

"On one occasion, in London, he broken into a gentleman's house, and had gathered together a number of valuables.

"This was when the family were at dinner below. To his chagrin, a lacquey entered the room, stared at him for a moment, and then, as if divining his purpose, bolted down the stairs.

"Peace got through the window by which he had entered, passed to the roof of an outbuilding, and dropped into the back yard. But the footman, for he was no other, had given the alarm to his master, and the latter, with presence of mind, had run to the kennel and unchained a large mastiff dog.

"The animal at once dashed towards Peace, but was shot dead on the spot by the intruder, the bullet entering its forehead, and the gentleman and his servant retreated indoors.

"On another occasion lights were observed through the upper windows of a house by the police on beat, who suspected that a burglar was at work in the upper rooms.

"The officers made their dispositions, and were confident that they had the depredator completely boxed. But the officers had 'reckoned without their host.'

"It was not a burglar of the ordinary stamp with whom they had to deal, but one who had gone through nearly every phase of life which it is possible for one who follows 'the profession' to experience.

"An alarm was raised, when, luckily for Peace, it proved that the occupants of the house were an old man and woman and the servant.

"He took good care they did not see him, but quickly made his way into the garret. The constables were admitted after some little demur, and a thorough search took place, but no intruder could be found. Still there was the fact that strange lights had been seen in the place, and the kitchen window had been broken open.

"One of the constables, however, raised the garret window, and on looking through saw a man sitting on the slates. He seemed determined to follow, and commenced to do so, but he found that he had no foothold, for the roof was of pantiles. Peace had slipped off his boots and left them on the roof.

"In great haste he scrambled away. His left foot came in contact with one of the broken tiles, and he cut it exceedingly severely. He got on some out-building, dropped into a garden, and escaped. He did not recover from his injuries, however, for some weeks after.

"On two separate occasions after the murder Peace was within a few yards of the clutches of the Hull detectives when they were actually in search of him.

"He had taken up his temporary quarters in a house there, and they must have suspected that he was lurking somewhere about it, for one day two detectives entered. He was in the back kitchen; so he quietly went upstairs and into the garret.

"The lower rooms were looked into, and also the bed-rooms, but there were no suspicious appearances, and the search was not proceeded with. On that occasion Peace was interrupted whilst in the enjoyment of a basin of soup.

"Shortly after that the detectives again visited the same place, for they still thought they might find some clue to him in the town which he had previously lived in. When they entered the front door Peace was again in the kitchen half stripped, washing himself at the sink. He had scarcely time to reach the top of the stairs before they were at the bottom of them, and he 'made' straight for the garret—this time to the roof also.

"He must have considered himself hardly pressed, for after going along the slates he got into another house through the window, and explained his presence in that condition to the wondering woman who occupied the house, by representing that the police were after him 'because he had deserted his family.'

"He said that he had only done it a week or so before through necessity, but had now got work, and intended to fetch his wife and the little ones. He was then allowed to remain in the house for the rest of the day—for this took place at noon.

"The detectives once more retired, after a fruitless search, and without the slightest knowledge that they had been so near to the one they wanted. That night had they apprehended a person who was dressed in female clothing, and who booked from Hull to Manchester, they would have caught Charles Peace, for it was disguised in this way that he effected his escape on that occasion from the town.

"From thence he went to Manchester, and afterwards to Nottingham. He was fruitful in his resources whenever danger was pressing, and, it will be seen, as cunning as he possibly could be.

"He had 'nerve,' however, and a run of good luck in almost all his proceedings.

"There was no doubt that the police were on a good track when they watched Hull closely, and though it may seem easy to say, 'They might have seen,' when the secret is known, they were not aware that they had nearly had the one they sought securely in their hand."

PEACE'S CAPTOR.

The proposed testimonial to Police-constable Robinson, the officer who captured Peace, prospered very satisfactorily. Subscriptions were received at the "Royal Hotel," Haymarket; the "Star," High-street; the "Exchange," Exchange-street; the "Elephant," Norfolk-street; "Bull's Head," Sheffield-moor; "Old Star Vaults," Old Haymarket; "Royal Hotel," High-field; "Little Angel," Westbar; "Hen and Chickens," Castle-green; "Queen," Sheaf-street.

Mr. George Dawson, a local phrenologist, sent the following letter:—

"Those who have or have not had the satisfaction to see Charles Peace are naturally desirous of seeing the man who was chiefly instrumental in capturing the great rascal, and who had so narrow an escape from being murdered by him.

"As many have asked me if I had seen him, the following brief sketch may be interesting:—Mr. Robinson is a good-looking, quiet, pleasant genial fellow, not unlike the Prince of Wales—has his type of features. He is rather florid, with light brown hair and beard. He is very finely developed physically, plump and muscular, with sufficient of adipose tissue to make him round in form and easy in manner.

"The bony and fibrous systems are less high in him than the vital and muscular. He is about 39 or 40 in. round the chest, 5 ft. 7½ in. high. He looks only a little man, but I am told he weighs 13 stone. He has a small head, measuring 21½ about, and his brain is mostly developed in the practical and observing and the moral faculties.

"He is quite firm and independent, but lacks self-esteem; has no desire or ability to show off—is very retiring. He is steady, cool, and rather harmonious, but has only moderate destructiveness and combativeness. Hence he is mild, kindly, and genial, the 'knotty' and 'quarrelsome' points being weak.

"He would hurt even a burglar only in self-defence. He is in almost every respect—bodily and mentally—the very opposite of Peace, though this is not the time to give a phrenological description of that gentleman. Sheffielders are pleased with the captor of their chief ruffian—and he is pleased with the heartiness and kindliness of Sheffielders."

EXTRAORDINARY COMMUNICATIONS.

Running away from Bannercross on the night of the murder, Peace accidentally or intentionally dropped a small bundle of notes and letters.

These were mentioned in the court of the proceedings at the trial, and they formed the subject of much of Mr. Clegg's cross-examination in court. It is contended by Peace that they were written to him by Mrs. Dyson. Mrs. Dyson, however, swears positively that they were not written by her, and that she never saw them until they were shown to her some time after they were found.

The theory of the prosecution was that the whole of the notes and letters were written by Peace for his own purpose. What those purposes were, of course can only be imagined.

It may have been to get Mrs. Dyson into his power. The notes were of an extraordinary character. Most of them were written in pencil on scraps of paper. As doubless this correspondence will be read with considerable interest, we give it in its entirety, following the spelling and other eccentricities of the writer :—

" Things are very bad for peple told him everything so the say you oat pick out for D. Do keep quiet, and don't let anyone see you. Money send me some.

" Send me a drink. I am nearly dead.

" be quick * * you * * he is out now.

" he is out now so be quick fanny as * * * let us have a look at you.

" Will you send me a shilling or two and a drope and keep very quiet, be quick.

" Give it to me up in the garret but don't talk for fear he is not going only his sister is coming, love to all.

" I will write you a note when I can perhaps to-morrow. You can give me something as a present if you like but I dont want to be covetous and take them from your wife and daughter.

" Mrs. Norton is raising hell about what I * * * * Could you settle it and send me a print that is I have and * * * * her to let me have a pint.

he is gone out come now for I must have a drink.

" After he is going out I won't go if I can help it so see for Janey.

" I have just run out of writing paper excuse the envelope. Many thanks for my book, don't mind framing the picture, let them have it without, as I have nothing to say in the matter. I will thank your wife as soon as I get a chance to see her for her kind present, tell her so, with my love. I was very sorry to hear your quarling, hope it is all settled now—and * * * * having to hear the readings you should be quiet. You have a good wife, be kind to her. This was written yesterday, but could not see you.

" He won't say when he is going. Not to-day any-how he is not very well. I will write you when I have a chance and put you in the work * * * *

" He only went for tobacco and he has not been out. I shall tell you when he does. You must not say I am Dr. when I am not for I don't thank you for for you form that opinion. I shall go to Ireland if you don't be——— I am washing to-day, so he won't be out perhaps. Get me paper. Love.

" If you have a note for me send now while he is out, but you must not venture for he is watching, and you cant be too careful. hope your foot is better, he went to Sheffi yesterday but I could not see you anywhere were you out love to Ja.

" Have you got your handkerchief I lost mine * * pocket hank and gloves * * * * thanks for this money * * * must be careful and not show anything or I will let you starve.

" I think I will go by 9 o'clock now, you must not go by train, go by trem because he will go down with me don't let him see anything. Meet me in the Wicker hope nothing will turn up to prevent it. Love to Janey.

" If you are not at home Janey will give you this do be careful you will get yourself into trouble about the empty house dont come until I tell you there is a man over the wall says he will give you hell now I tell you this as a friend so as you may be on the look out for your familyes.

" How well you never told that man. I looked at you out of the window. You left me to find out for myself, and would not put me on my guard, as I do yo you. Hope you won't omit again. Don't talk to Willie much, or give him any halfpegs. * * * * Don't be a fool. It looks as if you want people to know the way you and ———if you are not more careful we will have to say quits. I have told you not to say anything until * * * *

" Saturday Afternoon.

" I write you these few lines to thank you for all your kindness which I shall never forget from you and your wife she is a very good one does she know you are to give me the things or not how can you keep them concealed one thing I would wish you to do is to frame his mothers photo and send it in with my music book if you please do it when he is in. Many thanks for your kind advice I hope I shall benefit by it. I shall try to do right by every one if I can and shall always look on you as a friend, good bye I have not much time, burn this when you read it.

" Dear sir,—Are you at home or not, for I can't see you. I looked for you yesterday, when I went to Sheffield, but could not see you, and don't like to send if you are not in, because I know Janey have not seen you all day; but he has not been out. You are getting very with old Ned; don't blab anything to him, for it will be all over. Never speak of me. I will not send this till I know you are at home. Hope you are well, and don't fret; but I will give you the wink when the coast is clear; but you must not take notice till I tell you or you will make a mess of it, because he is always on the look out. Don't know when he will go out again, but will sure tell you. Love to G—— b——, burn this.

OTHER MURDERS BY PEACE.

The *Sheffield Telegraph* stated :—" ' Peace has committed many murders; he has done more than two, yes many !'

" Such were the words which fell from the lips of one who was placed in close communication with the convict, and who occupies a position which entitles his utterance to the fullest credence. We may go further and say that there is ample testimony that Peace has indeed pursued a career even more bloodstained than has yet been made known to the public, and that could he have been prevailed upon to state the whole of the fouler crimes that he has committed, there would indeed be a category so revolting that the community would scarcely believe such outrages could have been perpetrated, and the chief actor in them have escaped so long.

" He has not alone taken human life, in order to escape arrest, but he has taken it that he might effect robbery. Peace had accomplices in these deeds. There are those living who know, not only of their execution, but also of the planning of them, and have had a hand in the foul transaction.

" A statement like the foregoing is startling, but we have good grounds for saying that subsequent events will prove the truthfulness of them. It is also stated on high authority that more than one person is in prison suffering for the misdeeds of this man.

" We announced on the 11th instant that Peace had told his family on the previous day that one young man had already served seven years in penal servitude, having been respited after being condemned to death for wilful murder.

" We are told that Peace still holds to the statement, and says he will give such evidence as will clear the man. He gives further a strong intimation that he himself did the deed. The murder was committed at the close of 1871 or in 1872.

"We are also informed that on one occasion Peace premeditated a jewellery robbery in Chelsea, and that in order to carry it out he associated himself with a female paramour, who obeyed his instructions. This woman of set purpose sought the friendship of the jeweller, and became intimate with him, and on the night of the burglary assisted the chief actor in it.

"The jeweller offered a resistance, and was murdered, no person ever being convicted of the crime. The authorities are already using every means at their disposal for the discovery of Peace's principal movements during the past three years, and the recovery of some of the property stolen might lead to results of enormous consequence as affecting this revelation. There is now proof in hand that it was not with the bullet alone that Peace sent some of his victims on their last journey.

"It will be remembered that, when he was finally captured, a large knife was found in his possession, but on that occasion he never had the opportunity of using it. However, information has been given that on another occasion, whilst he was engaged in committing a robbery, he was surprised by a man, when he drew a knife from the pocket where he always kept it and stabbed his would-be captor.

"After that he gave the poor fellow a heavy downward blow with the weapon, and inflicted a wound from which the bowels protruded, and which ultimately caused the death of the victim. We have ground for stating also that more than one of his victims has been thrown into the Thames, although the murders have not taken place on its banks, if near to them.

"The convict has made use of certain expressions which leave no doubt that the worst part of his criminal career dates more than ten years back, probably fifteen, and though he is reticent on this point, it is believed that one of the greatest reasons for his disquietude of mind is the knowledge that more than one has suffered innocently because of his misdeeds.

"He has yet to state, should he carry out the intentions he has expressed, whether or not anyone has suffered on the gallows for murder done by him, and from the peculiar manner in which he has dealt with this subject it is feared that such is the case.

"It is thought also that the convict will throw some light on several tragedies in which he had not been personally concerned, but of which he has had a guilty knowledge. Should he do so—and it is a certainty he can if he likes—more tales of horror will be revealed, and some who are at liberty now will have to succumb to their merited fate.

"Allusion was made to the fact that Peace had accomplices in his crimes, and that they had a guilty knowledge of murder and of robberies which he committed. He has, however, gone even further.

"This week he made use of these extraordinary words: 'Yes, it was known what I was doing and what I have done, and before I die I will tell something and prove it too, which will show who knew.

"'Before I die I will make a revelation which will show what one man is, and it will place in the dock a man who occupies a far higher post than ever Micklejohn or Druscovitch did. Palmer never did anything like it.'

"Beyond the facts above recorded, we have further ground for saying that Peace was concerned in the Portland-street murder, London, when it will be remembered that a French lady, named Madame Riel, was found lying in a cupboard in her house having had her brains half knocked out. The unfortunate woman had also a thick rope entwined round her neck.

"The murder had been committed in the coal cellar, and the lady had been dragged upstairs to the cupboard, where her body lay all day, until it was found by her daughter and others.

"The cook, a Frenchwoman, absconded to Paris with some of Madame Riel's diamonds, and was apprehended in St. Denis by Druscovitch, the London detective, and some of the French gendarmerie.

"It then transpired that she had not committed the murder of her mistress alone, but was helped by more than one.

"Before the day of his execution, it is confidently believed that he will make such disclosures as will throw even the above revolting confessions into the shade."

The *Manchester Evening News* is responsible for the following story, which, whatever may be said of the facts it narrates, either does not relate to Peace, or is altogether mistaken as to time. Four years ago Peace, as is perfectly well known, was living in Scotland-street, whence, in the beginning of 1875, he removed to Darnall.

We have previously stated that when the transference of his picture-frame making business from Kenyon-alley to West-street proved a failure, he and his family went to live in Manchester, but that was in 1866, and he had not been there a fortnight before he was caught robbing a house, and was sentenced to eight years' penal servitude :—

"As our readers are well aware, Charles Peace, the man condemned to death for the Bannercross murder, on more than one occasion plied his many vocations in Manchester and the neighbourhood. From inquiries made in Levenshulme, it transpires that the notorious criminal resided in that pleasant suburb about four years ago.

"He stayed there only three months, and after he left the many freaks he committed gradually faded from the memory of the local residents. However, not many days ago a policeman took a photograph of Peace to the locality, and many tradesmen at once recognised him as the man who had formerly lived amongst them. In fact, he had for the time been quite a favourite in the district, and was well known to most of the inhabitants.

"He rented a small detached house called 'Olave Cottage,' in Rushford Park, which he had fairly well furnished. He gave his name as 'Mr. Thompson,' and he was accompanied by a woman who is supposed to be Mrs. Peace.

"He was never idle and always had some project on foot. He was constantly painting his cottage, and he took such trouble with the work that the neighbours took it for granted that he meant to remain there at least for some years.

"He was very affable and obliging to everybody, and was, until he decamped without paying his accounts, a great favourite with the tradesmen. To ladies he was especially polite and attentive. To every woman he met in a shop, he said, 'good morning' in the most agreeable tones, but usually accompanied his attentions by a wink at the shopman. He obtained considerable notoriety by his skill in contorting his features and assuming the appearance of a cripple. Subsequently he was known to have been the 'Burnage Bogie,' an apparition that had scared many people in Burnage-lane, and made numerous folks afraid to use that thoroughfare after nightfall.

"At the same time it is somewhat novel to learn that

he was never suspected of committing any robbery, nor has it been proved that he gave effect to his thieving propensity in the neighbourhood. If he did carry on any 'business' of that nature he certainly was never mistrusted on that ground, and even now not the slightest accusation is made against him on that score.

"Ostensibly he earned his livelihood as an acrobat, and was, we are informed, engaged at the Abbey Hey Grounds. In this capacity he was considered to be exceedingly clever, and our informant assures us that he could throw fifty-six pound weights about like pounds of sugar. He likewise performed publicly on the violin, and was regarded by the frequenters of the grounds as an able musician.

"As we have said, he was much esteemed whilst he lived as Levenshulme, owing chiefly to his unbounded spirits and his witticisms. He was respected as an honest, straightforward man, and no one anticipated that he would disappear so suddenly without paying sundry bills, and least of all was it thought that he would turn out to be one of the most remarkable criminals with which this country has become acquainted for many years."

PEACE'S AGE.

One of the most curious things about the personality of Peace is the conflict between his appearance and his age. He has been almost invariably spoken of as an old man, and no one seeing him could for a moment suppose that the age we have previously given, on the authority of the police notice issued after the Bannercross affair, is the correct one. That notice spoke of him as then forty-six years of age, but as looking ten years older. We have reason to believe that he is even now (two years afterwards) only forty-six, and will not be forty-seven until May next. He was born on the 14th of May, 1832, and it may, perhaps, be a convenience if we give the cardinal points of his career in brief chronological form:—

1832. May 14.—Born in Nursery-street.
1846.   „   Injured at Kelham Mills.
  „ to 1848.—Two years' illness.
1848 to 1851.—Employed by Mr. Edward Smith and in learning to play the violin.
1851. Oct. 26.—Robs Mrs. Ward's house.
  „ Dec. 13.—Sentenced to one month's imprisonment; age nineteen.
  „ to 1854.—Playing the violin at publichouses, &c.
1854. Sep. 7.—Robs Crookesmoor House.
  „ Sep. 20.—Robs Mr. Stuart's house, Brincliffe, and many similar robberies about the same time.
1854. Oct. 20, } Four years' penal servitude; age
  to   } 22.
1858.   }
1858 or 1859.—Marries Hannah Ward.
1859. Nov. 29} Daughter, Jane Ann, born.
  or 30.}
1859. Aug. 11,}
  to   } Penal servitude; age 27.
1864, June. }
1864 to 1866.—Picture-frame maker in Kenyon-alley and West-street.
1866. Dec. 3,}
  to   } Penal servitude; age 34.
1872, Aug. 8.}
1872 to 1875.—Picture-frame maker, in Brocco and Scotland-street.
1875, to Aug.,} Picture-frame maker at Darnall.
  1876.   }

1876. Aug. to} Provision shop keeper, in Hull.
  Nov.   }
1876. Nov. 14.—Leaves Hull suddenly.
1876. Nov. 29.—Shoots Mr. Dyson.
1876 to 1878.—Committing constant robberies at Nottingham, Hull, Lambeth, Greenwich, and Peckham.
1878. Oct. 10.—Captured by Police-constable Robinson while committing a burglary; gives name of John Ward.
  „ Nov. 6.—Identified in Newgate as Charles Peace.
  „ Nov. 19.—Penal servitude for life; age forty-six.
1879. Jan. 22.—Attempts to commit suicide by leaping from train.
  „ Jan. 24.—Committed for trial on a charge of wilful murder.

CHAPTER CLXXI.
EVENTS BEFORE THE EXECUTION—LETTER FROM THE HABRONS.

On Monday, February 24th, Mrs. Peace, Willie Ward, and Mr. and Mrs. Bolsover went to Leeds and had a final interview with Peace in his condemned cell in Armley Gaol.

It was their intention when they went on Friday to have taken their leave of him for ever in this world; but he begged (of them to come again on Monday, so that they might be the last of his relatives he would see before he was executed, and they promised him that they would do so.

They left Sheffield by the 10.50 train, and on arriving at Leeds they went to the Town Hall, where they found the orders ready for them to admit them to Armley. They got there soon after one o'clock, and after waiting for a short time they were conducted to the cell of the condemned man.

Peace was up and sitting at his little table writing a letter. He appeared better and more cheerful than he had been, although he complained of being very weak, and of suffering much pain, especially in his head.

When the chief warder conducted the party into the barred portion of the cell he called out, "Visitors, Peace!" The convict looked round and gave them a smile of recognition.

The two warders, who were in the cell with him, lifted him up—one taking hold of each arm, and then his chair was removed so close to the bars that when Peace was placed in it again he was able to rest his hand upon them.

Two chairs were then placed for the accommodation of Mrs. Peace and Mrs. Bolsover, and the two men were allowed to occupy the little seat that is always there. These were attentions that had not been shown to visitors on former occasions.

Peace was the first to speak, and beginning with his wife he addressed each by name, and asked how they were. Seeing that they were scarcely able to suppress their feelings, and to reply to him, he told them he hoped they would restrain their grief, or it would upset him. At present he said he felt very happy, and he did not want to be disturbed.

He then informed them that Messrs. Ford and Warren, solicitors, had been instructed to prepare another will and deed of gift, and that everything necessary had now been done to ensure their obtaining possession of whatever property he had.

They would now have no difficulty in claiming all he had possessed wherever they found it.

He next told them that Mr. Brion had been to see him, and had acknowledged to having in his custody their drawing-room suite, the model boat and case, cockatoo and cage, and that he would give them up to whoever might be legally entitled to receive them.

The chaplain and the warders had heard that statement and would corroborate it if necessary.

The goods were made over to Willie and Mrs. Bolsover, and he told them what he should like each to have; and how they were to proceed to recover the things.

While conversing on this point reference was made to Mrs. Thompson, and Peace said he wished her well, but he was afraid she was going the wrong road. It was his belief that the best that could be done for her would be to place her in a prison or a reformatory for a short time, so as to break her off her intense craving for drink. He was afraid she would make away with herself.

On one occasion, when living at Peckham, Mrs. Thompson attempted to strangle herself, and Peace then told her he " would rather die on the scaffold than live the life they were living." He now said he little thought when he made that remark that he should die on the scaffold.

Speaking of the articles he possessed when he was at Peckham, he said there was his small monument which was missing, the larger monument they had now at Darnall, the model boat, and his fiddle walking-stick—four of about as well made and curious things as could be seen anywhere.

The fiddle is a hollow bamboo cane, to which a tail piece, bridge, and screws can be attached, and then it can be played upon. Peace has played upon it many a time.

He told his friends if they could collect these four articles and have them exhibited at some music-hall in Sheffield as curiosities which had belonged to him, they might make money out of them.

Peace then alluded to the interview he had with the Rev. Mr. Littlewood, vicar of Darnall, and said he believed he had convinced that gentleman that it was really not him that stole the clock from Darnall school-room.

Mr. Littlewood had written to him for information about robberies which had been committed at Darnall and the neighbourhood, and he had replied to him, telling him that he never did a robbery at Darnall, Hardsworth, or any other place nearer than Sheffield.

Mr. Brion had asked him to send him a letter from the scaffold, and he had promised to do so, but he had not then had time to write it.

He said for several days he had done nothing else but write to his relatives and friends. He had got nearly all the letters ready, and he intended to take them with him to the scaffold.

" You know," he said, " my hands will be fastened behind me before I leave my cell, but I shall hold the letters, and when I reach the scaffold I shall ask the chaplain to take them out of my hand and to post them to you."

At this stage of the interview the sound of men hammering reached the cell. Peace listened for a moment, and then said, " That's a noise that would make some men fall on the floor! I hear they are working at my own scaffold. I have heard them before this morning."

The chief warder made answer, " You are mistaken, Peace; it is nothing of the sort."

Peace : No I am not. I have not worked so long with wood without knowing the sound of deals; and they don't have deals inside a prison for anything else than for scaffolds. I have heard them knocking the nails in, and I am sure I am right.

But (continued he), it does not matter much; it makes no difference to me. I should like to see my own coffin, and my own grave. It would not make the slightest difference to me, because I am prepared. I only look upon the scaffold as a short cut to Heaven. Alluding to the manner in which he would be buried, he said : I shall be thrown into my grave like a dog; but it won't matter; it will only be my poor body that will be there. My soul, I believe, will be in Heaven.

Peace then told his friends that he had received a letter from the father and mother of young William Habron, who was undergoing a sentence of penal servitude for life, for the murder of Police-constable Cock, asking him if he really had made a confession, and whether there was any probability of their son returning home to them.

Peace said he had written back to them at Manchester telling them that he had made a full confession of the murder, had drawn plans of the place where it occurred, and had sent them to the Home Secretary. He further told them that if their son had justice done to him he would be set at liberty.

Indeed he had no doubt that he would he restored to them.

He said he had asked the father and mother to forgive him for the great wrong he had done them, and had begged of them to ask their son when he came home to forgive him as well. He should be dead then; but he hoped to have the forgiveness of them all.

Since he had confessed to the crime he had been much happier than he was before; and he hoped his confession would be believed.

Suddenly arousing himself the convict said, " I have a good thing to tell you;" and he proceeded to relate the following remarkable incident :—

He said, " You have often heard ministers and others speak of the value of a soul and what sacrifices they would make to be the means of the conversion of one soul. I believe that, base and bad as I am, I have been the means of the conversion of one man. It occurred when I was brought down from Pentonville to Sheffield on the first occasion to be tried.

" There was a traveller to Manchester in the same train, and when we reached Sheffield he left his carriage and came out of mere curiosity to see me taken by the warders from the train to the cab.

" He went back to his carriage very much impressed with what he had seen of me and heard about me, and began to think about his own past life, and where such a life was likely to lead him. He could not shake off the feelings that had taken possession of him; he began to pray, and has since become a Christian.

" He has written to the chaplain, telling him all the story, and assuring him that through me he had believed, and had found salvation. He asked the chaplain if the prison rules would allow of it, to bring his letter and read it to me, and he has done so.

" Who would have thought," repeated Peace, " that a bad, base man as I am should have been the means of the conversion of anybody ? There is just that one good thing I have done, at any rate."

Peace then told them that he had received letters from several persons whose houses he had robbed, telling him that they forgave him, and that they were praying for him.

The recollection of such unexpected kindness seemed to quite overpower the convict, and he displayed more feeling than he had done throughout.

PEACE'S LAST BREAKFAST ON THE MORNING OF EXECUTION.

Commencing with his daughter, he asked each separately whether there was anything either wanted to ask him or to say to him. They were too much overcome to reply to him for a while; but presently Mrs. Peace said they had plenty to say to him, but not then.

He begged of her not to break down, and reminded her that that was the last time she would have an op-

portunity of speaking to him on this side of the grave.

He again asked her what she wished to say, and she reminded him that when there before he promised to pray with them when they came that day. He replied, "So I will."

The warders assisted him to kneel, and his friends knelt with him, and more than half an hour he prayed

No. 98.

with them. He remembered each of them separately, and was especially earnest in his petitions for the little babe that his daughter had with her.

He then prayed for young Habron, and asked that his innocence might be proved; and he prayed for Habron's father and mother.

With a choking voice, almost drowned by the sobs of his relatives, he prayed for the two men he had murdered, and for the relatives they had left behind; and, in conclusion, he prayed long and earnestly for himself that his sins might be forgiven him, and that he might meet them all in heaven.

There was not much more conversation when Peace and his friends rose from their knees, and then came the moment when the final separation had to to take place.

For the first time since he was sentenced to death Peace was allowed to shake hands with his family.

Taking the hand of each in turn he held it for several minutes while he blessed them, and prayed for them, and then kissed their hands.

When he saw the great distress of his wife and children, he broke down himself, and the last few moments they were altogether were truly sorrowful moments for them all.

Then they were conducted from the cell, and the interview, which had lasted nearly three hours, terminated.

The relatives came away with the belief that Peace had committed no other great crimes, or he would have confessed them.

FINAL INTERVIEW WITH HIS BROTHER AND OTHER RELATIVES.

On Saturday, Dan Peace, his wife, John Peace, and Ellen Peace, their son and daughter, and Tom Neil, a relative, had their final interview with him in Armley Gaol.

Cheerful, and apparently unconcerned at his fate hitherto, the condemned man, knowing that he was speaking to his brother and those who accompanied him for the last time, lost his old buoyancy of spirits, and, although he did not seem at all alarmed at the end awaiting him, appeared very much depressed in mind, and manifested considerable emotion.

His brother, Dan Peace, and the other relatives mentioned, were with him nearly two hours. The invitation was extended also to Mary Ann Neil, but she was not present at the gaol, as she did not arrive in Leeds in time for the interview.

The party had been specially invited by Peace, so that he could bid them farewell. They found the convict lying down, but as soon as he saw his brother, and the rest of the party, he struggled to raise himself to a sitting posture.

Finding it difficult to do this, he asked the warders to raise him.

The two warders, each getting on one side of the condemned man, took him by the arms, and lifted him up. So weak was he that even this alteration of position seemed to exhaust him, and, according to his brother Dan, he was " a pale, wretched, haggard man altogether," almost feeble as a child.

In answer to his brother, who asked, " How are you ?" he replied, "I am very, very ill, and very, very weak." And in the opinion of his relatives he certainly spoke the truth, for they affirm that he was very much weaker than he had ever previously appeared.

His head was still bandaged, and he told them that although the authorities were taking every possible care of him it seemed impossible to stop the discharge

from his wound, and that he felt very weak and depressed in consequence.

Suffering much physically, and the subject of much mental depression, he nevertheless made a great effort to welcome his brother and relatives cordially.

"I am very glad to see you," he said, and then remarked that he had also invited two friends—George Goodlad, and Arthur Cragg—to see him.

Being asked why they were not present, he said he had discovered that none but his own relatives could be admitted to the gaol.

He regretted this very much, and said he had got into some little trouble by persisting in asking to see these two friends.

He admitted now, however, that he had really no right to expect their admission ; yet, at the same time he stated that he was very, very sorry he should not be allowed to see them ; and, whilst speaking about his acquaintance with them, and the improbability of meeting them again on this side the grave, betrayed great emotion. " Give them my kind love," he said, " and tell them that I hope God will bless them, and that I shall meet them in heaven."

During the interview he became utterly exhausted, and was compelled to cease from speaking altogether for a few minutes; and even when he was able to converse, it was in such a low tone that his words were almost inaudible to his friends, although they were only a few feet away from him.

Dan said he understood that his brother was going to send them all a farewell letter. Peace replied that it was his intention to do so.

He was going to write several letters, take them to the scaffold with him, and on arriving there he should seal them up and hand them to the chaplain, with the request that he would gratify him by sending them to his friends by as early a post as he could after the execution was over.

He hoped, he said, that the letters would be delivered by the same evening's post, and then his relatives would have, before the day was over, his last thoughts about them.

The convict then went on to speak about his execution, mentioning details that made some of his relatives shudder, and all of them to grow sad.

He said : I am to die precisely at eight o'clock—so you will know when it is all over with me. After I am dead they will hold an inquest on my body, and I shall be buried, I expect about four o'clock in the afternoon.

Here he paused for a few minutes, partly because he seemed to be exhausted, and partly because he was overcome by his own feelings.

His relatives, seeing the distressed state he was in, broke down utterly, and for some little time there was nothing to be heard but their sobs.

Peace was the first to recover himself, and going on to speak of what would be done on Tuesday, he said : I shall be buried in my clothes, just as I am. They might, however, change my shirt, or something like that.

Then, again giving way and betraying more feeling than could possibly have been expected in a man who had led the life he had led, and committed the crimes to which he had confessed, he said : I shall be thrown into my grave, and there will be no service read over me ; no sermon preached ; nothing of that sort.

He again seemed exhausted and stopped speaking, and his relatives could only look at him and weep.

Peace after awhile aroused himself again, and alluding to the men he had murdered and the robberies he had committed, he said : I wish it was in my power to restore them to life, and to replace all the property I have stolen ; but, he added, that can never be.

His relatives asked him if he had any wish that they could carry out, or anything that they could do to please him ?

Peace replied with more animation than he had shown so far during the interview : Yes, there is one thing you can do, and I wish you would do it.

I want you on the day of my execution to go to the cemetery and plant a flower or a little tree on my mother's grave and on another grave that he named, and then when you see them think of me, and where I am, and where I am buried.

His relatives promised him that his wish in this respect should be gratified, and he seemed much pleased.

Peace, referring again to his execution, said he did hope he should have strength to walk to the scaffold, but he was afraid he should not be able to do so—he was so very weak.

Dan replied : Yes ; I should like thee to be able to walk. Stand it like a man !

Peace answered with much show of feeling—Dan, thee knows I shall do that if I can.

Dan afterwards asked him why he jumped out of the train when coming from London to Sheffield ; and he repeated what he had said before, that he wanted to commit suicide.

He said he neither wanted to spend his life in prison and then die there ; nor to pass through what he had had to pass through since. He thought if he had killed himself then he might have been buried amongst his friends at Darnall.

Much of the convict's conversation during the interview was on religious topics. He said he wished he could speak to all his friends, and then he would entreat them never to enter a public-house, or to gamble, or go to handicaps.

He made a personal appeal to Dan, and begged of him to change his mode of life and to become a good man ; or as he put it " to become religious." In this strain he talked for a long time ; at intervals resting from sheer exhaustion, and then going on again.

Much of what he said, however, they could not hear he spoke in so low a tone of voice. He made no further reference to either of the murders he had committed.

When the time came for the interview to terminate not only the condemned man, but Dan and all his friends were much affected, and as may be imagined the final farewell was a very sorrowful scene.

His last utterances to them were kind remembrances to George Goodlad and Cragg, and a promise that he would write to them both.

The relatives left the cell, feeling that they had indeed taken leave of a " poor, wretched, haggard man."

As the party were returning from Armley to Leeds they were accosted by Mrs. Brion and Mrs. Thompson who were urgent in their inquiries as to what had passed between them and " Dear Jack."

Dan, we understand, took no notice of them ; but the others conversed with the two women a short time. They were much impressed with Mrs. Thompson, and greatly astonished that she should ever have taken up with a man like him.

PEACE AS A PUBLIC PERFORMER.

An Ashton-under-Lyne correspondent telegraphs :— It is a well-known fact that Peace on more than one occasion plied his many vocations in Manchester and the neighbouring towns.

From inquiries made in Levenshulme it transpires that the notorious criminal resided in that suburb about four years ago.

He stayed there only four months, and after he left the local residents thought little more about him.

A day or two ago, however, a policeman took a photograph of Peace to the locality, and many tradesmen at once recognised the portrait as that of the man who had formerly lived among them, and for a time had been quite a favourite in the district.

He rented a small detached house called Olive-cottage, in Rushford-road Park, which he fairly well furnished.

He gave his name as Thompson, and he was accompanied by a woman supposed to have been Mrs. Peace.

He was never idle, and always had some project on foot. He was constantly painting his cottage, and took such trouble with the work that the neighbours took it for granted that he meant to remain there for some years.

He was very affable and obliging to everybody, and was, until he decamped without paying his accounts, a great favourite with the tradesmen.

To ladies he was especially polite and attentive, indeed almost too much so, for if he met a woman in a shop he would say " Good morning " in an agreeable tone, but usually accompanied his salutation by a wink at the shopman.

He obtained considerable notoriety by his skill in contorting his features and assuming the appearance of a cripple. Subsequently he was known to have been the " Burnage bogie," an apparition that had scared many people in Burnage-lane, and made folks afraid to use the thoroughfare after nightfall.

At the same time it is remarkable that he was never suspected of committing any robbery, nor has it been proved that he gave effect to his thievish prospensity in the neighbourhood.

Ostensibly he earned his livelihood as an acrobat, and was engaged at the Abbey Hey Park in this capacity.

He was considered exceedingly clever, and it is stated that he could throw half-hundred weights about like pounds of sugar.

He likewise performed publicly on the violin, and was regarded by frequenters of the grounds as an able musician.

A Bristol gentleman who was staying with Mr. Plimsoll, M.P., at the time Peace called upon him to submit plans for raising sunken vessels, said that these plans were introduced as a grand scheme for raising the " Vanguard," " Captain," and " Eurydice."

The stranger wished Mr. Plimsoll to introduce him to the First Lord of the Admiralty, and Mr. Samuda and Mr. Reed.

Mr. Plimsoll declined, desiring him, if he wished to communicate further with him, to do so in writing through his visitor from Bristol.

That gentleman afterwards received letters asking to be supplied with the names of the owners of any sunken vessels in the Bristol Channel or on the western coastline.

The writer was informed of the wreck on the Hook Sands of a Greek brig, for which the owner wanted £50. He thereupon asked Mr. Plimsoll's Bristol friend to pay the £50, assuring him that the money would be refunded ; but, as may be supposed, asked in vain.

The Ashton-under-Lyne correspondent of the Central News wrote :—" From inquiries made in Levenshulme it transpires that Peace, about four years ago, came to reside in that place, but stayed only three months.

"He had been forgotten, but several of the inhabitants, on seeing a portrait of the convict a day or two ago, recognised in him their neighbour, Mr. Thompson, who resided in a small detached house called Olive-cottage, in Rushford-road Park.

"He lived with a woman who is supposed to have been Mrs. Peace, and, being always affable and obliging, was a great favourite until he decamped without paying his accounts.

"He was never suspected of robbery, but in consequence of fancied apparations the people of the neighbourhood were afraid to use the thoroughfare close to his house after dark. He ostensibly earned his livelihood as an acrobat, and was considered extremely clever in this direction."

Peace's will was drawn by Deputy-Sheriff Ford, member of a local firm of solicitors.

It extended to but four or five lines, and bequeathe property to Hannah Ward, or Peace, his wife.

The text was not to be published until the day of his execution. In regard to the former will he made bequeathing everything to Mrs. Thompson, the latter's sister, it is said, burnt the document.

CHAPTER CLXXII.
THE EXECUTION OF CHARLES PEACE.

ON Tuesday, Feb. 25th, 1879, Peace was executed within the walls of Armley Gaol, Leeds, at eight o'clock in the morning. The convict had a short sleep just after eleven o'clock the night before. At half-past eleven the Governor of the Gaol (Mr. Keene) visited him and remained with him until twenty minutes past one. Immediately after the Governor left, the chaplain, the Rev. O. Cookson, came.

As Peace seemed drowsy and inclined for sleep, the chaplain retired. At two o'clock Peace slept calmly and soundly until a quarter to six next morning, when the chaplain again joined him.

Shortly afterwards he breakfasted, and was able to take a hearty meal of toast, bacon, and eggs and tea.

He had eaten well all throughout, especially during the previous few days, and had apparently become much stronger.

Between seven and eight o'clock a number of people began to assemble outside the prison walls. At first their numbers were not large, but as eight o'clock neared their strength increased largely.

The reporters arrived about seven o'clock; only four were present. They were conducted by two warders from the entrance office to the scaffold, which was erected on the west side of the prison, in an angle of the hospital, which stands apart from the prison.

Up to that time the morning had been clear and fair, but about ten minutes to eight there was a slight fall of snow, which did not last long. At a quarter to eight the prison bell began to toll, and continued tolling until a quarter past eight.

The scaffold was only within view from the western end of the corridor, at the other extremity of which the condemned cell is situated. The prisoners in this part of the prison were removed to another part of the building, in order that they might not witness the execution.

About five minutes to eight o'clock a procession emerged into the yard, taking a winding course to the prison wall to the scaffold.

First came the Under-Sheriff, Mr. Gray, and the governor of the gaol, Mr. Keene, bearing rods of office, then followed the chaplain in his canonicals, reading the Burial Service, but he selected passages from the Scriptures which form the usual service at the gaol on such occasions. Immediately behind Mr. Cookson came the prisoner. He was supported by two warders, and behind came Marwood.

As at the trial, he was dressed in yellowish drab, the Pentonville convict suit. His arms were pinioned. His step was weak and feeble, but he required less support than could have been anticipated.

There was no sign of terror or breaking down. He was very pale, but in his general appearance little altered from that which he presented when in the dock on his trial.

If anything, he looked in better health than at that time. Instead of looking on the ground and gazing vacantly, he peered round, as if looking for someone. The object of that was, perhaps, explained by what took place afterwards. The procession was brought up by six or eight warders.

Beyond the persons already enumerated and Mr. Price, the prison surgeon, no one else was present. The prisoner ascended the scaffold with a comparatively firm tread, although he had to be assisted up the steps. He was placed upon the drop with his head forward towards the spectators.

Whilst Marwood was tying his feet, the chaplain continued reading selected portions of the Scripture. The prisoner also kept repeating, "God, have mercy upon me! Christ, have mercy on me!"

As Marwood, who stood behind the culprit, was preparing the cap to pull over his face, the convict evinced slight signs of irritation at the unexpected haste, and again signified his wish to speak.

A brief space was accordingly allowed; and looking round amongst the small company before him, he addressed them in a clear, firm voice, the tones of which must have been heard outside the prison walls. He said—

"You gentlemen reporters, I wish you to notice the few words I am going to say. You know what my life has been. It has been base; and had I wished to ask the world, after you have seen my death, what man could die as I die if he did not die in the fear of the Lord.

"Tell all my friends that I feel sure that they sincerely forgive me, and that I am going into the Kingdom of Heaven, or else to that place prepared for us to rest until the day of judgment.

"I have no enemies that I feel to have on this earth. I wish all my enemies, or those that would be so, I wish them well; I wish them to come to the Kingdom of Heaven at last.

"And now, to one and all, I say, good-bye; Heaven bless you, and may you all come to the Kingdom of Heaven at last. Amen.

"Say that my last respects is to my dear children and to their dear mother. I hope that no paper will disgrace itself by taunting them and jeering them on my account, but will have mercy upon them. God bless you, my children; my children each good-bye, and Heaven bless you. Good-bye and Amen."

After the convict had thus delivered himself, Marwood drew the white cap over his face; and, whilst this was being done, Peace turned his head slightly towards the executioner, and said—

"I should like to have a drink. Have you a cup of water you could give me?"

No attention was paid to this request, and Marwood proceeded with his duty.

From beneath the cap, however, the voice of the culprit was again heard: "May I not have a drink?" and again, as the rope was being adjusted to his neck, he exclaimed: "Oh! that's too tight."

The voice of the chaplain was then heard saying: "In the midst of life we are in death. Of whom may we seek succour but of Thee, O Lord, who for our sins are justly displeased?"

Then was uttered the commendation: "Into thy hands, O Lord, we commend this soul, now about to depart from the body. Lord Jesus receive his spirit. Amen."

As those words were being uttered Marwood stepped forward and drew the bolt. The drop fell and the body disappeared. There was a distinct thud, but not the slightest quivering of the rope, and Mr. Price, the surgeon, said death must have been instantaneous.

The drop was 9 ft. 4 in. long. It was about four minutes past eight when the execution took place, and the black flag was immediately hoisted from the prison tower as an indication to the crowd outside that all was over.

Those who had been much with Peace during the last few days said that the speech from the scaffold was not altogether unexpected by them, because the convict was a man who talked much.

What he said during the previous few days was fully in keeping with what he said on the scaffold, and they believed what he said, and died penitent.

No confession was handed to any of the prison officials, and they had nothing to communicate except what had already been mentioned in the public press relating to the Whalley Range murder, the documents relative to which had been forwarded to the Home Office.

ANOTHER ACCOUNT.

The Press Association correspondent gave the following account:—One of the most extraordinary criminals reaped his well-merited reward at the hands of the common hangman at Armley gaol.

It is unnecessary to name the culprit, for the name of Peace has been before the public every morning for two or three months.

When on his trial, and as the curtain lifted from his life, he has gloated over his exploits, and notwithstanding his profession of penitence, few would doubt that if he had been left free he would have pursued the same murderous course.

There was a mingling with wonder and horror that a man who robbed houses two or three times a night, and for months successively in the districts where he prowled around as burglar, should have escaped the police; should have carried off his booty and sold it; should have passed as a respectable man in the neighbourhoods where he lived, and even palmed himself off as one interested in science.

Touching appeals to the reporters from the scaffold and the whining imploring way in which he begged Marwood to wait a bit when the noose was being adjusted, showed that he was wanting in courage.

One can hardly conceive that any man could really pity that monster of iniquity, who had lived in robbery through his life, and who had not scrupled, when interfered with in his nefarious deeds, to use his revolver in shooting down whomsoever he might chance to encounter.

He shot the policeman at Blackheath, he shot Constable Cock, at Manchester, and actually attended the trial and conviction of another man for the murder, whose sentence, however, was providentially commuted, and shortly after this he shot Mr. Dyson in as cold-blooded a murder as has ever been revealed, and, further, he was guilty of attempting to slur with dishonour the wife of the man he murdered. After his conviction he was removed from Wakefield to Armley gaol for greater security. The prison was considered by Lieutenant-Colonel Jebb, inspector of prisons, as the best and most substantial of its kind in the kingdom. It lies to the west of Leeds, about a mile and a half from the chief seat of the cloth trade. It is an imposing castellated stone structure, and its walls and towers are blackened with smoke from the neighbouring chimneys.

Standing on the crest of a ridge overlooking the valley of the Aire, it has at its base the Midland and Great Northern lines, and the Aire flowing sluggishly along, and viewed from its front or eastern side Leeds assumes a horseshoe shape, with its smoky chimneys, and to the north-west lies to the famous Kirkstall Abbey.

The prison is a conspicuous object for many miles around. It is worked on the silent system, and each prisoner has his or her work to do at the invisible results of the crank, or in making cocoa-matting, or in picking oakum.

It has four wings, which radiate from a common centre, and there is an exercising ground situate between each of the wings.

They are two stories in height, and they have cells underneath where prisoners are put on bread and water for punishment. It was built in 1847, and for many years Mr. Keene had been the governor.

In the murderer's cell of the prison, situate on the first floor of the wing radiating to the north-west, Peace had been kept in close confinement ever since January 29.

He was closely watched by the warders with a ceaseless vigilance from the day of his sentence up to the time of his execution.

His relatives were never allowed to pass the part of the prison room partitioned off with a few iron railings extending from the floor to the ceiling. His cell, including the part so partitioned off, was not more than six yards square, and visiting it a few minutes after Peace left it for the last time, one must have thought the warders, the chaplain, and the governor would be glad that their unceasing vigilance was at an end.

It contained a bed, a table, and two stools near the table fastened tightly to the ground, and here it was that two warders were at all times in attendance—the one sitting and the other patrolling, with the convict always in between them.

The guard was relieved about every three hours.

The room was only dimly lighted by two slits in the stone, opening into the courtyard, and about twenty yards from the scaffold which Peace must have known was being knocked together for him when the workmen were busy with it.

He had two rugs and two blankets on his camp bedstead, and here it is well to say that the reports about his not taking food were erroneous, for he always took kindly to whatever was provided for him.

It was feared that because he had made the desperate attempt to jump out of the express train that he would commit suicide, if he had a chance, in his cell.

The governor, however, whilst enforcing every precaution to prevent the convict succeeding in any attempt upon his life, considered that the criminal had not sufficient courage to do that, and certainly his conduct on the gallows corroborated that view.

He professed resignation and submissiveness, but these were not to be relied upon. His whole life had been a lie.

Often as he had been in prison (from 1854 to 1858, from 1859 to 1864, and from 1866 to 1872), he had conducted himself with such propriety as to earn the rewards of docility to gaol discipline, and the consequent shortening of his sentence.

But the moment he was freed confinement he plunged again into the desperate courses of a criminal career, stopping at nothing, not even at murder, to achieve his purpose of robbery.

He appeared cheerful and resolute, not in the demeanour of bravado, but in that of absolute submission to what he had felt, from the moment the death sentence, was passed, could not be averted by any accident of fortune or intercession of clemency.

The chaplain (the Rev. Mr. Oswald Cookson, M.A.) prayed with Peace daily, and gradually the culprit appeared to follow the prayers, for within the last few days of his life he had parted with his relations, his reputed wife, and step-son, and he had confessed the rascalities and atrocities of years of crime—from boasting of his deeds he pretended to have become penitent.

He was anxious to show that he had been pierced with contrition to such a depth as to give advice of a moral character to those who visited him. He stoutly maintained what he had said all along, that there was a struggle between him and Dyson, and that the revolver went off accidentally. The wretched man slept perfectly sound and calm on his last morning till a quarter to six, when the chaplain entered, and Peace woke up.

Devotional exercises were then engaged in for about an hour. He appeared to betray, by the fervour of his utterance to his responses to the prayers, that he feared the doom awaiting him within an hour.

This, however, did not prevent his partaking heartily of breakfast, which was now brought, consisting of eggs, slice of bacon, toast, and tea.

At a quarter to eight o'clock the prison bell began to toll with a dismal noise, and thus it continued to do till a quarter past eight o'clock.

Just then Marwood was introduced, the convict submitted to have a belt fastened round the waist tightly, and was securely attached to this belt by straps. The Under-Sheriff, Mr. William Gray, the governor, Mr. Keene, and the principal warders formed a group in the gloomy chamber, all standing in front of the criminal, who submitted passively to the pinioning process.

The death sentence was read to him, and then a procession was formed to go to the gallows. The gibbet was erected within twenty yards of the doomed man's cell, but he was compelled to travel the whole length of the corridor, about eighty yards, and on reaching the court-yard, owing to a number of dressed stones lying about, the procession skirted the outer wall of the prison, and traversed a distance of eighty yards before reaching the gibbet.

This latter was a black grim structure, let about six feet into a hollowed out piece of ground, the platform, only six feet from the level of the courtyard, being reached by half a dozen wooden steps.

The lower part of the structure was draped in black sacking, and the whole timber framework was painted black also. To this place, at twenty minutes to eight, the Press Association reporter and three other representatives of the press, who on this occasion became officials on duty to conform with the Private Execution Act, by signing their names as witnesses of the due carrying out of the law, were escorted by an inspector of warders.

We waited for a few minutes listening for the approach of the procession, which was now in readiness to start along the corridor, and then issue from the door beyond the snow-covered stones strewed about.

The procession was to take a beaten path, which, however, was very slippery with frozen snow and ice, and we were to keep by the scaffold.

At the front of the gaol where we entered, here and there were groups of three and four people.

On learning that the hanging would take place at the other side of the building, they made a circuit of the building through the fields.

We heard a hubbub of voices, and afterwards learned that not less than 1000 people had congregated outside.

The crowd consisted of men, women, and children, and as they could not see the scaffold, all eyes were turned to the centre tower, where a person was in readiness to hoist the black flag as soon as the fate of the criminal was sealed. Policemen were stationed to keep the people from the prison walls to prevent their hearing what was taking place; but a rush was made, and they crowded round the wall, from which place they could distinctly hear the chaplain going through the burial service, and Peace making his last dying speech from the scaffold.

Inside the gaol the north wind was blowing piercingly cold. At five minutes to eight a movement was made by the warders at the entrance of Peace's part of the building, and then issued forth the ceremonial procession in which Peace was principal actor.

First came the governor and under-sheriff abreast, carrying a white and black wand respectively, and at a few yards' distance behind the chaplain; slightly in front of Peace, who was supported by two warders, Marwood walking after them.

The procession was closed up by a number of warders walking two abreast. Peace was uncovered, and in his prison dress. He cast his eye towards the four reporters at the farther side of the courtyard, and then his quick piercing eyes seemed to fasten upon the scaffold, at which he gave a momentary shudder.

He still kept looking towards it, and partly in consequence of this he missed his footing two or three times on the slippery and undulating pathway.

Turning to within half-a-dozen yards of the scaffold, he cast an imploring look towards the reporters, and then he was helped up the steps on to the platform, where a new 2¼ in. rope was dangling in the centre overhead.

He was nervous and agitated. He stood with his hands strapped to his side, and now and then he opened and shut them with a nervous twitch.

Meanwhile the chaplain was reading the solemn burial service of the Church of England, and the governor, two warders, and the executioner Marwood took their stand round the murderer.

He looked ghastly pale; he had grown a little hair just behind his forehead, and he had a white moustache and a grey close-cropped beard.

Marwood took the rope down, and whilst the warders were placing Peace on the centre of the drop, he was keeping his eye on Marwood at his side, who seemed anxious to put the white cap over the culprit.

"Stop a minute," said Peace; "Let me hear this." The chaplain read on, "The Lord have mercy upon us!" to which Peace joined, "Oh God, have mercy upon me; Christ have mercy upon me!"

Marwood was about putting on the white cap, when the little nervous man excitedly turned his head to Marwood, and said: "I want to speak."

He then addressed the reporters in a clear voice.

Marwood instantly, on the conclusion of the speech, drew the cap over Peace's head, and finally adjusted the ring, the condemned crying out, "Almighty God, have mercy upon me !" and next ejaculated, "I should like to have a drink."

The chaplain continued, "In the midst of life we are in death ! To whom may we seek for succour but to Thee ?"

Peace was trembling, and his hands were being moved nervously, when he vehemently cried out, "Can't I have a drink ? Oh, it's too tight."

Marwood quietly remarked, "Keep still ; I won't hurt you a bit." The chaplain was repeating the words, "I am the Resurrection and the Life," to which Peace responded, "God bless you—good-bye."

Marwood stepped back, pulled a string, a bolt was removed, the platform fell, and the wretched murderer was launched into eternity. Marwood had done his work most effectively. The victim never quivered.

The bystanders looked down into the space beneath the scaffold, and then only a few officials were left on duty.

At nine o'clock he was cut down, very little altered in appearance so far as the bloodless face was concerned. The mark of the rope was clearly shown. The body was then conveyed to the deadhouse.

After the inquest the lid was adjusted to the coffin, and without mourners, without others than officials to bear the burden, the body was taken into the burial-yard of the prison, and lowered into the grave reserved for murderers.

Others are in company in the dust adjacent, who have suffered the same dread penalty and been borne to the same ignominious repose. Like others also, he had a stone erected, with his initials and date of the execution.

In his "Last hours of the Condemned," a great Frenchman shows us, after his fashion of mingled power and fantasy, the sentenced wretch more appalled by the retrospect of an evil life than by the doom fast darkening upon him.

The interest a master of sensational phrases contrives to enlist for his subject is paralleled in actual fact by the curiosity with which the last hours of the criminal Peace were regarded.

This curiosity was not unnatural. It had been stimulated by the startling rumours which had been in circulation respecting certain confessions it was said the prisoner intended to make before he suffered.

In the old Tyburn days the great attraction of the gallows was, for many, not so much the sight of a fellow-creature dangling from a rope, as his dying speech and confession.

The British public supped full with the mere horror of executions in times when stealing from the person any trifle value for twelve pence was grand larceny, punishable by death, and offenders were turned off every day.

But there was always the prospect that the criminal would "die game "—that is, meet his end with bravado and blasphemy.

If he died penitent, he denied himself his right to address the multitude from the drop; and, whether he spoke or perished in silence, the inventive writers who purveyed the literature of the gallows made his biography their care, and hawked his miserable chronicle among the eager crowd for whom his hanging made a holiday.

The brutal longing to hear the worst and last that could be learnt of an assassin or a highwayman can no more be gratified in the old ways.

Turpin, and Duval, and Gilderoy died, in spite of the law, like heroes of romance. Fair ladies shed tears upon their irons in the cells of Newgate, and when each fascinating scoundrel appeared with a noose on his neck and a bouquet in his button-hole, the male beholders cheered, while the women sobbed.

Justice had her revenge, but her victims lived in the ballad poetry of the nation ; for even at this very day the songs made upon some of these ancient marauders are sung in parts of Great Britain.

All that is over now, fortunately, and all the unhallowed glory in which formerly a villain died no longer demoralises.

If Peace were reserving himself for display (as for the "neck-verse of Hairibee," written of by Sir Walter Scott) he would have had to do without an audience.

A century since and such a man would have set London society crazy over his career. He would have made the most of his opportunities, seeing what a figure he had managed to preserve long after the novelty of his deeds might be supposed to have waned.

The publicity into which the man had been forced was largely responsible for his demoralising eminence. It was raking in the sink to publish every shred of correspondence which passed between the condemned brigand and his paramours.

He treated these women cruelly, it would seem ; they often had black eyes and bore the weals of a whip.

It is stated that Peace went always armed with a revolver and a knife. The manner in which he used his weapon against Dyson and Robinson proved that he was prepared to take human life on the least provocation, and gives a strong *prima facie* colour to the fearful tales that were told of him.

There is one good reason why it is well this man was eliminated from the community. He belonged, from all we know of him, to the most desperate and dangerous of his class.

Very few British highwaymen or burglars have shown themselves bloodthirsty as well as dishonest. Most of them, indeed, if they carried firearms, seldom had the heart to load them, and preferred losing their plunder to taking it by fatal violence. But Peace had the ferocious spirit of a Sicilian brigand. Mr. Dyson walked towards him, and he shot him. He was as murderously prompt with Policeman Robinson.

His method does not suit in England, and if there were some who admired the man and his career, it would be a corrective of their admiration to know that the peculiarities of procedure which gave their hero his notoriety are specially repugnant to the laws, and revolting to the people of this country.

THE MORAL OF PEACE'S CAREER.

The last days, the confession, the letters, the will, the dying speech, and the execution of Charles Peace will make a sensational history of the most dangerous description.

The large place which his villainy marked for him in the public attention for several weeks proved a stimulant to many a depraved appetite for notoriety.

All persons, in short, who have had occasion to watch the effect upon the public of the noisy passage of a great malefactor from the day of sentence to the morning of doom, must have remarked the extraordinary copiousness of the record of the sayings, doings, and writings of Charles Peace with positive alarm.

The rogue's march seemed to merge into a hymn of praise, and then into a chant of victory at the gallows.

People shuddered when the murderer's repulsive features were first displayed in the shops, in a row with the ostentatious beauties and the unabashed actresses of the day.

"No wonder," said the crowd, " that this monster is the hero of a string of crimes." Just as Sydney Smith said of a saintly man that he carried the ten commandments written in his face, might it have been remarked of Charles Peace that the "Newgate Calendar" was wrought in his.

But there is a fascination in the horrible as well as in the beautiful, and the people who were dismayed while they contemplated the brutal jaw, presently craved details of the crimes its owner had committed; of the manner in which he wrote and talked of the human creatures who had associated with—nay, loved him; of his appetite for the fare of the condemned cell, and his capacity for sleep, with Marwood for the subject of his dreams.

The poisonous food was forthcoming in large doses, and be it observed, its production is the inevitable, the forced, result of the demand.

The blame lies, not with the newspapers, but with the system of turning upon the murderer's cell a light as fierce as that which the poet tells us beats upon a throne.

The journalist is the servant of the public, and the appetite for news about the murderer's daily habits being strong, he has no choice but to provide all he can obtain.

He may condemn the publication of a rogue's correspondence with his wife, his mistress, and his pals; but he cannot prevent it.

It has often been our duty to comment with severity upon such a parade of crime as the career of the man who was hanged in Armley gaol-yard on that Tuesday afforded to the British public. In Peace's instance, however, the abuse was carried to the wildest excess. The public were with the Bannercross murderer night and day, from the hour when he was condemned, to the gallows.

The comings and goings of the unfortunate people connected with him were chronicled as methodically as the "Court Newsman" imparts to the public the airings and the dinners of the Royal family.

That on the fatal morning bacon and eggs were provided for him before his long journey; and that, albeit livid white, he ate with some relish before he sat down to write a parting letter to his wife—are facts in the biography of Charles Peace which the world that dotes on Newgate records would not willingly let die. We have chronicled them accordingly.

The culprit was even allowed to address a homily to the reporters, in the character of a man who had done with the wickedness of this world, and would be, in a few moments, among the angels.

He gave friends and foes his blessing, and wished they might follow him to Heaven. There are still people who, as the author of " The Fable for Critics " remarks—

> " ——think it looks odd
> To choke a poor scamp for the glory of God."

These old-fashioned folk may be also of the opinion that there is something very monstrous in this spectacle of a malefactor, speaking, with the rope round his neck, to " you reporters."

And they may go on their way pondering on the strangeness of a society, in which the honest and heroic poor die by the hundred unsolaced by the priest, while a holy man stands at the elbow of the murderer on the gallows, and as the hangman draws the bolt, cries—" Lord Jesus receive his soul !"

When Thurtell stood upon the scaffold at Tyburn, Championship of England was about to be decided;

and while the hangman was adjusting the fatal noose, the culprit expressed his regret that his execution could not be delayed for an hour or two, that before paying the penalty of his crimes he might have the satisfaction of knowing to which of the combatants the belt had been awarded.

Whether this great criminal's attitude in the presence of death contrasts favourably or unfavourably with that assumed upon the gallows by Charles Peace, is a question upon which we will not venture to express an opinion.

Both Thurtell and Peace, however, afford perhaps the most remarkable illustrations we could instance of the curious fact that great scoundrels apparently shuffle off the mortal coil more comfortably than honest people.

Possibly it is that long inurement to crime has so blunted their sensibilities that even conscience no longer makes cowards of them, and Hamlet's great query, " To die, to sleep, perchance to dream !" troubles them not.

But, in whatever way the phenomenon is to be accounted for, the fact remains that condemned culprits, as a rule, mount the scaffold with a firm step, and, while consenting to death, apparently conquer agony.

Charles Peace proved no exception to the rule. He slept well up to within an hour and a half of his execution, and on awaking partook of a hearty breakfast.

On emerging from the condemned cell to the courtyard in which the scaffold was erected, he heard the bell tolling for his own funeral without giving signs of terror.

Upon the scaffold he appeared to be in the same contented frame of mind as the celebrated essayist and father of English journalism, who on his deathbed requested his son to "come and see how a Christian could die." But, observed Thackeray, " unfortunately, he died of brandy !"

It must be confessed that it somewhat detracts from Peace's piety that he did not take refuge in the consolations of religion until he found there was no chance of his regaining his liberty.

We fear it would have been a dangerous experiment to have let him loose again upon society, even as a " converted man !"

There seems to be something repulsive in the idea of such a consummate rascal making sure of Heaven with so little effort, after having spent his whole life in the shameless violation of every law of God and man!

The wretch was so steeped in vice and crime that his death seems to remove him beyond the liberality of the old de mortuis injunction.

Had he been really repentant of his atrocious crimes rather than of the fearful consequences to which they had brought him, it would surely have been more becoming on his part had he humbled himself in the profoundest silence, and not run the risk of intensifying the enormity of his hypocrisy by palming himself off as a local preacher upon the scaffold.

When Christ converted people He told them to go home and keep quiet—" see thou sayest nothing to any man." But nowadays converts seem to be encouraged to advertise themselves as much as possible.

Charles Peace's demeanour in the presence of the hangman is, to our thinking, far from being edifying. The sooner all memory of the career of this cunning, cruel, and abject criminal is obliterated, the better it will be for society.

SCENE ON THE SCAFFOLD—MARWOOD PINIONING PEACE'S LEGS.

We may search in vain through the annals of crime to find the record of a more infamous life than his. The fellow's assumption of virtue was, perhaps, the most horrible thing about him.

"Now, sir," he is reported to have said to the Rev. Mr. Littlewood, "I want to tell you, and I want you to believe me when I say that I always made it a rule, during the whole of my career, never to take life if I could avoid it."

Virtuous man! "And it does seem odd," he further observed, "that in the end I should have to be hanged for having taken life—the very thing I was always so anxious to avoid."

It is a pity he forgot his intense respect for the

sanctity of human life on so many occasions. The vagabond who will talk like this, after having for years prowled about at night with a six-chambered revolver strapped to his wrist, must be an extraordinary combination of the heartless ruffian and the sneaking hypocrite.

In addition to this, Peace was perhaps the most accomplished burglar that ever necessitated the vigilance of the police.

But the terms murderer and burglar are scarcely adequate to paint the blackness of his character, for on his own confession this man actually sat in court at the Manchester Assizes and heard the sentence of death passed upon an innocent man for a murder which he himself had committed.

"I liked to attend trials," he said, "and I determined to be present. I left home for Manchester, not telling my family where I had gone. I attended the assizes for two days, and heard the youngest of the brothers, as I was told they were, sentenced to death. Now, sir, some people will say that I was a hardened wretch for allowing an innocent man to suffer for my crime."

Undoubtedly all people would. Peace, however, was too much satisfied with his good luck to permit his conscience to trouble him about the matter.

If capital punishment is justifiable, Marwood unquestionably did the State some service in ridding society of Charles Peace.

There is something terrible in the contemplation of a misspent life like his, and the wretched man's interment, after the terrible scene upon the gallows was enacted, would make sadder even the saddest of all cemeteries—namely, the burial-yard of a county prison.

The mercy which is infinite, and the repentance which secures it, invited Peace as they invite all other mortals, and upon the mystery of the felon's grave all comment is struck dumb.

It may be noted, however, that though the last utterances of the dying criminal were full of contrition and paternal solicitude, there is a certain tone in the whole speech which suggests that the man had in reality not awakened to a full estimate of the greatness of his offences. His demeanour throughout indicates the same moral defect.

There were in his character many signs of an idiosyncrasy which, like kleptomania and other depraved mental compulsions, dragged the possessed being into the vicious path and disabled the faculty of remorse.

Peace had the cunning of the rogue, plus that of the intelligent man he was. But until the eleventh hour he was playing a part.

First he shammed ill, then he had a spell of sullen silence, which was succeeded by that fit of communicativeness, oral and written, which has taken up so much space in the newspapers. He appears to have made a great many contradictory statements or confessions ; and, if all that have been published as such are really his, there is some difficulty in accepting as authentic even the most solemn of these avowals on the scaffold.

One of these confessions purported to be an admission of a series of murders, known and unknown, committed by him singly, or with accomplices, in London or the provinces.

If Peace reduced this horrid catalogue to two, and he in truth and in fact stated what appeared in print, would require clear corroborative evidence to sustain anything he asserted.

Peace declared in more than one of his many confessions that he murdered the policeman Cock at Whalley Range, near Manchester, in 1876. For this crime a young man named Habron was sentenced to death.

The sentence was commuted to penal servitude for life, and that terrible penalty the innocent and signally unfortunate man was still undergoing when Peace was first rendered amenable. The real assassin, according to his own avowal, was present in Court at the trial, and heard Habron sentenced.

The same night Peace shot Mr. Dyson. There can be little question, but he would have held his tongue to save his neck, had the poor man been permitted to suffer for his crime, and been put to death for it.

The one point of relief in an ugly picture is this, where we find justice done to the innocent by the detection of the guilty.

On the other hand, the vindication suggests grave reflections respecting the adequacy of trial by jury, and the security of our criminal procedure to place the guilt where it is charged on the guilty head, and save the innocent from destruction, by circumstantial evidence.

VISIT TO THE CONDEMNED CELL AFTER THE EXECUTION.

The *Central News* reporter telegraphed :—The prison chaplain was deeply affected on returning from the execution of Peace on Tuesday morning. Dr. Price, the gaol physician, escorted him to his official residence.

Under-sheriff Gray, his clerk, Mr. Waite, and the governor, together with the representatives of the press, in leaving the fatal spot passed into the wing of the gaol from which Peace had so recently emerged. The cell which the condemned man had occupied was also passed.

The gas was still burning in it, and the door was open. On the bed was a closed bible and a prayerbook, whilst the convict's shoes, slippers, wide-awake hat, and other articles of apparel were placed on the benches in the inner cell.

On the little table were a number of books and several sheets of paper, on which the convict had apparently been scribbling. A tin quart measure, nearly full of milk, also stood on the table.

SCENES OUTSIDE THE GAOL.

It was a fearful morning. The air was raw, and a searching wind pierced through one almost to the bone yet the fields dividing the gaol from the houses near seemed to be covered with people almost immediately.

They ran eagerly to get the best places that could be obtained. Everybody ran and everybody was anxious to get the best places. The peculiar coign of vantage, known only to the experienced, was said to be behind the prison, near the hospital.

This was where the scaffold had been erected, and it was said that outside the walls, at that point, the falling of the trap and the thud caused by the jerk to the rope could be distinctly heard.

It is no exaggeration to say that at least 500 people assembed at this spot, and that until the hoisting of the flag the most careful silence was preserved. Indeed, some of the people who were standing there declared that they heard Peace speaking, but could not make nt his words.

A large knot of people, numbering several hundred, appeared at the outer gates, without any warning, and undisturbed took up positions commanding a view of the flag-pole on the high tower.

About ten minutes to eight snow began to fall slightly, but it soon discontinued, and at five minutes to eight the weather was fine again.

What a rude, unsympathetic, ribald crowd that was! Drawn together merely by morbid curiosity, many of them laughed, smiled, and joked at the dread ordeal which the convict was even then undergoing.

They spoke of him as at that moment submitting to the pinions, and wondered with a fiendish glee how he liked the process. Women and girls vied with each other in depicting his agony as a subject for laughter, and the most horribly blasphemous expressions were used with respect to his penitence.

It might have been a crowd of citizenesses during the French revolution. There was an utter callousness, a cold-blooded nonchalance, and a frequency of oaths which made the crowd almost terrible as well as repulsive. There seemed to be not an atom of feeling amongst the lot. Everyone had something to say.

There was a continual hum of conversation, but amongst the Babel of words it was impossible to detect one which breathed kindly feeling, regret, or even seriousness.

But it is now five minutes to eight, and the first sign comes from the inside of the gaol. Upon the high tower a stalwart warder appears. At length the prison clock strikes the hour. The signal is given, and in another moment the black signal of death flutters in the clear fresh breeze.

A kind of shudder is observable among the people as the flag ascends, but the feeling soon passes away, and from a large number of the assembled crowd rises a fiendish and inhuman shout. The "cry for blood" was satisfied.

A stampede commenced immediately, and the hundreds of people streamed back into Leeds. A few still lingered about the place, gazing fitfully at the black signal, and talking together in knots of the strange and adventurous career which had just closed so ignominiously.

THE INQUEST AND VERDICT.

At eleven on the fatal morning the inquest on the body was held in the committee-room at the gaol, before Mr. J. C. Malcolm, the borough coroner. The verdict of the jury certified that the identity of the deceased as Charles Peace was proved, and that the sentence of death passed upon him had been carried out.

Peace's features were but little changed, and, excepting the usual swollen appearance of the face and neck, always observable in those hung, there was nothing to prevent anyone who had known him alive from identifying the remains as those of the convict.

THE INTERMENT.

The remains were subsequently taken to the murderers' graveyard, which is inside the walls, and were there unceremoniously interred. Rude stones mark the place of burial of previous victims of the law's highest penalty, and a headstone has been placed over Peace's grave similar to that of the others, on which are cut his initials and the date of his death.

PEACE AND HIS REVOLVERS.

The statement made by Mr. Woodward, the London gunsmith, to the effect that the manufacture of bullets like those found in the bodies of the policeman Cook and Mr. Dyson had been discontinued for more than five years, led to the inquiry where Peace could have obtained the bullets that he used.

It appears that Peace stole the revolver from the house of a gentleman at Manchester, in the early part of 1876; and with the revolver, which was in a case, he also stole a box of Eley's 442 pin-fire cartridges. The box was full, and contained probably 100 cartridges, several of which Peace used.

When the family at Peckham heard that Peace had been arrested at Blackheath, Mrs. Peace and Mrs. Thompson each packed up a large box of articles and left, the one for Nottingham and the other for Sheffield.

Mrs. Thompson put into her box Peace's other three revolvers, together with all the ammunition there was in the house, including the remainder of the box of pin-fire cartridges.

A short time after Mrs. Peace asked Mrs. Thompson what she had done with the revolvers and ammunition, and she replied that, being afraid to retain them in her possession, she had packed all in a basket and her sister had sunk them in the canal at Nottingham.

There is no reason to suppose, if properly gone about, that the sister would refuse to point out the spot where she put the basket. If that could be fished up from the bottom of the canal, and the pin-fire cartridges found, there would be further confirmation of the truth of Peace's confession that he shot policeman Cock.

PEACE'S LAST WILL AND TESTAMENT.

Some very erroneous statements have been made, not only as to the value of the property that was at Peace's disposal, but also as to the manner in which he had disposed of it.

At one of the interviews Peace had with his wife and family he signed a "deed of gift," in which he made over to them all he possessed.

They went to London in the hope of being able to obtain the property stated to belong to Peace; but not being successful, he had a will drawn up by Messrs. Warren and Ford, of Leeds, in which he left all he possessed to Willie Ward and his daughter, Mrs. Bolsover. The following is the full text of the will:—

"I, Charles Peace, at present lodged in Armley gaol, in the county of York, under sentence of death, do hereby revoke all wills, codicils, and other testamentary dispositions heretofore made by me, and declare this alone to be my last will and testament.

"I give, devise, and bequeath all my real estate, and all my money, securities for money, furniture, goods, chattels, and all other personal estate of which I shall die possessed, or over which I shall at my death have power to dispose by this my will unto William Ward, of Darnall, grocer's assistant, and Jane Ann Bolsover, of Darnall aforesaid, in equal shares as tenants in common, the share of the said Jane Ann Bolsover to be for her sole and separate use, and free from the control and debts of her present or any future husband.

"And I appoint the said William Ward and Jane Ann Bolsover executor and executrix of this my will. In witness whereof I have hereunto set my hand this twenty-fourth day of February, 1879."

The will is signed by Charles Peace, and witnessed by Osmond Cookson, M.A., chaplain of her Majesty's Prison, Leeds; and William Warren, solicitor, Leeds.

According to an old law the property of a felon became forfeit to the crown, and in consequence rich men who entered upon desperate enterprises often contrived, by deed or gift and other means, to outwit the avarice of the monarchy.

Practically, the law on this subject has long been obsolete, and hence we had the spectacle of a condemned murderer putting his house in order and making his will as if he were a respectable citizen dying in the odour of sanctity.

Mr. Charles Peace, temporarily residing in her Majesty's goal at Armley, had, with the commendable spirit of orderliness which were found to have marked all the known events of a singularly active and varied life, prepared his last will and testament, a document duly signed and attested by the governor of Armley gaol.

The contents of Mr. Peace's will had remained unknown until the testator left a world which only his most ardent admirers could contend that he adorned. However, there was not long to wait before the public learned the full particulars of the manner in which Mr. Peace disposed of what, if he had been half as careful as he was enterprising, might be a considerable personal estate. The chest full of jewellery and silver plate reported to have been discovered, buried in the railway embankment at Nunhead, was not included in the convict's belongings, for the simple reason that the chest and its contents never had any existence outside the imagination of the penny-a-liner who invented the story. Besides the duly attested will, Mr. Peace consigned to his wife a deed of gift, by which he disposed of certain effects in her favour, with the exception of a watch and his patent for raising sunken ships. Both watch and patent were conferred upon his step-son, Willie Ward, in the hope that he would make some use of the latter. So far as can be made out of the conflicting statements on all subjects appertaining to the interesting criminal, a half share in the patent for raising sunken ships belonged to Mr. Brion, the geographer. Such a slight matter of detail would not, however. affect a gentleman of Mr. Peace's proclivities in disposing by gift or otherwise of the entire property. A somewhat clouded comprehension of *meum* and *tuum* throughout marked his chequered career. Provided the Crown were willing to permit Mr. Peace the disposition of what he was pleased to call his property, surely the Government would feel some scruples in taking probate duty upon the results of crimes. If Mr. Peace's personalty were in cash, it would nothing but fair to opine that this particular money was essentually filthy lucre, with a genesis from the hands of a burglar, through those of a fence, and thence by the melting-pot back again to the possession of the criminal. Possibly the will itself might be, in some person's opinion, a bogus instrument, dealing with a fabulous estate. For it would seem if Mr. Peace were possessed of means he would have taken care for a satisfactory and complete defence. Assuming for the sake of argument that property belonging be the murderer had been hidden away somewhere, to be forthcoming after his execution, his heirs, executors, and assigns ought not to object to the £100 reward for his apprehension claimed by his "darling Sue" being paid out of his personalty. It would, under the circumstances, have been a hardship indeed if the country were saddled with the task of enriching such a creature as Mrs. Thompson.

CHAPTER CLXXIII.
THE EXECUTIONER'S STORY—A QUIET CHAT WITH MARWOOD.

SHORTLY after the execution of Charles Peace the following interview took place between a journalist and Marwood.

"The Irish call me the Prince of Executioners!" A gentleman of medium height, with a ruddy face, puckered in humorous wrinkles, and with bright eyes, shining with a merry light, utters these words to me in a voice sweet and low—almost gentle as a woman's.

It is Marwood, the executioner; he has just washed his hands of Peace's death, and now sits opposite me in the cozy drawing-room of a gentleman's villa, not far away from Armley gaol.

As he entered the room in his black suit of clerical

cut I had an idea that he dropped a carpet-bag in the passage—a bag containing the rope and straps by the aid of which he had taken the life of a fellow-being an hour ago; but he advanced towards me in such a pleasant way, and bowed so politely, that my dread soon vanished, and in a few minutes we were in the midst of a quiet chat on the subject of Peace's execution.

Without, the snow fell thickly, and a piercing wind swept round the house, with an angry, stormy sound; but within the curtains were drawn; a bright fire sent its glow throughout the room, and now and then gleamed on Marwood's face, making it look quite benevolent.

Seated by the fireside, conversing earnestly, we did not notice that the gentleman whose guest he was had tired of knocking, and entered the room to welcome his old friend.

Seeing him, Marwood immediately rose from the arm-chair in which he had been seated, and, bowing, said: "My kind regards. I pray that we may have happy lives, and that our work will be well done on earth."

A rosy-cheeked, chubby-face boy toddled into the room as he was speaking, and, seeing the little fellow, Marwood patted him on the head kindly, and with a smile on his face said: "I hope you will make a very good man."

A kind-hearted man enough, despite his profession, the executioner had promised me a private interview, and as soon as we were alone again he referred to the great skill he had attained in the science of hanging, and told me how Peace met his death.

"A firmer step never walked to the scaffold," he said. "I admired his bravery; he met his fate like a man; he acknowledged his guilt, and his hope in God with regard to his future was very good."

"But," I asked, "don't you think he feared death?"

"No," replied Marwood; "during the seven years I have officiated as executioner I never met a man who faced death with greater calmness."

"You mean to say then that he met his fate without a tremour?"

"Yes," responded the executioner. "It's true he shivered a bit; but not through fear. It was a bitter winter's morning, and he complained of the cold."

"It is not surprising," I said, "that a man like Peace, who has been face to face with danger so often should endeavour to die without betraying any weakness or timidity."

"The bravery was an outcome of his nature," replied Marwood. "He was ignorant alike of weakness and timidity. I will prove it to you. He had been suffering from a bad cough for some days. The night before his execution he said to one of his warders, 'I wonder whether Mr. Marwood can cure this bad cough of mine?' The warder replied, 'I have no doubt he could.' And I can tell you that a man who jokes about getting hanged to cure a cough is no coward.'

"Do you think he suffered much?" I asked.

"Not in the least; he was dead instantly. But perhaps I had better tell you what occurred just before the execution.

"It is a most curious thing. He had got hold of the idea that I should terribly punish him at the scaffold, and he repeatedly asked the chief warder to be sure and tell me that he wished for an interview about a quarter of an hour before he was led out to die.

"Accordingly at ten minutes to eight o'clock I went to the condemned cell, which stands about in the centre of the gaol, some hundred yards from the place where the scaffold was erected. Peace was seated—he was in his convict dress, and there were several officials attending upon him. The bandage had been removed from his head; and he did not wear spectacles.

"He was neither weak nor prostrate, but sat upright on his chair, as if he had never known a moment's illness. When I appeared in the doorway he seemed pleased, and holding out his hand said, 'I am glad to see you, Mr. Marwood. I wish to have a word with you. I do hope you will not punish me. I hope you will do your work quickly.'

"'You shall not suffer pain from my hand,' I replied; and then Peace, grasping my arm, said, 'God bless you. I hope to meet you all in Heaven. I am thankful to say my sins are all forgiven.'

"It was now time to pinion him," continued the executioner. "He stood up at my request, but did not really need the support of the two warders by his side. He was not at all nervous, and quietly submitted to my operations. Pinioning is a very ingenious process.

"I run a main strap round the body; and connected with it are two other straps, which take the small of the arm, so that the elbows are fastened close to the body and the hands are free.

"Peace complained, saying, 'The straps fit very tight.' I replied, 'It is better so; it will prevent you from suffering.' He made no further objection; and taking hold of the main strap, so as to keep my hand on him, we started for the scaffold.

"The governor and the under-sheriff went first, then came the chaplain; and I followed with the condemned man, two warders attending him, one on each side. They grasped him by the arms, but did not support him. He was bare-headed. His face was pale, but pinched with cold rather than fear.

"As he arrived near the scaffold he gave a very wistful look at my arrangements. They were all right, and seemed to satisfy him, for he made no remark. He went up the steps leading to the drop with a firm tread, whilst the chaplain read the burial service. I brought him to a proper stand under the crossbar, and then strapped his legs.

"When that was done he wished to say something to the reporters, and made a beautiful speech. Such a speech has never come from a condemned man I have executed.

"It was really a good speech. When he had finished it he asked for a drink; but you know that was unreasonable, and it could not be admitted, for the time fixed for the execution had fully expired.

"So I placed the cap over his face, and adjusted the rope, when he said—'I say, the rope fits very tight.' I replied, 'Never mind; it's all for the best; hold up your chin,' and he did so immediately, so that I could properly fix the rope. 'Good-bye, all; God bless you,' he kept repeating as I went towards the lever.

"At this time he did not require anyone to support him, but I told one of the warders to take hold of the back strap.

"Whilst he stood in this manner on the drop, with the noose around his neck, I pushed the lever forward; it withdrew the bolt from the swinging doors, and Peace's body fell through the aperture beneath the platform. The drop was exactly nine feet four inches.

"Peace was dead in a moment; he never moved a finger or a muscle after he fell; so I carried out my promise to do it well and quickly."

I must admit that I was rather astonished at the matter-of-fact and yet complacent way in which

Marwood described the execution, and modestly referred to his own dexterity; but I was anxious to know by what method he had obtained such success as an executioner, and endeavoured to glean from him the mysteries of his art.

The explanation is explicit, but rather embarrassing. The old system on which Calcraft rested his faith was, he told me, the system of strangulation, which frequently resulted in great suffering, especially when the short drop did not kill the man, and the executioner had to pull at his legs until the miserable being was lifeless.

"But my process is humane," says Marwood, "for it entails no suffering whatever. My principles are rapidity and dislocation.

"When the neck is dislocated the man does not suffer at all—at least, that is my opinion. I have no doubt that if you examined Peace you would find the spinal cord severed. It is done in this way. I attach the rope to the cross-bar; the noose at the opposite end is formed by a brass ring woven in the rope, and this is placed on the left side of the neck towards the chin."

Anxious to give me a correct idea of his process, he placed his finger on my own neck to signify the exact locality, and I began to grow nervous, and to wonder whether I had committed some diabolical murder or other, and was about to suffer for my sin. I suddenly became very wise as to the adjustment of the noose, and told Marwood that I had a very vivid idea of the perfection of the arrangement, with the intention of leading him to speak on some topic not quite so personal, but he said he had made this subject the study of his life, and he continued to point out the merits of the long drop, compared with the short drop, and to speak earnestly of the advantages derived from the alteration.

I am not very easily frightened, but I found this dissertation on the science of hanging oppress me. I had a desire to get outside the house—to get into a freer atmosphere.

I could almost imagine that if I didn't, and that speedily, I should not escape the long drop myself.

Still there was nothing terrible about Mr. Marwood, as he reclined in his easy chair, and spoke in his soft, pleasant tones of the strange experiences he had gone through.

"I am doing God's work," he said, "according to the Divine command, and the law of the British Crown. I do it simply as a matter of duty, and as a Christian, and I think no more of it than I do of chatting to you now."

Such is the affable man who executed Peace. Conscious that he is doing his duty, the character of the profession he follows has no influence upon him, and he claims to be a benefactor to society.

I asked him what induced him to adopt such a mode of gaining his livelihood, and he replied: "Oh, when I heard the old gentleman, Calcraft, was breaking down, and I saw the accounts of his bungling work, I thought if I could carry out the sentence of the law more mercifully it would be a service to the public.

"I always had a love of anatomy, and even when a boy was greatly interested in executions, but it is a most singular fact that I never saw an execution until I myself became an executioner. I do my duty with a kind hand, and with firmness, and believe I really render a benefit to society. I have been successful in every engagement, and I am respected wherever I go.

"I have told you that in Ireland I am known as ' the Prince of Executioners;' in Scotland I have received the kindest treatment, and if I were really a prince I could not be better served. In the past seven years more than 100 persons have died at my hand; but I cannot tell you the exact number, as I do not now keep a record."

"Are you ever haunted by the features of those you have executed?" I asked in desperation, thinking that perhaps I might surprise him into some expression of feeling.

"Bless your life, no," he said, smiling. I sleep as soundly as a child, and am never disturbed by phantoms. Where there is guilt there is bad sleeping, but I am not disturbed in the least, for I am conscious that I try to live a blameless life.

"The other night I slept in the warder's apartments in Armley gaol peacefully and undisturbed, although I had superintended the erection of the scaffold, and knew I had to execute Peace in the morning. It is a matter of duty with me entirely."

"Have all the criminals who have received your attentions acted courageously on the scaffold?"

"Well," Marwood replied, "taking them altogether they are a brave lot. The worst job I ever had was with a Spaniard, a sailor, at Usk, in Monmouth. He had murdered a man, his wife, and three children, and then set the house on fire. He was sentenced to death; and when he saw me enter the cell with the straps he fainted, and was saved from falling by two warders.

"I put the straps upon him; and said in an authoritative voice, 'Stand up, sir.' It was only a sham faint. I told him I would not have such nonsense, and he stood up immediately. With this lesson he walked out, and was hanged quietly. Peace, however, gave me no trouble of this kind, but met his fate like a man."

I now ventured to ask the executioner if he was not looked upon with some degree of loathing when he became the successor of Calcraft, and he freely admitted that such was the case.

"I was frequently jeered at," he said, "at first; but I put it down to people's ignorance, and now I am received with the greatest kindness wherever my services are needed."

"How does it affect you in your own town?" was the last question I put to Mr. Marwood.

"Oh!" he replied, "at Horncastle I was looked upon as one of the first men in the place. I was treated well by one and all. Detesting idleness, I passed my vacant time in business; and worked in my shoe-shop near the church day after day, until such time as I was required elsewhere. It would have been better for those I executed if they had preferred industry to idleness."

I had passed nearly two hours in the society of the hangman when our quiet chat was over, thanked him for his kindness, and bade him adieu. As I left the room he shook me heartily by the hand, then said, "Good-bye, God bless you," and bowed me out of the villa with that polished courtesy which is always so becoming in a Crown official.

CHAPTER CLXXIV.
CAPITAL PUNISHMENT—MERCIFUL AND MERCILESS MODES
IN DIFFERENT AGES.

IN this chapter we propose giving a short review of the methods by which obnoxious criminals have been, at various times, among various peoples, invited to "shuffle off this mortal coil."

Capital punishment, like Cleopatra's charms, has been of "infinite variety"—the variety, however, as a rule, being simply among the most horrible possible methods. No records remain to tell how the contem-

poraries of the Saurians and the Megatherium, the ingenious dwellers in caves, and warriors of the flint age, disposed of their malefactors, but the fullest accounts have been preserved of the proceedings of our more modern ancestors, since the days of Adam, in the way of executions.

The Jews, who led the bead-roll of antique nations, appear to have usually stoned the criminals of their own race—a democratic sort of penalty, where every good citizen had a finger in the pie, and hurled his righteous rock, and even the little Hebrew boys could enjoy the fun of the stoner. To the stoned it must have been something of a lingering torture, requiring much patience to bear. For their enemies they reserved the sharper practice of hewing them in pieces, or they burned them alive, or turned them to agricultural account, and fertilised the sites of their smoking cities by harrowing them in with considerable vehemence.

The Chinese, another ancient and highly cultured race, have been similarly merciless. It is singular how little difference there has been in this respect of ingenious cruelty between the most cultivated peoples and the wildest savages.

Decapitation is the mildest of Chinese extreme penalties, and is usually performed with much skill and sang-froid by means of a sword, the criminal, male and female, taking the matter most philosophically, and making no indecorous remonstrances at their summary taking off.

There is a tariff, too, for substitutes—a plan which might commend itself to our wealthier homicides. But our Celestial neighbours across the Pacific prefer killing the doomed by not allowing them to sleep, or starving them to death in cages or straightened limits, in which they are exhibited during the process of skeleton-formation, in peripatetic rambles on the shoulders of the local deputy sheriffs.

And chopping them deliberately into fragments, at intervals of an hour or so, is much to their taste. There is a cage, part of the spolia opima of the first Chinese war, among the archives of the Royal Artillery, at Madras, India, in which they carried about Colonel Rowlandson, and the London *Times* had a liberal annual payment on its pension list for the family of Mr. Bowles, a special correspondent, similarly disposed of just before the last Chinese war.

The torturing propensities of the pleasing red man, whom Cooper immortalised, and Custer has occasionally assisted to the happy hunting grounds, are too well known to require much notice.

The use of fire is a prominent feature in their social circles, complicated with the facetious tomahawk and the insinuating scalping-knife. But we know the Modocs, the Sioux, and others like them, only too well.

The Assyrians, Medes and Persians, ancient Egyptians, and other Orientals seemed to have employed similar agencies to their Israelitish neighbours for lopping off the rotten branches of their family trees.

The processes are faithfully depicted and chiselled on the walls of Thebes, Persepolis, and Nineveh.

The Greeks were somewhat tender-hearted in some cases; for instance, they allowed Socrates to poison himself comfortably among his friends.

They objected to parricides, however, and for them reserved a punishment adopted from the Egyptians, like their alphabet, and naturalised at a later date by the Romans. They confined the too impetuous slayer of his father in a bag with a snake, a monkey, and a cat, to keep him company, and then gently dropped the congenial party into the sea.

The Romans seem first to have hit on the idea of crucifixion, a singularly torturing refinement of internal, external, and mental pain.

It was esteemed an ignoble death, and must have been anguish to a sensitive mind; the cruel nails rending the flesh, barely supporting the weight of the writhing body, must have been severe, while the dreadful thirst of the fevered victim must have been a culminating horror.

The State criminals sometimes came floating over the Tarpeian rock, and smashed into pulp below.

This has been emulated by Theodore of Abyssinia, at his mountain fastness of Magdala, and by Tippoo Sahib at the Droorg, one of the peaks of the Neilgherry mountains in Southern India, where is a convenient precipice over 1000 feet clear of sheer natural wall.

The Roman taste for the joys of the circus stimulated their imagination to devise novel torment, and criminals or Christians, or simply prisoners of war, were exposed to combat wild beasts, or each other, to "grace a Roman holiday."

They sometimes, however, executed distinguished folks in polite fashion, merely sending a polite message for them to "stand not on the order of their going, but go" out of the world at their earliest convenience.

A good deal of bleeding to death in warm baths and sudden insertion of the "bare bodkin" resulted.

The chivalric Japanese custom of harikari is a similar concession to the conventionalities of society, and is also eminently useful as a duelling agent necessitating the absolute retirement of both disturbers of the peace and their friends' serenity.

It is hardly necessary to dilate on the ceremonious surroundings of these interesting occasions, when the accomplished gentleman who has offended the laws, or has been offended by a friend, calls his relatives and acquaintances together and, supported by a second, a veteran in the punctilio of the local code of honour, makes his little speech, drinks his farewell toast, and then proceeds to carve himself in the most approv d style, proudly feeling as he dies that he has done his duty to his country, his family, and the world at large, and that the gentleman he had the difficulty with cannot survive him.

The Druids, like the Huns, the Aztecs, and the Ashantees and Dahomeyans in the present day, were rather sanguinary.

Funerals were fittingly honoured by the sacrifice of a proportionate number of slaves and criminals, to form a retinue for the worthy departed in the world of spirits. The Druids usually burned a few hundreds in a great wicker image of the human figure.

It is recorded that many thousands of men, women, and children, with horses, jewels, arms, and domestic necessaries, were sacrificed when Attila, "the Scourge of God," died, and were buried with him in the bed of a river, diverted temporarily from its course for the purpose, and similar formalities are observed in the African kingdoms mentioned, on any one event, but repeated annually as a "custom," to keep the manes of the deceased in good humour by the polite remembrance implied by the observance.

But Christian Europe, in the Dark Ages, could vie with any race or century in the ingenuity and refined cruelty of capital punishment.

The preliminary tortures of the rack, the boots, the thumb-screws, the strappado, must have tended to make the recipient of these attentions desirous of death.

The noble Barons who harried each other, and re-

volted at brief intervals throughout their tumultous lives, pressed air, earth, fire, and water into their service for the purpose of execution.

Men were judicially pressed to death as late as the Titus Oates conspiracy, in the reign of Charles II. They were hanged in chains to starve; they were burned alive, half hanged, mutilated, and then burned; they were scorched with hot irons, their eyes seared out, their limbs plunged into molten lead or tar; they were spitted like cockchafers on stakes, they were drowned with unmerciful rapidity, or chained to stakes at low water to be more slowly suffocated by the rising tide; they were broken on the wheel, or torn apart by wild horses, while the axe for the noble kept up a perpetual refrain like the ticking of a clock.

The Inquisition, in the garb and under the name of religion, invented and applied more exquisite barbarities. To drive a man mad first and into a grave afterwards by the incessant trickling of a single drop of water was a torment worthy of Satan himself.

The thousands burned to death in Spain, France, England, China, India, Germany, attest the gusto with which the reverend brethren of the Holy Office snuffed in the flavour of roasting humanity, and were enraptured with the shrieks of the martyrs, as now-a-days we are when Capoul or Tamberlik rouses our enthusiasm with the ringing C in alt.

In those good old days men were slain for sneezing in improper places, for constructive disrespect, or for stealing a loaf, and the severity remained till within comparatively recent times.

Some of the middle-age methods still survive. In Naples, three years ago, of three women condemned for infanticide two were beheaded; the third, the principal culprit, was mazzolated, or knocked on the head with a mace, like an ox, her abdomen then slashed open, while the executioner executed a "pas de fascination" on the quivering trunk, spurting the blood out like a fountain.

In Spain, Spanish colonies, and the sister Republics who once owed allegiance to that haughty country, malefactors are garrotted, or strangled in an armchair with a steel cravat, which is jammed to the choking point by the dexterous twisting of a screw behind.

They also shoot considerably, evincing a peculiar fondness for shooting people in the back with a remarkably bad aim, and then finishing them with a shot in the ear at close quarters, or a dagger under the fifth rib.

It was in this way they disposed of William Walker, "the grey-eyed man of destiny," at Truxillo, in 1860. The French weakness for the guillotine, an aggravated edition of the domestic bread or meat chopper, has disposed of many multitudes of kings, queens, nobles, ragamuffins, petroleuses, and others, with business-like rapidity and cleanliness.

The baskets, sawdust, and brightly-polished cheese-knife employed are familiar, and almost inviting in comparison with the gallows adhered to by Anglo-Saxons.

Hanging nowadays seems a "lost art." The Americans have improved the machinery with patent drops and weights warranted to jerk up the hanged with satisfactory promptitude.

But the education of the hangman has been sadly neglected. The knot is rarely tied with scientific accuracy, or the rope in as good condition as it might be.

The consequence is, but a small proportion of the sufferers enjoy the sudden death they would prefer, if they must die in so hasty a manner, and instead of their necks being broken they are slowly strangled, if the rope does not break and necessitate a repetition of the performance.

Physicians and anatomists say this slow strangulation must be exquisitely painful.

Humanitarians have accordingly suggested " painless extinction." Chloroform applied long enough would soothe the slumberer to wake no more here below, with absolutely no pain.

An overdose of laudanum might be an improvement, as bestowing positive pleasure before he lapsed into unconsciousness.

Both these and other plans are warmly recommended, and discussed with some heat by their respective advocates. Some gentlemen have even hinted at the possibility of doing good at the same time by dissecting the brain of the living but unconscious subject, during the calm retreat from the sins and follies of his life.

Another method of painless extinction is by blowing the patient from a gun. This was invented by the Mahommedans of India, was employed by the British during the mutiny of 1857, and is still in favour with the Ameer of Afghanistan.

It has one great advantage as a preventive of crime in its application to Hindoos, as they believe, when a man's body is split into filaments, as it must be by such a process, that his chances of future existence are very slim.

Their ideas of resurrection are peculiar and Pythagorean, but they object to this total obliteration, and accordingly dread the blowing-from-gun procedure above all other penalties. Physically, it cannot hurt, however.

The conclusion and distribution of the fragments are so sudden and complete that pain must be entirely wanting as an element. Destroying a hanged Brahmin's body with quicklime is also objectionable to Hindoos, on account of similar doubts as to his future rehabilitation.

A Hindoo punishment, of gradually crushing a criminal under the foot of a trained elephant, is repulsive, and is discountenanced by the British Government. Any rajah who reverts to these ancestral amusements renders his tenure on the throne insecure. It has not been practised for some years.

The guillotine, of which such horrible use was made in the past French Revolution, has been said to be the most merciful mode of putting malefactors to death, but this is by no means certain.

Dr. Tuc and some German physicians and surgeons after him held that there does indubitably remain in the brain of a decapitated head some degree (*un reste*) of thought, and in the nerves something of sensibility, and the case of Mademoiselle Corday was alleged as proving that doctrine.

We abstain from any details of the thousands of murders by the guillotine at this time. One fact will enable our readers to understand something of its horrors.

It was proved on the trial of Fouquier Tinville that 160 persons of all ages and ranks, and of both sexes, were tried and executed on a charge of conspiracy, not merely false but absurd, visionary, and impossible—forty-five of these persons, who were utterly unknown to each other, were tried and condemned within twenty minutes, and executed on the same evening in almost as short a space. These executions were for many months the amusement—the spectacle of the people—we wish we could say the populace of Paris.

Chairs were stationed round the instrument of death, where women, in a station of life to be able to pay for that amusement, used to have seats, and sit, and chat, and work, while waiting for the tragedy, which they had looked at as a farce. We find in the *Revue Retrospective* a curious letter incidentally descriptive of this elegant scene of Parisian amusement.

"The Procureur-Général Rœderer to Citizen Guidon.
"13th May, 1793.

" I enclose, Citizen, the copy of a letter from Citizen Chaumette, solicitor to the Commune of Paris, by which you will perceive that complaints are made that, after these public executions, the blood of the criminals remains in pools upon the place, and that dogs come to drink it, and that crowds of men feed their eyes with this spectacle, which naturally instigates their hearts to ferocity and blood.

" I request you, therefore, to take the earliest and most convenient measures to remove from the eyes of men a sight so afflicting to humanity."

Our readers will observe the tender regret—not that all this blood was shed, but that it was not wiped up; and they will be startled when they recollect that at the date of this letter not above a dozen persons had been yet executed there, but that within one year the blood of a thousand victims had saturated the same small spot of ground.

In one of the foolish modern-antique processions of the Convention, the whole cortège was delayed and thrown into confusion because the cattle that were drawing some of their theatrical machines could neither be induced nor forced to traverse this blood-tainted place.

This Chaumette was one of the most impious and sanguinary of the whole tribe, and we could almost believe that he envied the dogs the blood they drank. He it was that bullied the wretched idiot Gobel, revolutionary Archbishop of Paris, to come to the bar of the Convention to abjure Christianity, and proclaim himself an impostor, at the head of a procession in which asses were insultingly decorated with the sacred emblems of religion.

Chaumette himself it was who introduced to the Convention a prostitute in the character of the Goddess of Reason. Robespierre sent this whole clique to the guillotine, and on the 13th of April, 1794, Chaumette's own blood flowed to increase the horrors of which he had complained.

The guillotine remained in permanence in the Place de la Révolution till the 8th of June, 1794, when the inhabitants of the streets through which the batches ("fournées"), as they were called, of sufferers used to pass, became at last tired of the agreeable sight, and solicited its removal.

Robespierre seems at this time to have adopted a new policy, to have formed some design of founding a dictatorial authority in his own person on the basis of religion and morals.

On the 7th June he made his famous report acknowledging " l'Etre Suprême," and appointed the 20th June for the great *fête* in the gardens of the Tuileries, which was to celebrate this recognition.

Of this ceremony Robespierre was to be the " Pontifex Maximus," and it can hardly be doubted that it was to remove the odious machines from the immediate scene of his glorification that it was—the day after the decree and ten days before the celebration—removed to the Place St. Antoine, in front of the ruins of the Bastile; but that a day might not be lost, it was removed on a Decade, the republican Sabbath.

In the forty-nine days in which it is said to have stood at the *Barrière du Trône* it despatched 1270 persons of both sexes, and of all ages and ranks, and it became necessary to build a kind of sanguiduct, to carry off the streams of blood; and on the very last day, when the tyrant had already fallen, and that the smallest interruption would have sufficed to have stopped the fatal procession, forty-nine persons passed almost unguarded through the stupified streets to the place of execution.

And here we have the last occasion to mention Sanson; and it is to his credit, as indeed all the personal details related of him seem to be. On the 9th Thermidor there was, about half-past three in the afternoon, just as this last batch of victims was about to leave the Conciergerie, a considerable commotion in the town, caused by the revolt against Robespierre.

At that moment Fouquier, on his way to dine with a neighbour, passed through the court where the prisoners were ascending the fatal carts. Sanson, whose duty it was to conduct the prisoners to execution, ventured to stop the Public Accuser, to represent to him that there were some rumours of a commotion, and to suggest whether it would not be prudent to postpone the execution till at least the next morning.

Fouquier roughly replied that the law must take its course. He went to dinner, and the forty-nine victims went to the scaffold, whither in due time he followed them.

After the accession of Louis Philippe, for whom the guillotine must have been an object of the most painful contemplation, sentences of death were also very rare, and certainly never executed where there was any possible room for mercy.

The executions, too, when forced upon him, took place at early hours, and in remote and uncertain places; and every humane art was used to cover the operations of the fatal instrument with a modest veil, not only from motives of general decency and humanity, but also, no doubt, from national pride and personal sensibility.

What Frenchman would not wish that the name and memory of the guillotine could be blotted from the history of mankind?

"The word *Guillotine*," says the author of *Les Festes de l'Anarchie*, "should be effaced from the language." But the revolutionary horrors which France is naturally so anxious to forget, it the more behoves us and the rest of Europe to remember and meditate.

Such massacres as we have been describing will probably never be repeated: they will, no doubt, stand unparalleled in the future, as they do in the former annals of the world; but they should never be forgotten as an example of the incalculable excesses of popular insanity.

The invention of this instrument of death (the guillotine) is thus described by a graphic writer:— Joseph Ignace Guillotin lived to deplore his own ingenuity in inventing or suggesting a machine which besides being effective for the immediate purpose intended, was the result of a really kind feeling. The stern irony of fate occasionally rewards inventors in this way.

Born in 1738, Guillotin received a medical training; he became a physician of much repute, and was chosen professor in one of the French universities. In 1789, when France was beginning to feel the first throes of the Revolution, Guillotin was elected member of the National Assembly, and took his seat among the Liberals or Reformers.

He proposed a resolution declaratory that capital punishment ought to bear no relation to the rank of the culprit; that when a criminal is condemned to death, for any crime whatever, the mode of execution should be the same whether he were peer or peasant.

Until then, nobles and privileged persons, when condemned to death, had the honour of being decapitated, either by the axe or by the sword; whereas the common people were left to the tender mercies of a hempen rope. Dr. Guillotin at the same time proposed a second resolution.

He wished to save the unhappy being from the additional punishment existing from the uncertainty, nervousness, or clumsiness of the executioner, whether axeman or swordsman.

He cited historical incidents in which two, three, or even more cuts were given, by the axe or the sword, before the head of the miserable sufferer was finally severed from the body. He proposed to do away alike with the gibbet, the sword, and the axe, and to substitute a decapitating machine, in which a sharp, heavy knife should descend on the neck of the condemned.

Feeling assured that bodily pain could not be felt during this brief operation, he was quite carried away by his subject, and said, enthusiastically, "I could cut off your head with my machine in the twinkling of an eye, without your suffering the smallest pain!"

Poor Dr. Guillotin had to bear the shafts of ridicule, always a terrible weapon to a Frenchman. Many of the members of the Assembly smiled at his ardent words; and the Royalists out of doors made rare fun of him. One of their journals gave a song, "On the inimitable machine of Dr. Guillotin for chopping off heads called after his name the Guillotine."

Poor Dr. Guillotin had to bear the shafts of ridicule, always a terrible weapon to a Frenchman. Many of the members of the Assembly smiled at his ardent words; and the Royalists out of doors made rare fun of him. One of their journals gave a song, "On the inimitable machine of Dr. Guillotin for chopping off heads called after his name."

This name, started in this bantering way, has clung to the machine from that day till now. The doctor protested against the designation, but in vain. He did not even invent the machine; he merely pointed out that the chopping action could easily be produced by a sharp, heavy blade descending from an upright frame.

The National Assembly, on receiving Dr. Guillotin's two propositions, at once adopted the first of them, by decreeing equality of punishment for all ranks of society; but left the mode of execution for further consideration. It was not till nearly two years afterwards, that, on the motion of MM. Lepelletier and Saint Fargeon, a decree was issued, declaring that the mode of capital punishment should be by decapitation. Even then the merits and demerits of the axe, the sword, and the falling knife were left in abeyance. In March, 1792, the Assembly sought the advice of Dr. Antoine Louis, a celebrated surgeon, and secretary of the Paris College of Surgeons.

He explained, scientifically, how far the various decapitating instruments acted like knives, and how far like scissors; and expressed himself decidedly in favour of a chopping machine.

He showed that the idea of such a machine was by no means a new one. An Italian book by Achille Bocchi, dated 1555, gives an engraving of an Italian nobleman being beheaded; a heavy blade, suspended by cords from a crossbar at the top of a frame, is represented as falling on the neck of the victim.

In 1632 some such apparatus was employed in Languedoc, for decapitating Duc Henry de Montmorenci. It was also ascertained that Scotland in the North, and Persia in the East, had employed machines bearing a resemblance to this.

Among the strange scenes of the French revolutionary days, not the least strange was that of the National Assembly listening gravely to the details given on these matters.

Dr. Louis conferred with Dr. Guillotin, and also with the famous executioner Sanson. Sanson specially urged that, if all executions henceforth were to be by beheading, a machine would be greatly needed, as he distrusted his own power of using the sword or the axe so frequently and so accurately as would be necessary.

After hearing all the explanations and suggestions, the Assembly passed a decree for the use of a decapitating machine, in substitution of the halter, the axe, the sword, and the various instruments of torture such as the rack.

One Schmidt, a German musical instrument maker, residing at Paris, was taken into council; and he, Guillotin, Louis, and Sanson, settled among them the details of the machine.

Nay, there was even a fifth adviser. The king, always fond of lock-making and amateur engineering, requested to have the designs shown to him; and he suggested an improvement which was practically adopted.

A sum of five thousand five hundred francs was paid for the machine, constructed for the National Assembly by Guidon, the carpenter. An attempt was made to give the name of Louisette, or Louison, to it, in honour of the learned doctor; but the name Guillotine had been current in the public mind for two or three years, and nothing could supplant it, although Dr. Guillotine certainly never sought to have his memory thus perpetuated.

The apparatus was first tried in decapitating the dead bodies of three men, and some live animals, at the prison of the Bicêtre. Dr. Louis, after seeing the efficacy of the invention tested in this way, died just before the terrible days of the revolution came on; and was therefore denied the pleasure, or spared the pain (whichever it might be), of seeing the guillotine employed as the most dreaded of political instruments.

The first victim was an ordinary criminal, an highwayman named Nicholas Jacques Pelletier, who was guillotined on the 25th of April, 1792.

The *Chronique de Paris*, in its next day's issue, stated that "The novelty in this mode of execution caused a considerable augmentation in the number of persons who usually witness such scenes.

"The machine is with good reason, preferred to other modes of putting to death. One human being is not directly employed in decapitating another; and the promptness with which the operation takes place is more consistent with the spirit of the law, which is often severe, but should never be cruel."

The first political guillotining took place four months later, when Louis David Collinot d'Augremont was executed by torchlight for the crime of having been among "the enemies of the people" on the 10th of August, the day on which "the people" broke into the Tuileries, expelled the royal family, and filled the palace and its surroundings with blood.

The National Assembly was succeeded by the National Convention, and by this Convention was founded the Revolutionary Tribunal, in April, 1793. Then, indeed, commenced the fearful period, always since recorded in history as the Reign of Terror, which lasted until July, 1794. How many unhappy persons were guillotined during these fifteen months is not accurately known; but in the final six weeks preceding the fall of Robespierre more than eleven hundred heads rolled in the dust of Paris alone.

Whether M. Guillotin had the heart to join in these discussions we do not know—he continued his practice as a physician, and was much respected. A popular notion prevails that he himself fell a victim to the machine which he had suggested—nay, that he was its first victim. Such was not the case; he was in prison as a "suspect" during the later days of the Terror; but the fall of Robespierre occurred just in the nick of time, and M. Guillotin survived to the days of the Consulate and the Empire

He wrote a portion of autobiography, marked by the omission of all notice of his much-regretted suggestion of a beheading machine. The indifference to death, induced by an almost daily familiarity with descriptions and spectacles relating to it, showed itself in ways which we in our quiet country and quiet times can hardly regard as credible.

During the Terror the guillotining of several persons every day—sometimes many scores a day—became so much a matter of course as to be treated by the Parisians as an ordinary element in city business. In the prison, to "play at guillotine" was a favourite amusement among the prisoners, and many jokes were manufactured about the "national razor."

Some of the shopkeepers went so far as to display earrings shaped like little guillotines. Two years before the fall of Robespierre, when violence had begun but had not yet assumed its more fearful aspect, aristocratic or royalist families kept a good deal within doors in their Parisian mansions, and sometimes amused themselves in a strangely morbid way.

Dolls or puppets were provided with features resembling those of the chief popular leaders. After dinner, during dessert, a small mahogany guillotine was introduced, and wheeled along the table from guest to guest; one by one the puppets were placed under the knife and their heads chopped off.

Inside the trunk or body of the puppet was a liquid, vinous and fragrant enough to be tasteful to the palate, but blood-red; this flowed out over the table, and the guests, including ladies, dipped their handkerchiefs into it, and applied it to their lips! In all probability this strange game was played but seldom, but opposition journalists magnified it into a regular habit of "les aristocrats."

They do these things differently in France, even as regards hanging and head chopping, to what we do in England, observes a writer while noticing the well-known work, entitled "The Memoirs of the Sansons."

There the office of public executioner is hereditary, and has been held by one of the same family from 1681 down to 1867.

Here, when Mr. Calcraft resigned his post, Mr. Marwood, a person in no way connected or related with his predecessor, succeeded him.

In this instance merit alone, and not hereditary right or title, we presume, assured to the present hangman his high office.

M. Sanson, whose memoirs are here translated from the French, is the last of his line. As the translator informs us, "he was the lineal descendant of a race of headsmen through whose hands every State victim, as well as every common criminal, had passed during two centuries. They had hung, beheaded, guillotined, quartered, and tortured, from father to son, without interruption."

The grandfather of the author executed King Louis the Sixteenth and his queen, besides a host of nobles and others.

He likewise had to carry into execution part of the sentence passed on Madame de la Motte, who had been found guilty of cheating two jewellers out of a valuable necklace on pretence that Queen Marie Antoinette had commissioned Cardinal de Rohan to purchase it for her.

She was sentenced to be whipped, branded, and imprisoned for life. M. Sanson thus describes how his grandfather performed the duties imposed on him :—

WOMAN-WHIPPING.

Madame de la Motte shuddered; she clenched her hands, looked down, and then raising her head, "Very well," she said. The two assistants, who had at first tried to secure her, came forward, but she motioned them away, and advanced before them.

When the procession reached the hall, where a parliamentary committee were sitting, the clerk read out the judgment. At the very first which proclaimed her guilt, the strongest emotion appeared on Madame de la Motte's face.

Her eyes rolled in their sockets; she bit her lips, and the hitherto pretty face now seemed to be the mask of fury.

Charles Henri foresaw a storm and approached her; and it was well that he did so, for as the clerk came to the penalties, the unhappy woman's rage burst out with extraordinary violence.

She fell backwards so suddenly that her head must have been fractured on the stones had not my grandfather caught her in his arms. Madame de la Motte's strength increased as the consciousness of her fate flashed through her mind; and a protracted struggle ensued between her and the assistants who attempted to pinion her.

She was at length carried down to the court. The scaffold was erected opposite the gate, which had been left open. But it was six o'clock in the morning, and only a limited number of persons were looking on.

She was stretched on the platform, and received twelve stripes. She never ceased shrieking while the punishment was being inflicted. She invoked vengeance on the head of Cardinal de Rohan; and she added that it was her own fault that she had suffered the disgrace which had been inflicted on her, since, had she said but one word, she would have been hanged instead of having been flogged.

The second part of the sentence had no doubt escaped her, for when she was seated on the platform she remained motionless, as if completely subdued and powerless. Charles Henri Sanson thought the moment was well chosen for the completion of the penalty.

Her dress had been torn, and her shoulders were bare; and he took an iron from the grate and applied it to her skin. Madame de la Motte uttered a wild shriek, and, writhing in the grasp of one of the assistants who were holding her, she bit his hand with such fury that she took a piece of flesh off.

She struggled again, and it was with the greatest difficulty that the iron could be applied to the other shoulder. Justice was now satisfied. Madame de la Motte was put into a fly, and taken to the Salpetriere. As she was alighting she tried to run under the wheels, and a few moments afterwards she thrust the sheet of her bed into her throat in a frenzied attempt to choke herself. Her imprisonment lasted for months.

AN AMATEUR HEADSMAN.

On August 20, 1792, the Tuileries were invaded, and the king incarcerated in the Temple. A revolutionary tribunal was instituted. This tribunal, although it numbered men like Fouquier-Tinville, used the guillotine with comparative moderation. It applied severe laws with severity; but it acted with justice, and respected the forms of law.

It had chiefly to deal with common malefactors. From 1771 to 1792 the number of raids on persons and property considerably increased. Paper-money, which was of recent creation, excited the cupidity of forgers. During a period of seven months, fifteen forgers were executed on the Place de Greve. On August 19, 1792, one Collot was condemned to death for forgery, and the guillotine was erected on the usual spot selected for executions.

The Place was, as usual, well attended. As the cart, in which were Charles Henri Sanson and the culprit, drove up, a tremendous clamour greeted their appearance, and my grandfather distinguished a cry of "To the Carrousel!" The horse continued to advance, but a man seized the bridle and asked the driver why he did not obey the popular order.

Charles Henri Sanson interposed; but the man declared that the will of the Commune was that the guillotine should henceforth be erected opposite the palace of the late king, and that he must immediately transfer his tools there. My grandfather replied that his duty was to carry out the orders which were transmitted to him, and not to meet the wishes of the magistrates before they were expressed. But the clamour became more vociferous, and the horse's head was turned in the direction of the Tuileries.

Charles Henri Sanson's position was very perplexing.

He asked, and at length obtained, leave to drive up to the Hotel de Ville to ask for instructions. After some hesitation the Procureur of the Commune authorised my grandfather to act according to the wishes of the mob.

The scaffold was taken down and transferred to the Place du Carrousel; and the cart repaired thither, escorted by the crowd. But a considerable time elapsed before the guillotine could be erected again; and the culprit, who had hitherto been calm, began to struggle violently.

As the carpenters had gone away the people helped my grandfather to reconstruct the instrument of death. This reconstruction, however, progressed so slowly that night came on before it was finished, and my grandfather, apprehending desperate resistance on the part of the doomed man, requested some of those who worked around him to go to the Commune and ask for an adjournment of the execution.

The request was received with jeers of anger and derision, and the public indignation became ominously threatening.

A beardless young man, who wore the red cap, came forward, shrieking that my grandfather was a traitor, and that he should taste of the guillotine himself unless he "operated" without more ado. Charles Henri retorted with some warmth that he could not execute the culprit without special assistance.

"Your assistants are drunk?" exclaimed the young man. "You can find as much help as you require here. The blood of aristocrats cement the happiness of the nation, and there is not one man in the crowd who is not ready to lend you a hand."

A general cry of assent followed these words; but the circle around the scaffold became wider, and it appeared obvious that few were prepared to stand by their word. My grandfather perceiving this, had hastened to prevent the first speaker from retreating, by accepting his offer.

The culprit was led to the steps of the scaffold, which he refused to mount, and Charles Henri was obliged to take him in his arms and carry him up the platform. When the unfortunate man saw the dark outline of the machine, his resistance became most desperate, and he shrieked for mercy. The crowd was now silent. The improvised executioner did not budge, but he was very pale.

At last, after a final struggle, the culprit was strapped to the plank, but his contortions were so violent that an assistant had to sit upon him.

Charles Henri Sanson now told the young man that he could not furnish a better proof of his patriotism than by taking a leading part in the execution; and he put in his hand the rope which communicated with the knife.

At his bidding the young man gave a tug; the knife fell, and the head rolled in the basket. This was not all; it was customary to show the head to the multitude after the decapitation, and loud cries reminded my grandfather of the custom. He explained to the young man what he was to do, at the same time proposing himself to do the horrible duty.

But his substitute refused; he took the head by the hair, and advanced to the edge of the scaffold; but as he was raising his arm to show the bloody trophy, he staggered and fell back. Charles Henri Sanson came to his assistance, thinking that he was fainting, but he discovered that he was dead! Violent emotion had brought on an apoplectic fit, which killed him instantaneously.

Notwithstanding all that had been said upon the efficacy of the guillotine, we much question its being a more merciful mode of death than Mr. Marwood's "long drop," as it is termed, as in many cases death has taken place instantaneously, and as a sequel to this chapter we subjoin a correct account of the leading phrenological characteristics of the present public executioner.

Mr. Max Greger, our local phrenologist, whose description of the "casts" of the convicts Wardlaw and Docherty was contributed at the time of the executions, has just added the following analysis of the phrenological characteristics of the "dread finisher of the law":—

General size of head—very large.

Temperament—fibrous-nervous.

Posterior lobe of the brain—small.

Anterior lobe of the brain—rather large.

Portion of the brain above Cautiousness—moderate.

Portion of the brain above Causality—moderate.

Circumference at the base—23¾ inches.

He is only 5 ft. 5 in. in height; as to age, he will be on the shady side of fifty; of remarkable muscular power, which is lost sight of in the face, the narrowness of which, compared with the enormous width of head, is strikingly peculiar—the disproportionate size of the latter giving a drooping posture to the body, and seemingly indicating that Nature had not intended this personage to hold up his head in society.

Though fully developed in the region of the reflective powers, those faculties which judge of the relative size, shape, and design of things, and which constitute the understanding proper, are conspicuous by their absence—accounted for in him by want of education and sedentary nature of previous calling (shoemaker). There is also a decided want of balancing power, which,

taken in conjunction with his possession of large imaginative powers, and stimulated by his active temperament, constitute him an enthusiast, and consequently he is naturally prone to an erratic course of life, and to be in some respects impracticable and visionary.

His large acquisitiveness denotes an inordinate desire to acquire wealth, while his enormous caution will assist in holding fast the same. His large reflective faculties will confer considerable penetration and perception of character and events. His sense of the ludicrous, with humour and mimicry, is large.

He, however, must be considered a somewhat grim joker, and he is not at all likely to desire to be made the subject of his own fun. He is ambitious of being thought knowing and deep. He has an inordinate amount of vanity and self-conceit—must be foremost in his business: "Better to reign in hell than serve in heaven."

Being highly sensitive to praise or the admiration of his fellow-men (which, however, he seldom gets), he is likely to consider the execution of Wainwright— a criminal of the first degree—as bringing both himself and his office still more prominently before the public; but this weakness, which is manifested in the manner in which he gloats over the *modus operandi* of his profession, may in time bring his office more and more into contempt, and thus defeat the very object he is anxious to attain.

From the development we find he is not wanting in energy, with considerable shrewdness and tact, and his mechanical and constructive talents would have enabled him to succeed in life either as a manufacturer, a machinist, or an agriculturist.

MARWOOD'S CARD.

The following is a copy of Mr. Marwood's professional card, in the last line of which there will be found a touch of grim—and, doubtless, unconscious— humour :—

WILLIAM MARWOOD,
EXECUTIONER,
CHURCH LANE,
HORNCASTLE,
LINCOLNSHIRE, ENGLAND.

ALL ORDERS PROMPTLY EXECUTED.

CHAPTER CLXXV.
CONCLUSION.

WE have seen the last of the miscreant whose career we have shadowed forth, and our task is all but completed.

The celebrated Peace, says a journalist, terminated his disgraceful career on Tuesday morning on the scaffold at Armley Gaol, Leeds. He seems to have kept up his pluck and his appetite to the very last, and concluded all by making a pious and edifying speech to the reporters. We should be sorry to criticise too closely a production which was given to the world under circumstances most trying to the nerves of its author. It would be obviously absurd to judge the statement of a man of Peace's antecedents by the canons of good taste; and as for the genuineness and sincerity of them they must be ascertained by a higher tribunal than public opinion. Nevertheless there is a little too much tendency to glorify a great criminal into a great hero. Peace was well aware of this and naturally acted consciously or unconsciously, upon the assumption. Several millions of people were kept from day to day in a perfect flutter of excitement to know all that the convict was saying, doing, writing, and almost thinking. Even the composition of his breakfasts and the way in which he enjoyed them were telegraphed for the information of an expectant public. For one who was not altogether insensible to his own merits as a professional burglar and murderer, there was a strong temptation to pose before the world. He was almost as closely watched as Louis XIV., who walked, ate, slept, dressed, and, Macaulay tells us, even vomited majestically before a crowd of distinguished spectators. With the knowledge that everybody's eyes were upon him, he may perhaps have been a little too self-conscious, and a little too solicitous not to spoil a reputation which he evidently considered splendid. His repentance may have been perfectly sincere, and his latest statements quite truthful. But it would be obviously unwise to take all his revelations for gospel verity without sifting them thoroughly. We trust that no pains will be spared in the investigation of his latest confessions, and that if they are found consistent, with known and undisputed facts, prompt reparation will be made to the man who has, or may have, suffered for his crimes. A more terrible fate than that of one who has been convicted and punished for an offence which he has not committed, on the strength of a chain of plausible circumstantial evidence, can hardly be conceived. The lawyers are, no doubt, right in their dictum that circumstantial evidence is the best of all evidence, always supposing that it is strong enough. But, after the recent statements of Peace, the public will naturally be tempted to re-open the question of the Whalley Range murder, in order to ascertain whether every link of the chain was complete; and if there is a single unsatisfied doubt, they will not remain content until the prisoner Habron receives the benefit of that doubt.

The last scene of what some exuberant journalists had delighted in calling Charles Peace's "life-drama" was thus enacted to the mild satisfaction of everybody whose hopes had not pictured a sensation of the type furnished by Mr. Meritt's "New Babylon."

There was the orthodox last dying speech and confession, ready to be turned into what has now become the fashionable literature of the period; there was the moribund posturising of nice old Newgate days; and, to increase the likeness to that Saturnian period, there was a crowd close at hand whose murmurs one could hear, and which the parson's and the patient's voices could reach.

The "celebrity" Mrs. Thompson so coyly deprecates, and which her paramour loved with all his little heart, was worthily crowned at the end.

The unkind prudishness of the prison officials refused to admit more than four reporters to the sickening ceremony; but those four were found quite sufficient to flood every newspaper in the land with funereal "flimsy."

The descriptions resulting from these reports were literary gems which, when he digs them up, will afford the coming New Zealander a curious insight into the niceties of contemporary taste and the peculiarities of contemporary syntax.

The most "thorough" descriptions took the convict very early indeed—in fact it might almost be alleged that they never quite let him go.

They informed us that his sleep was troubled and

his supper hearty; they dwelt on the poor wretch's feeble endeavour to emulate his betters in a silly and sickly "improving of the occasion—which apparently is achieved by an abundant use of the second person singular, and frequent references to the Gospel of St. Chadband; they hovered about his last sleep, and peered into the cups and egg-shells of his last breakfast.

And the occasion was one of such surpassing interest, the opportunity for distinguishing oneself in the appraisement of the criminal's linen, or the analysis of the criminal's countenance, that at least one gentleman, intoxicated with his sublimity, fairly forgot whether the subject of his essay was hanged or not, and used "he is" and "he was" in the same sentences with perplexing impartiality.

But that lucubration appeared in the *Daily Telegraph*, a journal which is happy in the possession of a class of readers who do not require good grammar to help down nasty stories. And this time the story was nasty enough to suit the palate of an epicure in Topsy-turvydom.

Every step, every pause on that vulgar *via dolorosa* that leads from the prison door to the scaffold was counted, criticised, described. Little scraps of the beautiful Burial Service were desecrated by being quoted beside the doomed man's call for drink.

The demeanour and voice of the hangman, the culprit's dress, his tremours, his appetite, his letters, his speeches, the scaffold itself, with its draping of black sacking or black glazed calico (authorities differ), all this forms as pretty a page of contemporary history as confirmed *Daily Telegraph* writers will ever care to dwell upon.

Well might the moribund hypocrite address his last whimpering to "you reporters;" the reporters make the "celebrity" of such as he was.

And we may add that the journalist just mentioned not only makes the celebrity but suggests imitation by its morbid habit of manufacturing monsters out of such sorry rascals as Charles Peace.

Its epitaph on the dead sinner is, "We hanged his detestable body because it was in the highest degree expedient to rid the world of a monster of iniquity." Common gratitude to a subject that has filled its most readable columns and suggested its most high-flown homilies for a long three months might have moved even the *Daily Telegraph* to tardy and temporary charity.

It is pleasant to record that the unfortunate young Irishman Habron has received her Majesty's pardon, and is at present in Ireland, a small yearly stipend having been settled upon him sufficient to support him in comparative comfort for the remainder of his life.

This is as it should be. A great wrong was done to the ill-fated young man, but every possible means has been taken to place him in a respectable position, for which it is understood he is duly grateful.

It will be needful before concluding to take a cursory glance at the other characters who have figured in this strange eventful history.

None of our hero's quondam companions was more pained and mortified on discovering the depth of guilt into which he had been plunged than "Bandy-Legged Bill," who, however, despite the overwhelming weight of evidence, stuck to his friend "Charlie" to the last, but after Peace's trial and conviction Bill Rawton became an altered man.

The change, we are happy to say, was for the better; Rawton reformed and became an altered character. He was never at any time what might be considered hopelessly bad; indeed, to say the truth, he possessed many good qualities, which, under different circumstances and conditions, might have done much to lift him out of the slough of despondency into which he had fallen, and in which he remained for so many dark and miserable years.

But Bill saw the errors of his way. Mrs. Bourne was very good to him, and strove as best she could to lead him towards the right path, and eventually succeeded. Bill Rawton is at the present time engaged as handy man in one of the travelling circus companies.

No one knew better than he how to manage horses, and by diligence, adroitness, and attention he has contrived to give general satisfaction in his new vocation.

Brickett still continues the obliging host of the " Old Carved Lion," but the halo of crime with which the name of Peace has become associated is still a puzzle to old Brickett, who, when the name of our hero is mentioned, shakes his head, heaves a sigh, and says he " can't make it out rightly—the fellow must have gone off his chump, or summat of the sort."

Mrs. Brickett's ghost is still said to haunt the precincts of the " Lion," and, in addition to this apparition, two others are at times visible in Marshgrove-lane; these being the spirits of the late Mr. Philip Jamblin and of Giles Chudley. This is, of course, only village gossip, or superstition; nevertheless, the rustics have full faith in the truth of the report.

Mr. Jakyl, full of years and honours, passed away tranquilly some months before the arrest of Peace; and the radiant footman (now radiant no longer) drives a prosperous business in the greengrocery line, and is the father of five pledges of affection.

Lord Ethalwood got himself into a host of entanglements, both monetary and amatory, and his life was none of the happiest for a very long time.

One night a strange circumstance happened to his lordship, which might, and indeed would, have proved fatal had it not been for a sudden and strange intervention. Lord Ethalwood had left Somerset-street after having paid a visit to Theresa Trieste.

He walked carelessly along until he reached Grosvenor-square. While crossing the road he was suddenly attacked by some person behind, who had aimed, what doubtless was intended to be, a fatal blow; but the point of the knife of the would-be assassin struck against the shoulder-blade, and did no further mischief than inflicting a long superficial gash, which proved afterwards to be painful and troublesome, but it was not dangerous.

Lord Ethalwood, young, active, and resolute, turned nimbly round upon his assailant, whom he struck several violent blows on the head and shoulders, at the same time shouting lustily for the police.

In a moment or so he was tripped up by another ruffian, who was evidently in league with the others, and it was equally clear (so his lordship thought) that their intention was murder.

He was not far out in his reckoning. The men who had been companions of the young mountaineer, Janot, had sworn to have Lionel Ethalwood's life, and for this purpose they had lain in wait for him.

What the issue would have been, had not timely assistance arrived, it would be impossible to say. Luckily, for his lordship, a passenger on the other side of the way saw the position he was in, and at once hastened to the rescue.

With one well-delivered blow he knocked down with his clenched fist one of the mountaineers. Upon the instant the other closed with him, and a short but desperate struggle ensued, the end of which was that both combatants fell, the stranger undermost and the mountaineer on the top.

Lord Ethalwood rose to his feet, whereupon both the foreigners scampered off without further ado. Now that the struggle was over two policemen came.

Lord Ethalwood was found to be bruised and wounded, but his rescuer was in a still worse plight; he was stretched on the pavement in a senseless condition, his head resting on the broad stone steps which led to the vestibule of a palatial mansion.

The policeman stooped down and examined the features of the stranger, from whose head a dark stream of blood was flowing. He was evidently a man slightly past the middle period of life. Lord Ethalwood was greatly concerned when he saw the lamentably prostrate condition of the gallant gentleman who had risked his own life to preserve his.

The stranger was taken to the accident ward of the nearest hospital, whereupon Lord Ethalwood jumped into a cab and proceeded at once to his own residence. The family doctor attended to his wound, and declared that his young patient had had a narrow escape.

In a few days, however, his lordship was convalescent. Not so, however, was the ill-fated man who had come so opportunely to his rescue. He had received from the fall a fracture of the skull, and for some days he alternated between life and death.

Earl Ethalwood was constant in his visits to the hospital where the patient lay, and it was on one of these occasions that a terrible and harrowing fact became manifest.

He discovered that his preserver was his own father, Tom Gatliffe, who, the reader will remember, had come upon the scene just in time to save his son. When the fact was clearly established the Earl was almost frantic.

Lady Batershall, Lady Marvlynn, and a host of other persons were in close attendance on the sufferer, who, despite skill and unremitting attention, breathed his last in the ward of a metropolitan hospital.

But very little now remains to be told. Mr. Kensett at his decease left all his worldly wealth to him whom we have known as Alf Purvis, who squandered his patrimony as he had heretofore squandered his ill-gotten gains, and died in poverty and wretchedness while yet in the springtime of his life.

Our story hath a mournful ending, but we trust that those who have perused these pages have yet been able to derive entertainment and instruction from the many noteworthy facts contained therein. One fact has been clearly established—

" A life of crime is always a life of sorrow and care, for the hearts of the guilty tremble for the past, for the present, and the future."

THE END.

CHARLES PEACE
THE
MASTER CRIMINAL

Regent Theatre

KINGS CROSS — LONDON. N.W.I.

PROPRIETORS: THE VARIETY THEATRES CONSOLIDATED LT?
LICENSED BY THE LORD CHAMBERLAIN TO WALTER PAYNE.

TELEPHONE   TERMINUS 6321 *(3 LINES)*

PROGRAMME

MARTIN SABINE

PRESENTS

The London Repertory Company

IN

THE MISDOINGS OF

CHARLEY PEACE

By EDWARD PERCY

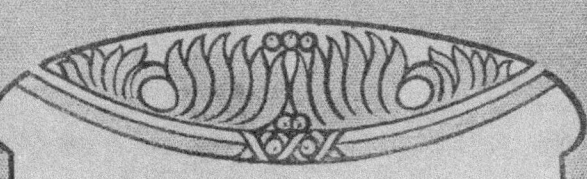

ONE PER DAY

REGENT THEATRE

KING'S CROSS. TERMINUS 6321
(3 LINES)

OUR NEXT PLAY

SATURDAY, NOVEMBER 2nd

YOUNG WOODLEY

By JOHN VAN DRUTEN

The Brilliant and Astounding Play of Modern School Life

ONE PER DAY!

Schweppes Lemon Squash

THE VARIETY THEATRES CONSOLIDATED LTD

LICENSED BY THE LORD CHAMBERLAIN TO

WALTER PAYNE.

Phone: TERMINUS 8321 (2 lines).

PROPRIETORS

REGENT THEATRE KING'S CROSS

Commencing SATURDAY, OCTOBER 26th, and EVERY EVENING at 6.30 & 8.40, SATURDAY 6.15

THE LONDON REPERTORY COMPANY and OSWALD DALE ROBERTS in

THE MISDOINGS OF

CHARLEY PEACE

By Edward Percy

By arrangement with WALTER PAYNE

MARTIN SABINE presents

NEXT SATURDAY

YOUNG WOODLEY

The Great Play of the Modern Schoolboy

Characters in the order of their appearance:

ACT I

SCENE 1—The Crossroads at Whalley Range, Manchester
1st August, 1876

Charley Peace	OSWALD DALE ROBERTS
P.C. Cock	PAGET HUNTER
P.C. Beanland	GEORGE WALKER
John Habron	G. EDWARD HALL
William Habron	BERNARD LEE
A Young Gentleman	HORACE CUSTINS

SCENE II—The Framers' and Gilders' shop at Darnall, Sheffield
3rd August, 1876

Hannah Peace	DOROTHY DEWHURST
Willie Ward	ROGER McCORMACK
Charley Peace	OSWALD DALE ROBERTS

SCENE III & IV—Manchester Assize Court, behind the Dock
27th & 28th November, 1876

North Countryman	WILLIAM DEWHURST
North Countrywoman	KAREN STANLEY ALDER
Bob	PAGET HUNTER
Charley Peace	OSWALD DALE ROBERTS
Official	CHRISTOPHER BENNETT
2nd Warder	FRANK NAPIER
1st Warder	EARLE D. DOUGLAS
William Habron	BERNARD LEE
John Habron	G. EDWARD HALL
Clerk of Arraigns	HORACE CUSTINS
Q.C. for Crown	GEORGE WALKER
The Judge	TERENCE MAXWELL

SCENE V—An Eating House at Hull

An Old Man	
Willie Ward	
Charley Peace	
Hannah Peace	
1st Customer	
2nd Customer	
1st Detective	
2nd Detective	

ACT I continued

30th November, 1876

	ALAN RANKIN
	ROGER McCORMACK
OSWALD DALE ROBERTS	
DOROTHY DEWHURST	
CHRISTOPHER BENNETT	
EARLE D. DOUGLAS	
FRANK NAPIER	
PAGET HUNTER	

INTERVAL, 8 MINUTES

ACT II

SCENE I—A Bar Parlour in South London
October, 1878

Mr. Ridgers	GEORGE WALKER
Mr. Trumble	TERENCE MAXWELL
Potman	WILLIAM DEWHURST
Potman	FRANK NAPIER
Miss Chase	JOYCE GIBSON
Mrs. Leeby	KAREN STANLEY ALDER
Mr. Forsey Brion	HORACE CUSTINS
Charley Peace	OSWALD DALE ROBERTS
Sue Thompson	AVERIL HALEY
Mr. Duffy	BERNARD LEE
Old Match Seller	DORA ALLEN

SCENE II—No. 5, East Terrace, Peckham
9th October, 1878

Charley Peace	OSWALD DALE ROBERTS
Mrs. Forsey Brion	DORA ALLEN
Mr. Forsey Brion	HORACE CUSTINS
Hannah Peace	DOROTHY DEWHURST
Sue Thompson	AVERIL HALEY
Willie Ward	ROGER McCORMACK

SCENE III—Garden of No. 2, St. John's Park, Blackheath
10th October, 1878

	BERNARD LEE
	G. EDWARD HALL
OSWALD DALE ROBERTS	

SCENE IV—No. 5, East Terrace, Peckham
November, 1878

Inspector Phillips	G. EDWARD HALL
Sergeant Brown	BERNARD LEE
Inspector Bonny	FRANK NAPIER
Mrs. Forsey Brion	DORA ALLEN
Mr. Forsey Brion	HORACE CUSTINS
Sue Thompson	AVERIL HALEY

SCENE V—The 5.15 a.m. Express from King's Cross to Sheffield
22nd January, 1879

Charley Peace	OSWALD DALE ROBERTS
Warder Robertson	CHRISTOPHER BENNETT
Chief Warder of Pentonville	WILLIAM DEWHURST

SCENE VI—The Railway Lines
22nd January, 1879

Charley Peace	OSWALD DALE ROBERTS
Railway Guard	EARLE D. DOUGLAS
Chief Warder of Pentonville	WILLIAM DEWHURST
Warder Robertson	CHRISTOPHER BENNETT

SCENE VII—The Condemned Cell at Armley Gaol
17th February, 1879

Charley Peace	OSWALD DALE ROBERTS
1st Warder	EARLE D. DOUGLAS
2nd Warder	ALAN RANKIN
Governor of Gaol	GEORGE WALKER
Rev. Mr. Littlewood	TERENCE MAXWELL
3rd Warder	CHRISTOPHER BENNETT
Hannah Peace	DOROTHY DEWHURST

The Play Produced by MARTIN SABINE

Manager for Regent Theatre   H. DAVIS

THE REGENT THEATRE ORCHESTRA

Musical Director—Frederick Grover

OVERTURE—Prelude   Rachmaninoff
SELECTION—"Cavalleria Rusticana"   Mascagni

NATIONAL SUNDAY LEAGUE CONCERT

SUNDAY, NOV. 3rd at 7 p.m.

THE FAMOUS ST. HILDA'S
PROFESSIONAL BAND

(Musical Director—Mr. James Oliver). Five times winners of the Crystal Palace 1,000 Guineas Trophy, and
the World's Championship. Miss Vera Siddons. Mr. Albert Edgar. Mr. Walter Barker,
Canadian. Mr. Geoffrey Dupree, Entertainer.

SEATS 6d. to 1/10   Bookable from
1/- to 1/10 at BOX OFFICE in ADVANCE

AT FIRST - - Completely
BANNED by the CENSOR

our Play Next Week

YOUNG
WOODLEY

By JOHN VAN DRUTEN

is undoubtedly, the

Outstanding Play of the Year

Brilliantly Written and more than
Absorbing, it tells a Daring Tale
of Modern School Life that has
astounded the World.   Mothers,
Fathers, Boys and Girls must see
this Play, for it is something

YOU   ALL   SHOULD   KNOW

Extract from the Rules made by the Lord Chamberlain

1.   The name of the actual and responsible Manager of the Theatre must be printed on every play bill.   2.   The Public can leave the Theatre at the end of the performance by all exit and entrance doors which must open outwards.   3.   Where there is a fire proof screen to the proscenium opening it must be lowered at least once during every performance to ensure its being in proper working order.   4.   All gangways, passages and staircases must be kept free from chairs or any other obstruction, whether permanent or temporary.

ONE PER DAY

THE LONDON
REPERTORY TRAINING SCHOOL

Special arrangements have been made for the

PRACTICAL TRAINING

of pupils for THE STAGE

Applications in writing to the Secretary, THE REPERTORY TRAINING SCHOOL, Regent Theatre.

3 REASONS WHY

You should join the London Co-operative Society, Ltd.

BECAUSE—

1. The Society is owned and controlled by its members.

2. Profits are returned to members IN CASH as Dividends.

3. Co-operative Goods are made and sold under trade union conditions.

Last Year our Sales exceeded £7,100,000, over £353,000 being returned in cash to our members.

Visit the Shops of the

LONDON CO-OPERATIVE SOCIETY, LTD.

See what the Society offers. Join without delay and share the prosperity of co-operative trade.

For full particulars of membership and benefits, apply to any branch, or write, 54, Maryland Street, E.15

LONDON CO-OPERATIVE SOCIETY, LTD.

www.ingramcontent.com/pod-product-compliance
Lightning Source LLC
Chambersburg PA
CBHW081137020726
47504CB00009B/1891